The Secret Pilgrim

Praise for The Secret Pilgrim

"Smiley is back! To have a new John le Carré is treat enough. But better still, as *The Secret Pilgrim* opens, the book seems to center on the formidable, wise and somehow rather cuddly spymaster, George Smiley.... Riveting . . . marvelous." —*The Philadephia Inquirer*

"Illumines the spiritual condition of being a spy."
—*The Washington Post Book World*

"Memorable . . . strongly romantic . . . One finishes the book confident that le Carré will find new spies and that they will find new arenas in which to practice their deceptions." —*Newsweek*

"No other contemporary novelist has more durably enjoyed [the] twin badges of being both well-read and well-regarded.... This book is like an old cop's fireside reminiscences of famous capers that he handled, with much the same charm. The stories Ned recalls along the way are good ones, suspenseful, telling, each one cleverly recounted." —SCOTT TUROW, *Chicago Tribune*

"John le Carré scales new heights."
—*The Christian Science Monitor*

"Wonderful ... *The Secret Pilgrim* [is] laced with lethal irony or occasional hope, with characters ranging from the heroic to the most banal form of evil. If John le Carré had to choose between his own espionage experience and his gifts as a writer, one strongly suspects he would bet on the latter." —*The Boston Globe*

"They keep calling him a spy novelist, but of course he is much more; he is, indeed, one of the half-dozen best novelists now working in English. . . . Here in *The Secret Pilgrim* are several old friends at twilight, telling tales to tomorrow morning's fresh class. . . . Anybody can write a novel. Nobody can write a le Carré novel."
—*Chicago Sun-Times*

"Powerful ... a highly absorbing tale written with le Carré's customary blend of deft characterization, scene-setting and dialogue, not to mention a new-found affinity for humor." —*Newsday*

"Riveting ... It's not only one of the author's best books, it's one of the best books, period." —*Cosmopolitan*

"*The Secret Pilgrim* bridges a gap between the recent past and the unforeseeable future. No longer able, because of the innate honesty that has characterized his storytelling career, to offer a full-blown cold war drama, le Carré pops out some discrete and satisfactorily chilling ice cubes."
—*Time*

By John le Carré

The
Secret Pilgrim

A Novel

JOHN LE CARRÉ

Ballantine Books
New York

2017 Ballantine Books Trade Paperback Edition

Copyright © 1990 by David Cornwell
Author essay copyright © 2001 by David Cornwell

Published in the United States by Ballantine Books, an imprint of Random House, a division of Penguin Random House LLC, New York.

BALLANTINE and the HOUSE colophon are registered trademarks of Penguin Random House LLC.

Originally published in hardcover in the United States by Alfred A. Knopf, an imprint of Random House, a division of Penguin Random House LLC, in 1990.

ISBN 978-0-345-50442-5

Printed in the United States of America on acid-free paper

randomhousebooks.com

13th Printing

Book design by Virginia Norey

*For Alec Guinness
with affection and thanks*

The Secret Pilgrim

Let me confess to you at once that if I had not, on the spur of the moment, picked up my pen and scribbled a note to George Smiley inviting him to address my passing-out class on the closing evening of their entry course—and had Smiley not, against all my expectations, consented—I would not be making so free to you with my heart.

At the most, I would be offering you the sort of laundered reminiscence with which, if I am honest, I was a bit too inclined to regale my students: feats of secret chivalry, of the dramatic, the resourceful and the brave. And always, of course, the useful. I would be enthralling you with memories of night drops into the Caucasus, hazardous crossings by fast boat, beach landings, winking shore lights, clandestine radio messages that ceased in midtransmission. Of silent heroes of the Cold War who, having made their contribution, modestly went to earth in the society they had protected. Of defectors-in-place snatched in the nick of time from the jaws of the opposition.

And to a point, yes, that is the life we lived. In our day we did those things, and some even ended well. We had good men in bad countries who risked their lives for us. And usually they were believed, and sometimes their intelligence was wisely used. I hope so, for the greatest spy on earth is worth nothing when it isn't.

And for the lighter note, over a second whisky in the Probationers' Mess, I would have picked out for them the occasion when a three-man reception team from the Circus, operating inside East Germany, and gallantly led by myself, lay freezing on a ridge in the Harz Mountains, praying for the flutter of an unmarked plane with its engines cut, and the blessed black parachute floating in its wake. And what did we find when our prayer was answered and we had slithered down an icefield to claim our treasure? Stones, I would tell my wide-eyed students. Chunks of honest Argyll granite. The despatchers at our Scottish airbase had sent us the training cannister by mistake.

That tale, at least, found a certain echo, even if some of my other offerings tended to lose their audience halfway through.

I suspect that my impulse to write to Smiley had been brewing in me longer than I realised. The idea was conceived during one of my regular visits to Personnel to discuss the progress of my students. Dropping in on the Senior Officers' Bar for a sandwich and a beer, I had bumped into Peter Guillam. Peter had played Watson to George's Sherlock Holmes in the long search for the Circus traitor, who turned out to be our Head of Operations, Bill Haydon. Peter had not heard from George for—oh, a year now, more. George had bought this cottage in North Cornwall somewhere, he said, and was indulging his dislike of the telephone. He had some kind of sinecure at Exeter University, and was allowed to use their library. Sadly I pictured the rest: George the lonely hermit on an empty landscape, taking his solitary walks and thinking his thoughts. George slipping up to Exeter for a little human warmth in his old age while he waited to take his place in the spies' Valhalla.

And Ann, his wife? I asked Peter, lowering my voice as one does when Ann's name comes up—for it was an open secret, and a painful one, that Bill Haydon had counted among Ann's many lovers.

Ann was Ann, said Peter, with a Gallic shrug. She had bits of family with grand houses on the Helford Estuary. Sometimes she stayed with them, sometimes she stayed with George.

I asked for Smiley's address. "Don't tell him I gave it you," said Peter as I wrote it down. With George, there had always been that certain kind of guilt about passing on his whereabouts—I still don't quite know why.

Three weeks later Toby Esterhase came down to Sarratt to give us his celebrated talk on the arts of clandestine surveillance on unfriendly soil. And of course he stayed for lunch, which was greatly enhanced for him by the presence of our first three girls. After a battle lasting as long as I had been at Sarratt, Personnel had finally decided that girls were all right after all.

And I heard myself trailing Smiley's name.

There have been times when I would not have entertained Toby in the woodshed, and others when I thanked my Maker I had him on my side. But with the years, I am pleased to notice, one settles to people.

"Oh look here, my God, Ned!" Toby cried in his incurably Hungarian English, smoothing back his carefully pomaded mane of silver hair. "You mean you haven't heard?"

"Heard what?" I asked patiently.

"My dear fellow, George is chairing the Fishing Rights Committee. Don't they tell you anything down here in the sticks? I think I better take this up with the Chief actually, one to one. A word in his ear at the Club."

"Perhaps you'd tell me first what the Fishing Rights Committee is," I suggested.

"Ned, you know what? I think I get nervous. Maybe they took you off the list."

"Maybe they did at that," I said.

He told me anyway, as I knew he would, and I duly acted astonished, which gave him an even greater sense of his importance. And there is a part of me that remains astonished to this day. The Fishing Rights Committee, Toby explained for the benefit of the unblessed, was an informal working party made up of officers from Moscow Centre and the Circus. Its job, said Toby—who I really believe had lost any capacity to be surprised— was to identify intelligence targets of interest to both services and thrash out a system of sharing. "The idea actually, Ned, was to target the world's trouble spots," he said with an air of maddening superiority.—"I think they fix first the Middle East. Don't quote me, Ned, okay?"

"And you're telling me Smiley *chairs* this committee?" I asked incredulously when I had attempted to digest this.

"Well, maybe not much longer, Ned—Anno Domini and so forth. But the Russians were so frightfully keen to meet him, we brought him in to snip the tape. Give the old fellow a treat, I say. Stroke him a bit. Bunch of fixers in an envelope."

I didn't know which to marvel at the more: the notion of Toby Esterhase tripping to the altar with Moscow Centre, or of George Smiley presiding over the marriage. A few days later, with Personnel's permission, I wrote to the Cornish address Guillam had given me, adding diffidently that if George loathed public speaking half as much as I did, he should on no account accept. I had been a bit in the dumps till then, but when his prim little card arrived by return declaring him delighted, I felt a probationer myself, and just as nervous.

Two weeks after that, wearing a brand-new country suit for the occasion, I was standing at the barrier at Paddington Station, watching the elderly trains disgorge their middle-aged commuters. I don't think I had ever been quite so aware of Smiley's anonymity. Wherever I looked, I seemed to see versions of him: tubby, bespectacled gentlemen of a certain seniority, and every one of them with George's air of being slightly late for something he would rather not be doing. Then suddenly we had shaken hands and he was sitting beside me in the back of a Head Office Rover, stockier than I remembered him, and white-haired, it was true, but of a vigour and good humour I had not seen in him since his wife had her fatal fling with Haydon.

"Well, well, Ned. How do you like being a schoolmaster?"

"How do you like retirement?" I countered, with a laugh. "I'll be joining you soon!"

Oh, he loved retirement, he assured me. Couldn't get enough of it, he said wryly; I should have no fears of it at all. A little tutoring here, Ned, the odd paper to deliver there; walks, he'd even acquired a dog.

"I hear they hauled you back to sit on some extraordinary committee," I said. "Conspiring with the Bear, they say, against the Thief of Baghdad."

George does not gossip, but I saw his smile broaden. "Do they now? And your source would be Toby, no doubt," he said, and beamed contentedly upon the dismal subtopian landscape while he launched into a diversionary story about two old ladies in his village who hated each other. One owned an antique shop, the other was very rich. But as the Rover continued its progress through once-rural Hertfordshire, I found myself thinking less about the ladies of George's village than about George himself. I was thinking that this was a Smiley reborn, who told stories about old ladies, sat on committees with Russian spies and gazed on the overt world with the relish of someone who has just come out of hospital.

That evening, squeezed into an elderly dinner jacket, the same man sat at my side at Sarratt high table, peering benignly round him at the polished plate candlesticks and old group photographs going back to God knows when. And at the fit, expectant faces of his young audience as they waited on the master's word.

"Ladies and gentlemen, Mr. George Smiley," I announced severely as I rose to introduce him. "A legend of the Service. Thank you."

"Oh, I don't think I'm a legend at all," Smiley protested as he clambered to his feet. "I think I'm just a rather fat old man wedged between the pudding and the port."

Then the legend began talking, and I realised that I had never heard Smiley address a social gathering before. I had assumed it was a thing he would be congenitally bad at, like forcing his opinions on people, or referring to a joe by his real name. So the sovereign way in which he addressed us surprised me before I had begun to fathom the content. I heard his first few sentences and I watched my students' faces—not always so obliging—lift and relax and light to him as they gave him first their attention, then their trust and finally their support. And I thought, with an inner smile of belated recognition: yes, yes, of course, this was George's other nature. This was the actor who had always lain hidden in him, the secret Pied Piper. This was the man Ann Smiley had loved and Bill Haydon had deceived and the rest of us had loyally followed, to the mystification of outsiders.

There is a wise tradition at Sarratt that our dinner speeches are not recorded and no notes are taken, and that no official reference may afterwards be made to what was said. The guest of honour enjoyed what Smiley in his Germanic way called "the fool's freedom," though I can think of few people less qualified for the privilege. But I am nothing if not a professional, trained to listen and remember, and you must understand also that Smiley had not spoken many words before I realised—as my students were not slow to notice—that he was speaking straight into my heretical heart. I refer to that other, less obedient person who is also inside me and whom, if I am honest, I had refused to acknowledge since I had embarked on this final lap of my career—to the secret questioner who had been my uncomfortable companion even before a reluctant joe of mine called Barley Blair had stepped across the crumbling Iron Curtain and, for reasons of love, and some sort of honour, had calmly kept on walking, to the incredulity of the Fifth Floor.

The better the restaurant, we say of Personnel, the worse the news. "It's time you handed on your wisdom to the new boys, Ned," he had told me over a suspiciously good lunch at the Connaught. "*And* to the new *girls,*" he added, with a loathsome smirk. "They'll be letting them into the Church next, I suppose." He returned to happier ground. "You know the tricks. You've kicked around. You've had an impressive last lap running Secretariat. Time to put it all to advantage. We think you should take over the Nursery and pass the torch to tomorrow's spies."

He had used a rather similar set of sporting metaphors, if I remembered rightly, when in the wake of Barley Blair's defection he had removed me from my post as Head of the Russia House and consigned me to that knacker's yard, the Interrogators' Pool.

He ordered up two more glasses of Armagnac. "How's your Mabel, by the way?" he continued, as if he had just remembered her. "Somebody told me she'd got her handicap down to twelve—ten, by God! Well. I trust you'll keep her away from me! So what do you say? Sarratt in the week, home to Tunbridge Wells at weekends, sounds to me like the triumphant crowning of a career. What do you say?"

So what *do* you say? You say what others have said before you. Those who can, do. Those who can't, teach. And what they teach is what they can't do any more, because either the body or the spirit or both have lost their singleness of purpose; because they have seen too much and suppressed too much and compromised too much, and in the end tasted too little. So they take to rekindling their old dreams in new minds, and warming themselves against the fires of the young.

And that brings me back to the opening bars of Smiley's speech that night, for suddenly his words were reaching out and grasping me. I had invited him because he was a legend of the past. Yet to the delight of all of us, he was turning out to be the iconoclastic prophet of the future.

I'll not bother you with the finer points of Smiley's introductory tour of the globe. He gave them the Middle East, which was obviously on his mind, and he explored the limits of colonial power in supposedly post-colonialist times. He gave them the Third World and the Fourth World and posited a Fifth World, and pondered aloud whether human despair and poverty were the serious concern of any wealthy nation. He seemed pretty confident they weren't. He scoffed at the idea that spying was a dying profession now that the Cold War had ended: with each new nation that came out of the ice, he said, with each new alignment, each rediscovery of old identities and passions, with each erosion of the old status quo, the spies would be working round the clock. He spoke, I discovered afterwards, for twice the customary length, but I didn't hear a chair creak or a glass clink—not even when they dragged him to the library and sat him in the throne of honour before the fire for more of the same, more heresy, more subversion. My children, hardened cases all of them, in love with George! I didn't hear a sound beyond the confident flow of Smiley's voice and the eager burst of laughter at some unexpected self-irony or confession of failure. You're only old once, I thought, as I listened with them, sharing their excitement.

He gave them case histories I had never heard, and which I was certain nobody in Head Office had cleared in advance—

certainly not our Legal Adviser Palfrey, who in response to the openness of our former enemies had been battening down and double-locking every useless secret he could lay his obedient hands on.

He dwelt on their future rôle as agent-runners and, applying it to the altered world, vested in it the traditional Service image of mentor, shepherd, parent and befriender, as prop and marriage counsellor, as pardoner, entertainer and protector; as the man or woman who has the gift of treating the outrageous premise as an everyday affair, and so becomes his agent's partner in illusion. None of that had changed, he said. None of it ever would. He paraphrased Burns: "A spy's a spy for all that."

But no sooner had he lulled them with this sweet notion than he warned them of the death of their own natures that could result from the manipulation of their fellow men, and the truncation of their natural feeling.

"By being all things to all spies, one does rather run the risk of becoming nothing to oneself," he confessed sadly. "Please don't ever imagine you'll be unscathed by the methods you use. The end may justify the means—if it wasn't supposed to, I dare say you wouldn't be here. But there's a price to pay, and the price does tend to be oneself. Easy to sell one's soul at your age. Harder later."

He mixed the deadly serious with the deadly frivolous and made the difference small. Betweenwhiles he seemed to be asking the questions I had been asking of myself for most of my working life, but had never managed to express, such as: "Did it do any good?" And "What did it do to me?" And "What will become of us now?" Sometimes his questions were answers: George, we used to say, never asked unless he knew.

He made us laugh, he made us feel and, by means of his inordinate deference, he shocked us with his contrasts. Better still, he put our prejudices at risk. He got rid of the acceptance in me and revived the slumbering rebel that my exile to Sarratt had silenced. George Smiley, out of a clear sky, had renewed my search and confused me wonderfully.

Frightened people never learn, I have read. If that is so, they certainly have no right to teach. I'm not a frightened man—or no more frightened than any other man who has looked at death and knows it is for him. All the same, experience and a little pain had made me a mite too wary of the truth, even towards myself. George Smiley put that right. George was more than a mentor to me, more than a friend. Though not always present, he presided over my life. There were times when I thought of him as some kind of father to replace the one I never knew. George's visit to Sarratt gave back the dangerous edge to my memory. And now that I have the leisure to remember, that's what I mean to do for you, so that you can share my voyage and ask yourself the same questions.

2

"There are some people," Smiley declared comfortably, favouring with his merry smile the pretty girl from Trinity Oxford whom I had thoughtfully placed across the table from him, "who, when their past is threatened, get frightened of losing everything they thought they had, and perhaps everything they thought they were as well. Now I don't feel that one bit. The purpose of *my* life was to end the time I lived in. So if my past were still around today, you could say I'd faded. But it's not around. We won. Not that the victory matters a damn. And perhaps we didn't win anyway. Perhaps they just lost. Or perhaps, without the bonds of ideological conflict to restrain us any more, our troubles are just beginning. Never mind. What matters is that a long war is over. What matters is the hope."

Removing his spectacles from his ears, he fumbled distractedly with his shirt front, looking for I could not imagine what, until I realised that it was the fat end of the necktie on which he was accustomed to polish his lenses. But an awkwardly assembled black bow tie provides no such conveniences, so he used the silk handkerchief from his pocket instead.

"If I regret anything at all, it's the way we wasted our time and skills. All the false alleys, and bogus friends, the misapplication of our energies. All the delusions we had about who we were." He replaced his spectacles and, as I fancied, turned his smile upon myself. And suddenly I felt like one of my own students. It was the sixties again. I was a fledgling spy, and George Smiley—tolerant, patient, clever George—was observing my first attempts at flight.

We were fine fellows in those days, and the days seemed longer. Probably no finer than my students today, but our patriotic vision was less clouded. By the end of my new-entry course I was ready to save the world if I had to spy on it from end to end. We were ten in my intake and after a couple of years of training—at the Sarratt Nursery, in the glens of Argyll and battle camps of Wiltshire—we waited for our first operational postings like thoroughbreds pining for the chase.

We too in our way had come to maturity at a great moment in history, even if it was the reverse of this one. Stagnation and hostility stared at us from every corner of the globe. The Red Peril was everywhere, not least on our own sacred hearth. The Berlin Wall had been up two years and by the looks of it would stay up for another two hundred. The Middle East was a volcano, just as it is now, except that in those days Nasser was our chosen British hate object, not least because he was giving Arabs back their dignity and playing hookey with the Russians into the bargain. In Cyprus, Africa and South East Asia the lesser breeds without the law were rising against their old colonial masters. And if we few brave British occasionally felt our power diminished by this—well, there was always Cousin America to cut us back into the world's game.

As secret heroes in the making, therefore, we had everything we needed: a righteous cause, an evil enemy, an indulgent ally, a seething world, women to cheer us, but only from the touchline, and best of all the Great Tradition to inherit, for the Circus in those days was still basking in its wartime glory. Almost all our leading men had earned their spurs by spying on the Germans. All of them, when questioned at our earnest, off-the-record seminars, agreed that when it came to protecting mankind against its own excesses, World Communism was an even darker menace than the Hun.

"You gentlemen have inherited a dangerous planet," Jack Arthur Lumley, our fabled Head of Training, liked to tell us. "And if you want my personal opinion, you're bloody lucky."

Oh, we wanted his opinion all right! Jack Arthur was a derring-do man. He had spent three years dropping in and out of Nazi-occupied Europe as if he were a regular house-guest. He had blown up bridges single-handed. He had been caught and escaped and caught again, no one knew how many times. He had killed men with his bare fingers, losing a couple in the fray, and when the Cold War came along to replace the hot one, Jack hardly noticed the difference. At the age of fifty-five he could still shoot you a grin on a man-sized target with a 9-millimetre Browning at twenty paces, pick your door lock with a paper clip, booby-trap a lavatory chain in thirty seconds or pin you helpless to the gym-mat in one throw. Jack Arthur had despatched us by parachute from Stirling bombers and landed us in rubber boats on Cornish beaches and drunk us under the table on mess nights. If Jack Arthur said it was a dangerous planet, we believed him to the hilt!

But it made the waiting all the harder. If I hadn't had Ben Arno Cavendish to share it with, it would have been harder still. There are only so many attachments you can serve around Head Office before your enthusiasm turns to gall.

Ben and I had been born under the same star. We were the same age, the same schooling, the same build, and within an inch of the same height. Trust the Circus to throw us together—we told each other excitedly; they probably knew it all along! We both had foreign mothers, though his was dead—the Arno came from his German side—and were both, perhaps by way of compensation, determinedly of the English extrovert classes—athletic, hedonistic, public-school, male, born to administer if not to rule. Though, as I look at the group photographs of our year, I see that Ben made a rather better job of the part than I did, for he possessed an air of maturity that in those days eluded me—he had the widow's peak and the confirmed jaw, a man superior to his youthfulness.

Which, for all I knew, was why Ben got the coveted Berlin job instead of me, running flesh-and-blood agents inside East Germany, while I was once more put on standby.

"We're lending you to the watchers for a couple of weeks, young Ned," said Personnel, with an avuncular complacency I was beginning to resent. "Be good experience for you, and they can do with a spare pair of hands. Plenty of cloak-and-dagger stuff. You like that."

Anything for a change, I thought, putting a brave face on it. For the past month I had bent my ingenuity to sabotaging the World Peace Conference in—let's say—Belgrade, from a dark desk on the Third Floor. Under the instruction of a slow-spoken superior who lunched for hours on end in the Senior Officers' Bar, I had enthusiastically re-routed delegates' trains, blocked their hotel plumbing and made anonymous bomb threats to their conference ball. For the month before that, I had crouched bravely in a stinking cellar next to the Egyptian Embassy at six every morning, waiting for a venal charlady to bring me, in exchange for a five-pound note, the contents of the Ambassadorial wastepaper basket from the previous day. By such modest standards, a couple of weeks riding around with the world's best watchers sounded like a free holiday.

"They're assigning you to Operation Fat Boy," Personnel said, and gave me the address of a safe house off Green Street in the

West End. I heard the sound of Ping-Pong as I walked in, and a cracked gramophone record playing Gracie Fields. My heart sank, and once again I sent a prayer of envy to Ben Cavendish and his heroic agents in Berlin, the spy's eternal city. Monty Arbuck, our section leader, briefed us the same evening.

Let me apologise for myself in advance. I knew very little of other ranks in those days. I was of the officer caste—literally for I had served with the Royal Navy—and found it perfectly natural that I had been born into the upper end of the social system. The Circus is nothing if not a little mirror of the England it protects, so it seemed equally right to me that our watchers and allied trades, such as burglars and eavesdroppers, should be drawn from the artisan community. You cannot follow a man for long in a bowler hat. A honed BBC voice is no passport to unobtrusiveness once you are outside London's golden mile, least of all if you are posing as a street hawker or a window cleaner or a post-office engineer. So you should see me, at best, as a callow young midshipman seated among his more experienced and less privileged shipmates. And you should see Monty not as he was, but as I saw him that evening, as a taut-minded gamekeeper with a chip on his shoulder. We were ten, including Monty: three teams of three, therefore, with a woman to each so that we could cover ladies' lavatories. That was the principle. And Monty our controller.

"Good evening, College," he said, placing himself before a blackboard and talking straight to me. "Always nice to have a touch of quality to raise the tone, I say."

Laughter all round, loudest from myself, a good sport to his men.

"Target for tomorrow, College, is His Right Royal Sovereign Highness Fat Boy, otherwise known as—"

Turning to the blackboard, Monty helped himself to a piece of chalk and laboriously scratched up a long Arab name.

"And the nature of our mission, College, is PR," he resumed. "I trust you know what PR is, do you? I have no doubt they teach you that at the spies' Eton?"

"Public Relations," I said, surprised to occasion so much merriment. For alas it turned out that in the watchers' vernacular the initials stood for Protect and Report, and that our task for tomorrow, and for as long as our royal visitor chose to remain our charge, was to ensure that no harm came to him, and to report to Head Office on his activities, whether social or commercial.

"College, you're with Paul and Nancy," Monty told me, when he had provided us with the rest of our operational intelligence. "You'll be number three in the section, College, and you'll kindly do *exactly* as you are told, irregardless."

But here I prefer to give you the background to Fat Boy's case not in Monty's words but in my own, and with the benefit of twenty-five years of hindsight. Even today, I can blush to think who I thought I was, and how I must have appeared to the likes of Monty, Paul and Nancy.

Understand first that licensed arms dealers in Britain regard themselves as some kind of rough-edged élite—did then, do now—and that they enjoy quite disproportionate privileges at the hands of the police, the bureaucracy and the intelligence services. For reasons I have never understood, their grisly trade puts them in a relationship of confidence with these bodies. Perhaps it's the illusion of reality they impart, of guns as the earthy truth of life and death. Perhaps, in the tethered minds of our officials, their wares suggest the same authority that is exerted by those who use them. I don't know. But I've seen enough of the street side of life in the years between to know that more men are in love with war than ever get a chance to fight one, and that more guns are bought to satisfy this love than for a pardonable purpose.

Understand also that Fat Boy was a most valued customer of this industry. And that our task of Protecting and Reporting was only one small part of a far larger undertaking; namely, the care and cultivation of a so-called friendly Arab state. By which was meant, and is meant to this day, currying favour, suborning and flattering its princelings with our English ways, wheedling favourable concessions in order to satisfy our oil addiction—and, along the way, selling enough British weaponry to keep the Satanic mills of Birmingham turning day and night. Which may have accounted for Monty's rooted distaste for our task. I like to think so anyway. Old watchers are famous for their moralising—and with reason. First they watch, later they think. Monty had reached the thinking stage.

As to Fat Boy, his credentials for this treatment were impeccable. He was the wastrel brother of the ruler of an oil-rich sheikdom. He was capricious, and prone to forget what he had bought before. And he arrived as billed, in the ruler's Boeing jet, at a military airport near London specially cleared for him, to have himself a little fun and do a little shopping—which we understood would include such fripperies as a couple of armoured Rolls-Royces for himself, half the trinkets at Cartier's for his women friends around the globe, a hundred or so of our not quite latest ground-to-air missile launchers, and a squadron or two of our not quite latest combat fighters for his royal brother. Not forgetting a succulent British government contract for spares, services and training which would keep the Royal Air Force and the arms manufacturers in clover for years to come. —Oh, and oil. We would have oil to burn. Naturally.

His retinue, apart from private secretaries, astrologers, flatterers, nannies, children and two tutors, comprised a personal doctor and three bodyguards.

Lastly there was Fat Boy's wife, and her codename is irrelevant because from Day One Monty's watchers dubbed her "the Panda" on account of the dark circles round her eyes when she was unveiled, and her wistful and solitary deportment, which gave the air of an endangered species. Fat Boy had a string of wives, but the Panda, though the oldest, was the most favoured, and perhaps the most tolerant of her husband's pleasures around town, for he liked nightclubs and he liked to gamble—tastes for which my fellow watchers cordially loathed him before he arrived, since it was known of him that he seldom went to bed before six in the morning, and never without losing about twenty times their combined annual salaries.

The party had rooms at a grand West End hotel, on two floors linked by a specially installed lift. Fat Boy, like many forty-year-old voluptuaries, was worried about his heart. He was also worried about microphones, and liked to use the lift as his safe room. So the Circus listeners had thoughtfully provided a microphone in the lift for him as well, which was where they reckoned to pick up their tidbits about the latest palace intrigues, or any unforeseen threat to Fat Boy's military shopping list.

And everything was running smoothly until Day Three, when one small unknown Arab man in a black overcoat with velvet collars appeared silently on our horizon. Or more accurately, in the ladies' lingerie department of a great Knightsbridge department store, where the Panda and her attendants were picking their way through a stack of frilly white undergarments spread over the glass counter. For the Panda also had her spies. And word had reached her that, on the day before, the Fat Boy himself had brooded fondly over the same articles, and even ordered a few dozen to be sent to an address in Paris where a favoured lady friend constantly awaited him in subsidised luxury.

* * *

Day Three, I repeat, and the morale of our three-strong unit under strain. Paul was Paul Skordeno, an inward man with a pocked complexion and a talent for ferocious invective. Nancy told me he was under a cloud, but wouldn't say what for.

"He *hit* a girl, Ned," she said, but I think now that she meant more than merely hit.

Nancy herself was all of five feet tall and in appearance a kind of licensed bag-lady. For her standard, as she called it, she wore lisle stockings and sensible rubber-soled walking shoes, which she seldom changed. What more she needed—scarves, raincoats, woollen hats of different colours—she took in a plastic carrier.

On surveillance duty our section worked eight-hour shifts always in the same formation, Nancy and Paul playing forward, young Ned trailing along behind as sweep. When I asked Skordeno whether we could vary the formation, he told me to get used to what I'd got. On our first day we had followed Fat Boy to Sandhurst, where a lunch had been organised in his honour. The three of us ate egg-and-chips in a café close to the main gates while Skordeno railed first against the Arabs, then against the Western exploitation of them, then to my distress against the Fifth Floor, whom he described as Fascist golfers.

"You a Freemason, College?"

I assured him I was not.

"Well, you'd best hurry up and join then, hadn't you? Haven't you noticed the saucy way Personnel shakes your hand? You'll never get to Berlin if you're not a Mason, College."

Day Two had been spent hanging around Mount Street while Fat Boy had himself measured for a pair of Purdy shotguns, first precariously brandishing a try-gun round the premises, then throwing a tantrum when he discovered he would have to wait two years before they were ready. Paul ordered me twice into the shop while this scene was unfolding, and seemed pleased when

I told him the staff were becoming suspicious of my frivolous enquiries.

"I'd have thought it was your kind of place," he said, with his skull-like grin. "Huntin', shootin' and fishin'—they like that on the Fifth Floor, College."

The same night had found us sitting three up in a van outside a shuttered whorehouse in South Audley Street, and Head Office in a state of near panic. Fat Boy had only been holed up there two hours when he had telephoned the hotel and ordered his personal doctor to attend immediately. His heart! we thought in alarm. Should we go in? While Head Office dithered, we entertained visions of our quarry dead of a heart attack in the arms of some over-conscientious whore before he had signed the cheque for his obsolete fighter planes. It was not till four o'clock that the listeners laid our fears to rest. Fat Boy had been afflicted by a spell of impotence, they explained, and his doctor had been summoned to inject an aphrodisiac into the royal rump. We returned home at five, Skordeno drunk with anger, but all of us consoled by the knowledge that Fat Boy was due in Luton at midday to attend a grand demonstration of the nearly latest British tank, and we could count on a day's rest. But our relief was premature.

"The Panda wants to buy herself some pretties," Monty announced to us benignly on our arrival in Green Street. "Your lot's on. Sorry about that, College."

Which brings us to the lingerie department of the great Knightsbridge store, and to my moment of glory. Ben, I was thinking; Ben, I would trade one day of yours for five of mine. Then suddenly I wasn't thinking of Ben any more and I had ceased to envy him. I had drawn back into the privacy of a doorway and was speaking into the mouthpiece of the cumbersome radio set, which in those days was the best there was. I had selected the channel which gave me a direct line to base. It was the one Skordeno had told me not to use.

"The Panda's got a monkey on her back," I informed Monty in my calmest voice, using the approved watchers' jargon to describe a mysterious follower. "Five five, black curly hair, heavy moustache, aged forty, black overcoat, rubber-soled black shoes, Arab appearance. He was at the airport when Fat Boy's plane came in. I remember him. It's the same man."

"Stay on him" came Monty's laconic reply. "Paul and Nancy stick with the Panda, you stick with the monkey. Which floor?"

"One."

"Stay on him wherever he goes, keep talking to me."

"He could be carrying," I said as my eyes again fixed surreptitiously on the subject of my call.

"You mean he's pregnant?"

I didn't think that very funny.

Let me set the scene precisely, for it was more complicated than you may suppose. Our trio was not alone in following the Panda's retinue on its snail-paced shopping expedition. Wealthy Arab princesses do not arrive unannounced at great Knightsbridge stores. In addition to a pair of floorwalkers in black jackets and striped trousers, two very obvious house detectives had placed themselves at either archway with their feet apart and their hands curled at their sides, ready at any moment to grapple with whirling dervishes. As if that were not enough, Scotland Yard had that morning taken upon itself to provide its own brand of protection in the form of an iron-faced man in a belted raincoat who insisted on placing himself beside the Panda and glowering at anyone who came near. And finally, you must see Paul and Nancy in their Sunday best, their backs turned to everyone while they affected to study trays of negligés, and watched our quarry in the mirrors.

And all of this again, you understand, set in the hushed and scented privacy of the harem; in a world of flimsy undergarments, deep-pile carpets and languorous half-naked dummies—

not to mention those kindly grey-haired lady attendants in black crêpe who, at a certain age, are deemed to have achieved a sufficiently unthreatening demeanour to reside over shrines of female intimacy.

Other men, I noticed, preferred not to enter the lingerie department at all, or hurried through it with averted gaze. My instinct would have been the same, had it not been for my recognition of this melancholy little man with his black moustache and passionate brown eyes, who unswervingly trailed the Panda's retinue at fifteen paces. If Monty had not appointed me sweep, I might not have seen him at all—or not then. But it was quickly clear that both he and I, by virtue of our different trades, were obliged to keep the same distance from our target—I with nonchalance, he with a kind of intense and mystical dependence. For his gaze never wavered from her. Even when he was unsighted by a pillar or a customer, he still contrived to crane his dark head this way or that until he had locked her once more in his zealous and—I was now convinced—fanatical gaze.

I had first sensed this fervour in him when I had spotted him in the arrivals hall at the airport, pressing himself on tiptoe against the long window as he wriggled to get a better view of the royal couple's approach. I had made nothing so special of him then. I was subjecting everyone to the same critical examination. He had seemed to be just another of the gaggle of diplomats, retainers and hangers-on who formed the royal welcome party. Nevertheless his intensity had struck a chord in me: So this is the Middle East, I had mused as I watched him squeeze his hollowed face against the glass. These are the heathen passions my Service must contain if we are to drive our cars and heat our houses and sell our weaponry in peace.

The monkey had taken a couple of steps forward and was peering at a cabinet of ribbons. His gait—exactly like that of his namesake—was wide but stealthy; he seemed to move entirely from the knees, in conspiratorial strides. I selected a display of garters next to him and peered into it while I again furtively examined him for tell-tale bulges round the waist and armpits. His black overcoat was of the classic gunman's cape: voluminous and without a belt, the kind of coat that covers effortlessly a long-barrelled pistol fitted with a suppressor, or a semi-automatic slung beneath the arm.

I studied his hands, my own nervously prickling. His left hung loosely at his side, but his right, which looked the stronger, kept travelling towards his chest and withholding, as if he were preparing himself to pluck up courage for the final act.

A right-handed cross draw, I thought; most likely to the armpit. Our weapons trainers had taught us all the combinations.

And his eyes—those dark, slow-burning, soulful zealot's eyes—even in profile they seemed fixed upon the afterlife. Had he sworn vengeance on her? On her household? Had fanatical mullahs promised him a place in Heaven if he did the deed? My knowledge of Islam was scant, and what there was of it was drawn from a couple of background lectures and the novels of P. C. Wren. Yet it was enough to warn me that I was in the presence of a desperate fanatic who counted his own life cheap.

As to myself, alas, I was unarmed. It was a sore point with me. Watchers would never dream of carrying weapons on normal duty, but covert protection work is a different type of watching, and Paul Skordeno had been allocated a sidearm from Monty's safe.

"One's enough, College," Monty had told me, with his old man's smile. "We don't want you starting World War Three, now do we?"

All that was left to me, therefore, as I rose and softly followed him again, was to select in advance one of the blows we had been taught to master in our silent-killing classes. Should I count on attacking him from behind—with a rabbit punch?—with a double simultaneous blow over the ears? Either method could kill him instantly, whereas a live one can still be questioned. Then would I do better breaking his right arm first, hoping to take him with his own weapon? Yet if I let him draw, might I myself not go down in a hail of bullets from the several bodyguards around the room?

She had seen him!

The Panda had looked straight into the eyes of the monkey, and the monkey had returned her stare!

Had she recognised him? I was certain she had. But had she recognised his purpose? And was she, perhaps, in some strange turn of Oriental fatalism, preparing herself for death? The lurid possibilities went racing through my mind as I continued to observe their mysterious exchange. Their eyes met, the Panda froze in mid-gesture. Her jewelled, crabby little hands, plundering the clothing on the counter, kept still—and then, as if to his command, slipped passively to her sides. After which she stood motionless, without will, without even the strength to detach herself from his penetrating stare.

At last, with a forlorn and strangely humble air, she turned away from him, murmured something to her lady companions and, holding out her hand to the counter, released whatever frilly thing she was still clutching in it. She was wearing brown that day—if she had been a man, I would be tempted to say a Franciscan habit—with wide sleeves longer than her arms, and a brown headband bound tightly across her brow.

I saw her sigh, then slowly and, I was sure, resignedly, she led her entourage towards the archway. After her went her personal bodyguard; after him the Scotland Yard policeman. Then came the ladies of her train, followed by the floorwalkers. And finally came Paul and Nancy, who, with a show of indecision, had torn themselves away from their study of the negligés and were sauntering like any shoppers in the party's wake. Paul, who had surely overheard my conversations with Monty, vouchsafed me not the smallest glance. Nancy, who prided herself on her amateur dramatics, was pretending to pick a marital dispute with him. I tried to see whether Paul had unbuttoned his jacket, for he too favoured the cross draw. But his broad back was turned away from me.

"All right, College, show me," said Money brightly into my left ear, appearing beside me as if by magic. How long had he been there? I had no idea. It was past midday and our time for standing down, but this was no moment to change the guard. The monkey was not five yards from us, stepping lightly but determinedly after the Panda.

"We can take him at the stairs," I murmured.

"Speak louder," Monty advised me, in the same unabashed voice. "Speak normally, no one listens to you. Mutter, mutter out of the corner of your mouth, they think you've come to rob the till."

Since we were on the first floor, the Panda's party was sure to take the lift, whether they went up or down. Beside the lift stood a pair of swing doors opening on to what in those days was a stone emergency staircase, rather dank and insanitary, with linoleum treads. My plan, which I outlined to Monty in staccato sentences as we followed the monkey towards the archway, was simplicity itself. As the party approached the lift, Monty and I would close on him from either side, grab an arm each and sweep him into the staircase. We would subdue him with a blow to the groin, remove his weapon, then spirit him to Green Street where we would invite him to make a voluntary statement. In training exercises we had done such things a dozen times—once, to our embarrassment, to an innocent bank clerk who was hurrying home to his wife and family, and whom we had mistaken for a member of the training staff.

But if Monty heard me, to my frustration he gave no sign of

having done so. He was watching the floorwalkers clear a path through the crowd to the lift so that the Panda's party could ride in privacy. And he was smiling like any casual commoner who stumbles on a glimpse of royalty.

"She's going down," he declared with satisfaction. "Pound to a penny it's the costume jewellery she's after. You'd think the Gulfies wouldn't bother with the artificial stuff, but they can't get enough of it; they think it's got to be a bargain. Come on, son. This is fun. Let's go and take a look."

I like to think that even in my perplexity I recognised the excellence of Monty's tradecraft. The Panda's exotic entourage, mostly in Arab dress, was arousing lively curiosity among the shoppers. Monty was just another punter, enjoying the spectacle. And yes, he was right again, their destination was the costume jewellery department, as the monkey also had divined, for as we emerged from our lift the monkey scampered ahead of the party to take up a favoured place alongside the glittering displays, his left shoulder nearest to the wall, exactly as required of a right-handed gunman who draws across his chest.

Yet, far from choosing a strategic position from which to return fire, Monty merely wandered after him, and, having placed himself next to him, beckoned me to join them, and in such a way that I had no alternative but to leave Monty, not the monkey, at the centre of our trio.

"This is why I always come to Knightsbridge, son," Monty was explaining, loudly enough for half the floor to hear. "You never know who you're going to meet. I brought your mother last time—*you* remember—we'd gone to the Harrods Food Hall. I thought: '*Hullo,* I know you, you're Rex Harrison.' I could have held out my hand and touched him but I didn't. It's the crossroads of the world, Knightsbridge is, don't you agree, sir?"— lifting his hat to the monkey, who smiled wanly in return. "Now I wonder where this lot would be from. Arabs, by the look of them, with the wealth of Solomon at their fingertips. And they don't even pay taxes, I dare say. Not royalty, well they wouldn't have to. There isn't a royal household in the world pays taxes to itself, it wouldn't be logical. See the big policeman there, son? He'll be Special Branch, you can tell by his stupid scowl."

The Panda's party meanwhile was distributing itself among the illuminated glass counters while the Panda, in barely concealed agitation, was requiring that the trays be taken out for her inspection. And soon, as in the lingerie department, she was picking out one object after another, turning it critically under the inspection light, then setting it down and taking up another. And yet again, as she continued to appraise and relinquish each piece in turn, I saw her worried gaze slip towards us, first to the monkey, then to myself, as if she had seen in me her one hope of protection.

Yet Monty, when I glanced at him for confirmation, was still smiling.

"That's exactly what happened in the lingerie department," I whispered, forgetting his instruction to speak normally.

But Monty continued his noisy monologue. "But underneath, son—I always say this—underneath, royals or not, they're the same as what we are, through and through. We're all born naked, we're all on our way to the grave. Your wealth is your health, better to be rich in friends than money, I say. We've all got the same appetites, the same little weaknesses and naughty ways." And on he ran, as if in deliberate contrast to my extreme alertness.

She had ordered up more trays. The counter was covered with sumptuous paste tiaras, bracelets and rings. Selecting a three-string necklace of imitation rubies, she held it to her throat, then took up a hand mirror to admire herself.

And was it my imagination? It was not! She was using the mirror to observe the monkey and ourselves! First one dark eye, then the other fixed upon us; then the two of them together, warning us, imploring us, before she set the mirror down again and turned her back to us, and swept as if in anger along the edge of the glass counter, where a fresh display awaited her.

At the same moment, the monkey took a step forward and I saw his hand rise to the opening of his overcoat. Throwing caution aside, I too stepped forward, my right arm drawn back, the fingers of my right hand flexed, palm parallel to the ground in the approved Sarratt manner. I had decided on an elbow to the heart, followed by a side-of-hand to the upper lip, to the point where the nose cartilage joins the top half of the jaw. A complicated network of nerves has its meeting point here, and a well-aimed blow can immobilise the victim for some while. The monkey was opening his mouth and breathing in. I anticipated a cry to Allah, or perhaps the screamed slogan of some fundamentalist sect—though I am no longer sure how much we knew or cared in those days about fundamentalist Arabs. I at once determined to scream myself, not only in order to confuse him, but because a deep breath would put more oxygen into my bloodstream and so increase my striking power. I was actually drawing this breath when I felt Monty's hand lock like an iron ring round my wrist and, with unpredicted power, immobilise me as he drew me back to him.

"Now don't do that, son, this gentleman was before you," he said in a matter-of-fact voice. "He's got a little confidential business to transact, haven't you, sir?"

He had indeed. And Monty's grasp did not release me until I had observed the nature of it. The monkey was speaking. Not to the Panda, not to her retinue, but to the two floorwalkers in striped trousers who were inclining their heads to listen to him, at first condescendingly, then with startled interest as their gaze switched to the Panda.

"Alas, gentlemen, Her Royal Highness prefers to make her purchases informally, you see," he was saying. "Without the inconvenience of a wrapping or an invoice, let us put it that way. It is her time of life. Three and four years ago, she was a most expert bargainer, you know. Oh yes. She would negotiate a most competitive discount for everything she wished to buy. But today, at her time of life, she is taking matters most literally into her own hands, you see. Or should I say into her sleeve, oh dear? I am therefore charged by His Royal Highness to make a most bountiful settlement for all such informal purchases, on the very clear understanding that no breath of publicity reaches the public ear, gentlemen, whether in the written or the spoken word, if you understand me."

Then from his pocket he drew not, alas, a deadly Walther automatic, not a Heckler & Koch sub-machine gun, not even one of our beloved standard Browning 9-millimetres, but a tooled Moroccan leather wallet stuffed with his master's banknotes in a variety of denominations.

"I counted, I believe, three fine rings, sir, one in artificial emerald, two in paste diamond, also a fine artificial ruby necklace, gentlemen, three strings. It is the wish of His Royal Highness that our settlement should take generous account of any inconvenience suffered by your most excellent staff, you see. Also commission to your good selves, on the understanding already stated regarding publicity."

Monty's grip on me had at last relaxed, and as we walked towards the hall I dared to glance at him, and saw to my relief that his expression, though thoughtful, was surprisingly gentle.

"That's the trouble in our job, Ned," he explained contentedly, using my Christian name for the first time. "Life's looking one way, we're looking the other. I like an honest-to-God enemy myself sometimes, I don't mind admitting. Take a lot of finding, though, don't they? Too many nice blokes about."

"Now do please remember," Smiley piously exhorted his young audience, in much the tone he might have selected if he had been asking them to put their offerings in the collection box as they were leaving, "that the privately educated Englishman—and Englishwoman, if you will allow me—is the greatest dissembler on earth." He waited for the laughter to subside. "Was, is now and ever shall be for as long as our disgraceful school system remains intact. Nobody will charm you so glibly, disguise his feelings from you better, cover his tracks more skilfully or find it harder to confess to you that he's been a damned fool. Nobody acts braver when he's frightened stiff, or happier when he's miserable; nobody can flatter you better when he hates you than your extrovert Englishman or woman of the supposedly privileged classes. He can have a Force Twelve nervous breakdown while he stands next to you in the bus queue, and you may be his best friend, but you'll never be the wiser. Which is why some of our best officers turn out to be our worst. And our worst, our best. And why the most difficult agent you will ever have to run is yourself."

In his own mind, I had no doubt, Smiley was talking about the greatest deceiver of us all, Bill Haydon. But for me, he was talking about Ben—and yes, though it's harder to admit, about the young Ned, and perhaps the old one too.

It was the afternoon of the day I had failed to immolate the Panda's bodyguard. Tired and dispirited, I arrived at my flat in Battersea to find the door on the latch and two men in grey suits sifting through the papers in my desk.

They barely looked at me as I burst in. The nearer of them was Personnel and the second an owlish, ageless, tubby man in circular spectacles who eyed me with a sort of baleful commiseration.

"When did you last hear from your friend Cavendish?" said Personnel, scarcely glancing at me before returning to my papers.

"He *is* your friend, isn't he?" said the owlish man unhappily while I struggled to collect myself. "Ben? Arno? Which do you call him?"

"Yes. He is. Ben is. What is this?"

"So when did you last hear from him?" Personnel repeated, shoving aside a pile of letters from my girlfriend of the time. "Does he ring you? How do you keep in touch?"

"I had a postcard from him a week ago. Why?"

"Where is it?"

"I don't know. I destroyed it. If it isn't in the desk. Will you kindly tell me what's going on?"

"Destroyed it?"

"Threw it away."

"*Destroy* sounds deliberate, doesn't it? What did it look like?" Personnel said, pulling out another drawer. "Stay where you are."

"It had a picture of a girl on one side and a couple of lines from Ben on the other. What does it matter what it had on it? Please get out of here."

"Saying?"

"Nothing. It said, this is my latest acquisition. 'Dear Ned, this is my new catch, so glad you're not here. Love, Ben.' Now get out!"

"What did he mean by that?"—pulling out another drawer.

"Glad I wouldn't cut him out with the girl, I suppose. It was a joke."

"Do you usually cut him out with his women?"

"We've no women in common. We never have had."

"What *do* you have in common?"

"Friendship," I said angrily. "What the hell are you looking for actually? I think you'd better leave at once. Both of you."

"I can't find it," Personnel complained to his fat companion as he tossed aside another wad of my private letters. "No postcard of any kind. You're not lying, are you, Ned?"

The owlish man had not taken his eyes off me. He continued to regard me with a wretched empathy, as if to say it comes to all of us and there's nothing we can do. "How was the postcard *delivered,* Ned?" he asked. His voice, like his demeanour, was tentative and regretful.

"By post, how else?" I replied rudely.

"The open mail, you mean?" the owlish man suggested sadly. "Not by Service bag, for instance?"

"By Forces mail," I replied. "Field Post Office. Posted Berlin with a British stamp on it. Delivered by the local postman."

"Do you remember the Field Post Office *number,* by any chance, Ned?" the owlish man enquired with enormous diffidence. "On the postmark, I mean?"

"It was the ordinary Berlin number, I imagine," I retorted, struggling to keep up my indignation in the face of someone so exquisitely deferential. "Forty, I think. Why's it so important? I've had enough of this."

"But you'd say it was definitely posted in Berlin anyway? I

mean, that was your impression at the time? So far as you recall it now? The Berlin number—you're sure?"

"It looked exactly like the others he'd sent me. I didn't submit it to a minute examination," I said, my anger rising again as I saw Personnel yank yet another drawer from my desk and tip out its contents.

"A *pin-up* sort of girl, Ned?" the owlish man enquired, with a hangdog smile, which was evidently intended to apologise for Personnel as well as for himself.

"A nude, yes. A tart, I assume, looking over her bare backside. That's why. I threw it away. Because of my cleaning lady."

"Oh, so you remember now!" Personnel cried, swinging round to face me. "'I threw it away.' Pity you didn't bloody say so at once!"

"Oh, I don't know, Rex," said the owlish man placatingly. "Ned was very confused when he came in. Who wouldn't be?" His worried gaze settled once more upon myself. "You're doing a stint with the watchers, isn't that right? Monty says you're rather good. Was she in colour, by the way? Your nude?"

"Yes."

"Did he always send postcards, or sometimes letters?"

"Only postcards."

"How many?"

"Three or four since he's been there."

"Always in colour?"

"I don't remember. Probably. Yes."

"And always of girls?"

"I think so."

"Oh, but you remember, really. Of course you do. And always naked too, I expect?"

"Yes."

"Where are the others?"

"I must have thrown them away too."

"Because of your cleaning lady?"

"Yes."

"To protect her sensitivities?"

"Yes!"

The owlish man took his time to consider this. "So the dirty postcards—forgive me, I don't mean that offensively, really not—they were a sort of running joke between you?"

"On his side, yes."

"But you didn't send him any in return? Please say if you did. Don't be embarrassed. There isn't time."

"I'm not embarrassed! I didn't send him any. Yes, they were a running joke. And they were getting increasingly *risqué*. If you want to know, I was becoming slightly bored with seeing them laid out on the hall table for my collection. So was Mr. Simpson. He's the landlord. He suggested I write to Ben and tell him to stop sending them. He said it was getting the house a bad name. Now will you please, one of you, tell me what the hell's going on?"

This time Personnel replied. "Well, that's what we thought you might be able to tell *us,*" he said in a mournful voice. "Ben Cavendish has disappeared. So have his agents, in a manner of speaking. A couple of them are featured in this morning's *Neues Deutschland*. British spy ring caught red-handed. The London evening papers are running the story in their late editions. He hasn't been seen for three days. This is Mr. Smiley. He wants to talk to you. You're to tell him whatever you know. And that means anything. I'll see you later."

I must have lost my bearings for a moment, because when I saw Smiley again he was standing at the centre of my carpet, gloomily peering round him at the havoc he and Personnel had wreaked.

"I've a house across the river in Bywater Street," he confessed, as if it were a great burden to him. "Perhaps we ought to pop round there, if it's all the same to you. It's not *terribly* tidy, but it is better than this."

We drove there in Smiley's humble little Austin, so slowly you would have supposed he was conveying an invalid, which was perhaps how he regarded me. It was dusk. The white lanterns of Albert Bridge floated at us like waterborne coachlights. Ben, I thought desperately, what have we done? Ben, what have they done to you?

Bywater Street was jammed, so we parked in a mews. Parking for Smiley was as complicated as docking a liner, but he managed it and we walked back. I remember how impossible it was to keep alongside him, how his thrusting roundarm waddle somehow ignored my existence. I remember how he steeled himself to turn the key of his own front door, and his alertness as he stepped into the hall. As if home were a dangerous place for him, as I know now that it was. There was a couple of days' milk in the hall and a half-eaten plate of chop and peas in the drawing room. The turntable of a gramophone was silently revolving. It didn't take a genius to surmise that he had been called out in a hurry—presumably by Personnel yesterday evening—while he was tucking into his chop and listening to a spot of music.

He wandered off to the kitchen in search of soda for our whiskies. I followed him. There was something about Smiley that made you responsible for his solitude. Open tins of food lay about and the sink was crammed with dirty plates. While he mixed our whiskies, I started clearing up, so he fished a teacloth from the back of the door and set to work drying and putting away.

"You and Ben were considerable partners, weren't you?" he asked.

"We shared a cabin at Sarratt, yes."

"So that's what—kitchen, couple of bedrooms, bathroom?"

"No kitchen."

"But you were twinned for your training course as well?"

"For the last year of it. You choose an oppo and learn to work to each other."

"Choose? Or have chosen for you?"

"Choose first, then they approve or break you up."

"And after that, you're landed with each other for better for worse?"

"Pretty much, yes."

"For the whole of the last year? For half the course, in fact? Day and night, as it were? A total marriage?"

I could not understand why he was pressing me about things he must have known.

"And you do everything together?" he continued. "Forgive me but it's some time since I was trained. Written, practical, physical, you mess together, share a cabin—a whole life, in fact."

"We do the syndicate work together, and the strong-arm stuff. That's automatic. It begins with being roughly the same weight and physical aptitude." Despite the disturbing tendency of his questions, I was beginning to feel a great need to talk to him. "Then the rest sort of follows naturally."

"Ah."

"Sometimes they split us up—say, for a special exercise if they think one person is relying too much on his oppo. But as long as it's fifty-fifty they're happy for you to keep together."

"And you won everything," Smiley suggested approvingly, helping himself to another wet plate. "You were the best pair. You and Ben."

"It was just that Ben was the best student," I said. "Whoever had him would have won."

"Yes, of course. Well, we all know people like that. Did you know each other before you joined the Service?"

"No. But we'd run parallel. We were at the same school, different houses. We were at Oxford, different colleges. We both read languages but we still never met. He did a short service commission in the army, I did the same in the navy. It took the Circus to bring us together."

Taking up a delicate bone-china cup, he peered doubtfully into it, as if searching for something I had missed. "Would *you* have sent Ben to Berlin?"

"Yes, of course I would. Why not?"

"Well, why?"

"He's got perfect German from his mother. He's bright. Resourceful. People do what he wants them to do. His father had this terrific war."

"So did your mother, as I remember." He was referring to my mother's work with the Dutch Resistance. "What did *he* do—Ben's father, I mean?" he continued, as if he really didn't know.

"He broke codes," I said, with Ben's pride. "He was a wrangler. A mathematician. A genius, apparently. He helped organise the double-cross system against the Germans—recruit their agents and play them back. My mother was very small beer by comparison."

"And Ben was impressed by that?"

"Who wouldn't be?"

"He talked of it, I mean," Smiley insisted. "Often? It was a big matter for him. You had that impression?"

"He just said it was something he had to live up to. He said it was the up-side of having a German mother."

"Oh dear," said Smiley unhappily. "Poor man. And those were his words? You're not embellishing?"

"Of course I'm not! He said that with a background like his, in England you had to run twice as fast as everyone else, just to keep up."

Smiley seemed genuinely upset. "Oh dear," he said again. "How unkind. And do you think he has the stamina, would you say?"

He had once more stopped me short. At our age, we really didn't think of stamina as being limited.

"What for?" I asked.

"Oh, I don't know. What kind of stamina would one need for running twice as fast as everyone else in Berlin? A double ration of nerves, I suppose—always a strain. A doubly good head for alcohol—*and* where women are concerned—never easy."

"I'm sure he's got whatever it takes," I said loyally.

Smiley hung his teacloth on a bent nail which looked like his own addition to the kitchen. "Did you ever talk politics, the two of you?" he asked as we took our whiskies to the drawing room.

"Never."

"Then I'm sure he's sound," he said, with a sad little laugh, and I laughed too.

Houses always seem to me, at first acquaintance, to be either masculine or feminine, and Smiley's was undoubtedly feminine, with pretty curtains and carved mirrors and clever woman's touches. I wondered who he was living with, or wasn't. We sat down.

"And is there any reason why you *mightn't* have sent Ben to Berlin?" he resumed, smiling kindly over the top of his glass.

"Well, only that I wanted to go myself. Everybody wants a Berlin break. It's the front line."

"He simply disappeared," Smiley explained, settling back and appearing to close his eyes. "We're not keeping anything from you. I'll tell you what we know. Last Thursday he crossed into East Berlin to meet his head agent, a gentleman named Hans Seidl—you can see his photograph in *Neues Deutschland*. It was Ben's first solo meeting with him. A big event. Ben's superior in the Berlin Station is Haggarty. Do you know Haggarty?"

"No."

"Have you heard of him?"

"No."

"Ben never mentioned him to you?"

"No. I told you. I've never heard his name."

"Forgive me. Sometimes an answer can vary with a context, if you follow me."

I didn't.

"Haggarty is second man in the Station under the Station Commander. Did you not know that either?"

"No."

"Has Ben a regular girlfriend?"

"Not that I know of."

"Irregular?"

"You only had to go to a dance with him, they were all over him."

"And after the dance?"

"He didn't brag. He doesn't. If he slept with them, he wouldn't say. He's not that kind of man."

"They tell me you and Ben took your bits of leave together. Where did you go?"

"Twickenham. Lord's. Bit of fishing. Mainly we stayed with one another's people."

"Ah."

I couldn't understand why Smiley's words were scaring me. Perhaps I was so scared for Ben that I was scared by everything. Increasingly I had the feeling Smiley assumed I was guilty of something, even if we had still to find out what. His recitation of events was like a summary of the evidence.

"First comes *Willis*," he said, as if we were following a difficult trail. "Willis is the Berlin Head of Station, Willis has overall command. Then comes *Haggarty*, and Haggarty is the senior field officer under Willis and Ben's direct boss. Haggarty is responsi-

ble for the day-to-day servicing of the Seidl network. The network is twelve agents strong, or was—that is to say, nine men
and three women, now all under arrest. An illegal network of
that size, communicating partly by radio and partly by secret
writing, requires a base team of at least the same number to
maintain it, and I'm not talking about evaluating or distributing
the product."

"I know."

"I'm sure you do, but let me tell you all the same," he continued at the same ponderous pace. "Then you can help me fill in the
gaps. Haggarty is a powerful personality. An Ulsterman. Off
duty, he drinks, he's noisy and unpleasant. But when he's working he's none of those things. He's a conscientious officer with a
prodigious memory. You're sure Ben never mentioned him to
you?"

"I told you. No."

I had not intended this to sound so adamant. There's always a
mystery about how often you can deny a thing without beginning
to sound like a liar, even to yourself; and of course this was the
very mystery Smiley was playing upon in order to bring hidden
things to the surface in me.

"Yes, well you *did* tell me no," he agreed with his habitual
courtesy. "And I did *hear* you say no. I merely wondered whether
I had jogged your memory?"

"No."

"Haggarty and Seidl were *friends*," he continued, speaking,
if it were possible, even more slowly. "So far as their business
allowed, they were *close* friends. Seidl had been a prisoner of war
in England, Haggarty in Germany. While Seidl was working as
a farm labourer near Cirencester in 1944, under the relaxed conditions for German prisoners of war that prevailed by then, he
succeeded in courting an English landgirl. His guards at the
camp took to leaving a bicycle for him outside the main gates

with an army greatcoat tossed over the handlebar to cover Seidl's prisoner-of-war tunic. As long as he was back in his own bed by reveille, the guards turned a blind eye. Seidl never forgot his gratitude to the English. When the baby came along, Seidl's guards and fellow prisoners came to the christening. Charming, isn't it? The English at their best. But the story doesn't ring a bell?"

"How could it? You're talking about a joe!"

"A blown joe. One of Ben's. Haggarty's experiences of German prison camp were not so uplifting. Never mind. In 1948, while Haggarty was nominally working with the Control Commission, he picked up Seidl in a bar in Hannover, recruited him and ran him back into East Germany, to his home town of Leipzig. He has been running him ever since. The Haggarty-Seidl friendship has been the linchpin of the Berlin Station for the last fifteen years. At the time of his arrest last week, Seidl was fourth man in the East German Foreign Ministry. He had served as their Ambassador in Havana. But you've never heard of him. Nobody ever mentioned him to you. Not Ben. Not anyone."

"No," I said, as wearily as I could manage.

"Once a month Haggarty was accustomed to going into East Berlin and debriefing Seidl—in a car, in a safe flat, on a park bench, wherever—the usual thing. After the Wall there was a suspension of service for a while, before the meetings were cautiously resumed. The game was to cross in a Four Power vehicle—say, an army jeep—introduce a substitute, hop out at the right moment and rejoin the vehicle at an agreed point. It sounds perilous and it was, but with practice it worked. If Haggarty was on leave or sick, there was no meeting. A couple of months ago Head Office ruled that Haggarty should introduce Seidl to be a successor. Haggarty is past retiring age, Willis has had Berlin so long he's blown sky high, and besides he knows far too many secrets to go wandering around behind the Curtain. Hence Ben's posting to Berlin. Ben was untarnished. Clean. Haggarty in person briefed him—I gather exhaustively. I'm sure he was not merciful. Haggarty is not a merciful man, and a twelve-strong network can be a complicated matter: who works to whom and why; who knows whose identity; the cut-outs, codes, couriers, covernames, symbols, radios, dead-letter boxes, inks, cars, salaries, children, birthdays, wives, mistresses. A lot to get into one's head all at once."

"I know."

"Ben told you, did he?"

I did not rise to him this time. I was determined not to. "We learned it on the course. *Ad infinitum,*" I said.

"Yes. Well, I suppose you did. The trouble is, the theory's never quite the same as the real thing, is it? Who's his best friend, apart from you?"

"I don't know." I was startled by his sudden change of tack. "Jeremy, I suppose."

"Jeremy who?"

"Galt. He was on the course."

"And women?"

"I told you. No one special."

"Haggarty wanted to take Ben into East Berlin with him, make the introduction himself," Smiley resumed. "The Fifth Floor wouldn't wear that. They were trying to wean Haggarty away from his agent, and they don't hold with sending two men into badland where one will do. So Haggarty took Ben through the rendezvous procedures on a street map, and Ben went into East Berlin alone. On the Wednesday, he did a dry run and reconnoitred the location. On the Thursday he went in again, this time for real. He went in legally, driven in a Control Commission Humber car. He crossed at Checkpoint Charlie at three in the afternoon and slipped out of the car at the agreed spot. His substitute rode in it for three hours, all as planned. Ben rejoined the car successfully at six-ten, and recrossed into West Berlin at six-fifty in the evening. His return was logged by the checkpoint. He had himself dropped at his flat. A faultless run. Willis and Haggarty were waiting for him at Station Headquarters, but he telephoned from his flat instead. He said the rendezvous had gone to plan, but he'd brought nothing back except a high temperature and a ferocious stomach bug. Could they postpone their debriefing till morning? Lamentably they could. They haven't seen him or heard from him since. He sounded cheerful despite his ailment, which they put down to nerves. Has Ben ever been ill on you?"

"No."

"He said their mutual friend had been in great form, real character and so forth. Obviously he could say no more on the open telephone. His bed wasn't slept in, he took no extra clothes with him. There's no proof that he was in his flat when he rang, there's no proof he's been kidnapped, there's no proof he hasn't been. If he was going to defect, why didn't he stay in East Berlin? They can't have turned him round and played him back at us or they wouldn't have arrested his network. And if they wanted to kidnap him, why not do it while he was their side of the Wall? There's no hard evidence that he left West Berlin by any of the approved corridors—train, autobahn, air. The controls are not efficient, and as you say, he was trained. For all we know, he hasn't left Berlin at all. On the other hand, we thought he might have come to you. Don't look so appalled. You're his friend, aren't you? His best friend? Closer to him than anyone? Young Galt doesn't compare. He told us so himself. 'Ben's great buddy was Ned,' he said. 'If Ben was going to turn to any of us, it would have to be Ned.' The evidence rather bears that out, I'm afraid."

"What evidence?"

No pregnant pause, no dramatic change of tone, no warning of any kind: just dear old George Smiley being his apologetic self.

"There's a letter in his flat, addressed to you," he said. "It's not dated, just thrown in a drawer. A scrawl rather than a letter. He was probably drunk. It's a love letter, I'm afraid." And, having handed me a photocopy to read, he fetched us both another whisky.

Perhaps I do it to help me look away from the discomfort of the moment. But always when I set that scene in my memory I find myself switching to Smiley's point of view. I imagine how it must have felt to be in his position.

What he had before him is easy enough to picture. See a striving trainee trying to look older than his years, a pipe-smoker, a sailor, a wise nodder, a boy who could not wait for middle age, and you have the young Ned of the early sixties.

But what he had behind him was not half so easy, and it was capable of altering his reading of me drastically. The Circus, though I couldn't know it at the time, was in low water, dogged by unaccountable failure. The arrest of Ben's agents, tragic in itself, was only the latest in a chain of catastrophes reaching across the globe. In northern Japan, an entire Circus listening station and its three-man staff had vanished into thin air. In the Caucasus, our escape lines had been rolled up overnight. We had lost networks in Hungary, Czechoslovakia and Bulgaria, all in a space of months. And in Washington our American Cousins were voicing ever-louder dissatisfaction with our reliability, and threatening to cut the special cord for good.

In such a climate, monstrous theories became daily fare. A bunker mentality develops. Nothing is allowed to be accidental, nothing random. If the Circus triumphed, it was because we were allowed to do so by our opponents. Guilt by association was rife. In the American perception, the Circus was nurturing not one mole but burrows of them, each cunningly advancing the career of every other. And what joined them was not so much their pernicious faith in Marx—though that was bad enough—it was their dreadful English homosexuality.

I read Ben's letter. Twenty lines long, unsigned, on white unwatermarked Service stationery, one side. Ben's handwriting but awry, no crossings out. So yes, probably he was drunk.

It called me "Ned my darling." It laid Ben's hands along my face and drew my lips to his. It kissed my eyelids and my neck and, thank God, on the physical front it stopped there.

It was without adjectives, without art, and the more appalling for its lack of them. It was not a period piece, it was not affected. It was not arch, Greek or nineteen-twenties. It was an unobstructed cry of homosexual longing from a man I had known only as my good companion.

But when I read it, I knew it was the real Ben who had written it. Ben in torment confessing feelings I had never been aware of, but which when I read them I accepted as true. Perhaps that already made me guilty—I mean, to be the object of his desire, even if I had never consciously attracted it, and did not desire him in return. His letter said sorry, then it ended. I didn't think it was unfinished. He had nothing more to say.

"I didn't know," I said.

I handed Smiley back the letter. He returned it to his pocket. His eyes didn't leave my face.

"Or you didn't know you knew," he suggested.

"I didn't know," I repeated hotly. "What are you trying to make me say?"

You must try to understand Smiley's eminence, the respect his name awoke in someone of my generation. He waited for me. I shall remember all my life the compelling power of his patience. A sudden shower of rain fell, with the handclap that London showers make in narrow sweets. If Smiley had told me he commanded the elements, I would not have been surprised.

"In England you can't tell anyway," I said sulkily, trying to collect myself. God alone knows what point I was trying to make. "Jack Arthur's not married, is he? Nowhere to go in the evenings. Drinks with the lads till the bar closes. Then drinks a bit more. No one says Jack Arthur's queer. But if they arrested him tomorrow in bed with two of the cooks, we'd say we'd known it all along. Or I would. It's imponderable." I stumbled on, all wrong, groping for a path and finding none. I knew that to protest at all was to protest too much, but I went on protesting all the same.

"Anyway, where was the letter found?" I demanded, trying to recover the initiative.

"In a drawer of his desk. I thought I told you."

"An empty drawer?"

"Does it matter?"

"Yes, it does! If it was jammed in among old papers, that's one thing. If it was put there to be found by you people, that's another. Maybe he was forced to write it."

"Oh, I'm sure he was forced," said Smiley. "It's just a question of what by. Did you know he was so lonely? If there was no one in his life but you, I'd have thought it would have been rather obvious."

"Then why wasn't it obvious to Personnel?" I said, bridling again. "My God, they grilled us for long enough before they appointed us. Sniffed round our friends and relations and teachers and dons. They know far more about Ben than I do."

"Why don't we just assume that Personnel fell down on the job? He's human, this is England, we're the clan. Let's begin again with the Ben who's disappeared. The Ben who wrote to you. There was no one close to him but you. Not anyone that you knew of, anyway. There could have been lots of people you *didn't* know of, but that's not your fault. As far as you knew, there was no one. We have that settled. Don't we?"

"Yes!"

"Very well then, let's talk about what you *did* know. How's that?"

Somehow he brought me down to earth and we talked into the small grey hours. Long after the rain had stopped and the starlings had begun, we were talking. Or I was—and Smiley was listening as only Smiley can, eyes half closed, chins sunk into his neck. I thought I was telling him everything I knew. Perhaps he thought I was too, though I doubt it, for he understood far better than I the levels of self-deception that are the means of our survival. The phone rang. He listened, muttered "Thank you" and rang off. "Ben's still missing and there are no new pointers," he said. "You're still the only clue." He took no notes that I remember and I don't know to this day whether he had a recorder running. I doubt it. He hated machines, and besides, his memory was more reliable than theirs.

I talked about Ben but I talked as much about myself, which was what Smiley wanted me to do: myself as the explanation for Ben's actions. I described again the parallel nature of our lives. How I had envied him his heroic father—I, who had no father to remember. I made no secret of our shared excitement, Ben's and mine, when we began to discover how much we had in common. No, no, I said again, I knew of no one woman—except his mother, who was dead. And I believed myself. I am sure I did.

In childhood, I told Smiley, I used to wonder whether somewhere in the world there was not another version of myself, some secret twin who had the same toys and clothes and thoughts that I did, even the same parents. Perhaps I'd read a book based on this story. I was an only child. So was Ben. I told Smiley all this because I was determined to talk directly to him from my thoughts and memories as they came to me, even if they incriminated me in his eyes. I only know that, consciously, I held nothing back from him, even if I reckoned it potentially ruinous to myself.

Somehow Smiley had convinced me that was the least I owed to
Ben. Unconsciously—well, that's another matter altogether. Who
knows what a man hides, even from himself, when he is telling
the truth for his survival?

I told him of our first meeting—mine and Ben's—in the Circus training house in Lambeth where the newly selected entrants
were convened. Until then, none of us had met any of his fellow
novices. We had hardly met the Circus either, for that matter,
beyond the recruiting officer, the selectors and the vetting team.
Some of us had only the haziest notion of what we'd joined.
Finally we were to be enlightened—about each other, and about
our calling—and we gathered in the waiting room like so many
characters in a Foreign Legion novel, each with his secret expectations and his secret reasons for being there, each with his overnight bag containing the same quantity of shirts and underpants,
marked in Indian ink with his personal number, in obedience to
the printed instructions on the unheaded notepaper. My number
was nine and Ben's was ten. There were two people ahead of me
when I walked into the waiting room, Ben and a stocky little Scot
called Jimmy. I nodded at Jimmy, but Ben and I recognised each
other at once—I don't mean from school or university but as people who bear a physical and temperamental similarity to one another.

"Enter the third murderer," he said, shaking my hand. It
seemed a wonderfully inappropriate moment to be quoting
Shakespeare. "I'm Ben, this is Jimmy. Apparently we've got no
surnames any more. Jimmy left his in Aberdeen."

So I shook Jimmy's hand as well, and waited on the bench beside Ben to see who came through the door next.

"Five to one he's got a moustache, ten to one a beard, thirty to
one green socks," said Ben.

"And evens on a cloak," I said.

I told Smiley about the training exercises in unfamiliar towns when we had to invent a cover story, meet a contact and withstand arrest and interrogation. I let him sense how such exploits deepened our companionship, just as sharing our first parachute jumps deepened it, or compass-trekking at night across the Scottish Highlands, or looking out dead-letter boxes in godforsaken inner cities, or making a beach landing by submarine.

I described to him how the directing staff would sometimes drop a veiled reference to Ben's father, just to emphasise their pride in having the son to teach. I told him about our leave weekends, how we would go once to my mother's house in Gloucestershire and once to his father's in Shropshire. And how, each parent being widowed, we had amused ourselves with the notion that we might broker a marriage between them. But the chances in reality were small, for my mother was stubbornly Anglo-Dutch, with jolly sisters and nephews and nieces who all looked like Breughel models, whereas Ben's father had become a scholarly recluse whose only known surviving passion was for Bach.

"And Ben reveres him," said Smiley, prodding again at the same spot.

"Yes. He adored his mother but she's dead. His father has become some sort of icon for him."

And I remember noticing to my shame that I had deliberately avoided using the word "love," because Ben had used it to describe his feelings for me.

I told him about Ben's drinking, though again I think he knew. How Ben normally drank little and often nothing at all, until an evening would come along—say, a Thursday and the weekend already looming—when he would drink insatiably, Scotch, vodka, anything, a shot for Ben, a shot for Arno. Then reel off to bed, speechless but inoffensive. And how on the morning after, he looked as if he had undergone a fortnight's cure at a health farm.

"And there was really nobody but you?" Smiley mused. "Poor you, what a burden, coping with all that charm alone."

I reminisced, I wandered, I told him everything as it came to me, but I knew he was still waiting for me to tell him something I was keeping back, if we could find out what it was. Was I conscious of withholding? I can only reply to you as I afterwards replied to myself: I did not know I knew. It took me a full twenty-four hours more of self-interrogation to winkle my secret out of its dark corner. At four A.M., he told me to go home and get some sleep. I was not to stray from my telephone without telling Personnel what I was up to.

"They'll be watching your flat, naturally," he warned me as we waited for my cab. "You won't take it personally, will you? If you imagine being on the loose yourself, there are really very few ports you'd feel safe to head for in a storm. Your flat could rank high on Ben's list. Assuming there isn't anybody else except his father. But he wouldn't go to him, would he? He'd be ashamed. He'd want you. So they watch your flat. It's natural."

"I understand," I said as a fresh wave of disgust swept over me.

"After all, there's no one of his age whom he seems to like better than you."

"It's all right. I understand," I repeated.

"On the other hand of course, he's not a fool, so he'll know how we're reasoning. And he could hardly imagine you would hide him in your priest-hole without telling us. Well, you wouldn't, would you?"

"No. I couldn't."

"Which if he's halfway rational he would also know, and that would rule you out for him. Still, he might drop by for advice or assistance, I suppose. Or a drink. It's unlikely, but it's not an assumption we can ignore. You must be far, far and away his best friend. Nobody to compare with you. Is there?"

I was wishing very much he would stop talking like this. Until now, he had shown the greatest delicacy in avoiding the topic of

Ben's declared love for me. Suddenly he seemed determined to reopen the wound.

"Of course he *may* have written to other people apart from you," he remarked speculatively. "Men or women, both. It's not so unlikely. There are times when one's so desperate that one declares one's love to all sorts of people. If one knows one's dying or contemplating some desperate act. The difference in their case would be, he posted the letters. Still, we can't go round Ben's chums asking them whether he's written them a steamy letter recently—it wouldn't be secure. Besides, where would one start? That's the question. You have to put yourself in Ben's position."

Did he deliberately plant the germ of self-knowledge in me? Later, I was certain he did. I remember his troubled, perspicacious gaze upon me as he saw me to the cab. I remember looking back as we turned the corner, and seeing his stocky figure standing in the centre of the street as he peered after me, ramming his last words into my departing head. "You have to put yourself in Ben's position."

I was in vortex. My day had begun in the small hours in South Audley Street and continued with barely pause for sleep through the Panda's monkey and Ben's letter until now. Smiley's coffee and my sense of being the prisoner of outrageous circumstance had done the rest. But the name of Stefanie, I swear it, was still nowhere in my head—not at the front, not at the back. Stefanie still did not exist. I have never, I am sure, forgotten anyone so thoroughly.

Back in my flat, my periodical spurts of revulsion at Ben's passion gave way to concern for his safety. In the living room I stared theatrically at the sofa where he had so often stretched out after a long day's street training in Lambeth: "Think I'll bunk down here if you don't mind, old boy. Jollier than home tonight. Arno can sleep at home. Ben sleeps here." In the kitchen I laid the palm of my hand on the old iron oven where I had fried him his midnight eggs: "Christ Almighty, Ned, is that a stove? Looks more like what we lost the Crimean War with!"

I remembered his voice, long after I had switched out my bedside light, rattling one crazy idea after another at me through the thin partition—the shared words we had, our insider language.

"You know what we ought to do with Brother Nasser?"

"No, Ben."

"Give him Israel. Know what we ought to do with the Jews?"

"No, Ben."

"Give them Egypt."

"Why, Ben?"

"People are only satisfied with what doesn't belong to them. Know the story of the scorpion and the frog crossing the Nile?"

"Yes, I do. Now shut up and go to sleep."

Then he'd tell me the story, nevertheless, as a Sarratt case history. The scorpion as penetration agent, needing to contact his stay-behind team on the opposite bank. The frog as double agent, pretending to buy the scorpion's cover story, then blowing it to his paymasters.

And in the morning he was gone, leaving behind him a one-line note saying, "See you at Borstal," which was his name for Sarratt. "Love, Ben."

Had we talked about Stefanie on those occasions? We hadn't. Stefanie was someone we discussed in motion, glancingly, not side by side through a stationary wall. Stefanie was a phantom shared on the run, an enigma too delightful to dissect. So perhaps that's why I didn't think of her. Or not yet. Not knowingly. There was no dramatic moment when a great light went up and I sprang from my bath shouting, *"Stefanie!"* It simply didn't happen that way, for the reason I'm trying to explain to you; somewhere in the no-man's-land between confession and self-preservation, Stefanie floated like a mythic creature who only existed when she was owned up to. As best I remember, the notion of her first came back to me as I was tidying up the mess left by Personnel. Stumbling on my last year's diary, I began flipping through it, thinking how much more of life we live than we remember. And in the month of June, I came on a line drawn diagonally through the two middle weeks, and the numeral "8" written neatly beside it—meaning Camp 8, North Argyll, where we did our paramilitary training. And I began to thank—or perhaps merely to sense—yes, of course, Stefanie.

And from there, still without any sudden Archimedean revelation, I found myself reliving our night drive over the moonlit Highlands. Ben at the wheel of the open Triumph roadster, and myself beside him making chatty conversation in order to keep him awake, because we were both happily exhausted after a week of pretending we were in the Albanian mountains raising a guerrilla army. And the June air rushing over our faces.

The rest of the intake were travelling back to London on the Sarratt bus. But Ben and I had Stefanie's Triumph roadster because Steff was a sport, Steff was selfless, Steff had driven it all the way from Oban to Glasgow just so that Ben could borrow it for the week and bring it back to her when the course restarted. And that was how Stefanie came back to me—exactly as she had come to me in the car—amorphously, a titillating concept, a shared woman—Ben's.

"So who or what *is* Stefanie, or do I get the usual loud silence?" I asked him as I pulled open the glove compartment and looked in vain for traces of her.

For a while I got the loud silence.

"Stefanie is a light to the ungodly and a paragon to the virtuous," he replied gravely. And then, more deprecatingly: "Steff's from the Hun side of the family." He was from it himself, he liked to say in his more acerbic moods. Steff was from the Arno side, he was saying.

"Is she pretty?" I asked.

"Don't be vulgar."

"Beautiful?"

"Less vulgar, but still not there."

"What is she, then?"

"She is perfection. She is luminous. She is peerless."

"So beautiful, then?"

"No, you lout. Exquisite. *Sans pareil.* Intelligent beyond the dreams of Personnel."

"And otherwise—to you—what is she? Apart from being Hun and the owner of this car?"

"She is my mother's eighteenth cousin dozens of times removed. After the war she came and lived with us in Shropshire and we grew up together."

"So she's your age, then?"

"If the eternal is to be measured, yes."

"Your proxy sister, as it were?"

"She was. For a few years. We ran wild together, picked mushrooms in the dawn, touched wee-wees. Then I went to boarding school and she returned to Munich to resume being a Hun. End of childhood idyll and back to Daddy and England."

I had never known him so forthcoming about any woman, nor about himself.

"And now?"

I feared he had switched off again, but finally he answered me. "Now is less funny. She went to art school, took up with a mad painter and settled in a dower house in the Western Isles of Scotland."

"Why's it less funny? Doesn't her painter like you?"

"He doesn't like anyone. He shot himself. Reasons unknown. Left a note to the local council apologising for the mess. No note to Steff. They weren't married, which made it more of a muddle."

"And now?" I asked him again.

"She still lives there."

"On the island?"

"Yes."

"In the dower house?"

"Yes."

"Alone?"

"Most of the time."

"You mean you go and see her?"

"I *see* her, yes. So I suppose I *go* too. Yes. I go and see her."

"Is it serious?"

"Everything to do with Steff is massively serious."

"What does she do when you're not there?"

"Same as she does when I'm there, I should think. Paints. Talks to the dickie birds. Reads. Plays music. Reads. Plays music. Paints. Thinks. Reads. Lends me her car. Do you want to know any more of my business?"

For a while we remained strangers, until Ben once more relented. "Tell you what, Ned. Marry her."

"Stefanie?"

"Who else, you idiot? That's a bloody good idea, come to think of it. I propose to bring the two of you together to discuss it. You shall marry Steff, Steff shall marry you, and I shall come and live with you both, and fish the loch."

My question sprang from a monstrous, culpable innocence: "Why don't you marry her yourself?" I asked.

Was it only now, standing in my flat and watching the slow dawn print itself on the walls, that I had the answer? Staring at the ruled-out pages of last June and remembering with a jolt his dreadful letter?

Or was it given to me already in the car, by Ben's silence as we sped through the Scottish night? Did I know even then that Ben was telling me he would never marry any woman?

And was this the reason why I had banished Stefanie from my conscious memory, planting her so deep that not even Smiley, for all his clever delving, had been able to exhume her?

Had I looked at Ben as I asked him my fatal question? Had I looked at him as he refused, and went on refusing, to reply? Had I deliberately not looked at him at all? I was used to his silences by then, so perhaps, having waited in vain, I punished him by entering my own thoughts.

All I knew for certain was that Ben never answered my question, and that neither of us ever mentioned Stefanie again.

Stefanie his dream woman, I thought as I continued to examine the diary. On her island. Who loved him. But should marry me.

Who had the taint of death about her that Ben's heroes always seemed to need.

Eternal Stefanie, a light to the ungodly, luminous, peerless, German Stefanie, his paragon and proxy sister—mother too, perhaps—waving to him from her tower, offering him sanctuary from his father.

You have to put yourself in Ben's position, Smiley had said.

Yet even now, the open diary in my hands, I did not allow myself the elusive moment of revelation. An idea was forming in me. Gradually it became a possibility. And only gradually again, as my state of physical and mental siege bore in on me, did it harden into conviction, and finally purpose.

It was morning at last. I hoovered the flat. I dusted and polished. I considered my anger. Dispassionately, you understand; I reopened the desk, pulled out my desecrated private papers and burned in the grate whatever I felt had been irrevocably sullied by the intrusion of Smiley and Personnel: the letters from Mabel, the exhortations from my former tutor to "do something a bit more fun" than mere research work at the War Office.

I did these things with the outside of myself while the rest of me grappled with the correct, the moral, the decent course of action.

Ben, my friend.

Ben, with the dogs after him.

Ben in anguish, and God knew what more besides.

Stefanie.

I took a long bath, then lay on my bed watching the mirror on the chest of drawers because the mirror gave me a view of the street. I could see a couple of men whom I took to be Monty's, dressed in overalls and doing something longwinded with a junction box. Smiley had said I shouldn't take them personally. After all, they only wanted to put Ben in irons.

It is ten o'clock of the same long morning as I stand purposefully to one side of my rear window, peering down into the squalid courtyard, with its creosoted shed that used to be the old privy, and its clapboard gate that opens on the dingy street. The street is empty. Monty is not so perfect after all.

The Western Isles, Ben had said. A dower house on the Western Isles.

But which isle? And Stefanie who? The only safe guess was that if she came from the German side of Ben's family and lived in Munich, and that since Ben's German relatives were grand, she was likely to be titled.

I rang Personnel. I might have rung Smiley but I felt safer lying to Personnel. He recognised my voice before I had a chance to state my business.

"Have you heard anything?" he demanded.

"Afraid not. I want to go out for an hour. Can I do that?"

"Where to?"

"I need a few things. Provisions. Something to read. Thought I'd just pop round to the library."

Personnel was famous for his disapproving silences.

"Be back by eleven. Ring me as soon as you get in."

Pleased by my cool performance, I went out by the front door, bought a newspaper and bread. Using shop windows, I checked my back. Nobody was following me, I was sure. I went to the public library and from the reference section drew an old copy of *Who's Who* and a tattered *Almanach de Gotha*. I did not pause to ask myself who on earth, in Battersea of all places, could have worn out the *Almanach de Gotha*. I consulted the *Who's Who* first and turned up Ben's father, who had a knighthood and a battery of decorations: *"1936, married the Gräfin Ilse Arno zu Lothringen, one son Benjamin Arno."* I switched to the *Almanach* and turned up the Arno Lothringens. They rated three pages, but it took me no time to identify the distant cousin whose first name was Stefanie. I boldly asked the librarian for a telephone directory for the Western Isles of Scotland. She hadn't one, but allowed me to call enquiries on her telephone, which was fortunate for I had no doubt my own was being tapped. By ten-forty-five I was back at the telephone in my flat talking to Personnel in the same relaxed tone as before.

"Where did you go?" he asked.

"To the newsagent. And the baker's."

"Didn't you do the library?"

"Library? Oh yes. Yes, I did."

"And what, pray, did you take out?"

"Nothing, actually. For some reason I find it hard to settle to anything at the moment. What do I do next?"

Waiting for him to reply, I wondered whether I had given too many answers but decided I had not.

"You wait. The same as the rest of us."

"Can I come in to Head Office?"

"Since you're waiting, you might as well wait there as here."

"I could go back to Monty, if you like."

It was probably my over-acute imagination at work, but I had a mental image of Smiley standing at his elbow, telling him how to answer me.

"Just wait where you are," he said curtly.

I waited, Lord knows how. I pretended to read. I dramatised myself and wrote a pompous letter of resignation to Personnel. I tore up the letter and burned the pieces. I watched television, and in the evening I lay on the bed observing the changing of Monty's guard in the mirror and thinking of Stefanie, then Ben, then Stefanie again, who was now firmly lodged in my imagination, always outside my reach, dressed in white, Stefanie the immaculate, Ben's protector. I was young, let me remind you, and in matters of women less experienced than you would have suspected if you had heard me speak of them. The Adam in me was still pretty much a child, not to be confused with the warrior.

I waited till ten, then slipped downstairs with a bottle of wine for Mr. Simpson and his wife, and sat with them while we drank it, watching more television. Then I took Mr. Simpson aside.

"Chris," I said. "I know it's daft but there's a jealous lady stalking me and I'd like to leave by the back way. Would you mind letting me out through your kitchen?"

An hour later, I was on the night sleeper to Glasgow. I had obeyed my counter-surveillance procedures to the letter and I was certain I was not being followed. At Glasgow Central Station, all the same, I took the precaution of dawdling over a pot of tea in the buffet while I cocked an eye for potential watchers. As a further precaution, I hired a cab to Helensburgh on the other side of the Clyde, before joining the Campbeltown bus to West Loch Tarbert. The ferry to the Western Isles sailed three days a week in those days, except for the short summer season. But my luck held: a boat was waiting, and she sailed as soon as I had boarded her, so that by early afternoon we had passed Jura, docked at Port Askaig and were heading out to the open sea again under a darkening northern sky. We were down to three passengers by then, an old couple and myself, and when I went up on deck to fend off their questions, the first mate cheerfully asked me more of his own: Was I on holiday now? Was I a doctor then? Was I married at all? Nevertheless, I was in my element. From the moment I take to the sea, everyone is clear to me, everything possible. Yes, I thought excitedly, surveying the great crags as they approached, and smiling at the shrieking of the gulls, yes, this is where Ben would hide! This is where his Wagnerian demons would find their ease!

You must understand and try to pardon my callow susceptibility in those days to all forms of Nordic abstraction. What Ben was driven by, I pursued. The mythic island—it should have been Ossian's!—the swirling clouds and tossing sea, the priestess in her solitary castle—I could not get enough of them. I was in the middle of my Romantic period, and my soul was lost to Stefanie before I met her.

The dower house was on the other side of the island, they told me at the shop, better ask young Fergus to take you in his jeep. Young Fergus turned out to be seventy, if a day. We passed between a pair of crumbling iron gates. I paid off young Fergus and rang the bell. The door opened; a fair woman stared at me.

She was tall and slim. If it was really true that she was my own age—and it was—she had an authority it would take me another lifetime to acquire. She wore, instead of white, a paint-smeared smock of dark blue. She held a palette knife in one hand, and as I spoke she raised it to her forehead and pushed away a stray bit of hair with the back of her wrist. Then lowered it again to her side, and stood listening to me long after I had finished speaking, while she pondered the resonance of my words inside her head and compared them with the man or boy who stood before her. But the strangest part of this moment is also the hardest for me to relate. It is that Stefanie came closer to the figure of my imagination than made sense. Her pallor, her air of uncorrupted truthfulness, of inner strength, coupled with an almost pitiable fragility, corresponded so exactly with my expectation that, had I bumped into her in another place, I would have known that she was Stefanie.

"My name's Ned," I said, speaking to her eyes. "I'm a friend of Ben's. Also a colleague. I'm alone. No one knows I'm here."

I had meant to go on. I had a pompous speech in my head that said something like "Please tell him that whatever he's done, it makes no difference to me." But the steadiness of her gaze prevented me.

"Why should it matter who knows that you are here and who does not?" she asked. She spoke without accent, but with a German cadence, making tiny hesitations before the open vowels. "He is not hiding. Who is looking for him except you? Why should he hide?"

"I understood he might be in some kind of trouble," I said, following her into the house.

The hall was half studio, half makeshift living room. Dust-sheets covered much of the furniture. The remains of a meal lay on the table: two mugs, two plates, both used.

"What kind of trouble?" she demanded.

"It's to do with his work in Berlin. I thought perhaps he would have told you about it."

"He has told me nothing. He has never talked to me about his work. Perhaps he knows I am not interested."

"May I ask what he does talk about?"

She considered this. "No." And then, as if relenting, "At present he does not talk to me at all. He seems to have become a Trappist. Why not? Sometimes he watches me paint, sometimes he fishes, sometimes we eat something or drink a little wine. Quite often he sleeps."

"How long's he been here?"

She shrugged. "Three days?"

"Did he come straight from Berlin?"

"He came on the boat. Since he does not speak, that's all I know."

"He disappeared," I said. "There's a hue and cry for him. They thought he might come to me. I don't think they know about you."

She was listening to me again, listening first to my words and then my silence. She seemed to be without embarrassment, like a listening animal. It's the authority of suffering, I thought, remembering her lover's suicide, she cannot be reached by small worries.

"*They,*" she repeated with puzzlement. "Who are *they*? What is there to *know* about me that is so particular?"

"Ben was doing secret work," I said.

"*Ben?*"

"Like his father," I said. "He was tremendously proud of following in his father's steps."

She was shocked and agitated. "What? Who for? Secret work? What a fool!"

"For British Intelligence. He was in Berlin, attached to the Military Adviser's office, but his real work was intelligence."

"*Ben?*" she said as the disgust and disbelief gathered in her face. "All those lies he must tell? Ben?"

"Yes, I'm afraid so. But it was duty."

"How *terrible*."

Her easel stood with its back to me. Placing herself the other side of it, she began mixing her paints.

"If I could just talk to him," I said, but she pretended to be too much lost to her painting to hear me.

The back of the house gave on to parkland, then a line of pines hunchbacked by the wind. Beyond the pines lay a loch surrounded by small mauve hills. On its far bank I made out a fisherman standing on a collapsed jetty. He was fishing but not casting. I don't know how long I watched him, but long enough to know that it was Ben, and that he had no interest in catching fish. I pushed open the French windows and stepped into the garden. A cold wind was ruffling the surface of the loch as I tiptoed along the jetty. He was wearing a tweed jacket that was too full for him. I guessed it had belonged to her dead lover. And a hat, a green felt hat that, like all hats with Ben, looked as though it had been made for him. He didn't turn, though he must have felt my footsteps. I placed myself beside him.

"The only thing you'll catch like that is pneumonia, you German ass," I said.

His face was turned against me, so I remained standing beside him, watching the water with him and sensing the nudge of his shoulder as the rocking jetty threw us carelessly together. I watched the water thicken and the sky turn grey behind the mountains. A few times I watched the red float of his line vanish below the oily surface. But if a fish had struck, Ben made no effort to play it or reel it in. I saw the lights go on in the house, and the figure of Stefanie standing at her easel, adding a brush stroke, then backing her wrist against her brow. The air turned cold and the night gathered, but Ben didn't move. We were in competition with each other, as we had been during our strongarm training. I was demanding, Ben was refusing. Only one of us could have his way. If it took me all night and all tomorrow, and if I starved in the process, I wasn't going to yield till he'd acknowledged me.

A half moon came up, and stars. The wind dropped and silver ground mist formed across the blackened heather. And still we stood there, waiting for one of us to surrender. I was nearly sleeping on my feet when I heard the rattle of his reel and saw the float lift from the water and the bare line after it, flashing in the moon-light. I didn't move and didn't speak. I let him reel in and make his hook fast. I let him turn to me, because he had to if he wanted to walk past me down the jetty.

We stood face-to-face in the moonlight. Ben looked down-wards, apparently studying my feet to see how he could step round them. His gaze travelled up to my face, but nothing changed in his expression. His locked features stayed locked. If they betrayed anything, it was anger.

"Well," he said. "Enter the third murderer."

This time neither of us laughed.

She must have sensed our approach and removed herself. I heard music playing in another part of the house. When we reached the hall, Ben headed for the stairs but I grabbed his arm.

"You've got to tell me," I said. "There's never going to be any-one better to tell. I broke ranks to come here. You've got to tell me what happened to the network."

There was a long drawing room beyond the hall, with shut-tered windows and more dustsheets over the sofas. It was cold, but Ben still had his jacket on and I my greatcoat. I opened the shutters and let the moonlight in. I had an instinct that anything brighter would disturb him. The music was not far away from us. I thought it was Grieg. I wasn't sure. Ben spoke without re-morse and without catharsis. He had confessed enough to him-self, all day and night, I knew. He talked in the dead tone of somebody describing a disaster he knows that nobody can under-stand who was not part of it, and the music kept playing below his voice. He had no use for himself. The glamorous hero had given up as one of life's contenders. Perhaps he was a little tired of his guilt. He spoke tersely. I think he wanted me to go.

"Haggarty's a shit," he said. "World class. He's a thief, he drinks, he rapes a bit. His one justification was the Seidl network. Head Office were trying to wheedle him away from it and give Seidl to new people. I was the first new person. Haggarty decided to punish me for taking away his network."

He described the studied insults, the successive night duties and weekends, the hostile reports passed back to Haggarty's supporters' club in Head Office.

"At first he wouldn't tell me anything about the network. Then Head Office bawled him out, so he told me everything. Fifteen years of it. Every tiny detail of their lives, even the joes who'd died on the job. He'd send files to me in pyramids, all flagged and cross-referred. Read this, remember that. Who's she? Who's he? Note this address, the name, these covernames, those symbols. Escape procedures. Fallbacks. The recognition codes and safety procedures for the radio. Then he'd test me. Take me to the safe room, sit me across the table, grill me. 'You're not up to it. We can't send you in till you know your stuff. You'd better stay in over the weekend and mug it up. I'll test you again on Monday.' The network was his life. He wanted me to feel inadequate. I did and I was."

But Head Office did not give in to Haggarty's bullying, neither did Ben. "I put myself on an exam footing," he said.

As the day of his first meeting with Seidl approached, Ben assembled for himself a system of mnemonics and acronyms that would enable him to encompass the network's fifteen years of history. Seated night and day in his office at Station Headquarters, he drew up consciousness charts and communications charts and devised systems for memorizing the aliases, covernames, home addresses and places of employment of its agents, subagents, couriers and collaborators. Then he transferred his data to plain postcards, writing on one side only. On the other, in one line, he wrote the subject "dead-letter boxes," "salaries," "safe houses." Each night, before going back to his flat or stretching out in the Station sickroom, he would play a game of memory with himself, first putting the cards face downward on his desk, then comparing what he had remembered with the data on the reverse side.

"I didn't sleep a lot but that's not unusual," he said. "As the day came up, I didn't sleep at all. I spent the whole night mugging up my stuff, then I lay on the couch staring at the ceiling. When I got up I couldn't remember any of it. Sort of paralysis. I went to my room, sat down at the desk, put my head in my hands and started to ask myself questions. 'If covername Margaret-stroke-two thinks he's under surveillance, whom does he contact how, and what does the contact then do?' The answer was a total blank.

"Haggarty wandered in and asked how I was feeling and I said 'fine.' To do him justice, he wished me luck and I think he meant it. I thought he'd shoot some trick question at me and I was going to tell him to go to hell. But he just said, *'Komm gut heim,'* and patted my shoulder. I put the cards in my pocket. Don't ask me why. I was scared of failure. That's why we do everything, isn't it? I was scared of failure and I hated Haggarty and Haggarty had put me to the torture. I've got about two hundred other reasons why I took the cards, but none of them help a great deal. Perhaps it was my way of committing suicide. I quite like that idea. I took them and I went across. We used a limousine, specially converted. I sat in the back with my double hidden under the seat. The Vopos weren't allowed to search us, of course. All the same, switching with a double as you turn a sharp corner is a bloody hairy game. You've got to sort of roll out of the car. Seidl had provided a bike for me. He believes in bicycles. His guards used to lend him one when he was a prisoner of war in England."

Smiley had told me the story already, but I let Ben tell it to me again.

"I had the cards in my jacket pocket," he went on. "My inside jacket pocket. It was one of those blazing-hot Berlin days. I think I unbuttoned my jacket while I bicycled. I don't know. When I try to remember, I sometimes unbuttoned it and I sometimes didn't. That's what happens to your memory when you work it to death. It does all the versions for you. I got to the rendezvous early, checked the cars, the usual bullshit, went in. It had all come back to me by then. Taking the cards with me had done the trick. I didn't need them. Seidl was fine. I was fine. We did our business, I briefed him, gave him some money—all just like Sarratt. I rode back to the pickup point, ditched the bike, dived into the car and as we crossed into West Berlin I realised I hadn't got the cards. I was missing the weight of them, or the pressure or something. I was in a panic but I always am. Deep down, I'm in a panic all the time. That's who I am. This was just a bigger panic. I made them drop me at my flat, rang Seidl's emergency number. No one answered. I tried the fallback. No answer. I tried his stand-in, a woman called Lotte. No answer. I took a cab to Tempelhof, made a discreet exit, came here."

Suddenly there was only Stefanie's music to listen to. Ben had finished his story. I didn't realise at first that this was all there was. I waited, staring at him, expecting him to go on. I had been wanting a kidnapping at least—savage East German secret police rising from the back of his car, sandbagging him, forcing a chloroformed mask on him while they rifled his pockets. It was only gradually that the appalling banality of what he had told me got through to me: that you could lose a network as easily as you could lose a bunch of keys or a cheque book or a pocket handkerchief. I was craving for a greater dignity, but he had none to offer me.

"So where did you last have them?" I said stupidly. I could have been talking to a child about his lost schoolbooks, but he didn't mind, he had no pride any more.

"The cards?" he said. "Maybe on the bicycle. Maybe rolling

out of the car. Maybe getting back into it. The bike has a security chain to lock round the wheel. I had to stoop down to put it on and take it off. Maybe then. It's like losing anything. Till you find it, you never know. Afterwards, it's obvious. But there hasn't been an afterwards."

"Do you think you were followed?"

"I don't know. I just don't know."

I wanted to ask him when he had written his love letter to me, but I couldn't bring myself to. Besides, I thought I knew it was in one of his drinking sessions when Haggarty was riding him hardest and he was in despair. What I really wanted him to tell me was that he had never written it. I wanted to put the clock back and make things the way they had been until a week ago. But the simple questions had died with the simple answers. Our childhoods were over for good.

They must have surrounded the house, and certainly they never rang the bell. Monty was probably standing outside the window when I opened the shutters to let the moonlight in, because when he needed to, he just stepped into the room, looking embarrassed but resolute.

"You did ever so nice, Ned," he said consolingly. "It was the public library gave you away. Your nice librarian lady took a real shine to you. I think she'd have come with us if we'd let her."

Skordeno followed him, and then Smiley appeared in the other doorway, wearing the apologetic air that frequently accompanied his most ruthless acts. And I recognised with no particular surprise that I had done everything he had wanted me to do. I had put myself in Ben's position and led them to my friend. Ben didn't seem particularly surprised either. Perhaps he was relieved. Monty and Skordeno moved into place either side of him, but Ben remained sitting among the dustsheets, his tweed jacket pulled around him like a rug. Skordeno tapped him on the shoulder; then Monty and Skordeno stooped and, like a pair of furniture removers used to one another's timing, lifted him gently to his feet. When I protested to Ben that I had not knowingly betrayed him, he shook his head to say it didn't matter. Smiley stepped aside to let them by. His myopic gaze was fixed on me enquiringly.

"We've arranged a special sailing," he said.

"I'm not coming," I replied.

I looked away from him and when I looked again he was gone. I heard the jeep disappearing down the track. I followed the music across the empty hall into a study crammed with books and magazines and what appeared to be the manuscript of a novel spread over the floor. She was sitting sideways in a deep chair. She had changed into a housecoat and her pale golden hair hung loose over her shoulders. She was barefoot, and did not lift her head as I entered. She spoke to me as if she had known me all her life, and I suppose in a way she had, in the sense that I was Ben's familiar. She switched off the music.

"Were you his lover?" she asked.

"No. He wanted me to be. I realise that now."

She smiled. "And I wanted him to be *my* lover, but that wasn't possible either, was it?" she said.

"It seems not."

"Have you had women, Ned?"

"No."

"Had Ben?"

"I don't know. I think he tried. I suppose it didn't work."

She was breathing deeply and tears were trickling down her cheeks and neck. She climbed to her feet, eyes pressed shut, and, like a blind woman, stretched out her arms for me to embrace her. Her body squeezed against me as she buried her head in my shoulder and shook and wept. I put my arms round her but she pushed me away and led me to the sofa.

"Who made him become one of you?" she said.

"No one. It was his own choice. He wanted to imitate his father."

"Is that a choice?"

"Of a sort."

"And you too, you are a volunteer?"

"Yes."

"Whom are *you* imitating?"

"No one."

"Ben had no capacity for such a life. They had no business to be charmed by him. He was too persuasive."

"I know."

"And you? Do you need them to make a man of you?"

"It's something that has to be done."

"To make a man of you?"

"The work. It's like emptying the dustbins or cleaning up in hospitals. Somebody has to do it. We can't pretend it isn't there."

"Oh, I think we can." She took my hand and wound her fingers stiffly into mine. "We pretend a lot of things aren't there. Or we pretend that other things are more important. That's how we survive. We shall not defeat liars by lying to them. Will you stay here tonight?"

"I have to go back. I'm not Ben. I'm me. I'm his friend."

"Let me tell you something. May I? It is very dangerous to play with reality. Will you remember that?"

I have no picture of our leavetaking, so I expect it was too painful and my memory has rejected it. All I know now is, I had to catch the ferry. There was no jeep waiting so I walked. I remember the salt of her tears and the smell of her hair as I hurried through the night wind, and the black clouds writhing round the moon and the thump of the sea as I skirted the rocky bay. I remember the headland and the stubby little lighted steamer starting to cast off. And I know that for the entire journey I stood on the foredeck and that for the last part of it Smiley stood beside me. He must have heard Ben's story by then, and come up on deck to offer me his silent consolation.

I never saw Ben again—they kept me from him as we disembarked—but when I heard he had been discharged from the Service I wrote to Stefanie and asked her to tell me where he was. My letter was returned marked "Gone Away."

I would like to be able to tell you that Ben did not cause the destruction of the network, because Bill Haydon had betrayed it long before. Or better, that the network had been set up for us by the East Germans or the Russians in the first place, as a means of keeping us occupied and feeding us disinformation. But I am afraid the truth is otherwise, for in those days Haydon's access was limited by compartmentation, and his work did not take him to Berlin. Smiley even asked Bill, after his capture, whether he had had a hand in it, and Bill had laughed.

"I'd been wanting to get my hooks on that network for years," he'd replied. "When I heard what had happened, I'd a bloody good mind to send young Cavendish a bunch of flowers, but I suppose it wouldn't have been secure."

The best I could tell Ben, if I saw him today, is that if he hadn't blown the network when he did, Haydon would have blown it for him a couple of years later. The best I could tell Stefanie is that she was right in her way, but then so was I, and that her words never left my memory, even after I had ceased to regard her as the fountain of all wisdom. If I never understood who she was—if she belonged, as it were, more to Ben's mystery than my own—she was nevertheless the first of the siren voices that sounded in my ear, warning me that my mission was an ambiguous one. Sometimes I wonder what I was for her, but I'm afraid I know only too well: a callow boy, another Ben, unversed in life, banishing weakness with a show of strength, and taking refuge in a cloistered world.

I went back to Berlin not long ago. It was a few weeks after the Wall had been declared obsolete. An old bit of business took me, and Personnel was pleased to pay my fare. I never was formally stationed there, as it worked out, but I had been a frequent visitor, and for us old cold warriors a visa to Berlin is like returning to the source. And on a damp afternoon I found myself standing at the grimy little bit of fencing known grandly as the Wall of the Unknown Ones, which was the memorial to those killed while trying to escape during the sixties, some of whom did not have the foresight to give their names in advance. I stood among a humble group of East Germans, mostly women, and I noticed that they were examining the inscriptions on the crosses: unknown man, shot on such-and-such a date, in 1965. They were looking for clues, fitting the dates to the little that they knew.

And the sickening notion struck me that they could even have been looking for one of Ben's agents who had made a dash for freedom at the eleventh hour and failed. And the notion was all the more bewildering when I reflected that it was no longer we Western Allies, but East Germany itself, which was struggling to snuff out its existence.

The memorial is gone now. Perhaps it will find a corner in a museum somewhere, but I doubt it. When the Wall came down—hacked to pieces, sold—the memorial came down with it, which strikes me as an appropriate comment on the fickleness of human constancy.

4

Somebody asked Smiley about interrogation, yet again. It was a question that cropped up often as the night progressed—mainly because his audience wanted to squeeze more case histories out of him. Children are merciless.

"Oh, there's *some* art to faulting the liar, of course there is," Smiley conceded doubtfully, and took a sip from his glass. "But the real art lies in recognising the truth, which is a great deal harder. Under interrogation, nobody behaves normally. People who are stupid act intelligent. Intelligent people act stupid. The guilty look innocent as the day, and the innocent look dreadfully guilty. And just occasionally people act as they are and tell the truth as they know it, and of course they're the poor souls who get caught out every time. There's nobody less convincing to our wretched trade than the blameless man with nothing to hide."

"Except possibly the blameless woman," I suggested under my breath.

George had reminded me of Bella and the ambiguous sea captain Brandt.

He was a big, rough flaxen fellow, at first guess Slav or Scandinavian, with the roll of a landed seaman and the far eyes of an adventurer. I first met him in Zurich where he was in hot water with the police. The city superintendent called me in the middle of the night and said, "Herr Konsul, we have somebody who says he has information for the British. We have orders to put him over the border in the morning."

I didn't ask which border. The Swiss have four, but when they are throwing somebody out they're not particular. I drove to the district prison and met him in a barred interviewing room: a caged giant in a roll-neck pullover who called himself Sea Captain Brandt, which seemed to be his personal version of *Kapitän zur See*.

"You're a long way from the sea," I said as I shook his great, padded hand.

As far as the Swiss were concerned, he had everything wrong with him. He had swindled a hotel, which in Switzerland is such a heinous crime it gets its own paragraph in the criminal code. He had caused a disturbance, he was penniless and his West German passport did not bear examination—though the Swiss refused to say this out loud, since a fake passport could prejudice their chances of getting rid of him to another country. He had been picked up drunk and vagrant and he blamed it on a girl. He had broken someone's jaw. He insisted on speaking to me alone.

"You British?" he asked in English, presumably in order to disguise our conversation from the Swiss, though they spoke better English than he did.

"Yes."

"Prove, please."

I showed him my official identity card, describing me as Vice-Consul for Economic Affairs.

"You work for British Intelligence?" he asked.

"I work for the British government."

"Okay, okay," he said, and in sudden weariness sank his head into his hand so that his long blond hair flopped forward, and he had to toss it back again with a sweep of his arm. His face was chipped and pitted like a boxer's.

"You ever been in prison?" he asked, staring at the scrubbed white table.

"No, thank God."

"Jesus," he said, and in bad English told me his story.

He was a Latvian, born in Riga of Latvian and Polish parents. He spoke Latvian, Russian, Polish and German. He was born to the sea, which I sensed immediately, for I was born to it myself. His father and grandfather had been sailors, he had served six years in the Soviet navy, sailing the Arctic out of Archangel, and the Sea of Japan out of Vladivostok. A year back he had returned to Riga, bought a small boat and taken up smuggling along the Baltic coast, running cheap Russian vodka into Finland with the help of Scandinavian fishermen. He was caught and put in prison near Leningrad, escaped and stowed away to Poland, where he lived illegally with a Polish girl student in Cracow. I tell you this exactly as he told it to me, as if stowing away to Poland from Russia were as self-evident as catching a number 11 bus or popping down the road for a drink. Yet even with my limited familiarity with the obstacles he had overcome, I knew it was an extraordinary feat—and no less so when he performed it a second time. For when the girl left him to marry a Swiss salesman, he headed back to the coast and got himself a ride to Malmö, then down to Hamburg where he had a distant cousin, but the cousin was distant indeed, and told him to go to hell. So he stole the cousin's passport and headed south to Switzerland, determined to get back his Polish girl. When her new husband wouldn't let her go, Brandt broke the poor man's jaw for him, so here he was, a prisoner of the Swiss police.

All this still in English, so I asked him where he'd learned it. From the BBC, when he was out smuggling, he said. From his Polish girl—she was a language student. I had given him a packet of cigarettes and he was devouring them one after another, making a gas chamber of our little room.

"So what's this information you've got for us?" I asked him.

As a Latvian, he said in preamble, he felt no allegiance to Moscow. He had grown up under the lousy Russian tyranny in Latvia, he had served under lousy Russian officers in the navy, he had been sent to prison by lousy Russians and hounded by lousy Russians, and he had no compunction about betraying them. He hated Russians. I asked him the names of the ships he had served on and he told me. I asked him what armament they carried and he described some of the most sophisticated stuff they possessed at that time. I gave him a pencil and paper and he made surprisingly impressive drawings. I asked him what he knew about signals. He knew a lot. He was a qualified signalman and had used their latest toys, even if his memory was a year old. I asked him, "Why the British?" and he replied that he had known "a couple of you guys in Leningrad"—British sailors on a goodwill visit. I wrote down their names and the name of their ship, returned to my office and sent a flash telegram to London because we only had a few hours' grace before they put him over the border. Next evening Sea Captain Brandt was undergoing rigorous questioning at a safe house in Surrey. He was on the brink of a dangerous career. He knew every nook and bay along the south Baltic coast; he had good friends who were honest Latvian fishermen, others who were black marketeers, thieves and disaffected drop-outs. He was offering exactly what London was looking for after our recent losses—the chance to build a new supply line in and out of northern Russia, across Poland into Germany.

I have to set the recent history for you here—of the Circus, and of my own efforts to succeed in it.

After Ben, it had been touch and go for me whether they promoted me or threw me out. I think today that I owed more to Smiley's backstairs intervention than I gave him credit for at the time. Left to himself, I don't think Personnel would have kept me five minutes. I had broken bounds while under house arrest, I had withheld my knowledge of Ben's attachment to Stefanie, and if I was not a willing recipient of Ben's amorous declarations, I was guilty by association, so to hell with me.

"We rather thought you might like to consider the British Council," Personnel had suggested nastily, at a meeting adorned not even by a cup of tea.

But Smiley interceded for me. Smiley, it appeared, had seen beyond my youthful impulsiveness, and Smiley commanded what amounted to his own modest private army of secret sources scattered around Europe. A further reason for my reprieve was provided—though not even Smiley could have known it at the time—by the traitor Bill Haydon, whose London Station was rapidly acquiring a monopoly of Circus operations worldwide. And if Smiley's questing eye had not yet focused on Bill, he was already convinced that the Fifth Floor was nursing a Moscow Centre mole to its bosom, and determined to assemble a team of officers whose age and access placed them beyond suspicion. By a mercy, I was one.

For a few months I was kept in limbo, devilling in large back rooms, evaluating and distributing low-grade reports to Whitehall clients. Friendless and bored, I was seriously beginning to wonder whether Personnel had decided to post me to death, when to my joy I was summoned to his office and in Smiley's presence offered the post of second man in Zurich, under a capable old trooper named Eddows, whose stated principle was to leave me to sink or swim.

Within a month I was installed in a small flat in the Altstadt, working round the clock eight days a week. I had a Soviet naval attaché in Geneva who loved Lenin but loved a French air hostess more, and a Czech arms dealer in Lausanne who was having a crisis of conscience about supplying the world's terrorists with weapons and explosives. I had a millionaire Albanian with a chalet in St. Moritz who was risking his neck by returning to his homeland and recruiting members of his former household, and a nervous East German physicist on attachment to the Max Planck Institute in Essen who had secretly converted to Rome. I had a beautiful little microphone operation running against the Polish Embassy in Bern and a telephone tap on a pair of Hungarian spies in Basel. And I was by now beginning to fancy myself seriously in love with Mabel, who had recently been transferred to Vetting Section, and was the toast of the Junior Officers' Bar.

And Smiley's faith in me was not misplaced, for by my own exertions in the field, and his insistence upon rigid need-to-know at home, we succeeded in netting valuable intelligence and even getting it into the right hands—and you would be surprised how rarely that combination is achieved.

So that when after two years of this the Hamburg slot came up—a one-man post, and working directly to London Station, now willy-nilly the operational hub of the Service—I had Smiley's generous blessing to apply for it, whatever his private reservations about Haydon's widening embrace. I angled, I was not brash, I reminded Personnel of my naval background. I let him infer, if I did not say it in as many words, that I was straining at the bonds of Smiley's old-world caution. And it worked. He gave me Hamburg Station on the Haydon ticket, and the same night, after a romantic dinner at Bianchi's, Mabel and I slept together, the first time for each of us.

My sense of the rightness of things was further increased when, on looking over my new stocklist, I saw to my amusement that one Wolf Dittrich, alias Sea Captain Brandt, was a leading player in my new cast of characters. We are talking of the late sixties now. Bill Haydon had three more years to run.

* * *

Hamburg had always been a good place to be English, now it was an even better place to spy. After the lakeside gentility of Zurich, Hamburg crackled with energy and sparkled with sea air. The old Hanseatic ties to Poland, northern Russia and the Baltic states were still very much alive. We had commerce, we had banking—well, so had Zurich. But we had shipping too, and immigrants and adventurers. We had brashness and vulgarity galore. We were the German capital of whoredom and the press. And on our doorstep we had the secretive lowlands of Schleswig-Holstein, with their horizontal rainstorms, red farms, green fields and cloudstacked skies. Every man has his price. To this day, my soul can be bought for a jar of Lübeck beer, a pickled herring and a glass of schnapps after a trudge along the dykes.

Everything else about the job was equally pleasing. I was Ned the Assistant Shipping Consul; my humble office was a pretty brick cottage with a brass plate, handy enough for the Consulate General, yet prudently apart from it. Two clerks on secondment from the Admiralty performed my cover work for me, and kept their mouths shut. I had a radio and a Circus cypher clerk. And if Mabel and I were not yet engaged to be married, our relationship had reached a stage when she was ready to clear her decks for me whenever I popped back to London for a consultation with Bill or one of his lieutenants.

To meet my joes, I had a safe flat in Wellingsbüttel overlooking the cemetery, on the upper floor of a flower shop managed by a retired German couple who had belonged to us in the war. Their busiest days were Sundays, and on Monday mornings a queue of kids from the housing estate sold them back the flowers they had sold the day before. I never saw a safer spot. Hearses, covered vans and funeral corteges rolled past us all day long. But at night the place was literally as quiet as the grave. Even the exotic figure of my sea captain became unremarkable when he donned his black hat and dark suit and swung into the brick archway of our shop and, with his commercial traveller's brief-case bouncing at his side, stomped up the stairs to our innocent front door marked *"Büro."*

I shall go on calling him Brandt. Some people, however much they change their names, have only one.

But the jewel in my crown was the *Margerite*—or, as we called her in English, the *Daisy*. She was a fifty-foot clinker-built, double-ended fishing boat converted to a cabin cruiser, with a wheelhouse, a main saloon and four berths in the foc's'le. She had a mizzen mast and sail to steady her from rolling. She had a dark-green hull with light-green gunnels and a white cabin roof. She was built for stealth, not speed. In poor light and choppy water, she was invisible to the naked eye. She had sparse top-hamper, and lay close to the water, which gave her a harmless image on the radar screens, particularly in heavy weather. The Baltic is a vengeful sea, shallow and tideless. Even in a mild wind, the waves come steep and nasty. At ten knots and full throttle, the *Daisy* pitched and rolled like a pig. The only speedy thing about her was the fourteen-foot Zodiac dinghy hoisted as the ship's lifeboat and lashed to the cabin roof, with a Johnson 50-horsepower to whisk our agents in and out.

For her berth she had the old fishing village of Blankenese on the river Elbe, just a few short miles out of Hamburg. And there she lay contentedly among her equals, as humble an example of her kind as you could wish. From Blankenese, when she was needed, she could slip upriver to the Kiel Canal, and crawl its sixty miles at five knots before hitting open sea.

She had a Decca navigator that took readings from slave sta-tions on the shore, but so did everyone. She had nothing inside or out that was not consistent with her modesty. Each of her three-man crew could turn his hand to everything. There were no specialists, though each had his particular love. When we needed expert despatchers or fitters, the Royal Navy was on hand to help us.

So you can see that, what with a new dynamic team to back me up at London Station, and a full hand of sources to test my versatility, and the *Daisy* and her crew to manage, I had everything that a Head of Station with salt water in his blood could decently inherit.

And of course I had Brandt.

Brandt's two years before the Circus mast had altered him in ways I at first found hard to define. It was not so much an aging or a hardening I observed in him, as that wearying alertness, that overwakefulness, which the secret world with time imprints upon even the most relaxed of its inhabitants. We met at the safe flat. He entered. He stopped dead and stared at me. His jaw fell open and he let out a great shout of recognition. He seized my arms in a sultan's greeting and nearly broke them. He laughed till the tears came, he held me away to look at, then hauled me back to hug against his black overcoat. But his spontaneity was strained by watchfulness. I knew the signs. I had seen them in other joes.

"God damn, why they don't tell me nothing, Herr Konsul?" he cried as he embraced me yet again. "What damn game they playing? Listen, we do some good things over there, hear me? We got good people, we beat those damn Russians to death, okay?"

"I know," I said, laughing back at him. "I heard."

And when night fell he insisted on seating me among the coils of rope in the back of his van and driving me at breakneck speed to the remote farmhouse that London had acquired for him. He was determined to introduce me to his crew and I looked forward to it. And I looked forward even more to getting a sight of his girlfriend Bella, because London Station was feeling a little queasy about her recent arrival in his life. She was twenty-two years old and had been with him three months. Brandt was looking hard at fifty. It was midsummer, I remember, and the inside of the van smelt of freesias, for he had bought her a bunch at the market.

"She's a number one girl," he told me proudly as we entered the house. "Cooks good, makes good love, learns English, everything. Hey, Bella, I brought you new boyfriend!"

Painters and sailors make the same kind of houses, and Brandt's was no exception. It was scant but homely, with brick floors and low, white-raftered ceilings. Even in the darkness it seemed to usher in the outside light. From the front door we stepped straight down into the drawing room. A wood fire smouldered in the hearth and a ship's lamp shone on the naked flank of a girl as she lay reading on a heap of cushions. Hearing us enter, she sprang excitedly to her feet. Twenty-two and going on eighteen, I thought as she grabbed my hand and gaily pumped it up and down. She was wearing a man's shirt and very short shorts. A gold amulet glinted at her throat, declaring Brandt's possession of her: this is my woman, wearing my badge of ownership. Her face was peasant and Slav and naturally happy, with clear, wide eyes, high cheeks and a tipped-up smile even when her lips were in repose. Her bare legs were long and tanned to the same gold colour as her hair. She had a small waist, high breasts and full hips. It was a very beautiful, very young body, and whatever Brandt was thinking, it belonged to no one of his age, or even mine.

She set his freesias in a vase and fetched black bread and pickles and a bottle of schnapps. She was carelessly provocative in her movements. Either she knew exactly, or not at all, the power of each slight gesture she made. She sat beside him at the table, smiled at me and threw her arm around him, letting her shirt gape. She took possession of his hand and showed me by comparison the slenderness of her own, while Brandt talked recklessly about the network, mentioning joes and places by name, and Bella measured me with her frank eyes.

"Listen," Brandt said, "we got to get Aleks another radio, hear me, Ned? They take it apart, they put new spares, batteries, that radio's lousy. That's a bad-luck radio."

When the phone rang, he answered it imperiously: "Listen, I'm busy, okay? . . . Leave the package with Stefan, I said. Listen, have you heard from Leonids?"

The room gradually filled up. First to enter was a darting, bandy-legged man with a drooping moustache. He kissed Bella rapturously but chastely on the lips, punched Brandt's forearm and helped himself to a plateful of food.

"That's Kazimirs," Brandt explained, with a jab of his thumb. "He's a bastard and I love him. Okay?"

"Very okay," I said heartily.

Kazimirs had escaped three years ago across the Finnish border, I remembered. He had killed two Soviet frontier guards along his way, and he was crazy about engines—never happier than when he was up to his elbows in oil. He was also the respected ship's cook.

After Kazimirs came the Durba brothers, Antons and Alfreds, stocky and pert like Welshmen, and blue-eyed like Brandt. The Durbas had sworn to their mother that they would never go to sea together, so they took it in turns, for the *Daisy* handled best with three, and we liked to leave space for cargo and unexpected passengers. Soon everyone was talking at once, shooting questions at me, not waiting for the answers, laughing, proposing toasts, smoking, reminiscing, conspiring. Their last run had been bad, really bad, said Kazimirs. That was three weeks ago. Daisy had hit a freak storm off the Gulf of Danzig and lost her mizzen. At Ujava on the Latvian coast, they had missed the light signal in the fog, said Antons Durba. They had fired a rocket and God help them, there was this whole damned reception party of crazy Latvians standing on the beach like a delegation of city fathers! Wild laughter, toasts, then a deep Nordic silence while everyone but myself was struck by the same solemn memory.

"To Valdemars," said Kazimirs, and we drank a toast to Valdemars, a member of their group who had died five years ago. Then Bella took Brandt's glass and drank too, a separate ceremony while she watched me over the brim. "Valdemars," she repeated softly, and her solemnity was as beguiling as her smile. Had she known Valdemars? Had he been one of her lovers? Or was she simply drinking to a brave fellow countryman who had died for the Cause?

But I have to tell you a little more about Valdemars—not whether he had slept with Bella or even how he had died, for no one knew for sure. All that was known was that he had been put ashore and never heard of again. One story said he had managed to swallow his pill, another that he had given orders to his bodyguard to shoot him if he walked into a trap. But the bodyguard had disappeared too. And Valdemars was not the only one who had disappeared during what was now remembered by the group as "the autumn of betrayal." In the next few months, as the anniversaries of their deaths came round, we drank to four other Latvian heroes who had perished unaccountably in the same ill-starred period—delivered, it was now believed, not to partisans in the forest, nor loyal reception parties on the beach, but straight into the hands of Moscow Centre's chief of Latvian operations. And if new networks had been cautiously rebuilt meanwhile, five years later the stigma of these betrayals still clung to the survivors, as Haydon had been at pains to warn me.

"They're a careless bunch of sods," he had said with his usual

irreverence, "and when they're not being careless, they're duplic-
itous. Don't be fooled by all that Nordic phlegm and backslap-
ping."

I was remembering his words as I continued my mental reconnaissance of Bella. Sometimes she listened resting her head on her
clenched fist, sometimes she laid her head on Brandt's forearm,
dreaming his thoughts for him while he plotted and drank. But
her big, light eyes never ceased visiting me, working me out, this
Englishman sent to rule our lives. And occasionally, like a warm
cat, she shook herself free of Brandt and took time to groom herself, recrossing her legs and primly correcting the fit of her shorts,
or twisting a hank of hair into a plait, or drawing her gold amulet
from between her breasts and examining it front and back. I
waited for a spark of complicity between herself and other members of the crew, but it was clear to me that Brandt's girl was holy
ground. Even the ebullient Kazimirs deadened his face to talk to
her. She fetched another bottle, and when she returned she sat
down beside me and took hold of my hand and opened my palm
on the table, examining it while she spoke in Latvian to Brandt,
who broke into a gust of laughter which the rest of them took up.

"You know what she say?"

"I'm afraid I don't."

"She says English make damn good husband. If I die, she
going to have you instead!"

She clambered back to him and, laughing, wriggled into his
embrace. She didn't look at me after that. It was as if she didn't
need to. So I avoided her eyes in return, and thought dutifully
about her history as told to London Station by Sea Captain
Brandt.

She was the daughter of a farmer from a village near Jelgava,
who had been shot dead when security police raided a secret
meeting of Latvian patriots, Brandt had said. The farmer was a
founder member of the group. The police wanted to shoot the

girl as well, but she escaped into the forest and joined up with a band of partisans and outlaws who passed her round among them for a summer, which did not seem to have upset her. By stages she had made her way to the coast and, by a route that was still mysterious to us, got word to Brandt, who, without troubling to mention her to London in advance, picked her off a beach while he was landing a new radio operator to replace another who had had a nervous breakdown. Radio operators are the opera star of every network. If they don't have breakdowns, they have shingles.

"Great guys," said Brandt enthusiastically as he drove me back to town. "You like them?"

"They're terrific," I said, and meant it, for there is no better company anywhere than men who love the sea.

"Bella want to work with us. She want to kill the guys who shoot her father. I say no. She's too young. I love her."

A fierce white moon shone on the flat meadows, and by its light I saw his craggy face in profile, as if set against the storm to come.

"And you knew him," I suggested, affecting to recapitulate something I vaguely remembered. "Her father. Feliks. He was a friend of yours."

"Sure I knew Feliks! I love him! He was a great guy! The bastards shot him dead."

"Did he die immediately?"

"They shoot him to pieces. Kalashnikovs. They shoot everybody. Seven guys. All shot."

"Did anyone see it happen?"

"One guy. He see it, run away."

"What became of the bodies?"

"Secret police take them. They're scared, those police guys. Don't want no trouble from the people. Shoot the partisans, throw them in a truck, drive away to hell."

"How well did you know him—her father?"

Brandt made his sweeping gesture with his forearm. "Feliks? He was my friend. Fought at Leningrad. Prisoner of war in Germany. Stalin didn't like those guys. When they came home from Germany, he sent them to Siberia, shot them, gave them a bad time. What the hell?"

But London Station had picked up a different story, even if at this stage it was only a whisper. The father had been the informant, said the whisper. Recruited in Siberian captivity and sent back to Latvia to penetrate the groups. He had called the meeting, tipped off his masters, then climbed out of the back window while the partisans were being slaughtered. As a reward, he was now managing a collective farm near Kiev, living under a different name. Somebody had recognised him and told somebody else who had told somebody else. The source was delicate, checking would be a lengthy process.

So I was warned. Watch out for Bella.

I was more than warned. I was disturbed. In the next weeks I saw Bella several times, and each time I was obliged to record my impressions on the encounter sheet which London Station now insisted must be completed each time she was sighted. I made a rendezvous with Brandt at the safe flat, and to my alarm he brought her with him. She had spent the day in town, he said. They were on their way back to the farmhouse, why not?

"Relax. She don't speak no English," he reminded me with a laugh, noticing my discomfort.

So I kept our business short, while she lounged on the sofa and smiled and listened to us with her eyes, but mostly she listened to me.

"My girl's studying," Brandt told me proudly, patting her on the backside as we prepared to separate. "One day she be a big professor. *Nicht wahr, Bella? Du wirst ein ganz grosser Professor, du!"*

A week later, when I took a discreet look at the *Daisy* at her berth in Blankenese, Bella was there again, wearing her shorts and scampering over the deck in her bare feet as if we were planning a Mediterranean cruise.

"For heaven's sake. We can't have girls abroad. London will go mad," I told Brandt that night. "So will the crew. You know how superstitious they are about having women on the ship. You're the same yourself."

He brushed me aside. My predecessor had raised no objection, he said. Why should I?

"Bella makes the boys happy," he insisted. "She's from home, Ned, she's a kid. She's a family for them, come on!"

When I checked the file, I discovered he was half right. My predecessor, a seconded naval officer, had reported that Bella was "conscious to" the *Daisy,* even adding that she seemed to "exert a benign influence as ship's mascot." And when I read between the lines of his report of the *Daisy*'s most recent operational mission, I realised that Bella had been there on the dockside to wave them off—and no doubt to wave them safely back as well.

Now of course operational security is always relative. I had never imagined that everything in the Brandt organisation was going to be played by Sarratt rules. I was aware that in the cloistered atmosphere of Head Office it was too easy to mistake our tortuous structures of codenames, symbols and cutouts for life on the ground, Cambridge Circus was one thing. A bunch of volatile Baltic patriots risking their necks was another.

Nevertheless the presence of an uncleared, unrecruited campfollower at the heart of our operation, privy to our plans and conversations, went beyond anything I had imagined—and all this in the wake of the betrayals five years earlier. And the more I worried over it, the more proprietorial, it seemed to me, did

Brandt's devotion to the girl become. His endearments grew increasingly lavish in my presence, his caresses more demonstrative. "A typical older man's infatuation for a young girl," I told London, as if I had seen dozens of such cases.

Meanwhile a new mission was being planned for the *Daisy,* the purpose to be revealed to us later. Twice, three times a week, I found myself of necessity driving out to the farmhouse, arriving after dark, then sitting for hours at the table while we studied charts and weather maps and the latest shore observation bulletins. Sometimes the full crew came, sometimes it was just the three of us. To Brandt it made no difference. He clasped Bella to him as if the two of them were in the throes of constant ecstasy, fondling her hair and neck, and once forgetting himself so far as to slip his hand inside her shirt and cup her naked breast while he gave her a prolonged kiss. Yet as I discreetly looked away from these disturbing scenes, what remained longest in my sight was Bella's gaze on me, as if she were telling me she wished that it was I, not Brandt, who was caressing her.

"Explicit embraces appear to be the norm," I wrote drily on the encounter sheet, Hamburg to London Station, late that night in my office. And in my nightly log: "Route, weather and sea conditions acceptable. We await firm orders from Head Office. Morale of crew high."

But my own morale was fighting for survival as one calamity followed upon another.

There was first the unfortunate business of my predecessor, full name Lieutenant Commander Perry de Mornay Lipton, D.S.O., R.N., retd., sometime hero of Jack Arthur Lumley's wartime irregulars. For ten years until my arrival, Lipton had cultivated the rôle of Hamburg character, by day acting the English bloody fool, sporting a monocle and hanging around the expatriate clubs ostensibly to pick up free advice on his investments. But come nightfall, he put on his secret hat and went to work briefing and debriefing his formidable army of secret agents. Or so the legend, as I had heard it from Head Office.

The only thing that had puzzled me was that there had been no formal handover between us, but Personnel had told me tersely Lipton was on a mission elsewhere. I was now admitted to the truth. Lipton had departed, not on some life-and-death adventure in darkest Russia, but to southern Spain, where he had set up house with a former Corporal of Horse named Kenneth, and two hundred thousand pounds of Circus funds, mainly in gold bars and Swiss francs, which he had paid out over several years to brave agents who did not exist.

The mistrust shed by this sad discovery now spilled into every operation Lipton had touched, including inevitably Brandt's. Was Brandt too a Lipton fiction, living high on our secret funds in exchange for ingeniously fabricated intelligence? Were his networks, were his vaunted collaborators and friends, many of whom were drawing liberal salaries?

And Bella—was Bella part of the deception? Had Bella softened his head and weakened his will? Was Brandt too feathering his nest before retiring with his loved one to the south of Spain?

A procession of Circus experts passed through the door of my little shipping office. First came an improbable man called Captain Plum. Crouched in the privacy of my safe room, Plum and I pored over the *Daisy*'s old fuel dockets and mileage records and compared them with the perilous routes that Brandt and the crew claimed to have steered on their missions along the Baltic coast. The ship's logs were sketchy at best, as most logs are, but we read them all, alongside Plum's records of signals intercepts, radar stations, navigational buoys and sightings of Soviet patrol boats.

A week later Plum was back, this time accompanied by a foulmouthed Mancunian called Rose, a former Malayan policeman who had made himself a name as a Circus sniffer dog. Rose questioned me as roughly as if I were myself a part of the deception.

But when I was about to lose my temper he disarmed me by declaring that, on the evidence available, the Brandt organisation was innocent of misdoing.

Yet in the minds of such people as this, suspicions of one kind only fired suspicions of another, and the question mark hanging over Bella's father, Feliks, had not gone away. If the father was bad, then the daughter must know it, went the reasoning. And if she knew and had not said it, then she was bad as well. Moscow Centre, like the Circus, was well known for recruiting entire families. A father-and-daughter team was eminently plausible. Soon, without any solid evidence I was aware of, London Station began to peddle the notion that Feliks had been responsible for the betrayals five years ago.

Inevitably, this placed Bella in an even more sinister light. There was talk of ordering her to London and grilling her, but here my authority as Brandt's case officer held sway. Impossible, I advised London Station. Brandt would never stand for it. Very well, came the answer—typical of Haydon's cavalier approach—bring them both over and Brandt can sit in while we interrogate the girl. This time I was sufficiently moved to fly back to London myself, where I insisted on stating my case personally to Bill. I entered his room to find him stretched out on a chaise longue, for he affected the eccentricity of never sitting at his desk. A joss stick was burning from an old ginger jar.

"Maybe Brother Brandt isn't as prickly as you think, Master Ned," he said accusingly, peering at me over his half-framed spectacles. "Maybe *you're* the prickly one?"

"He's besotted with her," I said.

"Are you?"

"If we start accusing his girl in front of him, he'll go crazy. He lives for her. He'd tell us to go to hell and dismantle the network, and I doubt whether anyone else could run it."

Haydon pondered this: "The Garibaldi of the Baltic. Well,

well. Still, Garibaldi wasn't much bloody good, was he?" He waited for me to answer but I preferred to take his question as rhetorical. "Those jokers she shacked up in the forest with," he drawled finally. "Does she talk about them?"

"She doesn't talk about any of it. Brandt does, she doesn't."

"So what does she talk about?"

"Nothing much. If she says anything of significance, it's usually in Latvian and Brandt translates or not as he thinks fit. Otherwise she just smiles and looks."

"At you?"

"At him."

"And she's quite a looker, I gather."

"She's attractive, I suppose. Yes."

Once more he took his time to consider this. "Sounds to me like the ideal woman," he pronounced. "Smiles and looks, keeps quiet, fucks—what more can you ask?" He again examined me quizzically over his spectacles. "Do you mean she doesn't even speak *German*? She must do, coming from up there. Don't be daft."

"She speaks German reluctantly when she's got no choice. Speaking Latvian's a patriotic act. German isn't."

"Good tits?"

"Not bad."

"Couldn't you get alongside her a bit more? Without rocking the lovers' boat, obviously. Just the answers to a few basic questions would be a help. Nothing dramatic. Just whether she's the real thing, or whether Brother Brandt smuggled her into the nest in a warming pan—or whether Moscow Centre did, of course. See what you can get out of her. He's not her natural father, you realise that, I suppose. He can't be."

"Who isn't?" For a confused moment I had thought he was still talking about Brandt.

"Her daddy. Feliks. The one who got shot or didn't. The

farmer. According to the record, she was born January '45, wasn't she?"

"Yes."

"Ergo, conceived around April '44. At which time—if Brother Brandt's to be believed—her supposed daddy was languishing in a prisoner-of-war camp in Germany. Mind you, we shouldn't be too straitlaced about it. No great feat of skill, I suppose, to get yourself knocked up while your old man's in the pen. Still every little detail helps when we're trying to decide whether to abort a network which may have run its course."

I was grateful for Mabel's company that night, even if we had not yet found our form as the great lovers we were so anxious to become. But of course I didn't tell her anything of my business, least of all about Bella. As a Vetting girl, Mabel was on the routine side of the Circus. It would have been quite improper for me to share my problems with her. If we had already been married— well, that might have been a different thing. Meanwhile, Bella must remain my secret.

And she did. Back in my solitary bed in Hamburg I thought of Bella and little else. The double mystery of her—as a woman and as a potential traitor—elevated her to an object of almost unlimited danger to me. I saw her no longer as a fringe figure of our organisation but its destiny. Her virtue as ours. If Bella was pure, so was the network. But if she was the plaything of another service—a deceiver planted on us to tempt and weaken and ultimately betray us—then the integrity of those round her was soiled with her own, and the network would indeed, as Haydon put it, have run its course.

I closed my eyes and saw her gaze upon me, sunny and beckoning. I felt again the softness of her kisses each time we greeted one another—always, as it seemed to me, held for a fraction longer than formality required. I pictured her liquid body in its different poses, and turned it over and over in my imagination in the same way that I contemplated the possibilities of her treason. I remembered Haydon's suggestion that I could try to "get alongside her," and discovered I was incapable of separating my sense of duty from my desires.

I retold myself the story of her escape, questioning it at every stage. Had she got away before the shooting or during it? And how? Had some lover among the security troops tipped her off? Had there been a shooting at all? And why did she not grieve more for her dead father, instead of making love to Brandt? Even her happiness seemed to speak against her. I imagined her in the forest, with the cut-throats and outlaws. Did each man take her at his will, or did she live now with this one, now with that? I dreamed of her, naked in the forest and myself naked with her. I awoke ashamed of myself and put through an early-morning call to Mabel.

Did I understand myself? I doubt it. I knew little about women, beautiful women least of all. I am sure it never occurred to me that finding fault with Bella might be my way of weakening her sexual hold on me. Determined on the straight path, I wrote to Mabel daily. Meanwhile I fixed on the *Daisy*'s forthcoming mission as the perfect opportunity to undertake a hostile questioning of Bella. The weather was turning foul, which was what suited the *Daisy* best. It was autumn and the nights were lengthening. The *Daisy* liked the dark too.

"Crew stand by to sail Monday," said London Station's first signal. The second, which did not arrive till Friday evening, gave their destination as the Narva Bay in northern Estonia, not a hundred miles west of Leningrad. Never before had the *Daisy* ventured so far along the Russian seaboard; only rarely had she been used in support of non-Latvian patriots.

"I would give my eyes," I told Brandt.

"You're too damn dangerous, Ned," he replied, clapping me on the shoulder. "Be seasick four days, lie in your bunk, get in the way, what the hell?"

We both knew it was impossible. The most Head Office had ever granted me was a night spin round the island of Bornholm, and even that had been like drawing teeth.

On the Saturday night we gathered in the farmhouse. Kazimirs and Antons Durba arrived together in the van. It was Antons's turn to go to sea. With such a small operational crew, everyone had to know everything, everyone had to be interchangeable. There was no more drink. From now on, they were a dry ship. Kazimirs had brought lobsters. He cooked them elaborately, with a sauce that he was famous for, while Bella played cabin girl to him, fetching and carrying and being decorative. When we had eaten, Bella cleared the table and I spread the charts under the hanging overhead lamp.

Brandt had said six days. It was an optimistic guess. From the Kieler Förde the *Daisy* would make for open sea, passing Bornholm on the Swedish side. On reaching the Swedish land of Gotland she would put in at Sundre on the southern tip, refuel and top up her provisions. While refuelling, she would be approached by two men, one of whom would ask if they had any herring. They were to reply: "Only in tins. There have been no herring in these waters for years." All such exchanges sound fatuous in cold blood, and this one reduced Antons and Kazimirs to fits of nervous laughter. Returning from the kitchen, Bella joined in.

One of the men would then ask to come aboard, I continued. He was an expert—I did not say in sabotage, because the crew had mixed feelings on the matter. His name for the trip would be Volodia. He would be carrying a leather suitcase and, in his coat pocket, a brown button and a white button as proof of his good faith. If he did not know his name, or carried no suitcase, or did not produce the buttons, they were to put him back on shore alive, but return to Kiel at once. There was an agreed radio signal for this eventuality. Otherwise they should make no signals whatever. A moment's silence gripped us, and I heard the sound of Bella's bare feet on the brick floor as she fetched more firewood.

From Gotland they should head northeast through international waters, I said, and steer a central course up the Gulf of Finland, until they were lying off the island of Hogland, where they should idle till dusk, then head due south for Narva Bay, reckoning to make landfall by midnight.

I had brought large-scale charts of the Bay and photographs of the sandy coastline. I spread them on the table and the men gathered to my side to look at them. As they did so, something made me glance up and I caught sight of Bella, curled up in her own corner of the room, her excited eye full upon me in the firelight.

I showed them the point on the beach that the Zodiac should make for, and the point on the headland where they should watch for signals. The landing party would be wearing ultra-violet glasses, I said; the Estonian reception party would be using an ultra-violet lamp. Nothing would be visible to the naked eye. After the passenger and his suitcase had been landed, the dinghy should wait no more than two minutes for any possible replacement before heading back for the *Daisy* at full speed. The dinghy should be crewed by one man only, so that if necessary he could take a second passenger on the return run. I recited the recognition signals to be exchanged with the reception party, and this time nobody laughed. I gave the shelving and gradients of the landing beach. There would be no moon. Bad weather was expected, and surely hoped for. Bella brought us tea, brushing carelessly against us as she set out the mugs. It was as if she were harnessing her sexuality to our cause. Reaching Brandt, who was still stooped over the beach chart, she gravely caressed his broad back with both hands as if filling him with her youthful strength.

I returned to my flat at five in the morning with no thought of

sleep. In the afternoon I rode with Brandt and Bella to Blankenese in the van. Antons and Kazimirs had been with the boat all
day. They were dressed for the voyage, in bobble hats and oilskin
trousers. Orange life jackets were airing on the deck. Shaking
hands with each man in turn, I passed round the seaproofed cap-
sules that contained their lethal pills of pure cyanide. A grey drizzle was falling; the little quay was deserted. Brandt walked to the
gangway, but when Bella made to follow him, he stopped her.

"No more," he told her. "You stay with Ned."

She was wearing his old duffle coat, and a woollen hat with
earflaps, which I suspected she had been wearing when he rescued her. He kissed her and she hugged him till he pushed her off
and went aboard, leaving her at my side. Antons stepped into the
engine house and we heard the engine cough and come to life.
Brandt and Kazimirs cast off. Nobody looked at us any more.
The *Daisy* cleared the quay and headed sedately for the centre of
the river. The three men's backs remained turned against us. We
heard the hoot of her ship's horn, and watched her until she had
slipped behind the curtain of grey mist.

Like abandoned children, Bella and I walked hand in hand up
the ramp to Brandt's parked van. Neither of us spoke. Neither of
us had anything to say. I glanced back for a last sight of the *Daisy,*
but the mist had swallowed her. I looked at Bella and saw that
her eyes were unusually bright, and that she was breathing fast.

"He'll be all right," I assured her, releasing her hand while I
unlocked the door. "They're very experienced. He's a great man."
Even in German, it sounded rather silly.

She got into the van beside me and took back my hand. Her
fingers were like separate lives inside my palm. Get alongside
her, Haydon had kept insisting. In my most recent signal, I had
assured him I would try.

* * *

At first we drove in companionable silence, joined and separated by our shared experience. I was driving cautiously because I was taut, but my hand still held hers to give her comfort, and when I was obliged to take a firmer grasp of the steering wheel, I saw that her hand stayed beside me, fingers upward, waiting for me to come back. Suddenly I was terribly concerned about where to take her. Absurdly so. I thought of an elegant basement restaurant with tiled alcoves where I took my banking joes. The elderly waiters would provide her with the kind of reassurance she needed. Then I remembered she was wearing Brandt's duffle coat, jeans and rubber boots. I was no better dressed myself. So where? I wondered anxiously. It was getting late. Through the mist, lights were coming on in the cottages.

"Are you hungry?" I asked.

She put her hand back on her lap.

"Should I find us somewhere to eat?" I asked.

She shrugged.

"Shall I take you to the farmhouse?" I suggested.

"What for?"

"Well I mean, how are you going to spend the next few days? What did you do the last time he was away?"

"I rested from him," she said, with a laugh I had not expected.

"Then tell me how you would like to wait for him," I suggested magnanimously, with a hint of rank. "Do you prefer to be alone? Meet up with other exiles and have gossips? What's best?"

"It's not important," she said, and moved away from me. "Tell me all the same. Help me."

"I shall go to cinemas. Look at shops. Read magazines. I shall listen to music. Try to study. Get bored."

I decided on the safe flat. There would be food in the fridge, I told myself. Give her a meal, a drink, get her talking. Then either drive her to the farmhouse or send her by cab.

We entered the city. I parked two streets away from the safe flat and took her arm as we walked along the tree-lined pavement. I would have done the same for any woman in a dark street, but there was something disturbing about feeling her bare arm inside Brandt's sleeve. The city was unfamiliar to me. In the lighted windows of the houses, people talked and laughed as if we didn't exist. She clasped my arm and drew my hand against her breast—to be precise, the underside of it, I could feel its shape precisely through the layers of clothing. I was remembering the Circus bar-room jokes about certain officers who picked up their best intelligence in bed. I was remembering Haydon asking me whether she had good tits. I felt ashamed, and took back my hand.

There was a man-door to one side of the cemetery gates. As I unlocked it and ushered her ahead of me, she turned and kissed me on the eyes, one after the other, while she held my face in both her hands. I gripped her waist and she seemed weightless. She was very happy. I could see her smile by the yellow cemetery lights.

"Everyone is dead," she whispered excitedly. "But we are alive."

I went ahead of her up the stairs. Halfway, I looked back to make sure she was following me. I was scared that she might have changed her mind. I was scared altogether—not because I was without experience—thanks to Mabel I was not—but because I knew already that I was encountering a different category of woman from any I had known before. She was standing right behind me, holding her shoes in her hands, still smiling.

I opened the door for her. She stepped through and kissed me again, laughing in merriment, just as if I had lifted her up and carried her across the threshold on our wedding day. I remembered stupidly that Russians never shake hands in doorways, and perhaps Latvians didn't either, and perhaps her kisses were some kind of ceremony of exorcism. I would have asked her, except that, near enough, I had lost my voice. I closed the door, then crossed the room to turn up the fire, an electric convector affair which, as long as the room was cold, blew out warm air with enormous vigour, but afterwards only fitfully, like an old dog dreaming.

I went to the kitchen to fetch some wine. When I returned she had disappeared and the light was on under the bathroom door. I set the table carefully with knives and forks and spoons and cheese and cold meat and glasses and paper napkins and anything else that I could possibly think of, because I was taking refuge in the distancing formalities of hospitality.

The bathroom door opened and she emerged wearing Brandt's coat wrapped round her as a dressing-gown and, to judge by her bare legs, little else. Her hair was brushed. In our safe flats, we always keep a brush and comb for hospitality.

And I remember thinking that if she was as bad as Haydon seemed to think she was, it was a pretty terrible thing for her to be wearing Brandt's coat in order to deceive the man she was already betraying, and a pretty terrible thing for me to be the man she had selected, while my agents were heading for high danger with lethal pills in their coat pockets. But I had no sense of guilt. I mention this in order to try to explain that my mind was zigzagging in any number of directions in its effort to still my desire for her.

I kissed her and took off her coat, and I never saw before or since anyone so beautiful. And the truth is that, at that moment and at that age, I had not yet acquired the power to distinguish between truth and beauty. They were one and the same to me, and I could only feel awe for her. If I had ever suspected her of anything, the sight of her naked body convinced me of her innocence.

After that, the images of my memory must tell you their own tale. Even today I see us as two other people, never as ourselves.

Bella naked by the half light of the fire, lying on her side as I had first seen her by the fire in the farmhouse. I had fetched the duvet from the bedroom.

"You're so beautiful," she whispered.

It had not occurred to me that I could fill her with a comparable wonder.

Bella at the window, the light from the cemetery making a perfect statue of her body, gilding her fleece and drawing light patterns on her breasts.

Bella kissing Ned's face, hundreds of small kisses as she brings him back to life. Bella laughing at the limitless beauty of herself, and of the two of us together. Bella taking laughter into love, a thing that had never happened to me before, until every part of each of us was a matter for celebration, to be kissed and suckled and admired in its own way.

Bella turning away from Ned to offer herself, thrusting back to accept him as she continues whispering to him. Her whispering stops. She begins her ascent, arching backward until she is upright. And suddenly she is crying out, crying to me and the dead, and she is the most living thing on earth.

Ned and Bella calm at last, standing at the window and gazing down into the graveyard.

There is Mabel, I say, but it seems too early to get married.

"It is always too early," she replies as we start to make love again.

Bella in the bath and myself crammed happily against the taps at the other end while she lazily fondles me under the water and talks about her childhood.

Bella on the duvet, drawing my head between her legs. Bella above me, riding me.

Bella kneeling over me, her secret garden open to my face as she transports me to places I have never imagined, not even lying in my wretched single bed, dreaming over and over of this moment and trying with far too little knowledge to ward off the unknown.

And betweenwhiles you may see Ned dozing on Bella's breast, our untouched food still on the table that I had set so formally in self-protection. With a mind made lucid by our lovemaking I ask whatever else I can think of that will satisfy Bill Haydon's curiosity, and my own.

I drove her home and reached my flat around seven in the morning. In no mood to sleep for the second night running, I sat down and wrote my encounter report instead, my pen flying because I was still in paradise. There was no message from the *Daisy* but I expected none. Come evening, I received an interim report on her progress. She had passed Kiel and was heading for the Kieler Förde. She would be hitting open sea in a couple of hours. I had a tame German journalist to see that night and a consular meeting in the morning, but I passed the news in veiled terms to Bella on the telephone and promised to come to her soon, for she was determined I should visit her at the farmhouse. When Brandt returned, she said, she wanted to be able to look at all the places in the house where we had made love, and think of me. I suppose it testifies to the power of love's illusion that I found nothing underhand in this, or paradoxical. We had created a world together and she wished to have it round her when I was taken away from her. That was all. She was Brandt's girl. She expected nothing of me but my love.

When I arrived, we made straight for the long drawing room, where this time it was she who had laid the table. We sat at it quite naked, which was what she wanted. She wanted to see me among the familiar furniture. Afterwards we made love in their bed. I suppose I should have been ashamed, but I felt only the excitement of being appointed to the most secret places of their lives. "These are his hairbrushes," she said. "These are his clothes, you are on his side of the bed." One day I will understand what this means, I thought. And then, more grimly: or is this the pleasure that she takes in betrayal?

Next evening I had arranged to visit an old Pole in Lübeck who had established a clandestine correspondence with a distant nephew in Warsaw. The boy was being trained for cypher work in the Polish diplomatic service, and wanted to spy for us in exchange for resettlement in Australia. London Station was considering a direct approach to him. I returned to Hamburg and slept like the dead. Next morning, while I was still writing my report, a signal from London announced that the *Daisy* had successfully refuelled in Sundre and was on course for the Finnish Gulf with passenger Volodia aboard. I phoned Bella and told her all was still well, and she said, "Please come to me."

I spent the morning in the Reeperbahn police station extricating a pair of drunk British merchant sailors who had broken up a brothel, and the afternoon at a ghastly consular wives' tea party to rally support for the Week of the Political Prisoner. I wished the merchant sailors had broken up that brothel too. I arrived at the farmhouse at eight in the evening and we went straight to bed. At two in the morning the phone rang and Bella answered it. It was my cypher clerk calling me from the shipping office: a decypher yourself, flash priority; I was required at once. I drove like the wind and made the office in forty minutes. As I sat down to the codebooks, I realised that Bella's smells were on my face and hands.

The signal had been transmitted over Haydon's symbol, personal to Head of Station, Hamburg. The *Daisy*'s landing party had come under heavy fire from prepared positions, it said. The dinghy was unaccounted for, and so was everyone aboard it, which meant Antons Durba and his passenger, and very likely whoever was waiting on the beach. There was no word of the

Estonian patriots. The *Daisy* had sighted ultraviolet-light signals from the shore, but only one completed series of the agreed pattern, and the assumption was that the Estonian team had been taken captive as soon as they had lured the landing party to its fate. It was a familiar story, even if it was five years old. The fallback radio in Tallinn was not replying.

I was to pass this information to nobody and return to London on the first flight of the morning. A seat had been reserved for me. Toby Esterhase would meet me at Heathrow. I drafted an acknowledgement and handed it to my clerk, who accepted it without comment. He knows, I thought. How could he not? He had telephoned me at the farmhouse and spoken to Bella. The rest he could see in my face and, for all I knew, he could smell it too.

This time there was no joss burning in Haydon's room and he was sitting at his desk. Roy Bland, his Head of Eastern Europe, sat one side of him, Toby Esterhase the other. Toby's jobs were never easily defined, for he liked to keep them vague in the hope that they would multiply. But in practice he was Haydon's poodle, a rôle which later cost him dear. And I was surprised to see George Smiley sitting unhappily apart from them on the edge of Haydon's chaise longue, even if the symbolism of his posture did not dawn on me till three years later.

"It's an inside job," Haydon said without preliminaries. "The mission was blown sky high in advance. If Durba hasn't gone down with the ship, he's already swinging by his thumbs, telling his all. Volodia doesn't know a lot, but that may be his tough luck, because his interrogators aren't going to believe him and he's got a hamper full of explosives to explain. Maybe he took the pill, but I doubt it—he's a ninny."

"Where's Brandt?" I said.

"Sitting under a bright light in the Sarratt interrogation wing and roaring like a bull. Somewhere somebody blundered. We're asking Brandt whether it might possibly be him. If not, who? It's a carbon-copy fuck-up from the last time round. Each member of the crew is being grilled separately."

"Where's the *Daisy*?"

"In Helsinki. We've put a navy crew aboard and they're under orders to get her out tonight. The Finns don't fancy being seen providing safe harbour for people teasing the Bear. If the press don't get to hear about it, it'll be a bloody miracle."

"I see," I said stupidly.

"Good. I don't. What do we do? You tell me. You've got thirty Baltic agents waiting on your every word. What do you say? Abort? Apologise? Act natural and look busy? All suggestions gratefully acknowledged."

"The Durbas weren't conscious to the Estonian network," I objected. "Antons can't blow what he doesn't know."

"So who blew Antons, pray? Who blew the landing party, the coordinates, the beach, the time? Who set us up? We asked Brandt the same question, funnily enough. We thought he might suggest Bella, the Baltic strumpet. He suggested it was one of us lot instead, the cheeky bastard."

He was furious and his fury was directed at me. I would never have imagined that lethargy could convert to such violent anger. Yet he still spoke quietly, in the nasal, upper-class drawl he had. He still managed to remain offhand. Even in passion he conveyed a deadly casualness, which made him all the more formidable.

"So what do *you* say?" he demanded of me.

"What about?"

"About *her*, sweetheart. Pouting Miss Latvia." He was holding up the encounter report that I had written after our first night together. "Christ Almighty, I asked for an assessment, not a bloody aria."

"I think she's innocent," I said. "I think she's a simple peasant kid. That's my assessment. I expect it's Brandt's too. She answered my questions, she gave a plausible account of herself."

Haydon had found his charm again. He could do that at the drop of a hat. He drew you and he repelled you. I remember that exactly. He danced all ways for you, playing your emotions against each other, because he had none of his own.

"Most spies *do* give a plausible account of themselves," he retorted as he turned the pages of my report. "The better ones do, anyway. Don't they, Tobe?"—favouring Esterhase.

"Absolutely, Bill. All the way, I would say," said Esterhase the pleaser.

The others had a copy too. Silence settled while they studied it, pausing at the passages Haydon had sidelined. Roy Bland lifted his head and peered at me. Bland had lectured to us at Sarratt. He was a North Countryman and former don who had spent years behind the Curtain under academic cover. His accent was broad and very flat.

"Bella admits her father's not her father, right, Ned? Her mother was raped by the Germans and got pregnant from it, so she's half German by origin. Right, Ned?"

"Yes. Right, Roy. That's what she told me."

"So when her father, as she calls him, when Feliks comes back from prisoner-of-war camp, and hears what's happened, he adopts the child. Her. Bella. Nice of him. She volunteered that to you. She made no secret of it. Right, Ned?"

"Yes. Right, Roy."

"Then why the fuck doesn't she tell Brandt the same tale as she tells you?"

I had asked her this myself, and so was able to answer him at once. "When he brought her to the West, she was afraid he wouldn't take her in if he knew she wasn't his best friend's natural daughter. They weren't lovers then. He was offering protection and a life. She was scared. She took it. She'd been living in the forest. It was her first time in the West. Her own father was dead, so she needed another father figure."

"Brandt, you mean?" said Bland slyly.

"Yes, of course."

"Well, don't you think it's pretty bloody odd then, Ned, that Brandt didn't know the truth about her anyway?" he demanded triumphantly. "If Brandt was her father's close buddy like he says he was, wouldn't he be bound to know all that? Come on, Ned!"

Smiley cut in, I thought in order to help me: "Brandt very probably *does* know, Roy. Would *you* tell your best friend's daughter that she was the illegitimate child of a German soldier if you thought she wasn't aware of it? I'm sure *I* wouldn't. *I'd* go to quite some lengths to protect her. Specially if the father was dead and I was in love with the daughter."

"Bugger love," said Haydon, turning another page of my report. "Brandt's a randy old goat. Who's this Tadeo she keeps talking about? 'Tadeo saw the bodies being loaded into the truck. Tadeo says he saw my father's body go in last. They'd shot most of the men in the face, but my father was shot in the chest and stomach, a machine gun had nearly cut him in two.' I mean, Christ, for a wilting violet she's bloody explicit when it helps her story, I will say."

"Tadeo was her first lover," I said.

"Jealous, are we?" Haydon asked me, drawing laughter from the satraps either side of him.

But not from Smiley. And not from me.

"Tadeo was a boy at her school," I said. "He'd been ordered to keep guard outside the house while the meeting took place, but he was making love with Bella in a field nearby. That's how she managed to escape. Tadeo told her to run for it, and who to ask for when she reached the partisans. Then he hid in a nearby house and watched what happened before joining her. It's in my report."

Toby Esterhase added his own kind of sneer, in his own kind of Austro-Hungarian English. "And Tadeo is most conveniently dead, of course, Ned. Being a witness in Bella's story is actually quite a risk business, I would say."

"He was shot by a frontier guard," I said. "He wasn't ever trying to cross. He was making a reconnaissance. She has the feeling everyone she touches dies," I added, thinking involuntarily of Ben.

"She could be right, at that," said Haydon.

Perversely, it seemed to me, Roy Bland now joined in my defence—for increasingly I had the feeling I was in the dock. "Mind you, Tadeo could be kosher *and* wrong about Feliks's death. Maybe the police faked his death. After all, he did go into the truck last. He'd have been covered with blood anyway in that slaughterhouse. They wouldn't have needed to splash the tomato ketchup on him, would they? It would have been done for them already."

Smiley took up Bland's cudgels. I was beginning to regret I had lobbied so hard to be posted out of his care.

"Is the father *really* so important to us, Bill?" he objected. "Feliks can be the Judas of all time, and still have a perfectly honest daughter, can't he?"

"I believe that too," I said. "She admires her father. She has no problem talking about him. She honours him. She's still in mourning for him."

I was remembering how she had looked down into the graveyard. I was remembering her determination to celebrate the gift of life. I refused to believe she had been pretending.

"All right," said Haydon impatiently, shoving a full-plate photograph at me across the desk. "We'll stretch a point and trust you. What the hell are we supposed to make of this lot?"

It was a much enlarged photograph and out of register. I guessed it was a photograph of a photograph. It was stamped in red along the top left corner with the one word "Witchcraft," which I had heard on the grapevine was London Station's most secret source.

Toby Esterhase's warning to me confirmed this: "You never saw this photograph actually, Ned," he told me over Haydon's shoulder, with the kind of smarminess people reserve for the young. "Also you never saw the word 'Witchcraft.' When you leave this room, your mind will be a blank, totally."

It was a group photograph of young men and women arranged against a background of what could have been a barracks, or the campus of a university. They were about sixty strong, and in civilian uniform, the men in suits and ties, the women in high white blouses and long skirts. A group of older men and an evil-looking woman stood to one side of them. The mood, like the clothes and the building and the background, was sullen.

"Second row of the chorus, third from the right," said Haydon, handing me a magnifying glass. "Good tits, same as the young man said."

It was Bella, there was no doubt of it. Bella three or four years younger it was true, and Bella with her hair swept back in what I guessed to be a bun. But Bella's broad, fair eyes and Bella's irrepressible smile, and the high, firm cheeks I adored.

"Did Bella ever whisper in your tiny shell-like ear that she'd been at language school in Kiev?" Haydon asked me.

"No."

"Did she give any account of her education at all, apart from how she'd had it off with Tadeo in the hay?"

"No."

"Of course Kiev *is* more of a holiday school than a school. Not a place many chaps talk about afterwards much. Unless they're confessing. Theoretically it's a school for tomorrow's interpreters but I'm afraid that in practice it's more a spawning ground for Moscow Centre hopefuls. Centre owns it, Centre staffs it, Centre skims the cream. The slops go to their Foreign Office, same as here."

"Has Brandt seen this?" I asked.

His levity fell from him. "You're joking, aren't you? Brandt's a hostile witness, so are they all."

"Can I see Brandt?"

"I wouldn't recommend it."

"Does that mean no?"

"Yes. It means no."

"Was Witchcraft also the source of the report against Bella's father?"

"Mind your own bloody business," he said, but I had caught Toby's startled eye and sensed that I was right.

"Does Moscow Centre always take class photographs of its white hopes?" I asked, emboldened as Smiley's head lifted to me in what I again took to be support.

"We take 'em at Sarratt," Haydon retorted. "Why shouldn't Moscow Centre?"

I could feel the sweat running down my back, and I knew my voice was slipping. But I floundered on. "Has anyone else in this photograph been identified?"

"As a matter of fact, yes."

"What as?"

"Never mind."

"What languages did she learn?"

Haydon had had enough of me. He lifted his eyes to Heaven as if appealing for the gift of patience. "Well, they *all* learn English, darling, if *that's* what you're asking," he drawled and, putting his chin in his hand, gave Smiley a long look.

I am not clairvoyant and I had no way of knowing what was passing between the two men, or what had passed already. But even allowing for the advantages of hindsight, I am sure I had the sensation of being caught between hostile camps. Even somebody as remote from Head Office politics as I was could not help hearing the rumble of the battle that was raging: how the great X had walked clean past the great Y in the corridor without so much as a "Good morning"; how A had refused to sit at the same table with B in the canteen. And how Haydon's London Station was becoming a service within a service, gobbling up the regional directorates, taking over the special sections, the watchers, the listeners, right the way down to such humble beings as our postmen, who sat in dripping sorting offices, loyally steaming open mail with gas kettles permanently on the boil. It was even hinted that the true clash of Titans was between Bill Haydon and the reigning Chief, the last to call himself Control, and that Smiley as Control's cupbearer was more on his master's side than Haydon's.

But then it was also hinted that Smiley himself was under sentence—or, put more tactfully—contemplating an academic appointment so that he could take more care of his marriage.

Haydon looked jauntily at Smiley, but the jaunty look became a chill stare as he waited for Smiley to return it. The rest of us waited too. The embarrassment was that Smiley didn't return it. He was like a man declining to acknowledge a salute. He sat on the chaise longue with his eyebrows lifted, and his long eyelids turned down, and his round head tilted, seeming to study the Persian prayer mat that was another eccentric feature of Bill's room. And he simply went on studying it as if he were unaware of Haydon's interest in him, though we all knew—even I knew— that he wasn't. Then he puffed out his cheeks and pulled a frown of disapproval. And finally he stood—not dramatically, for George never had that far to go—and gathered up his papers.

"Well, I think we've had the meat of this, don't you, Bill?" he said. "Control will see indoctrinated officers in one hour, please, if that's convenient, and we'll try to take a view. Ned, you and I have a small piece of Zurich history to clear up. Perhaps you'd drop by when Bill has done with you."

Twenty minutes later I was sitting in Smiley's office.

"Do you believe that photograph?" he asked, with no pretense of talking about Zurich.

"I suppose I have to."

"Why do you suppose that? Photographs can be faked. There is such a thing as disinformation. Moscow Centre has been known to go in for it now and then. They've even stooped to discrediting innocent people, I'm told. They have an entire department, as a matter of fact, devoted to little else. It runs to about five hundred officers."

"Then why frame Bella? Why not go for Brandt or one of the crew?"

"What's Bill told you to do?"

"Nothing. He says I'll get my orders in due course."

"You never answered his question. Do you think we should abort the network?"

"It's hard for me to say. I'm just the local link. The network's run direct from London Station."

"Nevertheless."

"We can't exfiltrate thirty agents. We'd start a war. If the supply lines are blown and the escape routes are closed, I don't see there's anything we can do for them at all."

"So they're dead anyway," he suggested, more in confirmation than question. A phone was ringing on his desk but he didn't pick it up. He continued to look at me with a merciful concern. "Well, if they *are* dead, will you please remember it's not your fault, Ned?" he added kindly. "Nobody expects you to take on Moscow Centre single-handed. It may be the Fifth Floor's fault, it may be mine. It certainly isn't yours."

He nodded me to the door. I closed it after me and heard his phone stop ringing.

* * *

I returned to Hamburg the same night. Bella sounded excited when I rang, and sad that I wasn't rushing round to her at once.

"Where's Brandt?" she asked. She had no notion of telephone security. I said Brandt was fine, just fine. I felt guilty talking to her when I knew so much and she so little. I was to be natural towards her, Haydon had said: "Whatever you did before, keep doing it or do it better. I don't want her guessing anything." I should tell her that Brandt loved her, which he was apparently insisting on. I guessed that in his travail he was asking to see me. I hoped so, because I trusted him and he was my responsibility.

I tried not to feel upset for myself when there were so many larger tragedies round me, but it was hard. Until a few days ago, Brandt and the crew had been mine to care for. I had been their spokesman and champion. Now one of them was dead or worse, and the rest had been taken out of my hands. The network, though it had worked to London, had been my proxy family. Now it was like the remnants of a ghostly army, out of touch, floating between life and death.

Worst of all was my sense of dislocation, of holding a dozen conflicting theories in my head at once, and favouring each in turn. One minute I was insisting to myself that Bella was innocent, just as I had maintained to Haydon. The next I was asking myself how she could have communicated with her masters. The answer was, only too easily. She shopped, she went to cinemas, she went to school. She could meet couriers, fill and empty dead-letter boxes to her heart's content.

But no sooner had I gone this far than I ran to her defence. Bella was not *bad*. The photograph was a plant and the story about her father amounted to nothing. Smiley had said as much. There were a hundred ways in which the mission could have been blown without Bella having the least thing to do with it. Our operational security was tight, but not as tight as I would have wished. My predecessor had turned out to be corrupt. Might he not, in addition to inventing agents, have sold a few as well? And even if he hadn't, was it really so unreasonable of Brandt to suggest that the leak could have come from our side of the fence, not his?

Now I would not have you think that, alone in his cot that night, the young Ned unravelled single-handed the skein of treachery that later took all George Smiley's powers to expose. A source can be a plant, a plant can be ignored, an experienced intelligence officer can take a wrong decision—all without the assistance of a traitor within the Fifth Floor's gates. I knew that. I was not a child, and not one of your grey-cheeked Circus conspiracy-theorists either.

Nevertheless I did ponder, as any of us might when he is stretched to the limits of his allegiance to his Service. I pieced together from my worm's-eye view all the rumours that had reached me on the Circus grapevine. Stories of unaccountable failure and repeated scandal, of the mounting anger of our American Cousins. Of meaningless reorganisations, wasteful rivalries between men who were today immortals and tomorrow had resigned. Horror stories of incompetence being taken as proof of grand betrayal—and unnerving evidence of betrayal dismissed as incompetence.

If there is such a thing as growing up, you may say that sometime that night I made one of those leaps into maturity. I realised that the Circus was much the same as any other British institution, except that it was more so, since it played its games in the safety of sealed rooms, with other people's lives for counters. Yet I was pleased to have made my recognition. It gave me back the responsibility for my actions, which hitherto I had been a little too willing to lay at other people's feet. If my career till now had been a constant battle between submission and identity, then you might say that submission had maintained the upper hand. But that night I crossed some sort of border. I decided that from then on, I would pay more heed to my own instincts and desires, and less to the harness that I seemed unable to dispense with.

We met at the safe flat. If there was neutral ground to be found anywhere, it was there. She still knew nothing of the catastrophe. I had told her only that Brandt had been summoned to England. We made love at once, blindly and hungrily; then I waited for the clarity of after-love to begin my interrogation.

I began playfully stroking her hair, smoothing it against her head. Then I swept it back with both my hands, and scooped it into a rough bun.

"This way you look very stern," I said, and kissed her, still holding it in place. "Have you ever worn it like this?" I kissed her again.

"When I was a girl."

"When was that?" I said, between our joined lips. "You mean before Tadeo? When?"

"Until I went to the forest. Then I cut it off. Another woman did it with a knife."

"Have you got a photograph of yourself like this?"

"In the forest we did not take photographs."

"I mean before. When you wore it like a stern lady."

She sat up. "Why?"

"Just tell me."

She was watching me with her almost colourless eyes. "At school, they took our photographs. Why?"

"In groups? In classes? What sort of photographs?"

"Why?"

"Just tell me, Bella. I need to know."

"They took photographs of us in our class, and they took photographs for our documents."

"What documents?"

"For identity. For our passports."

She did not mean a passport as we understand it. She meant a
passport for moving about inside the Soviet Union. No free citizen could cross the road without one.

"A full-face photograph? Not smiling?"

"Yes."

"What did you do with your old passport, Bella?"

She didn't remember.

"What did you wear for it—for the photograph?" I kissed her
breasts. "Not these. What did you wear?"

"A blouse and tie. What nonsense are you talking?"

"Bella, listen to me. Is there anyone you can think of, back at
home, a schoolfriend, an old boyfriend, a relation, who would
have a photograph of you with your hair back? Someone you
could write to, perhaps, who could be contacted?"

She considered for a moment, staring at me. "My aunt," she
said grumpily.

"What's her name?"

She told me.

"Where does she live?"

In Riga, she said. With Uncle Janek. I seized an envelope, sat
her still naked at a table and made her write out their full address. Then I put a piece of plain writing paper before her and
dictated a letter which she translated as she wrote.

"Bella." I lifted her to her feet and kissed her tenderly. "Bella,
tell me something else. Did you ever go to any school, of any
kind, except the schools in your own town?"

She shook her head.

"No holiday schools? Special schools? Language schools?"

"No."

"Did you learn English at school?"

"Of course not. Otherwise I would speak English. What's happening to you, Ned? Why are you asking me these stupid questions?"

"The *Daisy* sailed into trouble," I said, still face-to-face with her. "There was shooting. Brandt wasn't hurt but others were. That's all I'm allowed to tell you. We're to fly back to London tomorrow, you and I together. They need to ask us some questions and find out what went wrong."

She closed her eyes and began shaking. She opened her mouth and made a silent scream.

"I believe in you," I said. "I want to help you. And Brandt. That's the truth."

Gradually she came back to me and put her head on my chest while she wept. She was a child again. Perhaps she had always been one. Perhaps, by helping me to grow up, she had increased the distance between us. I had brought a British passport for her. She had no nationality of her own. I made her stay the night with me and she clutched me like a drowning girl. Neither of us slept.

On the plane she held my hand but we were already continents apart. Then she spoke in a voice that I had not heard from her before. A firm, adult voice of sadness and disillusionment that reminded me of Stefanie's when she had delivered her Sibyl's warning to me on the island.

"*Es ist ein reiner Unsinn,*" she said. It is a pure nonsense.

"What is?"

She had taken away her hand. Not in anger, but in a kind of worldly despair. "You tell them to put their feet into the water and you wait to see what happens. If they are not shot, they are heroes. If they are shot, they are martyrs. You gain nothing that is worth having and you encourage my people to kill themselves. What do you want us to do? Rise up and kill the Russian oppressor? Will you come and help us if we try? I don't think so. I think you are doing something because you cannot do nothing. I think you are not useful to us at all."

I could never forget what Bella said, for it was also a dismissal of my love. And today I think of her each morning as I listen to the news before walking my dog. I wonder what we thought we were promising to those brave Balts in those days, and whether it was the same promise which we are now so diligently breaking.

This time it was Peter Guillam who was waiting at the airport, which was a relief to me, because his good looks and breezy manners seemed to give her confidence. For a chaperone he had brought Nancy from the watchers, and Nancy had made herself motherly for the occasion. Between them they led Bella through immigration to a grey van which belonged to the Sarratt inquisitors. I wished that someone could have thought to send a less formidable vehicle, because when she saw the van she stopped and looked back to me in accusation before Nancy grabbed her by the arm and shoved her in.

In the turbulent life of a case officer, I was learning, there was not always such a thing as an elegant goodbye.

I can only tell you what I next did, and what I later heard. I made for Smiley's office, and spent most of my day trying to catch him between meetings. Circus protocol required me to go first to Haydon, but I had already exceeded Haydon's brief by the questions I had put to Bella, and suspected Smiley would give me a more sympathetic hearing. He listened to me; he took charge of Bella's letter and examined it.

"If we have it posted in Moscow and give a Finnish safe address for them to write back to, it might just work," I urged him.

But, as so often with Smiley, I had the impression that he was thinking beyond me into realms from which I was excluded. He dropped the letter in a drawer and closed it.

"I rather think it won't be necessary," he said. "Let us hope not anyway."

I asked him what they would do with Bella.

"I suppose much the same as they have done with Brandt," he replied, waking sufficiently from his absorption to give me a sad smile. "Take her through every detail of her life. Try to trip her up. Wear her down. They won't hurt her. Not physically. They won't tell her what they have against her. They'll just hope to break her cover. It seems that most of the men who looked after her in the forest were rounded up recently. That won't speak well for her, naturally."

"What will they do with her afterwards?"

"Well, I think we can still prevent the worst, even if we can't prevent much else these days," he replied, returning to his papers. "Time you went on to Bill, isn't it? He'll be wondering what you're up to."

And I remember the expression on his face as he dismissed me: the pain and frustration in it, and the anger.

Did Smiley have the letter posted as I suggested? Did the letter produce a photograph and did the photograph turn out to be the very one that Moscow Centre's forgers had dropped into their group photograph? I wish it were so neat, but in reality it never is, though I like to believe that my efforts on Bella's behalf had some influence on her release and resettlement in Canada, which occurred a few months later in circumstances that are a puzzle to me.

For Brandt refused to take her back, let alone go with her. Had Bella told him of our affair? Had someone else? I hardly think it possible, unless Haydon himself did it out of mischief. Bill hated all women and most men too, and liked nothing better than to turn people's affections inside out.

Brandt too was given a clean ticket and, after some resistance from the Fifth Floor, a gratuity to start him in a respectable walk of life. That is to say, he was able to buy a boat and take himself to the West Indies, where he resumed his old trade of smuggling, except that this time he chose arms to Cuba.

And the betrayal? The Brandt network had simply been too efficient for Haydon's stomach, Smiley told me later, so Bill had betrayed it as he had betrayed its predecessor, and tried to fix the blame on Bella. He had arranged for Moscow Centre to fake the evidence against her, which he then presented as coming from his spurious source Merlin, the provider of the Witchcraft material. Hard on the mole's tracks by then, Smiley had voiced his suspicions in high places, only to be sent into exile for being right. It took another two years for him to be brought back to clean the stable.

And there the story stood until our own internal *perestroika* began in earnest—in the winter of '89—when Toby Esterhase, the ubiquitous survivor, conducted a middle-ranking Circus delegation to Moscow Centre as a first step to what our blessed Foreign Office insisted on calling a "normalisation of the relationship between the two services."

Toby's team was welcomed at Dzerzhinsky Square and shown many of the appointments, though not, one gathers, the torture chambers of the old Lubyanka, or the roof on which certain careless prisoners had occasionally lost their footing. Toby and his men were wined and dined. They were shown, as the Americans say, a time. They bought fur hats and pinned facetious badges on them and had themselves photographed in Dzerzhinsky Square.

And on the last day, as a special gesture of goodwill, they were escorted to the gallery of Centre's huge communications hall, where reports from all sources are received and processed. And it was here, as they were leaving the gallery, says Toby, that he and Peter Guillam in the same moment spotted a tall, flaxen, thickset fellow in half silhouette at the further end of the corridor, emerging from what was apparently the men's lavatory, for there was only one other door in that part of the corridor, and it was marked for women.

He was a man of some age, yet he strode out of the doorway like a bull. He paused, and for a long beat stared straight at them, as if in two minds whether to come towards them and greet them or retreat. Then he lowered his head and, as it seemed to them, with a smile, swung away from them and disappeared into another corridor. But not before they had ample opportunity to remark his seamanly roll and wrestler's shoulders.

Nothing goes away in the secret world; nothing goes away in the real one. If Toby and Peter are right—and there are those who still maintain that Russian hospitality had got the better of them—then Haydon had an even stronger reason to point the finger of suspicion at Bella, and away from Sea Captain Brandt.

Was Brandt bad from the beginning? If so, I had unwittingly furthered his recruitment and our agents' deaths. It is a dreadful thought and sometimes in the cold grey hours as I lie at Mabel's side, it comes home to haunt me.

And Bella? I think of her as my last love, as the right turning I never took. If Stefanie had unlocked the door of doubt in me, Bella pointed me towards the open world while there was still time. When I think of my women since, they are aftercare. And when I think of Mabel, I can only explain her as the lure of domesticity to a man returned from the front line. But the memory of Bella remains as fresh for me as on our first night in the safe flat overlooking the cemetery—though in my dreams she is always walking away from me, and there is reproach even in her back.

5

"Are you saying we could be housing another Haydon *now?*" a student named Maggs called out amid the groans of his colleagues. "What's his motivation, Mr. Smiley? Who's paying him? What's his bag?"

I had had my doubts about Maggs ever since he had joined. He was earmarked for a cover career in journalism, and already had the worst characteristics of his future trade. But Smiley was unruffled.

"Oh well, I'm sure that in retrospect we owe Bill a great debt of thanks," he replied calmly. "He administered the needle to a Service that had been far too long a-dying." He made a fussy little frown of perplexity. "As to *new* traitors, I'm sure our present leader will have sown her discontents, won't she? Perhaps I'm one. I do find I become a great deal more radical in my old age."

But believe me, we didn't thank Bill at the time.

There was Before the Fall and there was After the Fall and the Fall was Haydon, and suddenly there was not a man or woman in the Circus who could not tell you where he was and what he was doing when he heard the dreadful news. Old hands tell each other to this day of the silence in the corridors, the numbed, averted faces in the canteen, the unanswered telephones.

The greatest casualty was trust. Only gradually, like dazed people after an air attack, did we step shyly, one by one, from our shattered houses, and set to work to reconstruct the citadel. A fundamental reform was deemed necessary, so the Circus abandoned its ancient nickname and the warren of Dickensian corridors and crooked staircases in Cambridge Circus that had housed its shame, and built itself instead a vile steel-and-glass affair not far from Victoria, where the windows still blow out in a gale and the corridors reek of stale cabbage from the canteen, and typewriter-cleaning fluid. Only the English punish themselves with quite such dreadful prisons. Overnight we became, in formal parlance, the Service, though the name "Circus" still occasionally crosses our lips in the same way as we speak of pounds, shillings and pence long after decimalisation.

The trust was broken because Haydon had been part of it. Bill was no upstart with a chip on his shoulder and a pistol in his pocket. He was exactly who he had always sneeringly described himself to be: Church and Spy Establishment, with uncles who sat on Tory Party committees, and a rundown estate in Norfolk with tenant farmers who called him "Mr. William." He was a strand of the finely spun web of English influence of which we had perceived ourselves the centre. And he had caught us in it.

In my own case—I still claim a certain distinction for this—I actually succeeded in hearing the news of Bill's arrest twenty-four hours after it had reached the rest of the Circus, for I was incarcerated in a windowless mediaeval cell at the back of a run of grand apartments in the Vatican. I was commanding a team of Circus eavesdroppers under the guidance of a hollow-eyed friar supplied to us by the Vatican's own secret service, who would rather have gone to the Russians themselves than seek the assistance of their secular colleagues a mile up the road in Rome. And our mission was to winkle a probe microphone into the audience room of a corrupt Catholic bishop who had got himself involved in a drugs-for-arms deal with one of our disintegrating colonies—well, why be coy? It was Malta.

With Monty and his boys flown in for the occasion, we had tiptoed through vaulted dungeons, up underground staircases, until we had reached this vantage point, from which we proposed to drill a fine hole through a course of old cement that ran between the blocks of a three-foot party wall. The hole by agreement was to be no more than two centimetres in diameter, wide enough for us to insert the elongated plastic drinking straw that would conduct the sound from the target room to our microphone, small enough to spare the hallowed masonry of the Papal palace. Today we would use more sophisticated equipment, but the seventies were the last of the steam age and probes were still the fashion. Besides, with the best will in the world, you don't show off your prize gadgets to an official Vatican liaison, let alone to a friar in a black habit who looks as though he has stepped straight out of the Inquisition.

We drilled, Monty drilled, the friar watched. We poured water onto red-hot drill-heads, and onto our sweating hands and faces. We muffled the drone of our drills with liquid foam, and every few minutes we took readings to make sure we hadn't drilled our way into the holy man's apartment by mistake. For the aim was to stop the drill-head a centimetre short of entry, and listen from inside the membrane of the wallpaper or surface plaster.

Suddenly we were through, but worse than through. We were in thin air. A hasty sampling by vacuum produced only exotic threads of silk. A bemused silence descended on us. Had we struck furniture? Drapes? A bed? Or the hem of some unsuspecting prelate's robe? Had the audience room been altered since we had taken the reconnaissance photographs?

At which low point the friar was inspired to remember, in an appalled whisper, that the good bishop was a collector of priceless needlework, and we realised that the shreds of cloth we were staring at were not pieces of sofa or curtain, or even some priest's finery, but fragments of Gobelin tapestry. Excusing himself, the friar fled.

Now the scene changes to the old Kentish town of Rye, where two sisters named the Misses Quayle ran a tapestry-restoration business, and by a mercy—or, you may say, by the ineluctable laws of English social connection—their brother Henry was a retired member of the Service. Henry was run to earth, the sisters were roused from their beds, an RAF jet plane wafted them to Rome's military airport, from where a car sped them to our side. Then Monty calmly returned to the front of the building and ignited a smoke bomb which cleared half the Vatican and gave our augmented team four desperate hours in the target room. By midafternoon of the same day, the Gobelin was passably patched and our probe microphone snugly in place.

The scene changes yet again to the grand dinner given by our Vatican hosts. Swiss Guards stand menacingly at the doors. Monty, a white napkin at his throat, is seated between the sedate Misses Quayle and wiping the last of his cannelloni from his plate with a piece of bread while he regales them with accounts of his daughter's latest accomplishments at her riding school.

"Now you won't know this, Rosie, and there's no reason why you should, but my Beckie has the best pair of hands for her age in the whole of South Croydon—"

Then Monty stops dead in his tracks. He is reading the note I have passed him, delivered to me by hand of a messenger from our Rome Station: *Bill Haydon, Director of Circus Clandestine Operations, has confessed to being a Moscow Centre spy.*

Sometimes I wonder whether that was the greatest of all Bill's crimes: to steal for good the lightness we had shared.

I returned to London to be told that when there was more to tell me I would be told. A few mornings later Personnel informed me that I had been classified "Tailor Halftone," which was Circus jargon for "unpostable to all but friendly countries." It was like being told I would spend the rest of my life in a wheelchair. I had done nothing wrong, I was in no disgrace, quite the contrary. But in the trade, cover is virtue, and mine was blown.

I packed up my desk and gave myself the rest of the day off. I drove into the country and I still don't remember the drive, but there is a walk I do on the Sussex Downs, over whaleback chalk hills with cliffs five hundred feet high.

It took another month before I heard my sentence. "You'll be back with the émigrés, I'm afraid," Personnel said, with his customary distaste. "And it's Germany again. Still, the allowances are quite decent, and the skiing isn't bad either, if you go high enough."

6

It was approaching midnight but Smiley's good spirits had increased with every fresh heresy. He's like a jolly Father Christmas, I thought, who hands round seditious leaflets with his gifts.

"Sometimes I think the most *vulgar* thing about the Cold War was the way we learned to gobble up our own propaganda," he said, with the most benign of smiles. "I don't mean to sound didactic, and of course in a way we'd done it all through our history. But in the Cold War, when our enemies lied, they lied to conceal the wretchedness of their system. Whereas when we lied, we concealed our virtues. Even from ourselves. We concealed the very things that made us right. Our respect for the individual, our love of variety and argument, our belief that you can only govern fairly with the consent of the governed, our capacity to see the other fellow's view—most notably in the countries we exploited, almost to death, for our own ends. In our supposed ideological rectitude, we sacrificed our compassion to the great god of indifference. We protected the strong against the weak, and we perfected the art of the public lie. We made enemies of decent reformers and friends of the most disgusting potentates. And we scarcely paused to ask ourselves how much longer we could defend our society by these means and remain a society worth defending." A glance to me again. "So it wasn't much wonder, was it, Ned, if we opened our gates to every con-man and charlatan in the anti-Communist racket? We got the villains we deserved. Ned knows. Ask Ned."

At which Smiley, to the general delight, burst out laughing—and I, after a moment's hesitation, joined in and assured my students that I would tell them about it some day.

Perhaps you caught the show, as they say in the States. Perhaps you were part of the appreciative audience at one of the many rousing performances they gave on their tireless trail through the American Midwest, as they pressed the flesh and worked the rubber-chicken luncheons of the lecture circuit, a hundred dollars a plate and every plate a sell-out. We called it the Teodor-Latzi show. Teodor was the Professor's first name.

Perhaps you joined in one of the numberless standing ovations as our two heroes humbly took centre stage, the Professor tall and resplendent in one of several costly new suits purchased for his tour, and the diminutive Latzi his chubby mute, his shallow eyes brimming with ideals. There were ovations before they started speaking and ovations when they had finished. No applause was loud enough for "two great American Hungarians who, single-handed, kicked themselves a hole in the Iron Curtain." I am quoting the Tulsa *Herald*.

Perhaps your all-American daughter dressed herself in the becoming costume of a Hungarian peasant girl and put flowers in her hair for the occasion—such things happened too. Perhaps you sent a donation to the League for the Liberation, Post Box something or other, Wilmington. Or did you read about our heroes in the *Reader's Digest* in your dentist's waiting room?

Or perhaps, like Peter Guillam, who was based in Washington at the time, you were honoured to be present at the grand world *première,* jointly stage-managed by our American Cousins, the Washington city police and the FBI, at no less a shrine of right-thinking than the austere and panelled Hay-Adams Hotel, just across the square from the White House. If so, you must have been rated a serious influence-maker. You had to be a front-line journalist or lobbyist at least to be admitted to the hushed conference room where every understated word had the authority of an engraved tablet, and men in bulging blazers watched tautly over your comfort and convenience. For who knew when the Kremlin would strike back? It was still that kind of time.

Or maybe you read their book, slipped by the Cousins to an obedient publisher on Madison Avenue and launched to a fanfare of docile critical acclaim before occupying the lower end of the non-fiction bestseller list for a spectacular two weeks. I hope you did, for though it appeared over their joint names, the fact is I wrote a slice of it myself, even if the Cousins took exception to my original title. The title of record was *The Kremlin's Killer.* I'll tell you what mine was later.

As usual, Personnel had got it wrong. For anybody who has lived in Hamburg, Munich is not Germany at all. It is another country. I never felt the remotest connection between the two cities, but when it came to spying, Munich like Hamburg was one of the unsung capitals of Europe. Even Berlin ran a poor second when it came to the size and visibility of Munich's invisible community. The largest and nastiest of our organisations was a body known best by the place that housed it, Pullach, where much too soon after 1945 the Americans had installed an unlovely assembly of old Nazi officers under a former general of Hitler's military intelligence. Their brief was to pay court to other old Nazis in East Germany and, by bribery, blackmail or an appeal to comradely sentiment, procure them for the West. It never seemed to occur to the Americans that the East Germans might be doing the same thing in reverse, though they did more of it and better.

So the German Service sat in Pullach, and the Americans sat with them, egging them on, then getting cold feet and egging them off. And where the Americans sat, there sat everybody else. And now and then frightful scandals broke, usually when one or other of this company of clowns literally forgot which side he was working for, or made a tearful confession in his cups, or shot his mistress or his boyfriend or himself, or popped up drunk on the other side of the Curtain to declare his loyalty to whomever he had not been loyal to so far. I never in my life knew such an intelligence bordello.

After Pullach came the codebreakers and security artists, and after these came Radio Liberty, Radio Free Europe and Radio Free Everywhere Else, and inevitably, since they were largely the same people, the émigré conspirators, who by now were feeling a little down on their luck but dared not say it. And much time was spent among these exiled bodies arguing out niceties about who would be Master of the Royal Horse when the monarchy was restored; and who would be awarded the Order of Saint Peter and the Hedgehog; or succeed to the Grand Duke's summer palace once the Communist chickens had been removed from its drawing rooms; or who would recover the crock of gold that had been sunk to the bottom of the Whatnotsee, always forgetting that the said lake had been drained thirty years ago by the Bolshevik usurpers, who had built a six-acre hydro-electric plant on the site before running out of water.

As if this were not enough, Munich played host to the wildest sort of All German aspiration, whose adherents regarded even the 1939 borders as a mere prelude to Greater German needs. East Prussians, Saxons, Pomeranians, Silesians, Baits and Sudeten Germans all protested the terrible injustice done to them, and drew fat pay-packets from Bonn for their grief. There were nights, as I trudged home to Mabel through the beery streets, when I fancied I could hear them singing their anthems behind Hitler's marching ghost.

Are they still in business as I write? Oh, I fear they are, and looking a lot less mad than in the days when it was my job to move among them. Smiley once quoted Horace Walpole to me, not a name that would otherwise have sprung naturally to my mind: This world is a comedy to those that think, said Walpole, a tragedy to those that feel. Well, for comedy Munich has her Bavarians. And for tragedy, she has her past.

My memory is patchy nearly twenty years later regarding the Professor's political antecedents. At the time, I fancied I understood them—indeed, I must have done, for most of my evenings with him were spent listening to his recitations of Hungarian history between the wars. And I am sure we put them into the book too—a chapter's worth, at least, if I could only lay my hands on a copy.

The problem was, he was so much happier evoking Hungary's past than her present. Perhaps he had learned, in a life of continual adjustment, that it is wise to limit one's concerns to issues safely consigned to history. There were the Legitimists, I remember, and they supported King Charles, who made a sudden return to Hungary in 1921, much to the consternation of the Allies, who ordered him smartly from the stage. I don't think the Professor could have been a day above five years old when this moving event occurred, but he spoke of it with tears in his enlightened eyes, and there was much in his bearing to suggest the transitory touch of monarchy. And when he mentioned the Treaty of Trianon, the refined white hand that held his wine glass trembled in restrained outrage.

"It was a *Diktat,* Herr Ned," he protested to me in courtly reproof. "Imposed upon us by you victors. You robbed us of two-thirds of our land under the Crown! You gave it to Czechoslovakia, Romania, Yugoslavia. Such scum you gave it to, Herr Ned! And we Hungarians were cultivated people! Why did you do it to us? For what?"

I could only apologise for my country's bad behaviour, just as I could only apologise for the League of Nations, which destroyed the Hungarian economy in 1931. Quite how the League achieved this reckless act I never understood, but I remember it had something to do with the wheat market, and the League's rigid policy of orthodox deflation.

Yet when we approached more contemporary matters, the Professor became strangely reticent in his opinions.

"It is another catastrophe" was all he would say. "It is all a consequence of Trianon and the Jews."

Shafts of evening sunlight sloped through the garden window on to Teodor's superb white head. He was a lion of a fellow, believe me, wide-browed and Socratic, like a grand conductor close to genius all the time, with sculpted hands and flowing locks, and a stoop of intellectual profundity. Nobody who looked so venerable could be shallow—not even when the learned eyes appeared a mite too small for their sockets, or slipped furtively to one side in the manner of a diner in a restaurant who catches sight of a better meal passing by.

No, no, he was a great, good man, and fifteen years our joe. If a man is tall, then clearly he has authority. If he has a golden voice, then his words are also golden. If he looks like Schiller, he must feel like Schiller. If the smile is remote and spiritual, then so for sure is the man within. Thus the visual society.

Except that just occasionally, as I think now, God amuses Himself by dealing us an entirely different man inside the shell. Some founder and are rumbled. Others expand until they meet the challenge of their looks. And a few do neither, but wear their splendours like a favour granted from above, blandly accepting the homage that is not their due.

* * *

The Professor's operational history is quickly told. Too quickly, for it was a mite banal. He was born in Debrecen, close to the Romanian border, an only son of indulgent parents of the small nobility who trimmed their sails to every wind. Through them, he inherited money and connections, a thing that happened more often in the so-called Socialist countries, even in those days, than you would suppose. He was a man of letters, a writer of articles for learned journals, a bit of a poet and a lover several times married. He wore his jackets like capes, the sleeves loose. All these luxuries he could well afford, on account of his privileges and discreet wealth.

In Budapest, where he taught a languid version of philosophy, he had acquired a modest following among his students, who discerned more fire in Teodor's words than he intended, for he was never cut out to be an orator, rhetoric being something for the rabble. Nevertheless, he had risen a certain distance to their needs. He had observed their passion, and as a natural conciliator he had responded by giving it a voice—moderate enough in all conscience, but a voice for all that, and one they respected, along with his beautiful manners and air of representing an older, better order. He was of an age, by then, to be warmed by youthful adulation, and he was always vain. And through vanity he allowed himself to be carried on the counter-revolutionary tide. So that when the Soviet tanks turned back from the border and surrounded Budapest on the terrible night of November 3, 1956, he had no choice but to run for his life, which he did, into the arms of British Intelligence.

The Professor's first act on arriving in Vienna was to telephone a Hungarian friend at Oxford, pressing him in his peremptory way for money, introductions and letters testifying to his excellence. This friend happened also to be a friend of the Circus, and it was the high season for recruitment.

Within months, the Professor was on the payroll. There was little courtship, no arch approach, no customary fan dance. The offer was made, and accepted as a due. Within a year, with generous American assistance, Professor Teodor had been set up in Munich, in a comfortable house beside the river, with a car and his devoted if distraught wife, Helena, who had escaped with him—one suspected, somewhat to his regret. Henceforth, and for an extraordinary length of time, Professor Teodor had been the unlikely spearhead of our Hungarian attack, and not even Haydon had unseated him.

His cover job was Radio Free Europe's patrician-at-large on the subject of Hungarian history and culture, and it fitted him like a glove. He had never been much else. In addition, he lectured a little and gave private tuition—mainly, I noticed, to girls. His clandestine job, for which, thanks to the Americans, he was remarkably well paid, was to foster his links with the friends and former students he had left behind, to be a focus for them and a rallying point and, under guidance, to shape them into an operational network, though none, to my knowledge, had ever quite emerged. It was a visionary operation, and better on the page perhaps than on the ground. Yet it ran and ran. It ran for five years, and then another five and by the time I took up the great man's file, it had completed an extraordinary fifteen years. Some operations are like that, and stagnation favours them. They are not expensive, they are not conclusive, they don't necessarily lead anywhere—but then neither does political stalemate—they are free of scandal. And each year when the annual audit is taken, they are waved through without a vote, until their longevity becomes their justification.

Now I won't say the Professor had achieved nothing for us in all that time. To say so would not only be unfair, it would be derogatory to Toby Esterhase, himself of Hungarian origin, who on his reinstatement After the Fall had become the desk officer handling the Professor's case. Toby had paid a heavy price for his blind support of Haydon, and when he was given the Hungary desk—never the most exalted of Iron Curtain slots—the Professor promptly became the most important player in Toby's personal rehabilitation programme.

"Teodor, I would say, Ned—Teodor is our absolutely total star," he had assured me before I left London, over a lunch he nearly paid for. "Old school, total discretion, lot of years in the saddle, loyal like a leech. Teodor is our ace, totally."

And certainly one of the Professor's more striking accomplishments had been to escape the Haydon axe—either because he had been lucky or, less charitably, because the Professor had never produced enough intelligence to merit the interest of a busy traitor. For I could not help noticing as I prepared myself for the takeover—my predecessor having dropped dead of a stroke while on leave in Ibiza—that whereas Teodor's personal file ran to several volumes, his product file was unusually slender. Partly this could be explained by the fact that his main function had been to spot talent rather than exploit it, partly that the few sources he had guided into our net over the long period he had been working for us were still relatively unproductive.

"Hungary, Ned, that's actually a damned hard target, I would say," Toby assured me when I delicately pointed this out to him. "It's too open. An open target, you get a lot of crap you know already. If you don't get the Crown jewels, you get the common knowledge—who needs it? What Teodor produces for the Americans, it's fantastic."

This seemed to be the nub. "So what *does* he produce for them actually?" I asked. "Apart from hearts and minds on the radio, and articles no one reads?"

Toby's smile became unpleasantly superior. "Sorry, Ned, old boy. 'Need to know,' I'm afraid. You're not on the list for this one."

A few days later, as protocol required, I called on Russell Sheriton in Grosvenor Square to say my goodbyes. Sheriton was the Cousins' Head of Station in London, but he was also responsible for their Western European operations. I bided my time, then dropped the name of Teodor.

"Ah now, that's for Munich to say, Ned," Sheriton said quickly. "You know me. Never trespass on another man's preserves."

"But is he doing you any good? That's all I want to know. I mean joes do burn out, don't they? Fifteen years."

"Well now, we thought he was doing *you* some good, Ned. To hear Toby speak, you'd think Teodor was propping up the free world single-handed."

No, I thought. To hear Toby speak, you'd think Teodor was propping up Toby single-handed. But I was not cynical. In spying, as in much of life, it is always easier to say no than yes. I arrived in Munich prepared to believe that Teodor was the star Toby had cracked him up to be. All I wanted was to be assured.

And I was. At first I was. He was magnificent. I thought my marriage to Mabel had ridded me of such swift enthusiasms, and in a way it had, until the evening when he opened the door to me and I decided I had walked in on one of those perfectly preserved relics of mid-European history, and that all I could decently do was sit at his feet like the rest of his disciples and drink in his wisdom. This is what the Service is for! I thought. Such a man is worth saving on his own account! The culture, I thought. The breadth. The years and years of service.

He received me warmly but with a certain distance, as became his age and distinction. He offered me a glass of fine Tokay and treated me to a discourse on its provenance. No, I confessed, I knew little about Hungarian wines, but I was keen to learn. He talked music, of which I am also sadly ignorant, and played a few bars for me on his treasured violin, the very one he had brought with him when he escaped from Hungary, he explained, and made not by Stradivarius but someone infinitely better, whose name has long escaped me. I thought it a wonderful privilege to be running an agent who had fled with his violin. He talked theatre. A Hungarian theatrical company was presently on tour in Munich with an extraordinary *Othello,* and though Mabel and I had yet to see the production, his opinion of it enchanted me. He was dressed in what Germans call a *Hausjacke,* black trousers and a pair of splendidly polished boots. We talked of God and the world, we ate the best *gulyás* of my life, served by the distraught Helena, who whispered her excuses and left us. She was a tall woman and must once have been beautiful, but she preferred to wear the signs of her neglect. We rounded off the meal with an apricot Palinká.

"Herr Ned, if I may call you so," said the Professor, "there is one matter which weighs heavily on my mind, and which you will permit me to raise with you at the outset of our professional relationship."

"Please do," I said generously.

"Unfortunately, your most recent predecessor—a good man, of course"—he broke off, evidently unable to speak ill of the recent dead—"and, like yourself, a man of culture—"

"Please," I repeated.

"It concerns my British passport."

"I didn't know you had one!" I exclaimed in surprise.

"That is the point. I haven't. One understands there are problems. It is so with all bureaucracies. Bureaucracies are the most evil of man's institutions, Herr Ned. They enshrine the worst of us and bring low the best of us. An exiled Hungarian living in Munich in the employment of an American organisation is not naturally eligible for British citizenship. I understand that. Nevertheless, after my many years of collaboration with your department; I am owed this passport. A temporary travel document is not a dignified alternative."

"But I understood the Americans were giving you a passport! Wasn't that the deal right from the beginning? The Americans to be responsible for your citizenship and resettlement? That includes a passport, surely. It must!"

I was upset that a man who had given us so much of his life should have been denied this simple dignity. But the Professor had learned a more philosophical attitude.

"The Americans, Herr Ned, are a young people and a mercenary people. Having used the best of me, they can scarcely regard me as a man of the future. For the Americans, I belong already to the garbage heap of obsolescence."

"But didn't they promise—subject to satisfactory service? I'm sure they did!"

He made a gesture I shall never forget. He lifted his hands from the table as if he were raising a prodigiously heavy rock. He brought them almost to the level of his shoulders, before letting them crash at full force back onto the table, the imaginary rock between them. And I remember his eyes, indignant from the exertion, accusing me in the silence. So much for your promises, he was saying. Yours and the Americans, both.

"Just get me my passport, Herr Ned."

As a loyal case officer, concerned to do the best for my joe, I threw myself upon the problem. Knowing Toby of old, I decided to take an official tone from the beginning: no half promises, no vaporous reassurances for me. I informed Toby of Teodor's request and asked for guidance. He was my desk officer after all, my London anchor. If it was true that the Americans were sliding out of their undertaking to give the Professor citizenship, the matter would have to be dealt with in London or Washington, I said, not Munich. And if, for reasons outside my knowledge, a British passport was to be granted after all, this too would require the energetic endorsement of the Fifth Floor. The days were gone for good when the Home Office handed out free British citizenship to every ex-Circus Tom, Dick and Teodor. The Fall had seen to that.

I did not signal my request, but sent it by bag, which in Circus lore gives greater formality. I wrote a fighting letter and a couple of weeks later followed it with a reminder. But when the Professor asked for a progress report, I was noncommittal. It's in the pipeline, I assured him; London does not take kindly to being hustled. But I still wondered why Toby took so long to answer.

Meanwhile, at my meetings with Teodor, I strove to unravel what precisely he was doing for us that made him the star of Toby's underpopulated firmament. My investigations were not made easier by the Professor's prickliness, and at first I wondered whether he was withholding his cooperation until the question of his passport was settled. Gradually I realised that where our secret work was concerned, this was his normal demeanour.

One of his more humdrum jobs was maintaining a one-roomed student flat in the Schwabing district, which he used as a safe address for receiving mail from certain of his Hungarian contacts. I persuaded him to take me there. He unlocked the door and there must have been a dozen envelopes lying on the mat, all with Hungarian stamps.

"My goodness, when did you last come here, Professor?" I asked him as I watched him gather them laboriously together.

He shrugged, I thought gracelessly.

"How many letters do you normally reckon to receive in a week, Professor?"

I took the envelopes from him and went through the postmarks. The oldest had been posted three weeks ago, the most recent, one. We moved to the tiny desk, which was covered in dust. With a sigh he settled himself in the chair, opened a drawer and withdrew a couple of bottles of chemicals and a paintbrush from a concealed recess. Taking up the first envelope, he examined it gloomily, then slit it open with a pocket knife.

"Who's it from?" I asked, with more curiosity than he appeared to consider warranted.

"Pali," he replied gloomily.

"Pali at the Agriculture Ministry?"

"Pali from Debrecen. He has been visiting Romania."

"What for? Not the toxic-weapons conference? That could be a scoop!"

"We shall see. An academic conference of some kind. His field is cybernetics. He is undistinguished."

I watched him dip the brush into the first bottle and paint the back of the handwritten letter with it. He rinsed the brush in water and applied the second chemical. And it seemed to me he was determined to demonstrate his disdain for such menial employment. He repeated the process for every letter, sometimes varying the routine by spreading open the envelope and treating the inside of it, or by painting between the lines of the visible handwriting. In the same slow motion, he sat himself at an upright Remington and wearily tapped out in translation the texts that had emerged: anticipated mineral and power deficiencies in the new industries ... bauxite quotas for mines in the Bakony Mountains ... low metal content of iron ore recently extracted in the region of Miskolc ... projected yield of maize and sugar-beet harvest in the region of somewhere else ... rumours of five-year plan to revitalise State railway network ... disruptive action against Party officials in Sopron ... I could almost hear the yawns of the Third Floor analysts as they waded through such turgid stuff. I remembered Toby's boast that Teodor was only interested in the highest quality of intelligence. If this was the highest, what in heaven's name was the lowest? Patience, I told myself. Great agents have to be humoured.

The next day I received a reply to my letter about the passport. The problem, Toby explained, was that there had been a lot of changes among the Cousins' Hungarian Section in recent years. An effort was now being made, he said—making suspicious use of the passive voice—to establish the terms of any undertakings given by the Americans or ourselves. Meanwhile I should avoid discussing the matter with Teodor, he added—as if it were I, not the Professor, who was making the running.

The matter was still in the air three weeks later when I lunched with Milton Wagner at the Cosmo. Wagner was an old hand and my American opposite number. Now he was winding up his career as the Cousins' Chief of Eastern Operations, Munich. The Cosmo was the kind of place Americans make anywhere, with crisp potato skins and garlic dip, and club sandwiches impaled on enormous plastic hairpins.

"How are you getting along with our distinguished academic friend?" he asked, in his southern drawl, after we had despatched our other business.

"Splendidly," I replied.

"Couple of our people seem to think Teodor's been having himself a free ride these how many years," said Wagner lazily.

This time I said nothing.

"The boys back home have been holding a retrospective of his work. Not good, Ned. Not good at all. Some of the 'Hello, Hungary' stuff he's been pushing out on the radio. It's been said before. They've found one passage makes a perfect fit with an article published in *Der Monat* back in '48. The original writer recognised his own words soon as he heard them on the air and flipped." He helped himself liberally to ketchup. "Could be any day now we haul him in for a full and frank exchange."

"Probably going through a bad patch," I said.

"Fifteen years is a long bad patch, Ned."

"Is he aware you're checking on him?"

"In Radio Free Europe, Ned? Among Hungarians? *Gossip?* You must be joking."

I could no longer contain my anxiety. "But why has nobody warned London? Why haven't *you*?"

"Understand we did, Ned. Understand the message fell on pretty deaf ears. Bad time for you boys. Don't we know it."

By now the momentous force of his news had got through to me. If the Professor was cheating with his broadcasts, whom else might he not be cheating?"

"Milt, can I ask you a silly question?"

"Be my guest, Ned."

"Has Teodor *ever* done good work for you? In all his time? Secret work? Very secret work, even?"

Wagner pondered this, determined to give the Professor the benefit of the doubt. "Can't say he has, Ned. We did consider using him as an intermediary for one of our big fish one time, but we kind of didn't like the old man's manners."

"Can I believe that?"

"Would I ever lie to you, Ned?"

So much for the fantastic work he's doing for the Americans, I thought. So much for the years of loyal service nobody can quite recall.

I signalled Toby straight away. I wasted time drafting different texts because my anger kept getting in the way. I understood only too well now why the Americans were refusing to give the Professor his passport, and why he had turned to us for one instead. I understood his air of last things, his listlessness, his lack of urgency: he was waiting to be sacked. I repeated Wagner's information and asked whether it was known to Head Office. If not, the Cousins were in default of their sharing agreement with us. If, on the other hand, the Cousins *had* warned us, why hadn't I been warned too?

Next morning I had Toby's slippery reply. It took a regal tone. I suspected he had got somebody to write it for him, for it was accent-free. The Cousins had given London a "non-specific warning" he explained, that the Professor might be facing "disciplinary enquiries at some future date on the subject of his broadcasts." Head Office—by which I suspected he meant himself—had "adopted the view" that the Professor's relationship with his American employers was not of direct concern to the Circus. Head Office also "took the point"—who but Toby could have made it?—that with so much operational work to occupy him, the Professor could be excused for any "small defects" in his cover work. If another cover job had to be found for the Professor, Head Office would "take steps at the appropriate time." One solution would be to place him with one of the tame magazines to which he was already an occasional contributor. But that was for the future. The Professor had fallen foul of his employers before, Toby reminded me, and he had ridden out the storm. This was true. A woman secretary had complained of his advances, and elements of the Hungarian community had taken exception to his anti-Semitic views.

For the rest, Toby advised me to cool down, bide my time, and—always a maxim of Toby's—act as if nothing had happened. Which was how matters stood one week and twelve hours later when the Professor telephoned me at ten at night, using the emergency wordcode and asking me in a strangled but imperious voice to come round to his house immediately, entering by way of the garden door.

My first thought was that he had killed someone, possibly his wife. I could not have been more wrong.

* * *

The Professor opened the back door, and closed it swiftly after me. The lights inside the house were dimmed. Somewhere in the gloom, a Biedermeier grandfather clock ticked like a big old bomb. At the entrance to the living room stood Helena, her hands to her mouth, smothering a scream. Twenty minutes had passed since Teodor's call, but the scream still seemed to be on the point of coming out of her.

Two armchairs stood before a dying fire. One was empty. I took it to be the Professor's. In the other, somewhat obscured from my line of sight, sat a silky, rounded man of forty, with a cap of soft black hair, and twinkling round eyes that said we were all friends, weren't we? His winged chair was high-backed and he had fitted himself into the angle of it like an aircraft passenger prepared for landing. His rather circular shoes stopped short of the floor, and it occurred to me they were East European shoes: marbled, of an uncertain leather, with moulded, heavy-treaded soles. His hairy brown suit was like a remodelled military uniform. Before him stood a table with a pot of mauve hyacinths on it, and beside the hyacinths lay a display of objects which I recognised as the instruments of silent killing: two garottes made of wooden toggles and lengths of piano wire; a screwdriver so sharpened that it was a stiletto; a Charter Arms .38 Undercover revolver with a five-shot cylinder, together with two kinds of bullet, six soft-nosed, and six rifled, with congealed powder squashed into the grooves.

"It is cyanide," the Professor explained, in answer to my silent perplexity. "It is an invention of the Devil. The bullet has only to graze the victim to destroy him utterly."

I found myself wondering how the poisonous powder was supposed to survive the intense heat of a gun barrel.

"This gentleman is named Ladislaus Kaldor," the Professor continued. "He was sent by the Hungarian secret police to kill us. He is a friend. Kindly sit down, Herr Ned."

With ceremony, Ladislaus Kaldor rose from his chair and pumped my hand as if we had concluded a profitable deal.

"Sir!" he cried happily, in English. "Latzi. I am sorry, sir. Don't worry anything. Everybody call me Latzi. Herr Doktor. My friend. Please sit down. Yes."

I remember how the scent of the hyacinths seemed to go so nicely with his smile. It was only slowly I began to realise I had no sense of danger. Some people convey danger all the time; others put it on when they are angry or threatened. But Latzi, when I was able to consult my instincts, conveyed only an enormous will to please. Which perhaps is all you need if you're a professional killer.

I did not sit down. A chorus of conflicting feelings was yelling in my head, but fatigue was not among them. The empty coffee cups, I was thinking. The empty plates with cake crumbs. Who eats cake and drinks coffee when his life is being threatened? Latzi was sitting again, smiling like a conjuror. The Professor and his wife were studying my face, but from different places in the room. They've quarrelled, I thought; crisis has driven them to their separate corners. An American revolver, I thought. But not the spare cylinder that serious players customarily carried. East European shoes, and with soles that leave a perfect print on every carpet or polished floor. Cyanide bullets that would burn off their cyanide in the barrel.

"How long's he been here?" I asked the Professor. He shrugged. I hated his shrugs. "One hour. Less."

"More than one hour," Helena contradicted him. Her indignant gaze was fixed upon me. Until tonight she had made a point of ignoring me, slipping past me like a ghost, smiling or scowling at the ground to show her disapproval. Suddenly she needed my support. "He rang the bell at eight-forty-five exactly. I was listening to the radio. The programme changed."

I glanced at Latzi. "You speak German?"

"*Jawohl,* Herr Doktor!"

Back to Helena. "Which programme?"

"The BBC World Service," she said.

I went to the radio and switched it on. A reedy Oxford academic of unknown gender was bleating about Keats. Thank you, BBC. I switched it off.

"He rang the bell—who answered it?" I said.

"I did," said the Professor.

"He did," said Helena.

"Please," said Latzi.

"And then?"

"He was standing on the doorstep, wearing a coat," said the Professor.

"A raincoat," Helena corrected him.

"He asked if I was Professor Teodor, I said yes. He gave his name, he said, 'Forgive me, Professor, I have come to kill you with a garotte or cyanide bullet but I do not wish to, I am your disciple and admirer. I wish, to surrender to you and remain in the West.'"

"He spoke Hungarian?" I asked.

"Naturally."

"So you invited him in?"

"Naturally."

Helena did not agree. "No! First Teodor asked for *me,*" she insisted. I had not heard her correct her husband before tonight. Now she had done so twice in as many minutes. "He calls to me and says, 'Helena, we have a guest.' I say, 'Good.' Then he asks Latzi into the house. I take his raincoat, I hang it in the hall, I make coffee. That is how it happened exactly."

"And cake," I said. "You made cake?"

"The cake was made already."

"Were you afraid?" I asked—for fear, like danger, was something else that was missing.

"I was disgusted, I was shocked," she replied. "Now I am afraid—yes, I am very afraid. We are all afraid."

"And you?" I said to the Professor.

He shrugged again, as if to say I was the last man on earth to whom he would confide his feelings.

"Why don't you take your wife to the study?" I said.

He was disposed to argue, then changed his mind. Strangers arm in arm, they marched from the room.

I was alone with Latzi. I stood, he sat. Munich can be a very silent city. Even in repose his face smiled at me ingratiatingly. His small eyes still twinkled, but there was nothing I could read in them. He gave me a nod of encouragement, his smile broadened. He said "Please," and eased himself more comfortably into his chair. I made the gesture every Middle European understands. I held out my hand, palm upward, and passed my thumb across the tip of my forefinger. Still smiling, he rummaged in his inside jacket pocket and handed me his papers. They were in the name of Egon Braubach of Passau, born 1933, occupation artist. I never saw anyone who looked less like a Bavarian artist. They comprised one West German passport, one driver's licence and one social security document. None of them, it seemed to me, carried the least conviction. Neither did his shoes.

"When did you enter Germany?"

"This afternoon, Herr Doktor, this afternoon at five. Please."

"Where from?"

"Vienna, please. Vienna," he repeated, in a breathless rush, as if making me a gift of the entire city, and gave another wriggling motion of his rump, apparently to achieve greater subservience. "I caught the first train to Munich this morning, Herr Doktor."

"At what time?"

"At eight o'clock, sir. The eight-o'clock train."

"When did you enter Austria?"

"Yesterday, Herr Doktor. It was raining. Please."

"Which papers did you present at the Austrian border?"

"My Hungarian passport, Your Excellency. In Vienna I was given German papers."

Sweat was forming on his upper lip. His German was fluent but unmistakably Balkan. He had travelled by train, he said: Budapest, Györ, Vienna, Herr Doktor. His masters had given him a cold chicken and a bottle of wine for the journey. With best pickles, Your Honour, and paprika. More smiles. Arriving in Vienna, he had checked in at the Altes Kaiserreich Hotel, near the railway station, where a room had been reserved for him. A humble room, a humble hotel, Your Excellency, but I am a humble man. It was at the hotel, late at night, that he was visited by a Hungarian gentleman whom he had not seen before—"But I suspect he was a diplomat, Herr Doktor. He was distinguished like yourself!" This gentleman gave him his money and documents, he explained—and the arsenal that lay before us on the table.

"Where are you staying in Munich?"

"It is a modest guesthouse on the edge of town, Herr Doktor," he replied, with an apologetic smile. "More a brothel. Yes, a brothel. One sees many men there, coming and going all the time." He told me its name, and I had half a notion he was going to recommend a girl as well.

"Did they tell you to stay there?"

"For the discretion, Herr Doktor. The anonymity. Please."

"Do you have luggage there?"

He gave the poor man's shrug, quite unlike the Professor's. "A toothbrush," he said. "Some clothes. A bag, sir. Modest materials."

In Hungary he was by vocation an agricultural journalist, he said, but he had made himself a second living working for the secret police, first as an informer, and more recently, for the money, as assassin. He had performed certain duties inside Hungary but preferred—forgive him, Excellency—not to say what these were until he was assured he would not be prosecuted in the West. The Professor was his first "foreign duty," but the thought of killing him had offended his sense of decorum.

"The Professor is a man of format, Herr Doktor! Of reputation! He is not some Jew or priest! Why should I kill this man? I'm a respectable human being, good heavens! I have my honour! Please!"

"Tell me your orders."

They were not complicated. He was to ring the Herr Professor's doorbell, they had said—so he had rung it. The Professor was sure to be at home, since on Wednesdays he gave private tuition until nine, they had said.—The Professor was indeed at home.—He should describe himself as a friend of Pali from Debrecen.—He had taken the liberty not to describe himself in these terms.—Once inside the house, he should kill the Herr Professor by whatever means seemed appropriate, but preferably the garotte, since it was sure and silent, though there was always a regrettable danger of decapitation. He should kill Helena also, they said—perhaps kill her first, depending on who opened the door to him, they were not particular. It was for this contingency that he had brought a second garotte. With a garotte, Herr Doktor, he explained helpfully, one could never be sure of being able to disentangle the instrument after use. He should then telephone a number in Bonn, ask for Peter, and report that "Susi will be staying with friends tonight"—Susi being the Professor's codename for the operation, Excellency. This was the signal for success, though in the present circumstance, Herr Doktor, it must be admitted that he had not been successful. Giggle.

"Telephone from here?" I asked.

"From this house, exactly. To Peter. Please. They are violent men, Herr Doktor. They threaten my family. I have no choice, naturally. I have a daughter. They gave me strict instructions: 'From the Professor's house you will telephone Peter.'"

This also surprised me. Since the Professor was identified to the Hungarian secret police as a Western asset—and had been for fifteen years—one might suppose they would be suspicious of his telephone.

"What do you do if you've failed?" I asked.

"If the duty cannot be fulfilled—if the Herr Professor has guests, or is for some reason not available—I am to ring from a phone box and say that Susi is on her way home."

"From any particular phone box?"

"All phone boxes are suitable, Herr Doktor, in the event of a non-completion. Peter may then give further instructions, he may not. If not, I return at once to Budapest. Alternatively, Peter may say, 'Try again tomorrow,' or he may say, 'Try in two days.' It is all in the hands of Peter in this case."

"What is the Bonn telephone number?"

He recited it.

"Turn out your pockets."

A khaki handkerchief, some badly printed family snaps, including some of a young girl, presumably his daughter, three East European condoms, an open packet of Russian cigarettes, a wobbly tin penknife of obvious Eastern manufacture, a stub of unpainted pencil, 960 West German marks, some small change. The return half of a second-class rail ticket, Vienna–Munich–Vienna. I never in my life saw such miserably assembled pockets. Did the Hungarian Service have no despatchers? Checkers? What the Devil were they thinking of?

"And your raincoat," I said, and watched him fetch it from the hall. It was brand-new. The pockets were empty. It was of Austrian manufacture and good quality. It must have cost serious Western money.

"Did you buy this in Vienna?"

"*Jawohl,* Herr Doktor. It was raining cats and dogs and I had no protection."

"When?"

"Please?"

"What with?"

"Please?"

I discovered he could anger me quite quickly. "You caught the first train this morning, right? It left Vienna before the shops opened, right? You didn't get your money till late last night when the Hungarian diplomat visited you. So when did you buy the coat and what did you use for money? Or did you steal it? Is that the answer?"

First he frowned, then he laughed indulgently at my breach of good manners. It was clear that he forgave me. He opened his hands to me in generosity. "But I bought it last night, Herr Doktor! When I arrived at the station! With my personal *Valuten* that I brought with me from Hungary for shopping, naturally! I am not a liar! Please!"

"Did you keep the receipt?"

He shook his head sagely, advice to a younger man. "To keep receipts, Herr Doktor? I give you this advice. To keep receipts is to invite questions about where you get your money. A receipt— it's like a spy in the pocket. Please."

Too many excuses, I thought, releasing myself from the brilliance of his smile. Too many answers in one paragraph. All my instincts told me to trust nobody and nothing about the story that was being told me. It was not so much the sloppiness of the assassination plan that strained my credulity—the implausible documents, the contents of the pockets, the shoes—not even the basic improbability of the mission. I had seen enough of low-level Soviet satellite operations to regard such amateurishness as the norm. What disturbed me about these people was the unreality of their behaviour in my company, the feeling there was one story for me and one for them; that I had been brought here to perform a function, and the collective will required me to shut up and get on with it.

Yet at the same time I was trapped. I had no choice, and no time, but to take everything they had told me at face value. I was in the position of a doctor who, while suspecting a patient of malingering, has no option but to treat his symptoms. By the laws of the game, Latzi was a prize. It was not every day that a Hungarian assassin offered to defect to the West, no matter how incompetent he was. By the same token, the man was in considerable danger, since it was unthinkable that an assassination operation of this consequence could be launched without separate surveillance.

When in doubt, says the handbook, take the operational line. Were they watching the house? It was necessary to assume so, though it was not an easy house to watch, which was what had commended it to Teodor's handlers fifteen years ago. It stood at the end of a leafy cul-de-sac and backed on to the river. The way into the garden led along a deserted tow-path. But the front porch was visible to anybody passing by, and Latzi could have already been observed entering it.

I went upstairs and from the landing window surveyed the road. The neighbouring houses were in darkness. I saw no sign of stray cars or people. My own car was parked in the next side-street, close to the river. I returned to the drawing room. The telephone was on the bookcase. I handed Latzi the receiver and watched him dial the number in Bonn. His hands were girlish and moist. Obligingly, he tilted the earpiece in my direction, and himself with it. He smelt of old blanket and Russian tobacco. The phone rang out, I heard a man's voice, very grumpy, speaking German. For somebody awaiting news of a killing, I thought, you're doing a good job of pretending you aren't.

A thick accent, presumably Hungarian: "Hullo? Yes? Who is it?"

I nodded to Latzi to go ahead.

"Good evening, sir. I wish, please to speak to Mr. Peter."

"What about?"

"Is this Mr. Peter, please? It is a private matter."

"What do you want?"

"Is this Peter?"

"My name is Peter!"

"It is regarding Susi, Mr. Peter," Latzi explained, with a side-ways wink at me. "Susi will not be coming home tonight, Mr. Peter. She will be staying with friends, I am afraid. Good friends. She will be looked after. Good night, Mr. Peter."

He was about to replace the receiver, but I stayed his hand long enough to hear a growl of contempt or incomprehension the other end before he rang off.

Latzi smiled at me, very pleased with himself. "He plays it well, Herr Doktor. A true professional, I would say. A fine actor, you agree?"

"Did you recognise the voice?"

"No, Herr Doktor. Alas, the voice is not familiar to me."

I shoved open the study door. The Professor sat at his desk, his fists in front of him. Helena sat on the tutorial sofa. I felt a need to acquaint the Professor with my scepticism. I stepped into the room, closing the door behind me.

"The man Latzi, as you call him, is a criminal," I said. "Either he's some kind of confidence trickster, or he's a self-confessed murderer who came to Germany on false papers in order to kill you and your wife. Either way, you're within your rights to turn him over to the West German police and be done with him. Do you want to do that? Or do you want to leave the decisions to us? Which?"

To my surprise, he appeared for the first time that evening

genuinely alarmed. Perhaps he had not expected to be challenged. Perhaps the proximity of his own death had dawned on him. Either way, I had the impression he was attaching more importance to my question than I understood. Helena had turned her eyes away from me and was watching him also. Critically. A woman waiting to be paid.

"Do whatever you must do," he muttered. "Then you must do as I ask. Both of you."

"We are cooperative. We shall be—yes, cooperative. We have been—cooperative—for many years. Too many."

I glanced at Helena.

"It will be my husband's responsibility," she said.

I had no time to ponder the mysteries of this ominous statement. "Then please put together some night things and be ready at the garden door in five minutes," I said, and returned to the drawing room and Latzi.

I think he had been standing at the door for he stepped quickly back as I entered, then clasped his hands to his chin and beamed at me, asking what was *gefällig*—what was my pleasure?

"Have you ever seen the Professor before tonight?"

"No, sir. Only photographs. One would admire him anywhere. A true aristocrat."

"And his wife?"

"She is known to me, sir. Naturally."

"How?"

"She was once an actress, Herr Doktor, one of the best in Budapest."

"And you saw her on the stage?"

Another pause. "No, sir."

"Then where did you see her?"

He was trying to read me. I had the impression he was wondering whether she might have told me something, and he was trimming his answers accordingly.

"Theatre bills, Your Excellency. When she was young, her famous face was on every street corner. All young men loved her—I was no exception."

"Where else?"

He saw that I had nothing. And I saw that he saw. "So sad about a woman's looks, Herr Doktor. A man, he can remain impressive until he is eighty. A woman—" he sighed.

I let him pack together his weapons, then took possession of them. I loaded the soft-nosed bullets into the revolver. As I did so, a thought occurred to me.

"When I walked in here, the cylinder was empty and the bullets were spread on the table."

"Correct, Excellency."

"When did you take the bullets out of the cylinder?" I asked.

"Before entering the house. So that I could demonstrate my peaceful intentions. Naturally."

"Naturally."

As we moved to the hall, I shoved the revolver into my waistband.

"If you take it into your head to run away, I shall shoot you in the back," I explained to him, and had the satisfaction of seeing his little eyes swivel in alarm. Professional assassins, it seemed, did not take kindly to their own medicine.

I tossed him his raincoat and glanced round the room for other traces of him. There were none. I ordered silence and led the three of them into the garden and along the tow-path to my car. A famous actress, I thought, and not a word about it on the file. I put the Professor and Helena in the back, and Latzi in the front beside me. Then we sat still for five minutes while I waited for the slightest sign that we were being watched. Nothing. It was by now midnight and a new moon had risen among the stars. I circled the town, keeping a watch on my mirror, then took the autobahn south-west to the Starnbergersee, where we kept a safe house for briefing and debriefing joes in passage. It lay close to the lake's edge and was manned by two murderous long-haired wonders left over from London Station's Lamplighters Section. They were called Jeffrey and Arnold. Arnold was hovering in the doorway by the time we reached it. One hand was in the pocket of his kaftan. The other hung threateningly to his side.

"It's me, you buffoon," I said softly.

Jeffrey showed the Professor and his wife to their bedroom while Arnold sat with Latzi in the drawing room. I went down the garden to the boat-house, where I was at last able to talk to Toby Esterhase on the safe telephone. He was amazingly composed. It was as if he had been expecting my call.

Toby arrived in Munich on the first flight from London next morning, wearing a beaver-lamb coat and a leather Trilby hat, and looking more the impresario than the beleaguered spy.

"Nedike, my God!" he cried, embracing me like a prodigal father. "Listen, you look fantastic, I would say. Congratulations, okay? Nothing like a little excitement to bring the blooms to your cheeks. How's Mabel, actually? A marriage, that's something you got to water, same as a flower."

I drove slowly and spoke, as best I could, dispassionately, giving him the fruits of my researches throughout the long night. I wanted him to know everything I knew by the time we reached the lake house.

Neither the Americans nor the West Germans had any trace of Latzi, I said. Neither, I gathered from Toby, had London.

"Latzi, that's an unwritten page, Ned. Totally," Toby agreed, surveying the passing landscape with every sign of approval.

There was also no trace of his Bavarian covername, or of any of the covernames that Latzi claimed to have used on his "duties" inside Hungary, I said.

Toby lowered his window to enjoy the fragrance of the fields.

Latzi's West German passport was a fake, I continued with determination, one of a batch recently run up by a low-grade forger in Vienna and sold on the private market.

Toby was mildly indignant. "I mean who buys that crap, for God's sake?" he protested, as we passed a pair of palomino horses grazing in a paddock. "With passports, these days, you get what you pay for actually. What you get for crap like that, it's six months in a stinking gaol." And he shook his head sadly like a man whose warnings go unheeded until it's too late.

I blundered on. The phone number in Bonn belonged to the Hungarian military attaché, I said, whose first name was indeed listed as Peter. He was an identified Hungarian Intelligence officer. I allowed myself a restrained irony:

"That's a new one for us, isn't it, Toby? A spy using his own name as a covername? I mean why bother any more? You're Toby, so we'll keep it a secret and call you Toby instead. Great."

But Toby was too set on enjoying his day in Bavaria to be disturbed by the implications of my words. "Nedike, believe me, those army guys, they're total idiots. Hungarian military intelligence, that's the same as Hungarian military music, know what I mean? They blow it out their arses actually."

I continued my recitation. West German Security had a permanent tap running on the Hungarian attaché's telephone, I said. A cassette of Latzi's conversation with Peter was on its way to my office. From what I understood, it offered no surprises except to underline that Peter appeared genuinely unprepared for the call. Peter had neither made nor received further calls last night, I said, nor had there been any burst of diplomatic signals traffic from the roof of the Hungarian Embassy in Bonn. Peter had, however, complained to the Protocol Department of the West German Foreign Office about telephone harassment on his home line. This was not, I suggested, the act of a conspirator. Toby was less sure.

"Could be one thing, Ned, could be the other," he said, leaning back in his seat and languidly tilting the flat of his hand both ways. "A man thinks he's been compromised? So maybe it's not so stupid he makes a formal complaint once, brushes over his traces—why not?"

I gave him the rest. I was determined to. Latzi's description of the putative diplomat in Vienna tallied with that of one Leo Bakocs, Commercial Secretary and, like Peter, an identified Hungarian Intelligence officer, I said. Cousin Wagner was getting hold of a photograph for us to show to Latzi later in the day.

The name Bakocs brought a fond smile to Toby's lips. "They drag *Leo* in on this? Listen, Leo's so vain he spies only on duchesses." He laughed in jolly disbelief. "Leo in some lousy hotel, handing over garottes to a smelly assassin? Tell me another, Ned. I mean."

"It isn't me who's telling you," I said. "It's Latzi."

Lastly, I said, I had despatched Jeffrey to the Munich whorehouse to pay Latzi's bill and collect his overnight bag. The only article of interest in his luggage was a set of pornographic photographs.

"It's the tension, Ned," Toby explained magnanimously. "In a foreign country, killing somebody you don't know, you need a little private company—know what I mean?"

In return, Toby had brought me nothing whatever, private or otherwise. I had imagined him on the phone all night, and perhaps he had been. But not in support of my enquiries.

"Maybe we have a party tonight," he proposed. "Harry Palfrey of Legal Department is coming over with a couple of guys from the Foreign Office. That's a nice fellow, Harry. Very English."

I was bewildered. "What branch of the Foreign Office?" I said. "Who? Why Palfrey?"

But as Toby would say, questions are never dangerous until you answer them. We arrived at the lake house to find Arnold cooking eggs and bacon. The Professor and Latzi sat at one end of the table. Helena, a vegetarian, sat at the other, eating a nut bar from her handbag.

Arnold was blond and lank. His hair was done in a knot at the back. "They had a bit of a dingdong, Ned," he confided to me disapprovingly while Toby fell about the Professor's neck. "The Professor and his missus, a real dogfight. I don't know who started it or what it was about, I wouldn't ask."

"Did Latzi join in?"

"He was going to, Ned, but I told him to keep quiet. I don't like a man who comes between husband and wife, I never did."

In retrospect, our discussions that day resemble an intricate minuet, beginning in our humble kitchen and ending in the courts of the Almighty Himself—more precisely in the beflagged conference room of the American Consulate General, where the inspiring features of President Nixon and Vice President Agnew smiled favourably on our endeavours.

For Toby, as I soon realised, far from doing nothing, had laid on an entire programme for himself, which he advanced from stage to stage with the dexterity of a ringmaster. In the kitchen, he listened to the whole story over again from Latzi and the Professor, while Helena chewed her nut bar. I had never seen Toby in full Hungarian flight before and found time to marvel at the transformation. With one sentence he had flung aside the unnatural corset of his Anglo-Saxon restraint and was back among his people. His eyes caught fire. He preened, and his back arched as if he were sitting on a parade horse.

"Ned, they say you have been quite fantastic actually," he called to me down the table in the midst of all this. "A tower of strength, they are saying, completely. I think maybe they will recommend you a Nobel prize!"

"Tell them to make it an Oscar, I'll accept," I said sourly, and took myself for a walk down to the lakeside to recover my temper.

I returned to the house to find Toby and the Professor closeted in the drawing room, talking volubly. Toby's high respect for the Professor seemed, if anything, to have increased. Latzi was helping Arnold with the washing-up and they were both sniggering. Latzi had evidently been telling a dirty joke. Helena was nowhere to be seen. Next, it was Latzi's turn to sit alone with Toby, while the Professor and his wife walked uneasily at the lakeside, pausing every few steps to remonstrate with each other, until the Professor turned on his heel and strode back to the house.

Seizing the moment, I slipped out and joined Helena. Her lips were pursed and her face was sickly-white—whether from fear, anger or fatigue, I couldn't tell. When she spoke, she had to stop and begin again before the words would come.

"He is a *liar*," she said. "It is all lies! Lie, lie! He is a liar!"

"Who is?"

"They are *both* liars. From the day of birth, they *lie*. On their deathbeds, they *lie*."

"So what's the truth?" I said.

"*Wait* is the truth!"

"Wait for what?"

"I have warned him. 'If you do this, I shall tell the English.' So we wait. If he does it, I shall tell you. If he repents, I shall spare him. I am his wife."

She walked to the house, a stately woman. As she entered it, a black limousine pulled up in the drive and Harry Palfrey, the Circus legal adviser, emerged, accompanied by two other members of the English governing classes. I recognised the taller of them as Alan Barnaby, luminary of the Foreign Office's misnomered Information and Research Department, which traded in Communist counterpropaganda at its sleaziest. Toby was shaking him warmly by the hand while with his other he beckoned me to join them. We went indoors and sat down.

At first I smouldered in silence. The players had been sent upstairs. Toby was doing the talking, the others listened to him with the special reverence their kind reserves for paupers or black men. I even found myself feeling a little protective of him—of Toby Esterhase, God help me, who protected no one but himself!

"What we are dealing with here, Alan, without talking out of turn actually, is a completely top source who is now expended," Toby explained. "A great joe, but his day is over."

"You mean the Prof," Barnaby said helpfully.

"They are on to him. They know his value too well. From certain clues I have obtained from Latzi, it's clear the Hungarians have a fat dossier on the Professor's operations. After all, I mean, why would they try to kill a fellow who is no use to us? A Hungarian assassination attempt—that's a *Good Housekeeping* certificate for the target, I would say."

"We can't be responsible for the Professor's safety indefinitely," Palfrey cautioned us with his loser's smile. "We can give him protection for a bit, naturally. But we can't accept a life interest in him. He has to know that. We may have to get him to sign something just to make the point."

The second Foreign Office man was round and shiny with a chain across his waistcoat. I had a childish urge to pull it and see if he squealed.

"Well, *I* think we may all be talking too much," he said silkily. "If the Americans agree to take the pair of 'em off our hands, the Prof and his missus, we shan't have to worry, shall we? Best keep our heads down and our powder dry, what?"

Palfrey demurred. "He should still sign a release for us, Norman. He has rather been playing us off against the Cousins in the last few years."

Ever the protector of his own, Toby gave a knowing smile. "All the best joes do this, I would say, Harry. One hand washes the other, even at Teodor's level. The question is, now that he is no longer usable, what have we got to lose except trouble actually? I mean, I am not the expert here," he added, with an ingratiating smile at Barnaby.

"What about the assassin fellow?" said the man called Norman. "Will he play ball as well? Bloody dangerous, isn't it, sitting up there like a duck in a tree?"

"Latzi is flexible," said Toby. "He is scared, he is also a complete patriot." I would not have backed him on either of these points, but I was too sickened to interrupt. "These *apparatchiks,* when they step out of the system, they are in shock. Latzi is coping with it. He agonises over his family, but he is reconciled. If Teodor accepts, Latzi will accept also. With guarantees, naturally."

"What *sort* of guarantees?" said the shiny Foreign Office man, so quickly that not even Harry Palfrey got in ahead of him.

Toby did not falter. "Well, naturally the usual. Latzi and Teodor don't want to be thrown on to the rubbish heap when this one's over, I would say. Nor does Helena. American passports, a good bit of money at the end of the road, assistance and protection—I mean, that's basic so to speak."

"The whole thing's a con," I blurted. I had had enough.

Everybody was smiling at me. They would have smiled whatever I had said. They were that sort of crowd. If I had said I was a Hungarian double agent, they would have smiled. If I had said I was Adolf Hitler's reincarnated younger brother, they would have smiled. All but Toby, that is, whose face had acquired the lifelessness of someone who knows that all he can safely be at this moment is nobody at all.

"Now why on earth do you say that, Ned?" Barnaby was asking, awfully interested.

"Latzi's not a trained killer," I said. "I don't know what he is, but he isn't a killer. He was carrying an unloaded gun. No professional in his right mind does that. He's posing as a Bavarian artist, but he's wearing Hungarian clothes and half the junk in his pockets is Hungarian. I was standing over him when he made his phone call to Bonn. Fine, the attaché's first name is Peter. It's in the diplomatic list as Peter. Peter wasn't expecting that call in a month of Sundays. Latzi laid it on him. Listen to the German tape of their conversation."

"Then what about the chap in Vienna, Ned?" said Barnaby, still determined to patronise me. "The chap who gave him his money and his hardware? Eh? Eh?"

"They never met. We showed Latzi the photograph and he was delighted. 'That's the man,' he said. Oh sure: he'd seen a photograph somewhere else. Ask Helena, she knows. She's not telling at the moment, but if we put pressure on her, I'm sure she will."

Toby came briefly alive. "Pressure, Ned? Helena? Pressure, that's something you use when you know you can squeeze harder than the other fellow. That woman is crazy about her husband. She defends him to the grave actually."

"The Professor's fallen foul of the Americans," I said. "They're rolling up his red carpet. He's desperate. If he didn't set up the assassination himself, Latzi did. The whole ploy is a device for him to cut his losses and make a new life."

They waited for me to continue, all of them. It was as if they were waiting for the punchline. Finally Toby spoke. He had rediscovered his form.

"Nedike, how long since you slept actually?" he asked with an indulgent smile. "Tell us, please."

"What's that got to do with it?"

Toby was ostentatiously studying his watch. "I think you have been now thirty hours without sleep, Ned. You took some pretty damn big decisions in that time—all good ones I would say. I don't think we can blame you for having a bit of a reaction."

It was as if I had never spoken. All heads had turned back to Toby.

"Well, *I* think it's rather important we take a peek at the cast," Barnaby was saying as I headed for the door. "Can we whistle them down, Toby? Question of how they'll shape up under the spotlights."

"I think there's news value in doing this thing straightaway, Barnaby," Palfrey was saying, as I headed for the garden and sanity. "Strike while the iron is hot. With me?"

"With you all the way, Harry. Hundred percent."

I refused to be present for the first audition. I sulked in the kitchen and let Arnold minister to me while I pretended to listen to some story about his mother walking out on the fellow she'd been with for twenty years and shacking up with her childhood sweetheart. I watched Toby skip upstairs to fetch his champions, and scowled when the three men descended some minutes later, Latzi with his black hair slicked into a parting, the Professor with his jacket outside his shoulders, his seer's head struck forward in contemplation and his white mane flowing becomingly.

Then Helena came into the kitchen with tears streaming down her cheeks, so Arnold gave her a hug and fetched a blanket for her, because the spring morning was crisp and she was shivering. Then Arnold made her a camomile tea, and sat with his arm round her till Toby bustled in to say we were all expected at the American Consulate in two hours.

"Russell Sheriton is flying in from London, Pete de May from Bonn. They are mustard for it, Ned. Totally mustard. Washington throws its cap in the air, completely." I do not recall whether Pete de May was grander than Sheriton or less grand. But grand enough. "Ned, that Teodor's fantastic," Toby assured me privately.

"Really? In what way?"

"You know what they told him? 'What you are doing is damn risky, Professor. Do you think you can handle it?' You know what he replied? 'Mr. Ambassador, risks are what we all take to protect civilised society.' He's quiet, he's dignified. Latzi too. Ned, after this you get some sleep, okay? I phone Mabel."

We rode in two cars, Toby with the Hungarians, myself with Palfrey and the Foreign Office. Opening the car door for me, Palfrey touched my arm and offered me some steel-edged advice. "I think from now on, it's all hands pulling together, Ned. Tired is one thing. Talk about con-tricks is something else. Yes? Agreed?"

We must have numbered twenty head. The Consul General presided. He was a pallid Midwesterner, an ex-lawyer like Palfrey, and kept talking anxiously about "reprocussions." Milton Wagner was seated between Sheriton and de May. It was clear to me that, whatever their private thoughts, Sheriton and Wagner had orders to keep their scepticism to themselves. Perhaps they too had recognised that there were worse ways of getting rid of useless agents than off-loading them onto the U.S. Information Services, who were represented by a quartet of troubled believers whose names I never learned.

Pullach was spoken for, naturally. Though not involved, they had sent their own observer, so we could be confident that our determinations would be the gossip of Potsdam by afternoon. They also insisted on making a voluble complaint about Vienna. It seemed that Pullach had a running battle with the Austrian police about forged passports, and suspected them of selling them to the Hungarians. Quite a lot of the meeting was taken up by an Oberst von-und-zu somewhere or other moaning about Austrian duplicity.

The three champions did not, of course, attend our deliberations, but sat in the waiting room. When sandwiches were passed round, a generous plate was sent out to them. And when they were finally called in, several of the lay members of the meeting broke into applause, which must have been the first of many times from then on when they heard the roar of the greasepaint.

But it was Helena's tears that stole the show. The Professor said his few words, and his halting dignity worked its predictable magic. Latzi followed him, and a cold chill fell over the room as he explained why he had carried the two garottes, which were then passed gingerly round the table with the rest of the exhibits. But when Helena stepped forward on the Professor's arm, I felt a lump rise to my throat, and knew that everyone in the room was feeling the same.

"I support my husband," was all the great actress could declaim.

But it was enough to bring the room to its feet.

It was late evening before I managed to speak to her alone. We were washed out by then; even the irrepressible Latzi was exhausted. The captains and the kings had departed, Toby had departed. I was sitting with Arnold in the drawing room of the lake house. An American van, with blackened windows and two plainclothes marines aboard, was waiting in the drive, but our stars were learning to keep their public waiting. The day had been spent preparing afternoon press announcements and signing Palfrey's releases, which he turned out to have brought with him in his briefcase.

She entered hesitantly, as if she expected me to strike her, but the anger had been drained out of me.

"We shall get our passports," she said, sitting down. "It is the new world."

Arnold slipped tactfully from the room, closing the door behind him.

"Who's Latzi?" I said.

"He is a friend of Teodor."

"What else is he?"

"He is an actor. A bad, oh a *bad* actor from Debrecen."

"Did he ever work for the secret police?"

She made a gesture of deprecation. "He had connections. When Teodor needed to arrange himself with the authorities, Latzi was the go-between."

"You mean, when Teodor needed to inform on his students?"

"Yes."

"Did Latzi supply Teodor with his information while you were in Munich?"

"At first only a little. But when none came from other sources, more. Then much more. Latzi prepared the material for Teodor. Teodor sold it to the British and Americans. Otherwise we would have had no money."

"Was Latzi getting help from the secret police to do this?"

"It was private. Things are changing in Hungary. It is no longer prudent to be involved with the authorities."

I unlocked the door and watched her make her exit, head erect.

A few weeks later, back in London, I faced Toby with her story. He was neither surprised nor contrite.

"Women, Ned, that's a criminal class actually. Better we eat the soup, not stir it."

A few weeks more and the Teodor-Latzi show was riding high. So was Toby. How much was he a part of it? How much did he know when? The whole of it? Did he dream up the entire piece of theatre in order to make the best of his imperilled agent and get him off his hands? I have often secretly suspected that the play was a three-hander, at the least, with Helena as the reluctant audience.

"Know what, Nedike?" Toby declared, throwing an affectionate arm around my shoulder. "If you can't ride two horses at once, you better stay out of the Circus."

You remember the pseudonymous Colonel Weatherby in the book? The master of disguises, at ease in seven European languages? Pimpernel leader of the East European resistance fighters? The man who "flitted back and forth across the Iron Curtain as if it were of frailest gossamer"? That was me. Ned. I didn't write that part, thank God. It was the work of some venal sports journalist from Baltimore recruited by the Cousins. Mine was the introductory pen portrait of the great man, printed under the caption "The Real Professor Teodor as I Knew Him," and gouged out of me by Toby and the Fifth Floor. My working title for the book was *Tricks of the Trade,* but the Fifth Floor said that might be misunderstood. They promoted me instead.

But not before I had taken my indignation to George Smiley, who had just given up his job as acting chief and was on the point of removing himself for the nearly last time to the shadows of academia. I was back in London on a mid-tour break. It was a

Friday evening and I ran him to earth in Bywater Street, packing for the weekend. He heard me out, he gave a small chuckle, then a larger chuckle. He muttered, *"Oh Toby,"* affectionately under his breath.

"But then they *do* assassinate, don't they, Ned," he objected as he laboriously folded a tweed suit. "The Hungarians, I mean. Even by East European standards, they're one of the foulest mobs there are, surely?"

Yes, I conceded, the Hungarians killed and tortured pretty much at will. But that didn't alter the fact that Latzi was a fake and Teodor was Latzi's accomplice, and as to Toby—

Smiley cut me short. "Now, Ned, I think you're being a little bit prissy. Every church needs its saints. The anti-Communist church is no exception. And saints as a bunch are a pretty bogus lot, when you come down to it. But no one would pretend they don't have their uses, once they get the job. Do you think this shirt will do, or must I give it another iron?"

We sat in his drawing room sipping our Scotches and listening to the clamour of party-goers in Bywater Street.

"And did the ghost of Stefanie stalk the Munich pavements for you, Ned?" Smiley enquired tenderly, just when I was beginning to wonder whether he had dozed off.

I had long ceased to marvel at his capacity to put himself in my shoes.

"Now and then," I replied.

"But not in the flesh? How sad."

"I once rang one of her aunts," I said. "I'd had some silly row with Mabel and gone to a hotel. It was late. I expect I was a bit drunk." I found myself wondering whether Smiley already knew, and decided I was being fanciful. "Or I *think* it was an aunt. It could have been a servant. No, it was an aunt."

"What did she say?"

" 'Fräulein Stefanie is not at home.' "

A long silence, but this time I did not make the mistake of thinking he had gone to sleep.

"Young voice?" he enquired thoughtfully.

"Quite."

"Then perhaps it was Stefanie who answered."

"Perhaps it was."

We listened again to the raised voices in the street. A girl was laughing. A man was cross. Somebody hooted a horn and drove away. The sounds died. Stefanie's my Ann, I thought, as I walked back across the river to Battersea, where I had kept my little flat: the difference is, I never had the courage to let her disappoint me.

7

Smiley had interrupted himself—some tale of a Central American diplomat with a passion for British model railways of a certain generation, and how the Circus had bought the man's lifelong allegiance with a Hornby Double-O shunting engine stolen from a London toy museum by Monty Arbuck's team. Everyone was laughing until this sudden reflective silence, while Smiley's troubled gaze fixed itself upon some point outside the room.

"And just occasionally we meet the reality we've been playing with," he said quietly. "Until it happens, we're spectators. The joes live out our dreams for us, and we case officers sit safe and snug behind our one-way mirrors, telling ourselves that seeing is feeling. But when the moment of truth strikes—if ever it does for you—well, from then on we become a little more humble about what we ask people to do for us."

He never once glanced at me as he said this. He gave no hint of who was in his mind. But I knew, and he knew. And each knew the other knew that it was Colonel Jerzy.

I saw him and I said nothing to Mabel. Perhaps I was too surprised. Or perhaps the old habits of dissembling die so hard that even today my first response at any unexpected event is to suppress the spontaneous reaction. We were watching the nine-o'clock news on television, which for Mabel and myself has become a kind of Evensong these days, don't ask me why. And suddenly I saw him. Colonel Jerzy. And instead of leaping from my chair and shouting, "My God! Mabel! Look, that fellow in the back there! That's Jerzy!"—which would have been the healthy reaction of any ordinary man—I went on watching the screen and sipping my whisky and soda. Then, as soon as I was alone, I slipped a fresh tape into the video machine so that I could be sure of catching the repeat when it came round on "Newsnight." Since when—the incident is now six weeks old—I must have watched it a dozen more times, for there is always some extra nuance to be relished.

But I shall leave that part of the story to the end where it belongs. Better to give you the events in the order they occurred, for there was more to Munich than Professor Teodor, and there was more to spying in the wake of Bill Haydon's exposure than waiting for the wounds to heal.

Colonel Jerzy was a Pole and I have never understood why so many Poles have a soft spot for us. Our repeated betrayals of their country have always seemed to me so disgraceful that if I were Polish, I would spit on every passing British shadow, whether I had suffered under the Nazis or the Russians—the British in their time having abandoned the poor Poles to both. And I would certainly be tempted to plant a bomb under the so-called "competent department" of the British Foreign Office. Dear heaven, what a phrase! As I write, the Poles are once more squeezed between the unpredictable Russian Bear and the rather more predictable German Ox. But you may be quite sure that if they should ever need a good friend to help them out, the same "competent department" of the British Foreign Office will send its treacly regrets and plead a more enticing function up the road.

Nevertheless, the record of my Service boasts a disproportionate rate of success in Poland, and an almost embarrassing number of Polish men and women who, with reckless Polish courage, have risked their necks and those of their families in order to spy for "England."

No wonder then if, in the aftermath of Haydon, the casualty rate among our Polish networks was correspondingly high. Thanks to Haydon, the British had added yet another betrayal to their long list. As each new loss followed the previous one with sickening inevitability, the air of mourning in our Munich Station became almost palpable, and our sense of shame was compounded by our helplessness. None of us had any doubt of what had happened. Until the Fall, Polish Security—ably led by their Chief of Operations, Colonel Jerzy—had held Haydon's treachery close to their chests, contenting themselves with penetrating our existing networks and using them as channels of disinformation—or, where they succeeded in turning them, playing them back at us with skill.

But After the Fall, the Colonel felt no further need of delicacy, and in the course of a few days savagely silenced those of our loyal agents whom till then he had allowed to remain in place. "Jerzy's hit list," we called it as the tally rose almost daily, and in our frustration we developed a personal hatred of the man who had murdered our beloved joes, sometimes not bothering with the formalities of a trial, but letting his interrogators have their fun until the end.

It may seem odd to think of Munich as a springboard to Poland. Yet for decades Munich had been the command centre for a range of Polish operations. From the roof of our Consular annexe in a leafy suburb, our antennae had listened night and day for our Polish agents' signals—often no more than a blip compressed between words spoken on the open radio. And in return, on pre-determined schedules, we had transmitted comfort and fresh orders to them. From Munich we had despatched our Polish letters, impregnated with secret writing. And if our sources managed to travel outside Poland, it was from Munich again that we flew off to debrief and feast them and listen to their worries.

It was from Munich also, when the need was great enough, that our Station officers would cross into Poland, always singly and usually in the guise of a visiting businessman bound for a trade fair or exhibition. And in some roadside picnic spot or backstreet café, our emissaries would come briefly face-to-face with our precious joes, transact their business and depart, knowing they had refilled the lamp. For nobody who has not led a joe's life can imagine what loneliness of faith it brings. A well-timed cup of bad coffee shared with a good case officer can raise a joe's morale for months.

Which is how it happened that, one winter's day soon after the beginning of the second half of my tour in Munich (and the welcome departure of Professor Teodor and his appendages to America), I found myself flying into Gdansk on a LOT Polish Airlines flight from Warsaw, with a Dutch passport in my pocket describing me as Franz Joost of Nijmegen, born forty years before. According to my businessman's visa application, my mission was to inspect prefabricated agricultural buildings on behalf of a West German farming consortium. For I have some basic grounding as an engineer, and certainly enough to exchange visiting cards with officials from their Ministry of Agriculture.

My other mission was more complicated. I was looking for a joe named Oskar, who had returned to life six months after being given up for dead. Out of the blue, Oskar had sent us a letter to an old cover address, using his secret writing equipment and describing everything he had done and not done from the day he had first heard of the arrests till now. He had kept his nerve. He had remained at his job. He had anonymously denounced some blameless *apparatchik* in his Archives Section in order to divert suspicion. He had waited, and after a few weeks the *apparatchik* disappeared. Encouraged, he waited again. Rumour reached him, that the *apparatchik* had confessed. Given Colonel Jerzy's tender ministrations, this was not surprising. As the weeks went by, he began to feel safe again. Now he was ready to resume work if someone would tell him what to do. In earnest of this, he had stuck microdots to the third, fifth and seventh full stop of the letter, which were the prearranged positions. Blown up, they amounted to sixteen pages of top-secret orders from the Polish Defence Ministry to Colonel Jerzy's department. The Circus analysts declared them "likely and presumed reliable," which, coming from them, was an ecstatic declaration of faith.

You must imagine now the excitement that Oskar's letter kindled in the Station, and even in myself, though I had never met him. Oskar! the believers cried. The old devil! Alive and kicking under the rubble! Trust Oskar to beat the rap! Oskar, our hardened Polish Admiralty clerk, based at Gdansk's coastal defence headquarters, one of the best the Station ever had!

Only the hardest-nosed, or those nearest to retirement, dismissed the letter as a lure. Saying "no" in such cases is easy. Saying "yes" takes nerve. Nevertheless, the nay-sayers are always heard the clearest, particularly after Haydon, and for a while there was a stalemate when no one had the nerve to jump either way. Buying time, we wrote to Oskar asking for more collateral. He wrote back angrily demanding to know whether he was trusted, and this time he insisted on a meeting. "A meeting or nothing," he said. And in Poland. Soon or never.

While Head Office continued to vacillate, I begged to be allowed to go to him. The unbelievers in my Station told me I was mad, the believers said it was the only decent thing to do.

I was convinced by neither side, but I wanted clarity. Perhaps I also wanted it for myself, for Mabel had recently shown signs of withdrawing herself from our relationship and I was not disposed to rate myself too highly. Head Office sided with the noes. I reminded them of my naval background. Head Office dithered and said "no, but maybe." I reminded them of my bilinguality and the tested strength of my Netherlands identity, which our Dutch liaison condoned in exchange for favours in another field. Head Office measured the risks and the alternatives, and finally said, "Yes, but only for two days." Perhaps they had concluded that, after Haydon, I hadn't that many secrets to give away anyway. Hastily I put together my cover and set off before they could change their minds again. It was six below as my plane touched down at Gdansk airport; thick snow was lying in the streets, more was falling and the quiet gave me a greater sense of safety than was prudent. But I was taking no risks, believe me. I might be looking for clarity, but I was nobody's innocent any more.

Gdansk hotels are of a uniform frightfulness and mine was no exception. The lobby stank like a disinfected urinal; checking-in was as complicated as adopting a baby and took longer. My room turned out to be someone else's and she spoke no known language. By the time I had found another room, and a maid to remove the grosser traces of its previous inhabitant, it was dusk and time for me to make my arrival known to Oskar.

Every joe has his handwriting. In summer, said the file, Oskar liked to fish, and my predecessor had held successful conversations with him along the river bank. They had even caught a couple of fish together, though the pollution had made them inedible. But this was deep-frozen winter, when only children and masochists fished. In winter Oskar's habits changed and he liked to play billiards at a club for small officials near the docks. And this club had a telephone. To initiate a meeting, my predecessor, who spoke Polish, had only to call him there and conduct a cheery conversation built round the fiction that he was an old naval friend named Lech. Then Oskar would say, "All right, I'll meet you tomorrow at my sister's for a drink," which meant "Pick me up in your car on the corner of so-and-so street in one hour's time."

But I spoke no Polish. And besides, the rules of post-Haydon tradecraft dictated that no agent should be reactivated by means of past procedures.

In his letter, Oskar had provided the telephone numbers of three cafés, and the times at which he would try to be available in each of them—three because there was always the likelihood that one of the phones would be out of order or occupied. If none of the phone calls worked, then we would resort to a car pick-up, and Oskar had told me which tram stop I should stand at, and at what time. He had provided the registration number of his new blue Trabant.

And if all of this seems to place me in a passive rôle, that is because the iron rule for such meetings is that the agent in the field is king, and it's the agent who decides what is the safest course for him, and the most natural to his lifestyle. What Oskar was suggesting was not what I would have suggested, nor did I understand why we had to speak on the telephone before we met. But perhaps Oskar understood. Perhaps he was afraid of a trap. Perhaps he wanted to sample the reassurance of my voice before he took the plunge.

Or perhaps there was some sidelight I had yet to learn of: he was bringing a friend with him; he wished to be evacuated at once; he had changed his mind. For there is a second rule of tradecraft as rigid as the first, which says that the outrageous is to be regarded at all times as the norm. The good case officer *expects* the entire Gdansk telephone system to fail the moment he begins his call. He expects the tram stop to be at the centre of a road works, or that Oskar will that morning have driven his car into a lamp-post or developed a temperature of a hundred and four, or that his wife will have persuaded him to demand a million dollars in gold before resuming contact with us, or that her baby will have decided to be premature. The whole art—as I told my students till they hated me for it—is to rely on Sod's Law and otherwise nothing.

It was with this maxim in mind that, having spent a fruitless hour telephoning the three cafés, I placed myself at the agreed tram stop at ten past nine that night, and waited for Oskar's Trabant to grope its way towards me down the street. For though the snow had by now ceased to fall, the street was still no more than a pair of black tracks at one side of the tramlines, and the few cars that passed had the wariness of survivors returning from the front.

There is old Danzig the stately Hanseatic port, and there is Gdansk the Polish industrial slum. The tram stop was in Gdansk. To left and right of me as I waited, dour, low-lit concrete apartment houses hunched under the smouldering orange sky. Looking up and down the street, I saw not the smallest sign of human love or pleasure. Not a café, not a cinema, not a pretty light. Even the pair of drunks slumped in a doorway across the street seemed afraid to speak. One peak of laughter, one shout of good-fellowship or pleasure would have been a crime against the drabness of this outdoor prison. A car slipped by but it was not blue and it was not a Trabant. Its side windows were caked with snow, and ever after it had passed I could not have told you how many people were inside. It stopped. Not at the side of the street, not on the pavement or in a turning or a layby, for mounds of snow blocked them all. It simply stopped in the twin black track of the road, and cut its engine, then its lights.

Lovers, I thought. If so, they were lovers blind to danger, for the road was two-way. A second car appeared, traveling in the same direction as the first. It too pulled up, but short of my tram stop. More lovers? Or merely a sensible drive allowing plenty of skidding distance between himself and the stationary car ahead of him? The effect was the same; there was one car to either side of me, and as I stood waiting, I saw that the two silent drunks were standing clear of their doorway and looking very sober. Then I heard the single footstep behind me, soft as a bedroom slipper in the snow, but close. And I knew that I must not make any sudden movement, certainly not a clever one. There was no springing free, there was no preemptive blow that would save me, because what I was beginning to fear in my imagination was either nothing or it was everything. And if it was everything, there was nothing I could do.

A man was standing to my left, close enough to touch me. He wore a fur coat and a leather hat and carried a collapsed umbrella that could have been a lead pipe shoved into a nylon sheath. Very well, like myself he was waiting for the tram. A second man was standing to my right. He smelt of horse. And very well, like his companion and myself, he too was waiting for the tram, even if he had ridden here on horseback. Then a man's voice spoke to me in mournful Polish English, and it came neither from my left nor my right, but from directly behind me, where I had heard the slippered footstep.

"Oskar will not be coming tonight, I am afraid, sir. He has been dead for six months."

But by then he had given me time to think. A whole age, in fact. I knew of no Oskar. Oskar who? Coming where? I was a Dutchman who spoke only a limited amount of English, with a thick Dutch accent like my uncles and aunts in Nijmegen. I paused while I let his words have their effect on me; then I turned—but slowly and incuriously.

"You are confusing me, sir, I think," I protested, in the slow singsong voice I had learned at my mother's knee. "My name is Franz Joost, from Holland, and I do not think that I am waiting for anyone except the tram."

And that was when the men on either side of me grabbed hold of me like good professionals, pinning my arms and knocking me off balance at the same moment, then dragging and toppling me all the way to the second car. But not before I had time to recognise the squat man who had addressed me, his damp grey jowls, and sodden night-clerk's eyes. It was our very own Colonel Jerzy, the much publicised hero of the Protection of the Polish People's Republic, whose expressionless photograph had graced the front pages of several illustrious Polish newspapers around the time that he was gallantly arresting and torturing our agents.

There are deaths we unconsciously prepare for, depending on our choice of trades. An undertaker contemplates his funerals, the richman his destitution, the gaoler his imprisonment, the debauchee his impotence. An actor's greatest terror, I am told, is to watch the theatre empty itself while he wrestles in a void for his lines, and what else is that but a premature vision of his dying? For the civil servant, it is the moment when his protective walls of privilege collapse around him and he finds himself no safer than the next man, exposed to the gaze of the overt world, answering like a lying husband for his laxities and evasions. And most of my intelligence colleagues, if I am honest, came into this category: their greatest fear was to wake up one morning to read their real names *en clair* in the newspapers; to hear themselves spoken of on the radio and television, joked and laughed about and, worse yet, questioned by the public they believed they served. They would have regarded such public scrutiny as a greater disaster than being outwitted by the opposition, or, blown to every kindred service round the globe. It would have been their death.

And for myself, the worst death, and therefore the greatest test, the one for which I had prepared myself ever since I passed through the secret door, was the one that was upon me now: to have my uncertain courage tested on the rack; to be reduced mentally and physically to my last component of endurance, knowing I had within me the power to stop the dying with a word—that what was going on inside me was mortal combat between my spirit and my body, and that those who were applying the pain were merely the hired mercenaries in this secret war within myself.

So that from the first blinding explosion of pain, my response was recognition: Hullo, I thought, you've come at last—my name is Joost, what's yours?

There was no ceremony, you see. He didn't sit me at a desk in the tried tradition of the screen and say, "Either talk to me or you'll be beaten. Here is your confession. Sign it." He didn't have them lock me in a cell and leave me to cook for a few days while I decided that confession was the better part of courage. They simply dragged me out of the car and through the gateway of what could have been a private house, then into a courtyard where the only footprints were our own, so that they had to topple me through the thick snow, slewing me on my heels, all three of them, punching me from one to the other, now in the face, now in the groin and stomach, now back to the face again, this time with an elbow or a knee. Then, while I was still double, kicking me like a half-stunned pig across the slithery cobble as if they couldn't wait to get indoors before they had me.

Then, once indoors, they became more systematic, as if the

elegance of the old bare room had instilled in them a sense of order. They took me in turns, like civilised men, two of them holding me and one hitting me, a proper democratic rota, except that when it was Colonel Jerzy's fifth or fiftieth turn, he hit me so regretfully and so hard that I actually did die for a while, and when I came round I was alone with him. He was seated at a folding desk, with his elbows on it, holding his unhappy head between his grazed hands as if he had a hangover, and reviewing with disappointment the answers I had given to the questions he had put to me between onslaughts, first lifting his head in order to study with disapproval my altered appearance, then shaking it painfully and sighing as if to say life really was unfair to him, he didn't know what more he could do to me to help me see the light. It dawned on me that more time had passed than I realised, perhaps several hours.

This was also the moment when the scene began to take on a resemblance to the one I had always imagined, with my tormentor sitting comfortably at a desk, brooding over me with a professional's concern, and myself spreadeagled against a scalding waterpipe, my arms handcuffed either side of a black concertina-style radiator; with corners that bit into the base of my spine like red-hot teeth. I had been bleeding from the mouth and nose and, I thought, from one ear as well, and my shirt front looked like a slaughterer's apron. But the blood had dried and I wasn't bleeding any more, which was another way of calculating the passage of time. How long does blood take to congeal in a big empty house in Gdansk when you are chained to a furnace and looking into the puppyish face of Colonel Jerzy?

It was terribly hard to hate him, and with the burning in my back it was becoming harder by the moment. He was my only saviour. His face stayed on me all the time now. Even when he turned his head downward to the table in private prayer, or got up and lit himself a filthy Polish cigarette and took a stretch around the room, his lugubrious gaze seemed to stay on me without reference to where the rest of him had gone. He turned his squat back to me. He gave me a view of his thick bald head and the pitted nape of his neck. Yet his eyes—treating with me, reasoning with me and sometimes, as it seemed, imploring me to ease his anguish—never left me for a second. And there was a part of me that really wanted to help him and it was becoming more and more strident with the burning. Because the burning was not a burning any more, it was pure pain, a pain indivisible and absolute, mounting like a scale that had no upper limit. So that I would have given almost anything to make him feel better—except myself. Except the part of me that made me separate from him, and was therefore my survival.

"What's your name?" he asked me, still in his Polish English.

"Joost." He had to bend over me to hear me. "Franz Joost."

"From Munich," he suggested, using my shoulder as a prop while he put his ear closer to my mouth.

"Born Nijmegen. Working for farmers in the Taunus, by Frankfurt."

"You've forgotten your Dutch accent." He shook me a little to wake me.

"You just don't hear it. You're a Pole. I want to see the Dutch Consul."

"You mean British Consul."

"Dutch." And then I think I repeated the same word "Dutch" several times, and went on repeating it till he threw cold water over me, then poured a little of it into my mouth to let me rinse and spit. I realised I was missing a tooth. Lower jaw front left. Two teeth perhaps. It was hard to tell.

"Do you believe in God?" he asked me.

When he stared down at me like this, his cheeks fell forward like a baby's and his lips formed themselves in a kiss, so that he looked like a puzzled cherub.

"Not at the moment," I said. "Why not?"

"Get me the Dutch Consul. You've got the wrong man."

I saw that he didn't like being told this. He wasn't used to being given orders or contradicted. He passed the back of his right hand across his lips, a thing he sometimes did before he hit me, and I waited for the blow. He began patting his pockets, I assumed for some instrument.

"No," he remarked, with a sigh. "You are mistaken. I have got the right man."

He knelt to me and I thought he was preparing to kill me because I had noticed that he was at his most murderous when he appeared most unhappy. But he was unlocking my handcuffs. When he had done so, he shoved his clenched fists under my armpits and hauled me—I almost thought helped me—to a spacious bathroom with an old, freestanding bath filled with warm water.

"Strip," he said, and watched me dejectedly while I dragged off what remained of my clothes, too exhausted to care about what he would do to me once I was in the water: drown me, or cook me or freeze me, or drop in an electric wire.

He had my suitcase from the hotel. While I lay in the bath, he picked out clean clothes and tossed them on to a chair.

"You leave on tomorrow's plane for Frankfurt via Warsaw. There has been a mistake," he said. "We apologise. We shall cancel your business appointments and say you were the victim of a hit-and-run car."

"I'll need more than an apology," I said.

The bath was doing me no good. I was afraid that if I lay flat any longer, I would die again. I hauled myself into a crouch. Jerzy held out his forearm. I clutched it and stood upright, swaying dangerously. Jerzy helped me out of the bath, then handed me a towel and watched me gloomily while I dried myself and pulled on the clean clothes he had laid out for me.

He led me from the house and across the courtyard, carrying my case in one hand and bearing my weight with the other, because the bath had weakened me as well as easing the pain. I peered round for the henchmen but saw none.

"The cold air will be good for you," he said, with the confidence of an expert.

He led me to a parked car, and it did not resemble either of the cars that had taken part in my arrest. A toy steering wheel lay on the backseat. We drove down empty streets. Sometimes I dozed. We reached a pair of white iron gates guarded by militia.

"Don't look at them," he ordered me, and showed them his papers, while I dozed again.

We got out of the car and stood on a grass clifftop. An inshore wind froze our faces. Mine felt big as two footballs. My mouth had moved into my left cheek. One eye had closed. There was no moon and the sea was a growl behind the salt mist. The only light came from the city, behind us. Occasionally phosphorous sparks slipped past us, or puffs of white spume spun away into the blackness. This is where I'm supposed to die, I thought as I stood beside him; first he beats me, then he gives me a warm bath, now he shoots me and shoves me over the cliff. But his hands were hanging glumly at his sides and there was no gun in them, and his eyes—what I could make out of them—were fixed on the starless darkness, not on me; so perhaps someone else was going to shoot me, someone already waiting in the dark. If I had had the energy, I could have killed Jerzy first. But I hadn't, and didn't feel the need. I thought of Mabel, but without any sense of loss or gain. I wondered how she'd manage living on a pension, whom she'd find. *Fräulein Stefanie is not at home,* I remembered. . . . *Then perhaps it was Stefanie who answered,* Smiley was saying. . . . So many unanswered prayers, I was thinking. But so many never offered, either. I was feeling very drowsy.

At last Jerzy spoke, his voice no less despondent than before. "I have brought you here because there isn't a microphone on earth can hear us. I wish to spy for your country. I need a good professional to act as intermediary. I have decided to choose you."

Once more I lost my sense of time and place. But perhaps he had lost his too, for he had turned his back on the sea and with his hand clutched to his leather hat to hold it against the wind, he had undertaken a mournful study of the inland lights, scowling at things that needed no scowling at, sometimes punching the windtears from his cheeks with his big fists.

"Why should anyone spy for Holland?" I asked him.

"Very well, I propose to spy for Holland," he replied wearily, indulging a pedant. "Therefore I need a good professional *Dutchman* who can keep his mouth shut. Knowing what fools you *Dutchmen* have employed against us in the past, I am understandably selective. However, you have passed the test. Congratulations. I select you."

I thought it best to say nothing. Probably I didn't believe him.

"In the false compartment of your suitcase you will find a wad of Polish secret documents," he continued, in a tone of dejection. "At Gdansk airport you will have no Customs problems, naturally. I have given orders for them not to examine your luggage. For all they know, you are by now my agent. In Frankfurt, you are on home ground. I shall work for you and nobody else. Our next meeting will be in Berlin on May 5th. I shall be attending the May Day celebrations to mark the glorious victory of the proletariat."

He was trying to light a fresh cigarette, but the wind kept putting out his matches. So he took his hat off and lit the cigarette inside the crown, lowering his fat face to it as if he were drinking water from a stream.

"Your people will wish to know my motive," he continued when he had taken a deep draught of cigarette smoke. "Tell them—" Suddenly at a loss, he sank his head into his shoulders and peered round at me as if pleading for advice on how to deal with idiots. "Tell them I'm bored. Tell them I'm sick of the work. Tell them the Party's a bunch of crooks. They know that anyway, but tell them. I'm a Catholic. I'm a Jew. I'm a Tartar. Tell them whatever the hell they want to hear."

"They may want to know why you have chosen to come to the *Dutch,*" I said. "Rather than to the Americans, or the French or whoever."

He thought about that too, puffing at his cigarette in the darkness. "You Dutch had some good joes," he said ruminatively. "I got to know some of them pretty well. They did a good job till that bastard Haydon came along." An idea occurred to him. "Tell them my father was a Battle of Britain pilot," he suggested. "Got himself shot down over Kent. That should please them. You know Kent?"

"Why should a Dutchman know Kent?" I said.

If I had weakened, I could have told him that, before our so-called "friendly" separation, Mabel and I had bought a house in Tunbridge Wells. But I didn't, which was as well, because when Head Office came to check the story out, there was no record of Jerzy's father having flown anything larger than a paper kite. And when I put this to Jerzy several years later—long after his loyalty to the perfidious British had been demonstrated beyond all doubt—he just laughed, and said his father was an old fool who cared for nothing but vodka and potatoes.

So why?

For five years Jerzy was my secret university of espionage, but his contempt for motive—his own particularly—never relaxed. First we idiots do what we want to do, he said; then we look round for justifications for having done it. All men were idiots to him, he told me, and we spies were the biggest idiots of all.

At first I suspected that he was spying for vengeance, and drew him out on the people above him in the hierarchy who might have slighted him. He hated them all, himself the most.

Then I decided he was spying for ideological reasons, and that his cynicism was a disguise for the finer yearnings he had discovered in his middle age. But when I attempted to use my wiles to break his cynicism down—"Your family, Jerzy, your mother, Jerzy. Admit you're proud to have become a grandfather"—I found only more cynicism beneath. He felt nothing for any of them, he retorted, but so icily that I concluded that he did indeed, as he maintained, hate the entire human race, and that his savagery, and perhaps his betrayal too, were the simple expression of this hatred.

As to the West, it was run by the same idiots who ran everything in the world, so what's the difference? And when I told him this simply was not so, he became as defensive of his nihilist creed as any other zealot, and I had to rein myself in for fear of angering him seriously.

So why? Why risk his neck, his life, his livelihood and the family he hated, to do something for a world he despised?

The Church? I asked him that too, and significantly, as I think now, he bridled. Christ was a manic depressive, he retorted. Christ needed to commit suicide in public, so he provoked the authorities until they did him the favour. "Those God-thumper guys are all the same," he said with contempt. "I've tortured them. I know."

Like most cynics, he was a Puritan, and this paradox repeated itself in him in several ways. When we offered to drop money for him, open a Swiss bank account, the usual, he flew into a rage and declared he was not some "cheap informant." When I picked a moment—on the instruction of Head Office—to assure him that if ever things went wrong, we would spare no effort to get him out and provide him with a new identity in the West, his contempt was absolute: "I'm a Polish creep, but I would rather face a firing squad of my fellow creeps than die a traitor in some capitalist pigsty."

As to life's other comforts, we could offer him nothing he had not got. His wife was a scold, he said, and going home after a heavy day at the office bored him. His mistress was a young fool, and after an hour with her he preferred a game of billiards to her conversation.

Then why? I kept asking myself when I had exhausted my checklist of the Service's standard-issue motives.

Meanwhile, Jerzy continued to fill our coffers. He was turning his Service inside out as neatly as Haydon had ever done with ours. When Moscow Centre gave him orders, we knew of them before he passed them to his underlings. He photographed everything that came within his reach; he took risks I begged him not to take. He was so heedless that sometimes he left me wondering whether, like the Christ he was so determined to deny, he was looking for a public death. It was only the unflagging efficiency of what we were pleased to call his cover work that protected him from suspicion. For that was the dark side of his balancing act: God help the Western agent, real or imagined, who was invited to make his voluntary confession at Jerzy's hands.

Only once in the five years that I ran him did he seem to let slip the clue I was searching for. He was tired to death. He had been attending a conference of Warsaw Pact Intelligence chiefs in Bucharest, in the midst of fighting off charges of brutality and corruption against his Service at home. We met in West Berlin, in a *pension* on the Kurfürstendamm which catered to the better type of representative. He was a really tired torturer. He sat on my bed, smoking and answering my follow-up questions about his last batch of material. He was red-eyed. When we had finished, he asked for a whisky, then another.

"No danger is no life," he said, tossing three more rolls of film on the counterpane. "No danger is dead." He took out a grimy brown handkerchief and carefully wiped his heavy face with it. "No danger, you do better stay home, look after the baby."

I preferred not to believe it was danger he was talking about. What he was talking about, I decided, was feeling, and his terror that by ceasing to feel he was ceasing to exist—which perhaps was why he was so devoted to instilling feeling in others. For that moment, I thought I caught a glimpse of why he was sitting with me in the room breaking every rule in his book. He was keeping his spirit alive at a time of his life when it was beginning to look like dying.

The same night I dined with Stefanie at an American restaurant ten minutes' walk from the *pension* where Jerzy and I had met. I had wangled her telephone number from a sister in Munich. She was as tall and beautiful as I remembered her, and determined to convince me she was happy. Oh, life was *perfect,* Ned, she declared. She was living with this *terribly* distinguished academic, not in his first youth any more—but look here, nor are we—and completely adorable and wise. She told me his name. It meant nothing to me. She said she was pregnant by him. It didn't show.

"And *you,* Ned, how did it go for *you?*" she asked, as if we were two generals reporting to each other from successful, but separate, campaigns.

I gave her my most confident smile, the one that had earned me the trust of my joes and colleagues in the years since I had seen her.

"Oh, I think it worked out pretty well actually, thanks, yes," I said, with seeming British understatement. "After all, you can't expect one person to be everything you need, can you? It's a pretty good partnership, I'd say. Good parallel living."

"And you still do that work?" she said. "Ben's work?"

"Yes."

It was the first time either of us had mentioned him. He was living in Ireland, she said. A cousin of his had bought a tumbledown estate in County Cork. Ben sort of caretook for him while he wasn't there, stocking the river and looking after the farm and so on.

I asked whether she ever saw him.

"No," she said. "He won't."

I would have driven her home, but she preferred a cab. We waited in the street till it came, and it seemed to take a terribly long time. As I closed the door on her, her head tipped forward, as if she had dropped something on the floor. I waved her out of sight but she didn't wave back.

The nine-o'clock news was showing us an outdoor meeting of Solidarity in Gdansk, where a Polish Cardinal was exhorting an enormous crowd to moderation. Losing interest, Mabel settled the *Daily Telegraph* on her lap and resumed her crossword. At first the crowd heard the Cardinal noisily. Then with the devotion Poles are famous for, they fell silent. After his address, the Cardinal moved among his flock, bestowing blessings and accepting homage. And as one dignitary after another was brought to him, I picked out Jerzy hovering in the background, like the ugly boy excluded from the feast. He had lost a lot of weight since he had retired, and I guessed that the social changes had not been kind to him. His jacket hung on him like someone else's; his once-formidable fists were hardly visible inside the sleeves.

Suddenly the Cardinal has spotted him, just as I had.

The Cardinal freezes as if in doubt of his own feelings, and for a moment makes himself neater somehow, almost in obedience, pressing in his elbows and drawing back his shoulders to attention. Then slowly his arms lift again and he gives an order to one of his attendants, a young priest who seems reluctant to obey it. The Cardinal repeats the order, the priest clears a path to Jerzy; the two men face each other, the secret policeman and the Cardinal. Jerzy winces, as if he has digestion pains. The Cardinal leans forward and speaks in Jerzy's ear. Awkwardly, Jerzy kneels to receive the Cardinal's blessing.

And each time I replay this moment I see Jerzy's eyes close apparently in pain. But what is he repenting? His brutality? His loyalty to a vanished cause? Or his betrayal of it? Or is squeezing the eyes shut merely the instinctive response of a torturer receiving the forgiveness of a victim?

I fish. I drop into my little reveries. My love of English landscape has, if possible, increased. I think of Stefanie and Bella, and my other half-had women. I lobby our Member of Parliament about the filthy river. He's a Conservative, but what on earth does he imagine he's conserving? I've joined one of the sounder environmentalist groups; I collect signatures on petitions. The petitions are ignored. I won't play golf, I never would. But I'll walk round with Mabel on a Wednesday afternoon, provided she's playing alone. I encourage her. The dog enjoys himself. Retirement is no time to be wandering lost, or puzzling how to reinvent mankind.

8

My students had decided to give Smiley a rough ride, just as they'd done to me from time to time. We'd be running along perfectly smoothly—a double session on natural cover, say, in the late afternoon—when one of them would start hectoring me, usually by adopting an anarchic stance which nobody, in his right mind could sustain. Then a second would chime in, then all of them, so that if I didn't have any sense of humour shining-ready—and I'm only human—they'd be trampling me till the bell rang for close of play. And next day all would be forgotten: they'd have fed whatever little demon had got hold of them and now they'd like to go back to learning, please, so where were we? At first I used to brood over these occasions, suspect conspiracy, hunt for ringleaders. Then cautiously I came to recognise them as spontaneous expressions of resistance to the unnatural harness that these children had chosen to put on.

But when they started in on Smiley, their guest of honour and mine, even questioning the entire purpose of his life's work, my tolerance ended with a snap. And this time the offender was not Maggs, either, but the demure Clare, his girlfriend, who had sat so adoringly opposite Smiley throughout dinner.

"No, no, Ned," Smiley protested, as I leapt angrily to my feet. "Clare has a valid point. Nine times out of ten a good journalist *can* tell us quite as much about a situation as the spies can. Very often they're sharing the same sources anyway. So why not scrap the spies and subsidise the newspapers? It's a point that should be answered in these changeable times. Why not?"

Reluctantly I resumed my seat, while Clare, snuggling close against Maggs, continued to gaze angelically at her victim while her colleagues smothered their grins.

But where I would have taken refuge in humour, Smiley elected to treat her sally seriously:

"It is perfectly true," he agreed, "that most of our work is either useless, or duplicated by overt sources. The trouble is, the spies aren't there to enlighten the public, but governments."

And slowly I felt his spell re-unite them. They had moved their chairs to him in a disordered half-circle. Some of the girls were sprawled becomingly on the floor.

"And governments, like anyone else, trust what they pay for, and are suspicious of what they don't," he said. Thus delicately passing beyond Clare's provocative question, he addressed a larger one: "Spying is eternal," he announced simply. "If governments *could* do without it, they never would. They adore it. If the day ever comes when there are no enemies left in the world, governments will invent them for us, so don't worry. Besides—who says we only spy on enemies? All history teaches us that today's allies are tomorrow's rivals. Fashion may dictate priorities, but foresight doesn't. For as long as rogues become leaders, we shall spy. For as long as there are bullies and liars, and madmen in the world we shall spy. For as long as nations compete, and politicians deceive, and tyrants launch conquests, and consumers need resources, and the homeless look for land, and the hungry for food, and the rich for excess, your chosen profession is perfectly secure, I can assure you."

And with the topic thus neatly turned back to their own future, he once more warned them of its perils:

"There's no career on earth more cockeyed than the one you've picked," he assured them, with every sign of satisfaction. "You'll be at your most postable while you're least experienced, and by the time you've learned the ropes, no one will be able to send you anywhere without a trade description round your necks. Old athletes know they've played their best games when they were in their prime. But spies in their prime are on the shelf, which is why they take so ungraciously to middle age, and start counting the cost of living how they've lived."

Though his hooded gaze to all appearance remained fixed upon his brandy, I saw him cast a sideways glance at me. "And then, at a certain age, you want the answer," he continued. "You want the rolled-up parchment in the inmost room that tells you who runs your lives and why. The trouble is, that by then you're the very people who know best that the inmost room is bare. Ned, you're not drinking. You're a brandy traitor. Fill him up, someone."

It is an uncomfortable truth of the period of my life that follows that I recall it as a single search the object of which was unclear to me. And that the object, when I found him, turned out to be the lapsed spy Hansen.

And that, although in reality I was pursuing quite other goals and people among my eastward journey, all of them in retrospect seem to have been stages on my journey to him. I can put it no other way. Hansen in his Cambodian jungle was my Kurtz at the heart of darkness. And everything that happened to me on the way was a preparation for our meeting. Hansen's was the voice I was waiting to hear. Hansen held the answer to the questions I did not know I was asking. Outwardly, I was my stolid, moderate, pipesmoking, decent self, a shoulder for weaker souls to rest their heads on. Inside, I felt a rampant incomprehension of my

uselessness; a sense that, for all my striving, I had failed to come
to grips with life; that in struggling to give freedom to others, I
had found none for myself. At my lowest ebb, I saw myself as ridiculous, a hero in the style not of Buchan but of Quixote.

I took to writing down sardonic versions of my life, so that
when, for instance, I reviewed the episodes I have described to
you this far, I gave them picaresque titles that emphasised their
futility: the Panda—I safeguard our Middle Eastern interests!
Ben—I run to earth a British defector! Bella—I make the
ultimate sacrifice! Teodor—I take part in a grand deception!
Jerzy—I play the game to the end! Though with Jerzy, I had to
admit, a positive purpose had been served, even if it was as short-
lived as most intelligence, and as irrelevant to the human forces
that have now engulfed his nation.

Like Quixote, I had set out in life vowing to check the flow of
evil. Yet in my lowest moments I was beginning to wonder
whether I had become a contributor to it. But I still looked to the
world to provide me with the chance to make my contribution—
and I blamed it for not knowing how to use me.

To understand this, you should know what has happened to
me after Munich. Jerzy, whatever else he did to me, brought me
a sort of prestige, and the Fifth Floor decided to invent a job for
me as roving operational fixer, sent out on short assignments "to
appraise, and where possible exploit opportunities outside the
remit of the local Station"—thus my brief, signed and returned
to maker.

Looking back, I realise that the constant travel this entailed—
Central America one week, Northern Ireland the next, Africa,
the Middle East, Africa again—soothed the restlessness that was
stalking me, and that Personnel in all likelihood knew this, for I
had recently embarked on a senseless love affair with a girl called
Monica, who worked in the Service's Industrial Liaison Section.

I had decided I needed an affair; I saw her in the canteen and cast her in the part. It was as banal as that. One night it was raining, and as I started to drive home, I saw her standing at a number 23 bus stop. Banality made flesh. I took her to her flat, I took her to her bed, I took her to dinner and we tried to work out what we had done, and came up with the convenient solution that we had fallen in love. It served us well for several months, until tragedy abruptly called me to my senses. By a mercy, I was back in London briefing myself for my next mission when word came that my mother was failing. By an act of divine ill taste, I was in bed with Monica when I took the call. But at least I was able to be present for the event, which was lengthy, but unexpectedly serene.

Nevertheless, I found myself unprepared for it. Somehow I had taken for granted that, in the same way that I had managed to negotiate myself round awkward hurdles in the past, I would do the same in the case of my mother's death. I could not have been more mistaken. Very few conspiracies, Smiley once remarked, survive contact with reality. And so it was with the conspiracy that I had made with myself to let my mother's death slip past me as a timely and necessary release from pain. I had not taken into my calculations that the pain could be my own.

I was orphaned and elated both at once. I can describe it no other way. My father had long been dead. Without my realising it, my mother had done duty for both parents. In her death I saw the loss, not only of my childhood, but of most of my adulthood as well. At last I stood unencumbered before life's challenges, yet many of them were already behind me—fudged, missed or botched. I was free to love at last, but whom? Not, I am afraid, Monica, however much I might protest the contrary and expect the reality to follow. Neither Monica nor my marriage offered me the magic it was henceforth my duty as a survivor to pursue. And when I looked at myself in the mirror of the undertaker's rose-tinted lavatory after my night's vigil, I was horrified by what I saw. It was the face of a spy branded by his own deception.

Have you seen it too, around you? On you? That face? In my case it was so much my everyday companion that I had ceased to notice it until the shock of death brought it home to me. We smile, but our withholding makes our smile false. When we are exhilarated, or drunk—or, even as I am told, make love—the reserve does not dissolve, the gyroscope stays vertical, the monitory voice reminds us of our calling. Until gradually our very withholding becomes so strident it is almost a security risk by itself. So that today—if I go to a reunion, say, or we have a Sarratt old-boys' night—I can actually look round the room and see how the secret stain has come out in every one of us. I see the overbright face or the underlit one, but inside each I see the remnants of a life withheld. I hear the hoot of supposedly abandoned laughter and I don't have to mark down the source of it to know that nothing has been abandoned—not its owner, nor its interior restrictions, nothing. In my younger days, I used to think it was just the inhibited British ruling classes who became that person. "They were born into captivity and had no option from then on," I would tell myself as I listened to their unconvincing courtesies, and returned their good-chap smiles. But, as only half a Briton, I had exempted myself from their misfortune—until that day in the undertaker's pink-tiled lavatory when I saw that the same shadow that falls across us all had fallen across me.

From that day on, I now believe, I saw only the horizon. I am starting too late! I thought. And from so far back! Life was to be searched, or nothing! But it was the fear that it was nothing that drove me forward. That's how I see it now. And so, please, must you see it, in the fragmented recollections that belong to this surreal passage of my life. In the eyes of the man I had become, every encounter was an encounter with myself. Every stranger's confession was my own, and Hansen's the most accusing—and therefore, ultimately, the most consoling. I buried my mother, I said goodbye to Monica and Mabel. The next day I departed for Beirut. Yet even that simple departure was attended by a disconcerting episode.

To brief myself for my mission, I had been sharing a room with a rather clever man called Giles Latimer, who had made a corner for himself in what was known as the "Mad Mullah department," studying the intricate and seemingly indecypherable web of Muslim fundamentalist groups operating out of Lebanon. The notion so beloved of the amateur terror industry that these bodies are all part of a super plot is nonsense. If only it were so, for then there might be some way to get at them! As it is, they slip about, grouping and regrouping like drops of water on a wet wall, and they are about as easy to pin down.

But Giles, who was an Arabist and a distinguished bridge player, had come as near to achieving the impossible as any one was likely to, and my job was to sit at his feet in order to prepare myself for my mission. He was tall, angular and woolly. He was of my intake. His boyish manner was given extra youthfulness by the redness of his cheeks, though this was actually the consequence of clusters of tiny broken blood vessels. He was indefatigably, painfully gentlemanly, forever opening doors and leaping to his feet for women. In the spring weather I twice saw him get drenched to the skin on account of his habit of lending his umbrella to whoever was proposing to venture out of doors without one. He was rich but frugal, and a thoroughly good man, with a thoroughly good wife, who organised Service bridge drives and remembered the names of the junior staff and their families. Which made it all the more bizarre when his files started disappearing.

It was I, inadvertently, who first noticed the phenomenon. I was tracking a German girl called Britta on her odyssey through the terrorist training camps in the Shuf Mountains, and I requested a contingent file which contained sensitive intercept material about her. The material was American and limited by a subscription list, but when I had gone through the rigmarole of signing myself in, nobody could find it. Nominally it was marked to Giles, but so was almost everything, because Giles was Giles and his name was on every list around.

But Giles knew nothing of it. He remembered reading it, he could quote from it; he thought he had passed it on to me. It must have gone to the Fifth Floor, he said, or back to Registry. Or somewhere.

So the file was posted missing and the Registry bloodhounds were informed, and everything ran along normally for a couple of days until the same thing happened again, though this time it was Giles's own secretary who started the hunt when Registry called in all three volumes on a misty group called the Brothers of the Prophet, supposedly based in Damour.

Once again, Giles knew nothing: he had neither seen nor touched them. The Registry bloodhounds showed him his signature on the receipt. He flatly disowned it. And when Giles denied something, you didn't feel like challenging him. As I say, he was a man of transparent rectitude.

By now, the hunt was up in earnest and inventories were being taken left and right. Registry was in its last days before computerisation, and could still find what it was looking for, or know for sure that it was lost. Today somebody would shake his head and phone for an engineer.

What Registry discovered was that thirty-two files marked out to Giles were missing. Twenty-one of them were standard top secret, five had higher gradings and six were of a category called RETAIN, which meant, I am afraid, that nobody of strong pro-

Jewish sentiments should be admitted as a signatory. Parse that how you will. It was a squalid limitation and there were few of us who were not embarrassed by it. But this was the Middle East.

My first intimation of the scale of the crisis came from Personnel. It was a Friday morning. Personnel always liked the shelter of the weekend when he was about to wield his axe.

"Has Giles been *well* lately, Ned?" he asked me, with old-boy intimacy.

"Perfectly," I said.

"He's a Christian, isn't he? Christian sort of chap. Pious."

"I believe so."

"Well, I mean we all are in a way, but he is a *heavy* sort of Christian, would you say, Ned? What's your opinion?"

"We've never discussed it."

"Are you?"

"No."

"Would you say, for example, he could be sympathetic to something like—say—the British-Israelite sect, or one of those sort of things, at all? Nothing against them, mind. Every man to his convictions, me."

"Giles is very orthodox, very down the middle, I am sure. He's some sort of lay dignitary at his parish church. I believe he gives the odd Lenten Address, and that's about it."

"That's what I've got down here," Personnel complained, tapping his knuckles on a closed file. "That's the picture I've got of him exactly, Ned. So what's up? Not always easy, my job, you know. Not always pleasant at all."

"Why don't you ask him yourself?"

"Oh I know, I know, I must. Unless you would, of course. You could take him out to lunch—my expense, obviously. Feel his bones. Tell me what you think."

"No," I said.

His old-boy manner gave way to something a lot harder. "I

thought you'd say that. I worry about you sometimes, Ned. You're putting yourself about with the women and you're a touch stubborn for your health. It's the Dutch blood in you. Well, keep your mouth shut. That's an order."

In the end it was Giles who took me out to lunch. Probably Personnel had played the game both ways, pitching some tale to Giles in reverse. Whether he had or not, at twelve-thirty Giles sprang suddenly to his feet and said, "To hell with it, Ned. It's Friday. Come on, I'll give you lunch. Haven't had a pissy lunch for years."

So we went to the Travellers', and sat at a table by the window and we drank a bottle of Sancerre very fast. And suddenly Giles began talking about a liaison trip he'd made recently to the FBI in New York. He kicked off quite normally. Then his voice seemed to get stuck on one note, and his eyes got fixed on something only he could see. I put it down to the wine at first. Giles didn't look like a drinker and didn't drink like one. Yet there was great conviction in the way he spoke and—as he continued—a visionary intensity.

"Peculiar chaps actually, the Americans, Ned, you want to watch out for them. One doesn't think they're after one at first. One's hotel, for instance. You can always read the clues in a hotel. Too much smiling when you sign in. Too much interest in your luggage. They're watching you. Damned great highrise greenhouse. Swimming pool on the top floor. You can look down on the helicopters going up the river. 'Welcome, Mr. Lambert, and have a nice day, sir.' I was using Lambert. I always do for America. The fourteenth floor they'd put me on. I'm a methodical chap. Always have been. Shoe-trees and that kind of thing. Can't help it. My father was the same. Shoes here, shirts there. Socks there. Suits in a certain order. We never have lightweight suits, do we, the English? You think they're lightweight. You choose lightweight. Your tailor tells you they're lightweight. 'Lightest we've got, sir. We don't go any lighter.' You'd think they'd have learned by now, the amount of American business they do. But they haven't. Cheers."

He drank and I drank with him. I poured him some mineral water. He was sweating.

"Next day I come back to the hotel. Meetings all day long. Lot of trying to like each other. And I do, I mean they're nice chaps. Just—well, different. Different attitudes. Carry guns. Want results. There can't be any, though, can there? We all know that. The more fanatics you kill, the more there are of them. I know that, they don't. My father was an Arabist too, you know."

I said I didn't. I said, "Tell me about him." I wanted to deflect him. I felt I would feel much better if he talked about his father instead of the hotel.

"So I walk in and they hand me the key. 'Hey, hang on,' I say. 'This isn't floor fourteen. This is floor twenty-one. Mistake.' I smile, naturally. Anyone can make a mistake. It's a woman this time. Very strong-looking woman. 'It is not a mistake, Mr. Lambert. You're on the twenty-first floor. You room is 2109.' 'No, no,' I say. 'It's 1409. Look here.' I had this identity card they give you somewhere and I looked for it. Turned out my pockets while she watched, but couldn't find it. 'Look,' I said. 'Believe me. I have that kind of memory. My room is 1409.' She gets out the guest list, shows it to me. Lambert, 2109. I go up in the lift, unlock the room, it's all there. Shoes here. Shirts there. Socks there. Suits in the same order. Everything where I'd put it in the other room down on the fourteenth floor. Know what they'd done?"

Again I said I didn't.

"Photographed it. Polaroid."

"Why would they do that?"

"They wanted to mike me—2109 was miked, 1409 was clean. No good to them, so they moved me up. They thought I was an Arab spy."

"Why would they think that?"

"Because of my father. He was a Lawrence man. They knew that. They'd decided. That's what they do. Photograph your room."

I scarcely remember the rest of lunch. I don't remember what we ate or what else we drank or anything at all. I have a recollection of Giles extolling Mabel at great length as the perfect Service wife, but perhaps that was my conscience. All I really remember is the two of us side by side in Giles's room back at Head Office, and Personnel standing in front of Giles's steel cupboard with the door removed, and the thirty-two missing files crammed higgledypiggledy into the shelves—all the files Giles hadn't been able to cope with while he was having what Smiley called his "Force Twelve nervous breakdown" in place.

And the reason for it, as I learned later? Giles too had found his Monica. What had unhinged him, ostensibly, was his passion for a twenty-year-old girl in his village. His love for her, his guilt and despair had dictated that he could no longer function. He had continued going through the day's motions—naturally, he was a soldier—but his mind wouldn't play anymore. It had acquired its own preoccupations, even if he wouldn't own to them.

What else had unhinged him, I leave that to you, and to our in-house shrinks who seem to be daily gaining ground. Something to do, perhaps, with the gap between our dreams and our realities. Something to do, perhaps, with the gap between what Giles longed for when he was young, and what he'd got now that he was nearly old. And the hard truth was, Giles had frightened me. I felt he had gone ahead of me down the road I myself was treading. I felt it as I drove to the airport; I felt it on the plane while I thought about my mother. And downed several in-flight whiskies in order not to feel it more.

I was still feeling it as I set out my own meagre wardrobe in

Room 607 at the Commodore Hotel, Beirut, and the telephone began ringing a few inches from my head. As I picked up the receiver, I had a wayward fancy I was going to hear Ahmed at the front desk telling me I had been allocated a new room on floor twenty-one. I was wrong. Surreal episode number two had just announced itself.

Shooting had started, semi-automatic on the move. Most likely a bunch of kids in a Japanese pickup hosing down the neighbourhood with AK 47s. It was one of those seasons in Beirut when you could set your watch by the first excitement of the evening. But I had never minded too much about the shooting. Shooting has a logic, if a haphazard one. It's directed at you, or away from you. My personal phobia was car bombs—never knowing, as you hurried along a pavement or dawdled in the sweating, crawling traffic, whether a parked car was going to take out the entire block with one huge heave, and leave you in such tiny shreds that there was nothing worth a body bag, let alone a burial. The thing you noticed about car bombs—I mean afterwards—was shoes. People blown clean out of them, but the shoes intact. So that even after the bits of body had been picked out and taken away, there was still the odd pair or two of wearable shoes among the broken glass and smashed false teeth and shreds of someone's suit. A little machine-gun fire, like now, or the odd hand-held rocket, didn't trouble me as much as it did some people.

I lifted the receiver and when I heard a woman's voice I quickened, not only because of my domestic ambiguities but because my errand was to trace a German woman—the same Britta who had been taking lessons in terror in the Shuf Mountains.

But it was not Britta. It was not Monica and not Mabel. The voice was middle-American and scared. And I was Peter, remember—Peter Carter, from a great British newspaper, even if its local correspondent had never heard of me. I was reminding myself of this as I listened to her.

"Peter, for Christ's sake, I need to be with you," she said in a single rush of breath. "Peter, where the fuck have you been?"

A rattle of heavy machine-gun fire broke out, to be promptly silenced by the smack of a rocket-propelled grenade. The voice on the phone resumed in greater agitation.

"Jesus, Peter, why don't you call me? Okay, I said some shitty things. I spoiled your copy. I'm sorry. I mean, Jesus, what are we? Children? You know how I hate this stuff."

A frenzy of rifle fire. Sometimes the kids just shot into the sky for effect.

Her voice rose steeply. "Talk to me, Peter! Tell me something funny, will you, please? Something funny must be happening *somewhere* in the world! Peter, will you please answer me? You're not dead, are you? You're not lying on the floor with your head blown off? Just nod for no. I don't want to die alone, Peter. I'm sociable. I love sociably, I die sociably. Peter, answer me. Please."

"What room are you calling?" I said.

Dead silence. The really dead silence that gathers between bursts of gunfire.

"Who is this?" she demanded.

"This is Peter, but I don't think I'm your Peter. What room are you calling?"

"This room."

"What number?"

"Room 607."

"I'm afraid he must have checked out. I arrived in Beirut this afternoon. This is the room they gave me."

A grenade exploded, answered by another. Out in the street, perhaps three blocks away, somebody screamed seriously. The scream ended.

"Is he dead?" she whispered.

I didn't answer.

"Could have been a woman," she said.

"Could have been," I agreed.

"Who are you? You British?"

"Yes." Peter is too, I thought, without knowing why.

"What do you do?"

"For a living?"

"Just talk to me. Keep talking."

"I'm a journalist," I said.

"Like Peter?"

"I don't know what kind of journalist he is."

"He's tough. The danger school. Are you tough?"

"Some things scare me, some don't."

"Mice?"

"Mice scare me stiff."

"Are you good?"

"As good as the news, I suppose. I don't write much any more. I'm editorial these days."

"Married?"

"Are you?"

"Yes."

"To Peter?"

"No, not Peter."

"How long have you known him?"

"My husband?"

"No. Peter," I said. I did not ask myself why I was more interested in her adultery than her marriage.

"You don't time things like that out here," she said. "A year, a couple of years—you don't talk that way. Not in Beirut. You're married too, aren't you? You didn't want to tell me till I told you first."

"Yes, I am."

"So tell me about her."

"My wife?"

"Sure. Do you love her? Is she tall? Great skin? Very British, stiff upper lip?"

I told her some harmless things about Mabel and invented some others, hating myself.

"I mean, who on earth can believe in sex after fifteen years of the same person?" she said.

I laughed but didn't answer.

"Are you faithful to her, Peter?"

"Infallibly," I said, after a delay.

"Okay, let's do work. Go back to work. What are you doing out here? Something special? Tell me what you're doing."

The spy in me dodged the question: "I think it's time you told me what *you* do," I said. "Are you a journalist too?"

A stream of tracer tore into the sky. The firing followed.

Her voice turned weary, as if the fear had worn her out. "I file copy, sure."

"Who for?"

"A lousy wire service, what else? Fifty cents a line, till some big prick steals it and makes two grand in an afternoon. What's new?"

"What's your name?" I asked.

"I don't know. Maybe Annie. Call me Annie. Listen, you're real nice, know that? What do you do if a Doberman humps your leg?"

"Bark?"

"Fake an orgasm. I'm scared, Peter. Maybe I didn't make that clear. I need a drink."

"Where are you?"

"Right here."

"Where's here?"

"In the hotel, for Christ's sake. The Commodore. Standing in the lobby, smelling Ahmed's garlic and getting eyeballed by the Greek."

"Who's the Greek?"

"Stavros. He pushes hard drugs and swears up and down they're soft. He's serious sleaze."

I listened, and for the first time made out the babble of voices in the background. The shooting was over.

"Peter?"

"Yes."

"Peter, put that light out."

She must have known there was only one light working in the room, a rickety bedside light with a tilted parchment shade. It lay on a locker between the two divans. I turned it off. There were stars again.

"Unlock your door and leave it ajar. One inch. Got booze?"

"A bottle of Scotch," I said.

"Vodka?"

"No."

"Ice?"

"No."

"I'll bring some. Peter?"

"Yes."

"You're a good man. Anybody ever told you that?"

"Not for a long time."

"Watch this space," she said, and rang off.

She never came to me.

You may imagine it any way you like, as I did, all ways, while I sat on the divan, watching the door in the darkness and watching my life go by while I waited to hear her tread in the corridor.

After an hour I went downstairs. I sat in the bar and listened to every female American voice I could find. None fitted. I looked for someone who might call herself Annie and proposition a man she had only talked to on the telephone. I bribed Ahmed to tell me who had used the house phone from the lobby at nine o'clock that night, but his memory, for whatever reason, did not stretch to an emotional American woman.

I went so far as to try to establish the identity of the previous occupant of my room, and whether his first name was Peter, but Ahmed became mysteriously vague and said he had been in Tripoli visiting his old mother, and the hotel kept no lists.

Did the real Peter return in the nick of time and sweep her off? Did Stavros the Greek? Was she a whore? Was I? Was Ahmed pimping her? Was the phone call some kind of elaborate trick she played on newcomers to the hotel, to hook them on their first nervous night alone?

Or was she, as I prefer to think, simply a frightened woman missing her boyfriend and craving a body to hold on to when the nightly thunder of the city started driving her mad?

Whatever mystery she presented, I had learned something about myself even if it disconcerted me. I had learned how perilous was my solitude, how available I was, how much I needed to give love and receive it; and how fickle in me was that virtue which the Service called "personal security," compared with my growing hunger for connection. I thought of Monica and my hollow protestations of love which so failed to move the gods they were addressed to. I thought of Giles Latimer and his hopeless passion. And somehow the woman who called herself Annie seemed to belong to the same line of anguished messengers, all speaking from inside myself.

After the faceless girl came the faceless boy. That happened the next evening.

* * *

Exhausted, I had settled myself in the hotel lobby and I was drinking my Scotch alone. I had been visiting the camps round Sidon and my hand was still shaking from just another day in southern Lebanon. Now it was the magic hour of dusk when Beirut's human animal kingdom agreed to put aside its feuds and assemble at the common watering hole. I have seen the same thing happen in the jungle. Perhaps you have too. At a single command, elephants, wart-hogs, gazelles, lions and giraffes tiptoe from the protective darkness of the trees and, mostly in silence, arrange themselves on the muddy flats. You could observe the Commodore lobby at the same hour, when the journalists came back from their day's excursions. As the electric glass doors, always a little too slow on their feet, sighed and grunted from their exertions, so the dark of the early Beirut night disgorged its motley: a Swedish television unit, fronted by a grey-faced blonde in designer denims; a photographer and correspondent from an American weekly; the wire men always in pairs; an elderly and utterly mysterious East German with his Japanese mistress. All had the same self-consciously undramatic way of entering, and pausing, and setting down the day's burden.

Not that their day was over. For the real journalists, there were films to be despatched, stories to be written and telexed and telephoned. Someone was missing and must be accounted for. So-and-so had taken a bad bullet, did his wife know? Nevertheless, with the closing of the glass doors behind them, their day was won back from the enemy. The hackpack was battening down the hatches for the night.

And as I watched, I waited—to meet a man who knew a man who knew another man who just might know the woman I had been sent to find. My day till then had yielded nothing, except another tour of the wretched of the earth.

Elsewhere in the lobby, other species were gathering, less glamorous but frequently more interesting to the observer: carpetbaggers and arms dealers and drug dealers and dark-suited minor diplomats, the pedlars in influence and information, switching at their worry-beads as their restless eyes darted from face to face about the room. And the spies—everyone's spies—trading openly, because in Beirut their trade was everyone's. There was not a man or woman in the place who had not got his source of inside information, if it was only Ahmed behind the counter, who for a few dollars and a smile would tell you the secrets of the universe.

But the figure who had caught my eye was exotic even by the standards of the Commodore's menagerie. I did not see him enter. He must have come in behind a group. I saw him inside the lobby, framed against the darkness of the glass doors, dressed in a striped football shirt and a clean white nurse's scarf tied lightly round his head. If he had not been slender and flat-chested, I would not have been certain, at first sight, whether he was a woman pretending to be a man, or a man pretending to be a woman.

The security man had noticed him too. So had Ahmed the concierge behind his formidable counter. His two Kalashnikovs were propped against the wall behind him, just below the pigeonholes where the room keys hung, and I saw Ahmed ease a half-step backward so that he had one within reach. A small hand-grenade in that lobby at that hour could have wiped out half the better rackets in the city.

But the apparition kept moving forward, either unaware or unheeding of the curiosity he was arousing. He was tall and young and agile, but rigid. He was like a person without will, summoned forward by his controller's voice. I saw him better now. He had dark glasses, black stubble and moustache. That was why his face had seemed so black. And the white nurse's scarf over his head. But it was the automaton's stiffness of his walk that set my skin tingling and made me wonder what kind of believer we might have on our hands.

He had reached the centre of the lobby. A few people made way for him. Some looked at him and looked away, others turned their backs in abstention, as if they knew and did not like him. Suddenly, under the brightness of the centre light, he seemed to be ascending. With his shrouded head forward and his arms barely moving, he was mounting his own scaffold on orders from above. I saw now that he was American. I saw it in the dipping knees and hanging wrists and slightly girlish hips. An all-American boy. His dark glasses were not dark enough, apparently, for a cloth eyeshade dangled from one long hand. It was of the kind that gamblers are supposed to wear, and night editors in forties films. He was six feet tall, at least. He wore sneakers, vestal white like his headscarf, and soundless.

An Arab freak? I wondered.

A crazed Zionist! There had been a few of those.

Stoned?

A high-school war tourist on the hippy trail, searching for kicks in the city of the damned?

Changing direction, he had begun talking to the receptionist, but at an angle facing into the lobby, already searching for the person he was enquiring for. Which was when I saw the red spots spattered over his cheeks and forehead, like hives or chicken pox, but more vivid. The bedbugs had eaten him in some stinking hostel, I decided. He had stuck his head through the windscreen of a clapped-out car. He started walking towards me. Stiffly again, without expression. Purposefully, a man used to being looked at. Angrily, the eyeshade dangling from his hand. Glowering at me blindly through his black glasses as I sat drinking. A woman had taken his arm. She wore a skirt and could have been the nurse who had given him his headscarf. They stood before me. Me and no one else.

"Sir? This is Sol, sir," she said—or Mort, or Syd, or whatever. "He's asking whether you're the journalist, sir."

I said I was a journalist.

"From London, sir, visiting? Are you the editor, sir? Are you influential, sir?"

Influential, I doubted, I said with a deprecating smile. I was on the managerial side, here on a brief swing. "And going back to London, sir? Soon?"

In Beirut you learn not to talk in advance about your movements. "Pretty soon," I conceded, though the truth was I was planning to return south again next day.

"Can Sol speak with you a moment, sir, just speak? Sol needs very much to speak with a person who has influence with the major Western newspapers. The journalists here, he feels they've seen it all, they're jaded. Sol needs a voice from outside."

I made space and she sat beside me while Sol very slowly lowered himself into a chair—this covered, silent, very clean man in his long football sleeves and headscarf. Seated finally, he laid his wrists over his knees, holding the eyeshade in both hands. Then he gave a long sigh and began to murmur to me.

"There's this thing I've written, sir. I'd like, please, to have it printed in your newspaper."

His voice, though soft, was educated and polite. But it was lifeless and, like his movements, economical, as if each word hurt him to produce. Inside the lenses of his very dark glasses I saw that his left eye was smaller than his right. Narrower. Not swollen, not closed by a punch, just altogether smaller than its partner, taken from a different face. And the spots were not bites, not hives, not cuts. They were craters, like pockmarks of small-arms fire on a Beirut wall, stamped with heat and speed. Like craters also, the skin around them had risen but not closed.

His story followed without my asking for it. He was a relief volunteer, sir, a third-year medical student from Omaha. He believed in peace, sir. And he had been in this bombing, down by the Corniche, in this restaurant that had been one of the worst-hit places, just wiped out, you should go down there and take a look, a place called Akhbar's, sir, where a lot of Americans went, there was this car bomb and car bombs are the worst. You can't get worse than car bombs for surprise.

I said I knew that.

Almost everyone in the restaurant had died except himself, sir, the people nearest the wall just blew apart, he continued, unaware that he had painted my own worst nightmare for me. And now he had this thing he had written, he felt he had to say it, sir, a sort of mild statement about peace; which he needed to print in my newspaper, maybe it would do some good, he was thinking of like this weekend or maybe Monday. He'd like to donate the fee to charity. He guessed it could be like a couple of hundred dollars, maybe more. In the Beirut hospitals, that still bought people a piece of hope.

"We need a pause, sir," he explained, in his dead voice as the woman fished a wad of typescript from his pocket for him. "A pause for moderation. Just a break between wars to find the middle way."

Only in the Commodore in Beirut could it have seemed natural that a bomb-shocked peace-seeker should be pleading a hopeless cause to a journalist who wasn't one. Nevertheless I promised to do what I could. When I had done my business with the man I was waiting for—who knew nothing, of course, had heard nothing, but perhaps, sir, if I spoke to Colonel Asme in Tyre?—I settled in my room and with a glass at my elbow began to read his offering, determined that if it had any reasonable chance of publication, I would twist the arm of one of our numberless Fleet Street friendlies when I returned to London, and see it done.

It was a tragic piece, and quickly it became unreadable: a rambling, emotional appeal to Jews, Christians and Muslims alike to remember their own mothers and children, and live together in love. It urged the middle ground of compromise and gave inaccurate examples from history. It proposed a new religion "like Joan of Arc would have given us only the English wouldn't let her, so they burned her alive, disregarding her screams and the will of the ordinary people." This great new movement, he said, would "bind the Semitic races in a spiritual brotherhood of love and tolerance." Then it lost its way completely, and resorted to capital letters, underlining, and rows of exclamation marks. So that by the time I reached the end, it had ceased to be what it set out to be at all, and was talking about "this whole family, kids, and grandparents, that was sitting up beside the wall nearest to the epicentre." And how they had all been blown to pieces, not once, but over and over again, each time Sol allowed himself to look into his anguished memory.

Suddenly I was writing the piece for him. To her. To Annie. First in my mind, then in the margin of his pages, then on a fresh sheet of A4 paper from my briefcase, which was quickly covered so I took another. I was sweating, the sweat was pouring off me like rain; it was that kind of Beirut night, quiet till now but with a damp, itchy heat rolling off the mountains and an evil grey smog like gunsmoke draping itself across the sea. I was writing, and wondering if she would ring again. I was writing as the bombed boy, to a girl I didn't know. I was writing—as I saw to my dismay when I awoke next morning—pretentious junk. I was proclaiming maverick affections, mouthing great sentiments, pontificating about the unbreakable cycle of human evil, about man's endless search for reasons to do the wrong thing.

A pause, the boy had said. A pause for moderation, a break between wars. I put him right on that. I put Annie right on it too. I told them that the only pauses in the history of human conflict had been pauses not for moderation but excess, pauses for the world to redivide itself, for the thugs and the victims to find each other, for greed and deprival to regroup. I wrote like an adolescent bleeding heart, and when the morning came and I saw the pages of my handwriting strewn over the floor around the empty whisky bottle, I could not believe this was the work of anyone I knew.

So I did the only thing I could think of. I put them in the hand-basin and cremated them, then broke up the ash and scattered it in the lavatory and flushed it into the body-blocked sewers of Beirut. And when I had done that, I took myself for a punishing pelt along the waterfront, running as hard as I could go from whatever was coming after me.

I was running towards Hansen, away from myself, but I had one more stop to make along the way.

My German girl, Britta, turned out to be in Israel, in the middle of the Negev Desert, in a compound of stark grey huts near a village called Revivim. The huts had a ploughed strip round them, and a double perimeter of barbed-wire fencing with a manned watchtower at each corner. If there were other European prisoners in the compound apart from her, I was not introduced to them. Her only companions that I saw were young Arab girls, mainly from poor villages in the West Bank or the Gaza, who had been talked or bullied by their Palestinian comrades into committing acts of savagery against the hated Zionist occupiers, most often planting bombs in marketplaces or tossing them into civilian buses.

I arrived there by jeep from Beersheeba, driven by a hardy young Colonel of Intelligence whose father, while still a boy, had been trained as a Night Raider by the eccentric General Wingate during the British Mandate. The Colonel's father remembered Wingate squatting naked in his tent by candlelight, drawing out the battle plan in the sand. Every Israeli soldier seems to talk about his father and a good few talk about the British. After the Mandate, they think they know us for what we probably still are:

anti-Semitic, ignorant and imperialist, with just enough exceptions to redeem us. Dimona, where the Israelis store their nuclear arsenal, was up the road.

My sense of unreality had not left me. To the contrary, it had intensified. It was as if I had lost the distance from the human condition that is essential to our trade. My feelings and the feelings of others seemed to count more with me than my observations. It is quite easy in the Lebanon, if you drop your guard, to develop an unreasoning hatred of Israel. But I had succumbed to a serious dose of the disease. Trudging through the mud and stench of the shattered camps, crouching in the sandbagged hovels, I convinced myself that the Israeli thirst for vengeance would not be stilled until the accusing eyes of the last Palestinian child had been closed for good.

Perhaps my young Colonel got a hint of this, for though I had flown in from Cyprus it was still only a few hours since I had left Beirut, and something of what I felt may still have been legible in my face.

"You get to see Arafat?" he asked, with a moody smile as we drove along the straight road.

"No, I didn't."

"Why not? He's a nice guy."

I let that go.

"Why do you want to see Britta?"

I told him. There was no point in not doing so. It had taken all London's powers of persuasion to get me the interview with her at all, and my hosts were certainly not going to let me speak to her alone.

"We think she may be willing to talk to us about an old boyfriend," I said.

"Why would she do that?"

"He jilted her. She was angry with him."

"Who's the 'boyfriend'?"—as if he didn't know.

"He's Irish. He has the rank of adjutant in the IRA. He briefs bombers, reconnoitres targets, supplies the equipment. She lived underground with him in Amsterdam and Paris."

"Like George Orwell, huh? *Down and Out?*"

"Like George Orwell."

"How long ago he jilted her?"

"Six months."

"Maybe she's not angry any more. Maybe she'll tell you go suck. For a girl like Britta, six months is a hell of a long time."

I asked whether she had talked much in her captivity. It was a delicate question, since the Israelis were still not saying how long they had been holding her, or how they had obtained her in the first place. The Colonel was broad-faced and brown-skinned. His family came originally from Russia. He wore parachute wings on his short-sleeved khaki shirt. He was twenty-eight, a Sabra, born in Tel Aviv, engaged to a Sephardi from Morocco. His father, the Night Raider, was now a dentist. All this he had told me in the first few minutes of our acquaintance, in a guttural English he had captured single-handed.

"Talked?" he repeated with a grim smile, in answer to my question. "Britta? That lady didn't stop talking since she became a resident."

Knowing a little of Israeli methods, I was not surprised, and I shuddered inwardly at the prospect of questioning a woman who had been subjected to them. It had happened to me in Ireland: a man buttoned to the neck who had stared at me like a dead man and confessed to everything.

"Do you interrogate her yourself?" I asked, noticing afresh his thick brown forearms and the uncompromising set of his jaw. And thinking, perhaps, of Colonel Jerzy.

He shook his head. "Impossible."

"Why?"

He seemed about to tell me something, then changed his mind.

"We got experts," he said. "Shin Bet guys, smart like Britta. Take their time with her. Family."

I had heard about this loving family too, though I didn't say so. The Zionists had lured her into a trap, a bloodshot-eyed informant had whispered to me in Tyre. She had left the camps and gone to Athens with her new boyfriend, Said, and three of Said's friends, he said. Good boys. All able. The plan had been to shoot down an El Al plane as it made its approach to Athens airport. The boys had got themselves a hand-held rocket launcher and a rented house on the flightpath. Britta's job, as an unsuspicious-looking European, was to stand in a phone box at the airport with a thirty-dollar shortwave receiver and relay the control tower's instructions to the boys on the roof as the plane came in. Everything had been set fair, said my bone-weary informant. The rehearsals had gone like a dream. But on the day, the operation had fouled up.

Listening to him, I had filled in the rest of the story for myself, imagining how the Service would have done the job if we'd had the foreknowledge: two teams to assault the roof and the phone box simultaneously; the target plane, forewarned and empty, landing safely at Athens airport; the plane's homeward journey to Tel Aviv with the terrorists chained in their seats. I wondered what they would do with her. Whether they would put her on trial or trade her for favours in return.

"What happened to the boys she was with in Athens?" I asked the Colonel, ignoring London's injunction to show no curiosity in such matters.

"Boys? She knows nothing from boys. Athens? Where's Athens already? She's an innocent German tourist on vacation in Eilat. We kidnapped her, we drugged her, we imprisoned her, now we're framing her for propaganda. She invites us to prove the contrary because she knows we can't. You want any more information? Ask Britta, be our guest."

His mood mystified me, the more so when, as we got out of the jeep, he laid a hand on my shoulder and wished me a sort of luck. "She's all yours," he said. *"Mazel tov."*

I was beginning to dread what I might find.

A dumpy little woman in army uniform received us in her clean office. Prison staff never go short of cleaners, I thought. She was Captain Levi and she was Britta's unlikely gaoler. She spoke English the way a small-town American schoolmistress might speak it, but more slowly, with greater care. She had twinkly eyes and short grey hair and a look of kindly resignation. She had the dusty complexion of prison life, but when she put her hands together you felt she ought to be knitting for her grandchildren.

"Britta is very intelligent," she said apologetically. "For an intelligent man to question an intelligent woman, that's sometimes difficult. Do you have a daughter, sir?"

I was not about to fill in my character profile for her so I said no, which happened also to be the truth.

"A pity. Never mind. Maybe you still get one. A man like you, you have time. You speak German?"

"Yes."

"Then you are lucky. You can communicate with her in her language. That way you get to know her better. Britta and I, we can speak only English together. I speak it like my late husband, who was American. Britta speaks it like her late lover, who was Irish. Tel Aviv says we are to allow you two hours. Will you be happy with two hours? If you need more, we shall ask them— maybe they say yes. Maybe two hours will be too much. We shall see."

"You are very kind," I said.

"Kind, I don't know. Maybe we should be less kind. Maybe we are making kind too much. You will see."

And with this she sent for coffee and for Britta, while the Colonel and myself took up our places along one side of the plain wood table.

But Captain Levi did not sit at the table, I supposed because she was not part of the interview. She sat beside the door on a straight kitchen chair, her eyes lowered as if in preparation for a concert. Even when Britta walked in between two young wardresses, she only lifted her eyes as far as was necessary to watch the three women's feet pass her to the centre of the room and halt. One wardress pulled back a chair for Britta, the second unlocked her handcuffs. The wardresses left, and we settled to the table.

And I would like to paint for you the scene exactly as I saw it from where I sat: with the Colonel to the right, and Britta opposite us across the table, and the bowed grey head of Captain Levi almost directly behind her, but slightly to the left, wearing a reminiscent expression that was half a smile. Throughout our discussion she stayed like that, still as a waxwork. Her part-smile of familiarity never altered and never went away. There was concentration in her pose, and something of effort, so that I wondered whether she was straining to pick out phrases and words she could identify, perhaps from a combined knowledge of Yiddish and English, for Britta, being a Bremen girl, spoke a clear and authoritarian German, which makes comprehension easier.

And Britta, without a doubt, was a fine sample of her breed. She was "blond as a bread roll," as they say up there, tall and deep-shouldered and well-grown, with wide rather insolent blue eyes and a strong, attractive jaw. She had Monica's youth and Monica's height as well, and, as I could not avoid speculating, Monica's sensuality. My suspicion that they had been maltreating her vanished as soon as she walked in. She held herself like a ballerina, but with more intelligence and more of life's reality than is to be found in most dancers. She would have looked well in tennis gear or in a *dirndl* dress, and I suspected that in her time she had worn both. Even her prison tunic did not diminish her, for she had made herself a cloth belt out of something, and tied it at the waist, and she had brushed her fair hair over her shoulders in a cape. Her first gesture when her hands were freed was to offer me one, at the same time dropping a schoolgirl bob, whether out of irony or respect it was too soon to tell. She wore no makeup but needed none.

"*Und mit wem hab' ich die Ehre?*" she enquired, either courteously or impishly. And whom do I have the honour to address?

"I'm a British official," I said.

"Your name, please?"

"It's unimportant."

"But you are very important!"

Prisoners when they are brought up from their cells often say silly things in their first flush, so I answered her with consideration.

"I'm working with the Israelis on aspects of your case. That's all you need to know."

"Case? I am a case? How amusing. I thought I was a human being. Please sit down, Mr. Nobody," she said, doing so herself.

So we sit as I have described, with Captain Levi's face behind her, a little out of focus like its expression. The Colonel had not stood up to greet Britta, and he barely bothered to look at her now she was sitting before him. He seemed suddenly to be without expectation. He glanced at his watch. It was of dull steel and like a weapon on his brown wrist. Britta's wrists were white and smooth like Monica's, but chafed with red rings from the handcuffs.

Suddenly she was lecturing me.

She began at once, as if she were resuming a tutorial, and in a sense she was, for I soon realised she lectured everyone this way, or everyone whom she had dismissed as bourgeois. She said she had a statement to make which she would like me to relay to my "colleagues," as she called them, since she felt that her position was not being sufficiently appreciated by the authorities. She was a prisoner of war, just as any Israeli soldier in Palestinian hands was a prisoner of war, and entitled to the treatment and privileges set out in the Geneva Convention. She was a tourist here, she had committed no crime against Israel; she had been arrested solely on the strength of her trumped-up record in other countries, as a deliberate act of provocation against the world proletariat.

I gave a quick laugh, and she faltered. She was not expecting laughter.

"But look here," I objected. "Either you're a prisoner of war or you're an innocent tourist. You can't be both."

"The struggle is between the innocent and the guilty," she retorted, without hesitation, and resumed her lecture. Her enemies were not limited to Zionism, she said, but what she called the dynamic of bourgeois domination, the repression of natural instincts, and the maintenance of despotic authority disguised as "democracy."

Again I tried to interrupt her, but this time she talked straight through me. She quoted Marcuse at me and Freud. She referred to the rebellion of sons in puberty against their fathers, and the disavowal of this rebellion in later years as the sons themselves became the fathers.

I glanced at the Colonel, but he seemed to be dozing.

The purpose of her "actions," she said, and those of her comrades, was to arrest this instinctual cycle of repression in all its forms—in the enslavement of labour to materialism, in the repressive principle of "progress" itself—and to allow the real forces of society to surge, like erotic energy, into new, unfettered forms of cultural creation.

"None of this is faintly interesting to me," I protested. "Just stop, please, and listen to my questions."

Acts of so-called "terrorism" had therefore two clear purposes, she continued, as if I had never spoken, of which the first was to disconcert the armies of the bourgeois-materialist conspiracy, and the second to instruct, by example, the pit-ponies of the earth, who had lost all knowledge of the light. In other words, to introduce ferment and awaken consciousness at the most repressed human levels.

She wished to add that though she was not an adherent of Communism, she preferred its teachings to those of Capitalism, since Communism provided a powerful negation of the ego-ideal which used property to construct the human prison.

She favoured free sexual expression and—for those who needed them—the use of drugs as a means of discovering the free self as contrasted with the unfree self that is castrated by aggressive tolerance.

I turned to the Colonel. There is an etiquette of interrogation as there is about everything else. "Do we have to go on listening to this nonsense? The lady is your prisoner, not mine," I said. For I could hardly lay the law down to her across his table.

The Colonel lifted his head high enough to glance at her with indifference. "You want to go back down, Britta?" he asked her. "You want bread and water for a couple of weeks?" His German was as bizarre as his English. He seemed suddenly a lot older than his age, and wiser.

"I have more to say, thank you."

"If you're going to stay up here, you answer his questions and you shut up," said the Colonel. "It's your choice. You want to leave now, it's fine by us." He added something in Hebrew to Captain Levi, who nodded distantly. An Arab prisoner entered with a tray of coffee—four cups and a plate of sugar biscuits— and handed them round meekly, a coffee cup for each of us and one for Captain Levi, the biscuits at the centre of the table. An air of lassitude had settled over us. Britta stretched out her long arm for a biscuit, lazily, as if she were in her own home. The Colonel's hand crashed on the table just ahead of her as he removed the plate from her reach.

"So what do you wish to ask me, please?" Britta enquired of me, as if nothing at all had happened. "Do you wish me to deliver the Irish to you? What other aspects of my case could interest the English, Mr. Nobody?"

"If you deliver us one particular Irishman, that will be fine," I said. "You lived with a man named Seamus for a year."

She was amused. I had provided her with an opening. She studied me, and seemed to see something in my face she recognised. "*Lived* with him? That is an exaggeration. I slept with him. Seamus was only for sex," she explained, with a mischievous smile. "He was a convenience, an instrument. A *good* instrument, I would say. I was the same for him. You like sex? Sometimes another boy would join us, maybe sometimes a girl. We make combinations. It was irrelevant but we had fun."

"Irrelevant to what?" I asked.

"To our work."

"What work?"

"I have already described our work to you, Mr. Nobody. I have told you of its aims, and of our motivations. Humanitarianism is not to be equated with non-violence. We must fight to be free. Sometimes even the highest causes can only be served by violent methods. Do you know that? Sex also can be violent."

"What kind of violent methods was Seamus involved in?" I asked.

"We are speaking not of wanton acts but of the people's right of resistance against acts committed by the forces of repression. Are you a member of those forces or are you in favour of spontaneity, Mr. Nobody? Perhaps you should free yourself and join us."

"He's a bomber," I said. "He blows up innocent people. His most recent target was a public house in southern England. He killed one elderly couple, the barman and the pianist, and I give you my word he didn't liberate a single deluded worker."

"Is that a question or a statement, Mr. Nobody?"

"It's an invitation to you to tell me about his activities."

"The public house was close to a British military camp," she replied. "It was providing infrastructure and comfort to Fascistic forces of oppression."

Again her cool eyes held me in their playful gaze. Did I say she was attractive? What is attraction in such circumstances? She was wearing a calico tunic. She was an enforced penitent of crimes that she did not repent. She was alert in every part of herself, I could feel it, and she knew I felt it, and the divide between us enticed her.

"My department is considering offering you a sum of money on your lease, payable, if you prefer, to somebody you nominate in the meantime," I said. "They want information that would lead to the arrest and conviction of your friend Seamus. They are interested in his past crimes, others he has yet to commit, safe addresses, contacts, habits and weaknesses." She waited for me to go on, so, perhaps unwisely, I did. "Seamus is not a hero. He's a pig. Not what you call a pig. A real pig. Nobody did bad things to him when he was young; his parents are decent people who run a tobacco shop in County Down. His grandfather was a policeman, a good one. Seamus is blowing people up for kicks because he's inadequate. That's why he treated you badly. He only exists when he's inflicting pain. The rest of the time he's a spoilt little boy."

I had not scratched the surface of her steady stare.

"Are you inadequate, Mr. Nobody? I think perhaps you are. In your occupation, that is normal. You should join us, Mr. Nobody. You should take lessons with us, and we shall convert you to our cause. Then you will be adequate."

You must understand that she did not raise her voice while she said this, or indulge in dramatics of any kind. She remained condescending and composed, even hospitable. The mischief in her lay deep and well-disguised. She had a healthy natural smile and it stayed with her all the time she spoke, while Captain Levi behind her continued to gaze into her own memories, perhaps because she did not understand what was being said.

The Colonel glanced at me in question. Not trusting myself to speak, I lifted my hands from the table, asking what's the point? The Colonel said something to Captain Levi, who in the disappointed manner of someone who has prepared a meal only to see it taken away uneaten, pressed a bell for the escort, Britta rose to her feet, smoothed her prison tunic over her breasts and hips and held out her hands for the handcuffs.

"How much money were they thinking of offering me, Mr. Nobody?" she enquired.

"None," I said.

She dropped me another bob and walked between her guards towards the door, her hips flowing inside her calico tunic, reminding me of Monica's inside her dressing-gown. I was afraid she would speak again but she didn't. Perhaps she knew she had won the day, and anything more would spoil the effect. The Colonel followed her out and I was alone with Captain Levi. The half smile had not left her face.

"There," she said. "Now you know a little of what it feels like to hear Britta's music."

"I suppose I do."

"Sometimes we communicate too much. Perhaps you should have spoken English to her. So long as she speaks English, I can care for her. She is a human being, she is a woman, she is in prison. And you may be sure she is in agony. She is courageous, and so long as she speaks English to me I can do my duty for her."

"And when she speaks German to you?"

"What would be the point, since she knows I cannot understand her?"

"But if she did—and if you could understand her? What then?"

Her smile twisted and became slightly shameful. "Then I think I would be frightened," she replied in her slow American. "I think if she ordered something of me, I would be tempted to obey her. But I do not let her order me. Why should I? I do not give her the power over me. I speak English and I stay the boss. I was for two years in concentration camp in Buchenwald, you see." Still smiling at me, she delivered the rest in German, in the clenched, hushed whisper of the campnik: *"Man hört so scheussliche Echos in ihrer Stimme, wissen Sie."* One hears such dreadful echoes in her voice, you see.

The Colonel was standing in the doorway waiting for me. As we walked downstairs, he put his hand once more on my shoulder. This time I knew why.

"Is she like that with all the boys?" I asked him.

"Captain Levi?"

"Britta."

"Sure. With you a bit more, that's all. Maybe that's because you're English."

Maybe it is, I thought, and maybe it's because she saw more in me than just my Englishness. Maybe she read my unconscious signals of availability. But whatever she saw in me, or didn't, Britta had provided the summation of my confusion until now. She had articulated my sense of trying to hold on to a world that was slipping away from me, my susceptibility to every stray argument and desire.

The summons to find Hansen arrived the same night, in the middle of a jolly diplomatic party given by my British Embassy host in Herzliyya.

9

Earnest Perigrew was quizzing Smiley about colonialism. Sooner or later, Perigrew quizzed everyone who came to Sarratt about colonialism, and his questions always hovered at the edge of outrage. He was a troubled boy, the son of British missionaries to West Africa, and one of those people the Service is almost bound to employ, on account of their rare knowledge and linguistic qualifications. He was sitting as usual alone, amid the shadows at the back of the library, his gaunt face thrust forward and one long hand held up as if to fend off ridicule. The question had started reasonably, then degenerated into a tirade against Britain's indifference towards her former enslaved subjects.

"Yes, well I think I rather agree with you," said Smiley courteously, to the general surprise, when he had heard Perigrew to the end. "The sad answer is, I'm afraid, that the Cold War produced in us a kind of *vicarious* colonialism. On the one hand we abandoned practically every article of our national identity to American foreign policy. On the other we bought ourselves a stay of execution for our vision of our colonial selves. Worse still, we encouraged the Americans to behave in the same way. Not that they needed our encouragement, but they were pleased to have it, naturally."

Hansen had said much the same. And in much the same language. But where Smiley had lost little of his urbanity, Hansen had glared into my face with eyes lit by the red hells from which he had returned.

I flew from Israel to Bangkok because Smiley said Hansen had gone mad and knew too many secrets; a decypher yourself signal, care of the Head of Station, Tel Aviv. Smiley had charge of Service security at the time, with the courtesy rank of deputy chief. Whenever I heard of him, he seemed to be scuttling round plugging another leak or another scandal. I spent the weekend in a heatwave sweating my way through the stack of hand-delivered files and an hour on the telephone placating Mabel, who had fallen at the last fence of her annual race to become ladies' captain of our local golf club and was scenting intrigue.

I don't know why they're so hard on Mabel. Perhaps it's her way of plain talking that puts them off. I did what I could. I told her that nothing I had come upon in the Service could compare with the skulduggery of those Kent wives. I promise her a splendid holiday when I returned. I forget where the holiday was going to be because we never took it.

Hansen's file gave me a portrait of a type I had grown familiar with because we used a good few of them. I was one myself and Ben was another: the crossbred Englishman who adopts the Service as his country and endows it with a bunch of qualities it hasn't really got.

Like myself, Hansen was half a Dutchman. Perhaps that was why Smiley had chosen me. He was born in the long night of the German Occupation of Holland and raised in the shadow of Delft Cathedral. His mother, a counter clerk at Thomas Cook's, was of English parents who urged her to go back to London with them when the war broke out. She refused, choosing instead to marry a Delft curate, who a year afterwards got himself shot by a

German firing squad, leaving his pregnant wife to fend for herself. Undaunted, she joined a British escape line and, by the time the war ended, had charge of a fully fledged network, with its own communications, informants, safe houses and the usual appointments. My mother's work with the Service had not been so different.

By what route the infant Hansen found his way to the Jesuits, the file did not relate. Perhaps the mother converted. Those were dark years still, and if expediency required it, she may have swallowed her Protestant convictions to buy the boy a decent education. Give the Jesuits his soul, she may have reasoned, and they will give him a brain. Or perhaps she sensed in her son from early on the mercurial nature that later ruled his life, and she determined to subordinate him to a stronger religious discipline than was offered by the easy-going Protestants. If so, she was wise. Hansen embraced the faith as he embraced everything else, with passion. The nuns had him, the brothers had him, the priests had him, the scholars had him. Till at twenty-one, schooled and devout but still a novice, he was packed off to a seminary in Indonesia to learn the ways of the heathen: Sumatra, Molucca, Java.

The Orient seems to have been an instinctive love of Hansen's as it is for many Dutchmen. The good Dutch, like Heine's proverbial pine tree, can stand on the shores of their flat little country and sniff the Asian scents of lemon grass and cooking pots on the chill sea air. Hansen arrived, he saw, he was conquered. Buddhism, Islam, the rites and superstitions of the remotest savages—he flung himself on all of them with a fervour that only intensified the deeper he penetrated into the jungle.

Languages also came naturally to him. To his native Dutch and English, he had effortlessly added French and German. Now he acquired Tamil, Khmer, Thai, Sanskrit and more than a smattering of Cantonese, often hiking hundreds of miles of hill country in his quest for a missing dialect or ritualistic link. He wrote papers on philology, marriage rites, illumination and monkeys. He discovered lost temples in the depths of the jungle, and won prizes the Society forbade him to accept. After six years of fearless exploring and enquiring, he was not only the kind of academic showpiece Jesuits are famous for; he was also a full priest.

But few secrets can survive six years. Gradually the stories about him began to acquire a seamy edge. Hansen the skin artist. Hansen's appetites. Don't look now but here comes one of Hansen's girls.

It was the scale as well as the duration that did for him: the fact that once they started probing, they found no corner to his life that was immune, no journey that did not have its detour. A woman here or there—a boy or two—well, from what I have seen of priesthood round the globe, such peccadilloes are to be found more in the observance than the breach.

But this wholesale indulgence, in every kampong, in every tawdry sidestreet, this indefatigable debauchery, flaunted, as they now discovered, beneath their noses for more than a decade, with girls who by Western standards were barely eligible for their First Communion, let alone the marriage bed—and many of them under the Church's own protection—made Hansen suddenly and dramatically untenable. Faced with the evidence of such prolonged and dedicated sinning, his Superior responded, more in grief than indignation. He ordered Hansen to return to Rome, and sent a letter ahead of him to the General of the Society. From Rome, he told Hansen sadly, he would most likely go to Loyola in Spain, where qualified Jesuit psychotherapists would help him come to terms with his regrettable weakness. After Loyola—well, a new beginning, perhaps a different hemisphere, a different decade.

But Hansen, like his mother before him, stubbornly declined to leave the place of his adoption.

At a loss, the Father Guardian packed him off to a distant mission in the hills run by a traditionalist of the sterner school. There Hansen suffered the barbarities of house arrest. He was watched over like a madman. He was forbidden to pass beyond the precincts of the house, denied books, paper, company, laughter. Men take to confinement in different ways, as they take differently to heights or cold or dying. Hansen took to it terribly, and after three months could bear no more. As his brother guardians escorted him to Mass, he hurled one of them down a staircase while the other fled. Then he headed back to Djakarta and, with neither money nor passport, went to ground in the brothels he knew well. The girls took him into their care, and in return he worked as pimp and bouncer. He gave out beer, washed glasses, ejected the unruly, heard confessions, gave succour, played with the children in the back room. I see him, as I know him now, doing all those things without fuss or complication. He was barely thirty and his desires burned bright as ever. Until one day, yielding as so often to an impulse, Hansen shaved, put on a clean shirt, and presented himself to the British Consul to claim his British soul.

And the Consul, being neither deaf nor blind, but a long-standing member of the Service, listened to Hansen's story, asked a humdrum question or two and, from behind a mask of apathy, sprang to action. For years he had been looking for a man of Hansen's gifts. Hansen's waywardness did not deter the Consul in the least. He liked it. He signalled London for background; he lent Hansen cautious sums of cash against receipts in triplicate, for he did not wish to show undue enthusiasm. When London came back with a white trace on Hansen's mother, indicating she was a former agent of the Service, the Consul's cup brimmed over.

Another month and Hansen was semi-conscious, which means he knew, but only half knew, but then again might not know, that he just could be half in touch with what one might loosely refer to as British Intelligence. Another two months and, restless as ever, he was taking a swing through southern Java ostensibly in search of ancient scrolls, in reality to report back to the Consul the strength of Communist subversion, which was his newly adopted anti-Christ. By the end of the year he was headed for London with the brand-new British passport he had wanted in his pocket, though not in his own name.

I turned to his potted training record, all six months of it. Clive Bellamy, a gangly, mischievous Etonian, was in charge of Sarratt. "Excellent at all things practical," he wrote in Hansen's end-of-course report. "Has a first-rate memory, fast reactions, is self-sufficient. Needs to be ridden hard. If there's ever a mutiny on my ship, Hansen will be the first man I'll flog. Needs a big canvas and a first-rate controller."

I turned to the operational record. No madness there either. Since Hansen was still Dutch, Head Office decided to keep him that way and play down his Englishness. Hansen bridled but they overruled him. At a time when the British abroad were being seen by everyone except themselves as Americans without the clout, Head Office would kill for a Swede and steal for a West German. Even Canadians, though more easily manufactured, were smiled on. Back in Holland, Hansen formalised his severance from the Jesuits and set about looking for new employment back East. A score of Oriental academic bodies were spread around the capitals of Western Europe in those days. Hansen did his rounds of them, gaining a promise here and a commitment there. A French Oriental news agency took him on as a stringer. A London weekly, nudged by Head Office, made a berth for him on condition they got him free. Till bit by bit his cover was complete—wide enough for him to have a reason to go anywhere and ask what questions he wanted, varied enough to be financially inscrutable, since no one would ever be able to tell which of his several employers were paying him how much for what. He was ready to be launched. British interests in South East Asia might have dwindled with her Empire, but the Americans were in there knee-deep with an official war running in Vietnam, an unofficial one in Cambodia and a secret one in Laos. In our unlovely rôle as camp follower, we were delighted to offer them Hansen's precious talents.

Espionage technology can do a lot. It can photograph crops and trenches, tanks and rocket sites and tyre-marks and the migration of the reindeer. It can flinch at the sound of a Russian fighter pilot breaking wind at forty thousand feet or a Chinese general belching in his sleep. But it can't replace human understanding. It can't tell you what's in the heart of a Cambodian farmer whose hill crops have been blown to smithereens by Dr. Kissinger's unmarked bombers, whose daughters have been sold into prostitution in the city, and whose sons have been lured into leaving the fields and fighting for an American puppet army, or urged, by way of family insurance, into the ranks of the Khmer Rouge. It can't read the lips of jungle fighters in black pyjamas whose most powerful weapon is the perverted Marxism of a blood-hungry Sorbonne-educated Cambodian psychopath. It can't sniff the exhaust fumes of an army that is unmechanised. Or break the codes of an army without radio. Or calculate the supplies of men who can nourish themselves on ground beetles and wood bark, or the morale of those who, having lost all they possess, have only the future to win.

But Hansen could. Hansen, the adopted Asian, could trek without food for a week, squat in the kampongs and listen to the murmur of the villagers, and Hansen could read the rising wind of their resistance long before it stirred the Stars and Stripes on the Embassy roofs of Phnom Penh and Saigon. And he could tell the bombers—and, to his later remorse, he did—he could tell the American bombers which villages were playing host to the Vietcong. He was a fisher of men, too. He could recruit helpers from every walk of life and instruct them how to see and hear and remember and report. He knew how little to tell them and how much, how to reward them and when not to.

For months, then years, Hansen functioned that way in the so-called "liberated areas" of northern Cambodia where the Khmer Rouge nominally held sway, until the day he vanished from the village he had made his home. Vanished soundlessly, taking the inhabitants with him. Soon to be given up for dead, another jungle disappearance.

And remained dead until a short time ago, when he had come alive in a brothel in Bangkok.

"Take your time, Ned," Smiley had urged me on the telephone to Tel Aviv. "If you want to add a couple of days for jet-lag, it's quite all right by me."

Which was Smiley-speak for "Get to him as fast as you can and tell me I haven't got another king-sized scandal on my hands."

Our Station Head in Bangkok was a bald, rude, moustachioed little tyrant called Rumbelow, whom I had never warmed to. The Service offers precious few prospects for men of fifty. Most are blown; many are too tired and disenchanted to care whether they are or not. Others head for private banking or big business, but the marriage seldom lasts. Something has happened to their way of thinking that unsuits them to the overt life. But a very few, of whom Toby Esterhase was one and Rumbelow another, pull off the trick of holding the Service hostage to their supposed assets.

Exactly what Rumbelow's were I never knew. Seedy, I am sure, for if he specialised in anything, it was human baseness. One rumour said he owned a couple of corrupt Thai generals who would work for him and for no one else. Another that he had managed to perform a grimy favour for a member of the royal household that was not transferable. Whatever his hold on them, the barons of the Fifth Floor would hear no ill of him. "And for God's sake, don't rub up Rumbelow the wrong way, Ned," Smiley had begged me. "I'm sure he's a pain in the neck, but we do need him."

I met him in my hotel room. To the overt world I was Mark Seymour, occupation accountant, and had no wish to parade myself at the Embassy or his house. I had been flying twenty hours. It was early evening. Rumbelow spoke like an Etonian bookmaker. Come to think of it, he looked like one as well.

"It was *sheerest* bloody coincidence we bumped into this bastard at all," he told me huffily. "One puts out one's feelers, naturally. One keeps one's ear on the proverbial ground. One knows the score. One's heard of other cases. One isn't insensitive. One doesn't like to think of one's joe trussed to a stick, being carted through the jungle for weeks on end, while the Khmer Rouge torture the hell out of him, naturally. Not an ostrich. Know the score. Your brown man doesn't obey the Queensberry Rules, you know," he assured me, as if I had implied the opposite. And, plucking a handkerchief from the sleeve of his sweat-patched suit, he pummelled his stupid moustache with it. "Your *average* joe would be yelling for a quick bullet after one night of it."

"Are you sure that's what happened to him?"

"Not sure of anything, thank you, old boy. Rumour, that's all. How *can* I be sure, if the bastard won't even talk to us? Threatens violence if we try! For all *I* know, the KR never had sight nor sound of him. Never did trust a Dutchman, not out here—they think they own the bloody place. Hansen wouldn't be the first joe to lie doggo when things got too hot for him, then come bouncing back when it's all over, asking for his gong and his pension, not by any means. Still in possession of all his fingers and thumbs, by all accounts. Not missing any other part of his anatomy either, to

judge by where he's holed out. Duffy Marchbanks spotted him.
Remember Duffy? Good chap."

With a sinking heart, yes, I remembered Duffy. I had remembered him when I saw his name in the file. He was a flamboyant
crook based in Hong Kong, with a taste for fast deals in anything
from opium to shellcases. For a few misguided years we had
financed his office.

"Purest chance, it was, on Duffy's part. He'd popped up here
on a flying visit. One day, that's all. One day, one night, then back
to the missus and a book. Offshore leisure consortium wanted
him to buy a hundred acres of prime coastland for them. Did his
business, then off they go to this girlie restaurant, Duffy, and a
bunch of his traders—Duffy's not averse to a bit of the other,
never has been. Place called The Sea of Happiness, slap in the
middle of the red-light quarter. Upmarket sort of establishment,
as they go, I'm told. Private rooms, decent food if you like Huna-
nese, a straight deal and the girls leave you alone unless you tell
'em not to."

At girlie restaurants, he explained, somehow contriving to
suggest he had never personally been to one, young hostesses,
dressed or undressed, sat between the guests and fed them food
and drink while the men talked high matters of business. In addition, The Sea of Happiness offered a massage parlour, a disco-
thèque and a live theatre on the ground floor.

"Duffy clinches the deal with the consortium, a cheque is
passed, he's feeling his oats. So he decides to do himself a favour
with one of the girls. Terms agreed, off they go to a cubicle. Girl
says she's thirsty, how about a bottle of champagne to get her
going? She's on commission, naturally—they all are. Never mind.
Duffy's feeling expansive, so he says why not. Girl presses a bell,
squawks into the intercom, next thing Duffy knows, in marches
this bloody great European chap with an ice bucket and a tray.

Sets it down, Duffy gives him twenty baht for himself, fellow says 'Thank you' in English, polite enough but no smiles, clears out. It's Hansen. Jungle Hansen. Not a portrait . . . himself!"

"How does Duffy know that?"

"Seen his photograph, hasn't he?"

"Why?"

"Because we showed Duffy the bloody photograph, for heaven's sake, when Hansen went missing! We showed it to everyone we knew, all over the bloody hemisphere! We didn't say why—we just said if you spot this man, holler. Head Office's orders, thank you, not *my* idea. I thought it was bloody insecure."

To calm himself, Rumbelow poured us both another whisky. "Duffy roars back to his hotel, phones me at home straight away. Three in the morning. 'It's your fellow,' he tells me. 'What fellow?' I say. 'Fellow you sent me that pretty picture of, back in Hongkers a year ago or more. He's potboy at a whorehouse called The Sea of Happiness.' You know how old Duffy talks. Loose. I sent Henry round next day. Bloody fool made a hash of it. You heard about that, I hope? Typical."

"Did Duffy speak to Hansen? Ask him who he was. Anything?"

"Not a dickie bird. Looked clean through him. Duffy's a trouper. Salt of the earth. Always was."

"Where's Henry?"

"Sitting downstairs in the lobby."

"Call him up."

Henry was Chinese, the son of a Kuomintang warlord in the Shan States and our resident chief agent, though I suspect he had long ago taken out reinsurance with the Thai police and was earning a quiet living playing both ends against the middle.

He was a podgy, over-eager, shiny fellow and he smiled too

much. He wore a gold chain round his neck and carried a smart leather notebook with a gold pen in it. His cover work was translator. No translator I had ever met sported a Gucci notebook, but Henry was different.

"Tell Mark how you made a bloody fool of yourself at The Sea of Happiness last Thursday evening," Rumbelow ordered menacingly.

"Sure, Mike."

"Mark," I said.

"Sure, Mark."

"His orders were to take a look. That's *all* he was to do," Rumbelow barged in before Henry could tell anything at all. "Take a look, sniff, get out, call me. Right, Henry? He was to spin the tale, sniff, *see* if he could spot Hansen anywhere, *not* approach him, report back to me. A discreet, no-contact reconnaissance. Sniff and tell. Now tell Mark what you did."

First Henry had had a drink at the bar, he said; then he had watched the show. Then he had sent for the Mama San, who hurried over assuming he had a special wish. The Mama San was a Chinese lady from the same province as Henry's father, so they had an immediate bond.

He had shown the Mama San his translator's card and said he was writing an article about her establishment—the superb food, the romantic girls, the high standards of sensitivity and hygiene, particularly the hygiene. He said he had a commission from a German travel magazine that recommended only the best places.

The Mama San took the bait and offered him the run of the house. She showed him the private dining rooms, the kitchens, cubicles, toilets. She introduced him to the girls—and offered him one on the house, which he declined—to the head chef, the doorman and the bouncers, but not, as it happened, to the enormous round-eye whom Henry had by then spotted three times, once as he carried a tray of glasses from the private dining rooms to the kitchens, once crossing a corridor pushing a trolley of bottles and once emerging from an open steel doorway which apparently led to the drinks store.

"But who is your *farang* who carries the bottles for you?" Henry had cried out with amusement to the Mama San. "Must he stay behind and work because he cannot pay his bill?"

The Mama San laughed also. Against *farangs,* or Westerners, all Asians feel naturally united. "The *farang* lives with one of our Cambodian girls," she replied with contempt, for Cambodians are rated even lower than *farangs* and Vietnamese in the Thai zoology. "He met her here and fell in love with her, so he tried to buy her and make a lady out of her. But she refused to leave us. So he brings her to work every day and stays until she is free to go home again."

"What kind of *farang* is he? German? English? Dutch?"

The Mama San shrugged. What was the difference? Henry pressed her. But a *farang* who brings his woman to the brothel and pushes drinks about while she goes with other men, he insisted, and then takes her home again to his bed. This must be quite some girl!

"She is number nineteen," said the Mama San, with a shrug. "Her house name is Amanda. Would you like her?"

But Henry was too excited by his journalistic coup to be sidetracked. "But the *farang,* what is his name? What is his history?" he cried in great amusement.

"He is called Ham Sin. He speaks Thai with us and Khmer with the girl but you must not put him in your magazine because he is illegal."

"I can disguise him. I can make it all disguised. Does the girl love him in return?"

"She prefers to be here at The Sea of Happiness with her friends," the Mama San said primly.

Henry could not resist taking a look. The girls who were not with clients lounged on plush benches behind a glass wall, wearing numbers round their necks and nothing else, while they chatted to each other or tended their fingernails or stared vacuously at an ill-tuned television set. As Henry watched, number 19 stood up in response to a summons, picked up her little handbag and a wrap and walked from the room. She was very young. Many girls lied about their age in order to defeat the regulations—penniless Cambodians particularly. But this girl, said Henry, had looked no more than fifteen.

It was here that Henry's excess of zeal began to lead him astray. He said his goodbyes to the Mama San and drove his car into an alley opposite the rear entrance, where he settled down to wait. Soon after one o'clock the staff began leaving, among them Hansen, twice the height of anyone else, leading number 19 on his arm. In the square, Hansen and the girl looked round for a cab and Henry had the temerity to pull up his car beside them. Pimps and illegal cab drivers thrive at that hour of night, and Henry in his time had been both, so perhaps the move came naturally to him.

"Where you want to go, sir?" he called to Hansen in English. "You want me to drive you?"

Hansen gave an address in a poor suburb five miles north. A price was agreed, Hansen and his girl got into the back of the car; they set off.

Now Henry began to lose his head in earnest. Flushed by his success, he decided for no reason he could afterwards explain that his best course of action would be to deliver his quarry and the girl to Rumbelow's house, which lay not north but west. He had not of course prepared Rumbelow for this bold manoeuvre; he had hardly prepared himself for it. He had no assurance that Rumbelow was at home, or in any condition, at one-thirty in the morning, to conduct a conversation with a former spy who had disappeared off the map for eighteen months. But reason, at that moment, did not predominate in Henry's mind. He was a joe, and there is not a joe in the world who does not, at one time or another in his life, do something totally daft.

"You like Bangkok?" Henry asked Hansen gaily, hoping to distract his passengers from the route he was taking.

No answer.

"You been here long?"

No answer.

"That's a nice girl. Very young. Very pretty. She your regular girl?"

The girl had her head on Hansen's shoulder. From what Henry could see in the mirror, she was already asleep. For some reason, this knowledge excited Henry further.

"You want a tailor, sir? All-night tailor, very good? I take you there. Good tailor."

And he drove wildly into a sidestreet, pretending to look for his wretched tailor while he hurried towards Rumbelow's house.

"Why are you going west?" said Hansen, speaking for the first time. "I don't want to go this way. I don't want a tailor. Get back on the main road."

The last of Henry's commonsense deserted him. He was suddenly terrified by Hansen's size and Hansen's tactical advantage in sitting behind him. What if Hansen was armed? Henry jammed on the brakes and stopped the car.

"Mr. Hansen, sir, I am your friend!" he cried in Thai, much as he might plead for mercy. "Mr. Rumbelow is your friend too. He's proud of you! He wants to give you a lot of money. You come with me, please. No problem. Mr. Rumbelow will be very happy to see you!"

That was the last speech Henry made that night, for the next thing he knew, Hansen had pushed the back of Henry's driving seat so hard that Henry's head nearly went through the windscreen. Hansen got out of the car and hauled Henry into the street. After that, Hansen lifted Henry to his feet and flung him across the road, to the dismay of a group of sleeping beggars, who began whimpering and clamouring while Hansen strode to where Henry lay and glared down at him.

"You tell Rumbelow, if he comes for me, I'll kill him," he said in Thai.

Then he led the girl up the road in search of a better cab, one arm round her waist while she dozed.

By the time I had heard the two men's story to the end, I was suddenly dreadfully tired.

I sent them away, telling Rumbelow to call me next morning. I said that before I did anything else I was going to sleep off my jet-lag. I lay down and was at once wide awake. An hour later, I was presenting myself at The Sea of Happiness and buying a ticket for fifty dollars. I removed my shoes, as custom required, and moments later I was standing in a neon-lit cubicle in my stockinged feet, staring into the passive, much painted features of girl number 19.

She wore a cheap silk wrap with tigers on it, but it was open from the neck down. Underneath it she was naked. A heavy Japanese-style makeup covered her complexion. She smiled at me and thrust her hand swiftly towards my groin, but I replaced it at her side. She was so slight it seemed a mystery that she was equal to the work. She was longer-legged than most Asian girls and her skin was unusually pale. She threw off her wrap and, before I could stop her, sprang on to the frayed chaise longue, where she arranged herself in what she imagined to be an erotic pose, caressing herself and uttering sighs of desire. She rolled on to her side with her rump thrust out, draping her black hair across her shoulder so that her tiny breasts poked through it. When I did not advance on her, she lay on her back and opened her thighs to me and bucked her pelvis, calling me "darling" and saying "please." She flung herself away from me so that I could admire her back view, keeping her legs apart in invitation.

"Sit up," I said, so she sat up and again waited for me to come to her.

"Put on your wrap," I said.

When she appeared not to understand, I helped her into it. Henry had written the message for me in Khmer. "I want to speak to Hansen," it read. "I am in a position to obtain Thai papers for yourself and your family." I handed it to her and watched her study it. Could she read? I had no way of telling. I held out a plain white envelope addressed to Hansen. She took it and opened it. The letter was typed and its tone was not gentle. It contained two thousand baht.

"As an old friend of Father Vernon," I had written, using the wordcode familiar to him, "I must advise you that you are in breach of your contract with our company. You have assaulted a Thai citizen and your girlfriend is an illegal Cambodian immigrant. We may have no alternative but to pass this information to the authorities. My car is parked across the street. Give the enclosed money to the Mama San as payment to release you for the night, and join me in ten minutes."

She left the cubicle, taking the letter with her. I had not realised till then how much noise there was in the corridor: the jangling music, the tinny laughter, the grumbles of desire, the swish of water down the ramshackle pipes.

I had left the car unlocked and he was sitting in the back, the girl beside him. Somehow I had not doubted he would bring the girl. He was big and powerful, which I knew already, and haggard. In the half darkness, with his black beard and hollowed eyes and his flattened hands curled tensely over the back of the passenger seat, he resembled one of the saints he had once worshipped, rather than the photographs on his file. The girl sat slumped and close to him, sheltering against his body. We had not gone a hundred metres before a rainburst crashed on us like a waterfall. I pulled in to the kerb while each of us stared through the drenched windscreen, watching the torrents of water swarm over the gutters and potholes.

"How did you get to Thailand?" I yelled in Dutch. The rain was thundering on the roof.

"I walked," Hansen replied in English.

"Where did you come over?" I yelled, in English also.

He mentioned a town. It sounded like "Orania Prathet." The downpour ended and I drove for three hours while the girl dozed and Hansen sat guard over her, alert as a cat, and silent. I had selected a beach hotel advertised in the Bangkok *Nation*. I wanted to get him out of his own setting, into one that I controlled. I drew the key and paid a night's lodging in advance. Hansen and the girl followed me down a concrete path to the beach. The bungalows stood in a half ring facing the sea. Mine was at one end. I unlocked the door and went ahead of them. Hansen followed, after him the girl. I switched on the light and the air-conditioning. The girl hovered near the door, but Hansen kicked off his shoes and placed himself at the centre of the room, casting round him with his hollowed eyes.

"Sit down," I said. I pulled open the refrigerator door. "Does she want a drink?" I asked.

"Give her a Coca-Cola," said Hansen. "Ice. Got any limes in there?"

"No."

He watched me on my knees in front of the refrigerator.

"How about you?" I asked.

"Water."

I searched again: glasses, mineral water, ice. As I did so, I heard Hansen say something tender to the girl in Khmer. She protested

and he overrode her. I heard her go into the bedroom and come
out again. Climbing to my feet, I saw the girl curled on the daybed that ran along one wall of the room, and Hansen bending
over her with a blanket, tucking her up. When he had finished,
he switched out the lamp above her and touched her cheek with
his fingertips before striding to the French window to stare at the
sea. A full red moon hung above the horizon. The rainclouds
made black mountains across the sky.

"What's your name?" he asked me.

"Mark," I said.

"Is that your real name? Mark?"

The surest knowledge we have of one another comes from instinct. As I watched Hansen's figure framed in the window and
gazing out to sea, and the moonlight picking out the lines and
hollows of his ravaged face, I knew that the lapsed priest had appointed me his confessor.

"Call me whatever you like," I said.

You must think of a strong but uneasy English voice, the tone
rich, the manner shocked, as if its owner never expected it to say
the things he is hearing. The slight accent is East Indian Dutch.
The bungalow is unlit, designed for fornication, and gives on to a
tiny illuminated swimming pool and concrete rockery. Beyond
this nonsense lies a superb and placid Asian sea, with a wide
moon-path, and stars sparkling in the water like sunspots. A couple of fishermen stand upright in their sampans, tossing their
round nets into the water and drawing them slowly out again.

In the foreground you must set the jagged, towering figure of
Hansen as he prowls the room in his bare feet, now pausing at the
French window, now perching himself on the arm of a chair before slipping soundlessly away to another corner. And always the
voice, now fierce, now ruminative, now shaken, and now, like his

body, resting itself for minutes on end while it gathers strength for the next ordeal.

Stretched on her daybed, the Cambodian girl lies wrapped in a blanket, her forearm crooked Asian style beneath her head. Was she awake? Did she understand what he was saying? Did she care? Hansen cared. He could not pass her without stopping to gaze down at her, or fiddle with the blanket at her neck. Once, dropping to the floor beside her, he stared ardently into her closed eyes while he laid his palm on her brow as if to test her temperature.

"She needs limes," he murmured. "Coca-Cola is nothing for her. Limes."

I had sent out for them already. They arrived, by hand of a boy from the front desk. There was business while Hansen squeezed them for her, then held her upright while she drank.

His first questions were a vague catechism about my standing in the Service. He wished to know with what authority had I been sent, with what instructions.

"I want no thanks for what I have done," he warned me. "There are no thanks for bombing villages."

"But you may need help," I said.

His response was to tell me formally that he would never again, in any circumstance, work for the Service. I could have told him that too, but I refrained. He had thought he was working for the British, he said, but he had been working for murderers. He had been another man when he did the things he did. He hoped the American pilots had been other men as well.

He asked after his sub-agents—the farmer so-and-so, the rice trader so-and-so. He asked about the staybehind network he had painstakingly built up against the certain day when the Khmer Rouge would break out of the jungle and help themselves to the cities, a thing that neither we nor the Americans, despite all the warnings, had ever quite believed would happen. But Hansen had believed it. Hansen was one of the warners. Hansen had told us time and again that Kissinger's bombs were dragon's teeth, even though Hansen had helped direct them to their targets.

"May I believe you?" he asked me when I assured him there had been no pattern of arrests among his sources.

"It's the truth," I said, responding to the supplication in his voice.

"Then I didn't betray them," he muttered in marvel. For a moment he sat and cupped his head in his hands, as if holding it together.

"If you were captured by the Khmer Rouge, nobody could expect you to stay silent, anyway," I said.

"Silent! My God." He almost laughed. "Silent!" And, standing sharply, he swung away to the window again.

By the moonlight I saw tears of sweat clinging to his great bearded face. I started to say something about the Service wishing to acquit itself honourably by him, but halfway through my speech he flung out his arms to their fullest extent, as if testing the limits of his confinement. Finding nothing to obstruct them, they fell back to his sides.

"The Service to hell," he said softly. "The West to bloody, bloody hell. We have no business making our wars here, peddling our religious recipes. We have sinned against Asia: the French, the British, the Dutch, now the Americans. We have sinned against the children of Eden. God forgive us."

My tape recorder lay on the table.

We are in Asia. Hansen's Asia. The Asia sinned against. Listen to the frenetic chatter of the insects. Thais and Cambodians alike have been known to bet large sums on the number of times a bullfrog will burp. The room is twilit, the hour forgotten, the room forgotten also; the moon has risen out of sight. The Vietnam

War is back with us, and we are in the Cambodian jungle with Hansen, and modern comforts are few, unless we include the American bombers that circle miles above us, like patient hawks, waiting for the computers to tell them what to destroy next: for instance, a team of oxen whose urine has been misread by secret sensors as the exhaust fumes of a military convoy; for instance, children whose chatter has been mistaken for military commands. The sensors have been hidden by American commandos along the supply routes Hansen has indicated to them—but unfortunately the sensors are not as well informed as Hansen is.

We are in what the American pilots call badland, though in the jungle definitions of good and bad are fluid. We are in a Khmer Rouge "liberated area" that provides sanctuary for Vietcong troops who wish to attack the Americans in the flank rather than head-on from the north. Yet despite these appearances of war, we are among people with no collective perception of their enemies, in a region unmapped except by fighters. To hear Hansen speak, the region is as close to paradise as makes no difference, whether he speaks as priest, sinner, scholar or spy.

A few miles up the trail by jeep is an ancient Buddhist temple which, with the help of villagers, Hansen has excavated from the depths of vegetation, and which is the apparent reason for his being there, and for the notes he takes, and the wireless messages he sends, and for the trickle of visitors who arrive usually just before nightfall, and depart at first light. The kampong where he lives is built on stilts in a clearing at the edge of a good river, in a plain of fertile fields that climb in steps to a rain forest. A blue mist is frequent. Hansen's house is set high up the slope in order to improve his radio reception and give a view of whatever enters and leaves the valley. In the wet season, it is his habit to leave the jeep in the village and trudge up to his house on foot. In the dry season, he drives into his compound, most often taking half the village children with him. As many as a dozen of them will be waiting to clamber over the tailboard for the five-minute ride from the village to his compound.

"Sometimes, my daughter was among them," Hansen said.

Neither Rumbelow nor the file had mentioned that Hansen had a daughter. If he had hidden her from us, he was gravely in breach of Service rules—though heaven knows, Service rules were about the last thing that mattered to either of us by then. Nevertheless he stopped speaking and glared at me in the darkness as if waiting for my reproof. But I preserved my silence, wishing to be the ear he had been waiting for, perhaps for years.

"While I was still a priest, I visited the temples of Cambodia," he said. "While I was there, I fell in love with a village woman and made her pregnant. In Cambodia it was the best time still. Sihanouk ruled. I remained with her until the child was born. A girl. I christened her Marie. I gave the mother money and returned to Djakarta, but I missed my child terribly. I sent more money. I sent money to the headman to look after them. I sent letters. I prayed for the child and her mother, and swore that one day I would care for them properly. As soon as I returned to Cambodia, I put the mother in my house, even though in the intervening years she had lost her beauty. My daughter had a Khmer name, but from the day she came to me I called her Marie. She liked that. She was proud to have me as her father."

He seemed concerned to make clear to me that Marie was at ease with her European name. It was not an American name, he said. It was European.

"I had other women in my household, but Marie was my only child and I loved her. She was more beautiful than I had imagined her. But if she had been ugly and ungracious I would have loved her no less." His voice acquired sudden strength and, as I heard it, warning. "No woman, no man, no child, ever claimed my love in such a way. You may say that Marie is the only woman I have loved purely except for my mother." He was staring at me in the darkness, challenging me to doubt his passion. But under Hansen's spell, I doubted nothing and had forgotten everything about myself, even my own mother's death. He was assuming me, occupying me.

"Once you have embarked upon the impossible concept of God, you will know that real love permits no rejection. Perhaps that is something only a sinner can properly understand. Only a sinner knows the scale of God's forgiveness."

I think I nodded wisely. I thought of Colonel Jerzy. I was wondering why Hansen needed to explain that he could not reject his daughter. Or why his sinfulness was a concern to him when he spoke of her.

"That evening when I drove home from the temple, there were no children waiting for me in the kampong, though it was the dry season. I was disappointed because we had made a good find that day and I wanted to tell Marie about it. They must be having a school festival, I thought, but I could not think which one. I drove up the hill to the compound and called her name. The compound was empty. The gatehouse empty. The women's cookpots empty under the stilts. I called Marie again, then my wife. Then anybody. No one came. I drove back to the village. I went into the house of one of Marie's friends, then another and another, calling Marie. Even the pigs and chickens had disappeared. I looked for blood, for traces of fighting. There were none. But I found footprints leading into the jungle. I drove back to the compound. I took a spade and cached my radio in the forest, halfway between two tall trees that made a line due west, close to an old ant-hill shaped like a man. I hated all my work for you, all my lies, for you and for the Americans. I still do. I walked back to the house, uncached my codepads and equipment and destroyed them. I was glad to. I hated them also. I put on boots and filled a rucksack with food for a week. With my revolver I sent three bullets through the jeep's engine to immobilise it; then

I followed the footprints into the jungle. The jeep was an insult to me, because you had bought it."

Alone, Hansen had set off in pursuit of the Khmer Rouge. Other men—even men who were not Western spies—might have thought twice and a third time, even with their wife and daughter taken hostage. Not Hansen. Hansen had one thought and, absolutist that he was, he acted on it.

"I could not allow myself to be separated from God's grace," he said. He was telling me, in case I did not know, that beyond the girl's survival lay the survival of his immortal soul.

I asked him how long he had marched for. He didn't know. To begin with he had marched only at night and lain up by day. But the daylight gnawed at him and gradually, against all jungle sense, it drew him forward. As he marched, he recalled every event of Marie's life from the night when he had lifted her from her mother's womb and, with a ritual bamboo stave, cut the cord and ordered the women in attendance to give him water so that he could wash her; and with the water, by his authority as priest and father, had christened her Marie after his own mother and the mother of Christ.

He remembered the nights when she had lain sleeping in his arms or in the rush crib at his feet. He saw her at her mother's breast in the firelight. He flailed himself for the dreadful years of separation in Djakarta and on his training course in England. He flailed himself for all the falsity of his work for the Service, and for his weakness, as he described it, his treachery against Asia. He was referring to his work of directing the American bombers.

He relived the hours he had spent telling her stories and singing her to sleep with English and Dutch songs. He cared only for his love for her, and his need of her, and for her need of him.

He was following the tracks because he had nothing else to

follow. He knew now what had happened. It had happened to other kampongs, though none in Hansen's region. The fighters had surrounded the kampong at night and waited till dawn, when the able-bodied left for the fields. They had taken the able-bodied, then crept into the village and taken the elderly and the children, afterwards the livestock. They were provisioning themselves but they were also adding to their ranks. They were in a hurry or they would have ransacked the houses, but they wanted to return to the jungle before they were discovered. Soon, by the light of a full moon, Hansen came upon the first grisly proofs of his theory: the naked bodies of an old storekeeper and his wife, their hands bound behind their backs. Had they been unable to keep up? Were they too ugly? Had they argued?

Hansen marched faster. He was thanking God that Marie looked like a full Asian. In most children of mixed blood, the European strain would have been there for every Asian to see, but Hansen, though a giant, was dark-skinned and slim-bodied, and somehow with his Asian soul he had succeeded in engendering an Asian girl.

Next night another corpse lay beside the trail and Hansen approached it fearfully. It was Ong Sai, the argumentative schoolmistress. Her mouth was wide open. Shot while protesting, Hansen diagnosed, and pressed anxiously forward. In search of Marie, his pure love, the earth mother who was his daughter, the only keeper of his grace.

He wondered which sort of unit he was following. The shy boys who banged on your door at night to ask a little rice for the fighters? The grim-jawed cadres who regarded the Asian smile as an emblem of Western decadence? And there were the zombies, he remembered: freebooting packs of homeless who had clubbed together from necessity, more outlaws than guerrillas. But already in the group ahead of him he had an intimation of discipline. A less organised gang would have stayed to loot the village. They would have made camp to eat a meal and congratu-late themselves. On the morning after he found Ong Sai, Hansen took special care to conceal himself while he slept.

"I had a premonition," he said.

In the jungle you ignored premonition at your peril. He bur-ied himself deep in the undergrowth and smeared himself with mud. He slept with his revolver in his hand. He woke at evening to the smell of woodsmoke and the shrill sound of shouting, and when he opened his eyes he found himself looking straight into the barrels of several automatic rifles.

He was talking about the chains. Jungle fighters, trained to travel light, humping a dozen sets of manacles for hundreds of kilometres—how had it happened? He was still mystified. Yet somebody had carried them, somebody had made a clearing and driven a stake into the centre of the clearing, and dropped the iron rings round the stake, and attached the twelve sets of chains to the twelve iron rings in order to tether twelve special prisoners to the rain and heat and cold and dark. Hansen described the pattern of the chains. To do so, he broke into French. I assumed he needed the protection of a different language. "... *une tringle collective sur laquelle étaient enfilés des étriers ... nous étions fixés par un pied ... j'avais été mis au bout de la chaîne parce que ma cheville trop grosse ne passait pas ...*"

I glanced at the girl. She lay, if it were possible, more inert than before. She could have been dead or in a trance. I realised Hansen was sparing her something he did not want her to hear.

By day, he said, still in French, our ankles were released, en-abling us to kneel and even crawl, though never far, because we were tethered to the stake and had each other's bodies to contend with. Only by night, when our foot irons were fixed to heavy poles that made up the circumference of the enclosure, were we able to stretch full length. The availability of chains determined the number of special prisoners, who were drawn exclusively from the village bourgeoisie, he said. He recognised two village elders, and a stringy forty-year-old widow called Ra who had a reputation for prophecy. And the three rice-dealing brothers Liu, who were famous misers, one of whom looked already dead, for he lay curled round his chains like a hairless hedgehog. Only the sound of his sobbing proved he was alive.

And Hansen, with his horror of captivity? How had he responded to his chains?

"Je les ai portées pour Marie," he answered in the swift, warning French I was learning to respect.

The prisoners who were not special were confined to a stockade at the clearing's edge, from which at intervals one of them was led or dragged to headquarters, a place out of sight behind a hillock. Questioning was brief. After a few hours' screaming, a single pistol shot would ring out and the uneasy quiet of the jungle would return. Nobody came back from questioning. The children, including Marie, were allowed to roam provided they did not approach the prisoners or venture up the hillock which hid the headquarters. The boldest of them had already struck up an acquaintance with the young fighters during the march, and were scurrying around them trying to perform errands or touch their guns.

But Marie had stayed apart from everyone. She sat in the dust of the clearing on the other side of the poles, watching over her father from dawn till night. Even when they hauled her mother from the stockade and her screams for Hansen rang out from behind the hillock, changing to screams for mercy and ending with the usual pistol shot, Marie's eyes never flinched from Hansen's face.

"Did she know?" I asked in French.

"The whole camp knew," he replied.

"Had she been fond of her mother?"

Was it my imagination or had Hansen closed his eyes in the darkness?

"I was the father of Marie," he replied. "I was not the father of their relationship."

How had I known that the mother and daughter had hated each other? Was it because I sensed that Hansen's love for Marie had been a jealous and demanding one—absolute, like all his loves, excluding rivals?

"I was not allowed to speak to her, nor she to me," he was saying. "Prisoners spoke to nobody on pain of death."

Even a groan was enough, as one of the luckless Liu brothers learned when the guards reduced him to permanent silence with their rifle butts, and replaced him next morning with a cringing leftover from the stockade. But between Marie and her father no words were necessary. The stoicism Hansen saw in his daughter's face was the impassioned determination of his own heart as he lay bound and helpless in his chains. With Marie to support him, he could bear anything. Each would be the salvation of the other. Her love for him was as fierce and single-minded as his for her. He did not doubt it. For all his loathing of captivity, he thanked God he had followed her.

A day passed and another, but Hansen remained chained to the stake, burning in the sun, shaking in the evening cold, stinking in his own filth, his gaze and spirit fixed always upon Marie.

In his head, meanwhile, he was wrestling with the tactics of his situation.

From the start it had been clear to him that he was a celebrity. If they had been planning to capture a European, they would have made their attack before Hansen left his house, and searched the house afterwards. He was unexpected treasure, and they were waiting to hear what should be done with him. Others on the stake were fetched and disappeared, all but the one surviving Liu brother and the woman fortune teller, who after days of noisy questioning reappeared as camp trusties, abusing their former companions and trying by every means to ingratiate themselves with the soldiers.

An indoctrination class was formed, and each evening the children and selected survivors sat in a circle in the shade to be harangued by a young commissar with a red headband. While Hansen burned and froze, he could hear the commissar's shrill squawk, hour by hour as he ranted against the hated imperialists. At first he resented these classes because they took Marie away from him. But when he made the effort, he could still lift his head high enough to see her straight body seated strictly at the far side of the circle, staring at him across the clearing. I will be your mother and your father and your friend, he told her. I will be your life, if I have to give up my own.

At other times he reproached himself with her spectacular beauty, regarding it as a punishment for his random lusts. Marie at twelve was without doubt the most beautiful in the camp, and though sex was forbidden to the cadres on the grounds that it was a bourgeois threat to their revolutionary will, Hansen could not help observe the effect that her thinly clothed figure had on the young fighters as they watched her pass; how their dulled eyes drank in her sprouting breasts and swinging haunches beneath the torn cotton frock, and their scowls darkened when they yelled at her. Worse still, he knew she was aware of their desire, and that her emerging womanhood responded to it.

Then a morning came when the routine of Hansen's captivity unaccountably improved, and his apprehensions deepened, for his benefactor was the young commissar in the red headband. Escorted by two soldiers, the commissar ordered Hansen to stand. When he was unable, the soldiers lifted him to his feet and, taking an arm each, let him stagger to a point along the river bank where an inlet made a natural pool.

"Wash," the young commissar ordered.

For days—ever since they had bound him—Hansen had been vainly demanding the right to clean himself. On his first evening he had roared at them, "Take me to the river." They had beaten him. The next morning he had flung himself about on his chains, risking more beatings, yelling for a responsible comrade, all to assert his right to remain a person whom his captors could respect and consequently preserve.

Under the gaze of the soldiers, Hansen sufficiently rallied his racked limbs to bathe and—though it was a crucifixion—rub himself with the fine river mud before being led back to the stake. On each journey, he passed within a few feet of his beloved Marie in her habitual place beyond the ring of poles. Though his heart leapt at her nearness and the courage in her eyes, he could not suppress the suspicion that it was his own child who had purchased the rare comfort he was now enjoying. And when the commissar grunted a greeting to her and Marie lifted her head and gave half a smile in return, the anguish of jealousy added itself to Hansen's pains.

After his bath, they brought him rice—more than they had given him in all the time he had been their prisoner. And instead of making him eat it from the bowl like a dog, they untied his hands and let him use his fingers, so that he was able to secrete a small amount in his palm, and drop it down the front of his tunic before they chained him again.

All day long he thought of nothing but the pellet of rice inside his shirt, making sure no movement of his body crushed it. I will win her back, he thought. I will supplant the commissar in her admiration. When evening came and they again led him to the river, he achieved the miracle he had been planning. Staggering more dramatically than was necessary, he succeeded in dropping a pellet of rice at Marie's feet, unnoticed by his guards. As he passed by her again on his way back, he saw to his secret ecstasy that it had vanished.

Yet her face told him nothing. Only her eyes, straight and sometimes lifeless in their devotion, told him she returned his absolute love. I was deluding myself, he decided, as they refastened his chains. She is learning the prisoner's tricks. She is chaste and will survive. That evening he listened with a new tolerance to the commissar's indoctrination class. Lead him on, he urged her in the telepathic dialogue he conducted with her constantly; lull him, bewitch him, gain his trust but give him nothing. And Marie must have heard him, because as the class broke up he saw the commissar beckon her over to him and rebuke her while she remained cowed and silent. He saw her head fall forward. He saw her walk away from him, her head still lowered.

Next day and for a week, Hansen repeated his trick, convinced he was unobserved except by Marie. The pellet of rice, rolling lightly over his stomach each time he shifted his body, became a source of vital comfort to him. I am nourishing her from my own breast. I am her guardian, the protector of her chastity. I am her priest, giving her Christ's Sacrament.

The rice was all that mattered to him. His concern was to contrive new ways to smuggle it to her, waiting till he was past her and flicking the pellet backward, letting it fall down the inside of his tattered trouser leg.

"I was inordinate," he said softly, in the tone of a penitent.

And because he had been inordinate, God took Marie from him. Suddenly one morning when they unchained him and led him to the pool, there was no Marie waiting to receive her Sacrament. At the evening indoctrination class, he saw that she had been elevated to the commissar's side, and he thought he heard her voice above the rest, intoning the liturgical responses with a new self-confidence. When night fell, he picked out her silhouette among the soldiers' fires—an accepted member of their company, sharing their rice like a comrade. Next day he did not see her at all, nor the day after.

"I wished to die," he said.

But in the evening as he waited in despair, prone and motionless, for the guards to chain his feet, it was the young commissar who marched towards him, and Marie, dressed in a black tunic, who trotted at his side.

"Is this man your father?" the commissar asked as they reached Hansen.

Marie's stare did not falter, but she seemed to be searching her memory for her reply. "Angka is my father," she said finally. "Angka is the father of all oppressed."

"Angka was the Party," Hansen explained for me, without my asking. "Angka was the Organisation that the Khmer Rouge prayed to. In the Khmer Rouge's ladder of beings, Angka was God."

"So who is your mother?" the commissar asked Marie.

"My mother is Angka. I have no mother but Angka."

"Who is this man?"

"He is an American agent," Marie replied. "He drops bombs on our villages. He kills our workers."

"Why does he pretend he is your father?"

"He wishes to trick us by claiming to be our comrade."

"Test the spy's chains. See that they are tight enough," the commissar commanded.

Marie knelt to Hansen's feet, exactly as he had taught her to kneel in prayer. For a moment, like the healing touch of Christ, her hand closed over his festering ankles.

"Can you insert your fingers between the chain and ankle?" the commissar asked.

In his panic, Hansen behaved as he always did when his feet were being chained. He flexed his ankle muscles, hoping to give himself more freedom when he relaxed. He felt her finger probe the chain.

"I can insert my little finger," she replied, holding it up while she kept her body in the line of sight between the commissar and Hansen's feet.

"Can you insert it with difficulty or easily?"

"I can insert my finger only with difficulty," she lied.

Watching them march away, Hansen noticed something that alarmed him. With her black tunic, Marie had put on the stealthy waddle of the jungle fighter. All the same, for the first time since his capture, Hansen slept soundly in his chains. She is joining them in order to deceive them, he assured himself. God is protecting us. Soon we shall escape.

The official interrogator arrived by boat, a smooth-cheeked student with an earnest, frowning manner. In Hansen's mind, that was how he named him: the student. A reception committee led by the commissar met him at the river bank and escorted him over the hillock to headquarters. Hansen knew he was the interrogator because he was the only one who did not turn his head to look at the last remaining prisoner rotting in the heat. But he looked at Marie. He stopped in front of her, obliging everybody to stop with him. He stood before her; he held his studious face close to her while he asked her questions. Hansen could not hear. He kept it there while he listened to her parrot answers. My daughter is the camp whore, thought Hansen in despair. But was she? Nothing he had ever heard about the Khmer Rouge suggested they appointed or even tolerated prostitutes in their midst. Everything suggested the contrary. *"Angka haït le sexuel,"* a French anthropologist had said to him once.

Then they are ravishing her with their puritanism, he decided. They have locked her to them in a passion that is worse than a debauching. He lay with his face in the earth, praying to be allowed to take her sins of innocence upon himself.

I have no coherent picture of Hansen's interrogation for the reason he had little himself. I remembered my own treatment at the hands of Colonel Jerzy, and it was child's play by comparison. But Hansen's recollections had the same imprecision. That they tortured him goes without saying. They had built a wooden grid for the purpose. Yet they were also concerned to keep him alive, because between sessions they gave him food and even, if he remembered rightly, allowed him visits to the river bank, though it may have been a single visit broken by spells of unconsciousness.

There were also the sessions of writing, for in the literal mind of the student, no confession was real until it was written down. And the writing grew harder and harder and became a punishment in itself, even though they unstrapped him from the grid to make him do it.

As an interrogator, the student seems to have proceeded simultaneously on two intellectual fronts. When he was checked on the one, he shifted to the other.

You are an American spy, he said, and an agent of the counterrevolutionary puppet Lon Nol, also an enemy of the revolution. Hansen disagreed.

But you're also a Roman Catholic masquerading as a Buddhist, a prisoner of minds, a promoter of anti-Party superstitions, and a saboteur of the popular enlightenment, the student screamed at him.

In general, the student seems to have preferred making statements to asking questions: "You will now please give all dates and places of your conspiratorial meetings with the counterrevolutionary puppet and American spy Lon Nol, naming all Americans present."

Hansen insisted that no such meetings had occurred. But this gave the student no satisfaction. As the agony increased, Hansen recalled the names from an English folksong that his mother had used to sing him: Tom Pearse ... Bill Brewer ... Jan Stewer ... Peter Gurney ... Peter Davey ... Dan Whiddon ... Harry Hawk ...

"You will now please write down the ringleader of this rabble," the student said, turning a page of his notebook. The student's eyes, said Hansen, were often nearly closed. I remembered that about Jerzy too.

"Cobbleigh," Hansen whispered, lifting his head from the desk where they had sat him. *Thomas Cobbleigh,* he wrote. *Tom for short. Covername Uncle.*

The dates were important because Hansen was concerned he would forget them once he had invented them, and be accused of inconsistency. He chose Marie's birthday and his mother's birthday and the date of his father's execution. He altered the year to suit Lon Nol's accession to power. For a conspiratorial place, he selected the walled gardens of Lon Nol's palace in Phnom Penh, which he had often admired on his way to a favourite *fumerie.*

His fear while he was confessing to this rubbish was that he would reveal true information by mistake, for it was by now clear to him that the student knew nothing about his real intelligence-gathering activities, and that the charges against him were based on the fact that he was a Westerner.

"You will please write down the name of each spy paid by you in the last five years, also each act of sabotage committed by you against the people."

Not in all the days and nights that Hansen had passed anticipating his ordeal had he imagined he might fail on the score of creativity. He recited the names of martyrs whose agonies he had contemplated in order to prepare himself, of Oriental scholars safely dead; of authors of learned works on philology and linguistics. Spies, he said. All spies. And wrote them down, his hand jerking on the paper to the convulsions of the pain that continued to rack him long after they switched off the machine.

Writing desperately, he made a list of T. E. Lawrence's officers in the desert, which he remembered from his many readings of *The Seven Pillars of Wisdom*. He described how on Lon Nol's personal orders he had organised the poisoning of crops and cattle by Buddhist priests. The student put him back on the grid and increased the pain.

He described the clandestine classes he had held in imperialism, and how he had encouraged the spread of bourgeois sentiment and family virtues. The student opened his eyes, offered his commiserations and again increased the pain.

He gave them nearly everything. He described how he had lit beacons to guide American bombers, and distributed rumours that the bombers were Chinese. He was on the brink of telling them who had helped him to lead American commandos to the supply trails, when mercifully he fainted.

But throughout his ordeal it was still Marie with whom he lived in his heart, to whom he cried out in his pain, whose hands drew him back to life when his body was begging to relinquish it, whose eyes watched over him in love and pity. It was Marie to whom he sacrificed his suffering and for whom he swore to survive. As he lay between life and death, he had a hallucination in which he saw himself stretched out in the well of the student's boat and Marie in her black tunic seated over him, paddling them upriver to Heaven. But he still was not dead. They have not killed me. I have confessed to everything and they have not killed me.

But he had not confessed to everything. He had remained true to his helpers and he had not told them about his radio. And when they dragged him back next day and strapped him once more to the grid, he saw Marie sitting at the student's side, a copy of his confession lying before her on the table. Her hair was cropped, her expression closed.

"Are you familiar with the statements of this spy?" the student asked her.

"I am familiar with his statements," she replied.

"Do the spy's statements accurately depict his lifestyle as you were able to observe it in his company?"

"No."

"Why not?" the student asked, opening his notebook.

"They are not complete."

"Explain why the spy Hansen's statements are not complete."

"The spy Hansen kept a radio in his house which he used for signalling to the imperialist bombers. Also the names he has mentioned in his confession are fictitious. They are taken from a bourgeois English song which he sang to me when he was pretending to be my father. Also he received imperialist soldiers at our house at night and led them into the jungle. Also he has failed to mention that he has an English mother."

The student appeared disappointed. "What else has he failed to mention?" he asked, flattening a fresh page with the edge of his small hand.

"During his confinement, he has been guilty of many breaches of regulation. He has hoarded food and attempted to buy the collaboration of comrades in his plans to escape."

The student sighed and made more notes. "What else has he failed to mention?" he asked patiently.

"He has been wearing his foot chains improperly. When the chains were being fastened, he braced his feet illegally, leaving the chains loose for his escape."

Until that moment Hansen had managed to persuade himself that Marie was playing a cunning game. No longer. The game was the reality.

"He is a whoremonger!" she screamed through her tears. "He debauches our women by bringing them to his house and drugging them. He pretends to make a bourgeois marriage, then forces his wife to tolerate his decadent practices. He sleeps with girls of my own age! He pretends he is the father of our children and that our blood is not Khmer! He reads us bourgeois literature in Western languages in order to deprave us! He seduces us by taking us for rides in his jeep and singing imperialist songs to us!"

He had never heard her scream before. Nor evidently had the student, who appeared embarrassed. But she would not be checked. She persisted in denying him. She told them how he had forbidden her mother to love her. She was expressing a hatred for him that he knew was unfeigned, as absolute and inordinate as his love for her. Her body shook with the pent-up hatred of a misused woman, her features were crumpled with hatred and guilt. Her arm struck out and she pointed at him in the classic posture of accusation. Her voice belonged to someone he had never known.

"Kill him!" she screamed. "Kill the despoiler of our people! Kill the corrupter of our Khmer blood! Kill the Western liar who tells us we are different from one another! Avenge the people!"

The student made a last note and ordered Marie to be led away.

"I prayed for her forgiveness," Hansen said.

In the bungalow, I realised, it was dawn. Hansen was standing at the window, his eyes fixed on the misty plateau of the sea. The girl lay on the daybed where she had lain all night, her eyes closed, the empty Coca-Cola can beside her, her head still supported by her arm. Her hand, hanging down, looked worn and elderly. A terseness had entered Hansen's voice, and for a moment I feared that with morning he had decided to resent me. Then I realised it was not me he was at odds with but himself. He was remembering his anger as they carried him, bound but not chained, to the stockade to sleep—if sleep is what you do when your body is dying of pain, and the blood is filling your ears and nose. Anger against himself that he had implanted in his child so much loathing.

"I was her father still," he said in French. "I blamed Marie for nothing, myself for everything. If only I had made my escape earlier, instead of counting on her to help me. If only I had fought my way out when I was strong, instead of placing my reliance in a child. I should never have worked for you. My secret work had endangered her. I cursed you all. I still do."

Did I speak? My concern was to say nothing that would obstruct his flow.

"She was drawn, to them," he said, making her excuses for her. "They were her own people, jungle fighters with a faith to die for. Why should she reject them?"

"I was the last obstacle to her acceptance by her people," he said, explaining her. "I was an intruder, a corrupter. Why should she believe I was her father when they were telling her I was not?"

Still lying in the stockade, he remembered her on the day the young commissar dressed her in her bridal black. He remembered her expression of distaste as she stared down at him, fouled and beaten, a beggar at her feet, a cringing Western spy. And beside her, the handsome commissar with his red headband. "I am wedded to the Angka," she was saying to him. "The Angka answers all my questions."

"I was alone," he said.

Darkness fell in the stockade, and he supposed that if they were going to shoot him they would wait for daylight. But the notion that Marie would go through life knowing she had ordered her father's death appalled him. He imagined her in middle age. Who would help her? Who would confess her? Who would give her release and absolution? The idea of his death became increasingly alarming to him. It will be her death too.

At some point he must have dozed, he said, for when dawn came he found a bowl of rice on the floor of the stockade and he knew it had not been there the night before; even in his agony he would have smelt it. Not rolled into pellets, the rice, not hoarded against the naked skin, but a white mound of it, enough for five days. At first he was too tired to be surprised. Lying on his stomach to eat, he noticed the quiet. By this hour the clearing should have been alive with the sounds of soldiers waking for the day: singsong voices and washing noises from the river bank, the clatter of pans and rifles, the chant of slogans led by the commissar. Yet when he paused to listen, even the birds and monkeys seemed to have stopped their shrieking and he heard no human sounds at all.

"They had gone," he said, from somewhere behind me. "They had decamped in the night, taking Marie with them."

He ate more rice and dozed again. Why have they not killed me? Marie has talked them out of it. Marie has bought me my life. Hansen set to work chafing his bonds against the wall of the stockade. By nightfall, covered in sores and flies, he was lying on the river bank, washing his wounds. He crawled back to the stockade to sleep, and next morning, with the remainder of his rice, he set off. This time, having no prisoners or livestock, they had left no tracks.

All the same, he went in search of her.

For months, Hansen thinks five or six, he remained in the jungle, moving from village to village, never settling, trusting no one— I suspect a little crazed. Wherever he could, he enquired after Marie's unit, but there was too little to describe it by and his quest became indiscriminate. He heard of units that had fighting girls. He heard of units that consisted of girls only. He heard of girls being sent into the towns as whores to gather information. He imagined Marie in all these situations. One night he crept back to his old house hoping she had taken refuge there. The village had been burned.

I asked him whether his cached wireless had been disturbed.

"I didn't look," he replied. "I didn't care. I hated you all."

Another night he called on Marie's aunt, who lived in a remote village, but she hurled pans at him and he had to flee. Yet his determination to rescue his daughter was stronger than ever, for he knew now that he must rescue her from herself. She is cursed with my absolutism, he thought. She is violent and headstrong; it is I who am to blame. I have locked her in the prison of my own impulses. Only a father's love could ever have blinded him to this knowledge. Now his eyes were open. He saw her drawn to cruelty and inhumanity as a means of proving her devotion. He saw her reliving his own erratic quest, yet deprived of his intellectual and religious disciplines—vaguely believing, like himself, that her assumption into a great vision would bring her self-fulfillment.

Of his walk to the Thai border he said little. He headed southwest towards Pailin. He had heard there was a camp there for Khmer refugees. He crossed mountains and malarial marshes. Once arrived, he besieged the tracing centres and pinned her description on camp noticeboards. How he achieved this without papers, money or connections, yet kept his presence in Thailand secret, is a mystery to me still. But Hansen was a trained and hardened agent, even if he denied us. He was not disposed to let much stop him. I asked why he did not turn to Rumbelow for help, but he shook off the idea contemptuously.

"I was not an imperialist agent any more. I believed in nothing but my daughter."

One day in the office of a relief organisation, he met an American woman who thought she remembered Marie.

"She left," she said cautiously.

Hansen pressed her. Marie was one of a group of half dozen girls, said the woman. They were whores but they had the assurance of fighters. When they were not entertaining men, they kept themselves apart from everyone and were tough to handle. One day they broke bounds. She had heard they were picked up by the Thai police. She never saw them again.

The woman who said this appeared unsure whether to say what else was on her mind, but Hansen gave her no choice.

"We were afraid for her," she said. "She gave different names for herself. She gave conflicting accounts of how she came to us. The doctors argued over whether she was mad. Somewhere along her journey, she had lost track of who she was."

Hansen presented himself to the Thai police and, by threats or animal persuasion, traced Marie to a police hostel run for the enjoyment of the officers. They never asked him who he was, it seems, or what he had for papers. He was a round-eye, a *farang*, who spoke Khmer and Thai. Marie had stayed three months, then vanished, they said. She was strange, said a kindly sergeant.

"What is strange?" Hansen asked.

"She would speak only English," the sergeant replied.

There was another girl, a friend of Marie's, who had stayed longer and married one of the corporals. Hansen obtained her name.

He had ceased speaking.

"And did you find her?" I asked after a long silence.

I knew the answer already, as I had known it from halfway through his story, without knowing that I knew. He was sitting at the girl's head, which he was gently stroking. Slowly she sat upright and with her little, old hands rubbed her eyes, pretending she had been asleep. I think she had listened to us all night.

"It was all she understood any more," Hansen explained in English, while he continued to stroke her head. He was speaking of the brothel where he had found her. "She wanted no big choices, did you, Marie? No big words, no promises." He pressed her to him. "She wishes only to be admired. By her own people. By us. All of us must love Marie. That is what comforts her."

I think he mistook my reticence for reproach, for his voice rose. "She wishes to be harmless. Is that so bad? She wishes to be left alone, as all of them wish. It would be a good thing if more of us wished the same. Your bombers and your spies and your big talk are not for her. She is not the child of Dr. Kissinger. She asks only for a small existence where she can give pleasure and hurt no one. Which is worse? Your brothel or hers? Get out of Asia. You should never have come, any of you. I am ashamed I ever helped you. Leave us alone."

"I shall tell Rumbelow very little of this," I said as I rose to leave.

"Tell him what you like."

From the doorway, I took a last look at them. The girl was staring at me as I believe she had stared at Hansen from outside the circle of chains, her eyes unflinching, deep and still. I thought I knew what was in her mind. I had paid her and not had her. She was wondering whether I want my money's worth.

Rumbelow drove me to the airport. Like Hansen, I would have preferred to do without him, but we had matters to discuss.

"You promised him *how* much?" he cried in horror.

"I told him he was entitled to a resettlement grant and all the protection we can give him. I told him you would be sending him a cashier's cheque for fifty thousand dollars."

Rumbelow was furious. "*Me* give *him* fifty thousand dollars? My dear man, he'll be drunk for six months and spill his life story all over Bangkok. What about that Cambodian whore of his? She's in the know, I'll bet."

"Don't worry," I said. "He turned me down."

This news astonished Rumbelow so profoundly that he ran out of indignation altogether, preserving instead a wounding silence that lasted us the rest of the journey.

On the plane I drank too much and slept too little. Once waking from a bad dream, I was guilty of a seditious thought about Rumbelow and the Fifth Floor. I wished I could pack off the whole tribe of them on Hansen's march into the jungle, Smiley included. I wished I could make them throw everything over for a flawed and impossible passion, only to see the object of it turn against them, proving there is no reward for love except the experience of loving, and nothing to be learned by it except humility.

Yet I was content, as I am content to this day whenever I think of Hansen. I had found what I was looking for—a man like myself, but one who in his search for meaning had discovered a worthwhile object for his life; who had paid every price and not counted it a sacrifice; who was paying it still and would pay it until he died; who cared nothing for compromise, nothing for ourselves or the opinion of others; who had reduced his life to the one thing that mattered to him, and was free. The slumbering subversive in me had met his champion. The would-be lover in me had found a scale by which to measure his own trivial preoccupations.

So that when a few years later I was appointed Head of the Russia House, only to watch my most valuable agent betray his country for his love, I could never quite muster the outrage required of me by my masters. Personnel was not all stupid when he packed me off to the Interrogators' Pool.

10

Maggs, my unpleasing crypto journalist, was trying to draw Smiley on the amoral nature of our work. He was wanting Smiley to admit that anything went, as long as you got away with it. I suspect he was actually wanting to hear this maxim applied to the whole of life, for he was ruthless as well as mannerless, and wished to see in our work some kind of licence to throw aside his few remaining scruples.

But Smiley would not give him this satisfaction. At first he appeared ready to be angry, which I hoped he would be. If so, he checked himself. He started to speak, but stopped again, and faltered, leaving me wondering whether it was time to call a halt to the proceedings. Until, to my relief, he rallied, and I knew he had merely been distracted by some private memory among the thousands that made up his secret self.

"You see," he explained—replying, as so often, to the spirit rather than the letter of the question—"it really is essential in a free society that the people who do our work should remain unreconciled. It's true that we are obliged to sup with the Devil, and not always with a very long spoon. And as everyone knows"—a sly glance at Maggs produced a gust of grateful laughter—"the Devil is often far better company than the Godly, isn't he? All the same, our obsession with virtue won't go away. Self-interest is so *limiting*. So is expediency." He paused again, still deep inside his own thoughts. "All I'm really saying, I suppose, is that if the temptation to humanity does assail you now and then, I hope you won't take it as a weakness in yourselves, but give it a fair hearing."

The cufflinks, I thought, in a flash of inspiration. George is remembering the old man.

For a long time I could not fathom why the story had continued to haunt me for so long. Then I realised I had happened upon it at a period when my relationship with my son Adrian had hit a low point. He was talking of not bothering with university, and getting himself a well-paid job instead. I mistook his restlessness for materialism and his dreams of independence for laziness, and one night I lost my temper and insulted him, and was duly ashamed of myself for weeks thereafter. It was during one of those weeks that I unearthed the story.

Then I remembered also that Smiley had had no children and that perhaps his ambiguous part in the affair was to some extent explained by this. I was slightly chilled by the thought that he might have been filling an emptiness in himself by redressing a relationship he had never had.

Finally I remembered that just a few days after coming upon the papers, I had received the letter that anonymously denounced poor Frewin as a Russian spy. And that there were certain mystical affinities between Frewin and the old man, to do with dogged loyalty and lost worlds. All this for context, you understand, for I never knew a case yet that was not made up of a hundred others.

Finally there was the fact that, as so often in my life, Smiley turned out once again to have been my precursor, for I had no sooner settled myself at my unfamiliar desk in the Interrogators' Pool than I found his traces everywhere: in our dusty archives, in backnumbers of our duty officer's log and in the reminiscent smiles of our senior secretaries, who spoke of him with the old vestal's treacly awe, part as God, part as teddy bear and part—though they were always quick to gloss over this aspect of his nature—as killer shark. They would even show you the bone-china cup and saucer by Thomas Goode of South Audley Street—where else?—a present to George from Ann, they explained dotingly, which George had bequeathed to the Pool after his reprieve and rehabilitation to Head Office—and, of course, like the Grail itself, the Smiley cup could never possibly be *drunk* from by a mere mortal.

The Pool, if you have not already gathered as much, is by way of being the Service's Siberia, and Smiley, I was comforted to discover, had served out not one exile there but two; the first, for his gall in suggesting to the Fifth Floor that it might be nursing a Moscow Centre mole to its bosom; and the second, a few years later, for being right. And the Pool has not only the monotony of Siberia but its remoteness also, being situated not in the main building but in a run of cavernous offices on the ground floor of a gabled pile in Northumberland Avenue at the northern end of Whitehall.

And, like so much of the architecture around it, the Pool has seen great days. It was set up in the Second World War to receive the offerings of strangers, to listen to their suspicions and calm their fears or—if they had indeed stumbled on a larger truth—misguide or scare them into silence.

If you thought you had glimpsed your neighbour late at night, for instance, crouched over a radio transmitter; if you had seen strange lights winking from a window and were too shy or untrusting to inform your local police station; if the mysterious foreigner on the bus who questioned you about your work had reappeared at your elbow in your local pub; if your secret lover confessed to you—out of loneliness or bravado or a desperate need to make himself more interesting in your eyes—that he was working for the German Secret Service—why then, after a correspondence with some spurious assistant to some unheard-of Whitehall Under-Secretary, you would quite likely, of an early evening, be summoned to brave the blitz, and find yourself being guided heart-in-mouth down the flaking, sandbagged corridor, on your way to Room 909, where a Major Somebody or a Captain Somebody Else, both bogus as three-dollar bills, would courteously invite you to state your matter frankly without fear of repercussion.

And occasionally, as the covert history of the Pool records, great things were born, and are still occasionally born today, of these inauspicious beginnings, though business is not a patch on what it used to be, and much of the Pool's work is now given over to such chores as unsolicited offers of service, anonymous denunciations like the one levelled at poor Frewin and even—in support of the despised security services—positive vetting enquiries, which are the worst Siberias of all, and about as far as you can get from the high-wire operations of the Russia House without quitting the Service altogether.

All the same, there is more than mere humility to be learned from these chastisements. An intelligence officer is nothing if he has lost the will to listen, and George Smiley, plump, troubled, cuckolded, unassuming, indefatigable George, forever polishing his spectacles on the lining of his tie, puffing to himself and sighing in his perennial distraction, was the best listener of us all.

Smiley could listen with his hooded, sleepy eyes; he could listen by the very inclination of his tubby body, by his stillness and his understanding smile. He could listen because with one exception, which was Ann, his wife, he expected nothing of his fellow souls, criticised nothing, condoned the worst of you long before you had revealed it. He could listen better than a microphone because his mind lit at once upon essentials; he seemed able to spot them before he knew where they were leading.

And that was how George had come to be listening to Mr. Arthur Wilfred Hawthorne of 12, The Dene, Ruislip, half a lifetime before me, in the very same Room 909 where I now sat, curiously turning the yellowed pages of a file marked "Destruction Pending" which I had unearthed from the shelves of the Pool's strongroom.

I had begun my quest idly—you may even say frivolously— much as one might pick up an old copy of the *Tatler* in one's club. And suddenly I realised I had stumbled on page after page of Smiley's familiar, guarded handwriting, with its sharp little German t's and twisted Greek e's, and signed with his legendary symbol. Where he was forced to appear in the drama in person— and you could feel him seeking any means to escape this vulgar ordeal—he referred to himself merely as "D.O.," short for Duty Officer. And since he was notorious for his hatred of initials, you are made once more aware of his reclusive, if not downright fugitive nature. If I had discovered a missing Shakespeare folio, I could not have been more excited. Everything was there: Hawthorne's original letter, transcripts of the microphoned interviews, initialled by Smiley himself, even Hawthorne's signed receipts for his travel money and out-of-pocket expenses.

My dull care was gone. My relegation no longer oppressed me, neither did the silence of the great empty house to which I was condemned. I was sharing them with George, waiting for the clip of Arthur Hawthorne's loyal boots as he was marched down the corridor and into Smiley's presence.

"Dear Sir," he had written to "The Officer in Charge of Intelligence, Ministry of Defence." And already, because we are British, his class is branded on the page—if only by the strangely imperious use of capitals so dear to uneducated people. I imagined much effort in the penning, and perhaps a dictionary at the elbow. "I wish, Sir, to Request an Interview with your Staff regarding a Person who has done Special Work for British Intelligence at the highest Level, and whose Name is as Important to my Wife and myself as it may be to your good Selves, and which I am accordingly forbidden to Mention in this Letter."

That was all. Signed "Hawthorne, A. W., Warrant Officer Class II, retired." Arthur Wilfred Hawthorne, in other words, as Smiley's researches revealed when he consulted the voters' list, and followed up his findings with an examination of the War Office files. Born 1915, Smiley painstakingly recorded on Hawthorne's personal particulars sheet. Enlisted 1939, served with the Eighth Army from Egypt to Italy. Ex–Sergeant Major Arthur Wilfred Hawthorne, twice wounded in battle, three commendations and one gallantry medal for his trouble, demobilised without a stain on his character, "the best example of the best fighting man in the world," wrote his commandant, in a glowing if hyperbolic commendation.

And I knew that Smiley, as a good professional, would have taken up his post well ahead of his client's arrival, just as I myself had done these last months: at the same scuffed yellow desk of wartime pine, singed brown along the leading edge—legend has it by the Hun; with the same mossy telephone, letters as well as numbers on the dial; the same hand-tinted photograph of the Queen, sitting on a horse when she was twenty. I see George frowning studiously at his watch, then pulling a sour face as he peered round him at the usual mess, for there had been a running battle for as long as anyone could remember about who was supposed to clean the place, the Ministry or ourselves. I see him tug a handkerchief from his sleeve—laboriously again, for no gesture ever came to George without a struggle—and wipe the grime off the seat of his wooden chair, then do the same in advance for Hawthorne on the other side of the desk. Then, as I had done myself a few times, perform a similar service for the Queen, setting her frame straight and bringing back the sparkle to her young, idealistic eyes.

For I imagined George already studying the feelings of his subject, as any good intelligence officer must. An ex–sergeant major would expect a certain order about him, after all. Then I see Hawthorne himself, punctual to the minute, as the janitor showed him in, his best suit buttoned like a battledress, the polished toecaps of his boots glistening like conkers in the gloom. Smiley's description of him on the encounter sheet was sparse but trenchant: height five seven, grey hair close cut, cleanshaven, groomed appearance, military bearing. Other characteristics: suppressed limp of the left leg, army boots.

"Hawthorne, sir," he snapped, and held himself to attention till Smiley with difficulty persuaded him to sit.

Smiley was Major Nottingham that day and had an impressive card with his photograph to prove it. In my pocket as I read his account of the case lay a similar card in the name of Colonel Ned Ascot. Don't ask me why Ascot except to note that, in choosing a place-name for my alias, I was yet again unconsciously copying one of Smiley's little habits.

"What regiment are you from, sir, if you don't mind my asking?" Hawthorne enquired of Smiley as he sat.

"The General List, I'm afraid," said Smiley, which is the only way we are allowed to answer.

But I am sure it came hard to Smiley, as it would to me, to have to describe himself as some kind of non-combatant.

As evidence of his loyalty, Hawthorne had brought his medals wrapped in a piece of gun cloth. Smiley obligingly went through them for him.

"It's about our son, sir," the old man said. "I've got to ask you. The wife—well, she won't hear of it any more, she says it's a load of his nonsense. But I told her I've got to ask you. Even if you refuse to answer, I told her, I won't have done my duty by my son if I didn't ask on his account."

Smiley said nothing but I am sure his silence was sympathetic.

"Ken was our only boy, you see, Major, so it's natural," said Hawthorne apologetically.

And still Smiley let him take his time. Did I not say he was a listener? Smiley could draw answers from you to questions he had never put, just by the sincerity of his listening.

"We're not asking for secrets, Major. We're not asking to know what can't be known. But Mrs. Hawthorne is failing, sir, and she needs to know whether it's true before she goes." He had prepared the question exactly. Now he put it. "Was our boy, or was he not—was Ken—in the course of what appeared to be a criminal career, operating behind enemy lines in Russia?"

And here you might say that for once I was ahead of Smiley, if only because after five years in the Russia House I had a pretty good idea of the operations we had conducted in the past. I felt a smile come to my face, and my interest in the story, if it was possible, increased.

But to Smiley's face, I am sure, came nothing at all. I imagine features settling into a Mandarin immobility. Perhaps he fiddled with his spectacles, which always gave the impression of belonging to a larger man. Finally he asked Hawthorne—but earnestly, never a hint of scepticism—why he supposed this might be the case.

"Ken told me he was, sir, that's why." And still nothing on Smiley's side, except an ever-open door. "Mrs. Hawthorne wouldn't visit Ken in prison, you see. I would. Every month. He was doing five years for grievous bodily harm, plus three more for being habitual. We had PD in those days, preventive deten-

tion. We're in the prison canteen there, me and Ken sitting together at a table. And suddenly Ken puts his head close to mine,
and he says to me in this low voice he's got, 'Don't come here
again, Dad. It's difficult for me. I'm not really locked up, you see.
I'm in Russia. They had to bring me back special, just to show me
to you. I'm working behind the lines, but don't tell Mum. Write
to me—that's not a problem, they'll send it on. And I'll write
back same as if I was a prisoner here, which is what I pretend to
be, because you can't get better cover than a prison. But the truth
is, Dad, I'm serving the old country just like you did when you
was with the Desert Rats, which is why the best of us are put on
earth.' I didn't ask to see Ken after that. I felt I had to obey orders.
I wrote to him, of course. In the prison. Hawthorne and then his
number. And three months later he'd write back on prison paper
like it was a different boy writing to me every time. Sometimes
the big heavy writing, like he was angry, sometimes small and
quick, like he hadn't had the time. Once or twice there was even
the foreign words in there that I didn't understand, crossed out
mainly, like he was having difficulty with his own language.
Sometimes he'd drop me a clue. 'I'm cold but safe,' he'd say. 'Last
week I had a bit more exercise than I needed,' he'd say. I didn't
tell the wife because he said I wasn't to. Besides, she wouldn't
have believed him. When I offered her his letters, she pushed
them away—they hurt too much. But when Ken died we went
and saw his body all cut to pieces in the prison morgue. Twenty
stab wounds and nobody to blame. She didn't weep, she doesn't,
but they might as well have stabbed her. And on the way home
on the bus I couldn't help it. 'Ken's a hero,' I said to her. I was
trying to wake her up because she'd gone all wooden. I got hold
of her by the sleeve and gave her a bit of a shake to make her listen. 'He's not a dirty convict,' I said. 'Not our Ken. He never was.
And it wasn't convicts who done him in, either. It was the Red

Russians.' I told her about the cufflinks too. 'Ken's romancing,' she said. 'Same as he always did. He doesn't know the difference, he never did, which has been his trouble all along.'"

Interrogators, like priests and doctors, have a particular advantage when it comes to concealing their feelings. They can ask another question, which is what I would have done myself.

"What cufflinks, Sergeant Major?" Smiley said, and I see him lowering his long eyelids and sinking his head into his neck as he once more prepared himself to listen to the old man's tale.

"'There's no medals, Dad,' Ken says to me. 'Medals wouldn't be secure. You have to be gazetted to get a medal, there'd be too many in the know. Otherwise I'd have a medal same as you. Maybe an even better one, if I'm honest, like the Victoria Cross, because they stretch us as far as we can go and sometimes further. But if you do right in the job, you earn your cufflinks and they keep them for you in a special safe. Then once a year there's this big dinner at a certain place I'm not allowed to mention, with the champagne and butlers you wouldn't believe, and all us Russia boys go to it. And we put on our tuxedos and we wear the cufflinks, same as a uniform but secret. And we have this party, with the speeches and the handshakes, like a special investiture, same as you had for your medals, I expect, in this place I'm not allowed to mention. And when the party's over, we hand the cufflinks back. We have to, for the security. So if ever I go missing, or if something happens to me, just you write to them at the Secret Service and ask them for the Russia cufflinks for your Ken. Maybe they'll say they never heard of me, maybe they'll say, "What cufflinks?" But maybe they'll make you a compassionate exception and let you have them, because they sometimes do. And *if* they do—you'll know that everything I ever did wrong was more right than you can imagine. Because I'm my dad's boy, right down the line, and the cufflinks will prove it to you. That's all I'm saying, and it's more than I'm allowed.'"

Smiley asked first for the boy's full name. Then for the boy's date of birth. Then he asked about his schooling and qualifications, which were predictably dismal, both. I see him acting quiet and businesslike as he takes down the details: Kenneth Branham Hawthorne, the old soldier told him—Branham, that was his mother's maiden name, sir; he sometimes used it for what they called his crimes—born Folkestone, July 14, 1946, sir, twelve months after I came back from the war. I wouldn't have a child earlier, although the wife wanted it, sir, I didn't think it right. I wanted our boy brought up in peace, sir, with both his living parents to look after him, Major, which is the right of any child, I say, even if it's not as usual as it ought to be.

Smiley's next task was not half as easy as it might seem, whatever the improbabilities of Kenneth Hawthorne's story. Smiley was never one to deny a good man, or even a bad one, the benefit of the doubt. The Circus of those days possesses no such thing as a reliable central index of its resources, and what passed for one was shamefully and often deliberately incomplete, for rival outfits guarded their sources jealously and poached from their neighbours when they saw the chance.

True, the old man's story bristled with unlikelihoods. In purist terms it was grotesque, for example, to imagine a group of secret agents meeting once a year to dine, thus breaking the most elementary rule of "need to know." But worse things could happen in the lawless world of the irregulars, as Smiley was aware. And it took all his powers of ingenuity and persuasion to satisfy himself that Hawthorne was nowhere on their books: not as a runner, not as a lamplighter or a scalphunter, not as a signalman and not as any other of the beloved tradenames with which these seedy operators glamourised their ranks.

And when he had exhausted the irregulars he returned to the armed services, the security services and the Royal Ulster Constabulary, any one of which might conceivably have employed—

if on some much more modest basis than the boy described—
a violent criminal of Ken Hawthorne's character.

For one thing at least seemed certain: the boy's criminal record
was a nightmare. It would have been hard to imagine a grimmer
record of persistent and often bestial behaviour. As Smiley crossed
and recrossed the boy's history, through childhood to adolescence,
reform school to prison, there seemed to be no transgression,
from pilfering to sadistic assault, that Kenneth Branham Hawthorne, born Folkestone 1946, had not stooped to.

Till at the end of a full week, Smiley appears reluctantly to
have admitted to himself what in another part of his head he
must have known all along. Kenneth Hawthorne, for whatever
sad reasons, had been an unredeemable and habitual monster.
The death he had suffered at the hands of his fellow prisoners
was no more than he deserved. His past was written and complete, and his tales of heroism on behalf of some mythical British
intelligence service were merely the last chapter in his lifelong
effort to steal his father's glory.

It was mid-winter. It was a foul grey, sleet-driven evening on
which to drag an old soldier back across London to a barren interviewing room in Whitehall. And Whitehall in the meagre
lighting of those days was a citadel still at war, even if its guns
were somewhere else. It was a place of military austerity, heart-
less and imperial, of lowered voices and blacked windows, of rare
and hurried footsteps and averted eyes. Smiley was in the War
too, remember, even if he was sitting behind German lines. I can
hear the puttering of the paraffin Aladdin stove which the Circus
had grudgingly approved to supplement the faulty ministerial
radiators. It has the sound of a wireless transmitter operated by a
freezing hand.

Hawthorne had not come alone to hear Major Nottingham's

reply. The old soldier had brought his wife, and I can even tell you how she looked, for Smiley had written of her in his log and my imagination has long painted in the rest.

She had a buckled sick body wrapped in Sunday best. She wore a brooch in the design of her husband's regimental badge. Smiley invited her to sit, but she preferred her husband's arm. Smiley stood across the desk from them, the same burned, yellowed desk where I had sat in exile these last months. I see him standing almost to attention, with his rounded shoulders uncharacteristically straightened. His stubby fingers curled at the seams of his trousers in traditional army manner.

Ignoring Mrs. Hawthorne, he addressed the old soldier man to man. "You understand I have absolutely nothing to say to you at all, Sergeant Major?"

"I do, sir."

"I never heard of your son, you understand? Kenneth Hawthorne is not a name to me, nor to any of my colleagues."

"Yes, sir." The old man's gaze was fixed parade-ground style above Smiley's head. But his wife had her eyes fiercely turned on Smiley's all the time, even if she found it hard to fix on them through the thick lenses of his spectacles.

"He has never in his life worked for any British department of government, whether secret or otherwise. He was a common criminal all his life. Nothing more. Nothing at all."

"Yes, sir."

"I deny absolutely that he was ever a secret agent in the service of the Crown."

"Yes, sir."

"You understand also that I can answer no questions, give you no explanations, and that you will never see me again or be received at this building?"

"Yes, sir."

"You understand finally that you may never speak of this moment to a living soul? However proud you may be of your son? That there are others still alive who must be protected?"

"Yes, sir. I understand, sir."

Opening the drawer of our desk, Smiley took out a small red Cartier box, which he handed to the old man. "I happened to find this in my safe," he said.

The old man passed the box to his wife without looking at it. With firm fingers, she forced it open. Inside lay a pair of superb gold cufflinks with a tiny English rose set discreetly in a corner, hand-engraved, a marvel of fine work. Her husband still did not look. Perhaps he didn't have to; perhaps he didn't trust himself. Closing the box, she parted the clasp of her scuffed purse and popped it inside. Then snapped the purse shut again, so loudly you would think she was slamming down the lid on her son's tomb. I have listened to the tape; it too is waiting to be destroyed.

The old man still said nothing. They were too proud to bother with Smiley as they left.

And the cufflinks? you ask—where did Smiley get the cufflinks from? I had my answer not from the yellowing records of Room 909 but from Ann Smiley herself, quite by chance one evening in a splendid Cornish castle near Saltash where we both happened to be guests. Ann was on her own, and chastened. Mabel had a golf tournament. It was long after the Bill Haydon business, but Smiley still could not bear to have her near him. When dinner was over, the guests dispersed themselves in groups, but Ann stayed close to me, I supposed as a substitute for being close to George. And I asked her, half intuitively, whether she had ever given George a pair of cufflinks. Ann was always at her most beautiful when she was alone.

"Oh those," she said, as if she scarcely remembered. "You mean the ones he gave to the old man."

Ann had given them to George on their first anniversary, she said. After her fling with Bill, he had decided they should be put to better use.

But *why,* exactly, did George decide that? I wondered.

At first it seemed perfectly clear to me. This was Smiley's soft centre. The old cold warrior was revealing his bleeding heart.

Like most things with George—maybe.

Or an act of vengeance against Ann perhaps? Or against his other faithless love, the Circus, at a time when the Fifth Floor was locking him out of the house?

Gradually I arrived at a slightly different theory, which I may as well pass on to you, since one thing is certain, and that is that George himself will not enlighten us.

Listening to the old soldier, Smiley recognised one of those rare moments when the Service could be of real value to real people. For once, the mythology of espionage would be used not to disguise yet another tale of incompetence or betrayal, but to leave an old couple with their dreams. For once, Smiley could look at an intelligence operation and say with absolute confidence that it had worked.

11

"And some interrogations," said Smiley, gazing into the dancing flames of the log fire, "are not interrogations at all, but communions between damaged souls."

He had been talking about his debriefing of the Moscow Centre spymaster, codename Karla, whose defection he had secured. But for me, he was talking only of poor Frewin, of whom, so far as I know, he had never heard.

The letter denouncing Frewin as a Soviet spy arrived on my desk on a Monday evening, posted first class in the S.W.I area of London on the Friday, opened by Head Office Registry on the Monday morning and marked by the Assistant Registrar on duty "HIP to see," HIP being the unlikely acronym of the Head of the Interrogators' Pool; in other words, myself, and in the opinion of some the "H" ought to be an "R"—you Rest in Peace at the Interrogators' Pool. It was five o'clock by the time the Head Office green van unloaded its humble package at Northumberland Avenue, and in the Pool such late intrusions were customarily ignored until next morning. But I was trying to change all that and, having anyway nothing else to do, I opened the envelope at once.

Two pink trace slips were pinned to the letter, each bearing a pencilled note. Head Office's notes to the Pool always had the ring of instructions addressed to an idiot. The first read, "FREWIN C presumed identical with FREWIN Cyril Arthur, Foreign Office cypher clerk," followed by Frewin's positive vetting reference and white file number, which was a cumbersome way of telling me there was nothing recorded against him. The second said, "MODRIAN S presumed identical with MODRIAN Sergei," followed by a further string of references, but I didn't bother with them. After my five years in the Russia House, Sergei Modrian was plain Sergei to me, as he had been to the rest of us: old Sergei, the crafty Armenian, head boy of Moscow Centre's generously over-staffed residence at the Soviet Embassy in London.

If I had had any lingering wish to postpone my reading of the letter till tomorrow, Sergei's name dispelled it. The letter might be bunkum, but I was playing on home ground.

To the Director,
The Security Department,
The Foreign Office,
Downing Street, SW.

Dear Sir,

This is to inform you, that C. Frewin, a Foreign Office
cypher clerk with constant and regular access to Top Secret
and Above, *has been keeping surreptitious company with*
S. Modrian, First Secretary at the Soviet Embassy in London,
for the last four years, and has not revealed same in his
annual vetting returns. Secret materials have been passed.
Mr. Modrian's whereabouts are no longer known, in view of
the fact that he has recently been recalled to the Soviet Union.
The said Frewin still resides at the Chestnuts, Beavor Drive,

Sutton, and Modrian has been present there at least on one occasion. C. Frewin is now living a highly solitary life.

Yours sincerely,
A. Patriot.

Electronically typed. Plain white A4 paper, no watermark. Dated, overpunctuated, accurately spelt and crisply folded. And no address of sender. There never is.

Having nothing much else to do that evening, I had a couple of Scotches at The Sherlock Holmes, then wandered round to Head Office, where I checked myself into the Registry reading room and drew the files. Next morning at the surgery hour of ten I took my place in Burr's waiting room, having first spelt my name to his glossy personal assistant, who seemed never to have heard of me. Brock, from Moscow Station, was ahead of me in the queue. We talked intently about cricket till his name was called, and managed not to refer to the fact that he had worked for me in the Russia House, most recently on the Blair case. A couple of minutes later, Peter Guillam drifted in clutching a bunch of files and looking hungover. He had recently become Head of Secretariat for Burr.

"Don't mind if I squeeze ahead of you, do you, old boy? I've been sent for urgently. Bloody man seems to expect me to work in my sleep. What's your problem?"

"Leprosy," I said.

There is nowhere quite like the Service—except possibly Moscow—for becoming an unperson overnight. In the upheavals that had followed Barley Blair's defection, not even Burr's predecessor, the nimble Clive, had kept his foothold on the slippery Fifth Floor deck. When last heard of, he was on his way to take up the salubrious post of Head of Station, Guyana. Only our craven legal adviser, Harry Palfrey, seemed as usual to have weathered the changes, and as I entered Burr's shiny executive suite, Palfrey was slipping stealthily out of the other door—but not quite quickly enough, so he treated me to a rhapsodic smile instead. He had recently grown himself a moustache for greater integrity.

"Ned! Marvellous! We must do that lunch," he breathed in an excited whisper, and disappeared below the waterline.

Like his office, Burr was all modern man. Where he came from was a mystery to me, but then I was no longer in the swim. Someone had told me advertising, someone else the City, someone else the Inns of Court. One wit in the Pool mailroom said he came from nowhere at all: that he had been born as found, smelling of aftershave and power, in his two-piece executive blue suit and his patent black shoes with side buckles. He was big and floating and absurdly young. Grasping his soft hand, you at once relaxed your grip for fear of denting it. He had Frewin's file in front of him on his executive desk, with my loose minute—written late last night—pinned to the cover.

"Where does the letter come from?" he demanded in his dry North Country cadence, before I had sat down.

"I don't know. It's well informed. Whoever wrote it did his homework."

"Probably Frewin's best friend," said Burr, as if that was what best friends were known for.

"He's got Modrian's dates right, he's got Frewin's access right," I said. "He knows the positive vetting routine."

"Not a work of art, though, is it? Not if you're an insider. Most likely a colleague. Or his girl. What do you want to ask me?"

I had not expected this quickfire interrogation. After six months in the Pool, I wasn't used to being hurried.

"I suppose I need to know whether you want me to pursue the case," I said.

"Why shouldn't I?"

"It's outside the Pool's normal league. Frewin's access is formidable. His section handles some of the most delicate signals traffic in Whitehall. I assumed you'd prefer to pass it to the Security Service."

"Why?"

"It's their bailiwick. If it's anything at all, it's a straight security enquiry."

"It's our information, our shout, our letter," Burr retorted with a bluntness that secretly warmed my heart. "To hell with them. When we know what we've got, we'll decide where we go with it. All that those churchy buggers across the Park can think of is a judgeproof prosecution and a bunch of medals to hand around. I collect intelligence for the marketplace. If Frewin's bad, maybe we can keep him going and turn him round. He might even get us alongside Brother Modrian back in Moscow. Who knows? The security artists don't, that's for sure."

"Then presumably you'd prefer to hand the case to the Russia House," I said doggedly.

"Why should I do that?"

I had assumed I would make an unappetising figure to him, for he was still of an age to find failure immoral. Yet he seemed to be asking me to tell him why he shouldn't count on me.

"The Pool has no charter to function operationally," I explained. "We run a front office and listen to the lonely hearts. We've no charter to conduct clandestine investigations or run agents, and no mandate to pursue suspects with Frewin's sort of access."

"You can run a phone tap, can't you?"

"If you get me a warrant I can."

"You can brief watchers, can't you? You've done that a few times, they say."

"Not unless you authorise it personally."

"Suppose I do? The Pool's also empowered to make vetting

enquiries. You can play Mr. Plod. You're good at it by all accounts. This is a vetting matter, right? And Frewin's due for a vetting top-up, right? So vet him."

"In positive vetting cases, the Pool is obliged to clear all enquiries with the Security Service in advance."

"Assume it's done."

"I can't do that unless I have it in writing."

"Oh yes you can. You're not a Service hack. You're the great Ned. You've broken as many rules as you've stuck to, you have, I've read you up. You know Modrian, too."

"Not well."

"How well?"

"I had dinner with him once and played squash with him once. That's hardly knowing him."

"Squash where?"

"At the Lansdowne."

"How did that come about?"

"Modrian was formally declared to us as the Embassy's Moscow Centre link. I was trying to put together a deal with him on Barley Blair. A swap."

"Why didn't you succeed?"

"Barley wouldn't go along with us. He'd done his own deal already. He wanted his girl, not us."

"What's his game like?"

"Tricky."

"Did you beat him?"

"Yes."

He interrupted his own flow while he looked me over. It was like being studied by a baby. "And you can handle it, can you? You're not under too much stress? You've done some good things in your time. You've a heart too, which is more than I can say for some of the capons in this outfit."

"Why should I be under stress?"

No answer. Or not yet. He seemed to be chewing at something just behind his thick lips.

"Who believes in marriage these days, for Christ's sake?" he demanded. His regional drawl had thickened. It was as if he had abandoned restraint. "If you want to live with your girl, live with her is my advice. We've cleared her, she's nobody's worry, she's not a bomb thrower or a secret sympathiser or a druggie, what's your bother? She's a nice girl in a nice way of life, and you're a lucky fellow. Do you want the case, or do you not?"

For a moment I was robbed of an answer. There was nothing surprising in Burr knowing of my affair with Sally. In our world you put those things on record before the record put them on you, and I had already endured my obligatory confessional with Personnel. No, it was Burr's capacity for intimacy that had silenced me, the speed with which he had got under my skin.

"If you'll cover me and give me the resources, of course I'll take it," I said.

"So get on with it, then. Keep me informed but not too much—don't bullshit me, always give me bad news straight. He's a man without qualities, our Cyril is. You've read Robert Musil, I dare say, haven't you?"

"I'm afraid I haven't."

He was pulling open Frewin's file. I say "pulling" because his doughy hands gave no impression of having done anything before: now we are going to see how this file opens; now we are going to address ourselves to this strange object called a pencil.

"He's got no hobbies, no stated interests beyond music, no wife, no girl, no parents, no money worries, not even any bizarre sexual appetites, poor devil," Burr complained, flipping to a different part of the file. When on earth had he found time to read it? I asked myself. I presumed the early hours. "And how the hell a man of your experience, whose job is dealing with modern civilisation and its discontentments, can manage without the wisdom of Robert Musil is a question which at a calmer moment I shall require you to answer." He licked his thumb and turned another page. "He's one of five," he said.

"I thought he was an only child."

"Not his brothers and sisters, you mug, his work. There's five clerks in his dreary cyphers office and he's one of them. They all handle the same stuff; they're all the same rank, work the same hours, think the same dirty thoughts." He looked straight at me, a thing he had not done before. "If he did it, what's his motive? The writer doesn't say. Funny, that. They usually do. Boredom—how about that? Boredom and greed, they're the only motives left these days. Plus getting even, which is eternal." He went back to the file. "Cyril's the only one not married, notice that? He's a poofter. So am I. I'm a poofter, you're a poofter. We're all poofters. It's just a question which bit of yourself ends on top. He's no hair, see that?" I caught a flash of Frewin's photograph as he waved it past me and talked on. He had a daunting energy. "Still that's no crime, I dare say, baldness, any more than marriage is. I should know, I've had three and I'm still not done. That's no normal denunciation, is it? That's why you're here. That letter knows what it's talking about. You don't think Modrian wrote it, do you?"

"Why should he have done?"

"I'm asking, Ned, don't fox with me. Wicked thoughts are what keep me going. Perhaps Modrian thought he'd leave a little confusion in his wake when he went back to Moscow. He's a scheming little monkey, Modrian, when he puts his mind to it. I've been reading him too."

When? I thought again. When on earth did you find the time?

For another twenty minutes he zigzagged back and forth tossing possibilities at me, seeing how they came back. And when I finally stepped exhausted into the anteroom, I walked straight into Peter Guillam again.

"Who the hell is Leonard Burr?" I asked him, still dazed.

Peter was astonished that I didn't know. "Burr? My dear chap. Leonard was Smiley's Crown Prince for years. George rescued him from a fate worse than death at All Souls."

Of Sally, my reigning extramarital girlfriend, what should I tell you? She was free, and spoke to the captive in me. Monica had been within my walls. Monica was a woman of the Service, bound and not bound to me by the same set of rules. But to Sally I was just a middle-aged civil servant who had forgotten to have any fun. She was a designer and sometime dancer whose passion was theatre, and she thought the rest of life unreal. She was tall and she was fair and rather wise, and sometimes I think she must have reminded me of Stefanie.

"Meet you, skipper?" Gorst cried over the telephone. "Top up our Cyril? It'll be my pleasure, sir!"

We met the next day in a Foreign Office interviewing room. I was Captain York, another dreary vetting officer doing his rounds. Gorst was head of Frewin's Cypher Section, which was better known as the Tank: a lecher in a beadle's suit, waddling, smirking man with prising elbows and a tiny mouth that wriggled like a worm. When he sat, he scooped up the skirts of his jacket as if he were exposing himself from behind. Then he kicked out a plump leg like a chorus girl, before laying it suggestively over the thigh of the other.

"Saint Cyril, that's what we call Mr. Frewin," he announced blithely. "Doesn't drink, doesn't smoke, doesn't swear, certified virgin. End of vetting interview." Extracting a cigarette from a packet of ten, he tapped the tip of it on his thumbnail, then moistened it with his busy tongue. "Music's his only weakness. Loves the *operah*. Goes to the *operah* regular as clockwork. Never cared for it myself. Can't make out whether it's actors singing or singers acting." He lit his cigarette. I could smell the lunchtime beer on his breath. "I'm not too fond of fat women, either, to be frank. Specially when they scream at me." He tipped his head back and blew out smoke rings, savouring them as if they were emblems of his authority.

"May I ask how Frewin gets on with the rest of the staff these days?" I said, playing the honest journeyman as I turned a page of my notebook.

"Swimmingly, your grace. Par-fectly."

"The archivists, registrars, secretaries—no trouble on that front?"

"Not a finger. Not a mini-digit."

"You all sit together?"

"In a big room and I'm the titular head of it. Very *tit*-ular indeed."

"And I've had it said to me he's something of a misogynist," I said, fishing.

Gorst gave a shrill laugh. "Cyril? A *misogynist*? Bollocks. He just hates the girls. Won't speak to them, not apart from good morning. Won't come to the pre-Christmas party if he can help it, in case he has to kiss them under the mistletoe." He recrossed his legs, indicating that he had decided to make a statement. "Cyril Arthur Frewin—Saint Cyril—is a highly reliable, eminently conscientious, totally bald, incredibly boring clerk of the old school. Saint Cyril, though punctilious to a fault, has in my view reached his natural promotion ceiling in his line of country or profession. Saint Cyril is set in his ways. Saint Cyril does what he does, one hundred percent. Amen."

"Politics?"

"Not in my house, thank you."

"And he's not workshy?"

"Did I say he was, squire?"

"No, to the contrary, I was quoting from the file. If there's extra work to be done, Cyril will always roll his sleeves up, stay on the lunch hour, the evenings and so forth. That's still the case, is it? No slackening off of his enthusiasm?"

"Our Cyril is ready to oblige at all hours, to the pleasure of those who have families, wives or a nice piece of Significant Other to return to. He'll do the early mornings, he'll do lunch hours, he'll do evening watch, except for *operah* nights, of course. Cyril never counts the cost. Latterly, I will admit, he has been slightly less inclined to martyr himself, but that is no doubt a purely temporary suspension of service. Our Cyril does have his little moods. Who does not, your eminence?"

"So recently a slackening off, you would say?"

"Not of his work, never. Cyril is your total workslave, always has been. Merely of his willingness to be put upon by his more human colleagues. Come five-thirty these days, Saint Cyril packs up his desk and goes home with the rest of us. He does not, for instance, offer to replace the late shift and remain solo incommunicado till nine o'clock and lock up, which was what he used to do."

"You can't put a date to that change of habit, can you?" I enquired as boringly as I could manage, turning dutifully to a fresh page of my notebook.

Curiously enough, Gorst could. He pursed his lips. He frowned. He raised his girlish eyebrows and pressed his chins into his grimy shirt collar. He made a vast show of ruminating. And he finally remembered. "The last time Cyril Frewin did young Burton's evening watch was Midsummer's Day. I keep a log, you see. Security. I also have quite an impressive memory, which I don't always care to reveal."

I was secretly impressed, but not by Gorst. Three days after Modrian left London for Moscow, Cyril Frewin had ceased to work late, I was thinking. I had other questions that were clamouring to be asked. Did the Tank boast electronic typewriters? Did the cypher clerks have access to them? Did Gorst? But I was afraid of arousing his suspicions.

"You mentioned his love of the opera," I said. "Could you tell me a little more about that?"

"No, I could not, since we do not get blow-by-blow accounts, and we do not ask for them. However, he does come in wearing a pressed dark suit on his *operah* days, if he doesn't bring his dinner jacket in a suitcase, and he does impart what I would refer to as a state of high if controlled excitement somewhat similar to other forms of anticipation, which I will not mention."

"But he has a regular seat, for instance? A subscription seat? It's only for the record. As you say, he's a bit short of relaxing pastimes otherwise."

"As I think I told you, squire, alas, me and *operah* were not made for each other. Put down 'opera buff' on his form and you're covered for your relaxing pastime is my advice."

"Thank you. I will." I turned another page. "And really no enemies that you can think of?" I said, my pencil hovering over my notebook.

Gorst became serious. The beer was wearing off. "Cyril is laughed at, Captain, I'll admit. But he takes it in good part. Cyril is not disliked."

"No one who would speak ill of him, for instance?"

"I can think of no single reason whatever why anyone should speak ill of Cyril Arthur Frewin. The British civil servant, he may be sullen but he's not malicious. Cyril does his duty, as we all do. We're a happy ship. I wouldn't mind if you put that down, too."

"I gather he went to Salzburg for Christmas this year. And previous years too, is that right?"

"That is correct. Cyril always takes his leave at Christmas. He goes to Salzburg, he hears the music. It's the one point on which he will make no concession to the rest of the Tank. There's some of the young ones try to complain about it, but I won't let them. 'Cyril makes it up to you in other ways,' I tell them. 'Cyril's got his seniority, he loves his trip to Salzburg for the music, he has his little ways, and that's how it's going to stay.'"

"Does he leave a holiday address behind when he goes?"

Gorst didn't know, but at my request he telephoned his personnel department and obtained it. The same hotel, the last four years running. He's been keeping company with Modrian for four years too, I thought, remembering the letter. Four years of Salzburg, four years of Modrian, ending in *a highly solitary life.*

"Does he take a friend, would you know?"

"Cyril never had a friend in his life, skipper." Gorst yawned. "Not one he'd take on holiday, that's for sure. Shall we do lunch next time? They tell me you boys have very nifty expense accounts when you care to give them a tickle."

"Does he talk about his Salzburg trips at all when he comes back? The fun he's had—the music he's heard—anything like that?" Thanks to Sally, I suppose, I had learned that people were expected to have fun.

Having made a brief show of thinking, Gorst shook his head. "If Cyril has fun, squire, it's very, very private," he said with a last smirk.

That wasn't Sally's idea of fun at all.

From my office at the Pool I booked a secure line to Vienna and spoke to Toby Esterhase, who with his infinite talent for survival had recently been made Head of Station.

"I want you to shake out the Weisse Rose in Salzburg for me, Toby. Cyril Frewin, British subject. Stayed there every Christmas for the last four years. I want to know when he arrived, how long he stayed, whether he's stayed there before, who with, how much the bills come to and what he gets up to. Concert tickets, excursions, meals, women, boys, celebrations—anything you can get. But don't raise local eyebrows, whatever you do. Be a divorce agent or something."

Toby was predictably appalled. "Ned, listen to me. Ned, this is actually completely impossible. I'm in Vienna, okay? Salzburg, that's like the other side of the globe. This city is buzzing like a beehouse. I need more staff, Ned. You got to tell Burr. He doesn't understand the pressures here. Get me two more guys, we do anything you want, no problem. Sorry."

He asked for a week. I said three days. He said he'd try his best and I believed him. He said he had heard a rumour that Mabel and I had broken up. I denied it.

Ever since I can remember, watchers have been most at home in condemned houses handy for bus routes and the airport. Monty's choice for his own headquarters was an unlikely Edwardian palazzo in Baron's Court. From the tiled hall, a stone staircase curled grandly through five pokey floors to a stained-glass sky-light. As I climbed, doors flew open and shut like a French farce as his strange crew, in varying stages of undress, scurried between changing room, cafeteria and briefing room, their eyes averted from the stranger. I arrived in a garret once a painter's studio. Somewhere a women's foursome was playing noisy Ping-Pong. Closer at hand, two male voices were singing Blake's "Jerusalem" under the shower.

I had not set eyes on Monty for a long time, but neither the years between nor his promotion to Head Watcher had aged him. A few grey hairs, a sharper edge to his hollow cheeks. He was not a natural conversationalist, and for a while we just sat and sipped our tea.

"Frewin, then," he said finally.

"Frewin," I said.

Like a marksman, Monty had a way of making his own particular area of quiet. "Frewin's a funny one, Ned. He's not being normal. Now of course we don't know what normal is, do we, not really, not for Cyril, not apart from what you pick up from hearsay and that. Postman, milkman, neighbours, the usual. Everyone talks to a window cleaner, you'd be amazed. Or a Telecom engineer who's lost his way with a junction box. We've only been on him two days, all the same."

With Monty, when he talked like this, you just pinned your ears back and bided your time.

"And nights, of course," he added. "If you count nights. Cyril's not sleeping, that's for sure. More prowling, judging by his windows and his teacups in the morning. And the music. One of his neighbours is thinking of complaining to him. She never has before, but she might this time. 'Whatever's come over him?' she says. 'Handel for breakfast is one thing, but Handel at three in the morning's a bit of another.' She thinks he's having his change. She says men get like that at his age, same as women. We wouldn't know about that, would we?"

I grinned. And again bided my time. "*She* does, though," Monty said reflectively. "Her old man's gone off with a supply teacher from the comprehensive. She's not at all sure she'll have him back. Nearly raped our pretty boy who'd come to read the meter. Here—how's Mabel?" he demanded.

I wondered whether he too had heard the rumour; but I decided that if he had, he would not have asked me. "Fine," I said.

"Cyril used to take a newspaper on the train. The *Telegraph,* need you ask. Cyril doesn't hold with Labour—he says they're common. But he doesn't buy a paper any more. He sits. Sits and stares. That's all he does. Our bloke had to give him a nudge yesterday when they pulled up at Victoria. He'd gone off in a daydream. Going home last night, he tapped out the whole score of an opera on his briefcase. Nancy says it was Vivaldi. I suppose she knows. Remember Pauli Skordeno?"

I said I did. Diversions were part of Monty's way. Like, "How's Mabel?" for instance.

"Pauli's doing seven years in Barbados for bothering a bank. What gets into them, Ned? He never put a foot wrong while he was watching. Never late, never naughty with his expenses, lovely memory, lovely eye, good nose. Burglaries galore we did. London, the Home Counties, the Midlands, the civil-rights boys, the disarmers, the Party, the naughty diplomats—we did the lot. Did Pauli ever get rumbled? Not once. The moment he goes private, he's all fingers and thumbs and boasting to the bloke next door to him in the bar. I think they *want* to be caught, that's my opinion. I think it's wanting recognition after all the years of being nobody."

He sipped his tea. "Cyril's other kick, apart from music, is his radio. He loves his radio. Only receiving, mind, as far as anybody knows. But he's got one of those fancy German sets with the fine tuning and big speakers for his concerts, and he didn't buy it locally because when it went on the blink the local shop had to send it off to Wiesbaden. Three months it took, and cost a fortune. He doesn't run a car, he doesn't hold with them. He shops by bus Saturday mornings, he's a stay-at-home except for his Christmases in Austria. No pets, he doesn't mix. Entertaining, forget it. No house-guests, lodgers, receives no mail except the bills, pays everything regular, doesn't vote, doesn't go to church, doesn't have a television. His cleaning lady says he reads a lot, mainly big books. She only comes once a week, usually when he's not there, and we didn't dare get close to her. A big book for her is anything bigger than a Bible-study pamphlet. His phone bills are modest, he's got six thousand in a building society, owns his house and maintains a well-managed bank account fluctuating between six and fourteen hundred, except Christmas times when it drops to around two hundred because of his holiday."

Monty's sense of the proprieties again required us to make a detour, this time to discuss our children. My son Adrian had just won a modern languages scholarship to Cambridge, I said. Monty was hugely impressed. Monty's only son had just passed his law exam with flying colours. We agreed that kids were what made life worth living.

"Modrian," I said when the formalities were once more over. "Sergei."

"I remember the gentleman well, Ned. We all do. We used to follow him round the clock some days. Except at Christmas, of course, when he took his home leave. . . . Hullo! Are you thinking what I'm thinking? We all take leave at Christmas?"

"It had crossed my mind," I said.

"We didn't even bother to pretend with Modrian, not after a while, you couldn't. *Oh,* he was a slippery eel, though. I could have walloped him sometimes, I really could. Pauli Skordeno got so angry with him once he let his tyres down outside the Victoria and Albert while he was inside sussing out a dead-letter box. I never reported it, I didn't have the heart."

"Am I not right in thinking Modrian was also an opera buff, Monty?"

Monty's eyes became quite round, and I had the rare pleasure of seeing him surprised.

"Oh my Lord, Ned," he exclaimed. "Oh dear, oh dear. You're right. Sergei was a Covent Garden subscriber—of course he was, same as Cyril. We must have taken him there and fetched him—oh, a dozen times. He could have used a cab if he'd had any mercy, but he never did. He liked wearing us out in the traffic."

"If we could know the performances he went to, and where he

sat—if you could get them—we could try and match them up with Frewin's."

Monty had fallen into a theatrical silence. He frowned, then scratched his head. "You don't think this is all a touch too *easy* for us, do you, Ned?" he asked. "I get suspicious when everything fits in a pretty pattern, don't you?"

"I won't be part of your pattern," Sally had said to me the night before. "Patterns are for breaking."

"He *sings,* Ned," Mary Lasselles murmured while she arranged my white tulips in a pickle jar. "He sings *all* the time. Night and day, it doesn't matter. I think he missed his vocation."

Mary was as pale as a nightnurse and as dedicated. A luminous virtue lit her unpowdered face and shone from her clear eyes. A shock of white, like the mark of early widowhood, capped her bobbed hair.

Of the many callings that comprise the over-world of intelligence, none requires as much devotion as that of the sisterhood of listeners. Men are no good at it. Only women are capable of such passionate espousal of the destiny of others. Condemned to windowless cellars, engulfed by tracks of grey-clad cable and banks of Russian-style tape recorders, they occupy a nether region populated by absent lives which they know more intimately than those of their closest friends or relations. They never see their quarries, never meet them, never touch them or sleep with them. Yet the whole force of their personalities is beamed upon these secret loves. On microphones and telephones they hear them blandish, weep, smoke, eat, argue and couple. They hear them cook, belch, snore and worry. They endure their children, in-laws and babysitters without complaint, as well as their tastes in television. These days, they even ride with them in cars, take them shopping, sit with them in cafés and bingo halls. They are the secret sharers of the trade.

Passing me a pair of earphones, Mary put on her own and, folding her hands beneath her chin, closed her eyes for better listening. So I heard Cyril Frewin's voice for the first time, singing himself a passage from *Turandot* while Mary Lasselles with her eyes shut smiled in her enchantment. His voice was mellow and, to my untutored ear, as pleasing as it clearly was to Mary.

I sat up straight. The singing had stopped. I heard a woman's voice in the background, then a man's, and they were speaking Russian.

"Mary, who the hell's that?"

"His teachers, darling. Radio Moscow's Olga and Boris, five days a week, six A.M. sharp. This is yesterday morning."

"You mean he's teaching himself *Russian*?"

"Well, he listens to it, darling. How much of it is going into his little head is anybody's guess. Every morning, sharp at six, Cyril does his Olga and Boris. They're visiting the Kremlin today. Yesterday they were shopping at Gum."

I heard Frewin mutter unintelligibly in the bath, I heard him call out "Mother" in the night, while he tossed restlessly in bed: FREWIN Ella, I remembered, deceased, mother to FREWIN Cyril Arthur, q.v. I have never understood why Registry insists on opening personal files for the dead relatives of suspected spies.

I listened to him arguing with the British Telecom engineers' department after he had waited the statutory twenty minutes to be connected with them. His voice was edgy, full of unexpected emphases.

"Well, *next* time you elect to identify a *fault* on my line, I would be *highly* grateful if you would kindly inform *me* as the subscriber *prior* to barging into my house when my cleaning woman happens to be in, and leaving particles of *wire* on the carpets and *boot*marks on the kitchen *floor* . . ."

I listened to him phone the Covent Garden opera house to say he would not be taking up his subscription ticket this Friday. This time his tone was self-pitying. He explained that he was ill. The kind lady on the other end said there was a lot of it about.

I listened to him talking to the butcher in anticipation of my visit, which Foreign Office Personnel had set for tomorrow morning at his house.

"Mr. Steele, this is Mr. Cyril Frewin. Good morning. I shall *not* be able to come *in* to you on Saturday, owing to the fact that I have a conference at my *house*. I would therefore be *grateful* if you would kindly deliver four *good* lamb chops for me on the Friday evening as you pass by on your way home. Will that be convenient, Mr. Steele? Also a jar of your pre-mixed mint *sauce*. No, I have red currant jelly already, thank you. Will you attach your *bill*, please?"

To my over-acute ear, he sounded like a man preparing to abandon ship.

"I'll take the engineers again, please, Mary," I said. Having twice more listened to Frewin's dogmatic tones of complaint to British Telecom, I gave her a distracted kiss and stepped into the evening air. Sally had said, "Come round," but I was in no mood to spend an evening professing love to her and listening to music I secretly detested.

I returned to the Pool. The Service laboratories had completed their examination of the anonymous letter. A Markus electronic, model number so-and-so, probably Belgian manufacture, new or little used, was the best they could suggest. They believed they would be able to identify another document issuing from the same machine. Could I get one? End of report. The laboratories were still wrestling with the characteristics of the new generation of machines.

I rang Monty at his lair in Baron's Court. Frewin's complaint to the engineers was still ringing in my memory: his pauses, like unnatural commas, his use of the word *highly,* his habit of punching the unlikely word to achieve vindictive emphasis.

"Did your fellows notice a typewriter in Cyril's house, Monty, by any chance, while they were kindly mending his telephone?" I asked.

"No, Ned. There was no typewriter, Ned—not one they saw, put it that way."

"Could they have missed it?"

"Easily, Ned. It was soft-pedalling only. No opening desks or cupboards, no photographing, not too much familiarity with his cleaning lady either, or she'll worry afterwards. It was 'See what you can, get out fast, and be sure you leave a mess or he'll smell a rat.'"

I thought of phoning Burr, but I didn't. My case officer's possessiveness was taking over, and I was damned if I was going to share Frewin with anyone, not even the man who had entrusted him to me. A hundred twisted threads were running through my head, from Modrian to Gorst to Boris and Olga to Christmas to Salzburg to Sally. In the end, I wrote Burr a minute setting out most of what I had discovered and confirming that I would "make a first reconnaissance" of Frewin tomorrow morning when I interviewed him for his routine vetting clearance.

To go home? To go to Sally? Home was a hateful little service flat in St. James's, where I was supposed to be sorting myself out—though that's the last thing any man does when he sits alone with a bottle of Scotch and a reproduction painting of *The Laughing Cavalier,* dithering between his dreams of freedom and his addiction to what holds him prisoner. Sally was my Alternative Life, but I knew already I was too set to jump the wall and reach it.

Preferring to remain at my desk, therefore, I fetched myself a whisky from the safe and browsed through Modrian's file. It told me nothing I didn't already know, but I wanted him at the front of my head. Sergei Modrian, tried and tested Moscow Centre professional. A charmer, a bit of a dancer, a befriender, a smiling Armenian with a mercury tongue. I had liked him. He had liked me. In our profession, since we may like no one beyond a point, we can forgive a lot for charm.

My direct line was ringing. I thought for a moment it would be Sally, for contrary to regulations I had given her the number. It was Toby and he sounded pleased with himself. He usually did. He didn't mention Frewin by name. He didn't mention Salzburg. I guessed he was ringing from his flat, and I'd a shrewd notion he was in bed and not alone.

"Ned? Your man's a joke. Books himself a single room for two weeks, checks in, pays his two weeks in advance, gives the staff their Christmas box, pats the kids, makes nice to everybody. Next morning he disappears, does it every year. Ned, can you hear me? Listen, the guy's crazy. No phone calls out, one meal, two *Apfelsaft,* no explanations, taxi to the station. Keep my room, don't let it, maybe I'll be back tomorrow, maybe in a few days, I don't know. After twelve days, back he comes, no explanations, tips the staff some more, everybody happy like a heathen. They call him 'the ghost.' Ned, you got to talk nice to Burr for me. You owe me now. Toby works his fingers to the bone, tell him. Old star like you, a young fellow like Burr, he'll listen to you, costs you nothing. I need another man out here, maybe two. Tell him, Ned, hear me? Cheers."

I stared at the wall, the one I couldn't scale; I stared at Modrian's file, I remembered Monty's dictum about too easy. I suddenly wanted Sally terribly, and had some cloudy notion that by solving the mystery of Frewin I would convert my recurring spurts for freedom into one bold leap. But as I reached for the phone to talk to her, it started to ring again.

"They fit," said Monty in a flat voice. He had managed to check Frewin's opera attendance. "It's Sergei and Cyril every time. When *he* goes, so does *he*. When *he* doesn't, neither does *he*. Maybe that's why *he* doesn't go any more. Got it?"

"And the seats?" I asked.

"Side by side, darling. What do you expect? Front to back?"

"Thanks, Monty," I said.

Do I have to tell you how I spent that interminable night? Have you never telephoned your own son, listened to his unhappy jibes and had to remind yourself that he is yours? Talked frankly to an understanding wife about your inadequacies, not knowing what on earth they were? Have you never reached out for your mistress, cried "I love you" and remained a mystified spectator to her untroubled fulfillment, before leaving her once more, to walk the London streets as if they were a foreign city? Have you never, from all the other sounds of dawn, picked out the wet chuckle of a magpie and fixed on it for your whole life long while you lie wide-eyed on your beastly single bed?

I arrived at Frewin's house at half past nine, having dressed myself as boringly as I could contrive, and that must have been boringly indeed, for I am not a natty dresser at the best of times, though Sally has appalling ideas about how she might improve my style. Frewin and I had agreed on ten but I told myself I wanted the element of surprise. Perhaps the truth was, I needed his company. A postman's van was parked up the street. A builder's truck with an aerial stood beyond it, telling me Monty's men were at their posts.

I forgot what month it was but I know it was autumn, both in my private life and in the prim cul-de-sac of steep brick houses. For I see a disc of white sun hanging behind the pollarded chestnut trees that had given the place its name, and I smell to this day the scent of bonfires and autumn air in my nostrils urging me to leave London, leave the Service, take to Sally and the world's real countryside. And I remember the whirr of small birds as they lifted from Frewin's telephone line on their way to somewhere better. And a cat in the next-door garden rising on its rear paws to box a drowsy butterfly.

I dropped the latch to the garden gate and crunched up the prim gravel path to the Seven Dwarfs semi-detached, with its bottle-glass windows and thatched porch. I reached out my hand for the bell, but the front door flew away from me. It was ribbed, and studded with fake coach bolts, and it shot back as if it had been blasted by a street bomb, almost sucking me after it into the dark tiled hall. Then the door stood still, and Frewin stood beside it, a bald centurion to his own endangered house.

He was taller than I had realised by a wrestler's head. His thick shoulders were braced to receive my attack, his eyes were fixed on me in scared hostility. Yet even at this first moment of encounter I sensed no contest in him, only a sort of heroic vulnerability made tragic by his bulk. I entered his house, and knew I was entering a madness. I had known it all night long. In desperation we find a natural kinship with the mad. I had known that for much longer.

"Captain York? Yes, well, welcome, sir. Welcome indeed. Personnel of their goodness *did* advise me you were coming. They don't always. But this time they did. Come in, please. You have your *duty* to do, Captain, as I have mine." His vast, soggy hands were lifted for my coat but seemed unable to grapple with it. So they hovered above my neck as if to strangle or embrace me while he went on talking. "We're all on the same side and no hard feelings, I say. I liken your job to airport security, personally, it's the same parameters. If they don't search *me,* they won't search the villains either, will they? It's the logical approach to the matter, in my view."

Heaven knows what lost original he thought he was copying as he delivered these over-prepared words, but at least they freed him from his frozen state. His hands descended to my coat and helped me out of it, and I can feel now the reverence with which they did so, as if unveiling something exciting to us both.

"You fly a lot then, do you, Mr. Frewin?" I asked.

He hung my coat on a hanger, and the hanger on a vile reproduction coat-tree. I waited for an answer but none came. I was thinking of his air travel to Salzburg, and I wonder whether he was too, and whether his conscience was speaking out of him in the tension of my arrival. He marched ahead of me to the drawing room, where by the light of the leaded bay window I was able to examine him at my ease, for he was already busy with the next article of his urgent hospitality: this time, an electric coffee percolator filled but not switched on—did I want the milk, or the sugar or the both, Captain? And the milk, Captain, was it hot or cold? And how about a home-made biscuit for you, Captain?

"You really made them yourself?" I asked as I fished one from the jar.

"Any fool who can read can cook," said Frewin, with a chaotic grin of superiority, and I could see at once why Gorst would loathe him.

"Well, I can read, but I certainly can't cook," I replied, with a rueful shake of my head.

"What's your first name, Captain?"

"Ned," I replied.

"Well, that's because you're married, Ned, I expect. Your wife has robbed you of your self-sufficiency. I've seen it too often in life. In comes the wife, out goes the independence. I'm Cyril."

And you're ducking my question about your air travel, I

thought, refusing to allow him this attempted incursion into my private territory.

"If *I* ran this country," Frewin announced over his shoulder to me while he poured, "which I am pleased to say I shall never have the opportunity to *do*"—his voice was acquiring the didactic drumbeat of his conversation with the engineers—"I would make an *absolute* law that *everyone,* regardless of colour, sex or creed, would take *cooking* as an obligatory subject *while* at school."

"Good idea," I said, accepting a mug of coffee, "very sound," and helped myself to sugar from the yellow beehive pot, which nestled like a missile in his damp paw. He had turned to me all at once, shoulders, waist and head together. His bare eyes, unfringed and unprotected, gazed down on me with a radiant and doting innocence.

"Play any games at all, Ned?" he enquired softly, tipping his head to one side for added confidentiality.

"A spot of golf, Cyril," I lied. "How about you?"

"Hobbies at all, Ned?"

"Well, I do like to do the odd watercolour when I'm on holiday," I said, borrowing again from Mabel.

"Drive a car, do you, Ned? I expect you boys have to have all the skills at your fingertips, don't you?"

"Just an old Rover."

"What year is it, then? What vintage, Ned? There's many a good tune played on an old fiddle, they say."

His energy was not just in his person, I realised as I gave him the first date that occurred to me; it spilled into every object that came within his sphere. Into the reproduction horse-brasses that glistened like military cap-badges from his vigorous polishing. Into the polished fire grate and wood fire and the resplendent surface of his dining table. Into the very chair where I now sat and meekly sipped my coffee, for its arms were concealed in linen covers so pressed and spotless that I was reluctant to put hands on them. And I knew without his telling me that, cleaning woman or none, he tended all these things himself, that he was their servant and dictator, in the kingdom of his boundless wasted energy.

"Where do you live then, Ned?"

"Me? Oh well, London, really."

"What part then, Ned? What district? Somewhere nice, or do you have to be slightly anonymous for your work?"

"Well, we're not really allowed to say, I'm afraid."

"London born, are you? Hastings, me."

"Sort of suburbs. You know. Pinner, say."

"You must retain your discretion, Ned. Always. Your discretion is your dignity. Let nobody take it from you. It's your professional integrity, discretion is. Remember that. It could come in handy."

"Thanks," I said, affecting a sheepish laugh. "I will."

He was feeding on me with his eyes. He reminded me of my dog Lizzie when she watches me for a signal—unblinking body ready to go. "Shall we start, then?" he said. "Want to sound the 'off'? As soon as it's official, tell me. 'Cyril. The red light's on.' That's all you have to say."

I laughed, shaking my head again, as if to say he was a card.

"It's only routine, Cyril," I said. "My goodness, you must know the questions by heart after all these years. Mind if I smoke?" I laboriously lit my pipe and dropped the match into the ashtray he was pressing on me. Then I resumed my study of his room. Along the walls, do-it-yourself shelves filled with do-it-yourself books, every one of them of global resonance: *The World's One Hundred Greatest Men; Gems of All the World's Literature; Music of the Great Ages in Three Volumes.* Next to them, his gramophone records in cases, all classical. And in the corner, the gramophone itself, a splendid teak affair with more control buttons than a simpleton like myself could master.

"Well now, if you like painting watercolours, Ned, why don't you try the music too?" he suggested, following my eye. "It's the finest consolation in the world, good music is, properly played, if you choose right. I could put you on the right lines if you wanted."

I puffed for a while. A pipe is a great weapon for playing slow against someone else's haste. "I rather think I'm tone deaf, actually, Cyril. I have made the occasional effort, but I don't know, I sort of lose heart really . . ."

My heresy—drawn, I am afraid, from inconclusive debates I had had with Sally—was already too much for him. He had sprung to his feet, his face a mask of horror and concern as he seized the biscuit jar and thrust it at me as if only food would save me.

"Now, Ned, that is not *right,* if I may say so! There is no such *thing* as a tone-deaf *person*! Take two, go on, there's plenty more in the kitchen."

"I'll stick to my pipe if you don't mind."

"Tone deafness, Ned, is merely a *term,* an expression, I will go so far as to say an excuse, designed to cover up, to disguise; a purely *temporary,* self-imposed *psychological* resistance to a certain world which your conscious mind is refusing you permission to enter! It is *merely* a fear of the unknown which is holding you *back*. Let me give you the example of certain acquaintances of mine . . ."

He ran on and I let him, while he dabbed at me with his forefinger, and with the other hand clutched the biscuit jar against his heart. I listened to him, I watched him, I expressed my admiration at the appropriate moments. I fished for my black notebook and removed the garter of black elastic from it as a signal to him that I was ready to begin, but he ignored me and ranted on. I imagined Mary Lasselles in her lair, smiling dreamily while her loved one lectured me. And Monty's boys and girls in their surveillance vans outside, cursing him and yawning while they waited to change shifts. For all I knew, Burr too—all of them hostages to Frewin's endless anecdote about a married couple he had had for neighbours when he lived in Surbiton, whom he had taught to share his musical appreciation.

"Anyway, I can tell my masters at PVHQ that music is still your great love," I suggested with a smile when he had finished.

"PV" for Positive Vetting, you understand, and "HQ" for Headquarters. My part as the downtrodden security workhorse required a higher authority than my own. Then, opening the notebook on my knee, I spread the pages, and with my unpainted government-issue pencil wrote the name FREWIN at the top of the left-hand page.

"Ah well, if you're talking about *love,* Ned—you *could* say music *was* my great love, yes. And music, to quote the bard, is the *food* of love. However, I'd *prefer* to say, it depends how you *define* love. What is love? That's your real question, Ned. *Define love*."

God's coincidences are sometimes too vulgar to be borne. "Well, I suppose *I* define it rather broadly," I said doubtfully, my pencil poised. "How do *you* define it?"

He shook his head and began energetically stirring his coffee, all his thick fingers gathered round the neck of one tiny Apostle spoon.

"Is this on the record?" he asked.

"It could be. Please yourself."

"Commitment is how *I* define love. A great *number* of people speak of *love* as if it were some kind of *nirvana*. It isn't. I happen to know that. Love is not *separate* from life. It's not *beyond* it or *superior* to it. Love is *within* life. Love is totally *integral* to life, and what you get out of it depends on the ways and means whereby you invest your *efforts* and your loyalty. Our Lord taught us that *perfectly* clearly, not that I'm a God-man personally, I'm a rationalist. Love is *sacrifice* and love is hard work. Love is *also* sweat and tears, exactly as your great music has to be in order to qualify. By that token, yes, I'll grant you, Ned, music is my first love, if you follow me."

I was following him only too well. I had made similar half-hearted representations to Sally, only to have them swept aside. I knew also that in his beleaguered state of mind there was no such thing to him as a casual question, let alone a casual answer—any more than there was to me, even if my systems of concealment were more sophisticated than his.

"I don't think I'll write that down," I said. "I think I'll regard it as what we call deep background." In earnest of which, I pencilled a couple of words in the notebook, as a memo to myself and a sign to him that we were going on the record. "All right, let's do the meat-and-potatoes-work first," I suggested, "or PVHQ will say I'm dragging my feet as usual. Have you joined the Communist Party since you were last spoken to by one of our representatives, Cyril, or have you managed to restrain yourself?"

"I have not," he said, with a smirk.

"Haven't joined or haven't restrained yourself?"

A broader smirk. "The first. I like you, Ned. I cherish wit when I find it, I always have done. Not that we're overburdened with it at my place of work. Where wit's concerned, I'd be inclined to refer to the Tank as a total desert."

"No friendship or peace groups?" I continued, affecting disappointment. "Fellow-travelling organisations? Taken out membership to any homosexual or otherwise deviant-oriented clubs, formed a secret passion for any under-age choirboys lately?"

"No to the lot, thank you," said Frewin, now smiling broadly.

"Run up vast debts, causing you to live beyond your means? Set up some tasteful redhead in the style to which she is not accustomed? Acquired a Ferrari motorcar on the hire purchase?"

"My needs remain as modest as they have always been, thank

you. I am not of a materialist or self-indulgent nature, as you may have gathered. I rather abhor materialism, frankly. There's too much of it these days. Far."

"And no to the rest?"

"All no."

I was jotting all the time, making annotations against an imaginary checklist.

"So you wouldn't be flogging secrets for money, then," I commented, turning a page and adding a couple of ticks. "And you have not launched yourself upon a course of foreign language instruction without first obtaining the consent of your employing department in writing, I take it?" My pencil was poised once more. "Sanskrit? Hebrew? Urdu? Serbo-Croat?" I suggested. "Russian?"

He was standing very still and staring at me, but I pretended to be unaware of this.

"Hottentot?" I continued facetiously. "Estonian?"

"Since when's *that* been on the list?" Frewin demanded aggressively.

"Hottentot?"

I waited.

"Languages. A language isn't a defect. It's an attribute. An accomplishment! You don't have to list all your accomplishments, just to get cleared!"

I tilted back my head in reminiscence. "Addendum to the Positive Vetting procedure, November, 1967," I recited. "I always remember that one. Fireworks Day. Special circular to all employing departments, yours included, requiring advance notice in writing of all intended language instruction courses. Recommended by Judicial Steering Committee, approved by Cabinet."

He had turned his back to me. "I regard this as a totally out-of-court question and I refuse to answer it in any shape or form. Write that down."

I puffed through my pipe smoke.

"I said write it down!"

"I wouldn't say that, Cyril, if I were you. They'll be cross with you."

"Let them be."

I drew on my pipe again. "I'll put it to you the way HQ put it to me, shall I? 'What's all this nonsense Cyril's been getting up to with his chums Boris and Olga?' they said. 'Ask him that one— then see what he comes up with.'"

Still turned away from me, he was scowling indignantly from place to place around the room, appealing to his polished world to witness my profanity. I waited for the explosion I was sure would come. But instead he peered at me in hurt reproach. *Us,* he was saying, *friends—and you do this to me.* And in the way that the brain in stress can handle a multitude of images at once, I saw before me, not Frewin, but a typist I had once interrogated in our Embassy in Ankara: how she had rolled back the sleeve of her cardigan and thrust out her arm at me and showed me the festering cigarette burns she had inflicted on herself the night before our interview. "Don't you think you have made me suffer enough?" she asked. Yet it was not I who had made her suffer; it was the twenty-five-year-old Polish diplomat for whom she had sacrificed every secret she possessed.

I took my pipe from my mouth and gave him a reassuring laugh. "Come on, Cyril. Aren't Boris and Olga two of the characters on this Russian course you're doing on the sly? Papering their house together? Going off to stay at Auntie Tanya's dacha, all that? You're doing the standard Radio Moscow language course, five days a week, six A.M. sharp, that's what they told me. 'Ask him about Boris and Olga,' they say. 'Ask him why he's learning Russian on the q.t.' So I'm asking you. That's all."

"They'd no business knowing I was doing that course," he muttered, still grappling with the implications of my question.

"Bloody sniffer dogs. It was private. Privately selected, privately pursued. They can get lost. So can you."

I laughed. But I was also put out. "Now don't be like that, Cyril. You know the rules as well as I do. It's not your style to ignore a regulation. It's not mine either. Russian is Russian, and reporting is reporting. It's only a matter of getting it down in writing. I didn't make up the regulations. I get a brief, the same as anyone else." I was talking to his back again. He had taken refuge at the bay window, and was gazing out at the rectangle that was his garden.

"What's their names?" he demanded.

"Olga and Boris," I repeated patiently.

This enraged him. "The people who brief you, idiot! I'm going to enter a complaint about them! Snooping, that's what it is. It's bloody brutal in this day and age. I'm holding you to blame too, frankly. What's their names?"

I still didn't answer him. I preferred to let the fury bank up in him.

"Number one," he announced in a louder voice, still staring at his mud patch. "Are you writing this down? Number one, I am not taking a language course within the meaning of the Act. A language course is going to a school or class, it is sitting on a bench with a bunch of snivelling typists with bad breath, it is submitting to the sneers of an uncouth instructor. Number two. I *do,* however, listen to *radio,* it being one of my *continuing* pleasures to scan the wavebands for examples of the quaint or esoteric. Write that down and I'll sign it. Finish, okay? Then take yourself off. I'm done with you, thank you up to here. Nothing personal. It's them."

"Which was how you stumbled on Boris and Olga," I suggested helpfully, writing again. "Got it. You scanned the wavebands and there they were. Boris and Olga. Nothing wrong in that, Cyril. Stick with it and you might even land yourself a language allowance, if you pass the test. It's only a few bob, I suppose, but it's better in your pocket than theirs, I always say." I continued writing, but slowly, letting him hear the maddening scratch of my government-issue pencil. "It's always the *not* reporting that bothers them most," I confided, apologising for the foibles of my masters. "'If he hasn't told us about Olga and Boris, what else hasn't he told us?' You can't blame them, I suppose. Their jobs are on the line, same as ours."

Turn another page. Lick tip of pencil. Make another annotation. I was beginning to feel the excitement of the chase. Love as commitment, he had said, love as part of life, love as effort, love as sacrifice. But love for whom? I drew a heavy pencil line and turned a page.

"Can we pass on to your Iron Curtains, please, Cyril?" I asked in my weariest voice. "HQ are devils for Iron Curtains. I wondered whether you'd any fresh names to add to the list of those you've already given us these past years. The last one"—I flipped to the back of the notebook—"my goodness, that was aeons ago. A gentleman from East Germany, a member of a local choral society you joined. Is there no one you can think of since at all? They're a bit after you now, Cyril, I'll admit, now that they've caught you not reporting the language course."

His disillusionment in me was again sliding into anger. Once again he began punching the unlikely words. But this time it was as if he were punching me.

"You will find *all* my Iron Curtain contacts, past and present, *such* as they are, *duly* listed and submitted *to* my superiors, according to regulations. *If* you had troubled yourself to *obtain* this data from Foreign Office Personnel Department *prior* to this interview—and I mean why they send me a hack like you—"

I decided to cut him short. I did not think it useful that he should be allowed to reduce me to nothing. To insignificance, yes. But not to nothing, for I was the servant of a higher authority. I pulled a sheet of paper from the back of my notebook. "Look, now, here you are, I've got them. All your Iron Curtains on one page. There's only been five ever, in your whole twenty years. HQ-cleared, I see, the lot. Well, so they would be, as long as you report them." I put the sheet back in my notebook. "Anyone to add, then? Who's to add? Think now, Cyril. Don't be hasty. They know an awful lot, my people. They shock me sometimes. Take your time."

He took his time. And more time. And more. Finally he took the line of self-pity.

"I'm not a *diplomat,* Ned," he complained in a small voice. "I'm not out doing the gay hurrah every night, Belgravia, Kensington, St. John's Wood, medals and white tie, rubbing shoulders with the great, am I? I'm a clerk. I'm not that man at all."

"What man's that, Cyril?"

"I like a treat, that's different. I like a friend best."

"I know you do, Cyril. HQ knows too."

A fresh resort to anger to mask his rising panic. Deafening body language as he clenches his great fists and lifts his elbows. "There is not a single *name* on that list that has *crossed* my path since I reported the *persons* concerned. The names in that list related *entirely* to the most *completely* casual encounters, which had no follow-up *whatsoever*."

"But, what about new people since?" I pleaded patiently. "You'll not get past them, Cyril. I don't, so why should you?"

"If there *was* anyone to add, any contact at all, even a Christmas card from someone, you may *rest* assured I would have been the first to add him. Finish. Done. Over. Next question, thank you."

Diplomat, I noted. *Him,* I noted; *Christmas.* Salzburg. I became if anything more laborious.

"That's not quite the answer they want, Cyril," I said as I wrote in my notebook. "That sounds a bit too much like flannel, frankly.

They want a 'yes' or a 'no,' or an 'if yes, who?' They want a straight answer and they're not settling for flannel. 'He didn't own up to his language, so why should we think he's owning up to his Iron Curtains?' That's what they're thinking, Cyril. That's what they're going to say to me too. It'll all come back on me in the end," I warned him, still writing.

Once again I could feel that my ponderousness was a torture to him. He was pacing, snapping his fingers at his sides. He was muttering, working his jaw menacingly, growling again about getting names. But I was far too busy writing in my notebook to notice any of this. I was old Ned, Burr's Mr. Plod, doing his duty by HQ.

"How's about this then, Cyril?" I said at last. And, holding up my notebook, I read aloud to him what I had written: "'I, Cyril Frewin, solemnly declare that I have not made the acquaintance, however briefly, of any Soviet or Eastern Bloc citizen, other than those already listed by me, in the last twelve months. Dated and signed Cyril.'"

I relit my pipe and studied the bowl in order to make quite sure it was drawing. I put the burned-out match in the matchbox, and the matchbox in my pocket. My voice, already slowed to a walking pace, now became a crawl.

"Alternatively, Cyril, and I say this advisedly, if there *is* anyone like that in your life, now's your chance to tell me. And them. I'll treat everything you say in confidence, so will they, depending what I tell them of it, which isn't always everything, not by any means. Nobody's a saint, after all. And HQ probably wouldn't clear them if they were."

Intentionally or otherwise, I had touched the fuse in him. He had been waiting for an excuse and now I had delivered it.

"Saint? Who's talking *saint*? Don't *you* call me bloody saint, I won't have it! Saint Cyril, they call me, did you know that? Of course you did, you're taunting me!"

Taut-faced and rude. Battering me with words. Frewin against the ropes, slugging anything that came at him. "If there *were* such a person—which there is not—I would *not* have told *you* or your snooping PV lot—I would have reported the matter *in writing,* according to regulations, to personnel department *at* the—"

For the second time, I allowed myself to cut him short. I didn't like him conducing the rhythm of our exchanges. "But there really isn't anyone, is that right?" I said, as pressingly as my passive rôle allowed. "There's no one? You haven't been to any functions—parties, get-togethers, meetings—official, unofficial—in London, outside London, abroad even—at which a citizen of an Iron Curtain country was remotely present?"

"Do I have to continue saying no?"

"Not if the answer's yes," I replied, with a smile he didn't like.

"The answer is no. No, no, no. Repeat no. Got it?"

"Thank you. So I can put *none,* can I? That means no one, not even a Russian. And you can sign it. Yes?"

"Yes."

"Meaning no?" I suggested, making another weak joke. "I'm sorry, Cyril, but we do have to be crystal clear, otherwise HQ will fall on us from a great height. Look, I've written it down for you. Sign it."

I handed him my pencil and he signed. I wanted to instill the habit in him. He handed back my notebook, smiling tragically at me. He had lied to me and he needed my comfort in his wretchedness. So I granted it to him—if only, I am afraid, because I wanted to take it away again very soon. I stowed the notebook in my inside pocket, stood up, and gave a big stretch as if announcing a break in our discussions, seeing that a tricky point was behind us. I rubbed my back a bit, an old man's ache.

"What's all that digging you've been doing out there, Cyril?" I said. "Building your own deep shelter, are you? Hardly necessary these days, I'd have thought."

Looking past him, my eye had fallen on a pile of new bricks stacked in a corner of the mud patch, with a tarpaulin tied over the top of them. An unfinished trench, about two feet deep, cut across the lawn towards them.

"I am *building a pond*," Frewin retorted, seizing gratefully on my facetious diversion. "I *happen* to be very fond of *water*."

"A goldfish pond, Cyril?"

"An *ornamental* pond." His good humour came sailing back. He relaxed, he smiled, and his smile was so warm and unaffected that I found myself smiling in return. "What I intend to do, Ned," he explained, drawing near to me in friendship, "is construct three separate levels of water, beginning four feet above the existing ground, descending over eighteen-inch intervals to that trench. I shall then illuminate each pool from beneath with the aid of a concealed lamp. I shall then pump the water with an electric pump. And at night, instead of drawing the curtains, I shall be able to look out on to my own private display of illuminated pools and waterfalls!"

"And play your music!" I cried, responding in full measure to his enthusiasm. "I think that's splendid, Cyril. Genius. I'm most impressed, I really am. I'd like my wife to see that. How was Salzburg, by the way?"

He actually reels, I thought, watching his head swing away from me. I hit him and he reels, and I wait till he recovers consciousness before I hit him again.

"You go to Salzburg for the music, they tell me. Quite a Mecca for you musicians, they tell me, Salzburg. Do they do opera at Christmas, or is it all carols and anthems you go for?"

They must have closed off the street, I thought, listening to the enormous silence. I wondered whether Frewin was thinking the same as he went on staring into the garden.

"Why should you care?" he answered. "You're a musical ignoramus. You said so. As well as being a very considerable snooper."

"Verdi? I've heard of Verdi. Mozart? He was Austrian, wasn't he? I saw the film. I'll bet they do you Mozart for Christmas. They'd have to. Which ones do they do?"

Silence again. I sat down and once again prepared myself to write to his dictation.

"Do you go alone?" I asked.

"Of course I do."

"Do you always?"

"Of course I do."

"Last time too?"

"Yes!"

"Do you stay alone?" I asked.

He laughed loudly. "Me? Not for one minute. Not me. There's dancing girls waiting for me in my room when I arrive. They're changed every day."

"But music night after night after night, the way you like it?"

"Who says what I like?"

"Fourteen nights of it. Twelve, I suppose, if you count the travel."

"Could be twelve. Could be fourteen. Could be thirteen. What does it matter?" He was still concussed. He was talking from a long way off.

"Which is what you go for. To Salzburg. And what you pay for. Yes? Yes, Cyril? Give me a signal, please, Cyril. I keep thinking I'm losing you. And it was what you went for this Christmas too?"

He nodded.

"Concerts, night after night? Opera? Carols?"

"Yes."

"Only the trouble is, you see, HQ says you only stayed the one night. You arrived on the first day as booked, they say, and you were off again next morning. You paid the full whack for your room, all two weeks, but the hotel never saw hide nor hair of you from your second day till you came back at the end of your holiday. So quite reasonably, really, HQ are asking where the bloody hell you went." I took my boldest leap so far. "And who with. They're asking whether you've got someone on the side. Like Boris and Olga, but real."

I turned a couple more pages of my notebook, and in the deep silence the rustle was like falling bricks. His terror was infecting me. It was like a shared evil. The truth lay a membrane from us, yet the dread of it seemed to be as terrible to the man who was trying to keep it outside the door as to myself, who was trying to let it in.

"All we need to do is get it down on paper, Cyril," I said. "Then we can forget it. Nothing like writing something down for getting it out of the way, I say. It's no crime to have a friend. Even a foreign one isn't a crime, as long as he's written down. He *is* foreign, I take it? Only, I notice a certain hesitation in you here. He must be quite some friend, I will say, if you gave up all that music for him."

"He's nowhere. He doesn't exist. He's gone. I was in his way."

"Well, he hadn't gone at Christmas time, had he? Not if you were together with him. Was he Austrian, Cyril?"

Frewin was lifeless. He was dead with his eyes open. I had hit him once too often.

"All right, then, he's French," I suggested more loudly, trying to jerk him from his introspection. "Was he a Frenchie, Cyril, your chum? . . . They wouldn't mind about a Frenchie, even if they don't like them. Come on, Cyril, how about a Yank then? They can't object to a Yank!" No answer. "Not Irish, was he? I hope not, for your sake!"

I did the laughing for him, but nothing stirred him from his melancholy. Still at the window, he had crooked his thumb and was boring the knuckle joint into his forehead, as if trying to make a bullet hole. Had he whispered something?

"I didn't catch you, Cyril!"

"He's above all that."

"Above nationality?"

"He's above it."

"You mean he's a diplomat."

"He didn't *come* to Salzburg, can't you bloody listen?" He swung round at me and began screaming. "You're bloody spastic, you know that? Never mind the answers, you can't even *ask* right! No wonder the country's in a mess! Where's your savvy gone? Where's your human understanding, for a change?"

I stood up again. Slowly. Keep him watching me. Give my back another rub. I wandered down the room. I shook my head as if to say this simply would not do.

"I'm trying to help you, Cyril. If you went to Salzburg and stayed there, that's one scenario. If you went on somewhere else—well, that's quite another. If your chum is Italian, say. And if you pretended to go to Salzburg but went—oh, I don't know—to Rome, say, or Milan, even Venice—well, that's another. I can't do it all for you. It's not fair and they wouldn't thank me if I did."

He was wide-eyed. He was transferring his madness to me, appointing himself the sane one. I refilled my pipe, giving it my entire attention while I went on talking.

"You're a hard man to please, Cyril"—tamping the tobacco with my forefinger—"you're a tease, if you want to know. 'Don't touch me here, take your hand away from there, you can do this but only once.' I mean, what *am* I allowed to talk about?"

I struck the match and held it to the bowl, and as I did so I saw that he had transferred his knuckles to his eyes in order not to be in the room. But I pretended not to notice. "All right, we'll forget Salzburg. If Salzburg is hurtful, put Salzburg aside and let's go back to your Iron Curtains. Yes? Agreed?"

His hands slipped slowly from his face. No answer, but no outright rejection either. I went on talking. He wanted me to. I could sense his reliance on my words as a bridge between the real world and the inner hell where he was living. He wanted me to do the talking for both of us. I felt I had to make his confession for him, which was why I decided to play my most perilous card.

"So suppose, for argument's sake, Cyril, we were to add the name of Sergei Modrian to this list and call it a day," I suggested carelessly, almost covering over my words in my efforts to sound unthreatening. "Just to be on the safe side," I added cheerfully. "What do you say?" His head was still hanging downward, his face cut off from me. Chatting cheerfully, I expanded on my latest helpful proposal for HQ. "'All right,' we say to them, 'so take your wretched Mr. Modrian. Don't play around with us any more, we'll come clean. Have him and go home. Ned and Cyril have got work to do.'"

He was dangling, smiling like a hanged man. In the profound silence that had settled over the neighbourhood, I had the sensation of hearing my words resounding from the rooftops. But Frewin seemed barely to have heard them.

"Modrian's the one they want you to own up to, Cyril," I continued reasonably. "They told me. If you say *yes* to Modrian—and if I write him down, which I'm doing, and you allow me to, and I notice you're not stopping me, are you?—nobody can accuse either one of us of being less than frank with them. 'Yes, I am a chum of Sergei Modrian and screw the lot of you'—how's that? '*And* I went with him to wherever we went, *and* we did this, we did that, we agreed to do certain other things, and we had a lovely time, or we didn't. And anyway, what's all the *glasnost* for, if I'm still being forbidden to associate with an extremely civilised Russian?' . . . How's that? Never mind the gaps for the moment, we can fill all those in later. Then, the way I see it, they can pack up the file for another year and we can all get on with our weekend."

"Why?"

I affected not to understand.

"Why can they pack up the file, then?" he demanded, as suspicions crowded in on him. "When they've been who they are? They're not going to turn round and say 'What's the point?' Nobody does. Not when they've been one thing. They stay who they are. They don't become other people. They can't."

"Come off it, Cyril!" He had sunk into his own thoughts and was becoming hard to reach. *"Cyril!"*

"What then? What's up? Don't shout."

"So what's wrong with being Russian these days? HQ would be *far* more worried if Sergei was a Frenchie! I only suggested Frenchie as a trap. I regret that now, I apologise. But a Russian these days—for heaven's sake, we're not just talking friendly nations, we're talking partners! *You* know HQ. They're always behind the times. So's Gorst. Our job's to set the trend. Are you hearing me, Cyril?"

And that was where, for a moment, I thought I had lost the whole game—lost his complicity, lost his dependence, lost the willing suspension of his disbelief. He wandered past me like a sleepwalker. He stood himself at his bay window again, here he remained contemplating his half-dug pool and all the other half-built dreams of his life, which he must have known by now would never be completed.

Then, to my relief, he started talking. Not about what he had done. Not about who he had done it with. But why.

"You don't know what it means, do you, to be locked up all day with a bunch of morons?"

I thought at first he was complaining of his future, till I realised he was talking about the Tank.

"Listening to their filthy jokes all day, choking on their fags and their BO? Not *you,* you're privileged, however humble you make yourself out. Day after day of it, sniggers about tits and knickers and periods and little bits on the side? 'Come on, Saint, tell us a naughty joke for a change! You're a deep one, I'll bet, Saint! What are you into—gym slips? Bit of the rough? What's the Saint's little fancy of a Saturday night?'" His energy had returned to him in full force, and with it, to my astonishment, an unexpected gift for mimicry. He was mincing at me, playing the music-hall queen, a ghastly soft grin twisting his hairless face. "'Heard the one about the Boy Scouts and the Girl Guides, Saint? The excitement was in tents. Get *you!*' You wouldn't know about that, would you? 'Do you pull it now and then, Saint? Give it a little jerk occasionally, just to make sure it's there? You'll go blind, you know. It'll drop off. I'll bet you've got a big one, haven't you? A real donkey knock, all the way down your leg and tucked into your garter'. . . . You've never had that, have you, all day long, in the office, in the canteen? You're a gentleman. Know what they gave me April Fool's Day? A top secret incoming from Paris, Frewin's eyes only, decypher yourself, manual, ha ha. *Flash priority,* get the joke? I didn't. So I go into the cubicle and get out the books, don't I? And I decypher it, don't I? Manual. Everyone's got his head down. Nobody laughing or spoiling it. I do the first six groups and it's filth, some filthy joke all about a French letter. Gorst had done it. He'd had the boys at the Paris Embassy send it specially as a joke. 'Steady on, Saint, keep your hair on, give us a smile. It was only a joke, Saint, can't you take a joke?' That's what Personnel said too, when I complained. Horseplay, they said. Pranks are good for morale. Think of it as a compliment, they said, show a little sporting instinct. If I hadn't had my music I'd have killed myself long ago. I considered it, I don't mind telling you. Trouble was, I wouldn't see their faces when they found out what they'd done."

A traitor needs two things, Smiley had once remarked bitterly to me at the time of Haydon's betrayal of the Circus: somebody to hate, and somebody to love. Frewin had told me whom he hated. Now he began to talk about whom he loved.

"I'd been all over the world that night—Puerto Rico, Cape Verde, Jo'burg—and there wasn't anything that took my fancy. I like the amateurs best, as a rule, the hacks. They've got more wit, which is what I like, I told you. I didn't even know it was morning. I've got these thick curtains up there, three hundred quids' worth, interlined. It's meat and drink to me after the Tank, the quiet is."

A different smile had come up on him, a small boy's smile on his birthday.

" 'Good morning to you, Boris, my friend,' says Olga. 'How are you feeling this morning?' Then she says it in Russian and Boris replies that he's feeling a bit low. He's often low, Boris is. He's prone to Slav depressions. Olga takes care of him, mind. She'll have a joke, but it's never cruelly meant. They have a fight now and then too—well, it's only natural, seeing they do everything together. But they always make it up in the same programme. They don't bear a grudge from day to day. Olga couldn't do that, to be frank. It's out with it and that's it, with Olga. Then they'll have a laugh together. That's how they are. Constructive. Friendly. Clean spoken. Musical too, naturally—well, they would be, being Russian. I wasn't that keen on Tchaikovsky till I heard them discussing him. But afterwards I came round to him straight away. Boris has got quite advanced tastes in music actually. Olga—well, she's a bit easy to please. Still, they're only actors, I suppose, reading their lines. But you forget that when you're listening to them, trying to learn the language. You believe in them."

And you send your written work in, he was saying.

For free correction and advice, he was saying.

You don't even have to write to Moscow after the first time. They've got this box number in Luxembourg.

He had fallen quiet but not dangerously so. Nevertheless I was becoming scared that his trance might end too soon. I took myself out of his line of sight, and stood in a corner of the room behind him.

"What address did you give them, Cyril?"

"This one, of course. What else have I got to give them, then? A country house in Shropshire? A villa in Capri?"

"Did you give them your own name, too?"

"Of course I didn't. Well, Cyril, yes. I mean anyone can be Cyril."

"Good man," I said approvingly. "Cyril who?"

"Nemo," he announced proudly. "Mr. C. Nemo. 'Nemo' is Latin for 'nobody,' in case you didn't know."

Mr. C. Nemo. Like Mr. A. Patriot, perhaps.

"Did you put your occupation?"

"Not my real one. You're being stupid again."

"So what did you put?"

"Musician."

"Did they ask for your age?"

"Of course they did. They had to. They had to know you were eligible, in case you won the prize. They can't give prizes to minors, can they? No one can."

"And status—married or single—you told them that too?"

"I *had* to put my status, didn't I, with the prize being available to *couples*! They can't give a *prize* to *one* person and leave his wife out, it wouldn't be gracious."

"What work did you send in—the first time round, for instance—do you remember?"

He decided to take further exception to my stupidity.

"Thickhead. What do you think I sent them? Bloody logarithms? You write in, you get the forms, you enrol, you get the Luxembourg box number, you get the book, you're one of them. After that you do what Boris and Olga tell you to do in the programme, don't you? 'Complete the exercise on page 9. Answer the questions on page 12.' Haven't you been to school then?"

"And you were good. HQ says you've got a mind like an encyclopaedia when you use it. They told me." I was beginning to learn how much he relished flattery.

"I was *more* than good, as a matter of fact, thank you, HQ. If you *wish* to know, I was in the nature of being their top pupil. Certain *notes* were sent to me by certain *tutors,* and some of them had a highly congratulatory *tone,*" he added, with the wild grin that came over him when he was praised. "It gave me quite a filip, if you wish to know, walking into the Tank of a Monday morning with one of their little notes in my pocket and not saying anything. I thought, I could tell some of you a tale if I wanted. I didn't, though. I preferred my privacy. I preferred my friendships. I wasn't going to have those animals making filthy comments about Olga and Boris, thank you."

"And you wrote back to these tutors?"

"Only as Nemo."

"But you didn't fool with them otherwise?" I asked, trying to fathom what restraints, if any, were in his mind as he embarked on this first illicit love affair. "I mean, if they asked you a plain question, you'd give them a plain answer. You weren't coy."

"I was *not* coy! I had no *cause* to be! I took great care to be courteous, the same as my tutors were. They were high professors, some of them, academicians. I was *grateful* and I was *diligent*. That was the least they deserved, considering there was no fee and it was voluntary and in the interests of human understanding."

The hunter in me again. I was calculating the moves they

would have made as they played him along. I was working out
how I would have played him myself, if the Circus had dreamed
up anything so perfect.

"And I suppose, as you improved, they passed you on from
plain printed exercises to the more ambitious stuff—composition,
essays?"

"When it was deemed by the Board of Tutors in Moscow that
I was ripe for it, yes, they moved me up to freestyle."

"Do you remember the subjects they set you?"

He laughed his superior laugh. "You think I'd forget them?
Five nights at each one of them with the dictionary? Two hours'
sleep if I'm lucky? Wake up, will you, Ned!"

I gave a rueful little laugh as I wrote to his dictation.

"'My Life' was the first one. I told them about the Tank, not
mentioning names, of course, or the nature of our work, naturally. Nevertheless, a certain element of social comment was present, I won't deny it. I thought the Board had a right to know,
specially with the glasnost in the pipeline and everything easing
up for the benefit of all mankind."

"What was the next one?"

"'My Home.' I told them about my plans for the pond. They
liked that. And my cooking. One of them was quite a major cook.
After that they gave me 'My Favourite Pastime,' which could
have been redundant but wasn't."

"You described your love of music, I suppose?"

"Wrong."

The rest of his answer rings in my ears today: as an accusation,
as a cry of sympathy from a fellow sufferer; as a blind prayer
flung into the ether by a man who, like myself, was desperate for
love before it was too late.

"I elected 'Good Company' as my favourite pastime, if you
really wish to know," he said as the wild smile came racing back
to his cheeks. "The fact that I had not *had* much good company in

my life hitherto did not *deter* me from relishing the few occasions when it *had* come my way." He seemed to forget that he had spoken, for he began again, in words I might have used of Sally: "I had a feeling I had *renounced* something in my life which I now wished to reclaim," he said.

"And did they admire your advanced work too? Were they impressed by it?" I asked as I diligently wrote this down.

He was smirking again. "Moderately, I assume. Marginally. Here and there. With reservations, naturally."

"Why do you assume that?"

"Because, unlike some, they had the grace and generosity to show their appreciation. That's why."

And they showed it, said Frewin—I scarcely needed to press him further—they showed it in the person of one Sergei Modrian, First Secretary Cultural, of the Soviet Embassy in London, in his capacity as Radio Moscow's devoted local emissary despatched to answer Frewin's prayer.

Like all good angels, Modrian arrived without warning, on Frewin's doorstep one dank November Saturday, bearing with him the gifts of his high office: one bottle of Moskovskaya vodka, one tin of Sevruga caviar, and one foully printed artbook about the Bolshoi Ballet. And one grandly typed letter appointing Mr. C. Nemo to be an Honorary Student of Moscow State University, in recognition of his unique progress in the Russian language.

But the greatest gift of all was Modrian's own magical person, custom-trained to provide the good company Frewin had so loudly craved in his prize-winning essay for the Board.

We had arrived at our destination. Frewin was calm, Frewin was in triumph; Frewin, for however long, was fulfilled. His voice had broken, free of its confinements; his plain face was lit with the smile of a man who had known true love and was longing to impart his luck. If there had been anyone in the world for whom I could ever have smiled in the same way, I would have been a different man.

"*Modrian,* Ned? Sergei Modrian? Oh, Ned, I mean we're talking the total top league here. One look at him, I knew. None of your half measures here, I thought. This one's the whole hog. We had the same sense of humour, of course, straight off. Acid. No wool across the eyes. The same interests too, right down to composers." He attempted a more detached tone, but in vain. "It is very *rare* in life, in my experience, for two human beings to be naturally compatible in each and every respect—bar women, where I have to admit that Sergei's experience far outran my own. Sergei's attitude to women"—he was trying hard to be disapproving—"I'll put it this way: if it had been anyone else behaving in that manner, I would have been hard put to it to approve."

"Did he introduce you to women, Cyril?"

His expression switched to one of adamant rejection. "He assuredly did not, thank you. Nor would I have permitted him to. Nor would he have regarded such introductions as coming within the ambit of our relationship."

"Not even on your trips to Russia together?" I ventured, taking another leap for him.

"Nowhere, thank you. It would have ruined them, as a matter of fact. Killed them stone dead."

"So it's all hearsay, what they say about his women?"

"No, it's not. It's what Sergei told me himself. Sergei Modrian had a totally ruthless attitude to women. His colleagues confirmed this to me privately. Ruthless."

I found time to marvel at Modrian's psychological dexterity—or was it the dexterity of his masters? Between Modrian the ruthless pursuer of women, and Frewin the ruthless rejecter of them, there was indeed a natural bond.

"So you met his colleagues too," I said. "In Moscow, presumably. At Christmas."

"Only the ones he trusted. Their respect for him was incredible. Or Leningrad. I wasn't fussy, I'd no right to be. I was an honoured guest. I went along with whatever they'd arranged for me."

I kept my eyes on my notebook. God knows what I was writing by then. Gobbledygook. Afterwards, there were whole tracts I couldn't read a word of. I selected my absolutely dullest tone.

"And was all this in honour of your remarkable linguistic abilities, Cyril? Or were you already providing informal services for Modrian by then? Like giving him information or whatever. Translating and so on. A lot do it, I'm told. They're not supposed to, of course. But you can't blame people—can you?—wanting to help the *glasnost* along, now it's come. We've waited long enough. Only, I've got to put the proper history to this, Cyril. They'll skin me otherwise."

I did not dare look up. I simply kept writing. I turned a page and wrote: *keep talking, keep talking, keep talking.* And still I did not look up.

I heard him whisper something I couldn't understand. I heard him mutter, "It's *not.* I didn't. I never bloody did." I heard him complain more loudly: "Don't *say* that, do you mind? Don't you ever say that again, you and your HQ. 'Giving him information'— what's all that about? They're wrong words. *I'm talking to you, Ned!*"

I looked up, sucking on my pipe and smiling. "Are you, Cyril? Of course you are. I'm sorry. You're my sixth in a week, to be honest. They're all doing the *glasnost* these days. It's the fashion. I'm beginning to feel my age."

He decided to comfort me. He sat down. Not in the chair, but on its arm. He put on an avuncular, friend-to-friend manner that reminded me of my preparatory-school headmaster.

"You're by way of being a liberal yourself, aren't you, Ned? You've got the face for it anyway, even if you are a bit of a toady for HQ."

"I suppose I'm a sort of free thinker in my way, yes," I conceded. "Though I do have my pension to consider, naturally."

"Of course you are! You favour a mixed economy, don't you? You don't like public poverty and private wealth any more than I do. Humanity above ideology, you believe in that? Stop the derailed tram of capitalism destroying all before it in its path? Of course you do! You've got a sensible concern for the environment, I dare say. Badgers, whales, fur coats, power stations. Even a vision of sharing, where it doesn't impinge. Brothers and sisters marching together towards common goals, culture and music for all! Freedom of movement and choice of allegiance! Peace! Well, then."

"Makes good sense to me," I said.

"You're not old enough to have done the thirties; neither am I. I wouldn't have held with them if I had been. We're *good men,* that's all we are. *Reasonable men.* That's what Sergei was too. You and Sergei—I can see it in your face, Ned, it's no good your trying to hide it, you're birds of a feather. So don't go painting me black and you white, because we're like minds, same as me and Sergei were. On the same side against the wickedness, the lack of culture, the filth. 'We're "the unrecognised aristocracy" '—that's what Sergei called us. He was right. You're one too, that's all I'm saying. I mean, who else is there? Who's the alternative to what we see around us every day, the degradation, the waste, the disrespect? Who are we going to listen to, up there in the attic at night, twiddling the dials? Not the yuppies, that's for sure. Not the pigs-in-clover lot—what have they got to say? Not the make-more spend-more be-more school, they're no help. Not the knickers-and-tits brigade, either. And we're not going to convert to Islam in a hurry, are we, not while they go round pinching countries off each other and doing the poison gas. So I mean what's the alternative for a feeling man, a man of conscience, now the Russians are abandoning their responsibilities right and left and putting on the hair shirt? Who's out there for us? Where's the vision any more? Where's the relief? The friendship? Someone's got to fill the gap. I can't be left in the air. I can't be without. Not after Sergei, Ned—I'd die. Sergei was the most important man on earth to me. Drink, meat and laughter, Sergei was. He was my total meaning. What's going to happen? That's what I want to know. There's some heads could roll, in my view. Sergei had the ideology. I don't see it in you—I don't think I do anyway. I get a glimpse of it, a longing here and there, then I'm not at all sure. I don't know you've got the quality."

"Try me," I said.

"I don't know you've got the wit. The dance. I thought that as you came in. I compared you with Sergei in my mind, and I'm afraid I found you seriously wanting. Sergei didn't shuffle in like a deadbeat; he took me by storm. Rings the bell, marches in as if he's bought the place, sits down where you're sitting, but more awake—not that he ever sat anywhere long. Sergei didn't, he was a shocking fidget, even at the opera. Then he grins like an elf and lifts up a glass of his own vodka. 'Congratulations, Mr. Nemo,' he says. 'Or may I call you C? You've won the competition and I'm the first prize.'"

He passed the back of his hand across his mouth, and realised that he was wiping away a grin. "He was a real flyer, Sergei was."

He was laughing, so I laughed with him. Modrian was his false freedom, I was thinking. As Sally is mine.

"He hadn't even taken his coat off," he continued. "He went straight into his pitch. 'Now the first thing we've got to talk about is the ceremony,' he says. 'Nothing flashy, Mr. Nemo, just a couple of friends of mine, who happen to be Boris and Olga, plus one or two high dignitaries from the Board, and a small reception for a few of your many admirers in Moscow.'

" 'At your Embassy?' I said. 'I'm not coming there. My office would kill me—you don't know Gorst.'

" 'No, no, Mr. Nemo,' he says. 'No, no, Mr. C. *I'm* not talking about the Embassy—who cares about the Embassy. *I'm* talking about Moscow State University foreign language school and the official inauguration of your honorary studentship with full civilian honours.'

"I thought I was dead at first. My heart had stopped beating. I could feel it. I'd never been beyond Dover in my life, let alone Russia, although I was Foreign Office. 'Come to Moscow?' I said.'You're off your head,' I said. 'I'm a cypher clerk, not a trade union leader with an ulcer. I can't come to Moscow at the drop of a hat,' I said. 'Even if there is a prize at the end of it, and Olga and Boris waiting to shake my hand, and studentships and I don't know what. You don't seem to understand the position at all. I'm in highly sensitive work,' I said. 'The people aren't that sensitive, but the work is. I've got constant and regular access to top secret and above. I'm not just anybody off the street, into your plane to Moscow and nobody's the wiser. I thought I put that in my essays, some of them.'

" 'Then come to Salzburg,' he says. 'Who's counting? Take a plane to Salzburg, say you're doing the music there, slip up to Vienna, I'll have the air tickets ready—all right, it's Aeroflot but it's only two hours—no nonsense with the passports when we arrive, we'll keep the ceremony family, who's the wiser?' Then he hands me this document like a scroll, all with the burned edges and that, the full formal invitation, signed by the whole Board, English one side, Russian the other. I read the English, I don't mind telling you. I wasn't going to sit in front of him with a dictionary for an hour, was I? I'd have looked a total idiot, me a top language student." He paused—a little shamefully, I thought. "Then I told him my name," he said. "I shouldn't have done, really, but I'd had enough of being Nemo. I wanted to be me."

Now you must lose me for a minute, as I lost Cyril. Until now, I had managed to stay abreast of his references. Where I had dared, I had even led them. Now suddenly he was running free and I was struggling to keep up with him. He was in Russia, but I wasn't. He'd given me no warning that he'd gone there. He was talking about Boris and Olga, not how they sounded any more, but how they looked; and how Boris had flung his arms round him, and how Olga had given him a demure but heartfelt Russian kiss—he didn't hold with kissing as a rule, Ned, but with the Russians it wasn't Gorst's kind of kissing at all, so you didn't mind. You even got to respect it, Ned, it being all part of what Russians regard as comradely. Frewin was looking twenty years younger and talking about being made a fuss of, all the birthdays, that he'd never had. Olga and Boris in the flesh, Ned, no side to them, just natural, same as they were in their lessons.

"'Congratulations, Cyril,' she says to me, 'on your completely phenomenal progress in the Russian language.' Well, through interpreters, naturally, I wasn't *that* far on, as I told her. Then Boris puts his arm round me. 'We're proud to be of assistance, Cyril,' he says. 'There's a lot of our students fall by the wayside, to be truthful, but those as don't make up for all the rest.'"

And by then at last I had pieced together the scene that he was painting for me in such broad, unpredicated strokes: his first Christmas in Russia, and for Frewin, I had no doubt, his first good Christmas anywhere, and Sergei Modrian playing ringmaster at his side. They are in a great room somewhere in Moscow, with chandeliers and speeches and a presentation and fifty handpicked extras from Moscow Central Casting, and Frewin in paradise, which is exactly where Modrian wishes him to be.

Then, as abruptly as Frewin had treated me to this memory he abandoned it. The light went out of his eyes, his head tipped to one side, and he beetled his eyebrows as if in judgment at his own behaviour.

Prudently, I returned him to time present. "So where is it?" I said. "The scroll he gave you. Here? The scroll, Cyril. Appointing you. Where?"

He stared, at me, slowly waking. "I had to give it back to Sergei. 'When we're in Moscow, Cyril,' he said, 'you shall have it hanging on your wall and framed in gold. Not here. I wouldn't put you in the danger.' He'd thought of everything, Sergei had, and he was quite right, what with you and your HQ snooping on me night and day."

I allowed no pause, no alteration in my voice, not even in the direction of casualness. I lowered my eyes again and dug once more in my inside pocket. I was his candidate as Sergei's replacement, and he was courting me. He was showing me his tricks and asking me to take him on. Instinct told me to make him work harder for me. I addressed myself to the notebook again, and I spoke exactly as if I were asking him the name of his maternal grandfather.

"So when did you start giving Sergei all these great British secrets?" I said. "Well, what we *call* secrets, anyway. Obviously what was secret a few years ago is not going to be the same as what's secret today, is it? We didn't win the Cold War by secrecy, did we? We won it with the openness. The *glasnost*."

It was the second time I had mentioned passing over secrets, but on this occasion, when I crossed the Rubicon for him, he came with me. Yet he seemed not even to notice he was on the other side.

"Correct. That's how we won it. And Sergei didn't even want the secrets at first, either. 'Secrets, Cyril, they're unimportant to me,' he said. 'Secrets, Cyril, in the changing world in which we live, I'm pleased to say, they're a drug on the market,' he said. 'I'd rather keep our friendship on a non-official basis. However, if I *do* require something in that line, you may count on me to let you know.' In the meantime, he said, it would be quite sufficient if I wrote him a few unofficial reports on the quality of Radio Moscow's programmes just to keep his bosses happy. Whether the reception was good enough, for example. You'd think they'd know that, really, but they don't. You never know with Russians where you're going to strike the ignorance in them, to be frank. That's not a criticism, it's a fact. He'd like my opinion of the course as well, he said, for standards of instruction generally, any suggestions I might have for Boris and Olga in the future, me being somewhat of an unusual pupil in my own right."

"So what changed it?"

"Changed what? Be lucid, please, Ned. I'm not nobody, you know. I'm not Mr. Nemo. I'm Cyril."

"What changed Sergei's reluctance to take secrets from you?" I said.

"His Embassy did. The diehards. The barbarians. They always do. They prevailed on him. They declined to recognize the course of history; they preferred to remain total troglodytes in their caves and continue with their ridiculous Cold War."

I said I did not understand him. I said he was a bit above my head.

"Yes, well I'm not surprised. I'll put it this way. There was lot of them in that Embassy didn't like the time given over to cultural friendship, for a start. There was this internal rivalry going on between the camps. I was an impotent spectator. The *doves,* they were in favour of the culture, naturally, and above all they

were in favour of the *glasnost*. They saw culture filling the vacuum left behind by the withdrawal hostilities. Sergei explained
that to me. But the hawks—*including* the Ambassador, I regret to
say—wanted Sergei concentrating more on the continuation of
old attitudes, what's left of them, gathering intelligence and generally acting in an aggressive and conspiratorial manner regardless of the changes in the world climate. The Embassy diehards
didn't care about Sergei being an idealist, not at all. Well, they
wouldn't, would they, any more than what Gorst does. Sergei
had to tread a highly precarious path, frankly, a bit for one side,
then a bit for the other. So did I, it was duty. We'd do our culture
together, a bit of language, a bit of art or music then we'd do some
secrets to satisfy the hawks. We had to justify ourselves to all parties, same as you with your HQ and me with the Tank."

He was fading, I was losing him. I had to use the whip. "So
when?" I asked impatiently.

"When what?"

"Don't be clever with me, Cyril, do you mind? I've got to get
this down. Look at the time. *When* did you start giving Sergei
Modrian information, *what* did you give him, what for, how
much for, when did it stop, and why, when it could perfectly well
have continued? I'd like a weekend, Cyril, if you don't mind. So
would my wife. I'd like to put my feet up in front of the telly. I'm
not paid overtime, you know. It's strictly piecework, what they
offer. One candidate's the same as another, when it comes to pay-
day. We're living in a time of cost effectiveness, in case you haven't
noticed. They tell me we could be privatised if we're not careful."

He didn't hear me. He didn't want to. He was wandering in
his body and in his mind, looking for distraction, for somewhere
to hide. My anger was not all simulated. I was beginning to hate
Modrian. I was angry about how much we depended on the credulity of the innocent in order to survive. It was sickening me

that a trickster like Modrian had contrived to turn Frewin's loneliness to treachery. I felt threatened by the notion of love as the
antithesis of duty.

I stood up smartly, anger still my ally. Frewin was perched listlessly on the edge of a carved Arthurian stool with the Royal
Navy's ensign stitched into the seat.

"Show me your toys," I ordered him.

"What toys? I'm a man, if you don't mind, not an infant. It's
my house. Don't tell me what to do."

I was remembering Modrian's tradecraft, the stuff he used, the
way he equipped his agents. I was remembering my own tradecraft, from the days when I had run Frewin's counterparts against
the Soviet target, even if they were not quite as bad as Frewin. I
was imagining how I would have handled a high-access walk-in
like Frewin, living on borrowed sanity.

"I want to see your camera, don't I?" I said petulantly. "Your
high-speed transmitter, right, Cyril? Your signals plan. Your
one-time codepads. Your crystals. Your white carbons for your
secret writing. Your concealment devices. I want to see them,
Cyril, I want to put them in my briefcase for Monday; then I
want to go home and watch Arsenal against United. That may
not be your taste, but it happens to be mine. So can we move this
along a bit and cut out the bullshit, *please*?"

The madness was running out, I could feel it. He was drained
and so was I. He sat head down and knees spread, staring dully at
his hands. I could sense the end beginning for him—the moment
when the penitent grows tired of his confession and of the emotions that compelled it.

"Cyril, I'm getting a bit edgy," I said.

And when he still didn't respond, I strode to his telephone, the
same one that Monty's fake engineer had made permanently live.
I dialled Burr's direct line and heard his fancy secretary on the
other end, the same one who hadn't known my name.

"Darling?" I said. "I'm going to be about another hour if I'm lucky. I've got a slow one. Yes, all right, I know, I'm sorry. Well, I said I'm sorry. Yes, of course."

I rang off and stared at him accusingly. He climbed slowly to his feet and led me upstairs. His attic was a spare bedroom roof high. His radio receiver stood on a table in the corner—German, just as Monty had said. I switched it on while he watched me, and we heard an accented female Russian voice talking indignantly about Moscow's criminal mafia.

"Why do they *do* that?" Frewin burst out at me, as if I were responsible. "The Russians. Why do they run down their own country all the time? They never used to. They were proud. I was proud too. All the cornfields, the classlessness, the chess, the cosmonauts, and ballet, the athletes. It was paradise till they started running it down. They've forgotten the good in themselves. It's bloody disgraceful. That's what I told Sergei."

"Then why do you still listen to them?" I said.

He was almost weeping, but I pretended not to notice.

"For the message, don't I?"

"Make it snappy, will you, Cyril!"

"Telling me I'm reactivated. That I'm wanted again. 'Come back, Cyril. All is forgiven, love, Sergei.' That's all I need to hear."

"How would they say that?"

"White paint."

"Go on."

" 'There's white paint on the dog, Olga.' . . . 'We need a spot of white paint on the bookshelf, Boris.' . . . 'Oh dear, oh dear, Olga, look at the cat, someone has dipped her tail in white paint. I hate cruelty,' says Boris. Why don't they say it when I'm listening?"

"Let's just stick to the method, can we? All right, you hear the message. On the radio. Olga or Boris says 'white paint.' Or they both do. *Then* what do you do?"

"Look in my signals plan."

I held out my hand, commanding him with my snapping fingers. "Hurry!" I said.

He hurried. He found a wooden hairbrush. Pulling the bristles from the casing, he shoved his big fingers into the gap and hauled out a piece of soft, flammable paper with times of the day and wavebands printed in parallel. He offered it to me, hoping it would satisfy. I took it from him without pleasure and snapped it into my notebook; glancing at my watch at the same moment.

"Thanks," I said curtly. "More, please, Cyril I need a codebook and a transmitter. Don't tell me you haven't got them, I'm not in the mood."

He was grappling with a tin of talcum powder, tugging at the base, trying desperately to please me. He talked nervously while he shook the powder into the handbasin.

"I was respected, you see, Ned, you don't get that a lot. There's three of these. Olga and Boris tell me which to use, like with the white paint except it was the composers. Tchaikovsky was number three, Beethoven was number two, Bach was one. They did them alphabetical to help me remember. You get the glimpses but you don't get the friends, not normally, do you? Not unless you meet Sergei or one of his lot."

The powder was all poured away. Three radio crystals lay in his palm, together with a tiny codepad and an eye-glass to enlarge it.

"He had all I'd got, Sergei did. I gave it to him. He'd tell me a thing, I'd add it to my life. I'd have a mood, he'd get me straight again. He understood. He could see right into me. It gave me a feeling of being known, which I liked. It's gone now. It's been posted back to Moscow."

His rambling was scaring me. So was his feverish desire to pacify me. If I had been his hangman, he would have been gratefully loosening his tie.

"Your transmitter," I snapped. "What the hell's the good of crystal and a codepad if you can't send!"

At the same terrible pace, he bent his swelled body to the floor and rolled back a corner of the tufted Wilton carpet.

"I haven't got a knife actually, Ned," he confessed.

Neither had I, but I dared not leave him, I dared not break my command over him. I crouched beside him. He was peering vaguely at a loose floorboard, trying to raise it with his thick fingertips. Clenching my fist, I punched one end of the board, and had the satisfaction of seeing the other end lift.

"Help yourself," I said.

It was old stuff, I could have guessed, nothing they cared about any more—a rig of grey boxes, a squash transmitter, a lash-up to be fitted to his receiver. Yet he handed it to me proudly, in its tangled mess.

A terrible anxiety had entered his eyes. "All I am now, you see, Ned, I'm a hole," he explained. "I don't mean to be morbid, do I, but I don't exist. This house isn't anything either. I used to love it. It looked after me, same as I looked after it. We'd have been nothing without each other, the house and me. It's hard for you to understand that, I dare say, if you have a wife, what a house is. She'd come between you. You and the house, I mean. Your wife. You and him. Modrian. I loved him, Ned. I was infatuated. 'You're too much, Cyril,' he used to say. 'Cool down. Relax. Take a holiday. You're hallucinating.' I couldn't. Sergei was my holiday."

"Camera," I ordered.

He didn't read me at once. He was obsessed with Modrian. He looked at me, but it was Modrian he saw.

"Don't be like that," he said, not understanding.

"Camera!" I yelled. "For Christ's sake, Cyril, don't you *ever* have a weekend?"

He stood at his wardrobe. Camelot sword blades carved on oak doors.

"Camera!" I shouted louder as he still hesitated. "How can you slip film to a good friend at the opera if you haven't photographed your files in the first place?"

"Take it easy, Ned. Cool down, will you? Please." Grinning in a superior way, he reached a hand into the wardrobe. But his eyes were ogling me, saying "Now watch this." He groped in the wardrobe, smiling at me mysteriously. He pulled out a pair of opera glasses and trained them on me, first the right way, then back to front. Then he handed them to me so that I could do the same to him. I took them in my hands and felt their unnatural weight at once. I turned the central dial until it clicked. He was nodding at me, encouraging me, saying "Yes, Ned, that's the way." He grabbed a book from the bookshelf and opened it at the centre, *All the World's Dancers*, illustrated. A young girl was doing a *pas de chat*. Sally too had been at ballet school. He unbuckled the neck strap and I saw that the short end did duty as a measuring chain. He took the binoculars from me and trained them on the book, measured the distance and turned the dial till it clicked.

"See?" he said proudly. "*Comprenez*, do you? They made it specially. For me. For opera nights. Sergei designed it personally. There's a lot of idleness in Russia, but Sergei had to have the best. I'd stay in late at the Tank. I'd photograph the whole weekly float for him if I felt like it, then give him the film while we were sitting in the stalls. I'd give it to him in one of the arias, usually—it was a sort of joke between us." He handed the binoculars back to me and drifted down the room, scrabbling his fingertips on his bare scalp as if he had a full head of hair. Then he held out his hands like someone testing the atmosphere for rain.

"Sergei had the best of me, Ned, and he's gone. *C'est la vie*, I say. Now it's up to you. Have you got the courage? Have you got the wit? That's why I wrote to you. I had to. I was empty. I didn't know you, but I needed you. I wanted a good man who understood me. A man I could trust again. It's up to you, Ned. Now's your chance. Jump out of yourself and live, I say, while there is yet time. That wife of yours is a bit of a bully, by the sound of her. You'd be well advised to tell her to live her own life instead of yours. I should have advertised, shouldn't I?" A terrible smile, which he turned full upon me. "Single man, non-smoker, fond of music and wit. I peruse those columns sometimes—who doesn't? I contemplate replying sometimes, except I'd never know how to break it off if I wasn't suited. So I wrote you a letter, didn't I? It was like writing to God in a way, till you came along in your shabby coat and asked a lot of spotty questions, no doubt drafted by HQ. It's time you stood on your own feet, Ned, same as me. You're cowed, that's your trouble. Your wife is partly to blame, in my opinion. I listened to your voice while you were apologising and I was not impressed. You won't reach out to take. Still, I reckon I could make something of you, and you could make something of me, too. You could help me dig my pool. I could show you music. That's evens, right? Nobody's impervious to music. I only did it because of Gorst." His voice leapt in horror. "*Ned!* Leave that alone, do you mind! Take your thieving hands off my property, Ned. *Now!*"

I was fingering his Markus typewriter. It was in the wardrobe where he kept his opera glasses, stowed under a few shirts. Signed A. Patriot, I thought. "A" standing for *Anyone's,* I thought. Anyone who loved him. I'd guessed already and he'd told me already, but the sight of it had excited both of us with a sense of ending.

"So why did you break it off with Sergei?" I asked him, still fingering the keys.

But this time he didn't rise to my flattery. "*I* didn't break it off. *He* did. I haven't ended it now, not if you're stepping into his shoes. Put that away. Cover it over the way you found it, thank you."

I did as he asked. I hid the evidence of the typewriter.

"What did he say?" I asked carelessly. "How did he break it to you? Or did he write and run?" I was thinking of Sally again.

"Not a lot. You don't need a lot of words when someone's stuck in London and you're in Moscow. The silence speaks for itself."

He wandered over to his radio and sat before it. I followed close on his heels, ready to restrain him.

"Let's plug her in, shall we, have a nice listen. I could still get a 'Come back, Cyril,' you never know."

I watched him set up his transmitter, then fling open the leaded window and toss out the hairline-aerial, which was like a fishing line with a lead sinker but no hook. I watched him peer at his signals plan and type out SOS and his callsign on his squash recorder. Then he linked the recorder to the transmitter and, with a *whizz,* sent it into the ether. He did this several times before he switched over to receive, but nothing came and he didn't expect it to; he was showing me that it never would again.

"He did *tell* me it was over," he said, staring at the dials. "I'm not accusing him. He did *say.*"

"*What* was over? Spying?"

"Oh no, not spying, that'll go on for ever, won't it? Communism, really. He said Communism was just another minority religion these days, but we hadn't woken up to the fact. 'Time to hang up your boots, Cyril. Better not come to Russia if you're rumbled, Cyril. You'd be a bit of an embarrassment to the new climate. We might have to give you back as a gesture. We're out of date, you see, you and me. Moscow Centre's decided. It's hard currency that talks to Moscow these days. They need all the pounds and dollars they can get. So I'm afraid we're on the shelf, you and me, we're *de trop* and slightly *déjà vu,* not to say a rather large embarrassment to all concerned. Moscow can't afford to be seen running Foreign Office cypher clerks with access to top secret and above, and they rather regard you and me as more of a liability than an asset, which is the reason why they're calling me home. My advice to you, Cyril, therefore, is to take a nice long holiday, see a doctor and get some sun and rest, because between you and me you're showing signs of being slightly barking. We'd like to do right by you but we're a bit strapped for hard currency, to be frank. If you'd like a modest couple of thousand, I'm sure we can do you a small something in a Swiss bank, but the larger sums are unavailable till further notice.' He was like a different person talking to me, to be honest, Ned," he continued, in a tone of valiant incomprehension. "We'd been these great friends and he didn't want me any more. 'Don't take life so hard, Cyril,' he says. He keeps telling me I'm under strain, too many people inside my head. He's right really, I suppose. I lived the wrong life, that's all. You don't know till it's too late, though, do you, sometimes? You think you're one person, you turn out to be another, same as opera. Still, not to worry, I say. Fight another day. Say not the struggle naught availeth. All grist to the mill. Yes."

He had pulled back his soft shoulders and inflated himself somehow, seeing himself as a person superior to events. "Right, then," he said, and we returned spryly to the drawing room.

We had finished. All that remained was to mop up the missing answers and obtain an inventory of what he had betrayed.

We had finished, but it was I, not Frewin, who was resisting the final step. Sitting on the arm of the sofa, he turned his head away from me, smiling over-brightly and offering me his long neck for the knife. But he was waiting for a strike that I was refusing to deliver. His round bald head was craned tensely upward while he leaned away from me as if saying, "Do it now, hit me here." But I couldn't do it. I made no move towards him. I had the notebook in my hand, and enough written down for him to sign and destroy himself. But I didn't move. I was on his stupid side, not theirs. Yet what side was that? Was love an ideology? Was loyalty a political party? Or had we, in our rush to divide the world, divided it the wrong way, failing to notice that the real battle lay between those who were still searching, and those who, in order to prevail had reduced their vulnerability to the lowest common factor of indifference? I was on the brink of destroying a man for love. I had led him to the steps of his own scaffold, pretending we were taking a Sunday stroll together.

"Cyril?"

I had to repeat his name.

"What is it?"

"I'm supposed to take a signed statement from you."

"You can tell HQ that I was furthering understanding be-tween great nations," he said helpfully. I had the feeling that if he had been able, he would have told them for me. "Tell them I was putting an end to the mindless and incredible hostility I had observed for many years in the Tank. That should keep them quiet."

"Well, they did guess it would be something like that," I said. "It's just that there's a bit more to it than you understand.

"Also, put in that I wish for a posting. I should like to leave the Tank forthwith and earn out my retirement in a non-classified appointment. I'll accept demotion, I've decided. I'm not short of a bob or two. I'm not proud. A change of work is better than a holiday, I say. Where are you going, Ned? The facilities are the other way."

I was heading for the door. I was heading for sanity and es-cape. It was as if my world had reduced itself to this dreadful room. "Just back to the office, Cyril. For an hour or so. I can't produce your statement out of a hat for you, you know. It's got to be properly drawn up on the right forms and so forth. Never mind about the weekend. I never like weekends anyway, to be truthful. Holes in the universe, if you want my secret opinion, weekends are." Why was I speaking with his cadences? "Not to worry, Cyril. I'll see myself out. You get some rest."

I wanted to escape before they came. Looking past Frewin's head to the window, I could see Monty and two of his boys climbing out of their van, and a black police car pulling up outside the house—for the Service, thank God, has no powers of arrest.

But Frewin was talking again, the way the dying go on talking after you think they're dead.

"I can't be left alone, Ned, you see. Not any more. I can't explain it to a stranger, Ned, what I've done, not all over again, no one can."

I heard a footfall on the gravel, then the ring of the doorbell. Frewin's head came up and his eyes found mine and I watched the knowledge dawn in them, and fade in disbelief, and dawn again. I kept my gaze on him while I opened the front door. Palfrey was standing at Monty's shoulder. Behind them stood two uniformed police officers and a man called Redman, better known as Bedlam, from the Service's team of shrinks.

"Marvellous, Ned," Palfrey murmured, in a hasty aside to me as the others brushed past us into the drawing room. "An absolute *coup*. You'll get a medal, I'll see to it."

They had put handcuffs on him. It had not occurred to me that they would do that. They had handcuffed his hands behind his back, which made him lift his chin. I walked with him to the van and helped him into it, but by then he had found some kind of dignity of his own, and was no longer bothering whose hand was on his elbow.

"It's not everyone can crack a Modrian-trained spook between breakfast and lunchtime," said Burr with dour satisfaction. We were eating a muted dinner at Cecconi's, where he had insisted on taking me the same evening. "Our dear brethren across the

Park are beside themselves with rage, anger, indignation and envy, which is never bad either." But he was speaking to me from a world I had temporarily taken leave of.

"He cracked himself," I said.

Burr looked sharply at me. "I won't have that, Ned. I've not seen a hand played better. You were a whore. You had to be. We're all whores. Whores who pay. I've had enough of your melancholy, come to think of it—sitting over there in Northumberland Avenue, sulking like a stormcloud, caught between your women. If you can't take a decision, that's a decision. Leave your little love and go back to Mabel, if you want my advice, which you don't. I went back to mine last week and it's bloody murder."

Despite myself I discovered I was laughing.

"So what I've decided is this," Burr continued when he had generously consented to another enormous plate of pasta. "You're to abandon sulking as a way of life, and you're to abandon the Interrogators' Pool, in which, in my humble opinion, you have been studying your own narcissistic reflection for somewhat too long. And you're to unroll your mat on the Fifth Floor and replace Peter Guillam as my Head of Secretariat, which will suit your Calvinist disposition and rid me of a thoroughly idle officer."

I did what he suggested—all of it. Not because he had suggested it, but because he had spoken into my mind. I told Sally of my decision the next night and, if nothing else, the wretchedness of the occasion served to ease my memories of Frewin. For a few months, at her request, I continued writing to her from Tunbridge Wells, but it became as difficult as writing home from school. Sally was the last of what Burr had called my little loves. Perhaps I had had a notion that, added together, they could make up one big one.

12

"So it's over," said Smiley. The glow of the dying fire lit the panelled library, gilding its gappy shelves of dusty books on travel and adventure, and the old, cracked leather of its armchairs, and the foxed photographs of its vanished battalions of uniformed officers with walking sticks, and finally our own assorted faces, turned to Smiley on his throne of honour. Four generations of the Service lounged about the room, but Smiley's quiet voice and the haze of cigar smoke seemed to bind us in a single family.

I did not remember ever quite inviting Toby to join us, but certainly the staff had been expecting him and the mess waiters had scurried out to greet him as he arrived. In his wide, watered-silk lapels and waistcoat with its Balkan frogging, he looked every inch the *Rittmeister*.

Burr had hastened directly from Heathrow, changing into his dinner jacket in the back of his chauffeur-driven Rover in deference to George. He had entered almost unremarked, with that soundless dancer's walk of his that big men seem to manage naturally. Then Monty Arbuck spotted him and at once gave up his seat. Burr had recently become the first man to make Coordinator before the age of thirty-five.

And at Smiley's feet lounged my last intake of students, the girls like cut flowers in their evening dresses, the boys keen and fresh-faced after their end-of-course exertions in Argyll.

"It's over," Smiley repeated.

Was it his sudden stillness that alerted us. His altered voice? Or some almost priestly gesture that he made, a stiffening of his tubby body in piety or resolution. I couldn't have told you then, I can't tell you now. But I know I caught no one's eye, yet with his words I felt at once a kind of tensing among us, as if Smiley were calling us to arms—yet what he was talking about had as much to do with laying them down as taking them up.

"It's over, and so am I. Absolutely over. Time you rang down the curtain on yesterday's cold warrior. And please don't ask me back, ever again. The new time needs new people. The worst thing you can do is imitate us."

I think he had intended to end there, but with George you do better not to guess. For all I know, he had committed his entire closing speech to memory before he came, worked on it, rehearsed it word for word. In either case our silence now commanded him, as did our need of ceremony. Indeed, so thorough was our dependence on him at that moment that if he had turned and walked from the room without offering us another word, our disappointment would have turned our love to gall.

"I only ever cared about the *man*," Smiley announced. And it was typical of his artfulness that he should have opened with a riddle, then waited a moment before setting out to explain it. "I never gave a fig for the ideologies, unless they were mad or evil, I never saw institutions as being worthy of their parts, or policies as much other than excuses for not feeling. *Man*, not the mass, is what our calling is about. It was *man* who ended the Cold War in case you didn't notice. It wasn't weaponry, or technology, or armies or campaigns. It was just man. Not even Western man either, as it happened, but our sworn enemy in the East, who went into the streets, faced the bullets and the batons and said:

we've had enough. It was *their* emperor, not ours, who had the nerve to mount the rostrum and declare he had no clothes. And the ideologies trailed after these impossible events like condemned prisoners, as ideologies do when they've had their day. Because they have no heart of their own. They're the whores and angels of our striving selves. One day, history may tell us who really won. If a democratic Russia emerges—why then, Russia will have been the winner. And if the West chokes on its own materialism, then the West may still turn out to have been the loser. History keeps her secrets longer than most of us. But she has one secret that I will reveal to you tonight in the greatest confidence. Sometimes there are no winners at all. And sometimes nobody needs to lose. You asked me how we should think of Russia today."

Was that really what we had asked him? What else explained his change of direction? We had talked loosely of the crumbling Soviet Empire, it was true; we had pondered the rise and rise of Japan and the historical shifts of economic power. And in the to-and-fro after dinner, yes, there had been a few passing references to my time in the Russia House, and a few questions touching on the Middle East and Smiley's work with the Fishing Rights Committee, which, thanks to Toby, had become common knowledge. But I don't think that was the question George was choosing to answer now.

"You ask," he went on, "can we ever trust the Bear? You seem to be amused, yet a bit unseated, by the notion that we can talk to the Russians like human beings and find common cause with them in many fields. I will give you several answers at once.

"The first is no, we can never trust the Bear. For one reason, the Bear doesn't trust himself. The Bear is threatened and the Bear is frightened and the Bear is falling apart. The Bear is disgusted with his past, sick of his present and scared stiff of his future. He often was. The bear is broke, lazy, volatile, incompetent, slippery, dangerously proud, dangerously armed, sometimes brilliant, often ignorant. Without his claws, he'd be just another chaotic member of the Third World. But he isn't without his claws, not by any means. And he can't pull his soldiers back from foreign parts overnight, for the good reason that he can't house them or feed them or employ them, and he doesn't trust them either. And since this Service is the hired keeper of our national mistrust, we'd be neglecting our duty if we relaxed for one second our watch on the Bear, or on any of his unruly cubs. That's the first answer.

"The second answer is yes, we can trust the Bear completely. The Bear has never been so trustworthy. The Bear is begging to be part of us, to submerge his problems in us, have his own bank account with us, to shop in our High Street and be accepted as a dignified member of our forest as well as his—all the more so because his society and economy are in tatters, his natural resources are pillaged and his managers incompetent beyond belief. The Bear needs us so desperately that we may safely trust him to need us. The Bear longs to wind back his dreadful history and emerge from the dark of the last seventy or seven hundred years. We are his daylight.

"The problem is, we Westerners do not find it in us naturally to trust the Bear, whether he's a White Bear or a Red Bear, or both kinds of bear at once, which is what he is at the moment. The Bear may be in perdition without us, but there are lots of us who believe that's exactly where he belongs. Just as there were people in 1945 who argued that a defeated Germany should remain a rubble desert for the rest of human history."

Smiley paused and seemed to wonder whether he had said enough. He glanced towards me but I refused to catch his eye. The waiting silence must have convinced him to go on.

"The Bear of the future will be whatever we make of him, and the reasons for making something of him are several. The first is common decency. When you've helped a man to escape from wrongful imprisonment, the least you can do is provide him with a bowl of soup and the means to take his place in a free world. The second is so obvious it makes me a little intemperate to have to mention it at all. Russia—even Russia alone, shorn of all her conquests and possessions—is a vast country with a vast population in a crucial part of the globe. Do we leave the Bear to rot?— encourage him to become resentful, backward, an over-armed nation outside our camp? Or make a partner of him in a world that's changing its shape every day?"

He picked up his balloon glass and peered thoughtfully into it while he swirled the last of his brandy. And I sensed that he was finding it harder to take his leave than he had expected.

"Yes. Well," he muttered, as if somehow defending himself against his own assertions. "It's not only our minds we're going to have to reconstruct, either. It's the over-mighty modern State we've built for ourselves as a bastion against something that isn't there any more. We've given up far too many freedoms in order to be free. Now we've got to take them back."

He gave a shy grin, and I knew that he was trying to break his own spell upon us.

"So while you're out there striving loyally for the State, perhaps you'll do me a small favour and lean on its pillars from time to time. It's got a lot too big for its boots of late. It would be nice if you would cut it down to size. Ned, I'm a bore. Time you sent me home."

He stood up abruptly, as if shaking himself free of something that threatened to hold him too tight. Then, very deliberately, he treated himself to a last slow look round the room—not at the students any more, but at the old photographs and trophies of his time, apparently committing them to memory. He was taking leave of his house after he had bequeathed it to his heirs. Then, with a great flurry, he launched a search for his spectacles, before he discovered he was wearing them. Then he drew back his shoulders and marched purposefully to the door as two students hastened to open it for him.

"Yes. Well. Goodnight. And thanks. Oh, and tell them to spy on the ozone layer, will you, Ned? It's dreadfully hot in St. Agnes for the time of year."

He left without looking back.

The rituals of retirement from the Service are probably no more harrowing than any other professional leave-taking, but they have their own poignancy. There are the ceremonies of remembering—lunches with old contacts, office parties, brave handshakes with tearful senior secretaries, courtesy visits to friendly services. And there are the ceremonies of forgetting, where snip by snip you sever yourself from the special knowledge not given to other mortals. For someone who has spent a lifetime in the Service, including three years in Burr's inmost Secretariat, these can be lengthy and repetitive affairs, even if the secrets themselves have retired long before you. Closeted in Palfrey's musty lawyer's office, mercifully quite often in the glow of a good lunch, I signed away one piece after another of my past, obediently mumbling after him the same shy little English oath, and listening each time to his insincere warnings of retribution should I be tempted by vanity or money to transgress.

And I would be deceiving us both if I pretended that the cumulative burden of these ceremonies did not slowly weigh me down, and make me wish that my day of execution could be brought forward—or, better still, regarded as accomplished. For day by day I began to feel like the man who is reconciled to death but has to spend the last of his energies consoling those who will survive him.

It was a considerable relief to me, therefore, when seated once more in Palfrey's wretched lair with three days still to go before my final freedom or imprisonment, I received a peremptory summons to Burr's presence.

"I've got a job for you. You'll hate it," he assured me, and slammed down the phone.

He was still fuming when I reached his gaudy modern office. "You're to read his file, then drive into the country and reason with him. You're not to offend him, but if you should happen to break his neck by accident you'll not find me over-critical."

"Who is he?"

"Some leftover relic of Percy Alleline's. One of those beer-bellied tycoons from the City that Percy liked to play his golf with."

I glanced at the cover of the top volume. "BRADSHAW," I read, "Sir Anthony Joyston." And in small letters underneath: "asset index," meaning that the fileholder was perceived as an ally of the Service.

"You're to crawl to him, that's an order. Appeal to his better nature," said Burr in the same acid tone. "Strike the elder statesman's note. Bring him back into the fold."

"Who says I am?"

"The sainted Foreign Office. Who do you think?"

"Why don't they do their own crawling?" I said, peering curiously at the career synopsis on page 1. "I thought that was what they were paid for."

"They tried. They sent a Junior Minister, cap in hand. Sir Anthony is crawlproof. He also knows too much. He can name names and point fingers. Sir Anthony Bradshaw"—Burr announced, raising his voice in a North Country salvo of indignation—"Sir Anthony *Joyston* Bradshaw," he corrected himself, "is one of England's natural shits, who in the course of affecting to be of service to his country has picked up more knowledge of the disreputable activities of Her Majesty's Government than HMG ever picked up from Sir Anthony in regard to her adversaries. He accordingly has HMG by the balls. Your brief is to invite him, very courteously, to relax his grip. Your weapons for this task are your grey locks and your palpable good nature, which I have observed that you are not above putting to perfidious use. He's expecting you at five this evening and he likes punctuality. Kitty's cleared a desk for you in the anteroom."

It was not long before Burr's outrage was explained to me. There are few things more riling in our trade than having to cope with the unappetising leftovers of one's predecessors, and Sir Anthony Joyston Bradshaw, self-styled merchant venturer and City magnate, was a gruesome example of the type. Alleline had befriended him—at his club, where else? Alleline had recruited him. Alleline had sponsored him through a string of shady transactions of dubious value to anybody but Sir Anthony, and there were uncomfortable suggestions that Alleline might have taken a cut. Where scandal had threatened, Alleline had sheltered Sir Anthony under the Circus's compendious umbrella. Worse still, many of the doors that Alleline had opened for Bradshaw appeared to have stayed open, for the reason that nobody had thought to close them. And it was through one of these that Bradshaw had now walked, to the shrill outrage of the Foreign Office and half of Whitehall.

I drew an Ordnance Survey map from Library and a Ford Granada from the car pool. At half past two, with the file pretty much in my head, I set off. Sometimes you forget how beautiful England is. I passed through Newbury and climbed a winding hill lined with beech trees whose long shadows were cut like trenches into the golden stubble. A smell of cricket fields filled the car. I mounted a crest, castles of white cloud waited to receive me. I must have been thinking of my childhood, I suppose, for I had a sudden urge to drive straight to them, a thing I had often dreamed of as a boy. The car dipped again and fell free, and suddenly a whole valley opened below me, strewn with hamlets, churches, folding fields and forests.

I passed a pub, and soon a great pair of closed and gilded gates appeared between stone gateposts capped by carved lions. Beside them stood a neat white gatehouse newly thatched. A fit young man lowered his face to my open window and studied me with sniper's eyes.

"To see Sir Anthony," I said.

"Name, sir?"

"Carlisle," I replied, using an alias for the last time.

The boy disappeared into the lodge; the gates opened, then closed as soon as I was through them. The park was bordered by a high brick wall—there must have been a couple of miles of it. Fallow deer lay in the shade of chestnut trees. The drive lifted and the house appeared before me. It was golden and immaculate and very large. The centre section was William and Mary. The wings looked later, but not much. A lake lay before it, vegetable gardens and greenhouses behind. The old stables had been converted to offices, with clever outside staircases and glazed external corridors. A gardener was watering the orangerie.

The drive skirted the lake and brought me to the front sweep. Two Arab mares and a llama eyed me over the fence of a lunging ring. A young butler came down the steps, dressed in black trousers and a linen jacket.

"Shall I park your car round the back, Mr. Carlisle, once you've been introduced?" he asked. "Sir Anthony does like a clear façade, when he can get one, sir."

I gave him the keys and followed him up the wide steps. There were nine, though I can't imagine why I counted, except that it was something we had taught on the Sarratt awareness course, and in recent weeks my life seemed to have become less a continuation than a mosaic of past ages and experiences. If Ben had come striding up to me and grasped my hand, I don't think I would have been particularly surprised. If Monica or Sally had appeared to accuse me, I would have had my answers ready.

I entered a huge hall. A splendid double staircase rose to an open landing. Portraits of noble ancestors, all men, stared down at me, but somehow I didn't believe they were of one family, or could have lived here long without their women. I passed through a billiards room and noticed that the table and cues were new. I suppose I saw everything so clearly because I was treating each experience as my last. I followed the butler through a stately drawing room and traversed a second room that was got up as a hall of mirrors, and a third that was supposed to be informal, with a television set the size of one of those old ice-cream tricycles that used to call at my preparatory school on sunny evenings just like this. I arrived at a pair of majestic doors and waited while the butler knocked. Then waited again for a response. If Bradshaw were an Arab, he would keep me standing here for hours, I thought, remembering Beirut.

Finally I heard a male voice drawl "Come," and the butler took a pace into the room and announced, "A Mr. Carlisle, Sir Anthony, from London."

I had not told him I had come from London.

The butler stepped aside and gave me a first view of my host, though it took a little longer before my host had his first view of Mr. Carlisle.

He was sitting at a twelve-foot desk with brass inlay and cabriole legs. Modern oil paintings of spoilt children hung behind him. His correspondence was stacked in trays of thick stitched hide. He was a big, well-nourished man, and clearly a big worker also, for he had stripped to his shirt, which was blue with a midwife's white collar, and he was working in his braces, which were red. Also he was too busy to acknowledge me. First he read, using a gold pen to guide his eye. Then he signed, using the gold pen to write. Then he meditated, still in a downward direction, using the tip of the gold pen as a focus for his great thoughts. His gold cufflinks were as big as old pennies. Then at last he laid the pen down and, with a wounded—even accusatory—air, he raised his head, first to discover me, then to measure me by standards I had yet to ascertain.

At the same moment, by a happy chance of nature, a shaft of low sunlight from the French windows landed on his face, and I was able to measure him in return: the self-sadness of his pouchy eyes, as if he should be pitied for his wealth, the straight small mouth set tense and crooked in the puckered chins, the air of resolution formed of weakness, of boyhood suspicions in a grown-up world. At forty-five, this fattened child was unappeased, blaming some absent parent for his comforts.

Suddenly, Bradshaw was walking towards me. Stalking? Wading? There is an English walk these days peculiar to men of power, and it is a confection of several things at once. Self-confidence is one, lazy sportiveness another. But there is also menace in it, and impatience, and a leisured arrogance, which comes with the crablike splaying of elbows that give way to no-body, and the boxer's slouch of the shoulders, and the playful springiness in the knees. You knew long before you shook his hand that he had no truck with a whole category of life that ranged from art to public transport. You were silently forewarned to keep your distance if you were that kind of fool.

"You're one of Percy's boys," he told me, in case I didn't know, while he sampled my hand, and was duly disappointed. "Well, well. Long time no see. Must be ten years. More. Have a drink. Have champagne. Have what you like." An order: "Summers. Get us a bottle of shampoo, bucket of ice, two glasses, then bugger off. And nuts!" he shouted after him. "Cashews. Brazils. Masses of fucking nuts—like nuts?" he enquired of me, with a sudden and disarming intimacy.

I said I did.

"Good. Me too. Love 'em. You've come to read me the riot act. Right? Go on. Not made of glass."

He was flinging open the French windows so that I could have a better view of what he owned. He had chosen a different walk for this manoeuvre, more march, more swinging the arms to the rhythm of unheard martial music. When he had opened the doors, he gave me his back to look at, and kept his arms up, palms propped against the door posts, like a martyr waiting for the arrow. And the City haircut, I thought: thick at the collar and little horns above the ears. In golds and browns and greens, the valley faded softly into eternity. A nanny and a small child were walking among the deer. She wore a brown hat with the brim up all the way round and a brown uniform like a Girl Guide's. The lawn was set for croquet.

"We're just appealing to you, that's all, Sir Anthony," I said. "Asking you another favour, like the ones you did for Percy. After all, it was Percy who got you your knighthood, wasn't it?"

"Fuck Percy. Dead, isn't he? Nobody gives me anything, thank you. Help myself to it. What do you want? Spit it out, will you? I've had one sermon already. Portly Savoury from the Foreign Office. Used to flog him when he was my fag at school. Wimp then, wimp now."

The arms stayed up there, the back was braced and aggressive. I might have spoken, but I felt strangely off key. Three days before my retirement, I was beginning to feel I hardly knew the real world at all. Summers brought champagne, uncorked it and filled two glasses, which he handed to us on a silver tray. Bradshaw snatched one and strode into the garden. I trailed after him

to the centre of a grass alley. Azaleas and rhododendrons grew
high to either side of us. At the farther end, a fountain played in
a stone pond.

"Did you get a lordship of the manor when you bought this
house?" I asked, thinking a little small talk might give me time to
collect myself.

"Suppose I did?" Bradshaw retorted, and I realised he did not
wish to be reminded that he had bought his house rather than
inherited it.

"Sir Anthony," I said.

"Well?"

"It's concerning your relationship with a Belgian company
called Astrasteel."

"Never heard of 'em."

"But you are associated with them, aren't you?" I said, with a
smile.

"Aren't now, never was. Told Savoury the same."

"But you have holdings in Astrasteel, Sir Anthony," I protested patiently.

"Zilch. Absolutely bugger all. Different bloke, wrong address.
Told him."

"But you do have a one hundred percent holding in a company
called Allmetal of Birmingham Limited, Sir Anthony. And Allmetal of Birmingham does own a company called Eurotech
Funding & Imports Limited of Bermuda, doesn't it? And Eurotech of Bermuda does own Astrasteel of Belgium, Sir Anthony.
So we may take it that a certain loose association might be said to
exist between yourself on the one hand, and this company that is
owned by the company you own on the other." I was still smiling,
still reasoning with him, joking him along.

"No holdings, no dividends, no influence over Astrasteel's affairs. Arm's length, whole thing. Told Savoury, tell the same to
you."

"Nevertheless, when you were invited by Alleline—back in the old days, I know, but not *so* long ago, was it?—to make deliveries of certain commodities to certain countries not strictly on the official shopping list for those commodities, Astrasteel *was* the company you used. And Astrasteel did what you told them to do. Because if they hadn't done, Percy would not have come to you—would he? You'd have been no use to him." My smile felt stiff on my face. "We're not *policemen,* Sir Anthony, we're not the *taxman.* I'm merely indicating to you certain relationships that stand—as you insist—beyond the law's reach, and were indeed designed—with Percy's active help—to do just that."

My speech sounded so ill composed to me, so unpointed that I assumed at first that Bradshaw did not propose to bother with it at all.

And in a way I was right, for he merely shrugged and said, "Fuck's that got to do with anything?"

"Well quite a lot actually." I could feel my blood beginning to rise, and there was nothing I could do to check it. "We're asking you to lay off. Stop. You've got your knighthood, you're worth a fortune, you have a duty to your country today just as you had twelve years ago. So get out of the Balkans and stop stirring it with the Serbs and stop stirring it in Central Africa, stop offering them guns galore on tick, and stop trying to cash in on wars that may never happen if you and other like-minded spirits keep your fingers out of them. You're British. You've more money in your pocket than most of us will touch in a lifetime. Stop. Just stop. That's all we're asking. Times have changed. We're not playing those games any more."

For a moment I fancied I had impressed him, for he turned his unlit gaze on me, and looked me over as if I were someone who might after all be worth buying. Then his interest flickered out again and he relapsed into despondency.

"It's your country talking to you, Bradshaw," I said, now with real anger. "For Christ's sake, man, what more do you *need*? Haven't you got even the vestige of a conscience?"

I will give you Bradshaw's reply as I transcribed it, for at Burr's request I had slipped a recorder into my jacket pocket and Bradshaw's sawing nasal tones ensured a perfect reproduction. I will give you his voice too, as nearly as I can write it down. He spoke English as if it were his second language, but it was the only one he had. He spoke in what my son Adrian tells me is called "slur," which is a slack-mouthed Belgravia cockney that contrives to make *mice* out of *mouse* and dispenses almost entirely with the formality of pronouns. It has a vocabulary, naturally: nothing rises but it *escalates,* no opportunity is without a *window,* no minor event occurs that is not *sensational.* It also has a pedantic inaccuracy which is supposed to distinguish it from the unwashed, and explains gems like "as for you and I." But even without my tape recorder, I like to think I would have remembered every word, for his speech was like an evening war-cry from a world I was leaving to itself.

"I'm sorry," he began, which was a lie to start with. "Did I understand you were appealing to my conscience? Good. Right. Make a statement for the record. Mind? Statement begins here. Point One. There *is* only one point actually. *I don't give a fart.* The difference between me and other charlies is, *I* admit it. If a horde of niggers—yes, I said *niggers,* I meant *niggers*—if these *niggers* shot each other dead with my toys tomorrow and I made a bob out of it, great news by me. Because if *I* don't sell 'em the goods, some *other* charlie will. Government used to understand that. If they've gone soft, tough titty on 'em. Point Two. Question: heard what the tobacco boys are up to these days? Flogging off high-toxic tobacco to the fuzzy-wuzzies and telling 'em it makes 'em horny and cures the common cold. Tobacco boys give a fart? Sit at home having nervous breakdowns about spreading lung cancer among the natives? The fuck they do. Doing a little creative selling, period. Take drugs. Don't use 'em personally. Don't need 'em. Never mind. If willing seller is doing business with willing buyer, my advice is step aside, let them slug it out, and bloody good luck to 'em. If drugs don't kill 'em, the atmosphere will or they'll get barbecued by the global warming. British, you said. Matter of fact, rather proud of it. Also rather proud of one's *school*. Empire man. Happens to be the tradition one's inherited. When people get in one's way, I break 'em. Or they break me. Discipline is rather up one's street too, actually. *Order.* Accepting responsibilities of one's class and education, and beating the foreigner at his own game. Thought you people were rather committed to that one, too. Error, apparently. Failure of communication. What one cares about is quality of life. *This* life. *Standards* actually. Old word. Don't care. *These* standards. Pompous, you're thinking. All right, I'm pompous. Fuck you. I'm Pharaoh, right? If a few thousand slaves have to die so that I can build this pyramid, nature. And if they can make *me* die for *their* fucking pyramid, bloody good on 'em. Know what I've got in my cellar? Iron rings. Rusty iron rings, built into the wall when this house was built. Know what they were for? Slaves. *That's* nature too. Original owner of this house—man who *built* this house— man who *paid* for it, man who sent his architect to Italy, learn his trade—that man owned slaves, and had his slave quarters in the cellar of this house. Think there aren't slaves today? Think capital doesn't *depend* on slaves. Jesus Christ, what kind of shop do you run? One doesn't normally talk philosophy, but I'm afraid one doesn't like being preached to either. Won't have it, you see. Not in my house, thank you. Annoys me. Don't bug easily, rather famous for one's cool. But one does have a certain view of nature; one gives work to people and one takes one's share."

I said nothing, and that is on the tape too.

In the face of an absolute, what can you say? All my life I had battled against an institutionalised evil. It had had a name and

most often a country as well. It had had a corporate purpose, and
had met a corporate end. But the evil that stood before me now
was a wrecking infant in our own midst, and I became an infant
in return, disarmed, speechless and betrayed. For a moment, it
was as if my whole life had been fought against the wrong enemy.
Then it was as if Bradshaw had personally stolen the fruits of my
victory. I remembered Smiley's aphorism about the right people
losing the Cold War, and the wrong people winning it, and I
thought of repeating it to him as some sort of insult, but I would
have been beating the air. I thought of telling him that now we
had defeated Communism, we were going to have to set about
defeating capitalism, but that wasn't really my point, the evil was
not in the system, but in the man. And besides, by then he was
asking me whether I wanted to stay to dinner, at which I politely
declined, and left.

In the event, it was Burr who gave me dinner, and I am pleased
to say I don't remember much about it. Two days later, I turned
in my Head Office pass.

You see your face. It's no one you remember. You wonder where
you put your love, what you found, what you were after. You
want to say: "I slew the dragon, I left the world a safer place."
You can't really, not these days. Perhaps you never could.

We have a good life, Mabel and I. We don't talk about things
we can't change. We don't cross each other. We're civilised. We've
bought a cottage on the coast. There's a long garden there I'd like
to get my hands on, plant a few trees, make a vista to the sea.
There's a sailing club for poor kids I'm involved in; we bring
them down from Hackney, they enjoy it. There's a move to draft
me for the local council. Mabel does the church. I go back to Holland now and then. I still have a few relations there.

Burr drops in from time to time. I like that in him. He gets on well with Mabel, as you'd expect. He doesn't try to be wise. He chats to her about her watercolours. He's not judgmental. We open a good bottle, cook a chicken. He brings me up to date, drives back to London. Of Smiley, nothing, but that's the way he wanted it. He hates nostalgia, even if he's part of other people's.

There's no such thing as retirement, really. Sometimes there's knowing too much, and not being able to do much about it, but that's just age, I'm sure. I think a lot. I'm stepping out with my reading. I talk to people, ride on buses. I'm a newcomer to the overt world but I'm learning.

An Essay by the Author

In *The Secret Pilgrim* I determined to make a last farewell of the Cold War, of George Smiley and all his people, and of certain elusive themes that had been nagging at me through two-and-a-half decades of writing. I wanted to consider who we had been and who we had become, and take a look at the future shape of the two superpowers, now that—with some reluctance on both sides—they had suspended, at least for the time being, their games of Russian roulette. I had already taken leave of the Cold War twice before, at least in my own mind: in *Smiley's People,* which ended for all time, as far as I was concerned, the standoff between Smiley and Karla; and in *A Perfect Spy,* in which the despairing protagonist doesn't know or care anymore whether he belongs to the East or West.

But the elusive themes still constituted unfinished business. Some of them remained unexplored until later books. Now that the West had dealt with rogue forms of communism, I wanted to ask, How was it going to deal with rogue forms of capitalism? In *The Secret Pilgrim,* Smiley pops the question, but I didn't really get round to addressing it until *Single & Single* and *The Constant Gardener.* A more banal theme that had always bugged me was the element of human incompetence in the world of espionage. Part of the baggage that a spywriter has to address is the conviction of the man on the street that spies are somehow smarter and more adept at life than are ordinary folk. Spies don't lose their car keys or forget the combinations to their safes or accidentally address their new wives by the names of their last ones. Well, of course they don't; they're spies, they're trained and all that—handpicked, aren't they? And we tell ourselves that despite the endless news stories of cock-up that reach us by way of disgruntled defectors like Shayler or Tomlinson, or through the daily press: briefcases stuffed with priceless secrets left on the London Underground, computer disks containing the names of informants picked up in secondhand radio stores, and so on.

Even when a Chinook helicopter crashes on its way from Northern Ireland, killing a galaxy of intelligence officers, we seem as a nation reluctant to ask ourselves how anyone could be such a purblind idiot as to put all these important people onto the same flight—even if we discount the fact that the perils of such flights had been abundantly clear to the evasive Ministry of Defence. *There must be a reason,* we tell ourselves, falling back on our faith in the occult. *Spies do things differently. They're not as daft as we are.* Whereas, as Arthur Koestler said famously of his fellow Jews, spies are the same as us, but more so.

But when from time to time I had tried—for instance in 1963 when I was writing *The Looking Glass War*—to use cock-up rather than conspiracy as the dramatic outline of my story, I failed to take the reader with me. And in a sense I had only myself to blame, for the book before it had been *The Spy Who Came in from the Cold,* in which conspiracy, and conspiracy only, ruled the plot. *First you tell us one thing, now you tell us the opposite* was the reader's justifiable grouse, and I paid a high price for my presumption, even if I never gave up my personal conviction that incompetence, not conspiracy, is what makes the secret world go round.

So in *The Secret Pilgrim,* you get a hyper-nervous young British intelligence officer who leaves a handwritten breakdown of his East German spy network on the roof of his car, and thereby destroys both himself and his luckless agents, and a pathologically solitary cypher clerk who deludes himself into believing he is a star Russian language student, and thus delivers himself to the KGB. The poor clerk wasn't the victim of a cock-up, exactly, but rather of the fatal triviality of human motive, of the hairline distinction between the harmlessly eccentric and the dangerously mad. Not nearly enough has been written about the phenomenon of seeming sanity among people who turn out to be barking mad. It will be years before anybody is brave enough to put a name to the motive that drove the recently unmasked senior FBI operative, [Robert] Hanssen, to betray his service for so long and with such extraordinary devotion, but the signs are that he was a seemingly sane man whose interior reality was mayhem.

But the character who haunts me most in these pages is neither the poor cypher clerk nor the Berlin trainee. Nor even the old soldier, Sergeant Major Hawthorne, who believed that his criminal thug of a son was a loyal British secret agent acting a part; and was allowed to persist in this belief by George Smiley, who gave him a pair of precious gold cufflinks as spurious proof of the boy's service before the secret mast.

It is Hansen. Not the wretched real-life Hanssen of the FBI to whom I have just referred, but Hansen my Dutchman and Asian scholar. Hansen my British agent and lapsed Jesuit priest, whose story you will find in chapter nine. Very few characters in my writing are drawn from actual people, and those that are tend to be a mishmash of several. Very few episodes have a basis in fact either, though I confess that the story of Smiley's cufflinks is descended from an incident attributed to Sir Maurice Oldfield, once chief of MI6.

But my character Hansen does for once have a real-life model and his name is François Bizot, a French scholar of Buddhism whom I first met in Cambodia and then in Thailand when I was researching *The Honourable Schoolboy,* and who generously gave me permission to adapt his true-life story to my spurious fictional purposes. And Bizot, I am delighted to say, last year published his own much-praised account of the events in his life that I have traduced. And Bizot's book, rightly hailed in France as a masterpiece, called *Le portail—The Gate*—and winner of a string of French literary prizes, will be published in English this year.

And it is a measure of the amoral ways of us fiction writers—of our secret thefts and wanton misrepresentations—that in my fictional story of Bizot's heroism I make of him precisely the person he empathically never was. He was not a Western lackey, he was not an imperialist spy masquerading as a Buddhist scholar, he was not the fascist running dog that Pol Pot and his henchman would have him be. He was Bizot, nobody's creature but his own—which was why, against all the probabilities of those dreadful times, his Khmer Rouge inquisitors let him go. By sheer determination and force of character, Bizot had convinced his would-be executioners of his innocence.

At the time of its publication I dedicated *The Secret Pilgrim* to Alec Guinness, in acknowledgment of his portrayal of George Smiley in the BBC television series, and of a modest friendship that persisted until his recent death. But Guinness was always humbled, as I am, by the gap between the world of the imagination and the world of the real. So he would certainly join me in raising a toast to Bizot, a real man among my cast of imaginary souls.

David Cornwell

JOHN LE CARRÉ was born in 1931. After attending the universities of Berne and Oxford, he taught at Eton and spent five years in the British Foreign Service. *The Spy Who Came in from the Cold,* his third book, secured him a worldwide reputation. He divides his time between England and the Continent.

johnlecarre.com
Facebook.com/johnlecarreofficial
Twitter: @lecarre_news

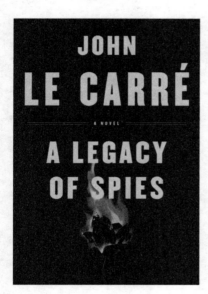

THE GEORGE SMILEY NOVELS

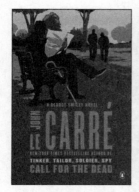
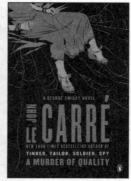

PENGUIN BOOKS

SMILEY'S PEOPLE

JOHN LE CARRÉ was born in 1931. For six decades, he wrote novels that came to define our age. The son of a con man, he spent his childhood between boarding school and the London underworld. At sixteen he found refuge at the university of Bern, then later at Oxford. A spell of teaching at Eton led him to a short career in British Intelligence (MI5&6). He published his debut novel, *Call for the Dead*, in 1961 while still a secret servant. His third novel, *The Spy Who Came in from the Cold*, secured him a worldwide reputation, which was consolidated by the acclaim for his trilogy *Tinker Tailor Soldier Spy*, *The Honourable Schoolboy*, and *Smiley's People*. At the end of the Cold War, le Carré widened his scope to explore an international landscape including the arms trade and the War on Terror. His memoir, *The Pigeon Tunnel*, was published in 2016 and the last George Smiley novel, *A Legacy of Spies*, appeared in 2017. He died on December 12, 2020.

ALSO BY JOHN LE CARRÉ

JOHN LE CARRÉ

SMILEY'S PEOPLE

PENGUIN BOOKS

PENGUIN BOOKS
An imprint of Penguin Random House LLC
penguinrandomhouse.com

First published in the United States of America by Franklin Library 1979
Published in the United States of America by Alfred A. Knopf 1980
Published in Penguin Books 2011

Grateful acknowledgment is made to Random House, Inc., and to Faber & Faber Ltd.
for permission to reprint a verse by W. H. Auden.

ISBN 9780143119777 (paperback)
ISBN 9781101535295 (ebook)
CIP data available

Printed in the United States of America
20th Printing

For my sons,
Simon, Stephen,
Timothy, and
Nicholas, with love
_____

INTRODUCTION

JOHN LE CARRÉ
Cornwall, October 2000

Smiley's People is the third and final novel in what became a trilogy recounting the duel of wits between George Smiley of the British Secret Service, which I called the Circus, and his rival and alter ego, code name Karla of the KGB, which I called Moscow Centre. The first novel of the trilogy was *Tinker, Tailor, Soldier, Spy*; the second, *The Honourable Schoolboy*. My grand ambition was to write not just three but a whole scad of them—ten or fifteen—describing an epic stand-off between my two protagonists that would cover every corner of the globe and collectively constitute a kind of *Comédie Humaine* of the cold war, told in terms of mutual espionage.

Spying, in all its different forms, was after all what the cold war had for a battlefield, and the spies were its ground troops. Hot wars like Korea and Vietnam might come and go, but spying was a continuum. The obsession of the two great economic systems with each other's identity, intentions, strengths, and weaknesses had produced by the 1970s a state of mutual watchfulness and paranoia that seemed to know no bounds. Each side was ready to pay any sum, take any risk, tell any lie, to gain a seeming intelligence advantage over the other. Neither seemed able to grasp the utter sterility of this situation. It is no wonder that, when the players were finally able to look at one another's cards, it tuned out that each had vastly exaggerated the other's strategic capability. In that sense, the quest for intelligence took on at its worst an almost mythic form, with the spies not so much required to report the truth about the enemy as paint him in a form monstrous enough to keep the alarm bells ringing for all eternity.

And at the heart of this war of fantasies lay the war between intelligence services of the opposing Blocs themselves—surely the most sterile, the least productive, and the most addictive of all the games spies play, since it neither enlightens nor benefits the real world which gives them their daily bread, and turns the basically very simple trade of espionage into a never-ending maze of mirrors to which only professionals are admitted, and nobody looks the wiser. Along the way, I had preachier notions I wanted to slip into my great *oeuvre*, provided I could find a way to dramatise them, even seditious ones—the moral corruption that the cold war was leaving in its wake in the Western as well as the Communist world, for instance; and how the cold war's cult of lying was permeating every area of Western public life so that in this country alone there was scarcely an organ of government, from the parish pump upwards, that couldn't invoke the spectre of national security to disguise its bias, incompetence, and corruption. And Smiley would be my champion, my mouthpiece, my knight errant. And my readers would listen to him where they wouldn't listen to me. Because he was a better man than I was, and part of a grand story. And if Smiley on the insistence of some secret loyalty board of American-inspired witch-hunters was one day hauled before a kangaroo court of his peers—such things happened in those days—and charged with harbouring sympathies incompatible with his secret work, then my readers would rush to his protection and send his accusers packing. In my head I had a lot of this stuff planned, and more of it in notebooks.

So what stopped me from fulfilling this grand design?

In part, Smiley did. The older I became, the more I wanted to write about younger passions and a changing society. There

had been a time when Smiley had been my proxy father, almost
my father confessor. But as my knight errant he cast too old an
eye on the world. Where he saw change, it pained him. And
where his corrosive eye and brave past had once provided me
with a voice and a disguise, I was beginning to find these very
assets a liability. Smiley was still my hero, but he had got above
his station. He was too patient for me. His radicalism was the
thinker's, not the doer's. Ultimately, whatever his misgivings,
he always knuckled down and did the job, even if he had to leave
his conscience outside the door. Which meant he and the reader
had the best of both worlds. Alec Guinness's superb portrayal of
him only added to my problems. When *Tinker, Tailor, Soldier,
Spy* was first shown on the BBC, the only independent channel
in those days obligingly staged a strike and for six precious
weeks the entire British viewing public had to choose between
BBC1 and BBC2. In consequence, we were pulling in audiences
of up to eleven million for each episode, and the series became a
kind of public institution, with endless chat on the radio about
who understood how much or how little of the plot, and George
Smiley briefly became a kind of myopic national hero, solving
crossword puzzles that defeated the rest of us.

The problem went further than that. George Smiley,
whether I liked it or not, *was* from then on Alec Guinness—
voice, mannerisms, the whole package. And I *did* like it. I liked
it enormously. Once in a writer's life, if he's lucky, an actor
plays one of his characters to perfection. And Alec did that. He
was as good at being Smiley as Cyril Cusack was at being Control in *The Spy Who Came In from the Cold*. Better. On the other
hand, I didn't at all enjoy the fact that Smiley had somehow
been taken over by my public. It was a thoroughly odd sensation, and not at all a pleasant one, when I went to get my character back after Alec had finished with him, to discover that I
had been given used goods. I think I even felt a little bit
betrayed.

Another thing that held me back from my great design was a drastic change in my writing methods for which to this day I can't quite account. Writing *Tinker, Tailor* had been a static exercise. I sat in Cornwall and scribbled. Though the story had scenes in Hong Kong, Delhi, and Prague, I had visited none of those places in order to write the novel. I had fed off my memory and imagination, and got away with it. Perhaps for this reason, when I came to write *The Honourable Schoolboy*, I took to the road in a very big way indeed. Basing myself in Hong Kong, I shot off to north-east Thailand, Laos, Cambodia, Vietnam, and Taiwan in quick order, and wrote, as it were, from the stirrup. Along the way, I tasted hot warfare for the first time, though mercifully very little of it, and by the time I'd seen what I set out to see, I was beginning to regard Smiley and Karla as superfluous baggage. *The Honourable Schoolboy* was kindly received, but I still believe it might have been a better novel without their presence.

For all these reasons then, *Smiley's People* was intended to be a requiem for the old spy, and to me that is what it remains. Smiley popped up again in *The Secret Pilgrim*, but only in a retrospective rôle. To provide him with a good send-off, I assembled all the usual suspects: Peter Guillam, Toby Esterhase, Connie Sachs, and, of course, the old fox himself, code name Karla. The grand finale takes place in divided Berlin. Where else could I choose? In *The Spy Who Came In from the Cold* it was at the Berlin Wall that Smiley was heard shouting at Alec Leamas not to go back for the girl Liz. For his last act, Smiley would return there, and in his heart beg Karla not to leave the East. Smiley wins, Karla loses. But at what cost to both of them? Facing each other, they are the two no-men of no-man's-land. Karla has sacrificed his political faith, Smiley his humanity.

I always remember the words of a Berlin comedian when, against all prediction, the Berlin Wall did finally come down.

"The right side lost but the wrong side won." He meant, I suppose, that having defeated Communism, we are left with the problem of how to tackle our own greed, and our indifference to human suffering in the world outside our own. I'll bet you that George Smiley, if he is still with us, is still agonising over the answer.

SMILEY'S PEOPLE

1

Two seemingly unconnected events heralded the summons of Mr. George Smiley from his dubious retirement. The first had for its background Paris, and for a season the boiling month of August, when Parisians by tradition abandon their city to the scalding sunshine and the bus-loads of packaged tourists.

On one of these August days—the fourth, and at twelve o'clock exactly, for a church clock was chiming and a factory bell had just preceded it—in a *quartier* once celebrated for its large population of the poorer Russian émigrés, a stocky woman of about fifty, carrying a shopping bag, emerged from the darkness of an old warehouse and set off, full of her usual energy and purpose, along the pavement to the bus-stop. The street was grey and narrow, and shuttered, with a couple of small *hôtels de passe* and a lot of cats. It was a place, for some reason, of peculiar quiet. The warehouse, since it handled perishable goods, had remained open during the holidays. The heat, fouled by exhaust fumes and unwashed by the slightest breeze, rose at her like the heat from a lift-shaft, but her Slavic features registered no complaint. She was neither dressed nor built for exertion on a hot day, being in stature very short indeed, and fat, so that she had to roll a little in order to get along. Her black dress, of ecclesiastical severity, possessed neither a waist nor any other relief except for a dash of white lace at the neck and a large metal cross, well fingered but of no intrinsic value, at the bosom.

Her cracked shoes, which in walking tended outwards at the points, set a stern tattoo rattling between the shuttered houses. Her shabby bag, full since early morning, gave her a slight starboard list and told clearly that she was used to burdens. There was also fun in her, however. Her grey hair was gathered in a bun behind her, but there remained one sprightly forelock that flopped over her brow to the rhythm of her waddle. A hardy humour lit her brown eyes. Her mouth, set above a fighter's chin, seemed ready, given half a reason, to smile at any time.

Reaching her usual bus-stop, she put down her shopping bag and with her right hand massaged her rump just where it met the spine, a gesture she made often these days though it gave her little relief. The high stool in the warehouse where she worked every morning as a checker possessed no back, and increasingly she was resenting the deficiency. "Devil," she muttered to the offending part. Having rubbed it, she began plying her black elbows behind her like an old town raven preparing to fly. "Devil," she repeated. Then, suddenly aware of being watched, she wheeled round and peered upward at the heavily built man towering behind her.

He was the only other person waiting, and indeed, at that moment, the only other person in the street. She had never spoken to him, yet his face was already familiar to her: so big, so uncertain, so sweaty. She had seen it yesterday, she had seen it the day before, and for all she knew, the day before that as well—my Lord, she was not a walking diary! For the last three or four days, this weak, itchy giant, waiting for a bus or hovering on the pavement outside the warehouse, had become a figure of the street for her; and what was more, a figure of a recognisable type, though she had yet to put her finger on which. She thought he looked *traqué*—hunted—as so many Parisians did these days. She saw so much fear in their faces; in the way they walked yet dared not greet each other. Perhaps it was the same everywhere, she wouldn't know. Also, more than once, she had felt *his* interest in *her.* She had wondered whether he was a policeman. She had even considered asking him, for she had this urban cockiness. His lugubrious build suggested the police, so did the sweaty suit and the needless raincoat that hung like a bit of old uniform from his forearm. If she was right, and he *was* police, then—high time too, the idiots were finally doing something about the spate of pilfering that had made a beargarden of her stock-checking for months.

By now the stranger had been staring down at her for some time, however. And he was staring at her still.

"I have the misfortune to suffer in my back, monsieur," she confided to him finally, in her slow and classically enunciated French. "It is not a large back but the pain is disproportionate. You are a doctor, perhaps? An osteopath?"

Then she wondered, looking up at him, whether he was ill, and her joke out of place. An oily gloss glistened on his jaw and neck, and there was an unseeing self-obsession about his pallid eyes. He seemed to see beyond her to some private trouble of his own. She was going to ask him this—You are perhaps in love, monsieur? Your wife is deceiving you?—and she was actually considering steering him into a café for a glass of water or a *tisane* when he abruptly swung away from her and looked behind him, then over her head up the street the other way. And it occurred to her that he really was afraid, not just *traqué* but frightened stiff; so perhaps he was not a policeman at all, but a thief—though the difference, she knew well, was often slight.

"Your name is Maria Andreyevna Ostrakova?" he asked her abruptly, as if the question scared him.

He was speaking French but she knew that it was not his mother tongue any more than it was her own, and his correct pronunciation of her name, complete with patronymic, already alerted her to his origin. She recognised the slur at once and the shapes of the tongue that made it, and she identified too late, and with a considerable inward start, the type she had not been able to put her finger on.

"If it is, who on earth are *you?*" she asked him in reply, sticking out her jaw and scowling.

He had drawn a pace closer. The difference in their heights was immediately absurd. So was the degree to which the man's features betrayed his unpleasing character. From her low position Ostrakova could read his weakness as clearly as his fear. His damp chin had set in a grimace, his mouth had twisted to make him look strong, but she knew he was only banishing an incurable cowardice. He is like a man steeling himself for a heroic act, she thought. Or a criminal one. He is a man cut off from all spontaneous acts, she thought.

"You were born in Leningrad on May 8, 1927?" the stranger asked.

Probably she said yes. Afterwards she was not sure. She saw his scared gaze lift and stare at the approaching bus. She saw an indecision near to panic seize him, and it occurred to her—which in the long run was an act of near clairvoyance—that he proposed to push her under it. He didn't, but he did put his next question in Russian—and in the brutal accents of Moscow officialdom.

"In 1956, were you granted permission to leave the Soviet Union for the purpose of nursing your sick husband, the traitor Ostrakov? Also for certain other purposes?"

"Ostrakov was not a traitor," she replied, cutting him off. "He was a patriot." And by instinct she took up her shopping bag and clutched the handle very tight.

The stranger spoke straight over this contradiction, and very loudly, in order to defeat the clatter of the bus: "Ostrakova, I bring you greetings from your daughter Alexandra in Moscow, also from certain official quarters! I wish to speak to you concerning her! Do not board this car!"

The bus had pulled up. The conductor knew her and was holding his hand out for her bag. Lowering his voice, the stranger added one more terrible statement: "Alexandra has serious problems which require the assistance of a mother."

The conductor was calling to her to get a move on. He spoke with pretended roughness, which was the way they joked. "Come on, mother! It's too hot for love! Pass us your bag and let's go!" cried the conductor.

Inside the bus there was laughter; then someone shouted an insult—old woman, keeps the world waiting! She felt the stranger's hand scrabbling inexpertly at her arm, like a clumsy suitor groping for the buttons. She pulled herself free. She tried to tell the conductor something but she couldn't; she opened her mouth but she had forgotten how to speak. The best she could manage was to shake her head. The conductor yelled at her again, then waved his hands and shrugged. The insults multiplied—old woman, drunk as a whore at midday! Remaining where she was, Ostrakova watched the bus out of sight, waiting for her vision to clear and her heart to stop its crazy cavorting. Now it is I who need a glass of water, she thought. From the strong I can protect myself. God preserve me from the weak.

She followed him to the café, limping heavily. In a forced-labour camp, exactly twenty-five years before, she had broken her leg in three places in a coal slip. On this August 4th—the date had not escaped her—under the extreme duress of the stranger's message, the old sensation of being crippled came back to her.

The café was the last in the street, if not in all Paris, to lack both a juke-box and neon lighting—and to remain open in August—though there were bagatelle tables that bumped and flashed from dawn till night. For the rest, there was the usual mid-morning hubbub, of grand politics, and horses, and whatever else Parisians talked; there was the usual trio of prostitutes murmuring among themselves, and a sullen young waiter in a soiled shirt who led them to a table in a corner that was reserved with a grimy Campari sign. A moment of ludicrous banality followed. The stranger ordered two coffees, but the waiter protested that at midday one does not reserve the best table in the house merely in order to drink coffee; the *patron* had to pay the rent, monsieur! Since the stranger did not follow this flow of patois, Ostrakova had to translate it for him. The stranger blushed and ordered two ham omelettes with *frites*, and two Alsatian beers, all without consulting Ostrakova. Then he took himself to the men's room to repair his courage—confident, presumably, she would not run away—and when he returned his face was dry and his ginger hair combed, but the stink of him, now they were indoors, reminded Ostrakova of Moscow subways, and Moscow trams, and Moscow interrogation rooms. More eloquently than anything he could ever have said to her, that short walk back from the men's room to their table had convinced her of what she already feared. He was one of them. The suppressed swagger, the deliberate brutalisation of the features, the ponderous style in which he now squared his forearms on the table and with feigned reluctance helped himself to a piece of bread from the basket as if he were dipping a pen in ink—they revived her worst memories of living as a disgraced woman under the weight of Moscow's malevolent bureaucracy.

"So," he said, and started eating the bread at the same time. He selected a crusty end. With hands like that he could have crushed it in a second, but instead he chose to prise ladylike flakes from it with his fat finger-ends, as if that were the official way of eating. While he nibbled, his eyebrows went up and he looked sorry for himself, me a stranger in this foreign land. "Do they know here that you have lived an immoral life in Russia?" he asked finally. "Maybe in a town full of whores they don't care."

Her answer lay ready on the tip of her tongue: *My life in Russia was not immoral. It was your system which was immoral.*

But she did not say it, she kept rigidly silent. Ostrakova had already sworn to herself that she would restrain both her quick temper and her quick tongue, and she now physically enjoined herself to this vow by grabbing a piece of skin on the soft inside of her wrist and pinching it through her sleeve with a fierce, sustained pressure under the table, exactly as she had done a hundred times before, in the old days, when such questionings were part of her daily life—When did you last hear from your husband, Ostrakov, the traitor? Name all persons with whom you have associated in the last three months! With bitter experience she had learned the other lessons of interrogation too. A part of her was rehearsing them at this minute, and though they belonged, in terms of history, to a full generation earlier, they appeared to her now as bright as yesterday and as vital: never to match rudeness with rudeness, never to be provoked, never to score, never to be witty or superior or intellectual, never to be deflected by fury, or despair, or the surge of sudden hope that an occasional question might arouse. To match dullness with dullness and routine with routine. And only deep, deep down to preserve the two secrets that made all these humiliations bearable: her hatred of them; and her hope that one day, after endless drips of water on the stone, she would wear them down, and by a reluctant miracle of their own elephantine processes, obtain from them the freedom they were denying her.

He had produced a notebook. In Moscow it would have been her file but here in a Paris café it was a sleek black leatherbound notebook, something that in Moscow even an official would count himself lucky to possess.

File or notebook, the preamble was the same: "You were born Maria Andreyevna Rogova in Leningrad on May 8, 1927," he repeated. "On September 1, 1948, aged twenty-one, you married the traitor Ostrakov Igor, a captain of infantry in the Red Army, born of an Estonian mother. In 1950, the said Ostrakov, being at the time stationed in East Berlin, traitorously defected to Fascist Germany through the assistance of reactionary Estonian émigrés, leaving you in Moscow. He took up residence, and later French citizenship, in Paris, where he continued his contact with anti-Soviet elements. At the time of his defection you had no children by this man. Also you were not pregnant. Correct?"

"Correct," she said.

In Moscow it would have been "Correct, Comrade Captain," or "Correct, Comrade Inspector," but in this clamorous French café such formality was out of place. The fold of skin on her wrist had gone numb. Releasing it, she allowed the blood to return, then took hold of another.

"As an accomplice to Ostrakov's defection you were sentenced to five years' detention in a labour camp, but were released under an amnesty following the death of Stalin in March, 1953. Correct?"

"Correct."

"On your return to Moscow, despite the improbability that your request would be granted, you applied for a foreign travel passport to join your husband in France. Correct?"

"He had cancer," she said. "If I had not applied, I would have been failing in my duty as his wife."

The waiter brought the plates of omelette and *frites* and the two Alsatian beers, and Ostrakova asked him to bring a *thé citron:* she was thirsty, but did not care for beer. Addressing the boy, she tried vainly to make a bridge to him, with smiles and with her eyes. But his stoniness repulsed her; she realised she was the only woman in the place apart from the three prostitutes. Holding his notebook to one side like a hymnal, the stranger helped himself to a forkful, then another, while Ostrakova tightened her grasp on her wrist, and Alexandra's name pulsed in her mind like an unstaunched wound, and she contemplated a thousand different *serious problems* that required *the assistance of a mother.*

The stranger continued his crude history of her while he ate. Did he eat for pleasure or did he eat in order not to be conspicuous again? She decided he was a compulsive eater.

"Meanwhile," he announced, eating.

"Meanwhile," she whispered involuntarily.

"Meanwhile, despite your pretended concern for your husband, the traitor Ostrakov," he continued through his mouthful, "you nevertheless formed an adulterous relationship with the so-called music student Glikman Joseph, a Jew with four convictions for anti-social behaviour whom you had met during your detention. You cohabited with this Jew in his apartment. Correct or false?"

"I was lonely."

"In consequence of this union with Glikman you bore a daughter, Alexandra, at The Lying-in Hospital of the October Revolution in Moscow. The certificate of parentage was signed by Glikman Joseph and Ostrakova Maria. The girl was registered in the name of the Jew Glikman. Correct or false?"

"Correct."

"Meanwhile, you persisted in your application for a foreign travel passport. Why?"

"I told you. My husband was ill. It was my duty to persist."

He ate again, so grossly that she had a sight of his many bad teeth. "In January, 1956, as an act of clemency you were granted a passport on condition the child Alexandra was left behind in Moscow. You exceeded the permitted time limit and remained in France, abandoning your child. Correct or false?"

The doors to the street were glass, the walls too. A big lorry parked outside them and the café darkened. The young waiter slammed down her tea without looking at her.

"Correct," she said again, and managed this time to look at her interrogator, knowing what would follow, forcing herself to show him that on this score at least she had no doubts, and no regrets.

"Correct," she repeated defiantly.

"As a condition of your application being favourably considered by the authorities, you signed an undertaking to the organs of State Security to perform certain tasks for them during your residence in Paris. One, to persuade your husband, the traitor Ostrakov, to return to the Soviet Union—"

"To *attempt* to persuade him," she corrected him, with a faint smile. "He was not amenable to this suggestion."

"Two, you undertook also to provide information concerning the activities and personalities of revanchist anti-Soviet émigré groups. You submitted two reports of no value and afterwards nothing. Why?"

"My husband despised such groups and had given up his contact with them."

"You could have participated in the groups without him. You signed the document and neglected its undertaking. Yes or no?"

"Yes."

"For this you abandon your child in Russia? To a Jew? In order to give your attention to an enemy of the people, a traitor of the State? For this you neglect your duty? Outstay the permitted period, remain in France?"

"My husband was dying. He needed me."

"And the child Alexandra? She did not need you? A dying husband is more important than a living child? A traitor? A conspirator against the people?"

Releasing her wrist, Ostrakova deliberately took hold of her tea and watched the glass rise to her face, the lemon floating on the surface. Beyond it, she saw a grimy mosaic floor and beyond the floor the loved, ferocious, and kindly face of Glikman pressing down on her, exhorting her to sign, to go, to swear to anything they asked. The freedom of one is more than the slavery of three, he had whispered; a child of such parents as ourselves cannot prosper in Russia whether you stay or go; leave and we shall do our best to follow; sign anything, leave, and live for all of us; if you love me, go. . . .

"They were the hard days, still," she said to the stranger finally, almost in a tone of reminiscence. "You are too young. They were the hard days, even after Stalin's death: still hard."

"Does the criminal Glikman continue to write to you?" the stranger asked in a superior, knowing way.

"He never wrote," she lied. "How could he write, a dissident, living under restriction? The decision to stay in France was mine alone."

Paint yourself black, she thought; do everything possible to spare those within their power.

"I have heard nothing from Glikman since I came to France more than twenty years ago," she added, gathering courage. "Indirectly, I learned that he was angered by my anti-Soviet behaviour. He did not wish to know me any more. Inwardly he was already wishing to reform by the time I left him."

"He did not write concerning your common child?"

"He did not write, he did not send messages. I told you this already."

"Where is your daughter now?"

"I don't know."

"You have received communications from her?"

"Of course not. I heard only that she had entered a State orphanage and acquired another name. I assume she does not know I exist."

The stranger ate again with one hand, while the other held the notebook. He filled his mouth, munched a little, then swilled his food down with the beer. But the superior smile remained.

"And now it is the criminal Glikman who is dead," the stranger announced, revealing his little secret. He continued eating.

Suddenly Ostrakova wished the twenty years were two hundred. She wished that Glikman's face had never, after all, looked down on her, that she had never loved him, never cared for him, never cooked for him, or got drunk with him day after day in his one-roomed exile where they lived on the charity of their friends, deprived of the right to work, to do anything but make music and love, get drunk, walk in the woods, and be cut dead by their neighbours.

"Next time I go to prison or you do, they will take her anyway.

Alexandra is forfeit in any case," Glikman had said. "But you can save yourself."

"I will decide when I am there," she had replied.

"Decide now."

"When I am there."

The stranger pushed aside his empty plate and once more took the sleek French notebook in both hands. He turned a page, as if approaching a new chapter.

"Concerning now your criminal daughter Alexandra," he announced, through his food.

"*Criminal?*" she whispered.

To her astonishment the stranger was reciting a fresh catalogue of crimes. As he did so, Ostrakova lost her final hold upon the present. Her eyes were on the mosaic floor and she noticed the husks of langoustine and crumbs of bread. But her mind was in the Moscow law court again, where her own trial was being repeated. If not hers, then Glikman's—yet not Glikman's either. Then whose? She remembered trials that the two of them had attended as unwelcome spectators. Trials of friends, if only friends by accident: such as people who had questioned the absolute right of the authorities; or had worshipped some unacceptable god; or had painted criminally abstract pictures; or had published politically endangering love-poems. The chattering customers in the café became the jeering claque of the State police; the slamming of the bagatelle tables, the crash of iron doors. On this date, for escaping from the State orphanage on something street, so many months' corrective detention. On that date, for insulting organs of State Security, so many more months, extended for bad behaviour, followed by so many years' internal exile. Ostrakova felt her stomach turn and thought she might be sick. She put her hands to her glass of tea and saw the red pinch marks on her wrist. The stranger continued his recitation and she heard her daughter awarded another two years for refusing to accept employment at the something factory, God help her, and why shouldn't she? Where had she learnt it? Ostrakova asked herself, incredulous. What had Glikman taught the child, in the short time before they took her away from him, that had stamped her in his mould and defeated all the system's efforts? Fear, exultation, amazement jangled in Ostrakova's mind, till something that the stranger was saying to her blocked them out.

"I did not hear," she whispered after an age. "I am a little distressed. Kindly repeat what you just said."

He said it again, and she looked up and stared at him, trying to think of all the tricks she had been warned against, but they were too many and she was no longer clever. She no longer had Glikman's cleverness—if she had ever had it—about reading their lies and playing their games ahead of them. She knew only that to save herself and be reunited with her beloved Ostrakov, she had committed a great sin, the greatest a mother can commit. The stranger had begun threatening her, but for once the threat seemed meaningless. In the event of her non-collaboration—he was saying—a copy of her signed undertaking to the Soviet authorities would find its way to the French police. Copies of her useless two reports (done, as he well knew, solely in order to keep the brigands quiet) would be circulated among the surviving Paris émigrés—though, God knows, there were few enough of *them* about these days! Yet why should she have to submit to *pressure* in order to accept a gift of such immeasurable value—when, by some inexplicable act of clemency, this man, this system, was holding out to her the chance to redeem herself, and her child? She knew that her nightly and daily prayers for forgiveness had been answered, the thousands of candles, the thousands of tears. She made him say it a third time. She made him pull his notebook away from his gingery face, and she saw that his weak mouth had lifted into a half smile and that, idiotically, he seemed to require her absolution, even while he repeated his insane, God-given question.

"Assuming it has been decided to rid the Soviet Union of this disruptive and unsocial element, how would you like your daughter Alexandra to follow your footsteps here to France?"

For weeks after that encounter, and through all the hushed activities that accompanied it—furtive visits to the Soviet Embassy, form-filling, signed affidavits, *certificats d'hébergement*, the laborious trail through successive French ministries— Ostrakova followed her own actions as if they were someone else's. She prayed often, but even with her prayers she adopted a conspiratorial attitude, dividing them among several Russian Orthodox churches so that in none would she be observed suffering an undue assault of piety. Some of the churches were no more than little private houses scattered round the 15th and 16th districts, with distinctive twice-struck crosses in plywood, and old, rain-sodden Russian notices on the doors, requesting cheap accommodation and offering instruction in the piano. She went to the Church of the Russian Abroad, and the Church of the Apparition of the Holy Virgin, and the Church of St. Seraphin of Sarov. She went everywhere. She rang the bells till someone came, a verger or a frail-faced woman in black; she gave them money, and they let her crouch in the damp cold before candle-lit icons, and breathe the thick incense till it made her half drunk. She made promises to the Almighty, she thanked Him, she asked Him for advice, she practically asked Him what *He* would have done if the stranger had approached Him in similar circumstances, she reminded Him that anyway she was under pressure, and they would destroy her if she did not obey. Yet at the same time, her indomitable common sense asserted itself, and she asked herself over and again *why* she of all people, wife of the traitor Ostrakov, lover of the dissident Glikman, mother—so she was given to believe—of a turbulent and anti-social daughter, should be singled out for such untypical indulgence?

In the Soviet Embassy, when she made her first formal

application, she was treated with a regard she would never have dreamed possible, which was suited neither to a defector and renegade spy nor to the mother of an untamable hell-raiser. She was not ordered brusquely to a waiting-room, but escorted to an interviewing-room, where a young and personable official showed her a positively Western courtesy, even helping her, where her pen or courage faltered, to a proper formulation of her case.

And she told nobody, not even her nearest—though her nearest was not very near. The gingery man's warning rang in her ears day and night: any indiscretion and your daughter will not be released.

And who was there, after all, apart from God, to turn to? To her half-sister Valentina, who lived in Lyons and was married to a car salesman? The very thought that Ostrakova had been consorting with a secret official from Moscow would send her rushing for her smelling-salts. In a *café*, Maria? In *broad daylight*, Maria? Yes, Valentina, and what he said is true. I had a bastard daughter by a Jew.

It was the nothingness that scared her most. The weeks passed; at the Embassy they told her that her application was receiving "favoured attention"; the French authorities had assured her that Alexandra would quickly qualify for French citizenship. The gingery stranger had persuaded her to back-date Alexandra's birth so that she could be represented as an Ostrakova, not a Glikman; he said the French authorities would find this more acceptable; and it seemed that they had done so, even though she had never so much as mentioned the child's existence at her naturalisation interviews. Now, suddenly, there were no more forms to fill in, no more hurdles to be cleared, and Ostrakova waited without knowing what she was waiting for. For the gingery stranger to reappear? He no longer existed. One ham omelette and *frites*, some Alsatian beer, two pieces of crusty bread had satisfied all his needs, apparently. What he was in relation to the Embassy she could not imagine: he had told her to present herself there, and that they would be expecting her; he was right. But when she referred to "your gentleman," even "your blond, large gentleman who first approached me," she met with smiling incomprehension.

Thus gradually whatever she was waiting for ceased to exist. First it was ahead of her, then it was behind her, and she had had no knowledge of its passing, no moment of fulfilment. Had Alexandra already arrived in France? Obtained her papers, moved on or gone to ground? Ostrakova began to think she might have done. Abandoned to a new and inconsolable sense of disappointment, she peered at the faces of young girls in the street, wondering what Alexandra looked like. Returning home, her eyes would fall automatically to the doormat in the hope of seeing a handwritten note or a *pneumatique:* "Mama, it is I. I am staying at the so-and-so hotel. . . ." A cable giving a flight number, arriving Orly tomorrow, tonight; or was it not Orly Airport but Charles de Gaulle? She had no familiarity with airlines, so she visited a travel agent, just to ask. It was both. She considered going to the expense of having a telephone installed so that Alexandra could ring her up. Yet what on earth was she expecting after all these years? Tearful reunions with a grown child to whom she had never been united? The wishful remaking, more than twenty years too late, of a relationship she had deliberately turned her back on? I have no right to her, Ostrakova told herself severely; I have only my debts and my obligations. She asked at the Embassy but they knew nothing more. The formalities were complete, they said. That was all they knew. And if Ostrakova wished to send her daughter money? she asked cunningly—for her fares, for instance, for her visa?—could they give her an address perhaps, an office that would find her?

We are not a postal service, they told her. Their new chilliness scared her. She did not go any more.

After that, she fell once more to worrying about the several muddy photographs, each the same, which they had given her to pin to her application forms. The photographs were all she had ever seen. She wished now that she had made copies, but she had never thought of it; stupidly, she had assumed she would soon be meeting the original. She had not had them in her hand above an hour! She had hurried straight from the Embassy to the Ministry with them, and by the time she left the Ministry the photographs were already working their way through another bureaucracy. But she had studied them! My Lord, how she had studied those photographs, whether they were each the same or not! On the Métro, in the Ministry waiting-room, even on the pavement before she went in, she had stared at the lifeless depiction of her child, trying with all her might to see in the expressionless grey shadows some hint of the man she had adored. And failing. Always, till then, whenever she had dared to wonder, she had imagined Glikman's features as clearly written on the growing child as they had been on the new-born baby. It had seemed impossible that a man so vigorous would not plant his imprint deeply and for good. Yet Ostrakova saw nothing of Glikman in that photograph. He had worn his Jewishness like a flag. It was part of his solitary revolution. He was not Orthodox, he was not even religious, he disliked Ostrakova's secret piety nearly as much as he disliked the Soviet bureaucracy—yet he had borrowed her tongs to curl his sideburns like the Hasidim, just to give focus, as he put it, to the anti-Semitism of the authorities. But in the face in the photograph she recognised not a drop of his blood, not the least spark of his fire—though his fire, according to the stranger, burned in her amazingly.

"If they had photographed a corpse to get that picture," thought Ostrakova aloud in her apartment, "I would not be surprised." And with this downright observation, she gave her first outward expression of the growing doubt inside her.

Toiling in her warehouse, sitting alone in her tiny apartment in the long evenings, Ostrakova racked her brains for

someone she could trust; who would not condone and not condemn; who would see round the corners of the route she had
embarked on; above all, who would not talk and thus wreck—
she had been assured of it—wreck her chances of being reunited
with Alexandra. Then one night, either God or her own striving memory supplied her with an answer: The General! she
thought, sitting up in bed and putting on the light. Ostrakov
himself had told her of him! Those émigré groups are a catastrophe, he used to say, and you must avoid them like the pest.
The only one you can trust is Vladimir the General; he is an
old devil, and a womaniser, but he is a man, he has connections
and knows how to keep his mouth shut.

But Ostrakov had said this some twenty years ago, and not
even old generals are immortal. And besides—Vladimir who?
She did not even know his other name. Even the name
Vladimir—Ostrakov had told her—was something he had put
on for his military service; since his real name was Estonian,
and not suitable for Red Army usage. Nevertheless, next day
she went down to the bookshop beside the Cathedral of St.
Alexander Nevsky, where information about the dwindling
Russian population was often to be had, and made her first
enquiries. She got a name and even a phone number, but no
address. The phone was disconnected. She went to the Post
Office, cajoled the assistants, and finally came up with a 1966
telephone directory listing the Movement for Baltic Freedom,
followed by an address in Montparnasse. She was not stupid.
She looked up the address and found no less than four other
organisations listed there also: the Riga Group, the Association of Victims of Soviet Imperialism, the Forty-Eight Committee for a Free Latvia, the Tallinn Committee of Freedom.
She remembered vividly Ostrakov's scathing opinions of such
bodies, even though he had paid his dues to them. All the
same, she went to the address and rang the bell, and the house
was like one of her little churches: quaint, and very nearly
closed for ever. Eventually an old White Russian opened the

door wearing a cardigan crookedly buttoned, and leaning on a walking-stick, and looking superior.

They've gone, he said, pointing his stick down the cobbled road. Moved out. Finished. Bigger outfits put them out of business, he added with a laugh. Too few of them, too many groups, and they squabbled like children. No wonder the Czar was defeated! The old White Russian had false teeth that didn't fit, and thin hair plastered all over his scalp to hide his baldness.

But the General? she asked. Where was the General? Was he still alive, or had he—?

The old Russian smirked and asked whether it was business.

It was not, said Ostrakova craftily, remembering the General's reputation for philandering, and contrived a shy woman's smile. The old Russian laughed, and his teeth rattled. He laughed again and said, "Oh, the General!" Then he came back with an address in London, stamped in mauve on a bit of card, and gave it to her. The General would never change, he said; when he got to Heaven, he'd be chasing after the angels and trying to up-end them, no question. And that night while the whole neighbourhood slept, Ostrakova sat at her dead husband's desk and wrote to the General with the frankness which lonely people reserve for strangers, using French rather than Russian as an aid to greater detachment. She told him about her love for Glikman and took comfort from the knowledge that the General himself loved women just as Glikman had. She admitted immediately that she had come to France as a spy, and she explained how she had assembled the two trivial reports that were the squalid price of her freedom. It was *à contre-cœur*, she said; invention and evasion, she said; a nothing. But the reports existed, so did her signed undertaking, and they placed grave limits on her freedom. Then she told him of her soul, and of her prayers to God all round the Russian churches. Since the gingery stranger's approach to her, she said, her days had become unreal; she had a feeling of being denied a natural explanation of her life, even if it had to be a painful one. She kept nothing back from him, for whatever guilty feelings she had, they did not relate to her efforts to bring Alexandra to the West, but rather to her decision to stay in Paris and take care of Ostrakov until he died—after which event, she said, the Soviets would not let her come back anyway; she had become a defector herself.

"But, General," she wrote, "if tonight I had to face my Maker in person, and tell Him what is deepest in my heart, I would tell Him what I now tell you. My child Alexandra was born in pain. Days and nights she fought me and I fought her back. Even in the womb she was her father's child. I had no time to love her; I only ever knew her as the little Jewish warrior her father made. But, General, this I do know: the child in the photograph is neither Glikman's, nor is she mine. They are putting the wrong egg into the nest, and though there is a part of this old woman that would like to be deluded, there is a stronger part that hates them for their tricks."

When she had finished the letter, she sealed it immediately in its envelope so that she would not read it and change her mind. Then she stuck too many stamps on it deliberately, much as she might have lit a candle to a lover.

For the next two weeks exactly, following the posting of this document, nothing happened, and in the strange ways of women the silence was a relief to her. After the storm had come the calm, she had done the little she could do—she had confessed her weaknesses and her betrayals and her one great sin—the rest was in the hands of God, and of the General. A disruption of the French postal services did not dismay her. She saw it rather as another obstacle that those who were shaping her destiny would have to overcome if their will was strong enough. She went to work contentedly and her back ceased to trouble her, which she took as an omen. She even managed to become philosophical again. It is this way or that way, she told herself; either Alexandra was in the West and better off—if indeed it *was* Alexandra—or Alexandra was where she had been before, and no worse off. But gradually, with another part of her, she saw through this false optimism. There was a third possibility, and that was the worst and by degrees the one she considered most likely: namely, that Alexandra was being used for a sinister and perhaps wicked purpose; that they were forcing her somehow, exactly as they had forced Ostrakova, misusing the humanity and courage that her father, Glikman, had given her. So that on the fourteenth night, Ostrakova broke into a profound fit of weeping, and with the tears streaming down her face walked half-way across Paris looking for a church, any church that was open, until she came to the Cathedral of St. Alexander Nevsky itself. It was open. Kneeling, she prayed for long hours to St. Joseph, who was after all a father and protector, and the giver of Glikman's first name, even if Glikman would have scoffed at the association. And on the day following these spiritual exertions, her prayer was answered. A letter came. It had no stamp or postmark. She had added her address at work as a precaution, and the letter was there waiting for her when she arrived, delivered by hand, presumably, some time in the night. It was a very short letter and carried neither the name of the sender nor his address. It was unsigned. Like her own, it was in a stilted French and handwritten, in the sprawl of an old and dictatorial hand, which she knew at once was the General's.

Madame!—it began, like a command—*Your letter has reached the writer safely. A friend of our cause will call upon you very soon. He is a man of honour and he will identify himself by handing to you the other half of the enclosed postcard. I urge you to speak to nobody concerning this matter until he arrives. He will come to your apartment between eight and ten o'clock in the evening. He will ring your doorbell three times. He has my absolute confidence. Trust him entirely, Madame, and we shall do everything to assist you.*

Even in her relief, she was secretly entertained by the writer's melodramatic tone. Why not deliver the letter directly to her flat? she wondered; and why should I feel safer because he gives me half an English picture? For the piece of postcard showed a part of Piccadilly Circus and was torn, not cut, with a deliberate roughness, diagonally. The side to be written on was blank.

To her astonishment the General's envoy came that night.

He rang the bell three times, as the letter promised, but he must have known she was in her apartment—must have watched her enter, and the lights go on—for all she heard was a snap of the letter-box, a snap much louder than it normally made, and when she went to the door she saw the piece of torn postcard lying on the mat, the same mat she had looked at so often when she was longing for word of her daughter Alexandra. Picking it up, she ran to the bedroom for her Bible, where her own half already lay, and yes, the pieces matched, God was on her side, St. Joseph had interceded for her. (But what a needless piece of nonsense, all the same!) And when she opened the door to him, he slipped past her like a shadow: a little hobgoblin of a fellow, in a black overcoat with velvet tabs on the collar, giving him an air of operatic conspiracy. They have sent me a midget to catch a giant, was her first thought. He had arched eyebrows and a grooved face and flicked-up horns of black hair above his pointed ears, which he prinked with his little palms before the hall mirror as he took off his hat—so bright and comic that on a different occasion Ostrakova would have laughed out loud at all the life and humour and irreverence in him.

But not tonight.

Tonight he had a gravity that she sensed immediately was not his normal way. Tonight, like a busy salesman who had just stepped off an aeroplane—she had the feeling also about him that he was brand new in town: his cleanliness, his air of travelling light—tonight he wished only to do business.

"You received my letter safely, madame?" He spoke Russian swiftly, with an Estonian accent.

"I had thought it was the General's letter," she replied,

affecting—she could not save herself—a certain sternness with him.

"It is I who brought it for him," he said gravely. He was delving in an inside pocket and she had a dreadful feeling that, like the big Russian, he was going to produce a sleek black notebook. But he drew out instead a photograph, and one look was quite enough: the pallid, glossy features, the expression that despised all womanhood, not just her own; the suggestion of longing, but not daring to take.

"Yes," she said. "That is the stranger."

Seeing his happiness increase, she knew immediately that he was what Glikman and his friends called "one of us"—not a Jew necessarily, but a man with heart and meat to him. From that moment on she called him in her mind "the magician." She thought of his pockets as being full of clever tricks, and of his merry eyes as containing a dash of magic.

For half the night, with an intensity she hadn't experienced since Glikman, she and the magician talked. First, she told it all again, reliving it exactly, secretly surprised to discover how much she had left out of her letter, which the magician seemed to know by heart. She explained her feelings to him, and her tears, her terrible inner turmoil; she described the crudeness of her perspiring tormentor. He was so *inept*—she kept repeating, in wonder—as if it were his first time, she said—he had no finesse, no assurance. So odd to think of the Devil as a fumbler! She told about the ham omelette and the *frites* and the Alsatian beer, and he laughed; about her feeling that he was a man of dangerous timidity and inhibition—not a woman's man at all—to most of which the little magician agreed with her cordially, as if he and the gingery man were already well acquainted. She trusted the magician entirely, as the General had told her to; she was sick and tired of suspicion. She talked, she thought afterwards, as frankly as she once had talked to Ostrakov when they were young lovers in her own home town, on the nights they thought they might never meet again, clutching each other under siege, whispering to the sound of approaching guns; or to Glikman, while they waited for the hammering on the door that would take him back to prison yet again. She talked to his alert and understanding gaze, to the laughter in him, to the suffering that she sensed immediately was the better side of his unorthodox and perhaps anti-social nature. And gradually, as she went on talking, her woman's instinct told her that she was feeding a passion in him—not a love this time, but a sharp and particular hatred that gave thrust and sensibility to every little question he asked. What or whom it was that he hated, exactly, she could not say, but she feared for any man, whether the gingery stranger or anybody else, who had attracted this tiny magician's fire. Glikman's passion, she recalled, had been a universal, sleepless passion against injustice, fixing itself almost at random upon a range of symptoms, small or large. But the magician's was a single beam, fixed upon a spot she could not see.

It is in any case a fact that by the time the magician left—my Lord, she thought, it was nearly time for her to go to work again!—Ostrakova had told him everything she had to tell, and the magician in return had woken feelings in her that for years, until this night, had belonged only to her past. Tidying away the plates and bottles in a daze, she managed, despite the complexity of her feelings regarding Alexandra, and herself, and her two dead men, to burst out laughing at her woman's folly.

"And I do not even know his name!" she said aloud, and shook her head in mockery. "How shall I reach you?" she had asked. "How can I warn you if he returns?"

She could not, the magician had replied. But if there was a crisis she should write to the General again, under his English name and at a different address. "Mr. Miller," he said gravely, pronouncing it as French, and gave her a card with a London address printed by hand in capitals. "But be discreet," he warned. "You must be indirect in your language."

All that day, and for many days afterwards, Ostrakova kept her last departing image of the magician at the forefront of her memory as he slipped away from her and down the ill-lit staircase. His last fervid stare, taut with purpose and excitement: "I promise to release you. Thank you for calling me to arms." His little white hand, running down the broad banister of the stairwell, like a handkerchief waved from a train window, round and round in a dwindling circle of farewell, till it disappeared into the darkness of the tunnel.

2

The second of the two events that brought George Smiley from his retirement occurred a few weeks after the first, in early autumn of the same year: not in Paris at all, but in the once ancient, free, and Hanseatic city of Hamburg, now almost pounded to death by the thunder of its own prosperity; yet it remains true that nowhere does the summer fade more splendidly than along the gold and orange banks of the Alster, which nobody as yet has drained or filled with concrete. George Smiley, needless to say, had seen nothing of its languorous autumn splendour. Smiley, on the day in question, was toiling obliviously, with whatever conviction he could muster, at his habitual desk in the London Library in St. James's Square, with two spindly trees to look at through the sash-window of the reading-room. The only link to Hamburg he might have pleaded—if he had afterwards attempted the connection, which he did not—was in the Parnassian field of German baroque poetry, for at the time he was composing a monograph on the bard Opitz, and trying loyally to distinguish true passion from the tiresome literary convention of the period.

The time in Hamburg was a few moments after eleven in the morning, and the footpath leading to the jetty was speckled with sunlight and dead leaves. A candescent haze hung over the flat water of the Aussenalster and through it the spires of the eastern bank were like green stains dabbed on the wet horizon.

Along the shore, red squirrels scurried, foraging for the winter. But the slight and somewhat anarchistic-looking young man standing on the jetty wearing a track suit and running shoes had neither eyes nor mind for them. His red-rimmed gaze was locked tensely upon the approaching steamer, his hollow face darkened by a two-day stubble. He carried a Hamburg news-paper under his left arm, and an eye as perceptive as George Smiley's would have noticed at once that it was yesterday's edi-tion, not today's. In his right hand he clutched a rush shopping basket better suited to the dumpy Madame Ostrakova than to this lithe, bedraggled athlete who seemed any minute about to leap into the lake. Oranges peeked out of the top of the basket, a yellow Kodak envelope with English printing lay on top of the oranges. The jetty was otherwise empty, and the haze over the water added to his solitude. His only companions were the steamer timetable and an archaic notice, which must have sur-vived the war, telling him how to revive the half-drowned; his only thoughts concerned the General's instructions, which he was continuously reciting to himself like a prayer.

The steamer glided alongside and the boy skipped aboard like a child in a dance game—a flurry of steps, then motion-less until the music starts again. For forty-eight hours, night and day, he had had nothing to think of but this moment: now. Driving, he had stared wakefully at the road, imagining, between glimpses of his wife and little girl, the many disas-trous things that could go wrong. He knew he had a talent for disaster. During his rare breaks for coffee, he had packed and repacked the oranges a dozen times, laying the envelope lengthways, sideways—no, this angle is better, it is more appro-priate, easier to get hold of. At the edge of town he had col-lected small change so that he would have the fare exactly—what if the conductor held him up, engaged him in casual conversa-tion? There was so little time to do what he had to do! He would speak no German, he had worked it out. He would mumble, smile, be reticent, apologise, but stay mute. Or he would say some of his few words of Estonian—some phrase from the Bible he could still remember from his Lutheran childhood, before his father insisted he learn Russian. But now, with the moment so close upon him, the boy suddenly saw a snag in this plan. What if his fellow passengers then came to his aid? In polyglot Hamburg, with the East only a few miles away, any six people could muster as many languages between them! Better to keep silent, be blank.

He wished he had shaved. He wished he was less conspicuous.

Inside the main cabin of the steamer, the boy looked at nobody. He kept his eyes lowered; *avoid eye contact*, the General had ordered. The conductor was chatting to an old lady and ignored him. He waited awkwardly, trying to look calm. There were about thirty passengers. He had an impression of men and women dressed alike in green overcoats and green felt hats, all disapproving of him. It was his turn. He held out a damp palm. One mark, a fifty-pfennig piece, a bunch of little brass tens. The conductor helped himself, not speaking. Clumsily, the boy groped his way between the seats, making for the stern. The jetty was moving away. They suspect me of being a terrorist, thought the boy. There was engine oil on his hands and he wished he'd washed it off. Perhaps it's on my face as well. *Be blank*, the General had said. *Efface yourself. Neither smile nor frown. Be normal.* He glanced at his watch, trying to keep the action slow. He had rolled back his left cuff in advance, specially to leave the watch free. Ducking, though he was not tall, the boy arrived suddenly in the stern section, which was open to the weather, protected only by a canopy. It was a case of seconds. Not of days or kilometres any more; not hours. Seconds. The timing hand of his watch flickered past the six. The next time it reaches six, you move. A breeze was blowing but he barely noticed it. The time was an awful worry to him. When he got excited—he knew—he lost all sense of time completely. He was afraid the seconds hand would race through a double circuit before he had realised, turning one minute into two. In the stern section all seats were vacant. He made jerkily for the last bench of all, holding the basket of oranges over his stomach in both hands, clamping the newspaper to his armpit at the same time: *it is I, read my signals.* He felt a fool. The oranges were too conspicuous by far. Why on earth should an unshaven young man in a track suit be carrying a basket of oranges and yesterday's newspaper? The whole boat must have noticed him! "Captain—that young man—there—he is a bomber! He has a bomb in his basket, he intends to hijack us or sink the ship!" A couple stood arm in arm at the railing with their backs to him, staring into the mist. The man was very small, shorter than the woman. He wore a black overcoat with a velvet collar. They ignored him. *Sit as far back as you can; be sure you sit next to the aisle,* the General had said. He sat down, praying it would work the first time, that none of the fall-backs would be needed. "Beckie, I do this for *you*," he whispered secretly, thinking of his daughter, and remembering the General's words. His Lutheran origins notwithstanding, he wore a wooden cross round his neck, a present to him from his mother, but the zip of his tunic covered it. Why had he hidden the cross? So that God would not witness his deceit? He didn't know. He wanted only to be driving again, to drive and drive till he dropped or was safely home.

Look nowhere, he remembered the General saying. He was to look nowhere but ahead of him: *You are the passive partner. You have nothing to do but supply the opportunity. No code word, nothing; just the basket and the oranges and the yellow envelope and the newspaper under your arm.* I should never have agreed to it, he thought. I have endangered my daughter Beckie. Stella will never forgive me. I shall lose my citizenship, I have put everything at risk. *Do it for our cause,* the General had said. General, I haven't got one: it was not my cause, it was your cause, it was my father's; that is why I threw the oranges overboard.

But he didn't. Laying the newspaper beside him on the slatted bench, he saw that it was drenched in sweat—that patches of print had worn off where he clutched it. He looked at his watch. The seconds hand was standing at ten. It's stopped! Fifteen seconds since I last looked—that simply is not possible! A frantic glance at the shore convinced him they were already in mid-lake. He looked at the watch again and saw the seconds hand jerking past eleven. Fool, he thought, calm yourself. Leaning to his right, he affected to read the newspaper while he kept the dial of his watch constantly in view. Terrorists. Nothing but terrorists, he thought, reading the headlines for the twentieth time. No wonder the passengers think I'm one of them. *Grossfahndung.* That was their word for massive search. It amazed him that he remembered so much German. *Do it for our cause.*

At his feet the basket of oranges was leaning precariously. *When you get up, put the basket on the bench to reserve your seat,* the General had said. What if it falls over? In his imagination he saw the oranges rolling all over the deck, the yellow envelope upside down among them, photographs everywhere, all of Beckie. The seconds hand was passing six. He stood up. *Now.* His midriff was cold. He tugged his tunic down to cover it and inadvertently exposed his mother's wooden cross. He closed the zip. *Saunter. Look nowhere. Pretend you are the dreamy sort,* the General had said. *Your father would not have hesitated a moment,* the General had said. *Nor will you.* Cautiously lifting the basket onto the bench, he steadied it with both hands, then leaned it towards the back to give it extra stability. Then tested it. He wondered about the *Abendblatt.* To take it, to leave it where it was? Perhaps his contact had still not seen the signal? He picked it up and put it under his arm.

He returned to the main cabin. A second couple moved into the stern section, presumably to take the air, older, very sedate. The first couple were a sexy pair, even from behind— the little man, the shapely girl, the trimness of them both. You knew they had a good time in bed, just to look at them. But this second couple were like a pair of policemen to him; the boy was certain they got no pleasure from their love-making at all. Where is my mind going? he thought crazily. To my wife, Stella, was the answer. To the long exquisite embraces we may never have again. Sauntering as he had been ordered to, he advanced down the aisle towards the closed-off area where the pilot sat. Looking at nobody was easy; the passengers sat with their backs to him. He had reached as far forward as passengers were allowed. The pilot sat to his left, on his raised platform. *Go to the pilot's window and admire the view. Remain there one minute exactly.* The cabin roof was lower here; he had to stoop. Through the big windscreen, trees and buildings on the move. He saw a rowing eight switch by, followed by a lone blonde goddess in a skiff. Breasts like a statue's, he thought. For greater casualness, he propped one running shoe on the pilot's platform. Give me a woman, he thought desperately as the moment of crisis came; give me my Stella, drowsy and desiring, in the half-light of early morning. He had his left wrist forward on the railing, his watch constantly in view.

"We don't clean boots here," the pilot growled.

Hastily the boy replaced his foot on the deck. Now he knows I speak German, he thought, and felt his face prickle in embarrassment. But they know anyway, he thought stupidly, for why else would I carry a German newspaper?

It was time. Swiftly standing to his full height again, he swung round too fast and began the return journey to his seat, and it was no use any more remembering not to stare at faces, because the faces stared at him, disapproving of his two days' growth of beard, his track suit, and his wild look. His eyes left one face, only to find another. He thought he had never seen such a chorus of mute ill-will. His track suit had parted at the midriff again and showed a line of black hair. Stella washes them too hot, he thought. He tugged the tunic down again and stepped into the air, wearing his wooden cross like a medal. As he did so, two things happened almost at the same time. On the bench, next to the basket, he saw the yellow chalk mark he was looking for, running over two slats, bright as a canary, telling him that the hand-over had taken place successfully. At the sight of it, a sense of glory filled him; he had known nothing like it in his life, a release more perfect than any woman could provide.

Why must we do it this way? he had asked the General; why does it have to be so elaborate?

Because the object is unique in the whole world, the General had replied. *It is a treasure without a counterpart. Its loss would be a tragedy to the free world.*

And he chose *me* to be his courier, thought the boy proudly: though he still, at the back of his mind, thought the old man was overdoing it. Serenely picking up the yellow envelope, he dropped it into his tunic pocket, drew the zip, and ran his finger down the join to make sure it had meshed.

At the same instant exactly, he realised he was being watched. The woman at the railing still had her back to him and he noticed again that she had very pretty hips and legs. But her sexy little companion in the black overcoat had turned all the way round to face him, and his expression put an end to all the good feelings the boy had just experienced. Only once had he seen a face like that, and that was when his father lay dying in their first English home, a room in Ruislip, a few months after they had reached England. The boy had seen nothing so desperate, so profoundly serious, so bare of all protection, in anyone else, ever. More alarming still, he knew—precisely as Ostrakova had known—that it was a desperation in contrast with the natural disposition of the features, which were those of a comedian—or as Ostrakova had it, a magician. So that the impassioned stare of this little, sharp-faced stranger, with its message of furious entreaty—"Boy, you have no idea what you are carrying! Guard it with your life!"—was a revelation of that same comedian's soul.

The steamer had stopped. They were on the other bank.

Seizing his basket, the boy leapt ashore and, almost running, ducked between the bustling shoppers from one side-street to another without knowing where they led.

All through the drive back, while the steering-wheel hammered his arms and the engine played its pounding scale in his ears, the boy saw that face before him in the wet road, wondering as the hours passed whether it was something he had merely imagined in the emotion of the hand-over. Most likely the real contact was someone completely different, he thought, trying to soothe himself. One of those fat ladies in the green felt hats—even the conductor. I was overstrung, he told himself. At a crucial moment, an unknown man turned round and looked at me and I hung an entire history on him, even imagining he was my dying father.

By the time he reached Dover, he almost believed he had put the man out of his mind. He had dumped the cursed oranges in a litter-bin; the yellow envelope lay snug in the pouch of his tunic, one sharp corner pricking his skin, and that was all that mattered. So he had formed theories about his secret accomplice? Forget them. And even if, by sheer coincidence, he was right and it *was* that hollowed, glaring face—*then* what? All the less reason to go blabbing about it to the General, whose concern with security the boy likened to the unchallengeable passion of a seer. The thought of Stella became an aching need to him. His desire sharpened with every noisy mile. It was early morning still. He imagined waking her with his caresses; he saw her sleepy smile slowly turn to passion.

The summons came to Smiley that same night, and it is a curious fact, since he had an overall impression of not sleeping at all well during this late period of his life, that the phone had to ring a long time beside the bed before he answered it. He had come home straight from the library, then dined poorly at an Italian restaurant in Kings Road, taking the *Voyages of Olearius* with him for protection. He had returned to his house in

Bywater Street and resumed work on his monograph with the devotion of a man who had nothing else to do. After a couple of hours he had opened a bottle of red Burgundy and drunk half of it, listening to a poor play on the radio. Then dozed, wrestling with troubled dreams. Yet the moment he heard Lacon's voice, he had the feeling of being hauled from a warm and treasured place, where he wished to remain undisturbed for ever. Also, though in fact he was moving swiftly, he had the sensation of taking a long time to dress; and he wondered whether that was what old men did when they heard about a death.

3

"Knew him personally at all, did you, sir?" the Detective Chief Superintendent of Police asked respectfully in a voice kept deliberately low. "Or perhaps I shouldn't enquire."

The two men had been together for fifteen minutes but this was the Superintendent's first question. For a while Smiley did not seem to hear it, but his silence was not offensive, he had the gift of quiet. Besides, there is a companionship about two men contemplating a corpse. It was an hour before dawn on Hampstead Heath, a dripping, misty, no-man's hour, neither warm nor cold, with a heaven tinted orange by the London glow, and the trees glistening like oilskins. They stood side by side in an avenue of beeches and the Superintendent was taller by a head: a young giant of a man, prematurely grizzled, a little pompous perhaps, but with a giant's gentleness that made him naturally befriending. Smiley was clasping his pudgy hands over his belly like a mayor at a cenotaph, and had eyes for nothing but the plastic-covered body lying at his feet in the beam of the Superintendent's torch. The walk this far had evidently winded him, for he puffed a little as he stared. From the darkness round them, police receivers crackled in the night air. There were no other lights at all; the Superintendent had ordered them extinguished.

"He was just somebody I worked with," Smiley explained after a long delay.

"So I was given to understand, sir," the Superintendent said.

He waited hopefully but nothing more came. "Don't even speak to him," the Deputy Assistant Commissioner (Crime and Ops) had said to him. "You never saw him and it was two other blokes. Just show him what he wants and drop him down a hole. Fast." Till now, the Detective Chief Superintendent had done exactly that. He had moved, in his own estimation, with the speed of light. The photographer had photographed, the doctor had certified life extinct, the pathologist had inspected the body *in situ* as a prelude to conducting his autopsy—all with an expedition quite contrary to the proper pace of things, merely in order to clear the way for the visiting *irregular*, as the Deputy Assistant Commissioner (Crime and Ops) had liked to call him. The irregular had arrived—with about as much ceremony as a meter-reader, the Superintendent noted—and the Superintendent had led him over the course at a canter. They had looked at footprints, they had tracked the old man's route till here. The Superintendent had made a reconstruction of the crime, as well as he was able in the circumstances, and the Superintendent was an able man. Now they were in the dip, at the point where the avenue turned, where the rolling mist was thickest. In the torchbeam the dead body was the centre-piece of everything. It lay face downward and spread-eagled, as if it had been crucified to the gravel, and the plastic sheet emphasized its lifelessness. It was the body of an old man, but broad-shouldered still, a body that had battled and endured. The white hair was cut to stubble. One strong, veined hand still grasped a sturdy walking-stick. He wore a black overcoat and rubber overshoes. A black beret lay on the ground beside him, and the gravel at his head was black with blood. Some loose change lay about, and a pocket handkerchief, and a small penknife that looked more like a keepsake than a tool. Most likely they had started to search him and given up, sir, the Superintendent had said. Most likely they were disturbed, Mr. Smiley, sir; and Smiley had wondered what it must be like to touch a warm body you had just shot.

"If I might possibly take a look at his face, Superintendent," Smiley said.

This time it was the Superintendent who caused the delay. "Ah, now are you sure about that, sir?" He sounded slightly embarrassed. "There'll be better ways of identifying him than *that*, you know."

"Yes. Yes, I am sure," said Smiley earnestly, as if he really had given the matter great thought.

The Superintendent called softly to the trees, where his men stood among their blacked-out cars like a next generation waiting for its turn.

"You there. Hall. Sergeant Pike. Come here at the double and turn him over."

Fast, the Deputy Assistant Commissioner (Crime and Ops) had said.

Two men slipped forward from the shadows. The elder wore a black beard. Their surgical gloves of elbow length shone ghostly grey. They wore blue overalls and thigh-length rubber boots. Squatting, the bearded man cautiously untucked the plastic sheet while the younger constable laid a hand on the dead man's shoulder as if to wake him up.

"You'll have to try harder than that, lad," the Superintendent warned in an altogether crisper tone.

The boy pulled, the bearded sergeant helped him, and the body reluctantly rolled over, one arm stiffly waving, the other still clutching the stick.

"Oh, Christ," said the constable. "Oh, bloody hell!"—and clapped a hand over his mouth. The sergeant grabbed his elbow and shoved him away. They heard the sound of retching.

"I don't hold with politics," the Superintendent confided to Smiley inconsequentially, staring downward still. "I don't hold with politics and I don't hold with politicians either. Licensed lunatics most of them, in my view. That's why I joined the Force, to be honest." The sinewy mist curled strangely in the steady beam of his torch. "You don't happen to know what did it, do you, sir? I haven't seen a wound like that in fifteen years."

"I'm afraid ballistics is not my province," Smiley replied after another pause for thought.

"No, I don't expect it would be, would it? Seen enough, sir?" Smiley apparently had not.

"Most people expect to be shot in the chest really, don't they, sir?" the Superintendent remarked brightly. He had learned that small talk sometimes eased the atmosphere on such occasions. "Your neat round bullet that drills a tasteful hole. That's what most people expect. Victim falls gently to his knees to the tune of celestial choirs. It's the telly that does it, I suppose. Whereas your real bullet these days can take off an arm or a leg, so my friends in brown tell me." His voice took on a more practical tone. "Did he have a moustache at all, sir? My sergeant fancied a trace of white whisker on the upper jaw."

"A military one," said Smiley after a long gap, and with his thumb and forefinger absently described the shape upon his own lip while his gaze remained locked upon the old man's body. "I wonder, Superintendent, whether I might just examine the contents of his pockets, possibly?"

"Sergeant Pike."

"Sir!"

"Put that sheet back and tell Mr. Murgotroyd to have his pockets ready for me in the van, will you, what they've left of them. At the double," the Superintendent added, as a matter of routine.

"Sir!"

"And come here." The Superintendent had taken the sergeant softly by the upper arm. "You tell that young Constable Hall that I can't stop him sicking up but I won't have his irreverent language." For the Superintendent on his home territory was a devoutly Christian man and did not care who knew it. "This way, Mr. Smiley, sir," he added, recovering his gentler tone.

As they moved higher up the avenue, the chatter of the radios faded, and they heard instead the angry wheeling of rooks and the growl of the city. The Superintendent marched briskly, keeping to the left of the roped-off area. Smiley hurried after him. A windowless van was parked between the trees, its back doors open, and a dim light burning inside. Entering, they sat on hard benches. Mr. Murgotroyd had grey hair and wore a grey suit. He crouched before them with a plastic sack like a transparent pillowcase. The sack had a knot at the throat, which he untied. Inside, smaller packages floated. As Mr. Murgotroyd lifted them out, the Superintendent read the labels by his torch before handing them to Smiley to consider.

"One scuffed leather coin purse Continental appearance. Half inside his pocket, half out, left-side jacket. You saw the coins by his body—seventy-two pence. That's all the money on him. Carry a wallet at all, did he, sir?"

"I don't know."

"Our guess is they helped themselves to the wallet, started on the purse, then ran. One bunch keys domestic and various, right-hand trousers. . . ." He ran on but Smiley's scrutiny did not relax. Some people *act* a memory, the Superintendent thought, noticing his concentration, others *have* one. In the Superintendent's book, memory was the better half of intelligence, he prized it highest of all mental accomplishments; and Smiley, he knew, possessed it. "One Paddington Borough Library Card in the name of V. Miller, one box Swan Vesta matches partly used, overcoat left. One Aliens' Registration Card, number as reported, also in the name of Vladimir Miller. One bottle tablets, overcoat left. What would the tablets be for, sir, any views on that at all? Name of Sustac, whatever that is, to be taken two or three times a day?"

"Heart," said Smiley.

"And one receipt for the sum of thirteen pounds from the Straight and Steady Minicab Service of Islington, North."

"May I look?" said Smiley, and the Superintendent held it out so that Smiley could read the date and the driver's signature, J. Lamb, in a copy-book hand wildly underlined.

The next bag contained a stick of school chalk, yellow and miraculously unbroken. The narrow end was smeared brown as if by a single stroke, but the thick end was unused.

"There's yellow chalk powder on his left hand too," Mr. Murgotroyd said, speaking for the first time. His complexion was like grey stone. His voice too was grey, and mournful as an undertaker's. "We did *wonder* whether he might be in the teaching line, actually," Mr. Murgotroyd added, but Smiley, either by design or oversight, did not answer Mr. Murgotroyd's implicit question, and the Superintendent did not pursue it.

And a second cotton handkerchief, proffered this time by Mr. Murgotroyd, part blooded, part clean, and carefully ironed into a sharp triangle for the top pocket.

"On his way to a party, we wondered," Mr. Murgotroyd said, this time with no hope at all.

"Crime and Ops on the air, sir," a voice called from the front of the van.

Without a word the Superintendent vanished into the darkness, leaving Smiley to the depressed gaze of Mr. Murgotroyd.

"You a specialist of some sort, sir?" Mr. Murgotroyd asked after a long sad scrutiny of his guest.

"No. No, I'm afraid not," said Smiley.

"Home Office, sir?"

"Alas, not Home Office either," said Smiley with a benign shake of his head, which somehow made him party to Mr. Murgotroyd's bewilderment.

"My superiors are a little worried about the press, Mr. Smiley," the Superintendent said, poking his head into the van again. "Seems they're heading this way, sir."

Smiley clambered quickly out. The two men stood face to face in the avenue.

"You've been very kind," Smiley said. "Thank you."

"Privilege," said the Superintendent.

"You don't happen to remember which pocket the *chalk* was in, do you?" Smiley asked.

"Overcoat left," the Superintendent replied in some surprise.

"And the searching of him—could you tell me again how you see *that* exactly?"

"They hadn't time or didn't care to turn him over. Knelt by him, fished for his wallet, pulled at his purse. Scattered a few objects as they did so. By then they'd had enough."

"Thank you," said Smiley again.

And a moment later, with more ease than his portly figure might have suggested him capable of, he had vanished among the trees. But not before the Superintendent had shone the torch full upon his face, a thing he hadn't done till now for reasons of discretion. And taken an intense professional look at the legendary features, if only to tell his grandchildren in his old age: how George Smiley, sometime Chief of the Secret Service, by then retired, had one night come out of the woodwork to peer at some dead foreigner of his who had died in highly nasty circumstances.

Not *one* face at all actually, the Superintendent reflected. Not when it was lit by the torch like that indirectly from below. More your whole range of faces. More your patchwork of different ages, people, and endeavours. Even—thought the Superintendent—of different faiths.

"The best I ever met," old Mendel, the Superintendent's onetime superior, had told him over a friendly pint not long ago. Mendel was retired now, like Smiley. But Mendel knew what he was talking about and didn't like Funnies any better than the Superintendent did—interfering la-di-da amateurs

most of them, and devious with it. But not Smiley. Smiley was
different, Mendel had said. Smiley was the best—simply the
best case man Mendel had ever met—and old Mendel knew
what he was talking about.

An abbey, the Superintendent decided. That's what he was,
an abbey. He would work that into his sermon the next time
his turn came around. An abbey, made up of all sorts of conflicting ages and styles and convictions. The Superintendent
liked that metaphor the more he dwelt on it. He would try it
out on his wife when he got home: man as God's architecture,
my dear, moulded by the hand of ages, infinite in his striving
and diversity. . . . But at this point the Superintendent laid a
restraining hand upon his own rhetorical imagination. Maybe
not, after all, he thought. Maybe we're flying a mite too high
for the course, my friend.

There was another thing about that face the Superintendent wouldn't easily forget either. Later, he talked to old Mendel about it, as he talked to him later about lots of things. The
moisture. He'd taken it for dew at first—yet if it was dew why
was the Superintendent's own face bone dry? It wasn't dew and
it wasn't grief either, if his hunch was right. It was a thing that
happened to the Superintendent himself occasionally and happened to the lads too, even the hardest; it crept up on them and
the Superintendent watched for it like a hawk. Usually in kids'
cases, where the pointlessness suddenly got through to you—
your child batterings, your criminal assaults, your infant rapes.
You didn't break down or beat your chest or any of those histrionics. No. You just happened to put your hand to your face
and find it damp and you wondered what the hell Christ bothered to die for, if He ever died at all.

And when you had *that* mood on you, the Superintendent
told himself with a slight shiver, the best thing you could do was
give yourself a couple of days off and take the wife to Margate,
or before you knew where you were you found yourself getting
a little too rough with people for your own good health.

"Sergeant!" the Superintendent yelled.

The bearded figure loomed before him.

"Switch the lights on and get it back to normal," the Super-intendent ordered. "And ask Inspector Hallowes to slip up here and oblige. At the double."

4

They had unchained the door to him, they had questioned him even before they took his coat: tersely and intently. Were there any compromising materials on the body, George? Any that would link him with us? My God, you've been a time! They had shown him where to wash, forgetting that he knew already. They had sat him in an armchair and there Smiley remained, humble and discarded, while Oliver Lacon, Whitehall's Head Prefect to the intelligence services, prowled the threadbare carpet like a man made restless by his conscience, and Lauder Strickland said it all again in fifteen different ways to fifteen different people, over the old upright telephone in the far corner of the room—"Then get me back to police liaison, woman, *at once*"—either bullying or fawning, depending on rank and clout. The Superintendent was a life ago, but in time ten minutes. The flat smelt of old nappies and stale cigarettes and was on the top floor of a scrolled Edwardian apartment house not two hundred yards from Hampstead Heath. In Smiley's mind, visions of Vladimir's burst face mingled with these pale faces of the living, yet death was not a shock to him just now, but merely an affirmation that his own existence too was dwindling; that he was living against the odds. He sat without expectation. He sat like an old man at a country railway station, watching the express go by. But watching all the same. And remembering old journeys.

This is how crises always were, he thought; ragtag conversations with no centre. One man on the telephone, another dead, a third prowling. The nervous idleness of slow motion.

He peered around, trying to fix his mind on the decaying things outside himself. Chipped fire extinguishers, Ministry of Works issue. Prickly brown sofas—the stains a little worse. But safe flats, unlike old generals, never die, he thought. They don't even fade away.

On the table before him lay the cumbersome apparatus of agent hospitality, there to revive the unrevivable guest. Smiley took the inventory. In a bucket of melted ice, one bottle of Stolichnaya vodka, Vladimir's recorded favourite brand. Salted herrings, still in their tin. Pickled cucumber, bought loose and already drying. One mandatory loaf of black bread. Like every Russian Smiley had known, the old boy could scarcely drink his vodka without it. Two Marks & Spencer vodka glasses, could be cleaner. One packet of Russian cigarettes, unopened: if he had come, he would have smoked the lot; he had none with him when he died.

Vladimir had none with him when he died, he repeated to himself, and made a little mental stammer of it, a knot in his handkerchief.

A clatter interrupted Smiley's reverie. In the kitchen, Mostyn the boy had dropped a plate. At the telephone Lauder Strickland wheeled round, demanding quiet. But he already had it again. What was Mostyn preparing anyway? Dinner? Breakfast? Seedcake for the funeral? And what was Mostyn? *Who* was Mostyn? Smiley had shaken his damp and trembling hand, then promptly forgotten what he looked like, except that he was so young. And yet for some reason Mostyn was known to him, if only as a type. Mostyn is our grief, Smiley decided arbitrarily.

Lacon, in the middle of his prowling, came to a sudden halt. "George! You look worried. Don't be. We're all in the clear on this. All of us!"

"I'm not worried, Oliver."

"You look as though you're reproaching yourself. I can tell!"

"When agents die—" said Smiley, but left the sentence incomplete, and anyway Lacon couldn't wait for him. He strode off again, a hiker with miles to go. Lacon, Strickland, Mostyn, thought Smiley as Strickland's Aberdonian brogue hammered on. One Cabinet Office factotum, one Circus fixer, one scared boy. Why not real people? Why not Vladimir's case officer, whoever he is? Why not Saul Enderby, their Chief?

A verse of Auden's rang in his mind from the days when he was Mostyn's age: *Let us honour if we can/The vertical man/Though we value none/But the horizontal one.* Or something.

And why Smiley? he thought. Above all, why me? Of all people, when as far as they're concerned I'm deader than old Vladimir.

"Will you have tea, Mr. Smiley, or something stronger?" called Mostyn through the open kitchen doorway. Smiley wondered whether he was naturally so pale.

"He'll have tea only, thank you, Mostyn!" Lacon blurted, making a sharp about-turn. "After shock, tea is a deal safer. With sugar, right, George? Sugar replaces lost energy. Was it *gruesome*, George? How perfectly awful for you."

No, it wasn't awful, it was the truth, thought Smiley. He was shot and I saw him dead. Perhaps you should do that too.

Apparently unable to leave Smiley alone, Lacon had come back down the room and was peering at him with clever, uncomprehending eyes. He was a mawkish creature, sudden but without spring, with youthful features cruelly aged and a raw unhealthy rash around his neck where his shirt had scuffed the skin. In the religious light between dawn and morning his black waistcoat and white collar had the glint of the soutane.

"I've hardly said hullo," Lacon complained, as if it were Smiley's fault. "George. Old friend. My goodness."

"Hullo, Oliver," said Smiley.

Still Lacon remained there, gazing down at him, his long

head to one side, like a child studying an insect. In his memory Smiley replayed Lacon's fervid phone call of two hours before.

It's an emergency, George. You remember Vladimir? George, are you awake? You remember the old General, George? Used to live in Paris?

Yes, I remember the General, he had replied. Yes, Oliver, I remember Vladimir.

We need someone from his past, George. Someone who knew his little ways, can identify him, damp down potential scandal. We need you, George. Now. George, wake up.

He had been trying to. Just as he had been trying to transfer the receiver to his better ear, and sit upright in a bed too large for him. He was sprawling in the cold space deserted by his wife, because that was the side where the telephone was.

You mean he's been shot? Smiley had repeated.

George, why can't you listen? Shot dead. This evening. George, for Heaven's sake wake up, we need you!

Lacon loped off again, plucking at his signet ring as if it were too tight. *I need you,* thought Smiley, watching him gyrate. *I love you, I hate you, I need you.* Such apocalyptic statements reminded him of Ann when she had run out of money or love. The heart of the sentence is the subject, he thought. It is not the verb, least of all the object. It is the ego, demanding its feed.

Need me what for? he thought again. To console them? Give them absolution? What have they done that they need my past to redress their future?

Down the room, Lauder Strickland was holding up an arm in Fascist salute while he addressed Authority.

"Yes, Chief, he's with us at this moment, sir. . . . I shall tell him that, sir. . . . Indeed, sir. . . . I shall convey to him that message. . . . Yes, sir. . . ."

Why are Scots so attracted to the secret world? Smiley wondered, not for the first time in his career. Ships' engineers,

Colonial administrators, spies. . . . Their heretical Scottish history drew them to distant churches, he decided.

"George!" Strickland, suddenly much louder, calling Smiley's name like an order. "Sir Saul sends you his warmest personal salutations, George!" He had swung round, still with his arm up. "At a quieter moment he will express his gratitude to you more fittingly." Back to the phone: "Yes, Chief, Oliver Lacon is also with me and his opposite number at the Home Office is at this instant in parley with the Commissioner of Police regarding our former interest in the dead man and the preparation of the D-notice for the press."

Former interest, Smiley recorded. A former interest with his face shot off and no cigarettes in his pocket. Yellow chalk. Smiley studied Strickland frankly: the awful green suit, the shoes of brushed pigskin got up as suède leather. The only change he could observe in him was a russet moustache not half as military as Vladimir's when he had still had one.

"Yes, sir, 'an extinct case of purely historic concern,' sir," Strickland went on, into the telephone. Extinct is right, thought Smiley. Extinct, extinguished, put out. "That is precisely the terminology," Strickland continued. "And Oliver Lacon proposes to have it included word for word in the D-notice. Am I on target there, Oliver?"

"*Historical*," Lacon corrected him irritably. "Not *historic* concern. That's the last thing we want! Historical." He stalked across the room, ostensibly to peer through the window at the coming day.

"It *is* still Enderby in charge, is it, Oliver?" Smiley asked, of Lacon's back.

"Yes, yes, it is still Saul Enderby, your old adversary, and he is doing marvels," Lacon retorted impatiently. Pulling at the curtain, he unseated it from its runners. "Not your style, I grant you—why should he be? He's an Atlantic man." He was trying to force the casement. "Not an easy thing to be under a government like this one, I can tell you." He gave the handle another savage shove. A freezing draught raced round Smiley's knees. "Takes a lot of footwork. Mostyn, where's tea? We seem to have been waiting for ever."

All our lives, thought Smiley.

Over the sound of a lorry grinding up the hill, he heard Strickland again, interminably talking to Saul Enderby. "I think the point with the press is not to play him down *too far*, Chief. Dullness is all, in a case like this. Even the private-life angle is a dangerous one, here. What we want is absolute lack of contemporary relevance of any sort. Oh, true, true, indeed, Chief, right—" On he droned, sycophantic but alert.

"Oliver—" Smiley began, losing patience. "Oliver, do you mind, just—"

But Lacon was talking, not listening. "How's Ann?" he asked vaguely, at the window, stretching his forearms on the sill. "With you and so forth, I trust? Not roaming, is she? *God*, I hate autumn."

"Fine, thank you. How's—" He struggled without success to remember the name of Lacon's wife.

"*Abandoned* me, dammit. Ran off with her pesky riding instructor, blast her. Left me with the children. The girls are farmed out to boarding-schools, thank God." Leaning over his hands, Lacon was staring up at the lightening sky. "Is that Orion up there, stuck like a golf ball between the chimney-pots?" he asked.

Which is another death, thought Smiley sadly, his mind staying briefly with Lacon's broken marriage. He remembered a pretty, unworldly woman and a string of daughters jumping ponies in the garden of their rambling house in Ascot.

"I'm sorry, Oliver," he said.

"Why should you be? Not *your* wife. She's mine. It's every man for himself in love."

"Could you close that window, please!" Strickland called, dialling again. "It's bloody arctic down this end."

Irritably slamming the window, Lacon strode back into the room.

Smiley tried a second time: "Oliver, what's going on?" he asked. "Why did you need me?"

"Only one who knew him, for a start. Strickland, are you nearly done? He's like one of those airport announcers," he told Smiley with a stupid grin. "*Never* done."

You could break, Oliver, thought Smiley, noticing the estrangement of Lacon's eyes as he came under the light. You've had too much, he thought in unexpected sympathy. We both have.

From the kitchen the mysterious Mostyn appeared with tea: an earnest, contemporary-looking child with flared trousers and a mane of brown hair. Seeing him set down the tray, Smiley finally placed him in the terms of his own past. Ann had had a lover like him once, an ordinand from Wells Theological College. She gave him a lift down the M-4 and later claimed to have saved him from going queer.

"What section are you in, Mostyn?" Smiley asked him.

"Oddbins, sir." He crouched, level to the table, displaying an Asian suppleness. "Since your day, actually, sir. It's a sort of operational pool. Mainly probationers waiting for overseas postings."

"I see."

"I heard you lecture at the Nursery at Sarratt, sir. On the new entrants' course. 'Agent Handling in the Field.' It was the best thing of the whole two years."

"Thank you."

But Mostyn's calf eyes stayed on him intently.

"Thank you," said Smiley again, more puzzled than before.

"Milk, sir, or lemon, sir? The lemon was for *him*," Mostyn added in a low aside, as if that were a recommendation for the lemon.

Strickland had rung off and was fiddling with the waistband of his trousers, making it looser or tighter.

"Yes, well, we have to temper truth, George!" Lacon bellowed suddenly, in what seemed to be a declaration of personal faith. "Sometimes people are innocent but the circumstances can make them appear quite otherwise. There was never a golden age. There's only a golden mean. We have to remember that. Chalk it on our shaving mirrors."

In yellow, Smiley thought.

Strickland was waddling down the room: "You. Mostyn. Young Nigel. You, sir!"

Mostyn lifted his grave brown eyes in reply.

"Commit nothing to paper whatever," Strickland warned him, wiping the back of his hand on his moustache as if one or the other were wet. "Hear me? That's an order from on high. There was no encounter, so you've no call to fill in the usual encounter sheet or any of that stuff. You've nothing to do but keep your mouth shut. Understand? You'll account for your expenses as general petty-cash disbursements. To me, direct. No file reference. Understand?"

"I understand," said Mostyn.

"And no whispered confidences to those little tarts in Registry, or I'll know. Hear me? Give us some tea."

Something happened inside George Smiley when he heard this conversation. Out of the formless indirection of these dialogues, out of the horror of the scene upon the Heath, a single shocking truth struck him. He felt a pull in his chest somewhere and he had the sensation of momentary disconnection from the room and the three haunted people he had found in it. *Encounter* sheet? No *encounter*? *Encounter* between Mostyn and Vladimir? *God in Heaven*, he thought, squaring the mad circle. *The Lord preserve, cosset, and protect us. Mostyn was Vladimir's case officer! That old man, a General, once our glory, and they farmed him out to this uncut boy!* Then another lurch, more violent still, as his surprise was swept aside in an explosion of internal fury. He felt his lips tremble, he felt his throat seize up in indignation, blocking his words, and when he turned to Lacon his spectacles seemed to be misting over from the heat.

"Oliver, I wonder if you'd mind finally telling me what I'm doing here," he heard himself suggesting for the third time, hardly above a murmur.

Reaching out an arm, he removed the vodka bottle from its bucket. Still unbidden, he broke the cap and poured himself a rather large tot.

Even then, Lacon dithered, pondered, hunted with his eyes, delayed. In Lacon's world, direct questions were the height of bad taste but direct answers were worse. For a moment, caught in mid-gesture at the centre of the room, he stood staring at Smiley in disbelief. A car stumbled up the hill, bringing news of the real world outside the window. Lauder Strickland slurped his tea. Mostyn was seating himself primly on a piano-stool to which there was no piano. But Lacon with his jerky gestures could only scratch about for words sufficiently elliptical to disguise his meaning.

"George," he said. A shower of rain crashed against the window, but he ignored it. "Where's Mostyn?" he asked.

Mostyn, no sooner settled, had flitted from the room to cope with a nervous need. They heard the thunder of the flush, loud as a brass band, and the gurgle of pipes all down the building.

Lacon raised a hand to his neck, tracing the raw patches. Reluctantly, he began: "Three years ago, George—let us start there—soon after you left the Circus—your successor Saul Enderby—your *worthy* successor—under pressure from a concerned Cabinet—by *concerned* I mean newly formed—decided on certain far-reaching changes of intelligence practice. I'm giving you the *background*, George," he explained, interrupting himself. "I'm doing this because you're who you are, because of old times, and because"—he jabbed a finger at the window—"because of out there."

Strickland had unbuttoned his waistcoat and lay dozing and replete like a first-class passenger on a night plane. But his small watchful eyes followed every pass that Lacon made. The door opened and closed, admitting Mostyn, who resumed his perch on the piano-stool.

"Mostyn, I expect you to close your ears to this. I am talking high, high policy. One of these *far-reaching* changes, George, was the decision to form an inter-ministerial Steering Committee. A *mixed* committee"—he composed one in the air with his hands—"part Westminster, part Whitehall, representing Cabinet as well as the major Whitehall customers. Known as the Wise Men. But placed—George—placed *between* the intelligence fraternity and Cabinet. As a channel, as a filter, as a brake." One hand had remained outstretched, dealing these metaphors like cards. "To look over the Circus's shoulder. To exercise control, George. Vigilance and accountability in the interest of a more open government. You don't like it. I can tell by your face."

"I'm out of it," Smiley said. "I'm not qualified to judge."

Suddenly Lacon's own face took on an appalled expression and his tone dropped to one of near despair.

"You should *hear* them, George, our new masters! You should *hear* the way they talk about the Circus! I'm their dog's-body, damn it; I *know*, get it every day! Gibes. Suspicion. Mistrust at every turn, even from Ministers who should know better. As if the Circus were some rogue animal outside their comprehension. As if British Intelligence were a sort of wholly owned subsidiary of the Conservative Party. Not their ally at all but some autonomous viper in their socialist nest. The thirties all over again. Do you know, they're even reviving all that talk about a British Freedom of Information Act on the American pattern? From *within* the Cabinet? Of open hearings, revelations, all for the public sport? You'd be shocked, George. Pained. Think of the effect such a thing would have on morale alone. Would Mostyn here have ever joined the Circus after that kind of notoriety in the press and wherever? Would you. Mostyn?"

The question seemed to strike Mostyn very deep, for his grave eyes, made yet darker by his sickly colour, became graver, and he lifted a thumb and finger to his lip. But he did not speak.

"Where was I, George?" Lacon asked, suddenly lost.

"The Wise Men," said Smiley sympathetically.

From the sofa, Lauder Strickland threw in his own pronouncement on that body: "Wise, my Aunt Fanny. Bunch of left-wing flannel merchants. Rule our lives for us. Tell us how to run the shop. Smack our wrists when we don't do our sums right."

Lacon shot Strickland a glance of rebuke but did not contradict him.

"One of the *less* controversial exercises of the Wise Men, George—one of their first duties—conferred upon them specifically by our masters—enshrined in a jointly drafted charter—was *stock-taking*. To review the Circus's resources worldwide and set them beside legitimate present-day targets. Don't ask me what constitutes a legitimate present-day target in their sight. That is a very moot point. However, I must not be disloyal." He returned to his text. "Suffice it to say that over a period of six months a review was conducted, and an axe duly laid." He broke off, staring at Smiley. "Are you with me, George?" he asked in a puzzled voice.

But it was hardly possible at that moment to tell whether Smiley was with anybody at all. His heavy lids had almost closed, and what remained visible of his eyes was clouded by the thick lenses of his spectacles. He was sitting upright but his head had fallen forward till his plump chins rested on his chest.

Lacon hesitated a moment longer, then continued: "Now as a result of this axe-laying—this stock-taking, if you prefer—on the part of the Wise Men, certain categories of clandestine operation have been ruled *ipso facto* out of bounds. *Verboten.* Right?"

Prone on his sofa, Strickland incanted the unsayable: "No coat-trailing. No honey-traps. No doubles. No stimulated defections. No émigrés. No bugger all."

"What's that?" said Smiley, as if sharply waking from a deep sleep. But such straight talk was not to Lacon's liking and he overrode it.

"Let us not be simplistic, please, Lauder. Let us reach things organically. Conceptual thinking is essential here. So the Wise Men composed a *codex*, George," he resumed to Smiley. "A catalogue of proscribed practices. Right?" But Smiley was waiting rather than listening. "Ranged the whole field—on the uses and abuses of agents, on our fishing rights in the Commonwealth countries—or lack of them—all sorts. Listeners, surveillance overseas, false-flag operations—a mammoth task, bravely tackled." To the astonishment of everyone but himself, Lacon locked his fingers together, turned down the palms, and cracked the joints in a defiant staccato.

He continued: "*Also* included in their forbidden list—and it *is* a crude instrument, George, no respecter of tradition—are such matters as the classic use of double agents. *Obsession*, our new masters were pleased to call it in their finding. The old games of coat-trailing—turning and playing back our enemies' spies—in your day the very meat and drink of counter-intelligence—today, George, in the collective opinion of the Wise Men—today they are ruled obsolete. Uneconomic. Throw them out."

Another lorry thundered giddily down the hill, or up it. They heard the bump of its wheels on the kerb.

"Christ," Strickland muttered.

"Or—for example—I strike another blow at random—the over-emphasis on exile groups."

This time there was no lorry at all: only the deep, accusing silence that had followed in its wake. Smiley sat as before, receiving not judging, his concentration only on Lacon, hearing him with the sharpness of the blind.

"Exile groups, you will want to know," Lacon went on, "or more properly the Circus's time-honoured connections with them—the Wise Men prefer to call it *dependence*, but I think that a trifle strong—I took issue with them, but was overruled—are today ruled provocative, anti-détente, inflammatory. An expensive indulgence. Those who tamper with them do so *on pain of excommunication*. I mean it, George. We have got thus far. This is the extent of their mastery. Imagine."

With a gesture of baring his breast for Smiley's onslaught, Lacon opened his arms and remained standing, peering down at him as he had done before, while in the background Strickland's Scottish echo once again told the same truth more brutally.

"The groups have been dustbinned, George," Strickland said. "The lot of them. Orders from on high. No contact, not even arm's length. The late Vladimir's death-and-glory artists included. Special two-key archive for 'em on the fifth floor. No officer access without consent in writing from the Chief. Copy to the weekly float for the Wise Men's inspection. Troubled times, George, I tell you true, troubled times."

"George, now steady," Lacon warned uneasily, catching something the others had not heard.

"What utter nonsense," Smiley repeated deliberately.

His head had lifted and his eyes had turned full on Lacon, as if emphasising the bluntness of his contradiction. "Vladimir wasn't *expensive*. He wasn't an indulgence either. Least of all was he uneconomic. You know perfectly well he loathed taking our money. We had to force it on him or he'd have starved. As to inflammatory—anti-détente, whatever those words mean—well, we had to hold him in check once in a while as one does with most good agents, but when it came down to it he took our orders like a lamb. You were a fan of his, Oliver. You know as well as I do what he was worth."

The quietness of Smiley's voice did not conceal its tautness.

Nor had Lacon failed to notice the dangerous points of colour in his cheeks.

Sharply, Lacon turned upon the weakest member present: "Mostyn, I expect you to forget all this. Do you hear? Strickland, tell him."

Strickland obliged with alacrity: "Mostyn, you will present yourself to Housekeepers this morning at ten-thirty precisely and sign an indoctrination certificate which I personally shall compose and witness!"

"Yes, sir," Mostyn said, after a slightly eerie delay.

Only now did Lacon respond to Smiley's point: "George, I admired the *man*. Never his Group. There is an absolute distinction here. The man, yes. In many ways, a heroic figure, if you will. But not the company he kept: the fantasists, the down-at-heel princelings. Nor the Moscow Centre infiltrators they enfolded so warmly to their breasts. Never. The Wise Men have a point and you can't deny it."

Smiley had taken off his spectacles and was polishing them with the thick end of his tie. By the pale light now breaking through the curtains, his plump face looked moist and undefended.

"Vladimir was one of the best agents we ever had," Smiley said baldly.

"Because he was yours, you mean?" Strickland sneered, behind Smiley's back.

"Because he was good!" Smiley snapped, and there was a startled silence everywhere while he recovered himself. "Vladimir's father was an Estonian and a passionate Bolshevik, Oliver," he resumed in a calmer voice. "A professional man, a lawyer. Stalin rewarded his loyalty by murdering him in the purges. Vladimir was born Voldemar but he even changed his name to Vladimir out of allegiance to Moscow and the Revolution. He still wanted to believe, despite what they had done to his father. He joined the Red Army and by God's grace missed being purged as well. The war prompted him, he fought like a

lion, and when it was over, he waited for the great Russian lib-
eralisation that he had been dreaming of, and the freeing of his
own people. It never came. Instead, he witnessed the ruthless
repression of his homeland by the government he had served.
Scores of thousands of his fellow Estonians went to the camps,
several of his own relatives among them." Lacon opened his
mouth to interrupt, but wisely closed it. "The lucky ones escaped
to Sweden and Germany. We're talking of a population of a
million sober, hard-working people, cut to bits. One night, in
despair, he offered us his services. Us, the British. In Moscow.
For three years after that he spied for us from the very heart of
the capital. Risked everything for us, every day."

"And needless to say, our George here ran him," Strickland
growled, still somehow trying to suggest that this very fact put
Smiley out of court. But Smiley would not be stopped. At his
feet, young Mostyn was listening in a kind of trance.

"We even gave him a medal, if you remember, Oliver. Not
to wear or possess, of course. But somewhere, on a bit of parchment that he was occasionally allowed to look at, there was a
signature very much like the Monarch's."

"George, this is history," Lacon protested weakly. "This is
not *today*."

"For three long years, Vladimir was the best source we ever
had on Soviet capabilities and intentions—and at the height of
the cold war. He was close to their intelligence community and
reported on that too. Then one day on a service visit to Paris,
he took his chance and jumped, and thank God he did, because
otherwise he'd have been shot a great deal sooner."

Lacon was suddenly quite lost. "What *do* you mean?" he
asked. "How *sooner?* What are you saying now?"

"I mean that in those days the Circus was largely run by a
Moscow Centre agent," Smiley replied with deadly patience.
"It was the sheerest luck that Bill Haydon happened to be stationed abroad while Vladimir was working for us. Another
three months and Bill would have been blown sky high."

Lacon found nothing to say at all, so Strickland filled in for him.

"Bill Haydon this, Bill Haydon that," he sneered. "Just because you had that extra involvement with him—" He was going to continue but thought better of it. "Haydon's dead, dammit," he ended sullenly, "so's that whole era."

"And so is Vladimir," said Smiley quietly, and once again there was a halt in the proceedings.

"George," Lacon intoned gravely, as if he had belatedly found his place in the prayer book. "We are *pragmatists*, George. We *adapt*. We are *not* keepers of some sacred flame. I ask you, I commend you, to remember this!"

Quiet but resolute, Smiley had not quite finished the old man's obituary, and perhaps he sensed already that it was the only one he was ever going to get.

"And when he did come out, all right, he was a declining asset, as all ex-agents are," he continued.

"I'll say," said Strickland *sotto voce*.

"He stayed on in Paris and threw himself whole-heartedly into the Baltic independence movement. All right, it was a lost cause. It so happens that to this very day, the British have refused *de jure* recognition to the Soviet annexation of the three Baltic States—but never mind that either. Estonia, you may not know, Oliver, maintains a perfectly respectable Legation and Consulate General in Queen's Gate. We don't mind supporting lost causes once they're fully lost, apparently. Not before." He drew a sharp breath. "And all right, in Paris he formed a Baltic Group, and the Group went downhill, as émigré groups and lost causes always will—let me go on Oliver, I'm not often long!"

"My dear fellow," said Lacon, and blushed. "Be as long as you like," he said, quelling another groan from Strickland.

"His Group split up, there were quarrels. Vladimir was in a hurry and wanted to bring all the factions under one hat. The factions had their vested interests and didn't agree. There was a pitched battle, some heads got broken, and the French threw him out. We moved him to London with a couple of his lieutenants. Vladimir in his old age returned to the Lutheran religion of his forefathers, exchanging the Marxist Saviour for the Christian Messiah. We're supposed to encourage that too, I believe. Or perhaps that is not policy any more. He has now been murdered. Since we are talking background, that is Vladimir's. Now why am I here?"

The ringing of the bell could not have been more timely. Lacon was still quite pink, and Smiley, breathing heavily, was once more polishing his spectacles. Reverently Mostyn the acolyte unchained the door and admitted a tall motor-cycle messenger dangling a bunch of keys in his gloved hand. Reverently, Mostyn bore the keys to Strickland, who signed for them and made an entry in his log. The messenger, after a long and even doting glance at Smiley, departed, leaving Smiley with the guilty feeling that he should have recognised him, even under all his paraphernalia. But Smiley had more pressing insights to concern him. With no reverence at all, Stickland dumped the keys into Lacon's open palm.

"All right, Mostyn, tell him!" Lacon boomed suddenly. "Tell him in your own words."

5

Mostyn sat with a quite particular stillness. He spoke softly. To hear him, Lacon had withdrawn to a corner and bunched his hands judicially under his nose. But Strickland had sat himself bolt upright and seemed, like Mostyn himself, to be patrolling the boy's words for lapses.

"Vladimir telephoned the Circus at lunch-time today, sir," Mostyn began, leaving some unclarity as to which "sir" he was addressing. "I happened to be Oddbins duty officer and took the call."

Strickland corrected him with unpleasant haste: "You mean *yesterday*. Be precise, can't you?"

"I'm sorry, sir. Yesterday," said Mostyn.

"Well, get it right," Strickland warned.

To be Oddbins duty officer, Mostyn explained, meant little more than covering the lunch-hour gap and checking desks and wastebins at closing time. Oddbins personnel were too junior for night duty, so there was just this roster for lunch-times and evenings.

And Vladimir, he repeated, came through in the lunch-hour, using the lifeline.

"*Lifeline?*" Smiley repeated in bewilderment. "I don't think I quite know what you mean."

"It's the system we have for keeping in touch with dead agents, sir," said Mostyn, then put his fingers to his temple and muttered, "Oh, my Lord." He started again: "I mean agents who have run their course but are still on the welfare roll, sir," said Mostyn unhappily.

"So he rang and you took the call," said Smiley kindly. "What time was that?"

"One-fifteen exactly, sir. Oddbins is like a sort of Fleet Street news-room, you see. There are these twelve desks and there's the section head's hen-coop at the end, with a glass partition between us and him. The lifeline's in a locked box and normally it's the section head who keeps the key. But in the lunch-hour he gives it to the duty dog. I unlocked the box and heard this foreign voice saying 'Hullo.'"

"Get on with it, Mostyn," Strickland growled.

"I said 'Hullo' back, Mr. Smiley. That's all we do. We don't give the number. He said, 'This is Gregory calling for Max. I have something very urgent for him. Please get me Max immediately.' I asked him where he was calling from, which is routine, but he just said he had plenty of change. We have no brief to trace incoming calls and anyway it takes too long. There's an electric card selector by the lifeline, it's got all the worknames on it. I told him to hold on and typed out 'Gregory.' That's the next thing we do after asking where they're calling from. Up it came on the selector. 'Gregory equals Vladimir, ex-agent, ex–Soviet General, ex-leader of the Riga Group.' Then the file reference. I typed out 'Max' and found you, sir." Smiley gave a small nod. "'Max equals Smiley.' Then I typed out 'Riga Group' and realised you were their last vicar, sir."

"Their *vicar?*" said Lacon, as if he had detected heresy. "Smiley their last *vicar*, Mostyn? What on earth—"

"I thought you had heard all this, Oliver," Smiley said, to cut him off.

"Only the essence," Lacon retorted. "In a crisis one deals only with essentials."

In his pressed-down Scottish, without letting Mostyn from his sight, Strickland provided Lacon with the required explanation: "Organisations such as the Group had by tradition two case officers. The postman, who did the nuts and bolts for them, and the vicar, who stood above the fight. Their father figure," he said, and nodded perfunctorily towards Smiley.

"And who was carded as his most recent postman, Mostyn?" Smiley asked, ignoring Strickland entirely.

"Esterhase, sir. Workname Hector."

"And he didn't ask for him?" said Smiley to Mostyn, speaking straight past Strickland yet again.

"I'm sorry, sir?"

"Vladimir didn't ask for Hector? His postman? He asked for me. Max. Only Max. You're sure of that?"

"He wanted you and nobody else, sir," said Mostyn earnestly.

"Did you make notes?"

"The lifeline is taped automatically, sir. It's also linked to a speaking clock, so that we get the exact timing as well."

"Damn you, Mostyn, that's a confidential matter," Strickland snapped. "Mr. Smiley may be a distinguished ex-member, but he's no longer family."

"So what did you do next, Mostyn?" Smiley asked.

"Standing instructions gave me very little latitude, sir," Mostyn replied, showing once again, like Smiley, a studied disregard for Strickland. "Both 'Smiley' and 'Esterhase' were wait-listed, which meant that they could be contacted only through the fifth floor. My section head was out to lunch and not due back till two-fifteen." He gave a light shrug. "I stalled. I told him to try again at two-thirty."

Smiley turned to Strickland. "I thought you said that all the émigré files had been consigned to special keeping?"

"Correct."

"Shouldn't there have been something on the selector card to that effect?"

"There should and there wasn't," Strickland said.

"That is just the point, sir," Mostyn agreed, talking only to Smiley. "At that stage there was no suggestion that Vladimir or his Group was out of bounds. From the card, he looked just like any other pensioned-off agent raising a wind. I assumed he wanted a bit of money, or company, or something. We get quite a few of those. Leave him to the section head, I thought."

"Who shall remain nameless, Mostyn," Strickland said. "Remember that."

It crossed Smiley's mind at this point that the reticence in Mostyn—his air of distastefully stepping round some danger-ous secret all the time he spoke—might have something to do with protecting a negligent superior. But Mostyn's next words dispelled this notion, for he went out of his way to imply that his superior was at fault.

"The trouble was, my section head didn't get back from lunch till three-fifteen, so that when Vladimir rang in at two-thirty, I had to put him off again. He was furious," said Mostyn. "Vladimir was, I mean. I asked whether there was anything I could do in the meantime and he said, 'Find Max. Just find me Max. Tell Max I have been in touch with certain friends, also through friends with neighbours.' There were a couple of notes on the card about his word code and I saw that 'neighbour' meant Soviet Intelligence."

A mandarin impassivity had descended over Smiley's face. The earlier emotion was quite gone.

"All of which you duly reported to your section head at three-fifteen?"

"Yes, sir."

"Did you play him the tape?"

"He hadn't time to hear it," said Mostyn mercilessly. "He had to leave straight away for a long week-end."

The stubborn brevity of Mostyn's speech was now so evi-dent that Strickland felt obliged to fill the gaps.

"Yes, well, there's no question but that if we're looking for scapegoats, George, that section head of Mostyn's made a mon-umental fool of himself, no question at all," Strickland declared brightly. "He omitted to send for Vladimir's papers—which would not, of course, have been forthcoming. He omitted to acquaint himself with standing orders on the handling of émigrés. He also appears to have succumbed to a severe dose of week-end fever, leaving no word of his whereabouts should he be required. God help him on Monday morning, says I. Oh, yes. Come, Mostyn, we're waiting, boy."

Mostyn obediently took back the story. Vladimir rang for the third and last time at three-forty-three, sir, he said, speaking even more slowly than before. It should have been quarter to four, but he jumped the gun by two minutes. Mostyn by then had a rudimentary brief from his section head, which he now repeated to Smiley: "He called it a bromide job. I was to find out what, if anything, the old boy really wanted and, if all else failed, make a rendezvous with him to cool him down. I was to give him a drink, sir, pat him on the back, and promise nothing except to pass on whatever message he brought me."

"And the 'neighbours'?" Smiley asked. "They were not an issue to your section head?"

"He rather thought that was just a bit of agent's histrionics, sir."

"I see. Yes, I see." Yet his eyes, in contradiction, closed completely for a moment. "So how did the dialogue with Vladimir go this third time?"

"According to Vladimir, it was to be an immediate meeting or nothing, sir. I tried out the alternatives on him as instructed— 'Write us a letter—is it money you want? Surely it can wait till Monday'—but by then he was shouting at me down the phone. 'A meeting or nothing. Tonight or nothing. Moscow Rules. I insist Moscow Rules. Tell this to Max—'"

Interrupting himself, Mostyn lifted his head and with unblinking eyes returned Lauder Strickland's hostile stare.

"Tell *what* to Max?" said Smiley, his gaze moving swiftly from one to the other of them.

"We were speaking French, sir. The card said French was his preferred second language and I'm only Grade B in Russian."

"Irrelevant," Strickland snapped.

"Tell *what* to Max?" Smiley persisted.

Mostyn's eyes searched out a spot on the floor a yard or two beyond his own feet. "He meant: Tell Max I insist it's Moscow Rules."

Lacon, who had stayed uncharacteristically quiet these last minutes, now chimed in: "There's an important point here, George. The Circus were not the suitors here. *He* was. The ex-agent. He was doing *all* the pressing, making *all* the running. If he'd accepted our suggestion, written out his information, none of this need ever have happened. He brought it on himself entirely. George, I insist you take the point!"

Strickland was lighting himself a fresh cigarette.

"Whoever heard of Moscow Rules in the middle of bloody Hampstead anyway?" Strickland asked, waving out the match.

"Bloody Hampstead is right," Smiley said quietly.

"Mostyn, wrap the story up," Lacon commanded, blushing scarlet.

They had agreed a time, Mostyn resumed woodenly, now staring at his left palm as if he were reading his own fortune in it: "Ten-twenty, sir."

They had agreed Moscow Rules, he said, and the usual contact procedures, which Mostyn had established earlier in the afternoon by consulting the Oddbins encounter index.

"And what *were* the contact procedures exactly?" Smiley asked.

"A copy-book rendezvous, sir," Mostyn replied. "The Sarratt training course all over again, sir."

Smiley felt suddenly crowded by the intimacy of Mostyn's respectfulness. He did not wish to be this boy's hero, or to be caressed by his voice, his gaze, his "sir"s. He was not prepared for the claustrophobic admiration of this stranger.

"There's a tin pavilion on Hampstead Heath, ten minutes' walk from East Heath Road, overlooking a games field on the south side of the avenue, sir. The safety signal was one new drawing-pin shoved high in the first wood support on the left as you entered."

"And the counter-signal?" Smiley asked.

But he knew the answer already.

"A yellow chalk line," said Mostyn. "I gather yellow was the sort of Group trade mark from the old days." He had adopted a tone of ending. "I put up the pin and came back here and waited. When he didn't show up, I thought, 'Well, if he's secrecy-mad I'll have to go up to the hut again and check out his counter-signal, then I'll know whether he's around and proposes to try the fallback.'"

"Which was what?"

"A car pick-up near Swiss Cottage underground at eleven-forty, sir. I was about to go out and take a look when Mr. Strickland rang through and ordered me to sit tight until further orders." Smiley assumed he had finished but this was not quite true. Seeming to forget everyone but himself, Mostyn slowly shook his handsome head. "I never met him," he said, in amazement. "He was my first agent, I never met him, I'll never know what he was trying to tell me," he said. "My first agent, and he's dead. It's incredible. I feel like a complete Jonah." His head continued shaking long after he had finished speaking.

Lacon added a brisk postscript: "Yes, well, Scotland Yard has a computer these days, George. The Heath Patrol found the body and cordoned off the area and the moment the name was fed into the computer a light came up or a lot of digits or something, and immediately they knew he was on our special watch list. From then on it went like clockwork. The Commissioner phoned the Home Office, the Home Office phoned the Circus—"

"And you phoned me," said Smiley. "Why, Oliver? Who suggested you bring me in on this?"

"George, does it matter?"

"Enderby?"

"If you insist, yes, it was Saul Enderby. George, listen to me."

* * *

It was Lacon's moment at last. The issue, whatever it might be, was before them, circumscribed if not yet actually defined. Mostyn was forgotten. Lacon was standing confidently over Smiley's seated figure and had assumed the rights of an old friend.

"George, as things now stand, I can go to the Wise Men and say: 'I have investigated and the Circus's hands are clean.' I can say that. 'The Circus gave no encouragement to these people, nor to their leader. For a whole year they have neither paid nor welfared him!' Perfectly honestly. They don't own his flat, his car, they don't pay his rent, educate his bastards, send flowers to his mistress, or have any other of the old—and lamentable—connections with him or his kind. His only link was with the past. His case officers have left the stage for good—yourself and Esterhase, both old 'uns, both off the books. I can say that with my hand on my breast. To the Wise Men, and if necessary to my Minister personally."

"I don't follow you," Smiley said with deliberate obtuseness. "Vladimir was our agent. He was trying to tell us something."

"Our *ex*-agent, George. How do we *know* he was trying to tell us something? We gave him no *brief*. He spoke of urgency—even of Soviet Intelligence—so do a lot of ex-agents when they're holding out their caps for a subsidy!"

"Not Vladimir," Smiley said.

But sophistry was Lacon's element. He was born to it, he breathed it, he could fly and swim in it, nobody in Whitehall was better at it.

"George, we cannot be held responsible for every ex-agent who takes an injudicious nocturnal walk in one of London's increasingly dangerous open spaces!" He held out his hands in appeal. "George. What is it to be? Choose. *You* choose. On the one hand, Vladimir asked for a chat with you. Retired buddies—a chin-wag about old times—why not? And in order to raise a bit of wind, as any of us might, he pretended he had something for you. Some nugget of information. Why not? They all do it. On that basis my Minister will back us. No heads need roll, no tantrums, Cabinet hysteria. He will help us bury the case. Not a cover-up, naturally. But he will use his judgment. If I catch him in the right mood, he may even decide that there is no point in troubling the Wise Men with it at all."

"Amen," Strickland echoed.

"On the other hand," Lacon insisted, mustering all his persuasiveness for the kill, "if things were to come unstuck, George, and the Minister got it into his head that we were engaging his good offices in order to clean up the traces of some unlicensed adventure which has aborted"—he was striding again, skirting an imaginary quagmire—"and there was a scandal, George, and the Circus were proved to be currently involved—your old service, George, one you still love, I am sure—with a notoriously revanchist émigré outfit—volatile, talkative, violently anti-détente—with all manner of anachronistic fixations—a total hangover from the worst days of the cold war—the very archetype of everything our masters have told us to avoid"—he had reached his corner again, a little outside the circle of light—"and there had been a death, George—and an attempted cover-up, as they would no doubt call it—with all the attendant publicity—well, it could be just one scandal too many. The service is a weak child still, George, a sickly one, and in the hands of these new people desperately delicate. At this stage in its rebirth, it could die of the common cold. If it does, your generation will not be least to blame. You have a duty, as we all do. A loyalty."

Duty to *what?* Smiley wondered, with that part of himself which sometimes seemed to be a spectator to the rest. Loyalty to *whom?* "There is no loyalty without betrayal," Ann liked to tell him in their youth when he had ventured to protest at her infidelities.

For a time nobody spoke.

"And the weapon?" Smiley asked finally, in the tone of

someone testing a theory. "How do you account for that, Oliver?"

"What weapon? There was no weapon. He was shot. By his own buddies most likely, knowing their cabals. Not to mention his appetite for other people's wives."

"Yes, he was shot," Smiley agreed. "In the face. At extremely close range. With a soft-nosed bullet. And cursorily searched. Had his wallet taken. That is the police diagnosis. But our diagnosis would be different, wouldn't it, Lauder?"

"No way," said Strickland, glowering at him through a cloud of cigarette smoke.

"Well, mine would."

"Then let's hear it, George," said Lacon handsomely.

"The weapon used to kill Vladimir was a standard Moscow Centre assassination device," Smiley said. "Concealed in a camera, a brief-case, or whatever. A soft-nosed bullet is fired at point-blank range. To obliterate, to punish, and to discourage others. If I remember rightly, they even had one on display at Sarratt in the black museum next to the bar."

"They still have. It's horrific," said Mostyn.

Strickland vouchsafed Mostyn a foul glance.

"But, George!" Lacon cried.

Smiley waited, knowing that in this mood Lacon could swear away Big Ben.

"These people—these émigrés—of whom this poor chap was one—don't they *come* from Russia? Haven't half of them been in *touch* with Moscow Centre—with or without our knowledge? A weapon like that—I'm not saying you're right, of course—a weapon like that, in their world, could be as common as cheese!"

Against stupidity, the gods themselves fight in vain, thought Smiley; but Schiller had forgotten the bureaucrats. Lacon was addressing Strickland.

"Lauder. There is the question of the D-notice to the Press

outstanding." It was an order. "Perhaps you should have another shot at them, see how far it's got."

In his stockinged feet, Strickland obediently padded down the room and dialled a number.

"Mostyn, perhaps you should take these things out to the kitchen. We don't want to leave needless traces, do we?"

With Mostyn also dismissed, Smiley and Lacon were suddenly alone.

"It's a yes or no, George," Lacon said. "There's cleaning up to be done. Explanations to be given to tradesmen, what do I know? Mail. Milk. Friends. Whatever such people have. No one knows the course as you do. No one. The police have promised you a head start. They will not be dilatory but they will observe a certain measured order about things and let routine play its part." With a nervous bound Lacon approached Smiley's chair and sat awkwardly on the arm. "George. You were their vicar. Very well, I'm asking you to go and read the Offices. He wanted *you*, George. Not us. You."

From his old place at the telephone, Strickland interrupted: "They're asking for a signature for that D-notice, Oliver. They'd like it to be yours, if it's all the same to you."

"Why not the chief's?" Lacon demanded warily.

"Seem to think yours will carry a spot more weight, I fancy."

"Ask him to hold a moment," Lacon said, and with a wind-mill gesture drove a fist into his pocket. "I may give you the keys, George?" He dangled them in front of Smiley's face. "On terms. Right?" The keys still dangled. Smiley stared at them and perhaps he asked "What terms?" or perhaps he just stared; he wasn't really in a mood for conversation. His mind was on Mostyn, and missing cigarettes; on phone calls about neighbours; on agents with no faces; on sleep. Lacon was counting. He attached great merit to numbering his paragraphs. "One, that you are a private citizen, Vladimir's executor, not ours. Two, that you are of the past, not the present, and conduct yourself accordingly. The *sanitised* past. That you will pour oil on the waters, not muddy them. That you will suppress your old professional interest in him, naturally, for that means ours. On those terms may I give you the keys? Yes? No?"

Mostyn was standing in the kitchen doorway. He was addressing Lacon, but his earnest eyes veered constantly towards Smiley.

"What is it, Mostyn?" Lacon demanded. "Be quick!"

"I just remembered a note on Vladimir's card, sir. He had a wife in Tallinn. I wondered whether she should be informed. I just thought I'd better mention it."

"The card is once more not accurate," said Smiley, returning Mostyn's gaze. "She was with him in Moscow when he defected, she was arrested and taken to a forced-labour camp. She died there."

"Mr. Smiley must do whatever he thinks fit about such things," Lacon said swiftly, anxious to avoid a fresh outbreak, and dropped the keys into Smiley's passive palm. Suddenly everything was in movement. Smiley was on his feet, Lacon was already half-way down the room, and Strickland was holding out the phone to him. Mostyn had slipped to the darkened hallway and was deftly unhooking Smiley's raincoat from the stand.

"What else did Vladimir say to you on the telephone, Mostyn?" Smiley asked quietly, dropping one arm into the sleeve.

"He said, 'Tell Max that it concerns the Sandman. Tell him I have two proofs and can bring them with me. Then perhaps he will see me.' He said it twice. It was on the tape but Strickland erased it."

"Do you know what Vladimir meant by that? Keep your voice down."

"No, sir."

"Nothing on the card?"

"No, sir."

"Do *they* know what he meant?" Smiley asked, tilting his hand swiftly towards Strickland and Lacon.

"I think Strickland may. I'm not sure."

"Did Vladimir really not ask for Esterhase?"

"No, sir."

Lacon was finishing on the phone. Strickland took back the receiver from him and spoke into it himself. Seeing Smiley at the door, Lacon bounded down the room to him.

"George! Good man! Fare you well! Listen. I want to talk to you about marriage some time. A seminar with no holds barred. I'm counting on you to tell me the art of it, George!"

"Yes. We must get together," Smiley said.

Looking down, he saw that Lacon was shaking his hand.

A bizarre postscript to this meeting confounds its conspiratorial purpose. Standard Circus tradecraft requires that hidden microphones be installed in safe houses. Agents in their strange way accept this, even though they are not informed of it, even though their case officers go through motions of taking notes. For his rendezvous with Vladimir, Mostyn had quite properly switched on the system in anticipation of the old man's arrival, and nobody, in the subsequent panic, thought to turn it off. Routine procedures brought the tapes to transcriber section, who in good faith put out several texts for the general Circus reader. The luckless head of Oddbins got a copy, so did the Secretariat, so did the heads of Personnel, Operations, and Finance. It was not till a copy landed in Lauder Strickland's in-tray that the explosion occurred and the innocent recipients were sworn to secrecy under all manner of dreadful threats. The tape is perfect. Lacon's restless pacing is there; so are Strickland's *sotto voce* asides, some of them obscene. Only Mostyn's flustered confessions in the hall escaped.

As to Mostyn himself, he played no further part in the affair. He resigned of his own accord a few months later, part of the wastage rate that gets everyone so worried these days.

6

The same uncertain light that greeted Smiley as he stepped gratefully out of the safe flat into the fresh air of that Hampstead morning greeted Ostrakova also, though the Paris autumn was further on, and only a last few leaves clung to the plane trees. Like Smiley's too, her night had not been restful. She had risen in the dark and dressed with care, and she had deliberated, since the morning looked colder, whether this was the day on which to get out her winter boots, because the draught in the warehouse could be cruel and affected her legs the most. Still undecided, she had fished them out of the cupboard and wiped them down, and even polished them, but she still had not been able to make up her mind whether to wear them or not. Which was how it always went with her when she had one big problem to grapple with: the small ones became impossible. She knew all the signs, she could feel them coming on, but there was nothing she could do. She would mislay her purse, botch her bookkeeping at the warehouse, lock herself out of the flat and have to fetch the old fool of a concierge, Madame la Pierre, who pecked and snuffled like a goat in a nettle patch. She could quite easily, when the mood was on her, after fifteen years of taking the same route, catch the wrong bus and finish up, furious, in a strange neighbourhood. She pulled on the boots finally—muttering to herself "old fool, cretin," and the like—and, carrying the heavy shopping bag that she had prepared the previous night, she set off along her usual route, passing her three usual shops and neglecting to enter any of them, while she tried to work out whether or not she was going off her head.

I am mad. I am not mad. Somebody is trying to kill me, somebody is trying to protect me. I am safe. I am in mortal danger. Back and forth.

In the four weeks since she had received her little Estonian confessor, Ostrakova had been aware of many changes in herself and for most of them she was not at all ungrateful. Whether she had fallen in love with him was neither here nor there: his appearance was timely, and the piracy in him had revived her sense of opposition at a moment when it was in danger of going out. He had rekindled her, and there was enough of the alley cat in him to remind her of Glikman and other men as well; she had never been particularly continent. And since, on top of this, she thought, the magician is a man of looks, and knows women, and steps into my life armed with a picture of my oppressor and the determination, apparently, to eliminate him—why then, it would be positively indecent, lonely old fool that I am, if I did *not* fall in love with him on the spot!

But it was his gravity that had impressed her even more than his magic. "You must not *decorate*," he had told her, with uncharacteristic sharpness, when for the sake of entertainment or variety she had allowed herself to deviate just a little from the version she had written to the General. "Merely because you yourself feel more at ease, do not make the mistake of supposing that the danger is over."

She had promised to improve herself.

"The danger is absolute," he had told her as he left. "It is not yours to make greater or make less."

People had talked to her about danger before, but when the magician talked about it, she believed him.

"Danger to my daughter?" she had asked. "Danger to Alexandra?"

"Your daughter plays no part in this. You may be sure she knows nothing of what is going on."

"Then danger to whom?"

"Danger to all of us who have knowledge of this matter," he had replied as she happily conceded, in the doorway, to their one embrace. "Danger most of all to you."

And now, for the last three days—or was it two? or was it ten?—Ostrakova swore she had seen the danger gather round her like an army of shadows at her own deathbed. The danger that was absolute; that was not hers to make greater or less. And she saw it again this Saturday morning as she clumped along in her polished winter boots, swinging the heavy shopping bag at her side: the same two men, pursuing her, the week-end notwithstanding. Hard men. Harder than the gingery man. Men who sit about at headquarters listening to the interrogations. And never speak a word. The one was walking five metres behind her, the other was keeping abreast of her across the street, at this moment passing the doorway of that vagabond Mercier the chandler, whose red-and-green awning hung so low it was a danger even to someone of Ostrakova's humble height.

She had decided, when she had first allowed herself to notice them, that they were the General's men. That was Monday, or was it Friday? General Vladimir has turned out his bodyguard for me, she thought with much amusement, and for a dangerous morning she plotted the friendly gestures she would make to them in order to express her gratitude: the smiles of complicity she would vouchsafe to them when there was nobody else looking; even the *soupe* she would prepare and take to them, to help them while away their vigil in the doorways. Two hulking great bodyguards, she had thought, just for one old lady! Ostrakov had been right: that General was a man! On the second day she decided they were not there at all, and that her desire to appoint such men was merely an extension of her desire to be reunited with the magician. I am looking for

links to him, she thought; just as I have not yet brought myself
to wash up the glass from which he drank his vodka, or to puff
up the cushions where he sat and lectured me on danger.

But on the third—or was it the fifth?—day she took a
different and harsher view of her supposed protectors. She
stopped playing the little girl. On whichever day it was, leaving her apartment early in order to check a particular consignment to the warehouse, she had stepped out of the sanctuary of
her abstractions straight into the streets of Moscow, as she had
too often known them in her years with Glikman. The ill-lit,
cobbled street was empty but for one black car parked twenty
metres from her doorway. Most likely it had arrived that minute. She had a notion, afterwards, of having seen it pull up,
presumably in order to deliver the sentries to their beat. Pull
up sharply, just as she came out. And douse its headlights. Resolutely she had begun walking down the pavement. "Danger
most of all to *you*," she kept remembering; "danger to all of us
who know."

The car was following her.

They think I am a whore, she thought vainly, one of those
old ones who work the early-morning market.

Suddenly her one aim had been to get inside a church. Any
church. The nearest Russian Orthodox church was twenty
minutes away, and so small that to pray in it at all was like a
séance; the very proximity of the Holy Family offered a forgiveness by itself. But twenty minutes was a lifetime. Non-
Orthodox churches she eschewed, as a rule, entirely—they
were a betrayal of her nationhood. That morning, however,
with the car crawling along behind her, she had suspended her
prejudice and ducked into the very first church she came to,
which turned out to be not merely Catholic, but *modern* Catholic as well, so that she heard the whole Mass twice through in
bad French, read by a worker-priest who smelt of garlic and
worse. But by the time she left, the men were nowhere to
be seen and that was all that mattered—even though when

she arrived at the warehouse she had to promise two extra hours to make up for the inconvenience she had caused by her lateness.

Then for three days nothing, or was it five? Ostrakova had become as incapable of hoarding time as money. Three or five, they had gone, they had never existed. It was all her "decoration," as the magician had called it, her stupid habit of seeing too much, looking too many people in the eye, inventing too much incident. Till today again, when they were back. Except that today was about fifty thousand times worse, because today was *now*, and the street today was as empty as on the last day or the first, and the man who was five metres behind her was drawing closer, and the man who had been under Mercier's outrageously dangerous awning was crossing the street to join him.

What happened next, in such descriptions or imaginings as had come Ostrakova's way, was supposed to happen in a flash. One minute you were upright, walking down the pavement, the next, with a flurry of lights and a wailing of horns, you were wafted to the operating table surrounded by surgeons in various coloured masks. Or you were in Heaven, before the Almighty, mumbling excuses about certain lapses that you did not really regret; and neither—if you understood Him at all—did He. Or worst of all, you came round, and were returned, as walking wounded, to your apartment, and your boring half-sister Valentina dropped everything, with an extremely ill grace, in order to come up from Lyons and be a non-stop scold at your bedside.

Not one of these expectations was fulfilled.

What happened took place with the slowness of an underwater ballet. The man who was gaining on her drew alongside her, taking the right, or inside, position. At the same moment, the man who had crossed the road from Mercier's came up on her left, walking not on the pavement but in the gutter, incidentally splashing her with yesterday's rain-water as he strode along. With her fatal habit of looking into people's eyes Ostrakova stared at her two unwished-for companions and saw faces she had already recognised and knew by heart. They had hunted Ostrakov, they had murdered Glikman, and in her personal view they had been murdering the entire Russian people for centuries, whether in the name of the Czar, or God, or Lenin. Looking away from them, she saw the black car that had followed her on her way to church heading slowly down the empty road towards her. Therefore she did exactly what she had planned to do all night through, what she had lain awake picturing. In her shopping bag she had put an old flat-iron, a bit of junk that Ostrakov had acquired in the days when the poor dying man had fancied he might make a few extra francs by dealing in antiques. Her shopping bag was of leather—green and brown in a patchwork—and stout. Drawing it back, she swung it round her with all her strength at the man in the gutter—at his groin, the hated centre of him. He swore—she could not hear in which language—and crumpled to his knees. Here her plan went adrift. She had not expected a villain on either side of her, and she needed time to recover her own balance and get the iron swinging at the second man. He did not allow her to do this. Throwing his arms round both of hers, he gathered her together like the fat sack she was, and lifted her clean off her feet. She saw the bag fall and heard the chime as the flat-iron slipped from it onto a drain cover. Still looking down, she saw her boots dangling ten centimetres from the ground, as if she had hanged herself like her brother Niki—his feet, exactly, turned into each other like a simpleton's. She noticed that one of her toe-caps, the left, was already scratched in the scuffle. Her assailant's arms now locked themselves even harder across her breast and she wondered whether her ribs would crack before she suffocated. She felt him draw her back, and she presumed that he was shaping to swing her into the car, which was now approaching at a good speed down the road: that she was being kidnapped. This notion terrified her. Nothing, least of all death, was as appalling to her at that moment as the thought that these pigs would take her back to Russia and subject her to the kind of slow, doctrinal prison death she was certain had killed Glikman. She struggled with all her force, she managed to bite his hand. She saw a couple of bystanders who seemed as scared as she was. Then she realised that the car was not slowing down, and that the men had something quite different in mind: not to kidnap her at all, but to kill her.

He threw her.

She reeled but did not fall, and as the car swerved to knock her down, she thanked God and all His angels that she had, after all, decided on the winter boots, because the front bumper hit her at the back of the shins, and when she saw her feet again, they were straight up in front of her face, and her bare thighs were parted as for childbirth. She flew for a while, then hit the road with everything at once—with her head, her spine, and her heels—then rolled like a sausage over the cobbles. The car had passed her but she heard it screech to a stop and wondered whether they were going to reverse and drive over her again. She tried to move but felt too sleepy. She heard voices and car doors slamming, she heard the engine roaring, and fading, so that either it was going away or she was losing her hearing.

"Don't touch her," someone said.

No, *don't*, she thought.

"It's a lack of oxygen," she heard herself say. "Lift me to my feet and I'll be all right."

Why on earth did she say that? Or did she only think it?

"*Aubergines*," she said. "Get the *aubergines*." She didn't know whether she was talking about her shopping, or the female traffic wardens for whom *aubergine* was the Paris slang.

Then a pair of woman's hands put a blanket over her, and a furious Gallic argument started about what one did next. Did anyone get the number? she wanted to ask. But she was really too sleepy to bother, and besides she had no oxygen—the fall had taken it out of her body for good. She had a vision of half-shot birds she had seen in the Russian countryside, flapping helplessly on the ground, waiting for the dogs to reach them. General, she thought, did you get my second letter? Drifting off, she willed him, begged him to read it, and to respond to its entreaty. General, read my second letter.

She had written it a week before in a moment of despair. She had posted it yesterday in another.

7

There are Victorian terraces in the region of Paddington Station that are painted as white as luxury liners on the outside, and inside are dark as tombs. Westbourne Terrace that Saturday morning gleamed as brightly as any of them, but the service road that led to Vladimir's part of it was blocked at one end by a heap of rotting mattresses, and by a smashed boom, like a frontier post, at the other.

"Thank you, I'll get out here," said Smiley politely, and paid the cab off at the mattresses.

He had come straight from Hampstead and his knees ached. The Greek driver had spent the journey lecturing him on Cyprus, and out of courtesy he had crouched on the jump seat in order to hear him over the din of the engine. Vladimir, we should have done better by you, he thought, surveying the filth on the pavements, the poor washing trailing from the balconies. The Circus should have shown more honour to its vertical man.

It concerns the Sandman, he thought. *Tell him I have two proofs and can bring them with me.*

He walked slowly, knowing that early morning is a better time of day to come out of a building than go into it. A small queue had gathered at the bus-stop. A milkman was going his rounds, so was a newspaper boy. A squadron of grounded sea-gulls scavenged gracefully at the spilling dustbins. If sea-gulls are taking to the cities, he thought, will pigeons take to the sea? Crossing the service road, he saw a motor-cyclist with a black official-looking side-car parking his steed a hundred yards down the kerb. Something in the man's posture reminded him of the tall messenger who had brought the keys to the safe flat—a similar fixity, even at that distance; a respectful attentiveness, of an almost military kind.

Shedding chestnut trees darkened the pillared doorway, a scarred cat eyed him warily. The doorbell was the topmost of thirty, but Smiley didn't press it and when he shoved the double doors they swung open too freely, revealing the same gloomy corridors painted very shiny to defeat graffiti writers, and the same linoleum staircase that squeaked like a hospital trolley. He remembered it all. Nothing had changed, and now nothing ever would. There was no light switch and the stairs grew darker the higher he climbed. Why didn't Vladimir's murderers steal his keys? he wondered, feeling them nudging against his hip with every step. Perhaps they didn't need them. Perhaps they had their own set already. He reached a landing and squeezed past a luxurious perambulator. He heard a dog howling and the morning news in German and the flushing of a communal lavatory. He heard a child screaming at its mother, then a slap and the father screaming at the child. *Tell Max it concerns the Sandman.* There was a smell of curry and cheap fat frying, and disinfectant. There was a smell of too many people with not much money jammed into too little air. He remembered that too. Nothing had changed.

If we'd treated him better, it would never have happened, Smiley thought. The neglected are too easily killed, he thought, in unconscious affinity with Ostrakova. He remembered the day they had brought him here, Smiley the vicar, Toby Esterhase the postman. They had driven to Heathrow to fetch him: Toby the fixer, dyed in all the oceans, as he would say of himself. Toby drove like the wind but they were almost late, even then. The plane had landed. They hurried to the barrier and there he was: silvered and majestic, towering stock-still in the temporary corridor from the arrivals bay, while the common peasants swept past him. He remembered their solemn embrace—"Max, my old friend, it is really you?" "It's me, Vladimir, they've put us together again." He remembered Toby spiriting them through the large back alleys of the immigration service, because the enraged French police had confiscated the old boy's papers before throwing him out. He remembered how they had lunched at Scott's, all three of them, the old boy too animated even to drink but talking grandly of the future they all knew he didn't have: "It will be Moscow all over again, Max. Maybe we even get a chance at the Sandman." Next day they went flat-hunting, "just to show you a few possibilities, General," as Toby Esterhase had explained. It was Christmas time and the resettlement budget for the year was used up. Smiley appealed to Circus Finance. He lobbied Lacon and the Treasury for a supplementary estimate, but in vain. "A dose of reality will bring him down to earth," Lacon had pronounced. "Use your influence with him, George. That's what you're there for." Their first dose of reality was a tart's parlour in Kensington, their second overlooked a shunting-yard near Waterloo. Westbourne Terrace was their third, and as they squeaked up these same stairs, Toby leading, the old man had suddenly halted, and put back his great mottled head, and wrinkled his nose theatrically.

Ah! So if I get hungry I have only to stand in the corridor and sniff and my hunger is gone! he had announced in his thick French. *That way I don't have to eat for a week!*

By then even Vladimir had guessed they were putting him away for good.

Smiley returned to the present. The next landing was musical, he noticed, as he continued his solitary ascent. Through one door came rock music played at full blast, through another Sibelius and the smell of bacon. Peering out of the window, he saw two men loitering between the chestnut trees who were not there when he had arrived. A team would do that, he thought. A team would post look-outs while the others went inside. Whose team was another question. Moscow's? The Superintendent's? Saul Enderby's? Farther down the road, the tall motor-cyclist had acquired a tabloid newspaper and was sitting on his bike reading it.

At Smiley's side a door opened and an old woman in a dressing-gown came out holding a cat against her shoulder. He could smell last night's drink on her breath even before she spoke to him.

"Are you a burglar, dearie?" she asked.

"I'm afraid not," Smiley replied with a laugh. "Just a visitor."

"Still, it's nice to be fancied, isn't it, dearie?" she said.

"It is indeed," said Smiley politely.

The last flight was steep and very narrow and lit by real daylight from a wired skylight on the slant. There were two doors on the top landing, both closed, both very cramped. On one, a typed notice faced him: "MR. V. MILLER, TRANSLATIONS." Smiley remembered the argument about Vladimir's alias now he was to become a Londoner and keep his head down. "Miller" was no problem. For some reason, the old boy found Miller rather grand. "Miller, *c'est bien*," he had declared. "Miller I like, Max." But "Mr." was anything but good. He pressed for General, then offered to settle for Colonel. But Smiley in his rôle as vicar was on this point unbudgeable: Mr. was a lot less trouble than a bogus rank in the wrong army, he had ruled.

He knocked boldly, knowing that a soft knock is more conspicuous than a loud one. He heard the echo, and nothing else. He heard no footfall, no sudden freezing of a sound. He called "Vladimir" through the letter-box as though he were an old friend visiting. He tried one Yale from the bunch and it stuck, he tried another and it turned. He stepped inside and closed the door, waiting for something to hit him on the back of the head but preferring the thought of a broken skull to having his face shot off. He felt dizzy and realised he was holding his breath. The same white paint, he noticed; the same prison emptiness exactly. The same queer hush, like a phone-box; the same mix of public smells.

This is where we stood, Smiley remembered—the three of us, that afternoon. Toby and myself like tugs, nudging at the old battleship between us. The estate agent's particulars had said "penthouse."

"Hopeless," Toby Esterhase had announced in his Hungarian French, always the first to speak, as he turned to open the door and leave. "I mean completely awful. I mean, I should have come and taken a look first, I was an idiot," said Toby when Vladimir still didn't budge. "General, please accept my apologies. This is a complete insult."

Smiley added his own assurances. We can do better for you than this, Vladi; much. We just have to persist.

But the old man's eyes were on the window, as Smiley's were now, on this dotty forest of chimney-pots and gables and slate roofs that flourished beyond the parapet. And suddenly he had thumped a gloved paw on Smiley's shoulder.

"Better you keep your money to shoot those swine in Moscow, Max," he had advised.

With the tears running down his cheeks, and the same determined smile, Vladimir had continued to stare at the Moscow chimneys; and at his fading dreams of ever again living under a Russian sky.

"*On reste ici*," he had commanded finally as if he were drawing up a last-ditch defence.

A tiny divan bed ran along one wall, a cooking ring stood on the sill. From the smell of putty Smiley guessed that the old man had kept whiting the place himself, painting out the damp and filling the cracks. On the table he used for typing and eating lay an old Remington upright and a pair of worn dictionaries. His translating work, he thought; the few extra pennies that fleshed out his allowance. Pressing back his elbows as if he were having trouble with his spine, Smiley drew himself to his full if diminutive height and launched himself upon the familiar death rites for a departed spy. An Estonian Bible lay on the pine bedside locker. He probed it delicately for cut cavities, then dangled it upside down for scraps of paper or photographs. Pulling open the locker drawer, he found a bottle of patent pills for rejuvenating the sexually jaded and three Red Army gallantry medals mounted on a chrome bar. So much for cover, thought Smiley, wondering how on earth Vladimir and his many paramours had managed on such a tiny bed. A print of Martin Luther hung at the bedhead. Next to it, a coloured picture called "The Red Roofs of Old Tallinn," which Vladimir must have torn from something and backed on cardboard. A second picture showed "The Kazari Coast," a third "Windmills and a Ruined Castle." He delved behind each. The bedside light caught his eye. He tried the switch and when it didn't work he unplugged it, took out the bulb, and fished in the wood base, but without result. Just a dead bulb, he thought. A sudden shriek from outside sent him pulling back against the wall but when he had collected himself he realised it was more of those land-borne sea-gulls: a whole colony had settled round the chimney-pots. He glanced over the parapet into the street again. The two loiterers had gone. They're on their way up, he thought; my head start is over. They're not police at all, he thought; they're assassins. The motor bike with its black side-car stood unattended. He closed the window, wondering whether there was a special Valhalla for dead spies where he and Vladimir would meet and he could put things right; telling himself he had lived a long life and that this moment was as good as any other for it to end. And not believing it for one second.

The table drawer contained sheets of plain paper, a stapler, a chewed pencil, some elastic bands, and a recent quarterly telephone bill, unpaid, for the sum of seventy-eight pounds, which struck him as uncharacteristically high for Vladimir's frugal lifestyle. He opened the stapler and found nothing. He put the phone bill in his pocket to study later and kept searching, knowing it was not a real search at all, that a real search

would take three men several days before they could say with
certainty they had found whatever was to be found. If he was
looking for anything in particular, then it was probably an
address book or a diary or something that did duty for one,
even if it was only a scrap of paper. He knew that sometimes
old spies, even the best of them, were a little like old lovers; as
age crept up on them, they began to cheat, out of fear that
their powers were deserting them. They pretended they had it
all in the memory, but in secret they were hanging on to their
virility, in secret they wrote things down, often in some home-
made code, which, if they only knew it, could be unbuttoned in
hours or minutes by anyone who knew the game. Names and
addresses of contacts, sub-agents. Nothing was holy. Routines,
times and places of meetings, worknames, phone numbers,
even safe combinations written out as social-security numbers
and birthdays. In his time Smiley had seen entire networks put
at risk that way because one agent no longer dared to trust his
head. He didn't believe Vladimir would have done that, but
there was always a first time.

Tell him I have two proofs and can bring them with me. . . .

He was standing in what the old man would have called his
kitchen: the window-sill with the gas ring on it, the tiny home-
made food-store with holes drilled for ventilation. We men
who cook for ourselves are half-creatures, he thought as he
scanned the two shelves, tugged out the saucepan and the
frying-pan, poked among the cayenne and paprika. Anywhere
else in the house—even in bed—you can cut yourself off, read
your books, deceive yourself that solitude is best. But in the
kitchen the signs of incompleteness are too strident. Half of
one black loaf. Half of one coarse sausage. Half an onion. Half
a pint of milk. Half a lemon. Half a packet of black tea. Half a
life. He opened anything that would open, he probed with his
finger in the paprika. He found a loose tile and prised it free,
he unscrewed the wooden handle of the frying-pan. About to
pull open the clothes cupboard, he stopped as if listening

again, but this time it was something he had seen that held him, not something he had heard.

On top of the food-store lay a parcel of Gauloises Caporal cigarettes, Vladimir's favourites when he couldn't get his Russians. Tipped, he noticed, reading the different legends. "Duty Free." "*Filtre.*" Marked "*Exportation*" and "Made in France." Cellophane-wrapped. He took them down. Of the ten original packets, one already missing. In the ashtray, three stubbed-out cigarettes of the same brand. In the air, now that he sniffed for it over the smell of food and putty, a faint aroma of French cigarettes.

And no cigarettes in his pocket, he remembered.

Holding the blue parcel in both hands, slowly turning it, Smiley tried to understand what it meant to him. Instinct—or better, a submerged perception yet to rise to the surface—signalled to him urgently that something about these cigarettes was wrong. Not their appearance. Not that they were stuffed with microfilm or high explosive or soft-nosed bullets or any other of those weary games.

Merely the fact of their presence, here and nowhere else, was wrong.

So new, so free of dust, one packet missing, three smoked.

And no cigarettes in his pocket.

He worked faster now, wanting very much to leave. The flat was too high up. It was too empty and too full. He had a growing sense of something being out of joint. Why didn't they take his keys? He pulled open the cupboard. It held clothes as well as papers but Vladimir possessed few of either. The papers were mostly cyclostyled pamphlets in Russian and English and in what Smiley took to be one of the Baltic languages. There was a folder of letters from the Group's old headquarters in Paris, and posters reading "REMEMBER LATVIA," "REMEMBER ESTONIA," "REMEMBER LITHUANIA," presumably for display at public demonstrations. There was a box of school chalk, yellow, a couple of pieces missing. And Vladimir's treasured

Norfolk jacket, lying off its hook on the floor. Fallen there, perhaps, as Vladimir closed the cupboard door too fast.

And Vladimir so vain? thought Smiley. So military in his appearance? Yet dumps his best jacket in a heap on the cupboard floor? Or was it that a more careless hand than Vladimir's had not replaced it on the hanger?

Picking the jacket up, Smiley searched the pockets, then hung it back in the cupboard and slammed the door to see if it fell off its hook.

It did.

They didn't take the keys, and they didn't search his flat, he thought. They searched Vladimir, but in the Superintendent's opinion they had been disturbed.

Tell him I have two proofs and can bring them with me.

Returning to the kitchen area, he stood before the food-store and took another studied look at the blue parcel lying on top of it. Then peered in the waste-paper basket. At the ashtray again, memorising. Then in the garbage bucket, just in case the missing packet, crumpled up, was there. It wasn't, which for some reason pleased him.

Time to go.

But he didn't, not quite. For another quarter of an hour, with his ear cocked for interruptions, Smiley delved and probed, lifting and replacing, still on the look-out for the loose floor-board, or the favoured recess behind the shelves. But this time he wanted *not* to find. This time, he wanted to confirm an absence. Only when he was as satisfied as circumstance allowed did he step quietly onto the landing and lock the door behind him. At the bottom of the first flight he met a temporary postman wearing a GPO armband emerging from another corridor. Smiley touched his elbow.

"If you've anything at all for flat 6B, I can save you the climb," he said humbly.

The postman rummaged and produced a brown envelope. Postmark Paris, dated five days ago, the 15th district. Smiley slipped it into his pocket. At the bottom of the second flight stood a fire-door with a push-bar to open it from the inside only. He had made a mental note of it on his way up. He pushed, the door yielded, he descended a vile concrete staircase and crossed an interior courtyard to a deserted mews, still pondering the omission. Why didn't they search his flat? he wondered. Moscow Centre, like any other large bureaucracy, had its fixed procedures. You decide to kill a man. So you station pickets outside his house, you stake out his route with static posts, you put in your assassination team, and you kill him. In the classic method. Then why not search his flat as well?—Vladimir, a bachelor, living in a building constantly overrun with strangers?—why not send in the pickets the moment he is on his way? *Because they knew he had it with him*, thought Smiley. And the body search, which the Superintendent regarded as so cursory? Suppose they were not disturbed, but had found what they were looking for?

He hailed a taxi, telling the driver, "Bywater Street in Chelsea, please, off Kings Road."

Go home, he thought. Have a bath, think it through. Shave. *Tell him I have two proofs and can bring them with me.*

Suddenly, leaning forward, he tapped on the glass partition and changed his destination. As they made the U-turn, the tall motor-cyclist screeched to a stop behind them, dismounted, and solemnly shunted his large black bike and side-car into the opposite lane. A footman, thought Smiley, watching him. A footman, wheeling in the trolley for tea. Like an official escort, arch-backed and elbows spread, the motor-cyclist followed them through the outer reaches of Camden, then, still at a regulation distance, slowly up the hill. The cab drew up, Smiley leaned forward to pay his fare. As he did so, the dark figure proceeded solemnly past them, one arm lifted from the elbow in a mail-fist salute.

8

He stood at the mouth of the avenue, gazing into the ranks of beech trees as they sank away from him like a retreating army into the mist. The darkness had departed reluctantly, leaving an indoor gloom. It could have been dusk already: tea-time in an old country house. The street lights either side of him were poor candles, illuminating nothing. The air felt warm and heavy. He had expected police still, and a roped-off area. He had expected journalists or curious bystanders. It never happened, he told himself, as he started slowly down the slope. No sooner had I left the scene than Vladimir clambered merrily to his feet, stick in hand, wiped off the gruesome make-up, and skipped away with his fellow actors for a pot of beer at the police station.

Stick in hand, he repeated to himself, remembering something the Superintendent had said to him. Left hand or right hand? "There's yellow chalk powder on his left hand too," Mr. Murgotroyd had said inside the van. "Thumb and first two fingers."

He advanced and the avenue darkened round him, the mist thickened. His footsteps echoed tinnily ahead of him. Twenty yards higher, brown sunlight burned like a slow bonfire in its own smoke. But down here in the dip the mist had collected in a cold fog, and Vladimir was very dead after all. He saw tyre marks where the police cars had parked. He noticed the absence of leaves and the unnatural cleanness of the gravel. What do they do? he wondered. Hose the gravel down? Sweep the leaves into more plastic pillowcases?

His tiredness had given way to a new and mysterious clarity. He continued up the avenue wishing Vladimir good morning and good night and not feeling a fool for doing so, thinking intently about drawing-pins and chalk and French cigarettes and Moscow Rules, looking for a tin pavilion by a playing field. Take it in sequence, he told himself. Take it from the beginning. Leave the Caporals on their shelf. He reached an intersection of paths and crossed it, still climbing. To his right, goal-posts appeared, and beyond them a green pavilion of corrugated iron, apparently empty. He started across the field, rain-water seeping into his shoes. Behind the hut ran a steep mud bank scoured with children's slides. He climbed the bank, entered a coppice, and kept climbing. The fog had not penetrated the trees and by the time he reached the brow it had cleared. There was still no one in sight. Returning, he approached the pavilion through the trees. It was a tin box, no more, with one side open to the field. The only furniture was a rough wood bench slashed and written on with knives, the only occupant a prone figure stretched on it, with a blanket pulled over his head and brown boots protruding. For an undisciplined moment Smiley wondered whether he too had had his face blown off. Girders held up the roof; earnest moral statements enlivened the flaking green paint. "Punk is destructive. Society does not need it." The assertion caused him a moment's indecision. "Oh, but society *does*," he wanted to reply; "society is an association of minorities." The drawing-pin was where Mostyn had said it was, at head height exactly, in the best Sarratt tradition of regularity, its Circus-issue brass head as new and as unmarked as the boy who had put it there.

Proceed to the rendezvous, it said; *no danger sighted.*

Moscow Rules, thought Smiley yet again. Moscow, where it could take a fieldman three days to post a letter to a safe address. Moscow, where all minorities are punk.

Tell him I have two proofs and can bring them with me....

Vladimir's chalked acknowledgment ran close beside the pin, a wavering yellow worm of a message scrawled all down the post. Perhaps the old man was worried about rain, thought Smiley. Perhaps he was afraid it could wash his mark away. Or perhaps in his emotional state he leaned too heavily on the chalk, just as he had left his Norfolk jacket lying on the floor. *A meeting or nothing,* he had told Mostyn . . . *Tonight or nothing* . . . *Tell him I have two proofs and can bring them with me....* Nevertheless only the vigilant would ever have noticed that mark, heavy though it was, or the shiny drawing-pin either, and not even the vigilant would have found them odd, for on Hampstead Heath people post bills and messages to each other ceaselessly, and not all of them are spies. Some are children, some are tramps, some are believers in God, some have lost pets, and some are looking for variations of love and having to proclaim their needs from a hilltop. And not all of them, by any means, get their faces blown off at point-blank range by a Moscow Centre assassination weapon.

And the purpose of this acknowledgment? In Moscow, when Smiley from his desk in London had had the ultimate responsibility for Vladimir's case—in Moscow these signs were devised for agents who might disappear from hour to hour; they were the broken twigs along a path that could always be their last. *I see no danger and am proceeding as instructed to the agreed rendezvous,* read Vladimir's last—and fatally mistaken—message to the living world.

Leaving the hut, Smiley moved a short distance back along the route he had just come. And as he walked, he meticulously called to mind the Superintendent's reconstruction of Vladimir's last journey, drawing upon his memory as if it were an archive.

Those rubber overshoes are a Godsend, Mr. Smiley, the Superintendent had declared piously: North British Century, diamond-pattern soles, sir, and barely walked on—why, you could follow him through a football crowd if you had to!

"I'll give you the authorised version," the Superintendent had said, speaking fast because they were short of time. "Ready, Mr. Smiley?"

Ready, Smiley had said.

The Superintendent changed his tone of voice. Conversation was one thing, evidence another. As he spoke, he shone his torch in phases onto the wet gravel of the roped-off area. A lecture with magic lantern, Smiley had thought; at Sarratt I'd have taken notes. "Here he is, coming down the hill now, sir. See him there? Normal pace, nice heel and toe movement, normal progress, everything above-board. See, Mr. Smiley?"

Mr. Smiley had seen.

"And the stick mark there, do you, in his right hand, sir?"

Smiley had seen that too, how the rubber-ferruled walking-stick had left a deep round rip with every second footprint.

"Whereas of course he had the stick in his *left* when he was shot, correct? You saw that, too, sir, I noticed. Happen to know which side his bad leg was at all, sir, if he had one?"

"The right," Smiley had said.

"Ah. Then most likely the right was the side he normally held the stick, as well. Down here, please, sir, that's the way! Walking normal still, please note," the Superintendent had added, making a rare slip of grammar in his distraction.

For five more paces the regular diamond imprint, heel and toe, had continued undisturbed in the beam of the Superintendent's torch. Now, by daylight, Smiley saw only the ghost of them. The rain, other feet, and the tyre tracks of illicit cyclists had caused large parts to disappear. But by night, at the Superintendent's lantern show, he had seen them vividly, as vividly as he saw the plastic-covered corpse in the dip below them, where the trail had ended.

"*Now*," the Superintendent had declared with satisfaction, and halted, the cone of his torchbeam resting on a single scuffed area of ground.

"How old did you say he was, sir?" the Superintendent asked.

"I didn't, but he owned to sixty-nine."

"Plus your recent heart attack, I gather. Now, sir. First he stops. In sharp order. Don't ask me why, perhaps he was spoken to. My guess is he heard something. Behind him. Notice the way the pace shortens, notice the position of the feet as he makes the half-turn, looks over his shoulder, or whatever? Anyway he *turns* and that's why I say 'behind him.' And whatever he saw or didn't see—or heard or didn't hear—he decides to run. Off he goes, look!" the Superintendent urged, with the sudden enthusiasm of the sportsman. "Wider stride, heels not hardly on the ground at all. A new print entirely, and going for all he's worth. You can even see where he shoved himself off with his stick for the extra purchase."

Peering now by daylight, Smiley no longer with any certainty *could* see, but he had seen last night—and in his memory saw again this morning—the sudden desperate gashes of the ferrule thrust downward, then thrust at an angle.

"Trouble was," the Superintendent commented quietly, resuming his courtroom style, "whatever killed him was out in front, wasn't it? Not behind him at all."

It was both, thought Smiley now, with the advantage of the intervening hours. They *drove* him, he thought, trying without success to recall the Sarratt jargon for this particular technique. They knew his route, and they *drove* him. The frightener behind the target drives him forward, the finger man loiters ahead undetected till the target blunders into him. For it was a truth known also to Moscow Centre murder teams that even the oldest hands will spend hours worrying about their backs, their flanks, the cars that pass and the cars that don't, the streets they cross, and the houses that they enter. Yet still fail, when the moment is upon them, to recognise the danger that greets them face to face.

"Still running," the Superintendent said, moving steadily nearer the body down the hill. "Notice how his pace gets a little longer because of the steeper gradient now? Erratic too, see that? Feet flying all over the shop. Running for dear life. Literally. And the walking-stick still in his right hand. See him veering now, moving towards the verge? Lost his bearings, I wouldn't wonder. Here we go. Explain *that* if you can!"

The torchbeam rested on a patch of footprints close together, five or six of them, all in a very small space at the edge of the grass between two high trees.

"Stopped again," the Superintendent announced. "Not so much a total *stop* perhaps, more your stutter. Don't ask me why. Maybe he just wrong-footed himself. Maybe he was worried to find himself so close to the trees. Maybe his heart got him if you tell me it was dicky. Then off he goes again same as before."

"With the stick in his left hand," Smiley had said quietly.

"Why? That's what I ask myself, sir, but perhaps you people know the answer. Why? Did he hear something again? Remember something? Why—when you're running for your life—why pause, do a duck-shuffle, change hands, and then run on again? Straight into the arms of whoever shot him? Unless of course whatever was behind him *overtook* him there, came round through the trees perhaps, made an arc as it were? Any explanation from *your* side of the street, Mr. Smiley?"

And with that question still ringing in Smiley's ears they had arrived at last at the body, floating like an embryo under its plastic film.

But Smiley, on this morning after, stopped short of the dip. Instead, by placing his sodden shoes as best he could upon each spot exactly, he set about trying to imitate the movements the old man might have made. And since Smiley did all this in slow motion, and with every appearance of concentration, under the eye of two trousered ladies walking their Alsatians, he was taken for an adherent of the new fad in Chinese martial exercises, and accounted mad accordingly.

First he put his feet side by side and pointed them down the hill. Then he put his left foot forward, and moved his right foot round until the toe pointed directly towards a spinney of

young saplings. As he did so, his right shoulder followed naturally, and his instinct told him that this would be the likely
moment for Vladimir to transfer the stick to his left hand. But
why? As the Superintendent had also asked, why transfer the
stick at all? Why, in this most extreme moment of his life, why
solemnly move a walking-stick from the right hand to the left?
Certainly not to defend himself—since, as Smiley remembered, he was right-handed. To defend himself, he would only
have seized the stick more firmly. Or clasped it with *both* his
hands, like a club.

Was it in order to leave his right hand free? But free for
what?

Aware this time of being observed, Smiley peered sharply
behind him and saw two small boys in blazers who had paused
to watch this round little man in spectacles performing strange
antics with his feet. He glowered at them in his most
school-masterly manner, and they moved hastily on.

To leave his right hand free for what? Smiley repeated to
himself. And why start running again a moment later?

Vladimir turned to the right, thought Smiley, once again
matching his action to the thought. Vladimir turned to the
right. He faced the spinney, he put his stick in his left hand.
For a moment, according to the Superintendent, he stood still.
Then he ran on.

Moscow Rules, Smiley thought, staring at his own right
hand. Slowly he lowered it into his raincoat pocket. Which was
empty, as Vladimir's right-hand coat pocket was also empty.

Had he meant to write a message perhaps? Smiley was teasing himself with the theory he was determined to hold at bay.
To write a message with the *chalk,* for instance? Had he recognised his pursuer, and wished to chalk a name somewhere, or a
sign? But what *on?* Not on these wet tree trunks for sure. Not
on the clay, the dead leaves, the gravel! Looking round him,
Smiley became aware of a peculiar feature of his location. Here,
almost between two trees, at the very edge of the avenue, at the

point where the fog was approaching its thickest, he was as good as out of sight. The avenue descended, yes, and lifted ahead of him. But it also curved, and from where he stood the upward line of sight in both directions was masked by tree trunks and a dense thicket of saplings. Along the whole path of Vladimir's last frantic journey—a path he knew well, remember, had used for similar meetings—this was the one point, Smiley realised with increasing satisfaction, where the fleeing man was out of sight from both ahead of him and behind him.

And had stopped.

Had freed his right hand.

Had put it—let us say—in his pocket.

For his heart tablets? No. Like the yellow chalk and the matches, they were in his left pocket, not his right.

For something—let us say—that was no longer in the pocket when he was found dead.

For what then?

Tell him I have two proofs and can bring them with me. . . . Then perhaps he will see me. . . . This is Gregory asking for Max. I have something for him, please. . . .

Proofs. Proofs too precious to post. He was bringing something. Two somethings. Not just in his head—in his pocket. And was playing Moscow Rules. Rules that had been drummed into the General from the very day of his recruitment as a defector in place. By Smiley himself, no less, as well as his case officer on the spot. Rules that had been invented for his survival; and the survival of his network. Smiley felt the excitement seize his stomach like a nausea. Moscow Rules decree that if you physically *carry* a message, you must also carry the means to discard it! That, however it is disguised or concealed—microdot, secret writing, undeveloped film, any one of the hundred risky, finicky ways—still as an *object* it must be the first and lightest thing that comes to hand, the least conspicuous when jettisoned!

Such as a medicine bottle full of tablets, he thought, calming a little. Such as a box of matches.

One box Swan Vesta matches partly used, overcoat left, he remembered. A smoker's match, note well.

And in the safe flat, he thought relentlessly—tantalising himself, staving off the final insight—there on the table waiting for him, one packet of cigarettes, Vladimir's favourite brand. And in Westbourne Terrace on the food-store, nine packets of Gauloises Caporal. Out of ten.

But no cigarettes in his pockets. None, as the good Superintendent would have said, on his person. Or not when they found him, that is to say.

So the premise, George? Smiley asked himself, mimicking Lacon—brandishing Lacon's prefectorial finger accusingly in his own intact face—the premise? The premise is thus far, Oliver, that a smoker, a habitual smoker, in a state of high nervousness, sets off on a crucial clandestine meeting equipped with matches but not even so much as an *empty* packet of cigarettes, though he possesses quite demonstrably a whole stock of them. So that either the assassins found it, and removed it—the proof, or proofs, that Vladimir was speaking of, or—or what? Or Vladimir changed his stick from his right hand to his left in time. And put his right hand in his pocket in time. And took it out again, also in time, at the very spot where he could not be seen. And got rid of it, or them, according to Moscow Rules.

Having satisfied his own insistence upon a logical succession, George Smiley stepped cautiously into the long grass that led to the spinney, soaking his trousers from the knees down. For half an hour or more he searched, groping in the grass and among the foliage, retreading his tracks, cursing his own blundering, giving up, beginning again, answering the fatuous enquiries of passersby, which ranged from the obscene to the excessively attentive. There were even two Buddhist monks from a local seminary, complete with saffron robes and lace-up boots and knitted woollen caps, who offered their assistance. Smiley courteously declined it. He found two broken kites, a quantity of Coca-Cola tins. He found scraps of the female body, some in colour, some in black-and-white, ripped from magazines. He found an old running shoe, black, and shreds of an old burnt blanket. He found four beer bottles, empty, and four empty cigarette packets so sodden and old that after one glance he discounted them. And in a branch, slipped into the fork just where it joined its parent trunk, the fifth packet—or better perhaps, the tenth—that was not even empty: a relatively dry packet of Gauloises Caporal, *Filtre* and Duty Free, high up. Smiley reached for it as if it were forbidden fruit, but like forbidden fruit it stayed outside his grasp. He jumped for it and felt his back rip: a distinct and unnerving parting of tissue that smarted and dug at him for days afterwards. He said "damn" out loud and rubbed the spot, much as Ostrakova might have done. Two typists, on their way to work, consoled him with their giggles. He found a stick, poked the packet free, opened it. Four cigarettes remained.

And behind those four cigarettes, half concealed, and protected by its own skin of cellophane, something he recognised but dared not even disturb with his wet and trembling fingers. Something he dared not even contemplate until he was free of this appalling place, where giggling typists and Buddhist monks innocently trampled the spot where Vladimir had died.

They have one, I have the other, he thought. I have shared the old man's legacy with his murderers.

Braving the traffic, he followed the narrow pavement down the hill till he came to South End Green, where he hoped for a café that would give him tea. Finding none open so early, he sat on a bench across from a cinema instead, contemplating an old marble fountain and a pair of red telephone-boxes, one filthier than the other. A warm drizzle was falling; a few shopkeepers had started lowering their awnings; a delicatessen store was taking delivery of bread. He sat with hunched shoulders, and the damp points of his mackintosh collar stabbed his unshaven cheeks whenever he turned his head. "For God's sake, mourn!" Ann had flung at Smiley once, infuriated by his apparent composure after yet another friend had died. "If you won't grieve for the dead, how can you love the living?" Sitting on his bench, pondering his next step, Smiley now transmitted to her the answer he had failed to find at the time. "You are wrong," he told her distractedly. "I mourn the dead sincerely, and Vladimir, at this moment, deeply. It's loving the living which is sometimes a bit of a problem."

He tried the two telephone-boxes and the second worked. By a miracle, even the S–Z directory was intact, and more amazing still, the Straight and Steady Minicab Service of Islington North had paid for the privilege of heavy type. He dialled the number and while it rang out he had a panic that he had forgotten the name of the signatory on the receipt in Vladimir's pocket. He rang off, recovering his twopence. Lane? Lang? He dialled again.

A female voice answered him in a bored singsong: "Straight-and-Stead-ee! Name-when-and-where-*to*-please?"

"I'd like to speak to Mr. J. Lamb, please, one of your drivers," Smiley said politely.

"Sorr-ee, no personal calls on this line," she sang and rang off.

He dialled a third time. It wasn't personal at all, he said huffily, now surer of his ground. He wanted Mr. Lamb to drive for him, and nobody but Mr. Lamb would do. "Tell him it's a long journey. Stratford-on-Avon"—choosing a city at random—"tell him I want to go to Stratford." *Sampson*, he replied, when she insisted on a name. Sampson with a "p."

He returned to his bench to wait again.

To ring Lacon? For what purpose? Rush home, open the cigarette packet, find out its precious contents? It was the first thing Vladimir threw away, he thought: in the spy trade we abandon first what we love the most. I got the better end of the bargain after all. An elderly couple had settled opposite him. The man wore a stiff Homburg hat and was playing war tunes on a tin whistle. His wife grinned inanely at the passers-by. To avoid her gaze, Smiley remembered the brown envelope from Paris, and tore it open, expecting what? A bill probably, some hangover from the old boy's life there. Or one of those cyclo-styled battle-cries that émigrés send each other like Christmas cards. But this was neither a bill nor a circular but a personal letter: an appeal, but of a very special sort. Unsigned, no address for the sender. In French, handwritten very fast. Smiley read it once and he was reading it a second time when an overpainted Ford Cortina, driven by a boy in a polo-neck pullover, skidded to a giddy halt outside the cinema. Returning the letter to his pocket, he crossed the road to the car.

"Sampson with a 'p'?" the boy yelled impertinently through the window, then shoved open the back door from inside. Smiley climbed in. A smell of aftershave mingled with stale cigarette smoke. He held a ten-pound note in his hand and he let it show.

"Will you please switch off the engine?" Smiley asked.

The boy obeyed, watching him all the time in the mirror. He had brown Afro hair. White hands, carefully manicured.

"I'm a private detective," Smiley explained. "I'm sure you get a lot of us and we're a nuisance but I would be happy to pay for a little bit of information. You signed a receipt yesterday for thirteen pounds. Do you remember who your fare was?"

"Tall party. Foreign. White moustache and a limp."

"Old?"

"Very. Walking-stick and all."

"Where did you pick him up?" Smiley asked.

"Cosmo Restaurant, Praed Street, ten-thirty, morning," the boy said, gabbling deliberately.

Praed Street was five minutes' walk from Westbourne Terrace.

"And where did you take him, please?"

"Charlton."

"Charlton in South-East London?"

"Saint Somebody's Church off of Battle-of-the-Nile Street. Ask for a pub called The Defeated Frog."

"Frog?"

"Frenchman."

"Did you leave him there?"

"One hour wait, then back to Praed Street."

"Did you make any other stops?"

"Once at a toy-shop going, once at a phone-box coming back. Party bought a wooden duck on wheels." He turned and, resting his chin on the back of the seat, insolently held his hands apart, indicating size. "Yellow job," he said. "The phone call was local."

"How do you know?"

"I lent him twopence, didn't I? Then he come back and borrows himself two ten p's, for in-case."

I asked him where he was calling from but he just said he had plenty of change, Mostyn had said.

Passing the boy the ten-pound note, Smiley reached for the door handle.

"You can tell your firm I didn't turn up," he said.

"Tell 'em what I bloody like, can't I?"

Smiley climbed quickly out, just managing to close the door before the boy drove away at the same frightful speed. Standing on the pavement, he completed his second reading of the letter, and by then he had it in his memory for good. A woman, he thought, trusting his first instinct. And she thinks she's going to die. Well, so do we all, and we're right. He was feigning lightheadedness to himself, indifference. Each man has only a quantum of compassion, he argued, and mine is used up for the day. But the letter scared him all the same, and recharged his sense of urgency.

General, I do not wish to be dramatic but some men are watching my house and I do not think they are your friends or mine. This morning I had an impression that they were trying to kill me. Will you not send me your magic friend once more?

He had things to hide. To *cache*, as they insisted on saying at Sarratt. He took busses, changing several times, watching his back, dozing. The black motor cycle with its side-car had not reappeared; he could discern no other surveillance. At a stationer's shop in Baker Street he bought a large cardboard box, some daily newspapers, some wrapping paper, and a reel of Scotch tape. He hailed a taxi, then crouched in the back making up his parcel. He put Vladimir's packet of cigarettes into the box, together with Ostrakova's letter, and he padded out the rest of the space with newspaper. He wrapped the box and got his fingers tangled in the Scotch tape. Scotch tape had always defeated him. He wrote his own name on the lid, "To be called for." He paid off the cab at the Savoy Hotel, where he consigned the box to the men's-cloakroom attendant, together with a pound note.

"Not heavy enough for a bomb, is it, sir?" the attendant asked, and facetiously held the parcel to his ear.

"I wouldn't be so sure," said Smiley, and they shared a good laugh together.

Tell Max that it concerns the Sandman, he thought. Vladimir, he wondered wistfully, what was your other proof?

9

The low skyline was filled with cranes and gasometers; lazy chimneys spouted ochre smoke into the rainclouds. If it had not been Saturday, Smiley would have used public transport but on Saturdays he was prepared to drive, though he lived on terms of mutual hatred with the combustion engine. He had crossed the river at Vauxhall Bridge. Greenwich lay behind him. He had entered the flat dismembered hinterland of the docks. While the wiper blades shuddered, large raindrops crept through the bodywork of his unhappy little English car. Glum children, sheltering in a bus-stop, said "Keep straight on, guv." He had shaved and bathed, but he had not slept. He had sent Vladimir's telephone bill to Lacon, requesting a breakdown of all traceable calls as a matter of urgency. His mind, as he drove, was clear, but prey to anarchic changes of mood. He was wearing a brown tweed overcoat, the one he used for travelling. He navigated a roundabout, mounted a rise, and suddenly a fine Edwardian pub stood before him, under the sign of a red-faced warrior. Battle-of-the-Nile Street rose away from it towards an island of worn grass, and on the island stood St. Saviour's Church, built of stone and flint, proclaiming God's message to the crumbling Victorian warehouses. Next Sunday's preacher, said the poster, was a female major in the Salvation Army, and in front of the poster stood the lorry: a sixty-foot giant trailer, crimson, its side windows fringed with football pennants and a motley of foreign registration stickers covering one door. It was the biggest thing in sight, bigger even than the church. Somewhere in the background he heard a motor-bike engine slow down and then start up again, but he didn't even bother to look back. The familiar escort had followed him since Chelsea; but fear, as he used to preach at Sarratt, is always a matter of selection.

Following the footpath, Smiley entered a graveyard with no graves. Lines of headstones made up the perimeter, a climbing frame and three standard-pattern new houses occupied the central ground. The first house was called Zion, the second had no name at all, the third was called Number Three. Each had wide windows but Number Three had lace curtains, and when he pushed the gate all he saw was one shadow upstairs. He saw it stationary, then he saw it sink and vanish as if it had been sucked into the floor, and for a second he wondered, in a quite dreadful way, whether he had just witnessed another murder. He rang the bell and angel chimes exploded inside the house. The door was made of rippled glass. Pressing his eye to it, he made out brown stair carpet and what looked like a perambulator. He rang the bell again and heard a scream. It started low and grew louder and at first he thought it was a child, then a cat, then a whistling kettle. It reached its zenith, held it, then suddenly stopped, either because someone had taken the kettle off the boil or because it had blown its nozzle off. He walked round to the back of the house. It was the same as the front, except for the drain-pipes and a vegetable patch, and a tiny goldfish pond made of pre-cast slab. There was no water in the pond, and consequently no goldfish either; but in the concrete bowl lay a yellow wooden duck on its side. It lay with its beak open and its staring eye turned to Heaven and two of its wheels were still going round.

"Party bought a wooden duck on wheels," the minicab driver had said, turning to illustrate with his white hands. "Yellow job."

The back door had a knocker. He gave a light tap with it

and tried the door handle, which yielded. He stepped inside and closed the door carefully behind him. He was standing in a scullery that led to a kitchen and the first thing he noticed in the kitchen was the kettle off the gas with a thin line of steam curling from its silent whistle. And two cups and a milk jug and a teapot on a tray.

"Mrs. Craven?" he called softly. "Stella?"

He crossed the dining-room and stood in the hall, on the brown carpet beside the perambulator, and in his mind he was making pacts with God: just no more deaths, no more Vladimirs, and I will worship You for the rest of our respective lives.

"Stella? It's me. Max," he said.

He pushed open the drawing-room door and she was sitting in the corner on an easy chair between the piano and window, watching him with cold determination. She was not scared, but she looked as if she hated him. She was wearing a long Asian dress and no make-up. She was holding the child to her, boy or girl he couldn't tell and couldn't remember. She had its tousled head pressed against her shoulder and her hand over its mouth to stop it making a noise, and she was watching him over the top of its head, challenging and defying him.

"Where's Villem?" he asked.

Slowly she took her hand away and Smiley expected the child to scream but instead it stared at him in salute.

"His name's William," she said quietly. "Get that straight, Max. That's his choice. William Craven. British to the core. Not Estonian, not Russian. British." She was a beautiful woman, black-haired and still. Seated in the corner holding her child, she seemed permanently painted against the dark background.

"I want to talk to him, Stella. I'm not asking him to do anything. I may even be able to help him."

"I've heard that before, haven't I? He's out. Gone to work where he belongs."

Smiley digested this.

"Then what's his lorry doing outside?" he objected gently.

"He's gone to the depot. They sent a car for him."

Smiley digested this also.

"Then who's the second cup for in the kitchen?"

"He's got nothing to do with it," she said.

He went upstairs and she let him. There was a door straight ahead of him and there were doors to his left and right, both open, one to the child's room, one to the main bedroom. The door ahead of him was closed and when he knocked there was no answer.

"Villem, it's Max," he said. "I have to talk to you, please. Then I'll go and leave you in peace, I promise."

He repeated this word for word, then went down the steep stairs again to the drawing-room. The child had begun crying loudly.

"Perhaps if you made that tea," he suggested between the child's sobs.

"You're not talking to him alone, Max. I'm not having you charm him off the tree again."

"I never did that. That was not my job."

"He still thinks the world of you. That's enough for me."

"It's about Vladimir," Smiley said.

"I know what it's about. They've been ringing half the night, haven't they?"

"Who have?"

"'Where's Vladimir? Where's Vladi?' What do they think William is? Jack the Ripper? He hasn't had sound nor sight of Vladi for God knows how long. Oh, Beckie, darling, *do* be quiet!" Striding across the room, she found a tin of biscuits under a heap of washing and shoved one forcibly into the child's mouth. "I'm not usually like this," she said.

"*Who's* been asking for him?" Smiley insisted gently.

"Mikhel, who else? Remember Mikhel, our Freedom Radio ace, Prime Minister designate of Estonia, betting tout? Three o'clock this morning while Beckie's cutting a tooth, the bloody phone goes. It's Mikhel doing his heavy-breathing act. 'Where's Vladi, Stella? Where's our leader?' I said to him: 'You're daft, aren't you? You think it's harder to tap the phone when people only whisper? You're barking mad,' I said to him. 'Stick to racehorses and get out of politics,' I told him."

"Why was he so worried?" Smiley asked.

"Vladi owed him money, that's why. Fifty quid. Probably lost it on a horse together, one of their many losers. He'd promised to bring it round to Mikhel's place and have a game of chess with him. In the middle of the night, mark you. They're insomniacs, apparently, as well as patriots. Our leader hadn't shown up. Drama. 'Why the hell should William know where he is?' I ask him. 'Go to sleep.' An hour later who's back on the line? Breathing as before? Our Major Mikhel once more, hero of the Royal Estonian Cavalry, clicking our heels and apologising. He's been round to Vladi's pad, banged on the door, rung the bell. There's nobody at home. 'Look, Mikhel,' I said. 'He's not here, we're not hiding him in the attic, we haven't seen him since Beckie's christening, we haven't heard from him. Right? William's just in from Hamburg, he needs sleep, and I'm not waking him.'"

"So he rang off again," Smiley suggested.

"Did he, hell! He's a leech. 'Villem is Vladi's favourite,' he says. 'What for?' I say. 'The three-thirty at Ascot? Look, go to bloody sleep!' 'Vladimir always said to me, if ever anything went wrong, I should go to Villem,' he said. 'So what do you want him to do?' I said. 'Drive up to town in the trailer and bang on Vladi's door as well?' Jesus!"

She sat the child on a chair. Where she stayed, contentedly cropping her biscuit.

There was the sound of a door slammed violently, followed by fast footsteps coming down the stairs.

"William's right out of it, Max," Stella warned, staring straight at Smiley. "He's not political and he's not slimy, and he's got over his dad being a martyr. He's a big boy now and he's going to stand on his own feet. Right? I said 'Right?'"

Smiley had moved to the far end of the room to give himself distance from the door. Villem strode in purposefully, still wearing his track suit and running shoes, about ten years Stella's junior and somehow too slight for his own safety. He perched himself on the sofa, at the edge, his intense gaze switching between his wife and Smiley as if wondering which of them would spring first. His high forehead looked strangely white under his dark, swept-back hair. He had shaved, and shaving had filled out his face, making him even younger. His eyes, red-rimmed from driving, were brown and passionate.

"Hullo, Villem," Smiley said.

"William," Stella corrected him.

Villem nodded tautly, acknowledging both forms.

"Hullo, Max," said Villem. On his lap, his hands found and held each other. "How you doing, Max? That's the way, huh?"

"I gather you've already heard the news about Vladimir," Smiley said.

"News? What news, please?"

Smiley took his time. Watching him, sensing his stress.

"That he's disappeared," Smiley replied quite lightly, at last. "I gather his friends have been ringing you up at unsocial hours."

"Friends?" Villem shot a dependent glance at Stella. "Old émigrés, drink tea, play chess all day, politics? Talk crazy dreams? Mikhel is not my friend, Max."

He spoke swiftly, with impatience for this foreign language, which was such a poor substitute for his own. Whereas Smiley spoke as if he had all day.

"But *Vladi* is your friend," he objected. "Vladi was your father's friend before you. They were in Paris together. Brothers-in-arms. They came to England together."

Countering the weight of this suggestion, Villem's small

body became a storm of gestures. His hands parted and made furious arcs, his brown hair lifted and fell flat again.

"Sure! Vladimir, he was my father's friend. His good friend. Also of Beckie the godfather, okay? But not for politics. Not any more." He glanced at Stella, seeking her approval. "Me, I am William Craven. I got English home, English wife, English kid, English name. Okay?"

"And an English job," Stella put in quietly, watching him.

"A good job! Know how much I earn, Max? We buy house. Maybe a car, okay?"

Something in Villem's manner—his glibness perhaps, or the energy of his protest—had caught the attention of his wife, for now Stella was studying him as intently as Smiley was, and she began to hold the baby distractedly, almost without interest.

"When did you last see him, William?" Smiley asked.

"Who, Max? See who? I don't understand you, please."

"Tell him, Bill," Stella ordered her husband, not moving her eyes from him for a moment.

"When did you last see Vladimir?" Smiley repeated patiently.

"Long time, Max."

"Weeks?"

"Sure. Weeks."

"Months?"

"Months. Six months! Seven! At christening. He was godfather, we make a party. But no politics."

Smiley's silences had begun to produce an awkward tension.

"And not since?" he asked at last.

"No."

Smiley turned to Stella, whose gaze had still not flinched.

"What time did William get back yesterday?"

"Early," she said.

"As early as ten o'clock in the morning?"

"Could have been. I wasn't here. I was visiting Mother."

"Vladimir drove down here yesterday by taxi," he explained, still to Stella. "I think he saw William."

Nobody helped him, not Smiley, not his wife. Even the child kept still.

"On his way here Vladimir bought a toy. The taxi waited an hour down the lane and took him away again, back to Paddington where he lives," Smiley said, still being very careful to keep the present tense.

Villem had found his voice at last. "Vladi is of Beckie the godfather!" he protested with another flourish, as his English threatened to desert him entirely. "Stella don't like him, so he must come here like a thief, okay? He bring my Beckie toy, okay? Is a crime already, Max? Is a law, an old man cannot bring to his godchild toys?"

Once again neither Smiley nor Stella spoke. They were both waiting for the same inevitable collapse.

"Vladi is old man, Max! Who knows when he sees his Beckie again? He is friend of family!"

"Not of this family," said Stella. "Not any more."

"He was friend of my father! Comrade! In Paris they fight together Bolshevism. So he brings to Beckie a toy. Why not, please? Why not, Max?"

"You said you bought the bloody thing yourself," said Stella. Putting a hand to her breast, she closed a button as if to cut him off.

Villem swung to Smiley, appealing to him: "Stella don't like the old man, okay? Is afraid I make more politics with him, okay? So I don't tell Stella. She goes to see her mother in Staines hospital and while she is away Vladi makes a small visit to see Beckie, say hullo, why not?" In desperation he actually leapt to his feet, flinging up his arms in too much protest. "Stella!" he cried. "Listen to me! So Vladi don't get home last night? Please, I am so sorry! But it is not my fault, okay? Max! That Vladi is an old man! Lonely. So maybe he finds a woman once. Okay? So he can't do much with her, but he still likes her company. For this he was pretty famous, I think! Okay? Why not?"

"And *before* yesterday?" Smiley asked, after an age. Villem seemed not to understand, so Smiley paced out the question again: "You saw Vladimir yesterday. He came by taxi and brought a yellow wooden duck for Beckie. On wheels."

"Sure."

"Very well. But before yesterday—not counting yesterday— when did you last see him?"

Some questions are hazard, some are instinct, some—like this one—are based on a premature understanding that is more than instinct, but less than knowledge.

Villem wiped his lips on the back of his hand. "Monday," he said miserably. "I see him Monday. He ring me, we meet. Sure."

Then Stella whispered, "Oh, William," and held the child upright against her, a little soldier, while she peered downward at the haircord carpet waiting for her feelings to right themselves.

The phone began ringing. Like an infuriated infant, Villem sprang at it, lifted the receiver, slammed it back on the cradle, then threw the whole telephone onto the floor and kicked the receiver clear. He sat down.

Stella turned to Smiley. "I want you to go," she said. "I want you to walk out of here and never come back. Please, Max. Now."

For a time Smiley seemed to consider this request quite seriously. He looked at Villem with avuncular affection; he looked at Stella. Then he delved in his inside pocket and pulled out a folded copy of the day's first edition of the *Evening Standard* and handed it to Stella rather than to Villem, partly because of the language barrier and partly because he guessed that Villem would break down.

"I'm afraid Vladi's disappeared for good, William," he said in a tone of simple regret. "It's in the papers. He's been shot dead. The police will want to ask you questions. I have to hear what happened and tell you how to answer them."

Then Villem said something hopeless in Russian, and Stella, moved by his tone if not his words, put down one child and went to comfort the other, and Smiley might not have been in the room at all. So he sat for a while quite alone, thinking of Vladimir's piece of negative film—indecipherable until he turned it to positive—nestling in its box in the Savoy Hotel with the anonymous letter from Paris that he could do nothing about. And of the second proof, wondering what it was, and how the old man had carried it, and supposing it was in his wallet; but believing also that he would never know.

Villem sat bravely as if he were already attending Vladimir's funeral. Stella sat at his side with her hand on his, Beckie the child lay on the floor and slept. Occasionally as Villem talked, tears rolled unashamedly down his pale cheeks.

"For the others I give nothing," said Villem. "For Vladi everything. I love this man." He began again: "After the death of my father, Vladi become father to me. Sometimes I even say him: 'my father.' Not uncle. Father."

"Perhaps we could start with Monday," Smiley suggested. "With the first meeting."

Vladi had telephoned, said Villem. It was the first time Villem had heard from him or from anybody in the Group for months. Vladi telephoned Villem at the depot, out of the blue, while Villem was consolidating his load and checking his transshipment papers with the office before leaving for Dover. That was the arrangement, Villem said, that was how it had been left with the Group. He was out of it, as they all were, more or less, but if he was ever urgently needed he could be reached at the depot on a Monday morning, not at home because of Stella. Vladi was Beckie's godfather and as godfather could ring the house any time. But not on business. Never.

"I ask him: 'Vladi! What you want? Listen, how are you?'"

Vladimir was in a call-box down the road. He wanted a personal conversation immediately. Against all the employers' regulations, Villem picked him up at the roundabout and Vladimir rode half the way to Dover with him: "black," said Villem—meaning "illegally." The old boy was carrying a rush

basket full of oranges, but Villem had not been of a mood to
ask him why he should saddle himself with pounds of oranges.
At first Vladimir had talked about Paris and Villem's father,
and the great struggles they had shared; then he talked about a
small favour Villem could do for him. For the sake of old times
a small favour. For the sake of Villem's dead father, whom
Vladimir had loved. For the sake of the Group, of which
Villem's father had once been such a hero.

"I tell him: 'Vladi, this small favour is impossible for me.
I promise Stella: is impossible!'"

Stella's hand left her husband's side and she sat alone, torn
between wishing to console him for the old man's death and
her hurt at his broken promise.

Just a small favour, Vladimir had insisted. Small, no trouble, no risk, but very helpful to our cause: also Villem's duty.
Then Vladi produced snaps he had taken of Beckie at the
christening. They were in a yellow Kodak envelope, the prints
on one side and the negatives in protective cellophane on the
other and the chemist's blue docket still stapled to the outside,
all as innocent as the day.

For a while they admired them till Vladimir said suddenly:
"It is for Beckie, Villem. What we do, we do for Beckie's
future."

Hearing Villem repeat this, Stella clenched her fists, and
when she looked up again she was resolute and somehow much
older, with islands of tiny wrinkles at the corner of each eye.

Villem went on with his story: "Then Vladimir tell to me,
'Villem. Every Monday you are driving to Hanover and Hamburg, returning Friday. How long you stay in Hamburg, please?'"

To which Villem had replied as short a time as possible,
depending on how long it took him to unload, depending on
whether he delivered to the agent or to the addressee, depending on what time of day he arrived and how many hours he
already had on his sheet. Depending on his return load, if he
had one. There were more questions of this sort, which Villem

now related, many trivial—where Villem slept on the journey, where he ate—and Smiley knew that the old man in a rather monstrous way was doing what he would have done himself; he was talking Villem into a corner, making him answer as a prelude to making him obey. And only after this did Vladimir explain to Villem, using all his military and family authority, just what he wished Villem to do.

"He say to me: 'Villem, take these oranges to Hamburg for me. Take this basket.' 'What for?' I ask him. 'General, why do I take this basket?' Then he give me fifty pounds. 'For emergencies,' he tell to me. 'In emergency, here is fifty pounds.' 'But why do I take this basket?' I ask him. 'What emergency is considered here, General?'"

Then Vladimir recited to Villem his instructions, and they included fall-backs and contingencies—even, if necessary, staying an extra night on the strength of the fifty pounds—and Smiley noticed how the old man had insisted upon Moscow Rules, exactly as he had with Mostyn, and how there was *too much*, as there always had been—the older he got, the more the old boy had tied himself up in the skeins of his own conspiracies. Villem should lay the yellow Kodak envelope containing Beckie's photographs on the top of the oranges, he should take his stroll down to the front of the cabin—all as Villem in the event had done, he said—and the envelope was the letter-box, and the sign that it had been filled would be a chalk mark, "also yellow like the envelope, which is the tradition of our Group," said Villem.

"And the safety signal?" Smiley asked. "The signal that says 'I am not being followed'?"

"Was Hamburg newspaper from yesterday," Villem replied swiftly—but on this subject, he confessed, he had had a small difference with Vladimir, despite all the respect he owed to him as a leader, as a General, and as his father's friend.

"He tell to me, 'Villem, you carry that newspaper in your pocket.' But I tell to him: 'Vladi, please, look at me, I have only track suit, no pockets.' So he say, 'Villem, then carry the news-paper under your arm.'"

"Bill," Stella breathed, with a sort of awe. "Oh, Bill, you stupid bloody fool." She turned to Smiley. "I mean, why didn't they just put it in the bloody post, whatever it is, and be done with it?"

Because it was a negative, and only negatives are acceptable under Moscow Rules. Because the General had a terror of betrayal, Smiley thought. The old boy saw it everywhere, in everyone around him. And if death is the ultimate judge, he was right.

"And it worked?" Smiley said finally to Villem with great gentleness. "The hand-over worked?"

"Sure! It work fine," Villem agreed heartily, and darted Stella a defiant glance.

"And did you have any idea, for instance, who might have been your contact at this meeting?"

Then with much hesitation, and after much prompting, some of it from Stella, Villem told that also: about the hol-lowed face that had looked so desperate and had reminded him of his father; about the warning stare, which was either real or he had imagined it because he was so excited. How sometimes, when he watched football on the television, which he liked to do very much, the camera caught someone's face or expression, and it stuck in your memory for the rest of the match, even if you never saw it again—and how the face on the steamer was of this sort exactly. He described the flicked horns of hair, and with his fingertips he lightly drew deep grooves in his own unmarked cheeks. He described the man's smallness, and even his sexiness—Villem said he could tell. He described his own feelings of being *warned* by the man, warned to take care of a precious thing. Villem would look the same way himself—he told Stella with a sudden flourish of imagined tragedy—if there was another war, and fighting, and he had to give away Beckie to a stranger to look after! And this was the cue for more tears, and more reconciliation, and more lamentations about the old man's death, to which Smiley's next question inevitably contributed.

"So you brought the yellow envelope back, and yesterday when the General came down with Beckie's duck, you handed him the envelope," he suggested, as mildly as he knew how, but it was still some while before a plain narrative emerged.

It was Villem's habit, he said, before driving home on Fridays, to sleep at the depot for a few hours in the cab, then shave and drink a cup of tea with the boys so that he arrived home feeling steady, rather than nervous and bad-tempered. It was a trick he had learned from the older hands, he said: not to rush home, you only regret it. But yesterday was different, he said, and besides—lapsing suddenly into monosyllabic names— Stell had taken Beck to Staines to see her mum. So he for once came straight home, rang Vladimir, and gave him the code word they had agreed on in advance.

"Rang him where?" Smiley asked, softly interrupting.

"At flat. He told me: 'Phone me only at flat. Never at library. Mikhel is good man, but he is not informed.'"

And, Villem continued, within a short time—he forgot how long—Vladimir had arrived at the house by minicab, a thing he had never done before, bringing the duck for Beck. Villem handed him the yellow envelope of snapshots and Vladimir took them to the window and very slowly, "like they were sacred from a church, Max," with his back to Villem, Vladimir held the negatives one after the other to the light till he apparently found the one he was looking for, and after that he went on gazing at it for a long time.

"Just one?" Smiley asked swiftly, his mind upon the two proofs again. "*One* negative?"

"Sure."

"One frame, or one strip?"

Frame: Villem was certain. One small frame. Yes, thirty-five

millimetre, like his own Agfa automatic. No, Villem had not
been able to see what it contained, whether writing or what.
He had seen Vladimir, that was all.

"Vladi was red, Max. Wild in the face, Max, bright with his
eyes. He was old man."

"And on your journey," Smiley said, interrupting Villem's
story to ask this crucial question. "All the way home from
Hamburg, you never once thought to look?"

"Was secret, Max. Was military secret."

Smiley glanced at Stella.

"He wouldn't," she said in answer to his unspoken question. "He's too straight."

Smiley believed her.

Villem took up his story again. Having put the yellow
envelope in his pocket, Vladimir took Villem into the garden
and thanked him, holding Villem's hand in both of his, telling
him that it was a great thing he had done, the best; that Villem was his father's son, a finer soldier even than his father—
the best Estonian stock, steady, conscientious, and reliable;
that with this photograph they could repay many debts and do
great damage to the Bolsheviks; that the photograph was a
proof, a proof impossible to ignore. But of what, he did not
say—only that Max would see it, and believe, and remember.
Villem didn't quite know why they had to go into the garden
but he supposed that the old man in his excitement had become
scared of microphones, for he was already talking a lot about
security.

"I take him to gate but not to taxi. He tell me I must not
come to taxi. 'Villem. I am old man,' he say to me. We speak
Russian. 'Next week maybe I fall dead. Who cares? Today we
have won great battle. Max will be greatly proud of us.'"

Struck by the aptness of the General's last words to him,
Villem again bounded to his feet in fury, his brown eyes smouldering. "Was Soviets!" he shouted. "Was Soviet spies, Max,
they kill Vladimir! He know too much!"

"So do you," said Stella, and there was a long and awkward silence. "So do we all," she added, with a glance at Smiley.

"That's all he said?" Smiley asked. "Nothing else, about the value of what you have done, for instance. Just that Max would believe?"

Villem shook his head.

"About there being other proofs, for instance?"

Nothing, said Villem; no more.

"Nothing to explain how he had communicated with Hamburg in the first place, set up the arrangements? Whether others of the Group were involved? Please think."

Villem thought, but without result.

"So whom have you told this to, William, apart from me?" Smiley asked.

"Nobody! Max, nobody!"

"He hasn't had time," said Stella.

"Nobody! On journey I sleep in cab, save ten pounds a night subsistence. We buy house with this money! In Hamburg I tell *nobody!* At depot *nobody!*"

"Had Vladimir told anyone—anyone that you know of, that is?"

"From the Group nobody only Mikhel, which was necessary, but not all, even to Mikhel. I ask to him: 'Vladimir, who knows I do this for you?' 'Only Mikhel a very little,' he say. 'Mikhel lends me money, lends me photocopier, he is my friend. But even to friends we cannot trust. Enemies I do not fear, Villem. But friends I fear greatly.'"

Smiley spoke to Stella: "If the police *do* come here," he said. "*If* they do, they will only know that Vladimir drove down here yesterday. They'll have got on to the cab driver, as I did."

She was watching him with her large shrewd eyes.

"So?" she asked.

"So don't tell them the rest. They know all they need. Any more could be an embarrassment to them."

"To them or to you?" Stella asked.

"Vladimir came here yesterday to see Beckie and bring her a present. That's the cover story, just as William first told it. He didn't know you'd taken her to see your mother. He found William here, they talked old times and strolled in the garden. He couldn't wait too long because of the taxi, so he left without seeing either you or his goddaughter. That's all there was."

"Were *you* here?" Stella was still watching him.

"If they ask about me, yes. I came here today and gave you the bad news. The police don't mind that Villem belonged to the Group. It's only the present that matters to them."

Smiley returned his attention to Villem. "Tell me, did you bring anything else for Vladimir?" he asked. "Apart from what was in the envelope? A present perhaps? Something he liked and couldn't buy himself?"

Villem concentrated energetically upon the question before replying. "Cigarettes!" he cried suddenly. "On boat, I buy him French cigarettes as gift. Gauloises, Max. He like very much! 'Gauloises Caporal, with filter, Villem.' Sure!"

"And the fifty pounds he had borrowed from Mikhel?" Smiley asked.

"I give back. Sure."

"All?" said Smiley.

"All. Cigarettes was gift. Max, I love this man."

Stella saw him to the door and at the door he gently took her arm and led her a few steps into the garden out of earshot of her husband.

"You're out of date," she told him. "Whatever it is you're doing, sooner or later one side or the other will have to stop. You're like the Group."

"Be quiet and listen," said Smiley. "Are you listening?"

"Yes."

"William's to speak to no one about this. Whom does he like to talk to at the depot?"

"The whole world."

"Well, do what you can. Did anybody else ring apart from Mikhel? A wrong-number call even? Ring—then ring off?"

She thought, then shook her head.

"Did anyone come to the door? Salesman, market researcher, religious evangelist. Canvasser. Anyone? You're sure?"

As she continued staring at him, her eyes seemed to acquire real knowledge of him, and appreciation. Then again she shook her head, denying him the complicity he was asking for.

"Stay away, Max. All of you. Whatever happens, however bad it is. He's grown up. He doesn't need a vicar any more."

She watched him leave, perhaps to make sure he really went. For a while as he drove, the notion of Vladimir's piece of negative film nestling in its box consumed him like hidden money—whether it was still safe, whether he should inspect it or convert it, since it had been brought through the lines at the cost of life. But by the time he approached the river he had other thoughts and purposes. Eschewing Chelsea, he joined the northbound Saturday traffic, which consisted mainly of young families with old cars. And one motor bike with a black side-car, clinging faithfully to his tail all the way to Bloomsbury.

10

The Free Baltic Library was on the third floor over a dusty antiquarian bookshop that specialised in the Spirit. Its little windows squinted down into a forecourt of the British Museum. Smiley reached the place by way of a winding wooden staircase, passing on his ponderous climb several aged hand-drawn signs pulling at their drawing-pins and a stack of brown toiletry boxes belonging to a chemist's shop next door. Gaining the top, he discovered himself thoroughly out of breath, and wisely paused before pressing the bell. Waiting, he was assailed in his momentary exhaustion by a hallucination. He had the delusion that he kept visiting the same high place over and over again: the safe flat in Hampstead, Vladimir's garret in Westbourne Terrace, and now this haunted backwater from the fifties, once a rallying point of the so-called Bloomsbury Irregulars. He fancied they were all a single place, a single proving ground for virtues not yet stated. The illusion passed, and he gave three short rings, one long, wondering whether they had changed the signal, doubting it; still worrying about Villem or perhaps Stella, or perhaps just the child. He heard a close creak of floorboards and guessed he was being examined through the spyhole by someone a foot away from him. The door swiftly opened, he stepped into a gloomy hall as two wiry arms hugged him in their grip. He smelt body-heat and sweat and cigarette smoke and an unshaven face pressed against his own—left cheek, right cheek, as if to bestow a medal—once more to the left for particular affection.

"Max," Mikhel murmured in a voice that was itself a requiem. "You came. I am glad. I had hoped but I did not dare expect. I was waiting for you nevertheless. I waited all day till now. He loved you, Max. You were the best. He said so always. You were his inspiration. He told me. His example."

"I'm sorry, Mikhel," Smiley said. "I'm really sorry."

"As we all are, Max. As we all are. Inconsolable. But we are soldiers."

He was dapper, and hollow-backed, and trim as the ex-major of horse he professed to be. His brown eyes, reddened by the night watch, had a becoming droopiness. He wore a black blazer over his shoulders like a cloak and black boots much polished, which could indeed have been for riding. His grey hair was groomed with military correctness, his moustache thick but carefully clipped. His face was at first glance youthful and only a close look at the crumbling of its pale surface into countless tiny deltas revealed his years. Smiley followed him to the library. It ran the width of the house and was divided by alcoves into vanished countries: Latvia, Lithuania, and—not least—Estonia, and in each alcove were a table and a flag and at several tables there were chess sets laid out for play, but nobody was playing, nobody was reading either; nobody was there, except for one blonde, broad woman in her forties wearing a short skirt and ankle socks. Her yellow hair, dark at the roots, was knotted in a severe bun, and she lounged beside a samovar, reading a travel magazine showing birch forests in the autumn. Drawing level with her, Mikhel paused and seemed about to make an introduction, but at the sight of Smiley she betrayed an intense and unmistakable anger. She looked at him, her mouth curled in contempt, she looked away through the rain-smeared window. Her cheeks were shiny from weeping and there were olive bruises under her heavy-lidded eyes.

"Elvira loved him also very much," Mikhel observed by

way of explanation when they were out of her hearing. "He was a brother to her. He instructed her."

"Elvira?"

"My wife, Max. After many years we are married. I resisted. It is not always good for our work. But I owe her this security."

They sat down. Around them and along the walls hung martyrs of forgotten movements. This one already in prison, photographed through wire. That one dead and—like Vladimir—they had pulled back the sheet to expose his bloodied face. A third, laughing, wore the baggy cap of a partisan and carried a long-barrelled rifle. From down the room they heard a small explosion followed by a rich Russian oath. Elvira, bride of Mikhel, was lighting the samovar.

"I'm sorry," Smiley repeated.

Enemies I do not fear, Villem, thought Smiley. *But friends I fear greatly.*

They were in Mikhel's private alcove that he called his office. An old-fashioned telephone lay on the table beside a Remington upright typewriter like the one in Vladimir's flat. Somebody must once have bought lots of them, thought Smiley. But the focus was a high hand-carved chair with barley-twist legs and a monarchic crest embroidered on the back. Mikhel sat on it primly, knees and boots together, a proxy king too small for his throne. He had lit a cigarette, which he held vertically from below. Above him a pall of tobacco smoke hung exactly where Smiley remembered it. In the waste-paper basket, Smiley noticed several discarded copies of *Sporting Life*.

"He was a leader, Max, he was a hero," Mikhel declared. "We must try to profit from his courage and example." He paused as if expecting Smiley to write this down for publication. "In such cases it is natural to ask oneself how one can possibly carry on. Who is worthy to follow him? Who has his stature, his honour, his sense of destiny? Fortunately our movement is a continuing process. It is greater than any one individual, even than any one group."

Listening to Mikhel's polished phrases, staring at his polished boots, Smiley found himself marvelling at the man's age. The Russians occupied Estonia in 1940, he recalled. To have been a cavalry officer then, Mikhel would now have to be sixty if a day. He tried to assemble the rest of Mikhel's turbulent biography—the long road through foreign wars and untrusted ethnic brigades, all the chapters of history contained in this one little body. He wondered how old the boots were.

"Tell me about his last days, Mikhel," Smiley suggested. "Was he active to the very end?"

"Completely active, Max, active in all respects. As a patriot. As a man. As a leader."

Her expression as contemptuous as before, Elvira put the tea before them, two cups with lemon, and small marzipan cakes. In motion she was insinuating, with fluid haunches and a sullen hint of challenge. Smiley tried to remember her background also, but it eluded him or perhaps he had never known it. *He was a brother to her*, he thought. *He instructed her.* But something from his own life had long ago warned him to mistrust explanations, particularly of love.

"As a member of the Group?" Smiley asked when she had left them. "Also active?"

"Always," said Mikhel gravely.

There was a small pause while each man politely waited for the other to continue.

"Who do you think did it, Mikhel? Was he betrayed?"

"Max, you know as well as I do who did it. We are all of us at risk. All of us. The call can come any time. Important is, we must be ready for it. Myself I am a soldier, I am prepared, I am ready. If I go, Elvira has her security. That is all. For the Bolshevites we exiles remain enemy number one. Anathema. Where they can, they destroy us. Still. As once they destroyed our churches and our villages and our schools and our culture.

And they are right, Max. They are right to be afraid of us. Because one day we shall defeat them."

"But why did they choose this particular moment?" Smiley objected gently after this somewhat ritualistic pronouncement. "They could have killed Vladimir years ago."

Mikhel had produced a flat tin box with two tiny rollers on it like a mangle, and a packet of coarse yellow cigarette-papers. Having licked a paper, he laid it on the rollers and poured in black tobacco. A snap, the mangle turned, and there on the silvered surface lay one fat, loosely packed cigarette. He was about to help himself to it when Elvira came over and took it. He rolled another and returned the box to his pocket.

"Unless Vladi was *up* to something, I suppose," Smiley continued after these staged manoeuvres. "Unless he *provoked* them in some way—which he might have done, knowing him."

"Who can tell?" Mikhel said, and blew some more smoke carefully into the air above them.

"Well, *you* can, Mikhel, if anyone can. Surely he confided in *you*. You were his right-hand man for twenty years or more. First Paris, then here. Don't tell me he didn't trust *you*," said Smiley ingenuously.

"Our leader was a secretive man, Max. This was his strength. He had to be. It was a military necessity."

"But not towards *you*, surely?" Smiley insisted, in his most flattering tone. "His Paris adjutant. His aide-de-camp. His confidential secretary? Come, you do yourself an injustice!"

Leaning forward in his throne, Mikhel placed a small hand strictly across his heart. His brown voice took on an even deeper tone.

"Max. Even towards me. At the end, even towards Mikhel. It was to shield me. To spare me dangerous knowledge. He said to me even: 'Mikhel, it is better that you—even you—do not know what the past has thrown up.' I implored him. In vain. He came to me one evening. Here. I was asleep upstairs. He gave the special ring on the bell: 'Mikhel, I need fifty pounds.'"

Elvira returned, this time with an empty ashtray, and as she put it on the table Smiley felt a surge of tension like the sudden working of a drug. He experienced it driving sometimes, waiting for a crash that didn't happen. And he experienced it with Ann, watching her return from some supposedly innocuous engagement and knowing—simply knowing—it was not.

"When was this?" he asked when she had left again.

"Twelve days ago. One week last Monday. From his manner I am able to discern immediately that this is an official affair. He has never before asked me for money. 'General,' I say to him. 'You are making a conspiracy. Tell me what it is.' But he shakes his head. 'Listen,' I tell him, 'if this is a conspiracy, take my advice, go to Max.' He refused. 'Mikhel,' he tells me, 'Max is a good man, but he does not have confidence any more in our Group. He wishes, even, that we end our struggle. But when I have landed the big fish I am hoping for, then I shall go to Max and claim our expenses and perhaps many things besides. But this I do afterwards, not before. Meanwhile I cannot conduct my business in a dirty shirt. Please, Mikhel. Lend me fifty pounds. In all my life this is my most important mission. It reaches far into our past.' His words exactly. In my wallet I had fifty pounds—fortunately I had that day made a successful investment—I give them to him. 'General,' I said. 'Take all I have. My possessions are yours. Please,'" said Mikhel and to punctuate this gesture—or to authenticate it—drew heavily at his yellow cigarette.

In the grimy window above them Smiley had glimpsed the reflection of Elvira standing half-way down the room, listening to their conversation. Mikhel had also seen her and had even shot her an evil frown, but he seemed unwilling, and perhaps unable, to order her away.

"That was very good of you," Smiley said after a suitable pause.

"Max, it was my duty. From the heart. I know no other law."

She despises me for not helping the old man, thought

Smiley. She was in on it, she knew, and now she despises me for not helping him in his hour of need. *He was a brother to her*, he remembered. *He instructed her.*

"And this approach to you—this request for operational funds," said Smiley. "It came out of the blue? There'd been nothing before, to tell you he was up to something big?"

Again Mikhel frowned, taking his time, and it was clear that Mikhel did not care too much for questions.

"Some months ago, perhaps two, he received a letter," he said cautiously. "Here, to this address."

"Did he receive so few?"

"This letter was special," said Mikhel, with the same air of caution, and suddenly Smiley realised that Mikhel was in what the Sarratt inquisitors called the loser's corner, because he did not know—he could only guess—how much or how little Smiley knew already. Therefore Mikhel would give up his information jealously, hoping to read the strength of Smiley's hand while he did so.

"Who was it from?"

Mikhel, as so often, answered a slightly different question.

"It was from Paris, Max, a long letter, many pages, handwritten. Addressed to the General personally, not Miller. To General Vladimir, most personal. On the envelope was written 'Most Personal,' in French. The letter arrived, I lock it in my desk; at eleven o'clock he walks in as usual. 'Mikhel, I salute you.' Sometimes, believe me, we even saluted each other. I hand him the letter, he sat"—he pointed towards Elvira's end of the room—"he sat down, opened it quite carelessly, as if he had no expectation from it, and I saw him gradually become preoccupied. Absorbed. I would say fascinated. Impassioned even. I spoke to him. He didn't answer. I spoke again—you know his ways—he ignored me totally. He went for a walk. 'I shall return,' he said."

"Taking the letter?"

"Of course. It was his fashion, when he had a great matter

to consider, to go for a walk. When he returned, I noticed a deep excitement in him. A tension. 'Mikhel.' You know how he spoke. All must obey. 'Mikhel. Get out the photocopier. Put some paper in it for me. I have a document to copy.' I asked him how many copies. One. I asked him how many sheets. 'Seven. Please stand at five paces' distance while I operate the machine,' he tells me. 'I cannot involve you in this matter.'"

Once again, Mikhel indicated the spot as if it proved the absolute veracity of his story. The black copier stood on its own table, like an old steam-engine, with rollers, and holes for pouring in the different chemicals. "The General was not mechanical, Max. I set up the machine for him—then I stood— here—so—calling out instructions to him across the room. When he had finished, he stood over the copies while they dried, then folded them into his pocket."

"And the original?"

"This also he put in his pocket."

"So you never read the letter?" Smiley said, in a tone of light commiseration.

"No, Max. I am sad to tell you I did not."

"But you saw the envelope. You had it here to give to him when he arrived."

"I told you, Max. It was from Paris."

"Which district?"

The hesitation again: "The fifteenth," said Mikhel. "I believe it was the fifteenth. Where many of our people used to be."

"And the date? Can you be more precise about it? You said about two months."

"Early September. I would say early September. Late August is possible. Say six weeks ago, around."

"The address on the envelope was also handwritten?"

"It was, Max. It was."

"What colour was the envelope?"

"Brown."

"And the ink?"

"I suppose blue."

"Was it sealed?"

"Please?"

"Was the envelope sealed with sealing-wax or adhesive tape? Or was it just gummed in the ordinary way?"

Mikhel shrugged, as if such details were beneath him.

"But the sender had put his name on the outside, presumably?" Smiley persisted lightly.

If he had, Mikhel was not admitting it.

For a moment Smiley allowed his mind to dwell upon the brown envelope cached in the Savoy cloakroom, and the passionate plea for help it had contained. *This morning I had an impression that they were trying to kill me. Will you not send me your magic friend once more?* Postmark Paris, he thought. The 15th district. After the first letter, Vladimir gave the writer his home address, he thought. Just as he gave his home telephone number to Villem. After the first letter, Vladimir made sure he bypassed Mikhel.

A phone rang and Mikhel answered it at once, with a brief "Yes," then listened.

"Then put me five each way," he muttered, and rang off with magisterial dignity.

Approaching the main purpose of his visit to Mikhel, Smiley took care to proceed with great respect. He remembered that Mikhel—who by the time he joined the Group in Paris had seen the inside of half the interrogation centres of Eastern Europe—had a way of slowing down when he was prodded, and by this means in his day had driven the Sarratt inquisitors half mad.

"May I ask you something, Mikhel?" Smiley said, instructively selecting a line that was oblique to the main thrust of his enquiry.

"Please."

"That evening when he called here to borrow money from

you, did he stay? Did you make him tea? Play a game of chess per-haps? Could you paint it for me a little, please, that evening?"

"We played chess, but not with concentration. He was pre-occupied, Max."

"Did he say any more about the big fish?"

The drooped eyes considered Smiley soulfully.

"Please, Max?"

"The big fish. The operation he said he was planning. I wondered whether he enlarged upon it in any way."

"Nothing. Nothing at all, Max. He was entirely secretive."

"Did you have the impression it involved another country?"

"He spoke only of having no passport. He was wounded—Max, I tell you this frankly—he was hurt that the Circus would not trust him with a passport. After such service, such devo-tion—he was hurt."

"It was for his own good, Mikhel."

"Max, *I* understand entirely. I am a younger man, a man of the world, flexible. The General was at times impulsive, Max. Steps had to be taken—even by those who admired him—to contain his energies. Please. But for the man himself, it was incomprehensible. An insult."

From behind him Smiley heard the thud of feet as Elvira stomped contemptuously back to her corner.

"So who did he think should do his travelling for him?" Smiley asked, again ignoring her.

"Villem," said Mikhel with obvious disapproval. "He does not tell me in many words but I believe he sends Villem. That was my impression. Villem would go. General Vladimir spoke with much pride of Villem's youth and honour. Also of his father. He even made an historical reference. He spoke of bringing in the new generation to avenge the injustices of the old. He was very moved."

"Where did he send him? Did Vladi give any hint of that?"

"He does not tell me. He tells me only, 'Villem has a pass-port, he is a brave boy, a good Balt, steady, he can travel, but it is also necessary to protect him.' I do not probe, Max. I do not pry. That is not my way. You know that."

"Still you did form an impression, I suppose," Smiley said. "The way one does. There are not so many places Villem would be free to go to, after all. Least of all on fifty pounds. There was Villem's job too, wasn't there? Not to mention his wife. He couldn't just step into the blue when he felt like it."

Mikhel made a very military gesture. Pushing out his lips till his moustache was almost on its back, he tugged shrewdly at his nose with his thumb and forefinger. "The General also asked me for maps," he said finally. "I was in two minds whether to tell you this. You are his vicar, Max, but you are not of our cause. But as I trust you, I shall."

"Maps of where?"

"Street maps." He flicked a hand towards the shelves as if ordering them closer. "City plans. Of Danzig. Hamburg. Lübeck. Helsinki. The northern seaboard. I asked him, 'General, sir. Let me help you,' I said to him. 'Please. I am your assistant for everything. I have a right. Vladimir. Let me help you.' He refused me. He wished to be entirely private."

Moscow Rules, Smiley thought yet again. Many maps and only one of them is relevant. And once again, he noted, towards his trusted Paris adjutant Vladimir was taking measures to obscure his purpose.

"After which he left?" he suggested.

"Correct."

"At what time?"

"It was late."

"Can you say how late?"

"Two. Three. Even four maybe. I am not sure."

Then Smiley felt Mikhel's gaze lift fractionally over his shoulder and beyond it and stay there, and an instinct that he had lived by for as long as he could remember made him ask: "Did Vladimir come here alone?"

"Of course, Max. Who would he bring?"

They were interrupted by a clank of crockery as Elvira at the other end of the room went clumsily back to her chores. Daring to glance at Mikhel just then, Smiley saw him staring after her with an expression he recognised but for a split second could not place: hopeless and affectionate at once, torn between dependence and disgust. Till, with sickening empathy, Smiley found himself looking into his own face as he had glimpsed it too often, red-eyed like Mikhel's, in Ann's pretty gilt mirrors in their house in Bywater Street.

"So if he wouldn't let you help him, what did you do?" Smiley asked with the same studied casualness. "Sit up and read—play chess with Elvira?"

Mikhel's brown eyes held him a moment, slipped away, and came back to him.

"No, Max," he replied with great courtesy. "I gave him the maps. He desired to be left alone with them. I wished him good night. I was asleep by the time he left."

But not Elvira, apparently, Smiley thought. Elvira stayed behind for instruction from her proxy brother. *Active as a patriot, as a man, as a leader*, Smiley rehearsed. *Active in all respects*.

"So what contact have you had with him since?" Smiley asked, and Mikhel came suddenly to yesterday. Nothing till yesterday, Mikhel said.

"Yesterday afternoon he called me on the telephone. Max, I swear to you I had not heard him so excited for many years. Happy, I would say ecstatic. 'Mikhel! Mikhel!' Max, that was a delighted man. He would come to me that night. Last night. Late maybe, but he will have my fifty pounds. 'General,' I tell him. 'What is fifty pounds? Are you well? Are you safe? Tell me.' 'Mikhel, I have been fishing and I am happy. Stay awake,' he says to me. 'I shall be with you at eleven o'clock, soon after. I shall have the money. Also it is necessary I beat you at chess to calm my nerves.' I stay awake, make tea, wait for him. And wait. Max, I am a soldier, for myself I am not afraid. But for the

General—for that old man, Max—I was afraid. I phone the
Circus, an emergency. They hang up on me. Why? Max, why
did you do that, please?"

"I was not on duty," Smiley said, now watching Mikhel as
intently as he dared. "Tell me, Mikhel," he began deliberately.

"Max."

"What did you think Vladimir was going to be doing after
he rang you with the good news—and before he came to repay
you fifty pounds?"

Mikhel did not hesitate. "Naturally I assumed he would be
going to Max," he said. "He had landed his big fish. Now he
would go to Max, claim his expenses, present him with his
great news. Naturally," he repeated, looking a little too straight
into Smiley's eyes.

Naturally, thought Smiley; and you knew to the minute
when he would leave his apartment, and to the metre the route
he would take to reach the Hampstead flat.

"So he failed to appear, you rang the Circus, and we were
unhelpful," Smiley resumed. "I'm sorry. So what did you do
next?"

"I phone Villem. First to make sure the boy is all right, also
to ask him where is our leader? That English wife of his bawled
me out. Finally I went to his flat. I did not like to—it was an
intrusion—his private life is his own—but I went. I rang the
bell. He did not answer. I came home. This morning at eleven
o'clock Jüri rings. I had not read the early edition of the evening papers, I am not fond of English newspapers. Jüri had
read them. Vladimir our leader was dead," he ended.

Elvira was at his elbow. She had two glasses of vodka on a
tray.

"Please," said Mikhel. Smiley took a glass, Mikhel the
other.

"To life!" said Mikhel, very loud, and drank as the tears
started to his eyes.

"To life," Smiley repeated while Elvira watched them.

She went with him, Smiley thought. She forced Mikhel to the old man's flat, she dragged him to the door.

"Have you told anyone else of this, Mikhel?" Smiley asked when she had once more left.

"Jüri I don't trust," said Mikhel, blowing his nose.

"Did you tell Jüri about Villem?"

"Please?"

"Did you mention Villem to him? Did you suggest to Jüri in any way that Villem might have been involved with Vladimir?"

Mikhel had committed no such sin, apparently.

"In this situation you should trust no one," Smiley said, in a more formal tone, as he prepared to take his leave. "Not even the police. Those are the orders. The police must not know that Vladimir was doing anything operational when he died. It is important for security. Yours as well as ours. He gave you no message otherwise? No word for Max, for instance?"

Tell Max that it concerns the Sandman, he thought.

Mikhel smiled his regrets.

"Did Vladimir mention Hector recently, Mikhel?"

"Hector was no good for him."

"Did Vladimir say that?"

"Please, Max. I have nothing against Hector personally. Hector is Hector, he is not a gentleman, but in our work we must use many varieties of mankind. This was the General speaking. Our leader was an old man. 'Hector,' Vladimir says to me. 'Hector is no good. Our good postman Hector is like the City banks. When it rains, they say, the banks take away your umbrella. Our postman Hector is the same.' Please. This is Vladimir speaking. Not Mikhel. 'Hector is no good.'"

"When did he say this?"

"He said it several times."

"Recently?"

"Yes."

"How recently?"

"Maybe two months. Maybe less."

"After he received the Paris letter, or before?"

"After. No question."

Mikhel escorted him to the door, a gentleman even if Toby Esterhase was not. At her place again beside the samovar, Elvira sat smoking before the same photograph of birch trees. And as he passed her, Smiley heard a sort of hiss, made through the nose or mouth, or both at once, as a last statement of her contempt.

"What will you do now?" he asked of Mikhel in the way one asks such things of the bereaved. Out of the corner of his eye he saw her head lift at his question and her fingers spread across the page.

A last thought struck him. "And you didn't recognise the handwriting?" Smiley asked.

"What handwriting is this, Max?"

"On the envelope from Paris?"

Suddenly he had no time to wait for an answer; suddenly he was sick of evasion.

"Goodbye, Mikhel."

"Go well, Max."

Elvira's head sank again to the birch trees.

I'll never know, Smiley thought, as he made his way quickly down the wooden staircase. None of us will. Was he Mikhel the traitor who resented the old man sharing his woman, and thirsted for the crown that had been denied him for too long? Or was he Mikhel the selfless officer and gentleman, Mikhel the ever-loyal servant? Or was he perhaps, like many loyal servants, both?

He thought of Mikhel's cavalry pride, as terribly tender as any other hero's manhood. His pride in being the General's keeper, his pride in being his satrap. His sense of injury at being excluded. His pride again—how it split so many ways! But how far did it extend? To a pride in giving nobly to each master, for instance? *Gentlemen, I have served you both well,* says the perfect double agent in the twilight of his life. And says it with pride, too, thought Smiley, who had known a number of them.

He thought of the seven-page letter from Paris. He thought of second proofs. He wondered who the photocopy had gone to—maybe Esterhase? He wondered where the original was. So who went to Paris? he wondered. If Villem went to Hamburg, who was the little magician? He was bone tired. His tiredness hit him like a sudden virus. He felt it in the knees, the hips, his whole subsiding body. But he kept walking, for his mind refused to rest.

11

To walk was just possible for Ostrakova, and to walk was all she asked. To walk and wait for the magician. Nothing was broken. Though her dumpy little body, when they had given her a bath, was shaping up to become as blackened and patchy as a map of the Siberian coalfields, nothing was broken. And her poor rump, which had given her that bit of trouble at the warehouse, looked already as though the assembled secret armies of Soviet Russia had booted her from one end of Paris to the other; still, nothing was broken. They had X-rayed every part of her, they had prodded her like questionable meat for signs of internal bleeding. But in the end, they had gloomily declared her to be the victim of a miracle.

They had wanted to keep her, for all that. They had wanted to treat her for shock, sedate her—at least for one night! The police, who had found six witnesses with seven conflicting accounts of what had happened (The car was grey, or was it blue? The registration number was from Marseilles, or was it foreign?), the police had taken one long statement from her, and threatened to come back and take another.

Ostrakova had nevertheless discharged herself.

Then had she at least children to look after her? they had asked. Oh, but she had a mass of them! she said. Daughters who would pander to her smallest whim, sons to assist her up and down the stairs! Any number—as many as they wished!

To please the sisters, she even made up lives for them, though her head was beating like a war-drum. She had sent out for clothes. Her own were in shreds and God Himself must have blushed to see the state she was in when they found her. She gave a false address to go with her false name; she wanted no follow-up, no visitors. And somehow, by sheer will-power, at the stroke of six that evening, Ostrakova became just another ex-patient, stepping cautiously and extremely painfully down the ramp of the great black hospital, to rejoin the very world which that same day had done its best to be rid of her for good. Wearing her boots, which like herself were battered but mysteriously unbroken; and she was quaintly proud of the way they had supported her.

She wore them still. Restored to the twilight of her own apartment, seated in Ostrakov's tattered armchair while she patiently wrestled with his old army revolver, trying to fathom how the devil it loaded, cocked, and fired itself, she wore them like a uniform. "I am an army of one." To stay alive: that was her one aim, and the longer she did it, the greater would be her victory. To stay alive until the General came, or sent her the magician.

To escape from them, like Ostrakov? Well, she had done that. To mock them, like Glikman, to force them into corners where they had no option but to contemplate their own obscenity? In her time, she liked to think, she had done a little of that as well. But to survive, as neither of her men had done; to cling to life, against all the efforts of that soulless, numberless universe of brutalised functionaries; to be a thorn to them every hour of the day, merely by staying alive, by breathing, eating, moving, and having her wits about her—that, Ostrakova had decided, was an occupation worthy of her mettle, and her faith, and of her two loves. She had set about it immediately, with appropriate devotion. Already she had sent the fool concierge to shop for her: disability had its uses.

"I have had a small *attack*, Madame la Pierre"—whether of

the heart, the stomach, or the Russian secret police she did not divulge to the old goat. "I am advised to leave off work for several weeks and rest completely. I am exhausted, madame— there are times when one wishes only to be alone. And here, take this, madame—not like the others, so grasping and over-vigilant." Madame la Pierre took the note in her fist, and looked at just one corner of it before tucking it away at her waist somewhere. "And listen, madame, if anyone asks for me, do me a favour and say I am away. I shall burn no lights on the street side. We women of sensitivity are entitled to a little peace, you agree? But, madame, please, remember who they are, these visitors, and tell me—the gasman, people from the charities—tell me everything. I like to hear that life is going on around me."

The concierge concluded she was mad, no doubt, but there was no madness to her money, and money was what the concierge liked best, and besides, she was mad herself. In a few hours, Ostrakova had become more cunning even than in Moscow. The concierge's husband came up—a brigand himself, worse than the old goat—and, encouraged by further payments, fixed chains to her front door. Tomorrow he would fit a peep-hole, also for money. The concierge promised to receive her mail for her, and deliver it only at certain agreed times—exactly eleven in the morning, six in the evening, two short rings—for money. By forcing open the tiny ventilator in the back lavatory and standing on a chair, Ostrakova could look down into the courtyard whenever she wanted, at whoever came and went. She had sent a note to the warehouse saying she was indisposed. She could not move her double bed, but with pillows and her feather coverlet she made up the divan and positioned it so that it pointed like a torpedo through the open door of the drawing-room at the front door beyond it, and all she had to do was lie on it with her boots aimed at the intruder and shoot down the line of them, and if she didn't blow her own foot off, she would catch him in the first moment of surprise as he attempted to burst in on her: she had worked it out. Her head throbbed and caterwauled, her eyes had a way of darkening over when she moved her head too fast, she had a raging temperature and sometimes she half fainted. But she had worked it out, she had made her dispositions, and till the General or the magician came, it was Moscow all over again. "You're on your own, you old fool," she told herself aloud. "You've nobody to rely on but yourself, so get on with it."

With one photograph of Glikman and one of Ostrakov on the floor beside her, and an icon of the Virgin under the coverlet, Ostrakova embarked upon her first night's vigil, praying steadily to a host of saints, not least of them St. Joseph, that they would send her her redeemer, the magician.

Not a single message tapped to me over the water-pipes, she thought. Not even a guard's insult to wake me up.

12

And still it was the same day; there was no end to it, no bed.
For a while after leaving Mikhel, George Smiley let his legs
lead him, not knowing where, too tired, too stirred to trust
himself to drive, yet bright enough to watch his back, to make
the vague yet sudden turnings that catch would-be followers
off guard. Bedraggled, heavy-eyed, he waited for his mind to
come down, trying to unwind, to step clear of the restless
thrust of his twenty-hour marathon. The Embankment had
him, so did a pub off Northumberland Avenue, probably The
Sherlock Holmes, where he gave himself a large whisky and
dithered over telephoning Stella—was she all right? Deciding
there was no point—he could hardly phone her every night
asking whether she and Villem were alive—he walked again
until he found himself in Soho, which on Saturday nights was
even nastier than usual. Beard Lacon, he thought. Demand
protection for the family. But he had only to imagine the scene
to know the idea was stillborn. If Vladimir was not the Circus's responsibility, then still less could Villem be. And how,
pray, do you attach a team of baby-sitters to a long-distance
Continental lorry driver? His one consolation was that Vladimir's assassins had apparently found what they were looking
for: that they had no other needs. Yet what about the woman
in Paris? What about the writer of the two letters?

Go home, he thought. Twice, from phone-boxes, he made

dummy calls, checking the pavement. Once he entered a cul-de-sac and doubled back, watching for the slurred step, the eye that ducked his glance. He considered taking a hotel room. Sometimes he did that, just for a night's peace. Sometimes his house was too much of a dangerous place for him. He thought of the piece of negative film: time to open the box. Finding himself gravitating by instinct towards his old headquarters at Cambridge Circus, he cut hastily away eastward, finishing by his car again. Confident that he was not observed, he drove to Bayswater, well off his beaten track, but he still watched his mirror intently. From a Pakistani ironmonger who sold everything, he bought two plastic washing-up bowls and a rectangle of commercial glass three and a half inches by five; and from a cash-and-carry chemist not three doors down, ten sheets of Grade 2 resin-coated paper of the same size, and a children's pocket torch with a spaceman on the handle and a red filter that slid over the lens when you pushed a nickel button. From Bayswater, by a painstaking route, he drove to the Savoy, entering from the Embankment side. He was still alone. In the men's cloakroom, the same attendant was on duty, and he even remembered their joke.

"I'm still waiting for it to explode," he said with a smile, handing back the box. "I thought I heard it ticking once or twice, and all."

At his front door the tiny wedges he had put up before his drive to Charlton were still in place. In his neighbours' windows he saw Saturday-evening candle-light and talking heads; but in his own, the curtains were still drawn as he had left them, and in the hall, Ann's pretty little grandmother clock received him in deep darkness, which he hastily corrected.

Dead weary, he nevertheless proceeded methodically.

First he tossed three fire-lighters into the drawing-room grate, lit them, shovelled smokeless coal over them, and hung Ann's indoor clothes-line across the hearth. For an overall he donned an old kitchen apron, tying the cord firmly round his ample midriff for additional protection. From under the stairs he exhumed a pile of green black-out material and a pair of kitchen steps, which he took to the basement. Having blacked out the window, he went upstairs again, unwrapped the box, opened it, and no, it was not a bomb, it was a letter and a packet of battered cigarettes with Vladimir's piece of negative film fed into it. Taking it out, he returned to the basement, put on the red torch, and went to work, though Heaven knows he possessed no photographic flair whatever, and could perfectly well—in theory—have had the job done for him in a fraction of the time, through Lauder Strickland, by the Circus's own photographic section. Or for that matter he could have taken it to any one of half a dozen "tradesmen," as they are known in the jargon: marked collaborators in certain fields who are pledged, if called upon at any time, to drop everything and, asking no questions, put their skills at the service's disposal. One such tradesman actually lived not a stone's throw from Sloane Square, a gentle soul who specialised in wedding photographs. Smiley had only to walk ten minutes and press the man's doorbell and he could have had his prints in half an hour. But he didn't. He preferred instead the inconvenience, as well as imperfection, of taking a contact print in the privacy of his home, while upstairs the telephone rang and he ignored it.

He preferred the trial and error of exposing the negative for too long, then for too little, under the main room light. Of using as a measure the cumbersome kitchen timer, which ticked and grumbled like something from *Coppélia*. He preferred grunting and cursing in irritation and sweating in the dark and wasting at least six sheets of resin-coated paper before the developer in the washing-up bowl yielded an image even half-way passable, which he laid in the rapid fixer for three minutes. And washed it. And dabbed it with a clean teacloth, probably ruining the cloth for good, he wouldn't know. And took it upstairs and pegged it to the clothesline. And for those who like a heavy symbol, it is a matter of history that the fire, despite the fire-lighters, was all but out, since the coal consisted in great measure of damp slag, and that George Smiley had to puff at the flames to prevent it from dying, crouching on all fours for the task. Thus it might have occurred to him—though it didn't, for with his curiosity once more aroused he had put aside his introspective mood—that the action was exactly contrary to Lacon's jangling order to douse the flames and not to fan them.

Next, with the point safely suspended over the carpet, Smiley addressed himself to a pretty marquetry writing-desk in which Ann kept her "things" with embarrassing openness. Such as a sheet of writing-paper on which she had written the one word "Darling" and not continued, perhaps uncertain which darling to write to. Such as book-matches from restaurants he had never been to and letters in handwriting he did not know. From among such painful bric-à-brac he extracted a large Victorian magnifying glass with a mother-of-pearl handle, which she employed for reading clues to crosswords never completed. Thus armed—the sequence of these actions, because of his fatigue, lacked the final edge of logic—he put on a record of Mahler, which Ann had given him, and sat himself in the leather reading chair that was equipped with a mahogany book-rest designed to swivel like a bed tray across the occupant's stomach. Tired to death again, he unwisely allowed his eyes to close while he listened, part to the music, part to the occasional *pat-pat* of the dripping photograph, and part to the grudging crackle of the fire. Waking with a start thirty minutes later, he found the print dry and the Mahler revolving mutely on its turntable.

He stared, one hand to his spectacles, the other slowly rotating the magnifying glass over the print.

The photograph showed a group, but it was not political, nor was it a bathing party, since nobody was wearing a swimming-suit. The group consisted of a quartet, two men and two women, and they were lounging on quilted sofas round a low table laden with bottles and cigarettes. The women were naked and young and pretty. The men, scarcely better covered, were sprawled side by side, and the girls had twined themselves dutifully around their elected mates. The lighting of the photograph was sallow and unearthly, and from the little Smiley knew of such matters he concluded that the negative was made on fast film, for the print was also grainy. Its texture, when he pondered it, reminded him of the photographs one saw too often of terrorists' hostages, except that the four in the photograph were concerned with each other, whereas hostages have a way of staring down the lens as if it were a gun barrel. Still in quest of what he would have called operational intelligence, he passed to the probable position of the camera and decided it must have been high above the subjects. The four appeared to be lying at the centre of a pit with the camera looking down on them. A shadow, very black—a balustrade, or perhaps it was a window-sill, or merely the shoulder of somebody in front—obtruded across the lower foreground. It was as if, despite the vantage point, only half the lens had dared to lift its head above the eye-line.

Here Smiley drew his first tentative conclusion. A step—not a large one, but he had enough large steps on his mind already. A technical step, call it: a modest technical step. The photograph had every mark of being what the trade called *stolen*. And stolen moreover with a view to *burning*, meaning "blackmail." But the blackmail of whom? To what end?

Weighing the problem, Smiley probably fell asleep. The telephone was on Ann's little desk, and it must have rung three or four times before he was aware of it.

"Yes, Oliver?" said Smiley cautiously.

"Ah. George. I tried you earlier. You got back all right, I trust?"

"Where from?" asked Smiley.

Lacon preferred not to answer this question. "I felt I owed

you a call, George. We parted on a sour note. I was brusque. Too much on my plate. I apologise. How are things? You are done? Finished?"

In the background Smiley heard Lacon's daughters squabbling about how much rent was payable on a hotel in Park Place. He's got them for the week-end, thought Smiley.

"I've had the Home Office on the line again, George," Lacon went on in a lower voice, not bothering to wait for his reply. "They've had the pathologist's report and the body may be released. An early cremation is recommended. I thought perhaps if I gave you the name of the firm that is handling things, you might care to pass it on to those concerned. Unattributably, of course. You saw the press release? What did you think of it? I thought it was apt. I thought it caught the tone exactly."

"I'll get a pencil," Smiley said and fumbled in the drawer once more until he found a pear-shaped plastic object with a leather thong, which Ann sometimes wore around her neck. With difficulty he prised it open, and wrote to Lacon's dictation: the firm, the address, the firm again, followed yet again by the address.

"Got it? Want me to repeat it? Or should you read it back to me, make assurance double sure?"

"I think I have it, thank you," Smiley said. Somewhat belatedly, it dawned on him that Lacon was drunk.

"Now, George, we have a date, don't forget. A seminar on marriage with no holds barred. I have cast you as my elder statesman here. There's a very decent steak-house downstairs and I shall treat you to a slap-up dinner while you give me of your wisdom. Have you a diary there? Let's pencil something in."

With dismal foreboding Smiley agreed on a date. After a lifetime of inventing cover stories for every occasion, he still found it impossible to talk his way out of a dinner invitation.

"And you found nothing?" Lacon asked, on a more cautious note. "No snags, hitches, loose ends. It was a storm in a teacup, was it, as we suspected?"

A lot of answers crossed Smiley's mind, but he saw no use to any of them.

"What about the phone bill?" Smiley asked.

"Phone bill? What phone bill? Ah, you mean *his*. Pay it and send me the receipt. No problem. Better still, slip it in the post to Strickland."

"I already sent it to you," said Smiley patiently. "I asked you for a breakdown of traceable calls."

"I'll get on to them at once," Lacon replied blandly. "Nothing else?"

"No. No, I don't think so. Nothing."

"Get some sleep. You sound all in."

"Good night," said Smiley.

With Ann's magnifying glass in his plump fist once more, Smiley went back to his examination. The floor of the pit was carpeted, apparently in white; the quilted sofas were formed in a horseshoe following the line of the drapes that comprised the rear perimeter. There was an upholstered door in the background and the clothes the two men had discarded—jackets, neckties, trousers—were hanging from it with hospital neatness. There was an ashtray on the table and Smiley set to work trying to read the writing round the edge. After much manipulation of the glass he came up with what the lapsed philologist in him described as the asterisk (or putative) form of the letters "A-C-H-T," but whether as a word in their own right—meaning "eight" or "attention," as well as certain other more remote concepts—or as four letters from a larger word, he could not tell. Nor did he at this stage exert himself to find out, preferring simply to store the intelligence in the back of his mind until some other part of the puzzle forced it into play.

Ann rang. Once again, perhaps, he had dozed off, for his recollection ever afterwards was that he did not hear the ring of the phone at all, but simply her voice as he slowly lifted the receiver to his ear: "George, George," as if she had been crying for him a long time, and he had only now summoned the energy or the caring to answer her.

They began their conversation as strangers, much as they began their love-making.

"How are you?" she asked.

"Very well, thank you. How are you? What can I do for you?"

"I meant it," Ann insisted. "How are you? I want to know."

"And I told you I was well."

"I rang you this morning. Why didn't you answer?"

"I was out."

Long silence while she appeared to consider this feeble excuse. The telephone had never been a bother to her. It gave her no sense of urgency.

"Out working?" she asked.

"An administrative thing for Lacon."

"He begins his administration early these days."

"His wife's left him," Smiley said by way of explanation.

No answer.

"You used to say she would be wise to," he went on. "She should get out fast, you used to say, before she became another Civil Service geisha."

"I've changed my mind. He needs her."

"But she, I gather, does not need him," Smiley pointed out, taking refuge in an academic tone.

"Silly woman," said Ann, and another longer silence followed, this time of Smiley's making while he contemplated the sudden unwished-for mountain of choice she had revealed to him.

To be together again, as she sometimes called it.

To forget the hurts, the list of lovers; to forget Bill Haydon, the Circus traitor, whose shadow still fell across her face each time he reached for her, whose memory he carried in him like a constant pain. Bill his friend, Bill the flower of their generation, the jester, the enchanter, the iconoclastic conformer; Bill the born deceiver, whose quest for the ultimate betrayal led him into the Russians' bed, and Ann's. To stage yet another honeymoon, fly away to the South of France, eat the meals, buy the clothes, all the let's pretend that lovers play. And for how long? How long before her smile faded and her eyes grew dull and those mythical relations started needing her to cure their mythical ailments in far-off places?

"Where are you?" he asked.

"Hilda's."

"I thought you were in Cornwall."

Hilda was a divorced woman of some speed. She lived in Kensington, not twenty minutes' walk away.

"So where's Hilda?" he asked when he had come to terms with this intelligence.

"Out."

"All night?"

"I expect so, knowing Hilda. Unless she brings him back."

"Well then, I suppose you must entertain yourself as well as you can without her," he said, but as he spoke he heard her whisper "George."

A profound and vehement fear seized hold of Smiley's heart. He glared across the room at the reading chair and saw the contact photograph still on the book-rest beside her magnifying glass; in a single surge of memory, he reconstructed all the things that had hinted and whispered to him throughout the endless day; he heard the drum-beats of his own past, summoning him to one last effort to externalise and resolve the conflict he had lived by; and he wanted her nowhere near him. *Tell Max that it concerns the Sandman.* Gifted with the clarity that hunger, tiredness, and confusion can supply, Smiley knew for certain she must have no part in what he had to do. He knew—he was barely at the threshold—yet he still knew that it was just possible, against all the odds, that he had been given, in late age, a chance to return to the rained-out contests of his

life and play them after all. If that was so, then no Ann, no
false peace, no tainted witness to his actions should disturb his
lonely quest. He had not known his mind till then. But now
he knew it.

"You mustn't," he said. "Ann? Listen. You mustn't come
here. It has nothing to do with choice. It's to do with practicalities. You mustn't come here." His own words rang strangely
to him.

"Then come here," she said.

He rang off. He imagined her crying, then getting out her
address book to see who from her First Eleven, as she called
them, might console her in his place. He poured himself a neat
whisky, the Lacon solution. He went to the kitchen, forgot
why, and wandered into his study. Soda, he thought. Too late.
Do without. I must have been mad, he thought. I'm chasing
phantoms, there is nothing there. A senile General had a
dream and died for it. He remembered Wilde: the fact that a
man dies for a cause does not make that cause right. A picture
was crooked. He straightened it, too much, too little, stepping
back each time. *Tell him it concerns the Sandman.* He returned
to the reading chair and his two prostitutes, fixing on them
through Ann's magnifying glass with a ferocity that would
have sent them scurrying to their pimps.

Clearly they were from the upper end of their profession, being
fresh-bodied and young and well-groomed. They seemed
also—but perhaps it was coincidence—to be deliberately distinguished from each other by whoever had selected them.
The girl at the left was blonde and fine and even classical in
build, with long thighs and small high breasts. Whereas her
companion was dark-haired and stubby, with spreading hips
and flared features, perhaps Eurasian. The blonde, he recorded,
wore earrings in the shape of anchors, which struck him as odd
because, in his limited experience of women, earrings were
what they took off first. Ann had only to go out of the house

without wearing them for his heart to sink. Beyond that he could think of nothing very clever to say about either girl and so, having swallowed another large gulp of raw Scotch, he transferred his attention to the men, once more—which was where it had been, if he would admit it, ever since he had started looking at the photograph in the first place. Like the girls, they were sharply differentiated from each other, though in the men—since they were a deal older—the differences had the appearance of greater depth and legibility of character. The man supporting the blonde girl was fair and at first sight dull, while the man supporting the dark girl was not merely dark-complexioned but had a Latin, even Levantine, alertness in his features, and an infectious smile that was the one engaging feature of the photograph. The fair man was large and sprawling, the dark man was small and bright enough to be his jester: a little imp of a fellow, with a kind face and flicked-up horns of hair above his ears.

A sudden nervousness—in retrospect perhaps foreboding—made Smiley take the fair man first. It was a time to feel safer with strangers.

The man's torso was burly but not athletic, his limbs ponderous without suggesting strength. The fairness of his skin and hair emphasised his obesity. His hands, one splayed on the girl's flank, the other round her waist, were fatty and artless. Lifting the magnifying glass slowly over the naked chest, Smiley reached the head. By the age of forty, someone clever had written ominously, a man gets the face he deserves. Smiley doubted it. He had known poetic souls condemned to life imprisonment behind harsh faces, and delinquents with the appearance of angels. Nevertheless, it was not an asset as a face, nor had the camera caught it at its most appealing. In terms of character, it appeared to be divided into two parts: the lower, which was pulled into a grin of crude high spirits as, open-mouthed, he addressed something to his male companion; the upper, which was ruled by two small and pallid eyes round which no mirth had gathered at all and no high spirits either, but which seemed to look out of their doughy surroundings with the cold, unblinking blandness of a child. The nose was flat, the hair-style full and mid-European.

Greedy, Ann would have said, who was given to passing absolute judgment on people merely by studying their portraits in the press. Greedy, weak, vicious. Avoid. A pity she had not reached the same conclusion about Haydon, he thought; or not in time.

Smiley returned to the kitchen and rinsed his face, then remembered that he had come to fetch water for his whisky. Settling again in the reading chair, he trained the magnifying glass on the second of the men, the jester. The whisky was keeping him awake, but it was also putting him to sleep. Why doesn't she ring again? he thought. If she rings again, I'll go to her. But in reality his mind was on this second face, because its familiarity disturbed him in much the way that its urgent complicity had disturbed Villem and Ostrakova before him. He gazed at it and his tiredness left him, he seemed to draw energy from it. Some faces, as Villem had suggested this morning, are known to us before we see them; others we see once and remember all our lives; others we see every day and never remember at all. But which was this?

A Toulouse-Lautrec face, Smiley thought, peering in wonder—caught as the eyes slid away to some intense and perhaps erotic distraction. Ann would have taken to him immediately; he had the dangerous edge she liked. A Toulouse-Lautrec face, caught as a stray shard of fair-ground light fired one gaunt and travelled cheek. A hewn face, peaked and jagged, of which the brow and nose and jaw seemed all to have succumbed to the same eroding gales. A Toulouse-Lautrec face, swift and attaching. A waiter's face, never a diner's. With a waiter's anger burning brightest behind a subservient smile. Ann would like that side less well. Leaving the print where it lay, Smiley clambered slowly to his feet in order to keep himself awake, and lumbered round the room, trying to place it, failing, wondering whether it was all imagining. Some people *transmit*, he thought. Some people—you meet them, and they bring you their whole past as a natural gift. Some people are intimacy itself.

At Ann's writing-table he paused to stare at the telephone again. Hers. Hers and Haydon's. Hers and everybody's. Trimline, he thought. Or was it Slimline? Five pounds extra to the Post Office for the questionable pleasure of its outmoded, futuristic lines. *My tart's phone*, she used to call it. *The little warble for my little loves, the loud woo-hoo for my big ones.* He realised it was ringing. Had been ringing a long while, the little warble for the little loves. He put down his glass, still staring at the telephone while it trilled. She used to leave it on the floor among her records when she was playing music, he remembered. She used to lie with it—there, by the fire, over there—one haunch carelessly lifted in case it needed her. When she went to bed, she unplugged it and took it with her, to comfort her in the night. When they made love, he knew he was the surrogate for all the men who hadn't rung. For the First Eleven. For Bill Haydon, even though he was dead.

It had stopped ringing.

What does she do now? Try the Second Eleven? *To be beautiful and Ann is one thing*, she had said to him not long ago; *to be beautiful and Ann's age will soon be another.* And to be ugly and mine is another again, he thought furiously. Taking up the contact print, he resumed, with fresh intensity, his contemplations.

Shadows, he thought. Smudges of light and dark, ahead of us, behind us, as we lurch along our ways. Imp's horns, devil's horns, our shadows so much larger than ourselves. Who is he? Who was he? I met him. I refused to. And if I refused to, how do I know him? He was a supplicant of some kind, a man with something to sell—intelligence, then? Dreams? Wakefully now, he stretched out on the sofa—anything rather than go upstairs to bed—and with the print before him, began plodding through the long galleries of his professional memory, holding the lamp to the half-forgotten portraits of charlatans, gold-markers, fabricators, pedlars, middlemen, hoods, rogues, and occasionally heroes who made up the supporting cast of his multitudinous acquaintance; looking for the one hollowed face that, like a secret sharer, seemed to have swum out of the little contact photograph to board his faltering consciousness. The lamp's beam flitted, hesitated, returned. I was deceived by the darkness, he thought. I met him in the light. He saw a ghastly, neon-lit hotel bedroom—Muzak and tartan wallpaper, and the little stranger perched smiling in a corner, calling him Max. A little ambassador—but representing what cause, what country? He recalled an overcoat with velvet tabs, and hard little hands jerking out their own dance. He recalled the passionate, laughing eyes, the crisp mouth opening and closing swiftly, but he heard no words. He felt a sense of loss—of missing the target—of some other, looming shadow being present while they spoke.

Maybe, he thought. Everything is maybe. Maybe Vladimir was shot by a jealous husband after all, he thought, as the front doorbell screamed at him like a vulture, two rings.

She's forgotten her key as usual, he thought. He was in the hall before he knew it, fumbling with the lock. Her key would do no good, he realised; like Ostrakova, he had chained the door. He fished at the chain, calling "Ann. Hang on!" and feeling nothing in his fingers. He slammed a bolt along its runner and heard the whole house tingle to the echo. "Just coming!" he shouted. "Wait! Don't go!"

He heaved the door wide open, swaying on the threshold, offering his plump face as a sacrifice to the midnight air, to the shimmering black leather figure, crash helmet under his arm, standing before him like death's sentinel.

* * *

"I didn't mean to alarm, sir, I'm sure," the stranger said. Clutching the doorway, Smiley could only stare at his intruder. He was tall and close cropped, and his eyes reflected unrequited loyalty.

"Ferguson, sir. You remember me, sir, Ferguson? I used to manage the transport pool for Mr. Esterhase's lamplighters."

His black motor cycle with its side-car was parked on the kerb behind him, its lovingly polished surfaces glinting under the street lamp.

"I thought lamplighter section had been disbanded," Smiley said, still staring at him.

"So they have, sir. Scattered to the four winds, I regret to say. The camaraderie, the spirit, gone for ever."

"So who employs you?"

"Well no one, sir. Not officially, as you might say. But still on the side of the angels, all the same."

"I didn't know we had any angels."

"No, well that's true, sir. All men are fallible, I do say. Specially these days." He was holding a brown envelope for Smiley to take. "From certain friends of yours, sir, put it that way. I understand it relates to a telephone account you were enquiring about. We get a good response from the Post Office generally, I will say. Good night, sir. Sorry to bother you. Time you had some shut-eye, isn't it? Good men are scarce, I always say."

"Good night," said Smiley.

But still his visitor lingered, like someone asking for a tip. "You did remember me really, didn't you, sir? It was just a lapse, wasn't it?"

"Of course."

There were stars, he noticed as he closed the door. Clear stars swollen by the dew. Shivering, he took out one of Ann's many photograph albums and opened it at the centre. It was her habit, when she liked a snap, to wedge the negative behind it. Selecting a picture of the two of them in Cap Ferrat—Ann

in a bathing-dress, Smiley prudently covered—he removed
the negative and put Vladimir's behind it. He tidied up his
chemicals and equipment and slipped the print into the twelfth
volume of his 1961 Oxford English Dictionary, under Y for
Yesterday. He opened Ferguson's envelope, glanced wearily
at the contents, registered a couple of entries and the word
"Hamburg," and tossed the whole lot into a drawer of the desk.
Tomorrow, he thought; tomorrow is another riddle. He
climbed into bed, never sure, as usual, which side to sleep on.
He closed his eyes and at once the questions bombarded him,
as he knew they would, in crazy uncoordinated salvoes.

Why didn't Vladimir ask for Hector? he wondered for the
hundredth time. Why did the old man liken Esterhase, alias
Hector, to the City banks who took your umbrella away when
it rained?

Tell Max it concerns the Sandman.

To ring her? To throw on his clothes and hurry round
there, to be received as her secret lover, creeping away with
the dawn?

Too late. She was already suited.

Suddenly, he wanted her dreadfully. He could not bear the
spaces round him that did not contain her, he longed for her
laughing trembling body as she cried to him, calling him her
only true, her best lover, she wanted none other, ever. "Women
are lawless, George," she had told him once, when they lay in
rare peace. "So what am I?" he had asked, and she said, "My
law." "So what was Haydon?" he had asked. And she laughed
and said, "My anarchy."

He saw the little photograph again, printed, like the little
stranger himself, in his sinking memory. A small man, with a
big shadow. He remembered Villem's description of the little
figure on the Hamburg ferry, the horns of flicked-up hair, the
grooved face, the warning eyes. *General*, he thought chaoti-
cally, *will you not send me your magic friend once more?*

Maybe. Everything is maybe.

Hamburg, he thought, and got quickly out of bed and put on his dressing-gown. Back at Ann's desk, he set to work seriously to study the breakdown of Vladimir's telephone account, rendered in the copperplate script of a post-office clerk. Taking a sheet of paper, he began jotting down dates and notes.

Fact: in early September, Vladimir receives the Paris letter, and removes it from Mikhel's grasp.

Fact: at about the same date, Vladimir makes a rare and costly trunk-call to Hamburg, operator-dialled, presumably so that he can later claim the cost.

Fact: three days after that again, the eighth, Vladimir accepts a reverse-charge call from Hamburg at a cost of two pounds eighty, origin, duration, and time all given, and the origin is the same number that Vladimir had called three days before.

Hamburg, Smiley thought again, his mind flitting once more to the imp in the photograph. The reversed telephone traffic had continued intermittently till three days ago; nine calls, totalling twenty-one pounds, and all of them from Hamburg to Vladimir. But who was calling him? From Hamburg? Who?

Then suddenly he remembered.

The looming figure in the hotel room, the imp's vast shadow, was Vladimir himself. He saw them standing side by side, both in black coats, the giant and the midget. The vile hotel with Muzak and tartan wallpaper was near Heathrow Airport, where the two men, so ill-matched, had flown in for a conference at the very moment of Smiley's life when his professional identity was crashing round his ears. *Max, we need you. Max, give us the chance.*

Picking up the telephone, Smiley dialled the number in Hamburg, and heard a man's voice at the other end: the one word "Yes," spoken softly in German, followed by a silence.

"I should like to speak to Herr Dieter Fassbender," Smiley said, selecting a name at random. German was Smiley's second language, and sometimes his first.

"We have no Fassbender," said the same voice coolly after a moment's pause, as if the speaker had consulted something in the meantime. Smiley could hear faint music in the background.

"This is Leber," Smiley persisted. "I want to speak to Herr Fassbender urgently. I'm his partner."

There was yet another delay.

"Not possible," said the man's voice flatly after another pause—and rang off.

Not a private house, thought Smiley, hastily jotting down his impressions—the speaker had too many choices. Not an office, for what kind of office plays soft background music and is open at midnight on a Saturday? A hotel? Possibly, but a hotel, if it was of any size, would have put him through to reception, and displayed a modicum of civility. A restaurant? Too furtive, too guarded—and surely they would have announced themselves as they picked up the phone?

Don't force the pieces, he warned himself. Store them away. Patience. But how to be patient when he had so little time?

Returning to bed, he opened a copy of Cobbett's *Rural Rides* and tried to read it while he loosely pondered, among other weighty matters, his sense of *civitas* and how much, or how little, he owed to Oliver Lacon: "Your *duty*, George." Yet who could seriously be Lacon's man? he asked himself. Who could regard Lacon's fragile arguments as Caesar's due?

"Émigrés in, émigrés out. Two legs good, two legs bad," he muttered aloud.

All his professional life, it seemed to Smiley, he had listened to similar verbal antics signalling supposedly great changes in Whitehall doctrine; signalling restraint, self-denial, always another reason for doing nothing. He had watched Whitehall's skirts go up, and come down again, her belts being tightened, loosened, tightened. He had been the witness, or victim—or even reluctant prophet—of such spurious cults as lateralism, parallelism, separatism, operational devolution, and now, if he remembered Lacon's most recent meanderings correctly, of integration. Each new fashion had been hailed as a panacea: "Now we shall vanquish, now the machine will work!" Each had gone out with a whimper, leaving behind it the familiar English muddle, of which, more and more, in retrospect, he saw himself as a lifelong moderator. He had forborne, hoping others would forbear, and they had not. He had toiled in back rooms while shallower men held the stage. They held it still. Even five years ago he would never have admitted to such sentiments. But today, peering calmly into his own heart, Smiley knew that he was unled, and perhaps unleadable; that the only restraints upon him were those of his own reason, and his own humanity. As with his marriage, so with his sense of public service. I invested my life in institutions—he thought without rancour—and all I am left with is myself.

And with Karla, he thought; with my black Grail.

He could not help himself: his restless mind would not leave him alone. Staring ahead of him into the gloom, he imagined he saw Karla standing before him, breaking and reforming in the shifting specks of dark. He saw the brown, attendant eyes appraising him, as once they had appraised him from the darkness of the interrogation cell in Delhi jail a hundred years before: eyes that at first glance were sensitive and seemed to signal companionship; then like molten glass slowly hardened till they were brittle and unyielding. He saw himself stepping onto the dust-driven runway of Delhi airport, and wincing as the Indian heat leapt up at him from the tarmac: Smiley alias Barraclough, or Standfast, or whatever name he had fished from the bag that week—he forgot. A Smiley of the Sixties, anyway, Smiley the commercial traveller, they called him, charged by the Circus to quarter the globe, offering resettlement terms to Moscow Centre officers who were thinking of jumping ship. Centre was holding one of its periodical purges at the time, and the woods were thick with Russian field officers scared of going home. A Smiley who was Ann's husband

and Bill Haydon's colleague, whose last illusions were still intact. A Smiley close to inner crisis all the same, for it was the year Ann lost her heart to a ballet dancer: Haydon's turn was yet to come.

Still in the darkness of Ann's bedroom, he relived the rattling, honking jeep-ride to the jail, the laughing children hanging to the tailboard; he saw the ox-carts and the eternal Indian crowds, the shanties on the brown river bank. He caught the smells of dung and ever-smouldering fires—fires to cook and fires to cleanse; fires to remove the dead. He saw the iron gateway of the old prison engulf him, and the perfectly pressed British uniforms of the warders as they waded knee-deep through the prisoners:

"This way, your honour, sir! Please be good enough to follow us, your excellency!"

One European prisoner, calling himself Gerstmann.

One grey-haired little man with brown eyes and a red calico tunic, resembling the sole survivor of an extinguished priesthood.

With his wrists manacled: "Please undo them, officer, and bring him some cigarettes," Smiley had said.

One prisoner, identified by London as a Moscow Centre agent, and now awaiting deportation to Russia. One little cold war infantryman, as he appeared, who knew—knew for certain—that to be repatriated to Moscow was to face the camps or the firing squad or both; that to have been in enemy hands was in Centre's eyes to have become the enemy himself: to have talked or kept his secrets was immaterial.

Join us, Smiley had said to him across the iron table.

Join us and we will give you life.

Go home and they will give you death.

His hands were sweating—Smiley's, in the prison. The heat was dreadful. Have a cigarette, Smiley had said—here, use my lighter. It was a gold one, smeared by his own damp hands. Engraved. A gift from Ann to compensate some misdemeanour.

To George from Ann with all my love. There are little loves and big loves, Ann liked to say, but when she had composed the inscription she awarded him both kinds. It was probably the only occasion when she did.

Join us, Smiley had said. Save yourself. You have no right to deny yourself survival. First mechanically, then with passion, Smiley had repeated the familiar arguments while his own sweat fell like raindrops onto the table. Join us. You have nothing to lose. Those in Russia who love you are already lost. Your return will make things worse for them, not better. Join us. I beg. Listen to me, listen to the arguments, the philosophy.

And waited, on and on, vainly, for the slightest response to his increasingly desperate entreaty. For the brown eyes to flicker, for the rigid lips to utter a single word through the billows of cigarette smoke—yes, I will join you. Yes, I will agree to be debriefed. Yes, I will accept your money, your promises of resettlement, and the leftover life of a defector. He waited for the freed hands to cease their restless fondling of Ann's lighter, to George from Ann with all my love.

Yet the more Smiley implored him, the more dogmatic Gerstmann's silence became. Smiley pressed answers on him, but Gerstmann had no questions to support them. Gradually Gerstmann's completeness was awesome. He was a man who had prepared himself for the gallows; who would rather die at the hands of his friends than live at the hands of his enemies. Next morning they parted, each to his appointed fate: Gerstmann, against all odds, flew back to Moscow to survive the purge and prosper. Smiley, with a high fever, returned to his Ann and not quite all her love; and to the later knowledge that Gerstmann was none other than Karla himself, Bill Haydon's recruiter, case officer, mentor; and the man who had spirited Bill into Ann's bed—this very bed where he now lay—in order to cloud Smiley's hardening vision of Bill's greater treason, against the service and its agents.

Karla, he thought, as his eyes bored into the darkness, what do you want with me now? *Tell Max it concerns the Sandman.*

Sandman, he thought: why do you wake me up when you are supposed to put me back to sleep?

Still incarcerated in her little Paris apartment, tormented equally in spirit and body, Ostrakova could not have slept even if she had wanted. Not all the Sandman's magic would have helped her. She turned on her side and her squeezed ribs screamed as if the assassin's arms were still flung round them while he prepared to sling her under the car. She tried her back and the pain in her rump was enough to make her vomit. And when she lay on her belly, her breasts became as sore as when she had tried to feed Alexandra in the months before she abandoned her, and she hated them.

It is God's punishment, she told herself, without too much conviction. Not till morning came and she was back in Ostrakov's armchair with his pistol across her knees did the waking world, for an hour or two, release her from her thoughts.

13

The gallery was situated in what the art trade calls the naughty end of Bond Street, and Smiley arrived on its doorstep that Monday morning long before any respectable art dealer was out of bed.

His Sunday had passed in mysterious tranquillity. Bywater Street had woken late, and so had Smiley. His memory had served him while he slept, and it continued to serve him in modest spasms of enlightenment throughout the day. In terms of memory at least, his black Grail had drawn a little nearer. His telephone had not rung once; a slight but persistent hangover had kept him in the contemplative mood. There was a club he belonged to, against his better judgment, near Pall Mall, and he lunched there in imperial solitude on warmed-up steak-and-kidney pie. Afterwards, from the head porter, he had requested his box from the club safe and discreetly abstracted a few illicit possessions, including a British passport in his former workname of Standfast, which he had never quite managed to return to Circus Housekeepers; an international driving licence to match; a sizeable sum of Swiss francs, his own certainly, but equally certainly retained in defiance of the Exchange Control Act. He had them in his pocket now.

The gallery had a dazzling whiteness and the canvases in its armoured glass window were much the same: white upon white, with just the faintest outline of a mosque or St. Paul's

Cathedral--or was it Washington?—drawn with a finger in the thick pigment. Six months ago the sign hanging over the pavement had proclaimed The Wandering Snail Coffee Shop. Today it read "ATELIER BENATI, GOÛT ARABE, PARIS, NEW YORK, MONACO," and a discreet menu on the door proclaimed the new chef's specialties: *"Islam classique-moderne. Conceptual Interior Design. Contracts catered. Sonnez."*

Smiley did as he was bidden, a buzzer screamed, the glass door yielded. A shop-worn girl, ash blonde and half awake, eyed him warily over a white desk.

"If I could just look round," said Smiley.

Her eyes lifted slightly towards an Islamic heaven. "The little red spots mean sold," she drawled, and, having handed him a typed price-list, sighed and went back to her cigarette and her horoscope.

For a few moments Smiley shuffled unhappily from one canvas to another till he stood in front of the girl again.

"If I could have a word with Mr. Benati," he said.

"Oh, I'm afraid Signor Benati is *fully* involved right now. That's the trouble with being international."

"If you could tell him it's Mr. Angel," Smiley proposed in the same diffident style. "If you could just tell him that. Angel, Alan Angel, he does know me."

He sat himself on the S-shaped sofa. It was priced at two thousand pounds and covered in protective cellophane, which squeaked when he moved. He heard her lift the phone and sigh into it.

"Got an angel for you," she drawled, in her pillow-talk voice. "As in Paradise, got it, angel?"

A moment later he was descending a spiral staircase into darkness. He reached the bottom and waited. There was a click and half a dozen picture lights sprang on to empty spaces where no pictures hung. A door opened revealing a small and dapper figure, quite motionless. His full white hair was swept back with bravado. He wore a black suit with a broad stripe and shoes with pantomime buckles. The stripe was definitely too big for him. His right fist was in his jacket pocket, but when he saw Smiley he drew it slowly out and held it at him like a dangerous blade.

"Why, Mr. Angel," he declared in a distinctly mid-European accent, with a sharp glance up the staircase as if to see who was listening. "What pure pleasure, sir. It has been far too long. Come in, please."

They shook hands, each keeping his distance.

"Hullo, Mr. Benati," Smiley said, and followed him to an inner room and through it to a second, where Mr. Benati closed the door and gently leaned his back against it, perhaps as a bulwark against intrusion. For a while after that, neither man spoke at all, each preferring to study the other in a silence bred of mutual respect. Mr. Benati's eyes were brown and they looked nowhere long and nowhere without a purpose. The room had the atmosphere of a sleazy boudoir, with a chaise longue and a pink hand-basin in one corner.

"So how's trade, Toby?" Smiley asked.

Toby Esterhase had a special smile for that question and a special way of tilting his little palm.

"We have been lucky, George. We had a good opening, we had a fantastic summer. Autumn, George"—the gesture again—"autumn I would say is on the slow side. One must live off one's hump actually. Some coffee, George? My girl can make some."

"Vladimir's dead," said Smiley after another longish gap. "Shot dead on Hampstead Heath."

"Too bad. That old man, huh? Too bad."

"Oliver Lacon has asked me to sweep up the bits. As you were the Group's postman, I thought I'd have a word with you."

"Sure," said Toby agreeably.

"You knew, then? About his death?"

"Read it in the papers."

Smiley let his eye wander round the room. There were no newspapers anywhere.

"Any theories about who did it?" Smiley asked.

"At *his* age, George? After a lifetime of disappointments, you might say? No family, no prospects, the Group all washed up—I assumed he had done it himself. Naturally."

Cautiously, Smiley sat himself on the chaise longue and, watched by Toby, picked up a bronze maquette of a dancer that stood on the table.

"Shouldn't this be *numbered* if it's a Degas, Toby?" Smiley asked.

"Degas, that's a very grey area, George. You got to know exactly what you are dealing with."

"But this one is genuine?" Smiley asked, with an air of really wishing to know.

"Totally."

"Would you sell it to me?"

"What's that?"

"Just out of academic interest. Is it for sale? If I offered to buy it, would I be out of court?"

Toby shrugged, slightly embarrassed.

"George, listen, we're talking thousands, know what I mean? Like a year's pension or something."

"When was the last time you had anything to do with Vladi's network, actually, Toby?" Smiley asked, returning the dancer to its table.

Toby digested this question at his leisure.

"Network?" he echoed incredulously at last. "Did I hear network, George?" Laughter in the normal run played little part in Toby's repertoire but now he did manage a small if tense outburst. "You call that crazy Group a network? Twenty cuckoo Balts, leaky like a barn, and they make a *network* already?"

"Well, we have to call them something," Smiley objected equably.

"Something, sure. Just not network, okay?"

"So what's the answer?"

"What answer?"

"When did you last have dealings with the Group?"

"Years ago. Before they sacked me. Years ago."

"How many years?"

"I don't know."

"Three?"

"May be."

"Two?"

"You trying to pin me down, George?"

"I suppose I am. Yes."

Toby nodded gravely as if he had suspected as much all along: "And have you forgotten, George, how it was with us in lamplighters? How overworked we were? How my boys and I played postman to half the networks in the Circus? Remember? In one week how many meetings, pick-ups? Twenty, thirty? In the high season once—forty? Go to Registry, George. If you've got Lacon behind you, go to Registry, draw the file, check the encounter sheets. That way you see exactly. Don't come here trying to trip me up, know what I mean? Degas, Vladimir—I don't like these questions. A friend, an old boss, my own house—it upsets me, okay?"

His speech having run for a deal longer than either of them apparently expected, Toby paused, as if waiting for Smiley to provide the explanation for his loquacity. Then he took a step forward, and turned up his palms in appeal.

"George," he said reproachfully. "George, my name is Benati, okay?"

Smiley seemed to have lapsed into dejection. He was peering gloomily at the stacks of grimy art catalogues strewn over the carpet.

"I'm not called Hector, definitely not Esterhase," Toby insisted. "I got an alibi for every day of the year—hiding from my bank manager. You think I want trouble round my neck? Émigrés, police even? This an interrogation, George?"

"You know me, Toby."

"Sure. I know you, George. You want matches so you can burn my feet?"

Smiley's gaze remained fixed upon the catalogues. "Before Vladimir died—hours before—he rang the Circus," he said. "He said he wanted to give us information."

"But this Vladimir was an old man, George!" Toby insisted—protesting, at least to Smiley's ear, altogether too much. "Listen, there's a lot of guys like him. Big background, been on the payroll too long; they get old, soft in the head, start writing crazy memoirs, seeing world plots everywhere, know what I mean?"

On and on, Smiley contemplated the catalogues, his round head supported on his clenched fists.

"Now why do you say that exactly, Toby?" he asked critically. "I don't follow your reasoning."

"What do you mean, why I say it? Old defectors, old spies, they get a bit cuckoo. They hear voices, talk to the dicky-birds. It's normal."

"Did Vladimir hear voices?"

"How should I know?"

"That's what I was asking you, Toby," Smiley explained reasonably, to the catalogues. "I told you Vladimir claimed to have news for us, and *you* replied to me that he was going soft in the head. I wondered how you knew. About the softness of Vladimir's head. I wondered how recent was your information about his state of mind. And why you pooh-poohed whatever he might have had to say. That's all."

"George, these are very old games you are playing. Don't twist my words. Okay? You want to ask me, ask me. Please. But don't twist my words."

"It wasn't suicide, Toby," Smiley said, still without a glance at him. "It *definitely* wasn't suicide. I saw the body, believe me. It wasn't a jealous husband either—not unless he was equipped with a Moscow Centre murder weapon. What we used to call them, those gun things? 'Inhumane killers,' wasn't it? Well, that's what Moscow used. An inhumane killer."

Smiley once more pondered, but this time—even if it was too late—Toby had the wit to wait in silence.

"You see, Toby, when Vladimir made that phone call to the Circus he demanded *Max*. Myself, in other words. Not his postman, which would have been you. Not Hector. He demanded his vicar, which for better or worse was me. Against all protocol, against all training, and against all precedent. Never done it before. I wasn't there of course, so they offered him a substitute, a silly little boy called Mostyn. It didn't matter because in the event they never met anyway. But can *you* tell me why he didn't ask for Hector?"

"George, I mean *really!* These are shadows you are chasing! Should I know why he *doesn't* ask for me? We are responsible for the omissions of others, suddenly? What is this?"

"Did you quarrel with him? Would that be a reason?"

"Why should I quarrel with Vladimir? He was being dramatic, George. That's how they are, these old guys when they retire." Toby paused as if to imply that Smiley himself was not above these foibles. "They get bored, they miss the action, they want stroking, so they make up some piece of mickey-mouse."

"But not all of them get shot, do they, Toby? That's the worry, you see: the cause and effect. Toby quarrels with Vladimir one day, Vladimir gets shot with a Russian gun the next. In police terms that's what one calls an embarrassing chain of events. In our terms too, actually."

"George, are you crazy? What the hell is quarrel? I told you: I never quarrel with the old man in my life!"

"Mikhel said you did."

"Mikhel? You go talking to *Mikhel?*"

"According to Mikhel, the old man was very bitter about you. 'Hector is no good,' Vladimir kept telling him. He quoted Vladimir's words exactly. 'Hector is no good.' Mikhel was very surprised. Vladimir used to think highly of you. Mikhel couldn't think what had been going on between the two of you that could produce such a severe change of heart. 'Hector is no good.' *Why* weren't you any good, Toby? What happened that made Vladimir so passionate about you? I'd like to keep it away from the police if I could, you see. For all our sakes."

But the fieldman in Toby Esterhase was by now fully awake, and he knew that interrogations, like battles, are never won but only lost.

"George, this is absurd," he declared with pity rather than hurt. "I mean it's so obvious you are fooling me. Know that? Some old man builds castles in the air, so you want to go to the police already? Is that what Lacon is hiring you for? Are these the bits you are sweeping up? George?"

This time, the long silence seemed to create some resolution in Smiley, and when he spoke again it was as if he had not much time left. His tone was brisk, even impatient.

"Vladimir came to see you. I don't know when but within the last few weeks. You met him or you talked to him over the phone—call-box to call-box, whatever the technique was. He asked you to do something for him. You refused. That's why he demanded Max when he rang the Circus on Friday night. He'd had Hector's answer already and it was no. That's also why Hector was 'no good.' You turned him down."

This time Toby made no attempt to interrupt.

"And if I may say so, you're scared," Smiley resumed, studiously not looking at the lump in Toby's jacket pocket. "You know enough about who killed Vladimir to think they might kill you too. You even thought it possible I wasn't the right Angel." He waited, but Toby didn't rise. His tone softened. "*You* remember what we used to say at Sarratt, Toby—about fear being information without the cure? How we should respect it? Well, I respect yours, Toby. I want to know more about it. Where it came from. Whether I should share it. That's all."

Still at the door, his little palms pressed flat against the panels, Toby Esterhase studied Smiley most attentively and without the smallest decline in his composure. He even contrived to suggest by the depth and question of his glance that his concern was now for Smiley rather than himself. Next, in line with this solicitous approach, he took a pace, then another, into the room—but tentatively, and somewhat as if he were visiting an ailing friend in hospital. Only then, with a passable imitation of a bedside manner, did he respond to Smiley's accusations with a most perceptive question, one that Smiley himself, as it happened, had been deliberating in some depth over the last two days.

"George. Kindly answer me something. Who is speaking here actually? Is it George Smiley? Is it Oliver Lacon? Mikhel? Who is speaking, please?" Receiving no immediate answer, he continued his advance as far as a grimy satin-covered stool where he perched himself with a catlike trimness, one hand over each knee. "Because for an official fellow, George, you are asking some pretty damn unofficial questions, it strikes me. You are taking rather an unofficial attitude, I think."

"You saw Vladimir and you spoke to him. What happened?" Smiley asked, quite undeflected by this challenge. "You tell me that, and I'll tell you who is speaking here."

In the farthest corner of the ceiling there was a yellowed patch of glass about a metre square and the shadows that played over it were the feet of passers-by in the street. For some reason Toby's eyes had fixed on this strange spot and he seemed to read his decision there, like an instruction flashed on a screen.

"Vladimir put up a distress rocket," Toby said in exactly the same tone as before, of neither conceding nor confiding. Indeed, by some trick of tone or inflection, he even managed to bring a note of warning to his voice.

"Through the Circus?"

"Through friends of mine," said Toby.

"When?"

Toby gave a date. Two weeks ago. A crash meeting. Smiley asked where it took place.

"In the Science Museum," Toby replied with new-found confidence. "The café on the top floor, George. We drank coffee, admired the old aeroplanes hanging from the roof. You going to report all this to Lacon, George? Feel free, okay? Be my guest. I got nothing to hide."

"And he put the proposition?"

"Sure. He put me a proposition. He wanted me to do a lamplighter job. To be his camel. That was our joke, back in the old Moscow days, remember? To collect, carry across the desert, to deliver. 'Toby, I got no passport. *Aidez-moi. Mon ami, aidez-moi.*' You know how he talked. Like de Gaulle. We used to call him that—'the other General.' Remember?"

"Carry what?"

"He was not precise. It was documentary, it was small, no concealment was needed. This much he tells me."

"For somebody putting out feelers, he seems to have told you a lot."

"He was asking a hell of a lot too," said Toby calmly, and waited for Smiley's next question.

"And the where?" Smiley asked. "Did Vladimir tell you that too?"

"Germany."

"Which one?"

"Ours. The north of it."

"Casual encounter? Dead-letter boxes? Live? What sort of meeting?"

"On the fly. I should take a train ride. From Hamburg north. The hand-over to be made on the train, details on acceptance."

"And it was to be a private arrangement. No Circus, no Max?"

"For the time being, very private, George."

Smiley picked his words with tact. "And the compensation for your labours?"

A distinct scepticism marked Toby's answer: "If we get the document—that's what he called it, okay? Document. If we get the document, and the document is genuine, which he swore it was, we win immediately a place in Heaven. We take first the document to Max, tell Max the story. Max would know its meaning, Max would know the crucial importance—of the document. Max would reward us. Gifts, promotion, medals, Max will put us in the House of Lords. Sure. Only problem was, Vladimir didn't know Max was on the shelf and the Circus has joined the Boy Scouts."

"Did he know that Hector was on the shelf?"

"Fifty-fifty, George."

"What does that mean?" Then, with a "never mind," Smiley cancelled his own question again and lapsed into prolonged thought.

"George, you want to drop this line of enquiry," Toby said earnestly. "That is my strong advice to you, abandon it," he said, and waited.

Smiley might not have heard. Momentarily shocked, he seemed to be pondering the scale of Toby's error.

"The point is, you sent him packing," he muttered, and remained staring into space. "He appealed to you and you slammed the door in his face. How could you do that, Toby? You of all people?"

The reproach brought Toby furiously to his feet, which was perhaps what it was meant to do. His eyes lit up, his cheeks coloured, the sleeping Hungarian in him was wide awake.

"And you want to hear why, maybe? You want to know why I told him, 'Go to hell, Vladimir. Leave my sight, please, you make me sick'? You want to know who his connect is out there—this magic guy in North Germany with the crock of gold that's going to make millionaires of us overnight, George—you want to know his full identity? Remember the name Otto Leipzig, by any chance? Holder many times of our Creep of the Year award? Fabricator, intelligence pedlar, confidence man, sex maniac, pimp, also various sorts of criminal? Remember *that* great hero?"

Smiley saw the tartan walls of the hotel again, and the dreadful hunting prints of Jorrocks in full cry; he saw the two black-coated figures, the giant and the midget, and the General's huge mottled hand resting on the tiny shoulder of his protégé. "*Max, here is my good friend Otto. I have brought him to tell his own story.*" He heard the steady thunder of the planes landing and taking off at Heathrow Airport.

"Vaguely," Smiley replied equably. "Yes, vaguely I do remember an Otto Leipzig. Tell me about him. I seem to remember he had rather a *lot* of names. But then so do we all, don't we?"

"About two hundred, but Leipzig he ended up with. Know why? Leipzig in East Germany; he liked the jail there. He was that kind of crazy joker. Remember the stuff he peddled, by any chance?" Believing he had the initiative, Toby stepped boldly forward and stood over the passive Smiley while he talked down at him: "George, do you not even remember the incredible and total bilge which year for year that creep would push out under fifteen different source names to our West European stations, mainly German? Our expert on the new Estonian order? Our top source on Soviet arms shipments out of Leningrad? Our inside ear at Moscow Centre, our principal Karla-watcher, even?" Smiley did not stir. "How he took our Berlin resident alone for two thousand Deutschmarks for a rewrite from *Stern* magazine? How he foxed that old General, worked on him like a sucking-leech, time and again—'us fellow Balts'—that line? 'General, I just got the Crown jewels for you—only trouble, I don't have the air fare'? Jesus!"

"It wasn't *all* fabrication, though, was it, Toby?" Smiley objected mildly. "Some of it, I seem to remember—in certain areas, at least—turned out to be rather good stuff."

"Count it on one finger."

"His Moscow Centre material, for instance. I don't remember that we faulted him on that, ever?"

"Okay! So Centre gave him some decent chicken-feed occasionally, so he could pass us the other crap! How else does anyone play a double, for God's sake?"

Smiley seemed about to argue this point, then changed his mind.

"I see," he said finally, as if overruled. "Yes, I see what you mean. A plant."

"Not a plant, a creep. A little of this, a little of that. A dealer. No principles. No standards. Work for anyone who sweetens his pie."

"I take the point," said Smiley gravely, in the same diminished tone. "And of course he settled in North Germany, too, didn't he? Up towards Travemünde somewhere."

"Otto Leipzig never settled anywhere in his life," said Toby with contempt. "George, that guy's a drifter, a total bum. Dresses like he was a Rothschild, owns a cat and a bicycle. Know what his last job was, this great spy? Night-watchman in some lousy Hamburg cargo house somewhere! Forget him."

"And he had a partner," Smiley said, in the same tone of innocent reminiscence. "Yes, that comes back to me too. An immigrant, an East German."

"Worse than East German: Saxon. Name of Kretzschmar, first name was Claus. Claus with a 'C,' don't ask me why. I mean these guys have got no logic at all. Claus was also a creep. They stole together, pimped together, faked reports together."

"But that was long ago, Toby," Smiley put in gently.

"Who cares? It was a perfect marriage."

"Then I expect it didn't last," said Smiley, in an aside to himself.

But perhaps Smiley had for once overdone his meekness; or perhaps Toby simply knew him too well. For a warning light had come up in his swift, Hungarian eye, and a tuck of suspicion formed on his bland brow. He stood back and, contemplating Smiley, passed one hand thoughtfully over his immaculate white hair.

"George," he said. "Listen, who are you fooling, okay?"

Smiley did not speak, but lifted the Degas, and turned it round, then put it down.

"George, listen to me once. Please! Okay, George? Maybe I give you once a lecture."

Smiley glanced at him, then looked away.

"George, I owe you. You got to hear me. So you pulled me from out the gutter once in Vienna when I was a stinking kid. I was a Leipzig. A bum. So you got me my job with the Circus. So we had a lot of times together, stole some horses. You remember the first rule of retirement, George? 'No moonlighting. No fooling with loose ends. No private enterprise ever'? You remember who preached this rule? At Sarratt? In the corridors? George Smiley did. 'When it's over, it's over. Pull down the shutters, go home!' So now what do you want to do, suddenly? Play kiss-kiss with an old crazy General who's dead but won't lie down and a five-sided comedian like Otto Leipzig! What is this? The last cavalry charge on the Kremlin suddenly? We're over, George. We got no licence. They don't want us any more. Forget it." He hesitated, suddenly embarrassed. "So okay, Ann gave you a bad time with Bill Haydon. So there's Karla, and Karla was Bill's big daddy in Moscow. George, I mean this gets very crude, know what I mean?"

His hands fell to his sides. He stared at the still figure before him. Smiley's eyelids were nearly closed. His head had dropped forward. With the shifting of his cheeks deep crevices had appeared round his mouth and eyes.

"We never faulted Leipzig's reports on Moscow Centre," Smiley said, as if he hadn't heard the last part. "I remember distinctly that we never faulted them. Nor on Karla. Vladimir trusted him implicitly. On the Moscow stuff, so did we."

"George, who ever faulted a report on Moscow Centre?

Please? So okay, once in a while we got a defector, he tells you: 'This thing is crap and that thing is maybe true.' So where's the collateral? Where's the hard base, you used to say? Some guy feeds you a story: 'Karla just built a new spy nursery in Siberia.' So who's to say he didn't? Keep it vague enough, you can't lose."

"That was why we put up with him," Smiley went on, as if he hadn't heard. "Where the Soviet service was involved, he played a straight game."

"George," said Toby softly, shaking his head. "You got to wake up. The crowds have all gone home."

"Will you tell me the rest of it now, Toby? Will you tell me exactly what Vladimir said to you? Please?"

So in the end, as a reluctant gift of friendship, Toby told it as Smiley asked, straight out, with a frankness that was like defeat.

The maquette that might have been by Degas portrayed a ballerina with her arms above her head. Her body was curved backward and her lips were parted in what might have been ecstasy and there was no question but that, fake or genuine, she bore an uncomfortable if superficial resemblance to Ann. Smiley had taken her in his hands again and was slowly turning her, gazing at her this way and that with no clear appreciation. Toby was back on his satin stool. In the ceiling window, the shadowed feet walked jauntily.

Toby and Vladimir had met in the café of the Science Museum on the aeronautical floor, Toby repeated. Vladimir was in a state of high excitement and kept clutching Toby's arm, which Toby didn't like; it made him conspicuous. Otto Leipzig had managed the impossible, Vladimir kept saying. It was the big one, the chance in a million, Toby; Otto Leipzig had landed the one Max had always dreamed of, "the full settlement of all our claims," as Vladimir had put it. When Toby asked him somewhat acidly what claims he had in mind, Vladimir either wouldn't or couldn't say: "Ask Max," he insisted. "If you do not believe me, ask Max, tell Max it is the big one."

"So what's the deal?" Toby had asked—knowing, he said, that where Otto Leipzig was concerned the bill came first and the goods a long, long way behind. "How much does he want, the great hero?"

Toby confessed to Smiley that he had found it hard to conceal his scepticism—"which put a bad mood on the meeting from the start." Vladimir outlined the terms. Leipzig had the story, said Vladimir, but he also had certain material proofs that the story was true. There was first a document, and the document was what Leipzig called a *Vorspeise*, or appetizer. There was also a second proof, a letter, held by Vladimir. There was then the story itself, which would be given by other materials, which Leipzig had entrusted to safe keeping. The document showed how the story was obtained, the materials themselves were incontrovertible.

"And the subject?" Smiley asked.

"Not revealed," Toby replied shortly. "To Hector, not revealed. Get Max, and okay—then Vladimir reveals the subject. But Hector for the time being got to shut up and run the errands."

For a moment Toby appeared about to launch upon a second speech of discouragement. "George, I mean look here, the old boy was just totally cuckoo," he began. "Otto Leipzig was taking him a complete ride." Then he saw Smiley's expression, so inward and inaccessible, and contented himself instead with a repetition of Otto Leipzig's totally outrageous demands.

"The document to be taken personally to Max by Vladimir, Moscow Rules at all points, no middle men, no correspondence. The preparations they made already on the telephone—"

"Telephone between London and Hamburg?" Smiley interrupted, suggesting by his tone that this was new and unwelcome information.

"They used word code, he tells me. Old pals, they know

how to fox around. But not with the proof, says Vladi; with the proof there's no foxing at all. No phones, no mails, no trucks, they got to have a camel, period. Vladi's security-crazy, okay, this we know already. From now on, only Moscow Rules apply."

Smiley remembered his own phone call to Hamburg of Saturday night, and wondered again what kind of establishment Otto Leipzig had been using as his telephone exchange.

"Once the Circus had declared its interest," Toby continued, "they pay a down payment to Otto Leipzig of five thousand Swiss for an audition fee. George! Five thousand Swiss! For openers! Just to be in the game! Next—George, you got to hear this—next, Otto Leipzig to be flown to a safe house in England for the audition. George, I mean I never heard such craziness. You want the rest? If, following the audition, the Circus wants to buy the material itself—you want to hear how much?"

Smiley did.

"Fifty grand Swiss. Maybe you want to sign me a cheque?"

Toby waited for a cry of outrage but none came.

"All for Leipzig?"

"Sure. They were Leipzig's terms. Who else would be so cuckoo?"

"What did Vladimir ask for himself?"

A small hesitation. "Nothing," said Toby reluctantly. Then, as if to leave that point behind, set off on a fresh wave of indignation.

"*Basta.* So now all Hector got to do is fly to Hamburg at his own expense, take a train north and play rabbit for some crazy entrapment game that Otto Leipzig has lined up for himself with the East Germans, the Russians, the Poles, the Bulgarians, the Cubans, and also no doubt, being modern, the Chinese. I said to him—George, listen to me—I said to him: 'Vladimir, old friend, excuse me, pay attention to me once. Tell me what in life is so important that the Circus pays five thousand Swiss from its precious reptile fund for one lousy audition with Otto Leipzig? Maria Callas never got so much and believe me she sang a damn lot better than Otto does.' He's holding my arm. Here." Demonstrating, Toby grasped his own biceps. "Squeezing me like I am an orange. That old boy had some strength still, believe me. 'Fetch the document for me, Hector.' He is speaking Russian. That's a very quiet place, that museum. Everyone has stopped to listen to him. I had a bad feeling. He is weeping. 'For the sake of God, Hector, I am an old man. I got no legs, no passport, no one I can trust but Otto Leipzig. Go to Hamburg and fetch the document. When he sees the proof, Max will believe me, Max has faith.' I try to console him, make some hints. I tell him émigrés are bad news these days, change of policy, new government. I advise him, 'Vladimir, go home, play some chess. Listen, I come round to the library one day, have a game maybe.' Then he says to me: 'Hector, I began this. It was me sent the order to Otto Leipzig telling him to explore the position. Me who sent the money to him for the groundwork, all I had.' Listen, that was an old, sad man. Past it."

Toby made a pause but Smiley did not stir. Toby stood up, went to a cupboard, poured two glasses of an extremely indifferent sherry, and put one on the table beside the Degas maquette. He said "Cheers" and drank back his glass, but still Smiley did not budge. His inertia rekindled Toby's anger.

"So I killed him, George, okay? It's Hector's fault, okay? Hector is personally and totally responsible for the old man's death. That's all I need." He flung out both hands, palms upward. "George! Advise me! George, for this story I should go to Hamburg, unofficial, no cover, no baby-sitter? Know where the East German border is up there? From Lübeck two kilometres? Less? Remember? In Travemünde you got to stay on the left of the street or you've defected by mistake." Smiley did not laugh. "And in the unlikely event I come back, I should call up George Smiley, go round to Saul Enderby with him, knock on the back door like a bum—'Let us in, Saul, please, we got hot information totally reliable from Otto Leipzig, only five grand Swiss for an audition concerning matters totally forbidden under the Boy Scout laws'? I should do this, George?"

From an inside pocket, Smiley drew a battered packet of English cigarettes. From the packet he drew the home-made contact print, which he passed silently across the table for Toby to look at.

"Who's the second man?" Smiley asked.

"I don't know."

"Not his partner, the Saxon, the man he stole with in the old days? Kretzschmar?"

Shaking his head, Toby Esterhase went on looking at the picture.

"So who's the second man?" Smiley asked again.

Toby handed back the photograph. "George, pay attention to me, please," he said quietly. "You listening?"

Smiley might have been and might not. He was threading the print back into the cigarette packet.

"People forge things like that these days, you know that? That's very easy done, George. I want to put a head on another guy's shoulders, I got the equipment, it takes me maybe two minutes. You're not a technical guy, George, you don't understand these matters. You don't buy photographs from Otto Leipzig, you don't buy Degas from Signor Benati, follow me?"

"Do they forge negatives?"

"Sure. You forge the print, then you photograph it, make a new negative—why not?"

"Is this a forgery?" Smiley asked.

Toby hesitated a long time. "I don't think so."

"Leipzig travelled a lot. How did we raise him if we needed him?" Smiley asked.

"He was strictly arm's length. Totally."

"So how did we raise him?"

"For a routine rendezvous the *Hamburger Abendblatt* marriage ads. Petra, aged twenty-two, blonde, petite, former singer—that crap. George, listen to me. Leipzig is a dangerous bum with very many lousy connections, mostly still in Moscow."

"What about emergencies? Did he have a house, a girl?"

"He never had a house in his life. For crash meetings, Claus Kretzschmar played key-holder. George, for God's sake, hear me once—"

"So how did we reach Kretzschmar?"

"He's got a couple of night-clubs. Cat houses. We left a message there."

A warning buzzer rang and from upstairs they heard the sound of voices raised in argument.

"I'm afraid Signor Benati has a conference in Florence today," the blonde girl was saying. "That's the trouble with being international."

But the caller refused to believe her; Smiley could hear the rising tide of his protest. For a fraction of a second Toby's brown eyes lifted sharply to the sound; then with a sigh he pulled open a wardrobe and drew out a grimy raincoat and a brown hat, despite the sunlight in the ceiling window.

"What's it called?" Smiley asked. "Kretzschmar's night-club—what's it called?"

"The Blue Diamond. George, don't do it, okay? Whatever it is, drop it. So the photo is genuine, then what? The Circus has a picture of some guy rolling in the snow courtesy of Otto Leipzig. You think that's a gold-mine suddenly? You think that makes Saul Enderby horny?"

Smiley looked at Toby, and remembered him, and remembered also that in all the years they had known each other and worked together, Toby had never once volunteered the truth, that information was money to him; even when he counted it valueless, he never threw it away.

"What else did Vladimir tell you about Leipzig's information?" Smiley asked.

"He said it was some old case come alive. Years of investment.

Some crap about the Sandman. He was a child again, remembering fairy tales, for God's sake. See what I mean?"

"What about the Sandman?"

"To tell you it concerned the Sandman. That's all. The Sandman is making a legend for a girl. Max will understand. George, he was weeping, for Christ's sake. He'd have said anything that came into his head. He wanted the action. He was an old spy in a hurry. You used to say they were the worst."

Toby was at the far door, already half-way gone. But he turned and came back despite the approaching clamour from upstairs, because something in Smiley's manner seemed to trouble him—"a definitely harder stare," he called it afterward, "like I'd completely insulted him somehow."

"George? George, this is Toby, remember? If you don't get the hell out of here, that guy upstairs will sequester you in part-payment, hear me?"

Smiley hardly did. "Years of investment and the Sandman was making a legend for a girl?" he repeated. "What else? Toby, what else!"

"He was behaving like a crazy man again."

"The General was? Vladi was?"

"No, the Sandman. George, listen. 'The Sandman is behaving like a crazy man again, the Sandman is making a legend for a girl, Max will understand.' *Finito*. The total garbage. I've told you every word. Go easy now, hear me?"

From upstairs, the sounds of argument grew still louder. A door slammed, they heard footsteps stamping towards the staircase. Toby gave Smiley's arm a last, swift pat.

"Goodbye, George. You want a Hungarian baby-sitter some day, call me. Hear that? You're messing around with a creep like Otto Leipzig, then you better have a creep like Toby look after you. Don't go out alone nights, you're too young."

Climbing the steel ladder back to the gallery, Smiley all but knocked over an irate creditor on his way down. But this was not important to Smiley; neither was the insolent sigh of the ash-blonde girl as he stepped into the street. What mattered was that he had put a name to the second face in the photograph; and to the name, the story, which like an undiagnosed pain had been nagging at his memory for the last thirty-six hours—as Toby might have said, the story of a legend.

And that, indeed, is the dilemma of those would-be historians who are concerned, only months after the close of the affair, to chart the interplay of Smiley's knowledge and his actions. Toby told him this much, they say, so he did that much. Or: if so-and-so had not occurred, then there would have been no resolution. Yet the truth is more complex than this, and far less handy. As a patient tests himself on coming out of the anaesthetic—this leg, that leg, do the hands still close and open?—so Smiley by a succession of cautious movements grew into his own strength of body and mind, probing the motives of his adversary as he probed his own.

14

He was driving on a high plateau and the plateau was above the tree-line because the pines had been planted low in the valley's cleft. It was early evening of the same day and in the plain the first lights were pricking the wet gloom. On the horizon lay the city of Oxford, lifted by ground mist, an academic Jerusalem. The view from that side was new to him and increased his sense of unreality, of being conveyed rather than determining his own journey; of being in the grasp of thoughts that were not his to command. His visit to Toby Esterhase had fallen, arguably, within the crude guide-lines of Lacon's brief; but this journey, he knew, led for better or for worse to the forbidden province of his secret interest. Yet he was aware of no alternative, and wanted none. Like an archaeologist who has delved all his life in vain, Smiley had begged for one last day, and this was it.

At first he had watched his rear-view mirror constantly, how the familiar motor cycle had hung behind him like a gull at sea. But when he left the last roundabout the man called Ferguson had not followed him, and when he pulled up to read the map nothing passed him either; so either they had guessed his destination or, for some arcane reason of procedure, they had forbidden their man to cross the county border. Sometimes, as he drove, a trepidation gripped him. Let her be, he thought. He had heard things; not much, but enough to guess the rest.

Let her be, let her find her own peace where she can. But he knew that peace was not his to give, that the battle he was involved in must be continuous to have any meaning at all.

The kennel sign was like a painted grin: "MERRILEE BOARD-ING ALL PETS WELCOME EGGS." A daubed yellow dog wearing a top hat pointed one paw down a cart-track; the track, when he took it, led so steeply downward that it felt like a free fall. He passed a pylon and heard the wind howling in it; he entered the plantation. First came the young trees; then the old ones dark-ened over him and he was in the Black Forest of his German childhood heading for some unrevealed interior. He switched on his headlights, rounded a steep bend, and another, and a third, and there was the cabin much as he had imagined it—her *dacha*, as she used to call it. Once she had had the house in Oxford and the *dacha* as a place away from it. Now there was only the *dacha;* she had quitted towns for ever. It stood in its own clear-ing of tree trunks and trodden mud, with a ramshackle veranda and a wood-shingle roof and a tin chimney with smoke coming out of it. The clapboard walls were blackened with creosote, a galvanised iron feed-tub almost blocked the front porch. On a bit of lawn stood a home-made bird-table with enough bread to feed an ark, and dotted round the clearing, like allotment huts, stood the asbestos sheds and wire runs that held the chickens and all the pets welcome without discrimination.

Karla, he thought. What a place to look for you.

He parked, and his arrival set loose a bedlam as dogs sobbed in torment and thin walls thundered to desperate bodies. He walked to the house, carrier-bag in hand, the bottles bumping against his legs. Above the din he heard his own feet rattling up the six steps of the veranda. A notice on the door read: "If OUT do NOT leave pets on spec." And underneath, seem-ingly added in a fury, "No bloody monkeys."

The bell-pull was a donkey's tail in plastic. He reached for it but the door had already opened and a frail pretty woman peered at him from the interior darkness of the cabin. Her eyes were timid and grey, she had that period English beauty which had once been Ann's: accepting, and grave. She saw him and stopped dead. "Oh, Lord," she whispered. "Gosh." Then looked downward at her brogues, brushing back her forelock with one finger, while the dogs barked themselves hoarse at him from behind their wire.

"I'm sorry, Hilary," said Smiley, with great gentleness. "It's only for an hour, I promise. That's all it is. An hour."

A deep, masculine voice, very slow, issued out of the darkness behind her. "What is it, Hils?" growled the voice. "Bogweevil, budgie, or giraffe?"

The question was followed by a slow thud like the movement of cloth over something hollow.

"It's human, Con," Hilary called over her shoulder, and went back to looking at her brogues.

"*She* human or the other thing?" the voice demanded.

"It's George, Con. Don't be cross, Con."

"*George?* Which *George?* George the Lorry, who waters my coal, or George the Meat, who poisons my dogs?"

"It's just some questions," Smiley assured Hilary in the same deeply compassionate tone. "An old case. Nothing momentous, I promise you."

"It doesn't matter, George," Hilary said, still looking downward. "Honestly. It's fine."

"Stop all that flirting!" the voice from inside the house commanded. "Unhand her, whoever you are!"

As the thudding drew gradually nearer, Smiley leaned past Hilary and spoke into the doorway. "Connie, it's me," he said. And once again, his voice did everything possible to signal his goodwill.

First came the puppies—four of them, probably whippets—in a fast pack. Next came a mangy old mongrel with barely life enough to reach the veranda and collapse. Then the door shuddered open to its fullest extent and revealed a mountainous woman propped crookedly between two thick wooden crutches, which she did not seem to hold. She had white hair clipped short as a man's, and watery, very shrewd eyes that held him fiercely in their stare. So long was her examination of him, in fact, so leisured and minute—his earnest face, his baggy suit, the plastic carrier-bag dangling from his left hand, his whole posture of waiting meekly to be admitted—that it gave her an almost regal authority over him, to which her stillness, and her troubled breathing, and her crippled state only contributed greater strength.

"Oh, my giddy aunts," she announced, still studying him, and blew out a stream of air. "Jumping whatevers. Damn you, George Smiley. Damn you and all who sail in you. Welcome to Siberia."

Then she smiled, and her smile was so sudden, and fresh, and little-girl, that it almost washed away the long questioning that had gone before it.

"Hullo, Con," said Smiley.

Her eyes, notwithstanding her smile, stayed on him still. They had the pallor of a new-born baby's.

"Hils," she said, at last. "I said *Hils!*"

"Yes, Con?"

"Go feed the doggie-wogs, darling. When you've done that, feed the filthy chickadees. Glut the brutes. When you've done that, mix tomorrow's meal, and when you've done *that*, bring me the humane killer so that I can dispatch this interfering whatsit to an early Paradise. George, follow me."

Hilary smiled but seemed unable to move till Connie softly pushed an elbow into her to get her going.

"Hoof it, darling. There's nothing he can do to you now. He's shot his bolt, and so have you, and, God knows, so have I."

It was a house of day and night at once. At the centre, on a pine table littered with the remains of toast and Marmite, an old oil lamp shed a globe of yellow light, intensifying the darkness round it. The gleam of blue rain clouds, streaked by sunset, filled the far French windows. Gradually, as Smiley followed Connie's agonisingly slow procession, he realised that this one wooden room was all there was. For an office, they had the roll-top desk laden with bills and flea powder; for a bedroom the brass double bedstead with its heap of stuffed toy animals lying like dead soldiers between the pillows; for a drawing-room Connie's rocking-chair and a crumbling wicker sofa; for a kitchen a gas ring fired from a cylinder; and for decoration the unclearable litter of old age.

"Connie's not coming back, George," she called as she hobbled ahead of him. "Wild horses can puff and blow their snivelling hearts out, the old fool has hung up her boots for good." Reaching her rocking-chair, she began the ponderous business of turning herself round until she had her back to it. "So if that's what you're after, you can tell Saul Enderby to shove it up his smoke and pipe it." She held out her arms to him and he thought she wanted him to kiss her. "Not *that*, you sex maniac. Batten on to my hands!"

He did so, and lowered her into the rocking-chair.

"That's not what I came for, Con," said Smiley. "I'm not trying to woo you away, I promise."

"For one good reason, she's dying," she announced firmly, not seeming to notice his interjection. "The old fool's for the shredder, and high time too. The leech tries to fool me, of course. That's because he's a funk. Bronchitis. Rheumatism. Touch of the weather. Balls, the lot of it. It's death, that's what I'm suffering from. The systematic encroachment of the big D. Is that booze you're toting in that bag?"

"Yes. Yes, it is," said Smiley.

"Goody. Let's have lots. How's the demon Ann?"

On the draining-board, amid a permanent pile of washing-up, he found two glasses, and half filled them.

"Flourishing, I gather," he replied.

Reciprocating, by his own kindly smile, her evident pleasure at his visit, he held out a glass to her and she grappled it between her mittened hands.

"You gather," she echoed. "Wish you *would* gather. Gather her up for good is what you should do. Or else put powdered glass in her coffee. All right, what are you after?" she demanded, all in the same breath. "I never knew you yet to do anything without a reason. Mud in your eye."

"And in yours, Con," said Smiley.

To drink, she had to lean her whole trunk towards the glass. And as her huge head lurched into the glare of the lamplight, he saw—he knew from too much experience—that she was telling no less than the truth, and her flesh had the leprous whiteness of death.

"Come on. Out with it," she ordered, in her sternest tone. "I'm not sure I'll help you, mind. I've discovered love since we parted. Addles the hormones. Softens the teeth."

He had wanted time to know her again. He was unsure of her.

"It's one of our old cases, Con, that's all," he began apologetically. "It's come alive again, the way they do." He tried to raise the pitch of his voice to make it sound casual. "We need more details. You know how you used to be about keeping records," he added, teasingly.

Her eyes did not stir from his face.

"*Kirov,*" he went on, pronouncing the name very slowly. "Kirov, first name Oleg. Ring a bell? Soviet Embassy, Paris, three or four years ago, Second Secretary? We thought he was some sort of Moscow Centre man."

"He was," she said, and sat back a little, still watching him.

She motioned for a cigarette. A packet of ten lay on the table. He wedged one between her lips and lit it, but still her eyes would not leave his face.

"Saul Enderby threw that case out of the window," she said and, forming her lips as if to play a flute, blew a lot of smoke straight downward in order to avoid his face.

"He ruled it should be dropped," Smiley corrected her.

"What's the difference?"

Smiley had not expected to find himself defending Saul Enderby.

"It ran awhile, then in the transition time between my tenure and his, he ruled, quite understandably, that it was unproductive," Smiley said, picking his words with measured care.

"And now he's changed his mind," she said.

"I've got bits, Con. I want it all."

"You always did," she said. "George," she muttered. "George Smiley. Lord alive. Lord bless us and preserve us. *George*." Her gaze was half possessive, half disapproving, as if he were an erring son she loved. It held him awhile longer, then switched to the French windows and the darkening sky outside.

"Kirov," he said again, reminding her, and waited, wondering seriously whether it was all up with her; whether her mind was dying with her body, and this was all there was.

"Kirov, Oleg," she repeated, in a musing tone. "Born Leningrad October, 1929, according to his passport, which doesn't mean a damn thing except that he probably never went near Leningrad in his life." She smiled, as if that were the way of the wicked world. "Arrived Paris June 1, 1974, in the rank and quality of Second Secretary, Commercial. Three to four years ago, you say? Dear Lord, it could be twenty. That's right, darling, he was a hood. 'Course he was. Identified by the Paris lodge of the poor old Riga Group, which didn't help us any, specially not on the fifth floor. What was his real name? *Kursky*. Of course it was. Yes, I think I remember Oleg Kirov né Kursky all right." Her smile returned, and was once more very pretty. "Must have been Vladimir's last case, near enough. How is the old stoat?" she asked, and her moist clever eyes waited for his answer.

"Oh, fighting fit," said Smiley.

"Still terrifying the virgins of Paddington?"

"I'm sure he is."

"Bless you, darling," said Connie, and turned her head till

it was in profile to him, very dark except for the one fine line from the oil lamp, while she again stared out of the French windows.

"Go and see how the mad bitch is, will you, heart?" she asked fondly. "Make sure the idiot hasn't thrown herself into the millrace or drunk the universal weed-killer."

Stepping outside, Smiley stood on the veranda, and in the thickening gloom made out the figure of Hilary loping awkwardly among the coops. He heard the clanking of her spoon on the bucket, and shreds of her well-bred voice on the night air as she called out childish names: "Come on Whitey, Flopsy, Bo."

"She's fine," said Smiley, coming back. "Feeding the chickens."

"I should tell her to bugger off, shouldn't I, George?" she remarked, ignoring his information entirely. "'Go forth into the world, Hils, my dear.' That's what I should say. 'Don't tie yourself to a rotting old hulk like Con. Marry a chinless fool, spawn brats, fulfil your foul womanhood.'" She had voices for everybody, he remembered: even for herself. She had them still. "I'll be damned if I will, George. I want her. Every gorgeous bit of her. I'd take her with me if I'd half a chance. You want to try it some time." A break. "How *are* all the boys and girls?"

For a second, he didn't understand her question; his thoughts were with Hilary still, and Ann.

"His Grace Saul Enderby is still top of the heap, I take it? Eating well, I trust? Not moulting?"

"Oh, Saul goes from strength to strength, thanks."

"That toad Sam Collins still head of Operations?"

There was an edge to her questions, but he had no choice except to answer.

"Sam's fine too," he said.

"Toby Esterhase still oiling round the corridors?"

"It's all pretty much as usual."

Her face was now so dark to him that he could not tell whether she was proposing to speak again. He heard her breathing and the rasp of her chest. But he knew he was still the object of her scrutiny.

"*You'd* never work for that bunch, George," she remarked at last, as if it were the most self-evident of platitudes. "Not you. Give me another drink."

Glad of the movement, Smiley went down the room again.

"*Kirov*, you said?" Connie called to him.

"That's right," said Smiley cheerfully, and returned with her glass replenished.

"That little ferret Otto Leipzig was the first hurdle," she remarked with relish, when she had taken a deep draught. "The fifth floor wouldn't believe *him*, would they? Not our little Otto—*oh*, no! Otto was a fabricator, and that was that!"

"But I don't think Leipzig ever lied to us about the *Moscow* target," Smiley said, taking up her tone of reminiscence.

"No, darling, he did *not*," she said with approval. "He had his weaknesses, I'll grant you. But when it came to the big stuff he always played a straight bat. And *you* understood that, alone of all your tribe, I'll say that for you. But you didn't get much support from the *other* barons, did you?"

"He never lied to Vladimir, either," Smiley said. "It was Vladimir's escape lines that got him out of Russia in the first place."

"Well, well," said Connie, after another long silence. "Kirov né Kursky, the Ginger Pig."

She said it again—"Kirov né Kursky"—a rallying call spoken to her own mountainous memory. As she did so, Smiley saw in his mind's eye the airport hotel room again, and the two strange conspirators seated before him in their black overcoats: the one so huge, the other tiny; the old General using all his bulk to enforce his passionate imploring; little Leipzig, an angry leash-dog at his side.

She was seduced.

The glow of the oil lamp had grown into a smoky light-ball, and Connie in her rocking-chair sat at the edge of it, Mother

Russia herself, as they had called her in the Circus, her wasting face hallowed with reminiscence as she unfolded the story of just one of her unnumbered family of erring children. Whatever suspicions she was harbouring about Smiley's motive in coming here, she had suspended them: this was what she had lived for; this was her song, even if it was her last; these monumental acts of recollection were her genius. In the old days, Smiley remembered, she would have teased him, flirted with her voice, taken huge arcs through seemingly extraneous chunks of Moscow Centre history, all to lure him nearer. But tonight her narrative had acquired an awesome sobriety, as if she knew she had very little time.

Oleg Kirov arrived in Paris direct from Moscow, she repeated—that June, darling, same as I told you—the one when it poured and poured and the annual Sarratt cricket match had to be scrapped three Sundays in a row. Fat Oleg was listed as single, and he didn't replace anyone. His desk was on the second floor overlooking the Rue Saint-Simon—trafficky but *nice*, darling—whereas the Moscow Centre Residency hogged the third and fourth, to the rage of the Ambassador, who felt he was being squeezed into a cupboard by his unloved neighbours. To outward appearances, therefore, Kirov looked at first sight like that rare creature of the Soviet diplomatic community—namely, a straight diplomat. But it was the practice in Paris in those days—and for all Connie knew in *these* days too, heart—whenever a new face showed up at the Soviet Embassy, to distribute his photograph among the émigré tribal chiefs. Brother Kirov's photograph duly found its way to the groups, and in no time that old devil Vladimir was banging on his case officer's door in a state of fine excitement—Steve Mackelvore had Paris in those days, bless him, and dropped dead of a heart attack soon after, but that's another story— insisting that "his people" had identified Kirov as a former *agent provocateur* named Kursky, who, while a student at Tallinn Polytechnical Institute, had formed a circle of dissident

Estonian dock workers, something called "the unaligned discussion club," then shopped its members to the secret police.
Vladimir's source, presently visiting Paris, had been one of
those unfortunate workers, and for his sins he had personally
befriended Kursky right up to the moment of his betrayal.

So far so good, except that Vladi's source—said Connie—
was none other than wicked little Otto, which meant that the
fat was in the fire from the start.

As Connie went on speaking, Smiley's memory once again
began to supplement her own. He saw himself in his last
months as caretaker Chief of the Circus, wearily descending
the rickety wooden staircase from the fifth floor for the
Monday meeting, a bunch of dog-eared files jammed under his
arm. The Circus in those days was like a bombed-out building, he remembered; its officers scattered, its budget ham-
strung, its agents blown or dead or laid off. Bill Haydon's
unmasking was an open wound in everyone's mind: they called
it the Fall and shared the same sense of primeval shame. In
their secret hearts, perhaps, they even blamed Smiley for having caused it, because it was Smiley who had nailed Bill's
treachery. He saw himself at the head of the conference, and
the ring of hostile faces already set against him as one by one
the week's cases were introduced, and subjected to the customary questions: Do we or do we not develop this? Shall we give
it another week? Another month? Another year? Is it a trap, is
it deniable, is it within our Charter? What resources will be
needed and are they better applied elsewhere? Who will authorise? Who will be informed? How much will it cost? He
remembered the intemperate outburst that the mere name, or
workname, of Otto Leipzig immediately called forth among
such uncertain judges as Lauder Strickland, Sam Collins, and
their kind. He tried to recall who else would have been there
apart from Connie and her cohorts from Soviet Research.
Director of Finance, director Western Europe, director Soviet

Attack, most of them already Saul Enderby's men. And Enderby himself, still nominally a Foreign Servant, put in by his own palace guard in the guise of Whitehall linkman, but whose smile was already their laughter, whose frown their disapproval. Smiley saw himself listening to the submission—Connie's own—much as she now repeated it, together with the results of her preliminary researches.

Otto's story figured, she had insisted. This far, it couldn't be faulted. She had shown her workings:

Her own Soviet Research Section had confirmed from printed sources that one Oleg Kursky, a law student, was at Tallinn Polytechnic during the relevant period, she said.

Foreign Office contemporary archives spoke of unrest in the docks.

A defector report from the American Cousins gave a Kursky query Karsky, lawyer, first name Oleg, as graduating from a Moscow Centre training course at Kiev in 1971.

The same source, though suspect, suggested Kursky had later changed his name on the advice of his superiors, "owing to his previous field experience."

Routine French liaison reports, though notoriously unreliable, indicated that for a Second Secretary, Commercial, in Paris, Kirov did indeed enjoy unusual freedoms, such as shopping alone and attending Third World receptions without the customary fifteen companions.

All of which, in short—Connie had ended, far too vigorously for the fifth-floor taste—all of which confirmed the Leipzig story, and the suspicion that Kirov had an intelligence rôle. Then she had slapped the file on the table and passed round her photographs—the very stills, picked up as a matter of routine by French surveillance teams, that had caused the original uproar in the Riga Group headquarters in Paris. Kirov enters an Embassy car. Kirov emerges from the Moscow Narodny carrying a brief-case. Kirov pauses at the window of a saucy bookshop in order to scowl at the magazine covers.

But none, Smiley reflected—returning to the present—
none showing Oleg Kirov and his erstwhile victim Otto
Leipzig disporting themselves with a pair of ladies.

"So that was the *case*, darling," Connie announced when she
had taken a long pull at her drink. "We had the evidence of little Otto with plenty on his file to prove him right. We had a
spot of collateral from other sources—not oodles, I grant you,
but a start. Kirov was a hood, he was newly appointed, but
what *sort* of hood was anybody's guess. And that made him
interesting, didn't it, darling?"

"Yes," Smiley said distractedly. "Yes, Connie, I remember
that it did."

"He wasn't residency mainstream, we knew that from day
one. He didn't ride about in residency cars, do night-shifts or
twin up with identified fellow hoods, or use their cipher room
or attend their weekly prayer-meetings or feed the residency
cat or whatever. On the other hand, Kirov wasn't Karla's man
either, was he, heart? That was the rum thing."

"Why not?" Smiley asked, without looking at her.

But Connie looked at Smiley all right. Connie made one of
her long pauses in order to consider him at her leisure, while
outside in the dying elms, the rooks wisely chose the sudden
lull to sound a Shakespearean omen of screams. "Because
Karla already *had* his man in Paris, darling," she explained
patiently. "As you are very well aware. That old stickler Pudin,
the assistant military attaché. *You* remember how Karla always
loved a soldier. Still does, for all I know." She broke off, in
order once more to study his impassive face. He had put his
chin in his hands. His eyes, half closed, were turned towards
the floor. "Besides, Kirov was an idiot, and the one thing Karla
never did like was idiots, did he? You weren't too kindly towards
them either, come to think of it. Oleg Kirov was foul-mannered,
stank, sweated, and stuck out like a fish in a tree wherever he

went. Karla would have run a *mile* before hiring an oaf like that." Again she paused. "So would you," she added.

Lifting a palm, Smiley placed it against his brow, fingers upward, like a child at an exam. "Unless," he said.

"Unless *what?* Unless he'd gone off his turnip, I suppose! That'll be the day, I must say."

"It was the time of the rumours," Smiley said from far inside his thoughts.

"What rumours? There were always rumours, you dunderhead."

"Oh, just defector reports," he said disparagingly. "Stories of strange happenings in Karla's court. Secondary sources, of course. But didn't they—"

"Didn't they what?"

"Well, didn't they suggest that he was taking rather strange people onto his pay-roll? Holding interviews with them at dead of night? It was all low-grade stuff, I know. I only mention it in passing."

"And we were ordered to discount them," Connie said very firmly. "Kirov was the target. Not Karla. That was the fifth-floor ruling, George, and you were party to it. 'Stop moon-gazing and get on with earthly matters,' says you." Twisting her mouth and putting back her head, she produced an uncomfortably realistic likeness of Saul Enderby: "'This service is in the business of collectin' intelligence,'" she drawled. "'*Not* conductin' feuds again the opposition.' Don't tell me he's changed his tune, darling. Has he? *George?*" she whispered. "Oh, *George*, you are bad!"

He fetched her another drink and when he came back he saw her eyes glistening with mischievous excitement. She was plucking at the tufts of her white hair the way she used to when she wore it long.

"The point is, we licensed the operation, Con," said Smiley, in a factual tone intended to rein her in. "We overruled the doubters, and we gave you permission to take Kirov to first base. How did it run after that?"

The drink, the memories, the revived excitement of the chase were driving her at a speed he could not control. Her breathing had quickened. She was rasping like an old engine with the restraints dangerously removed. He realised she was telling Leipzig's story the way Leipzig had told it to Vladimir. He had thought he was in the Circus with her still, with the operation against Kirov just about to be launched. But in her imagination she had leapt instead to the ancient city of Tallinn more than a quarter of a century earlier. In her extraordinary mind, she had been there; she had known both Leipzig and Kirov in the time of their friendship. A love story, she insisted. Little Otto and fat Oleg. This was the pivot, she said; let the old fool tell it the way it was, she said, and you pursue your wicked purposes as I go along, George.

"The tortoise and the hare, darling, that's who they were. Kirov the big sad baby, reading away at his law books at the Poly, and using the beastly secret police as Daddy; and little Otto Leipzig the proper devil, a finger in all the rackets, bit of prison behind him, working in the docks all day, at night preaching sedition to the unaligned. They met in a bar and it was love at first sight. Otto pulled the girls, Oleg Kirov slip-streamed along behind him, picking up his leavings. What are you trying to do, George? Joan-of-Arc me?"

He had lighted a fresh cigarette for her and put it into her mouth in the hope of calming her, but her feverish talking had already burned it low enough to scorch her. Taking it quickly from her, he stubbed it on the tin lid she used for an ashtray.

"They even shared a girl-friend for a time," she said, so loud she was nearly yelling. "And *one* day, if you can believe it, the poor ninny came to little Otto and warned him outright. 'Your fat friend is jealous of you and he's a toady of the secret police,' says she. 'The unaligned discussion club is for the high jump. Beware the Ides of March!'"

"Go easy, Con," Smiley warned her anxiously. "Con, come down!"

Her voice grew still louder: "Otto threw the girl out and a week later the whole bunch were arrested. Including fat Oleg, of course, who'd set them up—but they knew. Oh, *they* knew!" She faltered as if she had lost her way. "And the fool girl who'd tried to warn him died," she said. "Missing, believed interrogated. Otto combed the forests for her till he found someone who'd been with her in the cells. Dead as a dodo. Two dodos. Dead as I'll be, damn soon."

"Let's go on later," Smiley said.

He would have stopped her, too—made tea, talked weather, anything to halt the mounting speed of her. But she had taken a second leap and was already back in Paris, describing how Otto Leipzig, with the fifth floor's grudging approval and the old General's passionate help, set about arranging the reunion, after all those lost years, with Second Secretary Kirov, whom she dubbed the Ginger Pig. Smiley supposed it was her name for him at the time. Her face was scarlet and her breath was not enough for her story, so that it kept running out in a wheeze, but she forced herself to continue.

"Connie," he begged her again, but it was not enough either, and perhaps nothing would have been.

First, she said, in search of the Ginger Pig, little Otto trotted along to the various Franco-Soviet friendship societies that Kirov was known to frequent.

"That poor little Otto must have seen *The Battleship Potemkin* fifteen times, but the Ginger Pig never showed up once."

Word came that Kirov was showing a serious interest in émigrés, and even representing himself as their secret sympathiser, enquiring whether, as a junior official, there was anything he could do to help their families in the Soviet Union. With Vladimir's help Leipzig tried to put himself in Kirov's path, but once more luck was against him. Then Kirov started travelling—travelling everywhere, my dear, a positive Flying Dutchman—so that Connie and her boys began to wonder whether he was some sort of clerical administrator for Moscow Centre, not on the operational side at all: the accountant-auditor for a group of Western residencies, for instance, with Paris as their centre—Bonn, Madrid, Stockholm, Vienna.

"For Karla or for the mainstream?" Smiley asked quietly.

Whisper who dares, said Connie, but for her money, it was for Karla. Even though Pudin was already there. Even though Kirov was an idiot, and not a soldier; it still *had* to be for Karla, Connie said, perversely doubling back upon her own assertions to the contrary. If Kirov had been visiting the mainstream residencies, he would have been entertained and put up by identified intelligence officers. But instead, he lived his cover, and stayed only with his national counterparts in the Commercial sections, she said.

Anyway, the flying did it, said Connie. Little Otto waited till Kirov had booked himself on a flight to Vienna, made sure he was travelling alone, then boarded the same flight, and they were in business.

"A straight copybook honey-trap, that's what we were aiming for," Connie sang, very loud indeed. "Your real old-fashioned burn. A big operator might laugh it off, but not Brother Kirov, least of all if he was on Karla's books. Naughty photographs and information with menaces, that was what we were after. And when we'd done with him, and found out what he was up to, and who his nasty friends were, and who was giving him all that heady freedom, we'd either buy him in as a defector or bung him back in the pond, depending on how much was left of him!"

She stopped dead. She opened her mouth, closed it, drew some breath, held out her glass to him.

"Darling, get the old soak another drinkie, double-quick, will you? Connie's getting her lurgies. No, don't. Stay where you are."

For a fatal second, Smiley was lost.

"George?"

"Connie, I'm here! What is it?"

He was fast but not fast enough. He saw the stiffening of her face, saw her distorted hands fly out in front of her, and her eyes screw up in disgust, as if she had seen a horrible accident.

"Hils, quick!" she cried. "Oh, my hat!"

He embraced her and felt her forearms lock over the back of his neck to hold him tighter. Her skin was cold, she was shaking, but from terror not from chill. He stayed against her, smelling Scotch and medicated powder and old lady, trying to comfort her. Her tears were all over his cheeks, he could feel them and taste their salty sting as she pushed him away from her. He found her handbag and opened it for her, then went quickly back to the veranda and called to Hilary. She ran out of the darkness with her fists half clenched, elbows and hips rotating, in a way that makes men laugh. She hurried past him, grinning with shyness, and he stayed on the veranda, feeling the night cold pricking his cheeks while he stared at the gathering rain clouds and the pine trees silvered by the rising moon. The dogs' screaming had subsided. Only the wheeling rooks sounded their harsh warnings. Go, he told himself. Get out of here. Bolt. The car waited not a hundred feet from him, frost already forming on the roof. He imagined himself leaping into it and driving up the hill, through the plantation, and away, never to return. But he knew he couldn't.

"She wants you back now, George," Hilary said sternly from the doorway, with the special authority of those who nurse the dying.

But when he went back, everything was fine.

15

Everything was fine. Connie sat powdered and austere in her rocking-chair, and her eyes, as he entered, were as straight upon him as when he had first come here. Hilary had calmed her, Hilary had sobered her, and now Hilary stood behind her with her hands on Connie's neck, thumbs inward, while she gently massaged the nape.

"Spot of *timor mortis*, darling," Connie explained. "The leech prescribes Valium but the old fool prefers the juice. You won't mention that bit to Saul Enderby when you report back, will you, heart?"

"No, of course not."

"When *will* you be reporting back, by the by, darling?"

"Soon," said Smiley.

"Tonight, when you get home?"

"It depends what there is to tell."

"Con did write it all *up*, you know, George. The old fool's accounts of the case were very *full*, I thought. Very *detailed*. Very *circumstantial*, for once. But you haven't consulted them." Smiley said nothing. "They're lost. Destroyed. Eaten by mealy-bugs. You haven't had time. Well, well. And you such a devil for the paperwork. *Higher*, Hils," she ordered, without taking her gleaming eyes away from Smiley. "Higher, darling. The bit where the vertebrae get stuck in the tonsils."

Smiley sat down on the old wicker sofa.

"I used to love those double-double games," Connie confessed dreamily, rolling her head in order to caress Hilary's hands with it. "Didn't I, Hils? All human life was there. You wouldn't know that any more, would you? Not since you blew your gasket."

She returned to Smiley. "Want me to go on, dearie?" she asked in her East End tart's voice.

"If you could just take me through it briefly," Smiley said. "But not if it's—"

"Where were we? I know. Up in that aeroplane with the Ginger Pig. He's on his way to Vienna, he's got his trotters in a trough of beer. Looks up, and who does he see standing in front of him like his own bad conscience but his dear old buddy of twenty-five years ago, little Otto, grinning like Old Nick. What does Brother Kirov né Kursky *feel?* we ask ourselves, assuming he's got any feelings. Does Otto *know*—he wonders—that it was naughty me who sold him into the Gulag? So what does he do?"

"What does he do?" said Smiley, not responding to her banter.

"He decides to play it hearty, dearie. Doesn't he, Hils? Whistles up the caviare, and says 'Thank God.'" She whispered something and Hilary bent her head to catch it, then giggled. "'Champagne!' he says. And my God they have it, and the Ginger Pig pays for it, and they drink it, and they share a taxi into town, and they even have a quick snifter in a café before the Ginger Pig goes about his furtive duties. Kirov *likes* Otto," Connie insisted. "*Loves* him, doesn't he, Hils? They're a proper pair of raving whatsits, same as us. Otto's sexy, Otto's fun, Otto's dishy, and anti-authoritarian, and light on his feet—and—oh, everything the Ginger Pig could never be, not in a thousand years! Why did the fifth floor always think people had to have one motive only?"

"I'm sure I didn't," said Smiley fervently.

But Connie was back talking to Hilary, not to Smiley at all. "Kirov was *bored*, heart. Otto was life for him. Same as you are for me. You put the spring into my stride, don't you, lovey? Hadn't prevented him from shopping Otto, of course, but that's only nature, isn't it?"

Still gently swaying at Connie's back, Hilary nodded in vague assent.

"And what did Kirov mean to Otto Leipzig?" Smiley asked.

"Hate, my darling," Connie replied, without hesitation. "Pure, undiluted hatred. Plain, honest-to-God black loathing. Hate and money. Those were Otto's two best things. Otto always felt he was *owed* for all those years he'd spent in the slammer. He wanted to collect for the girl, too. His great dream was that one day he would sell Kirov né Kursky for lots of money. Lots and lots and *lots* of money. Then spend it."

A waiter's anger, Smiley thought, remembering the contact print. Remembering the tartan room again, at the airport, and Otto's quiet German voice with its caressing edge; remembering his brown, unblinking eyes that were like windows on his smouldering soul.

After the Vienna meeting, said Connie, the two men had agreed to meet again in Paris, and Otto wisely played a long hand. In Vienna, Otto had not asked a single question to which the Ginger Pig could take exception; Otto was a pro, said Connie. Was Kirov married? he had asked. Kirov had flung up his hands and roared with laughter at the question, indicating that he was prepared not to be at any time. *Married but wife in Moscow*, Otto had reported—which would make a honey-trap that much more effective. Kirov had asked Leipzig what his job was these days, and Leipzig had replied magnanimously "import-export," proposing himself as a bit of a wheeler-dealer, Vienna one day, Hamburg the next. In the event, Otto waited a whole month—after twenty-five years, said Connie, he could afford to take his time—and during that one month, Kirov was observed by the French to make three separate passes at elderly Paris-based Russian émigrés: one a taxi-driver, one a shopkeeper, one a restaurateur, all three with dependents in the Soviet Union. He offered to take letters, messages, addresses; he even offered to take money and, if they were not too bulky, gifts. And to operate a two-way service next time he returned. Nobody took him up. In the fifth week Otto rang Kirov at his flat, said he had just flown in from Hamburg, and suggested they have some fun. Over dinner, picking his moment, Otto said the night was on him; he had just made a big killing on a certain shipment to a certain country, and had money to burn.

"This was the bait we had worked out for him, darling," Connie explained, addressing Smiley directly at last. "And the Ginger Pig rose to it, didn't he, as they all do, don't they, bless them, salmon to the fly every time."

What sort of shipment? Kirov had asked Otto. What sort of country? For reply, Leipzig had drawn in the air a hooked nose on the end of his own, and broken out laughing. Kirov laughed too, but he was clearly very interested. To *Israel?* he said; then what sort of shipment? Leipzig pointed his same forefinger at Kirov and pretended to pull a trigger. *Arms* to Israel? Kirov asked in amazement, but Leipzig was a pro and would say no more. They drank, went to a strip club, and talked old times. Kirov even referred to their shared girl-friend, asking whether Leipzig knew what had become of her. Leipzig said he didn't. In the early morning, Leipzig had proposed they pick up some company and take it to his flat, but Kirov, to his disappointment, refused: not in Paris, too dangerous. In Vienna or Hamburg, sure. But not in Paris. They parted, drunk, at breakfast-time, and the Circus was a hundred pounds poorer.

"Then the bloody infighting started," said Connie, suddenly changing track completely. "The Great Head Office Debate. Debate, my arse. You were away, Saul Enderby put one manicured hoof in, and the rest of them promptly got the vapours—that's what happened." Her baron's voice again: "'Otto Leipzig's taking us for a ride. . . . We haven't cleared the operation with the Frogs. . . . Foreign Office worried about implications. . . . Kirov is a plant . . . the Riga Group a totally unsound base from which to make a ploy of this scale.' Where were you, anyway? Beastly Berlin, wasn't it?"

"Hong Kong."

"Oh, there," she said vaguely, and slumped in her chair while her eyelids drooped.

Smiley had sent Hilary to make tea, and she was clanking dishes at the other end of the room. He glanced at her, wondering whether he should call her, and saw her standing exactly as he had last seen her in the Circus the night they sent for him—her knuckles backed against her mouth, suppressing a silent scream. He had been working late—it was about that time; yes, he was preparing his departure to Hong Kong—when suddenly his internal phone rang and he heard a man's voice, very strained, asking him to come immediately to the cipher room, Mr. Smiley, sir, it's urgent. Moments later he was hurrying down a bare corridor, flanked by two worried janitors. They pushed open the door for him, he stepped inside, they hung back. He saw the smashed machinery, the files and card indices and telegrams flung around the room like rubbish at a football ground, he saw the filthy graffiti daubed in lipstick on the wall. And at the centre of it all, he saw Hilary herself, the culprit—exactly as she was now—staring through the thick net curtains at the free white sky outside: Hilary our Vestal, so well bred; Hilary our Circus bride.

"Hell are you up to, Hils?" Connie demanded roughly from her rocking-chair.

"Making tea, Con. George wants a cup of tea."

"To hell with what *George* wants," she retorted, flaring.

"George is *fifth floor*. George put the kibosh on the Kirov case and now he's trying to get it right, flying solo in his old age. Right, George? Right? Even lied to me about that old devil Vladimir, who walked into a bullet on Hampstead Heath, according to the newspapers, which he apparently doesn't read, any more than my reports!"

They drank the tea. A rainstorm was getting up. The first hard drops were hammering on the wood roof.

Smiley had charmed her, Smiley had flattered her, Smiley had willed her to go on. She had drawn the thread halfway out for him. He was determined that she should draw it all the way.

"I've got to have it all, Con," he repeated. "I've got to hear everything, just as you remember it, even if the end is painful."

"The end bloody well *is* painful," she retorted.

But already her voice, her face, the very lustre of her memory were flagging, and he knew it was a race against time.

Now it was Kirov's turn to play the classic card, she said wearily. At their next meeting, which was in Brussels a month later, Kirov referred to the Israeli arms shipment thing and said he had happened to mention their conversation to a friend of his in the Commercial Section of the Embassy who was contributing to a special study of the Israeli military economy, and even had funds available for researching it. Would Leipzig consider—no, but seriously, Otto!—talking to the fellow or, better still, giving the story to his old buddy Oleg here and now, who might even get a little credit for it on his own account? Otto said, "Provided it pays and doesn't hurt anyone." Then he solemnly fed Kirov a bag of chicken-feed prepared by Connie and the Middle Eastern people—all of it true, of course, and eminently checkable, even if it wasn't a lot of use to anyone—and Kirov solemnly wrote it all down, though both of them, as Connie put it, knew perfectly well that neither Kirov nor his master, whoever that was, had the smallest interest in Israel, or arms, or shipments, or her military economy—not in *this* case, anyway. What Kirov was aiming to do was create a conspiratorial relationship, as their next meeting back in Paris showed. Kirov evinced huge enthusiasm for the report, insisted that Otto accept five hundred dollars for it, against the minor formality of signing a receipt. And when Otto had done this, and was squarely hooked, Kirov sailed straight in with all the crudity he could command—which was a lot, said Connie—and asked Otto how well placed he was with the local Russian émigrés.

"Please, Con," he whispered. "We're almost there!" She was so near but he could feel her drifting farther and farther away.

Hilary was sitting on the floor with her head against Connie's knees. Absently, Connie's mittened hands had taken hold of her hair for comfort, and her eyes had fallen almost shut.

"Connie!" he repeated.

Opening her eyes, Connie gave a tired smile.

"It was only the fan dance, darling," she said. "The he-knows-I-know-you-know. The usual fan dance," she repeated indulgently, and her eyes closed again.

"So how did Leipzig answer him? *Connie!*"

"He did what we'd do, darling," she murmured. "Stalled. Admitted he was well in with the émigré groups, and hugger-mugger with the General. Then stalled. Said he didn't visit Paris that much. 'Why not hire someone local?' he said. He was teasing, Hils, darling, you see. Asked again: Would it hurt anyone? Asked what the job was, anyway. What did it pay? Get me some booze, Hils."

"No," said Hilary.

"Get it."

Smiley poured her two fingers of whisky and watched her sip.

"What did Kirov want Otto to do with the émigrés?" he said.

"Kirov wanted a legend," she replied. "He wanted a legend for a girl."

Nothing in Smiley's manner suggested he had heard the phrase from Toby Esterhase only a few hours ago. Four years before, Oleg Kirov wanted a legend, Connie repeated. Just as the Sandman, according to Toby and the General—thought Smiley—wanted one today. Kirov wanted a cover story for a female agent who could be infiltrated into France. That was the nub of it, Connie said. Kirov didn't say this, of course; he put it quite differently, in fact. He told Otto that Moscow had issued a secret instruction to all embassies announcing that split Russian families might in certain circumstances be reunited abroad. If enough families could be found who wished it, said the instruction, then Moscow would go public with the idea and thus enhance the Soviet Union's image in the field of human rights. Ideally, they wanted cases with a compassionate ring: daughters in Russia, say, cut off from their families in the West, single girls, perhaps of marriageable age. Secrecy was essential, said Kirov, until a list of suitable cases had been assembled—think of the outcry there would be, Kirov said, if the story leaked ahead of time!

The Ginger Pig made his pitch so badly, said Connie, that Otto had at first to deride the proposal simply for the sake of verisimilitude; it was too crazy, too hole-in-corner, he said— secret lists, what nonsense! Why didn't Kirov approach the émigré organisations themselves and swear them to secrecy? Why employ a total outsider to do his dirty work? As Leipzig teased, Kirov grew more heated. It was not Leipzig's job to make fun of Moscow's secret edicts, said Kirov. He began shouting at him, and somehow Connie discovered the energy to shout too, or at least to lift her voice above its weary level, and to give it the guttural Russian ring she thought Kirov ought to have: "'Where is your compassion?' he says. 'Don't you want to help people? Why do you sneer at a human gesture merely because it comes from Russia!'" Kirov said he had approached some families himself, but found no trust, and made no headway. He began to put pressure on Leipzig, first of a personal kind—"Don't you want to help me in my career?"—and when this failed, he suggested to Leipzig that since he had already supplied secret information to the Embassy for money, he might consider it prudent to continue, lest the West German authorities somehow get to hear of this connection and throw him out of Hamburg—maybe out of Germany altogether. How would Otto like that? And finally, said Connie, Kirov offered money, and that was where the wonder lay. "For each successful reunion effected, ten thousand U.S. dollars," she announced. "For each suitable candidate, whether a reunion takes place or not, one thousand U.S. on the nail. Cash-cash."

At which point, of course, said Connie, the fifth floor decided Kirov was off his head, and ordered the case abandoned immediately.

"And I returned from the Far East," said Smiley.

"Like poor King Richard from the Crusades, you did, darling!" Connie agreed. "*And* found the peasants in uproar and your nasty brother on the throne. Serves you right." She gave a gigantic yawn. "Case dustbinned," she declared. "The Kraut police wanted Leipzig extradited from France; we could perfectly well have begged them off but we didn't. No honey-trap, no dividend, no bugger-all. Fixture cancelled."

"And how did Vladimir take all that?" Smiley asked, as if he really didn't know.

Connie opened her eyes with difficulty. "Take what?"

"Cancelling the fixture."

"Oh, *roared*, what do you expect? Roar, roar. Said we'd spoilt the kill of the century. Swore to continue the war by other means."

"What *kind* of kill?"

She missed his question. "It's not a *shooting* war any more, George," she said as her eyes closed again. "That's the trouble. It's grey. Half-angels fighting half-devils. No one knows where the lines are. No bang-bangs."

Once again, Smiley in his memory saw the tartan hotel bedroom and the two black overcoats side by side as Vladimir appealed desperately to have the case reopened: "Max, hear us one more time, hear what has happened since you ordered us to stop!" They had flown from Paris at their own expense to tell him, because Finance Section on Enderby's orders had closed the case account. "Max, hear us, please," Vladimir had begged. "Kirov summoned Otto to his apartment late last night. They had another meeting, Otto and Kirov. Kirov got drunk and said amazing things!"

He saw himself back in his old room at the Circus, Enderby already installed at his desk. It was the same day, just a few hours later.

"Sounds like little Otto's last-ditch effort at keeping out of the hands of the Huns," Enderby said when he had heard Smiley out. "What do they want him for over there, theft or rape?"

"Fraud," Smiley had replied hopelessly, which was the wretched truth.

Connie was humming something. She tried to make a song of it, then a limerick. She wanted more drink but Hilary had taken away her glass.

"I want you to go," Hilary said, straight into Smiley's face.

Leaning forward on the wicker sofa, Smiley asked his last question. He asked it, one might have thought, reluctantly; almost with distaste. His soft face had hardened with determination, but not enough to conceal the marks of disapproval. "Do you remember a story old Vladimir used to tell, Con? One we never shared with anyone? Stored away, as a piece of private treasure? That Karla had a mistress, someone he loved?"

"His Ann," she said dully.

"That in all the world, she was his one thing, that she made him act like a crazy man?"

Slowly her head came up, and he saw her face clear, and his voice quickened and gathered strength.

"How that was the rumour they passed around in Moscow Centre—those in the know? Karla's invention—his creation, Con? How he found her when she was a child, wandering in a burnt-out village in the war? Adopted her, brought her up, fell in love with her?"

He watched her and despite the whisky, despite her deathly weariness, he saw the last excitement, like the last drop in the bottle, slowly rekindle her features.

"He was behind the German lines," she said. "It was the forties. There was a team of them, raising the Balts. Building networks, stay-behind groups. It was a big operation. Karla was boss. She became their mascot. They carted her from pillar to post. A kid. Oh, George!"

He was holding his breath to catch her words. The din on the roof grew louder, he heard the rising growl of the forest as the rain came down on it. His face was near to hers, very; its animation matched her own.

"And then what?" he said.

"Then he bumped her off, darling. That's what."

"Why?" He drew still closer, as if he feared her words might fail her at the crucial moment. "*Why*, Connie? Why kill her when he loved her?"

"He'd done everything for her. Found foster-parents for her. Educated her. Had her all got up to be his ideal hag. Played Daddy, played lover, played God. She was his toy. Then one day she ups and gets ideas above her station."

"What sort of ideas?"

"Soft on revolution. Mixing with bloody intellectuals. Wanting the State to wither away. Asking the big 'Why?' and the big 'Why not?' He told her to shut up. She wouldn't. She had a devil in her. He had her shoved in the slammer. Made her worse."

"And there was a child," Smiley prompted, taking her mittened hand in both of his. "He gave her a child, remember?" Her hand was between them, between their faces. "You researched it, didn't you, Con. One silly season, I gave you your head. 'Track it down, Con,' I said to you. 'Take it wherever it leads.' Remember?"

Under Smiley's intense encouragement, her story had acquired the fervour of a last love. She was speaking fast, eyes streaming. She was backtracking, zigzagging everywhere in her memory. Karla had this hag . . . yes, darling, that was the story, do you hear me?—Yes, Connie, go on, I hear you.—Then listen. He brought her up, made her his mistress, there was a brat, and the quarrels were about the brat. George, darling, do you love me like the old days?—Come on, Con, give me the rest, yes of course I do.—He accused her of warping its precious mind with dangerous ideas, like freedom, for instance. Or love. A girl, her mother's image, said to be a beauty. In the end the old despot's love turned to hatred and he had his ideal carted off and spavined: end of story. We had it from Vladimir first, then a few scraps, never the hard base. Name unknown, darling, because he destroyed all records of her, killed whoever might have heard, which is Karla's way, bless him, isn't it, darling, always was. Others said she wasn't dead at all, the story of her murder was disinformation to end the trail. There, she did it, didn't she? The old fool remembered!

"And the child?" Smiley asked. "The girl in her mother's image? There was a defector report—what was *that* about?" She didn't pause. She had remembered that as well, her mind was galloping ahead of her, just as her voice was outrunning her breath.

A don of some sort from Leningrad University, said Connie. Claimed he'd been ordered to take on a weird girl for special political instruction in the evenings, a sort of private patient who was showing anti-social tendencies, the daughter of a high official. Tatiana, he was only allowed to know her as Tatiana. She'd been raising hell all over town, but her father was a big beef in Moscow and she couldn't be touched. The girl tried to seduce him, probably did, then told him some story about how Daddy had had Mummy killed for showing insufficient faith in the historical process. Next day his professor called him in and said if he ever repeated a word of what had happened at that interview, he would find himself tripping on a very big banana skin. . . .

Connie ran on wildly, describing clues that led nowhere, the sources that vanished at the moment of discovery. It seemed impossible that her racked and drink-sodden body could have once more summoned so much strength.

"Oh, George, darling, take me with you! That's what you're after, I've got it! Who killed Vladimir, and why! I saw it in your ugly face the moment you walked in. I couldn't place it, now I can. You've got your Karla look! Vladi had opened up the vein again, so Karla had him killed! That's your banner, George. I can see you marching. Take me with you, George, for God's sake! I'll leave Hils, I'll leave anything, no more of the juice, I swear. Get me up to London and I'll find his hag for you, even if she doesn't exist, if it's the last thing I do!"

"Why did Vladimir call him the Sandman?" Smiley asked, knowing the answer already.

"It was his joke. A German fairy tale Vladi picked up in Estonia from one of his Kraut forebears. 'Karla is our Sandman. Anyone who comes too close to him has a way of falling asleep.' We never knew, darling, how could we? In the Lubianka, someone had met a man who'd met a woman who'd met her. Someone else knew someone who'd helped to bury her. That hag was Karla's shrine, George. And she betrayed him. Twin cities, we used to say you were, you and Karla, two halves of the same apple. George, darling, don't! Please!"

She had stopped, and he realised that she was staring up at him in fear, that her face was somehow beneath his own; he was standing, glaring down at her. Hilary was against the wall, calling "Stop, stop!" He was standing over her, incensed by her cheap and unjust comparison, knowing that neither Karla's methods nor Karla's absolutism were his own. He heard himself say "*No, Connie!*" and discovered that he had lifted his hands to the level of his chest, palms downward and rigid, as if he were pressing something into the ground. And he realised that his passion had scared her; that he had never betrayed so much conviction to her—or so much feeling—before.

"I'm getting old," he muttered, and gave a sheepish smile.

He relaxed, and as he did so, slowly Connie's own body became limp also, and the dream died in her. The hands that had clutched him seconds earlier lay on her lap like bodies in a trench.

"It was all bilge," she said sullenly. A deep and terminal listlessness descended over her. "Bored émigrés crying into their vodka. Drop it, George. Karla's beaten you all ends up. He foxed you, he made a fool of your time. *Our* time." She drank, no longer caring what she said. Her head flopped forward again and for a moment he thought she really was asleep. "He foxed *you*, he foxed *me*, and when you smelt a rat he got Bloody Bill Haydon to fox Ann and put you off the scent." With difficulty she lifted her head to stare at him one more time. "Go home, George. Karla won't give you back your past. Be like the old fool here. Get yourself a bit of love and wait for Armageddon."

She began coughing, hopelessly, one hacking retch after another.

The rain had stopped. Gazing out of the French windows, Smiley saw again the moonlight on the cages, touching the frost on the wire; he saw the frosted crowns of the fir trees climbing the hill into a black sky; he saw a world reversed, with the light things darkened into shadow, and the dark things picked out like beacons on the white ground. He saw a sudden moon, stepping clear before the clouds, beckoning him into seething crevices. He saw one black figure in Wellington boots and a headscarf running up the lane, and realised it was Hilary; she must have slipped out without his noticing. He remembered he had heard a door slam. He went back to Connie and sat on the sofa beside her. Connie wept and drifted, talking about love. Love was a positive power, she said vaguely—ask Hils. But Hilary was not there to ask. Love was a stone thrown into the water, and if there were enough stones and we all loved together, the ripples would eventually be strong enough to reach across the sea and overwhelm the haters and the cynics— "even beastly Karla, darling," she assured him. "That's what Hils says. Bilge, isn't it? It's bilge, Hils!" she yelled.

Then Connie closed her eyes again, and after a while, by her breathing, appeared to doze off. Or perhaps she was only pretending in order to avoid the pain of saying goodbye to him. He tiptoed into the cold evening. The car's engine, by a miracle, started; he began climbing the lane, keeping a look-out for Hilary. He rounded a bend and saw her in the headlights. She was cowering among the trees, waiting for him to leave before she went back to Connie. She had her hands to her face again and he thought he saw blood; perhaps she had scratched herself with her finger-nails. He passed her and saw her in the mirror, staring after him in the glow of his rear lights, and for a moment she resembled for him all those muddy ghosts who are the real victims of conflict: who lurch out of the smoke of war, battered and starved and deprived of all they ever had or loved. He waited until he saw her start down the hill again, towards the lights of the *dacha*.

At Heathrow Airport he bought his air ticket for the next morning, then lay on his bed in the hotel, for all he knew the same one, though the walls were not tartan. All night long the hotel stayed awake, and Smiley with it. He heard the clank of plumbing and the ringing of phones and the thud of lovers who would not or could not sleep.

Max, hear us one more time, he rehearsed; *it was the Sandman himself who sent Kirov to the émigrés to find the legend.*

16

Smiley arrived in Hamburg in mid-morning and took the airport bus to the city centre. Fog lingered and the day was very cold. In the Station Square, after repeated rejections, he found an old, thin terminus hotel with a lift licensed for three persons at a time. He signed in as Standfast, then walked as far as a car-rental agency, where he hired a small Opel, which he parked in an underground garage that played softened Beethoven out of loudspeakers. The car was his back door. He didn't know whether he would need it, but he knew it needed to be there. He walked again, heading for the Alster, sensing everything with a particular sharpness: the manic traffic, the toy-shops for millionaire children. The din of the city hit him like a fire-storm, causing him to forget the cold. Germany was his second nature, even his second soul. In his youth, her literature had been his passion and his discipline. He could put on her language like a uniform and speak with its boldness. Yet he sensed danger in every step he took, for Smiley as a young man had spent half the war here in the lonely terror of the spy, and the awareness of being on enemy territory was lodged in him for good. In boyhood he had known Hamburg as a rich and graceful shipping town, which hid its volatile soul behind a cloak of Englishness; in manhood as a city smashed into medieval darkness by thousand-bomber air raids. He had seen it in the first years of peace, one endless smouldering bombsite and the survivors tilling the rubble like fields. And he saw it today, hurtling into the anonymity of canned music, high-rise concrete, and smoked glass.

Reaching the sanctuary of the Alster, he walked the pleasant footpath to the jetty where Villem had boarded the steamer. On weekdays, he recorded, the first ferry was at 7:10, the last at 20:15, and Villem had been here on a weekday. There was a steamer due in fifteen minutes. Waiting for it, he watched the sculls and the red squirrels much as Villem had done, and when the steamer arrived he sat in the stern where Villem had sat, in the open air under the canopy. His companions consisted of a crowd of schoolchildren and three nuns. He sat with his eyes almost closed by the dazzle, listening to their chatter. Half-way across he stood, walked through the cabins to the forward window, looked out, apparently to confirm something, glanced at his watch, then returned to his seat until the Jungfernstieg, where he landed.

Villem's story tallied. Smiley had not expected otherwise, but in a world of perpetual doubt, reassurance never came amiss.

He lunched, then went to the main Post Office and studied old telephone directories for an hour, much as Ostrakova had done in Paris, though for different reasons. His researches complete, he settled himself gratefully in the lounge of the Four Seasons Hotel and read newspapers till dusk.

In a Hamburg guide to houses of pleasure, The Blue Diamond was not listed under night-clubs but under "amour" and earned three stars for exclusivity and cost. It was situated in St. Pauli, but discreetly apart from the main beat, in a cobbled alley that was tilted and dark and smelt of fish. Smiley rang the doorbell and it opened on an electric switch. He stepped inside and stood at once in a trim ante-room filled with grey machinery manned by a smart young man in a grey suit. On the wall grey reels of tape turned slowly, though the music they played was mostly somewhere else. On the desk an elaborate telephone system, also grey, flickered and ticked.

"I should like to pass some time here," Smiley said.

This is where they answered my phone call, he thought, when I telephoned Vladimir's Hamburg correspondent.

The smart young man drew a printed form from his desk and in a confiding murmur explained the procedure, much as a lawyer would, which possibly was his daytime profession anyway. Membership cost one hundred and seventy-five marks, he said softly. This was a one-time annual subscription entitling Smiley to enter free for a full year, as many times as he wished. The first drink would cost him a further twenty-five marks and thereafter prices were high but not unreasonable. A first drink was obligatory and, like the membership fee, payable before entry. All other forms of entertainment came without charge, though the girls received gifts appreciatively. Smiley should complete the form in whatever name he wished. It would be filed here by the young man personally. All he had to do on his next visit was remember the name under which he had joined and he would be admitted without formalities.

Smiley put down his money and added one more false name to the dozens he had used in his lifetime. He descended a staircase to a second door, which once more opened electronically, revealing a narrow passage giving on to a row of cubicles, still empty because in that world the night was only now beginning. At the end of the passage stood a third door and, once through it, he entered total darkness filled with the full blast of the music from the smart young man's tape-recorders. A male voice spoke to him, a pin-light led him to a table. He was handed a list of drinks. "Proprietor C. Kretzschmar," he read at the foot of the page in small print. He ordered whisky.

"I wish to remain alone. No company."

"I shall advise the house, sir," the waiter said with confiding dignity, and accepted his tip.

"Concerning Herr Kretzschmar. He is from Saxony, by any chance?"

"Yes, sir."

Worse than East German, Toby Esterhase had said. *Saxon. They stole together, pimped together, faked reports together. It was a perfect marriage.*

He sipped his whisky, waiting for his eyes to grow accustomed to the light. From somewhere a blue glow shone, picking out cuffs and collars eerily. He saw white faces and white bodies. There were two levels. The lower, where he sat, was furnished with tables and armchairs. The upper consisted of six *chambres séparées,* like boxes at the theatre, each with its own blue glow. It was in one of these, he decided, that, knowingly or not, the quartet had posed for its photograph. He recalled the angle from which the picture had been taken. It was from above— from well above. But "well above" meant somewhere in the blackness of the upper walls where no eye could penetrate, not even Smiley's.

The music died and over the same speakers a cabaret was announced. The title, said the *compère,* was Old Berlin, and the *compère's* voice was also Old Berlin: hectoring, nasal, and suggestive. The smart young man has changed the tape, thought Smiley. A curtain lifted revealing a small stage. By the light it released, he peered quickly upward again and this time saw what he was looking for: a small observation window of smoked glass set very high in the wall. The photographer used special cameras, he thought vaguely; these days, he had been told, darkness was no longer a hindrance. I should have asked Toby, he thought; Toby knows those gadgets by heart. On the stage, a demonstration of love making had begun, mechanical, pointless, dispiriting. Smiley turned his attention to his fellow members scattered round the room. The girls were beautiful and naked and young, in the way the girls in the photograph were young. Those who had partners sat entwined with them, seemingly delighted by their senility and ugliness. Those who had none sat in a silent group like American footballers waiting to be called. The noise from the speakers grew very loud, a mixture of music and hysterical narrative. And in Berlin they are playing Old Hamburg, Smiley thought. On the stage the couple increased their efforts, but to little account. Smiley wondered whether he would recognise the girls in the photograph if they should appear. He decided he would not. The curtain closed. He ordered another whisky in relief.

"Is Herr Kretzschmar in the house tonight?" he asked the waiter.

Herr Kretzschmar was a man of commitments, the waiter explained. Herr Kretzschmar was obliged to divide his time between several establishments.

"If he comes, have the goodness to let me know."

"He will be here at eleven exactly, sir."

At the bar, naked couples had begun dancing. He endured another half-hour of this before returning to the front office by way of the cubicles, some of which were now occupied. The smart young man asked whom he might announce.

"Tell him it's a special request," Smiley said.

The smart young man pressed a button and spoke extremely quietly, much as he had spoken to Smiley.

The upstairs office was clean as a doctor's surgery with a polished plastic desk and a lot more machinery. A closed-circuit television supplied a daylight version of the scene downstairs. The same observation window that Smiley had already noticed looked down into the *séparées*. Herr Kretzschmar was what the Germans call a serious person. He was fiftyish, groomed, and thickset, with a dark suit and a pale tie. His hair was straw blond like a good Saxon's, his bland face neither welcomed nor rejected. He shook Smiley's hand briskly and motioned him to a chair. He seemed well accustomed to dealing with special requests.

"Please," Herr Kretzschmar said, and the preliminaries were over.

There was nowhere to go but forward.

"I understand you were once business partner to an acquaintance of mine named Otto Leipzig," Smiley said, sounding a little too loud to himself. "I happen to be visiting Hamburg and I wondered whether you could tell me where he is. His address does not appear to be listed anywhere."

Herr Kretzschmar's coffee was in a silver pot with a paper napkin round the handle to protect his fingers when he poured. He drank and put his cup down carefully, to avoid collision.

"Who are you, please?" Herr Kretzschmar asked. The Saxon twang made his voice flat. A small frown enhanced his air of respectability.

"Otto called me Max," Smiley said.

Herr Kretzschmar did not respond to this information but he took his time before putting his next question. His gaze, Smiley noticed again, was strangely innocent. *Otto never had a house in his life,* Toby had said. *For crash meetings, Kretzschmar played key-holder.*

"And your business with Herr Leipzig, if I may ask?"

"I represent a large company," Smiley said. "Among other interests, we own a literary and photographic agency for freelance reporters."

"So?"

"In the distant past, my parent company has been pleased to accept occasional offerings from Herr Leipzig—through intermediaries—and pass them out to our customers for processing and syndication."

"So?" Herr Kretzschmar repeated. His head had lifted slightly, but his expression had not altered.

"Recently the business relationship between my parent company and Herr Leipzig was revived." He paused slightly. "Initially by means of the telephone," he said, but Herr Kretzschmar might never have heard of the telephone. "Through intermediaries again, he sent us a sample of his work, which we were pleased to place for him. I came here to discuss terms and to commission further work. Assuming, of course, that Herr Leipzig is in a position to provide it."

"Of what nature was this work, please—that Herr Leipzig sent you—please, Herr Max?"

"It was a negative photograph of erotic content. My firm always insists on negatives. Herr Leipzig knew this, naturally." Smiley pointed carefully across the room. "I rather think it must have been taken from that window. A peculiarity of the photograph is that Herr Leipzig himself was modelling in it. One therefore assumes that a friend or business partner may have operated the camera."

Herr Kretzschmar's blue gaze remained as direct and innocent as before. His face, though strangely unmarked, struck Smiley as courageous, but he didn't know why.

You're messing around with a creep like Leipzig, then you better have a creep like me look after you, Toby had said.

"There is another aspect," Smiley said.

"Yes?"

"Unhappily the gentleman who was acting as intermediary on this occasion met with a serious accident shortly after the negative was put into our care. The usual line of communication with Herr Leipzig was therefore severed."

Herr Kretzschmar did not conceal his anxiety. A frown of what seemed to be genuine concern clouded his smooth face and he spoke quite sharply.

"How so an accident? What sort of accident?"

"A fatal one. I came to warn Otto and talk to him."

Herr Kretzschmar owned a fine gold pencil. Taking it deliberately from an inside pocket, he popped out the point and, still frowning, drew a pure circle on the pad before him. Then he set a cross on top, then he drew a line through his creation, then he tutted and said "Pity," and when he had done all this he straightened up, and spoke tersely into a machine.

"No disturbances," he said. In a murmur, the voice of the grey receptionist acknowledged the instruction.

"You said Herr Leipzig was an old acquaintance of your parent company?" Herr Kretzschmar resumed.

"As I believe you yourself were, long ago, Herr Kretzschmar."

"Please explain this more closely," Herr Kretzschmar said, turning the pencil slowly in both hands as if studying the quality of the gold.

"We are talking old history, of course," said Smiley deprecatingly.

"This I understand."

"When Herr Leipzig first escaped from Russia, he came to Schleswig-Holstein," Smiley said. "The organisation which had arranged his escape was based in Paris, but as a Balt, he preferred to live in northern Germany. Germany was still occupied and it was difficult for him to make a living."

"For anyone," Herr Kretzschmar corrected him. "For anyone at all to make a living. Those were fantastically hard times. The young of today have no idea."

"None," Smiley agreed. "And they were particularly hard for refugees. Whether they came from Estonia or from Saxony, life was hard for them."

"This is absolutely correct. The refugees had it worst. Please continue."

"In those days there was a considerable industry in information. Of all kinds. Military, industrial, political, economic. The victorious powers were prepared to pay large sums of money for enlightening material about each other. My parent company was involved in this commerce, and kept a representative here whose task was to collect such material and pass it back to London. Herr Leipzig and his partner became occasional clients. On a free-lance basis."

News of the General's fatal accident notwithstanding, a swift and most unexpected smile passed like a breeze across the surface of Herr Kretzschmar's features.

"Free lance," he said, as if he liked the words, and were new to them. "Free lance," he repeated. "That's what we were."

"Such relationships are naturally of a temporary nature," Smiley continued. "But Herr Leipzig, being a Balt, had other interests and continued over a long period to correspond with my firm through intermediaries in Paris." He paused. "Notably a certain General. A few years ago, following a dispute, the General was obliged to move to London, but Otto kept in touch with him. And the General on his side remained the intermediary."

"Until his accident," Herr Kretzschmar put in.

"Precisely," Smiley said.

"It was a traffic accident? An old man—a bit careless?"

"He was shot," said Smiley, and saw Herr Kretzschmar's face once more wince with displeasure. "But murdered," Smiley added, as if to reassure him. "It wasn't suicide or an accident or anything like that."

"Naturally," said Herr Kretzschmar, and offered Smiley a cigarette. Smiley declined, so he lit one for himself, took a few puffs, and stubbed it out. His pale complexion was a shade paler.

"You have met Otto? You know him?" Herr Kretzschmar asked in the tone of one making light conversation.

"I have met him once."

"Where?"

"I am not at liberty to say."

Herr Kretzschmar frowned, but in perplexity rather than disapproval.

"Tell me, please. If your parent company—okay, London—wanted to reach Herr Leipzig directly, what steps did it take?" Herr Kretzschmar asked.

"There was an arrangement involving the *Hamburger Abendblatt*."

"And if they wished to contact him very urgently?"

"There was you."

"You are police?" Herr Kretzschmar asked quietly. "Scotland Yard?"

"No." Smiley stared at Herr Kretzschmar and Herr Kretzschmar returned his gaze.

"Have you brought me something?" Herr Kretzschmar asked. At a loss, Smiley did not immediately reply. "Such as a letter of introduction? A card, for instance?"

"No."

"Nothing to show? That's a pity."

"Perhaps when I have seen him, I shall understand your question better."

"But you have seen it evidently, this photograph? You have it with you, maybe?"

Smiley took out his wallet, and passed the contact print across the desk. Holding it by the edges, Herr Kretzschmar studied it for a moment, but only by way of confirmation, then laid it on the plastic surface before him. As he did so, Smiley's sixth sense told him that Herr Kretzschmar was about to make a statement, in the way that Germans sometimes do make statements—whether of philosophy, or personal exculpation, or in order to be liked, or pitied. He began to suspect that Herr Kretzschmar, in his own estimation at least, was a companionable if misunderstood man; a man of heart; even a good man; and that his initial taciturnity was something he wore like a professional suit, reluctantly, in a world that he frequently found unsympathetic to his affectionate character.

"I wish to explain to you that I run a decent house here," Herr Kretzschmar remarked when he had once more, by the clinical modern lamp, glanced at the print on his desk. "I am not in the habit of photographing clients. Other people sell ties, I sell sex. The important thing to me is to conduct my business in an orderly and correct manner. But this was not business. This was friendship."

Smiley had the wisdom to keep silent.

Herr Kretzschmar frowned. His voice dropped and became

confiding: "You knew him, Herr Max? That old General? You were personally connected with him?"

"Yes."

"He was something, I understand?"

"He was indeed."

"A lion, huh?"

"A lion."

"Otto was crazy about him. My name is Claus. 'Claus,' he would say to me. 'That Vladimir, I love that man.' You follow me? Otto is a very loyal fellow. The General too?"

"He was," said Smiley.

"A lot of people do not believe in Otto. Your parent company also, they do not always believe in him. This is understandable. I make no reproach. But the General, he believed in Otto. Not in every detail. But in the big things." Holding up his forearm, Herr Kretzschmar clenched his fist and it was suddenly a very big fist indeed. "When things got hard, the old General believed in Otto absolutely. I too believe in Otto, Herr Max. In the big things. But I am German, I am not political, I am a businessman. These refugee stories are finished for me. You follow me?"

"Of course."

"But not for Otto. Never. Otto is a fanatic. I can use that word. Fanatic. This is one reason why our lives have diverged. Nevertheless he is my friend. Anyone harms him, they get a bad time from Kretzschmar." His face clouded in momentary mystification. "You are sure you have nothing for me, Herr Max?"

"Beyond the photograph, I have nothing for you."

Reluctantly Herr Kretzschmar once more dismissed the matter, but it took him time; he was uneasy.

"The old General was shot in England?" he asked finally.

"Yes."

"But you consider nevertheless that Otto too is in danger?"

"Yes, but I think he has chosen to be."

Herr Kretzschmar was pleased with this answer and nodded energetically twice.

"So do I. I also. This is my clear impression of him. I told him many times: 'Otto, you should have been a high-wire acrobat.' To Otto, in my opinion, no day is worth living unless it threatens on at least six separate occasions to be his last. You permit me to make certain observations on my relationship with Otto?"

"Please," said Smiley politely.

Putting his forearms on the plastic surface, Herr Kretzschmar settled himself into a more comfortable posture for confession.

"There was a time when Otto and Claus Kretzschmar did everything together—stole a lot of horses, as we say. I was from Saxony, Otto came from the East. A Balt. Not Russia—he would insist—Estonia. He had had a tough time, studied the interior of a good few prisons, some bad fellow had betrayed him back in Estonia. A girl had died, and he was pretty mad about that. There was an uncle near Kiel but he was a swine. I may say that. A swine. We had no money, we were comrades and fellow thieves. This was normal, Herr Max."

Smiley acknowledged the instructive point.

"One of our lines of business was to sell information. You have said correctly that information was a valuable commodity in those days. For example, we would hear of a refugee who had just come over and had not yet been interviewed by the Allies. Or maybe a Russian deserted. Or the master of a cargo ship. We hear about him, we question him. If we are ingenious, we contrive to sell the same report in different versions to three or even four different buyers. The Americans, the French, the British, the Germans themselves, already back in the saddle, yes. Sometimes, as long as it was inaccurate, even five buyers." He gave a rich laugh. "But only if it was inaccurate, okay? On other occasions, when we were out of sources, we invented—no question. We had maps, good imagination, good contacts. Don't misunderstand me: Kretzschmar is an enemy of Communism. We are talking old history, like you said, Herr Max. It was necessary to survive. Otto had the idea, Kretzschmar did the work. Otto was not the inventor of work, I would say." Herr Kretzschmar frowned. "But in one respect Otto was a very serious man. He had a debt to settle. Of this he spoke repeatedly. Maybe against the fellow who betrayed him and killed his girl, maybe against the whole human race. What do I know? He had to be active. Politically active. So for this purpose he went to Paris, on many occasions. Many."

Herr Kretzschmar allowed himself a short period of reflection.

"I shall be frank," he announced.

"And I shall respect your confidence," said Smiley.

"I believe you. You are Max. The General was your friend, Otto told me this. Otto met you once, he admired you. Very well. I shall be frank with you. Many years ago Otto Leipzig went to prison for me. In those days I was not respectable. Now that I have money, I can afford to be. We stole something, he was caught, he lied and took the whole rap. I wanted to pay him. He said, 'What the hell? If you are Otto Leipzig, a year in prison is a holiday.' I visited him every week, I bribed the guards to take him special food—even once a woman. When he came out, I again tried to pay him. He declined my offers. 'One day I'll ask you something,' he said. 'Maybe your wife.' 'You shall have her,' I told him. 'No problem.' Herr Max, I assume you are an Englishman. You will appreciate my position."

Smiley said he did.

"Two months ago—what do I know, maybe more, maybe less—the old General comes through on the telephone. He needs Otto urgently. 'Not tomorrow, but tonight.' Sometimes he used to call that way from Paris, using code-names, all this nonsense. The old General is a secretive fellow. So is Otto. Like children, know what I mean? Never mind."

Herr Kretzschmar made an indulgent sweep of his big hand across his face, as if he were wiping away a cobweb. "'Listen,' I tell him. 'I don't know where Otto is. Last time I heard of him, he was in bad trouble with some business he started. I've got to find him, it will take time. Maybe tomorrow, maybe ten days.' Then the old man tells me, 'I sent you a letter for him. Guard it with your life.' Next day a letter comes, express for Kretzschmar, postmark London. Inside, a second envelope. 'Urgent and top secret for Otto.' *Top secret*, okay? So the old guy's crazy. Never mind. You know that big handwriting of his, strong like an army order?"

Smiley did.

"I find Otto. He's hiding from trouble again, no money. One suit he's got, but dresses like a film star. I give him the old man's letter."

"Which is a fat one," Smiley suggested, thinking of the seven pages of photocopy paper. Thinking of Mikhel's black machine parked like an old tank in the library.

"Sure. A long letter. He opened it while I was there—"

Herr Kretzschmar broke off and stared at Smiley, and from his expression seemed, reluctantly, to recognise a restraint.

"A long letter," he repeated. "Many pages. He read it, he got pretty excited. 'Claus,' he said. 'Lend me some money. I got to go to Paris.' I lend him some money, five hundred marks, no problem. After this I don't see him much for a time. A couple of occasions he comes here, makes a phone call. I don't listen. Then a month ago he came to see me." Again he broke off, and again Smiley felt his restraint. "I am being frank," he said, as if once again enjoining Smiley to secrecy. "He was—well, I would say excited."

"He wanted to use the night-club," Smiley suggested helpfully.

"'Claus,' he said. 'Do what I ask and you have paid your debt to me.' He called it a honey-trap. He would bring a man to the club, an Ivan, someone he knew well, had been cultivating for many years, he said, a very particular swine. This man was the target. He called him 'the target.' He said it was the chance of his life, everything he had waited for. The best girls, the best champagne, the best show. For one night, courtesy of Kretzschmar. The climax of his efforts, he said. The chance to pay old debts and make some money as well. He was owed, he said. Now he would collect. He promised there would be no repercussions. I said 'No problem.' 'Also, Claus, I wish you to photograph us,' he tells me. I said 'No problem' again. So he came. And brought his target."

Herr Kretzschmar's narrative had suddenly become uncharacteristically sparse. In the hiatus, Smiley slipped in a question, of which the purpose went far beyond the context: "What language did they speak?"

Herr Kretzschmar hesitated, frowned, but finally answered: "At first his target pretended to be French, but the girls did not speak much French so he spoke German to them. But with Otto he spoke Russian. He was disagreeable, this target. Smelt a lot, sweated a lot, and was in certain other ways not a gentleman. The girls did not like to stay with him. They came to me and complained. I sent them back but they still grumbled."

He seemed embarrassed.

"Another small question," said Smiley, as the awkwardness returned.

"Please."

"How could Otto Leipzig promise there would be no repercussions since he was presumably setting out to blackmail this man?"

"The target was not the *end*," Herr Kretzschmar said, pursing his lips to assist the intellectual point. "He was the means."

"The means to someone else?"

"Otto was not precise. 'A step on the General's ladder' was his expression. 'For me, Claus, the target is enough. The target and afterwards the money. But for the General, he is only a step on the ladder. For Max also.' For reasons I did not understand, the money was also dependent upon the General's satisfaction. Or perhaps yours." He paused, as if hoping Smiley might enlighten him. Smiley did not. "It was not my wish to ask questions or make conditions," Herr Kretzschmar continued, picking his words with much greater severity. "Otto and his target were admitted by the back entrance, and shown straight to a *séparée*. We arranged to display nothing that would indicate the name of the establishment. Not long ago, a night-club down the road went bankrupt," Herr Kretzschmar said, in a tone that suggested he might not be wholly desolated by the event. "Place called the Freudenjacht. I had bought certain equipment at the sale. Matches. Plates, we spread them around the *séparée*." Smiley remembered the letters "ACHT" on the ashtray in the photograph.

"Can you tell me what the two men discussed?"

"No." He changed his answer: "I have no Russian," he said. He made the same disowning wave of his hand. "In German they talked about God and the world. Everything."

"I see."

"That's all I know."

"How was Otto in his manner?" Smiley asked. "Was he still excited?"

"I never saw Otto like that before in my life. He was laughing like an executioner, speaking three languages at once, not drunk but extremely animated, singing, telling jokes, I don't know what. That's all I know," Herr Kretzschmar repeated, with embarrassment.

Smiley glanced discreetly at the observation window and at the grey boxes of machinery. He glimpsed once more in Herr Kretzschmar's little television screen the soundless twining and parting of the white bodies on the other side of the wall. He saw his last question, he recognised its logic, he sensed the wealth it promised. Yet the same lifetime's instinct that had brought him this far now held him back. Nothing at this moment, no short-term dividend, was worth the risk of alienating Kretzschmar, and closing the road to Otto Leipzig.

"And Otto gave you no other description of his target?" Smiley asked, for the sake of asking something; to help him run their conversation down.

"During the evening, he came to me once. Up here. He excused himself from the company and came up here to make sure the arrangements were in order. He looked at the screen there and laughed. 'Now I have taken him over the edge and he can't get back,' he said. I did not ask any more. That is all that happened."

Herr Kretzschmar was writing his instructions for Smiley on a leather-backed jotting pad with gold corners.

"Otto lives in bad circumstances," he said. "One cannot alter that. Giving him money does not improve his social standards. He remains"—Herr Kretzschmar hesitated—"he remains at heart, Herr Max, a *gypsy*. Do not misunderstand me."

"Will you warn him that I am coming?"

"We have agreed not to use the telephone. The official link between us is completely closed." He handed him the sheet of paper. "I strongly advise you to take care," Herr Kretzschmar said. "Otto will be very angry when he hears the old General has been shot." He saw Smiley to the door. "What did they charge you down there?"

"I'm sorry?"

"Downstairs. How much did they take from you?"

"A hundred and seventy-five marks for membership."

"With the drinks inside, at least two hundred. I'll tell them to give it back to you at the door. You English are poor these days. Too many trade unions. How'd you like the show?"

"It was very artistic," said Smiley.

Herr Kretzschmar was once again very pleased with Smiley's

answer. He patted Smiley on the shoulder: "Maybe you should have more fun in life."

"Maybe I should have done," Smiley agreed.

"Greet Otto for me," said Herr Kretzschmar.

"I will," Smiley promised.

Herr Kretzschmar hesitated, and the same momentary bewilderment came over him.

"And you have nothing for me?" he repeated. "No papers, for example?"

"No."

"Pity."

As Smiley left, Herr Kretzschmar was already at the telephone, attending to other special requests.

He returned to the hotel. A drunken night porter opened the door to him, full of suggestions about the wonderful girls he could send to Smiley's room. He woke, if he had ever slept, to the chime of church bells and the honk of shipping in the harbour, carried to him on the wind. But there are nightmares that do not go away with daylight, and as he drove northward over the fens in his hired Opel, the terrors that hovered in the mist were the same as those that had plagued him in the night.

17

The roads were as empty as the landscape. Through breaks in the mist, he glimpsed now a patch of cornfield, now a red farmhouse crouched low against the wind. A blue notice said "KAI." He swung sharply into a slip-road, dropping two flights, and saw ahead of him the wharf, a complex of low grey barracks dwarfed by the decks of cargo ships. A red-and-white pole guarded the entrance, there was a customs notice in several languages, but not a human soul in sight. Stopping the car, Smiley got out and walked lightly to the barrier. The red push-button was as big as a saucer. He pressed it and the shriek of its bell set a pair of herons flapping into the white mist. A control tower stood to his left on tubular legs. He heard a door slam and a ring of metal and watched a bearded figure in blue uniform stomp down the iron staircase to the bottom step. The man called to him, "What do you want then?" Not waiting for an answer, he released the boom and waved Smiley through. The tarmac was like a vast bombed area cemented in, bordered by cranes and pressed down by the fogged white sky. Beyond it, the low sea looked too frail for the weight of so much shipping. He glanced in the mirror and saw the spires of a sea town etched like an old print half-way up the page. He glanced out to sea and saw through the mist the line of buoys and winking lamps that marked the water border to East Germany and the start of seven and a half thousand miles of Soviet Empire. That's where the herons went, he thought. He was driving at a crawl between red-and-white traffic cones towards a container-park heaped with car tyres and logs. "Left at the container-park," Herr Kretzschmar had said. Obediently, Smiley swung slowly left, looking for an old house, though an old house in this Hanseatic dumping ground seemed a physical impossibility. But Herr Kretzschmar had said, "Look for an old house marked 'Office,'" and Herr Kretzschmar did not make errors.

He bumped over a railway track and headed for the cargo ships. Beams of morning sun had broken through the mist, making their white paintwork dazzle. He entered an alley comprised of control rooms for the cranes, each like a modern signal-box, each with green levers and big windows. And there at the end of the alley, exactly as Herr Kretzschmar had promised, stood the old tin house with a high tin gable cut like fretwork and crowned with a peeling flag-post. The electric wires that led into it seemed to hold it up; there was an old water pump beside it, dripping, with a tin mug chained to its pedestal. On the wooden door, in faded Gothic lettering, stood the one word "BUREAU," in the French spelling, not the German, above a newer notice saying "P.K. BERGEN, IMPORT-EXPORT." *He works there as the night clerk*, Herr Kretzschmar had said. *What he does by day only God and the Devil know.*

He rang the bell, then stood well back from the door, very visible. He was keeping his hands clear of his pockets and they were very visible too. He had buttoned his overcoat to the neck. He wore no hat. He had parked the car sideways to the house so that anyone indoors could see the car was empty. *I am alone and unarmed*, he was trying to say. *I am not their man, but yours.* He rang the bell again and called "Herr Leipzig!" An upper window opened, and a pretty woman looked out blearily, holding a blanket round her shoulders.

"I'm sorry," Smiley called up to her politely. "I was looking for Herr Leipzig. It's rather important."

"Not here," she replied, and smiled.

A man joined her. He was young and unshaven, with tattoo marks on his arms and chest. They spoke together a moment, Smiley guessed in Polish.

"*Nix hier*," the man confirmed guardedly. "*Otto nix hier.*"

"We're just the temporary tenants," the girl called down. "When Otto's broke, he moves to his country villa and rents us the apartment."

She repeated this to her man, who this time laughed.

"*Nix hier*," he repeated. "No money. Nobody has money."

They were enjoying the crisp morning, and the company.

"How long since you saw him?" Smiley asked.

More conference. Was it this day or that day? Smiley had the impression they had lost track of time.

"Thursday," the girl announced, smiling again.

"Thursday," her man repeated.

"I've got good news for him," Smiley explained cheerfully, catching her mood. He patted his side pocket. "Money. *Pinka-pinka*. All for Otto. He's earned it in commission. I promised to bring it to him yesterday."

The girl interpreted all this and the man argued with her, and the girl laughed again.

"My friend says don't give it to him or Otto will come back and move us out and we'll have nowhere to make love!"

Try the water camp, she suggested, pointing with her bare arm. Two kilometres along the main road, over the railway and past the windmill, then right—she looked at her hands, then curved one prettily towards her lover—yes, right; right towards the lake, though you don't see the lake till you get to it.

"What is the place called?" Smiley asked.

"It has no name," she said. "It's just a place. Ask for holiday houses to let, then drive on towards the boats. Ask for Walther. If Otto is around, Walther will know where to find him."

"Thank you."

"Walther knows everything!" she called. "He is like a professor!"

She translated this also, but this time her man looked angry. "*Bad* professor!" he called down. "Walther bad man!"

"Are you a professor too?" the girl asked Smiley.

"No. No, unfortunately not." He laughed and thanked them, and they watched him get into his car as if they were children at a celebration. The day, the spreading sunshine, his visit—everything was fun for them. He lowered the window to say goodbye and heard her say something he couldn't catch.

"What was that?" he called up to her, still smiling.

"I said, 'Then Otto is twice lucky, for a change!'" the girl repeated.

"Why?" asked Smiley, and stopped the engine. "Why is he twice lucky?"

The girl shrugged. The blanket was slipping from her shoulders and the blanket was all she wore. Her man put an arm round her and pulled it up again for decency.

"Last week the unexpected visit from the East," she said. "And today the money." She opened her hands. "Otto is Sunday's child for once. That's all."

Then she saw Smiley's face, and the laughter went clean out of her voice.

"Visitor?" Smiley repeated. "Who was the visitor?"

"From the East," she said.

Seeing her dismay, terrified she might disappear altogether, Smiley with difficulty resurrected his appearance of good humour.

"Not his brother, was it?" he asked gaily, all enthusiasm. He held out one hand, cupping it over the mythical brother's head. "A small chap? Spectacles like mine?"

"No, *no!* A big fellow. With a chauffeur. Rich."

Smiley shook his head, affecting light-hearted disappointment. "Then I don't know him," he said. "Otto's brother was certainly never rich." He succeeded in laughing outright. "Unless he was the chauffeur, of course," he added.

* * *

He followed her directions exactly, with the secret calmness of emergency. To be conveyed. To have no will of his own. To be conveyed, to pray, to make deals with your Maker. Oh, God, don't make it happen, not another Vladimir. In the sunlight the brown fields had turned to gold, but the sweat on Smiley's back was like a cold hand stinging his skin. He followed her directions seeing everything as if it were his last day, knowing that the big fellow with the chauffeur had gone ahead of him. He saw the farmhouse with the old horse-plough in the barn, the faulty beer sign with its neon blinking, the window-boxes of geraniums like blood. He saw the windmill like a giant pepper-mill and the field full of white geese all running with the gusty wind. He saw the herons skimming like sails over the fens. He was driving too fast. I should drive more often, he thought; I'm out of practice, out of control. The road changed from tarmac to gravel, gravel to dust, and the dust blew up round the car like a sandstorm. He entered some pine trees and on the other side of them saw a sign saying "HOLIDAY HOUSES TO LET," and a row of shuttered asbestos bungalows waiting for their summer paint. He kept going and in the distance saw a coppice of masts, and brown water low in its basin. He headed for the masts, bumped over a pot-hole, and heard a frightful crack from under the car. He supposed it was the exhaust, because the noise of his engine was suddenly much louder, and half the water birds in Schleswig-Holstein had taken fright at his arrival.

He passed a farm and entered the protective darkness of trees, then emerged in a stark and brilliant frame of whiteness of which a broken jetty and a few faint olive-coloured reeds made up the foreground, and an enormous sky the rest. The boats lay to his right, beside an inlet. Shabby caravans were parked along the track that led to them, grubby washing hung between the television aerials. He passed a tent in its own vegetable patch and a couple of broken huts that had once been military. On one, a psychedelic sunrise had been painted, and it was peeling. Three old cars and some heaped rubbish stood beside it. He parked and followed a mud path through the reeds to the shore. In the grass harbour lay a cluster of improvised houseboats, some of them converted landing-craft from the war. It was colder here, and for some reason darker. The boats he had seen were day boats, moored in a huddle apart, mostly under tarpaulins. A couple of radios played, but at first he saw nobody. Then he noticed a backwater, and a blue dinghy made fast in it. And, in the dinghy, one gnarled old man in a sailcloth jacket and a black peaked cap, massaging his neck as if he had just woken up.

"Are you Walther?" Smiley asked.

Still rubbing his neck, the old man seemed to nod.

"I'm looking for Otto Leipzig. They told me at the wharf I might find him here."

Walther's eyes were cut almond-shaped into the crumpled brown paper of his skin.

"*Isadora*," he said.

He pointed at a rickety jetty farther down the shore. The *Isadora* lay at the end of it, a forty-foot motor launch down on her luck, a Grand Hotel awaiting demolition. The portholes were curtained; one of them was smashed, another was repaired with Scotch tape. The planks of the jetty yielded alarmingly to Smiley's tread. Once he nearly fell, and twice, to bridge the gaps, he had to stride much wider than seemed safe to his short legs. At the end of the jetty, he realised that the *Isadora* was adrift. She had slipped her moorings at the stern and shifted twelve feet out to sea, which was probably the longest journey she would ever make. The cabin doors were closed, their windows curtained. There was no small boat.

The old man sat sixty yards off, resting on his oars. He had rowed out of the backwater to watch. Smiley cupped his hands and yelled: "How do I get to him?"

"If you want him, call him," the old man replied, not seeming to lift his voice at all.

Turning to the launch, Smiley called "Otto." He called softly, then more loudly, but inside the *Isadora* nothing stirred. He watched the curtains. He watched the oily water tossing against the rotting hull. He listened and thought he heard music like the music in Herr Kretzschmar's club, but it might have been echo from another boat. From the dinghy, Walther's brown face still watched him.

"Call again," he growled. "Keep calling, if you want him."

But Smiley had an instinct against being commanded by the old man. He could feel his authority and his contempt and he resented both.

"Is he in here or not?" Smiley called. "I said, 'Is he in here?'"

The old man did not budge.

"Did you see him come aboard?" Smiley insisted.

He saw the brown head turn, and knew the old man was spitting into the water.

"The wild pig comes and goes," Smiley heard him say. "What the hell do I care?"

"So when did he come last?"

At the sound of their voices a couple of heads had lifted out of other boats. They stared at Smiley without expression: the little fat stranger standing at the end of the broken jetty. On the shore a ragtag group had formed: a girl in shorts, an old woman, two blond teen-aged boys dressed alike. There was something that linked them in their disparity: a prison look; submission to the same bad laws.

"I'm looking for Otto Leipzig," Smiley called to all of them. "Can anyone tell me, please, whether he's around?" On a houseboat not too far away, a bearded man was lowering a bucket into the water. Smiley's eye selected him. "Is there anyone aboard the *Isadora?*" he asked.

The bucket gurgled and filled. The bearded man pulled it out, but didn't speak.

"You should see his car," a woman shouted shrilly from the shore, or perhaps it was a child. "They took it to the wood."

The wood lay a hundred yards back from the water, mostly saplings and birch trees.

"Who did?" Smiley asked. "Who took it there?"

Whoever had spoken chose not to speak again. The old man was rowing himself towards the jetty. Smiley watched him approach, watched him back the stern towards the jetty steps. Without hesitating, Smiley clambered aboard. The old man pulled him the few strokes to the *Isadora*'s side. A cigarette was jammed between his cracked old lips and, like his eyes, it shone unnaturally against the evil gloom of his weathered face.

"Come far?" the old man asked.

"I'm a friend of his," Smiley said.

There was rust and weed on the *Isadora*'s ladder, and as Smiley reached the deck it was slippery with dew. He looked for signs of life and saw none. He looked for footprints in the dew, in vain. A couple of fixed fishing-lines hung into the water, made fast to the rusted balustrade, but they could have been there for weeks. He listened, and heard again, very faintly, the strains of slow band music. From the shore? Or from farther out? From neither. The sound came from under his feet, and it was as if someone were playing a seventy-eight record on thirty-three.

He looked down and saw the old man in his dinghy, leaning back, and the peak of his cap pulled over his eyes, while he slowly conducted to the beat. He tried the cabin door and it was locked, but the door did not seem strong—nothing did—so he walked around the deck till he found a rusted screwdriver to use as a jemmy. He shoved it into the gap, worked it backwards and forwards, and suddenly to his surprise the whole door went, frame, hinges, lock, and everything else, with a bang like an explosion, followed by a shower of red dust from the rotten timber. A big slow moth thudded against his cheek and left it stinging strangely for a good while afterwards, till he began to wonder whether it was a bee. Inside, the cabin was pitch dark, but the music was a little louder. He was on the top rung of the ladder, and even with the daylight behind him the darkness below remained absolute. He pressed a light switch. It didn't work, so he stepped back and spoke down to the old man in his dinghy: "Matches."

For a moment Smiley nearly lost his temper. The peaked cap didn't stir, nor did the conducting cease. He shouted, and this time a box of matches landed at his feet. He took them into the cabin and lit one, and saw the exhausted transistor radio that was still putting out music with the last of its energy, and it was about the only thing intact, the only thing still functioning, in all the devastation round it.

The match had gone out. He pulled the curtains, but not on the landward side, before he lit another. He didn't want the old man looking in. In the grey sideways light, Leipzig was ridiculously like his tiny portrait in the photograph taken by Herr Kretzschmar. He was naked, he was lying where they had trussed him, even if there was no girl and no Kirov either. The hewn Toulouse-Lautrec face, blackened with bruising and gagged with several strands of rope, was as jagged and articulate in death as Smiley had remembered it in life. They must have used the music to drown the noise while they tortured him, Smiley thought. But he doubted whether the music would have been enough. He went on staring at the radio as a point of reference, a thing to go back to when the body became too much to look at before the match went out. Japanese, he noticed. Odd, he thought. Fix on the oddness of it. How odd of the technical Germans to buy Japanese radios. He wondered whether the Japanese returned the compliment. Keep wondering, he urged himself ferociously; keep your whole mind on this interesting economic phenomenon of the exchange of goods between highly industrialised nations.

Still staring at the radio, Smiley righted a folding stool and sat on it. Slowly, he returned his gaze to Leipzig's face. Some dead faces, he reflected, have the dull, even stupid look of a patient under anaesthetic. Others preserve a single mood of the once varied nature—the dead man as lover, as father, as car driver, bridge player, tyrant. And some, like Vladimir's, have ceased to preserve anything. But Leipzig's face, even with the ropes across it, had a mood, and it was anger: anger intensified by pain, turned to fury by it; anger that had increased and become the whole man as the body lost its strength.

Hate, Connie had said.

Methodically, Smiley peered about him, thinking as slowly as he could manage, trying, by his examination of the debris, to reconstruct their progress. First the fight before they overpowered him, which he deduced from the smashed table-legs and chairs and lamps and shelves, and anything else that could be ripped from its housing and either wielded or thrown. Then the search, which took place after they had trussed him and in the intervals while they questioned him. Their frustration was written everywhere. They had ripped out wall-boards and floor-boards, and cupboard drawers and clothes and mattresses and by the end anything that came apart, anything that was not a minimal component, as Otto Leipzig still refused to talk. He noticed also that there was blood in surprising places—in the wash-basin, over the stove. He liked to think it was not all Otto Leipzig's. And finally, in desperation, they had killed him, because those were Karla's orders, that was Karla's way. "The killing comes first, the questioning second," Vladimir used to say.

I too believe in Otto, Smiley thought stupidly, recalling Herr Kretzschmar's words. *Not in every detail but in the big things.* So do I, he thought. He believed in him, at that moment, as surely as he believed in death, and in the Sandman. As for Vladimir, so for Otto Leipzig: death had ruled that he was telling the truth.

From the direction of the shore, he heard a woman yelling: "What's he found? Has he found something? Who is he?"

He returned aloft. The old man had shipped his oars and let the dinghy drift. He sat with his back to the ladder, head hunched into his big shoulders. He had finished his cigarette and lit a cigar as if it were Sunday. And at the same moment as Smiley saw the old man, he also saw the chalk mark. It was in the same line of vision, but very close to him, swimming in the misted lenses of his spectacles. He had to lower his head and look over the top of them to fix on it. A chalk mark, sharp and yellow. One line, carefully drawn over the rust of the balustrade, and a foot away from it a reel of fishing-line, made fast with a sailor's knot. The old man was watching him; so, for all he knew, was the growing group of watchers on the shore, but he had no option. He pulled at the line and it was heavy. He pulled steadily, hand over hand, till the line changed to gut, and he found himself pulling that instead. The gut grew suddenly tight. Cautiously he kept pulling. The people on the shore had grown expectant; he could feel their interest even across the water. The old man had put back his head and was watching through the black shadow of his cap. Suddenly, with a plop, the catch jumped clear of the water and a peal of ribald laughter rose from the spectators: one old gym-shoe, green, with the lace still in it, and the hook that held it to the line was big enough to beach a shark. The laughter slowly died. Smiley unhooked the shoe. Then, as if he had other business there, he lumbered back into the cabin till he was out of sight, leaving the door ajar for light.

But happening to take the gym-shoe with him.

An oilskin packet was hand-stitched into the toe of the shoe. He pulled it out. It was a tobacco pouch, stitched along the top and folded several times. *Moscow Rules*, he thought woodenly. *Moscow Rules all the way.* How many more dead men's legacies must I inherit? he wondered. *Though we value none/But the horizontal one.* He had unpicked the stitching. Inside the pouch was another wrapping, this time a latex-rubber sheath knotted at the throat. And secreted inside the sheath, one hard wad of cardboard smaller than a book of matches. Smiley spread it open. It was half a picture postcard. Black-and-white, not even coloured. Half a dull picture of Schleswig-Holstein landscape with half a herd of Friesian cattle grazing in grey sunlight. Ripped with a deliberate jaggedness. No writing on the back, no address, no stamp. Just half a boring, unposted postcard; but they had tortured him, then killed him for it, and still not found it, or any of the treasures it unlocked. Putting it, together with its wrapping, into the inside pocket of his jacket, he returned to the deck. The old man in his dinghy had drawn alongside. Without a word, Smiley climbed slowly down the ladder. The crowd of camp people on the shore had grown still larger.

"Drunk?" the old man asked. "Sleeping it off?"

Smiley stepped into the dinghy and, as the old man pulled away, looked back at the *Isadora* once more. He saw the broken porthole, he thought of the wreckage in the cabin, the paper-thin sides that allowed him to hear the very shuffle of feet on the shore. He imagined the fight and Leipzig's screams filling the whole camp with their din. He imagined the silent group standing where they were standing now, without a voice or a helping hand between them.

"It was a party," the old man said carelessly while he made the dinghy fast against the jetty. "Lots of music, singing. They warned us it would be loud." He tugged at a knot. "Maybe they quarrelled. So what? Many people quarrel. They made some noise, played some jazz. So what? We are musical people here."

"They were police," a woman called from the group on the shore. "When police go about their business, it is the duty of the citizen to keep his trap shut."

"Show me his car," Smiley said.

They moved in a rabble, no one leading. The old man strode at Smiley's side, half custodian, half bodyguard, making a way for him with facetious ceremony. The children ran everywhere but they kept well clear of the old man. The Volkswagen stood in a coppice and it was ripped apart like the cabin of the *Isadora*. The roof lining hung in shreds, the seats had been pulled out and split open. The wheels were missing but Smiley guessed that had happened since. The camp people stood round it reverently, as if it were their show-piece. Someone had tried to burn it but the fire had not caught.

"He was scum," the old man explained. "They all are. Look at them. Polacks, criminals, subhumans."

Smiley's Opel stood where he had parked it, at the edge of the track, close to the dustbins, and the two blond boys who were dressed alike were standing over the boot beating the lid with hammers. As he walked towards them, he could see their forelocks bouncing with each blow. They wore jeans and black boots studded with love-daisies.

"Tell them to stop hitting my car," Smiley said to the old man.

The camp people were following at a distance. He could hear again the furtive shuffle of their feet, like a refugee army. He reached his car and had the keys in his hand, and the two boys were still bent over the back hitting with all their might. But when he walked round to take a look, all they had done was beat the lid of the boot right off its hinges, then fold it and beat it flat again till it lay like a crude parcel on the floor. He looked at the wheels but nothing seemed amiss. He didn't know what else to look for. Then he saw that they had tied a dustbin to the rear bumper with string. Keeping clear, he tugged at the string to break it, but it refused to yield. He tried it with his teeth, without success. The old man lent him a penknife and he cut it, keeping clear of the boys with their hammers. The camp people had made a half ring and they were holding up their children for the farewell. Smiley got into the car and the old man slammed the door after him with a tremendous heave. Smiley had the key in the ignition, but by the time he turned it, one of the boys had draped himself over the bonnet as languidly as a model at a motor show and the other was tapping politely at the window.

Smiley lowered the window. "What do you want?" he asked.

The boy held out his palm. "Repairs," he explained. "Your boot didn't shut properly. Time and materials. Overheads. Parking." He indicated his thumb-nail. "My colleague here hurt his hand. It could have been serious."

Smiley looked at the boy's face and saw no human instinct that he understood.

"You have repaired nothing. You have done damage. Ask your friend to get off the car."

The boys conferred, seeming to disagree. They did this under the full gaze of the crowd, in a reasoned manner, slowly pushing each other's shoulders and making rhetorical gestures that did not coincide with their words. They talked about nature and about politics, and their Platonic dialogue might have gone on indefinitely if the boy who was on the car had not stood up in order to make the best of a debating point. As he did so, he broke off a windscreen wiper as if it were a flower and handed it to the old man. Driving away, Smiley looked in his mirror and saw a ring of faces staring after him with the old man at their centre. Nobody waved goodbye.

He drove without haste, weighing the chances, while the car clanged like an old fire-engine. He supposed they had done something else to it as well, something he had failed to notice. He had left Germany before, he had come and gone illicitly, he had hunted while on the run, and though he was old now and in a different Germany, he felt as if he had been returned to the wild. He had no way of knowing whether anybody from the water camp had telephoned the police, but he took it for an accomplished fact. The boat was open and its secret out. Those who had looked away would now be the first to come forward as good citizens. He had seen that before as well.

He entered a sea town, the boot—if it *was* the boot—still clanking behind him. Or perhaps it's the exhaust, he thought; the pot-hole I crashed into on the way to the camp. A hot, unseasonable sun had replaced the morning mists. There were no trees. An amazing brilliance was opening around him. It was still early, and empty horse carriages stood waiting for the first tourists. The sand was a pattern of craters dug in the summer by sun-worshippers to escape the wind. He could hear the tinny echo of his own progress bouncing between the painted shop-fronts, and the sunlight seemed to make it even louder. Where he passed people, he saw their heads lift to stare after him because of the row the car made.

They'll know the car, he thought. Even if nobody at the water camp remembered the number, the smashed boot would give him away. He turned off the main street. The sun was really very bright indeed. "A man came, Herr Wachtmeister," they would be saying to the police patrol. "This morning, Herr Wachtmeister. He said he was a friend. He looked in the boat and then drove away. He asked us nothing, Captain. He was unmoved. He fished a shoe, Herr Wachtmeister. Imagine—a shoe!"

He was heading for the railway station, following the signs, looking for a place where you could park a car all day. The station was red brick and massive, he supposed from before the war. He passed it and found a big car-park to his left. A line of shedding trees ran through it, and there were leaves on some of the cars. A machine took his money and issued him a ticket to stick on his windscreen. He backed into the middle of a line, the boot as far out of sight as possible against a mud bank. He stepped out and the extraordinary sun hit him like a slap. There was not a breath of wind. He locked the car and put the keys in the exhaust-pipe, he didn't quite know why, except that he felt apologetic towards the hire company. He kicked up the leaves and sand till the front number-plate was almost hidden. In an hour, in this St. Luke's summer, there would be a hundred and more cars in the park.

He had noticed a men's clothes shop in the main street. He bought a linen jacket there but nothing more, because people who buy whole outfits are remembered. He did not wear it, but carried it in a plastic bag. In a side-street full of boutiques he bought a gaudy straw hat and, from a stationer's, a holiday map of the area, and a railway timetable of the region Hamburg, Schleswig-Holstein, and Lower Saxony. He didn't wear the hat either, but kept it in its bag like the jacket. He was sweating from the unexpected heat. The heat was upsetting him; it was as absurd as snow in summer. He went to a telephone-box and again consulted local directories. Hamburg had no Claus Kretzschmar, but one of the Schleswig-Holstein directories had a Kretzschmar who lived in a place Smiley had never heard of. He studied his map and found a small town by that name on the main railway line to Hamburg. This pleased him very much.

Calmly, all other thoughts bound down with iron bands, Smiley once more did his sums. Within moments of finding the car, the police would be talking to the hire firm in Hamburg. As soon as they had spoken to the hire firm and obtained his name and description, they would put a watch on the airport and other crossing places. Kretzschmar was a night-bird and would sleep late. The town where he lived was an hour away by stopping train.

He returned to the railway station. The main concourse was a Wagnerian fantasy of a Gothic court, with an arched roof and a huge stained-glass window that poured out coloured sunbeams onto the ceramic floor. From a telephone-box, he rang Hamburg Airport, giving his name as "Standfast, initial J," which was the name on the passport he had collected from his London club. The first available flight to London was this evening at six but only first-class was open. He booked a first-class seat and said he would upgrade his economy ticket on arrival at the airport. The girl said, "Then please come half an hour before check-in." Smiley promised he would—he wanted to make an impression—but no, alas, Mr. Standfast had no phone number where he could be reached meanwhile. There was nothing in her tone to suggest she had a security officer standing behind her with a Telex in his hand, whispering instructions in her ear, but he guessed that within a couple of hours Mr. Standfast's seat reservation was going to ring a lot of bells, because it was Mr. Standfast who had hired the Opel car. He stepped back into the concourse, and the shafts of coloured light. There were two ticket counters and two short queues. At the first, an intelligent girl attended him and he bought a second-class single ticket to Hamburg. But it was a deliberately laboured purchase, full of indecision and nervousness, and when he had made it he insisted on writing down times of departure and arrival: also on borrowing her ball-point and a pad of paper.

In the men's room, having first transferred the contents of his pockets, beginning with the treasured piece of postcard from Leipzig's boat, he changed into the linen jacket and straw hat, then went to the second ticket counter where, with a minimum of fuss, he bought a ticket on the stopping train to Kretzschmar's town. To do this, he avoided looking at the attendant at all, concentrating instead on the ticket and his change, from under the brim of his loud straw hat. Before leaving he took one last precaution. He made a wrong-number phone call to Herr Kretzschmar and established from an indignant wife that it was a scandal to telephone anybody so early. As a last measure, he folded the plastic carrier-bags into his pocket.

The town was leafy and secluded, the lawns large, the houses carefully zoned. Whatever there had been of country life had long fallen before the armies of suburbia, but the brilliant sunlight made everything beautiful. Number 8 was on the right-hand side, a substantial two-story residence with steep Scandinavian roofs, a double garage, and a wide selection of young trees planted much too close together. There was a

swing chair in the garden with a flowered plastic seat and a
new fish-pond in the romantic idiom. But the main attraction,
and Herr Kretzschmar's pride, was an outdoor swimming-pool
in its own patio of shrieking red tile, and it was there that
Smiley found him, in the bosom of his family, on this unlikely
autumn day, entertaining a few neighbours at an impromptu
party. Herr Kretzschmar himself, in shorts, was preparing
the barbecue and as Smiley dropped the latch on the gate he
paused from his labours and looked round to see who had
come. But the new straw hat and the linen jacket confused him
and he called instead to his wife.

Frau Kretzschmar strode down the path, bearing a champagne glass. She was clad in a pink bathing-dress and a diapha-
nous pink cape, which she allowed to flow behind her daringly.

"Who *is* that then? Who *is* the nice surprise?" she kept asking in a playful voice. She could have been talking to her puppy.

She stopped in front of him. She was tanned and tall and,
like her husband, built to last. He could see little of her face,
for she wore dark glasses with a white plastic beak to protect
her nose from burning.

"Here is family Kretzschmar, going about its pleasures,"
she said not very confidently when he had still not introduced
himself. "What can we do for you, sir? In what way can we
serve?"

"I have to speak to your husband," Smiley said. It was the
first time he had spoken since he bought his ticket, and his
voice was thick and unnatural.

"But Cläuschen does no business in the daytime," she said
firmly, still smiling. "In the daytime by family decree the
profit motive has its sleep. Shall I put handcuffs on him to
prove to you he is our prisoner till sunset?"

Her bathing-dress was in two parts and her smooth, full
belly was oily with lotion. She wore a gold chain round her
waist, presumably as a further sign of naturalness. And gold
sandals with very high heels.

"Kindly tell your husband that this is not business," Smiley said. "This is friendship."

Frau Kretzschmar took a sip of her champagne, then removed her dark glasses and beak, as if she were declaring herself at the *bal masqué*. She had a snub nose. Her face, though kindly, was a good deal older than her body.

"But how can it be friendship when I don't know your name?" she demanded, no longer certain whether to be winsome or discouraging.

But by then Herr Kretzschmar himself had walked down the path after her, and stopped before them, staring from his wife to Smiley, then at Smiley again. And perhaps the sight of Smiley's set face and manner, and the fixity of his gaze, warned Herr Kretzschmar of the reason for his coming.

"Go and take care of the cooking," he said curtly.

Guiding Smiley by the arm, Herr Kretzschmar led him to a drawing-room with brass chandeliers and a picture window full of jungle cacti.

"Otto Leipzig is dead," Smiley said without preliminary as soon as the door was closed. "Two men killed him at the water camp."

Herr Kretzschmar's eyes opened very wide; then unashamedly he swung his back to Smiley and covered his face with his hands.

"You made a tape-recording," Smiley said, ignoring this display entirely. "There was the photograph which I showed you, and somewhere there is also a tape-recording which you are keeping for him." Herr Kretzschmar's back showed no sign that he had heard. "You talked about it to me yourself last night," Smiley went on, in the same sentinel tone. "You said they discussed God and the world. You said Otto was laughing like an executioner, speaking three languages at once, singing, telling jokes. You took the photographs for Otto, but you also recorded their conversation for him. I suspect you also have the letter which you received on his behalf from London."

Herr Kretzschmar had swung round and he was staring at Smiley in outrage.

"Who killed him?" he asked. "Herr Max, I ask you as a soldier!"

Smiley had taken the torn piece of picture postcard from his pocket.

"Who killed him?" Herr Kretzschmar repeated. "I insist!"

"This is what you expected me to bring last night," said Smiley, ignoring the question. "Whoever brings it to you may have the tapes and whatever else you were keeping for him. That was the way he worked it out with you."

Kretzschmar took the card.

"He called it his Moscow Rules," Kretzschmar said. "Both Otto and the General insisted on it, though it struck me personally as ridiculous."

"You have the other half of the card?" Smiley asked.

"Yes," said Kretzschmar.

"Then make the match and give me the material. I shall use it exactly as Otto would have wished."

He had to say this twice in different ways before Kretzschmar answered. "You promise this?" Kretzschmar demanded.

"Yes."

"And the killers? What will you do with them?"

"Most likely they are already safe across the water," Smiley said. "They have only a few kilometres to drive."

"Then what good is the material?"

"The material is an embarrassment to the man who sent the killers," Smiley said, and perhaps at this moment the iron quietness of Smiley's demeanour advised Herr Kretzschmar that his visitor was as distressed as he was—perhaps, in his own very private fashion, more so.

"Will it kill him also?" Herr Kretzschmar asked.

Smiley took quite a time to answer this question. "It will do worse than kill him," he said.

For a moment Herr Kretzschmar seemed disposed to ask

what was worse than being killed; but he didn't. Holding the half postcard lifelessly in his hand, he left the room. Smiley waited patiently. A perpetual brass clock laboured on its captive course, red fish gazed at him from an aquarium. Kretzschmar returned. He held a white cardboard box. Inside it, padded in hygienic tissue, lay a folded wad of photocopy paper covered with a now familiar handwriting, and six miniature cassettes, blue plastic, of a type favoured by men of modern habits.

"He entrusted them to me," Herr Kretzschmar said.

"He was wise," said Smiley.

Herr Kretzschmar laid a hand on Smiley's shoulder. "If you need anything, let me know," he said. "I have my people. These are violent times."

From a call-box Smiley once more rang Hamburg Airport, this time to re-confirm Standfast's flight to London Heathrow. This done, he bought stamps and a strong envelope and wrote on it a fictional address in Adelaide, Australia. He put Mr. Standfast's passport inside it and dropped it in a letter-box. Then, travelling as plain Mr. George Smiley, profession clerk, he returned to the railway station, passing without incident across the border into Denmark. During the journey, he took himself to the lavatory and there read Ostrakova's letter, all seven pages of it, the copy made by the General himself on Mikhel's antiquated liquid copier in the little library next door to the British Museum. What he read, added to what he had that day already seen, filled him with a growing and almost uncontainable alarm. By train, ferry, and finally taxi, he hastened to Copenhagen's Castrup Airport. From Castrup he caught a mid-afternoon plane to Paris and, though the flight lasted only an hour, in Smiley's world it took a lifetime, conveying him across the entire range of his memories, emotions, and anticipations. His anger and revulsion at Leipzig's murder, till now suppressed, welled over, only to be set aside by his fears for Ostrakova: if they had done so much to Leipzig and the General, what would they not do to her? The dash through Schleswig-Holstein had given him the swiftness of revived youth, but now, in the anti-climax of escape, he was assailed by the incurable indifference of age. With death so close, he thought, so ever-present, what is the point of struggling any longer? He thought of Karla again, and of his absolutism, which at least gave point to the perpetual chaos that was life's condition; point to violence, and to death; of Karla for whom killing had never been more than the necessary adjunct of a grand design.

How can I win? he asked himself; alone, restrained by doubt and a sense of decency—how can any of us—against this remorseless fusillade?

The plane's descent—and the promise of the renewed chase—restored him. There are two Karlas, he reasoned, remembering again the stoic face, the patient eyes, the wiry body waiting philosophically upon its own destruction. There is Karla the professional, so self-possessed that he could allow, if need be, ten years for an operation to bear fruit: in Bill Haydon's case, twenty; Karla the old spy, the pragmatist, ready to trade a dozen losses for one great win.

And there is this other Karla, Karla of the heart after all, of the one great love, the Karla flawed by humanity. I should not be deterred if, in order to defend his weakness, he resorts to the methods of his trade.

Reaching in the compartment above him for his straw hat, Smiley happened to remember a cavalier promise he had once made concerning Karla's eventual downfall. "No," he had replied, in answer to a question much like the one he had just put to himself. "No, Karla is not fireproof. Because he's a fanatic. And one day, if I have anything to do with it, that lack of moderation will be his downfall."

Hastening to the cab rank, he recalled that his remark had been made to one Peter Guillam, who at this present moment happened to be much upon his mind.

18

Lying on the divan, Ostrakova glanced at the twilight and
seriously wondered whether it signalled the world's end.

All day long the same grey gloom had hung over the courtyard, consigning her tiny universe to a perpetual evening. At
dawn a sepia glow had thickened it; at midday, soon after the
men came, it was a celestial power-cut, deepening to a cavernous black in anticipation of her own end. And now, at evening,
fog had further strengthened the grip of darkness upon the
retreating forces of light. And so it goes with Ostrakova also,
she decided without bitterness: with my bruised, black-and-blue
body, and my siege, and my hopes for the second coming of
the redeemer; so it goes exactly, an ebbing of my own day.

She had woken this morning to find herself seemingly
bound hand and foot. She had tried to move one leg and, immediately, burning cords had tightened round her thighs and chest
and stomach. She had raised an arm, but only against the tugging of iron ligatures. She had taken a lifetime to crawl to the
bathroom and another to get herself undressed and into the
warm water. And when she entered it, she was frightened that
she had fainted from the pain, her flailed flesh hurt so terribly
where the road had grazed it. She heard a hammering and had
thought it was inside her head, till she realised it was the work
of a furious neighbour. When she counted the church clock's
chimes, they stopped at four; so no wonder the neighbour was

protesting at the thunder of running water in the old pipes. The labour of making coffee had exhausted her but sitting down was suddenly unbearable, lying down just as bad. The only way for her to rest was to lean herself forward, elbows on the draining-board. From there she could watch the courtyard, as a pastime and as a precaution, and from there she had seen the men, the two creatures of darkness, as she now thought of them, mouthing to the concierge, and the old goat of a concierge, Madame la Pierre, mouthing back, shaking her fool head—"No, Ostrakova is not here, not here"—not here in ten different ways, that echoed like an aria round the courtyard—*is not here*—drowning the clipping of carpet-beaters and the clatter of children and the gossip of the two turbaned old wives on the third floor, leaning out of their windows two metres apart—*is not here!* Till a child would not have believed her.

If she wanted to read, she had to put the book on the draining-board, which after the men came, was where she kept the gun as well, till she noticed the swivel on the butt-end, and with a woman's practicality improvised a lanyard out of kitchen string. In that way, with the pistol round her neck, she had both her arms free when she needed to hand herself across the room. But when it prodded her breasts she thought she would retch from the agony. After the men left again, she had started reciting aloud while she went about the chores she had promised herself she would observe during her imprisonment. "One *tall* man, one leather *coat*, one Homburg *hat*," she had murmured, helping herself to a generous ration of vodka to restore her. "One *broad* man, one balding *pate*, grey *shoes* with perforations!" Make songs of my memory, she had thought; sing them to the magician, to the General—oh, why don't they answer my second letter?

She was a child again, falling off her pony, and the pony came back and trampled her. She was a woman again, trying to be a mother. She remembered the three days of impossible pain in which Alexandra fiercely resisted being born into the grey and dangerous light of an unwashed Moscow nursing home—the same light that was outside her window now, and lay like unnatural dust over the polished floors of her apartment. She heard herself calling for Glikman—"Bring him to me, bring him to me." She remembered how it had seemed to her that sometimes it was he, Glikman her lover, whom she was bearing, and not their child at all—as if his whole sturdy, hairy body were trying to fight its way out of her—or was it into her?—as if to give birth at all would be to deliver Glikman into the very captivity she dreaded for him.

Why was he not there, why would he not come? she wondered, confusing Glikman with the General and the magician equally. Why don't they answer my letter?

She knew very well why Glikman had not come to her as she wrestled with Alexandra. She had begged him to keep away. "You have the courage to suffer, and that is enough," she had told him. "But you have not the courage to witness the suffering of others, and for that I love you also. Christ had it too easy," she told him. "Christ could cure the lepers, Christ could make the blind see and the dead come alive. He could even die in a sensible cause. But you are not Christ, you are Glikman, and there's nothing you can do about my pain except watch and suffer too, which does nobody any good whatever."

But the General and his magician were different, she argued, with some resentment; they have set themselves up as the physicians of my disease, and I have a right to them!

At her appointed time, the cretinous, braying concierge had come up, complete with her troglodyte husband with his screwdriver. They were full of excitement for Ostrakova, and joy at being able to bring such heartening news. Ostrakova had composed herself carefully for the visit, putting on music, making up her face, and heaping books beside the divan, all to create an atmosphere of leisured introspection.

"Visitors, madame, *men*. . . . No, they would not leave their names . . . here for a short visit from abroad . . . knew your *husband*, madame. Emigrés, they were like yourself. . . . No, they wished to keep it a *surprise*, madame. . . . They said they had *gifts* for you from relations, madame . . . a secret, madame, and one of them so big and strong and good-looking. . . . No, they will come back another time, they are here on business, many appointments, they said. . . . No, by taxi, and they kept it waiting—the expense, imagine!"

Ostrakova had laughed, and put her hand on the concierge's arm, physically drawing her into a great secret, while the troglodyte stood and puffed cigarette and garlic over both of them.

"Listen," she said. "Both of you. Attend to me, Monsieur and Madame la Pierre. I know very well who they are, these rich and handsome visitors. They are my husband's no-good nephews from Marseilles, lazy devils and great vagabonds. If they are bringing a present for me, you may be sure they will also want beds and most likely dinner too. Be so kind and tell them I am away in the country for a few more days. I love them dearly, but I must have my peace."

Whatever doubts or disappointments remained in their goatish heads, Ostrakova bought them away with money, and now she was alone again—the lanyard round her neck. She was stretched out on the divan, her hips hoisted into a position that was halfway tolerable. The gun was in her hand and pointed at the door, and she could hear the footsteps coming up the stairs, two pairs, the one heavy, the other light.

She rehearsed: "One *tall* man, one leather *coat* . . . One *broad* man, grey *shoes* with perforations . . ."

Then the knocking, timid as a childhood proposition of love. And the unfamiliar voice, speaking French with an unfamiliar accent, slow and classical like her husband Ostrakov's and with the same alluring tenderness.

"Madame Ostrakova. Please admit me. I am here to help you."

With a sense of everything ending, Ostrakova deliberately cocked her dead husband's pistol, and advanced with firm if painful steps, upon the door. She advanced crabwise and she wore no shoes and she mistrusted the fish-eye peep-hole. Nothing would convince her it couldn't peep in both directions. Therefore she made this detour round the room in the hope of escaping its eye-line, and on the way she passed Ostrakov's blurry portrait and resented very much that he had had the selfishness to die so early instead of staying alive so that he could protect her. Then she thought: No. I have turned the corner. I possess my own courage.

And she did possess it. She was going to war, every minute could be her last, but the pains had vanished, her body felt as ready as it had been for Glikman, always, any time; she could feel his energy running into her limbs like reinforcements. She had Glikman beside her and she remembered his strength without wishing for it. She had a Biblical notion that all his tireless lovemaking had invigorated her for this moment. She had the calm of Ostrakov and the honour of Ostrakov; she had his gun. But her desperate, solitary courage was finally her own, and it was the courage of a mother roused, and deprived, and furious: Alexandra! The men who had come to kill her were the same men who had taunted her with her secret motherhood, who had killed Ostrakov and Glikman, and would kill the whole poor world if she did not stop them.

She wanted only to aim before she fired, and she had realised that as long as the door was closed and chained and the peep-hole was in place, she could aim from very close—and the closer she aimed, the better, for she was sensibly modest about her marksmanship. She put her finger over the peep-hole to stop them looking in, then she put her eye to it to see who they were, and the first thing she saw was her own foolish concierge, very close, round as an onion in the distorted lens, with green hair from the glow of the ceramic tiles in the landing, and a huge rubber smile and a nose that came out like a duck's bill. And it occurred to Ostrakova that the light footsteps had been hers—lightness, like pain and happiness, being always relative to whatever has come before, or after. And the second thing she saw was a small gentleman in spectacles, who in the fish-eye was as fat as the Michelin tyre man. And while she watched him, he earnestly removed a straw hat that came straight out of a novel by Turgenev, and held it at his side as if he had just heard his national anthem being played. And she inferred from this gesture that the small gentleman was telling her that he knew she was afraid, and knew that a shadowed face was what she was afraid of most, and that by baring his head he was in some way revealing his goodwill to her.

His stillness and his gravity had a sense of dutiful submission about them, which, like his voice, again reminded her of Ostrakov; the lens might make him into a frog, but it could not take away his bearing. His spectacles also reminded her of Ostrakov, being as necessary to vision as a walking-stick to a cripple. All this, with a thumping heart but a very steady eye, Ostrakova took in at her first long inspection, while she kept the gun barrel clamped to the door and her finger on the trigger, and considered whether or not to shoot him then and there, straight through the door—"Take *that* for Glikman, *that* for Ostrakov, *that* for Alexandra!"

For, in her state of suspicion, she was ready to believe that they had selected the man for his very air of humanity; because they knew that Ostrakov himself had had this same capacity to be at once fat and dignified.

"I do not need help," Ostrakova called back at last, and watched in terror to see what effect her words would have on him. But while she watched, the fool concierge decided to start yelling on her own account.

"Madame, he is a gentleman! He is English! He is concerned for you! You are ill, madame, the whole street is frightened for you! Madame, you cannot lock yourself away like this any more." A pause. "He is a doctor, madame—aren't you, monsieur? A distinguished doctor for maladies of the spirit!"

Then Ostrakova heard the idiot whisper to him: "Tell her, monsieur. Tell her you're a doctor!"

But the stranger shook his head in disapproval, and replied: "No. It is not true."

"Madame, open up or I shall fetch the police!" the concierge cried. "A Russian, making such a scandal!"

"*I do not need help*," Ostrakova repeated, much louder.

But she knew already that help, more than anything else, was what she did need; that without it she would never kill, any more than Glikman would have killed. Not even if she had the Devil himself in her sights could she kill another woman's child.

As she continued her vigil, the little man took a slow step forward till his face, distorted like a face under water, was all she could see in the lens; and she saw for the first time the fatigue in it, the redness of the eyes behind the spectacles, the heavy shadows under them; and she sensed in him a passionate caring for herself that had nothing to do with death, but with survival; she sensed that she was looking at a face that was concerned, rather than one that had banished sympathy for ever. The face came closer still and the snap of the letter-box alone almost made her pull the trigger by mistake and this appalled her. She felt the convulsion in her hand and stayed it only at the very instant of completion; then stopped to pick the envelope from the mat. It was her own letter, addressed to the General—her second, saying "Someone is trying to kill me," written in French. As a last-ditch gesture of resistance, she pretended to wonder whether the letter was a trick, and they had intercepted it, or bought it, or stolen it, or done whatever deceivers do. But seeing her letter, recognising its opening words and its despairing tone, she became utterly weary of deceit, and weary of mistrust, and weary of trying to read evil where she wished more than anything to read good. She heard the fat man's voice again, and a French well-taught but a little rusty, and it reminded her of rhymes from school she half remembered. And if it was a lie he was telling, then it was the most cunning lie she had ever heard in her life.

"The magician is dead, madame," he said, fogging the fish-eye with his breath. "I have come from London to help you in his place."

For years afterwards, and probably for all his life, Peter Guillam would relate, with varying degrees of frankness, the story of his home-coming that same evening. He would emphasize that the circumstances were particular. He was in a bad temper—one—he had been so all day. Two—his Ambassador had publicly rebuked him at the weekly meeting for a remark of unseemly levity about the British balance of payments. He was newly married—three—and his very young wife was pregnant. Her phone call—four—came moments after he had decoded a long and extremely boring signal from the Circus reminding him for the fifteenth time that no, repeat *no* operations could be undertaken on French soil without advance permission in writing from Head Office. And—five—*le tout Paris* was having one of its periodical scares about kidnapping. Last, the post of Circus head resident in Paris was widely known to be a laying-out place for officers shortly to be buried, offering little more than the opportunity to lunch interminably with a variety of very corrupt, very boring chiefs of rival French Intelligence services who spent more time spying on each other than on their supposed enemies. All of these factors, Guillam would afterwards insist, should be taken into account before anyone accused him of impetuosity. Guillam, it may be added, was an athlete, half French, but more English on account of it; he was slender, and near enough handsome—but though he fought it every inch of the way, he was also close on fifty, which is the watershed that few careers of ageing field-men survive. He also owned a brand-new German Porsche car, which he had acquired, somewhat shamefacedly, at diplomatic rates, and parked, to the Ambassador's strident disapproval, in the Embassy car-park.

Marie-Claire Guillam, then, rang her husband at six exactly, just as Guillam was locking away his code-books. Guillam had two telephone lines to his desk, one of them in theory operational and direct. The second went through the Embassy switchboard. Marie-Claire rang on the direct line, a thing they had always agreed she would only ever do in emergency. She spoke French, which, true, was her native language, but they had recently been communicating in English in order to improve her fluency.

"Peter," she began.

He heard at once the tension in her voice.

"Marie-Claire? What is it?"

"Peter, there's someone here. He wants you to come at once."

"Who?"

"I can't say. It's important. Please come home at once," she repeated and rang off.

Guillam's chief clerk, a Mr. Anstruther, had been standing at the strong-room door when the call came, waiting for him to spin the combination lock before they each put in their keys. Through the open doorway to Guillam's office he saw him slam down the phone, and the next thing he knew, Guillam had tossed to Anstruther—a long throw, probably fifteen feet—the Head Resident's sacred *personal key*, near enough the symbol of his office, and Anstruther by a miracle had caught it: put up his left hand and caught it in his palm, like an American baseball player; he couldn't have done it again if he'd tried it a hundred times, he told Guillam later.

"Don't budge from here till I ring you!" Guillam shouted. "You sit at my desk and you man those phones. Hear me?"

Anstruther did, but by then Guillam was half-way down the absurdly elegant spiral staircase of the Embassy, barging between typists and Chancery guards and bright young men

setting out on the evening cocktail round. Seconds later, he
was at the wheel of his Porsche, revving the engine like a racing driver, which in another life he might well have been. Guillam's home was in Neuilly, and in the ordinary way these
sporting dashes through the rush-hour rather amused him,
reminding him twice a day—as he put it—that however mind-
bendingly boring the Embassy routine, life around him was
hairy, quarrelsome, and fun. He was even given to timing
himself over the distance. If he took the Avenue Charles de
Gaulle and got a fair wind at the traffic-lights, twenty-five
minutes through the evening traffic was not unreasonable.
Late at night or early in the morning, with empty roads and
CD plates, he could cut it to fifteen, but in the rush-hour
thirty-five minutes was fast going and forty the norm. That
evening, hounded by visions of Marie-Claire held at pistol
point by a bunch of crazed nihilists, he made the distance in
eighteen minutes cold. Police reports later submitted to the
Ambassador had him jumping three sets of lights and touching
around a hundred and forty kilometres as he entered the home
stretch; but these were of necessity something of a reconstruction, since no one felt inclined to try to keep up with him.
Guillam himself remembers little of the drive, beyond a near
squeak with a furniture van, and a lunatic cyclist who took it
into his head to turn left when Guillam was a mere hundred
and fifty metres behind him.

His apartment was in a villa, on the third floor. Braking
hard before he reached the entrance, he cut the engine and
coasted to a halt in the street outside, then pelted to the front
door as quietly as haste allowed. He had expected a car parked
somewhere close, probably with a get-away driver waiting at
the wheel, but to his momentary relief there was none in sight.
A light was burning in their bedroom, however, so that he now
imagined Marie-Claire gagged and tied to the bed, and her
captors sitting over her, waiting for Guillam to arrive. If it was
Guillam they wanted, he did not propose to disappoint them.

He had come unarmed; he had no choice. The Circus House-keepers had a holy terror of weapons, and his illicit revolver was in the bedside locker, where no doubt they had by now found it. He climbed the three flights silently and at the front door threw off his jacket and dropped it on the floor beside him. He had his door key in his hand, and now, as softly as he knew how, he fed it into the lock, then pressed the bell and called *"Facteur"*—postman—through the letter-box and then *"Exprès."* His hand on the key, he waited till he heard approaching footsteps, which he knew at once were not those of Marie-Claire. They were slow, even ponderous, and, to Guillam's ear, too self-assured by half. And they came from the direction of the bedroom. What he did next, he did all at once. To open the door from inside, he knew, required two distinct movements: first the chain must be shot, then the spring catch must be freed. In a half-crouch, Guillam waited till he heard the chain slip, then used his one weapon of surprise: he turned his own key and threw all his weight against the door and, as he did so, had the intense satisfaction of seeing a plump male figure spin wildly back against the hall mirror, knocking it clean off its moorings, while Guillam seized his arm and swung it into a vicious breaking lock—only to see the startled face of his lifelong friend and mentor, George Smiley, staring helplessly at him.

The aftermath of that encounter is described by Guillam somewhat hazily; he had, of course, no forewarning of Smiley's coming, and Smiley—perhaps out of fear of microphones—said little inside the flat to enlighten him. Marie-Claire was in the bedroom, but neither bound nor gagged; it was Ostrakova who, at Marie-Claire's insistence, was lying on the bed, still in her old black dress, and Marie-Claire was ministering to her in any way she could think of—jellied breast of chicken, mint tea, all the invalid foods she had diligently laid in for the wonderful day, alas not yet at hand, when Guillam would fall ill on her. Ostrakova, Guillam noticed (though he had yet to learn her name), seemed to have been beaten up. She had broad grey bruises round the eyes and lips, and her fingers were cut to bits where she had apparently tried to defend herself. Having briefly admitted Guillam to this scene—the battered lady tended by the anxious child bride—Smiley conducted Guillam to his own drawing-room and, with all the authority of Guillam's old chief, which he indeed had been, rapidly set out his requirements. Only now, it developed, was Guillam's earlier haste warranted. Ostrakova—Smiley referred to her only as "our guest"—should leave Paris tonight, he said. The station's safe house outside Orléans—he called it "our country mansion"—was not safe enough; she needed somewhere that provided care and protection. Guillam remembered a French couple in Arras, a retired agent and his wife, who in the past had provided shelter for the Circus's occasional birds of passage. It was agreed he would telephone them, but not from the apartment: Smiley sent him off to find a public call-box. By the time Guillam had made the necessary arrangements and returned, Smiley had written out a brief signal on a sheet of Marie-Claire's awful notepaper with its grazing bunnies, which he wished Guillam to have transmitted immediately to the Circus, "Personal for Saul Enderby, decipher yourself." The text, which Smiley insisted that Guillam should read (but not aloud), politely asked Enderby—"in view of a second death no doubt by now reported to you"—for a meeting at Ben's Place forty-eight hours hence. Guillam had no idea where Ben's Place was.

"And, Peter."

"Yes, George," said Guillam, still dazed.

"I imagine there exists an official directory of locally accredited diplomats. Do you happen to have such a thing in the house by any chance?"

Guillam did. Indeed, Marie-Claire lived by it. She had no memory for names at all, so it lay beside the bedroom telephone for every time a member of a foreign embassy telephoned her with yet another invitation to drinks, to dinner, or, most ghastly of all, to a National Day festivity. Guillam fetched it, and a moment later was peering over Smiley's shoulder. "Kirov," he read—but not, once more, aloud—as he followed the line of Smiley's thumb-nail—"Kirov, Oleg, Second Secretary (Commercial), Unmarried." Followed by an address in the Soviet Embassy ghetto in the 7th district.

"Ever bumped into him?" Smiley asked.

Guillam shook his head. "We took a look at him a few years back. He's marked 'hands off,'" he replied.

"When was this list compiled?" Smiley asked. The answer was printed on the cover: December of the previous year.

Smiley said, "Well, when you get to the office—"

"I'll take a look at the file," Guillam promised.

"There is also *this*," said Smiley sharply, and handed Guillam a plain carrier-bag containing, when he looked later, several micro-cassettes and a fat brown envelope.

"By first bag tomorrow, please," Smiley said. "The same grading and the same addressee as the telegram."

Leaving Smiley still poring over the list, and the two women cloistered in the bedroom, Guillam hastened back to the Embassy and, having released the bemused Anstruther from his vigil at the telephones, consigned the carrier-bag to him, together with Smiley's instructions. The tension in Smiley had affected Guillam considerably, and he was sweating. In all the years he had known George, he said later, he had never known him so inward, so intent, so elliptical, so desperate. Re-opening the strong-room, he personally encoded and dispatched the telegram, waiting only as long as it took him to receive the Head Office acknowledgment before drawing the file on Soviet Embassy movements and browsing through back numbers of old watch lists. He had not far to look. The third serial, copied to London, told him all that he needed to know. Kirov Oleg, Second Secretary Commercial, described this time as "married but wife not en poste," had returned to

Moscow two weeks ago. In the panel reserved for miscellaneous comments, the French liaison service had added that,
according to informed Soviet sources, Kirov had been "recalled
to the Soviet Ministry of Foreign Affairs at short notice in
order to take up a senior appointment which had become
vacant unexpectedly." The customary farewell parties had
therefore not been feasible.

Back in Neuilly, Smiley received Guillam's intelligence in
utter silence. He did not seem surprised, but he seemed in
some way appalled, and when he finally spoke—which did not
occur until they were all three in the car and speeding towards
Arras—his voice had an almost hopeless ring. "Yes," he
said—as if Guillam knew the whole history inside out. "Yes,
that is of course exactly what he *would* do, isn't it? He would
call Kirov back under the pretext of a promotion, in order to
make sure he really came."

George had not sounded that way, said Guillam—no doubt
with the wisdom of hindsight—since the night he unmasked
Bill Haydon as Karla's mole as well as Ann's lover.

Ostrakova also, in retrospect, had little coherent recollection
of that night, neither of the car journey, on which she contrived to sleep, nor of the patient but persistent questioning to
which the little plump man subjected her when she woke late
the next morning. Perhaps she had temporarily lost her capacity to be impressed—and, accordingly, to remember. She
answered his questions, she was grateful to him, she gave
him—without the zest or "decoration"—the same information
that she had given to the magician, though he seemed to possess most of it already.

"The magician," she said once. "Dead. My God."

She asked after the General, but scarcely heeded Smiley's
noncommittal reply. She was thinking of Ostrakov, then Glikman, now the magician—and she never knew his name. Her
host and hostess were kind to her also, but as yet made no

impression on her. It was raining and she could not see the distant fields.

Little by little, all the same, as the weeks passed, Ostrakova permitted herself an idyllic hibernation. The deep winter came early and she let its snows embrace her; she walked a little, and then a great deal, retired early, spoke seldom, and as her body repaired itself so did her spirit. At first a pardonable confusion reigned in her mind, and she found herself thinking of her daughter in the terms by which the gingery stranger had described her: as the tearaway dissenter and untameable rebel. Then slowly the logic of the matter presented itself to her. Somewhere, she argued, there was the real Alexandra who lived and had her being, as before. Or who, as before, did not. In either case, the gingery man's lies concerned a different creature altogether, one whom they had invented for their own needs. She even managed to find consolation in the likelihood that her daughter, if she lived at all, lived in complete ignorance of their machinations.

Perhaps the hurts which had been visited on her—of the mind as well as of the body—did what years of prayer and anxiety had failed to do, and purged her of her self-recriminations regarding Alexandra. She mourned Glikman at her leisure, she was conscious of being quite alone in the world, but in the winter landscape her solitude was not disagreeable to her. A retired brigadier proposed marriage to her but she declined. It turned out later that he proposed to everybody. Peter Guillam visited her at least every week and sometimes they walked together for an hour or two. In faultless French he talked to her mainly of landscape gardening, a subject on which he possessed an inexhaustible knowledge. That was Ostrakova's life, where it touched upon this story. And it was lived out in total ignorance of the events that her own first letter to the General had set in train.

19

"**D**o you know his name really *is* Ferguson?" Saul Enderby drawled in that lounging Belgravia cockney which is the final vulgarity of the English upper class.

"I never doubted it," Smiley said.

"He's about all we've got left of that whole lamplighter stable. Wise Men don't hold with domestic surveillance these days. Anti-Party or some damn thing." Enderby continued his study of the bulky document in his hand. "So what's *your* name, George? Sherlock Holmes dogging his poor old Moriarty? Captain Ahab chasing his big white whale? Who are you?"

Smiley did not reply.

"Wish I had an enemy, I must say," Enderby remarked, turning a few pages. "Been looking for one for donkey's years. Haven't I, Sam?"

"Night and day, Chief," Sam Collins agreed heartily, and sent his master a confiding grin.

Ben's Place was the back room of a dark hotel in Knightsbridge and the three men had met there an hour ago. A notice on the door said "MANAGEMENT STRICTLY PRIVATE" and inside was an ante-room for coats and hats and privacy, and beyond it lay this oak-panelled sanctum full of books and musk, which in turn gave on to its own rectangle of walled garden stolen from the park, with a fish-pond and a marble angel and a path for contemplative walks. Ben's identity, if he ever had one, was lost in the unwritten archives of Circus mythology. But this place of his remained, as an unrecorded perquisite of Enderby's appointment, and of George Smiley's before him—and as a trysting ground for meetings that afterwards have not occurred.

"I'll read it again, if you don't mind," Enderby said. "I'm a bit slow on the uptake this time of day."

"I think that would be jolly helpful, actually, Chief," said Collins.

Enderby shifted his half-lens spectacles, but only by way of peering over the top of them, and it was Smiley's secret theory that they were plain glass anyway.

"Kirov is doing the talking. This is after Leipzig has put the bite on him, right, George?" Smiley gave a distant nod. "They're still sitting in the cat house with their pants down, but it's five in the morning and the girls have been sent home. First we get Kirov's tearful how-could-you-do-this-to-me? 'I thought you were my friend, Otto!' he says. Christ, he picked a wrong 'un there! Then comes his statement, put into bad English by the translators. They've made a concordance—that the word, George? Um's and ah's omitted."

Whether it was the word or not, Smiley offered no answer. Perhaps he was not expected to. He sat very still in a leather armchair leaning forward over his clasped hands, and he had not taken off his brown tweed overcoat. A set of the Kirov typescripts lay at his elbow. He looked drawn, and Enderby remarked later that he seemed to have been on a diet. Sam Collins, head of Operations, sat literally in Enderby's shadow, a dapper man with a dark moustache and a flashy, ever-ready smile. There had been a time when Collins was the Circus hard-man, whose years in the field had taught him to despise the cant of the fifth floor. Now he was the poacher turned gamekeeper, nurturing his own pension and security in the way he had once nurtured his networks. A wilful blankness had overcome him; he was smoking brown cigarettes down to the half-way mark, then stubbing them into a cracked sea shell, while his doglike gaze rested faithfully on Enderby, his master. Enderby himself stood propped against the pillar of French windows, silhouetted by the light outside, and he was using a bit of matchstick to pick his teeth. A silk handkerchief peeked from his left sleeve and he stood with one knee forward and slightly bent as if he were in the members' enclosure at Ascot. In the garden, shreds of mist lay stretched like fine gauze across the lawn. Enderby put back his head and held the document away from him like a menu.

"Here we go. I'm Kirov. 'As a finance officer working in Moscow Centre from 1970 to 1974, it was my duty to unearth irregularities in the accounts of overseas residencies and bring the culprits to book.'" He broke off and peered over his glasses again. "This is all before Kirov was posted to Paris, right?"

"Dead right," said Collins keenly and glanced at Smiley for support, but got none.

"Just working it out, you see, George," Enderby explained. "Just getting my ducks in a row. Haven't got your little grey cells."

Sam Collins smiled brightly at his chief's show of modesty.

Enderby continued: "'As a result of conducting these extremely delicate and confidential enquiries, which in some cases led to the punishment of senior officers of Moscow Centre, I made the acquaintance of the head of the independent Thirteenth Intelligence Directorate, subordinated to the Party's Central Committee, who is known throughout Centre only by his workname Karla. This is a woman's name and is said to belong to the first network he controlled.' That right, George?"

"It was during the Spanish Civil War," said Smiley.

"The great playground. Well, well. To continue. 'The Thirteenth Directorate is a separate service within Moscow Centre, since its principal duty is the recruitment, training, and placing of illegal agents under deep cover in Fascist countries, known also as moles . . . blah . . . blah . . . blah. Often a mole will take many years to find his place inside the target country before he becomes active in secret work.' Shades of Bloody Bill Haydon. 'The task of servicing such moles is not entrusted to normal overseas residencies but to a Karla representative, as he is known, usually a military officer, whose daywork is to be an attaché of an embassy. Such representatives are handpicked by Karla personally and constitute an élite . . . blah . . . blah . . . enjoying privileges of trust and freedom not given to other Centre officers, also travel and money. They are accordingly objects of jealousy to the rest of the service.'"

Enderby affected to draw breath: "*Christ*, these translators!" he exclaimed. "Or maybe it's just Kirov being a perishing little bore. You'd think a man making his deathbed confession would have the grace to keep it brief, wouldn't you? But not our Kirov, oh no. How you doing, Sam?"

"Fine, Chief, fine."

"Here we go again," said Enderby, and resumed his ritual tone: "'In the course of my general investigations into financial irregularities, the integrity of a Karla resident came into question, the resident in Lisbon, Colonel Orlov. Karla convened a secret tribunal of his own people to hear the case, and as a result of my evidence Colonel Orlov was liquidated in Moscow on June 10, 1973.' That checks, you say, Sam?"

"We have an unconfirmed defector report that he was shot by firing-squad," said Collins breezily.

"Congratulations, Comrade Kirov, the embezzler's friend. Jesus. What a snake-pit. Worse than us." Enderby continued: "'For my part in bringing the criminal Orlov to justice I was personally congratulated by Karla, and also sworn to secrecy, since he considered the irregularity of Colonel Orlov a shame on his Directorate, and damaging to his standing within Moscow Centre. Karla is known as a comrade of high standards of integrity, and for this reason has many enemies among the ranks of the self-indulgent.'"

Enderby deliberately paused, and yet again glanced at Smiley over the top of his half-lenses.

"We all spin the ropes that hang us, right, George?"

"We're a bunch of suicidal spiders, Chief," said Collins heartily, and flashed an even broader smile at a place somewhere between the two of them.

But Smiley was lost in his reading of Kirov's statement and not accessible to pleasantries.

"Skip the next year of Brother Kirov's life and loves, and let's come to his next meeting with Karla," Enderby proposed, undeterred by Smiley's taciturnity. "The nocturnal summons . . . that's standard, I gather." He turned a couple of pages. Smiley, following Enderby, did the same. "Car pulls up outside Kirov's Moscow apartment—why can't they say *flat* for God's sake, like anyone else?—he's hauled out of bed and driven to an unknown destination. They lead a rum life, don't they, those gorillas in Moscow Centre, never knowing whether they're getting a medal or a bullet." He referred to the report again. "All that tallies, does it, George? The journey and stuff? Half an hour by car, small plane, and so forth?"

"The Thirteenth Directorate has three or four establishments, including a large training camp near Minsk," Smiley said.

Enderby turned some more pages.

"So here's Kirov back in Karla's presence again: middle of nowhere, the same night. Karla and Kirov totally alone. Small wooden hut, monastic atmosphere, no trimmings, no witnesses—or none visible. Karla goes straight to the nub. How would Kirov like a posting to Paris? Kirov would like one very much, sir—" He turned another page. "Kirov always admired the Thirteenth Directorate, sir, blah, blah—always been a great fan of Karla's—creep, crawl, creep. Sounds like you, Sam. Interesting that Kirov thought Karla looked tired—notice that point?—twitchy. Karla under stress, smoking like a chimney."

"He always did that," said Smiley.

"Did what?"

"He was always an excessive smoker," Smiley said.

"Was he, by God? Was he?"

Enderby turned another page. "Now Kirov's brief," he said. "Karla spells it out for him. 'For my daywork I should have the post of a Commercial officer of the Embassy, and for my special work I would be responsible for the control and conduct of financial accounts in all outstations of the Thirteenth Directorate in the following countries . . .' Kirov goes on to list them. They include Bonn, but not Hamburg. With me, Sam?"

"All the way, Chief."

"Not losing you in the labyrinth?"

"Not a bit, Chief."

"Clever blokes, these Russkies."

"Devilish."

"Kirov again: 'He impressed upon me the extreme importance of my task—blah, blah—reminded me of my excellent performance in the Orlov case, and advised me that in view of the great delicacy of the matters I was handling, I would be reporting directly to Karla's private office and would have a separate set of ciphers . . .' Turn to page fifteen."

"Page fifteen it is, Chief," Collins said.

Smiley had already found it.

"'In addition to my work as West European auditor to the Thirteenth Directorate outstations, however, Karla also warned me that I would be required to perform certain clandestine activities with a view to finding cover backgrounds, or legends for future agents. All members of his Directorate took a hand in this, he said, but legend work was extremely secret nevertheless, and I should not under any circumstances discuss it with anybody at all. Not my Ambassador, nor with Major Pudin, who was Karla's permanent operational representative inside our Embassy in Paris. I naturally accepted the appointment and, having attended a special course in security and communications, took up my post. I had not been in Paris long when a personal signal from Karla advised me that a legend was required urgently for a female agent, age about twenty-one years.' Now we're at the bone," Enderby commented with satisfaction. "'Karla's signal referred me to several émigré families who might be persuaded by pressure to adopt such an agent as their own child, since blackmail is considered by Karla a preferable technique to bribery.' Damn right it is," Enderby assented heartily. "At the present rate of inflation, blackmail's about the only bloody thing that keeps its value."

Sam Collins obliged with a rich laugh of appreciation.

"Thank you, Sam," said Enderby pleasantly. "Thanks very much."

A lesser man than Enderby—or a less thick-skinned one— might have skated over the next few pages, for they consisted mainly of a vindication of Connie Sachs's and Smiley's pleas of three years ago that the Leipzig-Kirov relationship should be exploited.

"Kirov dutifully trawls the émigrés, but without result," Enderby announced, as if he were reading out subtitles at the cinema. "Karla exhorts Kirov to greater efforts, Kirov strives still harder, and goofs again."

Enderby broke off, and looked at Smiley, this time very straight. "Kirov was no bloody good, was he, George?" he said.

"No," said Smiley.

"Karla couldn't trust his own chaps, that's your point. He had to go out into the sticks and recruit an irregular like Kirov."

"Yes."

"A clod. Sort of bloke who'd never make Sarratt."

"That's right."

"Having set up his apparatus, in other words, trained it to accept his iron rules, you might say, he didn't dare use it for this particular deal. That your point?"

"Yes," said Smiley. "That is my point."

Thus, when Kirov bumped into Leipzig on the plane to Vienna—Enderby resumed, paraphrasing Kirov's own account now—Leipzig appeared to him as the answer to all his prayers. Never mind that he was based in Hamburg, never mind that there'd been a bit of nastiness back in Tallinn: Otto was an émigré, in with the groups, Otto the Golden Boy. Kirov signalled urgently to Karla proposing that Leipzig be recruited as an émigré source and talent-spotter. Karla agreed.

"Which is another rum thing, when you work it out," Enderby remarked. "Jesus, I mean who'd back a horse with Leipzig's record when he was sober and of sound mind? Specially for a job like that?"

"Karla was under stress," Smiley said. "Kirov said so and we have it from elsewhere also. He was in a hurry. He had to take risks."

"Like bumping chaps off?"

"That was more recent," Smiley said, in a tone of such casual exoneration that Enderby glanced at him quite sharply.

"You're bloody forgiving these days, aren't you, George?" said Enderby suspiciously.

"Am I?" Smiley sounded puzzled by the question. "If you say so, Saul."

"And bloody meek too." He returned to the transcript. "Page twenty-one and we're home free." He read slowly to give the passage extra point. "Page twenty-one," he repeated. "'Following the successful recruitment of Ostrakova, and the formal issuing of a French permit to her daughter Alexandra, I was instructed to set aside immediately ten thousand American dollars a month from the Paris imprest for the purpose of servicing this new mole, who was henceforth awarded the workname KOMET. The agent KOMET also received the highest classification of secrecy within the Directorate, requiring all communications regarding her to be sent to the Director personally, using person-to-person ciphers, and without intermediaries. Preferably, however, such communications should go by courier, since Karla is an opponent of the excessive use of radio.' Any truth in that one, George?" Enderby asked casually.

"It was how we caught him in India," said Smiley without lifting his head from the script. "We broke his codes and he later swore that he would never use radio again. Like most promises, it was subject to review."

Enderby bit off a bit of matchstick, and smeared it onto the back of his hand. "Don't you want to take your coat off, George?" he asked. "Sam, ask him what he wants to drink."

Sam asked, but Smiley was too absorbed in the script to answer.

Enderby resumed his reading aloud: "'I was also instructed to make sure that no reference to KOMET appeared on the annual accounts for Western Europe which, as auditor, I was obliged to sign and present to Karla for submission to the Collegium of Moscow Centre at the close of each financial year. . . . No, I never met the agent KOMET, nor do I know what became of her, or in which country she is operating. I know only that she is living under the name of Alexandra Ostrakova, the daughter of naturalised French parents. . . .'" More turning of pages. "'The monthly payment of ten thousand dollars was not expended by myself, but transferred to a bank in Thun in the Swiss canton of Berne. The transfer is made by standing orders to the credit of a Dr. Adolf Glaser. Glaser is the nominal account holder, but I believe that Dr. Glaser is only the workname for a Karla operative at the Soviet Embassy in Berne, whose real name is Grigoriev. I believe this because once when I sent money to Thun, the sending bank made an error and it did not arrive; when this became known to Karla, he ordered me to send a second sum immediately to Grigoriev personally while bank enquiries were continuing. I did as I was ordered and later recovered the duplicated amount. This is all I know. Otto, my friend, I beg you to preserve these confidences, they could kill me.' He's bloody right. They did." Enderby chucked the transcript onto a table, and it made a loud slap. "Kirov's last will and testament, as you might say. That's it. George?"

"Yes, Saul."

"Really no drink?"

"Thank you, I'm fine."

"I'm still going to spell it out because I'm thick. Watch my arithmetic. It's nowhere near as good as yours. Watch my *every move*." Recalling Lacon, he held up a white hand and spread the fingers as a prelude to counting on them.

"One, Ostrakova writes to Vladimir. Her message rings old bells. Probably Mikhel intercepted and read it, but we'll never know. We could sweat him, but I doubt if it would help, and it would most certainly put the cat among Karla's pigeons in a big way if we did." He grabbed a second finger. "Two, Vladimir sends a copy of Ostrakova's letter to Otto Leipzig, urging him to rewarm the Kirov relationship double-quick. Three, Leipzig roars off to Paris, sees Ostrakova, gets himself alongside his dear old buddy Kirov, tempts him to Hamburg—where Kirov is free to go, after all, since Leipzig is still down in Karla's books as Kirov's agent. Now there's a thing, George."

Smiley waited.

"In Hamburg, Leipzig burns Kirov rotten. Right? Proof right here in our sweaty hands. But I mean—how?"

Did Smiley really not follow, or was he merely intent upon making Enderby work a little harder? In either case, he preferred to take Enderby's question as rhetorical.

"*How* does Leipzig burn him precisely?" Enderby insisted. "What's the pressure? Dirty pix—well, okay. Karla's a puritan, so's Kirov. But I mean, Christ, this isn't the fifties, is it? Everyone's allowed a bit of leg-sliding these days, what?"

Smiley offered no comment on Russian mores; but on the subject of pressure he was as precise as Karla might have been: "It's a different ethic to ours. It suffers no fools. We think of ourselves as more susceptible to pressure than the Russians. It's not true. It's simply not true." He seemed very sure of this. He seemed to have given the matter a lot of recent thought:

"Kirov had been incompetent and indiscreet. For his indiscretion alone, Karla would have destroyed him. Leipzig had the proof of that. You may remember that when we were running the original operation against Kirov, Kirov got drunk and talked out of turn about Karla. He told Leipzig that it was Karla personally who had ordered him to compose the legend for a female agent. You discounted the story at the time, but it was true."

Enderby was not a man to blush, but he did have the grace to pull a wry grin before fishing in his pocket for another matchstick.

"*And he that rolleth a stone, it will return upon him*," he remarked contentedly, though whether he was referring to his own dereliction or to Kirov's was unclear. "Tell us the rest, buddy, or I'll tell Karla what you've told me already, says little Otto to the fly. Jesus, you're right, he really *did* have Kirov by the balls!"

Sam Collins ventured a soothing interjection. "I think George's point meshes pretty neatly with the reference on page two, Chief," he said. "There's a passage where Leipzig actually refers to 'our discussions in Paris.' Otto's twisting the Karla knife there, no question. Right, George?"

But Sam Collins might have been speaking in another room for all the attention either of them paid him.

"Leipzig also had Ostrakova's letter," Smiley added. "Its contents did not speak well for Kirov."

"Another thing," said Enderby.

"Yes, Saul?"

"Four years, right? It's fully four years since Kirov made his original pass at Leipzig. Suddenly he's all over Ostrakova, wanting the same thing. Four years later. You suggesting he's been swanning around with the same brief from Karla all this time, and got no forrarder?"

Smiley's answer was curiously bureaucratic. "One can only suppose that Karla's requirement ceased and was then revived," he replied primly, and Enderby had the sense not to press him.

"Point is, Leipzig burns Kirov rotten and gets word to Vladimir that he's done so," Enderby resumed as the spread fingers came up again for counting. "Vladimir dispatches Villem to play courier. Meanwhile back at the Moscow ranch, Karla is either smelling a rat or Mikhel has peached, probably the latter. In either case, Karla calls Kirov home under the pretext of promotion and swings him by his ears. Kirov sings, as I would, fast. Karla tries to put the toothpaste back in the tube. Kills Vladimir while he's on the way to our rendezvous armed with Ostrakova's letter. Kills Leipzig. Takes a pot at the old lady, and fluffs it. What's his mood now?"

"He's sitting in Moscow waiting for Holmes or Captain Ahab to catch up with him," Sam Collins suggested, in his velvet voice, and lit yet another of his brown cigarettes.

Enderby was unamused. "So why doesn't Karla dig up his treasure, George? Put it somewhere else? If Kirov has confessed to Karla what he's confessed to Leipzig, Karla's first move should be to brush over the traces!"

"Perhaps the treasure is not movable," Smiley replied. "Perhaps Karla's options have run out."

"But it would be daylight madness to leave that bank account intact!"

"It was daylight madness to use a fool like Kirov," Smiley said, with unusual harshness. "It was madness to let him recruit Leipzig and madness to approach Ostrakova, and madness to believe that by killing three people he could stop the leak. Presumptions of sanity are therefore not given. Why should they be?" He paused. "And Karla *does* believe it, apparently, or Grigoriev would not still be in Berne. Which you say he is, I gather?" The smallest glance at Collins.

"As of today he's sitting pretty," Collins said through his all-weather grin.

"Then moving the bank account would hardly be a logical step," Smiley remarked. And he added: "Even for a madman."

And it was strange—as Collins and Enderby afterwards

privily agreed—how everything that Smiley said seemed to pass through the room like a chill; how in some way that they failed to understand, they had removed themselves to a higher order of human conduct for which they were unfit.

"So who's his dark lady?" Enderby demanded outright. "Who's worth ten grand a month and his whole damn career? Forcing him to use boobies instead of his own regular cut-throats? Must be quite a gal."

Again there is mystery about Smiley's decision not to reply to this question. Perhaps only his wilful inaccessibility can explain it; or perhaps we are staring at the stubborn refusal of the born case man to reveal anything to his controller that is not essential to their collaboration. Certainly there was philosophy in his decision. In his mind already, Smiley was accountable to nobody but himself: why should he act as if things were otherwise? "The threads lead all of them into my own life," he may have reasoned. "Why pass the ends to my adversary merely so that he can manipulate me?" Again, he may well have assumed—and probably with justice—that Enderby was as familiar as Smiley was with the complexities of Karla's background; and that even if he was not, he had had his Soviet Research Section burrowing all night until they found the answers he required.

In any case, the fact is that Smiley kept his counsel.

"George?" said Enderby, finally.

An aeroplane flew over quite low.

"It's simply a question of whether you want the product," Smiley said at last. "I can't see that anything else is ultimately of very much importance."

"Can't you, by God!" said Enderby, and pulled his hand from his mouth and the matchstick with it. "Oh, I *want* him all right," he went on, as if that were only half the point. "I *want* the Mona Lisa, and the Chairman of the Chinese People's

Republic, and next year's winner of the Irish Sweep. I *want* Karla sitting in the hot seat at Sarratt, coughing out his life story to the inquisitors. I *want* the American Cousins to eat out of my hand for years to come. I *want* the whole ball game, of course I do. Still doesn't get me off the hook."

But Smiley seemed curiously unconcerned by Enderby's dilemma.

"Brother Lacon told you the facts of life, I suppose? The stalemate and all?" Enderby asked. "Young, idealistic Cabinet, mustard for détente, preaching open government, all that balls? Ending the conditioned reflexes of the cold war? Sniffing Tory conspiracies under every Whitehall bed, ours specially? Did he? Did he tell you they're proposing to launch a damn great Anglo-Bolshie peace initiative, yet another, which will duly fall on its arse around Christmas next?"

"No. No, he didn't tell me that part."

"Well, they are. And we're not to jeopardise it, tra-la. Mind you, the very chaps who go hammering the peace-drums are the ones who scream like hell when we don't deliver the goods. I suppose that stands to reason. They're already asking what the Soviet posture will be, even now. Was it always like that?"

Smiley took so long to answer that he might have been passing the Judgment of Ages. "Yes. I suppose it was. I suppose that in one form or another it always *was* like that," he said at last, as if the answer mattered to him deeply.

"Wish you'd warned me."

Enderby sauntered back towards the centre of the room and poured himself some plain soda from the sideboard; he stared at Smiley with what seemed to be honest indecision. He stared at him, he shifted his head and stared again, showing all the signs of being faced with an insoluble problem.

"It's a tough one, Chief, it really is," said Sam Collins, unremarked by either man.

"And it's not all a wicked Bolshie plot, George, to lure us to our ultimate destruction—you're sure of *that?*"

"I'm afraid we're no longer worth the candle, Saul," Smiley said, with an apologetic smile.

Enderby did not care to be reminded of the limitations of British grandeur, and for a moment his mouth set into a sour grimace.

"All right, Maud," he said finally. "Let's go into the garden."

They walked side by side. Collins, on Enderby's nod, had stayed indoors. Slow rain puckered the surface of the pool and made the marble angel glisten in the dusk. Sometimes a breeze passed and a chain of water slopped from the hanging branches onto the lawn, soaking one or the other of them. But Enderby was an English gentleman, and while God's rain might be falling on the rest of mankind, he was damned if it was going to fall on him. The light came at them in bits. From Ben's French windows, yellow rectangles fell across the pond. From over the brick wall, they had the sickly green glow of a modern street lamp. They completed a round in silence before Enderby spoke.

"Led us a proper dance, you did, George, I'll tell you that for nothing, Villem, Mikhel, Toby, Connie. Poor old Ferguson hardly had time to fill in his expense claims before you were off again. 'Doesn't he ever sleep?' he asked me. 'Doesn't he ever drink?'"

"I'm sorry," said Smiley, for something to say.

"Oh, no, you're not," said Enderby, and came to a sudden halt. "*Bloody* laces," he muttered, stooping over his boot, "they always do this with suède. Too few eyeholes, that's the problem. You wouldn't think even the bloody Brits would manage to be mean with *holes*, would you?"

Enderby replaced one foot and lifted the other.

"I want his body, George, hear me? Hand me a live, talking Karla and I'll accept him and make my excuses later. Karla asks for asylum? Well, um, yes, most reluctantly he can have it. By the time the Wise Men are loading their shot-guns for me, I'll have enough out of him to shut them up for good. His body or nothing, you got me?"

They were strolling again, Smiley trailing behind, but Enderby, though he was speaking, did not turn his head.

"Don't you ever go thinking they'll go away, either," he warned. "When you and Karla are stuck on your ledge on the Reichenbach Falls and you've got your hands round Karla's throat, Brother Lacon will be right there behind you holding your coat-tails and telling you not to be beastly to the Russians. Did you get that?"

Smiley said yes, he had got it.

"What have you got on him so far? Misuse of the facilities of his office, I suppose. Fraud. Peculation of public funds, the very thing he topped that Lisbon fellow for. Unlawful operations abroad, including a couple of assassination jobs. I suppose there's a whole bloody bookful when you work it out. *Plus* all those jealous beavers at Centre longing for an excuse to knife him. He's right: blackmail's a *bloody* sight better than bribery."

Smiley said yes, it seemed so.

"You'll need people. Baby-sitters, lamplighters, all the forbidden toys. Don't talk to me about it, find your own. Money's another matter. I can lose you in the accounts for years the way these clowns in Treasury work. Just tell me when and how much and where, and I'll do a Karla for you and fiddle the accounts. How about passports and stuff? Need some addresses?"

"I think I can manage, thank you."

"I'll watch you day and night. If the ploy aborts and there's a scandal, I'm not going to have people telling me I should have staked you out. I'll say I suspected you might be slipping the leash on the Vladimir thing and I decided to have you checked in case. I'll say the whole catastrophe was a ludicrous piece of private enterprise by a senile spy who's lost his marbles."

Smiley said he thought that was a good idea.

"I may not have much to put on the street, but I can still tap your phone, steam open your mail, and if I want to, I'll bug your bedroom too. We've been listening in since Saturday as it is. Nothing, of course, but what do you expect?"

Smiley gave a small nod of sympathy.

"If your departure abroad strikes me as hasty or mysterious I shall report it. I also need a cover story for your visits to the Circus Registry. You'll go at night but you may be recognised and I'm not having *that* catch up with me, either."

"There was a project once to commission an in-house history of the service," Smiley said helpfully. "Nothing for publication, obviously, but some sort of continuing record which could be available to new entrants and certain liaison services."

"I'll send you a formal letter," Enderby said. "I'll bloody well backdate it too. If you happen to misuse your licence while you're inside the building, it's no fault of mine. That chap in Berne whom Kirov mentioned. Grigoriev, Commercial Counsellor. The chap who's been getting the cash?"

Smiley seemed lost in thought. "Yes, yes, of course," he said. "Grigoriev?"

"I suppose he's your next stop, is he?"

A shooting star ran across the sky and for a second they both watched it.

Enderby pulled a plain piece of folded paper from his inside pocket. "Well, that's Grigoriev's pedigree, far as we know it. He's clean as a whistle. One of the very rare ones. Used to be an economics don at some Bolshie university. Wife's a harridan."

"Thank you," said Smiley politely. "Thank you very much."

"Meanwhile, you have my totally deniable blessing," said Enderby as they started back towards the house.

"Thank you," said Smiley again.

"Sorry you've become an instrument of the imperial hypocrisy but there's rather a lot of it about."

"Not at all," said Smiley.

Enderby stopped to let Smiley draw up beside him.

"How's Ann?"

"Well, thank you."

"How much—" He was suddenly off his stroke. "Put it this way, George," he suggested, when he had savoured the night air for a moment. "You travelling on business, or for pleasure in this thing? Which is it?"

Smiley's reply was also slow in coming, and as indirect: "I was never conscious of pleasure," he said. "Or perhaps I mean: of the distinction."

"Karla still got that cigarette-lighter she gave you? It's true, isn't it? That time you interviewed him in Delhi—tried to get him to defect—they say he pinched your cigarette-lighter. Still got it, has he? Still using it? Pretty grating, I'd find that, if it was mine."

"It was just an ordinary Ronson," Smiley said. "Still, they're made to last, aren't they?"

They parted without saying goodbye.

20

In the weeks that followed this encounter with Enderby, George Smiley found himself in a complex and variable mood to accompany his many tasks of preparation. He was not at peace; he was not, in a single phrase, definable as a single person, beyond the one constant thrust of his determination. Hunter, recluse, lover, solitary man in search of completion, shrewd player of the Great Game, avenger, doubter in search of reassurance—Smiley was by turns each one of them, and sometimes more than one. Among those who remembered him later—old Mendel, the retired policeman, one of his few confidants; a Mrs. Gray, the landlady of the humble bed-and-breakfast house for gentlemen only, in Pimlico, which for security reasons he made his temporary headquarters; or Toby Esterhase, alias Benati, the distinguished dealer in Arab art—most, in their various ways, spoke of an ominous *going in*, a *quietness*, an economy of word and glance, and they described it according to their knowledge of him, and their station in life.

Mendel, a loping, dourly observant man with a taste for keeping bees, said outright that George was pacing himself before his big fight. Mendel had been in the amateur ring in his time, he had boxed middleweight for the Division, and he claimed to recognise the eve-of-match signs: a sobriety, a clarifying loneliness, and what he called a staring sort of look, which showed that Smiley was "thinking about his hands."

Mendel seems to have taken him in occasionally, and fed him meals. But Mendel was too perceptive not to observe the other sides of him also: the perplexity, often cloaked as social inhibition; his habit of slipping away, on a frail excuse, as if the sitting-still had suddenly become too long for him; as if he needed movement in order to escape himself.

To his landlady, Mrs. Gray, Smiley was, quite simply, bereaved. She knew nothing of him as a man, except that his name was Lorimer and he was a retired librarian by trade. But she told her other gentlemen she could feel he had had a *loss*, which was why he left his bacon, why he went out a lot but always alone, and why he slept with his light on. He reminded her of her father, she said, "after Mother went." And this was perceptive of Mrs. Gray, for the aftermath of the two violent deaths hung heavily on Smiley in the lull, though it did the very reverse of slow his hand. She was also right when she called him *divided*, constantly changing his mind about small things; like Ostrakova, Smiley found life's lesser decisions increasingly difficult to take.

Toby Esterhase, on the other hand, who dealt with him a great deal, took a more informed view, and one that was naturally brightened by Toby's own excitement at being back in the field. The prospect of playing Karla "at the big table," as he insisted on describing it, had made a new man of Toby. Mr. Benati had become international indeed. For two weeks, he toured the byways of Europe's seedier cities, mustering his bizarre army of discarded specialists—the pavement artists, the sound-thieves, the drivers, the photographers—and every day, from wherever he happened to be, using an agreed word code, he telephoned Smiley at a succession of numbers within walking distance of the boarding-house in order to report his progress. If Toby was passing through London, Smiley would drive to an airport hotel and debrief him in one of its now familiar bedrooms. George—Toby declared—was making a *Flucht nach vorn*, which nobody has ever quite succeeded in translating.

Literally it means "an escape forward," and it implies a desperation certainly, but also a weakness at one's back, if not an actual
burning of boats. Quite what this weakness was, Toby could
not describe. "Listen," he would say. "George always bruised
easy, know what I mean? You see a lot—your eyes get very painful. George saw too much, maybe." And he added, in a phrase
which found a modest place in Circus folklore—"George has
got too many heads under his hat." Of his generalship, on the
other hand, Toby had no doubt whatever. "Meticulous to a
fault," he declared respectfully—even if the fault included
checking Toby's imprest down to the last Swiss *Rappen*, a discipline he accepted with a rueful grace. George was nervous, he
said, as they all were; and his nervousness came to a natural
head as Toby began concentrating his teams, in twos and threes,
on the target city of Berne, and very, very cautiously taking the
first steps towards the quarry. "He got too detailed," Toby complained. "Like he wanted to be on the pavement with us. A case
man, he finds it hard to delegate, know what I mean?"

Even when the teams were all assembled, all accounted for
and briefed, Smiley from his London base still insisted on
three days of virtual inactivity while everybody "took the temperature of the city," as he called it, acquired local clothes and
transport, and rehearsed the systems of communication. "It's
lace curtain all the way, Toby," he repeated anxiously. "For
every week that nothing happens, Karla will feel that much
more secure. But frighten the game just once, and Karla will
panic and we're done for." After the first operational swing
Smiley summoned Toby home to report yet again: "Are you
sure there was no eye contact? Did you ring the changes
enough? Do you need more cars, more people?" Then, said
Toby, he had to take him through the whole manoeuvre yet
again, using street maps and still photographs of the target
house, explaining exactly where the static posts were laid,
where the one team had peeled off to make room for the
next. "Wait till you've got his pattern," said Smiley as they

parted. "When you've got his behaviour pattern, I'll come. Not before."

Toby says he made damn sure to take his time.

Of Smiley's visits to the Circus during this trying period there is, naturally, no official memory at all. He entered the place like his own ghost, floating as if invisible down the familiar corridors. At Enderby's suggestion he arrived at a quarter past six in the evening, just after the day-shift had ended, and before the night staff had got into its stride. He had expected barriers; he had queasy notions of janitors he had known for twenty years telephoning the fifth floor for clearance. But Enderby had arranged things differently, and when Smiley presented himself, passless, at the hardboard chicane, a boy he had never seen before nodded him carelessly to the open lift. From there, he made his way unchallenged to the basement. He got out, and the first thing he saw was the welfare club notice-board and they were the same notices from his own days exactly, word for word: free kittens available to good home; the junior staff drama group would read *The Admirable Crichton*, misspelt, on Friday in the canteen. The same squash competition, with players enrolled under worknames in the interest of security. The same ventilators emitting their troubled hum. So that, by the time he pushed the wired-glass door of Registry and scented the printing-ink and library dust, he half expected to see his own rotund shape bowed over the corner desk in the glow of the chipped green reading-lamp, as it had been often enough in the days when he was charting Bill Haydon's rampages of betrayal, and trying, by a reverse process of logic, to point to the weaknesses in Moscow Centre's armour.

"Ah, now, you're writing up our glorious past, I hear," the night registrar sang indulgently. She was a tall girl and county, with Hilary's walk: she seemed to topple even when she sat. She plonked an old tin deed-box on the table. "Fifth floor sent you this lot with their love," she said. "Squeal if you need ferrying around, won't you?"

The label on the handle read "Memorabilia." Lifting the lid, Smiley saw a heap of old buff files bound together with green string. Gently, he untied and lifted the cover of the first volume, to reveal Karla's misted photograph staring up at him like a corpse from the darkness of its coffin. He read all night, he hardly stirred. He read as far into his own past as into Karla's, and sometimes it seemed to him that the one life was merely the complement to the other; that they were causes of the same incurable malady. He wondered, as so often before, how he would have turned out if he had had Karla's childhood, had been fired in the same kilns of revolutionary upheaval. He tried but, as so often before, failed to resist his own fascination at the sheer scale of the Russian suffering, its careless savagery, its flights of heroism. He felt small in the face of it, and soft by comparison, even though he did not consider his own life wanting in its pains. When the night-shift ended, he was still there, staring into the yellow pages "the way a horse sleeps standing up," said the same night registrar, who rode in gymkhanas. Even when she took the files from him to return them to the fifth floor, he went on staring till she gently touched his elbow.

He came the next night and the next; he disappeared, and returned a week later without explanation. When he had done with Karla, he drew the files on Kirov, on Mikhel, on Villem, and on the Group at large, if only to give, in retrospect, a solid documentary heart to all he had heard and remembered of the Leipzig-Kirov story. For there was yet another part of Smiley, call it pedant, call it scholar, for which the file was the only truth, and all the rest a mere extravagance until it was matched and fitted to the record. He drew the files on Otto Leipzig and the General, too, and, as a service to their memory, if nothing else, added to each a memorandum that calmly set out the true circumstances of his death. The last file he drew was Bill Haydon's. There was hesitation at first about releasing it, and the fifth-floor duty officer, whoever he was that night, called Enderby out of a private ministerial dinner party in order to clear it with him. Enderby, to his credit, was furious: "God Almighty, man, he *wrote* the damn thing in the first place, didn't he? If George can't read his own reports, who the hell can?" Smiley didn't really *read* it, even then, the registrar reported, who had a secret watching brief on everything he drew. It was more *browsing*, she said—and described a slow and speculative turning of the pages, "like someone looking for a picture they'd seen and couldn't find again." He only kept the file for an hour or so, then gave it back with a polite "Thank you very much." He did not come again after that, but there is a story the janitors tell that some time after eleven on the same night, when he had tidied away his papers and cleared his desk space and consigned his few scribbled notes to the bin for secret waste, he was observed to stand for a long time in the rear courtyard—a dismal place, all white tiles and black drain-pipes and a stink of cat—staring at the building he was about to take his leave of, and at the light that was burning weakly in his former room, much as old men will look at the houses where they were born, the schools where they were educated, and the churches where they were married. And from Cambridge Circus—it was by then eleven-thirty—he startled everybody, took a cab to Paddington and caught the night sleeper to Penzance, which leaves just after midnight. He had not bought a ticket in advance, or ordered one by telephone; nor did he have any night things with him, not even a razor, though in the morning he did manage to borrow one from the attendant. Sam Collins had put together a ragtag team of watchers by then, an amateurish lot admittedly, and all they could say afterwards was that he made a call from a phone-box, but there was no time for them to do anything about it.

"Bloody queer moment to take a holiday, isn't it?" Enderby remarked petulantly when this intelligence was brought to him, together with a string of moans from the staff-side about overtime, travelling time, and allowances for unsocial hours.

Then he remembered, and said, "Oh, my Christ, he's visiting his bitch goddess. Hasn't he got enough problems, taking on Karla single-handed?" The whole episode annoyed Enderby strangely. He fumed all day and insulted Sam Collins in front of everyone. As a former diplomat, he had great contempt for abstracts, even if he took refuge in them constantly.

The house stood on a hill, in a coppice of bare elms still waiting for the blight. It was granite and very big, and crumbling, with a crowd of gables that clustered like torn black tents above the tree-tops. Acres of smashed greenhouses led to it; collapsed stables and an untended kitchen garden lay below it in the valley. The hills were olive and shaven, and had once been hill-forts. "Harry's Cornish heap," she called it. Between the hills ran the line of the sea, which that morning was hard as slate under the lowering cloud banks. A taxi took him up the bumpy drive, an old Humber like a wartime staff car. This is where she spent her childhood, thought Smiley; and where she adopted mine. The drive was very pitted; stubs of felled trees lay like yellow tombstones either side. She'll be in the main house, he thought. The cottage where they had passed their holidays together lay over the brow, but on her own she stayed in the house, in the room she had had as a girl. He told the driver not to wait, and started towards the front porch, picking his way between the puddles with his London shoes, giving the puddles all his attention. It's not my world any more, he thought. It's hers, it's theirs. His watcher's eyes scanned the many windows of the front façade, trying to catch a glimpse of her shadow. She'd have picked me up at the station, only she muddled the time, he thought, giving her the benefit of the doubt. But her car was parked in the stables with the morning frost still on it; he had spotted it while he was still paying off the taxi. He rang the bell and heard her footsteps on the flagstones, but it was Mrs. Tremedda who opened the door and showed him to one of the drawing-rooms—smoking-room, morning-room, drawing-room, he had never worked them out. A log fire was burning.

"I'll get her," Mrs. Tremedda said.

At least I haven't got to talk about Communists to mad Harry, Smiley thought while he waited. At least I haven't got to hear how all the Chinese waiters in Penzance are standing by for the order from Peking to poison their customers. Or how the bloody strikers should be put up against a wall and shot—where's their sense of service, for Christ's sake? Or how Hitler may have been a blackguard but he had the right idea about the Jews. Or some similar monstrous, but seriously held, conviction.

She's told the family to keep clear, he thought.

He could smell honey through the wood-smoke and wondered, as he always did, where it came from. The furniture wax? Or was there, somewhere in the catacombs, a honey room, just as there was a gunroom and a fishing-room and a box-room and, for all he knew, a love room? He looked for the Tiepolo drawing that used to hang over the fireplace, a scene of Venice life. They've sold it, he thought. Each time he came, the collection had dwindled by one more pretty thing. What Harry spent the money on was anybody's guess—certainly not the upkeep of the house.

She crossed the room to him and he was glad it was she who was doing the walking, not himself, because he would have stumbled into something. His mouth was dry and he had a lump of cactus in his stomach; he didn't want her near him, her reality was suddenly too much for him. She was looking beautiful and Celtic, as she always did down here, and as she came towards him her brown eyes scanned him, looking for his mood. She kissed him on the mouth, putting her fingers along the back of his neck to guide him, and Haydon's shadow fell between them like a sword.

"You didn't think to pick up a morning paper at the station, did you?" she enquired. "Harry's stopped them again."

She asked whether he had breakfasted and he lied and said he had. Perhaps they could go for a walk instead, she suggested, as if he were someone wanting to see round the estate. She took him to the gunroom where they rummaged for boots that would do. There were boots that shone like conkers and boots that looked permanently damp. The coast footpath led in both directions out of the bay. Periodically, Harry threw barbed-wire barricades across it, or put up notices saying "DANGER LAND-MINES." He was fighting a running battle with the Council for permission to make a camping site, and its refusal sometimes drove him to a fury. They chose the north shoulder and the wind, and she had taken his arm to listen. The north was windier, but on the south you had to go single file through the gorse.

"I'm going away for a bit, Ann," he said, trying to use her name naturally. "I didn't want to tell you over the telephone." It was his wartime voice and he felt an idiot when he heard himself using it. "I'm going off to blackmail a lover," he should have said.

"Away to somewhere particular, or just away from me?"

"There's a job I have to do abroad," he said, still trying to escape his Gallant Pilot rôle, and failing. "I don't think you should go to Bywater Street while I'm away."

She had locked her fingers through his own, but then she did those things: she handled people naturally, all people. Below them in the rocks' cleft, the sea broke and formed itself furiously in patterns of writhing foam.

"And you've come all this way just to tell me the house is out of bounds?" she asked.

He didn't answer.

"Let me try it differently," she proposed when they had walked a distance. "If Bywater Street had been *in* bounds, would you have suggested that I *did* go there? Or are you telling me it's out of bounds for good?"

She stopped and gazed at him, and held him away from her,

trying to read his answer. She whispered, "For goodness' sake," and he could see the doubt, the pride, and the hope in her face all at once, and wondered what she saw in his, because he himself had no knowledge of what he felt, except that he belonged nowhere near her, nowhere near this place; she was like a girl on a floating island that was swiftly moving away from him with the shadows of all her lovers gathered round her. He loved her, he was indifferent to her, he observed her with the curse of detachment, but she was leaving him. If I do not know myself, he thought, how can I tell who you are? He saw the lines of age and pain and striving that their life together had put there. She was all he wanted, she was nothing, she reminded him of someone he had once known a long time ago; she was remote to him, he knew her entirely. He saw the gravity in her face and one minute wondered that he could ever have taken it for profundity; the next, he despised her dependence on him, and wanted only to be free of her. He wanted to call out "Come back" but he didn't do it; he didn't even put out a hand to stop her from slipping away.

"You used to tell me never to stop looking," he said. The statement began like the preface to a question, but no question followed.

She waited, then offered a statement of her own. "I'm a comedian, George," she said. "I need a straight man. I need you."

But he saw her from a long way off.

"It's the job," he said.

"I can't live with them. I can't live without them." He supposed she was talking about her lovers again. "There's one thing worse than change and that's the status quo. I hate the choice. I love you. Do you understand?" There was a gap while he must have said something. She was not relying on him, but she was leaning on him while she wept, because the weeping had taken away her strength. "You never knew how free you were, George," he heard her say. "I had to be free for both of us."

She seemed to realise her own absurdity and laughed.

She let go his arm and they walked again while she tried to right the ship by asking plain questions. He said weeks, perhaps longer. He said "In a hotel," but didn't say which city or country. She faced him again, and the tears were suddenly running anywhere, worse than before, but they still didn't move him as he wished they would.

"George, this is all there is, I promise you," she said, halting to make her entreaty. "The whistle's gone, in your world and in mine. We're landed with each other. There isn't any more. According to the averages we're the most contented people on earth."

He nodded, seeming to take the point that she had been somewhere he had not, but not regarding it as conclusive. They walked a little more, and he noticed that when she didn't speak he was able to relate to her, but only in the sense that she was another living creature moving along the same path as himself.

"It's to do with the people who ruined Bill Haydon," he said to her, either as a consolation, or an excuse for his retreat. But he thought: "who ruined you."

He had missed his train and there were two hours to kill. The tide was out so he walked along the shore near Marazion, scared by his own indifference. The day was grey, the seabirds were very white against the slate sea. A couple of brave children were splashing in the surf. I am a thief of the spirit, he thought despondently. Faithless, I am pursuing another man's convictions; I am trying to warm myself against other people's fires. He watched the children, and recalled some scrap of poetry from the days when he read it:

> *To turn as swimmers into cleanness leaping,*
> *Glad from a world grown old and cold and weary.*

Yes, he thought glumly. That's me.

*   *   *

"Now, George," Lacon demanded. "Do you think we set our women up too high, is *that* where we English middle-class chaps go wrong? Do you think—I'll put it this way—that we English, with our traditions and our schools, expect our womenfolk to stand for *far* too much, then *blame* them for not standing up at all—if you follow me? We see them as *concepts*, rather than flesh and blood. Is that our hangup?"

Smiley said it might be.

"Well, if it *isn't*, why does Val *always* fall for shits?" Lacon snapped aggressively, to the surprise of the couple sitting at the next-door table.

Smiley did not know the answer to that either.

They had dined, appallingly, in the steak-house Lacon had suggested. They had drunk Spanish burgundy out of a carafe, and Lacon had raged wildly over the British political dilemma. Now they were drinking coffee and a suspect brandy. The anti-Communist phobia was overdone; Lacon had declared himself sure of it. Communists were only *people*, after all. They weren't red-toothed monsters, not any more. Communists wanted what everyone wanted: prosperity and a bit of peace and quiet. A chance to take a breather from all this damned hostility. And if they didn't—well, what could we do about it anyway? he had asked. Some problems—take Ireland—were insoluble, but you would never get the Americans to admit *anything* was insoluble. Britain was ungovernable; so would everywhere else be in a couple of years. Our future was with the collective, but our survival was with the individual, and the paradox was killing us every day.

"Now, George, how do *you* see it? You're out of harness after all. You have the objective view, the overall perspective."

Smiley heard himself muttering something inane about a spectrum.

And now the topic that Smiley had dreaded all evening was finally upon them: their seminar on marriage had begun.

"*We* were always taught that women had to be cherished," Lacon declared resentfully. "If one didn't make 'em feel loved every minute of the day, they'd go off the rails. But this chap Val's with—well, if she annoys him, or speaks out of turn, he'll like as not give her a black eye. You and I never do that, do we?"

"I'm sure we don't," said Smiley.

"Look here. Do you reckon if I went and saw her—bearded her in his house—took a really tough line—threatened legal action and so forth—it might tip the scales? I mean I'm bigger than he is, God knows. I'm not without clout, whichever way you read me!"

They stood on the pavement under the stars, waiting for Smiley's cab.

"Well, have a good holiday anyway. You've deserved it," Lacon said. "Going somewhere warm?"

"Well, I thought I might just take off and wander."

"Lucky you. My God, I envy you your freedom! Well, you've been jolly useful, anyway. I shall follow your advice to the letter."

"But, Oliver, I didn't *give* you any advice," Smiley protested, slightly alarmed.

Lacon ignored him. "And that other thing is all squared away, I hear," he said serenely. "No loose ends, no messiness. Good of you, that, George. Loyal. I'm going to see if we can get you a bit of recognition for it. What have you got already, I forget? Some chap the other day in the Athenaeum was saying you deserve a K."

The cab came, and to Smiley's embarrassment Lacon insisted on shaking hands. "George. Bless you. You've been a brick. We're birds of a feather, George. Both patriots, givers, not takers. Trained to our services. Our country. We must pay the price. If Ann had been your agent instead of your wife, you'd probably have run her pretty well."

* * *

The next afternoon, following a telephone call from Toby to say that "the deal was just about ready for completion," George Smiley quietly left for Switzerland, using the workname Barraclough. From Zurich Airport he took the Swissair bus to Berne and made straight for the Bellevue Palace Hotel, an enormous, sumptuous place of mellowed Edwardian quiet, which on clear days looks across the foothills to the glistening Alps, but that evening was shrouded in a cloying winter fog. He had considered smaller places; he had considered using one of Toby's safe flats. But Toby had persuaded him that the Bellevue was best. It had several exits, it was central, and it was the first place in Berne where anyone would think to find him, and therefore the last where Karla, if he was looking out for him, would expect him to be. Entering the enormous hall, Smiley had the feeling of stepping onto an empty liner far out at sea.

21

His room was a tiny Swiss Versailles. The *bombé* writing-desk had brass inlay and a marble top, and a Bartlett print of Lord Byron's Childe Harold hung above the pristine twin beds. The fog outside the window made a grey wall. He unpacked and went downstairs again to the bar where an elderly pianist was playing a medley of hits from the Fifties, things that had been Ann's favourites, and, he supposed, his. He ate some cheese and drank a glass of Fendant, thinking: *Now*. Now is the beginning. From now on there is no shrinking back, no space for hesitation. At ten he made his way to the old city, which he loved. The streets were cobbled; the freezing air smelt of roast chestnuts and cigar. The ancient fountains advanced on him through the fog, the medieval houses were the backdrop to a play he had no part in. He entered the arcades, passing art galleries and antique shops and doorways tall enough to ride a horse through. At the Nydegg Bridge he came to a halt, and stared into the river. So many nights, he thought. So many streets till here. He thought of Hesse: *strange to wander in the fog . . . no tree knows another.* The frozen mist curled low over the racing water; the weir burned creamy yellow.

An orange Volvo estate car drew up behind him, Berne registration, and briefly doused its lights. As Smiley started towards it, the passenger door was pushed open from inside, and by the interior light he saw Toby Esterhase in the driving seat, and in the back, a stern-looking woman in the uniform of a Bernese housewife, dandling a child on her knee. He's using them for cover, Smiley thought; for what the watchers called the silhouette. They drove off and the woman began talking to the child. Her Swiss German had a steady note of indignation: "See there the crane, Eduard. . . . Now we are passing the bear pit, Eduard. . . . Look, Eduard, a tram . . ." Watchers are always dissatisfied, he remembered; it's the fate of every voyeur. She was moving her hands about, directing the child's eye to anything. *A family evening, Officer,* said the scenario. *We are going visiting in our fine orange Volvo, Officer. We are going home.* And the men, naturally, Officer, seated in the front.

They had entered Elfenau, Berne's diplomatic ghetto. Through the fog, Smiley glimpsed tangled gardens white with frost, and the green porticoes of villas. The headlights picked out a brass plate proclaiming an Arab state, and two bodyguards protecting it. They passed an English church and a row of tennis-courts; they entered an avenue lined with bare beeches. The street lights hung in them like white balloons.

"Number eighteen is five hundred metres on the left," said Toby softly. "Grigoriev and his wife occupy the ground floor." He was driving slowly, using the fog as his excuse.

"Very rich people live here, Eduard!" the woman was singing from behind them. "All from foreign places."

"Most of the Iron Curtain crowd live in Muri, not Elfenau," Toby went on. "It's a commune, they do everything in groups. Shop in groups, go for walks in groups, you name it. The Grigorievs are different. Three months ago, they moved out of Muri and rented this apartment on a personal basis. Three thousand five hundred a month, George, he pays it in person to the landlord."

"Cash?"

"Monthly in one-hundred notes."

"How are the rest of the Embassy hirings paid for?"

"Through the Mission accounts. Not Grigoriev's. Grigoriev is the exception."

A police-patrol car overtook them with the slowness of a river barge; Smiley saw its three heads turned to them.

"Look, Eduard, police!" the woman cried, and tried to make the child wave at them.

Toby too was careful not to stop talking. "The police boys are worried about bombs," he explained. "They think the Palestinians are going to blow the place sky high. That's been good and bad for us, George. If we're clumsy, Grigoriev can tell himself we're local angels. The same doesn't go for the police. One hundred metres, George. Look for a black Mercedes in the forecourt. Other staff use the Embassy car pool. Not Grigoriev. Grigoriev drives his own Mercedes."

"When did he get it?" Smiley asked.

"Three months ago, second-hand. Same time as he moved out of Muri. That was a big leap for him, George. Like a birthday, so many things. The car, the house, promotion from First Secretary to Counsellor."

It was a stucco villa, set in a large garden that had no back because of the fog. In a bay window at the front Smiley glimpsed a light burning behind curtains. There was a children's slide in the garden, and what appeared to be an empty swimming-pool. On the gravel sweep stood a black Mercedes with CD plates.

"All Soviet Embassy car numbers end with 73," said Toby. "The Brits have 72. Grigorieva got herself a driving licence two months ago. There are only two women in the Embassy with licences. She's one and she's a terrible driver, George. And I mean terrible."

"Who occupies the rest of the house?"

"The landlord. A professor at Berne University, a creep. A while ago the Cousins got alongside him and said they'd like to run a couple of probe mikes into the ground floor, offered him money. The professor took the money and reported them to the Bundespolizei like a good citizen. The Bundespolizei got a scare. They'd promised the Cousins to look the other way in exchange for a sight of the product. Operation abandoned. Seems the Cousins had no particular interest in Grigoriev, it was just routine."

"Where are the Grigoriev children?"

"In Geneva at Soviet Mission School, weekly boarders. They get home Friday nights. Week-ends the family make excursions. Romp in the woods, langlauf, play badminton. Collect mushrooms. Grigorieva's a fresh-air freak. Also they have taken up bicycling," he added, with a glance.

"Does Grigoriev go with the family on these excursions?"

"Saturdays he works, George—and, I am certain, only to escape them." Toby had formed decided views on the Grigoriev marriage, Smiley noticed. He wondered whether it had echoes of one of Toby's own.

They had left the avenue and entered a side-road. "Listen, George," Toby was saying, still on the subject of Grigoriev's week-ends. "Okay? Watchers imagine things. They got to, it's their job. There's a girl works in the Visa Section. Brunette and, for a Russian, sexy. The boys call her 'little Natasha.' Her real name's something else but for them she's Natasha. Saturdays she comes in to the Embassy. To work. Couple of times, Grigoriev drives her home to Muri. We took some pictures, not bad. She got out of the car short of her apartment and walked the last five hundred metres. Why? Another time he took her nowhere—just a drive round the Gurten, but talking very cosy. Maybe the boys just want it to be that way, on account of Grigorieva. They like the guy, George. You know how watchers are. It's love or hate all the time. They like him."

He was pulling up. The lights of a small café glowed at them through the fog. In its courtyard stood a green Citroën *deuxchevaux*, Geneva registration. Cardboard boxes were heaped on the back seat like trade samples. A foxtail dangling from the radio aerial. Springing out, Toby pulled open the flimsy door and hustled Smiley into the passenger seat: then handed him a trilby hat, which he put on. For himself, Toby

had a Russian-style fur. They drove off again, and Smiley saw
their Bernese matron climbing into the front of the orange
Volvo they had just abandoned. Her child waved at them
despondently through the back window as they left.

"How is everyone?" Smiley said.

"Great. Pawing the earth, George, every one of them. One
of the Sartor brothers had a sick kid, had to go home to Vienna.
It nearly broke his heart. Otherwise great. You're Number
One for all of them. This is Harry Slingo coming up on the
right. Remember Harry? Used to be my sidekick back in
Acton."

"I read that his son had won a scholarship to Oxford," Smiley said.

"Physics. Wadham, Oxford. The boy's a genius. Keep looking down the road, George, don't move your head."

They passed a van with "*Auto-Schnelldienst*" painted in
breezy letters on the side, and a driver dozing at the wheel.

"Who's in the back?" Smiley asked when they were clear.

"Pete Lusty, used to be a scalp-hunter. Those guys have
been having it very bad, George. No work, no action. Pete
signed up for the Rhodesian Army. Killed some guys, didn't
care for it, came back. No wonder they love you."

They were passing Grigoriev's house again. A light was
burning in the other window.

"The Grigorievs go to bed early," Toby said in a sort of awe.

A parked limousine lay ahead of them with Zurich consular
plates. In the driving seat, a chauffeur was reading a paperback
book.

"That's Canada Bill," Toby explained. "Grigoriev leaves
the house, turns right, he passes Pete Lusty. Turns left, he
passes Canada Bill. They're good boys. Very vigilant."

"Who's behind us?"

"The Meinertzhagen girls. The big one got married."

The fog made their progress private, very quiet. They
descended a gentle hill, passing the British Ambassador's resi-

dence on their right, and his Rolls-Royce parked in the sweep. The road led left and Toby followed it. As he did so, the car behind overtook them and conveniently put up its headlights. By their beam, Smiley found himself looking into a wooded cul-de-sac ending in a pair of tall closed gates guarded on the inside by a small huddle of men. The trees cut off the rest entirely.

"Welcome to the Soviet Embassy, George," Toby said, very softly. "Twenty-four diplomats, fifty other ranks—cipher clerks, typists, and some very lousy drivers, all home-based. The trade delegation's in another building, Schanzeneck-strasse 17. Grigoriev visits there a lot. In Berne we got also Tass and Novosti, mostly mainstream hoods. The parent residency is Geneva, U.N. cover, about two hundred strong. This place is a side-show: twelve, fifteen altogether, growing but only slow. The Consulate is tacked onto the back of the Embassy. You go into it through a door in the fence, like it was an opium den or a cat house. They got a closed-circuit television camera on the path and scanners in the waiting-room. Try applying for a visa once."

"I think I'll give it a miss, thanks," said Smiley, and Toby gave one of his rare laughs.

"Embassy grounds," Toby said as the headlights flashed over steep woods falling away to the right. "That's where Grigorieva plays her volley-ball, gives political instruction to the kids. George, believe me, that's a very distorting woman. Embassy kindergarten, the indoctrination classes, the Ping-Pong club, women's badminton—that woman runs the whole show. Don't take my word for it, hear my boys talk about her." As they turned out of the cul-de-sac, Smiley lifted his glance towards the upper window of the corner house and saw a light go out, and then come on again.

"And that's Pauli Skordeno saying 'Welcome to Berne,'" said Toby. "We managed to rent the top floor last week. Pauli's a Reuters stringer. We even faked a press pass for him. Cable cards, everything."

Toby had parked near the Thunplatz. A modern clock tower was striking eleven. Fine snow was falling but the fog had not dispersed. For a moment neither man spoke.

"Today was a model of last week, last week was a model of the week before, George," said Toby. "Every Thursday it's the same. After work he takes the Mercedes to the garage, fills it with petrol and oil, checks the batteries, asks for a receipt. He goes home. Six o'clock, a little after, an Embassy car arrives at his front door and out gets Krassky, the regular Thursday courier from Moscow. Alone. That's a very itchy fellow, a professional. In all other situations, Krassky don't go anywhere without his companion Bogdanov. Fly together, carry together, eat together. But to visit Grigoriev, Krassky breaks ranks and goes alone. Stays half an hour, leaves again. Why? That's very irregular in a courier, George. Very dangerous, if he hasn't got the backing, believe me."

"So what do you make of Grigoriev, Toby?" Smiley asked. "What is he?"

Toby made his tilting gesture with his outstretched palm. "A trained hood Grigoriev isn't, George. No tradecraft, actually a complete catastrophe. But he's not straight either. A half-breed, George."

So was Kirov, Smiley thought.

"Do you think we've got enough on him?" Smiley asked.

"Technically no problem. The bank, the false identity, little Natasha even: technically we got a hand of aces."

"And you think he'll burn," said Smiley, more as confirmation than a question.

In the darkness, Toby's palm once more tilted, this way, that way.

"Burning, George, that's always a hazard, know what I mean? Some guys get heroic and want to die for their countries suddenly. Other guys roll over and lie still the moment you put the arm on them. Burning, that touches the stubbornness in certain people. Know what I mean?"

"Yes. Yes, I think I do," said Smiley. And he remembered Delhi again, and the silent face watching him through the haze of cigarette smoke.

"Go easy, George. Okay? You got to put your feet up now and then."

"Good night," said Smiley.

He caught the last tram back to the town centre. By the time he had reached the Bellevue, the snow was falling heavily: big flakes, milling in the yellow light, too wet to settle. He set his alarm for seven.

22

The young woman they called Alexandra had been awake one hour exactly when the morning bell sounded for assembly, but when she heard it she immediately drew up her knees inside her calico night-suit, crammed her eyelids together, and swore to herself she was still asleep, a child who needed rest. The assembly bell, like Smiley's alarm clock, went off at seven, but already at six she had heard the chiming of the valley clocks, first the Catholics, then the Protestants, then the Town Hall, and she didn't believe in any of them. Not this God, not that God, and least of all the burghers with their butchers' faces, who at the annual festival had stood to attention with their stomachs stuck out while the fire-brigade choir moaned patriotic songs in dialect.

She knew about the annual festival because it was one of the few Permitted Expeditions, and she had recently been allowed to attend it as a privilege—her first, and to her huge amusement it was devoted to the celebration of the common onion. She had stood between Sister Ursula and Sister Beatitude and she knew they were both alert in case she tried to run away or snap inside and start a fit, and she had watched an hour of the most boring speechifying ever, then an hour's singing to the accompaniment of boring martial music by the brass band. Then a march past of people dressed in village costume and carrying strings of onions on long sticks, headed by the village flag-swinger, who on other days brought the milk to the lodge and—if he could slip by—right up to the hostel door, in the hope of getting a sight of a girl through the window, or perhaps it was just Alexandra trying to get a sight of him.

After the village clocks had chimed the six, Alexandra from deep, deep in her bed had decided to count the minutes till eternity. In her self-imposed rôle as child, she had done this by counting each second in a whisper: "One thousand and *one*, one thousand and *two*." At twelve minutes past, by her childish reckoning, she heard Mother Felicity on her way back from Mass, her pompous Moped snorting down the drive, telling everyone that Felicity-Felicity—pop-pop—and no one else— pop-pop—was our Superintendent and Official Starter of the Day; nobody else—pop-pop—would do. Which was funny because her real name was not Felicity at all; Felicity was what she had chosen for the other nuns. Her real name, she had told Alexandra as a secret, was Nadezhda, meaning "Hope." So Alexandra had told Felicity that *her* real name was Tatiana, not Alexandra at all. Alexandra was a *new* name, she explained, put on to wear in Switzerland specially. But Felicity-Felicity had told her sharply not to be a silly girl.

After Mother Felicity's arrival, Alexandra had held the white bed sheet to her eyes and decided that time was not passing at all, that she was in a child's white limbo where everything was shadowless, even Alexandra, even Tatiana. White light bulbs, white walls, a white iron bed frame. White radiators. Through the high windows, white mountains against a white sky.

Dr. Rüedi, she thought, here is a new dream for you when we have our next little Thursday talk, or is it Tuesday?

Now listen carefully, Doctor. Is your Russian good enough? Sometimes you pretend to understand more than you really do. Very well, I will begin. My name is Tatiana and I am standing in my white night-suit in front of the white Alpine landscape, trying to write on the mountain face with a stick of Felicity-Felicity's white chalk, whose real name is Nadezhda. I am wearing nothing underneath. You pretend you are indifferent to such things, but when I talk to you about how I love my body you pay close attention, don't you, Dr. Rüedi? I scribble with the chalk in the mountain face. I stub with it like a cigarette. I think of the filthiest words I know—yes, Dr. Rüedi, *this* word, *that* word—but I fear your Russian vocabulary is unlikely to include them. I try to write them also, but white on white, what impact can a little girl make, I ask you, Doctor?

Doctor, it's terrible, you must never have my dreams. Do you know I was once a whore called Tatiana? That I can do no wrong? That I can set fire to things, even myself, vilify the State, and *still* the wise ones in authority will not punish me? But instead, let me out of the back door—"Go, Tatiana, go"— did you know this?

Hearing footsteps in the corridor, Alexandra pulled herself deeper under the bedclothes. The French girl is being led to the toilets, she thought. The French girl was the most beautiful in the place. Alexandra loved her, just for her beauty. She beat the whole system with it. Even when they put her in the coat—for clawing or messing herself or smashing something— her angel's face still gazed at them like one of their own icons. Even when she wore her shapeless night-suit with no buttons, her breasts lifted it up in a crisp bridge and there was nothing anyone could do, not even the most jealous, not even Felicity-Felicity whose secret name was Hope, to prevent her from looking like a film star. When she tore her clothes off, even the nuns stared at her with a kind of covetous terror. Only the American girl had matched her for looks, and the American girl had been taken away, she was too bad. The French girl was bad enough with her naked tantrums and her wrist-cutting and her fits of rage at Felicity-Felicity, but she was nothing beside the American girl by the time she left. The sisters had to fetch Kranko from the lodge to hold her down, just for the sedation. They had to close the entire rest-wing while they did it, but when the van took the American girl off, it was like a death in the family and Sister Beatitude wept all through evening prayers. And afterwards, when Alexandra forced her to tell, she called her by her pet name, Sasha, a sure sign of her distress. "The American girl has gone to Untersee," she said through her tears when Alexandra forced her to tell. "Oh, Sasha, Sasha, promise me you will never go to Untersee." Just as in the life she could not mention, they had begged her: "Tatiana, do not do these mad and dangerous things!"

After that, Untersee became Alexandra's worst terror, a threat that silenced her at any time, even her naughtiest: "If you are bad, you will go to Untersee, Sasha. If you tease Dr. Rüedi, pull up your skirt, and cross your legs at him, Mother Felicity will have to send you to Untersee. Hush, or they'll send you to Untersee."

The footsteps returned along the corridor. The French girl was being taken to be dressed. Sometimes she fought them and ended up in the coat instead. Sometimes Alexandra would be sent to calm her, which she did by brushing the French girl's hair over and over again, not talking, till the French girl relaxed and started to kiss her hands. Then Alexandra would be taken away again, because love was not, was not, was *not* on the curriculum.

The door flew open and Alexandra heard Felicity-Felicity's courtly voice, harrying her like an old nurse in a Russian play: "Sasha! You must get up immediately! Sasha, wake up immediately! Sasha, wake up! Sasha!"

She came a step nearer. Alexandra wondered whether she was going to pull back the sheets and yank her to her feet. Mother Felicity could be rough as a soldier, for all her aristocratic blood. She was not a bully, but she was blunt and easily provoked.

"Sasha, you will be late for breakfast. The other girls will look at you and laugh and say that we stupid Russians are always late. Sasha? Sasha, do you want to miss prayers? God will be very angry with you, Sasha. He will be sad and He will cry. He may have to think of ways of punishing you."

Sasha, do you want to go to Untersee?

Alexandra pressed her eyelids closer together. I am six years old and need my sleep, Mother Felicity. God make me five, God make me four. I am three years old and need my sleep, Mother Felicity.

"Sasha, have you forgotten it is your special day? Sasha, have you forgotten you have your *visitor* today?"

God make me two, God make me one, God make me nothing and unborn. No, I have not forgotten my visitor, Mother Felicity. I remembered my visitor before I went to sleep, I dreamt of him, I have thought of nothing else since I woke. But, Mother Felicity, I do not want my visitor today, or any other day. I cannot, cannot live the lie, I don't know how, and that is why I shall not, shall not, *shall* not let the day begin!

Obediently, Alexandra clambered out of bed.

"*There*," said Mother Felicity, and gave her a distracted kiss before bustling off down the corridor, calling "Late again! Late again!" and clapping her hands—"Shoo, shoo!"—just as she would to a flock of silly hens.

23

The train journey to Thun took half an hour and from the station Smiley drifted, window-shopping, making little detours. *Some guys get heroic and want to die for their countries*, he thought. . . . *Burning, that touches the stubbornness in people*. . . . He wondered what it would touch in himself.

It was a day of darkening blankness. The few pedestrians were slow shadows against the fog, and lake steamers were frozen in the locks. Occasionally the blankness parted enough to offer him a glimpse of castle, a tree, a piece of city wall. Then swiftly closed over them again. Snow lay in the cobble and in the forks of the knobbly spa trees. The few cars drove with their lights on, their tyres crackling in the slush. The only colours were in shop-windows: gold watches, ski clothes like national flags. "Be there by eleven earliest," Toby had said; "eleven is already too early, George, they won't arrive till twelve." It was only ten-thirty but he wanted the time, he wanted to circle before he settled; time, as Enderby would say, to get his ducks in a row. He entered a narrow street and saw the castle lift directly above him. The arcade became a pavement, then a staircase, then a steep slope, and he kept climbing. He passed an English Tea-Room, an American-Bar, an Oasis Night-Club, each hyphenated, each neon-lit, each a sanitised copy of a lost original. But they could not destroy his love of Switzerland. He entered a square and saw the bank, the

very one, and straight across the road the little hotel exactly as
Toby had described it, with its café-restaurant on the ground
floor and its barracks of rooms above. He saw the yellow mail
van parked boldly in the no-parking bay, and he knew it was
Toby's static post. Toby had a lifelong faith in mail vans; he
stole them wherever he went, saying nobody noticed or remembered them. He had fitted new number-plates but they looked
older than the van. Smiley crossed the square. A notice on the
bank door said "OPEN MONDAY TO THURSDAY 07.45–17.00, FRIDAY
07.45–18.15." "Grigoriev likes the lunch-hour because in Thun
nobody wastes his lunch-hour going to the bank," Toby had
explained. "He has completely mistaken quiet for security,
George. Empty places, empty times, Grigoriev is so conspicuous he's embarrassing." He crossed a foot-bridge. The time
was ten to eleven. He crossed the road and headed for the
little hotel with its unencumbered view of Grigoriev's bank.
Tension in a vacuum, he thought, listening to the clip of his
own feet and the gurgle of water from the gutters; the town
was out of season and out of time. *Burning, George, that's always
a hazard.* How would Karla do it? he wondered. What would
the absolutist do which we are not doing ourselves? Smiley
could think of nothing, short of straight physical abduction.
Karla would collect the operational intelligence, he thought,
then he would make his approach—risking the hazard. He
pushed the café door and the warm air sighed to him. He made
for a window table marked "RESERVED." "I'm waiting for Mr.
Jacobi," he told the girl. She nodded disapprovingly, missing
his eye. The girl had a cloistered pallor, and no expression at
all. He ordered *café-crème* in a glass, but she said that if it came
in a glass, he would have to have schnapps with it.

"Then in a cup," he said, capitulating.

Why had he asked for a glass in the first place?

Tension in a vacuum, he thought again, looking round.
Hazard in a blank place.

The café was modern Swiss antique. Crossed plastic lances

hung from stucco pillars. Hidden speakers played harmless music; the confiding voice changed language with each announcement. In a corner, four men played a silent game of cards. He looked out of the window, into the empty square. Rain had started again, turning white to grey. A boy cycled past wearing a red woollen cap, and the cap went down the road like a torch until the fog put it out. The bank's doors were double, he noticed, opened by electronic eye. He looked at his watch. Eleven-ten. A till murmured. A coffee machine hissed. The card-players were dealing a new hand. Wooden plates hung on the wall: dancing couples in national costume. What else was there to look at? The lamps were wrought iron but the illumination came from a ring of strip lighting round the ceiling and it was very harsh. He thought of Hong Kong, with its Bavarian beer cellars on the fifteenth floor, the same sense of waiting for explanations that would never be supplied. And today is only preparation, he thought: today is not even the approach. He looked at the bank again. Nobody entering, nobody leaving. He remembered waiting all his life for something he could no longer define: call it resolution. He remembered Ann, and their last walk. Resolution in a vacuum. He heard a chair squeak and saw Toby's hand held out for him, Swiss style, to shake, and Toby's bright face sparkling as if he'd just come in from a run.

"The Grigorievs left the house in Elfenau five minutes ago," he said quietly. "Grigorieva's driving. Most likely they die before they get here."

"And the bicycles?" Smiley said anxiously.

"Like normal," said Toby, pulling up a chair.

"Did she drive last week?"

"Also the week before. She insists. George, I mean that woman is a monster." The girl brought him a coffee unbidden. "Last week, she actually hauled Grigoriev out of the driving seat, then drove the car into the gatepost, clipped the wing. Pauli and Canada Bill were laughing so much we thought we'd get static on the whisperers." He put a friendly hand on

Smiley's shoulder. "Listen, it's going to be a nice day. Believe me. Nice light, a nice layout, all you got to do is sit back and enjoy the show."

The phone rang, and the girl called, "Herr Jacobi!" Toby walked easily to the counter. She handed him the receiver and blushed at something he whispered to her. From the kitchen, the chef came in with his small son: "Herr Jacobi!" The chrysanthemums on Smiley's table were plastic but someone had put water in the vase.

"*Ciao*," Toby called cheerfully into the phone, and came back. "Everyone in position, everyone happy," he announced with satisfaction. "Eat something, okay? Enjoy yourself, George. This is Switzerland."

Toby stepped gaily into the street. *Enjoy the show*, thought Smiley. That's right. I wrote it, Toby produced it, and all I can do now is watch. No, he thought, correcting himself: Karla wrote it, and sometimes that worried him quite a lot.

Two girls in hiking kit were entering the double doors of the bank. A moment later and Toby had followed them in. He's packing the bank, thought Smiley. He'll man every counter two-deep. After Toby, a young couple, arm in arm, then a stubby woman with two shopping bags. The yellow mail van had not budged: nobody moves a mail van. He noticed a public phone-box, and two figures huddled into it, perhaps sheltering from the rain. Two people are less conspicuous than one, they liked to say at Sarratt, and three are less conspicuous than a pair. An empty tour coach passed. A clock struck twelve and, right on cue, a black Mercedes lurched out of the fog, its dipped headlights glittering on the cobble. Bumping clumsily onto the kerb, it stopped outside the bank, six feet from Toby's mail van. *Soviet Embassy car numbers end with 73*, Toby had said. *She drops him and drives round the block a couple of times till he comes out.* But today, in the filthy weather, the Grigorievs had apparently decided to flout the parking laws and Karla's laws too, and rely on their CD plates to keep them out of trouble. The passenger door opened and a stocky figure in a dark suit and spectacles scampered for the bank entrance, carrying a brief-case. Smiley had just time to record the thick grey hair and rimless spectacles of Grigoriev's photographs before a lorry masked his view. When it moved on, Grigoriev had disappeared, but Smiley had a clear sight of the formidable bulk of Grigorieva herself, with her red hair and learner-driver scowl, seated alone at the steering-wheel. *George, believe me, that's a very distorting woman.* Seeing her now, her set jaw, her bullish glare, Smiley was able for the first time, if cautiously, to share Toby's optimism. If fear was the essential concomitant of a successful burn, Grigorieva was certainly someone to be afraid of.

In his mind's eye Smiley now imagined the scene that was playing inside the bank, exactly as he and Toby had planned. The bank was a small one, a team of seven could flood it. Toby had opened a private account for himself: Herr Jacobi, a few thousand francs. Toby would take one counter and occupy it with small transactions. The foreign-exchange desk was also no problem. Two of Toby's people, armed with a spread of currencies, could keep them on the run for minutes. He imagined the hubbub of Toby's hilarity, causing Grigoriev to raise his voice. He imagined the two girl hikers doing a double act, one rucksack dumped carelessly at Grigoriev's feet, recording whatever he happened to say to the cashier; and the hidden cameras snapping away from toggle bags, rucksacks, brief-cases, bedrolls, or wherever they were stowed. "It's the same as the firing-squad, George," Toby explained when Smiley said he was worried about the shutter noise. "Everybody hears the click except the quarry."

The bank doors slid open. Two businessmen emerged, adjusting their raincoats as if they had been to the lavatory. The stubby woman with the two shopping bags followed them out, and Toby came after her, chatting volubly to the girl hikers. Next came Grigoriev himself. Oblivious of everything, he hopped into the black Mercedes and planted a kiss on his wife's cheek before she had time to turn away. He saw her mouth show criticism of him, and Grigoriev's placatory smile as he replied. Yes, Smiley thought, he certainly has something to be guilty about; yes, he thought, remembering the watchers' affection for him; yes, I understand that too. But the Grigorievs did not leave; not yet. Grigoriev had hardly closed his door before a tall, vaguely familiar woman in a green Loden coat came striding down the pavement, tapped fiercely on the passenger window, and delivered herself of what seemed to be a homily upon the sins of parking on pavements. Grigoriev was embarrassed, Grigorieva leaned across him and bawled at her—Smiley even heard the word *Diplomat* in heavy German rise above the sound of the traffic—but the woman remained where she was, her handbag under her arm, still swearing at them as they drove away. She'll have snapped them in the car with the bank doors in the background, he thought. They photograph through perforations: half a dozen pin-holes and the lens can see perfectly.

Toby had returned and was sitting beside him at the table. He had lit a small cigar. Smiley could feel him trembling like a dog after the chase.

"Grigoriev drew his normal ten thousand," he said. His English had become a little rash. "Same as last week, same as the week before. We got it, George, the whole scene. The boys are very happy, the girls too. George, I mean they are fantastic. Completely the best. I never had so good. What do you think of him?"

Surprised to be asked, Smiley actually laughed.

"He's certainly henpecked," he agreed.

"And a nice fellow, know what I mean? Reasonable. I think he'll act reasonable too. That's my view, George. The boys are the same."

"Where do the Grigorievs go from here?"

A sharp male voice interrupted him. "Herr Jacobi!"

But it was only the chef, holding up a glass of schnapps to drink Toby's health. Toby returned the toast.

"Lunch at the station buffet, first-class," he continued. "Grigorieva takes pork chop and chips, Grigoriev steak, a glass of beer. Maybe they take also a couple of vodkas."

"And after lunch?"

Toby gave a brisk nod, as if the question required no elucidation.

"Sure," he said. "That's where they go. George, cheer up. That guy will fold, believe me. You never had a wife like that. And Natasha's a cute kid." He lowered his voice. "Karla's his meal ticket, George. You don't always understand the simple things. You think she'd let him give up the new apartment? The Mercedes?"

Alexandra's weekly visitor arrived, always punctual, always at the same time, which was on Fridays after rest. At one o'clock came lunch, which on Fridays consisted of cold meat and *Rösti* and *Kompott* of apples or perhaps plums, depending on the season, but she couldn't eat it and sometimes she made a show of sicking it up or running to the lavatory or calling Felicity-Felicity and complaining, in the basest language, about the quality of the food. This never failed to annoy her. The hostel took great pride in growing its own fruit, and the hostel's brochures in Felicity-Felicity's office contained many photographs of fruit and blossom and Alpine streams and mountains indiscriminately, as if God, or the sisters, or Dr. Rüedi, had grown the whole lot specially for the inmates. After lunch came an hour's rest and on Fridays this daily hour was Alexandra's worst, her worst of the whole week, when she had to lie on the white iron bedstead and pretend she was relaxing, while she prayed to any God that would have her that Uncle Anton might be run over or have a heart attack, or, best of all, cease to exist—locked away with her own past and her own secrets and her own name of Tatiana. She thought of his rimless spectacles and in her imagination she drove them into his head and out the other side, taking his eyes with them, so that instead of his soggy gaze to stare at, she would see straight through him to the world outside.

And now at last rest had ended, and Alexandra stood in the empty dining hall in her best frock, watching the lodge through the window while two of the Marthas scoured the tiled floor. She felt sick. Crash, she thought. Crash on your silly bicycle. Other girls had visitors, but they came on Saturdays and none had Uncle Anton, few had men of any sort; it was mainly wan aunts and bored sisters who attended. And none got Felicity-Felicity's study to sit in, either, with the door closed and nobody present but the visitor; that was a privilege which Alexandra and Uncle Anton enjoyed alone, as Sister Beatitude never tired of pointing out. But Alexandra would have traded all of those privileges, and a good few more besides, for the privilege of not having Uncle Anton's visit at all.

The lodge gates opened and she began trembling on purpose, shaking her hands from the wrists as if she had seen a mouse, or a spider, or a naked man aroused for her. A tubby figure in a brown suit began cycling down the drive. He was not a natural cyclist, she could tell from his self-consciousness. He had not cycled here from any distance, bringing a breath of outside. It could be baking hot, but Uncle Anton neither sweated nor burned. It could be raining heavily, but Uncle Anton's mackintosh and hat, when he reached the main door, would scarcely be wet, and his shoes were never muddied. Only when the giant snowfall had come, three weeks ago, or call it years, and put a metre's thickness of extra padding round the dead castle, did Uncle Anton look anything like a real man living in the real elements; in his thick knee boots and anorak and fur hat, skirting the pine trees as he plodded up the track, he stepped straight out of the memories she was never to mention. And when he had embraced her, calling her "my little daughter," slapping his big gloves down on Felicity-Felicity's highly polished table, she felt such a surge of kinship and hope that she would catch herself smiling for days afterwards.

"He was so warm," she confided to Sister Beatitude in her bit of French. "He held me like a friend! Why does the snow make him so fond?"

But today there was only sleet and fog and big floppy flakes that would not settle on the yellow gravel.

He comes in a car, Sasha—Sister Beatitude told her once—with a *woman*, Sasha. Beatitude had seen them. Twice. Watched them, naturally. They had two bicycles strapped to the roof of the car, upside down, and the woman did the driving, a big strong woman, a bit like Mother Felicity but not so Christian, with hair red enough to scare a bull. When they reached the edge of the village, they parked the car behind Andreas Gertsch's barn, and Uncle Anton untied his bicycle and rode it to the lodge. But the woman stayed in the car and smoked, and read *Schweizer Illustrierte*, sometimes scowling at the mirror, and her bicycle never left the roof; it stayed there like an upturned sow while she read her magazine! And guess what! Uncle Anton's bicycle was *illegal!* The bicycle—as a good Swiss, Sister Beatitude had checked the point quite naturally—Uncle Anton's bicycle had no *plaque*, no licence, he was a criminal at large, and so was the woman, though she was probably too fat to ride it!

But Alexandra cared nothing for illegal bicycles. It was the car she wanted to know about. What type? Rich or poor? What colour, and above all, where did it come from? Was it from Moscow, from Paris, where? But Sister Beatitude was a country girl and simple, and in the world beyond the mountains most foreign places were alike to her. Then what letters were on the number-plate, for goodness' sake, silly? Alexandra had cried. Sister Beatitude had not noticed such matters. Sister Beatitude shook her head like the dumb dairymaid she was. Bicycles and cows she understood. Cars were beyond her mark.

Alexandra watched Grigoriev arrive, she waited for the moment when he leaned his head forward over the handle-bars and raised his ample bottom in the air and swung one short leg over the crossbars as if he were climbing off a woman. She saw how the short ride had reddened his face, she watched him unfasten the brief-case from the rack over the back wheel. She ran to the door and tried to kiss him, first on the cheek, then on the lips, for she had an idea of putting her tongue into his mouth as an act of welcome, but he scurried past her with his head down as if he were already going back to his wife.

"Greetings, Alexandra Borisovna," she heard him whisper, all of a flurry, uttering her patronymic as if it were a state secret.

"Greetings, Uncle Anton," she replied; then Sister Beatitude caught her by the arm, and whispered to her to behave herself or else.

Mother Felicity's study was at once both sparse and sumptuous. It was small and bare and very hygienic, and the Marthas scrubbed it and polished it every day so that it smelt like a swimming-pool. Yet her little pieces of Russia glistened like caskets. She had icons, and she had richly framed sepia photographs of princesses she had loved, and bishops she had served, and on her saint's day—or was it her birthday or the bishop's?—she had taken them all down and made a theatre of them with candles and a Virgin and a Christ-child. Alexandra knew this because Felicity had called her in to sit with her, and had read old Russian prayers to her aloud, and chanted bits of liturgy in a marching rhythm to her, and given her sweet cake and a glass of sweet wine, all to have Russian company on her saint's day—or was it Easter or Christmas? Russians were the best in the world, she said. Gradually, though she had had a lot of pills, Alexandra had realised that Felicity-Felicity was stone drunk, so she lifted up her old feet and put a pillow for her, and kissed her hair and let her fall asleep on the tweed sofa where parents sat when they came to enrol fresh patients. It was the same sofa where Alexandra sat now, staring at Uncle Anton while he pulled the little notebook from his pocket. He was having one of his brown days, she noticed: brown suit, brown tie, brown shirt.

"You should buy yourself brown cycle clips," she told him in Russian.

Uncle Anton did not laugh. He kept a piece of black elastic like a garter round his notebook and he was unwinding it with a shrewd, reluctant air while he moistened his official lips. Sometimes Alexandra thought he was a policeman, sometimes a priest disguised, sometimes a lawyer or schoolmaster, sometimes even a special kind of doctor. But whatever he was, he clearly wished her to know, by means of the elastic and the notebook, and by the expressions of nervous benevolence, that there was a Higher Law for which neither he nor she was personally responsible, that he did not mean to be her jailer, that he wished her forgiveness—if not her actual love—for locking her away. She knew also that he wished her to know that he was sad and even lonely, and assuredly that he was fond of her, and that in a better world he would have been the uncle who brought her birthday presents, Christmas presents faithfully, and each year chucked her under the chin, "My-*my*, Sasha, aren't you growing up," followed by a restrained pat on some rounded part of her, meaning "My-*my*, Sasha, you'll soon be ready for the pot."

"How is your reading progressing, Alexandra?" he asked her while he flattened the notebook in front of him and turned the pages looking for his list. This was small talk. This was not the Higher Law. This was like talk about the weather, or what a pretty dress she was wearing, or how happy she appeared today—not at all like last week.

"My name is Tatiana and I come from the moon," she replied.

Uncle Anton acted as though this statement had not been made, so perhaps she only said it to herself, silently in her mind, where she said a lot of things.

"You have finished the novel by Turgenev I brought you?" he asked. "You were reading *Torrents of Spring*, I think."

"Mother Felicity was reading it to me but she has a sore throat," said Alexandra.

"So."

This was a lie. Felicity-Felicity had stopped reading to her as a punishment for throwing her food on the floor.

Uncle Anton had found the page of his notebook with the list on it, and he had found his pencil too, a silver one with a top you pressed; he appeared inordinately proud of it.

"So," he said. "*So* then, Alexandra!"

Suddenly Alexandra did not want to wait for his questions. Suddenly she could not. She thought of pulling down his trousers and making love to him. She thought of messing in a corner like the French girl. She showed him the blood on her hands where she had chewed them. She needed to explain to him, through her own divine blood, that she did not want to hear his first question. She stood up, holding out one hand for him while she dug her teeth into the other. She wanted to demonstrate to Uncle Anton, for once and for ever, that the question he had in mind was obscene to her, and insulting, and unacceptable, and mad, and to do this she had chosen Christ's example as the nearest and best: did He not hang on Felicity-Felicity's wall, straight ahead of her, with blood running down His wrists? *I have shed this for you, Uncle Anton,* she explained, thinking of Easter now, of Felicity-Felicity going round the castle breaking eggs. *Please. This is my blood, Uncle Anton. I have shed it for you.* But with her other hand jammed in her mouth, all she could manage in her speaking voice was a sob. So finally she sat down, frowning, with her hands linked on her lap, not actually *bleeding,* she noticed, but at least wet with her saliva.

Uncle Anton held the notebook open with his right hand and was holding the pop-top pencil in his left. He was the first left-handed man she had known and sometimes, watching him write, she wondered whether he was a mirror image, with the real version of him sitting in the car behind Andreas Gertsch's barn. She thought what a wonderful way that would be of handling what Dr. Rüedi called the "divided nature"—to send one half away on a bicycle while the other half stayed put in the car with the redheaded woman who drove him. Felicity-Felicity, if you lend me your pop-pop bicycle, I will send the bad part of me away on it.

Suddenly she heard herself talking. It was a wonderful sound. It made her like all the strong healthy voices around her: politicians on the radio, doctors when they looked down on her in bed.

"Uncle Anton, where do you come from, please?" she heard herself enquire, with measured curiosity. "Uncle Anton, pay attention to me, please, while I make a statement. Until you have told me who you are and whether you are my real uncle, and what is the registration number of your big black car, I shall refuse to answer any of your questions. I regret this, but it is necessary. Also, is the redheaded woman your wife or is she Felicity-Felicity with her hair dyed, as Sister Beatitude advises me?"

But too often Alexandra's mind spoke words which her mouth did not transmit, with the result that the words stayed flying around inside her and she became their unwilling jailer, just as Uncle Anton pretended to be hers.

"Who gives you the money to pay Felicity-Felicity for my detention here? Who pays Dr. Rüedi? Who dictates what questions go into your notebook every week? To whom do you pass my answers which you so meticulously write down?"

But once again, the words flew around inside her skull like the birds in Kranko's greenhouse in the fruit season, and there was nothing that Alexandra could do to persuade them to come out.

"*So*, then?" said Uncle Anton a third time, with the watery smile that Dr. Rüedi wore when he was about to give her an injection. "Now first you must please tell me your full name, Alexandra."

Alexandra held up three fingers and counted on them like a good child. "Alexandra Borisovna Ostrakova," she said in an infantile voice.

"Good. And how have you been feeling this week, Sasha?"

Alexandra smiled politely in response: "Thank you, Uncle Anton. I have been feeling much better this week. Dr. Rüedi tells me that my crisis is already far behind me."

"Have you received by any means—post, telephone, or word of mouth—any communication from outside persons?"

Alexandra had decided she was a saint. She folded her hands on her lap, and tilted her head to one side, and imagined she was one of Felicity-Felicity's Russian Orthodox saints on the wall behind the desk. Vera, who was faith; Liubov, who was love; Sofia, Olga, Irina, or Xenia—all the names that Mother Felicity had taught her during that evening when she had confided that her own real name was Hope—whereas Alexandra's was Alexandra or Sasha, but never, never Tatiana, and just remember it. Alexandra smiled at Uncle Anton and she knew her smile was sublime, and tolerant, and wise; and that she was hearing God's voice, not Uncle Anton's; and Uncle Anton knew it too, for he gave a long sigh and put away his notebook, then reached for the bell button to summon Mother Felicity for the ceremony of the money.

Mother Felicity came hastily and Alexandra guessed she had not been far from the other side of the door. She had the account ready in her hand. Uncle Anton considered it and frowned, as he always did, then counted notes onto the desk, blue ones and orange ones singly, so that each was for a moment transparent under the beam of the reading lamp. Then Uncle Anton patted Alexandra on the shoulder as if she were fifteen instead of twenty-five, or twenty, or however old she was when she had clipped away the forbidden bits of her life. She watched him waddle out of the door again and onto his bike. She watched his rump strive and gather rhythm as he rode away from her, through the lodge, past Kranko, and away down the hill towards the village. And as she watched she saw a strange thing, a thing that had never happened before: not to Uncle Anton, at least. From nowhere, two purposeful figures materialised—a man and a woman, wheeling a motor bike. They must have been sitting on the summer bench the other side of the lodge, keeping out of sight, perhaps in order to make love. They moved into the lane, and stared after him, but they didn't mount the motor bike, not yet. Instead, they waited till Uncle Anton was almost out of sight before setting off after him down the hill. Then Alexandra decided to scream, and this time she found her talking voice and the scream split the whole house from roof to floor before Sister Beatitude bore down on her to quell her with a heavy smack across the mouth.

"They're the same people," Alexandra shrieked.

"Who are?" Sister Beatitude demanded, drawing back her hand in case she needed to use it again. "Who are the same people, you bad girl?"

"They're the people who followed my mother before they dragged her away to kill her."

Sister Beatitude gave a snort of disbelief. "On black horses, I suppose!" she sneered. "Dragged her on a sledge, too, didn't he, all across Siberia!"

Alexandra had spun these tales before. How her father was a secret prince more powerful than the Czar. How he ruled at night, as the owls rule while the hawks are at rest. How his secret eyes followed her wherever she went, how his secret ears heard every word she spoke. And how, one night, hearing her mother praying in her sleep, he sent his men for her and they took her into the snow and she was never seen again: not even by God, He was looking for her still.

24

The burning of Tricky Tony, as it afterwards became known in the Circus mythology—such being Grigoriev's whimsical code-name among the watchers—was one of those rare operations where luck, timing, and preparation come together in a perfect marriage. They had all known from early on that the problem would be to find Grigoriev alone at a moment that allowed for his speedy reintroduction into normal life a few hours later. Yet by the week-end following the coverage of the Thun bank, intensive researches into Grigoriev's behaviour pattern had produced no obvious pointers as to when this moment might be. In desperation Skordeno and de Silsky, Toby's hard men, dreamed up a wildcat scheme to snatch him on his way to work, along the few hundred metres of pavement between his house and the Embassy. Toby killed it at once. One of the girls offered herself as a decoy: perhaps she could hitch a lift from him somehow? Her altruism was applauded, but it did not answer the practicalities.

The main problem was that Grigoriev was under double guard. Not only did the Embassy security staff keep check on him as a matter of routine; so did his wife. The watchers had no doubt that she suspected him of a tenderness for little Natasha. Their fears were confirmed when Toby's listeners contrived to tamper with the junction box at the corner of the road. In one day's watch, Grigorieva telephoned her husband no less than three times, to no apparent purpose other than to establish that he was indeed at the Embassy.

"George, I mean that woman is a total monster," Toby stormed when he heard this. "Love—I mean, all right. But possession, for its own sake, this I absolutely condemn. It's a matter of principle for me."

The one chink was Grigoriev's Thursday-afternoon drives to the garage, when he took the Mercedes to have it checked. If a practised car coper such as Canada Bill could introduce an engine fault during the Wednesday night—one that kept the car mobile, but only just—then might not Grigoriev be snatched from the garage while he was waiting for the mechanic to trace it? The plan bristled with imponderables. Even if everything worked, how long would they have Grigoriev to themselves? Then again, on Thursdays Grigoriev must be back home in time to receive his weekly visit from the courier Krassky. Nevertheless, it remained the only plan they had—their worst except for the others, said Toby—and accordingly they settled to an apprehensive wait of five days while Toby and his team leaders plotted fall-backs for the many unpleasant contingencies should the plot abort: everyone to be signed out of his hotel and packed; escape papers and money to be carried at all times; radio equipment to be boxed and cached under American identity in the vaults of one of the major banks, so that any clues left behind would point to the Cousins rather than themselves; no forms of assembly other than walk-and-talk encounters on the pavement; wavelengths to be changed every four hours. Toby knew his Swiss police, he said. He had hunted here before. If the balloon went up, he said, then the fewer of his boys and girls around to answer questions, the better. "I mean thank God the Swiss are only neutral, know what I mean?"

As a somewhat forlorn consolation, and as a boost to the delicate morale of the watchers, Smiley and Toby decreed that the surveillance of Grigoriev should be kept at full pitch throughout the expected days of waiting. The observation post in the Brunnadernrain would be manned round the clock; car and cycle patrols would be increased; everyone should be on his toes for the remote chance that God, in an uncharacteristic moment, would favour the just.

What God did, in fact, was send idyllic Sunday weather, and it proved decisive. By ten o'clock that Sunday it was as if the Alpine sun had come down from the Oberland to brighten the lives of the fog-ridden lowlanders. In the Bellevue Palace, which on Sundays has a quite overwhelming calm, a waiter had just spread a napkin on Smiley's lap for him. He was drinking a leisurely coffee, trying to concentrate on the week-end edition of the *Herald Tribune*, when, looking up, he saw the gentle figure of Franz the head porter standing before him.

"Mr. Barraclough, sir, the telephone, I am sorry. A Mr. Anselm."

The cabins were in the main hall, the voice was Toby's, and the name Anselm signified urgency: "The Geneva bureau has just advised us that the managing director is on his way to Berne at this very moment."

The Geneva bureau was word code for the Brunnadernrain observation post.

"Is he bringing his wife?" said Smiley.

"Unfortunately, Madame is obliged to make an excursion with the children," Toby replied. "Perhaps if you could come down to the office, Mr. Barraclough?"

Toby's office was a sun pavilion situated in an ornamental garden next to the Bundeshaus. Smiley was there in five minutes. Below them lay the ravine of the green river. In the distance, under a blue sky, the peaks of the Bernese Oberland lifted splendidly in the sunlight.

"Grigoriev left the Embassy on his own five minutes ago, wearing a hat and coat," Toby said as soon as Smiley arrived. "He's heading for the town on foot. It's like the first Sunday we watched him. He walks to the Embassy, ten minutes later he sets off for the town. He's going to watch the chess game, George, no question. What do you say?"

"Who's with him?"

"Skordeno and de Silsky on foot, a back-up car behind, two more ahead. One team's heading for the Cathedral Close right now. Do we go, George, or don't we?"

For a moment, Toby was aware of that disconnection which seemed to afflict Smiley whenever the operation gathered speed: less indecision, then a mysterious reluctance to advance.

He pressed him: "The green light, George? Or not? George, please! We are speaking of seconds here!"

"Is the house still covered for when Grigorieva and the children get back?"

"Completely."

For a moment longer Smiley hesitated. For a moment, he weighed the method against the prize, and the grey and distant figure of Karla seemed actually to admonish him.

"The green light, then," said Smiley. "Yes. Go."

He had barely finished speaking before Toby was standing in the telephone kiosk not twenty metres from the pavilion. "With my heart going like a complete steam engine," as he later claimed. But also with the light of battle in his eyes.

There is even a scale model of the scene at Sarratt, and occasionally the directing staff will dig it out and tell the tale.

The old city of Berne is best described as a mountain, a fortress, and a peninsula all at once, as the model shows. Between the Kirchenfeld and Kornhaus bridges, the Aare runs in a horseshoe cut into a giddy cleft, and the old city roosts prudently inside it, in rising foothills of medieval streets, till it reaches the superb late-Gothic spire of the Cathedral, which is both the mountain's peak and its glory. Next to the Cathedral, at the same height, stands the Platform, from whose southern perimeter the unwary visitor may find himself staring down a hundred feet of sheer stone face, straight into the swirling river. It is a place to draw suicides and no doubt there have been some. It is a place where, according to popular history, a pious man was thrown from his horse and, though he fell the whole awesome distance, survived by God's deliverance to serve the church for another thirty years, dying peacefully at a great age. The rest of the Platform makes a tranquil spot, with benches and ornamental trees and a children's playground—and, in recent years, a place for public chess. The pieces are two feet or more in height, light enough to move, but heavy enough to withstand the occasional thrust of a south wind that whips off the surrounding hills. The scale model even runs to replicas of them.

By the time Toby Esterhase arrived there that Sunday morning, the unexpected sunshine had drawn a small but tidy body of the game's enthusiasts, who stood or sat around the chequered pavement. And at their centre, a mere six feet from where Toby stood, as oblivious to his surroundings as could be wished, stood Counsellor (Commercial) Anton Grigoriev of the Soviet Embassy in Berne, a truant from both work and family, intently following, through his rimless spectacles, each move the players made. And behind Grigoriev stood Skordeno and his companion de Silsky, watching Grigoriev. The players were young and bearded and volatile—if not art students, then certainly they wished to be taken for them. And they were very conscious of fighting a duel under the public gaze.

Toby had been this close to Grigoriev before, but never when the Russian's attention was so firmly locked elsewhere. With the calm of impending battle, Toby appraised him and confirmed what he had all along maintained: Anton Grigoriev was not a fieldman. His rapt attention, the unguarded frankness of his expressions as each move was played or contemplated, had an innocence that could never have survived the infighting of Moscow Centre.

Toby's personal appearance was another of those happy chances of the day. Out of respect for the Bernese Sunday, he had donned a dark overcoat and his black fur hat. He was therefore, at this crucial moment of improvisation, looking exactly as he would have wished had he planned everything to the last detail: a man of position takes his Sunday relaxation.

Toby's dark eyes lifted to the Cathedral Close. The get-away cars were in position.

A ripple of laughter went out. With a flourish, one of the bearded players lifted his queen and, pretending it was a most appalling weight, reeled with it a couple of steps and dumped it with a groan. Grigoriev's face darkened into a frown as he considered this unexpected move. On a nod from Toby, Skordeno and de Silsky drew one to either side of him, so close that Skordeno's shoulder was actually nudging the quarry's, but Grigoriev paid no heed. Taking this as their signal, Toby's watchers began sauntering into the crowd, forming a second echelon behind de Silsky and Skordeno. Toby waited no longer. Placing himself directly in front of Grigoriev, he smiled and lifted his hat. Grigoriev returned the smile—uncertainly, as one might to a diplomatic colleague half-remembered—and lifted his hat in return.

"How are you today, Counsellor?" Toby asked in Russian, in a tone of quiet jocularity.

More mystified than ever, Grigoriev said thank you, he was well.

"I hope you enjoyed your little excursion to the country on Friday," said Toby in the same easy but very quiet voice, as he slipped his arm through Grigoriev's. "The old city of Thun is not sufficiently appreciated, I believe, by members of our distinguished diplomatic community here. In my view it is to be recommended both for its antiquity, and its banking facilities. Do you not agree?"

This opening sally was long enough, and disturbing enough, to carry Grigoriev unresisting to the crowd's edge. Skordeno and de Silsky were packing close behind.

"My name is Kurt Siebel, sir," Toby confided in Grigoriev's

ear, his hand still on his arm. "I am chief investigator to the Bernese Standard Bank of Thun. We have certain questions relating to Dr. Adolf Glaser's private account with us. You would do well to pretend you know me." They were still moving. Behind them, the watchers followed in a staggered line, like rugger players poised to block a sudden dash. "Please do not be alarmed," Toby continued, counting the steps as Grigoriev kept up his progress. "If you could spare us an hour, sir, I am sure we could arrange matters without troubling your domestic or professional position. Please."

In the world of a secret agent, the wall between safety and extreme hazard is almost nothing, a membrane that can be burst in a second. He may court a man for years, fattening him for the pass. But the pass itself—the "will you, won't you?"—is a leap from which there is either ruin or victory, and for a moment Toby thought he was looking ruin in the face. Grigoriev had finally stopped dead and turned round to stare at him. He was pale as an invalid. His chin lifted, he opened his mouth to protest a monstrous insult. He tugged at his captive arm in order to free himself, but Toby held it firm. Skordeno and de Silsky were hovering, but the distance to the car was still fifteen metres, which was a long way, in Toby's book, to drag one stocky Russian. Meanwhile, Toby kept talking; all his instinct urged him to.

"There are irregularities, Counsellor. Grave irregularities. We have a dossier upon your good self which makes lamentable reading. If I placed it before the Swiss police, not all the diplomatic protests in the world would protect you from the most acute public embarrassment. I need hardly mention the consequence to your professional career. Please. I said *please*."

Grigoriev had still not budged. He seemed transfixed with indecision. Toby pushed at his arm, but Grigoriev stood rock solid and seemed unaware of the physical pressure on him. Toby shoved harder, Skordeno and de Silsky drew closer, but

Grigoriev had the stubborn strength of the demented. His mouth opened, he swallowed, his gaze fixed stupidly on Toby.

"What irregularities?" he said at last. Only the shock and the quietness in his voice gave cause for hope. His thick body remained rigidly set against further movement. "Who is this Glaser you speak of?" he demanded huskily, in the same stunned tone. "I am not Glaser. I am a diplomat, Grigoriev. The account you speak of has been conducted with total propriety. As Commercial Counsellor I have immunity. I also have the right to own foreign bank accounts."

Toby fired his only other shot. *The money and the girl*, Smiley had said. *The money and the girl are all you have to play with*.

"There is also the delicate matter of your marriage, sir," Toby resumed with a show of reluctance. "I must advise you that your philanderings in the Embassy have put your domestic arrangements in grave danger." Grigoriev started, and was heard to mutter "*banker*"—whether in disbelief or derision will never be sure. His eyes closed and he was heard to repeat the word, this time—according to Skordeno—with a particularly vile obscenity. But he started walking again. The rear door of the car stood open. The back-up car waited behind it. Toby was talking some nonsense about the withholding tax payable on the interest accruing from Swiss bank accounts, but he knew that Grigoriev was not really listening. Slipping ahead, de Silsky jumped into the back of the car and Skordeno threw Grigoriev straight in after him, then sat down beside him and slammed the door. Toby took the passenger seat; the driver was one of the Meinertzhagen girls. Speaking German, Toby told her to go easy and for God's sake remember it was a Bernese Sunday. No English in Grigoriev's hearing, Smiley had said.

Somewhere near the station Grigoriev must have had second thoughts, because there was a short scuffle and when Toby looked in the mirror Grigoriev's face was contorted with pain and he had both hands over his groin. They drove to the

Länggass-strasse, a long dull road behind the university. The door of the apartment house opened as they pulled up outside it. A thin housekeeper waited on the doorstep. She was Millie McCraig, an old Circus trooper. At the sight of her smile, Grigoriev bridled, and now it was speed, not cover, that mattered. Skordeno jumped onto the pavement, seized one of Grigoriev's arms, and nearly pulled it out of its socket; de Silsky must have hit him again, though he swore afterwards it was an accident, for Grigoriev came out doubled up, and between them they carried him over the threshold like a bride, and burst into the drawing-room in a bunch. Smiley was seated in a corner waiting for them. It was a room of brown chintzes and lace. The door closed, the abductors allowed themselves a brief show of festivity. Skordeno and de Silsky burst out laughing in relief. Toby took off his fur hat and wiped the sweat away.

"*Ruhe*," he said softly, ordering quiet. They obeyed him instantly.

Grigoriev was rubbing his shoulder, seemingly unaware of anything but the pain. Studying him, Smiley took comfort from this gesture of self-concern: subconsciously, Grigoriev was declaring himself to be one of life's losers. Smiley remembered Kirov, his botched pass at Ostrakova and his laborious recruitment of Otto Leipzig. He looked at Grigoriev and read the same incurable mediocrity in everything he saw: in the new but ill-chosen striped suit that emphasised his portliness; in the treasured grey shoes, punctured for ventilation but too tight for comfort; in the prinked, waved hair. All these tiny, useless acts of vanity communicated to Smiley an aspiration to greatness which he knew—as Grigoriev seemed to know—would never be fulfilled.

A former academic, he remembered, from the document Enderby had handed him at Ben's Place. *Appears to have abandoned university teaching for the larger privileges of officialdom.*

A pincher, Ann would have said, weighing his sexuality at a single glance. *Dismiss him.*

But Smiley could not dismiss him. Grigoriev was a hooked fish: Smiley had only moments in which to decide how best to land him. He wore rimless spectacles and was running to fat round the chin. His hair oil, warmed by the heat of his body, gave out a lemon vapour. Still kneading his shoulder, he started peering round at his captors. Sweat was falling from his face like raindrops.

"Where am I?" he demanded truculently, ignoring Smiley and selecting Toby as the leader. His voice was hoarse and high pitched. He was speaking German, with a Slav sibilance.

Three years as First Secretary, Commercial, Soviet Mission to Potsdam, Smiley remembered. *No apparent intelligence connection.*

"I demand to know where I am. I am a senior Soviet diplomat. I demand to speak to my Ambassador immediately."

The continuing action of his hand upon his injured shoulder took the edge off his indignation.

"I have been kidnapped! I am here against my will! If you do not immediately return me to my Ambassador there will be a grave international incident!"

Grigoriev had the stage to himself, and he could not quite fill it. Only George will ask questions, Toby had told his team. Only George will answer them. But Smiley sat still as an undertaker; nothing, it seemed, could rouse him.

"You want ransom?" Grigoriev called, to all of them. An awful thought appeared to strike him. "You are terrorists?" he whispered. "But if you are terrorists, why do you not bind my eyes? Why do you let me see your faces?" He stared round at de Silsky, then at Skordeno. "You must cover your faces. Cover them! I want no knowledge of you!"

Goaded by the continuing silence, Grigoriev drove a plump fist into his open palm and shouted "I demand" twice. At which point Smiley, with an air of official regret, opened a note-book on his lap, much as Kirov might have done, and gave a small, very official sigh: "You are Counsellor Grigoriev of the Soviet Embassy in Berne?" he asked in the dullest possible voice.

"Grigoriev! I am Grigoriev! Yes, well done, I am Grigoriev! Who are you, please? Al Capone? Who are you? Why do you rumble at me like a commissar?"

Commissar could not have described Smiley's manner better: it was leaden to the point of indifference.

"Then, Counsellor, since we cannot afford to delay, I must ask you to study the incriminating photographs on the table behind you," Smiley said, with the same studied dullness.

"Photographs? What photographs? How can you incriminate a diplomat? I demand to telephone my Ambassador immediately!"

"I would advise the Counsellor to look at the photographs first," said Smiley, in a glum, regionless German. "When he has looked at the photographs, he is free to telephone whomever he wants. Kindly start at the left," he advised. "The photographs are arranged from left to right."

A blackmailed man has the dignity of all our weaknesses, Smiley thought, covertly watching Grigoriev shuffling along the table as if he were inspecting one more diplomatic buffet. A blackmailed man is any one of us caught in the door as we try to escape the trap. Smiley had arranged the layout of the pictures himself; he had imagined, in Grigoriev's mind, an orchestrated succession of disasters. The Grigorievs parking their Mercedes outside the bank. Grigorieva, with her perpetual scowl of discontent, waiting alone in the driving seat, clutching the wheel in case anyone tried to take it from her. Grigoriev and little Natasha in long shot, sitting very close to each other on a bench. Grigoriev inside the bank, several pictures, culminating in a superb over-the-shoulder shot of Grigoriev signing a cashier's receipt, the full name Adolf Glaser clearly typed on the line above his signature. There was Grigoriev, looking uncomfortable on his bicycle, about to enter the sanatorium; there was Grigorieva roosting crossly in the car again, this time beside Gertsch's barn, her own bicycle still strapped to the roof. But the photograph that held Grigoriev longest, Smiley noticed, was the muddy long shot stolen by the Meinertzhagen girls. The quality was not good but the two heads in the car, though they were locked mouth to mouth, were recognisable enough. One was Grigoriev's. The other, pressed down on him as if she would eat him alive, was little Natasha's.

"The telephone is at your disposal, Counsellor," Smiley called to him quietly, when Grigoriev still did not move.

But Grigoriev remained frozen over this last photograph, and to judge by his expression, his desolation was complete. He was not merely a man found out, thought Smiley; he was a man whose very dream of love, till now vested in secrecy, had suddenly become public and ridiculous.

Still using his glum tone of official necessity, Smiley set about explaining what Karla would have called the pressures. Other inquisitors, says Toby, would have offered Grigoriev a choice, thereby inevitably mustering the Russian obstinacy in him, and the Russian penchant for self-destruction: the very impulses, he says, which could have invited catastrophe. Other inquisitors, he insists, would have menaced, raised their voices, resorted to histrionics, even physical abuse. Not George, he says: never. George acted out the low-key official time-server, and Grigoriev, like Grigorievs the world over, accepted him as his unalterable fate. George bypassed choice entirely, says Toby. George calmly made clear to Grigoriev why it was that he had no choice at all: The important thing, Counsellor— said Smiley, as if he were explaining a tax demand—was to consider what impact these photographs would have in the places where they would very soon be studied if nothing was done to prevent their distribution. There were first the Swiss authorities, who would obviously be incensed by the misuse of a Swiss passport on the part of an accredited diplomat, not to mention the grave breach of banking laws, said Smiley. They would register the strongest official protest, and the Grigorievs would be returned to Moscow overnight, all of them, never again to enjoy the fruits of a foreign posting. Back in Moscow, however, Grigoriev would not be well regarded either, Smiley explained. His superiors in the Foreign Ministry would take a dismal view of his behaviour, "both in the private and professional spheres." Grigoriev's prospects for an official career would be ended. He would be an *exile* in his own land, said Smiley, and his family with him. All his family. "Imagine facing the wrath of Grigorieva twenty-four hours a day in the wastes of outer Siberia," he was saying in effect.

At which Grigoriev slumped into a chair and clapped his hands on to the top of his head, as if scared it would blow off.

"But finally," said Smiley, lifting his eyes from his notebook, though only for a moment—and what he read there, said Toby, God knows, the pages were ruled but otherwise blank— "finally, Counsellor, we have also to consider the effect of these photographs upon certain organs of State Security."

And here Grigoriev released his head and drew the handkerchief from his top pocket and began wiping his brow, but as hard as he wiped, the sweat came back again. It fell as fast as Smiley's own in the interrogation cell in Delhi, when he had sat face to face with Karla.

Totally committed to his part as bureaucratic messenger of the inevitable, Smiley signed once more and primly turned to another page of his notebook.

"Counsellor, may I ask you what time you expect your wife and family to return from their picnic?"

Still dabbing with the handkerchief, Grigoriev appeared too preoccupied to hear.

"Grigorieva and the children are taking a picnic in the Elfenau woods," Smiley reminded him. "We have some questions to ask you, but it would be unfortunate if your absence from home were to cause concern."

Grigoriev put away the handkerchief. "You are spies?" he whispered. "You are Western spies?"

"Counsellor, it is better that you do not know who we are,"

said Smiley earnestly. "Such information is a dangerous burden. When you have done as we ask, you will walk out of here a free man. You have our assurance. Neither your wife, nor even Moscow Centre, will ever be the wiser. Please tell me what time your family returns from Elfenau—" Smiley broke off.

Somewhat half-heartedly, Grigoriev was affecting to make a dash for it. He stood up, he took a bound towards the door. Paul Skordeno had a languid air for a hard-man, but he caught the fugitive in an armlock even before he had taken a second step, and returned him gently to his chair, careful not to mark him. With another stage groan, Grigoriev flung up his hands in vast despair. His heavy face coloured and became convulsed, his broad shoulders started heaving as he broke into a mournful torrent of self-recrimination. He spoke half in Russian, half in German. He cursed himself with a slow and holy zeal, and after that, he cursed his mother, his wife and his bad luck and his own dreadful frailty as a father. He should have stayed in Moscow, in the Trade Ministry. He should never have been wooed away from academia merely because his fool wife wanted foreign clothes and music and privileges. He should have divorced her long ago but he could not bear to relinquish the children, he was a fool and a clown. He should be in the asylum instead of the girl. When he was sent for in Moscow, he should have said no, he should have resisted the pressure, he should have reported the matter to his Ambassador when he returned.

"Oh, Grigoriev!" he cried. "Oh, Grigoriev! You are so weak, so weak!"

Next, he delivered himself of a tirade against conspiracy. Conspiracy was anathema to him, several times in the course of his career he had been obliged to collaborate with the hateful "neighbours" in some crackpot enterprise, every time it was a disaster. Intelligence people were criminals, charlatans, and fools, a masonry of monsters. Why were Russians so in love with them? Oh, the fatal flaw of secretiveness in the Russian soul!

"Conspiracy has replaced religion!" Grigoriev moaned to all of them, in German. "It is our mystical substitute! Its agents are our Jesuits, these swine, they ruin everything!"

Bunching his fists now, he pushed them into his cheeks, pummelling himself in his remorse, till with a movement of the notepad on his lap, Smiley brought him dourly back to the matter in hand:

"Concerning Grigorieva and your children, Counsellor," he said. "It really is essential that we know what time they are due to return home."

In every successful interrogation—as Toby Esterhase likes to pontificate concerning this moment—there is one slip which cannot be recovered; one gesture, tacit or direct, even if it is only a half smile, or the acceptance of a cigarette, which marks the shift away from resistance, towards collaboration. Grigoriev, in Toby's account of the scene, now made his crucial slip.

"She will be home at one o'clock," he muttered, avoiding both Smiley's eye, and Toby's.

Smiley looked at his watch. To Toby's secret ecstasy, Grigoriev did the same.

"But perhaps she will be late?" Smiley objected.

"She is never late," Grigoriev retorted moodily.

"Then kindly begin by telling me of your relationship with the girl Ostrakova," said Smiley, stepping right into the blue— says Toby—yet contriving to imply that his question was the most natural sequel to the issue of Madame Grigorieva's punctuality. Then he held his pen ready, and in such a way, says Toby, that a man like Grigoriev would feel positively obliged to give him something to write down.

For all this, Grigoriev's resistance was not quite evaporated. His *amour propre* demanded at least one further outing. Opening his hands, therefore, he appealed to Toby: "*Ostrakova!*" he repeated with exaggerated scorn. "He asks me about some woman called *Ostrakova?* I know no such person. Perhaps he does, but I do not. I am a diplomat. Release me immediately. I have important engagements."

But the steam, as well as the logic, was fast going out of his protests. Grigoriev knew this as well as anyone.

"Alexandra Borisovna Ostrakova," Smiley intoned, while he polished his spectacles on the fat end of his tie. "A Russian girl, but has a French passport." He replaced his spectacles. "Just as you are Russian, Counsellor, but have a Swiss passport. Under a false name. Now how did you come to get involved with her, I wonder?"

"*Involved?* Now he tells me I was *involved* with her! You think I am so base I sleep with mad girls? I was blackmailed. As you blackmail me now, so I was *blackmailed*. Pressure! Always pressure, always Grigoriev!"

"Then tell me how they blackmailed you," Smiley suggested, with barely a glance at him.

Grigoriev peered into his hands, lifted them, but let them drop back onto his knees again, for once unused. He dabbed his lips with his handkerchief. He shook his head at the world's iniquity.

"I was in Moscow," he said, and in Toby's ears, as he afterwards declares, angel choirs sang their hallelujahs. George had turned the trick, and Grigoriev's confession had begun.

Smiley, on the other hand, betrayed no such jubilation at his achievement. To the contrary, a frown of irritation puckered his plump face.

"The *date*, please, Counsellor," he said, as if the place were not the issue. "Give the *date* when you were in Moscow. Henceforth, please give dates at all points."

This too is classic, Toby likes to explain: the wise inquisitor will always light a few false fires.

"September," said Grigoriev, mystified.

"Of which year?" said Smiley, writing.

Grigoriev looked plaintively to Toby again. "Which year! I say September, he asks me *which* September. He is a historian? I think he is a historian. *This* September," he said sulkily to Smiley. "I was recalled to Moscow for an urgent commercial conference. I am an expert in certain highly specialized economic fields. Such a conference would have been meaningless without my presence."

"Did your wife accompany you on this journey?"

Grigoriev let out a hollow laugh. "Now he thinks we are capitalists!" he commented to Toby. "He thinks we go flying our wives around for two-week conferences, first-class Swissair."

"'In September of this year, I was ordered to fly alone to Moscow in order to attend a two-week economic conference,'" Smiley proposed, as if he were reading Grigoriev's statement aloud. "'My wife remained in Berne.' Please describe the purpose of the conference."

"The subject of our high-level discussions was extremely secret," Grigoriev replied with resignation. "My Ministry wished to consider ways of giving teeth to the official Soviet attitude towards nations who were selling arms to China. We were to discuss what sanctions could be used against the offenders."

Smiley's faceless style, his manner of regretful bureaucratic necessity, were by now not merely established, says Toby, they were perfected: Grigoriev had adopted them wholesale, with philosophic, and very Russian, pessimism. As to the rest of those present, they could hardly believe, afterwards, that he had not been brought to the flat already in a mood to talk.

"Where was the conference held?" Smiley asked, as if secret matters concerned him less than formal details.

"At the Trade Ministry. On the fourth floor . . . in the conference room. Opposite the lavatory," Grigoriev retorted, with hopeless facetiousness.

"Where did you stay?"

At a hostel for senior officials, Grigoriev replied. He gave the address and even, in sarcasm, his room number. Sometimes, our discussions ended late at night, he said, by now liberally volunteering information; but on the Friday, since it was still summer weather and very hot, they ended early in order to enable those who wished, to leave for the country. But Grigoriev had no such plans. Grigoriev proposed to stay in Moscow for the week-end, and with reason: "I had arranged to pass two days in the apartment of a girl called Evdokia, formerly my secretary. Her husband was away on military service," he explained, as if this were a perfectly normal transaction among men of the world; one which Toby at least, as a fellow soul, would appreciate, even if soulless commissars would not. Then, to Toby's astonishment, he went straight on. From his dalliance with Evdokia, he passed without warning or preamble to the very heart of their enquiry:

"Unfortunately, I was prevented from adhering to these arrangements by the intervention of members of the Thirteenth Directorate of Moscow Centre, known also as the Karla Directorate. I was summoned to attend an interview immediately."

At which moment, the telephone rang. Toby took the call, rang off, and spoke to Smiley.

"She's arrived back at the house," he said, still in German.

Without demur, Smiley turned straight to Grigoriev: "Counsellor, we are advised that your wife has returned home. It has now become necessary for you to telephone her."

"Telephone her?" Horrified, Grigoriev swung round on Toby. "He tells me, telephone her! What do I say? 'Grigorieva, here is loving husband! I have been kidnapped by Western spies!' Your commissar is mad! Mad!"

"You will please tell her you are unavoidably delayed," Smiley said.

His placidity added fuel to Grigoriev's outrage: "I tell this to my wife? To Grigorieva? You think she will believe me? She will report me to the Ambassador immediately. 'Ambassador, my husband has run away! Find him!'"

"The courier Krassky brings your weekly orders from Moscow, does he not?" Smiley asked.

"The commissar knows everything," Grigoriev told Toby, and wiped his hand across his chin. "If he knows everything, why doesn't he speak to Grigorieva himself?"

"You are to adopt an official tone with her, Counsellor," Smiley advised. "Do not refer to Krassky by name, but suggest that he has ordered you to meet him for a conspiratorial discussion somewhere in the town. An emergency. Krassky has changed his plans. You have no idea when you will be back, or what he wants. If she protests, rebuke her. Tell her it is a secret of State."

They watched him worry, they watched him wonder. Finally, they watched a small smile settle over his face.

"A secret," Grigoriev repeated, to himself. "A secret of State. Yes."

Stepping boldly to the telephone, he dialled a number. Toby stood over him, one hand discreetly poised to slam the cradle should he try some trick, but Smiley with a small shake of the head signalled him away. They heard Grigorieva's voice saying "Yes?" in German. They heard Grigoriev's bold reply, followed by his wife—it is all on tape—demanding sharply to know where he was. They saw him stiffen and lift his chin, and put on an official face; they heard him snap out a few short phrases, and ask a question to which there was apparently no answer. They saw him ring off again, bright-eyed and pink with pleasure, and his short arms fly in the air with delight, like someone who has scored a goal. The next thing they knew, he had burst out laughing, long, rich gusts of Slav laughter, up and down the scale. Uncontrollably, the others began laughing with him—Skordeno, de Silsky, and Toby. Grigoriev was shaking Toby's hand.

"Today I like very much conspiracy!" Grigoriev cried, between further gusts of cathartic laughter. "Conspiracy is very good today!"

Smiley had not joined in the general festivity, however. Having cast himself deliberately as the killjoy, he sat turning the pages of his notebook, waiting for the fun to end.

"You were describing how you were approached by members of the Thirteenth Directorate," Smiley said, when all was quiet again. "Known also as the Karla Directorate. Kindly continue with your narrative, Counsellor?"

25

Did Grigoriev sense the new alertness round him—the discreet freezing of gestures? Did he notice how the eyes of Skordeno and de Silsky, both, hunted out Smiley's impassive face and held it in their gaze? How Millie McCraig slipped silently to the kitchen to check her tape recorders yet again, in case, by an act of a malevolent god, both the main set and the reserve had failed at once? Did he notice Smiley's now almost Oriental self-effacement—the very opposite of interest—the retreat of his whole body into the copious folds of his brown tweed travelling coat, while he patiently licked his thumb and finger and turned a page?

Toby, at least, noticed these things. Toby in his dark corner by the telephone had a grandstand seat from which he could observe everyone and remain as good as unobserved himself. A fly could not have crossed the floor, but Toby's watchful eyes would have recorded its entire odyssey. Toby even describes his own symptoms—a hot feeling around the neckband, he says, a knotting of the throat and stomach muscles—Toby not only endured these discomforts, but remembered them faithfully. Whether Grigoriev was responsive to the atmosphere is another matter. Most likely he was too consumed by his central rôle. The triumph of the telephone call had stimulated him, and revived his self-confidence; and it was significant that his first statement, when he once more had the floor, con-

cerned not the Karla Directorate, but his prowess as the lover
of little Natasha: "Fellows of our age *need* a girl like that," he
explained to Toby with a wink. "They make us into young
men again, like we used to be!"

"Very well, you flew to Moscow alone," Smiley said, quite
snappishly. "The conference got under way, you were approached
for an interview. Please continue from there. We have not got
all afternoon, you know."

The conference started on the Monday, Grigoriev agreed,
obediently resuming his official statement. When the Friday
afternoon came, I returned to my hostel in order to fetch my
belongings and take them to Evdokia's apartment for our little
week-end together. Instead of this, however, I was met by three
men who ordered me into their car with even less explanation
than you did—a glance at Toby—saying to me only that I was
required for a special task. During the journey they advised
me that they were members of the Thirteenth Directorate of
Moscow Centre, which everybody in official Moscow knows
to be the élite. I formed the impression that they were intelligent men, above the common run of their profession, which,
saving your presence, sir, is not high. I had the impression they
could be officers rather than mere lackeys. Nevertheless I was
not unduly worried. I assumed that my professional expertise
was being required for some secret matter, that was all. They
were courteous and I was even somewhat flattered . . .

"How long was the journey?" Smiley interrupted, as he
continued writing.

Across town, Grigoriev replied vaguely. Across town, then
into countryside till dark. Till we reached this one little man like
a monk, sitting in a small room, who seemed to be their master.

Once again, Toby insists on bearing witness here to Smiley's
unique mastery of the occasion. It was the strongest proof
yet of Smiley's tradecraft, says Toby—as well as of his command of Grigoriev altogether—that throughout Grigoriev's

protracted narrative, he never once, whether by an over-hasty
follow-up question or the smallest false inflection of his voice,
departed from the faceless rôle he had assumed for the interrogation. By his self-effacement, Toby insists, George held the
whole scene "like a thrush's egg in his hand." The slightest
careless movement on his part could have destroyed everything, but he never made it. And as the crowning example,
Toby likes to offer this crucial moment, when the actual figure
of Karla was for the first time introduced. Any other inquisitor, he says, at the very mention of a "little man like a monk
who seemed to be their master," would have pressed for a
description—his age, rank, what was he wearing, smoking,
how did you know he was their master? Not Smiley. Smiley
with a suppressed exclamation of annoyance tapped his ballpoint pen on his pad, and in a long-suffering voice invited
Grigoriev, then and for the future, kindly *not* to foreshorten
factual detail:

"Let me put the question again. How long was the journey?
Please describe it precisely as you remember it and let us proceed from there."

Crestfallen, Grigoriev actually apologised. He would say
they drove for four hours at speed, sir; perhaps more. He
remembered now that they twice stopped to relieve themselves. After four hours they entered a guarded area—no, sir, I
saw no shoulder-boards, the guards wore plain clothes—and
drove for at least another half hour into the heart of it. Like a
nightmare, sir.

Yet again, Smiley objected, determined to keep the temperature as low as possible. How could it have been a nightmare, he wanted to know, since Grigoriev had only a moment
before claimed that he was not frightened?

Well, not a nightmare exactly, sir, more a dream. At this
stage, Grigoriev had had an impression he was being taken to
the *landlord*—he used the Russian word, and Toby translated
it—while he himself felt increasingly like a poor peasant.

Therefore he was not frightened, sir, because he had no control over events, and accordingly nothing for which to reproach himself. But when the car finally stopped, and one of the men put a hand on his arm, and addressed a warning to him: at this point, his attitude changed entirely, sir: "You are about to meet a great Soviet fighter and a powerful man," the man told him. "If you are disrespectful to him, or attempt to tell lies, you may never again see your wife and family."

"What is the name of this man?" Grigoriev had asked.

But the men replied, without smiling, that this great Soviet fighter had no name. Grigoriev asked whether he was Karla himself; knowing that Karla was the code name for the head of the Thirteenth Directorate. The men only repeated that the great fighter had no name.

"So that was when the dream became a nightmare, sir," said Grigoriev humbly. "They told me also that I could say good-bye to my week-end of love. Little Evdokia would have to get her fun elsewhere, they said. Then one of them laughed."

Now a great fear had seized Grigoriev, he said, and by the time he had entered the first room and advanced upon the second door, he was so scared his knees were shaking. He even had time to be scared for his beloved Evdokia. Who could this supernatural person be, he wondered in awe, that he could know almost before Grigoriev himself knew, that he was pledged to meet Evdokia for the week-end?

"So you knocked on the door," said Smiley, as he wrote.

And I was ordered to enter! Grigoriev went on. His enthusiasm for confession was mounting; so was his dependence upon his interrogator. His voice had become louder, his gestures more free. It was as if, says Toby, he was trying physically to coax Smiley out of his posture of reticence; whereas in reality it was Smiley's feigned indifference which was coaxing Grigoriev into the open. And I found myself not in a large and splendid office at all, sir, as became a senior official and a great Soviet fighter, but in a room so barren it would have done duty for a prison cell, with a bare wood desk at the centre, and a hard chair for a visitor to sit on:

"Imagine, sir, a great Soviet fighter and a powerful man! And all he had was a bare desk, which was illuminated only by a most inferior light! And behind it sat this priest, sir, a man of no affectation or pretence at all—a man of deep experience, I would say—a man from the very roots of his country—with small, straight eyes, and short grey hair, and a habit of holding his hands together while he smoked."

"Smoked *what?*" Smiley asked, writing.

"Please?"

"What did he smoke? The question is plain enough. A pipe, cigarettes, cigar?"

"Cigarettes. American, and the room was full of their aroma. It was like Potsdam again, when we were negotiating with the American officers from Berlin. 'If this man smokes American all the time,' I thought, 'then he is certainly a man of influence.'" Rounding on Toby again in his excitement, Grigoriev put the same point to him in Russian. To smoke American, chain smoke them, he said: imagine the cost, the influence necessary to obtain so many packets!

Then Smiley, true to his pedantic manner, asked Grigoriev to demonstrate what he meant by "holding his hands together" while he smoked. And he looked on impassively while Grigoriev took a brown wood pencil from his pocket and linked his chubby hands in front of his face, and held the pencil in both of them, and sucked at it in caricature, like someone drinking two-handed from a mug.

"So!" he explained, and with another volatile switch of mood, shouted something in high laughter to Toby in Russian, which Toby did not see fit, at the time, to translate, and in the transcription is rendered only as "obscene."

The priest ordered Grigoriev to sit, and for ten minutes described to him the most intimate details of Grigoriev's love affair with Evdokia, and also of his indiscretions with two other girls, who had both worked for him as secretaries, one in Potsdam and one in Bonn, and had ended up, unknown to Grigorieva, by sharing his bed. At which point, if Grigoriev was to be believed, he made a show of courage, and rose to his feet, demanding to know whether he had been brought halfway across Russia in order to attend a court of morals: "To sleep with one's secretary was not an unknown phenomenon, I told him, even in the Politburo! I assured him that I had never been indiscreet with foreign girls, only Russians. 'This too I know,' he says. 'But Grigorieva is unlikely to appreciate the distinction.'"

And then, to Toby's continuing amazement, Grigoriev gave vent to another burst of throaty laughter; and though both de Silsky and Skordeno discreetly joined in, Grigoriev's mirth outlived everybody's, so that they had to wait for it to run down.

"Kindly tell us, please, why the man you call the priest summoned you," Smiley said, from deep in his brown overcoat.

"He advised me that he had special work for me in Berne on behalf of the Thirteenth Directorate. I should reveal it to nobody, not even to my Ambassador, it was too secret for any of them. 'But,' says the priest, 'you shall tell your wife. Your personal circumstances render it impossible for you to make a conspiracy without the knowledge of your wife. This I know, Grigoriev. So tell her.' And he was right," Grigoriev commented. "This was wise of him! This was clear evidence that the man was familiar with the human condition."

Smiley turned a page and continued writing. "Go on, please," he said.

First, said the priest, Grigoriev was to open a Swiss bank account. The priest handed him a thousand Swiss francs in one hundred notes and told him to use them as the first payment. He should open the account not in Berne, where he was known, nor in Zurich, where there was a Soviet trade bank.

"The Vozhod," Grigoriev explained gratuitously. "This bank is used for many official and unofficial transactions."

Not in Zurich, then, but in the small town of Thun, a few kilometres outside Berne. He should open the account under the name of Glaser, a Swiss subject: "But I am a Soviet diplomat!" Grigoriev had objected. "I am not Glaser, I am Grigoriev!"

Undeterred, the priest handed him a Swiss passport in the name of Adolf Glaser. Every month, said the priest, the account would be credited with several thousand Swiss francs, sometimes even ten or fifteen. Grigoriev would now be told what use to make of them. It was very secret, the priest repeated patiently, and to the secrecy belonged both a reward and a threat. Very much as Smiley himself had done an hour before, the priest baldly set out each in turn. "Sir, you should have observed his composure towards me," Grigoriev told Smiley incredulously. "His calmness, his authority in all circumstances! In a chess game he would win everything, merely by his nerves."

"But he was not playing chess," Smiley objected drily.

"Sir, he was not," Grigoriev agreed, and with a sad shake of his head resumed his story.

A reward, and a threat, he repeated.

The threat was that Grigoriev's parent Ministry would be advised that he was unreliable on account of his philandering, and that he should therefore be barred from further foreign postings. This would cripple Grigoriev's career, also his marriage. So much for the threat.

"This would be extremely terrible for me," Grigoriev added, needlessly.

Next the reward, and the reward was substantial. If Grigoriev acquitted himself well, and with absolute secrecy, his career would be furthered, his indiscretions overlooked. In Berne he would have an opportunity to move to more agreeable quarters, which would please Grigorieva; he would be given funds with which to buy himself an imposing car which would be greatly to Grigorieva's taste; also he would be independent of Embassy drivers, most of whom were "neighbours," it was true, but were not admitted to this great secret. Lastly, said the priest, his promotion to Counsellor would be accelerated in order to explain the improvement in his living standards.

Grigoriev looked at the heap of Swiss francs lying on the desk between them, then at the Swiss passport, then at the priest. And he asked what would happen to him if he said he would rather not take part in this conspiracy. The priest nodded his head. He too, he assured Grigoriev, had considered this third possibility, but unfortunately the urgency of the need did not provide for such an option.

"So tell me what I must do with this money," Grigoriev had said.

It was routine, the priest replied, which was another reason why Grigoriev had been selected: "In matters of routine, I am told you are excellent," he said. Grigoriev, though he was by now scared half-way out of his skin by the priest's words, had felt flattered by this commendation.

"He had heard good reports of me," he explained to Smiley with pleasure.

Then the priest told Grigoriev about the mad girl.

Smiley did not budge. His eyes as he wrote were almost closed, but he wrote all the time—though God knows *what* he wrote, says Toby, for George would never have dreamed of consigning anything of even passing confidentiality to a notepad. Now and then, says Toby, while Grigoriev continued talking, George's head lifted far enough out of his coat collar for him to study the speaker's hands, or even his face. In every other respect he appeared remote from everything and everybody inside the room. Millie McCraig was in the doorway, de Silsky and Skordeno kept still as statues, while Toby prayed only for Grigoriev to "keep talking, I mean talking at any price, who cares? We were hearing of Karla's tradecraft from the horse's mouth."

The priest proposed to conceal nothing, he assured

Grigoriev—which, as everyone in the room but Grigoriev at once recognised, was a prelude to concealing something.

In a private psychiatric clinic in Switzerland, said the priest, there was confined a young Russian girl who was suffering from an advanced state of schizophrenia: "In the Soviet Union this form of illness is not sufficiently understood," said the priest. Grigoriev recalled being strangely touched by the priest's finality. "Diagnosis and treatment are too often complicated by political considerations," the priest went on. "In four years of treatment in our hospitals, the child Alexandra has been accused of many things by her doctors. 'Paranoid reformist and delusional ideas . . . An over-estimation of her own personality . . . Poor adaptation to the social environment . . . Over-inflation of her capabilities . . . A bourgeois decadence in her sexual behaviour.' Soviet doctors have repeatedly ordered her to renounce her incorrect ideas. This is not medicine," said the priest unhappily to Grigoriev. "It is politics. In Swiss hospitals, a more advanced attitude is taken to such matters. Grigoriev, it was essential that the child Alexandra should go to Switzerland!"

It was by now clear to Grigoriev that the high official was personally committed to the girl's problem, and familiar with every aspect of it. Grigoriev himself was already beginning to feel sad for her. She was the daughter of a Soviet hero—said the priest—and a former official of the Red Army who, in the guise of a traitor to Russia, was living in penurious circumstances among counter-revolutionary Czarists in Paris.

"His name," the priest said now, admitting Grigoriev to the greatest secret of all, "his name," he said, "is Colonel Ostrakov. He is one of our finest and most active secret agents. We rely on him totally for our information regarding counter-revolutionary conspirators in Paris."

Nobody in the room, says Toby, showed the least surprise at this sudden deification of a dead Russian deserter.

The priest, said Grigoriev, now proceeded to sketch the manner of the heroic agent Ostrakov's life, at the same time initiating Grigoriev into the mysteries of secret work. In order to escape the vigilance of imperialist counter-intelligence, the priest explained, it was necessary to invent for an agent a legend or false biography that would make him acceptable to anti-Soviet elements. Ostrakov was therefore in appearance a Red Army defector who had "escaped" into West Berlin, and thence to Paris, abandoning his wife and one daughter in Moscow. But in order to safeguard Ostrakov's standing among the Paris émigrés, it was logically necessary that the wife should suffer for the traitorous actions of the husband.

"For after all," said the priest, "if imperialist spies were to report that Ostrakova, the wife of a deserter and renegade, was living in good standing in Moscow—receiving her husband's salary, for example, or occupying the same apartment—imagine the effect this would have upon the credibility of Ostrakov!"

Grigoriev said he could imagine this well. The priest, he explained in parenthesis, was in no sense authoritarian in his manner, but rather treated Grigoriev as an equal, doubtless out of respect for his academic qualifications.

"Doubtless," Smiley said, and made a note.

Therefore, said the priest somewhat abruptly, Ostrakova and her daughter Alexandra, with the full agreement of her husband, were transferred to a far province and given a house to live in, and different names, and even—in their modest and selfless way—of necessity, their own legend also. Such, said the priest, was the painful reality of those who devoted themselves to special work. And consider, Grigoriev—he went on intently—consider the effect that such deprivation, and subterfuge, and even duplicity, might have upon a sensitive and perhaps already unbalanced daughter: an absent father whose very name had been eradicated from her life! A mother, who before being removed to safety, was obliged to endure the full brunt of public disgrace! Picture to yourself, the priest insisted—you, a father—the strains upon the young and delicate nature of a maturing girl!

Bowing to such forceful eloquence, Grigoriev was quick to say that as a father he could picture such strains easily; and it occurred to Toby at that moment, and probably to everybody else as well, that Grigoriev was exactly what he claimed to be: a humane and decent man caught in the net of events beyond his understanding or control.

For the last several years, the priest continued in a voice heavy with regret, the girl Alexandra—or, as she used to call herself, Tatiana—had been, in the Soviet province where she lived, a wanton and a social outcast. Under the pressures of her situation she had performed a variety of criminal acts, including arson and theft in public places. She had sided with pseudo-intellectual criminals and the worst imaginable anti-social elements. She had given herself freely to men, often several in a day. At first, when she was arrested, it had been possible for the priest and his assistants to stay the normal processes of law. But gradually, for reasons of security, this protection had to be withdrawn, and Alexandra had more than once been confined to State psychiatric clinics that specialised in the treatment of congenital social malcontents—with the negative results the priest had already described.

"She has also on several occasions been detained in a common prison," said the priest in a low voice. And, according to Grigoriev, he summed up this sad story as follows: "You will readily appreciate, dear Grigoriev, as an academic, a father, as a man of the world, how tragically the ever-worsening news of his daughter's misfortunes affected the usefulness of our heroic agent Ostrakov in his lonely exile in Paris."

Yet again, Grigoriev had been impressed by the remarkable sense of feeling—he would call it even a sense of direct personal responsibility—that the priest, through his story, inspired.

His voice arid as ever, Smiley made another interruption.

"And the mother is by now *where*, Counsellor, according to your priest?" he asked.

"Dead," Grigoriev replied. "She died in the province. The province to which she had been sent. She was buried under another name, naturally. According to the story as he told it to me, she died of a broken heart. This also placed a great burden on the priest's heroic agent in Paris," he added. "And upon the authorities in Russia."

"Naturally," said Smiley, and his solemnity was shared by the four motionless figures stationed round the room.

At last, said Grigoriev, the priest came to the precise reason why Grigoriev had been summoned. Ostrakova's death, coupled with the dreadful fate of Alexandra, had produced a grave crisis in the life of Moscow's heroic foreign agent. He was even for a short time tempted to give up his vital work in Paris in order to return to Russia and take care of his deranged and motherless child. Eventually, however, a solution was agreed upon. Since Ostrakov could not come to Russia, his daughter must come to the West, and be cared for in a private clinic where she was accessible to her father whenever he cared to visit her. France was too dangerous for this purpose, but in Switzerland, across the border, treatment could take place far from the suspicious eye of Ostrakov's counter-revolutionary companions. As a French citizen, the father would claim the girl and obtain the necessary papers. A suitable clinic had already been located and it was a short drive from Berne. What Grigoriev must now do was take over the welfare of this child, from the moment she arrived there. He must visit her, pay the clinic, and report weekly to Moscow on her progress, so that the information could at once be relayed to her father. This was the purpose of the bank account, and of what the priest referred to as Grigoriev's Swiss identity.

"And you agreed," said Smiley, as Grigoriev paused, and they heard his pen scratching busily over the paper.

"Not immediately. I asked him first two questions," said

Grigoriev, with a queer flush of vanity. "We academics are not deceived so easily, you understand. First, I naturally asked him why this task could not be undertaken by one of the many Swiss-based representatives of our State Security."

"An excellent question," Smiley said, in a rare mood of congratulation. "How did he reply to it?"

"It was too secret. Secrecy, he said, was a matter of compartments. He did not wish the name of Ostrakov to be associated with the people of the Moscow Centre mainstream. As things were now, he said, he would know that if ever there was a leak, Grigoriev alone was personally responsible. I was not grateful for this distinction," said Grigoriev, and smirked somewhat wanly at Nick de Silsky.

"And what was your second question, Counsellor?"

"Concerning the father in Paris: how often he would visit. If the father was visiting frequently, then surely my own position as a substitute father was redundant. Arrangements could be made to pay the clinic directly, the father could visit from Paris every month and concern himself with his own daughter's welfare. To this the priest replied that the father could come only very seldom and should never be spoken of in discussions with the girl Alexandra. He added, without consistency, that the topic of the daughter was also acutely painful to the father and that conceivably he would never visit her at all. He told me I should feel honoured to be performing an important service on behalf of a secret hero of the Soviet Union. He grew stern. He told me it was not my place to apply the logic of an amateur to the craft of professionals. I apologised. I told him I indeed felt honoured. I was proud to assist however I could in the anti-imperialist struggle."

"Yet you spoke without inner conviction?" Smiley suggested, looking up again and pausing in his writing.

"That is so."

"Why?"

At first, Grigoriev seemed unsure why. Perhaps he had never before been invited to speak the truth about his feelings.

"Did you perhaps not *believe* the priest?" Smiley suggested.

"The story had many inconsistencies," Grigoriev repeated with a frown. "No doubt in secret work this was inevitable. Nevertheless I regarded much of it as unlikely or untrue."

"Can you explain why?"

In the catharsis of confession, Grigoriev once more forgot his own peril, and gave a smile of superiority.

"He was emotional," he said. "I asked myself. Afterwards, with Evdokia, next day, lying at Evdokia's side, discussing the matter with her, I asked myself: What was it between the priest and this Ostrakov? Are they brothers? Old comrades? This great man they had brought me to see, so powerful, so secret—all over the world he is making conspiracies, putting pressure, taking special action. He is a ruthless man, in a ruthless profession. Yet when I, Grigoriev, am sitting with him, talking about some fellow's deranged daughter, I have the feeling I am reading this man's most intimate love letters. I said to him: 'Comrade. You are telling me too much. Don't tell me what I do not need to know. Tell me only what I must do.' But he says to me: 'Grigoriev, you must be a friend to this child. Then you will be a friend to me. Her father's twisted life has had a bad effect on her. She does not know who she is or where she belongs. She speaks of freedom without regard to its meaning. She is the victim of pernicious bourgeois fantasies. She uses foul language not suitable to a young girl. In lying, she has the genius of madness. None of this is her fault.' Then I ask him: 'Sir, have you met this girl?' And he says to me only, 'Grigoriev, you must be a father to her. Her mother was in many ways not an easy woman either. You have sympathy for such matters. In her later life she became embittered, and even supported her daughter in some of her anti-social fantasies.'"

Grigoriev fell silent a moment and Toby Esterhase, still reeling from the knowledge that Grigoriev had discussed Karla's proposition with his occasional mistress within hours of its being made, was grateful for the respite.

"I felt he was dependent on me," Grigoriev resumed. "I felt he was concealing not only facts, but feelings."

There remained, said Grigoriev, the practical details. The priest supplied them. The overseer of the clinic was a White Russian woman, a nun, formerly of the Russian Orthodox community in Jerusalem, but a good-hearted woman. In these cases, we should not be too scrupulous politically, said the priest. This woman had herself met Alexandra in Paris and escorted her to Switzerland. The clinic also had the services of a Russian-speaking doctor. The girl, thanks to the ethnic connections of her mother, also spoke German, but frequently refused to do so. These factors, together with the remoteness of the place, accounted for its selection. The money paid into the Thun bank would be sufficient for the clinic's fees, for medical attention up to one thousand francs a month, and as a hidden subsidy for the Grigorievs' new life-style. More money was available if Grigoriev thought it necessary; he should keep no bills or receipts; the priest would know soon enough if Grigoriev was cheating. He should visit the clinic weekly to pay the bill and inform himself of the girl's welfare; the Soviet Ambassador in Berne would be informed that the Grigorievs had been entrusted with secret work, and that he should allow them flexibility.

The priest then came to the question of Grigoriev's communication with Moscow.

"He asked me: 'Do you know the courier Krassky?' I reply, naturally I know this courier; Krassky comes once, sometimes twice a week to the Embassy in the company of his escort. If you are friendly with him, he will maybe bring you a loaf of black bread direct from Moscow."

In future, said the priest, Krassky would make a point of

meeting Grigoriev privately each Thursday evening during his regular visit to Berne, either in Grigoriev's house or in Grigoriev's room in the Embassy, but preferably his house. No conspiratorial discussions would take place, but Krassky would hand to Grigoriev an envelope containing an apparently personal letter from Grigoriev's aunt in Moscow. Grigoriev would take the letter to a safe place and treat it at prescribed temperatures with three chemical solutions freely available on the open market—the priest named them and Grigoriev now repeated them. In the writing thus revealed, said the priest, Grigoriev would find a list of questions he should put to Alexandra on his next weekly visit. At the same meeting with Krassky, Grigoriev should hand him a letter to be delivered to the same aunt, in which he would pretend to be writing in detail about his wife Grigorieva's welfare, whereas in fact he would be reporting to the priest on the welfare of the girl Alexandra. This was called word code. Later, the priest would if necessary supply Grigoriev with materials for a more clandestine communication, but for the time being the word-code letter to Grigoriev's aunt would do.

The priest then handed Grigoriev a medical certificate, signed by an eminent Moscow doctor.

"While here in Moscow, you have suffered a minor heart attack as a consequence of stress and overwork," said the priest. "You are advised to take up regular cycling in order to improve your physical condition. Your wife will accompany you."

By arriving at the clinic by bicycle or on foot, the priest explained, Grigoriev would be able to conceal the diplomatic registration of his car.

The priest then authorised him to purchase two second-hand bicycles. There remained the question of which day of the week would be best suited for Grigoriev's visits to the clinic. Saturday was the normal visiting day but this was too dangerous; several of the inmates were from Berne and there was always the risk that "Glaser" would be recognised. The overseer had therefore been advised that Saturdays were impracticable, and had consented, exceptionally, to a regular Friday-afternoon visit. The Ambassador would not object, but how would Grigoriev reconcile his Friday absences with Embassy routine?

There was no problem, Grigoriev replied. It was always permissible to trade Fridays for Saturdays, so Grigoriev would merely apply to work on Saturdays instead; then his Fridays would be free.

His confession over, Grigoriev treated his audience to a swift, over-lit smile.

"On Saturdays, a certain young lady also happened to be working in the Visa Section," he said, with a wink at Toby. "It was therefore possible we could enjoy some privacy together."

This time the general laughter was not quite as hearty as it might have been. Time, like Grigoriev's story, was running out.

They were back where they had started, and suddenly there was only Grigoriev himself to worry about, only Grigoriev to administer, only Grigoriev to secure. He sat smirking on the sofa, but the arrogance was ebbing from him. He had linked his hands submissively and he was looking from one to the other of them, as if expecting orders.

"My wife cannot ride a bicycle," he remarked with a sad little smile. "She tried many times." Her failure seemed to mean whole volumes to him. "The priest wrote to me from Moscow: 'Take your wife to her. Maybe Alexandra needs a mother, also.'" He shook his head, bemused. "She cannot ride it," he said to Smiley. "In such a great conspiracy, how can I tell Moscow that Grigorieva cannot ride a bicycle?" Perhaps there was no greater test of Smiley's rôle as the responsible functionary in charge, than the way in which he now almost casually transformed Grigoriev the onetime source into Grigoriev the defector-in-place.

"Counsellor, whatever your long-term plans may be, you will please remain at the Embassy for at least another two weeks," he announced, precisely closing his notepad. "If you do as I propose, you will find a warm welcome should you elect to make a new life somewhere in the West." He dropped the pad into his pocket. "But next Friday you will on no account visit the girl Alexandra. You will tell your wife that this was the substance of today's meeting with Krassky. When Krassky the courier brings you Thursday's letter, you will accept it normally but you will afterwards continue to maintain to your wife that Alexandra is not to be visited. Be mysterious towards her. Blind her with mystery."

Accepting his instructions, Grigoriev nodded uneasily.

"I must warn you, however, that if you make the smallest error or, on the other hand, try some trick, the priest will find out and destroy you. You will also forfeit your chances of a friendly reception in the West. Is that clear to you?"

There were telephone numbers for Grigoriev to ring, there were call-box to call-box procedures to be explained, and against all the laws of the trade, Smiley allowed Grigoriev to write the whole lot down, for he knew that he would not remember them otherwise. When all this was done, Grigoriev took his leave in a spirit of brooding dejection. Toby drove him to a safe dropping point, then returned to the flat and held a curt meeting of farewell.

Smiley was in his same chair, hands clasped on his lap. The rest of them, under Millie McCraig's orders, were busily tidying up the traces of their presence, polishing, dusting, emptying ashtrays and waste-paper baskets. Everyone present except himself and Smiley was getting out today, said Toby, the surveillance teams as well. Not tonight, not tomorrow. Now. They were sitting on a king-sized time bomb, he said: Grigoriev might at this very moment, under the continued impulse of confession, be describing the entire episode to his awful wife. If he had told Evdokia about Karla, who was to say he would not tell Grigorieva, or for that matter little Natasha, about his pow-wow with George today? Nobody should feel discarded, nobody should feel left out, said Toby. They had done a great job, and they would be meeting again soon to set the crown on it. There were handshakes, even a tear or two, but the prospect of the final act left everybody cheerful at heart.

And Smiley, sitting so quiet, so immobile, as the party broke up around him, what did he feel? On the face of it, this was a moment of high achievement for him. He had done everything he had set out to do, and more, even if he had resorted to Karla's techniques for the purpose. He had done it alone; and today, as the record would show, he had broken and turned Karla's hand-picked agent in the space of a couple of hours. Unaided, even hampered by those who had called him back to service, he had fought his way through to the point where he could honestly say he had burst the last important lock. He was in late age, yet his tradecraft had never been better; for the first time in his career, he held the advantage over his old adversary.

On the other hand, that adversary had acquired a human face of disconcerting clarity. It was no brute whom Smiley was pursuing with such mastery, no unqualified fanatic after all, no automaton. It was a man; and one whose downfall, if Smiley chose to bring it about, would be caused by nothing more sinister than excessive love, a weakness with which Smiley himself, from his own tangled life, was eminently familiar.

26

To every clandestine operation, says the folklore, belong more days of waiting than are numbered in Paradise, and for both George Smiley and Toby Esterhase, in their separate ways, the days and nights between Sunday evening and Friday seemed often numberless, and surely bore no relation to the Hereafter.

They lived not so much by Moscow Rules, says Toby, as by George's war rules. Both changed hotels and identities that same Sunday night, Smiley decamping to a small *hôtel garni* in the old town, the Arca, and Toby to a distasteful motel outside the town. Thereafter the two men communicated between call-boxes according to an agreed rota, and if they needed to meet, they selected crowded outdoor places, walking a short distance together before parting. Toby had decided to change his tracks, he said, and was using cars as sparingly as possible. His task was to keep the watch on Grigoriev. All week he clung to his stated conviction that, having so recently enjoyed the luxury of one confession, Grigoriev was sure to treat himself to another. To forestall this, he kept Grigoriev on as short a rein as possible, but to keep up with him at all was a nightmare. For example, Grigoriev left his house at quarter to eight each morning and had a five-minute walk to the Embassy. Very well: Toby would make one car sweep down the road at seven-fifty exactly. If Grigoriev carried his brief-case in his right hand, Toby would know that nothing was happening. But the left hand meant "emergency," with a crash meeting in the gardens of the Elfenau palace and a fall-back in the town. On the Monday and Tuesday, Grigoriev went the distance using his right hand only. But on the Wednesday it was snowing, he wished to clear his spectacles, and therefore he stopped to locate his handkerchief, with the result that Toby first saw the brief-case in his left hand, but when he raced round the block again to check, Grigoriev was grinning like a madman and waving the brief-case at him with his right. Toby, according to his own account, had "a total heart attack." The next day, the crucial Thursday, Toby achieved a car meeting with Grigoriev in the little village of Allmendingen, just outside the town, and was able to talk to him face to face. An hour earlier, the courier Krassky had arrived, bringing Karla's weekly orders: Toby had seen him enter the Grigoriev residence. So where were the instructions from Moscow? Toby asked. Grigoriev was cantankerous and a little drunk. He demanded ten thousand dollars for the letter, which so enraged Toby that he threatened Grigoriev with exposure then and there; he would make a citizen's arrest and take him straight down to the police station and charge him personally with posing as a Swiss national, abusing his diplomatic status, evading Swiss tax laws, and about fifteen other things, including venery and espionage. The bluff worked, Grigoriev produced the letter, already treated, with the secret writing showing between the hand-written lines. Toby took several photographs of it, then returned it to Grigoriev.

Karla's questions from Moscow, which Toby showed to Smiley late that night in a rare meeting at a country inn, had a beseeching ring: ". . . report more fully on Alexandra's appearance and state of mind. . . . Is she lucid? Does she laugh and does her laughter make a happy or a sad impression? Is she clean in her personal habits, clean finger-nails, brushed hair? What is the doctor's latest diagnosis; does he recommend some other treatment?"

But Grigoriev's main preoccupations at their rendezvous in Allmendingen turned out not to be with Krassky, or with the letter, or its author. His lady-friend of the Visa Section had been demanding outright to know about his Friday excursions, he said. Hence his depression and drunkenness. Grigoriev had answered her vaguely, but now he suspected her of being a Moscow spy, put there either by the priest or, worse, by some other frightful organ of Soviet Security. Toby, as it happened, shared this belief, but did not feel that much would be served by saying so.

"I have told her I shall not make love to her again until I completely trust her," Grigoriev said earnestly. "Also I have not yet decided whether she shall be permitted to accompany me in my new life in Australia."

"George, this is a madhouse!" Toby told Smiley in a furious mixture of images, while Smiley continued to study Karla's solicitous questions, even though they were written in Russian. "Listen, I mean how long can we hold the dam? This guy is a total crazy!"

"When does Krassky return to Moscow?" Smiley asked.

"Saturday midday."

"Grigoriev must arrange a meeting with him before he leaves. He's to tell Krassky he will have a special message for him. An urgent one."

"Sure," said Toby. "Sure, George." And that was that.

Where had George gone in his mind? Toby wondered, watching him vanish into the crowd once more. Karla's instructions to Grigoriev seemed to have upset Smiley quite absurdly. "I was caught between one total loony and one complete depressive," Toby claims of this taxing period.

While Toby, however, could at least agonise over the vagaries of his master and his agent, Smiley had less substantial fare with which to occupy his time, which may have been his problem. On the Tuesday, he took a train to Zurich and lunched at

the Kronenhalle with Peter Guillam, who had flown in by way
of London at Saul Enderby's behest. Their discussion was
restrained, and not merely on the grounds of security. Guillam
had taken it upon himself to speak to Ann while he was in
London, he said, and was keen to know whether there was any
message he might take back to her. Smiley said icily that there
was none, and came as near as Guillam could remember to
bawling him out. On another occasion—he suggested—
perhaps Guillam would be good enough to keep his damned
fingers out of Smiley's private affairs? Guillam switched the
topic hastily to business. Concerning Grigoriev, he said, Saul
Enderby had a notion to sell him to the Cousins as found
rather than process him at Sarratt. How did George feel about
that one? Saul had a sort of hunch that the glamour of a senior
Russian defector would give the Cousins a much-needed lift in
Washington, even if he hadn't anything to tell, while Grigoriev in London might, so to speak, mar the pure wine to
come. How did George feel on that one, actually?

"Quite," said Smiley.

"Saul also rather wondered whether your plans for next
Friday were strictly necessary," said Guillam, with evident
reluctance.

Picking up a table-knife, Smiley stared along the blade.

"She's worth his career to him," he said at last, with a most
unnerving tautness. "He steals for her, lies for her, risks his
neck for her. He has to know whether she cleans her finger-
nails and brushes her hair. Don't you think we owe her a look?"

Owe to whom? Guillam wondered nervously as he flew
back to London to report. Had Smiley meant that he owed it
to himself? Or did he mean to Karla? But he was far too cautious to air these theories to Saul Enderby.

From a distance, it might have been a castle, or one of those
small farmsteads that sit on hilltops in the Swiss wine country,
with turrets, and moats with covered bridges leading to inner

courtyards. Closer to, it took on a more utilitarian appearance, with an incinerator, and an orchard, and modern outbuildings with rows of small windows rather high. A sign at the edge of the village pointed to it, praising its quiet position, its comfort, and the solicitude of its staff. The community was described as "interdenominational Christian theosophist," and foreign patients were a speciality. Old, heavy snow cluttered fields and roof-tops, but the road that Smiley drove was clear. The day was all white; sky and snow had merged into a single, uncharted void. From the gatehouse a dour porter telephoned ahead of him and, receiving somebody's permission, waved him through. There was a bay marked "DOCTORS" and a bay marked "VISITORS" and he parked in the second. When he pressed the bell, a dull-looking woman in a grey habit opened the door to him, blushing even before she spoke. He heard crematorium music, and the clanking of crockery from a kitchen, and human voices all at once. It was a house with hard floors and no curtains.

"Mother Felicity is expecting you," said Sister Beatitude in a shy whisper.

A scream would fill the entire house, thought Smiley. He noticed potted plants out of reach. At a door marked "OFFICE" his escort thumped lustily, then shoved it open. Mother Felicity was a large, inflamed-looking woman with a disconcerting worldliness in her gaze. Smiley sat opposite her. An ornate cross rested on her large bosom, and while she spoke, her heavy hands consoled it with a couple of touches. Her German was slow and regal.

"So," she said. "So, you are Herr *Lachmann*, and Herr Lachmann is an acquaintance of Herr *Glaser*, and Herr Glaser is this week indisposed." She played on these names as if she knew as well as he did they were lies. "He was not so indisposed that he could not telephone, but he was so indisposed that he could not bicycle. That is correct?"

Smiley said it was.

"Please do not lower your voice merely because I am a nun. We run a noisy house here and nobody is the less pious for it. You look pale. You have a flu?"

"No. No, I am well."

"Then you are better off than Herr Glaser, who has succumbed to a flu. Last year we had an Egyptian flu, the year before it was an Asian flu, but this year the *malheur* seems to be our own entirely. Does Herr Lachmann have documents, may I ask, which legitimise him for who he is?"

Smiley handed her a Swiss identity card.

"Come. Your hand is shaking. But you have no flu. By occupation, *professor*," she read aloud. "Herr Lachmann hides his light. He is *Professor* Lachmann. Of which subject is he professor, may one ask?"

"Of philology."

"So. Philology. And Herr *Glaser*, what is *his* profession? He has never revealed it to me."

"I understand he is in business," Smiley said.

"A businessman who speaks perfect Russian. You also speak perfect Russian, Professor?"

"Alas, no."

"But you are friends." She handed back the identity card. "A Swiss-Russian businessman and a modest professor of philology are friends. So. Let us hope the friendship is a fruitful one."

"We are also neighbours," Smiley said.

"We are all neighbours, Herr Lachmann. Have you met Alexandra before?"

"No."

"Young girls are brought here in many capacities. We have godchildren. We have wards. Nieces. Orphans. Cousins. Aunts, a few. A few sisters. And now a professor. But you would be very surprised how few *daughters* there are in the world. What is the family relationship between Herr Glaser and Alexandra, for example?"

"I understand he is a friend of Monsieur Ostrakov."

"Who is in Paris. But is invisible. As also is Madame Ostrakova. Invisible. As also, today, is Herr Glaser. You see how difficult it is for us to come to grips with the world, Herr Lachmann? When we ourselves scarcely know who we are, how can we tell *them* who *they* are? You must be very careful with her." A bell was ringing for the end of rest. "Sometimes she lives in the dark. Sometimes she sees too much. Both are painful. She has grown up in Russia. I don't know why. It is a complicated story, full of contrasts, full of gaps. If it is not the cause of her malady, it is certainly, let us say, the framework. You do not think Herr Glaser is the father, for instance?"

"No."

"Nor do I. Have you *met* the invisible Ostrakov? You have not. Does the invisible Ostrakov exist? Alexandra insists he is a phantom. Alexandra will have a quite different parentage. Well, so would many of us!"

"May I ask what you have told her about me?"

"All I know. Which is nothing. That you are a friend of Uncle Anton, whom she refuses to accept as her uncle. That Uncle Anton is ill, which appears to delight her, but probably it worries her very much. I have told her it is her father's wish to have someone visit her every week, but she tells me her father is a brigand and pushed her mother off a mountain at dead of night. I have told her to speak German but she may still decide that Russian is best."

"I understand," said Smiley.

"You are lucky, then," Mother Felicity retorted. "For I do not."

Alexandra entered and at first he saw only her eyes: so clear, so defenceless. In his imagination, he had drawn her, for some reason, larger. Her lips were full at the centre, but at the corners already thin and too agile, and her smile had a dangerous luminosity. Mother Felicity told her to sit, said something in Russian, gave her a kiss on her flaxen head. She left, and they

heard her keys jingle as she strode off down the corridor, yelling at one of the sisters in French to have this mess cleared up.
Alexandra wore a green tunic with long sleeves gathered at the
wrists and a cardigan over her shoulders like a cape. She seemed
to carry her clothes rather than wear them, as if someone had
dressed her for the meeting.

"Is Anton dead?" she asked, and Smiley noticed that there
was no natural link between the expression on her face and the
thoughts in her head.

"No, Anton has a bad flu," he replied.

"Anton says he is my uncle but he is not," she explained.
Her German was good, and he wondered, despite what Karla
had said to Grigoriev, whether she had that from her mother
too, or whether she had inherited her father's gift for languages, or both. "He also pretends he has no car." As her father
had once done, she watched him without emotion, and without
commitment. "Where is your list?" she asked. "Anton always
brings a list."

"Oh, I have my questions in my head."

"It is forbidden to ask questions without a list. Questions
out of the head are all completely forbidden by my father."

"Who is your father?" Smiley asked.

For a time he saw only her eyes again, staring at him out of
their private lonely place. She picked up a roll of Scotch tape
from Mother Felicity's desk, and lightly traced the shiny surface with her finger.

"I saw your car," she said. "'BE' stands for 'Berne.'"

"Yes, it does," said Smiley.

"What kind of car does Anton have?"

"A Mercedes. A black one. Very grand."

"How much did he pay for it?"

"He bought it second-hand. About five thousand francs, I
should imagine."

"Then why does he come and see me on a bicycle?"

"Perhaps he needs the exercise."

"No," she said. "He has a secret."

"Have *you* got a secret, Alexandra?" Smiley asked.

She heard his question, and smiled at it, and nodded a couple of times as if to someone a long way off. "My secret is called Tatiana," she said.

"That's a good name," said Smiley. "*Tatiana*. How did you come by that?"

Raising her head, she smiled radiantly at the icons on the wall. "It is forbidden to talk about it," she said. "If you talk about it, nobody will believe you, but they put you in a clinic."

"But you are in a clinic already," Smiley pointed out.

Her voice did not lift, it only quickened. She remained so absolutely still that she seemed not even to draw breath between her words. Her lucidity and her courtesy were awesome. She respected his kindness, she said, but she knew that he was an extremely dangerous man, more dangerous than teachers or police. Dr. Rüedi had invented property and prisons, and many of the clever arguments by which the world lived out its lies, she said. Mother Felicity was too close to God, she did not understand that God was somebody who had to be ridden and kicked like a horse till he took you in the right direction.

"But you, Herr Lachmann, represent the forgiveness of the authorities. Yes, I am afraid you do."

She sighed, and gave him a tired smile of indulgence, but when he looked at the table he saw that she had seized hold of her thumb, and was forcing it back upon itself till it looked like snapping.

"Perhaps *you* are my father, Herr Lachmann," she suggested with a smile.

"No, alas, I have no children," Smiley replied.

"Are you God?"

"No, I'm just an ordinary person."

"Mother Felicity says that in every ordinary person, there is a part that is God."

This time it was Smiley's turn to take a long while to reply. His mouth opened, then with uncharacteristic hesitation closed again.

"I have heard it said too," he replied, and looked away from her a moment.

"You are supposed to ask me whether I have been feeling better."

"Are you feeling better, Alexandra?"

"My name is Tatiana," she said.

"Then how does Tatiana feel?"

She laughed. Her eyes were delightfully bright. "Tatiana is the daughter of a man who is too important to exist," she said. "He controls the whole of Russia, but he does not exist. When people arrest her, her father arranges for her to be freed. He does not exist but everyone is afraid of him. Tatiana does not exist either," she added. "There is only Alexandra."

"What about Tatiana's mother?"

"She was punished," said Alexandra calmly, confiding this information to the icons rather than to Smiley. "She was not obedient to history. That is to say, she believed that history had taken a wrong course. She was mistaken. The people should not attempt to change history. It is the task of history to change the people. I would like you to take me with you, please. I wish to leave this clinic."

Her hands were fighting each other furiously while she continued to smile at the icons.

"Did Tatiana ever meet her father?" he asked.

"A small man used to watch the children walk to school," she replied. He waited but she said no more.

"And then?" he asked.

"From a car. He would lower the window but he looked only at me."

"Did you look at him?"

"Of course. How else would I know he was looking at me?"

"What was his appearance? His manner? Did he smile?"

"He smoked. Feel free, if you wish. Mother Felicity likes a cigarette occasionally. Well, it's only natural, isn't it? Smoking calms the conscience, I am told."

She had pressed the bell: reached out and pressed it for a long time. He heard the jingle of Mother Felicity's keys again, coming towards them down the bare corridor, and the shuffle of her feet at the door as she paused to unlock it, just like the sounds of any prison in the world.

"I wish to come with you in your car," said Alexandra.

Smiley paid her bill and Alexandra watched him count the notes out under the lamp, exactly the way Uncle Anton did it. Mother Felicity intercepted Alexandra's studious look and perhaps she sensed trouble, for she glanced sharply at Smiley as if she suspected some misconduct in him. Alexandra accompanied him to the door and helped Sister Beatitude open it, then shook Smiley's hand in a very stylish way, lifting her elbow up and outward, and bending her front knee. She tried to kiss his hand but Sister Beatitude prevented her. She watched him to the car and she began waving, and he was already moving when he heard her screaming from very close, and saw that she was trying to open the car door and travel with him, but Sister Beatitude hauled her off and dragged her, still screaming, back into the house.

Half an hour later in Thun, in the same café from which he had observed Grigoriev's visit to the bank a week before, Smiley silently handed Toby the letter he had prepared. Grigoriev was to give it to Krassky tonight or whenever they met, he said.

"Grigoriev wants to defect tonight," Toby objected.

Smiley shouted. For once in his life, shouted. He opened his mouth very wide, he shouted, and the whole café sat up with a jolt—which is to say that the barmaid looked up from her marriage advertisements, and of the four card-players in the corner, one at least turned his head.

"*Not yet!*"

Then, to show that he had himself completely under control, he repeated the words quietly: "Not yet, Toby. Forgive me. Not yet."

Of the letter that Smiley sent to Karla by way of Grigoriev, no copy exists, which is perhaps what Smiley intended, but there can be little doubt of the substance, since Karla himself was anyway a self-professed exponent of the arts of what he liked to call pressure. Smiley would have set out the bare facts: that Alexandra was known to be his daughter by a dead mistress of manifest anti-Soviet tendencies, that he had arranged her illegal departure from the Soviet Union by pretending that she was his secret agent; that he had misappropriated public money and resources; that he had organised two murders and perhaps also the conjectured official execution of Kirov, all in order to protect his criminal scheme. Smiley would have pointed out that the accumulated evidence of this was quite sufficient, given Karla's precarious position within Moscow Centre, to secure his liquidation by his peers in the Collegium; and that if this were to happen, his daughter's future in the West— where she was residing under false pretences—would be uncertain, to say the least. There would be no money for her, and Alexandra would become a perpetual and ailing exile, ferried from one public hospital to another, without friends, proper papers, or a penny to her name. At worst, she would be brought back to Russia, to have visited upon her the full wrath of her father's enemies.

After the stick, Smiley offered Karla the same carrot he had offered him more than twenty years before, in Delhi: save your skin, come to us, tell us what you know, and we will make a home for you. A straight replay, said Saul Enderby later, who liked a sporting metaphor. Smiley would have promised Karla immunity from prosecution for complicity in the murder of Vladimir, and there is evidence that Enderby obtained a similar concession through his German liaison regarding the murder of Otto Leipzig. Without question, Smiley also threw in general guarantees about Alexandra's future in the West—treatment, maintenance, and, if necessary, citizenship. Did he take the line of kinship, as he had done before, in Delhi? Did he appeal to Karla's humanity, now so demonstrably on show? Did he add some clever seasoning, calculated to spare Karla humiliation and, knowing his pride, head him off perhaps from an act of self-destruction?

Certainly he gave Karla very little time to make up his mind. For that too is an axiom of pressure, as Karla was well aware: time to think is dangerous, except that in this case, there is reason to suppose that it was dangerous to Smiley also, though for vastly different reasons: he might have relented at the eleventh hour. Only the immediate call to action, says the Sarratt folklore, will force the quarry to slip the ropes of his restraint and, against every impulse born or taught to him, sail into the blue. The same, on this occasion, may be said to have applied equally to the hunter.

27

It's like putting all your money on black, thought Guillam, staring out of the window of the café: everything you've got in the world, your wife, your unborn child. Then waiting, hour by hour, for the croupier to spin the wheel.

He had known Berlin when it was the world capital of the cold war, when every crossing point from East to West had the tenseness of a major surgical operation. He remembered how on nights like these, clusters of Berlin policemen and Allied soldiers used to gather under the arc lights, stamping their feet, cursing the cold, fidgeting their rifles from shoulder to shoulder, puffing clouds of frosted breath into each other's faces. He remembered how the tanks waited, growling to keep their engines warm, their gun barrels picking targets on the other side, feigning strength. He remembered the sudden wail of the alarm klaxons and the dash to the Bernauerstrasse or wherever the latest escape attempt might be. He remembered the fire-brigade ladders going up; the orders to shoot back; the orders not to; the dead, some of them agents. But after tonight, he knew that he would remember it only like this: so dark you wanted to take a torch with you into the street, so still you could have heard the cocking of a rifle from across the river.

"What cover will he use?" he asked.

Smiley sat opposite him across the little plastic table, a cup of cold coffee at his elbow. He looked somehow very small inside his overcoat.

"Something humble," Smiley said. "Something that fits in. Those who cross here are mostly old-age pensioners, I gather." He was smoking one of Guillam's cigarettes and it seemed to take all his attention.

"What on earth do pensioners want here?" Guillam asked.

"Some work. Some visit dependents. I didn't enquire very closely, I'm afraid."

Guillam remained dissatisfied.

"We pensioners tend to keep ourselves to ourselves," Smiley added, in a poor effort at humour.

"You're telling me," said Guillam.

The café was in the Turkish quarter because the Turks are now the poor whites of West Berlin, and property is worst and cheapest near the Wall. Smiley and Guillam were the only foreigners. At a long table sat a whole Turkish family, chewing flat bread and drinking coffee and Coca-Cola. The children had shaven heads and the wide, puzzled eyes of refugees. Islamic music was playing from an old tape-recorder. Strips of coloured plastic hung from the hardboard arch of an Islamic doorway.

Guillam returned his gaze to the window, and the bridge. First came the piers of the overhead railway, next the old brick house that Sam Collins and his team had discreetly requisitioned as an observation centre. His men had been moving in surreptitiously these last two days. Then came the halo of sodium arc lights, and behind it lay a barricade, a pillbox, then the bridge. The bridge was for pedestrians only, and the only way over it was a corridor of steel fencing like a bird walk, sometimes one man's width and sometimes three. Occasionally one crossed, keeping a meek appearance and a steady pace in order not to alarm the sentry tower, then stepping into the sodium halo as he reached the West. By daylight the bird walk was grey; by night for some reason yellow, and strangely bright. The pillbox was a yard or two inside the border, its roof just mastering the barricade, but it was the tower that dominated everything, one iron-black rectangular pillar at the bridge's centre. Even the snow avoided it. There was snow on the concrete teeth that blocked the bridge to traffic, snow swarmed round the halo and the pillbox and made a show of settling on the wet cobble; but the sentry tower was immune, as if not even the snow would go near it of its own free will. Just short of the halo, the bird walk narrowed to a last gateway and a cattle pen. But the gateway, said Toby, could be closed electrically at a moment's notice from inside the pillbox.

The time was ten-thirty but it could have been three in the morning, because along its borders, West Berlin goes to bed with the dark. Inland, the island-city may chat and drink and whore and spend its money; the Sony signs and rebuilt churches and conference halls may glitter like a fair-ground; but the dark shores of the border-land are silent from seven in the evening. Close to the halo stood a Christmas tree, but only the upper half of it was lit, only the upper half was visible from across the river. It is a place of no compromise, thought Guillam, a place of no third way. Whatever reservations he might occasionally have about the Western freedom, here, at this border, like most other things, they stopped dead.

"George?" said Guillam softly, and cast Smiley a questioning glance.

A labourer had lurched into the halo. He seemed to rise into it as they all did the moment they stepped out of the bird walk, as if a burden had fallen from their backs. He was carrying a small brief-case and what looked like a rail man's lamp. He was slight of build. But Smiley, if he had noticed the man at all, had already returned to the collar of his brown overcoat and his lonely, faraway thoughts. "If he comes, he'll come on time," Smiley had said. Then why do we get here two hours early? Guillam had wanted to ask. Why do we sit here, like two strangers, drinking sweet coffee out of little cups, soaked in the steam of this wretched Turkish kitchen, talking platitudes? But he knew the answer already. Because we *owe*, Smiley would have said if he had been in a talking mood. Because we owe the caring and the waiting, we owe this vigil over one man's effort to escape the system he has helped create. For as long as he is trying to reach us, we are his friends. Nobody else is on his side.

He'll come, Guillam thought. He won't. He may. If this isn't prayer, he thought, what is?

"More coffee, George?"

"No, thank you, Peter. No, I don't think so. No."

"They seem to have soup of some sort. Unless that was the coffee."

"Thank you, I think I've consumed about all I can manage," said Smiley, in quite a general tone, as if anyone who wished to hear was welcome.

"Well, maybe I'll just order something for rent," said Guillam.

"Rent? I'm sorry. Of course. God knows what they must live on."

Guillam ordered two more coffees and paid for them. He was paying as he went, deliberately, in case they had to leave in a hurry.

Come for George's sake, he thought; come for mine. Come for all our damn sakes, and be the impossible harvest we have dreamed of for so long.

"When did you say the baby was due, Peter?"

"March."

"Ah. March. What will you call it?"

"We haven't really thought."

Across the road, by the glow of a furniture shop that sold reproduction wrought iron and brocade and fake muskets and pewter, Guillam made out the muffled figure of Toby Esterhase in his Balkan fur hat, affecting to study the wares. Toby and his team had the streets, Sam Collins had the observation post: that was the deal. For the escape cars, Toby had insisted on taxis, and there they stood, three of them, suitably shabby, in the darkness of the station arches, with notices in their windscreens saying "OUT OF SERVICE," and their drivers standing at the *Imbiss*-stand, eating sausages in sweet sauce out of paper dishes.

The place is a total minefield, Peter, Toby had warned. *Turks, Greeks, Yugoslavs, a lot of crooks—even the damn cats are wired, no exaggeration.*

Not a whisper anywhere, Smiley had ordered. *Not a murmur, Peter. Tell Collins.*

Come, thought Guillam urgently. We're all rooting for you. Come.

From Toby's back, Guillam lifted his gaze slowly to the top-floor window of the old house where Collins's observation post was sited. Guillam had done his Berlin stint, he had been part of it a dozen times. The telescopes and cameras, the directional microphones, all the useless hardware that was supposed to make the waiting easier; the crackle of the radios, the stink of coffee and tobacco; the bunk-beds. He imagined the co-opted West German policeman who had no idea why he had been brought here, and would have to stay till the operation was abandoned or successful—the man who knew the bridge by heart and could tell the regulars from the casuals and spot the smallest bad omen the moment it occurred: the silent doubling of the watch, the Vopo sharpshooters easing softly into place.

And if they shoot him? thought Guillam. If they arrest him? If they leave him—which they would surely like to, and had done before to others—bleeding to death, face downward in the bird walk not six feet from the halo?

Come, he thought, less certainly, willing his prayers into the black skyline of the East. Come all the same.

A fine, very bright pin-light flitted across the west-facing upper window of the observation house, bringing Guillam to his feet. He turned round to see Smiley already half-way to the door. Toby Esterhase was waiting for them on the pavement.

"It's only a possibility, George," he said softly, in the tone of a man preparing them for disappointment. "Just a thin chance, but he could be our man."

They followed him without another word. The cold was ferocious. They passed a tailor's shop with two dark-haired girls stitching in the window. They passed wall posters offering cheap ski holidays, death to Fascists, and to the Shah. The cold made them breathless. Turning his face from the swirling snow, Guillam glimpsed a children's adventure playground made of old railway sleepers. They passed between black, dead buildings, then right, across the cobbled road, in pitch-frozen darkness to the river bank, where an old timber bullet-shelter with rifle slits offered them the whole span of the bridge. To their left, black against the hostile river, a tall wooden cross, garnished with barbed wire, bore memory to an unknown man who had not quite escaped.

Toby silently extracted a pair of field-glasses from his overcoat and handed them to Smiley.

"George. Listen. Good luck, okay?"

Toby's hand closed briefly over Guillam's arm. Then he darted away again, into the darkness.

The shelter stank of leaf-mould and damp. Smiley crouched to the rifle slit, the skirt of his tweed coat trailing in the mud, while he surveyed the scene before him as if it held the very reaches of his own long life. The river was broad and slow, misted with cold. Arc lights played over it, and the snow danced in their beams. The bridge spanned it on fat stone piers, six or eight of them, which swelled into crude shoes as they reached the water. The spaces between them were arched, all but the centre, which was squared off to make room for shipping, but the only ship was a grey patrol boat moored at the eastern bank, and the only commerce it offered was death. Behind the bridge, like its vastly bigger shadow, ran the railway viaduct, but like the river it was derelict, and no trains ever crossed. The warehouses of the far bank stood monstrous as the hulks of an earlier barbaric civilisation, and the bridge with its yellow bird walk seemed to leap from half-way up them, like a fantastic light-path out of darkness. From his vantage point, Smiley could scan the whole length of it with his field-glasses, from the floodlit white barrack house on the eastern bank, up to the black sentry tower at the crest, then slightly downhill again towards the western side: to the cattle pen, the pillbox that controlled the gateway, and finally the halo.

Guillam stood but a few feet behind him, yet Guillam could have been back in Paris for all the awareness Smiley had of him: he had seen the solitary black figure start his journey; he had seen the glimmer of the cigarette-end as he took one last pull, the spark of it comet towards the water as he tossed it over the iron fencing of the bird walk. One small man, in a worker's half-length coat, with a worker's satchel slung across his little chest, walking neither fast nor slowly, but walking like a man who walked a lot. One small man, his body a fraction too long for his legs, hatless despite the snow. That is all that happens, Smiley thought; one little man walks across a bridge.

"Is it him?" Guillam whispered. "George, tell me! Is it Karla?"

Don't come, thought Smiley. *Shoot*, Smiley thought, talking to Karla's people, not to his own. There was suddenly something terrible in his foreknowledge that this tiny creature was about to cut himself off from the black castle behind him. Shoot him from the sentry tower, shoot him from the pillbox, from the white barrack hut, from the crow's-nest on the prison warehouse, slam the gate on him, cut him down, your own traitor, kill him! In his racing imagination, he saw the scene unfold: the last-minute discovery by Moscow Centre of Karla's infamy; the phone calls to the frontier—"Stop him at any cost!" And the shooting, never too much—enough to hit a man a time or two, and wait.

"It's him!" Guillam whispered. He had taken the binoculars from Smiley's unresisting hand. "It's the same man! The photograph that hung on your wall in the Circus! George, you miracle!"

But Smiley in his imagination saw only the Vopo's searchlights converging on Karla as if he were a hare in the headlights, so dark against the snow; and Karla's hopeless old man's run before the bullets threw him like a rag doll over his own feet. Like Guillam, Smiley had seen it all before. He looked across the river into the darkness again, and an unholy vertigo seized him as the very evil he had fought against seemed to reach out and possess him and claim him despite his striving, calling him a traitor also; mocking him, yet at the same time applauding his betrayal. On Karla has descended the curse of Smiley's compassion; on Smiley the curse of Karla's fanaticism. I have destroyed him with the weapons I abhorred, and they are his. We have crossed each other's frontiers, we are the no-men of this no-man's-land.

"Just keep moving," Guillam was murmuring. "Just keep moving, let nothing stop you."

Approaching the blackness of the sentry tower, Karla took a couple of shorter steps and for a moment Smiley really thought he might change his mind and give himself up to the East Germans. Then he saw a cat's tongue of flame as Karla lit a fresh cigarette. With a match or a lighter? he wondered. *To George from Ann with all my love.*

"Christ, he's cool!" said Guillam.

The little figure set off again, but at a slower pace, as if he had grown weary. He is stoking up his courage for the last step, thought Smiley, or he is trying to damp his courage down. He thought again of Vladimir and Otto Leipzig and the dead Kirov; he thought of Haydon and his own life's work ruined; he thought of Ann, permanently stained for him by Karla's cunning and Haydon's scheming embrace. He recited in his despair a whole list of crimes—the tortures, the killings, the endless ring of corruption—to lay upon the frail shoulders of this one pedestrian on the bridge, but they would not stay there: he did not want these spoils, won by these methods. Like a chasm, the jagged skyline beckoned to him yet again, the swirling snow made it an inferno. For a second longer, Smiley stood on the brink, at the smouldering river's edge.

They had started walking along the tow-path, Guillam leading, Smiley reluctantly following. The halo burned ahead of them, growing as they approached it. *Like two ordinary pedestrians*, Toby had said. *Just walk to the bridge and wait, it's normal.* From the darkness around them, Smiley heard whispered voices and the swift, damped sounds of hasty movement under tension. "George," someone whispered. "George." From a yellow phone-box, an unknown figure lifted a hand in discreet salute, and he heard the word "triumph" smuggled to him on the wet freezing air. The snow was blurring his glasses, he found it hard to see. The observation post stood to their right, not a light burning in the windows. He made out a van parked at the entrance, and realised it was a Berlin mail van, one of Toby's favourites. Guillam was hanging back. Smiley heard something about "claiming the prize."

They had reached the edge of the halo. An orange rampart blocked the bridge and the chicane from sight. They were out of the eye-line of the sentry-box. Perched above the Christmas tree, Toby Esterhase was standing on the observation scaffold with a pair of binoculars, calmly playing the cold-war tourist. A plump female watcher stood at his side. An old notice warned them they were there at their own risk. On the smashed brick viaduct behind them Smiley picked out a forgotten armorial crest. Toby made a tiny motion with his hand: *thumbs up, it's our man now.* From beyond the rampart, Smiley heard light footsteps and the vibration of an iron fence. He caught the smell of an American cigarette as the icy wind wafted it ahead of the smoker. There's still the electric gateway, he thought; he waited for the clang as it slammed shut, but none came. He realised he had no real name by which to address his enemy:

only a code-name, and a woman's at that. Even his military rank was a mystery. And still Smiley hung back, like a man refusing to go on stage.

Guillam had drawn alongside him and seemed to be trying to edge him forward. He heard soft footsteps as Toby's watchers gathered to the edge of the halo, safe from view in the shelter of the rampart, waiting with bated breath for a sight of the catch. And suddenly, there he stood, like a man slipping into a crowded hall unnoticed. His small right hand hung flat and naked at his side, his left held the cigarette timidly across his chest. One little man, hatless, with a satchel. He took a step forward and in the halo Smiley saw his face, aged and weary and travelled, the short hair turned to white by a sprinkling of snow. He wore a grimy shirt and a black tie: he looked like a poor man going to the funeral of a friend. The cold had nipped his cheeks low down, adding to his age.

They faced each other; they were perhaps a yard apart, much as they had been in Delhi jail. Smiley heard more footsteps and this time it was the sound of Toby padding swiftly down the wooden ladder of the scaffold. He heard soft voices and laughter; he thought he even heard the sound of gentle clapping, but he never knew; there were shadows everywhere, and once inside the halo, it was hard for him to see out. Paul Skordeno slipped forward and stood himself one side of Karla; Nick de Silsky stood the other. He heard Guillam telling someone to get that bloody car up here before they come over the bridge and get him back. He heard the ring of something metal falling onto the icy cobble, and knew it was Ann's cigarette-lighter, but nobody else seemed to notice it. They exchanged one more glance and perhaps each for that second did see in the other something of himself. He heard the crackle of car tyres and the sounds of doors opening, while the engine kept running. De Silsky and Skordeno moved towards it, and Karla went with them though they didn't touch him; he seemed to have acquired already the submissive manner of a prisoner;

he had learned it in a hard school. Smiley stood back and the three of them marched softly past him, all somehow too absorbed by the ceremony to pay attention to him. The halo was empty. He heard the quiet closing of the car's doors and the sound of it driving away. He heard two other cars leave after it, or with it. He didn't watch them go. He felt Toby Esterhase fling his arms round his shoulders, and saw that his eyes were filled with tears.

"George," he began. "All your life. Fantastic!"

Then something in Smiley's stiffness made Toby pull away, and Smiley himself stepped quickly out of the halo, passing very close to Ann's lighter on his way. It lay at the halo's very edge, tilted slightly, glinting like fool's gold on the cobble. He thought of picking it up, but somehow there seemed no point and no one else appeared to have seen it. Someone was shaking his hand, someone else was clapping him on the shoulder. Toby quietly restrained them.

"Take care, George," Toby said. "Go well, hear me?"

Smiley heard Toby's team leave one by one until only Peter Guillam remained. Walking a short way back along the embankment, almost to where the cross stood, Smiley took another look at the bridge, as if to establish whether anything had changed, but clearly it had not, and though the wind appeared a little stronger, the snow was still swirling in all directions.

Peter Guillam touched his arm.

"Come on, old friend," he said. "It's bedtime."

From long habit, Smiley had taken off his spectacles and was absently polishing them on the fat end of his tie, even though he had to delve for it among the folds of his tweed coat.

"George, you won," said Guillam, as they walked slowly towards the car.

"Did I?" said Smiley. "Yes. Yes, well I suppose I did."

Silverview
A Novel

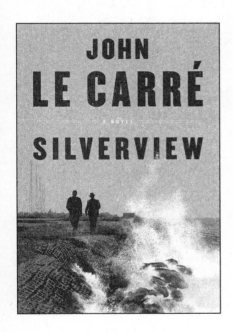

Julian Lawndsley has renounced his high-flying job in the city for a simpler life running a bookshop in a small English seaside town. But Edward, a Polish émigré living in Silverview, the big house on the edge of town, seems to know a lot about Julian's family and is quite interested in his new career. When a London spy chief receives a letter warning him of a dangerous leak, the investigations lead him to this quiet town. In his inimitable voice, John le Carré seeks to answer the question of what we truly owe to the people we love.

"The plot unfolds with as much cryptic cunning as a reader could want . . . Enjoyable throughout, written with grace, and a welcome gift from the past." —*The Wall Street Journal*

VIKING PENGUIN BOOKS

PENGUIN BOOKS

THE HONOURABLE SCHOOLBOY

JOHN LE CARRÉ was born in 1931. For six decades, he wrote novels that came to define our age. The son of a con man, he spent his childhood between boarding school and the London underworld. At sixteen he found refuge at the university of Bern, then later at Oxford. A spell of teaching at Eton led him to a short career in British Intelligence (MI5&6). He published his debut novel, *Call for the Dead*, in 1961 while still a secret servant. His third novel, *The Spy Who Came in from the Cold*, secured him a worldwide reputation, which was consolidated by the acclaim for his trilogy *Tinker Tailor Soldier Spy*, *The Honourable Schoolboy*, and *Smiley's People*. At the end of the Cold War, le Carré widened his scope to explore an international landscape including the arms trade and the War on Terror. His memoir, *The Pigeon Tunnel*, was published in 2016 and the last George Smiley novel, *A Legacy of Spies*, appeared in 2017. He died on December 12, 2020.

ALSO BY JOHN LE CARRÉ

JOHN LE CARRÉ

THE HONOURABLE SCHOOLBOY

PENGUIN BOOKS

PENGUIN BOOKS
An imprint of Penguin Random House LLC
penguinrandomhouse.com

First published in the United States of America by Alfred A. Knopf,
an imprint of Penguin Random House LLC, 1977
Published in Penguin Books 2011

22nd Printing

Grateful acknowledgment is made to Random House, Inc., and to Faber & Faber Ltd.
for permission to reprint four lines of "September 1, 1939" from *The Collected
Poetry of W. H. Auden* by W. H. Auden. Copyright 1940 by W. H. Auden.

PUBLISHER'S NOTE
This is a work of fiction. Names, characters, places, and incidents are either the product
of the author's imagination or are used fictitiously, and any resemblance to actual persons, living
or dead, business establishments, events, or locales is entirely coincidental.

ISBN 9780143119739 (paperback)
ISBN 9781101528754 (ebook)
CIP data available

Printed in the United States of America

For Jane, who bore the brunt,
put up with my presence and
absence alike, and made it all possible

I and the public know
What all schoolchildren learn,
Those to whom evil is done
Do evil in return.

—W. H. AUDEN

FOREWORD

Cornwall, 1977

I offer my warm thanks to the many generous and hospitable people who found time to help me with my research for this novel.

In Singapore, Alwyne (Bob) Taylor, the *Daily Mail* correspondent; Max Vanzi, of U.P.I.; Peter Simms, then of *Time;* and Bruce Wilson, of the *Melbourne Herald.*

In Hong Kong, Sydney Liu, of *Newsweek;* Bing Wong, *of Time;* H. D. S. Greenway, of the *Washington Post;* Anthony Lawrence, of the B.B.C.; Richard Hughes, then of the *Sunday Times;* Donald A. Davis and Vic Vanzi, of U.P.I.; and Derek Davies and his staff at the *Far Eastern Economic Review,* notably Leo Goodstadt. I must also acknowledge with gratitude the exceptional co-operation of Major General Penfold and his team at the Royal Hong Kong Jockey Club, who gave me the run of Happy Valley Racecourse and showed me much kindness without once seeking to know my purpose. I wish I could also name the several officials of the Hong Kong government, and members of the Royal Hong Kong Police, who opened doors for me at some risk of embarrassment to themselves.

In Phnom Penh, my genial host Baron Walther von Marschall took marvellous care of me, and I could never have managed without the wisdom of Kurt Furrer and Madame Yvette Pierpaoli, both of Suisindo Shipping & Trading Co., and currently in Bangkok.

But my special thanks must be reserved for those who put up with me the longest: for my friend David Greenway, of the *Washington Post*, who allowed me to follow in his distinguished shadow through Laos, North East Thailand, and Phnom Penh; and for Peter Simms, who, before settling in Hong Kong, guided my eye through unfamiliar territory and helped me with much of the legwork. To them, to Bing Wong, and to certain Hong Kong Chinese friends who, I believe, will prefer to remain anonymous, I owe a great debt.

Last there is the great Dick Hughes, whose outward character and mannerisms I have shamelessly exaggerated for the part of old Craw. Some people, once met, simply elbow their way into a novel and sit there till the writer finds them a place. Dick is one. I am sorry I could not obey his urgent exhortation to libel him to the hilt. My cruellest efforts could not prevail against the affectionate nature of the original.

And since none of these good people had any more notion than I did, in those days, of how the book would turn out, I must be quick to absolve them from my misdemeanours.

Terry Mayers, a veteran of the British Karate Team, advised me on certain alarming skills. And for Miss Nellie Adams, for her stupendous bouts of typing, no praise is enough.

INTRODUCTION

John le Carré

July 1989

A clever English writer once remarked that he wrote in order to have something to read in his old age. At fifty-seven I have yet to count myself old, but there is no doubt that in the thirteen years since I began this book, history has aged perceptibly. Thirteen years ago the Soviet Union was still locked in the ice of a slothful and corrupt oligarchy, and the puritanically minded leaders of the new China had turned their backs on their old ally and mentor in contempt. Today it is the Soviet Union which is in the throes of redefining the great Proletarian Revolution, if there ever really was one, while the blood of heroic young Chinese men and women who asked peaceably for similar redefinition of their political identity lies thick on Tiananmen Square, however many times the Army's water-cannons try to wash it away.

So if you read this book, be warned. You are reading an historical novel, written on the hoof, in a climate so altered that I for one would not know how to recapture any part of it if I were to try to tell you the same story in recollection today.

There is another reason why I might be tempted back to this book in my old age, and that is its fragile recognition of the man I was at the time. *The Honourable Schoolboy* was the first book I wrote on location, and the first, but not the last, for which I put on the non-uniform of a field reporter in order to obtain my experiences and my information. It commemorates the first time I saw shots exchanged in the heat of battle, or succoured a wounded soldier, or smelt the stench of old blood in the fields. It tells therefore of a certain growing up, but also of a certain growing down, for war is nothing if not a return to childhood.

Thus when Jerry Westerby, my hero, takes his taxi-ride to the battle front a few kilometres outside Phnom Penh, and involuntarily finds himself behind Khmer Rouge lines, I was sitting much where he sat, in the same taxi, with my heart in my mouth, drumming my fingers on the same dashboard and offering the same prayers to my Maker. When Jerry visits an opium den or entrusts himself to the flying skills of an intoxicated Chinese opium pilot in an aeroplane that would not have passed muster in a scrap-auction, he is the beneficiary of my own timid adventurings. Which means only that, in the space of a few months, I shared the perils that any good reporter will take in his stride in a single afternoon.

I remember only one occasion when I chickened, but it does duty for those other occasions I have conveniently forgotten. With H. D. S. Greenway, then of the *Washington Post*, I was proposing to take a train from Nakhomphenom, in North-East Thailand, back to Bangkok. We had come from Laos and had been roughing it for a week. We had shared some rich but unnerving encounters in the insurgency area, not least with an American-trained Thai colonel of Special Forces whom you will meet in the later chapters of the book and who carried more armament on his person than anybody I have ever seen before or since. As we approached the ticket office, Greenway asked me wearily whether my quest for material required us to travel in the poorest part of the train. I was still hesitating when he came up with the solution: "Tell you what. We'll travel First and leave Smiley to sweat it out in Third." And so we did, and consequently arrived in Bangkok in good enough shape to celebrate the publication of *Tinker, Tailor, Soldier, Spy*.

Why else might I pick up this book ten years from now? The answer is like a sad smile in my memory. For the vanished Cambodia. For the vanished Phnom Penh, the last of Joseph Conrad's river ports to go to the devil. For the scent of cooking oil and night flowers and the clamour of the bullfrogs as we ate our ridiculously wonderful French-Khmer meals just a few miles from the predatory armies that were about to devastate the city. For the insinuating murmur of the street girls perched up in the backs of their cyclos, as they ticked past us in the hot dark. For the memory, in short, of the dying days of French colonialism, before the vengeance of the terrible Pol Pot and his Khmer Rouge swept it all away for good or bad.

As to Hong Kong—is that all history too? Even as I write, Mrs. Thatcher's Foreign Secretary is in the Colony, bravely explaining why Britain can do nothing for a people she has dined off for a hundred and fifty years. Only betrayal, it seems, is timeless.

THE HONOURABLE
SCHOOLBOY

PART I

Winding the Clock

1

How the Circus Left Town

Afterwards, in the dusty little corners where London's secret servants drink together, there was argument about where the Dolphin case history should really begin. One crowd, led by a blimpish fellow in charge of microphone transcription, went so far as to claim that the fitting date was some sixty years ago, when "that arch-cad Bill Haydon" was born into the world under a treacherous star. Haydon's very name struck a chill into them. It does so even today. For it was this same Haydon who, while still at Oxford, was recruited by Karla the Russian as a "mole" or "sleeper"—or, in English, agent of penetration—to work against them. And who with Karla's guidance entered their ranks and spied on them for thirty years or more. And whose eventual discovery—thus the line of reasoning—brought the British so low that they were forced into a fatal dependence upon their American sister service, whom they called in their own strange jargon "the Cousins." The Cousins changed the game entirely, said the blimpish fellow, much as he might have deplored power tennis or bodyline bowling. And ruined it too, said his seconds.

To less-flowery minds, the true genesis was Haydon's unmasking by George Smiley and Smiley's consequent appointment as caretaker chief of the betrayed service, which occurred in the late November of 1973. Once George had got Karla under his skin, they said, there was no stopping him; the rest was inevitable. Poor old George: but what a mind under all that burden!

One scholarly soul, a researcher of some sort—in the jargon, a "burrower"—even insisted, in his cups, upon January 26, 1841, as the natural date, when a certain Captain Elliot of the Royal Navy took a landing party to a fog-laden rock called Hong Kong at the mouth of the Pearl River and a few days later proclaimed it a British colony. With Elliot's arrival, said the scholar, Hong Kong became the headquarters of Britain's opium trade to China, and in consequence one of the pillars of the Imperial economy. If the British had not invented the opium market—he said, not entirely serious—then there would have been no case, no ploy, no dividend; and therefore no renaissance of the Circus following Bill Haydon's traitorous depredations.

Whereas the hard men—the grounded fieldmen, the trainers, and the case officers who made their own murmured caucus always—they saw the question solely in operational terms. They pointed to Smiley's deft footwork in tracking down Karla's paymaster in Vientiane; to Smiley's handling of the girl's parents; and to his wheeling and dealing with the reluctant barons of Whitehall, who held the operational purse strings and dealt out rights and permissions in the secret world. Above all, to the wonderful moment where he turned the operation round on its own axis. For these pros, the case was a victory of technique. Nothing more. They saw the shot-gun marriage with the Cousins as just another skilful bit of tradecraft in a long and delicate poker game. As to the final outcome: to hell. The king is dead, so long live the next one.

The debate continues wherever old comrades meet, though the name of Jerry Westerby, understandably, is seldom mentioned. Occasionally, it is true, somebody does, out of foolhardiness or sentiment or plain forgetfulness, dredge it up, and there is atmosphere for a moment; but it passes. Only the other day a young probationer just out of the Circus's refurbished training school at Sarratt—in the jargon again, "the Nursery"—piped it out in the under-thirties bar, for instance. A watered-down version of the Dolphin case had recently been introduced at Sarratt as material for syndicate discussion—even playlets—and the poor boy, still very green, was brimming with excitement to discover he was in the know. "But my *God*," he protested, enjoying the kind of fool's freedom sometimes granted to naval midshipmen in the wardroom, "my *God*, why does nobody seem to recognise Westerby's part in the affair? If *anybody* carried the load, it was Jerry Westerby. He was the spearhead. Well, wasn't he? Frankly?" Except, of course, he did not utter the name "Westerby," or "Jerry" either, not least because he did not know them; but used instead the cryptonym allocated to Jerry for the duration of the case.

Peter Guillam fielded this loose ball. Guillam is tall and tough and graceful, and probationers awaiting first posting tend to look up to him as some sort of Greek god.

"Westerby was the stick that poked the fire," he declared curtly, ending the silence. "Any fieldman would have done as well, some a damn sight better."

When the boy still did not take the hint, Guillam rose and went over to him and, very pale, snapped into his ear that he should fetch himself another drink, if he could hold it, and thereafter guard his tongue for several days or weeks. Whereupon the conversation returned once more to the topic of dear old George Smiley, surely the last of the *true* greats, and what was he doing with himself these days, back in retirement? So many lives he had led; so much to recollect in tranquillity, they agreed.

"George went five times round the moon to our one," someone declared loyally, a woman.

Ten times, they agreed. Twenty! *Fifty!* With hyperbole, Westerby's shadow mercifully receded. As in a sense, so did George Smiley's. Well, George had a marvellous innings, they would say. At *his* age what could you expect?

* * *

Perhaps a more realistic point of departure is a certain typhoon Saturday in mid-1974, three o'clock in the afternoon, when Hong Kong lay battened down waiting for the next onslaught. In the bar of the Foreign Correspondents' Club, a score of journalists, mainly from former British colonies—Australian, Canadian, American—fooled and drank in a mood of violent idleness, a chorus without a hero. Thirteen floors below them, the old trams and double-deckers were caked in the mud-brown sweat of building dust and smuts from the chimney stacks in Kowloon. The tiny ponds outside the high-rise hotels prickled with slow, subversive rain. And in the men's room, which provided the Club's best view of the harbour, young Luke, the Californian, was ducking his face into the hand-basin, washing the blood from his mouth.

Luke was a wayward, gangling tennis player, an old man of twenty-seven who, until the American pull-out, had been the star turn in his magazine's Saigon stable of war reporters. When you knew he played tennis, it was hard to think of him doing anything else, even drinking. You imagined him at the net, uncoiling and smashing everything to kingdom come; or serving aces between double faults. His mind, as he sucked and spat, was fragmented by drink and mild concussion— Luke would probably have used the war word "fragged"—into several lucid parts. One part was occupied with a Wanchai bar-girl called Ella, for whose sake he had punched the pig policeman on the jaw and suffered the inevitable consequences. With the minimum necessary force, Superintendent Rockhurst, known otherwise as "the Rocker," who was this minute relaxing in a corner of the bar after his exertions, had knocked Luke cold and kicked him smartly in the ribs. Another part of Luke's mind was on something his Chinese landlord had said to him this morning when he called to complain of the noise of Luke's gramophone, and had stayed to drink a beer.

A scoop of some sort, definitely. But what sort?

He retched again, then peered out of the window. The junks were lashed behind the barriers and the Star Ferry had stopped running. A veteran British frigate lay at anchor, and Club rumours said Whitehall was selling it.

"Should be putting to sea," he muttered confusedly, recalling some bit of naval lore he had picked up in his travels. "Frigates put to sea in typhoons. Yes, *sir*."

The hills were slate under the stacks of black cloud-bank. Six months ago, the sight would have had him cooing with pleasure. The harbour, the din, even the skyscraper shanties that clambered from the sea's edge upwards to the Peak: after Saigon, Luke had ravenously embraced the whole scene. But all he saw today was a smug, rich British rock run by a bunch of plum-throated traders whose horizons went no farther than their belly-lines. The Colony had therefore become for him exactly what it was already for the rest of the journalists: an air-field, a telephone, a laundry, a bed. Occasionally—but never for long—a woman. Where even experience had to be imported. As to the wars which for so long had been his addiction, they were as remote from Hong Kong as they were from London or New York. Only the Stock Exchange showed a token sensibility, and on Saturdays it was closed anyway.

"Think you're going to live, ace?" asked the shaggy Canadian cowboy, coming to the stall beside him. The two men had shared the pleasures of the Tet offensive.

"Thank you, dear, I feel perfectly topping," Luke replied, in his most exalted English accent.

Luke decided it really was important for him to remember what Jake Chiu had said to him over the beer this morning, and suddenly, like a gift from heaven, it came to him.

"I remember!" he shouted. "Jesus, cowboy, I remember! Luke, you remember! My brain! It works! Folks, give ear to Luke!"

"Forget it," the cowboy advised. "That's badland out there today, ace. Whatever it is, forget it."

But Luke kicked open the door and charged into the bar, arms flung wide.

"Hey! Hey! *Folks!*"

Not a head turned. Luke cupped his hands to his mouth.

"Listen, you drunken bums, I got *news.* This is fantastic. Two bottles of Scotch a day and a brain like a razor. Someone give me a bell."

Finding none, he grabbed a tankard and hammered it on the bar rail, spilling the beer. Even then, only the dwarf paid him the slightest notice.

"So what's happened, Lukie?" whined the dwarf, in his queeny Greenwich Village drawl. "Has Big Moo gotten hiccups again? I can't bear it."

Big Moo was Club jargon for the Governor, and the dwarf was Luke's chief of bureau. He was a pouchy, sullen creature, with disordered hair that wept in black strands over his face, and a silent way of popping up beside you. A year back, two Frenchmen, otherwise rarely seen there, had nearly killed him for a chance remark he had made on the origins of the mess in Vietnam. They took him to the lift, broke his jaw and several of his ribs, then dumped him in a heap on the ground floor and came back to finish their drinks. Soon afterwards the Australians did a similar job on him when he made a silly accusation about their token military involvement in the war. He suggested that Canberra had done a deal with President Johnson to keep the Australian boys in Vung Tau, which was a picnic, while the Americans did the real fighting elsewhere. Unlike the French, the Australians didn't even bother to use the lift. They just beat the hell out of the dwarf where he stood, and when he fell they added a little more of the same. After that, he learned when to keep clear of certain people in Hong Kong. In times of persistent fog, for instance. Or when the water was cut to four hours a day. Or on a typhoon Saturday.

Otherwise the Club was pretty much empty. For reasons of prestige, the top correspondents steered clear of the place anyway. A few businessmen, who came for the flavour pressmen give; a few girls, who came for the men. A couple of war tourists in fake battle-drill. And in his customary corner, the awesome Rocker, Superintendent of Police, ex-Palestine, ex-Kenya, ex-Malaya, ex-Fiji, an implacable war-horse, with a beer, one set of slightly reddened knuckles, and a weekend copy of the *South China Morning Post*. The Rocker, people said, came for the class.

At the big table at the centre, which on weekdays was the preserve of United Press International, lounged the Shanghai Junior Baptist Conservative Bowling Club, presided over by mottled old Craw, the Australian, enjoying its usual Saturday tournament. The aim of the contest was to pitch a screwed-up napkin across the room and lodge it in the wine rack. Every time you succeeded, your competitors bought you the bottle and helped you drink it. Old Craw growled the orders to fire, and an elderly Shanghainese waiter, Craw's favourite, wearily manned the butts and served the prizes. The game was not a zestful one that day, and some members were not bothering to throw. Nevertheless this was the group Luke selected for his audience.

"Big Moo's *wife's* got hiccups!" the dwarf insisted. "Big Moo's wife's *horse* has got hiccups! Big Moo's wife's horse's *groom's* got hiccups! Big Moo's wife's horse's—"

Striding to the table, Luke leapt straight onto it with a crash, breaking several glasses and cracking his head on the ceiling in the process. Framed up there against the south window in a half-crouch, he was out of scale to everyone: the dark mist, the dark shadow of the Peak behind it, and this giant filling the whole foreground. But they went on pitching and drinking as if they hadn't seen him. Only the Rocker glanced in Luke's direction, once, before licking a huge thumb and turning to the cartoon page.

"Round three," Craw ordered, in his rich Australian accent. "Brother Canada, prepare to fire. *Wait*, you slob. Fire."

A screwed-up napkin floated toward the rack, taking a high trajectory. Finding a cranny, it hung a moment, then flopped to the ground. Egged on by the dwarf, Luke began stamping on the table and more glasses fell. Finally he wore his audience down.

"Your Graces," said old Craw, with a sigh. "Pray silence for my son. I fear he would have parley with us. Brother Luke, you have committed several acts of war today and one more will meet with our severe disfavour. Speak clearly and concisely omitting no detail, however slight, and thereafter hold your water, sir."

In their tireless pursuit of legends about one another, old Craw was their Ancient Mariner. Craw had shaken more sand out of his shorts, they told each other, than most of them would walk over; and they were right. In Shanghai, where his career had started, he had been teaboy and city editor to the only English-speaking journal in the port. Since then, he had covered the Communists against Chiang Kai-shek and Chiang against the Japanese and the Americans against practically everyone. Craw gave them a sense of history in this rootless place. His style of speech, which at typhoon times even the hardiest might pardonably find irksome, was a genuine hangover from the thirties, when Australia provided the bulk of journalists in the Orient, and the Vatican, for some reason, the jargon of their companionship.

So Luke, thanks to old Craw, finally got it out.

"Gentlemen! Dwarf, you damn Polack, let go of my foot! Gentlemen." He paused to dab his mouth with a handkerchief. "The house known as High Haven is for sale and His Grace Tufty Thesinger has flown the coop."

Nothing happened, but he didn't expect much anyway. Journalists are not given to cries of amazement or even incredulity.

"High Haven," Luke repeated sonorously, "is up for grabs. Mr. Jake Chiu, the well-known and popular real-estate entrepreneur, more familiar to you as my personal irate landlord, has been charged by Her Majesty's majestic government to *dispose* of High Haven. To wit, peddle. Let me go, you Polish bastard, I'll kill you!"

The dwarf had toppled him. Only a flailing, agile leap saved him from injury. From the floor, Luke hurled more abuse at his assailant. Meanwhile, Craw's large head had turned to Luke, and his moist eyes fixed on him a baleful stare that seemed to go on forever. Luke began to wonder which of Craw's many laws he might have sinned against. Beneath his various disguises, Craw was a complex and solitary figure, as everyone round the table knew. Under the willed roughness of his manner lay a love of the East which seemed sometimes to string him tighter than he could stand, so that there were months when he would disappear from sight altogether and, like a sulky elephant, go off on his private paths until he was once more fit to live with.

"Don't burble, Your Grace, do you mind?" said Craw at last, and tilted back his big head imperiously. "Refrain from spewing low-grade bilge into highly salubrious water, will you, Squire? High Haven's the spookhouse. Been the spookhouse for years. Lair of the lynx-eyed Major Tufty Thesinger, formerly of Her Majesty's Rifles, presently Hong Kong's Lestrade of the Yard. Tufty wouldn't fly the coop. He's a hood, not a tit. Give my son a drink, Monsignor"—this to the Shanghainese barman—"he's wandering."

Craw intoned another fire order and the Club returned to its intellectual pursuits. The truth was, there was little new to these great spy scoops by Luke. He had a long reputation as a failed spook-watcher, and his leads were invariably disproved. Since Vietnam, the stupid lad saw spies under every carpet. He believed the world was run by them, and much of his spare time, when he was sober, was spent hanging round the Colony's numberless battalions of thinly disguised China-watchers, and worse, who infested the enormous American Consulate up the hill. So if it hadn't been such a listless day, the matter would probably have rested there. As it was, the dwarf saw an opening to amuse, and seized it.

"Tell us, Lukie," he suggested, with a queer upward twisting of the hands, "are they selling High Haven with *contents* or *as found?*"

The question won him a round of applause. Was High
Haven worth more with its secrets or without?

"Do they sell it with *Major Thesinger?*" the South African
photographer pursued, in his humourless singsong, and there
was more laughter still, though it was no more affectionate. The
photographer was a disturbing figure, crew cut and starved, and
his complexion was pitted like the battlefields he loved to haunt.
He came from Cape Town, but they called him Deathwish the
Hun. The saying was, he would bury all of them, for he stalked
them like a mute.

For several diverting minutes now, Luke's point was lost
entirely under a spate of Major Thesinger stories and Major
Thesinger imitations, in which all but Craw joined. It was
recalled that the Major had made his first appearance in the
Colony as an importer, with some fatuous cover down among
the docks; only to transfer, six months later, quite improbably,
to the services' list and, complete with his staff of pallid clerks
and doughy, well-bred secretaries, decamp to the said spookhouse as somebody's replacement.

In particular, the Major's *tête-à-tête* luncheons were described,
to which, as it now turned out, practically every journalist listening had at one time or another been invited. And which
ended with laborious proposals over brandy, including such
wonderful phrases as: "Now, look here, old man, if you should
ever bump into an interesting Chow from over the river, you
know—one with *access*, follow me?—just you remember High
Haven!" Then the magic telephone number—the one that
"rings spot on my desk, no middle men, tape-recorders, nothing, right?"—which a good half-dozen of them seemed to have
in their diaries: "Here, pencil this one on your cuff; pretend
it's a date or a girl-friend or something. Ready for it? Hong
Kong-side five zero two four . . ."

Having chanted the digits in unison, they fell quiet. Somewhere a clock chimed for three-fifteen. Luke slowly stood up
and brushed the dust from his jeans. The old Shanghainese

waiter gave up his post by the racks and reached for the menu, in the hope that someone might eat. For a moment, uncertainty overcame them. The day was forfeit. It had been so since the first gin.

In the background, a low growl sounded as the Rocker ordered himself a generous luncheon: "And bring me a cold beer, *cold*, you hear, boy? *Muchee coldee. Chop chop.*" The Superintendent had his way with natives and said this every time. The quiet returned.

"Well, there you are, Lukie," the dwarf called, moving away. "That's how you win your Pulitzer, I guess. Congratulations, darling. Scoop of the year."

"Ah, go impale yourselves, the bunch of you," said Luke carelessly and started to make his way down the bar to where two sallow blond girls sat, army daughters on the prowl. "Jake Chiu showed me the damn letter of instruction, didn't he? On Her Majesty's damn Service, wasn't it? Damn crest on the top, lion screwing a goat. Hi, sweethearts, remember me? I'm the kind man who bought you the lollipops at the fair."

"Thesinger don't answer," Deathwish the Hun sang mournfully from the telephone. "Nobody don't answer. Not Thesinger, not his duty man. They disconnected the line." In the excitement, or the monotony, no one had noticed Deathwish slip away.

Till now, old Craw the Australian had lain dead as a dodo. Now he looked up sharply.

"Dial it again, you fool," he ordered, tart as a drill sergeant.

With a shrug, Deathwish dialled Thesinger's number a second time, and a couple of them went to watch him do it. Craw stayed put, watching from where he sat. There were two instruments. Deathwish tried the second, but with no better result.

"Ring the operator," Craw ordered across the room to them. "Don't stand there like a pregnant banshee. Ring the operator, you African ape!"

Number disconnected, said the operator.

"Since when, man?" Deathwish demanded, into the mouth-piece.

No information available, said the operator.

"Maybe they got a new number then, right, man?" Death-wish howled, still at the luckless operator. No one had ever seen him so involved. Life for Deathwish was what happened at the end of a viewfinder: such passion was only attributable to the typhoon.

No information available, said the operator.

"Ring Shallow Throat," Craw ordered, now quite furious. "Ring every damned striped-pants in the Colony!"

Deathwish shook his long head uncertainly. Shallow Throat was the official government spokesman, a hate-object to them all. To approach him for anything was bad face.

"Here, give him to me," said Craw and, rising to his feet, shoved them aside to get to the phone and embark on the lugu-brious courtship of Shallow Throat. "Your devoted Craw, sir, at your service. How's Your Eminence in mind and health? Charmed, sir, charmed. And the wife and veg, sir? All eating well, I trust? No scurvy or typhus? Good. Well now, perhaps you'll have the benison to advise me why the hell Tufty Thesinger's flown the coop?"

They watched him, but his face had set like rock, and there was nothing more to read there.

"And the same to you, sir!" he snorted finally, and slammed the phone back on its cradle so hard the whole table bounced. Then he turned to the old Shanghainese waiter. "Monsignor Goh, sir, order me a petrol donkey and oblige! Your Graces, get off your arses, the pack of you!"

"What the hell for?" said the dwarf, hoping to be included in the command.

"For a story, you snotty little Cardinal, for a story, Your lech-erous, alcoholic Eminences. For wealth, fame, women, and lon-gevity!"

His black mood was indecipherable to any of them.

"But what did Shallow Throat say that was so damn bad?" the shaggy Canadian cowboy asked, mystified.

The dwarf echoed him. "Yeah, so what did he say, Brother Craw?"

"He said, 'No comment,'" Craw replied with fine dignity, as if the words were the vilest slur upon his professional honour.

So up the Peak they went, leaving only the silent majority of drinkers to their peace: restive Deathwish the Hun went, long Luke, then the shaggy Canadian cowboy, very striking in his Mexican revolutionary moustache, the dwarf, attaching as ever, and finally old Craw and the two army girls—a plenary session of the Shanghai Junior Baptist Conservative Bowling Club, therefore, with ladies added, though the Club was sworn to celibacy. Amazingly, the jolly Cantonese driver took them all, a triumph of exuberance over physics. He even consented to give three receipts for the full fare, one for each of the journals represented, a thing no Hong Kong taxi-driver had been known to do before or since. It was a day to break all precedents. Old Craw sat in the front wearing his famous soft straw hat with Eton colours on the ribbon, bequeathed to him by an old comrade in his will. The dwarf was squeezed over the gear lever, the other three men sat in the back, and the two girls sat on Luke's lap, which made it hard for him to dab his mouth.

The Rocker did not see fit to join them. He had tucked his napkin into his collar in preparation for the Club's roast lamb and mint sauce and a lot of potatoes: "And another beer! But *cold* this time—hear that, boy? *Muchee coldee,* and bring it *chop chop.*"

But once the coast was clear, the Rocker also made use of the telephone, and spoke to Someone in Authority, just to be on the safe side, though they agreed there was nothing to be done.

The taxi was a red Mercedes, quite new, but nowhere kills a car faster than the Peak, climbing at no speed forever, air-conditioners at full blast. The weather continued awful. As the car sobbed slowly up the concrete cliffs, they were engulfed by a fog thick enough to choke on. When they got out, it was even worse. A hot, unbudgeable curtain had spread itself across the summit, reeking of petrol and crammed with the din of the valley. The moisture floated in hot fine swarms. On a clear day they would have had a view both ways, one of the loveliest on earth: northward to Kowloon and the blue mountains of the New Territories, which hid from sight the eight hundred million Chinese who lacked the privilege of British rule; southward to Repulse and Deep Water Bays and the open China Sea. High Haven, after all, had been built by the Royal Navy in the twenties in all the grand innocence of that service, to receive and impart a sense of power.

But that afternoon, if the house had not been set among the trees, and in a hollow where the trees grew tall in their effort to reach the sky, and if the trees had not kept the fog out, they would have had nothing to look at but the two white concrete pillars—one bearing bell buttons marked "DAY" and "NIGHT"—and the chained gates they supported. Thanks to the trees, however, they saw the house clearly, though it was set back fifty yards. They could pick out the drain-pipes, fire-escapes, and washing lines and they could admire the green dome which the Japanese army had added during their four years' tenancy.

Hurrying to the front in his desire to be accepted, the dwarf pressed the bell marked "DAY." A speaker was let into the pillar and they all stared at it, waiting for it to say something or, as Luke would have it, puff out pot-smoke. At the roadside, the Cantonese driver had switched on his radio full, and it was playing a whining Chinese love song, on and on. The second pillar was blank except for a brass plate announcing the Inter Services Liaison Staff, Thesinger's threadbare cover. Death-wish the Hun had produced a camera and was photographing as methodically as if he were on one of his native battlefields.

"Maybe they don't work Saturdays," Luke suggested while they continued to wait, at which Craw told him not to be bloody silly; spooks worked seven days a week and round the clock, he said. Also they never ate, apart from Tufty.

"*Good* afternoon to you," said the dwarf.

Pressing the night bell, he had put his twisted red lips to the vents of the speaker and affected an upper-class English accent, which, to give him credit, he managed surprisingly well.

"My name is Michael Hanbury-Steadly-Heamoor, and I'm personal bumboy to Big Moo. I should like, *pliss*, to speak to Major Thesinger on a matter of some urgency, *pliss*. There is a mushroom-shaped cloud the Major may not have noticed; it *appearce* to be forming over the *Pearl* River and it's spoiling Big Moo's golf. *Thenk* you. Will you kindly open the gate?"

One of the blond girls gave a titter.

"I didn't know he was a *Steadly*-Heamoor," she said.

Abandoning Luke, they had tethered themselves to the shaggy Canadian's arm, and spent a lot of time whispering in his ear.

"He's Rasputin," said one of the girls admiringly, stroking the back of his thigh. "I've seen the film. He's the spitten image, aren't you, Canada?"

Now everybody had a drink from Luke's flask while they regrouped and wondered what to do. From the direction of the parked cab, the driver's Chinese love song continued dauntlessly, but the speakers on the pillars said nothing at all. The dwarf pressed both bells at once, and tried an Al Capone threat.

"Now see here, Thesinger, we know you're in there. You come out with your hands raised, uncloaked, throw down your daggers—*Hey, watch it, you stupid cow!*"

The imprecation was addressed neither to the Canadian nor to old Craw—who was sidling toward the trees, apparently to meet a call of nature—but to Luke, who had decided to beat his way into the house. The gateway stood in a muddy service bay sheltered by dripping trees. On the far side was a pile of refuse, some new. Sauntering over to this in search of an illuminating clue, Luke had unearthed a piece of pig-iron made in the shape of an "S." Having carted it to the gate, though it must have weighed thirty pounds or more, he was holding it two-handed above his head and driving it against the staves, at which the gate tolled like a cracked bell.

Deathwish had sunk to one knee, his hollowed face clawed into a martyr's smile as he shot.

"Counting five, Tufty!" Luke yelled, with another shattering heave. "One . . ." He struck again. "Two . . ."

Overhead an assorted flock of birds, some very large, lifted out of the trees and flew in slow spirals, but the thunder of the valley and the boom of the gate drowned their screams. The taxi-driver was dancing about, clapping and laughing, his love song forgotten. Stranger still, in view of the menacing weather, an entire Chinese family appeared, pushing not one pram but two, and they began laughing, also—even the smallest child—holding their hands across their mouths to conceal their teeth. Till suddenly the Canadian cowboy let out a cry, shook off the girls, and pointed through the gates.

"For Lord's sakes, what the heck's Craw doing? Old buzzard's jumped the wire."

By now, whatever sense of normal scale there might have been had vanished. A collective madness had seized everyone. The drink, the black day, the claustrophobia had gone to their heads entirely. The girls fondled the Canadian with abandon, Luke continued his hammering, the Chinese were hooting with laughter, until with divine timeliness the fog lifted, temples of blue-black cloud soared directly above them, and a torrent of rain crashed into the trees. A second longer and it hit them, drenching them in the first swoop. The girls, suddenly half naked, flew laughing and shrieking for the Mercedes, but the male ranks held firm—even the dwarf held firm—staring through the films of water at the unmistakeable figure of the old Australian in his Etonian hat, standing in the shelter of the house under a rough porch that looked as if it were made for bicycles, though no one but a lunatic would bicycle up the Peak.

"Craw!" they screamed. "Monsignor! The bastard's scooped us!"

The din of the rain was deafening; the branches seemed to be cracking under its force. Luke had thrown aside his mad hammer. The shaggy cowboy went first, Luke and the dwarf followed, Deathwish with his smile and his camera brought up the tail, crouching and hobbling as he continued photographing blindly. The rain poured off them as it wanted, sloshing in red rivulets round their ankles as they pursued Craw's trail up a slope where the screech of bullfrogs added to the row. They scaled a bracken ridge, slithered to a halt before a barbed-wire fence, clambered through the parted strands, and crossed a low ditch. By the time they reached him, Craw was gazing at the green cupola, while the rain—despite the straw hat—ran busily off his jaw, turning his trim fawn suit into a blackened, shapeless tunic. He stood as if mesmerised, staring upward.

Luke, who loved him best, spoke first. "Your Grace? Hey, wake up! It's me—Romeo. Jesus Christ, what the hell's eating him?"

Suddenly concerned, Luke gently touched his arm. But still Craw didn't speak.

"Maybe he died standing up," the dwarf suggested, while grinning Deathwish photographed him on this happy off chance.

Like an old prize-fighter, Craw slowly rallied. "Brother Luke, we owe you a handsome apology, sir," he muttered.

"Get him back to the cab," said Luke, and began clearing a way for him, but the old boy refused to move.

"Tufty Thesinger. A good scout. Not a flyer—not sly enough for flight—but a good scout."

"Tufty Thesinger rest in peace," said Luke impatiently. "Let's go. Dwarf, move your ass."

"He's stoned," said the cowboy.

"Consider the clues, Watson," Craw resumed, after another pause for meditation, while Luke tugged at his arm and the rain came on still faster. "Remark first the empty cages over the window, whence air-conditioners have been untimely ripped. Parsimony, my son, a commendable virtue—especially, if I may say so, in a spook. Notice the dome there? Study it carefully, sir. Scratch marks. Not, alas, the footprints of a gigantic hound, but the scratch marks of wireless aerials removed by the frantic hand of round-eyes. Ever heard of a spookhouse without a wireless aerial? Might as well have a cathouse without a piano."

The rainfall had reached a crescendo. Huge drops thumped around them like shot. Craw's face was a mix of things Luke could only guess at. Deep in his heart it occurred to him that Craw really might be dying. Luke had seen little of natural death, and was very much on the alert for it.

"Maybe they just got rock-fever and split," he said, trying again to coax him to the car.

"Very possibly, Your Grace, very possibly indeed. It is certainly the season for rash, ungovernable acts."

"Home," said Luke, and pulled firmly at his arm. "Make a path there, will you? Stretcher party."

But the old man still lingered stubbornly for a last look at the English spookhouse flinching in the storm.

The Canadian cowboy filed first, and his piece deserved a better fate. He wrote it that night, while the girls slept in his bed. He guessed the story would go best as a magazine piece rather than straight news, so he built it round the Peak in general and only used Thesinger as a peg. He explained how the Peak was traditionally Hong Kong's Olympus—"the higher you lived on it, the higher you stood in society"—and how the rich British opium traders, Hong Kong's founding fathers, fled there to avoid the cholera and fever of the town; how even a couple of decades ago a person of Chinese race required a pass before he could set foot there. He described the history of High Haven, and lastly its reputation, fostered by the Chinese-language press, as a witches' kitchen of British Imperialist plots against Mao. Overnight the kitchen had closed and the cooks had vanished.

"Another conciliatory gesture?" he asked. "Appeasement? All part of Britain's low-profile policy toward the mainland? Or simply one more sign that in South East Asia, as everywhere else in the world, the British were having to come down from their mountaintop?"

His mistake was to select a heavy English Sunday paper, which occasionally ran his pieces. The D notice forbidding all reference to these events was there ahead of him. "REGRET YOUR NICE HAVEN STORY UNPLACED," the editor cabled, and shoved it straight on the spike. A few days later, returning to his room, the cowboy found it ransacked. Also, for several weeks his telephone developed a sort of laryngitis, so that he never used it without including an obscene reference to Big Moo and his retinue.

Luke went home full of ideas, bathed, drank a lot of black coffee, and set to work. He telephoned airlines, government contacts, and a whole host of pale, over-brushed acquaintances in the U.S. Consulate, who infuriated him with arch and Delphic answers. He pestered furniture-removal firms which specialised in handling government contracts. By ten that night, he had, in his own words to the dwarf, whom he also telephoned several times, "proof-cooked five different ways" that Thesinger, his wife, and all the staff of High Haven had left Hong Kong by charter in the early hours of Thursday morning, bound for London. Thesinger's boxer dog, he learned by a happy chance, would follow by air cargo later in the week. Having made a few notes, Luke crossed the room, settled to his typewriter, bashed out a few lines, and dried up, as he knew he would.

He began in a rush, fluently: "Today a fresh cloud of scandal hangs over the embattled and non-elected government of

Britain's one remaining Asian colony. Hot on the latest revelations of graft in the police and civil service comes word that the Island's most hush-hush establishment, High Haven, base for Britain's cloak-and-dagger ploys against Red China, has been summarily shut down."

There, with a blasphemous sob of impotence, he stopped and pressed his face into his open hands. Nightmares: those he could stand. To wake, after so much war, shaking and sweating from unspeakable visions, with his nostrils filled with the stink of napalm on human flesh: in a way, it was a consolation to him to know that after all that pressing down, the floodgates of his feeling had burst. There had been times, experiencing those things, when he longed for the leisure to recover his powers of disgust. If nightmares were necessary in order to restore him to the ranks of normal men and women, then he could embrace them with gratitude. But not in the worst of his nightmares had it occurred to him that having written the war, he might not be able to write the peace. For six night hours, Luke fought with this awful deadness. Sometimes he thought of old Craw, standing there with the rain running off him, delivering his funeral oration: maybe *that* was the story? But whoever hung a story on the strange humour of a fellow hack?

Nor did the dwarf's own hashed-out version meet with much success, which made him very scratchy. On the face of it, the story had everything they asked for. It spoofed the British, it had *spy* written large, and for once it got away from the notion of America as the hangman of South East Asia. But all he had for a reply, after a five-day wait, was a terse instruction to stay on his rostrum and leave off trying to play the trumpet.

Which left old Craw. Though a mere side-show by comparison with the thrust of the main action, the timing of what Craw did, and did not do, remains to this day impressive. He filed nothing for three weeks. There was small stuff he should have handled but he didn't bother. To Luke, who was seriously concerned for him, he seemed at first to continue his mysterious decline. He lost his bounce and his love of fellowship entirely. He became snappish and at times downright unkind, and he barked bad Cantonese at the waiters—even at his favourite, Goh. He treated the Shanghai Bowlers as if they were his worst enemies, and recalled alleged slights they had long forgotten. Sitting alone at his window-seat, he was like an old boulevardier fallen on hard times, waspish, inward, slothful.

Then one day he disappeared, and when Luke called apprehensively at his apartment the old amah told him that "Whisky Papa runrun London fastee." She was a strange little creature and Luke was inclined to doubt her. A dull North German stringer for *Der Spiegel* reported sighting Craw in Vientiane, carousing at the Constellation bar, but again Luke wondered. Craw-watching had always been something of an insider sport, and there was prestige in adding to the general fund.

Till a Monday came, and around midday the old boy strolled into the Club wearing a new beige suit and a very fine buttonhole, all smiles and anecdotes once more, and went to work on the High Haven story. He spent money, more than his paper would normally have allowed him. He ate several jovial lunches with well-dressed Americans from vaguely titled United States agencies, some of them known to Luke. Wearing his famous straw hat, he took each separately to quiet, well-chosen restaurants. In the Club, he was reviled for diplomat-crawling, a grave crime, and this pleased him.

Next, a China-watchers' conference summoned him to Tokyo, and with hindsight it is fair to assume he used that visit to check out other parts of the story that was shaping for him. Certainly he asked old friends at the conference to unearth bits of fact for him when they got home to Bangkok, or Singapore, or Taipei, or wherever they came from, and they obliged because they knew he would have done the same for them. In an eerie way, he seemed to know what he was looking for before they found it.

The result appeared in its fullest version in a Sydney morning newspaper, which was beyond the long arm of Anglo-American censorship. By common consent, it recalled the master's vintage years. It ran to two thousand words. Typically, he did not lead with the High Haven story at all, but with the "mysteriously empty wing" of the British Embassy in Bangkok, which till a month ago had housed a strange body called the Seato Coordination Unit, as well as a Visa Section boasting six second secretaries. Was it the pleasures of the Soho massage parlours, the old Australian enquired sweetly, which lured the Thais to Britain in such numbers that six second secretaries were needed to handle their visa applications? Strange too, he mused, that since their departure and the closure of that wing, long queues of aspirant travellers had *not* formed outside the Embassy.

Gradually—he wrote at ease, but never carelessly—a surprising picture unfolded before his readers. He called British intelligence "the Circus." He said the name derived from the address of that organisation's secret headquarters, which overlooked a famous intersection of London streets. The Circus had not merely pulled out of High Haven, he said, but out of Bangkok, Singapore, Saigon, Tokyo, Manila, and Djakarta as well. And Seoul. Even solitary Taiwan was not immune, where an unsung British Resident was discovered to have shed three clerk-drivers and two secretarial assistants only a week before the article went to press.

"A hoods' Dunkirk," Craw called it, "in which charter DC-3s replaced the Kentish fishing fleets."

What had prompted such an exodus? Craw offered several nimble theories. Were we witnessing yet one more cut in British government spending? The writer was sceptical. In times of travail, Britain's tendency was to rely more, not less, on spies. Her entire Empire history urged her to do so. The thinner her trade routes, the more elaborate her clandestine efforts to protect them. The more feeble her colonial grip, the more desperate her subversion of those who sought to loosen it. No: Britain might be on the breadline, but the spies would be the last of her luxuries to go. Craw set up other possibilities and knocked them down. A gesture of *détente* toward mainland China? he suggested, echoing the cowboy's point. Certainly Britain would do anything under the sun to keep Hong Kong clear of Mao's anti-colonial zeal—short of giving up her spies.

Thus old Craw arrived at the theory he liked best: "Right across the Far Eastern chequerboard," he wrote, "the Circus is performing what is known in the spy-trade as a duck-dive."

But why?

The writer now quoted his "senior American prebends of the intelligence church militant in Asia." American intelligence agents generally, he said, and not just in Asia, were "hopping mad about lax security in the British organisations." They were hopping highest about the recent discovery of a top Russian spy—he threw in the correct trade name of "mole"—inside the Circus's London headquarters: a British traitor, whom they declined to name, but who, in the words of the senior prebends, had "compromised every Anglo-American clandestine operation worth a dime for the last twenty years." Where was the mole now? the writer had asked his sources. To which, with undiminished spleen, they had replied: "Dead. In Russia. And hopefully both."

Craw had never wanted for a wrap-up, but this one, to Luke's fond eye, had a real sense of ceremony about it. It was almost an assertion of life itself, if only of the secret life:

"Is Kim, the boy spy, vanished for good, then, from the legends of the East?" he asked. "Shall the English pundit never again stain his skin, slip into native costume, and silently take his place beside the village fires? Do not fear," he insisted, "the British will be back! The time-honoured sport of spot-the-spook will be with us once again! The spy is not dead: he sleepeth."

The piece appeared. In the Club, it was fleetingly admired, envied, forgotten. A local English-language paper with strong

American connections reprinted it in full, with the result that
the mayfly, after all, enjoyed another day of life. The old boy's
charity benefit, they said: a doffing of the cap before he passes
from the stage. Then the overseas network of the B.B.C. ran it,
and finally the Colony's own torpid radio network ran a version
of the B.B.C.'s version, and for a full day there was debate about
whether Big Moo had decided to take the muzzle off the local
news services. Yet even with this protracted billing, nobody—
not Luke, not even the dwarf—saw fit to wonder how the devil
the old man had known the back way into High Haven.

Which merely proved, if proof were ever needed, that journalists are no quicker than anybody else at spotting what goes
on under their noses. It was a typhoon Saturday, after all.

Within the Circus itself, as Craw had correctly called the seat
of British intelligence, reactions to Craw's piece varied according to how much was known by those who were doing the
reacting. In Housekeeping Section, for instance, which was
responsible for such tatters of cover as the Circus could gather
to itself these days, the old boy released a wave of pent-up fury
that can only be understood by those who have tasted the
atmosphere of a secret department under heavy siege. Even
otherwise tolerant spirits became savagely retributive. Treachery! Breach of contract! Block his pension! Put him on the
watch list! Prosecution the moment he returns to England!

Down the market a little, those less rabid about their security took a kindlier view, though it was still uninformed. Well,
well, they said a little ruefully, that was the way of it; name us a
joe who didn't blow his top now and then, and specially one
who'd been left in ignorance for as long as poor old Craw had.
And after all, he'd disclosed nothing that wasn't generally available, now had he? Really, those housekeeper people should show
a *little* moderation. Look how they went for poor Molly Meakin
the other night, sister to Mike and hardly out of ribbons, just
because she left a bit of blank stationery in her waste basket!

Only those at the inmost point saw things differently. To them, old Craw's article was a discreet masterpiece of disinformation; George Smiley at his best, they said. Clearly, the story had to come out, and all were agreed that censorship at any time was objectionable. Much better therefore to let it come out in the manner of our choosing. The right timing, the right amount, the right tone: a lifetime's experience, they agreed, in every brushstroke. But that was not a view which passed outside their set.

Back in Hong Kong—clearly, said the Shanghai Bowlers, the old boy, like the dying, had had a prophetic instinct of this— Craw's High Haven story turned out to be his swan-song. A month after it appeared, he had retired, not from the Colony but from his trade as a scribbler and from the Island too. Renting a cottage in the New Territories, he announced that he proposed to expire under a slant-eye heaven. For the Bowlers, he might as well have chosen Alaska. It was just too damn far, they said, to drive back when you were drunk. There was a rumour—untrue, since Craw's appetites did not run in that direction—that he had got himself a pretty Chinese boy as a companion. That was the dwarf's work: he did not like to be scooped by old men.

Only Luke refused to put him out of mind. Luke drove out to see him one mid-morning after night-shift. For the hell of it, and because the old buzzard meant a lot to him. Craw was happy as the day is long, he reported; quite his former vile self, but a bit dazed to be bearded by Luke without warning. He had a friend with him, not a Chinese boy, but a visiting fireman whom he introduced as George: a podgy, ill-sighted little body in very round spectacles who had apparently dropped in unexpectedly. Aside, Craw explained to Luke that this George was a back-room boy on a British newspaper syndicate he used to work for in the dark ages.

"Handles the geriatric side, Your Grace. Taking a swing through Asia."

Whoever he was, it was clear that Craw stood in awe of the podgy man, for he even called him "Your Holiness." Luke had felt he was intruding and left without getting drunk.

So there it was: Thesinger's moonlight flit; old Craw's near death and resurrection; his swan-song in defiance of so much hidden censorship; Luke's restless preoccupation with the secret world; the Circus's inspired exploitation of a necessary evil. Nothing planned but, as life would have it, a curtain-raiser to much that happened later. A typhoon Saturday; a ripple on the plunging, fetid, sterile, swarming pool that is Hong Kong; a bored chorus, still without a hero. And curiously, a few months afterwards, it fell once more to Luke, in his role of Shakespearean messenger, to announce the hero's coming. The news came over the house wire while he was on stand-by, and he published it to a bored audience with his customary fervour.

"Folks! Give ear! I have news! Jerry Westerby's back on the beat, men! Heading out East again, hear me, stringing for that same damn comic!"

"His Lordship," the dwarf cried at once, in mock ecstasy. "A desh of blue blood, I say, to raise the vulgar tone! 'Oorah for quality, I say." With a profane oath, he threw a napkin at the wine rack. "Jesus," he said, and emptied Luke's glass.

2

The Great Call

On the afternoon the telegram arrived, Jerry Westerby was hacking at his typewriter on the shaded side of the balcony of his run-down farmhouse, a sack of old books dumped at his feet. The envelope was brought by the black-clad person of the post-mistress, a craggy and ferocious peasant who, with the ebbing of traditional forces, had become the headman of the ragtag Tuscan hamlet. She was a wily creature, but today the drama of the occasion had the better of her, and despite the heat she fairly scampered up the arid track. In her ledger the historic moment of delivery was later put at six past five, which was a lie but gave it force. The real time was five exactly. Indoors, Westerby's scrawny girl, whom the village called "the orphan," was hammering at a stubborn piece of goat's meat, vehemently, the way she attacked everything. The greedy eye of the postmistress spotted her at the open window and from a good way off: elbows stuck out all ways and her top teeth jammed onto her lower lip—scowling, no doubt, as usual.

Whore, thought the postmistress passionately; now you have what you have been waiting for!

The radio was blaring Verdi; the orphan would hear only classical music, as the whole village had learned from the scene she had made at the tavern the evening when the blacksmith tried to choose rock music on the juke-box. She had thrown a

pitcher at him. So what with the Verdi, and the typewriter, and
the goat, said the postmistress, the row was so deafening that
even an Italian would have heard it.

Jerry sat like a locust on the wood floor, she recalled—
maybe he had one cushion—and he was using the book-sack as
a footstool. He sat splay-footed, typing between his knees. He
had bits of fly-blown manuscript spread round him, which
were weighted with stones against the red-hot breezes that
plagued his scalded hilltop, and a wicker flask of the local red
at his elbow, no doubt for the moments, known even to the
greatest artists, when natural inspiration failed him. He typed
the eagle's way, she told them later amid admiring laughter:
much circling before he swooped.

He wore what he always wore, whether he was loafing fruit-
lessly around his bit of paddock tilling the dozen useless olive
trees which the rogue Marcello had palmed off on him, or paddling down to the village with the orphan to shop, or sitting in
the tavern over a sharp one before embarking on the long climb
home: buckskin boots, which the orphan never brushed and
were consequently worn shiny at the toe; ankle socks, which she
never washed; a filthy shirt, once white; and grey shorts, which
looked as though they had been frayed by hostile dogs and
which an honest woman would long ago have mended. And he
greeted the postmistress with that familiar burry rush of words,
at once bashful and enthusiastic, which she did not understand
in detail, but only generally, like a news broadcast, and could
copy, through the black gaps of her decrepit teeth, with surprising flashes of fidelity.

"Mama Stefano, gosh, super, must be boiling. Here, sport,
wet your whistle," he exclaimed, while he slopped down the
brick steps with a glass of wine for her, grinning like a schoolboy, which was his nickname in the village: the schoolboy—a
telegram for the schoolboy, urgent from London! In nine
months, no more than a wad of paperback books and the weekly
scrawl from his child, and now out of a blue sky this monument

of a telegram, short like a demand, but fifty words prepaid for the reply! Imagine, fifty, the cost alone! Only natural that as many as possible should have tried their hand at reading it.

They had choked at first over "Honourable." "The *Honourable* Gerald Westerby." Why? The baker, who had been a prisoner of war in Birmingham, produced a battered dictionary: "having honour, title of courtesy given to the son of a nobleman." Of course. Signora Sanders, who lived across the valley, had already declared the schoolboy to be of noble blood. The second son of a press baron, she had said: *Lord* Westerby, a newspaper proprietor, dead. First the paper had died, then its owner—thus Signora Sanders, a wit; they had passed the joke round. Next "regret," which was easy. So was "advise." The postmistress was gratified to discover, against all expectation, how much good Latin the English had assimilated despite their decadence. The word "guardian" came harder, for it led to "protector," thence inevitably to unsavoury jokes among the menfolk, which the postmistress angrily quelled.

Till at last, step by step, the code was broken and the story out. The schoolboy had a guardian, meaning a substitute father. This guardian lay dangerously ill in hospital, demanding to see the schoolboy before he died. He wanted nobody else. Only Honourable Westerby would do. Quickly they filled in the rest of the picture for themselves: the sobbing family gathered at the bedside, the wife prominent and inconsolable, refined priests administering the last sacraments, valuables being locked away, and all over the house—in corridors, back kitchens—the same whispered words, "Westerby—where is Honourable Westerby?"

Lastly the telegram's signatories remained to be interpreted. There were three and they called themselves "solicitors," a word which triggered one more burst of dirty innuendo before "notary" was arrived at, and faces abruptly hardened. Holy Maria. If three notaries were involved, then so were large sums of money. And if all three had insisted upon signing, and prepaid that fifty-word reply to boot, then not just large but mountainous sums! Acres! Wagonloads! No wonder the orphan had clung to him so—the whore! Suddenly everyone was clamouring to make the hill-climb. Guido's Lambretta would take him as far as the water tank; Mario could run like a fox; Manuela, the chandler's girl, had a tender eye—the shadow of bereavement sat well on her. Repulsing all volunteers, and handing Mario a sharp cuff for his presumption, the postmistress locked the till and left her idiot son to mind the shop, though it meant twenty sweltering minutes and—if that cursed furnace of a wind was blowing up there—a mouthful of red dust for her toil.

They had not made enough of Jerry at first. She regretted this now as she laboured through the olive groves, but the error had its reasons. First, he had arrived in winter when the cheap buyers come. He arrived alone, but wearing the furtive look of someone who has recently dumped a lot of human cargo, such as children, wives, mothers; the postmistress had known men in her time, and she had seen that wounded smile too often not to recognise it in Jerry. "I am married but free," it said, and neither claim was true.

Second, the scented English major had brought him, a known pig who ran a property agency for exploiting peasants—yet another reason to spurn the schoolboy. The scented major showed him several desirable farmhouses, including one in which the postmistress herself had an interest—also, by coincidence, the finest—but the schoolboy settled instead for the pederast Franco's hovel stuck on this forsaken hilltop she was now ascending. The devil's hill, they called it; the devil came up here when hell became too cool for him. Slick Franco, of all people, who watered his milk and his wine and spent his Sundays simpering with popinjays in the town square! The inflated price was half a million lire, of which the scented major tried to steal a third, merely because there was a contract.

"And everyone knows why the major favoured slick Franco," she hissed through her frothing teeth, and her pack of supporters made knowing "tch-tch" noises at each other, till she again ordered them to shut up.

Also, as a shrewd woman, she distrusted something in Jerry's make-up. A hardness buried in the lavishness. She had seen it with Englishmen before, but the schoolboy was in a class by himself, and she distrusted him; she held him dangerous through his restless charm. Today, of course, one could put down those early failings to the eccentricity of a noble English writer, but at the time the postmistress had shown him no such indulgence.

"Wait till the summer," she had warned her customers in a snarl, soon after his first shambling visit to her shop—pasta, bread, fly-killer. "In the summer he'll find out what he's bought, the cretin." In the summer, slick Franco's mice would storm the bedroom, Franco's fleas would devour him alive, and Franco's pederastic hornets would chase him round the garden and the devil's red-hot wind would burn his parts to a frazzle. The water would run out, he would be forced to defecate in the fields like an animal. And when winter came round again the scented pig major could sell the house to another fool, at a loss to everyone but himself.

As to celebrity, in those first weeks the schoolboy showed not a shred of it. He never bargained, he had never heard of discounts, there was not even pleasure in robbing him. And when, in the shop, she drove him beyond his few miserable phrases of kitchen Italian, he did not raise his voice and bawl at her like the real English but shrugged happily and helped himself to whatever he wanted. A *writer*, they said; well, who was not? Very well, he bought quires of foolscap from her. She ordered more, he bought them. Bravo. He possessed books: a mildewed lot, by the look of them, which he carried in a grey jute sack like a poacher's, and before the orphan came they would see him striding off into the middle of nowhere, the book-sack slung over his shoulder, for a reading session. Guido had happened on him in the Contessa's forest, perched on a log like a toad and leafing through them one after another, as if they were all one

book and he had lost his place. He also possessed a typewriter
of which the filthy cover was a patchwork of worn-out luggage
labels: bravo again. Just as any long-hair who buys a paint pot
calls himself an artist: *that* sort of writer. In the spring, the
orphan came and the postmistress hated her too.

A redhead, which was half-way to whoredom for a start. Not
enough breast to nurse a rabbit, and worst of all a fierce eye for
arithmetic. They said he found her in the town: whore again.
From the first day, she had not let him out of her sight. Clung
to him like a child. Ate with him, and sulked; drank with him,
and sulked; shopped with him, picking up the language like a
thief, till they became a minor local sight together, the English
giant and his sulking wraith whore, trailing down the hill with
their rush basket—the schoolboy, in his tattered shorts, grinning at everyone, and the scowling orphan, in her whore's sack-
cloth with nothing underneath, so that though she was plain as
a scorpion the men stared after her to see her hard haunches
rock through the fabric. She walked with all her fingers locked
round his arm and her cheek against his shoulder, and she only
let go of him to pay out meanly from the purse she now controlled. When they met a familiar face, he greeted it for both
of them, flapping his vast free arm like a Fascist. And God help
the man who, on the rare occasion when she went alone, ventured a fresh word or a wolf call: she would turn and spit like a
gutter-cat, and her eyes burned like the devil's.

"And now we know why!" cried the postmistress very loud
as, still climbing, she mounted a false crest. "The orphan is
after his inheritance. Why else would a whore be loyal?"

It was the visit of Signora Sanders to her shop which had caused
Mama Stefano's dramatic reappraisal of the schoolboy's worth,
and of the orphan's motive. The Sanders was rich and bred
horses farther up the valley, where she lived with a lady friend,
known as the man-child, who wore close-cut hair and chain
belts. Their horses won prizes everywhere. The Sanders was

sharp and intelligent, and frugal in a way Italians liked, and she knew whoever was worth knowing of the few moth-eaten English scattered over the hills. She called ostensibly to buy a ham—a month ago, it must have been—but her real quest was for the schoolboy. Was it true? she asked. Signor *Gerald* Westerby, and living here in the village? A large man, pepper and salt hair, athletic, full of energy, an aristocrat, shy? Her father, the General, had known the family in England, she said; they had been neighbours in the country for a spell, the schoolboy's father and her own. The Sanders was considering paying him a visit. What were the schoolboy's circumstances? The postmistress muttered something about the orphan, but the Sanders was unperturbed.

"Oh, the Westerbys are *always* changing their women," she said with a laugh, and turned toward the door.

Dumfounded, the postmistress detained her, then showered her with questions.

But who was he? What had he done with his youth? A journalist, said the Sanders, and gave what she knew of the family background. The father, a flamboyant figure, fair-haired like the son, kept racehorses; she had met him again not long before his death and he was still a man. Like the son, he was never at peace: women and houses, changing them all the time; always roaring at someone, if not at his son then at someone across the street. The postmistress pressed harder. But in his own right— was the schoolboy distinguished in his own right? Well, he had certainly worked for some distinguished newspapers, put it that way, said the Sanders, her smile mysteriously broadening.

"It is not the English habit, as a rule, to accord distinction to journalists," she explained, in her classic Roman way of talking.

But the postmistress needed more, far more. His writing, his book, what was all *that* about? So long! So much thrown away! Basketsful, the rubbish carter had told her—for no one in his right mind would light a fire up there in summertime. Beth Sanders understood the intensity of isolated people, and knew that in barren places their intelligence must fix on tiny matters. So she tried, she really tried to oblige. Well, he certainly had *travelled* incessantly, she said, coming back to the counter and putting down her parcel. Today all journalists were travellers, of course—breakfast in London, lunch in Rome, dinner in Delhi—but Signor Westerby had been exceptional even by that standard. So perhaps it was a travel book, she ventured.

But *why* had he travelled, the postmistress insisted, for whom no journey was without a goal; *why?*

For the wars, the Sanders replied patiently; for wars, pestilence, and famine. "What else has a journalist to do these days, after all, but report life's miseries?" she asked.

The postmistress shook her head wisely, all her senses fixed upon the revelation: the son of a blond equestrian lord who bellowed, a mad traveller, a writer in distinguished newspapers! And was there a particular theatre? she asked—a corner of God's earth—in which he was a specialist? He was mostly in the East, the Sanders said after a moment's reflection. He had been everywhere, but there is a kind of Englishman for whom only the East is home. No doubt that was why he had come to Italy; some men go dull without the sun.

And some women too, the postmistress shrieked, and they had a good laugh.

Ah, the East, said the postmistress, with a tragic rolling of the head—war upon war, why didn't the Pope stop it? As Mama Stefano ran on this way, the Sanders seemed to remember something. She smiled slightly at first, and her smile grew. An exile's smile, the postmistress reflected, watching her; she is like a sailor remembering the sea.

"He used to drag a sackful of books around," she said. "We used to say he stole them from the big houses."

"He carries it now!" the postmistress cried, and told how Guido had stumbled on him in the Contessa's forest, the schoolboy, reading on the log.

"He had notions of becoming a *novelist*, I believe," the

Sanders continued, in the same vein of private reminiscence. "I remember his father telling us. He was *frightfully* angry. Roared all over the house."

"The schoolboy? The *schoolboy* was angry?" Mama Stefano exclaimed, now quite incredulous.

"No, no. The father." The Sanders laughed aloud; in the English social scale, she explained, novelists rated even worse than journalists. "Does he also paint still?"

"Paint? He is a painter?"

He tried, said the Sanders, but the father forbade that also. Painters were the lowest of *all* creatures, she said, amid fresh laughter; only the successful ones were remotely tolerable.

Soon after this multiple bombshell, the blacksmith—the same blacksmith who had been the target of the orphan's pitcher—reported having seen Jerry and the girl at the Sanders's stud, twice in one week, then three times, also eating there. And that the schoolboy had shown a great talent for horses, lunging and walking them with natural understanding—even the wildest. The orphan took no part, said the blacksmith. She sat in the shade with the man-child, either reading from the book-sack or watching him with her jealous, unblinking eyes; waiting, as they all now knew, for the guardian to die. And today the telegram!

Jerry had seen Mama Stefano from a long way off. He had that instinct; there was a part of him that never ceased to watch. A black figure hobbling inexorably up the dust path like a lame beetle in and out of the ruled shadows of the cedars, up the dry watercourse of slick Franco's olive groves, into their own bit of Italy, as he called it, all two hundred square metres of it, but big enough to hit a tethered tennis-ball round a pole on cool evenings when they felt athletic. He had seen very early the blue envelope she was waving, and he had even heard the sound of her mewing carrying crookedly over the other sounds of the valley: the Lambrettas and the band-saws. And his first gesture, without stopping his typing, was to steal a glance at the house to make sure the girl had closed the kitchen window to keep out the heat and the insects. Then, just as the postmistress later described, he went quickly down the steps to her, wineglass in hand, in order to head her off before she came too near.

He read the telegram slowly, once, bending over it to get the writing into shadow, and his face as Mama Stefano watched it became gaunt, and private, and an extra huskiness entered his voice as he laid one huge, cushioned hand on her arm.

"*La sera*," he managed, as he guided her back along the path. He would send his reply this evening, he meant. "*Molto grazie*, Mama. Super. Thanks very much. Terrific."

The other English managed *grazie tanto*, but not the schoolboy.

As they parted, she was still chattering wildly, offering him every service under the sun—taxis, porters, phone calls to the airport—and Jerry was vaguely patting the pockets of his shorts for small or large change; he had momentarily forgotten, apparently, that the girl looked after the money.

The schoolboy had received the news with bearing, the postmistress reported to the village. Graciously, to the point of escorting her part of the way back; bravely, so that only a woman of the world—and one who knew the English—would have read the aching grief beneath; distractedly, so that he had neglected to tip her. Or was he already acquiring the extreme parsimony of the very rich?

But how did the *orphan* behave, they asked. Did she not sob and cry to the Virgin, pretending to share his distress?

"He has yet to tell her," the postmistress whispered, recalling wistfully her one short glimpse of her, side-view, hammering at the meat. "He has *yet* to consider her position."

The village settled, waiting for the evening, and Jerry sat in the hornet field, gazing at the sea and winding the book-bag round and round, till it reached its limit and unwound itself.

First there was the valley, and above it stood the five hills in a half-ring, and above the hills ran the sea, which at that time of day was no more than a flat brown stain in the sky. The hornet field where he sat was a long terrace shored by stones, with a ruined barn at one corner which had given them shelter to picnic and sunbathe unobserved until the hornets nested in the wall. She had seen them when she was hanging out washing, and had run in to Jerry to tell him, and Jerry had unthinkingly grabbed a bucket of mortar from slick Franco's place and filled in all their entrances. Then called her down so that she could admire his handiwork: my man, how he protects me. In his memory he saw her exactly: shivering at his side, arms huddled across her body, staring at the new cement and listening to the crazed hornets inside and whispering, "Jesus, Jesus," too frightened to budge.

Maybe she'll wait for me, he thought.

He remembered the day he met her. He told himself that story often, because good luck was rare in Jerry's life where women were concerned, and when it happened he liked to roll it around the tongue, as he would say. A Thursday. He'd taken his usual lift to town in order to do a spot of shopping, or maybe to see a fresh set of faces and get away from the novel for a while; or maybe just to bolt from the screaming monotony of that empty landscape, which more often was like a prison to him, and a solitary one at that. Or conceivably he might just hook himself a woman, which occasionally he brought off by hanging round the bar of the tourist hotel. So he was sitting reading in the *trattoria* in the town square—a carafe, plate of ham, olives— and suddenly he became aware of this skinny, rangy kid, red-head, sullen face, and a brown dress like a monk's habit and a shoulder-bag made out of carpet stuff.

Looks naked without a guitar, he'd thought.

Vaguely, she reminded him of his daughter Cat, short for Catherine, but only vaguely, because he hadn't seen Cat for ten years, which was when his first marriage fell in. Quite why he hadn't seen her, he could even now not say. In the first shock of separation a confused sense of chivalry told him Cat would do better to forget him. Best if she writes me off. Put her heart where her home is. When her mother remarried, the case for self-denial seemed all the stronger. But sometimes he missed her very badly, and most likely that was why, having caught his interest, the girl held it. Did Cat go round like that, alone and spiked with tiredness? Had Cat got her freckles still, and a jaw like a pebble?

Later, the girl told him she'd jumped the wall. She'd got herself a governess job with some rich family in Florence. Mother was too busy with the lovers to worry about the kids, but the husband had lots of time for the governess. She'd grabbed what cash she could find and bolted, and here she was: no luggage, the police alerted, and using her last chewed banknote to buy herself one square meal before perdition.

There was not a lot of talent in the square that day—there never was, really—and by the time she sat down, that kid had got just about every able-bodied fellow in town giving her the treatment, from the waiters upwards, purring "beautiful missus" and much rougher stuff besides, of which Jerry missed the precise drift, but it had them all laughing at her expense. Then one of them tried to tweak her breast, at which Jerry got up and went over to her table. He was no great hero—quite the reverse, in his secret view—but a lot of things were going around in his mind, and it might just as well have been Cat who was getting shoved into a corner. So, yes: anger. He therefore clapped one hand on the shoulder of the small waiter who had made the dive for her, and one hand on the shoulder of the big one who had applauded such bravado, and he explained to them, in bad Italian, but in a fairly reasonable way, that they really must stop being pests and let the beautiful missus eat her meal in peace. Otherwise he would break their greasy little necks.

The atmosphere wasn't too good after that, and the little one seemed actually to be squaring for a fight, for his hand kept travelling toward a back pocket, and hitching at his jacket, till a final look at Jerry changed his mind for him. Jerry dumped some money on the table, picked up her bag for her, went back to collect his book-sack, and led her by the arm, all but lifting her off the ground, across the square to the Apollo.

"Are you English?" she asked on the way.

"Pips, core, the lot," Jerry snorted furiously, which was the first time he saw her smile. It was a smile definitely worth working for; her bony little face lit up like an urchin's through the grime.

So, simmered down, Jerry fed her, and with the advent of calm he began spinning the tale a bit, because after all those weeks without a focus it was natural he should make an effort to amuse. He explained that he was a newshound out to grass and now writing a novel, that it was his first shot, that he was scratching a long-standing itch, and that he had a dwindling pile of cash from a comic that had paid him redundancy—which was a giggle, he said, because he had been redundant all his life.

"Kind of golden handshake," he said. He had put a bit down for the house, loafed a bit, and now there was precious little gold left over. That was the second time she smiled. Encouraged, he touched on the solitary nature of the creative life: "But, Christ, you wouldn't believe the sweat of really—well, *really* getting it all to come *out*, sort of thing—"

"Wives?" she asked, interrupting him. For a moment, he had assumed she was tuning to the novel. Then he saw her waiting, suspicious eyes, so he replied cautiously, "None active," as if wives were volcanoes, which in Jerry's world they had been.

After lunch as they drifted, somewhat plastered, across the empty square, with the sun pelting straight down on them, she made her one declaration of intent: "Everything I own is in this bag, got it?" she asked. It was the shoulder-bag made out of carpet stuff. "That's the way I'm going to keep it. So just don't anybody give me anything I can't carry. Got it?"

When they reached his bus-stop she hung around, and when the bus came she climbed aboard after him and let him buy her a ticket, and when she got out at the village she climbed the hill with him, Jerry with his book-sack, the girl with her shoulder-bag, and that's how it was. Three nights and most of the days she slept, and on the fourth night she came to him. He was so unprepared for her that he had actually left his bedroom door locked; he had a bit of a thing about doors and windows, specially at night. So that she had to hammer on the door and shout, "I want to come into your bloody cot, for Christ's sake!" before he opened up.

"Just never lie to me," she warned, scrambling into his bed as if they were sharing a dormitory feast. "No words, no lies. Got it?"

As a lover, she was like a butterfly, he remembered—could have been Chinese. Weightless, never still, so unprotected he despaired of her. When the fireflies came out, the two of them knelt on the window-seat and watched them, and Jerry thought about the East. The cicadas shrieked and the frogs burped, and the lights of the fireflies ducked and parried round a central pool of blackness, and they would kneel there naked for an hour or more, watching and listening, while the hot moon drooped into the hill-crests. They never spoke on those occasions, or reached any conclusions that he was aware of. But he gave up locking his door.

The music and the hammering had stopped, but a din of church bells had started—he supposed for evensong. The valley was never quiet, but the bells sounded heavier because of the dew. He sauntered over to the swing-ball, teasing the rope away from the metal pillar, then with his old buckskin boot kicked at the grass around the base, remembering her lithe little body flying from shot to shot and the monk's habit billowing.

"*Guardian* is the big one," they had said to him. "*Guardian* means the road back." For a moment longer Jerry hesitated, gazing downward again into the blue plain where the very road, not figurative at all, led shimmering and straight as a canal toward the city and the airport.

Jerry was not what he would have called a thinking man. A childhood spent listening to his father's bellowing had taught him early the value of big ideas, and big words as well. Perhaps that was what had joined him to the girl in the first place, he thought. That's what she was on about: "Don't give me anything I can't carry."

Maybe. Maybe not. She'll find someone else. They always do.

It's time, he thought. Money gone, novel stillborn, girl too young. Come on. It's *time*.

Time for what?

Time! Time she found herself a young bull instead of wearing out an old one. Time to let the wanderlust stir. Strike camp. Wake the camels. On your way. Lord knows, he had done it before once or twice. Pitch the old tent, stay a little, move on; sorry, sport.

It's an order, he told himself. Ours not to reason. Whistle goes, the lads rally. End of argument. *Guardian.*

Rum how he'd had a feeling it was coming, all the same, he thought, still staring into the blurred plain. No great presentiment, any of that tripe; simply, yes, a sense of time. It was due. A sense of season. But in place of a gay upsurge of activity, a deep sluggishness seized hold of his body. He suddenly felt too tired, too fat, too sleepy ever to move again. He could have lain down just here, where he stood. He could have slept on the harsh grass till she woke him or the darkness came.

Tripe, he told himself. Sheer tripe. Taking the telegram from his pocket, he strode vigorously into the house, calling her name.

"Hey, sport! Old thing! Where are you hiding? Spot of bad news." He handed it to her. "Doomsville," he said, and went to the window rather than watch her read it.

He waited till he heard the flutter of the paper landing on

the table. Then he turned round because there was nothing else
for it. She hadn't said anything, but she had wedged her hands
under her armpits and sometimes her body-talk was deafening.
He saw how the fingers waved blindly about, trying to lock on
to something.

"Why not shove off to Beth's place for a bit?" he suggested.
"She'll have you like a shot, old Beth. Thinks the world of you.
Have you long as you like, Beth would."

She kept her arms folded till he went down the hill to send
his telegram. By the time he came back she had got his suit out,
the blue one they had always laughed about—his prison gear,
she called it—but she was trembling and her face had turned
white and ill, the way it went when he dealt with the hornets.
When he tried to kiss her, she was cold as marble, so he let her
be. At night they slept together and it was worse than being
alone.

Mama Stefano announced the news at lunch-time, breathlessly. The honourable schoolboy had left, she said. He wore
his suit. He carried a grip, his typewriter, and the book-sack.
Franco had taken him to the airport in the van. The orphan
had gone with them, but only as far as the slip-road to the
autostrada. When she got out, she didn't even say goodbye—
just sat beside the road like the trash she was. For a while, after
they dumped her, the schoolboy had remained very quiet and
private. He scarcely noticed Franco's ingenious and pointed
questions, and he pulled at his tawny forelock a lot—the Sanders had called it pepper and salt. At the airport, with an hour
to kill before the plane left, they had a flask together, also a
game of dominoes, but when Franco tried to rob him for the
fare, the schoolboy showed an unusual harshness, haggling at
last like the true rich.

Franco had told her, she said; her bosom friend. Franco,
maligned as a pederast. Had she not always defended him,
Franco the elegant? Franco, the father of her idiot son? They

had had their differences—who had not?—but let them only name for her, if they could, in the whole valley, a more upright, diligent, graceful, better-dressed man than Franco, her friend and lover!

The schoolboy had gone back for his inheritance, she said.

3

Mr. George Smiley's Horse

Only George Smiley, said Roddy Martindale, a fleshy Foreign Office wit, could have got himself appointed captain of a wrecked ship. Only Smiley, he added, could have compounded the pains of that appointment by choosing the same moment to abandon his beautiful, if occasionally errant wife.

At first or even second glance, George Smiley was ill-suited to either part, as Martindale was quick to note. He was tubby, and in small ways hopelessly unassertive. A natural shyness made him from time to time pompous, and to men of Martindale's flamboyance his unobtrusiveness acted as a standing reproach. He was also myopic, and to see him in those first days after the holocaust—in his round spectacles and his civil-servant weeds, attended by his slender, tight-mouthed cupbearer Peter Guillam, discreetly padding the marshier bypaths of the Whitehall jungle; or stooped over a heap of papers at any hour of day or night in his scruffy throne-room on the fifth floor of the Edwardian mausoleum in Cambridge Circus, which he now commanded—you would think it was he, and not the dead Haydon, the Russian spy, who deserved the trade name "mole." After such long hours of work in that cavernous and half-deserted building, the bags beneath his eyes turned to bruises, he smiled seldom, though he was by no means humourless, and there were times when the mere exertion of rising from his chair seemed to leave him winded. Reaching the upright posi-

tion, he would pause, mouth slightly open, and give a little, frica-
tive "uh" before moving off. Another mannerism had him
polishing his spectacles distractedly on the fat end of his tie,
which left his face so disconcertingly naked that one very senior secretary—in the jargon, these ladies were known as
"mothers"—was on more than one occasion assailed by a barely
containable urge, of which psychiatrists would have made all
sorts of heavy weather, to start forward and shelter him from
the impossible task he seemed determined to perform.

"George Smiley isn't just cleaning the stable," the same
Roddy Martindale remarked, from his luncheon table at the
Garrick. "He's carrying his horse up the hill as well. Haw haw."

Other rumours, favoured mainly by departments which had
entered bids for the charter of the foundered service, were less
respectful of his travail.

"George is living on his reputation," they said, after a few
months of this. "Catching Bill Haydon was a fluke."

Anyway, they said, it had been an American tip-off, not
George's *coup* at all; the Cousins should have had the credit,
but they had waived it diplomatically. No, no, said others, it
was the Dutch. The Dutch had broken Moscow Centre's code
and passed the take through liaison; ask Roddy Martindale—
Martindale, of course, being a professional trafficker in Circus
misinformation. And so, back and forth, while Smiley, seemingly oblivious, kept his counsel and dismissed his wife.

They could hardly believe it.

They were stunned.

Martindale, who had never loved a woman in his life, was
particularly affronted. He made a positive *thing* of it at the
Garrick.

"The gall! Him a complete nobody and her half a Sawley!
Pavlovian, that's what I call it. Sheer Pavlovian cruelty. After
years of putting up with her perfectly healthy peccadilloes—
driving her to them, you mark my words—what does the little
man do? Turns round and with quite *Napoleonic* brutality kicks

her in the teeth! It's a scandal. I shall tell everyone it's a scandal. I'm a tolerant man in my way—not unworldly, I think—but Smiley has gone too far. Oh, yes."

For once, as occasionally occurred, Martindale had the picture straight. The evidence was there for all to read. With Haydon dead and the past buried, the Smileys had made up their differences, and together, with some small ceremony, the reunited couple had moved back into their little Chelsea house in Bywater Street. They had even made a stab at being in society. They had gone out, they had entertained in the style befitting George's new appointment; the Cousins, the odd parliamentary Minister, a variety of Whitehall barons all dined and went home full. They had even for a few weeks made a modestly exotic couple around the higher bureaucratic circuit. Till overnight, to his wife's unmistakeable discomfort, George Smiley had removed himself from her sight and set up camp in the meagre attics behind his throne-room in the Circus. Soon the gloom of the place seemed to work itself into the fabric of his face, like dust into the complexion of a prisoner. While, in Chelsea, Ann Smiley pined, taking very hardly to her unaccustomed rôle of wife abandoned.

Dedication, said the knowing. Monkish abstinence. George is a saint. And at *his* age.

Balls, the Martindale faction retorted. Dedication to *what?* What was there left, in that dreary red-brick monster, that could possibly command such an act of self-immolation? What was there *anywhere* in beastly Whitehall—or, Lord help us, in beastly *England*—that could command it any more?

Work, said the knowing.

But *what* work? came the falsetto protests of these self-appointed Circus-watchers, handing round, like Gorgons, their little scraps of sight and hearing. What did he do up there, shorn of three-quarters of his staff, all but a few old biddies to brew his tea, his networks blown to smithereens? His foreign residencies, his reptile fund frozen solid by the Treasury (they meant his operational accounts), and not a friend in Whitehall or Washington to call his own? Unless you counted that loping prig Lacon at the Cabinet Office to be his friend, always so determined to go down the line for him at every conceivable opportunity. And naturally *Lacon* would put up a fight for him; what else had he? The Circus was Lacon's power base. Without it, he was—well, what he was already, a capon. Naturally, *Lacon* would sound the battle cry.

"It's a scandal," Martindale announced huffily as he cropped his smoked eel and steak-and-kidney and the club's own claret, up another twenty pence a crack. "I shall tell everybody."

Between the villagers of Whitehall and the villagers of Tuscany, there was sometimes surprisingly little to choose.

Time did not kill the rumours. To the contrary, they multiplied, taking colour from his isolation, and calling it obsession.

It was remembered that Bill Haydon had not merely been George Smiley's colleague, but Ann's cousin and something more besides. Smiley's fury against him, they said, had not stopped at Haydon's death; he was positively dancing on Bill's grave. For example, George had personally supervised the clearing of Haydon's fabled pepper-pot room overlooking the Charing Cross Road, and the destruction of every last sign of him, from the indifferent oil-paintings by his own hand to the left-over oddments in the drawers of his desk; even the desk itself, which he had ordered sawn up and burned. And when *that* was done, they maintained, he had called in Circus workmen to tear down the partition walls. Oh, yes.

Or, for another example, and frankly a most unnerving one, take the photograph which hung on the wall of Smiley's dingy throne-room—a passport photograph by the look of it, but blown up far beyond its natural size, so that it had a grainy and, some said, spectral look. One of the Treasury boys spotted it during an *ad hoc* conference about scrapping the operational bank accounts.

"Is that Control's portrait, by the by?" he had asked of Peter Guillam, purely as a bit of social chit-chat. No sinister intent behind the question. Well, surely one was allowed to *ask?* Control, other names still unknown, was the legend of the place. He had been Smiley's guide and mentor for all of thirty years. Smiley had actually buried him, they said; for the very secret, like the very rich, have a tendency to die unmourned.

"No, it bloody well *isn't* Control," Guillam, the cupbearer, had retorted, in that offhand, supercilious way of his. "It's Karla."

And who was Karla when he was at home?

Karla, my dear, was the work name of the Soviet case officer who had recruited Bill Haydon in the first place, and had the running of him thereafter. "A different sort of legend *entirely,* to say the least," said Martindale, all a-quiver. "It seems we've a real vendetta on our hands. How puerile can you get, I wonder?"

Even Lacon was a mite bothered by that picture: "Now, seriously, why do you hang him there, George?" he demanded, in his bold, head prefect's voice, dropping in on Smiley one evening on his way home from the Cabinet Office. "What does he mean to you, I wonder? Have you thought about that one? It isn't a little macabre, you don't think? The victorious enemy? I'd have thought he would get you down, gloating over you all up there?"

"Well, Bill's *dead,*" said Smiley, who had a habit sometimes of giving a clue to an argument, rather than the argument itself.

"And Karla's alive, you mean?" Lacon prompted. "And you'd rather have a live enemy than a dead one? Is that what you mean?"

But questions of George Smiley at a certain point had a habit of passing him by—even, said his colleagues, of appearing to be in bad taste.

An incident which provided more substantial fare around the Whitehall bazaars concerned the "ferrets," or electronic sweepers. A worse case of favouritism could not be remembered anywhere. My *God*, those hoods had a nerve sometimes! Martindale, who had been waiting a year to have *his* room done, sent a complaint to his Under-Secretary. By hand. To be opened personally by. So did his Brother-in-Christ at Defence and so, nearly, did Hammer of Treasury, but Hammer either forgot to post his or thought better of it at the last moment. It wasn't just a question of priorities—not at all. Not even of principle. *Money* was involved. *Public* money. Treasury had already had half the Circus rewired on George's insistence. His paranoia about eavesdropping knew no limits, apparently. Add to that, the ferrets were short-staffed, there had been industrial disputes about unsocial hours—oh, any number of angles! Dynamite, the whole subject.

Yet what had happened in the event? Martindale had the details at his manicured fingertips. George went to Lacon on a Thursday—the day of the freak heat wave, you remember, when everyone practically *expired*, even at the Garrick—and by the Saturday—a Saturday, *imagine* the overtime!—the brutes were swarming over the Circus, enraging the neighbours with their din, and tearing the place apart. A more *gross* case of blind preference had not been met with since—well, since they allowed Smiley to have back that mangy old Russian researcher of his—Sachs, Connie Sachs—the don woman from Oxford, against all reason, calling her a mother when she wasn't.

Discreetly, or as discreetly as he could manage, Martindale went to quite some lengths to find out whether the ferrets had actually discovered anything, but met a blank wall. In the secret world, information is money, and by that standard at least, though he might not know it, Roddy Martindale was a pauper, for the inside to this inside story was known only to the smallest few. It was true that Smiley called on Lacon in his panelled room overlooking St. James's Park on the Thursday, and that the day was uncommonly hot for autumn. Rich shafts of sunlight poured on to the representational carpet, and the dust specks played in them like tiny tropical fish. Lacon had even removed his jacket, though of course not his tie.

"Connie Sachs has been doing some arithmetic on Karla's handwriting in analogous cases," Smiley announced.

"Handwriting?" Lacon echoed, as if handwriting were a vice.

"Tradecraft. Karla's habits of technique. It seems that where it was operable, he ran moles and sound-thieves in tandem."

"Once more now, in English, George—do you mind?"

Where circumstance allowed, said Smiley, Karla had backed up his agent operations with microphones. Though Smiley was satisfied that nothing had been said within the building which could compromise any "present plans," as he called them, the implications were unsettling.

Lacon was getting to know Smiley's handwriting too: "Any collateral for that rather academic theory?" he enquired, examining Smiley's expressionless features over the top of his pencil, which he held between his two index fingers, like a rule.

"We've been making an inventory of our own audio stores," Smiley confessed with a puckering of his brow. "There's a quantity of house equipment missing. A lot seems to have disappeared during the alterations of 'sixty-six." Lacon waited, dragging it out of him. "Haydon was on the building committee responsible for having the work carried out," Smiley ended, as a final sop. "He was the driving force, in fact. It's just—well, if the Cousins ever got to hear of it, I fear it would be the last straw."

Lacon was no fool, and the Cousins' wrath just when everyone was trying to smooth their feathers was a thing to be avoided at any cost. If he had had his way, he would have ordered the ferrets out the same day. Saturday was a compromise, and without consulting anybody he dispatched the entire team, all twelve of them, in two grey vans painted "PEST CONTROL."

It was true that they tore the place apart; hence the silly rumours about the destruction of the pepper-pot room. They were angry because it was the weekend, and perhaps therefore needlessly violent; the tax they paid on overtime was frightful.

But their mood changed fast enough when they bagged eight radio microphones in the first sweep, every one of them Circus standard-issue from audio stores. Haydon's distribution of them was classic, as Lacon agreed when he called to make his own inspection. One in a drawer of a disused desk, as if innocently left there and forgotten about, except that the desk happened to be in the coding room. One collecting dust on top of an old steel cupboard in the fifth-floor conference room—or, in the jargon, rumpus room. And one, with typical Haydon flair, wedged behind the cistern in the senior officers' lavatory next door. A second sweep, to include load-bearing walls, threw up three more embedded in the fabric during the building work. Probes, with plastic snorkel-straws to pipe the sound back to them. The ferrets laid them out like a game-line. Extinct, of course, as all the devices were, but put there by Haydon nevertheless, and tuned to frequencies the Circus did not use.

"Maintained at Treasury cost, too, I declare," said Lacon, with the driest of smiles, fondling the leads which had once connected the probe microphones with the mains power supply. "Or used to be, till George rewired the place. I must be sure to tell Brother Hammer. He'll be thrilled." Hammer, a Welshman, being Lacon's most persistent enemy.

On Lacon's advice, Smiley now staged a modest piece of theatre. He ordered the ferrets to reactivate the radio microphones in the conference room and to modify the receiver on one of the Circus's few remaining surveillance cars. Then he invited three of the least bending Whitehall desk jockeys, including the Welsh Hammer, to drive in a half-mile radius round the building, while they listened to a pre-scripted discussion between two of Smiley's shadowy helpers sitting in the rumpus room. Word for word. Not a syllable out of place.

After which, Smiley himself swore them to absolute secrecy, and for good measure made them sign a declaration, drafted by the housekeepers expressly to inspire awe.

Peter Guillam reckoned it would keep them quiet for about a month. "Or less if it rains," he added, sourly.

Yet if Martindale and his colleagues in the Whitehall outfield lived in a state of primeval innocence about the reality of Smiley's world, those closer to the throne felt equally removed from him. The circles around him grew smaller as they grew nearer, and precious few in the early days reached the centre. Entering the brown and dismal doorway of the Circus, with its temporary barriers manned by watchful janitors, Smiley shed none of his habitual privacy. For nights and days at a time, the door to his tiny office suite stayed closed and his only company was Peter Guillam, and a hovering dark-eyed factotum named Fawn, a sleek, diminutive creature who had shared with Guillam the job of baby-sitting for Smiley during the smoking-out of Haydon.

Sometimes Smiley disappeared by the back door with no more than a nod, taking Fawn with him and leaving Guillam to field the phone calls and get hold of him in emergency. The mothers likened his behaviour to the last days of Control, who had died in harness, thanks to Haydon, of a broken heart. By the organic processes of a closed society, a new word was added to the jargon. The unmasking of Haydon now became the "fall," and Circus history was divided into before the fall and after it. To Smiley's comings and goings, the physical fall of the building itself—three-quarters empty and, since the visit of the ferrets, in a wrecked condition—lent a sombre sense of ruin which at low moments became symbolic to those who had to live with it. What the ferrets destroy they do not put together; and the same, they felt perhaps, was true of Karla, whose dusty features, nailed there by their elusive chief, continued to watch over them from the shadows of his Spartan throne-room.

The little they did know was appalling. Such humdrum matters as personnel, for example, took on a horrific dimension. Smiley had blown staff to dismiss, and blown residencies to dismantle; poor Tufty Thesinger's in Hong Kong, for one—though, being pretty far removed from the anti-Soviet scene, Hong Kong was among the last to go.

Round Whitehall—a terrain which, like Smiley, they deeply distrusted—they heard of him engaged in bizarre and rather terrible arguments over terms of severance and resettlement. There were cases, it seemed—poor Tufty Thesinger in Hong Kong once more supplied the readiest example—where Bill Haydon had deliberately encouraged the over-promotion of burnt-out officers who could be counted on not to mount private initiatives. Should they be paid off at their natural value, or at the inflated one Haydon had mischievously set on them? There were others where Haydon, for his own preservation, had confected reasons for dismissal. Should they receive full pension? Had they a claim to reinstatement? Perplexed young Ministers, new to power since the elections, made brave and contradictory rulings. In consequence, a sad stream of deluded Circus field officers, both men and women, passed through Smiley's hands, and the housekeepers were ordered to make sure that for reasons of security and perhaps aesthetics, none of these returnees from foreign residencies should set foot inside the main building.

Nor would Smiley tolerate any contact between the damned and the reprieved. Accordingly, with grudging Treasury support from the Welsh Hammer, the housekeepers opened a temporary reception point in a rented house in Bloomsbury, under cover of a language school ("Regret No Callers Without Appointment"), and manned it with a quartet of pay-and-personnel officers. This body became inevitably the Bloomsbury Group, and it was known that sometimes for a spare hour or so Smiley made a point of slipping down there and, rather in the manner of a hospital visitor, offering his condolences to faces frequently unknown to him. At other times, depending on his mood, he would remain entirely silent, preferring to perch unexplained and Buddha-like in a corner of the dusty interviewing room.

What drove him? What was he looking for? If anger was
the root, then it was an anger common to them all in those
days. They could be sitting together in the rumpus room after
a long day's work, joking and gossiping; but if someone should
let slip the names of Karla or his mole Haydon, a silence of
angels would descend on them, and not even cunning old Connie Sachs, the Moscow-gazer, could break the spell.

Even more affecting in the eyes of his subordinates were
Smiley's efforts to save something of the agent networks from
the wreck. Within a day of Haydon's arrest, all nine of the
Circus's Soviet and East European networks had gone cold.
Radio links stopped dead, courier lines dried up, and there was
every reason to say that if there had been any genuinely Circus-
owned agents left among them, they had been rolled up overnight. But Smiley fiercely opposed that easy view, just as he
refused to accept that Karla and Moscow Centre between
them were invincibly efficient, or tidy, or logical.

He pestered Lacon, he pestered the Cousins in their vast
annexes in Grosvenor Square, he insisted that agent radio frequencies continue to be monitored, and, despite bitter protest
by the Foreign Office (Roddy Martindale, as ever, to the fore),
he had open-language messages put out by the overseas services of the B.B.C. ordering any live agent who should happen
to hear them and know the code word to abandon ship immediately. And, little by little, to their amazement, came tiny flut-
terings of life, like garbled messages from another planet.

First, the Cousins, in the person of their suspiciously bluff
local station chief Martello, reported from Grosvenor Square
that an American escape line was passing two British agents, a
man and a woman, to the old holiday resort of Sochi on the
Black Sea, where a small boat was being fitted in readiness for
what Martello's quiet men insisted on calling an "exfiltration
assignment." By his description, he was referring to the
Churayevs, linchpins of the Contemplate network, which had
covered Georgia and the Ukraine. Without waiting for Trea-

sury sanction, Smiley resurrected from retirement one Roy Bland, a burly ex-Marxist dialectician and sometime field agent, who had been the network's case officer. To Bland, who had come down heavily in the fall, he entrusted the two Russian leash-dogs, de Silsky and Kaspar, also in moth-balls, also former Haydon protégés, to make up a stand-by reception party. They were still sitting in their R.A.F. transport plane when word came through that the couple had been shot dead as they were leaving harbour. The exfiltration assignment had fallen through, said the Cousins. In sympathy, Martello personally telephoned Smiley with the news. He was a kindly man by his own lights and, like Smiley, old school. It was night-time, and raining furiously.

"Now, don't go taking this too hard, George," he warned in his avuncular way. "Hear me? There's fieldmen and there's deskmen and it's up to you and me to see that the distinction is preserved. Otherwise we all go crazy. Can't go down the line for every one of them. That's generalship. So you just remember that."

Peter Guillam, who was at Smiley's shoulder when he took the call, swore later that Smiley showed no particular reaction; and Guillam knew him well. Nevertheless, ten minutes later, unobserved by anybody, he was gone, and his voluminous mackintosh was missing from its peg. He returned after dawn, drenched to the skin, still carrying the mackintosh over his arm. Having changed, he returned to his desk, but when Guillam, unbidden, tiptoed in to him with tea, he found his master, to his embarrassment, sitting rigidly before an old volume of German poetry, fists clenched either side of it, while he silently wept.

Bland, Kaspar, and de Silsky begged for reinstatement. They pointed to little Toby Esterhase the Hungarian, who had somehow gained readmittance, and demanded the same treatment. In vain. They were stood down and not spoken of again. To injustice belongs injustice. Though tarnished, they might have been useful, but Smiley would not hear their names; not then; not later; not ever. Of the immediate post-fall period, that was the lowest point. There were those who seriously believed—inside the Circus, as well as out—that they had heard the last beat of the secret English heart.

A few days after this catastrophe, as it happened, luck handed Smiley a small consolation. In Warsaw, in broad daylight, a Circus head agent on the run picked up the B.B.C. signal and walked straight into the British Embassy. Thanks to ferocious lobbying by Lacon and Smiley between them, he was flown home to London the same night disguised as a diplomatic courier, Martindale notwithstanding. Mistrusting his cover story, Smiley turned the man over to the Circus inquisitors, who, deprived of other meat, nearly killed him but afterwards declared him clean. He was resettled in Australia.

Next, still at the very genesis of his rule, Smiley was compelled to pass judgment on the Circus's blown domestic outstations. His instinct was to shed everything: the safe houses, now totally unsafe; the Sarratt Nursery, where traditionally the briefing and training of agents and new entrants was conducted; the experimental audio laboratories in Harlow; the stinks-and-bangs school in Argyll; the water school in the Helford Estuary, where passe sailors practised the black arts of small-boat seacraft like the ritual of some lost religion; and the long-arm radio-transmission base at Canterbury. He would even have done away with the wranglers' headquarters in Bath, where the code-breaking went on.

"Scrap the lot," he told Lacon, calling on him in his rooms.

"And then what?" Lacon enquired, puzzled by his vehemence, which since the Sochi failure was more marked in him.

"Start again."

"I see," said Lacon, which meant, of course, that he didn't. Lacon had sheets of Treasury figures before him and was studying them while he spoke.

"The Sarratt Nursery, for some reason which I fail to understand, is carried on the *military* budget," he observed reflectively. "Not on your reptile fund at all. The Foreign Office pays for Harlow—and I'm sure has long forgotten the fact. Argyll is under the wing of the Ministry of Defence, who most certainly won't know of its existence. The Post Office has Canterbury and the Navy has Helford. Bath, I'm pleased to say, is also supported from Foreign Office funds, over the particular signature of Martindale, appended six years ago and similarly faded from official memory. So they don't eat a thing. Do they?"

"They're dead wood," Smiley insisted. "And while they exist we shall never replace them. Sarratt went to the devil long ago, Helford is moribund, Argyll is farcical. As to the wranglers, for the last five years they've been working practically full time for Karla."

"By Karla you mean Moscow Centre?"

"I mean the department responsible for Haydon and half a dozen—"

"I know what you mean. But I think it safer to stay with institutions, if you don't mind. In that way we are spared the embarrassment of personalities. After all, that's what institutions are *for*, isn't it?" Lacon tapped the back of his pencil rhythmically on his desk. Finally he looked up, and considered Smiley quizzically. "Well, well, you *are* the root-and-bough man these days, George. I dread to think what would happen if you were ever to wield your axe round *my* side of the garden. Those outstations are gilt-edged stock. Do away with them now and you'll never get them back. Later, if you like, when you're on the road again, you can cash them in and buy yourself something better. You mustn't sell when the market's low, you know. You must wait till you can take a profit."

Reluctantly, Smiley bowed to his advice.

As if all these headaches were not enough, there came one bleak Monday morning when a Treasury audit pointed up serious discrepancies in the conduct of the Circus reptile fund over the period of five years before it was frozen by the fall. Smiley was forced to hold a kangaroo court, at which an elderly clerk in Finance Section, hauled from retirement, broke down and confessed to a shameful passion for a girl in Registry who had led him by the nose. In a ghastly fit of remorse, the old man went home and hanged himself. Against all Guillam's advice, Smiley insisted on attending the funeral.

Yet it is a matter of record that from these quite dismal beginnings, and indeed from his very first weeks in office, George Smiley went over to the attack.

The base from which this attack was launched was in the first instance philosophical, in the second theoretical, and only in the last instance, thanks to the dramatic appearance of the egregious gambler Sam Collins, human.

The philosophy was simple. The task of an intelligence service, Smiley announced firmly, was not to play chase games but to deliver intelligence to its customers. If it failed to do this, those customers would resort to other, less scrupulous sellers or, worse, indulge in amateurish self-help. And the service itself would wither. Not to be seen in the Whitehall markets was not to be desired, he went on. Unless the Circus produced, it would also have no wares to barter with the Cousins, or with other sister services with whom reciprocal deals were traditional. Not to produce was not to trade, and not to trade was to die.

Amen, they said.

His theory—he called it his "premise"—on how intelligence could be produced with no resources was the subject of an informal meeting held in the rumpus room, not two months after his accession, between himself and the tiny inner circle which made up, to a point, his team of confidants. They were, in all, five: Smiley himself; Peter Guillam his cupbearer; big, flowing Connie Sachs the Moscow-gazer; Fawn the dark-eyed factotum, who wore black gym shoes and manned the Russian-style copper samovar and gave out biscuits; and lastly Doc di Salis, known as "the Mad Jesuit," the Circus's head China-watcher. When God had finished making Connie

Sachs, said the wags, He needed a rest, so He ran up Doc di Salis from the remnants.

The Doc was a patchy, grubby little creature, more like Connie's monkey than her counterpart, and his features, it was true, from the spiky silver hair that strayed over his grimy collar to the moist misshapen fingertips, which picked like chicken beaks at everything around them, had an unquestionably ill-begotten look. If Beardsley had drawn him, he would have had him chained and hirsute, peeping round the corner of her enormous caftan. Yet di Salis was a notable Orientalist, a scholar, and something of a hero too, for he had spent a part of the war in China, recruiting for God and the Circus, and another part in Changi jail, for the pleasure of the Japanese.

That was the team: the group of five. In time it expanded, but to start with, these five alone made up the famous cadre, and to have been one of them, said di Salis afterwards, was "like holding a Communist Party card with a single-figure membership number."

First, Smiley reviewed the wreck, and that took some while, in the way that sacking a city takes some while, or liquidating great numbers of people. He simply drove through every back alley the Circus possessed, demonstrating quite ruthlessly how, by what method, and often exactly when Haydon had laid bare its secrets to his Soviet masters. He had, of course, the advantage of his own interrogation of Haydon, and of the original researches which had led him to Haydon's discovery. He knew the track. Nevertheless, his peroration was a minor *tour de force* of destructive analysis.

"So no illusions," he ended tersely. "This service will never be the same again. It may be better, but it will be different."

Amen again, they said, and took a doleful break to stretch their legs.

It was odd, Guillam recalled later, how the important scenes of those early months seemed all to play at night. The rumpus room was long and raftered, with high dormer windows which gave on to nothing but orange night sky and a coppice of rusted radio aerials, war relics no one had seen fit to remove.

The premise, said Smiley when they had resettled, was that Haydon had done nothing against the Circus that was not directed, and that the direction came from one man personally: Karla.

The premise was that in briefing Haydon, Karla was exposing the gaps in Moscow Centre's knowledge; that in ordering Haydon to suppress certain intelligence which came the Circus's way, in ordering him to downgrade or distort it, to deride it, or even to deny it circulation altogether, Karla was indicating which secrets he did not want revealed.

"So we can take the back-bearings, can't we, darling?" murmured Connie Sachs, whose speed of uptake put her, as usual, a good length ahead of the rest of the field.

"That's right, Con. That's exactly what we can do," said Smiley gravely. "We can take the back-bearings." He resumed his lecture, leaving Guillam, for one, more mystified than before.

By minutely charting Haydon's path of destruction (his pug marks, as Smiley called them); by exhaustively recording his selection of files; by reassembling—after aching weeks of research, if necessary—the intelligence culled in good faith by Circus outstations, and balancing it, in every detail, against the intelligence distributed by Haydon to the Circus's customers in the Whitehall market-place, it would be possible to take back-bearings (as Connie so rightly called them) and establish Haydon's, and therefore Karla's, point of departure. Said Smiley.

Once a correct back-bearing had been taken, surprising doors of opportunity would open, and the Circus, against all outward likelihood, would be in a position to go over to the initiative—or, as Smiley put it, "to *act*, and not merely to *react*."

The premise, to use Connie Sachs's joyous description later, meant "Looking for another bloody Tutankhamun, with

George Smiley holding the light and us poor Charlies doing the digging."

At that time, of course, Jerry Westerby was not even a twinkle in their operational eye.

They went into battle next day, huge Connie to one corner, the crabbed little di Salis to his. As di Salis said, in a nasal, deprecating tone that had a savage force, "At least we do finally know why we're here." Their families of pasty burrowers carved the archive in two. To Connie and "my Bolshies," as she called them, went Russia and the Satellites. To di Salis and his "yellow perils" China and the Third World. What fell between— source reports on the nation's theoretical Allies, for instance— was consigned to a special wait-bin for later evaluation.

They worked, like Smiley himself, impossible hours. The canteen complained, the janitors threatened to walk out, but gradually the sheer energy of the burrowers infected even the ancillary staff, and they shut up. A bantering rivalry developed. Under Connie's influence, back-room boys and girls who till now had scarcely been seen to smile learned suddenly to chaff each other in the language of their great familiars in the world outside the Circus. Czarist imperialist running dogs drank tasteless coffee with divisive, deviationist, chauvinist Stalinists and were proud of it.

But the most impressive blossoming was unquestionably in di Salis, who interrupted his nocturnal labours with short but vigorous spells at the Ping-Pong table, where he would challenge all comers, leaping about like a lepidopterist after rare specimens. Soon the first fruits appeared, and gave them fresh impetus. Within a month, three reports had been nervously distributed, under extreme limitation, and even found favour with the sceptical Cousins. A month later, a hard-bound summary wordily entitled "Interim Report on Lacunae in Soviet Intelligence Regarding Nato Sea-to-Air Strike Capacity" earned grudging applause from Martello's parent factory in

Langley, Virginia, and an exuberant phone call from Martello himself.

"George, I *told* them!" he yelled, so loud that the telephone line seemed an unnecessary extravagance. "I told them, 'The Circus will deliver.' Did they believe me? Did they hell!"

Meanwhile, sometimes with Guillam for company, sometimes with silent Fawn to baby-sit, Smiley conducted his own dark peregrinations and marched till he was half dead with tiredness. And, still without reward, kept marching. By day and often by night as well, he trailed the home counties and points beyond, questioning past officers of the Circus and former agents out to grass.

In Chiswick, perched meekly in the office of a cut-price travel agent and talking in murmurs to a former Polish colonel of cavalry resettled as a clerk there, he thought he had glimpsed it; but like a mirage, the promise dissolved as he advanced on it. In a second-hand radio shop in Sevenoaks, a Sudeten Czech held out the same hope to him, but when he and Guillam hurried back to confirm the story from Circus records, they found the actors dead and no one left to lead him further. At a private stud in Newmarket, to Fawn's near-violent fury, he suffered insult at the hand of a tweedy and opinionated Scot, a protégé of Smiley's predecessor Alleline, all in the same elusive cause. Back home, he called for the papers, only once more to see the light go out.

For this was the last and unspoken conviction of the premise Smiley had outlined in the rumpus room: that the snare with which Haydon had trapped himself was not unique. That in the end analysis, it was not Haydon's paperwork which had caused his downfall, not his meddling with reports, or his "losing" of inconvenient records. It was Haydon's panic. It was Haydon's spontaneous intervention in a field operation, where the threat to himself, or perhaps to another Karla agent, was suddenly so grave that his one hope was to suppress it despite the risk.

This was the trick which Smiley longed to find repeated. And this was the question which never directly, but by inference, Smiley and his helpers in the Bloomsbury reception centre canvassed: "Can you remember any incident during your service in the field when in your opinion you were unreasonably restrained from following an operational lead?"

And it was dapper Sam Collins, in his dinner-jacket, with his brown cigarette and his trim moustache and his Mississippi dandy's smile, summoned for a quiet chat one day, who breezed in to say, "Come to think of it, yes, old boy, I can."

But behind this question again, and Sam's crucial answer, stalked the formidable person of Miss Connie Sachs and her pursuit of Russian gold.

And behind Connie again, as ever, the permanently misted photograph of Karla.

"Connie's got one, Peter," she whispered to Guillam over the internal telephone late one night. "She's got one, sure as boots."

It was not her first find, by any means, not her tenth, but her devious instinct told her straight away it was "the genuine article, darling, mark old Connie's words." So Guillam told Smiley and Smiley locked up his files and cleared his desk and said, "All right, send her in."

She was a huge, crippled, cunning woman, a don's daughter, a don's sister, herself some sort of academic, and known to the older hands as Mother Russia. The folklore said Control had recruited her over a rubber of bridge while she was still a débutante, on the night Neville Chamberlain promised "peace in our time." When Haydon came to power in the slip-stream of his protector Alleline, one of his first and most prudent moves was to have Connie put out to grass.

For Connie knew more about the byways of Moscow Centre than most of the wretched brutes, as she called them, who toiled there, and Karla's private army of moles and recruiters had always been her very special joy. Not a Soviet defector, in the old days, but his debriefing report had passed through Mother Russia's arthritic fingers; not a coat-trailer who had manoeuvred himself alongside an identified Karla talent-spotter, but Connie greedily rehearsed him in every detail of the quarry's choreography; not a scrap of hearsay over nearly forty years on the beat that had not been assumed into her pain-wracked body, and lodged there among the junk of her compendious memory, to be turned up the moment she rummaged for it. Connie's mind, said Control once, in a kind of despair, was like the back of one enormous envelope.

Dismissed, she went back to Oxford and the devil. At the time Smiley reclaimed her, her only recreation was the *Times* crossword and she was running at a comfortable bottle of gin a day.

But that night, that modestly historic night, as Connie hauled her great frame along the fifth-floor corridor toward George Smiley's inner room, she sported a clean grey caftan, she had daubed a pair of rosy lips not far from her own, and she had taken nothing stronger than a vile peppermint cordial all day long—of which the reek lingered in her wake. A sense of occasion, they all decided afterwards, was stamped on her from the first. She carried a heavy plastic shopping bag, for she would countenance no leather. In her lair on a lower floor, her mongrel dog, christened Trot and recruited on a wave of remorse for its late predecessor, whimpered disconsolately from beneath her desk, to the lively fury of her roommate di Salis, who would often privily lash at the beast with his foot; or in more jovial moments content himself with reciting to Connie the many tasty ways in which the Chinese prepared their dogs for the pot. Outside the Edwardian dormers, as she passed them one by one, a racing late-summer rain was falling, ending a long drought, and she saw it—she told them all later—as symbolic, if not Biblical. The drops rattled like pellets on the slate roof, flattening the dead leaves which had settled there. In that ante-room, the mothers continued stonily with their business, accustomed to Connie's pilgrimages, and not liking them the better for it.

"Darlings," Connie murmured, waving her hand to them like royalty. "So loyal. So *very* loyal."

There was one step down into the throne-room—the uninitiated tended to stumble on it despite the faded warning notice—and Connie, with her arthritis, negotiated it as if it were a ladder while Guillam held her arm.

Smiley watched her, plump hands linked on his desk, as she began solemnly unpacking her offerings from the carrier: not eye of newt, or the finger of a birth-strangled babe—Guillam speaking once more—but files, a string of them, flagged and annotated, the booty of yet another of her impassioned skirmishes through the Moscow Centre archive, which until her return from the dead a few months before had, thanks to Haydon, lain gathering dust for all of three long years. As she pulled them out, and smoothed the notes that she had pinned on them like markers in her paper-chase, she smiled that brimming smile of hers—Guillam again, for curiosity had obliged him to down tools and come and watch—and she was muttering, "There, you little devil," and, "Now where did *you* get to, you wretch?" not to Smiley or Guillam, of course, but to the documents themselves, for Connie had the affectation of assuming everything was alive and potentially recalcitrant, whether it was Trot her dog or a chair that obstructed her passage, or Moscow Centre, or finally Karla himself.

"A guided tour, darlings," she announced; "that's what Connie's been having. *Super* fun. Reminded me of Easter, when Mother hid painted eggs round the house and sent us gals off hunting for them."

For perhaps three hours after that, interspersed with coffee and sandwiches and other unwanted treats, which dark Fawn insisted on bringing to them, Guillam struggled to follow the twists and impulsions of Connie's extraordinary journey, to which her subsequent research had by now supplied the solid basis. She dealt Smiley papers as if they were playing cards, shoving them down and snatching them back with her crumpled hands almost before he had had a chance to read them. Over it all she was keeping up what Guillam called "her fifth-rate conjurer's patter," the abracadabra of the obsessive burrower's trade.

At the heart of her discovery, so far as Guillam could make out, lay what Connie called a Moscow Centre "gold seam"; a Soviet laundering operation to move clandestine funds into open-air channels. The charting of it was not complete. Israeli liaison had supplied one section, the Cousins another, Steve Mackelvore, head resident in Paris, now dead, a third. From Paris the trail turned East, by way of the Banque de l'Indochine. At this point also, the papers had been put up to Haydon's London Station, as the operational directorate was called, together with a recommendation from the Circus's depleted Soviet research section that the case be thrown open to full-scale enquiry in the field.

London Station killed the suggestion stone dead: "Potentially prejudicial to a highly delicate source," wrote one of Haydon's minions, and that was that.

"File and forget," Smiley muttered, distractedly turning pages. "File and forget. We always have good reasons for doing nothing."

Outside, the world was fast asleep.

"*Exactly*, dear," said Connie very softly, as if she were afraid to wake him.

Files and folders were by then strewn all over the throne-room. The scene looked a lot more like a disaster than a triumph. For an hour longer, Guillam and Connie gazed silently into space or at Karla's photograph while Smiley conscientiously retraced her steps, his anxious face stooped to the reading-lamp, its pudgy lines accentuated by the beam, his hands skipping over the papers and occasionally lifting to his mouth so that he could lick his thumb. Once or twice, he started to glance at her or open his mouth to speak, but Connie had the answer ready before he put his question. In her mind, she was walking beside him along the path.

When he had finished he sat back, and took off his spectacles and polished them—not on the fat end of his tie, for once, but on a new silk handkerchief in the top pocket of his black jacket, for he had spent most of the day cloistered with the Cousins on another fence-mending mission. While he did this, Connie beamed at Guillam and mouthed "Isn't he a love?"—a favourite dictum when she was talking of her Chief, which drove Guillam nearly mad with rage.

Smiley's next utterance had the ring of mild objection: "All the same, Con, a formal search request *did* go out from London Station to our residency in Vientiane."

"Happened before Bill had time to get his hoof on it," she replied.

Not seeming to hear, Smiley picked up an open file and held it to her across the desk. "And Vientiane *did* send a lengthy reply. It's all marked up in the index. We don't seem to have that. Where is it?"

Connie had not bothered to receive the offered file. "In the *shredder*, darling," she said, and beamed contentedly at Guillam.

The morning had come. Guillam strolled round switching out the lights.

The same afternoon, he dropped in at the quiet West End gaming club where, in the permanent night-time of his elected trade, Sam Collins endured the rigours of retirement. Expecting to find him overseeing his usual afternoon game of chemin de fer, Guillam was surprised at being shown to a sumptuous room marked "Management." Sam was roosting behind a fine desk, smiling prosperously through the smoke of his habitual brown cigarette.

"What the hell have you done, Sam?" Guillam demanded in a stage whisper, affecting to look round nervously. "Taken over the Mafia? Jesus!"

"Oh, that wasn't necessary," said Sam, with the same raffish smile. Slipping a mackintosh over his dinner-jacket, he led Guillam down a passage and through a fire door into the street, where the two men hopped into the back of Guillam's waiting cab, while Guillam still secretly marvelled at Sam's new-found eminence.

Fieldmen have different ways of showing no emotion, and Sam's was to smile, smoke slower, and fill his eyes with a dark glow of particular indulgence, fixing them intently on his partner in discussion. Sam was an Asian hand, old Circus, with a lot of time behind him in the field: five years in Borneo, six in Burma, five more in Northern Thailand and latterly three in the Laotian capital of Vientiane, all under natural cover as a general trader. The Thais had sweated him twice but let him go. He'd had to leave Sarawak in his socks. When he was in the mood, he had stories to tell about his journeying among the northern hill tribes of Burma and the Shans, but he was seldom in the mood. Sam was a Haydon casualty. There had been a moment, five years back, when Sam's lazy brilliance had made him a serious contender for promotion to the fifth floor—even, said some, to the post of Chief itself, had not Haydon put his weight behind the preposterous Percy Alleline. So in place of power, Sam was left to moulder in the field until Haydon contrived to recall him, and have him sacked for a trumped-up misdemeanour.

"Sam! How good of you! Take a pew," said Smiley, all conviviality for once. "Will you drink? Where are you in your day? Perhaps we should be offering you breakfast?"

At Cambridge, Sam had taken a dazzling first, thus confounding his tutors, who till then had dismissed him as a near idiot. He had done it, the dons afterwards told each other consolingly, entirely on memory. The more worldly tongues told a different tale, however. According to them, Sam had trailed a love affair with a plain girl at the Examination Schools, and obtained from her a preview of the papers.

4

The Castle Wakes

Now at first Smiley tested the water with Sam—and Sam, who liked a poker hand himself, tested the water with Smiley. Some fieldmen, and particularly the clever ones, take a perverse pride in not knowing the whole picture. Their art consists in the deft handling of loose ends, and stops there stubbornly. Sam was inclined that way. Having raked a little in his dossier, Smiley tried him out on several old cases, which had no sinister look at all but which gave a clue to Sam's present disposition and confirmed his ability to remember accurately. He received Sam alone because with other people present it would have been a different game—either more or less intense, but different.

Later, when the story was out in the open and only follow-up questions remained, he did summon Connie and Doc di Salis from the nether regions, and let Guillam sit in too. But that was later, and for the time being Smiley plumbed Sam's mind alone, concealing from him entirely the fact that all case papers had been destroyed, and that since Mackelvore was dead, Sam was at present the only witness to certain key events.

"Now, Sam, do you remember at all," Smiley asked, when he finally judged the moment right, "a request that came in to you in Vientiane once, from here in London, concerning certain money drafts from Paris? Just a standard request it would have been, asking for 'unattributable field enquiries please, to confirm or deny'—that sort of thing? Ring a bell, by any chance?"

He had a sheet of notes before him, so that this was just one more question in a slow stream. As he spoke, he was actually marking something with his pencil, not looking at Sam at all. But in the same way that we hear better with our eyes closed, Smiley did sense Sam's attention harden; which is to say, Sam stretched out his legs a little, and crossed them, and slowed his gestures almost to a halt.

"Monthly transfers to the Banque de l'Indochine," said Sam after a suitable pause. "Hefty ones. Paid out of a Canadian overseas account with their Paris affiliate." He gave the number of the account. "Payments made on the last Friday of every month. Start date January 'seventy-three or thereabouts. It rings a bell, sure."

Smiley detected immediately that Sam was settling to a long game. His memory was clear but his information meagre: more like an opening bid than a frank reply.

Still stooped over the papers, Smiley said, "Now can we just wander over the course here a little, Sam? There's some discrepancy on the filing side, and I'd like to get your part of the record straight."

"Sure," said Sam again, and drew comfortably on his brown cigarette. He was watching Smiley's hands, and occasionally, with studied idleness, his eyes—though never for too long. Whereas Smiley, for his part, fought only to keep his mind open to the devious options of a fieldman's life. Sam might easily be defending something quite irrelevant. He had fiddled a little bit on his expenses, for example, and was afraid he'd been caught out. He had fabricated his report rather than go out and risk his neck; Sam was of an age, after all, where a fieldman looks first to his own skin.

Or it was the opposite situation. Sam had ranged a little wider in his enquiries than Head Office had sanctioned. Hard pressed, he had gone to the pedlars rather than file a nil return.

He had fixed himself a side-deal with the local Cousins. Or the local security services had blackmailed him—in Sarratt jargon the angels had put a burn on him—and he had played the case both ways in order to survive and smile and keep his Circus pension. To read Sam's moves, Smiley knew that he must stay alert to these and countless other options. A desk is a dangerous place from which to watch the world.

So, as Smiley proposed, they wandered. London's request for field enquiries, said Sam, reached him in standard form, much as Smiley had described. It was shown to him by old Mac who, until his Paris posting, was the Circus's linkman in the Vientiane Embassy. An evening session at their safe house. Routine, though the Russian aspect stuck out from the start, and Sam actually remembered saying to Mac that early, "London must think it's Moscow Centre reptile money," because he had spotted the cryptonym of the Circus's Soviet research section mixed in with the prelims on the signal. (Smiley noted that Steve Mackelvore had no business showing Sam the signal.) Sam also remembered Mac's reply to his observation. "They should never have given old Connie Sachs the shove," he had said. Sam had agreed wholeheartedly.

As it happened, said Sam, the request was pretty easy to meet; Sam already had a contact at the Indochine, a good one—call him Johnny.

"Filed here, Sam?" Smiley enquired politely.

Sam avoided answering that question directly and Smiley respected his reluctance. The fieldman who files all his contacts with Head Office, or even clears them, was not yet born. As illusionists cling to their mystique, so fieldmen for different reasons are congenitally secretive about their sources.

Johnny was reliable, said Sam emphatically. He had an excellent track record on several arms-dealing and narcotics cases, and Sam would swear by him anywhere.

"Oh, you handled those things, too, did you, Sam?" Smiley asked respectfully.

So Sam had moonlighted for the local narcotics bureau on the side, Smiley noted. A lot of fieldmen did that, some even with Head Office consent; in their world, they likened it to selling off industrial waste. It was a perk. Nothing dramatic therefore, but Smiley stored away the information all the same.

"Johnny was okay," Sam repeated, with a warning in his voice.

"I'm sure he was," said Smiley with the same courtesy.

Sam continued with his story. He had called on Johnny at the Indochine and sold him a cock-and-bull cover to keep him quiet, and a few days later, Johnny, who was just a humble counter clerk, had checked the ledgers and unearthed the dockets and Sam had the first leg of the connection cut and dried.

The routine went this way, said Sam: "On the last Friday of each month, a telexed money order arrived from Paris to the credit of a Monsieur Delassus presently staying at the Hotel Condor, Vientiane, payable on production of passport, number quoted." Once again, Sam effortlessly recited the figures. "The bank sent out the advice, Delassus called first thing on the Monday, drew the money in cash, stuffed it in a brief-case, and walked out with it. End of connection," said Sam.

"How much?"

"Started small and grew fast. Then went on growing, then grew a little more."

"Ending where?"

"Twenty-five thousand U.S., in big ones," said Sam without a flicker.

Smiley's eyebrows lifted slightly. "A month?" he said, in humorous surprise.

"The big table," Sam agreed, and lapsed into a leisurely silence. There is a particular intensity about clever men whose brains are under-used, and sometimes there is no way they can control their emanations. In that sense, they are a great deal more at risk under the bright lights than their more stupid colleagues. "You checking me against the record, old boy?" Sam asked.

"I'm not checking you against anything, Sam. You know how it is at times like this. Clutching at straws, listening to the wind."

"Sure," said Sam sympathetically and, when they had exchanged further glances of mutual confidence, once more resumed his narrative.

So Sam enquired at the Hotel Condor, he said. The porter there was a stock sub-source to the trade; everybody owned him. No Delassus staying there, but the front desk cheerfully admitted to receiving a little something for providing him with an accommodation address. The very next Monday—which happened to follow the last Friday of the month, said Sam—with the help of his contact Johnny, Sam duly hung around the bank "cashing traveller's cheques and whatnot," and had a grandstand view of the said Monsieur Delassus marching in, handing over his French passport, counting the money into a brief-case, and retreating with it to a waiting taxi.

Taxis, Sam explained, were rare beasts in Vientiane. Anyone who was anyone had a car and a driver, so the presumption was that Delassus didn't want to be anyone.

"So far, so good," Sam concluded, watching with interest while Smiley wrote.

"So far, so *very* good," Smiley corrected him. Like his predecessor Control, Smiley never used pads—just single sheets of paper, one at a time, and a glass top to press on, which Fawn polished twice a day.

"Do I fit the record or do I deviate?" asked Sam.

"I'd say you were right on course, Sam," Smiley said. "It's the *detail* I'm enjoying. You know how it is with records."

The same evening, Sam said, hugger-mugger with his linkman Mac once more, he took a long cool look at the rogues' gallery of local Russians, and was able to identify the unlovely

features of a Second Secretary (Commercial) at the Soviet
Embassy, Vientiane, mid-fifties, military bearing, no previous
convictions, full names given but unpronounceable, and known
therefore around the diplomatic bazaars as "Commercial Boris."

But Sam, of course, had the unpronounceable names ready
in his head and spelt them out for Smiley slowly enough for
him to write them down in block capitals.

"Got it?" he enquired helpfully.

"Thank you, yes."

"Somebody left the card index on a bus, have they, old
boy?" Sam asked.

"That's right," Smiley said, with a laugh.

When the crucial Monday came round again a month later,
Sam went on, he decided he would tread wary. So instead of
gumshoeing after Commercial Boris himself, he stayed home
and briefed a couple of locally based leash-dogs who specialised
in pavement work.

"A lace-curtain job," said Sam. "No shaking the tree, no
branch lines, no nothing. Laotian boys."

"Our own?"

"Three years at the mast," said Sam. "And *good*," added the
fieldman in him, for whom all his geese are swans.

The said leash-dogs watched the brief-case on its next journey. The taxi, a different one from the month before, took
Boris on a tour of the town and after half an hour dropped him
back near the main square, not far from the Indochine. Commercial Boris walked a short distance, ducked into a second
bank, a local one, and paid the entire sum straight across the
counter to the credit of another account.

"So tra-la," said Sam, and lit a fresh cigarette, not bothering to conceal his amused bewilderment that Smiley was
rehearsing orally a case so fully documented.

"Tra-la indeed," Smiley murmured, writing hard.

After that, said Sam, they were home and dry. Sam lay low

for a couple of weeks to let the dust settle, then put in his girl assistant to deliver the final blow. "Name?"

Sam gave it. A home-based senior girl, Sarratt trained, sharing his commercial cover. This senior girl waited ahead of Boris in the local bank, let him complete his paying-in forms, then raised a small scene.

"How did she do that, Sam?"

"Demanded to be served first," said Sam, with a grin. "Brother Boris, being a male chauvinist pig, thought he had equal rights and objected. Words passed."

The paying-in slip lay on the counter, said Sam, and while the senior girl did her number she read it upside down. Twenty-five thousand American dollars to the credit of the overseas account of a mickey-mouse aviation company called Indocharter Vientiane S.A.: "Assets, a handful of clapped-out DC-3s, a tin hut, a stack of fancy letter-paper, one dumb blonde for the front office, and a wildcat Mexican pilot known round town as Tiny Ricardo on account of his considerable height," said Sam. He added, "And the usual anonymous bunch of diligent Chinese in the back room, of course."

Smiley's ears were so sharp at that moment that he could have heard a leaf fall; but what he heard, metaphorically, was the sound of barriers being erected, and he knew at once, from the cadence, from the tightening of the voice, from the tiny facial and physical things which make up an exaggerated show of throwaway, that he was closing on the heart of Sam's defences.

So in his mind he put in a marker, deciding to remain with the mickey-mouse aviation company for a while.

"Ah," he said lightly, "you mean you knew the firm already?"

Sam tossed out a small card. "Vientiane's not exactly your giant metropolis, old boy."

"But you knew of it? That's the point."

"Everybody in town knew Tiny Ricardo," said Sam, grinning more broadly than ever, and Smiley knew at once that

Sam was throwing sand in his eyes. But he played Sam along all the same.

"Tell me about Ricardo," he suggested.

"One of the ex-Air America clowns. Vientiane was stiff with them. Fought the secret war in Laos."

"And lost it," Smiley said, writing again.

"Single-handed," Sam agreed, watching Smiley put aside one sheet and take another from his drawer. "Ricardo was local legend. Flew with Captain Rocky and that crowd. Credited with a couple of joy-rides into Yunnan Province for the Cousins. When the war ended, he kicked around a bit, then took up with the Chinese. We used to call those outfits Air Opium. By the time Bill hauled me home, they were a flourishing industry."

Still Smiley let Sam run. As long as Sam thought he was leading Smiley from the scent, he would talk the hind legs off a donkey; whereas if Sam thought Smiley was getting too close, he would put up the shutters at once.

"Fine," he said amiably, therefore, after yet more careful writing. "Now let's go back to what Sam did next, may we? We have the money, we know whom it's paid to, we know who handles it. What's your next move, Sam?"

Well, if Sam remembered rightly, he took stock for a day or two. There were *angles*, Sam explained, gathering confidence; there were little things that caught the eye. First, you might say, there was the strange case of Commercial Boris. Boris, as Sam had indicated, was held to be a bona-fide diplomat, if such a thing existed: no known connection with any other firm. Yet he rode around alone, had sole signing rights over a pot of money, and in Sam's limited experience, either one of these things spelt hood on one hand.

"Not just hood, a blasted supremo. A red-toothed four-square paymaster—colonel or upwards, right?"

"What other *angles*, Sam?" Smiley asked, keeping Sam on the same long rein; still making no effort to go for what Sam regarded as the centre of things.

"The money wasn't mainstream," said Sam. "It was odd-ball. Mac said so. I said so. We all said so."

Smiley's head lifted even more slowly than before.

"Why?" he asked, looking very straight at Sam.

"The above-the-line Soviet residency in Vientiane ran three bank accounts round town. The Cousins had all three wired. They've had them wired for years. They knew every cent the residency drew, and even, from the account number, whether it was for intelligence-gathering or subversion. The residency had its own money-carriers, and a triple-signature system for any drawing over a thousand bucks. Christ, George, I mean it's all in the record, you know!"

"Sam, I want you to pretend that record doesn't exist," said Smiley gravely, still writing. "All will be revealed to you in due season. Till then, bear with us."

"Whatever you say," said Sam, breathing much more easily, Smiley noticed; he seemed to feel he was on firmer ground.

It was at this point that Smiley proposed they get old Connie to come and lend an ear, and perhaps Doc di Salis, too, since South East Asia was, after all, Doc's patch. Tactically, he was content to bide his time with Sam's little secret; and strategically, the force of Sam's story was already of burning interest. So Guillam was sent to whip them in while Smiley called a break and the two men stretched their legs.

"How's trade?" Sam asked politely.

"Well, a *little* depressed," Smiley admitted. "Miss it?"

"That's Karla, is it?" said Sam, studying the photograph.

Smiley's tone became at once donnish and vague.

"Who? Ah, yes, yes it is. Not much of a likeness, I'm afraid, but the best we can do as yet."

They might have been admiring an early water-colour.

"You've got some personal thing about him, haven't you?" said Sam ruminatively.

At this point, Connie, di Salis, and Guillam filed in, led by Guillam, with little Fawn needlessly holding open the door.

* * *

With the enigma temporarily set aside therefore, the meeting became something of a war party: the hunt was up. First Smiley recapitulated for Sam, incidentally making it clear in the process that they were *pretending* there were no records—which was a veiled warning to the new-comers. Then Sam took up the tale where he had left off: about the *angles*, the little things that caught the eye; though really, he insisted, there was not a lot more to say. Once the trail led to Indocharter Vientiane S.A., it stopped dead.

"Indocharter was an overseas Chinese company," said Sam, with a glance at Doc di Salis. "Mainly Swatownese."

At the name "Swatownese" di Salis gave a cry, part laughter, part lament. "Oh, they're the *very* worst," he declared, meaning the most difficult to crack.

"It was an overseas Chinese outfit," Sam repeated for the rest of them, "and the loony-bins of South East Asia are jam-packed with honest fieldmen who have tried to unravel the life-style of hot money once it entered the maw of the overseas Chinese." Particularly, he added, of the Swatownese or Chiu Chow, who were a people apart, and controlled the rice monopolies in Thailand, Laos, and several other spots as well. Of which league, said Sam, Indocharter Vientiane S.A. was classic. His trade cover had evidently allowed him to investigate it in some depth.

"First, the *société anonyme* was registered in Paris," he said. "Second, the *société*, on reliable information, was the property of a discreetly diversified overseas Shanghainese trading company based in Manila, which was itself owned by a Chiu Chow company registered in Bangkok, which in turn paid its dues to a totally amorphous outfit in Hong Kong called China Airsea, quoted on the local Stock Exchange, which owned everything from junk-fleets to cement factories to racehorses to restaurants. China Airsea was, by Hong Kong standards, a blue-chip trading house, long-established and in good standing," said Sam, "and probably the only connection between Indocharter and China Airsea was that somebody's fifth elder brother had an aunt who was at school with one of the shareholders and owed him a favour."

Di Salis gave another swift, approving nod and, linking his awkward hands, thrust them over one crooked knee and drew it to his chin.

Smiley had closed his eyes and seemed to have dozed off. But in reality he was hearing precisely what he had expected to hear: when it came to the full staffing of the firm of Indocharter Vientiane S.A., Sam Collins trod very lightly round a certain personality.

"But I think you mentioned there were also two *non*-Chinese in the firm, Sam," Smiley reminded him. "A dumb blonde, you said, and a pilot: Ricardo."

Sam lightly brushed the objection aside. "Ricardo was a madcap March Hare," he said. "The Chinese wouldn't have trusted him with the stamp money. The real work was all done in the back room. If cash came in, that's where it was handled, that's where it was lost. Whether it was Russian cash, opium cash, or whatever."

Di Salis, pulling frantically at one ear-lobe, was prompt to agree. "Reappearing at will in Vancouver, Amsterdam, or Hong Kong, or wherever it suited somebody's very Chinese purpose," he declared, and writhed in pleasure at his own perception.

Once again, thought Smiley, Sam had got himself off the hook. "Well, well," he said. "And how did it go from there, Sam, in your authorised version?"

"London scrubbed the case."

From the dead silence, Sam must have realised in a second that he had touched a considerable nerve. His sign language indicated as much, for he did not peer round at their faces, or register any curiosity at all. Instead, out of a sort of theatrical modesty, he studied his shiny evening shoes and his elegant dress socks, and drew thoughtfully on his brown cigarette.

"When did they do that then, Sam?" asked Smiley.

Sam gave the date.

"Go back a little. Still forgetting the record, right? How much did London know of your enquiries as you went along? Tell us that. Did you send progress reports from day to day? Did Mac?"

If the mothers next door had set a bomb off, said Guillam afterwards, nobody would have taken his eyes off Sam.

Well, said Sam easily, as if humouring Smiley's whim, he was an old dog. His principle in the field had always been to do it first and apologise afterwards. Mac's, too. Operate the other way round and soon you have London refusing to let you cross the street without changing your nappies first, said Sam.

"So?" said Smiley patiently.

So the first word they sent London on the case was, you might say, their last. Mac acknowledged the enquiry, reported the sum of Sam's findings, and asked for instructions.

"And London? What did London do, Sam?"

"Sent Mac a top-priority shriek pulling us both off the case and ordering him to cable back immediately confirming I had understood and obeyed the order. For good measure, they threw in a rocket telling us not to fly solo again."

Guillam was doodling on the sheet of paper before him: a flower, then petals, then rain falling on the flower. Connie was beaming at Sam as if it were his wedding day, and her baby eyes were brimming tears of excitement. Di Salis, as usual, was jiggling and fiddling like an old engine, but his gaze also, as much as he could fix it anywhere, was upon Sam.

"You must have been rather cross," said Smiley.

"Not really."

"Didn't you have any wish to see the case through? You'd made a considerable strike."

"I was irked, sure."

"But you went along with London's instruction?"

"I'm a soldier, George. We all are in the field."

"Very laudable," said Smiley, considering Sam once more, how he lounged smooth and charming in his dinner-jacket.

"Orders is orders," said Sam, with a smile.

"Indeed. And when you eventually got back to London, I wonder," Smiley went on, in a controlled, speculative way, "and you had your 'welcome-home-well-done' session with Bill, did you happen to mention the matter casually at all, to Bill?"

"Asked him what the hell he thought he was up to," Sam agreed, just as leisurely.

"And what did Bill have to answer there, Sam?"

"Blamed the Cousins. Said they had got in on the act ahead of us. Said it was their case and their parish."

"Had you any reason to believe that?"

"Sure. Ricardo."

"You guessed he was the Cousins' man?"

"He'd flown for them. He was on their books already. He was a natural. All they had to do was keep him in play."

"I thought we were agreed that a man like Ricardo would have no access to the real operations of the company?"

"Wouldn't stop them using him. Not the Cousins. Still be their case, even if Ricardo was a bummer. The hands-off pact would apply either way."

"Let's go back to the moment when London pulled you off the case. You received the order 'Drop everything.' You obeyed. But it was some while yet before you returned to London, wasn't it? Was there an aftermath of any kind?"

"Don't quite follow you, old boy."

Once again, at the back of his mind, Smiley made a scrupulous record of Sam's evasion.

"For example your friendly contact at the Banque de l'Indochine. Johnny. You kept up with him, of course?"

"Sure," said Sam.

"And did Johnny happen to mention to you, as a matter of history, what happened to the gold seam after you'd received your hands-off telegram? Did it continue to come in month by month, just as it had before?"

"Stopped dead. Paris turned the tap off. No Indocharter, no nothing."

"And Commercial Boris, of no previous convictions? Does he live happily ever after?"

"Went home."

"Was he due to?"

"Done three years."

"They usually do more."

"Specially the hoods," Sam agreed, smiling.

"And Ricardo, the madcap Mexican flyer whom you suspect of being the Cousins' agent—what became of him?"

"Died," said Sam, eyes on Smiley all the while. "Crashed up on the Thai border. The boys put it down to an overload of heroin."

Pressed, Sam had that date too.

"Was there moaning at the bar about that, so to speak?"

"Not much. General feeling seemed to be that Vientiane would be a safer place without Ricardo emptying his pistol through the ceiling of the White Rose or Madame Lulu's."

"Where was that feeling expressed, Sam?"

"Oh, at Maurice's place."

"Maurice?"

"Constellation Hotel. Maurice is the proprietor."

"I see. Thank you."

Here there was a definite gap, but Smiley seemed disinclined to fill it. Watched by Sam and his three assistants and Fawn the factotum, Smiley plucked at his spectacles, tilted them, straightened them, and returned his hands to the glass-top desk. Then he took Sam all the way through the story again, rechecked dates and names and places, very laboriously in the way of trained interrogators the world over, listening by long habit for the tiny flaws and the chance discrepancies and the omissions and the changes of emphasis, and apparently not finding any.

And Sam, in his sense of false security, let it all happen, watching with the same blank smile with which he watched cards slip across the baize, or the roulette wheel tease the white ball from one bay to another.

"Sam, I wonder whether you could possibly manage to stay the night with us?" Smiley said when they were once more just the two of them. "Fawn will do you a bed and so on. Do you think you could swing that with your club?"

"My dear fellow," said Sam generously.

Then Smiley did a rather unnerving thing. Having handed Sam a bunch of magazines, he phoned for Sam's personal dossier, all volumes, and with Sam sitting there before him he read them in silence from cover to cover.

"I see you're a ladies' man," he remarked at last, as the dusk gathered at the window.

"Here and there," Sam agreed, still smiling. "Here and there." But the nervousness was quite apparent in his voice.

When night came, Smiley sent the mothers home and issued orders through Housekeeping Section to have the archives cleared of all burrowers by eight at the latest. He gave no reason. He let them think what they wanted. Sam should lie up in the rumpus room to be on call, and Fawn should keep him company and not let him stray. Fawn took this instruction literally. Even when the hours dragged out and Sam appeared to doze, Fawn stayed folded like a cat across the threshold, but with his eyes always open.

Then the four of them cloistered themselves in Registry— Connie, di Salis, Smiley, and Guillam—and began the long, cautious paper-chase. They looked first for the operational case papers which properly should have been housed in the South East Asian cut, under the dates Sam had given them. There was no card in the index and there were no case papers either, but this was not yet significant. Haydon's London Station had been in the habit of waylaying operational files and confining them to its own restricted archive. So they plodded across the basement, feet clapping on the brown linoleum tiles, till they came to a barred alcove like an antechapel where the remains of what was formerly London Station's archive were laid to rest. Once again, they found no card and no papers.

"Look for the telegrams," Smiley ordered, so they checked the signals ledgers, both incoming and outgoing, and for a moment Guillam at least was ready to suspect Sam of lying, till Connie pointed out that the relevant traffic sheets had been typed with a different typewriter: a machine, as it later turned out, that had not been acquired by housekeepers till six months after the date on the paper.

"Look for floats," Smiley ordered.

Circus floats were duplicated copies of main serials, which Registry ran off when case papers threatened to be in constant action. They were banked in loose-leaf folders like back numbers of magazines and indexed every six weeks. After much delving, Connie Sachs unearthed the South East Asian folder covering the six-week period immediately following Collins's trace request. It contained no reference to a suspected Soviet gold seam and none to Indocharter Vientiane S.A.

"Try the P.F.s," said Smiley, with a rare use of initials, which he otherwise detested. So they trailed to another corner of Registry and sorted through drawers of cards, looking first for personal files on Commercial Boris, then for Ricardo, then under aliases for Tiny, believed dead, whom Sam had apparently mentioned in his original ill-fated report to London Station. Now and then, Guillam was sent upstairs to ask Sam some small point, and found him reading *Field* and sipping a large Scotch, watched unflinchingly by Fawn, who occasionally varied his routine—Guillam learned later—with press-ups, first on two knuckles of each hand, then on his fingertips. In the case of Ricardo, they mapped out phonetic variations and ran them across the index also.

"Where are the organisations filed?" Smiley asked.

But of the *société anonyme* known as Indocharter Vientiane, the organisations index contained no card either.

"Look up the liaison material."

Dealings with the Cousins in Haydon's day were handled entirely through the London Station Liaison Secretariat, of which he himself for obvious reasons had personal command and which held its own file copies of all inter-service correspondence. Returning to the antechapel, they once more drew a blank. To Peter Guillam the night was taking on surreal dimensions. Smiley had become all but wordless. His plump face turned to rock. Connie in her excitement had forgotten her arthritic aches and pains and was hopping around the shelves like a teenager at the ball. Not by any means a born paper man, Guillam scrambled after her pretending to keep up with the pack, and secretly grateful for his trips up to Sam.

"We've *got* him, George, darling," Connie kept saying under her breath. "Sure as boots we've *got* the beastly toad."

Doc di Salis had danced away in search of Indocharter's Chinese directors—Sam, astonishingly, had the names of two still in his head—and was wrestling with their names first in Chinese, then in Roman script, and finally in Chinese commercial code. Smiley sat in a chair reading the files on his knee like a man in a train, doughtily ignoring the passengers. Sometimes he lifted his head, but the sounds he heard were not from inside the room.

Connie, on her own initiative, had launched a search for cross-references to files with which the case papers should theoretically have been linked. There were subject files on mercenaries, and on free-lance aviators. There were method files on Centre's techniques for laundering agent payments, and even a treatise, which she herself had written long ago, on the subject of below-the-line paymasters responsible for Karla's illegal networks run unbeknown to the mainstream residencies. Commercial Boris's unpronounceable last names had not been added to the appendix. There were background files on the Banque de l'Indochine and its links with the Moscow Narodny Bank, and statistical files on the growing scale of Centre's activities in South East Asia, and study files on the Vientiane residency itself. But the negatives only multiplied, and as they multiplied they proved the affirmative: nowhere in their whole pursuit of Haydon had they come upon such a systematic and wholesale brushing-over of the traces. It was the back-bearing of all time.

And it led inexorably East.

Only one clue that night pointed to the culprit. They came on it somewhere between dawn and morning while Guillam was dozing on his feet. Connie sniffed it out, Smiley laid it silently on the table, and three of them peered at it together under the reading-light as if it were the clue to buried treasure: a clip of destruction certificates, a dozen in all, with the authorising cryptonym scribbled in black felt-tip along the middle line, giving a pleasing effect of charcoal. The condemned files related to "top-secret correspondence with H/Annexe"; that is to say, with the Cousins' Head of Station—then, as now, Smiley's Brother-in-Christ Martello. The reason for destruction was the same as that which Haydon had given to Sam Collins for abandoning the field enquiries in Vientiane: "Risk of compromising delicate American operation." The signature consigning the files to the incinerator was in Haydon's work name.

Returning upstairs, Smiley invited Sam once more to his room. Sam had removed his bow-tie, and the stubble of his jaw against his open-necked white shirt made him a lot less smooth.

First, Smiley sent Fawn out for coffee. He let it arrive and he waited till Fawn had flitted away again before pouring two cups, black for both of them, sugar for Sam, a saccharin for Smiley on account of his weight problem. Then he settled in a soft chair at Sam's side rather than have a desk between them, in order to affiliate himself to Sam.

"Sam, I think I ought to hear a little about the girl," he said very softly, as if he were breaking sad news. "Was it chivalry that made you miss her out?"

Sam seemed rather amused. "Lost the files, have you, old boy?" he enquired, with the same men's-room intimacy.

Sometimes, in order to obtain a confidence, it is necessary to impart one.

"*Bill* lost them," Smiley replied gently.

Elaborately, Sam lapsed into deep thought. Curling one card-player's hand, he surveyed his fingertips, lamenting their grimy state.

"That club of mine practically runs itself these days," he reflected. "I'm getting bored with it, to be frank. Money, money. Time I had a change, made something of myself."

Smiley understood, but he had to be firm: "I've no resources, Sam. I can hardly feed the mouths I've hired already."

Sam sipped his black coffee ruminatively, smiling through the steam.

"Who is she, Sam? What's it all about? No one minds how bad it is. It's water under the bridge, I promise you."

Standing, Sam sank his hands in his pockets, shook his head, and, rather as Jerry Westerby might have done, began meandering round the room, peering at the odd gloomy things that hung on the wall: group war photographs of dons in uniform; a framed and handwritten letter from a dead Prime Minister; Karla's portrait again, which this time he studied from very close, on and on.

"'Never throw your chips away,'" he remarked, so close to Karla that his breath dulled the glass. "That's what my old mother used to tell me. 'Never make a present of your assets. We get very few in life. Got to dole them out sparingly.' Not as if there isn't a game going, is it?" he enquired. With his sleeve he wiped the glass clean. "Very hungry mood prevails in this house of yours. Felt it the moment I walked in. The big table, I said to myself. Baby will eat tonight."

Arriving at Smiley's desk, he sat himself in the chair as if testing it for comfort. The chair swivelled as well as rocked. Sam tried both movements. "I need a search request," he said.

"Top right," said Smiley, and watched while Sam opened the drawer, pulled out a yellow flimsy, and laid it on the glass to write.

For a couple of minutes Sam composed in silence, pausing occasionally for artistic consideration, then writing again.

"Call me if she shows up," he said and, with a facetious wave to Karla, took his leave.

When he had gone, Smiley took the form from the desk, sent for Guillam, and handed it to him without a word.

On the staircase Guillam paused to read the text: "Worthington Elizabeth, alias Lizzie, alias Ricardo Lizzie." That was the top line. Then the details: "Age about twenty-seven. Nationality British. Status: married, details of husband unknown, maiden name also unknown. 1972/3 common-law wife of Ricardo Tiny, now dead. Last known place of residence: Vientiane, Laos. Last known occupation: typist-receptionist with Indocharter Vientiane S.A. Previous occupations: night-club hostess, whisky saleswoman, high-class tart."

Performing its usual dismal rôle these days, Registry took about three minutes to regret "no trace repeat no trace of subject." Beyond this, the Queen Bee took issue with the term "high class." She insisted that "superior" was the proper way to describe that kind of tart.

Curiously enough, Smiley was not deterred by Sam's reticence. He seemed happy to accept it as part and parcel of the trade. Instead, he requested copies of all source reports which Sam had originated from Vientiane or elsewhere over the last ten years odd, and which had escaped Haydon's clever knife. And thereafter, in leisure hours, such as they were, he browsed through these and allowed his questing imagination to form pictures of Sam's murky world.

* * *

At this hanging moment in the affair Smiley showed a quite lovely sense of tact, as all later agreed. A lesser man might have stormed round to the Cousins and asked, as a matter of the highest urgency, that Martello look out the American end of the destroyed correspondence and grant him a sight of it, but Smiley wanted nothing stirred, nothing signalled. So instead he chose his humblest emissary.

Molly Meakin was a prim, pretty graduate, a little blue-stocking, perhaps, a little inward, but already with a modest name as a capable desk officer, and Old Circus by virtue of both her brother and her father. At the time of the fall, she was still a probationer, cutting her milk-teeth in Registry. After it, she was kept on as skeleton staff and promoted, if that is the word, to Vetting Section, whence no man, let alone woman, says the folklore, returns alive. But Molly possessed, perhaps by hered-ity, what the trade calls a natural eye. While those around her were still exchanging anecdotes about exactly where they were and what they were wearing when the news of Haydon's arrest was broken to them, Molly was setting up an unsung channel to her opposite number at the Annexe in Grosvenor Square, one which bypassed the laborious procedures laid down by the Cousins since the fall.

Molly's greatest ally was routine. Her visiting day was a Friday. Every Friday she drank coffee with Ed, who manned the computer; and talked classical music with Marge, who doubled for Ed; and sometimes she stayed for Old Tyme danc-ing or a game of shuffleboard or tenpin bowling at the Twi-light Club in the basement. Friday was also the day, quite incidentally, when she took along her little shopping list of trace requests. Even if she had none outstanding, Molly was careful to invent some in order to keep the channel open, and on this particular Friday, at Smiley's behest, Molly Meakin included the name of Tiny Ricardo in her selection. "But I don't want him sticking out in any way, Molly," said Smiley anxiously.

"Of course not," said Molly.

For smoke, as she called it, Molly chose a dozen other "R"s, and when she came to Ricardo she wrote down "Richards query Rickard query Ricardo, profession teacher query aviation instructor," so that the real Ricardo would only be thrown up as a possible identification. "Nationality Mexican query Arab," she added; and she threw in the extra information that he might anyway be dead.

It was once more late in the evening before Molly returned to the Circus. Guillam was exhausted. Forty is a difficult age at which to stay awake, he decided. At twenty or at sixty the body knows what it's about, but forty is an adolescence where one sleeps to grow up or to stay young. Molly was twenty-three. She came straight to Smiley's room, sat down primly with her knees pressed tight together, and began unpacking her handbag, watched intently by Connie Sachs, and even more intently by Peter Guillam, though for different reasons.

She was sorry she'd been so long, she said severely, but Ed had insisted on taking her to a rerun of *True Grit*, a great favourite in the Twilight Club, and afterwards she had had to fight him off, but hadn't wished to give offence, least of all tonight. She handed Smiley an envelope and he opened it and drew out a long buff computer card. So did she fight him off or not? Guillam wanted to ask.

"How did it play?" was Smiley's first question.

"Quite straightforward," she replied.

"What an extraordinary-looking script," Smiley exclaimed next. But as he went on reading, his expression changed slowly to a rare and wolfish grin.

Connie was less restrained. By the time she had passed the card to Guillam, she was laughing outright.

"Oh, *Bill!*" she cried. "Oh, you wicked lovely man! Talk about pointing everybody in the wrong direction! Oh, the devil!"

In order to silence the Cousins, Haydon had reversed his original lie. Deciphered, the lengthy computer print-out told the following enchanting story.

Anxious lest the Cousins might have been duplicating the Circus's enquiries into Indocharter Vientiane S.A., Bill Haydon, in his capacity as Head of London Station, had sent to the Annexe a pro-forma hands-off notice, under the standing bilateral agreement between the services. This advised the Americans that Indocharter Vientiane S.A. was presently under scrutiny by London and that the Circus had an agent in place. Accordingly, the Americans consented to drop any interest they might have in the case in exchange for a share of the eventual take. As an aid to the British operation, the Cousins did however mention that their link with the pilot Tiny Ricardo was extinct.

In short, as neat an example of playing both ends against the middle as anybody had met with.

"Thank you, Molly," said Smiley politely, when everyone had had a chance to marvel. "Thank you very much indeed."

"Not at all," said Molly, prim as a nursemaid. "And Ricardo is definitely dead, Mr. Smiley," she ended, and she quoted the same date of death which Sam Collins had already supplied. With that, she snapped together the clasp of her handbag, pulled her skirt over her admirable knees, and walked delicately from the room, well observed once more by Peter Guillam.

A different pace, a different mood entirely, now overtook the Circus. The frantic search for a trail, any trail, was over. They could march to a purpose, rather than gallop in all directions. The amiable distinctions between the two families largely fell away: the Bolshies and the yellow perils became a single unit under the joint direction of Connie and the Doc, even if they kept their separate skills. Joy after that, for the burrowers, came in bits, like water-holes on a long and dusty trek, and sometimes they all but fell at the wayside.

Connie took no more than a week to identify the Soviet paymaster in Vientiane who had supervised the transfer of funds to Indocharter Vientiane S.A.—the Commercial Boris. He was the former soldier Zimin, a long-standing graduate of Karla's private training school outside Moscow. Under the previous alias of Smirnov, this Zimin was on record as having played paymaster to an East German *apparat* in Switzerland six years ago. Using the name Kursky, he had surfaced before that in Vienna. As a secondary skill, he offered sound-stealing and entrapment, and some said he was the same Zimin who had sprung the successful honey-trap in West Berlin against a certain French senator who later sold half his country's secrets down the river. He had left Vientiane exactly a month after Sam's report had hit London.

After that small triumph, Connie set herself the apparently impossible task of defining what arrangements Karla, or his paymaster Zimin, might have made to replace the interrupted gold seam. Her touchstones were several. First, the known conservatism of enormous intelligence establishments, and their attachment to proven trade routes. Second, Centre's presumed need, since large payments were involved, to replace the old system with a new one fast. Third, Karla's complacency, both before the fall, when he had the Circus tethered, and since the fall, when it lay gasping and toothless at his feet. Lastly, quite simply, she relied upon her own encyclopaedic grasp of the subject. Gathering together the heaps of unprocessed raw material which had lain deliberately neglected during the years of her exile, Connie's team made huge arcs through the files, revised, conferred, drew charts and diagrams, pursued the individual handwriting of known operators, had migraines, argued, played Ping-Pong, and occasionally, with agonising caution and Smiley's express consent, undertook timid investigations in the field. A friendly contact in the City was persuaded to visit an old acquaintance who specialised in offshore Hong Kong companies. A Cheapside currency broker opened his books to

Toby Esterhase, the sharp-eyed Hungarian survivor who was all that remained of the Circus's once glorious travelling army of couriers and pavement artists.

So it went on, at a snail's pace; but at least the snail knew where it wanted to go. Doc di Salis, in his distant way, took the overseas Chinese path, working his passage through the arcane connections of Indocharter Vientiane S.A. and its elusive echelons of parent companies. His helpers were as uncommon as himself, either language students or elderly recycled China hands. With time they acquired a collective pallor, like inmates of the same dank seminary.

Meanwhile, Smiley himself advanced no less cautiously, if anything down yet more devious avenues, and through a greater number of doors.

Once more he sank from view. It was a time of waiting and he spent it in attending to the hundred other things that needed his urgent attention. His brief burst of team-work over, he withdrew to the inner regions of his solitary world. Whitehall saw him; so did Bloomsbury still; so did the Cousins. At other times the throne-room door stayed closed for days at a time, and only dark Fawn the factotum was permitted to flit in and out in his gym shoes, bearing steaming cups and plates of biscuits and occasional written memoranda, to or from his master.

Smiley had always loathed the telephone, and now he would take no calls whatever, unless in Guillam's view they concerned matters of great urgency, and none did. The only instrument Smiley could not switch off controlled the direct line from Guillam's desk, but when he was in one of his moods he went so far as to put a tea-cosy over it in an effort to quell the ring. The invariable procedure was for Guillam to say that Smiley was out, or in conference, and would return the call in an hour's time. He then wrote out a message, handed it to Fawn, and eventually, with the initiative on his side, Smiley would ring back.

He conferred with Connie, sometimes with di Salis, sometimes with both, but Guillam was not required. The Karla file was transferred from Connie's research section to Smiley's personal safe for good—all seven volumes. Guillam signed for them and took them in to him, and when Smiley looked up from the desk and saw them, the quiet of recognition came over him, and he reached forward as if to receive an old friend. The door closed again, and more days passed.

"Any word?" Smiley would ask occasionally of Guillam. He meant "Has Connie rung?"

The Hong Kong residency was evacuated around this time, and, too late, Smiley was advised of the housekeepers' elephantine efforts at repressing the High Haven story. He at once drew Craw's dossier, and again called Connie in for consultation. A few days later, Craw himself appeared in London for a forty-eight-hour visit. Guillam had heard him lecture at Sarratt and detested him.

A couple of weeks afterwards, the old man's celebrated article finally saw the light of day. Smiley read it intently, then passed it to Guillam, and for once he actually offered an explanation for his action: Karla would know very well what the Circus was up to, he said. Back-bearings were a time-honoured pastime. However, Karla would not be human if he didn't sleep after such a big kill.

"I want him to hear from everyone just how dead we are," Smiley explained.

Soon this broken-wing technique was extended to other spheres, and one of Guillam's more entertaining tasks was to make sure that Roddy Martindale was well supplied with woeful stories about the Circus's disarray.

And still the burrowers toiled. They called it afterwards "the phoney peace." They had the map, Connie said later, and they had the directions, but there were still mountains to be moved in spoonfuls. Waiting, Guillam took Molly Meakin to long and costly dinners, but they ended inconclusively. He played squash with her and admired her eye, he swam with her and admired her body, but she warded off closer contact with a mysterious and private smile, turning her head away and downward while she went on holding him.

Under the continued pressure of idleness, Fawn the factotum took to acting strangely. When Smiley disappeared and left him behind, he literally pined for his master's return. Catching him by surprise in his little den one evening, Guillam was shocked to find him in a near-foetal crouch, winding a handkerchief round and round his thumb like a ligature, in order to hurt himself.

"For God's sake, it's nothing personal, man!" Guillam cried. "George doesn't need you for once, that's all. Take a few days' leave or something. Unwind."

But Fawn referred to Smiley as the Chief, and looked askance at those who called him George.

It was toward the end of this barren phase that a new and wonderful gadget appeared on the fifth floor. It was brought in suitcases by two crew-cut technicians and installed over three days: a green telephone destined, despite his prejudices, for Smiley's desk and connecting him directly with the Annexe. It was routed by way of Guillam's room, and linked to all manner of anonymous grey boxes, which hummed without warning. Its presence only deepened the general mood of nervousness. What use was a machine, they asked each other, if they had nothing to put into it?

But they had something.

Suddenly the word was out. What Connie had found she wasn't saying, but news of the discovery ran like wildfire through the building: "Connie's *home!* The burrowers are *home!* They've found the new gold seam! They've traced it all the way through!"

Through what? To whom? Where did it end? Connie and di Salis still kept mum. For a day and a night, they trailed in and out of the throne-room laden with files, no doubt once more in order to show Smiley their workings.

Then Smiley disappeared for three days, and Guillam only

learned much later that "in order to screw down every bolt," as he called it, he had visited both Hamburg and Amsterdam for discussions with certain eminent bankers of his acquaintance. These gentlemen spent a great while explaining to him that the war was over and they could not possibly offend against their code of ethics; and then they gave him the information he so badly needed, though it was only the final confirmation of all that the burrowers had deduced. Smiley returned, but Peter Guillam still remained shut out, and he might well have continued in this private limbo indefinitely had it not been for dinner at the Lacons'.

Guillam's inclusion was pure chance. So was the dinner. Smiley had asked Lacon for an afternoon appointment at the Cabinet Office, and spent several hours in cahoots with Connie and di Salis preparing for it. At the last moment, Lacon was summoned by his parliamentary masters, and proposed potluck at his ugly mansion at Ascot instead. Smiley detested driving and there was no duty car. In the end, Guillam offered to chauffeur him in his draughty old Porsche, having first put a rug over him, which he was keeping in case Molly Meakin consented to a picnic.

On the drive Smiley attempted small talk, which came hard to him, but he was nervous. They arrived in rain and there was muddle on the doorstep about what to do with the unexpected underling. Smiley insisted that Guillam would make his own way and return at ten-thirty; the Lacons that he *must* stay, there was simply *masses* of food.

"It's up to you," said Guillam to Smiley.

"Oh, of course. No, I mean really, if it's all right with the Lacons, naturally," said Smiley huffily, and in they went.

So a fourth place was laid, and the over-cooked steak was cut into bits till it looked like dry stew, and a daughter was dispatched on her bicycle with a pound to fetch a second bottle of wine from the pub up the road. Mrs. Lacon was doe-like and fair and blushing, a child bride who had become a child mother.

The table was too long for four. She sat Smiley and her husband one end and Guillam next to her. Having asked him whether he liked madrigals, she embarked on an endless account of a concert at her daughters' private school. She said it was absolutely *ruined* by the rich foreigners they were taking in to balance the books. Half of them couldn't sing in a Western way at all.

"I mean who wants one's child brought up with a lot of Persians when they all have six wives apiece?" she said.

Stringing her along, Guillam strove to catch the dialogue at the other end of the table. Lacon seemed to be bowling and batting at once.

"First, you petition *me*," he boomed. "You are doing that now, very properly. At this stage, you should give no more than a preliminary outline. Traditionally, Ministers like nothing that cannot be written on a postcard. Preferably a *picture* postcard," he said, and took a prim sip at the vile red wine.

Mrs. Lacon, whose intolerance had a beatific innocence about it, began complaining about Jews.

"I mean they don't even eat the same *food* as we do," she said. "Penny says they get special herring things for lunch."

Guillam again lost the thread till Lacon raised his voice in warning.

"Try to keep 'Karla' out of this, George. I've asked you before. Learn to say 'Moscow' instead, will you? They don't like personalities—however dispassionate your hatred of him. Nor do I."

"Moscow, then," Smiley said.

"It's not that one *dislikes* them," Mrs. Lacon said. "They're just different."

Lacon picked up some earlier point: "When you say a *large* sum, how large is large?"

"We are not yet in a position to say," Smiley replied.

"Good. More enticing. Have you no panic factor?"

Smiley didn't follow that question any better than Guillam did.

"What alarms you most about your discovery, George? What do you fear for here, in your rôle of watch-dog?"

"The security of a British Crown Colony?" Smiley suggested after some thought.

"They're talking about Hong Kong," Mrs. Lacon explained to Guillam. "My uncle was Political Secretary. On Daddy's side," she added. "Mummy's brothers never did anything brainy at all."

She said Hong Kong was nice but smelly.

Lacon had become a little pink and erratic. "Colony—my God, hear that, Val?" he called down the table, taking time off to educate her. "Richer than we are by half, I should think, and from where *I* sit, enviably more secure as well. A full twenty years their treaty has to run, even if the Chinese enforce it. More. At this rate, they should see us out in comfort!"

"Oliver thinks we're *doomed*," Mrs. Lacon explained to Guillam excitedly, as if she were admitting him to a family secret, and shot her husband an angelic smile.

Lacon resumed his former confiding tone, but he continued to blurt, and Guillam guessed he was showing off to his squaw. "You would also make the point to me, wouldn't you—as background to the postcard, as it were—that a major Soviet intelligence presence in Hong Kong would be an appalling embarrassment to the Colonial government in her relations with Peking?"

"Before I went as far as that—"

"On whose magnanimity," Lacon pursued, "she depends from hour to hour for her survival—correct?"

"It's because of these very implications—" Smiley said.

"Oh, Penny, you're naked!" Mrs. Lacon cried indulgently. Providing Guillam with a glorious respite, she bounded off to calm an unruly small daughter who had appeared at the doorway. Lacon meanwhile had filled his lungs for an aria.

"We are therefore not only protecting Hong Kong from the *Russians*—which is bad enough, I grant you, but perhaps not *quite* bad enough for some of our higher-minded Ministers—we are protecting her from the wrath of Peking, which is universally held to be awful. Right, Guillam? *However*," said Lacon, and to emphasise the volte-face went so far as to arrest Smiley's arm with his long hand so that he had to put down his glass. "*However*," he warned, as his erratic voice swooped and rose again, "whether our masters will swallow all that is quite another matter altogether."

"I would not consider asking them to until I had obtained corroboration of our data," Smiley said sharply.

"Ah, but you can't, can you?" Lacon warned, changing hats. "You can't go beyond domestic research. You haven't the charter."

"Without a reconnaissance of the information—"

"Ah, but what does that *mean*, George?"

"Putting in an agent."

Lacon lifted his eyebrows and turned away his head, reminding Guillam irresistibly of Molly Meakin.

"Method is not my affair, nor are the details. Clearly you can do nothing to embarrass, since you have no money and no resources." He poured more wine, spilling some. "Val!" he yelled. "Cloth!"

"I do have *some* money."

"But not for that purpose." The wine had stained the table-cloth. Guillam poured salt on it while Lacon lifted the cloth and shoved his napkin-ring under it to spare the polish.

A long silence followed, broken by the slow pat of wine falling on the parquet floor.

Finally Lacon said, "It is entirely up to you to define what is chargeable under your mandate."

"May I have that in writing?"

"No, sir."

"May I have your authority to take what steps are needed to corroborate the information?"

"No, sir."

"But you won't block me?"

"Since I know nothing of method, and am not required to, it is hardly my province to dictate to you."

"But since I make a formal approach—" Smiley began.

"Val, *do* bring a cloth! Once you make a formal approach, I shall wash my hands of you entirely. It is the Intelligence Steering Group, not myself, who determine your scope of action. You will make your pitch. They will hear you out. From then on, it's between you and them. I am just the midwife. Val, bring a cloth—it's everywhere!"

"Oh, it's my head on the block, not yours," said Smiley, almost to himself. "You're impartial. I know all about that."

"*Oliver's* not impartial," said Mrs. Lacon gaily as she returned with the girl over her shoulder, brushed and wearing a nightdress. "He's *terrifically* in favour of you, aren't you, Olly?" She handed Lacon a cloth and he began mopping. "He's become a real *hawk* these days. Better than the Americans. Now say good night to everyone, Penny, come on." She was offering the child to each of them in turn. "Mr. Smiley first . . . Mr. Guillam . . . now Daddy. . . . How's Ann, George; not off to the country again, I hope?"

"Oh, very bonny, thank you."

"Well, make Oliver give you what you want. He's getting *terribly* pompous, aren't you, Olly?"

She danced off, chanting her own rituals to the child: "Hitty pitty *without* the wall . . . hitty pitty *within* the wall . . . and *bumps* goes Pottifer!"

Lacon proudly watched her go.

"Now, will you bring the Americans into it, George?" he demanded airily. "That's a great catchpenny, you know. Wheel in the Cousins and you'd carry the committee without a shot fired. Foreign Office would eat out of your hand."

"I would prefer to stay my decision on that, if you don't mind."

The green telephone, thought Guillam, might never have existed.

Lacon ruminated, twiddling his glass.

"Pity," he pronounced finally. "Pity. No Cousins, no panic factor—" He gazed at the dumpy, unimpressive figure before him. Smiley sat, eyes closed, seemingly half asleep. "And no credibility, either," Lacon went on, apparently as a direct comment upon Smiley's appearance. "Defence won't lift a finger for you, I'll tell you that for a start. Nor will the Home Office. The Treasury's a toss-up, and the Foreign Office—depends who they send to the meeting and what they had for breakfast." Again he reflected. "George."

"Yes?"

"Let me send you an advocate. Somebody who can ride point for you, draft your submission, carry it to the barricades."

"Oh, I think I can manage, thank you!"

"Make him rest more," Lacon advised Guillam, in a deafening whisper as they walked to the car. "And try and get him to drop those black jackets and stuff. They went out with bustles. Goodbye, George! Ring me tomorrow if you change your mind and want help. Now drive carefully, Guillam. Remember you've been drinking."

As they passed through the gates, Guillam said something very rude indeed, but Smiley was too deep inside the rug to hear.

"So it's Hong Kong, then?" Guillam said.

No answer; but no denial, either.

"And who's the lucky fieldman?" Guillam asked a little later, with no real hope of getting an answer. "Or is that all part of foxing around with the Cousins?"

"We're not foxing around with them at all," Smiley retorted, stung for once. "If we cut them in, they'll swamp us. If we don't, we've no resources. It's simply a matter of balance."

Smiley dived back into the rug.

But the very next day, lo and behold, they were ready.

At ten, Smiley convened an operational directorate. Smiley

talked, Connie talked, and di Salis fidgeted and scratched himself like a verminous court tutor in a Restoration comedy till it was his turn to speak out, in his cracked, clever voice.

The same evening still, Smiley sent his telegram to Italy: a real one, not just a signal, code word "Guardian," copy to the fast-growing file. Smiley wrote it out, Guillam gave it to Fawn, who whisked it off triumphantly to the all-night post office at Charing Cross. From the air of ceremony with which he departed, one might have supposed that the little buff form was the highest point so far of his sheltered life. This was not so. Before the fall, Fawn had worked under Guillam as a scalp-hunter based in Brixton. By actual trade though, he was a silent killer.

5

A Walk in the Park

Throughout that whole sunny week, Jerry Westerby's leave-taking had a bustling, festive air which never once let up. If London was holding its summer late, then so, one might have thought, was Jerry. Stepmothers, vaccinations, travel touts, literary agents, and Fleet Street editors—Jerry, though he loathed London like the pest, took them all in his cheery pounding stride.

He even had a London persona to go with the buckskin boots: a suit, not Savile Row exactly, but undeniably a suit. His prison gear, as the orphan called it, was a washable, blue-faded affair, the creation of a twenty-four-hour tailor named Pontschak Happy House of Bangkok, who guaranteed it "unwrinkable" in radiant silk letters on the tag. In the mild midday breezes, it billowed as weightlessly as a frock on Brighton pier. His silk shirt from the same source had a yellowed, locker-room look recalling Wimbledon or Henley. His tan, though Tuscan, was as English as the famous cricketing tie which flew from him like a patriotic flag. Only his expression, to the very discerning, had that certain watchfulness, which also Mama Stefano, the postmistress, had noticed and which the instinct describes as "professional" and leaves at that. Sometimes, if he anticipated waiting, he carted the book-sack with him, which gave him a bumpkin air: Dick Whittington had come to town.

He was based, if anywhere, in Thurloe Square where he

lodged with his stepmother, the third Lady Westerby, in a tiny frilly flat crammed with huge antiques salvaged from abandoned houses. She was a painted, hen-like woman—snappish, as old beauties sometimes are—and she would often curse him for real or imagined crimes, such as smoking her last cigarette or bringing in mud from his caged rambles in the park. Jerry took it all in good part. Sometimes, returning as late as three or four in the morning but still not sleepy, he would hammer on her door to wake her, though often she was awake already; and when she had put on her make-up, he set her on his bed in her frou-frou dressing-gown with a king-sized *crème de menthe frappée* in her little claw, while Jerry himself sprawled over the whole floor space, among a magic mountain of junk, getting on with what he called his packing.

The mountain was made of everything that was useless: old press cuttings, heaps of yellowed newspapers, legal deeds tied in green ribbon, and even a pair of custom-made riding boots, treed but green with mildew. In theory, Jerry was deciding what he would need of all this for his journey, but he seldom got much further than a keepsake of some kind, which set the two of them off on a chain of memories. One night, for example, he unearthed an album of his earliest stories.

"Hey, Pet, here's a good one! Westerby really rips the mask off this one! Make your heart beat faster, does it, sport? Get the old blood stirring?"

"You should have gone into your uncle's business," she retorted, turning the pages with great satisfaction. The uncle in question was a gravel king, whom Pet used freely to emphasise old Sambo's improvidence.

Another time, they found a copy of the old man's will from years back—"I, Samuel, also known as Sambo, Westerby"— jammed in with a bunch of bills and solicitors' correspondence addressed to Jerry, in his function as executor, all stained with whisky, or quinine, and beginning "We regret."

"Bit of a turn-up, that one," Jerry muttered uncomfortably

when it was too late to re-bury the envelope in the mountain. "Reckon we could bung it down the old whatnot, don't you, sport?"

Her boot-button eyes glowed furiously.

"Aloud," she ordered, in a booming theatrical voice, and in no time they were wandering together through the insoluble complexities of trusts that endowed grandchildren, educated nephews and nieces, the income to this wife for her lifetime, the capital to so-and-so on death or marriage; codicils to reward favours, others to punish slights.

"Hey, know who that was? Dread cousin Aldred, the one who went to jug! Jesus, why'd he want to leave *him* money? Blow it in one night!"

And codicils to take care of the racehorses, who might otherwise come under the axe: "My horse Rosalie in Maison Laffitte, together with two thousand pounds a year for stabling . . . my horse Intruder, presently under training in Dublin, to my son Gerald for their respective lifetimes, on the understanding he will support them to their natural deaths. . . ."

Old Sambo, like Jerry, dearly loved a horse.

Also for Jerry: stock. Only for Jerry: the company's stock in millions. A mantle, power, responsibility; a whole grand world to inherit and romp around in—a world offered, promised even, then withheld: "my son to manage all the newspapers of the group according to the style and codes of practice established in my lifetime." Even a bastard was owned to: a sum of twenty thousands, free of duty, payable to Miss Mary Something of The Green, Chobham, the mother of my acknowledged son Adam. The only trouble was: the cupboard was bare. The figures on the account sheet wasted steadily away from the day the great man's empire tottered into liquidation. Then changed to red and grew again into long bloodsucking insects, swelling by a nought a year.

"Ah well, Pet," said Jerry, in the unearthly silence of early dawn, as he tossed the envelope back on the magic mountain.

"Shot of him now, aren't you, sport?" Rolling onto his side, he grabbed the pile of faded newspapers—last editions of his father's brainchildren—and, as only old pressmen can, fumbled his way through all of them at once. "Can't go chasing the dolly-birds where *he* is, can he, Pet?"—a huge rustle of paper—"Wouldn't put it past him, mind. Wouldn't be for want of trying, I daresay." And in a quieter voice, as he turned back to glance at the little still doll on the edge of his bed, her feet barely reaching the carpet: "You were always his *tai-tai*, sport, his number one. Always stuck up for you. Told me. 'Most beautiful girl in the world, Pet is.' Told me. Very words. Bellowed it at me across Fleet Street once. 'Best wife I ever had.'"

"Damn devil," said his stepmother, in a soft, sudden rush of pure North Country dialect, as the creases collected like a surgeon's pins round the red scar of her lips. "Rotten devil, I hate every inch of him." And for a while they stayed that way, neither of them speaking, Jerry lying pottering with his junk and yanking up his forelock, she sitting, joined in some kind of love for Jerry's father.

"You should have sold ballast for your Uncle Paul," she sighed, with the insight of a much-deceived woman.

On their last night, Jerry took her out to dinner, and afterwards, back in Thurloe Square, she served him coffee in what was left of her Sèvres service. The gesture led to disaster. Wedging his broad forefinger unthinkingly into the handle of his cup, Jerry broke it off with a faint *putt* which mercifully escaped her notice. By dexterous palming, he contrived to conceal the damage from her until he was able to gain the kitchen and make a swap. God's wrath is inescapable, alas. When Jerry's plane staged in Tashkent (he had wangled himself a concession on the trans-Siberian route), he found to his surprise that the Russian authorities had opened a bar at one end of the waiting-room—in Jerry's view, amazing evidence of the country's liberalization. Groping in his jacket pocket for hard currency to pay for a large vodka, he came instead on the pretty little porcelain question mark with its snapped-off edges. He forswore the vodka.

In business matters he was equally amenable, equally compliant. His literary agent was an old cricketing acquaintance, a snob of uncertain origins called Mencken, known as Ming, one of those natural fools for whom English society, and the publishing world in particular, is ever ready to make a comfortable space. Mencken—his famous name could have been his one invention—was bluff and gusty and sported a grizzled beard, perhaps in order to suggest he wrote the books he trafficked in. They lunched in Jerry's club, a grand, grubby place which owed its survival to amalgamation with humbler clubs, and repeated appeals through the post. Huddled in the half-empty dining-room, under the marble eyes of Empire builders, they lamented Lancashire's lack of fast bowlers. Jerry wished Kent would "hit the damn ball, Ming, not peck at it." Middlesex, they agreed, had some good young ones coming on. But "Lord help us, *look* at the way they pick 'em," said Ming, shaking his head and cutting his food all at once.

"Pity you ran out of steam," Ming bawled to Jerry and anyone else who cared to listen. "Nobody's brought off the Eastern novel recently, my view. Greene managed it, if you can take Greene, which I can't—too much popery. Malraux, if you like philosophy, which I don't. Maugham you can *have*, and before that it's back to Conrad. Cheers. Mind my saying something?" Jerry filled Ming's glass. "Go easy on the Hemingway stuff. All that grace under pressure, love with your balls shot off. They don't like it, my view. It's been *said*."

Jerry saw Ming to his cab.

"Mind my saying something?" Mencken repeated. "Longer sentences. Moment you journalist chappies turn your hand to novels, you write too short. Short paragraphs, short sentences, short chapters. You see the stuff in column inches, 'stead of across the page. Hemingway was just the same. Always

trying to write novels on the back of a matchbox. Spread yourself, my view."

"Cheero, Ming. Thanks."

"Cheero, Westerby. Remember me to your old father, mind.
Must be getting on now, I suppose. Still, it comes to us all."

Even with Stubbs, Jerry near enough preserved the same
sunny temper; though Stubbs, as Connie Sachs would have
said, was a known pig.

Pressmen, like other travelling people, make the same mess
everywhere, and Stubbs, as the group's managing editor, was
no exception. His desk was littered with tea-stained proofs and
ink-stained cups and the remains of a ham sandwich that had
died of old age. Stubbs himself sat scowling at Jerry from the
middle of it all as if Jerry had come to take it away from him.

"Stubbsie. Pride of the profession," Jerry murmured, shoving open the door, and leaned against the wall with his hands
behind him as if to keep them in check.

Stubbs bit something hard and nasty on the tip of his
tongue before returning to the file he was studying at the top
of the muck on his desk. Stubbs made all the weary jokes about
editors come true. He was a resentful man with heavy grey
jowls and heavy eyelids that looked as though they had been
rubbed with soot. He would stay with the daily until the ulcers
got him, and then they would send him to the Sunday. Another
year, he would be farmed out to the women's magazines to take
orders from children till he had served his time. Meanwhile he
was devious, and listened to incoming phone calls from correspondents without telling them he was on the line.

"Saigon," Stubbs growled, and with a chewed ballpoint
marked something in a margin. His London accent was complicated by a half-hearted twang left over from the days when
Canadian was the Fleet Street sound. "Christmas, three years
back. Ring a bell?"

"What bell's that, old boy?" Jerry asked, still pressed against
the wall.

"A *festive* bell," said Stubbs, with a hangman's smile. "Fellowship and good cheer in the bureau, when the group was fool enough to maintain one out there. A Christmas party. You gave it." He read from a file. "'To Christmas luncheon, Hotel Continental, Saigon.' Then you list the guests, just the way we ask you to. Stringers, photographers, drivers, secretaries, messenger boys—what the hell do I know? Cool seventy pounds changed hands in the interest of public relations and festive cheer. Recall that?" He went straight on. "Among the guests, you have Smoothie Stallwood entered. He was *there*, was he? Stallwood? His usual act? Oiling up to the ugliest girls, saying the right things?"

Waiting, Stubbs nibbled again at whatever it was he had on the tip of his tongue. But Jerry propped up the wall, ready to wait all day.

"We're a left-wing group," said Stubbs, launching on a favourite dictum. "That means we disapprove of fox-hunting and rely for our survival on the generosity of one illiterate millionaire. Records say Stallwood ate his Christmas lunch in Phnom Penh, lashing out hospitality on dignitaries of the Cambodian government, God help him. I've spoken to Stallwood, and he seems to think that's where he was. Phnom Penh."

Jerry slouched over to the window and settled his rump against an old black radiator. Outside, not six feet from him, a grimy clock hung over the busy pavement, a present to Fleet Street from the founder. It was mid-morning, but the hands were stuck at five to six. In a doorway across the street, two men stood reading a newspaper. They wore hats, and the newspaper obscured their faces, and Jerry reflected how lovely life would be if watchers only looked like that in reality.

"Everybody screws this comic, Stubbsie," he said thoughtfully after another longish silence. "You included. You're talking about three bloody years ago. Stuff it, sport. That's my advice. Pop it up the old back passage. Best place for that one."

"It's not a comic, it's a rag. Comic's a colour supplement."

"Comic to me, sport. Always was, always will be."

"Welcome," Stubbs intoned, with a sigh. "Welcome to the Chairman's choice." He took up a printed form of contract. "Name: Westerby, Clive Gerald," he declaimed, pretending to read from it. "Profession: aristocrat. Welcome to the son of old Sambo." He tossed the contract on the desk. "You take the both. The Sunday and the daily. Seven-day coverage, wars to tit-shows. No tenure or pension, expenses at the meanest possible level. Laundry in the field only, and that doesn't mean the whole week's wash. You get a cable card but don't use it. Just air-freight your story and wire the number of the way-bill and we'll put it on the spike for you when it arrives. Further payment by results. The B.B.C. is also graciously pleased to take voice interviews from you at the usual derisory rates. Chairman says it's good for prestige, whatever the hell that means. For syndication—"

"Alleluia," said Jerry in a long outward breath.

Ambling to the desk, he took up the chewed ballpoint, still wet from Stubbs's lick, and without a glance at its owner, or the wording of the contract, scrawled his signature in a slow zigzag along the bottom of the last page, grinning lavishly. At the same moment, as if summoned to interrupt this hallowed event, a girl in jeans unceremoniously kicked open the door and dumped a fresh sheaf of galleys on the desk. The phones rang—perhaps they had been ringing for some while—the girl departed, balancing absurdly on her enormous platform heels, an unfamiliar head poked round the door and yelled "Old man's prayer-meeting, Stubbsie," an underling appeared, and moments later Jerry was being marched down the chicken run: administration, foreign desk, editorial, pay, diary, sports, travel, the ghastly women's magazines. His guide was a twenty-year-old bearded graduate, and Jerry called him "Cedric" all the way through the ritual. On the pavement Jerry paused, rocking slightly, heel to toe and back, as if he were drunk, or punch-drunk.

"Super," he muttered, loud enough for a couple of girls to turn and stare at him as they passed. "Excellent. Marvellous.

Splendid. Perfect." With that, he dived into the nearest watering-hole, where a bunch of old hands were propping up the bar, mainly the industrial and political caucus, boasting about how they nearly had a page 5 lead.

"Westerby! It's the Earl himself! It's the *suit!* The same suit! And Early-bird's inside it, for Christ's sake!"

Jerry stayed till "time" was called. He drank frugally, nevertheless, for he liked to keep a clear head for his walks in the park with George Smiley.

To every closed society there is an inside and an outside, and Jerry was on the outside. To walk in the park with George Smiley, in those days; or—free of the professional jargon—to make a clandestine rendezvous with him; or, as Jerry himself might have expressed it (if he ever, which God forbid, put a name to the larger issues of his destiny), "to take a dive into his other, better life," required him to saunter from a given point of departure, usually some rather under-populated area like the recently extinguished Covent Garden, and arrive still on foot at a given destination at a little before six. By which time, he assumed, the Circus's depleted team of pavement artists had taken a look at his back and declared it clean. On the first evening, his destination was the embankment side of Charing Cross underground station, as it was still called that year, a busy, scrappy spot where something awkward always seems to be happening to the traffic. On the last evening, it was a multiple bus-stop on the southern pavement of Piccadilly where it borders Green Park.

There were, in all, four occasions: two in London and two at the Nursery. The Sarratt stuff was operational—the obligatory rebore in tradecraft to which fieldmen must periodically submit—and included much to be memorised, such as phone numbers, word codes, and contact procedures; such as open-code phrases for insertion into plain-language telex messages to the comic; such as fall-backs and emergency action in certain, it was hoped, remote contingencies. Like many sportsmen,

Jerry had a clear, easy memory for facts, and when the inquisitors tested him they were pleased. Also they rehearsed him in
the strong-arm stuff, with the result that his back bled from
hitting the worn matting once too often.

The sessions in London consisted of one very simple briefing and one very short farewell.

The pick-ups were variously contrived. At Green Park, by
way of a recognition signal, he carried a Fortnum & Mason
carrier-bag and managed, however long the bus queue became,
by a series of grins and shuffles, to remain neatly at the back of
it. Hovering at the embankment, on the other hand, he clutched
an out-of-date copy of *Time* magazine, bearing by coincidence
the nourished features of Chairman Mao on the cover, of which
the red lettering and border on a white field stood out strongly
in the slanting sunlight. Big Ben struck six and Jerry counted
the chimes, but the ethic of such meetings requires they do not
happen on the hour or on the quarter, but in the vaguer spaces
in between, which are held to be less conspicuous. Six o'clock
was the witching hour, when the smells of every wet and leaf-
blown country cricket field in England were wafted up-river
with the damp shreds of dusk, and Jerry passed the time in a
pleasurable half-trance, scenting them thoughtlessly and keeping his left eye, for some reason, wedged tight shut.

The van, when it lumbered up to him, was a battered green
Bedford, with a ladder on the roof and "HARRIS BUILDER"
painted out but still legible on the side: an old surveillance
horse put out to grass, with steel flaps over the windows. Seeing it pull up, Jerry started forward at the same moment that
the driver, a sour boy with a harelip, shoved his spiky head
through the open window.

"Where's Wilf, then?" the boy demanded rudely. "They
said you got Wilf with you."

"You'll have to make do with me," Jerry retorted with spirit.
"Wilf's on a job." And, opening the back door, he clambered

straight in and slammed it, for the passenger seat in the front cab was deliberately crammed with lengths of plywood, so that there was no room for him to sit there.

That was the only conversation they had, ever.

In the old days, when the Circus had a natural noncommissioned class, Jerry would have counted on some amiable small talk. No longer. When he went to Sarratt, the procedure was little different except that they bounced along for fifteen miles or so, and if he was lucky, the boy remembered to throw in a cushion to prevent the total rupture of Jerry's backside. The driver's cab was blocked off from the belly of the van where Jerry crouched, and all he had to look through, as he slid up and down the wooden bench and clutched the grab handles, were the cracks at the edges of the steel window screens, which gave at best a perforated view of the world outside, though Jerry was quick enough to read the landmarks.

On the Sarratt run, he passed depressing segments of out-of-date factories resembling poorly whitewashed cinemas in the twenties, and a brick road-house with "WEDDING RECEPTIONS CATERED FOR" in red neon. But his feelings were at their most intense on the first evening, and on the last, when he visited the Circus. On the first evening, as he approached the fabled turrets—the moment never failed him—a sort of muddled saintliness came over him: "This is what service is all about." A smear of red brick was followed by the blackened stems of plane trees, a salad of coloured lights came up, a gateway flung past him, and the van thudded to a stop. The van doors were slammed open from outside at the same time that he heard the gates close and a male, sergeant-major voice shout, "Come on, man, *move* it, for Christ's sake," and that was Guillam, having a bit of fun.

"Hullo, Peter boy, how's *trade? Jesus*, it's cold!"

Not bothering to reply, Peter Guillam slapped Jerry on the shoulder briskly, as if starting him on a race, closed the door fast, locked it top and bottom, pocketed the keys, and led him off at a trot down a corridor which the ferrets must have ripped apart in fury. Plaster was hacked away in clumps, exposing the lath beneath; doors had been torn from their hinges; joists and lintels were dangling; dust-sheets, ladders, rubble lay everywhere.

"Had the Irish in, have you?" Jerry yelled. "Or just an all-ranks dance?"

His questions were lost in the clatter. The two men climbed fast and competitively, Guillam bounding ahead and Jerry on his heels, laughing breathlessly, their feet thundering and scraping like lively animals on the bare wood steps. A door delayed them, and Jerry waited while Guillam fiddled with the locks. Then waited again the other side while he reset them.

"Welcome aboard," said Guillam more quietly.

They had reached the fifth floor. They trod quietly now, no more romping, English subalterns called to order. The corridor turned left, then right again, then rose by a few narrow steps. A cracked fish-eye mirror, steps again, two up, three down, till they came to a janitor's desk, unmanned. To their left lay the rumpus room, empty, with the chairs pulled into a rough ring and a good fire burning in the grate. Thus to a long, brown-carpeted room marked "Secretariat" but in fact the ante-room, where three mothers, in pearls and twin sets, quietly typed by the glow of reading-lamps. At the far end of this room, one more door, shut, unpainted, and very grubby round the handle. No finger-plate, no escutcheon for the lock. Just the screw holes, he noticed, and the halo where one had been. Pushing it open without knocking, Guillam shoved his head through the gap and announced something quietly into the room. Then he backed away and quickly ushered Jerry past him: Jerry Westerby, into the presence.

"Gosh, super, George, hullo."

"And don't ask him about his wife," Guillam warned, in a fast, soft murmur that hummed in Jerry's ear for a good spell afterwards.

* * *

Father and son? That kind of relationship? Brawn to brain? More exact, perhaps, would be a son to his adopted father, which in the trade is held to be the strongest tie of all.

"Sport," Jerry muttered, and gave a husky laugh.

English friends have no real way of greeting each other, least of all across a glum civil-service office with nothing more lovely to inspire them than a deal desk. For a fraction of a second, Jerry laid his cricketer's fist alongside Smiley's soft, hesitant palm, then lumbered after him at a distance to the fireside, where two armchairs awaited them: old leather, cracked, and much sat in. Once again, in this erratic season, a fire burned in the Victorian grate, but very small by comparison with the fire in the rumpus room.

"And how was Lucca?" Smiley enquired, filling two glasses from a decanter.

"Lucca was great."

"Oh, dear. Then I expect it was a wrench to leave."

"Gosh, no. Super. Cheers."

"Cheers."

They sat down.

"Now, why *super*, Jerry?" Smiley enquired, as if "super" were not a word he was familiar with. There were no papers on the desk and the room was bare, more like a spare room than his own.

"I thought I was done for," Jerry explained. "Out to grass for good. Telegram took the wind right out of my sails. I thought, Well, Bill's blown me sky high. Blew everyone else, so why not me?"

"Yes," Smiley said, as if sharing Jerry's doubts, and peered at him a moment in frank speculation. "Yes, yes, quite. However, on balance it seems he never got around to blowing the Occasionals. We've traced him to pretty well every other corner of the archive, but the Occasionals were filed under 'friendly contacts' in the Territorials' cut, in a separate archive altogether, one to which he had no natural access. It's not that he didn't think you important enough," he added hastily, "it's simply that other claims on him took priority."

"I can live with it," said Jerry, with a grin.

"I'm glad," said Smiley, missing the joke. Rising, he refilled their glasses, then went to the fire and, taking up a brass poker, began stabbing thoughtfully at the coals. "Lucca. Yes. Ann and I went there. Oh, eleven, twelve years ago, it must have been. It rained." He gave a little laugh. In a cramped bay at the farther end of the room, Jerry glimpsed a narrow, bony-looking campbed with a row of telephones at the head.

"We visited the *bagno*, I remember," Smiley went on. "It was the fashionable cure. Lord alone knows what we were curing." He attacked the fire again, and this time the flames flew alive, daubing the rounded contours of his face with strokes of orange and making gold pools of his thick spectacles. "Did you know the poet Heine had a great adventure there? A romance? I rather think it must be why we went, come to think of it. We thought some of it would rub off."

Jerry grunted something, not too certain, at that moment, who Heine was.

"He went to the *bagno*, he took the waters, and while doing so he met a lady whose name alone so impressed him that he made his wife use it from then on." The flames held him for a moment longer. "And you had an adventure there, too, didn't you?"

"Just a flutter. Nothing to write home about."

Beth Sanders, Jerry thought automatically as his world rocked, then righted itself. A natural, Beth was. Father a retired general, High Sheriff of the County. Old Beth must have an aunt in every secret office in Whitehall.

Stooping again, Smiley propped the poker in a corner, laboriously, as if he were laying a wreath. "We're not necessarily in competition with affection. We simply like to know where it lies." Jerry said nothing. Over his shoulder Smiley glanced at Jerry, and Jerry pulled a grin to please him.

"The name of Heine's lady-love, I may tell you, was Irwin Mathilde," Smiley resumed, and Jerry's grin became an awkward laugh. "Yes, well, it does sound better in German, I confess. And the novel—how will that fare? I'd hate to think we'd scared away your muse. I don't think I'd forgive myself, I'm sure."

"No problem," said Jerry.

"Finished?"

"Well, you know."

For a moment there was no sound but the mothers' typing and the rumble of traffic from the street below.

"Then we shall make it up to you when this is over," Smiley said. "I insist. How did the Stubbs scene play?"

"No problem," said Jerry again.

"Nothing more we need do for you to smooth your path?"

"Don't think so."

From beyond the ante-room they heard the shuffle of footsteps all in one direction. It's a war party, Jerry thought, a gathering of the clans.

"And you're game, and so on?" Smiley asked. "You're—well, *prepared?* You have the will?"

"No problem." Why can't I say something different? he asked himself. Bloody needle's stuck.

"A lot of people haven't these days. The will. Specially in England. A lot of people see *doubt* as a legitimate philosophical posture. They think of themselves in the middle, whereas, of course, really they're nowhere. No battle was ever won by spectators, was it? We understand that in this service. We're lucky. Our war began in nineteen seventeen, with the Bolshevik Revolution. It hasn't changed yet."

Smiley had taken up a new position, across the room from him, not far from the bed. Behind him an old and grainy photograph glittered in the new firelight. Jerry had noticed it as he came in. Now, in the strain of the moment, he felt himself to be the object of a double scrutiny: by Smiley, and by the blurred eyes of the portrait dancing in the firelight behind the glass. The sounds of preparation multiplied. They heard voices and snatches of laughter, the squeak of chairs.

"I read somewhere," Smiley said, "an historian, I suppose he was—an American, anyway—he wrote of generations that are born into debtors' prisons and spend their lives buying their way to freedom. I think ours is such a generation. Don't you? I still feel strongly that I owe. Don't you? I've always been grateful to this service, that it gave me a chance to pay. Is that how *you* feel? I don't think we should be afraid of . . . devoting ourselves. Is that old-fashioned of me?"

Jerry's face clamped tight shut. He always forgot this part of Smiley when he was away from him, and remembered it too late when he was with him. There was a bit of the failed priest in old George, and the older he grew, the more prominent it became. He seemed to assume that the whole blasted Western world shared his worries and had to be talked round to a proper way of thinking.

"In that sense, I think we may legitimately congratulate ourselves on being a trifle old-fashioned—"

Jerry had had enough. "Sport," he expostulated, with a clumsy laugh, as the colour rose to his face. "For heaven's sake. You point me and I'll march. Okay? You're the owl, not me. Tell me the shots, I'll play them. World's chock-a-block with milk-and-water intellectuals armed with fifteen conflicting arguments against blowing their blasted noses. We don't need another. Okay? I mean, Christ."

A sharp knock at the door announced the reappearance of Guillam.

"Peace pipes all lit, Chief."

To his surprise, over the clatter of this interruption, Jerry thought he caught the term "ladies' man," but whether it was a reference to himself or the poet Heine, he could not say, nor did he particularly care. Smiley hesitated, frowned, then seemed to wake again to his surroundings. He glanced at Guillam, then once more at Jerry; then his eyes settled on that middle distance which is the special preserve of English academics.

"Well then, yes, let's start winding the clock," he said in a withdrawn voice.

As they trooped out, Jerry paused to admire the photograph on the wall, hands in pockets, grinning at it, hoping Guillam would hang back, too, which he did.

"Looks as though he's swallowed his last sixpence," said Jerry. "Who is he?"

"Karla," said Guillam. "Recruited Bill Haydon. Russian hood."

"Sounds more like a girl's name. How you keeping?"

"It's the code-name of his first network. There's a school of thought that says it's also the name of his one love."

"Bully for him," said Jerry carelessly and, still grinning, padded beside him toward the rumpus room. Perhaps deliberately, Smiley had gone ahead, out of earshot of their conversation. "Still with that loony girl, the flute-player, are you?" Jerry asked.

"She got less loony," said Guillam. They took a few more paces.

"Bolted?" Jerry enquired sympathetically.

"Something like that."

"And he's all right, is he?" Jerry asked dead casually, nodding at the solitary figure ahead of them. "Eating well, good coat, all that stuff?"

"Never been better. Why?"

"Just asked," said Jerry, very pleased.

From the airport, Jerry rang his daughter Cat, a thing he rarely did, but this time he had to. He knew it was a mistake before he put the money in, but he still persisted, and not even the terribly familiar voice of the early wife could put him off.

"Gosh, hullo! It's me, actually. Super. Listen: how's Phillie?"

Phillie was her husband, a civil servant nearly eligible for a pension, though younger than Jerry by about thirty muddled lives.

"Perfectly well, thank you," she retorted, in the frosty tone with which old wives defend new mates. "Is that why you rang?"

"Well, I did just think I might chat up old Cat, actually. Going out East for a bit, back in harness," he said. He felt he should apologise. "It's just the comic needs a hack out there," he said, and heard a clatter as the receiver hit the hall chest. Oak, he remembered. Barley-twist legs. Another of old Sambo's left-overs.

"Daddy?"

"Hi!" he yelled, as if the line were bad, as if she had taken him by surprise. "Cat? Hullo, hey, listen, *sport*, did you get my postcards and stuff?" He knew she had. She had thanked him regularly in her weekly letters.

Hearing nothing but "Daddy" repeated in a questioning voice, Jerry asked jovially, "You do still collect stamps, don't you? Only I'm going that way, you see. East."

Planes were called, others landed, whole worlds were changing places, but Jerry Westerby, speaking to his daughter, was motionless in the procession.

"You used to be a demon for stamps," he reminded her.

"I'm seventeen."

"Sure, sure, what do you collect now? Don't tell me. Boys!" With the brightest humour, he kept it going while he danced from one buckskin boot to the other, making his own jokes and supplying his own laughter. "Listen, I'm sending you some money—Blatt & Rodney are fixing it, sort of birthday and Christmas put together—better talk to Mummy before spending it. Or maybe Phillie, what? He's a sound sort of bloke, isn't he? Turn Phillie loose on it, kind of thing he likes to get his teeth into." He opened the kiosk door to raise an artificial flurry. "'Fraid they're calling my flight there, Cat," he bellowed over the clatter. "Look, mind how you go, d'you hear? Watch yourself. Don't give yourself too easy. Know what I mean?"

He queued for the bar awhile, but at the last moment the old Eastern hand in him woke up and he moved across to the cafeteria. It might be some time before he got his next glass of fresh cow's milk. Standing in the queue, Jerry had a sensation of being watched. No trick to that; at an airport everyone watches everyone, so what the hell? He thought of the orphan and wished he'd had time to get himself a girl before he left, if only to take the bad taste out of his mouth.

Smiley walked, one round little man in a raincoat. Social journalists with more class than Jerry, shrewdly observing his progress through the purlieus of the Charing Cross Road, would have recognised the type at once: the mackintosh brigade personified, cannon-fodder of the mixed-sauna parlours and the naughty bookshops. These long tramps had become a habit for him; with his new-found energy he could cover half the length of London and not notice it. From Cambridge Circus, now that he knew the byways, he could take any of twenty routes and never cross the same path twice. Having selected a beginning, he would let luck and instinct guide him while his other mind plundered the remoter regions of his soul.

But this evening his journey had a pull to it, drawing him south and westward, and Smiley yielded. The air was damp and cold, hung with a harsh fog that had never seen the sun. Walking, he took his own island with him, and it was crammed with images, not people. Like an extra mantle, the white walls encased him in his thoughts. In a doorway, two murderers in leather coats were whispering; under a streetlamp, a dark-haired boy angrily clutched a violin case. Outside a theatre, a waiting crowd burned in the blaze of lights from the awning overhead, and the fog curled round them like fire smoke.

Never had Smiley gone into battle knowing so little and expecting so much. He felt lured, and he felt pursued. Yet when he tired, and drew back for a moment, and considered the logic of what he was about, it almost eluded him. He glanced back and saw the jaws of failure waiting for him. He peered forward and through his moist spectacles saw the phantoms of great hopes dancing in the mist. He blinked around him and knew there was nothing for him where he stood. Yet he advanced without the ultimate conviction.

It was no answer to rehearse the steps that had brought him to this point—the Russian gold seam, the imprint of Karla's private army, the thoroughness of Haydon's efforts to extinguish knowledge of them. Beyond the limits of these external reasons, Smiley perceived in himself the existence of a darker motive, infinitely more obscure, one which his rational mind continued to reject. He called it Karla, and it was true that somewhere in him, like a leftover legend, there burned the embers of hatred toward the man who had set out to destroy the temples of his private faith, whatever remained of them: the service that he loved, his friends, his country, his concept of a reasonable balance in human affairs. It was true also that a lifetime or two ago, in a sweltering Indian jail, the two men had actually faced each other, Smiley and Karla, across an iron table, though Smiley had no reason at the time to know he was in the presence of his destiny. Karla's head was on the block in Moscow; Smiley had tried to woo him to the West, and Karla had kept silent, preferring death or worse to an easy defection. And it was true that now and then the memory of that encounter, of Karla's unshaven face and watchful, inward eyes, came at him like a spectre out of the murk of his little room while he slept fitfully on his bunk.

But hatred was really not an emotion he could sustain for any length of time, unless it was the obverse side of love.

He was approaching the King's Road in Chelsea. The fog was heavier because of the closeness of the river. Above him, the globes of streetlamps hung like Chinese lanterns in the bare branches of the trees. The traffic was sparse and cautious. Crossing the road, he followed the pavement till he came to Bywater Street and turned in to it: a cul-de-sac of neat flat-fronted terrace cottages. He trod discreetly now, keeping to the west side, and the shadow of the parked cars. It was the cocktail hour, and in other windows he saw talking heads and shrieking, silent mouths. Some he recognised, some she even had names for: "Felix the cat," "Lady Macbeth," "the Puffer."

He drew level with his own house. For their reunion, she had had the shutters painted blue and they were blue still. The curtains were open because she hated to be enclosed. She sat alone at her escritoire, and she might have composed the scene for him deliberately: the beautiful and conscientious wife, ending her day, attends to matters of administration. She was listening to music, and he caught the echo of it carried on the fog: Sibelius. Smiley wasn't good at music, but he knew all her records and he had several times praised the Sibelius out of politeness. He couldn't see the gramophone but he knew it lay on the floor, where it had lain for Bill Haydon when she was trailing her affair with him. He wondered whether the German dictionary lay beside it, and her anthology of German poetry. Several times, over the last decade or two, usually during reconciliations, she had made a show of learning German so that Smiley would be able to read aloud to her.

As he watched, she got up, crossed the room, paused in front of the pretty gilt mirror to adjust her hair. The notes she wrote to herself were jammed into the frame. What was it this time, he wondered. "Blast garage." "Cancel lunch Madeleine." "Destroy butcher." Sometimes, when things were tense, she had sent him messages that way: "Force George to smile, apologise insincerely for lapse." In very bad times, she wrote whole letters to him, and posted them there for his collection.

To his surprise, she had put out the light. He heard the bolts slide on the front door. Drop the chain, he thought automatically. Double-lock the Banhams. How many times do I have to tell you bolts are as weak as the screws that hold them in place? Odd, all the same; he had somehow supposed she would leave the bolts open in case he might return. Then the bedroom light went on, and he saw her body framed in silhouette in the window as, angel-like, she stretched her arms to the curtains. She drew them almost to her, stopped, and momentarily he feared she had seen him, till he remembered her shortsightedness and her refusal to wear glasses. She's going out, he thought; she's going to doll herself up. He saw her head half turn as if she had been addressed. He saw her lips move, and break into a puckish smile as her arms lifted again, this time to the back of her neck, and she began to unfasten the top button of her housecoat. In the same moment, the gap between the curtains was abruptly closed by other, impatient hands.

Oh, *no*, thought Smiley hopelessly. Please! Wait till I've gone!

For a minute, perhaps longer, standing on the pavement, he stared in disbelief at the blacked-out window, till anger, shame, and finally self-disgust broke in him together like a physical anguish and he turned and hurried blindly back toward the King's Road. Who was it this time? Another beardless ballet dancer, performing some narcissistic ritual? Her vile cousin Miles, the career politician? Or a one-night Adonis spirited from the nearby pub?

When the outside telephone rang, Peter Guillam was sitting alone in the rumpus room a little drunk, languishing equally for Molly Meakin's body and George Smiley's return. He lifted the receiver at once and heard Fawn, out of breath and furious.

"I've lost him!" he shouted. "He's bilked me!"

"Then you're a bloody idiot," Guillam retorted with satisfaction.

"Idiot nothing! He heads for home, right? Our usual ritual. I'm waiting for him, I stand off, he's coming back to the main road, looks at me. Like I'm dirt. Just *dirt*. Next thing I know, I'm on my own. How does he do it? Where does he go? I'm his friend, aren't I? Who the hell does he think he is? Fat little runt, I'll kill him!"

Guillam was still laughing as he rang off.

6

The Burning of Frost

In Hong Kong it was Saturday again, but the typhoons were forgotten and the day burned hot and clear and breathless. In the Hong Kong Club a serenely Christian clock struck eleven and the chimes tinkled in the panelled quiet like spoons dropped on a distant kitchen floor. The better chairs were already taken by readers of last Thursday's *Telegraph*, which gave a quite dismal picture of the moral and economic miseries of their homeland.

"Pound's in the soup again," a crusted voice growled through a pipe. "Electricians out. Railways out. Pilots out."

"Who's *in?* More the question," said another, just as crusted.

"If I was the Kremlin, I'd say we were doing a first-class *job*," said the first speaker, barking out the final word to give it a military indignation, and with a sigh ordered up a couple of dry martinis. Neither man was above twenty-five years old, but being an exiled patriot in search of a quick fortune can age you pretty fast.

The Foreign Correspondents' Club, by contrast, was having one of its churchy days when burghers far outnumbered newsmen. Without old Craw to hold them together, the Shanghai Bowlers had dispersed and several had left the Colony altogether. The photographers had been lured to Phnom Penh by the promise of some great new fighting now the wet season was ended. The cowboy was in Bangkok for an expected revival of student riots, Luke was at the bureau, and his boss the dwarf was slouched grumpily at the bar surrounded by sonorous British suburbanites in dark trousers and white shirts discussing the 1100 gearbox.

"But *cold* this time. Hear that? *Muchee coldee* and bring it *chop chop!*"

Even the Rocker was muted. He was attended this morning by his wife, a former Bible School teacher from Borneo, a dried-out shrew in bobbed hair and ankle socks who could spot a sin before it was committed.

And a couple of miles eastward on Cloudview Road, a thirty-cent ride on the one-price city bus—in what is said to be the most populated corner of our planet, on North Point, just where the city swells toward the Peak—on the sixteenth floor of a high-rise block called 7A, Jerry Westerby was lying on a mattress after a short but dreamless sleep, singing his own words to the tune of "Miami Sunrise" and watching a beautiful girl undress.

The mattress was seven feet long, intended to be used the other way on by an entire Chinese family, and for about the first time in his life his feet didn't hang over the end. It was longer than Pet's cot by a mile, longer even than the bed in Tuscany, though in Tuscany it hadn't mattered, because he had a real girl to curl round and with a girl you don't lie so straight. Whereas the girl he was watching was framed in a window opposite his own, ten yards or miles out of reach, and on every one of the nine mornings he had woken here, she had stripped and washed herself this way, to his considerable enthusiasm, even applause. When he was lucky, he followed the whole ceremony, from the moment when she tipped her head sideways to let her black hair fall to her waist, until she chastely wound a sheet about her and rejoined her ten-strong family in the next room where they all lived. He knew the family intimately. Their washing habits. Their tastes in music, cooking, and lovemaking, their celebrations, their flaring, dangerous rows. The only thing he wasn't sure of was whether she was two girls or one.

She vanished, but he went on singing. He felt eager, which was how it took him every time, whether he was about to gumshoe down a back alley in Prague to swap little packages with a terror-stricken joe in a doorway or—his finest hour, and for an Occasional unprecedented—row three miles in a blackened dinghy to scrape a radio operator off a Caspian beach. As the clamps tightened, Jerry discovered the same surprising mastery of himself, the same jollity, and the same alertness. And the same barking funk, not necessarily a contradiction. It's today, he thought. The kissing's over.

There were three tiny rooms and they were parquet-floored all through. That was the first thing he noted every morning, because there was no furniture anywhere, except the mattress and the kitchen chair and the table where his typewriter sat, the one dinner plate, which did duty as an ashtray, and the girlie calendar, vintage 1960, of a redhead whose charms had long since lost their bloom. He knew the type exactly: green eyes, a temper, and a skin so sensitive it looked like a battlefield every time you laid a finger on it. Add one telephone, one ancient record-player for 78s only, and two very real opium pipes suspended from business-like nails on the wall, and he had a complete inventory of the wealth and interests of Deathwish the Hun, now in Cambodia, from whom Jerry had rented the apartment. And one book-sack, his own, beside the mattress.

The gramophone had run down. He climbed happily to his feet, tightening the makeshift sarong around his stomach. As he did so, the telephone began ringing, so he sat again and, grabbing the wire, dragged the instrument toward him across the floor. It was Luke, as usual wanting to play.

"Sorry, sport. Doing a story. Try solo whist."

Dialling the speaking clock, Jerry heard a Chinese squawk, then an English squawk, and set his watch by the second. Then he went to the gramophone and put on "Miami Sunrise" again,

loud as it would go. It was the only record, but it drowned the
gurgle of the useless air-conditioner. Still humming, he pulled
open the one wardrobe, and from an old leather grip on the
floor picked out his father's yellowed tennis racquet, vintage
1930-odd, with "S.W." in marking ink on the pommel. Unscrew-
ing the handle, he fished from the recess four lozenges of
subminiature film, a worm of grey wadding, and a battered subminiature camera with measuring chain, which the conservative in him preferred to the flashier models that the Sarratt
smudgers had tried to press on him. He loaded a cassette into
the camera, set the film speed, and took three sample light-
readings of the redhead's bosom before slopping to the kitchen
in his sandals, where he lowered himself devoutly to his knees
before the fridge and loosened the Free Foresters tie that held
the door in place. With a wild tearing noise he passed his right
thumb-nail down the rotted rubber strips, took out three eggs,
and re-tied the tie. Waiting for them to boil, he lounged at the
window, elbows on the sill, peering fondly through the burglar wire at his beloved roof-tops, which descended like giant
stepping-stones to the sea's edge.

The roof-tops were a civilisation for themselves, a breath-
taking theatre of survival against the raging of the city. Within
their barbed-wire compounds, sweat-shops turned out anor-
aks, religious services were held, mah-jong was played, and
fortune-tellers burned joss and consulted huge brown volumes. Ahead of him lay a formal garden made of smuggled
earth. Below, three old women fattened chow puppies for the
pot. There were schools for dancing, reading, ballet, recreation, and combat; there were schools in culture and the wonders of Mao, and this morning, while Jerry's eggs boiled, an
old man completed his long rigmarole of calisthenics before
opening the tiny folding chair where he performed his daily
reading of the great man's Thoughts.

The wealthier poor, if they had no roof, built themselves
giddy crow's-nests, two feet by eight, on home-made cantile-

vers driven into their drawing-room floors. Deathwish maintained there were suicides all the time. That was what grabbed him about the place, he said. When he wasn't fornicating, he liked to hang out of the window with his Nikon, hoping to catch one, but he never did. Down to the right lay the graveyard, which Deathwish said was bad luck and knocked a few dollars off the rent.

While he was eating, the phone rang again.

"What story?" said Luke.

"Wanchai whores have hijacked Big Moo," Jerry said. "Taken him to Stonecutters Island and are holding him to ransom."

Other than Luke, it tended to be Deathwish's women who called, but they didn't want Jerry instead. The shower had no curtain, so Jerry had to squat in a tiled corner, like a boxer, in order not to flood the bathroom. Returning to the bedroom, he put on his suit, grabbed a bread knife, and counted twelve wood blocks from the corner of the room. With the knife blade he dug up the thirteenth. In a hollowed recess cut into the tar-like under-surface lay one plastic bag containing a roll of American bills of large and small denominations; one escape passport, driving licence, and air-travel card in the name of Worrell, contractor; and one small-arm, which, in defiance of every Circus regulation under the sun, Jerry had procured from Deathwish, who did not care to take it on his travels. From this treasure chest he extracted five one-hundred-dollar bills and, leaving the rest untouched, replaced the wood block.

He dropped the camera and two spare cassettes into his pockets, then, whistling, stepped onto the tiny landing. His front door was guarded by a white-painted grille which would have delayed a decent burglar for ninety seconds. Jerry had picked the lock when he had nothing better to do, and that was how long it took him. He pressed the button for the lift, and it arrived full of Chinese, who all got out. It happened every time; Jerry was just too big for them, too ugly, and too foreign.

From scenes like these, thought Jerry, with willed cheerfulness as he plunged into the pitch darkness of the city-bound bus, St. George's children go forth to save the Empire.

Time spent in preparation is never time wasted runs the Nursery's laborious maxim on counter-surveillance.

Sometimes Jerry became Sarratt man and nothing else. By the ordinary logic of things he could have gone to his destination directly; he had every right. By the ordinary logic of things there was no reason on earth, particularly after their revelries of last night, why Jerry should not have taken a cab to the front door, barged gaily in, bearded his new-found bosom friend, and be done with it. But this was not the ordinary logic of things, and in the Sarratt folklore Jerry was approaching the operational moment of truth: the moment when the back door closed on him with a bang, after which there was no way out but forward. The moment when every one of his twenty years of tradecraft rose in him and shouted "caution." If he was walking into a trap, this was where the trap was sprung. Even if they knew his route in advance, still the static posts would be staked out ahead of him, in cars and behind windows, and the surveillance teams locked on to him in case of fumble or branch lines. If there was ever a last opportunity to test the water before he jumped, it was now. Last night, around the haunts, he could have been watched by a hundred local angels and still not have known for certain he was their quarry. But here he could weave and count the shadows; here, in theory at least, he had a chance to know.

He glanced at his watch. Exactly twenty minutes to go, and even at Chinese rather than European pace he needed seven. So he sauntered, but never idly. In other countries, in almost any place in the world outside Hong Kong, he would have given himself far longer. Behind the Curtain, Sarratt lore said, half a day, preferably more. He'd have posted himself a letter, just so that he could walk half-way down the street, stop dead at the post-box, and double back, checking the feet that faltered and the faces that ducked away; looking for the classic

formations, a two this side, a three across the road, a front tail
who floats ahead of you.

But paradoxically, though this morning he zealously went
through the steps, another side of him knew he was wasting his
time; knew that in the East a round-eye could live all his life
in the same block and never have the smallest notion of the
secret tic-tac on his doorstep. At every corner of each teeming
street he entered, men waited, lounged, and watched, strenuously employed in doing nothing. The beggar who suddenly
stretched his arms and yawned; the crippled shoeshine boy who
dived for his escaping feet and, having missed them, drove the
backs of his brushes together in a crack; the old hag selling
bi-racial pornography who cupped her hand and shrieked one
word into the bamboo scaffolding above her: though in his
mind Jerry recorded them, they were as obscure to him today
as they had been when he first came East—twenty?—Lord help
us, twenty-five years ago. Pimps? Numbers boys? Dope pedlars
pushing the coloured twists of candy paper—"Yellow two dollar, blue five dollar? You chase dragon, like quick-shot?" Or
were they ordering up a bowl of rice from the food stalls across
the way? In the East, sport, survival is knowing you don't know.

He was using the reflections in the marble facing of the
shops: shelves of amber, shelves of jade, credit-card signs, electrical gadgets, and pyramids of black luggage nobody ever
seemed to carry. At Cartier's, a beautiful girl was laying pearls
on a velvet tray, putting them to bed for the day. Sensing his
presence, she lifted her eyes to him; and in Jerry, despite his
preoccupation, the old Adam briefly stirred. But one glance at
his shambler's grin and his shabby suit and his buckskin boots
told her all she needed to know: Jerry Westerby was not a
potential customer. There was news of fresh battles, Jerry
noticed, passing a news-stand. The Chinese-language press
carried front-page photographs of decimated children, screaming mothers, and troops in American-style helmets. Whether
Vietnam, or Cambodia, or Korea, or the Philippines, Jerry

couldn't tell. The red characters of the headline had the effect of splashed blood. Maybe Deathwish was in luck.

Thirsty from last night's booze, Jerry cut through the Mandarin and plunged into the twilight of the Captain's Bar, but he only drank water in the Gents. Back in the lobby, he bought a copy of *Time* but didn't like the way the plain-clothes crushers looked at him, and left. Joining the crowds again, he sauntered toward the post office, built 1911 and since pulled down, but in those days a rare and hideous antique made beautiful by the clumsy concrete of the buildings round it; then he doubled through the arches into Pedder Street, passing under a green corrugated bridge where mailbags trailed like turkeys on the gibbet. Doubling yet again, he crossed to the Connaught Centre, using the foot-bridge to thin out the field.

In the glittering steel lobby, a peasant woman was scrubbing out the teeth of a stationary escalator with a wire brush, and on the promenade a group of Chinese students gazed in respectful silence at Henry Moore's "Oval with Points." Looking back, Jerry glimpsed the brown dome of the old law courts dwarfed by the Hilton's beehive walls: *Regina versus Westerly,* he thought, "and the prisoner is charged with blackmail, corruption, pretended affection, and a few others we shall dream up before the day is out, my Lord." The harbour was alive with shipping, most of it small. Beyond it, the New Territories, pocked with excavation, shoved vainly against muddy clouds of smog. At their feet, new godowns, and factory chimneys belching brown smoke.

Retracing his steps, he passed the big Scottish business houses: Jardines, Swire, old opium money washed moderately clean. Must be a holiday, he thought. Ours or theirs? In Statue Square a leisurely carnival was taking place, with fountains, beach umbrellas, Coca-Cola sellers, and about half a million Chinese who stood in groups or shuffled past him like a barefoot army, darting glances at his size. Loudspeakers, building drills, wailing music. He crossed Jackson Road and the noise level fell a little.

Ahead of him, on a patch of perfect English lawn, fifteen white-clad figures lounged. The all-day cricket match had just begun. At the receiving end, a lank, disdainful figure in an out-dated cap was fiddling with his batting gloves. Pausing, Jerry watched, grinning in fond familiarity. The bowler bowled. Medium pace, bit of inswing, dead wicket. The batsman played a gracious stroke, missed, and took a leg-bye in slow motion. Jerry foresaw a long dull innings to no applause. He wondered who was playing whom, and decided it was the usual Peak mafia playing itself. On the leg boundary, across the road, rose the Bank of China, a vast and fluted cenotaph festooned with crimson slogans loving Mao. At its base, granite lions looked on sightlessly while flocks of white-shirted Chinese photographed each other against their flanks.

But the bank which Jerry had his eye on stood directly behind the bowler's arm. A Union Jack was posted at its pinnacle, an armoured van more confidently at its base. The doors stood open and their burnished surfaces glittered like fool's gold. While Jerry continued his shambling arc toward it, a gang of helmeted guards, escorted by tall Indians with elephant guns, emerged suddenly from the interior blackness and nursed three black money boxes down the wide steps as if they held the Host itself. The armoured van drove away, and for a sickening moment Jerry had visions of the bank's doors closing after it.

Not logical visions. Not nervous visions, either. Merely that for a moment Jerry expected fumble with the same trained pessimism with which a gardener foresees drought or an athlete a foolish sprain on the eve of a great match; or a fieldman with twenty years on the clock foresees just one more unpredictable frustration. But the doors stayed open, and Jerry veered away to the left. Give the guards time to relax, he thought. Shepherding the money will have made them jumpy. They'll see too sharply, they'll remember things.

Turning, he began a slow, dreamy stroll toward the Hong Kong Club: Wedgwood porticoes, striped blinds, and a smell

of stale English food at the doorway. Cover is not a lie, they
tell you. Cover is what you believe. Cover is who you are. *On
Saturday morning Mr. Gerald Westerby, the not very distinguished
journalist, heads for a favourite watering-hole.* . . . On the Club
steps, Jerry paused, patted his pockets, then turned full circle
and struck out purposefully for his destination, making two
long sides of the square as he watched for the last time for the
slurring feet and turned-down glances. *Mr. Gerald Westerby,
discovering he is short of weekend cash, decides on a quick visit to the
bank.* Elephant guns slung carelessly at their shoulders, the
Indian guards studied him without interest.

  Except, Mr. Gerald Westerby doesn't!

  Cursing himself for being a damned fool, Jerry remembered that the time was after twelve o'clock, and that at twelve
sharp the banking halls were closed. After twelve it was upstairs
only, and that was the way he had planned it.

  Relax, he thought. You're thinking too much. Don't think:
do. *In the beginning was the deed.* Who had said that to him
once? Old George, for God's sake, quoting Goethe. Coming
from him, of all people!

  As he began the run-in, a wave of dismay hit him, and he
knew it was fear. He was hungry. He was tired. Why had
George left him alone like this? Why did he have to do
everything for himself? Before the fall they'd have posted
baby-sitters ahead of him—even someone inside the bank—
just to watch for rain. They'd have had a reception team to
skim the take almost before he left the building, and an escape
car in case he had to slip away in his socks. And in London, he
thought sweetly, talking himself down, they'd have had dear
old Bill Haydon—wouldn't they?—passing it all to the Russians, bless him.

  Thinking this, Jerry willed upon himself an extraordinary
hallucination, quick as the flash of a camera, and as slow to fade.
God had answered his prayers, he thought. The old days were
here again, after all, and the street was alive with a grand-slam

supporting cast. Behind him a blue Peugeot had pulled up and two bullish round-eyes sat in it studying a Happy Valley race-card. Radio aerial, the works. From his left, American matrons sauntered by, laden with guidebooks and a positive obligation to observe. And from the bank itself, as he advanced swiftly on its portals, a couple of solemn money-men emerged, wearing just that grim stare watchers sometimes use in order to discourage an enquiring eye.

Senility, Jerry told himself. You're over the hill, sport, no question. Dotage and funk have brought you to your knees. He bounded up the steps, jaunty as a cock robin on a hot spring day.

The lobby was big as a railway station, the canned music as martial. The banking area was barred and he saw no one lurking, not even a phantom stand-off man. The lift was a gold cage with a spittoon filled with sand for cigarettes, but by the ninth floor the largeness of downstairs had all gone. Space was money. A narrow cream corridor led to an empty reception desk. Jerry strolled easily, marking the emergency exit and the service lift, which the bearleaders had already charted for him in case he had to do a duck-dive. Queer how they knew so much, he thought, with so few resources; must have dug out an architect's drawing from somewhere.

On the counter, one teak sign reading "Trustee Department Enquiries." Beside it, one grimy paperback on fortune-telling by the stars, open and much annotated. But no receptionist, because Saturdays are different. On Saturdays you get the best ride, they had said. He looked cheerfully round, nothing on his conscience. A second corridor ran the width of the building, office doors to the left, soggy vinyl-covered partitions to the right. From behind the partitions came the slow pat of an electric typewriter as someone typed a legal document, and the slow Saturday singsong of Chinese secretaries without a lot to do except wait for lunch and the free afternoon.

There were four glazed doors with penny-sized eyeholes

for looking in or out. Jerry ambled down the corridor, glancing through each as if glancing were his recreation, hands in
pockets, a slightly daft smile aloft. The fourth on the left, they
had said, one door, one window. A clerk walked past him, then
a secretary on dinky, clicking heels, but Jerry, though scruffy,
was European and wore a suit, and neither challenged him.

"Morning, gang," he muttered, and they wished him "Good
day, sir," in return.

There were iron bars at the end of the corridor and iron
bars over the windows. A blue night-light was fixed to the ceiling, he supposed for security but he didn't know: fire, space
protection—he didn't know, the bearleaders hadn't mentioned
it, and stinks and bangs were not his thing. The first room was
an office, unoccupied except for a few dusty sports trophies on
the window-sill and an embroidered coat of arms of the bank
athletics club on the pegboard wall. He passed a pile of apple
boxes marked "Trustee." They seemed to be full of deeds and
wills. The cheese-paring tradition of the old China trading
houses died hard, apparently. A notice on the wall read "Private" and another "By Appointment Only."

The second door gave on to a corridor and a small archive,
which was likewise empty. The third was a "Directors Only" lavatory; the fourth had a staff notice-board mounted directly
beside it and a red light bulb on the jamb and an important
name-plate in Letraset saying "J. Frost, Deputy Chief Trustee,
Appointments Only, Do *Not* Enter When Light Is *On.*" But the
light was not on, and the penny-sized eyehole showed one man at
his desk alone, and the only company he had was a heap of files,
and scrolls of costly paper bound in green silk on the English
legal pattern, and two closed-circuit television sets for the Stock
Exchange prices, dead, and the harbour view, mandatory to the
higher-executive image, sliced into pencil-grey lines by mandatory Venetian blinds. One shiny, podgy, prosperous little man in
a sporty linen suit of Robin Hood green, working far too conscientiously for a Saturday. Moisture on his brow, black crescents

beneath his arms, and—to Jerry's informed eye—the leaden immobility of a man recovering very slowly from debauch.

A corner room, thought Jerry. One door only, this one. One shove and you're away. He took a last glance up and down the empty corridor. Jerry Westerby on stage, he thought. If you can't talk, dance. The door gave immediately. He stepped gaily inside wearing his best shy smile.

"Gosh, Frostie, hullo, *super.* Am I early or late? Sport—I say—most *extraordinary* thing back there. In the corridor—nearly fell over them—lot of apple boxes full of legal bumf. 'Who's Frostie's client?' I asked myself. 'Cox's Orange Pippins? Or Beauty of Bath?' Beauty of Bath, knowing you. Thought it was rather a giggle, after last night's high jinks round the parlours."

All of which, feeble though it might have sounded to the astonished Frost, got him into the room with the door closed, fast, while his broad back masked the only eyehole and his soul sent prayers of gratitude to Sarratt for a soft landing, and prayers of preservation to his Maker.

A moment of theatricality followed Jerry's entry. Frost lifted his head slowly, keeping his eyes half shut, as if the light were hurting them, which it probably was. Spotting Jerry, he winced and looked away, then looked at him again to confirm that he was flesh. Then he wiped his brow with his handkerchief.

"Christ," he said. "It's his nibs. What the hell are you doing here, you disgusting aristocrat?"

To which Jerry, still at the door, responded with another large grin, and a lifting of one hand in a Red Indian salute, while he marked down the worry points precisely: the two telephones, the grey box for inter-office speaking, and the wardrobe safe with a keyhole but no combination lock.

"How did they let you in? I suppose you flashed your Honourable at them. What do you mean by it, barging in here?" Not half as displeased as his words suggested, Frost had left his desk and was waddling down the room. "This isn't a cathouse, you know. This is a respectable bank. More or less."

Arriving at Jerry's considerable bulk, he stuck his hands on his hips and gazed at him, shaking his head in wonder. Then patted Jerry's arm, then prodded him in the stomach, amid more shaking of the head.

"You alcoholic, dissolute, lecherous, libidinous . . ."

"Newshound," Jerry prompted.

Frost was not above forty, but nature had already printed on him the crueller marks of littleness, such as a floor-walker's fussiness about the cuffs and fingers, and a moistening of his lips and pursing of them all at once. What redeemed him was a transparent sense of fun, which leapt to his damp cheeks like sunlight.

"Here," said Jerry. "Poison yourself," and offered him a cigarette.

"Christ," said Frost again, and with a key from his chain opened an old-fashioned walnut cupboard, full of mirror and rows of cocktail sticks with artificial cherries, and trick tankards with pin-ups and pink elephants.

"Bloody Mary do you?"

"Bloody Mary would slip down grateful, sport," Jerry assured him.

On the key chain, one brass Chubb key. The safe was also Chubb, a fine one, with a battered gold medallion fading into the old green paint.

"I'll say one thing for you blue-blooded rakes," Frost called while he poured and shook the ingredients like a chemist. "You do know the haunts. Drop you blindfold in the middle of Salisbury Plain, I reckon you'd find a cathouse in thirty seconds flat. My virgin sensitive nature took yet another grave jolt last night. Rocked to its frail little bearings, it was—say when!—I'll take a few addresses off you sometime, when I'm healed. If I ever am, which I doubt."

Sauntering over to Frost's desk, Jerry riffled idly through his correspondence, then began playing with the switches of the speaking-box, patting them up and down one by one with his enormous index finger, but getting no answers. A separate button was marked "ENGAGED." Pressing it, Jerry saw a rose gleam in the eyehole as the caution-light went on in the corridor.

"As to those girls," Frost was saying, his back still turned to Jerry while he rattled the sauce bottle. "Wicked they were. Shocking." Laughing delightedly, Frost advanced across the room, holding the glasses wide. "What were their names? Oh, dear, oh, dear!"

"Seven and twenty-four," said Jerry distractedly.

He was stooping as he spoke, looking for the alarm button he knew would be somewhere on the desk.

"Seven and twenty-four!" Frost repeated rapturously. "What poetry! What a memory!"

At knee level Jerry had found a grey box screwed to the drawer pillar. The key was vertical, at the off position. He pulled it out and dropped it into his pocket.

"I said what a wonderful memory," Frost repeated, rather puzzled.

"You know newshounds, sport," said Jerry, straightening. "Worse than wives, us newshounds are, when it comes to memories."

"Here. Come off there. That's holy ground."

Picking up Frost's large desk diary, Jerry was studying it for the day's engagements.

"Jesus," he said. "It's all go, isn't it? Who's N, sport? N, eight to twelve? Not your mother-in-law, is she?"

Ducking his mouth to the glass, Frost drank greedily, swallowed, then made a farce of choking, writhing, and recovering. "Keep her out of this, do you mind? You nearly gave me a heart attack. Bung-ho."

"N for nuts? N for Napoleon? Who's N?"

"Natalie. My secretary. Very nice. Legs go right up to its bottom, so they tell me. Never been there myself, so I don't know. My one rule. Remind me to break it sometime. Bung-ho," he said again.

"She in?"

"I think I heard her dulcet tread, yes. Want me to give her a buzz? I'm told she puts on a very nice turn for the upper classes."

"No, thanks," said Jerry and, setting down the diary, looked at Frost four square, man to man, though the fight was uneven, for Jerry was a whole head taller than Frost, and a lot broader.

"Incredible," Frost declared reverently, still beaming at Jerry. "Incredible, that's what it was." His manner was devoted, even possessive. "Incredible girls, incredible company. I mean why should a bloke like me bother with a bloke like you? A mere Honourable, at that? Dukes are my level. Dukes and tarts. Let's do it again tonight. Come on."

Jerry laughed.

"I mean it. Scout's honour. Let's die of it before we're too old. On me this time, the whole treat." In the corridor heavy footsteps sounded, coming nearer. "Know what *I'm* going to do? Try me. I'm going to go back to the Meteor with you, and I'm going to call Madame Whoosit, and I'm going to insist on a—What's eating you?" he said, catching Jerry's expression.

The footsteps slowed, then stopped. A black shadow filled the eyehole and stayed.

"Who is he?" said Jerry quietly.

"Milky."

"Who's Milky?"

"Milky Way, my boss," said Frost as the footsteps moved away. Closing his eyes, he crossed himself devoutly. "Going home to his very lovely lady wife, the distinguished Mrs. Way, alias Moby Dick. Six foot eight and a cavalry moustache. Not him. Her." Frost giggled.

"Why didn't he come in?"

"Thought I had a client, I suppose," said Frost carelessly, again puzzled by Jerry's watchfulness, and by his quiet. "Apart from the fact that Moby Dick would kick him to death if she caught him with the smell of alcohol on his evil lips at this hour of the day. Cheer up, you've got me to look after you. Have the other half. You look a bit pious today. Gives me the creeps."

When you get in there, go, the bearleaders had said. *Don't feel his bones too long; don't let him get comfy with you.*

"Hey, Frostie," Jerry said when the footsteps had quite faded. "How's the missis?" Frost had his hand out for Jerry's glass. "Your missis. How's she doing?"

"Still ailing nicely, thank you," said Frost uncomfortably.

"Ring the hospital, did you?"

"This morning? You're crazy. I wasn't coherent till eleven o'clock. If then. She'd have smelt my breath."

"When are you next visiting?"

"Look. Shut up. Shut up about her. Do you mind?"

With Frost watching him, Jerry drifted to the safe. He tried the big handle but it was locked. On the top, covered in dust, lay a heavy riot stick. Taking it in both hands, he played a couple of distracted cricket shots and put it back, while Frost's puzzled stare followed him alertly.

"I want to open an account, Frostie," said Jerry, still at the safe.

"You?"

"Me."

"From all you told me last night, you haven't the resources to open a bloody piggy bank. Not unless your distinguished dad kept a bit in the mattress, which I somehow doubt." Frost's world was slipping fast but he tried desperately to hold on to it. "Look, get yourself a bloody drink and stop playing Boris Karloff on a wet Wednesday, will you? Let's go to the gee-gees. Happy Valley, here we come. I'll buy you lunch."

"I didn't mean we'd open *my* account exactly, sport. I meant someone else's," Jerry explained.

In a slow, sad comedy, the fun drained out of Frost's little face, and he muttered, "Oh, *no*. Oh, Jerry," under his breath, as if he were witnessing an accident in which Jerry, not Frost, were the victim. For the second time, footsteps approached down the corridor. A girl's, short and quick. Then a sharp knock. Then silence.

"Natalie?" said Jerry quietly. Frost nodded. "If I was a client, would you introduce me?" Frost shook his head. "Let her in."

Frost's tongue, like a scared pink snake, peeked out from between his lips, looked quickly round, then vanished.

"Come!" he called in a hoarse voice, and a tall Chinese girl with thick glasses collected some letters from his out-tray.

"Enjoy your weekend, Mr. Frost," she said.

"See you Monday," said Frost.

The door closed again.

Coming across the room, Jerry put an arm round Frost's shoulders and guided him, unresisting, quickly to the window.

"A trust account, Frostie. Lodged in your incorruptible hands. Sharpish."

In the square, the carnival continued. On the cricket field, somebody was out. The lank batsman in the outmoded cap had dropped into a crouch and was patiently repairing the pitch. The fieldsmen lay about and chatted.

"You set me up," said Frost simply, trying to get used to the notion. "I thought I had a friend at last, and now you want to screw me. And you a lord."

"Shouldn't mingle with newshounds, Frostie. Rough bunch. No sporting instinct. Shouldn't have shot your mouth off. Where do you keep the records?"

"Friends *do* shoot their mouths off," Frost protested. "That's what friends are for! To *tell* each other!"

"Then tell me."

Frost shook his head. "I'm a Christian," he said stupidly. "I go every Sunday, I never miss. I'm afraid it's quite out of the question. I'd rather lose my place in society than commit a breach of confidence. It's known of me, right? No go. Sorry about that."

Jerry edged closer along the sill, till their arms were all but touching. The big window-pane was trembling from the traffic. The Venetian blinds were red with building smuts. Frost's face worked pitifully as he wrestled with the news of his bereavement.

"Here's the deal, sport," said Jerry, very quietly. "Listen carefully. Right? It's a stick-and-carrot job. If you don't play, the comic will blow the whistle on you. Front-page mug shot, banner headlines, continued back page, col six, the works. 'Would you buy a second-hand trust account from this man?' Hong Kong the cesspit of corruption and Frostie the slavering monster: that line. We'd tell them how you play round-eye musical beds at the young bankers' club, just the way you told it to me, and how till recently you maintained a wicked love-nest over on Kowloon-side, only it went sour on you because she wanted more bread. Before they did all that, of course, they'd check the story out with your Chairman and maybe with your missis, too, if she's well enough."

A rainstorm of sweat had broken on Frost's face without warning. One moment his sallow features had shown an oily moistness and that was all. The next they were drenched and the sweat was running unchecked off his plump chin and falling on his Robin Hood suit.

"It's the booze," he said stupidly, trying to staunch it with his handkerchief. "I always get this when I drink. Bloody climate—I shouldn't be exposed to it. No one should. Rotting out here. I hate it."

"That's the *bad* news," Jerry continued. They were still at the window, side by side, like two men loving the view. "The good news is five hundred U.S. into your hot little hand, compliments of Grub Street, no one any the wiser, and Frostie for Chairman. So why not sit back and enjoy it? See what I mean?"

"And may I *enquire*," Frost said at last, with a disastrous shot at sarcasm, "to what end or purpose you wish to peruse this file in the first place?"

"Crime and corruption, sport. The Hong Kong connection.

Grub Street names the guilty men. Account number four four two. Do you keep it here?" Jerry asked, indicating the safe.

Frost made a "No" with his lips, but no sound came out.

"Both the fours, then the two. Where is it?"

"Look," Frost muttered. His face was a hopeless mess of fear and disappointment. "Do me a favour, will you? Keep me out of it. Bribe one of my Chinese clerks, okay? That's the proper way. I mean I've got a position here."

"You know the saying, Frostie. In Hong Kong even the daisies talk. I want *you*. You're here, and you're better qualified. Is it in the strong-room?"

You have to keep it moving, they said. *You have to raise the threshold all the time. Lose the initiative once and you lose it forever.*

As Frost dithered, Jerry affected to lose patience. With one very large hand, he seized hold of Frost's shoulder and spun him round, and backed him till his little shoulders were flat against the safe.

"Is it in the strong-room?"

"How should I know?"

"I'll tell you how," Jerry promised, and nodded hard at Frost so that his forelock flopped up and down. "I'll tell you, sport," he repeated, tapping Frost's shoulder lightly with his free hand. "Because otherwise you're forty and on the road, with a sick wife, and bambinos to feed, and school fees, and the whole catastrophe. It's one thing or t'other, and the moment's now. Not five minutes on, but now. I don't care how you do it, but make it sound normal and keep Natalie out of it."

Jerry guided him back into the middle of the room, where his desk stood, and the telephone. There are parts in life which are impossible to play with dignity. Frost's that day was one. Lifting the receiver, he dialled a single digit.

"Natalie? Oh, you haven't gone. Listen, I'll be staying on for an hour yet; I've just had a client on the phone. Tell Syd to leave the strong-room on the key. I'll close up when I go, right?"

He slumped into his chair.

"Straighten your hair," said Jerry, and returned to the window while they waited.

"Crime and corruption, my arse," Frost muttered. "All right, suppose he cuts a few corners. Name me a Chinese who doesn't. Name me a Brit who doesn't. Do you think that brings the Island to its feet?"

"Chinese, is he?" said Jerry very sharply.

Coming back to the desk, Jerry himself dialled Natalie's number. No answer. Lifting Frost gently to his feet, Jerry led him to the door.

"Now, don't go locking up," he warned. "We'll need to put it back before you leave."

Frost had returned. He sat glumly at the desk, three folders before him on the blotter. Jerry poured him a vodka.

Standing at his shoulder while Frost drank it, Jerry explained how a collaboration of this sort worked. Frostie wouldn't feel a thing, he said. All he had to do was leave everything where it lay, then step into the corridor, closing the door carefully after him. Beside the door was a staff notice-board; Frostie had no doubt observed it often. Frostie should place himself before this notice-board and read the notices diligently, all of them, until he heard Jerry give two knocks from within, when he could return. While reading, he should take care to keep his body at such an angle as to obscure the peep-hole, so that Jerry would know he was still there, and passersby would not be able to see in. Frost could also console himself with the thought that he had betrayed no confidences, Jerry explained. The worst that Higher Authority could ever say—or the client, for that matter—was that by abandoning his room when Jerry was inside it, he had committed a technical breach of the bank's security regulations.

"How many papers are there in the folders?"

"How should I know?" asked Frost, slightly emboldened by his unexpected innocence.

"Count 'em, will you, sport? Attaboy."

There were fifty exactly, which was a great deal more than Jerry had bargained for. There remained the fall-back against the eventuality that Jerry, despite these precautions, might be disturbed.

"I'll need application forms," he said.

"What bloody application forms? I don't keep forms," Frost retorted. "I've got *girls* who bring me forms. No, I haven't. They've gone home."

"To open my trust account with your distinguished house, Frostie. Spread here on the table, with your hospitality gold-plated fountain-pen—will you? You're taking a break while I fill them in. And that's the first installment," he said. Drawing a little wad of American money from his hip pocket, he tossed it on the table with a pleasing slap. Frost eyed the money but did not pick it up.

Alone, Jerry worked fast. He disentangled the papers from the clasp and laid them out in pairs, photographing them two pages to a shot, keeping his big arms close to his body for stillness and his big feet slightly apart for balance, like a slip-catch at cricket, and the measuring chain just brushing the papers for distance. When he was not satisfied he repeated a shot. Sometimes he bracketed the exposure. Often he turned his head and glanced at the circle of Robin Hood green in the eyehole to make sure Frost was at his post and not, even now, calling in the guards armoured.

Once, Frost grew impatient and tapped on the glass, and Jerry growled at him to shut up. Occasionally he heard footsteps approach, and when that happened he left everything on the table with the money and the application forms, put the camera in his pocket, and ambled to the window to gaze at the harbour and yank at his hair, like a man contemplating the great decisions of his life. And once, which is a fiddly game when you have big fingers and you're under stress, he changed the cassette, wishing the old camera's action a shade more quiet.

By the time he called Frost back, the folders were once more on his desk, the money was beside the folders, and Jerry was feeling cold and just a little murderous.

"You're a bloody fool," Frost announced, feeding the five hundred dollars into the button-down pocket of his tunic.

"Sure," he said. He was looking round, brushing over his traces.

"You're out of your dirty little mind," Frost told him. His expression was oddly resolute. "You think you can bust a man like him? You might as well try and take Fort Knox with a jemmy and a box of firecrackers as take the lid off that crowd."

"Mr. Big himself. I like that."

"No, you won't, you'll hate it."

"Know him, do you?"

"We're like ham and eggs," said Frost sourly. "I'm in and out of his place every day. You know my passion for the high and mighty."

"Who opened his account for him?"

"My predecessor."

"Been here, has he?"

"Not in my day."

"Ever seen him?"

"Canidrome in Macao."

"The *where?*"

"Macao dog races. Losing his shirt. Mixing with the common crowd. I was with my little Chinese bird—the one before last. She pointed him out to me. 'Him?' I said. 'Him? Oh, yes—well, he's a client of mine.' Very impressed she was." A flicker of his former self appeared in Frost's subdued features. "I'll tell you one thing; *he* wasn't doing badly for himself. Very nice blond party he had with him. Round-eye. Film star, by the look of her. Swedish. Lot of conscientious work on the casting couch. Here—" Frost managed a ghostly smile.

"Hurry, sport. What is it?"

"Let's make it up. Come on. We'll go on the town. Blow

my five hundred bucks. You're not really like that, are you? It's just something you do for your living."

Groping in his pocket, Jerry dug out the alarm key and dropped it into Frost's passive hand.

"You'll need this," he said.

On the great steps as he left stood a slender, well-dressed young man in low-cut American slacks. He was reading a serious-looking book in the hardback edition; Jerry couldn't see what. He had not got very far into it, but he was reading it intently, like somebody determined upon improving his mind.

Sarratt man, once more; the rest blanked out.

Heeltap, said the bearleaders. Never go there straight. If you can't cache the take, at least queer the scent. He took taxis, but always to somewhere specific. To the Queen's Pier, where he watched the out-island ferries loading and the brown junks skimming between the liners. To Aberdeen, where he meandered with the sightseers gawping at the boat people and the floating restaurants. To Stanley village, and along the public beach, where pale-bodied Chinese bathers, a little stooped as if the city were still weighing on their shoulders, chastely paddled with their children. Chinese never swim after the moon festival, he reminded himself automatically, but he couldn't remember off-hand when the moon festival was.

He had thought of dropping the camera at the hat-check room at the Hilton Hotel. He had thought of night safes, and posting a parcel to himself; of special messengers under journalistic cover. None worked for him—more particularly, none worked for the bearleaders. It's a solo, they had said; it's a do-it-yourself or nothing. So he bought something to carry: a plastic shopping bag and a couple of cotton shirts to flesh it out. When you're hot, said the doctrine, make sure you have a distraction. Even the oldest watchers fall for it. And if they flush you and you drop it, who knows? You may even hold off the dogs long enough to get out in your socks.

He kept clear of people, all the same. He had a living terror of the chance pickpocket. In the hire garage on Kowloon-side, they had the car ready for him. He felt calm—he was coming down—but his vigilance never relaxed. He felt victorious and the rest of what he felt was of no account. Some jobs are grubby.

Driving, he watched particularly for Hondas, which in Hong Kong are the poor bloody infantry of the watching trade. Before leaving Kowloon, he made a couple of passes through side-streets. Nothing. At Junction Road he joined the picnic convoy and continued toward Clear Water Bay for another hour, grateful for the really bad traffic; there is nothing harder than unobtrusively ringing the changes between a trio of Hondas caught in a fifteen-mile snarl-up. The rest was watching mirrors, driving, getting there—flying solo. The afternoon heat stayed fierce. He had the air-conditioning full on but couldn't feel it. He passed acres of potted plants, Seiko signs, then quilts of paddies and plots of young peach trees growing for the new-year market.

He came to a narrow sand lane to his left and turned sharply in to it, watching his mirror. He pulled up, parked for a while with the rear lid up, pretending to let the engine cool. A pea-green Mercedes slid past him, smoked windows, one driver, one passenger in front. It had been behind him for some time. But it stuck to the main road. He crossed the road to the café, dialled a number, let the phone ring four times, and rang off. He dialled the number again; it rang six times and as the receiver was lifted he rang off again.

He drove on, lumbering through remnants of fishing villages to a lake-side where the rushes were threaded far out into the water, and doubled by their own straight reflection. Bull-frogs bellowed and light pleasure yachts switched in and out of the heat haze. The sky was dead white and reached right into the water. He got out. As he did so, an old Citroën van hobbled down the road, several Chinese aboard: Coca-Cola hats, fishing tackle, kids; but two men, no women, and the men ignored him. He made for a row of clapboard balcony houses, very run-down and fronted with concrete lattice walls like houses on an English sea front, but the paint on them paler because of the sun. Their names were done in heavy poker-work on bits of ship's timber: "Driftwood," "Susy May," "Dun-romin." There was a marina at the end of the track, but it was closed down and the yachts now harboured somewhere else.

Approaching the houses, Jerry glanced casually at the upper windows. In the second from the left stood a lurid vase of dried flowers, their stems wrapped in silver paper. All clear, it said. Pushing open the little gate, he pressed the bell. The Citroën had stopped at the lake-side. He heard the doors slam at the same time that he heard the misused electronics over the entry-phone loudspeaker.

"What bastard's that?" a gravel voice demanded, its rich Australian tones thundering through the atmospherics, but the catch on the door was already buzzing, and when Jerry shoved it he saw the gross figure of old Craw in his kimono planted at the top of the staircase, hugely pleased, calling him "Monsignor" and "you thieving pommy dog," and exhorting him to haul his ugly, upper-class backside up here and put a bloody drink under his belt.

The house reeked of burning joss. From the shadows of a ground-floor doorway a toothless amah grinned at him, the same strange little creature whom Luke had questioned while Craw was absent in London. The drawing-room was on the first floor, the grimy panelling strewn with curling photographs of Craw's old pals, journalists he'd worked with for all of fifty years of crazy Oriental history. At the centre stood a table with a battered Remington where Craw was supposed to be composing his life's memoirs. The rest of the room was sparse. Craw, like Jerry, had kids and wives left over from half a dozen existences, and after meeting the immediate needs there wasn't much money for furniture.

The bathroom had no window.

Beside the hand-basin, a developing tank and brown bottles of fixer and developer. Also a small editor with a ground-glass screen for reading negatives. Craw switched off the light, and for numberless years in space laboured in the total darkness, grunting and cursing and appealing to the Pope. Beside him, Jerry sweated and tried to chart the old man's actions by his swearing. Now, he guessed, Craw was feeding the narrow ribbon from the cassette onto the spool. Jerry imagined him holding it too lightly for fear of marking the emulsion. In a moment he'll be doubting whether he's holding it at all, thought Jerry. He'll be having to will his fingertips into continuing the movement. He felt sick. In the darkness old Craw's cursing grew much louder, but not loud enough to drown the scream of water birds from the lake. He's deft, thought Jerry, reassured. He can do it in his sleep. He heard the grinding of bakelite as Craw screwed down the lid, and a muttered "Go to bed, you little heathen bastard," then the strangely dry rattle as he cautiously shook the air bubbles out of the developer. Then the safety light went on with a snap as loud as a pistol-shot, and there was old Craw himself once more, red as a parrot from the glow, stooped over the sealed tank, quickly pouring in the hypo, then confidently overturning the tank and setting it right again while he watched the old kitchen timer stammer through the seconds.

Half stifled with nerves and heat, Jerry returned alone to the drawing-room, poured himself a beer, and slumped into a cane chair, looking nowhere while he listened to the steady running of the tap. From the window came the bubbling of Chinese voices. At the lake's edge the two fishermen had set up their tackle. The children were watching them, sitting in the dust. From the bathroom came the scratching of the lid again, and Jerry leapt to his feet, but Craw must have heard him, for he growled "Wait" and closed the door.

Airline pilots, journalists, spies, the Sarratt doctrine warned, *it's the same drag. Bloody inertia interspersed with bouts of bloody frenzy.*

He's taking first look, thought Jerry; in case it's fumble. In the pecking order, it was Craw, not Jerry, who had to make his peace with London. Craw who, in the worst contingency, would order him to take a second bite of Frost.

"What are you doing in there, for Christ's sake?" Jerry yelled. "What goes on?"

Perhaps he's having a pee, he thought absurdly.

Slowly the door opened. Craw's gravity was awesome.

"They haven't come out," said Jerry.

He had the feeling of not reaching Craw at all. He was going to repeat himself, in fact, loudly. He was going to dance about and make a damn scene. So that Craw's answer, when it finally came, came just in time.

"To the contrary, my son." The old boy took a step forward, and Jerry could see the films now, hanging behind him like black wet worms from Craw's little clothes-line, pink pegs holding them in place. "To the contrary, sir," he said, "every frame is a bold and disturbing masterpiece."

7

More About Horses

In the Circus, the first scraps of news on Jerry's progress arrived in the early morning, in a deadly quiet, and thereafter set the weekend upside down. Knowing what to expect, Guillam had taken himself to bed at ten and slumbered fitfully between bouts of anxiety for Jerry, and frankly lustful visions of Molly Meakin with and without her sedate swimming-suit. Jerry was due to present himself to Frost just after 4 a.m. London time, and by three-thirty Guillam was clattering in his old Porsche through the foggy streets toward Cambridge Circus. It could have been dawn or dusk. He arrived at the rumpus room to find Connie completing the *Times* crossword and Doc di Salis reading the meditations of Thomas Traherne, plucking his ear, and jiggling his foot all at the same time, like a one-man percussion band. Restless as ever, Fawn flitted between them, dusting and tidying, a headwaiter impatient for the next sitting. Now and then he sucked his teeth and let out a breathy "*tah*," in barely controlled frustration. A pall of tobacco smoke hung like a rain cloud across the room and there was the usual stink of rank tea from the samovar.

Smiley's door was closed and Guillam saw no cause to disturb him. He opened a copy of *Country Life*. Like waiting at the bloody dentist, he thought, and sat staring mindlessly at photographs of great houses till Connie softly put down her crossword, sat bolt upright, and said "Listen." Then he heard a quick snarl from the

Cousins' green telephone before Smiley picked it up. Through the open doorway to his own room Guillam glanced at the row of electronic boxes. On one, a green caution-light burned for as long as the conversation lasted. Then the pax rang in the rumpus room—"pax" being jargon for internal phone—and this time Guillam reached it before Fawn.

"He's entered the bank," Smiley announced cryptically.

Guillam relayed the message to the gathering. "He's gone into the bank," he said, but he might have been talking to the dead: nobody gave the slightest sign of hearing.

By five, Jerry had come out of the bank. Nervously contemplating the options, Guillam felt physically sick. Burning was a dangerous game, and like most pros Guillam hated it, though not for reasons of scruple. First there was the quarry or, worse, the local security angels. Second there was the burn itself, and not everybody responded logically to blackmail. You got heroes, you got liars, you got hysterical virgins who put their heads back and screamed blue murder even if they were enjoying it. But the real danger came now, when the burn was over and Jerry had to turn his back on the smoking bomb and run. Which way would Frost jump? Would he telephone the police? His mother? His boss? His wife? "Darling, I'll confess all. Save me and we'll turn over a new leaf." Guillam did not even rule out the ghastly possibility that Frost might go directly to his client. "Sir, I have come to purge myself of a gross breach of bank confidence."

In the fusty eeriness of early morning Guillam shuddered, and fixed his mind resolutely on Molly.

On the next occasion the green phone sounded, Guillam didn't hear it. George must have been sitting right over the thing; suddenly the pin-light in Guillam's room was glowing, and it continued glowing for fifteen minutes. It went out and they waited, all eyes fixed on Smiley's door, willing him from his seclusion. Fawn was frozen in mid-movement, holding a plate of brown marmalade sandwiches, which nobody would ever eat.

Then the handle tipped and Smiley appeared with a common-or-garden search-request form in his hand, already completed in his own neat script and flagged "Stripe," which meant "Urgent for Chief" and was the top priority. He gave it to Guillam and asked him to take it straight to the Queen Bee in Registry and stand over her while she looked up the name. Receiving it, Guillam recalled an earlier moment when he had been presented with a similar form, made out in the name of Worthington Elizabeth, alias Lizzie, and ending "high-class tart." And as he departed, he heard Smiley quietly inviting Connie and di Salis to accompany him to the throne-room, while Fawn was packed off to the unclassified library in search of the current edition of *Who's Who in Hong Kong*.

The Queen Bee had been specially summoned for the dawn shift, and when Guillam walked in on her, her lair looked like a tableau of "The Night London Burned," complete with an iron bunk and a small primus stove, though there was a coffee machine in the corridor. All she needs is a boiler suit and a portrait of Winston Churchill, he thought. The details on the trace read "Ko forename Drake other names unknown, date of birth 1925 Shanghai, present address Seven Gates, Headland Road, Hong Kong, occupation Chairman and Managing Director of China Airsea Ltd., Hong Kong." The Queen Bee launched herself on an impressive paper-chase, but all she finally came up with was the information that Ko had been appointed to the Order of the British Empire under the Hong Kong list in 1966 for "social and charitable services to the Colony," and that the Circus had responded "Nothing recorded against" to a vetting enquiry from the Governor's office before the award was passed up for approval.

Hurrying upstairs with this glad intelligence, Guillam was awake enough to remember that China Airsea Ltd., Hong Kong, had been described by Sam Collins as the ultimate owner of that mickey-mouse airline in Vientiane, which had been the beneficiary of Commercial Boris's bounty. This struck Guillam as a most orderly connection. Pleased with himself, he returned to the throne-room to be greeted by funereal silence. Strewn over the floor lay not just the current edition of *Who's Who* but several back numbers as well; Fawn, as usual, had overreached himself. Smiley sat at his desk and he was staring at a sheet of notes in his own handwriting, Connie and di Salis were staring at Smiley, but Fawn was absent again, presumably on another errand. Guillam handed Smiley the trace form with the Queen Bee's findings written along the middle in her best Kensington copperplate. At the same moment, the green phone crackled again. Lifting the receiver, Smiley began jotting on the sheet before him.

"Yes. Thanks, I have that. Go on, please. Yes, I have that also." And so on for ten minutes, till he said, "Good. Till this evening, then," and rang off.

Outside in the street, an Irish milkman was enthusiastically proclaiming that he never would be the wild rover no more.

"Westerby's landed the complete file," Smiley said finally—though, like everyone else, he referred to him by his cryptonym. "All the figures." He nodded as if agreeing with himself, still studying the paper. "The film won't be here till tonight but the shape is already clear. Everything that was originally paid through Vientiane has found its way to the account in Hong Kong. Right from the very beginning. Hong Kong was the final destination of the gold seam. All of it. Down to the last cent. No deductions, not even for bank commission. It was at first a humble figure, then rose steeply—why, we may only guess. All as Collins described. Till it stopped at twenty-five thousand a month and stayed there. When the Vientiane arrangement ended, Centre didn't miss a single month. They switched to the alternative route immediately. You're right, Con. Karla never does anything without a fall-back."

"He's a professional, darling," Connie Sachs murmured. "Like you."

"Not like me." He continued studying his jottings. "It's a lock-away account," he declared, in the same matter-of-fact tone. "Only one name is given and that's the founder of the trust. Ko. 'Beneficiary unknown,' they say. Perhaps we shall see why tonight. Not a penny has been drawn," he said, singling out Connie Sachs. He repeated that: "Since the payments started over two years ago, not a single penny has been drawn from the account. The balance stands in the order of half a million American dollars. With compound interest, it's naturally rising fast."

To Guillam, this last piece of intelligence was daylight madness. What the hell was the point to a million-dollar gold seam if the money was not even used when it reached the other end? To Connie Sachs and di Salis, on the other hand, it was patently of enormous significance. A crocodile smile spread slowly across Connie's face and her baby eyes fixed on Smiley in silent ecstasy.

"Oh, *George*," she breathed at last, as the revelation gathered in her. "Darling. *Lock-away!* Well, that's quite a different kettle of fish. Well, of course it had to be, didn't it! It had all the signs. From the very first *day*. And if fat, stupid Connie hadn't been so blinkered and old and doddery and idle, she'd have read them off *long* ago! You leave me alone, Peter Guillam, you lecherous young toad." She was pulling herself to her feet, her crippled hands clamped over the chair arms. "But who can be worth so much? Would *it* be a network? No, no, they'd never do it for a *network*. No precedent. Not a wholesale thing, that's unheard of. So who can it be? Whatever can he *deliver* that would be worth so much?" She was hobbling toward the door, tugging the shawl over her shoulders, slipping already from their world to her own. "*Karla* doesn't pay out money like that." They heard her mutterings follow her. She passed the mothers' lane of covered typewriters, muffled sentinels in the gloom. "*Karla's* such a mean prig he thinks his agents should work for him for *nothing!* 'Course he does. *Pennies*, that's what he pays them. Pocket-money. Inflation is all very well, but half a million dollars for one little mole—I never heard such a thing!"

In his quirkish way, di Salis was no less impressed than

Connie. He sat with the top part of his crabbed, uneven body tilted forward, and he was stirring feverishly in the bowl of his pipe with a silver knife as if it were a cook pot which had caught on the flame. His silver hair stood wry as a cockscomb over the dandruffed collar of his crumpled black jacket.

"Well, well, no wonder Karla wanted the bodies buried," he blurted suddenly, as if the words had been jerked out of him. "No wonder. Karla's a China hand, too, you know. It's attested. I have it from Connie." He clambered to his feet, holding too many things in his hands: pipe, tobacco tin, his penknife, and his Thomas Traherne. "Not sophisticated, naturally. Well, one doesn't expect that. Karla's no scholar, he's a soldier. But not blind, either—not by a long chalk, she tells me. *Ko.*" He repeated the name at several different levels: "Ko. *Ko.* I must see the character. It depends entirely on the character. *Height . . . Tree* even, yes I can see *tree . . .* or can I? . . . oh, and several other concepts. 'Drake' is mission school, of course. Shanghainese mission boy. Well, well. Shanghai was where it all started, you know. First party cell *ever* was in Shanghai. Why did I say that? *Drake Ko.* Wonder what his real names are. We shall find that all out very shortly, no doubt. Yes, good. Well, I think I might go back to my reading, too. Smiley, do you think I might have a coal-scuttle in my room? Without the heating on, one simply freezes up. I've asked the housekeepers a dozen times and had nothing but impertinence for my pains. *Anno Domini,* I'm afraid, but the winter is almost upon us, I suppose. You'll show us the raw material as soon as it arrives, I trust? One doesn't like to work too long on potted versions. I shall make a *curriculum vitae.* That will be my first thing. Ko. Ah, thank you, Guillam."

He had dropped his Thomas Traherne. Accepting it, he dropped his tobacco tin, so Guillam picked that up as well. "Drake Ko. Shanghainese doesn't mean a thing, of course. Shanghai was the real melting-pot. Chiu Chow's the answer, judging by what we know. Still, mustn't jump the gun. Baptist. Well, the Chiu Chow Christians mostly are, aren't they? Swa-

townese: where did we have that? Yes, the intermediate company in Bangkok. Well, that figures well enough. Or Hakka.
They're not mutually exclusive, not by any means."

He stalked after Connie into the corridor, leaving Guillam
alone with Smiley, who rose and, going to an armchair, slumped
into it staring sightlessly at the fire.

"Odd," he remarked finally. "One has no sense of shock.
Why is that, Peter? You know me. Why is it?"

Guillam had the wisdom to keep quiet.

"A big fish. In Karla's pay. Lock-away accounts, the threat
of Russian spies at the very centre of the Colony's life. So why
no sense of shock?"

The green telephone was barking again; this time Guillam
took the call. As he did so, he was surprised to see a fresh folder
of Sam Collins's Far Eastern reports lying open on the desk.

That was the weekend. Connie and di Salis sank without trace;
Smiley set to work preparing his submission; Guillam smoothed
feathers, called in the mothers, and arranged for typing in shifts.
On the Monday, carefully briefed by Smiley, he telephoned
Lacon's private secretary. He did it very well. "No drum-beats,"
Smiley had warned. "Keep it very idle." And Guillam did just
that. There had been talk over dinner the other evening—he
said—of a prima-facie case for convening the Intelligence Steering Group.

"The case has firmed up a little, so perhaps it would be sensible to fix a date. Give us the batting order and we'll circulate
the document in advance."

"A *batting order*? *Firmed up*? Where *ever* do you people learn
your English?"

Lacon's private secretary was a fat voice called Pym. Guillam
had never met him, but he loathed him quite unreasonably.

"I can only tell him," Pym warned. "I can tell him and I can
see what he says and I can ring you back. His card is *very* heavily marked this month."

"It's just one little waltz, if he can manage it," said Guillam, and rang off in a fury.

You bloody well wait and see what hits you, he thought.

When London is having its baby, the folklore says, the field-man can only pace the waiting-room. Airline pilots, news-hounds, spies—Jerry was back with the bloody inertia.

"We're in moth-balls," Craw announced. "The word is well done and hold your water."

They talked every two days at least, limbo calls between two third-party telephones, usually one hotel lobby to another. They disguised their language with a mix of Sarratt word code and journalistic mumbo-jumbo.

"Your story is being checked out on high," Craw said. "When our editors have wisdom, they will impart it in due season. Mean-while, slap your hand over it and keep it there. That's an order."

Jerry had no idea how Craw talked to London and he didn't care as long as it was safe. He assumed some co-opted official from the huge, untouchable above-the-line intelligence frater-nity was playing linkman; but he didn't care.

"Your job is to put in mileage for the comic and tuck some spare copy under your belt, which you can wave at Brother Stubbs when the next crisis comes," Craw said to him. "Noth-ing else, hear me?"

Drawing on his jaunts with Frost, Jerry bashed out a piece on the effect of the American military pull-out upon the night-life of Wanchai: "What's happened to Susie Wong since war-weary G.I.s with bulging wallets have ceased to flock in for rest and recreation?" He fabricated a "dawn interview" with a disconsolate and fictitious bar-girl who was reduced to accept-ing Japanese customers, air-freighted his piece, and got Luke's bureau to wire through the number of the way-bill, all as Stubbs had ordered.

Jerry was by no means a bad reporter, but just as pressure brought out the best in him, sloth brought out the worst. Astonished by Stubbs's prompt and even gracious acceptance (a "herogram," Luke called it, phoning through the text from the bureau), he cast around for other heights to scale. A couple of sensational corruption trials were attracting good houses, starring the usual crop of misunderstood policemen, but after taking a look at them, Jerry concluded they hadn't the scale to travel. England had her own these days. A "please-matcher" ordered him to chase a story floated by a rival comic about the alleged pregnancy of Miss Hong Kong, but a libel suit got there ahead of him.

He attended an arid government press briefing by Shallow Throat, himself a humourless reject from a Northern Irish daily; idled away a morning researching successful stories from the past that might stand re-heating; and, on the strength of a rumour about army economy cuts, spent an afternoon being trailed round the Gurkha garrison by a public-relations major who looked about eighteen. And no, the major *didn't* know, thank you, in reply to Jerry's cheerful enquiry, what his men would do for sex when their families were sent home to Nepal. They would be visiting their villages about once every three years, he thought; and he seemed to think that was quite enough for anyone. Stretching the facts till they read as if the Gurkhas were already a community of military grass widowers ("COLD SHOWERS IN A HOT CLIMATE FOR BRITAIN'S MERCENARIES"), Jerry triumphantly landed himself an inside lead. He banked a couple more stories for a rainy day, lounged away the evenings at the Club, and inwardly gnawed his head off while he waited for the Circus to produce its baby.

"For Christ's sake," he protested to Craw. "The bloody man's practically public property."

"All the same," said Craw firmly.

So Jerry said "Yes, sir," and a few days later, out of sheer boredom, began his own entirely informal investigation into the life and loves of Mr. Drake Ko, O.B.E., Steward of the Royal Hong Kong Jockey Club, millionaire, and citizen above

suspicion. Nothing dramatic; nothing, in Jerry's book, dis-
obedient; for there is not a fieldman born who does not at one
time or another stray across the borders of his brief. He began
tentatively, like journeys to a forbidden biscuit box. As it happened, he had been considering proposing to Stubbs a three-part
series on the Hong Kong super-rich. Browsing in the reference
shelves of the Foreign Correspondents' Club before lunch one
day, he unconsciously took a leaf from Smiley's book and
turned up "Ko, Drake" in the current edition of *Who's Who in
Hong Kong*: married; one son, died 1968; sometime law student
of Gray's Inn, London, but not a successful one, apparently,
for there was no record of his having been called to the bar.
Then a run-down of his twenty-odd directorships. Hobbies:
horseracing, cruising, and jade. Well, whose aren't? Then the
charities he supported, including a Baptist church, a Chiu Chow
Spirit Temple, and the Drake Ko Free Hospital for Children.
Backed all the possibilities, Jerry reflected with amusement.
The photograph showed the usual soft-eyed, twenty-year-old
beautiful soul, rich in merit as well as goods, and was otherwise
unrecognisable.

The dead son's name was Nelson, Jerry noticed: Drake and
Nelson, British admirals. He couldn't get it out of his mind
that the father should be named after the first British sailor to
enter the China Seas, and the son after the hero of Trafalgar.

Jerry had a lot less difficulty than Peter Guillam in making
the connection between China Airsea in Hong Kong and Indocharter S.A. in Vientiane, and he was amused to read in the
China Airsea company prospectus that its business was described
as a "wide spread of trading and transportation activities in the
South East Asian theatre"—including rice, fish, electrical goods,
teak, real estate, and shipping.

Devilling at Luke's bureau, he took a bolder step; the sheerest accident shoved the name of Drake Ko under his nose. True,
he had looked up Ko in the card index. Just as he had looked up
a dozen or twenty other wealthy Chinese in the Colony; just as

he had asked the Chinese clerk, in perfectly good faith, who *she* thought were the most exotic Chinese millionaires for his purpose. And while Drake might not have been one of the absolute front runners, it took very little to draw the name from her, and consequently the papers. Indeed, as he had already protested to Craw, there was something flattening, not to say dream-like, about pursuing by hole-and-corner methods a man so publicly evident. Soviet intelligence agents, in Jerry's limited experience of the breed, normally came in more modest versions. Ko seemed king-sized by comparison.

Reminds me of old Sambo, Jerry thought. It was the first time this intimation struck him.

The most detailed offering appeared in a glossy periodical called *Golden Orient*, now out of print. In one of its last editions, an eight-page illustrated feature titled "The Red Knights of Nanyang" concerned itself with the growing number of overseas Chinese with profitable trade relations with Red China, commonly known as "fat cats." Nanyang, as Jerry knew, meant the realms south of China, and implied to the Chinese a kind of eldorado of peace and wealth. To each chosen personality the feature devoted a page and a photograph, generally shot against a background of personal possessions. The hero of the Hong Kong interview—there were pieces from Bangkok, Manila, and Singapore as well—was that "much-loved sporting personality and Jockey Club Steward," Mr. Drake Ko, President, Chairman, Managing Director, and chief shareholder of China Airsea Ltd., and he was shown with his horse Lucky Nelson at the end of a successful season in Happy Valley. The horse's name momentarily arrested Jerry's Western eye. He found it macabre that a father should christen a horse after his dead son.

The accompanying photograph revealed much more than the spineless mug shot in *Who's Who*. Ko looked jolly, even exuberant, and he appeared, despite his hat, to be hairless. The hat was at this stage the most interesting thing about Ko, for it was one which no Chinese, in Jerry's firm opinion, had ever been seen to wear before. It was a beret, worn sloping, putting Ko somewhere between a British soldier and a French onion seller; but above all, it had, for a Chinese, the rarest quality of all—self-mockery. He was apparently tall, he was wearing a Burberry, and his long hands stuck out of the sleeves like twigs. He seemed genuinely to like the horse, and one arm rested easily on its back.

Asked why he still ran a junk-fleet when these were commonly held to be unprofitable, he replied: "My people are Hakka from Chiu Chow. We breathed the water, farmed the water, slept on the water. Boats are my element." He was fond also of describing his journey from Shanghai to Hong Kong in 1951. At that time, the border was still open and there were no effective restrictions on immigration. Nevertheless, Ko chose to make the trip by fishing junk—pirates, blockades, and bad weather notwithstanding—which was held at the very least to be eccentric.

"I'm a very lazy fellow," he was reported as saying. "If the wind will blow me for nothing, why should I walk? Now I've got a sixty-foot cruiser but I still love the sea."

Famous for his sense of humour, said the article.

A good agent must have entertainment value, say the Sarratt bearleaders; that was something Moscow Centre also understood.

There being no one watching, Jerry ambled over to the card index and a few minutes later had taken possession of a thick folder of press cuttings, the bulk of which concerned a share scandal in 1965, in which Ko and a group of Swatownese had played a shady part. The Stock Exchange enquiry, not surprisingly, proved inconclusive and was shelved. The following year Ko got his O.B.E. "If you buy people," old Sambo used to say, "buy them thoroughly."

In Luke's bureau they kept a bunch of Chinese researchers, among them a convivial Cantonese named Jimmy who often appeared at the Club and was paid at Chinese rates to be the oracle on Chinese matters. Jimmy said the Swatownese were a people apart, "like Scots or Jews," hardy, clannish, and notoriously thrifty, who lived near the sea so that they could run for it when they were persecuted or starving or in debt. He said their women were sought-after, being beautiful, diligent, frugal, and lecherous.

"Writing yourself another novel, your Lordship?" the dwarf asked endearingly, coming out of his office to find out what Jerry was up to. Jerry had wanted to ask why a Swatownese should have been brought up in Shanghai, but he thought it wiser to bend course toward a less delicate topic.

Next day Jerry borrowed Luke's battered car. Armed with a standard-size 35-millimetre camera, he drove to Headland Road, a millionaire's ghetto between Repulse Bay and Stanley, where he made a show of rubbernecking at the outside of the villas there, as many idle tourists do. His cover story was still that feature for Stubbs on the Hong Kong super-rich; even now, even to himself, he would scarcely have admitted going there on account of Drake Ko.

"He's raising Cain in Taipei," Craw had told him casually in one of their limbo calls. "Won't be back till Thursday." Once again, Jerry accepted without question Craw's lines of communication.

He did not photograph the house called Seven Gates, but he took several long, stupid gazes at it. He saw a low, pantiled villa set well back from the road, with a big verandah on the seaward side and a pergola of white-painted pillars cut against the blue horizon. Craw had told him that Drake must have chosen the name because of Shanghai, whose old city walls were pierced with seven gates. "Sentiment, my son. Never underrate the power of sentiment upon a slant-eye, and never count on it either. Amen." He saw lawns—including, to his amusement, a croquet lawn. He saw a fine collection of azaleas and hibiscus. He saw a model junk about ten feet long set on a concrete sea, and he saw a garden bar, round like a bandstand, with a blue-and-white striped awning over it, and a ring of empty white chairs presided over by a boy in a white coat and trousers and white shoes. The Kos were evidently expecting company. He saw other houseboys washing a tobacco-coloured Rolls-Royce Phantom saloon. The long garage was open, and he recorded a Chrysler station-wagon of some kind, and a Mercedes, black, with the licence plates removed, presumably as part of some repair. But he was meticulous about giving equal attention to the other houses in Headland Road, and photographed three of them.

Continuing to Deep Water Bay, he stood on the shore gazing at the small armada of stockbroker junks and launches which bobbed at anchor on the choppy sea, but was not able to pick out *Admiral Nelson*, Ko's celebrated ocean-going cruiser—the ubiquity of the name Nelson was becoming positively oppressive. About to give up, he heard a cry from below him, and walking down a rickety wooden causeway, he found an old woman in a sampan grinning up at him and pointing to herself with a yellow chicken leg she had been sucking with her toothless gums.

Clambering aboard, he indicated the boats and she took him on a tour of them, laughing and chanting while she skulled, and keeping the chicken leg in her mouth. *Admiral Nelson* was sleek and low-lined. Three more boys in white ducks were diligently scouring the decks. Jerry tried to calculate Ko's monthly housekeeping bill, just for staff alone.

On the drive back he paused to examine the Drake Ko Free Hospital for Children and established, for what it was worth, that that too was in excellent repair.

Next morning early, Jerry placed himself in the lobby of a chintzy high-rise office building in Central, and read the brass plates of the business companies housed there. China Airsea Ltd. and its affiliates occupied the top three floors, but somewhat predictably there was no mention of Indocharter Vientiane S.A., the former recipient of twenty-five thousand U.S. dollars on the last Friday of every month.

The cuttings folder in Luke's bureau had contained a cross-reference to U.S. Consulate archives. Jerry called there next day, ostensibly to check out his story on the American troops in Wanchai. Under the eyes of an unreasonably pretty girl, Jerry drifted, picked at a few things, then settled on some of the oldest stuff they had, which dated from the very early fifties when Truman had put a trade embargo on China and North Korea. The Hong Kong Consulate had been ordered to report infringements, and this was the record of what they had unearthed. The favourite commodity, next to medicines and electrical goods, was oil, and "the United States Agencies," as they were styled, had gone for it in a big way, setting traps, putting out gunboats, interrogating defectors and prisoners, and finally placing huge dossiers before Congressional and Senate sub-committees.

The year in question was 1951, two years after the Communist take-over in China and the year Ko sailed to Hong Kong from Shanghai without a cent to his name. The operation to which the bureau's reference directed him was Shanghainese, and to begin with, that was the only connection it had with Ko. Many Shanghainese immigrants in those days lived in a crowded, insanitary hotel on the Des Voeux Road. The introduction said that they were like one enormous family, welded together by shared suffering and squalor. Some had escaped together from the Japanese before escaping from the Communists.

"After enduring so much at Communist hands," one culprit told his interrogators, "the least we could do was make a little money out of them."

Another was more aggressive: "The Hong Kong fat cats are making millions out of this war. Who sells the Reds their electronic equipment, their penicillin, their rice?"

In '51 there were two methods open to them, said the report. One was to bribe the frontier guards and truck the oil across the New Territories and over the border. The other was taking it by ship, which meant bribing the harbour authorities.

An informant again: "Us Hakka know the sea. We find boat, three hundred tons, we rent. We fill with drums of oil, make false manifest and false destination. We reach international waters, run like hell for Amoy. Reds call us brother, profit one hundred percent. After a few runs we buy boat."

"Where did the original money come from?" the interrogator demanded.

"Ritz Ballroom" was the disconcerting answer. The Ritz was a high-class pick-up spot right down the King's Road on the waterfront, said a footnote. Most of the girls were Shanghainese. The same footnote named members of the gang. Drake Ko was one.

"Drake Ko was very tough boy," said a witness's statement given in fine print in the appendix. "You don't tell no fairy story to Drake Ko. He don't like politician people one piece. Chiang Kai-shek. Mao. He say they all one person. He say he keen supporter of Chiang Mao-shek. One day Mr. Ko lead our gang."

As to gangs, the investigation turned up nothing. It was a matter of history that Shanghai, by the time it fell to Mao in '49, had emptied three-quarters of its underworld into Hong Kong; that the Red Gang and the Green Gang had fought enough battles over the Hong Kong protection rackets to make Chicago in the twenties look like child's play. But not a witness could be found who admitted to knowing anything about gangs, triads, or any other criminal organisation.

Not surprisingly, by the time Saturday came round and Jerry was on his way to Happy Valley races, he possessed quite a detailed portrait of his quarry.

The taxi charged double because it was the races, and Jerry paid because he knew it was the form. He had told Craw he was going and Craw had not objected. He had brought Luke along for the ride, knowing that sometimes two are less conspicuous than one. He was nervous of bumping into Frost, because round-eye Hong Kong is a very small city indeed. At the main entrance, he telephoned the management to raise some influence, and in due course a Captain Grant appeared, a young official to whom Jerry explained that this was work: he was writing the place up for the comic.

Grant was a witty, elegant man who smoked Turkish cigarettes through a holder, and everything Jerry said seemed to amuse him in a fond, if rather remote way.

"You're the son, then," he said finally.

"Did you know him?" said Jerry, grinning.

"Only *of* him," Captain Grant replied; but he seemed to like what he had heard.

He gave them badges and offered them drinks later. The second race was just over. While they talked, they heard the roar of the crowd set to and rise and die like an avalanche. Waiting for the lift, Jerry checked the notice-board to see who had taken the private boxes. The hardy annuals were the Peak mafia: The Bank—as the Hong Kong & Shanghai Bank liked to call itself—Jardine Matheson, the Governor, the Commander British Forces. Mr. Drake Ko, O.B.E., though a Steward of the Club, was not among them.

"Westerby! Good *God*, man, who the hell ever let you in here? Listen, is it true your dad went bust before he died?"

Jerry hesitated, grinning, then belatedly drew the card from his memory: Clive Somebody, pigs-in-clover solicitor, house in Repulse Bay, overpowering Scot, all false affability and an open reputation for crookedness. Jerry had used him for background in a Macao-based gold swindle and concluded that Clive had had a slice of the cake.

"Gosh, Clive, super, marvellous."

They exchanged banalities, still waiting for the lift.

"Here. Give us your card. Come on! I'll make your fortune yet." Porton, thought Jerry; Clive Porton. Tearing the racecard from Jerry's hand, Porton licked his big thumb, turned to a centre page, and ringed a horse's name in ballpoint. "Number seven in the third—you can't go wrong," he breathed. "Put your shirt on it, okay? Not every day I give away money, I'll tell you."

"What did the slob sell you?" Luke enquired when they were clear of him.

"Thing called Open Space."

Their ways divided. Luke went off to place bets and wangle his way into the American Club upstairs. Jerry, on an impulse, took a hundred dollars' worth of Lucky Nelson and set a hasty course for the Hong Kong Club's luncheon room. If I lose, he thought drily, I'll chalk it up to George.

The double doors were open and he walked straight in. The atmosphere was of dowdy wealth: a Surrey golf-club on a wet weekend, except that those brave enough to risk the pickpockets wore real jewels. A group of wives sat apart, like expensive unused equipment, scowling at the closed-circuit television and moaning about servants and muggings. There was a smell of cigar smoke and sweat and departed food. Seeing him shamble in—the awful suit, the buckskin boots, "press" written all over him—their scowls darkened. The trouble with being exclusive in Hong Kong, their faces said, was that not enough people are thrown out.

A school of serious drinkers had gathered at the bar, mainly carpet-baggers from the London merchant banks, with curdled accents, beer bellies, and fat necks before their time. With them, the Jardine Matheson second eleven, not yet grand enough for the firm's private box: groomed, unloveable innocents for whom heaven was money and promotion. Apprehensively, he glanced round for Frostie, but either the gee-gees hadn't drawn him today or he was with some other crowd.

With one grin and a vague flap of the hand for all of them, Jerry winkled out the under-manager, saluted him like a lost friend, talked airily of Captain Grant, slipped him twenty bucks for himself, signed up for the day in defiance of every regulation, and stepped gratefully onto the balcony with eighteen minutes still before the "off": sun, the stink of dung, the feral rumble of a Chinese crowd, and Jerry's own quickening heartbeat that whispered "horses."

For a moment Jerry hung there, grinning, taking in the view, because every time he saw it was the first time.

The grass at Happy Valley Racecourse must be the most valuable crop on earth. There was very little of it. A narrow ring ran round the edge of what looked like a London borough recreation ground which sun and feet have beaten into dirt. Eight scuffed football pitches, one rugger pitch, one hockey gave an air of municipal neglect. But the thin green ribbon which surrounded this dingy package in that year alone was likely to attract a cool hundred million sterling through legal betting, and the same amount again in the shade. The place was less a valley than a fire-bowl—glistening white stadium one side, brown hills the other—while ahead of Jerry and to his left lurked the other Hong Kong: a card-house Manhattan of grey skyscraper slums crammed so tight they seemed to lean on one another in the heat. From each tiny balcony, a bamboo pole stuck out like a pin put in to brace the structure; from each pole hung innumerable flags of black laundry, as if something huge had brushed against the building leaving these tatters in its wake. It was from places like these, for all but the tiniest few that day, that Happy Valley offered the gambler's dream of instantaneous salvation.

Away to the right of Jerry shone newer, grander buildings. There, he remembered, the illegal bookies pitched their offices and by a dozen obscure methods—tic-tac, walkie-talkie, flashing lights; Sarratt would have been entranced by them—kept up their dialogue with legmen round the course. Higher again ran the spines of shaven hilltop slashed by quarries and littered with the ironmongery of electronic eavesdropping. Jerry had heard somewhere that the saucers had been put there for the Cousins, so that they could track the sponsored over-flights of Taiwanese U-2s. Above the hills, dumplings of white cloud which no weather ever seemed to clear away. And above the cloud, that day, the bleached China sky aching in the sun, and one hawk slowly wheeling. All this Jerry took in at a single, grateful draught.

For the crowd it was the aimless time. The focus of attention, if anywhere, was on the four fat Chinese women in fringed Hakka hats and black pyjama suits who were marching down the track with rakes, prinking the precious grass where the galloping hoofs had mussed it. They moved with the dignity of total indifference; it was as if the whole of Chinese peasantry were depicted in their gestures. For a second, in the way crowds have, a tremor of collective affinity reached out to them, and was forgotten.

The betting put Clive Porton's Open Space third favourite. Drake Ko's Lucky Nelson was in with the field at forty to one, which meant nowhere. Edging his way past a bunch of festive Australians, Jerry reached the corner of the balcony and, craning, peered steeply downward over the tiers of heads to the owners' box, cut off from the common people by a green iron gate and a security guard. Shading his eyes and wishing he had brought binoculars, he made out one fat, hard-looking man in a suit and dark glasses, accompanied by a young and very pretty girl. He looked half Chinese, half Latin, and Jerry put him down as Filipino. The girl was the best that money could buy.

Must be with his horse, thought Jerry, recalling old Sambo. Most likely in the paddock, briefing his trainer and the jockey.

Striding back through the luncheon room to the main lobby, he dropped into a wide back-stairway for two floors and crossed a hall to the viewing gallery, which was filled with a vast and thoughtful Chinese crowd, all men, staring downward in devotional silence into a covered sand-pit filled with noisy sparrows and three horses, each led by his permanent male groom, the mafoo. The mafoos held their charges miserably, as if sick with nerves. The elegant Captain Grant was looking on; so was an old White Russian trainer called Sacha, whom Jerry loved. Sacha sat on a tiny folding chair, leaning slightly forward as if he were fishing. Sacha had trained Mongolian ponies in the treaty days of Shanghai, and Jerry could listen to him all night: how Shanghai had had three racecourses, British, International, and Chinese; how the British merchant princes kept sixty—even a hundred—horses apiece and sailed them up and down the coast, competing like madmen with each other from port to port. Sacha was a gentle, philosophical fellow with far-away blue eyes and an all-in wrestler's jaw. He was also the trainer of Lucky Nelson. He sat alone, watching what Jerry took to be a doorway out of his own line of sight.

A sudden hubbub from the stands caused Jerry to turn sharply toward the sunlight. A roar sounded, then one high, strangled shriek as the crowd on one tier swayed and an axe-head of grey-and-black uniforms tore into it. An instant later and a swarm of police was dragging some wretched pick-pocket, bleeding and coughing, into the tunnel stairway for a voluntary statement. Dazzled, Jerry returned his gaze to the interior darkness of the sand-paddock, and took a moment to focus on the fogged outline of Mr. Drake Ko.

The identification was nowhere near immediate. The first person Jerry noticed was not Ko at all, but the young Chinese jockey standing at old Sacha's side: tall boy, thin as wire where his silks were nipped into his breeches. He was slapping his whip against his boot as if he had seen the gesture in an English sporting print; he was wearing Ko's colours—"sky blue and sea grey, quartered," said the article in *Golden Orient*—and, like Sacha, he was staring at something out of Jerry's sight.

Next, from under the platform where Jerry stood, came a bay griffin, led by a giggly fat mafoo in filthy grey overalls. His number was hidden by a rug, but Jerry knew the horse already from its photograph, and he knew it even better now; he knew it really well, in fact. There are some horses that are simply superior to their class, and Lucky Nelson, to Jerry's eye, was one. Bit of quality, he thought, nice long rein, a bold eye. None of your

jail-bait chestnut with a light mane and tail that take the wom-
en's vote in every race. Given the local form, which is heavily
restricted by the climate, Lucky Nelson was as sound as anything he'd seen here. Jerry was sure of it. For one bad moment
he was anxious about the horse's condition: sweating, too much
gloss on the flanks and quarters. Then he looked again at the
bold eye, and the slightly unnatural sweat lines, and his heart
revived. Cunning devil's had him hosed down to make him look
poorly, he thought, in joyous memory of old Sambo.

It was only at that late point, therefore, that Jerry moved
his eye from the horse to its owner.

Mr. Drake Ko, O.B.E., the recipient to date of a cool half
million of Moscow Centre's American dollars, the avowed supporter of Chiang Mao-shek, stood apart from everyone, in the
shadow of a white concrete pillar ten feet in diameter: an ugly
but inoffensive figure at first glance, tall, with a stoop that
should have been occupational—a dentist, or a cobbler. He was
dressed in an English way, in baggy grey flannels and a black
double-breasted blazer too long in the waist, so that it emphasised the disjointedness of his legs and gave a crumpled look to
his spare body. His face and neck were as polished as old leather
and as hairless, and the many creases looked sharp as ironed
pleats. His complexion was darker than Jerry had expected; he
would almost have suspected Arab or Indian blood. He wore
the same unsuitable hat of the photograph, a dark blue beret,
and his ears stuck out from under it like pastry roses. His very
narrow eyes were stretched still finer by its pressure. Brown
Italian shoes, white shirt, open neck. No props, not even binoculars: but a marvellous half-million-dollar smile, ear to ear,
partly gold, that seemed to relish everyone's good fortune as
well as his own.

Except there was a hint—some men have it, it is like a tension; headwaiters, doormen, journalists can spot it at a glance;
old Sambo *almost* had it—there was a hint of resources instantly

available. If things were needed, hidden people would bring them at the double.

The picture sprang to life. Over the loudspeaker the clerk of the course ordered the jockeys to mount. The giggly mafoo pulled off the rug, and Jerry, to his pleasure, noticed that Ko had had the bay's coat back-brushed to emphasise his supposedly poor condition. The thin jockey made the long awkward journey to the saddle and, with nervous friendliness, called down to Ko on the other side of him.

Ko, already moving away, swung round and snapped something back, one inaudible syllable, without looking where he spoke or who picked it up. A rebuke? An encouragement? An order to a servant? The smile had lost none of its exuberance, but the voice was hard as a whipcrack. Horse and rider took their leave. Ko took his. Jerry raced back up the stairs, through the lunch-room to the balcony, waded to the corner, and looked down.

By then Ko was no longer alone, but married.

Whether they arrived together on the stand, whether she followed him at a moment's distance, Jerry was never sure. She was so small. He spotted a glitter of black silk and a movement round it as men deferred—the stand was filling up—but at first he looked too high and missed her. Her head was at the level of their chests. He picked her up again at Ko's side, a tiny, immaculate Chinese wife, sovereign, elderly, pale, so groomed you could never imagine she had been any other age or worn any clothes but these Paris-tailored black silks, frogged and brocaded like a hussar's. *Wife's a handful*, Craw had said, extemporising as they sat bemused in front of the tiny projector. *Pinches from the big stores. Ko's people have to get in ahead of her and promise to pay for whatever she nicks.*

The article in *Golden Orient* referred to her as "an early business partner." Reading between the lines, Jerry guessed she'd been one of the girls at the Ritz Ballroom.

The crowd's roar had gathered throat.

"Did you do him, Westerby? Did you do him, man?" Scottish Clive Porton was bearing down on him, sweating heavily from drink. "Open Space, for God's sake! Even at those odds you'll make a dollar or two! Go on, man, it's a cert!"

The "off" spared him a reply. The roar choked, lifted, and swelled. All round him a pitter-patter of names and numbers fluttered in the stands; the horses sprang from their traps, drawn forward by the din. The lazy first furlong had begun. Wait: frenzy will follow the inertia. In the dawn light when they train, Jerry remembered, their hoofs are muffled in order to spare the residents their slumbers. Sometimes in the old days, drying out between war stories, Jerry would get up early and come down here just to watch them and, if he was lucky and found an influential friend, go back with them to the air-conditioned, multistorey stables where they lived, to watch the grooming and the cosseting. Whereas, by day the howl of traffic drowned their thunder entirely and the glittering cluster that advanced so slowly made no sound at all, but floated on the thin emerald river.

"Open Space all the way," Clive Porton announced uncertainly as he watched through his glasses. "The favourite's done it. Well done, Open Space, well done, lad." They began the long turn before the final straight. "*Come* on, Open Space, stretch for it man, *ride!* Use your whip, you cretin!" Porton screamed, for by now it was clear even to the naked eye that the sky-blue and sea-grey colours of Lucky Nelson were heading for the front, and that his competitors were courteously making way for him. A second horse put up a show of challenging, then flagged, but Open Space was already three lengths behind while his jockey worked furiously with his whip on the air around his mount's quarters.

"Objection!" Porton was shouting. "Where's the stewards, for God's sake? That horse was pulled! I never saw a horse so pulled in my life!"

As Lucky Nelson loped gracefully past the post, Jerry

quickly turned his gaze to the right again, and down. Ko appeared unmoved. It was not Oriental inscrutability; Jerry had never subscribed to that myth. Certainly it was not indifference. It was merely that he was observing the satisfactory unfolding of a ceremony: Mr. Drake Ko watches a march-past of his troops. His little mad wife stood poker-backed beside him as if, after all the struggles of her life, they were finally playing her anthem. For a second Jerry was reminded of old Pet in her prime. Just the way Pet looked, thought Jerry, when Sambo's pride came in a good eighteenth. Just the way she stood, and coped with failure.

The Presentation was a moment for dreams.

While the scene lacked a cake stall, the sunshine was certainly far beyond the expectation of the most sanguine organiser of an English village fête, and the silver cups were a great deal more lavish than the scratched little beaker presented by the squire for excellence in the three-legged race. The sixty uniformed policemen were also perhaps a trifle ostentatious. But the gracious lady in a 1930s turban who presided over the long white table was as mawkish and arrogant as the most exacting patriot would have wished. She knew the form exactly. The Chairman of the Stewards handed her the cup, and she quickly held it away from her as if it were too hot for her hands. Drake Ko and his wife—both grinning hugely, Ko still in his beret—emerged from a cluster of delighted supporters and grabbed the cup, but they tripped so fast and merrily back and forth across the roped-off patch of grass that the photographer was caught unprepared and had to ask the actors to re-stage the moment of consummation. This annoyed the gracious lady quite a lot, and Jerry caught the words "bloody bore" drawled out over the chatter of the onlookers. The cup was finally Ko's, the gracious lady took sullen delivery of six hundred dollars' worth of gardenias, and East and West returned gratefully to their separate cantonments.

"Do him?" Captain Grant enquired amiably. They were sauntering back toward the stands.

"Well, *yes*, actually," Jerry confessed with a grin. "Bit of a turnup, wasn't it?"

"Oh, it was Drake's race, all right," said Grant drily. They walked a little. "Clever of you to spot it. More than we did. Do you want to talk to him?"

"Talk to who?"

"Ko. While he's flushed with victory. Perhaps you'll get something out of him, for once," said Grant, with that fond smile. "Come, I'll introduce you."

Jerry did not falter. As a reporter, he had every reason to say yes. As a spy—well, sometimes they say at Sarratt that nothing is insecure but thinking makes it so. They sauntered back to the group. The Ko party had formed a rough circle round the cup and the laughter was very loud. At the centre, closest to Ko, stood the fat Filipino with his beautiful girl, and Ko was clowning with the girl, kissing her on both cheeks, then kissing her again, while everyone laughed except Ko's wife, who withdrew deliberately to the edge and began talking to a Chinese woman her own age.

"That's Arpego," said Grant, in Jerry's ear and indicating the fat Filipino. "He owns Manila and most of the out-islands."

Arpego's paunch sat forward over his belt like a rock stuffed inside his shirt.

Grant did not make straight for Ko, but singled out a burly, bland-faced Chinese in an electric-blue suit, who seemed to be some kind of aide. Jerry stood off, waiting. The plump Chinese came over to him, Grant at his side.

"This is Mr. Tiu," said Grant quietly. "Mr. Tiu, meet Mr. Westerby, son of the famous one."

"You wanna talk to Mr. Ko, Mr. Wessby?"

"If it's convenient."

"Sure it's convenient," said Tiu euphorically. His chubby hands floated restlessly in front of his stomach. He wore a gold watch on his right wrist. His fingers were curled, as if to scoop water. He was sleek and shiny, and he could have been thirty or sixty. "Mr. Ko win a horse-race, everything's convenient. I bring him over. Stay here. What your father's name?"

"Samuel," said Jerry.

"*Lord* Samuel," said Grant firmly, and inaccurately.

"Who is he?" Jerry asked aside, as plump Tiu returned to the noisy Chinese group.

"Ko's major-domo. Manager, chief bag-carrier, bottle-washer, fixer. Been with him since the start. They ran away from the Japanese together in the war."

And his chief crusher, too, Jerry thought, watching Tiu waddle back with his master.

Grant began again with the introductions. "Sir," he said, "this is Westerby, whose famous father had a lot of very slow horses. He also bought several racecourses for the bookmakers."

"What paper?" asked Ko. His voice was harsh and powerful and deep, yet to Jerry's surprise he could have sworn he caught a trace of an English North Country accent, reminiscent of old Pet's.

Jerry told him.

"That the paper with the girls!" Ko cried gaily. "I used to read that paper when I was in London, during my residence there for the purpose of legal study at the famous Gray's Inn of Court. Do you know why I read your paper, Mr. Westerby? It is my sound opinion that the more papers which are printing pretty girls in preference to politics today, the more chance we get of a damn sight better world, Mr. Westerby," Ko declared, in a vigorous mixture of misused idiom and boardroom English. "Kindly tell that to your paper from me, Mr. Westerby. I give it to you as free advice."

With a laugh, Jerry opened his notebook. "I backed your horse, Mr. Ko. How does it feel to win?"

"Better than losing, I think."

"Doesn't wear off?"

"I like it better every time."

"Does the same go for business?"

"Naturally."

"Can I speak to Mrs. Ko?"

"She's busy."

Jotting, Jerry was disconcerted by a familiar smell. It was of a musky, very pungent French soap, a blend of almonds and rose-water favoured by an early wife; and also, apparently, by the shiny Tiu for his greater allure.

"What's your formula for winning, Mr. Ko?"

"Hard work. No politics. Plenty sleep."

"Are you a lot richer than you were ten minutes ago?"

"I was pretty rich ten minutes ago. You may tell your paper also I am a great admirer of the British way of life."

"Even though we don't work hard? And make a lot of politics?"

"Just tell them," Ko said straight at him, and that was an order.

"What makes you so lucky, Mr. Ko?"

Ko appeared not to hear this question, except that his smile slowly vanished. He was staring at Jerry, measuring him through his very narrow eyes, and his face had hardened remarkably.

"What makes you so lucky, sir?" Jerry repeated.

There was a long silence.

"No comment," Ko said, still into Jerry's face.

The temptation to press the question had become irresistible. "Play fair, Mr. Ko," Jerry urged, grinning largely. "The world's full of people who dream of being as rich as you are. Give them a clue, won't you? What makes you so lucky?"

"Mind your own damn business," Ko told him, and without the smallest ceremony turned his back on him and walked away. At the same moment, Tiu took a leisurely half-pace forward, arresting Jerry's line of advance with one soft hand on his upper arm.

"You going to win next time round, Mr. Ko?" Jerry called over Tiu's shoulder at his departing back.

"You betta ask the horse, Mr. Wessby," Tiu suggested with a chubby smile, his hand still on Jerry's arm.

He might as well have done so, for Ko had already rejoined his friend Mr. Arpego, the Filipino, and they were laughing and talking just as before. *Drake Ko was very tough boy*, Jerry remembered the witness saying. *You don't tell no fairy story to Drake Ko.* Tiu doesn't do so badly either, he thought.

As they walked back toward the grandstand, Grant was laughing quietly to himself.

"Last time Ko won, he wouldn't even lead the horse into the paddock after the race," he recalled. "Waved it away. Didn't want it."

"Why the hell not?"

"Hadn't expected it to win, that's why. Hadn't told his Chiu Chow friends. Bad face. Maybe he felt the same when you asked him about his luck."

"How did he get to be a Steward?"

"Oh, had Tiu buy the votes for him, no doubt. The usual thing. Cheers. Don't forget your winnings."

Then it happened: Ace Westerby's unforeseen scoop.

The last race was over, Jerry was four thousand dollars to the good, and Luke had disappeared. Jerry tried the American Club, the Club Lusitano, and a couple of others, but either they hadn't seen him or they'd thrown him out. From the enclosure there was only one gate, so Jerry joined the march. The traffic was chaotic. Rolls-Royces and Mercedes vied for curb space and the crowds were shoving from behind.

Deciding not to join the fight for taxis, Jerry started along the narrow pavement and saw, to his surprise, Drake Ko alone, emerging from a gateway across the road. Reaching the roadside, he seemed undecided whether to cross, then settled for where he was, gazing at the on-coming traffic. He's waiting for the Rolls-Royce Phantom, thought Jerry, remembering the fleet in the garage at Headland Road. Or the Merc, or the Chrysler.

Suddenly Jerry saw him whip off the beret and, clowning, hold it into the road as if to draw rifle fire. The wrinkles flew up around his eyes and jaw, his gold teeth glittered in welcome; but instead of a Rolls-Royce, or a Merc, or a Chrysler, a long red Jaguar E-type with a soft top folded back screeched to a stop beside him, oblivious of the other cars. Jerry couldn't have missed it if he'd wanted to; the noise of the tyres alone turned every head along the pavement. His eye read the number, his mind recorded it. Ko climbed aboard with all the excitement of someone who might never have ridden in an open car before, and he was already talking and laughing before they pulled away.

But not before Jerry had seen the driver: her fluttering blue headscarf, dark glasses, long blond hair, and enough of her body, as she leaned across Drake to lock his door, to know that she was a hell of a lot of woman. Drake's hand was resting on her bare back, fingers splayed; his spare hand was waving about while he no doubt gave her a blow-by-blow account of his victory, and as they set off together he planted a very un-Chinese kiss on her cheek, and then for good measure two more: but all somehow with a great deal more sincerity than he had brought to the business of kissing Mr. Arpego's escort.

On the other side of the road stood the gateway Ko had just come out of, and the iron gate was still open. His mind spinning, Jerry dodged the traffic and walked through. He was in the old Colonial Cemetery, a lush place scented with flowers and shaded by heavy overhanging trees. Jerry had never been here and he was shocked to enter such seclusion. It was built up an opposing slope round an old chapel that was gently falling into disuse. Its cracking walls glinted in the speckled evening light. Beside it, from a chicken-wire kennel, an emaciated Alsatian dog howled at him in fury.

Jerry peered round, not knowing why he was here or what

he was looking for. The graves were of all ages and races and sects. There were White Russian graves, and their orthodox headstones were dark and scrolled with Czarist grandeur. Jerry imagined heavy snow on them and their shape still coming through. Another stone described a restless sojourn of a Russian princess and Jerry paused to read it: Tallin to Peking, with dates; Peking to Shanghai, dates again; to Hong Kong in '49, to die. "And estates in Sverdlovsk," the inscription ended defiantly. Was Shanghai the connection? Was Drake here on some pilgrimage to old friends?

He rejoined the living: three old men in blue pyjama suits sat on a shaded bench, not talking. They had hung their cagebirds in the branches overhead, close enough to hear one another's song above the noise of traffic and cicadas. Two grave-diggers in steel helmets were filling a new grave. No mourners watched. Still not knowing what he wanted, Jerry reached the chapel steps. He peered through the door. Inside was pitch dark after the sunlight. An old woman glared at him. He drew back. The Alsatian dog howled at him still louder. A sign said "Verger" and he followed it. The shriek of the cicadas was deafening, even drowning the dog's barking. The scent of flowers was steamy and a little rotten. An idea had struck him, almost an intimation. He was determined to pursue it.

The verger was a kindly distant man and spoke no English. The ledgers were very old; the entries resembled old bank accounts. Jerry sat at a desk slowly turning the heavy pages, reading the names, the dates of birth, death, and burial; lastly the map reference—the zone and the number. Having found what he was looking for, he stepped into the air again and made his way along a different path, through a cloud of butterflies, up the hill toward the cliff-side. A bunch of schoolgirls watched him from a foot-bridge, giggling. He took off his jacket and trailed it over his shoulder.

He passed between high shrubs and entered a slanted coppice of yellow grass where the headstones were very small, the

mounds only a foot or two long. Jerry sidled past them, reading the numbers, till he found himself in front of a low iron
gate marked 728. The gate was part of a rectangular perimeter, and as Jerry lifted his eyes he found himself looking at the
statue of a small boy in Victorian knickerbockers and an Eton
jacket, life size, with tousled stone curls and rosebud stone lips,
reading or singing from an open stone book while real butterflies dived giddily round his head. He was an entirely English
child, and the inscription read "Nelson Ko in loving memory."
A lot of dates followed, and it took Jerry a second to understand their meaning: ten successive years with none left out,
and the last 1968. Then he realised they were the ten years the
boy had lived, each one to be relished. On the bottom step of
the plinth lay a large bunch of orchids, still in their paper.

Ko was thanking Nelson for his win. Now, at least, Jerry
understood why he did not care to be invaded with questions
about his luck.

There is a kind of fatigue, sometimes, which only fieldmen
know: a temptation to gentleness that can be the kiss of death.
Jerry lingered a moment longer, staring at the orchids and the
stone boy, and setting them in his mind beside everything he
had seen and learned of Ko till now. And he had an overwhelming feeling—only for a moment, but dangerous at any
time—of completeness, as if he had met a family, only to discover it was his own. He had a feeling of arrival. Here was a
man, housed this way, married that way, striving and playing
in ways Jerry effortlessly understood. A man of no particular
persuasion, yet Jerry saw him in that moment more clearly
than he had ever seen himself. A Chiu Chow poor-boy who
becomes a Jockey Club Steward with an O.B.E., and hoses
down his horse before a race. A Hakka water-gypsy who gives
his child a Baptist burial and an English effigy. A capitalist
who hates politics. An incomplete lawyer, a gang boss, a builder
of hospitals who runs an opium airline. A supporter of spirit
temples who plays croquet and rides about in a Rolls-Royce.

An American bar in his Chinese garden, and Russian gold in his trust account.

Such complex and conflicting insights did not at that moment alarm Jerry in the least; they presaged no foreboding or paradox. Rather he saw them welded by Ko's own harsh endeavour into a single but many-sided man not too unlike old Sambo. Stronger still—for the few seconds that it lasted—he had an irresistible feeling of being in good company, a thing he had always liked. He returned to the gate in a mood of calm munificence, as if he, not Ko, had won the race.

The traffic had cleared and he found a taxi straight away. They had driven a hundred yards when he saw Luke performing lonely pirouettes along the curb. Jerry coaxed him aboard and dumped him outside the Foreign Correspondents' Club. From the Furama Hotel he rang Craw's home number, let it ring twice, rang it again, and heard Craw's voice demanding "Who the bloody hell is that?" He asked for a Mr. Savage, received a foul rebuke and the information that he was ringing the wrong number, allowed Craw half an hour to get to another phone, then walked over to the Hilton to field the return call.

Our friend had surfaced in person, Jerry told him. Been put on public view on account of a big win. When it was over, a very nice blond party gave him a lift in her sports car. Jerry gave the licence number. They were definitely friends, he said. Very demonstrative and un-Chinese. At *least* friends, he would say.

"Round-eye?"

"Of course she was bloody well round-eye! Who the hell ever heard of a—"

"Jesus," said Craw softly, and rang off before Jerry even had a chance to tell him about little Nelson's shrine.

8

The Barons Confer

The waiting-room of the pretty Foreign Office conference house in Carlton Gardens was slowly filling up. People in twos and threes, ignoring each other, like mourners for a funeral. A printed notice hung on the wall saying "Warning, no confidential matter to be discussed." Smiley and Guillam perched disconsolately beneath it, on a bench of salmon velvet. The room was oval, the style Ministry of Works Rococo. Across the painted ceiling Bacchus pursued nymphs who were a lot more willing to be caught than Molly Meakin. Empty fire-buckets stood against the wall, and two government messengers guarded the door to the interior. Outside the curved sash windows, autumn sunlight filled the park, making each leaf crisp against the next.

Saul Enderby strode in, leading the Foreign Office contingent. Guillam knew him only by name. He was a former Ambassador to Indonesia, now chief pundit on South East Asia and said to be a great supporter of the American hard line. In tow, one obedient Parliamentary Under-Secretary, a trade-union appointment, and one flowery, overdressed figure who advanced on Smiley on tiptoe, hands held horizontal, as if he had caught him napping.

"Can it be?" he whispered exuberantly. "Is it? It *is!* George Smiley, all in your feathers. My dear, you've lost simply pounds.

Who's your nice boy? Don't tell me. Peter Guillam. I've heard all about him. *Quite* unspoilt by failure, I'm told."

"Oh, *no!*" Smiley cried involuntarily. "Oh, Lord. *Roddy.*"

"What do you mean 'Oh, no. Oh, Lord. Roddy,'" Martindale demanded, wholly undeterred, in the same vibrant murmur. "'Oh, *yes*' is what you mean! 'Yes, Roddy. Divine to see you, Roddy!' Listen. Before the riff-raff come. How is the exquisite Ann? For my very own ears. Can I make a dinner for the two of you? You shall choose the guests. How's that? And yes, I *am* on the list, if that's what's going through your rat-like little mind, young Peter Guillam. I've been translated, I'm a goodie, our new masters adore me. So they should, the fuss I've made of them."

The interior doors opened with a bang. One of the messengers shouted "Gentlemen!" and those who knew the form stood back to let the women file ahead. There were two. The men followed and Guillam brought up the tail. For a few yards it might have been the Circus: a makeshift bottle-neck at which each face was checked by janitors, then a makeshift corridor leading to what resembled a builders' cabin parked at the centre of a gutted stair-well—except that it had no windows and was suspended from wires and held tight by guy-ropes. Guillam had lost sight of Smiley entirely, and as he climbed the hardboard steps and entered the safe room he saw only shadows hovering under a blue night-light.

"Do *do* something, somebody," Enderby growled, in the tones of a bored diner complaining about the service. "Lights, for God's sake. *Bloody* little men."

The door slammed behind Guillam's back, a key turned in the lock, an electronic hum did the scale and whined out of earshot, and three strip-lights stammered to life, drenching everyone in their sickly pallor.

"Hoorah," said Enderby, and sat down. Later Guillam wondered how he had been so sure it was Enderby calling in the darkness, but there are voices you can hear before they speak.

The conference table was covered in a ripped green baize like a billiards table in a youth club. The Foreign Office sat one end, the Colonial Office at the other. The separation was visceral rather than legal. For six years, the two departments had been formally married under the grandiose awnings of the Diplomatic Service, but no one in his right mind took the union seriously.

Guillam and Smiley sat at the centre, shoulder to shoulder, each with empty chairs to the other side of him. Examining the cast, Guillam was absurdly aware of costume. The Foreign Office had come sharply dressed in charcoal suits and the secret plumage of privilege: both Enderby and Martindale wore Old Etonian ties. The Colonialists had the home-weave look of country people come to town, and the best they could offer in the way of ties was one Royal Artilleryman: honest Wilbraham, their leader, a fit lean schoolmasterly figure with crimson veins on his weather-beaten cheeks. A tranquil woman in church-organ brown supported him, and to the other side a freshly minted boy with freckles and a shock of ginger hair.

The rest of the committee sat across from Smiley and Guillam and had the air of seconds in a duel they disapproved of. They had come in twos for protection: dark Pretorius of the Security Service with one nameless woman bag-carrier; two grim warriors from Defence; two Treasury bankers, one of them Welsh Hammer. Oliver Lacon was alone and had set himself apart from everyone, for all the world the person least engaged.

Before each pair of hands lay Smiley's submission in a pink-and-red folder marked "Top Secret Withhold," like a souvenir programme. The "Withhold" meant keep it away from the Cousins. Smiley had drafted it, the mothers had typed it, Guillam himself had watched the eighteen pages come off the duplicators and supervised the hand-stitching of the twenty-four copies. Now their handiwork lay tossed around the torn baize, among the water-glasses and the ashtrays. Lifting a copy six inches above the table, Enderby let it fall with a slap.

"All read it?" he asked. All had.

"Then let's go," said Enderby, and peered round the table with bloodshot, arrogant eyes. "Who'll start the bowling? Oliver? You got us here. You shoot first."

It crossed Guillam's mind that Martindale, the great scourge of the Circus and its works, was curiously subdued. His eyes were turned dutifully to Enderby, and his mouth sagged unhappily.

Lacon meanwhile was setting out his defences: "Let me say first that I'm as much taken by surprise in this as anyone else," he said. "This is a real body-blow, George. It would have been helpful to have had a little preparation. It's a little uncomfortable for *me*, I have to tell you, to be the link to a service which has rather cut its links of late."

Wilbraham said, "Hear, hear." Smiley preserved a mandarin silence. Pretorius of the competition frowned in agreement.

"It also comes at an awkward time," Lacon added portentously. "I mean the thesis, your thesis *alone*, is—well, momentous. A lot to swallow. A lot to face up to, George."

Having thus secured his back way out, Lacon made a show of pretending there might not be a bomb under the bed at all.

"Let me try to summarise the summary. May I do that? In bald terms, George. A prominent Hong Kong Chinese citizen is under suspicion of being a Russian spy. That's the nub?"

"He is known to receive very large Russian subventions," Smiley corrected him, but talking to his hands.

"From a secret fund devoted to financing penetration agents?"

"Yes."

"*Solely* for financing them? Or does this fund have other uses?"

"To the best of our knowledge, it has no other use at all," said Smiley in the same lapidary tone as before.

"Such as—propaganda—the informal promotion of trade—kickbacks, that kind of thing? No?"

"To the best of our knowledge: no," Smiley repeated.

"Ah, but how good's their knowledge?" Wilbraham called from below the salt. "Hasn't been too good in the past, has it?"

"You see what I'm getting at?" Lacon asked.

"We would want *far* more corroboration," the Colonial lady in church brown said, with a heartening smile.

"So would we," Smiley agreed mildly. One or two heads lifted in surprise. "It is in order to obtain corroboration that we are asking for rights and permissions."

Lacon resumed the initiative. "Accept your thesis for a moment. A secret intelligence fund, all much as you say."

Smiley gave a remote nod.

"Is there any suggestion that he subverts the Colony?"

"No."

Lacon glanced at his notes. It occurred to Guillam that he had done a lot of homework.

"He is not, for example, preaching the withdrawal of their sterling reserves from London? Which would put us a further nine hundred million pounds in the red?"

"To my knowledge, no."

"He is not telling us to get off the Island. He is not whipping up riots or urging amalgamation with the mainland, or waving the wretched treaty in our faces?"

"Not that we know."

"He's not a leveller. He's not demanding effective trade unions, or a free vote, or a minimum wage, or compulsory education, or racial equality, or a separate parliament for the Chinese instead of their tame assemblies, whatever they're called?"

"Legco and Exco," Wilbraham snapped. "And they're not tame."

"No, he isn't," said Smiley.

"Then what *is* he doing?" Wilbraham interrupted excitedly. "Nothing. That's the answer. They've got it all wrong. It's a goose-chase."

"For what it's worth," Lacon proceeded, as if he hadn't heard, "he probably does as much to enrich the Colony as any other wealthy and respected Chinese businessman. Or as little. He dines with the Governor, but he is not known to rifle the contents of his safe, I assume. In fact, to all outward purposes, he is something of a Hong Kong prototype: Steward of the Jockey Club, supports the charities, pillar of the integrated society, successful, benevolent, has the wealth of Croesus and the commercial morality of the whore-house."

"I say, that's a bit hard!" Wilbraham objected. "Steady on, Oliver. Remember the new housing estates."

Again Lacon ignored him: "Short of the Victoria Cross, a war-disability pension, and a baronetcy, therefore, it is hard to see how he could be a less suitable subject for harassment by a British service, or recruitment by a Russian one."

"In my world, we call that good cover," said Smiley.

"*Touché*, Oliver," said Enderby with satisfaction.

"Oh, everything's cover these days," said Wilbraham mournfully, but it didn't get Lacon off the hook.

Round 1 to Smiley, thought Guillam in delight, recalling the dreadful Ascot dinner. "Hitty-pitty within the wall, and bumps goes Pottifer," he chanted inwardly, with due acknowledgment to his hostess.

"Hammer?" said Enderby, and the Treasury had a brief fling in which Smiley was hauled over the coals for his financial accounts, but no one except the Treasury seemed to find Smiley's transgressions relevant.

"This is not the purpose for which you were granted a secret float," Hammer kept insisting, in Welsh outrage. "That was postmortem funds only—"

"Fine, fine, so Georgie's been a naughty boy," Enderby interrupted in the end, closing him down. "Has he thrown his money down the drain or has he made a cheap killing? That's the question. Chris, time the Empire had its shout."

Thus bidden, Colonial Wilbraham formally took the floor, backed by his lady in church brown and his red-haired assistant, whose young face was already set bravely in protection of his headmaster.

Wilbraham was one of those men who are unconscious of how much time they take to think. "Yes," he began after an age. "Yes. Yes—well, I'd like to stay with the money, if I may, much as Lacon did, to begin with." It was already clear that he regarded the submission as an assault upon his territory. "Since the money is all we've got to go on," he remarked pointedly, turning back a page in his folder. "Yes." And there followed another interminable hiatus. "You say here the money first of all came from Paris through Vientiane." Pause. "Then the Russians switched systems, so to speak, and it was paid through a different channel altogether. A Hamburg-Vienna-Hong Kong tie-up. Endless complexities, subterfuges, all that—we'll take your word for it—right. Same amount, different hat, so to speak. Right. Now, why d'you think they did that, so to speak?"

"So to speak," Guillam recorded, who was very susceptible to verbal ticks.

"It is sensible practice to vary the routine from time to time," Smiley replied, repeating the explanation he had already offered in the submission.

"*Tradecraft*, Chris," Enderby put in, who liked his bit of jargon, and Martindale, still *piano*, shot him a glance of admiration.

Again Wilbraham slowly wound himself up.

"We've got to be guided by what Ko *does*," he declared with puzzled fervour, and rattled his knuckles on the baize table. "Not by what he *gets*. That's my argument. After all, I mean—dash it—it's not Ko's own money, is it? Legally it's nothing to do with him." The point caused a moment's puzzled silence. "Page two, top. Money's all in trust." A general shuffle as everyone but Smiley and Guillam reached for their folders. "I mean, not only is none of it being *spent*, which in itself is jolly odd—I'll come to that in a bit—it's *not Ko's money*. It's in trust, and when the claimant comes along, whoever he or she is, it will be the claimant's money. Till then, it's the trust's money. So to speak. So, I mean, *what's Ko done wrong?* Opened a trust? No law against that. Done every day. Specially in Hong Kong. The *beneficiary* of the trust—oh, well, he could be anywhere! In Moscow or Timbuctoo or—" He didn't seem to be able to think of a third place, so he dried up, to the discomfort of his ginger-headed assistant, who scowled straight at Guillam as if to challenge him. "Point is: what's against *Ko?*"

Enderby was holding a matchstick to his mouth, and rolling it between his front teeth. Conscious perhaps that his adversary had made a good point badly—whereas his own speciality tended to be the reverse—he took the matchstick out and contemplated the wet end.

"Hell's all this balls about thumb-prints, George?" he asked, perhaps in an effort to deflate Wilbraham's success. "Like something out of Phillips Oppenheim."

Belgravia cockney, thought Guillam: the last stage of linguistic collapse.

Smiley's answers contained about as much emotion as a speaking clock: "The use of thumb-prints is old banking practice along the China coast. It dates from the days of widespread illiteracy. Many overseas Chinese prefer to use British banks rather than their own, and the structure of this account is by no means extraordinary. The beneficiary is not named, but identifies himself by a visual means, such as the torn half of a banknote—or in this case his left thumb-print, on the assumption that it is less worn by labour than the right. The bank is unlikely to raise an eyebrow provided that whoever founded the trust has indemnified the bank against charges of accidental or wrongful payment."

"Thank you," said Enderby, and did more delving with the matchstick. "Could be Ko's *own* thumb-print, I suppose," he suggested. "Nothing to stop him doing that, is there? *Then* it would be his money all right. If he's trustee and beneficiary all at once, of *course* it's his own damn money."

To Guillam, the issue had already taken a quite ludicrous wrong turning.

"That's pure supposition," Wilbraham said after the usual two-minute silence. "Suppose Ko's doing a favour for a chum. Just suppose that for a moment. And this chum's on a fiddle, so to speak, or doing business with the Russians at several removes. Your Chinese *loves* a conspiracy. Get up to *all* the tricks, even the nicest of 'em. Ko's no different, I'll be bound."

Speaking for the first time, the red-haired boy ventured direct support.

"The submission rests on a fallacy," he declared bluntly, speaking at this stage more to Guillam than to Smiley. Sixth-form puritan, thought Guillam; thinks sex weakens you and spying is immoral. "*You* say Ko is on the Russian payroll. *We* say that's not demonstrated. We say the trust *may* contain Russian money, but that Ko and the trust are separate entities." In his indignation he went on too long: "You're talking about guilt. Whereas *we* say Ko's done nothing wrong under Hong Kong law and should enjoy the due rights of a Colonial subject."

Several voices pounced at once. Lacon's won. "No one is talking about guilt," he retorted. "Guilt doesn't enter into it in the least degree. We're talking about security. Solely. Security, and the desirability or otherwise of investigating an apparent threat."

Welsh Hammer's Treasury colleague was a bleak Scot, as it turned out, with a style as bald as the sixth-former's.

"Nobody's sizing up to infringe Ko's Colonial rights, either," he snapped. "He hasn't any. There's nothing in Hong Kong law *whatever* which says the Governor cannot steam open Mr. Ko's mail, tap Mr. Ko's telephone, suborn his maid, or bug his house to kingdom come. Nothing whatever. There are a few other things the Governor can do too, if he feels like it."

"Also speculative," said Enderby, with a glance to Smiley. "Circus has no local facilities for those high jinks, and anyway in the circumstances they'd be insecure."

"They would be scandalous," said the red-haired boy unwisely, and Enderby's gourmet eye, yellowed by a lifetime's luncheons, lifted to him, and marked him down for future treatment.

So that was the second, inconclusive skirmish. They hacked about in this way till coffee break, no victor and no corpses. Round 2 a draw, Guillam decided. He wondered despondently how many rounds there would be.

"What's it all about?" he asked Smiley under the buzz. "They won't make it go away by talking. It's a monstrous notion. What's wrong with them?"

"They have to reduce it to their own size," Smiley explained uncritically. Beyond that, he seemed bent on Oriental self-effacement, and no prodding from Guillam was going to shake him out of it. Enderby demanded fresh ashtrays.

The parliamentary Under-Secretary said they should try to make progress. "Think what it's costing the taxpayer, just having us sit here," he urged proudly. Lunch was still two hours away.

Opening round 3, Enderby moved the ticklish issue of whether to advise the Hong Kong government of the intelligence regarding Ko. This was impish of him, in Guillam's view, since the position of the shadow Colonial Office (as Enderby referred to his homespun confrères) was still that there was no crisis, and consequently nothing for anyone to be advised of.

But honest Wilbraham, failing to see the trap, walked into it and said, "Of course we should advise Hong Kong! They're self-administering. We've no alternative."

"Oliver?" said Enderby with the calm of a man who holds good cards. Lacon glanced up, clearly irritated at being drawn into the open. "Oliver?" Enderby repeated.

"I'm *tempted* to reply that it's Smiley's case and Wilbraham's Colony and we should let them fight it out," he said, remaining firmly on the fence.

Which left Smiley: "Oh, well, if it were the Governor and

nobody else I could hardly object," he said. "That is, if you feel it's not too much for him," he added dubiously, and Guillam saw the redhead stoke himself up again.

"Why the dickens should it be too much for the Governor?" Colonial Wilbraham demanded, genuinely perplexed. "Experienced administrator, shrewd negotiator. Find his way through anything. Why's it too much?"

This time, it was Smiley who made the pause. "He would have to encode and decode his own telegrams, of course," he mused, as if he were even now working his way obliviously through all the implications. "We couldn't have him cutting his staff in on the secret, naturally. That's asking too much of anyone. Personal code-books—well, we can fix him up with those, no doubt. Brush up his coding, if he needs it. There is also the problem, I suppose, of the Governor being forced into the position of *agent provocateur* if he continues to receive Ko socially—which he obviously must. We can't frighten the game at this stage. Would he mind that? Perhaps not. Some people take to it quite naturally." He glanced at Enderby.

Wilbraham was already expostulating: "But good heavens, man—if Ko's a Russian spy, which we say he isn't anyway—if the Governor has him to dinner, and perfectly naturally, in confidence, commits some minor indiscretion—Well, it's damned unfair. It could ruin the man's career. Let alone what it could do to the Colony! He *must* be told!"

Smiley looked sleepier than ever. "Well, of course, if he's given to being indiscreet," he murmured meekly, "I suppose one *might* argue that he's not a suitable person to be informed anyway."

In the icy silence, Enderby once more languidly took the matchstick from his mouth. "Bloody odd it would be, wouldn't it, Chris," he called cheerfully down the table to Wilbraham, "if Peking woke up one morning to the glad news that the Governor of Hong Kong, Queen's representative and what have you, head of the troops and so forth, made a point of entertaining

Moscow's ace spy at his dinner table once a month. *And* gave him a medal for his trouble. *What's* he got so far? Not a K, is it?"

"An O.B.E.," said somebody *sotto voce*.

"Poor chap. Still, he's on his way, I suppose. He'll work his way up, same as we all do."

Enderby, as it happened, had his knighthood already, whereas Wilbraham was stuck in the bulge, owing to the growing shortage of colonies.

"There is no case, " said Wilbraham stoutly, and laid a hairy hand flat over the lurid folder before him.

A free-for-all followed, to Guillam's ear an *intermezzo*, in which by tacit understanding the minor parts were allowed to chime in with irrelevant questions in order to get themselves a mention in the minutes. The Welsh Hammer wished to establish *here and now* what would happen to Moscow Centre's half million dollars of reptile money if by any chance they fell into British hands. There could be no question of their simply being recycled through the Circus, he warned. Treasury would have sole rights. Was that clear?

It was clear, Smiley said.

Guillam began to discern a gulf. There were those who assumed, even if reluctantly, that the investigation was a *fait accompli*; and those who continued to fight a rear-guard action against its taking place. Hammer, he noticed to his surprise, seemed reconciled to an investigation.

A string of questions on "legal" and "illegal" residencies, though wearisome, served to entrench the fear of a Red peril. Luff, the parliamentarian, wanted the difference spelt out to him. Smiley patiently obliged. A "legal" or "above-the-line" resident, he said, was an intelligence officer living under official or semi-official protection. Since the Hong Kong government, out of deference to Peking's sensitivities about Russia, had seen fit to banish all forms of Soviet representation from the Colony—embassy, consular, Tass, Radio Moscow, Novosti,

Aeroflot, Intourist, and the other flags of convenience which legals traditionally sailed under—then by definition it followed that any Soviet activity on the Colony had to be carried out by an illegal or below-the-line apparatus.

It was this presumption which had directed the efforts of the Circus's researches toward discovering the replacement money route, he said, avoiding the jargon "gold seam."

"Ah, well, then, we've forced the Russians into it," said Luff with satisfaction. "We've only ourselves to thank. We victimise the Russians, they bite back. Well, who's surprised by that? It's the *last* government's hash we're settling. Not ours at all. Go in for Russian-baiting, you get what you deserve. Natural. We're just reaping the whirlwind, as usual."

"What have the Russians got up to in Hong Kong *before* this?" asked a clever back-room boy from the Home Office.

The Colonialists at once sprang to life. Wilbraham began feverishly leafing through a folder, but seeing his red-headed assistant straining at the leash, he muttered, "You'll do that one, then, John, will you? Good," and sat back looking ferocious. The brown-clad lady smiled wistfully at the baize cloth. So the sixth-former made his second disastrous sally.

"We consider the precedents here very enlightening indeed," he began aggressively. "Moscow Centre's previous attempts to gain a toe-hold on the Colony have been one and all, without exception, abortive and completely low grade." He reeled off a bunch of boring instances.

Five years ago, he said, a bogus Russian Orthodox archimandrite flew in from Paris in an effort to make links with remnants of the White Russian community.

"This gentleman tried to press-gang an elderly restaurateur into Moscow Centre's service and was promptly arrested. More recently, we have had cases of ship's crew coming ashore from Russian freighters which have put in to Hong Kong for repair. They have made ham-fisted attempts to suborn longshoremen and dock workers whom they consider to be leftist oriented. They have been arrested, questioned, made complete fools of by the press, and duly confined to their ship for the rest of its stay." He gave other equally milk-and-water examples and everyone grew sleepy, waiting for the last lap. "Our policy has been *exactly* the same each time. As soon as they're caught, right away, culprits are put on public show. Press photographs? As many as you like, gentlemen. Television? Set up your cameras. Result? Peking hands us a nice pat on the back for containing Soviet imperialist expansionism."

Thoroughly over-excited, he found the nerve to address himself directly to Smiley. "So you see, as to your networks of illegals, to be frank, we discount them. Legal, illegal, above-the-line, below it—our view is, the Circus is doing a bit of special pleading in order to get its nose back under the wire!"

Opening his mouth to deliver a suitable rebuke, Guillam felt a restraining touch on his elbow and closed it again.

There was a long silence, in which Wilbraham looked more embarrassed than anybody.

"Sounds more like *smoke* to me, Chris," said Enderby drily.

"What's he driving at?" Wilbraham demanded nervously.

"Just answering the point your bully-boy made for you, Chris. Smoke. Deception. Russians are waving their sabres where you can watch 'em, and while your heads are all turned the wrong way, they get on with the dirty work t'other side of the Island. To wit, Brother Ko. Right, George?"

"Well, that is our view, yes," Smiley conceded. "And I suppose I *should* remind you—it's in the submission, actually— that Haydon himself was always very keen to argue that the Russians had nothing going in Hong Kong."

"Lunch," Martindale announced without much optimism. They ate it upstairs, glumly, off plastic catering trays delivered by van. The partitions were too low, and Guillam's custard flowed into his meat.

* * *

Thus refreshed, Smiley availed himself of the after-luncheon torpor to raise what Lacon had called the panic factor. More accurately, he sought to entrench in the meeting a sense of logic behind a Soviet presence in Hong Kong, even if, as he put it, Ko did not supply the example.

How Hong Kong, as mainland China's largest port, handled 40 percent of her foreign trade.

How an estimated one out of every five Hong Kong residents travelled legally in and out of China every year, though many-time travellers doubtless raised the average.

How Red China maintained in Hong Kong, *sub rosa* but with the full connivance of the authorities, teams of first-class negotiators, economists, and technicians to watch over Peking's interest in trade, shipping, and development; and how every man jack of them constituted a natural intelligence target for "enticement, or other forms of secret persuasion," as he put it.

How Hong Kong's fishing fleets and junk-fleets enjoyed dual registration in Hong Kong and along the China coast, and passed freely in and out of China waters—

Interrupting, Enderby drawled a supporting question: "And Ko owns a junk-fleet. Didn't you say he's one of the last of the brave?"

"Yes, yes, he does."

"But he doesn't visit the mainland himself?"

"No, never. His assistant goes, but not Ko, we gather."

"Assistant?"

"He has a manager body named Tiu. They've been together for twenty years. Longer. They share the same background— Hakka, Shanghai, and so forth. Tiu's his front man on several companies."

"And Tiu goes to the mainland regularly?"

"Once a year, at least."

"All over?"

"Canton, Peking, Shanghai are on record. But the record is not necessarily complete."

"But Ko stays home. Queer."

There being no further questions or comments on that score, Smiley resumed his Cook's tour of the charms of Hong Kong as a spy base. Hong Kong was unique, he stated simply. Nowhere on earth offered a tenth of the facilities for getting a toe-hold on China.

"*Facilities!*" Wilbraham echoed. "Temptations, more like."

Smiley shrugged. "If you like, temptations," he agreed. "The Soviet service is not famous for resisting them." And amid some knowing laughter, he went on to recount what was known of Centre's attempts till now against the China target as a whole: a joint précis by Connie and di Salis. He described Centre's efforts to attack from the north, by means of the wholesale recruitment and infiltration of her own ethnic Chinese. Abortive, he said. He described a huge network of listening-posts all along the 4,500-mile Sino-Soviet land border: unproductive, he said, since the yield was military, whereas the threat was political. He recounted the rumours of Soviet approaches to Taiwan, proposing common cause against the China threat through joint operations and profit-sharing: rejected, he said, and probably designed for mischief to annoy Peking, rather than to be taken at face value. He gave instances of the Russian use of talent-spotters among overseas Chinese communities in London, Amsterdam, Vancouver, and San Francisco; and touched on Centre's veiled proposals to the Cousins some years ago for the establishment of an "intelligence pool" available to China's common enemies. Fruitless, he said. The Cousins wouldn't play. Lastly he referred to Centre's long history of savage burning and bribery operations against Peking officials in overseas posts: product indeterminate, he said.

When he had done all this, he sat back and restated the thesis that was causing all the trouble:

"Sooner or later," he repeated, "Moscow Centre has to come to Hong Kong."

Which brought them to Ko once more, and to Roddy Martindale, who, under Enderby's eagle eye, made the next real passage of arms.

"Well, what do *you* think the money's for, George? I mean we've heard all the things it *isn't* for, and we've heard it's not being spent. But we're no *forrarder*, are we, bless us? We don't seem to *know* anything. It's the same old question: how's the money being earned, how's it being spent, what should we *do?*"

"That's three questions," said Enderby cruelly under his breath.

"It is *because* we don't know," said Smiley woodenly, "that we are asking permission to find out."

Someone from the Treasury benches said, "Is half a million a lot?"

"In my experience, unprecedented," said Smiley. "Moscow Centre"—dutifully he avoided "Karla"—"detests having to buy loyalty at any time. For them to buy it on this scale is unheard of."

"But *whose* loyalty are they buying?" someone complained.

Martindale, the gladiator, back to the charge: "You're selling us short, George. I know you are. You have an inkling—of course you have. Now cut us in on it. Don't be so coy."

"Yes, can't you kick a few ideas around for us?" said Lacon, equally plaintively.

"Surely you can go down the line a *little*," Hammer pleaded.

Even under this three-pronged attack Smiley still did not waver. The panic factor was finally paying off; Smiley himself had triggered it. Like scared patients they were appealing to him for a diagnosis. And Smiley was declining to provide one, on the grounds that he lacked the data.

"Really, I cannot do more than give you the facts as they stand. For me to speculate aloud at this stage would not be useful."

For the first time since the meeting had begun, the Colonial lady in brown opened her mouth and asked a question. Her voice was melodious and intelligent.

"On the matter of precedents then, Mr. Smiley—?" Smiley ducked his head in a quaint little bow. "Are there, for instance, precedents for secret Russian moneys being paid to a stake-holder? In other theatres, for instance?"

Smiley did not immediately answer. Seated only a few inches from him, Guillam swore he sensed a sudden tension, like a surge of energy, passing through his neighbour. But when he glanced at the impassive profile, he saw only a deepening somno-lence in his master, and a slight lowering of the weary eyelids.

"There have been a few cases of what we call *alimony*," he conceded finally.

"*Alimony*, Mr. Smiley?" the Colonial lady echoed, while her red-haired companion scowled more terribly, as if divorce were something else he disapproved of.

Smiley picked his way with extreme care. "Clearly there are agents, working in hostile countries—hostile from the Soviet point of view—who for reasons of cover cannot enjoy their pay while they are in the field." The brown-clad lady del-icately nodded her understanding. "The normal practice in such cases is to bank the money in Moscow and make it avail-able to the agent when he is free to spend it. Or to his depen-dents if—"

"If he gets the chop," said Martindale with relish.

"But Hong Kong is not Moscow," the Colonial lady reminded him with a smile.

Smiley had all but come to a halt. "In rare cases where the incentive is money, and the agent perhaps has no stomach for eventual resettlement in Russia, Moscow Centre has been known, under duress, to make a comparable arrangement in, say, Switzerland."

"But not in Hong Kong?" she persisted.

"No. Not. And it is unimaginable, on past showing, that Moscow would contemplate parting with alimony on such a scale. For one thing, it would be an inducement to the agent to retire from the field."

There was laughter, but when it died, the brown-clad lady had her next question ready.

"But the payments began modestly," she persisted pleasantly. "The inducement is only of relatively recent date?"

"Correct," said Smiley.

Too damn correct, thought Guillam, starting to get alarmed.

"Mr. Smiley, if the dividend were of sufficient value to them, do you think the Russians *would* be prepared to swallow their objections and pay such a price? After all, in absolute terms the money is entirely trivial beside the value of a great intelligence advantage."

Smiley had simply stopped. He made no particular gesture. He remained courteous, he even managed a small smile, but he was plainly finished with conjecture. It took Enderby, with his blasé drawl, to blow the question away.

"Look, children, we'll be doing the theoreticals all day if we're not careful," he said, looking at his watch. "Chris, do we wheel the Americans in here? If we're not telling the Governor, where do we stand on telling the gallant Allies?"

George saved by the bell, thought Guillam.

At the mention of the Americans, Colonial Wilbraham came in like an angry bull. Guillam guessed he had sensed the issue looming, and determined to kill it immediately it showed its head.

"Vetoed, I'm afraid," he snapped. "Absolutely. Whole host of grounds. Demarcation for one. Hong Kong's our patch. Americans have no fishing rights there. None. Ko's a British subject, for another, and entitled to some protection from us. I suppose that's old-fashioned. Don't care too much, to be frank. Americans would go clean overboard. Seen it before. God knows where it would end. Three: small point of protocol." He meant this ironically. He was appealing to the instincts of an ex-Ambassador, trying to rouse his sympathy. "Just a small point, Enderby. Telling the Americans and not telling the Governor—if *I* was the Governor, put in that position, I'd turn in my badge. That's all I can say. You would, too. Know you would. You do. I do."

"Assuming you found out," Enderby corrected him.

"Don't worry. I'd find out. I'd have 'em ten deep crawling over his house with microphones, for a start. One or two places in Africa where we let them in. Disaster. Total." Plonking his forearms on the table, one over the other, he stared at them furiously.

A vehement chugging, as if from an outboard motor, announced a fault in one of the electronic bafflers. It choked, recovered, and zoomed out of hearing again.

"Be a brave man who diddled you on that one, Chris," Enderby murmured, with a long admiring smile, into the strained silence.

"Endorsed," Lacon blurted out of the blue.

They know, thought Guillam simply. George has squared them. They know he's done a deal with Martello, and they know he won't say so because he's determined to lie dead. But Guillam saw nothing clearly that day. While the Treasury and Defence factions cautiously concurred on what seemed to be a straight issue—"keep the Americans out of it"—Smiley himself appeared mysteriously unwilling to toe the line.

"But there does *remain* the headache of what to do with the raw intelligence," he said. "Should you decide that my service may not proceed, I mean," he added doubtfully, to the general confusion.

Guillam was relieved to find Enderby equally bewildered: "Hell's that mean?" he demanded, running with the hounds for a moment.

"Ko has financial interests all over South East Asia," Smiley reminded them. "Page one of my submission." Business; clatter of papers. "We have information, for example, that he controls through intermediaries and straw men such oddities

as a string of Saigon night-clubs, a Vientiane-based aviation
company, a piece of a tanker fleet in Thailand. . . . Several of
these enterprises could well be seen to have political overtones
which are *far* within the American sphere of influence. I would
have to have your written instruction, naturally, if I were to
ignore our side of the existing bilateral agreements."

"Keep talking," Enderby ordered, and pulled a fresh match
from the box in front of him.

"Oh, I think my point is made, thank you," said Smiley
politely. "Really, it's a very simple one. Assuming we don't proceed, which Lacon tells me is the balance of probability today,
what am I to do? Throw the intelligence on the scrap-heap? Or
pass it to our Allies under the existing barter arrangements?"

"Allies," Wilbraham exclaimed bitterly. "Allies? You're putting a pistol at our heads, man!"

Smiley's iron reply was all the more startling for the passivity which had preceded it: "I have a standing instruction from
this committee to repair our American liaison. It is written into
my charter, by yourselves, that I am to do everything possible to
nurture the special relationship and revive the spirit of mutual
confidence which existed before—Haydon. 'To get us back to
the top table,' you said. . . ." He was looking directly at Enderby.

"*Top table*" someone echoed—a quite new voice. "Sacrificial
altar, if you ask me. We've already burned the Middle East and
half Africa on it. All for the special relationship."

But Smiley seemed not to hear. He had relapsed once more
into his posture of mournful reluctance. Sometimes, his sad
face said, the burdens of his office were simply too much for
him to bear.

A fresh bout of post-luncheon sulkiness set in. Someone complained of the tobacco smoke. A messenger was summoned.

"Devil's happened to the extractors?" Enderby demanded
crossly. "We're stifling."

"It's the parts," the messenger said. "We put in for them

months ago, sir. Before Christmas it was, sir—nearly a year, come to think of it. Still, you can't blame delay, can you, sir?"

"Christ," said Enderby.

Tea was sent for. It came in paper cups which leaked onto the baize. Guillam gave his thoughts to Molly Meakin's peerless figure.

It was almost four o'clock when Lacon rode disdainfully in front of the armies and invited Smiley to state "just exactly what it is you're asking for in practical terms, George. Let's have it all on the table and try to hack out an answer."

Enthusiasm would have been fatal. Smiley seemed to understand that.

"One, we need rights and permissions to operate in the South East Asian theatre—deniably. So that the Governor can wash his hands of us"—a glance at the Parliamentary Under-Secretary—"and so can our masters here. Two, to conduct certain domestic enquiries."

Heads shot up. The Home Office at once grew fidgety. Why? Who? How? *What* enquiries? If it's domestic, it should go to the competition. Pretorius, of the Security Service, was already in a ferment.

"Ko read law in London," Smiley insisted. "He has connections here, social and business. We should naturally have to investigate them." He glanced at Pretorius. "We would show the competition all our findings," he promised.

He resumed his bid. "As regards money, my submission contains a full breakdown of what we need at once, as well as supplementary estimates for various contingencies. Finally we are asking permission, at local as well as Whitehall level, to reopen our Hong Kong residency as a forward base for the operation."

A stunned silence greeted this last item, to which Guillam's own amazement contributed. Nowhere, in any of the preparatory discussions at the Circus, or with Lacon, had anybody—not even Smiley himself, to Guillam's knowledge—raised the

slightest question of reopening High Haven or establishing its
successor. A fresh clamour started.

"Failing that," he ended, overriding the protests, "if we
cannot have our residency, we request at the very least blind-eye
approval to run our own below-the-line agents on the Colony.
No local awareness, but approval and protection by London.
Any existing sources to be retrospectively legitimised. In writing," he ended, with a hard glance at Lacon, and stood up.

Glumly, Guillam and Smiley sat themselves once more in the
waiting-room on the same salmon bench where they had begun,
side by side, like passengers travelling in the same direction.

"*Why?*" Guillam muttered once, but asking questions of
George Smiley was not merely in bad taste that day; it was a
pastime expressly forbidden by the cautionary notice that hung
above them on the wall.

Of all the damn-fool ways of overplaying one's hand, thought
Guillam dismally. You've thrown it, he thought. Poor old sod:
finally past it. The one operation which could put us back in the
game. Greed, that's what it was. The greed of an old spy in a
hurry. I'll stick with him, thought Guillam. I'll go down with the
ship. We'll open a chicken farm together. Molly can keep the
accounts, and Ann can have bucolic tangles with the labourers.

"How do you feel?" he asked.

"It's not a matter of feeling," Smiley replied.

Thanks very much, thought Guillam.

The minutes turned to twenty. Smiley had not stirred. His
chin had fallen on to his chest, his eyes had closed; he might
have been at prayer.

"Perhaps you should take an evening off," said Guillam.

Smiley only frowned.

A messenger appeared, inviting them to return. Lacon was
now at the head of the table, and his manner was prefectorial.
Enderby sat two away from him, conversing in murmurs with
the Welsh Hammer. Pretorius glowered like a storm cloud,

and his nameless lady pursed her lips in an unconscious kiss of disapproval.

Lacon rustled his notes for silence and, like a teasing judge, began reading off the committee's detailed findings before he delivered the verdict. The Treasury had entered a serious protest, on the record, regarding the misuse of Smiley's management account. Smiley should also bear in mind that any requirement for domestic rights and permissions should be cleared with the Security Service in advance and not "sprung on them like a rabbit out of a hat in the middle of a full-dress meeting of the committee." There could be no earthly question of reopening the Hong Kong residency. Simply on the issue of time alone, such a step was impossible. It was really a quite shameful proposal, he implied. Principle was involved, consultation would have to be at the highest level, and since Smiley had already moved specifically against advising the Governor of his findings—Lacon's doff of the cap to Wilbraham here—it was going to be very hard to make a case for re-establishing a residency in the foreseeable future, particularly bearing in mind the unhappy publicity attaching to the evacuation of High Haven.

"I must accept that view with great reluctance," said Smiley gravely.

Oh, for God's sake, thought Guillam; let's at least go down fighting!

"Accept it how you like," said Enderby—and Guillam could have sworn he saw in the eyes of both Enderby and the Welsh Hammer a gleam of victory.

Bastards, he thought simply. No free chickens for you. In his mind he was taking leave of the whole pack of them.

"Everything else," said Lacon, putting down a sheet of paper and taking up another, "with certain limiting conditions and safeguards regarding desirability, money, and the duration of the licence, is granted."

* * *

The park was empty. The lesser commuters had left the field to the professionals. A few lovers lay on the damp grass like soldiers after the battle. A few flamingoes dozed. At Guillam's side, as he sauntered euphorically in Smiley's wake, Roddy Martindale was singing Smiley's praises. "I think George is simply marvellous. Indestructible. And *grip*. I adore grip. Grip is my favourite human quality. George has it in spades. One takes quite a different view of these things when one's translated. One grows to the scale of them, I admit. Your father was an Arabist, I recall?"

"Yes," said Guillam, his mind yet again on Molly, wondering whether dinner was still possible.

"And frightfully *Almanack de Gotha*. Now was he an A.D. man or a B.C. man?"

About to give a thoroughly obscene reply, Guillam realised just in time that Martindale was enquiring after nothing more harmful than his father's scholarly preferences.

"Oh, B.C. B.C. all the way," he said. "He'd have gone back to Eden if he could have done."

"Come to dinner."

"Thanks."

"We'll fix a date. Now, who's *fun* for a change? Who do you like?"

Ahead of them, floating on the dewy air, they heard the drawling voice of Enderby applauding Smiley's victory.

"Nice little meeting. Lot achieved. Nothing given away. Nicely played hand. Land this one and you can just about build an extension, I should think. And the Cousins will play ball, will they?" He was bellowing as if they were still inside the safe room. "You've tested the water there? They'll carry your bags for you and not hog the match? Bit of a cliff-hanger that one, I'd have thought, but I suppose you're up to it. You tell Martello to wear his crêpe soles, if he's got any, or we'll be in deep trouble with the Colonials in no time. Pity about old Wilbraham. He'd have run India rather well."

Beyond them again, almost out of sight among the trees, the little Welsh Hammer was making energetic gestures to Lacon, who was stooping to catch his words.

Nice little conspiracy too, thought Guillam. He glanced back and was surprised to see Fawn, the baby-sitter, hurrying after them. He seemed at first a long way off. Shreds of fog obscured his legs entirely. Only the top of him reached above the sea. Then suddenly he was much closer, and Guillam heard his familiar plaintive bray calling "Sir, sir," trying to catch Smiley's attention. Quickly placing Martindale out of earshot, Guillam strode up to him.

"What the devil's the matter? Why are you bleating like that?"

"They've found a girl! Miss Sachs, sir, she sent me to tell him specially." His eyes shone bright and slightly crazy. "'Tell the Chief they've found the girl.' Her very words, personal for Chief."

"Do you mean she *sent* you here?"

"Personal for Chief, immediate," Fawn replied evasively.

"I said, 'Did she send you here?'" Guillam was seething. "Answer, 'No, sir, she did not.' You bloody little drama queen, racing round London in your gym shoes! You're out of your mind." Snatching the crumpled note from Fawn's hand, he read it cursorily. "It's not even the same name. Hysterical bloody nonsense. You go straight back to your hutch, do you hear? The Chief will give the matter his attention when he returns. Don't you dare stir things up like that again."

"*Whoever* was he?" Martindale enquired, quite breathless with excitement, as Guillam returned. "What a darling little creature! Are all spies as pretty as that? How positively Venetian. I shall volunteer at once."

The same night, a ragged conference was held in the rumpus room, and the quality was not improved by the euphoria—in Connie's case, alcoholic—brought on by Smiley's triumph at the steering conference. After the constraints and tensions of the last months, Connie charged in all directions. The girl! The girl was the clue! Connie had shed all her intellectual bonds. Send Toby Esterhase to Hong Kong, house her, photograph her, trace her, search her room! Get Sam Collins in, *now!*

Di Salis fidgeted, simpered, puffed at his pipe, and jiggled his feet, but for that evening he was entirely under Connie's spell. He even spoke once of "a natural line to the heart of things"—meaning, yet again, the mystery girl. No wonder little Fawn had been infected by their zeal. Guillam felt almost apologetic for his outburst in the park. Indeed, without Smiley and Guillam to put the dampers on, an act of collective folly could very easily have taken place that night, and God knows where it might not have led. The secret world has plenty of precedents of sane people breaking out that way, but this was the first time Guillam had seen the disease in action.

So it was ten o'clock or more before a brief could be drafted for old Craw, and half past before Guillam blearily bumped into Molly Meakin on his way to the lift. In consequence of this happy coincidence—or had Molly planned it? He never knew—a beacon was lit in Peter Guillam's life that burned fiercely from then on. With her customary acquiescence, Molly consented to be driven home, though she lived in Highgate, miles out of his way, and when they reached her doorstep she as usual invited him in for a quick coffee. Anticipating the familiar frustrations ("no-Peter-please-Peter-*dear*-I'm-sorry"), Guillam was on the brink of declining, when something in her eye—a certain calm resolution, as it seemed to him—caused him to change his mind. Once inside her flat, she closed the door and put it on the chain. Then she led him demurely to her bedroom, where she astonished him with a joyous and refined carnality.

9

Craw's Little Ship

In Hong Kong it was forty-eight hours later, and a Sunday evening. In the alley Craw walked carefully. Dusk had come early with the fog, but the houses were jammed too close to let it in, so it hung a few floors higher, with the washing and the cables, spitting hot polluted raindrops which raised smells of orange in the food-stalls and ticked on the brim of Craw's straw hat. He was in China here, at sea-level, the China he loved most, and China was waking for the festival of night: singing, honking, wailing, beating gongs, bargaining, cooking, playing tinny tunes through twenty different instruments; or watching motionless from doorways how delicately the fancy-looking foreign devil picked his way among them. Craw loved it all; but most tenderly he loved his "little ships," as the Chinese called their secret whisperers, and of these Miss Phoebe Wayfarer, whom he was on his way to visit, was a classic, if modest example.

He breathed in, savouring the familiar pleasures. The East had never failed him: "We colonise them, Your Graces, we corrupt them, we exploit them, we bomb them, sack their cities, ignore their culture, and confound them with the infinite variety of our religious sects. We are hideous not only in their sight, Monsignors, but in their nostrils as well—the stink of the round-eye is abhorrent to them and we're too thick even to know it. Yet when we have done our worst, and more than our worst, my sons, we have barely scratched the surface of the Asian smile."

Other round-eyes might not have come here so willingly alone. The Peak mafia would not have known this place existed; the embattled British wives in their government housing ghettoes in Happy Valley would have found here everything they hated most about their billet. It was not a bad part of town, but it was not Europe either: the Europe of Central and Pedder Street half a mile away, of electric doors that sighed for you as they admitted you to the air-conditioning. Other round-eyes, in their apprehension, might have cast inadvertent glares, and that was dangerous. In Shanghai, Craw had known more than one man die of an accidental bad look. Whereas Craw's look was at all times kindly; he deferred, he was modest in his manner, and when he stopped to make a purchase, he offered respectful greetings to the stall-holder in bad but robust Cantonese. And he paid without carping at the surcharge befitting his inferior race.

He bought orchids and lamb's liver. He bought them every Sunday, distributing his custom fairly between rival stalls and—when his Cantonese ran out—lapsing into his own ornate version of English.

He pressed the bell. Phoebe, like old Craw himself, had an entry phone. Head Office had decreed they should be standard issue. She had twisted a piece of heather into her mail-box for good joss, and this was the safety signal.

"Hi," a girl's voice said, over the speaker. It could have been American or it could have been Cantonese, offering an interrogative "Yes?"

"Larry calls me Pete," Craw said.

"Come on up, I have Larry with me at this moment."

The staircase was pitch dark and stank of vomit, and Craw's heels clanked like tin on the stone treads. He pressed the time-switch but no light went on, so he had to grope his way for three floors. There had been a move to find her somewhere better, but it had died with Thesinger's departure and now there was no hope and, in a way, no Phoebe either.

"Bill," she murmured, closing the door after him, and kissed him on both mottled cheeks, the way pretty girls may kiss kind uncles, though she was not pretty. Craw gave her the orchids. His manner was gentle and solicitous.

"My dear," he said. "My *dear*."

She was trembling. There was a bed-sitting-room with a cooker and a hand-basin; there was a separate lavatory with a shower. That was all. He walked past her to the basin, unwrapped the liver, and gave it to the cat.

"Oh, you spoil her, Bill," said Phoebe, smiling at the flowers. He had laid a brown envelope on the bed, but neither of them mentioned it.

"How's *William?*" she said, playing with the sound of his name.

Craw had hung his hat and stick on the door and was pouring Scotch: neat for Phoebe, soda for himself.

"How's Pheeb? That's more to the point. How's it been out there, the cold long week? Eh, Pheeb?"

She had ruffled the bed and laid a frilly night dress on the floor, because so far as the block was concerned, Phoebe was the half-*kwailo* bastard who whored with the fat foreign devil. Over the crushed pillows hung her picture of Swiss Alps, the picture every Chinese girl seemed to have, and on the bedside locker the photograph of her English father, the only picture she had ever seen of him: a clerk from Dorking in Surrey, just after his arrival on the Island—rounded collars, moustache, and staring, slightly crazy eyes. Craw sometimes wondered whether it was taken after he was shot.

"It's all right *now*," said Phoebe. "It's fine *now*, Bill."

She stood at his shoulder, filling the vase, and her hands were shaking badly, which they usually did on Sundays. She wore a grey tunic dress in honour of Peking, and the gold necklace given to her to commemorate her first decade of service to the Circus. In a ridiculous spurt of gallantry, Head Office had decided to have it made at Asprey's, then sent out by bag, with a personal letter to her signed by Percy Alleline, George

Smiley's luckless predecessor, which she had been allowed to look at but not keep. Having filled the vase, she tried to carry it to the table but it slopped, so Craw took it.

"*Hey*, now, take it easy, won't you?"

She stood for a moment, still smiling at him, then breathed out, a long slow sob of reaction, and slumped into a chair. Sometimes she wept, sometimes she sneezed, or was very loud and laughed too much, but always she saved the moment for his arrival, however it took her.

"Bill, I get so frightened sometimes."

"I know, dear, I know." He sat at her side, holding her hand.

"That new boy in Features. He *stares* at me, Bill, he watches everything I do. I'm sure he works for someone. Bill, who does he work for?"

"Maybe he's a little amorous," said Craw, in his softest tone, as he rhythmically patted her shoulder. "You're an attractive woman, Phoebe. Don't you forget that, my dear. You can exert an influence without knowing it." He affected a paternal sternness. "Now, have you been flirting with him? There's another thing. A woman like you can flirt without being conscious of the fact. A man of the world can spot these things, Phoebe. He can tell."

Last week, it was the janitor downstairs; she said he was writing down the hours she came and went. The week before, it was a car she kept seeing, an Opel, always the same one, green. The trick was to calm her fears without discouraging her vigilance; because one day—as Craw never allowed himself to forget—one day, she was going to be right.

Producing a bunch of handwritten notes from the bedside, she began her own debriefing, but so suddenly that Craw was over-run. She had a pale large face that missed being beautiful in either race. Her trunk was long, her legs were short, and her hands Saxon, ugly, and strong. Sitting on the edge of the bed, she looked suddenly matronly. She had put on thick spectacles to read. Canton was sending a student commissar to address Tuesday's cadre, she said, so the Thursday meeting was closed and Ellen Tuo had once more lost her chance to be secretary for an evening—

"Hey steady down, now," Craw cried, laughing. "Where's the fire, for God's sake!"

Opening a notebook on his knee, he tried to catch up with her. But Phoebe would not be checked, not even by Bill Craw, though she had been told he was, in fact, a colonel—even higher. She wanted it behind her, the whole confession. One of her routine targets was a leftist intellectual group of university students and Communist journalists, which had somewhat superficially accepted her. She had reported on it weekly without much progress. Now, for some reason, the group had flared into activity. Billy Chan had been called to Kuala Lumpur for a special conference, she said, and Johnny and Belinda Fong were being asked to find a safe store for a printing press. The evening was approaching fast. While she ran on, Craw discreetly rose and put on the lamp so that the electric light would not shock her once the day faded altogether.

There was talk of joining up with the Fukienese in North Point, she said, but the academic comrades were opposed as usual. "They're opposed to *everything*," said Phoebe savagely, "the snobs. And anyway that stupid bitch Belinda is months behind on her dues, and we may quite well chuck her out of the Party unless she stops gambling."

"And quite right too, my dear," said Craw sedately.

"Johnny Fong says Belinda's pregnant and it isn't his. Well, I hope she is; it will shut her up," said Phoebe, and Craw thought, We had that trouble a couple of times with *you* if I remember rightly, and it didn't shut you up, did it?

Craw wrote obediently, knowing that neither London nor anyone else would ever read a word of it. In the days of its wealth, the Circus had penetrated dozens of such groups, hoping in time to break into what was idiotically referred to as "the Peking-Hong Kong shuttle" and so get a foot in the mainland. The ploy had withered and the Circus had no brief to act as

watch-dog for the Colony's security, a rôle Special Branch jealously guarded for itself. But little ships, as Craw knew very well,
cannot change course as easily as the winds that drive them.

Craw played her along, pitching in with the follow-up questions, checking sources and sub-sources. Was it hearsay, Pheeb?
Well, where did Billy Lee get *that* one from, Pheeb? Was it possible Billy Lee was needling the story a bit—for face, Pheeb,
giving it the old needle? He used the journalistic term because,
like Jerry and Craw himself, Phoebe was in her other profession a journalist, a free-lance gossip writer feeding the local
English-language press with tid-bits about life-styles of the
local Chinese aristocracy.

Listening, waiting—vamping, as the actors call it—Craw
told himself her story, just as he had told it on the refresher
course at Sarratt five years ago, when he was back there getting
a rebore in the black arts. The triumph of the fortnight, they
had told him afterwards. They had made it a plenary session in
anticipation. Even the directing staff had come to hear him.
Those who were off duty had asked for a special van to bring
them in early from their Watford housing estate. Just to hear
old Craw, the Eastern hand, sitting under the antlers in the
converted library, sum up a lifetime in the game. "Agents Who
Recruit Themselves" ran the title. There was a lectern on the
podium but he didn't use it. Instead, he sat on a plain chair, with
his jacket off and his belly hanging out and his knees apart and
shadows of sweat darkening his shirt, and he told it to them the
way he would have told it to the Shanghai Bowlers, on a typhoon
Saturday in Hong Kong, if only circumstance had allowed.

"'Agents Who Recruit Themselves,' Your Graces."

No one knew the job better, they told him—and he believed
them. If the East was Craw's home, the little ships were his
family, and he lavished on them all the fondness for which the
overt world had somehow never given him an outlet. He raised
and trained them with a love that would have done credit to a
father; and it was the hardest moment in an old man's life when

Tufty Thesinger did his moonlight flit and left Craw unwarned, temporarily without a purpose or a lifeline.

Some people are agents from birth, Monsignors—he told them—appointed to the work by the period of history, the place, and their own natural dispositions. In their cases, it was simply a question of who got to them first, Your Eminences: "Whether it's us, whether it's the opposition, or whether it's the bloody missionaries."

Laughter.

Then the case histories with names and places changed, and among them none other than code-name Susan, a little ship of the female gender, Monsignors, South East Asian theatre, born in the year of turmoil 1941, of mixed blood. He was referring to Phoebe Wayfarer.

"Father a penniless clerk from Dorking, Your Graces. Came East to join one of the Scottish houses that plundered the coast six days a week and prayed to Calvin on the seventh. Too broke to get himself a European wife, lads, so he takes a forbidden Chinese girl and sets her up for a few pence, and code-name Susan is the result. Same year the Japanese appear on the scene. Call it Singapore, Hong Kong, Malaya—the story's the same, Monsignors. They appear overnight. To stay. In the chaos, code-name Susan's father does a very noble thing: 'To hell with caution, Your Eminences,' he says. 'This is the time for good men and true to stand up and be counted.' So he marries the lady, Your Graces, a course of action I would not normally counsel, but he does, and when he's married her he christens his daughter code-name Susan and joins the Volunteers, which was a fine body of heroic fools who formed a local Home Guard against the Nipponese hordes. The very next day, not being a natural man-at-arms, Your Graces, he gets his arse shot off by the Japanese invader and promptly expires. Amen. May the clerk from Dorking rest in peace, Your Graces."

As old Craw crosses himself, gusts of laughter sweep the room. Craw does not laugh with them, but plays the straight man. There are fresh faces in the front two rows, uncut, unlined, television faces; Craw guesses they are new entrants whipped in to hear the Great One. Their presence sharpens his performance. Henceforth he has a special eye for the front rows.

"Code-name Susan is still in rompers when her good father meets his quietus, lads, but all her life she's going to remember: when the chips are down, the British stand by their commitments. Every year that passes, she's going to love that dead hero a little more. After the war, her father's old trading house remembers her for a year or two, then conveniently forgets her. Never mind. At fifteen, she's ill from having to keep her sick mother and work the ballrooms to finance her own schooling. Never mind. A welfare worker takes up with her—fortunately, a member of our distinguished brethren, Your Reverends—and he guides her in our direction." Craw mops his brow. "Code-name Susan's rise to wealth and godliness has begun, Your Graces," he declares. "Under journalist cover we bring her into play, give her Chinese newspapers to translate, send her on little errands, involve her, complete her education, and train her in nightwork. A little money, a little patronage, a little love, a little patience, and it's not too long before our Susan has seven legal trips to mainland China to her credit, including some very windy tradecraft. Skilfully performed, Your Graces. She has played courier, and made one crash approach to an uncle in Peking, which paid off. All this, lads, despite the fact she's half a *kwailo* and not naturally trusted by the Chinese.

"And who did she think the Circus was, all that time?" Craw bellowed at his enthralled audience. "Who did she think we were, lads?" The old magician drops his voice, and lifts a fat forefinger. "Her father," he says, in the silence. "We're that dead clerk from Dorking. Saint George, that's who we are. Cleansing the overseas Chinese communities of 'harmful elements,' whatever the hell they are. Breaking the triads and the rice cartels and the opium gangs and the child prostitution. She even saw us, when she had to, as the secret ally of Peking, because we, the

Circus, had the interest of all *good* Chinese at heart." Craw ran a ferocious eye over the rows of child faces longing to be stern.

"Do I see someone smiling, Your Graces?" he demanded, in a voice of thunder. He didn't.

"Mind you, Squires," Craw ended, "there's a part of her knew damn well it was all baloney. That's where *you* come in. That's where your fieldman is ever at the ready. Oh, yes! We're keepers of the faith, lads. When it shakes, we stiffen it. When it falls, we've got our arms out to catch it." He had reached his zenith. In counterpoint, he let his voice fall to a mellow murmur. "Be the faith ever so crackpot, Your Graces, never despise it. We've precious little else to offer them these days. Amen."

All his life, in his unashamedly emotional way, old Craw would remember the applause.

Her debriefing finished, Phoebe was hunched forward, her forearms on her knees, the knuckles of her big hands backed loosely against each other like tired lovers. Craw rose solemnly, took her notes from the table, and burnt them at the gas ring.

"Bravo, my dear," he said quietly. "A sterling week, if I may say so. Anything else?"

She shook her head.

"I mean to burn," he said.

She shook her head again.

Craw studied her. "Pheeb, my dear," he declared at last, as if he had reached a momentous decision. "Get off your hunkers. It's time I took you out to dinner." She looked around at him, confused. The drink had raced to her head, as it always did. "An amiable dinner between fellow scribblers, once in a while, is not inconsistent with cover, I venture to suggest. How about it?"

She made him look at the wall while she put on a pretty frock. She used to have a humming-bird but it died. He bought her another but it died too, so they agreed the flat was bad luck for humming-birds and gave up on them.

"One day I'll take you skiing," he said as she locked the front door behind them. It was a joke between them, to do with her snow scene over the bed.

"Only for one day?" she replied. Which was also a joke, part of the same habitual repartee.

In that year of turmoil, as Craw would say, it was still clever to eat in a sampan on Causeway Bay. The smart set had not discovered it; the food was cheap and unlike food elsewhere. Craw took a gamble and by the time they reached the waterfront the fog had lifted and the night sky was clear. He chose the sampan farthest out to sea, deep in among a cluster of small junks. The cook squatted at the charcoal brazier and his wife served; the hulls of the junks loomed over them, blotting out the stars, and the boat children scampered like crabs from one deck to another while their parents chanted slow funny catechisms across the black water. Craw and Phoebe crouched on wood stools under the furled canopy, two feet above the sea, eating mullet by lamplight. Beyond the typhoon shelters, ships slid past them, lighted buildings on the march, and the junks hobbled in their wakes. Inland, the Island whined and clanged and throbbed, and the huge slums twinkled like jewel boxes opened by the deceptive beauty of the night. Presiding over them, glimpsed between the dipping finger of the masts, sat the black Peak, Victoria, her sodden face shrouded with moonlit skeins; the goddess, the freedom, the lure of all that wild striving in the valley.

They talked the arts. Phoebe was doing what Craw thought of as her cultural number. It was very boring. One day, she said drowsily, she would direct a film, perhaps two, on the *true*, the *real* China. Recently she had seen an historical romance made by Run Run Shaw, all about the palace intrigues. She considered it excellent but a little too—well—*heroic*. Theatre, now. Had Craw heard the good news that the Cambridge Players might be bringing a new revue to the Colony in December? At present it was only a rumour, but she hoped it would be confirmed next week.

"*That* should be fun, Pheeb," said Craw heartily.

"It will *not* be fun at all," Phoebe retorted sternly. "The Players specialise in biting social satire."

In the darkness Craw smiled and poured Phoebe more beer. You can always learn, he told himself; Monsignors, you can always learn.

Till with no prompting that she could have been aware of, Phoebe began talking about her Chinese millionaires, which was what Craw had been waiting for all evening. In Phoebe's world, the Hong Kong rich were royalty. Their foibles and excesses were handed round as freely as in other places the lives of actresses or footballers. Phoebe knew them by heart.

"So who's pig of the week this time, Pheeb?" Craw asked genially.

Phoebe was unsure. "Whom shall we elect?" she said, affecting coquettish indecision. There was the pig P.K. of course: his sixty-eighth birthday on Tuesday, a third wife half his age, and how does P.K. celebrate? Out on the town with a twenty-year-old slut.

Disgusting, Craw agreed. "P.K.," he repeated. "P.K. was the fellow with the gateposts, wasn't he?"

One hundred thousand Hong Kong, said Phoebe. Dragons nine feet high, cast in fibreglass and perspex so that they lit up from inside.

Or it might be the pig Y.Y., she reflected judiciously, changing her mind. Y.Y. was certainly a candidate. Y.Y. had married one month ago exactly, that nice daughter of J. J. Haw, of Haw & Chan, the tanker kings, a thousand lobsters at the wedding. Night before last, he turned up at a reception with a brand-new mistress, bought with his wife's money, a nobody except that he had dressed her at Saint Laurent and decked her out in a four-string choker of Mikimoto pearls—hired, of course, not given.

Despite herself, Phoebe's voice faltered and softened. "Bill," she breathed, "that kid looked completely fantastic beside the old frog. You should have seen."

Or maybe Harold Tan, she pondered dreamily. Harold had been specially nasty. Harold Tan had flown his kids home from their Swiss finishing schools for the festival, first class return from Geneva. At four in the morning, they were all cavorting naked round the pool, the kids and their friends, drunk, pouring champagne into the water, while Harold Tan tried to photograph the action.

Craw waited, in his mind holding the door wide open for her, but still she wouldn't pass through, and Craw was far too old a dog to push her. Chiu Chow were best, he said archly. "Chiu Chow wouldn't get up to all that nonsense. Eh, Pheeb? Very long pockets, the Chiu Chow have, and very short arms," he advised her. "Make a Scotsman blush, your Chiu Chow would—eh, Pheeb?"

Phoebe had no place for irony. "Do not believe it," she retorted demurely. "Many Chiu Chow are both generous and high-minded."

He was willing the man on her, like a conjurer willing a card, but still she hesitated, walked around it, reached for the alternatives.

She mentioned this one, that one, lost the thread, wanted more beer, and when he had all but given up she remarked, quite dreamily, "And as for Drake Ko, he is a complete *lamb*. Against Drake Ko, no bad words at *all*, please."

Now it was Craw's turn to walk away. What did Phoebe think of old Andrew Kwok's divorce, he asked; Christ, *that* must have been a costly one! They say she would have given him the push long ago, but she wanted to wait till he'd made his pile and was really worth divorcing. Any truth in that one, Pheeb? And so on, three, five names, before he allowed himself to take the bait.

"Have you ever heard of old Drake Ko keeping a round-eye mistress at any time? They were talking about it in the Hong Kong Club, only the other day. Blond party, said to be quite a dish."

Phoebe liked to think of Craw in the Hong Kong Club. It satisfied her colonial yearnings.

"Oh, *everyone* has heard," she said wearily, as if Craw, as usual, was light-years behind the hunt. "There was a time when *all* the boys had them—didn't you know? P.K. had two, of course. Harold Tan had one, till Eustace Chow stole her, and Charlie Wu tried to take *his* to dinner at the Governor's, but his *tai-tai* wouldn't let the chauffeur pick her up."

"Where'd they get them from, for Christ's sakes?" Craw asked with a laugh. "Lane Crawford?"

"From the airlines, where do you think," Phoebe retorted with heavy disapproval. "Air hostesses moonlighting on their stopovers, five hundred U.S. a night for a white-woman whore. *And* including the English lines—don't deceive yourself, the English were the worst by far. Then Harold Tan liked his so much he made an arrangement with her, and the next thing they were all moving into flats and walking round the stores like duchesses any time they came to Hong Kong for four days—enough to make you *sick*.

"Mind you, Liese is a different class entirely. Liese has class. She is extremely aristocratic, her parents own fabulous estates in the South of France and also an out-island in the Bahamas, and it is purely for reasons of moral independence that she refuses to accept their wealth. You only have to look at her bone structure."

"Liese," Craw repeated. *"Liese?* Kraut, eh? Don't hold with Krauts. No racial prejudices but don't care for Krauts, I'm afraid. Now, what's a nice Chiu Chow boy like Drake doing with a hateful Hun for a concubine, I ask myself. Still, you should know, Pheeb, you're the expert, it's your bailiwick, my dear—who am I to criticise?"

They had moved to the back of the sampan and were lying in the cushions side by side.

"Don't be utterly ridiculous. Liese is an aristocratic English girl."

"Tra-la-la," said Craw, and for a while gazed at the stars.

"She has a most positive and refining influence on him."

"Who does?" said Craw, as if he had lost the thread.

Phoebe spoke through gritted teeth. "*Liese* has a refining influence on *Drake Ko*. Bill, listen! Are you asleep? Bill, I think you should take me home. Take me home, please."

Craw gave a low sigh. These lovers' tiffs between them were six-monthly events, at least, and had a cleansing effect on their relationship.

"My dear. Phoebe. Give ear to me, will you? For one moment, right? No English girl, high-born, fine-boned, or knock-kneed, can possibly be named Liese unless there is a Kraut at work somewhere. That's for openers. What's her other name?"

"Worth."

"Worth what? All right, that was a joke. Forget it. Elizabeth, that's what she is. Contracted to Lizzie. Or Liza. Liza of Lambeth. You misheard. There's blood for you, if you like: Miss Elizabeth Worth. I could see the bone structure there all right. Not Liese, dear. Lizzie."

Phoebe became openly furious: "Don't you tell me how to pronounce *anything!*" she flung at him. "Her name is Liese, pronounced 'Leesa' and written 'L-i-e-s-e,' because I *asked* her and I wrote it *down* and I have printed that name in—Oh, Bill." Her forehead fell on his shoulder. "Oh, Bill. Take me home."

She began weeping. Craw cuddled her against him, gently patting her shoulder.

"Ah, now, cheer up, my dear. The fault was mine, not yours. I should have known that she was a friend of yours. A fine society woman like Liese, a woman of beauty and fortune, locked in romantic attachment to one of the Island's new nobility— how could a diligent newshound like Phoebe fail to befriend her? I was blind. Forgive me." He allowed a decent interval. "What happened?" he asked indulgently. "You interviewed her, did you?"

For the second time that night, Phoebe dried her eyes with Craw's handkerchief.

"She begged me. She's not my friend. She is far too grand to be my friend. How could she be? She begged me not to print her name. She is here incognito. Her life depends upon it. If her parents know she is here, they will send for her at once. They are fantastically influential. They have private planes, everything. The minute they know she is living with a Chinese man, they would bring fantastic pressure to bear just to get her back. 'Phoebe,' she said. 'Of all people in Hong Kong, you will understand best what it means to live under the shadow of intolerance.' She appealed to me. I promised."

"Quite right," said Craw stoutly. "Don't you ever break that promise, Pheeb. A promise is a bond." He gave an admiring sigh. "Life's byways, I always maintain, are ever stranger than life's highways. If you put that in your paper, your editor would say you were soft in the head, I daresay. And yet it's true. A shining wonderful example of human integrity for its own sake." Her eyes had closed, so he gave her a jolt in order to keep them open. "Now, where does a match like that have its genesis, I ask myself. What star, what happy chance could bring together two such needful souls? In Hong Kong too, for God's sake."

"It was fate. She was not even living here. She had withdrawn from the world altogether after an unhappy love affair, and she had decided to spend the rest of her life making exquisite jewellery in order to give the world something beautiful among all its suffering. She flew in for a day or two just to buy some gold, and quite by chance, at one of Sally Cale's fabulous receptions, she met Drake Ko and that was that."

"And thereafter the course of true love ran sweet, eh?"

"Certainly not. She met him. She loved him. But she was determined not to get embroiled, and returned home."

"*Home?*" Craw echoed, mystified. "Where's home for a woman of her integrity?"

Phoebe laughed. "Not to the South of France, silly. To Vientiane. To a city no one ever visits. A city without high life, or any of the luxuries to which she was accustomed from birth. That was her chosen place. Her island. She had friends there, she was interested in Buddhism and art and antiquity."

"And where does she hang out now? Still in some humble croft, is she, clinging to her notions of abstinence? Or has Brother Ko converted her to less frugal paths?"

"Don't be sarcastic. Drake has given her a most beautiful apartment, naturally."

That was Craw's limit; he knew it at once. He covered the card with others, he told her stories about old Shanghai. But he didn't take another step toward the elusive Liese Worth, though Phoebe might have saved him a lot of legwork.

"Behind every painter," he liked to say, "and behind every fieldman, lads, there should be a colleague standing with a mallet, ready to hit him over the head when he has gone far enough."

In the taxi home, she was calm again but shivering. He saw her right to the door in style. He had forgiven her entirely. On the doorstep he made to kiss her, but she held him back from her.

"Bill. Am I really any use? Tell me. When I'm no use, you must throw me out, I insist. Tonight was nothing. You are sweet, you pretend, I try. But it was still nothing. If there is other work for me, I will take it. Otherwise you must throw me aside. Ruthlessly."

"There'll be other nights," he assured her, and only then did she let him kiss her.

"Thank you, Bill," she said.

"So there you are, Your Graces," Craw reflected happily, as he took the taxi on to the Hilton. "Code-name Susan toiled and span and she was worth a little less each day, because agents are only ever as good as the target they're pointed at, and that's the truth of them. And the one time she gave us gold, pure gold, Monsignors"—in his mind's eye, he held up that same fat forefinger, one message for the uncut boys spellbound in the forward rows—"the *one time*—she didn't even know she'd done it, and she *never could!*"

The best jokes in Hong Kong, Craw had once written, are seldom laughed at because they are too serious. That year there was the Tudor pub in the unfinished high-rise building, for instance, where genuine, sour-faced English wenches in period *décolleté* served genuine English beer at twenty degrees below its English temperature, while outside in the lobby sweating coolies in yellow helmets toiled round the clock to finish off the elevators. Or you could visit the Italian *taverna* where a cast-iron spiral staircase pointed to Juliet's balcony but ended instead in a blank plaster ceiling; or the Scottish inn with kilted Chinese Scots who occasionally rioted in the heat or when the fares rose on the Star Ferry. Craw had even attended an opium divan with air-conditioning and Muzak churning out "Greensleeves." But the most bizarre, the most contrary, for Craw's money, was this roof-top bar overlooking the harbour, with its four-piece Chinese band playing Noël Coward, and its straight-faced Chinese barmen in periwigs and frock-coats looming out of the darkness and enquiring, in good Americanese, what was his "drinking pleasure?"

"A beer," Craw's guest growled, helping himself to a handful of salted almonds. "But *cold*. Hear that? *Muchee coldee*. And bring it *chop chop*."

"Life smiles upon Your Eminence?" Craw enquired.

"Drop all that, d'you mind? Gets on my wick."

The Superintendent's embattled face had one expression only, and that was of a bottomless cynicism. If man had a choice between good and evil, his baleful scowl said, he chose evil any time; and the world was cut down the middle, between those who knew this, and accepted it, and those long-haired pansies in Whitehall who believed in Father Christmas.

"Found her file yet?" Craw enquired.

"No."

"She calls herself Worth. She's had her syllables removed."

"I know what she bloody calls herself. She can call herself bloody Mata Hari, for all I care. There's still no file on her."

"But there was?"

"Right, cobber, there *was*," the Rocker simpered furiously, mimicking Craw's accent. "There was, and now there isn't. Do I make myself clear or shall I write it in invisible ink on a carrier pigeon's arse for you, you heathen bloody Aussie?"

Craw sat quiet awhile, sipping his drink in steady, repetitive movements.

"Would Ko have done that?"

"Done what?" The Rocker was being wilfully obtuse.

"Had her file nicked?"

"Could have done."

"The missing-record malady appears to be spreading," Craw commented after further pause for refreshment. "London sneezes and Hong Kong catches the cold. My professional sympathies, Monsignor. My fraternal commiserations." He lowered his voice to a toneless murmur. "Tell me: is the name Sally Cale music to Your Grace's ear?"

"Never heard of her."

"What's her racket?"

"Chichi antiquities limited, Kowloon-side. Pillaged art treasures, quality fakes, images of the Lord Buddha."

"Where from?"

"Real stuff comes from Burma, way of Vientiane. Fakes are home produce. Sixty-year-old dyke," he added sourly, addressing himself cautiously to another beer. "Keeps Alsatians and chimpanzees. Just up your street."

"Any form?"

"You're joking."

"I am advised that it was Cale who introduced the girl to Ko."

"So what? Cale pimps the round-eye lay. The Chows like her for it, and so do I. I asked her to fix me up once. Said she hadn't got anything small enough, cheeky sow."

"Our frail beauty was here allegedly on a gold-buying kick. Does that figure?"

The Rocker looked at Craw with fresh loathing and Craw looked at the Rocker, and it was a collision of two immovable objects.

"'Course it bloody figures," said the Rocker contemptuously. "Cale had the corner in bent gold from Macao, didn't she?"

"So where did Ko fit in the bed?"

"Ah, come off it, don't pussyfoot around. Cale was the front man. It was Ko's racket all along. That fat bulldog of his went in as partner with her."

"Tiu?"

The Rocker had lapsed once more into beery melancholy, but Craw would not be deflected, and put his mottled head very close to the Rocker's battered ear: "My Uncle George will be highly appreciative of all available intelligence on the said Cale. Right? He will reward merit richly. He is particularly interested in her as of the fateful moment when she introduced my little lady to her Chow protector, and up to the present day. Names, dates, track record, whatever you've got in the fridge. Hear me?"

"Well, you tell your Uncle George he'll get me five bloody years in Stanley jail."

"And you won't want for company there, either, will you, Squire?" said Craw pointedly.

This was an unkind reference to recent sad events in the Rocker's world. Two of his senior colleagues had been sent down for several years apiece, and there were others dolefully waiting to join them.

"Corruption," the Rocker muttered in disgust. "They'll be discovering bloody steam next."

Craw had heard it all before, but he heard it again now, for he had the golden gift of listening, which at Sarratt they prize far higher than communication.

"Thirty thousand bloody Europeans and four million bloody slant-eyes, a different bloody morality, some of the best-organised bloody crime syndicates in the bloody world. What do they expect me to do? We can't stop crime, so how do we control it? We dig out the big boys and we do a deal with them, of course we do. 'Right, boys. No casual crime, no territorial infringements, everything clean and decent, and my daughter can walk down the street any time of day or night. I want plenty of arrests to keep the judges happy and earn me my pathetic pension, and God help anybody who breaks the rules or is disrespectful to authority.' All right, they pay a little squeeze. Name me one person on this whole benighted Island who doesn't pay a little squeeze along the line. If there's people *paying* it, there's people *getting* it. Stands to reason. And if there's people getting it . . . Besides," said the Rocker, suddenly bored by his own theme, "George knows it all already."

Craw's lion's head lifted slowly, until his dreadful eye was fixed squarely on the Rocker's averted face.

"George knows *what*, may I enquire?"

"Sally bloody Cale. We turned her inside out for you people years ago. Planning to subvert the bloody pound sterling or some damn thing. Bullion-dumping on the Zurich gold markets, I ask you. Load of old cobblers as usual, if you want my view."

It was another half-hour before the Australian climbed wearily to his feet, wishing the Rocker long life and felicity.

"And you keep your arse to the sunset," the Rocker growled.

Craw did not go home that night. He had friends, an American lawyer and his wife, who owned one of Hong Kong's two hundred-odd private houses, an elderly rambling place on Pollock's Path high up on the Peak, and they had given him a key. A consular car was parked in the driveway, but Craw's friends were known for their addiction to the diplomatic whirl. Entering his room, Craw seemed not at all surprised to find a respectful young American seated in the wicker armchair reading a heavy novel: a blond, trim boy in a neat diplomatic-looking suit. Craw did not greet this person, or remark his presence in any way, but instead placed himself at the glass-topped writing-desk and, on a single sheet of paper, in the best tradition of his papal mentor, began blocking out a message in capital letters, personal for His Holiness, heretical hands keep off. Afterwards, on another sheet, he set out the key to match it. When he had finished, he handed both to the boy, who with great deference put them in his pocket and departed swiftly without a word. Left alone, Craw waited till he heard the growl of the limousine before opening and reading the signal the boy had left for him. Then he burned it and washed the ash down the sink before stretching himself gratefully on the bed.

A Gideon's day, but I can surprise them yet, he thought. He was tired. Christ, he was tired. He saw the serried faces of the Sarratt children. But we progress, Your Graces. Inexorably we progress. Albeit at the blind man's speed, as we tap-tap along in the dark. Time I smoked a little opium, he thought. Time I had a nice little girl to cheer me up. Christ, he was tired.

Smiley was equally tired, perhaps, but the text of Craw's message, when he received it an hour later, quickened him remarkably: the more so since the file on Miss Cale, Sally—last known address Hong Kong, art faker, illicit bullion dealer, and occasional heroin trafficker—was, for once, alive and well and intact in the Circus archives. Not only that. The cryptonym of Sam Collins, in his capacity as the Circus's below-the-line resident in Vientiane, was blazoned all over it like the bunting of a long-awaited victory.

10

Tea and Sympathy

It has been laid at Smiley's door more than once since the curtain was rung down on the Dolphin case that now was the moment when George should have gone back to Sam Collins and hit him hard and straight just where it hurt. George could have cut a lot of corners that way, say the knowing; he could have saved vital time.

They are talking simplistic nonsense.

In the first place, time was of no account. The Russian gold seam, and the operation it financed, whatever that was, had been running for years, and undisturbed would presumably run for many more. The only people who were demanding action were the Whitehall barons, the Circus itself, and indirectly Jerry Westerby, who had to eat his head off with boredom for a couple more weeks while Smiley meticulously prepared his next move. Also, Christmas was approaching, which makes everyone impatient. Ko, and whatever show he was controlling, showed no sign of development.

"Ko and his Russian money stood like a mountain before us," Smiley wrote later, in his departing paper on Dolphin: "We could visit the case whenever we wished, but we could not move it. The problem was going to be not how to stir ourselves but how to stir Ko to the point where we could read him."

The lesson is clear: long before anyone else, except perhaps Connie Sachs, Smiley already saw the girl as a potential lever and, as such, the most important single character in the cast—far more important, for instance, than Jerry Westerby, who was at any time replaceable. This was just one of many good reasons why Smiley made it his business to get as close to her as security considerations allowed.

Another was that the whole nature of the link between Sam Collins and the girl still floated in uncertainty. It's so easy now to turn round and say "obvious," but at that time the issue was anything but cut and dried. The Cale file gave an indication. Smiley's intuitive feeling for Sam's footwork helped fill in some blanks; hasty back-bearings by Registry produced clues and the usual batch of analogous cases; the anthology of Sam's field reports was illuminating. The fact still remains that the longer Smiley held Sam off, the closer he came to an independent understanding of the relationship between the girl and Ko, and between the girl and Sam; and the stronger his bargaining power when he and Sam next sat down together.

And who on earth could honestly say how Sam would have reacted under pressure, had Smiley allowed it to be applied? The Sarratt inquisitors have had their successes, true, but also their failures. And Sam was a very hard nut.

One more consideration also weighed with Smiley, though in his farewell paper he is too gentlemanly to mention it. A lot of ghosts walked in those post-fall days, and one of them was a fear that, buried somewhere in the Circus, lay Bill Haydon's chosen successor: that Bill had brought him on, recruited and educated him against the very day when he himself, one way or another, would fade from the scene. Sam was originally a Haydon nominee. His later victimisation by Haydon could easily have been a put-up job. Who was to say, in that very jumpy atmosphere, that Sam Collins, manoeuvring for readmission, was not the heir elect to Haydon's treachery?

For all these reasons, George Smiley put on his raincoat and got himself out on the street. Besides, at heart, he was still a case man. Even his detractors give him that.

*   *   *

In the district of old Barnsbury, in the London borough of
Islington, on the day that Smiley finally made his discreet
appearance there, the rain was taking a mid-morning pause.
On the slate roof-tops of Victorian cottages, the dripping
chimney-pots huddled like bedraggled birds among the television aerials. Behind them, held up by scaffolding, rose the outline of a public housing estate abandoned for want of funds.

"Mr.—?"

"Standfast," Smiley replied politely, from beneath his umbrella.

Honourable men recognise each other instinctively. Mr.
Peter Worthington had only to open his front door and run
his eye over the plump, rain-soaked figure on the step—the
black official brief-case, with "E II R" embossed on the bulging plastic flap, the diffident and slightly shabby air—for an
expression of friendly welcome to brighten his kindly face.

"That's it. Jolly decent of you to come. Foreign Office is in
Downing Street these days, isn't it? What did you do? Tube
from Charing Cross, I suppose? Come on in, have a cuppa."

He was a public-school man who had gone into state education because it was more rewarding. His voice was moderate
and consoling and loyal. Even his clothes, Smiley noticed, following him down the slim corridor, had a sort of faithfulness.
Peter Worthington might be only thirty-four years old, but
his heavy tweed suit would stay in fashion—or out of it—for as
long as its owner needed.

There was no garden. The study backed straight on to a concrete playground. A stout grille protected the window, and the
playground was divided in two by a high wire fence. Beyond it
stood the school itself, a scrolled Edwardian building not unlike
the Circus, except that it was possible to see in. On the ground
floor, Smiley noticed children's paintings hanging on the walls.
Higher up, test-tubes in wooden racks.

It was playtime, and in their own half girls in gym-slips
were racing after a handball. But on the other side of the wire

the boys stood in silent groups, like pickets at a factory gate, blacks and whites separate. The study was knee deep in exercise books. A pictorial guide to the kings and queens of England hung on the chimney-breast. Dark clouds filled the sky and made the school look rusty.

"Hope you don't mind the noise," Peter Worthington called from the kitchen. "I don't hear it any more, I'm afraid. Sugar?"

"No, no. No sugar, thank you," said Smiley, with a confessive grin.

"Watching the calories?"

"Well, a little, a little."

Smiley was acting himself, but more so, as they say at Sarratt. A mite homelier, a mite more care-worn: the gentle, decent civil servant who had reached his ceiling by the age of forty, and stayed there ever since.

"There's lemon if you want it!" Peter Worthington called from the kitchen, clattering dishes inexpertly.

"Oh, no, thank you! Just the milk."

On the threadbare study floor lay evidence of yet another, smaller child: bricks, and a scribbling book with "D"s and "A"s scrawled endlessly. From the lamp hung a Christmas star in cardboard. On the drab walls Magi and sleds and cotton wool. Peter Worthington returned carrying a tea-tray. He was big and rugged, with wiry brown hair going early to grey. After all the clattering, the cups were still not very clean.

"Clever of you to choose my free period," he said, with a nod at the exercise books. "If you can call it free, with that lot to correct."

"I do think you people are very underrated," Smiley said, mildly shaking his head. "I have friends in the profession myself. They sit up half the night just correcting the work, so they assure me, and I've no reason to doubt them."

"They're the conscientious ones."

"I trust I may include you in that category."

Peter Worthington grinned, suddenly very pleased. "Afraid

so. If a thing's worth doing, it's worth doing well," he said, helping Smiley out of his raincoat.

"I could wish that view were a little more widely held, to be frank."

"You should have been a teacher yourself," said Peter Worthington, and they both laughed.

"What do you do with your little boy?" said Smiley, sitting down.

"Ian? Oh, he goes to his gran's. My side, not hers," he added as he poured. He handed Smiley a cup. "You married?" he asked.

"Yes, yes, I am, and very happily so, too, if I may say so."

"Kids?"

Smiley shook his head, allowing himself a small frown of disappointment. "Alas," he said.

"That's where it hurts," said Peter Worthington, entirely reasonably.

"I'm sure it does," said Smiley. "Still, we'd have liked the experience. You feel it more, at our age."

"You said on the phone there was some news of Elizabeth," said Peter Worthington. "I'd be awfully grateful to hear it, I must say."

"Well, nothing to be excited about," said Smiley cautiously.

"But hopeful. One must have hope."

Smiley stooped to the official black plastic brief-case and unlocked the cheap clasp.

"Well, now, I wonder whether you'll oblige me," he said. "It's not that I'm holding back on you, but we do like to be *sure*. I'm a belt-and-braces man myself, and I don't mind admitting it. We do exactly the same with our foreign deceases. We never commit ourselves until we're *absolutely sure*. Forenames, surname, full address, date of birth, if we can get it. We go to no end of trouble. Just to be safe. Not *cause*, of course, we don't do *cause*—that's up to the local authorities."

"Shoot ahead," said Peter Worthington heartily. Noticing

the exaggeration in his tone, Smiley glanced up, but Peter Worthington's honest face was turned away and he seemed to be studying a pile of old music stands heaped in a corner.

Licking his thumb, Smiley laboriously opened a file on his lap and turned some pages. It was the Foreign Office file, marked "Missing Person," and obtained by Lacon on a pretext to Enderby.

"Would it be asking too much if I went through the details with you from the beginning? Only the salient ones, naturally, and only what you wish to tell me—I don't have to say that, do I? My headache is, you see, I'm actually not the normal person for this work. My colleague Wendover, whom you met, is sick, I'm afraid—and well, we don't always like to put *everything* on paper, do we? He's an admirable fellow, but when it comes to report writing I do find him a little *terse*. Not sloppy, far from it, but sometimes a little wanting on the human-picture side."

"I've always been absolutely frank. Always," said Peter Worthington rather impatiently to the music stands. "I believe in that."

"And for *our* part, I can assure you we at the Office do respect a confidence."

A sudden lull descended. It had not occurred to Smiley, till this moment, that the scream of children could be soothing; yet as it stopped, and the playground emptied, he had a sense of dislocation which took him a moment to get over.

"Break's finished," said Peter Worthington, with a smile.

"I'm sorry?"

"Break. Milk and buns. What you pay your taxes for."

"Now first of all, there is no question here, according to my colleague Wendover's notes—nothing against him, I hasten to say—that Mrs. Worthington left under any kind of constraint. . . . Just a minute. Let me explain what I mean by that. Please. She left voluntarily. She left alone. She was not unduly prevailed upon, lured, or in any wise the victim of unnatural pressure. Pressure, for instance, which, let us say, might in due course be the subject of a legal court action by yourself or others against a third party not so far named?"

Long-windedness, as Smiley knew, creates in those who must put up with it an almost unbearable urge to speak. If they do not interrupt directly, they at least counter with pent-up energy; and as a schoolmaster, Peter Worthington was not by any means a natural listener.

"She left alone, absolutely alone, and my entire position is, was, and always has been that she was free to do so. If she had *not* left alone, if there had been others involved—men, God knows we're all human—it would have made no difference. Does that satisfy your question? Children have a right to both parents," he ended, stating a maxim.

Smiley was writing diligently but very slowly. Peter Worthington drummed his fingers on his knee, then cracked them, one after another, in a quick impatient salvo.

"Now in the interim, Mr. Worthington, can you please tell me whether a custody order has been applied for in respect of—"

"We always knew she'd wander. That was understood. I was her anchor. She called me 'my anchor.' Either that or 'schoolmaster.' I didn't mind. It wasn't badly meant. It was just she couldn't bear to say *Peter*. She loved me as a *concept*. Not as a figure, perhaps, a body, a mind, a person, not even as a partner. As a concept, a necessary adjunct to her personal, human completeness. She had an urge to please; I understand that. It was part of her insecurity, she longed to be admired. If she paid a compliment, it was because she wished for one in return."

"I see," said Smiley, and wrote again, as if physically subscribing to this view.

"I mean nobody could have a girl like Elizabeth as a wife and expect to have her all to himself. It wasn't natural. I've come to terms with that now. Even little Ian had to call her Elizabeth. Again I understand. She couldn't bear the chains of 'Mummy.' Child running after her calling 'Mummy.' Too much for her.

That's all right. I understand that too. I can imagine it might be hard for you, as a childless man, to understand how a woman of any stamp, a mother—well cared for and loved and looked after, not even having to earn—can literally walk out on her own son and not even send him a postcard from that day to this. Probably that worries, even disgusts you. Well, I take a different view, I'm afraid. At the time, I grant you—yes, it was hard."

He glanced toward the wired playground. He spoke quietly with no hint at all of self-pity. He might have been talking to a pupil. "We try to teach people freedom here. Freedom within citizenship. Let them develop their individuality. How could *I* tell *her* who *she* was? I wanted to be there, that's all. To be Elizabeth's friend. Her longstop—that was another of her words for me. 'My longstop.' The point is she didn't *need* to go. She could have done it all here. At my side. Women need a prop, you know. Without one—"

"And you still have not received any direct word of her?" Smiley enquired meekly. "Not a letter, not even that postcard to Ian, nothing?"

"Not a sausage."

"Mr. Worthington, to your knowledge, has your wife ever used another name?" For some reason, the question threatened to annoy Peter Worthington quite considerably; he flared, as if he were responding to impertinence in class, and his finger shot up to command silence. But Smiley hurried on. "Her *maiden* name, for instance? Perhaps an abbreviation of her married one, which in a non-English-speaking country *could* create difficulties with the natives—"

"Never. Never, *never.* You have to understand basic human behavioural psychology. She was a textbook case. She couldn't wait to get rid of her father's name. One very good reason why she married me was to have a *new* father and a *new* name. Once she'd got it, why should she give it up? It was the same with her romancing, her wild, *wild* story-telling. She was trying to escape from her environment. Having done so, having succeeded, having found *me*, and the stability which I represent, she naturally no longer needed to *be* someone else. She *was* someone else. She was fulfilled. So *why* go?"

Again Smiley took his time. He looked at Peter Worthington as if in uncertainty; he looked at his file; he turned to the last entry, tipped his spectacles and read it, obviously not by any means for the first time.

"Mr. Worthington, if our information is correct, and we have good reason to believe it is—I'd say our estimate was a conservative eighty percent sure, I'd go *that* far—your wife is at present using the surname Worth. And she is using a forename with a German spelling, curiously enough 'L-i-e-s-e.' Pronounced not 'Liza,' I am told, but 'Leesa.' I wondered whether you were in a position to confirm or deny this suggestion, also the suggestion that she is actively connected with a Far Eastern jewellery business with ramifications extending to Hong Kong and other major centres. She appears to be living in a style of affluence and good social appearance, moving in quite high circles."

Peter Worthington seemed to absorb very little of this. He had taken a position on the floor but seemed unable to lower his knees. Cracking his fingers once more, he glared impatiently at the music stands crowded like skeletons into the corner of the room, and was already trying to speak before Smiley had ended.

"Look. This is what I want. That whoever approaches her should make the right kind of point. I don't want any passionate appeals, no appeals to conscience. All that's out. Just a straight statement of what's offered, and she's welcome. That's all."

Smiley took refuge in the file: "Well, before we come to *that*, if we could just continue going through the facts, Mr. Worthington—"

"There *aren't* facts," said Peter Worthington, thoroughly irritated again. "There are just two people. Well, three, with Ian. There *aren't* facts in a thing like this. Not in *any* marriage. That's what life teaches us. Relationships are *entirely* subjective. I'm sitting on the floor. *That's* a fact. You're writing. *That's* a fact. Her mother was behind it. *That's* a fact. Follow me? Her father is a raving criminal lunatic. *That's* a fact. Elizabeth is *not* the daughter of the Queen of Sheba *or* the natural grandchild of Lloyd George. Whatever she may say. She has *not* got a degree in Sanskrit, which she chose to tell the headmistress, who still believes it to this day. 'When are we going to see your charming Oriental wife again?' She knows no more about jewellery than I do. *That's* a fact."

"Dates and places," Smiley murmured to the file. "If I could just check those for a start."

"Absolutely," said Peter Worthington handsomely, and from a green tin teapot refilled Smiley's cup. Blackboard chalk was worked into his large fingertips. It was like the grey in his hair.

"It really was the mother that messed her up, I'm afraid, though," he went on, in the same entirely reasonable tone. "All that urgency about putting her on the stage, then ballet, then trying to get her into television. Her mother just wanted Elizabeth to be admired. As a substitute for herself, of course. It's perfectly natural, psychologically. Read Berne. Read anyone. That's just *her* way of defining *her* individuality. Through her daughter. One must respect that those things happen. I understand all that now. She's okay, I'm okay, the world's okay, Ian's okay, then suddenly she's off."

"Do you happen to know whether she communicates with her mother, incidentally?"

Peter Worthington shook his head.

"Absolutely not, I'm afraid. She'd seen through her entirely by the time she left. Broken with her completely. The one hurdle I can safely say I helped her over. My one contribution to her happiness—"

"I don't think we have her mother's address here," said Smiley, leafing doggedly through the pages of the file. "You don't—"

Peter Worthington gave it to him rather loud, at dictation speed.

"And now the dates and places," Smiley repeated. *"Please."*

She had left him two years ago. Peter Worthington recited not just the date but the hour. There had been no scene—Peter Worthington didn't hold with scenes; Elizabeth had had too many with her mother—they'd had a happy evening, as a matter of fact, *particularly* happy. For a diversion, he'd taken her to the kebab house.

"Perhaps you spotted it as you came down the road? The Knossos, it's called, next door to the Express Dairy?"

They'd had wine and a real blow-out, and Andrew Wiltshire, the new English master, had come along to make a three. Elizabeth had introduced this Andrew to yoga only a few weeks before; they had gone to classes together at the Sobell Centre and become great buddies.

"She was really *into* yoga," he said, with an approving nod of the grizzled head. "It was a real *interest* for her. Andrew was just the sort of chap to bring her out. Extrovert, unreflective, physical . . . perfect for her," he said determinedly.

The three of them had returned to the house at ten, because of the baby-sitter, he said: himself, Andrew, and Elizabeth. He'd made coffee, they'd listened to music, and around eleven Elizabeth gave them both a kiss and said she was going over to her mother's to see how she was.

"I had understood she had broken with her mother," Smiley objected mildly, but Peter Worthington chose not to hear.

"Of course, *kisses* mean nothing with her," Peter Worthington explained, as a matter of information. "She kisses everybody, the pupils, her girl-friends—she'd kiss the dustman, anyone. She's *very* outgoing. Once again, she can't leave anyone alone. I mean *every* relationship has to be a conquest. With her child, the waiter at the restaurant . . . Then when she's won them, they bore her. Naturally. She went upstairs, looked at Ian, and—I've no doubt—used the moment to collect her passport and the house-keeping money from the bedroom. She left a note saying 'sorry' and I haven't seen her since. Nor's Ian," said Peter Worthington.

"Er, has *Andrew* heard from her?" Smiley enquired, with another tilt of his spectacles.

"Why should he have done?"

"You said they were friends, Mr. Worthington. Sometimes third parties become intermediaries in these affairs."

On the word "affair," he looked up and found himself staring directly into Peter Worthington's honest, abject eyes; and for a moment the two masks slipped simultaneously. Was Smiley observing? Or was he being observed? Perhaps it was only his embattled imagination—or did he sense, in himself and in this weak boy across the room, the stirring of an embarrassed kinship? *There should be a* league *for deceived husbands who feel sorry for themselves. You've all got the same boring, awful charity!* Ann had once flung at him. You never knew your Elizabeth, Smiley thought, still staring at Peter Worthington; and I never knew my Ann.

"That's all I can remember, really," said Peter Worthington. "After that, it's a blank."

"Yes," said Smiley, inadvertently taking refuge in Worthington's own repeated assertion: "Yes, I understand."

He rose to leave. A little boy was standing in the doorway. He had a shrouded, hostile stare. A placid, heavy woman stood behind him, holding him by both wrists above his head, so that he seemed to swing from her, though really he was standing by himself.

"Look, there's Daddy," said the woman, gazing at Worthington with brown, attaching eyes.

"Jenny, hi. This is Mr. Standfast from the Foreign Office."

"How do you do?" said Smiley politely, and after a few minutes' meaningless chatter, and a promise of further information in due course should any become available, he quietly took his leave.

"Oh, and Happy Christmas," Peter Worthington called from the steps.

"Ah, yes. And to you, too. To all of you. Happy indeed and many more of them."

In the transport café they put in sugar unless you asked them not to, and each time the Indian woman made a cup, the tiny kitchen filled with steam. In twos and threes, not talking, men ate breakfast, lunch, or supper, depending on the point they had reached in their separate days. Here also Christmas was approaching. Six greasy coloured glass balls dangled over the counter for festive cheer; and a net stocking appealed for help for spastic kids.

Smiley stared at an evening paper, not reading it. In a corner, not twelve feet from him, little Fawn had taken up the baby-sitter's classic position. His dark eyes smiled agreeably on the diners and on the doorway. He lifted his cup with his left hand, while his right idled close to his chest. Did Karla sit like this, Smiley wondered. Did Karla take refuge among the unsuspecting?

Control had. Control had made a whole second, third, or fourth life for himself in a two-room upstairs flat, beside the Western bypass, under the plain name of Matthews, not filed with housekeepers as an alias. Well, "whole" life was an exaggeration. But he had kept clothes there, and a woman—Mrs. Matthews herself—even a cat. And taken golf lessons at an artisans' club on Thursday mornings early, while from his desk in the Circus he poured scorn on the great unwashed, and on golf, and on love, and on any other piffling human pursuit which secretly might tempt him. He had even rented a garden allotment, Smiley remembered, down by a railway siding. Mrs. Matthews had insisted on driving Smiley to see it in her groomed Morris car on the day he broke the sad news to her. It was as big a mess as anyone else's allotment: standard roses, winter vegetables they hadn't used, a tool-shed crammed with hose-pipe and seed boxes.

Mrs. Matthews was a widow, pliant but capable. "All I want to know," she had said, having read the figure on the cheque.

"All I want to be sure of, Mr. Standfast, is he *really* dead, or has he gone back to his wife?"

"He is really dead," Smiley assured her, and she believed him gratefully. He forbore from adding that Control's wife had gone to her grave eleven years ago, still believing her husband was something in the Coal Board.

Did Karla have to scheme in committees? Fight cabals, deceive the stupid, flatter the clever, look in distorting mirrors of the Peter Worthington variety, all in order to do the job?

He glanced at his watch, then at Fawn. The coin-box stood next to the lavatory. But when Smiley asked the proprietor for change, he refused it on the grounds that he was too busy.

"Hand it over, you awkward bastard," shouted a long-distance driver all in leather. The proprietor briskly obliged.

"How did it go?" Guillam asked, taking the call on the direct line.

"Good background," Smiley replied.

"Hooray," said Guillam coolly.

Another of the charges later levelled against Smiley was that he wasted time on menial matters, instead of delegating them to his subordinates.

There are blocks of flats near the Town and Country Golf Course on the northern fringes of London that are like the superstructure of permanently sinking ships. They lie at the end of long lawns where the flowers are never quite in flower; the husbands man the lifeboats all in a flurry at about eight-thirty in the morning, and the women and children spend the day keeping afloat until their men-folk return too tired to sail anywhere. These buildings were built in the thirties and have stayed a grubby white ever since. Their oblong, steel-framed windows look on to the lush billows of the links, where women in eye-shades wander like lost souls.

One such block is called Arcady Mansions, and the Pellings lived in number 7, with a cramped view of the ninth green which vanished when the beeches were in leaf. When Smiley rang the bell, he heard nothing except the thin electric tinkle: no footsteps, no dog, no music. The door opened and a man's cracked voice said "Yes?" from the darkness, but it belonged to a woman. She was tall and stooping. A cigarette hung from her hand.

"My name is Oates," Smiley said, offering a big green card encased in cellophane. To a different cover belongs a different name.

"Oh, it's you, is it? Come in. Dine, see the show. You sounded younger on the telephone," she boomed, in a curdled voice striving for refinement. "He's in here. He thinks you're a spy," she said, squinting at the green card. "You're not, are you?"

"No," said Smiley. "I'm afraid not. Just a snooper."

The flat was all corridors. She led the way, leaving a vapour trail of gin. One leg slurred as she walked, and her right arm was stiff. Smiley guessed she had had a stroke. She dressed as if nobody had ever admired her height or sex. And as if she didn't care. She wore flat shoes and a mannish pullover with a belt that made her shoulders broad.

"He says he's never heard of you. He says he's looked you up in the telephone directory and you don't exist."

"We like to be discreet," Smiley said.

She pushed open a door. "He exists," she reported loudly, ahead of her into the room. "And he's not a spy, he's a snooper."

In a far chair a man was reading the *Daily Telegraph*, holding it in front of his face so that Smiley only saw the bald head, and the dressing-gown, and the short crossed legs ending in leather bedroom slippers; but somehow he knew at once that Mr. Pelling was the kind of small man who would only ever marry tall women. The room carried everything he could need in order to survive alone: his television, his bed, his gas fire, a table to eat at, and an easel for painting by numbers. On the wall hung an over-coloured portrait photograph of a very beautiful girl, with an inscription scribbled diagonally across one corner in the way that film stars wish love to the unglamorous. Smiley recognised it as Elizabeth Worthington; he had seen a lot of photographs already.

"Mr. Oates, meet Nunc," she said, and all but curtsied.

The *Daily Telegraph* came down with the slowness of a garrison flag, revealing an aggressive, glittering little face with thick brows and managerial spectacles.

"Yes. Well, just who are you precisely?" said Mr. Pelling. "Are you Secret Service or aren't you? Don't shilly-shally, out with it and be done. I don't hold with snooping, you see. What's that?" he demanded.

"His *card*," said Mrs. Pelling, offering it. "Green in hue."

"Oh, we're exchanging notes, are we? *I* need a card too then, Cess, don't I? Better get some printed, my dear. Slip down to Smith's, will you?"

"Do you like *tea?*" Mrs. Pelling asked, peering down at Smiley with her head on one side.

"What are you giving him tea for?" Mr. Pelling demanded, watching her plug in the kettle. "He doesn't need tea. He's not a guest. He's not even intelligence. I didn't ask him. Stay the week," he said to Smiley. "Move in if you like. Have her bed. 'Bullion Universal Security Advisors,' my Aunt Fanny."

"He wants to talk about Lizzie, darling," said Mrs. Pelling, setting a tray for her husband. "Now be a father for a change."

"Fat lot of good her bed would do *you*, mind," said Mr. Pelling, taking up his *Telegraph* again.

"For those kind words," said Mrs. Pelling, and gave a laugh. It consisted of two notes like a bird-call, and was not meant to be funny. A disjointed silence followed.

Mrs. Pelling handed Smiley a cup of tea. Accepting it, he addressed himself to the back of Mr. Pelling's newspaper. "Sir, your daughter Elizabeth is being considered for an important appointment with a major overseas corporation. My organisation has been asked in confidence—as a normal but very necessary formality these days—to approach friends and relations in this country and obtain character references."

"That's *us*, dear," Mrs. Pelling explained, in case her husband hadn't understood.

The newspaper came down with a snap.

"Are you suggesting my daughter is of bad character? Is that what you're sitting here, drinking my tea, suggesting?"

"No, sir," said Smiley.

"No, sir," said Mrs. Pelling unhelpfully.

A long silence followed, which Smiley was at no great pains to end.

"Mr. Pelling," he said finally, in a firm and patient voice. "I understand that you spent many years in the Post Office and rose to a high position."

"Many *many* years," Mrs. Pelling agreed.

"I worked," said Mr. Pelling from behind his newspaper once more. "There's too much talk in the world. Not enough work done."

"Did you employ criminals in your department?"

The newspaper rattled, then held still.

"Or Communists?" said Smiley, equally gently.

"If we did, we damn soon got rid of them," said Mr. Pelling, and this time the newspaper stayed down.

Mrs. Pelling snapped her fingers. "Like *that*," she said.

"Mr. Pelling," Smiley continued, in the same bedside manner, "the position for which your daughter is being considered is with one of the major Eastern companies. She will be specialising in air transport, and her work will give her advance knowledge of large gold shipments to and from this country, as well as the movement of diplomatic couriers and classified mails. It carries an extremely high remuneration. I don't think it unreasonable—and I don't think you do—that your daughter should be subject to the same procedures as any other candidate for such a responsible—and desirable—post."

"Who employs *you*," said Mr. Pelling. "That's what I'm getting at. Who says *you're* responsible?"

"Nunc," Mrs. Pelling pleaded. "Who says anyone is?"

"Don't *Nunc* me! Give him some more tea. You're hostess, aren't you? Well, act like one. It's high time Lizzie was rewarded and I'm frankly displeased that it hasn't occurred before now, seeing what they owe her."

Mr. Pelling resumed his reading of Smiley's impressive green card: "'Correspondents in Asia, U.S.A., and the Middle East.' Pen-friends, I suppose *they* are. Head Office in South Molton Street. Any enquiries, telephone blah-blah-blah. Who do I get then? Your partner in crime, I suppose."

"If it's South Molton Street, he *must* be all right," said Mrs. Pelling.

"Authority without responsibility," Mr. Pelling said, dialling the number. He spoke as if someone were holding his nostrils. "I don't hold with it, I'm afraid."

"*With* responsibility," Smiley corrected him. "We as a company are pledged to indemnify our customers against any dishonesty on the part of staff we recommend. We are insured accordingly."

The number rang five times before the Circus switchboard answered it, and Smiley hoped to God there wasn't going to be a muddle.

"Give me the Managing Director," Mr. Pelling ordered. "*I* don't care if he's in conference! Has he got a name? Well, what is it? Well, you tell Mr. Andrew Forbes-Lisle that Mr. Humphrey Pelling desires a personal word with him. Now." Long wait. Well done, thought Smiley; nice touch. "Pelling here. I've a man calling himself Oates sitting in front of me. Short, fat, and worried. What do you want me to do with him?"

In the background, Smiley heard Peter Guillam's resonant, officer-like tones all but ordering Pelling to stand up when he addressed him. Mollified, Mr. Pelling rang off.

"Does Lizzie know you're talking to us?" he asked.

"She'd laugh her head off if she did," said his wife.

"She may not even know she is being considered for the post," said Smiley. "More and more, the tendency these days is to make the approach after clearance has been obtained."

"It's for Lizzie, Nunc," Mrs. Pelling reminded him. "You know you love her, although we haven't heard of her for a year."

"You don't write to her at all?" Smiley asked sympathetically.

"She doesn't want it," said Mrs. Pelling, with a glance at her husband.

The tiniest grunt escaped Smiley's lips. It could have been regret, but it was actually relief.

"Give him more tea," her husband ordered. "He's wolfed that lot already." He stared quizzically at Smiley yet again. "I'm still not *sure* he's not Secret Service, even now," he said. "He may not be glamour, but that could be deliberate."

Smiley had brought forms. The Circus printer had run them up last night, on buff paper—which was fortunate, for in Mr. Pelling's world, it turned out, forms were the legitimisation of everything, and buff was the respectable colour. So the men worked together, like two friends solving a crossword, Smiley perched at his side, and Mr. Pelling doing the pencil work while his wife sat smoking and staring through the grey net curtains, turning her wedding ring round and round. They did date and place of birth: "Up the road at the Alexandra Nursing Home. Pulled it down now, haven't they, Cess? Turned it into one of those ice-cream blocks." They did education, and Mr. Pelling gave his views on that subject.

"I never let one school have her too long, did I, Cess? Keep her mind alert. Don't let it get into a rut. A change is worth a holiday, I said. Didn't I, Cess?"

"He's read books on education," said Mrs. Pelling.

"We married late," he said, as if explaining her presence.

"We wanted her on the stage," she said. "He wanted to be her manager, among other things."

He gave other dates. There was a drama school and there was a secretarial course.

"Grooming," Mr. Pelling said. "Preparation, not education, that's what I believe in. Throw a bit of everything at her. Make her worldly. Give her deportment."

"Oh, she's got the deportment," Mrs. Pelling agreed, and with a click of her throat blew out a lot of cigarette smoke. "*And* the worldliness."

"But she never finished secretarial college?" Smiley asked, pointing to the panel. "Or the drama."

"Didn't need to," said Mr. Pelling.

They came to previous employers. Mr. Pelling listed half a dozen in the London area, all within eighteen months of one another.

"All bores," said Mrs. Pelling pleasantly.

"She was looking around," said her husband airily. "She was taking the pulse before committing herself. I made her, didn't I, Cess? They all wanted her but I wouldn't fall for it." He flung out an arm at her. "And don't say it didn't pay off in the end!" he yelled. "Even if we aren't allowed to talk about it!"

"She liked the ballet best," said Mrs. Pelling. "Teaching the children. She *adores* children. *Adores* them."

This annoyed Mr. Pelling very much. "She's making a *career*, Cess!" he shouted, slamming the form on his knee. "God Almighty, you cretinous woman, do you want her to go back to him?"

"Now, what was she doing in the Middle East exactly?" Smiley asked.

"Taking courses. Business schools. Learning Arabic," said Mr. Pelling, acquiring a sudden largeness of view. To Smiley's surprise, he even stood and, gesticulating imperiously, roamed the room. "What got her there in the first place, I don't mind telling you, was an unfortunate marriage."

"Jesus," said Mrs. Pelling.

Upright, he had a prehensile sturdiness which made him formidable. "But we got her back. Oh, yes. Her room's always ready when she wants it. Next door to mine. She can find me any time. Oh, yes. We helped her over that hurdle, didn't we, Cess? Then one day I said to her——"

"She came with a darling English teacher with curly hair," his wife interrupted. "Andrew."

"Scottish," Mr. Pelling corrected her automatically.

"Andrew was a *nice* boy but no match for Nunc, was he, darling?"

"He wasn't enough for her. All that Yogi Bear stuff. Swinging by your tail is what I call it. Then one day I said to her, 'Lizzie: Arabs. That's where your future is.'" He snapped his fingers, pointing at an imaginary daughter. "'Oil. Money. Power. Away you go. Pack. Get your ticket. Off.'"

"A night-club paid her fare," said Mrs. Pelling. "It took her for one hell of a ride too."

"It did no such thing!" Mr. Pelling retorted, hunching his broad shoulders to yell at her, but Mrs. Pelling continued as if he weren't there.

"She answered this advertisement, you see. Some woman in Bradford with a soft line of talk. A bawd. 'Hostesses needed, but not what you'd think,' she said. They paid her air fare and the moment she landed in Bahrein they made her sign a contract giving over all her salary for the rent of her flat. From then on they'd got her, hadn't they? There was nowhere she could go, was there? The Embassy couldn't help her, no one could. She's beautiful, you see."

"You stupid bloody hag! We're talking about a *career!* Don't you love her? Your own daughter? You unnatural mother! My God!"

"She's got her career," said Mrs. Pelling complacently. "The best in the world."

In desperation Mr. Pelling turned to Smiley. "Put down 'reception work and picking up the language,' and put down——"

"Perhaps you could tell me," Smiley interjected mildly as he licked his thumb and turned the page. "This might be the way to do it—of any experience she has had in the transportation industry."

"And put down"—Mr. Pelling clenched his fists and stared first at his wife, then at Smiley, and he seemed in two minds as to whether to go on or not—"put down 'working for the British Secret Service in a high capacity.' Undercover. Go on, put it down! There. It's out now." He swung back at his wife. "He's in security, he said so. He's got a right to know and she's got a right to have it known of her. No daughter of mine's going to be an *unsung heroine! Or* unpaid! She'll get the George Medal before she's done, you mark my words!"

"Oh, balls," said Mrs. Pelling wearily. "That was just one of her *stories*. You know that."

"Could we *possibly* take things one by one?" Smiley asked in a tone of gentle forbearance. "We were talking, I think, of experience in the transportation industry."

Sage-like, Mr. Pelling put his thumb and forefinger to his chin.

"Her first *commercial* experience," he began ruminatively, "running her own show entirely, you understand—when everything came together, and jelled, and really began to pay off—apart from the intelligence side I'm referring to—employing staff and handling large quantities of cash and exercising the responsibility she's capable of—came in—how do you pronounce it?"

"Vi-ent-iane," his wife droned, with perfect Anglicisation.

"Capital of La-os," said Mr. Pelling, pronouncing the word to rhyme with "chaos."

"And what was the name of the firm, please?" Smiley enquired, pencil poised over the appropriate panel.

"A distilling company," said Mr. Pelling grandly. "My daughter Elizabeth owned and managed one of the major distilling concessions in that war-torn country."

"And the name?"

"She was selling kegs of unbranded whisky to American layabouts," said Mrs. Pelling, to the window. "On commission, twenty percent. They bought their kegs and left them to mature in Scotland as an investment to be sold off later."

"*They*, in this case, being—?" Smiley asked.

"Then her lover went and filched the money," Mrs. Pelling said. "It was a racket. Rather a good one."

"Sheer unadulterated balderdash!" Mr. Pelling shouted. "The woman's insane. Disregard her."

"And what was her address at that time, please?" Smiley asked.

"Put down 'representative,'" said Mr. Pelling, shaking his head as if things were quite out of hand. "'Distiller's representative and secret agent.'"

"She was living with a pilot," said Mrs. Pelling. "Tiny, she called him. If it hadn't been for Tiny, she'd have starved. He was gorgeous but the war had turned him inside out. Well, of *course* it would! Same with *our* boys, wasn't it? Missions night after night, day after day." Putting back her head, she screamed very loud, "'*Scramble!*'"

"She's mad," Mr. Pelling explained.

"Nervous wrecks at eighteen, half of them. But they stuck it. They loved Churchill, you see. They loved his *guts*."

"Blind mad," Mr. Pelling repeated. "Barking."

"I'm sorry," said Smiley, writing busily. "Tiny who? The pilot? What was his name?"

"Ricardo. Tiny Ricardo. A *lamb*. He died, you know," she said, straight at her husband. "Lizzie was *heart-broken*, wasn't she, Nunc? Still, it was probably the best way."

"She wasn't living with *anyone*, you anthropoid ape! It was a put-up, the whole thing. She was working for the British Secret Service!"

"Oh, my Christ," said Mrs. Pelling hopelessly.

"*Not* your Christ. *My* Mellon. Take that down, Oates. Let

me see you write it down. Mellon. The name of her commanding officer in the British Secret Service was M-e-l-l-o-n. Like
the fruit but twice the l's. Mellon. Pretending to be a plain simple trader. *And* making quite a decent thing of it. Naturally, an
intelligent man, he would. But underneath"—Mr. Pelling drove
a fist into his open palm, making an astonishingly loud noise—
"but underneath the bland and affable exterior of a British businessman, this same Mellon, two l's, was fighting a secret and
lonely war against Her Majesty's enemies, and my Lizzie was
helping him do it. Drug dealers, Chinese, homosexuals, every
single foreign element sworn to the subversion of our island
nation, my gallant daughter Lizzie and her friend Colonel Mellon between them fought to check their insidious progress!
And that's the honest truth."

"*Now* ask me where she gets it from," said Mrs. Pelling and,
leaving the door open, trailed away down the corridor grumbling to herself. Glancing after her, Smiley saw her pause and
seem to tilt her head, beckoning to him from the gloom. They
heard a distant door slam shut.

"It's true," said Pelling stoutly, but more quietly. "She did,
she did, she did. My daughter was a senior and respected operative of our British intelligence."

Smiley did not reply at first, he was too intent on writing;
so for a while there was no sound but the slow scratch of his
pen on paper, and the rustle as he turned the page.

"Good. Well, then, I'll just take those details, too, if I may.
In confidence, naturally. We come across quite a lot of it in our
work, I don't mind telling you."

"*Right*," said Mr. Pelling and, sitting himself vigorously on
a plastic-covered stool, he pulled a single sheet of paper from
his wallet and thrust it into Smiley's hand. It was a letter, handwritten, one and a half sides long, and very badly spelt; the
script was at once grandiose and childish, with high, curled "I"s
for the first person, while the other characters appeared more
cautiously.

It began "My dearest darling Pops," and it ended "Your One True Daughter Elizabeth," and the message between, the bulk of which Smiley committed to his memory, ran like this: "I have arrived in Vientiane which is a flat town, a bit French and wild but don't wory, I have important news for you which I have to impart immediately. It is possible you may not hear from me for a bit but don't worry even if you hear bad things. I'm all right and cared for and doing it for a Good Cause you would be proud of. As soon as I arrived I contacted the British Trade Counsul Mister Mackervoor (British) and he sent me for a job to Mellon. I'm not aloud to tell you so you'll have to trust me but Mellon is his name and he's a well-off English trader here but that's only half the story. Mellon is Dispatching me on a mision to Hong Kong and I'm to investgate Bullion and Drugs, pretending otherwise, and he's got men everywhere to look after me and his real name isn't Mellon. Mackervoor is in on it only secretly. If anything happens to me it will be worth it anyway because you and I know the Country matters and what's one life among so many in Asia where life counts for nought anyway? This is good Work, Dad, the kind we dreamed of you and me and specially you when you were in the war fighting for your family and loved ones. Pray for me and look after Mum. I will always love even in prison."

Smiley handed back the letter.

"There's no date," he objected flatly. "Can you give me the date, Mr. Pelling? Even approximately?"

Pelling gave it not approximately but exactly; not for nothing had he spent his working life handling the Royal Mails.

"She's never written to me since," said Mr. Pelling proudly, folding the letter back into his wallet. "Not a word, not a peep have I had out of her from that day to this. Totally unnecessary. We're one. It was said, I never alluded to it, neither did she. She'd tipped me the wink. I knew. She knew I knew. You'll never get finer understanding between daughter and father than that. Everything that followed: Ricardo, whatever his name was—

alive, dead, who cares? Some Chinaman she's on about—forget him. Men friends, girl-friends, business—disregard everything you hear. It's cover, the lot. They own her, they control her completely. She works for Mellon and she loves her father. Finish."

"You've been very kind," said Smiley, packing together his papers. "Please don't worry, I'll see myself out."

"See yourself how you like," Mr. Pelling said with a flash of his old wit.

As Smiley closed the door, he had resumed his armchair, and was ostentatiously looking for his place in the *Daily Telegraph*.

In the dark corridor the smell of drink was stronger. Smiley had counted nine paces before the door slammed, so it must have been the last door on the left, and the farthest from Mr. Pelling. It might have been the lavatory, except the lavatory was marked with a sign saying "Buckingham Palace Rear Entrance," so he called her name very softly and heard her yell, "Get out!"

He stepped inside and found himself in her bedroom, and Mrs. Pelling sprawled on the bed with a glass in her hand, riffling through a heap of picture postcards. The room itself, like her husband's, was fitted up for a separate existence, with a cooker and a sink and a pile of unwashed plates. Round the walls were snapshots of a tall and very pretty girl, some with boy-friends, some alone, mainly against Oriental backgrounds. The smell was of gin and cat.

"He won't leave her alone," Mrs. Pelling said. "Nunc won't. Never could. He tried but he never could. She's beautiful, you see," she explained for the second time, and rolled on to her back while she held a postcard above her head to read it.

"Will he come in here?"

"Not if you dragged him, darling."

Smiley closed the door, sat in a chair, and once more took out his notebook.

"She's got a dear sweet Chinaman," she said still gazing at

the postcard upside down. "She went to him to save Ricardo and then she fell in love with him. He's a real father to her, the first she ever had. It's all come out all right after all. All the bad things. They're over. He calls her 'Liese,'" she said. "He thinks it's prettier for her. Funny, really. We don't like Germans. We're patriotic. And now he's fiddling her a lovely job, isn't he?"

"I understand she prefers the name Worth, rather than Worthington. Is there a reason for that, that you know of?"

"Cutting that boring schoolmaster down to size, I should think."

"When you say she did it to *save* Ricardo, you mean of course that—"

Mrs. Pelling let out a stage groan of pain.

"*Oh,* you men. When? Who? Why? How? In the bushes, dear. In a telephone box, dear. She bought Ricardo his life, darling, with the only currency she has. She did him proud, then left him. What the hell, he was a slug." She took up another postcard and studied the picture of palm trees and an empty beach. "My little Lizzie went behind the hedge with half of Asia before she found her Drake. But she found him."

As if hearing a noise, she sat up sharply and stared at Smiley most intently while she straightened her hair. "I think you'd better go, dear," she said, in the same low voice, while she turned herself toward the mirror. "You give me the galloping creeps, to be honest. I can't do with trustworthy faces round me. Sorry, darling, know what I mean?"

At the Circus, Smiley took no more than a couple of minutes to confirm what he already knew: that Mellon was the work name of Sam Collins.

11

Shanghai Express

In the scheme of things as they are now conveniently remembered, there is at this point a deceptive condensation of events. Somewhere around here in Jerry's life, Christmas came and went in a succession of aimless drinking sessions at the Foreign Correspondents' Club, and a series of last-minute parcels to Cat clumsily wrapped in holly paper at all hours of the night. A revised trace request on Ricardo was submitted formally to the Cousins, and Smiley took it to the Annexe in person in order to explain himself more fully to Martello. But the request got snarled up in the Christmas rush—not to mention the impending collapse of Vietnam and Cambodia—and didn't complete its round of the American departments till well into the New Year, as the dates in the Dolphin file show. Indeed, the crucial meeting with Martello and his friends on the Drug Enforcement side did not take place till early February.

The wear of this prolonged delay on Jerry's nerves was appreciated intellectually within the Circus, but not, in the continued mood of crisis, felt or acted on. For that, one may again blame Smiley, depending where one stands, but it is very hard to see what more he could have done short of calling Jerry home, particularly since Craw continued to report favourably on his general disposition. The fifth floor was working flat out all the time, and Christmas was hardly noticed apart from a rather battered sherry party at midday on the twenty-fifth, and a break later while Connie and the mothers played the Queen's speech very loud in order to shame heretics like Guillam and Molly Meakin, who found it hilarious and did bad imitations of it in the corridors.

The formal induction of Sam Collins to the Circus's meagre ranks took place on a really freezing day in mid-January, and it had a light side and a dark side. The light side was his arrest. He arrived at ten exactly, on a Monday morning, not in a dinner-jacket but in a dapper grey overcoat with a rose in the buttonhole, looking miraculously youthful in the cold. But Smiley and Guillam were out, cloistered with the Cousins, and neither the janitors nor the housekeepers had any brief to admit him, so they locked him in a basement for three hours where he shivered and fumed till Smiley returned to verify the appointment. There was more comedy about his room. Smiley had put him on the fourth floor next to Connie and di Salis, but Sam wouldn't wear that and wanted the fifth. He considered it more suitable to his acting rank of co-ordinator. The poor janitors humped furniture up and down stairs like coolies.

The dark side was harder to describe, though several tried. Connie said Sam was "frigid," a disturbing choice of adjective. To Guillam he was "hungry," to the mothers "shifty," and to the burrowers "too smooth by half." The strangest thing, to those who did not know the background, was his self-sufficiency. He drew no files, he made no bids for this or that responsibility, and he scarcely used the telephone, except to place gambling bets or oversee the running of his club. But his smile went with him everywhere. The typists declared that he slept in it, and hand-washed it at weekends. Smiley's interviews with him took place behind closed doors, and bit by bit the product of them was communicated to the team.

Yes, the girl had fetched up in Vientiane with a couple of hippies who had overrun the Katmandu trail. Yes, when they dumped her she had asked Mackelvore to find her a job. And yes, Mackelvore had passed her on to Sam, thinking that on looks alone she must be exploitable: all, reading between the lines, much as the girl had described in her letter home. Sam had a couple of low-grade drug ploys mouldering on his books and was otherwise, thanks to Haydon, becalmed, so he thought he might as well put her alongside the flying boys and see what came up. He didn't tell London, because London at that point was killing everything. He just went ahead with her on trial and paid her out of his management fund. What came up was Ricardo. He also let her follow an old lead to the bullion racket in Hong Kong; but that was all before he realised she was a total disaster. It was a positive relief to Sam, he said, when Ricardo took her off his hands and got her a job with Indocharter.

"So what else does he know?" Guillam demanded indignantly. "That's not much of a ticket, is it, for screwing up the pecking order, horning in on our meetings."

"He knows *her*," said Smiley patiently, and resumed his study of Jerry Westerby's file, which of late had become his principal reading. "We are not above a little blackmail ourselves from time to time," he added with maddening tolerance, "and it is perfectly reasonable that we should have to submit to it occasionally." Whereas Connie, with unwonted coarseness, startled everyone by paraphrasing—apparently—President Johnson on the subject of J. Edgar Hoover. "George would rather have Sam Collins inside the tent pissing out than outside the tent pissing in," she declared, and gave a schoolgirl giggle at her own audacity.

And most particularly, it was not till mid-January, in the course of his continued excursions into the minutiae of the Ko background, that Doc di Salis unveiled his amazing discovery of the survival of a certain Mr. Hibbert, a China missionary in the Baptist interest, whom Ko had mentioned as a referee when he applied to read law in London.

All much more spread out, therefore, than the contemporary

memory conveniently allows—and the strain on Jerry accordingly all the greater.

"There's the possibility of a knighthood," Connie Sachs said. They had said it already on the telephone.

It was a very sober scene. Connie had bobbed her hair. She wore a dark brown hat and a dark brown suit, and she carried a dark brown handbag to contain the radio microphone. Outside in the little drive, in a blue cab with the engine and the heater on, Toby Esterhase, the Hungarian pavement artist, wearing a peak cap, pretended to doze while he received and recorded the conversation on the instruments beneath his seat. Connie's extravagant shape had acquired a prim discipline. She held a Stationery Office notebook handy, and a Stationery Office ball-point pen between her arthritic fingers. As to the remote di Salis, the art had been to modernise him a little. Under protest, he wore one of Guillam's striped shirts, with a dark tie to match. The result, somewhat surprisingly, was quite convincing.

"It's *extremely* confidential," Connie said to Mr. Hibbert, speaking loud and clear. She had said that on the telephone as well.

"Enormously," di Salis muttered in confirmation, and flung his arms about till one elbow settled awkwardly on his knobbly knee, and a crabbed hand enclosed his chin, then scratched it.

The Governor had recommended one, she said, and now it was up to the Board to decide whether or not they would pass the recommendation on to the Palace. And on the word "Palace" she cast a restrained glance at di Salis, who at once smiled brightly but modestly, like a celebrity at a chat show. His strands of grey hair were slicked down with cream, and looked (said Connie later) as though they had been basted for the oven.

"So you *will* understand," said Connie, in the precise accents of a female news-reader, "that in order to protect our noblest institutions against embarrassment, a very thorough enquiry has to be made."

"The *Palace*," Mr. Hibbert echoed, with a wink in di Salis's direction. "Well, I'm blowed. The Palace—hear that, Doris?" He was very old. The record said eighty-one, but his features had reached the age where they were once more unweathered. He wore a clerical dog-collar, a tan cardigan with worn leather patches on the elbows, and a shawl around his shoulders. The background of the grey sea made a halo round his white hair. "Sir Drake Ko," he said. "That's one thing I'd not thought of, I will say." His North Country accent was so pure that, like his snowy hair, it could have been put on. "Sir Drake," he repeated. "Well, I'm blowed. Eh, Doris?"

A daughter sat with them, thirty to forty-odd, blond, and she wore a yellow frock and powder but no lipstick. Since girlhood, nothing seemed to have happened to her face beyond a steady fading of its hopes. When she spoke, she blushed, but she rarely spoke. She had made pastries, and sandwiches as thin as handkerchiefs, and seed-cake on a doily; to strain the tea she used a piece of muslin with beads to weight it stitched around the border.

From the ceiling hung a pronged parchment lampshade made in the shape of a star. An upright piano stood along one wall with the score of "Lead, Kindly Light" open on its stand. A sampler of Kipling's "If" hung over the empty fire grate, and the velvet curtains on either side of the sea window were so heavy they might have been there to screen off an unused part of life. There were no books; there was not even a Bible. There was a very big colour television set and there was a long line of Christmas cards hung laterally over string, wings downward, like shot birds halfway to hitting the ground. There was nothing to recall the China coast, unless it was the shadow of the winter sea. It was a day of no weather and no wind. In the garden, cacti and shrubs waited dully in the cold. Walkers went quickly on the promenade.

They would like to take notes, Connie added. For it is Circus folklore that when the sound is being stolen, notes should be taken, both as fall-back and for cover.

"Oh, you write away," Mr. Hibbert said encouragingly. "We're not all elephants, are we, Doris? Doris is, mind—wonderful her memory is, good as her mother's."

"So what we'd like to do first," said Connie—careful all the same to match the old man's pace—"if we may, is what we do with all character witnesses, as we call them. We'd like to establish exactly how long you've known Mr. Ko, and the circumstances of your relationship with him."

Describe your access to Dolphin, she was saying, in a somewhat different language.

Talking of others, old men talk about themselves, studying their image in vanished mirrors.

"I was born to the calling," Mr. Hibbert said. "My grandfather, he was called. My father, he had—oh, a big parish in Macclesfield. My uncle died when he was twelve, but he still took the Pledge, didn't he, Doris? I was in missionary training school at twenty. By twenty-four, I'd set sail for Shanghai to join the Lord's Life Mission. The *Empire Queen*, she was called. We'd more waiters than passengers, the way I remember it. Oh, dear."

He aimed to spend a few years in Shanghai teaching and learning the language, he said, and then with luck transfer to the China Inland Mission and move to the interior.

"I'd have liked that. I'd have liked the challenge. I've always liked the Chinese. The Lord's Life wasn't posh, but it did a job. Now, those *Roman* schools—well, they were more like your monasteries, *and* with all that that entails," said Mr. Hibbert.

Di Salis, the sometime Jesuit, gave a dim smile.

"Now, we'd got *our* kids in from the streets," he said. "Shanghai was a rare old hotchpotch, I can tell you. We'd everything and everyone. Gangs, corruption, prostitution galore, we'd politics, money and greed and misery. All human life was there, wasn't it, Doris? She wouldn't remember, really. We went back after the war, didn't we, but they soon chucked us out again. She wasn't above eleven, even then, were you? There weren't the places left after that—well, not like Shanghai—so we came back here. But we *like* it, don't we, Doris?" said Mr. Hibbert, very conscious of speaking for both of them. "We like the *air*. That's what we like."

"Very much," said Doris, and cleared her throat with a cough into her large fist.

"So we'd fill up with whatever we could get, that's what it came to," he resumed. "We had old Miss Fong. Remember Daisy Fong, Doris? 'Course you do—Daisy and her bell? Well, she wouldn't really. My, how the time goes, though. A Pied Piper, that's what Daisy was, except it was a bell, and her not a man, and she was doing God's work even if she did fall later. Best convert I ever had, till the Japs came. She'd go down the streets, Daisy would, ringing the daylights out of that bell. Sometimes old Charlie Wan would go along with her, sometimes I'd go. We'd choose the docks or the night-club areas— behind the Bund maybe—Blood Alley we called that street, remember, Doris?—she wouldn't really—and old Daisy would ring her bell, ring, ring!"

He burst out laughing at the memory; he saw her before him quite clearly, for his hand was unconsciously making the vigorous movements of the bell. Di Salis and Connie politely joined in his laughter, but Doris only frowned.

"Rue de Jaffe, that was the worst spot. In the French concession, not surprisingly, where the houses of sin were. Well, they were everywhere, really. Shanghai was jam-packed with them. Sin City they called it. And they were right. Then a few kids gathered and she'd ask them, 'Any of you lost your mothers?' And you'd get a couple. Not all at once, here one, there one. Some would try it on, like for the rice supper, then get sent home with a cuff. But we'd always a *few* real ones, hadn't we, Doris? And bit by bit we got a school going, forty-four we had by the end, hadn't we? Some boarders, not all. Bible Class, the three Rs, a bit of geography and history. That's all we could do, really. No, we weren't a posh place."

Restraining his impatience, di Salis had fixed his gaze on the grey sea and kept it there. But Connie had arranged her expression in a steady smile of admiration, and her eyes never left the old man's face.

"That's how Daisy found the Kos," he went on, oblivious of his erratic sequence. "Down in the docks, didn't she, Doris, looking for their mother.

"They'd come up from Swatow, the two of them. When was that? Nineteen thirty-six, I suppose. Young Drake was ten or eleven, and his brother Nelson was eight—thin as wire, they were, hadn't had a square meal for weeks. They became rice Christians overnight, I can tell you! Mind you, they hadn't names in those days—not English, naturally. They were boat people, Chiu Chow. We never really found out about the mother, did we, Doris? 'Killed by the guns,' they said. 'Killed by the guns.' Could have been Japanese guns, could have been Kuomintang. We never got to the bottom of it; why should we? The Lord had her and that was that. Might as well stop all the questions and get on with it.

"Little Nelson had his arm all messed. Shocking, really. Broken bone sticking through his sleeve—I suppose the guns did that as well. Drake, he was holding Nelson's good hand, and he wouldn't let it go for love nor money at first, not even for the lad to eat. We used to say they'd one good hand between them—remember, Doris? Drake would sit there at table clutching on to him, shovelling rice into him for all he was worth. We had the doctor in: *he* couldn't separate them. We just had to put up with it. 'You'll be Drake,' I said, 'and you'll be Nelson, because you're both brave sailors, how's that?' It was your mother's idea, wasn't it, Doris? She'd always wanted boys."

Doris looked at her father, started to say something, and changed her mind.

"They used to stroke her hair," the old man said, in a slightly mystified voice. "Stroke your mother's hair and ring old Daisy's bell, that's what they liked. They'd never seen blond hair before.

"Here, Doris, how about a drop more *saw?* Mine's run cold, so I'm sure theirs has. *Saw* is Shanghainese for tea," he explained. "In Canton they call it *cha*. We've kept some of the old words, I don't know why."

With an exasperated hiss, Doris bounded from the room, and Connie seized the opportunity to speak.

"Now, Mr. Hibbert, we have no note of a *brother* till now," she said, in a slightly reproachful tone. "He was younger, you say. Two years younger? Three?"

"No note of Nelson?" The old man was amazed. "Why, he loved him! Drake's whole life, Nelson was. Do anything for him. No note of *Nelson*, Doris?"

But Doris was in the kitchen, fetching *saw*.

Referring to her notes, Connie gave a strict smile.

"I'm afraid it's we who are to blame, Mr. Hibbert. I see here that Government House has left a blank against 'Brothers and sisters.' There'll be one or two red faces in Hong Kong quite shortly, *I* can tell you. You don't happen to remember Nelson's date of birth, I suppose? Just to short-cut things?"

"No, my goodness! Daisy Fong would remember, of course, but she's long gone. Gave them all birthdays, Daisy did, even when they didn't know them theirselves."

Di Salis hauled on his ear-lobe, pulling his head down. "Or his Chinese forenames?" he blurted in his high voice. "*They* might be useful, if one's checking."

Mr. Hibbert was shaking his head. "No note of Nelson! Bless my soul! You can't really think of Drake, not without little Nelson at his side. Went together like bread and cheese, we used to say. Being orphans, naturally."

From the hall they heard a telephone ringing, and to the secret surprise of both Connie and di Salis a distinct "Oh, *hell*" from Doris in the kitchen as she dashed to answer it. They heard clippings of angry conversation against the mounting whimper of a tea-kettle: "Well, *why* isn't it? Well, if it's the bloody brakes, *why* say it's the clutch? No, we *don't* want a new car. We want the old one repaired, for God's sake." With a loud "Christ" she rang off and returned to the kitchen and the screaming kettle.

"Nelson's Chinese forenames," Connie prompted gently, through her smile, but the old man shook his head.

"You'd have to ask old Daisy that," he said. "And she's long in heaven, bless her." Di Salis seemed about to contest the old man's claim to ignorance, but Connie shut him up with a look: *Let him run*, she was urging. *Force him and we'll lose the whole match.*

The old man's chair was on a swivel. Unconsciously, he had worked his way clockwise, and now he was talking to the sea.

"They were like chalk and cheese," Mr. Hibbert said. "I never saw two brothers so different, nor so faithful, and that's a fact."

"Different in what *way?*" Connie asked invitingly.

"Little Nelson, now, he was frightened of the cockroaches. That was the first thing. We didn't have your modern sanitation, naturally. We had to send them down to the hut, and—oh, dear, those cockroaches, they flew about that hut like bullets! Nelson wouldn't go near the place. His arm was mending well enough, he was eating like a fighting cock, but that lad would hold himself in for days on end rather than go inside the hut. Your mother promised him the moon if he'd go. Daisy Fong took a stick to him, and I can see his eyes still. He'd look at you sometimes and clench his one good fist, and you'd think he'd turn you to stone. That Nelson was a rebel from the day he was born.

"Then one day we looked out of the window and there they were. Drake with his arm round little Nelson's shoulder, leading him down the path to keep him company while he did his business. Notice how they walk different, the boat children?"

he asked brightly, as if he saw them now. "Bow-legged from the cramp, they both were."

The door was barged open and Doris came in with a tray of fresh tea, making a clatter as she set it down.

"Singing was just the same," he said, and fell silent again, gazing at the sea.

"Singing *hymns?*" Connie prompted brightly, glancing at the polished piano with its empty candle-holders.

"Drake, he'd belt anything out as long as your mother was at the piano. Carols. 'There Is a Green Hill.' Cut his own throat for your mother, Drake would. But young Nelson, I never heard him sing one note."

"You heard him later all right," Doris reminded him harshly, but he preferred not to notice her.

"You'd take his lunch away, his supper, but he'd not even say his Amens. He'd a real quarrel with God from the start." He laughed with sudden freshness. "Well, those are your real believers, I always say. The others are just polite. There's no true conversion, not without a quarrel."

"Damn garage," Doris muttered, still fuming after her telephone call, as she hacked at the seed-cake.

"Here! Is your driver all right?" Mr. Hibbert cried. "Shall Doris take out to him? He must be freezing to death out there! Bring him in, go on!" But before either of them could answer, Mr. Hibbert had started talking about his war. Not Drake's war, or Nelson's, but his own, in unjoined scraps of graphic memory.

"Funny thing, there was a lot who thought the Japs were just the ticket. Teach those upstart Chinese Nationalists where to get off. Let alone the Communists, of course. Oh, it took quite a while for the scales to fall, I can tell you. Even after the bombardments started. European shops closed. Taipans evacuated their families, Country Club became a hospital. But there were still the ones who said 'Don't worry.' Then one day, *bang*, they'd locked us up, hadn't they, Doris? *And* killed your mother into the bargain. She'd not the stamina, had she, not after her tuberculosis. Still, those Ko brothers were better off than most, for all that."

"Oh. Why was that?" Connie enquired, all interest.

"They'd the knowledge of Jesus to guide and comfort them, hadn't they?"

"Of course," said Connie.

"Naturally," di Salis chimed, linking his fingers and hauling at them. "*Indeed* they had," he said unctuously.

So with the Japs, as he called them, the mission closed and Daisy Fong with her handbell led the children to join the stream of refugees, who by cart, bus, or train, but mostly on foot, were taking the trail to Shangjao and finally to Chungking, where Chiang's Nationalists had set up their temporary capital.

"He can't go on too long," Doris warned at one point, in an aside to Connie. "He gets gaga."

"Oh, yes, I can, dear," Mr. Hibbert corrected her, with a fond smile. "I've had my share of life now. I can do what I like."

With his wife's death, he somehow said, his own life had ended too; he was marking time until he joined her. He had had a living in the North of England for a while. After that he'd done a bit of work in London, propagating the Bible.

"Then we came south, didn't we, Doris? I don't know why."

"For the air," she said.

"There'll be a party, will there, at the Palace?" Mr. Hibbert asked. "I suppose Drake might even put us down for invites. Think of that, Doris. You'd like that: a Royal Garden Party. Hats."

"But you did return to Shanghai," Connie reminded him eventually, shuffling her notes to call him back. "The Japanese were defeated, Shanghai was reopened, and back you went. Without your wife, of course, but you returned all the same."

"Oh, ay, we went."

"So you saw the Kos again. You all met up and you had a marvellous old natter, I'm sure. Is that what happened, Mr. Hibbert?"

For a moment it seemed he hadn't taken in the question, but suddenly with a delayed action he laughed. "By Jove and weren't they real little men by then, too! Fly as fly they were! *And* after the girls, saving your presence, Doris. I always say Drake would have married you, dear, if you'd given him any hope."

"Oh, *honestly*, Dad," Doris muttered, and scowled at the floor.

"And Nelson—on, *my*, he was the firebrand!" He drank his tea with the spoon, carefully, as if he were feeding a bird. "'Where Missie?' His first question that was, Drake's. He wanted your mother. 'Where Missie?' He'd forgotten all his English, so'd Nelson. I'd to give them lessons later. So I told him. He'd seen enough of death by then, *that* was for sure. Wasn't as if he didn't believe in it.

"'Missie dead,' I said. Nothing else to say. 'She's dead, Drake, and she's with God.' I never saw him weep before or since, but he wept then and I loved him for it. 'I lose two mothers,' he says to me. 'Mother dead, now Missie dead.' We prayed for her, what else can you do? Little Nelson, now he didn't cry or pray. Not him. He never took to her the way Drake did. Nothing personal. She was enemy. We all were."

"*We* being who precisely, Mr. Hibbert?" di Salis asked coaxingly.

"Europeans, capitalists, missionaries: all of us exploiters who were there for their souls, or their labour, or their silver. All of us," Mr. Hibbert repeated, without the least hint of rancour. "Exploiters. That's how he saw us. Right, in a way too." The conversation hung awkwardly for a moment till Connie carefully retrieved it.

"So, anyway," she said, "you reopened the mission, and you stayed till the Communist take-over of 'forty-nine, I assume, and for those four years at least you were able to keep a fatherly eye on Drake and Nelson. Is that how it went, Mr. Hibbert?" she asked, pen poised.

"Oh, we hung the lamp on the door again, yes. In 'forty-five, we were jubilant, same as anyone else. The fighting had stopped, the Japs were beaten, the refugees could come home. Hugging in the street, there was, the usual. We'd money—reparation, I suppose, a grant. Daisy Fong came back, but not for long. For the first year or two the surface held, but not really, even then. We were there as long as Chiang Kai-shek could govern—well, he was never much of a one for that, was he? By 'forty-seven we'd the Communism out on the streets—and by 'forty-nine it was there to stay. International Settlement long gone, of course—concessions, too, and a good thing. The rest went slowly.

"You got the blind ones, as usual, who said the old Shanghai would go on forever, same as you did with the Japs. Shanghai had corrupted the Manchus, they said; the war-lords, the Kuomintang, the Japanese, the British. Now she'd corrupt the Communists. They were wrong, of course. Doris and me—well, we didn't believe in corruption, did we, not as a solution to China's problems—nor did your mother. So we came home."

"And the Kos?" Connie reminded him, while Doris noisily hauled some knitting out of a brown-paper bag.

The old man hesitated, and this time it was not senility, perhaps, which slowed his narrative, but doubt. "Well, yes," he conceded, after an awkward gap. "Yes, rare adventures those two had, *I* can tell you."

"*Adventures,*" Doris echoed angrily as she clicked her knitting needles. "Rampages, more like."

The light was clinging to the sea, but inside the room it was dying and the gas fire puttered like a distant motor.

Several times, escaping from Shanghai, Drake and Nelson were separated, the old man said. When they couldn't find each other, they ate their hearts out till they did. Nelson, the young

one, got all the way to Chungking without a scratch, surviving
starvation, exhaustion, and hellish air bombardments which
killed thousands of civilians. But Drake, being older, was drafted
into Chiang's army, though Chiang did nothing but run away,
hoping that the Communists and the Japanese would kill each
other.

"Charged all over the shop, Drake did, trying to find the
front and worrying himself to death about Nelson. And, of
course, Nelson—well, he was twiddling his thumbs in Chungking, wasn't he, boning up on his ideological reading. They'd
even the *New China Daily* there, he told me afterwards, *and*
published with Chiang's agreement. Fancy that! There was a
few others of his mind around, and in Chungking they got
their heads together rebuilding the world for when the war
ended, and one day, thank God, it did."

In 1945, said Mr. Hibbert simply, their separation was ended
by a miracle. "One chance in thousands, it was—millions. That
road back littered with streams of lorries, carts, troops, guns all
pouring toward the coast, and there was Drake running up and
down like a madman: 'Have you seen my brother?'"

The drama of the instant touched the preacher in him, and
his voice lifted: "And one little dirty fellow put his arm on
Drake's elbow. 'Here. You. Ko.' Like he's asking for a light.
'Your brother's two trucks back, talking the hind legs off a
bunch of Hakka Communists.' Next thing, they're in each
other's arms and Drake won't let Nelson out of his sight till
they're back in Shanghai, and *then* not!"

"So they came to see you," Connie suggested cosily.

"When Drake got back to Shanghai, he'd one thing in his
mind and one only. Brother Nelson should have a formal education. Nothing else on God's good earth mattered to Drake
except Nelson's schooling. *Nothing.* Nelson must go to school."
The old man's hand thudded on the chair arm. "*One* of the
brothers at least would make the grade. Oh, he was adamant,
Drake was! *And* he did it," said the old man. "Drake swung it.

He would. He was a real fixer by then. Drake was nineteen years of age, odd, when he came back from the war. Nelson, he was going on seventeen, and worked night and day, too—on his studies, of course. Same as Drake did, but Drake worked with his body."

"He was bent," Doris said under her breath. "He joined a gang and stole. When he wasn't pawing *me*."

Whether Mr. Hibbert heard her or whether he was simply answering a standard objection in her was not clear. "Now, Doris, you must see those triads in perspective," he corrected her. "Shanghai was a city-state. It was run by a bunch of merchant princes, robber barons, and worse. There were no unions, no law and order, life was cheap and hard, and I doubt Hong Kong's that different today once you scratch the surface. Some of those so-called English gentlemen would have made your Lancashire mill-owner into a shining example of Christian charity by comparison."

The mild rebuke administered, he returned to Connie and his narrative. Connie was familiar to him: the archetypal lady in the front pew, big, attentive, in a hat, listening indulgently to the old man's every word.

"They'd come round to tea, see, five o'clock, the brothers. I'd to have everything ready, the food on the table—lemonade they liked, called it soda. Drake came in from the docks, Nelson from his books, and they'd eat not hardly talking; then back to work, wouldn't they, Doris? They'd dug out some legendary hero, the scholar Che Yin. Che Yin was so poor he'd had to teach himself to read and write by the light of the fireflies. They'd go on about how Nelson was to emulate him. 'Come on, Che Yin,' I'd say. 'Have another bun to keep your strength up.' They'd laugh a bit and away they'd go again. 'Bye-bye, Che Yin, off you go.'

"Now and then, when his mouth wasn't too full, Nelson would have a go at me on the politics. *My*, he'd some ideas! Nothing *we* could have taught him, I can tell you—we didn't know enough. Money the root of all evil—well, I'd never deny *that!* I'd been preaching it myself for years! Brotherly love, comradeship, religion the opiate of the masses—well, I couldn't go along with that, but clericalism, High Church baloney, popery, idolatry—well, he wasn't too far wrong there either, the way I saw it. He'd a few bad words against us British too, not but what we deserved them, I daresay."

"Didn't stop him eating your food, did it?" Doris said, in another low-toned aside. "*Or* renouncing his religious background. Or smashing the mission to pieces."

But the old man only smiled patiently. "Doris, my dear, I have told you before and I'll tell you again. The Lord reveals himself in many ways. So long as good men are prepared to go out and seek for truth and justice and brotherly love, He'll not be kept waiting too long outside the door."

Colouring, Doris dug away at her knitting.

"She's right, of course. Nelson *did* smash up the mission. Renounced his religion too." A cloud of grief threatened his old face for a moment, till laughter suddenly triumphed. "And my billy-oh, didn't Drake make him smart for it! Didn't he give him a dressing down, though! Oh dear, oh dear! 'Politics,' says Drake. 'You can't eat them, you can't sell them, and'—saving Doris's presence—'you can't sleep with them! All you can do with them is smash temples and kill the innocent!' I've never seen him so angry. *And* gave Nelson a hiding, he did! Drake had learned a thing or two down in the docks, *I* can tell you!"

"And you *must*," di Salis hissed, snake-like in the gloom. "You must tell us *everything*. It's your duty."

"A student procession," Mr. Hibbert resumed. "Torchlight, after the curfew, group of Communists out on the streets for a shindy. Early 'forty-nine—spring it would have been, I suppose—things were just beginning to hot up." In contrast to his earlier ramblings, Mr. Hibbert's narrative style had become unexpectedly concise.

"We were sitting by the fire, weren't we, Doris? Fourteen, Doris was, or was it fifteen? We used to love a fire, even when there wasn't the need—took us home to Macclesfield. And we hear this clattering and chanting outside: cymbals, whistles, gongs, bells, drums—oh, a shocking din. I'd a notion something like this might have been happening. Little Nelson, he was forever warning me in his English lessons. 'You go home, Mr. Hibbert. You're a good man,' he used to say, bless him. 'You're a good man, but when the floodgates burst the water will cover the good and the bad alike.' He'd a lovely turn of phrase, Nelson, when he wanted. It went with his faith. Not invented. *Felt.*

"'Daisy,' I said—Daisy Fong, that was; she was sitting with us—'Daisy, you and Doris go to the back courtyard, I think we're about to have company.' Next thing I knew, *smash*, someone had tossed a stone through the window. We heard voices, of course, shouting, and I picked out young Nelson even then, just from his voice. He'd the Chiu Chow *and* the Shanghainese, of course, but he was using Shanghainese to the lads, naturally. 'Condemn the imperialist running dogs!' he's yelling. 'Down with the religious hyenas!' Oh, the slogans they dream up! They sound all right in the Chinese but shove 'em into English and they're rubbish. Then the door goes and in they come."

"They smashed the cross," said Doris, pausing to glare at her pattern.

It was Hibbert this time, not his daughter, who startled his audience with his earthiness: "They smashed a damn sight more than that, Doris! They smashed the lot. Pews, the Table, the piano, chairs, lamps, hymn-books, Bibles. Oh, they'd a real old go, *I* can tell you. Proper little pigs, they were. 'Go on,' I says. 'Help yourselves. What man hath put together will perish, but you'll not destroy God's word, not if you chop the whole place up for matchwood.' Nelson, he wouldn't look at me, poor lad. I could have wept for him.

"When they'd gone, I looked round and I saw old Daisy

Fong standing there in the doorway and Doris behind her. She'd been watching, had Daisy. Enjoying it. I could see it in her eyes. She was one of them, at heart. Happy. 'Daisy,' I said. 'Pack your things and go. In this life you can give yourself or withhold yourself as you please, my dear. But never lend yourself. That way you're worse than a spy.'"

While Connie beamed her agreement, di Salis gave a squeaky, offended wheeze.

But the old man was really enjoying himself. "Well, so we sat down, me and Doris here, and we'd a bit of a cry together, I don't mind admitting, hadn't we, Doris? I'm not ashamed of tears, never have been. We missed your mother sorely. Knelt down, had a pray. Then we started clearing up. Difficult to know where to begin, really.

"Then in comes Drake!" He shook his head in wonder. "'Good evening Mr. Hibbert,' he says, in that deep voice of his, plus a bit of my North Country that always made us laugh. And behind him, there's little Nelson standing with a brush and pan in his hand. He'd still his crooked arm—I suppose he has now—smashed in the bombs when he was little, but it didn't stop him brushing, I can tell you. That's when Drake went for him—oh, cursing him like a navvy! I'd never heard him like it. Well, he *was* a navvy, wasn't he, in a manner of speaking?" He smiled serenely at his daughter. "Lucky he spoke the Chiu Chow, eh, Doris? I only understand the half of it myself, not that, but my *hat!* Effing and blinding like I don't know what."

He paused and closed his eyes a moment, either in prayer or tiredness. "It wasn't Nelson's fault, of course. Well, we knew that already. He was a leader. Face was involved. They'd started marching, nowhere much in mind, then somebody calls to him, 'Hey! Mission boy! Show us where your loyalties are now!' So he did. He had to. Didn't stop Drake lamming into him, all the same. They cleaned up, we went to bed, and the two lads slept on the chapel floor in case the mob came back. Came down in the morning, there were the hymn-books all piled up neatly, those that had survived, same with the Bibles. They'd fixed a cross up, fashioned it theirselves. Even patched up the piano, though not to tune it, naturally."

Winding himself into a fresh knot, di Salis put a question. Like Connie, he had a notebook open, but he had not yet written anything in it.

"What was Nelson's *discipline* at this time?" he demanded, in his nasal, indignant way, and held his pen ready to write.

Mr. Hibbert gave a puzzled frown: "Why, the Communist Party, naturally."

As Doris whispered "Oh, *Daddy*" into her knitting, Connie hastily translated: "What was Nelson studying, Mr. Hibbert, and where?"

"Ah, *discipline*. *That* kind of discipline!" Mr. Hibbert resumed his plainer style.

He knew the answer exactly. What else, he asked, had he and Nelson to talk about in their English lessons—apart from the Communist gospel—but Nelson's own ambitions? Nelson's passion was engineering. Nelson believed that technology, not Bibles, would lead China out of feudalism.

"Shipbuilding, roads, railways, factories: that was Nelson. The Angel Gabriel with a slide-rule and a white collar, and a degree. That's who *he* was, in his mind."

Mr. Hibbert did not stay in Shanghai long enough to see Nelson achieve this happy state, he said, because Nelson did not graduate till '51.

Di Salis's pen scratched wildly on the notebook.

"But Drake, who'd scraped and scrounged for him those six years," said Mr. Hibbert—over Doris's renewed references to the triads—"Drake stuck it out, and he had his reward, same as Nelson did. He saw that vital piece of paper go into Nelson's hand, and he knew his job was done and he could get out, just like he'd always planned."

Di Salis in his excitement was growing positively avid. His

ugly face had sprung fresh patches of colour and he was fidgeting desperately on his chair.

"And *after* graduating—what then?" he said urgently. "What did he *do?* What became of him? Go on, please. *Please* go on."

Amused by such enthusiasm, Mr. Hibbert smiled. Well, according to Drake, he said, Nelson had first joined the shipyards as a draughtsman, working on blueprints and building-projects, and learning like mad whatever he could from the Russian technicians who'd poured in since Mao's victory. Then in '53, if Mr. Hibbert's memory served him correctly, Nelson was privileged to be chosen for further training at the Leningrad University in Russia, and he stayed on there till—well, late fifties anyway.

"Oh, he was like a dog with two tails, Drake was, by the sound of him." Mr. Hibbert could not have looked more proud if it had been his own son he was talking of.

Di Salis suddenly leaned forward, even presuming, despite cautionary glances from Connie, to jab his pen in the old man's direction. "So *after* Leningrad: what did they do with him *then?*"

"Why, he came back to Shanghai, naturally," said Mr. Hibbert with a laugh. "*And* promoted, he was, after the learning he'd acquired, and the standing: a shipbuilder, Russian taught, a technologist, an administrator! Oh, he loved those Russians! Specially after Korea. They'd machines, power, ideas, philosophy. His promised land, Russia was. He looked up to them like—"

His voice and his zeal both died. "Oh, dear," he muttered, and stopped, unsure of himself for the second time since they had listened to him. "But that couldn't last forever, could it? Admiring Russia—how long was that fashionable in Mao's new wonderland? Doris dear, get me a shawl."

"You're wearing it," Doris said.

Yet still, tactlessly, stridently, di Salis bore in on him. He cared for nothing now except the answers—not even for the notebook open on his lap.

"He returned," he piped. "Very well. He rose in the hierarchy. He was Russia trained, Russia oriented. Very well. *What comes next?*"

Mr. Hibbert looked at di Salis for a long time. There was no guile in his face, and none in his gaze. He looked at him as a clever child might, without the hindrance of sophistication; and it was suddenly clear that Mr. Hibbert didn't trust di Salis any more, and indeed that he didn't like him.

"He's dead, young man," Mr. Hibbert said finally, and, swivelling his chair, stared at the sea view. In the room it was already half dark, and most of the light came from the gas fire. The grey beach was empty. On the wicket gate a single sea-gull perched black and vast against the last strands of the evening sky.

"You said he still had his crooked arm," di Salis snapped straight back. "You said you supposed he had. You said it about *now;* I heard it in your voice."

"Well, now, *I* think we have taxed Mr. Hibbert quite enough," said Connie brightly and, with a sharp glance at di Salis, stooped for her bag. But di Salis would have none of it.

"I don't believe him!" he cried in his shrill voice. "When did Nelson die? Give us the dates!"

But the old man only drew his shawl more closely round him, and kept his eyes to the sea.

"We were in Durham," Doris said, still looking at her knitting, though there was not the light to knit by. "Drake drove up and saw us in his big chauffeur-driven car. He took his henchman with him, the one he calls Tiu. They were fellow crooks together in Shanghai. Wanted to show off. Brought me a platinum cigarette-lighter, and a thousand pounds in cash for Dad's church and flashed his O.B.E. at us in its case; took me into a corner and asked me to come to Hong Kong and be his mistress, right under Dad's nose. Bloody sauce!

"He wanted Dad's signature on something. A guarantee.

Said he was going to read law at Gray's Inn. At his age, I ask you! Forty-two! Talk about mature student! He wasn't, of course. It was all just face and talk, as usual. Dad said to him, 'How's Nelson?' and—"

"Just one minute, please." Di Salis had made yet another ill-judged interruption. "The date? *When* did all this happen, please? I must have *dates!*"

"'Sixty-seven. Dad was almost retired, weren't you, Dad?" The old man did not stir.

"All right, 'sixty-seven. What month? Be precise, please!"

He all but said "Be precise, *woman*," and he was making Connie seriously anxious. But when she tried to restrain him, he again ignored her.

"April," Doris said, after some thought. "We'd just had Dad's birthday. That's why he brought the thousand quid for the church. He knew Dad wouldn't take it for himself, because Dad didn't like the way Drake made his money."

"All right. Good. Well done. April. So Nelson died pre-April, 'sixty-seven. What details did Drake supply of the circumstances? Do you remember that?"

"None. No details. I told you. Dad asked, and he just said 'dead,' as if Nelson was a dog. So much for brotherly love. Dad didn't know where to look. It nearly broke his heart and there was Drake not giving a hoot. 'I have no brother. Nelson is dead.' And Dad still praying for Nelson, weren't you, Dad?"

"I prayed for Nelson and I pray for him still," he said bluntly. "When he was alive, I prayed that one way or another he would do God's work in the world. I believed he had it in him to do great things. Drake—he'd manage anywhere. He's tough. But the light on the door at the Lord's Life Mission would not have burned in vain, I used to think, if Nelson Ko succeeded in helping to lay the foundation of a just society in China. Nelson might *call* it Communism. Call it what he likes. But for three long years your mother and I gave him our Christian love, and

I won't have it said, Doris, not by you or anyone, that the light of God's love can be put out forever—not by politics, not by the sword."

He drew a long breath. "And now he's dead I pray for his soul, same as I do for your mother's," he said, sounding strangely less convinced. "If that's popery, I don't care."

Connie had actually risen to go. She knew the limits, she had the eye, and she was scared of the way di Salis was hammering on. But di Salis on the scent knew no limits at all.

"So it was a *violent* death, was it? Politics and the sword, you said. *Which* politics? Did Drake tell you that? Actual *killings* were relatively rare, you know. I think you're holding out on us!"

Di Salis also was standing, but at Mr. Hibbert's side, and he was yapping these questions down at the old man's white head as if he were acting in a Sarratt playlet on interrogation.

"You've been so *very* kind," said Connie gushingly to Doris. "Really, we've all we could possibly need *and* more. I'm sure it will all go through with the knighthood," she said, in a voice pregnant with message for di Salis. "Now, away we go and thank you both *enormously.*"

But this time it was the old man himself who frustrated her. "And the year after, he lost his other Nelson, too, God help him, his little boy," he said. "He'll be a lonely man, will Drake. That was his last letter to us, wasn't it, Doris? 'Pray for my little Nelson, Mr. Hibbert,' he wrote. And we did.

"Wanted me to fly over and conduct the funeral. I couldn't do it, I don't know why. I never much held with money spent on funerals, to be honest."

At this di Salis literally pounced, and with a truly terrible glee. He stooped right over the old man, and he was so animated that he grabbed a fistful of shawl in his feverish little hand.

"Ah! Ah, *now!* But did he ever ask you to pray for Nelson *senior?* Answer me that."

"No," the old man said simply. "No, he didn't."

"Why not? Unless he wasn't really dead, of course! There

are more ways than one of dying in China, aren't there, and not all of them fatal! 'Disgraced'—is that a better expression?"

His squeaky words flew about the firelit room like ugly spirits.

"They're to go, Doris," the old man said calmly to the sea. "See that driver right, won't you, dear? I'm sure we should have taken out to him, but never mind."

They stood in the hall, making their goodbyes. The old man had stayed in his chair, and Doris had closed the door on him.

Sometimes Connie's sixth sense was frightening. "The name *Liese* doesn't mean anything to you, does it, Miss Hibbert?" she asked, buckling her enormous plastic coat. "We have a reference to a Liese in Mr. Ko's life."

Doris's powdered face made an angry scowl.

"That's Mum's name," she said. "She was German Lutheran. The swine stole that too, did he?"

With Toby Esterhase at the wheel, Connie Sachs and Doc di Salis hurried home to George with their amazing news. At first, on the way, they squabbled about di Salis's lack of restraint. Toby Esterhase particularly was shocked, and Connie seriously feared the old man might write to Ko. But soon the import of their discovery overwhelmed their apprehensions, and they arrived triumphant at the gates of their secret city.

Safely inside the walls, it was now di Salis's hour of glory. Summoning his family of yellow perils once more, he set in motion a whole variety of enquiries, which sent them scurrying all over London on one false pretext or another, and to Cambridge too. At heart di Salis was a loner: no one knew him, except Connie perhaps; and if Connie didn't care for him, then no one liked him either. Socially, he was discordant and frequently absurd. But neither did anyone doubt his hunter's will.

He scoured old records of the Shanghai University of Communications—in Chinese the Chiao Tung—which had a reputation for student Communist militancy after the 1939–45

war, and concentrated his interest upon the Department of
Marine Studies, which included both administration and ship-
building in its curriculum. He drew lists of Party cadre members of both before and after '49, and pored over the scant
details of those entrusted with the take-over of big enterprises
where technological know-how was required—in particular
the Kiangnan shipyard, a massive affair from which the
Kuomintang elements had repeatedly to be purged.

Having drawn up lists of several thousand names, he opened
files on all those who were known to have continued their studies at Leningrad University and afterwards reappeared at the
shipyard in improved positions. A course of shipbuilding at
Leningrad took three years. By di Salis's computation, Nelson
should have been there from '53 to '56, and afterwards formally
assigned to the Shanghai municipal department in charge of
marine engineering, which would then have returned him to
the Kiangnan.

Accepting that Nelson not only possessed Chinese forenames which were still unknown, but quite possibly had chosen
a new surname for himself into the bargain, di Salis warned his
helpers that Nelson's biography might be split into two parts,
each under a different name. They should watch for dovetailing. He cadged lists of graduates and lists of enrolled students
both at Chiao Tung and at Leningrad and set them side by side.

China-watchers are a fraternity apart, and their common
interests transcend protocol and national differences. Di Salis
had connections not only in Cambridge, and in every Oriental
archive, but in Rome, Tokyo, and Munich as well. He wrote to
all of them, concealing his goal in a welter of other questions.
Even the Cousins, it turned out later, had unwittingly opened
their files to him. He made other enquiries even more devious.
He dispatched burrowers to the Baptists, to delve among
records of old pupils at the mission schools, on the off chance
that Nelson's Chinese names had, after all, been taken down

and filed. He tracked down any chance records of the deaths of middle-ranking Shanghai officials in the shipping industry.

That was the first leg of his labours. The second began with what Connie called the Great Beastly Cultural Revolution of the mid-sixties and the names of such Shanghainese officials who, in consequence of criminal pro-Russian leanings, had been officially purged, humiliated, or sent to a May 7th school to rediscover the virtues of peasant labour. He also consulted lists of those sent to labour reform camps, but with no great success. He looked for any references among the Red Guards' harangues to the wicked influence of a Baptist upbringing upon this or that disgraced official, and he played complicated games with the name of Ko, for it was at the back of his mind that, in changing his name, Nelson might have hit upon a different character which retained an internal kinship with the original— either homophonic or symphonetic. But when he tried to explain this to Connie, he lost her.

For Connie Sachs was pursuing a different line entirely. Her interest centred on the activities of known Karla-trained talent-spotters working among overseas students at the University of Leningrad in the fifties; and on rumours, never proven, that Karla, as a young Comintern agent, had been lent to the Shanghai Communist underground after the war to help them rebuild their secret apparatus.

It was in the middle of all this fresh burrowing that a small bombshell was delivered from Grosvenor Square. Mr. Hibbert's intelligence was still fresh from the presses, in fact, and the researchers of both families were still frantically at work when Peter Guillam walked in on Smiley with an urgent message. He was, as usual, deep in his own reading, and as Guillam entered he slipped a file into a drawer and closed it.

"It's the Cousins," Guillam said gently. "About Brother Ricardo, your favourite pilot. They want to meet with you at the Annexe as soon as possible. I'm to ring back by yesterday."

"They want *what?*"

"To meet you. But they use the preposition."

"*Do* they? Do they *really?* Good Lord. I suppose it's the German influence. Or is it Old English? Meet *with*. Well, I must say." And he lumbered off to his bathroom to shave.

Returning to his own room, Guillam found Sam Collins sitting in the soft chair, smoking one of his beastly brown cigarettes, and smiling his washable smile.

"Something up?" Sam asked, very leisurely.

"Get the hell out of here," Guillam snapped. Sam was nosing around a lot too much for Guillam's liking, but that day he had a firm reason for distrusting him. Calling on Lacon at the Cabinet Office to deliver the Circus's monthly imprest account for his inspection, he had been astonished to see Sam emerging from his private office, joking easily with Lacon and Saul Enderby of the Foreign Office.

12

The Resurrection of Ricardo

Before the fall, studiously informal meetings of intelligence partners to the special relationship were held as often as monthly and followed by what Smiley's predecessor Alleline had liked to call "a jar." If it was the American turn to play host, then Alleline and his cohorts—among them the popular Bill Haydon—would be shepherded to a vast roof-top bar, known within the Circus as "the planetarium," to be regaled with dry martinis and a view of West London they could not otherwise have afforded. If it was the British turn, then a trestle-table was set up in the rumpus room, and a darned damask table-cloth spread over it, and the American delegates were invited to pay homage to the last bastion of clubland spying, and incidentally the birthplace of their own service, while they sipped South African sherry disguised by cut-glass decanters on the grounds that they wouldn't know the difference. For the discussions there was no agenda and by tradition no notes were taken. Old friends had no need of such devices, particularly since hidden microphones stayed sober and did the job better.

Since the fall, these niceties had for a while stopped dead. Under orders from Martello's headquarters at Langley, Virginia, the "British liaison," as they knew the Circus, was placed on the arm's-length list, equating it with Yugoslavia and Lebanon, and for a while the two services in effect passed each other on opposite sidewalks, scarcely lifting their eyes. They were like an estranged couple in the middle of divorce proceedings. But by the time that grey winter's morning had come along when Smiley and Guillam, in some haste, presented themselves at the front doors of the Legal Advisor's Annexe in Grosvenor Square, a marked thaw was already discernible everywhere, even in the rigid faces of the two Marines who frisked them.

The doors, incidentally, were double, with black grilles over black iron, and gilded feathers on the grilles. The cost of them alone would have kept the entire Circus ticking over for a couple of days at least. Once inside them, Smiley and Guillam had the sensation of coming from a hamlet to a metropolis.

Martello's room was very large. There were no windows and it could have been midnight. Above an empty desk, an American flag, unfurled as if by a breeze, occupied half the end wall. At the centre of the floor, a ring of airport chairs was clustered round a fake rosewood table, and in one of these sat Martello himself, a burly, cheerful-looking Yale man in a country suit which seemed always out of season. Two quiet men flanked him, each as sallow and sincere as the other.

"George, this is good of you," said Martello heartily, in his warm, confiding voice, as he came quickly forward to receive them. "I don't need to tell you. I *know* how busy you are. I *know*.

"Sol," he said, turning to two strangers sitting across the room so far unnoticed: the one young like Martello's quiet men, if less smooth; the other squat and tough and much older, with a slashed complexion and a crew cut, a veteran of something. "Sol," Martello repeated in a voice of hushed ceremony, "I want you to meet one of the true legends of our profession. Sol: Mr. George Smiley. George, this is Sol Eckland, who's high in our fine Drug Enforcement Administration, formerly the Bureau of Narcotics and Dangerous Drugs, now rechristened— right, Sol? Sol, say hello to Pete Guillam."

The elder of the two men put out a hand, and Smiley and Guillam each shook it, and it felt like dried bark.

"Sure," said Martello, looking on with the satisfaction of a matchmaker. "George, ah, remember Ed Ristow, also in narcotics, George? Paid a courtesy call on you over there a few months back? Well, Sol has taken over from Ristow. He has the South East Asian sphere. Cy here is with him."

Nobody remembers names like the Americans, thought Guillam.

Cy was the young one of the two. He had sideburns and a gold watch and he looked like a Mormon missionary: devout, but defensive. He smiled as if smiling had been part of his course, and Guillam smiled in return.

"What happened to Ristow?" Smiley asked as they sat down.

"Coronary," growled Sol in a voice as dry as his hand. His hair was like wire wool crimped into small trenches. When he scratched it, which he did a lot, it rasped.

"I'm sorry," said Smiley.

"Could be permanent," said Sol, not looking at him, and drew on his cigarette.

Here, for the first time, it passed through Guillam's mind that something fairly momentous was in the air. He caught a hint of real tension between the two American camps. Unheralded replacements, in Guillam's experience of the American scene, were seldom caused by anything as banal as illness. He went so far as to wonder in what way Sol's predecessor might have blotted his copy-book.

"Enforcement, ah, naturally has a strong interest in our little joint venture, ah, George," Martello said, and with this unpromising fanfare the Ricardo connection was indirectly announced, though Guillam detected there was still a mysterious urge, on the American side, to pretend their meeting was about something different—as witness Martello's vacuous opening comments.

"George, our people in Langley like to work very closely indeed with their good friends in narcotics," he declared, with all the warmth of a diplomatic *note verbale*.

"Cuts both ways," Sol, the veteran, said in confirmation and expelled more cigarette smoke while he scratched his iron-grey hair. He seemed to Guillam at root a shy man, not comfortable here at all. Cy, his young sidekick, was a lot smoother.

"It's parameters, Mr. Smiley, sir. On a deal like this, you get some areas, they overlap entirely." Cy's voice was a little too high for his size.

"Cy and Sol have hunted with us before, George," Martello said, offering yet further reassurance. "Cy and Sol are family—take my word for it. Langley cuts Enforcement in, Enforcement cuts Langley in. That's the way it goes. Right, Sol?"

"Right," said Sol.

If they don't go to bed together soon, thought Guillam, they just *may* claw each other's eyes out instead. He glanced at Smiley and saw that he too was conscious of the strained atmosphere. He sat like his own effigy, a hand on each knee, eyes almost closed as usual, and he seemed to be willing himself into invisibility while the explanation was acted out for him.

"Maybe we should all just get ourselves up to date on the latest details first," Martello now suggested, as if he were inviting everyone to wash.

First before what? Guillam wondered.

One of the quiet men used the work name Murphy. Murphy was so fair he was nearly albino. Taking a folder from the rosewood table, Murphy began reading from it aloud with great respect in his voice. He held each page singly between his clean fingers.

"Sir, Monday subject flew to Bangkok with Cathay Pacific Airlines, flight details given, and was picked up at the airport by Tan Lee, our reference given, in his personal limousine. They proceeded directly to the Airsea permanent suite at the Hotel Erawan." He glanced at Sol. "Tan is managing director of Asian Rice & General, sir, that's Airsea's Bangkok subsidiary, file references appended. They spent three hours in the suite and—"

"Ah, Murphy," said Martello, interrupting.

"Sir?"

"All that 'reference given,' 'reference appended.' Leave that out, will you? We all know we have files on these guys. Right?"

"Right, sir."

"Ko alone?" Sol demanded.

"Sir, Ko took his manager Tiu along with him. Tiu goes with him most everywhere."

Here, chancing to look at Smiley again, Guillam intercepted an enquiring glance from him directed at Martello. Guillam had a notion he was thinking of the girl—had *she* gone, too?—but Martello's indulgent smile didn't waver, and after a moment Smiley seemed to accept this, and resumed his attentive pose.

Sol meanwhile had turned to his assistant and the two of them had a brief private exchange.

"Why the hell doesn't somebody bug the damn hotel suite, Cy? What's holding everyone up?"

"We already suggested that to Bangkok, Sol, but they've got problems with the party walls—they've got no proper cavities or something."

"Those Bangkok clowns are drowsy with too much ass. That the same Tan we tried to nail last year for heroin?"

"No, that was Tan *Ha*, Sol. This one's Tan *Lee*. They have a lot of Tans out there. Tan Lee's just a front man. He plays link to Fatty Hong in Chiang Mai. It's Hong who has the connections to the growers and the big brokers."

"Somebody ought to go out and shoot that bastard," Sol said. Which bastard wasn't quite clear.

Martello nodded at pale Murphy to go on.

"Sir, the three men then drove down to Bangkok port—that's Ko and Tan Lee and Tiu, sir—and they looked at twenty or thirty small coasters tied up along the bank. Then they drove back to Bangkok airport and subject flew to Manila, Philippines, for a cement conference at the Hotel Eden and Bali."

"Tiu didn't go to Manila?" Martello asked, buying time.

"No, sir. Flew home," Murphy replied, and once more Smiley glanced at Martello.

"Cement, my ass," Sol exclaimed. "Those the boats that do the run up to Hong Kong, Murphy?"

"Yes, sir."

"We know those boats," expostulated Sol. "We've been going for those boats for years. Right, Cy?"

"Right."

Sol had rounded on Martello as if he were personally to blame: "They leave harbour clean. They don't take the stuff aboard till they're at sea. Nobody knows which boat will carry, not even the captain of the selected vessel, until the launch pulls alongside, gives them the dope. When they hit Hong Kong waters, they drop the dope overboard with markers and the junks scoop it in." He spoke slowly, as if speaking hurt him, forcing each word out hoarsely. "We've been screaming at the Brits for years to shake those junks out, but the bastards are all on the take."

"That's all we have, sir," said Murphy, and put down his report.

They were back to the awkward pauses. A pretty girl, armed with a tray of coffee and biscuits, provided a temporary reprieve, but when she left the silence was worse.

"Why don't you just tell him?" Sol snapped finally. "Otherwise maybe I will."

Which was when, as Martello would have said, they finally got down to the nitty-gritty.

Martello's manner became both grave and confiding, a family solicitor reading a will to the heirs. "George, ah, at our request Enforcement here took a kind of a second look at the background and the record of the missing pilot Ricardo, and as we half surmised, they've dug up a fair quantity of material which till now has not come to light as it should have done, owing to various factors. There's no profit, in my view, to pointing the finger at anyone, and besides Ed Ristow is a sick man. Let's just agree that, however it happened, the Ricardo thing fell into a small gap between Enforcement and ourselves. That gap has since closed and we'd like to rectify the information for you."

"Thank you, Marty," said Smiley patiently.

"Seems Ricardo's alive, after all," Sol declared. "Seems like it's a prime snafu."

"A *what?*" Smiley asked sharply, perhaps before the full significance of Sol's statement had sunk in.

Martello was quick to translate: "Error, George. Human error. Happens to all of us. Snafu. Even you, okay?"

Guillam was studying Cy's shoes, which had a rubbery gloss and thick welts. Smiley's eyes had lifted to the side wall, where the benevolent features of President Nixon gazed down encouragingly on the triangular union. Nixon had resigned a good six months ago, but Martello seemed touchingly determined to tend his lamp. Murphy and his mute companion sat as still as confirmands in the presence of the bishop. Only Sol was forever on the move, alternately scratching at his crimped scalp or sucking on his cigarette, like an athletic version of di Salis. He never smiles, thought Guillam extraneously; he's forgotten how.

Martello continued: "Ricardo's death is formally recorded in our files as on or around August twenty-first, nineteen seventy-three, George, correct?"

"Correct," said Smiley.

Martello drew a breath and tilted his head the other way as he read his notes. "However, on September second—couple of weeks after his death, right?—it, ah, seems Ricardo made personal contact with one of the narcotics bureaus in the Asian theatre, then known as B.N.D.D. but primarily the same house, okay? Sol would, ah, prefer not to mention *which* bureau, and I respect that."

The mannerism "ah," Guillam decided, was Martello's way of continuing to talk while he thought.

Martello went on: "Ricardo offered the bureau his services on a sell-and-tell basis regarding an, ah, opium mission he claimed to have received to fly right over the border into, ah, Red China."

A cold hand seemed to seize hold of Guillam's stomach at this moment and stay there. His sense of occasion was all the greater following the slow lead-in through so much unrelated detail. He told Molly afterwards that it was as if "all the threads of the case had suddenly wound themselves together in a single skein" for him; but that was hindsight and he was boasting a little. Nevertheless the shock—after all the tiptoeing and the speculation, and the paper-chases—the plain shock of being almost physically projected into the Chinese mainland: that certainly was real, and required no exaggeration.

Martello was doing his worthy-solicitor act again.

"George, I have to fill you in on, ah, a little of the family background here. During the Laos thing the Company used a few of the northern hill tribes for combat purposes—maybe you knew that. Right up there in Burma—know those parts, the Shans? Volunteers, follow me? Lot of those tribes were one-crop communities, ah, opium communities, and in the interests of the war there, the Company had to, ah—well, turn a blind eye to what we couldn't change, follow me? These good people have to live and many knew no better and saw nothing wrong in, ah, growing that crop. Follow me?"

"Jesus Christ," said Sol under his breath. "Hear that, Cy?"

"I heard, Sol."

Smiley said he followed.

"This policy, conducted, ah, by the Company, caused a very brief and very temporary rift between the Company on the one side and the, ah, Enforcement people here, formerly the Bureau of Narcotics. Because—well, while Sol's boys were out to, well, ah, suppress the abuse of drugs, and quite rightly and, ah, ride down the shipments, which is their job, George, and their duty, it was in the Company's best interest—in the best interest of the war, that is—at this point in time, you follow, George—to, well, ah, turn a blind eye."

"Company played godfather to the hill tribes," Sol growled. "Menfolk were all out fighting the war, Company people flew up to the villages, pushed their poppy crops, screwed their women, and flew their dope."

Martello was not so easily thrown. "Well, we think that's overstating things a little, Sol, but the, ah, rift was there and that's the point as far as our friend George is concerned. Ricardo—well, he's a tough cookie. He flew a lot of missions for the Company in Laos, and when the war ended, the Company resettled him and kissed him off and pulled up the ladder. Nobody messes around with those boys when there's no war for them any more. So, ah, maybe at that time, the, ah, gamekeeper Ricardo turned into the, ah, poacher Ricardo, if you follow me—"

"Well, not *absolutely*," Smiley confessed mildly.

Sol had no such scruples about unpalatable truths. "Long as the war was on," he said, "Ricardo carried dope for the Company to keep the home fires burning up in the hill villages. War ended, he carried it for himself. He had the connects and he knew where the bodies were buried. He went independent, that's all."

"Thank you," said Smiley, and Sol went back to scratching his crew cut.

For the second time, Martello backed toward the story of Ricardo's embarrassing resurrection.

They must have done a deal between them, thought Guillam: Martello does the talking. "Smiley's our contact," Martello would have said. "We play him our way."

On the second of September, 1973, said Martello, an "unnamed narcotics agent in the South East Asian theatre," as he insisted on describing him, "a young man quite new to the field, George," received a nocturnal telephone call at his home from a self-styled Captain Tiny Ricardo, hitherto believed dead, formerly a Laos mercenary with Captain Rocky. Ricardo offered a sizeable quantity of raw opium at standard buy-in rates. In addition to the opium, however, he was offering hot information at what he called a bargain-basement price for a quick sale. That is to say, fifty thousand U.S. dollars in small notes and a West German passport for a one-time journey out. "The unnamed narcotics agent met Ricardo later that night at a parking lot, and they quickly agreed on the sale of the opium."

"You mean he *bought* it?" Smiley asked, most surprised.

"Sol tells me there is a, ah, fixed tariff for such deals—right Sol?—known to everyone in the game, George, and, ah, based upon a percentage of the street value of the haul, right?" Sol growled an affirmative. "The, ah, unnamed agent had a standing authority to buy in at that tariff, and he exercised it. No problem. The agent also, ah, expressed himself willing, subject to higher consent, to supply Ricardo with quick-expiry documentation, George" (he meant, it turned out later, a West German passport with only a few days to run) "in the event, George—an event not yet realised, you follow me—that Ricardo's information prove to be of value, since policy is to encourage informants at all costs. But he made it clear, the agent, that the whole deal—the passport and the payment for the information—was subject to the ratification, and authority, of Sol's people back at headquarters. So he bought the opium, but he held on the information. Right Sol?"

"On the button," Sol growled.

"Sol, ah, maybe you should handle this part," Martello said.

When Sol spoke, he kept the rest of himself still for once. Just his mouth moved. "Our agent asked Ricardo for a teaser so's the information could be evaluated back home. What we call taking it to first base. Ricardo comes up with the story he's been ordered to fly the dope over the border into Red China and bring back an unspecified load in payment. That's what he said.

His teaser. He said he knew who was behind the deal; he said he knew the Mr. Big of all time, but that's what every informant says, and very few do. He said he embarked on his journey for the China mainland, chickened out, and hedge-hopped home over Laos, ducking the radar screens. That's what he said, no more, no less.

"He didn't say where he set out from. He said he owed a favour to the people who sent him, and if they ever found him they'd kick his teeth right up his throat. That's what's in the protocol, word for word. His teeth up his throat. So he was in a hurry, hence the favourable price of fifty grand. He didn't say who the people were, he did not produce one scrap of positive collateral apart from the opium, but he said he had the plane still hidden, a Beechcraft, and he offered to show this plane to our agent at the next occasion of their meeting, subject to there being serious interest back at headquarters," said Sol, and devoted himself to his cigarette. "Opium was a couple of hundred kilos. Good stuff."

Martello deftly took back the ball: "So the unnamed narcotics agent filed his story, George. He took down the teaser and he sent it back to headquarters and he told Ricardo to lie low till he heard back from his people. See you in ten days, maybe fourteen. Here's your opium-money, but for information-money you have to wait a little. There's regulations. Follow me?"

Smiley nodded sympathetically, and Martello nodded back at him while he went on talking: "So here it is. Here's where you get your human error, right? It could be worse, but not much. In our game there's two views of history: conspiracy and fuck-up. Here's where we get the fuck-up, no question at all. Sol's predecessor Ed, now ill, evaluated the material and on the evidence—now, you met him George, Ed Ristow, a good sound guy—and on the evidence available to him, Ed decided, understandably but wrongly, not to proceed. Ricardo wanted fifty grand. Well, for a major haul I understand that's chickenfeed.

But Ricardo, he wanted payment on the nail. A one-time, and out. And Ed—well Ed had responsibilities, and a lot of family trouble, and Ed just didn't see his way to investing that sum of public American money in a character like Ricardo, when no haul is guaranteed, who has all the passes, knows all the fast steps, and is maybe squaring up to take that field agent of Ed's, who is only a young guy, for one hell of a journey. So Ed killed it. No further action. File and forget. All squared away. Buy the opium, but not the story."

Maybe it was a real coronary after all, Guillam reflected, marvelling. But with another part of him he knew it could have happened to himself, and even had: the pedlar who has the big one, and you let it through your fingers.

Rather than waste time in recrimination, Smiley had quietly moved ahead to the remaining possibilities.

"Where is Ricardo now, Marty?" he asked.

"Not known."

His next question was much longer in coming, and was scarcely a question so much as a piece of thinking aloud. "To bring back an 'unspecified load in payment,'" he repeated. "Are there any theories as to what type of load that might have been?"

"We guessed gold. We don't have second vision, any more than you do," Sol said harshly.

Here Smiley simply ceased to take part in the proceedings for a time. His face set, his expression became anxious and, to anyone who knew him, inward, and suddenly it was up to Guillam to keep the ball rolling. To do this, like Smiley, he addressed Martello.

"Ricardo did not give any hint of where he was to deliver his return load?"

"I told you, Pete; that's all we have."

Smiley was still non-combatant. He sat staring mournfully at his folded hands.

Guillam hunted for another question. "And no hint of the anticipated *weight* of the return load, either?" he asked.

"Jesus Christ," said Sol and, misreading Smiley's attitude, slowly shook his head in wonder at the kind of dead-beat company he was obliged to keep.

"But you *are* satisfied it was Ricardo who approached your agent?" Guillam asked, still in there throwing punches.

"One hundred percent," said Sol.

"Sol," Martello suggested, leaning across to him. "Sol, why don't you just give George a blind copy of that original field report? That way he has everything we have."

Sol hesitated, glanced at his sidekick, shrugged, and finally with some reluctance drew a flimsy sheet of India paper from a folder on the table beside him, from which he solemnly tore off the signature.

"Off the record," he growled.

At this point Smiley abruptly revived, and, receiving the report from Sol's hand, studied both sides intently for a while in silence.

"And where, please, is the unnamed narcotics agent who wrote this document?" he enquired finally, looking first at Martello, then at Sol.

Sol scraped his scalp. Cy began shaking his head in disapproval. Whereas Martello's two quiet men showed no curiosity whatever. Pale Murphy continued reading among his notes, and his colleague gazed blankly at the former President.

"Shacked up in a hippie commune north of Katmandu," Sol growled through a gush of cigarette smoke. "Bastard joined the opposition."

Martello's bright end-piece was wonderfully irrelevant: "So, ah, that's the reason, George, why *our* computer has Ricardo dead and buried, George, when the over-all record—on reconsideration by our Enforcement friends—gives no grounds for that, ah, assumption."

So far, it had seemed to Guillam that the boot was all on Martello's foot. Sol's boys had made fools of themselves, he was saying, but the Cousins were nothing if not magnanimous and they were willing to kiss and make up. In the post-coital calm which followed Martello's revelations, this false impression prevailed a little longer.

"So, ah, George, I would say that henceforward, we may count—you, we, Sol here—on the fullest co-operation of all our agencies. I would say there was a very positive side to this. Right, George? Constructive?"

But Smiley in his renewed distraction only lifted his eyebrows and pursed his lips.

"Something on your mind, George?" Martello asked. "I said is there something on your mind?"

"Oh. Thank you. Beechcraft," Smiley said. "Is that a single-engined plane?"

"Jesus," said Sol under his breath.

"Twin, George, twin," said Martello. "Kind of executive runabout kind of thing."

"And the weight of the opium load was four hundred kilos, the report says."

"Just short of half of one ton, George," said Martello at his most solicitous. "A *metric* ton," he added doubtfully, to Smiley's shadowed face. "Not your English ton, George, naturally. Metric."

"And it would be carried where—the opium, I mean?"

"Cabin," said Sol. "Most likely unscrewed the spare seats. Beechcrafts come different shapes. We don't know which this was, because we never got to see it."

Smiley peered once more at the flimsy which he still clutched in his pudgy hand. "Yes," he muttered. "Yes, I suppose they would have done." And with a gold lead-pencil he wrote a small hieroglyphic in the margin before relapsing into his private reverie.

"Well," said Martello brightly. "Guess us worker bees had better get back to our hives and see where that gets us—right, Pete?"

Guillam was half-way to his feet as Sol spoke. Sol had the rare and rather terrible gift of natural rudeness. Nothing had changed in him. He was in no way out of control. This was the way he talked, this was the way he did business, and other ways patently bored him.

"Jesus *Christ*, Martello," he said. "What kind of a game are we playing round here? This is the big one, right? We have put our finger on maybe the most important single narcotics target in the entire South East Asian scene. Okay, so there's liaison. Okay, so we have a hands-off deal with the Brits on Hong Kong. But Thailand's ours, so's the Philippines, so's Taiwan, so's the whole damn theatre, so's the war, and the Brits are on their ass. Four months ago the Brits came in and made their pitch. Great, so we roll it to the Brits. What they been doing all that time? Rubbing soap into their pretty faces. So when do they get to shave, for God's sakes?

"We got money riding on this. We got a whole apparatus standing by, ready to shake out Ko's connections across the hemisphere. We been looking *years* for a guy like this. And we can nail him. We have enough legislation—boy, do we have legislation!—to pin a ten-to-thirty on him and *then* some! We got drugs on him, we got arms, we got embargoed goods, we got the biggest damn load of Red gold we ever saw Moscow hand to one man in our *lives*, and we got the first proof ever, if this guy Ricardo is telling a correct story, of a Moscow-subsidised drug-subversion programme which is ready and willing to carry the battle into Red China in the hopes of doing the same for them as they're already doing for us."

The outburst had woken Smiley like a douche of water. He was sitting forward on the edge of his chair, the narcotics agent's report crumpled in his hand, and he was staring appalled, first at Sol, finally at Martello.

"Marty," he muttered, "oh, my Lord. *No*."

Guillam showed greater presence of mind. At least he threw

in an objection: "You'd have to spread half a ton awfully *thin*, wouldn't you, Sol, to hook eight hundred million Chinese?"

But Sol had no use for humour, or objections either, least of all from some pretty-faced Brit. "And do we go for his jugular?" he demanded, keeping straight on course. "Do we, hell. We pussyfoot. We stand on the sidelines. 'Play it delicate. It's a British ball game. Their territory, their joe, their party.' So we weave, we dance around. We float like a butterfly and sting like one. Jesus, if *we'd* been handling this thing, we'd have had that bastard trussed over a barrel months ago."

Slapping the table with his palm, he used the rhetorical trick of repeating his point in different language. "For the first time ever, we have gotten ourselves a sabre-toothed Soviet Communist corrupter in our sights, pushing dope and screwing up the area and taking Russian money and we can *prove* it!" It was all addressed to Martello; Smiley and Guillam might not have been there at all.

"And you just remember another thing," he advised Martello in conclusion. "We got big people wanting mileage out of this. Impatient people. Influential. People very angry with the dubious part your Company has indirectly played in the supply and merchandising of narcotics to our boys in Vietnam, which is why you cut us in on this in the first place. So maybe you better tell some of those limousine liberals back in Langley, Virginia, it's time for them to shit or get off the pot. Pot in *both senses*," he ended, in a humourless—and to Guillam, pointless—pun.

Smiley had turned so pale that Guillam was genuinely afraid for him; he wondered whether he had had a heart attack, or was going to faint. From where Guillam sat, his cheeks and complexion were suddenly an old man's, and his eyes, as he too addressed Martello only, had an old man's fire.

"However, there is an agreement," Smiley said. "And so long as it stands, I trust that you will stick to it. We have your general declaration that you will abstain from operations in British areas unless our permission has been granted. We have your particular promise that you will leave to us the entire development of this case, outside surveillance and communication, regardless of where the development leads. That was the contract: a complete hands-off in exchange for a complete sight of the product. I take that to mean this: *no* action by Langley and *no* action by any other American agency. I take that to be your absolute word. And I take your word to be still good, and I regard that understanding as irreducible."

"Tell him," said Sol, and walked out, followed by Cy, his sallow Mormon sidekick. At the door Sol turned and jabbed a finger in Smiley's direction.

"You ride our wagon, we tell you where to get off and where to stay topsides," he said.

The Mormon nodded. "Sure do," he said, and smiled at Guillam as if in invitation. On Martello's nod, Murphy and his fellow quiet man followed them out of the room.

Martello was pouring drinks. In his office, the walls were also rosewood—a fake laminate, Guillam noticed, not the real thing—and when Martello pulled a handle he revealed an ice machine that vomited a steady flow of pellets in the shape of rugby balls. He poured three whiskies without asking the others what they wanted. Smiley looked all in. His plump hands were still cupped over the ends of his airport chair, but he was leaning back like a spent boxer between rounds, staring at the ceiling, which was perforated by twinkling lights. Martello set the glasses on the table.

"Thank you, sir," Guillam said. Martello liked a "sir."

"You bet," said Martello.

"Whom else have your headquarters told?" Smiley said, to the stars. "The Revenue Service? The Customs Service? The Mayor of Chicago? Their twelve best friends? Do you realise that not even my masters know we are in collaboration with you? God in heaven."

"Ah, come on now, George. We have politics, same as you. We have promises to keep. Mouths to buy. Enforcement's out for our blood. That dope story's gotten a lot of air time on the Hill. Senators, the House sub-committees, the whole garbage. Kid comes back from the war a screaming junkie, first thing his pa does is write to his congressman. Company doesn't care for all those bad rumours. It likes to have its friends on its own side. That's showbiz, George."

"Could I please just know what the deal is?" Smiley asked. "Could I have it in plain words, at least?"

"Oh, now, there's no *deal*, George. Langley can't deal with what she doesn't own, and this is *your* case, your property, your . . . We fish for him—you do, with a little help from us, maybe—we do our best and then if, ah, we don't come up with anything—why, Enforcement will get in on the act a little and, on a very friendly and controllable basis, try their hand."

"At which point it's open season," Smiley said. "My goodness, what a way to run a case."

When it came to pacification, Martello was a very old hand indeed.

"George. *George.* Suppose they nail Ko. Suppose they fall on him out of the trees next time he leaves the Colony. If Ko's going to languish in Sing Sing on a ten-to-thirty rap—why, we can pick him clean at will. Is that so very terrible, suddenly?"

Yes it bloody well is, thought Guillam, till it suddenly dawned on him, with a quite malignant glee, that Martello himself was not "witting" on the subject of brother Nelson, and that George had kept his best card to his chest.

Smiley was still sitting forward. The ice in his whisky had put a damp frost round the outside of the glass, and for a time he stared at it, watching the tears slide onto the rosewood table.

"So how long have we got on our own?" Smiley asked.

"What's our head start before the narcotics people come barging in?"

"It's not rigid, George. It's not *like* that! It's parameters, like Cy said."

"Three months?"

"That's generous, a little generous."

"Less than three months?"

"Three months, inside of three months, ten to twelve weeks—in that area, George. It's fluid. It's between friends. Three months outside, I would say."

Smiley breathed out in a long slow sigh: "Yesterday we had all the time in the world."

Martello dropped the veil an inch or two. "Sol is not that conscious, George," he said, careful to use Circus jargon rather than his own. "Ah, Sol has blank areas," he said, half by way of admission. "We don't just throw him the whole carcass, know what I mean?"

Martello paused, then said, "Sol goes to first echelon. No further. Believe me."

"And what does first echelon mean?"

"He knows Ko is in funds from Moscow. Knows he pushes opium. That's all."

"Does he know of the girl?"

"Now, she's a case in point, George. The girl. That girl went with him on the trip to Bangkok. Remember Murphy describing the Bangkok trip? She stayed in the hotel suite with him. She flew on with him to Manila. I saw you read me there. I caught your eye. But we had Murphy delete that section of the report. Just for Sol's benefit."

Very slightly, Smiley seemed to revive. "Deal stands, George," Martello assured him munificently. "Nothing's added, nothing's subtracted. You play the fish, we'll help you eat it. Any help along the way, you just have to pick up that green line and holler."

He went so far as to lay a consoling hand on Smiley's shoulder, but sensing that Smiley disliked the gesture, abandoned it rather quickly. "However, if you ever *do* want to pass us the oars—why, we would merely reverse that arrangement and—"

"Steal our thunder and get yourselves thrown off the Colony into the bargain," said Smiley, completing the sentence for him. "I want one more thing made clear. I want it written down. I want it to be the subject of an exchange of letters between us."

"Your party, you choose the games," said Martello expansively.

"My service will play the fish," Smiley insisted, in the same direct tone. "We will also land it, if that is the angling expression. I'm not a sportsman, I'm afraid."

"Land it, beach it, hook it, sure."

Martello's good will, to Guillam's suspicious eye, was tiring a little at the edges.

"I insist on it being *our* operation. Our man. I insist on first rights. To have and to hold, until we see fit to pass him on."

"No problem, George, no problem at all. You take him aboard, he's yours. Soon as you want to share him, call us. It's simple as that."

"I'll send round a written confirmation in the morning."

"Oh, don't bother to do that, George. We have people. We'll have them collect it for you."

"I'll send it round," said Smiley.

Martello stood up. "George, you just got yourself a deal."

"I had a deal already," Smiley said. "Langley broke it."

They shook hands.

The case history has no other moment like this. In the trade it goes under various smart phrases. "The day George reversed the controls," is one—though it took him a good week, and brought Martello's deadline that much nearer. But to Guillam the process had something far more stately about it, far more beautiful than a mere technical retooling. As his understanding of Smiley's intention slowly grew, as he looked on fascinated while Smiley laid down each meticulous line, summoned this or that collaborator, put out a hook here, and took in a cleat there, Guillam had the sensation of watching the turn-round of some large ocean-going vessel as it is coaxed and nosed and gentled into facing back along its own course.

They returned to the Circus without a word spoken. Smiley took the last flight of stairs slowly enough to revive Guillam's fears for his health, so that as soon as he was able he rang the Circus doctor and gave him a run-down of the symptoms as he saw them—only to be told that Smiley had been round to see him a couple of days ago on an unrelated matter and showed every sign of being indestructible.

The throne-room door closed and Fawn, the baby-sitter, once more had his beloved Chief to himself. Smiley's needs, where they filtered through, had the smack of alchemy. Beech-craft aeroplanes: he wished for plans and catalogues, and also—provided they could be obtained unattributably—any details of owners, sales, and purchases in the South East Asian region. Toby Esterhase duly disappeared into the murky thickets of the aircraft sales industry, and soon afterwards Fawn handed to Molly Meakin a daunting heap of back numbers of a journal called *Transport World* with handwritten instructions from Smiley in the traditional green ink of his office to mark down any advertisements for Beechcraft planes which might have caught the eye of a potential buyer during the six-month period before the pilot Ricardo's abortive opium mission into Red China.

Again on Smiley's written orders, Guillam discreetly visited several of di Salis's burrowers and, without the knowledge of their temperamental superior, established that they were still far from putting the finger on Nelson Ko. One old fellow went so far as to suggest that Drake Ko had spoken no less than the truth in his last meeting with old Hibbert, and that brother Nelson was dead indeed. But when Guillam took this news to Smiley he shook his head impatiently and handed him a signal for transmission to Craw, telling him to obtain from his local police source, preferably on a pretext, all recorded details of the travel movements of Ko's manager, Tiu, in and out of mainland China.

Craw's long answer was on Smiley's desk forty-eight hours later, and it appeared to give him a rare moment of pleasure, for he ordered out the duty driver and had himself taken to Hampstead, where he walked alone over the Heath for an hour, through sunlit frost and, according to Fawn, stood gawping at the ruddy squirrels before returning to the throne-room.

"But don't you *see?*" Smiley protested to Guillam, in an equally rare fit of excitement that evening. "Don't you *understand*, Peter?" He shoved Craw's dates under Guillam's nose, actually stubbing his finger on one entry. "Tiu went to Shanghai six weeks before Ricardo's mission. How long did he stay there? Forty-eight hours. Oh, you are a dunce!"

"I'm nothing of the kind," Guillam retorted. "I just don't happen to have a direct line to God, that's all."

In the cellars, cloistered with Millie McCraig, the head listener, Smiley replayed old Hibbert's monologues, scowling occasionally—said Millie—at di Salis's clumsy bullying. Otherwise he read and prowled, and talked to Sam Collins in short, intensive bursts. These encounters, Guillam noticed, cost Smiley a lot of spirit, and his bouts of ill temper—which Lord knows were few enough for a man with Smiley's burdens—always occurred after Sam's departure. And even when they had blown over, he looked more strained and lonely than ever, till he had taken one of his long night walks.

Then on about the fourth day, which in Guillam's life was a crisis day for some reason—probably the argument with Treasury, who resented paying Craw a bonus—Toby Esterhase somehow slipped through the net of both Fawn and Guillam, and gained the throne-room undetected, where he presented Smiley with a bunch of Xeroxed contracts of sale for one brand-new four-seater Beechcraft to the Bangkok firm of Aerosuis & Co., registered in Zurich, details pending. Smiley was particularly jubilant about the fact that there were four seats. The two at the rear were removable, but the pilot's and co-pilot's were fixed. As to the actual sale of the plane, it had been completed on the twentieth of July: a scant month, therefore, before the crazy Ricardo set off to infringe Red China's airspace and then changed his mind.

"Even Peter can make *that* connection," Smiley declared, with heavy skittishness. "Sequence, Peter, sequence, come on!"

"The plane was sold two weeks after Tiu returned from Shanghai," Guillam replied reluctantly.

"And so?" Smiley demanded. "And so? What do we look at next?"

"We ask ourselves who owns the firm of Aerosuis," Guillam snapped, really quite irritated.

"Precisely. Thank you," said Smiley in mock relief. "You restore my faith in you, Peter. Now, then: whom do we discover at the helm of Aerosuis, do you think? The Bangkok representative, no less?"

Guillam glanced at the notes on Smiley's desk, but Smiley was too quick and clapped his hands over them.

"Tiu," Guillam said, actually blushing.

"Hoorah. Yes. Tiu. Well done."

But by the time Smiley sent again for Sam Collins that evening, the shadows had returned to his pendulous face.

Still the lines were thrown out. After his success in the aircraft industry, Toby Esterhase, the pavement artist, was reassigned to the liquor trade and flew to the Western Isles of Scotland, under the guise of a value-added-tax inspector, where he spent three days making a spot check of the books of a house of whisky distillers who specialised in the forward selling of unmatured kegs. He returned—to quote Connie—leering like a successful bigamist.

The multiple climax of all this activity was an extremely long signal to Craw, drafted after a full-dress meeting of the operational directorate—the Golden Oldies, to quote Connie yet again—with Sam Collins added. The meeting followed an extended ways-and-means session with the Cousins, at which Smiley refrained from all mention of the elusive Nelson Ko, but requested certain additional facilities of surveillance and communication in the field.

To his collaborators Smiley explained his plans this way: Till now the operation had been limited to obtaining intelligence about Ko and the ramifications of the Soviet gold seam. Much care had been taken to prevent Ko from becoming aware of the Circus's interest in him.

He then summarised the intelligence they had so far collected: Nelson, Ricardo, Tiu, the Beechcraft, the dates, the inferences, the Swiss-registered aviation company—which, as it now turned out, possessed no premises and no other aircraft. He would prefer, he said, to wait for the positive identification of Nelson, but every operation was a compromise and time, partly thanks to the Cousins, was running out.

He made no mention at all of the girl, and he never once looked at Sam Collins while he delivered his address.

Then he came to what he modestly called "the next phase."

"Our problem is to break the stalemate. There are operations which run better for not being resolved. There are others which are worthless until they *are* resolved, and the Dolphin case is one of these."

He gave a studious frown, and blinked, then whipped off his spectacles and, to the secret delight of everyone, unconsciously subscribed to his own legend by polishing them on the fat end of his tie. "I propose to do this by turning our tactic inside out. In other words, by declaring to Ko our interest in his affairs."

It was Connie, as ever, who put an end to the suitably stunned silence. Her smile was also the fastest—and the most knowing. "He's smoking him out," she whispered to them all in ecstasy. "Same as he did with Bill, the clever hound! Lighting a fire on his doorstep, aren't you, darling, and seeing which way he runs. Oh, *George*, you lovely, lovely man—the best of all my boys, I do declare!"

Smiley's signal to Craw used a different metaphor to describe the plan: one which fieldmen favour. He referred to "shaking Ko's tree," and it was clear from the remainder of the text that, despite the considerable dangers, he proposed to use the broad back of Jerry Westerby to do it.

As a footnote to all this: a couple of days later, Sam Collins vanished. Everyone was very pleased. He ceased to come in and Smiley did not refer to him. His room, when Guillam sneaked in covertly to look it over, contained nothing personal to Sam at all except a couple of unbroken packs of playing-cards and some garish book matches advertising a West End night-club. When he sounded out the housekeepers, they were for once unusually forthcoming: his price was a kiss-off gratuity, they said, and a promise to have his pension rights reconsidered. He had not really had much to sell at all. A flash in the pan, they said, never to reappear. Good riddance.

All the same, Guillam could not rid himself of a certain unease about Sam, which he often conveyed to Molly Meakin over the next few weeks. It was not just about bumping into him at Lacon's office. He was bothered about the business of Smiley's exchange of letters with Martello confirming their oral understanding. Rather than have the Cousins collect it, with the consequent parade of a limousine and even a motor-cycle outrider in Cambridge Circus, Smiley had ordered Guillam to run it round to Grosvenor Square himself, with Fawn baby-sitting. But Guillam was snowed under with work, as it happened, and Sam as usual was spare. So when Sam volunteered to take it for him, Guillam let him, and wished to God he never had. He wished it still, devoutly. Because instead of handing George's letter to Murphy or his faceless running mate, said Fawn, Sam had insisted on going in to Martello personally, and spent more than an hour with him alone.

PART II

Shaking the Tree

13

LIESE

Star Heights was the newest and tallest apartment block in the Midlevels, built on the round, and by night jammed like a huge lighted pencil into the soft darkness of the Peak. A winding causeway led to it, but the only pavement was a line of curbstone six inches wide between the causeway and the cliff. At Star Heights, pedestrians were in bad taste. It was early evening and the social rush hour was nearing its height.

As Jerry edged his way along the curb, the Mercedes and Rolls-Royces brushed against him in their haste to deliver and collect. He carried a bunch of orchids wrapped in tissue: larger than the bunch Craw had presented to Phoebe Wayfarer, smaller than the one Drake Ko had given the dead boy Nelson. These orchids were for nobody. "When you're my size, sport, you have to have a hell of a good reason for whatever you do."

He felt tense but also relieved that the long, long wait was over.

A straight foot-in-the-door operation, Your Grace, Craw had advised him at yesterday's protracted briefing. *Shove your way in there and start pitching and don't stop till you're out the other side.*

A striped awning led to the entrance hall and a perfume of women hung in the air, like a foretaste of his errand. *And just remember Ko owns the building,* Craw had added sourly, as a parting gift. The interior decoration was not quite finished. Plates of marble were missing round the mail-boxes. A fibreglass fish

should have been spewing water into a terrazzo fountain, but
the pipes had not yet been connected and bags of cement were
heaped in the basin.

He headed for the lifts. A glass booth was marked "Reception" and the Chinese porter was watching him from inside it.
Jerry only saw the blur of him. He had been reading when Jerry
arrived, but now he was staring at Jerry, undecided whether to
challenge him, but half reassured by the orchids. A couple of
American matrons in full war-paint arrived and took up a position near him.

"Great flowers," they said, poking in the tissue.

"Super, aren't they? Here, have them. Present! Come on!
Beautiful woman. Naked without them!"

Laughter. The English are a race apart. The porter returned
to his reading and Jerry was authenticated. A lift arrived. A herd
of diplomats, businessmen, and their squaws shuffled into the
lobby, sullen and bejewelled. Jerry ushered the American matrons
ahead of him. Cigar smoke mingled with the scent. Slovenly
canned music hummed forgotten melodies. The matrons pressed
the button for twelve.

"You visiting with the Hammersteins too?" they asked,
still looking at the orchids.

At the fifteenth, Jerry made for the fire stairs. They stank of
cat, and rubbish from the chute. Descending, he met an amah
carrying a nappy bucket. She scowled at him till he greeted her,
then laughed uproariously. He kept going till he reached the
eighth floor where he stepped back into the plush of the residents' landing. He was at the end of a corridor. A small rotunda
gave on to two gold lift doors. There were four flats, each a
quadrant of the circular building, and each with its own corridor. He took up a position in the B corridor with only the flowers to protect him. He was watching the rotunda, his attention
on the mouth of the corridor marked C. The tissue round the
orchids was damp where he'd been clutching it too tight.

"It's a firm weekly date," Craw had assured him. "Every

Monday, flower arrangement at the American Club. Regular as clockwork. She meets a girl-friend there, Nellie Tan, works for Airsea. They take in the flower arrangement and stay for dinner afterwards."

"So where's Ko meanwhile?"

"In Bangkok. Trading."

"Well, let's bloody well hope he stays there."

"Amen, sir. Amen."

With a shriek of new hinges unoiled, the door at his ear was yanked open and a slim young American in a dinner-jacket stepped into the corridor, stopped dead, and stared at Jerry and the orchids. He had blue, steady eyes and he carried a brief-case.

"You looking for me with those things?" he enquired, with a Boston society drawl. He looked rich and assured. Jerry guessed diplomacy or Ivy League banking.

"Well, I don't think so, actually," Jerry confessed, playing the English bloody fool. "Cavendish," he said. Over the American's shoulder Jerry saw the door quietly close on a packed book shelf. "Friend of mine asked me to give these to a Miss Cavendish at 9D. Waltzed off to Manila, left me holding the orchids, sort of thing."

"Wrong floor," said the American, strolling toward the lift. "You want one up. Wrong corridor, too. D's over on the other side. Thattaway."

Jerry stood beside him, pretending to wait for an up lift. The down lift came first, the young American stepped easily into it, and Jerry resumed his post. The door marked C opened; he saw her come out, and turn to double-lock it. Her clothes were everyday. Her hair was long and ash blond but she had tied it in a pony-tail at the nape. She wore a plain halter-neck dress and sandals, and though he couldn't see her face he knew already she was beautiful. She walked to the lift, still not seeing him, and Jerry had the illusion of looking in on her through a window from the street.

There were women in Jerry's world who carried their bodies

as if they were citadels to be stormed only by the bravest, and Jerry had married several; or perhaps they grew that way under his influence. There were women who seemed determined to hate themselves, hunching their backs and locking up their hips. And there were women who had only to walk toward him to bring him a gift. They were the rare ones, and for Jerry at that moment she led the pack.

She had stopped at the gold doors and was watching the lighted numbers. He reached her side as the lift arrived and she still hadn't noticed him. It was packed, as he had hoped it would be. He entered crabwise, intent on the orchids, apologising, grinning, and making a show of holding them high. She had her back to him, and he was standing at her shoulder. It was a strong shoulder, and bare either side of the halter, and Jerry could see small freckles and a down of tiny gold hairs disappearing down her spine. Her face was in profile below him. He peered down at it.

"Lizzie?" he said uncertainly. "Hey, *Lizzie*. It's me, Jerry."

She turned sharply and stared up at him. He wished he could have backed away from her, because he knew her first response would be physical fear of his size, and he was right. He saw it momentarily in her grey eyes, which flickered before holding him in their stare.

"Lizzie *Worthington!*" he declared more confidently. "How's the whisky, remember me? One of your proud investors. Jerry. Chum of Tiny Ricardo's. One fifty-gallon keg with my name on the label. All paid and above-board."

He had kept it quiet on the assumption that he might be raking up a past she was keen to disown. He had kept it so quiet that their fellow passengers heard either "Raindrops Keep Fallin' on My Head" over the Muzak or the grumbling of an elderly Greek who thought he was boxed in.

"Why, of course," she said, and gave a bright, air-hostess smile. "Jerry!" Her voice faded as she pretended to have it on the tip of her tongue: "Jerry—er—" She frowned and looked upward like a repertory actress doing forgetfulness. The lift stopped at the sixth floor.

"Westerby," he said promptly, getting her off the hook. "Newshound. You put the bite on me in the Constellation bar. I wanted a spot of loving comfort and all I got was a keg of whisky."

Somebody next to him laughed.

"Of *course!* Jerry *darling!* How could I possibly . . . So, I mean, what are you doing in Hong Kong? My *God!*"

"Usual beat. Fire and pestilence, famine. How about you? Retired, I should think, with your sales methods. Never had my arm twisted so thoroughly in my life."

She laughed delightedly. The doors had opened at the third floor. An old woman shuffled in on two walking-sticks.

Lizzie Worthington sold in all a cool fifty-five kegs of the blushful Hippocrene, Your Grace, old Craw had said. *Every one of them to a male buyer and a fair number of them, according to my advisers, with service thrown in. Gives a new meaning to the term "good measure," I venture to suggest.*

They had reached the ground floor. She got out first and he walked beside her. Through the main doors he saw her red sports car, with its roof up, waiting in the bay, jammed among the glistening limousines. She must have phoned down and ordered them to have it ready, he thought; if Ko owns the building, he'll make damn sure she gets the treatment. She was heading for the porter's window. As they crossed the hall, she went on chattering, pivoting to talk to him, one arm held wide of her body, palm upward, like a fashion model. He must have asked her how she liked Hong Kong, though he couldn't remember doing so.

"I adore it, Jerry, I simply *adore* it. Vientiane seems—oh, centuries away. You know Ric died?" She threw this in heroically, as if she and death weren't strangers to each other. "After Ric, I thought I'd never care for anywhere again. I was completely wrong, Jerry. Hong Kong *has* to be the most fun city in the world. Lawrence, darling, I'm sailing my red submarine. It's hen night at the club."

Lawrence was the porter, and the key to her car dangled from a large silver horseshoe which reminded Jerry of Happy Valley races.

"Thank you, Lawrence," she said sweetly, and gave him a smile that would last him all night. "The *people* here are so marvellous, Jerry," she confided to him in a stage whisper as they moved toward the main entrance. "To *think* what we used to say about the Chinese in Laos! Yet here they're just the most marvellous and outgoing and inventive people ever." She had slipped into a stateless foreign accent, he noticed. Must have picked it up from Ricardo and stuck to it for chic. "People think to themselves: Hong Kong—fabulous shopping—tax-free cameras—restaurants. But honestly, Jerry, when you get under the surface, and meet the *true* Hong Kong, and the *people*—it's got everything you could possibly want from life. Don't you adore my new car?"

"So that's how you spend the whisky profits."

He held out his open palm, and she dropped the keys into it so that he could unlock the door for her. Still in dumb show, he gave her the orchids to hold. Behind the black Peak a full moon, not yet risen, glowed like a forest fire. She climbed in, he handed her the keys, and this time he felt the contact of her hand and remembered Happy Valley again, and Ko's kiss as they drove away.

"Mind if I ride on the back?" he asked.

She laughed and pushed open the passenger door for him. "Where are you going with those gorgeous orchids, anyway?"

She started the engine, but Jerry gently switched it off again, so that she stared at him in surprise.

"Sport," he said quietly. "I cannot tell a lie. I'm a viper in your nest, and before you drive me anywhere, you'd better fasten your seat-belt and hear the grisly truth."

He had chosen this moment carefully, because he didn't want her to feel threatened. She was in the driving seat of her own car, under the lighted awning of her own apartment block, within sixty feet of Lawrence, the porter, and he was playing the humble sinner in order to increase her sense of security.

"Our chance reunion was not entire chance. That's point one. Point two, not to put too fine an edge on it, my paper told me to run you to earth and besiege you with many searching questions regarding your late chum Ricardo."

She was still watching him, still waiting. On the point of her chin she had two small parallel scars like claw marks, quite deep. He wondered who had made them, and what with.

"But Ricardo's dead," she said, much too early.

"Sure," said Jerry consolingly. "No question. However, the comic is in possession of what they're pleased to call a hot tip that he's alive after all, and it's my job to humour them."

"But that's absolutely absurd!"

"Agreed. Totally. They're out of their minds. The consolation prize is two dozen well-thumbed orchids and the best dinner in town."

Turning away from him, she gazed through the windscreen, her face in the full glare of the overhead lamp, and Jerry wondered what it must be like to inhabit such a beautiful body, living up to it twenty-four hours a day. Her grey eyes opened a little wider, and he had a shrewd suspicion that he was supposed to notice the tears brimming and the way her hands grasped the steering-wheel for support.

"Forgive me," she murmured. "It's just—when you love a man—give everything up for him—and he dies—then one evening, out of the blue—"

"Sure," said Jerry. "I'm sorry."

She started the engine. "Why should you be sorry? If he's alive, that's bonus. If he's dead, nothing's changed. We're on a pound to nothing." She laughed. "Ric always said he was indestructible."

It's like stealing from a blind beggar, he thought. She shouldn't be let loose.

She drove well but stiffly, and he guessed—because she

inspired guesswork—that she had only recently passed her test and that the car was her prize for doing so. It was the calmest night in the world. As they sank into the city, the harbour lay like a perfect mirror at the centre of the jewel box. They talked places. Jerry suggested the Peninsula, but she shook her head.

"Okay. Let's go get a drink first," he said. "Come on, let's blow the walls out!"

To his surprise, she reached across and gave his hand a squeeze. Then he remembered Craw: she did that to everyone, he'd said.

She was off the leash for a night: he had that overwhelming sensation. He remembered taking his daughter out from school when she was young, and how they had to do lots of different things in order to make the afternoon longer.

At a dark disco on Kowloon-side, they drank Rémy Martin with ice and soda. He guessed it was Ko's drink and she had picked up the habit to keep him company. It was early and there were maybe a dozen people, no more. The music was loud and they had to yell to hear each other, but she didn't mention Ricardo. She preferred the music, and listening with her head back. Sometimes she held his hand, and once put her head on his shoulder, and once she blew him a distracted kiss and drifted onto the floor to perform a slow, solitary dance, eyes closed, slightly smiling. The men ignored their own girls and undressed her with their eyes, and the Chinese waiters brought fresh ashtrays every three minutes so that they could look down her dress.

After two drinks and half an hour, she announced a passion for the Duke and the big-band sound, so they raced back to the Island to a place Jerry knew where a live Filipino band gave a fair rendering of Ellington. Cat Anderson was the best thing since sliced bread, she said. Had he heard Armstrong and Ellington together? Weren't they just the greatest? More Rémy Martin while she sang "Mood Indigo" to him.

"Did Ricardo dance?" Jerry asked.

"Did he dance?" she replied softly as she tapped her foot and lightly clicked her fingers to the rhythm.

"Thought Ricardo had a limp," Jerry objected.

"*That* never stopped him," she said, still absorbed by the music. "I'll never go back to him, you understand. Never. That chapter's closed. And how."

"How'd he pick it up?"

"Dancing?"

"The limp."

With her finger curled round an imaginary trigger, she fired a shot into the air.

"It was either the war or an angry husband," she said. He made her repeat it, her lips close to his ear.

She knew a new Japanese restaurant where they served fabulous Kobe beef.

"Tell me how you got those scars," he asked as they were driving there. He touched his own chin. "The left and the right. What did it?"

"Oh, hunting poor innocent foxes," she said with a light smile. "My dear papa was horse mad. He still is, I'm afraid."

"Where does he live?"

"Daddy? Oh, the usual tumbledown schloss in Shropshire. *Miles* too big but they won't move. No staff, no money, ice cold three-quarters of the year. Mummy can't even boil an egg."

He was still reeling when she remembered a bar where they gave heavenly curry canapés, so they drove around until they found it and she kissed the barman. There was no music, but for some reason he heard himself telling her all about the orphan, till he came to the reasons for their breakup, which he deliberately fogged over.

"Ah, but Jerry, darling," she said sagely. "With twenty-five years between you and her, what else can you expect?"

And with nineteen years and a Chinese wife between you and Drake Ko, what can *you* expect? he thought.

They left—more kisses for the barman—and Jerry was not

so intoxicated by her company, or by the brandy-sodas, to miss
the point that she made a phone call, allegedly to cancel her
date, that the call took a long time, and that when she returned
from it she looked rather solemn. In the car again, he caught
her eye and thought he read a shadow of mistrust.

"Jerry?"

"Yes?"

She shook her head, laughed, ran her palm along his face,
then kissed him. "It's fun," she said.

He guessed she was wondering whether, if she had really
sold him that keg of unbranded whisky, she would so thoroughly have forgotten him. He guessed she was also wondering
whether, in order to sell him the keg, she had thrown in any
fringe benefits of the sort Craw had so coarsely referred to. But
that was her problem, he reckoned. Had been from the start.

In the Japanese restaurant they were given the corner table,
thanks to Lizzie's smile and other attributes. She sat looking into
the room, and he sat looking at Lizzie, which was fine with Jerry
but would have given Sarratt the bends. By the candle-light he
saw her face very clearly and was conscious for the first time of the
signs of wear: not just the claw marks on her chin, but her lines of
travel, and of strain, which to Jerry had a determined quality
about them, like honourable scars from all the battles against her
bad luck and her bad judgment. She wore a gold bracelet, new, and
a bashed tin watch with a Walt Disney dial on it and scratched
gloved hands pointing to the numerals. Her loyalty to the old
watch impressed him and he wanted to know who gave it to her.

"Daddy," she said distractedly.

A mirror was let into the ceiling above them, and he could
see her gold hair and the swell of her breasts among the scalps
of other diners, and the gold-dust of the hairs on her back.
When he tried to hit her with Ricardo, she turned guarded. It
should have occurred to Jerry, but it didn't, that her attitude
had changed since she made the phone call.

"What guarantee do I have that you will keep my name out of your paper?" she asked.

"Just my promise."

"But if your editor knows I was Ricardo's girl, what's to stop him putting it in for himself?"

"Ricardo had lots of girls. You know that. They came in all shapes and sizes and ran concurrently."

"There was only one of *me*," she said firmly, and he saw her glance toward the door; but then she had that habit anyway, wherever she was, of looking round the room all the time for someone who wasn't there. He let her keep the initiative.

"You said your paper had a hot tip," she said. "What do they mean by that?"

He had boned up his answer to this with Craw. It was one they had actually rehearsed. He delivered it therefore with force if not conviction.

"Ric's crash was eighteen months ago in the hills near Pailin on the Thai-Cambodian border. That's the official line. No one found a body, no one found wreckage, and there's talk he was doing an opium run. The insurance company never paid up and Indocharter never sued them. Why not? Ricardo had an exclusive contract to fly for them. For that matter, why doesn't someone sue Indocharter? You, for instance. You were his woman. Why not go for damages?"

"That is a *very* vulgar suggestion," she said, in her duchess voice.

"Beyond that, there's rumours he's been seen recently around the haunts a little. He's grown a beard but he can't cure the limp, they say, nor his habit of sinking a bottle of Scotch a day, nor— saving your presence—chasing after everything that wears a skirt within a five-mile radius of wherever he happens to be standing."

She was forming up to argue, but he gave her the rest while he was about it. "Head porter at the Rincome Hotel, Chiang Mai, confirmed the identification from a photograph, beard notwithstanding. All right, us round-eyes all look the same to them. Nevertheless he was pretty sure. Then only last month a fifteen-year-old girl in Bangkok, particulars to hand, took her little bundle to the Mexican Consulate and named Ricardo as the lucky father. I don't believe in eighteen-month pregnancies and I assume you don't. And don't look at *me* like that, sport. It's not my idea, is it?"

It's London's, he might have added: as neat a blend of fact and fiction as ever shook a tree. But she was actually looking past him, at the door again.

"Another thing I'm to ask you about is the whisky racket," he said.

"It was *not* a racket, Jerry. It was a perfectly valid business enterprise!"

"Sport. *You* were straight as a die. No breath of scandal attaches. Etcetera. But if *Ric* cut a few too many corners, now, that *would* be a reason for doing the old disappearing act, wouldn't it?"

He seriously regretted her discomfort. It ran quite contrary to the feelings he would have wished for her in other circumstances. He watched her and he knew that argument was something she always lost; it planted a hopelessness in her, a resignation to defeat.

"That wasn't Ric's way," she said finally, without any conviction at all. "He liked to be the big man around town. It wasn't his way to run."

"For example," Jerry continued—as her head fell forward in submission—"were we to prove that your Ric, in flogging *his* kegs, had stuck to the cash and instead of passing it back to the distillery—pure hypothesis, no shred of evidence—then in that case—"

"By the time our partnership was wound up, *every* investor had a certificated contract with interest from the date of purchase. Every penny we borrowed was duly accounted for."

Till now, it all had been footwork. Now he saw his goal looming, and he made for it fast.

"Not *duly*, sport," he corrected her, while she continued to stare down at her uneaten food. "Not duly at all. Those settlements were made six months *after* the due date. *Un*duly. That's a very eloquent point, in my view. Question: who bailed Ric out? According to *our* information, the whole world was going for him. The distillers, the creditors, the law, the local community— every one of them had the knife sharpened for him. Till one day—*bingo!* Writs withdrawn, shades of the prison bars recede. How? Ric was on his knees. Who's the mystery angel? Who bought his debts?"

She had lifted her head while he was speaking and now to his astonishment a radiant smile suddenly lit her face, and the next thing he knew, she was waving over his shoulder at someone he couldn't see till he looked into the ceiling mirror and caught the glitter of an electric-blue suit and a full head of black hair well greased; and between the two, a foreshortened chubby Chinese face set on a pair of powerful shoulders, and two curled hands held out in a fighter's greeting while Lizzie piped him aboard.

"Mr. Tiu! What a marvellous coincidence. Come on over! Try the beef. It's *gorgeous*. Mr. Tiu, this is Jerry, from Fleet Street. Jerry, this is a very good friend of mine who helps look after me. He's interviewing me, Mr. Tiu! Me! It's most exciting. All about Vientiane and a poor pilot I tried to help a hundred years ago. Jerry knows everything about me. He's a miracle!"

"We met," said Jerry, with a broad grin.

"Sure," said Tiu, equally happy, and as he spoke, Jerry once more caught the familiar smell of almonds and rose-water mixed, the one his early wife had so much liked. "Sure," Tiu repeated. "You the horse-writer, okay?"

"Okay," Jerry agreed, stretching his smile to breaking-point.

Then of course Jerry's vision of the world turned several somersaults, and he had a whole lot of business to worry about: such as appearing to be as tickled as everybody else by the amazing good luck of Tiu's appearance; such as shaking hands, which was like a mutual promise of future settlement; such as drawing up a chair and calling for drinks, beef and chopsticks, and all the rest. But the thing that stuck in his mind even while he did all this—the memory that lodged there as permanently as later events allowed—had little to do with Tiu or his hasty arrival; or not directly. It was the expression on Lizzie's face as she first caught sight of him, for the fraction of a second before the lines of courage drew the gay smile out of her. It explained to him as nothing else could have done the paradoxes that comprised her: her prisoner's dreams, her borrowed personalities which were like disguises in which she could momentarily escape her destiny. Of course she had summoned Tiu: she had no choice. It amazed him that neither the Circus nor he himself had predicted it. The Ricardo story, whatever the truth of it, was far too hot for her to handle by herself. But the expression in her grey eyes as Tiu entered the restaurant was not relief, but resignation: the doors had slammed on her again; the fun was over. "We're like those bloody glow-worms," the orphan had whispered to him once, raging about her childhood, "carting the bloody fire round on our backs."

Operationally of course, as Jerry recognised immediately, Tiu's appearance was a gift from the gods. If information was to be fed back to Ko, then Tiu was an infinitely more impressive channel for it than Lizzie Worthington could ever hope to be.

She had finished kissing Tiu, so she handed him to Jerry.

"Mr. Tiu, you're my witness," she declared, making a great conspiracy of it. "You must remember every word I say. Jerry, go straight on *just* as if he wasn't here. I mean Mr. Tiu's as silent as the *grave*, aren't you. *Darling*," she said, and kissed him again. "It's *so* exciting," she repeated, and they all settled down for a friendly chat.

"So what you looking for, Mr. Wessby?" Tiu enquired, perfectly affably, while he tucked into his beef. "You a horse-writer, why you bother pretty girls, okay?"

"Good point, sport! Good point! Horses much safer, right?"
They all laughed richly, avoiding one another's eyes.

The waiter put a half-bottle of Black Label Scotch in front of
Tiu. He unscrewed it and sniffed at it critically before pouring.

"He's looking for *Ricardo*, Mr. Tiu. Don't you understand?
He thinks Ricardo is *alive*. Isn't that wonderful? I mean I have
no vestige of feeling for him now, naturally, but it would be
lovely to have him back with us. Think of the party we could
give!"

"Liese tell you that?" Tiu asked, pouring himself two
inches of Scotch. "She tell you Ricardo still around?"

"Who, old boy? Didn't get you. Didn't get the first name."

Tiu jabbed a chopstick at Lizzie. "She tell you he's alive?
This pilot guy? This Ricardo? Liese tell you that?"

"I never reveal my sources, Mr. Tiu," said Jerry, just as archly.
"That's a journalist's way of saying he's made something up," he
explained.

"A horse-writer's way, okay?"

"That's it, that's it!"

Again Tiu laughed, and this time Lizzie laughed even louder.
She was slipping out of control again. Maybe it's the drink,
thought Jerry, or maybe she goes for the stronger stuff and the
drink has stoked the fire. And if he calls me horse-writer again,
maybe I'll take defensive action.

Lizzie again, a party-piece: "Oh, Mr. Tiu, Ricardo was so
lucky! Think who he had. Indocharter—me—everyone. There I
was, working for this little airline—some dear Chinese people
Daddy knew—and Ricardo, like all the pilots, was a shocking
businessman—got into the most *frightful* debt." With a wave of
her hand, she brought Jerry into the act. "My God, he even tried
to involve *me* in one of his schemes, can you imagine!—selling
whisky, if you please—and suddenly my lovely, dotty Chinese
friends decided they needed another charter pilot. They settled
his debts, put him on a salary, they gave him an old banger to
fly—"

Jerry now took the first of several irrevocable steps. "When Ricardo went missing, he wasn't flying an old banger, sport. He was flying a brand-new Beechcraft," he corrected her deliberately. "Indocharter never had a Beechcraft to their name. They haven't now. My editor's checked it right through—don't ask me how. Indocharter never hired one, never leased one, never crashed one."

Tiu gave another jolly whoop of laughter.

Tiu is a very cool bishop, Your Eminence, Craw had warned. *Ran Monsignor Ko's San Francisco diocese with exemplary efficiency for five years, and the worst the narcotics artists could hang on him was washing his Rolls-Royce on a saint's day.*

"Hey, Mr. Wessby, maybe Liese stole them one!" Tiu cried in his half-American accent. "Maybe she go out nights steal aircraft from other airlines!"

"Mr. Tiu, that's very naughty of you!" Lizzie declared.

"How you like that, horse-writer? How you like?"

The merriment at their table was by now so loud for three people that several heads turned to peer at them. Jerry saw them in the mirrors, where he half expected to spot Ko himself, with his crooked boat people's walk, swaying toward them through the wicker doorway. Lizzie plunged wildly on.

"Oh, it was a complete fairy tale! One moment Ric can scarcely eat, *and* owed all of us money—Charlie's savings, my allowance from Daddy—Ric practically ruined us all. Of course everyone's money just naturally belonged to him—and the next thing we knew, Ric had work, he was in the clear, life was a ball again. All those other poor pilots grounded, and Ric and Charlie flying all over the place like—"

"Like blue-arsed flies," Jerry suggested, at which Tiu was so doubled with hilarity that he was obliged to hold on to Jerry's shoulder to keep himself afloat—while Jerry had the uncomfortable feeling of being physically measured for the knife.

"Hey listen, that pretty good! Blue-arse fly! I like that! You pretty funny fellow, horse-writer!"

It was at this point, under the pressure of Tiu's cheerful insults, that Jerry used very good footwork indeed. Afterwards, Craw said the best. He ignored Tiu entirely and picked up that other name which Lizzie had let slip:

"Yeah, whatever happened to old Charlie, by the way?" he asked, not having the least idea who Charlie was. "What became of him after Ric did his disappearing number? Don't tell me he went down with his ship as well?"

Once more she floated away on a fresh wave of narrative, and Tiu patently enjoyed everything he heard, chuckling and nodding while he ate.

He's here to find out the score, Jerry thought. He's much too sharp to put the brakes on Lizzie. It's me he's worried about, not her.

"Oh, Charlie's indestructible, *completely* immortal," Lizzie declared, and once more selected Tiu as her foil: "Charlie *Marshall*, Mr. Tiu," she explained. "Oh, you should meet him, a fantastic half-Chinese, all skin and bones and opium and a completely brilliant pilot. His father's old Kuomintang, a terrific brigand, and lives up in the Shans. His mother was some poor Corsican girl—you know how the Corsicans flocked into Indo-China—but really he is an utterly fantastic character. Do you know why he calls himself Marshall? His father wouldn't give him his own name. So what does Charlie do? Gives himself the highest rank in the army instead. 'My dad's a general but I'm a marshal,' he'd say. Isn't that cute? And *far* better than *admiral*, I mean."

"Super," Jerry agreed. "Marvellous. Charlie's a prince."

"Liese some pretty utterly fantastic character herself, Mr. Wessby," Tiu remarked handsomely, so on Jerry's insistence they drank to that—to her fantastic character.

"Hey, what's all this 'Liese' thing, actually?" Jerry asked as he put down his glass. "You're *Lizzie*. Who's this Liese? Mr. Tiu, I don't know the lady. Why am I left out of the joke?"

Here Lizzie did definitely turn to Tiu for guidance, but

Tiu had ordered himself some raw fish and was eating it rapidly and with total devotion.

"Some horse-writer ask pretty damn questions," he remarked, through a full mouth.

"New town, new leaf, new name," Lizzie said finally, with an unconvincing smile. "I wanted a change, so I chose a new name. Some girls get a new hair-do, I get a new name."

"Got a new fellow to go with it?" Jerry asked.

She shook her head, eyes down, while Tiu let out a whoop of laughter.

"What's happened to this town, Mr. Tiu?" Jerry demanded, instinctively covering for her. "Chaps all gone blind or something? Crikey, I'd cross continents for her, wouldn't you? Whatever she calls herself, right?"

"Me, I go from Kowloon-side to Hong Kong-side, no further!" said Tiu, hugely entertained by his own wit. "Or maybe I stay Kowloon-side and call her up, tell her come over see me one hour!" At which Lizzie's eyes stayed down and Jerry thought it would be quite fun, on another occasion when they all had more time, to break Tiu's fat neck in several places.

Unfortunately, however, breaking Tiu's neck was not at present on Craw's shopping list.

The money, Craw had said. *When the moment's right, open up one end of the gold seam and that's your grand finale.*

So he started her off about Indocharter. Who were they, what was it like to work for them? She rose to it so fast he began to wonder whether she enjoyed this knife-edge existence more than he had realised.

"Oh, it was a fabulous adventure, Jerry! You can't begin to imagine it, I assure you." Ric's multinational accent again. "'Airline'—just the word is so absurd. I mean don't for a minute think of your bright new planes and your glamorous hostesses and champagne and caviar or anything like that *at all*. This was work. This was pioneering, which is what drew me in the first place. I could *perfectly* well have simply lived off Daddy, or my aunts. I mean mercifully I'm totally independent, but *who* can resist challenge? All we started out with was a couple of dreadful old DC-3s *literally* stuck together with string and chewing-gum. We even had to *buy* the safety certificates. Nobody would issue them. After that we flew literally anything. Hondas, vegetables, pigs—oh, the boys had such a story about those poor pigs. They broke loose, Jerry. They came into the first class, even into the cabin, imagine!"

"Like passengers," Tiu explained, with his mouth full. "She fly first-class pigs, okay, Mr. Wessby?"

"What routes?" Jerry asked when they had recovered from their laughter.

"You can see how he interrogates me, Mr. Tiu? I never knew I was so glamorous! So mysterious! We flew everywhere, Jerry. Bangkok, Cambodia sometimes. Battambang, Phnom Penh, Kampong Cham when it was open. Everywhere. Awful places."

"And who were your customers? Traders, taxi jobs—who were the regulars?"

"Absolutely anyone we could get. Anyone who could pay. Preferably in advance, naturally."

Pausing from his Kobe beef, Tiu felt inspired to offer social chit-chat.

"Your father some big lord, okay, Mr. Wessby?"

"More or less," said Jerry.

"Lords some pretty rich fellows. Why you gotta be a horse-writer, okay?"

Ignoring Tiu entirely, Jerry played his trump card and waited for the ceiling mirror to crash on to their table.

"There's a story that you people had some local Russian Embassy link," he said easily, straight at Lizzie. "That ring a bell at all, sport? Any Reds under your bed at all, if I may ask?"

Having resumed his eating, Tiu was taking care of his rice, holding the bowl under his chin and shovelling it non-stop; but this time, significantly, Lizzie didn't give him half a glance.

"*Russians?*" she repeated, puzzled. "Why on earth should Russians come to *us?* They had regular Aeroflot flights in and out of Vientiane every week."

Though he would have sworn, then or later, that she was telling the truth, Jerry acted not quite satisfied. "Not even *local* runs?" he insisted. "Fetching and carrying, courier service, or whatever?"

"Never. How could we? Besides, the Chinese simply *loathe* the Russians, don't they, Mr. Tiu?"

"Russians pretty bad people, Mr. Wessby," Tiu agreed. "They stink pretty bad."

So do you, thought Jerry, catching a fresh waft of that early wife's body-water.

Jerry laughed at his own absurdity. "I've got editors like other people have stomach-aches," he protested. "He's *convinced* we can do a Red-under-the-bed job. 'Ricardo's Soviet paymasters' . . . 'Did Ricardo take a dive for the Kremlin?'"

"Paymaster?" Lizzie repeated, utterly mystified. "Ric never received a penny from the Russians. What *are* they talking about?"

Jerry again: "But Indocharter did, didn't they? Unless my lords and masters have been sold a total pup, which I suspect they have been, as usual. They drew money from the local Russian Embassy and piped it down to Hong Kong in U.S. dollars. That's *London's* story and they're sticking to it."

"They're mad," she said confidently. "I've never heard such nonsense."

To Jerry she seemed even relieved that the conversation had taken this improbable course. Ricardo alive—there she was drifting through a minefield. Ko as her lover—that secret was Ko's or Tiu's to dispense, not hers. But Russian money—Jerry was as certain as he dared be that she knew nothing and feared nothing about it.

He offered to ride back with her to Star Heights, but Mr. Tiu lived that way, she said.

"See you again pretty soon, Mr. Wessby," Tiu promised.

"Look forward to it, sport," said Jerry.

"You wanna stick to horse-writing, hear that? In my opinion, you get more money that way, Mr. Wessby, okay?" There was no menace in his voice or in the friendly way he patted Jerry's upper arm. Tiu did not even speak as if he expected his advice to be taken as any more than a confidence between friends.

Then suddenly it was over. Lizzie kissed the headwaiter, but not Jerry. She sent Jerry, not Tiu, for her coat, so that she wouldn't be alone with him. She scarcely looked at him as she said goodbye.

Dealing with beautiful women, Your Grace, Craw had warned, *is like dealing with known criminals, and the lady you are about to solicit undoubtedly falls within that category.*

Wandering home through the moonlit streets—the long trek, beggars, eyes in doorways notwithstanding—Jerry subjected Craw's dictum to closer scrutiny. On "criminal" he really couldn't rule at all: "criminal" seemed a pretty variable sort of standard at the best of times, and neither the Circus nor its agents existed to uphold some parochial concept of the law. Craw had told him that in slump periods Ricardo had made her carry little parcels for him over frontiers. Big deal. Leave it to the owls. "Known" criminal, however, was quite a different matter. "Known" he would go along with absolutely. Remembering Elizabeth Worthington's caged stare at Tiu, he reckoned he had known that face, that look, and that dependence in one guise or another for the bulk of his waking life.

It has been whispered once or twice by certain trivial critics of George Smiley that at this juncture he should somehow have seen which way the wind was blowing with Jerry, and hauled him out of the field. Effectively, Smiley was Jerry's case officer, after all. Smiley alone kept Jerry's file, welfared and briefed him. Had George been at his peak, they say, instead of half-way down the other side, he would have read the warning signals between the lines of Craw's reports and headed Jerry off in time. They might just as well have complained that he was a second-rate fortune-teller. The facts, as they came to Smiley, are these.

On the morning following his "pass" at Lizzie Worth or Worthington—the jargon has no sexual connotation—Craw debriefed Jerry for more than three hours on a car pick-up, and his report describes Jerry as being, quite reasonably, in a state of "anti-climactic gloom." He appeared, said Craw, to be afraid that Tiu, or even Ko, might blame the girl for her "guilty knowledge" and even lay hands on her. Jerry referred more than once to Tiu's patent contempt for the girl—and for himself, and, he suspected, for all Europeans—and repeated his comment about travelling from Kowloon-side to Hong Kong-side for her and no further. Craw countered by pointing out that Tiu could at any time have shut her up; and that her knowledge, on Jerry's own testimony, did not extend even as far as the Russian gold seam, let alone to brother Nelson.

Jerry, in short, was producing the standard post-operational manifestations of a fieldman. A sense of guilt, coupled with foreboding, an involuntary movement of affiliation toward the target person—these are as predictable as a burst of tears in an athlete after the big race.

At their next contact—an extended limbo call on the second day, at which, to buoy him up, Craw passed on Smiley's warm personal congratulations somewhat ahead of receiving them from the Circus—Jerry sounded in altogether better case, but he was worried about his daughter Cat. He had forgotten her birthday—he said it was tomorrow—and wished the Circus to send her at once a Japanese cassette player with a bunch of cassettes to start off her collection. Craw's telegram to Smiley named the cassettes, asked for immediate action by housekeepers, and requested that Shoemaker Section—the Circus forgers, in other words—run up an accompanying card in Jerry's handwriting, text given: "Darling Cat. Asked a friend of mine to post this in London. Look after yourself, my dearest, love to you now and ever, Pa."

Smiley authorised the purchase, instructing housekeepers to dock the cost from Jerry's pay at source. He personally checked the parcel before it was sent, and approved the forged card. He also verified what he and Craw already suspected: that it was not Cat's birthday, or anywhere near. Jerry simply had a strong urge to make a gesture of affection: once more, a normal symptom of temporary field fatigue. Smiley cabled Craw to stay close to him but the initiative was with Jerry, and Jerry made no further contact till the night of the fifth day, when he demanded—and got—a crash meeting within the hour. This took place at their standing after-dark emergency rendezvous, an all-night road-side café in the New Territories, under the guise of a casual encounter between old colleagues. Craw's letter, marked "Personal to Smiley only," was a follow-up to his telegram. It arrived at the Circus by hand of the Cousins' courier two days after the episode it describes: on day seven therefore. Writing on the assumption that the Cousins would contrive to read the text despite the seal and other devices, Craw crammed it with evasions, work names, and cryptograph, which are here restored to their real meaning:

> Westerby was very angry. He demanded to know what the hell Sam Collins was doing in Hong Kong and in what way Collins was involved in the Ko case. I have not seen him so disturbed before. I asked him what made him think Collins was around. He replied that he had seen him that very night—eleven-fifteen exactly—sitting in a parked car in the Midlevels, on a terrace just below Star Heights, under a streetlamp, reading a newspaper. The position Collins had taken up, said Westerby, gave him a clear view to Lizzie Worthington's windows on the eighth floor, and it was Westerby's assumption that he was engaged in some sort of

surveillance. Westerby, who was on foot at the time, insists
that he "damn nearly went up to Sam and asked him outright." But Sarratt discipline held firm, and he kept going
down the hill on his own side of the road. But he does claim
that as soon as Collins saw him, he started the car and drove
up the hill at speed. Westerby has the licence number, and of
course it is the correct one. Collins confirms the rest.

In accordance with our agreed position in this contingency (your signal of Feb. 15th), I gave Westerby the following answers:

1. Even if it *was* Collins, the Circus had no control over his
movements. Collins had left the Circus under a cloud, before
the fall, he was a known gambler, drifter, wheeler-dealer, etc.,
and the East was his natural stomping-ground. I told Westerby he was being a fat-headed idiot to assume that Collins
was still on the payroll, or, worse, had any part in the Ko case.

2. Collins is facially a *type*, I said: regular-featured, mous-
tached, etc., looked like half the pimps in London. I doubted
whether, from across a road at eleven-fifteen at night, Westerby could be certain of his identification. Westerby retorted
that he had A-1 vision and that Sam had his newspaper open
at the racing page.

3. Anyway, what was Westerby himself doing, I enquired,
round Star Heights at eleven-fifteen at night? Answer, returning from drinking with the U.P.I. mob and hoping for a cab.
At this I pretended to explode, and said that nobody who had
been on a U.P.I. thrash could see an elephant at five yards, let
alone Sam Collins at twenty-five, in a car, at dead of night.
Over and out—I hope.

That Smiley was seriously concerned about this incident
goes without saying. Only four people knew of the Collins
ploy: Smiley, Connie Sachs, Craw, and Sam himself. That

Jerry should have stumbled on him provided an added anxiety in an operation already loaded with imponderables.

But Craw was deft, and Craw believed he had talked Jerry down, and Craw was the man on the spot. Just possibly in a perfect world, Craw might have made it his business to find out whether there had really been a U.P.I. party in the Midlevels that night—and on learning that there had not, he might have challenged Jerry again to explain his presence in the region of Star Heights, and in that case Jerry would probably have thrown a tantrum and produced some other story that was not checkable: that he had been with a woman, for instance, and Craw could mind his bloody business. Of which the net result would have been needless bad blood and the same take-it-or-leave-it situation as before.

It is also tempting, but unreasonable, to expect of Smiley that with so many other pressures upon him—the continued and unabating quest for Nelson, daily sessions with the Cousins, rear-guard actions round the Whitehall corridors—he should have drawn the inference closest to his own lonely experience: namely, that Jerry, having no taste for sleep or company that evening, had wandered the night pavements till he found himself standing outside the building where Lizzie lived, and hung about, as Smiley did, without exactly knowing what he wanted, beyond the off chance of a sight of her. The rush of events which carried Smiley along was far too powerful to permit of such fanciful abstractions. Not only did the eighth day, when it came, put the Circus effectively on a war footing; it is also the pardonable vanity of lonely people everywhere to assume that they have no counterparts.

14

The Eighth Day

The jolly mood of the fifth floor was a great relief after the depression of the previous gathering. "A burrowers' honeymoon," Guillam called it, and tonight was its highest point, its attenuated star-burst of a consummation, and it came exactly eight days, in the chronology which historians afterwards impose on things, after Jerry and Lizzie and Tiu had had their full and frank exchange of views on the subject of Tiny Ricardo and the Russian gold seam—to the great delight of the Circus planners. Guillam had wangled Molly along specially.

They had run in all directions, these shady night animals, down old paths and new paths and old paths grown over till they were rediscovered; and now at last, behind their twin leaders—Connie Sachs alias Mother Russia, and di Salis alias the Doc—they crammed themselves, all twelve of them, into the very throne-room itself, under Karla's portrait, in an obedient half-circle round their chief, Bolshies and yellow perils together. A plenary session, then: for people unused to such drama, a monument of history indeed. And Molly primly at Guillam's side, her hair brushed long to hide the bite marks on her neck.

Di Salis does most of the talking. The other ranks feel this to be appropriate. After all, Nelson Ko is the Doc's patch entirely: Chinese to the sleeve-ends of his tunic. Reining himself right in—his spiky wet hair, his knees and feet and fussing fingers all but still for once—he keeps things in a low and almost deprecating key of which the inexorable climax is accordingly more thrilling. The climax even has a name. It is Ko Sheng-hsiu—alias Ko, Nelson—later known also as Yao Kai-sheng, under which name he was still later disgraced in the Cultural Revolution.

"But within these walls, gentlemen," pipes the Doc, whose awareness of the female sex is inconsistent, "we shall continue to call him Nelson." Born 1928 of humble proletarian stock, in Swatow—to quote the official sources, says the Doc—and soon afterwards removed to Shanghai. No mention, in either official or unofficial handouts, of Mr. Hibbert's Lord's Life Mission school, but a sad reference to "exploitation at the hands of Western Imperialists in childhood," who poisoned him with religion. When the Japanese reached Shanghai, Nelson joined the refugee trail to Chungking, all as Mr. Hibbert has described.

From an early age, the Doc continues, once more according to official records, Nelson secretly devoted himself to seminal revolutionary reading and took an active part in clandestine Communist groups, despite the oppression of the loathsome Chiang Kai-shek rabble. On the refugee trail he also attempted "on many occasions" to escape to Mao, but his extreme youth held him back. Returning to Shanghai, he became, already as a student, a leading cadre member of the outlawed Communist movement and undertook special assignments in and around the Kiangnan shipyards to subvert the pernicious influence of K.M.T. Fascist elements. At the University of Communications he appealed publicly for a united front of students and peasants. Graduated with conspicuous excellence in 1951. . . .

Di Salis interrupts himself, and in a sharp release of tension throws up one arm and clenches the hair at the back of his head.

"The usual unctuous portrait, Chief, of a student hero who sees the light before his time," he sings.

"What about Leningrad?" Smiley asks, from his desk, while he jots the occasional note.

"Nineteen fifty-three to six."

"Yes, Connie?"

Connie is in her wheelchair again. She blames the freezing month and that toad Karla, jointly.

"We have a Brother Bretlev, darling. Bretlev, Ivan Ivanovitch, Academician, Leningrad faculty of shipbuilding, old-time China hand, devilled in Shanghai for Centre's China hounds. Revolutionary war-horse, latter-day Karla-trained university talent-spotter trawling the overseas students for likely lads and lasses."

For the burrowers on the Chinese side—the yellow perils—this intelligence is new and thrilling, and produces an excited crackle of chairs and papers till at a sign from Smiley, di Salis lets go his head and takes up his narrative once more.

"Nineteen fifty-seven returned to Shanghai and was put in charge of a railway workshop—"

Smiley again: "But his dates at Leningrad were 'fifty-three to 'fifty-six?"

"Correct," says di Salis.

"Then there seems to be a missing year."

Now no papers crackle and no chairs, either.

"A tour of Soviet shipyards is the official explanation," says di Salis, with a smirk at Connie and a mysterious, knowing writhe of the neck.

"Thank you," says Smiley and makes another note. "'Fifty-seven," he repeats. "Was that before or after the Sino-Soviet split, Doc?"

"Before. The split started in earnest in 'fifty-nine."

Smiley asks here whether Nelson's brother receives a mention anywhere; or is Drake as much disowned in Nelson's China as Nelson is in Drake's?

"In one of the earliest biographies, Drake is referred to, but not by name. In the later ones, a brother is said to have died during the Communist take-over of 'forty-nine."

Smiley makes a rare joke, which is followed by dense, relieved laughter. "This case is littered with people pretending to be dead," he complains. "It will be a positive relief to me to find a real corpse somewhere."

Only hours later, this *mot* was remembered with a shudder.

"We also have a note that Nelson was a model student at Leningrad," di Salis goes on. "At least in Russian eyes. They sent him back with the highest references."

Connie from her iron chair allows herself another interjection. She has brought Trot, her mangy mongrel, with her. He lies mis-shapenly across her vast lap, stinking and occasionally sighing, but not even Guillam, who is a dog-hater, has the nerve to banish him.

"Oh, and so they would, dear, wouldn't they?" she cries. "The Russians would praise Nelson's talents to the skies, 'course they would, specially if Brother Ivan Ivanovitch Bretlev has snapped him up at university, and Karla's lovelies have spirited him off to training school and all! Bright little mole like Nelson, give him a decent start in life for when he gets home to China! Didn't do him much good later though, did it, Doc? Not when the Great Beastly Cultural Revolution got him in the neck! The generous admiration of Soviet imperialist running dogs wasn't at all the thing to be wearing in your cap *then*, was it?"

Of Nelson's fall, few details are available, the Doc proclaims, speaking louder in response to Connie's outburst. "One must assume that it was violent, and as Connie has pointed out, those who were highest in Russian favour fell the hardest."

He glances at the sheet of paper which he holds crookedly before his blotched face. "I won't give you all his appointments at the time of his disgrace, Chief, because he lost them anyway. But there is no doubt that he did indeed have effective management of most of the shipbuilding in Kiangnan, and consequently of a large part of China's naval tonnage."

"I see," says Smiley quietly. Jotting, he purses his lips as if in disapproval, while his eyebrows lift very high.

"His post at Kiangnan also procured him a string of seats on the naval planning committees and in the field of communications and strategic policy. By 'sixty-three his name is beginning to pop up regularly in the Cousins' Peking watch reports."

"Well done, Karla," Guillam says quietly from his place at Smiley's side, and Smiley, still writing, actually echoes this sentiment with a "Yes."

"The only one, Peter dear!" Connie yells, suddenly unable to contain herself. "The only one of all those toads to see it coming! A voice in the wilderness, wasn't he, Trot? 'Look out for the yellow peril,' he told 'em. 'One day they're going to turn round and bite the hand that's feeding 'em, sure as eggs. And when that happens you'll have eight hundred million new enemies banging on your own back door. *And* your guns will all be pointing the wrong way. Mark my words.'

"Told 'em," she repeats, hauling at the mongrel's ear in her emotion. "Put it all in a paper, 'Threat of Deviation by Emerging Socialist Partner.' Circulated every little brute in Moscow Centre's Collegium. Drafted it word for word in his clever little mind while he was doing a spot of time in Siberia for Uncle Joe Stalin, bless him. 'Spy on your friends today, they're certain to be your enemies tomorrow,' he told them. Oldest maxim of the trade, Karla's favourite. When he was given his job back, he practically nailed it on the door in Dzerzhinski Square. No one paid a blind bit of notice. Not a scrap. Fell on barren ground, my dear. Five years later, he was proved right, and the Collegium didn't thank him for that, either, *I* can tell you! He's been right a sight too often for their liking, the boobies—hasn't he, Trot! *You* know, don't you, darling, *you* know what the old fool-woman's on about!" At which she lifts the puling dog a few inches in the air by its forepaws and lets it flop back onto her lap again.

Connie can't bear old Doc hogging the limelight, they secretly agree. She sees the logic of it, but the woman in her can't abide the reality.

"Very well, he was purged, Doc," Smiley says quietly, restoring calm. "Let's go back to 'sixty-seven, shall we?" And puts his chin back in his hand.

In the gloom, Karla's portrait peers stodgily down as di Salis resumes. "Well, the usual grim story, one supposes, Chief," he chants. "The dunce's cap, no doubt. Spat on in the street. Wife and children kicked and beaten up. Indoctrination camps, labour education 'on a scale commensurate with the crime.' Urged to reconsider the peasant virtues. One report has him sent to a rural commune to test himself. And when he came crawling back to Shanghai they'd have made him start at the bottom again, driving bolts into a railway line or whatever. As far as the *Russians* were concerned—if that's what we're talking about"—he hurries on before Connie can interrupt again—"he was a wash-out. No access, no influence, no friends."

"How long did it take him to climb back?" Smiley enquires, with a characteristic lowering of the eyelids.

"About three years ago he started to be functional again. In the long run he has what they need most: brains, technical know-how, experience. But his *formal* rehabilitation didn't really occur till the beginning of 'seventy-three."

While di Salis goes on to describe the stages of Nelson's ritual reinstatement, Smiley quietly draws a folder to him and refers to certain other dates which, for reasons as yet unexplained, are suddenly acutely relevant to him.

"The payments to Drake have their beginnings in January 'seventy-three," he murmurs. "They rise steeply in mid-'seventy-three."

"With Nelson's *access*, darling," Connie whispers after him, like a prompter from the wings. "The more he knows, the more he tells, and the more he tells, the more he gets. Karla only pays for goodies, and even then it hurts like blazes."

"By 'seventy-three," says di Salis, "Nelson, having made all the proper confessions, has been embraced into the Shanghai municipal revolutionary committee, and appointed responsible person in a naval unit of the People's Liberation Army. Six months later—"

"Date?" Smiley interrupts.

"July."

Six months later, di Salis continues, Nelson is seen to be acting in an unknown capacity with the Central Committee of the Chinese Communist Party.

"Holy *smoke*," says Guillam softly, and Molly Meakin gives his hand a hidden squeeze.

"And a report from the Cousins," says di Salis, "undated as usual but well attested, has Nelson down as an informal adviser to the Munitions and Ordnance Committee of the Ministry of Defence."

Rather than orchestrate this revelation with his customary range of mannerisms, di Salis again contrives to keep rock-still to great effect.

"In terms of *eligibility*, Chief," he goes on quietly, "from an *operational* standpoint, we on the China side of your house would regard this as one of the key positions in the whole of the Chinese administration. If we could pick ourselves one slot for an agent inside the mainland, Nelson's might well be the one."

"Reasons?" Smiley enquires, still alternating between his jottings and the open folder before him.

"The Chinese navy is still in the Stone Age. We do have a formal interest in Chinese technical intelligence, naturally, but our real priorities—like those of Moscow, no doubt—are strategic and political. Beyond that, Nelson could supply us with the total capacity of all Chinese shipyards. Beyond that again, he could tell us the Chinese submarine potential, which has been frightening the daylights out of the Cousins for years. And of ourselves too, I may add, off and on."

"So think what it's doing for Moscow," an old burrower murmurs out of turn.

"The Chinese are supposedly developing their own version of the Russian G-2 class submarine," di Salis explains. "No one knows a lot about it. Have they their own design? Have they two or four tubes? Are they armed with sea-to-air missiles or sea-to-sea? What is the financial appropriation for them? There's talk of a Han class. We had word they laid one down in 'seventy-one. We've never had confirmation. In Dairen in 'sixty-four, they allegedly built a G class armed with ballistic missiles but it still hasn't been officially sighted. And so forth and so on," he says deprecatingly, for, like most of the Circus, he has a rooted dislike of military matters and would prefer the more artistic targets.

"For hard and fast detail on those subjects the Cousins would pay a fortune," di Salis says. "In a couple of years, Langley could spend hundreds of millions in research, over-flights, satellites, listening devices, and God knows what—and still not come up with an answer half as good as one photograph. So if Nelson—" He lets the sentence hang, which is somehow a lot more effective than making it finite.

Connie whispers, "Well *done*, Doc," but still for a while nobody else speaks; they are held back by Smiley's jotting, and his continued examination of the folder.

"Good as Haydon," Guillam mutters. "Better. China's the last frontier. Toughest nut in the trade."

Smiley sits back, his calculations apparently finished.

"Ricardo made his trip a few months after Nelson's formal rehabilitation," he says.

Nobody sees fit to question this.

"Tiu travels to Shanghai, and six weeks later Ricardo—"

In the far background, Guillam hears the bark of the Cousins' telephone switched through to his room, and it is a thing he afterwards avers most strongly—whether in truth or with hindsight—that the unloveable image of Sam Collins was at this point conjured out of his subconscious memory like a djinni out of a lamp, and that he wondered yet again how he could ever have been so unthinking as to let Sam Collins deliver that vital letter to Martello.

"Nelson has one more string to his bow, Chief," di Salis continues, just as everyone is assuming he is done. "I hesitate to offer it with any confidence, but in the circumstances I dare not omit it altogether. A barter report from the West Germans, dated a few weeks ago. According to *their* sources, Nelson is lately a member of what we have for want of information dubbed the Peking Tea Club, an embryonic body which we believe has been set up to co-ordinate the Chinese intelligence effort. He came in first as an adviser on electronic surveillance, and was then co-opted as a full member. It functions, so far as we can fathom, somewhat as our own Intelligence Steering Group. But I must emphasise that this is a shot in the dark. We know absolutely nothing about the Chinese services, and nor do the Cousins."

For once at a loss for words, Smiley stares at di Salis, opens his mouth, closes it, then pulls off his glasses and polishes them.

"And Nelson's *motive?*" he asks, still oblivious to the steady bark of the Cousins' bell. "A shot in the dark, Doc? How would you see that?"

Di Salis gives an enormous shrug, so that his tallow hair bucks like a floor-mop. "Oh, anybody's guess," he says waspishly. "Who believes in *motive* these days? It would have been perfectly natural for him to respond to Centre's recruitment overtures while a student in Leningrad, of course, provided they were made in the right way. Not a disloyal thing at all. Not doctrinally, anyway. Russia was China's big elder brother. Nelson needed merely to be told he had been chosen as one of a special vanguard of vigilantes. I see no great art to that."

Outside the room, the green phone just goes on ringing, which is remarkable. Martello is not usually so persistent. Only Guillam and Smiley are allowed to pick it up. But Smiley has not heard it, and Guillam is damned if he will budge while di Salis is extemporising on Nelson's possible reasons for becoming Karla's mole.

"When the Cultural Revolution came, many people in Nelson's position believed that Mao had gone mad," di Salis explains, still reluctant to theorise. "Even some of his own generals thought so. The humiliations Nelson suffered made him conform outwardly—while inwardly, perhaps, he remained bitter—who knows?—and vengeful."

"The alimony payments to Drake started at a time when Nelson's rehabilitation was barely complete," Smiley objects mildly. "What is the presumption there, Doc?"

All this is just too much for Connie, and once again she brims over. "Oh, George, how can you be so naïve? *You* can find the line, dear, *'course* you can! Those poor Chinese can't afford to hang a top technician in the cupboard half his life and not use him! Karla saw the drift, didn't he, Doc? He read the wind and went with it. He kept his poor little Nelson on a string and as soon as he started to come out of the wilderness again he had his legmen get alongside him: 'It's *us*, remember? Your friends! *We* don't let you down! *We* don't spit on you in the street! Let's get back to business!' You'd play it just the same way yourself, you know you would!"

"And the money?" Smiley asks. "The half million?"

"Stick and carrot! Blackmail implicit, rewards enormous. Nelson's hooked both ways."

But it is di Salis, Connie's outburst notwithstanding, who has the last word: "He's Chinese. He's pragmatic. He's Drake's brother. He can't get out of China—"

"Not yet," says Smiley softly, glancing at the folder again.

"—and he knows very well his market value to the Russian service. 'You can't eat politics, you can't sell them, and you can't sleep with them,' Drake liked to say. So you might as well make money out of them."

"Against the day when you *can* leave China and spend it," Smiley concludes and, as Guillam tiptoes from the room, silently closes the folder and takes up his sheet of jottings. "Drake tried to get him out and failed, so he took the Russians' money till . . . till what? Till Drake has better luck, perhaps."

In the background, the insistent snarling of the green telephone has finally ceased.

"Nelson is Karla's mole," Smiley remarks at last, once more almost himself. "He's sitting on a priceless crock of Chinese intelligence. That alone we could do with. He's acting on Karla's orders. The orders themselves are of inestimable value to us. They would show us precisely how much the Russians know about their Chinese enemy, and even what they intend toward him. We could take back-bearings galore. Yes, Peter?"

In the breaking of tragic news there is no transition. One minute a concept stands, the next it lies smashed, and for those affected the world has altered irrevocably. As a cushion, however, Guillam had used official Circus stationery and the written word. By writing his message to Smiley in signal form, he hoped that the sight of it would prepare him in advance. Walking quietly to the desk, the form in his hand, he laid it on the glass sheet and waited.

"About *Charlie Marshall*, the other pilot, by the way," Smiley asked of the gathering, still oblivious. "Have the Cousins run him to earth yet, Molly?"

"His record is much the same as Ricardo's," Molly Meakin replied, glancing queerly at Guillam. Still at Smiley's side, he looked suddenly grey and middle-aged and ill. "Like Ricardo, he flew for the Cousins in the Laos war, Mr. Smiley. They were contemporaries at Langley's secret aviation school in Oklahoma. They dumped him when Laos ended and have no further word on him. Enforcement say he has ferried opium, but they say that of all of the Cousins' pilots."

"I think you should read that," Guillam said, pointing firmly at the message.

"Marshall must be our next step," Smiley said. "We have to maintain the pressure."

Picking up the signal form at last, he held it critically to his left side, where the reading-light was brightest. He read with his eyebrows raised and his lids lowered. As always, he read twice. His expression did not change, but those nearest him said the movement went out of his face.

"Thank you, Peter," he said quietly, laying the paper down again. "And thank you everyone else. Connie and the Doc, perhaps you'd stay behind. I trust the rest of you will get a good night's sleep."

Among the younger sparks this hope was greeted with cheerful laughter, for it was well past midnight already.

The girl from upstairs slept, a neat brown doll along the length of one of Jerry's legs, plump and immaculate by the orange night-light of the rain-soaked Hong Kong sky. She was snoring her head off, and Jerry was staring through the window thinking of Lizzie Worthington. He thought of the twin claw marks on her chin and wondered again who had put them there. He thought of Tiu, imagining him as her jailer, and he rehearsed the name horse-writer until it really annoyed him. He wondered how much more waiting there was, and whether at the end of it he might have a chance with her, which was all he asked: a chance. The girl stirred, but only to scratch her rump. From next door, Jerry heard a ritual clicking as the habitual mah-jong party washed the pieces before distributing them.

The girl had not been unduly responsive to Jerry's courtship at first—a gush of impassioned notes jammed through her letter-box at all hours of the previous few days—but she did need to pay her gas bill. Officially, she was the property of a businessman, but recently his visits had become fewer and most recently had ceased altogether, with the result that she could afford neither the fortune-teller nor mah-jong, nor the stylish clothes she had set her heart on for the day she broke into Kung Fu films. So she succumbed, but on a clear financial understanding.

Her main fear was of being known to consort with the hideous *kwailo*, and for this reason she had put on her entire outdoor equipment to descend the one floor: a brown raincoat with transatlantic brass buckles on the epaulettes, plastic yellow boots, and a plastic umbrella with red roses. Now this equipment lay around the parquet floor like armour after the battle, and she slept with the same noble exhaustion. So that when the phone rang her only response was a drowsy Cantonese oath.

Lifting the receiver, Jerry nursed the idiotic hope it might be Lizzie, but it wasn't.

"Get your ass down here fast," Luke said. "And Stubbsie will *love* you. *Move* it. I'm doing you the favour of our career."

"Where's here?" Jerry asked.

"Downstairs, you ape."

He rolled the girl off him but she still didn't wake.

The roads glittered with unexpected rain and a thick halo ringed the moon. Luke drove as if they were in a jeep: in high gear with hammer changes on the corners. Fumes of whisky filled the car.

"What have you got, for Christ's sake?" Jerry demanded. "What's going on?"

"Great meat. Now shut up."

"I don't want meat. I'm suited."

"You'll want this one. *Man*, you'll want this one."

They were heading for the harbour tunnel. A flock of cyclists without lights lurched out of a side turning, and Luke had to mount the central reservation to avoid them.

"Look for a damn great building site," Luke said. A patrol car overtook them, all lights flashing. Thinking he was going to be stopped, Luke lowered his window.

"We're *press*, you idiots!" he screamed. "We're *stars*, hear me?"

Inside the patrol car as it passed they had a glimpse of a Chinese sergeant and his driver, and an august-looking European perched in the back like a judge. Ahead of them, to the right of the carriage-way, the promised building site sprang into view: a cage of yellow girders and bamboo scaffolding alive with sweating coolies. Cranes, glistening in the wet, dangled over them like whips. The floodlighting came from the ground and poured wastefully into the mist.

"Look for a low place just near," Luke ordered, slowing down to sixty. "White. Look for a white place."

Jerry pointed to it: a two-storey complex of weeping stucco, neither new nor old, with a twenty-foot stand of bamboos by the entrance, and an ambulance. The ambulance stood open and the three attendants lounged in it, smoking, watching the police who milled around the forecourt as if it were a riot they were handling.

"He's giving us an hour's start over the field."

"Who?"

"Rocker. Rocker is. Who do you think?"

"Why?"

"Because he hit me, I guess. He loves me. He loves you, too. He said to bring you specially."

"Why?"

The rain fell steadily.

"*Why? Why? Why?*" Luke echoed, furious. "Just hurry!"

The bamboos were out of scale, higher than the wall. A couple of orange-clad priests were sheltering against them, clapping cymbals. A third held an umbrella. There were flower stalls and hearses and from somewhere out of sight the sounds of leisurely incantation. The entrance lobby was a jungle swamp reeking of formaldehyde.

"Big Moo's special envoy," said Luke.

"Press," said Jerry.

The police nodded them through, not looking at their cards.

"Where's the Superintendent?" said Luke.

The smell of formaldehyde was awful. A young sergeant led them. They pushed through a glass door to a room where old men and women, maybe thirty of them, mostly in pyjama suits, waited phlegmatically as if for a late train, under shadowless neon lights and an electric fan. One old man was clearing out his throat, snorting onto the green tiled floor. Seeing the giant *kwailos*, they stared in polite amazement. The pathologist's office was yellow. Yellow walls; yellow blinds, closed; an air-conditioner that wasn't working. The same green tiles, easily washed down.

"Great *smell*," said Luke.

"Like home," Jerry agreed.

Jerry wished it was battle. Battle was easier. The sergeant told them to wait while he went ahead. They heard the squeak of trolleys, low voices, the clamp of a freezer door, the low hiss of rubber soles. A volume of *Gray's Anatomy* lay next to the telephone. Jerry turned the pages, staring at the illustrations. Luke perched on a chair. An assistant in short rubber boots and overalls brought tea. White cups, green rims, and the Hong Kong monogram with a crown.

"Can you tell the sergeant to hurry, please?" said Luke. "You'll have the whole damn town here in a minute."

"Why us?" said Jerry again.

Luke poured some tea onto the tiled floor, and while it ran into the gutter he topped up the cup from his whisky flask. The sergeant returned, beckoning quickly with his slender hand. They followed him back through the waiting-room. This way there was no door, just a corridor, and a turn like a public lavatory, and they were there.

The first thing Jerry saw was the trolley chipped to hell; there's nothing older or more derelict than worn-out hospital equipment, he thought. The walls were covered in green mould, green stalactites hung from the ceiling, a battered spittoon was filled with used tissues. They clean out the noses, he remembered, before they pull down the sheet to show you. It's a courtesy, so that you aren't shocked. The fumes of formaldehyde made his eyes run. A Chinese pathologist was sitting at the window, making notes on a pad. A couple of attendants were hovering, and more police. There seemed to be a general sense of apology around; Jerry couldn't make it out.

The Rocker was ignoring them. He was in a corner, murmuring to the august-looking gentleman from the back of the patrol car, but the corner wasn't far away and Jerry heard "slur on our reputation" spoken twice, in an indignant, nervous tone. Over the body lay a white sheet with a blue cross on it, made in two equal lengths. So that they can use it either way round, Jerry thought. It was the only trolley in the room. The only sheet. The rest of the exhibition was inside the two big freezers with the wooden doors, walk-in size, big as a butcher's shop. Luke was going out of his mind with impatience.

"Jesus, Rocker!" he called across the room. "How much longer you going to keep the lid on this? We got work to do."

No one bothered with him. Tired of waiting, Luke yanked back the sheet. Jerry looked, and looked away. The autopsy room was next door, and he could hear the sound of sawing, like the snarling of a dog.

No wonder they're all so apologetic, Jerry thought stupidly. Bringing a round-eye corpse to a place like this.

"Jesus *Christ*," Luke was saying. "Holy *Christ*. Who did it to him? How do you *make* those marks? That's a triad thing. *Jesus*."

The dampened window gave on to the courtyard. Jerry could see the bamboos rocking in the rain and the liquid shadows of an ambulance delivering another customer, but he doubted whether any of them looked like this. A police photographer had appeared and there were flashes. A telephone extension hung on the wall. The Rocker was talking into it. He still hadn't looked at Luke, or at Jerry.

"I want him out of here," the august gentleman said.

"Soon as you like," said the Rocker. He returned to the telephone. "In the Walled City, sir. . . . Yes, sir. . . . In an alley, sir. Stripped. Lot of alcohol. . . . The forensic pathologist recognised him immediately, sir. . . . Yes, sir, the bank's here already, sir." He rang off. "Yes, sir, no, sir, three bags full, sir." He dialled a number.

Luke was making notes. "Jesus," he kept saying in awe. "Jesus. They must have taken *weeks* to kill him. Months."

He had died twice, Jerry decided. Once to make him talk and once to shut him up. The things they had done to him first were all over his body, in big and small patches, the way fire hits a carpet, eats holes, then suddenly gives up. Then there was the thing round his neck, a different, faster death altogether. They had done that last, when they didn't want him any more.

Luke called to the pathologist. "Turn him over, will you? Would you mind please turning him over, *sir?*"

The Superintendent had put down the phone.

"What's the story?" said Jerry, straight at him. "Who is he?"

"Name of Frost," the Rocker said, staring back with one eyelid drooping. "Senior official of the South Asian & China. Trustee Department."

"Who killed him?" Jerry asked.

"Yeah, who did it? That's the point," said Luke, writing hard.

"Mice," said the Rocker.

"Hong Kong has no triads, no Communists, and no Kuomintang. Right, Rocker?"

"And no whores," the Rocker said.

The august gentleman spared the Rocker further reply. "A vicious case of mugging," he declared over the policeman's shoulder. "A filthy, vicious mugging, exemplifying the need for public vigilance at all times. He was a loyal servant of the bank."

"That's not a mugging," said Luke, looking at Frost again. "That's a *party.*"

"He certainly had some damned odd friends," the Rocker said, still staring at Jerry.

"What's that supposed to mean?" said Jerry.

"What's the story so far?" said Luke.

"He was on the town till midnight. In the company of a couple of Chinese males. One cathouse after another. Then we lose him. Till tonight."

"The bank's offering a reward of fifty thousand dollars," said the august man.

"Hong Kong or U.S.?" said Luke, writing.

The august man said, "Hong Kong," very tartly.

"Now, you boys go easy," the Rocker warned. "There's a sick wife in Stanley Hospital, and there's kids—"

"And there's the reputation of the bank," said the august man.

"That will be our first concern," said Luke.

They left half an hour later, still ahead of the field.

"Thanks," said Luke to the Superintendent.

"For nothing," said the Rocker. His drooping eyelid, Jerry noticed, leaked when he was tired.

We've shaken the tree, thought Jerry as they drove away. Boy, oh, boy, have we shaken the tree!

They sat in the same attitudes, Smiley at his desk, Connie in her wheelchair, di Salis gazing into the languid smoke-coil of his pipe. Guillam stood at Smiley's side, the grate of Martello's voice still in his ears. Smiley, with a slight circular movement of his thumb, was polishing his spectacles with the fat end of his tie.

Di Salis, the Jesuit, spoke first. Perhaps he had the most to disown. "There is nothing in logic to link us with this incident. Frost was a libertine. He kept Chinese women, he was manifestly corrupt. He took our bribe without demur. Heaven knows what bribes he has not taken in the past. I will not have it laid at my door."

"Oh, *stuff*," Connie muttered. She sat expressionless and the dog lay sleeping on her lap. Her crippled hands lay over his brown back for warmth. In the background Fawn was pouring tea. Smiley took neither milk nor sugar.

Smiley spoke to the signal form. Nobody had seen his face since he had first looked down to read it.

"Connie, I want the arithmetic," he said.

"Yes, dear."

"Outside these four walls, who is conscious that we leaned on Frost?"

"Craw. Westerby. Craw's policeman. And if they've any mind, the Cousins will have guessed."

"Not Lacon, not Whitehall."

"And *not* Karla, dear," Connie declared, with a sharp look at the murky portrait.

"No. Not Karla. I believe that." From his voice, they could feel the intensity of the conflict as his intellect forced its will upon his emotions. "For Karla, it would be a most exaggerated response. If a bank account is blown, all he need do is open another elsewhere. He doesn't need *this*." With the tips of his fingers, he precisely moved the signal form an inch up the glass. "The ploy went as planned. The response was simply—" He began again. "The response was more than we expected. Operationally nothing is amiss. Operationally we have advanced the case."

"We've *drawn* them, dear," Connie said firmly.

Di Salis blew up completely. "I insist you do not speak as if we were all of us accomplices here. There is no proven link and I consider it invidious that you should suggest there is."

Smiley remained remote in his response: "*I* would consider it invidious if I suggested anything else. I ordered this initiative. I refuse not to look at the consequences merely because they are ugly. Put it on my head. But don't let's deceive ourselves."

"Poor devil didn't know enough, did he?" Connie mused, seemingly to herself. At first nobody took her up. Then Guillam did: what did she mean by that?

"Frost had nothing to betray, darling," she explained. "That's the worst that can happen to anyone. What could he give them? One zealous journalist, name of Westerby. They had that already, little dears. So of course, they went on. And on." She turned to Smiley's direction. He was the only one who shared so much history with her. "We used to make it a *rule*—remember, George—when the boys went in? We always gave them something they could confess."

With loving care, Fawn set down a paper cup on Smiley's desk, a slice of lemon floating on the tea. His skull-like grin moved Guillam to repressed fury.

"When you've handed that round, get out," he snapped in his ear. Still smirking, Fawn left.

"Where is Ko, in his mind, at this moment?" Smiley asked, still talking to the signal form. He had locked his fingers under his chin and might have been praying.

"Funk and fuzzy-headedness," Connie declared with confidence. "Fleet Street on the prowl, Frost dead and he's still no further forward."

"Yes. Yes, he'll dither. 'Can he hold the dam? Can he plug the leaks? Where *are* the leaks, anyway?' . . . That's what we wanted. We've got it." He made the smallest movement of his bowed head, and it pointed toward Guillam. "Peter, you will please ask the Cousins to step up their surveillance on Tiu. Static posts only, tell them. No street-work, no frightening the game, no nonsense of that kind. Telephone, mail, the easy things only. Doc, when did Tiu last visit the mainland?"

Di Salis grudgingly gave a date.

"Find out the route he travelled and where he bought his ticket. In case he does it again."

"It's on record already," di Salis retorted sulkily and made a most unpleasing sneer, looking to heaven and writhing with his lips and shoulders.

"Then kindly be so good as to make me a separate note of it," Smiley replied with unshakeable forbearance. "Westerby," he went on in the same flat voice, and for a second Guillam had the sickening feeling that Smiley was suffering from some kind of hallucination, and thought that Jerry was in the room with him, to receive his orders like the rest of them. "I pull him out—I can do that. His paper recalls him, why shouldn't it? Then what? Ko waits. He listens. He hears nothing. And he relaxes."

"And enter the narcotics heroes," Guillam said, glancing at the calendar.

"Or I pull him out and I replace him, and another fieldman takes up the trail. Is he any less at risk than Westerby is now?"

"It never works," Connie muttered. "Changing horses. Never. You know that. Briefing, training, re-gearing, new relationships. Never."

"I don't see that he *is* at risk!" di Salis asserted shrilly.

Swinging angrily round, Guillam started to slap him down, but Smiley spoke ahead of him: "Why not, Doc?"

"Accepting your hypothesis—which I don't—Ko is not a man of violence. He's a successful businessman and his maxims are face, and expediency, and merit, and hard work. I won't have him spoken of as if he were some kind of thug. I grant you he has people, and perhaps his people are less nice than he when it comes to method. Much as we are Whitehall's people. That doesn't make blackguards of Whitehall, I trust."

For Christ's sake, out with it! thought Guillam.

"Westerby is not a Frost," di Salis persisted, in the same didactic, nasal whine. "Westerby is not a dishonest servant. Westerby has not betrayed Ko's confidence, or Ko's money, or Ko's brother. In Ko's eyes, Westerby represents a large newspaper. And Westerby has let it be known—both to Frost and to Tiu, I understand—that his paper possesses a greater degree of knowledge in the matter than he himself. Ko understands the world. By removing one journalist, he will not remove the risk. To the contrary, he will bring out the whole pack."

"Then what is in his mind?" said Smiley.

"Uncertainty. Much as Connie said. He cannot gauge the threat. The Chinese have little place for abstracts, less still for abstract situations. He would like the threat to blow over, and if nothing concrete occurs, he will assume it has done so. That is not a habit confined to the Occident. I am extending your hypothesis." He stood up. "I am not endorsing it. I refuse to. I dissociate myself from it absolutely."

He stalked out. On Smiley's nod, Guillam followed him. Only Connie stayed behind.

Smiley had closed his eyes and his brow was drawn into a rigid knot above the bridge of his nose. For a long while Connie said nothing at all. Trot lay as dead across her lap, and she gazed down at him, fondling his belly.

"Karla wouldn't give two pins, would he, dearie?" she murmured. "Not for one dead Frost, nor for ten. That's the difference, really. We can't write it much larger than that, can we, not these days? Who was it who used to say, 'We're fighting for the survival of Reasonable Man'? Steed-Asprey? Or was it Control? I loved that. It covered it all. Hitler. The new thing. That's who we are: reasonable. Aren't we, Trot? We're not just English. We're reasonable."

Her voice fell a little. "Darling, what about Sam? Have you had *thoughts?*"

It was still a long while before Smiley spoke, and when he did so, his voice was harsh, like a voice to keep her at a distance.

"He's to stand by. Do nothing till he has the green light. He knows that. He's to wait till the green light." He drew in a deep breath and let it out again. "He may not even be needed. We may quite well manage without him. It all depends how Ko jumps."

"George, darling, *dear* George."

In silent ritual, she pushed herself to the grate, took up the poker, and with a huge effort stirred the coals, clinging to the dog with her free hand.

Jerry stood at the kitchen window, watching the yellow dawn cut up the harbour mist. Last night there had been a storm, he remembered. Must have hit an hour before Luke telephoned.

He had watched it from the mattress while the girl lay snoring along his leg. First the smell of vegetation, then the wind rustling guiltily in the palm trees, dry hands rubbed together. Then the hiss of rain like tons of molten shot being shaken into the sea. Finally the sheet lightning rocking the harbour in long slow breaths while salvos of thunder cracked over the dancing roof-tops. I killed him, he thought. Give or take a little, it was me who gave him the shove. "It's not just the generals, it's every man who carries a gun." Quote source and context.

The phone was ringing. Let it ring, he thought. Probably Craw, wetting his pants. He picked up the receiver. Luke, sounding even more than usually American.

"Hey, man! Big drama! Stubbsie just came through on the wire. Personal for Westerby. Eat before reading. Want to hear it?"

"No."

"A swing through the war zones. Cambodia's airlines and the siege economy. Our man amid shot and shell! You're in luck, sailor! They want you to get your ass shot off!"

And leave Lizzie to Tiu, he thought, ringing off.

And for all I know, to that bastard Collins too, lurking in her shadow like a white slaver. Jerry had worked to Sam a couple of times while Sam was plain Mr. Mellon of Vientiane, an uncannily successful trader, headman of the local round-eye crooks. He reckoned him one of the most unappetising operators in the game.

He returned to his place at the window thinking of Lizzie again, up there on her own giddy roof-top. Thinking of little Frost, and of his fondness for being alive. Thinking of the smell that had greeted him when he returned here, to his flat. It was everywhere. It overrode the reek of the girl's deodorant, the stale cigarette smoke, the smell of gas, and the smell of cooking oil from the mah-jong players next door. It even overrode the memory of Frost's formaldehyde. Catching it, Jerry had actually charted in his imagination the route Tiu had taken as he foraged: where he had lingered, and where he had skimped on his journey through Jerry's clothes, Jerry's pantry, and Jerry's few possessions. A smell of rose-water and almonds mixed, favoured by an early wife.

15

Siege Town

When you leave Hong Kong, it ceases to exist. When you have passed the last Chinese policeman in British ammunition boots and puttees, and held your breath as you race sixty feet above the roofs of the grey slums, when the out-islands have dwindled into the blue mist, you know that the curtain has been rung down, the props cleared away, and the life you lived there was all illusion. But this time for once, Jerry couldn't rise to that feeling: he carried the memory of the dead Frost and the live girl with him, and they were still beside him as he reached Bangkok.

As usual it took him all day to find what he was looking for; as usual he was about to give up. In Bangkok, in Jerry's view, that happened to everyone: a tourist looking for a *wat*, a journalist for a story—or Jerry for Ricardo's friend and partner Charlie Marshall—your prize sits down the far end of some damned alley, jammed between a silted *klong* and a pile of concrete trash, and it costs you five dollars U.S. more than you expected. Also, though this was theoretically Bangkok's dry season, Jerry could not remember ever being here except in rain, which cascaded in unheralded bursts from the polluted, burning sky. Afterwards people always told him he got the one wet day. He started at the airport, because he was already there and because he reasoned that in the South East no one can fly for long without flying through Bangkok. Charlie wasn't around any more, they said; someone even assured him Charlie had stopped being a pilot after Ric died. Someone else said he was in jail, someone else again that he was most likely in "one of the dens." A ravishing Air Vietnam hostess said with a giggle that he was making freight hops to Saigon; she only ever saw him in Saigon.

"Out of where?" Jerry asked.

"Maybe Phnom Penh, maybe Vientiane," she said—but Charlie's destination, she insisted, was always Saigon and he never hit Bangkok. Jerry checked the telephone directory and there was no Indocharter listed. On an off chance he looked up Marshall too, discovered one—even a Marshall, C.—called him, but found himself talking not to the son of a Kuomintang war-lord who had christened himself with high military rank but to a puzzled Scottish trader who kept saying, "Listen, but *do* come round."

He went to the jail where the *farangs* are locked up when they can't pay or have been rude to a general, and checked the record. He walked along the balconies and peered through the cage doors and spoke to a couple of crazed hippies. But while they had a good deal to say about being locked up, they hadn't seen Charlie Marshall and they hadn't heard of him, and to put it delicately they didn't care about him either. In a black mood he drove to the so-called sanatorium where addicts enjoy their cold turkey, and there was great excitement because a man in a strait-jacket had succeeded in putting his own eyes out with his fingers, but it wasn't Charlie Marshall, and no, they had no pilots, no Corsicans, no Corsican Chinese, and *certainly* no son of a Kuomintang general.

So Jerry started on the hotels where pilots might hang out in transit. He didn't like the work, because it was deadening and, more particularly, he knew that Ko had a big outfit here. He had no serious doubt that Frost had blown him; he knew that most rich overseas Chinese legitimately run several passports and the Swatownese more than several; he knew that Ko had a Thai passport in his pocket and probably a couple of Thai generals as well. And he knew that when they were cross the Thais killed a great deal sooner and more thoroughly than almost everyone else, even though when they condemned a man to the firing-squad, they shot him through a stretched bed sheet in order not to offend the laws of the Lord Buddha. For that reason among a good few others, Jerry felt less than comfortable shouting Charlie Marshall's name all over the big hotels.

He tried the Erawan, the Hyatt, the Miramar, and the Oriental and about thirty others, and at the Erawan he trod specially lightly, remembering that China Airsea had a suite there and Craw said Ko used it often. He formed a picture of Lizzie with her blond hair, playing hostess for him or stretched out at the poolside sunning her long body while the tycoons sipped their Scotches and wondered how much would buy an hour of her time.

While he rode round, a sudden rainstorm pelted fat drops so foul with soot that they blackened the gold of the street temples. The taxi-driver aquaplaned on the flooded roads, missing the water-buffaloes by inches, the garish buses jingled and charged at them, blood-stained Kung Fu posters screamed at them; but Marshall—Charlie Marshall—*Captain* Marshall—was not a name to anyone, though Jerry dispensed coffee money liberally. Charlie's got a girl, thought Jerry. He's got a girl and uses her place, just as I would.

At the Oriental he tipped the porter and arranged to collect messages and use the telephone, and best of all he obtained a receipt for two nights' lodging with which to taunt Stubbs. But his trail round the hotels had scared him, he felt exposed and at risk, so to sleep, for a dollar a night, he took a prepaid room in a nameless backstreet doss-house where the formalities of registration were dispensed with: a place like a row of beach huts, with all the room doors opening straight on to the pavement in order to make fornication easier, and open garages with plastic curtains that screened the number of your car.

By the evening he was reduced to stomping the air-freight agencies, asking about a firm called Indocharter, though he wasn't too keen to do that either, and he was seriously wondering whether to believe the Air Vietnam hostess and take up the trail in Saigon, when a Chinese girl in one of the agencies said, "Indocharter? That's Captain Marshall's line."

She directed him to a bookshop where Charlie Marshall bought his literature and collected his mail whenever he was in town. The shop was also run by Chinese, and when Jerry mentioned Marshall the old proprietor burst out laughing and said Charlie hadn't been in for months. The old man was very small, with false teeth that grimaced.

"He owe you money? Charlie Marshall owe you money, clash a plane for you?" He once more hooted with laughter and Jerry joined in.

"Super. Great. Listen, what do you do with all the mail when he doesn't come here? Do you send it on?"

Charlie Marshall, he didn't get no mail, the old man said.

"Ah, but, sport, if a letter comes tomorrow, where will you send it?"

To Phnom Penh, the old man said, pocketing his five dollars, and fished a scrap of paper from his desk so that Jerry could copy down the address.

"Maybe I should buy him a book," said Jerry, looking round. "What does he like?"

"Flench," the old man said automatically and, taking Jerry upstairs, showed him his sanctum for round-eye culture: for the English, pornography printed in Brussels; for the French, row after row of tattered classics—Voltaire, Montesquieu, Hugo. Jerry bought a copy of *Candide* and slipped it into his pocket. Visitors to this room were *ex officio* celebrities apparently, for the old man produced a visitor's book and Jerry signed it: "J. Westerby, newshound." The comments column was played for laughs, so he wrote, "A most distinguished emporium."

Then he looked back through the pages and asked, "Charlie Marshall sign here too, sport?"

The old man showed him Charlie Marshall's signature a couple of times—"Address: here," he had written.

"How about his friend?"

"Flend?"

"Captain Ricardo."

At this the old man grew very solemn and gently took away the book.

He went round to the Foreign Correspondents' Club at the Oriental, and it was empty except for a troop of Japanese who had just returned from Cambodia. They told him the state of play there as of yesterday, and he got a little drunk. And as he was leaving, to his momentary horror, the dwarf appeared, in town for consultation with the local bureau. He had a Thai boy in tow, which made him particularly pert. "Why, *Westerby!* But *how's* the Secret Service today?" He played this joke on pretty well everyone, but it didn't improve Jerry's peace of mind.

At the doss-house he drank a lot more Scotch but the exertions of his fellow guests kept him awake. Finally, in self-defence he went out and found himself a girl, a soft little creature from a bar up the road, but when he lay alone his thoughts once more homed on Lizzie: like it or not, she was his bed companion.

How much was she consciously involved with them? he wondered. Did she know what she was playing with when she set Jerry up for Tiu? Did she know what Drake's boys had done to Frost? Did she know they might do it to Jerry? It even entered his mind that she had been there while they did it, and that thought appalled him. No question: Frost's body was still very fresh in his memory. It was one of the worst.

By two in the morning he decided he was going to have a bout of fever, he was sweating and turning so much. Once, he heard sounds of soft footsteps inside the room and flung himself into a corner, clutching a teak table-lamp ripped from its socket. At four he was woken by that amazing Asian hubbub: pig-like hawking sounds, bells, cries of old men *in extremis*, the crowing of a thousand roosters echoing in the tile and concrete corridors. He fought with the broken plumbing and began the laborious business of getting clean from a thin trickle of cold water. At five the radio was turned on full blast to get him out of bed, and a whine of Asian music announced that the day had begun in earnest. By then he had shaved as if it were his wedding day, and at eight he cabled his plans to the comic for the Circus to intercept.

At eleven he caught the plane to Phnom Penh. As he climbed aboard the Air Cambodge Caravelle, the ground hostess turned her lovely face to him and, in her best lilting English, melodiously wished him a "nice fright."

"Thanks. Yes. Super," he said, and chose the seat over the wing where you stood the best chance. As they slowly took off, he saw a group of fat Thais playing lousy golf on perfect links just beside the runway.

There were eight names on the flight manifest when Jerry read it at the check-in, but only one other passenger boarded the plane, a black-clad American boy with a brief-case. The rest was cargo, stacked aft in brown gunny bags and rush boxes. A siege plane, Jerry thought automatically. You fly in with the goods, you fly out with the lucky. The stewardess offered him an old *Jours de France* and a barley sugar. He read the *Jours de France* to put some French back into his mind, then remembered *Candide* and read that. He had brought the book-bag, and in the book-bag he had Conrad. In Phnom Penh he always read Conrad; it tickled him to remind himself he was sitting in the last of the true Conrad river ports.

To land, they flew in high, then pancaked in a tight uneasy spiral to avoid random small-arms fire from the jungle. There was no ground control, but Jerry hadn't expected any. The stewardess didn't know how close the Khmer Rouge were to the town, but the Japanese had said fifteen kilometres on all fronts and less where there were no roads. The Japanese had said the airport was under fire but only from rockets and sporadically. No 105s. Not yet, but there's always a beginning, thought Jerry.

Then olive earth leapt at them and Jerry saw bomb craters spattered like egg-spots, and the yellow lines from the tyre tracks of the convoys. As they landed feather-light on the pitted runway, the inevitable naked brown children splashed contentedly in a mud-filled crater.

He stepped on to the tarmac and as the heat hit him with a slap, so did the roar of transport planes taking off and landing. Yet for all that, he had the illusion of arriving on a calm summer's day: for in Phnom Penh, like nowhere else Jerry had ever been, war took place in an atmosphere of peace. He remembered the last time he was here, before the bombing halt. A group of Air France passengers bound for Tokyo had been dawdling curiously on the apron, not realising they had landed in a battle. No one told them to take cover, no one was with them. F-4s and 111s were screaming over the airfield, there was shooting from the perimeter, Air America choppers were landing the dead in nets like frightful catches from some red sea, and a Boeing 707, in order to take off, had to crawl across the entire airfield, running the gauntlet in slow motion. Spellbound, Jerry had watched her lollop out of range of the ground fire, and all the way he had waited for the thump that would tell him she had been hit in the tail. But she had kept going as if the innocent were immune, and disappeared into the untroubled horizon.

Now ironically, with the end so close, he noticed that the accent was on the cargo of survival. On the farther side of the airfield huge chartered all-silver American transport planes, 707s and four-engined turbo-prop C-130s marked "Trans World," "Bird Airways," or not marked at all, were landing and taking off in a clumsy, dangerous shuttle as they brought the ammunition and rice in from Thailand and Saigon. On his hasty walk to the terminal Jerry saw two landings, and each time held his breath waiting for the late back-charge of the jets as they fought and shivered to a halt inside the *revêtement* of earth-filled ammunition boxes at the soft end of the landing-strip. Even before they stopped, flight handlers in flack-jackets and helmets had converged like unarmed platoons to wrest their precious sacks from the holds.

Yet even these bad omens could not destroy his pleasure at being back.

"*Vous restez combien de temps, Monsieur?*" the immigration officer enquired.

"*Toujours*, sport," said Jerry. "Long as you'll have me. Longer." He thought of asking after Charlie Marshall then and there, but the airport was stiff with police and spooks of every sort, and as long as he didn't know what he was up against it seemed wise not to advertise his interest. There was a colourful array of old aircraft with new insignia, but he couldn't see any belonging to Indocharter, whose registered markings, Craw had told him at the valedictory briefing just before he left Hong Kong, were believed to be Ko's racing colours: sea grey and sky blue.

He took a taxi and rode in front, gently declining the driver's courteous offers of girls, shows, clubs, boys. The *flamboyants* made a luscious arcade of orange against the slate monsoon sky. He stopped at a haberdasher to change money *au cours flexible*, a term he loved. The money-changers used to be Chinese, Jerry remembered. This one was Indian: the Chinese get out early, but the Indians stay to pick the carcass. Shanty towns lay left and right of the road. Refugees crouched everywhere, cooking, dozing in silent groups. A ring of small children sat passing round a cigarette.

"*Nous sommes un village avec une population des millions,*" said the driver in his schoolroom French.

An army convoy drove at them, headlights on, sticking to the centre of the road. The taxi-driver obediently pulled into the dirt. An ambulance brought up the rear, both doors

open. The bodies were stacked feet outward, legs like pigs'
trotters, marbled and bruised. Dead or alive, it scarcely mattered. They passed a cluster of stilt houses smashed by rockets,
and entered a provincial French square: a restaurant, an *épice-
rie*, a *charcuterie*, advertisements for Byrrh and Coca-Cola. On
the curb, children squatted, watching over litre winebottles
filled with stolen petrol. Jerry remembered that too: that was
what had happened in the shellings. The shells touched off the
petrol and the result was a blood-bath. It would happen again
this time. Nobody learned anything, nothing changed, the
offal was cleared away by morning.

"Stop!" said Jerry and on the spur of the moment handed
the driver the piece of paper on which he had written down the
Bangkok bookshop's address for Charlie Marshall. He had
imagined he should creep up on the place at dead of night, but
in the sunlight there seemed no point any more.

"*Y aller?*" the driver asked, turning to look at him in surprise.

"That's it, sport."

"*Vous connaissez cette maison?*"

"Chum of mine."

"*A vous? Un ami à vous?*"

"Press," said Jerry, which explains any lunacy.

The driver shrugged and pointed the car down a long boulevard, past the French cathedral, into a mud road lined with
courtyard villas which became quickly dingier as they approached the edge of town. Twice Jerry asked the driver what
was special about the address, but the driver had lost his charm
and shrugged away the questions. When they stopped, he insisted on being paid off, and drove away racing the gear changes
in rebuke.

It was just another villa, the lower half hidden behind a wall
pierced with a wrought-iron gate. Jerry pushed the bell and
heard nothing. When he tried to force the gate, it wouldn't
move. He heard a window slam and thought, as he looked
quickly up, that he saw a brown face slip away behind the mos-

quito wire. Then the gate buzzed and yielded, and he walked up a few steps to a tiled verandah and another door, this one of solid teak with a tiny shaded grille for looking out but not in. He waited, then hammered heavily on the knocker, and heard the echoes bounding all over the house. The door was double, with a join at the centre. Pressing his face to the gap, he saw a strip of tiled floor and two steps, presumably the last two steps of a staircase. On the lower of these stood two smooth brown feet, naked, and two bare shins, but he saw no farther than the knees.

"Hullo!" he yelled, still at the gap. "*Bonjour!* Hullo!" And when the legs still did not move: "*Je suis un ami de Charlie Marshall! Madame, Monsieur, je suis un ami anglais de Charlie Marshall! Je veux lui parler.*"

He took out a five-dollar bill and shoved it through the gap but nothing happened, so he took it back and instead tore a piece of paper from his notebook. He headed his message "To Captain C. Marshall" and introduced himself by name as "a British journalist with a proposal to our mutual interest," and gave the address of his hotel. Threading this note also through the gap, he looked for the brown legs again but they had vanished, so he walked till he found a *cyclo*, then rode in the *cyclo* till he found a cab: and no, thank you, no, thank you, he didn't want a girl—except that, as usual, he did.

The hotel used to be the Royal. Now it was *Le Phnom*. A flag was flying from the mast-head, but its grandeur already looked desperate. Signing himself in, he saw living flesh basking round the courtyard pool and once more thought of Lizzie. For the girls, this was the hard school, and if she'd carried little packets for Ricardo, then ten to one she'd been through it. The prettiest belonged to the richest, and the richest were Phnom Penh's Rotarian crooks: the gold and rubber smugglers, the police chiefs, the big-fisted Corsicans who made neat deals with the Khmer Rouge in mid-battle.

There was a letter waiting for him, the flap not sealed. The receptionist, having read it himself, politely watched Jerry do the same. A gilt-edged invitation card with an Embassy crest invited him to dinner. His host was someone he had never heard of. Mystified, he turned the card over. A scrawl on the back read "Knew your friend George of the *Guardian*," and "guardian" was the word that introduced. Dinner and dead-letter boxes, he thought: what Sarratt scathingly called the great Foreign Office disconnection.

"*Téléphone?*" Jerry enquired.

"*Il est foutu, Monsieur.*"

"*Electricité?*"

"*Aussi foutue, Monsieur, mais nous avons beaucoup de l'eau.*"

"Keller!" said Jerry with a grin.

"*Dans la cour, Monsieur.*"

He walked into the gardens. Among the flesh sat a bunch of warries from the Fleet Street Heavies, drinking Scotch and exchanging hard stories. They looked like boy pilots in the Battle of Britain fighting a borrowed war, and they watched him in collective contempt for his upper-class origins. One wore a white kerchief, and lank hair bravely tossed back.

"Christ, it's the Duke," he said. "How'd you get here? Walk on the Mekong?"

But Jerry didn't want them, he wanted Keller. Keller was permanent. He was a wireman and he was American and Jerry knew him from other wars. More particularly, no *uitlander* newsman came to town without putting his cause at Keller's feet, and if Jerry was to have credibility, then Keller's chop would supply it, and credibility was increasingly dear to him. He found Keller in the car-park. Broad shoulders, grey-headed, one sleeve rolled down. He was standing with his sleeved arm stuffed into his pocket, watching a driver hose out the inside of a Mercedes.

"Max. Super."

"Ripping," said Keller after glancing at him, then went back to his watching. Beside him stood a pair of slim Khmer boys looking like fashion photographers, in high-heeled boots and bell-bottoms and cameras dangling over their glittering, unbuttoned shirts. As Jerry looked on, the driver stopped hosing and began scrubbing the upholstery with an army pack of lint which turned brown the more he rubbed. Another American joined the group and Jerry guessed he was Keller's newest stringer. Keller went through stringers fairly fast.

"What happened?" said Jerry as the driver began hosing again.

"Two-dollar hero caught very expensive bullet," said the stringer. "That's what happened." He was a pale Southerner with an air of being amused, and Jerry was prepared to dislike him.

"Right, Keller?" Jerry asked.

"Photographer," Keller said.

"One of Keller's native picture-warriors," said the Southerner, still grinning.

Keller's wire service ran a stable of them. All the big services did: Cambodian boys, like the couple standing here. They paid them two U.S. to go to the front and twenty for every photo printed. Jerry had heard that Keller was losing them at the rate of one a week.

"Took it clean through the shoulder while he was running and stooping," said the stringer. "Lost it through the lower back. Went through him like grass through a goose." He seemed impressed.

"Where is he?" said Jerry for something to say, while the driver continued to mop and hose and scrub.

"Dying right up the road there. What happened, see, couple of weeks back those bastards in the New York bureau dug their toes in about medication. We used to ship them to Bangkok. Not now. Man, not now. Know something? Up the road they lie on the floor and have to bribe the nurses to take them water. Right, boys?"

The two Cambodians smiled politely.

"Want something, Westerby?" Keller asked.

Keller's face was grey and pitted. Jerry knew him best from the sixties in the Congo, where Keller had burned his hand pulling a kid out of a lorry. Now the fingers were welded like a

webbed claw, but otherwise he looked the same. Jerry remembered that incident best because he had been holding the other
end of the kid.

"Comic wants me to take a look round," Jerry said.

"Can you still do that?"

Jerry laughed and Keller laughed, and they drank Scotch in
the bar till the car was ready, chatting about old times. At the
main entrance, they picked up a girl who had been waiting all
day, just for Keller, a tall Californian with too much camera
and long, restless legs. As the phones weren't working, Jerry
insisted on stopping off at the British Embassy so that he could
reply to his invitation.

Keller wasn't very polite: "You some kinda spook or something these days, Westerby, slanting your stories, arse-licking
for deep background and a pension on the side or something?"
There were people who said that was roughly Keller's position,
but there are always people.

"Sure," said Jerry amiably. "Been at it for years."

The sandbags at the entrance were new and new anti-
grenade wires glistened in the teeming sunlight. In the lobby,
with the spine-breaking irrelevance which only diplomats can
quite achieve, a big partitioned poster recommended "British
High Performance Cars" to a city parched of fuel, and supplied cheerful photographs of several unavailable models.

"I will tell the Counsellor you have accepted," said the
receptionist solemnly.

The Mercedes still smelt a little warm from the blood, but
the driver had turned up the air-conditioning.

"What do they do in there, Westerby?" Keller asked. "Knit
or something?"

"Or something." Jerry smiled, mainly to the Californian girl.

Jerry sat in front, Keller and the girl in the back.

"Okay. So hear this," said Keller.

"Sure," said Jerry.

Jerry had his notebook open and scribbled while Keller

talked. The girl wore a short skirt and Jerry and the driver could see her thighs in the mirror. Keller had his good hand on her knee. Her name of all things was Lorraine and, like Jerry, she was formally taking a swing through the war zones for her group of Midwest dailies. Soon they were the only car. Soon even the *cyclos* stopped, leaving them peasants, and bicycles, and buffaloes, and the flowered bushes of the approaching countryside.

"Heavy fighting on all the main highways," Keller intoned at near dictation speed. "Rocket attacks at night, *plastics* during the day, Lon Nol still thinks he's God, and the U.S. Embassy has hot flushes supporting him then trying to throw him out." He gave statistics, ordnance, casualties, the scale of U.S. aid. He named generals known to be selling American arms to the Khmer Rouge, and generals who ran phantom armies in order to claim the troops' pay, and generals who did both.

"The usual snafu," he went on. "Bad guys are too weak to take the towns, good guys are too crapped out to take the countryside, and nobody wants to fight except the Corns. Students ready to set fire to the place soon as they're no longer exempt from the war, food riots any day now, corruption like there was no tomorrow, no one can live on his salary, fortunes being made, and the place bleeding to death. Palace is unreal and the Embassy is a nut-house, more spooks than straight guys and all pretending they've got a secret. Want more?"

"How long do you give it?"

"A week. Ten years."

"How about the airlines?"

"Airlines is all we have. Mekong's good as dead, so's the roads. Airlines have the whole ballpark. We did a story on that. You see it? They ripped it to pieces. Jesus," he said to the girl. "Why do I have to give a rerun for the poms?"

"More," said Jerry, writing.

"Six months ago this town had five registered airlines. Last three months we got thirty-four new licences issued and there's like another dozen in the pipeline. Going rate is three million

riels to the Minister personally and two million spread around
his people. Less if you pay gold, less still if you pay abroad.
We're working route thirteen," he said to the girl. "Thought
you'd like to take a look."

"Great," said the girl and pressed her knees together, entrap-
ping Keller's good hand.

They passed a statue with its arm shot off and after that the
road followed the river bend.

"That's if Westerby here can handle it," Keller added as an
afterthought.

"Oh, I think I'm in pretty good shape," said Jerry, and the
girl laughed, changing sides a moment.

"K.R. got themselves a new position out on the far bank
there, hon," Keller explained, talking to the girl in preference.
Across the brown, fast water, Jerry saw a couple of T-28s, poking around looking for something to bomb. There was a fire,
quite a big one, and the smoke column rose straight into the
sky like a virtuous offering.

"Where do the overseas Chinese come in?" Jerry asked.
"In Hong Kong no one's heard of this place."

"Chinese control eighty percent of our commerce and that
includes airlines. Old or new. Cambodian's lazy, see, hon? Your
Cambodian's content to take his profit out of American aid. Your
Chinese aren't like that. Oh, no, siree. Chinese like to work,
Chinese like to turn their cash over. They fixed our money market, our transport monopoly, our rate of inflation, our siege
economy. War's getting to be a wholly owned Hong Kong subsidiary. Hey, Westerby, you still got that wife you told me about,
the cute one with the eyes?"

"Took the other road," Jerry said.

"Too bad. She sounded real great. He had this great wife,"
said Keller to the girl.

"How about you?" asked Jerry.

Keller shook his head and smiled at the girl. "Care if I
smoke, hon?" he asked confidingly.

There was a gap in Keller's welded claw which could have been drilled specially to hold a cigarette, and the rim of it was brown with nicotine. Keller put his good hand back on her thigh. The road turned to track, and deep ruts appeared where the convoys had passed. They entered a short tunnel of trees, and as they did so a thunder of shell-fire opened to their right and the trees arched like trees in a typhoon.

"*Wow!*" the girl yelled. "Can we slow down a little?" And she began hauling at the straps of her camera.

"Be my guest. Medium artillery," said Keller. "Ours," he added as a joke. The girl lowered the window and shot off some film. The barrage continued, the trees danced, but the peasants in the paddy didn't even lift their heads. When it died, the bells of the water-buffaloes went on ringing like an echo. They drove on. On the near river-bank, two kids had an old bike and were swapping rides. In the water, a shoal of them were diving in and out of an inner tube, brown bodies glistening. The girl photographed them too.

"You still speak French, Westerby? Me and Westerby did a thing together in the Congo awhile back," he explained to the girl.

"I heard," she said knowingly.

"Poms get education," Keller explained. Jerry hadn't remembered him so talkative. "They get *raised*. That right, Westerby? Specially lords, right? Westerby's some kind of lord."

"That's us, sport. Scholars to a man. Not like you hayseeds."

"Well, you speak to the driver, right? We got instructions for him, you do the saying. He hasn't had time to learn English yet. Go left."

"*A gauche,*" said Jerry.

The driver was a boy, but he already had the guide's boredom.

In the mirror Jerry noticed that Keller's white claw was shaking as he drew on the cigarette. He wondered if it always did. They passed through a couple of villages. It was very quiet.

He thought of Lizzie and the claw marks on her chin. He longed to do something plain with her, like taking a walk over English fields. Craw said she was a suburban drag-up. It touched him that she had a fantasy about horses.

"Westerby."

"Yes, sport?"

"That thing you have with your fingers. Drumming them. Mind not doing that? Bugs me. It's repressive, somehow." He turned to the girl. "They been pounding this place for years, hon," he said expansively. "Years." He blew out a gust of cigarette smoke.

"About the airline thing," Jerry suggested, pencil ready to write again. "What's the arithmetic?"

"Most of the companies take dry-wing leases out of Vientiane. That includes maintenance, pilot, depreciation, but not fuel. Maybe you knew that. Best is own your own plane. That way you have the two things. You milk the siege and you get your ass out when the end comes. Watch for the kids, hon," he told the girl as he drew again on his cigarette. "While there's kids around there won't be trouble. When the kids disappear it's bad news. Means they've hidden them. Always watch for kids."

The girl Lorraine was fiddling with her camera again. They had reached a rudimentary check-point. A couple of sentries peered in as they passed, but the driver didn't even slow down. They approached a fork and the driver stopped.

"The river," Keller ordered. "Tell him to stay on the river-bank."

Jerry told him. The boy seemed surprised; seemed even about to object, then changed his mind.

"Kids in the villages," Keller was saying, "kids at the front. No difference. Either way, kids are a weather-vane. Khmer soldiers take their families with them to war as a matter of course. If the father dies, there'll be nothing for the family anyway, so they might as well come along with the military where there's food. Another thing, hon, another thing is, the widows must be right on hand to claim evidence of the father's death, right? That's a human-interest thing for you—right, Westerby? If they don't claim, the commanding officer will deny it and steal the man's pay for himself. Be my guest," he said as she wrote. "But don't think anyone will print it. This war's over. Right, Westerby?"

"*Finito*," Jerry agreed.

She would be funny, he decided. If Lizzie were here, she would definitely see a funny side and laugh at it. Somewhere among all her imitations, he reckoned, there was a lost original, and he definitely intended to find it. The driver drew up beside an old woman and asked her something in Khmer, but she put her face in her hands and turned her head away.

"Why'd she do *that*, for God's sakes?" the girl cried angrily. "We didn't want anything bad. Jesus!"

"Shy," said Keller in a flattening voice.

Behind them the artillery barrage fired another salvo and it was like a door slamming, barring the way back. They passed a *wat* and entered a market square made of wooden houses. Saffron-clad monks stared at them, but the girls tending the stalls ignored them and the babies went on playing with the bantams.

"So what was the check-point for?" the girl asked as she photographed. "Are we somewhere dangerous now?"

"Getting there, hon, getting there. Now shut up."

Ahead of them Jerry could hear the sound of automatic fire, M-16s and AK-47s mixed. A jeep raced at them out of the trees and at the last second veered, banging and tripping over the ruts. At the same moment the sunshine went out. Till now they had accepted it as their right, a liquid, vivid light washed clean by the rainstorms. This was March and the dry season; this was Cambodia, where war, like cricket, was played in decent weather. But now black clouds collected, the trees closed round them like winter, and the wooden houses pulled into the dark.

"What do the Khmer Rouge dress like?" the girl asked in a quieter voice. "Do they have *uniforms?*"

"Feathers and a G-string," Keller roared. "Some are even bottomless." As he laughed, Jerry heard the taut strain in his voice, and glimpsed the trembling claw as he drew on his cigarette. "Hell, hon, they dress like farmers, for Christ's sake. They just have these black pyjamas."

"Is it always so empty?"

"Varies," said Keller.

"And Ho Chi Minh sandals," Jerry put in distractedly.

A pair of green water birds lifted across the track. The sound of firing was no louder.

"Didn't you have a daughter or something? What happened there?" Keller said.

"She's fine. Great."

"Called what?"

"Catherine," said Jerry.

"Sounds like we're going away from it," Lorraine said, disappointed. They passed an old corpse with no arms. The flies had settled on the face wounds in a black lava.

"Do they always do that?" the girl asked, curious.

"Do what, hon?"

"Take off the boots?"

"Sometimes they take the boots off, sometimes they're the wrong damn size," said Keller in another queer snap of anger. "Some cows got horns, some cows don't, and some cows is horses. Now shut up, will you? Where you from?"

"Santa Barbara," said the girl.

Abruptly the trees ended. They turned a bend and were in the open again, with the brown river right beside them. Unbidden, the driver stopped, then gently backed into the trees.

"Where's he going?" the girl asked. "Who told him to do that?"

"I think he's worried about his tyres, sport," said Jerry, making a joke of it.

"At thirty bucks a day?" said Keller, also as a joke.

They had found a little battle. Ahead of them, dominating

the river bend, stood a smashed village on high waste ground without a living tree near it. The ruined walls were white and the torn edges yellow. With so little vegetation the place looked like the remnants of a Foreign Legion fort, and perhaps it was just that. Inside the walls brown lorries clustered, like lorries at a building site. They heard a few shots, a light rattle. It could have been huntsmen shooting at the evening flight. Tracer flashed, a trio of mortar bombs struck, the ground shook, the car vibrated, and the driver quietly unwound his window while Jerry did the same. But the girl had opened her door and was getting out, one classic leg after the other. Rummaging in a black air-bag, she produced a telefoto lens, screwed it into her camera, and studied the enlarged image.

"That's all there is?" she asked doubtfully. "Shouldn't we see the enemy as well? I don't see anything but our guys and a lot of dirty smoke."

"Oh, they're out on the other side there, hon," Keller said.

"Can't we see?" There was a small silence while the two men conferred without speaking.

"Look," said Keller. "This was just a tour, okay, hon? The detail of the thing gets very varied. Okay?"

"I just think it would be great to see the enemy. I want confrontation, Max. I really do. I like it."

They started walking.

Sometimes you do it to save face, thought Jerry, other times you just do it because you haven't done your job unless you've scared yourself to death. Other times again, you go in order to remind yourself that survival is a fluke. But mostly you go because the others go—for machismo—and because in order to belong you must share.

In the old days perhaps, Jerry had gone for more select reasons. In order to know himself: the Hemingway game. In order to raise his threshold of fear. Because in battle, as in love, desire escalates. When you have been machine-gunned, single rounds seem trivial. When you've been shelled to pieces, the machine-gunning's child's play, if only because the impact of plain shot leaves your brain in place, where the clump of a shell blows it through your ears. And there is a peace: he remembered that too. At bad times in his life—money, children, women all adrift—there had been a sense of peace that came from realising that staying alive was his only responsibility. But this time, he thought, this time it's the most damn-fool reason of all, and that's because I'm looking for a drugged-out pilot who knows a man who used to have Lizzie Worthington for his mistress.

They were walking slowly because the girl in her short skirt had difficulty picking her way over the slippery ruts.

"Great chick," Keller murmured.

"Made for it," Jerry agreed dutifully.

With embarrassment Jerry remembered how in the Congo they used to be confidants, confessing their loves and weaknesses. To steady herself on the rutted ground, the girl was swinging her arms about.

Don't point, thought Jerry; for Christ's sake, don't point. That's how photographers get theirs.

"Keep walking, hon," Keller said shrilly. "Don't think of anything. Walk. Want to go back, Westerby?"

They stepped round a little boy playing privately with stones in the dust. Jerry wondered whether he was gun-deaf. He glanced back. The Mercedes was still parked in the trees. Ahead he could pick out men in low firing positions among the rubble, more men than he had realised.

The noise rose suddenly. On the far bank a couple of bombs exploded in the middle of the fire: the T-28s were trying to spread the flames. A ricochet tore into the bank below them, flinging up wet mud and dust. A peasant rode past them on his bicycle, serenely. He rode into the village, through it, and out again, slowly past the ruins and into the trees beyond. No one shot at him, no one challenged him. He could be theirs or ours, thought Jerry. He came into town last night, tossed a *plastic* into a cinema, and now he's returning to his kind.

"Jesus," cried the girl, with a laugh, "why didn't *we* think of bicycles?"

With a clatter of bricks falling, a volley of machine-gun bullets slapped all round them. Below them in the river-bank, by the grace of God, ran a line of empty leopard spots, shallow firing positions dug into the mud. Jerry had picked them out already. Grabbing the girl, he threw her down. Keller was already flat. Lying beside her, Jerry discerned a deep lack of interest. Better a bullet or two here than getting what Frostie got.

The bullets threw up screens of mud and whined off the road. They lay low, waiting for the firing to tire. The girl was looking excitedly across the river, smiling. She was blue-eyed and flaxen and Aryan. A mortar bomb landed behind them on the verge, and for the second time Jerry shoved her flat. The blast swept over them, and when it was past feathers of earth drifted down like a propitiation. But she came up smiling. When the Pentagon thinks of civilisation, thought Jerry, it thinks of you.

In the fort the battle had suddenly thickened. The lorries had disappeared, a dense pall had gathered, the flash and din of mortar was incessant, light machine-gun fire challenged and answered itself with increasing swiftness. Keller's pocked face appeared white as death over the edge of his leopard spot.

"K.R.'s got them by the balls!" he yelled. "Across the river, ahead, and now from the other flank. We should have taken the other lane!"

Christ, Jerry thought, as the rest of the memories came back to him, Keller and I once fought over a girl too. He tried to remember who she was and who had won.

They waited, the firing died. They walked back to the car and gained the fork in time to meet the retreating convoy. Dead and wounded were littered along the roadside, and women crouched among them, fanning the stunned faces with palm leaves.

They got out of the car again. Refugees trundled buffaloes and handcarts and one another, while they screamed at their pigs and children. One old woman screamed at the girl's camera, thinking the lens was a gun barrel. There were sounds Jerry couldn't place, like the ringing of bicycle bells and wailing, and sounds he could, like the drenched sobs of the dying and the clump of approaching mortar fire. Keller was running beside a lorry, trying to find an English-speaking officer; Jerry loped beside him yelling the same questions in French.

"Ah, to hell," said Keller, suddenly bored. "Let's go home." His English lordling's voice: "The *people* and the *noise*," he explained. They returned to the Mercedes.

For a while they were stuck in the column, with the lorries cutting them to the side and the refugees politely tapping at the window asking for a ride. Once Jerry thought he saw Deathwish the Hun riding pillion on an army motor-bike. At the next fork Keller ordered the driver to turn left.

"More private," he said, and put his good hand back on the girl's knee. But Jerry was thinking of Frost in the mortuary, and the whiteness of his screaming jaw.

"My old mother *always* told me," Keller declared in a folksy drawl, "Son, don't never go back through the jungle the same way as you came. Hon?"

"Yes?"

"Hon, you just lost your cherry. My humble congratulations." The hand slipped a little higher.

From all round them came the sound of pouring water like so many burst pipes as a sudden torrent of rain fell. They passed a settlement full of chickens running in a flurry. A barber's chair stood empty in the rain. Jerry turned to Keller.

"This siege economy thing," he resumed as they settled to one another again. "Market forces and so forth. You reckon that story will go?"

"Could do," said Keller airily. "It's been done a few times. But it travels."

"Who are the main operators?"

Keller named a few.

"Indocharter?"

"Indocharter's one," said Keller.

Jerry took a long shot: "There's a clown called Charlie Marshall flies for them, half Chinese. Somebody said he'd talk. Met him?"

"Nope."

He reckoned that was far enough: "What do most of them use for machines?"

"Whatever they can get. DC-4s, you name it. One's not enough. You need two at least—fly one, cannibalise the second for parts. Cheaper to ground a plane and strip it than bribe the customs to release the spares."

"What's the profit?"

"Unprintable."

"Much opium around?"

"There's a whole damn refinery out on the Bassac, for Christ's sakes. Looks like something out of Prohibition times. I can arrange a tour if that's what you're after."

The girl Lorraine was at the window, staring at the rain. "I don't see any kids, Max," she announced. "You said to look out for no kids, that's all. Well, I've been watching and they've disappeared." The driver stopped the car. "It's raining, and I read somewhere that when it rains Asian kids like to come out and play. So, you know, where's the kids?" she said, but Jerry wasn't listening to what she'd read. Ducking and peering through the windscreen all at once, he saw what the driver saw, and it made his throat dry.

"You're the boss, sport," he said to Keller quietly. "Your car, your war, and your girl."

In the mirror, to his pain, Jerry watched Keller's pumice-stone face torn between experience and incapacity.

"Drive at them slowly," Jerry said, when he could wait no longer. "*Lentement.*"

"That's right," Keller said. "Do that."

Fifty yards ahead of them, shrouded by the teeming rain, a grey lorry had pulled broadside across the track, blocking it. In the mirror, a second had pulled out behind them, blocking their retreat.

"Better show our hands," said Keller in a hoarse rush. With his good one he wound down his window. The girl and Jerry did the same. Jerry wiped the windscreen clear of mist and put his hands on the console. The driver held the wheel at the top.

"Don't smile at them, don't speak to them," Jerry ordered.

"Jesus Christ," said Keller. "Holy God."

All over Asia, thought Jerry, pressmen had their favourite stories of what the Khmer Rouge did to you, and most of them were true. Even Frost at this moment would have been grateful for his relatively peaceful end. He knew newsmen who carried poison, or a concealed gun, to save themselves from just this moment. If you're caught, the first night is the only night to get out, he remembered: before they take your shoes, and your health, and God knows what other parts of you. The first night is your only chance, said the folklore. He wondered whether he should repeat it for the girl, but he didn't want to hurt Keller's feelings.

The Mercedes was ploughing forward in first gear, engine whining. The rain was flying all over the car, thundering on the roof, smacking the bonnet, and darting through the open windows. If we bog down, we're finished, Jerry thought. Still the lorry ahead had not moved and it was no more than fifteen yards away, a glistening monster in the downpour. In the dark of the lorry's cab they saw thin faces watching them. At the last minute it lurched backward into the foliage, leaving just enough room to pass. The Mercedes tilted. Jerry had to hold the door pillar to stop himself rolling onto the driver. The two offside wheels skidded and whined, the bonnet swung and all but lurched onto the fender of the lorry.

"No licence plates," Keller breathed. "Holy Christ."

"Don't hurry," Jerry warned the driver. *"Toujours lentement.* Don't put on your lights." He was watching in the mirror.

"And those were the black pyjamas?" the girl said excitedly. "And you wouldn't even let me take a picture?"

No one spoke.

"What did they want? Who are they trying to ambush?" she insisted.

"Somebody else," said Jerry. "Not us."

"Some bum following us," said Keller. "Who cares?"

"Shouldn't we warn someone?"

"There isn't the apparatus," said Keller.

They heard shooting behind them but they kept going.

"Fucking rain," Keller breathed, half to himself. "Why the hell do we get rain suddenly?"

It had all but stopped.

"But Christ, Max," the girl protested, "if they've got us pinned out on the floor like this, why don't they just finish us off?"

Before Keller could reply, the driver did it for him in French, softly and politely, though only Jerry understood.

"When they want to come, they will come," he said, smiling at her in the mirror. "In the bad weather. While the Americans are adding another five metres of concrete to the Embassy roof, and the soldiers are crouching in capes under their trees, and the journalists are drinking whisky, and the generals are at the opium houses, the Khmer Rouge will come out of the jungle and cut our throats."

"What did he say?" Keller demanded. "Translate that, Westerby."

"Yeah, what *was* all that?" said the girl. "It sounded really great. Like a proposition or something."

"Didn't quite get it actually, sport. Sort of outgunned me."

They all broke out laughing, too loud, the driver as well.

And all through it, Jerry realised, he had thought of nobody but Lizzie. Not to the exclusion of danger—quite the contrary.

Like the new, glorious sunshine which suddenly engulfed them, she was the prize of his survival.

At *Le Phnom*, the same sun was beating gaily on the poolside. There had been no rain in the town, but a bad rocket near the girls' school had killed eight or nine children. The Southern stringer had that moment returned from counting them.

"So how did Maxie make out at the bang-bangs?" he asked Jerry as they met in the hall. "Seems to me like his nerve is creaking at the joints a little these days."

"Take your grinning little face out of my sight," Jerry advised. "Otherwise actually I'll smack it." Still grinning, the Southerner departed.

"We could meet tomorrow," the girl said to Jerry. "Tomorrow's free all day."

Behind her, Keller was making his way slowly up the stairs, a hunched figure in a one-sleeved shirt, pulling himself by the bannister rail.

"We could even meet tonight, if you wanted," Lorraine said.

For a while, Jerry sat alone in his room writing postcards for Cat. Then he set course for Max's bureau. He had a few more questions about Charlie Marshall; and besides, he had a notion old Max would appreciate his company.

His duty done, he took a *cyclo* and rode up to Charlie Marshall's house again, and though he pummelled on the door and yelled, all he could see was the same bare brown legs motionless at the bottom of the stairs, this time by candle-light. But the page torn from his notebook had disappeared.

He returned to the town and, still with an hour to kill, settled at a pavement café in one of a hundred empty chairs and drank a long Pernod, remembering how once the girls of the town had ticked past him here on their little wicker carriages, whispering clichés of love in singsong French. Tonight the darkness trembled to nothing more lovely than the thud of occasional gun-fire, while the town huddled, waiting for the blow.

Yet it was not the shelling but the silence that held the greatest fear. Like the jungle itself, silence, not gun-fire, was the natural element of the approaching enemy.

When a diplomat wants to talk, the first thing he thinks of is food, and in diplomatic circles one dined early because of the curfew. Not that diplomats were subject to such rigours, but it is a charming arrogance of diplomats the world over to suppose they set an example—to whom, or of what, the devil himself will never know. The Counsellor's house was in a flat, leafy enclave bordering Lon Nol's palace. In the driveway as Jerry arrived, an official limousine was emptying its occupants, watched over by a jeep stiff with militia. It's either royalty or religion, Jerry thought as he got out; but it was no more than a senior American diplomat and his wife arriving for a meal.

"Ah. You must be Mr. Westerby," said his hostess.

She was tall and Harrods and amused by the idea of a journalist, as she was amused by anyone who was not a diplomat, and of counsellor rank at that. "John has been *dying* to meet you," she declared brightly, and Jerry supposed she was putting him at his ease. He followed the trail upstairs. His host stood at the top, a wiry man with a moustache and a stoop and a boyishness which Jerry more usually associated with the clergy.

"Oh, well done! Smashing. You're the cricketer. Well done. Mutual friends, right? We're not allowed to use the balcony tonight, I'm afraid," he said, with a naughty glance toward the American corner. "Good men are too scarce, apparently. Got to stay under cover. Seen where you are?" He stabbed a commanding finger at a leather-framed placement chart showing the seating arrangement. "Come and meet some people. Just a minute." He drew him slightly aside, but only slightly. "It all goes through me, right? I've made that absolutely clear. Don't let them get you into a corner, right? Quite a little *squall* running, if you follow me. Local thing. Not your problem."

The senior American appeared at first sight small, being

dark and tidy, but when he stood to shake Jerry's hand, he was nearly Jerry's height. He wore a tartan jacket of raw silk and he held a walkie-talkie radio in a black plastic case. His brown eyes were intelligent but over-respectful, and as they shook hands, a voice inside Jerry said "Cousin."

"Glad to know you, Mr. Westerby. I understand you're from Hong Kong. Your Governor there is a very good friend of mine. Beckie, this is Mr. Westerby, a friend of the Governor of Hong Kong and a good friend of John, our host."

He indicated a large woman bridled in dull hand-beaten silver from the market. Her bright clothes flowed in an Asian medley.

"Oh, Mr. *Westerby*," she said. "From Hong Kong. *Hello*."

The remaining guests were a mixed bag of local traders. Their womenfolk were Eurasian, French, and Corsican. A houseboy hit a silver gong. The dining-room ceiling was concrete, but as they trooped in Jerry saw several eyes lift to make sure. A silver card holder told him he was "The Honourable G. Westerby," a silver menu holder promised him *le roast beef à l'anglaise*, silver candle-sticks held long candles of a devotional kind, Cambodian boys flitted and backed at the half-crouch with trays of food cooked this morning while the electricity was on. A much travelled French beauty sat to Jerry's right with a lace handkerchief between her breasts. She held another in her hand, and each time she ate or drank she dusted her little mouth. Her name card called her Countess Sylvia.

"*Je suis très, très diplomée*," she whispered to Jerry as she pecked and dabbed. "*J'ai fait la science politique, mécanique, et l'électricité générale*. In January I have a bad heart. Now I recover."

"Ah, well now, me, I'm not qualified at *anything*," Jerry insisted, making far too much of a joke of it. "Jack of all trades, master of none, that's us." To put this into French took him quite some while, and he was still labouring at it when from somewhere fairly close a burst of machine-gun fire sounded, far too long for the health of the gun. There were no answering shots. The conversation hung.

"Some bloody idiot shooting at the geckos, I should think," said the Counsellor, and his wife laughed at him fondly down the table, as if the war were a little side-show they had laid on between them for their guests. The silence returned, more pregnant than before. The little Countess put her fork on her plate and it clanged like a tram in the night.

"*Dieu,*" she said.

At once, everyone started talking. The American wife asked Jerry where he was *raised*, and when they had been through that she asked him where his *home* was, so Jerry gave Thurloe Square, old Pet's place, because he didn't feel like talking about Tuscany.

"We own land in Vermont," she said firmly. "But we haven't built on it yet."

Two rockets fell at the same time. Jerry reckoned they were east about half a mile. Glancing round to see whether the windows were closed, Jerry caught the brown gaze of the American husband fixed on him with mysterious urgency.

"You have plans for tomorrow, Mr. Westerby?" he asked.

"Not particularly."

"If there's anything we can do, let me know."

"Thanks," said Jerry, but he had the feeling that wasn't the point of the question.

A Swiss trader with a wise face had a funny story. He used Jerry's presence to repeat it.

"Some time back, the whole town was alight with shooting, Mr. Westerby," he said. "We were all going to die. Oh, *definitely.* Tonight we die! Everything—shells, tracer—poured into the sky, one million dollars' worth of ammunition, we heard afterwards. Hours on end. Some of my friends went round shaking hands with one another." An army of black ants emerged from under the table and began marching in single column across the perfectly laundered damask cloth, making a careful detour round the silver candle-sticks and the silver flower bowl brimming with hibiscus. "The Americans radioed around, hopped up and down, we all considered very carefully our position on the evacuation list, but a funny thing, you know: the telephones were working and we even had electricity. What did the target turn out to be?" The others were already laughing hysterically. "Frogs! Some very greedy *frogs!*"

"Toads," somebody corrected him, but it didn't stop the laughter.

The American diplomat, a model of courteous self-criticism, supplied the amusing epilogue.

"The Cambodians have an old superstition, Mr. Westerby," he said. "When there's an eclipse of the moon, you must make a lot of noise. You must shoot off fireworks, you must bang tin cans, or, best still, fire off a million dollars' worth of ordnance. Because if you don't—why, the frogs will gobble up the moon. We *should* have known, but we *didn't* know, and in consequence we were made to look very, very silly indeed," he said proudly.

"Yes, I'm afraid you boobed there, old boy," the Counsellor said with satisfaction.

But though the American's smile remained frank and open his eyes continued to impart something far more pressing— such as a message between professionals.

Someone talked about servants and their amazing fatalism. An isolated detonation, loud and seemingly quite near, ended the performance. As the Countess Sylvia reached for Jerry's hand, their hostess smiled interrogatively at her husband down the table.

"John, darling," she asked in her most hospitable voice, "was that incoming or outgoing?"

"Outgoing," he replied, with a laugh. "Oh, outgoing definitely. Ask our journalist friend if you don't believe me. He's been through a few wars, haven't you, Westerby?"

At which the silence, yet again, joined them like a forbidden topic. The American lady clung to that piece of land in Vermont: perhaps, after all, they *should* build on it. Perhaps, after all, it was time.

"Maybe we should just *write* to that architect," she said.

"Maybe we should," her husband agreed, and at that moment they were flung into a pitched battle. From very close a prolonged burst of pom-poms lit the washing in the courtyard and a cluster of machine-guns—as many as twenty—crackled in a sustained and desperate fire. By the flashes they saw the servants scurry into the house, and over the firing they heard orders given and replied to, scream for scream, and the crazy ringing of hand-gongs.

Inside the room, nobody moved except the American diplomat, who lifted his walkie-talkie to his lips, drew out the aerial, and murmured something before putting it to his ear. Jerry glanced downward and saw the Countess's hand battened trustingly to his own. Her cheek brushed his shoulder. The firing faltered. He heard the clump of a small bomb close. No vibration, but the flames of the candles tilted in salute and on the mantelshelf a couple of heavy invitation cards flopped over with a slap and lay still, the only recognisable casualties. Then as a last and separate sound, they heard the grizzle of a departing single-engined plane like the distant grousing of a child.

It was capped by the Counsellor's easy laughter as he addressed his wife. "Ah, well now, that *wasn't* the eclipse, I'm afraid, was it, Hills? That was the advantage of having Lon Nol as our neighbour. One of his pilots gets fed up with not being paid now and then, so he takes up a plane and has a pot-shot at the palace. Darling, are you going to take the gels off to powder their noses and do whatever you all do?"

It's anger, Jerry decided, catching the senior American's eye again. He's like a man with a mission to the poor who has to waste his time with the rich.

* * *

Downstairs Jerry, the Counsellor, and the American stood alone in the ground-floor study. The Counsellor had acquired a wolfish shyness.

"Yes, well," he said. "Now I've put you both on the map, perhaps I should leave you to it. Whisky in the decanter, right, Westerby?"

"Right, John," said the American, but the Counsellor didn't seem to hear.

"Just remember, Westerby: the mandate's *ours*, right? We're keeping the bed warm. Right?" With a knowing wag of the finger, he disappeared.

The study was candle-lit, a small masculine room with no mirrors or pictures, just a ribbed teak ceiling and a green metal desk. The geckos and the bullfrogs would have baffled the most sophisticated microphone.

"Hey, let me get that," said the American, arresting Jerry's progress to the sideboard, and made a show of getting the mix just right for him: water or soda, don't let me drown it.

"Seems kind of a long way round to bring two friends together," the American said, in a taut, chatty tone, from the sideboard as he poured.

"Does rather."

"John's a great guy, but he's kind of a stickler for protocol. Your people have no resources here right now but they have certain rights, so John likes to make sure that the ball doesn't slip out of his court for good. I can understand his point of view. Just that things take a little longer sometimes."

He handed Jerry a long brown envelope from inside the tartan jacket, and with the same pregnant intensity as before watched while he broke the seal. The paper had a smeared and photographic quality.

Somewhere a child moaned, and was silenced. The garage, Jerry thought: the servants have filled the garage with refugees and the Counsellor is not to know.

ENFORCEMENT SAIGON reports Charlie MARSHALL rpt MAR-
SHALL scheduled hit Battambang ETA 1930 tomorrow via
Pailin . . . converted DC-4 Carvair, Indocharter markings
manifest quotes miscellaneous cargo . . . scheduled continue
Phnom Penh.

Then he read the time and date of transmission and anger
hit him like a wind storm. He remembered yesterday's foot-
slogging in Bangkok and today's harebrained taxi ride with
Keller and the girl, and with a "Jesus *Christ*" he slammed the
message back on the table between them: "How long have you
been sitting on this? That's not tomorrow. That's tonight!"

"Unfortunately our host could not arrange the wedding
any earlier. He has an extremely crowded social programme.
Good luck."

Just as angry as Jerry, he quietly took back the signal,
slipped it into the pocket of his jacket, and disappeared upstairs
to his wife, who was busy admiring her hostess's indifferent
collection of pilfered Buddhas.

He stood alone. A rocket fell and this time it was close. The
candles went out and the night sky seemed finally to be split-
ting with the strain of this illusory, Gilbertian war. Mindlessly
the machine-guns joined the clatter. The little bare room with
its tiled floor rattled and sang like a sound machine.

Only as suddenly to stop again, leaving the town to the
silence.

"Something wrong, old boy?" the Counsellor enquired genially from the doorway. "Yank rub you up the wrong way, did
he? They seem to want to run the world single-handed these
days."

"I'll need six-hour options," Jerry said. The Counsellor
didn't quite follow. Having explained to him how they worked,
Jerry stepped quickly into the night.

"Got transport, have you, old boy? That's the way. They'll
shoot you, otherwise. Mind how you go."

* * *

He strode quickly, driven by his irritation and disgust. It was long after curfew. There were no streetlamps, no stars. The moon had vanished, and the squeak of his crêpe soles ran with him like an unwanted companion. The only light came from the perimeter of the palace across the road, but none spilled onto Jerry's side of the street. High walls blocked off the inner building, high wires crowned the walls, and barrels of the light anti-aircraft guns gleamed bronze against the black and sound-less sky. Young soldiers dozed in groups and as Jerry strode past them a fresh roll of gong-beats sounded: the master of the guard was keeping the sentries awake. There was no traffic, but between the sentry posts the refugees had made up their own night villages in a long column down the pavement. Some had draped themselves with strips of brown tarpaulin, some had plank bunks, and some were cooking by tiny flames, though God alone knew what they had found to eat. Some sat in neat social groups, facing in upon each other. On an ox-cart a girl lay with a boy, children Cat's age when he last had seen her in the flesh. But from the hundreds of them not one sound came, and after he had gone a distance he actually turned and peered to make sure they were there. If they were, the dark-ness and the silence hid them. He thought of the dinner party. It had taken place in another land, another universe entirely. He was irrelevant here, yet somehow he had contributed to the disaster.

For no reason that he knew of, the sweat began running off him and the night air made no cooling impact. The dark was as hot as the day. Ahead of him in the town a stray rocket struck carelessly. They creep into the paddies until they're within range, he thought. They lie up, hugging their bits of drain-pipe and their little bomb, then fire and run like hell for the jungle. The palace was behind him. A battery fired a salvo and for a few seconds he was able to see his way by the flashes. The road was broad, a boulevard, and as best he could he kept to the crown. Occasionally he made out the gaps of the side-streets passing him in geometric regularity. If he stooped, he could even see the tree-tops retreating into the paler sky. Once a *cyclo* pattered by, toppling nervously out of the turning, hitting the curb, then steadying. He thought of shouting to it but he preferred to keep on striding.

A male voice greeted him doubtfully out of the darkness—a whisper, nothing indiscreet: *"Bon soir? Monsieur? Bon soir?"*

The sentries stood every hundred metres in ones or twos, holding their carbines in both hands. Their murmurs came to him like invitations, but Jerry was always careful and kept his hands wide of his pockets where they could watch them. Some, seeing the enormous sweating round-eye, laughed and waved him on. Others stopped him at pistol point and gazed up at him earnestly by the light of bicycle lamps while they asked him questions in order to practise their French. Some requested cigarettes and these he gave. He tugged off his drenched jacket and opened his shirt to the waist, but still the air wouldn't cool him and he wondered again whether he had a fever and whether, like last night in Bangkok, he would wake up in his bedroom crouching in the darkness waiting to brain someone with a table-lamp.

The moon appeared, lapped by the foam of the rain clouds. By its light his hotel resembled a locked fortress. He reached the garden wall and followed it leftwards along the trees until it turned again. He threw his jacket over the wall and with difficulty climbed after it. He crossed the lawn to the steps, pushed open the door to the lobby, and stepped back with a surge of disgust. The lobby was in pitch blackness except for a single moonbeam, which shone like a spotlight on a huge luminous chrysalis spun around the naked brown larva of a human body.

It was the night watchman in his hammock, asleep under a mosquito net.

"Vous désirez, Monsieur?" a voice asked softly.

The boy handed him a key and a note, and silently accepted

his tip. Jerry struck his lighter and read the note: "Darling, I'm in room 28 and lonely. Come and see me. L."

What the hell? he thought; maybe it'll put the bits back together again. He climbed the stairs to the second floor, forgetting her terrible banality, thinking only of her long legs and her tilting rump as she negotiated the ruts along the river-bank; her cornflower eyes and her regular all-American gravity as she lay in the leopard spot; thinking only of his own yearning for human touch. Who gives a damn about Keller? he thought. To hold someone is to exist. Perhaps she's frightened too. He knocked on the door, waited, gave it a shove.

"Lorraine? It's me. Westerby."

Nothing happened. He lurched toward the bed, conscious of the absence of any female smell, even face powder or deodorant. On his way there he saw by the same moonlight the dreadfully familiar sight of blue jeans, heavy bean-boots, and a tattered Olivetti portable not unlike his own.

"Come one step nearer and it's statutory rape," said Luke, uncapping the whisky bottle on his bedside table.

16

Friends of Charlie Marshall

He crept out before light, having slept on Luke's floor. He took his typewriter and shoulder-bag, though he expected to use neither. He left a note for Keller asking him to wire Stubbs that he was following the siege story out to the provinces. His back ached from the floor and his head from the bottle.

Luke had come for the bang-bangs, he said; bureau was giving him a rest from Big Moo. Also Jake Chiu, his irate landlord, had finally thrown him out of his apartment.

"I'm destitute, Westerby!" he had cried, and began wailing round the room, *"Destitute,"* till Jerry, to buy himself some sleep and stop the neighbour's banging, slipped his spare flat-key off its ring and flung it at him.

"Until I get back," he warned. "Then *out*. Understood?"

Jerry asked about the Frost thing. Luke had forgotten all about it and had to be reminded. Ah, *him*, he said. *Him*. Yeah, well there were stories he'd been cheeky to the triads and maybe in a hundred years they would all come true, but meanwhile who gave a damn?

But sleep hadn't come so easy even then. They discussed today's arrangements. Luke had proposed to do whatever Jerry was doing. Dying alone was a bore, he had insisted. Better they got drunk and found some whores. Jerry had replied that Luke would have to wait awhile before the two of them went into the sunset together, because he was going fishing for the day and he was going alone.

"Fishing for what, for hell's sakes? If there's a story, share it. Where can you go that is not more beautiful for Brother Lukie's presence?"

Pretty well anywhere, Jerry had said unkindly, and managed to leave without waking him.

He made first for the market and sipped a *soupe chinoise*, studying the stalls and shop fronts. He selected a young Indian who was offering nothing but plastic buckets, water-bottles, and brooms, yet looking very prosperous on the profits.

"What else do you sell, sport?"

"Sir, I sell all things to all gentlemen."

They foxed around. No, said Jerry, it was nothing to smoke that he wanted, and nothing to swallow, nothing to sniff and nothing for the wrists, either. And no, thank you, with all respect to the many beautiful sisters, cousins, and young men of his circle, Jerry's other needs were also taken care of.

"Then, oh, gladness, sir, you are a most happy man."

"I was *really* looking for something for a friend," said Jerry.

The Indian boy looked sharply up and down the street and he wasn't foxing any more.

"A *friendly* friend, sir?"

"Not very."

They shared a *cyclo*. The Indian had an uncle who sold Buddhas in the silver market, and the uncle had a back room with locks and bolts on the door. For thirty American dollars Jerry bought a neat brown Walther automatic with twenty rounds of ammunition. The Sarratt bearleaders, he reckoned as he climbed back into the *cyclo*, would have fallen into a deep swoon. First for what they called improper dressing, a crime of crimes. Second because they preached the hardy nonsense that small guns gave more trouble than use. But they'd have had a bigger fit still if he'd carted his Hong Kong Webley through customs to Bangkok and thence to Phnom Penh, so in Jerry's view they could count themselves lucky, because he wasn't walking into this one naked whatever their doctrine of the week.

At the airport there was no plane to Battambang, but there was never a plane to anywhere. There were the silver rice jets howling on and off the landing-strip, and there were new *revêtements* being built after a fresh fall of rockets in the night. Jerry watched the earth arriving in lorry-loads, and the coolies filling ammunition boxes frantically. In another life, he decided, I'll go into the sand business and flog it to besieged cities.

In the waiting-room Jerry found a group of stewardesses drinking coffee and laughing, and in his breezy way he joined them. A tall girl who spoke English made a doubtful face and disappeared with his passport and five dollars.

"*C'est impossible,*" they all assured him while they waited for her. "*C'est tout occupé.*"

The girl returned smiling. "The pilot is *very* susceptible," she said. "If he don't like you, he don't take you. But I show him your photograph and he has agreed to *surcharger.* He is allowed to take only thirty-one *personnes* but he take you, he don't care, he do it for friendship if you give him one thousand five hundred riels."

The plane was two-thirds empty, and the bullet-holes in the wings wept dew like undressed wounds.

At that time, Battambang was the safest town left in Lon Nol's dwindling archipelago, and Phnom Penh's last farm. For an hour they lumbered over supposedly Khmer Rouge-infested territory without a soul in sight. As they circled, someone shot lazily from the paddies and the pilot pulled a couple of token turns to avoid being hit, but Jerry was more concerned to mark the ground layout before they landed: the park-bays; which runways were civil and which were military; the wired-off enclave which contained the freight huts. They landed in an air of pastoral affluence. Flowers grew round the gun emplace-ments, fat brown chickens scurried in the shell-holes, water and electricity abounded, though a telegram to Phnom Penh already took a week.

Jerry trod very carefully now. His instinct for cover was stronger than ever. *The Honourable Gerald Westerby, the distinguished hack, reports on the siege economy.* When you're my size, sport, you have to have a hell of a good reason for whatever you're doing. So he put out smoke, as the jargon goes.

At the enquiry desk, watched by several quiet men, he asked for the names of the best hotels in town and wrote down a couple while he continued to study the groupings of planes and buildings. Meandering from one office to another, he asked what facilities existed to air-freight news copy to Phnom Penh and no one had the least idea. Continuing his discreet reconnaissance, he waved his cable card around and enquired how to get to the governor's palace, implying that he might have business with the great man personally. By now he was the most distinguished reporter who had ever been to Battambang. Meanwhile he noted the doors marked "Crew" and the doors marked "Private," and the position of the men's rooms, so that later, when he was clear, he could make himself a sketch plan of the entire concourse, with emphasis on the exits to the wired-off part of the airfield.

Finally he asked who was in town just now among the pilots. He was friendly with several, he said, so his simplest plan— should it become necessary—was probably to ask one of them to take his copy in his flight-bag. A stewardess gave names from a list, and while she did this Jerry gently turned the list round and read off the rest. The Indocharter flight was listed but no pilot was mentioned.

"Captain Andreas still flying for Indocharter?" he enquired. *"Le capitaine qui, Monsieur?"*

"Andreas. We used to call him André. Little fellow, always wore dark glasses. Did the Kampong Cham run."

She shook her head. Only Captain Marshall and Captain Ricardo, she said, flew for Indocharter, but Captain Ric had immolated himself in an accident. Jerry affected no interest but established in passing that Captain Marshall's Carvair was due to take off in the afternoon, as forecast in last night's signal, but there was no freight space available; everything was taken, Indocharter was always fully contracted.

"Know where I can reach him?"

"Captain Marshall never flies in the mornings, Monsieur."

He took a cab into town. The best hotel was a flea-bitten dug-out in the main street. The street itself was narrow, stinking, and deafening: an Asian boom town in the making, pounded by the din of Hondas and crammed with the frustrated Mercedes of the quick rich. Keeping his cover going, he took a room and paid for it in advance, to include *service spécial*, which meant nothing more exotic than clean sheets as opposed to those which still bore the marks of other bodies. He told his driver to return in an hour. By force of habit he secured an inflated receipt. He showered, changed, and listened courteously while the houseboy showed him where to climb in after curfew; then he went out to find breakfast because it was still only nine in the morning.

He carried his typewriter and shoulder-bag with him. He saw no other round-eyes. He saw basket-makers, skin-sellers, and fruit-sellers, and once again the inevitable bottles of stolen petrol laid along the pavement waiting for an attack to touch them off. In a mirror hung in a tree he watched a dentist extract teeth from a patient tied in a high chair, and he watched the red-tipped tooth being solemnly added to the thread that displayed the day's catch.

All of these things Jerry recorded in his notebook, as became a zealous reporter of the social scene. And from a pavement café, as he consumed cold beer and fresh fish, he watched the dingy half-glazed offices marked "Indocharter" across the road and waited for someone to come and unlock the door. No one did. *Captain Marshall never flies in the mornings, Monsieur.*

At a chemist's shop that specialised in children's bicycles, he bought a roll of sticking-plaster and back in his room taped the Walther to his ribs rather than have it waving around in his waistband. Thus equipped, the intrepid journalist set forth to live some more cover, which sometimes, in the psychology of a fieldman, is no more than a gratuitous act of self-legitimisation as the heat begins to gather.

The governor lived on the edge of town, behind a verandah and French colonial portals, and a secretariat seventy strong. The vast concrete hall led to a waiting-room never finished, and to much smaller offices behind, and in one of these, after a fifty-minute wait, Jerry was admitted to the presence of a tiny, very senior black-suited Cambodian sent by Phnom Penh to handle noisome correspondents. Word said he was the son of a general and managed the Battambang end of the family opium business. His desk was much too big for him. Several attendants lounged about and they all looked very severe. One wore a uniform with a lot of medal ribbons.

Jerry asked for deep background and made a list of several charming dreams: that the Communist enemy was all but beaten; that there was serious discussion about reopening the entire national road system; that tourism was the growth industry of the province. The general's son spoke slow and beautiful French, and it clearly gave him great pleasure to hear himself, for he kept his eyes half closed and smiled as he spoke, as if listening to beloved music.

"I may conclude, Monsieur, with a word of warning to your country. You are American?"

"English."

"It is the same. Tell your government, sir. If you do not help us to continue the fight against the Communists, we shall go to the Russians and ask them to replace you in our struggle."

Oh, Mother, thought Jerry. Oh, boy. Oh, God.

"I will give them that message," he promised, and made to go.

"*Un instant, Monsieur,*" said the senior official sharply, and there was a stirring among his dozing courtiers. He opened a drawer and pulled out an imposing folder. Frost's will, Jerry thought. My death warrant. Stamps for Cat.

"You are a writer?"

"Yes."

Ko's putting the arm on me. Prison tonight, and wake up with my throat cut tomorrow.

"You were at the Sorbonne, Monsieur?" the official enquired.

"Oxford."

"Oxford in London?"

"Yes."

"Then you have read the great French poets, Monsieur?"

"With intense pleasure," Jerry replied fervently. The courtiers were looking extremely grave.

"Then perhaps Monsieur will favour me with his opinion of the following few verses." In his dignified French, the little official began to read aloud, slowly conducting with his palm.

> *"Deux amants assis sur la terre*
> *Regardaient la mer,"*

he began, and continued for perhaps twenty excruciating lines while Jerry listened in mystification.

"*Voilà,*" said the official finally and put the file aside. "*Vous l'aimez?*" he enquired, severely fixing his eye upon a neutral part of the room.

"*Superbe,*" said Jerry with a gush of enthusiasm. "*Merveilleux.* The sensitivity."

"They are by whom, would you think?"

Jerry grabbed a name at random: "By Lamartine?"

The senior official shook his head. The courtiers were observing Jerry even more closely.

"Victor Hugo?" Jerry ventured.

"They are by me," said the official, and with a sigh returned his poems to the drawer. The courtiers relaxed. "See that this literary person has every facility," he ordered.

* * *

Jerry returned to the airport to find it a milling, dangerous chaos. Mercedes raced up and down the approach as if someone had invaded their nest, the forecourt was a turmoil of beacons, motorcycles, and sirens; and the hall, when he argued his way through the cordon, was jammed with scared people fighting to read notice-boards, yell at each other, and hear the blaring loudspeakers all at the same time.

Forcing a path to the information desk, Jerry found it closed. He leapt on the counter and saw the airfield through a hole in the anti-blast board. A squad of armed soldiers was jog-trotting down the empty runway toward a group of white poles where the national flags drooped in the windless air. They lowered two of the flags to half-mast, and inside the hall the loudspeakers interrupted themselves to blare a few bars of the national anthem. Over the seething heads Jerry searched for someone he might talk to. He selected a lank missionary with cropped yellow hair and glasses and a six-inch silver cross pinned to the pocket of his brown shirt. A pair of Cambodians in dog-collars stood miserably beside him.

"*Vous parlez français?*"

"Yes, but I also speak English!"

A lilting, corrective tone. Jerry guessed he was a Dane.

"I'm press. What's the fuss?" He was shouting at the top of his voice.

"Phnom Penh is closed," the missionary bellowed in reply. "No planes may leave or land."

"Why?"

"Khmer Rouge have hit the ammunition dump in the airport. The town is closed till morning at the least!"

The loudspeaker began chattering again. The two priests listened. The missionary stooped nearly double to catch their murmured translation.

"They have made a great damage and devastated half a dozen planes already. They have laid them waste entirely. The authority is also suspecting sabotage. Maybe she also takes some prisoners. Why are they putting an ammunition house inside the airport in the first case? That was most dangerous. What is the reason here?"

"Good question," Jerry agreed.

He ploughed across the hall. His master plan was already dead, as his master plans usually were. The "Crew Only" door was guarded by a pair of very serious crushers, and in the tension he saw no chance of brazening his way through. The thrust of the crowd was toward the passenger exit, where harassed ground staff were refusing to accept boarding tickets, and harassed police were being besieged with letters of *laissez-passer* designed to put the prominent outside their reach. He let it carry him. At the edges, a team of French traders was screaming for a refund, and the elderly were preparing to settle for the night. But the centre pushed and peered and exchanged fresh rumours, and the momentum carried him steadily to the front. Reaching it, Jerry discreetly took out his cable card and climbed over the improvised barrier. The senior policeman was sleek and well covered and he watched Jerry disdainfully while his subordinates toiled. Jerry strode straight up to him, his shoulder-bag dangling from his hand, and pressed the cable card under his nose.

"*Sécurité américaine,*" he roared in awful French and, with a snarl at the two men on the swing-doors, barged his way onto the tarmac and kept going, while his back waited all the time for a challenge or a warning shot or, in the trigger-happy atmosphere, a shot that was not even a warning. He walked angrily, with rough authority, swinging his shoulder-bag Sarratt-style to distract. Ahead of him—sixty yards, soon fifty—stood a row of single-engined military trainers without insignia. Beyond lay the caged enclosure and the freight huts, numbered nine to eighteen, and beyond the freight huts Jerry saw a cluster of hangars and park-bays marked "Prohibited" in just about every language except Chinese.

Reaching the trainers, Jerry strode imperiously along the line of them as if he were carrying out an inspection. They were anchored with bricks on wires. Pausing but not stopping, he stabbed irritably at a brick with his buckskin boot, yanked at an aileron, and shook his head. From their sandbagged emplacement, to his left, an anti-aircraft gun crew watched him indolently.

"Qu'est-ce que vous faites?"

Half turning, Jerry cupped his hands to his mouth. "Watch the damn sky, for Christ's sakes," he yelled in good American, pointing angrily to heaven, and kept going till he reached the high cage. It was open and the huts lay ahead of him. Once past them he would be out of sight of both the terminal and the control tower. He was walking on smashed concrete with couch-grass in the cracks. There was nobody in sight. The huts were weather-board, thirty feet long, ten high, with palm roofs. He reached the first. The boarding on the windows read "Bomb Cluster Fragmentation Without Fuses." A trodden dust path led to the hangars on the other side. Through the gap Jerry glimpsed the parrot colours of parked cargo planes.

"Got you," Jerry muttered aloud as he emerged on the safe side of the huts, because there ahead of him, clear as day, like a first sight of the enemy after months of lonely marching, a battered blue-grey DC-4 Carvair, fat as a frog, squatted on the crumbling tarmac with her nose-cone open. Diesel oil was dripping in a fast black rain from both her starboard engines, and a spindly Chinese in a sailing cap laden with military insignia stood smoking under the loading bay while he marked an inventory. Two coolies scurried back and forth with sacks, and a third worked the ancient loading lift. At his feet, chickens scrabbled petulantly. And on the fuselage, in flaming crimson against Drake Ko's faded racing colours, ran the letters "OCHART." The others had been lost in a repair job.

Oh, Charlie's indestructible, completely immortal! Charlie

Marshall, *Mr. Tiu, a fantastic half-Chinese, all skin and bones and opium and a completely brilliant pilot.* . . .

He'd bloody well better be, sport, thought Jerry with a shudder, as the coolies loaded sack after sack through the open nose and into the battered belly of the plane.

The Reverend Ricardo's lifelong Sancho Panza, Your Grace, Craw had said, in extension of Lizzie's description. *Half Chow, as the good lady advised us, and the proud veteran of many futile wars.*

Jerry remained standing, making no attempt to conceal himself, dangling the bag from his fist, and wearing the apologetic grin of an English stray. Coolies now seemed to be converging on the plane from several points at once: there were many more than two. Turning his back on them, Jerry repeated his routine of strolling along the line of huts, much as he had walked along the line of trainers, or along the corridor toward Frost's room, peering through cracks in the weather-board and seeing nothing but the occasional broken packing-case. *The concession to operate out of Battambang costs half a million U.S. renewable,* Keller had said. At that price, who pays for redecoration?

The line of huts broke and he came on four army lorries loaded high with fruit, vegetables, and unmarked gunny bags. Their tailboards faced the plane and they sported artillery insignia. Two soldiers stood in each lorry, handing the gunny bags down to the coolies. The sensible thing would have been to drive the lorries onto the tarmac, but a mood of discretion prevailed. *The army likes to be in on things,* Keller had said. *The navy can make millions out of one convoy down the Mekong, the air force is sitting pretty. Bombers fly fruit and the choppers can airlift the rich Chinese instead of the wounded out of the siege towns. Only the fighter boys go hungry, because they have to land where they take off. But the army really has to scratch around to make a living.*

Jerry was closer to the plane now and could hear the squawking as Charlie Marshall fired commands at the coolies.

The huts began again. Number 18 had double doors and the name "Indocharter" daubed in green down the woodwork so that from any distance the letters looked like Chinese characters. In the gloomy interior a Chinese peasant couple squatted on the dust floor. A tethered pig lay with its head on the old man's slippered foot. Their other possession was a long rush parcel meticulously bound with string. It could have been a corpse. A water jar stood in one corner with two rice-bowls at its base. There was nothing else in the hut. Welcome to the Indocharter transit lounge, Jerry thought. With the sweat running down his ribs he tagged himself to the line of coolies till he drew alongside Charlie Marshall, who went on squawking in Khmer at the top of his voice while his shaking pen checked each load on the inventory.

He wore an oily white short-sleeved shirt with enough gold stripes on the epaulettes to make a full general in anybody's air force. Two American combat patches were stitched to his shirt front, amid an amazing collection of medal ribbons and Communist red stars. One patch read "Kill a Commie for Christ," and the other "Christ Was a Capitalist at Heart." His head was turned down and his face was in the shadow of his huge sailing cap, which slopped freely over his ears.

Jerry waited for him to look up. The coolies were already yelling for Jerry to move on, but Charlie Marshall kept his head turned stubbornly down while he added and wrote on the inventory and squawked furiously back at them.

"Captain Marshall, I'm doing a story on Ricardo for a London newspaper," said Jerry quietly. "I want to ride with you as far as Phnom Penh and ask you some questions."

As he spoke, he gently laid the volume of *Candide* on top of the inventory, with three one-hundred-dollar bills poking outward in a discreet fan. When you want a man to look one way, says the Sarratt school of illusionists, always point him in the other.

"They tell me you like Voltaire," he said.

"I don't like anybody," Charlie Marshall retorted in a scratchy falsetto at the inventory, while the cap slipped still lower over his face. "I hate the whole human race, hear me?" His vituperation, despite its Chinese cadence, was unmistakeably French-American. "Jesus Christ, I hate mankind so damn much that if it don't hurry and blow itself to pieces, I'm personally going to buy some bombs and go out there *myself!*"

He had lost his audience. Jerry was half-way up the steel ladder before Charlie Marshall had completed his thesis.

"Voltaire didn't know a damn bloody thing!" he screamed at the next coolie. "He fought the wrong damn war, hear me? Put it over there, you lazy coon, and grab another handful! *Dépêche-toi, crétin, oui?*"

But all the same he jammed Voltaire into the back pocket of his baggy trousers.

The inside of the plane was dark and roomy and as cool as a cathedral. The seats had been removed, and perforated green shelves like meccano had been fitted to the walls. Carcasses of pig and guinea-fowl hung from the roof. The rest of the cargo was stowed in the gangway, starting from the tail-end, which gave Jerry no good feeling about taking off, and consisted of fruit and vegetables and the gunny bags Jerry had spotted in the army trucks, marked "GRAIN," "RICE," "FLOUR," in letters large enough for the most illiterate narcotics agent to read. But the sticky smell of yeast and molasses that already filled the hold required no labels at all.

Some of the bags had been arranged in a ring, to make a sitting area for Jerry's fellow passengers. Chief of these were two austere Chinese men, dressed very poorly in grey, and from their sameness and their demure superiority Jerry at once inferred an expertise of some kind; he remembered explosives-wallahs and pianists he had occasionally ferried thanklessly in and out of badland. Next to them, but respectfully apart, four hillsmen armed to the teeth sat smoking and cropping from their rice-bowls. Jerry guessed Meo or one of the Shan tribes from the northern borders where Charlie Marshall's father had his army, and he guessed from their ease that they were part of the permanent help.

In a separate class altogether sat the quality: the colonel of artillery himself, who had thoughtfully supplied the transport and the troop escort, and his companion, a senior officer of customs, without whom nothing could have been achieved. They reclined regally in the gangway on chairs specially provided, watching proudly while the loading continued, and they wore their best uniforms, as the ceremony demanded.

There was one other member of the party and he lurked alone on top of the cases in the tail, head almost against the roof, and it was not possible to make him out in any detail. He sat with a bottle of whisky to himself, and even a glass to himself. He wore a Fidel Castro hat and a full beard. Gold links glittered on his dark arms, known in those days (to all but those who wore them) as C.I.A. bracelets, on the happy assumption that a man ditched in hostile country could buy his way to safety by doling out a link at a time. But his eyes, as they watched Jerry along the well-oiled barrel of an AK-47 automatic rifle, had a fixed brightness.

He was covering me through the nose-cone, Jerry thought. He had a bead on me from the moment I left the hut.

The two Chinese were cooks, he decided in a moment of inspiration—"cooks" being the underworld nickname for chemists. Keller had said that the Air Opium lines had taken to bringing in the raw base and refining it in Phnom Penh, but were having hell's own job persuading the cooks to come and work in siege conditions.

"Hey, you! Voltaire!"

Jerry hurried forward to the edge of the hold. Looking down, he saw the old peasant couple standing at the bottom of the ladder and Charlie Marshall trying to wrench the pig from them while he shoved the old woman up the steel ladder.

"When she come up, you gotta reach out and grab her, hear me?" he called, holding the pig in his arms. "She fall down and break her arse, we gotta whole lot more trouble with the coons. You some crazy narcotics hero, Voltaire?"

"No."

"Well, you grab hold of her completely, hear me?"

She started up the ladder. When she had gone a few rungs, she began croaking and Charlie Marshall contrived to get the pig under his arm while he gave her a sharp crack on the rump and screamed at her in Chinese. The husband scurried up after her, and Jerry hauled them both to safety.

Finally Charlie Marshall's own clown's head appeared through the cone, and though it was swamped by the hat, Jerry had his first glimpse of the face beneath: skeletal and brown, with sleepy Chinese eyes and a big French mouth which twisted all ways when he squawked. He shoved the pig through, Jerry grabbed it and carted it, screaming and wriggling, to the old peasants. Then Charlie hauled his own fleshless frame aboard, like a spider climbing out of a drain. At once the officer of customs and the colonel of artillery stood up, brushed the seats of their uniforms, and progressed swiftly along the gangway to the shadowed man in the Castro hat squatting on the packing-cases. Reaching him, they waited respectfully, like sidesmen taking the offertory to the altar.

The link bracelets flashed, an arm reached down, once, twice, and a devout silence descended while the two men carefully counted a lot of banknotes and everybody watched. In rough unison, they returned to the top of the ladder where Charlie Marshall waited with the manifest. The officer of customs signed it, the colonel of artillery looked on approvingly; then they both saluted and disappeared down the ladder. The nose-cone juddered to an almost closed position, Charlie Marshall gave it a kick, flung some matting across the gap, and clambered quickly over the packing-cases to an inside stairway leading to the cabin.

Jerry clambered after him and, having settled himself into the co-pilot's seat, silently totted up his blessings: We're about five hundred tons overweight. We're leaking oil. We're carrying an armed bodyguard. We're forbidden to take off. We're forbidden to land, and Phnom Penh airport's probably got a hole in it the size of Buckinghamshire. We have an hour and a half of Khmer Rouge between us and salvation, and if anybody turns sour on us at the other end, ace operator Westerby is caught with his knickers round his ankles and about two hundred gunny bags of opium base in his arms.

"You know how to fly this thing?" Charlie Marshall yelled as he struck at a row of mildewed switches. "You some kinda great flying hero, Voltaire?"

"I hate it all."

"Me too."

Seizing a swatter, Charlie Marshall flung himself upon a huge bottle-fly that was buzzing round the windscreen, then started the engines one by one, until the whole dreadful plane was heaving and rattling like a London bus on its last journey home up Clapham Hill. The radio crackled and Charlie Marshall took time off to give an obscene instruction to the control tower, first in Khmer and afterwards, in the best aviation tradition, in English. Heading for the far end of the runway, they passed a couple of gun emplacements and for a moment Jerry expected an over-zealous crew to loose off at the fuselage, till in gratitude he remembered the army colonel and his lorries and his pay-off.

Another bottle-fly appeared and this time Jerry took possession of the fly-swatter. The plane seemed to be gathering no speed at all, but half the instruments read zero, so he couldn't be sure. The din of the wheels on the runway seemed louder than the engines. Jerry remembered old Sambo's chauffeur driving him back to school: the slow, inevitable progress down the Western bypass toward Slough and finally Eton.

A couple of the hillsmen had come forward to see the fun and were laughing their heads off. A clump of palm trees came hopping toward them, but the plane kept its feet firmly on the ground. Charlie Marshall absently pulled back the stick and retracted the landing-gear. Uncertain whether the nose had really lifted, Jerry thought of school again, and competing in the long jump, and recalled the same sensation of not rising, yet ceasing to be on the earth.

He felt the jolt and heard the swish of leaves as the under-belly cropped the trees. Charlie Marshall was screaming at the plane to pull itself into the damn air, and for an age they made no height at all but hung and wheezed a few feet above a winding road which climbed inexorably toward a ridge of hills. Charlie Marshall was lighting a cigarette, so Jerry held the wheel in front of him and felt the live kick of the rudder. Taking back the controls, Charlie Marshall put the plane into a slow bank toward the lowest point of the range. He held the turn, crested the range, and went on to make a complete circle. As they looked down on the brown roof-tops and the river and the airport, Jerry reckoned they had an altitude of a thousand feet. As far as Charlie Marshall was concerned, that was a comfortable cruising height, for now at last he took his hat off and, with the air of a man who had done a good job well, treated himself to a large glass of Scotch from the bottle at his feet. Below them dusk was gathering, and the brown earth was fading softly into mauve.

"Thanks," said Jerry, accepting the bottle. "Yes, I think I might."

Jerry kicked off with a little small talk—if it is possible to talk small while you are shouting at the top of your voice.

"Khmer Rouge just blew up the airport ammunition dump!" he bellowed. "It's closed for landing and take-off."

"They did?" For the first time since Jerry had met him, Charlie Marshall seemed both pleased and impressed.

"They say you and Ricardo were great buddies."

"We bomb everything. We killed half the human race already. We see more dead people than alive people. Plain of Jars, Danang—we're such big damn heroes that when we die Jesus Christ going to come down personally with a chopper and fish us out the jungle."

"They tell me Ric was a great guy for business!"

"Sure! He the greatest! Know how many offshore companies we got, me and Ricardo? Six. We got foundations in Liechtenstein, corporations in Geneva, we got a bank manager in the Dutch Antilles, lawyers, Jesus. Know how much money I got?" He slapped his back pocket. "Three hundred U.S. exactly. Charlie Marshall and Ricardo killed half the whole damn human race together. Nobody give us no money. My father killed the other half and he got plenty *plenty* money. Ricardo, he always got these crazy schemes always. Shell cases. Jesus. We're going to pay the coons to collect up all the shell cases in Asia, sell 'em for the next war!"

The nose dropped and he hauled it up again with a foul French oath. "Latex! We gotta steal all the latex out of Kampong Cham! We fly to Kampong Cham, we got big choppers, red crosses. So what do we do? We bring out the damn wounded. Hold still, you crazy bastard, hear me?" He was talking to the plane again. In the nose-cone, Jerry noticed a long line of bullet-holes which had not been very well patched. Tear here, he thought absurdly.

"Human hair. We were gonna be millionaires out of hair. All the coon girls in the villages got to grow long hair and we're going to cut it off and fly it to Bangkok for wigs."

"Who was it paid Ricardo's debts so that he could fly for Indocharter?"

"Nobody!"

"Somebody told me it was Drake Ko."

"I never heard of Drake Ko. On my deathbed, I tell my mother, my father: bastard Charlie, the General's boy, he never heard of Drake Ko in his life."

"What did Ricardo do for Ko that was so special that Ko paid all his debts?"

Charlie Marshall drank some whisky straight from the bottle, then handed it to Jerry. His fleshless hands shook wildly whenever he took them off the stick, and his nose ran all the while. Jerry wondered how many pipes a day he was up to. He had once known a *pied-noir* hotelier in Luang Prabang who needed sixty to do a good day's work. *Captain Marshall never flies in the mornings*, he thought.

"Americans always in a hurry," Charlie Marshall complained, shaking his head. "Know why we gotta take this stuff to Phnom Penh now? Everybody impatient. Everybody want quick-shot these days. Nobody got time to smoke. Everybody got to turn on quick. You wanta kill the human race, you gotta take time, hear me?"

Jerry tried again. One of the four engines had given up, but another had developed a howl as if from a broken silencer, so that he had to yell even louder than before.

"What did Ricardo do for all that money?" he repeated.

"Listen, Voltaire, okay? I don't like politics, I'm just a simple opium smuggler, okay? You like politics you go back below and talk to those crazy Shans. 'You can't eat politics. You can't screw politics. You can't smoke politics.' He tell my father."

"Who did?"

"Drake Ko tell my father, my father tell me, and me—I tell the whole damn human race! Drake Ko some philosopher, hear me?"

For its own reasons, the plane had begun falling steadily till it was a couple of hundred feet above the paddies. They saw a village, and cooking fires burning, and figures running wildly toward the trees, and Jerry wondered seriously whether Charlie Marshall had noticed. But at the last minute, like a patient jockey, he hauled and leaned and finally got the horse's head up, and they both had some more Scotch.

"You know him well?"

"Who?"

"Ko."

"I never met him in my life, Voltaire. You wanna talk about Drake Ko, you go ask my father. He cut your throat."

"How about Tiu? Tell me, who's the couple with the pig?" Jerry yelled, to keep the conversation going while Charlie took back the bottle for another pull.

"Haw people, down from Chiang Mai. They worried about their lousy son in Phnom Penh. They think he too damn hungry, so they take him a pig."

"So how about Tiu?"

"I never heard of Mr. Tiu, hear me?"

"Ricardo was seen up in Chiang Mai three months ago," Jerry yelled.

"Yeah—well, Ric's a damn fool," said Charlie Marshall with feeling. "Ric's gotta keep his ass out of Chiang Mai or somebody shoot it right off. Anybody lying dead they gotta keep their damn mouth shut, hear me? I say to him, 'Ric, you my partner. Keep your damn mouth shut and your ass out of sight or certain people get personally pretty mad with you.'"

The plane entered a rain cloud and at once began losing height fast. Rain raced over the iron deck and down the insides of the windows. Charlie Marshall flicked some switches up and down; there was a bleeping from the controls panel and a couple of pin-lights came on, which no amount of swearing could put out. To Jerry's amazement they began climbing again, though in the racing cloud he doubted his judgment of the angle. Glancing behind him in order to check, he was in time to glimpse the bearded figure of the dark-skinned paymaster in the Fidel Castro cap retreating down the cabin ladder, holding his AK-47 by the barrel.

They continued climbing, the rain ended, and the night surrounded them like another country. The stars broke suddenly above them, they jolted over the moonlit crevasses of the cloud-tops, they lifted again, the cloud vanished for good, and

Charlie Marshall put on his hat and announced that both starboard engines had now ceased to play any part in the festivities. In this moment of respite, Jerry asked his maddest question.

"So where's Ricardo now, sport? Got to find him, see. Promised my paper I'd have a word with him. Can't disappoint them, can we?"

Charlie Marshall's sleepy eyes had all but closed. He was sitting in a half-trance with his head against the seat and the brim of his hat over his nose.

"What's that, Voltaire? You speak at all?"

"Where is Ricardo now?"

"Ric?" Charlie Marshall repeated, glancing at Jerry in a sort of wonder. "Where Ricardo is, Voltaire?"

"That's it, sport. Where is he? I'd like to have an exchange of views with him. That's what the three hundred bucks were about. There's another five hundred if you could find the time to arrange an introduction."

Springing suddenly to life, Charlie Marshall delved for the *Candide* and slammed it into Jerry's lap while he delivered himself of a furious outburst.

"I don't know where Ricardo is *ever,* hear me? I never don't want a friend in my life. If I see that crazy Ricardo, I shoot his balls right off in the street, hear me? He dead. So he can stay dead till he dies. He tell everyone he got killed. So maybe for once in my life I'm going to believe that bastard!"

Pointing the plane angrily into the cloud, he let it fall toward the slow flashes of Phnom Penh's artillery batteries to make a perfect three-point landing in what to Jerry was pitch darkness. He waited for the burst of machine-gun fire from the ground defences, he waited for the sickening free fall as they nosedived into a mammoth crater, but all he saw, quite suddenly, was a newly assembled *revêtement* of the familiar mud-filled ammunition boxes, arms open and palely lit, waiting to receive them. As they taxied toward it, a brown jeep pulled in front of them with a green light winking on the back, like a flashlight being turned on and off by hand. The plane was humping over grass. Hard beside the *revêtement* Jerry could see a pair of green lorries and a tight knot of waiting figures looking anxiously toward them, and behind them the dark shadow of a twin-engined sports plane. They parked, and Jerry heard at once from the hold beneath their penthouse the creak of the nose-cone opening, followed by the clatter of feet on the iron ladder and the quick call and answer of voices. The speed of their departure took him by surprise. But he heard something else that turned his blood cold and made him charge down the steps to the belly of the plane.

"Ricardo!" he yelled. "Stop! Ricardo!"

But the only passengers left were the old couple clutching their pig and their parcel. Seizing the steel ladder, he let himself fall, jolting his spine as he hit the tarmac with his heels. The jeep had already left with the Chinese cooks and their Shan bodyguard. As he ran forward, Jerry could see the jeep racing for an open gateway at the perimeter of the airfield. It passed through, and two sentries slammed the gates and took up their position as before. Behind him the helmeted flight-handlers were swarming toward the Carvair. A couple of lorry-loads of police looked on, and for a moment the Western fool in Jerry was seduced into thinking they might be playing some restraining rôle, till he realised they were Phnom Penh's guard of honour for a three-ton load of opium. But his eye was for one figure only, and that was the tall bearded man with the Fidel Castro hat and the AK-47 and the heavy limp that sounded like a hard-soft drum-beat as the rubber-soled flying boots hobbled down the steel ladder.

Jerry saw him just. The door of the little Beechcraft waited open for him, and there were two ground crew poised to help him in. As he reached them, they held out their hands for the rifle but Ricardo waved them aside. He had turned and was looking for Jerry. For a second they saw each other. Jerry was falling and Ricardo was lifting the gun, and for twenty seconds

Jerry reviewed his life from birth till now while a few more bullets ripped and whined round the battle-torn airfield. By the time Jerry looked up again, the firing had stopped, Ricardo was inside the plane, and his helpers were pulling away the chocks. As the little plane lifted into the flashes, Jerry ran like the devil for the darkest part of the perimeter before anybody else decided that his presence was obstructive to good trading.

Just a lovers' tiff, he told himself, sitting in a taxi-cab, and he held his hands over his head and tried to damp down the wild shaking of his chest. That's what you get for trying to play footsie-footsie with an old flame of Lizzie Worthington's. Somewhere a rocket fell and he didn't give a damn.

He allowed Charlie Marshall two hours, though he reckoned one was generous. It was past curfew but the day's crisis had not ended with the dark; there were traffic checks all the way to Le Phnom, and the sentries held their machine-pistols at the ready. In the square two men were screaming at each other by torchlight before a gathering crowd. Farther down the boulevard, troops had surrounded a floodlit house and were leaning against the wall of it, fingering their guns. The driver said the secret police had made an arrest there. A colonel and his people were still inside with a suspected agitator. In the hotel forecourt tanks were parked, and in his bedroom Jerry found Luke lying on the bed drinking contentedly.

"Any water?" Jerry asked.

"Yip."

He turned on the bath and started to undress until he remembered the Walther.

"Filed?" he asked.

"Yip," said Luke again. "And so have you."

"Ha ha."

"I had Keller cable Stubbsie under your byline."

"The airport story?"

Luke handed him a tear-sheet. "Added some true Westerby

colour. How the buds are bursting in the cemeteries. Stubbsie
loves you."

"Well, thanks."

In the bathroom, Jerry unstuck the Walther from the plaster and slipped it in the pocket of his jacket where he would be
able to get at it.

"Where we going tonight?" Luke called through the closed
door.

"Nowhere."

"What the hell's that mean?"

"I've got a date."

"A woman?"

"Yes."

"Take Lukie. Three in a bed."

Jerry sank gratefully into the tepid water. "No."

"Call her. Tell her to whip in a whore for Lukie. Listen, there's
that hooker from Santa Barbara downstairs. I'm not proud. I'll
bring her."

"No."

"For Christ's sakes!" Luke shouted, now serious. "Why the
hell not?" He had come right to the locked door to make his
protest.

"Sport, you've got to get off my back," Jerry advised.
"Honest. I love you, but you're not everything to me, right? So
stay off."

"Thorn in your breeches, huh?" Long silence. "Well don't
get your ass shot off, pardner, it's a stormy night out there."

When Jerry returned to the bedroom, Luke was back on
the bed staring at the wall and drinking methodically.

"You know, you're worse than a bloody woman," Jerry told
him, pausing at the door to look back at him.

The whole childish exchange would not have caused him
another moment's thought had it not been for the way things
turned out afterwards.

* * *

This time Jerry didn't bother with the bell on the gate, but climbed the wall and grazed his hands on the broken glass that ran along the top of it. He didn't make for the front door either, or go through the formality of watching the brown legs waiting on the bottom stair. Instead he stood in the garden waiting for the thump of his heavy landing to fade and for his eyes and ears to catch a sign of habitation from the big villa which loomed darkly above him with the moon behind it.

A car drew up without lights and two figures got out, by their size and quietness Cambodian. They pressed the gate bell and at the front door murmured the magic password through the crack, and were instantly, silently admitted. Jerry tried to fathom the layout. It puzzled him that no telltale smell escaped either from the front of the house or into the garden where he stood. There was no wind. He knew that for a large *divan* secrecy was vital, not because the law was punitive, but because the bribes were. The villa possessed a chimney and a courtyard and two floors: a place to live comfortably as a French *colon*, with a little family of concubines and half-caste children. The kitchen, he guessed, would be given over to preparation. The safest place to smoke would undoubtedly be upstairs in rooms which faced the courtyard. And since there was no smell from the front door, Jerry reckoned that they were using the rear of the courtyard rather than the wings or the front.

He trod soundlessly till he came to the paling that marked the rear boundary. It was lush with flowers and creeper. A barred window gave a first foothold to his buckskin boot, an overflow pipe a second, a high extractor fan a third, and as he climbed past it to the upper balcony he caught the smell he expected: warm and sweet and beckoning. On the balcony there was still no light, though the two Cambodian girls who squatted there were easily visible in the moonlight and he could see their scared eyes fixing him as he appeared out of the sky. Beckoning them to their feet, he walked them ahead of him, led by the smell.

The shelling had stopped, leaving the night to the geckos. Jerry remembered that Cambodians liked to gamble on the number of times they cheeped: tomorrow will be a lucky day; tomorrow won't; tomorrow I will take a bride; no, the day after. The girls were very young and they must have been waiting for the customers to send for them. At the rush door they hesitated and stared unhappily back at him. Jerry signalled and they began pulling aside layers of matting until a pale light gleamed onto the balcony, no stronger than a candle. He stepped inside, keeping the girls ahead of him.

The room must once have been the master bedroom, with a second, smaller room connecting. He had his hand on the shoulder of one girl. The other followed submissively. Twelve customers lay in the first room, all men. A few girls lay between them, whispering. Barefooted coolies ministered, moving with great deliberation from one recumbent body to the next, threading a pellet onto the needle, lighting it and holding it across the bowl of the pipe while the customer took a long steady draught and the pellet burned itself out. The conversation was slow and murmured and intimate, broken by soft ripples of grateful laughter. Jerry recognised the wise Swiss from the Counsellor's dinner party. He was chatting to a fat Cambodian. No one was interested in Jerry; like the orchids he carried at Lizzie Worthington's apartment block, the girls authenticated him.

"Charlie Marshall," Jerry said quietly. A coolie pointed to the next room. Jerry dismissed the two girls and they slipped away. The second room was smaller and Charlie Marshall lay in the corner, while a Chinese girl in an elaborate cheongsam crouched over him preparing his pipe. Jerry supposed she was the daughter of the house and that Charlie Marshall was getting the grand treatment because he was both an habitué and a supplier. He knelt the other side of him. An old man was watching from the doorway. The girl watched also, the pipe still in her hands.

"What you want, Voltaire? Why don't you leave me be?"

"Just a little stroll, sport. Then you can come back."

Taking his arm, Jerry lifted him gently to his feet, while the girl helped.

"How much has he had?" he asked the girl. She held up three fingers.

"And how much does he like?" he asked.

She lowered her head, smiling. A whole lot more, she was saying.

Charlie Marshall walked shakily at first, but by the time they reached the balcony he was prepared to argue, so Jerry lifted him up and carried him across his body like a fire victim, down the wooden steps and across the courtyard. The old man bowed them obligingly through the front door, a grinning coolie held the gate onto the street, and both were clearly very thankful to Jerry for showing so much tact. They had gone perhaps fifty yards when a pair of Chinese boys came rushing down the road at them, yelling and waving sticks like small paddles. Setting Charlie Marshall upright but holding him firmly with his left hand, Jerry let the first boy strike, deflected the paddle, then hit him at half strength with a two-knuckle punch just below the eye. The boy ran away, his friend after him. Still clutching Charlie Marshall, Jerry walked him till they came to the river and a heavy patch of darkness. Then he sat him down on the bank like a puppet in the sloped, dry grass.

"You gonna blow my brains out, Voltaire?"

"We're going to have to leave that to the opium, sport," said Jerry.

Jerry liked Charlie Marshall, and in a perfect world he would have been glad to spend an evening with him at the *fumerie* and hear the story of his wretched but extraordinary life. But now his fist grasped Charlie Marshall's tiny arm remorselessly lest he took it into his hollow head to bolt; for he had a feeling Charlie could run very fast when he became desperate. He half lay therefore, much as he had lounged among the magic mountain of possessions in old Pet's place, on his left haunch and his left elbow, holding Charlie Marshall's wrist into the mud, while Charlie Marshall lay flat on his back. From the river thirty feet below them came the murmured chant of the sampans as they drifted like long leaves across the golden moon path. From the sky—now in front of them, now behind—came the occasional ragged flashes of outgoing gun-fire as some bored battery commander decided to justify his existence. And sometimes from much nearer came the lighter, sharper snap as the Khmer Rouge replied, but only as tiny interludes between the racket of the geckos and the greater silence just beyond. By the moonlight Jerry looked at his watch, then at the crazed face, trying to calculate the strength of Charlie Marshall's cravings. If Charlie was a night smoker and slept in the mornings, then his needs must come on fast. The wet on his face was already unearthly. It flowed from the heavy pores and from the stretched eyes, and from the sniffing, weeping nose. It channelled itself meticulously along the engraved creases, making neat reservoirs in the caverns.

"Jesus, Voltaire. Ricardo's my friend. He got a lot of philosophy, that guy. You want to hear him talk, Voltaire. You wanna hear his ideas."

"Yes," Jerry agreed. "I do."

Charlie Marshall grabbed hold of Jerry's hand.

"Voltaire, these are good guys, hear me? Mr. Tiu . . . Drake Ko. They don't want to hurt nobody. They wanna do business. They got something to sell, they got people buying it! It's a service! Nobody gets his rice-bowl broken. Why you want to screw that up? You're a nice guy yourself. I saw. You carry the old boy's pig, okay? Whoever saw a round-eye carry a slant-eye pig before? But Jesus, Voltaire, you screw it out of me, they will kill you very completely, because that Mr. Tiu, he's a business-like and very philosophical gentleman, hear me? They kill *me*, they kill *Ricardo*, they kill *you*, they kill the whole damn human race!"

The artillery fired a barrage, and this time the jungle replied with a small salvo of missiles, perhaps six, which hissed over their heads like whirring boulders from a catapult. Moments later they heard the detonations somewhere in the centre of the town. After them, nothing. Not the wail of a fire engine, not the siren of an ambulance.

"Why would they kill *Ricardo*?" Jerry asked. "What's *Ricardo* done wrong?"

"Voltaire! Ricardo's my friend! Drake Ko my father's friend! Those old men big brothers. They fight some lousy war together in Shanghai about two hundred and fifty years ago, okay? I go see my father. I tell him, 'Father you gotta love me once. You gotta quit calling me your spider bastard, and you gotta tell your good friend Drake Ko to take the heat off Ricardo. You gotta say, "Drake Ko, that Ricardo and my Charlie, they are like you and me. They brothers, same as us. They learn fly together in Oklahoma, they kill the human race together. And they some pretty good friends. And that's a fact."' My father hate me very bad, okay?"

"Okay."

"But he send Drake Ko a damn long personal message all the same."

Charlie Marshall breathed in, on and on, as if his little breast could scarcely hold enough air to feed him. "That Lizzie. She some woman. Lizzie, she go personally to Drake Ko herself. Also on a very private basis. And she say to him, 'Mr. Ko, you gotta take the heat off Ric.' That's a very delicate situation there, Voltaire. We all got to hold on to each other tight or we fall off the crazy mountaintop, hear me? Voltaire, let me go. I beg! I completely beg, for Christ's sake, *je m'abîme*, hear me? That's all I know!"

Watching him, listening to his wracked outbursts, how he collapsed and rallied and broke again and rallied less, Jerry felt he was witnessing the last martyred writhing of a friend. His instinct was to lead Charlie slowly and let him ramble. His dilemma was that he didn't know how much time he had before whatever happens to an addict happened. He asked questions, but often Charlie didn't seem to hear them. At other times he appeared to answer questions Jerry hadn't put. And sometimes a delayed-action mechanism threw out an answer to a question which Jerry had long abandoned. At Sarratt the inquisitors said a broken man was dangerous because he paid you money he didn't have in order to buy your love. But for whole precious minutes Charlie could pay nothing at all.

"Drake Ko never went to Vientiane in his life!" Charlie yelled suddenly. "You crazy, Voltaire! A big guy like Ko bothering with a dirty little Asian town? Drake Ko some philosopher, Voltaire! You wanna watch that guy pretty careful!" Everyone, it seemed, was some philosopher—or everyone but Charlie Marshall. "In Vientiane nobody even heard Ko's name! Hear me, Voltaire?"

At another point, Charlie Marshall wept and seized Jerry's hands and enquired between sobs whether Jerry also had a father.

"Yes, sport, I did," said Jerry patiently. "And in his way he was a general too."

Over the river two white flares shed an amazing daylight, inspiring Charlie to reminisce on the hardships of their early days together in Vientiane. Sitting bolt upright, he drew a house in diagram in the mud. That's where Lizzie and Ric and Charlie Marshall lived, he said proudly: in a stinking flea-hut on the edge of town, a place so lousy even the geckos got sick from it. Ric and Lizzie had the royal suite, which was the only room this flea-hut contained, and Charlie's job was to keep out of the way and pay the rent and fetch the booze. But the memory of their dreadful economic plight moved Charlie to a fresh storm of tears.

"So what did you live on, sport?" Jerry asked, expecting nothing from the question. "Come on. It's over now. What did you live on?"

More tears while Charlie confessed to a monthly allowance from his father, whom he loved and revered.

"That crazy Lizzie," said Charlie through his grief, "that crazy Lizzie, she make trips to Hong Kong for Mellon."

Somehow Jerry contrived to keep himself steady in order not to shake Charlie from his course: "Mellon? Who's this Mellon?" he asked. But the soft tone made Charlie sleepy, and he started playing with the mud house, adding a chimney and smoke.

"Come on, damn you! *Mellon! Mellon!*" Jerry shouted straight into Charlie's face, trying to shock him into replying. "*Mellon*, you hashed-out wreck! Trips to Hong Kong!" Lifting Charlie to his feet, he shook him like a rag doll, but it took a lot more shaking to produce the answer, and in the course of it Charlie Marshall implored Jerry to understand what it was like to love, really to love, a crazy round-eye hooker and know you could never have her, even for a night.

Mellon was a creepy English trader, nobody knew what he did. A little of this, a little of that, Charlie said. People were scared of him. Mellon said he could get Lizzie into the big-time heroin trail. "With your passport and your body," Mellon had told her, "you can go in and out of Hong Kong like a princess."

Exhausted, Charlie sank to the ground and crouched before his mud house. Squatting beside him, Jerry fastened his fist to the back of Charlie's collar, careful not to hurt him.

"So she did that for him, did she, Charlie? Lizzie carried for Mellon." With his palm, he gently tipped Charlie's head round till his lost eyes were staring straight at him.

"Lizzie don't carry for *Mellon*, Voltaire," Charlie corrected him. "Lizzie carry for *Ricardo*. Lizzie don't love Mellon. She love *Ric* and *me*."

Staring glumly at the mud house, Charlie burst suddenly into raucous dirty laughter, which then petered out with no explanation.

"You louse it up, Lizzie!" Charlie called teasingly, poking a finger into the mud door. "You louse it up as usual, honey! You talk too much. Why you tell everyone you Queen of England? Why you tell everyone you some great spook-lady? Mellon get very very mad with you, Lizzie. Mellon throw you out, right out on your ass. Ric got pretty mad too, remember? Ric smash you up real bad and Charlie have to take you to the doctor in the middle of the damn night, remember? You got one hell of a big mouth, Lizzie, hear me? You my sister, but you got the biggest damn mouth *ever!*"

Till Ricardo closed it for her, Jerry thought, remembering the grooves on her chin. Because she spoiled the deal with Mellon.

Still crouching at Charlie's side and clutching him by the scruff, Jerry watched the world around him vanish, and in place of it he saw Sam Collins sitting in his car below Star Heights, with a clear view of the eighth floor, while he studied the racing page of the newspaper at eleven o'clock at night. Not even the clump of a rocket falling quite close could distract him from that freezing vision. And he heard Craw's voice above the mortar fire, intoning on the subject of Lizzie's criminality. When funds were low, Craw had said, Ricardo had made her carry little parcels across frontiers for him.

And how did London town learn *that*, Your Grace—Jerry would have liked to ask old Craw—if not from Sam Collins alias Mellon himself?

A three-second rainstorm had washed away Charlie's mud house and he was furious about it. He was splashing around on all fours looking for it, weeping and cursing frantically. The fit passed and he started talking about his father again, and how the old man had found employment for his natural son with a certain distinguished Vientiane airline—though Charlie till then had been quite keen to get out of flying for good on account of losing his nerve.

One day, it seemed, the General just lost patience with Charlie. He called together his bodyguard and came down from his hilltop in the Shans to a little opium town called Fang, not far inside the Thai border. There, after the fashion of patriarchs the world over, the General rebuked Charlie for his spendthrift ways.

Charlie had a special squawk for his father and a special way of puffing out his wasted cheeks in military disapproval.

"'So you better do some proper damn work, for a change— hear me, you *kwailo* spider bastard? You better stay away from horse gambling, hear me, and strong liquor, and opium. And you better take those Commie stars off your tits and sack that stink friend Ricardo of yours. And you better cease financing his woman, hear me? Because I don't gonna keep you one day more, not one *hour*, you spider bastard, and I hate you so much one day I kill you because you remind me of that Corsican whore your mother!'"

Then to the job itself—Charlie's father, the General, still speaking: "'Certain very fine Chiu Chow gentlemen who are pretty good friends of pretty good friends of mine, hear me, happen to have a controlling interest in a certain aviation company. Also I got certain shares in that company. Also this company happens to bear the distinguished title of Indocharter Aviation. So these good friends, they do me a favour to assist me in my disgrace for my three-legged spider-bastard son and I pray sincerely you may fall out of the sky and break your *kwailo* neck.'"

So Charlie flew his father's opium for Indocharter—one, two flights a week at first, but regular, honest work and he liked it. His nerve came back, he steadied down, and he felt real gratitude toward his old man. He tried, of course, to get the Chiu Chow boys to take Ricardo too, but they wouldn't. After a few months they did agree to pay Lizzie twenty bucks a week to sit in the front office and sweet-mouth the clients. These were the golden days, Charlie implied. Charlie and Lizzie earned the money, Ricardo wasted it on ever crazier enterprises, everybody was happy, everybody was employed.

Till one evening, like a nemesis, Tiu appeared and screwed the whole thing up. He appeared just as they were locking up the company's offices, straight off the pavement without an appointment, asking for Charlie Marshall by name and describing himself as part of the company's Bangkok management. The Chiu Chow boys came out of the back office, took one look at Tiu, vouched for his good faith, and made themselves scarce.

Charlie broke off in order to weep on Jerry's shoulder.

"Now listen to me carefully, sport," Jerry urged. "Listen. This is the bit I like, okay? You tell me this bit carefully and I'll take you home. Promise. *Please*."

But Jerry had it wrong. It was no longer a matter of making Charlie talk. Jerry was now the drug on which Charlie Marshall depended. It was no longer a matter of holding him down, either. Charlie Marshall clutched Jerry's breast as if it were the last raft on his lonely sea, and their conversation had become a desperate monologue from which Jerry stole his facts while Charlie Marshall cringed and begged and howled for his tormentor's attention, making jokes and laughing at them through his tears. Downriver one of Lon Nol's machine-guns which had not yet been sold to the Khmer Rouge was firing tracer into the jungle by the light of another flare. Long golden bolts flowed in streams above and below the water, and lit a small cave where they disappeared into the trees.

Charlie's sweat-soaked hair was pricking Jerry's chin and Charlie was gabbling and dribbling all at the same time.

"Mr. Tiu don't wanna talk in no office, Voltaire. Oh, no! Mr. Tiu don't dress too good, either. Tiu very Chiu Chow person, he use Thai passport like Drake Ko, he use crazy name and keep very very low appearance when he come to Vientiane.

'Captain Marshall,' he say to me, 'how you like earn a lot of extra cash by performing certain interesting and varied work outside the company's hours, tell me? How you like fly a certain unconventional journey for me once? They tell me you some pretty damn fine pilot these days, very steady. How you like earn yourself not less than maybe four to five thousand U.S. for one day's work, not even a whole day? How would that personally attract you, Captain Marshall?' 'Mr. Tiu,' I tell him"—Charlie is shouting hysterically now—"'without in any way prejudicing my negotiating position, Mr. Tiu, for five thousand bucks U.S. in my present serene mood I go down to hell for you and I bring you the devil's balls back!' Tiu say he come back one day and I gotta keep my damn mouth shut."

Suddenly Charlie had changed to his father's voice, and he was calling himself a spider bastard and the son of a Corsican whore—till gradually it dawned on Jerry that Charlie was describing the next episode in the story.

Amazingly, it turned out, Charlie had kept to himself the secret of Tiu's offer until he next saw his father, this time in Chiang Mai for a celebration of the Chinese New Year. He had not told Ric and he had not even told Lizzie—maybe because at this point they weren't getting on too well any more, and Ric was having himself a lot of women on the side.

The General's counsel was not encouraging: "'Don't you touch that horse! That Tiu, he got some pretty highly big connections, and they all a bit too special for a crazy little spider bastard like you, hear me! Jesus Christ, who ever heard of a Swatownese give five thousand dollar to a lousy half-*kwailo* to improve his mind with travel!'"

"So you passed the deal to Ric, right?" said Jerry quickly. "Right, Charlie? You told Tiu, 'Sorry, but try Ricardo.' Is that how it went?"

But Charlie Marshall was missing—believed dead. He had fallen straight off Jerry's chest and lay flat in the mud with his eyes closed, and only his occasional gulps for breath—greedy, rasping draughts of it—and the crazy beating of his pulse where Jerry held his wrist testified to the life inside the frame.

"Voltaire," Charlie whispered. "On the Bible, Voltaire. You're a good man. Take me home. Jesus, take me home, Voltaire."

Stunned, Jerry stared at the prone and broken figure and knew that he had to ask one more question, even if it was the last in both their lives. Reaching down, he dragged Charlie to his feet for the last time. And there for an hour in the black road, struggling on his arm, while more aimless barrages stabbed the darkness, Charlie Marshall screamed, and begged, and swore he would love Jerry always if only he didn't have to reveal what arrangements his friend Ricardo had made for his survival. But Jerry explained that without that, the mystery was not even half revealed. And perhaps Charlie Marshall, in his ruin and despair, as he sobbed out the forbidden secrets, understood Jerry's reasoning: that in a city about to be given back to the jungle, there was no destruction unless it was complete.

As gently as he could, Jerry carried Charlie Marshall down the road, back to the villa and up the steps, where the same silent faces gratefully received him. I should have got more, he thought. I should have told him more as well; I didn't tend the two-way traffic in the way they ordered. I stayed too long with the business of Lizzie and Sam Collins. I did it upside down, I foozled my shopping list, I loused it up like Lizzie. He tried to feel sorry about that but he couldn't, and the things he remembered best were the things that weren't on the list at all, and they were the same things that stood up in his mind like monuments while he typed his message to dear old George.

He typed with the door locked and the gun in his belt. There was no sign of Luke, so Jerry assumed he had gone off to a whore-house, still in his drunken sulk. It was a long signal, the longest of his career: "Know this much in case you don't hear from me again." He reported his contact with the Counsellor, he gave his next port of call and gave Ricardo's address, and a portrait of Charlie Marshall and of the three-sided household in the flea-hut, but only in the most formal terms, and he left out entirely his new-found knowledge regarding the rôle played by the unsavoury Sam Collins. After all, if they knew it already what was the point of telling it to them again? He left out the place-names and the proper names and made a separate key of them, then spent another hour putting the two messages into a first-base code that wouldn't fool a cryptographer for five minutes, but was beyond the ken of ordinary mortals, and of mortals like his host the British Counsellor. He ended with a reminder to housekeepers to check whether Blatt & Rodney had made that latest money draft to Cat. He burned the *en clair* texts, rolled the encoded versions into a newspaper, then lay on the newspaper and dozed, the gun awkwardly at his side.

At six he shaved, transferred his signals to a paperback novel which he felt able to part with, and took himself for a walk in the morning quiet. In the *place*, the Counsellor's car was parked conspicuously. The Counsellor himself was parked equally conspicuously on the terrace of a pretty bistro, wearing a Riviera straw hat reminiscent of Craw's, and treating himself to hot croissants and *café au lait*. Seeing Jerry, he gave an elaborate wave.

Jerry wandered over to him: "Morning," he said.

"Ah, you've got it! Good man!" the Counsellor cried, bounding to his feet. "Been *longing* to read it ever since it came out!"

Parting with the signal, conscious only of its omissions, Jerry had a feeling of end-of-term. He might come back, he might not, but things would never be quite the same again.

The exact circumstances of Jerry's departure from Phnom Penh are relevant because of Luke, later.

For the first part of the morning that remained, Jerry pursued

his obsessional search for cover, which was the natural antidote, perhaps, to his increasing sense of nakedness. Diligently
he went on the stomp for refugee and orphan stories, which he
filed through Keller at midday, together with a quite decent
atmosphere piece on his visit to Battambang, which, though
never used, has at least a place in his dossier. There were two
refugee camps at that time, both blossoming, one in an enormous hotel on the Bassac, Sihanouk's personal and unfinished
dream of paradise; one in the railway-yards near the airport,
two or three families packed into each carriage. He visited both
and they were the same: young Australian heroes struggling
with the impossible, the only water filthy, a rice hand-out twice
a week, and the children chirruping "Hi" and "Bye-bye" after
him while he trailed his Cambodian interpreter up and down
their lines, besieging everyone with questions, acting large,
and looking for that extra something that would melt Stubbsie's
heart.

At a travel office he noisily booked a passage to Bangkok.
Making for the airport, he had a sudden sense of *déjà vu*. Last
time I was here, I went water-skiing, he thought. The round-eye
traders kept houseboats moored along the Mekong. And for
a moment he saw himself—and the city—in the days when
the Cambodian war still had a certain ghastly innocence: ace
operator Westerby, risking mono, bouncing boyishly over the
brown water of the Mekong, towed by a jolly Dutchman in a
speed launch that burned enough petrol to feed a family for a
week. The greatest hazard was the two-foot wave, he remembered, which rolled down the river every time the guards on the
bridge let off a depth-charge to prevent the Khmer Rouge div-
ers from blowing it up. But now the river was theirs, so was the
jungle. And so, tomorrow or the next day, was the town.

At the airport, he ditched the Walther in a rubbish bin and
at the last minute bribed his way aboard a plane to Saigon,
which was his destination. Taking off, he wondered who had the
longer expectation of survival, himself or the city.

* * *

Luke, on the other hand, with the key to Deathwish the Hun's flat nestling in his pocket, flew to Bangkok, and as luck had it he flew under Jerry's name, since Jerry was on the flight list and Luke was not, and the remaining places were all taken. In Bangkok he attended a hasty bureau conference at which the magazine's local manpower was carved up between various bits of the crumbling Vietnam front. Luke got Hué and Danang and accordingly left for Saigon next day, thence north by connecting midday plane.

Contrary to later rumour, the two men did not meet in Saigon.

Nor did they meet in the course of the northern roll-back.

The last they saw of each other, in any mutual sense, was on that final evening in Phnom Penh, when Jerry had bawled Luke out and Luke had sulked: and that's fact—a commodity which was afterwards notoriously hard to come by.

17

RICARDO

At no time in the entire case did George Smiley hold the ring with such tenacity as now. In the Circus, nerves were stretched to snapping-point. The bloody inertia and the bouts of frenzy which Sarratt habitually warned against became one and the same. Each day that brought no hard news from Hong Kong was another day of disaster. Jerry's long signal was put under the microscope and held to be ambiguous, then neurotic.

Why had he not pressed Marshall harder? Why had he not raised the Russian spectre again? He should have grilled Charlie about the gold seam; he should have carried on where he left off with Tiu. Had he forgotten that his main job was to sow alarm and only afterwards to obtain information? As to his obsession with that wretched daughter of his—God Almighty, doesn't the fellow *know* what signals cost? (They seemed to forget it was the Cousins who were footing the bill.) And what was all this about having no more to do with British Embassy officials standing proxy for the absent Circus resident? All right, there had been a delay in the pipeline in getting the signal across from the Cousins' side of the house. Jerry had still run Charlie Marshall to earth, hadn't he? It was absolutely no part of a fieldman's job to dictate the "do"s and "don't"s to London. Housekeeping Section, who had arranged the contact, wanted him rebuked by return.

Pressure from outside the Circus was even fiercer. Colonial

Wilbraham's faction had not been idle, and the Steering Group, in a startling about-turn, decided that the Governor of Hong Kong should after all be informed of the case, and soon. There was high talk of calling him back to London on a pretext. The panic had arisen because Ko had once more been received at Government House, this time at one of the Governor's talk-in suppers, at which influential Chinese were invited to air their opinions off the record.

By contrast Saul Enderby and his fellow hard-liners pulled the opposite way: "To hell with the Governor. What we want is full partnership with the Cousins immediately!" George should go to Martello *today*, said Enderby, and make a clean breast of the whole case and invite them to take over the last stage of development. He should stop playing hide-and-seek about Nelson, he should admit that he had no resources, he should let the Cousins compute the possible intelligence dividend for themselves, and if they brought the job off, so much the better: let them claim the credit on Capitol Hill, to the confusion of their enemies. The result of this generous and timely gesture, Enderby argued—coming bang in the middle of the Vietnam fiasco—would be an indissoluble intelligence partnership for years to come, a view which in his shifty way Lacon seemed to support. Caught in the cross-fire, Smiley suddenly found himself saddled with a double reputation. The Wilbraham set branded him as anti-Colonial and pro-American, while Enderby's men accused him of ultra-conservatism in the handling of the special relationship.

Much more serious however was Smiley's impression that some hint of the row had reached Martello by other routes, and that he would be able to exploit it. For example, Molly Meakin's sources spoke of a burgeoning relationship between Enderby and Martello at the personal level, and not just because their children were all being educated at the Lycée in South Kensington. It seemed that the two men had taken to fishing together at weekends in Scotland, where Enderby had a bit of water. Martello supplied the plane, said the joke later, and Enderby supplied the fish. Smiley also learned around this time, in his unworldly way, what everyone else had known from the beginning and assumed he knew too. Enderby's third and newest wife was American and rich. Before their marriage she had been a considerable hostess of the Washington establishment, a rôle she was now repeating with some success in London.

But the underlying cause of everybody's agitation was finally the same. On the Ko front, nothing ultimately was happening. Worse still, there was an agonising shortage of operational intelligence. Every day now, at ten o'clock, Smiley and Guillam presented themselves at the Annexe and every day came away less satisfied. Tiu's domestic telephone line was tapped, so was Lizzie Worthington's. The tapes were locally monitored, then flown back to London for detailed processing. Jerry had sweated Charlie Marshall on a Wednesday. On the Friday, Charlie was sufficiently recovered from his ordeal to ring Tiu from Bangkok and pour out his heart to him. But after listening for less than thirty seconds, Tiu cut him short with an instruction to "get in touch with Harry right away," which left everybody mystified: nobody had a Harry anywhere.

On the Saturday there was drama because the watch on Ko's home number had him cancelling his regular Sunday-morning golf date with Mr. Arpego. Ko pleaded a pressing business engagement. This was it! This was the breakthrough! Next day, with Smiley's consent, the Hong Kong Cousins locked a surveillance van, two cars, and a Honda on to Ko's Rolls-Royce as it entered town. What secret mission at five-thirty on a Sunday morning was so important to Ko that he would abandon his weekly golf? The answer turned out to be his fortune-teller, a venerable old Swatownese who operated from a seedy spirit temple in a side-street off the Hollywood Road. Ko spent more than an hour with him before returning home, and though some zealous child inside the Cousins' van trained a concealed directional microphone on the temple window for the entire session, the only sounds he recorded apart from the traffic turned out to be cluckings from the old man's hen-house. Back at the Circus, di Salis was called in. What on earth would anyone be going to the fortune-teller at six in the morning for, least of all a millionaire?

Greatly amused by their perplexity, di Salis twirled his hair in delight. A man of Ko's standing would insist on being the first client in a fortune-teller's day, he said, while the great man's mind was still clear to receive the intimations of the spirits.

Then nothing happened for five weeks. Nothing. The mail and phone checks spewed out wads of indigestible raw material which, when refined, produced not a single intelligence lead. Meanwhile the artificial deadline imposed by the Enforcement Agency drew steadily nearer, on which day Ko should become open game for whoever could pin something on him soonest.

Yet Smiley kept his head. He resisted all recriminations, both of his own handling of the case and of Jerry's. The tree had been shaken, he maintained, Drake Ko was running scared, and time would show they were right. He refused to be hustled into some dramatic gesture to Martello, and he held resolutely to the terms of the deal that he had outlined in his letter, and of which a copy now lodged with Lacon. He also refused, as his charter allowed him, to enter into any discussion of operational detail, either with the Steering Group or with Enderby personally, except where issues of protocol or local mandate were concerned. To give way on this, he knew very well, would only have meant providing the doubters with fresh ammunition with which to shoot him down.

He held this line for five weeks, and on the thirty-sixth day, either God or the forces of logic—or better, the forces of Ko's human chemistry—delivered to Smiley a substantial if mysterious consolation. Ko took to the water. Accompanied by Tiu and an unknown Chinese later identified as the lead captain of

Ko's junk-fleet, he spent the better part of three days touring the Hong Kong out-islands, returning each evening at dusk. Where they went, there was as yet no telling. Martello proposed a series of helicopter over-flights to observe their course, but Smiley turned down the suggestion flat. Static surveillance from the quayside confirmed that they apparently left and returned by a different route each day, and that was all. And on the last day, the fourth, the boat did not return at all.

Panic. Where had it gone? Martello's masters in Langley, Virginia, flew into a complete spin and decided that Ko and the *Admiral Nelson* had deliberately strayed into China waters. Even that they had been abducted. Ko would never be seen again, and Enderby, going downhill fast, actually telephoned Smiley and told him it would be "your damn fault if Ko pops up in Peking yelling the odds about Secret Service persecution." Even Smiley, for one agonising day, secretly wondered whether, against all reason, Ko had indeed gone to join his brother.

Then of course, next morning early, the launch sailed back into the main harbour looking as if it had just returned from a regatta, and Ko gaily disembarked, following his beautiful Liese down the gangway.

It was this intelligence which, after very long thought and a renewed and detailed reading of Ko's file—not to mention much tense debate with Connie and di Salis—determined Smiley to take two decisions at once or, in gambler's terms, to play the only two cards that were left to him.

One: Jerry should advance to the "last stage," by which Smiley meant Ricardo. He hoped by this step to maintain the pressure on Ko, and provide Ko, if he needed it, with the final proof that he must act.

Two: Sam Collins should "go in."

This second decision was reached in consultation with Connie Sachs alone. It finds no mention in Jerry's main dossier, but only in a secret appendix later released, with deletions, for wider scrutiny.

The fragmenting effect upon Jerry of these delays and hesitations was something not the greatest intelligence chief on earth could have included in his calculations. To be aware of it was one thing—and Smiley undoubtedly was, and even took one or two steps to forestall it. To be guided by it, to set it on the same plane as the factors of high policy which he was having daily fired at him, would have been downright irresponsible. A general is nothing without priorities.

The fact remains that Saigon was the worst place on earth for Jerry to be kicking his heels. Periodically, as the delays dragged on, there was talk at the Circus of sending him somewhere more salubrious—for instance, to Singapore or Kuala Lumpur—but the arguments of expediency and cover always kept him where he was; besides, tomorrow everything might change. There was also the matter of his personal safety. Hong Kong was not to be considered, and in both Singapore and Bangkok, Ko's influence was sure to be strong. Then, cover again: with the collapse approaching, where more natural than Saigon?

Yet it was a half-life Jerry lived, and in a half-town. For forty years, give or take, war had been Saigon's staple industry, but the American pull-out of '73 had produced a slump from which, to the end, the city never properly recovered, so that even this long-awaited final act, with its cast of millions, was playing to quite poor audiences. Even when he took his obligatory rides to the sharp end of the fighting, Jerry had a sense of watching a rained-off cricket match where the contestants wanted only to go back to the pavilion. The Circus forbade him to leave Saigon on the grounds that he might be needed elsewhere at any moment, but the injunction, literally observed, would have made him look ridiculous, and he ignored it. Xuan Loc was a boring French rubber town fifty miles out, on what was now the city's tactical perimeter. For this was a different war entirely from Phnom Penh's, more technical and more European in inspiration. Where the Khmer Rouge had no armour, the North Vietnamese had Russian tanks and 130 millimetre artillery, which they drew up on the classic Russian pattern, wheel to wheel, as if they were about to storm Berlin under Marshal Zhukov, and nothing would move till the last gun was laid and primed. He found the town half deserted, and the Catholic church empty except for one French priest.

"*C'est terminé*," the priest explained to him simply. The South Vietnamese would do what they always did, he said. They would stop the advance, then turn and run.

They drank wine together staring at the empty square.

Jerry filed a story saying the rot this time was irreversible, and Stubbsie shoved it on the spike with a laconic "PREFER PEOPLE TO PROPHECIES STUBBS."

Back in Saigon, on the steps of the Hotel Caravelle, begging children peddled useless garlands of flowers. Jerry gave them money and to save them face took their flowers, then dumped them in the waste-paper basket in his room. When he sat downstairs, they tapped on the window and sold him *Stars & Stripes*. In the almost empty bars where he drank, the girls collected to him desperately as if he were their last chance before the end. Only the police were in their element. They stood at every corner in white helmets and fresh white gloves, as if already waiting to direct the victorious enemy traffic when it arrived. They rode like monarchs past the refugees in their bird-coops on the pavement.

Jerry returned to his hotel room and Hercule rang, his favourite Vietnamese, whom he had been avoiding for all he was worth. Hercule, as he called himself, was anti-establishment and anti-Thieu and had made a quiet living supplying British journalists with information on the Vietcong, on the questionable grounds that the British were not involved in the war. "The British are my friends!" he begged into the phone. "Get me out! I need papers, I need money!"

Jerry said, "Try the Americans," and rang off hopelessly.

The Reuters office, when Jerry filed his stillborn copy, was a monument to forgotten heroes and the romance of failure. Under the glass desk-tops lay the photographed heads of tousled boys, on the walls famous rejection slips and samples of editorial fury; in the air a stink of old newsprint, and the Somewhere-in-England sense of makeshift habitation which enshrines the secret nostalgia of every exiled correspondent. There was a travel agent just round the corner, and later it turned out that Jerry had twice in that period booked himself passages to Hong Kong, then not appeared at the airport. He was serviced by an earnest young Cousin named Pike, who had Information cover and occasionally came to the hotel with signals in yellow envelopes marked "RUSH PRESS" for authenticity. But the message inside was the same: no decision, stand by, no decision. He read Ford Madox Ford and a truly terrible novel about old Hong Kong. He read Greene and Conrad and T. E. Lawrence, and still no word came. The shellings sounded worst at night, and the panic was everywhere, like a spreading plague. In search of Stubbsie's people not prophecies, he went down to the American Embassy where ten thousand-odd Vietnamese were beating at the doors in an effort to prove their American citizenship. As he watched, a South Vietnamese officer rode up in a jeep, leapt out, and began yelling at the women, calling them whores and traitors—picking, as it happened, a group of bona-fide U.S. wives to bear the brunt.

Again Jerry filed and again Stubbs threw his story out, which no doubt added to his depression. A few days later the Circus planners lost their nerve. As the rout continued, and worsened, they signalled Jerry to fly at once to Vientiane and keep his head down till ordered otherwise by a Cousins' postman. So he took a room at the Constellation, where Lizzie had liked to hang out, and he drank at the bar where Lizzie had liked to drink, and he occasionally chatted to Maurice the proprietor, and he waited. The bar was of concrete, two feet deep, so that if the need arose it could do duty as a bomb shelter or firing position. Each night in the gloomy dining room attached to it, one old *colon* ate and drank fastidiously, a napkin tucked into his collar. Jerry sat reading at another table. They were the only diners ever, and they never spoke. In the streets, the Pathet Lao—not long down from the hills—walked righteously in pairs and in great number, wearing Maoist caps and tunics and avoiding the glances of the girls. They had commandeered the corner villas and the villas along the road to the airport. They had camped in immaculate tents which peeked over the walls of overgrown gardens.

"Will the coalition hold?" Jerry asked Maurice once.

Maurice was not a political man. He gave a huge shrug. "It's the way it is," he replied in a stage French accent, and in silence handed Jerry a ballpoint pen as a consolation. It had "Läwenbröu" written on it: Maurice owned the concession for the whole of Laos, selling—it was said—several bottles a year. Jerry avoided absolutely the street that housed the Indocharter offices, just as he restrained himself from taking a look, out of curiosity, at the flea-hut on the edge of town which, on Charlie Marshall's testimony, had housed their *ménage à trois*. When asked, Maurice said there were very few Chinese left in town these days: "Chinese do not like," he said with another smile, tilting his head at the Pathet Lao on the pavement outside.

There remains the mystery of the telephone transcripts. Did Jerry ring Lizzie from the Constellation, or not? And if he did ring her, did he mean to talk to her, or only to listen to her voice? And if he intended to talk to her, then what did he propose to say? Or was the very act of making the phone call—like the act of booking airline passages in Saigon—in itself sufficient catharsis to hold him back from the reality?

What is certain is that nobody—neither Smiley nor Connie nor anyone else who read the crucial transcripts—can be seriously accused of failing in their duty, for the entry was at best ambivalent:

0055 hrs HK time. Incoming overseas call, personal for subject. Operator on the line. Subject accepts call, says "hullo" several times.

Operator: "Speak up, please, caller!"

(repeated in French and ? Lao)

Subject: "Hullo? Hullo?"

Operator: "Can you hear me, caller? Speak up, please!"

(repeated in French and ? Lao)

Subject: "Hullo? Liese Worth here. Who's calling, please?"

Call disconnected from caller's end.

The transcript nowhere mentions Vientiane as the place of origin and it is even doubtful whether Smiley saw it, since his cryptonym does not appear in the signing panel.

Anyway, whether it was Jerry who made that call or someone else, the next day a pair of Cousins, not one, brought him his marching orders and at long long last the welcome relief of action. The bloody inertia, however many interminable weeks of it, had ended—as it happened for good.

Jerry spent the afternoon fixing himself visas and transport, and next morning at dawn he crossed the Mekong into North East Thailand, carrying his shoulder-bag and his typewriter. The long wooden ferry boat was crammed with peasants and shrieking pigs. At the shack that controlled the crossing point, he pledged himself to return to Laos by the same route. Documentation would otherwise be impossible, the officials warned him severely. If I return at all, he thought. Looking back to the receding shores of Laos, he saw an American car parked on the tow-path, and beside it two slender, stationary figures watching. The Cousins we have always with us.

On the Thai bank everything was immediately impossible. Jerry's visa was not enough, his photographs bore no likeness, the whole area was forbidden to *farangs*. Ten dollars secured a revised opinion. After the visa, the car. Jerry had insisted on an English-speaking driver and the rate had been fixed accordingly, but the old man who waited for him spoke nothing but Thai, and little of that. By bawling English phrases into the nearby rice shop, Jerry finally hooked a fat supine boy who had some English and said he could drive.

A laborious contract was drawn up. The old man's insurance did not cover another driver, and anyway it was out of date. An exhausted travel clerk issued a new policy while the boy went home to make his arrangements. The car was a clapped-out red Ford with bald tyres. Of all the ways Jerry didn't intend to die in the next day or two, this was one of them. They haggled, Jerry put up another twenty dollars. At a garage full of chickens he watched every move of the mechanics till the new tyres were in place.

Having thus wasted an hour, they set out at a breakneck speed south-eastwards over flat farm country. The boy played "The lights are always out in Massachusetts" five times before Jerry asked for silence.

The road was tarmac but deserted. Occasionally a yellow bus came side-winding down the hill toward them, and at once the driver accelerated and stayed on the crown till the bus had yielded a foot and thundered past. Once while he was dozing, Jerry was startled by the crunch of bamboo fencing and woke in time to see a fountain of splinters lift into the sunlight just ahead of him, and a pick-up truck rolling into the ditch in slow motion. He saw the door float upward like a leaf and the flailing driver follow it through the fence and into the high grass. The boy hadn't even slowed down, though his laughter made them swerve all over the road. Jerry shouted "Stop!" but the boy would have none of it.

"You want to get blood on your suit? You leave that to the doctors," he advised sternly. "I look after you, okay? This very bad country here. Lot of Commies."

"What's your name?" said Jerry resignedly.

It was unpronounceable, so they settled on Mickey.

It was two more hours before they hit the first barrier. Jerry dozed again, rehearsing his lines. There's always one more door you have to put your foot in, he thought. He wondered whether a day would come—for the Circus—for the comic—when the old entertainer would not be able to pull the gags any more; when just the sheer energy of bare-arsing his way over the threshold would defeat him, and he would stand there flaccid, sporting his friendly salesman's grin while the words died in his throat. Not this time, he thought hastily. Dear God, not this time please.

They stopped, and a young monk scurried out of the trees with a *wat* bowl and Jerry dropped a few *baht* into it. Mickey opened the boot. A police sentry peered inside, then ordered Jerry out and led him and Mickey over to a captain, who sat in a shaded hut all his own. The captain took a long while to notice Jerry at all.

"He ask you American?" said Mickey.

Jerry produced his papers.

On the other side of the barrier the perfect tarmac road ran straight as a pencil over the flat scrub land.

"He says what you want here?" Mickey said.

"Business with the colonel."

Driving on, they passed a village and a cinema. Even the latest films up here are silents, Jerry recalled. He had once done a story about them. Local actors made the voices and invented whatever plots came into their heads. He remembered John Wayne with a squeaky Thai voice, and the audience ecstatic, and the interpreter explaining to him that they were hearing an imitation of the local mayor, who was a famous queen.

They were passing forest, but the shoulders of the road had been cleared fifty yards on either side to cut the risk of ambush. Occasionally they came on sharp white lines which had nothing to do with earth-bound traffic. The road had been laid by the Americans with an eye to auxiliary landing-strips.

"You know this colonel guy?" Mickey asked.

"No," said Jerry.

Mickey laughed in delight. "Why you want?"

Jerry didn't bother to answer.

The second road-block came twenty miles later, in the centre of a small village given over to police. A cluster of grey trucks stood in the courtyard of the *wat*; four jeeps were parked beside the road-block. The village lay at a junction. At right angles to their road a yellow dust path crossed the plain and snaked into the hills on either side.

This time Jerry took the initiative, leaping from the car immediately with a merry cry of "Take me to your leader!" Their leader turned out to be a nervous young captain with the anxious frown of a man trying to keep abreast of matters beyond his learning. He sat in the police station with his pistol on the desk. The police station was temporary, Jerry noticed. Out of the window he saw the bombed ruins of what he took to be the last one.

"My colonel is a busy man," the captain said, through Mickey the driver.

"He is also a very brave man," Jerry said.

There was dumb show till they had established "brave."

"He has shot many Communists," Jerry said. "My paper wishes to write about this brave Thai colonel."

The captain spoke for quite a while, and suddenly Mickey began hooting with laughter: "The captain say we don't got no Commies. We only got Bangkok! Poor people up here don't know nothing, because Bangkok don't give them no schools, so the Commies come talk to them in the night and the Commies tell them all their sons go Moscow, learn be big doctors, so they blow up the police station."

"Where can I find the colonel?"

"Captain say we stay here."

"Will he ask the colonel to come to us?"

"Colonel very busy man."

"Where is the colonel?"

"He next village."

"What is the name of the next village?"

The driver once more collapsed with laughter. "It don't got no name. That village all dead."

"What was the village called before it died?"

Mickey said a name.

"Is the road open as far as this dead village?"

"Captain say military secret. That mean he don't know."

"Will the captain let us through to take a look?"

A long exchange followed. "Sure," said Mickey finally. "He say we go. Okay."

"Will the captain radio the colonel and tell him we are coming?"

"Colonel very busy man."

"Will he radio him?"

"Sure," said the driver, as if only a hideous *farang* could have made a meal of such a patently obvious detail.

They climbed back into the car. The boom lifted and they continued along the perfect tarmac road with its cleared shoulders and occasional landing marks. For twenty minutes they drove without seeing another living thing, but Jerry wasn't consoled by the emptiness. He had heard that for every Communist guerrilla fighting with a gun in the hills, it took five in the plains to produce the rice, the ammunition, and the infrastructure, and these were the plains. They came to a dust path on their right, and the dust of it was smeared across the tarmac from recent use. Mickey swung down it, following the heavy tyre tracks, playing "The lights are always out in Massachusetts" again, and singing the words very loud, Jerry notwithstanding.

"This way the Commies think we plenty people," he explained amid more laughter, thus making it impossible for him to object. To Jerry's surprise he also produced a huge, long-barrelled .45 target pistol from the bag beneath his seat. Jerry ordered him sharply to shove it back where it came from.

Minutes later they smelt burning, then they drove through
wood-smoke, then they reached what was left of the village:
clusters of cowed people, a couple of acres of burnt teak trees
like a petrified forest, three jeeps, twenty-odd police, and a
stocky lieutenant-colonel at their centre. Villagers and police
alike were gazing at a patch of smouldering ash sixty yards
across, in which a few charred beams sketched the outline of
the burned houses.

The colonel watched them park and he watched them
walk over. He was a fighting man. Jerry saw it immediately. He
was squat and strong, and he neither smiled nor scowled. He was
swarthy and greying, and he could have been Malay, except
that he was thicker in the trunk. He wore parachute wings and
flying wings and a couple of rows of medal ribbons. He wore
battle-drill and a regulation automatic in a leather holster on
his right thigh, and the restraining straps hung open.

"You the newsman?" he asked Jerry in flat, military American.

"That's right."

The colonel turned to the driver. He said something, and
Mickey walked hastily back to the car, got into it, and stayed
there.

"What do you want?"

"Anybody die here?"

"Three people. I just shot them. We got thirty-eight million." His functional American-English, all but perfect, came
as a growing surprise.

"Why did you shoot them?"

"At night the C.T.s held classes here. People come from all
around to hear the C.T.s."

Communist terrorists, thought Jerry. He had an inkling it
was originally a British phrase. A string of lorries was nosing
down the dust path. Seeing them, the villagers began picking
up their bedrolls and children. The colonel gave an order, and

his men formed them into a rough file while the lorries turned round.

"We find them a better place," the colonel said. "They start again."

"Who did you shoot?"

"Last week two of my men got bombed. The C.T.s operated from this village." He picked out a sullen woman at that moment clambering on the lorry and called her back so that Jerry could take a look at her. She stood with her head bowed.

"They stay in her house," he said. "This time I shoot her husband. Next time I shoot her."

"And the other two?" Jerry asked.

He asked because to keep asking is to stay punching, but it was Jerry, not the colonel, who was under interrogation. The colonel's eyes were hard and appraising and held a lot in reserve. They looked at Jerry enquiringly but without anxiety.

"One of the C.T.s sleep with a girl here," he said simply. "We're not only the police. We're the judge and courts as well. There's no one else. Bangkok don't care for a lot of public trials up here. That's the way it is."

The villagers had boarded the lorries. They drove away without looking back. Only the children waved over the tailboards. The jeeps followed, leaving the three of them, and the two cars, and a boy, perhaps fifteen.

"Who's he?" said Jerry.

"He comes with us. Next year—year after, maybe—I shoot him too."

Jerry rode in the jeep beside the colonel, who drove. The boy sat impassively in the back, murmuring yes and no while the colonel lectured him in a firm, mechanical tone. Mickey followed in the car. On the floor of the jeep, between the seat and the pedals, the colonel kept four grenades in a cardboard carton. A small machine-gun lay along the rear seat, and the colonel didn't bother to move it for the boy. Above the driving mirror beside the votive pictures hung a postcard portrait of John Kennedy, with the legend "Ask not what your country can do for you. Ask rather what you can do for your country." Jerry had taken his notebook out. The lecture to the boy continued.

"What are you saying to him?"

"I am explaining the principles of democracy."

"What are they?"

"No Communism and no generals," he replied, and laughed.

At the main road they turned right, farther into the interior, Mickey following in the red Ford.

"Dealing with Bangkok is like climbing that big tree," the colonel said to Jerry, pointing at the forest. "You climb one branch, go up a bit, change branches, the branch breaks, you go up again. Maybe one day you get to the top general. Maybe never."

Two small kids flagged them down, and the colonel stopped to let them squeeze in beside the boy.

"I don't do that too often," he said with a smile. "I do that to show you I'm a nice guy. The C.T.s get to know you stop for kids, they put out kids to stop you. You got to vary yourself. That way you stay alive."

He had turned in to forest again. They drove a few miles and let the small children out, but not the sullen boy. The trees stopped and gave way to desolate scrub land. The sky grew white, with the shadows of the hills just breaking through the mist.

"What's he done?" Jerry asked.

"Him? He's a C.T.," the colonel said. "We catch him." In the forest Jerry saw a flash of gold, but it was only a *wat*. "Last week one of my police turns informer to C.T. I send him on patrol, shoot him, make him a big hero. I fix the wife a pension, I buy a big flag for the body, I make a great funeral, and the village gets a bit richer. That guy's not an informer any more. He's a folk hero. You got to win the hearts and minds of the people."

"No question," Jerry agreed.

They had reached a wide dry paddy-field with two women hoeing at the centre and otherwise nothing in sight but a far hedge and rocky dune land fading into the white sky. Leaving Mickey in the Ford, Jerry and the colonel began walking across the field, the sullen boy trailing behind him.

"You British?"

"Yes."

"I was at Washington International Police Academy," said the colonel. "Very nice place. I studied law enforcement at Michigan State. They showed us a good time. You want to keep clear of me a little?" he asked politely as they trod meticulously over the plough. "They shoot me, not you. They shoot a *farang*, they get too much trouble here. They don't want that. Nobody shoots a *farang* in my territory."

They had reached the women. The colonel spoke to them, walked a distance, stopped, looked back at the sullen boy, and returned to the women and spoke to them a second time.

"What's that about?" said Jerry.

"I ask them if there's any C.T.s around. They tell me no. Then I think, Maybe the C.T.s want this boy back. So I go back and tell them, 'If anything goes wrong, we shoot you women first.'" They had reached the hedge. The dunes lay ahead of them, overgrown with high bushes and palms like sword blades. The colonel cupped his hands and yelled until an answering call came.

"I learned that in the jungle," he explained with another smile. "When you're in the jungle, always call first."

"What jungle was that?" said Jerry.

"Stand near to me now please. Smile when you speak to me. They like to see you very clear."

They had reached a small river. Around it, a hundred or more males, some even younger than the boy, picked indifferently at the rocks with axes and spades, or humped bags of cement from one vast pile to another. A handful of armed police looked negligently on. The colonel called up the boy and spoke to him, and the boy bowed his head and the colonel boxed him sharply on the ears. The boy muttered something and the colonel hit him again, then patted him on the shoulder, whereupon like a freed but crippled bird the boy scuffled away to join the labour force.

"You write about C.T.s, you write about my dam, too," the colonel ordered as they started their return talk. "We're going to make this fine pasture here. They will name it after me."

"What jungle did you fight in?" Jerry repeated.

"Laos. Very hard fighting."

"You volunteered?"

"Sure. I got kids, need the money. I joined PARU. Heard of PARU? Police Aerial Reinforcement Unit. The Americans ran it. They got it made. I write a letter resigning from the Thai police. They put it in a drawer. If I get killed, they pull out the letter to prove I resigned before I joined PARU."

"That where you met Ricardo?"

"Sure. Ricardo's my friend. We fought together, shoot a lot of bad guys."

"I want to see him," said Jerry. "I met a girl of his in Saigon. She told me he had a place up here. I want to make him a business proposition."

They passed the women again. The colonel waved at them but they ignored him. Jerry was watching his face but he could as soon have watched a boulder back on the dunes. The colonel climbed into the jeep. Jerry got in after him.

"I thought maybe you could take me to him. I could even make him rich for a few days."

"This for your paper?"

"It's private."

"A private business proposition?" the colonel asked.

"That's right."

As they drove back to the road, two cement-mixer lorries came toward them and the colonel had to back to let them pass. Automatically Jerry noticed the name painted on the yellow sides. As he did so, he caught the colonel's eye watching him.

They continued toward the interior, driving as fast as the jeep would go, in order to beat anybody's bad intentions along the way. Faithfully Mickey followed behind.

"Ricardo is my friend and this is my territory," the colonel repeated. The statement, though familiar, was this time an entirely explicit warning. "He lives here under my protection, according to an arrangement we have made. Everybody around here knows that. The villagers know it, C.T. knows it. Nobody hurts Ricardo or I'll shoot every C.T. on the dam."

As they turned off the main road into the dust path again, Jerry saw the light skid marks of a small plane written on the tarmac.

"This where he lands?"

"Only in the rainy season." The colonel continued outlining his ethical position in the matter: "If Ricardo kills you, that's his business. One *farang* shoots another on my territory, that's natural." He could have been explaining basic arithmetic to a child. "Ricardo is my friend," he repeated without embarrassment. "My comrade."

"He expecting me?"

"Please pay attention to him. Captain Ricardo is sometimes a sick man."

Tiu make a special place for him, Charlie Marshall had said, *a place where only crazy people go. Tiu say to him, "You stay alive, you keep the plane, you ride shot-gun for Charlie Marshall any time you like, carry money for him, if that's the way Charlie wants it. That's the deal and Drake Ko don't never break a deal," he say. But if Ric make trouble, or if Ric louses up, or if Ric shoot his big mouth off about certain matters, Tiu and his people kill that crazy bastard so completely he don't never know who he is.*

"Why doesn't Ric just take the plane and run for it?" Jerry had asked.

Tiu got Ric's passport, Voltaire. Tiu buy Ric's debts and his business enterprises and his police record. Tiu pinned about fifty tons of opium on him and Tiu got the proof all ready for the narcs for if ever he need it. Ric, he's free to walk out any damn time he wants. They got prisons waiting for him everywhere.

The house stood on stilts at the centre of a wide dust path, with a balcony all round it and a small stream beside it and a couple of Thai girls under it, and one of them was feeding her baby while the other stirred a cook pot. Behind the house lay a flat brown field with a shed at one end big enough to house a small plane—say, a Beechcraft—and there was a silvered track of pressed grass down the field where one might recently have landed. There were no trees near the house and it stood on a small rise. It had all-round vision and broad windows not very high, which Jerry guessed had been altered to provide a wide angle of fire from inside.

Short of the house the colonel told Jerry to get out, and walked back with him to Mickey's car. He spoke to Mickey and Mickey leapt out and unlocked the boot. The colonel reached under the car seat and pulled out the target pistol and tossed it contemptuously into the jeep. He frisked Jerry, then he frisked Mickey; then he searched the car for himself. Then he told them both to wait and climbed the steps to the first floor. The girls ignored him.

"He fine colonel," said Mickey.

They waited.

"England rich country," said Mickey.

"England a very *poor* country," Jerry retorted as they continued to watch the house.

"Poor country, rich people," said Mickey. He was still shaking with laughter at his own good joke as the colonel came out of the house, climbed into the jeep, and drove away.

"Wait here," said Jerry. He walked slowly to the foot of the steps, cupped his hands to his mouth, and called upwards.

"My name's Westerby. You may remember shooting at me in Phnom Penh a few weeks ago. I'm a poor journalist with expensive ideas."

"What do you want, Voltaire? Somebody told me you were dead already."

A Latin-American voice, deep and feathered, from the darkness above.

"I want to blackmail Drake Ko. I reckon that between us we could sting him for a couple of million bucks and you could buy your freedom."

In the darkness of the trap above him Jerry saw a single gun barrel, like a Cyclopean eye, wink, then settle its gaze on him again.

"*Each*," Jerry called. "Two for you, two for me. I've got it all worked out. With my brains and your information and Lizzie Worthington's figure, I reckon it's a dead cert."

He started walking slowly up the steps. Voltaire, he thought; when it came to spreading the word, Charlie Marshall didn't hang around. As to being dead already—give it a little time, he thought.

As Jerry climbed through the trap he moved from the dark into the light, and the Latin-American voice said, "Stay right there." Doing as he was told, Jerry was able to look round the room, which was a mix between a small armaments museum and an American P.X. On the centre table on a tripod stood an AK-47 similar to the one Ricardo had already fired at him, and as Jerry had suspected, it covered all four approaches through the windows. But in case it didn't, there were a couple of spares and beside each gun a decent pile of ammunition clips. Grenades lay about like fruit, in clusters of three and four, and on the hideous walnut cocktail cabinet under a plastic effigy of the Madonna lay a selection of pistols and automatics for all occasions.

There was only one room but it was large, with a low bed with japanned and lacquered ends, and Jerry had a silly moment wondering how the devil Ricardo had ever got it into his Beech-craft. There were two refrigerators and an ice-maker, and there were painfully worked oil paintings of nude Thai girls, drawn with the sort of erotic inaccuracy that usually comes with too little access to the subject. There was a filing cabinet with a Luger on it and there was a book shelf with works on company law, international taxation, and sexual technique. On the walls hung several locally carved icons of saints, the Virgin, and the Christ-child. On the floor lay a steel scaffold of a rowing-boat, with a sliding seat for improving the figure.

At the centre of all this, in much the same pose in which Jerry had first set eyes on him, sat Ricardo in a senior executive's swivel chair, wearing his C.I.A. bracelets and a sarong and a gold cross on his handsome bare chest. His beard was a lot less full than when Jerry had seen it last, and he guessed the girls had clipped it for him. He wore no cap, and his crinkly black hair was threaded into a small gold ring at the back of his neck. He was broad-shouldered and muscular and his skin was tanned and oily and his chest was matted with hair.

He also had a bottle of Scotch at his elbow, and a jug of water, but no ice because there was no electricity for the refrigerators.

"Take off your jacket please, Voltaire," Ricardo ordered, so Jerry did, and with a sigh Ricardo stood up, and picked an automatic from the table, and walked slowly round Jerry, studying his body while he gently probed it for weapons.

"You play tennis?" he enquired from behind him, running one hand very lightly down Jerry's back. "Charlie said you got muscles like a gorilla." But Ricardo did not really ask questions of anyone but himself. "I like very much tennis. I am an extremely good player. I win always. Here unfortunately I have little opportunity."

He sat down again. "Sometimes you got to hide with the enemy to get away from your friends. I ride horses, box, shoot, I got degrees, I fly an aeroplane, I know a lot of things about life, I'm very intelligent, but, owing to unforeseen circumstances, I live in the jungle like a monkey." The automatic lay casually in his left hand. "That what you call a paranoid, Voltaire? Somebody who think everybody his enemy?"

"I rather think it is."

To produce the well-trodden witticism, Ricardo laid a finger to his bronzed and oiled breast: "Well, this paranoid got real enemies," he said.

"With two million bucks," said Jerry, still standing where Ricardo had left him, "I'm sure most of them could be eliminated."

"Voltaire, I must tell you honestly that I regard your business proposition as crap."

Ricardo laughed. That was to say he made a fine display of his white teeth against his newly clipped beard, and flexed his stomach muscles a little, and kept his eyes fixed dead level on Jerry's face while he sipped his glass of whisky. He's got a brief, thought Jerry, same as I have. *If he shows up, you hear him out,* Tiu had no doubt said to him. And when Ricardo had heard him out—then what?

"I definitely understood you had had an accident, Voltaire," said Ricardo sadly and shook his head as if complaining about the poor quality of his information. "You want a drink?"

"Thanks, I'll pour it for myself," said Jerry. The glasses were in a cabinet, all different colours and sizes. Deliberately Jerry walked over to it and helped himself to a long pink tumbler with a dressed girl outside and a naked girl inside. He poured a couple of fingers of Scotch into it, added a little water, and sat down opposite Ricardo at the table, while Ricardo studied him with interest.

"You do exercises, weight-lifting, something?" Ricardo enquired confidingly.

"Just the odd bottle," said Jerry.

Ricardo laughed inordinately, still examining him very closely with his flickering bedroom eyes.

"That was a very bad thing you did to little Charlie, you

know that? I don't like you to sit on my friend's head in the
darkness while he catch cold turkey. Charlie going to take a
long while to recover. That's no way to make friends with
Charlie's friends, Voltaire. They say you even been rude to
Mr. Ko. Took my little Lizzie out to dinner. That true?"

"I took her out to dinner."

"You screw her?"

Jerry didn't answer. Ricardo gave another burst of laughter,
which stopped as suddenly as it had started. He took a long
draught of whisky and sighed.

"Well, I hope she's grateful, that's all." Ricardo was at once
a much misunderstood man. "I forgive her. Okay? You see
Lizzie again, tell her I, Ricardo, forgive her. I train her. I put
her on the right road. I tell her a lot of things—art, culture,
politics, business, religion—I teach her how to make love, and
I send her into the world. Where would she be without my
connections? Where? Living in the jungle with Ricardo like a
monkey. She owes me everything.

"Pygmalion—know that movie? Well, I'm the professor. I
tell her some things—know what I mean?—I tell her things no
man can tell her but Ricardo. Seven years in Vietnam. Two
years in Laos. Four thousand dollars a month from C.I.A., and
me a Catholic. You think I can't tell her some things, a girl like
that from nowhere, an English scrubber? She got a kid, you
know that? Little boy in London. She walk out on him, imagine. Such a mother, huh? Worse than a whore."

Jerry found nothing useful to say. He was looking at the two
large rings side by side on the middle fingers of Ricardo's heavy
right hand, and in his memory measuring them against the
twin scars on Lizzie's chin. It was a downward blow, he decided,
a right cross while she was below him. It seemed strange he
hadn't broken her jaw. Perhaps he had, and she'd had a lucky
mend.

"You gone deaf, Voltaire? I said outline to me your business proposition. Without prejudice, you understand. Except I don't believe a word of it."

Jerry helped himself to some more whisky: "I thought maybe if you told me what it was Drake Ko wanted you to do that time you flew for him, and if Lizzie could get me alongside Ko, and we all kept our hands on the table, we'd have a good chance of taking him to the cleaners."

Now he said it, it sounded even lamer than when he had rehearsed it, but he didn't particularly care.

"You crazy, Voltaire. Crazy. You're making pictures in the air."

"Not if Ko was asking you to fly into the China mainland for him, I'm not. Ko can own the whole of Hong Kong for all I care, but if the Governor ever got to hear of that little adventure, I reckon he and Ko would stop kissing overnight. That's for openers. There's more."

"What are you talking about, Voltaire? China? What nonsense is this you are telling me about the China *mainland?*" He shrugged his glistening shoulders and drank, smirking into his glass. "I do not read you, Voltaire. You talk through your ass. What makes you think I fly to China for Ko? Ridiculous. Laughable."

As a liar, Jerry reckoned, Ricardo was about three leagues lower down the chart than Lizzie, which was saying quite a lot.

"My editor makes me think it, sport. My editor is a very sharp fellow. Lot of influential and knowledgeable friends. They tell him things. Now, for instance, my editor has a very good hunch that not long after you died so tragically in that air crash of yours you sold a damn great load of raw opium to a friendly American purchaser engaged in the suppression of dangerous drugs. Another hunch of his tells him it was Ko's opium, not yours to sell at all, and that it was addressed to the China mainland. Only you decided to play the angles instead."

He went straight on, while Ricardo's eyes watched him over

the top of his whisky glass. "Now, if that were so, and Ko's ambition were, let us say, to reintroduce the opium habit to the mainland—slowly, but gradually creating new markets, you follow me—well, I reckon he would go a very long distance to prevent that information making the front pages of the world's press. That's not all either. There are other aspects altogether, for us even more lucrative."

"What's that, Voltaire?" Ricardo asked and continued watching him as fixedly as if he had him in the sights of his rifle. "What are these other aspects you refer to? Kindly tell me, please."

"Well, I think I'll hold back on that," said Jerry with a frank smile. "I think I'll keep it warm while you give me a little something in return."

A girl came silently up the stairs carrying bowls of rice and lemon grass and boiled chicken. She was trim and entirely beautiful. They could hear voices from underneath the house, including Mickey's, and the sound of the baby laughing.

"Who you got down there, Voltaire?" Ricardo asked vaguely, half waking from his reverie. "You got some damn bodyguard or something?"

"Just the driver."

"He got guns?"

Receiving no reply, Ricardo shook his head in wonder. "You're some crazy fellow," he remarked, as he waved at the girl to get out. "You're some really crazy fellow." He handed Jerry a bowl and chopsticks. "Holy Maria. That Tiu, he's a pretty rough guy. I'm a pretty rough guy myself. But those Chinese can be very hard people, Voltaire. You mess with a guy like Tiu, you get pretty big trouble."

"We'll beat them at their own game," said Jerry. "We'll use English lawyers. We'll stack it so high a board of bishops couldn't knock it down. We'll collect witnesses. You, Charlie Marshall, whoever else knows. Give dates and times of what he said and did. We'll show him a copy and we'll bank the others and we'll make a contract with him. Signed, sealed, and delivered. Legal as hell. That's what he likes. Ko's a very legal-minded man. I've been into his business affairs. I've seen his bank statements, his assets. The story's pretty good as it stands. But with the other aspects I'm talking about, I reckon it's cheap at five million. Two for you. Two for me. One for Lizzie."

"For her, nothing."

Ricardo was stooping over the filing cabinet. Pulling open a drawer, he began picking through the contents, studying brochures and correspondence.

"You ever been to Bali, Voltaire?"

Solemnly pulling on a pair of reading glasses, Ricardo sat at the table again and began studying the file. "I bought some land there a few years back. A deal I made. I make many deals. Walk, ride, I got a Honda seven fifty there, a girl. In Laos we kill everybody, in Vietnam we burn the whole damn countryside, so I buy this land in Bali, bit of land we don't burn for once and a girl we don't kill, know what I mean? Fifty acres of scrub. Here, come here."

Peering over his shoulder, Jerry saw a planner's mimeographed diagram of an isthmus broken into numbered building plots, and in the bottom left corner the words "Ricardo & Worthington Ltd., Dutch Antilles."

"You come into business with me, Voltaire. We develop this thing together, okay? Build fifty houses, have one each, nice people, put Charlie Marshall out there as manager, get some girls, make a colony maybe—artists, concerts sometimes—you like music, Voltaire?"

"I need hard facts," Jerry insisted firmly. "Dates, times, places, witnesses' statements. When you've told me, I'll trade you. I'll explain those other aspects to you—the lucrative ones. I'll explain the whole deal."

"Sure," said Ricardo distractedly, still studying the map. "We screw him. Sure we do."

This is how they lived together, Jerry thought: with one foot in fairyland and the other in jail, bolstering each other's fantasies, a beggars' opera with a cast of three.

For a while now Ricardo fell in love with his sins and there was nothing Jerry could do to stop him. In Ricardo's simple world, to talk about himself was to get to know the other person better.

So he talked about his big soul, about his great sexual potency and his concern for its continuation, but most of all he talked about the horrors of war, a subject on which he considered himself uniquely well informed.

"In Vietnam I fall in love with a girl, Voltaire. I, Ricardo, I fall in love. This is very rare and holy to me. Black hair, straight back, face like a Madonna, little tits. Each morning I stop the jeep as she walks to school, each morning she says 'No.' 'Listen,' I tell her. 'Ricardo is not American. He is Mexican.' She never even heard of Mexico. I go crazy, Voltaire. For weeks I, Ricardo, live like a monk. The other girls, I don't touch them any more. Every morning. Then one day I'm in first gear already and she throws up her hand—stop! She gets in beside me. She leaves school, goes out to live in a kampong, I tell you one day the name.

"The B-52s go in and flatten the village. Some hero doesn't read the map. Little villages, they're like stones on the beach, each one the same. I'm in the chopper behind. Nothing's stopping me. Charlie Marshall's beside me and he's screaming me I'm crazy. I don't care. I go down, land, I find her. The whole village dead. I find her. She's dead too, but I find her. I get back to base, the military police beat me up, I get seven weeks in solitary, lose my service stripes. Me. Ricardo."

"You poor thing," said Jerry, who had played these games before and hated them—disbelieved or believed them, but always hated them.

"You are right," said Ricardo, acknowledging Jerry's homage with a bow. "'Poor' is the correct word. They treat us like peasants. Me and Charlie, we fly everything. We were never properly rewarded. Wounded, dead, bits of bodies, dope. For nothing. Jesus, that was shooting, that war. Twice I fly into Yunnan Province. I am fearless. Totally. Even my good looks do not make me afraid for myself."

"Counting Drake Ko's trip," Jerry reminded him, "you would have been there three times, wouldn't you?"

"I train pilots for the Cambodian air force. For nothing. The Cambodian air force, Voltaire! Eighteen generals, fifty-four planes—and Ricardo. End of your time, you get the life insurance—that's the deal. A hundred thousand U.S. Only you. Ricardo die, his next of kin get nothing—that's the deal. Ricardo make it, he get it all. I talk to some friends from the French Foreign Legion once. They know the racket, they warn me. 'Take care, Ricardo. Soon they send you to bad spots you can't get out of. That way they don't have to pay you.' Cambodians want me to fly on half fuel. I got wing tanks and refuse. Another time they fix my hydraulics. I engineer the plane myself. That way they don't kill me. Listen, I snap my fingers, Lizzie come back to me. Okay?"

Lunch was over.

"So how did it go with Tiu and Drake?" said Jerry. With confession, they say at Sarratt, all you have to do is tilt the stream a little.

For the first time, it seemed to Jerry, Ricardo stared at him with the full intensity of his animal stupidity.

"You confuse me, Voltaire. If I tell you too much, I have to shoot you. I'm a very talkative person, you follow me? I get lonely up here, it is my disposition always to be lonely. I like a guy, I talk to him, then I regret myself. I remember my business commitments, follow me?"

An inner stillness came over Jerry now, as Sarratt man became Sarratt recording angel with no part to play but to receive and to remember. Operationally, he knew, he stood close to journey's

end: even if the journey back was, at best, imponderable. Operationally, by any precedents he understood, muted bells of triumph should have been sounding in his awe-struck ear. But
that didn't happen. And the fact that it didn't was an early warning to him even then, that his quest was no longer, in every
respect, on all fours with that of the Sarratt bearleaders.

At first—with allowances for Ricardo's vaunting ego—the
story went much as Charlie Marshall had said it went. Tiu came
to Vientiane dressed like a coolie and smelling of cat scent and
asked around for the finest pilot in town, and naturally he was
at once referred to Ricardo, who as it happened was resting
between business commitments and available for certain specialised and highly rewarded work in the aviation field.

Unlike Charlie Marshall, Ricardo told his story with a studious directness, as if he expected to be dealing with intellects
inferior to his own. Tiu introduced himself as a person with
wide contacts in the aviation industry, mentioned his unde-
fined link with Indocharter, and went over the ground he had
already covered with Charlie Marshall. Finally he came to the
project in hand—which is to say that, in fine Sarratt style, Tiu
fed Ricardo the cover story. A certain major Bangkok trading
company, with which Tiu was proud to be associated, was in
the throes of an extremely legitimate deal with certain officials
in a neighbouring friendly foreign country.

"I ask him, Voltaire, very seriously, 'Mr. Tiu, maybe you
just discovered the moon. I never heard yet an Asian country
with a friendly foreign neighbour.' Tiu laughed at my joke. He
naturally considered it a witty contribution," said Ricardo very
seriously, in one of his strange outbreaks of business-school
English.

Before consummating their profitable and legitimate deal,
however, Tiu explained, in Ricardo's language, his business
associates were faced with the problem of paying off certain
officials and other parties inside that friendly foreign country
who had cleared away tiresome bureaucratic obstacles.

"Why was this a problem?" Ricardo had asked, not unnaturally.

Suppose, said Tiu, the country was Burma. Just suppose. In modern Burma officials were not allowed to enrich themselves, nor could they easily bank money. In such a case some other means of payment would have to be found.

Ricardo suggested gold. Tiu, said Ricardo, regretted himself: in the country he had in mind, even gold was difficult to negotiate. The currency selected in this case was therefore to be opium, he said: four hundred kilos of it. The distance was not great, the inside of a day would see Ricardo there and back; the fee was five thousand dollars, and the remaining details would be vouchsafed to him just before departure in order to avoid "a needless erosion of the memory," as Ricardo put it, in another of those bizarre linguistic flourishes which must have formed a major part of Lizzie's education at his hands. Upon Ricardo's return from what Tiu was certain would be a painless and instructive flight, five thousand U.S. dollars in convenient denominations would at once be his—subject, of course, to Ricardo producing, in whatever form should prove convenient, confirmation that the consignment had reached its destination.

A receipt, for example.

Ricardo, as he described his own footwork, now showed a crude cunning in his dealings with Tiu. He told him he would think about this offer. He spoke of other pressing commitments and his ambitions to open his own airline. Then he set to work to find out who the hell Tiu was. He discovered at once that, following their interview, Tiu had returned not to Bangkok but to Hong Kong on the direct flight. He made Lizzie pump the Chiu Chow boys at Indocharter, and one of them let slip that Tiu was a big cat in China Airsea, because when he was in Bangkok he stayed in the China Airsea suite at the Erawan Hotel. By the time Tiu returned to Vientiane to hear Ricardo's answer, Ricardo therefore knew a lot more about him—even, though he made little of it, that Tiu was right-hand man to Drake Ko.

Five thousand U.S. dollars for a one-day trip, he now told
Tiu at this second interview, was either too little or too much.
If the job was as soft as Tiu insisted, it was too much. If it was
as totally crazy as Ricardo suspected, it was too little. Ricardo
suggested a different arrangement: a "business compromise,"
he said. He was suffering, he explained—in a phrase he had no
doubt used often—from "a temporary problem of liquidity." In
other words (Jerry interpreting) he was broke as usual, and the
creditors were at his throat. What he required immediately was
a regular income, and this was best obtained by Tiu arranging
for him to be taken on by Indocharter as a pilot-consultant for
a year at an agreed salary of twenty-five thousand U.S. dollars.

Tiu did not seem too shocked by the idea, said Ricardo.
Upstairs in the stilt-house, the room grew very quiet.

Secondly, instead of being paid five thousand dollars on
delivery of the consignment, Ricardo wanted an advance of
twenty thousand U.S. dollars now, with which to settle his outstanding commitments. Ten thousand would be considered
earned as soon as he had delivered the opium, and the other ten
thousand would be deductible "at source"—another Ricardo
nom de guerre—from his Indocharter salary over the remaining
months of his employment. If Tiu and his associates couldn't
manage this, Ricardo explained, then unfortunately he would
have to leave town before he could make the opium delivery.

Next day, with variations, Tiu agreed to the terms. Rather
than advance Ricardo twenty thousand dollars, Tiu and his associates proposed to buy Ricardo's debts directly from his creditors.
That way, he explained, they would feel more comfortable. The
same day, the arrangement was *sanctified*—Ricardo's religious
convictions were never far away—by a formidable contract,
drawn in English and signed by both parties. Ricardo—Jerry
silently recorded—had just sold his soul.

"What did Lizzie think of the deal?" Jerry asked.

He shrugged his smooth shoulders. "Women," Ricardo said.

"Sure," said Jerry, returning his knowing smile.

Ricardo's future thus secured, he resumed a "suitable professional life-style," as he called it. A scheme to float an all-Asian football pool claimed his attention, so did a fourteen-year-old girl in Bangkok named Rosie, whom on the strength of his Indocharter salary he periodically visited for the purpose of training her for life's great stage.

Occasionally but not often, he flew the odd run for Indocharter, but nothing demanding: "Chiang Mai couple of times. Saigon. Couple of times into the Shans, visit Charlie Marshall's old man, collect a little mud maybe, take him a few guns, rice, gold. Battambang maybe."

"Where's Lizzie meanwhile?" Jerry asked in the same easy, man-to-man tone as before.

The same contemptuous shrug: "Sitting in Vientiane. Does her knitting. Scrubs a little at the Constellation. That's an old woman already, Voltaire. I need youth. Optimism. Energy. People who respect me. It is my nature to give. How can I give to an old woman?"

"Until?" Jerry repeated.

"Huh?"

"So when did the kissing stop?"

Misunderstanding the phrase, Ricardo looked suddenly very dangerous, and his voice dropped to a low warning: "What the hell you mean?"

Jerry soothed him with the friendliest of smiles. "How long did you draw your pay and kick around before Tiu collected on the contract?"

Six weeks, said Ricardo, recovering his composure. Maybe eight. Twice the trip was on, then cancelled. Once, it seemed, he was ordered to Chiang Mai and loafed for a couple of days till Tiu called to say the people at the other end weren't ready. Increasingly Ricardo had the feeling he was mixed up in something deep, he said, but history, he implied, had always cast him for the great rôles of life and at least the creditors were off his back.

Ricardo broke off and once more studied Jerry closely, scratching his beard in contemplation. Finally he sighed and, pouring them both a whisky, pushed a glass across the table. Below them the perfect day was preparing its own slow death. The green trees had grown heavy; the wood-smoke from the girls' cook pot smelt damp.

"Where you go from here, Voltaire?"

"Home," said Jerry.

Ricardo let out a fresh burst of laughter. "You stay the night, I send you one of my girls."

"I'll make my own damn way, actually, sport," Jerry said. Like fighting animals, the two men surveyed each other, and for a moment the spark of battle was very close indeed.

"You some crazy fellow, Voltaire," Ricardo muttered.

But Sarratt man prevailed. "Then one day the trip was on, right?" Jerry said. "And nobody cancelled. Then what? Come on sport, let's have the story."

"Sure," said Ricardo. "Sure, Voltaire," and drank, still watching him. "How it happened," he said. "Listen, I tell you how it happened, Voltaire."

And then I'll kill you, said his eyes.

Ricardo was in Bangkok. Rosie was being demanding. Tiu had insisted Ricardo should always be within reach, and one morning early, maybe five o'clock, a messenger arrived at their love-nest summoning him to the Erawan immediately. Ricardo was impressed by the suite. He would have wished it for himself.

"Ever seen Versailles, Voltaire? A desk so big as a B-52. This Tiu is a very different human individual to the cat-scent coolie who came to Vientiane, okay? This is a very influential person. 'Ricardo,' he tell me. 'This time is for certain. This time we deliver.'"

Tiu's orders were simple. In a few hours there was a commercial flight to Chiang Mai. Ricardo should take it. Rooms had been booked for him at the Hotel Rincome. He should stay the night there. Alone. No drink, no women, no society.

"'You better take plenty to read, Mr. Ricardo,' he tell me. 'Mr. Tiu,' I tell him. 'You tell me where to fly. You don't tell me where to read. Okay?' This guy is very arrogant behind his big desk—understand me, Voltaire? I am obliged to teach him manners."

Next morning, someone would call for Ricardo at six o'clock at his hotel announcing himself as a friend of Mr. Johnny. Ricardo should go with him.

Things went as planned. Ricardo flew to Chiang Mai, spent an abstemious night at the Rincome, and at six o'clock two Chinese, not one, called for him and drove him north for some hours till they came to a Hakka village. Leaving the car, they walked for half an hour till they reached an empty field with a hut at one end of it. Inside the hut stood "a dandy little Beechcraft," brand new, and inside the Beechcraft sat Tiu, with a lot of maps and documents on his lap, in the seat beside the pilot's. The rear seats had been removed to make space for the gunny bags. A couple of Chinese crushers stood off watching, and the over-all mood, Ricardo implied, was not all he would have liked.

"First I got to empty my pockets. My pockets are very personal to me, Voltaire. They are like a lady's handbag. Mementoes. Letters. Photographs. My Madonna. They retain everything. My passport, my pilot's licence, my money . . . even my bracelets," he said and lifted his brown arms so that the gold links jingled.

After that, he said with a frown of disapproval, there were yet more documents to sign. Such as a power of attorney, signing over whatever bits of Ricardo's life were left to him after his Indocharter contract. Such as various confessions to "previous technically illegal undertakings," several of them—Ricardo asserted in considerable outrage—performed on behalf of

Indocharter. One of the Chinese crushers even turned out to be a lawyer. Ricardo considered this particularly unsporting.

Only then did Tiu unveil the maps, and the instructions, which Ricardo now reproduced in a blend of his own style and Tiu's: "'You head north, Mr. Ricardo, and you keep heading north. Maybe you clip the edge off Laos, maybe you stay over the Shans, I don't give a damn. Flying is your business, not mine. Fifty miles inside the China border you pick up the Mekong and follow it. Then you keep going north till you find a little hill town called Tienpao stuck on a tributary of that very famous river. Head due east twenty miles, you find a landing-strip—one white flare, one green—you do me a favour please. You land there. A man will be waiting for you. He speaks very lousy English, but he speaks it. Here is half one-dollar bill. This man will have the other half. Unload the opium. This man will give you a package, and certain particular instructions. The package is your receipt, Mr. Ricardo. When you return, bring it with you and obey all instructions most absolutely, including especially your place of landing. Do you understand me entirely, Mr. Ricardo?'"

"What kind of package?" Jerry asked.

"He don't say and I don't care. 'You do that,' he tell me, 'and keep your big mouth shut, Mr. Ricardo, and my associates will look after you all your life like you are their son. Your children, they look after—your girls. Your girl in Bali. All your life they will be grateful men. But you screw them, or you go big-mouthing round town, they definitely kill you, Mr. Ricardo, believe me. Not tomorrow maybe, not the next day, but they definitely kill you. We got a contract, Mr. Ricardo. My associates don't never break a contract. They are very legal men.' I got sweat on me, Voltaire. I am in perfect condition, a fine athlete, but I sweat. 'Don't you worry, Mr. Tiu,' I tell him. 'Mr. Tiu, sir. Any time you want to fly opium into Red China, Ricardo's your man.' Voltaire, believe me, I was very concerned."

Ricardo squeezed his nose as if it were smarting with sea water.

"Hear this, Voltaire. Listen most attentively. When I was young and crazy, I flew twice into Yunnan Province for the Americans. To be a hero, one must do certain crazy things, and if you crash, maybe one day they get you out. But each time I flew, I look down at the lousy brown earth and I see Ricardo in a wood cage. No women, extremely lousy food, no place to sit, no place to stand or sleep, chains on my arms, no status or position assured to me. 'See the imperialist spy and running dog.' Voltaire, I do not like this vision. To be locked all my life in China for running opium? I am not enthusiastic. 'Sure, Mr. Tiu! Bye-bye! See you this afternoon!' I have to consider most seriously."

The brown haze of the sinking sun suddenly filled the room. On Ricardo's chest, despite the perfection of his condition, the same sweat had gathered. It lay in beads over the matted black hair and on his oiled shoulders.

"Where was Lizzie in all this?" Jerry asked again.

Ricardo's answer was nervous and already angry. "In Vientiane! On the moon! In bed with Charlie! What the hell do I care?"

"Did she know of the deal with Tiu?"

Ricardo gave only a scowl of contempt.

Time to go, Jerry thought. Time to light the last fuse and run. Below, Mickey was making a great hit with Ricardo's women. Jerry could hear his singsong chattering, broken by their high-pitched laughter, like the laughter of a whole class at girls' school.

"So away you flew," he said. He waited, but Ricardo remained lost in thought.

"You took off and headed north," Jerry said.

Lifting his eyes a little, Ricardo held Jerry in a bullish, furious stare, till the invitation to describe his own heroic feat finally got the better of him.

"I never flew so good in my life. Never. I was magnificent. That little black Beechcraft. North a hundred miles because I don't trust nobody. Maybe those clowns have got me locked on a radar screen somewhere? I don't take no chances. Then east, but very slowly, very low over the mountains, Voltaire. I fly between the cow's legs, okay? In the war we have little landing-strips up there, crazy listening places in the middle of badland. I flew those places, Voltaire. I know them. I find one right at the top of a mountain, you can reach it only from the air. I take a look, I see the fuel dump, I land, I refuel, I take a sleep, it's crazy. But Jesus, Voltaire, it's not Yunnan Province, okay? It's not China—and Ricardo, the American war criminal and opium smuggler, is not going to spend the rest of his life hang-ing from a hen-hook in Peking, okay? Listen, I brought that plane back south again. I know places, I know places I could lose a whole air force, believe me."

Ricardo became suddenly very vague about the next few months of his life. He had heard of the Flying Dutchman, and he said that was what he became; he flew, hid again, flew, resprayed the Beechcraft, changed the registration once a month, sold the opium in small lots in order not to be conspic-uous, a kilo here, fifty there, bought a Spanish passport from an Indian but had no faith in it, kept away from everyone he knew, including Rosie in Bangkok, and even Charlie Marshall. It was also the time, Jerry remembered from his briefing by old Craw, when Ricardo sold Ko's opium to the Enforcement heroes but got the cold shoulder on his story. On Tiu's orders, said Ricardo, the Indocharter boys had been quick to post him dead, and changed his flight route southwards to distract atten-tion. Ricardo heard of this and did not object to being dead.

"What did you do about Lizzie?" Jerry asked.

Again Ricardo flared. "Lizzie, Lizzie! You got some fixa-tion about that scrubber, Voltaire, that you throw *Lizzie* in my face all the time? I never knew a woman so irrelevant. Listen, I give her to Drake Ko, okay? I make her fortune."

Seizing his whisky glass, he drank from it, still glowering.

She was lobbying for him, Jerry thought. She and Charlie Marshall. Plodding the pavements trying to buy Ricardo's neck for him.

"You referred boastingly to other lucrative aspects of the case," Ricardo said in a peremptory resumption of his business-school English. "Kindly advise me what they are, Voltaire."

Sarratt man had this part off pat. "Number one: Ko was being paid large sums by the Russian Embassy in Vientiane. The money was syphoned through Indocharter and ended up in a slush account in Hong Kong. We've got the proof. We've got photostats of the bank statements."

Ricardo pulled a face as if his whisky didn't taste right, then went on drinking.

"Whether the money was for reviving the opium habit in Red China or for some other service, we don't yet know," said Jerry. "But we will. Point two. Do you want to hear it or am I keeping you awake?"

Ricardo had yawned.

"Point two," Jerry continued. "Ko has a younger brother in Red China. Used to be called Nelson. Ko pretends he's dead but he's a big beef with the Peking administration. Ko's been trying to get him out for years. Your job was to take in opium and bring out a package. The package was brother Nelson. That's why Ko was going to love you like his own son if you brought him back. And that's why he was going to kill you if you didn't. If that's not a five-million-dollar touch, what is?"

Nothing much happened to Ricardo as Jerry watched him in the failing light, except that the slumbering animal in him visibly woke. To set down his glass, he leaned forward slowly, but he couldn't conceal the tautness of his shoulders or the knotting of the muscles of his stomach. To flash a smile of exceptional good will at Jerry, he turned quite languidly, but his eyes had a brightness that was like a signal to attack. So that when he reached out and patted Jerry's cheek affectionately with his right hand, Jerry was quite ready to fall straight back with it if necessary, on the off chance he would manage to throw Ricardo across the room.

"Five million bucks, Voltaire!" Ricardo exclaimed with steely-bright excitement. "Five million! Listen—we got to do something for poor old Charlie Marshall, okay? For love. Charlie's always broke. Maybe we put him in charge of the football pool once. Wait a minute. I get some more Scotch, we celebrate." He stood up, his head tilted to one side; he held out his naked arms. "Voltaire," he said softly. "*Voltaire!*" Affectionately, he took Jerry by the cheeks and kissed him. "Listen, that's some research you guys did! That's some pretty smart editor you work for. You be my business partner. Like you say. Okay? I need an Englishman in my life. I got to be like Lizzie once, marry a schoolmaster. You do that for Ricardo, Voltaire? You hold me down a little?"

"No problem," said Jerry, smiling back.

"You play with the guns a minute, okay?"

"Sure."

"I got to tell those girls some little thing."

"Sure."

"Personal family thing."

"I'll be here."

From the top of the trap Jerry looked urgently down after him. Mickey, the driver, was dandling the baby on his arm, chucking it under the ear. In a mad world you keep the fiction going, he thought; stick to it till the bitter end and leave the first bite to him. Returning to the table, Jerry took Ricardo's pencil and his pad of paper and wrote out a non-existent address in Hong Kong where he could be reached at any time. Ricardo had still not returned, but when Jerry stood he saw him coming out of the trees behind the car. He likes contracts, he thought; give him something to sign. He took a fresh sheet of paper. "I, Jerry Westerby, do solemnly swear to share with my friend

Captain Tiny Ricardo all proceeds relating to our joint exploitation of his life story," he wrote, and signed his name.

Ricardo was coming up the steps. Jerry thought of helping himself from the private armoury, but he guessed Ricardo was waiting for him to do just that. While Ricardo poured more whisky, Jerry handed him the two sheets of paper.

"I'll draft a legal deposition," he said, looking straight into Ricardo's burning eyes. "I have an English lawyer in Bangkok whom I trust entirely. I'll have him check it over and bring it back to you to sign. After that we'll plan the march route and I'll talk to Lizzie. Okay?"

"Sure. Listen, it's dark out there. They got a lot of bad guys in that forest. You stay the night. I talk to the girls. They like you. They say you very strong man. Not so strong as me, but strong."

Jerry said something about not wasting time. He'd like to make Bangkok by tomorrow, he said. To himself he sounded as lame as a three-legged mule—good enough to get in maybe, but never to get out. But Ricardo seemed content to the point of serenity. Maybe it's the ambush deal, thought Jerry, something the colonel is arranging.

"Go well, horse-writer. Go well, my friend."

Ricardo put both hands on the back of Jerry's neck and let his thumb-prints settle into Jerry's jaw, then drew Jerry's head forward for another kiss, and Jerry let it happen. Though his heart thumped and his wet spine felt sore against his shirt, Jerry let it happen.

Outside it was half dark. Ricardo did not see them to the car but watched them indulgently from under the stilts, the girls sitting at his feet, while he waved with both naked arms.

From the car Jerry turned and waved back. The last sun lay dying in the teak trees. My last ever, he thought.

"Don't start the engine," he told Mickey quietly. "I want to check the oil."

Perhaps it's just me who's mad. Perhaps I really got myself a deal, he thought.

Sitting in the driver's seat, Mickey released the catch and Jerry pulled up the bonnet but there was no little *plastic*, no leaving-present from his new friend and partner. He pulled up the dipstick and pretended to read it.

"You want oil, horse-writer?" Ricardo yelled down the dust path.

"No, we're all right. So long!"

"So long."

He had no torch, but when he crouched and groped under the chassis in the gloom, he again found nothing.

"You lost something, horse-writer?" Ricardo called again, cupping his hands to his mouth.

"Start the engine," Jerry said and got into the car.

"Lights on, Mister?"

"Yes, Mickey. Lights on."

"Why he call you horse-writer?"

"Mutual friends."

If Ricardo has tipped off the C.T.s, thought Jerry, it won't make any damn difference either way. Mickey put on the lights, and inside the car the American dashboard lit up like a small city.

"Let's go," said Jerry.

"Quick-quick?"

"Yes, quick-quick."

They drove five miles, seven, nine. Jerry was watching them on the indicator, reckoning twenty to the first check-point and forty-five to the second. Mickey had hit seventy and Jerry was in no mood to complain. They were on the crown of the road and the road was straight, and beyond the ambush strips the tall teaks slid past them like orange ghosts.

"Fine man," Mickey said. "He plenty fine lover. Those girls say he some pretty fine lover."

"Watch for wires," Jerry said.

On the right the trees broke and a red dust track disappeared into the cleft.

"He get pretty good time in there," said Mickey. "Girls, he get kids, he get whisky. He get real good time."

"Pull in, Mickey. Stop the car. Here in the middle of the road where it's level. Just do it, Mickey."

Mickey began laughing.

"Girls get good time, too," Mickey said. "Girls get candy, little baby get candy, everybody get candy!"

"Stop the damn car!"

At his own leisurely pace, Mickey brought the car to a halt, still giggling about the girls.

"Is that thing accurate?" Jerry asked, his finger pressed to the petrol gauge.

"Accurate?" Mickey echoed, puzzled by the English.

"Petrol. Gas. Full? Or half full? Or three-quarters? Has it been reading right on the journey?"

"Sure. He right."

"When we arrived at the burnt village, Mickey, you had half-full gas. You still have half-full gas."

"Sure."

"You put any in? From a can? You fill car?"

"No."

"Get out."

Mickey began protesting, but Jerry leaned across him, opened his door, shoved Mickey straight through it onto the tarmac, and followed him. Seizing Mickey's arm, he jammed it into his back and frog-marched him at a gallop across the road to the edge of the wide soft shoulder and twenty yards into it, then threw him into the scrub and fell half beside him, half onto him, so that the wind went out of Mickey's stomach in a single astonished hiccup, and it took him all of half a minute before he was able to give vent to an indignant "Why for?"

But Jerry by that time was pushing his face into the earth to keep it out of the blast.

The old Ford seemed to burn first and explode afterwards, finally lifting into the air in one last assertion of life, before collapsing dead and flaming on its side. While Mickey gasped in admiration, Jerry looked at his watch. Eighteen minutes since they had left the stilt house. Maybe twenty. Should have happened sooner, he thought. Not surprising Ricardo was keen for us to go. At Sarratt they wouldn't even have seen it coming; this was an Eastern treat, and Sarratt's natural soul was with Europe and the good old days of the cold war— Czecho, Berlin, and the old fronts. Jerry wondered which brand of grenade it was. The Vietcong preferred the American type; they loved its double action. All you needed, they said, was a wide throat to the petrol tank. You took out the pin, you put an elastic band over the spring, you slipped the grenade into the petrol tank, and you waited patiently for the petrol to eat its way through the rubber. The result was one of those Western inventions it took the Vietcong to discover. Ricardo must have used fat elastic bands, he decided.

They made the first check-point in four hours, walking on the road. Mickey was extremely happy about the insurance situation, assuming that since Jerry had paid the premium, the money was automatically theirs to squander. Jerry could not deter him from this view. But Mickey was also scared: first of C.T.s, then of ghosts, then of the colonel. So Jerry explained to him that neither the ghosts nor the C.T.s would venture near the road after that little episode. As for the colonel—though Jerry didn't mention this to Mickey—well, he was a father and a soldier and he had a dam to build. Not for nothing was he building it with Drake Ko's cement and China Airsea's transport.

At the check-point they eventually found a truck to take Mickey home. Riding with him a distance, Jerry promised the comic's support in any insurance haggle, but Mickey in his euphoria was deaf to doubts. Amid much laughter they exchanged addresses and many hearty handshakes; then Jerry dropped off at a roadside café to wait half a day for the bus that would carry him eastwards toward a fresh field of war.

Need Jerry have ever gone to Ricardo in the first place? Would the outcome, for himself, have been different if he had not? Or did Jerry, as Smiley's defenders to this day insist, by his pass at Ricardo, supply the last crucial heave which shook the tree and caused the coveted fruit to fall?

For the George Smiley Supporters' Club there is no question: the visit to Ricardo was the final straw, and Ko's back broke under it. Without it he might have gone on dithering until the open season started, by which time Ko himself, and the intelligence on him, would be up for grabs. End of argument. And on the face of it, the facts demonstrate a wonderful causality. For this is what happened.

A mere six hours after Jerry and his driver Mickey had picked themselves out of the dust of that roadside in North East Thailand, the whole of the Circus fifth floor exploded into a blaze of ecstatic jubilation which would have outshone the pyre of Mickey's borrowed Ford car any night. In the rumpus room, where Smiley announced the news, Doc di Salis actually danced a stiff little jig, and Connie would unquestionably have joined him if her arthritis had not held her to that wretched chair. Trot howled, Guillam and Molly embraced, and only Smiley amid so much revelry preserved his usual slightly startled air, though Molly swore she saw him redden as he blinked around the company.

He had just had word, he said. A flash communication from the Cousins. At seven this morning, Hong Kong time, Tiu had telephoned Ko at Star Heights, where he had been spending the night relaxing with Lizzie Worth. Lizzie herself took the call in the first instance, but Ko came in on the extension and sharply ordered Lizzie to ring off, which she did. Tiu had proposed breakfast in town at once: "At George's place," said Tiu, to the great entertainment of the transcribers. Three hours later Tiu was on the phone to his travel agent making hasty plans for a business trip to mainland China. His first stop would be Canton, where China Airsea kept a representative, but his ultimate destination was Shanghai.

So how did Ricardo get through to Tiu so fast without the telephone? The most likely theory is the colonel's police link to Bangkok. And from Bangkok? Heaven knows. Trade telex, the exchange-rate network—anything is possible. The Chinese have their own ways of doing these things.

On the other hand, it may just be that Ko's patience chose this moment to snap of its own accord, and that the breakfast at George's place was about something entirely different. Either way, it was the breakthrough they had all been dreaming of, the triumphant vindication of Smiley's footwork. By lunch-time Lacon had called in person to offer his congratulations, and by early evening Saul Enderby had made a gesture nobody from the wrong side of Trafalgar Square had ever made before. He had sent round a crate of champagne from Berry Brothers & Rudd, a vintage Krug, a real beauty. Attached to it was a note to George saying "To the first day of summer." And indeed, though late April, it seemed to be just that. Through the thick net curtains of the lower floors, the plane trees were already in leaf. Higher up a cluster of hyacinths had bloomed in Connie's window-box. "Red," she said as she drank Saul Enderby's health. "Karla's favourite colour, bless him."

18

The River Bend

The air base was neither beautiful nor victorious. Technically—since it was in North East Thailand—it was under Thai command, and in practice the Thais were allowed to collect the garbage and occupy the stockade close to the perimeter. The check-point was a separate town. Amid smells of charcoal, urine, pickled fish, and Calor gas, chains of collapsing tin hovels plied the historic trades of military occupation. The brothels were manned by crippled pimps, the tailor shops offered wedding tuxedos, the bookshops offered pornography and travel, the bars were called Sunset Strip, Hawaii, and Lucky Time. At the M.P. hut, Jerry asked for Captain Urquhart of public relations, and the black sergeant squared to throw him out when he said he was press. On the base telephone Jerry heard a lot of clicking and popping before a slow Southern voice said, "Urquhart isn't around just now. My name is Masters. Who's this again?"

"We met last summer at General Crosse's briefing," Jerry said.

A long silence followed, presumably while the code words "Urquhart" and "Crosse" were hunted down in the contingency book.

"Well now, so we did, man," said the same amazingly slow voice, reminding him of Deathwish. "Pay off your cab. Be right down. Blue jeep. Wait for the whites of its eyes."

A flow of air-force personnel was drifting in and out of the camp, blacks and whites, in scowling segregated groups. A white officer passed. The blacks gave him the black-power salute. The officer warily returned it. The enlisted men wore Charlie Marshall-style patches on their uniforms, mostly in praise of drugs. The mood was sullen, defeated, and innately violent. The Thai troops greeted nobody. Nobody greeted the Thais.

A blue jeep with lights flashing and siren wailing pulled up with a ferocious skid on the other side of the boom. The sergeant waved Jerry through. A moment later he was careering over the runway at breakneck speed toward a long string of low white huts at the centre of the airfield. His driver was a lanky boy with all the signs of a probationer.

"You Masters?" Jerry asked.

"No, sir. Sir, I just carry the Major's bags," he said.

They passed a ragged baseball game, siren wailing all the time, lights still flashing.

"Great cover," said Jerry.

"What's that, sir?" the boy yelled above the din.

"Forget it."

It was not the biggest base. Jerry had seen larger. They passed lines of Phantoms and helicopters, and as they approached the white huts he realised that they comprised a separate spook encampment, with their own compound and aerial masts and their own cluster of little black-painted small planes—"weirdos," they used to be called—which before the pull-out had dropped and collected God knew whom in God knew where.

They entered by a side door which the boy unlocked. The short corridor was empty and soundless. A door stood ajar at the end of it, made of traditional fake rosewood. Masters wore a short-sleeved air-force uniform with few insignia. He had medals and the rank of major and Jerry guessed he was the paramilitary type of Cousin, maybe not even career. He was sallow and wiry, with resentful tight lips and hollow cheeks. He stood before a fake fireplace, under an Andrew Wyeth reproduction, and there was something strangely still about him, and disconnected. He was like a man being deliberately slow when everyone else was in a hurry. The boy made the introductions and hesitated. Masters stared at him until he left, then turned his colourless gaze to the table where the coffee was.

"Look like you need breakfast," Masters said. He poured coffee and proffered a plate of doughnuts, all in slow motion.

"Facilities," he said.

"Facilities," Jerry agreed.

An electric typewriter lay on the desk, and plain paper beside it. Masters walked stiffly to a chair and perched on the arm. Taking up a copy of *Stars & Stripes*, he held it in front of him while Jerry settled at the desk.

"Hear you're going to win it all back for us single-handed," said Masters to his *Stars & Stripes*. "Well now."

Jerry set up his portable in preference to the electric, and stabbed out his report in a series of quick smacks, which to his own ear grew louder as he laboured. Perhaps to Masters's ear also, for he looked up frequently, though only as far as Jerry's hands and the toy-town portable.

Jerry handed him his copy.

"Your orders are to remain here," Masters said, articulating each word with great deliberation. "Your orders are to remain here while we dispatch your signal. Man, will we dispatch that signal. Your orders are to stand by for confirmation and further instructions. That figure? Does that figure, *sir?*"

"Sure," said Jerry.

"Heard the glad news by any chance?" Masters enquired. They were facing each other. Not three feet lay between them. Masters was staring at Jerry's signal, but his eyes did not appear to be scanning the lines.

"What news is that, sport?"

"We just lost the war, Mr. Westerby. Yes, sir. Last of the brave just had themselves scraped off the roof of the Saigon

Embassy by chopper, like a bunch of rookies caught with their pants down in a whore-house. Maybe that doesn't affect you. Ambassador's dog survived, you'll be relieved to hear. Newsman took it out on his damn lap. Maybe that doesn't affect you either. Maybe you're not a dog-lover. Maybe you feel about dogs the same way I personally feel about newsmen, Mr. Westerby, sir."

Jerry had caught the smell of brandy on Masters's breath, which no amount of coffee could conceal, and he guessed he had been drinking for a long time without succeeding in getting drunk.

"Mr. Westerby, sir?"

"Yes, old boy."

Masters held out his hand. "*Old boy*, I want you to shake me by the hand."

The hand stuck between them, thumb upward.

"What for?" said Jerry.

"I want you to extend to me the hand of welcome, sir. The United States of America has just applied to join the club of second-class powers, of which I understand your own fine nation to be chairman, president, and oldest member. *Shake it!*"

"Proud to have you aboard," said Jerry and obligingly shook the Major's hand.

He was at once rewarded by a brilliant smile of false gratitude.

"Why, sir, I call that *real* handsome of you, Mr. Westerby. Anything we can do to make your stay with us more comfortable, I invite you to let me know. If you want to rent the place, no reasonable offer refused, we say."

"You could shove a little Scotch through the bars," Jerry said, pulling a dead grin.

"*Mah pleasure*," said Masters, in a drawl so long it was like a slow punch. "Man after my own heart. Yes, sir."

Masters left him with a half-bottle of J & B from the cupboard, and some back numbers of *Playboy*.

"We keep these handy for English gentlemen who didn't see fit to lift a damn finger to help us," he explained confidingly.

"Very thoughtful of you," said Jerry.

"I'll go send your letter home to Mummy. How *is* the Queen, by the way?"

Masters didn't turn a key, but when Jerry tested the door handle it was locked. The windows overlooking the airfield were smoked and double glazed. On the runway aircraft landed and took off without making a sound. This is how they tried to win, Jerry thought: from inside sound-proof rooms, through smoked glass, using machines at arm's length. This is how they lost. He drank, feeling nothing. . . . Waiting. So it's over, he thought, and that was all. So what was his next stop? Charlie Marshall's old man? Little swing through the Shans, heart-to-heart chat with the General's bodyguard? He waited, his thoughts crowding formlessly. He sat down, then lay on the sofa and for a while slept. He woke abruptly to the sound of canned music occasionally interrupted by an announcement of homely-wise assurance. Would Captain somebody do so and so? Once the speaker offered higher education. Once cut-price washing-machines. Once prayer. Jerry prowled the room, made nervous by the crematorium quiet and the music.

He crossed to the other window, and in his mind Lizzie's face bobbed along at his shoulder, the way the orphan's once had, but no longer. He drank more whisky. I should have slept in the truck, he thought. Altogether I should sleep more. So they've lost the war at last. It seemed a long time since he'd slept the way he'd like to. Old Frostie had rather put an end to that. His hand was shaking: Christ, look at that. He thought of Luke. Time we went on a bender together. He must be back by now, if he hasn't had his arse shot off. Got to stop the old brain a bit, he thought. But sometimes the old brain hunted on its own these days. Bit too much, actually. Got to tie it down, he told himself sternly. *Man.*

He thought of Ricardo's grenades. Hurry up, he thought.

Come on, let's have a decision. *Where* next? *Who* now? No whys. His face was dry and hot, and his hands moist. He had a headache just above the eyes. Bloody music, he thought. Bloody, bloody end-of-world music. He was casting round urgently for somewhere to switch it off when he saw Masters standing in the doorway, an envelope in his hand and nothing in his eyes. Jerry read the signal. Masters settled on the chair arm again.

"'Son, come home,'" Masters intoned, mocking his own Southern drawl. "'Come directly home. Do not pass *go*. Do not collect two hundred dollars.' The Cousins will fly you to Bangkok. From Bangkok you will proceed immediately to London, England, *not* repeat not London, Ontario, by a flight of *your* own choosing. You will on no account return to Hong Kong. You will not! No *sir!* Mission accomplished, *son*. Thank you and well done. Her Majesty is so *thrilled*. So hurry home to dinner, we got hominy grits and turkey, and blueberry pie. Sounds like a bunch of fairies you're working for, man."

Jerry read the signal a second time.

"Plane leaves for Bangkok one one hundred," Masters said. He wore his watch on the inside of his wrist, so that its information was private to himself. "Hear me?"

Jerry grinned. "Sorry, sport. Slow reader. Thanks. Too many big words. Lot to get the old mind round. Look, left my things at the hotel."

"My houseboys are at your royal command."

"Thanks, but if you don't mind, I'd prefer to avoid the official connection."

"Please yourself, sir, please yourself."

"I'll find a cab at the gates. There and back in an hour. Thanks," he repeated.

"Thank *you*."

Sarratt man provided a smart piece of tradecraft for the kiss-off. "Mind if I leave that there?" he asked, nodding to his scruffy portable where it lay beside Masters's golf-ball I.B.M.

"Sir, it shall be our most treasured possession."

If Masters had bothered to look at him at that moment, he might have hesitated when he saw the purposeful brightness in Jerry's eye. If he had known Jerry's voice better perhaps, or noticed its particularly friendly huskiness, he might also have hesitated. If he had seen the way Jerry clawed at his forelock, arm across his body in an attitude of instinctive self-concealment, or responded to Jerry's sheepish grin of thanks as the probationer returned to drive him to the gates in the blue jeep—well, again he might have had his doubts. But Major Masters was not only an embittered professional with a lot of disillusionment to his credit. He was a Southern gentleman suffering the stab of defeat at the hands of unintelligible savages; and he hadn't too much time just then for the contortions of a bone-weary overdue Brit using his expiring spookhouse as a post office.

A mood of festivity attended the leavetaking of the Circus's Hong Kong operations party, and it was only enriched by the secrecy of the arrangements. The news of Jerry's reappearance triggered it. The content of his signal intensified it and coincided with word from the Cousins that Drake Ko had cancelled all his social and business engagements and withdrawn to the seclusion of his house, Seven Gates, in Headland Road. A photograph of Ko, taken in long shot from the Cousins' surveillance van, showed him in quarter-profile, standing in his own large garden, at the end of an arbour of rose-trees, staring out to sea. The concrete junk was not visible, but he was wearing his floppy beret.

"Like a latter-day Jay Gatsby, my dear!" Connie Sachs cried in delight as they all pored over it. "Mooning at the blasted light at the end of the pier, or whatever the ninny did!"

When the van returned that way two hours later, Ko was in the identical pose, so they didn't bother to re-shoot. More significant was the fact that Ko had ceased to use the telephone altogether—or at least those lines on which the Cousins ran a tap.

Sam Collins also sent a report, the third in a stream, but by far his longest to date. As usual it arrived in a special cover addressed to Smiley personally, and as usual he discussed its contents with nobody but Connie Sachs. And at the very moment when the party was leaving for London Airport, a last-minute message from Martello advised them that Tiu had returned from China and was at present closeted with Ko in Headland Road.

But the most important ceremony, then and later in Guillam's recollection, and the most disturbing, was a small war party held in Martello's rooms in the Annexe, which, exceptionally, was attended not only by the usual quintet of Martello, his two quiet men, Smiley, and Guillam, but also by Lacon and Saul Enderby as well, who significantly arrived in the same official car. The purpose of the ceremony—called by Smiley—was the formal handing over of the keys. Martello was now to receive a complete portrait of the Dolphin case, including the all-important link with Nelson. He was to be indoctrinated, with certain minor omissions which only showed up later, as a full partner in the enterprise.

How Lacon and Enderby muscled in on the occasion, Guillam never quite knew and Smiley was afterwards understandably reticent about it. Enderby declared in a fat voice that he had come along in the "interest of good order and military discipline." Lacon looked more than usually wan and disdainful. Guillam had the strongest impression they were up to something, and this was further strengthened by his observation of the interplay between Enderby and Martello: in short, these buddies cut each other so dead they put Guillam in mind of two secret lovers meeting at communal breakfast in a country house, a situation in which he often found himself.

It was the *scale* of the thing, Enderby explained at one point. Case was blowing up so big he really thought there ought to be a few official flies on the wall. It was the Colonial lobby, he explained at another. Wilbraham was raising a stink with Treasury.

"All right, so we've heard the dirt," said Enderby, when Smiley had finished his lengthy summary and Martello's praises had all but brought the roof down. "Now whose finger's on the trigger, George, point one?" he demanded to know, and after that the meeting became very much Enderby's show, as meetings with Enderby usually did. "Who calls the shots when it gets hot? You, George? Still? I mean you've done a good planning job, I grant you, but it's old Marty here who's providing the artillery, isn't it?"

At which Martello had another bout of deafness, while he beamed upon all the great and lovely British people he was privileged to be associated with, and let Enderby go on doing his hatchet-work for him.

"Marty, how do *you* see this one?" Enderby pressed, as if he really had no idea; as if he never went fishing with Martello, or gave lavish dinners for him, or discussed top-secret matters out of school.

A strange insight came to Guillam at this moment, though he kicked himself afterwards for making too little of it. *Martello knew.* The revelations about Nelson, which Martello had affected to be dazzled by, were not revelations at all, but restatements of information that he and his quiet men already possessed. Guillam read it in their pale, wooden faces and their watchful eyes. He read it in Martello's fulsomeness. *Martello knew.*

"Ah, technically this is George's show, Saul," Martello reminded Enderby loyally, in answer to his question, but with just enough spin on the "technically" to put the rest in doubt. "George is on the bridge, Saul. We're just there to stoke the engines."

Enderby staged an unhappy frown and shoved a matchstick between his teeth. "George, how does that grab *you?* You content to let that happen, are you? Let Marty chuck in the cover, the accommodation out there, communications, all the cloak-and-dagger stuff, surveillance, charging round Hong

Kong and what-not? While you call the shots? Bit like wearing someone else's dinner-jacket, I'd have thought."

Smiley was firm enough but, to Guillam's eye, a deal too concerned with the question and not nearly concerned enough with the thinly veiled collusion.

"Not at all," said Smiley. "Martello and I have a clear understanding. The spearhead of the operation will be shared by ourselves. If supportive action is required, Martello will supply it. The product is then halved. If one is thinking in terms of a dividend for the American investment, it comes with the partition of the product. The responsibility for obtaining it remains ours." He ended strongly: "The letter of agreement setting all this out has of course long been on file."

Enderby glanced at Lacon. "Oliver, you said you'd send me that. Where is it?"

Lacon put his long head on one side and pulled a dreary smile at nothing in particular. "Kicking around your Third Room, I should think, Saul."

Enderby tried another tack: "And you two guys can see the deal holding up in all contingencies, can you? I mean, who's handling the safe houses, all that? Burying the body sort of thing?"

Smiley again: "Housekeeping Section has already rented a cottage in the country, and is preparing it for occupation," he said stolidly.

Enderby took the wet matchstick from his mouth and broke it into the ashtray. "Could have had my place if you'd asked," he muttered absently. "Bags of room. Nobody ever there. Staff. Everything." But he went on worrying at his theme. "Look here. Answer me this one. Your man panics. He cuts and runs through the back streets of Hong Kong. Who plays cops-and-robbers to get him back?"

Don't answer it. Guillam prayed. He has absolutely no business to plumb around like this! Tell him to get lost!

Smiley's answer, though effective, lacked the fire Guillam longed for. "Oh, I suppose one can always invent a *hypothesis*," he objected mildly. "I think the best one can say is that Martello and I would at that stage pool our thoughts and act for the best."

"George and I have a fine working relationship, Saul," Martello declared handsomely. "Just fine."

"Much *tidier*, you see, George," Enderby resumed, through a fresh matchstick. "Much *safer* if it's an all-Yank do. Marty's people make a hash and all they do is apologise to the Governor, post a couple of blokes to Walla Walla, and promise not to do it again. That's it. What everyone expects of 'em anyway. Advantage of a disgraceful reputation—right, Marty? Nobody's surprised if you screw the housemaid."

"Why, *Saul*," said Martello, and laughed richly at the great British sense of humour.

"Much more tricky if *we're* the naughty boys, George," Enderby went on. "Or *you* are, rather. Governor could blow you down with one puff, the way it's set up at the moment. Wilbraham's crying all over his desk already."

Against Smiley's distracted obduracy, there was however no progress to be made, so for the while Enderby bowed out and they resumed their discussion of the "meat and potatoes," which was Martello's amusing phrase for modalities. But before they finished, Enderby had one last shot at dislodging Smiley from his primacy, choosing again the issue of the efficient handling and after-care of the catch.

"George, who's going to manage all the grilling and stuff? You using that funny little Jesuit of yours, the one with the smart name?"

"Di Salis will be responsible for the Chinese aspects of the debriefing and our Soviet research section the Russian."

"That the crippled don woman, is it, George? The one Bill shoved out to grass for drinking?"

"It is they, between them, who have brought the case this far," said Smiley.

Inevitably Martello sprang into the breach: "Ah, now, George, I won't have that! Sir, I will not! Saul, Oliver, I wish you to know that I regard the Dolphin case, in all its aspects, Saul, as a personal triumph for George here and for George *alone!*"

With a big hand all round for dear old George, they made their way back to Cambridge Circus.

"Gunpowder, treason, and plot!" Guillam expostulated. "Why's Enderby selling you down the river? What's all that tripe about losing the letter?"

"Yes," said Smiley at last, but from far away. "Yes, that's very careless of them. I thought I'd send them a copy, actually. Blind, by hand, for information only. Enderby seemed so *woolly*, didn't he? Will you attend to that, Peter, ask the mothers?"

The mention of the letter of agreement—*heads* of agreement, as Lacon called it—revived Guillam's worst misgivings. He remembered how he had foolishly allowed Sam Collins to be the bearer of it, and how, according to Fawn, he had spent more than an hour cloistered with Martello under the pretext of delivering it. He remembered Sam Collins also as he had glimpsed him in Lacon's ante-room, the mysterious confidant of Lacon and Enderby, lazing around Whitehall like a blasted Cheshire cat. He remembered Enderby's taste for backgammon, which he played for very high stakes, and it even passed through his head, as he tried to sniff out the conspiracy, that Enderby might be a client of Sam Collins's club. From that notion he soon pulled back, discounting it as too absurd. But ironically it later turned out to be true. And he remembered his fleeting conviction—based on little but the physiognomy of the three Americans, and therefore soon also to be dismissed—that they knew already what Smiley had come to tell them.

But Guillam did not pull back from the notion of Sam Col-

lins as the ghost at that morning's feast, and as he boarded the
plane at London Airport, exhausted by his long and energetic
farewell from Molly, the same ghost grinned at him through
the smoke of his infernal brown cigarette.

The flight was uneventful except in one respect. They were
three strong, and in the seating arrangements Guillam had
won a small battle in his running war with Fawn. Over Housekeeping Section's dead body, Guillam and Smiley flew first
class, while Fawn, the baby-sitter, took an aisle seat at the front
of the tourist compartment, cheek by jowl with the airline
security guards, who slept innocently for most of the journey
while Fawn sulked. There had never been any suggestion, fortunately, that Martello and his quiet men would fly with them,
for Smiley was determined that that should not happen on any
account. As it was, Martello flew west, staging in Langley for
instructions and continuing through Honolulu and Tokyo in
order to be on hand in Hong Kong for their arrival.

As an unconsciously ironic footnote to their departure,
Smiley left a long handwritten note to Jerry, to be presented to
him on his arrival at the Circus, congratulating him on his
first-rate performance. The carbon copy is still in Jerry's dossier. Nobody has thought to remove it. Smiley speaks of Jerry's
"unswerving loyalty" and of "setting the crown on more than
twenty years of service." He includes an apocryphal message
from Ann, "who joins me in wishing you an equally distinguished career in letters." And he winds up rather awkwardly
with the sentiment that "one of the privileges of our work is
that it provides us with such wonderful colleagues. I must tell
you that we all think of you in those terms."

Certain people do still ask why no anxious word about Jerry's
whereabouts had reached the Circus before take-off. He was,
after all, several days overdue. Once more they look for ways of
blaming Smiley, but there is no evidence of a lapse on the Circus's side. For the transmission of Jerry's report from the air

base in North East Thailand—his last—the Cousins had cleared
a line through Bangkok direct to the Annexe in London. But
the arrangement was valid for one signal and one answer-back
only, and a follow-up was not envisaged.

Accordingly, the grizzle, when it came, was routed first to
Bangkok on the military network, thence to the Cousins in
Hong Kong on *their* network—since Hong Kong was held to
have a total lien on all Dolphin-starred material—and only
then, marked "Routine," repeated by Hong Kong to London,
where it kicked around in several rosewood in-trays before
anybody noted its significance. And it must be admitted that
the languid Major Masters had attached very little significance
to the no-show, as he later called it, of some travelling English
fairy. "ASSUME EXPLANATION YOUR END," his message ends.
Major Masters now lives in Norman, Oklahoma, where he
runs a small automobile repair business.

Nor did Housekeeping Section have any reason to panic—or
so they still plead. Jerry's instructions on reaching Bangkok
were to find himself a plane, any plane, using his air-travel card,
and get himself to London. No date was mentioned and no airline. The whole purpose was to leave things fluid. Most likely
he had stopped over somewhere for a bit of relaxation. Many
homing fieldmen do, and Jerry was on record as sexually oriented. So they kept their usual watch on flight lists and made a
provisional booking at Sarratt for the two weeks' drying-out
and recycling ceremony, then returned their attention to the
far more urgent business of setting up the Dolphin safe house.

This was a charming mill-house, quite remote, though situated in the commuter town of Maresfield, Sussex, and on
most days they found a reason for going down there. As well as
di Salis and a sizeable part of his Chinese archive, a small army
of interpreters and transcribers had to be accommodated, not
to mention technicians, baby-sitters, and a Chinese-speaking
doctor. In no time at all the residents were complaining noisily
to the police about the influx of Japanese. The local paper car-

ried a story that they were a visiting dance troupe. Housekeeping Section had inspired the leak.

Jerry had nothing to collect at the hotel—and, as it happened, no hotel—but he reckoned he had an hour to get clear, perhaps two. He had no doubt the Americans had the whole town wired, and he knew there would be nothing easier, if London asked for it, than for Major Masters to have Jerry's name and description broadcast as an American deserter travelling on a false-flag passport. Once his taxi was clear of the gates, therefore, he took it to the southern edge of town, waited, then took a second taxi and pointed it due north.

A wet haze lay over the paddies and the straight road ran into it endlessly. The radio pumped out female Thai voices like a slow-motion nursery rhyme. They passed an American electronics base, a circular grid a quarter of a mile wide floating in the haze and known locally as the Elephant Cage. Giant bodkins marked the perimeter, and at the middle, surrounded by webs of strung wire, burned a single infernal light like the promise of a future war. He had heard there were twelve hundred language students inside the place, but not one soul was to be seen.

He needed time, and in the event he helped himself to more than a week. Even now, he needed that long to bring himself to the point, because Jerry at heart was a soldier and voted with his feet. *In the beginning was the deed*, Smiley liked to say to him, in his failed-priest mood, quoting from Goethe. For Jerry that simple statement had become a pillar of his uncomplicated philosophy. What a man thinks is his own business. What matters is what he does.

Reaching the Mekong by early evening, he selected a village and for a couple of days strolled idly up and down the river-bank, trailing his shoulder-bag and kicking at an empty Coca-Cola tin with the toe of his buckskin boot. Across the river, behind the brown anthill mountains, lay the Ho Chi

Minh trail. He had once watched a B-52 strike from this very point, three miles away in central Laos. He remembered how the ground shook under his feet and the sky emptied and burned, and he had known—he had really for a moment known—what it was like to be in the middle of it.

In this same spot, to use Frost's jolly phrase, Jerry Westerby blew the walls out, much along the lines the housekeepers expected of him, if not in quite the circumstances. In a riverside bar where they played old tunes on a nickelodeon, he drank black-market P.X. Scotch and night after night drove himself into oblivion, leading one laughing girl after another up the unlit staircase to a tattered bedroom, till finally he stayed there sleeping and didn't come down.

Waking with a jolt, clear-headed at dawn, to the screaming of roosters and the clatter of the river traffic, Jerry would force himself to think long and generously of his chum and mentor, George Smiley. It was an act of will that made him do this, almost an act of obedience. He wished, quite simply, to rehearse the articles of his creed, and his creed till now had been old George. At Sarratt they have a very worldly and relaxed attitude to the motives of a fieldman, and no patience at all for the fiery-eyed zealot who grinds his teeth and says, "I hate Communism." If he hates it that much, they argue, he's most likely half-way in love with it already. What they really like—and what Jerry possessed, what he *was*, in effect—was the fellow who hadn't a lot of time for flannel but loved the service and knew—though God forbid he should make a fuss of it—that *we* were right. *We* being a necessarily flexible notion, but to Jerry it meant George and that was that.

Old George. Super. Good morning.

He saw him as he liked to remember him best, the first time they met, at Sarratt soon after the war. Jerry was still an army subaltern, his time nearly up and Oxford looming, and he was bored stiff. The course was for London Occasionals: people who, having done the odd bit of skulduggery without going formally onto the Circus payroll, were being groomed as an auxiliary reserve. Jerry had already volunteered for full-time employment, but Circus personnel had turned him down, which scarcely helped his mood.

So when Smiley waddled into the paraffin-heated lecture hut in his heavy overcoat and spectacles, Jerry inwardly groaned and prepared himself for another creaking fifty minutes of boredom—on good places to look for dead-letter boxes, most likely, followed by a sort of clandestine nature ramble through Rickmansworth, trying to spot hollow trees in graveyards. There was comedy while the Directing Staff cranked the lectern lower so that George could see over the top. In the end he stood himself a little fussily at the side of it and declared that his subject this afternoon was "Problems of Maintaining Courier Lines Inside Enemy Territory." Slowly it dawned on Jerry that he was talking not from the textbook but from experience: that this little pedant with the diffident voice and the blinking, apologetic manner had sweated out three years in some benighted German town, holding the threads of a very respectable network, while he waited for the boot through the door panel or the pistol butt across the face that would introduce him to the pleasures of interrogation.

When the meeting was over, Smiley asked to see him. They met in a corner of an empty bar, under the antlers where the darts board hung.

"I'm so sorry we couldn't have you," Smiley said. "I think our feeling was you needed a little more time *outside* first." Which was their way of saying he was immature. Too late, Jerry remembered Smiley as one of the non-speaking members of the Selection Board that had failed him. "Perhaps if you could get your degree and make your way a little in a different walk of life, they would change their way of thinking. Don't lose touch, will you?"

After which, somehow, old George had always been there. Never surprised, never out of patience, old George had gently but firmly rejigged Jerry's life till it was Circus property. His father's empire collapsed: George was waiting with his hands out to catch him. His marriages collapsed: George would sit all night for him, hold his head.

"I've always been grateful to this service that it gave me a chance to pay," Smiley had said. "I'm sure one should feel that. I don't think we should be afraid of . . . devoting ourselves. Is that old-fashioned of me?"

"You point me, I'll march," Jerry had replied. "Tell me the shots and I'll play them."

There was still time. He knew that. Train to Bangkok, hop on a plane home, and the worst he would get was a flea in his ear for jumping ship for a few days. "Home," he repeated to himself. Bit of a problem. Home to Tuscany and the yawning emptiness of the hilltop without the orphan? Home to old Pet, sorry about the teacup? Home to dear old Stubbsie, key appointment as desk jockey with special responsibility for the spike? Or home to the Circus: "We think you'd be happiest in Banking Section." Even—great thought—home to Sarratt, training job, winning the hearts and minds of new entrants while he commuted dangerously from a maisonette in Watford.

On the third or fourth morning he woke very early. Dawn was just rising over the river, turning it first red, then orange, now brown. A family of water-buffaloes wallowed in the mud, their bells jingling. In mid-stream three sampans were linked in a long and complicated trawl. He heard a hiss and saw a net curl, then fall like hail on the water.

Yet it's not for want of a future that I'm here, he thought. It's for want of a present.

Home's where you go when you run out of homes, he thought. Which brings me to Lizzie. Vexed issue. Shove it on the back burner. Spot of breakfast.

Sitting on the teak balcony munching eggs and rice, Jerry remembered George breaking the news to him about Haydon: El Vino's bar, Fleet Street, a rainy midday. Jerry had never found it possible to hate anyone for very long, and after the initial shock there had really not been much more to say.

"Well, no point in crying in the old booze, is there, sport? Can't leave the ship to the rats. Soldier on, that's the thing."

To which Smiley agreed; yes, that was the thing, to soldier on, grateful for the chance to pay. Jerry had even found a sort of rum comfort in the fact that Bill was one of the clan. He had never seriously doubted, in his vague way, that his country was in a state of irreversible decline, or that his own class was to blame for the mess. "We *made* Bill," ran his argument, "so it's right we should carry the brunt of his betrayal." Pay, in fact. Pay. What old George was on about.

Pottering beside the river again, breathing the free warm air, Jerry chucked flat stones to make them bounce.

Lizzie, he thought. Lizzie Worthington, suburban bolter. Ricardo's pupil and punch-ball. Charlie Marshall's big sister and earth mother and unattainable whore. Drake Ko's cagebird. My dinner companion for all of four hours. And to Sam Collins—to repeat the question—what had she been to him? For Mr. Mellon, Charlie's "creepy English trader" of eighteen months ago, she was a courier working the Hong Kong heroin trail. But she was more than that. Somewhere along the line, Sam had shown her a bit of ankle and told her she was working for Queen and country. Which glad news Lizzie had promptly shared with her admiring circle of friends. To Sam's fury, and he dropped her like a hot brick. So Sam had set her up as a patsy of some kind. A coat-trailer on probation. In one way this thought amused Jerry very much, for Sam had a reputation as an ace operator, whereas Lizzie Worthington might well star at Sarratt as the archetypal Woman Never to Be Recruited as Long as She Can Speak or Breathe.

Less funny was the question of what she meant to Sam *now*. What kept him skulking in her shadow like a patient murderer, smiling his grim iron smile? That question worried Jerry very much. Not to put too fine a point on it, he was obsessed by it. He definitely did not wish to see Lizzie taking another of her dives. If she went anywhere from Ko's bed, it was going to be into Jerry's. For some while, off and on—ever since he had met her, in fact—he had been thinking how much Lizzie would benefit from the bracing Tuscan air. And while he didn't know how or why Sam Collins came to be in Hong Kong, or even what the Circus at large intended for Drake Ko, he had the strongest possible impression—and here was the nub of the thing—that by pushing off to London at this moment, far from carting Lizzie away on his white charger, Jerry was leaving her sitting on a very large bomb.

Which struck him as unacceptable. In other times, he might have been prepared to leave that problem to the owls, as he had left so many other problems in his day. But these were not other times. This time, as he now realised, it was the Cousins who were paying the piper, and while Jerry had no particular quarrel with the Cousins, their presence made it a much rougher ball game. So that whatever vague notions he had about George's humanity did not apply.

Also he cared about Lizzie. Urgently. There was nothing imprecise in his feelings at all. He ached for her, warts and all. She was his kind of loser, and he loved her. He had worked it out and drawn the line, and that, after several days of counting on beads, was his net unalterable solution. He was a little awed, but very pleased by it.

Gerald Westerby, he told himself. You were present at your birth. You were present at your several marriages and at some of your divorces, and you will certainly be present at your funeral. High time, in our considered view, that you were present at certain other crucial moments in your history.

Taking a bus up-river a few miles, he walked again, rode on *cyclos*, sat in bars, made love to the girls, thinking only of Lizzie. The inn where he stayed was full of children and one morning he woke to find two of them sitting on his bed, marvelling at the enormous length of the *farang*'s legs and giggling at the way his bare feet hung over the end. Maybe I'll just stay here, he thought. But by then he was fooling, because he knew that he had to go back and ask her, even if the answer was a custard pie. From the balcony he launched paper aeroplanes for the children, and they clapped and danced, watching them float away.

He found a boatman and, when evening came, crossed the river to Vientiane, avoiding the formalities of immigration. Next morning, also without formality, he wangled himself aboard an unscheduled Royal Air Lao DC-8, and by afternoon he was airborne and in possession of a delicious warm whisky and chatting merrily to a couple of friendly opium dealers. As they landed, black rain was falling and the windows of the airport bus were foul with dust. Jerry didn't mind at all. For the first time in his life, returning to Hong Kong was quite like coming home after all.

Inside the reception area nevertheless, Jerry played a cautious hand. No trumpets, he told himself: definitely. The few days' rest had done wonders for his presence of mind. Having taken a good look round, he made for the men's room instead of the immigration desks and lay up there till a big load of Japanese tourists arrived, then barged over to them and asked who spoke English. Having cut out four of them, he showed them his Hong Kong press card, and while they stood in line waiting for their passport check he besieged them with questions about why they were here and what they proposed to do, and with whom, and wrote wildly on his pad before choosing four more and repeating the process. Meanwhile he waited for the police on duty to change watch. At four o'clock they did, and he at once made for a door marked "No Entry," which he had noted earlier. He banged on it till it was opened, and started to walk through to the other side.

"Where the hell are you going?" asked an outraged Scottish police inspector.

"Home to the comic, sport. Got to file the dirt on our friendly Japanese visitors."

He showed his press card.

"Well go through the damn gates, like everyone else."

"Don't be bloody silly. I haven't got my passport. That's why your distinguished colleague brought me through this way in the first place."

Bulk, a ranking voice, a patently British appearance, an affecting grin, won him a space in a city-bound bus five minutes later. Outside his apartment block he dawdled but saw no one suspicious, but this was China and who could tell?

The lift as usual emptied for him. Riding in it, he hummed Deathwish the Hun's one record in anticipation of a hot bath and change of clothes. At his front door he had a moment's anxiety when he noticed the tiny wedges he had left in place lying on the floor, till he belatedly remembered Luke and smiled at the prospect of their reunion. He unlocked the burglar door, and as he did so he heard the sound of humming from inside, a droning monotone, which could have been an air-conditioner but not Deathwish's. Bloody idiot Luke has left the gramophone on, he thought, and it's about to brew up. Then he thought, I'm doing him an injustice; it's that fridge.

Then he opened the door and saw Luke's dead body strewn across the floor with half his head shot to pieces, and half the flies in Hong Kong swarming over it and round it; and all he could think of to do, as he quickly closed the door behind him and jammed his handkerchief over his mouth, was run into the kitchen in case there was still someone there. Returning to the living-room, he pushed Luke's feet aside and dug up the parquet brick where he had cached his forbidden side-arm and his escape kit, and put them in his pocket before he vomited.

Of course, he thought. That's why Ricardo was so certain the horse-writer was dead.

Join the club, he thought, as he stood out in the street again, with rage and grief pounding in his ears and eyes: Nelson Ko's dead, but he's running China. Ricardo's dead, but Drake Ko says he can stay alive as long as he sticks to the shady side of the street. Jerry Westerby the horse-writer is also completely dead, except that Ko's stupid pagan vicious bastard of a henchman, Mr. Tiu, was so thick he shot the wrong round-eye.

19

Golden Thread

The inside of the American Consulate in Hong Kong could have been the inside of the Annexe, right down to the ever-present fake rosewood and the bland courtesy and the airport chairs and the heartening portrait of the President, even if this time it was Ford. Welcome to your Howard Johnson spookhouse, Guillam thought. The section they worked in was called the isolation ward and had its own doorway to the street, guarded by two Marines. They had passes in false names—Guillam's was Gordon—and for the duration of their stay there, except on the telephone, they never spoke to a soul inside the building except one another. "We're not just deniable, gentlemen," Martello had told them proudly in the briefing, "we're also invisible." That was how it was going to be played, he said. The U.S. Consul General could put his hand on the Bible and swear to the Governor they weren't there and his staff were not involved, said Martello; "Blind eye right down the line." After that, he handed over to George, because "George, this is your show from soup to nuts."

Downhill they had five minutes' walk to the Hilton, where Martello had booked them rooms. Uphill, though it would have been hard going, they had ten minutes' walk to Lizzie Worth's apartment block. They had been here five days and now it was evening, but they had no way of telling because there were no windows in the operations room; there were maps and sea charts instead, and a couple of telephones manned by Martello's quiet men, Murphy and his friend. Martello and Smiley had a big desk each; Guillam, Murphy, and his friend shared the table with the telephones, and Fawn sat moodily at the centre of an empty row of cinema chairs along the back wall, like a bored critic at a preview, sometimes picking his teeth and sometimes yawning but refusing to take himself off as Guillam repeatedly advised him. Craw had been spoken to but ordered to keep clear of everything—a total duck-dive. Smiley was frightened for him since Frost's death and would have preferred him evacuated, but the old boy wouldn't leave.

It was also for once the hour of the quiet men: "Our final detailed briefing," Martello had called it. "Ah, that's if it's okay by *you*, George." Pale Murphy, wearing a white shirt and blue trousers, was standing on the raised podium before a wall chart, soliloquising from pages of detailed notes. The rest of them sat at his feet and listened mainly in silence, including Smiley and Martello. Murphy could have been describing a vacuum cleaner, and to Guillam that made his monologue the more hypnotic.

The chart showed largely sea, but at the top and to the left hung a lace-fringe of the South China coast. Behind Hong Kong the spattered outskirts of Canton were just visible below the batten which held the chart in place, and due south of Hong Kong at the very mid-point of the chart stretched the green outline of what looked to be a cloud divided into four sections, marked A, B, C, and D. These, said Murphy reverently, were the fishing beds and the cross at the centre was Centre Point, sir. Murphy spoke only to Martello, whether it was George's show from soup to nuts or not.

"Sir, basing on the last occasion Drake exited Red China, sir, and updating our assessment to the situation as of now, we and navy int. between us, sir—"

"Murphy, Murphy," put in Martello quite kindly, "ease off a little, will you, friend? This isn't training school any more, okay? Loosen your girdle, will you, son?"

"Sir. One. Weather," Murphy said, quite untouched by this appeal. "April and May are the transitional months, sir, between the north-east monsoons and the beginning of the south-west monsoons. Forecasts day-to-day are unpredictable, sir, but no extreme conditions are foreseen for the trip." He was using the pointer to show the line from Swatow southward to the fishing beds, then from the fishing beds north-west past Hong Kong up the Pearl River to Canton.

"Fog?" Martello said.

"Fog is traditional for the season, and cloud is anticipated at six to seven oktas, sir."

"What the hell's an okta, Murphy?"

"One okta is one eighth of sky area covered, sir. Oktas have replaced the former tenths. No typhoons have been recorded in April for over fifty years and navy int. calls typhoons unlikely. Wind is easterly, nine to ten knots, but any fleet that runs with it must count on periods of calm—also contrary winds too, sir. Humidity around eighty percent, temperature fifteen to twenty-four centigrade. Sea conditions calm with a small swell. Currents around Swatow tend to run north-east through the Taiwan Strait, at around three sea miles per day. But farther westward—on *this* side, sir—"

"That's one thing I *do* know, Murphy," Martello put in sharply. "I know where west is, dammit." Then he grinned at Smiley as if to say "these young whipper-snappers."

Murphy was again unmoved. "We have to be prepared to calculate the speed factor and consequently the progress of the fleet at any one point in its journey, sir."

"Sure, sure."

"Moon, sir," Murphy continued. "Assuming the fleet to have exited Swatow on the night of Friday, April twenty-fifth, the moon would be three days off of full—"

"Why do we assume that, Murphy?"

"Because that's when the fleet exited Swatow, sir. We had confirmation from navy int. one hour ago. Column of junks

sighted at the eastern end of fishing bed C and easing westward with the wind, sir. Positive identification of the lead junk
confirmed."

There was a prickly pause. Martello coloured.

"You're a clever boy, Murphy," Martello said in a warning
tone. "But you should have given me that information a little
earlier."

"Yes, sir. Assuming also that the intention of the junk containing Nelson Ko is to hit Hong Kong waters on the night of
May fourth, the moon will be in its last quarter, sir. If we follow precedents right down the line—"

"We do," said Smiley firmly. "The escape is to be an exact
repetition of Drake's own journey in 'fifty-one."

Once more, no one doubted him, Guillam noticed. Why
not? It was utterly bewildering.

"—then our junk should hit the southernmost out-island of
Po Toi at twenty hundred hours tomorrow, and rejoin the fleet
up along the Pearl River in time to make Canton harbour
between zero ten-thirty and twelve hundred hours the following day, May fifth, sir."

While Murphy droned on, Guillam covertly kept his eye on
Smiley, thinking, as he often did, that he knew him no better
today than when he first met him back in the dark days of the
cold war in Europe. Where did he slip away to at all odd hours?
Mooning about Ann? About Karla? What company did he keep
that brought him back to the hotel at four in the morning?
Don't tell me George is having a second spring, he thought.

Last night at eleven there had been a scream from London, so
Guillam had trailed up here to unbutton it. Westerby adrift,
they said. They were terrified Ko had had him murdered—or,
worse, abducted and tortured—and that the operation would
abort in consequence. Guillam thought it more likely Jerry
was holed up with a couple of air hostesses somewhere en route
to London, but with that priority on the signal he had no option

but to wake Smiley and tell him. He rang his room and got no answer, so he dressed and banged on Smiley's door, and finally he was reduced to picking the lock, for now it was Guillam's turn to panic: he thought Smiley might be ill.

But Smiley's room was empty and his bed unslept in, and when Guillam went through his things he was fascinated to see that the old fieldman had gone to the length of sewing false name-tapes in his shirts. That was all he discovered, however. So he settled in Smiley's chair and dozed and didn't wake till four, when he heard a tiny flutter and opened his eyes to see Smiley stooped and peering at him from about six inches away; how he got into the room so silently, God alone knew.

"Gordon?" he asked softly. "What can I do for you?"—for they were on an operational footing of course, and lived with the assumption the rooms were bugged. For the same reason Guillam did not speak but handed Smiley the envelope containing Connie's message, which he read and reread, then burned. Guillam was impressed how seriously he took the news. Even at that hour he insisted on going straight up to the Consulate to attend to it, so Guillam went along to carry his bags.

"Instructive evening?" he asked lightly as they plodded the short way up the hill.

"I? Oh, to a point, thank you, to a point," Smiley replied, doing his disappearing act, and that was all Guillam or anyone could get out of him about his nocturnal or other ambles. Meanwhile, without the smallest explanation of his source, George was bringing in hard operational data in a manner that brooked no enquiry from anyone.

"Ah, George, we can count on that, can we?" Martello asked in bewilderment, on the first occasion that this happened.

"What? Oh yes, yes, indeed you may."

"Great. Great footwork, George. I admire you," said Martello heartily after a further puzzled silence, and from then on they had gone along with it. They had no choice. For nobody, not even Martello, quite dared to challenge Smiley's authority.

* * *

"How many days' fishing is that, Murphy?" Martello was asking.

"Fleet will have had seven days' fishing and hopefully make Canton with full holds, sir."

"That figure, George?"

"Yes, oh yes—nothing to add, thank you."

Martello asked what time the fleet would have to leave the fishing beds in order for Nelson's junk to make tomorrow evening's rendezvous on time.

"I have put it at eleven tomorrow morning," Smiley said without looking up from his notes.

"Me too," said Murphy.

"This rogue junk, Murphy," Martello said, with another deferential glance at Smiley.

"Yes, sir," said Murphy.

"Can it break away from the pack that easy? What would be its cover for entering Hong Kong waters, Murphy?"

"Happens all the time, sir. Red Chinese junk-fleets operate a collective catch system without profit motivation, sir. Consequence of that, you get the single junks that break away at night-time and come in without lights and sell their fish to the out-islanders for money."

"*Literally* moonlighting!" Martello exclaimed, much amused by the felicity of the expression.

Smiley had turned to the map of Po Toi island on the other wall and was tilting his head in order to intensify the magnification of his spectacles.

"What size of junk are we talking about here?" Martello asked.

"Twenty-eight-man long-liners, sir, baited for shark, golden thread, and conger."

"Did Drake use that type also?"

"Yes," said Smiley, still watching the map. "Yes, he did."

"And she can come that close in, can she? Provided the weather allows?"

Again it was Smiley who answered. Till today, Guillam had not heard him so much as speak of a boat in his life.

"The draw of a long-liner is very modest," he remarked. "She can come in pretty well as close as she wishes, provided always that the sea is not too rough."

From the back bench Fawn gave an immoderate laugh. Wheeling round in his chair, Guillam shot him a foul look. Fawn leered and shook his head, marvelling at his master's omniscience.

"How many junks make up a fleet?" Martello asked.

"Twenty to thirty," said Smiley.

"Check," said Murphy meekly.

"So what does Nelson *do*, George? Kind of get out to the edge of the pack there and stray a little?"

"He'll hang back," said Smiley. "The fleets like to move in column astern. Nelson will tell his skipper to take the rear position."

"Will he, by God," Martello muttered under his breath. "Murphy, what identifications are traditional?"

"Very little known in that area, sir. Boat people are notoriously evasive. They have no respect for marine regulations. Out to sea, they show no lights at all, mostly for fear of pirates."

Smiley was lost to them again. He had sunk into a wooden immobility, and though his eyes stayed fixed on the big sea chart, his mind, Guillam knew, was anywhere but with Murphy's dreary recitation of statistics. Not so Martello.

"How much coastal trade do we have over all, Murphy?"

"Sir, there are no controls and no data."

"Any quarantine checks as the junks enter Hong Kong waters, Murphy?" Martello asked.

"Theoretically all vessels should stop and have themselves checked, sir."

"And in practice, Murphy?"

"Junks are a law to themselves, sir. Technically, Chinese junks are forbidden to sail between Victoria Island and Kowloon point, sir, but the last thing the Brits want is a hassle with the mainland over rights of way. Sorry, sir."

"Not at all," said Smiley politely, still gazing at the chart. "Brits we are and Brits we shall remain."

It's his Karla expression, Guillam decided; the one that comes over him when he looks at the photograph. He catches sight of it, it surprises him, and for a while he seems to study its contours, its blurred and sightless gaze. Then the light slowly goes out of his eyes, and somehow the hope as well, and you feel he's looking inward, in alarm.

"Murphy, did I hear you mention navigation lights?" Smiley enquired, turning his head slightly but still staring toward the chart.

"Yes, sir."

"I expect Nelson's junk to carry three," said Smiley. "Two green lights vertically on the stern mast and one red light to starboard."

"Yes, sir."

Martello tried to catch Guillam's eye but Guillam wouldn't play.

"But it may not," Smiley warned as an afterthought. "It may carry none at all, and simply signal from close in."

Murphy resumed. A new heading: Communications.

"Sir, in the communications area, sir, few junks have their own transmitters but most all have receivers. Once in a while you get a skipper who buys a cheap walkie-talkie with range about one mile to facilitate the trawl, but they've been doing it so long they don't have much call to speak to each other, I guess. Then as to finding their way—well, navy int. says that's near enough a mystery. We have reliable information that many long-liners operate on a primitive compass, a hand lead and line, or even just a rusty alarm clock for finding true north."

"Murphy, how the *hell* do they work *that*, for God's sakes?" Martello cried.

"Line with a lead plumb and wax stuck to it, sir. They sound the bed and know where they are from what sticks to the wax."

"Well, they *really* do it the hard way," Martello declared.

A phone rang. Martello's other quiet man took the call, listened, then put his hand over the mouthpiece.

"Quarry Worth's just gotten back, sir," he said to Smiley. "Party drove around for an hour, now she's checked in her car back at the block. Mac says sounds like she's running a bath, so maybe she plans going out again later."

"And she's alone," Smiley said impassively. It was a question.

"She alone there, Mac?" He gave a hard laugh. "I'll bet you would, you dirty bastard. Yes, *sir*, lady's all alone taking a bath, and Mac there says when will we ever get to use video as well. Is the lady *singing* in the bath, Mac?" He rang off. "She's not singing."

"Murphy, get on with the war," Martello snapped.

Smiley would like the interception plans rehearsed once more, he said.

"Why, George! Please! It's your show, remember?"

"Perhaps we could look again at the big map of Po Toi island, could we? And then Murphy could break it down for us, would you mind?"

"*Mind*, George, *mind?*" Martello cried, so Murphy began again, this time using a pointer. "Navy int. observation posts *here*, sir . . . constant two-way communication with base, sir . . . no presence at all within two sea miles of the landing zone. . . . Navy int. to advise base the moment the Ko launch starts back for Hong Kong, sir. . . . Interception will take place by regular British police vessel as the Ko launch enters harbour. . . . U.S. to supply op. int. and stand off only, for unforeseen supportive situation. . . ."

Smiley monitored every detail with a prim nod of his head.

"After all, Marty," he put in at one point, "once Ko has Nelson aboard, there's nowhere else he *can* go, is there? Po Toi is right at the edge of China waters. It's us or nothing."

One day, thought Guillam, as he continued listening, one of two things will happen to George. He'll cease to care or the paradox will kill him. If he ceases to care, he'll be half the operator he is. If he doesn't, that little chest will blow up from the struggle of trying to find the explanation for what we do. Smiley himself, in a disastrous off-the-record chat to senior officers, had put the names to his dilemma, and Guillam with some embarrassment recalled them to this day. To be *inhuman in defence of our humanity*, he had said, *harsh in defence of compassion*. To be *single-minded in defence of our disparity*. They had filed out in a veritable ferment of protest; why didn't George just do the job and shut up instead of taking his faith out and polishing it in public till the flaws showed? Connie had even murmured a Russian aphorism in Guillam's ear, which she insisted on attributing to Karla. "There'll be no war, will there, Peter darling?" she had said reassuringly, squeezing his hand as he led her along the corridor. "But in the struggle for peace not a single stone will be left standing, bless the old fox. I'll bet they didn't thank him for *that* one in the Collegium, either."

A thud made Guillam swing round. Fawn was changing cinema seats again. Seeing Guillam, he flared his nostrils in an insolent sneer.

He's off his head, thought Guillam with a shiver.

Fawn too, for different reasons, was now causing Guillam serious anxiety. Two days ago, in Guillam's company, he had been the author of a disgusting incident. Smiley as usual had gone out alone. To kill time Guillam had hired a car and driven Fawn up to the China border. Returning, they were waiting at some country traffic-lights when a Chinese boy drew alongside on a Honda. Guillam was driving. Fawn had the passenger seat. Fawn's window was lowered; he had taken his jacket off and was resting his left arm on the door where he could admire a new gilt watch he had bought himself in the Hilton shopping concourse.

As they pulled away, the Chinese boy ill-advisedly made a

dive for the watch, but Fawn was much too quick for him. Catching hold of the boy's wrist instead, he held on to it, towing him beside the car while the boy struggled vainly to break free. Guillam had driven fifty yards or so before he realised what had happened, and he at once stopped the car, which was what Fawn was waiting for. He hopped out before Guillam could stop him, lifted the boy straight off his Honda, led him to the side of the road, and broke both his arms for him, then returned smiling to the car. Terrified of a scandal, Guillam drove rapidly from the scene, leaving the boy screaming and staring at his dangling arms. He reached Hong Kong determined to report Fawn to George immediately, but luckily for Fawn it was eight hours before Smiley surfaced, and by then Guillam reckoned George had enough on his plate already.

Another phone was ringing, the red. Martello took the call himself. He listened a moment, then burst into a loud laugh.

"They found him," he told Smiley, holding the phone to him.

"Found whom?"

The phone hovered between them.

"Your *man*, George. Your Weatherby—"

"Westerby," Murphy corrected him, and Martello shot him a venomous look.

"They got him," said Martello.

"Where is he?"

"Where *was* he, you mean! George, he just had himself the time of his life in two cathouses up along the Mekong. If our people are not exaggerating, he's the hottest thing since Barnum's baby elephant left town in 'forty-nine!"

"And where is he now, please?"

Martello handed him the phone. "Why don't you just have 'em read you the signal, okay? They have some story that he crossed the river." He turned to Guillam and winked. "They tell me there's a couple of places in Vientiane where he might find himself a little action too," he said, and went on laughing richly while Smiley sat patiently with the telephone to his ear.

* * *

Jerry chose a cab with two wing mirrors and sat in the front. In Kowloon he hired a car from the biggest outfit he could find, using the escape passport and driving licence because marginally he thought the false name was safer if only by an hour. As he headed up the Midlevels, it was dusk and still raining and huge haloes hung from the neon lights that lit the hillside. He passed the American Consulate and drove past Star Heights twice, half expecting to see Sam Collins, and on the second occasion he knew for sure he had found her flat and that her light was burning: an arty Italian affair by the look of it, that hung across the picture window in a gracious droop, three hundred dollars' worth of pretension. Also the frosted glass of a bathroom window was lit. The third time he passed, he saw her pulling a wrap over her shoulders, and instinct or something about the formality of her gesture told him she was once more preparing to go out for the evening but that this time she was dressed to kill.

Every time he allowed himself to remember Luke, a darkness covered his eyes and he imagined himself doing the noble useless things like telephoning Luke's family in California, or the dwarf at the bureau, or even for whatever purpose the Rocker. Later, he thought. Later, he promised himself, he would mourn Luke in fitting style.

He coasted slowly into the driveway that led to the entrance till he came to the slip-road to the car-park. The park was three tiers deep and he idled round it till he found her red Jaguar stowed in a safe corner behind a chain to discourage careless neighbours from approaching its peerless paint-work. She had put a mock leopard-skin cover on the steering-wheel. She just couldn't do enough for the damn car. Get pregnant, he thought, in a burst of fury; buy a dog. Keep mice. For two pins he'd have smashed the front in, but those two pins had held Jerry back more times than he liked to count. If she's not using it, then he's sending a limousine for her, he thought. Maybe with Tiu

riding shot-gun, even. Or maybe he'll come himself. Or maybe
she's just getting herself dolled up for the evening sacrifice and
not going out at all. He wished it was Sunday. He remembered
Craw saying that Drake Ko spent Sundays with his family, and
that on Sundays Lizzie had to make her own running. But it
wasn't Sunday, and neither did he have dear old Craw at his
elbow telling him—on what evidence Jerry could only guess—
that Ko was away in Bangkok or Timbuctoo conducting his
business.

Grateful that the rain was turning to fog, he headed back
up the slipway to the drive and at the junction found a narrow
piece of shoulder where, if he parked hard against the barrier,
the other traffic could complain but squeeze past. He grazed
the barrier and didn't care. From where he now sat, he could
watch the pedestrians coming in and out under the striped
awning of the block, and the cars joining or leaving the main
road. He felt no sense of caution at all. He lit a cigarette and
the limousines crackled past him both ways, but none belonged
to Ko. Occasionally as a car edged by him, the driver paused to
hoot or shout a complaint and Jerry ignored him. Every few
seconds his eyes took in the mirrors, and once when a plump
figure not unlike Tiu padded guiltily up behind him, he actually dropped the safety catch of the pistol in his jacket pocket
before admitting to himself that the man lacked Tiu's brawn.
Probably been collecting gambling debts from the *pak-pai*
drivers, he thought, as the figure went by him.

He remembered being with Luke at Happy Valley. He remembered being with Luke.

He was still looking in the mirror when the red Jaguar
hissed up the slipway behind him, just the driver, and the roof
closed, no passenger. The one thing he hadn't thought of was
that she might take the lift right down to the car-park and collect the car herself rather than have the porter bring it to the
door for her as he did before. Pulling out after her, he glanced
up and saw the lights still burning in her window. Had she left

somebody behind? Or did she propose to come back shortly? Then he thought, Don't be so damn clever. She's just careless about lights.

The last time I spoke to Luke, it was to tell him to get out of my hair, he thought, and the last time he spoke to me was to tell me he'd covered my back with Stubbsie.

She had turned down the hill toward the town. He headed down after her, and for a space nothing followed him, which seemed unnatural, but these were unnatural hours and Sarratt man was dying in him faster than he could handle. She was heading for the brightest part of town. He supposed he still loved her, though just now he was prepared to suspect anybody of anything. He kept close behind her, remembering that she used her mirror seldom. In this dusky fog she would only see his head-lights anyway. The fog hung in patches and the harbour looked as if it were on fire, with the shafts of crane-light playing like water hoses on the crawling smoke. In Central she ducked into another basement garage, and he drove straight in after her and parked six bays away, but she didn't notice him. Remaining in the car, she paused to repair her make-up and he actually saw her working on her chin, powdering the scars. Then she got out and went through the ritual of locking, though a kid with a razor-blade could have cut through the soft top in one easy movement. She was dressed in a silk cape of some kind and a long silk dress, and as she walked toward the stone spiral stair she raised both her hands and carefully lifted her hair, which was gathered at the neck, and laid the pony-tail down the outside of the cape. Getting out after her, he followed her as far as the hotel lobby and turned aside in time to avoid being photographed by a bisexual drove of chattering fashion journalists in satins and bows.

Hanging back in the comparative safety of the corridor, Jerry pieced the scene together. It was a large private party, and Lizzie had joined it from the blind side. The other guests were arriving at the front entrance, where the Rolls-Royces

were so thick on the ground that nobody was special. A woman
with blue-grey hair presided, doing absolutely nothing but
swaying about and speaking gin-sodden French. A prim Chinese public-relations girl with a couple of assistants made up
the receiving line, and as the guests filed in, the girl and her
cohorts came forward frightfully cordially and asked for names
and sometimes invitation cards before consulting a list and saying "Oh, yes, of *course*." The blue-grey woman smiled and
growled. The cohorts handed out lapel pins for the men and
orchids for the women, then lighted on the next arrivals.

Lizzie Worthington went through this screening woodenly. Jerry gave her a minute to clear, watched her through
the double doors marked *"Soirée"* with a Cupid's arrow, then
attached himself to the queue. The public-relations girl was
bothered by his buckskin boots. His suit was disgusting enough,
but it was the boots that bothered her. On her course of training, he decided while she stared at them, she had been taught to
place a lot of value on shoes. Millionaires may be tramps from
the socks up but a pair of two-hundred-dollar Guccis is a passport not to be missed. She frowned at his press card, then at her
guest list, then at his press card again, and once more at his
boots, and she threw a lost glance at the blue-grey lush, who
kept on smiling and growling. Jerry guessed she was drugged
clean out of her mind. Finally the girl put up her own special
smile for the marginal consumer and handed him a disc the
size of a coffee saucer painted fluorescent pink with "PRESSE" an
inch high in white.

"Tonight we are making *everybody* beautiful, Mr. Westerby,"
she said.

"Have a job with me, sport."

"You like my *parfum*, Mr. Westerby?"

"Sensational," said Jerry.

"It is called Juice of the Vine, Mr. Westerby, one hundred
Hong Kong for a little bottle, but tonight Maison Flaubert
gives free samples to all our guests. Madame Montifiori . . .

oh ... of *course*, welcome to House of Flaubert. You like my *parfum*, Madame Montifiori?"

A Eurasian girl in a cheongsam held out a tray and whispered, "Flaubert wishes you an exotic night."

"For Christ's sake," Jerry said.

Inside the double doors a second receiving line was manned by three pretty boys flown in from Paris for their charm, and a posse of security men that would have done credit to a President. For a moment he thought they might frisk him, and he knew that if they tried he was going to pull down the temple with him. They eyed Jerry without friendliness, counting him part of the help, but he was light-haired and they let him go.

"The press is in the third row back from the catwalk," said a hermaphrodite blond in a cowboy leather suit, handing him a press kit. "You have no camera, Monsieur?"

"I just do the captions," Jerry said, jamming a thumb over his shoulder. "Spike here does the pictures." He walked into the reception room peering round him, grinning extravagantly, waving at whoever caught his eye.

The pyramid of champagne glasses was six feet tall, with black satin steps so that the waiters could take them from the top. In sunken ice coffins lay magnums awaiting burial. There was a wheelbarrow full of cooked lobsters and a wedding cake of pâté de foie gras, with "Maison Flaubert" done in aspic on the top. Space music was playing and there was even conversation under it, if only the bored drone of the extremely rich. The catwalk stretched from the foot of the long window to the centre of the room. The window faced the harbour but the fog broke the view into patches. The air-conditioning was turned up so that the women could wear their mink without sweating. Most of the men wore dinner-jackets but the young Chinese playboys sported New York-style slacks and black shirts and gold chains. The British taipans stood in one sodden circle with their womenfolk, like bored officers at a garrison get-together.

Feeling a hand on his shoulder, Jerry swung fast, but all he found in front of him was a little Chinese queer called Graham who worked for one of the local gossip rags. Jerry had once helped him out with a story he was trying to sell to the comic. Rows of armchairs faced the catwalk in a rough horseshoe, and Lizzie was sitting in the front between Mr. Arpego and his wife or paramour. Jerry recognised them from Happy Valley. They looked as though they were chaperoning Lizzie for the evening. The Arpegos talked to her, but she seemed barely to hear them. She sat straight and beautiful and she had taken off her cape, and from where Jerry sat she could have been stark naked except for her pearl collar and her pearl earrings. At least she's still intact, he thought. She hasn't rotted or got cholera or had her head shot off. He remembered the line of gold hairs running down her spine as he stood over her that first evening in the lift. Queer Graham sat next to Jerry, and Phoebe Wayfarer sat two along. He knew her only vaguely but gave her a fat wave.

"Gosh. Super. Pheeb. You look terrific. Should be up there on the catwalk, sport, showing a bit of leg."

He thought she was a bit tight, and perhaps she thought he was, though he'd drunk nothing since the plane. He took out a pad and wrote on it, playing the professional, trying to rein himself in. Easy as you go. Don't frighten the game. When he read what he had written, he saw the words "Lizzie Worthington" and nothing else. Chinese Graham read it too, and laughed.

"My new byline," said Jerry, and they laughed together, too loud, so that people in front turned their heads as the lights began to dim. But not Lizzie, though he thought she might have recognised his voice.

Behind them the doors were being closed, and as the lights went lower Jerry had a mind to fall asleep in this soft and kindly chair. The space music gave way to a jungle beat brushed out on a cymbal, till only a single chandelier flickered over the black catwalk, answering the churned and patchy lights of the harbour in the window behind. The drum-beat rose in a slow crescendo from amplifiers everywhere. It went on a long time, just drums very well played, very insistent, till gradually grotesque human shadows became visible against the harbour window. The drum-beats stopped. In a wracked silence two black girls strode flank against flank down the catwalk, wearing nothing but jewels. Their skulls were shaven and they wore round ivory earrings and diamond collars like the iron rings of slave girls. Their oiled limbs shone with clustered diamonds, pearls, and rubies. They were tall, and beautiful, and lithe, and utterly unexpected, and for a moment they cast over the whole audience the spell of absolute sexuality. The drums recovered and soared, spotlights raced over jewels and limbs. They writhed out of the steaming harbour and advanced on the spectators with the anger of sensuous enslavement. They turned and walked slowly away, challenging and disdaining with their haunches.

Lights came on, there was a crash of nervous applause followed by laughter and drinks. Everyone was talking at once and Jerry was talking loudest: to Miss Lizzie Worthington, the well-known aristocratic society beauty whose mother couldn't even boil an egg, and to the Arpegos who owned Manila and one or two of the out-islands, as Captain Grant of the Jockey Club had once assured him. Jerry was holding his notebook like a headwaiter.

"Lizzie Worthington, *gosh*, all Hong Kong at your feet, Madame, if I may say so. My paper is doing an exclusive on this event, Miss Worth or Worthington, and we're hoping to feature you, your dresses, your fascinating life-style, and your even more fascinating friends. My photographers are bringing up the rear." He bowed to the Arpegos. "Good evening, Madame. Sir. Proud to have you with us, I'm sure. This your first visit to Hong Kong?"

He was doing his big-puppy number, the boyish soul of the party. A waiter brought champagne and he insisted on transferring the glasses to their hands rather than let them help themselves. The Arpegos were much amused by this performance. Craw said they were crooks. Lizzie was staring at him and there was something in her eyes he couldn't make out, something real and appalled, as if she, not Jerry, had just opened the door on Luke.

"Mr. Westerby has already done one story on me, I understand," she said. "I don't think it was ever printed, was it, Mr. Westerby?"

"Who you write for?" Mr. Arpego demanded suddenly. He wasn't smiling any more. He looked dangerous and ugly, and she had clearly reminded him of something he had heard about and didn't like. Something Tiu had warned him of, for instance.

Jerry told him.

"Then go write for them. Leave this lady alone. She don't give interviews. You got work to do, you work somewhere else. You didn't come here to play. Earn your money."

"Couple of questions for *you* then, Mr. Arpego. Just before I go. How can I write you down, sir? As a rude Filipino millionaire? Or only half a millionaire?"

"For God's sake," Lizzie breathed, and by a mercy the lights went out again, the drum-beat began, everyone went back to his corner, and a woman's voice with a French accent began a soft commentary on the loudspeaker. At the back of the catwalk the two black girls were performing long insinuating shadow dances. As the first model appeared, Jerry saw Lizzie stand up ahead of him in the darkness, pull her cape over her shoulders, and walk fast and softly up the aisle past him and toward the doors, head bowed. Jerry went after her. In the lobby she half turned as if to look at him, and it crossed his mind she was expecting him. Her expression was the same and it reflected his own mood. She looked haunted and tired and utterly confused.

"Lizzie!" he called as if he had just sighted an old friend, and ran quickly to her side before she could reach the powder-room door. "Lizzie! My God! It's been years! A lifetime! Super!"

A couple of security guards looked on meekly as he flung his arms round her for the kiss of long friendship. He had slipped his left hand under her cape, and as he bent his laughing face to hers he laid the small revolver against the bare flesh of her back, the barrel just below her nape, and in that way, linked to her with bonds of old affection, led her straight into the street, chatting gaily all the way, and hailed a cab. He hadn't wanted to produce the gun but he couldn't risk having to manhandle her. That's the way it goes, he thought: you come back to tell her you love her and end up by marching her at gunpoint.

She was shivering and furious but he didn't think she was afraid, and he didn't even think she was sorry to be leaving that awful gathering.

"That's all I need," she said as they wound up the hill again, through the fog. "Perfect. Bloody perfect."

She wore a scent that was strange to him, but it smelt a deal better than Juice of the Vine.

Guillam was not bored exactly, but neither was his capacity for concentration infinite, as George's appeared to be. When he wasn't wondering what the devil Jerry Westerby was up to, he found himself basking in the erotic deprival of Molly Meakin or else remembering the Chinese boy with his arms inside out, whining like a half-shot hare after the disappearing car. Murphy's theme was now the island of Po Toi and he was dilating on it remorselessly.

Volcanic, sir, he said.

Hardest rock substance of the whole Hong Kong group, sir, he said.

And the most southerly of the islands, he said.

Seven hundred and ninety feet high, sir; fishermen use it as a navigation point from far out to sea, sir, he said.

Technically not one island but a group of six islands, the other five being barren and treeless and uninhabited.

Fine temple, sir. Great antiquity. Fine wood carvings but little natural water.

"Jesus Christ, Murphy, we're not *buying* the damn place, are we?" Martello expostulated. With action close and London far away, Martello had lost a lot of his gloss, Guillam noticed, and all his Englishness. His tropical suits were honest-to-cornball American, and he needed to talk to people, preferably his own. Guillam suspected that even London was an adventure for him, and Hong Kong was already enemy territory. Whereas under stress Smiley went quite the other way; he became private and rigidly polite.

Po Toi itself has a shrinking population of one hundred and eighty farmers and fishermen, mostly Communist, three living villages and three dead ones, sir, said Murphy. He droned on. Smiley continued to listen intently but Martello impatiently doodled on his pad.

"And *tomorrow*, sir," said Murphy, "tomorrow is the night of Po Toi's annual festival intended to pay homage to Tin Hau, the goddess of the sea, sir."

Martello stopped doodling: "These people really believe that crap?"

"Everybody has a right to his religion, sir."

"They teach you that at training college too, Murphy?" Martello returned to his doodling.

There was an uncomfortable silence before Murphy valiantly took up his pointer and laid the tip on the southern edge of the island's coastline.

"This festival of Tin Hau, sir, is concentrated in the one main harbour, sir, right here on the south-west point where the ancient temple is situated. Mr. Smiley's informed prediction, sir, has the Ko landing operation taking place *here*, away from the main bay, in a small cove on the east side of the island. By landing on that side of the island, which has *no* habitation, *no* natural access to the sea, at a point in time when the diversion of the island festival in the *main* bay—"

Guillam never heard the ring. He just heard the voice of Martello's other quiet man answering the call: "Yes, Mac," then the squeak of his airport chair as he sat bolt upright, staring at Smiley. "Right, Mac. Sure, Mac. Right now. Yes. Hold it. Right beside me. Hold everything."

Smiley was already standing over him, his hand held out for the phone. Martello was watching Smiley. On the podium Murphy had his back turned while he pointed out further intriguing features of Po Toi, not quite registering the interruption.

"This island is also known to seamen as Ghost Rock, sir," he explained, in the same dreary voice. "But nobody seems to know why."

Smiley listened briefly then put down the telephone. "Thank you, Murphy," he said courteously. "That was very interesting."

He stood dead still a moment, his fingers to his upper lip in a Pickwickian posture of deliberation. "Yes," he repeated. "Yes, very."

He walked as far as the door then paused again.

"Marty, forgive me, I shall have to leave you for a while. Not above an hour or two, I trust. I shall telephone you in any event."

He reached for the door handle, then turned to Guillam.

"Peter, I think you had better come along too—would you mind? We may need a car and you seem admirably unmoved by the Hong Kong traffic. Did I see Fawn somewhere? Ah, there you are."

On Headland Road the flowers had a hairy brilliance, like ferns sprayed for Christmas. The pavement was narrow and seldom used, except by amahs to exercise the children, which they did without talking to them, as if they were walking dogs. The Cousins' surveillance van was a deliberately forgettable brown Mercedes lorry, battered-looking, with clay dust on the wings and "H. K. DEVP. & BLDG. SURVEY LTD." sprayed on one side. An old aerial with Chinese streamers trailing from it drooped over the cab, and as the lorry nosed its lugubrious way past the Ko residence—for the second, or was it the fourth time that morning?—nobody gave it a thought. In Headland Road, as everywhere in Hong Kong, somebody is always building.

Stretched inside the lorry on leather bunks fitted for the purpose, the two men watched intently from among a forest of lenses, cameras, and radio-telephone appliances. For them also, their progress past Seven Gates was becoming something of a routine.

"No change?" said the first.

"No change," the second confirmed.

"No change," the first repeated into the radio-telephone, and heard the assuring voice of Murphy at the other end, acknowledging the message.

"Maybe they're waxworks," said the first, still watching. "Maybe we should go give them a prod and see if they holler."

"Maybe we should, at that," said the second.

In all their professional lives, they were agreed, they had never followed anything that kept so still. Ko stood where he always stood, at the end of the rose-arbour, his back to them as he stared out to sea. His little wife sat apart from him, dressed as usual in black, on a white garden chair, and she seemed to be staring at her husband. Only Tiu made any movement. He also was sitting, but to Ko's other side, and he was munching what looked like a doughnut.

Reaching the main road, the lorry lumbered toward Stanley, pursuing for cover reasons its fictional reconnaissance of the region.

20

Liese's Lover

Her apartment was big and unreconciled: a mix of hotel lounge, executive suite, and tart's boudoir. The drawing-room ceiling was raked to a lopsided point like the nave of a subsiding church. The floor changed levels restlessly; the carpet was as thick as grass, and Lizzie and Jerry left shiny footprints where they walked. The enormous windows gave limitless but lonely views, and when she closed the blinds and drew the curtains, the two of them were suddenly in a suburban bungalow with no garden. The amah had gone to her room behind the kitchen, and when she appeared Lizzie sent her back there. She crept out scowling and hissing. "Wait till I tell the master," she was saying.

He put the chains across the front door, and after that he took her with him, steering her from room to room, making her walk a little ahead of him on his left side, open the doors for him and even the cupboards. The bedroom was a television stage-set for a *femme fatale*, with a round, quilted bed and a sunken round bath behind Spanish screens. He looked through the bedside lockers for a small-arm because, though Hong Kong is not particularly gun-ridden, people who have lived in Indo-China usually have something. Her dressing-room looked as though she'd emptied one of the smart Scandinavian décor shops in Central by telephone. The dining-room was done in smoked glass, polished chrome and leather, with fake

Gainsborough ancestors staring at the empty chairs—all the
mummies who couldn't boil eggs, he thought. Black tiger-skin
steps led to Ko's den, and here Jerry lingered, staring round,
fascinated despite himself, seeing the man in everything,
and—for all his rather awful crimes at first remove—his kinship with old Sambo. The king-sized desk with the *bombé* legs
and ball-and-claw feet, the Presidential cutlery. The ink-wells,
the sheathed paper-knife and scissors, the untouched works of
legal reference, the very ones old Sambo trailed around with
him: Simons on tax, Charlesworth on company law. The
framed testimonials on the wall. The citation for his Order of
the British Empire, beginning "Elizabeth the Second by the
Grace of God . . ." The medal itself, embalmed in satin like
the arms of a dead knight. Group photographs of Chinese
elders on the steps of a spirit temple. Victorious racehorses.
Lizzie laughing to him. Lizzie in a swim-suit, looking stun-
ning. Lizzie in Paris.

Gently he pulled open the desk drawers and discovered the
embossed stationery of a dozen different companies. In the
cupboards, empty files, an I.B.M. electric typewriter with no
plug on it, an address book with no addresses entered. Lizzie
naked from the waist up, glancing round at him over her long
back. Lizzie, God help her, in a wedding dress, clutching a
posy of gardenias. Ko must have sent her to a bridal parlour for
the photograph.

There were no photographs of gunny bags of opium.

The executive sanctuary, thought Jerry, still standing there.
Old Sambo had several, he remembered: girls who had flats
from him—one even a house—yet saw him only a few times a
year. But always this one secret special room, with the desk
and the unused telephones and the instant mementoes, a physical corner carved off someone else's life, a shelter from his
other shelters.

"Where is he?" Jerry asked, remembering Luke again.
"Drake?"

"No, Father Christmas."

"You tell me."

He followed her to the bedroom. "Do you often not know?" he asked.

She was pulling off her earrings, dropping them in a jewellery box. Then her clasp, her necklace and bracelets.

"He rings me wherever he is, night or day, we never care. This is the first time he's cut himself off."

"Can you ring him?"

"*Any* bloody time," she said with savage sarcasm. "'Course I can. Number One Wife and me get on just *great*."

"What about at the office?"

"He's not going to the office."

"What about Tiu?"

"Sod Tiu."

"Why?"

"Because he's a pig," she snapped, pulling open a cupboard.

"He could pass on messages for you."

"If he felt like it, which he doesn't."

"Why not?"

"How the hell should I know?" She hauled out a pullover and some jeans and chucked them on the bed. "Because he resents me. Because he doesn't trust me. Because he doesn't like round-eyes horning in on Big Sir. Get out while I change."

So he wandered into the dressing-room again, keeping his back to her, hearing the rustle of silk and skin.

"I saw Ricardo," he said. "We had a full and frank exchange of views."

He needed very much to hear whether they had told her. He needed to absolve her from Luke. He listened, then went on:

"Charlie Marshall gave me his address, so I popped up and had a chat with him."

"Great. So now you're family."

"They told me about Mellon. Said you carried dope for him."

She didn't speak so he turned to look at her, and she was

sitting on the bed with her head in her hands. In the jeans and pullover she looked about fifteen years old, and half a foot shorter.

"What the hell do you want?" she whispered at last, so quietly she might have been putting the question to herself.

"You," he said. "For keeps."

He didn't know whether she heard because all she did was let out a long breath and whisper "Oh, Jesus" at the end of it.

"Mellon a friend of yours?" she asked finally.

"No."

"Pity. He needs a friend like you."

"Does Arpego know where Ko is?"

She shrugged.

"When did you last hear from him?"

"A week."

"What did he say?"

"He had things to arrange."

"What things?"

"For Christ's sake, stop asking questions! The whole sodding world is asking questions, so just don't join the queue, right?"

He stared at her and her eyes were alight with anger and despair. He opened the balcony door and stepped outside.

I need a brief, he thought bitterly. Sarratt bearleaders, where are you now I need you? It hadn't dawned on him till now that when he cut the cable, he was also dropping the pilot.

The balcony ran along three sides. The fog had temporarily cleared. Behind him hung the Peak, its shoulders festooned in gold lights. Banks of running cloud made changing caverns round the moon. The harbour had dug out all its finery. At its centre an American aircraft carrier, floodlit and dressed overall, basked like a pampered woman amid a cluster of attendant launches. On her deck, a line of helicopters and small fighters reminded him of the air base in Northern Thailand. A column of ocean-going junks drifted past her, headed for Canton.

"Jerry," she called.

She was standing in the open doorway, watching him down a line of tub trees.

"Come on in. I'm hungry," she said.

It was a kitchen where nobody cooked or ate, but it had a Bavarian corner, with pine settles, Chinese-style alpine pictures, and ashtrays saying "Carlsberg." She gave him coffee from an ever-ready percolator, and he noticed how when she was on guard she kept her shoulders forward and her forearms across her body, the way the orphan used to. She was shivering. He thought she had been shivering ever since he laid the gun on her and he wished he hadn't done that, because it was beginning to dawn on him that she was in as bad a state as he was, and perhaps a damn sight worse, and that the mood between them was like two people after a disaster, each in a separate hell. He made her a brandy and soda and the same for himself and sat her in the drawing-room where it was warmer, and he watched her while she hugged herself and drank the brandy, staring at the carpet.

"Music?" he asked.

She shook her head.

"I represent myself," he said. "No connection with any other firm."

She might not have heard.

"I'm free and willing," he said. "It's just that a friend of mine died."

He saw her nod, but only in sympathy; he was sure it rang no bell with her at all.

"The Ko thing is getting very grubby," he said. "It's not going to work out well. They're very rough boys you're mixed up with. I thought maybe you'd like a leg out of it all. That's why I came back. My Galahad act. It's just I don't quite know what's gathering round you. Mellon—all that. Maybe we should unbutton it together and see what's there."

After which not very articulate explanation, the telephone

rang. It had one of those throttled croaks designed to spare the nerves.

The telephone was across the room on a gilded trolley. A pin-light winked on it with each dull note, and the rippled glass shelves picked up the reflection. She glanced at it, then at Jerry, and her face was at once alert with hope. Jumping to his feet, he pushed the trolley over to her and its wheels stammered in the deep pile. The wire uncoiled behind him as he walked, till it was like a child's scribble across the room. She lifted the receiver quickly and said "Worth" in the slightly rude tone women learn when they live alone. He thought of telling her the line was bugged but he didn't know what he was warning her against; he had no position any more, this side or that side. He didn't know what the sides were, but his head was suddenly full of Luke again and the hunter in him was wide awake.

She had the telephone to her ear but she hadn't spoken. Once she said "Yes," as if she were acknowledging instructions, and once she said "No" strongly. Her expression had turned blank, her voice told him nothing. But he sensed obedience and he sensed concealment, and as he did so, the anger lit in him completely and nothing else mattered.

"No," she said to the phone. "I left the party early."

He knelt beside her, trying to listen, but she kept the receiver pressed hard against her.

Why didn't she ask him where he was? Why didn't she ask when she would see him? Whether he was all right? Why he hadn't phoned? Why did she look at Jerry like this, show no relief?

His hand on her cheek, he forced her head round and whispered to the other ear.

"Tell him you *must* see him! You'll come to him. *Anywhere*."

"Yes," she said again into the phone. "All right. Yes."

"Tell him! Tell him you must see him!"

"I must see you," she said finally. "I'll come to you wherever you are."

The receiver was still in her hand. She made a shrug, asking for instruction, and her eyes were still turned to Jerry—not as her Sir Galahad but as just another part of a hostile world that encircled her.

"*I love you!*" he whispered. "Say what you say!"

"I love you," she said shortly, with her eyes closed, and rang off before he could stop her.

"He's coming here," she said. "And damn you."

Jerry was still kneeling beside her. She stood up in order to get clear of him.

"Does he know?" Jerry asked.

"Know what?"

"That I'm here?"

"Perhaps." She lit a cigarette.

"Where is he now?"

"I don't know."

"When will he be here?"

"He said soon."

"Is he alone?"

"He didn't say."

"Does he carry a gun?"

She was across the room from him. Her strained grey eyes still held him in their furious, frightened glare. But Jerry was indifferent to her mood. A feverish urge for action had overcome all other feelings.

"Drake Ko. The nice man who set you up here. Does he carry a gun? Is he going to shoot me? Is Tiu with him? Just questions, that's all."

"He doesn't wear it in bed, if that's what you mean."

"Where are you going?"

"I thought you two men would prefer to be left alone."

Leading her back to the sofa, he sat her facing the double doors at the far end of the room. They were panelled with frosted glass, and on the other side of them lay the hall and the front entrance. He opened them, clearing her line of view to anybody coming in.

"Do you have rules about letting people in, you two?" She didn't follow his question. "There's a peep-hole here. Does he insist you check every time before you open?"

"He'll ring on the house phone from downstairs. Then he'll use his door key."

The front door was laminated hardboard, not solid, but solid enough. Sarratt folklore said, "If you are taking a lone intruder unawares, don't get behind the door or you'll never get out again." For once Jerry was inclined to agree. Yet to keep to the open side was to be a sitting duck for anyone aggressively inclined, and Jerry was by no means sure that Ko was either unaware or alone. He considered going behind the sofa, but if there was to be shooting he didn't want the girl to be in the line of it; he definitely didn't. Her passivity, her lethargic stare did nothing to reassure him. His brandy glass was beside hers on the table, and he put it quietly out of sight behind a vase of plastic orchids. He emptied the ashtray and set an open copy of *Vogue* in front of her on the table.

"You play music when you're alone?"

"Sometimes."

He chose Ellington.

"Too loud?"

"Louder," she said. Suspicious, he turned down the sound, watching her. As he did so, the house phone whistled twice from the hall.

"Take care," he warned and, gun in hand, moved to the open side of the front door, the sitting-duck position, three feet from the arc, close enough to spring forward, far enough to shoot and throw himself, which was what he had in mind as he dropped into a half-crouch. He held the gun in his left hand and nothing in his right, because at that distance he couldn't miss with either hand, whereas if he had to strike he wanted his right hand free. He remembered the way Tiu carried his hands curled, and he warned himself not to get in close. Whatever he did, to do it from a distance. A groin kick but don't follow it in; stay outside those hands.

"You say 'Come on up,'" he told her.

"Come on up," Lizzie repeated into the phone. She rang off and unhooked the chain.

"When he comes in, smile for the camera. Don't shout."

"Go to hell," she said.

From the lift-well, to his sharpened ear, came the clump of a lift arriving and the monotonous "ping" of the bell. He heard footsteps approaching the door, one pair only, steady, and remembered Drake Ko's comic, slightly ape-like gait at Happy Valley, how the knees tipped through the grey flannels. A key slid into the lock, one hand came round the door, and the rest with no apparent forethought followed. By then Jerry had sprung with all his weight, flattening the unresisting body against the wall. A picture of Venice fell, the glass smashed, he slammed the door, all in the same moment that he found a throat and jammed the barrel of the pistol straight into the deep flesh. Then the door was unlocked a second time from outside, very fast, the wind went out of his body, his feet flew upward, a crippling shock of pain spread from his kidneys and felled him on the thick carpet, a second blow caught him in the groin and made him gasp as he jerked his knees to his chin. Through his streaming eyes he saw the little, furious figure of Fawn the baby-sitter standing over him, shaping for a third strike, and the rigid grin of Sam Collins as he peered calmly over Fawn's shoulder to see what the damage was. And still in the doorway, wearing an expression of grave apprehension as he straightened his collar after Jerry's unprovoked assault on him, the flustered figure of his one-time guide and mentor, Mr. George Smiley, breathlessly calling his leash-dogs to order.

* * *

Jerry was able to sit, but only if he leaned forward. He held both hands in front of him, his forearms jammed into his lap. The pain was all over his body, like poison spreading from a central source. The girl watched from the hall doorway. Fawn was lurking, hoping for another excuse to hit him. Sam Collins was at the other end of the room, sitting in a winged armchair with his legs crossed as if he were at home here and the chair his favourite. Smiley had poured Jerry a neat brandy and was stooping over him, poking the glass into his hand.

"What are you doing here, Jerry?" Smiley said. "I don't understand."

"Courting," said Jerry and closed his eyes as a wave of black pain swept over him. "Developed an unscheduled affection for our hostess, here. Sorry about that."

"That was a very dangerous thing to do, Jerry," Smiley objected. "You could have wrecked the entire operation. Suppose I had been Ko. The consequences would have been disastrous."

"I'll say they would." He drank some brandy. "Luke's dead. Lying in my flat with his head shot off."

"Who's Luke?" Smiley asked, forgetting their meeting at Craw's house.

"No one. Just a friend." He drank again. "American journalist. A drunk. No loss to anyone."

Smiley glanced at Sam Collins, but Sam shrugged. "Nobody *we* know," he said.

"Ring them, all the same," said Smiley.

Sam picked up the mobile telephone and walked out of the room with it because he knew the layout.

"Put the burn on her, have you?" Jerry said, with a nod of his head toward Lizzie. "About the only thing left in the book that hasn't been done to her, I should think." He called over to her. "How are you doing there, sport? Sorry about the tussle. Didn't break anything, did we?"

"No," she said.

"Put the bite on you about your wicked past, did they? Stick and carrot? Promised to wipe the slate clean? Silly girl, Lizzie. Not allowed a past in this game. Can't have a future either. *Verboten.*"

He turned back to Smiley. "That's all it was, George. No philosophy to it. Old Lizzie got under my skin."

Tilting back his head, he studied Smiley's face through half-closed eyes. And with the clarity which pain sometimes brings, he felt somehow that by his action he had put Smiley's own existence under threat.

"Don't worry," he said gently. "Won't happen to you, that's for sure."

"Jerry," said Smiley.

"Yes, sir," said Jerry and made a show of sitting to attention.

"Jerry, you don't understand what's going on. How much you could upset things. Billions of dollars and thousands of men could not obtain a part of what we stand to gain from this one operation. A war general would laugh himself silly at the thought of such a tiny sacrifice for such an enormous dividend."

"Don't ask *me* to get you off the hook, old boy," Jerry said, looking up into his face again. "You're the owl, remember? Not me."

Sam Collins returned. Smiley glanced at him in question.

"He's not one of theirs either," said Sam.

"They were aiming for me," said Jerry. "They got Lukie instead. He's a big bloke. Or was."

"And he's in your flat?" Smiley asked. "Dead. Shot. And in your flat?"

"Been there some while."

Smiley to Collins: "We shall have to brush over the traces, Sam. We can't risk a scandal."

"I'll get back to them now," Collins said.

"And find out about planes," Smiley called after him. "Two first-class seats."

Collins nodded.

"Don't like that fellow one bit," Jerry confessed. "Never did. Must be his moustache." He shoved a thumb toward Lizzie. "What's she got that's so hot for you all, anyway, George? Ko doesn't whisper his inmost secrets to her. She's a round-eye." He turned to Lizzie. "Does he?"

She shook her head.

"If he did, she wouldn't remember," he went on. "She's thick as hell about those things. She's probably never even heard of Nelson." He called to her again. "You. Who's Nelson? Come on, who is he? Ko's little dead son, isn't he? That's right. Named his boat after him, didn't he? And his gee-gee." He turned back to Smiley. "See? Thick. Leave her out of it, that's my advice."

Collins had returned with a note of flight times. Smiley read it, frowning through his spectacles. "We shall have to send you home at once, Jerry," he said. "Guillam's waiting downstairs with a car. Fawn will go along as well."

"I'd just like to be sick again if you don't mind."

Reaching upward, Jerry took hold of Smiley's arm for support, and at once Fawn sprang forward, but Jerry shot out a warning finger at him as Smiley ordered him back.

"You keep your distance, you poisonous little leprechaun," Jerry advised. "You're allowed one bite and that's all. The next one won't be so easy."

He moved in a crouch, trailing his feet slowly, hands latched over his groin. Reaching the girl, he stopped in front of her.

"Did they have powwows up here, Ko and his lovelies? Ko bring his boy-friends up here for a natter, did he?"

"Sometimes."

"And you helped with the mikes, did you, like the good little housewife? Let the sound boys in, tended the lamp? I bet you did."

She nodded.

"Still not enough," he objected as he hobbled to the bathroom. "Still doesn't answer my question. Must be more to it than that. *Far* more."

In the bathroom he held his face under cold water, drank some, and immediately vomited. On the way back, he looked for the girl again. She was in the drawing-room, and in the way that people under stress look for trivial things to do, she was sorting the gramophone records, putting each in its proper sleeve. In a distant corner, Smiley and Collins were quietly conferring. Closer at hand Fawn was waiting at the door.

"Bye, sport," he said to her. Putting his hand on her shoulder, he drew her round till her grey eyes looked straight at him.

"Goodbye," she said and kissed him, not in passion exactly, but at least with more deliberation than the waiters got.

"I was a sort of accessory before the fact," he explained. "I'm sorry about that. I'm not sorry about anything else. You'd better look after that sod Ko too. Because if they don't manage to kill him, I may."

He touched the lines on her chin, then shuffled toward the door where Fawn stood, and turned round to take his leave of Smiley, who was alone again; Collins had been sent off to telephone. Smiley stood as Jerry remembered him best, his short arms slightly lifted from his sides, his head back a little, his expression at once apologetic and enquiring, as if he'd just left his umbrella on the underground. The girl had turned away from both of them and was still sorting the records.

"Love to Ann, then," Jerry said.

"Thank you."

"You're wrong, sport. Don't know how, don't know why, but you're wrong. Still, too late for that, I suppose." He felt sick again and his head was shrieking from the pains in his body. "You come any nearer than that," he said to Fawn, "and I will definitely break your bloody neck, you understand?" He turned back to Smiley, who stood in the same posture and gave no sign of having heard.

"Season of the year to you, then," said Jerry.

With a last nod, but none to the girl, Jerry limped into the corridor, Fawn following. Waiting for the lift, he saw the elegant American standing at his open doorway, watching his departure.

"Ah, yeah, I forgot about you," he called very loudly. "You're running the bug on her flat, aren't you? The Brits blackmail her and the Cousins bug her—lucky girl gets it all ways."

The American vanished, closing the door quickly after him. The lift came and Fawn shoved him in.

"Don't do that," Jerry warned him. "This gentleman's name is Fawn," he told the other occupants of the lift in a very loud voice. They mostly wore dinner-jackets and sequinned dresses. "He's a member of the British Secret Service and he's just kicked me in the balls. The Russians are coming," he added, to their doughy, indifferent faces. "They're going to take away all your bloody money."

"Drunk," said Fawn in disgust.

In the lobby Lawrence the porter watched with keen interest. In the forecourt a Peugeot saloon waited, blue. Peter Guillam was sitting in the driving seat.

"Get in," he snapped.

The passenger door was locked. He climbed into the back, Fawn after him.

"What the hell do you think you're up to?" Guillam demanded through clenched teeth. "Since when did half-arsed London Occasionals cut anchor in mid-operation?"

"Keep clear," Jerry warned Fawn. "Just the hint of a frown from you right now is enough to get me going. I mean that. I warn you. Official."

The ground fog had returned, rolling over the bonnet. The passing city offered itself like the framed glimpses of a junk yard: a painted sign, a shop-window, strands of cable strung across a neon sign, a clump of suffocated foliage; the inevitable building site, floodlit. In the mirror Jerry saw a black Mercedes following, male passenger, male driver.

"Cousins bringing up the tail," he announced.

A spasm of pain in the abdomen almost blacked him out, and for a moment he actually thought Fawn had hit him again, but it was only an after-effect of the first time. In Central he made Guillam pull up and was sick in the gutter in full public view, leaning his head through the window while Fawn crouched tensely over him. Behind them the Mercedes stopped too.

"Nothing like a spot of pain," he exclaimed, settling in the car again, "for getting the old brain out of moth-balls once in a while. Eh, Peter?"

Guillam made an obscene answer.

You don't understand what's going on, Smiley had said. *How much you could upset things. Billions of dollars and thousands of men could not obtain a part of what we stand to gain . . .*

How? he kept asking himself. Gain *what?* His knowledge of Nelson's position inside Chinese affairs was sketchy. Craw had told him only the minimum he needed to know: *Nelson has access to the Crown jewels of Peking, Your Grace. Whoever gets his hooks on Nelson has earned a lifetime's merit for himself and his noble house.*

They were skirting the harbour, heading for the tunnel. From sea-level the American aircraft carrier looked strangely small against the merry backdrop of Kowloon.

"How's Drake getting him out, by the way?" he asked Guillam chattily. "Not trying to fly him again, *that's* for sure. Ricardo put the lid on that one for good, didn't he?"

"Suction," Guillam snapped—which was very silly of him, thought Jerry jubilantly; he should have kept his mouth shut.

"Swimming?" Jerry asked. "Nelson on the Mirs Bay ticket. *That's* not Drake's way, is it? Nelson's too old for that one, anyway. Freeze to death, even if the sharks didn't get his whatnots. How about the pig train, come out with the grunters? Sorry you've got to miss the big moment, sport, all on account of me."

"So am I, as a matter of fact. I'd like to kick your teeth in."

Inside Jerry's brain, the sweet music of rejoicing sounded. It's true! he told himself. That's what's happening! Drake's bringing Nelson out and they're all queueing up for the finish!

Behind Guillam's lapse—just one word, but in Sarratt terms totally unforgivable, indivisibly wrong—there lay nevertheless a revelation as dazzling as anything which Jerry was presently enduring, and in some respects vastly more bitter. If anything mitigates the crime of indiscretion, and in Sarratt terms nothing does, then Guillam's experiences of the last hour—half of it spent driving Smiley frantically through rush-hour traffic and half of it waiting, in desperate indecision, in the car outside Star Heights—would surely qualify. Everything he had feared in London, the most Gothic of his apprehensions regarding the Enderby-Martello connection, and the supporting rôles of Lacon and Sam Collins, had in these sixty minutes been proved to him beyond all reasonable doubt as right and true and justified—and if anything somewhat understated.

They had driven first to Bowen Road in the Midlevels, to an apartment block so blank and featureless and large that even those who lived there must have had to look twice at the number before they were sure they were entering the right one. Smiley pressed a bell marked "Mellon," and, idiot that he was, Guillam asked "Who's Mellon?" at the same moment he remembered that it was Sam Collins's work name. Then he did a double take and asked himself—but not Smiley; they were in the lift by now—what maniac, after Haydon's ravages, could conceivably award himself the same work name which he had used before the fall? Then Collins opened the door to them, wearing his Thai silk dressing-gown, a brown cigarette jammed into a holder, and his washable non-iron smile, and the next thing was they were grouped in a parquet drawing-room with bamboo chairs and Sam had switched two transistor radios to different programmes, one voice, the other music, to provide rudimentary anti-bug security while they talked. Sam listened, ignoring Guillam entirely, then promptly phoned Martello direct—Sam had a *direct line* to him, please note, no dialling, nothing; a straight land-line, apparently—to ask in veiled language how things stood with chummy. Chummy—Guillam learned later—being gambling slang for a mug. Martello replied that the surveillance van had just reported in. Chummy and Tiu were presently sitting in Causeway Bay aboard the *Admiral Nelson*, said the watchers, and the directional mikes (as usual) were picking up so much bounce from the water that the transcribers would need days, if not weeks, to clean off the extraneous sound and find out whether the two men had ever said anything interesting. Meanwhile they had dropped one man at the quayside as a static post, with orders to advise Martello immediately should the boat weigh anchor or either of the two quarries disembark.

"Then we must go there at once," said Smiley, so they piled back into the car, and while Guillam drove the short distance to Star Heights, seething and listening impotently to their terse conversation, he became with every moment more convinced that he was looking at a spider's web, and that only George Smiley, obsessed by the promise of the case and the image of Karla, was myopic enough, and trusting enough—and, in his own paradoxical way, innocent enough—to bumble straight into the middle of it.

George's age, thought Guillam. Enderby's political ambitions, his fondness for the hawkish, pro-American stance—not to mention the crate of champagne and his outrageous courtship of the fifth floor. Lacon's tepid support of Smiley, while he secretly cast around for a successor. Martello's stopover in Langley. Enderby's attempt *only days ago* to prise Smiley away from the case and hand it to Martello on a plate. And now, most eloquent and ominous of all, the reappearance of Sam Collins as the joker in the pack with a private line to Martello! And

Martello, heaven help us, acting dumb about where George got his information from—the direct line notwithstanding.

To Guillam all these threads added up to one thing only, and he could not wait to take Smiley aside and, by any means at his command, deflect him sufficiently from the operation, just for one moment, for him to see where he was heading. To tell him about the letter. About Sam's visit to Lacon and Enderby in Whitehall.

Instead of which? He was to return to England. Why was he to return to England? Because a genial thick-skulled hack named Westerby had had the gall to slip the leash.

Even without his crying awareness of impending disaster, the disappointment to Guillam would have been scarcely supportable. He had endured a great deal for this moment. Disgrace and exile to Brixton under Haydon, poodling for old George instead of getting back to the field, putting up with George's obsessive secretiveness, which Guillam privately considered both humiliating and self-defeating—but at least it had been a journey with a destination, till Jerry bloody Westerby, of all people, had robbed him even of that. But to return to London knowing that, for the next twenty-two hours at least, he was leaving Smiley and the Circus to a bunch of wolves, without even the chance to warn him—to Guillam it was the crowning cruelty of a frustrated career, and if blaming Jerry helped, then damn him, he would blame Jerry or anybody else.

"Send Fawn!"

"Fawn's not a gentleman," Smiley would have replied—or words that meant the same.

You can say *that* again too, thought Guillam, remembering the broken arms.

Jerry was equally conscious of abandoning someone to the wolves, even if it was Lizzie Worthington rather than George Smiley. As he gazed through the rear window of the car, it seemed to him that the very world that he was moving through had also been abandoned. The street markets were deserted, the pavements, even the doorways. Above them the Peak loomed fitfully, its crocodile spine daubed by a ragged moon.

It's the Colony's last day, he decided: Peking has made its proverbial telephone call. "Get out, party over." The last hotel was closing; he saw the empty Rolls-Royces lying like scrap around the harbour, and the last blue-rinse round-eye matron, laden with her tax-free furs and jewellery, tottering up the gangway of the last cruise ship; the last China-watcher frantically feeding his last miscalculations into the shredder; the looted shops, the empty city waiting like a carcass for the hordes. For a moment it was all one vanishing world; here, Phnom Penh, Saigon, London—a world on loan, with the creditors standing at the door, and Jerry himself, in some unfathomable way, a part of the debt that was owed.

I've always been grateful to this service, that it gave me a chance to pay. Is that how you feel?

Yes, George, he thought. Put the words into my mouth, old boy. That's *exactly* how I feel, sport. But perhaps not quite in the sense *you* mean it, however. He saw Frost's cheerful, fond little face as they drank and fooled. He saw it the second time, locked in that awful scream. He felt Luke's friendly hand upon his shoulder and saw the same hand lying on the floor, flung back over his head to catch a ball that would never come, and he thought, Trouble is, sport, the paying is actually done by the other poor sods.

Like Lizzie, for instance.

He'd mention that to George one day, if they ever, over a jar, should get back to that sticky little matter of just why we climb the mountain. He'd make a point there—nothing aggressive, not rocking the boat, you understand, sport— about the selfless and devoted way in which we sacrifice other people, such as Luke and Frost and Lizzie. George would have a perfectly good answer, of course. Reasonable. Measured. Apologetic. George saw the bigger picture. Understood the imperatives. Of course he did. He was an owl.

The harbour tunnel was approaching and he was thinking of her shivering last kiss, and remembering the drive to the mortuary all at the same time, because the scaffold of a new building rose ahead of them out of the fog and, like the scaffold on the way to the mortuary, it was floodlit and glistening coolies were swarming over it in yellow helmets.

Tiu doesn't like her either, he thought. Doesn't like round-eyes who spill the beans on Big Sir.

Forcing his mind in other directions, he tried to imagine what they would do with Nelson: stateless, homeless, a fish to be devoured or thrown back into the sea at will. Jerry had seen a few of those fish before: he had been present for their capture; at their swift interrogation. He had led more than one of them back across the border they had so recently crossed, for hasty *recycling*, as the Sarratt jargon had it—"quick before they notice he has left home." And if they didn't put him back? If they kept him, this great prize they all so coveted? Then after the years of his debriefing—two, three even; he had heard some ran for five—Nelson would become one more Wandering Jew of the spy-trade, to be hidden, and moved again, and hidden, to be loved not even by those to whom he had betrayed his trust.

And what will Drake do with Lizzie, he wondered, while that little drama unfolds? Which particular scrap-heap is she headed for this time?

They were at the mouth of the tunnel and they had slowed almost to a halt. The Mercedes lay right behind them. Jerry let his head fall forward. He put both hands over his groin while he rocked himself and grunted in pain. From an improvised police box, like a sentry post, a Chinese constable watched curiously.

"If he comes over to us, tell him we've got a drunk on our hands," Guillam snapped. "Show him the sick on the floor."

They crawled into the tunnel. Two lanes of north-bound traffic were bunched nose to bumper by the bad weather. Guillam had taken the right-hand stream. The Mercedes drew up beside them on their left. In the mirror, through half-closed eyes, Jerry saw a brown lorry grind down the hill after them.

"Give me some change," Guillam said. "I'll need change as I come out."

Fawn delved in his pockets, but using one hand only.

The tunnel pounded to the roar of engines. A hooting match started. Others began joining in. To the encroaching fog was added the stench of exhaust fumes. Fawn closed his window. The din rose and echoed till the car trembled to it.

Jerry put his hands to his ears. "Sorry, sport. Going to bring up again, I'm afraid."

But this time he leaned toward Fawn, who, with a muttered "Filthy bastard," started hastily to wind his window down again, until Jerry's head crashed into the lower part of his face and Jerry's elbow hacked down in his groin. For Guillam, caught between driving and defending himself, Jerry had one pounding chop on the point where the shoulder socket meets the collar-bone. He started the strike with the arm quite relaxed, converting the speed into power at the last possible moment. The impact made Guillam scream "Christ!" and lifted him straight out of his seat as the car veered to the right.

Fawn had an arm round Jerry's neck and with his other hand he was trying to press Jerry's head over it, which would definitely have killed him. But there is a blow they teach at Sarratt for cramped spaces that is called "the tiger's claw" and is delivered by driving the heel of the hand upwards into the opponent's windpipe, keeping the arm crooked and the fingers pressed back for tension. Jerry did that now, and Fawn's head hit the back window so hard that the safety glass starred. In the Mercedes the two Americans went on looking ahead of them, as if they were driving to a state funeral. He thought of squeezing Fawn's windpipe with his finger and thumb but it didn't seem necessary. Recovering his gun from Fawn's waistband, Jerry opened the right-hand door. Guillam made one desperate dive for him, ripping the sleeve of his faithful but very old suit to the elbow. Jerry swung the gun onto his arm and saw his face contort with pain. Fawn got a leg out, but Jerry slammed the door on it and heard him shout "Bastard!" again, and after that he just kept running back toward town, against the stream.

Bounding and weaving between the land-locked cars, he pelted out of the tunnel and up the hill until he reached the little sentry hut. He thought he heard Guillam yelling. He thought he heard a shot, but it could have been a car backfiring. His groin was hurting amazingly, but he seemed to run faster under the impetus of the pain. A policeman on the curb shouted at him, another held out his arms, but Jerry brushed them aside, and they gave him the final indulgence of the round-eye. He ran until he found a cab. The driver spoke no English so he had to point the way. "That's it, sport. Up there. Left, you bloody idiot. That's it—" until they reached her block.

He didn't know whether Smiley and Collins were still there, or whether Ko had turned up, perhaps with Tiu, but there was very little time to play games finding out. He didn't ring the bell because he knew the mikes would pick it up. Instead he fished a card from his wallet, scribbled on it, shoved it through the letter-box, and waited in a crouch, shivering and sweating and panting like a dray-horse while he listened for her tread and nursed his groin. He waited an age, and finally the door opened and she stood there staring at him while he tried to get upright.

"Christ, it's Galahad," she muttered. She wore no make-up and Ricardo's claw marks were deep and red. She wasn't crying; he didn't think she did that, but her face looked older than the rest of her. To talk, he drew her into the corridor and she didn't resist. He showed her the door leading to the fire steps.

"Meet me the other side of it in five seconds flat, hear me? *Don't* telephone anybody, *don't* make a clatter leaving, and *don't* ask any bloody silly questions. Bring some warm clothes. Now do it, sport. Don't dither. *Please*."

She looked at him, at his torn sleeve, and sweat-stained jacket; at his mop of forelock hanging over one eye.

"It's me or nothing," he said. "And believe me, it's a big nothing."

She walked back to her flat alone, leaving the door ajar. But she came out much faster, and for safety's sake she didn't even close the door. On the fire stairs he led the way. She carried a shoulder-bag and wore a leather coat. She had brought a cardigan for him to replace the torn jacket—he supposed Drake's, because it was miles too small, but he managed to squeeze into it. He emptied his jacket pockets into her bag and chucked the jacket down the rubbish chute.

She was so quiet following him that he twice looked back to make sure she was still there. Reaching the ground floor, he peered through the window and drew back in time to see the Rocker in person, accompanied by a heavy subordinate, approach the porter in his kiosk and show him his police pass. They followed the stair as far as the car-park, and she said, "Let's take the red canoe."

"Don't be bloody stupid, we left it in town."

Shaking his head, he led her past the cars into a squalid open-air compound full of refuse and building junk, like the backyard at the Circus. From here, between walls of weeping concrete, a giddy stairway fell toward the town, overhung by black branches and cut into sections by the winding road. The jarring of the downward steps hurt his groin a lot. The first time they reached the road, Jerry took her straight across it. The second time, alerted by the blood-red flash of an alarm light in the distance, he hauled her into the trees to avoid the beam of a police car whining down the hill at speed. At the underpass they found a *pak-pai* and Jerry gave the address.

"Where the hell's that?" she asked.

"Somewhere you don't have to register," said Jerry. "Just

shut up and let me be masterful, will you? How much money have you got with you?"

She opened her bag and counted from a fat wallet. "I won it off Tiu at mah-jong," she said, and for some reason he sensed she was romancing.

The driver dropped them at the end of the alley and they walked the short distance to the low gateway. The house had no lights, but as they approached the front door it opened and another couple flitted past them out of the darkness. They entered the hall and the door closed behind them, and they followed a hand-borne pin-light through a short maze of brick walls until they reached a smart interior lobby in which piped music played. On the serpentine sofa in the centre sat a trim Chinese lady with a pencil and a notebook on her lap, to all the world a model chatelaine. She saw Jerry and smiled; she saw Lizzie and her smile broadened.

"For the whole night," said Jerry.

"Of course," she replied.

They followed her upstairs to a small corridor. The open doors gave glimpses of silk counterpanes, low lights, mirrors. The woman was murmuring prices in Jerry's ear. Jerry chose the least suggestive, declined the offer of a second girl to make up the numbers, gave her money, and ordered a bottle of Rémy Martin. Lizzie followed him in, chucked her shoulder-bag on the bed, and, while the door was still open, broke into a taut laugh of relief.

"Lizzie Worthington," she announced, "this is where they said you'd end up, you brazen bitch, and blow me if they weren't right!"

There was a chaise longue and Jerry lay on it, staring at the ceiling, feet crossed, the brandy glass in his hand. Lizzie took the bed and for a time neither spoke. The place was very still. Occasionally, from the floor above, they heard a cry of pleasure or muffled laughter, once of protest. She went to the window and peered out.

"What's out there?" he asked.

"Bloody brick wall, about thirty cats, stacks of empties."

"Foggy?"

"Vile."

She sauntered to the bathroom, poked around, came out again.

"Sport," said Jerry quietly.

She paused, suddenly wary.

"Are you sober and of sound judgment?"

"Why?"

"I want you to tell me everything you told them. When you've done that, I want you to tell me everything they asked you, whether you could answer it or not. And when you've done that, we'll try to take a little thing called a back-bearing and work out where those bastards all are in the scheme of the universe."

"It's a replay," she said finally.

"What of?"

"I don't know: it's all to be exactly the way it happened before."

"So what happened before?"

"Whatever it was," she said wearily, "it's going to happen again."

21

Nelson

It was one in the morning. She had bathed. She came out of the bathroom wearing a white wrap and no shoes and her hair in a towel.

"They've even got those bits of paper stretched across the loo," she said. "And tooth-mugs in cellophane bags."

She dozed on the bed and he on the sofa, and once she said, "I'd like to, but it doesn't work," and he replied that after being kicked where Fawn had kicked him the libido tended to be a bit quiescent anyway. She told him about her schoolmaster—Mr. Bloody Worthington, she called him—and "her one shot at going straight," and about the child she had borne him out of politeness. She talked about her terrible parents, and about Ricardo and what a sod he was, and how she had loved him, and how a girl in the Constellation bar had advised her to poison him with laburnum, so one day after he had beaten her half to death she put a "damn great dose in his coffee." But perhaps she hadn't got the right stuff, she said, because all that happened was that he was sick for days and "the one thing worse than Ricardo healthy was Ricardo at death's door." How another time she actually got a knife into him while he was in the bath, but all he did was stick a bit of plaster over it and swipe her again.

How when Ricardo did his disappearing act she and Charlie Marshall refused to accept that he was dead, and mounted a

"Ricardo Lives!" campaign as they called it, and how Charlie went and badgered his old man, all just as he had described to Jerry. And how Lizzie packed up her rucksack and went down to Bangkok, where she barged straight into the China Airsea suite at the Erawan, intending to beard Tiu, and found herself face to face with Ko instead, having met him only once before, very briefly—at a bun-fight in Hong Kong given by one Sally Cale, an old bull-dyke in the antique trade who pushed heroin on the side. And how that was quite a scene she played, beginning with Ko's sharp instruction to get out, and ending with "nature taking her course," as she put it cheerfully: "Another step on Lizzie Worthington's unswerving road to perdition." So that slowly and deviously, with Charlie Marshall's old man pulling, "and Lizzie pushing, as you might say," they put together a very Chinese contract, to which the main signatories were Ko and Charlie's old man, and the commodities to be transacted were, one, Ricardo and, two, his recently retired life partner, Lizzie.

In which said contract, Jerry learned with no particular surprise, both she and Ricardo gratefully acquiesced.

"You should have let him rot," said Jerry, remembering the twin rings on his right hand, and the Ford car blown to bits.

But Lizzie hadn't seen it that way at all, and she didn't now. "He was one of us," she said. "Although he was a sod."

But having bought his life, she felt free of him.

"Chinese arrange marriages every day. So why shouldn't Drake and Liese?"

What was all the "Liese" stuff? Jerry asked. Why Liese instead of Lizzie?

She didn't know. Something Drake didn't talk about, she said. There had once been a Liese in his life, he told her, and his fortune-teller had promised him that one day he would get another, and he reckoned Lizzie was near enough, so they gave it a shove and called it Liese and while she was about it she pared her surname to plain Worth.

"Blond bird," she said absently.

The name-change had a practical purpose, too, she said. Having chosen a new name for her, Ko took the trouble to have the local police record of her old one destroyed. "Till that sod Mellon marches in and says he'll get them to rewrite it, with a special mention about me carrying his bloody heroin," she said.

Which brought them back to where they were now. And why.

To Jerry, their sleepy wanderings occasionally had the calm of after-love. He lay on the divan, wide awake, but Lizzie talked between dozes, taking up her story dreamily where she had left it when she fell asleep, and he knew that near enough she was telling him the truth, because it made nothing of her that he did not already know, and understand. He realised also that with time Ko had become another anchor for her, somewhat as the schoolmaster had. He gave her the authority from which to survey her odyssey.

"Drake never broke a promise in his life," she said once, as she rolled over and sank back into a fitful sleep. Jerry remembered the orphan: just never lie to me.

Hours, lifetimes later, she was woken by a squawk of ecstasy next door.

"Christ," she declared appreciatively, "she *really* hit the moon." The squawk repeated itself. She changed her mind. "No go," she said disapprovingly. "She's faking it." Silence. "You awake?" she asked.

"Yes."

"What are you going to do?"

"Tomorrow?"

"Yes."

"I don't know," he said.

"Join the club," she whispered, and seemed to fall asleep again.

I need that Sarratt brief again, he thought. Very badly I need it. Put in a limbo call to Craw, he thought. Ask dear old

George for a spot of that philosophical advice he's taken to doling out these days. He must be around. Somewhere.

Smiley was around, but at that moment he could not have given Jerry any help at all. He would have traded all his knowledge for a little understanding. The isolation ward had no night-time, so they lay or lounged under the punctured daylight of the ceiling, the three Cousins and Sam on one side of the room, Smiley and Guillam on the other, and Fawn striding up and down the line of the cinema seats, looking caged and furious and squeezing what appeared to be a squash-ball in each fist. His lips were black and swollen and one eye was shut. A clot of blood under his nose refused to go away. Guillam had his right arm strapped to his shoulder and his eyes were on Smiley all the while. But so were the eyes of everyone—or everyone but Fawn. A phone rang, but it was the communications room upstairs saying Bangkok had reported Jerry traced for certain as far as Vientiane.

"Tell them the trail's cold, Murphy," Martello ordered, his eyes still on Smiley. "Tell them any damn thing. Just get them off our backs. Right, George?"

Smiley nodded.

"Right," said Guillam firmly, speaking for him.

"The trail's cold, honey," Murphy echoed into the phone. The "honey" came as a surprise. Murphy had not till now shown such signs of human tenderness. "You want to make a signal or do I have to do it for you? We're not interested, right? Kill it."

He rang off.

"Rockhurst has found her car," Guillam said for the second time, while Smiley still stared ahead of him. "In an underground car-park in Central. There is a hire-car down there too. Westerby rented it. Today. In his work name. George?"

Smiley gave a nod so slight it might have been no more than an attack of sleepiness he had staved away.

"At least he's doing something, George," said Martello

pointedly down the room from his own small caucus of Collins and the quiet men. "Some people would say, when you have a rogue elephant, best thing to do is go out there and shoot him."

"You have to find him first," snapped Guillam, whose nerves were at breaking-point.

"I'm not even sure George wants to do that, Peter," Martello said, in a reprise of his avuncular style. "I think George may be lifting his eye from the ball a little on this, to the grave peril of our common enterprise."

"What do you want George to do?" Guillam rejoined tartly. "Walk the streets till he finds him? Have Rockhurst circulate his name and description, so that every journalist in town knows there's a man-hunt for him?"

At Guillam's side Smiley remained hunched and inert like an old man.

"Westerby's a professional," Guillam insisted. "He's not a natural, but he's good. He can lie up for months in a town like this and Rockhurst wouldn't get a scent of him."

"Not even with the girl in tow?" said Murphy.

His strapped arm notwithstanding, Guillam stooped to Smiley: "It's your operation," he whispered urgently. "If you say we've got to wait, we'll wait. Just give the order. All these people want is an excuse to take over. Anything but a vacuum. Anything."

Prowling the line of the cinema chairs, Fawn gave vent to a sarcastic murmur: "Talk, talk, talk. That's all they can do."

Martello tried again: "George. Is this island British or is it not? You guys can shake this town out any time." He pointed to a windowless wall. "We have a man out there—your man— who seems bent on running amok. Nelson Ko is the biggest catch you or I are ever likely to land. The biggest of my career, and—I will stake my wife, my grandmother, and the deeds of my plantation—the biggest even of yours."

"No takers," said Sam Collins, the gambler, through his grin.

Martello stuck to his guns: "Are we going to let him rob us of the prize, George, sit here passively asking one another how it came about that Jesus Christ was born on Christmas Day and not on December twenty-sixth or twenty-seventh?"

Smiley peered at Martello at last, then up at Guillam, who stood stiffly at his side, tipping back his shoulders to support the sling, and finally he looked downward at his own, locked, conflicting hands, and for a period quite meaningless in time he studied himself in his mind, and reviewed his quest for Karla, whom Ann called his "black Grail." He thought of Ann and her repeated betrayals of him in the name of her own Grail, which she called love. He recalled how against his better judgment he had tried to share her faith and, like a true believer, renew it each day, despite her anarchic interpretations of its meaning. He thought of Haydon, steered at Ann by Karla. He thought of Jerry and the girl, and he thought of Peter Worthington, her husband, and the dog-like look of kinship which Worthington had bestowed on him when he called to interview him in the terrace house in Islington: "You and I are the ones they leave behind," ran the message.

He thought of Jerry's other tentative loves along his untidy trail, the half-paid bills the Circus had picked up for him, and it would have been handy to lump Lizzie in with them as just one more, but he couldn't do that. He was not Sam Collins, and he had not the smallest doubt that at this moment Jerry's feeling for the girl was a cause Ann would warmly have espoused. But he was not Ann either. For a cruel moment nevertheless, as he sat still locked in indecision, he did honestly wonder whether Ann was right and his striving had become nothing other than a private journey among the beasts and villains of his own insufficiency, in which he ruthlessly involved simplistic minds like Jerry's.

You're wrong, sport. Don't know how, don't know why, but you're wrong.

The fact that I am wrong, Smiley had once replied to Ann, in the mid-stream of one of their endless arguments, *does not make you right*.

He heard Martello again, speaking in present time: "George, we have people waiting with *open arms* for what we can give them. What Nelson can."

A phone was ringing. Murphy took the call and relayed the message to the silent room: "Land-line from the aircraft carrier, sir. Navy int. has the junks dead on schedule, sir. South wind favourable and good fishing along the way. Sir, I don't even think Nelson's riding with them. I don't see why he should."

The focus shifted abruptly to Murphy, who had never before been heard to express an opinion.

"What the hell's *that*, Murphy?" Martello demanded quite astonished. "You been to the fortune-teller too, son?"

"Sir, I was down on the carrier this morning and those people have a lot of data. They can't figure why anybody who lives in Shanghai would ever want to exit out of Swatow. They would do it all different, sir. They would fly or train to Canton, then take the bus maybe to Waichow. They say that's a lot safer, sir."

"These are Nelson's people," Smiley said as the heads swung sharply back on him. "They're his clan. He would rather be at sea with them, even if he's at risk. He trusts them." He turned to Guillam. "We'll do this," he said. "Tell Rockhurst to distribute a description of Westerby and the girl together. You say he hired the car under his work name? Used his escape papers?"

"Yes."

"Worrell?"

"Yes."

"The police are looking for a Mr. and Mrs. Worrell then, British. No photographs, and make sure the descriptions are vague enough not to arouse suspicion. Marty."

Martello was all attentiveness.

"Is Ko still on his boat?" Smiley asked.

"Nestled right in there with Tiu, George."

"It's just possible Westerby may try to reach him. You have a static post at the quayside. Put more men down there."

"What are they looking for?"

"Trouble. The same goes for surveillance on his house. Tell me—" He sank into his thoughts a moment, but Guillam need not have worried. "Tell me, can you simulate a fault on Ko's home telephone line?"

Martello glanced at Murphy.

"Sir, we don't have the apparatus handy," Murphy said, "but I guess we could. . . ."

"Then cut it," Smiley said simply. "Cut the whole cable if necessary. Try and do it near some road-works."

Having dispensed his orders, Martello came lightly across the room and sat himself at Smiley's side.

"Ah, George, about tomorrow, now. Do you think we might, ah, put a little hardware on stand-by as well?" From the desk where he was telephoning Rockhurst, Guillam watched the dialogue most intently. From across the room so did Sam Collins. "Just seems there's no telling what your man Westerby might do, George. We have to be prepared for all emergencies, right?"

"By all means stand anything by. But for the time being, if you don't mind, we'll leave the interception plans as they are. And the competence with me."

"Sure, George. Sure," said Martello fulsomely, and with the same church-like reverence tiptoed back to his own camp.

"What did he want?" Guillam demanded in a low voice, crouching at Smiley's side. "What's he trying to get you to agree to?"

"I will not have it, Peter," Smiley warned, also under his breath. He was suddenly very angry. "I shall not hear you again. I shall not tolerate your Byzantine notions of a palace plot. These people are our hosts and our Allies. We have a written agreement with them. We have quite enough to worry about already without grotesque and—I may tell you honestly— paranoid fancies. Now please—"

"I tell *you!*" Guillam began, but Smiley closed him down.

"I want you to get hold of Craw. Call on him, if necessary. Perhaps the journey would do you good. Tell him Westerby's on the rampage. He's to let us know at once if he has word of him. He'll know what to do."

Still walking the line of seats, Fawn watched Guillam leave, while his fists continued restlessly kneading whatever was inside them.

In Jerry's world it was also three in the morning, and the madame had found him a razor, but no fresh shirt. He had shaved and cleaned himself up as best he could, but his body still ached from head to toe. He stood over Lizzie where she lay on the bed and promised to be back in a couple of hours, but he doubted whether she even heard him. *The more papers which are printing pretty girls in preference to politics today,* he remembered Ko saying, *the more chance we get of a damn sight better world.*

He took *pak-pais*, knowing they were less under the thumb of the police. Otherwise he walked, and the walking helped his body and his mystical process of decision-taking, because back there on the divan it had suddenly become impossible. He needed to move in order to find direction. He was heading for Deep Water Bay, and he knew he was entering badland. Now that he was on the loose, they would be on to that launch like leeches. He wondered who they had, what they were using. If it was the Cousins, he would look for too much hardware, and overmanning.

Rain was coming on and he feared it would clear the fog. Above him the moon was already partly free, and as he padded silently down the hill he could make out by its pale light the nearest stock-broker junks groaning and tugging at their moorings. A south-east wind, he noticed, and rising. If it's a static observation post, they'll go for height, he thought, and sure enough there on the promontory to his right he saw a battered-looking Mercedes van tucked between the trees, and the aerial with its Chinese streamers.

He waited, watching the fog roll, till a car came down the hill with its lights full on, and as soon as it was past him he darted across the road, knowing that not all the hardware in the world would enable them to see him behind the advancing head-lights. At the water's level the visibility was down to zero, and he had to grope in order to pick out the rickety wooden causeway he remembered from his previous reconnaissance.

Then he found what he was looking for. The same toothless old woman sat in her sampan, grinning up at him through the fog.

"Ko," he whispered. *"Admiral Nelson.* Ko?"

The echo of her cackle bounded away across the water. "Po Toi!" she shouted. "Tin Hau! Po Toi!"

"Today?"

"Today!"

"Tomorrow?"

"Tomollow!"

He tossed her a couple of dollars and her laughter followed him as he crept away.

I'm right, Lizzie's right, *we're* right, he thought. He's going to the festival. He hoped to God Lizzie was staying put. If she woke up, he wouldn't put it past her to wander.

He walked, trying to stamp away the aching in his groin and back. Take it stage by stage, he thought. Nothing big. Just play it as it comes. The fog was like a corridor leading to different rooms. Once he met an invalid car crawling along the curb as its owner exercised his dog. Once he saw two old men in undervests performing their morning exercises. In a public garden small children stared at him from a rhododendron bush they seemed to have made their home, for their clothes were draped over the branches and they were as naked as the refugee kids in Phnom Penh.

She was sitting up waiting for him when he returned, and she looked terrible.

"Don't do that again," she warned, and shoved her arm through his as they set out to find some breakfast and a boat. "Don't ever bloody walk out on me without waving."

Hong Kong at first possessed no boats at all that day. Jerry would not contemplate the big out-island ferries which took the trippers. He knew the Rocker would have them sewn up. He refused to go down to the bays and make conspicuous enquiries. When he telephoned the listed water-taxi firms, whatever they had was either rented or too small for the voyage. Then he remembered Luigi Tan, the fixer, who was a myth at the Foreign Correspondents' Club; Luigi could get you anything from a Korean dance troupe to a cut-price air ticket faster than any fixer in town. They took a taxi to the other side of Wanchai, where Luigi had his lair, then walked. It was eight in the morning but the hot fog had not lifted. The unlit signs sprawled over the narrow lanes like spent fireworks: "Happy Boy," "Lucky Place," "Americana." The crowded foodstalls added their warm smells to the reek of petrol fumes and soot. Through splits in the wall they sometimes glimpsed a canal. "Anyone tell you where to find me," Luigi Tan liked to say. "Ask for the big guy with one leg."

They found him behind the counter of his shop, just tall enough to look over it, a tiny, darting half-Portuguese who had once earned a living Chinese-boxing in the grimy booths of Macao. The front of the shop was six feet wide. His wares were new motor-bikes and relics of the old China service, which he called antiques: daguerreo-types of hatted ladies in tortoiseshell frames, a battered travelling box, an opium clipper's log.

Luigi knew Jerry already but he liked Lizzie much better, and insisted that she go ahead so that he could study her hind quarters while he ushered them under a washing line to an outhouse marked "Private," with three chairs and a telephone on the floor. Crouching till he was rolled into a neat ball, Luigi talked Chinese to the telephone and English to Lizzie. He was a grandfather, he said, but virile, and had four sons, all good. Even Number Four son was off his hands. All good drivers, good workers, and good husbands. Also, he said to Lizzie, he had a Mercedes complete with stereo.

"Maybe I take you ride in it one day," he said.

Jerry wondered whether she realised that he was proposing marriage, or perhaps something slightly less.

And yes, Luigi thought he had a boat as well.

After two phone calls he knew he had a boat, which he only ever lent to friends, at a nominal cost. He gave Lizzie his credit-card case to count the number of cards, then his wallet to admire the family snaps, one of which showed a lobster caught by Number Four son on the day of his recent wedding, though the son was not visible.

"Po Toi bad place," said Luigi Tan to Lizzie, still on the telephone. "Very dirty place. Rough sea, lousy festival, bad food. Why you want to go there?"

For Tin Hau of course, Jerry said patiently, answering for her. For the famous temple and the festival.

Luigi Tan preferred to speak to Lizzie.

"You go Lantau," he advised. "Lantau good island. Nice food, good fish, nice people. I tell them you go Lantau, eat at Charlie's. Charlie my friend."

"Po Toi," said Jerry firmly.

"Po Toi hell of a lot of cash."

"We've got a hell of a lot of cash," said Lizzie with a lovely smile, and Luigi looked at her again, contemplatively, the long up-and-down look.

"Maybe I come with you," he said to her.

"No," said Jerry.

Luigi drove them to Causeway Bay and rode with them on the sampan. The boat was a fourteen-foot power boat, common as driftwood, but Jerry reckoned she was sound and Luigi said she had a deep keel. A boy lounged on the stern, trailing one foot in the water.

"My nephew," said Luigi, ruffling the boy's hair proudly. "He got mother in Lantau. He take you Lantau, eat Charlie's place, give you good time. You pay me later."

"Old boy," said Jerry patiently. "Sport. We don't want Lantau. We want Po Toi. Only Po Toi. Po Toi or nothing. Drop us there and go."

"Po Toi bad weather, bad festival. Bad place. Too near China. Lot of Commies."

"Po Toi or nothing," Jerry said.

"Boat too small," said Luigi with a frightful loss of face, and it took all Lizzie's charm to build him up again.

For another hour the boys primed the boat, and all Jerry and Lizzie could do was sit in the half-cabin keeping out of sight and sip judicious shots of Rémy Martin. Periodically one or the other of them sank into a private reverie. When Lizzie did this, she hugged herself and rocked slowly on her haunches, head down. Whereas Jerry yanked at his forelock, and once he yanked so hard she touched his arm to stop him, and he laughed.

Almost carelessly they pulled away from the harbour.

"Stay out of sight," Jerry ordered and for safety's sake put his arm round her to keep her in the meagre shelter of the open cabin.

The American aircraft carrier had stripped off her ornamental garb and lay grey and menacing, like an unsheathed knife, above the water. At first they had nothing but the same sticky calm. On the shore, shelves of fog pressed on the grey high-rises, and brown smoke columns slid into a white expressionless sky. On the flat water their boat felt high as a balloon. But as they slipped the shelter and headed east, the waves slapped her sides hard enough to wind her, the bow pitched and cracked, and they had to brace themselves to keep upright. With the little bow lifting and tugging like a bad horse, they tumbled past cranes and godowns and factories and the stumps of quarried hillsides.

They were running straight into the wind and spray was flying on all sides. The coxswain at the wheel was laughing and crowing to his mate, and Jerry supposed it was the mad round-eyes they were laughing at, who chose to do their courting in a pitching tub. A giant tanker passed them, not seeming to move, brown junks running in her wake. From the dockyards, where a freighter was laid to, the white flashes of the welders' lamps signalled to them across the water.

The boys' laughter eased and they began to talk sensibly because they were at sea. Looking back between the swaying walls of transport ships, Jerry saw the Island drawing slowly away from him, cut like a table mountain by the cloud. Once more Hong Kong was ceasing to exist.

They passed another headland. As the sea roughened, the pitching steadied and the cloud above them dropped until its base was only a few feet above their mast, and for a while they stayed in this lower, unreal world, advancing under cover of its protective blanket. The fog ended suddenly and left them in dancing sunlight. Southward, on hills of violent lushness, an orange navigation lamp winked at them through the clear air.

"What do we do now?" she asked softly, looking through the porthole.

"Smile and pray," said Jerry.

A pilot's launch was pulling alongside and for a moment he definitely expected to see the hideous face of the Rocker glowering down on him, but the crew ignored them entirely.

"Who are they?" she whispered. "What do you think?"

"It's routine," said Jerry. "It's meaningless."

The launch veered away. That's it, thought Jerry, with no particular feeling; they've spotted us.

"You sure it was just routine?" she asked.

"Hundreds of boats go to the festival," he said.

The boat bucked violently and kept bucking. Great seawor-
thiness, he thought, hanging on to Lizzie. Great keel. If this
goes on, we won't have anything to decide. The sea will do it
for us. It was one of those trips where if you made it, nobody
noticed, and if you didn't, they'd say you threw your life away.
The east wind could swirl right round on itself at any moment,
he thought. In the season between monsoons, nothing was ever
sure. He listened anxiously to the erratic galloping of the
engine. If it gives up, we'll finish on the rocks.

Suddenly his nightmares multiplied unreasonably. The
butane, he thought; Christ, the butane! While the boys were
preparing the boat, he had glimpsed two cylinders stowed in
the front hold beside the water tanks, presumably for cooking
Luigi's lobsters. Fool that he was, he had made nothing of them
till now. He worked it out. Butane is heavier than air. All cylinders leak. It's just a question of degree. With this sea pounding the bows, they leak faster, and the escaped gas will now be
lying in the bilge about two feet from the spark of the engine,
with a nice blend of oxygen to assist combustion.

Lizzie had slipped from his grasp and stood astern. The sea
was suddenly crowded. Out of nowhere, a fleet of fishing junks
had gathered, and she was gazing at them earnestly. Grabbing
her arm, he hauled her back to the cover of the cabin.

"Where do you think you are?" he shouted. "Bloody Cowes?"

She studied him a moment, then gently kissed him, then
kissed him again.

"You calm down," she warned. She kissed him a third time,
muttered *"Yes,"* as if her expectations had been fulfilled, then
sat quiet for a while, looking at the deck but keeping hold of his
hand.

Jerry reckoned they were making five knots into the wind.
A small plane zoomed overhead. Holding her out of sight, he
looked up sharply, but was too late to read the markings.

And good morning to *you*, he thought.

They were rounding the last point, tossing and groaning in

the spray. Once, the propellers lifted clean out of the water with a roar. As they hit the sea again, the engine faltered, choked, but decided to stay alive. Touching Lizzie's shoulder, Jerry pointed ahead of them to where the bare, steep island of Po Toi loomed like a cut-out against the cloud-torn sky: two peaks, sheer from the water, the larger to the south, and a saddle between.

The sea had turned iron blue and the wind ripped over it, slapping the breath from their mouths and hurling spray at them like hail. On the port bow lay Beaufort Island: a lighthouse, a jetty, no inhabitants. The wind dropped as though it had never been. Not a breeze greeted them as they entered the unruffled water of the island's lee. The sun's heat was direct and harsh. Ahead of them, perhaps a mile, lay the mouth of Po Toi's main bay, and behind it the low brown ghosts of China's islands.

Soon they could make out a whole untidy fleet of junks and cruise boats jamming the bay. The first jingle of drums and cymbals and unco-ordinated chanting floated to them across the water. On the hill behind lay the shanty village, its tin roofs twinkling, and on its own small headland stood one solid building, the temple of Tin Hau, with a bamboo scaffold lashed round it in a rudimentary grandstand, and a large crowd with a pall of smoke hanging over it and dabs of gold between.

"Which side was it?" he asked her.

"I don't know. We climbed to a house and walked from there."

Each time he spoke to her, he looked at her, but now she avoided his gaze. Tapping the coxswain on the shoulder, he pointed the course he wanted him to take. The boy at once began protesting. Squaring to him, Jerry showed him a bunch of money, pretty well all he had left. With an ill grace the boy swung across the mouth of the harbour, weaving between the boats toward a small granite headland where a tumbledown jetty offered a risky landing. The din of the festival was much louder. They could smell charcoal and suckling pig, and hear concerted bursts of laughter, but for the time being the crowd was out of sight to them, as they were to the crowd.

"Here!" Jerry yelled. "Put in here. Now! *Now!*"

The jetty leaned drunkenly as they clambered onto it. They had not even reached land before their boat had turned for home. Nobody said goodbye. They climbed up the rock hand in hand and walked straight into a money game that was being watched by a large and laughing crowd. At the centre stood a clownish old man with a bag of coins, and he was throwing them down the rock one by one while barefooted boys hurled themselves after them, pushing each other almost to the cliff-edge in their zeal.

"They took a boat," Guillam said. "Rockhurst has interviewed the proprietor. The proprietor is a friend of Westerby's, and yes it was Westerby and a beautiful girl, and they wanted to go to Po Toi for Tin Hau."

"And how did Rockhurst play that?" Smiley asked.

"Said in that case it wasn't the couple he was looking for. Bowed out. Disappointed. The harbour police have also belatedly reported sighting it on course for the festival."

"Want us to put up a spotter plane, George?" Martello asked nervously. "Navy int. have all sorts standing by."

Murphy had a bright suggestion: "Why don't we just go right in with choppers and scoop Nelson off that end junk?" he demanded.

"Murphy, shut up," Martello said.

"They're making for the island," Smiley said firmly. "We know they are. I don't think we need air cover to prove it."

Martello was not satisfied. "Then maybe we should send a couple of people out to that island, George. Maybe we ought to do a little interfering, finally."

Fawn was standing stock-still. Even his fists had stopped working.

"No," said Smiley.

At Martello's side Sam Collins grinned a little thinly.

"Any reason?" Martello asked.

"Right up to the last minute, Ko has one sanction. He can signal his brother not to come ashore," Smiley said. "The merest hint of a disturbance on the island could persuade him to do that."

Martello gave a nervous, angry sigh. He had put aside the pipe he sometimes smoked and was drawing heavily on Sam's supply of brown cigarettes, which seemed to be endless.

"George, what does this man *want?*" he demanded in exasperation. "Is this a blackmail thing now, a disruption? I don't see a category here." A dreadful thought struck him. His voice dropped and he pointed with the full length of his arm across the room. "Now just don't tell me we got one of these *new* ones on our hands, for Christ's sakes! Don't tell me he's one of those cold-war converts with a middle-aged mission to wash his soul in public. Because if he is, and if we are going to read this guy's frank life story in the *Washington Post* next week, George, I personally am going to put the whole Fifth Fleet on that island, if that's what it takes to hold him down." He turned to Murphy. "I have contingencies, right?"

"Right."

"George, I want a landing party on stand-by. You guys can come aboard or stay home. Please yourselves."

Smiley stared at Martello, then at Guillam, with his strapped and useless arm, then at Fawn, who was poised like a diver at the end of a spring-board, eyes half closed and heels together, while he lifted himself slowly up and down on his toes.

"Fawn and Collins," Smiley said at last.

"You two boys take them to the aircraft carrier and hand them right over to the people there. Murphy comes back."

A smoke cloud marked the place where Collins had been sitting. Where Fawn had stood, two squash-balls slowly rolled a distance before coming to a halt.

"God help us all," somebody murmured fervently. It was Guillam, but Smiley ignored him.

The lion was three men long and the crowd was laughing because it nipped at them and because self-appointed picadors were prodding it with sticks while it lolloped in dance steps down the narrow path, to the clatter of the drums and cymbals. Reaching the headland, the procession slowly turned itself and started to retrace its steps, and at this point Jerry drew Lizzie quickly into the middle of it, bending low in order to make less of his height. At first the track was mud and full of puddles, but soon the dance was leading them past the temple and down concrete steps toward a sand beach where the suckling pigs were being roasted.

"Which way?" he asked her.

She led him quickly left, out of the dance, along the back of a shanty village and over a wooden bridge across an inlet. They climbed along a fringe of cypress trees, Lizzie leading, until they were alone again, standing over the perfect horseshoe bay, looking down on Ko's *Admiral Nelson* where she lay at the very centre point, like a grand lady among the hundreds of pleasure boats and junks around her. There was nobody visible on deck, not even crew. A clutch of grey police boats, five or six of them, was anchored farther out to sea.

And why not, thought Jerry, since this was a festival?

She had let go his hand, and when he turned to her, she was still staring at Ko's launch and he saw the shadow of confusion in her face.

"Is this really the way he brought you?" he asked.

It was the way, she said; and turned to him, to look; to confirm or weigh things in her mind. Then with her forefinger she gravely traced his lips as if examining the point where she had kissed them. "Jesus," she said, and as gravely shook her head.

They started climbing again. Glancing up, Jerry saw the brown island peak deceptively near, and on the hillside groups

of rice terraces gone to ruin. They entered a small village populated by nothing but surly dogs, and the bay vanished from sight.
The schoolhouse was open and empty. Through the doorway
they saw charts of fighting aircraft. Washing jars stood on the
step. Cupping her hands, Lizzie rinsed her face. The huts were
slung with wire and brick to anchor them against typhoons.
The path turned to sand and the going grew harder.

"Still right?" he asked.

"It's just *up*," she said, as if she were sick of telling him. "It's
just *up*, and then the *house*, and bingo. I mean Christ, what do
you think I am, a bloody nitwit?"

"I didn't say a thing," said Jerry. He put his arm round her
and she pressed in to him, giving herself exactly as she had
done on the dance floor.

They heard a blare of music from the temple as somebody
tested the loudspeakers, and after it the wail of a slow tune.
The bay was in view again. A crowd had gathered on the shore.
Jerry saw more puffs of smoke and, in the windless heat of this
side of the island, caught a whiff of joss. The water was blue
and clear and calm. Round it, white lights burned on poles.
The Ko launch had not stirred, nor had the police.

"See him?" he asked.

She stood apart from him. She was studying the crowd. She
shook her head. "Probably having a kip after lunch," she said.

The beating of the sun was ferocious. When they entered
the shadow of the hillside it was like a sudden dusk, and when
they reached the sunlight it stung their faces like the heat of a
close fire. The air was alive with dragonflies, the hillside
strewn with big boulders, but where bushes grew they wound
and straggled, producing rich trumpets, red and white and yellow. Old picnic cans lay in profusion.

"And that's the house?"

"I told you," she said.

It was a ruin: a broken villa with gaping walls and a view. It
had been built with some grandeur above a dried-up stream

and was reached by a concrete foot-bridge. The mud stank and hummed with insects. Between palms and bracken the remains of a verandah gave a vast prospect of the sea and of the bay. As they crossed the foot-bridge, he took her arm.

"So let's play it from here," he said. "No interrogations. Just tell."

"We walked up here. Like I said. Me, Drake, and bloody Tiu. The boys brought a basket and the booze. I said 'Where are we going?' and he said 'Picnic.' Tiu didn't want me but Drake said I could come. 'You *hate* walking,' I said. 'I've never even seen you even cross a *road* before!' 'Today we walk,' he says, doing his Captain of Industry act. So I tag along and shut up."

A thick cloud was already obscuring the peak above them and rolling slowly down the hill. The sun had vanished. In moments the cloud reached them and they were alone at the world's end, unable to see even their feet. They groped their way into the house. She sat apart from him on a roof beam. Chinese slogans were daubed in red paint down the door pillars. The floor was littered with picnic refuse and long twists of lining paper.

"He tells the boys to hop it, so they hop it," she went on. "Him and Tiu have a long earnest natter in whatever they're speaking this week, and half-way through lunch he breaks into English and tells me Po Toi's *his* island. It's where he first landed when he left China. The boat people dumped him here. 'My people,' he calls them. That's why he comes to the festival every year and that's why he gives money to the temple, and that's why we've sweated up the bloody hill for a picnic. Then they go back into Chinese and I get the feeling Tiu is tearing him off a strip for talking too much, but Drake's all excited and little-boy and he won't listen. Then they go on up."

"*Up?*"

"Up to the top. 'Old ways are the best,' he says to me. 'We shall stick to what is proven.' Then his Baptist bit—'Hold fast to that which is good, Liese. That is what God likes.'"

Jerry glanced into the fog-bank above him, and he could have sworn he heard the crackle of a small plane, but at that moment he didn't mind too much whether it was there or not, because he had the two things he most badly needed. He had the girl with him, and he had the information: for now he finally understood exactly what she had been worth to Smiley and Sam Collins, and how she had unconsciously betrayed to them the vital clue to Ko's intentions.

"So they went on to the top. Did you go with them?"

"No."

"Did you see where they went?"

"To the top. I told you."

"Then what?"

"They looked down the other side. Talked. Pointed. More talk, more pointing. Then down they come again and Drake's even more excited, the way he gets when he's brought off a big deal and Number One's not there to disapprove. Tiu looks dead solemn, and that's the way he gets when Drake acts fond of me. Drake wants to stay and have a couple of brandies, so Tiu goes back to Hong Kong in a huff. Drake gets amorous and decides we'll spend the night on the boat and go home in the morning, so that's what we do."

"Where does he moor the boat? Here? In the bay?"

"No."

"Where?"

"Off Lantau."

"You went straight there, did you?"

She shook her head. "We did a round of the island."

"*This* island?"

"There was a place he wanted to look at in the dark. A bit of coast round the other side. The boys had to shine the lamps on it. 'That's where I land in 'fifty-one,' he says. 'The boat people were frightened to put in to the main harbour. They were frightened of police and ghosts and pirates and customs men. They say the islanders will cut their throats.'"

"And in the night?" said Jerry. "While you were moored off Lantau?"

"He told me he had a brother and loved him."

"That was the first time he told you?"

She nodded.

"He tell you where the brother was?"

"No."

"But you knew?"

This time she didn't even nod.

From below, the clatter of the festival rose through the cloud. He lifted her gently to her feet.

"Bloody questions," she muttered.

"They're nearly over," he promised. He kissed her and she let him, but did not otherwise take part.

"Let's go up there and take a look," he said.

Ten minutes more and the sunlight returned and blue sky opened above them. With Lizzie leading, they scrambled quickly over several false peaks toward the saddle. The sounds from the bay stopped and the colder air filled with screaming, wheeling gulls. They approached the crest, the path widened, they walked side by side. A few steps more and the wind hit them with a force that made them gasp and reel back. They were at the knife-edge, looking down into an abyss. At their very feet the cliff fell vertical to a boiling sea, and the foam smothered the headlands. Dumpling clouds were blowing from the east and behind them the sky was black. Two hundred metres down lay an inlet which the breakers did not cover. Fifty yards out from it, a shoal of rock checked the sea's force, and the spume washed it in white rings.

"That it?" he yelled above the wind. "He landed there? That bit of coast?"

"Yes."

"Shone the lights on it?"

"Yes."

Leaving her where she stood, he moved slowly up the knife-edge, crouching almost double while the wind rushed over his ears and covered his face in a sticky salt sweat and his stomach screamed in pain from what he supposed was a punctured gut or internal bleeding or both. At the inmost point before the cliff cut back into the sea, he looked down once more, and now he thought he could just make out a skimpy path, sometimes no more than a seam of rock or a ridge of rough grass, ekeing its way cautiously toward the inlet. There was no sand in the inlet but some of the rocks looked dry. Returning to her, he led her away from the knife-edge. The wind dropped and they heard the din of the festival again, much louder than before. The snap of firecrackers made a toy war.

"It's his brother Nelson," he explained. "In case you hadn't gathered. Ko's bringing him out of China. Tonight's the night. Trouble is, he's a much sought-after character. Lot of people would like a chat with him. That's where Mellon came in." He took a breath. "My view is that you should get the hell out of here. How do you see that? Drake's not going to want you around, that's for sure."

"Is he going to want you?" she asked.

"I think what you should do, you should go back to the harbour. Are you listening?"

She managed "Of course I am."

"You look for a nice friendly-looking round-eye family. Choose the woman, for once, not the bloke. Tell her you've had a row with your boy-friend and can they take you home in their boat? If they'll have you, stay the night with them; otherwise go to a hotel. Spin them one of your stories. Christ, that's no problem, is it?"

A police helicopter pattered overhead in a long curve, presumably to observe the festival. Instinctively he grabbed her shoulders and drew her back to the rock.

"Remember the second place we went—the big-band sound—the bar?" He was still holding her.

She said, "Yes."

"I'll pick you up there tomorrow night."

"I don't know," she said.

"Be there at seven. At seven, got it?"

She pushed him gently away from her, as if she were determined to stand alone.

"Tell him I kept faith," she said. "It's what he cares about most. I stuck to the deal. If you see him, tell him, 'Liese stuck to the deal.'"

"Sure."

"Not *sure*. *Yes*. Tell him. He did everything he promised. He said he'd look after me. He did. He said he'd let Ric go. He did that, too. He always stuck to a deal."

She was looking down. He raised her head, holding it with both his hands, but she insisted on going on.

"And tell him—and tell him—tell him they made it impossible. They fenced me in."

"Be there from seven on," he said. "Even if I'm a bit late. Now come on, that's not too difficult, is it? You don't need a university degree to hoist that aboard." He was gentling her, battling for a smile, striving for a last complicity before they separated.

She wanted to say something but it didn't work. She took a few steps, turned and looked back at him, and he waved—one big flap of the arm. She took a few more and kept going till she was below the line of the hill, but he did hear her shout "Seven, then," or thought he did. Having watched her out of sight, Jerry returned to the knife-edge, where he sat down for a bit of a breather before the Tarzan stuff. A snatch of John Donne came back to him, one of the few things he had picked up at school, though somehow he never got quotations completely right:

On a huge hill
Cragged and steep, Truth stands, and he that will
Reach her, about must, and about must go.

Or something.

For an hour, deep in thought—two hours—he lay in the lee of the rock and watched the daylight turn to dusk over the Chinese islands a few miles into the sea. Then he pulled off his buckskin boots and re-threaded the laces in a herring-bone, the way he used to thread them for his cricket boots. Then he put them on again and tied them as tight as they would go. It could be Tuscany again, he thought, and the five hills which he used to look at from the hornet field. Except that this time he wasn't proposing to walk out on anyone. Not the girl. Not Luke. Not himself. Even if it took a lot of footwork.

"Navy int. has the junk-fleet making around six knots and dead on course," Murphy announced. "Quit the beds right on one one hundred, just like they were following our projection."

From somewhere he had scrounged a set of bakelite toy boats which he could fix to the chart. Standing, he pointed them proudly in a single column at Po Toi island.

Murphy had returned but his colleague had stayed with Sam Collins and Fawn, so they were four.

"And Rockhurst has found the girl," said Guillam quietly, putting down the other phone. His shoulder was acting up and he was extremely pale.

"Where?" said Smiley.

Still at the chart, Murphy turned.

At his desk, where he was keeping a log of events, Martello put down his pen.

"Picked her up at Aberdeen harbour as she landed," Guillam went on. "She'd cadged a lift back from Po Toi with a clerk and his wife from the Hong Kong & Shanghai Bank."

"So what's the story?" Martello demanded before Smiley could speak. "Where's Westerby?"

"She doesn't know," said Guillam.

"Ah, come on!" Martello protested.

"She says they had a row and left in different boats. Rock-hurst says give him another hour with her."

Smiley spoke. "And Ko?" he asked. "Where's he?"

"His launch is still in Po Toi harbour," Guillam replied. "Most of the other boats have already left. But Ko's is where it was this morning. Sitting pretty, Rockhurst says, and everyone below."

Smiley peered at the sea chart, then at Guillam, then at the map of Po Toi.

"If she told Westerby what she told Collins," he said, "then he's stayed on the island."

"With what in mind?" Martello demanded very loud. "George, for what purpose is *that* man remaining on *that* island?"

An age went by for all of them.

"He's waiting," Smiley said.

"For *what*, may I enquire?" Martello persisted in the same determined tone.

Nobody saw Smiley's face. It had found its own bit of shadow. They saw his shoulders hunch, they saw his hand rise to his spectacles as if to remove them, they saw it fall back empty in defeat onto the rosewood table.

"Whatever we do, we must let Nelson land," he said firmly.

"And whatever *do* we do?" Martello demanded, getting up and coming round the table. "Westerby's not *here*, George. He never entered the Colony. He can leave by the same damn route!"

"Please don't shout at me," Smiley said.

Martello ignored him. "Which is it going to be, that's all? The conspiracy or the fuck-up?"

Guillam was standing his height, barring the way, and for an extraordinary moment it seemed possible that, broken shoulder notwithstanding, he proposed physically to restrain Martello from coming any closer to where Smiley sat.

"Peter," Smiley said quietly. "I see there's a telephone behind you. Perhaps you'd be good enough to pass it to me."

*   *   *

With the full moon, the wind had dropped and the sea settled. Jerry had not descended all the way to the inlet but made a last camp thirty feet above it, in the cover of a shrub, where he had protection. His hands and knees were cut, and a branch had grazed his cheek, but he felt good: hungry and alert. In the sweat and danger of the scramble he had forgotten his pain. The inlet was larger than he had imagined when he looked down on it from higher up, and the granite cliffs at sea-level were pierced with caves. He was trying to guess Ko's plan. He had been trying all day. What Ko had to do he would do from the sea, because he was not capable of the nightmarish climb down the cliff. Jerry had wondered at first whether Ko might try to intercept Nelson before he landed, but could see no safe way for Nelson to slip the fleet and make a sea-meeting with his brother.

The sky darkened, the stars came, and the path of the moon grew brighter. And Westerby? he thought. What does A do now? A was one hell of a long way from the syndicate solutions of Sarratt, *that* was for sure.

Ko would also be a fool to attempt to bring his launch to this side of the island, he decided. She was unwieldy and drew too much water to come inshore on a windward coast. A small boat was better, and a sampan or a rubber dinghy best. Clambering down the cliff till his boots hit pebbles, Jerry huddled against the rock, watching the breakers thump and the sparks of phosphorus riding with the spume.

She'll be back by now, he thought. With any luck, she's talked her way into someone's house and is charming the kids and wrapping herself round a cup of Bovril. "Tell him I kept faith," she said.

The moon lifted and still Jerry waited, training his eyes on the darkest spots in an effort to improve his vision. Then, over the clatter of the sea, he could have sworn he heard the

awkward slap of water on a wooden hull and the short grumble
of an engine switched on and off again. He saw no light. Edging his way along the shadowed rock, he crept as close to the
water's edge as he dared and once more crouched, waiting. As a
wave of surf soaked him to the thighs, he saw what he was waiting for: against the moon path, not twenty yards from him, the
arched cabin and curled prow of a single sampan rocking on its
anchor. He heard a splash and a muffled order, and as he sank
as low as the slope allowed, he picked out the unmistakeable
shape of Drake Ko, in his Anglo-French beret, wading cautiously ashore, followed by Tiu carrying an M-16 across both
arms. So there you are, thought Jerry. End of the long trail.
Luke's killer, Frostie's killer—whether by proxy or in the flesh
is immaterial—Lizzie's lover, Nelson's father, Nelson's brother.
Welcome to the man who never broke a deal in his life.

Ko also had a burden but it was less ferocious, and Jerry
knew long before he made it out that it was a lamp and a power
pack, pretty much like those he had used in the Circus water
games on the Helford Estuary, except that the Circus favoured
ultraviolet, and shoddy wire-framed spectacles which were useless in rain or spray.

Reaching the beach, the two men made their way over the
shingle until they reached the highest point; then, like Jerry,
they merged against the black rock. He reckoned they were
sixty feet from him. He heard a grunt and saw the flame of a
cigarette lighter, then the red glow of two cigarettes followed
by the murmur of Chinese voices. Wouldn't mind one myself,
thought Jerry. Stooping, he spread out one large hand and began
loading it with pebbles until it was full, then padded as stealthily as he could manage along the base of the rock toward the
two red embers. By his calculation he was eight paces from
them. He had the pistol in his left hand and the pebbles in his
right, and he was listening to the clump of the waves, how they
gathered, tottered, and fell, and he was thinking that it was

going to be a lot easier to have a chat with Drake once Tiu was out of the way.

Very slowly, in the classic posture of the outfielder, he leaned back, raised his left elbow in front of him, and crooked his right arm behind him, prepared for a throw at full stretch. A wave fell, he heard the shuffle of the undertow, the grumble as another gathered. Still he waited, right arm back, palm sweating as he clasped the pebbles. Then as the wave reached its height he hurled the pebbles high up the cliff, using all his strength, before ducking to a crouch, gaze fixed upon the embers of the two cigarettes. He waited, then heard the pebbles patter against the rock above him and the hailstorm gather as they tumbled down. In the next instant he heard Tiu's short curse and saw one red ember fly into the air as he leapt to his feet, M-16 in hand, barrel lifted to the cliff and his back to Jerry. Ko was scrambling for cover.

First Jerry hit Tiu very hard with the pistol, taking care to keep his fingers inside the guard. Then he hit him again with his closed right hand, a two-knuckle strike at full force, "with the fist turned down and turning," as they say at Sarratt, and a lot of follow-through at the end. As Tiu went down, Jerry caught his cheek-bone with the whole weight of his swinging right boot and heard the snap of his closing jaw. And as he stooped to pick up the M-16 he smashed the butt of it into Tiu's kidneys, thinking angrily of both Luke and Frost, but also of the cheap crack Tiu had made about Lizzie not rating more than the journey from Kowloon-side to Hong Kong-side. Greetings from the horse-writer, he thought. Then he looked toward Ko, who, having stepped forward, was still no more than a black shape against the sea: a crooked silhouette with piecrust ears sticking out below the line of his odd beret. A strong wind had risen again, or perhaps Jerry was only now aware of it. It rattled in the rocks behind them and made Ko's broad trousers billow.

"That Mr. Westerby, the English newsman?" he enquired, in precisely the deep, harsh tones he had used at Happy Valley.

"The same," said Jerry.

"You're a very political man, Mr. Westerby. What the hell do you want here?"

Jerry was recovering his breath, and for a moment he didn't feel quite ready to answer.

"Mr. Ricardo tells my people it is your aim to blackmail me. Is money your aim, Mr. Westerby?"

"Message from your girl," Jerry said, feeling he should discharge that promise first. "She says she keeps faith. She's on your side."

"I don't have a side, Mr. Westerby. I'm an army of one. What do you want? Mr. Marshall tells my people you are some kind of hero. Heroes are very political persons, Mr. Westerby. I don't care for heroes."

"I came to warn you. They want Nelson. You mustn't take him back to Hong Kong. They've got him all sewn up. They've got plans that will last him the rest of his life. And you as well. They're queueing up for both of you."

"What do you *want*, Mr. Westerby?"

"A deal."

"Nobody wants a deal. They want a commodity. The deal obtains for them the commodity. What do you want?" Ko repeated, raising his voice in command. "Tell me, please."

"You bought yourself the girl with Ricardo's life," said Jerry. "I thought I might buy her back with Nelson's. I'll speak to them for you. I know what they want. They'll settle."

That's the last foot in the last door for me, he thought, forever and a day.

"A *political* settlement, Mr. Westerby? With *your* people? I made many political settlements with them. They told me God loved children. Did you ever notice God love an Asian child, Mr. Westerby? They told me God was a *kwailo* and his mother had yellow hair. They told me God was a peaceful man, but I read once that there have never been so many civil wars as in the kingdom of Christ. They told me—"

"Your brother's right behind you, Mr. Ko."

Ko swung round. On their left, heading from the east, a dozen or more junks in full sail trembled southward across the moon path in ragged column, lights prickling in the water. Dropping to his knees, Ko began frantically groping for the lamp. Jerry found the tripod, wrenched it open; Ko stood the lamp on it, but his hands were shaking wildly and Jerry had to help him. Jerry seized the wires, struck a match, and clipped the cables to the terminals. They were staring out to sea, side by side. Ko flashed the lamp once, then again, first red then green.

"Wait," Jerry said softly. "You're too soon. Go easy or you'll muck it all up."

Moving him gently aside, Jerry bent to the eyepiece and scanned the line of boats: "Which one?"

"The last," said Ko.

Holding the last junk in view, though it was still only a shadow, Jerry signalled again, one red, one green, and a moment later heard Ko let out a cry of joy as an answering flicker darted back across the water.

"Can he fix on that?" said Jerry.

"Sure," said Ko, still looking out to sea. "Sure. He will fix on that."

"Then leave it alone. Don't do any more."

Ko turned to him, and Jerry saw the excitement in his face, and felt his dependence.

"Mr. Westerby, I am advising you sincerely: if you have played a trick on me for my brother Nelson, your Christian Baptist hell will be a very comfortable place by comparison with what my people do to you. But if you help me I give you everything. That is my contract and I never broke a contract in my life. My brother also made certain contracts." He looked out to sea. "I am pleased to advise you that he has seen the error of his ways."

The forward junks were out of sight. Only the tail-enders remained. From far away Jerry fancied he heard the uneven rumble of an engine, but he knew his mind was all over the place and it could have been the tumble of the waves. The moon passed behind the peak and the shadow of the mountain fell like a black knife-point onto the sea, leaving the far fields silver. Stooped to the lamp, Ko gave another cry of pleasure.

"Here! Here! Take a look, Mr. Westerby."

Through the eyepiece Jerry made out a single phantom junk, unlit except for three pale lamps, two green ones on the mast and a red one to starboard, making its way toward them. It passed from the silver into the blackness and he lost it. From behind him, he heard a groan from Tiu. Ignoring it, Ko remained stooped to the eyepiece, one arm held wide like a Victorian photographer while he began calling softly in Chinese. Running up the shingle, Jerry pulled the pistol from Tiu's belt, picked up the M-16 again, and, taking both to the sea's edge, chucked them in. Ko was preparing to repeat the signal but mercifully he couldn't find the button and Jerry was in time to stop him.

Once more Jerry thought he heard the rumble, not of one engine but two. Running out onto the headland, he peered anxiously north and south in search of a patrol boat, but again he saw nothing and again he blamed the surf and his strained imagination. The junk was nearer, beating in toward the island, her brown batwing sail suddenly tall and terribly conspicuous against the sky. Ko had run to the water's edge and was waving and yelling across the sea.

"Keep your voice down!" Jerry whispered from beside him.

But Jerry had become an irrelevance: Drake Ko's whole life was for Nelson. From the shelter of the near headland, the sampan tottered alongside the rocking junk. The moon came out of hiding, and for a moment Jerry forgot his anxiety as a

little grey-clad figure, small and sturdy, in stature Drake's antithesis, in a kapok coat and bulging proletarian cap, lowered himself over the side and leapt for the waiting arms of the sampan's
crew. Drake Ko gave another cry; the junk filled its sails and
slid behind the headland till only the green lights on its mast-
head remained visible above the rocks, and then they too vanished. The sampan was making for the beach, and Jerry could
see Nelson's stocky frame as he stood on the bow waving with
both hands and Drake Ko in his beret wild on the beach, dancing like a madman, waving back.

The throb of engines grew steadily louder, but still Jerry
couldn't place them. The sea was empty, and when he looked
upwards he saw only the hammer-head cliff and its peak black
against the stars. The brothers met and embraced and stayed
locked in each other's arms, not moving.

In a burst of realisation Jerry seized hold of both of them,
began pummelling them, and cried out for all his life, "Get
back in the boat! Hurry!"

They saw no one but each other. Running back to the water's
edge, Jerry grabbed the sampan's prow and held it, still calling
to them as he saw the sky behind the peak turn yellow, then
quickly brighten as the throb of the engines swelled to a roar
and three blinding searchlights burst on them from blackened
helicopters. The rocks danced to the whirl of landing lights,
the sea furrowed, pebbles bounced and flew around in storms.
For a fraction of a second Jerry saw Drake Ko's face turn to him
beseeching help, as if too late he had recognised where help lay.
He mouthed something but the din drowned it.

Jerry hurled himself forward, not for Nelson's sake, still
less for Drake's; but for what linked them, and for what linked
him to Lizzie. But long before he reached them a dark swarm
closed on the two men, tore them apart, and bundled the baggy
shape of Nelson into the hold of one of the helicopters. In the
mayhem Jerry had drawn his gun and held it in his hand. He
was screaming, though he could not hear himself above the

hurricanes of war. The helicopter was lifting. A single figure remained in the open doorway, looking down, and perhaps it was Fawn, for he looked dark and mad. Then an orange flash broke from in front of him, then a second and a third, and after that Jerry wasn't calling any more. In fury he threw up his hands, his mouth still open, his face still silently imploring. Then he fell and lay there. Soon there was once more no sound but the surf flopping on the beach and Drake Ko's hopeless, choking grief against the victorious armadas of the West, which had stolen his brother and left their hard-pressed soldier dead at his feet.

22

Born Again

In the Circus a mood of wild triumph broke out when the grand news came through from the Cousins. Nelson landed, Nelson bagged! Not a hair of his head injured! For two days there was speculation about medals, knighthoods, and promotions. They must do *something* for George at last, they *must!* Not so, said Connie shrewdly from the touch-line. They would never forgive him for raking up Bill Haydon.

The euphoria was followed by certain perplexing rumours. Connie and Doc di Salis, for instance, who were eagerly ensconced in the Maresfield safe house, now dubbed the Dolphinarium, waited a full week for their body to arrive, and waited in vain. So did the interpreters, transcribers, inquisitors, baby-sitters, and allied trades who made up the rest of the reception and interrogation unit there.

The match was rained off, said the housekeepers. Another date would be fixed. Stand by, they said. But quite soon a source at the local estate agent in the neighbouring town of Uckfield revealed that the housekeepers were trying to renege on the lease. Sure enough, after another week the team was stood down "pending policy decisions." It was never reassembled.

Next, word filtered out that Enderby and Martello jointly— the combination even then seemed odd—were chairing an Anglo-American processing committee. It would meet alternately in Washington and London and have responsibility for simultaneous distribution of the Dolphin product, code-name Whitebait, on either side of the Atlantic.

Quite incidentally it emerged that Nelson was somewhere in the United States, in an armed compound already prepared for him in Philadelphia. The explanation was even slower in coming. It was *felt*—presumably *by* somebody, but feelings are hard to trace among so many corridors—that Nelson would be safer there. Physically safer. Think of the Russians. Think of the Chinese. Also, the housekeepers insisted, the Cousins' processing and evaluation units were more of a scale to handle the unprecedented take that was expected. Also, they said, the Cousins could afford the cost. *Also*—

"Also gammon and spinach!" Connie stormed when she heard the news.

She and di Salis waited moodily to be invited to join the Cousins' team. Connie even got herself the injections to be ready, but no call came.

More explanations. The Cousins had a new man at Harvard, the housekeepers said, when Connie sailed in on them in her wheelchair.

"Who?" she demanded in a fury.

A professor somebody, young, a Moscow-gazer. He had made a *life specialty* of the dark side of Moscow Centre, they said, and had recently published a paper for private distribution only, but based on Company archives, in which he had referred to the "mole principle" and even in veiled terms to Karla's private army.

"Of course he did, the maggot!" she blurted at them, through her bitter tears of frustration. "And he hogged it all from Connie's blasted reports, didn't he? Culpepper, that's his name, and he knows as much about Karla as my left toe!"

The housekeepers were unmoved however by thoughts of Connie's toe. It was Culpepper, not Sachs, who had the new committee's vote.

"Wait till George gets back!" Connie warned them. The threat left them strangely unaffected.

Di Salis fared no better. China-watchers were two a penny in Langley, he was told. A glut on the market, old boy. Sorry, but Enderby's orders, said the housekeepers.

"*Enderby's?*" di Salis echoed.

The committee's, they said vaguely. It was a joint decision.

So di Salis took his cause to Lacon, who liked to think of himself as a poor man's ombudsman in such matters, and Lacon in turn took di Salis to luncheon, at which they split the bill down the middle because Lacon did not hold with civil servants treating one another at the taxpayers' expense.

"How do you all *feel* about Enderby, by the by?" he asked at some point in the meal, interrupting di Salis's plaintive monologue about his familiarity with the Chiu Chow and Hakka dialects. *Feeling* was playing a large part just at the moment. "Does he go down well over there? I'd have thought you liked his way of seeing things. Isn't he rather sound, wouldn't you say?"

"Sound" in the Whitehall vocabulary in those days meant hawkish.

Rushing back to the Circus, di Salis duly reported this amazing question to Connie Sachs—as Lacon of course wished him to—and Connie was thereafter seen little. She spent her time quietly "packing her trunk," as she called it: that is to say, preparing her Moscow Centre archive for posterity. There was a new young burrower she favoured, a goatish but obliging youth called Doolittle. She made this Doolittle sit at her feet while she gave him of her wisdom.

"The old order's hoofing it," she warned whoever would listen. "That twerp Enderby is oiling through the back door. It's a pogrom."

They treated her at first with much the same derision that Noah had to put up with when he started building his ark. No slouch at tradecraft still, Connie meanwhile secretly took

Molly Meakin aside and persuaded her to put in a letter of resignation. "Tell the housekeepers you're looking for something more fulfilling, dear," she advised, with much winking and pinching. "They'll give you a rise at the very least."

Molly had fears of being taken at her word, but Connie knew the game too well. So she wrote her letter and was at once ordered to stay behind after hours. Certain changes were in the air, the housekeepers told her in great confidence. There was a move to create a younger and more vigorous service, with closer links to Whitehall. Molly solemnly promised to reconsider her decision, and Connie Sachs resumed her packing with fresh determination.

Then where *was* George Smiley all this while? In the Far East? No, in Washington! Nonsense! He was back home and skulking down in the country somewhere—Cornwall was his favourite—taking a well-earned rest and mending his fences with Ann!

Then one of the housekeepers let slip that George might be "suffering from a spot of strain," and his phrase struck a chill everywhere, for even the dimmest little gnome in Banking Section knew that strain, like old age, was a disease for which there was only one known remedy, and it did not entail recovery.

Guillam came back eventually, but only to sweep Molly off on leave, and he refused to say anything at all. Those who saw him on his swift passage through the fifth floor said he looked shot-about, and obviously in need of a break. Also he seemed to have had an accident to his collar-bone; his right shoulder was all strapped up. From the housekeepers it became known that he had spent a couple of days in the care of the Circus leech at his private clinic in Manchester Square. But still there was no Smiley, and the housekeepers showed only a steely bonhomie when asked when he would return. The housekeepers in these cases become the Star Chamber, feared but needed. Unobtrusively Karla's portrait disappeared, the wits said for cleaning.

What was odd, and in a way rather terrible, was that none of them thought to drop in on the little house in Bywater Street and simply ring the doorbell. If they had done so they would have found Smiley there, most likely in his dressing-gown, either clearing up plates or preparing food he didn't eat. Sometimes, usually at dusk, he took himself for a solitary walk in the park and peered at people as if he half recognised them, so that they peered in return, and then looked down. Or he would go and sit himself in one of the cheaper cafés in the King's Road, taking a book for company and sweet tea for refreshment—for he had abandoned his good intentions about saccharin for his waistline. They would have noticed that he spent a deal of time looking at his hands, and polishing his spectacles on his tie, or re-reading the letter Ann had left for him, which was very long, but only because of repetitions.

Lacon called on him and so did Enderby, and once Martello came along with them, dressed in his London character again; for everyone agreed, and none with greater sincerity than Smiley, that in the interest of the service the hand-over should be as smooth and painless as possible. Smiley made certain requests regarding staff and these were carefully noted by Lacon, who let him understand that toward the Circus—if toward no one else—Treasury was at present in a spending mood. In the secret world at least, sterling was on the up. It was not merely the success of the Dolphin affair which accounted for this change of heart, Lacon said. The American enthusiasm for Enderby's appointment had been overwhelming. It had been felt even at the highest diplomatic levels. "Spontaneous applause" was how Lacon described it.

"Saul really knows how to talk to them," he said.

"Oh, does he. Ah, good. Well, good," Smiley said and bucked his head in approval, as the deaf do.

Even when Enderby confided to Smiley that he proposed to appoint Sam Collins as his head of operations, Smiley showed nothing but courtesy toward the suggestion. Sam was a hustler,

Enderby explained, and hustlers were what Langley liked these days.

"Ah, yes. No doubt," said Smiley.

The two men agreed that Roddy Martindale, though he had bags of entertainment value, was *not* cut out for the game. Old Roddy really was *too* queer, said Enderby, and the Minister was scared stiff of him. Nor did he exactly go down swimmingly with the Americans, even the ones that happened to be that way themselves. Also, Enderby was a bit chary of taking in any more Etonians. Gave the wrong impression.

A week later the housekeepers reopened Sam's old room on the fifth floor and removed the furniture. Collins's ghost laid for good, said certain unwise voices with relish. Then on the Monday an ornate desk arrived, with a red leather top, and several fake hunting prints from the walls of Sam's club, which was in the process of being taken over by one of the larger gambling syndicates, to the satisfaction of all parties.

Little Fawn was not seen again. Not even when several of the more muscular London outstations were revived, including the Brixton scalp-hunters, to whom he had formerly belonged, and the Acton lamplighters under Toby Esterhase. But he was not missed either. Like Sam Collins somehow, he had stalked the story without ever quite belonging to it; but unlike Sam, he stayed in the thickets when it ended, and never reappeared.

To Sam Collins, on his first day back in harness, fell the task of breaking the sad news of Jerry's death. He did it in the rumpus room, just a small, unaffected speech, and everyone agreed he did it well. They had not thought he had it in him.

"For fifth-floor ears only," he told them. His audience was stunned, then proud. Connie wept and tried to claim Jerry as another of Karla's victims, but she was held back in this for want of information about who or what had killed him. It was operational, went the word, and it was noble.

* * *

Back in Hong Kong, the Foreign Correspondents' Club showed much initial concern for its missing children Luke and Westerby. Thanks to heavy lobbying by its members, a full-scale confidential enquiry was set up, under the chairmanship of the vigilant Superintendent Rockhurst, to solve the double riddle of their disappearance. The authorities promised full publication of all findings, and the United States Consul General offered five thousand dollars of his own money to anyone coming forward with helpful information. As a gesture to local feeling he included Jerry Westerby's name in the offer.

The two became known as "the missing newsmen," and suggestions of a disgraceful attachment between them were rampant. Luke's bureau matched the five-thousand-dollar figure, and the dwarf, though he was inconsolable, entered a strong bid to have the moneys paid to him. It was he, after all, working on both fronts at once, who had learned from Deathwish that the Cloudview Road apartment, which Luke had last used, had been redecorated from floor to ceiling before the Rocker's sharp-eyed investigators got round to visiting it. Who ordered this? Who paid? Nobody knew. It was the dwarf also who collected first-hand reports that Jerry had been seen at Kai Tak airport interviewing Japanese package tourists. But the Rocker's committee of enquiry was obliged to reject these reports. The Japanese concerned were "willing but unreliable witnesses," they said, when it came to identifying a round-eye who sprang at them after a long journey.

As to Luke—well, the way he had been going, they said, he was heading for some kind of breakdown anyway. The knowing spoke of amnesia brought on by alcohol and fast living. After a while even the best stories grow cold. Rumours went out that the two men had been seen hunting together during the Hué collapse—or was it Danang?—and drinking together in Saigon. Another had them sitting side by side on the waterfront at Manila.

"Holding hands?" the dwarf asked.

"Worse" was the reply.

The Rocker's name was also in wide circulation, thanks to his success in a recent spectacular narcotics trial mounted with the help of the American Drug Enforcement Administration. Several Chinese and a glamorous English adventuress, a heroin carrier, were featured, and though as usual the Mr. Big was never brought to justice, it was said the Rocker came within an ace of nailing him. "Our tough but honest trouble-shooter," wrote the *South China Morning Post* in an editorial praising his astuteness. "Hong Kong could do with more like him."

For other distractions the Club could turn to the dramatic reopening of High Haven behind a twenty-foot floodlit wire perimeter patrolled by guard dogs. But there were no free lunches any more and the joke soon faded.

As to old Craw, for months he was not seen and not spoken of. Till one night he appeared, looking much aged and soberly dressed, and sat in his former corner gazing into space. A few were still left who recognised him. The Canadian cowboy suggested a rubber of Shanghai bowling, but he declined. Then a strange thing happened. An argument broke out concerning a silly point of Club protocol. Nothing serious at all: whether some item of tradition about signing chits was still useful to the Club's running. As trifling as that. But for some reason it made the old fellow absolutely furious. Rising to his feet, he stomped toward the lifts, tears pouring down his face, while he hurled one insult after another at them.

"Don't change anything," he advised them, shaking his stick in fury. "The old order changeth *not*, let it all run on. You won't stop the wheel—not together, not divided—you snivelling, arse-licking novices! You're a bunch of suicidal tits to try!"

Past it, they agreed, as the doors closed on him. Poor fellow. Embarrassing.

* * *

Was there really a conspiracy against Smiley, of the scale that Guillam supposed? If so, how was it affected by Westerby's own maverick intervention? No information is available and even those who trust each other well are not disposed to discuss the question. Certainly there was a secret understanding between Enderby and Martello, that the Cousins should have first bite of Nelson—as well as joint credit for procuring him—against their championship of Enderby for chief. Certainly Lacon and Collins, in their vastly different spheres, were party to it. But at what point they proposed to seize Nelson for themselves and by what means—for instance, the more conventional recourse of a concerted *démarche* at ministerial level in London—will probably never be known. But there can be no doubt, as it turned out, that Westerby was a blessing in disguise. He gave them the excuse they were looking for.

And did Smiley *know* of the conspiracy, deep down? Was he aware of it, and did he secretly even welcome the solution? Peter Guillam, who has since had two good years in exile in Brixton to consider his opinion, insists that the answer to both questions is a firm *yes*. There is a letter George wrote to Ann Smiley—he says—in the heat of the crisis, presumably in one of the long waiting periods in the isolation ward. Guillam leans heavily on it for his theory. Ann showed it to him when he called on her in Wiltshire, in the hope of bringing about a reconciliation, and though the mission failed, she produced it from her handbag in the course of their talk. Guillam memorised a part, he claims, and wrote it down as soon as he got back to the car. Certainly the style flies a lot higher than anything Guillam would aspire to for himself:

I honestly do wonder, without wishing to be morbid, how I reached this present pass. So far as I can ever remember of my youth, I chose the secret road because it seemed to lead

straightest and furthest toward my country's goal. The enemy
in those days was someone we could point at and read about
in the papers. Today, all I know is that I have learned to interpret the whole of life in terms of conspiracy. That is the sword
I have lived by, and as I look round me now I see it is the
sword I shall die by as well. These people terrify me, but I am
one of them. If they stab me in the back, then at least that is
the judgment of my peers.

As Guillam points out, the letter was essentially from Smiley's blue period.

These days, he says, the old boy is much more himself.
Occasionally he and Ann have lunches, and Guillam personally is convinced that they will simply get together one day and
that will be that. But George never mentions Westerby. And
nor does Guillam, for George's sake.

PENGUIN BOOKS

TINKER, TAILOR, SOLDIER, SPY

JOHN LE CARRÉ was born in 1931. For six decades, he wrote novels that came to define our age. The son of a con man, he spent his childhood between boarding school and the London underworld. At sixteen he found refuge at the university of Bern, then later at Oxford. A spell of teaching at Eton led him to a short career in British Intelligence (MI5&6). He published his debut novel, *Call for the Dead*, in 1961 while still a secret servant. His third novel, *The Spy Who Came in from the Cold*, secured him a worldwide reputation, which was consolidated by the acclaim for his trilogy *Tinker Tailor Soldier Spy*, *The Honourable Schoolboy*, and *Smiley's People*. At the end of the Cold War, le Carré widened his scope to explore an international landscape including the arms trade and the War on Terror. His memoir, *The Pigeon Tunnel*, was published in 2016 and the last George Smiley novel, *A Legacy of Spies*, appeared in 2017. He died on December 12, 2020.

BY JOHN LE CARRÉ

Call for the Dead
A Murder of Quality
The Spy Who Came in from the Cold
The Looking Glass War
A Small Town in Germany
The Naïve and Sentimental Lover
Tinker, Tailor, Soldier, Spy
The Honourable Schoolboy
The Little Drummer Girl
A Perfect Spy
The Russia House
The Secret Pilgrim
The Night Manager
Our Game
The Tailor of Panama
Single & Single
The Constant Gardener
Absolute Friends
The Mission Song
A Most Wanted Man
Our Kind of Traitor
A Delicate Truth
The Pigeon Tunnel
A Legacy of Spies
Agent Running in the Field
Silverview

JOHN LE CARRÉ

TINKER, TAILOR, SOLDIER, SPY

PENGUIN BOOKS

PENGUIN BOOKS
An imprint of Penguin Random House LLC
penguinrandomhouse.com

First published in the United States of America by Alfred A. Knopf 1974
Published in Penguin Books 2011

Grateful acknowledgment is made to The Clarendon Press for permission to reprint the
eight-line rhyme and descriptive paragraph from page 404 of the *Oxford Dictionary of Nursery
Rhymes*, edited by Iona and Peter Opie (1951).

ISBN 9780143119784 (paperback)
CIP data available

Printed in the United States of America
27th Printing
Set in Janson Text

For James Bennett
and Dusty Rhodes,
in memory

TINKER,
TAILOR,
SOLDIER,
SAILOR,
RICH MAN,
POOR MAN,
BEGGARMAN,
THIEF.

Small children's fortune-telling rhyme used when counting cherry stones, waistcoat buttons, daisy petals, or the seeds of the Timothy grass.

—from the *Oxford Dictionary of Nursery Rhymes*

INTRODUCTION

JOHN LE CARRÉ

July 1991

I have always wanted to set a novel in Cornwall, and to this day *Tinker Tailor* is as near as I ever came to doing so. The unfinished version that had lain in my desk drawer for years before I started writing the story in earnest did not contain George Smiley at all, but opened instead with a solitary and embittered man living alone on a Cornish cliff, staring up at a single black car as it wove down the hillside towards him. I had chosen in my imagination a spot not unlike the little harbour of Porthgwarra in West Cornwall, where the cottages lie low on the sea's edge, and the hills behind seem to be pressing them into the sea. My man was holding a bucket in his hand, on his way to feeding his chickens. He had a limp, as Jim Prideaux has a limp in the version you are about to read, and like Jim he was a former British agent who had walked into a trap set for him by a traitor inside his own service, called "The Circus."

My original plan was for the Circus investigators to put this figure back into harness, in a way that would provoke the unknown traitor to try his hand again, and thus reveal himself. I wanted the entire story to play in contemporary time and not in the flashbacks I later resorted to. But when I got down to writing the book for real, I discovered that I was painting myself into a corner. I could think of no plausible way to pursue a linear path forward while at the same time peering back down the path that had brought my man to the point where the story began. So one day, after months of frustration, I took the whole manuscript into the garden and burned it, and began again.

I had also saddled myself with another headache. I was determined to describe something that in those days was still new to my readers and perhaps, despite all the press revelations about the penetration of our secret services, still is even now: namely, the inside-out logic of a double-agent operation, and the sheer scale of the mayhem that can be visited on an enemy service when its intelligence-gathering efforts fall under the control of its opponent.

Oh, we knew vaguely that Kim Philby had once been head of the counter-intelligence section of the British secret service and privy to American efforts to penetrate the KGB. We knew that at one time he was in line to become chief of the entire British service. Perhaps we even knew that he had personally advised the CIA's foremost Moscow Centre watcher, James Jesus Angleton, on double-agent cases, in which Philby was held to possess exceptional expertise. We had read perhaps that George Blake, another KGB traitor inside SIS, had betrayed a number of British agents to his Soviet masters—he now claims hundreds, and who is to deny the wretched man his boast? His cause, like his victims, is dead. But what very few people managed to understand was the pushme-pullyou nature of the double-agent's trade.

For while on one side the secret traitor will be doing his damnedest to frustrate the efforts of his own service, on the other he will be building himself a successful career in it, providing it with the coups and grace-notes that it needs to justify its existence, and generally passing himself off as a capable and trustworthy fellow, a good man on a dark night. The art of the game—best described in J. C. Masterman's account of the British double-cross system operated against Germany in wartime—is therefore a balancing act between what is good for the double agent in his role as loyal member of his service, and what is good for your own side in its unrelenting efforts to pervert that service to the point where it is doing more harm to the country that employs it than good; or, as Smiley has it, where it has been pulled inside out.

Such an abject state of affairs was certainly reached by SIS in the high days of Blake and Philby, just as it was self-inflicted on the CIA by the paranoid influence of Angleton himself, who, in the aftermath of discovering that he had been eating out of the hand of the KGB's most successful double agent, spent the rest of his life trying to prove that the Agency, like SIS, was being controlled by Moscow; and that its occasional successes were consequently no more than sweeteners tossed to it by the fiendish manipulators of the KGB. Angleton was wrong, but his effect on the CIA was as disastrous as if he had been right. Both services would have done much less damage to their countries, moral and financial, if they had simply been disbanded.

I never knew either Blake or Philby, but I always had a quite particular dislike for Philby, and an unnatural sympathy for Blake. The reasons, I fear, have much to do with the inverted snobbery of my class and generation. I disliked Philby because he had so many of my attributes. He was public-school educated, the son of a wayward and dictatorial father—the explorer and adventurer, St. John Philby—he drew people easily to him and he was adept at hiding his feelings, in particular, his seething distaste for the bigotries and prejudices of the English ruling classes. I'm afraid that all of these characteristics have at one time or another been mine. I felt I understood him too well, and in some odd way he seems to have sensed this, for in his last interview before he died he told his interviewer, Phil Knightley, that he had the feeling I knew something discreditable about him. And in a way, he was right: I knew what it was like, as he did, to be brought up by a man so oversized that your only resort as his child was to subterfuge and deceit. And I knew, or thought I knew, how easily the anger and inwardness thus born could turn themselves into a love-hate relationship with the father images of society, and finally with society itself, so that the childish avenger becomes the adult predator, a thing I touched upon in my most autobiographical novel, *A Perfect Spy*. I knew, if you like, that Philby had taken a road that was dangerously open to myself, though I had resisted it. I knew that he represented one of the—thank God, unrealised—possibilities of my nature.

I warmed to Blake, on the other hand, because he was half a Dutchman and half a Jew, and in both capacities a most unlikely recruit to the secret ranks of the British Establishment. Where Philby had been born inside the fortress and spent his life borrowing beneath its ramparts, Blake had been born in the wastes of foreign and ethnic disadvantage, and had gone to great lengths to gain acceptance by those who secretly despised him: his employers. So that when I started putting together my little bestiary of suspects, I made sure that there were at least two of them—Bland and Esterhase and perhaps Jim Prideaux also—who were alienated by birth from the class structure that they served.

So much for the documentary background. The rest is an informed fantasy. The origin of my use of the word "mole" to describe a long-term penetration agent is a small mystery to me, as it was to the editors of the Oxford English Dictionary, who wrote to me asking whether I had invented it. I could not say for certain. I had a memory that it was current KGB jargon in the days when I was briefly an intelligence officer. I even thought I had seen it written down, in an annexe to the Royal Commission report on the Petrovs, who defected to the Australians in Canberra some time in the Fifties. But the OED couldn't find the trace and neither could I, so for a long time, I thought perhaps I had. Then one day, I received a letter from a reader, referring me to page 240 of Francis Bacon's *Historie of the Reigne of King Henry the Seventh*, published in 1641:

> As for his secret Spialls, which he did imploy both at home and abroad, by them to discover what Practices and Conspiracies were against him, surely his Case required it: Hee had such Moles perpetually working and casting to undermine him.

Well, I certainly hadn't read Francis Bacon on moles. Where did he have them from? Or was he just having fun with an apt metaphor?

The other bits of jargon—lamplighter, scalp-hunter, baby-sitter, honey trap and the rest—were all invented, but they too, I am told, have at least in part since been adopted by the professionals. I made no particular cult of them as I wrote: I wished merely to underline the fact that spying for those who do it is a trade like any other, and that, like other trades, it has its little bits of language. The Russians were always more imaginative in this respect, living in daily contact with shoe-makers (forgers), neighbours (members of a sister service), pia-nists (radio operators) and the like. My clandestine vocabulary was therefore a small conceit, but when the BBC's television version reached the screen, it became for a while a national amusement, for which I was duly grateful.

How do I remember the book now, sixteen years on? Partly, I suppose, for the luck that followed it—the exposure of Blunt, the TV series, Alec Guinness triumphant as George Smiley, not to mention the marvellous direction and casting. And partly, because it restored my spirits after the miserable critical recep-tion given to its predecessor, *The Naive and Sentimental Lover.* But mostly I remember it for the little boy Bill Roach, who had his counterpart in my own days as a schoolmaster, and later in *A Perfect Spy* as poor Pym's son. Roach was not his name, of course, and he did not, so far as I know, spy on mem-bers of the staff. But I remember his watchfulness as if it had been my own, and I remember how deeply he got under my skin, perhaps because I could not help thinking of him as myself, when I was fifteen years younger.

And I remember Connie Sachs, too, my Circus researcher, an archetype for the last generation of secret service vestals— clever, unhappy ladies of the English upper classes, who, having joined the service in the war, stayed on to fight the peace, making a kind of granary of their extraordinary memories for us young turks to plunder.

It is odd, in these altered days, to discover that *Tinker Tailor* is already an historical novel, but I don't think that makes it irrelevant, and I hope you have as much pleasure with it as I do myself, when I dip into it.

TINKER, TAILOR, SOLDIER, SPY

PART I

1

The truth is, if old Major Dover hadn't dropped dead at Taunton races Jim would never have come to Thursgood's at all. He came in mid-term without an interview—late May, it was, though no one would have thought it from the weather—employed through one of the shiftier agencies specialising in supply teachers for prep schools, to hold down old Dover's teaching till someone suitable could be found. "A linguist," Thursgood told the common-room, "a temporary measure," and brushed away his forelock in self-defence. "Priddo." He gave the spelling, "P-r-i-d"—French was not Thursgood's subject so he consulted the slip of paper—"e-a-u-x, first name James. I think he'll do us very well till July." The staff had no difficulty in reading the signals. Jim Prideaux was a poor white of the teaching community. He belonged to the same sad bunch as the late Mrs. Loveday, who had a Persian-lamb coat and stood in for junior divinity until her cheques bounced, or the late Mr. Maltby, the pianist who had been called from choir practice to help the police with their enquiries, and as far as anyone knew was helping them to this day, for Maltby's trunk still lay in the cellar awaiting instructions. Several of the staff, but chiefly Marjoribanks, were in favour of opening that trunk. They said it contained notorious missing treasures: Aprahamian's silver-framed picture of his Lebanese mother, for instance; Best-Ingram's Swiss army penknife and Matron's

watch. But Thursgood set his creaseless face resolutely against
their entreaties. Only five years had passed since he had inherited the school from his father, but they had taught him already
that some things are best locked away.

Jim Prideaux arrived on a Friday in a rainstorm. The rain
rolled like gun-smoke down the brown combes of the Quantocks, then raced across the empty cricket fields into the sandstone of the crumbling façades. He arrived just after lunch,
driving an old red Alvis and towing a second-hand trailer that
had once been blue. Early afternoons at Thursgood's are tranquil, a brief truce in the running fight of each school day. The
boys are sent to rest in their dormitories, the staff sit in the
common-room over coffee reading newspapers or correcting
boys' work. Thursgood reads a novel to his mother. Of the
whole school, therefore, only little Bill Roach actually saw Jim
arrive, saw the steam belching from the Alvis's bonnet as it
wheezed its way down the pitted drive, windscreen wipers
going full pelt and the trailer shuddering through the puddles
in pursuit.

Roach was a new boy in those days and graded dull, if not
actually deficient. Thursgood's was his second prep school in
two terms. He was a fat round child with asthma, and he spent
large parts of his rest kneeling on the end of his bed, gazing
through the window. His mother lived grandly in Bath; his
father was agreed to be the richest in the school, a distinction
which cost the son dear. Coming from a broken home, Roach
was also a natural watcher. In Roach's observation Jim did not
stop at the school buildings but continued across the sweep to
the stable yard. He knew the layout of the place already. Roach
decided later that he must have made a reconnaissance or
studied maps. Even when he reached the yard, he didn't stop
but drove straight onto the wet grass, travelling at speed to
keep the momentum. Then over the hummock into the Dip,
head-first and out of sight. Roach half expected the trailer to
jackknife on the brink, Jim took it over so fast, but instead it

just lifted its tail and disappeared like a giant rabbit into its hole.

The Dip is a piece of Thursgood folklore. It lies in a patch of wasteland between the orchard, the fruit house, and the stable yard. To look at, it is no more than a depression in the ground, grass covered, with hummocks on the northern side, each about boy height and covered in tufted thickets which in summer grow spongy. It is these hummocks that give the Dip its special virtue as a playground and also its reputation, which varies with the fantasy of each new generation of boys. They are the traces of an open-cast silver mine, says one year, and digs enthusiastically for wealth. They are a Romano-British fort, says another, and stages battles with sticks and clay missiles. To others the Dip is a bomb-crater from the war and the hummocks are seated bodies buried in the blast. The truth is more prosaic. Six years ago, and not long before his abrupt elopement with a receptionist from the Castle Hotel, Thursgood's father had launched an appeal for a swimming pool and persuaded the boys to dig a large hole with a deep and a shallow end. But the money that came in was never quite enough to finance the ambition, so it was frittered away on other schemes, such as a new projector for the art school, and a plan to grow mushrooms in the school cellars. And even, said the cruel ones, to feather a nest for certain illicit lovers when they eventually took flight to Germany, the lady's native home.

Jim was unaware of these associations. The fact remains that by sheer luck he had chosen the one corner of Thursgood's academy which, as far as Roach was concerned, was endowed with supernatural properties.

Roach waited at the window but saw nothing more. Both the Alvis and the trailer were in dead ground, and if it hadn't been for the wet red tracks across the grass he might have wondered whether he had dreamed the whole thing. But the tracks were real, so when the bell went for the end of rest he put on his rubber boots and trudged through the rain to the top of the Dip and peered down, and there was Jim dressed in an army raincoat and a quite extraordinary hat, broadbrimmed like a safari hat but hairy, with one side pinned up in a rakish piratical curl and the water running off it like a gutter.

The Alvis was in the stable yard; Roach never knew how Jim spirited it out of the Dip, but the trailer was right down there, at what should have been the deep end, bedded on platforms of weathered brick, and Jim was sitting on the step drinking from a green plastic beaker, and rubbing his right shoulder as if he had banged it on something, while the rain poured off his hat. Then the hat lifted and Roach found himself staring at an extremely fierce red face, made still fiercer by the shadow of the brim and by a brown moustache washed into fangs by the rain. The rest of the face was criss-crossed with jagged cracks, so deep and crooked that Roach concluded in another of his flashes of imaginative genius that Jim had once been very hungry in a tropical place and filled up again since. The left arm still lay across his chest, the right shoulder was still drawn high against his neck. But the whole tangled shape of him was stock-still, he was like an animal frozen against its background: a stag, thought Roach, on a hopeful impulse; something noble.

"Who the hell are you?" asked a very military voice.

"Sir, Roach, sir. I'm a new boy."

For a moment longer, the brick face surveyed Roach from the shadow of the hat. Then, to his intense relief, its features relaxed into a wolfish grin, the left hand, still clapped over the right shoulder, resumed its slow massage while at the same time he managed a long pull from the plastic beaker.

"New boy, eh?" Jim repeated into the beaker, still grinning. "Well, that's a lucky break, I will say."

Rising now, and turning his crooked back on Roach, Jim set to work on what appeared to be a detailed study of the trailer's four legs, a very critical study that involved much rocking of the suspension, and much tilting of the strangely garbed head, and the emplacement of several bricks at different angles and points. Meanwhile the spring rain was clattering down on everything: his coat, his hat, and the roof of the old trailer. And Roach noticed that throughout these manoeuvres Jim's right shoulder had not budged at all but stayed wedged high against his neck like a rock under the mackintosh. Therefore he wondered whether Jim was a sort of giant hunchback and whether all hunch backs hurt as Jim's did. And he noticed as a generality, a thing to store away, that people with bad backs take long strides; it was something to do with balance.

"New boy, eh? Well, *I'm* not a new boy," Jim went on, in altogether a much more friendly tone, as he pulled at a leg of the trailer. "I'm an old boy. Old as Rip van Winkle, if you want to know. Older. Got any friends?"

"No, sir," said Roach simply, in the listless tone that school-boys always use for saying "no," leaving all positive response to their interrogators. Jim, however, made no response at all, so that Roach felt an odd stirring of kinship suddenly, and of hope.

"My other name's Bill," he said. "I was christened Bill but Mr. Thursgood calls me William."

"Bill, eh. The unpaid Bill. Anyone ever call you that?"

"No, sir."

"Good name, anyway."

"Yes, sir."

"Known a lot of Bills. They've all been good'uns."

With that, in a manner of speaking, the introduction was made. Jim did not tell Roach to go away, so Roach stayed on the brow peering downward through his rain-smeared spec-tacles. The bricks, he noticed with awe, were pinched from the cucumber frame. Several had been loose already and Jim must have loosened them a bit more. It seemed a wonderful thing to Roach that anyone just arrived at Thursgood's should be so self-possessed as to pinch the actual fabric of the school for his own purposes, and doubly wonderful that Jim had run a lead off the hydrant for his water, for that hydrant was the subject of a special school rule: to touch it at all was a beatable offence.

"Hey, you, Bill. You wouldn't have such a thing as a marble on you, by any chance?"

"A, sir, what, sir?" Roach asked, patting his pockets in a dazed way.

"Marble, old boy. Round glass marble, little ball. Don't boys play marbles any more? We did when I was at school."

Roach had no marble, but Aprahamian had had a whole collection flown in from Beirut. It took Roach about fifty seconds to race back to the school, secure one against the wildest undertakings, and return panting to the Dip. There he hesitated, for in his mind the Dip was already Jim's and Roach required leave to descend it. But Jim had disappeared into the trailer, so, having waited a moment, Roach stepped gingerly down the bank and offered the marble through the doorway. Jim didn't spot him at once. He was sipping from the beaker and staring out the window at the black clouds as they tore this way and that over the Quantocks. This sipping movement, Roach noticed, was actually quite difficult, for Jim could not easily swallow standing up straight; he had to tilt his whole twisted trunk backward to achieve the angle. Meanwhile the rain came on really hard again, rattling against the trailer like gravel.

"Sir," said Roach, but Jim made no move.

"Trouble with an Alvis is, no damn springs," said Jim at last, more to the window than to his visitor. "You drive along with your rump on the white line, eh? Cripple anybody." And, tilting his trunk again, he drank.

"Yes, sir," said Roach, much surprised that Jim should assume he was a driver.

Jim had taken off his hat. His sandy hair was close-cropped; there were patches where someone had gone too low with the scissors. These patches were mainly on one side, so that Roach guessed that Jim had cut the hair himself with his good arm, which made him even more lopsided.

"I brought you a marble," said Roach.

"Very good of you. Thanks, old boy." Taking the marble, he slowly rolled it round his hard, powdery palm, and Roach knew at once that he was very skillful at all sorts of things; that he was the kind of man who lived on terms with tools and objects generally. "Not level, you see, Bill," he confided, still intent upon the marble. "Skewy. Like me. Watch," and turned purposefully to the larger window. A strip of aluminium beading ran along the bottom, put there to catch the condensation. Laying the marble in it, Jim watched it roll to the end and fall on the floor.

"Skewy," he repeated. "Listing in the stern. Can't have that, can we? Hey, hey, where d'you get to, you little brute?"

The trailer was not a homey place, Roach noticed, stooping to retrieve the marble. It might have belonged to anyone, though it was scrupulously clean. A bunk, a kitchen chair, a ship's stove, a calor gas cylinder. Not even a picture of his wife, thought Roach, who had not yet met a bachelor, with the exception of Mr. Thursgood. The only personal things he could find were a webbing kit-bag hanging from the door, a set of sewing things stored beside the bunk, and a homemade shower made from a perforated biscuit tin and neatly welded to the roof. And on the table one bottle of colourless drink, gin or vodka, because that was what his father drank when Roach went to his flat for weekends in the holidays.

"East-west looks okay, but north-south is undoubtedly skewy," Jim declared, testing the other window ledge. "What are you good at, Bill?"

"I don't know, sir," said Roach woodenly.

"Got to be good at something, surely; everyone is. How about football? Are you good at football, Bill?"

"No, sir," said Roach.

"Are you a grind, then?" Jim asked carelessly, as he lowered himself with a short grunt onto the bed and took a pull from the beaker. "You don't look a grind, I must say," he added politely. "Although you're a loner."

"I don't know," Roach repeated, and moved half a pace towards the open door.

"What's your best thing, then?" He took another long sip. "Must be good at something, Bill; everyone is. My best thing was ducks and drakes. Cheers."

Now this was an unfortunate question to ask of Roach just then, for it occupied most of his waking hours. Indeed he had recently come to doubt whether he had any purpose on earth at all. In work and play he considered himself seriously inadequate; even the daily routine of the school, such as making his bed and tidying his clothes, seemed to be beyond his reach. Also he lacked piety: old Mrs. Thursgood had told him so; he screwed up his face too much at chapel. He blamed himself very much for these shortcomings, but most of all he blamed himself for the break-up of his parents' marriage, which he should have seen coming and taken steps to prevent. He even wondered whether he was more directly responsible; whether, for instance, he was abnormally wicked or divisive or slothful, and that his bad character had wrought the rift. At his last school he had tried to explain this by screaming, and feigning fits of cerebral palsy, which his aunt had. His parents conferred, as they frequently did in their reasonable way, and changed his school. Therefore this chance question, levelled at him in the cramped trailer by a creature at least halfway to divinity—a fellow solitary, at that—brought him suddenly very near disaster. He felt the heat charging to his face; he watched his spectacles mist over and the trailer begin to dissolve into a sea of grief. Whether Jim noticed this, Roach never knew, for suddenly he had turned his crooked back on him, moved away to the table, and was helping himself from the plastic beaker while he threw out saving phrases.

"You're a good watcher, anyway, I'll tell you that for nothing, old boy. Us singles always are—no one to rely on, what? Nobody else spotted me. Gave me a real turn up there, parked on the horizon. Thought you were a juju man. Best watcher in the unit, Bill Roach is, I'll bet. Long as he's got his specs on. What?"

"Yes," Roach agreed gratefully, "I am."

"Well, you stay here and watch, then," Jim commanded, clapping the safari hat back on his head, "and I'll slip outside and trim the legs. Do that?"

"Yes, sir."

"Where's damn marble?"

"Here, sir."

"Call out when she moves, right? North, south, whichever way she rolls. Understand?"

"Yes, sir."

"Know which way's north?"

"That way," said Roach promptly, and struck out his arm at random.

"Right. Well, you call when she rolls," Jim repeated, and disappeared into the rain. A moment later, Roach felt the ground swaying under his feet and heard another roar either of pain or anger, as Jim wrestled with a recalcitrant leg.

In the course of that same summer term, the boys paid Jim the compliment of a nickname. They had several shots before they were happy. They tried "Trooper," which caught the bit of military in him, his occasional, quite harmless cursing, and his solitary rambles in the Quantocks. All the same, "Trooper" didn't stick, so they tried "Pirate" and for a while "Goulash." "Goulash" because of his taste for hot food, the smell of curries and onions and paprika that greeted them in warm puffs as they filed past the Dip on their way to evensong. "Goulash" for his perfect French, which was held to have a slushy quality. Spikely, of Five B, could imitate it to a hair: "You heard the question, Berger. What is Emile looking at?"—a convulsive jerk of the right hand—"Don't gawp at me, old boy, I'm not a juju man. *Qu'est-ce qu'il regarde, Emile dans le tableau que tu as sous le nez? Mon cher Berger,* if you do not very soon summon one lucid sentence of French, *je te mettrai tout de suite à la porte, tu comprends*, you beastly toad?"

But these terrible threats were never carried out, either in French or in English. In a quaint way, they actually added to the aura of gentleness which quickly surrounded him, a gentleness only possible in big men seen through the eyes of boys.

Yet "Goulash" did not satisfy them, either. It lacked the hint of strength contained. It took no account of Jim's passionate Englishness, which was the only subject where he could be relied on to waste time. Toad Spikely had only to venture one disparaging comment on the monarchy, extol the joys of some foreign country, preferably a hot one, for Jim to colour sharply and snap out a good three minutes' worth on the privilege of being born an Englishman. He knew they were teasing him but he was unable not to rise. Often he ended his homily with a rueful grin, and muttered references to red herrings, and red faces too, when certain people would have to come in for extra work and miss their football. But England was his love; when it came down to it, no one suffered for her.

"Best place in the whole damn world!" he bellowed once. "Know why? Know why, toad?"

Spikely did not, so Jim seized a crayon and drew a globe. To the west, America, he said, full of greedy fools fouling up their inheritance. To the east, China-Russia; he drew no distinction: boiler suits, prison camps, and a damn long march to nowhere. In the middle . . .

Finally they hit on "Rhino."

Partly this was a play on "Prideaux," partly a reference to his taste for living off the land and his appetite for physical exercise, which they noted constantly. Shivering in the shower queue first thing in the morning, they would see the Rhino pounding down Combe Lane with a rucksack on his crooked back as he returned from his morning march. Going to bed, they could glimpse his lonely shadow through the plastic roof of the fives court as the Rhino tirelessly attacked the concrete wall. And sometimes, on warm evenings, from their dormitory windows they would covertly watch him at golf, which he played with a dreadful old iron, zigzagging across the playing fields, often after reading to them from an extremely English adventure book: Biggles, Percy Westerman, or Jeffrey Farnol, grabbed haphazard from the dingy library. At each stroke they waited for the grunt as he started his backswing, and they were seldom disappointed. They kept a meticulous score. At the staff cricket match he made twenty-five before dismissing himself with a ball deliberately lofted to Spikely at square leg. "Catch, toad, catch it—go on. Well done, Spikely, good lad—that's what you're there for."

He was also credited, despite his taste for tolerance, with a sound understanding of the criminal mind. There were several examples of this, but the most telling occurred a few days before the end of term, when Spikely discovered in Jim's waste-basket a draft of the next day's examination paper, and rented it to candidates at five new pence a time. Several boys paid their shilling and spent an agonised night memorising answers by torchlight in their dormitories. But when the exam came round Jim presented a quite different paper.

"You can look at this one for nothing," he bellowed as he sat down. And, having hauled open his *Daily Telegraph*, he calmly gave himself over to the latest counsels of the juju men, which they understood to mean almost anyone with intellectual pretension, even if he wrote in the Queen's cause.

There was lastly the incident of the owl, which had a separate place in their opinion of him, since it involved death, a phenomenon to which children react variously. The weather continuing cold, Jim brought a bucket of coal to his classroom and one Wednesday lit it in the grate, and sat there with his back to the warmth, reading a *dictée*. First some soot fell, which he ignored; then the owl came down, a full-sized barn owl which had nested up there, no doubt, through many unswept winters and summers of Dover's rule, and was now smoked out, dazed and black from beating itself to exhaustion in the flue. It fell over the coals and collapsed in a heap on the wooden floorboard with a clatter and a scuffle, then lay like an emissary of the devil, hunched but breathing, wings stretched, staring straight out at the boys through the soot that caked its eyes. There was no one who was not frightened; even Spikely, a hero, was frightened. Except for Jim, who had in a second folded the beast together and taken it out the door without a word. They heard nothing, though they listened like stowaways, till the sound of running water from down the corridor as Jim evidently washed his hands. "He's having a pee," said Spikely, which earned a nervous laugh. But as they filed out of the classroom they discovered the owl still folded, neatly dead and awaiting burial, on top of the compost heap beside the Dip. Its neck, as the braver ones established, was snapped. Only a gamekeeper, declared Sudeley, who had one, would know how to kill an owl so well.

Among the rest of the Thursgood community, opinion regarding Jim was less unanimous. The ghost of Mr. Maltby, the pianist, died hard. Matron, siding with Bill Roach, pronounced him heroic and in need of care: it was a miracle he managed with that back. Marjoribanks said he had been run over by a bus when he was drunk. It was Marjoribanks also, at the staff match where Jim so excelled, who pointed out the sweater. Marjoribanks was not a cricketer but he had strolled down to watch with Thursgood.

"Do you think that sweater's kosher," he asked in a high, jokey voice, "or do you think he pinched it?"

"Leonard, that's very unfair," Thursgood scolded, hammering at the flanks of his Labrador. "Bite him, Ginny, bite the bad man."

By the time he reached his study, however, Thursgood's laughter had quite worn off and he became extremely nervous. Bogus Oxford men he could deal with, just as in his time he had known classics masters who had no Greek and parsons who had no divinity. Such men, confronted with proof of their deception, broke down and wept and left, or stayed on half-pay. But men who withheld genuine accomplishment—these were a breed he had not met but he knew already that he did not like them. Having consulted the university calendar, he telephoned the agency—a Mr. Stroll, of the house of Stroll & Medley.

"What precisely do you want to know?" Mr. Stroll asked with a dreadful sigh.

"Well, nothing *precisely*." Thursgood's mother was sewing at a sampler and seemed not to hear. "Merely that if one asks for a written *curriculum vitae* one likes it to be complete. One doesn't like gaps. Not if one pays one's fee."

At this point Thursgood found himself wondering rather wildly whether he had woken Mr. Stroll from a deep sleep to which he had now returned.

"Very patriotic bloke," Mr. Stroll observed finally.

"I did not employ him for his patriotism."

"He's been in dock," Mr. Stroll whispered on, as if through frightful draughts of cigarette smoke. "Laid up. Spinal."

"Quite so. But I assume he has not been in hospital for the whole of the last twenty-five years. *Touché*," he murmured to his mother, his hand over the mouthpiece, and once more it crossed his mind that Mr. Stroll had dropped off to sleep.

"You've only got him till the end of term," Mr. Stroll breathed. "If you don't fancy him, chuck him out. You asked for temporary, temporary's what you've got. You said cheap, you've got cheap."

"That's as may be," Thursgood retorted gamely. "But I've paid you a twenty-guinea fee; my father dealt with you for many years and I'm entitled to certain assurances. You've put here—may I read it to you?—you've put here: 'Before his injury, various overseas appointments of a commercial and prospecting nature.' Now that is hardly an enlightening description of a lifetime's employment, is it?"

At her sewing his mother nodded her agreement. "It is *not*," she echoed aloud.

"That's my first point. Let me go on a little."

"Not too much, darling," warned his mother.

"I happen to know he was up at Oxford in 1938. Why didn't he finish? What went wrong?"

"I seem to recall there was an interlude round about then," said Mr. Stroll after another age. "But I expect you're too young to remember it."

"He can't have been in prison *all* the time," said his mother after a very long silence, still without looking up from her sewing.

"He's been somewhere," said Thursgood morosely, staring across the windswept gardens towards the Dip.

All through the summer holidays, as he moved uncomfortably between one household and another, embracing and rejecting, Bill Roach fretted about Jim: whether his back was hurting; what he was doing for money now that he had no one to teach and only half a term's pay to live on; worst of all, whether he would be there when the new term began, for Bill had a feeling he could not describe that Jim lived so precariously on the world's surface that he might at any time fall off it into a void; he feared that Jim was like himself, without a natural gravity to hold him on. He rehearsed the circumstances of their first meeting, and in particular Jim's enquiry regarding friendship, and he had a holy terror that just as he had failed his parents in love, so he had failed Jim, largely owing to the disparity in their ages. And that therefore Jim had moved on and was already looking somewhere else for a companion, scanning other schools with his pale eyes. He imagined also that, like himself, Jim had had a great attachment that had failed him and that he longed to replace. But here Bill Roach's speculation met a dead end: he had no idea how adults loved each other.

There was so little he could do that was practical. He consulted a medical book and interrogated his mother about hunchbacks and he longed but did not dare to steal a bottle of his father's vodka and take it back to Thursgood's as a lure. And when at last his mother's chauffeur dropped him at the hated steps, he did not pause to say goodbye but ran for all he was worth to the top of the Dip, and there to his immeasurable joy was Jim's trailer in its same spot at the bottom, a shade dirtier than before, and a fresh patch of earth beside it, he supposed for winter vegetables. And Jim sitting on the step, grinning up at him as if he had heard Bill coming and got the grin of welcome ready before he appeared at the brink.

That same term, Jim invented a nickname for Roach. He dropped "Bill" and called him "Jumbo" instead. He gave no reason for this and Roach, as is common in the case of christenings, was in no position to object. In return, Roach appointed himself Jim's guardian; a regent-guardian was how he thought of the appointment; a stand-in replacing Jim's departed friend, whoever that friend might be.

2

Unlike Jim Prideaux, Mr. George Smiley was not naturally equipped for hurrying in the rain, least of all at dead of night. Indeed, he might have been the final form for which Bill Roach was the prototype. Small, podgy, and at best middle-aged, he was by appearance one of London's meek who do not inherit the earth. His legs were short, his gait anything but agile, his dress costly, ill-fitting, and extremely wet. His overcoat, which had a hint of widowhood about it, was of that black loose weave which is designed to retain moisture. Either the sleeves were too long or his arms were too short, for, as with Roach, when he wore his mackintosh, the cuffs all but concealed the fingers. For reasons of vanity he wore no hat, believing rightly that hats made him ridiculous. "Like an egg-cosy," his beautiful wife had remarked not long before the last occasion on which she left him, and her criticism, as so often, had endured. Therefore the rain had formed in fat, unbanishable drops on the thick lenses of his spectacles, forcing him alternately to lower or throw back his head as he scuttled along the pavement that skirted the blackened arcades of Victoria Station. He was proceeding west, to the sanctuary of Chelsea, where he lived. His step, for whatever reason, was a fraction uncertain, and if Jim Prideaux had risen out of the shadows demanding to know whether he had any friends, he would probably have answered that he preferred to settle for a taxi.

"Roddy's such a windbag," he muttered to himself as a fresh deluge dashed itself against his ample cheeks, then trickled downward to his sodden shirt. "Why didn't I just get up and leave?"

Ruefully, Smiley once more rehearsed the reasons for his present misery, and concluded with a dispassion inseparable from the humble part of his nature that they were of his own making.

It had been from the start a day of travail. He had risen too late after working too late the night before, a practice that had crept up on him since retirement last year. Discovering he had run out of coffee, he queued at the grocer's till he ran out of patience also, then haughtily decided to attend to his personal administration. His bank statement, which had arrived with the morning's post, revealed that his wife had drawn the lion's share of his monthly pension: very well, he decreed, he would sell something. The response was irrational, for he was quite decently off and the obscure City bank responsible for his pension paid it with regularity. Wrapping up an early edition of Grimmelshausen, nevertheless, a modest treasure from his Oxford days, he solemnly set off for Heywood Hill's bookshop in Curzon Street, where he occasionally contracted friendly bargains with the proprietor. On the way he became even more irritable, and from a call-box sought an appointment with his solicitor for that afternoon.

"George, how can you be so vulgar? Nobody divorces Ann. Send her flowers and come to lunch."

This advice bucked him up and he approached Heywood Hill with a merry heart only to walk slap into the arms of Roddy Martindale emerging from Trumper's after his weekly haircut.

Martindale had no valid claim on Smiley either professionally or socially. He worked on the fleshy side of the Foreign Office and his job consisted of lunching visiting dignitaries whom no one else would have entertained in his woodshed. He

was a floating bachelor with a grey mane and that nimbleness
which only fat men have. He affected buttonholes and pale
suits, and he pretended on the flimsiest grounds to an intimate
familiarity with the large back rooms of Whitehall. Some
years ago, before it was disbanded, he had adorned a Whitehall
working party to co-ordinate intelligence. In the war, having a
certain mathematical facility, he had also haunted the fringes
of the secret world; and once, as he never tired of telling, he
had worked with John Landsbury on a Circus coding operation of transient delicacy. But the war, as Smiley sometimes
had to remind himself, was thirty years ago.

"Hullo, Roddy," said Smiley. "Nice to see you."

Martindale spoke in a confiding upper-class bellow of the
sort that, on foreign holidays, had more than once caused
Smiley to sign out of his hotel and run for cover.

"My dear boy, if it isn't the maestro himself! They told me
you were locked up with the monks in Saint Gallen or somewhere, poring over manuscripts! Confess to me at once. I want
to know all you've been doing, every little bit. Are you well?
Do you love England still? How's the delicious Ann?" His
restless gaze flicked up and down the street before lighting on
the wrapped volume of Grimmelshausen under Smiley's arm.
"Pound to a penny that's a present for her. They tell me you
spoil her outrageously." His voice dropped to a mountainous
murmur: "I say, you're not back on the beat, are you? Don't tell
me it's all cover, George, *cover?*" His sharp tongue explored
the moist edges of his little mouth, then, like a snake, vanished
between its folds.

So, fool that he was, Smiley bought his escape by agreeing
to dine that same evening at a club in Manchester Square to
which they both belonged but which Smiley avoided like the
pest, not least because Roddy Martindale was a member. When
evening came, he was still full of luncheon at the White Tower,
where his solicitor, a very self-indulgent man, had decided that

only a great meal would recover George from his doldrums. Martindale, by a different route, had reached the same conclusion, and for four long hours over food Smiley did not want they had bandied names as if they were forgotten footballers. Jebedee, who was Smiley's old tutor: "*Such* a loss to us, bless him," murmured Martindale, who so far as Smiley knew had never clapped eyes on Jebedee. "And what a talent for the game, eh? One of the real greats, I always say." Then Fielding, the French mediaevalist from Cambridge: "Oh, but what a *lovely* sense of humour. Sharp mind, sharp!" Then Sparke from the School of Oriental Languages, and lastly Steed-Asprey, who had founded that very club in order to escape from bores like Roddy Martindale.

"I knew his poor brother, you know. Half the mind and twice the brawn, bless him. Brain went all the other way."

And Smiley through a fog of drink had listened to this nonsense, saying "yes" and "no" and "what a pity" and "no, they never found him," and once, to his abiding shame, "oh, come, you flatter me," till with lugubrious inevitability Martindale came to more recent things—the change of power and Smiley's withdrawal from the service.

Predictably, he started with the last days of Control: "Your old boss, George, bless him, the only one who ever kept his name a secret. Not from you, of course, he never had *any* secrets from you, George, did he? Close as thieves, Smiley and Control were, so they say, right to the end."

"They're very complimentary."

"Don't flirt, George; I'm an old trooper, you forget. You and Control were just like that." Briefly the plump hands made a token marriage. "That's why you were thrown out—don't deceive me, that's why Bill Haydon got your job. That's why he's Percy Alleline's cup-bearer and you're not."

"If you say so, Roddy."

"I do. I say more than that. *Far* more."

As Martindale drew closer, Smiley caught the odour of one of Trumper's most sensitive creations.

"I say something else: Control never died at all. He's been seen." With a fluttering gesture he silenced Smiley's protests. "Let me finish. Willy Andrewartha walked straight into him in Jo'burg airport, in the waiting-room. Not a ghost. Flesh. Willy was at the bar buying a soda for the heat; you haven't seen Willy recently but he's a balloon. He turned round, and there was Control beside him dressed up like a ghastly Boer. The moment he saw Willy he bolted. How's that? So now we know. Control never died at all. He was driven out by Percy Alleline and his three-piece band, so he went to ground in South Africa, bless him. Well, you can't blame him, can you? You can't blame a man for wanting a drop of peace in the evening of his life. I can't."

The monstrosity of this, reaching Smiley through a thickening wall of spiritual exhaustion, left him momentarily speechless.

"That's ridiculous! That's the most idiotic story I ever heard! Control is dead. He died of a heart attack after a long illness. Besides, he hated South Africa. He hated everywhere except Surrey, the Circus, and Lords Cricket Ground. Really, Roddy, you mustn't tell stories like that." He might have added: I buried him myself at a hateful crematorium in the East End, last Christmas Eve, alone. The parson had a speech impediment.

"Willy Andrewartha was always the most God-awful liar," Martindale reflected, quite unruffled. "I said the same to him myself: 'The sheerest nonsense, Willy; you should be ashamed of yourself.'" And straight on, as if never by thought or word had he subscribed to that silly view: "It was the Czech scandal that put the final nail into Control's coffin, I suppose. That poor fellow who was shot in the back and got himself into the newspapers, the one who was so thick with Bill Haydon always, so we hear. *Ellis*, we're to call him, and we still do, don't we, even if we know his real name as well as we know our own."

Shrewdly Martindale waited for Smiley to cap this, but Smiley had no intention of capping anything, so Martindale tried a third tack.

"Somehow I can never quite believe in Percy Alleline as Chief, can you? Is it age, George, or is it just my natural cynicism? Do tell me, you're so good at people. I suppose power sits poorly on those we've grown up with. Is that a clue? There are so few who can carry it off for me these days and poor Percy's such an *obvious* person, I always think, specially after that little serpent, Control. That heavy good fellowship—how can one take him seriously? One has only to think of him in the old days lolling in the bar of the Travellers', sucking away on that log pipe of his and buying drinks for the moguls; well, really, one does like one's perfidy to be subtle, don't you agree? Or don't you care as long as it's successful? What's his knack, George, what's his secret recipe?" He was speaking most intently, leaning forward, his eyes greedy and excited. Only food could otherwise move him so deeply. "Living off the wits of his subordinates—well, maybe that's leadership these days."

"Really, Roddy, I can't help you," said Smiley weakly. "I never knew Percy as a force, you see. Only as a—" He lost the word.

"A striver," Martindale suggested, eyes glistening. "With his sights on Control's purple, day and night. Now he's wearing it and the mob loves him. So who's his strong left arm, George? Who's earning him his reputation? Wonderfully well he's doing, we hear it from all sides. Little reading rooms at the Admiralty, little committees popping up with funny names, red carpet for Percy wherever he goes in the Whitehall corridors, junior ministers receiving special words of congratulation from on high, people one's never heard of getting grand medals for nothing. I've seen it all before, you know."

"Roddy, I can't help you," Smiley insisted, making to get up. "You're out of my depth, truly." But Martindale was physically restraining him, holding him at the table with one damp hand while he talked still faster.

"So who's the cleverboots? Not Percy, that's for sure. And don't tell me the Americans have started trusting us again, either." The grip tightened. "Dashing Bill Haydon, our latter-day Lawrence of Arabia, bless him; there you are—it's Bill, your old rival." Martindale's tongue poked out its head again, reconnoitred and withdrew, leaving a thin smile like a trail. "I'm told that you and Bill shared *everything* once upon a time," he said. "Still, he never was orthodox, was he? Genius never is."

"Anything further you require, Mr. Smiley?" the waiter asked.

"Then it's Bland: the shop-soiled white hope, the redbrick don." Still he would not release him. "And if those two aren't providing the speed, it's someone in retirement, isn't it? I mean someone pretending to be in retirement, don't I? And if Control's dead, who is there left? Apart from you."

They were putting on their coats. The porters had gone home; they had to fetch them for themselves from the empty brown racks.

"Roy Bland's not redbrick," Smiley said loudly. "He was at Saint Antony's College, Oxford, if you want to know."

Heaven help me, it was the best I could do, thought Smiley.

"Don't be silly, dear," Martindale snapped. Smiley had bored him: he looked sulky and cheated; distressing downward folds had formed on the lower contours of his cheeks. "Of course Saint Antony's is redbrick; it makes no difference there's a little bit of sandstone in the same street, even if he was your protégé. I expect he's Bill Haydon's now—don't tip him, it's my party, not yours. Father to them all, Bill is—always was. Draws them like bees. Well, he has the glamour, hasn't he; not like some of us. Star quality I call it, one of the few. I'm told the women literally bow down before him, if that's what women do."

"Good night, Roddy."

"Love to Ann, mind."

"I won't forget."

"Well, don't."

And now it was pouring with rain, Smiley was soaked to the skin, and God as a punishment had removed all taxis from the face of London.

3

"Sheer lack of will-power," he told himself as he courteously declined the suggestions of a lady in a doorway. "One calls it politeness, whereas in fact it is nothing but weakness. You *featherhead*, Martindale. You pompous, bogus, effeminate, nonproductive—" He stepped widely to avoid an unseen obstacle. "Weakness," he resumed, "and an inability to live a self-sufficient life independent of institutions"—a puddle emptied itself neatly into his shoe—"and emotional attachments that have long outlived their purpose. *Viz.*, my wife; *viz.*, the Circus; *viz.*, living in London. Taxi!"

Smiley lurched forward but was already too late. Two girls, giggling under one umbrella, clambered aboard in a flurry of arms and legs. Uselessly pulling up the collar of his black overcoat, he continued his solitary march. "Shop-soiled white hope," he muttered furiously. "Little bit of sandstone in the street. You bombastic, inquisitive, impertinent—"

And then, of course, he remembered far too late that he had left the Grimmelshausen at his club.

"Oh, damn!" he cried *sopra voce*, halting in his tracks for greater emphasis. "Oh, damn—oh, *damn*—oh, damn."

He would sell his London house: he had decided. Back there under the awning, crouching beside the cigarette machine, waiting for the cloudburst to end, he had taken this grave decision. Property values in London had risen out of proportion; he had heard it from every side. Good. He would sell and with a part of the proceeds buy a cottage in the Cotswolds. Burford? Too much traffic. Steeple Aston—that was a place. He would set up as a mild eccentric, discursive, withdrawn, but possessing one or two lovable habits such as muttering to himself as he bumbled along pavements. Out of date, perhaps, but who wasn't these days? Out of date, but loyal to his own time. At a certain moment, after all, every man chooses: will he go forward, will he go back? There was nothing dishonourable in not being blown about by every little modern wind. Better to have worth, to entrench, to be an oak of one's own generation. And if Ann wanted to return—well, he would show her the door.

Or not show her the door, according to—well, how much she wanted to return.

Consoled by these visions, Smiley arrived at the King's Road, where he paused on the pavement as if waiting to cross. To either side, festive boutiques. Before him, his own Bywater Street, a cul-de-sac exactly 117 of his own paces long. When he had first come to live here, these Georgian cottages had a modest, down-at-heel charm, with young couples making do on fifteen pounds a week and a tax-free lodger hidden in the basement. Now steel screens protected their lower windows, and for each house three cars jammed the curb. From long habit, Smiley passed these in review, checking which were familiar, which were not; of the unfamiliar, which had aerials and extra mirrors, which were the closed vans that watchers like. Partly he did this as a test of memory to preserve his mind from the atrophy of retirement, just as on other days he learnt the names of the shops along his bus route to the British Museum; just as he knew how many stairs there were to each flight of his own house and which way each of the twelve doors opened.

But Smiley had a second reason, which was fear, the secret fear that follows every professional to his grave. Namely, that one day, out of a past so complex that he himself could not remember all the enemies he might have made, one of them would find him and demand the reckoning.

At the bottom of the street, a neighbour was exercising her dog; seeing him, she lifted her head to say something, but he ignored her, knowing it would be about Ann. He crossed the road. His house was in darkness; the curtains were as he had left them. He climbed the six steps to the front door. Since Ann's departure, his cleaning woman had also left: no one but Ann had a key. There were two locks, a Banham deadlock and a Chubb Pipekey, and two splinters of his own manufacture, splits of oak each the size of a thumbnail, wedged into the lintel above and below the Banham. They were a hangover from his days in the field. Recently, without quite knowing why, he had started using them again; perhaps he didn't want her to take him by surprise. With the tips of his fingers he discovered each in turn. The routine over, he unlocked the door, pushed it open, and felt the midday mail slithering over the carpet.

What was due? he wondered. *German Life and Letters? Philology? Philology*, he decided; it was already overdue. Putting on the hall light, he stooped and peered through his post. One "account rendered" from his tailor for a suit he had not ordered but that he suspected was one of those presently adorning Ann's lover; one bill from a garage in Henley for her petrol (what, pray, were they doing in Henley, broke, on the ninth of October?); one letter from the bank regarding a local cashing facility in favour of the Lady Ann Smiley at a branch of the Midland Bank in Immingham.

And what the devil, he demanded of this document, are they doing in Immingham? Who ever had a love affair in Immingham, for goodness' sake? Where *was* Immingham?

He was still pondering the question when his gaze fell upon an unfamiliar umbrella in the stand, a silk one with a stitched leather handle and a gold ring with no initial. And it passed through his mind with a speed which has no place in time that since the umbrella was dry it must have arrived there before six-fifteen when the rain began, for there was no moisture in the stand either. Also that it was an elegant umbrella and the ferrule was barely scratched, though it was not new. And that therefore the umbrella belonged to someone agile—even young, like Ann's latest swain. But that since its owner had known about the wedges and known how to put them back once he was inside the house, and had the wit to lay the mail against the door after disturbing and no doubt reading it, then most likely he knew Smiley, too; and was not a lover but a professional like himself, who had at some time worked closely with him and knew his handwriting, as it is called in the jargon.

The drawing-room door was ajar. Softly he pushed it further open.

"Peter?" he said.

Through the gap he saw by the light of the street two suède shoes, lazily folded, protruding from one end of the sofa.

"I'd leave that coat on if I were you, George, old boy," said an amiable voice. "We've got a long way to go."

Five minutes later, dressed in a vast brown travelling coat, a gift from Ann and the only one he had that was dry, George Smiley was sitting crossly in the passenger seat of Peter Guillam's extremely draughty sports car, which he had parked in an adjoining square. Their destination was Ascot, a place famous for women and horses. And less famous, perhaps, as the residence of Mr. Oliver Lacon, of the Cabinet Office, a senior adviser to various mixed committees and a watchdog of intelligence affairs. Or, as Guillam had it less reverentially, Whitehall's head prefect.

While, at Thursgood's school, wakefully in bed, Bill Roach was contemplating the latest wonders that had befallen him in the course of his daily vigil over Jim's welfare. Yesterday Jim had amazed Latzy. Thursday he had stolen Miss Aaronson's mail. Miss Aaronson taught violin and scripture; Roach courted her for her tenderness. Latzy, the assistant gardener, was a D.P., said Matron, and D.P.s spoke no English, or very little. D.P. meant Different Person, said Matron, or anyway, foreign from the war. But yesterday Jim had spoken to Latzy, seeking his assistance with the car club, and he had spoken to him in D.P., or whatever D.P.s speak, and Latzy had grown a foot taller on the spot.

The matter of Miss Aaronson's mail was more complex. There were two envelopes on the staffroom sideboard Thursday morning after chapel when Roach called for his form's exercise books, one addressed to Jim and one to Miss Aaronson. Jim's was typewritten. Miss Aaronson's was handwritten, in a hand not unlike Jim's own. The staffroom, while Roach made these observations, was empty. He helped himself to the exercise books and was quietly taking his leave when Jim walked in by the other door, red and blowing from his early walk.

"On your way, Jumbo, bell's gone," stooping over the sideboard.

"Yes, sir."

"Foxy weather, eh, Jumbo?"

"Yes, sir."

"On your way, then."

At the door, Roach looked round. Jim was standing again, leaning back to open the morning's *Daily Telegraph*. The sideboard was empty. Both envelopes had gone.

Had Jim written to Miss Aaronson and changed his mind? Proposing marriage, perhaps? Another thought came to Bill Roach. Recently, Jim had acquired an old typewriter, a wrecked Remington that he had put right with his own hands. Had he typed his own letter on it? Was he so lonely that he wrote himself letters, and stole other people's as well? Roach fell asleep.

4

Guillam drove languidly but fast. Smells of autumn filled the car, a full moon was shining, strands of mist hung over open fields, and the cold was irresistible. Smiley wondered how old Guillam was and guessed forty, but in that light he could have been an undergraduate sculling on the river; he moved the gear lever with a long flowing movement as if he were passing it through water. In any case, Smiley reflected irritably, the car was far too young, for Guillam. They had raced through Runnymede and begun the run up Egham Hill. They had been driving for twenty minutes and Smiley had asked a dozen questions and received no answer worth a penny, and now a nagging fear was waking in him that he refused to name.

"I'm surprised they didn't throw you out with the rest of us," he said, not very pleasantly, as he hauled the skirts of his coat more tightly round him. "You had all the qualifications: good at your work, loyal, discreet."

"They put me in charge of scalp-hunters."

"Oh, my Lord," said Smiley with a shudder, and, pulling up his collar round his ample chins, he abandoned himself to that memory in place of others more disturbing: Brixton, and the grim flint schoolhouse that served the scalp-hunters as their headquarters. The scalp-hunters' official name was Travel. They had been formed by Control on Bill Haydon's suggestion in the pioneer days of the cold war, when murder and kidnapping and crash blackmail were common currency, and their first commandant was Haydon's nominee. They were a small outfit, about a dozen men, and they were there to handle the hit-and-run jobs that were too dirty or too risky for the residents abroad. Good intelligence work, Control had always preached, was gradual and rested on a kind of gentleness. The scalp-hunters were the exception to his own rule. They weren't gradual and they weren't gentle either, thus reflecting Haydon's temperament rather than Control's. And they worked solo, which was why they were stabled out of sight behind a flint wall with broken glass and barbed wire on the top.

"I asked whether 'lateralism' was a word to you."

"It most certainly is not."

"It's the 'in' doctrine. We used to go up and down. Now we go along."

"What's that supposed to mean?"

"In your day, the Circus ran itself by regions. Africa, satellites, Russia, China, South East Asia, you name it: each region was commanded by its own juju man; Control sat in heaven and held the strings. Remember?"

"It strikes a distant chord."

"Well, today everything operational is under one hat. It's called London Station. Regions are out, lateralism is in. Bill Haydon's Commander London Station, Roy Bland's his number two, Toby Esterhase runs between them like a poodle. They're a service within a service. They share their own secrets and don't mix with the proles. It makes us more secure."

"It sounds a very good idea," said Smiley, studiously ignoring the innuendo.

As the memories once more began seething upward into his conscious mind, an extraordinary feeling passed over him: that he was living the day twice, first with Martindale in the club, now again with Guillam in a dream. They passed a plantation of young pine trees. The moonlight lay in strips between them.

Smiley began, "Is there any word of—" Then he asked, in a more tentative tone, "What's the news of Ellis?"

"In quarantine," said Guillam tersely.

"Oh, I'm sure. Of course. I don't mean to pry. Merely, can he get around and so on? He did recover; he can walk? Backs can be terribly tricky, I understand."

"The word says he manages pretty well. How's Ann, I didn't ask."

"Fine. Just fine."

It was pitch dark inside the car. They had turned off the road and were passing over gravel. Black walls of foliage rose to either side, lights appeared, then a high porch, and the steepled outline of a rambling house lifted above the treetops. The rain had stopped, but as Smiley stepped into the fresh air he heard all round him the restless ticking of wet leaves.

Yes, he thought, it was raining when I came here before, when the name Jim Ellis was headline news.

They had washed and, in the lofty cloakroom, inspected Lacon's climbing kit mawkishly dumped on the Sheraton chest of drawers. Now they sat in a half-circle facing one empty chair. It was the ugliest house for miles around and Lacon had picked it up for a song. "A Berkshire Camelot," he had once called it, explaining it away to Smiley, "built by a teetotal millionaire." The drawing-room was a great hall with stained-glass windows twenty feet high and a pine gallery over the entrance. Smiley counted off the familiar things: an upright piano littered with musical scores, old portraits of clerics in gowns, a wad of printed invitations. He looked for the Cambridge University oar and found it slung over the fireplace. The same fire was burning, too mean for the enormous grate. An air of need prevailing over wealth.

"Are you enjoying retirement, George?" Lacon asked, as if blurting into the ear trumpet of a deaf aunt. "You don't miss the warmth of human contact? I rather would, I think. One's work, one's old buddies."

He was a string bean of a man, graceless and boyish: church and spy establishment, said Haydon, the Circus wit. His father was a dignitary of the Scottish church and his mother something noble. Occasionally the smarter Sundays wrote about him, calling him "new-style" because he was young. The skin of his face was clawed from hasty shaving.

"Oh, I think I manage very well, really, thank you," said Smiley politely. And to draw it out: "Yes. Yes, I'm sure I do. And you? All goes well with you?"

"No big changes, no. All very smooth. Charlotte got her scholarship to Roedean, which was nice."

"Oh, good."

"And your wife, she's in the pink and so on?"

His expressions were also boyish.

"Very bonny, thank you," said Smiley, trying gallantly to respond in kind.

They were watching the double doors. From far off they heard the jangle of footsteps on a ceramic floor. Smiley guessed two people, both men. The doors opened and a tall figure appeared half in silhouette. For the fraction of a moment, Smiley glimpsed a second man behind him, dark, small, and attentive; but only the one man stepped into the room before the doors were closed by unseen hands.

"Lock us in, please," Lacon called, and they heard the snap of the key. "You know Smiley, don't you?"

"Yes, I think I do," said the figure as he began the long walk towards them out of the far gloom. "I think he once gave me a job, didn't you, Mr. Smiley?"

His voice was as soft as a southerner's drawl, but there was no mistaking the colonial accent. "Tarr, sir. Ricki Tarr from Penang."

A fragment of firelight illuminated one side of the stark smile and made a hollow of one eye. "The lawyer's boy, remember? Come on, Mr. Smiley, you changed my first nappies."

And then, absurdly, they were all four standing, and Guillam and Lacon looked on like godparents while Tarr shook Smiley's hand once, then again, then once more for the photographs.

"How are you, Mr. Smiley? It's real nice to see you, sir."

Relinquishing Smiley's hand at last, he swung away in the direction of his appointed chair, while Smiley thought, Yes, with Ricki Tarr it could have happened. With Tarr, anything could have happened. My God, he thought; two hours ago I was telling myself I would take refuge in the past. He felt thirsty, and supposed it was fear.

Ten? Twelve years ago? It was not his night for understanding time. Among Smiley's jobs in those days was the vetting of recruits: no one taken on without his nod, no one trained without his signature on the schedule. The cold war was running high, scalp-hunters were in demand, the Circus's residencies abroad had been ordered by Haydon to look out for likely material. Steve Mackelvore from Djakarta came up with Tarr. Mackelvore was an old pro with cover as a shipping agent, and he had found Tarr angry drunk, kicking round the docks looking for a girl called Rose, who had walked out on him.

According to Tarr's story, he was mixed up with a bunch of Belgians running guns between the islands and up-coast. He disliked Belgians and he was bored with gunrunning and he was angry because they'd stolen Rose. Mackelvore reckoned he would respond to discipline and was young enough to train for the type of mailfist operation that the scalp-hunters undertook from behind the walls of their glum Brixton schoolhouse. After the usual searches, Tarr was forwarded to Singapore for a second look, then to the Nursery at Sarratt for a third. At that point Smiley came into the act as moderator at a succession of interviews, some hostile. Sarratt Nursery was the training compound, but it had space for other uses.

Tarr's father was an Australian solicitor living in Penang, it seemed. The mother was a small-time actress from Bradford who came East with a British drama group before the war. The father, Smiley recalled, had an evangelical streak and preached in local gospel halls. The mother had a small criminal record in England, but Tarr's father either didn't know or didn't care. When the war came, the couple evacuated to Singapore for the sake of their young son. A few months later, Singapore fell and Ricki Tarr began his education in Changi jail under Japanese supervision. In Changi the father preached God's charity to everyone in sight, and if the Japs hadn't persecuted him his fellow prisoners would have done the job for them. With Liberation, the three of them went back to Penang. Ricki tried to read for the law but more often broke it, and the father turned some rough preachers loose on him to beat the sin out of his soul. Tarr flew the coop to Borneo. At eighteen he was a fully paid-up gunrunner playing all seven ends against the middle around the Indonesian islands, and that was how Mackelvore stumbled on him.

By the time he had graduated from the Nursery, the Malayan emergency had broken. Tarr was played back into gunrunning. Almost the first people he bumped into were his old Belgian friends. They were too busy supplying guns to the Communists to bother where he had been, and they were shorthanded. Tarr ran a few shipments for them in order to blow their contacts, then one night got them drunk, shot four of them, including Rose, and set fire to their boat. He hung around Malaya and did a couple more jobs before being called back to Brixton and refitted for special operations in Kenya—or, in less sophisticated language, hunting Mau Mau for bounty.

After Kenya, Smiley pretty much lost sight of him, but a couple of incidents stuck in his memory because they might have become scandals and Control had to be informed. In

1964, Tarr was sent to Brazil to make a crash offer of a bribe to an armaments minister known to be in deep water. Tarr was too rough; the minister panicked and told the press. Tarr had Dutch cover and no one was wiser except Netherlands intelligence, who were furious. In Spain a year later, acting on a tip-off supplied by Bill Haydon, Tarr blackmailed—or burned, as the scalp-hunters would say—a Polish diplomat who had lost his heart to a dancer. The first yield was good; Tarr won a commendation and a bonus. But when he went back for a second helping the Pole wrote a confession to his ambassador and threw himself, with or without encouragement, from a high window.

In Brixton, they used to call him accident-prone. Guillam, by the expression on his immature but aging face, as they sat in their half-circle round the meagre fire, called him a lot worse than that.

"Well, I guess I'd better make my pitch," Tarr said pleasantly as he settled his easy body into the chair.

5

"It happened around six months ago," Tarr began.

"April," Guillam snapped. "Just keep it precise, shall we, all the way along?"

"April, then," Tarr said equably. "Things were pretty quiet in Brixton. I guess there must have been half a dozen of us on standby. Pete Sembrini, he was in from Rome; Cy Vanhofer had just made a hit in Budapest"—he gave a mischievous smile—"Ping-Pong and snooker in the Brixton waiting room. Right, Mr. Guillam?"

"It was the silly season."

When out of the blue, said Tarr, came a flash requisition from Hong Kong residency.

"They had a low-grade Soviet trade delegation in town, chasing up electrical goods for the Moscow market. One of the delegates was stepping wide in the nightclubs. Name of Boris; Mr. Guillam has the details. No previous record. They'd had the tabs on him for five days, and the delegation was booked in for fourteen more. Politically it was too hot for the local boys to handle but they reckoned a crash approach might do the trick. The yield didn't look that special, but so what? Maybe we'd just buy him for stock—right, Mr. Guillam?"

Stock meant sale or exchange with another intelligence service: a commerce in small-time defectors handled by the scalp-hunters.

Ignoring Tarr, Guillam said, "South East Asia was Tarr's parish. He was sitting around with nothing to do, so I ordered him to make a site inspection and report back by cable."

Each time someone else spoke, Tarr sank into a dream. His gaze settled upon the speaker, a mistiness entered his eyes, and there was a pause like a coming back before he began again.

"So I did what Mr. Guillam ordered," he said. "I always do, don't I, Mr. Guillam? I'm a good boy really, even if I am impulsive."

He flew the next night—Saturday, March 31st—with an Australian passport describing him as a car salesman and with two virgin Swiss escape passports hidden in the lining of his suitcase. These were contingency documents to be filled in as circumstances demanded: one for Boris, one for himself. He made a car rendezvous with the Hong Kong resident not far from his hotel, the Golden Gate on Kowloon.

Here Guillam leaned over to Smiley and murmured, "Tufty Thesinger, buffoon. Ex-major, King's African Rifles. Percy Alleline's appointment."

Thesinger produced a report on Boris's movements based on one week's surveillance.

"Boris was a real oddball," Tarr said. "I couldn't make him out. He'd been boozing every night without a break. He hadn't slept for a week and Thesinger's watchers were folding at the knees. All day he trailed round after the delegation, inspecting factories, chiming in at discussions, and being the bright young Soviet official."

"How young?" Smiley asked.

Guillam threw in: "His visa application gave him born Minsk 1946."

"Evening time, he'd go back to the Alexandra Lodge, an old shanty house out on North Point where the delegation had holed out. He'd eat with the crew; then around nine he'd ease out the side entrance, grab a taxi, and belt down to the main-line night spots around Pedder Street. His favourite haunt was

the Cat's Cradle in Queen's Road, where he bought drinks for
local businessmen and acted like Mr. Personality. He might
stay there till midnight. From the Cradle he cut right down to
Aberdeen Harbour, a place called Angelika's, where the drink
was cheaper. Alone. It's mainly floating restaurants and the big
spenders down there, but Angelika's is a landbound café with a
hellhole in the basement. He'd have three or four drinks and
keep the receipts. Mainly he drank brandy but now and then
he'd have a vodka to vary his diet. He'd had one tangle with a
Eurasian girl along the way, and Thesinger's watchers got after
her and bought the story. She said he was lonely and sat on the
bed moaning about his wife for not appreciating his genius.
That was a real breakthrough," he added sarcastically as Lacon
noisily swooped on the little fire and stirred it, one coal against
the other, into life. "That night I went down to the Cradle and
took a look at him. Thesinger's watchers had been sent to bed
with a glass of milk. They didn't want to know."

Sometimes as Tarr spoke, an extraordinary stillness came
over his body, as if he were hearing his own voice played back
to him.

"He arrived ten minutes after me and he brought his own
company, a big blond Swede with a Chinese broad in tow. It
was dark, so I moved into a table nearby. They ordered Scotch,
Boris paid, and I sat six feet away watching the lousy band and
listening to their conversation. The Chinese kid kept her
mouth shut and the Swede was doing most of the running.
They talked English. The Swede asked Boris where he was
staying, and Boris said the Excelsior, which was a damn lie
because he was staying at the Alexandra Lodge with the rest of
the church outing. All right, the Alexandra is down the list;
the Excelsior sounds better. About midnight the party breaks
up. Boris says he's got to go home and tomorrow's a busy day.
That was the second lie, because he was no more going home
than—what's the one, Jekyll and Hyde, right!—the regular

doctor who dressed up and went on the razzle. So Boris was who?"

For a moment no one helped him.

"Hyde," said Lacon to his scrubbed red hands. Sitting again, he had clasped them on his lap.

"Hyde," Tarr repeated. "Thank you, Mr. Lacon; I always saw you as a literary man. So they settle the bill and I traipse down to Aberdeen to be there ahead of him when he hits Angelika's. By this time I'm pretty sure I'm in the wrong ball game."

On dry long fingers, Tarr studiously counted off the reasons: first, he never knew a Soviet delegation that didn't carry a couple of security gorillas whose job was to keep the boys out of the fleshpots. So how did Boris slip the leash night after night? Second, he didn't like the way Boris pushed his foreign currency around. For a Soviet official, that was against nature, he insisted: "He just doesn't have any damn currency. If he does, he buys beads for his squaw. And three, I didn't like the way he lied. He was a sight too glib for decency."

So Tarr waited at the Angelika, and sure enough half an hour later his Mr. Hyde turned up all on his own. "He sits down and calls for a drink. That's all he does. Sits and drinks like a damn wallflower!"

Once more it was Smiley's turn to receive the heat of Tarr's charm: "So what's it all about, Mr. Smiley? See what I mean? It's *little* things I'm noticing," he confided, still to Smiley. "Just take the way he sat. Believe me, sir, if we'd been in that place ourselves we couldn't have sat better than Boris. He had the pick of the exits and the stairway; he had a fine view of the main entrance and the action; he was right-handed and he was covered by a left-hand wall. Boris was a professional, Mr. Smiley; there was no doubt of it whatsoever. He was waiting for a connect, working a letter-box, maybe, or trailing his coat and looking for a pass from a mug like me. Well, now listen: it's one thing to burn a small-time trade delegate. It's quite a different ball game to swing your legs at a Centre-trained hood—right, Mr. Guillam?"

Guillam said, "Since the reorganisation, scalp-hunters have no brief to trawl for double agents. They must be turned over to London Station on sight. The boys have a standing order, over Bill Haydon's own signature. If there's even a smell of the opposition, abandon." He added, for Smiley's special ear, "Under lateralism our autonomy is cut to the bone."

"And I've been in double-double games before," Tarr confessed in a tone of injured virtue. "Believe me, Mr. Smiley, they are a can of worms."

"I'm sure they are," said Smiley, and gave a prim tug at his spectacles.

Tarr cabled Guillam "no sale," booked a flight home, and went shopping. However, since his flight didn't leave till Thursday, he thought that before he left, just to pay his fare, he might as well burgle Boris's room.

"The Alexandra's a real ramshackle old place, Mr. Smiley, off Marble Road, with a stack of wooden balconies. As for the locks—why, sir, they give up when they see you coming."

In a very short time, therefore, Tarr was standing inside Boris's room with his back against the door, waiting for his eyes to grow accustomed to the dark. He was still standing there when a woman spoke to him in Russian drowsily from the bed.

"It was Boris's wife," Tarr explained. "She was crying. Look, I'll call her Irina, right? Mr. Guillam has the details."

Smiley was already objecting: wife was impossible, he said. Centre would never let them both out of Russia at the same time; they'd keep one and send the other—

"Common-law marriage," Guillam said dryly. "Unofficial but permanent."

"There's a lot that are the other way round these days," said Tarr with a sharp grin at no one, least of all Smiley, and Guillam shot him another foul look.

6

From the outset of this meeting, Smiley had assumed for the main a Buddha-like inscrutability from which neither Tarr's story nor the rare interjections of Lacon and Guillam could rouse him. He sat leaning back with his short legs bent, head forward, and plump hands linked across his generous stomach. His hooded eyes had closed behind the thick lenses. His only fidget was to polish his glasses on the silk lining of his tie, and when he did this his eyes had a soaked, naked look that was embarrassing to those who caught him at it. His interjection, however, and the donnish, inane sound that followed Guillam's explanation, now acted like a signal upon the rest of the gathering, bringing a shuffling of chairs and a clearing of throats.

Lacon was foremost: "George, what are your drinking habits? Can I get you a Scotch or anything?" He offered drink solicitously, like aspirin for a headache. "I forgot to say it earlier," he explained. "George, a bracer: come. It's winter, after all. A nip of something?"

"I'm fine, thank you," Smiley said.

He would have liked a little coffee from the percolator but somehow he didn't feel able to ask. Also he remembered it was terrible.

"Guillam?" Lacon proceeded. No; Guillam also found it impossible to accept alcohol from Lacon.

He didn't offer anything to Tarr, who went straight on with his narrative.

Tarr took Irina's presence calmly, he said. He had worked up his fallback before he entered the building, and now he went straight into his act. He didn't pull a gun or slap his hand over her mouth or any of that tripe, as he put it, but he said he had come to speak to Boris on a private matter; he was sorry and he was damn well going to sit there till Boris showed up. In good Australian, as became an outraged car salesman from down under, he explained that while he didn't want to barge into anyone's business he was damned if he was going to have his girl and his money stolen in a single night by a lousy Russian who couldn't pay for his pleasures. He worked up a lot of outrage but managed to keep his voice down, and then he waited to see what she did.

And that, said Tarr, was how it all began.

It was eleven-thirty when he made Boris's room. He left at one-thirty with a promise of a meeting next night. By then the situation was all the other way: "We weren't doing anything improper, mind. Just pen friends—right, Mr. Smiley?"

For a moment, that bland sneer seemed to lay claim to Smiley's most precious secrets.

"Right," he assented vapidly.

There was nothing exotic about Irina's presence in Hong Kong and no reason why Thesinger should have known of it, Tarr explained. Irina was a member of the delegation in her own right. She was a trained textile buyer: "Come to think of it, she was a sight better qualified than her old man, if I can call him that. She was a plain kid, a bit blue-stocking for my taste, but she was young and she had one hell of a pretty smile when she stopped crying." Tarr coloured quaintly. "She was good company," he insisted, as if arguing against a trend. "When Mr. Thomas from Adelaide came into her life, she was at the end of the line from worrying what to do about the demon Boris. She thought I was the Angel Gabriel. Who could she talk to about her husband who wouldn't turn the dogs on him? She'd no chums on the delegation; she'd no one she trusted even back in Moscow, she said. Nobody who hadn't been through it would ever know what it was like trying to keep a ruined relationship going while all the time you're on the move." Smiley was once more in a deep trance. "Hotel after hotel, city after city, not even allowed to speak to the natives in a natural way or get a smile from a stranger—that's how she described her life. She reckoned it was a pretty miserable state of affairs, Mr. Smiley, and there was a lot of God-thumping and an empty vodka bottle beside the bed to show for it. Why couldn't she be like normal people? she kept saying. Why couldn't she enjoy the Lord's sunshine like the rest of us? She loved sightseeing, she loved foreign kids; why couldn't she have a kid of her own? A kid born free, not in captivity. She kept saying that: born in captivity, born free. 'I'm a jolly person, Thomas. I'm a normal, sociable girl. I like people: why should I deceive them when I like them?' And then she said, the trouble was that long ago she had been chosen for work that made her frozen like an old woman and cut her off from God. So that's why she'd had a drink and why she was having a cry. She'd kind of forgotten her husband by then; she was apologising for having a fling, more." Again he faltered. "I could scent it, Mr. Smiley. There was gold in her. I could scent it from the start. Knowledge is power, they say, sir, and Irina had the power, same as she had the quality. She was hellbent maybe, but she could still give her all. I can sense generosity in a woman where I meet it, Mr. Smiley. I have a talent for it. And this lady was generous. Jesus, how do you describe a hunch? Some people can smell water under the ground . . ."

He seemed to expect some show of sympathy, so Smiley said, "I understand," and plucked at the lobe of his ear.

Watching him with a strange dependence in his expression, Tarr kept silent a stretch longer. "First thing next morning, I cancelled my flight and changed my hotel," he said finally.

Abruptly Smiley opened his eyes wide. "What did you tell London?"

"Nothing."

"Why not?"

"Because he's a devious fool," said Guillam.

"Maybe I thought Mr. Guillam would say, 'Come home, Tarr,'" he replied, with a knowing glance at Guillam that was not returned. "You see, long ago when I was a little boy I made a mistake and walked into a honey trap."

"He made an ass of himself with a Polish girl," said Guillam.

"He sensed her generosity, too."

"I knew Irina was no honey trap, but how could I expect Mr. Guillam to believe me? No way."

"Did you tell Thesinger?"

"Hell, no."

"What reason did you give London for postponing your flight?"

"I was due to fly Thursday. I reckoned no one back home would miss me till Tuesday. Specially with Boris being a dead duck."

"He didn't give a reason and the housekeepers posted him absent without leave on the Monday," said Guillam. "He broke every rule in the book. And some that aren't. By the middle of that week, even Bill Haydon was beating his war drums. And I was having to listen," he added tartly.

However that was, Tarr and Irina met next evening. They met again the evening after that. The first meeting was in a café and it limped. They took a lot of care not to be seen, because Irina was frightened stiff not just of her husband but of the security guards attached to the delegation—the gorillas, as Tarr called them. She refused a drink and she was shaking. The second evening Tarr was still waiting on her generosity. They took the tram up to Victoria Peak, jammed between American matrons in white socks and eyeshades. The third he hired a car and drove her round the New Territories till she suddenly got the heebies about being so close to the Chinese border, so they had to run for harbour. Nevertheless she loved that trip, and often spoke of the tidy beauty of it, the fish ponds and the paddy fields. Tarr also liked the trip because it proved to both of them that they weren't being watched. But Irina had still not unpacked, as he put it.

"Now I'll tell you a damn odd thing about this stage of the game. At the start, I worked Thomas the Aussie to death. I fed her a lot of smoke about a sheep station outside Adelaide and a big property in the high street with a glass front and 'Thomas' in lights. She didn't believe me. She nodded and fooled around and waited till I'd said my piece; then she said, 'Yes, Thomas,' 'No, Thomas,' and changed the subject."

On the fourth evening, he drove her into the hills overlooking North Shore, and Irina told Tarr that she had fallen in love with him and that she was employed by Moscow Centre, she and her husband both, and that she knew Tarr was in the trade, too; she could tell by his alertness and the way he listened with his eyes.

"She'd decided I was an English colonel of intelligence," said Tarr with no smile at all. "She was crying one minute and laughing the next, and in my opinion she was three-quarters of the way to being a basket case. Half, she talked like a pocket-book loony heroine, half like a nice up-and-down suburban kid. The English were her favourite people. Gentlemen, she kept saying. I'd brought her a bottle of vodka and she drank half of it in about fifteen seconds flat. Hooray for English gentlemen. Boris was the lead and Irina was the backup girl. It was a his-and-hers act, and one day she'd talk to Percy Alleline and tell him a great secret all for himself. Boris was on a trawl for Hong Kong businessmen and had a post-box job on the side for the local Soviet residency. Irina ran courier, boiled down the microdots, and played radio for him on a high-speed squirt to beat the listeners. That was how it read on paper, see? The two nightclubs were rendezvous and fallback for his local connect, in that order. But all Boris really wanted to do was drink and chase the dancing girls and have depressions. Or else go for five-hour walks because he couldn't stand being in the same room with his wife. All Irina did was wait around crying and getting plastered, and fancy herself sitting alone at Percy's fireside, telling him all she knew. I kept her there talking, up on the hill, sitting in the car. I didn't move because I didn't want to break the spell. We watched the dusk fall on the harbour and the lovely moon come up there, and the peasants slipping by with their long poles and kerosene lamps. All we needed was Humphrey Bogart in a tuxedo. I kept my foot on the vodka bottle and let her talk. I didn't move a muscle. Fact, Mr. Smiley. Fact," he declared, with the defencelessness of a man longing to be believed, but Smiley's eyes were closed and he was deaf to all appeal.

"She just completely let go," Tarr explained, as if it were suddenly an accident, a thing he had had no part in. "She told me her whole life story, from birth to Colonel Thomas; that's me. Mummy, Daddy, early loves, recruitment, training, her lousy half-marriage, the lot. How her and Boris were teamed at training and had been together ever since: one of the great unbreakable relationships. She told me her real name, her workname, and the cover names she'd travelled and transmitted by; then she hauled out her handbag and started showing me her conjuring set: recessed fountain pen, signal plan folded up inside; concealed camera—the works. 'Wait till Percy sees that,' I tell her—playing her along, like. It was production-line stuff, mind, nothing coach-built, but grade-one material all the same. To round it off, she starts barking the dirt about the Soviet Hong Kong set-up: legmen, safe houses, letter-boxes, the lot. I was going crazy trying to remember it all."

"But you did," said Guillam shortly.

Yes, Tarr agreed; near on, he did. He knew she hadn't told him the whole truth, but he knew truth came hard to a girl who'd been a hood since puberty, and he reckoned that for a beginner she was doing pretty nice.

"I kind of felt for her," he said with another flash of that false confessiveness. "I felt we were on the same wave-length, no messing."

"Quite so," said Lacon in a rare interjection. He was very pale, but whether that was anger or the effect of the grey light of early morning creeping through the shutters, there was no way to tell.

7

"Now I was in a queer situation. I saw her next day and the day after, and I reckoned that if she wasn't already schizoid she was going to be that way damn soon. One minute talking about Percy giving her a top job in the Circus working for Colonel Thomas, and arguing the hell with me about whether she should be a lieutenant or a major. Next minute saying she wouldn't spy for anybody ever again and she was going to grow flowers and rut in the hay with Thomas. Then she had a convent kick: Baptist nuns were going to wash her soul. I nearly died. Who the hell ever heard of Baptist nuns, I ask her. Never mind, she says, Baptists are the greatest; her mother was a peasant and knew. That was the second biggest secret she would ever tell me. 'What's the biggest, then?' I ask. No dice. All she's saying is, we're in mortal danger, bigger than I could possibly know: there's no hope for either of us unless she has that special chat with Brother Percy. 'What danger, for Christ's sake? What do you know that I don't?' She was vain as a cat but when I pressed her she clammed up, and I was frightened to death she'd belt home and sing the lot to Boris. I was running out of time, too. Then it was Wednesday already and the delegation was due to fly home to Moscow Friday. Her tradecraft wasn't all lousy but how could I trust a nut like her? You know how women are when they fall in love, Mr. Smiley. They can't hardly—"

Guillam had already cut him off. "You just keep your head down, right?" he ordered, and Tarr sulked for a space.

"All I knew was Irina wanted to defect—talk to Percy, as she called it. She had three days left, and the sooner she jumped the better for everybody. If I waited much longer, she was going to talk herself out of it. So I took the plunge and walked in on Thesinger, first thing while he was opening up the shop."

"Wednesday, the eleventh," Smiley murmured. "In London the early hours of the morning."

"I guess Thesinger thought I was a ghost," Tarr said. " 'I'm talking to London, personal for Head of London Station,' I said. He argued like hell but he let me do it. I sat at his desk and coded up the message myself from a one-time pad while Thesinger watched me like a sick dog. We had to top and tail it like trade code because Thesinger has export cover. That took me an extra half hour. I was nervy, I really was. Then I burnt the whole damn pad and typed out the message on the ticker machine. At that point, there wasn't a soul on earth but me who knew what the numbers meant on that sheet of paper— not Thesinger, nobody but me. I applied for full defector treatment for Irina on emergency procedure. I held out for all the goodies she'd never even talked about: cash, nationality, a new identity, no limelight, and a place to live. After all, I was her business representative in a manner of speaking, wasn't I, Mr. Smiley?"

Smiley glanced up as if surprised to be addressed. "Yes," he said quite kindly. "Yes, I suppose in a manner of speaking that's what you were."

"He also had a piece of the action, if I know him," said Guillam under his breath.

Catching this or guessing the meaning of it, Tarr was furious.

"That's a damn lie!" he shouted, colouring deeply. "That's a—" After glaring at Guillam a moment longer, he went back to his story.

"I outlined her career to date and her access, including jobs she'd had at Centre. I asked for inquisitors and an Air Force plane. She thought I was asking for a personal meeting with Percy Alleline on neutral ground, but I reckoned we'd cross that bridge when we were past it. I suggested they should send out a couple of Esterhase's lamplighters to take charge of her, maybe a tame doctor as well."

"Why lamplighters?" Smiley asked sharply. "They're not allowed to handle defectors."

The lamplighters were Toby Esterhase's pack, based not in Brixton but in Acton. Their job was to provide the support services for mainline operations: watching, listening, transport, and safe houses.

"Ah, well, Toby's come up in the world since your day, Mr. Smiley," Tarr explained. "They tell me even his pavement artists ride around in Cadillacs. Steal the scalp-hunters' bread out of their mouths, too, if they get the chance—right, Mr. Guillam?"

"They've become the general footpads for London Station," Guillam said shortly. "Part of lateralism."

"I reckoned it would take half a year for the inquisitors to clean her out, and for some reason she was crazy about Scotland. She had a great wish to spend the rest of her life there, in fact. With Thomas. Raising our babies in the heather. I gave it the London Station address group; I graded it flash and by hand of officer only."

Guillam put in: "That's the new formula for maximum limit. It's supposed to cut out handling in the coding rooms."

"But not in London Station?" said Smiley.

"That's their affair."

"You heard Bill Haydon got that job, I suppose?" said Lacon, jerking round on Smiley. "Head of London Station? He's effectively their chief of operations, just as Percy used to be when Control was there. They've changed all the names, that's the thing. You know how your old buddies are about names. You ought to fill him in, Guillam, bring him up to date."

"Oh, I think I have the picture, thank you," Smiley said politely. Of Tarr, with a deceptive dreaminess, he asked, "She spoke of a great secret, you said?"

"Yes, sir."

"Did you give any hint of this in your cable to London?"

He had touched something, there was no doubt of it; he had found a spot where touching hurt, for Tarr winced, and darted a suspicious glance at Lacon, then at Guillam.

Guessing his meaning, Lacon at once sang out a disclaimer: "Smiley knows nothing beyond what you have so far told him in this room," he said. "Correct, Guillam?" Guillam nodded yes, watching Smiley.

"I told London the same as she'd told me," Tarr conceded grumpily, like someone who has been robbed of a good story.

"What form of words, precisely?" Smiley asked. "I wonder whether you remember that."

"'Claims to have further information crucial to the well-being of the Circus, but not yet disclosed.' Near enough, anyhow."

"Thank you. Thank you very much."

They waited for Tarr to continue.

"I also requested Head of London Station to inform Mr. Guillam here that I'd landed on my feet and wasn't playing hookey for the hell of it."

"Did that happen?" Smiley asked.

"Nobody said anything to me," said Guillam dryly.

"I hung around all day for an answer, but by evening it still hadn't come. Irina was doing a normal day's work. I insisted on that, you see. She wanted to stage a light dose of fever to keep her in bed but I wouldn't hear of it. The delegation had factories to visit on Kowloon and I told her to tag along and look intelligent. I made her swear to keep off the bottle. I didn't want her involved in amateur dramatics at the last moment. I wanted it normal right up to when she jumped. I waited till evening, then cabled a flash follow-up."

Smiley's shrouded gaze fixed upon the pale face before him. "You had an acknowledgement, of course?" he asked.

"'We read you.' That's all. I sweated out the whole damn night. By dawn I still didn't have an answer. I thought, Maybe that R.A.F. plane is already on its way. London's playing it long, I thought, tying all the knots before they bring me in. I mean when you're that far away from them you *have* to believe they're good. Whatever you think of them, you *have* to believe that. And I mean now and then they are—right, Mr. Guillam?"

No one helped him.

"I was worried about Irina, see? I was damn certain that if she had to wait another day she would crack. Finally the answer did come. It wasn't an answer at all. It was a stall: 'Tell us what sections she worked in, names of former contacts and acquaintances inside Moscow Centre, name of her present boss, date of intake into Centre.' Jesus, I don't know what else. I drafted a reply fast because I had a three o'clock date with her down by the church—"

"What church?" Smiley again.

"English Baptist." To everyone's astonishment, Tarr was once again blushing. "She liked to visit there. Not for services, just to sniff around. I hung around the entrance looking natural but she didn't show. It was the first time she'd broken a date. Our fallback was for three hours later on the hilltop, then a one-minute-fifty descending scale back at the church till we met up. If she was in trouble, she was going to leave her bathing suit on her window-sill. She was a swimming nut, swam every day. I shot round to the Alexandra: no bathing suit. I had two and a half hours to kill. There was nothing I could do any more except wait."

Smiley said, "What was the priority of London Station's telegram to you?"

"Immediate."

"But yours was flash?"

"Both of mine were flash."

"Was London's telegram signed?"

Guillam put in: "They're not any more. Outsiders deal with London Station as a unit."

"Was it decypher yourself?"

"No," said Guillam.

They waited for Tarr to go on.

"I kicked around Thesinger's office but I wasn't too popular there; he doesn't approve of scalp-hunters and he has a big thing going on the Chinese mainland that he seemed to think I was going to blow for him. So I sat in a café and I had this idea I just might go down to the airport. It was an idea: like you might say, "Maybe I'll go to a movie." I took the Star Ferry, hired a cab, and told the driver to go like hell. It got like a panic. I barged the Information queue and asked for all departures to Russia, or connections in. I nearly went mad going through the flight lists, yelling at the Chinese clerks, but there wasn't a plane since yesterday and none till six tonight. But now I had this hunch. I had to know. What about charters, what about the unscheduled flights, freight, casual transit? Had nothing, but *really* nothing, been routed for Moscow since yesterday morning? Then this little girl comes through with the answer, one of the Chinese hostesses. She fancies me, see. She's doing me a favour. An unscheduled Soviet plane had taken off two hours ago. Only four passengers boarded. The centre of attraction was a woman invalid. A lady. In a coma. They had to cart her to the plane on a stretcher, and her face was wrapped in bandages. Two male nurses went with her and one doctor—that was the party. I called the Alexandra as a last hope. Neither Irina nor her so-called husband had checked out of their room, but there was no reply. The lousy hotel didn't even know they'd left."

Perhaps the music had been going on a long time and Smiley only noticed it now. He heard it in imperfect fragments from different parts of the house: a scale on a flute, a child's tune on a recorder, a violin piece more confidently played. The many Lacon daughters were waking up.

8

"Perhaps she *was* ill," said Smiley stolidly, speaking more to Guillam than anyone else. "Perhaps she *was* in a coma. Perhaps they were real nurses who took her away. By the sound of her, she was a pretty good mess, at best." He added, with half a glance at Tarr: "After all, only twenty-four hours had elapsed between your first telegram and Irina's departure. You can hardly lay it at London's door on that timing."

"You can *just*," said Guillam, looking at the floor. "It's extremely fast, but it does just work, if somebody in London—" They were all waiting. "If somebody in London had very good footwork. And in Moscow, too, of course."

"Now, that's exactly what I told myself, sir," said Tarr proudly, taking up Smiley's point and ignoring Guillam's. "My very words, Mr. Smiley. 'Relax, Ricki,' I said; 'you'll be shooting at shadows if you're not damn careful.'"

"Or the Russians tumbled to her," Smiley said. "The security guards found out about your affair and removed her. It would be a wonder if they *hadn't* found out, the way you two carried on."

"Or she told her husband," Tarr suggested. "I understand psychology as well as the next man, sir. I know what can happen between a husband and wife when they have fallen out. She wishes to annoy him. To goad him, to obtain a reaction, I thought. 'Want to hear what I've been doing while you've been out boozing and cutting the rug?'—like that. Boris peels off and tells the gorillas; they sandbag her and take her home. I went through all those possibilities, Mr. Smiley, believe me. I really worked on them, truth. Same as any man does whose woman walks out on him."

"Let's just have the story, shall we?" Guillam whispered, furious.

Well, now, said Tarr, he would agree that for twenty-four hours he went a bit berserk: "Now, I don't often get that way— right, Mr. Guillam?"

"Often enough."

"I was feeling pretty physical. Frustrated, you could almost say."

His conviction that a considerable prize had been brutally snatched away from him drove him to a distracted fury that found expression in a rampage through old haunts. He went to the Cat's Cradle, then to Angelika's, and by dawn he had taken in half a dozen other places besides, not to mention a few girls along the way. At some point he crossed town and raised a spot of dust around the Alexandra. He was hoping to have a couple of words with those security gorillas. When he sobered down, he got thinking about Irina and their time together, and he decided before he flew back to London to go round their dead letter-boxes to check whether by any chance she had written to him before she left.

Partly it was something to do. "Partly, I guess, I couldn't bear to think of a letter of hers kicking around in a hole in a wall while she sweated it out in the hot seat," he added, the ever-redeemable boy.

They had two places where they dropped mail for one another. The first was not far from the hotel on a building site.

"Ever seen that bamboo scaffolding they use? Fantastic. I've seen it twenty storeys high and the coolies swarming over it with slabs of precast concrete." A bit of discarded piping, he said, handy at shoulder height. It seemed most likely, if Irina was in a hurry, that the piping was the letter-box she would use, but when Tarr went there it was empty. The second was back by the church, "in under where they stow the pamphlets," as he put it. "This stand was part of an old wardrobe, see. If you kneel in the back pew and grope around, there's a loose board. Behind the board there's a recess full of rubbish and rat's mess. I tell you, it made a real lovely drop, the best ever."

There was a short pause, illuminated by the vision of Ricki Tarr and his Moscow Centre mistress kneeling side by side in the rear pew of a Baptist church in Hong Kong.

In this dead letter-box, Tarr said, he found not a letter but a whole damn diary. The writing was fine and done on both sides of the paper, so that quite often the black ink came through. It was fast urgent writing with no erasures. He knew at a glance that she had maintained it in her lucid periods.

"This isn't it, mind. This is only my copy."

Slipping a long hand inside his shirt, he had drawn out a leather purse attached to a broad thong of hide. From it he took a grimy wad of paper.

"I guess she dropped the diary just before they hit her," he said. "Maybe she was having a last pray at the same time. I made the translation myself."

"I didn't know you spoke Russian," said Smiley—a comment lost to everyone but Tarr, who at once grinned.

"Ah, now, a man needs a qualification in this profession, Mr. Smiley," he explained as he separated the pages. "I may not have been too great at law but a further language can be decisive. You know what the poets say, I expect?" He looked up from his labours and his grin widened. "'To possess another language is to possess another soul.' A great king wrote that, sir, Charles the Fifth. My father never forgot a quotation, I'll say that for him, though the funny thing is he couldn't speak a damn thing but English. I'll read the diary aloud to you, if you don't mind."

"He hasn't a word of Russian to his name," said Guillam.

"They spoke English all the time. Irina had done a three-year English course."

Guillam had chosen the ceiling to look at, Lacon his hands. Only Smiley was watching Tarr, who was laughing quietly at his own little joke.

"All set?" he enquired. "Right, then, I'll begin. 'Thomas, listen, I am talking to you.' She called me by my surname," he explained. "I told her I was Tony, but it was always Thomas, right? 'This diary is my gift for you in case they take me away before I speak to Alleline. I would prefer to give you my life, Thomas, and naturally my body, but I think it more likely that this wretched secret will be all I have to make you happy. Use it well!'" Tarr glanced up. "It's marked Monday. She wrote the diary over the four days." His voice had become flat, almost bored. "'In Moscow Centre there is more gossip than our superiors would wish. Especially the little fellows like to make themselves grand by appearing to be in the know. For two years before I was attached to the Trade Ministry, I worked as a supervisor in the filing department of our headquarters in Dzerzhinsky Square. The work was so dull, Thomas, the atmosphere was not happy, and I was unmarried. We were encouraged to be suspicious of one another; it is such a strain never to give your heart, not once. Under me was a clerk named Ivlov. Though Ivlov was not socially or in rank my equal, the oppressive atmosphere brought out a mutuality in our temperaments. Forgive me, sometimes only the body can speak for us—you should have appeared earlier, Thomas! Several times Ivlov and I worked night shifts together, and eventually we agreed to defy regulations and meet outside the building. He was blond, Thomas, like you, and I wanted him. We met in a café in a poor district of Moscow. In Russia we are taught that Moscow has no poor districts, but this is a lie. Ivlov told me that his real name was Brod but he was not a Jew. He brought me some coffee sent to him illicitly by a comrade in Teheran—he was very sweet—also some stockings. Ivlov told me that he admired me greatly

and that he had once worked in a section responsible for recording the particulars of all the foreign agents employed by Centre. I laughed and told him that no such record existed; it was
an idea of dreamers to suppose so many secrets would be in one
place. Well, we were both dreamers I suppose.'"

Again Tarr broke off. "We get a new day," he announced.
"She kicks off with a lot of 'good morning Thomas's,' prayers,
and a bit of love-talk. A woman can't write to the air, she says,
so she's writing to Thomas. Her old man's gone out early; she's
got an hour to herself. Okay?"

Smiley grunted.

"'On the second occasion with Ivlov, I met him in the room
of a cousin of Ivlov's wife, a teacher at Moscow State University.
No one else was present. The meeting, which was extremely
secret, involved what in a report we would call an incriminating
act. I think, Thomas, you yourself once or twice committed
such an act! Also at this meeting Ivlov told me the following
story to bind us in even closer friendship. Thomas, you must
take care. Have you heard of Karla? He is an old fox, the most
cunning in the Centre, the most secret; even his name is not a
name that Russians understand. Ivlov was extremely frightened to
tell me this story, which according to Ivlov concerned a great
conspiracy, perhaps the greatest we have. The story of Ivlov is
as follows. You should tell it only to *most trustworthy people*,
Thomas, because of its extremely conspiratorial nature. You
must tell no one in the Circus, for no one can be trusted until
the riddle is solved. Ivlov said it was not true that he once
worked on agent records. He had invented this story only to
show me the great depth of his knowledge concerning the Centre's affairs and to assure me that I was not in love with a
nobody. The truth was he had worked for Karla as a helper in
one of Karla's great conspiracies and he had actually been stationed in England in a conspiratorial capacity, under the cover
of being a driver and assistant coding clerk at the Embassy. For
this task he was provided with the workname Lapin. Thus Brod

became Ivlov and Ivlov became Lapin: of this poor Ivlov was extremely proud. (I did not tell him what Lapin means in French.) That a man's wealth should be counted by the number of his names! Ivlov's task was to service a mole. A mole is a deep-penetration agent so called because he burrows deep into the fabric of Western imperialism, in this case an Englishman. Moles are very precious to the Centre because of the many years it takes to place them, often fifteen or twenty. Most of the English moles were recruited by Karla before the war and came from the higher bourgeoisie, even aristocrats and nobles who were disgusted with their origins, and became secretly fanatic, much more fanatic than their working-class English comrades, who are slothful. Several were applying to join the Party when Karla stopped them in time and directed them to special work. Some fought in Spain against Franco Fascism, and Karla's talent-spotters found them there and turned them over to Karla for recruitment. Others were recruited in the war during the alliance of expediency between Soviet Russia and Britain. Others afterwards, disappointed that the war did not bring Socialism to the West . . .' It kind of dries up here," Tarr announced without looking anywhere but at his own manuscript. "I wrote down, 'dries up.' I guess her old man came back earlier than she expected. The ink's all blotted. God knows where she stowed the damn thing. Under the mattress maybe."

If this was meant as a joke, it failed.

" 'The mole whom Lapin serviced in London was known by the code name Gerald. He had been recruited by Karla and was the object of extreme conspiracy. The servicing of moles is performed only by comrades with a very high standard of ability, said Ivlov. Thus while in appearance Ivlov-Lapin was at the Embassy a mere nobody, subjected to many humiliations on account of his apparent insignificance, such as standing with women behind the bar at functions, by right he was a great man, the secret assistant to Colonel Gregor Viktorov, whose workname at the Embassy is Polyakov.' "

Here Smiley made his one interjection, asking for the spelling. Like an actor disturbed in midflow, Tarr answered rudely, "P-o-l-y-a-k-o-v, got it?"

"Thank you," said Smiley with unshakeable courtesy, in a manner which conveyed conclusively that the name had no significance for him whatever. Tarr resumed.

"'Viktorov is himself an old professional of great cunning, said Ivlov. His cover job is cultural attaché and that is how he speaks to Karla. As Cultural Attaché Polyakov, he organises lectures to British universities and societies concerning cultural matters in the Soviet Union, but his nightwork as Colonel Gregor Viktorov is briefing and debriefing the mole Gerald on instruction from Karla at Centre. For this purpose, Colonel Viktorov-Polyakov uses legmen and poor Ivlov was for a while one. Nevertheless it is Karla in Moscow who is the real controller of the mole Gerald.'"

"Now it really changes," said Tarr. "She's writing at night and she's either plastered or scared out of her pants, because she's going all over the damn page. There's talk about footsteps in the corridor and the dirty looks she's getting from the gorillas. Not transcribed—right, Mr. Smiley?" And, receiving a small nod, he went on: "'The measures for the mole's security were remarkable. Written reports from London to Karla at Moscow Centre even after coding were cut in two and sent by separate couriers, others in secret inks underneath orthodox Embassy correspondence. Ivlov told me that the mole Gerald produced at times more conspiratorial material than Viktorov-Polyakov could conveniently handle. Much was on undeveloped film, often thirty reels in a week. Anyone opening the container in the wrong fashion at once exposed the film. Other material was given by the mole in speeches, at extremely conspiratorial meetings, and recorded on special tape that could only be played through complicated machines. This tape was also wiped clean by exposure to light or to the wrong machine. The meetings were of the crash type, always

different, always sudden, that is all I know except that it was
the time when the Fascist aggression in Vietnam was at its
worst; in England the extreme reactionaries had again taken
the power. Also that according to Ivlov-Lapin, the mole Gerald
was a high functionary in the Circus. Thomas, I tell you this
because, since I love you, I have decided to admire all English,
you most of all. I do not wish to think of an English gentleman
behaving as a traitor, though naturally I believe he was right to
join the workers' cause. Also I fear for the safety of anyone
employed by the Circus in a conspiracy. Thomas, I love you;
take care with this knowledge—it could hurt you also. Ivlov
was a man like you, even if they called him Lapin . . .'" Tarr
paused diffidently. "There's a bit at the end which . . ."

"Read it," Guillam murmured.

Lifting the wad of paper slightly sideways, Tarr read in the
same flat drawl: " 'Thomas, I am telling you this also because I
am afraid. This morning when I woke, he was sitting on the
bed, staring at me like a madman. When I went downstairs for
coffee, the guards Trepov and Novikov watched me like animals, eating very carelessly. I am sure they had been there
hours; also from the Residency, Avilov sat with them, a boy.
Have you been indiscreet, Thomas? Did you tell more than
you let me think? Now you see why only Alleline would do.
You need not blame yourself; I can guess what you have told
them. In my heart I am free. You have seen only the bad things
in me—the drink, the fear, the lies we live. But deep inside me
burns a new and blessed light. I used to think that the secret
world was a separate place and that I was banished for ever to
an island of half-people. But, Thomas, it is not separate. God
has shown me that it is here, right in the middle of the real
world, all round us, and we have only to open the door and step
outside to be free. Thomas, you must always long for the light
which I have found. It is called love. Now I shall take this to
our secret place and leave it there while there is still time.

Dear God, I hope there is. God give me sanctuary in His

Church. Remember it: I loved you there also.'" Tarr was extremely pale, and his hands, as he pulled open his shirt to return the diary to its purse, were trembling and moist. "There's a last bit," he said. "It goes: 'Thomas, why could you remember so few prayers from your boyhood? Your father was a great and good man.' Like I told you," he explained, "she was crazy."

Lacon had opened the blinds and now the full white light of day was pouring into the room. The windows looked onto a small paddock where Jackie Lacon, a fat little girl in plaits and a riding hat, was cautiously cantering her pony.

9

Before Tarr left, Smiley asked a number of questions of him. He was gazing not at Tarr but myopically into the middle distance, his pouchy face despondent from the tragedy.

"Where is the original of that diary?"

"I put it straight back in the dead letter-box. Figure it this way, Mr. Smiley: by the time I found the diary, Irina had been in Moscow twenty-four hours. I guessed she wouldn't have a lot of breath when it came to the interrogation. Most likely they'd sweated her on the plane, then a second going over when she touched down, then question one as soon as the big boys had finished their breakfast. That's the way they do it to the timid ones: the arm first and the questions after, right? So it might be only a matter of a day or two before Centre sent along a footpad to take a peek round the back of the church, okay?" Primly again: "Also I had my own welfare to consider."

"He means that Moscow Centre would be less interested in cutting his throat if they thought he hadn't read the diary," said Guillam.

"Did you photograph it?"

"I don't carry a camera. I bought a dollar notebook. I copied the diary into the notebook. The original I put back. The whole job took me four hours flat." He glanced at Guillam, then away from him. In the fresh daylight, a deep inner fear was suddenly apparent in Tarr's face. "When I got back to the hotel, my room was a wreck; they'd even stripped the paper off the walls. The manager told me, 'Get the hell out.' He didn't want to know."

"He's carrying a gun," said Guillam. "He won't part with it."

"You're damn right I won't."

Smiley offered a dyspeptic grunt of sympathy. "These meetings you had with Irina: the dead letter-boxes, the safety signals, and fallbacks. Who proposed the tradecraft, you or she?"

"She did."

"What were the safety signals?"

"Body-talk. If I wore my collar open, she knew I'd had a look around and I reckoned the coast was clear. If I wore it closed, scrub the meeting till the fallback."

"And Irina?"

"Handbag. Left hand, right hand. I got there first and waited up somewhere she could see me. That gave her the choice: whether to go ahead or split."

"All this happened more than six months ago. What have you been doing since?"

"Resting," said Tarr rudely.

Guillam said, "He panicked and went native. He bolted to Kuala Lumpur, then lay up in one of the hill villages. That's his story. He has a daughter called Danny."

"Danny's my little kid."

"He shacked up with Danny and her mother," said Guillam, talking, as was his habit, clean across anything Tarr said. "He's got wives scattered across the globe, but she seems to lead the pack just now."

"Why did you choose this particular moment to come to us?"

Tarr said nothing.

"Don't you want to spend Christmas with Danny?"

"Sure."

"So what happened? Did something scare you?"

"There was rumours," said Tarr sullenly.

"What sort of rumours?"

"Some Frenchman turned up in K.L. telling them all I owed him money. Wanted to get some lawyer hounding me. I don't owe anybody money."

Smiley returned to Guillam. "At the Circus he's still posted as a defector?"

"Presumed."

"What have they done about it so far?"

"It's out of my hands. I heard on the grapevine that London Station held a couple of war parties over him a while back, but they didn't invite me and I don't know what came of them. Nothing, I should think, as usual."

"What passport's he been using?"

Tarr had his answer ready: "I threw away Thomas the day I hit Malaya. I reckoned Thomas wasn't exactly the flavour of the month in Moscow and I'd do better to kill him off right there. In K.L. I had them run me up a British." He handed it to Smiley. "Name of Poole. It's not bad for the money."

"Why didn't you use one of your Swiss escapes?"

Another wary pause.

"Or did you lose them when your hotel room was searched?"

Guillam said, "He cached them as soon as he arrived in Hong Kong. Standard practice."

"So why didn't you use them?"

"They were numbered, Mr. Smiley. They may have been blank but they were numbered. I was feeling a mite windy, frankly. If London had the numbers, maybe Moscow did, too, if you take my meaning."

"So what did you do with your Swiss escapes?" Smiley repeated pleasantly.

"He says he threw them away," said Guillam. "He sold them, more likely. Or swapped them for that one."

"How? Threw them away how? Did you burn them?"

"That's right, I burned them," said Tarr with a nervy ring to his voice, half a threat, half fear.

"So when you say this Frenchman was enquiring for you—"

"He was looking for Poole."

"But who else ever heard of Poole, except the man who faked this passport?" Smiley asked, turning the pages. Tarr said nothing. "Tell me how you travelled to England," Smiley suggested.

"Soft route from Dublin. No problem." Tarr lied badly under pressure. Perhaps his parents were to blame. He was too fast when he had no answer ready, too aggressive when he had one up his sleeve.

"How did you get to Dublin?" Smiley asked, checking the border stamps on the middle page.

"Roses." He had recovered his confidence. "Roses all the way. I've got a girl who's an air hostess with South African. A pal of mine flew me cargo to the Cape; at the Cape my girl took care of me, then hitched me a free ride to Dublin with one of the pilots. As far as anyone back East knows, I never left the peninsula."

"I'm doing what I can to check," said Guillam to the ceiling.

"Well, you be damn careful, baby," Tarr snapped down the line to Guillam. "Because I don't want the wrong people on my back."

"Why did you come to Mr. Guillam?" Smiley enquired, still deep in Poole's passport. It had a used, well-thumbed look, neither too full nor too empty. "Apart from the fact that you were frightened, of course."

"Mr. Guillam's my boss," said Tarr virtuously.

"Did it cross your mind he might just turn you straight over to Alleline? After all, you're something of a wanted man as far as the Circus top brass is concerned, aren't you?"

"Sure. But I don't figure Mr. Guillam's any fonder of the new arrangement than you are, Mr. Smiley."

"He also loves England," Guillam explained with mordant sarcasm.

"Sure. I got homesick."

"Did you ever consider going to anyone else but Mr. Guillam? Why not one of the overseas residencies, for instance, where you were in less danger? Is Mackelvore still headman in Paris?" Guillam nodded. "There you are, then: you could have gone to Mr. Mackelvore. He recruited you, you can trust him: he's old Circus. You could have sat safely in Paris instead of risking your neck over here. Oh, dear God. Lacon, quick!"

Smiley had risen to his feet, the back of one hand pressed to his mouth as he stared out the window. In the paddock Jackie Lacon was lying on her stomach screaming while a riderless pony careered between the trees. They were still watching as Lacon's wife, a pretty woman with long hair and thick winter stockings, bounded over the fence and gathered the child up.

"They're often taking tumbles," Lacon remarked, quite cross. "They don't hurt themselves at that age." And scarcely more graciously: "You're not responsible for everyone, you know, George."

Slowly they settled again.

"And if you had been making for Paris," Smiley resumed, "which route would you have taken?"

"The same till Ireland, then Dublin-Orly, I guess. What do you expect me to do—walk on the damn water?"

At this Lacon coloured and Guillam with an angry exclamation rose to his feet. But Smiley seemed quite unbothered.

Taking up the passport again, he turned slowly back to the beginning.

"And how did you get in touch with Mr. Guillam?"

Guillam answered for him, speaking fast: "He knew where I garage my car. He left a note on it saying he wanted to buy it and signed it with his workname Trench. He suggested a place to meet and put in a veiled plea for privacy before I took my trade elsewhere. I brought Fawn along to baby-sit—"

Smiley interrupted: "That was Fawn at the door just now?"

"He watched my back while we talked," Guillam said. "I've kept him with us ever since. As soon as I'd heard Tarr's story, I rang Lacon from a call-box and asked for an interview... George, why don't we talk this over among ourselves?"

"Rang Lacon down here or in London?"

"Down here," said Lacon.

There was a pause till Guillam explained. "I happened to remember the name of a girl in Lacon's office. I mentioned her name and said she had asked me to speak to him urgently on an intimate matter. It wasn't perfect but it was the best I could think of on the spur of the moment." He added, filling the silence, "Well, damn it, there was no *reason* to suppose the phone was tapped."

"There was every reason."

Smiley had closed the passport and was examining the binding by the light of a tattered reading lamp at his side. "This is rather good, isn't it?" he remarked lightly. "Really very good indeed. I'd say that was a professional product. I can't find a blemish."

"Don't worry, Mr. Smiley," Tarr retorted, taking it back; "it's not made in Russia." By the time he reached the door, his smile had returned. "You know something?" he said, addressing all three of them down the aisle of the long room. "If Irina is right, you boys are going to need a whole new Circus. So if we all stick together I guess we could be in on the ground floor." He gave the door a playful tap. "Come on, darling, it's me. Ricki."

"Thank you! It's all right now! Open up, please," Lacon shouted, and a moment later the key was turned, the dark figure of Fawn the baby-sitter flitted into view, and then the footsteps faded into the big hollows of the house, to the distant accompaniment of Jackie Lacon's crying.

10

On another side of the house, away from the pony paddock, a grass tennis court was hidden among the trees. It was not a good tennis court; it was mown seldom. In spring the grass was sodden from the winter and no sun got in to dry it, in summer the balls disappeared into the foliage, and this morning it was ankle deep in frosted leaves that had collected from all over the garden. But round the outside, roughly following the wire rectangle, a footpath wandered between some beech trees and here Smiley and Lacon wandered also. Smiley had fetched his travelling coat but Lacon wore only his threadbare suit. For this reason, perhaps, he chose a brisk, if unco-ordinated, pace which with each stride took him well ahead of Smiley, so that he had constantly to hover, shoulders and elbows lifted, waiting till the shorter man caught up. Then he promptly bounded off again, gaining ground. They completed two laps in this way before Lacon broke the silence.

"When you came to me a year ago with a similar suggestion, I'm afraid I threw you out. I suppose I should apologise. I was remiss." There was a suitable silence while he pondered his dereliction. "I instructed you to abandon your enquiries."

"You told me they were unconstitutional," Smiley said mournfully, as if he were recalling the same sad error.

"Was that the word I used? Good Lord, how very pompous of me!"

From the direction of the house came the sound of Jackie's continued crying.

"You never had any, did you?" Lacon piped at once, his head lifted to the sound.

"I'm sorry?"

"Children. You and Ann."

"No."

"Nephews, nieces?"

"One nephew."

"On your side?"

"Hers."

Perhaps I never left the place, Smiley thought, peering around him at the tangled roses, the broken swings and sodden sandpits, the raw red house so shrill in the morning light. Perhaps we're still here from last time.

Lacon was apologising again: "Dare I say I didn't absolutely trust your motives? It rather crossed my mind that Control had put you up to it, you see. As a way of hanging on to power and keeping Alleline out"—swirling away again, long strides, wrists outward.

"Oh, no, I assure you Control knew nothing about it at all."

"I realise that now. I didn't at the time. It's a little difficult to know when to trust you people and when not. You do live by rather different standards, don't you? I mean you have to. I accept that. I'm not being judgemental. Our aims are the same, after all, even if our methods are different"—bounding over a cattle ditch. "I once heard someone say morality was method. Do you hold with that? I suppose you wouldn't. You would say that morality was vested in the aim, I expect. Difficult to know what one's aims *are*, that's the trouble, specially if you're British. We can't expect you people to determine *our policy* for us, can we? We can only ask you to further it. Correct? Tricky one, that."

Rather than chase after him, Smiley sat on a rusted swing seat and huddled himself more tightly in his coat, till finally

Lacon stalked back and perched beside him. For a while they rocked together to the rhythm of the groaning springs.

"Why the devil did she choose Tarr?" Lacon muttered at last, fiddling his long fingers. "Of all the people in the world to choose for a confessor, I can imagine none more miserably unsuitable."

"I'm afraid you'll have to ask a woman that question, not us," said Smiley, wondering again where Immingham was.

"Oh, indeed," Lacon agreed lavishly. "All that's a complete mystery. I'm seeing the Minister at eleven," he confided, in a lower tone. "I have to put him in the picture. Your parliamentary cousin," he added, forcing an intimate joke.

"Ann's cousin, actually," Smiley corrected him, in the same absent tone. "Far removed I may add, but cousin for all that."

"And Bill Haydon is also Ann's cousin? Our distinguished Head of London Station." They had played this game before as well.

"By a different route, yes, Bill is also her cousin." He added quite uselessly: "She comes from an old family with a strong political tradition. With time it's rather spread."

"The tradition?"—Lacon loved to nail an ambiguity.

"The family."

Beyond the trees, Smiley thought, cars are passing. Beyond the trees lies a whole world, but Lacon has this red castle and a sense of Christian ethic that promises him no reward except a knighthood, the respect of his peers, a fat pension, and a couple of charitable directorships in the City.

"Anyway I'm seeing him at eleven." Lacon had jerked to his feet and they were walking again. Smiley caught the name "Ellis" floating backward to him on the leafy morning air. For a moment, as in the car with Guillam, an odd nervousness overcame him.

"After all," Lacon was saying, "we both held perfectly honourable positions. You felt that Ellis had been betrayed and you wanted a witch-hunt. My Minister and I felt there had been gross incompetence on the part of Control—a view which to put it mildly the Foreign Office shared—and we wanted a new broom."

"Oh, I quite understood *your* dilemma," said Smiley, more to himself than to Lacon.

"I'm glad. And don't forget, George: you were Control's man. Control preferred you to Haydon, and when he lost his grip towards the end—and launched that whole extraordinary adventure—it was you who fronted for him. No one but you, George. It's not every day that the head of one's secret service embarks on a private war against the Czechs." It was clear that the memory still smarted. "In other circumstances, I suppose, Haydon might have gone to the wall, but you were in the hot seat and—"

"And Percy Alleline was the Minister's man," said Smiley, mildly enough for Lacon to slow himself and listen.

"It wasn't as if you had a suspect, you know! You didn't point the finger at anyone! A directionless enquiry can be extraordinarily destructive!"

"Whereas a new broom sweeps cleaner."

"Percy Alleline has produced intelligence instead of scandals, he has stuck to the letter of his charter and won the trust of the customers. And he has not, to my knowledge, invaded Czechoslovak territory. All in all he has done extremely well."

"With Bill Haydon to field for him, who wouldn't?"

"Control, for one," said Lacon, with punch.

They had drawn up at an empty swimming pool and now stood staring into the deep end. From its grimy depths Smiley fancied he heard again the insinuating tones of Roddy Martindale: "Little reading rooms at the Admiralty, little committees popping up with funny names . . ."

"Is that special source of Percy's still running?" Smiley enquired. "The Witchcraft material, or whatever it's called these days?"

"I didn't know you were on the list," Lacon said, not at all pleased. "Since you ask, yes. Source Merlin's our mainstay and

Witchcraft is still the name of his product. The Circus hasn't turned in such good material for years. Since I can remember, in fact."

"And still subject to all that special handling?"

"Certainly, and now that this has happened I've no doubt that we shall take even more rigorous precautions."

"I wouldn't do that if I were you. Gerald might smell a rat."

"That's the point, isn't it?" Lacon observed quickly. His strength was improbable, Smiley reflected. One minute he was like a thin, drooping boxer whose gloves were too big for his wrists; the next he had reached out and rocked you against the ropes, and was surveying you with Christian compassion. "We can't move. We can't investigate because all the instruments of enquiry are in the Circus's hands, perhaps in the mole Gerald's. We can't watch, or listen, or open mail. To do any one of those things would require the resources of Esterhase's lamplighters, and Esterhase like anyone else must be suspect. We can't interrogate; we can't take steps to limit a particular person's access to delicate secrets. To do any of these things would be to run the risk of alarming the mole. It's the oldest question of all, George. Who can spy on the spies? Who can smell out the fox without running with him?" He made an awful stab at humour: "Mole, rather," he said, in a confiding aside.

In a fit of energy Smiley had broken away and was pounding ahead of Lacon down the path that led towards the paddock.

"Then go to the competition," he called. "Go to the security people. They're the experts; they'll do you a job."

"The Minister won't have that. You know perfectly well how he and Alleline feel about the competition. Rightly, too, if I may say so. A lot of ex-colonial administrators ploughing through Circus papers: you might as well bring in the army to investigate the navy!"

"That's no comparison at all," Smiley objected.

But Lacon as a good civil servant had his second metaphor ready: "Very well, the Minister would rather live with a damp

roof than see his castle pulled down by outsiders. Does that
satisfy you? He has a perfectly good point, George. We do
have agents in the field, and I wouldn't give much for their
chances once the security gentlemen barge in."

Now it was Smiley's turn to slow down. "How many?"

"Six hundred, give or take a few."

"And behind the Curtain?"

"We budget for a hundred and twenty." With numbers,
with facts of all sorts, Lacon never faltered. They were the
gold he worked with, wrested from the grey bureaucratic
earth. "So far as I can make out from the financial returns,
almost all of them are presently active." He took a long bound.
"So I can tell him you'll do it, can I?" he sang quite casually, as
if the question were mere formality, check the appropriate box.
"You'll take the job, clean the stables? Go backwards, go forwards, do whatever is necessary? It's your generation, after all.
Your legacy."

Smiley had pushed open the paddock gate and slammed it
behind him. They were facing each other over its rickety frame.
Lacon, slightly pink, wore a dependent smile.

"Why do I say Ellis?" he asked conversationally. "Why do
I talk about the Ellis affair when the poor man's name was
Prideaux?"

"Ellis was his workname."

"Of course. So many scandals in those days, one forgets the
details." Hiatus. Swinging of the right forearm. Lunge. "And
he was Haydon's friend, not yours?" Lacon enquired.

"They were at Oxford together before the war."

"And stablemates in the Circus during and after. The
famous Haydon-Prideaux partnership. My predecessor spoke
of it interminably." He repeated, "But you were never close to
him?"

"To Prideaux? No."

"Not a cousin, I mean?"

"For heaven's sake," Smiley breathed.

Lacon grew suddenly awkward again, but a dogged purpose kept his gaze on Smiley. "And there's no emotional or other reason which you feel might debar you from the assignment? You must speak up, George," he insisted anxiously, as if speaking up were the last thing he wanted. He waited a fraction, then threw it all away: "Though I see no real case. There's always a part of us that belongs to the public domain, isn't there? The social contract cuts both ways; you always knew that, I'm sure. So did Prideaux."

"What does that mean?"

"Well, good Lord, he was shot, George. A bullet in the back is held to be quite a sacrifice, isn't it, even in your world?"

Alone, Smiley stood at the further end of the paddock, under the dripping trees, trying to make sense of his emotions while he reached for breath. Like an old illness, his anger had taken him by surprise. Ever since his retirement, he had been denying its existence, steering clear of anything that could touch it off: newspapers, former colleagues, gossip of the Martindale sort. After a lifetime of living by his wits and his considerable memory, he had given himself full time to the profession of forgetting. He had forced himself to pursue scholarly interests which had served him well enough as a distraction while he was at the Circus, but which now that he was unemployed were nothing, absolutely nothing. He could have shouted: Nothing!

"Burn the lot," Ann had suggested helpfully, referring to his books. "Set fire to the house. But don't rot."

If by rot, she meant conform, she was right to read that as his aim. He had tried, really tried, as he approached what the insurance advertisements were pleased to call the evening of his life, to be all that a model *rentier* should be; though no one, least of all Ann, thanked him for the effort. Each morning as he got out of bed, each evening as he went back to it, usually alone, he had reminded himself that he never was and never had been indispensable. He had schooled himself to admit that in those last wretched months of Control's career, when disasters followed one another with heady speed, he had been guilty of seeing things out of proportion. And if the old professional Adam rebelled in him now and then and said: You *know* the place went bad, you *know* Jim Prideaux was betrayed—and what more eloquent testimony is there than a bullet, two bullets, in the back? Well, he had replied, suppose he did? And suppose he was right? "It is sheer vanity to believe that one fat middle-aged spy is the only person capable of holding the world together," he would tell himself. And other times: "I never heard of anyone yet who left the Circus without some unfinished business."

Only Ann, though she could not read his workings, refused to accept his findings. She was quite passionate, in fact, as only women can be on matters of business, really driving him to go back, take up where he had left off, never to veer aside in favour of the easy arguments. Not of course that she knew anything, but what woman was ever stopped by a want of information? She felt. And despised him for not acting in accordance with her feelings.

And now, at the very moment when he was near enough beginning to believe his own dogma, a feat made no easier by Ann's infatuation for an out-of-work actor, what happens but that the assembled ghosts of his past—Lacon, Control, Karla, Alleline, Esterhase, Bland, and finally Bill Haydon himself—barge into his cell and cheerfully inform him, as they drag him back to this same garden, that everything he had been calling vanity is truth?

"Haydon," he repeated to himself, no longer able to stem the tides of memory. Even the name was like a jolt. "I'm told that you and Bill shared *everything* once upon a time," said Martindale. He stared at his chubby hands, watching them shake. Too old? Impotent? Afraid of the chase? Or afraid of what he might unearth at the end of it? "There are always a dozen reasons for doing nothing," Ann liked to say—it was a

favourite apologia, indeed, for many of her misdemeanours—
"There is only one reason for doing *something*. And that's
because you want to." Or have to? Ann would furiously deny it:
coercion, she would say, is just another word for doing what
you want; or for not doing what you are afraid of.

Middle children weep longer than their brothers and sisters.
Over her mother's shoulder, stilling her pains and her injured
pride, Jackie Lacon watched the party leave. First, two men
she had not seen before: one tall, one short and dark. They
drove off in a small green van. No one waved to them, she
noticed, or even said goodbye. Next, her father left in his own
car; lastly a blond, good-looking man and a short fat one in an
enormous overcoat like a pony blanket made their way to a
sports car parked under the beech trees. For a moment she
really thought there must be something wrong with the fat
one, he followed so slowly and so painfully. Then, seeing the
handsome man hold the car door for him, he seemed to wake,
and hurried forward with a lumpy skip. Unaccountably, this
gesture upset her afresh. A storm of sorrow seized her and her
mother could not console her.

11

Peter Guillam was a chivalrous fellow whose conscious loyalties were determined by his affections. The others had been made over long ago to the Circus. His father, a French businessman, had spied for a Circus *réseau* in the war while his mother, an Englishwoman, did mysterious things with codes. Until eight years ago, under the cover of a shipping clerk, Guillam himself had run his own agents in French North Africa, which was considered a murderous assignment. He was blown, his agents were hanged, and he entered the long middle age of the grounded pro. He did hackwork in London, sometimes for Smiley, ran a few home-based operations, including a network of girlfriends who were not, as the jargon has it, inter-conscious, and when Alleline's crowd took over he was shoved out to grass in Brixton—he supposed because he had the wrong connections, among them Smiley. That, resolutely, was how until last Friday he would have told the story of his life. Of his relationship with Smiley he would have dwelt principally upon the end.

Guillam was living mainly in London docks in those days, where he was putting together low-grade Marine networks from whatever odd Polish, Russian, and Chinese seamen he and a bunch of talent-spotters occasionally managed to get their hands on. Betweenwhiles he sat in a small room on the first floor of the Circus and consoled a pretty secretary called

Mary, and he was quite happy except that no one in authority would answer his minutes. When he used the phone, he got "engaged" or no answer. He had heard vaguely there was trouble, but there was always trouble. It was common knowledge, for instance, that Alleline and Control had locked horns, but they had been doing little else for years. He also knew, like everyone else, that a big operation had aborted in Czechoslovakia, that the Foreign Office and the Defence Ministry had jointly blown a gasket, and that Jim Prideaux—head of scalphunters, the oldest Czecho hand, and Bill Haydon's lifelong stringer—had been shot up and put in the bag. Hence, he assumed, the loud silence and the glum faces. Hence also Bill Haydon's manic anger, of which the news spread like a nervous thrill through all the building: like God's wrath, said Mary, who loved a full-scale passion. Later he heard the catastrophe called Testify. Testify, Haydon told him much later, was the most incompetent bloody operation ever launched by an old man for his dying glory, and Jim Prideaux was the price of it. Bits made the newspapers, there were parliamentary questions, and even rumours, never officially confirmed, that British troops in Germany had been put on full alert.

Eventually, by sauntering in and out of other people's offices, he began to realise what everyone else had realised some weeks before. The Circus wasn't just silent, it was frozen. Nothing was coming in, nothing was going out; not at the level on which Guillam moved, anyhow. Inside the building, people in authority had gone to earth, and when pay day came round there were no buff envelopes in the pigeon-holes because, according to Mary, the housekeepers had not received the usual monthly authority to issue them. Now and then somebody would say they had seen Alleline leaving his club and he looked furious. Or Control getting into his car and he looked sunny. Or that Bill Haydon had resigned, on the grounds that he had been overruled or undercut, but Bill was always resigning. This time, said the rumour, the grounds were somewhat different, however: Haydon was furious that the Circus would not pay the Czech price for Jim Prideaux's repatriation; it was said to be too high in agents, or prestige. And that Bill had broken out in one of his fits of chauvinism and declared that any price was fair to get one loyal Englishman home: give them everything, only get Jim back.

Then, one evening, Smiley peered round Guillam's door and suggested a drink. Mary didn't realise who he was and just said "Hullo" in her stylish classless drawl. As they walked out of the Circus side by side, Smiley wished the janitors good night with unusual terseness, and in the pub in Wardour Street he said, "I've been sacked," and that was all.

From the pub they went to a wine bar off Charing Cross, a cellar with music playing and no one there. "Did they give any reason?" Guillam enquired. "Or is it just because you've lost your figure?"

It was the word "reason" that Smiley fixed on. He was by then politely but thoroughly drunk, but reason, as they walked unsteadily along the Thames embankment, reason got through to him.

"Reason as logic, or reason as motive?" he demanded, sounding less like himself than Bill Haydon, whose pre-war, Oxford Union style of polemic seemed in those days to be in everybody's ears. "Or reason as a way of life?" They sat on a bench. "They don't have to give *me* reasons. I can write my own damn reasons. And that is not the same," he insisted as Guillam guided him carefully into a cab, gave the driver the money and the address, "that is not the same as the half-baked tolerance that comes from no longer caring."

"Amen," said Guillam, fully realising as he watched the cab pull into the distance that by the rules of the Circus their friendship, such as it was, had that minute ended. Next day Guillam learned that more heads had rolled and that Percy Alleline was to stand in as night watchman with the title of acting chief, and that Bill Haydon, to everyone's astonishment, but most likely out of persisting anger with Control, would serve under him; or, as the wise ones said, over him.

By Christmas, Control was dead. "They'll get you next," said Mary, who saw these events as a second storming of the Winter Palace, and she wept when Guillam departed for the siberias of Brixton, ironically to fill Jim Prideaux's slot.

Climbing the four steps to the Circus that wet Monday afternoon, his mind bright with the prospect of felony, Guillam passed these events in review and decided that today was the beginning of the road back.

He had spent the previous night at his spacious flat in Eaton Place in the company of Camilla, a music student with a long body and a sad, beautiful face. Though she was not more than twenty, her black hair was streaked with grey, as if from a shock she never talked about. As another effect, perhaps, of the same undescribed trauma, she ate no meat, wore no leather, and drank nothing alcoholic; only in love, it seemed to Guillam, was she free of these mysterious restraints.

He had spent the morning alone in his extremely dingy room in Brixton photographing Circus documents, having first drawn a subminiature camera from his own operational stores, a thing he did quite often to keep his hand in. "Daylight or electric?" the storeman asked, and they had a friendly discussion about film grain. He told his secretary he didn't want to be disturbed, closed his door, and set to work according to Smiley's precise instructions. The windows were high in the wall. Even sitting, he could see only the sky and the tip of the new school up the road.

He began with works of reference from his personal safe. Smiley had given him priorities. First the staff directory, on issue to senior officers only, which supplied the home addresses, telephone numbers, names, and worknames of all home-based Circus personnel. Second, the handbook on staff duties, including the fold-in diagram of the Circus's reorganisation under Alleline. At its centre lay Bill Haydon's London Station, like a giant spider in its own web. "After the Prideaux fiasco," Bill had reputedly fumed, "we'll have no more damned private armies, no more left hand not knowing what the right hand is doing." Alleline, he noticed, was billed twice: once as Chief, once as Director Special Sources. According to rumour, it was those sources that kept the Circus in business. Nothing else, in Guillam's view, could account for the Circus's inertia at working level and the esteem it enjoyed in Whitehall. To these documents, at Smiley's insistence, he added the scalp-hunters' revised charter, in the form of an Alleline letter beginning "Dear Guillam," and setting out in detail the diminution of his powers. In several cases, the winner was Toby Esterhase, head of Acton lamplighters, the one outstation that had actually grown fatter under lateralism.

Next he moved to his desk and photographed, also on Smiley's instruction, a handful of routine circulars that might be useful as background reading. These included a belly-ache from Admin., on the state of safe houses in the London area (*"Kindly* treat them as if they were your *own"*), and another about the misuse of unlisted Circus telephones for private calls. Lastly a very rude personal letter from documents warning him "for the last time of asking" that his workname driving licence was out of date, and that unless he took the trouble to renew it "his name would be forwarded to the housekeepers for appropriate disciplinary action."

He put away the camera and returned to his safe. On the bottom shelf lay a stack of lamplighter reports issued over Toby Esterhase's signature and stamped with the code word "Hatchet." These supplied the names and cover jobs of the two or three hundred identified Soviet intelligence officers operating in London under legal or semi-legal cover: trade, Tass, Aeroflot, Radio Moscow, consular, and diplomatic. Where appropriate, they also gave the dates of lamplighter investigations and names of branch lines, which is jargon for contacts thrown up in the course of surveillance and not necessarily run to earth. The reports came in a main annual volume and monthly supplements. He consulted the main volume first, then the supplements. At eleven-twenty he locked his safe, rang London Station on the direct line, and asked for Lauder Strickland, of Banking Section.

"Lauder, this is Peter from Brixton; how's trade?"

"Yes, Peter, what can we do for you?"

Brisk and blank. We of London Station have more important friends, said the tone.

It was a question of washing some dirty money, Guillam explained, to finance a ploy against a French diplomatic courier who seemed to be for sale. In his meekest voice, he wondered whether Lauder could possibly find the time for them to meet and discuss it. Was the project cleared with London Station, Lauder demanded. No, but Guillam had already sent the papers to Bill by shuttle. Lauder Strickland came down a peg. Guillam pressed his cause: "There are one or two tricky aspects, Lauder; I think we need your sort of brain."

Lauder said he could spare him half an hour.

On his way to the West End, he dropped his films at the meagre premises of a chemist called Lark, in the Charing Cross Road. Lark, if it was he, was a very fat man with tremendous fists. The shop was empty.

"Mr. Lampton's films, to be developed," said Guillam. Lark took the package to the back room, and when he returned he said "All done" in a gravel voice, then blew out a lot of air at once, as if he were smoking, which he wasn't. He saw Guillam to the door and closed it behind him with a clatter. Where on God's earth does George find them, Guillam wondered. He had bought some throat pastilles. Every move must be accountable, Smiley had warned him: assume that the Circus has the dogs on you twenty-four hours a day. So what's new about that, Guillam thought; Toby Esterhase would put the dogs on his own mother if it bought him a pat on the back from Alleline.

From Charing Cross he walked up to Chez Victor for lunch with his head man, Cy Vanhofer, and a thug calling himself Lorimer, who claimed to be sharing his mistress with the East German ambassador in Stockholm. Lorimer said the girl was ready to play ball but she needed British citizenship and a lot of money on delivery of the first take. She would do anything, he said: spike the ambassador's mail, bug his rooms, or "put broken glass in his bath," which was supposed to be a joke. Guillam reckoned Lorimer was lying, and he was inclined to wonder whether Vanhofer was too, but he was wise enough to realise that he was in no state to say which way anyone was leaning just then. He liked Chez Victor but had no recollection of what he ate, and now as he entered the lobby of the Circus he knew the reason was excitement.

"Hullo, Bryant."

"Nice to see you, sir. Take a seat, sir, please, just for a moment, sir, thank you," said Bryant, all in one breath, and Guillam perched on the wooden settle thinking of dentists and Camilla. She was a recent and somewhat mercurial acquisition; it was a while since things had moved quite so fast for him. They met at a party and she talked about truth, alone in a corner over a carrot juice. Guillam, taking a long chance, said he wasn't too good at ethics, so why didn't they just go to bed together? She considered for a while, gravely; then fetched her coat. She'd been hanging around ever since, cooking nut rissoles and playing the flute.

The lobby looked dingier than ever. Three old lifts, a wooden barrier, a poster for Mazawattee tea, Bryant's glass-fronted sentry box with a "Scenes of England" calendar, and a line of mossy telephones.

"Mr. Strickland *is* expecting you, sir," said Bryant as he emerged, and in slow motion stamped a pink chit with the time of day: "14:55, P. Bryant, Janitor." The grille of the centre lift rattled like a bunch of dry sticks.

"Time you oiled this thing, isn't it?" Guillam called as he waited for the mechanism to mesh.

"We keep asking," said Bryant, embarking on a favourite lament. "They never do a thing about it. You can ask till you're blue in the face. How's the family, sir?"

"Fine," said Guillam, who had none.

"That's right," said Bryant. Looking down, Guillam saw the creamy head vanish between his feet. Mary called him strawberry and vanilla, he remembered: red face, white hair, and mushy.

In the lift he examined his pass. "Permit to enter L.S.," ran the headline. "Purpose of visit: Banking Section. This document to be handed back on leaving." And a space, marked "host's signature," blank.

"Well met, Peter. Greetings. You're a trifle late, I think, but never mind."

Lauder was waiting at the barrier—all five foot nothing of him, white collared and secretly on tiptoe—to be visited. In Control's day this floor had been a thoroughfare of busy people. Today a barrier closed the entrance and a rat-faced janitor scrutinised his pass.

"Good God, how long have you had that monster?" Guillam asked, slowing down before a shiny new coffee machine. A couple of girls, filling beakers, glanced round and said "Hullo, Lauder," looking at Guillam. The tall one reminded him of Camilla: the same slow-burning eyes, censuring male insufficiency.

"Ah, but you've no notion how many man-hours it saves!" Lauder cried at once. "Fantastic. Quite fantastic," and all but knocked over Bill Haydon in his enthusiasm.

He was emerging from his room, an hexagonal pepper pot overlooking New Compton Street and the Charing Cross Road. He was moving in the same direction as they were but at about half a mile an hour, which for Bill indoors was full throttle. Outdoors was a different matter; Guillam had seen that, too—on training games at Sarratt, and once on a night drop in Greece. Outdoors he was swift and eager; his keen face, in this clammy corridor shadowed and withdrawn, seemed in the free air to be fashioned by the outlandish places where he had served. There was no end to them: no operational theatre, in Guillam's admiring eyes, that did not bear the Haydon imprint somewhere. Over and again in his own career, he had made the same eerie encounter with Bill's exotic progress. A year or two back, still working on Marine intelligence and having as one of his targets the assembly of a team of coast-watchers for the Chinese ports of Wenchow and Amoy, Guillam discovered to his amazement that there were actually Chinese stay-behind agents living in those very towns, recruited by Bill Haydon in the course of some forgotten wartime exploit, rigged out with cached radios and equipment, with whom contact might be made. Another time, raking through war records of Circus strong-arm men, more out of nostalgia for the period than present professional optimism, Guillam stumbled twice on Haydon's workname in as many minutes: in 1941 he was running French fishing smacks out of the Helford Estuary; in the same year, with Jim Prideaux as his stringer, he was laying down courier lines across southern Europe from the Balkans to Madrid. To Guillam, Haydon was of that unrepeatable, fading Circus generation, to which his parents and George Smiley also belonged—exclusive and, in Haydon's case, blue-blooded—which had lived a dozen leisured lives to his own hasty one, and still, thirty years later, gave the Circus its dying flavour of adventure.

Seeing them both, Haydon stood rock-still. It was a month since Guillam had spoken to him; he had probably been away on unexplained business. Now, against the light of his own open doorway, he looked strangely black and tall. He was carrying something—Guillam could not make out what it was—a magazine, a file, or a report; his room, split by his own shadow, was an undergraduate mayhem, monkish and chaotic. Reports, flimsies, and dossiers lay heaped everywhere; on the wall a baize noticeboard jammed with postcards and press cuttings; beside it, askew and unframed, one of Bill's old paintings, a rounded abstract in the hard flat colours of the desert.

"Hullo, Bill," said Guillam.

Leaving his door open—a breach of housekeeper regulations—Haydon fell in ahead of them, still without a word. He was dressed with his customary dottiness. The leather patches of his jacket were stitched on like diamonds, not squares, which from behind gave him a harlequin look. His spectacles were jammed up into his hair like goggles. For a moment they followed him uncertainly, till, without warning, he suddenly turned himself round, all of him at once like a statue being slowly swivelled on its plinth, and fixed his gaze on Guillam. Then he grinned, so that his crescent eyebrows went straight up like a clown's, and his face became handsome and absurdly young.

"What the hell are you doing here, you pariah?" he enquired pleasantly.

Taking the question seriously, Lauder started to explain about the Frenchman and the dirty money.

"Well, mind you lock up the spoons," said Bill, talking straight through him. "Those bloody scalp-hunters will steal the gold out of your teeth. Lock up the girls, too," he added as an afterthought, his eyes still on Guillam, "if they'll let you. Since when did scalp-hunters wash their own money? That's our job."

"Lauder's doing the washing. We're just spending the stuff."

"Papers to me," Haydon said to Strickland, with sudden curtness. "I'm not crossing any more bloody wires."

"They're already routed to you," said Guillam. "They're probably in your in-tray now."

A last nod sent them on ahead, so that Guillam felt Haydon's pale blue gaze boring into his back all the way to the next dark turning.

"Fantastic fellow," Lauder declared, as if Guillam had never met him. "London Station could not be in better hands. Incredible ability. Incredible record. Brilliant."

Whereas you, thought Guillam savagely, are brilliant by association. With Bill, with the coffee machine, with banks. His meditations were interrupted by Roy Bland's caustic cockney voice, issuing from a doorway ahead of them.

"Hey, Lauder, hold on a minute: have you seen Bloody Bill anywhere? He's wanted urgently."

Followed at once by Toby Esterhase's faithful mid-European echo from the same direction: "Immediately, Lauder; actually, we have put out an alert for him."

They had entered the last cramped corridor. Lauder was perhaps three paces on and was already composing his answer to this question as Guillam arrived at the open doorway and looked in. Bland was sprawled massively at his desk. He had thrown off his jacket and was clutching a paper. Arcs of sweat ringed his armpits. Tiny Toby Esterhase was stooped over him like a headwaiter, a stiff-backed miniature ambassador with silvery hair and a crisp unfriendly jaw, and he had stretched out one hand towards the paper as if to recommend a speciality. They had evidently been reading the same document when Bland caught sight of Lauder Strickland passing.

"Indeed I have seen Bill Haydon," said Lauder, who had a trick of rephrasing questions to make them sound more seemly. "I suspect Bill is on his way to you this moment. He's a way back there down the corridor; we were having a brief word about a couple of things."

Bland's gaze moved slowly to Guillam and settled there; its chilly appraisal was uncomfortably reminiscent of Haydon's. "Hullo, Pete," he said. At this, Tiny Toby straightened up and turned his eyes also directly towards Guillam; brown and quiet like a pointer's.

"Hi," said Guillam, "what's the joke?"

Their greeting was not merely frosty; it was downright hostile. Guillam had lived cheek by jowl with Toby Esterhase for three months on a very dodgy operation in Switzerland and Toby had never smiled once, so his stare came as no surprise. But Roy Bland was one of Smiley's discoveries, a warmhearted and impulsive fellow for that world, red-haired and burly, an intellectual primitive whose idea of a good evening was talking Wittgenstein in the pubs round Kentish Town. He'd spent ten years as a Party hack, plodding the academic circuit in Eastern Europe, and now, like Guillam, he was grounded, which was even something of a bond. His usual style was a big grin, a slap on the shoulder, and a blast of last night's beer; but not today.

"No joke, Peter, old boy," said Roy, mustering a belated smile. "Just surprised to see you, that's all. We're used to having this floor to ourselves."

"Here's Bill," said Lauder, very pleased to have his prognostication so promptly confirmed. In a strip of light, as he entered it, Guillam noticed the queer colour of Haydon's cheeks. A blushing red, daubed high on the bones, but deep, made up of tiny broken veins. It gave him, thought Guillam in his heightened state of nervousness, a slightly Dorian Gray look.

His meeting with Lauder Strickland lasted an hour and twenty minutes; Guillam spun it out that long, and throughout it his mind went back to Bland and Esterhase and he wondered what the hell was eating them.

"Well, I suppose I'd better go and clear all this with the Dolphin," he said at last. "We all know how she is about Swiss banks." The housekeepers lived two doors down from Banking. "I'll leave this here," he added and tossed the pass on to Lauder's desk.

Diana Dolphin's room smelt of fresh deodorant; her chainmail handbag lay on the safe beside a copy of the *Financial Times*. She was one of those groomed Circus brides whom no one ever marries. Yes, he said wearily, the operational papers were already on submission to London Station. Yes, he understood that freewheeling with dirty money was a thing of the past.

"Then we shall look into it and let you know," she announced, which meant she would go and ask Phil Porteous, who sat next door.

"I'll tell Lauder, then," said Guillam, and left.

Move, he thought.

In the men's room he waited thirty seconds at the basins, watching the door in the mirror and listening. A curious quiet had descended over the whole floor. Come on, he thought, you're getting old; move. He crossed the corridor, stepped boldly into the duty officers' room, closed the door with a slam, and looked round. He reckoned he had ten minutes, and he reckoned that a slammed door made less noise in that silence than a door surreptitiously closed. Move.

He had brought the camera but the light was awful. The net-curtained window looked onto a courtyard full of blackened pipes. He couldn't have risked a brighter bulb even if he'd had one with him, so he used his memory. Nothing much seemed to have changed since the takeover. In the daytime the place was used as a restroom for girls with the vapours, and to judge by the smell of cheap scent it still was. Along one wall lay the imitation-leather divan, which at night made into a rotten bed; beside it the first-aid chest with the red cross peeling off the front, and a clapped-out television. The steel cupboard stood in its same place between the switchboard and the locked telephones, and he made a beeline for it. It was an old cupboard and he could have opened it with a tin opener. He had brought his picks and a couple of light alloy tools. Then he remembered that the combination used to be 31-22-11 and he tried it, four anti, three clock, two anti, clockwise till she springs. The dial was so jaded it knew the way. When he opened the door, dust rolled out of the bottom in a cloud, crawled a distance, then slowly lifted towards the dark window. At the same moment, he heard what sounded like a single note played on a flute: it came from a car, most likely, braking in the street outside; or the wheel of a file trolley squeaking on linoleum. But for that moment it was one of those long, mournful notes which made up Camilla's practice scales. She played exactly when she felt like it. At midnight, in the early morning, or whenever. She didn't give a damn about the neighbours; she seemed quite nerveless altogether. He remembered her that first evening: "Which is your side of the bed? Where shall I put my clothes?" He prided himself on his delicate touch in such things, but Camilla had no use for it; technique was already a compromise, a compromise with reality— she would say an escape from it. All right, so get me out of this lot.

The duty logbooks were on the top shelf, in bound volumes with the dates pasted on the spines. They looked like family account books. He took down the volume for April and studied the list of names on the inside cover, wondering whether anyone could see him from the dupe-room across the courtyard, and if they could, would they care? He began working through the entries, searching for the night of the tenth and eleventh, when the signals traffic between London Station and Tarr was supposed to have taken place. Hong Kong was eight hours ahead, Smiley had pointed out: Tarr's telegram and London's first answer had both happened out of hours.

From the corridor came a sudden swell of voices, and for a second he even fancied he could pick out Alleline's growling border brogue lifted in humourless banter, but fancies were two a penny just now. He had a cover story and a part of him believed it already. If he was caught, the whole of him would believe it; and if the Sarratt inquisitors sweated him, he had a fallback—he never travelled without one. All the same, he was terrified. The voices died, and the ghost of Percy Alleline with them. Sweat was running over his ribs. A girl tripped past humming a tune from *Hair*. If Bill hears you, he'll murder you, he thought; if there's one thing that sends Bill spare it's humming. "What are you doing here, you pariah?"

Then, to his fleeting amusement, he actually heard Bill's infuriated roar, echoing from God knows what distance: "Stop that moaning. Who *is* the fool?"

Move. Once you stop, you never start again: there is a special stage-fright that can make you dry up and walk away, that burns your fingers when you touch the goods and turns your stomach to water. Move. He put back the April volume and drew four others at random: February, June, September, and October. He flicked through them fast, looking for comparisons, returned them to the shelf, and dropped into a crouch. He wished to God the dust would settle; there seemed to be no end to it. Why didn't someone complain? Always the same when a lot of people use one place: no one's responsible, no one gives a hoot. He was looking for the night janitors' attendance lists. He found them on the bottom shelf, jammed in with the tea-bags and the condensed milk: sheafs of them in envelope-type folders. The janitors filled them in and brought them to you twice in your twelve-hour tour of duty: at midnight and again at 6 A.M. You vouched for their correctness—God knows how, since the night staff were scattered all over the building— signed them off, kept the third copy, and chucked it in the cupboard, no one knew why. That was the procedure before the Flood, and it seemed to be the procedure now.

Dust and tea-bags on one shelf, he thought. How long since anyone made tea?

Once again he fixed his sights on April 10th–11th. His shirt was clinging to his ribs. What's happened to me? Christ, I'm over the hill. He turned forward and back, forward again, twice, three times, then closed the cupboard on the lot. He waited, listened, took a last worried look at the dust, then stepped boldly across the corridor, back to the safety of the men's room. On the way the clatter hit him: coding machines, the ringing of the telephones, a girl's voice calling "Where's that damn float—I had it in my hand," and that mysterious piping again, but no longer like Camilla's in the small hours. Next time I'll get her to do the job, he thought savagely; without compromise, face to face, the way life should be.

In the men's room he found Spike Kaspar and Nick de Silsky standing at the hand basins and murmuring at each other into the mirror: legmen for Haydon's Soviet networks, they'd been around for years, known simply as "the Russians." Seeing Guillam, they at once stopped talking.

"Hullo, you two. Christ, you really *are* inseparable."

They were blond and squat and they looked more like Russians than the real ones. He waited till they'd gone, rinsed the dust off his fingers, then drifted back to Lauder Strickland's room.

"Lord save us, that Dolphin does talk," he said carelessly.

"Very able officer. Nearest thing to indispensable we have around here. Extremely competent, you can take my word for it," said Lauder. He looked closely at his watch before he signed the chit, then led Guillam back to the lifts. Toby Esterhase was at the barrier, talking to an unfriendly young janitor.

"You are going back to Brixton, Peter?" His tone was casual, his expression as usual impenetrable.

"Why?"

"I have a car outside, actually. I thought maybe I could run you. We have some business out that way."

Run you: Tiny Toby spoke no known language perfectly, but he spoke them all. In Switzerland, Guillam had heard his French and it had a German accent; his German had a Slav accent and his English was full of stray flaws and stops and false vowel sounds.

"It's all right, Tobe, I think I'll just go home. Night."

"Straight home? I would run you, that's all."

"Thanks, I've got shopping to do. All those bloody godchildren."

"Sure," said Toby as if he hadn't any, and stuck in his little granite jaw in disappointment.

What the hell does he want, Guillam thought. Tiny Toby and Big Roy, both: why were they giving me the eye? Was it something they were reading or something they ate?

Out in the street he sauntered down the Charing Cross Road peering at the windows of the bookshops while his other mind checked both sides of the pavement. It had turned much colder, a wind was getting up, and there was a promise to people's faces as they bustled by. He felt elated. Till now he had been living too much in the past, he decided. Time to get my eye in again. In Zwemmer's he examined a coffee-table book called *Musical Instruments Down the Ages* and remembered that Camilla had a late lesson with Dr. Sand, her flute-teacher. He walked back as far as Foyle's, glancing down bus queues as he went. Think of it as abroad, Smiley had said. Remembering the duty room and Roy Bland's fishy stare, Guillam had no difficulty. And Bill, too: was Haydon party to their same suspicion? No. Bill was his own category, Guillam decided, unable to resist a surge of loyalty to Haydon. Bill would share nothing that was not his own in the first place. Set beside Bill, those other two were pygmies.

In Soho he hailed a cab and asked for Waterloo Station. At Waterloo, from a reeking phone box, he telephoned a number in Mitcham, Surrey, and spoke to an Inspector Mendel, formerly of Special Branch, known to both Guillam and Smiley from other lives. When Mendel came on the line, Guillam asked for Jenny and heard Mendel tell him tersely that no Jenny lived there. He apologised and rang off. He dialed the time and feigned a pleasant conversation with the automatic announcer because there was an old lady outside waiting for him to finish. By now he should be there, he thought. He rang off and dialed a second number in Mitcham, this time a call-box at the end of Mendel's avenue.

"This is Will," said Guillam.

"And this is Arthur," said Mendel cheerfully. "How's Will?" He was a quirkish, loping tracker of a man, sharp-faced and sharp-eyed, and Guillam had a very precise picture of him just then, leaning over his policeman's notebook with his pencil poised.

"I want to give you the headlines now in case I go under a bus."

"That's right, Will," said Mendel consolingly. "Can't be too careful."

He gave his message slowly, using the scholastic cover they had agreed on as a last protection against random interception: exams, students, stolen papers. Each time he paused, he heard nothing but a faint scratching. He imagined Mendel writing slowly and legibly and not speaking till he had it all down.

"I got those happy snaps from the chemist, by the by," said Mendel finally, when he had checked it all back. "Come out a treat. Not a miss among them."

"Thanks. I'm glad."

But Mendel had already rung off.

I'll say one thing for moles, thought Guillam: it's a long dark tunnel all the way. As he held open the door for the old lady, he noticed the telephone receiver lying on its cradle, how the sweat crawled over it in drips. He considered his message to Mendel; he thought again of Roy Bland and Toby Esterhase staring at him through the doorway; he wondered quite urgently where Smiley was, and whether he was taking care. He returned to Eaton Place needing Camilla badly, and a little afraid of his reasons. Was it really age that was against him suddenly? Somehow, for the first time in his life, he had sinned against his own notions of nobility. He had a sense of dirtiness, even of self-disgust.

12

There are old men who go back to Oxford and find their youth beckoning to them from the stones. Smiley was not one of them. Ten years ago he might have felt a pull. Not now. Passing the Bodleian, he vaguely thought, I worked there. Seeing the house of his old tutor in Parks Road, he remembered that before the war in its long garden Jebedee had first suggested he might care to talk to "one or two people I know in London." And hearing Tom Tower strike the evening six, he found himself thinking of Bill Haydon and Jim Prideaux, who must have arrived here the year that he went down, and were then gathered up by the war; and he wondered idly how they must have looked together then; Bill, the painter, polemicist, and socialite; Jim, the athlete, hanging on his words. In their heyday together in the Circus, he reflected, that distinction had all but evened out: Jim grew nimble at the brainwork and Bill in the field was no man's fool. Only at the end, the old polarity asserted itself: the workhorse went back to his stable, the thinker to his desk.

Spots of rain were falling but he couldn't see them. He had travelled by rail and walked from the station, making detours all the way: Blackwell's, his old college, anywhere, then north. Dusk had come here early because of the trees.

Reaching a cul-de-sac, he once more dawdled, once more took stock. A woman in a shawl rode past him on a push-bike, gliding through the beams of the streetlamps where they pierced the swathes of mist. Dismounting, she pulled open a gate and vanished. Across the road a muffled figure was walking a dog—man or woman, he couldn't tell. Otherwise the road was empty, so was the phone box. Then abruptly two men passed him, talking loudly about God and war. The younger one did most of the talking. Hearing the older one agree, Smiley supposed he was the don.

He was following a high paling that bulged with shrubs. The gate of number 15 was soft on its hinges, a double gate but only one side used. When he pushed it, the latch was broken. The house stood a long way back; most of the windows were lit. In one, high up, a young man stooped over a desk. At another, two girls seemed to be arguing; at a third, a very pale woman was playing the viola but he couldn't hear the sound. The ground-floor windows were also lit but the curtains were drawn. The porch was tiled, the front door panelled with stained glass; on the jamb was pinned an old notice: "After 11 P.M. use side door only." Over the bells, more notices: "Prince, three rings," "Lumby, two rings," "Buzz: out all evening, see you, Janet." The bottom bell said "Sachs" and he pressed it. At once dogs barked and a woman started yelling.

"Flush, you *stupid* boy, it's only a dunderhead. Flush, shut up, you fool. Flush!"

The door opened part way, held on a chain; a body swelled into the opening. While Smiley in the same instant gave his whole effort to seeing who else was inside the house, two shrewd eyes, wet like a baby's, appraised him, noted his briefcase and his spattered shoes, flickered upward to peer past his shoulder down the drive, then once more looked him over. Finally the white face broke into a charming smile, and Miss Connie Sachs, formerly queen of research at the Circus, registered her spontaneous joy.

"George Smiley," she cried, with a shy trailing laugh as she drew him into the house. "Why, you lovely darling man, I thought you were selling me a Hoover, bless you, and all the time it's George!"

She closed the door after him, fast.

She was a big woman, bigger than Smiley by a head. A tangle of white hair framed her sprawling face. She wore a brown jacket like a blazer and trousers with elastic at the waist and she had a low belly like an old man's. A coke fire smouldered in the grate. Cats lay before it and a mangy grey spaniel, too fat to move, lounged on the divan. On a trolley were the tins she ate from and the bottles she drank from. From the same adapter she drew power for her radio, her electric ring, and her curling tongs. A boy with shoulder-length hair lay on the floor, making toast. Seeing Smiley, he put down his brass trident.

"Oh, Jingle, darling, *could* it be tomorrow?" Connie implored. "It's not often my oldest, oldest lover comes to see me." He had forgotten her voice. She played with it constantly, pitching it at all odd levels. "I'll give you a whole free hour, dear, all to himself: will you? One of my dunderheads," she explained to Smiley, long before the boy was out of earshot. "I still teach, I don't know why. *George*," she murmured, watching him proudly across the room as he took the sherry bottle from his briefcase and filled two glasses. "Of all the lovely darling men I ever knew. *He walked*," she explained to the spaniel. "Look at his boots. Walked all the way from London, didn't you, George? Oh, *bless*, God bless."

It was hard for her to drink. Her arthritic fingers were turned downward, as if they had all been broken in the same accident, and her arm was stiff. "Did you walk alone, George?" she asked, fishing a loose cigarette from her blazer pocket. "Not accompanied, were we?"

He lit the cigarette for her and she held it like a peashooter, fingers along the top, then watched him down the line of it with her shrewd, pinkish eyes. "So what does he want from Connie, you bad boy?"

"Her memory."

"What part?"

"We're going back over some old ground."

"Hear that, Flush?" she yelled to the spaniel. "First they chuck us out with an old bone, then they come begging to us. Which *ground*, George?"

"I've brought a letter for you from Lacon. He'll be at his club this evening at seven. If you're worried, you're to call him from the phone box down the road. I'd prefer you not to do that, but if you must he'll make the necessary impressive noises."

She had been holding him, but now her hands flopped to her sides and for a good while she floated round the room, knowing the places to rest and the holds to steady her, and cursing, "Oh, damn George Smiley and all who sail in him." At the window, perhaps out of habit, she parted the edge of the curtain but there seemed to be nothing to distract her.

"Oh, George, damn you so," she muttered. "How could you let a *Lacon* in? Might as well let in the competition, while you're about it."

On the table lay a copy of the day's *Times*, crossword uppermost. Each square was inked in laboured letters. There were no blanks.

"Went to the soccer today," she sang from the dark under the stairs as she cheered herself up from the trolley. "Lovely Will took me. My favourite dunderhead, wasn't that super of him?" Her little-girl voice; it went with an outrageous pout: "Connie got *cold*, George. Froze solid, Connie did, toes an' all."

He guessed she was crying, so he fetched her from the dark and led her to the sofa. Her glass was empty and he filled it half. Side by side on the sofa, they drank while Connie's tears ran down her blazer onto his hands.

"Oh, George," she said. "Do you know what she told me when they threw me out? That personnel cow?" She was holding one point of Smiley's collar, working it between her finger and thumb while she cheered up. "You know what the cow said?" Her sergeant-major voice: "'You're losing your sense of

proportion, Connie. It's time you got out into the real world.'
I *hate* the real world, George. I like the Circus and all my
lovely boys." She took his hands, trying to interlace her fingers
with his.

"Polyakov," he said quietly, pronouncing it in accordance
with Tarr's instruction. "Aleksey Aleksandrovich Polyakov,
cultural attaché, Soviet Embassy, London. He's come alive again,
just as you predicted."

A car was drawing up in the road; he heard only the sound
of the wheels, the engine was already switched off. Then footsteps, very lightly.

"Janet, smuggling in her boyfriend," Connie whispered,
her pink-rimmed eyes fixed on his while she shared his distraction. "She thinks I don't know. Hear that? Metal quarters on
his heels. Now, wait." The footsteps stopped, there was a small
scuffle. "She's giving him the key. He thinks he works it more
quietly than she can. He can't." The lock turned with a heavy
snap. "Oh, you men," Connie breathed with a hopeless smile.
"Oh, George. Why do you have to drag up Aleks?" And for a
while she wept for Aleks Polyakov.

Her brothers were dons, Smiley remembered; her father
was a professor of something. Control had met her at bridge
and invented a job for her.

She began her story like a fairy-tale: "Once upon a time, there
was a defector called Stanley, way back in 1963," and she applied
to it the same spurious logic—part inspiration, part intellectual opportunism—born of a wonderful mind that had never
grown up. Her formless white face took on the grandmother's
glow of enchanted reminiscence. Her memory was as compendious as her body and surely she loved it more, for she had put
everything aside to listen to it: her drink, her cigarette, even
for a while Smiley's passive hand. She sat no longer slouched
but strictly, her big head to one side as she dreamily plucked
the white wool of her hair. He had assumed she would begin at

once with Polyakov, but she began with Stanley; he had for-gotten her passion for family trees. Stanley, she said; the inquisitors' cover name for a fifth-rate defector from Moscow Centre. March, 1963. The scalp-hunters bought him second-hand from the Dutch and shipped him to Sarratt, and proba-bly if it hadn't been the silly season and if the inquisitors hadn't happened to have time on their hands—well, who knows whether any of it would ever have come to light? As it was, Brother Stanley had a speck of gold on him, one teeny speck, and they found it. The Dutch missed it but the inquisitors found it, and a copy of their report came to Connie, "which was a whole *other* miracle in itself," Connie bellowed huffily, "considering that everyone, and *specially* Sarratt, made an abso-lute *principle* of leaving research off their distribution lists."

Patiently Smiley waited for the speck of gold, for Connie was of an age where the only thing a man could give her was time.

Now, Stanley had defected while he was on a mailfist job in The Hague, she explained. He was by profession an assassin of some sort and had been sent to Holland to murder a Russian émigré who was getting on Centre's nerves. Instead, he decided to give himself up. "Some *girl* had made a fool of him," said Connie with great contempt. "The Dutch set him a honey trap, my dear, and he barged in with his eyes wide shut."

To prepare him for the mission, Centre had posted him to one of their training camps outside Moscow for a brush-up in the black arts: sabotage and silent killing. The Dutch, when they had him, were shocked by this and made it the focal point of their interrogation. They put his picture in the newspapers and had him drawing pictures of cyanide bullets and all the other dreary weaponry Centre so adored. But at the Nursery the inquisitors knew that stuff by heart, so they concentrated on the camp itself, which was a new one, not much known: "Sort of a millionaires' Sarratt," she explained. They made a sketch-plan of the compound, which covered several hundred acres of forest and lakeland, and put in all the buildings Stanley could remember: laundries, canteens, lecture huts, ranges, all the dross. Stanley had been there several times and remembered a lot. They thought they were about finished when Stanley went very quiet. He took a pencil and in the north west corner he drew five more huts and a double fence round them for the guard dogs, bless him. These huts were new, said Stanley, built in the last few months. You reached them by a private road; he had seen them from a hilltop when he was out walking with his instructor, Milos. According to Milos (who was Stanley's *friend*, said Connie with much innuendo), they housed a special school recently founded by Karla for training military officers in conspiracy.

"So, my dear, there we were," Connie cried. "For *years* we'd been hearing rumours that Karla was trying to build a private army of his own inside Moscow Centre but, poor lamb, he hadn't the power. We knew he had agents scattered round the globe, and *naturally* he was worried that as he grew older and more senior he wouldn't be able to manage them alone. We knew that, like everyone else, he was *dreadfully* jealous of them and couldn't bear the idea of handing them over to the legal residencies in the target countries. Well, *naturally* he wouldn't: you know how he hated residencies—overstaffed, insecure. Same as he hated the old guard. 'Flat-earthers,' he called them. Quite right. Well, now he had the power and he was doing something about it, as any real man would. March, 1963," she repeated, in case Smiley had missed the date.

Then nothing, of course. "The usual game: sit on your thumbs, get on with other work, whistle for a wind." She sat on them for three years, until Major Mikhail Fedorovich Komarov, assistant military attaché in the Soviet Embassy in Tokyo, was caught *in flagrante* taking delivery of six reels of top-secret intelligence procured by a senior official in the Japanese Defence Ministry. Komarov was the hero of her second fairy-tale: not a defector but a soldier with the shoulder boards of the artillery.

"And medals, my dear! Medals galore!"

Komarov himself had to leave Tokyo so fast that his dog got locked in his flat and was later found starved to death, which was something Connie could *not* forgive him for. Whereas Komarov's Japanese agent was, of course, duly interrogated and by a happy chance the Circus was able to buy the report from the Toka.

"Why, George, come to think of it, it was you who arranged the deal!"

With a quaint pout of professional vanity, Smiley conceded that it might well have been.

The essence of the report was simple. The Japanese defence official was a mole. He had been recruited before the war in the shadow of the Japanese invasion of Manchuria, by one Martin Brandt, a German journalist who seemed to be connected with the Comintern. Brandt, said Connie, was one of Karla's names in the nineteen-thirties. Komarov himself had never been a member of the official Tokyo residency inside the Embassy; he'd worked solo, with one legman and a direct line to Karla, whose brother officer he had been in the war. Better still, before he arrived in Tokyo he had attended a special training course at a new school outside Moscow set up specially for Karla's handpicked pupils. "Conclusion," Connie sang. "Brother Komarov was our first and, alas, *not* very distinguished graduate of the Karla training school. He was shot, poor lamb," she added, with a dramatic fall of her voice. "They never *hang*, do they: too impatient, the little horrors."

Now Connie had felt able to go to town, she said. Knowing what signs to look for, she tracked back through Karla's file. She spent three weeks in Whitehall with the army's Moscow-gazers combing Soviet Army posting bulletins for disguised entries until, from a host of suspects, she reckoned she had three new, identifiable Karla trainees. All were military men, all were personally acquainted with Karla, all were ten to fifteen years his junior. She gave their names as Bardin, Stokovsky, and Viktorov—all colonels.

At the mention of this third name, Smiley's eyes turned very tired, as if he were staving off boredom.

"So what became of them all," he asked.

"Bardin changed to Sokolov, then Rusakov. Joined the Soviet Delegation to the United Nations in New York. No overt connection with the local residency, no involvement in bread-and-butter operations, no coat-trailing, no talent-spotting—a good solid cover job. Still there, for all I know."

"Stokovsky?"

"Went illegal, set up a photographic business in Paris as Grodescu, French Rumanian. Formed an affiliate in Bonn, believed to be running one of Karla's West German sources from across the border."

"And the third? Viktorov?"

"Sunk without trace."

"Oh, dear," said Smiley, and his boredom seemed to deepen.

"Trained and disappeared off the face of the earth. May have died, of course. One does *tend* to forget the natural causes."

"Oh, indeed," Smiley agreed; "oh, quite."

He had that art, from miles and miles of secret life, of listening at the front of his mind; of letting the primary incidents unroll directly before him while another, quite separate faculty wrestled with their historical connection. The connection ran through Tarr to Irina, through Irina to her poor lover who was so proud of being called Lapin, and of serving one Colonel Gregor Viktorov "whose workname at the Embassy is Polyakov." In his memory, these things were like part of a childhood: he would never forget them.

"Were there photographs, Connie?" he asked glumly. "Did you land physical descriptions at all?"

"Of Bardin at the United Nations, naturally. Of Stokovsky, perhaps. We had an old press picture from his soldiering days, but we could never quite nail the verification."

"And of Viktorov, who sank without trace?" Still, it might

have been any name. "No pretty picture of him, either?" Smiley asked, going down the room to fetch more drink.

"Viktorov, Colonel Gregor," Connie repeated with a fond distracted smile. "Fought like a terrier at Stalingrad. No, we never had a photograph. Pity. They said he was yards the best." She perked up: "Though, of course, we don't *know* about the others. Five huts and a two-year course: well, my dear, that adds up to a sight more than three graduates after all these years!"

With a tiny sigh of disappointment, as if to say there was nothing so far in that whole narrative, let alone in the person of Colonel Gregor Viktorov, to advance him in his laborious quest, Smiley suggested they should pass to the wholly unrelated phenomenon of Polyakov, Aleksey Aleksandrovich, of the Soviet Embassy in London, better known to Connie as dear Aleks Polyakov, and establish just where he fitted into Karla's scheme of things and why it was that she had been forbidden to investigate him further.

13

She was much more animated now. Polyakov was not a fairy-tale hero; he was her lover Aleks, though she had never spoken to him, probably never seen him in the flesh. She had moved to another seat closer to the reading lamp, a rocking-chair that relieved certain pains: she could sit nowhere for long. She had tilted her head back so that Smiley was looking at the white billows of her neck and she dangled one stiff hand coquettishly, recalling indiscretions she did not regret; while to Smiley's tidy mind her speculations, in terms of the acceptable arithmetic of intelligence, seemed even wilder than before.

"*Oh*, he was so good," she said. "Seven long years Aleks had been here before we even had an inkling. Seven years, my dear, and not so much as a *tickle!* Imagine!"

She quoted his original visa application, those nine years ago: Polyakov, Aleksey Aleksandrovich, graduate of Leningrad State University, cultural attaché with second-secretary rank, married but not accompanied by wife, born March 3, 1922, in the Ukraine, son of a transporter, early education not supplied. She ran straight on, a smile in her voice as she gave the lamplighters' first routine description: "Height, five foot eleven; heavy build; colour of eyes, green; colour of hair, black; no other visible distinguishing marks. Jolly giant of a bloke," she declared with a laugh. "Tremendous joker. Black tuft of hair, here, over the right eye. I'm sure he was a bottom pincher, though we never caught him at it. I'd have offered him one or two bottoms of our own if Toby had played ball, which he wouldn't. Not that Aleksey Aleksandrovich would have fallen for *that*, mind. Aleks was *far* too artful," she said proudly. "Lovely voice. Mellow like yours. I often used to play the tapes twice, just to listen to him speaking. Is he really still around, George? I don't even like to ask, you see. I'm afraid they'll all change and I won't know them any more."

He was still there, Smiley assured her. The same cover, the same rank.

"And still occupying that dreadful little suburban house in Highgate that Toby's watchers hated so? Forty Meadow Close, top floor. Oh, it was a *pest* of a place. I love a man who really lives his cover, and Aleks did. He was the busiest culture vulture that Embassy ever had. If you wanted something done fast—lecturer, musician, you name it—Aleks cut through the red tape faster than any man."

"How did he manage that, Connie?"

"Not how *you* think, George Smiley," she sang as the blood shot to her face. "*Oh*, no. Aleksey Aleksandrovich was nothing but what he said he was—so there; you ask Toby Esterhase or Percy Alleline. Pure as the driven snow, he was. Unbesmirched in any shape or form—Toby will put you right on that!"

"Hey," Smiley murmured, filling her glass. "Hey, steady, Connie. Come down."

"*Fooey*," she shouted, quite unmollified. "Sheer unadulterated *fooey*. Aleksey Aleksandrovich Polyakov was a six-cylinder Karla-trained hood if ever I saw one, and they wouldn't even listen to me! 'You're seeing spies under the bed,' says Toby. 'Lamplighters are fully extended,' says Percy"—her Scottish brogue—"'We've no place for luxuries here.' Luxuries my foot!" She was crying again. "Poor George," she kept saying. "Poor George. You tried to help but what could you do? You were on the down staircase yourself. Oh, George, don't go hunting with the Lacons. Please don't."

Gently he guided her back to Polyakov, and why she was so sure he was Karla's hood, a graduate of Karla's special school.

"It was Remembrance Day," she sobbed. "We photographed his medals—'course we did."

Year one again, year one of her seven-year love affair with Aleks Polyakov. The curious thing was, she said, that she had her eye on him from the moment he arrived:

"Hullo, I thought. I'm going to have a bit of fun with you."

Quite why she thought that she didn't know. Perhaps it was his self-sufficiency, perhaps it was his poker walk, straight off the parade-ground: "Tough as a button. Army written all over him." Or perhaps it was the way he lived: "He chose the one house in London those lamplighters couldn't get within fifty yards of." Or perhaps it was his work: "There were three cultural attachés already: two of them were hoods and the only thing the third did was cart the flowers up to Highgate Cemetery for poor Karl Marx."

She was a little dazed, so he walked her again, taking the whole weight of her when she stumbled. Well, she said, at first Toby Esterhase agreed to put Aleks on the A list and have his Acton lamplighters cover him for random days, twelve out of every thirty, and each time they followed him he was as pure as the driven snow.

"My dear, you'd have thought I'd rung him up and told him, 'Aleks Aleksandrovich, mind your "p"s and "q"s because I'm putting Tiny Toby's dogs on you. So just you live your cover and no monkey business.'"

He went to functions, lectures, strolled in the park, played a little tennis, and short of giving sweets to the kids he couldn't have been more respectable. Connie fought for continued coverage but it was a losing battle. The machinery ground on and Polyakov was transferred to the B list: to be topped up every six months or as resources allowed. The six-monthly top-ups produced nothing at all, and after three years he was graded Persil: investigated in depth and found to be of no intelligence interest. There was nothing Connie could do, and really she had almost begun to live with the assessment when one gorgeous November day lovely Teddy Hankie telephoned her rather breathlessly from the Laundry at Acton to say Aleks Polyakov had blown his cover and run up his true colours at last. They were splashed all over the masthead.

"Teddy was an old *old* chum. Old Circus and a perfect pet; I don't care if he's ninety. He'd finished for the day and was on his way home when the Soviet Ambassador's Volga drove past going to the wreath-laying ceremony, carrying the three service attachés. Three others were following in a second car. One was Polyakov and he was wearing more medals than a Christmas tree. Teddy shot down to Whitehall with his camera and photographed them across the street. My dear, *everything* was on our side: the weather was perfect, a bit of rain and then some lovely afternoon sunshine; he could have got the smile on a fly's backside at three hundred yards. We blew up the photographs and there they were: two gallantry and four campaign. Aleks Polyakov was a war veteran and he'd never told a soul in seven years. Oh, I was excited! I didn't even need to plot the campaigns. 'Toby,' I said—I rang him straight away—'You just listen to me for a moment, you Hungarian poison dwarf. This is one of the occasions when ego has finally got the better of cover. I want you to turn Aleks Aleksandrovich *inside out* for me, no "if"s or "but"s. Connie's little hunch has come home trumps.'"

"And what did Toby say?"

The grey spaniel let out a dismal sigh, and dropped off to sleep again.

"Toby?" Connie was suddenly very lonely. "Oh, Tiny Toby gave me his dead-fish voice and said Percy Alleline was now head of operations, didn't he? It was Percy's job, not his, to allocate resources. I knew straight away something was wrong but I thought it was Toby." She fell silent. "Damn fire," she muttered morosely. "You only have to turn your back and it goes out." She had lost interest. "You know the rest. Report went to Percy. 'So what?' Percy says. 'Polyakov used to be in the Russian Army. It was a biggish army and not everybody who fought in it was Karla's agent.' Very funny. Accused me of unscientific deduction. 'Whose expression is that?' I said to him. 'It's not deduction at all,' he says, 'it's induction.' 'My dear Percy, wherever have you been learning words like that; you sound just like a beastly doctor or someone.' *My dear*, he was cross! As a sop, Toby puts the dogs on Aleks and nothing happens. 'Spike his house,' I said. 'His car, everything! Rig a mugging, turn him inside out, put the listeners on him! Fake a mistaken identity, search him. Anything, but for God's *sake* do something, because it's a pound to a rouble Aleks Polyakov is running an English mole!' So Percy sends for me, all lofty,"—the brogue again: "'You're to leave Polyakov alone. You're to put him out of your silly woman's mind, do you understand? You and your blasted Polly what's-'is-name are becoming a damned nuisance, so lay off him.' Follows it up with a rude letter. 'We spoke and you agreed,' copy to head cow. I wrote, 'yes repeat no' on the bottom and sent it back to him." She switched to her sergeant-major voice: "'You're losing your sense of proportion, Connie. Time you got out into the real world.'"

Connie was having a hangover. She was sitting again, slumped over her glass. Her eyes had closed and her head kept falling to one side.

"Oh, God," she whispered, waking up again. "Oh, my Lordy be."

"Did Polyakov have a legman?" Smiley asked.

"Why should he? He's a culture vulture. Culture vultures don't need legmen."

"Komarov had one in Tokyo. You said so."

"Komarov was military," she said sullenly.

"So was Polyakov. You saw his medals."

He held her hand, waiting. Lapin the rabbit, she said, clerk driver at the Embassy, twerp. At first she couldn't work him out. She suspected him of being one Ivlov, but she couldn't prove it and no one would help her anyway. Lapin the rabbit spent most of his day padding round London looking at girls and not daring to talk to them. But gradually she began to pick up the connection. Polyakov gave a reception, Lapin helped pour the drinks. Polyakov was called in late at night, and half an hour later Lapin turned up presumably to unbutton a telegram. And when Polyakov flew to Moscow, Lapin the rabbit actually moved into the Embassy and slept there till he came back. "He was doubling up," said Connie firmly. "Stuck out a mile."

"So you reported that, too?"

"'Course I did."

"And what happened?"

"Connie was sacked and Lapin went home," Connie said with a giggle. "Couple of weeks later, Jimmy Prideaux got shot in the bot, George Smiley was pensioned off, and Control . . ." She yawned. "Hey, ho," she said. "Halcyon days. Landslide. Did I start it, George?"

The fire was quite dead. From somewhere above them came a thud; perhaps it was Janet and her lover. Gradually, Connie began humming, then swaying to her own music.

He stayed, trying to cheer her up. He gave her more drink and finally it brightened her.

"Come on," she said, "I'll show you *my* bloody medals."

Dormitory feasts again. She had them in a scuffed attaché case, which Smiley had to pull out from under the bed. First a real medal in a box and a typed citation calling her by her workname Constance Salinger and putting her on the Prime Minister's list.

"'Cause Connie was a good girl," she explained, her cheek against his. "And loved all her gorgeous boys."

Then photographs of past members of the Circus: Connie in Wren's uniform in the war, standing between Jebedee and old Bill Magnus, the wrangler, taken somewhere in England; Connie with Bill Haydon one side and Jim Prideaux the other, the men in cricket gear and all three looking very-nicely-thank-you, as Connie put it, on a summer course at Sarratt, the grounds stretching out behind them, mown and sunlit, and the sight screens glistening. Next an enormous magnifying glass with signatures engraved on the lens: from Roy, from Percy, from Toby and lots of others, "To Connie with love and never say goodbye!"

Lastly, Bill's own special contribution: a caricature of Connie lying across the whole expanse of Kensington Palace Gardens while she peered at the Soviet Embassy through a telescope: "With love and fond memories, dear, dear Connie."

"They still remember him here, you know," she said. "The golden boy. Christ Church common-room has a couple of his paintings. They take them out quite often. Giles Langley stopped me in the High only the other day: did I ever hear from Haydon? Don't know what I said: Yes. No. Does Giles's sister still do safe houses, do you know?" Smiley did not. "'We miss his flair,' says Giles, 'they don't breed them like him any more.' Giles must be a hundred and eight in the shade. Says he taught Bill modern history, in the days before 'Empire' became a dirty word. Asked after Jim, too. 'His alter ego, we might say, hem hem, hem hem.' You never liked Bill, did you?" Connie ran on vaguely, as she packed it all away again in plastic bags and bits of cloth. "I never knew whether you were jealous of him or he was jealous of you. Too glamorous, I suppose. You always distrusted looks. Only in men, mind."

"My dear Connie, don't be absurd," Smiley retorted, off guard for once. "Bill and I were perfectly good friends. What on earth makes you say that?"

"Nothing." She had almost forgotten it. "I heard once he had a run round the park with Ann, that's all. Isn't he a cousin of hers, or something? I always thought you'd have been so good together, you and Bill, if it could have worked. You'd have brought back the old spirit. Instead of that Scottish twerp. Bill rebuilding Camelot"—her fairy-tale smile again—"and George—"

"George picking up the bits," said Smiley, vamping for her, and they laughed, Smiley falsely.

"Give me a kiss, George. Give Connie a kiss."

She showed him through the kitchen garden, the route her lodgers used; she said he would prefer it to the view of the filthy new bungalows the Harrison pigs had flung up in the next door garden. A thin rain was falling, a few stars glowed big and pale in the mist; on the road lorries rumbled northward through the night. Clasping him, Connie grew suddenly frightened.

"You're very naughty, George. Do you hear? Look at me. Don't look that way, it's all neon lights and Sodom. Kiss me. All over the world, beastly people are making our time into nothing; why do you help them? Why?"

"I'm not helping them, Connie."

"'Course you are. Look at me. It was a good time, do you hear? A real time. Englishmen could be proud then. Let them be proud now."

"That's not quite up to me, Connie."

She was pulling his face onto her own, so he kissed her full on the lips.

"Poor loves." She was breathing heavily, not perhaps from any one emotion but from a whole mess of them, washed around in her like mixed drinks. "Poor loves. Trained to Empire, trained to rule the waves. All gone. All taken away. Bye-bye, world. You're the last, George, you and Bill. And filthy Percy a bit." He had known it would end like this; but not quite so awfully. He had had the same story from her every Christmas at the little drinking parties that went on in corners round the Circus. "You don't know Millponds, do you?" she was asking.

"What's Millponds?"

"My brother's place. Beautiful Palladian house, lovely grounds, near Newbury. One day a road came. Crash. Bang. Motorway. Took all the grounds away. I grew up there, you see. They haven't sold Sarratt, have they? I was afraid they might."

"I'm sure they haven't."

He longed to be free of her but she was clutching him more fiercely; he could feel her heart thumping against him.

"If it's bad, don't come back. Promise? I'm an old leopard and I'm too old to change my spots. I want to remember you all as you were. Lovely, lovely boys."

He did not like to leave her there in the dark, swaying under the trees, so he walked her halfway back to the house, neither of them talking. As he went down the road, he heard her humming again, so loud it was like a scream. But it was nothing to the mayhem inside him just then, the currents of alarm and anger and disgust at this blind night walk, with God knew what bodies at the end.

He caught a stopping train to Slough, where Mendel was waiting for him with a hired car. As they drove slowly towards the orange glow of the city, he listened to the sum of Peter Guillam's researches. The duty officers' ledger contained no record of the night of April 10th–11th, said Mendel. The pages had been excised with a razor blade. The janitors' returns for the same night were also missing, as were the signals' returns.

"Peter thinks it was done recently. There's a note scribbled on the next page, saying, 'All enquiries to Head of London Station.' It's in Esterhase's handwriting and dated Friday."

"*Last* Friday?" said Smiley, turning so fast that his seat belt let out a whine of complaint. "That's the day Tarr arrived in England."

"It's all according to Peter," Mendel replied stolidly.

And finally, concerning Lapin alias Ivlov, and Cultural Attaché Aleksey Aleksandrovich Polyakov, both of the Soviet

Embassy in London, Toby Esterhase's lamplighter reports carried no adverse trace whatever. Both had been investigated, both were graded Persil: the cleanest category available. Lapin had been posted back to Moscow a year ago.

In a briefcase, Mendel had also brought Guillam's photographs, the result of his foray at Brixton, developed and blown up to full-plate size. Close to Paddington Station, Smiley got out and Mendel held the case out to him through the doorway.

"Sure you don't want me to come with you?" Mendel asked.

"Thank you. It's only a hundred yards."

"Lucky for you there's twenty-four hours in the day, then."

"Yes, it is."

"Some people sleep."

"Good night."

Mendel was still holding onto the briefcase. "I may have found the school," he said. "Place called Thursgood's, near Taunton. He did half a term's supply work in Berkshire first, then seems to have hoofed it to Somerset. Got a trailer, I hear. Want me to check?"

"How will you do that?"

"Bang on his door. Sell him a magazine, get to know him socially."

"I'm sorry," said Smiley, suddenly worried. "I'm afraid I'm jumping at shadows. I'm sorry, that was rude of me."

"Young Guillam's jumping at shadows, too," said Mendel firmly. "Says he's getting funny looks around the place. Says there's something up and they're all in it. I told him to have a stiff drink."

"Yes," said Smiley after further thought. "Yes, that's the thing to do. Jim's a pro," he explained. "A fieldman of the old school. He's good, whatever they did to him."

Camilla had come back late. Guillam had understood her flute lesson with Sand ended at nine, yet it was eleven by the time she let herself in, and he was accordingly short with her; he couldn't help it. Now she lay in bed, with her grey-black hair spread over the pillow, watching him as he stood at the unlit window staring into the square.

"Have you eaten?" he said.

"Dr. Sand fed me."

"What on?"

Sand was a Persian, she had told him.

No answer. Dreams, perhaps? Nut steak? Love? In bed she never stirred except to embrace him. When she slept, she barely breathed; sometimes he would wake and watch her, wondering how he would feel if she were dead.

"Are you fond of Sand?" he asked.

"Sometimes."

"Is he your lover?"

"Sometimes."

"Maybe you should move in with him instead of me."

"It's not like that," said Camilla. "You don't understand."

No. He didn't. First there had been a loving couple necking in the back of a Rover, then a lonely queer in a trilby exercising his Sealyham; then a girl made an hour-long call from the phone box outside his front door. There need be nothing to any of it, except that the events were consecutive, like a changing of the guard. Now a van had parked and no one got out. More lovers, or a lamplighters' night team? The van had been there ten minutes when the Rover drove away.

Camilla was asleep. He lay awake beside her, waiting for tomorrow when, at Smiley's request, he intended to steal the file on the Prideaux affair, otherwise known as the Ellis scandal or—more locally—Operation Testify.

14

It had been, till that moment, the second happiest day of Bill Roach's short life. The happiest was shortly before the dissolution of his household, when his father discovered a wasps' nest in the roof and recruited Bill to help him smoke them out. His father was not an outdoor man—not even handy—but after Bill had looked up wasps in his encyclopaedia they drove to the chemist together and bought sulphur, which they burned on a charger under the eave, and did the wasps to death.

Whereas today had seen the formal opening of Jim Prideaux's car-club rally. Till now they had only stripped the Alvis down, refurbished her, and put her together again, but today, as the reward, they had laid out—with the help of Latzy, the D.P.—a slalom of straw bales on the stony side of the drive. Then each in turn had taken the wheel and, with Jim as time-keeper, puffed and shunted through the gates to the tumult of their supporters. "Best car England ever made" was how Jim had introduced his car. "Out of production, thanks to Socialism." She was now repainted, she had a racing Union Jack on the bonnet, and she was undoubtedly the finest, fastest car on earth. In the first round, Roach had come third out of fourteen, and now in the second he had reached the chestnut trees without once stalling, and was all set for the home lap and a record time. He had never imagined that anything could give him so much pleasure. He loved the car, he loved Jim, and he even loved the school, and for the first time in his life he loved trying to win. He could hear Jim yelling, "Easy, Jumbo," and he could see Latzy leaping up and down with the improvised chequered flag; but as he clattered past the post he already knew that Jim wasn't watching him any more but glaring down the course towards the beech trees.

"Sir, how long, sir?" he asked breathlessly, and there was a small hush.

"Timekeeper!" sang Spikely, chancing his luck. "Time, please, Rhino."

"Was very good, Jumbo," Latzy said, also looking at Jim.

For once, Spikely's impertinence, like Roach's entreaty, found no response. Jim was staring across the field, towards the lane that formed the eastern border. Beside him stood a boy named Coleshaw, whose nickname was Cole Slaw. He was a lag from Three B, and famous for sucking up to staff. The ground lay very flat just there before lifting to the hills; often after a few days' rain it flooded. For this reason there was no good hedge beside the lane but a post-and-wire fence; and no trees, either—just the fence, the flats, and sometimes the Quantocks behind, which today had vanished in the general whiteness. The flats could have been a marsh leading to a lake, or simply to the white infinity. Against this washed-out background strolled a single figure, a trim, inconspicuous pedestrian, male and thin-faced, in a trilby hat and grey raincoat, carrying a walking stick that he barely used. Watching him also, Roach decided that the man wanted to walk faster but was going slowly for a purpose.

"Got your specs on, Jumbo?" asked Jim, staring after the man, who was about to draw level with the next post.

"Yes, sir."

"Who is he, then? Looks like Solomon Grundy."

"Don't know, sir."

"Never seen him before?"

"No, sir."

"Not staff, not village. So who is he? Beggarman? Thief? Why doesn't he look this way, Jumbo? What's wrong with us? Wouldn't you, if you saw a bunch of boys flogging a car round a field? Doesn't he like cars? Doesn't he like boys?"

Roach was still thinking up an answer to all these questions when Jim started speaking to Latzy in D.P., using a murmured, level sort of tone, which at once suggested to Roach that there was a complicity between them, a special foreign bond. The impression was strengthened by Latzy's reply, plainly negative, which had the same unstartled quietness.

"Sir, please, sir, I think he's to do with the church, sir," said Cole Slaw. "I saw him talking to Wells Fargo, sir, after chapel."

The vicar's name was Spargo and he was very old. It was Thursgood legend that he was in fact the great Wells Fargo in retirement. At this intelligence, Jim thought awhile and Roach, furious, told himself that Coleshaw was making the story up.

"Hear what they talked about, Cole Slaw?"

"Sir, no, sir. They were looking at pew lists, sir. But I could ask Wells Fargo, sir."

"*Our* pew lists? Thursgood pew lists?"

"Yes, sir. School pew lists. Thursgood's. With all the names, sir, where we sit."

And where the staff sit, too, thought Roach sickly.

"Anybody sees him again, let me know. Or any other sinister bodies, understand?" Jim was addressing them all, making light of it now. "Don't hold with odd bods hanging about the school. Last place I was at, we had a whole damn gang. Cleared the place out. Silver, money, boys' watches, radios—God knows what they didn't pinch. He'll pinch the Alvis next. Best car England ever made, and out of production. Colour of hair, Jumbo?"

"Black, sir."

"Height, Cole Slaw?"

"Sir, six foot, sir."

"Everybody looks six foot to Cole Slaw, sir," said a wit, for Coleshaw was a midget, reputedly fed on gin as a baby.

"Age, Spikely, you toad?"

"Ninety-one, sir."

The moment dissolved in laughter; Roach was awarded a re-drive and did badly, and the same night lay in an anguish of jealousy that the entire car club, not to mention Latzy, had been recruited wholesale to the select rank of watcher. It was poor consolation to assure himself that their vigilance would never match his own; that Jim's order would not outlive the day; or that from now on he must increase his efforts to meet what was clearly an advancing threat.

The thin-faced stranger disappeared, but next day Jim paid a rare visit to the churchyard; Roach saw him talking to Wells Fargo before an open grave. Thereafter Bill Roach noticed a steady darkening of Jim's face, and an alertness which at times was like an anger in him, as he stalked through the twilight every evening, or sat on the hummocks outside his trailer, indifferent to the cold or wet, smoking his tiny cigar and sipping his vodka as the dusk closed on him.

PART II

15

The Hotel Islay in Sussex Gardens—where, on the day after his visit to Ascot, George Smiley under the name of Barraclough had set up his operational headquarters—was a very quiet place, considering its position, and perfectly suited to his needs. It lay a hundred yards south of Paddington Station, one of a terrace of elderly mansions cut off from the main avenue by a line of plane trees and a parking patch. The traffic roared past it all night. But the inside, though it was a fire-bowl of clashing wallpapers and copper lampshades, was a place of extraordinary calm. Not only was there nothing going on in the hotel, there was nothing going on in the world, either, and this impression was strengthened by Mrs. Pope Graham, the proprietor, a major's widow with a terribly langorous voice that imparted a sense of deep fatigue to Mr. Barraclough or anyone else who sought her hospitality. Inspector Mendel, whose informant she had been for many years, insisted that her name was plain Graham. The Pope had been added for grandeur or out of deference to Rome.

"Your father wasn't a Green Jacket, was he, dear?" she enquired, with a yawn, as she read Barraclough in the register. Smiley paid her fifty pounds' advance for a two-week stay, and she gave him Room 8 because he wanted to work. He asked for a desk and she gave him a rickety card table; Norman, the boy, brought it. "It's Georgian," she said with a sigh, supervising its delivery. "So you will love it for me, won't you, dear? I shouldn't lend it to you, really; it was the Major's."

To the fifty, Mendel privately had added a further twenty on account, from his own wallet—"dirty oncers," as he called them—which he later recovered from Smiley. "No smell to nothing, is there?" he said.

"You could say so," Mrs. Pope Graham agreed, demurely stowing the notes among her nether garments.

"I'll want every scrap," Mendel warned, seated in her basement apartment over a bottle of the one she liked. "Times of entry and exit, contacts, life-style, and most of all," he said, lifting an emphatic finger, "most of all—and more important than you can possibly know, this is—I'll want suspicious persons taking an interest or putting questions to your staff under a pretext." He gave her his state-of-the-nation look. "Even if they say they're the Guards Armoured and Sherlock Holmes rolled into one."

"There's only me and Norman," said Mrs. Pope Graham, indicating a shivery boy in a black overcoat to which had been stitched a velvet collar of beige. "And they'll not get far with Norman—will they, dear; you're too sensitive."

"Same with his incoming letters," said the Inspector. "I'll want postmarks and times posted where legible, but no tampering or holding back. Same with his objects." He allowed a hush to fall as he eyed the substantial safe that formed such a feature of the furnishings. "Now and then, he's going to ask for objects to be lodged. Mainly they'll be papers, sometimes books. There's only one person allowed to look at those objects apart from him." He pulled a sudden piratical grin: "Me. Understand? No one else can even know you've got them. And don't fiddle with them, or he'll know because he's sharp. It's got to be expert fiddling. I'm not saying any more," Mendel concluded. Though he did remark to Smiley, soon after returning from Somerset, that if twenty quid was all it cost them,

Norman and his protectress were the cheapest baby-sitting service in the business.

In which boast he was pardonably mistaken, for he could hardly be expected to know of Jim's recruitment of the entire car club; or the means by which Jim was able subsequently to trace the path of Mendel's wary investigations. Nor could Mendel, or anyone else, have guessed the state of electric alertness to which anger, and the strain of waiting, and perhaps a little madness, had seemingly brought Jim.

Room 8 was on the top floor. Its window looked onto the parapet. Beyond the parapet lay a side street with a shady bookshop and a travel agency called Wide World. The hand towel was embroidered "Swan Hotel Marlow." Lacon stalked in that evening carrying a fat briefcase containing the first consignment of papers from his office. To talk, the two men sat side by side on the bed while Smiley played a transistor wireless to drown the sound of their voices. Lacon took this mawkishly; he seemed somehow too old for the picnic. Next morning on his way to work, Lacon reclaimed the papers and returned the books that Smiley had given him to pad out his briefcase. In this role Lacon was at his worst. His manner was offended and off-hand; he made it clear he detested the irregularity. In the cold weather, he seemed to have developed a permanent blush. But Smiley could not have read the files by day, because they were on call to Lacon's staff and their absence would have caused an uproar. Nor did he want to. He knew better than anyone that he was desperately short of time. Over the next three days this procedure varied very little. Each evening on his way to take the train from Paddington, Lacon dropped in his papers, and each night Mrs. Pope Graham furtively reported to Mendel that the sour gangly one had called again—the one who looked down his nose at Norman. Each morning, after three hours' sleep and a disgusting breakfast of undercooked sausage and overcooked tomato—there was no other menu—Smiley waited for Lacon to arrive, then slipped gratefully into the cold winter's day to take his place among his fellow men.

They were extraordinary nights for Smiley, alone up there on the top floor. Thinking of them afterwards—though his days between were just as fraught, and on the surface more eventful—he recalled them as a single journey, almost a single night. "And you'll do it," Lacon had piped shamelessly in the garden. "Go forwards, go backwards?" As Smiley retraced path after path into his own past, there was no longer any difference between the two: forwards or backwards, it was the same journey and its destination lay ahead of him. There was nothing in that room, no object among that whole magpie collection of tattered hotel junk, that separated him from the rooms of his recollection. He was back on the top floor of the Circus, in his own plain office with the Oxford prints, just as he had left it a year ago. Beyond his door lay the low-ceilinged anteroom where Control's grey-haired ladies, the mothers, softly typed and answered telephones; while here in the hotel an undiscovered genius along the corridor night and day tapped patiently at an old machine. At the anteroom's far end—in Mrs. Pope Graham's world there was a bathroom there, and a warning not to use it—stood the blank door that led to Control's sanctuary: an alley of a place, with old steel cupboards and old red books, a smell of sweet dust and jasmine tea. Behind the desk Control himself, a carcass of a man by then, with his lank grey forelock and his smile as warm as a skull.

This mental transposition was so complete in Smiley that when his phone rang—the extension was an extra, payable in cash—he had to give himself time to remember where he was. Other sounds had an equally confusing effect on him, such as the rustle of pigeons on the parapet, the scraping of the television mast in the wind, and—in rain—the sudden river gurgling in the roof valley. For these sounds also belonged to his past, and in Cambridge Circus were heard by the fifth floor only. His ear selected them, no doubt, for that very reason: they were the background jingle of his past. Once in the early morning, hearing a footfall in the corridor outside his room, Smiley actually went to the bedroom door expecting to let in the Circus night coding clerk. He was immersed in Guillam's photographs at the time, puzzling out, from far too little information, the likely Circus procedure under lateralism for handling an incoming telegram from Hong Kong. But instead of the clerk he found Norman, barefooted in pyjamas. Confetti was strewn over the carpet and two pairs of shoes stood outside the opposite door, a man's and a girl's, though no one at the Islay—least of all Norman—would ever clean them.

"Stop prying and go to bed," said Smiley. And when Norman only stared: "Oh, do go away, will you?"—And nearly, but he stopped himself in time, "You grubby little man."

"Operation Witchcraft," read the title on the first volume Lacon had brought to him that first night. "Policy regarding distribution of Special Product." The rest of the cover was obliterated by warning labels and handling instructions, including one that quaintly advised the accidental finder to "return the file UNREAD" to the Chief Registrar at the Cabinet Office. "Operation Witchcraft," read the second. "Supplementary estimates to the Treasury, special accommodation in London, special financing arrangements, bounty, etc." "Source Merlin," read the third, bound to the first with pink ribbon. "Customer Evaluations, cost effectiveness, wider exploitation; see also Secret Annexe." But the secret annexe was not attached, and when Smiley asked for it there was a coldness.

"The Minister keeps it in his personal safe," Lacon snapped.

"Do you know the combination?"

"Certainly not," he retorted, now furious.

"What is the title of it?"

"It can be of no possible concern to you. I entirely fail to see why you should waste your time chasing after this material in the first place. It's highly secret and we have done everything humanly possible to keep the readership to the minimum."

"Even a secret annexe has to have a title," said Smiley mildly.

"This has none."

"Does it give the identity of Merlin?"

"Don't be ridiculous. The Minister would not want to know, and Alleline would not want to tell him."

"What does 'wider exploitation' mean?"

"I refuse to be interrogated, George. You're not family any more, you know. By rights, I should have you specially cleared, as it is."

"Witchcraft-cleared?"

"Yes."

"Do we have a list of people who have been cleared in that way?"

It was in the policy file, Lacon retorted, and all but slammed the door on him before coming back, to the slow chant of "Where Have All the Flowers Gone?" introduced by an Australian disc-jockey. "The Minister—" He stopped, and began again. "He doesn't like devious explanations. He has a saying: he'll only believe what can be written on a postcard. He's very impatient to be given something he can get his hands on."

Smiley said, "You won't forget Prideaux, will you? Just anything you have on him at all; even scraps are better than nothing."

With that, Smiley left Lacon to glare awhile, then make a second exit: "You're not going fey, are you, George? You realise that Prideaux had most likely never even *heard* of Witchcraft before he was shot? I really do fail to see why you can't stick with the primary problem instead of rootling around in . . ." But by this time he had talked himself out of the room.

Smiley turned to the last of the batch: "Operation Witchcraft, correspondence with Department." "Department" being one of Whitehall's many euphemisms for the Circus. This volume was conducted in the form of official minutes between the Minister on the one side, and on the other—recognisable at once by his laborious schoolboy hand—Percy Alleline, at that time still consigned to the bottom rungs of Control's ladder of beings.

A very dull monument, Smiley reflected, surveying these much-handled files, to such a long and cruel war.

16

It was this long and cruel war that in its main battles Smiley now relived as he embarked upon his reading. The files contained only the thinnest record of it; his memory contained far more. Its protagonists were Alleline and Control, its origins misty. Bill Haydon—a keen, if saddened, follower of those events—maintained that the two men learned to hate each other at Cambridge during Control's brief spell as a don and Alleline's as an undergraduate. According to Bill, Alleline was Control's pupil and a bad one, and Control taunted him, which he certainly might have.

The story was grotesque enough for Control to play it up: "Percy and I are blood brothers, I hear. We romped together in punts, imagine!" He never said whether it was true.

To half-legend of that sort, Smiley could add a few hard facts from his knowledge of the two men's early lives. While Control was no man's child, Percy Alleline was a lowland Scot and a son of the Manse; his father was a Presbyterian hammer, and if Percy did not have his faith, he had surely inherited the faculty of bullish persuasion. He missed the war by a year or two and joined the Circus from a City company. At Cambridge he had been a bit of a politician (somewhat to the right of Genghis Khan, said Haydon who was himself, Lord knows, no milk-and-water liberal) and a bit of an athlete. He was recruited by a figure of no account called Maston, who for a short time contrived to build himself a corner in counter-intelligence. Maston saw a great future in Alleline and, having peddled his name furiously, fell from grace. Finding Alleline an embarrassment, Circus personnel packed him off to South America, where he did two full tours under consular cover without returning to England.

Even Control later admitted that Percy did extremely well there, Smiley recalled. The Argentinians, liking his tennis and the way he rode, took him for a gentleman—Control speaking—and assumed he was stupid, which Percy never quite was. By the time he handed over to his successor, he had put together a string of agents along both seaboards and was spreading his wings northward as well. After home leave and a couple of weeks' briefing, he was moved to India, where his agents seemed to regard him as the reincarnation of the British Raj. He preached loyalty to them, paid them next to nothing, and—when it suited him—sold them down the river. From India he went to Cairo. That posting should have been difficult for Alleline, if not impossible, for the Middle East till then had been Haydon's favourite stamping-ground. The Cairo networks looked on Bill quite literally in the terms which Martindale had used of him that fateful night in his anonymous dining-club: as a latter-day Lawrence of Arabia. They were all set to make life hell for his successor. Yet somehow Percy bulldozed his way through and, if he had only steered clear of the Americans, might have gone down in memory as a better man than Haydon. Instead there was a scandal and an open row between Percy and Control.

The circumstances were still obscure: the incident occurred long before Smiley's elevation as Control's high chamberlain. With no authority from London, it appeared, Alleline had involved himself in a silly American plot to replace a local potentate with one of their own. Alleline had always had a fatal reverence for the Americans. From Argentina he had observed with admiration their rout of left-wing politicians around the hemisphere; in India he had delighted in their skill at dividing the forces of centralisation. Whereas Control, like most of the Circus, despised them and all their works, which he frequently sought to undermine.

The plot aborted, the British oil companies were furious, and Alleline, as the jargon happily puts it, had to leave in his socks. Later, Alleline claimed that Control had urged him on, then pulled the rug out from under; even that he had deliberately blown the plot to Moscow. However it was, Alleline reached London to find a posting order directing him to the Nursery, where he was to take over the training of greenhorn probationers. It was a slot normally reserved for rundown contract men with a couple of years to go before their pension. There were just so few jobs left in London those days for a man of Percy's seniority and talents, explained Bill Haydon, then head of personnel.

"Then you'll damn well have to invent me one," said Percy. He was right. As Bill frankly confessed to Smiley some while later, he had reckoned without the power of the Alleline lobby.

"But who are these people?" Smiley used to ask. "How can they force a man on you when you don't want him?"

"Golfers," Control snapped. Golfers and conservatives, for Alleline in those days was flirting with the opposition and was received with open arms, not least by Miles Sercombe, Ann's lamentably unremoved cousin and now Lacon's Minister. Yet Control had little power to resist. The Circus was in the doldrums and there was loose talk of scrapping the existing outfit entirely and starting elsewhere with a new one. Failures in that world occur traditionally in series, but this had been an exceptionally long run. Product had slumped; more and more of it had turned out to be suspect. In the places where it mattered, Control's hand was none too strong.

This temporary incapacity did not mar Control's joy in the drafting of Percy Alleline's personal charter as Operational Director. He called it Percy's Fool's Cap.

There was nothing Smiley could do. Bill Haydon was in Washington by then, trying to renegotiate an intelligence treaty with what he called the Fascist puritans of the American agency. But Smiley had risen to the fifth floor, and one of his tasks was to keep petitioners off Control's back. So it was to Smiley that Alleline came to ask "Why?" Would call on him in his office when Control was out, invite him to that dismal flat of his, having first sent his paramour to the cinema, and interrogate him in his plaintive brogue. "Why?" He even invested in a bottle of a malt whisky, which he forced on Smiley liberally while sticking to the cheaper brand himself.

"What have I done to him, George, that's so damn special? We'd a brush or two—what's so unusual to that, if you'll tell me? Why does he pick on me? All I want is a place at the top table. God knows my record entitles me to that!"

By top table, he meant the fifth floor.

The charter which Control had drafted for him, and which at a glance had a most impressive shape, gave Alleline the right to examine all operations before they were launched. The small print made this right conditional upon the consent of the operational sections, and Control made sure that this was not forthcoming. The charter invited him to "co-ordinate resources and break down regional jealousies," a concept Alleline had since achieved with the establishment of London Station. But the resources sections, such as the lamplighters, the forgers, the listeners, and the wranglers, declined to open their books to him and he lacked the powers to force them. So Alleline starved; his trays were empty from lunchtime onwards.

"I'm mediocre, is that it? We've all to be geniuses these days, prima donnas and no damn chorus; old men, at that." For Alleline, though it was easily forgettable in him, was still a young man to be at the top table, with eight or ten years to brandish over Haydon and Smiley, and more over Control.

Control was immovable: "Percy Alleline would sell his mother for a knighthood and this service for a seat in the

House of Lords." And later, as his hateful illness began creeping over him: "I refuse to bequeath my life's work to a parade horse. I'm too vain to be flattered, too old to be ambitious, and I'm ugly as a crab. Percy's quite the other way and there are enough witty men in Whitehall to prefer his sort to mine."

Which was how, indirectly, Control might be said to have brought Witchcraft upon his own head.

"George, come in here," Control snapped one day over the buzzer. "Brother Percy's trying to twist my tail. Come in here or there'll be bloodshed."

It was a time, Smiley remembered, when unsuccessful warriors were returning from foreign parts. Roy Bland had just flown in from Belgrade, where with Toby Esterhase's help he had been trying to save the wreck of a dying network; Paul Skordeno, at that time head German, had just buried his best Soviet agent in East Berlin; and as to Bill, after another fruitless trip he was back in his pepper pot room fuming about Pentagon arrogance, Pentagon idiocy, Pentagon duplicity, and claiming that "the time had come to do a deal with the bloody Russians instead."

And in the Islay it was after midnight; a late guest was ringing the bell. Which will cost him ten bob to Norman, thought Smiley, for whom the revised British coinage was still something of a puzzle. With a sigh, he drew towards him the first of the Witchcraft files, and, having vouchsafed a gingerly lick to his right finger and thumb, set to work matching the official memory with his own.

"We spoke," wrote Alleline, only a couple of months after that interview, in a slightly hysterical personal letter addressed to Ann's distinguished cousin the Minister and entered on Lacon's file. "Witchcraft reports derive from a source of extreme sensitivity. To my mind, no existing method of Whitehall distribution meets the case. The dispatch-box system which we used for GADFLY fell down when keys were lost by Whitehall customers, or in one disgraceful case when an overworked Under-Secretary gave his key to his personal assistant. I have already spoken to Lilley, of naval intelligence, who is prepared to put at our disposal a special reading-room in the Admiralty main building where the material is made available to customers and watched over by a senior janitor of this service. The reading-room will be known, for cover purposes, as the conference room of the Adriatic Working Party, or the A.W.P. room for short. Customers with reading rights will not have passes, since these also are open to abuse. Instead they will identify themselves personally to my janitor"—Smiley noted the pronoun—"who will be equipped with an indoctrination list illustrated with customers' photographs."

Lacon, not yet convinced, to the Treasury through his odious master, the Minister, on whose behalf his submissions were invariably made:

> Even allowing that this is necessary, the reading-room will have to be extensively rebuilt.
>
> 1. Will you authorise cost?
> 2. If so, the cost should seem to be borne by the Admiralty. Department will covertly reimburse.
> 3. There is also the question of extra janitors, a further expense . . .

And there is the question of Alleline's greater glory, Smiley commented as he slowly turned the pages. It shone already like a beacon everywhere: Percy is heading for the top table and Control might already be dead.

From the stairwell came the sound of rather beautiful singing. A Welsh guest, very drunk, was wishing everyone good night.

Witchcraft, Smiley recalled—his memory again, the files knew nothing so plainly human—Witchcraft was by no means Percy Alleline's first attempt, in his new post, at launching his own operation; but since his charter bound him to obtain Control's approval, its predecessors had been stillborn. For a while, for instance, he had concentrated on tunnelling. The Americans had built audio tunnels in Berlin and Belgrade; the French had managed something similar against the Americans. Very well, under Percy's banner the Circus would get in on the market. Control looked on benignly, an inter-services committee was formed (known as the Alleline Committee), and a team of boffins from nuts and bolts made a survey of the foundations of the Soviet Embassy in Athens, where Alleline counted on the unstinted support of the latest military régime which, like its predecessors, he greatly admired. Then, very gently, Control knocked over Percy's bricks and waited for him to come up with something new. Which, after several shots between, was exactly what Percy was doing that grey morning when Control peremptorily summoned Smiley to the feast.

Control was sitting at his desk, Alleline was standing at the window; between them lay a plain folder, bright yellow and closed.

"Sit over there and take a look at this nonsense."

Smiley sat in the easy chair and Alleline stayed at the window resting his big elbows on the sill, staring over the rooftops to Nelson's Column and the spires of Whitehall beyond.

Inside the folder was a photograph of what purported to be a high-level Soviet naval dispatch fifteen pages long.

"Who made the translation?" Smiley asked, thinking that it looked good enough to be Roy Bland's work.

"God," Control replied. "God made it, didn't he, Percy? Don't ask him anything, George, he won't tell you."

It was Control's time for looking exceptionally youthful. Smiley remembered how Control had lost weight, how his cheeks were pink, and how those who knew him little tended to congratulate him on his good appearance. Only Smiley, perhaps, ever noticed the tiny beads of sweat that in those days habitually followed his hairline.

Precisely, the document was an appreciation, allegedly prepared for the Soviet High Command, of a recent Soviet naval exercise in the Mediterranean and Black Sea. In Lacon's file it was entered simply as Report No. 1, under the title "Naval." For months the Admiralty had been screaming at the Circus for anything relating to this exercise. It therefore had an impressive topicality, which at once, in Smiley's eyes, made it suspect. It was detailed but it dealt with matters that Smiley did not understand even at a distance: shore-to-sea strike power, radio activation of enemy alert procedures, the higher mathematics of the balance of terror. If it was genuine it was gold-dust, but there was no earthly reason to suppose it was genuine. Every week the Circus processed dozens of unsolicited so-called Soviet documents. Most were straight pedlar material. A few were deliberate plants by allies with an axe to grind; a few more were Russian chicken-feed. Very rarely, one turned out to be sound, but usually after it had been rejected.

"Whose initials are these?" Smiley asked, referring to some annotations pencilled in Russian in the margin. "Does anyone know?"

Control tilted his head at Alleline. "Ask the authority. Don't ask me."

"Zharov," said Alleline. "Admiral, Black Sea Fleet."

"It's not dated," Smiley objected.

"It's a draft," Alleline replied complacently, his brogue richer than usual. "Zharov signed it Thursday. The finished dispatch with those amendments went out on circulation Monday, dated accordingly."

Today was Tuesday.

"Where does it come from?" Smiley asked, still lost.

"Percy doesn't feel able to tell," said Control.

"What do our own evaluators say?"

"They've not seen it," said Alleline, "and what's more they're not going to."

Control said icily, "My brother in Christ, Lilley, of naval intelligence, has passed a preliminary opinion, however, has he not, Percy? Percy showed it to him last night—over a pink gin, was it, Percy, at the Travellers'?"

"At the Admiralty."

"Brother Lilley, being a fellow Caledonian of Percy's, is as a rule sparing in his praise. However, when he telephoned me half an hour ago he was positively fulsome. He even congratulated me. He regards the document as genuine and is seeking our permission—Percy's, I suppose I should say—to apprise his fellow sea-lords of its conclusions."

"Quite impossible," said Alleline. "It's for his eyes only, at least for a couple more weeks."

"The stuff is so hot," Control explained, "that it has to be cooled off before it can be distributed."

"But where does it come from?" Smiley insisted.

"Oh, Percy's dreamed up a cover name, don't you worry. Never been slow on cover names, have we, Percy?"

"But what's the access? Who's the case officer?"

"You'll enjoy this," Control promised, aside. He was extraordinarily angry. In their long association Smiley could not remember him so angry. His slim, freckled hands were shaking and his normally lifeless eyes were sparkling with fury.

"Source Merlin," Alleline said, prefacing the announcement with a slight but very Scottish sucking of the teeth, "is a highly placed source with access to the most sensitive levels of Soviet policy-making." And, as if he were royalty: "We have dubbed his product 'Witchcraft.'"

He had used the identical form of words, Smiley noticed, in a top-secret and personal letter to a fan at the Treasury, requesting for himself greater discretion in *ad hoc* payments to agents.

"He'll be saying he won him at the football pool next," Control warned, who despite his second youth had an old man's inaccuracy when it came to popular idiom. "Now get him to tell you why he won't tell you."

Alleline was undeterred. He, too, was flushed, but with triumph, not disease. He filled his big chest for a long speech, which he delivered entirely to Smiley, tonelessly, rather as a Scottish police sergeant might give evidence before the courts.

"The identity of Source Merlin is a secret which is not mine to divulge. He's the fruit of a long cultivation by certain people in this service. People who are bound to me, as I am to them. People who are not at all entertained, either, by the failure rate around this place. There's been too much blown. Too much lost, wasted, too many scandals. I've said so many times, but I might as well have spoken to the wind for all the damn care he paid me."

"He's referring to me," Control explained from the sidelines. "I am *he* in this speech—you follow, George?"

"The ordinary principles of tradecraft and security have gone to the wall in this service. Need to know: where is it? Compartmentation at all levels: where is it, George? There's too much regional backbiting, stimulated from the top."

"Another reference to myself," Control put in.

"Divide and rule, that's the principle at work these days. Personalities who should be helping to fight Communism are all at one another's throats. We're losing our top partners."

"He means the Americans," Control explained.

"We're losing our livelihood. Our self-respect. We've had enough." He took back the report and jammed it under his arm. "We've had a bellyful, in fact."

"And like everyone who's had enough," said Control as Alleline noisily left the room, "he wants more."

Now for a while Lacon's files, instead of Smiley's memory, once more took up the story. It was typical of the atmosphere of those last months that, having been brought in on the affair at the beginning, Smiley should have received no subsequent word of how it had developed. Control detested failure as he detested illness, and his own failures most. He knew that to recognise failure was to live with it; that a service that did not struggle did not survive. He detested the silk-shirt agents, who hogged large chunks of the budget to the detriment of the bread-and-butter networks in which he put his faith. He loved success, but he detested miracles if they put the rest of his endeavour out of focus. He detested weakness as he detested sentiment and religion, and he detested Percy Alleline, who had a dash of most of them. His way of dealing with them was literally to close the door: to withdraw into the dingy solitude of his upper rooms, receive no visitors, and have all his phone calls fed to him by the mothers. The same quiet ladies fed him jasmine tea and the countless office files that he sent for and returned in heaps. Smiley would see them piled before the door as he went about his own business of trying to keep the rest of the Circus afloat. Many were old, from the days before Control led the pack. Some were personal, the biographies of past and present members of the service.

Control never said what he was doing. If Smiley asked the mothers, or if Bill Haydon sauntered in, favourite boy, and made the same enquiry, they only shook their heads or silently raised their eyebrows towards paradise: "A terminal case," said these gentle glances. "We are humouring a great man at the end of his career." But Smiley—as he now patiently leafed through file after file, and in a corner of his complex mind rehearsed Irina's diary to Ricki Tarr—Smiley knew, and in a quite real way took comfort from the knowledge, that he was not after all the first to make this journey of exploration; that Control's ghost was his companion into all but the furthest reaches; and might even have stayed the whole distance if Operation Testify, at the eleventh hour, had not stopped him dead.

* * *

Breakfast again, and a much-subdued Welshman not drawn by undercooked sausage and overcooked tomato.

"Do you want these back," Lacon demanded, "or have you done with them? They can't be very enlightening, since they don't even contain the reports."

"Tonight, please, if you don't mind."

"I suppose you realise you look a wreck."

He didn't realise, but at Bywater Street, when he returned there, Ann's pretty gilt mirror showed his eyes red-rimmed and his plump cheeks clawed with fatigue. He slept a little, then went his mysterious ways. When evening came, Lacon was actually waiting for him. Smiley went straight on with his reading.

For six weeks, according to the files, the naval dispatch had no successor. Other sections of the Ministry of Defence echoed the Admiralty's enthusiasm for the original dispatch; the Foreign Office remarked that "this document sheds an extraordinary sidelight on Soviet aggressive thinking," whatever that meant; Alleline persisted in his demands for special handling of the material, but he was like a general with no army. Lacon referred frostily to "the somewhat delayed follow-up," and suggested to his Minister that he should "defuse the situation with the Admiralty." From Control, according to the file, nothing. Perhaps he was lying low and praying it would blow over. In the lull, a Treasury Moscow-gazer sourly pointed out that Whitehall had seen plenty of this in recent years: an encouraging first report, then silence or, worse, a scandal.

He was wrong. In the seventh week, Alleline announced publication of three new Witchcraft reports all on the same day. All took the form of secret Soviet interdepartmental correspondence, though the topics differed widely.

Witchcraft No. 2, according to Lacon's summary, described tensions inside Comecon and spoke of the degenerative effect of Western trade deals on its weaker members. In Circus terms, this was a classic report from Roy Bland territory, covering the very target that the Hungarian-based Aggravate network had been attacking in vain for years. "Excellent *tour d'horizon*," wrote a Foreign Office customer, "and backed by good collateral."

Witchcraft No. 3 discussed revisionism in Hungary and Kadar's renewed purges in political and academic life: the best way to end loose talk in Hungary, said the author of the paper, borrowing a phrase coined by Khrushchev long before, would be to shoot some more intellectuals. Once again this was Roy Bland territory. "A salutary warning," wrote the same Foreign Office commentator, "to all those who like to think the Soviet Union is going soft on satellites."

These two reports were both in essence background, but Witchcraft No. 4 was sixty pages long and held by the customers to be unique. It was an immensely technical Soviet Foreign Service appreciation of the advantages and disadvantages of negotiating with a weakened American President. The conclusion, on balance, was that by throwing the President a bone for his own electorate, the Soviet Union could buy useful concessions in forthcoming discussions on multiple nuclear warheads. But it seriously questioned the desirability of allowing the United States to feel too much the loser, since this could tempt the Pentagon into a retributive or preemptive strike. The report was from the very heart of Bill Haydon territory. But, as Haydon himself wrote in a touching minute to Alleline (promptly copied, without Haydon's knowledge, to the Minister and entered on the Cabinet Office file), in twenty-five years of attacking the Soviet nuclear target he had not laid his hands on anything of this quality.

"Nor," he concluded, "unless I am extremely mistaken, have our American brothers-in-arms. I know that these are early days, but it does occur to me that anyone taking this material to Washington could drive a very hard bargain in return. Indeed, if Merlin maintains the standard, I would venture to predict that we could buy anything there is to have in the American agency's shop."

Percy Alleline had his reading-room; and George Smiley made himself a coffee on the derelict burner beside the washstand. Midway the meter ran out, and in a temper he called for Norman and ordered five pounds' worth of shillings.

17

With mounting interest, Smiley continued his journey through Lacon's meagre records from that first meeting of protagonists until the present day. At the time, such a mood of suspicion had gripped the Circus that even between Smiley and Control the subject of Source Merlin became taboo. Alleline brought up the Witchcraft reports and waited in the anteroom while the mothers took them to Control, who signed them at once in order to demonstrate that he had not read them. Alleline took back the file, poked his head round Smiley's door, grunted a greeting, and clumped down the staircase. Bland kept his distance, and even Bill Haydon's breezy visits—traditionally a part of the life up there, of the "talking shop" that Control in the old days had liked to foster among his senior lieutenants—became fewer and shorter, then ceased entirely.

"Control's going potty," Haydon told Smiley with contempt. "And if I'm not mistaken he's also dying. It's just a question of which gets him first."

The customary Tuesday meetings were discontinued, and Smiley found himself constantly harassed by Control either to go abroad on some blurred errand or to visit the domestic outstations—Sarratt, Brixton, Acton, and the rest—as his personal envoy. He had a growing feeling that Control wanted him out of the way. When they talked, he felt the heavy strain

of suspicion between them, so that even Smiley seriously wondered whether Bill was right and Control was unfit for his job.

The Cabinet Office files made it clear that those next three
months saw a steady flowering of the Witchcraft operation,
without any help from Control. Reports came in at the rate of
two or even three a month, and the standard, according to the
customers, continued excellent, but Control's name was seldom mentioned and he was never invited to comment. Occasionally the evaluators produced quibbles. More often they
complained that corroboration was not possible, since Merlin
took them into uncharted areas: could we not ask the Americans to check? We could not, said the Minister. Not yet, said
Alleline; who in a confidential minute seen by no one, added,
"When the time is ripe we shall do more than barter our material for theirs. We are not interested in a one-time deal. Our
task is to establish Merlin's track record beyond all doubt.
When that is done, Haydon can go to market . . ."

There was no longer any question of it. Among the chosen
few who were admitted to the chambers of the Adriatic
Working Party, Merlin was already a winner. His material was
accurate; often other sources confirmed it retrospectively. A
Witchcraft committee formed, with the Minister in the chair.
Alleline was vice-chairman. Merlin had become an industry,
and Control was not even employed. Which was why in desperation he had sent out Smiley with his beggar's bowl: "There
are three of them and Alleline," he said. "Sweat them, George.
Tempt them, bully them, give them whatever they eat."

Of those meetings also, the files were blessedly ignorant,
for they belonged in the worst rooms of Smiley's memory. He
had known already that there was nothing left in Control's lar-
der that would satisfy their hunger.

It was April. Smiley had come back from Portugal, where
he had been burying a scandal, to find Control living under
siege. Files lay strewn over the floor; new locks had been fitted

to the windows. He had put the tea-cosy over his one tele-phone and from the ceiling hung a baffler against electronic eavesdropping—a thing like an electric fan, which constantly varied its pitch. In the three weeks Smiley had been away, Control had become an old man.

"Tell them they're buying their way in with counterfeit money," he ordered, barely looking up from his files. "Tell them any damn thing. I need time."

"There are three of them and Alleline," Smiley now repeated to himself, seated at the Major's card table and studying Lacon's list of those who had been Witchcraft-cleared. Today there were sixty-eight licensed visitors to the Adriatic Work-ing Party's reading-room. Each, like a member of the Commu-nist Party, was numbered according to the date of his admission. The list had been retyped since Control's death; Smiley was not included. But the same four founding fathers still headed the list: Alleline, Bland, Esterhase, and Bill Haydon. Three of them and Alleline, Control had said.

Suddenly Smiley's mind, open as he read to every inference, every oblique connection, was assailed by a quite extraneous vision: of himself and Ann walking the Cornish cliffs. It was the time immediately after Control's death, the worst time Smiley could remember in their long, puzzled marriage. They were high on the coast, somewhere between Lamorna and Porth-curno; they had gone there out of season ostensibly for Ann to take the sea air for her cough. They had been following the coast path, each lost in his thoughts: she to Haydon, he sup-posed; he to Control, to Jim Prideaux and Testify, and the whole mess he had left behind him on retirement. They shared no har-mony. They had lost all calmness in one another's company; they were a mystery to each other, and the most banal conversa-tion could take strange, uncontrollable directions. In London, Ann had been living quite wildly, taking anyone who would have her. He knew she was trying to bury something that hurt or worried her very much; but he knew no way to reach her.

"If *I* had died," she demanded suddenly, "rather than Control, say, how would you feel towards Bill?"

Smiley was still pondering his answer when she threw in: "I sometimes think I safeguard your opinion of him. Is that possible? That I somehow keep the two of you together. Is that possible?"

"It's possible." He added, "Yes, I suppose I'm dependent on him, too, in a way."

"Is Bill still important in the Circus?"

"More than he was, probably."

"And he still goes to Washington, wheels and deals with them, turns them upside down?"

"I expect so. I hear so."

"Is he as important as you were?"

"I suppose."

"I suppose," she repeated. "I expect. I hear. Is he *better*, then? A better performer than you, better at the arithmetic? Tell me. Please tell me. You must."

She was strangely excited. Her eyes, tearful from the wind, shone desperately upon him; she had both hands on his arm and, like a child, was dragging on him for an answer.

"You've always told me that men aren't to be compared," he replied awkwardly. "You've always said you didn't think in that category of comparison."

"Tell me!"

"All right: no, he's not better."

"As good?"

"No."

"And if I wasn't there, what would you think of him then? If Bill were not my cousin, not my anything? Tell me, would you think more of him, or less?"

"Less, I suppose."

"Then think less *now*. I divorce him from the family, from our lives, from everything. Here and now. I throw him into the sea. There. Do you understand?"

He understood only: go back to the Circus, finish your business. It was one of a dozen ways she had of saying the same thing.

Still disturbed by this intrusion on his memory, Smiley stood up in rather a flurry and went to the window, his habitual lookout when he was distracted. A line of sea-gulls, a half dozen of them, had settled on the parapet. He must have heard them calling, and remembered that walk to Lamorna.

"I cough when there are things I can't say," Ann had told him once. What couldn't she say then, he asked glumly of the chimney-pots across the street. Connie could say it, Martindale could say it; so why couldn't Ann?

"Three of them and Alleline," Smiley muttered aloud. The sea-gulls had gone, all at once, as if they had spotted a better place. "Tell them they're buying their way in with counterfeit money." And if the banks accept the money? If the experts pronounce it genuine, and Bill Haydon praises it to the skies? And the Cabinet Office files are full of plaudits for the brave new men of Cambridge Circus, who have finally broken the jinx?

He had chosen Esterhase first because Toby owed Smiley his career. Smiley had recruited him in Vienna, a starving student living in the ruins of a museum of which his dead uncle had been curator. He drove down to Acton and bearded him at the Laundry across his walnut desk with its row of ivory telephones. On the wall, kneeling Magi, questionable Italian seventeenth century. Through the window, a closed courtyard crammed with cars and vans and motorbikes, and rest-huts where the teams of lamplighters killed time between shifts. First Smiley asked Toby about his family: there was a son who went to Westminster and a daughter at medical school, first year. Then he put it to Toby that the lamplighters were two months behind on their worksheets, and when Toby hedged he asked him outright whether his boys had been doing any special jobs recently, either at home or abroad, which for good reasons of security Toby didn't feel able to mention in his returns.

"Who would I do that for, George?" Toby had asked, dead-eyed. "You know in my book that's completely illegal." And idiom, in Toby's book, had a way of being ludicrous.

"Well, I can see you doing it for Percy Alleline, for one," Smiley suggested, feeding him the excuse: "After all, if Percy *ordered* you to do something and not to record it, you'd be in a very difficult position."

"What sort of something, though, George, I wonder?"

"Clear a foreign letter-box, prime a safe house, watch someone's back, spike an embassy. Percy's Director of Operations, after all. You might think he was acting on instructions from the fifth floor. I can see that happening quite reasonably."

Toby looked carefully at Smiley. He was holding a cigarette, but apart from lighting it he hadn't smoked it at all. It was a hand-rolled affair, taken from a silver box, but once lit, it never went into his mouth. It swung around, along the line or away to the side; sometimes it was poised to take the plunge, but it never did. Meanwhile Toby made his speech: one of Toby's personal statements, supposedly definitive about where he stood at this point in his life.

Toby liked the service, he said. He would prefer to remain in it. He felt sentimental about it. He had other interests and at any time they could claim him altogether, but he liked the service best. His trouble was, he said, promotion. Not that he wanted it for any greedy reason. He would say his reasons were social.

"You know, George, I have so many years' seniority I feel actually quite embarrassed when these young fellows ask me to take orders from them. You know what I mean? Acton, even— just the name of Acton for them is ridiculous."

"Oh," said Smiley mildly. "Which young fellows are these?"

But Esterhase had lost interest. His statement completed, his face settled again into its familiar blank expression, his doll's eyes fixed on a point in the middle distance.

"Do you mean Roy Bland?" Smiley asked. "Or Percy? Is Percy young? Who, Toby?"

It was no good, Toby regretted: "George, when you are overdue for promotion and working your fingers to the bones, anyone looks young who's above you on the ladder."

"Perhaps Control could move you up a few rungs," Smiley suggested, not much caring for himself in this role.

Esterhase's reply struck a chill. "Well, actually, you know, George, I am not too sure he is able these days. Look here"—opening a drawer—"I give Ann something. When I heard you were coming, I phone a couple of friends of mine; something beautiful, I say, something for a faultless woman; you know I never forget her since we met once at Bill Haydon's cocktail?"

So Smiley carried off the consolation prize—a costly scent, smuggled, he assumed, by one of Toby's homing lamplighters—and took his beggar bowl to Bland, knowing as he did so that he was coming one step nearer to Haydon.

Returning to the Major's table, Smiley searched through Lacon's files till he came to a slim volume marked "Operation Witchcraft, direct subsidies," which recorded the earliest expenses incurred through the running of Source Merlin. "For reasons of security it is proposed," wrote Alleline in yet another personal memo to the Minister, this one dated almost two years ago, "to keep the Witchcraft financing *absolutely separate* from all other Circus imprests. Until some proper cover can be found, I am asking you for *direct subventions from Treasury funds* rather than mere supplementaries to the Secret Vote, which in due course *are certain to find their way into the mainstream of Circus accounting*. I shall then account to you personally."

"Approved," wrote the Minister a week later, "provided always . . ."

There were no provisions. A glance at the first row of figures showed Smiley all he needed to know: already by May of that year, when that interview at Acton took place, Toby Esterhase had personally made no fewer than eight trips on the Witchcraft budget, two to Paris, two to The Hague, one to Helsinki, and three to Berlin. In each case the purpose of the journey was curtly described as "Collecting product." Between May and November, when Control faded from the scene, he made a further nineteen. One of these took him to Sofia, another to Istanbul. None required him to be absent for more than three full days. Most took place at weekends. On several such journeys, he was accompanied by Bland.

Not to put too fine an edge on it, Toby Esterhase, as Smiley had never seriously doubted, had lied in his teeth. It was nice to find the record confirming his impression.

Smiley's feelings towards Roy Bland had at that time been ambivalent. Recalling them now, he decided they still were. A don had spotted him, Smiley had recruited him; the combination was oddly akin to the one that had brought Smiley himself into the Circus net. But this time there was no German monster to fan the patriotic flame, and Smiley had always been a little embarrassed by protestations of anti-Communism. Like Smiley, Bland had no real childhood. His father was a docker, a passionate trade-unionist, and a Party member. His mother died when Bland was a boy. His father hated education as he hated authority, and when Bland grew clever the father took it into his head that he had lost his son to the ruling class and beat the life out of him. Bland fought his way to grammar school and in the holidays worked his fingers, as Toby would say, to the bones, in order to raise the extra fee. When Smiley met him in his tutor's rooms at Oxford, he had the battered look of someone just arrived from a bad journey.

Smiley took him up, and over several months edged closer to a proposition, which Bland accepted—largely, Smiley assumed, out of animosity towards his father. After that he passed out of Smiley's care. Subsisting on odd grants undescribed, Bland toiled in the Marx Memorial Library and wrote leftish papers for tiny magazines that would have died long ago had the Circus not subsidized them. In the evenings he disputed loud and long at smoky meetings in pubs and school halls. In the vacations he went to the Nursery, where a fanatic called Thatch ran a charm school for outward-bound penetration agents, one pupil at a time. Thatch trained Bland in tradecraft and carefully nudged his progressive opinions nearer to his father's Marxist camp. Three years to the day after his recruitment, partly thanks to his proletarian pedigree, and his father's influence at King Street, Bland won a year's appointment as assistant lector in economics at the University of Poznan. He was launched.

From Poland he applied successfully for a post at the Budapest Academy of Sciences, and for the next eight years he lived the nomadic life of a minor left-wing intellectual in search of light, often liked but never trusted. He staged in Prague, returned to Poland, did a hellish two semesters in Sofia and six in Kiev, where he had a nervous breakdown, his second in as many months. Once more the Nursery took charge of him, this time to dry him out. He was passed as clean, his networks were given to other fieldmen, and Roy himself was brought into the Circus to manage, mainly from a desk, the networks he had recruited in the field. Recently, it had seemed to Smiley, Bland had become very much Haydon's colleague. If Smiley chanced to call on Roy for a chat, like as not Bill was lounging in his armchair surrounded by papers, charts, and cigarette smoke; if he dropped in on Bill, it was no surprise to find Bland, in a sweat-soaked shirt, padding heavily back and forth across the carpet. Bill had Russia, Bland the satellites; but already in those early days of Witchcraft, the distinction had all but vanished.

They met at a pub in St. John's Wood—still May—half past five on a dull day and the garden empty. Roy brought a child, a boy of five or so, a tiny Bland, fair, burly, and pink-faced. He didn't explain the boy, but sometimes as they talked he shut off and watched him where he sat on a bench away from them, eating nuts. Nervous breakdowns or not, Bland still bore the imprimatur of the Thatch philosophy for agents in the enemy camp: self-faith, positive participation, Pied Piper appeal, and all those other uncomfortable phrases which in the high day of the cold-war culture had turned the Nursery into something close to a moral-rearmament centre.

"So what's the deal?" Bland asked affably.

"There isn't one really, Roy. Control feels that the present situation is unhealthy. He doesn't like to see you getting mixed up in a cabal. Nor do I."

"Great. So what's the deal?"

"What do you want?"

On the table, soaked from the earlier rain fall, was a cruet set left over from lunchtime, with a bunch of paper-wrapped cellulose toothpicks in the centre compartment. Taking one, Bland spat the paper onto the grass and began working his back teeth with the fat end.

"Well, how about a five-thousand-quid backhander out the reptile fund?"

"And a house and a car?" said Smiley, making a joke of it.

"And the kid to Eton," Bland added, and winked across the concrete paving to the boy while he went on working with the toothpick. "I've paid, see, George. You know that. I don't know what I've bought with it but I've paid a hell of a lot. I want some back. Ten years' solitary for the fifth floor; that's big money at any age. Even yours. There must have been a reason why I fell for all that spiel, but I can't quite remember what it was. Must be your magnetic personality."

Smiley's glass was still going, so Bland fetched himself another from the bar, and something for the boy as well.

"You're an educated sort of swine," he announced easily as he sat down again. "An artist is a bloke who can hold two fundamentally opposing views and still function: who dreamed that one up?"

"Scott Fitzgerald," Smiley replied, thinking for a moment that Bland was proposing to say something about Bill Haydon.

"Well, Fitzgerald knew a thing or two," Bland affirmed. As he drank, his bulging eyes slid sideways toward the fence, as if in search of someone. "And I'm definitely functioning, George. As a good Socialist, I'm going for the money. As a good capitalist, I'm sticking with the revolution, because if you can't beat it spy on it. Don't look like that, George. It's the name of the game these days: you scratch my conscience, I'll drive your Jag, right?" He was already lifting an arm as he said this. "With you in a minute!" he called across the lawn. "Set one up for me!"

Two girls were hovering on the other side of the wire fence.

"Is that Bill's joke?" Smiley asked, suddenly quite angry.

"Is what?"

"Is that one of Bill's jokes about materialist England, the pigs-in-clover society?"

"Could be," said Bland, and finished his drink. "Don't you like it?"

"Not too much, no. I never knew Bill before as a radical reformer. What's come over him all of a sudden?"

"That's not radical," Bland retorted, resenting any devaluation of his Socialism, or of Haydon. "That's just looking out the bloody window. That's just England now, man. Nobody wants that, do they?"

"So how do you propose," Smiley demanded, hearing himself at his pompous worst, "to destroy the acquisitive and competitive instincts in Western society without also destroying . . ."

Bland had finished his drink; and the meeting, too. "Why should you be bothered? You've got Bill's job. What more do you want? Long as it lasts."

And Bill's got my wife, Smiley thought as Bland rose to go; and, damn him, he's told you.

The boy had invented a game. He had laid a table on its side and was rolling an empty bottle onto the gravel. Each time, he started the bottle higher up the table-top. Smiley left before it smashed.

* * *

Unlike Esterhase, Bland had not even bothered to lie. Lacon's files made no pretence of his involvement with the Witchcraft operation:

"Source Merlin," wrote Alleline, in a minute dated soon after Control's departure, "is in every sense a committee operation . . . I cannot honestly say which of my three assistants deserves most praise. The energy of Bland has been an inspiration to us all . . ." He was replying to the Minister's suggestion that those responsible for Witchcraft should be honoured in the New Year's list. "While Haydon's operational ingenuity is at times little short of Merlin's own," he added. The medals went to all three; Alleline's appointment as Chief was confirmed, and with it his beloved knighthood.

18

Which left me Bill, thought Smiley.

In the course of most London nights, there is one respite from alarm. Ten, twenty minutes, thirty, even an hour, and not a drunk groans or a child cries or a car's tyres whine into a collision. In Sussex Gardens it happens around three. That night it came early, at one, as Smiley stood once more at his dormer window peering down like a prisoner at Mrs. Pope Graham's sand patch, where a Bedford van had recently parked. Its roof was daubed with slogans: "Sydney 90 Days," "Athens Non-Stop," "Mary Lou Here We Come." A light glowed inside, and he presumed some children were sleeping there in unmarried bliss. "Kids," he was supposed to call them. Curtains covered the windows.

Which left me Bill, he thought, still staring at the closed curtains of the van and its flamboyant globe-trotting proclamations; which left me Bill, and our friendly little chat in Bywater Street—just the two of us, old friends, old comrades-at-arms, "sharing everything," as Martindale had it so elegantly, but Ann sent out for the evening so that the men could be alone. "Which left me Bill," he repeated hopelessly, and felt the blood rise, and the colours of his vision heighten, and his sense of moderation begin its dangerous slide.

Who was he? Smiley had no focus on him any more. Each time he thought of him, he drew him too large, and different.

Until Ann's affair with him, he thought he knew Bill pretty well, his brilliance and its limitations. He was of that pre-war set that seemed to have vanished for good, which managed to be disreputable and high-minded at the same time. His father was a high court judge, two of his several beautiful sisters had married into the aristocracy; at Oxford he favoured the unfashionable right rather than the fashionable left, but never to the point of strain. From his late teens he had been a keen explorer and amateur painter of brave, if over-ambitious, stamp; several of his paintings now hung in Miles Sercombe's fatuous palace in Carlton Gardens. He had connections in every embassy and consulate across the Middle East and he used them ruthlessly. He took up remote languages with ease, and when 1939 came, the Circus snapped him up; they had had their eye on him for years. He had a dazzling war. He was ubiquitous and charming; he was unorthodox and occasionally outrageous. He was probably heroic. The comparison with Lawrence was inevitable.

And it was true, Smiley conceded, that Bill in his time had fiddled with substantial pieces of history; had proposed all sorts of grand designs for restoring England to influence and greatness—like Rupert Brooke, he seldom spoke of Britain. But Smiley, in his rare moments of objectivity, could remember few that ever got off the ground.

It was the other side of Haydon's nature, by contrast, that as a colleague he had found easier to respect: the slow-burning skills of the natural agent runner; his rare sense of balance in the playing back of double agents and the mounting of deception operations; his art of fostering affection, even love, though it ran against the grain of other loyalties.

As witness, thank you, my wife.

Perhaps Bill really *is* out of scale, Smiley thought hopelessly, still grappling for a sense of proportion. Picturing him now, and putting him beside Bland, Esterhase, even Alleline, it did truthfully seem to Smiley that all of them were, to a great or small extent, imperfect imitations of that one original, Haydon. That their affectations were like steps towards the same unobtainable ideal of the rounded man, even if the ideal was itself misconceived, or misplaced; even if Bill was utterly unworthy of it. Bland in his blunt impertinence, Esterhase in his lofty artificial Englishness, Alleline with his shallow gift of leadership—without Bill they were a disarray. Smiley also knew, or thought he knew—the idea came to him now as a mild enlightenment—that Bill in turn was also very little by himself: that while his admirers (Bland, Prideaux, Alleline, Esterhase, and all the rest of the supporters' club) might find in him completeness, Bill's real trick was to use them, to live through them to complete himself, here a piece, there a piece, from their passive identities, thus disguising the fact that he was less, far less, than the sum of his apparent qualities . . . and finally submerging this dependence beneath an artist's arrogance, calling them the creatures of his mind . . .

"That's quite enough," said Smiley aloud.

Withdrawing abruptly from this insight, dismissing it irritably as yet another theory about Bill, he cooled his overheated mind with the recollection of their last meeting.

"I suppose you want to grill me about bloody Merlin," Bill began. He looked tired and nervy; it was his time for commuting to Washington. In the old days he would have brought an unsuitable girl and sent her to sit with Ann upstairs while they talked their business; expecting Ann to bolster his genius to her, thought Smiley cruelly. They were all of the same sort: half his age, bedraggled art school, clinging, surly; Ann used to say he had a supplier. And once, to shock, he brought a ghastly youth called Steggie, an assistant barman from one of the Chelsea pubs, with an open shirt and a gold chain round his midriff.

"Well, they do say you write the reports," Smiley explained.

"I thought that was Bland's job," said Bill with his foxy grin.

"Roy makes the translations," said Smiley. "You draft the covering reports; they're typed on your machine. The material's not cleared for typists at all."

Bill listened carefully, brows lifted, as if at any moment he might interrupt with an objection or a more congenial topic, then hoisted himself from the deep armchair and ambled to the bookcase, where he stood a full shelf higher than Smiley. Fishing out a volume with his long fingers, he peered into it, grinning.

"Percy Alleline won't do," he announced, turning a page. "Is that the premise?"

"Pretty well."

"Which means that Merlin won't do, either. Merlin would do if he were *my* source, wouldn't he? What would happen if Bloody Bill here pottered along to Control and said he'd hooked a big fish and wanted to play him alone? 'That's very nifty of you, Bill, boy,' Control would say. 'You do it just the way you want, Bill, boy—'course you do. Have some filthy tea.' He'd be giving me a medal by now, instead of sending you snooping round the corridors. We used to be rather a classy bunch. Why are we so vulgar these days?"

"He thinks Percy's on the make," Smiley said.

"So he is. So am I. I want to be head boy. Did you know that? Time I made something of myself, George. Half a painter, half a spy—time I was *all* something. Since when was ambition a sin in our beastly outfit?"

"Who runs him, Bill?"

"Percy? Karla does—who else? Lower-class bloke with upper-class sources, must be a bounder. Percy's sold out to Karla; it's the only explanation." He had developed the art, long ago, of deliberately misunderstanding. "Percy's our house mole," he said.

"I meant who runs Merlin? Who *is* Merlin? What's going on?"

Leaving the bookcase, Haydon took himself on a tour of Smiley's drawings. "This is a Callot, isn't it," unhooking a small gilt frame and holding it to the light. "It's nice." He tilted his spectacles to make them magnify. Smiley was certain he had looked at it a dozen times before. "It's *very* nice. Doesn't anyone think *my* nose should be out of joint? I am supposed to be in charge of the Russian target, you know. Given it my best years, set up networks, talent-spotters, all mod cons. You chaps on the fifth floor have forgotten what it's like to run an operation where it takes you three days to post a letter and you don't even get an answer for your trouble."

Smiley, dutifully: Yes, I have forgotten. Yes, I sympathise. No, Ann is nowhere in my thoughts. We are colleagues, after all, and men of the world; we are here to talk about Merlin and Control.

"Along comes this upstart Percy, damn Caledonian street-merchant, no shadow of class, shoving a whole wagonload of Russian goodies. Bloody annoying, don't you think?"

"Very."

"Trouble is, my networks aren't very good. Much easier to spy on Percy than—" He broke off, tired of his own thesis. His attention had settled on a tiny van Mieris head in chalk. "And I fancy this *very* much," he said.

"Ann gave it me."

"Amends?"

"Probably."

"Must have been quite a sin. How long have you had it?"

Even now, Smiley remembered noticing how silent it was in the street. Tuesday? Wednesday? And he remembered thinking: No, Bill. For you I have so far received no consolation prize at all. As of this evening, you don't even rate a pair of bedroom slippers . . . Thinking but not saying.

"Is Control dead yet?" Haydon asked.

"Just busy."

"What does he do all day? He's like a hermit with the clap, scratching around all on his own in that cave up there. All those bloody files he reads—what's he about, for God's sake?

Sentimental tour of his unlovely past, I'll bet. He looks sick as a cat. I suppose that's Merlin's fault, too, is it?"

Again Smiley said nothing.

"Why doesn't he eat with the cooks? Why doesn't he join us instead of grubbing around for truffles up there? What's he after?"

"I didn't know he was after anything," said Smiley.

"Ah, stop flirting around. Of course he is. I've got a source up there—one of the mothers, didn't you know? Tells me indiscretions for chocolate. Control's been toiling through personal dossiers of old Circus folk heroes, sniffing out the dirt, who was pink, who was a queen. Half of them are under the earth already. Making a study of all our failures. Can you imagine? And for why? Because we've got a success on our hands. He's mad, George. He's got the big itch: senile paranoia, take my word for it. Ann ever tell you about wicked Uncle Fry? Thought the servants were bugging the roses to find out where he'd hidden his money. Get away from him, George. Death's a bore. Cut the cord, move down a few floors. Join the proles."

Ann had still not returned, so they sauntered side by side down the King's Road looking for a cab while Bill enunciated his latest vision of politics, and Smiley said "Yes, Bill," "No, Bill," and wondered how he was going to break it to Control. He forgot now which particular vision it was. The year before, Bill had been a great hawk. He had wanted to run down conventional forces in Europe and replace them outright with nuclear weapons. He was about the only person left in Whitehall who believed in Britain's independent deterrent. This year, if Smiley remembered rightly, Bill was an aggressive English pacifist and wanted the Sweden solution but without the Swedes.

No cab came; it was a beautiful night, and like old friends they went on walking, side by side.

"By the by, if you ever want to sell that Mieris, let me know, will you? I'll give you a bloody decent price for it."

Thinking Bill was making another bad joke, Smiley rounded on him, at last prepared to be angry. Haydon was not even conscious of his interest. He was gazing down the street, his long arm raised at an approaching cab.

"Oh, Christ, look at them," he shouted irritably. "Full of bloody Jews going to Quag's."

"Bill's backside must look like a damn gridiron," Control muttered next day, barely looking up from his reading. "The years he's spent sitting on the fence."

For a moment he stared at Smiley in an unfocused way, as if looking through him to some different, less fleshy prospect; then ducked his eyes and seemed to resume his reading. "I'm glad he's not *my* cousin," he said.

The following Monday, the mothers had surprising news for Smiley. Control had flown to Belfast for discussions with the army. Later, checking the travel imprests, Smiley nailed the lie. No one in the Circus had flown to Belfast that month, but there was a charge for a first-class return to Vienna and the issuing authority was given as G. Smiley.

Haydon, also looking for Control, was cross: "So now what's the pitch? Dragging Ireland into the net, creating an organisational diversion, I suppose. Jesus, your man's a bore!"

The light in the van went out, but Smiley continued to gaze at its garish roof. How do they live? he wondered. What do they do for water, money? He tried to fathom the logistics of a troglodyte life in Sussex Gardens: water, drains, light. Ann would work them out all right; so would Bill.

Facts. What were the facts?

Facts were that one balmy pre-Witchcraft summer evening, I returned unexpectedly from Berlin to find Bill Haydon stretched on the drawing-room floor and Ann playing Liszt on the gramophone. Ann was sitting across the room from him in her dressing gown, wearing no make-up. There was no scene; everyone behaved with painful naturalness. According to Bill, he had dropped by on his way from the airport, having just flown in from Washington; Ann had been in bed but insisted on getting up to receive him. We agreed it was a pity we hadn't shared a car from Heathrow. Bill left; I asked "What did he want?" And Ann said: "A shoulder to cry on." Bill was having girl trouble, wanted to pour out his heart, she said.

"There's Felicity in Washington, who wants a baby, and Jan in London, who's having one."

"Bill's?"

"God knows. I'm sure Bill doesn't."

Next morning, without even wishing to, Smiley established that Bill had been back in London two days, not one. Following the episode, Bill showed an uncharacteristic deference towards Smiley, and Smiley reciprocated with acts of courtesy which normally belong to a newer friendship. In due course Smiley noticed that the secret was out, and he was still mystified by the speed with which that had happened. He supposed Bill had boasted to someone, perhaps Bland. If the word was correct, Ann had broken three of her own rules. Bill was Circus and he was Set—her word for family and ramifications. On either count he would be out of bounds. Thirdly, she had received him at Bywater Street, an agreed violation of territorial decencies.

Withdrawing once more into his own lonely life, Smiley waited for Ann to say something. He moved into the spare room and arranged for himself plenty of evening engagements in order that he would not be too aware of her comings and goings. Gradually it dawned on him that she was deeply unhappy. She lost weight, she lost her sense of play, and if he didn't know her better he would have sworn she was having a bad bout of the guilts, even of self-disgust. When he was gentle with her, she fended him off; she showed no interest in Christmas shopping and developed a wasting cough, which he knew was her signal of distress. If it had not been for Operation Testify, they would have left for Cornwall earlier. As it was, they had to postpone the trip till January, by which time Control was dead, Smiley was unemployed, the scale had tipped; and Ann, to his mortification, was covering the Haydon card with as many others as she could pull from the pack.

So what happened? Did she break off the affair? Did Haydon? Why did she never speak of it? Did it matter, anyway— one among so many? He gave up. Like the Cheshire cat, the face of Bill Haydon seemed to recede as soon as he advanced upon it, leaving only the smile behind. But he knew that some- how Bill had hurt her deeply, which was the sin of sins.

19

Returning with a grunt of distaste to the unlovable table, Smiley resumed his reading of Merlin's progress since his own enforced retirement from the Circus. The new régime of Percy Alleline, he at once noticed, had immediately produced several favourable changes in Merlin's life-style. It was like a maturing, a settling down. The night dashes to European capitals ceased; the flow of intelligence became more regular and less nervy. There were headaches, certainly. Merlin's demands for money—requirements, never threats—continued, and with the steady decline in the value of the pound these large payments in foreign currency caused the Treasury much agony. There was even a suggestion at one point, never pursued, that "since we are the country of Merlin's choice, he should be ready to shoulder his portion of our financial vicissitudes." Haydon and Bland exploded, apparently: "I have not the face," wrote Alleline with rare frankness to the Minister, "to mention this subject to my staff again."

There was also a row about a new camera, which at great expense was broken into tubular components by nuts and bolts section and fitted into a standard lamp of Soviet manufacture. The lamp, after screams of pain—this time from the Foreign Office—was spirited to Moscow by diplomatic bag. The problem was then the drop. The residency could not be informed of Merlin's identity, nor did it know the contents of the lamp. The lamp was unwieldy, and would not fit the boot of the resident's car. After several shots, an untidy handover was achieved, but the camera never worked and there was bad blood between the Circus and its Moscow residency as a result. A less ambitious model was taken by Esterhase to Helsinki, where it was handed— thus Alleline's memo to the Minister—to "a trusted intermediary whose frontier crossings would go unchallenged."

Suddenly, Smiley sat up with a jolt.

"We spoke," wrote Alleline to the Minister, in a minute dated February 27th this year. "You agreed to submit a supplementary estimate to the Treasury for a London house to be carried on the Witchcraft budget."

He read it once, then again more slowly. The Treasury had sanctioned sixty thousand pounds for the freehold and another ten for furniture and fittings. To cut costs, it wanted its own lawyers to handle the conveyance. Alleline refused to reveal the address. For the same reason there was an argument about who should keep the deeds. This time the Treasury put its foot down and its lawyers drew up instruments to get the house back from Alleline should he die or go bankrupt. But he still kept the address to himself, as also the justification for this remarkable, and costly, adjunct to an operation that was supposedly taking place abroad.

Smiley searched eagerly for an explanation. The financial files, he quickly confirmed, were scrupulous to offer none. They contained only one veiled reference to the London house, and that was when the rates were doubled: Minister to Alleline: "I assume the London end is still necessary?" Alleline to Minister: "Eminently. I would say more than ever. I would add that the circle of knowledge has not widened since our conversation." What knowledge?

It was not till he went back to the files which appraised the Witchcraft product that he came on the solution. The house was paid for in late March. Occupancy followed immediately. From the same date exactly, Merlin began to acquire a personality, and it was shaped here in the customers' comments. Till now, to Smiley's suspicious eye, Merlin had been a machine: faultless in tradecraft, eerie in access, free of the strains that make most agents such hard going. Now, suddenly, he was having a tantrum.

"We put to Merlin your follow-up question about the prevailing Kremlin view on the sale of Russian oil surpluses to the United States. We suggested to him, at your request, that this was at odds with his report last month that the Kremlin is presently flirting with the Tanaka government for a contract to sell Siberian oil on the Japanese market. Merlin saw no contradiction in the two reports and declined to forecast which market might ultimately be favoured."

Whitehall regretted its temerity.

"Merlin will not, repeat not, add to his report on the repression of Georgian nationalism and the rioting in Tbilisi. Not being himself a Georgian, he takes the traditional Russian view that all Georgians are thieves and vagabonds, and better behind bars . . ."

Whitehall agreed not to press.

Merlin had suddenly drawn nearer. Was it only the acquisition of a London house that gave Smiley this new sense of Merlin's physical proximity? From the remote stillness of a Moscow winter, Merlin seemed suddenly to be sitting here before him in the tattered room; in the street outside his window, waiting in the rain, where now and then, he knew, Mendel kept his solitary guard. Here out of the blue was a Merlin who talked and answered back and gratuitously offered his opinions, a Merlin who had time to be met. Met here in London? Fed, entertained, debriefed in a sixty-thousand-pound house while he threw his weight about and made jokes about Georgians? What was this circle of knowledge that had now formed itself even within the wider circle of those initiated into the secrets of the Witchcraft operation?

At this point, an improbable figure flitted across the stage: one J.P.R., a new recruit to Whitehall's growing band of

Witchcraft evaluators. Consulting the indoctrination list, Smiley established that his full name was Ribble, and that he was a member of Foreign Office Research Department. J. P. Ribble was puzzled.

J.P.R. to the Adriatic Working Party (A.W.P.): "May I respectfully draw your attention to an apparent discrepancy concerning dates? Witchcraft No. 104 (Soviet-French discussions on joint aircraft production) is dated April 21st. According to your covering minute, Merlin had this information directly from General Markov on the day after the negotiating parties agreed to a secret exchange of notes. But on that day, April 21st, according to our Paris Embassy, Markov was still in Paris, and Merlin, as witness your Report No. 109, was himself visiting a missile research establishment outside Leningrad . . ."

The minute cited no fewer than four similar "discrepancies," which, put together, suggested a degree of mobility in Merlin that would have done credit to his miraculous namesake.

J. P. Ribble was told in as many words to mind his own business. But in a separate minute to the Minister, Alleline made an extraordinary admission that shed an entirely new light on the nature of the Witchcraft operation.

"Extremely secret and personal. We spoke. Merlin, as you have known for some time, is not one source but several. While we have done our best for security reasons to disguise this fact from your readers, the sheer volume of material makes it increasingly difficult to continue with this fiction. Might it not be time to come clean, at least on a limited basis? By the same token it would do the Treasury no harm to learn that Merlin's ten thousand Swiss francs a month in salary, and a similar figure for expenses and running costs, are scarcely excessive when the cloth has to be cut so many ways."

But the minute ended on a harsher note: "Nevertheless, even if we agree to open the door this far, I regard it as paramount that knowledge of the existence of the London house, and the purpose for which it is used, remain absolutely at a minimum. Indeed, once Merlin's plurality is published among our readers, the delicacy of the London operation is increased."

Totally mystified, Smiley read this correspondence several times. Then, as if struck by a sudden thought, he looked up, his face a picture of confusion. So far away were his thoughts, indeed, so intense and complex, that the telephone rang several times inside the room before he responded to the summons. Lifting the receiver, he glanced at his watch; it was six in the evening; he had been reading barely an hour.

"Mr. Barraclough? This is Lofthouse from finance, sir."

Peter Guillam, using the emergency procedure, was asking by means of the agreed phrases for a crash meeting, and he sounded shaken.

20

The Circus Archives were not accessible from the main entrance. They rambled through a warren of dingy rooms and half-landings at the back of the building, more like one of the second-hand bookshops that proliferate round there than the organised memory of a large department. They were reached by a dull doorway in the Charing Cross Road, jammed between a picture-framer and an all-day café that was out of bounds to staff. A plate on the door read, "Town and Country Language School, Staff Only," and another, "C & L Distribution, Ltd." To enter, you pressed one or other bell and waited for Alwyn, an effeminate Marine who spoke only of weekends. Till Wednesday or so, he spoke of the weekend past; after that he spoke of the weekend to come. This morning, a Tuesday, he was in a mood of indignant unrest.

"Here, what about that storm, then?" he demanded as he pushed the book across the counter for Guillam to sign. "Might as well live in a lighthouse. All Saturday, all Sunday. I said to my friend: 'Here we are in the middle of London and listen to it.' Want me to look after that for you?"

"You should have been where I was," said Guillam, consigning the brown canvas grip into Alwyn's waiting hands. "Talk about listen to it, you could hardly stand upright."

Don't be over-friendly, he thought, talking to himself.

"Still, I do like the country," Alwyn confided, stowing the grip in one of the open lockers behind the counter. "Want a number, then? I'm supposed to give you one—the Dolphin would kill me if she knew."

"I'll trust you," said Guillam. Climbing the four steps, he pushed open the swing doors to the reading-room. The place was like a makeshift lecture hall: a dozen desks all facing the same way, a raised area where the archivist sat. Guillam took a desk near the back. It was still early—ten-ten by his watch—and the only other reader was Ben Thruxton, of research, who spent most of his time here. Long ago, masquerading as a Latvian dissident, Ben had run with revolutionaries through the streets of Moscow calling death to the oppressors. Now he crouched over his papers like an old priest, white-haired and perfectly still.

Seeing Guillam standing at her desk, the archivist smiled. Quite often, when Brixton was dead, Guillam would spend a day here searching through old cases for one that could stand refiring. She was Sal, a plump, sporting girl who ran a youth club in Chiswick and was a judo black-belt.

"Break any good necks this weekend?" he asked, helping himself to a bunch of green requisition slips.

Sal handed him the notes she kept for him in her steel cupboard.

"Couple. How about you?"

"Visiting aunts in Shropshire, thank you."

"Some aunts," said Sal.

Still at her desk, he filled in slips for the next two references on his list. He watched her stamp them, tear off the flimsies, and post them through a slot on her desk.

"D corridor," she murmured, handing back the top copies. "The two-eights are halfway on your right, the three-ones are next alcove down."

Pushing open the far door, he entered the main hall. At the centre an old lift like a miner's cage carried files into the body of the Circus. Two bleary juniors were feeding it; a third stood by to operate the winch. Guillam moved slowly along the shelves reading the fluorescent number cards.

"Lacon swears he holds no file on Testify at all," Smiley had explained in his usual worried way. "He has a few resettlement papers on Prideaux and nothing else." And, in the same lugubrious tone: "So I'm afraid we'll have to find a way of getting hold of whatever there is in Circus Registry."

For "getting hold," in Smiley's dictionary, read "steal."

One girl stood on a ladder. Oscar Allitson, the collator, was filling a laundry basket with wrangler files; Astrid, the maintenance man, was mending a radiator. The shelves were wooden, deep as bunks, and divided into pigeon-holes by panels of ply. He knew already that the Testify reference was 4482E which meant alcove 44, where he now stood. "E" stood for "extinct" and was used for dead operations only. Guillam counted to the eighth pigeon-hole from the left. Testify should be second from the left, but there was no way of making certain because the spines were unmarked. His reconnaissance complete, he drew the two files he had requested, leaving the green slips in the steel brackets provided for them.

"There won't be much, I'm sure," Smiley had said, as if thinner files were easier. "But there ought to be something, if only for appearances." That was another thing about him that Guillam didn't like just then: he spoke as if you followed his reasoning, as if you were inside his mind all the time.

Sitting down, he pretended to read but passed the time thinking of Camilla. What was he supposed to make of her? Early this morning as she lay in his arms, she told him she had once been married. Sometimes she spoke like that, as if she'd lived about twenty lives. It was a mistake, so they packed it in.

"What went wrong?"

"Nothing. We weren't right for each other."

Guillam didn't believe her.

"Did you get a divorce?"

"I expect so."

"Don't be damn silly; you must know whether you're divorced or not!"

His parents handled it, she said; he was foreign.

"Does he send you money?"

"Why should he? He doesn't owe me anything."

Then the flute again, in the spare room, long questioning notes in the half-light while Guillam made coffee. Is she a fake or an angel? He'd half a mind to pass her name across the records. She had a lesson with Sand in an hour.

Armed with a green slip with a 43 reference, he returned the two files to their places and positioned himself at the alcove next to Testify.

Dry run uneventful, he thought.

The girl was still up her ladder. Allitson had vanished but the laundry basket was still there. The radiator had already exhausted Astrid and he was sitting beside it reading the *Sun*. The green slip read "4343," and he found the file at once because he had already marked it down. It had a pink jacket like Testify. Like Testify, it was reasonably thumbed. He fitted the green slip into the bracket. He moved back across the aisle, again checked Allitson and the girls, then reached for the Testify file and replaced it very fast with the file he had in his hand.

"I think the vital thing, Peter"—Smiley speaking—"is not to leave a gap. So what I suggest is, you requisition a comparable file—*physically* comparable, I mean—and pop it into the gap which is left by—"

"I get you," Guillam said.

Holding the Testify file casually in his right hand, title inward to his body, Guillam returned to the reading-room and again sat at his desk. Sal raised her eyebrows and mouthed something. Guillam nodded that all was well, thinking that was what she was asking, but she beckoned him over. Momentary panic. Take the file with me or leave it? What do I usually do? He left it on the desk.

"Juliet's going for coffee," Sal whispered. "Want some?"

Guillam laid a shilling on the counter.

He glanced at the clock, then at his watch. Christ, stop looking at your damn watch! Think of Camilla, think of her starting her lesson, think of those aunts you didn't spend the weekend with, think of Alwyn not looking in your bag. Think of anything but the time. Eighteen minutes to wait. "Peter, if you have the smallest reservation, you really mustn't go ahead with it. Nothing is as important as that." Great, so how do you spot a reservation when thirty teenage butterflies are mating in your stomach and the sweat is like a secret rain inside your shirt? Never, he swore, never had he had it this bad.

Opening the Testify file, he tried to read it.

It wasn't all that thin, but it wasn't fat, either. It looked pretty much like a token volume, as Smiley had said: the first serial was taken up with a description of what wasn't there. "Annexes 1 to 8 held London Station, cross-refer to P.F.s ELLIS Jim, PRIDEAUX Jim, HAJEK Vladimir, COLLINS Sam, HABOLT Max . . ." and a whole football team besides. "For these files, consult H/London Station or C.C.," standing for Chief of Circus and his appointed mothers. Don't look at your watch; look at the clock and do the arithmetic, you idiot. Eight minutes. Odd to be pinching files about one's predecessor. Odd to have Jim as a predecessor, come to think of it, and a secretary who held a wake over him without ever mentioning his name. The only living trace Guillam had ever found of him, apart from his workname on the files, was his squash racket jammed behind the safe in his room, with "J.P." hand-done in poker-work on the handle. He showed it to Ellen, a tough old biddy who could make Cy Vanhofer quail like a schoolboy, and she broke into floods of tears, wrapped it, and sent it to the house-keepers by the next shuttle, with a personal note to the Dolphin insisting that it be returned to him "if humanly possible." How's your game these days, Jim, with a couple of Czech bullets in your shoulder-bone?

Still eight minutes.

"Now, if you could contrive," said Smiley, "I mean if it wouldn't be too much bother, to take your car in for a service at your local garage. Using your home phone to make the appointment, of course, in the *hope* that Toby is listening . . ."

In the hope. Mother of Pearl. And all his cosy chats with Camilla? Still eight minutes.

The rest of the file seemed to be Foreign Office telegrams, Czech press cuttings, monitoring reports on Prague radio, extracts from a policy file on the resettlement and rehabilitation of blown agents, draft submissions to the Treasury, and a postmortem by Alleline that blamed Control for the fiasco. Sooner you than me, George.

In his mind, Guillam began measuring the distance from his desk to the rear door, where Alwyn dozed at the reception counter. He reckoned it was five paces and he decided to make a tactical staging post. Two paces from the door stood a chart chest like a big yellow piano. It was filled with oddments of reference: large-scale maps, back copies of *Who's Who*, old Baedekers. Putting a pencil between his teeth, he picked up the Testify file, wandered to the chest, selected a telephone directory of Warsaw, and began writing names on a sheet of paper. My hand! a voice screamed inside him: my hand is shaking all over the page; look at those figures—I might be drunk! Why has no one noticed? . . . The girl Juliet came in with a tray and put a cup on his desk. He blew her a distracted kiss. He selected another directory—he thought for Poznan—and laid it beside the first. When Alwyn came through the door, he didn't even look up.

"Telephone, sir," he murmured.

"Oh, to hell," said Guillam, deep in the directory. "Who is it?"

"Outside line, sir. Someone rough. The garage, I think, regarding your car. Said he'd got some bad news for you," said Alwyn, very pleased.

Guillam was holding the Testify file in both hands, apparently cross-referring with the directory. He had his back to Sal and he could feel his knees shaking against his trouser legs. The pencil was still jammed in his mouth. Alwyn went ahead and held the swing door for him, and he passed through it reading the file. Like a damned choirboy, he thought. He waited for lightning to strike him, Sal to call murder, old Ben the superspy to leap suddenly to life, but it didn't happen. He felt much better: Alwyn is my ally, I trust him, we are united against the Dolphin, I can move. The swing doors closed; he went down the four steps and there was Alwyn again, holding open the door to the telephone cubicle. The lower part was panelled, the upper part glass. Lifting the receiver, he laid the file at his feet and heard Mendel tell him he needed a new gear-box; the job could cost anything up to a hundred quid. They'd worked this up for the benefit of the housekeepers or whoever read the transcripts, and Guillam kept it going nicely to and fro till Alwyn was safely behind his counter, listening like an eagle. It's working, he thought; I'm flying, it's working after all. He heard himself say, "Well, at least get on to the main agents first and find out how long they'll take to supply the damn thing. Have you got their number?" And irritably: "Hang on."

He half-opened the door and he kept the mouthpiece jammed against his backside because he was very concerned that this part should not go on tape. "Alwyn, chuck me that bag a minute, will you?"

Alwyn brought it over keenly, like the first-aid man at a football match. "All right, Mr. Guillam, sir? Open it for you, sir?"

"Just dump it there, thanks."

The bag was on the floor outside the cubicle. Now he stooped, dragged it inside, and unzipped it. At the middle, among his shirts and a lot of newspaper, were three dummy files, one buff, one green, one pink. He took out the pink dummy and his address book and replaced them with the Testify file. He closed the zip, and stood up and read Mendel a telephone number— actually the right one. He rang off, handed Alwyn the bag, and returned to the reading-room with the dummy file. He dawdled at the chart chest, fiddled with a couple more directories, then sauntered to the archive carrying the dummy file. Allitson was going through a comedy routine, first pulling then pushing the laundry basket.

"Peter, give us a hand, will you—I'm stuck."

"Half a sec."

Recovering the 43 file from the Testify pigeon-hole, he replaced it with the dummy, restored it to its rightful place in the 43 alcove, and removed the green slip from the bracket. God is in His heaven and the first night was a wow. He could have sung out loud: God is in His heaven and I can still fly.

He took the slip to Sal, who signed it and put it on a spike as she always did. Later today she would check. If the file was in its place, she would destroy both the green slip and the flimsy from the box, and not even clever Sal would remember that he had been alongside the 44 alcove. He was about to return to the archive to give old Allitson a hand when he found himself looking straight into the brown, unfriendly eyes of Toby Esterhase.

"Peter," said Toby, in his not quite perfect English. "I am so sorry to disturb you but we have a tiny crisis and Percy Alleline would like quite an urgent word with you. Can you come now? That would be very kind." And at the door, as Alwyn let them out: "Your opinion he wants, actually," he remarked with the officiousness of a small but rising man. "He wishes to consult you for an opinion."

In a desperately inspired moment, Guillam turned to Alwyn and said, "There's a midday shuttle to Brixton. You might just give transport a buzz and ask them to take that thing over for me, will you?"

"Will do, sir," said Alwyn. "Will do. Mind the step, sir."

And you pray for me, thought Guillam.

21

"Our Shadow Foreign Secretary," Haydon called him. The janitors called him "Snow White" because of his hair. Toby Esterhase dressed like a male model, but the moment he dropped his shoulders or closed his tiny fists he was unmistakably a fighter. Following him down the fourth-floor corridor—noting the coffee machine again, and Lauder Strickland's voice explaining that he was unobtainable—Guillam thought, Christ, we're back in Berne and on the run.

He'd half a mind to call this out to Toby, but decided the comparison was unwise.

Whenever he thought of Toby, that was what he thought of: Switzerland eight years ago, when Toby was just a humdrum watcher with a growing reputation for informal listening on the side. Guillam was kicking his heels after North Africa, so the Circus packed them both off to Berne on a one-time operation to spike a pair of Belgian arms dealers who were using the Swiss to spread their wares in unpopular directions. They rented a villa next door to the target house, and the following night Toby opened up a junction box and rearranged things so that they overheard the Belgians' conversations on their own phone. Guillam was boss and legman, and twice a day he dropped the tapes on the Berne residency, using a parked car as a letter-box. With the same ease, Toby bribed the local postman to give him a first sight of the Belgians' mail before he delivered it, and the cleaning lady to plant a radio mike in the drawing room where they held most of their discussions. For diversion, they went to the Chikito and Toby danced with the youngest girls. Now and then he brought one home, but by morning she was always gone and Toby had the windows open to get rid of the smell.

They lived this way for three months and Guillam knew him no better at the end than he had on the first day. He didn't even know his country of origin. Toby was a snob, and knew the places to eat and be seen. He washed his own clothes and at night he wore a net over his snow white hair, and on the day the police hit the villa and Guillam had to hop over the back wall, he found Toby at the Bellevue Hotel munching *pâtisseries* and watching the *thé dansant*. He listened to what Guillam had to say, paid his bill, tipped first the bandleader, then Franz, the head porter, and then led the way along a succession of corridors and staircases to the underground garage where he had cached the escape car and passports. There also, punctiliously, he asked for his bill. Guillam thought, If you ever want to get out of Switzerland in a hurry, you pay your bills first. The corridors were endless, with mirror walls and Versailles chandeliers, so that Guillam was following not just one Esterhase but a whole delegation of them.

It was this vision that came back to him now, though the narrow wooden staircase to Alleline's rooms was painted mud-green and only a battered parchment lampshade recalled the chandeliers.

"To see the Chief," Toby announced portentously to the young janitor who beckoned them through with an insolent nod. In the anteroom at four grey typewriters sat the four grey mothers, in pearls and twin-sets. They nodded to Guillam and ignored Toby. A sign over Alleline's door said "Engaged." Beside it, a six-foot wardrobe safe, new. Guillam wondered how on earth the floor took the strain. On its top, bottles of

South African sherry; glasses, plates. Tuesday, he remembered: London Station's informal lunch meeting.

"I'll have no phone calls, tell them," Alleline shouted as Toby opened the door.

"The Chief will take no calls, please, ladies," said Toby elaborately, holding back the door for Guillam. "We are having a conference."

One of the mothers said, "We heard."

It was a war party.

Alleline sat at the head of the table in the megalomaniac's throne, reading a two-page document, and he didn't stir when Guillam came in. He just growled, "Down there with you. By Paul. Below the salt," and went on reading with heavy concentration.

The chair to Alleline's right was empty, and Guillam knew it was Haydon's by the posture-curve cushion tied to it with string. To Alleline's left sat Roy Bland, also reading, but he looked up as Guillam passed, and said "Wotcher, Peter," then followed him all the way down the table with his bulging eyes. Next to Bill's empty chair sat Mo Delaware, London Station's token woman, in bobbed hair and a brown tweed suit. Across from her, Phil Porteous, the head housekeeper, a rich servile man with a big house in suburbia. When he saw Guillam, he stopped his reading altogether, ostentatiously closed the folder, laid his sleek hands over it, and smirked.

"'Below the salt' means next to Paul Skordeno," said Phil, still smirking.

"Thanks. I can see it."

Across from Porteous came Bill's Russians, last seen in the fourth-floor men's room, Nick de Silsky and his boyfriend Kaspar. They couldn't smile, and for all Guillam knew they couldn't read, either, because they had no papers in front of them; they were the only ones who hadn't. They sat with their four thick hands on the table as if somebody were holding a gun behind them, and they just watched him with their four brown eyes.

Downhill from Porteous sat Paul Skordeno, now reputedly Roy Bland's fieldman on the satellite networks, though others said he ran between wickets for Bill. Paul was thin and mean and forty, with a pitted brown face and long arms. Guillam had once paired with him on a tough-guy course at the Nursery and they all but killed each other.

Guillam moved the chair away from him and sat down, so Toby sat next along like the other half of a bodyguard. Guillam thought, What the hell do they expect me to do—make a mad dash for freedom? Everyone was watching Alleline fill his pipe when Bill Haydon upstaged him. The door opened and at first no one came in. Then a slow shuffle and Bill appeared, clutching a cup of coffee in both hands, the saucer on top. He had a striped folder jammed under his arm and his glasses were over his nose, for a change, so he must have done his reading elsewhere. They've all been reading it except me, thought Guillam, and I don't know what it is. He wondered whether it was the same document that Esterhase and Roy were reading yesterday, and decided on no evidence at all that it was; that yesterday it had just come in, that Toby had brought it to Roy, and that he had disturbed them in their first excitement—if excitement was the word.

Alleline had still not looked up. Down the table Guillam had only his rich black hair to look at, and a pair of broad tweedy shoulders. Mo Delaware was pulling at her fringe while she read. Percy had two wives, Guillam remembered, as Camilla once more flitted through his teeming mind, and both were alcoholics, which must mean something. He had met only the London edition. Percy was forming his supporters' club and gave a drinks party at his sprawling panelled flat in Buckingham Palace Mansions. Guillam arrived late and he was taking off his coat in the lobby when a pale blond woman loomed timidly towards him holding out her hands. He took her for the maid wanting his coat.

"I'm Joy," she said, in a theatrical voice, like "I'm Virtue" or "I'm Continence." It wasn't his coat she wanted but a kiss. Yielding to it, Guillam inhaled the joint pleasures of Je Reviens and a high concentration of inexpensive sherry.

"Well, now, young Peter Guillam"—Alleline speaking—"are you ready for me finally or have you other calls to make about my house?" He half looked up and Guillam noticed two tiny triangles of fur on each weathered cheek. "What are you getting up to out there in the sticks these days"—turning a page—"apart from chasing the local virgins, if there are any in Brixton, which I severely doubt—if you'll pardon my freedom, Mo—and wasting public money on expensive lunches?"

This banter was Alleline's one instrument of communication; it could be friendly or hostile, reproachful or congratulatory, but in the end it was like a constant tapping on the same spot.

"Couple of Arab ploys look quite promising. Cy Vanhofer's got a lead to a German diplomat. That's about it."

"Arabs," Alleline repeated, pushing aside the folder and dragging a rough pipe from his pocket. "Any bloody fool can burn an Arab—can't he, Bill? Buy a whole damn Arab Cabinet for half a crown, if you've a mind to." From another pocket Alleline took a tobacco pouch, which he tossed easily onto the table. "I hear you've been hobnobbing with our late-lamented Brother Tarr. How is he these days?"

A lot of things went through Guillam's mind as he heard himself answer. That the surveillance on his flat did not begin till last night—he was sure of it. That over the weekend he was in the clear unless Fawn, the captive baby-sitter, had doubled, which would have been hard for him. That Roy Bland bore a close resemblance to the late Dylan Thomas: Roy had always reminded him of someone and till this moment he'd never been able to pin down the connection; and that Mo Delaware had only passed muster as a woman because of her brownie mannishness. He wondered whether Dylan Thomas had had Roy's extraordinary blue eyes. That Toby Esterhase was helping himself to a cigarette from his gold case, and that Alleline didn't as a rule allow cigarettes but only pipes, so Toby must stand pretty well with Alleline just now. That Bill Haydon was looking strangely young and that Circus rumours about his love-life were not after all so laughable: they said he went both ways. That Paul Skordeno had one brown palm flat on the table and the thumb slightly lifted in a way that hardened the hitting surface on the outside of the hand. He thought also of his canvas case: had Alwyn put it on the shuttle? Or had he gone off for his lunch leaving it in Registry, waiting to be inspected by one of the new young janitors busting for promotion? And Guillam wondered—not for the first time—just how long Toby had been hanging around Registry before Guillam noticed him.

He selected a facetious tone: "That's right, Chief. Tarr and I have tea at Fortnum's every afternoon."

Alleline was sucking at his empty pipe, testing the packing of the tobacco.

"Peter Guillam," he said deliberately, in his pert brogue. "You may not be aware of this, but I am of an extremely forgiving nature. I am positively seething with goodwill, in fact. All I require is the matter of your discussion with Tarr. I do not ask for his head, nor any other part of his damned anatomy, and I will restrain my impulse personally to strangle him. Or you." He struck a match and lit his pipe, making a monstrous flame. "I would even go so far as to consider hanging a gold chain about your neck and bringing you into the palace from hateful Brixton."

"In that case, I can't wait for him to turn up," said Guillam.

"And there's a free pardon for Tarr till I get my hands on him."

"I'll tell him. He'll be thrilled."

A great cloud of smoke rolled out over the table.

"I'm very disappointed with you, young Peter. Giving ear to gross slanders of a divisive and insidious nature. I pay you honest money and you stab me in the back. I consider that extremely poor reward for keeping you alive. Against the entreaties of my advisers, I may tell you."

Alleline had a new mannerism, one that Guillam had noticed often in vain men of middle age: it involved taking hold of a tuck of flesh under the chin and massaging it between finger and thumb in the hope of reducing it.

"Tell us some more about Tarr's circumstances just now," said Alleline. "Tell us about his emotional state. He has a daughter, has he not? A wee daughter name of Danny. Does he talk of her at all?"

"He used to."

"Regale us with some anecdotes about her."

"I don't know any. He was very fond of her, that's all I know."

"Obsessively fond?" His voice rose suddenly in anger. "What's that shrug for? What the hell are you shrugging at me like that for? I'm talking to you about a defector from your own damn section; I'm accusing you of playing hookey with him behind my back, of taking part in damn-fool parlour games when you don't know the stakes involved, and all you do is shrug at me down the table. There's a *law*, Peter Guillam, against consorting with enemy agents. Maybe you didn't know that. I've a good mind to throw the book at you!"

"But I haven't been seeing him," said Guillam as anger came also to his rescue. "It's not me who's playing parlour games. It's you. So get off my back."

In the same moment he sensed the relaxation round the table, like a tiny descent into boredom, like a general recognition that Alleline had shot off all his ammunition and the target was unmarked. Skordeno was fidgeting with a bit of ivory, some lucky charm he carried round with him. Bland was reading again and

Bill Haydon was drinking his coffee and finding it terrible, for he made a sour face at Mo Delaware and put down the cup. Toby Esterhase, chin in hand, had raised his eyebrows and was gazing at the red cellophane that filled the Victorian grate. Only the Russians continued to watch him unblinkingly, like a pair of terriers not wanting to believe that the hunt was over.

"So he used to chat to you about Danny, eh? And he told you he loved her," said Alleline, back at the document before him. "Who's Danny's mother?"

"A Eurasian girl."

Now Haydon spoke for the first time. "Unmistakably Eurasian, or could she pass for something nearer home?"

"Tarr seems to think she looks full European. He thinks the kid does, too."

Alleline read aloud: "Twelve years old, long blond hair, brown eyes, slim. Is that Danny?"

"I should think it could be. It sounds like her."

There was a long silence and not even Haydon seemed inclined to break it.

"So if I told you," Alleline resumed, choosing his words extremely carefully: "if I told you that Danny and her mother were due to arrive three days ago at London Airport on the direct flight from Singapore, I may take it you would share our perplexity."

"Yes, I would."

"You would also keep your mouth shut when you got out of here. You'd tell no one but your twelve best friends?"

From not far away came Phil Porteous's purr: "The source is extremely secret, Peter. It may sound to you like ordinary flight information but it isn't that at all. It's ultra, *ultra* sensitive."

"Ah, well, in that case I'll try to keep my mouth *ultra* shut," said Guillam to Porteous, and while Porteous coloured Bill Haydon gave another schoolboy grin.

Alleline came back. "So what would you make of this information? Come on, Peter—" the banter again—"Come on, you were his boss, his guide, philosopher, and his friend. Where's your psychology, for God's sake? Why is Tarr coming to England?"

"That's not what you said at all. You said Tarr's girl and her daughter Danny were expected in London three days ago. Perhaps she's visiting relations. Perhaps she's got a new boyfriend. How should I know?"

"Don't be obtuse, man. Doesn't it occur to you that where little Danny is, Tarr himself is unlikely to be far behind? If he's not here already, which I'm inclined to believe he is, that being the manner of men to come first and bring their impedimenta later. Pardon me, Mo Delaware, a lapse."

For the second time, Guillam allowed himself a little temperament. "Till now it had not occurred to me, no. Till now Tarr was a defector. Housekeepers' ruling as of seven months ago. Right or wrong, Phil? Tarr was sitting in Moscow and everything he knew should be regarded as blown. Right, Phil? That was also held to be a good enough reason for turning the lights out in Brixton and giving one chunk of our workload to London Station and another to Toby's lamplighters. What's Tarr supposed to be doing now, redefecting to us?"

"Redefecting would be a damned charitable way of putting it, I'll tell you that for nothing," Alleline retorted, back at the paper before him. "Listen to me. Listen exactly, and remember. Because I've no doubt that, like the rest of my staff, you've a memory like a sieve—all you prima donnas are the same. Danny and her mother are travelling on fake British passports in the name of Poole, like the harbour. The passports are Russian fakes. A third went to Tarr himself, the well-known *Mr.* Poole. Tarr is already in England but we don't know where. He left ahead of Danny and her mother and came here by a different route; our investigations suggest a black one. He instructed his wife or mistress or whatever"—he said this as if he had neither—"pardon again, Mo, to follow him in one week, which they have not yet done, apparently. This information only reached us yesterday, so we've a lot of footwork to do yet. Tarr instructed them, Danny and her mother, that if by any chance he failed to make contact with them, they should throw themselves on the mercy of one Peter Guillam. That's you, I believe."

"If they were due three days ago, what's happened to them?"

"Delayed. Missed their plane. Changed their plans. Lost their tickets. How the hell do I know?"

"Or else the information's wrong," Guillam suggested.

"It isn't," Alleline snapped.

Resentment, mystification: Guillam clung to them both. "All right. The Russians have turned Tarr round. They've sent his family over—God knows why; I'd have thought they'd put them in the bank—and they've sent him, too. Why's it all so hot? What sort of plant can he be when we don't believe a word he says?"

This time, he noticed with exhilaration, his audience was watching Alleline, who seemed to Guillam to be torn between giving a satisfactory but indiscreet answer or making a fool of himself.

"Never mind what sort of plant! Muddying pools. Poisoning wells, maybe. That damn sort. Pulling the rug out when we're all but home and dry." His circulars read that way, too, thought Guillam. Metaphors chasing each other off the page. "But just you remember this. At the first peep, before the first peep, at the first whisper of him or his lady or his wee daughter, young Peter Guillam, you come to one of us grown-ups. Anyone you see at this table. But not another damn soul. Do you follow that injunction perfectly? Because there are more damn wheels within wheels here than you can possibly guess or have any right to know . . ."

It became suddenly a conversation in movement. Bland had plugged his hands into his pockets and slouched across the room to lean against the far door. Alleline had relit his pipe and was putting out the match with a long movement of his arm while he glowered at Guillam through the smoke. "Who are you courting these days, Peter—who's the lucky wee lady?" Porteous was sliding a sheet of paper down the table for Guillam's signature. "For you, Peter, if you please." Paul Skordeno was whispering something into the ear of one of the Russians, and Esterhase was at the door giving unpopular orders to the mothers. Only Mo Delaware's brown, unassuming eyes still held Guillam in their gaze.

"Read it first, won't you," Porteous advised silkily.

Guillam was halfway through the form already: "I certify that I have today been advised of the contents of Witchcraft Report No. 308, Source Merlin," ran the first paragraph. "I undertake not to divulge any part of this report to other members of the service, nor will I divulge the existence of Source Merlin. I also undertake to report at once any matter which comes to my notice which appears to bear on this material."

The door had stayed open and, as Guillam signed, the second echelon of London Station filed in, led by the mothers with trays of sandwiches. Diana Dolphin, Lauder Strickland looking taut enough to blow up, the girls from distribution, and a sour-faced old war-horse called Haggard, who was Ben Thruxton's overlord. Guillam left slowly, counting heads because he knew Smiley would want to know who was there. At the door, to his surprise, he found himself joined by Haydon, who seemed to have decided that the remaining festivities were not for him.

"Stupid bloody cabaret," Bill remarked, waving vaguely at the mothers. "Percy's getting more insufferable every day."

"He does seem to," said Guillam heartily.

"How's Smiley these days? Seen much of him? You used to be quite a chum of his, didn't you?"

Guillam's world, which was showing signs till then of steadying to a sensible pace, plunged violently. "Afraid not," he said; "he's out of bounds."

"Don't tell me you take any notice of that nonsense," Bill said, snorting. They had reached the stairs. Haydon went ahead.

"How about you?" Guillam called. "Have you seen much of him?"

"And Ann's flown the coop," said Bill, ignoring the question. "Pushed off with a sailor-boy or a waiter or something." The door to his room was wide open, the desk heaped with secret files. "Is that right?"

"I didn't know," said Guillam. "Poor old George."

"Coffee?"

"I think I'll get back, thanks."

"For tea with Brother Tarr?"

"That's right. At Fortnum's. So long."

In Archives Section, Alwyn was back from lunch. "Bag's all gone, sir," he said gaily. "Should be over in Brixton by now."

"Oh, damn," said Guillam, firing his last shot. "There was something in it I needed."

A sickening notion had struck him: it seemed so neat and so horribly obvious that he could only wonder why it had come to him so late. Sand was Camilla's husband. She was living a double life. Now whole new vistas of deceit opened before him. His friends, his loves, even the Circus itself; joined and re-formed in endless patterns of intrigue. A line of Mendel's came back to him, dropped two nights ago as they drank beer in some glum suburban pub: "Cheer up, Peter, old son. Jesus Christ only had twelve, you know, and one of them was a double."

Tarr, he thought. That bastard Ricki Tarr.

22

The bedroom was long and low, once a maid's room, built into the attic. Guillam was standing at the door; Tarr sat on the bed motionless, his head tilted back against the sloped ceiling, hands to either side of him, fingers wide. There was a dormer window above him, and from where Guillam stood he could see long reaches of black Suffolk countryside and a line of black trees traced against the sky. The wallpaper was brown with large red flowers. The one light hung from a black oak truss, lighting their two faces in strange geometric patterns, and when either one of them moved, Tarr on the bed or Smiley on the wooden kitchen chair, they seemed by their movement to take the light with them a distance before it resettled.

Left to himself, Guillam would have been very rough with Tarr, he had no doubt of it. His nerves were all over the place, and on the drive down he had touched ninety before Smiley sharply told him to go steady. Left to himself, he would have been tempted to beat the daylights out of Tarr, and if necessary he would have brought Fawn in to lend a hand; driving, he had a very clear picture of opening the front door of wherever Tarr lived and hitting him in the face several times, with love from Camilla and her ex-husband, the distinguished doctor of the flute. And perhaps in the shared tension of the journey Smiley had received the same picture telepathically, for the little he said was clearly directed to talking Guillam down. "Tarr has not lied to us, Peter. Not in any material way. He has simply done what agents do the world over: he has failed to tell us the whole story. On the other hand, he has been rather clever." Far from sharing Guillam's bewilderment, he seemed curiously confident—even complacent—to the extent of allowing himself a sententious aphorism from Steed-Asprey on the arts of double-cross; something about not looking for perfection, but for advantage, which again had Guillam thinking about Camilla. "Karla has admitted us to the inner circle," Smiley announced, and Guillam made a bad joke about changing at Charing Cross. After that Smiley contented himself with giving directions and watching the wing mirror.

They had met at Crystal Palace, a van pick-up with Mendel driving. They drove to Barnsbury, straight into a car-body repair shop at the end of a cobbled alley full of children. There they were received with discreet rapture by an old German and his son, who had stripped the plates off the van almost before they got out of it and led them to a souped-up Vauxhall ready to drive out of the far end of the workshop. Mendel stayed behind with the Testify file, which Guillam had brought from Brixton in his night-bag; Smiley said, "Find the A12." There was very little traffic but short of Colchester they hit a cluster of lorries and Guillam suddenly lost patience. Smiley had to order him to pull in. Once they met an old man driving at twenty in the fast lane. As they overtook him on the inside, he veered wildly towards them, drunk or ill, or just terrified. And once, with no warning, they hit a fog wall; it seemed to fall on them from above. Guillam drove clean through it, afraid to brake because of black ice. Past Colchester they took small lanes. On the signposts were names like Little Horkesley, Wormingford, and Bures Green; then the signposts stopped and Guillam had a feeling of being nowhere at all.

"Left here and left again at the dower house. Go as far as you can but park short of the gates."

They reached what seemed to be a hamlet but there were no lights, no people, and no moon. As they got out, the cold hit them and Guillam smelt a cricket field and wood-smoke and Christmas all at once; he thought he had never been anywhere so quiet or so cold or so remote. A church tower rose ahead of them, a white fence ran to one side, and up on the slope stood what he took to be the rectory, a low rambling house, part thatched; he could make out the fringe of gable against the sky. Fawn was waiting for them; he came to the car as they parked, and climbed silently into the back.

"Ricki's been that much better today, sir," he reported. He had evidently done a lot of reporting to Smiley in the last few days. He was a steady, soft-spoken boy with a great will to please, but the rest of the Brixton pack seemed to be afraid of him, Guillam didn't know why. "Not so nervy—more relaxed, I'd say. Did his pools this morning—loves the pools, Ricki does—this afternoon we dug up fir trees for Miss Ailsa, so's she could drive them into market. This evening we had a nice game of cards and early bed."

"Has he been out alone?" asked Smiley.

"No, sir."

"Has he used the telephone?"

"Gracious, no, sir, not while I'm around, and I'm sure not while Miss Ailsa was, either."

Their breath had misted the windows of the car, but Smiley would not have the engine on, so there was no heater and no de-mister.

"Has he mentioned his daughter Danny?"

"Over the weekend he did a lot. Now he's sort of cooled off about them. I think he's shut them out of his mind, in view of the emotional side."

"He hasn't talked about seeing them again?"

"No, sir."

"Nothing about arrangements for meeting when all this is over?"

"No, sir."

"Or bringing them to England?"

"No, sir."

"Nor about providing them with documents?"

"No, sir."

Guillam chimed in irritably: "So what has he talked about, for heaven's sake?"

"The Russian lady, sir. Irina. He likes to read her diary. He says when the mole's caught, he's going to make Centre swap him for Irina. Then we'll get her a nice place, sir—like Miss Ailsa's but up in Scotland where it's nicer. He says he'll see me right, too. Give me a big job in the Circus. He's been encouraging me to learn another language to increase my scope."

There was no telling, from the flat voice behind them in the dark, what Fawn made of this advice.

"Where is he now?"

"In bed, sir."

"Close the doors quietly."

Ailsa Brimley was waiting in the front porch for them: a grey-haired lady of sixty with a firm, intelligent face. She was old Circus, Smiley said, one of Lord Landsbury's coding ladies from the war, now in retirement but still formidable. She wore a trim brown suit. She shook Guillam by the hand and said "How do you do," bolted the door, and when he looked again she had gone. Smiley led the way upstairs. Fawn should wait on the lower landing in case he was needed.

"It's Smiley," he said knocking on Tarr's door. "I want a chat with you."

Tarr opened the door fast. He must have heard them coming, and been waiting just the other side. He opened it with his left hand, holding the gun in his right, and he was looking past Smiley down the corridor.

"It's only Guillam," said Smiley.

"That's what I mean," said Tarr. "Babies can bite."

They stepped inside. He wore slacks and some sort of cheap Malay wrap. Spelling cards lay spread over the floor and in the air hung a smell of curry that he had cooked for himself on a ring.

"I'm sorry to be pestering you," said Smiley with an air of sincere commiseration. "But I must ask you again what you did with those two Swiss escape passports you took with you to Hong Kong."

"Why?" said Tarr at last.

The jauntiness was all gone. He had a prison pallor; he had lost weight and as he sat on the bed with the gun on the pillow beside him, his eyes sought them out nervously, each in turn, trusting nothing.

Smiley said, "Listen. I want to believe your story. Nothing is altered. Once we know, we'll respect your privacy. But we have to know. It's terribly important. Your whole future stands by it."

And a lot more besides, thought Guillam, watching; a whole chunk of devious arithmetic was hanging by a thread, if Guillam knew Smiley at all.

"I told you I burned them. I didn't fancy the numbers. I reckoned they were blown. Might as well put a label round your neck 'Tarr, Ricki Tarr, Wanted' soon as use those passports."

Smiley's questions were terribly slow in coming. Even to Guillam it was painful waiting for them in the deep silence of the night.

"What did you burn them with?"

"What the hell does that matter?"

But Smiley apparently did not feel like giving reasons for his enquiries; he preferred to let the silence do its work, and he seemed confident that it would. Guillam had seen whole inter-rogations conducted that way: a laboured catechism swathed in deep coverings of routine; wearying pauses as each answer was written down in longhand and the suspect's brain besieged itself with a thousand questions to the interrogator's one; and his hold on his story weakened from day to day.

"When you bought your British passport in the name of Poole," Smiley asked, after another age, "did you buy any other passports from the same source?"

"Why should I?"

But Smiley did not feel like giving reasons.

"Why should I?" Tarr repeated. "I'm not a damn collector, for Christ's sake; all I wanted was to get out from under."

"And protect your child," Smiley suggested, with an understanding smile. "And protect her mother, too, if you could. I'm sure you gave a lot of thought to that," he said in a flattering tone. "After all, you could hardly leave them behind to the mercy of that inquisitive Frenchman, could you?"

Waiting, Smiley appeared to examine the lexicon cards, reading off the words longways and sideways. There was nothing to them: they were random words. One was misspelt; Guillam noticed "epistle" with the last two letters back to front. What's he been doing up there, Guillam wondered, in that stinking flea-pit of a hotel? What furtive little tracks has his mind been following, locked away with the sauce bottles and the commercial travellers?

"All right," said Tarr sullenly, "so I got passports for Danny and her mother. Mrs. Poole, Miss Danny Poole. What do we do now, cry out in ecstasy?"

Again it was the silence that accused.

"Now why didn't you tell us that before?" Smiley asked in the tone of a disappointed father. "We're not monsters. We don't wish them harm. Why didn't you tell us? Perhaps we could even have helped you," and went back to his examination of the cards. Tarr must have used two or three packs; they lay in rivers over the coconut carpet. "Why didn't you tell us?" he repeated. "There's no crime in looking after the people one loves."

If they'll let you, thought Guillam, with Camilla in mind.

To help Tarr answer, Smiley was making helpful suggestions: "Was it because you dipped into your operational expenses to buy these British passports? Was that the reason you didn't tell us? Good heavens, no one here is worried about money. You've brought us a vital piece of information. Why should we quarrel about a couple of thousand dollars?" And the time ticked away again without anyone using it.

"Or was it," Smiley suggested, "that you were ashamed?"

Guillam stiffened, his own problems forgotten.

"Rightly ashamed in a way, I suppose. It wasn't a very gallant act, after all, to leave Danny and her mother with blown passports, at the mercy of that so-called Frenchman who was looking so hard for Mr. Poole? While you yourself escaped to all this V.I.P. treatment? It is horrible to think of," Smiley agreed, as if Tarr, not he, had made the point. "It is horrible to contemplate the lengths Karla would go to in order to obtain your silence. Or your services."

The sweat on Tarr's face was suddenly unbearable. There was too much of it; it was like tears all over. The cards no longer interested Smiley; his eye had settled on a different game. It was a toy, made of two steel rods like the shafts of a pair of tongs. The trick was to roll a steel ball along them. The further you rolled it, the more points you won when it fell into one of the holes underneath.

"The other reason you might not have told us, I suppose, is that you burnt them. You burnt the *British* passports, I mean, not the Swiss ones."

Go easy, George, thought Guillam, and softly moved a pace nearer to cover the gap between them. Just go easy.

"You knew that Poole was blown, so you burnt the Poole passports you had bought for Danny and her mother, but you kept your own because there was no alternative. Then you made travel bookings for the two of them in the name of

Poole in order to convince everybody that you still believed in
the Poole passports. By everybody, I think I mean Karla's footpads, don't I? You doctored the Swiss escapes, one for Danny,
one for her mother, took a chance that the numbers wouldn't
be noticed, and you made a different set of arrangements which
you didn't advertise. Arrangements which matured earlier
than those you made for the Pooles. How would that be? Such
as staying out East, but somewhere else, like Djakarta: somewhere you have friends."

Even from where he stood, Guillam was too slow. Tarr's
hands were at Smiley's throat; the chair toppled and Tarr fell
with him. From the heap, Guillam selected Tarr's right arm
and flung it into a lock against his back, bringing it very near
to breaking as he did so. From nowhere Fawn appeared, took
the gun from the pillow, and walked back to Tarr as if to give
him a hand. Then Smiley was straightening his suit and Tarr
was back on the bed, dabbing the corner of his mouth with a
handkerchief.

Smiley said, "I don't know where they are. As far as I know,
no harm has come to them. You believe that, do you?"

Tarr was staring at him, waiting. His eyes were furious, but
over Smiley a kind of calm had settled, and Guillam guessed it
was the reassurance he had been hoping for.

"Maybe you should keep a better eye on your own damn
woman and leave mine alone," Tarr whispered, his hand across
his mouth. With an exclamation, Guillam sprang forward but
Smiley restrained him.

"As long as you don't try to communicate with them,"
Smiley continued, "it's probably better that I shouldn't know.
Unless you want me to do something about them. Money or
protection or comfort of some sort?"

Tarr shook his head. There was blood in his mouth, a lot of
it, and Guillam realised Fawn must have hit him but he couldn't
work out when.

"It won't be long now," Smiley said. "Perhaps a week. Less, if I can manage it. Try not to think too much."

By the time they left, Tarr was grinning again, so Guillam guessed that the visit, or the insult to Smiley or the smash in the face, had done him good.

"Those football-pool coupons," Smiley said quietly to Fawn as they climbed into the car: "You don't post them anywhere, do you?"

"No, sir."

"Well, let's hope to God he doesn't have a win," Smiley remarked in a most unusual fit of jocularity, and there was laughter all round.

The memory plays strange tricks on an exhausted, overladen brain. As Guillam drove, one part of his conscious mind upon the road and another still wretchedly grappling with even more gothic suspicions of Camilla, odd images of this and other long days drifted freely through his memory. Days of plain terror in Morocco as one by one his agent lines went dead on him, and every footfall on the stair had him scurrying to the window to check the street; days of idleness in Brixton when he watched that poor world slip by and wondered how long before he joined it. And suddenly the written report was there before him on his desk: duplicated on blue flimsy because it was traded, source unknown, and probably unreliable, and every word of it came back to him in letters a foot high:

According to a recently released prisoner from Lubianka, Moscow Centre held a secret execution in the punishment block in July. The victims were three of its own functionaries. One was a woman. All three were shot in the back of the neck.

"It was stamped 'internal,' " Guillam said dully. They had parked in a layby beside a roadhouse hung with fairy lights.

"Somebody from London Station had scribbled on it: 'Can anyone identify the bodies?'"

By the coloured glow of the lights, Guillam watched Smiley's face pucker in disgust.

"Yes," he agreed at last. "Yes, well now, the woman was Irina, wasn't she? Then there was Ivlov and then there was Boris, her husband, I suppose." His voice remained extremely matter-of-fact. "Tarr mustn't know," he continued, as if shaking off lassitude. "It is vital that he should have no wind of this. God knows what he would do, or not do, if he knew that Irina was dead." For some moments neither moved; perhaps for their different reasons neither had the strength just then, or the heart.

"I ought to telephone," said Smiley, but he made no attempt to leave the car.

"George?"

"I have a phone call to make," Smiley muttered. "Lacon."

"Then make it."

Reaching across him, Guillam pushed open the door. Smiley clambered, walked a distance over the tarmac, then seemed to change his mind and came back.

"Come and eat something," he said through the window, in the same preoccupied tone. "I don't think even Toby's people would follow us in here."

It was once a restaurant, now a transport café with trappings of old grandeur. The menu was bound in red leather and stained with grease. The boy who brought it was half asleep.

"I hear the *coq au vin* is always reliable," said Smiley, with a poor effort at humour as he returned from the telephone booth in the corner. And in a quieter voice, that fell short and echoed nowhere: "Tell me, how much do you know about Karla?"

"About as much as I know about Witchcraft and Source Merlin, and whatever else it said on the paper I signed for Porteous."

"Ah, well, now, that's a very good answer, as it happens. You meant it as a rebuke, I expect, but as it happens, the analogy was most apt." The boy reappeared, swinging a bottle of Burgundy like an Indian club. "Would you please let it breathe a little?"

The boy stared at Smiley as if he were mad.

"Open it and leave it on the table," said Guillam curtly.

It was not the whole story Smiley told. Afterwards Guillam did notice several gaps. But it was enough to lift his spirits from the doldrums where they had strayed.

23

"It is the business of agent runners to turn themselves into legends," Smiley began, rather as if he were delivering a trainee lecture at the Nursery. "They do this first to impress their agents. Later they try it out on their colleagues and, in my personal experience, make rare asses of themselves in consequence. A few go so far as to try it on themselves. Those are the charlatans and they must be got rid of quickly, there's no other way."

Yet legends were made and Karla was one of them. Even his age was a mystery. Most likely Karla was not his real name. Decades of his life were not accounted for, and probably never would be, since the people he worked with had a way of dying off or keeping their mouths shut.

"There's a story that his father was in the Okhrana and later reappeared in the Cheka. I don't think it's true but it may be. There's another that he worked as a kitchen boy on an armoured train against Japanese Occupation troops in the East. He is said to have learnt his tradecraft from Berg—to have been his ewe lamb, in fact—which is a bit like being taught music by . . . oh, name a great composer. So far as I am concerned, his career began in Spain in 1936, because that at least is documented. He posed as a White Russian journalist in the Franco cause and recruited a stable of German agents. It was a most intricate operation, and for a young man remarkable. He popped up next in the Soviet counter-offensive against Smolensk in the autumn of 1941 as an intelligence officer under Konev. He had the job of running networks of partisans behind the German lines. Along the way he discovered that his radio operator had been turned round and was transmitting radio messages to the enemy. He turned him back and from then on played a radio game which had them going in all directions."

That was another part of the legend, said Smiley: at Yelnya, thanks to Karla, the Germans shelled their own forward line.

"And between these two sightings," he continued, "in 1936 and 1941, Karla visited Britain; we think he was here six months. But even today we don't know—that's to say, *I* don't know— under what name or cover. Which isn't to say Gerald doesn't. But Gerald isn't likely to tell us, at least not on purpose."

Smiley had never talked to Guillam this way. He was not given to confidences or long lectures; Guillam knew him as a shy man, for all his vanities, and one who expected very little of communication.

"In '48-odd, having served his country loyally, Karla did a spell in prison and later in Siberia. There was nothing personal about it. He simply happened to be in one of those sections of Red army intelligence which, in some purge or other, ceased to exist."

And certainly, Smiley went on, after his post-Stalin reinstatement, he went to America; because when the Indian authorities in the summer of '55 arrested him in Delhi on vague immigration charges, he had just flown in from California. Circus gossip later linked him with the big treason scandals in Britain and the States.

Smiley knew better: "Karla was in disgrace again. Moscow was out for his blood, and we thought we might persuade him to defect. That was why I flew to Delhi. To have a chat with him."

There was a pause while the weary boy slouched over and enquired whether everything was to their satisfaction. Smiley, with great solicitude, assured him that it was.

"The story of my meeting with Karla," he resumed, "belonged very much to the mood of the period. In the mid-fifties, Moscow Centre was in pieces on the floor. Senior officers were being shot or purged wholesale and its lower ranks were seized with a collective paranoia. As a first result, there was a crop of defections among Centre officers stationed overseas. All over the place—Singapore, Nairobi, Stockholm, Canberra, Washington, I don't know where—we got this same steady trickle from the residencies: not just the big fish, but the legmen, drivers, cypher clerks, typists. Somehow we had to respond—I don't think it's ever realised how much the industry stimulates its own inflation—and in no time I became a kind of commercial traveller, flying off one day to a capital city, the next to a dingy border outpost—once even to a ship at sea—to sign up defecting Russians. To seed, to stream, to fix the terms, to attend to debriefing and eventual disposal."

Guillam was watching him all the while, but even in that cruel neon glow Smiley's expression revealed nothing but a slightly anxious concentration.

"We evolved, you might say, three kinds of contract for those whose stories held together. If the client's access wasn't interesting, we might trade him to another country and forget him. Buy him for stock, as you would say, much as the scalp-hunters do today. Or we might play him back into Russia—that's assuming his defection had not already been noticed there. Or, if he was lucky, we took him; cleaned him of whatever he knew and resettled him in the West. London decided, usually. Not me. But remember this. At that time Karla—or Gerstmann, as he called himself—was just another client. I've told his story back to front; I didn't want to be coy with you, but you have to bear in mind now, through anything that happened between us—or didn't happen, which is more to the point—that all I or anyone in the Circus knew when I flew to Delhi was that a man calling himself Gerstmann had been setting up a radio link between Rudnev, head of illegal networks at Moscow Centre, and a Centre-run apparatus in California that was lying fallow for want of a means of communication. That's all. Gerstmann had smuggled a transmitter across the Canadian border and lain up for three weeks in San Francisco breaking in the new operator. That was the assumption, and there was a batch of test transmissions to back it up."

For these test transmissions between Moscow and California, Smiley explained, a book code was used: "Then, one day, Moscow signalled a straight order—"

"Still on the book code?"

"Precisely. That is the point. Owing to a temporary inattention on the part of Rudnev's cryptographers, we were ahead of the game. The wranglers broke the code and that's how we got our information. Gerstmann was to leave San Francisco at once and head for Delhi for a rendezvous with the Tass correspondent, a talent-spotter who had stumbled on a hot Chinese lead and needed immediate direction. Why they dragged him all the way from San Francisco to Delhi, why it had to be Karla and no one else—well, that's a story for another day. The only material point is that when Gerstmann kept the rendezvous in Delhi, the Tass man handed him an aeroplane ticket and told him to go straight home to Moscow. No questions. The order came from Rudnev personally. It was signed with Rudnev's workname and it was brusque even by Russian standards."

Whereupon the Tass man fled, leaving Gerstmann standing on the pavement with a lot of questions and twenty-eight hours until take-off.

"He hadn't been standing there long when the Indian authorities arrested him at our request and carted him off to Delhi jail. As far as I remember, we had promised the Indians a piece of the product. I *think* that was the deal," he remarked and, like someone suddenly shocked by the faultiness of his own memory, fell silent and looked distractedly down the steamy room. "Or perhaps we said they could have him when we'd done with him. Dear, oh dear."

"It doesn't really matter," Guillam said.

"For once in Karla's life, as I say, the Circus was ahead of him," Smiley resumed, having taken a sip of wine and made a face. "He couldn't know it but the San Francisco network which he had just serviced had been rolled up hide and hair the day he left for Delhi. As soon as Control had the story from the wranglers, he traded it to the Americans on the understanding that they missed Gerstmann but hit the rest of the Rudnev network in California. Gerstmann flew on to Delhi unaware, and he was still unaware when I arrived at Delhi jail to sell him a piece of insurance, as Control called it. His choice was very simple. There could not be the slightest doubt, on present form, that Gerstmann's head was on the block in Moscow, where to save his own neck Rudnev was busy denouncing him for blowing the San Francisco network. The affair had made a great splash in the States, and Moscow was very angry at the publicity. I had with me the American press photographs of the arrest, even of the radio set Karla had imported and the signal plans he had cached before he left. You know how prickly we all become when things get into the papers."

Guillam did; and with a jolt remembered the Testify file, which he had left with Mendel earlier that evening.

"To sum it up, Karla was the proverbial cold-war orphan. He had left home to do a job abroad. The job had blown up in his face, but he couldn't go back: home was more hostile than abroad. We had no powers of permanent arrest, so it was up to Karla to ask us for protection. I don't think I had ever come across a clearer case for defection. I had only to convince him of the arrest of the San Francisco network—wave the press photographs and cuttings from my briefcase at him—talk to him a little about the unfriendly conspiracies of Brother Rudnev in Moscow, and cable the somewhat overworked inquisitors in Sarratt, and with any luck I'd make London by the weekend. I rather think I had tickets for Sadler's Wells. It was Ann's great year for ballet."

Yes, Guillam had heard about that, too: a twenty-year-old Welsh Apollo, the season's wonder boy. They had been burning up London for months.

The heat in the jail was appalling, Smiley continued. The cell had an iron table at the centre and iron cattle rings let into the wall. "They brought him manacled, which seemed silly because he was so slight. I asked them to free his hands and when they did, he put them on the table in front of him and watched the blood come back. It must have been painful but he didn't comment on it. He'd been there a week and he was wearing a calico tunic. Red. I forget what red meant. Some piece of prison ethic." Taking a sip of wine, he again pulled a face, then slowly corrected the gesture as the memories once more bore in upon him.

"Well, at first sight, he made little impression on me. I would have been hard put to it to recognise in the little fellow before me the master of cunning we have heard about in Irina's diary, poor woman. I suppose it's also true that my nerve-ends had been a good deal blunted by so many similar encounters in the last few months, by travel, and well by—well, by things at home."

In all the time Guillam had known him, it was the nearest Smiley had ever come to acknowledging Ann's infidelities.

"For some reason, it hurt an awful lot." His eyes were still open but his gaze had fixed upon an inner world. The skin of his brow and cheeks was drawn smooth as if by the exertion of his memory; but nothing could conceal from Guillam the loneliness evoked by this one admission. "I have a theory which I suspect is rather immoral," Smiley went on, more lightly. "Each of us has only a quantum of compassion. That if we lavish our concern on every stray cat, we never get to the centre of things. What do you think of it?"

"What did Karla look like?" Guillam asked, treating the question as rhetorical.

"Avuncular. Modest, and avuncular. He would have looked very well as a priest: the shabby, gnomic variety one sees in

small Italian towns. Little wiry chap, with silvery hair and
bright brown eyes and plenty of wrinkles. Or a schoolmaster,
he could have been a schoolmaster: tough—whatever that
means—and sagacious within the limits of his experience; but
the small canvas, all the same. He made no other initial impression, except that his gaze was straight and it fixed on me from
early in our talk. If you can call it a talk, seeing that he never
uttered a word. Not one, the whole time we were together; not
a syllable. Also it was stinking hot and I was travelled to death."

Out of a sense of manners rather than appetite, Smiley set
to work on his food, eating several mouthfuls joylessly before
resuming his narrative. "There," he muttered, "that shouldn't
offend the cook. The truth is, I was slightly predisposed
against Mr. Gerstmann. We all have our prejudices and radio
men are mine. They're a thoroughly tiresome lot, in my experience, bad fieldmen and overstrung, and disgracefully unreliable when it comes down to doing the job. Gerstmann, it
seemed to me, was just another of the clan. Perhaps I'm looking for excuses for going to work on him with less"—he
hesitated—"less care, less caution, than in retrospect would
seem appropriate." He grew suddenly stronger. "Though I'm
not at all sure I need make any excuses," he said.

Here Guillam sensed a wave of unusual anger, imparted by
a ghostly smile that crossed Smiley's pale lips. "To hell with
it," Smiley muttered.

Guillam waited, mystified.

"I also remember thinking that prison seemed to have
taken him over very fast in seven days. He had that white dust
in the skin and he wasn't sweating. I was, profusely. I trotted
out my piece, as I had a dozen times that year already, except
that there was obviously no question of his being played back
into Russia as our agent. 'You have the alternative. It's no one
else's business but your own. Come to the West and we can
give you, within reason, a decent life. After questioning, at
which you are expected to cooperate, we can help you to a new

start, a new name, seclusion, a certain amount of money. On the other hand, you can go home and I suppose they'll shoot you or send you to a camp. Last month they sent Bykov, Shur, and Muranov. Now why don't you tell me your real name?' Something like that. Then I sat back and wiped away the sweat and waited for him to say, 'Yes, thank you.' He did nothing. He didn't speak. He simply sat there stiff and tiny under the big fan that didn't work, looking at me with his brown, rather jolly eyes. Hands out in front of him. They were very calloused. I remember thinking I must ask him where he had been doing so much manual labour. He held them—like this—resting on the table, palms upward and fingers a little bent, as if he were still manacled."

The boy, thinking that by this gesture Smiley was indicating some want, came lumbering over, and Smiley again assured him that all was doubly well, and the wine in particular was exquisite—he really wondered where they had it from; till the boy left grinning with secret amusement and flapped his cloth at an adjoining table.

"It was then, I think, that an extraordinary feeling of unease began to creep over me. The heat was really getting to me. The stench was terrible and I remember listening to the *pat-pat* of my own sweat falling onto the iron table. It wasn't just his silence; his physical stillness began to get under my skin. Oh, I had known defectors who took time to speak. It can be a great wrench for somebody trained to secrecy even towards his closest friends suddenly to open his mouth and spill secrets to his enemies. It also crossed my mind that the prison authorities might have thought it a courtesy to soften him up before they brought him to me. They assured me they hadn't, but of course one can never tell. So at first, I put his silence down to shock. But this stillness—this intense, watchful stillness—was a different matter. Specially when everything inside me was so much in motion: Ann, my own heartbeats, the effects of heat and travel . . ."

"I can understand," said Guillam quietly.

"Can you? Sitting is an eloquent business; any actor will tell you that. We sit according to our natures. We sprawl and straddle, we rest like boxers between rounds, we fidget, perch, cross and uncross our legs, lose patience, lose endurance. Gerstmann did none of those things. His posture was finite and irreducible, his little jagged body was like a promontory of rock; he could have sat that way all day, without stirring a muscle. Whereas I—" Breaking out in an awkward, embarrassed laugh, Smiley tasted the wine again, but it was no better than before. "Whereas I longed to have something before me— papers, a book, a report. I think I am a restless person, fussy, variable. I thought so then, anyway. I felt I lacked philosophic repose. Lacked philosophy, if you like. My work had been oppressing me much more than I realised; till now. But in that foul cell I really felt aggrieved. I felt that the entire responsibility for fighting the cold war had landed on my shoulders. Which was tripe, of course; I was just exhausted and a little bit ill." He drank again.

"I tell you," he insisted, once more quite angry with himself. "No one has any business to apologise for what I did."

"What did you do?" Guillam asked, with a laugh.

"So anyway there came this gap," Smiley resumed, disregarding the question. "Hardly of Gerstmann's making, since he was all gap; so of mine, then. I had said my piece; I had flourished the photographs, which he ignored—I may say, he appeared quite ready to take my word for it that the San Francisco network was blown. I restated this part, that part, talked a few variations, and finally I dried up. Or, rather, sat there sweating like a pig. Well, any fool knows that if ever that happens, you get up and walk out. 'Take it or leave it,' you say. 'See you in the morning'; anything. 'Go away and think for an hour.'

"As it was, the next thing I knew, I was talking about Ann." He left no time for Guillam's muffled exclamation. "Oh, not about *my* Ann, not in as many words. About *his* Ann. I assumed he had one. I had asked myself—lazily, no doubt—what would a man think of in such a situation, what would I? And my mind came up with a subjective answer: his woman. Is it called 'projection' or 'substitution'? I detest those terms but I'm sure one of them applies. I exchanged my predicament for his, that is the point, and as I now realise I began to conduct an interrogation with myself—he didn't speak, can you imagine? There were certain externals, it is true, to which I pinned the approach. He *looked* connubial; he *looked* like half a union; he *looked* too complete to be alone in all his life. Then there was his passport, describing Gerstmann as married; and it is a habit in all of us to make our cover stories, our assumed personae, at least parallel with the reality." He lapsed again into a moment of reflection. "I often thought that. I even put it to Control: we should take the opposition's cover stories more seriously, I said. The more identities a man has, the more they express the person they conceal. The fifty-year-old who knocks five years off his age. The married man who calls himself a bachelor; the fatherless man who gives himself two children . . . Or the interrogator who projects himself into the life of a man who does not speak. Few men can resist expressing their appetites when they are making a fantasy about themselves."

He was lost again, and Guillam waited patiently for him to come back. For while Smiley might have fixed his concentration upon Karla, Guillam had fixed his on Smiley; and just then would have gone anywhere with him, turned any corner, in order to remain beside him and hear the story out.

"I also knew from the American observation reports that Gerstmann was a chain-smoker: Camels. I sent out for several packs of them—'packs' is the American word?—and I remember feeling very strange as I handed money to a guard. I had the impression, you see, that Gerstmann saw something symbolic in the transaction of money between myself and the

Indian. I wore a money belt in those days. I had to grope and peel off a note from a bundle. Gerstmann's gaze made me feel like a fifth-rate imperialist oppressor." He smiled. "And that I assuredly am *not*. Bill, if you like. Percy. But not I." He called to the boy, in order to send him away: "May we have some water, please? A jug and two glasses? Thank you." Again he picked up the story: "So I asked him about Mrs. Gerstmann. I asked him: where was she? It was a question I would dearly have wished answered about Ann. No reply but the eyes unwavering. To either side of him, the two guards, and their eyes seemed so light by comparison. She must make a new life, I said; there was no other way. Had he no friend he could count on to look after her? Perhaps we could find methods of getting in touch with her secretly? I put it to him that his going back to Moscow would do nothing for her at all. I was listening to myself, I ran on, I couldn't stop. Perhaps I didn't want to. I was really thinking of leaving Ann, you see; I thought the time had come. To go back would be a quixotic act, I told him, of no material value to his wife or anyone—quite the reverse. She would be ostracised; at best, she would be allowed to see him briefly before he was shot. On the other hand, if he threw in his lot with us, we might be able to trade her; we had a lot of stock in those days, remember, and some of it was going back to Russia as barter; though why in God's name we should have used it up for that purpose is beyond me. Surely, I said, she would prefer to know him safe and well in the West, with a fair chance that she herself would join him, than shot or starving to death in Siberia? I really harped upon her: his expression encouraged me. I could have sworn I was getting through to him, that I had found the chink in his armour; when of course all I was doing—all I was doing was showing him the chink in mine. And when I mentioned Siberia, I touched something. I could feel it, like a lump in my own throat; I could feel in Gerstmann a shiver of revulsion. Well, naturally I did," Smiley commented sourly; "since it was only recently that he had been made an inmate. Finally, back came the guard with the cigarettes, armfuls of them, and dumped them with a clatter on the iron table. I counted the change, tipped him, and in doing so again caught the expression in Gerstmann's eyes; I fancied I read amusement there, but really I was no longer in a state to tell. I noticed that the boy refused my tip; I suppose he disliked the English. I tore open a packet and offered Gerstmann a cigarette. 'Come,' I said, 'you're a chain-smoker, everyone knows that. And this is your favourite brand.' My voice sounded strained and silly, and there was nothing I could do about it. Gerstmann stood up and politely indicated to the warders that he would like to return to his cell."

Taking his time, Smiley pushed aside his half-eaten food, over which white flakes of fat had formed like seasonable frost.

"As he left the cell, he changed his mind and helped himself to a packet of cigarettes and the lighter from the table—my lighter, a gift from Ann. 'To George from Ann with all my love.' I would never have dreamed of letting him take it in the ordinary way; but this was not the ordinary way. Indeed I thought it thoroughly appropriate that he should take her lighter; I thought it—Lord help me—expressive of the bond between us. He dropped the lighter and the cigarettes into the pouch of his red tunic, then put out his hand for handcuffs. I said, 'Light one now, if you want.' I told the guards, 'Let him light a cigarette, please.' But he didn't make a movement. 'The intention is to put you on tomorrow's plane to Moscow unless we come to terms,' I added. He might not have heard me. I watched the guards lead him out, then returned to my hotel; someone drove me—to this day I couldn't tell you who. I no longer knew what I felt. I was more confused and more ill than I would admit, even to myself. I ate a poor dinner, drank too much, and ran a soaring temperature. I lay on my bed sweating, dreaming about Gerstmann. I wanted him terribly to stay. Lightheaded as I was, I had really set myself to keep him, to remake his life—if possible to set him up again with his wife in idyllic circumstances. To make him free; to get him out of the war for good. I wanted him desperately not to go back." He glanced up with an expression of self-irony. "What I am saying, Peter, is it was Smiley, not Gerstmann, who was stepping out of the conflict that night."

"You were ill," Guillam insisted.

"Let us say tired. Ill or tired; all night, between aspirin and quinine and treacly visions of the Gerstmann marriage resurrected, I had a recurring image. It was of Gerstmann, poised on the sill, staring down into the street with those fixed brown eyes, and myself talking to him, on and on, 'Stay, don't jump, stay.' Not realising, of course, that I was dreaming of my own insecurity, not his. In the early morning a doctor gave me injections to bring down the fever. I should have dropped the case, cabled for a replacement. I should have waited before going to the prison, but I had nothing but Gerstmann in mind; I needed to hear his decision. By eight o'clock I was already having myself escorted to the accommodation cells. He was sitting stiff as a ramrod on a trestle bench; for the first time, I guessed the soldier in him, and I knew that, like me, he hadn't slept all night. He hadn't shaved and there was a silver down on his jaw which gave him an old man's face. On other benches Indians were sleeping, and with his red tunic and this silvery colouring he looked very white among them. He was holding Ann's lighter in his hands; the packet of cigarettes lay beside him on the bench, untouched. I concluded that he had been using the night, and the forsworn cigarettes, to decide whether he could face prison and interrogation, and death. One look at his expression told me that he had decided he could. I didn't beseech him," Smiley said, going straight on. "He would never have been swayed by histrionics. His plane left in the mid-morning; I still had two hours. I am the worst advocate in the world, but in those two hours I tried to summon all the reasons I knew for his not flying to Moscow. I believed, you see, that I had seen something in his face that was superior to mere dogma, not realising that it was my own reflection. I had convinced myself that Gerstmann ultimately was accessible to ordinary human arguments coming from a man of his own age and profession and—well, durability. I didn't promise him wealth and women and Cadillacs and cheap butter; I accepted that he had no use for those things. I had the wit by then, at least, to steer clear of the topic of his wife. I didn't make speeches to him about freedom—whatever that means—or the essential goodwill of the West; besides, they were not favourable days for selling that story, and I was in no clear ideological state myself. I took the line of kinship. 'Look,' I said, 'we're getting to be old men, and we've spent our lives looking for the weaknesses in one another's systems. I can see through Eastern values just as you can see through our Western ones. Both of us, I am sure, have experienced *ad nauseam* the technical satisfactions of this wretched war. But now your own side is going to shoot you. Don't you think it's time to recognise that there is as little worth on your side as there is on mine? Look,' I said, 'in our trade we have only negative vision. In that sense, neither of us has anywhere to go. Both of us when we were young subscribed to *great* visions—' Again I felt an impulse in him— Siberia—I had touched a nerve. 'But not any more. Surely?' I urged him just to answer me this: did it not occur to him that he and I by different routes might well have reached the same conclusions about life? Even if my conclusions were what he would call unliberated, surely our workings were identical? Did he not believe, for example, that the political generality was meaningless? That only the particular in life had value for him now? That in the hands of politicians grand designs achieve nothing but new forms of the old misery? And that therefore his life, the saving of it from yet another meaningless firing squad, was more important—morally, ethically more important—than the sense of duty, or obligation, or commitment, or whatever it was that kept him on this present path of self-destruction? Did it not occur to him to question—after all the travels of his life—to question the integrity of a system that proposed cold-bloodedly to shoot him down for misdemeanours he had never committed? I begged him—yes, I did beseech him, I'm afraid; we were on the way to the airport and he still had not addressed a word to me—I begged him to consider whether he really believed; whether faith in the system he had served was honestly possible to him at this moment."

For a while now, Smiley sat silent.

"I had thrown psychology to the winds, such as I possess; tradecraft, too. You can imagine what Control said. My story amused him, all the same; he loved to hear of people's weakness. Mine especially, for some reason." He had resumed his factual manner. "So there we are. When the plane arrived, I climbed aboard with him and flew part of the distance: in those days it wasn't all jet. He was slipping away from me and I couldn't do anything to stop him. I'd given up talking but I was there if he wanted to change his mind. He didn't. He would rather die than give me what I wanted; he would rather die than disown the political system to which he was committed. The last I saw of him, so far as I know, was his expressionless face framed in the cabin window of the aeroplane, watching me walk down the gangway. A couple of very Russian-looking thugs had joined us and were sitting in the seats behind him, and there was really no point in my staying. I flew home, and Control said: 'Well, I hope to God they do shoot him,' and restored me with a cup of tea. That filthy China stuff he drinks, lemon jasmine or whatever; he sends out for it to that grocer's round the corner. I mean he used to. Then he sent me on three months' leave without the option. I like you to have doubts,' he said. 'It tells me where you stand. But don't make a cult of them or you'll be a bore.' It was a warning. I heeded it. And he told me to stop thinking about the Americans so much; he assured me that he barely gave them a thought."

Guillam gazed at him, waiting for the resolution. "But what do *you* make of it?" he demanded, in a tone that suggested he had been cheated of the end. "Did Karla ever really think of staying?"

"I'm sure it never crossed his mind," said Smiley with disgust. "I behaved like a soft fool. The very archetype of a flabby Western liberal. But I would rather be my kind of fool than his, for all that. I am sure," he repeated vigorously, "that neither my arguments nor his own predicament at Moscow Centre would ultimately have swayed him in the least. I expect he spent the night working out how he would outgun Rudnev when he got home. Rudnev was shot a month later, incidentally. Karla got Rudnev's job and set to work reactivating his old agents. Among them Gerald, no doubt. It's odd to reflect that all the time he was looking at me, he could have been thinking of Gerald. I expect they've had a good laugh about it since."

The episode had one other result, said Smiley. Since his San Francisco experience, Karla had never once touched illegal radio. He cut it right out of his handwriting. "Embassy links are a different matter. But in the field his agents aren't allowed to go near it. And he still has Ann's cigarette lighter."

"Yours," Guillam corrected him.

"Yes. Yes, mine. Of course. Tell me," he continued, as the waiter took away his money, "was Tarr referring to anyone in particular when he made that unpleasant reference to Ann?"

"I'm afraid he was. Yes."

"The rumour is as precise as that?" Smiley enquired. "And it goes that far down the line? Even to Tarr?"

"Yes."

"And what does it say, precisely?"

"That Bill Haydon was Ann Smiley's lover," said Guillam, feeling that coldness coming over him which was his protection when he broke bad news such as: you're blown; you're sacked; you're dying.

"Ah. I see. Yes. Thank you."

There was a very awkward silence.

"And was there—is there a Mrs. Gerstmann?" Guillam asked.

"Karla once made a marriage with a girl in Leningrad, a student. She killed herself when he was sent to Siberia."

"So Karla is fireproof," Guillam asked finally. "He can't be bought and he can't be beaten?"

They returned to the car.

"I must say that was rather expensive for what we had," Smiley confessed. "Do you think the waiter robbed me?"

But Guillam was not disposed to chat about the cost of bad meals in England. Driving again, the day once more became a nightmare to him, a milling confusion of half-perceived dangers, and suspicions.

"So who's Source Merlin?" he demanded. "Where could Alleline have had that information from, if not from the Russians themselves?"

"Oh, he had it from the Russians all right."

"But for God's sake, if the Russians sent Tarr—"

"They didn't. Nor did Tarr use the British passports, did he? The Russians got it wrong. What Alleline had was the proof that Tarr had fooled them. That is the vital message we have learned from that whole storm in a teacup."

"So what the hell did Percy mean about 'muddying pools'? He must have been talking about Irina, for heaven's sake."

"And Gerald," Smiley agreed.

Again they drove in silence, and the gap between them seemed suddenly unbridgeable.

"Look, I'm not quite there myself, Peter," Smiley said quietly. "But nearly I am. Karla's pulled the Circus inside out; that much I understand, so do you. But there's a last clever knot, and I can't undo it. Though I mean to. And if you want a sermon, Karla is not fireproof, because he's a fanatic. And one day, if I have anything to do with it, that lack of moderation will be his downfall."

It was raining as they reached Stratford tube station; a bunch of pedestrians was huddled under the canopy.

"Peter, I want you to take it easy from now on."

"Three months without the option?"

"Rest on your oars a bit."

Closing the passenger door after him, Guillam had a sudden urge to wish Smiley good night or even good luck, so he leaned across the seat and lowered the window and drew in his breath to call. But Smiley was gone. He had never known anyone who could disappear so quickly in a crowd.

Through the remainder of that same night, the light in the dormer window of Mr. Barraclough's attic room at the Islay Hotel burned uninterrupted. Unchanged, unshaven, George Smiley remained bowed at the Major's card table, reading, comparing, annotating, cross-referring—all with an intensity that, had he been his own observer, would surely have recalled for him the last days of Control on the fifth floor at Cambridge Circus. Shaking the pieces, he consulted Guillam's leave rosters and sick-lists going back over the last year, and set these beside the overt travel pattern of Cultural Attaché Aleksey Aleksandrovich Polyakov, his trips to Moscow, his trips out of London, as reported to the Foreign Office by Special Branch and the immigration authorities. He compared these again with the dates when Merlin apparently supplied his information and, without quite knowing why he was doing it, broke down the Witchcraft reports into those which were demonstrably topical at the time they were received and those which could have been banked a month, two months before, either by Merlin or his controllers, in order to bridge empty periods: such as think pieces, character studies of prominent members of the administration, and scraps of Kremlin tittle-tattle which could have been picked up any time and saved for a rainless day. Having listed the topical reports, he set down their dates in a single column and threw out the rest. At this point, his mood could be best compared with that of a scientist who senses by instinct that he is on the brink of a discovery and is awaiting any minute the logical connection. Later, in conversation with Mendel, he called it "shoving everything into a test-tube and seeing if it exploded." What fascinated him most, he said, was the very point that Guillam had made regarding Alleline's grim warnings about muddied pools: he was looking, in other terms, for the "last clever knot" that Karla had tied in order to explain away the precise suspicions to which Irina's diary had given shape.

He came up with some curious preliminary findings. First, that on the nine occasions when Merlin had produced a topical report, either Polyakov had been in London or Toby Esterhase had taken a quick trip abroad. Second, that over the crucial period following Tarr's adventure in Hong Kong this year, Polyakov was in Moscow for urgent cultural consultations; and that soon afterwards Merlin came through with some of his most spectacular and topical material on the "ideological penetration" of the United States, including an appreciation of Centre's coverage of the major American intelligence targets.

Backtracking again, he established that the converse was also true: that the reports he had discarded on the grounds that they had no close attachment to recent events were those which most generally went into distribution while Polyakov was in Moscow or on leave.

And then he had it.

No explosive revelation, no flash of light, no cry of "Eureka," phone calls to Guillam, Lacon, "Smiley is a world champion." Merely that here before him, in the records he had examined and the notes he had compiled, was the corroboration of a theory which Smiley and Guillam and Ricki Tarr had that day from their separate points of view seen demonstrated: that between the mole Gerald and the Source Merlin there was an interplay which could no longer be denied; that Merlin's proverbial versatility allowed him to function as Karla's instrument as well as Alleline's. Or should he rather say, Smiley reflected—tossing a towel over his shoulder and hopping blithely into the corridor for a celebratory bath—as Karla's agent? And that at the heart of this plot lay a device so simple that it left him genuinely elated by its symmetry. It had even a physical presence: here in London, a house, paid for by the Treasury, all sixty thousand pounds of it; and often coveted, no doubt, by the many luckless tax-payers who daily passed it by, confident they could never afford it and not knowing that they had already paid for it.

It was with a lighter heart than he had known for many months that he took up the stolen file on Operation Testify.

24

To her credit, Matron had been worried about Roach all week, ever since she had spotted him alone in the washroom, ten minutes after the rest of his dormitory had gone down to breakfast, still in his pyjama trousers, hunched over a basin while he doggedly scrubbed his teeth. When she questioned him, he avoided her eye. "It's that wretched father of his," she told Thursgood. "He's getting him down again." And by the Friday: "You *must* write to the mother and tell her he's having a spell."

But not even Matron, for all her motherly perception, would have hit on plain terror as the diagnosis.

Whatever could he do—he, a child? That was his guilt. That was the threat that led directly back to the misfortune of his parents. That was the predicament that threw upon his hunched shoulders the responsibility night and day for preserving the world's peace. Roach, the watcher—"best watcher in the whole damn unit," to use Jim Prideaux's treasured words—had finally watched too well. He would have sacrificed everything he possessed—his money, his leather photograph case of his parents, whatever gave him value in the world—if it would buy him release from the knowledge that had consumed him since Sunday evening.

He had put out signals. On Sunday night, an hour after lights out, he had gone noisily to the lavatory, probed his throat, gagged, and finally vomited. But the dormitory monitor, who was supposed to wake and raise the alarm—"Matron, Roach's been sick"—slept stubbornly through the whole charade. Roach clambered miserably back to bed. From the call-box outside the staffroom next afternoon, he had dialled the menu for the day and whispered strangely into the mouthpiece, hoping to be overheard by a master and taken for mad. No one paid him any attention. He had tried mixing up reality with dreams, in the hope that the event would be converted into something he had imagined; but each morning as he passed the Dip he saw again Jim's crooked figure stooping over the spade in the moonlight; he saw the black shadow of his face under the brim of his old hat, and heard the grunt of effort as he dug.

Roach should never have been there. That also was his guilt: that the knowledge was acquired by sin. After a cello lesson on the far side of the village, he had returned to school with deliberate slowness in order to be too late for evensong, and Mrs. Thursgood's disapproving eye. The whole school was worshipping, all but himself and Jim: he heard them sing the *Te Deum* as he passed the church, taking the long route so that he could skirt the Dip, where Jim's light was glowing. Standing in his usual place, Roach watched Jim's shadow move slowly across the curtained window. He's turning in early, he decided with approval as the light suddenly went out; for Jim had recently been too absent for his taste, driving off in the Alvis after rugger and not returning till Roach was asleep. Then the trailer door opened and closed, and Jim was standing at the vegetable patch with a spade in his hand and Roach in great perplexity was wondering what on earth he should be wanting to dig for in the dark. Vegetables for his supper? For a moment Jim stood very still, listening to the *Te Deum;* then glared slowly round and straight at Roach, though he was out of sight against the blackness of the hummocks. Roach even thought of calling to him, but felt too sinful on account of missing chapel.

Finally Jim began measuring. That, at least, was how it seemed to Roach. Instead of digging, he had knelt at one corner of the patch and laid the spade on the earth, as if aligning it with something that was out of sight to Roach: for instance, the church spire. This done, Jim strode quickly to where the blade lay, marked the spot with a thud of his heel, took up the spade, and dug fast—Roach counted twelve times—then stood back, taking stock again. From the church, silence; then prayers. Quickly stooping, Jim drew a package from the ground, which he at once smothered in the folds of his duffel coat. Seconds later, and much faster than seemed possible, the trailer door slammed, the light went on again, and in the boldest moment of his life Bill Roach tiptoed down the Dip to within three feet of the poorly curtained window, using the slope to give himself the height he needed to look in.

Jim stood at the table. On the bunk behind him lay a heap of exercise books, a vodka bottle, and an empty glass. He must have dumped them there to make space. He had a penknife ready but he wasn't using it. Jim would never have cut string if he could avoid it. The package was a foot long and made of yellowy stuff like a tobacco pouch. Pulling it open, he drew out what seemed to be a monkey wrench wrapped in sacking. But who would bury a monkey wrench, even for the best car England ever made? The screws or bolts were in a separate yellow envelope; he spilled them on to the table and examined each in turn. Not screws: pen-tops. Not pen-tops, either; but they had sunk out of sight.

And not a monkey wrench, not a spanner—nothing, but absolutely nothing, for the car.

Roach had blundered wildly to the brow. He was running between the hummocks, making for the drive, but running slower than he had ever run before; running through sand and deep water and dragging grass, gulping the night air, sobbing it out again, running lopsidedly like Jim, pushing now with this leg, now with the other, flailing with his head for extra speed. He had no thought for where he was heading. All his awareness was behind him, fixed on the black revolver and the bands of chamois leather; on the pen-tops that turned to bullets as Jim threaded them methodically into the chamber, his lined face tipped towards the lamplight, pale and slightly squinting in the dazzle.

25

"I won't be quoted, George," the Minister warned, in his lounging drawl. "No minutes, no pack-drill. I got voters to deal with. You don't. Nor does Oliver Lacon, do you, Oliver?"

He had also, thought Smiley, the American violence with auxiliary verbs. "Yes, I'm sorry about that," he said.

"You'd be sorrier still if you had my constituency," the Minister retorted.

Predictably, the mere question of where they should meet had sparked a silly quarrel. Smiley had pointed out to Lacon that it would be unwise to meet at his room in Whitehall, since it was under constant attack by Circus personnel, whether janitors delivering dispatch boxes or Percy Alleline dropping in to discuss Ireland. Whereas the Minister declined both the Islay Hotel and Bywater Street, on the arbitrary grounds that they were insecure. He had recently appeared on television and was proud of being recognised. After several more calls back and forth, they settled for Mendel's semi-detached Tudor residence in Mitcham, where the Minister and his shiny car stuck out like a sore thumb. There they now sat, Lacon, Smiley, and the Minister, in the trim front room with net curtains and fresh salmon sandwiches, while their host stood upstairs watching the approaches. In the lane, children tried to make the chauffeur tell them whom he worked for.

Behind the Minister's head ran a row of books on bees. They were Mendel's passion, Smiley remembered: he used the word "exotic" for bees that did not come from Surrey. The Minister was a young man still, with a dark jowl that looked as though it had been knocked off-true in some unseemly fracas. His head was bald on top, which gave him an unwarranted air of maturity, and a terrible Eton drawl. "All right, so what are the decisions?" He also had the bully's art of dialogue.

"Well first, I suppose, you should damp down whatever recent negotiations you've been having with the Americans. I was thinking of the untitled secret annexe which you keep in your safe," said Smiley, "the one that discusses the further exploitation of Witchcraft material."

"Never heard of it," said the Minister.

"I quite understand the incentives, of course; it's always tempting to get one's hands on the cream of that enormous American service, and I can see the argument for trading them Witchcraft in return."

"So what are the arguments *against?*" the Minister enquired as if he were talking to his stockbroker.

"If the mole Gerald exists," Smiley began. Of all her cousins, Ann had once said proudly, only Miles Sercombe was without a single redeeming feature. For the first time, Smiley really believed she was right. He felt not only idiotic but incoherent. "If the mole exists, which I assume is common ground among us . . ." He waited, but no one said it wasn't. "If the mole exists," he repeated, "it's not only the Circus that will double its profits by the American deal. Moscow Centre will, too, because they'll get from the mole whatever you buy from the Americans."

In a gesture of frustration, the Minister slapped his hand on Mendel's table, leaving a moist imprint on the polish.

"God damn it, I do *not* understand," he declared. "That Witchcraft stuff is bloody marvellous! A month ago it was buying us the moon. Now we're disappearing up our orifices and saying the Russians are cooking it for us. What the hell's happening?"

"Well, I don't think that's quite as illogical as it sounds, as a matter of fact. After all, we've run the odd Russian network from time to time, and though I say it myself we ran them rather well. We gave them the best material we could afford. Rocketry, war planning. You were in on that yourself"—this to Lacon, who threw a jerky nod of agreement. "We tossed them agents we could do without; we gave them good communications, safed their courier links, cleared the air for their signals so that we could listen to them. That was the price we paid for running the opposition—what was your expression?—'for knowing how they briefed their commissars.' I'm sure Karla would do as much for us if he was running our networks. He'd do more, wouldn't he, if he had his eye on the American market, too?" He broke off and glanced at Lacon. "Much, much more. An American connection—a big American dividend, I mean—would put the mole Gerald *right* at the top table. The Circus, too, by proxy of course. As a Russian, one would give almost anything to the English if . . . well, if one could buy the Americans in return."

"Thank you," said Lacon quickly.

The Minister left, taking a couple of sandwiches with him to eat in the car and failing to say goodbye to Mendel, presumably because he was not a constituent.

Lacon stayed behind.

"You asked me to look out for anything on Prideaux," he announced at last. "Well, I find that we do have a few papers on him, after all."

He had happened to be going through some files on the internal security of the Circus, he explained, "Simply to clear my decks." Doing so, he had stumbled on some old positive vetting reports. One of them related to Prideaux.

"He was cleared absolutely, you understand. Not a shadow. However"—an odd inflexion of his voice caused Smiley to glance at him—"I think it might interest you, all the same. Some tiny murmur about his time at Oxford. We're all entitled to be a bit pink at that age."

"Indeed, yes."

The silence returned, broken only by the soft tread of Mendel upstairs.

"Prideaux and Haydon were really very close indeed, you know," Lacon confessed. "I hadn't realised."

He was suddenly in a great hurry to leave. Delving in his briefcase, he hauled out a large plain envelope, thrust it into Smiley's hand, and went off to the prouder world of Whitehall; and Mr. Barraclough to the Islay Hotel, where he returned to his reading of Operation Testify.

26

It was lunchtime next day. Smiley had read and slept a little, read again and bathed, and as he climbed the steps to that pretty London house he felt pleased, because he liked Sam.

The house was brown brick and Georgian, just off Grosvenor Square. There were five steps and a brass doorbell in a scalloped recess. The door was black, with pillars either side. He pushed the bell and he might as well have pushed the door; it opened at once. He entered a circular hallway with another door the other end, and two large men in black suits who might have been ushers at Westminster Abbey. Over a marble chimney-piece, horses pranced and they might have been Stubbs. One man stood close while he took off his coat; the second led him to a Bible desk to sign the book.

"Hebden," Smiley murmured as he wrote, giving a work-name Sam could remember.

"Adrian Hebden."

The man who had his coat repeated the name into a house telephone:

"Mr. Hebden—Mr. Adrian Hebden."

"If you wouldn't mind waiting one second, sir," said the man by the Bible desk. There was no music, and Smiley had the feeling there should have been; also a fountain.

"I'm a friend of Mr. Collins's, as a matter of fact," said Smiley. "If Mr. Collins is available. I think he may even be expecting me."

The man at the telephone murmured, "Thank you," and hung it on the hook. He led Smiley to the inner door and pushed it open. It made no sound at all, not even a rustle on the silk carpet.

"Mr. Collins is over there, sir," he murmured respectfully. "Drinks are with the courtesy of the house."

The three reception rooms had been run together, with pillars and arches to divide them optically, and mahogany panelling. In each room was one table, the third was sixty feet away. The lights shone on meaningless pictures of fruit in colossal gold frames, and on the green baize tablecloths. The curtains were drawn, the tables about one third occupied, four or five players to each, all men, but the only sounds were the click of the ball in the wheel, the click of the chips as they were redistributed, and the very low murmur of the croupiers.

"Adrian Hebden," said Sam Collins, with a twinkle in his voice. "Long time no see."

"Hullo, Sam," said Smiley, and they shook hands.

"Come down to my lair," said Sam, and nodded to the only other man in the room who was standing, a very big man with blood pressure and a chipped face. The big man nodded, too.

"Care for it?" Sam enquired as they crossed a corridor draped in red silk.

"It's very impressive," said Smiley politely.

"That's the word," said Sam. "Impressive. That's what it is." He was wearing a dinner jacket. His office was done in Edwardian plush, his desk had a marble top and ball-and-claw feet, but the room itself was very small and not at all well ventilated—more like the back room of a theatre, Smiley thought, furnished with leftover props.

"They might even let me put in a few pennies of my own later, give it another year. They're toughish boys, but very go-ahead, you know."

"I'm sure," said Smiley.

"Like we were in the old days."

"That's right."

He was trim and lighthearted in his manner and he had a trim black moustache. Smiley couldn't imagine him without it. He was probably fifty. He had spent a lot of time out East, where they had once worked together on a catch-and-carry job against a Chinese radio operator. His complexion and hair were greying but he still looked thirty-five. His smile was warm and he had a confiding, messroom friendliness. He kept both hands on the table as if he were at cards, and he looked at Smiley with a possessive fondness that was paternal or filial or both.

"If chummy goes over five," he said, still smiling, "give me a buzz, Harry, will you? Otherwise keep your big mouth shut; I'm chatting up an oil king." He was talking into a box on his desk. "Where is he now?"

"Three up," said a gravel voice. Smiley guessed it belonged to the chipped man with blood pressure.

"Then he's got eight to lose," said Sam blandly. "Keep him at the table, that's all. Make a hero of him." He switched off and grinned. Smiley grinned back.

"Really, it's a great life," Sam assured him. "Better than selling washing machines, anyway. Bit odd, of course, putting on the dinner jacket at ten in the morning. Reminds one of diplomatic cover." Smiley laughed. "Straight, too, believe it or not," Sam added with no change to his expression. "We get all the help we need from the arithmetic."

"I'm sure you do," said Smiley, once more with great politeness.

"Care for some music?"

It was canned and came out of the ceiling. Sam turned it up as loud as they could bear.

"So what can I do you for?" Sam asked, the smile broadening.

"I want to talk to you about the night Jim Prideaux was shot. You were duty officer."

Sam smoked brown cigarettes that smelt of cigar. Lighting one, he let the end catch fire, then watched it die to an ember. "Writing your memoirs, old boy?" he enquired.

"We're reopening the case."

"What's this *we*, old boy?"

"I, myself, and me, with Lacon pushing and the Minister pulling."

"All power corrupts but some must govern, and in that case Brother Lacon will reluctantly scramble to the top of the heap."

"It hasn't changed," said Smiley.

Sam drew ruminatively on his cigarette. The music switched to phrases of Noël Coward.

"It's a dream of mine, actually," said Sam Collins through the smoke. "One of these days Percy Alleline walks through that door with a shabby brown suitcase and asks for a flutter. He puts the whole of the secret vote on red and loses."

"The record's been filleted," said Smiley. "It's a matter of going to people and asking what they remember. There's almost nothing on file at all."

"I'm not surprised," said Sam. Over the phone he ordered sandwiches. "Live on them," he explained. "Sandwiches and canapés. One of the perks."

He was pouring coffee when the red pinlight glowed between them on the desk.

"Chummy's even," said the gravel voice.

"Then start counting," said Sam, and closed the switch.

He told it plainly but precisely, the way a good soldier recalls a battle, not to win or lose any more, but simply to remember. He had just come back from abroad, he said; a three-year stint in Vientiane. He'd checked in with personnel and cleared himself with the Dolphin; no one seemed to have any plans for him, so he was thinking of taking off for the South of France for a month's leave when MacFadean, that old janitor who was practically Control's valet, scooped him up in the corridor and marched him to Control's room.

"This was which day, exactly?" said Smiley.

"October 19th."

"The Thursday."

"The Thursday. I was thinking of flying to Nice on Monday. You were in Berlin. I wanted to buy you a drink but the mothers said you were *occupé*, and when I checked with Movements they told me you'd gone to Berlin."

"Yes, that's true," Smiley said simply. "Control sent me there."

To get me out of the way, he might have added; it was a feeling he had had even at the time.

"I hunted round for Bill but Bill was also in baulk. Control had packed him up-country somewhere," said Sam, avoiding Smiley's eye.

"On a wild goose chase," Smiley murmured. "But he came back."

Here Sam tipped a sharp, quizzical glance in Smiley's direction, but he added nothing on the subject of Bill Haydon's journey.

"The whole place seemed dead. Damn nearly caught the first plane back to Vientiane."

"It pretty much *was* dead," Smiley confessed, and thought, Except for Witchcraft.

And Control, said Sam, looked as though he'd had a five-day fever. He was surrounded by a sea of files, his skin was yellow, and as he talked he kept breaking off to wipe his forehead with a handkerchief. He scarcely bothered with the usual fan-dance at all, said Sam. He didn't congratulate him on three good years in the field, or make some snide reference to his private life, which was at that time messy; he simply said he wanted

Sam to do weekend duty instead of Mary Masterman; could Sam swing it?

"'Sure I can swing it,' I said. 'If you want me to do duty officer, I'll do it.' He said he'd give me the rest of the story on Saturday. Meanwhile I must tell no one. I mustn't give a hint anywhere in the building, even that he'd asked me this one thing. He needed someone good to man the switchboard in case there was a crisis, but it had to be someone from an out-station or someone like me who'd been away from head office for a long time. And it had to be an old hand."

So Sam went to Mary Masterman and sold her a hard-luck story about not being able to get the tenant out of his flat before he went on leave on Monday; how would it be if he did her duty for her and saved himself the hotel? He took over at nine on Saturday morning with his toothbrush and six cans of beer in a briefcase, which still had palm-tree stickers on the side. Geoff Agate was slated to relieve him on Sunday evening.

Once again Sam dwelt on how dead the place was. Back in the old days, Saturdays were much like any other day, he said. Most regional sections had a deskman working weekends, some even had night staff, and when you took a tour of the building you had the feeling that, warts and all, this was an outfit that had a lot going. But that Saturday morning the building might have been evacuated, said Sam; which in a way, from what he heard later, it had been—on orders from Control. A couple of wranglers toiled on the second floor; the radio and code rooms were going strong, but those boys worked all the hours anyway. Otherwise, said Sam, it was the big silence. He sat around waiting for Control to ring but nothing happened. He fleshed out another hour teasing the janitors, whom he reckoned the idlest lot of so-and-so's in the Circus. He checked their attendance lists and found two typists and one desk officer marked in but absent, so he put the head janitor, a new boy called Mellows, on report. Finally he went upstairs to see if Control was in.

"He was sitting all alone, except for MacFadean. No mothers, no you—just old Mac peeking around with jasmine tea and sympathy. Too much?"

"No, just go on, please. As much detail as you can remember."

"So then Control peeled off another veil. Half a veil. Someone was doing a special job for him, he said. It was of great importance to the service. He kept saying that: to the service. Not Whitehall or sterling or the price of fish, but us. Even when it was all over, I must never breathe a word about it. Not even to you. Or Bill or Bland or anyone."

"Nor Alleline?"

"He never mentioned Percy once."

"No," Smiley agreed. "He scarcely could at the end."

"I should regard him, for the night, as Director of Operations. I should see myself as cut-out between Control and whatever was going on in the rest of the building. If anything came in—a signal, a phone call, however trivial it seemed—I should wait till the coast was clear, then whip upstairs and hand it to Control. No one was to know, now or later, that Control was the man behind the gun. In no case should I phone him or minute him; even the internal lines were taboo. Truth, George," said Sam, helping himself to a sandwich.

"Oh, I do believe you," said Smiley with feeling.

If outgoing telegrams had to be sent, Sam should once more act as Control's cut-out. He need not expect much to happen till this evening; even then it was most unlikely anything would happen. As to the janitors and people like that, as Control put it, Sam should do his damnedest to act natural and look busy.

The séance over, Sam returned to the duty room, sent out for an evening paper, opened a can of beer, selected an outside telephone line, and set about losing his shirt. There was steeplechasing at Kempton, which he hadn't watched for years. Early evening, he took another walk around the lines and tested the alarm pads on the floor of the general registry. Three out of fifteen didn't work, and by this time the janitors were really loving him. He cooked himself an egg, and when he'd eaten it he trotted upstairs to take a pound off old Mac and give him a beer.

"He'd asked me to put him a quid on some nag with three left feet. I chatted with him for ten minutes, went back to my post, wrote some letters, watched a rotten movie on the telly, then turned in. The first call came just as I was getting to sleep. Eleven-twenty, exactly. The phones didn't stop ringing for the next ten hours. I thought the switchboard was going to blow up in my face."

"Arcadi's five down," said a voice over the box.

"Excuse me," said Sam, with his habitual grin and, leaving Smiley to the music, slipped upstairs to cope.

Sitting alone, Smiley watched Sam's brown cigarette slowly burning away in the ashtray. He waited, Sam didn't return, and he wondered whether he should stub it out. Not allowed to smoke on duty, he thought; house rules.

"All done," said Sam.

The first call came from the Foreign Office resident clerk on the direct line, said Sam. In the Whitehall stakes, you might say, the Foreign Office won by a curled lip.

"The Reuters headman in London had just called him with a story of a shooting in Prague. A British spy had been shot dead by Russian security forces, there was a hunt out for his accomplices, and was the F.O. interested? The duty clerk was passing it to us for information. I said it sounded bunkum, and rang off just as Mike Meakin, of wranglers, came through to say that all hell had broken out on the Czech air: half of it was coded, but the other half was *en clair*. He kept getting garbled accounts of a shooting near Brno. Prague or Brno? I asked. Or both? Just Brno. I said keep listening, and by then all five buzzers were going. Just as I was leaving the room, the resident clerk came back on the direct. The Reuters man had corrected his story, he said: for Prague read Brno. I closed the door and it was like leaving a wasps' nest in your drawing-room. Control was standing at his desk as I came in. He'd heard me coming up the stairs. Has Alleline put a carpet on those stairs, by the way?"

"No," said Smiley. He was quite impassive. "George is like a swift," Ann had once told Haydon in his hearing. "He cuts down his body temperature till it's the same as the environment. Then he doesn't lose energy adjusting."

"You know how quick he was when he looked at you. He checked my hands to see whether I had a telegram for him, and I wished I'd been carrying something but they were empty. 'I'm afraid there's a bit of a panic,' I said. I gave him the gist, he looked at his watch; I suppose he was trying to work out what should have been happening if everything had been plain sailing. I said, 'Can I have a brief, please?' He sat down; I couldn't see him too well—he had that low green light on his desk. I said again, 'I'll need a brief. Do you want me to deny it? Why don't I get someone in?' No answer. Mind you, there wasn't anyone to get, but I didn't know that yet. 'I must have a brief.' We could hear footsteps downstairs and I knew the radio boys were trying to find me. 'Do you want to come down and handle it yourself?' I said. I went round to the other side of the desk, stepping over these files, all open at different places; you'd think he was compiling an encyclopaedia. Some of them must have been pre-war. He was sitting like this."

Sam bunched the fingers of one hand, put the tips to his forehead, and stared at the desk. His other hand was laid flat, holding Control's imaginary fob watch. "'Tell MacFadean to get me a cab, then find Smiley.' 'What about the operation?' I asked. I had to wait all night for an answer. 'It's deniable,' he says. 'Both men had foreign documents. No one could know they were British at this stage.' 'They're only talking about one man,' I said. Then I said, 'Smiley's in Berlin.' That's what I think I said, anyway. So we have another two-minute silence. 'Anyone will do. It makes no difference.' I should have been sorry for him, I suppose, but just then I couldn't raise much sympathy. I was having to hold the baby and I didn't know a damn thing. MacFadean wasn't around so I reckoned Control could find his own cab, and by the time I got to the bottom of the steps I must have looked like Gordon at Khartoum. The duty harridan from monitoring was waving bulletins at me like flags, a couple of janitors were yelling at me, the radio boy was clutching a bunch of signals, the phones were going—not just my own, but half a dozen of the direct lines on the fourth floor. I went straight to the duty room and switched off all the lines while I tried to get my bearings. The monitor—what's that woman's name, for God's sake, used to play bridge with the Dolphin?"

"Purcell. Molly Purcell."

"That's the one. Her story was at least straightforward. Prague radio was promising an emergency bulletin in half an hour's time. That was quarter of an hour ago. The bulletin would concern an act of gross provocation by a Western power, an infringement of Czechoslovakia's sovereignty, and an outrage against freedom-loving people of all nations. Apart from that," said Sam dryly, "it was going to be laughs all the way. I rang Bywater Street, of course; then I made a signal to Berlin telling them to find you and fly you back by yesterday. I gave Mellows the main phone numbers and sent him off to find an outside line and get hold of whoever was around of the top brass. Percy was in Scotland for the weekend and out to dinner. His cook gave Mellows a number; he rang it, spoke to his host. Percy had just left."

"I'm sorry," Smiley interrupted. "Rang Bywater Street, what for?" He was holding his upper lip between his finger and thumb, pulling it out like a deformity, while he stared into the middle distance.

"In case you'd come back early from Berlin," said Sam.

"And had I?"

"No."

"So who did you speak to?"

"Ann."

Smiley said, "Ann's away just now. Could you remind me how it went, that conversation?"

"I asked for you and she said you were in Berlin."

"And that was all?"

"It was a crisis, George," Sam said, in a warning tone.

"So?"

"I asked her whether by any chance she knew where Bill Haydon was. It was urgent. I gathered he was on leave but might be around. Somebody once told me they were cousins." He added: "Besides, he's a friend of the family, I understood."

"Yes. He is. What did she say?"

"Gave me a shirty 'no' and rang off. Sorry about that, George. War's war."

"How did she sound?" Smiley asked, after letting the aphorism lie between them for some while.

"I told you: shirty."

Roy Bland was at Leeds University talent-spotting, said Sam, and not available.

Between calls, Sam was getting the whole book thrown at him. He might as well have invaded Cuba. The military were yelling about Czech tank movements along the Austrian border; the wranglers couldn't hear themselves think for the radio traffic round Brno; and as for the Foreign Office, the resident clerk was having the vapours and yellow fever all in one. "First Lacon, then the Minister were baying at the doors, and at half past twelve we had the promised Czech news bulletin, twenty minutes late but none the worse for that. A British spy named Jim Ellis, travelling on false Czech papers and assisted by Czech counter-revolutionaries, had attempted to kidnap an unnamed Czech general in the forests near Brno and smuggle him over the Austrian border. Ellis had been shot but they didn't say killed; other arrests were imminent. I looked Ellis up in the workname index and found Jim Prideaux. And I thought, just as Control must have thought, If Jim is shot and has Czech papers, how the hell do they know his workname, and how do they know he's British? Then Bill Haydon arrived, white as a sheet. Picked up the story on the ticker-tape at his club. He turned straight round and came to the Circus."

"At what time was that, exactly?" Smiley asked, with a vague frown. "It must have been rather late."

Sam looked as if he wished he could make it easier. "One-fifteen," he said.

"Which is late, isn't it, for reading club ticker-tapes."

"Not my world, old boy."

"Bill's the Savile, isn't he?"

"Don't know," said Sam doggedly. He drank some coffee. "He was a treat to watch, that's all I can tell you. I used to think of him as an erratic sort of devil. Not that night, believe me. All right, he was shaken. Who wouldn't be? He arrived knowing there'd been a God-awful shooting party and that was about all. But when I told him that it was Jim who'd been shot, he looked at me like a madman. Thought he was going to go for me. 'Shot. Shot how? Shot dead?' I shoved the bulletins into his hand and he tore through them one by one—"

"Wouldn't he have known already from the ticker-tape?" Smiley asked, in a small voice. "I thought the news was everywhere by then: Ellis shot. That was the lead story, wasn't it?"

"Depends which news bulletin he saw, I suppose," Sam shrugged it off. "Anyway, he took over the switchboard and by morning he'd picked up what few pieces there were and introduced something pretty close to calm. He told the Foreign Office to sit tight and hold its water; he got hold of Toby Esterhase and sent him off to pull in a brace of Czech agents, students at the London School of Economics. Bill had been letting them hatch till then; he was planning to turn them round and play them back into Czecho. Toby's lamplighters sandbagged the pair of them and locked them up in Sarratt. Then Bill rang the Czech head resident in London and spoke to him like a sergeant major: threatened to strip him so bare he'd be the laughing-stock of the profession if a hair of Jim Prideaux's head was hurt. He invited him to pass that on to his masters. I felt I was watching a street accident and Bill was the only doctor. He rang a press contact and told him in strict confidence that Ellis was a Czech mercenary with an American contract; he could use the story unattributably. It actually made the late editions. Soon as he could, he slid off to Jim's rooms to make sure he'd left nothing around that a journalist might pick on if a journalist were clever enough to make the connection, Ellis to Prideaux. I guess he did a thorough cleaning-up job. Dependents, everything."

"There weren't any dependents," Smiley said. "Apart from Bill, I suppose," he added, half under his breath.

Sam wound it up: "At eight o'clock Percy Alleline arrived; he'd cadged a special plane off the Air Force. He was grinning all over. I didn't think that was very clever of him, considering Bill's feelings, but there you are. He wanted to know why I was doing duty, so I gave him the same story I'd given to Mary Masterman: no flat. He used my phone to make a date with the Minister, and was still talking when Roy Bland came in, hopping mad and half plastered, wanting to know who the hell had been messing on his patch and practically accusing me. I said, 'Christ, man, what about old Jim? You could pity him while you were about it,' but Roy's a hungry boy and likes the living better than the dead. I gave him the switchboard with my love, went down to the Savoy for breakfast, and read the Sundays. The most any of them did was run the Prague radio reports and a pooh-pooh denial from the Foreign Office."

Finally Smiley said, "After that you went to the South of France?"

"For two lovely months."

"Did anyone question you again—about Control, for instance?"

"Not till I got back. You were out on your ear by then; Control was ill in hospital." Sam's voice deepened a little. "He didn't do anything *silly*, did he?"

"He just died. What happened?"

"Percy was acting head boy. He called for me and wanted to know why I'd done duty for Masterman and what communication I'd had with Control. I stuck to my story and Percy called me a liar."

"So that's what they sacked you for: lying?"

"Alcoholism. The janitors got a bit of their own back. They'd counted five beer cans in the waste-basket in the duty officer's lair and reported it to the housekeepers. There's a standing order: no booze on the premises. In the due process of time, a disciplinary body found me guilty of setting fire to the Queen's dockyards so I joined the bookies. What happened to you?"

"Oh, much the same. I didn't seem to be able to convince them I wasn't involved."

"Well, if you want anyone's throat cut," said Sam as he saw him quietly out through a side door into a pretty mews, "give me a buzz." Smiley was sunk in thought. "And if you ever want a flutter," Sam went on, "bring along some of Ann's smart friends."

"Sam, listen. Bill was making love to Ann that night. No, listen. You phoned her, she told you Bill wasn't there. As soon as she'd rung off, she pushed Bill out of bed and he turned up at the Circus an hour later knowing that there had been a shooting in Czecho. If you were giving me the story from the shoulder—on a postcard—that's what you'd say?"

"Broadly."

"But you didn't tell Ann about Czecho when you phoned her—"

"He stopped at his club on the way to the Circus."

"If it was open. Very well: then why didn't he know that Jim Prideaux had been shot?"

In the daylight, Sam looked briefly old, though the grin had not left his face. He seemed about to say something, then changed his mind. He seemed angry, then thwarted, then blank again. "Cheeribye," he said. "Mind how you go," and withdrew to the permanent night-time of his elected trade.

27

When Smiley had left the Islay for Grosvenor Square that morning, the streets had been bathed in harsh sunshine and the sky was blue. Now as he drove the hired Rover past the unlovable façades of the Edgware Road, the wind had dropped, the sky was black with waiting rain, and all that remained of the sun was a lingering redness on the tarmac. He parked in St. John's Wood Road, in the forecourt of a new tower block with a glass porch, but he did not enter by the porch. Passing a large sculpture describing, as it seemed to him, nothing but a sort of cosmic muddle, he made his way through icy drizzle to a descending outside staircase marked "Exit Only." The first flight was of terrazzo tile and had a bannister of African teak. Below that, the contractor's generosity ceased. Rough-rendered plaster replaced the earlier luxury and a stench of uncollected refuse crammed the air. His manner was cautious rather than furtive, but when he reached the iron door he paused before putting both hands to the long handle and drew himself together as if for an ordeal. The door opened a foot and stopped with a thud, to be answered by a shout of fury, which echoed many times like a shout in a swimming pool.

"Hey, why you don't look out once?"

Smiley edged through the gap. The door had stopped against the bumper of a very shiny car, but Smiley wasn't looking at the car. Across the garage two men in overalls were hosing down a Rolls-Royce in a cage. Both were looking in his direction.

"Why you don't come other way?" the same angry voice demanded. "You tenant here? Why you don't use tenant lift? This stair for fire."

It was not possible to tell which of them was speaking, but whichever it was, he spoke in a heavy Slav accent. The light in the cage was behind them. The shorter man held the hose.

Smiley walked forward, taking care to keep his hands clear of his pockets. The man with the hose went back to work, but the taller stayed watching him through the gloom. He wore white overalls and he had turned the collar-points upwards, which gave him a rakish air. His black hair was swept back and full.

"I'm not a tenant, I'm afraid," Smiley conceded. "But I wonder if I might just speak to someone about renting a space. My name's *Carmichael*," he explained, in a louder voice. "I've bought a flat up the road."

He made a gesture as if to produce a card, as if his documents would speak better for him than his insignificant appearance. "I'll pay in advance," he promised. "I could sign a contract or whatever is necessary, I'm sure. I'd want it to be above-board, naturally. I can give references, pay a deposit, anything within reason. As long as it's above-board. It's a Rover. A new one. I won't go behind the company's back, because I don't believe in it. But I'll do anything else within reason. I'd have brought it down, but I didn't want to presume. And—well, I know it sounds silly but I didn't like the look of the ramp. It's so new, you see."

Throughout this protracted statement of intent, which he delivered with an air of fussy concern, Smiley had remained in the downbeam of a bright light strung from the rafter: a supplicant, rather abject figure, one might have thought, and easily visible across the open space. The attitude had its effect. Leaving the cage, the white figure strode towards a glazed kiosk, built between two iron pillars, and with his fine head beckoned Smiley to follow. As he went, he pulled the gloves off his hands. They were leather gloves, hand-stitched and quite expensive.

"Well, you want mind out how you open door," he warned in the same loud voice. "You want use lift, see, or maybe you pay couple pounds. Use lift you don't make no trouble."

"Max, I want to talk to you," said Smiley once they were inside the kiosk. "Alone. Away from here."

Max was broad and powerful with a pale boy's face, but the skin of it was lined like an old man's. He was handsome and his brown eyes were very still. He had altogether a rather deadly stillness.

"Now? You want talk now?"

"In the car. I've got one outside. If you walk to the top of the ramp, you can get straight into it."

Putting his hand to his mouth, Max yelled across the garage. He was half a head taller than Smiley and had a roar like a drum major's. Smiley couldn't catch the words. Possibly they were Czech. There was no answer, but Max was already unbuttoning his overall.

"It's about Jim Prideaux," Smiley said.

"Sure," said Max.

They drove up to Hampstead and sat in the shiny Rover, watching the kids breaking the ice on the pond. Real rain had held off, after all; perhaps because it was so cold.

Above ground Max wore a blue suit and a blue shirt. His tie was blue but carefully differentiated from the other blues: he had taken a lot of trouble to get the shade. He wore several rings and flying boots with zips at the side.

"I'm not in it any more. Did they tell you?" Smiley asked. Max shrugged. "I thought they would have told you," Smiley said.

Max was sitting straight; he didn't use the seat to lean on; he was too proud. He did not look at Smiley. His eyes were turned fixedly to the pool and the kids fooling and skidding in the reeds.

"They don't tell me nothing," he said.

"I was sacked," said Smiley. "I guess at about the same time as you."

Max seemed to stretch slightly, then settle again. "Too bad, George. What you do, steal money?"

"I don't want them to know, Max."

"You private—I private, too," said Max, and from a gold case offered Smiley a cigarette, which he declined.

"I want to hear what happened," Smiley went on. "I wanted to find out before they sacked me but there wasn't time."

"That why they sack you?"

"Maybe."

"You don't know so much, huh?" said Max, his gaze nonchalantly on the kids.

Smiley spoke very simply, watching all the while in case Max didn't understand. They could have spoken German but Max wouldn't have that, he knew. So he spoke English and watched Max's face.

"I don't know anything, Max. I had no part in it at all. I was in Berlin when it happened; I knew nothing of the planning or the background. They cabled me, but when I arrived in London it was too late."

"Planning," Max repeated. "That was some planning." His jaw and cheeks became suddenly a mass of lines and his eyes turned narrow, making a grimace or a smile. "So now you got plenty time, eh, George? Jesus, that was some planning."

"Jim had a special job to do. He asked for you."

"Sure. Jim ask for Max to baby-sit."

"How did he get you? Did he turn up in Acton and speak to Toby Esterhase, and say, 'Toby, I want Max'? How did he get you?"

Max's hands were resting on his knees. They were groomed and slender—all but the knuckles, which were very broad.

Now, at the mention of Esterhase, he turned the palms slightly inwards and made a light cage of them as if he had caught a butterfly.

"What the hell?" Max asked.

"So what did happen?"

"Was private," said Max. "Jim private, I private. Like now."

"Come," said Smiley. "Please."

Max spoke as if it were any mess: family or business or love. It was a Monday evening in mid-October—yes, the sixteenth. It was a slack time, he hadn't been abroad for weeks, and he was fed up. He had spent all day making a reconnaissance of a house in Bloomsbury where a pair of Chinese students was supposed to live; the lamplighters were thinking of mounting a burglary against their rooms. He was on the point of returning to the Laundry in Acton to write his report when Jim picked him up in the street with a chance-encounter routine and drove him up to Crystal Palace, where they sat in the car and talked, like now, except they spoke Czech. Jim said there was a special job going, something so big, so secret that no one else in the Circus, not even Toby Esterhase, was allowed to know that it was taking place. It came from the very top of the tree and it was hairy. Was Max interested?

"I say, 'Sure, Jim. Max interested.' Then he ask me: 'Take leave. You go to Toby, you say, Toby, my mother sick, I got to take some leave.' I don't got no mother. 'Sure,' I say, 'I take leave. How long for, please, Jim?'"

The whole job shouldn't last more than the weekend, said Jim. They should be in on Saturday and out on Sunday. Then he asked Max whether he had any current identities running for him: best would be Austrian, small trade, with driving licence to match. If Max had none handy at Acton, Jim would get something put together in Brixton.

"'Sure,' I say. 'I have Hartmann, Rudi, from Linz, Sudeten émigré.'"

So Max gave Toby a story about girl trouble up in Bradford and Toby gave Max a ten-minute lecture on the sexual mores of the English; and on the Thursday, Jim and Max met in a safe house that the scalp-hunters ran in those days, a rackety old place in Lambeth. Jim had brought the keys. A three-day hit, Jim repeated; a clandestine conference outside Brno. Jim had a big map and they studied it. Jim would travel Czech, Max would go Austrian. They would make their separate ways as far as Brno. Jim would fly from Paris to Prague, then train from Prague. He didn't say what papers he would be carrying himself, but Max presumed Czech because Czech was Jim's other side; Max had seen him use it before. Max was Hartmann Rudi, trading in glass and ovenware. He was to cross the Austrian border by van near Mikulov, then head north to Brno, giving himself plenty of time to make a six-thirty rendezvous on Saturday evening in a side street near the football ground. There was a big match that evening starting at seven. Jim would walk with the crowd as far as the side street, then climb into the van. They agreed times, fallbacks, and the usual contingencies; and besides, said Max, they knew each other's handwriting by heart.

Once out of Brno, they were to drive together along the Bilovice road as far as Krtiny, then turn east towards Racice. Somewhere along the Racice road they would pass on the left side a parked black car, most likely a Fiat. The first two figures of the registration would be 99. The driver would be reading a newspaper. They would pull up; Max would go over and ask whether he was all right. The man would reply that his doctor had forbidden him to drive more than three hours at a stretch. Max would say it was true that long journeys were a strain on the heart. The driver would then show them where to park the van and take them to the rendezvous in his own car.

"Who were you meeting, Max? Did Jim tell you that as well?"

No, that was all Jim told him.

As far as Brno, said Max, things went pretty much as planned. Driving from Mikulov, he was followed for a while by a couple of civilian motorcyclists who interchanged every ten minutes, but he put that down to his Austrian number plates and it didn't bother him. He made Brno comfortably by mid-afternoon, and to keep things shipshape he booked into the hotel and drank a couple of coffees in the restaurant. Some stooge picked him up and Max talked to him about the vicissitudes of the glass trade and about his girl in Linz who'd gone off with an American. Jim missed the first rendezvous but he made the fallback an hour later. Max supposed at first the train was late, but Jim just said, "Drive slowly," and he knew then that there was trouble.

This was how it was going to work, said Jim. There'd been a change of plan. Max was to stay right out of it. He should drop Jim short of the rendezvous, then lie up in Brno till Monday morning. He was not to make contact with any of the Circus's trade routes: no one from Aggravate, no one from Plato, least of all with the Prague residency. If Jim didn't surface at the hotel by eight on Monday morning, Max should get out any way he could. If Jim did surface, Max's job would be to carry Jim's message to Control: the message could be very simple; it might be no more than one word. When he got to London, he should go to Control personally, make an appointment through old MacFadean, and give him the message—was that clear? If Jim didn't show up, Max should take up life where he left off and deny everything, inside the Circus as well as out.

"Did Jim say why the plan had changed?"

"Jim worried."

"So something had happened to him on his way to meet you?"

"Maybe. I say Jim: 'Listen, Jim, I come with. You worried, I be baby-sitter. I drive for you, shoot for you, what the hell?' Jim get damn angry, okay?"

"Okay," said Smiley.

They drove to the Racice road and found the car parked without lights facing a track over a field, a Fiat, 99 on the number plates, black. Max stopped the van and let Jim out. As Jim walked towards the Fiat, the driver opened the door an inch in order to work the courtesy light. He had a newspaper opened over the steering wheel.

"Could you see his face?"

"Was in shadow."

Max waited; presumably they exchanged word codes, Jim got in, and the car drove away over the track, still without lights. Max returned to Brno. He was sitting over a schnapps in the restaurant when the whole town started rumbling. He thought at first the sound came from the football stadium; then he realised it was lorries, a convoy racing down the road. He asked the waitress what was going on, and she said there had been a shooting in the woods—counter-revolutionaries were responsible. He went out to the van, turned on the radio, and caught the bulletin from Prague. That was the first he had heard of a general. He guessed there were cordons everywhere, and anyway he had Jim's instructions to lie up in the hotel till Monday morning.

"Maybe Jim send me message. Maybe some guy from resistance come to me."

"With this one word," said Smiley quietly.

"Sure."

"He didn't say what sort of word it was?"

"You crazy," said Max. It was either a statement or a question.

"A Czech word or an English word or a German word?"

No one came, said Max, not bothering to answer craziness.

On Monday he burned his entry passport, changed the plates on his van, and used his West German escape. Rather than head south he drove south west, ditched the van, and crossed the border by bus to Freistadt, which was the softest route he knew. In Freistadt he had a drink and spent the night with a girl because he felt puzzled and angry and he needed to catch his breath. He got to London on Tuesday night, and despite Jim's orders he thought he'd better try and contact Control. "That was quite damn difficult," he commented.

He tried to telephone but only got as far as the mothers. MacFadean wasn't around. He thought of writing but he remembered Jim, and how no one else in the Circus was allowed to know. He decided that writing was too dangerous. The rumour at the Acton Laundry said that Control was ill. He tried to find out what hospital, but couldn't.

"Did people at the Laundry seem to know where you'd been?"

"I wonder."

He was still wondering when the housekeepers sent for him and asked to look at his Rudi Hartmann passport. Max said he had lost it, which was after all pretty near true. Why hadn't he reported the loss? He didn't know. When had the loss occurred? He didn't know. When did he last see Jim Prideaux? He couldn't remember. He was sent down to the Nursery at Sarratt but Max felt fit and angry, and after two or three days the inquisitors got tired of him or somebody called them off.

"I go back Acton Laundry; Toby Esterhase give me hundred pound, tell me go to hell."

A scream of applause went up round the pond. Two boys had sunk a great slab of ice and now the water was bubbling through the hole.

"Max, what happened to Jim?"

"What the hell?"

"You hear these things. It gets around among the émigrés. What happened to him? Who mended him, how did Bill Haydon buy him back?"

"Emigrés don't speak Max no more."

"But you have heard, haven't you?"

This time it was the white hands that told him. Smiley saw the spread of fingers, five on one hand, four on the other and already he felt the sickness before Max spoke.

"So they shoot Jim from behind. Maybe Jim was running away, what the hell? They put Jim in prison. That's not so good for Jim. For my friends also. Not good." He started counting: "Pribyl," he began, touching his thumb. "Bukova Mirek, from Pribyl's wife the brother," he took a finger. "Also Pribyl's wife," a second finger. A third: "Kolin Jiri. Also his sister, mainly dead. This was network Aggravate." He changed hands. "After network Aggravate come network Plato. Come lawyer Rapotin, come Colonel Landkron, and typists Eva Krieglova and Hanka Bilova. Also mainly dead. That's damn big price, George"—holding the clean fingers close to Smiley's face—"that's damn big price for one Englishman with bullet-hole." He was losing his temper. "Why you bother, George? Circus don't be no good for Czecho. Allies don't be no good for Czecho. No rich guy don't get no poor guy out of prison! You want know some history? How you say '*Märchen*,' please, George?"

"Fairy tale," said Smiley.

"Okay, so don't tell me no more damn fairy tale how English got to save Czecho no more!"

"Perhaps it wasn't Jim," said Smiley after a long silence. "Perhaps it was someone else who blew the networks. Not Jim."

Max was already opening the door. "What the hell?" he asked.

"Max," said Smiley.

"Don't worry, George. I don't got no one to sell you to. Okay?"

"Okay."

Sitting in the car still, Smiley watched him hail a taxi. He did it with a flick of the hand, as if he were summoning a waiter.

He gave the address without bothering to look at the driver. Then rode off sitting very upright again, staring straight ahead of him, like royalty ignoring the crowd.

As the taxi disappeared, Inspector Mendel rose slowly from a bench, folded together his newspaper, walked over to the Rover.

"You're clean," he said. "Nothing on your back, nothing on your conscience."

Not so sure of that, Smiley handed him the keys to the car, then walked to the bus stop, first crossing the road in order to head west.

28

His destination was in Fleet Street, a ground-floor cellar full of wine barrels. In other areas, three-thirty might be considered a little late for a pre-luncheon apéritif, but as Smiley gently pushed open the door a dozen shadowy figures turned to eye him from the bar. And at a corner table, as unremarked as the plastic prison arches or the fake muskets on the wall, sat Jerry Westerby with a very large pink gin.

"Old boy," said Jerry Westerby shyly, in a voice that seemed to come out of the ground. "Well, I'll be damned. Hey, Jimmy!" His hand, which he laid on Smiley's arm while he signalled for refreshment with the other, was enormous and cushioned with muscle, for Jerry had once been wicketkeeper for a county cricket team. In contrast to other wicketkeepers he was a big man, but his shoulders were still hunched from keeping his hands low. He had a mop of sandy grey hair and a red face and he wore a famous sporting tie over a cream silk shirt. The sight of Smiley clearly gave him great joy, for he was beaming with pleasure.

"Well, I'll be damned," he repeated. "Of all the amazing things. Hey, what are you doing these days," dragging him forcibly into the seat beside him. "Sunning your fanny, spitting at the ceiling? Hey"—a most urgent question—"what'll it be?"

Smiley ordered a Bloody Mary.

"It isn't *complete* coincidence, Jerry," Smiley confessed. There was a slight pause between them, which Jerry was suddenly concerned to fill.

"Listen, how's the demon wife? All well? That's the stuff. One of the great marriages, that one—always said so."

Jerry Westerby himself had made several marriages but few that had given him pleasure.

"Do a deal with you, George," he proposed, rolling one great shoulder towards him. "I'll shack up with Ann and spit at the ceiling, you take my job and write up the women's Ping-Pong. How's that? God bless."

"Cheers," said Smiley good-humouredly.

"Haven't seen many of the boys and girls for a while, matter of fact," Jerry confessed awkwardly with an unaccountable blush. "Christmas card from old Toby last year, that's about my lot. Guess they've put me on the shelf as well. Can't blame them." He flicked the rim of his glass. "Too much of this stuff, that's what it is. They think I'll blab. Crack up."

"I'm sure they don't," said Smiley, and the silence reclaimed them both.

"Too much firewater not good for braves," Jerry intoned solemnly. For years they had had this Red Indian joke running, Smiley remembered with a sinking heart.

"*How,*" said Smiley.

"*How,*" said Jerry, and they drank.

"I burnt your letter as soon as I'd read it," Smiley went on in a quiet, unbothered voice. "In case you wondered. I didn't tell anyone about it at all. It came too late, anyway. It was all over."

At this, Jerry's lively complexion turned a deep scarlet.

"So it wasn't the letter you wrote me that put them off you," Smiley continued in the same very gentle voice, "if that's what you were thinking. And, after all, you did drop it in to me by hand."

"Very decent of you," Jerry muttered. "Thanks. Shouldn't have written it. Talking out of school."

"Nonsense," said Smiley as he ordered two more. "You did it for the good of the service."

To himself, saying this, Smiley sounded like Lacon. But the only way to talk to Jerry was to talk like Jerry's newspaper: short sentences; facile opinions.

Jerry expelled some breath and a lot of cigarette smoke. "Last job—oh, year ago," he recalled with a new airiness. "More. Dumping some little packet in Budapest. Nothing to it, really. Phone box. Ledge at the top. Put my hand up. Left it there. Kid's play. Don't think I muffed it or anything. Did my sums first—all that. Safety signals. 'Box ready for emptying. Help yourself.' The way they taught us, you know. Still, you lads know best, don't you? You're the owls. Do one's bit, that's the thing. Can't do more. All part of a pattern. Design."

"They'll be beating the doors down for you soon," said Smiley consolingly. "I expect they're resting you up for a season. They do that, you know."

"Hope so," said Jerry with a loyal, very diffident smile. His glass shook slightly as he drank.

"Was that the trip you made just before you wrote to me?" Smiley asked.

"Sure. Same trip, actually; Budapest, then Prague."

"And it was in Prague that you heard this story? The story you referred to in your letter to me?"

At the bar a florid man in a black suit was predicting the imminent collapse of the nation. He gave it three months, he said, then curtains.

"Rum chap, Toby Esterhase," said Jerry.

"But good," said Smiley.

"Oh, my God, old boy, first rate. Brilliant, my view. But rum, you know. *How.*" They drank again, and Jerry Westerby loosely poked a finger behind his head, in imitation of an Apache feather.

"Trouble is," the florid man at the bar was saying over the top of his drink, "we won't even know it's happened."

They decided to lunch straight away, because Jerry had a
story to file for tomorrow's edition about some top footballer
who'd been caught shoplifting. They went to a curry house
where the management was content to serve beer at teatime,
and they agreed that if anyone bumped into them Jerry would
introduce George as his bank manager, a notion that tickled
him repeatedly throughout his hearty meal. There was background music, which Jerry called the connubial flight of the
mosquito, and at times it threatened to drown the fainter notes
of his husky voice. Which was probably just as well, for while
Smiley made a brave show of enthusiasm for the curry, Jerry
was launched, after his initial reluctance, upon quite a different story, concerning one Jim Ellis: the story that dear old
Toby Esterhase had refused to let him print.

Jerry Westerby was that extremely rare person, the perfect
witness. He had no fantasy, no malice, no personal opinion.
Merely, the thing was rum. He couldn't get it off his mind and,
come to think of it, he hadn't spoken to Toby since.

"Just this card, you see, 'Happy Christmas, Toby'—picture
of Leadenhall Street in the snow." He gazed in great perplexity at the electric fan. "Nothing *special* about Leadenhall Street,
is there, old boy? Not a spy-house or a meeting place or something, is it?"

"Not that I know of," said Smiley, with a laugh.

"Couldn't think why he chose Leadenhall Street for a
Christmas card. Damned odd, don't you think?"

Perhaps he just wanted a snowy picture of London, Smiley
suggested; Toby, after all, was quite foreign in lots of ways.

"Rum way to keep in touch, I must say. Used to send me a
crate of Scotch regular as clockwork." Jerry frowned and drank
from his krug. "It's not the Scotch I mind," he explained with
that puzzlement that often clouded the greater visions of his
life; "buy my own Scotch any time. It's just that when you're

on the outside, you think everything has a meaning, so presents are important—see what I'm getting at?"

It was a year ago—well, December. The Restaurant Sport in Prague, said Jerry Westerby, was a bit off the track of your average Western journalist. Most of them hung around the Cosmo or the International, talking in low murmurs and keeping together because they were jumpy. But Jerry's local was the Sport, and ever since he had taken Holotek, the goalie, along after the winning match against the Tartars, Jerry had had the big hand from the barman, whose name was Stanislaus or Stan.

"Stan's a perfect prince. Does just what he damn well pleases. Makes you suddenly think Czecho's a free country."

Restaurant, he explained, meant bar. Whereas bar in Czecho meant nightclub, which was rum. Smiley agreed that it must be confusing.

All the same, Jerry always kept an ear to the ground when he went there; after all, it was Czecho, and once or twice he'd been able to bring back the odd snippet for Toby or put him onto the track of someone.

"Even if it was just currency-dealing, black-market stuff. All grist to the mill, according to Tobe. These little scraps add up—that's what Tobe said, anyway."

Quite right, Smiley agreed. That was the way it worked.

"Tobe was the owl, what?"

"Sure."

"I used to work straight to Roy Bland, you see. Then Roy got kicked upstairs, so Tobe took me over. Bit unsettling, actually, changes. Cheers."

"How long had you been working to Toby when this trip took place?"

"Couple of years, not more."

There was a pause while food came and krugs were refilled and Jerry Westerby with his enormous hands shattered a popadam onto the hottest curry on the menu, then spread a crimson sauce over the top. The sauce, he said, was to give it bite. "Old Khan runs it up for me specially," he explained, aside. "Keeps it in a deep shelter."

So anyway, he resumed, that night in Stan's bar there was this young boy with the pudding-bowl haircut and the pretty girl on his arm.

"And I thought, Watch out, Jerry, boy; that's an army haircut. Right?"

"Right," Smiley echoed, thinking that in some ways Jerry was a bit of an owl himself.

It turned out the boy was Stan's nephew, and very proud of his English. "Amazing what people will tell you if it gives them a chance of showing off their languages." He was on leave from the army and he'd fallen in love with this girl; he'd eight days to go and the whole world was his friend, Jerry included. Jerry particularly, in fact, because Jerry was paying for the booze.

"So we're all sitting hugger-mugger at the big table in the corner—students, pretty girls, all sorts. Old Stan had come round from behind the bar and some laddie was doing a fair job with a squeeze-box. Bags of *Gemütlichkeit*, bags of booze, bags of noise."

The noise was specially important, Jerry explained, because it let him chat to the boy without anyone else paying attention. The boy was sitting next to Jerry; he'd taken a shine to him from the start. He had one arm slung round the girl and one arm round Jerry.

"One of those kids who can touch you without giving you the creeps. Don't like being touched, as a rule. Greeks do it. Hate it, personally."

Smiley said he hated it, too.

"Come to think of it, the girl looked a bit like Ann," Jerry reflected. "Foxy—know what I mean? Garbo eyes, lots of oomph."

So while everyone was carrying on, singing and drinking and playing kiss-in-the-ring, this lad asked Jerry whether he would like to know the truth about Jim Ellis.

"Pretended I'd never heard of him," Jerry explained to Smiley. " 'Love to,' I said. 'Who's Jim Ellis when he's at home?' And the boy looks at me as if I'm daft and says, 'A British spy.' Only no one else heard, you see; they were all yelling and singing saucy songs. He had the girl's head on his shoulder, but she was half cut and in her seventh heaven, so he just went on talking to me, proud of his English, you see."

"I get it," said Smiley.

" 'British spy.' Yells straight into my ear-hole. 'Fought with Czech partisans in the war. Came here calling himself Hajek and was shot by the Russian secret police.' So I just shrugged and said, 'News to me, old boy.' Not pushing, you see. Mustn't be pushy, ever. Scares them off."

"You're absolutely right," said Smiley wholeheartedly, and for an interlude patiently parried further questions about Ann, and what it was like to love—really to love—the other person all your life.

"I am a conscript," the boy began, according to Jerry Westerby. "I have to serve in the army or I can't go to university." In October he had been on basic-training manoeuvres in the forests near Brno. There was always a lot of military in the woods there; in summer the whole area was closed to the public for a month at a time. He was on a boring infantry exercise that was supposed to last two weeks, but on the third day it was called off for no reason and the troops were ordered back to town. That was the order: pack now and get back to barracks. The whole forest was to be cleared by dusk.

"Within hours, every sort of daft rumour was flying around," Jerry went on. "Some fellow said the ballistics research station at Tisnov had blown up. Somebody else said the training battalions had mutinied and were shooting up the Russian soldiers. Fresh uprising in Prague, Russians taken over the government, the Germans had attacked—God knows what hadn't happened. You know what soldiers are. Same everywhere, soldiers. Gossip till the cows come home."

The reference to the army moved Jerry Westerby to ask after certain acquaintances from his military days, people Smiley had dimly known, and forgotten. Finally they resumed.

"They broke camp, packed the lorries, and sat about waiting for the convoy to get moving. They'd gone half a mile when everything stopped again and the convoy was ordered off the road. Lorries had to duckshuffle into the trees. Got stuck in the mud, ditches, every damn thing. Chaos, apparently."

It was the Russians, said Westerby. They were coming from the direction of Brno, and they were in a very big hurry and everything that was Czech had to get out of the light or take the consequences.

"First came a bunch of motorcycles tearing down the track with lights flashing and the drivers screaming at them. Then a staff car and civilians—the boy reckoned six civilians altogether. Then two lorryloads of special troops armed to the eyebrows and wearing combat paint. Finally a truck full of tracker dogs. All making a most God-awful row. Not boring you am I, old boy?"

Westerby dabbed the sweat from his face with a handkerchief and blinked like someone coming round. The sweat had come through his silk shirt as well; he looked as if he had been under a shower. Curry not being a food he cared for, Smiley ordered two more krugs to wash away the taste.

"So that was the first part of the story. Czech troops out, Russian troops in. Got it?"

Smiley said yes, he thought he had his mind round it so far.

Back in Brno, however, the boy quickly learned that his unit's part in the proceedings was nowhere near done. Their convoy was joined up with another, and the next night for eight or ten hours they tore round the countryside with no apparent destination. They drove west to Trebic, stopped and waited while the signals section made a long transmission; then they cut back south east nearly as far as Znojmo on the Austrian border, signalling like mad as they went. No one knew who had ordered the route; no one would explain a thing. At one point they were ordered to fix bayonets; at another they pitched camp, then packed up all their kit again and pushed off. Here and there they met up with other units: near Breclav marshalling-yards, tanks going round in circles, once a pair of self-propelled guns on pre-laid track. Everywhere the story was the same: chaotic, pointless activity. The older hands said it was a Russian punishment for being Czech. Back in Brno again, the boy heard a different explanation. The Russians were after a British spy called Hajek. He'd been spying on the research station and tried to kidnap a general and the Russians had shot him.

"So the boy asked, you see," said Jerry. "Sassy little devil asked his sergeant, 'If Hajek is already shot, why do we have to tear round the countryside creating an uproar?' And the sergeant told him, 'Because it's the army.' Sergeants all over the world, what?"

Very quietly Smiley asked, "We're talking about two nights, Jerry. Which night did the Russians move into the forest?"

Jerry Westerby screwed up his face in perplexity. "That's what the boy wanted to tell me, you see, George. That's what he was trying to put over in Stan's bar. What all the rumours were about. The Russians moved in on Friday. They didn't shoot Hajek till Saturday. So the wise lads were saying: there you are, Russians were waiting for Hajek to turn up. Knew he was coming. Knew the lot. Lay in wait. Bad story, you see. Bad for our reputation—see what I mean? Bad for big chief. Bad for tribe. *How.*"

"*How,*" said Smiley, into his beer.

"That's what Toby felt, too, mind. We saw it the same way; we just reacted differently."

"So you told all to Toby," said Smiley lightly, as he passed Jerry a large dish of dal. "You had to see him anyway to tell him you'd dropped the package for him in Budapest, so you told him the Hajek story, too."

Well, that was just it, said Jerry. That was the thing that had bothered him, the thing that was rum, the thing that made him write to George, actually. "Old Tobe said it was tripe. Got all regimental and nasty. First he was keen as mustard, clapping me on the back, and Westerby for mayor. He went back to the shop, and next morning he threw the book at me. Emergency meeting, drove me round and round the park in a car, yelling blue murder. Said I was so plastered these days I didn't know fact from fiction. All that stuff. Made me a bit shirty, actually."

"I expect you wondered who he'd been talking to in between," said Smiley sympathetically. "What did he say *exactly*," he asked, not in any intense way but as if he just wanted to get it all crystal clear in his mind.

"Told me it was most likely a put-up ploy. Boy was a provocateur. Disruption job to make the Circus chase its own tail. Tore my ears off for disseminating half-baked rumours. I said to him, George: 'Old boy,' I said. 'Tobe, I was only reporting, old boy. No need to get hot under the collar. Yesterday you thought I was the cat's whiskers. No point in turning round and shooting the messenger. If you've decided you don't like the story, that's your business.' Wouldn't sort of listen any more—know what I mean? Illogical, I thought it was. Bloke like that. Hot one minute and cold the next. Not his best performance—know what I mean?"

With his left hand Jerry rubbed the side of his head, like a schoolboy pretending to think. " 'Okie-dokie,' I said, 'forget it. I'll write it up for the rag. Not the part about the Russians getting there first. The other part. "Dirty work in the forest," that sort of tripe.' I said to him, 'If it isn't good enough for the Circus, it'll do for the rag.' Then he went up the wall again.

Next day some owl rings the old man. Keep that baboon Westerby off the Ellis story. Rub his nose in the D notice: formal warning. 'All further references to Jim Ellis alias Hajek against the national interest, so put 'em on the spike.' Back to women's Ping-Pong. Cheers."

"But by then you'd written to me," Smiley reminded him.

Jerry Westerby blushed terribly. "Sorry about that," he said. "Got all xenophobe and suspicious. Comes from being on the outside: you don't trust your best friends. Trust them— well, less than strangers." He tried again: "Just that I thought old Tobe was going a bit haywire. Shouldn't have done it, should I? Against the rules." Through his embarrassment he managed a painful grin. "Then I heard on the grapevine that the firm had given you the heave-ho, so I felt an even bigger damn fool. Not hunting alone, are you, old boy? Not . . ." He left the question unasked; but not, perhaps, unanswered.

As they parted, Smiley took him gently by the arm.

"If Toby should get in touch with you, I think it better if you don't tell him we met today. He's a good fellow but he does tend to think people are ganging up on him."

"Wouldn't dream of it, old boy."

"And if he *does* get in touch in the next few days," Smiley went on—in that remote contingency, his tone suggested— "you could even warn me, actually. Then I can back you up. Don't ring *me*, come to think of it, ring this number."

Suddenly Jerry Westerby was in a hurry; that story about the shoplifting footballer couldn't wait. But as he accepted Smiley's card he did ask with a queer, embarrassed glance away from him, "Nothing untoward going on is there, old boy? No dirty work at the crossroads?" The grin was quite terrible. "Tribe hasn't gone on the rampage or anything?"

Smiley laughed and lightly laid a hand on Jerry's enormous, slightly hunched shoulder.

"Any time," said Westerby.

"I'll remember."

"I thought it was you, you see: you who telephoned the old man."

"It wasn't."

"Maybe it was Alleline."

"I expect so."

"Any time," said Westerby again. "Sorry, you know. Love to Ann." He hesitated.

"Come on, Jerry, out with it," said Smiley.

"Toby had some bad story about her and Bill the Brain. I told him to stuff it up his shirt-front. Nothing to it, is there?"

"Thanks, Jerry. So long. *How.*"

"I knew there wasn't," said Jerry, very pleased, and lifting his finger to denote the feather, padded off into his own reserves.

29

Waiting that night, alone in bed at the Islay but not yet able to sleep, Smiley once more took up the file that Lacon had given him in Mendel's house. It dated from the late fifties, when the Circus, like other Whitehall departments, was being pressed by the competition to take a hard look at the loyalty of its staff. Most of the entries were routine: telephone intercepts, surveillance reports, endless interviews with dons, friends, and nominated referees. But one document held Smiley like a magnet; he could not get enough of it. It was a letter, entered baldly on the index as "Haydon to Fanshawe, February 3, 1937." More precisely it was a handwritten letter, from the undergraduate Bill Haydon to his tutor Fanshawe, a Circus talent-spotter, introducing the young Jim Prideaux as a suitable candidate for recruitment to British intelligence. It was prefaced by a wry *explication de texte*. The Optimates were "an upper-class Christ Church Club, mainly old Etonian," wrote the unknown author. Fanshawe (P.R. de T. Fanshawe, Légion d'Honneur, O.B.E., Personal File so-and-so) was its founder; Haydon (countless cross-references) was in that year its leading light. The political complexion of the Optimates, to whom Haydon's father had also in his day belonged, was unashamedly conservative. Fanshawe, now long dead, was a passionate Empire man and "the Optimates were his private selection tank for The Great Game," ran the preface. Curiously enough, Smiley dimly remembered Fanshawe from his own day: a thin eager man with rimless spectacles, a Neville Chamberlain umbrella, and an unnatural flush to his cheeks as if he were still teething. Steed-Asprey called him the fairy godfather.

"My dear Fan, I suggest you stir yourself to make a few enquiries about the young gentleman whose name is appended on the attached fragment of human skin." [Inquisitors' super-fluous note: Prideaux] "You probably know Jim—if you know him at all—as an *athleticus* of some accomplishment. What you do not know but ought to is that he is no mean linguist nor yet a total idiot either . . ." [Here followed a biographical sum-mary of surprising accuracy: . . . Lycée Lakanal in Paris, put down for Eton, never went there, Jesuit day-school Prague, two semesters Strasbourg, parents in European banking, small aristo, live apart . . .]

"Hence our Jim's wide familiarity with parts foreign, and his rather parentless look, which I find irresistible. By the way: though he is made up of all different bits of Europe, make no mistake: the completed version is devoutly our own. At present, he is a bit of a striver and a puzzler, for he has just noticed that there is a World Beyond the Touchline and that world is me.

"But you must first hear how I met him.

"As you know, it is my habit (and your command) now and then to put on Arab costume and go down to the bazaars, there to sit among the great unwashed and give ear to the word of their prophets, that I may in due course better confound them. The juju man *en vogue* that evening came from the bosom of Mother Russia herself: one Academician Khlebnikov, pres-ently attached to the Soviet Embassy in London, a jolly, rather infectious little fellow, who managed some quite witty things among the usual nonsense. The bazaar in question was a debat-ing club called the Populars—our rival, dear Fan, and well known to you from other forays I have occasionally made. After the sermon a wildly proletarian coffee was served, to the accompaniment of a dreadfully democratic bun, and I noticed this large fellow sitting alone at the back of the room, apparently too shy to mingle. His face was familiar from the cricket field; it turns out we both played in some silly scratch team without exchanging a word. I don't quite know how to describe him. He has it, Fan. I am serious now."

Here the handwriting, till now ill-at-ease, spread out as the writer got into his stride:

"He has that heavy quiet that commands. Hard-headed, quite literally. One of those shrewd quiet ones that lead the team without anyone noticing. Fan, you know how hard it is for me to *act*. You have to remind me all the time, intellectually remind me, that unless I sample life's dangers I shall never know its mysteries. But Jim acts from instinct . . . he is functional . . . He's my other half; between us we'd make one marvellous man, except that neither of us can sing. And, Fan, you know that feeling when you just have to go out and find someone new or the world will die on you?"

The writing steadied again.

" 'Yavas Lagloo,' says I, which I understand is Russian for meet me in the woodshed or something similar, and he says 'Oh, hullo,' which I think he would have said to the Archangel Gabriel if he'd happened to be passing.

" 'What is your dilemma?' says I.

" 'I haven't got one,' says he, after about an hour's thought.

" 'Then what are you doing here? If you haven't a dilemma, how did you get in?'

"So he gives a big placid grin and we saunter over to the great Khlebnikov, shake his tiny paw for a while, then toddle back to my rooms. Where we drink. And drink. And, Fan, he drank everything in sight. Or perhaps I did, I forget. And come the dawn, do you know what we did? I will tell you, Fan. We walked solemnly down to the Parks, I sit on a bench with a stop-watch, and big Jim gets into his running kit and lopes twenty circuits. Twenty. I was quite exhausted.

"We can come to you any time; he asks nothing better than to be in my company or that of my wicked, divine friends. In short, he has appointed me his Mephistopheles and I am vastly tickled by the compliment. By the by, he is virgin, about eight feet tall, and built by the same firm that did Stonehenge. Do not be alarmed."

The file died again. Sitting up, Smiley turned the yellowed pages impatiently, looking for stronger meat. The tutors of both men aver (twenty years later) that it is inconceivable that the relationship between the two was "more than purely friendly" . . . Haydon's evidence was never called . . . Jim's tutor speaks of him as "intellectually omnivorous after long starvation"—dismisses any suggestion that he was "pink." The confrontation, which takes place at Sarratt, begins with long apologies, particularly in view of Jim's superb war record. Jim's answers breathe a pleasing straightforwardness after the extravagance of Haydon's letter. One representative of the competition present, but his voice is seldom heard. No, Jim never again met Khlebnikov or anyone representing himself as his emissary . . . No, he never spoke to him but on that one occasion. No, he had no other contact with Communists or Russians at that time; he could not remember the name of a single member of the Populars . . .

Q: *(Alleline)* Shouldn't think that keeps you awake, does it?
A: As a matter of fact, no. *(Laughter)*

Yes, he had been a member of the Populars just as he had been a member of his college drama club, the philatelic society, the modern language society, the Union and the historical society, the ethical society and the Rudolf Steiner study group . . . It was a way of getting to hear interesting lectures, and of meeting people, particularly the second. No, he had never distributed left-wing literature, though he did for a while take *Soviet Weekly* . . . No, he had never paid dues to any political party, at Oxford or later; as a matter of fact, he had never even used his vote . . . One reason why he joined so many clubs at Oxford was that after a messy education abroad he had no natural English contemporaries from school . . .

By now the inquisitors are one and all on Jim's side; everyone is on the same side against the competition and its bureaucratic meddling.

Q: *(Alleline)* As a matter of interest, since you were overseas so much, do you mind telling us where you learned your off-drive? *(Laughter)*

A: Oh, I had an uncle, actually, with a place outside Paris. He was cricket mad. Had a net and all the equipment. When I went there for holidays, he bowled at me non-stop.

[Inquisitors' note: Comte Henri de Sainte-Yvonne, dec. 1942, P.F. AF64-7.] End of interview. Competition representative would like to call Haydon as a witness but Haydon is abroad and not available. Fixture postponed *sine die* . . .

Smiley was nearly asleep as he read the last entry on the file, tossed in haphazard long after Jim's formal clearance had come through from the competition. It was a cutting from an Oxford newspaper of the day giving a review of Haydon's one-man exhibition in June, 1938, headed "Real or Surreal? An Oxford Eye."

Having torn the exhibition to shreds, the critic ended on this gleeful note: "We understand that the distinguished Mr. James Prideaux took time off from his cricket in order to help hang the canvases. He would have done better, in our opinion, to remain in the Banbury Road. However, since his role of Dobbin to the arts was the only heartfelt thing about the whole occasion, perhaps we had better not sneer too loud . . ."

He dozed, his mind a controlled clutter of doubts, suspicions, and certainties. He thought of Ann, and in his tiredness cherished her profoundly, longing to protect her frailty with his own. Like a young man, he whispered her name aloud and imagined her beautiful face bowing over him in the half-light, while Mrs. Pope Graham yelled prohibition through the keyhole. He thought of Tarr and Irina, and pondered uselessly on love and loyalty; he thought of Jim Prideaux and what tomorrow held. He was aware of a modest sense of approaching conquest. He had been driven a long way; he had sailed backwards and forwards. Tomorrow, if he was lucky, he might spot land: a peaceful little desert island, for instance. Somewhere Karla had never heard of. Just for himself and Ann. He fell asleep.

PART III

30

In Jim Prideaux's world, Thursday had gone along like any other, except that some time in the small hours of the morning the wounds in his shoulder-bone started leaking, he supposed because of the inter-house run on Wednesday afternoon. He was woken by the pain, and by the draught on the wet of his back where the discharge flowed. The other time this happened he had driven himself to Taunton General, but the nurses took one look at him and slapped him into emergency to wait for doctor somebody and an X-ray, so he filched his clothes and left. He'd done with hospitals and he'd done with medicos. English hospitals, other hospitals—Jim had done with them. They called the discharge a "track."

He couldn't reach the wound to treat it, but after last time he had hacked himself triangles of lint and stitched strings to the corners. Having put these handy on the draining board and prepared the hibitane, he heated hot water, added half a packet of salt, and gave himself an improvised shower, crouching to get his back under the jet. He soaked the lint in the hibitane, flung it across his back, strapped it from the front, and lay face down on the bunk with a vodka handy. The pain eased and a drowsiness came over him, but he knew if he gave way to it he would sleep all day, so he took the vodka bottle to the window and sat at the table correcting Five B French while Thursday's dawn slipped into the Dip and the rooks started their clatter in the elms.

Sometimes he thought of the wound as a memory he couldn't keep down. He tried his damnedest to patch it over and forget, but even his damnedest wasn't always enough.

He took the correcting slowly because he liked it, and because correcting kept his mind in the right places. At six-thirty, seven, he was done so he put on some old flannel bags and a sports coat and walked quietly down to the church, which was never locked. There he knelt a moment in the centre aisle of the Curtois antechapel, which was a family monument to the dead from two wars, and seldom visited by anyone. The cross on the little altar had been carved by sappers at Verdun. Still kneeling, Jim groped cautiously under the pew until his fingertips discovered the line of several pieces of adhesive tape, and following these, a casing of cold metal. His devotions over, he bashed up Combe Lane to the hilltop, jogging a bit to get a sweat running, because the warm did him wonders while it lasted, and rhythm soothed his vigilance.

After his sleepless night and the early-morning vodka, he was feeling a bit light-headed, so when he saw the ponies down the combe, gawping at him with their fool faces, he yelled at them in bad Somerset—"Git 'an there! Damned old fools, take your silly eyes off me!"—before pounding down the lane again for coffee, and a change of bandage.

First lesson after prayers was Five B French, and there Jim all but lost his temper: doled out a silly punishment to damn-fool Clements, draper's son; had to take it back at the end of class. In the common-room he went through another routine, of the sort he had followed in the church: quickly, mindlessly, no fumble and out. It was a simple enough notion, the mail check, but it worked. He'd never heard of anyone else who used it, among the pros, but then pros don't talk about their game. "See it this way," he would have said. "If the opposition is watching you, it's certain to be watching your mail, because mail's the easiest watch in the game—easier still if the opposition is the home side and has the co-operation of the postal service. So what do you do? Every week, from the same post-box, at the same time, at the same rate, you post one envelope to yourself and a second to an innocent party at the same address. Shove in a bit of trash—charity Christmas-card literature, come-on from local supermarket—be sure to seal envelope, stand back and compare times of arrival. If your letter turns up later than the other feller's, you've just felt someone's hot breath on you—in this case, Toby's."

Jim called it, in his odd, chipped vocabulary, water-testing, and once again the temperature was unobjectionable. The two letters clocked in together, but Jim arrived too late to pinch back the one addressed to Marjoribanks, whose turn it was to act as unwitting running mate. So, having pocketed his own, Jim snorted at the *Daily Telegraph* while Marjoribanks, with an irritable "Oh, to hell," tore up a printed invitation to join the Bible Reading Fellowship. From there, school routine carried him again till junior rugger versus St. Ermin's, which he was billed to referee. It was a fast game and when it was over his back acted up again, so he drank vodka till first bell, which he'd promised to take for young Elwes. He couldn't remember why he'd promised, but the younger staff and specially the married ones relied on him a lot for odd jobs and he let it happen. The bell was an old ship's tocsin, something Thursgood's father had dug up and now part of the tradition. As Jim rang it, he was aware of little Bill Roach standing right beside him, peering up at him with a white smile, wanting his attention, as he wanted it half a dozen times each day.

"Hullo, there, Jumbo, what's your headache this time?"

"Sir, please, sir."

"Come on, Jumbo, out with it."

"Sir, there's someone asking where you live, sir," said Roach.

Jim put down the bell.

"What sort of someone, Jumbo? Come on, I won't bite you, come on, hey . . . hey! What sort of someone? Man someone?

Woman? Juju man? Hey! Come on, old feller," he said softly, crouching to Roach's height. "No need to cry. What's the matter, then? Got a temperature?" He pulled a handkerchief from his sleeve. "What sort of someone?" he repeated in the same low voice.

"He asked at Mrs. McCullum's. He said he was a friend. Then he got back into his car; it's parked in the churchyard, sir." A fresh gust of tears. "He's just sitting in it."

"Get the hell away, damn you!" Jim called to a bunch of seniors grinning in a doorway. "Get the hell!" He went back to Roach. "Tall friend?" he asked softly. "Sloppy tall kind of fellow, Jumbo? Eyebrows and a stoop? Thin feller? Bradbury, come here and stop gawping! Stand by to take Jumbo up to Matron! Thin feller?" he asked again, very steady.

But Roach had run out of words. He had no memory any more, no sense of size or perspective; his faculty of selection in the adult world had gone. Big men, small men, old, young, crooked, straight—they were a single army of indistinguishable dangers. To say no to Jim was more than he could bear; to say yes was to shoulder the whole awful responsibility of disappointing him. He saw Jim's eyes on him; he saw the smile go out and he felt the merciful touch of a big hand upon his arm.

"Attaboy, Jumbo. Nobody ever watched like you, did they?"

Laying his head hopelessly against Bradbury's shoulder, Bill Roach closed his eyes. When he opened them, he saw through his tears that Jim was already halfway up the staircase.

Jim felt calm; almost easy. For days he had known there was someone. That also was part of his routine: to watch the places where the watchers asked. The church, where the ebb and flow of the local population is a ready topic; county hall, register of electors; tradesmen, if they kept customer accounts; pubs, if the quarry didn't use them. In England, he knew these were the natural traps that watchers automatically patrolled before they closed on you. And, sure enough, in Taunton two days ago, chatting pleasantly with the assistant librarian, Jim had come across the footprint he was looking for. A stranger, apparently down from London, had been interested in village wards; yes, a political gentleman—well, more in the line of political research, he was—professional, you could tell—and one of the things he had wanted—fancy that, now—was the up-to-date record of Jim's very village—yes, the voters' list—as they were thinking of making a door-to-door survey of a really out-of-the-way community, specially new immigrants . . . Yes, fancy that, Jim agreed, and, from then on, made his dispositions. He bought railway tickets to places—Taunton to Exeter, Taunton to London, Taunton to Swindon, valid one month—because he knew that if he were on the run again, tickets would be hard to come by. He had uncached his old identities and his gun, and hid them handily above ground; he dumped a suit-case full of clothes in the boot of the Alvis, and kept the tank full. These precautions eased his fears a little, made sleep a possibility; or would have done, before his back.

"Sir, who won, sir?"

Prebble, a new boy, in dressing gown and toothpaste, on his way to surgery. Sometimes boys spoke to Jim for no reason; his size and crookedness were a challenge.

"Sir, the match, sir, versus Saint Ermin's."

"Saint *Vermin's*," another boy piped. "Yes, sir, who won, actually?"

"Sir, *they* did, sir," Jim barked. "As you'd have known, *sir*, if you'd been watching, *sir*," and swinging an enormous fist at them in a slow feinted punch, he propelled both boys across the corridor to Matron's dispensary.

"Night, sir."

"Night, you toads," Jim sang, and stepped the other way into the sick-bay for a view of the church and the cemetery. The sick-bay was unlit; it had a look and a stink he hated. Twelve boys lay in the gloom, dozing between supper and temperatures.

"Who's that?" asked a hoarse voice.

"Rhino," said another. "Hey, Rhino, who won against Saint Vermin's?"

To call Jim by his nickname was insubordinate, but boys in sick-bay feel free from discipline.

"Rhino? Who the hell's *Rhino?* Don't know him. Not a name to me," Jim snorted, squeezing between two beds. "Put that torch away—not allowed. Damn walk-over, that's who won. Eighteen to nothing for Vermin's." That window went down almost to the floor. An old fireguard protected it from boys. "Too much damn fumble in the three-quarter line," he muttered, peering down.

"I hate rugger," said a boy called Stephen.

The blue Ford was parked in the shadow of the church, close in under the elms. From the ground floor it would have been out of sight but it didn't look hidden. Jim stood very still, a little back from the window, studying it for telltale signs. The light was fading fast, but his eyesight was good and he knew what to look for: discreet aerial, second inside mirror for the legman, burn marks under the exhaust. Sensing the tension in him, the boys became facetious.

"Sir, is it a bird, sir? Is she any good, sir?"

"Sir, are we on fire?"

"Sir, what are her legs like?"

"Gosh, sir, don't say it's Miss *Aaronson?*" At this everyone started giggling, because Miss Aaronson was old and ugly.

"Shut up," Jim snapped, quite angry. "Rude pigs, shut up." Downstairs in assembly, Thursgood was calling senior roll before prep.

Abercrombie? Sir. Astor? Sir. Blakeney? Sick, sir.

Still watching, Jim saw the car door open and George Smiley climb cautiously out, wearing a heavy overcoat.

Matron's footsteps sounded in the corridor. He heard the squeak of her rubber heels and the rattle of thermometers in a paste pot.

"My good Rhino, whatever are you doing in my sick-bay? And close that curtain, you bad boy—you'll have the whole lot of them dying of pneumonia. William Merridew, sit up at once."

Smiley was locking the car door. He was alone and he carried nothing, not even a briefcase.

"They're screaming for you in Grenville, Rhino."

"Going, gone," Jim retorted briskly and with a jerky "Night, all," he humped his way to Grenville dormitory, where he was pledged to finish a story by John Buchan. Reading aloud, he noticed that there were certain sounds he had trouble pronouncing; they caught somewhere in his throat. He knew he was sweating, he guessed his back was seeping, and by the time he had finished there was a stiffness round his jaw that was not just from reading aloud. But all these things were small symptoms beside the rage that was mounting in him as he plunged into the freezing night air. For a moment, on the overgrown terrace, he hesitated, staring at the church. It would take him three minutes, less, to untape the gun from underneath the pew, shove it into the waistband of his trousers, left side, butt inward to the groin . . .

But instinct advised him "no," so he set course directly for the trailer, singing "Hey, diddle-diddle" as loud as his tuneless voice would carry.

31

Inside the motel room, the state of restlessness was constant. Even when the traffic outside went through one of its rare lulls, the windows continued vibrating. In the bathroom the tooth glasses also vibrated, while from either wall and above them they could hear music, thumps, and bits of conversation or laughter. When a car arrived in the forecourt, the slam of the door seemed to happen inside the room, and the footsteps too. Of the furnishings, everything matched. The yellow chairs matched the yellow pictures and the yellow carpet. The candlewick bedspreads matched the orange paintwork on the doors, and by coincidence the label on the vodka bottle. Smiley had arranged things properly. He had spaced the chairs and put the vodka on the low table, and now as Jim sat glaring at him he extracted a plate of smoked salmon from the tiny refrigerator, and brown bread already buttered. His mood in contrast to Jim's was noticeably bright, his movements swift and purposeful.

"I thought we should at least be comfortable," he said, with a short smile, setting things busily on the table. "When do you have to be at school again? Is there a particular time?" Receiving no answer, he sat down. "How do you like teaching? I seem to remember you had a spell of it after the war—is that right? Before they hauled you back? Was that also a prep school? I don't think I knew."

"Look at the file," Jim barked. "Don't you come here playing cat-and-mouse with me, George Smiley. If you want to know things, read my file."

Reaching across the table, Smiley poured two drinks and handed one to Jim.

"Your personal file at the Circus?"

"Get it from housekeepers. Get it from Control."

"I suppose I should," said Smiley doubtfully. "The trouble is Control's dead and I was thrown out long before you came back. Didn't anyone bother to tell you that when they got you home?"

A softening came over Jim's face at this, and he made in slow motion one of those gestures which so amused the boys at Thursgood's. "Dear God," he muttered, "so Control's gone," and passed his left hand over the fangs of his moustache, then upward to his moth-eaten hair. "Poor old devil," he muttered. "What did he die of, George? Heart? Heart kill him?"

"They didn't even tell you this at the debriefing?" Smiley asked.

At the mention of a debriefing, Jim stiffened and his glare returned.

"Yes," said Smiley. "It was his heart."

"Who got the job?"

Smiley laughed. "My goodness, Jim, what *did* you all talk about at Sarratt, if they didn't even tell you that?"

"God damn it, who got the job? Wasn't you, was it—threw you out! Who got the job, George?"

"Alleline got it," said Smiley, watching Jim very carefully, noting how the right forearm rested motionless across the knees. "Who did you want to get it? Have a candidate, did you, Jim?" And after a long pause: "And they didn't tell you what happened to the Aggravate network, by any chance? To Pribyl, to his wife, and brother-in-law? Or the Plato network? Landkron, Eva Krieglova, Hanka Bilova? You recruited some of those, didn't you, in the old days before Roy Bland? Old Landkron even worked for you in the war."

There was something terrible just then about the way Jim would not move forward and could not move back. His red face was twisted with the strain of indecision and the sweat had gathered in studs over his shaggy ginger eyebrows.

"God damn you, George, what the devil do you want? I've drawn a line. That's what they told me to do. Draw a line, make a new life, forget the whole thing."

"Which *they* is this, Jim? Roy? Bill, Percy?" He waited. "Did they tell you what happened to Max, whoever they were? Max is all right, by the way." Rising, he briskly refreshed Jim's drink, then sat again.

"All right, come on, so what's happened to the networks?"

"They're blown. The story is you blew them to save your own skin. I don't believe it. But I have to know what happened." He went on, "I know Control made you promise by all that's holy, but that's finished. I know you've been questioned to death and I know you've pushed some things so far down you can hardly find them any more or tell the difference between truth and cover. I know you've tried to draw a line under it and say it didn't happen. I've tried that, too. Well, after tonight you can draw your line. I've brought a letter from Lacon and if you want to ring him he's standing by. I don't want to silence you. I'd rather you talked. Why didn't you come and see me at home when you got back? You could have done. You tried to see me before you left, so why not when you got back? Wasn't just the rules that kept you away."

"Didn't anyone get out?" Jim said.

"No. They seem to have been shot."

They had telephoned Lacon and now Smiley sat alone sipping his drink. From the bathroom he could hear the sound of running taps and grunts as Jim sluiced water in his face.

"For God's sake, let's get somewhere we can breathe," Jim whispered when he came back, as if it were a condition of his talking. Smiley picked up the bottle and walked beside him as they crossed the tarmac to the car.

They drove for twenty minutes, Jim at the wheel. When they parked, they were on the plateau, this morning's hilltop free of fog, and a long view down the valley. Scattered lights reached into the distance. Jim sat as still as iron, right shoulder high and hands hung down, gazing through the misted windscreen at the shadow of the hills. The sky was light and Jim's face was cut sharp against it. Smiley kept his first questions short. The anger had left Jim's voice and little by little he spoke with greater ease. Once, discussing Control's tradecraft, he even laughed, but Smiley never relaxed; he was as cautious as if he were leading a child across the street. When Jim ran on, or bridled, or showed a flash of temper, Smiley gently drew him back until they were level again, moving at the same pace and in the same direction. When Jim hesitated, Smiley coaxed him forward over the obstacle. At first, by a mixture of instinct and deduction, Smiley actually fed Jim his own story.

For Jim's first briefing by Control, Smiley suggested, they had made a rendezvous outside the Circus? They had. Where? At a service flat in St. James's, a place proposed by Control. Was anyone else present? No one. And to get in touch with Jim in the first place, Control had used MacFadean, his personal janitor? Yes, old Mac came over on the Brixton shuttle with a note asking Jim for a meeting that night. Jim was to tell Mac yes or no and give him back the note. He was on no account to use the telephone, even the internal line, to discuss the arrangement. Jim had told Mac yes and arrived at seven.

"First, I suppose, Control cautioned you?"

"Told me not to trust anyone."

"Did he name particular people?"

"Later," said Jim. "Not at first. At first, he just said trust nobody. Specially nobody in the mainstream. George?"

"Yes."

"They were shot all right, were they? Landkron, Krieglova, Bilova, the Pribyls? Straight shooting?"

"The secret police rolled up both networks the same night. After that no one knows, but next of kin were told they were dead. That usually means they are."

To their left, a line of pine trees like a motionless army climbed out of the valley.

"And then, I suppose, Control asked you what Czech identities you had running for you," Smiley resumed. "Is that right?"

He had to repeat the question.

"I told him Hajek," said Jim finally. "Vladimir Hajek, Czech journalist based on Paris. Control asked me how much longer the papers were good for. 'You never know,' I said. 'Sometimes they're blown after one trip.'" His voice went suddenly louder, as if he had lost his hold on it. "Deaf as an adder, Control was, when he wanted to be."

"So then he told you what he wanted you to do," Smiley suggested.

"First, we discussed deniability. He said if I was caught, I should keep Control out of it. A scalp-hunter ploy, bit of private enterprise. Even at the time I thought, Who the hell will ever believe that? Every word he spoke was letting blood," said Jim. "All through the briefing, I could feel his resistance to telling me anything. He didn't want me to know but he wanted me well briefed. 'I've had an offer of service,' Control says. 'Highly placed official, cover name Testify.' 'Czech official?' I ask. 'On the military side,' he says. 'You're a military minded man, Jim, you two should hit it off pretty well.' That's how it went, the whole damn way. I thought, If you don't want to tell me, don't, but stop dithering."

After more circling, said Jim, Control announced that Testify was a Czech general of artillery. His name was Stevcek; he was known as a pro-Soviet hawk in the Prague defence hierarchy, whatever that was worth; he had worked in Moscow on liaison and was one of the very few Czechs the Russians trusted. Stevcek had conveyed to Control, through an intermediary whom Control had personally interviewed in Austria, his desire to talk to a ranking officer of the Circus on matters of mutual interest. The emissary must be a Czech speaker, somebody able to take decisions. On Friday, October 20th, Stevcek would be inspecting the weapon research station at Tisnov, near Brno, about a hundred miles north of the Austrian border. From there he would be visiting a hunting-lodge for the weekend, alone. It was a place high up in the forests not far from Racice. He would be willing to receive an emissary there on the evening of Saturday, the twenty-first. He would also supply an escort to and from Brno.

Smiley asked, "Did Control have any suggestions about Stevcek's motive?"

"A girlfriend," Jim said. "Student he was going with, having a last spring, Control said; twenty years' age difference between them. She was shot during the uprising of summer '68. Till then, Stevcek had managed to bury his anti-Russian feelings in favour of his career. The girl's death put an end to all that: he was out for their blood. For four years he'd lain low acting friendly and salting away information that would really hurt them. Soon as we gave him assurances and fixed the trade routes, he was ready to sell."

"Had Control checked any of this?"

"What he could. Stevcek was well enough documented. Hungry desk general with a long list of staff appointments. Technocrat. When he wasn't on courses, he was sharpening his teeth abroad: Warsaw, Moscow, Peking for a year, spell of military attaché in Africa, Moscow again. Young for his rank."

"Did Control tell you what you were to expect in the way of information?"

"Defence material. Rocketry. Ballistics."

"Anything else?" said Smiley, passing the bottle.

"Bit of politics."

"Anything else?"

Not for the first time, Smiley had the distinct sense of stumbling not on Jim's ignorance but on the relic of a willed determination not to remember. In the dark, Jim Prideaux's breathing became suddenly deep and greedy. He had lifted his hands to the top of the wheel and was resting his chin on them, peering blankly at the frosted windscreen.

"How long were they in the bag before being shot?" Jim demanded to know.

"I'm afraid, a lot longer than you were," Smiley confessed.

"Holy God," said Jim. With a handkerchief taken from his sleeve, he wiped away the perspiration and whatever else was glistening on his face.

"The intelligence Control was hoping to get out of Stevcek," Smiley prompted, ever so softly.

"That's what they asked me at the interrogation."

"At Sarratt?"

Jim shook his head. "Over there." He nodded his untidy head towards the hills. "They knew it was Control's operation from the start. There was nothing I could say to persuade them it was mine. They laughed."

Once again Smiley waited patiently till Jim was ready to go on.

"Stevcek," said Jim. "Control had this bee in his bonnet: Stevcek would provide the answer, Stevcek would provide the key. 'What key?' I asked. 'What key?' Had his bag, that old brown music case. Pulled out charts, annotated all in his own handwriting. Charts in coloured inks, crayons. 'Your visual aid,' he says. 'This is the fellow you'll be meeting.' Stevcek's career plotted year by year: took me right through it. Military academies, medals, wives. 'He's fond of horses,' he says. 'You used to ride yourself, Jim. Something else in common— remember it.' I thought, That'll be fun, sitting in Czecho with the dogs after me, talking about breaking thoroughbred mares." He laughed a little strangely, so Smiley laughed, too.

"The appointments in red were for Stevcek's Soviet liaison work. Green were his intelligence work. Stevcek had had a finger in everything. Fourth man in Czech army intelligence, chief boffin on weaponry, secretary to the national internal security committee, military counsellor of some sort to the Praesidium, Anglo-American desk in the Czech military intelligence set-up. Then Control comes to this patch in the mid-sixties, Stevcek's second spell in Moscow, and it's marked green and red fifty-fifty. Ostensibly, Stevcek was attached to the Warsaw Pact Liaison staff as a colonel general, says Control, but that was just cover. 'He'd nothing to do with the Warsaw Pact Liaison staff. His real job was in Moscow Centre's England section. He operated under the workname of Minin,' he says. 'His job was dovetailing Czech efforts with Centre's. This is the treasure,' Control says. 'What Stevcek really wants to sell us is the name of Moscow Centre's mole inside the Circus.'"

It might be only one word, Smiley thought, remembering Max, and felt again that sudden wave of apprehension. In the end, he knew, that was all it would be: a name for the mole Gerald, a scream in the dark.

"'There's a rotten apple, Jim,' Control said, 'and he's infecting all the others.'" Jim was going straight on. His voice had stiffened, his manner also. "Kept talking about elimination, how he'd backtracked and researched and was nearly there. There were five possibilities, he said. Don't ask me how he dug them up. 'It's one of the top five,' he says. 'Five fingers to a hand.' He gave me a drink and we sat there like a pair of school-boys making up a code, me and Control. We used Tinker, Tailor. We sat there in the flat putting it together, drinking that cheap Cyprus sherry he always gave. If I couldn't get out, if there was any fumble after I'd met Stevcek, if I had to go underground, I must get the one word to him, even if I had to go to Prague and chalk it on the Embassy door or ring the Prague resident and yell it at him down the phone. Tinker, Tailor, Soldier, Sailor. Alleline was Tinker, Haydon was Tailor, Bland was Soldier, and Toby Esterhase was Poorman. We dropped Sailor because it rhymed with Tailor. You were Beggarman," Jim said.

"Was I, now? And how did you take to it, Jim, to Control's theory? How did the idea strike you, over-all?"

"Damn silly. Poppycock."

"Why?"

"Just damn silly," he repeated in a tone of military stubbornness. "Think of any one of you—mole—*mad!*"

"But did you believe it?"

"No! Lord alive, man, why do you—"

"Why not? Rationally we always accepted that sooner or
later it would happen. We always warned one another: be on
your guard. We've turned up enough members of other outfits: Russians, Poles, Czechs, French. Even the odd American.
What's so special about the British, all of a sudden?"

Sensing Jim's antagonism, Smiley opened his door and let
the cold air pour in.

"How about a stroll?" he said. "No point in being cooped
up when we can walk around."

With movement, as Smiley had anticipated, Jim found a
new fluency of speech.

They were on the western rim of the plateau, with only a
few trees standing and several lying felled. A frosted bench was
offered, but they ignored it. There was no wind, the stars were
very clear, and as Jim took up his story they went on walking
side by side, Jim adjusting always to Smiley's pace, now away
from the car, now back again. Occasionally they drew up,
shoulder to shoulder, facing down the valley.

First Jim described his recruitment of Max and the manoeuvres he went through in order to disguise his mission from the
rest of the Circus. He let it leak that he had a tentative lead to
a high-stepping Soviet cypher clerk in Stockholm, and booked
himself to Copenhagen in his old workname Ellis. Instead, he
flew to Paris, switched to his Hajek papers, and landed by
scheduled flight at Prague airport at ten on Saturday morning.
He went through the barriers like a song, confirmed the time
of his train at the terminus, then took a walk because he had a
couple of hours to kill and thought he might watch his back a
little before he left for Brno. That autumn there had been

freak bad weather. There was snow on the ground and more falling.

In Czecho, said Jim, surveillance was not usually a problem. The security services knew next to nothing about street-watching, probably because no administration in living memory had ever had to feel shy about it. The tendency, said Jim, was still to throw cars and pavement artists around like Al Capone, and that was what Jim was looking for: black Skodas and trios of squat men in trilbies. In the cold, spotting these things is marginally harder because the traffic is slow, the people walk faster, and everyone is muffled to the nose. All the same, till he reached Masaryk Station—or Central, as they're pleased to call it these days—he had no worries. But at Masaryk, said Jim, he got a whisper, more instinct than fact, about two women who'd bought tickets ahead of him.

Here, with the dispassionate ease of a professional, Jim went back over the ground. In a covered shopping arcade beside Wenceslaus Square he had been overtaken by three women, of whom the one in the middle was pushing a pram. The woman nearest the curb carried a red plastic handbag and the woman on the inside was walking a dog on a lead. Ten minutes later two other women came towards him, arm in arm, both in a hurry, and it crossed his mind that if Toby Esterhase had had the running of the job, an arrangement like this would be his handwriting; quick profile changes from the pram, backup cars standing off with short-wave radio or bleep, with a second team lying back in case the forward party overran. At Masaryk, looking at the two women ahead of him in the ticket queue, Jim was faced with the knowledge that it was happening now. There is one garment that a watcher has neither time nor inclination to change, least of all in sub-Arctic weather, and that is his shoes. Of the two pairs offered for his inspection in the ticket queue, Jim recognised one: furlined plastic, black, with zips on the outside and soles of a thick brown composition that sang slightly in the snow. He had seen them once already that morning, in the Sterba passage, worn with different top clothes by the woman who had pushed past him with the pram. From then on, Jim didn't suspect. He knew, just as Smiley would have known.

At the station bookstall, Jim bought himself a *Rude Pravo* and boarded the Brno train. If they had wanted to arrest him, they would have done so by now. They must be after the branch lines: they were following Jim in order to house his contacts. There was no point in looking for reasons, but Jim guessed that the Hajek identity was blown and they'd primed the trap the moment he booked himself on the plane. As long as they didn't know he had flushed them, he still had the edge, said Jim; and for a moment Smiley was back in occupied Germany, in his own time as a field agent, living with terror in his mouth, naked to every stranger's glance.

He was supposed to catch the thirteen-eight arriving Brno sixteen-twenty-seven. It was cancelled, so he took some wonderful stopping train, a special for the football match, which called at every other lamp-post, and each time Jim reckoned he could pick out the hoods. The quality was variable. At Chocen, a one-horse place if ever he saw one, he got out and bought himself a sausage, and there were no fewer than five, all men, spread down the tiny platform with their hands in their pockets, pretending to chat to one another and making damn fools of themselves.

"If there's one thing that distinguishes a good watcher from a bad one," said Jim, "it's the gentle art of doing damn all convincingly."

At Svitavy two men and a woman entered his carriage and talked about the big match. After a while Jim joined the conversation; he had been reading up the form in his newspaper. It was a club replay, and everyone was going crazy about it. By Brno, nothing more had happened, so he got out and sauntered through shops and crowded areas where they had to stay close for fear of losing him.

He wanted to lull them, demonstrate to them that he suspected nothing. He knew now that he was the target of what Toby would call a grand-slam operation. On foot they were working teams of seven. The cars changed so often he couldn't count them. The over-all direction came from a scruffy green van driven by a thug. The van had a loop aerial and a chalk star scrawled high on the back where no child could reach. The cars, where he picked them out, were declared to one another by a woman's handbag on the gloveboard and a passenger sun visor turned down. He guessed there were other signs but those two were good enough for him. He knew from what Toby had told him that jobs like this could cost a hundred people and were unwieldy if the quarry bolted. Toby hated them for that reason.

There is one store in Brno main square that sells everything, said Jim. Shopping in Czecho is usually a bore because there are so few retail outlets for each state industry, but this place was new and quite impressive. He bought children's toys, a scarf, some cigarettes, and tried on shoes. He guessed his watchers were still waiting for his clandestine contact. He stole a fur hat and a white plastic raincoat and a carrier bag to put them in. He loitered at the men's department long enough to confirm that two women who formed the forward pair were still behind him but reluctant to come too close. He guessed they had signalled for men to take over, and were waiting. In the men's lavatory he moved very fast. He pulled the white raincoat over his overcoat, stuffed the carrier bag into the pocket, and put on the fur hat. He abandoned his remaining parcels, then ran like a madman down the emergency staircase, smashed open a fire door, pelted down an alley, strolled up another, which was one-way, stuffed the white raincoat into the carrier bag, sauntered into another store, which was just closing, and there bought a black raincoat to replace the white one. Using the departing shoppers for cover, he squeezed into a crowded tram, stayed aboard till the last stop but one, walked for an hour, and made the fallback with Max to the minute.

Here he described his dialogue with Max and said they nearly had a standing fight.

Smiley asked, "It never crossed your mind to drop the job?"

"No. It did not," Jim snapped, his voice rising in a threat.

"Although, right from the start, you thought the idea was poppycock?" There was nothing but deference in Smiley's tone. No edge, no wish to score: only a wish to have the truth, clear under the night sky. "You just kept marching. You'd seen what was on your back, you thought the mission absurd, but you still went on, deeper and deeper into the jungle."

"I did."

"Had you perhaps changed your mind about the mission? Did curiosity draw you, after all—was that it? You wanted passionately to know who the mole was, for instance? I'm only speculating, Jim."

"What's the difference? What the hell does my motive matter in a damn mess like this?"

The half-moon was free of cloud and seemed very close. Jim sat on the bench. It was bedded in loose gravel, and while he spoke he occasionally picked up a pebble and flicked it backhand into the bracken. Smiley sat beside him, looking nowhere but at Jim. Once, to keep him company, he took a pull of vodka and thought of Tarr and Irina drinking on their hilltop in Hong Kong. It must be a habit of the trade, he decided: we talk better when there's a view.

Through the window of the parked Fiat, said Jim, the word code passed off without a hitch. The driver was one of those stiff, muscle-bound Czech Magyars with an Edwardian moustache and a mouthful of garlic. Jim didn't like him but he hadn't expected to. The two back doors were locked and there was a row about where he should sit. The Magyar said it was insecure for Jim to be in the back. It was also undemocratic. Jim told him to go to hell. He asked Jim whether he had a gun, and Jim said no, which was not true, but if the Magyar didn't believe him he didn't dare say so. He asked whether Jim had brought instructions for the General. Jim said he had brought nothing. He had come to listen.

Jim felt a bit nervy, he said. They drove and the Magyar said his piece. When they reached the lodge, there would be no lights and no sign of life. The General would be inside. If there was any sign of life—a bicycle, a car, a light, a dog—if there was any sign that the hut was occupied, then the Magyar would go in first and Jim would wait in the car. Otherwise Jim should go in alone and the Slav would do the waiting. Was that clear?

Why didn't they just go in together? Jim asked. Because the General didn't want them to, said the Slav.

They drove for half an hour by Jim's watch, heading north east at an average of thirty kilometres an hour. The track was winding and steep and tree-lined. There was no moon and he could see very little except occasionally against the skyline more forest, more hilltops. The snow had come from the north, he noticed; it was a point that was useful later. The track was clear but rutted by heavy lorries. They drove without lights. The Magyar had begun telling a dirty story and Jim guessed it was his way of being nervous. The smell of garlic was awful. He seemed to chew it all the time. Without warn-ing, he cut the engine. They were running downhill, but more slowly. They had not quite stopped when the Magyar reached for the handbrake and Jim smashed his head against the window-post and took his gun. They were at the opening to a side-path. Thirty yards down this path lay a low wooden hut. There was no sign of life.

Jim told the Magyar what he would like him to do. He would like him to wear Jim's fur hat and Jim's coat and take the walk for him. He should take it slowly, keeping his hands linked behind his back, and walking at the centre of the path. If he failed to do either of those things, Jim would shoot him. When he reached the hut, he should go inside and explain to the Gen-eral that Jim was indulging in an elementary precaution. Then he should walk back slowly, report to Jim that all was well, and that the General was ready to receive him. Or not, as the case might be.

The Magyar didn't seem very happy about this but he didn't have much choice. Before he got out, Jim made him turn the car round and face it down the path. If there was any monkey business, Jim explained, he would put on the headlights and shoot him along the beam, not once but several times, and not in the legs. The Magyar began his walk. He had nearly reached the hut when the whole area was floodlit: the hut, the path, and a large space around. Then a number of things happened at once. Jim didn't see everything, because he was busy turning the car. He saw four men fall out of the trees, and so far as he could work out, one of them had sandbagged the Magyar. Shooting started but none of the four paid it any attention; they were standing back while somebody took photographs. The shooting seemed to be directed at the clear sky behind the floodlights. It was very theatrical. Flares exploded, Very lights went up, even tracers, and as Jim raced the Fiat down the track, he had the impression of leaving a military tattoo at its climax. He was almost clear—he really felt he *was* clear—when from the woods to his right someone opened up with a machine-gun at close quarters. The first burst shot off a back wheel and turned the car over. He saw the wheel fly over the bonnet as the car took to the ditch on the left. The ditch might have been ten feet deep but the snow let him down kindly. The car didn't burn so he lay behind it and waited, facing across the track hoping to get a shot at the machine-gunner. The next burst came from behind him and threw him up against the car. The woods must have been crawling with troops. He knew that he had been hit twice. Both shots caught him in the right shoulder and it seemed amazing to him, as he lay there watching the tattoo, that they hadn't taken off the arm. A klaxon sounded, maybe two or three. An ambulance rolled down the track and there was still enough shooting to frighten the game for years. The ambulance reminded him of those old Hollywood fire engines, it was so upright. A whole mock battle was taking place, yet the ambulance boys stood gazing at him without a care in the world. He was losing consciousness as he heard a second car arrive, and men's voices, and more photographs were taken, this time of the right man. Someone gave orders, but he couldn't tell what they were because they were given in Russian. His one thought, as they dumped him on the stretcher and the lights went out, concerned going back to London. He imagined himself in the St. James's flat, with the coloured charts and the sheaf of notes, sitting in the armchair and explaining to Control how in their old age the two of them had walked into the biggest sucker's punch in the history of the trade. His only consolation was that they had sandbagged the Magyar, but looking back Jim wished very much he'd broken his neck for him: it was a thing he could have managed very easily, and without compunction.

32

The describing of pain was to Jim an indulgence to be dispensed with. To Smiley, his stoicism had something awesome about it, the more so because he seemed unaware of it. The gaps in his story came mainly where he passed out, he explained. The ambulance drove him, so far as he could fathom, further north. He guessed this from the trees when they opened the door to let the doctor in: the snow was heaviest when he looked back. The surface was good and he guessed they were on the road to Hradec. The doctor gave him an injection; he came round in a prison hospital with barred windows high up, and three men watching him. He came round again after the operation, in a different cell with no windows at all, and he thought probably the first questioning took place there, about seventy-two hours after they'd patched him up, but time was already a problem and of course they'd taken away his watch.

They moved him a lot. Either to different rooms, depending on what they were going to do with him, or to other prisons, depending on who was questioning him. Sometimes they just moved to keep him awake, walking him down cell corridors at night. He was also moved in lorries, and once by a Czech transport plane, but he was trussed for the flight and hooded, and passed out soon after they took off. The interrogation which followed this flight was very long. Otherwise he had little sense of progression from one questioning to another and thinking didn't get it any straighter for him—rather the reverse. The thing that was still strongest in his memory was the plan of campaign he formed while he waited for the first interrogation to begin. He knew silence would be impossible and that for his own sanity, or survival, there had to be a dialogue, and at the end of it they had to think he had told them what he knew, all he knew. Lying in hospital, he prepared his mind into lines of defence behind which, if he was lucky, he could fall back stage by stage until he had given the impression of total defeat. His forward line, he reckoned, and his most expendable, was the bare bones of Operation Testify. It was anyone's guess whether Stevcek was a plant, or had been betrayed. But whichever was the case, one thing was certain: the Czechs knew more about Stevcek than Jim did. His first concession, therefore, would be the Stevcek story, since they had it already; but he would make them work for it. First he would deny everything and stick to his cover. After a fight, he would admit to being a British spy and give his workname Ellis, so that if they published it, the Circus would at least know he was alive and trying. He had little doubt that the elaborate trap and the photographs augured a lot of ballyhoo. After that, in accordance with his understanding with Control, he would describe the operation as his own show, mounted without the consent of his superiors, and calculated to win him favour. And he would bury, as deep as they could go and deeper, all thoughts of a spy inside the Circus.

"No mole," said Jim, to the black outlines of the Quantocks. "No meeting with Control, no service flat in St. James's."

"No Tinker, Tailor."

His second line of defence would be Max. He proposed at first to deny that he had brought a legman at all. Then he might say he had brought one but didn't know his name. Then, because everyone likes a name, he would give them one: the wrong one first, then the right one. By that time Max must be clear, or underground, or caught.

Now came in Jim's imagination a succession of less strongly held positions: recent scalp-hunter operations, Circus tittle-tattle—anything to make his interrogators think he was broken and talking free and that this was all he had, they had passed the last trench. He would rack his memory for back scalp-hunter cases, and if necessary he would give them the names of one or two Soviet and satellite officials who had recently been turned or burned; of others who in the past had made a one-time sale of assets and, since they had not defected, might now be considered to be in line for burning or a second bite. He would throw them any bone he could think of—sell them, if necessary, the entire Brixton stable. And all of this would be the smokescreen to disguise what seemed to Jim to be his most vulnerable intelligence, since they would certainly expect him to possess it: the identity of members of the Czech end of the Aggravate and Plato networks.

"Landkron, Krieglova, Bilova, the Pribyls," said Jim.

Why did he choose the same order for their names? Smiley wondered.

For a long time Jim had had no responsibility for these networks. Years earlier, before he took over Brixton, he had helped establish them, recruited some of the founder members; since then, a lot had happened to them in the hands of Bland and Haydon of which he knew nothing. But he was certain that he still knew enough to blow them both sky high. And what worried him most was the fear that Control, or Bill, or Percy Alleline, or whoever had the final say these days, would be too greedy, or too slow, to evacuate the networks by the time Jim, under forms of duress he could only guess at, had no alternative but to break completely.

"So that's the joke," said Jim, with no humour whatever. "They couldn't have cared less about the networks. They asked me half a dozen questions about Aggravate, then lost interest. They knew damn well that Testify wasn't my private brain-child and they knew all about Control buying the

Stevcek pass in Vienna. They began exactly where I wanted to end: with the briefing in St. James's. They didn't ask me about a legman; they weren't interested in who had driven me to the rendezvous with the Magyar. All they wanted to talk about was Control's rotten-apple theory."

One word, thought Smiley again, it might be just one word. He said, "Did they actually know the St. James's address?"

"They knew the brand of the bloody sherry, man."

"And the charts?" asked Smiley quickly. "The music case?"

"No." He added, "Not at first. No."

Thinking inside out, Steed-Asprey used to call it. They knew because the mole Gerald had told them, thought Smiley. The mole knew what the housekeepers had succeeded in getting out of old MacFadean. The Circus conducts its post-mortem: Karla has the benefit of its findings in time to use them on Jim.

"So I suppose by now you were beginning to think Control was right: there *was* a mole," said Smiley.

Jim and Smiley were leaning on a wooden gate. The ground sloped sharply away from them in a long sweep of bracken and fields. Below them lay another village, a bay, and a thin ribbon of moonlit sea.

"They went straight to the heart of it. 'Why did Control go it alone? What did he hope to achieve?' 'His come-back,' I said. So they laugh: 'With tinpot information about military emplacements in the area of Brno? That wouldn't even buy him a square meal in his club.' 'Maybe he was losing his grip,' I said. If Control was losing his grip, they said, who was stamping on his fingers? Alleline, I said, that was the buzz; Alleline and Control were in competition to provide intelligence. But in Brixton we only got the rumours, I said. 'And what is Alleline producing that Control is *not* producing?' 'I don't know.' 'But you just said that Alleline and Control are in competition to provide intelligence.' 'It's rumour. I don't know.' Back to the cooler."

Time, said Jim, at this stage lost him completely. He lived either in the darkness of the hood, or in the white light of the cells. There was no night or day, and to make it even more weird they kept the noises going most of the time.

They were working him on the production-line principle, he explained: no sleep, relays of questions, a lot of disorientation, a lot of muscle, till the interrogation became to him a slow race between going a bit dotty, as he called it, and breaking completely. Naturally, he hoped he'd go dotty but that wasn't something you could decide for yourself, because they had a way of bringing you back. A lot of the muscle was done electrically.

"So we start again. New tack. 'Stevcek was an important general. If he asked for a senior British officer, he could expect him to be properly informed about all aspects of his career. Are you telling us you did not inform yourself?' 'I'm saying I got my information from Control.' 'Did you read Stevcek's dossier at the Circus?' 'No.' 'Did Control?' 'I don't know.' 'What conclusions did Control draw from Stevcek's second appointment in Moscow? Did Control speak to you about Stevcek's role in the Warsaw Pact Liaison Committee?' 'No.' They stuck to that question and I suppose I stuck to my answer, because after a few more 'no's they got a bit crazy. They seemed to lose patience. When I passed out, they hosed me down and had another crack."

Movement, said Jim. His narrative had become oddly jerky. Cells, corridors, car . . . at the airport V.I.P. treatment and a mauling before the aeroplane . . . on the flight, dropped off to sleep and was punished for it. "Came round in a cell again, smaller, no paint on the walls. Sometimes I thought I was in Russia. I worked out by the stars that we had flown east. Sometimes I was in Sarratt, back on the interrogation resistance course."

For a couple of days they let him alone. Head was muzzy. He kept hearing the shooting in the forest and he saw the tattoo again, and when finally the big session started—the one he remembered as the marathon—he had the disadvantage of feeling half defeated when he went in.

"Matter of health, much as anything," he explained, very tense now.

"We could take a break if you want," Smiley said, but where Jim was, there were no breaks, and what he wanted was irrelevant.

That was the long one, Jim said. Sometime in the course of it, he told them about Control's notes and his charts and the coloured inks and crayons. They were going at him like the devil and he remembered an all-male audience, at one end of the room, peering like a lot of damn medicos and muttering to one another, and he told them about the crayons just to keep the talk alive, to make them stop and listen. They listened but they didn't stop.

"Once they had the colours, they wanted to know what the colours meant. 'What did blue mean?' 'Control didn't have blue.' 'What did red mean? What did red stand for? Give us an example of red on the chart. What did red mean? What did red mean? What did red mean?' Then everybody clears out except a couple of guards and one cold little fellow, stiff back, seemed to be head boy. The guards take me over to a table, and this little fellow sits beside me like a bloody gnome with his hands folded. He's got two crayons in front of him, red and green, and a chart of Stevcek's career."

It wasn't that Jim broke exactly; he just ran out of invention. He couldn't think up any more stories. The truths that he had locked away so deeply were the only things that suggested themselves.

"So you told him about the rotten apple," Smiley suggested. "And you told him about Tinker, Tailor."

Yes, Jim agreed, he did. He told him that Control believed Stevcek could identify a mole inside the Circus. He told him about the Tinker, Tailor code and who each of them was, name by name.

"What was his reaction?"

"Thought for a bit, then offered me a cigarette. Hated the damn thing."

"Why?"

"Tasted American. Camel, one of those."

"Did he smoke one himself?"

Jim gave a short nod. "Bloody chimney," he said.

Time, after that, began once more to flow, said Jim. He was taken to a camp, he guessed outside a town, and lived in a compound of huts with a double perimeter of wire. With the help of a guard, he was soon able to walk; one day they even went for a stroll in the forest. The camp was very big; his own compound was only a part of it. At night he could see the glow of a city to the east. The guards wore denims and didn't speak, so he still had no way of telling whether he was in Czecho or in Russia, but his money was heavily on Russia, and when the surgeon came to take a look at his back he used a Russian-English interpreter to express his contempt for his predecessor's handiwork. The interrogation continued sporadically, but without hostility. They put a fresh team on him but it was a leisurely crowd by comparison with the first eleven. One night he was taken to a military airport and flown by R.A.F. fighter to Inverness. From there he went by small plane to Elstree, then by van to Sarratt; both were night journeys.

Jim was winding up fast. He was already launched on his experiences at the Nursery, in fact, when Smiley asked, "And the headman, the little cold one: you never saw him again?"

Once, Jim conceded; just before he left.

"What for?"

"Gossip." Much louder. "Lot of damned tripe about Circus personalities, matter of fact."

"Which personalities?"

Jim ducked that question. Tripe about who was on the up staircase, he said, who was on the down. Who was next in line for Chief: "'How should I know,' I said. 'Bloody janitors hear it before Brixton does.'"

"So who came in for the tripe, precisely?"

Mainly Roy Bland, said Jim sullenly. How did Bland reconcile his left-wing leanings with his work at the Circus? He hasn't got any left-wing leanings, said Jim, that's how. What was Bland's standing with Esterhase and Alleline? What did Bland think of Bill's paintings? Then how much Roy drank and what would become of him if Bill ever withdrew his support for him? Jim gave meagre answers to these questions.

"Was anyone else mentioned?"

"Esterhase," Jim snapped, in the same taut tone. "Bloody man wanted to know how anyone could trust a Hungarian."

Smiley's next question seemed, even to himself, to cast an absolute silence over the whole black valley.

"And what did he say about me?" He repeated: "What did he say about me?"

"Showed me a cigarette lighter. Said it was yours. Present from Ann. 'With all my love.' Her signature. Engraved."

"Did he mention how he came by it? What did he say, Jim? Come on, I'm not going to weaken at the knees just because some Russian hood made a bad joke about me."

Jim's answer came out like an army order. "He reckoned that after Bill Haydon's fling with her, she might care to redraft the inscription." He swung away towards the car. "I told him," he shouted furiously. "Told him to his wrinkled little face. You can't judge Bill by things like that. Artists have totally different standards. See things we can't see. Feel things that are beyond us. Bloody little man just laughed. 'Didn't know his pictures were that good,' he said. I told him, George. 'Go to hell. Go to bloody hell. If you had one Bill Haydon in your damned outfit, you could call it set and match.' I said to him: 'Christ Almighty,' I said, 'what are you running over here? A service or the bloody Salvation Army?' "

"That was well said," Smiley remarked at last, as if commenting on some distant debate. "And you'd never seen him before?"

"Who?"

"The little frosty chap. He wasn't familiar to you—from long ago, for instance? Well, you know how we are. We're trained, we see a lot of faces, photographs of Centre personalities, and sometimes they stick. Even if we can't put a name to them any more. This one didn't, anyway. I just wondered. It occurred to me you had a lot of time to think," he went on, conversationally. "You lay there recovering, waiting to come home, and what else had you to do, but think?" He waited. "So what did you think of, I wonder? The mission. Your mission, I suppose."

"Off and on."

"With what conclusions? Anything useful? Any suspicions, insights, any hints for me to take away?"

"Damn all, thank you," Jim snapped, very hard. "You know me, George Smiley. I'm not a juju man, I'm a—"

"You're a plain fieldman who lets the other chaps do his thinking. Nevertheless, when you know you have been led into a king-sized trap, betrayed, shot in the back, and have nothing to do for months but lie or sit on a bunk, or pace a Russian cell, I would guess that even the most dedicated man of action"—his voice had lost none of its friendliness—"might put his mind to wondering how he landed in such a scrape. Let's take Operation Testify a minute," Smiley suggested to the motionless figure before him. "Testify ended Control's career. He was disgraced and he couldn't pursue his mole, assuming there was one. The Circus passed into other hands. With a sense of timeliness, Control died. Testify did something else, too. It revealed to the Russians—through you, actually—the exact reach of Control's suspicions. That he'd narrowed the field to five, but apparently no further. I'm not suggesting you should have fathomed all that for yourself in your cell, waiting. After all, you had no idea, sitting in the pen, that Control had been thrown out—though it might have occurred to you that the

Russians laid on that mock battle in the forest in order to raise a wind. Did it?"

"You've forgotten the networks," said Jim dully.

"Oh, the Czechs had the networks marked down long before you came on the scene. They only rolled them up in order to compound Control's failure."

The discursive, almost chatty tone with which Smiley threw out these theories found no resonance in Jim. Having waited in vain for him to volunteer some word, Smiley let the matter drop. "Well, let's just go over your reception at Sarratt, shall we? To wrap it up?"

In a rare moment of forgetfulness, he helped himself to the vodka bottle before passing it to Jim.

To judge by his voice, Jim had had enough. He spoke fast and angrily, with that same military shortness which was his refuge from intellectual incursions.

For four days Sarratt was limbo, he said: "Ate a lot, drank a lot, slept a lot. Walked round the cricket ground." He'd have swum, but the pool was under repair, as it had been six months before: damned inefficient. He had a medical, watched television in his hut, and played a bit of chess with Cranko, who was running reception.

Meanwhile he waited for Control to show up, but he didn't. The first person from the Circus to visit him was the resettlement officer, talking about a friendly teaching agency; next came some pay wallah to discuss his pension entitlement; then the doctor again to assess him for a gratuity. He waited for the inquisitors to appear but they never did, which was a relief because he didn't know what he would have told them until he had the green light from Control and he'd had enough of questions. He guessed Control was holding them off. It seemed mad that he should keep from the inquisitors what he had already told the Russians and the Czechs, but until he heard from Control, what else could he do? When Control still sent no word, he formed notions of presenting himself to Lacon and telling his story. Then he decided that Control was waiting for him to get clear of the Nursery before he contacted him. He had a relapse for a few days, and when it was over Toby Esterhase turned up in a new suit, apparently to shake him by the hand and wish him luck. But in fact to tell him how things stood.

"Bloody odd fellow to send, but he seemed to have come up in the world. Then I remembered what Control said about only using chaps from outstations."

Esterhase told him that the Circus had very nearly gone under as a result of Testify and that Jim was currently the Circus's Number One leper. Control was out of the game and a reorganisation was going on in order to appease Whitehall.

"Then he told me not to worry," said Jim.

"In what way not worry?"

"About my special brief. He said a few people knew the real story, and I needn't worry because it was being taken care of. All the facts were known. Then he gave me a thousand quid in cash to add to my gratuity."

"Who from?"

"He didn't say."

"Did he mention Control's theory about Stevcek? Centre's spy inside the Circus?"

"The facts were known," Jim repeated, glaring. "He *ordered* me not to approach anyone or try to get my story heard, because it was all being taken care of at the highest level and anything I did might spoil the kill. The Circus was back on the road. I could forget Tinker, Tailor and the whole damn game—moles, everything. 'Drop out,' he said. 'You're a lucky man, Jim,' he kept saying. 'You've been ordered to become a lotus-eater.' I could forget it. Right? Forget it. Just behave as if it had never happened." He was shouting. "And that's what I've been doing: obeying orders and forgetting!"

The night landscape seemed to Smiley suddenly innocent; it was like a great canvas on which nothing bad or cruel had ever been painted. Side by side, they stared down the valley over the clusters of lights to a tor raised against the horizon. A single tower stood at its top and for a moment it marked for Smiley the end of the journey.

"Yes," he said. "I did a bit of forgetting, too. So Toby actually mentioned Tinker, Tailor to you. However did he get hold of *that* story, unless . . . And no word from Bill?" he went on. "Not even a postcard."

"Bill was abroad," said Jim shortly.

"Who told you that?"

"Toby."

"So you never saw Bill; since Testify, your oldest, closest friend, he disappeared."

"You heard what Toby said. I was out of bounds. Quarantine."

"Bill was never much of a one for regulations, though, was he?" said Smiley, in a reminiscent tone.

"And you were never one to see him straight," Jim barked.

"Sorry I wasn't there when you called on me, before you left for Czecho," Smiley remarked after a small pause. "Control had pushed me over to Germany to get me out of the light and when I came back—what was it that you wanted, exactly?"

"Nothing. Thought Czecho might be a bit hairy. Thought I'd give you the nod, say goodbye."

"Before a mission?" cried Smiley in mild surprise. "Before such a *special* mission?" Jim showed no sign that he had heard. "Did you give anyone else the nod? I suppose we were all away. Toby, Roy—Bill; did he get one?"

"No one."

"Bill was on leave, wasn't he? But I gather he was around, all the same."

"No one," Jim insisted, as a spasm of pain caused him to lift his right shoulder and rotate his head. "All out," he said.

"That's very unlike you, Jim," said Smiley in the same mild tone, "to go round shaking hands with people before you go on vital missions. You must have been getting sentimental in your old age. It wasn't . . ." he hesitated. "It wasn't advice or anything that you wanted, was it? After all, you did think the mission was poppycock, didn't you? And that Control was losing his grip. Perhaps you felt you should take your problem to a third party? It all had rather a mad air, I agree."

Learn the facts, Steed-Asprey used to say, then try on the stories like clothes.

With Jim still locked in a furious silence, they returned to the car.

At the motel Smiley drew twenty postcard-sized photographs from the recesses of his coat and laid them out in two lines across the ceramic table. Some were snaps, some portraits; all were of men and none of them looked English. With a grimace Jim picked out two and handed them to Smiley. He was sure of the first, he muttered, less sure of the second. The first was the headman, the cool little man. The second was one of the swine who watched from the shadows while the thugs took Jim to pieces. Smiley returned the photographs to his pocket. As he topped up their glasses for a nightcap, a less tortured observer than Jim might have noticed a sense not of triumph but of ceremony about him; as though the drink were putting a seal on something.

"So when was the last time you saw Bill, actually? To talk to," Smiley asked, just as one might about any old friend. He had evidently disturbed Jim in other thoughts, for he took a moment to lift his head and catch the question.

"Oh, round about," he said carelessly. "Bumped into him in the corridors, I suppose."

"And to talk to? Never mind." For Jim had returned to his other thoughts.

Jim would not be driven all the way to school. Smiley had to drop him short, at the top of the tarmac path that led through the graveyard to the church. He had left some workbooks in the antechapel, he said. Momentarily, Smiley felt disposed to disbelieve him, but could not understand why. Perhaps because he had come to the opinion that after thirty years in the trade, Jim was still a rather poor liar. The last Smiley saw of him was that lopsided shadow striding towards the Norman porch as his heels cracked like gunshot between the tombs.

Smiley drove to Taunton and from the Castle Hotel made a string of telephone calls. Though exhausted, he slept fitfully between visions of Karla sitting at Jim's table with two crayons, and Cultural Attaché Polyakov alias Viktorov, fired by concern for the safety of his mole Gerald, waiting impatiently in the interrogation cell for Jim to break. Lastly of Toby Esterhase bobbing into Sarratt in place of the absent Haydon, cheerfully advising Jim to forget all about Tinker, Tailor, and his dead inventor, Control.

The same night, Peter Guillam drove west, clean across England to Liverpool, with Ricki Tarr as his only passenger. It was a tedious journey in beastly conditions. For most of it, Tarr boasted about the rewards he would claim, and the promotion, once he had carried out his mission. From there he talked about his women: Danny, her mother, Irina. He seemed to envisage a *ménage à quatre* in which the two women would jointly care for Danny, and for himself.

"There's a lot of the mother in Irina. That's what frustrates her, naturally." Boris, he said, could get lost; he would tell Karla to keep him. As their destination approached, his mood changed again and he fell silent. The dawn was cold and foggy. In the suburbs they had to drop to a crawl and cyclists overtook them. A reek of soot and steel filled the car.

"Don't hang about in Dublin, either," said Guillam suddenly. "They expect you to work the soft routes, so keep your head down. Take the first plane out."

"We've been through all that."

"Well, I'm going through it all again," Guillam retorted. "What's Mackelvore's workname?"

"For Christ's sake," Tarr breathed, and gave it.

It was still dark when the Irish ferry sailed. There were soldiers and police everywhere: this war, the last, the one before. A fierce wind was blowing off the sea and the going looked rough. At the dockside, a sense of fellowship briefly touched the small crowd as the ship's lights bobbed quickly into the gloom. Somewhere a woman was crying, somewhere a drunk was celebrating his release.

He drove back slowly, trying to work himself out: the new Guillam who starts at sudden noises, has nightmares, and not only can't keep his girl but makes up crazy reasons for distrusting her. He had challenged Camilla about Sand, and the hours she kept, and about her secrecy in general. After listening with her grave brown eyes fixed on him, she told him he was a fool, and left. "I am what you think I am," she said, and fetched her things from the bedroom. From his empty flat he telephoned Toby Esterhase, inviting him for a friendly chat later that day.

33

Smiley sat in the Minister's Rolls, with Lacon beside him. In Ann's family the car was called the black bedpan, and hated for its flashiness. The chauffeur had been sent to find himself breakfast. The Minister sat in the front and everyone looked forward down the long bonnet, across the river to the foggy towers of Battersea Power Station. The Minister's hair was full at the back, and licked into small black horns around the ears.

"If you're right," the Minister declared, after a funereal silence. "I'm not saying you're not, but if you are, how much porcelain will he break at the end of the day?"

Smiley did not quite understand.

"I'm talking about scandal. Gerald gets to Moscow. Right, so then what happens? Does he leap on a soap-box and laugh his head off in public about all the people he's made fools of over here? I mean, Christ, we're all in this together, aren't we? I don't see why we should let him go just so's he can pull the bloody roof down over our heads and the competition sweep the bloody pool."

He tried a different tack. "I mean to say, just because the Russians know our secrets, doesn't mean everyone else has to. We got plenty of other fish to fry apart from them, don't we? What about all the black men: are they going to be reading the gory details in the Walla Walla *News* in a week's time?"

Or his constituents, Smiley thought.

"I think that's always been a point the Russians accept," said Lacon. "After all, if you make your enemy look a fool, you lose the justification for engaging him." He added, "They've never made use of their opportunities so far, have they?"

"Well, make sure they toe the line. Get it in writing. No, don't. But you tell them what's sauce for the goose is sauce for the gander. We don't go round publishing the batting order at Moscow Centre, so they can bloody well play ball, too, for once."

Declining a lift, Smiley said the walk would do him good.

It was Thursgood's day for duty and he felt it badly. Headmasters, in his opinion, should be above the menial tasks; they should keep their minds clear for policy and leadership. The flourish of his Cambridge gown did not console him, and as he stood in the gymnasium watching the boys file in for morning line-up, his eye fixed on them balefully, if not with downright hostility. It was Marjoribanks, though, who dealt the death-blow.

"He said it was his mother," he explained, in a low murmur to Thursgood's left ear. "He'd had a telegram and proposed to leave at once. He wouldn't even stay for a cup of tea. I promised to pass on the message."

"It's monstrous, absolutely monstrous," said Thursgood.

"I'll take his French, if you like. We can double up Five and Six."

"I'm furious," said Thursgood. "I can't think, I'm so furious."

"And Irving says he'll take the rugger final."

"Reports to be written, exams, rugger finals to play off. What's supposed to be the matter with the woman? Just a flu, I suppose, a seasonal flu. Well, we've all got that, so have our mothers. Where does she live?"

"I rather gathered from what he said to Sue that she was dying."

"Well, that's *one* excuse he won't be able to use again," said Thursgood, quite unmollified, and with a sharp bark quelled the noise and read the roll.

"Roach?"

"Sick, sir."

That was all he needed to fill his cup. The school's richest boy having a nervous breakdown about his wretched parents, and the father threatening to remove him.

34

It was almost four o'clock on the afternoon of the same day.
Safe houses I have known, thought Guillam, looking round
the gloomy flat. He could write of them the way a commercial
traveller could write about hotels: from your five-star hall of
mirrors in Belgravia, with Wedgwood pilasters and gilded oak
leaves, to this two-room scalp-hunters' shakedown in Lexham
Gardens, smelling of dust and drains, with a three-foot fire
extinguisher in the pitch-dark hall. Over the fireplace, cava-
liers drinking out of pewter. On the nest of tables, sea-shells
for ashtrays; and in the grey kitchen, anonymous instructions
to "Be Sure and Turn Off the Gas Both Cocks." He was crossing the hall when the house bell rang, exactly on time. He
lifted the phone and heard Toby's distorted voice howling in
the earpiece. He pressed the button and heard the clunk of the
electric lock echoing in the stairwell. He opened the front
door but left it on the chain till he was sure Toby was alone.

"How are we?" said Guillam cheerfully, letting him in.

"Fine, actually, Peter," said Toby, pulling off his coat and
gloves.

There was tea on a tray: Guillam had prepared it, two cups.
To safe houses belongs a certain standard of catering. Either
you are pretending that you live there or that you are adept
anywhere; or simply that you think of everything. In the trade,

naturalness is an art, Guillam decided. That was something Camilla could not appreciate.

"Actually, it's quite strange weather," Esterhase announced, as if he had really been analysing its qualities. Safe-house small-talk was never much better. "One walks a few steps and is completely exhausted already. So we are expecting a Pole?" he said, sitting down. "A Pole in the fur trade who you think might run courier for us."

"Due here any minute."

"Do we know him? I had my people look up the name but they found no trace."

My people, thought Guillam: I must remember to use that one. "The Free Poles made a pass at him a few months back and he ran a mile," he said. "Then Karl Stack spotted him round the warehouses and thought he might be useful to the scalp-hunters." He shrugged. "I liked him but what's the point? We can't even keep our own people busy."

"Peter, you are very generous," said Esterhase reverently, and Guillam had the ridiculous feeling he had just tipped him. To his relief, the front doorbell rang and Fawn took up his place in the doorway.

"Sorry about this, Toby," Smiley said, a little out of breath from the stairs. "Peter, where shall I hang my coat?"

Turning him to the wall, Guillam lifted Toby's unresisting hands and put them against it, then searched him for a gun, taking his time. Toby had none.

"Did he come alone?" Guillam asked. "Or is there some little friend waiting in the road?"

"Looked all clear to me," said Fawn.

Smiley was at the window, gazing down into the street. "Put the light out a minute, will you?" he said.

"Wait in the hall," Guillam ordered, and Fawn withdrew, carrying Smiley's coat. "Seen something?" he asked Smiley, joining him at the window.

Already the London afternoon had taken on the misty pinks and yellows of evening. The square was Victorian residential; at the centre, a caged garden, already dark. "Just a shadow, I suppose," said Smiley with a grunt, and turned back to Esterhase. The clock on the mantelpiece chimed four. Fawn must have wound it up.

"I want to put a thesis to you, Toby. A notion about what's going on. May I?"

Esterhase didn't move an eyelash. His little hands rested on the wooden arms of his chair. He sat quite comfortably, but slightly to attention, toes and heels of his polished shoes together.

"You don't have to speak at all. There's no risk to listening, is there?"

"Maybe."

"It's two years ago. Percy Alleline wants Control's job, but he has no standing in the Circus. Control has made sure of that. Control is sick and past his prime but Percy can't dislodge him. Remember the time?"

Esterhase gave a neat nod.

"One of those silly seasons," said Smiley, in his reasonable voice. "There isn't enough work outside so we start intriguing around the service, spying on one another. Percy's sitting in his room one morning with nothing to do. He has a paper appointment as Operational Director, but in practice he's a rubber stamp between the regional sections and Control, if that. Percy's door opens and somebody walks in. We'll call him Gerald—it's just a name. 'Percy,' he says, 'I've stumbled on a major Russian source. It could be a gold-mine.' Or perhaps he doesn't say anything till they're outside the building, because Gerald is very much a fieldman; he doesn't like to talk with walls and telephones around. Perhaps they take a walk in the park or a drive in a car. Perhaps they eat a meal somewhere, and at this stage there isn't much Percy can do but listen.

Percy's had very little experience of the European scene, remember, least of all Czecho or the Balkans. He cut his teeth in South America and after that he worked the old possessions: India, the Middle East. He doesn't know a lot about Russians or Czechs or what you will; he's inclined to see red as red and leave it at that. Unfair?"

Esterhase pursed his lips and frowned a little, as if to say he never discussed a superior.

"Whereas Gerald is an expert on those things. His operational life has been spent weaving and ducking round the Eastern markets. Percy's out of his depth but keen. Gerald's on his home ground. This Russian source, says Gerald, could be the richest the Circus has had for years. Gerald doesn't want to say too much but he expects to be getting some trade samples in a day or two, and when he does, he'd like Percy to run his eye over them just to get a notion of the quality. They can go into source details later. 'But why me?' says Percy. 'What's it all about?' So Gerald tells him. 'Percy,' he says, 'some of us in the regional sections are worried sick by the level of operational losses. There seems to be a jinx around. Too much loose talk inside the Circus and out. Too many people being cut in on distribution. Out in the field, our agents are going to the wall, our networks are being rolled up or worse, and every new ploy ends up a street accident. We want you to help us put that right.' Gerald is not mutinous, and he's careful not to suggest that there's a traitor inside the Circus who's blowing all the operations, because you and I know that once talk like that gets around the machinery grinds to a halt. Anyway the last thing Gerald wants is a witch-hunt. But he does say that the place is leaking at the joints, and that slovenliness at the top is leading to failures lower down. All balm to Percy's ear. He lists the recent scandals and he's careful to lean on Alleline's own Middle East adventure, which went so wrong and nearly cost Percy his career. Then he makes his proposal. This is what he says. In my thesis, you understand—it's just a thesis."

"Sure, George," said Toby, and licked his lips.

"Another thesis would be that Alleline was his own Gerald, you see. It just happens that I don't believe it; I don't believe Percy is capable of going out and buying himself a top Russian spy and manning his own boat from then on. I think he'd mess it up."

"Sure," said Esterhase, with absolute confidence.

"So this, in my thesis, is what Gerald says to Percy next. 'We—that is, myself and those like-minded souls who are associated with this project—would like you to act as our father figure, Percy. We're not political men, we're operators. We don't understand the Whitehall jungle. But you do. You handle the committees, we'll handle Merlin. If you act as our cut-out, and protect us from the rot that's set in, which means in effect limiting knowledge of the operation to the absolute minimum, we'll supply the goods.' They talk over ways and means in which this might be done; then Gerald leaves Percy to fret for a bit. A week, a month, I don't know. Long enough for Percy to have done his thinking. One day Gerald produces the first sample. And of course it's very good. Very, very good. Naval stuff, as it happens, which couldn't suit Percy better, because he's very well in at the Admiralty; it's his supporters' club. So Percy gives his naval friends a sneak preview and they water at the mouth. 'Where does it come from? Will there be more?' There's plenty more. As to the identity of the source— well, that's a big big mystery at this stage, but so it should be. Forgive me if I'm a little wide of the mark here and there, but I've only the file to go by."

The mention of a file, the first indication that Smiley might be acting in some official capacity, produced in Esterhase a discernible response. The habitual licking of the lips was accompanied by a forward movement of the head and an expression of shrewd familiarity, as if Toby by all these signals was trying to indicate that he, too, had read the file, whatever file it was, and entirely shared Smiley's conclusions. Smiley had broken off to drink some tea.

"More for you, Toby?" he asked over his cup.

"I'll get it," said Guillam with more firmness than hospitality.

"Tea, Fawn," he called through the door. It opened at once and Fawn appeared on the threshold, cup in hand.

Smiley was back at the window. He had parted the curtain an inch, and was staring into the square.

"Toby?"

"Yes, George?"

"Did you bring a baby-sitter?"

"No."

"No one?"

"George, why should I bring baby-sitters if I am just going to meet Peter and a poor Pole?"

Smiley returned to his chair. "Merlin as a source," he resumed. "Where was I? Yes, well, conveniently Merlin wasn't just one source, was he, as little by little Gerald explained to Percy and the two others he had by now drawn into the magic circle. Merlin was a Soviet agent, all right, but, rather like Alleline, he was also the spokesman of a dissident group. We love to see ourselves in other people's situations, and I'm sure Percy warmed to Merlin from the start. This group, this caucus of which Merlin was the leader, was made up of, say, half a dozen like-minded Soviet officials, each in his way well-placed. With time, I suspect, Gerald gave his lieutenants, and Percy, a pretty close picture of these sub-sources, but I don't know. Merlin's job was to collate their intelligence and get it to the West, and over the next few months he showed remarkable versatility in doing just that. He used all manner of methods, and the Circus was only too willing to feed him the equipment. Secret writing, microdots stuck over full stops on innocent-looking letters, dead letter-boxes in Western capitals, filled by God knows what brave Russian, and dutifully cleared by Toby Esterhase's brave lamplighters. Live meetings, even, arranged and watched over by Toby's baby-sitters"—a minute pause as Smiley glanced again towards the window—"a couple of drops in Moscow that had to be fielded by the local residency, though they were never allowed to know their benefactor. But no clandestine radio; Merlin doesn't care for it. There was a proposal once—it even got as far as the Treasury—to set up a permanent long-arm radio station in Finland, just to service him, but it all foundered when Merlin said, 'Not on your nelly.' He must have been taking lessons from Karla, mustn't he? You know how Karla hates radio. The great thing is, Merlin has mobility: that's his biggest talent. Perhaps he's in the Moscow Trade Ministry and can use the travelling salesmen. Anyway, he has the resources and he has the leads out of Russia. And that's why his fellow conspirators look to him to deal with Gerald and agree to the terms, the financial terms. Because they do want money. Lots of money. I should have mentioned that. In that respect, secret services and their customers are like anyone else, I'm afraid. They value most what costs most, and Merlin costs a fortune. Ever bought a fake picture?"

"I sold a couple once," said Toby with a flashy, nervous smile, but no one laughed.

"The more you pay for it, the less inclined you are to doubt it. Silly, but there we are. It's also comforting for everyone to know that Merlin is venal. That's a motive we all understand— right, Toby? Specially in the Treasury. Twenty thousand francs a month into a Swiss bank: well, there's no knowing who wouldn't bend a few egalitarian principles for money like that. So Whitehall pays him a fortune, and calls his intelligence priceless. And some of it *is* good," Smiley conceded. "Very good, I do think, and so it should be. Then, one day, Gerald admits Percy to the greatest secret of all. The Merlin caucus has a London end. It's the start, I should tell you now, of a very, very clever knot."

Toby put down his cup and with his handkerchief primly dabbed the corners of his mouth.

"According to Gerald, a member of the Soviet Embassy here in London is actually ready and able to act as Merlin's London representative. He is even in the extraordinary position of being able to use, on rare occasions, the Embassy facilities to talk to Merlin in Moscow, to send and receive messages. And if every imaginable precaution is taken, it is even possible now and then for Gerald to arrange clandestine meetings with this wonder-man, to brief and debrief him, to put follow-up questions and receive answers from Merlin almost by return of post. We'll call this Soviet official Aleksey Aleksandrovich Polyakov, and we'll pretend he's a member of the cultural section of the Soviet Embassy. Are you with me?"

"I didn't hear anything," said Esterhase. "I gone deaf."

"The story is, he's been a member of the London Embassy quite a while—nine years, to be precise—but Merlin's only recently added him to the flock. While Polyakov was on leave in Moscow, perhaps?"

"I'm not hearing nothing."

"Very quickly Polyakov becomes important, because before long Gerald appoints him linchpin of the Witchcraft operation and a lot more besides. The dead drops in Amsterdam and Paris, the secret inks, the microdots—they all go on, all right, but at less of a pitch. The convenience of having Polyakov right on the doorstep is too good to miss. Some of Merlin's best material is smuggled to London by diplomatic bag; all Polyakov has to do is slit open the envelopes and pass them to his counterpart in the Circus—Gerald or whomever Gerald nominates. But we must never forget that this part of the Merlin operation is deathly, deathly secret. The Witchcraft committee itself is, of course, secret, too, but large. That's inevitable. The operation is large, the take is large; processing and distribution alone require a mass of clerical supervision—transcribers, translators, codists, typists, evaluators, and God knows what. None of that worries Gerald at all, of course: he likes it, in fact, because the art of being Gerald is to be one of a crowd. Is the Witchcraft committee led from below? From the middle or from the top? I rather like Karla's description of committees, don't you? Is it Chinese? A committee is an animal with four back legs.

"But the London end—Polyakov's leg—that part is confined to the original magic circle. Skordeno, de Silsky, all the pack: they can tear off abroad and devil like mad for Merlin away from home. But here in London, the operation involving Brother Polyakov, the way that knot is tied—that's a very special secret, for very special reasons. You, Percy, Bill Haydon, and Roy Bland. You four are the magic circle. Right? Now let's just speculate about how it works, in detail. There's a house, we know that. All the same, meetings there are very elaborately arranged; we can be sure of that, can't we? Who meets him, Toby? Who has the handling of Polyakov? You? Roy? Bill?"

Taking the fat end of his tie, Smiley turned the silk lining outwards and polished his glasses. "Everyone does," he said, answering his own question. "How's that? Sometimes Percy meets him. I would guess Percy represents the authoritarian side with him: 'Isn't it time you took a holiday? Have you heard from your wife this week?' Percy would be good at that. But the Witchcraft committee uses Percy sparingly. Percy's the big gun and he must have rarity value. Then there's Bill Haydon; Bill meets him. That would happen more often, I think. Bill's impressive on Russia and he has entertainment value. I have a feeling that he and Polyakov would hit it off pretty well. I would think Bill shone when it came to the briefing and the follow-up questions, wouldn't you? Making certain that the right messages went to Moscow? Sometimes he takes Roy Bland with him, sometimes he sends Roy on his own. I expect that's something they work out between themselves. And Roy, of course, is an economic expert, as well as top man on satellites, so there'll be lots to talk about in that department also.

And sometimes—I imagine birthdays, Toby, or a Christmas, or special presentations of thanks and money—there's a small fortune written down to entertainment, I notice, let alone bounties. Sometimes, to make the party go, you all four trot along, and raise your glasses to the king across the water: to Merlin, through his envoy, Polyakov. Finally, I suppose, Toby himself has things to talk to friend Polyakov about. There's tradecraft to discuss; there are the useful snippets about goings on inside the Embassy, which are so handy to the lamplighters in their bread-and-butter surveillance operations against the residency. So Toby also has his solo sessions. After all, we shouldn't overlook Polyakov's local potential, quite apart from his role as Merlin's London representative. It's not every day we have a tame Soviet diplomat in London eating out of our hands. A little training with a camera and Polyakov could be very useful just at the straight domestic level. Provided we all remember our priorities."

His gaze had not left Toby's face. "I can imagine that Polyakov might run to quite a few reels of film, can't you? And that one of the jobs of whoever was seeing him might be to replenish his stock: take him little sealed packets. Packets of film. Unexposed film, of course, since it came from the Circus. Tell me, Toby— could you, please—is the name Lapin familiar to you?"

A lick, a frown, a smile, a forward movement of the head: "Sure, George, I know Lapin."

"Who ordered the lamplighter reports on Lapin destroyed?"

"I did, George."

"On your own initiative?"

The smile broadened a fraction. "Listen, George, I made some rungs up the ladder these days."

"Who said Connie Sachs had to be pushed downhill?"

"Look, I think it was Percy—okay? Say it was Percy, maybe Bill. You know how it is in a big operation. Shoes to mend, pots to clean, always a thing going." He shrugged. "Maybe it was Roy, huh?"

"So you take orders from all of them," said Smiley lightly. "That's very indiscriminate of you, Toby. You should know better."

Esterhase didn't like that at all.

"Who told you to cool off Max, Toby? Was it the same three people? Only I have to report all this to Lacon, you see. He's being awfully pressing just at the moment. He seems to have the Minister on his back. Who was it?"

"George, you been talking to the wrong guys."

"One of us has," Smiley agreed pleasantly. "That's for sure. They also want to know about Westerby: just who put the muzzle on him. Was it the same person who sent you down to Sarratt with a thousand quid in cash and a brief to put Jim Prideaux's mind at rest? It's only facts I'm after, Toby, not scalps. You know me—I'm not the vindictive sort. Anyway, what's to say you're not a very loyal fellow? It's just a question of who to." He added, "Only they do badly want to know, you see. There's even some ugly talk of calling in the competition. Nobody wants that, do they? It's like going to solicitors when you've had a row with your wife: an irrevocable step. Who gave you the message for Jim about Tinker, Tailor? Did you know what it meant? Did you have it straight from Polyakov, was that it?"

"For God's sake," Guillam whispered, "let me sweat the bastard."

Smiley ignored him. "Let's keep talking about Lapin. What was his job over here?"

"He worked for Polyakov."

"His secretary in the cultural department?"

"His legman."

"But, my dear Toby, what on earth is a cultural attaché doing with his own legman?"

Esterhase's eyes were on Smiley all the time. He's like a dog, thought Guillam; he doesn't know whether to expect a kick or a bone. They flickered from Smiley's face to his hands, then back to his face, constantly checking the telltale places.

"Don't be damn silly, George," Toby said carelessly. "Polyakov is working for Moscow Centre. You know that as well as I do." He crossed his little legs and, with a resurgence of all his former insolence, sat back in his chair and took a sip of cold tea.

Whereas Smiley, to Guillam's eye, appeared momentarily set back; from which Guillam in his confusion dryly inferred that he was doubtless very pleased with himself. Perhaps because Toby was at last doing the talking.

"Come on, George," Toby said. "You're not a child. Think how many operations we ran this way. We buy Polyakov, okay? Polyakov's a Moscow hood but he's our Joe. But he's got to pretend to his own people that he's spying on us. How else does he get away with it? How does he walk in and out of that house all day, no gorillas, no baby-sitters, everything so easy? He comes down to our shop, so he got to take home the goodies. So we give him goodies. Chicken-feed, so he can pass it home and everyone in Moscow claps him on the back and tells him he's a big guy—happens every day."

If Guillam's head by now was reeling with a kind of furious awe, Smiley's seemed remarkably clear.

"And that's pretty much the standard story, is it, among the four initiated?"

"Well, standard I wouldn't know," said Esterhase, with a very Hungarian movement of the hand, a spreading of the palm and a tilting either way.

"So who is Polyakov's agent?"

The question, Guillam saw, mattered very much to Smiley: he had played the whole long hand in order to arrive at it. As Guillam waited, his eyes now on Esterhase, who was by no means so confident any more, now on Smiley's mandarin face, he realised that he, too, was beginning to understand the shape of Karla's last clever knot, as Smiley had called it—and of his own gruelling interview with Alleline.

"What I'm asking you is very simple," Smiley insisted. "Notionally, who is Polyakov's agent inside the Circus? Good heavens, Toby, don't be obtuse. If Polyakov's cover for meeting you people is that he is spying on the Circus, then he must have a Circus spy, mustn't he? So who is he? He can't come back to the Embassy after a meeting with you people, loaded with reels of Circus chicken-feed, and say, 'I got this from the boys.' There has to be a story—and a good one, at that: a whole history of courtship, recruitment, clandestine meetings, money, and motive. Doesn't there? Heavens, this isn't just Polyakov's cover story: it's his life-line. It's got to be thorough. It's got to be convincing; I'd say it was a very big issue in the game. So who is he?" Smiley enquired pleasantly. "You? Toby Esterhase masquerades as a Circus traitor in order to keep Polyakov in business? My hat, Toby, that's worth a whole handful of medals."

They waited while Toby thought.

"You're on a damn long road, George," Toby said at last. "What happens you don't reach the other end?"

"Even with Lacon behind me?"

"You bring Lacon here. Percy, too; Bill. Why you come to the little guy? Go to the big ones, pick on them."

"I thought you *were* a big guy these days. You'd be a good choice for the part, Toby. Hungarian ancestry, resentment about promotion, reasonable access but not too much . . . quick-witted, likes money . . . With you as his agent, Polyakov would have a cover story that really sits up and works. The big three give you the chicken-feed, you hand it to Polyakov, Centre thinks Toby is all theirs, everyone's served, everyone's content. The only problem arises when it transpires that you've been handing Polyakov the crown jewels and getting Russian chicken-feed in return. If that *should* turn out to be the case, you're going to need pretty good friends. Like us. That's how my thesis runs—just to complete it. That Gerald is a Russian mole, run by Karla. And he's pulled the Circus inside out."

Esterhase looked slightly ill. "George, listen. If you're wrong, I don't want to be wrong too, get me?"

"But if he's right, you want to be right," Guillam suggested, in a rare interruption. "And the sooner you're right, the happier you'll be."

"Sure," said Toby, quite unaware of any irony. "Sure. I mean George got a nice idea, but Jesus, there's two sides to everyone, George, agents specially, and maybe it's you who got the wrong one. Listen: who ever called Witchcraft chickenfeed? No one. Never. It's the best. You get one guy with a big mouth starts shouting the dirt, and you dug up half London already. Get me? Look, I do what they tell me. Okay? They say act the stooge for Polyakov, I act him. Pass him this film, I pass it. I'm in a very dangerous situation," he explained. "For me, very dangerous indeed."

"I'm sorry about that," said Smiley at the window, where through a chink in the curtain he was once more studying the square. "Must be worrying for you."

"Extremely," Toby agreed. "I get ulcers, can't eat. Very bad predicament."

For a moment, to Guillam's fury, they were all three joined in a sympathetic silence over Toby Esterhase's bad predicament.

"Toby, you wouldn't be lying about those baby-sitters, would you?" Smiley enquired, still from the window.

"George, I cross my heart, I swear you."

"What would you use for a job like this? Cars?"

"Pavement artists. Put a bus back by the air terminal, walk them through, turn 'em over."

"How many?"

"Eight, ten. This time of year—six, maybe. We get a lot ill. Christmas," he said morosely.

"And one man alone?"

"Never. You crazy. One man! You think I run a toffee shop these days?"

Leaving the window, Smiley sat down again.

"Listen, George, that's a terrible idea you got there, you know that? I'm a patriotic fellow. Jesus," Toby repeated.

"What is Polyakov's job in the London residency?" Smiley asked.

"Polly works solo."

"Running his master spy inside the Circus?"

"Sure. They take him off regular work, give him a free hand so's he can handle Toby, master spy. We work it all out; hours on end I sit with him. 'Listen,' I say. 'Bill is suspecting me, my wife is suspecting me, my kid got measles, and I can't pay the doctor.' All the crap that agents give you, I give it to Polly so's he can pass it home for real."

"And who's Merlin?"

Esterhase shook his head.

"But at least you've heard he's based in Moscow," Smiley said. "And a member of the Soviet intelligence establishment, whatever else he isn't?"

"That much they tell me," Esterhase agreed.

"Which is how Polyakov can communicate with him. In the Circus's interest, of course. Secretly, without his own people becoming suspicious?"

"Sure." Toby resumed his lament, but Smiley seemed to be listening to sounds that were not in the room.

"And Tinker, Tailor?"

"I don't know what the hell it is. I do what Percy tells me."

"And Percy told you to square Jim Prideaux?"

"Sure. Maybe it was Bill. Or Roy, maybe. Listen, it was Roy. I got to eat, George, understand? I don't cut my throat two ways, follow me?"

"It is the perfect fix; you see that, don't you, Toby, really?" Smiley remarked in a quiet, rather distant way. "Assuming it *is* a fix. It makes everyone wrong who's right: Connie Sachs, Jerry Westerby . . . Jim Prideaux . . . even Control. Silences the doubters before they've even spoken out . . . The permutations are infinite, once you've brought off the basic lie. Moscow Centre must be allowed to think she has an important Circus source; Whitehall on no account must get wind of the same notion. Take it to its logical conclusion and Gerald would have us strangling our own children in their beds. It would be beautiful in another context," he remarked almost dreamily. "Poor Toby; yes, I do see. What a time you must have been having, running between them all."

Toby had his next speech ready: "Naturally, if there is anything I can do of a practical nature, you know me, George, I am always pleased to help—no trouble. My boys are pretty well trained; you want to borrow them, maybe we can work a deal. Naturally, I have to speak to Lacon first. All I want, I want to get this thing cleared up. For the sake of the Circus, you know. That's all I want. The good of the firm. I'm a modest man; I don't want anything for myself—okay?"

"Where's this safe house you keep exclusively for Polyakov?"

"Five Lock Gardens, Camden Town."

"With a caretaker?"

"Mrs. McCraig."

"Lately a listener?"

"Sure."

"Is there built-in audio?"

"What do you think?"

"So Millie McCraig keeps house and mans the recording instruments."

She did, said Toby, ducking his head with great alertness.

"In a minute, I want you to telephone her and tell her I'm staying the night and I'll want to use the equipment. Tell her I've been called in on a special job and she's to do whatever I ask. I'll be round about nine. What's the procedure for contacting Polyakov if you want a crash meeting?"

"My boys have a room on Haverstock Hill. Polly drives

past the window each morning on the way to the Embassy, each night going home. If they put up a yellow poster protesting against traffic, that's the signal."

"And at night? At weekends?"

"Wrong-number phone call. But nobody likes that."

"Has it ever been used?"

"I don't know."

"You mean you don't listen to his phone?"

No answer.

"I want you to take the weekend off. Would that raise eyebrows at the Circus?" Enthusiastically, Esterhase shook his head. "I'm sure you'd prefer to be out of it, anyway, wouldn't you?" Esterhase nodded. "Say you're having girl trouble or whatever sort of trouble you're in these days. You'll be spending the night here, possibly two. Fawn will look after you; there's food in the kitchen. What about your wife?"

While Guillam and Smiley looked on, Esterhase dialled the Circus and asked for Phil Porteous. He said his lines perfectly: a little self-pity, a little conspiracy, a little joke. Some girl who was passionate about him up north, Phil, and threatening wild things if he didn't go and hold her hand.

"Don't tell me, I know it happens to you every day, Phil. Hey, how's that gorgeous new secretary of yours? And listen, Phil, if Mara phones from home, tell her Toby's on a big job, okay? Blowing up the Kremlin, back on Monday. Make it nice and heavy, huh? Cheers, Phil."

He rang off and dialled a number in north London. "Mrs. M., hullo, this is your favourite boyfriend—recognise the voice? Good. Listen, I'm sending you a visitor tonight—an old, old friend, you'll be surprised. She hates me," he explained to them, his hand over the mouthpiece. "He wants to check the wiring," he went on. "Look it all over, make sure it's working okay, no bad leaks—all right?"

"If he's any trouble," Guillam said to Fawn with real venom as they left, "bind him hand and foot."

In the stairwell, Smiley lightly touched his arm. "Peter, I want you to watch my back. Will you do that for me? Give me a couple of minutes, then pick me up on the corner of Marloes Road, heading north. Stick to the west pavement."

Guillam waited, then stepped into the street. A thin drizzle lay on the air, which had an eerie warmness like a thaw. Where lights shone, the moisture shifted in fine clouds, but in shadow he neither saw nor felt it: simply, a mist blurred his vision, making him half close his eyes. He completed one round of the gardens, then entered a pretty mews well south of the pick-up point. Reaching Marloes Road, he crossed to the west pavement, bought an evening paper, and began walking at a leisurely rate past villas set in deep gardens. He was counting off pedestrians, cyclists, cars, while out ahead of him, steadily plodding the far pavement, he picked out George Smiley, the very prototype of the homegoing Londoner. "Is it a team?" Guillam had asked. Smiley could not be specific. "Short of Abingdon Villas, I'll cross over," he said. "Look for a solo. But look!"

As Guillam watched Smiley pulled up abruptly, as if he had just remembered something, stepped perilously into the road, and scuttled between the angry traffic to disappear at once through the doors of a liquor store. As he did so, Guillam saw, or thought he saw, a tall crooked figure in a dark coat step out after him, but at that moment a bus drew up, screening both Smiley and his pursuer; and when it pulled away, it must have taken his pursuer with it, for the only survivor on that strip of pavement was an older man in a black plastic raincoat and cloth cap lolling at the bus stop while he read his evening paper; and when Smiley emerged from the store with his brown bag, the man did not so much as lift his head from the sporting pages. For a short while longer, Guillam trailed Smiley through the smarter reaches of Victorian Kensington as he slipped from one quiet square to another, sauntered into a mews and out again by the same route. Only once, when Guillam forgot

Smiley and out of instinct turned upon his own tracks, did he have a suspicion of a third figure walking with them: a fanged shadow thrown against the broadloom brickwork of an empty street, but when he started forward, it was gone.

The night had its own madness after that; events ran too quickly for him to fasten on them singly. Not till days afterwards did he realise that the figure, or the shadow of it, had struck a chord of familiarity in his memory. Even then, for some time, he could not place it. Then one early morning, waking abruptly, he had it clear in his mind: a barking, military voice, a gentleness of manner heavily concealed, a squash racket jammed behind the safe of his room in Brixton, which brought tears to the eyes of his unemotional secretary.

35

Probably the only thing which Steve Mackelvore did wrong that same evening, in terms of classic tradecraft, was blame himself for leaving the passenger door of his car unlocked. Climbing in from the driver's side, he put it down to his own negligence that the other lock was up. Survival, as Jim Prideaux liked to recall, is an infinite capacity for suspicion. By that purist standard, Mackelvore should have suspected that in the middle of a particularly vile rush-hour, on a particularly vile evening, in one of those blaring side streets that feed into the lower end of the Elysées, Ricki Tarr would unlock the passenger door and hold him up at gunpoint. But life in the Paris residency these days did little to keep a man's wits sharp, and most of Mackelvore's working day had been taken up with filing his weekly expenses and completing his weekly returns of staff for the housekeepers. Only lunch, a longish affair with an insincere anglophile in the French security labyrinth, had broken the monotony of that Friday.

His car, parked under a lime tree that was dying of exhaust fumes, had an extraterritorial registration and "C.C." plastered on the back, for the residency cover was consular, though no one took it seriously. Mackelvore was a Circus elder, a squat, white-haired Yorkshireman with a long record of consular appointments which in the eyes of the world had brought him no advancement. Paris was the last of them. He did not care particularly for Paris, and he knew from an operational lifetime in the Far East that the French were not for him. But as a prelude to retirement it could not be bettered. The allowances were good, the billet was comfortable, and the most that had been asked of him in the ten months he had been here was to welfare the occasional agent in transit, put up a chalk-mark here and there, play postman to some ploy by London Station, and show a time to the visiting firemen.

Until now, that was, as he sat in his own car with Tarr's gun jammed against his rib-cage, and Tarr's hand resting affectionately on his right shoulder, ready to wrench his head off if he tried any monkey business. A couple of feet away, girls hurried past on their way to the Metro, and six feet beyond that the traffic had come to a standstill; it could stay that way for an hour. None was faintly stirred by the sight of two men having a cosy chat in a parked car.

Tarr had been talking ever since Mackelvore sat down. He needed to send a message to Alleline, he said. It would be personal and decypher yourself, and Tarr would like Steve to work the machine for him while Tarr stood off with the gun.

"What the hell have you been up to, Ricki?" Mackelvore complained, as they walked arm in arm back to the residency. "The whole service is looking for you—you know that, don't you? They'll skin you alive if they find you. We're supposed to do blood-curdling things to you on sight."

He thought of turning into the hold and smacking Tarr's neck, but he knew he hadn't the speed and Tarr would kill him.

The message would run to about two hundred groups, said Tarr, as Mackelvore unlocked the front door and put on the lights. When Steve had transmitted them, they would sit on the machine and wait for Percy's answer. By tomorrow, if Tarr's instinct was correct, Percy would be coming over to Paris hotfoot to have a conference with Ricki. This conference would also take place in the residency, because Tarr reckoned it was marginally less likely that the Russians would try to kill him on British consular premises.

"You're berserk, Ricki. It's not the Russians who want to kill you. It's us."

The front room was called Reception; it was what remained of the cover. It had an old wooden counter and out-of-date "Notices to British Subjects" hanging on the grimy wall. Here, with his left hand, Tarr searched Mackelvore for a weapon but found none. It was a courtyard house and most of the sensitive stuff was across the yard: the cypher-room, the strong-room, and the machines.

"You're out of your mind, Ricki," Mackelvore warned monotonously, as he led the way through a couple of empty offices and pressed the bell to the cypher-room. "You always thought you were Napoleon Bonaparte and now it's got you completely. You'd too much religion from your dad."

The steel message hatch slid back and a mystified, slightly silly face appeared in the opening. "You can go home, Ben, boy. Go home to your missus but stay close to your phone in case I need you, there's a lad. Leave the books where they are and put the keys in the machines. I'll be talking to London presently, under my own steam."

The face withdrew and they waited while the boy unlocked the door from inside: one key, two keys, a spring lock.

"This gentleman's from out East, Ben," Mackelvore explained as the door opened. "He's one of my most distinguished connections."

"Hullo, sir," said Ben. He was a tall, mathematical-looking boy with spectacles and an unblinking gaze.

"Get along with you, Ben. I'll not dock it against your duty pay. You've the weekend free on full rates, and you'll not owe me time, either. Off you go, then."

"Ben stays here," said Tarr.

In Cambridge Circus the lighting was quite yellow and from where Mendel stood, on the third floor of the clothes shop, the wet tarmac glistened like cheap gold. It was nearly midnight

and he had been standing three hours. He stood between a net
curtain and a clothes-horse. He stood the way coppers stand
the world over: weight on both feet equally, legs straight, leaning slightly backward over the line of balance. He had pulled
his hat low and turned up his collar to keep the white of his
face from the street, but his eyes as they watched the front
entrance below him glittered like a cat's eyes in a coal-hole. He
would wait another three hours or another six: Mendel was
back on the beat; the scent of the hunt was in his nostrils. Better still, he was a night bird; the darkness of that fitting room
woke him wonderfully. Such light as reached him from the
street lay upside down in pale pieces on the ceiling. All the
rest—the cutting-benches, the bolts of cloth, the draped
machines, the steam iron, the signed photographs of princes of
the blood—these were there because he had seen them on his
reconnaissance that afternoon; the light did not reach them
and even now he could barely make them out.

From his window he covered most of the approaches: eight
or nine unequal roads and alleys that for no good reason had
chosen Cambridge Circus as their meeting point. Between
them, the buildings were gimcrack, cheaply fitted out with bits
of Empire: a Roman bank, a theatre like a vast desecrated
mosque. Behind them, high-rise blocks advanced like an army
of robots. Above, a pink sky was slowly filling with fog.

Why was it so quiet? he wondered. The theatre had long
emptied but why didn't the pleasure trade of Soho, only a
stone's throw from his window, fill the place with taxis, groups
of loiterers? Not a single fruit lorry had rumbled down Shaftes-
bury Avenue on its way to Covent Garden.

Through his binoculars Mendel once more studied the
building straight across the road from him. It seemed to sleep
even more soundly than its neighbours. The twin doors of the
portico were closed and no light was visible in the ground-floor
windows. Only on the fourth floor, out of the second window
from the left, a pale glow issued, and Mendel knew it was the

duty officer's room; Smiley had told him. Briefly he raised the glasses to the roof, where a plantation of aerials made wild patterns against the sky, then down a floor to the four blackened windows of the radio section.

"At night everyone uses the front door," Guillam had said. "It's an economy measure to cut down on janitors."

In those three hours, only three events had rewarded Mendel's vigil; one an hour is not much. At half past nine a blue Ford Transit delivered two men carrying what looked like an ammunition box. They unlocked the door for themselves and closed it as soon as they were inside, while Mendel murmured his commentary into the telephone. At ten o'clock the shuttle arrived; Guillam had warned him of this, too. The shuttle collected hot documents from the outstations and stored them for safekeeping at the Circus over the weekend. It called at Brixton, Acton, and Sarratt, in that order, said Guillam, lastly at the Admiralty, and it made the Circus by about ten. In the event, it arrived on the dot of ten, and this time two men from inside the building came out to help unload; Mendel reported that, too, and Smiley acknowledged with a patient "Thank you."

Was Smiley sitting down? Was he in the darkness like Mendel? Mendel had a notion he was. Of all the odd coves he had known, Smiley was the oddest. You thought, to look at him, that he couldn't cross the road alone, but you might as well have offered protection to a hedgehog. Funnies, Mendel mused. A lifetime of chasing villains and how do I end up? Breaking and entering, standing in the dark and spying on the Funnies. He'd never held with Funnies till he met Smiley. Thought they were an interfering lot of amateurs and college boys; thought they were unconstitutional; thought the best thing the Special Branch could do, for its own sake and the public's, was say "Yes, sir," "No, sir" and lose the correspondence. Come to think of it, with the notable exception of Smiley and Guillam, that's exactly what he thought tonight.

Shortly before eleven, just an hour ago, a cab arrived. A plain licensed London hackney cab, and it drew up at the theatre. Even that was something Smiley had warned him about: it was the habit within the service not to take taxis to the door. Some stopped at Foyle's, some in Old Compton Street or at one of the shops; most people had a favourite cover destination and Alleline's was the theatre. Mendel had never seen Alleline, but he had their description of him and as he watched him through the glasses he recognised him without a doubt, a big lumbering fellow in a dark coat; he even noticed how the cabby pulled a bad face at his tip and called something after him as Alleline delved for his keys.

The front door is not secured, Guillam had explained; it is only locked. The security begins inside, once you have turned left at the end of the corridor. Alleline lives on the fifth floor. You won't see his windows light up but there's a skylight and the glow should catch the chimney-stack. Sure enough, as he watched, a patch of yellow appeared on the grimy bricks of the chimney: Alleline had entered his room.

And young Guillam needs a holiday, thought Mendel. He'd seen *that* happen before, too: the tough ones who crack at forty. They lock it away, pretend it isn't there, lean on grown-ups who turn out not to be so grown up after all; then one day it's all over them, and their heroes come tumbling down and they're sitting at their desks with the tears pouring onto the blotter.

He had laid the receiver on the floor. Picking it up, he said, "Looks like Tinker's clocked in."

He gave the number of the cab, then went back to waiting.

"How did he look?" Smiley murmured.

"Busy," said Mendel.

"So he should be."

That one won't crack, though, Mendel decided with approval; one of your flabby oak trees, Smiley was. Think you could blow him over with one puff, but when it comes to the storm he's the only one left standing at the end of it. At this point in his reflections a second cab drew up, squarely at the front entrance, and a tall slow figure cautiously climbed the steps one at a time, like a man who takes care of his heart.

"Here's your Tailor," Mendel murmured into the telephone. "Hold on, here's Soldier-boy, too. Proper gathering of the clans, by the look of it. I say, take it easy."

An old Mercedes 190 shot out of Earlham Street, swung directly beneath his window, and held the curve with difficulty as far as the northern outlet of the Charing Cross Road, where it parked. A young heavy fellow with ginger hair clambered out, slammed the door, and clumped across the street to the entrance without even taking the key out of the dash. A moment later another light went up on the fourth floor as Roy Bland joined the party.

All we need to know now is who comes out, thought Mendel.

36

Lock Gardens, which presumably drew its name from the Camden and Hampstead Road Locks nearby, was a terrace of four flat-fronted nineteenth-century houses built at the centre of a crescent, each with three floors and a basement and a strip of walled back garden running down to the Regent's Canal. The numbers ran 2 to 5: number 1 had either fallen down or never been built. Number 5 made up the north end, and as a safe house it could not have been improved, for there were three approaches in thirty yards and the canal towpath offered two more. To the north lay Camden High Street for joining traffic; south and west lay the parks and Primrose Hill. Better still, the neighbourhood possessed no social identity and demanded none. Some of the houses had been turned into one-room flats, and had ten doorbells laid out like a typewriter. Some were got up grandly and had only one. Number 5 had two: one for Millie McCraig and one for her lodger, Mr. Jefferson.

Mrs. McCraig was churchy and collected for everything, which was incidentally an excellent way of keeping an eye on the locals, though that was scarcely how they viewed her zeal. Jefferson, her lodger, was known vaguely to be foreign and in oil and away a lot. Lock Gardens was his *pied-à-terre*. The neighbours, when they bothered to notice him, found him shy and respectable. They would have formed the same impression of George Smiley if they had happened to spot him in the dim light of the porch at nine that evening, as Millie McCraig admitted him to her front room and drew the pious curtains. She was a wiry Scottish widow with brown stockings and bobbed hair and the polished, wrinkled skin of an old man. In the interest of God and the Circus, she had run Bible schools in Mozambique and a seaman's mission in Hamburg, and though she had been a professional eavesdropper for twenty years since then, she was still inclined to treat all menfolk as transgressors. Smiley had no way of telling what she thought. Her manner, from the moment he arrived, had a deep and lonely stillness; she showed him round the house like a chatelaine whose guests had long since died.

First the semi-basement, where she lived herself, full of plants and that medley of old postcards, brass table-tops, and carved black furniture which seems to attach itself to travelled British ladies of a certain age and class. Yes, if the Circus wanted her at night they rang her on the basement phone. Yes, there was a separate line upstairs, but it was only for outgoing calls. The basement phone had an extension in the upstairs dining-room. Then up to the ground floor, a veritable shrine to the costly bad taste of the housekeepers: loud Regency stripes, gilded reproduction chairs, plush sofas with roped corners. The kitchen was untouched and squalid. Beyond it lay a glass outhouse, half conservatory, half scullery, which looked down to the rough garden and the canal. Strewn over the tiled floor: an old mangle, a copper tub, and crates of tonic water.

"Where are the mikes, Millie?" Smiley had returned to the drawing-room.

They were in pairs, Millie murmured, bedded behind the wallpaper: two pairs to each room on the ground floor, one to each room upstairs. Each pair was connected with a separate recorder. He followed her up the steep stairs. The top floor was unfurnished save for an attic bedroom that contained a grey steel frame with eight tape machines, four up, four down.

"And Jefferson knows all about this?"

"Mr. Jefferson," said Millie primly, "is run on a basis of trust." That was the nearest she came to expressing her disapproval of Smiley, or her devotion to Christian ethics.

Downstairs again, she showed him the switches that controlled the system. An extra switch was fitted in each finger panel. Any time Jefferson or one of the boys, as she put it, wanted to go over to record, he had only to get up and turn down the left-hand light switch. From then on, the system was voice-activated; that is to say, the tape deck did not turn unless somebody was speaking.

"And where are you while all this goes on, Millie?"

She remained downstairs, she said, as if that were a woman's place.

Smiley was pulling open cupboards, lockers, walking from room to room. Then back to the scullery again, with its view to the canal. Taking out a pocket torch, he signalled one flash into the darkness of the garden.

"What are the safety procedures?" Smiley asked as he thoughtfully fingered the end light switch by the drawing-room door.

Her reply came in a liturgical monotone. "Two full milk bottles on the doorstep, you may come in and all's well. No milk bottles and you're not to enter."

From the direction of the sunroom came a faint tapping. Returning to the scullery, Smiley opened the glazed door and after a hastily murmured conversation reappeared with Guillam.

"You know Peter, don't you, Millie?"

Millie might, she might not; her little hard eyes had fixed on him with scorn. He was studying the switch panel, feeling in his pocket as he did so.

"What's he doing? He's not to do that. Stop him."

If she was worried, said Smiley, she should ring Lacon on the basement phone. Millie McCraig didn't stir, but two red bruises had appeared on her leathery cheeks and she was snapping her fingers in anger. With a small screwdriver Guillam had cautiously removed the screws from either side of the plastic panel, and was peering at the wiring behind. Now, very carefully, he turned the end switch upside down, twisting it on its wires, then screwed the plate back in position, leaving the remaining switches undisturbed.

"We'll just try it," said Guillam, and while Smiley went upstairs to check the tape deck, Guillam sang "Old Man River," in a low Paul Robeson growl.

"Thank you," said Smiley with a shudder, coming down again. "That's more than enough."

Millie had gone to the basement to ring Lacon. Quietly, Smiley set the stage. He put the telephone beside an armchair in the drawing-room, then cleared his line of retreat to the scullery. He fetched two full bottles of milk from the icebox and placed them on the doorstep to signify, in the eclectic language of Millie McCraig, that you may come in and all's well. He removed his shoes and took them to the scullery, and having put out all the lights, took up his post in the armchair just as Mendel made his connecting call.

On the canal towpath, meanwhile, Guillam had resumed his vigil of the house. The footpath is closed to the public one hour before dark: after that it can be anything from a trysting place for lovers to a haven for down-and-outs; both, for different reasons, are attracted by the darkness of the bridges. That cold night Guillam saw neither. Occasionally an empty train raced past, leaving a still greater emptiness behind. His nerves were so taut, his expectations so varied, that for a moment he saw the whole architecture of that night in apocalyptic terms: the signals on the railway bridge turned to gallows; the Victorian warehouses to gigantic prisons, their windows barred and arched against the misty sky. Closer at hand, the ripple of rats and the stink of still water. Then the drawing-room lights went out; the house stood in darkness except for the chinks of yellow to either side of Millie's basement window. From the scullery a pin of light winked at him down the unkempt garden. Taking a pen torch from his pocket, he slipped out the silver hood, sighted it with shaking fingers at the point from which the light had come, and signalled back. From now on, they could only wait.

Tarr tossed the incoming telegram back to Ben, together with the one-time pad from the safe.

"Come on," he said, "earn your pay. Unbutton it."

"It's personal for you," Ben objected. "Look. 'Personal from Alleline decypher yourself.' I'm not allowed to touch it. It's the tops."

"Do as he asks, Ben," said Mackelvore, watching Tarr.

For ten minutes, no word passed between the three men. Tarr was standing across the room from them, very nervous from the waiting. He had jammed the gun in his waistband. His jacket lay over a chair. The sweat had stuck his shirt to his back all the way down. Ben was using a ruler to read off the number groups, then carefully writing his findings on the block of graph paper before him. To concentrate, he put his tongue against his teeth, and now he made a small click as he withdrew it. Putting aside his pencil, he offered Tarr the tearsheet.

"Read it aloud," Tarr said.

Ben's voice was kindly, and a little fervent. " 'Personal for Tarr from Alleline decypher yourself. I positively require clarification and/or trade samples before meeting your request. Quote information vital to safeguarding of the service unquote does not qualify. Let me remind you of your bad position here following your disgraceful disappearance stop urge you confide Mackelvore immediately repeat immediately stop Chief.' "

Ben had not quite finished before Tarr began laughing in a strange, excited way.

"That's the way, Percy boy!" he cried. "Yes repeat no! Know why he's stalling, Ben, darling? He's sizing up to shoot me in the bloody back! That's how he got my Russki girl. He's playing the same tune, the bastard." He was ruffling Ben's hair, shouting at him, laughing. "I warn you, Ben: there's some damn lousy people in this outfit, so don't you trust the one of them, I'm telling you, or you'll never grow up strong!"

Alone in the darkness of the drawing-room, Smiley also waited, sitting in the housekeeper's uncomfortable chair, his head propped awkwardly against the earpiece of the telephone. Occasionally he would mutter something and Mendel would mutter back; most of the time they shared the silence. His mood was subdued, even a little glum. Like an actor, he had a sense of approaching anti-climax before the curtain went up, a sense of great things dwindling to a small, mean end; as death itself seemed small and mean to him after the struggles of his life. He had no sense of conquest that he knew of. His thoughts, as often when he was afraid, concerned people. He had no theories or judgements in particular. He simply wondered how everyone would be affected; and he felt responsible. He thought of Jim and Sam and Max and Connie and Jerry Westerby, and personal loyalties all broken; in a separate category he thought of Ann and the hopeless dislocation of their talk on the Cornish cliffs; he wondered whether there was any love between human beings that did not rest upon some sort of self-delusion; he wished he could just get up and walk out before it happened, but he couldn't. He worried, in a quite paternal way, about Guillam, and wondered how he would take the late strains of growing up. He thought again of the day he buried Control. He thought about treason and wondered whether there was mindless treason in the same way, supposedly, as there was mindless violence. It worried him that he felt so bankrupt; that whatever intellectual or philosophical precepts he clung to broke down entirely now that he was faced with the human situation.

"Anything?" he asked Mendel, into the telephone.

"A couple of drunks," said Mendel, "singing 'See the jungle when it's wet with rain.'"

"Never heard of it."

Changing the telephone to his left side, he drew the gun from the wallet pocket of his jacket, where it had already ruined the excellent silk lining. He discovered the safety catch, and for a moment played with the idea that he didn't know which way was on and which way off. He snapped out the magazine and put it back, and remembered doing this hundreds of times on the trot, in the night range at Sarratt before the war; he remembered how you always shot with two hands, sir, one to hold the gun and one the magazine, sir; and how there was a piece of Circus folklore which demanded that he should lay his index finger along the barrel and pull the trigger with his second. But when he tried it the sensation was ridiculous and he forgot about it.

"Just taking a walk," he murmured, and Mendel said "Righty-ho."

The gun still in his hand, he returned to the scullery, listening for a creak in the floorboards that might give him away, but the floor must have been concrete under the tatty carpet; he could have jumped and caused not even a vibration. With his torch he signalled two short flashes, a long delay, then two more. At once Guillam replied with three short.

"Back again."

"Got you," said Mendel.

He settled, thinking glumly of Ann: to dream the impossible dream. He put the gun in his pocket. From the canal side, the moan of a hooter. At night? Boats moving at night? Must be a car. What if Gerald has a whole emergency procedure that we know nothing about? A call-box to call-box, a car pick-up? What if Polyakov has after all a legman, a helper whom Connie never identified? He'd been through that already. This system was built to be watertight, to accommodate meetings in all contingencies. When it comes to tradecraft, Karla is a pedant.

And his fancy that he was being followed? What of that? What of the shadow he never saw, only felt, till his back seemed to tingle with the intensity of his watcher's gaze; he saw nothing, heard nothing, only felt. He was too old not to heed the warning. The creak of a stair that had not creaked before; the rustle of a shutter when no wind was blowing; the car with a different number plate but the same scratch on the offside wing; the face on the Metro that you know you have seen somewhere before: for years at a time these were signs he had lived by; any one of them was reason enough to move, change towns, identities. For in that profession there is no such thing as coincidence.

"One gone," said Mendel suddenly. "Hullo?"

"I'm here."

Somebody had just come out of the Circus, said Mendel. Front door, but he couldn't be certain of the identification. Mackintosh and hat. Bulky and moving fast. He must have ordered a cab to the door and stepped straight into it.

"Heading north, your way."

Smiley looked at his watch. Give him ten minutes, he thought. Give him twelve; he'll have to stop and phone Polyakov on the way. Then he thought, Don't be silly, he's done that already from the Circus.

"I'm ringing off," said Smiley.

"Cheers," said Mendel.

On the footpath, Guillam read three long flashes. The mole is on his way.

In the scullery Smiley had once more checked his thoroughfare, shoved some deck-chairs aside, and pinned a string to the mangle to guide him because he saw badly in the dark. The string led to the open kitchen door, and the kitchen led to the drawing-room and dining-room both; it had the two doors side by side. The kitchen was a long room, actually an annexe to the house before the glass scullery was added. He had thought of using the dining-room but it was too risky, and besides from the dining-room he couldn't signal to Guillam. So he waited in the scullery, feeling absurd in his stockinged feet, polishing his spectacles because the heat of his face kept misting them. It was much colder in the scullery. The drawing-room was close and over-heated but the scullery had these outside walls, and this glass and this concrete floor beneath the matting, which made his feet feel wet. The mole arrives first, he thought; the mole plays host: that is protocol, part of the pretence that Polyakov is Gerald's agent.

A London taxi is a flying bomb.

The comparison rose in him slowly, from deep in his unconscious memory. The clatter as it barges into the crescent, the metric *tick-tick* as the bass notes die. The cut-off: where has it stopped, which house—when all of us on the street are waiting in the dark, crouching under tables or clutching at pieces of string—which house? Then the slam of the door, the explosive anti-climax: if you can hear it, it's not for you.

But Smiley heard it, and it was for him.

He heard the tread of one pair of feet on the gravel, brisk and vigorous. They stopped. It's the wrong door, Smiley thought absurdly; go away. He had the gun in his hand; he had dropped the catch. Still he listened, heard nothing. You're suspicious, Gerald, he thought. You're an old mole, you can sniff there's something wrong. Millie, he thought; Millie has taken away the milk bottles, put up a warning, headed him off. Millie's spoilt the kill. Then he heard the latch turn, one turn, two; it's a Banham lock, he remembered—my God, we must keep Banham's in business. Of course: the mole had been patting his pockets, looking for his key. A nervous man would have it in his hand already, would have been clutching it, cosseting it in his pocket all the way in the taxi; but not the mole. The mole might be worried but he was not nervous. At the same moment the latch turned, the bell chimed—housekeepers' taste again: high tone, low tone, high tone. That will mean it's one of us, Millie had said; one of the boys, her boys, Connie's boys, Karla's boys. The front door opened, someone stepped into the house, he heard the shuffle of the mat, he heard the door close, he heard the light switches snap and saw a pale line appear under the kitchen door. He put the gun in his pocket and wiped the palm of his hand on his jacket, then took it out again and in the same moment he heard a second flying bomb, a second taxi pulling up, and footsteps fast. Polyakov didn't just have the key ready, he had his taxi money ready, too: do Russians tip, he wondered, or is tipping undemocratic? Again the bell rang, the front door opened and closed, and Smiley heard the double chink as two milk bottles were put on the hall table in the interest of good order and sound tradecraft.

Lord save me, thought Smiley in horror as he stared at the old icebox beside him; it never crossed my mind: suppose he had wanted to put them back in the fridge?

The strip of light under the kitchen door grew suddenly brighter as the drawing-room lights were switched on. An extraordinary silence descended over the house. Holding the string, Smiley edged forward over the icy floor. Then he heard voices. At first they were indistinct. They must still be at the far end of the room, he thought. Or perhaps they always begin in a low tone. Now Polyakov came nearer: he was at the trolley, pouring drinks.

"What is our cover story in case we are disturbed?" he asked in good English.

"Lovely voice," Smiley remembered; "mellow like yours. I often used to play the tapes twice, just to listen to him speaking." Connie, you should hear him now.

From the further end of the room still, a muffled murmur answered each question. Smiley could make nothing of it. "Where shall we regroup?" "What is our fallback?" "Have you anything on you that you would prefer me to be carrying during our talk, bearing in mind I have diplomatic immunity?"

It must be a catechism, Smiley thought; part of Karla's school routine.

"Is the switch down? Will you please check? Thank you. What will you drink?"

"Scotch," said Haydon, "a bloody great big one."

With a feeling of utter disbelief, Smiley listened to the familiar voice reading aloud the very telegram that Smiley himself had drafted for Tarr's use only forty-eight hours ago.

Then, for a moment, one part of Smiley broke into open revolt against the other. The wave of angry doubt that had swept over him in Lacon's garden, and that ever since had pulled against his progress like a worrying tide, drove him now on to the rocks of despair, and then to mutiny: I refuse. Nothing is worth the destruction of another human being. Somewhere the path of pain and betrayal must end. Until that happened, there was no future; there was only a continued slide into still more terrifying versions of the present. This man was my friend and Ann's lover, Jim's friend and—for all I know—Jim's lover, too; it was the treason, not the man, that belonged to the public domain.

Haydon had betrayed. As a lover, a colleague, a friend; as a patriot; as a member of that inestimable body that Ann loosely called the Set: in every capacity, Haydon had overtly pursued one aim and secretly achieved its opposite. Smiley knew very well that even now he did not grasp the scope of that appalling duplicity; yet there was a part of him that rose already in Haydon's defence. Was not Bill also betrayed? Connie's lament rang in his ears: "Poor loves. Trained to Empire, trained to rule the waves . . . You're the last, George, you and Bill." He saw with painful clarity an ambitious man born to the big canvas, brought up to rule, divide and conquer, whose visions and vanities all were fixed, like Percy's, upon the world's game; for whom the reality was a poor island with scarcely a voice that would carry across the water. Thus Smiley felt not only disgust, but, despite all that the moment meant to him, a surge of resentment against the institutions he was supposed to be protecting: "The social contract cuts both ways, you know," said Lacon. The Minister's lolling mendacity, Lacon's tight-lipped moral complacency, the bludgeoning greed of Percy Alleline:

such men invalidated any contract—why should anyone be loyal to them?

He knew, of course. He had always known it was Bill. Just as Control had known, and Lacon in Mendel's house. Just as Connie and Jim had known, and Alleline and Esterhase; all of them had tacitly shared that unexpressed half-knowledge which was like an illness they hoped would go away if it was never owned to, never diagnosed.

And Ann? Did Ann know? Was that the shadow that fell over them that day on the Cornish cliffs?

For a space, that was how Smiley stood: a fat, barefooted spy, as Ann would say, deceived in love and impotent in hate, clutching a gun in one hand, a bit of string in the other, as he waited in the darkness. Then, gun still in hand, he tiptoed backward as far as the window, from which he signalled five short flashes in quick succession. Having waited long enough to read the acknowledgement, he returned to his listening post.

Guillam raced down the canal towpath, the torch jolting wildly in his hand, till he reached a low arched bridge and a steel stairway that led upward in zigzags to Gloucester Avenue. The gate was closed and he had to climb it, ripping one sleeve to the elbow. Lacon was standing at the corner of Princess Road, wearing an old country coat and carrying a briefcase.

"He's there. He's arrived," Guillam whispered. "He's got Gerald." "I won't have bloodshed," Lacon warned. "I want absolute calm."

Guillam didn't bother to reply. Thirty yards down the road Mendel was waiting in a tame cab. They drove for two minutes, not so much, and stopped the cab short of the crescent. Guillam was holding Esterhase's door key. Reaching number 5, Mendel and Guillam stepped over the gate, rather than risk the noise of it, and kept to the grass verge. As they went, Guillam glanced back and thought for a moment he saw a figure watching them—man or woman, he couldn't tell—from

the shadow of a doorway across the road; but when he drew
Mendel's attention to the spot there was nothing there, and
Mendel ordered him quite roughly to calm down. The porch
light was out. Guillam went ahead; Mendel waited under an
apple tree. Guillam inserted the key, felt the lock ease as he
turned it. Damn fool, he thought triumphantly, why didn't you
drop the latch? He pushed open the door an inch and hesitated. He was breathing slowly, filling his lungs for action.
Mendel moved forward another bound. In the street two
young boys went by, laughing loudly because they were nervous of the night. Once more Guillam looked back but the
crescent was clear. He stepped into the hall. He was wearing
suede shoes and they squeaked on the parquet; there was no
carpet. At the drawing-room door he listened long enough for
the fury to break in him at last.

His butchered agents in Morocco, his exile to Brixton, the
daily frustration of his efforts as daily he grew older and youth
slipped through his fingers; the drabness that was closing
round him; the truncation of his power to love, enjoy, and
laugh; the constant erosion of the standards he wished to live
by; the checks and stops he had imposed on himself in the
name of tacit dedication—he could fling them all in Haydon's
sneering face. Haydon, once his confessor; Haydon, always
good for a laugh, a chat, and a cup of burnt coffee; Haydon, a
model on which he built his life.

And more. Now that he saw, he knew. Haydon was more
than his model, he was his inspiration, the torch-bearer of a
certain kind of antiquated romanticism, a notion of English
calling which—for the very reason that it was vague and understated and elusive—had made sense of Guillam's life till now.
In that moment, Guillam felt not merely betrayed but
orphaned. His suspicions, his resentments for so long turned
outward on the real world—on his women, his attempted
loves—now swung upon the Circus and the failed magic that
had formed his faith. With all his force he shoved open the

door and sprang inside, gun in hand. Haydon and a heavy man with black hair were seated either side of a small table. Polyakov—Guillam recognised him from the photographs—was smoking a very English pipe. He wore a grey cardigan with a zip down the front, like the top half of a track suit. He had not even taken the pipe from his mouth before Guillam had Haydon by the collar. With a single heave he lifted him straight out of his chair. He had thrown away his gun and was hurling Haydon from side to side, shaking him, and shouting. Then suddenly there seemed no point. After all, it was only Bill and they had done a lot together. Guillam had drawn back long before Mendel took his arm, and he heard Smiley, politely as ever, inviting "Bill and Colonel Viktorov," as he called them, to raise their hands and place them on their heads till Percy Alleline arrived.

"There was no one out there, was there, that you noticed?" Smiley asked of Guillam, while they waited.

"Quiet as the grave," said Mendel, answering for both of them.

37

There are moments that are made up of too much stuff for them to be lived at the time they occur. For Guillam and all those present, this was one. Smiley's continued distraction and Haydon's indifference; his frequent cautious glances from the window; Polyakov's predictable fit of indignation, his demands to be treated as became a member of the Diplomatic Corps—demands that Guillam from his place on the sofa tersely threatened to meet; the flustered arrival of Alleline and Bland; more protestations and the pilgrimage upstairs, where Smiley played the tapes; the long glum silence that followed their return to the drawing-room; the arrival of Lacon and finally of Esterhase and Fawn; Millie McCraig's silent ministrations with the teapot: all these events and cameos unrolled with a theatrical unreality that, much like the trip to Ascot an age before, was intensified by the unreality of the hour of day. It was also true that these incidents, which included at an early point the physical constraint of Polyakov—and a stream of Russian abuse directed at Fawn for hitting him, heaven knows where, despite Mendel's vigilance—were like a silly subplot against Smiley's only purpose in convening the assembly: to persuade Alleline that Haydon offered Smiley's one chance to treat with Karla, and to save, in humanitarian if not professional terms, whatever was left of the networks that Haydon had betrayed. Smiley was not empowered to conduct these transactions, nor did he seem to want to; perhaps he reckoned that between them Esterhase and Bland and Alleline were better placed to know what agents were still theoretically in being. In any event he soon took himself upstairs, where Guillam heard him once more restlessly padding from one room to the other as he continued his vigil from the windows.

So while Alleline and his lieutenants withdrew with Polyakov to the dining-room to conduct their business alone, the rest of them sat in silence in the drawing-room, either looking at Haydon or deliberately away from him. He seemed unaware that they were there. Chin in hand, he sat apart from them in a corner, watched over by Fawn, and he looked rather bored. The conference ended, they all trooped out of the dining-room and Alleline announced to Lacon, who insisted on not being present at the discussions, that an appointment had been made three days hence at this address, by which time "the Colonel will have had a chance to consult his superiors." Lacon nodded. It might have been a board meeting.

The departures were even stranger than the arrivals. Between Esterhase and Polyakov in particular, there was a curiously poignant farewell. Esterhase, who would always rather have been a gentleman than a spy, seemed determined to make a gallant occasion of it, and offered his hand, which Polyakov struck petulantly aside. Esterhase looked round forlornly for Smiley, perhaps in the hope of ingratiating himself further with him, then shrugged and flung an arm across Bland's broad shoulder. Soon afterwards they left together. They didn't say goodbye to anybody, but Bland looked dreadfully shaken and Esterhase seemed to be consoling him, though his own future at that moment could hardly have struck him as rosy. Soon afterwards a radio cab arrived for Polyakov and he, too, left without a nod to anyone. By now, the conversation had died entirely; without the Russian present, the show became wretchedly parochial. Haydon remained in his familiar bored pose, still watched by Fawn and Mendel, and stared at in mute

embarrassment by Lacon and Alleline. More telephone calls
were made, mainly for cars. At some point Smiley reappeared
from upstairs and mentioned Tarr. Alleline phoned the Circus
and dictated one telegram to Paris saying that he could return
to England with honour, whatever that meant; and a second to
Mackelvore saying that Tarr was an acceptable person, which
again seemed to Guillam a matter of opinion.

Finally, to the general relief, a windowless van arrived from
the Nursery, and two men got out whom Guillam had never
seen before, one tall and limping, the other doughy and
fair-haired. With a shudder Guillam realised they were inquisitors. Fawn fetched Haydon's coat from the hall, went through
the pockets, and respectfully helped him into it. At this point,
Smiley gently interposed himself and insisted that Haydon's
walk from the front door to the van should take place without
the hall light on, and that the escort should be large. Guillam,
Fawn, even Alleline, were pressed into service, and finally,
with Haydon at its centre, the whole motley group shuffled
through the garden to the van.

"It's simply a precaution," Smiley insisted. No one was disposed to argue with him. Haydon climbed in, and the inquisitors followed, locking the grille from inside. As the doors
closed, Haydon lifted one hand in an amiable, if dismissive,
gesture directed at Alleline.

So it was only afterwards that separate things came back to
Guillam and single people came forward for his recollection:
the unqualified hatred, for instance, which Polyakov directed
against everyone present, from poor little Millie McCraig
upwards, and which actually distorted him; his mouth curved
in a savage, uncontrollable sneer, he turned white and trembled, but not from fear and not from anger. It was just plain
hatred, of the sort that Guillam could not visit on Haydon, but
then Haydon was of his own kind.

For Alleline, in the moment of his defeat, Guillam discovered a sneaking admiration: Alleline at least had shown a

certain bearing. But later Guillam was not so sure whether Percy realised, on that first presentation of the facts, quite what the facts were: after all, he was still Chief, and Haydon was still his Iago.

But the strangest thing to Guillam, the insight that he took away with him and thought over much more deeply than was commonly his policy, was that despite his banked-up anger at the moment of breaking into the room, it required an act of will on his own part—and quite a violent one, at that—to regard Bill Haydon with much other than affection. Perhaps, as Bill would say, he had finally grown up. Best of all, on the same evening he climbed the steps to his flat and heard the familiar notes of Camilla's flute echoing in the well. And if Camilla that night lost something of her mystery, at least by morning he had succeeded in freeing her from the toils of double-cross to which he had latterly consigned her.

In other ways also, over the next few days, his life took on a brighter look. Percy Alleline had been dispatched on indefinite leave; Smiley had been asked to come back for a while and help sweep up what was left. For Guillam himself there was talk of being rescued from Brixton. It was not till much, much later that he learned that there had been a final act; and he put a name and a purpose to that familiar shadow which had followed Smiley through the night streets of Kensington.

38

For the next two days George Smiley lived in limbo. To his neighbours, when they noticed him, he seemed to have lapsed into a wasting grief. He rose late and pottered round the house in his dressing gown, cleaning things, dusting, cooking himself meals and not eating them. In the afternoon, quite against the local by-laws, he lit a coal fire and sat before it reading among his German poets or writing letters to Ann, which he seldom completed and never posted. When the telephone rang, he went to it quickly, only to be disappointed. Outside the window the weather continued foul, and the few passers-by—Smiley studied them continuously—were huddled in Balkan misery. Once Lacon called with a request from the Minister that Smiley should "stand by to help clear up the mess at Cambridge Circus, were he called upon to do so"—in effect, to act as night watchman till a replacement for Percy Alleline could be found. Replying vaguely, Smiley prevailed on Lacon to take extreme care of Haydon's physical safety while he was at Sarratt.

"Aren't you being a little dramatic?" Lacon retorted. "The only place he can go is Russia, and we're sending him there anyway."

"When? How soon?"

The details would take several more days to arrange. Smiley disdained, in his state of anti-climactic reaction, to ask how the interrogation was progressing meanwhile, but Lacon's manner suggested that the answer would have been "badly." Mendel brought him more solid fare.

"Immingham railway station's shut," he said. "You'll have to get out at Grimsby and hoof it or take a bus."

More often, Mendel simply sat and watched him, as one might an invalid. "Waiting won't make her come, you know," he said once. "Time the mountain went to Mohammed. Faint heart never won fair lady, if I may say so."

On the morning of the third day, the doorbell rang and Smiley answered it so fast that it might have been Ann, having mislaid her key as usual. It was Lacon. Smiley was required at Sarratt, he said; Haydon insisted on seeing him. The inquisitors had got nowhere and time was running out. The understanding was that if Smiley would act as confessor, Haydon would give a limited account of himself.

"I'm assured there has been no coercion," Lacon said.

Sarratt was a sorry place after the grandeur that Smiley remembered. Most of the elms had gone with the disease; pylons burgeoned over the old cricket field. The house itself, a sprawling brick mansion, had also come down a lot since the heyday of the cold war in Europe, and most of the better furniture seemed to have disappeared, he supposed into one of Alleline's houses. He found Haydon in a Nissen hut hidden among the trees.

Inside, it had the stink of an army guardhouse, black-painted walls and high-barred windows. Guards manned the rooms to either side and they received Smiley respectfully, calling him "sir." The word, it seemed, had got around. Haydon was dressed in denims, he was trembling, and he complained of dizziness. Several times he had to lie on his bed to stop the nosebleeds he was having. He had grown a half-hearted beard: apparently there was a dispute about whether he was allowed a razor.

"Cheer up," said Smiley. "You'll be out of here soon."

He had tried, on the journey down, to remember Prideaux, and Irina, and the Czech networks, and he even entered Haydon's

room with a vague notion of public duty: somehow, he thought,
he ought to censure him on behalf of right-thinking men. He
felt instead rather shy; he felt he had never known Haydon at
all, and now it was too late. He was also angry at Haydon's
physical condition, but when he taxed the guards they professed mystification. He was angrier still to learn that the additional security precautions he had insisted on had been relaxed
after the first day. When he demanded to see Craddox, head of
Nursery, Craddox was unavailable and his assistant acted dumb.

Their first conversation was halting and banal.

Would Smiley please forward the mail from his club, and
tell Alleline to get a move on with the horse-trading with
Karla? And he needed tissues, paper tissues for his nose. His
habit of weeping, Haydon explained, had nothing to do with
remorse or pain; it was a physical reaction to what he called the
pettiness of the inquisitors, who had made up their minds that
Haydon knew the names of other Karla recruits, and were
determined to have them before he left. There was also a
school of thought which held that Fanshawe, of the Christ
Church Optimates, had been acting as a talent-spotter for
Moscow Centre as well as for the Circus, Haydon explained.
"Really, what can one do with asses like that?" He managed,
despite his weakness, to convey that his was the only level head
around. They walked in the grounds, and Smiley established
with something close to despair that the perimeter was not
even patrolled any more, either by night or by day. After one
circuit, Haydon asked to go back to the hut, where he dug
up a piece of floorboard and extracted some sheets of paper
covered in hieroglyphics. They reminded Smiley forcibly of
Irina's diary. Squatting on the bed, he sorted through them,
and in that pose, in that dull light, with his long forelock dangling almost to the paper, he might have been lounging in
Control's room, back in the sixties, propounding some wonderfully plausible and quite inoperable piece of skulduggery
for England's greater glory. Smiley did not bother to write

anything down, since it was common ground between them that their conversation was being recorded anyway. The statement began with a long apologia, of which he afterwards recalled only a few sentences.

"We live in an age where only fundamental issues matter . . .

"The United States is no longer capable of undertaking its own revolution . . .

"The political posture of the United Kingdom is without relevance or moral viability in world affairs . . ."

With much of it, Smiley might, in other circumstances, have agreed; it was the tone, rather than the music, that alienated him.

"In capitalist America economic repression of the masses is institutionalised to a point which not even Lenin could have foreseen . . .

"The cold war began in 1917 but the bitterest struggles lie ahead of us, as America's death-bed paranoia drives her to greater excesses abroad . . ."

He spoke not of the decline of the West, but of its death by greed and constipation. He hated America very deeply, he said, and Smiley supposed he did. Haydon also took it for granted that secret services were the only real measure of a nation's political health, the only real expression of its subconscious.

Finally he came to his own case. At Oxford, he said, he was genuinely of the right, and in the war it scarcely mattered where one stood as long as one was fighting the Germans. For a while, after '45, he said, he had remained content with Britain's part in the world, till gradually it dawned on him just how trivial this was. How and when was a mystery. In the historical mayhem of his own lifetime he could point to no one occasion; simply he knew that if England were out of the game, the price of fish would not be altered by a farthing. He had often wondered which side he would be on if the test ever came; after prolonged reflection he had finally to admit that if either monolith had to win the day, he would prefer it to be the East.

"It's an aesthetic judgement as much as anything," he explained, looking up. "Partly a moral one, of course."

"Of course," said Smiley politely.

From then on, he said, it was only a matter of time before he put his efforts where his convictions lay.

That was the first day's take. A white sediment had formed on Haydon's lips, and he had begun weeping again. They agreed to meet tomorrow at the same time.

"It would be nice to go into the detail a little, if we could, Bill," Smiley said as he left.

"Oh, and look—tell Jan, will you?" Haydon was lying on the bed, staunching his nose again. "Doesn't matter a hoot what you say, long as you make it final." Sitting up, he wrote out a cheque and put it in a brown envelope. "Give her that for the milk bill."

Realising, perhaps, that Smiley was not quite at ease with this brief, he added, "Well, I can't take her with me, can I? Even if they let her come, she'd be a bloody millstone."

The same evening, following Haydon's instructions, Smiley took a tube to Kentish Town and unearthed a cottage in an unconverted mews. A flat-faced fair girl in jeans opened the door to him; there was a smell of oil paint and baby. He could not remember whether he had met her at Bywater Street, so he opened with "I'm from Bill Haydon. He's quite all right but I've got various messages from him."

"Jesus," said the girl softly. "About bloody time and all."

The drawing-room was filthy. Through the kitchen door he saw a pile of dirty crockery and he knew she used everything until it ran out, then washed it all at once. The floorboards were bare except for long psychedelic patterns of snakes and flowers and insects painted over them.

"That's Bill's Michelangelo ceiling," she said conversationally. "Only he's not going to have Michelangelo's bad back. Are you government?" she asked, lighting a cigarette. "He works for government, he told me." Her hand was shaking and she had yellow smudges under her eyes.

"Oh, look, first I'm to give you that," said Smiley, reaching in an inside pocket, and handing her the envelope with the cheque.

"Bread," said the girl, and put the envelope beside her.

"Bread," said Smiley, answering her grin; then something in his expression, or the way he echoed that one word, made her take up the envelope and rip it open. There was no note, just the cheque, but the cheque was enough; even from where Smiley sat, he could see it had four figures.

Not knowing what she was doing, she walked across the room to the fireplace and put the cheque with the grocery bills in an old tin on the mantelpiece. She went into the kitchen and mixed two cups of Nescafé, but she came out with only one.

"Where is he?" she said. She stood facing him. "He's gone chasing after that snotty little sailor-boy again. Is that it? And this is the pay-off, is that it? Well, you bloody tell him from me—"

Smiley had had scenes like this before, and now absurdly the old words came back to him.

"Bill's been doing work of national importance. I'm afraid we can't talk about it, and nor must you. A few days ago he went abroad on a secret job. He'll be away some while. Even years. He wasn't allowed to tell anyone he was leaving. He wants you to forget him. I really am most awfully sorry."

He got that far before she burst out. He didn't hear all she said, because she was blurting and screaming, and when the baby heard her it started screaming, too, from upstairs. She was swearing—not at him, not even particularly at Bill, just swearing dry-eyed—and demanding to know who the hell, who the bloody bloody hell believed in government any more? Then her mood changed. Round the walls, Smiley noticed Bill's other paintings, mainly of the girl; few were finished, and they had a cramped, condemned quality by comparison with his earlier work.

"You don't like him, do you? I can tell," she said. "So why do you do his dirty work for him?"

To this question also there seemed no immediate answer. Returning to Bywater Street, he again had the impression of being followed, and tried to telephone Mendel with the number of a cab which had twice caught his eye, and to ask him to make immediate enquiries. For once, Mendel was out till after midnight: Smiley slept uneasily and woke at five. By eight he was back at Sarratt, to find Haydon in a festive mood. The inquisitors had not bothered him; he had been told by Craddox that the exchanges had been agreed and he should expect to travel tomorrow or the next day. His requests had a valedictory ring: the balance of his salary and the proceeds of any odd sales made on his behalf should be forwarded to him care of the Moscow Narodny Bank, which would also handle his mail. The Arnolfini Gallery in Bristol had a few pictures of his, including some early water-colours of Damascus, which he coveted. Could Smiley please arrange? Then, the cover for his disappearance:

"Play it long," he advised. "Say I've been posted, lay on the mystery, give it a couple of years, then run me down . . ."

"Oh, I think we can manage something, thank you," Smiley said.

For the first time since Smiley had known him, Haydon was worried about clothes. He wanted to arrive *looking* like someone, he said; first impressions were so important. "Those Moscow tailors are unspeakable. Dress you up like a bloody beadle."

"Quite," said Smiley, whose opinion of London tailors was no better.

Oh, and there was a boy, he added carelessly, a sailor friend, lived in Notting Hill. "Better give him a couple of hundred to shut him up. Can you do that out of the reptile fund?"

"I'm sure."

He wrote out an address. In the same spirit of good fellowship, Haydon then entered into what Smiley had called the details.

He declined to discuss any part of his recruitment or of his lifelong relationship with Karla. "Lifelong?" Smiley repeated quickly. "When did you meet?" The assertions of yesterday appeared suddenly nonsensical; but Haydon would not elaborate.

From about 1950 onwards, if he was to be believed, Haydon had made Karla occasional selected gifts of intelligence. These early efforts were confined to what he hoped would directly advance the Russian cause over the American; he was "scrupulous not to give them anything harmful to ourselves," as he put it, or harmful to our agents in the field.

The Suez adventure in '56 finally persuaded him of the inanity of the British situation, and of the British capacity to spike the advance of history while not being able to offer anything by way of contribution. The sight of the Americans sabotaging the British action in Egypt was, paradoxically, an additional incentive. He would say therefore that from '56 on, he was a committed, full-time Soviet mole with no holds barred. In 1961 he formally received Soviet citizenship, and over the next ten years two Soviet medals—quaintly, he would not say which, though he insisted that they were "top stuff." Unfortunately, overseas postings during this period limited his access; and since he insisted on his information being acted upon wherever possible—"rather than being chucked into some daft Soviet archive"—his work was dangerous as well as uneven. With his return to London, Karla sent him Polly (which seemed to be the house name for Polyakov) as a helpmate, but Haydon found the constant pressure of clandestine meetings difficult to sustain, particularly in view of the quantity of stuff he was photographing.

He declined to discuss cameras, equipment, pay, or tradecraft during this pre-Merlin period in London, and Smiley was conscious all the while that even the little Haydon was telling him was selected with meticulous care from a greater, and perhaps somewhat different truth.

Meanwhile both Karla and Haydon were receiving signals that Control was smelling a rat. Control was ill, of course, but clearly he would never willingly give up the reins while there was a chance that he was making Karla a present of the service. It was a race between Control's researches and his health. Twice he had very nearly struck gold—again Haydon declined to say how—and if Karla had not been quick on his feet, the mole Gerald would have been trapped. It was out of this nervy situation that first Merlin and finally Operation Testify were born. Witchcraft was conceived primarily to take care of the succession: to put Alleline next to the throne, and hasten Control's demise. Secondly, of course, Witchcraft gave Centre absolute autonomy over the product flowing into Whitehall. Thirdly—and in the long run most important, Haydon insisted—it brought the Circus into position as a major weapon against the American target.

"How much of the material was genuine?" Smiley asked.

Obviously the standard varied according to what one wanted to achieve, said Haydon. In theory, fabrication was very easy: Haydon had only to advise Karla of Whitehall's areas of ignorance and the fabricators would write for them. Once or twice, for the hell of it, said Haydon, he had written the odd report himself. It was an amusing exercise to receive, evaluate, and distribute one's own work. The advantages of Witchcraft in terms of tradecraft were, of course, inestimable. It placed Haydon virtually out of Control's reach, and gave him a cast-iron cover story for meeting Polly whenever he wished. Often months would pass without their meeting at all. Haydon would photograph Circus documents in the seclusion of his room—under cover of preparing Polly's chicken-feed—hand it over to Esterhase with a lot of other rubbish, and let him cart it down to the safe house in Lock Gardens.

"It was a classic," Haydon said simply. "Percy made the running, I slipstreamed behind him, Roy and Toby did the legwork."

Here Smiley asked politely whether Karla had ever thought of having Haydon actually take over the Circus himself: why bother with a stalking-horse at all? Haydon stalled and it occurred to Smiley that Karla, like Control, might well have considered Haydon better cast as a subordinate.

Operation Testify, said Haydon, was rather a desperate throw. Haydon was certain that Control was getting very warm indeed. An analysis of the files he was drawing produced an uncomfortably complete inventory of the operations that Haydon had blown, or otherwise caused to abort. He had also succeeded in narrowing the field to officers of a certain age and rank . . .

"Was Stevcek's original offer genuine, by the way?" Smiley asked.

"Good Lord, no," said Haydon, actually shocked. "It was a fix from the start. Stevcek existed, of course. He was a distinguished Czech general. But he never made an offer to anyone."

Here Smiley sensed Haydon falter. For the first time, he actually seemed uneasy about the morality of his behaviour. His manner became noticeably defensive.

"Obviously, we needed to be certain Control would rise, and how he would rise . . . and who he would send. We couldn't have him picking some half-arsed little pavement artist; it had to be a big gun to make the story stick. We knew he'd only settle for someone outside the mainstream and someone who wasn't Witchcraft-cleared. If we made it a Czech, he'd have to choose a Czech speaker, naturally."

"Naturally."

"We wanted old Circus: someone who could bring down the temple a bit."

"Yes," said Smiley, remembering that heaving, sweating figure on the hilltop. "Yes, I see the logic of that."

"Well, damn it, I got him back," Haydon snapped.

"Yes, that was good of you. Tell me, did Jim come to see you before he left on that Testify mission?"

"Yes, he did, as a matter of fact."

"To say what?"

For a long, long while Haydon hesitated, then did not answer. But the answer was written there, all the same: in the sudden emptying of his eyes, in the shadow of guilt that crossed his face. He came to warn you, Smiley thought; because he loved you. To warn you; just as he came to tell me that Control was mad, but couldn't find me because I was in Berlin. Jim was watching your back for you right till the end.

Also, Haydon resumed, it had to be a country with a recent history of counter-revolution: Czecho was honestly the only place.

Smiley appeared not quite to be listening.

"Why did you bring him back?" he asked. "For friendship's sake? Because he was harmless and you held all the cards?"

It wasn't just that, Haydon explained. As long as Jim was in a Czech prison (he didn't say Russian), people would agitate for him and see him as some sort of key. But once he was back, everyone in Whitehall would conspire to keep him quiet; that was the way of it with repatriations.

"I'm surprised Karla didn't just shoot him. Or did he hold back out of delicacy towards you?"

But Haydon had drifted away again into half-baked political assertions.

Then he began speaking about himself, and already, to Smiley's eye, he seemed visibly to be shrinking to something quite small and mean. He was touched to hear that Ionesco had recently promised us a play in which the hero kept silent and everyone round him spoke incessantly. When the psychologists and fashionable historians came to write their apologias for him, he hoped they would remember that that was how he saw himself. As an artist he had said all he had to say at the age of seventeen, and one had to do something with one's later years. He was awfully sorry he couldn't take some of his friends with him. He hoped Smiley would remember him with affection.

Smiley wanted at that point to tell him that he would not remember him in those terms at all, and a good deal more besides, but there seemed no point and Haydon was having another nosebleed.

"Oh, I'm to ask you to avoid publicity, by the way. Miles Sercombe made quite a thing of it."

Here Haydon managed a laugh. Having messed up the Circus in private, he said, he had no wish to repeat the process in public.

Before he left, Smiley asked the one question he still cared about.

"I'll have to break it to Ann. Is there anything particular you want me to pass on to her?"

It required discussion for the implication of Smiley's question to get through to him. At first, he thought Smiley had said "Jan," and couldn't understand why he had not yet called on her.

"Oh, *your* Ann," he said, as if there were a lot of Ann's around.

It was Karla's idea, he explained. Karla had long recognised that Smiley represented the biggest threat to the mole Gerald. "He said you were quite good."

"Thank you."

"But you had this one price: Ann. The last illusion of the illusionless man. He reckoned that if I were known to be Ann's lover around the place you wouldn't see me very straight when it came to other things." His eyes, Smiley noticed, had become very fixed. Pewtery, Ann called them. "Not to strain it or anything but, if it was possible, join the queue. Point?"

"Point," said Smiley.

For instance, on the night of Testify, Karla was adamant that if possible Haydon should be dallying with Ann. As a form of insurance.

"And wasn't there in fact a small hitch that night?" Smiley asked, remembering Sam Collins and the matter of whether Ellis had been shot. Haydon agreed that there had been. If everything had gone according to plan, the first Czech bulletins should have broken at ten-thirty. Haydon would have had a chance to read his club ticker-tape after Sam Collins had rung Ann, and before he arrived at the Circus to take over. But because Jim had been shot, there was fumble at the Czech end and the bulletin was released after his club had closed.

"Lucky no one followed it up," he said, helping himself to another of Smiley's cigarettes. "Which one was I, by the way?" he asked conversationally. "I forget."

"Tailor. I was Beggarman."

By then Smiley had had enough, so he slipped out, not bothering to say goodbye. He got into his car and drove for an hour anywhere, till he found himself on a side road to Oxford doing eighty, so he stopped for lunch and headed back for London. He still couldn't face Bywater Street, so he went to a cinema, dined somewhere, and got home at midnight, slightly drunk, to find both Lacon and Miles Sercombe on the doorstep, and Sercombe's fatuous Rolls, the black bedpan, all fifty feet of it, shoved up on the curb in everyone's way.

They drove to Sarratt at a mad speed, and there, in the open night under a clear sky, lit by several hand torches and stared at by several white-faced inmates of the Nursery, sat Bill Haydon on a garden bench facing the moonlit cricket field. He was wearing striped pyjamas under his overcoat; they looked more like prison clothes. His eyes were open and his head was propped unnaturally to one side, like the head of a bird when its neck has been expertly broken.

There was no particular dispute about what had happened. At ten-thirty Haydon had complained to his guards of sleeplessness and nausea: he proposed to take some fresh air. His case being regarded as closed, no one thought to accompany him and he walked out into the darkness alone. One of the guards remembered him making a joke about "examining the state of the wicket." The other was too busy watching the television to remember anything. After half an hour they became apprehensive, so the senior guard went off to take a look while his assistant stayed behind in case Haydon should return. Haydon was found where he was now sitting; the guard thought at first that he had fallen asleep. Stooping over him, he caught the smell of alcohol—he guessed gin or vodka—and decided that Haydon was drunk, which surprised him since the Nursery was officially dry. It wasn't till he tried to lift him that his head flopped over, and the rest of him followed as dead weight. Having vomited (the traces were over there by the tree), the guard propped him up again and sounded the alarm.

Had Haydon received any messages during the day? Smiley asked.

No. But his suit had come back from the cleaners and it was possible a message had been concealed in it—for instance inviting him to a rendezvous.

"So the Russians did it," the Minister announced with satisfaction to Haydon's unresponsive form. "To stop him peaching, I suppose. Bloody thugs."

"No," said Smiley. "They take pride in getting their people back."

"Then who the hell *did?*"

Everyone waited on Smiley's answer, but none came. The torches went out and the group moved uncertainly towards the car.

"Can we lose him just the same?" the Minister asked on the way back.

"He was a Soviet citizen. Let them have him," said Lacon.

They agreed it was a pity about the networks. Better see whether Karla would do the deal anyhow.

"He won't," said Smiley.

39

Recalling all this in the seclusion of his first-class compartment, Smiley had the curious sensation of watching Haydon through the wrong end of a telescope. He had eaten very little since last night, but the bar had been open for most of the journey.

Leaving King's Cross, he had had a wistful notion of liking Haydon and respecting him: Bill was a man, after all, who had had something to say and had said it. But his mental system rejected this convenient simplification. The more he puzzled over Haydon's rambling account of himself, the more conscious he was of the contradictions. He tried at first to see Haydon in the romantic newspaper terms of a thirties intellectual, for whom Moscow was the natural Mecca. "Moscow was Bill's discipline," he told himself. "He needed the symmetry of an historical and economic solution." This struck him as too sparse, so he added more of the man whom he was trying to like: "Bill was a romantic and a snob. He wanted to join an elitist vanguard and lead the masses out of darkness." Then he remembered the half-finished canvases in the girl's drawing-room in Kentish Town: cramped, over-worked, and condemned. He remembered also the ghost of Bill's authoritarian father—Ann had called him simply the Monster—and he imagined Bill's Marxism making up for his inadequacy as an artist and for his loveless childhood. Later, of course, it hardly mattered if the doctrine wore thin. Bill was set on the road and Karla would know how to keep him there. Treason is very much a matter of habit, Smiley decided, seeing Bill again stretched out on the floor in Bywater Street, while Ann played him music on the gramophone.

Bill had loved it, too. Smiley didn't doubt that for a moment. Standing at the middle of a secret stage, playing world against world, hero and playwright in one: oh, Bill had loved that, all right.

Smiley shrugged it all aside, distrustful as ever of the standard shapes of human motive. He settled instead for a picture of one of those wooden Russian dolls that open up, revealing one person inside the other, and another inside him. Of all men living, only Karla had seen the last little doll inside Bill Haydon. When was Bill recruited, and how? Was his right-wing stand at Oxford a pose, or was it paradoxically the state of sin from which Karla summoned him to grace?

Ask Karla: pity I didn't.

Ask Jim: I never shall.

Over the flat East Anglian landscape as it slid slowly by, the unyielding face of Karla replaced Bill Haydon's crooked death mask. "But you had this one price: Ann. The last illusion of the illusionless man. He reckoned that if I were known to be Ann's lover around the place you wouldn't see me very straight when it came to other things."

Illusion? Was that really Karla's name for love? And Bill's?

"Here," said the guard very loudly, and perhaps for the second time. "Come on with it, you're for Grimsby, aren't you?"

"No, no—Immingham." Then he remembered Mendel's instructions and clambered onto the platform.

There was no cab in sight, so, having enquired at the ticket office, he made his way across the empty forecourt and stood beside a green sign marked "Queue." He had hoped she might collect him, but perhaps she hadn't received his wire. Ah well: the post office at Christmas: who could blame them? He wondered how she would take the news about Bill; till, remembering her frightened face on the cliffs in Cornwall, he realised that by then Bill was already dead for her. She had sensed the coldness of his touch, and somehow guessed what lay behind it.

Illusion? He repeated to himself. Illusionless?

It was bitterly cold. He hoped very much that her wretched lover had found her somewhere warm to live.

He wished he had brought her fur boots from the cupboard under the stairs.

He remembered the copy of Grimmelshausen, still uncollected at Martindale's club.

Then he saw her: her disreputable car shunting towards him down the lane marked "Buses Only" and Ann at the wheel staring the wrong way. Saw her get out, leaving the indicator winking, and walk into the station to enquire: tall and puckish, extraordinarily beautiful, essentially another man's woman.

For the rest of that term, Jim Prideaux behaved in the eyes of Roach much as his mother had behaved when his father went away. He spent a lot of time on little things, like fixing up the lighting for the school play and mending the soccer nets with string, and in French he took enormous pains over small inaccuracies. But big things, like his walks and solitary golf, he gave up altogether, and in the evenings stayed in and kept clear of the village. Worst of all was his staring empty look when Roach caught him unaware, and the way he forgot things in class, even red marks for merit. Roach had to remind him to hand them in each week.

To support him, Roach took the job of dimmer man on the lighting. Thus at rehearsals Jim had to give him a special signal—to Bill and no one else. He was to raise his arm and drop it to his side when he wanted the footlights to fade.

With time, Jim seemed to respond to treatment, however. His eye grew clearer and he became alert again, as the shadow of his mother's death withdrew. By the night of the play, he was more light-hearted than Roach had ever known him. "Hey, Jumbo, you silly toad, where's your mac—can't you see it's raining?" he called out as, tired but triumphant, they trailed back to the main building after the performance. "His real name is Bill," he heard him explain to a visiting parent. "We were new boys together."

The gun, Bill Roach had finally convinced himself, was, after all, a dream.

Silverview
A Novel

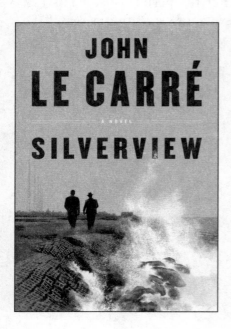

Julian Lawndsley has renounced his high-flying job in the city for a simpler life running a bookshop in a small English seaside town. But Edward, a Polish émigré living in Silverview, the big house on the edge of town, seems to know a lot about Julian's family and is quite interested in his new career. When a London spy chief receives a letter warning him of a dangerous leak, the investigations lead him to this quiet town. In his inimitable voice, John le Carré seeks to answer the question of what we truly owe to the people we love.

"The plot unfolds with as much cryptic cunning as a reader could want . . . Enjoyable throughout, written with grace, and a welcome gift from the past." —*The Wall Street Journal*

Praise for John le Carré

"There are those writer[s] . . . who themselves should be immortal. . . . I would suggest immortality for John le Carré, who I believe one of the most intelligent and entertaining writers. . . . May he write forever!"
—Alan Cheuse, *Chicago Tribune*

"No other contemporary novelist has more durably enjoyed the twin badges of being both well-read and well-regarded."
—Scott Turow

"A brilliant linguistic artist with a keen eye for the exotic and not-so-exotic locale, a crafty moralizer."
—*The Wall Street Journal*

"Le Carré is simply the world's greatest fictional spymaster."
—*Newsweek*

"Le Carré's work is . . . the gold standard of espionage fiction and the author is . . . a master of any sort of fiction, no matter the genre."
—*The Seattle Times*

"Le Carré's execution is perfect."
—*The New York Times Book Review*

"Le Carré has a great talent for entangling his audience in the sticky tape of complexity, paradox, and irony, and much of the pleasure in his stories is following the same dense, dark path as his characters."
—*New York Daily News*

"He has reinvented the realistic spy story as the supreme theater of paradox, where heroism breeds vice, and virtue is a quite accidental by-product of impudent crimes."
—*Time*

PENGUIN BOOKS

THE LOOKING GLASS WAR

JOHN LE CARRÉ was born in 1931 and attended the universities of Bern and Oxford. He taught at Eton and served briefly in British Intelligence during the Cold War. For the last 50 years he has lived by his pen. He divides his time between London and Cornwall.

JOHN LE CARRÉ

THE LOOKING GLASS WAR

PENGUIN BOOKS

PENGUIN BOOKS
Published by the Penguin Group
Penguin Group (USA) Inc., 375 Hudson Street, New York, New York 10014, USA
Penguin Group (Canada), 90 Eglinton Avenue East, Suite 700,
Toronto, Ontario M4P 2Y3, Canada (a division of Pearson Penguin Canada Inc.)
Penguin Books Ltd, 80 Strand, London WC2R 0RL, England
Penguin Ireland, 25 St Stephen's Green, Dublin 2, Ireland (a division of Penguin Books Ltd)
Penguin Group (Australia), 707 Collins Street, Melbourne, Victoria 3008, Australia
(a division of Pearson Australia Group Pty Ltd)
Penguin Books India Pvt Ltd, 11 Community Centre,
Panchsheel Park, New Delhi–110 017, India
Penguin Group (NZ), 67 Apollo Drive, Rosedale, Auckland 0632,
New Zealand (a division of Pearson New Zealand Ltd)
Penguin Books (South Africa), Rosebank Office Park, 181 Jan Smuts Avenue,
Parktown North 2193, South Africa
Penguin China, B7 Jiaming Center, 27 East Third Ring Road North,
Chaoyang District, Beijing 100020, China

Penguin Books Ltd, Registered Offices:
80 Strand, London WC2R 0RL, England

First published in Great Britain by William Heinemann Ltd. 1965
First published in the United States of America by Coward-McCann, Inc. 1965
Published in Penguin Books 2012

11th Printing

Copyright © le Carré Productions, 1965
Copyright renewed © David Cornwell, 1993
All rights reserved

LIBRARY OF CONGRESS CATALOGING-IN-PUBLICATION DATA
Le Carré, John, 1931–
The looking glass war / John Le Carré.
p. cm.
ISBN 978-0-14-312259-3
1. Smiley, George (Fictitious character)—Fiction.   2. Intelligence officers—Fiction.
3. Cold War.   4. Spy stories.   I. Title.
PR6062.E33L6 2013
823'.914—dc23   2012038483

Printed in the United States of America

To James Kennaway

'I wouldn't mind being a Pawn, if only I might join.'

Alice

FOREWORD

None of the characters, clubs, institutions nor intelligence organisations I have described here or elsewhere exists, or has existed to my knowledge in real life. I wish to make that very clear.

My thanks are due to the Radio Society of Great Britain and to Mr R. E. Molland, to the editors and staff of *Aviation Week & Space Technology* and Mr Ronald Coles, all of whom provided me with valuable technical advice; and to Miss Elizabeth Tollinton for her secretarial help.

I must thank above all my wife for her untiring cooperation.

JOHN LE CARRÉ,
Agios Nikolaos,
Crete
May, 1964

CONTENTS

'The carrying of a very heavy weight such as a large suitcase or trunk, immediately before sending practice, renders the muscles of the forearm, wrist and fingers too insensitive to produce good Morse.'

F. Tait's *The Complete Morse Instructor*, Pitman.

INTRODUCTION

JOHN LE CARRÉ

July 1991

Any writer who imagines he has a career is the fool of fashion and circumstance. He has his books, and he has his artistic conscience, which, if he is any good, is a great deal more rigorous than anybody else's judgment.

I learned this the hard way with *The Looking Glass War*, which I wrote in the aftermath of *The Spy Who Came in from the Cold*, and which was received, in Britain, with such wholesale derision from the critical community that, had I taken it to heart, would have persuaded me to follow a different profession, such as window-cleaning, or literary journalism.

After the success of *The Spy* I felt I had earned the right to experiment with the more fragile possibilities of the spy story than those I had explored till now. For the truth was, that the realities of spying as I had known them on the ground had been far removed from the fiendishly clever conspiracy that had entrapped my hero and heroine in *The Spy*. I was eager to find a way of illustrating the muddle and futility that were so much closer to life. Indeed, I felt I had to: for while *The Spy* had been heralded as the book that ripped the mask off the spy business, my private view was that it had glamorised the spy business to Kingdom Come. The brilliance of my British Intelligence mastermind, Control, was like a fan letter to the British secret establishment; the shared death of my doomed lovers at the Berlin Wall was a device of intense romantic satisfaction.

So this time, I thought, I'll tell it the hard way. This time, cost what it will, I'll describe a Secret Service that is really not very good at all; that is eking out its wartime glory; that is feeding itself on Little England fantasies; is isolated, directionless, overprotected and destined ultimately to destroy itself.

Such an outfit, if I got it right, would speak not only for the British Intelligence community of the 'sixties, with its internecine feuds and betrayals, its class distinctions and its obsessive vision of the American oaf, trespassing on our precious colonial turf. It would presume to speak also for Little England itself, the England of the Suez campaign, the same England that in those days was being hilariously torn to shreds by the *Beyond the Fringe* team, and by the revolutionary 'getting-out-from-under' music of the Beatles. In a word, I would use the spy story to tell a *roman noir* in which the British Intelligence Service would be portrayed as a political somnambulant, tapping about in the after-lunch haze of victory, uncertain any more whether it is fighting the Russians or the Germans, but fighting anyway, because not to fight is to wake up. In that sense, *The Looking Glass War* would be a deliberate reversal, if not an actual parody, of *The Spy*.

My error, I now believe, was not to have gone far enough down this dangerous path. I should not, as I see it now, have bothered with the Circus or George Smiley at all. I should not have taken counsel from my American editor, the gifted Jack Geoghegan. I should not have pulled my punches. I should have let the Department exist where I was convinced that Britain herself existed, and in some eerie way contrives to exist until this very day: in a vapour of self-delusion and class arrogance, in a gung-ho world of 'we've-never-had-it-so-good' bordered on one side by our supposed external enemies—the Europeans, the Russians, you name it—and on the other by an illusory conviction that our island can live off its colonial heritage and the favour of its American Cousins for all time.

But my British critics absolutely didn't see the joke. Or if they did see it, they didn't find it faintly funny. They wanted *A Spy at Easter*, *A Spy at Christmas*, *Alec Leamas Rides Again*. They wanted anything but the bad, sad news. Thus the book at first found favour only among people who knew us from outside: in Europe, and to my relief in America, where John Kenneth Galbraith wrote that it evoked for him memories of the abortive Bay of Pigs invasion, which was also based on self-delusion; and Allen Dulles, who had recently retired from his post of Director of the Central Intelligence Agency, that this was how the spy world really was. But here in Britain, at least to begin with, I had to live with the pained disappointment of many readers and the outright abuse of the critics. I was duly hurt, and I duly survived. And so, to my surprise, did the book, which little by little clambered its way back into favour with my public.

It is certainly a sad book, but as I flip through it now I find it a rather beautiful one. I wrote it on the island of Crete, whither I had fled after the clamour of *The Spy*, in the hope of repairing a marriage that had suffered too much from the blows of success. Stuck on a solitary Cretan peninsula, and feeling somewhat directionless myself, I suppose I naturally identified with the forlorn loves of my two male protagonists: Avery's, for his estranged wife, and Leiser's for a world that no longer existed.

I cannot tell, even now, how well or badly the novel works. Perhaps, as Joseph Conrad remarked of one of his characters, it stands for so much that it doesn't stand up. What I do know is that it was an honest book, and perhaps a brave one. Above all, it was the best I could do at the time.

THE LOOKING GLASS WAR

PART I

Taylor's Run

'A fool lies here who tried to hustle the East.'

KIPLING

1

Snow covered the airfield.

It had come from the north, in the mist, driven by the night wind, smelling of the sea. There it would stay all Winter, threadbare on the grey earth, an icy, sharp dust; not thawing and freezing, but static like a year without seasons. The changing mist, like the smoke of war, would hang over it, swallow up now a hangar, now the radar hut, now the machines; release them piece by piece, drained of colour, black carrion on a white desert.

It was a scene of no depth, no recession and no shadows. The land was one with the sky; figures and buildings locked in the cold like bodies in an icefloe.

Beyond the airfield there was nothing; no house, no hill, no road; not even a fence, a tree; only the sky pressing on the dunes, the running fog that lifted on the muddy Baltic shore. Somewhere inland were the mountains.

A group of children in school caps had gathered at the long observation window, chatting in German. Some wore ski clothes. Taylor gazed dully past them, holding a glass in his gloved hand. A boy turned round and stared at him, blushed and whispered to the other children. They fell silent.

He looked at his watch, making a wide arc with his arm, partly to free the sleeve of his overcoat and partly because it was his style; a military man, he wished you to say, decent regiment, decent club, knocked around in the war.

Ten to four. The plane was an hour late. They would have to

announce the reason soon over the loudspeaker. He wondered what they would say: delayed by fog, perhaps; delayed take-off. They probably didn't even know – and they certainly would not admit – that she was two hundred miles off course, and south of Rostock. He finished his drink, turned to get rid of the empty glass. He had to admit that some of these foreign hooches, drunk in their own country, weren't at all bad. On the spot, with a couple of hours to kill and ten degrees of frost the other side of the window, you could do a lot worse than Steinhäger. He'd make them order it at the Alias Club when he got back. Cause quite a stir.

The loudspeaker was humming; it blared suddenly, faded out and began again, properly tuned. The children stared expectantly at it. First, the announcement in Finnish, then in Swedish, now in English. Northern Air Services regretted the delay to their charter flight two-nine-zero from Düsseldorf. No hint of how long, no hint of why. They probably didn't know themselves.

But Taylor knew. He wondered what would happen if he sauntered over to that pert little hostess in the glass box and told her: two-nine-zero will be a bit of time yet, my dear, she's been blown off course by heavy northerly gales over the Baltic, bearings all to Hades. The girl wouldn't believe him, of course, she'd think he was a crank. Later she'd know better. She'd realise he was something rather unusual, something rather special.

Outside it was already growing dark. Now the ground was lighter than the sky; the swept runways stood out against the snow like dykes, stained with the amber glow of marking lights. In the nearest hangars neon tubes shed a weary pallor over men and aeroplanes; the foreground beneath him sprang briefly to life as a beam from the control tower flicked across it. A fire engine had pulled away from the workshops on the left and joined the three ambulances already parked short of the centre runway. Simultaneously they switched on their blue rotating lights, and stood in line patiently flashing out their warning. The children pointed at them, chattering excitedly.

The girl's voice began again on the loudspeaker, it could

only have been a few minutes since the last announcement. Once more the children stopped talking and listened. The arrival of flight two-nine-zero would be delayed at least another hour. Further information would be given as soon as it became available. There was something in the girl's voice, midway between surprise and anxiety, which seemed to communicate itself to the half-dozen people sitting at the other end of the waiting-room. An old woman said something to her husband, stood up, took her handbag and joined the group of children. For a time she peered stupidly into the twilight. Finding no comfort there, she turned to Taylor and said in English, 'What is become of the Düsseldorf plane?' Her voice had the throaty, indignant lilt of a Dutchwoman. Taylor shook his head. 'Probably the snow,' he replied. He was a brisk man; it went with his military way.

Pushing open the swing door, Taylor made his way downstairs to the reception hall. Near to the main entrance he recognised the yellow pennant of the Northern Air Services. The girl at the desk was very pretty.

'What's happened to the Düsseldorf flight?' His style was confiding; they said he had a knack with little girls. She smiled and shrugged her shoulders.

'I expect it is the snow. We are often having delays in Autumn.'

'Why don't you ask the boss?' he suggested, indicating with a nod the telephone in front of her.

'They will tell it on the loudspeaker,' she said, 'as soon as they know.'

'Who's the skipper, dear?'

'Please?'

'Who's the skipper, the captain?'

'Captain Lansen.'

'Is he any good?'

The girl was shocked. 'Captain Lansen is a very experienced pilot.'

Taylor looked her over, grinned and said, 'He's a very *lucky* pilot anyway, my dear.' They said he knew a thing or two, old Taylor did. They said it at the Alias on Friday nights.

Lansen. It was odd to hear a name spoken out like that. In the outfit they simply never did it. They favoured circumlocution, cover names, anything but the original: Archie boy, our flying friend, our friend up north, the chappie who takes the snapshots; they would even use the tortuous collection of figures and letters by which he was known on paper; but never in any circumstances the name.

Lansen. Leclerc had shown him a photograph in London: a boyish thirty-five, fair and good-looking. He'd bet those hostesses went mad about him; that's all they were, anyway, cannonfodder for the pilots. No one else got a look in. Taylor ran his right hand quickly over the outside of his overcoat pocket just to make sure the envelope was still there. He'd never carried this sort of money before. Five thousand dollars for one flight; seventeen hundred pounds, tax free, to lose your way over the Baltic. Mind you, Lansen didn't do that every day. This was special, Leclerc had said so. He wondered what she would do if he leant across the counter and told her who he was; showed her the money in that envelope. He'd never had a girl like that, a real girl, tall and young.

He went upstairs again to the bar. The barman was getting to know him. Taylor pointed to the bottle of Steinhäger on the centre shelf and said, 'Give me another of those, d'you mind? That's it, the fellow just behind you; some of your local poison.'

'It's German,' the barman said.

He opened his wallet and took out a banknote. In the Cellophane compartment there was a photograph of a girl, perhaps nine years old, wearing glasses and holding a doll. 'My daughter,' he explained to the barman, and the barman gave a watery smile.

His voice varied a lot, like the voice of a commercial traveller. His phoney drawl was more extravagant when he addressed his own class, when it was a matter of emphasising a distinction which did not exist; or as now, when he was nervous.

He had to admit: he was windy. It was an eerie situation for a man of his experience and age, going over from routine courier work to operational stuff. This was a job for those swine in the Circus, not for his outfit at all. A different kettle of fish altogether, this was, from the ordinary run-of-the-mill stuff he was used to; stuck out on a limb, miles from nowhere. It beat him how they ever came to put an airport in a place like this. He quite liked the foreign trips as a rule: a visit to old Jimmy Gorton in Hamburg, for instance, or a night on the tiles in Madrid. It did him good to get away from Joanie. He'd done the Turkish run a couple of times, though he didn't care for wogs. But even that was a piece of cake compared to this: first-class travel and the bags on the seat beside him, a Nato pass in his pocket; a man had status, doing a job like that; good as the diplomatic boys, or nearly. But this was different, and he didn't like it.

Leclerc had said it was big, and Taylor believed him. They had got him a passport with another name. Malherbe. Pronounced Mallaby, they said. Christ alone knew who'd chosen it. Taylor couldn't even spell it; made a botch of the hotel register when he signed in that morning. The subsistence was fantastic, of course: fifteen quid a day operational expenses, no vouchers asked for. He'd heard the Circus gave seventeen. He could make a good bit on that, buy something for Joanie. She'd probably rather have the money.

He'd told her, of course: he wasn't supposed to, but Leclerc didn't know Joanie. He lit a cigarette, drew from it and held it in the palm of his hand like a sentry smoking on duty. How the hell was he supposed to push off to Scandinavia without telling his wife?

He wondered what those kids were doing, glued to the window all this time. Amazing the way they managed the foreign language. He looked at his watch again, scarcely noticing the time, touched the envelope in his pocket. Better not have another drink; he must keep a clear head. He tried to guess what Joanie was doing now. Probably having a sit-down with a gin and something. A pity she had to work all day.

He suddenly realised that everything had gone silent. The

barman was standing still, listening. The old people at the table were listening too, their silly faces turned towards the observation window. Then he heard it quite distinctly, the sound of an aircraft, still far away, but approaching the airfield. He made quickly for the window, was halfway there when the loudspeaker began; after the first few words of German the children, like a flock of pigeons, fluttered away to the reception lounge. The party at the table had stood up; the women were reaching for their gloves, the men for their coats and briefcases. At last the announcer gave the English. Lansen was coming in to land.

Taylor stared into the night. There was no sign of the plane. He waited, his anxiety mounting. It's like the end of the world, he thought, the end of the bloody world out there. Supposing Lansen crashed; supposing they found the cameras. He wished someone else were handling it. Woodford, why hadn't Woodford taken it over, or sent that clever college boy Avery? The wind was stronger; he could swear it was far stronger; he could tell from the way it stirred the snow, flinging it over the runway; the way it tore at the flares; the way it made white columns on the horizon, dashing them vehemently away like a hated creation. A gust struck suddenly at the windows in front of him, making him recoil, and there followed the rattle of ice grains and the short grunt of the wooden frame. Again he looked at his watch; it had become a habit with Taylor. It seemed to help, knowing the time.

Lansen will never make it in this, never.

His heart stood still. Softly at first, then rising swiftly to a wail, he heard the klaxons, all four together, moaning out over that godforsaken airfield like the howl of starving animals. Fire . . . the plane must be on fire. He's on fire and he's going to try and land . . . he turned frantically, looking for someone who could tell him.

The barman was standing beside him, polishing a glass, looking through the window.

'What's going on?' Taylor shouted. 'Why are the sirens going?'

'They always make the sirens in bad weather,' he replied. 'It is the law.'

'Why are they letting him land?' Taylor insisted. 'Why don't they route him farther south? It's too small, this place; why don't they send him somewhere bigger?'

The barman shook his head indifferently. 'It's not so bad,' he said indicating the airfield. 'Besides, he is very late. Maybe he has no petrol.'

They saw the plane low over the airfield, her lights alternating above the flares; her spotlights scanned the runway. She was down, safely down, and they heard the roar of her throttle as she began the long taxi to the reception point.

The bar had emptied. He was alone. Taylor ordered a drink. He knew his drill: stay put in the bar, Leclerc had said, Lansen will meet you in the bar. He'll take a bit of time; got to cope with his flight documents, clear his cameras. Taylor heard the children singing downstairs, and a woman leading them. Why the hell did he have to be surrounded by kids and women? He was doing a man's job, wasn't he, with five thousand dollars in his pocket and a phoney passport?

'There are no more flights today,' the barman said. 'They have forbidden all flying now.'

Taylor nodded. 'I know. It's bloody shocking out there, shocking.'

The barman was putting away bottles. 'There was no danger,' he added soothingly. 'Captain Lansen is a very good pilot.' He hesitated, not knowing whether to put away the Steinhäger.

'Of course there wasn't any danger,' Taylor snapped. 'Who said anything about danger?'

'Another drink?' the barman said.

'No, but you have one. Go on, have one yourself.'

The barman reluctantly gave himself a drink, locked the bottle away.

'All the same, how do they do it?' Taylor asked. His voice was conciliatory, putting it right with the barman. 'They can't see a thing in weather like this, not a damn thing.' He smiled knowingly. 'You sit there in the nose and you might just as well have your eyes shut for all the good they do. I've seen it,' Taylor added, his hands loosely cupped in front of him as though he were at the controls. 'I know what I'm talking about . . . and they're the first to catch it, those boys, if something *does* go wrong.' He shook his head. 'They can keep it,' he declared. 'They're entitled to every penny they earn. Specially in a kite that size. They're held together with string, those things; string.'

The barman nodded distantly, finished his drink, washed up the empty glass, dried it and put it on the shelf under the counter. He unbuttoned his white jacket.

Taylor made no move.

'Well,' said the barman with a mirthless smile, 'we have to go home now.'

'What do you mean *we*?' Taylor asked, opening his eyes wide and tilting back his head. 'What do you mean?' He'd take on anyone now; Lansen had landed.

'I have to close the bar.'

'Go home indeed. Give us another drink, come on. You can go home if you like. I happen to live in London.' His tone was challenging, half playful, half resentful, gathering volume. 'And since your aircraft companies are unable to *get* me to London, or any other damn place until tomorrow morning, it's a bit silly of you to tell me to go there, isn't it, old boy?' He was still smiling, but it was the short, angry smile of a nervous man losing his temper. 'And next time you accept a drink from me, chum, I'll trouble you to have the courtesy . . .'

The door opened and Lansen came in.

This wasn't the way it was supposed to happen; this wasn't the way they'd described it at all. Stay in the bar, Leclerc had said, sit at the corner table, have a drink, put your hat and coat on the other chair as if you're waiting for someone. Lansen always has a beer when he clocks in. He likes the public lounge, it's Lansen's style. There'll be people milling about, Leclerc said. It's a small place but there's always something going on at these airports. He'll look around for somewhere to sit – quite open and above board – then he'll come over and ask you if anyone's using the chair. You'll say you kept it free for a friend but the friend hadn't turned up: Lansen will ask if he can sit there. He'll order a beer, then say, 'Boy friend or girl friend?' You'll tell him not to be indelicate, and you'll both laugh a bit and get talking. Ask the two questions: height and airspeed. Research Section must know the height and airspeed. Leave the money in your overcoat pocket. He'll pick up your coat, hang his own beside it and help himself quietly, without any fuss, taking the envelope and dropping the film into your coat pocket. You finish your drinks, shake hands, and Bob's your uncle. In the morning you fly home. Leclerc had made it sound so simple.

Lansen strode across the empty room towards them, a tall, strong figure in a blue mackintosh and cap. He looked briefly at Taylor and spoke past him to the barman: 'Jens, give me a beer.' Turning to Taylor he said, 'What's yours?'

Taylor smiled thinly. 'Some of your local stuff.'

'Give him whatever he wants. A double.'

The barman briskly buttoned up his jacket, unlocked the cupboard and poured out a large Steinhäger. He gave Lansen a beer from the cooler.

'Are you from Leclerc?' Lansen inquired shortly. Anyone could have heard.

'Yes.' He added tamely, far too late, 'Leclerc and Company, London.'

Lansen picked up his beer and took it to the nearest table. His hand was shaking. They sat down.

'Then you tell me,' he said fiercely, 'which damn fool gave me those instructions?'

'I don't know.' Taylor was taken aback. 'I don't even know what your instructions were. It's not my fault. I was sent to collect the film, that's all. It's not even my job, this kind of thing. I'm on the overt side – courier.'

Lansen leant forward, his hand on Taylor's arm. Taylor could feel him trembling. 'I was on the overt side too. Until today. There were kids on that plane. Twenty-five German schoolchildren on Winter holidays. A whole load of kids.'

'Yes.' Taylor forced a smile. 'Yes, we had the reception committee in the waiting-room.'

Lansen burst out, 'What were we *looking* for, that's what I
don't understand. What's so exciting about Rostock?'

'I tell you I'm nothing to do with it.' He added inconsist-
ently: 'Leclerc said it wasn't Rostock but the area south.'

'The triangle south: Kalkstadt, Langdorn, Wolken. You
don't have to tell me the area.'

Taylor looked anxiously towards the barman.

'I don't think we should talk so loud,' he said. 'That fellow's
a bit anti.' He drank some Steinhäger.

Lansen made a gesture with his hand as if he were brushing
something from in front of his face. 'It's finished,' he said. 'I
don't want any more. It's finished. It was OK when we just
stayed on course photographing whatever there was; but this is
too damn much, see? Just too damn, damn much altogether.'
His accent was thick and clumsy, like an impediment.

'Did you get any pictures?' Taylor asked. He must get the
film and go.

Lansen shrugged, put his hand in his raincoat pocket and,
to Taylor's horror, extracted a zinc container for thirty-five-
millimetre film, handing it to him across the table.

'What was it?' Lansen asked again. 'What were they after in
such a place? I went under the cloud, circled the whole area. I
didn't see any atom bombs.'

'Something important, that's all they told me. Something
big. It's got to be done, don't you see? You can't make illegal
flights over an area like that.' Taylor was repeating what someone had said. 'It has to be an airline, a registered airline, or nothing. There's no other way.'

'Listen. They picked us up as soon as we got into the place.
Two MIGs. Where did they come from, that's what I want to
know? As soon as I saw them I turned into cloud; they followed
me. I put out a signal, asking for bearings. When we came out
of the cloud, there they were again. I thought they'd force me
down, order me to land. I tried to jettison the camera but it was

stuck. The kids were all crowding the windows, waving at the MIGs. They flew alongside for a time, then peeled off. They came close, very close. It was bloody dangerous for the kids.' He hadn't touched his beer. 'What the hell did they want?' he asked. 'Why didn't they order me down?'

'I told you: it's not my fault. This isn't my kind of work. But whatever London are looking for, they know what they're doing.' He seemed to be convincing himself; he needed to believe in London. 'They don't waste their time. Or yours, old boy. They know what they're up to.' He frowned, to indicate conviction, but Lansen might not have heard.

'They don't believe in unnecessary risks either,' Taylor said. 'You've done a good job, Lansen. We all have to do our bit . . . take risks. We all do. I did in the war, you know. You're too young to remember the war. This is the same job; we're fighting for the same thing.' He suddenly remembered the two questions. 'What height were you doing when you took the pictures?'

'It varied. We were down to six thousand feet over Kalkstadt.'

'It was Kalkstadt they wanted most,' Taylor said with appreciation. 'That's first-class, Lansen, first-class. What was your airspeed?'

'Two hundred . . . two forty. Something like this. There was nothing there, I'm telling you, nothing.' He lit a cigarette.

'It's the end now,' Lansen repeated. 'However big the target is.' He stood up. Taylor got up too; he put his right hand in his overcoat pocket. Suddenly his throat went dry: the money, where was the money?

'Try the other pocket,' Lansen suggested.

Taylor handed him the envelope. 'Will there be trouble about this? About the MIGs, I mean?'

Lansen shrugged. 'I doubt it, it hasn't happened to me before. They'll believe me once; they'll believe it was the weather. I went off course about halfway. There could have been a fault in the ground control. In the hand-over.'

'What about the navigator? What about the rest of the crew? What do they think?'

'That's my business,' said Lansen sourly. 'You can tell London it's the end.'

Taylor looked at him anxiously. 'You're just upset,' he said, 'after the tension.'

'Go to hell,' said Lansen softly. 'Go to bloody hell.' He turned away, put a coin on the counter and strode out of the bar, stuffing carelessly into his raincoat pocket the long buff envelope which contained the money.

After a moment Taylor followed him. The barman watched him push his way through the door and disappear down the stairs. A very distasteful man, he reflected; but then he never had liked the English.

Taylor thought at first that he would not take a taxi to the hotel. He could walk it in ten minutes and save a bit on subsistence. The airline girl nodded to him as he passed her on his way to the main entrance. The reception hall was done in teak; blasts of warm air rose from the floor. Taylor stepped outside. Like the thrust of a sword the cold cut through his clothes; like the numbness of an encroaching poison it spread swiftly over his naked face, feeling its way into his neck and shoulders. Changing his mind, he looked round hastily for a taxi. He was drunk. He suddenly realised: the fresh air had made him drunk. The rank was empty. An old Citroën was parked fifty yards up the road, its engine running. He's got the heater on, lucky devil, thought Taylor and hurried back through the swing doors.

'I want a cab,' he said to the girl. 'Where can I get one, d'you know?' He hoped to God he looked all right. He was mad to have drunk so much. He shouldn't have accepted that drink from Lansen.

She shook her head. 'They have taken the children,' she said. 'Six in each car. That was the last flight today. We don't have many taxis in Winter.' She smiled. 'It's a very *little* airport.'

'What's that up the road, that old car? Not a cab, is it?' His voice was indistinct.

She went to the doorway and looked out. She had a careful balancing walk, artless and provocative.

'I don't see any car,' she said.

Taylor looked past her. 'There was an old Citroën. Lights on. Must have gone. I just wondered.' Christ, it went past and he'd never heard it.

'The taxis are all Volvos,' the girl remarked. 'Perhaps one will come back after he has dropped the children. Why don't you go and have a drink?'

'Bar's closed,' Taylor snapped. 'Barman's gone home.'

'Are you staying at the airport hotel?'

'The Regina, yes. I'm in a hurry, as a matter of fact.' It was easier now. 'I'm expecting a phone call from London.'

She looked doubtfully at his coat; it was of rainproof material in a pebble weave. 'You could walk,' she suggested. 'It is ten minutes, straight down the road. They can send your luggage later.'

Taylor looked at his watch, the same wide gesture. 'Luggage is already at the hotel. I arrived this morning.'

He had that kind of crumpled, worried face which is only a hair's breadth from the music halls and yet is infinitely sad; a face in which the eyes are paler than their environment, and the contours converge upon the nostrils. Aware of this, perhaps, Taylor had grown a trivial moustache, like a scrawl on a photograph, which made a muddle of his face without concealing its shortcomings. The effect was to inspire disbelief, not because he was a rogue but because he had no talent for deception. Similarly he had tricks of movement crudely copied from some lost original, such as an irritating habit which soldiers have of arching his back suddenly, as if he had discovered himself in an unseemly posture, or he would affect an agitation about the knees and elbows which feebly caricatured an association with horses. Yet the whole was dignified by pain, as if he were holding his little body stiff against a cruel wind.

'If you walk quickly,' she said, 'it takes less than ten minutes.'

Taylor hated waiting. He had a notion that people who waited were people of no substance: it was an affront to be seen waiting. He pursed his lips, shook his head, and with an ill-tempered 'Goodnight, lady,' stepped abruptly into the freezing air.

Taylor had never seen such a sky. Limitless, it curved downward to the snowbound fields, its destiny broken here and there by films of mist which frosted the clustered stars and drew a line round the yellow half-moon. Taylor was frightened, like a landsman frightened by the sea. He hastened his uncertain step, swaying as he went.

He had been walking about five minutes when the car caught him up. There was no footpath. He became aware of its headlights first, because the sound of its engine was deadened by the snow, and he only noticed a light ahead of him, not realizing where it came from. It traced its way languidly over the snowfields and for a time he thought it was the beacon from the airport. Then he saw his own shadow shortening on the road, the light became suddenly brighter, and he knew it must be a car. He was walking on the right, stepping briskly along the edge of the icy rubble that lined the road. He observed that the light was unusually yellow and he guessed the headlamps were masked according to the French rule. He was rather pleased with this little piece of deduction; the old brain was pretty clear after all.

He didn't look over his shoulder because he was a shy man in his way and did not want to give the impression of asking for a lift. But it did occur to him, a little late perhaps, that on the continent they actually drove on the right, and that therefore strictly speaking he was walking on the wrong side of the road, and ought to do something about it.

The car hit him from behind, breaking his spine. For one dreadful moment Taylor described a classic posture of anguish, his head and shoulders flung violently backwards, fingers extended. He made no cry. It was as if his entire body and soul were concentrated in this final attitude of pain, more articulate in death than any sound the living man had made. It is quite possible that the driver was unaware of what he had done; that the impact of the body on the car was not to be distinguished from a thud of loose snow against the axle.

The car carried him for a yard or two then threw him aside, dead on the empty road, a stiff, wrecked figure at the fringe of the wilderness. His trilby hat lay beside him. A sudden blast seized it, carrying it across the snow. The shreds of his pebble-weave coat fluttered in the wind, reaching vainly for the zinc capsule as it rolled gently with the camber to lodge for a moment against the frozen bank, then to continue wearily down the slope.

PART II

Avery's Run

'There are some things that no one has a right to ask of any white man.'

<small>JOHN BUCHAN,</small> *Mr Standfast*

2

Prelude

It was three in the morning.

Avery put down the telephone, woke Sarah and said, 'Taylor's dead.' He shouldn't have told her, of course.

'Who's Taylor?'

A bore, he thought; he only remembered him vaguely. A dreary English bore, straight off Brighton pier.

'A man in courier section,' he said. 'He was with them in the war. He was rather good.'

'That's what you always say. They're all good. How did he die, then? How did he die?' She had sat up in bed.

'Leclerc's waiting to hear.' He wished she wouldn't watch him while he dressed.

'And he wants you to help him wait?'

'He wants me to go to the office. He wants me. You don't expect me to turn over and go back to sleep, do you?'

'I was only asking,' Sarah said. 'You're always so considerate to Leclerc.'

'Taylor was an old hand. Leclerc's very worried.' He could still hear the triumph in Leclerc's voice: 'Come at once, get a taxi; we'll go through the files again.'

'Does this often happen? Do people often die?' There was indignation in her voice, as if no one ever told her anything; as if she alone thought it dreadful that Taylor had died.

'You're not to tell anyone,' said Avery. It was a way of keeping her from him. 'You're not even to say I've gone out in the middle of the night. Taylor was travelling under another name.' He added, 'Someone will have to tell his wife.' He was looking for his glasses.

She got out of bed and put on a dressing-gown. 'For God's sake stop talking like a cowboy. The secretaries know; why can't the wives? Or are they only told when their husbands die?' She went to the door.

She was of medium height and wore her hair long, a style at odds with the discipline of her face. There was a tension in her expression, an anxiety, an incipient discontent, as if tomorrow would only be worse. They had met at Oxford; she had taken a better degree than Avery. But somehow marriage had made her childish; dependence had become an attitude, as if she had given him something irredeemable, and were always asking for it back. Her son was less her projection than her excuse; a wall against the world and not a channel to it.

'Where are you going?' Avery asked. She sometimes did things to spite him, like tearing up a ticket for a concert. She said, 'We've got a child, remember?' He noticed Anthony crying. They must have woken him.

'I'll ring from the office.'

He went to the front door. As she reached the nursery she looked back and Avery knew she was thinking they hadn't kissed.

'You should have stuck to publishing,' she said.

'You didn't like that any better.'

'Why don't they send a car?' she asked. 'You said they had masses of cars.'

'It's waiting at the corner.'

'Why, for God's sake?'

'More secure,' he replied.

'Secure against what?'

'Have you got any money? I seem to have run out.'

'What for?'

'Just money, that's all! I can't run around without a penny in my pocket.' She gave him ten shillings from her bag. Closing the door quickly behind him he went down the stairs into Prince of Wales Drive.

He passed the ground-floor window and knew without looking that Mrs Yates was watching him from behind her curtain, as she watched everybody night and day, holding her cat for comfort.

It was terribly cold. The wind seemed to come from the river, across the park. He looked up and down the road. It was empty. He should have telephoned the rank at Clapham but he wanted to get out of the flat. Besides, he had told Sarah the car was coming. He walked a hundred yards or so towards the Power Station, changed his mind and turned back. He was sleepy. It was a curious illusion that even in the street he still heard the telephone ringing. There was a cab that hung round Albert Bridge at all hours; that was the best bet. So he passed the entrance to his part of the Mansions, glanced up at the nursery window, and there was Sarah looking out. She must have been wondering where the car was. She had Anthony in her arms and he knew she was crying because he hadn't kissed her. He took half an hour to find a taxi to Blackfriars Road.

Avery watched the lamps come up the street. He was quite young, belonging to that intermediate class of contemporary Englishman which must reconcile an Arts degree with an uncertain provenance. He was tall and bookish in appearance, slow-eyed behind his spectacles, with a gently self-effacing manner which endeared him to his elders. The motion of the taxi comforted him, as rocking consoles a child.

He reached St George's Circus, passed the Eye Hospital and entered Blackfriars Road. Suddenly he was upon the house, but told the driver to drop him at the next corner because Leclerc had said to be careful.

'Just here,' he called. 'This will do fine.'

The Department was housed in a crabbed, sooty villa of a place with a fire extinguisher on the balcony. It was like a house eternally for sale. No one knew why the Ministry put a wall round it; perhaps to protect it from the gaze of the people, like the wall round a cemetery; or the people from the gaze of the dead. Certainly not for the garden's sake, because nothing grew in it but grass which had worn away in patches like the coat of an old mongrel. The front door was painted dark green; it was never opened. By day anonymous vans of the same colour occasionally passed down the shabby drive, but they transacted their business in the back yard. The neighbours, if they referred to the place at all, spoke of the Ministry House, which was not accurate, for the Department was a separate entity, and the Ministry its master. The building had that unmistakable air of controlled dilapidation which characterises government hirings all over the world. For those who worked in it, its mystery was like the mystery of motherhood, its survival like the mystery of England. It shrouded and contained them, cradled them and, with sweet anachronism, gave them the illusion of nourishment.

Avery could remember it when the fog lingered contentedly against its stucco walls, or in the Summer, when the sunlight would briefly peer through the mesh curtains of his room, leaving no warmth, revealing no secrets. And he would remember it on that Winter dawn, its façade stained black, the street lights catching the raindrops on the grimy windows. But however he remembered it, it was not as a place where he worked, but where he lived.

Following the path to the back, he rang the bell and waited for Pine to open the door. A light shone in Leclerc's window.

He showed Pine his pass. Perhaps both were reminded of the war: for Avery a vicarious pleasure, while Pine could look back on experience.

'A lovely moon, sir,' said Pine.

'Yes.' Avery stepped inside. Pine followed him in, locking up behind him.

'Time was, the boys would curse a moon like this.'

'Yes, indeed,' Avery laughed.

'Heard about the Melbourne test, sir? Bradley's out for three.'

'Oh dear,' said Avery pleasantly. He disliked cricket.

A blue lamp glowed from the hall ceiling like the night light in a Victorian hospital. Avery climbed the staircase; he felt cold and uneasy. Somewhere a bell rang. It was odd how Sarah had not heard the telephone.

Leclerc was waiting for him: 'We need a man,' he said. He spoke involuntarily, like someone waking. A light shone on the file before him.

He was sleek, small and very bland; a precise cat of a man, clean-shaven and groomed. His stiff collars were cut away; he favoured ties of one colour, knowing perhaps that a weak claim was worse than none. His eyes were dark and quick; he smiled as he spoke, yet conveyed no pleasure. His jackets had twin vents, he kept his handkerchief in his sleeve. On Fridays he wore suede shoes, and they said he was going to the country. No one seemed to know where he lived. The room was in half-darkness.

'We can't do another overflight. This was the last; they warned me at the Ministry. We'll have to put a man in. I've been going through the old cards, John. There's one called Leiser, a Pole. He would do.'

'What happened to Taylor? Who killed him?'

Avery went to the door and switched on the main light. They looked at one another awkwardly. 'Sorry. I'm still half asleep,' Avery said. They began again, finding the thread.

Leclerc spoke up. 'You took a time, John. Something go wrong at home?' He was not born to authority.

'I couldn't get a cab. I phoned the rank at Clapham but they didn't reply. Nor Albert Bridge; nothing there either.' He hated to disappoint Leclerc.

'You can charge for it,' Leclerc said distantly, 'and the phone calls, you realise. Your wife all right?'

'I told you: there was no reply. She's fine.'

'She didn't mind?'

'Of course not.'

They never talked about Sarah. It was as if they shared a
single relationship to Avery's wife, like children who are able to
share a toy they no longer care for. Leclerc said, 'Well, she's got
that son of yours to keep her company.'

'Yes, rather.'

Leclerc was proud of knowing it was a son and not a daughter.

He took a cigarette from the silver box on his desk. He had
told Avery once: the box was a gift, a gift from the war. The
man who gave it to him was dead, the occasion for giving it was
past; there was no inscription on the lid. Even now, he would
say, he was not entirely certain whose side the man had been on,
and Avery would laugh to make him happy.

Taking the file from his desk, Leclerc now held it directly
under the light as if there was something in it which he must
study very closely.

'John.'

Avery went to him, trying not to touch his shoulder.

'What do you make of a face like that?'

'I don't know. It's hard to tell from photographs.'

It was the head of a boy, round and blank, with long, fair hair
swept back.

'Leiser. He *looks* all right, doesn't he? That was twenty years
ago, of course,' Leclerc said. 'We gave him a very high rating.'
Reluctantly he put it down, struck his lighter and held it to the
cigarette. 'Well,' he said briskly, 'we seem to be up against something. I've no idea what happened to Taylor. We have a routine
consular report, that's all. A car accident apparently. A few details, nothing informative. The sort of thing that goes out to
next of kin. The Foreign Office sent us the teleprint as it came
over the wire. They knew it was one of our passports.' He
pushed a sheet of flimsy paper across the desk. He loved to make
you read things while he waited. Avery glanced at it: 'Malherbe?
Was that Taylor's cover name?'

'Yes. I'll have to get a couple of cars from the Ministry pool,'
Leclerc said. 'Quite absurd not having our own cars. The Circus
has a whole fleet.' And then, 'Perhaps the Ministry will believe

me now. Perhaps they'll finally accept we're still an operational department.'

'Did Taylor collect the film?' Avery asked. 'Do we know whether he got it?'

'*I've* no inventory of his possessions,' Leclerc replied indignantly. 'At the moment, all his effects are impounded by the Finnish police. Perhaps the film is among them. It's a small place and I imagine they like to stick to the letter of the law.' And casually, so that Avery knew it mattered, 'The Foreign Office is afraid there may be a muddle.'

'Oh dear,' said Avery automatically. It was their practice in the Department: antique and understated.

Leclerc looked directly at him now, taking interest. 'The Resident Clerk at the Foreign Office spoke to the Assistant half an hour ago. They refuse to involve themselves. They say we're a clandestine service and must do it our own way. Somebody's got to go out there as next of kin; that is the course they favour. To claim the body and effects and get them back here. I want you to go.'

Avery was suddenly aware of the pictures round the room, of the boys who had fought in the war. They hung in two rows of six, either side of the model of a Wellington bomber, rather a dusty one, painted black with no insignia. Most of the photographs had been taken out of doors. Avery could see the hangars behind, and between the young, smiling faces the half-hidden fuselages of parked aircraft.

Beneath each photograph were signatures, already brown and faded, some fluent and racy, others – they must have been the other-ranks – self-conscious and elaborate, as if the writers had come unnaturally to fame. There were no surnames, but sobriquets from children's magazines: Jacko, Shorty, Pip and Lucky Joe. Only the Mae West was uniform, the long hair and the sunny, boyish smile. They seemed to like having their photographs taken, as if being together were an occasion for laughter which might not be repeated. The men in front were crouching comfortably, like men used to crouching in gun turrets, and those behind had put their arms carelessly over one another's shoulders. There was no affectation but a spontaneous goodwill which does not seem to survive war or photographs.

One face was common to every picture, right to the end; the face of a slim, bright-eyed man in a duffel coat and corduroy trousers. He wore no life jacket and stood a little apart from the men as if he were somehow extra. He was smaller than the rest, older. His features were formed; he had a purpose about him which the others lacked. He might have been their schoolmaster. Avery had once looked for his signature to see if it had altered in the nineteen years, but Leclerc had not signed his name. He was still very like his photographs: a shade more set around the jaw perhaps, a shade less hair.

'But that would be an operational job,' said Avery uncertainly.

'Of course. We're an operational department, you know.' A little buck of the head. 'You are entitled to operational subsistence. All you have to do is collect Taylor's stuff. You're to bring back everything except the film, which you deliver to an address in Helsinki. You'll be instructed about that separately. You come back and you can help me with Leiser—'

'Couldn't the Circus take it on? I mean, couldn't they do it more simply?'

This smile came slowly. 'I'm afraid that wouldn't answer at all. It's our show, John: the commitment is within our competence. A military target. I would be shirking our responsibility if I gave it to the Circus. Their charter is political, exclusively political.'

His small hand ran over his hair, a short, concise movement, tense and controlled. 'So it's our problem. Thus far, the Ministry approves my reading' – a favourite expression – 'I can send someone else if you prefer – Woodford or one of the older men. I thought you'd enjoy it. It's an important job, you know; something new for you to tackle.'

'Of course. I'd like to go . . . if you trust me.'

Leclerc enjoyed that. Now he pushed a piece of blue draft paper into Avery's hand. It was covered with Leclerc's own writing, boyish and rounded. He had written 'Ephemeral' at the top and underlined it. In the left-hand margin were his initials, all four, and beneath them the word *Unclassified*. Once more Avery began reading.

'If you follow it carefully,' he said, 'you'll see that we don't specifically state that you *are* next of kin; we just quote from Taylor's application form. That's as far as the Foreign Office people are prepared to go. They've agreed to send this to the local consulate via Helsinki.'

Avery read: 'Following from Consular Department. Your Teleprint re Malherbe. John Somerton Avery, holder of British passport no—, half-brother of deceased, is named in Malherbe's passport application as next of kin. Avery informed and proposes to fly out today take over body and effects. NAS flight 201 via Hamburg, ETA 1820 local time. Please provide usual facilities and assistance.'

'I didn't know your passport number,' Leclerc said. 'The plane leaves at three this afternoon. It's only a small place; I imagine the Consul will meet you at the airport. There's a flight from Hamburg every other day. If you don't have to go to Helsinki you can take the same plane back.'

'Couldn't I be his brother?' Avery asked lamely. 'Half-brother looks fishy.'

'There's no time to rig the passport. The Foreign Office are being very sticky about passports. We had a lot of trouble about Taylor's.' He had returned to the file. 'A *lot* of trouble. It would mean calling *you* Malherbe as well, you see. I don't think they'd like that.' He spoke without attention, paying out rope.

The room was very cold.

Avery said, 'What about our Scandinavian friend . . . ?' Leclerc looked uncomprehending. 'Lansen. Shouldn't someone contact him?'

'I'm attending to that.' Leclerc, hating questions, replied cautiously as if he might be quoted.

'And Taylor's wife?' It seemed pedantic to say widow. 'Are you attending to her?'

'I thought we'd go round first thing in the morning. She's not on the telephone. Telegrams are so cryptic.'

'We?' said Avery. 'Do we both need to go?'

'You're my aide, aren't you?'

It was too quiet. Avery longed for the sound of traffic and the buzz of telephones. By day they had people about them, the tramp of messengers, the drone of Registry trolleys. He had the feeling, when alone with Leclerc, that the third person was missing. No one else made him so conscious of behaviour, no one else had such a disintegrating effect on conversation. He wished Leclerc would give him something else to read.

'Have you heard anything about Taylor's wife?' Leclerc asked. 'Is she a secure sort of person?'

Seeing that Avery did not understand, he continued:

'She could make it awkward for us, you know. If she decided to. We shall have to tread carefully.'

'What will you say to her?'

'We shall play it by ear. The way we did in the war. She won't know, you see. She won't even know he was abroad.'

'He might have told her.'

'Not Taylor. Taylor's an old hand. He had his instructions and knew the rules. She must have a pension, that's most important. Active service.' He made another brisk, finite gesture with his hand.

'And the staff; what will you tell them?'

'I shall hold a meeting this morning for Heads of Sections. As for the rest of the Department, we shall say it was an accident.'

'Perhaps it was,' Avery suggested.

Leclerc was smiling again; an iron bar of a smile, like an affliction.

'In which case we shall have told the truth; and have more chance of getting that film.'

There was still no traffic in the street outside. Avery felt hungry. Leclerc glanced at his watch.

'You were looking at Gorton's report,' Avery said.

He shook his head, wistfully touched a file, revisiting a favourite album. 'There's nothing there. I've read it over and over again. I've had the other photographs blown up to every conceivable size. Haldane's people have been on them night and day. We just can't get any farther.'

Sarah was right: to help him wait.

Leclerc said – it seemed suddenly the point of their meeting– 'I've arranged for you to have a short talk with George Smiley at the Circus after this morning's conference. You've heard of him?'

'No,' Avery lied. This was delicate ground.

'He used to be one of their best men. Typical of the Circus in some ways, of the better kind. He resigns, you know, and he comes back. His conscience. One never knows whether he's there or not. He's a bit past it now. They say he drinks a good deal. Smiley has the North European desk. He can brief you about dropping the film. Our own courier service is disbanded, so there's no other way: the FO don't want to know us; after Taylor's death I can't allow you to run around with the thing in your pocket. How much do you know about the Circus?' He might have been asking about women, wary, an older man without experience.

'A bit,' said Avery. 'The usual gossip.'

Leclerc stood up and went to the window. 'They're a curious crowd. Some good, of course. Smiley was good. But they're cheats,' he broke out suddenly. 'That's an odd word, I know, to use about a sister service, John. Lying's second nature to them. Half of them don't know any longer when they're telling the truth.' He was inclining his head studiously this way and that to catch sight of whatever moved in the waking street below. 'What wretched weather. There was a lot of rivalry during the war, you know.'

'I heard.'

'That's all over now. I don't grudge them their work. They've more money and more staff than we have. They do a bigger job. However, I doubt whether they do a better one. Nothing can touch our Research Section, for example. Nothing.' Avery suddenly had the feeling that Leclerc had revealed something intimate, a failed marriage or a discreditable act, and that now it was all right.

'When you see Smiley, he may ask you about the operation. I don't want you to tell him *anything*, do you see, except that you are going to Finland and you may be handling a film for urgent dispatch to London. If he presses you, suggest it is a training matter. That's all you're authorised to say. The background, Gorton's report, future operations; none of that concerns them in the least. A training matter.'

'I realise that. But he'll know about Taylor, won't he, if the FO knows?'

'Leave that to me. And don't be misled into believing the Circus has a monopoly of agent running. We have the same right. We just don't use it unnecessarily.' He had restated his text.

Avery watched Leclerc's slim back against the lightening sky outside; a man excluded, a man without a card, he thought.

'Could we light a fire?' he asked, and went into the corridor where Pine had a cupboard for mops and brushes. There was kindling wood and some old newspaper. He came back and knelt in front of the fireplace, keeping the best pieces of cinder and coaxing the ash through the grate, just as he would in the flat at Christmas. 'I wonder if it was really wise to let them meet at the airport,' he asked.

'It was urgent. After Jimmy Gorton's report, it was very urgent. It still is. We haven't a moment to lose.'

Avery held a match to the newspaper and watched it burn. As the wood caught, the smoke began to roll gently into his face, causing his eyes to water behind his glasses. 'How could they know Lansen's destination?'

'It was a scheduled flight. He had to get clearance in advance.'

Tossing more coal on to the fire, Avery got up and rinsed his hands at the basin in the corner, drying them on his handkerchief.

'I keep asking Pine to put me out a towel,' said Leclerc. 'They haven't enough to do, that's half the trouble.'

'Never mind.' Avery put the wet handkerchief in his pocket. It felt cold against his thigh. 'Perhaps they will have now,' he added without irony.

'I thought I'd get Pine to make me up a bed here. A sort of ops room.' Leclerc spoke cautiously, as if Avery might deprive him of the pleasure. 'You can ring me here tonight from Finland. If you've got the film, just say the deal's come off.'

'And if not?'

'Say the deal's off.'

'It sounds rather alike,' Avery objected. 'If the line's bad, I mean. "Off" and "Come off".'

'Then say they're not interested. Say something negative. You know what I mean.'

Avery picked up the empty scuttle. 'I'll give this to Pine.'

He passed the duty-room. An Air Force clerk was half asleep beside the telephones. He made his way down the wooden staircase to the front door.

'The Boss wants some coal, Pine.' The porter stood up, as he always did when anyone spoke to him, at attention by his bed in a barrack-room.

'I'm sorry, sir. Can't leave the door.'

'For God's sake, I'll look after the door. We're freezing up there.'

Pine took the scuttle, buttoned his tunic and disappeared down the passage. He didn't whistle these days.

'And a bed made up in his room,' he continued when Pine returned. 'Perhaps you'd tell the duty clerk when he wakes up. Oh, and a towel. He must have a towel by his basin.'

'Yes, sir. Wonderful to see the old Department on the march again.'

'Where can we get breakfast round here? Is there anywhere near by?'

'There's the Cadena,' Pine replied doubtfully, 'but I don't

know whether it would do for the Boss, sir.' A grin. 'We had the canteen in the old days. Slinger and wadge.'

It was quarter to seven. 'When does the Cadena open?'

'Couldn't say, sir.'

'Tell me, do you know Mr Taylor at all?' He nearly said 'did'.

'Oh yes, sir.'

'Have you met his wife?'

'No, sir.'

'What's she like? Have you any idea? Heard anything?'

'Couldn't say, I'm sure, sir. Very sad business indeed, sir.'

Avery looked at him in astonishment. Leclerc must have told him, he thought, and went upstairs. Sooner or later he would have to telephone Sarah.

3

They breakfasted somewhere. Leclerc refused to go into the Cadena and they walked interminably until they found another café, worse than the Cadena and more expensive.

'I can't remember him,' Leclerc said. 'That's the absurd thing. He's a trained radio operator apparently. Or was in those days.'

Avery thought he was talking about Taylor. 'How old did you say he was?'

'Forty, something over. That's a good age. A Danzig Pole. They speak German, you know. Not as mad as the pure Slav. After the war he drifted for a couple of years, pulled himself together and bought a garage. He must have made a nice bit.'

'Then I don't suppose he'll . . .'

'Nonsense. He'll be grateful, or should be.'

Leclerc paid the bill and kept it. As they left the restaurant he said something about subsistence, and putting in a bill to Accounts. 'You can claim for night duty as well, you know. Or time in lieu.' They walked down the road. 'Your air ticket is booked. Carol did it from her flat. We'd better make you an advance for expenses. There'll be the business of having his body sent and that kind of thing. I understand it can be very costly. You'd better have him flown. We'll do a post-mortem privately over here.'

'I've never seen a dead man before,' Avery said.

They were standing on a street corner in Kennington, looking for a taxi; a gas works on one side of the road, nothing on the other: the sort of place they could wait all day.

'John, you've got to keep very quiet about that side of it; about putting a man in. No one's to know, not even in the Department, no one at all. I though we'd call him Mayfly. Leiser, I mean. We'll call him Mayfly.'

'All right.'

'It's very delicate; a question of timing. I've no doubt there'll be opposition, within the Department as well as outside.'

'What about my cover and that kind of thing?' Avery asked. 'I'm not quite—' A taxi with its flag up passed them without stopping.

'Bloody man,' Leclerc snapped. 'Why didn't he pick us up?'

'He lives out here, I expect. He's making for the West End. About cover,' he prompted.

'You're travelling under your own name. I don't see that there's any problem. You can use your own address. Call yourself a publisher. After all you *were* one. The Consul will show you the ropes. What are you worried about?'

'Well – just the details.'

Leclerc, coming out of his reverie, smiled. 'I'll tell you something about cover; something you'll learn for yourself. Never volunteer information. People don't *expect* you to explain yourself. After all, what is there to explain? The ground's prepared; the Consul will have our teleprint. Show your passport and play the rest by ear.'

'I'll try,' said Avery.

'You'll succeed,' Leclerc rejoined with feeling, and they both grinned shyly.

'How far is it to the town?' Avery asked. 'From the airport?'

'About three miles. It feeds the main ski resorts. Heaven knows what the Consul does all day.'

'And to Helsinki?'

'I told you. A hundred miles. Perhaps more.'

Avery proposed they took a bus but Leclerc wouldn't queue, so they remained standing at the corner. He began talking about official cars again. 'It's utterly absurd,' he said. 'In the old days we had a pool of our own, now we have two vans and the

Treasury won't let us pay the driver overtime. How can I run a Department under those conditions?'

In the end they walked. Leclerc had the address in his head; he made a point of remembering such things. It was awkward for Avery to walk beside him for long, because Leclerc adjusted his pace to that of the taller man. Avery tried to keep himself in check, but sometimes he forgot and Leclerc would stretch uncomfortably beside him thrusting upwards with each stride. A fine rain was falling. It was still very cold.

There were times when Avery felt for Leclerc a deep, protective love. Leclerc had that indefinable quality of arousing guilt, as if his companion but poorly replaced a departed friend. Somebody had been there, and gone; perhaps a whole world, a generation; somebody had made him and disowned him, so that while at one moment Avery could hate him for his transparent manipulation, detest his prinking gestures as a child detests the affectations of a parent, at the next he ran to protect him, responsible and deeply caring. Beyond all the vicissitudes of their relationship, he was somehow grateful that Leclerc had engendered him; and thus they created that strong love which exists between the weak; each became the stage to which the other related his actions.

'It would be a good thing,' Leclerc said suddenly, 'if you shared the handling of Mayfly.'

'I'd like to.'

'When you get back.'

They had found the address on the map. Thirty-four Roxburgh Gardens; it was off Kennington High Street. The road soon became dingier, the houses more crowded. Gas lights burnt yellow and flat like paper moons.

'In the war they gave us a hostel for the staff.'

'Perhaps they will again,' Avery suggested.

'It's twenty years since I did an errand like this.'

'Did you go alone then?' Avery asked, and wished at once that he had not. It was so easy to inflict pain on Leclerc.

'It was simpler in those days. We could say they'd died for

their country. We didn't have to tell them the details; they didn't
expect that.' So it *was* we, thought Avery. Some other boy, one
of those laughing faces on the wall.

'They died every day then, the pilots. We did reconnaissance, you know, as well as special operations . . . I'm ashamed
sometimes: I can't even remember their names. They were so
young, some of them.'

There passed across Avery's mind a tragic procession of
horror-struck faces; mothers and fathers, girl friends and wives,
and he tried to visualize Leclerc standing among them, naïve
yet footsure, like a politician at the scene of a disaster.

They stood at the top of a rise. It was a wretched place. The
road led downward into a line of dingy, eyeless houses; above
them rose a single block of flats: Roxburgh Gardens. A string
of lights shone on to the glazed tiles, dividing and redividing
the whole structure into cells. It was a large building, very ugly
in its way, the beginning of a new world, and at its feet lay the
black rubble of the old: crumbling, oily houses, haunted by sad
faces which moved through the rain like driftwood in a forgotten harbour.

Leclerc's frail fists were clenched; he stood very still.

'There?' he said. 'Taylor lived there?'

'What's wrong? It's part of a scheme, redevelopment . . .'
Then Avery understood. Leclerc was ashamed. Taylor had disgracefully deceived him. This was not the society they protected, these slums with their Babel's Tower: they had no place
in Leclerc's scheme of things. To think that a member of Leclerc's
staff should daily trudge from the breath and stink of such a
place to the sanctuary of the Department: had he no money, no
pension? Had he not a little bit beside, as we all have, just a hundred or two, to buy himself out of this squalor?

'It's no worse than Blackfriars Road,' Avery said involuntarily; it was meant to comfort him.

'Everyone knows we used to be in Baker Street,' Leclerc
retorted.

They made their way quickly to the base of the block, past

shop windows filled with old clothes and rusted electric fires, all
the sad muddle of useless things which only the poor will buy.
There was a chandler; his candles were yellow and dusty like
fragments of a tomb.

'What number?' Leclerc asked.

'You said thirty-four.'

They passed between heavy pillars crudely ornamented with
mosaics, followed plastic arrows marked with pink numbers;
they squeezed between lines of aged, empty cars, until finally
they came to a concrete entrance with cartons of milk on the
step. There was no door, but a flight of rubberized steps which
squeaked as they trod. The air smelt of food and that liquid soap
they give in railway lavatories. On the heavy stucco wall a hand-
painted notice discouraged noise. Somewhere a wireless played.
They continued up two flights, and stopped before a green door,
half glazed. Mounted on it in letters of white Bakelite was the
number thirty-four. Leclerc took off his hat and wiped the sweat
from his temples. He might have been entering church. It had
been raining more than they realised; their coats were quite wet.
He pressed the bell. Avery was suddenly very frightened; he
glanced at Leclerc and thought: this is your show; you tell her.

The music seemed louder. They strained their ears to catch
some other sound, but there was none.

'Why did you call him Malherbe?' Avery asked suddenly.

Leclerc pressed the bell again; and then they heard it, both of
them, a whimper midway between the sob of a child and the
whine of a cat, a throttled, metallic sigh. While Leclerc stepped
back, Avery seized the bronze knocker on the letter box and
banged it violently. The echo died away and they heard from
inside the flat a light, reluctant tread; a bolt was slid from its
housing, a spring lock disengaged. Then they heard again, much
louder and more distinctly, the same plaintive monotone. The
door opened a few inches and Avery saw a child, a frail, pallid rag
of a girl not above ten years old. She wore steel-rimmed spectacles, the kind Anthony wore. In her arms, its pink limbs splayed
stupidly about it, its painted eyes staring from between fringes

of ragged cotton, was a doll. Its daubed mouth was lolling open, its head hung sideways as if it were broken or dead. It is called a talking doll, but no living thing uttered such a sound.

'Where is your mother?' asked Leclerc. His voice was aggressive, frightened.

The child shook her head. 'Gone to work.'

'Who looks after you, then?'

She spoke slowly as if she were thinking of something else. 'Mum comes back tea-times. I'm not to open the door.'

'Where is she? Where does she go?'

'Work.'

'Who gives you lunch?' Leclerc insisted.

'What?'

'Who gives you dinner?' Avery said quickly.

'Mrs Bradley. After school.'

Then Avery asked, 'Where's your father?' and she smiled and put a finger to her lips.

'He's gone on an aeroplane,' she said. 'To get money. But I'm not to say. It's a secret.'

Neither of them spoke. 'He's bringing me a present,' she added.

'Where from?' said Avery.

'From the North Pole, but it's a secret.' She still had her hand on the doorknob. 'Where Father Christmas comes from.'

'Tell your Mother some men were here,' Avery said. 'From your Dad's office. We'll come again tea-time.'

'It's important,' said Leclerc.

She seemed to relax when she heard they knew her father.

'He's on an aeroplane,' she repeated. Avery felt in his pocket and gave her two half-crowns, the change from Sarah's ten shillings. She closed the door, leaving them on that damned staircase with the wireless playing dreamy music.

4

They stood in the street not looking at one another. Leclerc said, 'Why did you ask that question, the question about her father?'

When Avery did not reply he added incongruously, 'It isn't a matter of liking people.'

Sometimes Leclerc seemed neither to hear nor to feel; he drifted away, listening for a sound, like a man who having learnt the steps had been deprived of the music; this mood read like a deep sadness, like the bewilderment of a man betrayed.

'I'm afraid I shan't be able to come back here with you this afternoon,' Avery said gently. 'Perhaps Bruce Woodford would be prepared—'

'Bruce is no good.' He added: 'You'll be at the meeting; at ten forty-five?'

'I may have to leave before the end to get to the Circus and collect my things. Sarah hasn't been well. I'll stay at the office as long as I can. I'm sorry I asked that question, I really am.'

'I don't want anyone to know. I must speak to her mother first. There may be some explanation. Taylor's an old hand. He knew the rules.'

'I shan't mention it, I promise I shan't. Nor Mayfly.'

'I must tell Haldane about Mayfly. He'll object, of course. Yes, that's what we'll call it . . . the whole operation. We'll call it Mayfly.' The thought consoled him.

They hurried to the office, not to work but for refuge; for anonymity, a quality they had come to need.

His room was one along from Leclerc's. It had a label on the door saying, 'Director's Aide'. Two years ago Leclerc had been invited to America, and the expression dated from his return. Within the Department, staff were referred to by the function they fulfilled. Hence Avery was known simply as Private Office; though Leclerc might alter the title every week, he could not alter the vernacular.

At a quarter to eleven Woodford came into his room. Avery guessed he would: a little chat before the meeting began, a quiet word about some matter not strictly on the agenda.

'What's it all about, John?' He lit his pipe, tilted back his large head and extinguished the match with long, swinging movements of his hand. He had once been a schoolmaster; an athletic man.

'You tell me.'

'Poor Taylor.'

'Precisely.'

'I don't want to jump the gun,' he said, and settled himself on the edge of the desk, still absorbed in his pipe.

'I don't want to jump the gun, John,' he repeated. 'But there's another matter we ought to look at, tragic as Taylor's death is.' He stowed the tobacco tin in the pocket of his green suit and said, 'Registry.'

'That's Haldane's parish. Research.'

'I've got nothing against old Adrian. He's a good scout. We've been working together for over twenty years.' And therefore you're a good scout too, thought Avery.

Woodford had a way of coming close when he spoke; riding his heavy shoulder against you like a horse rubbing itself against a gate. He leant forward and looked at Avery earnestly: a plain man perplexed, he was saying, a decent man choosing between friendship and duty. His suit was hairy, too thick to crease, forming rolls like a blanket; rough-cut buttons of brown bone.

'John, Registry's all to the devil; we both know that. Papers

aren't being entered, files aren't brought up on the right dates.'
He shook his head in despair. 'We've been missing a policy
file on marine freight since mid-October. Just vanished into
thin air.'

'Adrian Haldane put out a search notice,' Avery said. 'We
were all involved, not just Adrian. Files do get lost – this is the
first since April, Bruce. I don't think that's bad, considering the
amount we handle. I thought Registry was one of our best things.
The files are immaculate. I understand our Research index is
unique. That's all Adrian's doing, isn't it? Still, if you're worried
why not speak to Adrian about it?'

'No, no. It's not *that* important.'

Carol came in with the tea. Woodford had his in a pottery
jumbo-cup, with his initials drawn large, embossed like icing.
As Carol put it down, she remarked, 'Wilf Taylor's dead.'

'I've been here since one,' Avery lied, 'coping with it. We've
been working all night.'

'The Director's very upset,' she said.

'What was his wife like, Carol?' She was a well-dressed girl,
a little taller than Sarah.

'Nobody's met her.'

She left the room, Woodford watching her. He took his pipe
from his mouth and grinned. Avery knew he was going to say
something about sleeping with Carol and suddenly he'd had
enough.

'Did your wife make that cup, Bruce?' he asked quickly. 'I
hear she's quite a potter.'

'Made the saucer as well,' he said. He began talking about
the classes she went to, the amusing way it had caught on in
Wimbledon, how his wife was tickled to death.

It was nearly eleven; they could hear the others gathering in
the corridor.

'I'd better go next door,' Avery said, 'and see if he's ready.
He's taken quite a beating in the last eight hours.'

Woodford picked up his mug and took a sip of tea. 'If you get
a chance, mention that Registry business to the Boss, John. I don't

want to drag it up in front of everyone else. Adrian's getting a bit past it.'

'The Director's very tied up at the moment, Bruce.'

'Oh, quite.'

'He hates to interfere with Haldane, you know that.' As they reached the door of his room he turned to Woodford and asked, 'Do you remember a man called Malherbe in the Department?'

Woodford stopped dead. 'God, yes. A young chap, like you. In the war. Good Lord.' And earnestly, but quite unlike his usual manner: 'Don't mention that name to the Boss. He was very cut up about young Malherbe. One of the special fliers. The two of them were quite close in a way.'

Leclerc's room by daylight was not so much drab as of an impermanent appearance. You would think its occupant had requisitioned it hastily, under conditions of emergency, and had not known how long he would be staying. Maps lay sprawled over the trestle table, not in threes or fours but dozens, some of a scale large enough to show streets and buildings. Teletape, pasted in strips on pink paper, hung in batches on the notice board, fastened with a heavy bulldog clip like galley proofs awaiting correction. A bed had been put in one corner with a counterpane over it. A clean towel hung beside the basin. The desk was new, of grey steel, Government issue. The walls were filthy. Here and there the cream paint had peeled, showing dark green beneath. It was a small, square room with Ministry of Works curtains. There had been a row about the curtains, a question of equating Leclerc's rank to the Civil Service scale. It was the one occasion, so far as Avery knew, when Leclerc had made any effort to improve the disorder of the room. The fire was nearly out. Sometimes when it was very windy the fire would not burn at all, and all through the day Avery could hear from next door the soot falling in the chimney.

Avery watched them come in; Woodford first, then Sandford, Dennison and McCulloch. They had all heard about Taylor. It was easy to imagine the news going round the Department, not as headlines, but as a small and gratifying sensation, passed from room to room, lending a briskness to the day's activity, as it had to these men; giving them a moment's optimism, like a rise in pay. They would watch Leclerc, watch him as prisoners watch a warder. They knew his routine by instinct, and they waited for him to break it. There would not be a man or woman in the Department but knew they had been called in the middle of the night, and that Leclerc was sleeping in the office.

They settled themselves at the table, putting their cups in front of them noisily like children at a meal, Leclerc at the head, the others on either side, an empty chair at the farther end. Haldane came in, and Avery knew as soon as he saw him that it would be Leclerc versus Haldane.

Looking at the empty chair, he said, 'I see I'm to take the draughtiest place.'

Avery rose, but Haldane had sat down. 'Don't bother, Avery. I'm a sick man already.' He coughed, just as he coughed all year. Not even the Summer could help him, apparently; he coughed in all seasons.

The others fidgeted uncomfortably; Woodford helped himself to a biscuit. Haldane glanced at the fire. 'Is that the best the Ministry of Works can manage?' he asked.

'It's the rain,' Avery said. 'The rain disagrees with it. Pine's had a go but he made no difference.'

'Ah.'

Haldane was a lean man with long, restless fingers; a man locked in himself, slow in his movements, agile in his features; balding, spare, querulous and dry; a man seemingly contemptuous of everything, keeping his own hours and his own counsel; addicted to crossword puzzles and nineteenth-century water colours.

Carol came in with files and maps, putting them on Leclerc's desk, which in contrast to the remainder of his room was very tidy. They waited awkwardly until she had gone. The door securely closed, Leclerc passed his hand cautiously over his dark hair as if he were not quite familiar with it.

'Taylor's been killed. You've all heard it by now. He was

killed last night in Finland, travelling under another name.' Avery noticed he never mentioned Malherbe. 'We don't know the details. He appears to have been run over. I've told Carol to put it about that it was an accident. Is that clear?'

Yes, they said, it was quite clear.

'He went to collect a film from . . . a contact, a Scandinavian contact. You know whom I mean. We don't normally use the routine couriers for operational work, but this was different; something very special indeed. I think Adrian will back me up there.' He made a little upward gesture with his open hands, freeing the wrists from his white cuffs, laying the palms and fingers vertically together; praying for Haldane's support.

'Special?' Haldane repeated slowly. His voice was thin and sharp like the man himself, cultivated, without emphasis and without affectation; an enviable voice. 'It was different, yes. Not least because Taylor died. We should never have used him, never,' he observed flatly. 'We broke a first principle of intelligence. We used a man on the overt side for a clandestine job. Not that we have a clandestine side any more.'

'Shall we let our masters be the judges of that?' Leclerc suggested demurely. 'At least you'll agree the Ministry is pressing us daily for results.' He turned to those on either side of him, now to the left, now to the right, bringing them in like shareholders. 'It is time you all knew the details. We are dealing with something of exceptional security classification, you understand. I propose to limit to Heads of Sections. So far, only Adrian Haldane and one or two of his staff in Research have been initiated. And John Avery as my aide. I wish to emphasize that our sister service knows nothing whatever about it. Now about our own arrangements. The operation has the codeword Mayfly.' He was speaking in his clipped, effective voice. 'There is one action file, which will be returned to me personally, or to Carol if I am out, at the end of each day; and there is a library copy. That is the system we used in the war for operational files and I think you are all familiar with it. It's the system we shall use henceforth. I shall add Carol's name to the subscription list.'

Woodford pointed at Avery with his pipe, shaking his head. Not young John there; John was not familiar with the system. Sandford, sitting beside Avery, explained. The library copy was kept in the cypher-room. It was against regulations to take it away. All new serials were to be entered on it as soon as they were made; the subscription list was the list of persons author-ised to read it. No pins were allowed; all the papers had to be fast. The others looked on complacently.

Sandford was Administration; he was a fatherly man in gold-rimmed spectacles and came to the office on a motorbike. Leclerc had objected once, on no particular grounds, and now he parked it down the road opposite the hospital.

'Now, about the operation,' Leclerc said. The thin line of his joined hands bisected his bright face. Only Haldane was not watching him; his eyes were turned away towards the window. Outside, the rain was falling gently against the buildings like Spring rain in a dark valley.

Abruptly Leclerc rose and went to a map of Europe on the wall. There were small flags pinned to it. Stretching upwards with his arm, riding on his toes to reach the northern hemi-sphere, he said, 'We're having a spot of trouble with the Ger-mans.' A little laugh went up. 'In the area south of Rostock; a place called Kalkstadt, just here.' His finger traced the Baltic coastline of Schleswig-Holstein, moved east and stopped an inch or two south of Rostock.

'To put it in a nutshell, we have three indicators which suggest – I cannot say prove – that something big is going on there in the way of military installations.'

He swung round to face them. He would remain at the map and say it all from there, to show he had the facts in his memory and didn't need the papers on the table.

'The first indicator came exactly a month ago when we received a report from our representative in Hamburg, Jimmy Gorton.'

Woodford smiled: good God, was old Jimmy still going?

'An East German refugee crossed the border near Lübeck,

swam the river; a railwayman from Kalkstadt. He went to our
Consulate and offered to sell them information about a new
rocket site near Rostock. I need hardly tell you the Consulate
threw him out. Since the Foreign Office will not even give us the
facilities of its bag service it is unlikely' – a thin smile – 'that they
will assist us by buying military information.' A nice murmur
greeted this joke. 'However, by a stroke of luck Gorton got to
hear of the man and went to Flensburg to see him.'

Woodford would not let this pass. Flensburg? Was not that
the place where they had located German submarines in 'forty-
one? Flensburg had been a hell of a show.

Leclerc nodded at Woodford indulgently, as if he too had
been amused by the recollection. 'The wretched man had been
to every Allied office in North Germany, but no one would look
at him. Jimmy Gorton had a chat with him.' Implicit in Leclerc's
way of describing things was an assumption that Gorton was
the only intelligent man among a lot of fools. He crossed to his
desk, took a cigarette from the silver box, lit it, picked up a file
with a heavy red cross on the cover and laid it noiselessly on the
table in front of them. 'This is Jimmy's report,' he said. 'It's a
first-class bit of work by any standard.' The cigarette looked
very long between his fingers. 'The defector's name,' he added
inconsequentially, 'was Fritsche.'

'Defector?' Haldane put in quickly. 'The man's a low-grade
refugee, a railwayman. We don't usually talk about men like
that *defecting*.'

Leclerc replied defensively, 'The man's not only a railwayman. He's a bit of a mechanic and a bit of a photographer.'

McCulloch opened the file and began methodically turning
over the serials. Sandford watched him through his gold-
rimmed spectacles.

'On the first or second of September – we don't know which
because he can't remember – he happened to be doing a double
shift in the dumping sheds at Kalkstadt. One of his comrades
was sick. He was to work from six till twelve in the morning,
and four till ten at night. When he arrived to report for work

there were a dozen Vopos, East German people's police, at the station entrance. All passenger traffic was forbidden. They checked his identity papers against a list and told him to keep away from the sheds on the eastern side of the station. They said,' Leclerc added deliberately, 'that if he approached the eastern sheds he was liable to be shot.'

This impressed them. Woodford said it was typical of the Germans.

'It's the Russians we're fighting,' Haldane put in.

'He's an odd fish, our man. He seems to have argued with them. He told them he was as reliable as they were, a good German and a Party member. He showed them his union card, photographs of his wife and Heaven knows what. It didn't do any good, of course, because they just told him to obey orders and keep away from the sheds. But he must have caught their fancy because when they brewed up some soup at ten o'clock they called him over and offered him a cup. Over the soup he asked them what was going on. They were cagey, but he could see they were excited. Then something happened. Something very important,' he continued. 'One of the younger ones blurted out that whatever they had in the sheds could blow the Americans out of West Germany in a couple of hours. At this point an officer came along and told them to get back to work.'

Haldane coughed a deep, hopeless cough, like an echo in an old vault.

What sort of officer, someone asked, was he German or Russian?

'German. That is most relevant. There were no Russians in evidence at all.'

Haldane interrupted sharply. 'The refugee saw none. That's all we know. Let us be accurate.' He coughed again. It was very irritating.

'As you wish. He went home and had lunch. He was disgruntled at being ordered around in his own station by a lot of young fellows playing soldiers. He had a couple of glasses of schnapps and sat there brooding about the dumping shed. Adrian, if your

cough is troubling you . . . ?' Haldane shook his head. 'He remembered that on the northern side it abutted with an old stor-
age hut, and that there was a shutter-type ventilator let into the
party wall. He formed the notion of looking through the ventilator to see what was in the shed. As a way of getting his own
back on the soldiers.'

Woodford laughed.

'Then he decided to go one further and photograph whatever was there.'

'He must have been mad,' Haldane commented. 'I find this
part impossible to accept.'

'Mad or not, that's what he decided to do. He was cross because they wouldn't trust him. He felt he had a right to know what
was in the shed.' Leclerc missed a beat then took refuge in technique. 'He had an Exa-two camera, single lens reflex. East German
manufacture. It's cheap housing but takes all the Exakta-range
lenses; far fewer speeds than the Exakta, of course.' He looked in-
quiringly at the technicians, Dennison and McCulloch. 'Am I
right, gentlemen?' he asked. 'You must correct me.' They smiled
sheepishly because there was nothing to correct. 'He had a good
wide-angle lens. The difficulty was the light. His next shift didn't
begin till four, by which time dusk would be falling and there
would be even less light inside the shed. He had one fast Agfa film
which he'd been keeping for a special occasion; it had a DIN speed
of twenty-seven. He decided to use that.' He paused, more for
effect than for questions.

'Why didn't he wait till next morning?' Haldane asked.

'In the report,' Leclerc continued blandly, 'you'll find a very
full account by Gorton of how the man got into the hut, stood
on an oil drum and took his photographs through the ventilator. I'm not going to repeat all that now. He used the maximum
aperture of two point eight, speeds ranging from a quarter of a
second to two seconds. A fortunate piece of German thoroughness.' No one laughed. 'The speeds were guesswork, of course.
He was bracketing an estimated exposure time of one second.
Only the last three frames show anything. Here they are.'

Leclerc unlocked the steel drawer of his desk and extracted a set of high-gloss photographs twelve inches by nine. He was smiling a little, like a man looking at his own reflection. They gathered round, all but Haldane and Avery, who had seen them before.

Something was there.

You could see it if you looked quickly; something hidden in the disintegrating shadows; but keep looking and the dark closed in and the shape was gone. Yet something was there; the muffled form of a gun barrel, but pointed and too long for its carriage, the suspicion of a transporter, a vague glint of what might have been a platform.

'They would put protective covers over them, of course,' Leclerc commented, studying their faces hopefully, waiting for their optimism.

Avery looked at his watch. It was twenty past eleven. 'I shall have to go soon, Director,' he said. He still hadn't rung Sarah. 'I have to see the accountant about my air ticket.'

'Stay another ten minutes,' Leclerc pleaded, and Haldane asked, 'Where's he going?'

Leclerc replied, 'To take care of Taylor. He has a date at the Circus first.'

'What do you mean, take care of him? Taylor's dead.'

There was an uncomfortable silence.

'You know very well that Taylor was travelling under an alias. Somebody has to collect his effects; recover the film. Avery is going out as next of kin. The Ministry has already given its approval; I wasn't aware that I needed yours.'

'To claim the body?'

'To get the film,' Leclerc repeated hotly.

'That's an operational job; Avery's not trained.'

'They were younger than he in the war. He can look after himself.'

'Taylor couldn't. What will he do when he's got it; bring it back in his sponge bag?'

'Shall we discuss that afterwards?' Leclerc suggested, and

addressed himself once more to the others, smiling patiently as if to say old Adrian must be humoured.

'That was all we had to go on till ten days ago. Then came the second indicator. The area round Kalkstadt had been declared a prohibited area.' There was an excited murmur of interest. 'For a radius of – as far as we can establish – thirty kilometres. Sealed off; closed to all traffic. They brought in frontier guards.' He glanced round the table. 'I then informed the Minister. I cannot tell even you all the implications. But let me name one.' He said the last sentence quickly, at the same time flicking upwards the little horns of greying hair that grew above his ears.

Haldane was forgotten.

'What puzzled us in the beginning' – he nodded at Haldane, a conciliatory gesture at a moment of victory, but Haldane ig-nored it – 'was the absence of Soviet troops. They have units in Rostock, Witmar, Schwerin.' His finger darted among the flags. 'But none – this is confirmed by other agencies – none in the immediate area of Kalkstadt. If there *are* weapons there, weap-ons of high destructive capacity, why are there no Soviet troops?'

McCulloch made a suggestion: might there not be techni-cians, Soviet technicians in civilian dress?

'I regard that as unlikely.' A demure smile. 'In comparable cases where tactical weapons were being transported we have always identified at least one Soviet unit. On the other hand, five weeks ago a few Russian troops *were* seen at Gustweiler, far-ther south.' He was back to the map. 'They billeted for one night at a pub. Some wore artillery flashes; others had no shoulder-boards at all. One might conclude they had brought something, left it and gone away again.'

Woodford was becoming restless. What did it all add up to, he wanted to know, what did they make of it over at the Ministry? Woodford had no patience with riddles.

Leclerc adopted his academic tone. It had a bullying qual-ity as if facts were facts and could not be disputed. 'Research Section have done a magnificent job. The overall length of the object in these photographs – they can compute it pretty exactly – is equal to the length of a Soviet middle-range rocket. On present information' – he lightly tapped the map with his knuckles so that it swung sideways on its hook – 'the Ministry believes it is *conceivable* we are dealing with Soviet missiles under East German control. Research,' he added quickly, 'are not prepared to go so far. Now if the Ministry view prevails, if they are right, that is, we would have on our hands' – this was his moment – 'a sort of Cuba situation all over again, only' – he tried to sound apologetic, to make it a throw-away line – 'more dangerous.'

He had them.

'It was at this point,' Leclerc explained, 'that the Ministry felt entitled to authorize an overflight. As you know, for the last four years the Department has been limited to aerial photographs along orthodox civilian or military air routes. Even these required Foreign Office approval.' He drifted away. 'It really was too bad.' His eyes seemed to be searching for something not in the room. The others watched him anxiously, waiting for him to continue.

'For once the Ministry agreed to waive the ruling, and I am pleased to say the task of mounting the operation was given to this Department. We selected the best pilot we could find on our books: Lansen.' Someone looked up in surprise; agents' names were never used that way. 'Lansen undertook, for a price, to go off course on a charter flight from Düsseldorf to Finland. Taylor was dispatched to collect the film; he died at the landing field. A road accident, apparently.'

Outside they could hear the sound of cars moving through the rain like the rustling of paper in the wind. The fire had gone out; only the smoke remained, hanging like a shroud over the table.

Sandford had raised his hand. What kind of missile was this supposed to be?

'A Sandal, Medium Range. I am told by Research that it was first shown in Red Square in November 'sixty-two. It has achieved a certain notoriety since then. It was the Sandal which

the Russians installed in Cuba. The Sandal is also' – a glance at
Woodford – 'the linear descendant of the wartime German V2.'

He fetched other photographs from the desk and laid them
on the table.

'Here is a Research Section photograph of the Sandal missile. They tell me it is distinguished by what is called a flared
skirt' – he pointed to the formation at the base – 'and by small
fins. It is about forty foot long from base to cone. If you look
carefully you will see tucks near the clamp – just here – which
hold the protective cloth cover in position. There is, ironically,
no extant picture of the Sandal in protective covers. Possibly the
Americans have one, but I don't feel able to approach them at
this stage.'

Woodford reacted quickly. 'Of course not,' he said.

'The Minister was anxious that we shouldn't alarm them
prematurely. One only has to *suggest* rockets to the Americans
to get the most drastic reaction. Before we know where we are
they'll be flying U2s over Rostock.' Encouraged by their laughter, Leclerc continued: 'The Minister made another point which
I think I might pass on to you. The country which comes under
maximum threat from these rockets – they have a range of
around eight hundred miles – might well be our own. It is certainly not the United States. Politically, this would be a bad
moment to go hiding our faces in the Americans' skirts. After
all, as the Minister put it, we still *have* one or two teeth of our
own.'

Haldane said sarcastically, 'That is a charming notion,' and
Avery turned on him with all the anger he had fought away.

'I think you might do better than that,' he said. He nearly
added: have a little mercy.

Haldane's cold gaze held Avery for a moment, then released
him, his case not forgiven but suspended.

Someone asked what they would do next: suppose Avery did not
find Taylor's film? Suppose it just wasn't there? Could they mount
another overflight?

'No,' Leclerc replied. 'Another overflight is out of the question. Far too dangerous. We shall have to try something else.' He seemed disinclined to go further, but Haldane said, 'What, for instance?'

'We may have to put a man in. It seems to be the only way.'

'This Department?' Haldane asked incredulously. 'Put a man in? The Ministry would never tolerate such a thing. You mean, surely, you'll ask the Circus to do it?'

'I have already told you the position. Heaven knows, Adrian, you're not going to tell me we can't do it?' He looked appealingly round the table. 'Every one of us here except young Avery has been in the business twenty years or more. You yourself have forgotten more about agents than half those people in the Circus ever knew.'

'Hear, hear!' Woodford cried.

'Look at your own section, Adrian; look at Research. There must have been half a dozen occasions in the last five years when the Circus actually came to you, asked you for advice, used your facilities and skills. The time may come when they do the same with agents! The Ministry granted us an overflight. Why not an agent too?'

'You mentioned a third indicator. I don't follow you. What was that?'

'Taylor's death,' said Leclerc.

Avery got up, nodded goodbye and tiptoed to the door. Haldane watched him go.

5

There was a note on his desk from Carol: 'Your wife rang.'

He walked into her office and found her sitting at her typewriter but not typing. 'You wouldn't talk about poor Wilf Taylor like that,' she said, 'if you'd known him better.'

'Like what? I haven't talked about him at all.'

He thought he should comfort her, because sometimes they touched one another; he thought she might expect that now.

He bent forward, advancing until the sharp ends of her hair touched his cheek. Inclining his head inwards so that their temples met, he felt her skin travel slightly across the flat bone of her skull. For a moment they remained thus, Carol sitting upright, looking straight ahead of her, her hands either side of the typewriter, Avery awkwardly stooping. He thought of putting his hand beneath her arm and touching her breast, but did not; both gently recoiling, they separated and were alone again. Avery stood up.

'Your wife telephoned,' she said. 'I told her you were at the meeting. She wants to talk to you urgently.'

'Thanks. I'm on my way.'

'John, what *is* going on? What's all this about the Circus? What's Leclerc up to?'

'I thought you knew. He said he'd put you on the list.'

'I don't mean that. Why's he lying to them again? He's dictated a memorandum to Control about some training scheme and you going abroad. Pine took it round by hand. He's gone mad about her pension; Mrs Taylor's; looking up precedents and Heaven knows what. Even the application is Top Secret. He's building one of his card houses, John, I know he is. Who's Leiser, for instance?'

'You're not supposed to know. He's an agent; a Pole.'

'Does he work for the Circus?' She changed her tack. 'Well, why are *you* going? That's another thing I don't understand. For that matter, why did Taylor have to go? If the Circus has couriers in Finland, why couldn't we have used them in the first place? Why send poor Taylor? Even now the FO could iron it out. I'm sure they could. He just won't give them a chance: he *wants* to send you.'

'You don't understand,' Avery said shortly.

'Another thing,' she demanded as he was going, 'why does Adrian Haldane hate you so?'

He visited the accountant then took a taxi to the Circus. Leclerc had said he could claim for it. He was cross that Sarah had tried to reach him at such a moment. He had told her never to ring him at the Department. Leclerc said it was insecure.

'What did you read at Oxford? It was Oxford, wasn't it?' Smiley asked, and gave him a cigarette, rather a muddled one from a packet of ten.

'Languages.' Avery patted his pockets for a match. 'German and Italian.' When Smiley said nothing he added, 'German principally.'

Smiley was a small, distracted man with plump fingers and a shadowy, blinking way with him which suggested discomfort. Whatever Avery had expected, it was not this.

'Well, well.' Smiley nodded to himself, a very private comment. 'It's a question of a courier, I believe, in Helsinki. You want to give him a film. A training scheme.'

'Yes.'

'It's a most unusual request. You're sure . . . do you know the *size* of the film?'

'No.'

A long pause.

'You should try to find out that kind of thing,' Smiley said kindly. 'I mean, the courier may want to conceal it, you see.'

'I'm sorry.'

'Oh, it doesn't matter.'

Avery was reminded of Oxford, and reading essays to his tutor.

'Perhaps,' said Smiley thoughtfully, 'I might say one thing. I'm sure Leclerc has already had it from Control. We want to give you all the help we can – *all* the help. There used to be a time,' he mused, with that curious air of indirection which seemed to characterise all his utterances, 'when our departments *competed*. I always found that very painful. But I wondered whether you could tell me a *little*, just a little . . . Control was so anxious to help. We should hate to do the wrong thing out of ignorance.'

'It's a training exercise. Full dress. I don't know much about it myself.'

'We want to help,' Smiley repeated simply. 'What is your target country, your *putative* target?'

'I don't know. I'm only playing a small part. It's training.'

'But if it's training, why so much secrecy?'

'Well, Germany,' Avery said.

'Thank you.'

Smiley seemed embarrassed. He looked at his hands folded lightly on the desk before him. He asked Avery whether it was still raining. Avery said he was afraid so.

'I'm sorry to hear about Taylor,' he said. Avery said yes he was a good man.

'Do you know what time you'll have your film? Tonight? Tomorrow? Leclerc rather thought tonight, I gather.'

'I don't know. It depends how it goes. I just can't tell at the moment.'

'No.' There followed a long, unexplained silence. He's like an old man, thought Avery, he forgets he's not alone. 'No, there are so many imponderables. Have you done this kind of thing before?'

'Once or twice.' Again Smiley said nothing and did not seem to notice the gap.

'How *is* everyone in Blackfriars Road? Do you know Haldane at all?' Smiley asked. He didn't care about the reply.

'He's Research now.'

'Of course. A good brain. Your Research people enjoy quite a reputation, you know. We have consulted them ourselves more than once. Haldane and I were contemporaries at Oxford. Then in the war we worked together for a while. A Greats man. We'd have taken him here after the war; I think the medical people were worried about his chest.'

'I hadn't heard.'

'Hadn't you?' The eyebrows rose comically. 'There's a hotel in Helsinki called the Prince of Denmark. Opposite the main station. Do you know it by any chance?'

'No. I've never been to Helsinki.'

'Haven't you, now?' Smiley peered at him anxiously. 'It's a very *strange* story. This Taylor: was he training too?'

'I don't know. But I'll find the hotel,' Avery said with a touch of impatience.

'They sell magazines and postcards just inside the door. There's only the one entrance.' He might have been talking about the house next door. 'And flowers. I think the best arrangement would be for you to go there once you have the film. Ask the people at the flower stall to send a dozen red roses to Mrs Avery at the Imperial Hotel at Torquay. Or half a dozen would be enough, we don't want to waste money, do we? Flowers are so expensive up there. Are you travelling under your own name?'

'Yes.'

'Any particular reason? I don't mean to be curious,' he added hastily, 'but one has such a short life anyway . . . I mean before one's blown.'

'I gather it takes a bit of time to get a fake passport. The Foreign Office . . .' He shouldn't have answered. He should have told him to mind his own business.

'I'm sorry,' said Smiley, and frowned as if he had made an error of tact. 'You can always come to us, you know. For passports, I mean.' It was meant as a kindness. 'Just send the flowers. As you leave the hotel, check your watch by the hall clock. Half an hour later return to the main entrance. A taxi driver will recognize you and open the door of his car. Get in, drive around, give him the film. Oh, and pay him, please. Just the ordinary fare. It's so easy to forget the *little* things. What *kind* of training precisely?'

'What if I don't get the film?'

'In that case do nothing. Don't go near the hotel. Don't go to Helsinki. Forget about it.' It occurred to Avery that his instructions had been remarkably clear.

'When you were reading German, did you touch on the seventeenth century by any chance?' Smiley inquired hopefully as Avery rose to go. 'Gryphius, Lohenstein; those people?'

'It was a special subject. I'm afraid I didn't.'

'*Special*,' muttered Smiley. 'What a *silly* word. I suppose they mean extrinsic; it's a very impertinent notion.'

As they reached the door he said, 'Have you a briefcase or anything?'

'Yes.'

'When you have that film, put it in your pocket,' he suggested, 'and carry the briefcase in your hand. If you *are* followed, they tend to watch the briefcase. It's natural, really. If you just drop the briefcase somewhere, they may go looking for that instead. I don't think the Finns are very *sophisticated* people. It's only a training hint, of course. But don't *worry*. It's such a mistake, I always feel, to put one's trust in *technique*.' He saw Avery to the door, then made his way ponderously along the corridor to Control's room.

Avery walked upstairs to the flat, guessing how Sarah would react. He wished he had telephoned after all because he hated to find her in the kitchen, and Anthony's toys all over the drawing-room carpet. It never worked, turning up without warning. She took fright as if she expected him to have done something dreadful.

He did not carry a key; Sarah was always in. She had no friends of her own as far as he knew; she never went to coffee parties or took herself shopping. She seemed to have no talent for independent pleasure.

He pressed the bell, heard Anthony calling Mummy, Mummy, and waited to hear her step. The kitchen was at the end of the passage, but this time she came from the bedroom, softly as though she were barefooted.

She opened the door without looking at him. She was wearing a cotton nightdress and a cardigan.

'God, you took your time,' she said, turned and walked uncertainly back to the bedroom. 'Something wrong?' she asked over her shoulder. 'Someone else been murdered?'

'What's the matter, Sarah? Aren't you well?'

Anthony was running about shouting because his father had come home. Sarah climbed back into bed. 'I rang the doctor. *I* don't know what it is,' she said, as if illness were not her subject.

'Have you a temperature?'

She had put a bowl of cold water and the bathroom flannel beside her. He wrung out the flannel and laid it on her head. 'You'll have to cope,' she said. 'I'm afraid it's not as exciting as spies. Aren't you going to ask me what's wrong?'

'When's the doctor arriving?'

'He has surgery till twelve. He'll turn up after that, I suppose.'

He went to the kitchen, Anthony following. The breakfast things were still on the table. He telephoned her mother in Reigate and asked her to come straight away.

It was just before one when the doctor arrived. A fever, he said; some germ that was going the rounds.

He thought she would weep when he told her he was going abroad; she took it in, reflected for a while and then suggested he went and packed.

'Is it important?' she said suddenly.

'Of course. Terribly.'

'Who for?'

'You, me. All of us, I suppose.'

'And for Leclerc?'

'I told you. For all of us.'

He promised Anthony he would bring him something.

'Where are you going?' Anthony asked.

'In an aeroplane.'

'Where?'

He was going to tell him it was a great secret when he re-membered Taylor's little girl.

He kissed her goodbye, took his suitcase to the hall and put it on the mat. There were two locks on the door for Sarah's sake and they had to be turned simultaneously. He heard her say:

'Is it dangerous too?'

'I don't know. I only know it's very big.'

'You're really sure of that, are you?'

He called almost in despair, 'Look, how far am I supposed to think? It isn't a question of politics, don't you see? It's a question of fact. Can't you believe? Can't you tell me for once in my life that I'm doing something good?' He went into the bedroom, rea-soning. She held a paperback in front of her and was pretending to read. 'We all have to, you know, we all have to draw a line round our lives. It's no good asking me the whole time, "Are you sure?" It's like asking whether we should have children, whether we should have married. There's just no point.'

'Poor John,' she observed, putting down the book and ana-lysing him. 'Loyalty without faith. It's very hard for you.' She said this with total dispassion as if she had identified a social evil. The kiss was like a betrayal of her standards.

Haldane watched the last of them leave the room: he had ar-rived late, he would leave late, never with the crowd.

Leclerc said, 'Why do you do that to me?' He spoke like an actor tired from the play. The maps and photographs were strewn on the table with the empty cups and ashtrays.

Haldane didn't answer.

'What are you trying to prove, Adrian?'

'What was that you said about putting a man in?'

Leclerc went to the basin and poured himself a glass of water from the tap. 'You don't care for Avery, do you?' he asked.

'He's young. I'm tired of that cult.'

'I get a sore throat, talking all the time. Have some yourself. Do your cough good.'

'How old is Gorton?' Haldane accepted the glass, drank, and handed it back.

'Fifty.'

'He's more. He's our age. He was our age in the war.'

'One forgets. Yes, he must be fifty-five or six.'

'Established?' Haldane persisted.

Leclerc shook his head. 'He's not qualified. Broken service. He went to the Control Commission after the war. When that packed up he wanted to stay in Germany. German wife, I think. He came to us and we gave him a contract. We could never afford to keep him there if he were established.' He took a sip of water, delicately, like a girl. 'Ten years ago we'd thirty men in the field. Now we've nine. We haven't even got our own couriers, not clandestine ones. They all knew it this morning; why didn't they say so?'

'How often does he put in a refugee report?'

Leclerc shrugged. 'I don't see all his stuff,' he said. 'Your people should know. The market's dwindling, I suppose, now they've closed the Berlin border.'

'They only put the better reports up to me. This must be the first I've seen from Hamburg for a year. I always imagined he had some other function.'

Leclerc shook his head. Haldane asked, 'When does his contract come up for renewal?'

'I don't know. I just don't know.'

'I suppose he must be fairly worried. Does he get a gratuity on retirement?'

'It's just a three-year contract. There's no gratuity. No frills.

He has the chance of going on after sixty, of course, if we want him. That's the advantage of being a temporary.'

'When was his contract last renewed?'

'You'd better ask Carol. It must be two years ago. Maybe longer.'

Haldane said again, 'You talked about putting a man in.'

'I'm seeing the Minister again this afternoon.'

'You've sent Avery already. You shouldn't have done that, you know.'

'Somebody had to go. Did you want me to ask the Circus?'

'Avery was very impertinent,' Haldane observed.

The rain was running in the gutters, tracing grey tracks on the dingy panes. Leclerc seemed to want Haldane to speak, but Haldane had nothing to say. 'I don't know yet what the Minister thinks about Taylor's death. He'll ask me this afternoon and I shall give him my opinion. We're all in the dark, of course.' His voice recovered its strength. 'But he may instruct me – it's on the cards, Adrian – he may *instruct* me to get a man in.'

'Well?'

'Suppose I asked you to form an operations section, make the research, prepare papers and equipment; suppose I asked you to find, train and field the agent. Would you do it?'

'Without telling the Circus?'

'Not in detail. We may need their facilities from time to time. That doesn't mean we need tell them the whole story. There's the question of security: *need to know.*'

'Then without the Circus?'

'Why not?'

Haldane shook his head. 'Because it isn't our work. We're just not equipped. Give it to the Circus and help them out with the military stuff. Give it to an old hand, someone like Smiley or Leamas . . .'

'Leamas is dead.'

'All right then, Smiley.'

'Smiley is blown.'

Haldane coloured. 'Then Guillam or one of the others. One of the pros. They've got a big enough stable these days. Go and see Control, let him have the case.'

'No,' Leclerc said firmly, putting the glass on the table. 'No, Adrian. You've been in the Department as long as I have, you know our brief. *Take all necessary steps* – that's what it says – *all necessary steps for the procurement, analysis and verification of military intelligence in those areas where the requirement cannot be met from conventional military resources.*' He beat out the words with his little fist as he spoke. 'How else do you think I got authority for the overflight?'

'All right,' Haldane conceded. 'We have our brief. But things have changed. It's a different game now. In those days we were top of the tree – rubber boats on a moonless night; a captured enemy plane; wireless and all that. You and I know; we did it together. But it's changed. It's a different war; a different kind of fighting. They know that at the Ministry perfectly well.' He added, 'And don't place too much trust in the Circus; you'll get no charity from those people.'

They looked at one another in surprise, a moment of recognition. Leclerc said, his voice scarcely above a whisper: 'It began with the networks, didn't it? Do you remember how the Circus swallowed them up one by one? The Ministry would say: "We're in danger of duplication on the Polish desks, Leclerc. I've decided Control should look after Poland." When was that? July 'forty-eight. Year after year it's gone on. Why do you think they patronize your Research Section? Not just for your beautiful files; they've got us where they want us, don't you see? Satellites! Non-operational! It's a way of putting us to sleep! You know what they call us in Whitehall these days? The Grace and Favour boys.'

There was a long silence.

Haldane said, 'I'm a collator, not an operational man.'

'You *used* to be operational, Adrian.'

'So did we all.'

'You know the target. You know the whole background. There's no one else. Take whom you want – Avery, Woodford, whoever you want.'

'We're not used to people any more. Handling them, I mean.' Haldane had become unusually diffident. 'I'm a Research man. I work with files.'

'We've had nothing else to give you until now. How long is it? Twenty years.'

'Do you know what it means, a rocket site?' Haldane demanded. 'Do you know how much mess it makes? They need launch pads, blast shields, cable troughs, control buildings; they need bunkers for storing the warheads, trailers for fuel and oxidizers. All those things come first. Rockets don't creep about in the night; they move like a travelling fair; we'd have other indicators before now; or the Circus would. As for Taylor's death—'

'For Heaven's sake, Adrian, do you think Intelligence consists of unassailable philosophical truths? Does every priest have to *prove* that Christ was born on Christmas Day?'

His little face was thrust forward as he tried to draw from Haldane something he seemed to know was there. 'You can't do it all by sums, Adrian. We're not academics, we're Civil Servants. We have to deal with things as they are. We have to deal with people, with events!'

'Very well, events then: if he swam the river, how did he preserve the film? How did he *really* take the pictures? Why isn't there any trace of camera shake? He'd been drinking, he was balancing on tiptoe; they're long enough exposures, you know, time exposures, he said.' Haldane seemed afraid, not of Leclerc, not of the operation, but of himself. 'Why did he give Gorton for nothing what he'd offered elsewhere for money? Why did he risk his life at all, taking those photographs? I sent Gorton a list of supplementaries. He's still trying to find the man, he says.'

His eyes drifted to the model aeroplane and the files on Leclerc's desk. 'You're thinking of Peenemünde, aren't you?' he continued. 'You want it to be like Peenemünde.'

'You haven't told me what you'll do if I get those instructions.'

'You never will. You never, never will.' He spoke with great finality, almost triumph. 'We're dead, don't you see? You said it yourself. They want us to go to sleep, not go to war.' He stood up. 'So it doesn't matter. It's all academic, after all. Can you *really* imagine Control would help us?'

'They've agreed to help us with a courier.'

'Yes. I find that most odd.'

Haldane stopped before a photograph by the door. 'That's Malherbe, isn't it? The boy who died. Why did you choose that name?'

'I don't know. It just came into my head. One's memory plays odd tricks.'

'You shouldn't have sent Avery. We've no business to use him for a job like that.'

'I went through the cards last night. We've got a man who'd do. A man we could send, I mean.' Daring, he added, 'An agent. Trained wireless operator, German speaker, unmarried.' Haldane stood quite still.

'Age?' he asked at last.

'Forty. A bit over.'

'He must have been very young.'

'He put up a good show. They caught him in Holland and he got away.'

'How did he get caught?'

The slightest pause. 'It isn't recorded.'

'Intelligent?'

'He seems quite well qualified.'

The same long silence.

'So am I. Let's see what Avery brings back.'

'Let's see what the Ministry says.'

Leclerc waited till the sound of coughing had faded down the corridor before he put on his coat. He would go for a walk, take some fresh air and have lunch at his club; the best they had. He wondered what it would be; the place had gone off badly in the last few years. After lunch he would go round to Taylor's widow. Then to the Ministry.

Woodford, lunching with his wife at Gorringe's, said, 'Young Avery's on his first run. Clarkie sent him. He should make a good job of it.'

'Perhaps he'll get himself killed, too,' she said nastily. She was off the drink, doctor's orders. 'Then you can have a real ball. Christ, that would be a party and a half! Come to the Black Friars' Ball!' Her lower lip was quivering. 'Why are the young ones always so bloody marvellous? We were young, weren't we? ... Christ, we still are! What's wrong with us? We can't wait to grow old, can we? We can't—'

'All right, Babs,' he said. He was afraid she might cry.

6

Take-off

Avery sat in the aeroplane remembering the day when Haldane failed to appear. It was, by coincidence, the first of the month, July it must have been, and Haldane did not come to the office. Avery knew nothing of it until Woodford rang him on the internal telephone to tell him. Haldane was probably ill, Avery had said; some personal matter had cropped up. But Woodford was adamant. He had been to Leclerc's room, he said, and had looked at the leave roster: Haldane was not due for leave till August.

'Telephone his flat, John, telephone his flat,' he had urged. 'Speak to his wife. Find out what's become of him.' Avery was so astonished that he did not know what to say: those two had worked together for twenty years, and even he knew Haldane was a bachelor.

'Find out where he is,' Woodford had persisted. 'Go on, I order you: ring his flat.'

So he did. He might have told Woodford to do it himself, but he hadn't the heart. Haldane's sister answered. Haldane was in bed, his chest was playing him up; he had refused to tell her the Department's telephone number. As Avery's eye caught the calendar, he realised why Woodford had been so agitated: it was the beginning of a quarter. Haldane might have got a new job and left the Department without telling Woodford. A day or two later, when Haldane returned, Woodford was uncommonly warm towards him, bravely ignoring his sarcasm; he was grateful to him for coming back. For some time after that, Avery had been frightened. His faith shaken, he examined more closely its object.

He noticed that they ascribed – it was a plot in which all but Haldane compounded – legendary qualities to one another. Leclerc, for instance, would seldom introduce Avery to a member of his parent Ministry without some catchword. 'Avery is the brightest of our new stars' – or, to more senior men, 'John is my memory. You must ask John.' For the same reason they lightly forgave one another their trespasses, because they dared not think, for their own sakes, that the Department had room for fools. He recognised that it provided shelter from the complexities of modern life, a place where frontiers still existed. For its servants, the Department had a religious quality. Like monks, they endowed it with a mystical identity far away from the hesitant, sinful band which made up its ranks. While they might be cynical of the qualities of one another, contemptuous of their own hierarchical preoccupations, their faith in the Department burnt in some separate chapel and they called it patriotism.

For all that, as he glanced at the darkening sea beneath him, at the cold sunlight slanting on the waves, he felt his heart thrilling with love. Woodford with his pipe and his plain way became part of that secret élite to which Avery now belonged; Haldane, Haldane above all, with his crosswords and his eccentricities, fitted into place as the uncompromising intellectual, irritable and aloof. He was sorry he had been rude to Haldane. He saw Dennison and McCulloch as the matchless technicians, quiet men, not articulate at meetings, but tireless and, in the end, right. He thanked Leclerc, thanked him warmly, for the privilege of knowing these men, for the excitement of this mission; for the opportunity to advance from the uncertainty of the past towards experience and maturity, to become a man, shoulder to shoulder with the others, tempered in the fire of war; he thanked him for the precision of command, which made order out of the anarchy of his heart. He imagined that when Anthony grew up, he too might be led into those dowdy corridors, and be presented to old Pine, who with tears in his eyes would stand up in his box and warmly grasp the child's tender hand.

It was a scene in which Sarah played no part.

Avery lightly touched a corner of the long envelope in his inside pocket. It contained his money: two hundred pounds in a blue envelope with the Government crest. He had heard of people in the war sewing such things into the lining of their clothes, and he rather wished they had done that for him. It was a childish conceit, he knew; he even smiled to discover himself given to such fancies.

He remembered Smiley that morning; in retrospect he was just a little frightened of Smiley. And he remembered the child at the door. A man must steel himself against sentiment.

'Your husband did a very good job,' Leclerc was saying, 'I cannot tell you the details. I am sure that he died very gallantly.'

Her mouth was stained and ugly. Leclerc had never seen anyone cry so much; it was like a wound that would not close.

'What do you mean, gallantly?' She blinked. 'We're not fighting a war. That's finished, all that fancy talk. He's dead,' she said stupidly, and buried her face in her crooked arm, slouching across the dining-room table like a puppet abandoned. The child was staring from a corner.

'I trust,' Leclerc said, 'that I have your permission to apply for a pension? You must leave all that to us. The sooner we take care of it the better. A pension,' he declared, as if it were the maxim of his house, 'can make a lot of difference.'

The Consul was waiting beside the Immigration Officer; he came forward without a smile, doing his duty. 'Are you Avery?' he asked. Avery had the impression of a tall man in a trilby and a dark overcoat; red-faced and severe. They shook hands.

'You're the British Consul, Mr Sutherland.'

'H. M. Consul, actually,' he replied, a little tartly. 'There's a difference, you know.' He spoke with a Scottish accent. 'How did you know my name?'

They walked together towards the main entrance. It was all very simple. Avery noticed the girl at the desk; fair and rather pretty.

'It's kind of you to come all this way,' Avery said.

'It's only three miles from the town.' They got into the car.

'He was killed just up the road,' said Sutherland. 'Do you want to see the spot?'

'I might as well. To tell my mother.' He was wearing a black tie.

'Your name *is* Avery, isn't it?'

'Of course it is; you saw my passport at the desk.' Sutherland didn't like that, and Avery rather wished he hadn't said it. He started the engine. They were about to pull into the centre of the road when a Citroën swung out and overtook them.

'Damn fool,' Sutherland snapped. 'Roads are like ice. One of these pilots, I suppose. No idea of speed.' They could see a peaked cap silhouetted against the windscreen as the car hurried down the long road across the dunes, throwing up a small cloud of snow behind it.

'Where do you come from?' he asked.

'London.'

Sutherland pointed straight ahead: 'That's where your brother died. Up there on the brow. The police reckon the driver must have been tight. They're very hot on drunken driving here, you know.' It sounded like a warning. Avery stared at the flat reaches of snowbound country on either side and thought of lonely, English Taylor struggling along the road, his weak eyes streaming from the cold.

'We'll go to the police afterwards,' said Sutherland. 'They're expecting us. They'll tell you all the details. Have you booked yourself a room here?'

'No.'

As they reached the top of the rise Sutherland said with grudging deference, 'It was just here, if you want to get out.'

'It's all right.'

Sutherland accelerated a little as if he wanted to get away from the place.

'Your brother was walking to the hotel. The Regina, just here. There was no taxi.' They descended the slope on the other side; Avery caught sight of the long lights of a hotel across the valley.

'No distance at all, really,' Sutherland commented. 'He'd have done it in fifteen minutes. Less. Where does your mother live?'

The question took Avery by surprise.

'Woodbridge, in Suffolk.' There was a by-election going on there; it was the first town that came into his head, though he had no interest in politics.

'Why didn't he put her down?'

'I'm sorry, I don't understand.'

'As next of kin. Why didn't Malherbe put his mother down instead of you?'

Perhaps it was not meant as a serious question; perhaps he just wanted to keep Avery talking because he was upset; nevertheless, it was unnerving. He was still strung up from the journey, he wanted to be taken for granted, not subjected to this interrogation. He realised, too, that he had not sufficiently worked out the supposed relationship between Taylor and himself. What had Leclerc written in the teleprint; half-brother or step-brother? Hastily he tried to visualise a train of family events, death, remarriage or estrangement, which would lead him to the answer to Sutherland's question.

'There's the hotel,' the Consul said suddenly, and then, 'It's nothing to do with me, of course. He can put down whoever he wants.' Resentment had become a habit of speech with Sutherland, a philosophy. He spoke as if everything he said were the contradiction of a popular view.

'She's old,' Avery replied at last. 'It's a question of protecting her from shock. I expect that's what he had in mind when he filled in his passport application. She's been ill; a bad heart. She's had an operation.' It sounded very childish.

'Ah.'

They had reached the outskirts of the town.

'There has to be a post-mortem,' Sutherland said. 'It's the law here, I'm afraid, in the case of violent death.'

Leclerc was going to be angry about that. Sutherland continued, 'For us, it makes the formalities more complicated. The Criminal Police take over the body until the post-mortem is complete. I asked them to be quick, but one can't insist.'

'Thanks. I thought I'd have the body flown back.' As they turned off the main road into the market square, Avery asked casually, as if he had no personal interest in the outcome, 'What about his effects? I'd better take them with me, hadn't I?'

'I doubt whether the police will hand them over until they've had the go-ahead from the public prosecutor. The post-mortem report goes to him; he gives clearance. Did your brother leave a will?'

'I've no idea.'

'You'd not happen to know whether you're an executor?'

'No.'

Sutherland gave a dry, patient laugh. 'I can't help feeling you're a little premature. Next of kin is not quite the same as executor,' he said. 'It gives you no legal rights, I'm afraid, apart from the disposal of the body.' He paused, looking back over his seat while he reversed the car into a parking space. 'Even if the police hand your brother's effects over to me, I'm not allowed to release them until I've had instructions from the Office, and *they*,' he continued quickly, for Avery was about to interrupt him, 'won't issue such instructions to *me* until a grant of probate has been made or a Letter of Administration issued. But I can give you a death certificate,' he added consolingly, opening his door, 'if the insurance companies require it.' He looked at Avery sideways, as if wondering whether he stood to inherit anything. 'It'll cost you five shillings for the Consular registration and five shillings per certified copy. What was that you said?'

'Nothing.' Together they climbed the steps to the police station.

'We'll be seeing Inspector Peersen,' Sutherland explained. 'He's quite well disposed. You'll kindly let me handle him.'

'Of course.'

'He's been a lot of help with my DBS problems.'

'Your what?'

'Distressed British Subjects. We get one a day in Summer. They're a disgrace. Did your brother drink a lot, incidentally? There's some suggestion he was—'

'It's possible,' Avery said. 'I hardly knew him in the last few years.' They entered the building.

Leclerc himself was walking carefully up the broad steps of the Ministry. It lay between Whitehall Gardens and the river; the doorway was large and new, surrounded with that kind of Fascist statuary which is admired by local authorities. Partly modernised, the building was guarded by sergeants in red sashes and contained two escalators; the one which descended was full, for it was half past five.

'Under Secretary,' Leclerc began diffidently. 'I shall have to ask the Minister for another overflight.'

'You'll be wasting your time,' he replied with satisfaction. 'He was most apprehensive about the last one. He's made a policy decision; there'll be no more.'

'Even with a target like this?'

'Particularly with a target like this.'

The Under Secretary lightly touched the corners of his in-tray as a bank manager might touch a statement. 'You'll have to think of something else,' he said. 'Some other way. Is there no *painless* method?'

'None. I suppose we could try to stimulate a defection from the area. That's a lengthy business. Leaflets, propaganda broadcasts, financial inducements. It worked well in the war. We would have to approach a lot of people.'

'It sounds a most improbable notion.'

'Yes. Things are different now.'

'What other ways are there, then?' he insisted.

Leclerc smiled again, as if he would like to help a friend, but could not work miracles. 'An agent. A short-term operation. In and out: a week altogether perhaps.'

The Under Secretary said, 'But who could you find for a job like that? These days?'

'Who indeed? It's a very long shot.'

The Under Secretary's room was large but dark, with rows of bound books. Modernisation had encroached as far as his Private Office, which was done in the contemporary style, but there the process had stopped. They could wait till he retired to do his room. A gas fire burnt in the marble fireplace. On the wall hung an oil painting of a battle at sea. They could hear the sound of barges in the fog. It was an oddly maritime atmosphere.

'Kalkstadt's pretty close to the border,' Leclerc suggested. 'We wouldn't have to use a scheduled airline. We could do a training flight, lose our way. It's been done before.'

'Precisely,' said the Under Secretary, then: 'This man of yours who died.'

'Taylor?'

'I'm not concerned with names. He was murdered, was he?'

'There's no proof,' Leclerc said.

'But you assume it?'

Leclerc smiled patiently. 'I think we both know, Under Secretary, that it is very dangerous to make broad assumptions when decisions of policy are involved. I'm still asking for another overflight.'

The Under Secretary coloured.

'I told you it's out of the question. No! Does that make it clear? We were talking of alternatives.'

'There's one alternative, I suppose, which would scarcely touch on my Department. It's more a matter for yourselves and the Foreign Office.'

'Oh?'

'Drop a hint to the London newspapers. Stimulate publicity. Print the photographs.'

'And?'

'Watch them. Watch the East German and Soviet diplomacy, watch their communications. Throw a stone into the nest and see what comes out.'

'I can tell you exactly what would come out. A protest from

the Americans that would ring through these corridors for another twenty years.'

'Of course. I was forgetting that.'

'Then you're very lucky. You suggested putting an agent in.'

'Only tentatively. We've no one in mind.'

'Look,' said the Under Secretary, with the finality of a man
much tried. 'The Minister's position is very simple. You have produced a report. If it is true, it alters our entire defence position. In
fact it alters everything. I detest sensation, so does the Minister.
Having put up the hare, the least you can do is have a shot at it.'

Leclerc said, 'If I found a man there's the problem of resources. Money, training and equipment. Extra staff perhaps.
Transport. Whereas an overflight . . .'

'Why do you raise so many difficulties? I understood you
people existed for this kind of thing.'

'We have the expertise, Under Secretary. But I cut down, you
know. I have cut down a lot. Some of our functions have lapsed:
one must be honest. I have never tried to put the clock back. This
is, after all' – a delicate smile – 'a slightly *anachronistic* situation.'

The Under Secretary glanced out of the window at the lights
along the river.

'It seems pretty contemporary to me. Rockets and that kind
of thing. I don't think the Minister considers it anachronistic.'

'I'm not referring to the target but the method of attack: it
would have to be a crash operation at the border. That has
scarcely been done since the war. Although it is a form of clandestine warfare with which my Department is traditionally at
home. Or used to be.'

'What are you getting at?'

'I'm only thinking aloud, Under Secretary. I wonder whether
the Circus might not be better equipped to deal with this. Perhaps you should approach Control. I can promise him the support of my armaments people.'

'You mean you don't think you can handle it?'

'Not with my existing organisation. Control can. As long,
that is, as the Minister doesn't mind bringing in another

Department. Two, really. I didn't realise you were so worried about publicity.'

'Two?'

'Control will feel bound to inform the Foreign Office. It's his duty. Just as I inform you. And from then on, we must accept that it will be their headache.'

'If *those* people know,' the Under Secretary said with contempt, 'it'll be round every damned club by tomorrow.'

'There is that danger,' Leclerc conceded. 'More particularly, I wonder whether the Circus has the *military* skills. A rocket site is a complicated affair: launch pads, blast shields, cable troughs; all these things require proper processing and evaluation. Control and I could combine forces, I suppose—'

'That's out of the question. You people make poor bedfellows. Even if you succeeded in cooperating, it would be against policy: no monolith.'

'Ah yes. Of course.'

'Assume you do it yourself, then; assume you find a man, what would that involve?'

'A supplementary estimate. Immediate resources. Extra staff. A training establishment. Ministerial protection; special passes and authority.' The knife again: 'And *some* help from Control . . . we could obtain that under a pretext.'

A foghorn echoed mournfully across the water.

'If it's the only way . . .'

'Perhaps you'd put it to the Minister,' Leclerc suggested.

Silence. Leclerc continued, 'In practical terms we need the best part of thirty thousand pounds.'

'Accountable?'

'Partially. I understood you wanted to be spared details.'

'Except where the Treasury's concerned. I suggest that you make a minute about costs.'

'Very well. Just an outline.'

The silence returned.

'That is hardly a large sum when set against the risk,' the Under Secretary said, consoling himself.

'The potential risk. We want to clarify. I don't pretend to be convinced. Merely suspicious, heavily suspicious.' He couldn't resist adding, 'The Circus would ask twice as much. They're very free with money.'

'Thirty thousand pounds, then, and our protection?'

'And a man. But I must find him for myself.' A small laugh.

The Under Secretary said abruptly: 'There are certain details the Minister will not want to know. You realise that?'

'Of course. I imagine you will do most of the talking.'

'I imagine the Minister will. You've succeeded in worrying him a good deal.'

Leclerc remarked with impish piety, 'We should never do that to our master; our common master.'

The Under Secretary did not seem to feel they had one. They stood up.

'Incidentally,' Leclerc said, 'Mrs Taylor's pension. I'm making an application to the Treasury. They feel the Minister should sign it.'

'Why, for God's sake?'

'It's a question of whether he was killed in action.'

The Under Secretary froze. 'That is most presumptuous. You're asking for Ministerial confirmation that Taylor was murdered.'

'I'm asking for a widow's pension,' Leclerc protested gravely. 'He was one of my best men.'

'Of course. They always are.'

The Minister did not look up as they came in.

But the Police Inspector rose from his chair, a short, plump man with a shaven neck. He wore plain clothes. Avery supposed him to be a detective. He shook their hands with an air of professional bereavement, sat them in modern chairs with teak arms and offered cigars out of a tin. They declined, so he lit one himself, and used it thereafter both as a prolongation of his short fingers when making gestures of emphasis, and as a drawing instrument to describe in the smoke-filled air objects of

which he was speaking. He deferred frequently to Avery's grief
by thrusting his chin downwards into his collar and casting
from the shadow of his lowered eyebrows confiding looks of
sympathy. First he related the circumstances of the accident,
praised in tiresome detail the efforts of the police to track down
the car, referred frequently to the personal concern of the President of Police, whose anglophilia was a byword, and stated his
own conviction that the guilty man would be found out, and
punished with the full severity of Finnish law. He dwelt for
some time on his own admiration of the British, his affection
for the Queen and Sir Winston Churchill, the charms of Finnish neutrality and finally he came to the body.

The post-mortem, he was proud to say, was complete, and
Mr Public Prosecutor (his own words) had declared that the circumstances of Mr Malherbe's death gave no grounds for suspicion despite the presence of a considerable amount of alcohol in
the blood. The barman at the airport accounted for five glasses
of Steinhäger. He returned to Sutherland.

'Does he want to see his brother?' he inquired, thinking it
apparently a delicacy to refer the question to a third party.

Sutherland was embarrassed. 'That's up to Mr Avery,' he said,
as if the matter were outside his competence. They both looked
at Avery.

'I don't think so,' Avery said.

'There is one difficulty. About the identification,' Peersen said.

'Identification?' Avery repeated. 'Of my brother?'

'You saw his passport,' Sutherland put in, 'before you sent it
up to me. What's the difficulty?'

The policeman nodded. 'Yes, yes.' Opening a drawer he took
out a handful of letters, a wallet and some photographs.

'His name was Malherbe,' he said. He spoke fluent English
with a heavy American accent which somehow suited the cigar.
'His passport was Malherbe. It was a *good* passport, wasn't it?'
Peersen glanced at Sutherland. For a second Avery thought he detected in Sutherland's clouded face a certain honest hesitation.

'Of course.'

Peersen began to sort through the letters, putting some in a file before him and returning others to the drawer. Every now and then, as he added to the pile, he muttered: 'Ah, so,' or 'Yes, yes.' Avery could feel the sweat running down his body; it drenched his clasped hands.

'And your brother's name was Malherbe?' he asked again, when he had finished his sorting.

Avery nodded. 'Of course.'

Peersen smiled. 'Not of course,' he said, pointing his cigar and nodding in a friendly way as if he were making a debating point. 'All his possessions, his letters, his clothes, driving licence, all belong to a Mr Taylor. You know anything of Taylor?'

A dreadful block was forming in Avery's mind. The envelope, what should he do with the envelope? Go to the lavatory, destroy it now before it was too late? He doubted whether it would work: the envelope was stiff and shiny. Even if he tore it, the pieces would float. He was aware of Peersen and Sutherland looking at him, waiting for him to speak and all he could think of was the envelope weighing so heavily in his inside pocket.

He managed to say, 'No, I don't. My brother and I . . .' Stepbrother or half-brother? '. . . my brother and I did not have much to do with one another. He was older. We didn't really grow up together. He had a lot of different jobs, he could never quite settle down to anything. Perhaps this Taylor was a friend of his . . . who . . .' Avery shrugged, bravely trying to imply that Malherbe had been something of a mystery to him also.

'How old are you?' Peersen asked. His respect for the bereaved seemed to be dwindling.

'Thirty-two.'

'And Malherbe?' he threw out conversationally. 'He was how many years older, please?'

Sutherland and Peersen had seen his passport and knew his age. One remembers the age of people who die. Only Avery, his brother, had no idea how old the dead man was.

'Twelve,' he hazarded. 'My brother was forty-four.' Why did he have to say so much?

Peersen raised his eyebrows. 'Only forty-four? Then the passport is wrong as well.'

Peersen turned to Sutherland, poked his cigar towards the door at the far end of the room and said happily, as if he had ended an old argument between friends, 'Now you are seeing why I have a problem about identification.'

Sutherland was looking very angry.

'It would be nice if Mr Avery looked at the body,' Peersen suggested, 'then we can be sure.'

Sutherland said, 'Inspector Peersen. The identity of Mr Malherbe has been established from his passport. The Foreign Office in London has ascertained that Mr Avery's name was quoted by Mr Malherbe as his next of kin. You tell me there is nothing suspicious about the circumstances of his death. The customary procedure is now for you to release his effects to me for custody pending the completion of formalities in the United Kingdom. Mr Avery may presumably take charge of his brother's body.'

Peersen seemed to deliberate. He extracted the remainder of Taylor's papers from the steel drawer of his desk, added them to the pile already in front of him. He telephoned somebody and spoke in Finnish. After some minutes an orderly brought in an old leather suitcase with an inventory which Sutherland signed. Throughout all this, neither Avery nor Sutherland exchanged a word with the Inspector.

Peersen accompanied them all the way to the front door. Sutherland insisted on carrying the suitcase and papers himself. They went to the car. Avery waited for Sutherland to speak, but he said nothing. They drove for about ten minutes. The town was poorly lit. Avery noticed there was a chemical on the road, in two lanes. The crown and gutters were still covered with snow. He was reminded of riding in the Mall, a thing he had never done. The street lamps were neon, shedding a sickly light which seemed to shrink before the gathering darkness. Now and then Avery was aware of steep timbered roofs, the clanging of a tram or the tall white hat of a policeman.

Occasionally he stole a glance through the rear window.

7

Woodford stood in the corridor smoking his pipe, grinning at the staff as they left. It was his hour of magic. The mornings were different. Tradition demanded that the junior staff arrived at half past nine; officer grades at ten or quarter past. Theoretically, senior members of the Department stayed late in the evening, clearing their papers. A gentleman, Leclerc would say, never watched the clock. The custom dated from the war, when officers spent the early hours of the morning debriefing reconnaissance pilots back from a run, or the late hours of the night dispatching an agent. The junior staff had worked shift in those days, but not the officers, who came and went as their work allowed. Now tradition fulfilled a different purpose. Now there were days, often weeks, when Woodford and his colleagues scarcely knew how to fill the time until five thirty; all but Haldane, who supported on his stooping shoulders the Department's reputation for research. The rest would draft projects which were never submitted, bicker gently among themselves about leave, duty rosters and the quality of their official furniture, give excessive attention to the problems of their section staff.

Berry, the cypher clerk, came into the corridor, stooped and put on his bicycle clips.

'How's the missus, Berry?' Woodford asked. A man must keep his finger on the pulse.

'Doing very nicely, thank you, sir.' He stood up, ran a comb through his hair. 'Shocking about Wilf Taylor, sir.'

'Shocking. He was a good scout.'

'Mr Haldane's locking up Registry, sir. He's working late.'

'Is he? Well, we all have our hands full now.'

Berry lowered his voice. 'And the Boss is sleeping in, sir. Quite a crisis, really. I hear he's gone to see the Minister. They sent a car for him.'

'Goodnight, Berry.' They hear too much, Woodford reflected with satisfaction, and began sauntering along the passage.

The illumination in Haldane's room came from an adjustable reading-lamp. It threw a brief, intense beam on to the file in front of him, touching the contours of his face and hands.

'Working late?' Woodford inquired.

Haldane pushed one file into his out-tray and picked up another.

'Wonder how young Avery's faring; he'll do well, that boy. I hear the Boss isn't back yet. Must be a long session.' As he spoke Woodford settled himself in the leather armchair. It was Haldane's own, he had brought it from his flat and sat in it to do his crossword after luncheon.

'Why should he do well? There is no particular precedent,' Haldane said, without looking up.

'How did Clarkie get on with Taylor's wife?' Woodford now asked. 'How'd she take it?'

Haldane sighed and put his file aside.

'He broke it to her. That's all I know.'

'You didn't hear how she took it? He didn't tell you?'

Woodford always spoke a little louder than necessary, for he was used to competing with his wife.

'I've really no idea. He went alone, I understand. Leclerc prefers to keep these things to himself.'

'I thought perhaps with you . . .'

Haldane shook his head. 'Only Avery.'

'It's a big thing, this, isn't it, Adrian . . . could be?'

'It could be. We shall see,' Haldane said gently. He was not always unkind towards Woodford.

'Anything new on the Taylor front?'

'The Air Attaché at Helsinki has located Lansen. He confirms that he handed Taylor the film. Apparently the Russians intercepted him over Kalkstadt; two MIGs. They buzzed him, then let him go.'

'God,' said Woodford stupidly. 'That clinches it.'

'It does nothing of the kind; it's consistent with what we know. If they declare the area closed why shouldn't they patrol it? They probably closed it for manoeuvres, ground-air exercises. Why didn't they force Lansen down? The whole thing is entirely inconclusive.'

Leclerc was standing in the doorway. He had put on a clean collar for the Minister and a black tie for Taylor.

'I came by car,' he said. 'They've given us one from the Ministry pool on indefinite loan. The Minister was quite distressed to hear we hadn't one. It's a Humber, chauffeur-driven like Control's. They tell me the chauffeur is a secure sort of person.' He looked at Haldane. 'I've decided to form Special Section, Adrian. I want you to take it over. I'm giving Research to Sandford for the time being. The change will do him good.' His face broke into a smile as if he could contain himself no longer. He was very excited. 'We're putting a man in. The Minister's given his consent. We go to work at once. I want to see Heads of Sections first thing tomorrow. Adrian, I'll give you Woodford and Avery. Bruce, you keep in touch with the boys; get on to the old training people. The Minister will support three-month contracts for temporary staff. No peripheral liabilities, of course. The usual programme: wireless, weapon training, cyphers, observation, unarmed combat and cover. Adrian, we'll need a house. Perhaps Avery could go into that when he comes back. I'll approach Control about documentation; the forgers all went over to him. We'll want frontier records for the Lübeck area, refugee reports, details of minefields and obstructions.' He glanced at his watch. 'Adrian, shall we have a word?'

'Tell me one thing,' Haldane said. 'How much does the Circus know about this?'

'Whatever we choose to tell them. Why?'

'They know Taylor is dead. It's all over Whitehall.'

'Possibly.'

'They know Avery's picking up a film in Finland. They may very well have noticed the Air Safety Centre report on Lansen's plane. They have a way of noticing things . . .'

'Well?'

'So it isn't only a question of what we tell them, is it?'

'You'll come to tomorrow's meeting?' Leclerc asked a little pathetically.

'I think I have the meat of my instructions. If you have no objection I would like to make one or two inquiries. This evening and tomorrow perhaps.'

Leclerc, bewildered, said, 'Excellent. Can we help you?'

'Perhaps I might have the use of your car for an hour?'

'Of course. I want us all to use it – to our common benefit. Adrian – this is for you.'

He handed him a green card in a Cellophane folder.

'The Minister signed it, personally.' He implied that, like a Papal blessing, there were degrees of authenticity in a Ministerial signature. 'Then you'll do it, Adrian? You'll take the job?'

Haldane might not have heard. He had reopened the file and was looking curiously at the photograph of a Polish boy who had fought the Germans twenty years ago. It was a young, strict face; humourless. It seemed to be concerned not with living but with survival.

'Why, Adrian,' Leclerc cried with sudden relief, 'you've taken the second vow!'

Reluctantly Haldane smiled, as if the phrase had called to mind something he thought he had forgotten. 'He seems to have a talent for survival,' he observed, finally indicating the file. 'Not an easy man to kill.'

'As next of kin,' Sutherland began, 'you have the right to state your wishes concerning the disposal of your brother's body.'

'Yes.'

Sutherland's house was a small building with a picture

window full of potted plants. Only these distinguished it, either externally or internally, from its model in the dormitory areas of Aberdeen. As they walked down the drive, Avery caught sight of a middle-aged woman in the window. She wore an apron and was dusting something. She reminded him of Mrs Yates and her cat.

'I have an office at the back,' said Sutherland, as if to emphasise that the place was not wholly given over to luxury. 'I suggest we tie up the rest of the details now. I shan't keep you long.' He was telling Avery he needn't expect to stay to supper. 'How do you propose to get him back to England?'

They sat down either side of the desk. Behind Sutherland's head hung a watercolour of mauve hills reflected in a Scottish loch.

'I should like it flown home.'

'You know that is an expensive business?'

'I should like him flown all the same.'

'For burial?'

'Of course.'

'It isn't "of course" at all,' Sutherland countered with distaste. 'If your brother' – he said it in inverted commas now, but he would play the game to the end – 'were to be cremated, the flight regulations would be totally different.'

'I see. I'm sorry.'

'There is a firm of undertakers in the town, Barford and Company. One of the partners is English, married to a Swedish girl. There is a substantial Swedish minority here. We do our best to support the British community. In the circumstances I would prefer you to return to London as soon as you can. I suggest you empower me to use Barford.'

'All right.'

'As soon as he has taken over the body, I will provide him with your brother's passport. He will have to obtain a medical certificate regarding the cause of death. I'll put him in touch with Peersen.'

'Yes.'

'He will also require a death certificate issued by a local

registrar. It is cheaper if one attends to that side of things one-self. If money matters to your people.'

Avery said nothing.

'When he has found out a suitable flight he will look after the freight warrant and bill of lading. I understand these things are usually moved at night. The freight rate is cheaper and . . .'

'That's all right.'

'I'm glad. Barford will make sure the coffin is airtight. It may be of metal or wood. He will also append his own certifi-cate that the coffin contains nothing but the body – and the same body as that to which the passport and the death certifi-cate refer. I mention this for when you take delivery in London. Barford will do all this very quickly. I shall see to that. He has some pull with the charter companies here. The sooner he—'

'I understand.'

'I'm not sure you do.' Sutherland raised his eyebrows, as if Avery had been impertinent. 'Peersen has been very reasonable. I don't wish to test his patience. Barford will have a correspond-ent firm in London – it is London, isn't it?'

'London, yes.'

'I imagine he will expect some payment in advance. I suggest you leave the money with me against a receipt. As regards your brother's effects, I take it that whoever sent you wished you to recover these letters?' He pushed them across the table.

Avery muttered, 'There was a film, an undeveloped film.' He put the letters in his pocket.

Deliberately Sutherland extracted a copy of the inventory which he had signed at the police station, spread it out before him and ran his finger down the left-hand column, suspiciously, as if he were checking someone else's figures.

'There is no film entered here. Was there a camera too?'

'No.'

'Ah.'

He saw Avery to the door. 'You'd better tell whoever sent you that Malherbe's passport was not valid. The Foreign Office sent out a circular about a group of numbers, twenty-odd. Your brother's was one of them. There must have been a slip-up. I was about to report it when a Foreign Office teleprint arrived empowering you to take over Malherbe's effects.' He gave a short laugh. He was very angry. 'That was nonsense, of course. The Office would never have sent that on their own. They've no authority, not unless you'd Letters of Administration, and you couldn't have got *those* in the middle of the night. Have you somewhere to stay? The Regina's quite good, near the airport. Out of town, too. I assume you can find your own way. I gather you people get excellent subsistence.'

Avery made his way quickly down the drive, carrying in his memory the indelible image of Sutherland's thin, bitter face set angrily against the Scottish hills. The wooden houses beside the road shone half white in the darkness like shadows round an operating table.

Somewhere not far from Charing Cross, in the basement of one of those surprising eighteenth-century houses between Villiers Street and the river, is a club with no name on the door. You reach it by descending a curving stone staircase. The railing, like the woodwork of the house in Blackfriars Road, is painted dark green and needs replacing.

Its members are an odd selection. Some of a military kind, some in the teaching profession, others clerical; others again from that no-man's-land of London society which lies between the bookmaker and the gentleman, presenting to those around them, and perhaps even to themselves, an image of vacuous courage; conversing in codes and phrases which a man with a sense of language can only listen to at a distance. It is a place of old faces and young bodies; of young faces and old bodies; where the tensions of war have become the tensions of peace, and voices are raised to drown the silence, and glasses to drown the loneliness; it is the place where the searchers meet, finding no one but each other and the comfort of a shared pain; where the tired watchful eyes have no horizon to observe. It is their battle-field still; if there is love, they find it here in one another, shyly like adolescents, thinking all the time of other people.

From the war, none but the dons were missing.

It is a small place, run by a thin, dry man called Major Dell; he has a moustache and a tie with blue angels on a black background. He stands the first drink, and they buy him the others. It is called the Alias Club, and Woodford was a member.

It is open in the evenings. They come at about six, detaching themselves with pleasure from the moving crowd, furtive but determined, like men from out of town visiting a disreputable theatre. You notice first the things that are not there: no silver cups behind the bar, no visitors' book nor list of membership; no insignia, crest or title. Only on the whitewashed brick walls a few photographs hang, framed in passe-partout, like the photographs in Leclerc's room. The faces are indistinct, some enlarged, apparently from a passport, taken from the front with both ears showing according to the regulation; some are of women, a few of them attractive, with high square shoulders and long hair after the fashion of the war years. The men are wearing a variety of uniforms; Free French and Poles mingle with their British comrades. Some are fliers. Of the English faces one or two, grown old, still haunt the club.

When Woodford came in everyone looked round and Major Dell, much pleased, ordered his pint of beer. A florid, middle-aged man was talking about a sortie he once made over Belgium but he stopped when he lost the attention of his audience.

'Hello, Woodie,' somebody said in surprise. 'How's the lady?'

'Fit,' Woodford smiled genially. 'Fit.' He drank some beer. Cigarettes were passed round. Major Dell said, 'Woodie's jolly shifty tonight.'

'I'm looking for someone. It's all a bit top secret.'

'We know the form,' the florid man replied. Woodford glanced round the bar and asked quietly, a note of mystery in his voice, 'What did Dad do in the war?'

A bewildered silence. They had been drinking for some time.

'Kept Mum, of course,' said Major Dell uncertainly and they all laughed.

Woodford laughed with them, savouring the conspiracy, re-living the half-forgotten ritual of secret mess nights somewhere in England.

'And where did he keep her?' he demanded, still in the same confiding tone: this time two or three voices called in unison, 'Under his blooming hat!'

They were louder, happier.

'There was a man called Johnson,' Woodford continued quickly, 'Jack Johnson. I'm trying to find out what became of him. He was a trainer in wireless transmission; one of the best. He was at Bovingdon first with Haldane until they moved him up to Oxford.'

'Jack Johnson!' the florid man cried excitedly. 'The WT man? I bought a car radio from Jack two weeks ago! Johnson's Fair Deal in the Clapham Broadway, that's the fellow. Drops in here from time to time. Amateur wireless enthusiast. Little bloke, speaks out of the side of his face?'

'That's him,' someone else said. 'He knocks off twenty per cent for the old gang.'

'He didn't for me,' the florid man said.

'That's Jack; he lives at Clapham.'

The others took it up; that was the fellow and he ran this shop, at Clapham; king of ham radio, been a ham before the war even when he was a kid; yes, on the Broadway, hung out there for years; must be worth a ransom. Liked to come into the club round Christmas time. Woodford, flushed with pleasure, ordered drinks.

In the bustle that followed, Major Dell took Woodford gently by the arm and guided him to the other end of the bar.

'Woodie, is it true about Wilf Taylor? Has he really bought it?'

Woodford nodded, his face grave. 'He was on a job. We think someone's been a little bit naughty.'

Major Dell was all solicitude. 'I haven't told the boys. It would only worry them. Who's caring for the Missus?'

'The Boss is taking that up now. It looks pretty hopeful.'

'Good,' said the Major. 'Good.' He nodded, patting Woodford's arm in a gesture of consolation. 'We'll keep it from the boys, shall we?'

'Of course.'

'He had one or two bills. Nothing very big. He liked to drop in Friday nights.' The Major's accent slipped from time to time like a made-up tie.

'Send them along. We'll take care of those.'

'There was a kid, wasn't there? A little girl?' They were moving back to the bar. 'How old was she?'

'Eightish. Maybe more.'

'He talked about her a lot,' said the Major.

Somebody called, 'Hey, Bruce, when are you chaps going to take another crack at the Jerries? They're all over the bloody place. Took the wife to Italy in the Summer – full of arrogant Germans.'

Woodford smiled. 'Sooner than you think. Now let's try this one.' The conversation died. Woodford was real. He still did the job.

'There was an unarmed-combat man, a staff sergeant; a Welshman. He was short too.'

'Sounds like Sandy Lowe,' the florid man suggested.

'Sandy, that's him!' They all turned to the florid man in admiration. 'He was a Taffy. Randy Sandy we called him.'

'Of course,' said Woodford contentedly. 'Now didn't he go off to some public school as a boxing instructor?' He was looking at them narrowly, holding a good deal back, playing it long because it was so secret.

'That's him, that's Sandy!'

Woodford wrote it down, taking care because he had learnt from experience that he tended to forget things which he entrusted to memory.

As he was going, the Major asked, 'How's Clarkie?'

'Busy,' Woodford said. 'Working himself to death, as always.'

'The boys talk about him a lot, you know. I wish he'd come here now and then; give them a hell of a boost, you know. Perk them up.'

'Tell me,' said Woodford. They were by the door. 'Do you remember a fellow called Leiser? Fred Leiser, a Pole? Used to be with our lot. He was in the Holland show.'

'Still alive?'

'Yes.'

'Sorry,' said the Major vaguely. 'The foreigners have stopped coming; I don't know why. I don't discuss it with the boys.'

Closing the door behind him, Woodford stepped into the London night. He looked about him, loving all he saw – the mother city in his rugged care. He walked slowly, an old athlete on an old track.

8

Avery, on the other hand, walked fast. He was afraid. There is no terror so consistent, so elusive to describe, as that which haunts a spy in a strange country. The glance of a taxi driver, the density of people in the street, the variety of official uniform – was he a policeman or a postman? – the obscurity of custom and language, and the very noises which comprised the world into which Avery had moved contributed to a state of constant anxiety, which, like a nervous pain, became virulent now that he was alone. In the shortest time his spirit ranged between panic and cringing love, responding with unnatural gratitude to a kind glance or word. It was part of an effeminate dependence upon those whom he deceived. Avery needed desperately to win from the uncaring faces around him the absolution of a trusting smile. It was no help that he told himself: you do them no harm, you are their protector. He moved among them like a hunted man in search of rest and food.

He took a cab to the hotel and asked for a room with a bath. They gave him the register to sign. He had actually put his pen to the page when he saw, not ten lines above, done in a laborious hand, the name Malherbe, broken in the middle as if the writer could not spell it. His eye followed the entry along the line: Address, London; Profession, Major (retired); Destination, London. His last vanity, Avery thought, a false profession, a false rank, but little English Taylor had stolen a moment's glory. Why not Colonel? Or Admiral? Why not give himself a peerage and an address in Park Lane? Even when he dreamt, Taylor had known his limits.

The concierge said, 'The valet will take your luggage.'

'I'm sorry,' said Avery, a meaningless apology, and signed his name, while the man watched him curiously.

He gave the valet a coin and it occurred to him as he did so that he had given him eight and six. He closed the bedroom door. For a while he sat on his bed. It was a carefully planned room but bleak and without sympathy. On the door was a notice in several languages warning against the perils of theft, and by the bed another which explained the financial disadvantages of failing to breakfast in the hotel. There was a magazine about travel on the writing-desk, and a Bible bound in black. There was a small bathroom, very clean, and a built-in wardrobe with one coat-hanger. He had forgotten to bring a book. He had not anticipated having to endure leisure.

He was cold and hungry. He thought he would have a bath. He ran it and undressed. He was about to get into the water when he remembered Taylor's letters in his pocket. He put on a dressing-gown, sat on the bed and looked through them. One from his bank about an overdraft, one from his mother, one from a friend which began Dear Old Wilf, the rest from a woman. He was suddenly frightened of the letters: they were evidence. They could compromise him. He determined to burn them all. There was a second basin in the bedroom. He put all the papers into it and held a match to them. He had read somewhere that was the thing to do. There was a membership card for the Alias Club made out in Taylor's name so he burnt that too, then broke up the ash with his fingers and turned on the water; it rose swiftly. The plug was a built-in metal affair operated by a lever between the taps. The sodden ash was packed beneath it. The basin was blocked.

He looked for some instrument to probe under the lip of the plug. He tried his fountain pen but it was too fat, so he fetched the nail file. After repeated attempts he persuaded the ash into the outlet. The water ran away, revealing a heavy brown stain on the enamel. He rubbed it, first with his hand then with the scrubbing brush, but it wouldn't go. Enamel didn't stain like that, there must have been some quality in the paper, tar or something. He went into the bathroom, looking vainly for a detergent.

As he re-entered his bedroom he became aware that it was filled with the smell of charred paper. He went quickly to the window and opened it. A blast of freezing wind swept over his naked limbs. He was gathering the dressing-gown more closely about him when there was a knock on the door. Paralysed with fear, he stared at the door handle, heard another knock, called, watched the handle turn. It was the man from Reception.

'Mr Avery?'

'Yes?'

'I'm sorry. We need your passport. For the police.'

'Police?'

'It's the customary procedure.'

Avery had backed against the basin. The curtains were flapping wildly beside the open window.

'May I close the window?' the man asked.

'I wasn't well. I wanted some fresh air.'

He found his passport and handed it over. As he did so, he saw the man's gaze fixed upon the basin, on the brown mark and the small flakes which still clung to the sides.

He wished as never before that he was back in England.

The row of villas which lines Western Avenue is like a row of pink graves in a field of grey; an architectural image of middle age. Their uniformity is the discipline of growing old, of dying without violence and living without success. They are houses which have got the better of their occupants, whom they change at will, and do not change themselves. Furniture vans glide respectfully among them like hearses, discreetly removing the dead and introducing the living. Now and then some tenant will raise his hand, expending pots of paint on the woodwork or labour on the garden, but his efforts no more alter the house than flowers a hospital ward, and the grass will grow its own way, like grass on a grave.

Haldane dismissed the car and turned off the road towards South Park Gardens, a crescent five minutes from the Avenue. A school, a post office, four shops and a bank. He stooped a little as he walked; a black briefcase hung from his thin hand. He made his way quietly along the pavement; the tower of a modern church rose above the houses; a clock struck seven. A grocer's on the corner, new façade, self-service. He looked at the name: Smethwick. Inside, a youngish man in a brown overall was completing a pyramid of cereal foods. Haldane rapped on the glass. The man shook his head and added a packet to the pyramid. He knocked again, sharply. The grocer came to the door.

'I'm not allowed to sell you anything,' he shouted, 'so it's no good knocking, is it?' He noticed the briefcase and asked, 'Are you a rep, then?'

Haldane put his hand in his inside pocket and held something to the window – a card in a Cellophane wrapper like a season ticket. The grocer stared at it. Slowly he turned the key.

'I want a word with you in private,' Haldane said, stepping inside.

'I've never seen one of those,' the grocer observed uneasily. 'I suppose it's all right.'

'It's quite all right. A security inquiry. Someone called Leiser, a Pole. I understand he worked here long ago.'

'I'll have to call my Dad,' the grocer said. 'I was only a kid then.'

'I see,' said Haldane, as if he disliked youth.

It was nearly midnight when Avery rang Leclerc. He answered straight away. Avery could imagine him sitting up in the steel bed, the Air Force blankets thrown back, his small, alert face anxious for the news.

'It's John,' he said cautiously.

'Yes, yes, I know who you are.' He sounded cross that Avery had mentioned his name.

'The deal's off I'm afraid. They're not interested . . . negative. You'd better tell the man I saw; the little, fat man . . . tell
him we shan't need the services of his friend here.'

'I see. Never mind.' He sounded utterly uninterested.

Avery didn't know what to say; he just didn't know. He
needed desperately to go on talking to Leclerc. He wanted to
tell him about Sutherland's contempt and the passport that
wasn't right. 'The people here, the people I'm negotiating with,
are rather worried about the whole deal.'

He waited.

He wanted to call him by his name but he had no name for
him. They did not use 'Mister' in the Department; the elder
men addressed one another by their surnames and called the
juniors by their Christian names. There was no established
style of addressing one's superior. So he said, 'Are you still
there?' and Leclerc replied, 'Of course. Who's worried? What's
gone wrong?' Avery thought: I could have called him 'Director',
but that would have been insecure.

'The representative here, the man who looks after our
interests . . . he's found out about the deal,' he said. 'He seems to
have guessed.'

'You stressed it was highly confidential?'

'Yes, of course.' How could he ever explain about Sutherland?

'Good. We don't want any trouble with the Foreign Office
just now.' In an altered tone Leclerc continued, 'Things are going
very well over here, John, very well. When do you get back?'

'I've got to cope with the . . . with bringing our friend home.
There are a lot of formalities. It's not as easy as you'd think.'

'When will you be finished?'

'Tomorrow.'

'I'll send a car to meet you at Heathrow. A lot's happened in
the last few hours; a lot of improvements. We need you badly.'
Leclerc added, throwing him a coin, 'And well done, John, well
done indeed.'

'All right.'

He expected to sleep heavily that night, but after what might have been an hour he woke, alert and watchful. He looked at his watch; it was ten past one. Getting out of bed he went to the window and looked on to the snow-covered landscape, marked by the darker lines of the road which led to the airport; he thought he could discern the little rise where Taylor had died.

He was desolate and afraid. His mind was obsessed by confused visions: Taylor's dreadful face, the face he so nearly saw, drained of blood, wide-eyed as if communicating a crucial discovery; Leclerc's voice, filled with vulnerable optimism; the fat policeman, staring at him in envy, as if he were something he could not afford to buy. He realised he was a person who did not take easily to solitude. Solitude saddened him, made him sentimental. He found himself thinking, for the first time since he had left the flat that morning, of Sarah and Anthony. Tears came suddenly to his tired eyes when he recalled his boy, the steel-rimmed spectacles like tiny irons; he wanted to hear his voice, he wanted Sarah, and the familiarity of his home. Perhaps he could telephone the flat, speak to her mother, ask after her. But what if she were ill? He had suffered enough pain that day, he had given enough of his energy, fear and invention. He had lived a nightmare: he could not be expected to ring her now. He went back to bed.

Try as he might, he could not sleep. His eyelids were hot and heavy, his body deeply tired, but still he could not sleep. A wind rose, rattling the double windows; now he was too hot, now too cold. Once he dozed, only to be woken violently from his uneasy rest by the sound of crying, it might have been in the next room, it might have been Anthony, or it might have been – since he did not hear it properly, but only half knew in waking what kind of a sound it had been – the metallic sobbing of a child's doll.

And once, it was shortly before dawn, he heard a footfall outside his room, a single tread in the corridor, not imagined but real, and he lay in chill terror waiting for the handle of his door to turn or the peremptory knocking of Inspector Peersen's men. As he strained his ears he swore he detected the faintest rustle of clothing, the subdued intake of human breath, like a tiny sigh; then silence. Though he listened for minutes on end, he heard nothing more.

Putting on the light, he went to the chair, felt in his jacket for his fountain pen. It was by the basin. From his briefcase he took a leather holdall which Sarah had given him.

Settling himself at the flimsy table in front of the window, he began writing a love letter to a girl, it might have been to Carol. When at last morning came, he destroyed it, tearing it into small pieces and flushing them down the lavatory. As he did so he caught sight of something white on the floor. It was a photograph of Taylor's child carrying a doll; she was wearing glasses, the kind Anthony wore. It must have been among his papers. He thought of destroying it but somehow he couldn't. He slipped it into his pocket.

9

Homecoming

Leclerc was waiting at Heathrow as Avery knew he would be, standing on tiptoe, peering anxiously between the heads of the waiting crowd. He had squared the customs somehow, he must have got the Ministry to do it, and when he saw Avery he came forward into the hall and guided him in a managing way as if he were used to being spared formalities. This is the life we lead, Avery thought; the same airport with different names; the same hurried, guilty meetings; we live outside the walls of the town, black friars from a dark house in Lambeth. He was desperately tired. He wanted Sarah. He wanted to say sorry, make it up with her, get a new job, try again, play with Anthony more. He felt ashamed.

'I'll just make a telephone call. Sarah wasn't too well when I left.'

'Do it from the office,' Leclerc said. 'Do you mind? I have a meeting with Haldane in an hour.' Thinking he detected a false note in Leclerc's voice, Avery looked at him suspiciously, but the other's eyes were turned away towards the black Humber standing in the privilege car park. Leclerc let the driver open the door for him; a silly muddle took place until Avery sat on his left as protocol apparently demanded. The driver seemed tired of waiting. There was no partition between him and themselves.

'This is a change,' Avery said, indicating the car.

Leclerc nodded in a familiar way as if the acquisition were no longer new. 'How are things?' he asked, his mind elsewhere.

'All right. There's nothing the matter, is there? With Sarah, I mean.'

'Why should there be?'

'Blackfriars Road?' the driver inquired, without turning his head, as a sense of respect might have indicated.

'Headquarters, yes, please.'

'There was a hell of a mess in Finland,' Avery observed brutally. 'Our friend's papers . . . Malherbe's . . . weren't in order. The Foreign Office had cancelled his passport.'

'Malherbe? Ah yes. You mean Taylor. We know all about that. It's all right now. Just the usual jealousy. Control is rather upset about it, as a matter of fact. He sent round to apologise. We've a lot of people on our side now, John, you've no idea. You're going to be very useful, John; you're the only one who's seen it on the ground.' Seen what? Avery wondered. They were together again. The same intensity, the same physical unease, the same absences. As Leclerc turned to him Avery thought for one sickening moment he was going to put a hand on his knee. 'You're tired, John, I can tell. I know how it feels. Never mind – you're back with us now. Listen, I've good news for you. The Ministry's woken up to us in a big way. We're to form a special operational unit to mount the next phase.'

'Next phase?'

'Of course. The man I mentioned to you. We can't leave things as they are. We're clarifiers, John, not simply collators. I've revived Special Section; do you know what that is?'

'Haldane ran it during the war; training . . .'

Leclerc interrupted quickly for the driver's sake: '. . . training the travelling salesmen. And he's going to run it again now. I've decided you're to work with him. You're the two best brains I've got.' A sideways glance.

Leclerc had altered. There was a new quality to his bearing, something more than optimism or hope. When Avery had seen him last he had seemed to be living against adversity; now he had a freshness about him, a purpose, which was either new or very old.

'And Haldane accepted?'

'I told you. He's working night and day. You forget, Adrian's a professional. A real technician. Old heads are the best for a job like this. With one or two young heads among them.'

Avery said, 'I want to talk to you about the whole operation . . . about Finland. I'll come to your office after I've rung Sarah.'

'Come straight away, then I can put you in the picture.'

'I'll phone Sarah first.'

Again Avery had the unreasonable feeling that Leclerc was trying to keep him from communicating with Sarah.

'She *is* all right, isn't she?'

'So far as I know. Why do you ask?' Leclerc went on, charming him: 'Glad to be back, John?'

'Yes, of course.'

He sank back into the cushions of the car. Leclerc, noticing his hostility, abandoned him for a time; Avery turned his attention to the road and the pink, healthy villas drifting past in the light rain.

Leclerc was talking again, his committee voice. 'I want you to start straight away. Tomorrow if you can. We've got your room ready. There's a lot to be done. This man: Haldane has him in play. We should hear something when we get home. From now on you're Adrian's creature. I trust that pleases you. Our masters have agreed to provide you with a special Ministry pass. The same kind of thing that they have in the Circus.'

Avery was familiar with Leclerc's habit of speech; there were times when he resorted entirely to oblique allusion, offering a raw material which the consumer, not the purveyor, must refine.

'I want to talk to you about the whole thing. When I've rung Sarah.'

'That's right,' Leclerc replied nicely. 'Come and talk to me about it. Why not come now?' He looked at Avery, offering his whole face; a thing without depth, a moon with one side. 'You've done well,' he said generously, 'I hope you'll keep it up.' They entered London. 'We're getting some help from the Circus,' he added. 'They seem to be quite willing. They don't know the whole picture of course. The Minister was very firm on that point.'

They passed down Lambeth Road, where the God of Battles presides; the Imperial War Museum one end, schools the other, hospitals in between; a cemetery wired off like a tennis court. You cannot tell who lives there. The houses are too many for the people, the schools too large for the children. The hospitals may be full, but the blinds are drawn. Dust hangs everywhere, like the dust of war. It hangs over the hollow façades, chokes the grass in the graveyard: it has driven away the people, save those who loiter in the dark places like the ghosts of soldiers, or wait sleepless behind their yellow-lighted windows. It is a road which people seem to have left often. The few who returned brought something of the living world, according to their voyages. One a piece of field, another a broken Regency terrace, a warehouse or dumping yard; or a pub called the Flowers of the Forest.

It is a road filled with faithful institutions. Over one presides our Lady of Consolation, over another, Archbishop Amigo. Whatever is not hospital, school, pub or seminary is dead, and the dust has got its body. There is a toyshop with a padlocked door. Avery looked into it every day on the way to the office; the toys were rusting on the shelves. The window looked dirtier than ever; the lower part was striped with children's finger-marks. There is a place that mends your teeth while you wait. He glimpsed them now from the car, counting them off as they drove past, wondering whether he would ever see them again as a member of the Department. There are warehouses with barbed wire across their gates, and factories which produce nothing. In one of them a bell rang but no one heard. There is a broken wall with posters on it. You are somebody today in the Regular Army. They rounded St George's Circus and entered Blackfriars Road for the home run.

As they approached the building, Avery sensed that things had changed. For a moment he imagined that the very grass on the wretched bit of lawn had thickened and revived during his brief absence; that the concrete steps leading to the front door, which even in Midsummer managed to appear moist and dirty, were now clean and inviting. Somehow he knew, before he entered the building at all, that a new spirit had infected the Department.

It had reached the most humble members of the staff. Pine, impressed no doubt by the black staff car and the sudden passage of busy people, looked spruce and alert. For once he said nothing about cricket scores. The staircase was daubed with wax polish.

In the corridor they met Woodford. He was in a hurry. He was carrying a couple of files with red caution notices on the cover.

'Hullo, John! You've landed safely, then? Good party?' He really did seem pleased to see him. 'Sarah all right now?'

'He's done well,' said Leclerc quickly. 'He had a very difficult run.'

'Ah yes; poor Taylor. We shall need you in the new section. Your wife will have to spare you for a week or two.'

'What was that about Sarah?' Avery asked. Suddenly he was frightened. He hastened down the corridor. Leclerc was calling but he took no notice. He entered his room and stopped dead. There was a second telephone on his desk, and a steel bed like Leclerc's along the side wall. Beside the new telephone was a piece of military board with a list of emergency telephone numbers pinned to it. The numbers for use during the night were printed in red. On the back of the door hung a two-colour poster depicting in profile the head of a man. Across his skull was written, 'Keep it here', and across his mouth, 'Don't let it out here'. It took him a moment or two to realise that the poster was an exhortation to security, and not some dreadful joke about Taylor. He lifted the receiver and waited. Carol came in with a tray of papers for signature.

'How did it go?' she asked. 'The Boss seems pleased.' She was standing quite close to him.

'Go? There's no film. It wasn't among his things. I'm going to resign; I've decided. What the hell's wrong with this phone?'

'They probably don't know you're back. There's a thing from Accounts about your claim for a taxi. They've queried it.'

'Taxi?'

'From your flat to the office. The night Taylor died. They say it's too much.'

'Look, go and stir up the exchange, will you, they must be fast asleep.'

Sarah answered the telephone herself.

'Oh, thank God it's you.'

Avery said yes, he had got in an hour ago. 'Sarah, look, I've had enough, I'm going to tell Leclerc—' But before he could finish she burst out, 'John, for *God's* sake, what *have* you been doing? We had the police here, detectives; they want to talk to you about a body that's arrived at London Airport; somebody called Malherbe. They say it was sent from Finland on a false passport.'

He closed his eyes. He wanted to put down the receiver, he held it away from his ear but he still heard her voice, saying John, John. 'They say he's your brother; it's addressed to *you*, John; some London undertaker was supposed to be doing it all for you . . . John, John, are you still there?'

'Listen,' he said, 'it's all right. I'll take care of it now.'

'I told them about Taylor: I had to.'

'Sarah!'

'What else could I do? They thought I was a criminal or something; they didn't believe me, John! They asked how they could get hold of you; I had to say I didn't know; I didn't even know which country or which plane; I was ill, John, I felt awful, I've got this damn 'flu and I'd forgotten to take my pills. They came in the middle of the night, two of them. John, why did they come in the night?'

'What did you tell them? For Christ's sake, Sarah, what else did you say to them?'

'Don't swear at me! I should be swearing at you and your beastly Department! I said you were doing something secret;

you'd had to go abroad for the Department – John, I don't even know its *name*! – that you'd been rung in the night and you'd gone away. I said it was about a courier called Taylor.'

'You're mad,' Avery shouted, 'you're absolutely mad. I told you never to say!'

'But, John, they were *policemen*! There can't be any harm in telling them.' She was crying, he could hear the tears in her voice. 'John, *please* come back. I'm so frightened. You've got to get out of this, go back to publishing; I don't care what you do but . . .'

'I can't. It's terribly big. More important than you can possibly understand. I'm sorry, Sarah. I just can't leave the office.' He added savagely, a useful lie, 'You may have wrecked the whole thing.'

There was a very long silence.

'Sarah, I'll have to sort this out. I'll ring you later.'

When at last she answered he detected in her voice the same flat resignation with which she had sent him to pack his things. 'You took the cheque book. I've no money.'

He told her he would send it round. 'We've got a car,' he added, 'specially for this thing, chauffeur-driven.' As he rang off he heard her say, 'I thought you'd got lots of cars.'

He ran into Leclerc's room. Haldane was standing behind the desk; his coat still wet from the rain. They were bent over a file. The pages were faded and torn.

'Taylor's body!' he blurted out. 'It's at London Airport. You've messed the whole thing up. They've been on to Sarah! In the middle of the night!'

'Wait!' It was Haldane who spoke. 'You have no business to come running in here,' he declared furiously. 'Just wait.' He did not care for Avery.

He returned to the file, ignoring him. 'None at all,' he muttered, adding to Leclerc: 'Woodford has already had some success, I gather. Unarmed combat's all right; he's heard of a wireless operator, one of the best. I remember him. The garage is called the King of Hearts; it is clearly prosperous. We inquired at the bank; they were quite helpful if not specific. He's unmarried. He has a reputation for women; the usual Polish style. No political interests, no known hobbies, no debts, no complaints. He seems to be something of a nonentity. They say he's a good mechanic. As for character—' he shrugged. 'What do we know about anybody?'

'But what did they *say*? Good Heavens, you can't be fifteen years in a community without leaving *some* impression. There was a grocer wasn't there – Smethwick? – he lived with them after the war.'

Haldane allowed himself a smile. 'They said he was a good worker and very polite. Everyone says he's polite. They remember one thing only: he had a passion for hitting a tennis ball round their back yard.'

'Did you take a look at the garage?'

'Certainly not. I didn't go near it. I propose to call there this evening. I don't see that we have any other choice. After all, the man's been on our cards for twenty years.'

'Is there nothing more you can find out?'

'We would have to do the rest through the Circus.'

'Then let John Avery clear up the details.' Leclerc seemed to have forgotten Avery was in the room. 'As for the Circus, I'll deal with them myself.' His interest had been arrested by a new map on the wall, a town plan of Kalkstadt showing the church and railway station. Beside it hung an older map of Eastern Europe. Rocket bases whose existence had already been confirmed were here related to the putative site south of Rostock. Supply routes and chains of command, the order of battle of supporting arms, were indicated with lines of thin wool stretched between pins. A number of these led to Kalkstadt.

'It's good, isn't it? Sandford put it together last night,' Leclerc said. 'He does that kind of thing rather well.'

On his desk lay a new whitewood pointer like a giant bodkin threaded with a loop of barrister's ribbon. He had a new telephone, green, smarter than Avery's, with a notice on it saying

'Speech on this telephone is NOT secure.' For a time Haldane and Leclerc studied the map, referring now and then to a file of telegrams which Leclerc held open in both hands as a choirboy holds a psalter.

Finally Leclerc turned to Avery and said, 'Now, John.' They were waiting for him to speak.

He could feel his anger dying. He wanted to hold on to it but it was slipping away. He wanted to cry out in indignation: how dare you involve my wife? He wanted to lose control, but he could not. His eyes were on the map.

'Well?'

'The police have been round to Sarah. They woke her in the middle of the night. Two men. Her mother was there. They came about the body at the airport: Taylor's body. They knew the passport was phoney and thought she was involved. They woke her up,' he repeated lamely.

'We know all about that. It's straightened out. I wanted to tell you but you wouldn't let me. The body's been released.'

'It was wrong to drag Sarah in.'

Haldane lifted his head quickly: 'What do you mean by that?'

'We're not competent to handle this kind of thing.' It sounded very impertinent. 'We shouldn't be doing it. We ought to give it to the Circus. Smiley or someone – they're the people, not us.' He struggled on: 'I don't even believe that report. I don't believe it's true! I wouldn't be surprised if that refugee never existed; if Gorton made the whole thing up! I don't believe Taylor was murdered.'

'Is that all?' Haldane demanded. He was very angry.

'It's not something I want to go on with. The operation, I mean. It isn't right.'

He looked at the map and at Haldane, then laughed a little stupidly. 'All the time I've been chasing a dead man you've been after a live one! It's easy here, in the dream factory ... but they're people out there, real people!'

Leclerc touched Haldane lightly on the arm as if to say he

would handle this himself. He seemed undisturbed. He might almost have been gratified to recognise symptoms which he had previously diagnosed. 'Go to your room, John, you're suffering from strain.'

'But what do I tell Sarah?' He spoke with despair.

'Tell her she won't be troubled any more. Tell her it was a mistake . . . tell her whatever you like. Get some hot food and come back in an hour. These airline meals are useless. Then we'll hear the rest of your news.' Leclerc was smiling, the same neat, bland smile with which he had stood among the dead fliers. As Avery reached the door he heard his name called softly, with affection: he stopped and looked back.

Leclerc raised one hand from the desk and with a semicircular movement indicated the room in which they were standing.

'I'll tell you something, John. During the war we were in Baker Street. We had a cellar and the Ministry fixed it up as an emergency operations room. Adrian and I spent a lot of time down there. A *lot* of time.' A glance at Haldane. 'Remember how the oil lamp used to swing when the bombs fell? We had to face situations where we had one rumour, John, no more. One indicator and we'd take the risk. Send a man in, two if necessary, and maybe they wouldn't come back. Maybe there wouldn't be anything there. Rumours, a guess, a hunch one follows up; it's easy to forget what intelligence consists of: luck, and speculation. Here and there a windfall, here and there a scoop. Sometimes you stumbled on a thing like this: it could be very big, it could be a shadow. It may have been from a peasant in Flensburg, or it may come from the Provost of King's, but you're left with a possibility you dare not discount. You get instructions: find a man, put him in. So we did. And many *didn't* come back. They were sent to resolve doubt, don't you see? We sent them because we didn't know. All of us have moments like this, John. Don't think it's always easy.' A reminiscent smile. 'Often we had scruples like you. We had to overcome them. We used to call that the second vow.' He leant against the desk, informally. 'The second vow,' he repeated.

'Now, John, if you want to wait until the bombs are falling, till people are dying in the street . . .' He was suddenly serious, as if revealing his faith. 'It's a great deal harder, I know, in peacetime. It requires courage. Courage of a different kind.'

Avery nodded. 'I'm sorry,' he said.

Haldane was watching him with distaste.

'What the Director means,' he said acidly, 'is that if you wish to stay in the Department and do the job, do it. If you wish to cultivate your emotions, go elsewhere and do so in peace. We are too old for your kind here.'

Avery could still hear Sarah's voice, see the rows of little houses hanging in the rain; he tried to imagine his life without the Department. He realised that it was too late, as it always had been, because he had gone to them for the little they could give him, and they had taken the little he had. Like a doubting cleric, he had felt that whatever his small heart contained was safely locked in the place of his retreat: now it was gone. He looked at Leclerc, then at Haldane. They were his colleagues. Prisoners of silence, the three of them would work side by side, breaking the arid land all four seasons of the year, strangers to each other, needing each other, in a wilderness of abandoned faith.

'Did you hear what I said?' Haldane demanded.

Avery muttered: 'Sorry.'

'You didn't fight in the war, John,' Leclerc said kindly. 'You don't understand how these things take people. You don't understand what real duty is.'

'I know,' said Avery. 'I'm sorry. I'd like to borrow the car for an hour . . . send something round to Sarah, if that's all right.'

'Of course.'

He realised he had forgotten Anthony's present. 'I'm sorry,' he said again.

'Incidentally—' Leclerc opened a drawer of the desk and took out an envelope. Indulgently he handed it to Avery. 'That's your pass, a special one from the Ministry. To identify yourself. It's in your own name. You may need it in the weeks to come.'

'Thanks.'

'Open it.'

It was a piece of thick pasteboard bound in Cellophane, green, the colour washed downwards, darker at the bottom. His name was printed across it in capitals with an electric typewriter: Mr John Avery. The legend entitled the bearer to make inquiries on behalf of the Ministry. There was a signature in red ink.

'Thanks.'

'You're safe with that,' Leclerc said. 'The Minister signed it. He uses red ink, you know. It's tradition.'

He went back to his room. There were times when he confronted his own image as a man confronts an empty valley, and the vision propelled him forward again to experience, as despair compels us to extinction. Sometimes he was like a man in flight, but running towards the enemy, desperate to feel upon his vanishing body the blows that would prove his being; desperate to imprint upon his sad conformity the mark of real purpose, desperate perhaps, as Leclerc had hinted, to abdicate his conscience in order to discover God.

PART III

Leiser's Run

'To turn, as swimmers into cleanness leaping,
Glad from a world grown old and cold and weary'

RUPERT BROOKE, '1914'

10

Prelude

The Humber dropped Haldane at the garage.

'You needn't wait. You have to take Mr Leclerc to the Ministry.'

He picked his way reluctantly over the tarmac, past the yellow petrol pumps and the advertisement shields rattling in the wind. It was evening; there was rain about. The garage was small but very smart; showrooms one end, workshops the other, in the middle a tower where somebody lived. Swedish timber and open plan; lights on the tower in the shape of a heart, changing colour continuously. From somewhere came the whine of a metal lathe. Haldane went into the office. It was empty. There was a smell of rubber. He rang the bell and began coughing wretchedly. Sometimes when he coughed he held his chest, and his face betrayed the submissiveness of a man familiar with pain. Calendars with showgirls hung on the wall beside a small handwritten notice, like an amateur advertisement, which read, 'St Christopher and all his angels, please protect us from road accidents. F.L.' At the window a budgerigar fluttered nervously in its cage. The first drops of rain thumped lazily against the panes. A boy came in, about eighteen, his fingers black with engine oil. He wore an overall with a red heart sewn on to the breast pocket with a crown above it.

'Good evening,' said Haldane. 'Forgive me. I'm looking for an old acquaintance; a friend. We knew one another long ago. A Mr Leiser. Fred Leiser. I wondered if you had any idea . . .'

'I'll get him,' the boy said, and disappeared.

Haldane waited patiently, looking at the calendars and wondering whether it was the boy or Leiser who had hung them there. The door opened a second time. It was Leiser. Haldane recognised him from his photograph. There was really very little change. The twenty years were not drawn in forceful lines but in tiny webs beside each eye, in marks of discipline around the mouth. The light above him was diffuse and cast no shadow. It was a face which at first sight recorded nothing but loneliness. Its complexion was pale.

'What can I do for you?' Leiser asked. He stood almost at attention.

'Hullo, I wonder if you remember me?'

Leiser looked at him as if he were being asked to name a price, blank but wary.

'Sure it was me?'

'Yes.'

'It must have been a long time ago,' he said at last. 'I don't often forget a face.'

'Twenty years.' Haldane coughed apologetically.

'In the war then, was it?'

He was a short man, very straight; in build he was not unlike Leclerc. He might have been a waiter. His sleeves were rolled up a little way, there was a lot of hair on the forearms. His shirt was white and expensive; a monogram on the pocket. He looked like a man who spent a good deal on his clothes. He wore a gold ring; a golden wristband to his watch. He took great care of his appearance; Haldane could smell the lotion on his skin. His long brown hair was full, the line along the forehead straight. Bulging a little at the sides, the hair was combed backwards. He wore no parting; the effect was definitely Slav. Though very upright, he had about him a certain swagger, a looseness of the hips and shoulders, which suggested a familiarity with the sea. It was here that any comparison with Leclerc abruptly ceased. He looked, despite himself, a practical man, handy in the house or starting the car on a cold day; and he looked an innocent man, but travelled. He wore a tartan tie.

'Surely you remember me?' Haldane pleaded.

Leiser stared at the thin cheeks, touched with points of high colour, at the hanging, restless body and the gently stirring hands, and there passed across his face a look of painful recognition, as if he were identifying the remains of a friend.

'You're not Captain Hawkins, are you?'

'That's right.'

'God Christ,' said Leiser, without moving. 'You're the people who've been asking about me.'

'We're looking for someone with your experience, a man like you.'

'What do you want him for, sir?'

He still hadn't moved. It was very hard to tell what he was thinking. His eyes were fixed on Haldane.

'To do a job, one job.'

Leiser smiled, as if it all came back to him. He nodded his head towards the window. 'Over there?' He meant somewhere beyond the rain.

'Yes.'

'What about getting back?'

'The usual rules. It's up to the man in the field. The war rules.'

He pushed his hands into his pockets, discovered cigarettes and a lighter. The budgerigar was singing.

'The war rules. You smoke?' He gave himself a cigarette and lit it, his hands cupped round the flame as if there were a high wind. He dropped the match on to the floor for someone else to pick up.

'God Christ,' he repeated. 'Twenty years. I was a kid in those days, just a kid.'

Haldane said, 'You don't regret it, I trust. Shall we go and have a drink?' He handed Leiser a card. It was newly printed: Captain A. Hawkins. Written underneath was a telephone number.

Leiser read it and shrugged. 'I don't mind,' he said and went to fetch his jacket. Another smile, incredulous this time. 'But you're wasting your time, Captain.'

'Perhaps you know someone. Someone else from the war who might take it on.'

'I don't know a lot of people,' Leiser replied. He took the jacket from its peg and a nylon raincoat of dark blue. Going ahead of Haldane to the door, he opened it elaborately as if he valued formality. His hair was laid carefully upon itself like the wings of a bird.

There was a pub on the other side of the Avenue. They reached it by crossing a footbridge. The rush hour traffic thundered beneath them; the cold, plump raindrops seemed to go with it. The bridge trembled to the drumming of the cars. The pub was Tudor with new horse brasses and a ship's bell very highly polished. Leiser asked for a White Lady. He never drank anything else, he said. 'Stick to one drink, Captain, that's my advice. Then you'll be all right. Down the hatch.'

'It's got to be someone who knows the tricks,' Haldane observed. They sat in a corner near the fire. They might have been talking about trade. 'It's a very important job. They pay far more than in the war.' He gave a gaunt smile. 'They pay a lot of money these days.'

'Still, money's not everything, is it?' A stiff phrase, borrowed from the English.

'They remembered you. People whose names you've forgotten, if you even knew them.' An unconvincing smile of reminiscence crossed his thin lips: it might have been years since he had lied. 'You left quite an impression behind you, Fred; there weren't many as good as you. Even after twenty years.'

'They remember me then, the old crowd?' He seemed grateful for that, but shy, as if it were not his place to be held in memory. 'I was only a kid then,' he repeated. 'Who's there still, who's left?'

Haldane, watching him, said, 'I warned you: we play the same rules, Fred. *Need to know*, it's all the same.' It was very strict.

'God Christ,' Leiser declared. 'All the same. Big as ever, then, the outfit?'

'Bigger.' Haldane fetched another White Lady. 'Take much interest in politics?'

Leiser lifted a clean hand and let it fall.

'You know the way we are,' he said. 'In Britain, you know.' His voice carried the slightly impertinent assumption that he was as good as Haldane.

'I mean,' Haldane prompted, 'in a *broad* sense.' He coughed his dusty cough. 'After all, they took over your country, didn't they?' Leiser said nothing. 'What did you think of Cuba, for instance?'

Haldane did not smoke, but he had bought some cigarettes at the bar, the brand Leiser preferred. He removed the Cellophane with his slim, ageing fingers, and offered them across the table. Without waiting for an answer, he continued, 'The point was, you see, in the Cuba thing the Americans *knew*. It was a matter of information. Then they could act. Of course *they* made over-flights. One can't always do that.' He gave another little laugh. 'One wonders what they would have done without them.'

'Yes, that's right.' He nodded his head like a dummy. Haldane paid no attention.

'They might have been stuck,' Haldane suggested and sipped his whisky. 'Are you married, by the way?'

Leiser grinned, held his hand out flat, tipped it briskly to left and right, like a man talking about aeroplanes. 'So, so,' he said. His tartan tie was fastened to his shirt with a heavy gold pin in the shape of a riding crop against a horse's head. It was very incongruous.

'How about you, Captain?'

Haldane shook his head.

'No,' Leiser observed thoughtfully. 'No.'

'Then there have been other occasions,' Haldane went on, 'where very serious mistakes were made because they hadn't the *right* information, or not enough. I mean not even we can have people permanently everywhere.'

'No, of course,' Leiser said politely.

The bar was filling up.

'I wonder whether you know of a different place where we might talk?' Haldane inquired. 'We could eat, chat about some of the old gang. Or have you another engagement?' The lower classes eat early.

Leiser glanced at his watch. 'I'm all right till eight,' he said. 'You want to do something about that cough, sir. It can be dangerous, a cough like that.' The watch was of gold; it had a black face and a compartment for indicating phases of the moon.

The Under Secretary, similarly conscious of the time, was bored to be kept so late.

'I think I mentioned to you,' Leclerc was saying, 'that the Foreign Office has been awfully sticky about providing operational passports. They've taken to consulting the Circus in every case. We have no status, you understand; it's hard for me to make myself unpleasant about these things – they have only the vaguest notion of how we work. I wondered whether the best system might not be for my Department to route passport requisitions through your Private Office. That would save the bother of going to the Circus every time.'

'What do you mean, sticky?'

'You will remember we sent poor Taylor out under another name. The Office revoked his operational passport a matter of hours before he left London. I fear the Circus made an administrative blunder. The passport which accompanied the body was therefore challenged on arrival in the United Kingdom. It gave us a lot of trouble. I had to send one of my best men to sort it out,' he lied. 'I'm sure that if the Minister insisted, Control would be quite agreeable to a new arrangement.'

The Under Secretary jabbed a pencil at the door which led to his Private Office. 'Talk to them in there. Work something out. It sounds very stupid. Who do you deal with at the Office?'

'De Lisle,' said Leclerc with satisfaction, 'in General Department. He's the Assistant. And Smiley at the Circus.'

The Under Secretary wrote it down. 'One never knows *who* to talk to in that place; they're so top-heavy.'

'Then I may have to approach the Circus for technical resources. Wireless and that kind of thing. I propose to use a cover story for security reasons: a notional training scheme is the most appropriate.'

'Cover story? Ah yes: a lie. You mentioned it.'

'It's a precaution, no more.'

'You must do as you think fit.'

'I imagined you would prefer the Circus not to know. You said yourself: no monolith. I have proceeded on that assumption.'

The Under Secretary glanced again at the clock above the door. 'He's been in rather a difficult mood: a dreary day with the Yemen. I think it's partly the Woodbridge by-election: he gets so upset about the marginals. How's this thing going, by the way? It's been very worrying for him, you know. I mean, what's he to believe?' He paused. 'It's these Germans who terrify me . . . You mentioned you'd found a fellow who fitted the bill.' They moved to the corridor.

'We're on to him now. We've got him in play. We shall know tonight.'

The Under Secretary wrinkled his nose very slightly, his hand on the Minister's door. He was a churchman and disliked irregular things.

'What makes a man take on a job like that? Not you; him, I mean.'

Leclerc shook his head in silence, as if the two of them were in close sympathy. 'Heaven knows. It's something we don't even understand ourselves.'

'What kind of person is he? What sort of class? Only generally, you appreciate.'

'Intelligent. Self-educated. Polish extraction.'

'Oh, I see.' He seemed relieved. 'We'll keep it gentle, shall

we? Don't paint it too black. He loathes drama. I mean any fool
can see what the *dangers* are.'

They went in.

Haldane and Leiser took their places at a corner table, like
lovers in a coffee bar. It was one of those restaurants which rely
on empty Chianti bottles for their charm and on very little else
for their custom. It would be gone tomorrow, or the next day,
and scarcely anyone would notice, but while it was there and
new and full of hope, it was not at all bad. Leiser had steak, it
seemed to be habit, and sat primly while he ate it, his elbows
firmly at his side.

At first Haldane pretended to ignore the purpose of his visit.
He talked badly about the war and the Department; about
operations he had half forgotten until that afternoon, when he
had refreshed his memory from the files. He spoke – no doubt it
seemed desirable – mainly of those who had survived.

He referred to the courses Leiser had attended; had he kept
up his interest in radio at all? Well, no, as a matter of fact. How
about unarmed combat? There hadn't been the opportunity,
really.

'You had one or two rough moments in the war, I remember,' Haldane prompted. 'Didn't you have some trouble in
Holland?' They were back to vanity and old times' sake.

A stiff nod. 'I had a spot of trouble,' he conceded. 'I was
younger then.'

'What happened exactly?'

Leiser looked at Haldane, blinking, as if the other had woken
him, then began to talk. It was one of those wartime stories
which have been told with variations since war began, as remote
from the neat little restaurant as hunger or poverty, less credible
for being articulate. He seemed to tell it at second hand. It might
have been a big fight he had heard on the wireless. He had been
caught, he had escaped, he had lived for days without food, he
had killed, been taken into refuge and smuggled back to England. He told it well; perhaps it was what the war meant to him

now, perhaps it was true, but as with a Latin widow relating the manner of her husband's death, the passion had gone out of his heart and into the telling. He seemed to speak because he had been told to; his affectations, unlike Leclerc's, were designed less to impress others than to protect himself. He seemed a very private man whose speech was exploratory; a man who had been a long time alone and had not reckoned with society; poised, not settled. His accent was good but exclusively foreign, lacking the slur and the elision which escapes even gifted imitators; a voice familiar with its environment, but not at home there.

Haldane listened courteously. When it was over he asked, 'How did they pick you up in the first place, do you know?' The space between them was very great.

'They never told me,' he said blankly, as if it were not proper to inquire.

'Of course you *are* the man we need. You've got the German background, if you understand me. You know them, don't you; you have the German experience.'

'Only from the war,' Leiser said.

They talked about the training school. 'How's that fat one? George somebody. Little sad bloke.'

'Oh . . . he's well, thank you.'

'He married a pretty girl.' He laughed obscenely, raising his right forearm in an Arab gesture of sexual prowess. 'God Christ,' he said, laughing again. 'Us little blokes! Go for anything.' It was an extraordinary lapse. It seemed to be what Haldane had been waiting for.

He watched Leiser for a long time. The silence became remarkable. Deliberately he stood up; he seemed suddenly very angry; angry at Leiser's silly grin and this whole cheap, incompetent flirtation; at these meaningless repetitive blasphemies and this squalid derision of a person of quality.

'Do you mind not saying that? George Smiley happens to be a friend of mine.'

He called the waiter and paid the bill, stalked quickly from the restaurant, leaving Leiser bewildered and alone, his White

Lady held delicately in his hand, his brown eyes turned anxiously towards the doorway through which Haldane had so abruptly vanished.

Eventually he left, making his way back by the footbridge, slowly through the dark and the rain, staring down on the double alley of streetlamps and the traffic passing between them. Across the road was his garage, the line of illuminated pumps, the tower crowned with its neon heart of sixty-watt bulbs alternating green and red. He entered the brightly lit office, said something to the boy, walked slowly upstairs towards the blare of music.

Haldane waited till he had disappeared from sight, then hurried back to the restaurant to order a taxi.

She had put the gramophone on. She was listening to dance music, sitting in his chair, drinking.

'Christ, you're late,' she said. 'I'm starving.'

He kissed her.

'You've eaten,' she said. 'I can smell the food.'

'Just a snack, Bett. I had to. A man called; we had a drink.'

'Liar.'

He smiled. 'Come off it, Betty. We've got a dinner date, remember?'

'What man?'

The flat was very clean. Curtains and carpets were flowered, the polished surfaces protected with lace. Everything was protected; vases, lamps, ashtray, all were carefully guarded, as if Leiser expected nothing from nature but stark collision. He favoured a suggestion of the antique: it was reflected in the scrolled woodwork of the furniture and the wrought iron of the lamp brackets. He had a mirror framed in gold and a picture made of fretwork and plaster; a new clock with weights which turned in a glass case.

When he opened the cocktail cabinet it played a brief tune on a music box.

He mixed himself a White Lady, carefully, like a man

making up medicine. She watched him, moving her hips to the record, holding her glass away to one side as if it were her partner's hand, and the partner were not Leiser.

'What man?' she repeated.

He stood at the window, straight-backed like a soldier. The flashing heart on the roof played over the houses, caught the staves of the bridge and quivered in the wet surface of the Avenue. Beyond the houses was the church, like a cinema with a spire, fluted brick with vents where the bells rang. Beyond the church was the sky. Sometimes he thought the church was all that remained, and the London sky was lit with the glow of a burning city.

'Christ, you're really gay tonight.'

The church bells were recorded, much amplified to drown the noise of traffic. He sold a lot of petrol on Sundays. The rain was running harder against the road; he could see it shading the beams of the car lights, dancing green and red on the tarmac.

'Come on, Fred, dance.'

'Just a minute, Bett.'

'Oh, for Christ's sake, what's the matter with you? Have another drink and forget it.'

He could hear her feet shuffling across the carpet to the music; the tireless jingle of her charm bracelet.

'Dance, for Christ's sake.'

She had a slurred way of talking, slackly dragging the last syllable of a sentence beyond its natural length; it was the same calculated disenchantment with which she gave herself, sullenly, as if she were giving money, as if men had all the pleasure and women the pain.

She stopped the record, careless as she pulled the arm. The needle scratched in the loudspeaker.

'Look, what the hell goes on?'

'Nothing, I tell you. I've just had a hard day, that's all. Then this man called, somebody I used to know.'

'I keep asking you: who? Some woman, wasn't it? Some tart.'

'No, Betty, it was a man.'

She came to the window, nudging him indifferently. 'What's so bloody marvellous about the view, anyway? Just a lot of rotten little houses. You always said you hated them. Well, who was it?'

'He's from one of the big companies.'

'And they want you?'

'Yes . . . they want to make me an offer.'

'Christ, who'd want a bloody Pole?'

He hardly stirred. 'They do.'

'Someone came to the bank, you know, asking about you. They all sat together in Mr Dawnay's office. You're in trouble, aren't you?'

He took her coat and helped her into it, very correct, elbows wide.

She said: 'Not that new place with waiters, for Christ's sake.'

'It's nice there, isn't it? I thought you fancied it there. You can dance too; you like that. Where do you want to go then?'

'With you? For Christ's sake! Somewhere where there's a bit of life, that's all.'

He stared at her. He was holding the door open. Suddenly he smiled.

'OK, Bett. It's your night. Slip down and start the car, I'll book a table.' He gave her the key. 'I know a place, a real place.'

'What the hell's come over you now?'

'You can drive. We'll have a night out.' He went to the telephone.

It was shortly before eleven when Haldane returned to the Department. Leclerc and Avery were waiting for him. Carol was typing in the Private Office.

'I thought you'd be here earlier,' Leclerc said.

'It's no good. He said he wouldn't play. I think you'd better try the next one yourself. It's not my style any more.' He seemed undisturbed. He sat down. They stared at him incredulously.

'Did you offer money?' Leclerc asked finally. 'We have clearance for five thousand pounds.'

'Of course I offered money. I tell you he's just not interested. He was a singularly unpleasant person.'

'I'm sorry.' He didn't say why.

They could hear the tapping of Carol's typewriter. Leclerc said, 'Where do we go from here?'

'I have no idea.' He glanced restlessly at his watch.

'There must be others, there must be.'

'Not on our cards. Not with his qualifications. There are Belgians, Swedes, Frenchmen. But Leiser was the only German-speaker with technical experience. On paper, he's the only one.'

'Still young enough. Is that what you mean?'

'I suppose so. It would have to be an old hand. We haven't the time to train a new man, nor the facilities. We'd better ask the Circus. They'll have someone.'

'We can't do that,' Avery said.

'What kind of man was he?' Leclerc persisted, reluctant to abandon hope.

'Common, in a Slav way. Small. He plays the *Rittmeister*. It's most unattractive.' He was looking in his pockets for the bill. 'He dresses like a bookie, but I suppose they all do that. Do I give this to you or Accounts?'

'Secure?'

'I don't see why not.'

'And you spoke about the urgency? New loyalties and that kind of thing?'

'He found the old loyalties more attractive.' He put the bill on the table.

'And politics . . . some of these exiles are very . . .'

'We spoke about politics. He's not that sort of exile. He considers himself integrated, naturalised British. What do you expect him to do? Swear allegiance to the Polish royal house?' Again he looked at his watch.

'You never wanted to recruit him!' Leclerc cried, angered by Haldane's indifference. 'You're pleased, Adrian, I can see it in your face! Good God, what about the Department! Didn't that mean anything to him? You don't believe in it any more, you don't care! You're sneering at me!'

'Who of us does believe?' asked Haldane with contempt. 'You said yourself: we do the job.'

'I believe,' Avery declared.

Haldane was about to speak when the green telephone rang. 'That will be the Ministry,' Leclerc said. 'Now what do I tell them?' Haldane was watching him.

He picked up the receiver, put it to his ear then handed it across the table. 'It's the exchange. Why on earth did they come through on green? Somebody asking for Captain Hawkins. That's you, isn't it?'

Haldane listened, his thin face expressionless. Finally he said, 'I imagine so. We'll find someone. There should be no difficulty. Tomorrow at eleven. Kindly be punctual,' and rang off. The light in Leclerc's room seemed to ebb towards the thinly curtained window. The rain fell ceaselessly outside.

'That was Leiser. He's decided he'll do the job. He wants to know whether we can find someone to take care of his garage while he's away.'

Leclerc looked at him in astonishment. Pleasure spread comically over his face. 'You expected it!' he cried. He stretched out his small hand. 'I'm sorry, Adrian. I misjudged you. I congratulate you warmly.'

'Why did he accept?' Avery asked excitedly. 'What made him change his mind?'

'Why do agents ever do anything? Why do any of us?' Haldane sat down. He looked old but inviolate, like a man whose friends had already died. 'Why do they consent or refuse, why do they lie or tell the truth? Why do any of us?' He began coughing again. 'Perhaps he's under-employed. It's the Germans: he hates them. That's what he says. I place no value on that. Then he said he couldn't let us down. I assume he means himself.'

To Leclerc he added, 'The war rules: that was right, wasn't it?'

But Leclerc was dialling the Ministry.

Avery went into the Private Office. Carol was standing up.

'What's going on?' she said quickly. 'What's the excitement?'

'It's Leiser.' Avery closed the door behind him. 'He's agreed to go.' He stretched out his arms to embrace her. It would be the first time.

'Why?'

'Hatred of the Germans, he says. My guess is money.'

'Is that a good thing?'

Avery grinned knowingly. 'As long as we pay him more than the other side.'

'Shouldn't you go back to your wife?' she said sharply. 'I can't believe you need to sleep here.'

'It's operational.' Avery went to his room. She did not say goodnight.

Leiser put down the telephone. It was suddenly very quiet. The lights on the roof went out, leaving the room in darkness. He went quickly downstairs. He was frowning, as if his entire mental force were concentrated on the prospect of eating a second dinner.

11

They chose Oxford as they had done in the war. The variety of nationalities and occupations, the constant coming and going of visiting academics and the resultant anonymity, the proximity of open country, all perfectly suited their needs. Besides, it was a place they could understand. The morning after Leiser had rung, Avery went ahead to find a house. The following day he telephoned Haldane to say he had taken one for a month in the north of the town, a large Victorian affair with four bedrooms and a garden. It was very expensive. It was known in the Department as the Mayfly house and carded under Live Amenities.

As soon as Haldane heard, he told Leiser. At Leiser's suggestion it was agreed that he should put it about that he was attending a course in the Midlands.

'Don't give any details,' Haldane had said. 'Have your mail sent *poste restante* to Coventry. We'll get it picked up from there.' Leiser was pleased when he heard it was Oxford.

Leclerc and Woodford had searched desperately for someone to run the garage in Leiser's absence; suddenly they thought of McCulloch. Leiser gave him power of attorney and spent a hasty morning showing him the ropes. 'We'll offer you some kind of guarantee in return,' Haldane said.

'I don't need it,' Leiser replied, explaining quite seriously, 'I'm working for English gentlemen.'

On the Friday night Leiser had telephoned his consent; by

the Wednesday preparations were sufficiently advanced for Leclerc to convene a meeting of Special Section and outline his plans. Avery and Haldane were to be with Leiser in Oxford; the two of them would leave the following evening, by which time he understood that Haldane would be ready with his syllabus. Leiser would arrive in Oxford a day or two later, as soon as his own arrangements were complete. Haldane was to supervise his training, Avery to act as Haldane's assistant. Woodford would remain in London. Among his tasks was that of consulting with the Ministry (and Sandford of Research) in order to assemble instructional material on the external specifications of short- and medium-range rockets, and thus provided come himself to Oxford.

Leclerc had been tireless, now at the Ministry to report on progress, now at the Treasury to argue the case for Taylor's widow, now, with Woodford's aid, engaging former instructors in wireless transmission, photography and unarmed combat.

Such time as remained to Leclerc he devoted to Mayfly Zero: the moment at which Leiser was to be infiltrated into Eastern Germany. At first he seemed to have no firm idea of how this was to be done. He talked vaguely of a sea operation from Denmark; small fishing craft and a rubber dinghy to evade radar detection; he discussed illegal frontier crossing with Sand-ford and telegraphed Gorton for information on the border area round Lübeck. In veiled terms he even consulted the Circus. Control was remarkably helpful.

All this took place in that atmosphere of heightened activity and optimism which Avery had observed on his return. Even those who were kept, supposedly, in ignorance of the operation were infected by the air of crisis. The little lunch group that gathered daily at a corner table of the Cadena café was alive with rumours and speculation. It was said, for instance, that a man named Johnson, known in the war as Jack Johnson, a wire-less instructor, had been taken on to boost the strength of the Department. Accounts had paid him subsistence and – most in-triguing of all – they had been asked to draft a three-month contract for submission to the Treasury. Who ever heard, they asked, of a three-month contract? Johnson had been concerned with the French drops during the war; a senior girl remembered him. Berry, the cypher clerk, had asked Mr Woodford what Johnson was up to (Berry was always the cheeky one) and Mr Woodford had grinned and told him to mind his own business, but it was for an operation, he'd said, a very secret one they were running in Europe . . . northern Europe, as a matter of fact, and it might interest Berry to know that poor Taylor had not died in vain.

There was now a ceaseless traffic of cars and Ministry messengers in the front drive; Pine requested and received from another Government establishment a junior whom he treated with sovereign brutality. In some oblique way he had learnt that Germany was the target, and the knowledge made him diligent.

It was even rumoured among the local tradesmen that the Ministry House was changing hands; private buyers were named and great hopes placed upon their custom. Meals were sent for at all hours, lights burnt day and night; the front door, hitherto permanently sealed for reasons of security, was opened, and the sight of Leclerc with bowler hat and briefcase entering his black Humber became a familiar one in Blackfriars Road.

And Avery, like an injured man who would not look at his own wound, slept within the walls of his little office, so that they became the boundary of his life. Once he sent out Carol to buy Anthony a present. She came back with a toy milk lorry with plastic bottles. You could lift the caps off and fill the bottles with water. They tried it out one evening, then sent it round to Battersea in the Humber.

When all was ready Haldane and Avery travelled to Oxford first class on a Ministry Warrant. At dinner on the train they had a table to themselves. Haldane ordered half a bottle of wine and drank it while he completed *The Times* crossword. They sat in silence, Haldane occupied, Avery too diffident to interrupt him.

Suddenly Avery noticed Haldane's tie; before he had time to think, he said, 'Good Lord, I never knew you were a cricketer.'

'Did you expect me to tell you?' Haldane snapped. 'I could hardly wear it in the office.'

'I'm sorry.'

Haldane looked at him closely. 'You shouldn't apologise so much,' he observed. 'You both do it.' He helped himself to some coffee and ordered a brandy. Waiters noticed Haldane.

'Both?'

'You and Leiser. He does it by implication.'

'It's going to be different with Leiser, isn't it?' Avery said quickly. 'Leiser's a professional.'

'Leiser is not one of us. Never make that mistake. We touched him long ago, that's all.'

'What's he like? What sort of man is he?'

'He's an agent. He's a man to be handled, not known.' He returned to his crossword.

'He must be loyal,' Avery said. 'Why else would he accept?'

'You heard what the Director said: the two vows. The first is often quite frivolously taken.'

'And the second?'

'Ah, that is different. We shall be there to help him take it.'

'But why did he accept the first time?'

'I mistrust reasons. I mistrust words like loyalty. And above all,' Haldane declared, 'I mistrust *motive*. We're running an agent; the arithmetic is over. You read German, didn't you? In the beginning was the deed.'

Shortly before they arrived Avery ventured one more question.

'Why *was* that passport out of date?'

Haldane had a way of inclining his head when addressed.

'The Foreign Office used to allocate a series of passport numbers to the Department for operational purposes. The arrangement ran from year to year. Six months ago the Office said they wouldn't issue any more without reference to the Circus. It seems Leclerc had been making insufficient claims on the facility and Control cut him out of the market. Taylor's passport was one of the old series. They revoked the whole lot three days before he left. There was no time to do anything about it. It might never have been noticed. The Circus has been very devious.' A pause. 'Indeed I find it hard to understand what Control *is* up to.'

They took a taxi to North Oxford and got out at the corner of their road. As they walked along the pavement Avery looked at the houses in the half-darkness, glimpsed grey-haired figures moving across the lighted windows, velvet-covered chairs trimmed with lace, Chinese screens, music stands and a bridge four sitting like bewitched courtiers in a castle. It was a world he had known about once; for a time he had almost fancied he was part of it; but that was long ago.

They spent the evening preparing the house. Haldane said Leiser should have the rear bedroom overlooking the garden, they themselves would take the rooms on the street side. He had sent some academic books in advance, a typewriter and some imposing files. These he unpacked and arranged on the dining-room table for the benefit of the landlord's housekeeper who would come each day. 'We shall call this room the study,' he said. In the drawing-room he installed a tape recorder.

He had some tapes which he locked in a cupboard, meticulously adding the key to his key ring. Other luggage was still waiting in the hall: a projector, Air Force issue, a screen, and a suitcase of green canvas, securely fastened, with leather corners.

The house was spacious and well kept; the furniture was of mahogany, with brass inlay. The walls were filled with pictures of some unknown family: sketches in sepia, miniatures, photographs faded with age. There was a bowl of potpourri on the sideboard and a palm cross pinned to the mirror; chandeliers hung from the ceiling, clumsy, but inoffensive; in one corner, a bible table; in another a small cupid, very ugly, its face turned to the dark. The whole house gently asserted an air of old age; it had a quality, like incense, of courteous but inconsolable sadness.

By midnight they had finished unpacking. They sat down in

the drawing-room. The marble fireplace was supported by blackamoors of ebony; the light of the gas fire played over the gilded rose-chains which linked their thick ankles. The fireplace came from an age, it might have been the seventeenth century, it might have been the nineteenth, when blackamoors had briefly replaced borzois as the decorative beasts of society; they were quite naked, as a dog might be, and chained with golden roses. Avery gave himself a whisky, then went to bed, leaving Haldane sunk in his own thoughts.

His room was large and dark; above the bed hung a light shade of blue china; there were embroidered covers on the tables and a small enamelled notice saying, 'God's blessing on this house'; beside the window was a picture of a child saying its prayers while his sister ate breakfast in bed.

He lay awake, wondering about Leiser; it was like waiting for a girl. From across the passage he could hear Haldane's solitary cough, on and on. It had not ended when he fell asleep.

Leclerc thought Smiley's club a very strange place; not at all the kind of thing he had expected. Two half-basement rooms and a dozen people dining at separate tables before a large fire. Some of them were vaguely familiar. He suspected they were connected with the Circus.

'This is rather a good spot. How do you join?'

'Oh, you don't,' said Smiley apologetically, then blushed and continued, 'I mean, they don't have new members. Just one generation . . . several went in the war, you know, some have died or gone abroad. What was it you had in mind, I wonder?'

'You were good enough to help young Avery out.'

'Yes . . . yes of course. How did that go, by the way? I never heard.'

'It was just a training run. There was no film in the end.'

'I'm sorry,' Smiley spoke hastily, covering up, as if someone were dead and he had not known.

'We didn't really expect there would be. It was just a precaution. How much did Avery tell you, I wonder? We're training up one or two of the old hands . . . and some of the new boys too. It's something to do,' Leclerc explained, 'during the slack season . . . Christmas, you know. People on leave.'

'I know.'

Leclerc noticed that the claret was very good. He wished he had joined a smaller club; his own had gone off terribly. They had such difficulty with staff.

'You have probably heard,' Leclerc added, officially, as it were, 'that Control has offered me full assistance for training purposes.'

'Yes, yes, of course.'

'My Minister was the moving spirit. He likes the idea of a pool of trained agents. When the plan was first mooted I went and spoke to Control myself. Later, Control called on me. You knew that, perhaps?'

'Yes. Control wondered . . .'

'He has been most helpful. Don't think I am unappreciative. It has been agreed – I think I should give you the background, your own office will confirm it – that if the training is to be effective, we must create as nearly as possible an operational atmosphere. What we used to call battle conditions.' An indulgent smile. 'We've chosen an area in Western Germany. It's bleak and unfamiliar ground, ideal for frontier-crossing exercises and that kind of thing. We can ask for the Army's cooperation if we need it.'

'Yes, indeed. What a good idea.'

'For elementary reasons of security, we all accept that your office should only be briefed in the aspects of this exercise in which you are good enough to help.'

'Control told me,' said Smiley. 'He wants to do whatever he can. He didn't know you touched this kind of thing any more. He was pleased.'

'Good,' Leclerc said shortly. He moved his elbows forward a little across the polished table. 'I thought I might pick your brains . . . quite informally. Rather as you people from time to time have made use of Adrian Haldane.'

'Of course.'

'The first thing is false documents. I looked up our old forgers in the index. I see Hyde and Fellowby went over to the Circus some years ago.'

'Yes. It was the change in emphasis.'

'I've written down a personal description of a man in our employment; he is supposedly resident at Magdeburg for the purposes of the scheme. One of the men under training. Do you think they could prepare documents, Identity Card, Party Membership and that kind of thing? Whatever is necessary.'

'The man would have to sign them,' Smiley said. 'We would then stamp on top of his signature. We'd need photographs too. He'd have to be briefed on how the documents worked; perhaps Hyde could do that on the spot with your agent?'

A slight hesitation. 'No doubt. I have selected a cover name. It closely approximates his own; we find that a useful technique.'

'I might just make the point,' Smiley said, with a rather comic frown, 'since this is such an *elaborate* exercise, that forged papers are of very *limited* value. I mean, one telephone call to the Magdeburg Town Administration and the best forgery in the world is blown sky high . . .'

'I think we know about that. We want to teach them cover, submit them to interrogation . . . you know the kind of thing.'

Smiley sipped his claret. 'I just thought I'd make the point. It's so easy to get hypnotised by *technique*. I didn't mean to imply . . . How is Haldane, by the way? He read Greats, you know. We were up together.'

'Adrian is well.'

'I liked your Avery,' Smiley said politely. His heavy small face contracted in pain. 'Do you realise,' he asked impressively, 'they *still* don't include the Baroque period in the German syllabus? They call it a special subject.'

'Then there is the question of clandestine wireless. We haven't used that kind of thing much since the war. I understand it has all become a great deal more sophisticated. High-speed transmission and so on. We want to keep up with the times.'

'Yes. Yes, I believe the message is taped on a miniature recorder and sent over the air in a matter of seconds.' He sighed. 'But no one really tells us much. The technical people hold their cards very close to their chests.'

'Is that a method in which our people could profitably be trained . . . in a month, say?'

'And use under operational conditions?' Smiley asked in astonishment. 'Straight away, after a month's training?'

'Some are technically minded, you understand. People with wireless experience.'

Smiley was watching Leclerc incredulously. 'Forgive me. Would he, would they,' he inquired, 'have *other* things to learn in that month as well?'

'For some it's more a refresher course.'

'Ah.'

'What do you mean?'

'Nothing, nothing,' Smiley said vaguely and added, 'I don't *think* our technical people would be very keen to part with this kind of equipment unless . . .'

'Unless it were their own training operation?'

'Yes,' Smiley blushed. 'Yes, that's what I mean. They're very particular, you know; jealous.'

Leclerc lapsed into silence, lightly tapping the base of his wine glass on the polished surface of the table. Suddenly he smiled and said, as if he had shaken off depression, 'Oh well. We shall just have to use a conventional set. Have direction-finding methods also improved since the war? Interception, location of an illegal transmitter?'

'Oh yes. Yes, indeed.'

'We would have to incorporate that. How long can a man remain on the air before they spot him?'

'Two or three minutes, perhaps. It depends. Often it's a matter of luck how soon they hear him. They can only pin him down while he's transmitting. Much depends on the frequency. Or so they tell me.'

'In the war,' said Leclerc reflectively, 'we gave an agent several crystals. Each vibrated at a fixed frequency. Every so often he changed the crystal; that was usually a safe enough method. We could do that again.'

'Yes. Yes, I remember that. But there was the headache of re-tuning the transmitter . . . possibly changing the coil . . . matching the aerial.'

'Suppose a man is used to a conventional set. You tell me the chances of interception are greater now than they were in the war? You say allow two or three minutes?'

'Or less,' said Smiley, watching him. 'It depends on a lot of things . . . luck, reception, amount of signal traffic, density of population . . .'

'Supposing he changed his frequency after every two and a half minutes on the air. Surely that would meet the case?'

'It could be a slow business.' His sad, unhealthy face was wrinkled in concern. 'You're quite sure this is only training?'

'As far as I remember,' Leclerc persisted, courting his own idea, 'these crystals are the size of a small matchbox. We could give them several. We're only aiming at a few transmissions; perhaps only three or four. Would you consider my suggestion impractical?'

'It's hardly my province.'

'What is the alternative? I asked Control; he said speak to you. He said you'd help, find me the equipment. What else can I do? Can I *talk* to your technical people?'

'I'm sorry. Control rather agreed with the technical side, that we should give all the help we can, but not compromise new equipment. *Risk* compromising it, I mean. After all, it is only training. I think he felt that if you hadn't full technical resources you should . . .'

'Hand over the commitment?'

'No, no,' Smiley protested, but Leclerc interrupted him. 'These people would eventually be used against military targets,' he said angrily. 'Purely military. Control accepts that.'

'Oh quite.' He seemed to have given up. 'And if you want a conventional set, no doubt we can dig one up.'

The waiter brought a decanter of port. Leclerc watched Smiley pour a little into his glass, then slide the decanter carefully across the polished table.

'It's quite good, but I'm afraid it's nearly finished. When this is gone we shall have to break into the younger ones. I'm seeing Control first thing tomorrow. I'm sure he'll have no objection. About the documents, I mean. And crystals. We could advise you on frequencies, I'm sure. Control made a point of that.'

'Control's been very good,' Leclerc confessed. He was slightly drunk. 'It puzzles me sometimes.'

12

Two days later, Leiser arrived at Oxford. They waited anxiously for him on the platform, Haldane peering among the hurrying faces in the crowd. It was Avery, curiously, who saw him first: a motionless figure in a camel-hair coat at the window of an empty compartment.

'Is that him?' Avery asked.

'He's travelling first class. He must have paid the difference.' Haldane spoke as if it were an affront.

Leiser lowered the window and handed out two pigskin cases shaped for the boot of a car, a little too orange for nature. They greeted one another briskly, shaking hands for everyone to see. Avery wanted to carry the luggage to the taxi, but Leiser preferred to take it himself, a piece in each hand, as if it were his duty. He walked a little away from them, shoulders back, staring at the people as they went by, startled by the crowd. His long hair bounced with each step.

Avery, watching him, felt suddenly disturbed.

He was a man; not a shadow. A man with force to his body and purpose to his movement, but somehow theirs to direct. There seemed to be nowhere he would not walk. He was recruited; and had assumed already the anxious, brisk manner of an enlisted man. Yet, Avery accepted, no single factor wholly accounted for Leiser's recruitment. Avery was already familiar, during his short association with the Department, with the phenomenon of organic motivation; with operations which had

no discernible genesis and no conclusion, which formed part of
an unending pattern of activity until they ceased to have any
further identity; with that progress of fruitless courtships
which, in the aggregate, passed for an active love life. But as he
observed this man bobbing beside him, animate and quick, he
recognised that hitherto they had courted ideas, incestuously
among themselves; now they had a human being upon their
hands, and this was he.

They climbed into the taxi, Leiser last because he insisted. It
was mid-afternoon, a slate sky behind the plane trees. The
smoke rose from the North Oxford chimneys in ponderous columns like proof of a virtuous sacrifice. The houses were of a
modest stateliness; romantic hulls redecked, each according to a
different legend. Here the turrets of Avalon, there the carved
trellis of a pagoda; between them the monkey-puzzle trees, and
the half-hidden washing like butterflies in the wrong season.
The houses sat decently in their own gardens, the curtains
drawn, first lace and then brocade, petticoats and skirts. It was
like a bad water-colour, the dark things drawn too heavy, the
sky grey and soiled in the dusk, the paint too worked.

They dismissed the taxi at the corner of the street. A smell
of leaf mould lingered in the air. If there were children they
made no noise. The three men walked to the gate. Leiser, his
eyes on the house, put down his suitcases.

'Nice place,' he said with appreciation. He turned to Avery:
'Who chose it?'

'I did.'

'That's nice.' He patted his shoulder. 'You did a good job.'
Avery, pleased, smiled and opened the gate; Leiser was determined that the others should pass through first. They took him
upstairs and showed him his room. He still carried his own
luggage.

'I'll unpack later,' he said. 'I like to make a proper job of it.'

He walked through the house in a critical way, picking things
up and looking at them; he might have come to bid for the place.

'It's a nice spot,' he repeated finally; 'I like it.'

'Good,' said Haldane, as if he didn't give a damn.

Avery went with him to his room to see if he could help.

'What's your name?' Leiser asked. He was more at ease with Avery; more vulgar.

'John.'

They shook hands again.

'Well, hullo, John; glad to meet you. How old are you?'

'Thirty-four,' he lied.

A wink. 'Christ, I wish I was thirty-four. Done this kind of thing before, have you?'

'I finished my own run last week.'

'How did it go?'

'Fine.'

'That's the boy. Where's your room?'

Avery showed him.

'Tell me, what's the set-up here?'

'What do you mean?'

'Who's in charge?'

'Captain Hawkins.'

'Anyone else?'

'Not really. I shall be around.'

'All the time?'

'Yes.'

He began unpacking. Avery watched. He had brushes backed with leather, hair lotion, a whole range of little bottles of things for men, an electric shaver of the newest kind and ties, some in tartan, others in silk, to match his costly shirts. Avery went downstairs. Haldane was waiting. He smiled as Avery came in. 'Well?'

Avery shrugged, too big a gesture. He felt elated, ill at ease. 'What do *you* make of him?' he asked.

'I hardly know him,' Haldane said drily. He had a way of terminating conversations. 'I want you to be always in his company. Walk with him, shoot with him, drink with him if you must. He's not to be alone.'

'What about his leave in between?'

'We'll see about that. Meanwhile, do as I say. You will find he enjoys your company. He's a very *lonely* man. And remember he's British: British to the core. One more thing – this is most important – do not let him think we have changed since the war. The Department has remained exactly as it was: that is an illusion you must foster even' – he did not smile – 'even though you are too young to make the comparison.'

They began next morning. Breakfast over, they assembled in the drawing-room and Haldane addressed them.

The training would be divided into two periods of a fortnight each, with a short rest in between. The first was to be a refresher course; in the second, old skills, now revived, would be related to the task which lay ahead. Not until the second period would Leiser be told his operational name, his cover and the nature of his mission; even then, the information would reveal neither the target area nor the means by which he was to be infiltrated.

In communications as in all other aspects of his training he would graduate from the general to the particular. In the first period he would familiarise himself once more with the technique of cyphers, signal plans and schedules. In the second he would spend much time actually transmitting under semi-operational conditions. The instructor would arrive during that week.

Haldane explained all this with pedagogic acrimony while Leiser listened carefully, now and then briskly nodding his assent. Avery found it strange that Haldane took so little care to conceal his distaste.

'In the first period we shall see what you remember. We shall give you a lot of running about, I'm afraid. We want to get you fit. There'll be small-arms training, unarmed combat, mental exercises, tradecraft. We shall try to take you walking in the afternoons.'

'Who with? Will John come?'

'Yes. John will take you. You should regard John as your adviser on all minor matters. If there is anything you wish to discuss, any complaint or anxiety, I trust you will not hesitate to mention it to either one of us.'

'All right.'

'On the whole, I must ask you not to venture out alone. I should prefer John to accompany you if you wish to go to the cinema, do some shopping or whatever else the time allows. But I fear you may not have much chance of recreation.'

'I don't expect it,' Leiser said; 'I don't need it.' He seemed to mean he didn't want it.

'The wireless instructor, when he comes, will not know your name. That is a customary precaution: please observe it. The daily woman believes we are participating in an academic conference. I cannot imagine you will have occasion to talk to her, but if you do, remember that. If you wish to make inquiries about your business, kindly consult me first. You should not telephone without my consent. Then there will be other visitors: photographers, medical people, technicians. They are what we call ancillaries and are not in the picture. Most of them believe you're here as part of a wider training scheme. Please remember this.'

'OK,' said Leiser. Haldane looked at his watch.

'Our first appointment is at ten o'clock. A car will collect us from the corner of the road. The driver is not one of us: no conversation on the journey, please. Have you no other clothes?' he asked. 'Those are scarcely suitable for the range.'

'I've got a sports coat and a pair of flannels.'

'I could wish you less conspicuous.'

As they went upstairs to change, Leiser smiled wryly at Avery. 'He's a real boy, isn't he? The old school.'

'But good,' Avery said.

Leiser stopped. 'Of course. Here, tell me something. Was this place always here? Have you used it for many people?'

'You're not the first,' Avery said.

'Look, I know you can't tell me much. Is the outfit still like it was . . . people everywhere . . . the same set-up?'

'I don't think you'd find much difference. I suppose we've expanded a bit.'

'Are there many young ones like you?'

'Sorry, Fred.'

Leiser put his open hand on Avery's back. He used his hands
a lot.

'You're good, too,' he said. 'Don't bother about me. Not to
worry, eh, John?'

They went to Abingdon: the Ministry had made arrangements
with the parachute base. The instructor was expecting them.

'Used to any particular gun, are you?'

'Browning three-eight automatic, please,' Leiser said, like a
child ordering groceries.

'We call it the nine-millimetre now. You'll have had the
Mark One.'

Haldane stood in the gallery at the back while Avery helped
wind in the man-sized target to a distance of ten yards and paste
squares of gum-strip over the old holes.

'You call me "Staff",' the instructor said and turned to Avery.
'Like to have a go as well, sir?'

Haldane put in quickly, 'Yes, they are both shooting, please,
Staff.'

Leiser took first turn. Avery stood beside Haldane while
Leiser, his long back towards them, waited in the empty range,
facing the plywood figure of a German soldier. The target was
black, framed against the crumbling whitewash of the walls;
over its belly and groin a heart had been crudely described in
chalk, its interior extensively repaired with fragments of paper.
As they watched, he began testing the weight of the gun, raising
it quickly to the level of his eye, then lowering it slowly; pushing
home the empty magazine, taking it out and thrusting it in
again. He glanced over his shoulder at Avery, with his left hand
brushing from his forehead a strand of brown hair which threatened to impede his view. Avery smiled encouragement, then said
quickly to Haldane, talking business, 'I still can't make him out.'

THE LOOKING GLASS WAR

'Why not? He's a perfectly ordinary Pole.'

'Where does he come from? What part of Poland?'

'You've read the file. Danzig.'

'Of course.'

The instructor began. 'We'll just try it with the empty gun first, both eyes open, and look along the line of sight, feet nicely apart now, thank you, that's lovely. Relax now, be nice and comfy, it's not a drill movement, it's a firing position, oh yes, we've done *this* before! Now traverse the gun, point it but never aim. Right!' The instructor drew breath, opened a wooden box and took out four magazines. 'One in the gun and one in the left hand,' he said and handed the other two up to Avery, who watched with fascination as Leiser deftly slipped a full magazine into the butt of the automatic and advanced the safety catch with his thumb.

'Now cock the gun, pointing it at the ground three yards ahead of you. Now take up a firing position, keeping the arm straight. Pointing the gun but not aiming it, fire off one magazine, two shots at a time, remembering that we don't regard the automatic as a weapon of science but more in the order of a stopping weapon for close combat. Now slowly, very slowly . . .'

Before he could finish the range was vibrating with the sound of Leiser's shooting – he shot fast, standing very stiff, his left hand holding the spare magazine precisely at his side like a grenade. He shot angrily, a mute man finding expression. Avery could feel with rising excitement the fury and purpose of his shooting; now two shots, and another two, then three, then a long volley, while the haze gathered round him and the plywood soldier shook and Avery's nostrils filled with the sweet smell of cordite.

'Eleven out of thirteen on the target,' the instructor declared. 'Very nice, very nice indeed. Next time, stick to two shots at a time, please, and wait till I give the fire order.' To Avery, the subaltern, he said, 'Care to have a go, sir?'

Leiser had walked up to the target and was lightly tracing the bullet holes with his slim hands. The silence was suddenly oppressive. He seemed lost in meditation, feeling the plywood here and there, running a finger thoughtfully along the outline of the German helmet, until the instructor called:

'Come on. We haven't got all day.'

Avery stood on the gym mat, measuring the weight of the gun. With the instructor's help he inserted one magazine, clutching the other nervously in his left hand. Haldane and Leiser looked on.

Avery fired, the heavy gun thudding in his ears, and he felt his young heart stir as the silhouette flicked passively to his shooting.

'Good shot, John, good shot!'

'Very good,' said the instructor automatically. 'A very good first effort, sir.' He turned to Leiser: 'Do you mind not shouting like that?' He knew a foreigner when he saw one.

'How many?' Avery asked eagerly, as he and the sergeant gathered round the target, touching the blackened perforations scattered thinly over the chest and belly. 'How many, Staff?'

'You'd better come with me, John,' Leiser whispered, throwing his arm over Avery's shoulder. 'I could do with you over there.' For a moment Avery recoiled. Then, with a laugh, he put his own arm round Leiser, feeling the warm, crisp cloth of his sports jacket in the palm of his hand.

The instructor led them across the parade ground to a brick barrack like a theatre with no windows, tall at one end. There were walls half crossing one another like the entrance to a public lavatory.

'Moving targets,' Haldane said, 'and shooting in the dark.'

At lunch they played the tapes.

The tapes were to run like a theme through the first two weeks of his training. They were made from old gramophone records; there was a crack in one which recurred like a metronome. Together, they comprised a massive parlour game in which things to be remembered were not listed but mentioned, casually, obliquely, often against a distracting background of other noises, now contradicted in conversation, now corrected or con-

tested. There were three principal voices, one female and two
male. Others would interfere. It was the woman who got on their
nerves.

She had that antiseptic voice which air hostesses seem to acquire. In the first tape she read from lists, quickly; first it was
a shopping-list, two pounds of this, one kilo of that; without
warning she was talking about coloured skittles – so many green
so many ochre; then it was weapons, guns, torpedoes, ammunition of this and that calibre; then a factory with capacity, waste
and production figures, annual targets and monthly achieve-
ments. In the second tape she had not abandoned these topics,
but unfamiliar voices distracted her and led the dialogue into
unexpected paths.

While shopping she entered into an argument with the grocer's wife about certain merchandise which did not meet with
her approval; eggs that were not sound, the outrageous cost of
butter. When the grocer himself attempted to mediate he was
accused of favouritism; there was talk of points and ration cards,
the extra allowance of sugar for jam-making; a hint of undis-
closed treasures under the counter. The grocer's voice was
raised in anger but he stopped when the child intervened, talking about skittles. 'Mummy, Mummy, I've knocked over the
three green ones, but when I tried to put them up, seven black
ones fell down; Mummy, why are there only eight black ones
left?'

The scene shifted to a public house. It was the woman again.
She was reciting armaments statistics; other voices joined in.
Figures were disputed, new targets stated, old ones recalled; the
performance of a weapon – a weapon unnamed, undescribed –
was cynically questioned and heatedly defended.

Every few minutes a voice shouted 'break!' – it might have
been a referee – and Haldane stopped the tape and made Leiser
talk about football or the weather, or read aloud from a newspaper for five minutes by his watch (the clock on the mantelpiece was broken). The tape recorder was switched on again,
and they heard a voice, vaguely familiar, trailing a little like a

parson's; a young voice, deprecating and unsure, like Avery's:
'Now here are the four questions. Discounting those eggs which
were not sound, how many has she bought in the last three
weeks? How many skittles are there altogether? What was the
annual overall output of proved and calibrated gun barrels for
the years 1937 and 1938? Finally, put in telegraph form any information from which the length of the barrels might be
computed.'

Leiser rushed into the study – he seemed to know the game –
to write down his answers. As soon as he had left the room
Avery said accusingly, 'That was you. That was your voice speaking at the end.'

'Was it?' Haldane replied. He might not have known.

There were other tapes too, and they had the smell of death;
the running of feet on a wooden staircase, the slamming of a
door, a click, and a girl's voice asking – she might have been offering lemon or cream – 'Catch of a door, cocking of a gun?'

Leiser hesitated. 'A door,' he said. 'It was just the door.'

'It was a gun,' Haldane retorted. 'A Browning nine-millimetre
automatic. The magazine was being slid into the butt.'

In the afternoon they went for their first walk, the two of
them, Leiser and Avery, through Port Meadow and into the
country beyond. Haldane had sent them. They walked fast,
striding over the whip grass, the wind catching at Leiser's hair
and throwing it wildly about his head. It was cold but there was
no rain; a clear, sunless day when the sky above the flat fields
was darker than the earth.

'You know your way round here, don't you?' Leiser asked.
'Were you at school here?'

'I was an undergraduate here, yes.'

'What did you study?'

'I read languages. German principally.'

They climbed a stile and emerged in a narrow lane.

'You married?' he asked.

'Yes.'

'Kids?'

'One.'

'Tell me something, John. When the Captain turned up my card . . . what happened?'

'What do you mean?'

'What does it look like, an index for so many? It must be a big thing in an outfit like ours.'

'It's in alphabetical order,' Avery said helplessly. 'Just cards. Why?'

'He said they remembered me: the old hands. I was the best, he said. Well, *who* remembered?'

'They all did. There's a special index for the best people. Practically everyone in the Department knows Fred Leiser. Even the new ones. You can't have a record like yours and get forgotten, you know.' He smiled. 'You're part of the furniture, Fred.'

'Tell me something else, John. I don't want to rock the boat, see, but tell me this . . . Would I be any good on the inside?'

'The inside?'

'In the office, with you people. I suppose you've got to be born to it really, like the Captain.'

'I'm afraid so, Fred.'

'What cars do you use up there, John?'

'Humbers.'

'Hawk or Snipe?'

'Hawk.'

'Only four-cylinder? The Snipe's a better job, you know.'

'I'm talking about non-operational transport,' Avery said. 'We've a whole range of stuff for the special work.'

'Like the van?'

'That's it.'

'How long before . . . how long does it take to train you? You, for instance; you just did a run. How long before they let you go?'

'Sorry, Fred. I'm not allowed . . . not even you.'

'Not to worry.'

They passed a church set back on a rise above the road,

skirted a field of plough and returned, tired and radiant, to the cheerful embrace of the Mayfly house and the gas fire playing on the golden roses.

In the evening, they had the projector for visual memory: they would be in a car, passing a marshalling yard; or in a train beside an airfield; they would be taken on a walk through a town, and suddenly they would become aware that a vehicle or a face had reappeared, and they had not remembered its features. Sometimes a series of disconnected objects were flashed in rapid succession on to the screen, and there would be voices in the background, like the voices on the tape, but the conversation was not related to the film, so that the student must consult both his senses and retain what was valuable from each.

Thus the first day ended, setting the pattern for those that followed: carefree, exciting days for them both, days of honest labour and cautious but deepening attachment as the skills of boyhood became once more the weapons of war.

For the unarmed combat they had rented a small gymnasium near Headington which they had used in the war. An instructor had come by train. They called him Sergeant.

'Will he be carrying a knife at all? Not wanting to be curious,' he asked respectfully. He had a Welsh accent.

Haldane shrugged. 'It depends what he likes. We don't want to clutter him up.'

'There's a lot to be said for a knife, sir.' Leiser was still in the changing-room. 'If he knows how to use it. And the Jerries don't like them, not one bit.' He had brought some knives in a hand-case, and he unpacked them in a private way, like a traveller unpacking his samples. 'They never could take cold steel,' he explained. 'Nothing too long, that's the trick of it, sir. Something flat with the two cutting edges.' He selected one and held it up. 'You can't do much better than this, as a matter of fact.' It was wide and flat like a laurel leaf, the blade unpolished, the handle waisted like an hourglass, cross-hatched to prevent slip.

Leiser was walking towards them, smoothing a comb through his hair.

'Used one of these, have you?'

Leiser examined the knife and nodded. The sergeant looked at him carefully. 'I know you, don't I? My name's Sandy Lowe. I'm a bloody Welshman.'

'You taught me in the war.'

'Christ,' said Lowe softly, 'so I did. You haven't changed much, have you?' They grinned shyly at one another, not knowing whether to shake hands. 'Come on, then, see what you remember.' They walked to the coconut matting in the centre of the floor. Lowe threw the knife at Leiser's feet and he snatched it up, grunting as he bent.

Lowe wore a jacket of torn tweed, very old. He stepped quickly back, took it off and with a single movement wrapped it round his left forearm, like a man preparing to fight a dog. Drawing his own knife he moved slowly round Leiser, keeping his weight steady but riding a little from one foot to the other. He was stooping, his bound arm held loosely in front of his stomach, fingers outstretched, palm facing the ground. He had gathered his body behind the guard, letting the blade play restlessly in front of it while Leiser kept steady, his eyes fixed upon the sergeant. For a time they feinted back and forth; once Leiser lunged and Lowe sprang back, allowing the knife to cut the cloth of the jacket on his arm. Once Lowe dropped to his knees, as if to drive the knife upwards beneath Leiser's guard, and it was Leiser's turn to spring back, but too slowly, it seemed, for Lowe shook his head, shouted 'Halt!' and stood upright.

'Remember that?' He indicated his own belly and groin, pressing his arms and elbows in as if to reduce the width of his body. 'Keep the target small.' He made Leiser put his knife away and showed him holds, crooking his left arm round Leiser's neck and pretending to stab him in the kidneys or the stomach. Then he asked Avery to stand as a dummy, and the two of them moved round him with detachment, Lowe indicating the places with his knife and Leiser nodding, smiling occasionally when a particular trick came back to him.

'You didn't weave with the blade enough. Remember thumb on top, blade parallel to the ground, forearm stiff, wrist loose. Don't let his eye settle on it, not for a moment. And left hand in over your own target, whether you've got the knife or not. Never be generous about offering the body, that's what I say to my daughter.' They laughed dutifully, all but Haldane.

After that, Avery had a turn. Leiser seemed to want it. Removing his glasses, he held the knife as Lowe showed him, hesitant, alert, while Leiser trod crabwise, feinted and darted lightly back, the sweat running off his face, his small eyes alight with concentration. All the time Avery was conscious of the sharp grooves of the haft against the flesh of his palm, the aching in his calves and buttocks as he kept his weight forward on his toes, and Leiser's angry eyes searching his own. Then Leiser's foot had hooked round his ankle; as he lost his balance he felt the knife being wrenched from his hand; he fell back, Leiser's full weight upon him, Leiser's hand clawing at the collar of his shirt.

They helped him up, all laughing, while Leiser brushed the dust from Avery's clothes. The knives were put away while they did physical training; Avery took part.

When it was over Lowe said: 'We'll just have a spot of unarmed combat and that will do nicely.'

Haldane glanced at Leiser. 'Have you had enough?'

'I'm all right.'

Lowe took Avery by an arm and stood him in the centre of the gym mat. 'You sit on the bench,' he called to Leiser, 'while I show you a couple of things.'

He put a hand on Avery's shoulder. 'We're only concerned with five marks, whether we got a knife or not. What are they?'

'Groin, kidneys, belly, heart and throat,' Leiser replied wearily.

'How do you break a man's neck?'

'You don't. You smash his windpipe at the front.'

'What about a blow on the back of the neck?'

'Not with the bare hand. Not without a weapon.' He had put his face in his hands.

'Correct.' Lowe moved his open palm in slow motion towards Avery's throat. 'Hand open, fingers straight, right?'

'Right,' Leiser said.

'What else do you remember?'

A pause. 'Tiger's Claw. An attack on the eyes.'

'Never use it,' the sergeant replied shortly. 'Not as an attacking blow. You leave yourself wide open. Now for the strangle holds. All from behind, remember? Bend the head back, so, hand on the throat, so, and *squeeze*.' Lowe looked over his shoulder: 'Look this way, please. I'm not doing this for my own benefit . . . come on, then, if you know it all, show us some throws!'

Leiser stood up, locking arms with Lowe, and for a while they struggled back and forth, each waiting for the other to offer an opening. Then Lowe gave way, Leiser toppled and Lowe's hand slapped the back of his head, thrusting it down so that Leiser fell face forward heavily on to the mat.

'You fall a treat,' said Lowe with a grin, and then Leiser was upon him, twisting Lowe's arm savagely back and throwing him very hard so that his little body hit the carpets like a bird hitting the windscreen of a car.

'You play fair!' Leiser demanded. 'Or I'll damn well hurt you.'

'Never lean on your opponent,' Lowe said shortly. 'And don't lose your temper in the gym.'

He called across to Avery. 'You have a turn now, sir; give him some exercise.'

Avery stood up, took off his jacket and waited for Leiser to approach him. He felt the strong grasp upon his arms and was suddenly conscious of the frailty of his body when matched against this adult force. He tried to seize the forearms of the older man, but his hands could not encompass them; he tried to break free, but Leiser held him; Leiser's head was against his own, filling his nostrils with the smell of hair oil. He felt the damp stubble of his cheek and the close, rank heat of his thin, straining body. Putting his hands on Leiser's chest he forced himself back, throwing all his energy into one frantic effort to escape the suffocating constriction of the man's embrace. As he drew away they caught sight of one another, it might have been for the first time, across the heaving cradle of their entangled arms; Leiser's face, contorted with exertion, softened into a smile; the grip relaxed.

Lowe walked over to Haldane. 'He's foreign, isn't he?'

'A Pole. What's he like?'

'I'd say he was quite a fighter in his day. Nasty. He's a good build. Fit too, considering.'

'I see.'

'How are you these days, sir, in yourself? All right, then?'

'Yes, thank you.'

'That's right. Twenty years. Amazing really. Kiddies all grown up.'

'I'm afraid I have none.'

'Mine, I mean.'

'Ah.'

'See any of the old crowd, then, sir? How about Mr Smiley?'

'I'm afraid I have not kept in touch. I am not a gregarious kind of person. Shall we settle up?'

Lowe stood lightly to attention while Haldane prepared to pay him; travelling money, salary and thirty-seven and six for the knife, plus twenty-two shillings for the sheath, a flat metal one with a spring to facilitate extraction. Lowe wrote him a receipt, signing it S.L. for reasons of security. 'I got the knife at cost,' he explained. 'It's a fiddle we work through the sports club.' He seemed proud of that.

Haldane gave Leiser a trenchcoat and wellingtons and Avery took him for a walk. They went by bus as far as Headington, sitting on the top deck.

'What happened this morning?' Avery asked.

'I thought we were fooling about, that's all. Then he threw me.'

'He remembered you, didn't he?'

'Of course he did: then why did he hurt me?'

'He didn't mean to.'

'Look, it's all right, see.' He was still upset.

They got out at the terminus and began trudging through the rain. Avery said, 'It's because he wasn't one of us; that's why you didn't like him.'

Leiser laughed, slipped his arm through Avery's. The rain, drifting in slow waves across the empty street, ran down their faces and trickled into the collars of their mackintoshes. Avery pressed his arm to his side, holding Leiser's hand captive, and they continued their walk in shared contentment, forgetting the rain or playing with it, treading in the deepest parts and not caring about their clothes.

'Is the Captain pleased, John?'

'Very. He says it's going fine. We begin the wireless soon, just the elementary stuff. Jack Johnson's expected tomorrow.'

'It's coming back to me, John, the shooting and that. I hadn't forgotten.' He smiled. 'The old three-eight.'

'Nine-millimetre. You're doing fine, Fred. Just fine. The Captain said so.'

'Is that what he said, John, the Captain?'

'Of course. And he's told London. London's pleased too. We're only afraid you're a bit too . . .'

'Too what?'

'Well – too English.'

Leiser laughed. 'Not to worry, John.'

The inside of Avery's arm, where he held Leiser's hand, felt dry and warm.

They spent a morning on cyphers. Haldane acted as instructor. He had brought pieces of silk cloth imprinted with a cypher of the type Leiser would use, and a chart backed with cardboard for converting letters into numerals. He put the chart on the chimney-piece, wedging it behind the marble clock, and lectured them, rather as Leclerc would have done, but without affectation. Avery and Leiser sat at the table, pencils in hand, and under Haldane's tuition converted one passage after another into numbers according to the chart, deducted the result from figures on the silk cloth, finally re-translating into letters. It was a process which demanded application rather than concentration, and perhaps because Leiser was trying too hard he became bothered and erratic.

'We'll have a timed run over twenty groups,' Haldane said, and dictated from the sheet of paper in his hand a message of eleven words with the signature Mayfly. 'From next week you will have to manage without the chart. I shall put it in your room and you must commit it to memory. Go!'

He pressed the stopwatch and walked to the window while the two men worked feverishly at the table, muttering almost in unison while they jotted elementary calculations on the scrap paper in front of them. Avery could detect the increasing flurry of Leiser's movements, the suppressed sighs and imprecations, the angry erasures; deliberately slowing down, he glanced over the other's arm to ascertain his progress and noticed that the stub of pencil buried in his little hand was smeared with sweat. Without a word, he silently changed his paper for Leiser's. Haldane, turning round, might not have seen.

Even in these first few days, it had become apparent that Leiser looked to Haldane as an ailing man looks to his doctor; a sinner to his priest. There was something terrible about a man who derived his strength from such a sickly body.

Haldane affected to ignore him. He adhered stubbornly to the habits of his private life. He never failed to complete his crossword. A case of burgundy was delivered from the town, half-bottles, and he drank one alone at each meal while they listened to the tapes. So complete, indeed, was his withdrawal that one might have thought him revolted by the man's proximity. Yet the more elusive, the more aloof Haldane became, the more surely he drew Leiser after him. Leiser, by some obscure standards of his own, had cast him as the English gentleman, and whatever Haldane did or said only served, in the eyes of the other, to fortify him in the part.

Haldane grew in stature. In London he was a slow-walking man; he picked his way pedantically along the corridors as if he were looking for footholds; clerks and secretaries would hover impatiently behind him, lacking the courage to pass. In Oxford he betrayed an agility which would have astonished his London colleagues. His parched frame had revived, he held himself erect. Even his hostility acquired the mark of command. Only the cough remained, that racked, abandoned sob too heavy for such a narrow chest, bringing dabs of red to his thin cheeks and causing Leiser the mute concern of a pupil for his admired master.

'Is the Captain sick?' he once asked Avery, picking up an old copy of Haldane's *Times*.

'He never speaks of it.'

'I suppose that would be bad form.' His attention was suddenly arrested by the newspaper. It was unopened. Only the crossword had been done, the margins round it sparsely annotated with permutations of a nine-letter anagram. He showed it to Avery in bewilderment.

'He doesn't read it,' he said. 'He's only done the competition.'

That night, when they went to bed, Leiser took it with him, furtively as if it contained some secret which study could reveal.

So far as Avery could judge, Haldane was content with Leiser's progress. In the great variety of activities to which Leiser was now subjected, they had been able to observe him more closely; with the corrosive perception of the weak they discovered his failings and tested his power. He acquired, as they gained his trust, a disarming frankness; he loved to confide. He was their creature; he gave them everything, and they stored it away as the poor do. They saw that the Department had provided direction for his energy: like a man of uncommon sexual appetite, Leiser had found in his new employment a love which he could illustrate with his gifts. They saw that he took pleasure in their command, giving in return his strength as homage for fulfilment. They even knew perhaps that between them they constituted for Leiser the poles of absolute authority: the one by his bitter adherence to standards which Leiser could never achieve, the other by his youthful accessibility, the apparent sweetness and dependence of his nature.

He liked to talk to Avery. He talked about his women or the war. He assumed – it was irritating for Avery, but nothing more – that a man in his middle thirties, whether married or not, led an intense and varied love life. Later in the evening when the two of them had put on their coats and hurried to the pub at the end of the road, he would lean his elbows on the small table, thrust his bright face forward and relate the smallest detail of his exploits, his hand beside his chin, his slim fingertips rapidly parting and closing in unconscious imitation of his mouth. It was not vanity which made him thus but friendship. These betrayals and confessions, whether truth or fantasy, were the simple coinage of their intimacy. He never mentioned Betty.

Avery came to know Leiser's face with an accuracy no longer related to memory. He noticed how its features seemed structurally to alter shape according to his mood, how when he was tired or depressed at the end of a long day the skin on his cheekbones was drawn upwards rather than down, and the corners of his eyes and mouth rose tautly so that his expression was at once more Slav and less familiar.

He had acquired from his neighbourhood or his clients certain turns of phrase which, though wholly without meaning, impressed his foreign ear. He would speak, for instance, of 'some measure of satisfaction', using an impersonal construction for the sake of dignity. He had assimilated also a variety of clichés. Expressions like 'not to worry', 'don't rock the boat', 'let the dog see the rabbit', came to him continually, as if he were aspiring after a way of life which he only imperfectly understood, and these were the offerings that would buy him in. Some expressions, Avery remarked, were out of date.

Once or twice Avery suspected that Haldane resented his intimacy with Leiser. At other times it seemed that Haldane was deploying emotions in Avery over which he himself no longer disposed. One evening at the beginning of the second week, while Leiser was engaged in that lengthy toilet which preceded almost any recreational engagement, Avery asked Haldane whether he did not wish to go out himself.

'What do you expect me to do? Make a pilgrimage to the shrine of my youth?'

'I thought you might have friends there; people you still know.'

'If I do, it would be insecure to visit them. I am here under another name.'

'I'm sorry. Of course.'

'Besides' – a dour smile – 'we are not all so prolific in our friendships.'

'You told me to stay with him!' Avery said hotly.

'Precisely; and you have. It would be churlish of me to complain. You do it admirably.'

'Do what?'

'Obey instructions.'

At that moment the door bell rang and Avery went downstairs to answer it. By the light of the streetlamp he could see the familiar shape of a Department van in the road. A small, homely figure stood on the doorstep. He was wearing a brown suit and overcoat. There was a high shine on the toes of his brown shoes. He might have come to read the meter.

'Jack Johnson's my name,' he said uncertainly. 'Johnson's Fair Deal, that's me.'

'Come in,' Avery said.

'This is the right place, isn't it? Captain Hawkins . . . and all that?'

He carried a soft leather bag which he laid carefully on the

floor as if it contained all he possessed. Half closing his umbrella he shook it expertly to rid it of the rain, then placed it on
the stand beneath his overcoat.

'I'm John.'

Johnson took his hand and squeezed it warmly.

'Very pleased to meet you. The Boss has talked a lot about
you. You're quite the blue-eyed boy, I hear.'

They laughed.

He took Avery by the arm in a quick confiding gesture.
'Using your own name, are you?'

'Yes. Christian name.'

'And the Captain?'

'Hawkins.'

'What's he like, Mayfly? How's he bearing up?'

'Fine. Just fine.'

'I hear he's quite a one for the girls.'

While Johnson and Haldane talked in the drawing-room
Avery slipped upstairs to Leiser.

'It's no go, Fred. Jack's come.'

'Who's Jack?'

'Jack Johnson, the wireless chap.'

'I thought we didn't start that till next week.'

'Just the elementary this week, to get your hand in. Come
down and say hullo.'

He was wearing a dark suit and held a nail file in one hand.

'What about going out, then?'

'I told you; we can't tonight, Fred; Jack's here.'

Leiser went downstairs and shook Johnson briefly by the
hand, without formality, as if he did not care for latecomers.
They talked awkwardly for a quarter of an hour until Leiser,
protesting tiredness, went sullenly to bed.

Johnson made his first report. 'He's slow,' he said. 'He hasn't
worked a key for a long time, mind. But I daren't try him on a set
till he's quicker on the key. I know it's all of twenty years, sir; you
can't blame him. But he *is* slow, sir, very.' He had an attentive,

nursery-rhyme way of talking as if he spent much time in the company of children. 'The Boss says I'm to play him all the time – when he starts the job, too. I understand we're all going over to Germany, sir.'

'Yes.'

'Then we shall have to get to know each other,' he insisted, 'Mayfly and me. We ought to be together a lot, sir, the moment I begin working him on the set. It's like handwriting, this game, we've got to get used to one another's handwriting. Then there's schedules, times for coming up and that; signal plans for his frequencies. Safety devices. That's a lot to learn in a fortnight.'

'Safety devices?' Avery asked.

'Deliberate mistakes, sir; like a misspelling in a particular group, an E for an A or something of that kind. If he wants to tell us he's been caught and is transmitting under control, he'll miss the safety device.' He turned to Haldane. 'You know the kind of thing, Captain.'

'There was talk in London of teaching him high-speed transmission on tape. Do you know what became of that idea?'

'The Boss did mention it to me, sir. I understand the equipment wasn't available. I can't say I know much about it, really; since my time, the transistorised stuff. The Boss said we were to stick to the old methods but change the frequency every two and a half minutes, sir; I understand the Jerries are very hot on the direction-finding these days.'

'What set did they send down? It seemed very heavy for him to carry about.'

'It's the kind Mayfly used in the war, sir, that's the beauty of it. The old B2 in the waterproof casing. If we've only got a couple of weeks there doesn't hardly seem time to go over anything else. Not that he's ready to work it yet—'

'What does it weigh?'

'About fifty pound, sir, all in. The ordinary suitcase set. It's the waterproofing that adds the weight, but he's got to have it if he's going over rough country. Specially at this time of year.' He hesitated. 'But he's slow on his Morse, sir.'

'Quite. Do you think you can bring him up to scratch in the time?'

'Can't tell yet, sir. Not till we really get cracking on the set. Not till the second period, when he's had his little bit of leave. I'm just letting him handle the buzzer at present.'

'Thank you,' said Haldane.

13

At the end of the first two weeks they gave him forty-eight hours' leave of absence. He had not asked for it and when they offered it to him he seemed puzzled. In no circumstances was he to visit his own neighbourhood. He could depart for London on the Friday but he said he preferred to go on Saturday. He could return on Monday morning but he said it depended and he might come back late on Sunday. They stressed that he was to keep clear of anyone who might know him, and in some curious fashion this seemed to console him.

Avery, worried, went to Haldane.

'I don't think we should send him off into the blue. You've told him he can't go back to South Park; or visit his friends, even if he's got any; I don't see quite where he can go.'

'You think he'll be lonely?'

Avery blushed. 'I think he'll just want to come back all the time.'

'We can hardly object to that.'

They gave him subsistence money in old notes, fives and ones. He wanted to refuse it, but Haldane pressed it on him as if a principle were involved. They offered to book him a room but he declined. Haldane assumed he was going to London, so in the end he went, as if he owed it to them.

'He's got some woman,' said Johnson with satisfaction.

He left on the midday train, carrying one pigskin suitcase

and wearing his camel-hair coat; it had a slightly military cut, and leather buttons, but no person of breeding could ever have mistaken it for a British warm.

He handed in his suitcase to the depository at Paddington Station and wandered out into Praed Street because he had nowhere to go. He walked about for half an hour, looking at the shop windows and reading the tarts' advertisements on the glazed notice boards. It was Saturday afternoon: a handful of old men in trilby hats and raincoats hovered between the pornography shops and the pimps on the corner. There was very little traffic: an atmosphere of hopeless recreation filled the street.

The cinema club charged a pound and gave him a predated membership card because of the law. He sat among ghost figures on a kitchen chair. The film was very old; it might have come over from Vienna when the persecutions began. Two girls, quite naked, took tea. There was no sound track and they just went on drinking tea, changing position a little as they passed their cups. They would be sixty now, if they had survived the war. He got up to go because it was after half past five and the pubs were open. As he passed the kiosk at the doorway, the manager said: 'I know a girl who likes a gay time. Very young.'

'No, thanks.'

'Two and a half quid; she likes foreigners. She gives it foreign if you like. French.'

'Run away.'

'Don't you tell me to run away.'

'Run away.' Leiser returned to the kiosk, his small eyes suddenly alight. 'Next time you offer me a girl, make it something English, see.'

The air was warmer, the wind had dropped, the street emptied; pleasures were indoors now. The woman behind the bar said, 'Can't mix it for you now, dear, not till the rush dies down. You can see for yourself.'

'It's the only thing I drink.'

'Sorry, dear.'

He ordered gin and Italian instead and got it warm with no cherry. Walking had made him tired. He sat on the bench which ran along the wall, watching the darts four. They did not speak, but pursued their game with quiet devotion, as if they were deeply conscious of tradition. It was like the film club. One of them had a date, and they called to Leiser, 'Make a four, then?'

'I don't mind,' he said, pleased to be addressed, and stood up; but a friend came in, a man called Henry, and Henry was preferred. Leiser was going to argue but there seemed no point.

Avery too had gone out alone. To Haldane he had said he was taking a walk, to Johnson that he was going to the cinema. Avery had a way of lying which defied rational explanation. He found himself drawn to the old places he had known; his college in the Turl; the bookshops, pubs and libraries. The term was just ending. Oxford had a smell of Christmas about it, and acknowledged it with prudish ill will, dressing the shop windows with last year's tinsel.

He took the Banbury Road until he reached the street where he and Sarah had lived for the first year of marriage. The flat was in darkness. Standing before it, he tried to detect in the house, in himself, some trace of the sentiment, or affection, or love, or whatever it was that explained their marriage, but it was not to be found and he supposed it had never been. He sought desperately, wanting to find the motive of youth; but there was none. He was staring into an empty house. He hastened home to the place where Leiser lived.

'Good film?' Johnson asked.

'Fine.'

'I thought you were going for a walk,' Haldane complained, looking up from his crossword.

'I changed my mind.'

'Incidentally,' Haldane said, 'Leiser's gun. I understand he prefers the three-eight.'

'Yes. They call it the nine-millimetre now.'

'When he returns he should start to carry it with him; take it everywhere, unloaded of course.' A glance at Johnson. 'Particularly when he begins transmission exercises on any scale. He must have it on him all the time; we want him to feel lost without it. I have arranged for one to be issued; you'll find it in your room, Avery, with various holsters. Perhaps you'd explain it to him, would you?'

'Won't you tell him yourself?'

'You do it. You get on with him so nicely.'

He went upstairs to telephone Sarah. She had gone to stay with her mother. Conversation was very formal.

Leiser dialled Betty's number, but there was no reply.

Relieved, he went to a cheap jeweller's, near the station, which was open on Saturday afternoon and bought a gold coach and horses for a charm bracelet. It cost eleven pounds, which was what they had given him for subsistence. He asked them to send it by registered mail to her address in South Park. He put a note in saying 'Back in two weeks. Be good', signing it, in a moment of aberration, F. Leiser, so he crossed it out and wrote 'Fred'.

He walked for a bit, thought of picking up a girl, and finally booked in at the hotel near the station. He slept badly because of the noise of traffic. In the morning he rang her number again; there was no reply. He replaced the receiver quickly; he might have waited a little longer. He had breakfast, went out and bought the Sunday papers, took them to his room and read the football reports till lunch time. In the afternoon he went for a walk, it had become a habit, right through London, he hardly knew where. He followed the river as far as Charing Cross and found himself in an empty garden filled with drifting rain. The tarmac paths were strewn with yellow leaves. An old man sat on the bandstand, quite alone. He wore a black overcoat and a rucksack of green webbing like the case of a gas mask. He was asleep, or listening to music.

He waited till evening in order not to disappoint Avery, then caught the last train home to Oxford.

Avery knew a pub behind Balliol where they let you play bar billiards on Sundays. Johnson liked a game of bar billiards. Johnson was on Guinness, Avery was on whisky. They were laughing a good deal; it had been a tough week. Johnson was winning; he went for the lower numbers, methodically, while Avery tried cushion shots at the hundred pocket.

'I wouldn't mind a bit of what Fred's having,' Johnson said with a snigger. He played a shot; a white ball dropped dutifully into its hole. 'Poles are dead randy. Go up anything, a Pole will. Specially Fred, he's a real terror. He's got the walk.'

'Are you that way, Jack?'

'When I'm in the mood. I wouldn't mind a little bit now, as a matter of fact.'

They played a couple of shots, each lost in an alcoholic euphoria of erotic fancy.

'Still,' said Johnson gratefully, 'I'd rather be in our shoes, wouldn't you?'

'Any day.'

'You know,' Johnson said, chalking his cue, 'I shouldn't be speaking to you like this, should I? You've had college and that. You're different class, John.'

They drank to each other, both thinking of Leiser.

'For Christ's sake,' Avery said. 'We're fighting the same war, aren't we?'

'Quite right.'

Johnson poured the rest of the Guinness out of the bottle. He took great care, but a little ran over the side on to the table.

'Here's to Fred,' Avery said.

'To Fred. On the nest. And bloody good luck to him.'

'Good luck, Fred.'

'I don't know how he'll manage the B2,' Johnson murmured. 'He's got a long way to go.'

'Here's to Fred.'

'Fred. He's a lovely boy. Here: do you know this bloke Woodford, the one who picked me up?'

'Of course. He'll be coming down next week.'

'Met his wife at all; Babs? She was a girl, she was; give it to
anyone . . . Christ! Past it now, I suppose. Still, many a good
tune, eh?'

'That's right.'

'To him that hath shalt be given,' Johnson declared.

They drank; that joke went astray.

'She used to go with the admin bloke, Jimmy Gorton. What
happened to him then?'

'He's in Hamburg. Doing very well.'

They got home before Leiser. Haldane was in bed.

It was after midnight when Leiser hung his wet camel-hair
coat in the hall, on a hanger because he was a precise man: tiptoed to the drawing-room and put on the light. His eye ran fondly
over the heavy furniture, the tallboy elaborately decorated with
fretwork and heavy brass handles; the escritoire and the bible
table. Lovingly he revisited the handsome women at croquet,
handsome men at war, disdainful boys in boaters, girls at Cheltenham; a whole long history of discomfort and not a breath of
passion. The clock on the chimney-piece was like a pavilion in
blue marble. The hands were of gold, so ornate, so fashioned, so
flowered and spreading that you had to look twice to see where
the points of them lay. They had not moved since he went away,
perhaps not since he was born, and somehow that was a great
achievement for an old clock.

He picked up his suitcase and went upstairs. Haldane was
coughing but no light came from his room. He tapped on Avery's
door.

'You there, John?'

After a moment he heard him sit up. 'Nice time, Fred?'

'You bet.'

'Woman all right?'

'Just the job. See you tomorrow, John.'

'See you in the morning. Night, Fred. Fred . . .'

'Yes, John?'

'Jack and I had a bit of a session. You should have been there.'

'That's right, John.'

Slowly he made his way along the corridor, content in his weariness, entered his room, took off his jacket, lit a cigarette and threw himself gratefully into the armchair. It was tall and very comfortable, with wings on the side. As he did so he caught sight of something. A chart hung on the wall for turning letters into figures, and beneath it, on the bed, lying in the middle of the eiderdown, was an old suitcase of continental pattern, dark green canvas with leather on the corners. It was open; inside were two boxes of grey steel. He got up, staring at them in mute recognition; reached out and touched them, wary as if they might be hot; turned the dials, stooped and read the legend by the switches. It could have been the set he had in Holland: transmitter and receiver in one box; power unit, key and earphones in the other. Crystals, a dozen of them, in a bag of parachute silk with a green drawstring threaded through the top. He tested the key with his finger; it seemed much smaller than he remembered.

He returned to the armchair, his eyes still fixed upon the suitcase; sat there, stiff and sleepless, like a man conducting a wake.

He was late for breakfast. Haldane said, 'You spend all day with Johnson. Morning and afternoon.'

'No walk?' Avery was busy with his egg.

'Tomorrow perhaps. From now on we're concerned with technique. I'm afraid walks take second place.'

Control quite often stayed in London on Monday nights, which he said was the only time he could get a chair at his club; Smiley suspected he wanted to get away from his wife.

'I hear the flowers are coming out in Blackfriars Road,' he said. 'Leclerc's driving around in a Rolls-Royce.'

'It's a perfectly ordinary Humber,' Smiley retorted. 'From the Ministry pool.'

'Is that where it comes from?' Control asked, his eyebrows very high. 'Isn't it fun? So the black friars have won the pool.'

14

'You know the set, then?' Johnson asked.

'The B2.'

'OK. Official title, Type three, Mark two; runs on AC or a six-volt car battery, but you'll be using the mains, right? They've queried the current where you're going and it's AC. Your mains consumption with this set is fifty-seven watts on transmit and twenty-five on receive. So if you *do* end up somewhere and they've only got DC, you're going to have to borrow a battery, right?'

Leiser did not laugh.

'Your mains lead is provided with adaptors for all continental sockets.'

'I know.'

Leiser watched Johnson prepare the set for operation. First he linked the transmitter and receiver to the power pack by means of six-pin plugs, adjusting the twin claws to the terminals; having plugged in the set and turned it on, he joined the miniature Morse key to the transmitter and the earphones to the receiver.

'That's a smaller key than we had in the war,' Leiser objected. 'I tried it last night. My fingers kept slipping.'

Johnson shook his head.

'Sorry, Fred; same size.' He winked. 'Perhaps your finger's grown.'

'All right, come on.'

Now he extracted from the spares box a coil of multistranded wire, plastic covered, attaching one end to the aerial terminals. 'Most of your crystals will be around the three megacycle mark, so you may not have to change your coil – get a nice stretch on your aerial and you'll be a hundred per cent, Fred; specially at night. Now watch the tuning. You've connected up your aerial, earth, key, headphones and power pack. Look at your signal plan and see what frequency you're on; fish out the corresponding crystal, right?' He held up a small capsule of black bakelite, guided the pins into the double socket – 'Shoving the male ends into the doodahs, like so. All right so far, Fred? Not hurrying you, am I?'

'I'm watching. Don't keep asking.'

'Now turn the crystal selector dial to "fundamental all crystals", and adjust your wave band to match your frequency. If you're on three and a half megs you want the wave-band knob on three to four, like so. Now insert your plug-in coil either way round, Fred; you've got a nice overlap there.'

Leiser's head was supported in his hand as he tried desperately to remember the sequence of movements which once had come so naturally to him. Johnson proceeded with the method of a man born to his trade. His voice was soft and easy, very patient, his hands moving instinctively from one dial to another with perfect familiarity. All the time the monologue continued:

'TRS switch on T for tune; put your anode tuning and aerial matching on ten; now you can switch on your power pack, right?' He pointed to the meter window. 'You should get the three hundred reading, near enough, Fred. Now I'm ready to have a go: I shove my meter selector on three and twiddle the PA tuning till I get maximum meter reading; now I put her on six—'

'What's PA?'

'Power Amplifier, Fred: didn't you know that?'

'Go on.'

'Now I move the anode tuning knob till I get my minimum value – here you are! She's a hundred with the knob on two, right? Now push your TRS over to S – S for send, Fred – and you're ready to tune the aerial. Here – press the key. That's right, see? You get a bigger reading because you're putting power into the aerial, follow it?'

Silently he performed the brief ritual of tuning the aerial until the meter obediently dipped to the final reading.

'And Bob's your uncle!' he declared triumphantly. 'Now it's Fred's turn. Here, your hand's sweating. You must have had a week-end, you must. Wait a minute, Fred!' He left the room, returning with an oversized white pepperpot, from which he carefully sprinkled French chalk over the black lozenge on the key lever.

'Take my advice,' Johnson said, 'just leave the girls in peace, see, Fred? Let it grow.'

Leiser was looking at his open hand. Particles of sweat had gathered in the grooves. 'I couldn't sleep.'

'I'll bet you couldn't.' He slapped the case affectionately. 'From now on you sleep with *her*. She's Mrs Fred, see, and no one else!' He dismantled the set and waited for Leiser to begin. With childish slowness Leiser painfully reassembled the equipment. It was all so long ago.

Day after day Leiser and Johnson sat at the small table in the bedroom tapping out their messages. Sometimes Johnson would drive away in the van leaving Leiser alone, and they would work back and forth till early morning. Or Leiser and Avery would go – Leiser was not allowed out alone – and from a borrowed house in Fairford they would pass their signals, encoding, sending and receiving *en clair* trivialities disguised as amateur transmissions. Leiser discernibly changed. He became nervy and irritable; he complained to Haldane about the complications of transmitting on a series of frequencies, the difficulty of constant retuning, the shortage of time. His relationship to Johnson was always uneasy. Johnson had arrived late, and for some reason Leiser insisted on treating him as an outsider, not admitting him properly to the companionship which he fancied to exist between Avery, Haldane and himself.

There was a particularly absurd scene one breakfast. Leiser

raised the lid of a jam-pot, peered inside and, turning to Avery, asked, 'Is this bee-honey?'

Johnson leant across the table, knife in one hand, bread and butter in the other.

'We don't say that, Fred. We just call it honey.'

'That's right, honey. Bee-honey.'

'Just honey,' Johnson repeated. 'In England we just call it honey.'

Leiser carefully replaced the lid, pale with anger. 'Don't you tell me what to say.'

Haldane looked up sharply from his paper. 'Be quiet, Johnson. Bee-honey is perfectly accurate.'

Leiser's courtesy had something of the servant, his quarrels with Johnson something of the backstairs.

Despite such incidents as this, like any two men engaged daily upon a single project, they came gradually to share their hopes, moods and depressions. If a lesson had gone well, the meal that followed it would be a happy affair. The two of them would exchange esoteric remarks about the state of the ionosphere, the skip distance on a given frequency, or an unnatural meter reading which had occurred during tuning. If badly, they would speak little or not at all, and everyone but Haldane would hasten through his food for want of anything to say. Occasionally Leiser would ask whether he might not take a walk with Avery, but Haldane shook his head and said there was no time. Avery, a guilty lover, made no move to help.

As the two weeks neared their end, the Mayfly house was several times visited by specialists of one kind or another from London. A photographic instructor came, a tall, hollow-eyed man, who demonstrated a sub-miniature camera with interchangeable lenses; there was a doctor, benign and wholly incurious, who listened to Leiser's heart for minutes on end. The Treasury had insisted upon it; there was the question of compensation. Leiser declared he had no dependants, but he was examined all the same to satisfy the Treasury.

With the increase in these activities Leiser came to derive

great comfort from his gun. Avery had given it to him after his
week-end's leave. He favoured a shoulder holster (the drape of
his jackets nicely concealed the bulge) and sometimes at the end
of a long day he would draw the gun and finger it, looking down
the barrel, raising it and lowering it as he had done on the range.
'There isn't a gun to beat it,' he would say. 'Not for the size. You
can have your continental types any time. Women's guns, they
are, like their cars. Take my advice, John, a three-eight's best.'

'Nine-millimetre they call it now.'

His resentment of strangers reached its unexpected climax
HYDE in the visit of Hyde, a man from the Circus. The morning had
gone badly. Leiser had been making a timed run, encoding and
transmitting forty groups; his bedroom and Johnson's were now
linked on an internal circuit; they played back and forth behind
closed doors. Johnson had taught him a number of international
code signs: QRJ, your signals are too weak to read; QRW, send
faster; QSD, your keying is bad; QSM, repeat the last message;
QSZ, send each word twice; QRU, I have nothing for you. As
Leiser's transmission became increasingly uneven, Johnson's
comments, thus cryptically expressed, added to his confusion,
until with a shout of irritation he switched off his set and stalked
downstairs to Avery. Johnson followed him.

'It's no good giving up, Fred.'

'Leave me alone.'

'Look, Fred, you did it all wrong. I *told* you to send the
number of groups *before* you send the message. You can't remember a thing, can you—'

'Look, leave me alone, I said!' He was about to add something
when the door bell rang. It was Hyde. He had brought an assistant,
a plump man who was sucking something against the weather.

They did not play the tapes at lunch. Their guests sat side by
side, eating glumly as if they had the same food every day because of the calories. Hyde was a meagre, dark-faced man without a trace of humour who reminded Avery of Sutherland. He
had come to give Leiser a new identity. He had papers for him to
sign, identity documents, a form of ration card, a driving licence,

a permit to enter the border zone along a specified area, and an old shirt in a briefcase. After lunch he laid them all out on the drawing-room table while the photographer put up his camera.

They dressed Leiser in the shirt and took him full face with both ears showing according to the German regulations, then led him to sign the papers. He seemed nervous.

'We're going to call you Freiser,' Hyde said, as if that were an end to the matter.

'Freiser? That's like my own name.'

'That's the idea. That's what your people wanted. For signatures and things, so that there's no slip-up. You'd better practise it a bit before you sign.'

'I'd rather have it different. Quite different.'

'We'll stick to Freiser, I think,' said Hyde. 'It's been decided at high level.' Hyde was a man who leant heavily upon the Passive Voice.

There was an uncomfortable silence.

'I want it different. I don't like Freiser and I want it different.' He didn't like Hyde either, and in half a minute he was going to say so.

Haldane intervened. 'You're under instructions. The Department has taken the decision. There is no question of altering it now.'

Leiser was very pale.

'Then they can bloody well change the instructions. I want a different name, that's all. Christ, it's only a little thing, isn't it? That's all I'm asking for: another name, a proper one, not a half-cock imitation of my own.'

'I don't understand,' Hyde said. 'It's only training, isn't it?'

'You don't have to understand! Just change it, that's all. Who the hell d'you think you are, coming in here and ordering me about?'

'I'll telephone London,' Haldane said, and went upstairs. They waited awkwardly until he came down.

'Will you accept Hartbeck?' Haldane inquired. There was a note of sarcasm in his voice.

Leiser smiled. 'Hartbeck. That's fine.' He spread out his hands in a gesture of apology. 'Hartbeck's fine.'

Leiser spent ten minutes practising a signature then signed the papers, with a little flourish each time as if there were dust on them. Hyde gave them a lecture on the documents. It took a very long time. There were no actual ration cards in East Germany, Hyde said, but there existed a system of registration with food shops, who provided a certificate. He explained the principle of travel permits and the circumstances under which they were granted, he talked at length about the obligation on Leiser to show his identity card, unasked, when he bought a railway ticket or put up at an hotel. Leiser argued with him and Haldane attempted to terminate the meeting. Hyde paid no attention. When he had finished he nodded and went away with his photographer, folding the old shirt into his briefcase as if it were part of his equipment.

This outburst of Leiser's appeared to cause Haldane some concern. He telephoned to London and ordered his assistant, Gladstone, to go over Leiser's file for any trace of the name Freiser; he had a search made in all the indices, but without success. When Avery suggested Haldane was making too much of the incident the other shook his head. 'We're waiting for the second vow,' he said.

Following upon Hyde's visit, Leiser now received daily briefings about his cover. Stage by stage he, Avery and Haldane constructed in tireless detail the background of the man Hartbeck, establishing him in his work, his tastes and recreations, in his love life and choice of friends. Together, they entered the most obscure corners of the man's conjectured existence, gave him skills and attributes which Leiser himself barely possessed.

Woodford came with news of the Department.

'The Director's putting up a marvellous show.' From the way he spoke, Leclerc might have been fighting an illness. 'We leave for Lübeck a week today. Jimmy Gorton's been on to the German frontier people – he says they're pretty reliable. We've got a crossing point lined up and we've taken a farmhouse on the outskirts of the town. He's let it be known that we're a team of academics wanting a quiet time and a bit of fresh air.' Woodford looked confidingly at Haldane. 'The Department is working wonderfully. As one man. And what a *spirit*, Adrian! No watching the clock these days. And no *rank*. Dennison, Sandford ... we're just a single team. You should see the way Clarkie's going for the Ministry about poor Taylor's pension. How's Mayfly bearing up?' he added in a low voice.

'All right. He's doing wireless upstairs.'

'Any more signs of nerves? Outbreaks or anything?'

'None so far as I know,' Haldane replied, as if he were unlikely to know anyway.

'Is he getting frisky? Sometimes they want a girl about now.'

Woodford had brought drawings of Soviet rockets. They had been made by Ministry draughtsmen from photographs held in Research Section, enlarged to about two foot by three, neatly mounted on showcards. Some were stamped with a security classification. Prominent features were marked with arrows; the nomenclature was curiously childish: fin, cone, fuel compartment, payload. Beside each rocket stood a gay little figure like a penguin in a flying helmet, and printed beneath him: 'size of average man'. Woodford arranged them round the room as if they were his own work; Avery and Haldane watched in silence.

'He can look at them after lunch,' Haldane said. 'Put them together till then.'

'I've brought along a film to give him some background. Launchings, transportation, a bit about destructive capacity. The Director said he should have an idea what these things can do. Give him a shot in the arm.'

'He doesn't need a shot in the arm,' Avery said.

Woodford remembered something. 'Oh – and your little Gladstone wants to talk to you. He said it was urgent – didn't know how to get hold of you. I told him you'd give him a ring when you had time. Apparently you asked him to do a job on the Mayfly area. Industry, was it, or manoeuvres? He says he's got the answer ready for you in London. He's the best type of NCO, that fellow.' He glanced at the ceiling. 'When's Fred coming down?'

Haldane said abruptly, 'I don't want you to meet him, Bruce.' It was unusual in Haldane to use a Christian name. 'I'm afraid you must take luncheon in the town. Charge it to Accounts.'

'Why on earth not?'

'Security. I see no point in his knowing more of us than is strictly necessary. The charts speak for themselves; so, presumably, does the film.'

Woodford, profoundly insulted, left. Avery knew then that Haldane was determined to preserve Leiser in the delusion that the Department housed no fools.

For the last day of the course, Haldane had planned a full-scale exercise to last from ten in the morning until eight in the evening, a combined affair including visual observation in the town, clandestine photography and listening to tapes. The information which Leiser assembled during the day was to be made into a report, encoded and communicated by wireless to Johnson in the evening. A certain hilarity infected the briefing that morning. Johnson made a joke about not photographing the Oxford Constabulary by mistake; Leiser laughed richly and even Haldane allowed himself a wan smile. It was the end of term; the boys were going home.

The exercise was a success. Johnson was pleased; Avery enthusiastic; Leiser manifestly delighted. They had made two faultless transmissions, Johnson said, Fred was steady as a rock. At eight o'clock they assembled for dinner wearing their best suits. A special menu had been arranged. Haldane had presented the rest of his burgundy; toasts were made; there was talk of an annual reunion in years to come. Leiser looked very smart in a dark blue suit and a pale tie of watered silk.

Johnson got rather drunk and insisted on bringing down Leiser's wireless set, raising his glass to it repeatedly and calling it Mrs Hartbeck. Avery and Leiser sat together: the estrangement of the last week over.

The next day, a Saturday, Avery and Haldane returned to London. Leiser was to remain in Oxford with Johnson until the whole party left for Germany on Monday. On the Sunday, an Air Force van would call at the house to collect the suitcase. This would be independently conveyed to Gorton in Hamburg together with Johnson's own base equipment, and thence to the farmhouse near Lübeck from which Operation Mayfly would be launched. Before he left the house Avery took a last look round, partly for reasons of sentiment, and partly because he had signed the lease and was concerned about the inventory.

Haldane was ill at ease on the journey to London. He was still waiting, apparently, for some unknown crisis in Leiser.

15

It was the same evening. Sarah was in bed. Her mother had brought her to London.

'If you ever want me,' he said, 'I'll come to you, wherever you are.'

'You mean when I'm dying.' Analysing, she added, 'I'll do the same for you, John. Now can I repeat my question?'

'Monday. There's a group of us going.' It was like children: parallel playing.

'Which part of Germany?'

'Just Germany, West Germany. For a conference.'

'More bodies?'

'Oh, for God's sake, Sarah, do you think I want to keep it from you?'

'Yes, John, I do,' she said simply. 'I think if you were allowed to tell me you wouldn't care about the job. You've got a kind of licence I can't share.'

'I can only tell you it's a big thing . . . a big operation. With agents. I've been training them.'

'Who's in charge?'

'Haldane.'

'Is that the one who confides in you about his wife? I think he's utterly disgusting.'

'No, that's Woodford. This man's quite different. Haldane's odd. Donnish. Very good.'

'But they're all good, aren't they? Woodford's good too.'

Her mother came in with tea.

'When are you getting up?' he asked.

'Monday, probably. It depends on the doctor.'

'She'll need quiet,' her mother said, and went out.

'If you believe in it, do it,' Sarah said. 'But don't . . .' she broke off, shook her head, little girl now.

'You're jealous. You're jealous of my job and the secrecy. You don't *want* me to believe in my work!'

'Go on. Believe in it if you can.'

For a while they did not look at one another. 'If it weren't for Anthony I really would leave you,' Sarah declared at last.

'What for?' Avery asked hopelessly, and then, seeing the opening, 'Don't let Anthony stop you.'

'You never talk to me: any more than you talk to Anthony. He hardly knows you.'

'What is there to talk about?'

'Oh, God.'

'I can't talk about my work, you know that. I tell you more than I should as it is. That's why you're always sneering at the Department, isn't it? You can't understand it, you don't want to; you don't *like* it being secret but you despise me when I break the rules.'

'Don't go over that again.'

'I'm not coming back,' Avery said. 'I've decided.'

'This time, perhaps you'll remember Anthony's present.'

'I bought him that milk lorry.'

They sat in silence again.

'You ought to meet Leclerc,' said Avery; 'I think you ought to talk to him. He keeps suggesting it. Dinner . . . he might convince you.'

'What of?'

She found a piece of cotton hanging from the seam of her bed-jacket. Sighing, she took a pair of nail scissors from the drawer in the bedside table and cut it off.

'You should have drawn it through at the back,' Avery said. 'You ruin your clothes that way.'

'What are they like?' she asked. 'The agents? Why do they do it?'

'For loyalty, partly. Partly money, I suppose.'

'You mean you bribe them?'

'Oh shut up!'

'Are they English?'

'One of them is. Don't ask me any more, Sarah; I can't tell you.' He advanced his head towards her. 'Don't ask me, Sweet.' He took her hand; she let him.

'And they're all men?'

'Yes.'

Suddenly she said, it was a complete break, no tears, no precision, but quickly, with compassion, as if the speeches were over and this were the choice: 'John, I want to know, I've got to know, now, before you go. It's an awful, unEnglish question, but all the time you've been telling me something, ever since you took this job. You've been telling me people don't matter, that *I* don't, Anthony doesn't; that the agents don't. You've been telling me you've found a vocation. Well, who calls you, that's what I mean: what *sort* of vocation? That's the question you never answer: that's why you hide from me. Are you a martyr, John? Should I admire you for what you're doing? Are you making sacrifices?'

Flatly, avoiding her, Avery replied, 'It's nothing like that. I'm doing a job. I'm a technician; part of the machine. You want me to say double-think, don't you? You want to demonstrate the paradox.'

'No. You've said what I want you to say. You've got to draw a circle and not go outside it. That's not double-think, it's unthink. It's very humble of you. Do you really believe you're that small?'

'You've made me small. Don't sneer. You're making me small now.'

'John, I swear it, I don't mean to. When you came back earlier in the evening you looked as though you'd fallen in love. The kind of love that gives you comfort. You looked free and at peace. I thought for a moment you'd found a woman. That's why

I asked, really it is, whether they were all men . . . I thought you were in love. Now you tell me you're nothing, and you seem proud of that too.'

He waited, then smiling, the smile he gave Leiser, he said, 'Sarah, I missed you terribly. When I was in Oxford I went to the house, the house in Chandos Road, remember? It was fun there, wasn't it?' He gave her hand a squeeze. 'Real fun. I thought about it, our marriage and you. And Anthony. I love you, Sarah; I love you. For everything . . . the way you bring up our baby.' A laugh. 'You're both so vulnerable, sometimes I can hardly tell you apart.'

She remained silent, so he continued, 'I thought perhaps if we lived in the country, bought a house . . . I'm established now: Leclerc would arrange a loan. Then Anthony could run about more. It's only a matter of increasing our range. Going to the theatre, like we used to at Oxford.'

She said absently, 'Did we? We can't go to the theatre in the country, can we?'

'The Department gives me something, don't you understand? It's a real job. It's important, Sarah.'

She pushed him gently away. 'My mother's asked us to Reigate for Christmas.'

'That'll be fine. Look . . . about the office. They owe me something now, after all I've done. They accept me on equal terms. As a colleague. I'm one of them.'

'Then you're not responsible, are you? Just one of the team. So there's no sacrifice.' They were back to the beginning. Avery, not realising this, continued softly, 'I can tell him, can't I? I can tell him you'll come to dinner?'

'For pity's sake, John,' she snapped, 'don't try to run me like one of your wretched agents.'

Haldane, meanwhile, sat at his desk, going through Gladstone's report.

There had twice been manoeuvres in the Kalkstadt area; in 1952 and 1960. On the second occasion the Russians had staged an infantry attack on Rostock with heavy armoured support but no air cover. Little was known of the 1952 exercise, except that a large detachment of troops had occupied the town of Wolken. They were believed to be wearing magenta shoulder-boards. The report was unreliable. On both occasions the area had been declared closed; the restriction had been enforced as far as the northern coast. There followed a long recitation of the principal industries. There was some evidence – it came from the Circus, who refused to release the source – that a new refinery was being constructed on a plateau to the east of Wolken, and that the machinery for it had been transported from Leipzig. It was conceivable (but unlikely) that it had come by rail and been sent by way of Kalkstadt. There was no evidence of civil or industrial unrest, nor of any incident which could account for a temporary closure of the town.

A note from Registry lay in his in-tray. They had put up the files he had asked for, but some were Subscription Only; he would have to read them in the library.

He went downstairs, opened the combination lock on the steel door of General Registry, groped vainly for the light switch. Finally he made his way in the dark between the shelves to the small, windowless room at the back of the building where documents of special interest or secrecy were kept. It was pitch dark. He struck a match, put on the light. On the table were two sets of files: *Mayfly*, heavily restricted, now in its third volume, with a subscription list pasted on the cover, and Deception (*Soviet and East Germany*), an immaculately kept collection of papers and photographs in hard folders.

After glancing briefly at the Mayfly files he turned his attention to the folders, thumbing his way through the depressing miscellany of rogues, double agents and lunatics who in every conceivable corner of the earth, under every conceivable pretext, had attempted, sometimes successfully, to delude the Western intelligence agencies. There was the boring similarity of technique; the grain of truth carefully reconstructed, culled from newspaper reports and bazaar gossip; the follow-up, less carefully done, betraying the deceiver's contempt for the deceived; and finally the flight of fancy, the stroke of artistic impertinence which wantonly terminated a relationship already under sentence.

On one report he found a flag with Gladstone's initials; written above them in his cautious, rounded hand were the words: 'Could be of interest to you.'

It was a refugee report of Soviet tank trials near Gustweiler. It was marked: 'Should not issue. Fabrication.' There followed a long justification citing passages in the report which had been abstracted almost verbatim from a 1949 Soviet military manual. The originator appeared to have enlarged every dimension by a third, and added some ingenious flavouring of his own. Attached were six photographs, very blurred, purporting to have been taken from a train with a telephoto lens. On the back of the photographs was written in McCulloch's careful hand: 'Claims to have used Exa-two camera, East German manufacture. Cheap housing. Exakta-range lens. Low shutter speed. Negatives very blurred owing to camera shake from train. Fishy.' It was all very inconclusive. The same make of camera, that was all. He locked up the Registry and went home. Not his duty, Leclerc had said, to prove that Christ was born on Christmas Day; any more, Haldane reflected, than it was his business to prove that Taylor had been murdered.

Woodford's wife added a little soda to her Scotch, a splash: it was habit rather than taste.

'Sleep in the office, my foot,' she said. 'Do you get operational subsistence?'

'Yes, of course.'

'Well, it *isn't* a conference then, is it? A conference isn't operational. Not unless,' she added with a giggle, 'you're having it in the Kremlin.'

'All right, it's not a conference. It's an operation. That's why I'm getting subsistence.'

She looked at him cruelly. She was a thin, childless woman, her eyes half shut from the smoke of the cigarette in her mouth.

'There's nothing going on at all. You're making it up.' She began laughing, a hard false laugh. 'You poor sod,' she said and laughed again, derisively. 'How's little Clarkie? You're all scared of him, aren't you? Why don't you ever say anything against him? Jimmy Gorton used to: *he* saw through him.'

'Don't mention Jimmy Gorton to me!'

'Jimmy's *lovely*.'

'Babs, I warn you!'

'Poor Clarkie. Do you remember,' his wife asked reflectively, 'that nice little dinner he gave us in his club? The time he remembered it was our turn for welfare? Steak and kidney and frozen peas.' She sipped her whisky. 'And warm gin.' Something struck her. 'I wonder if he's ever had a woman,' she said. 'Christ, I wonder why I never thought of that before?'

Woodford returned to safer ground.

'All right, so nothing's going on.' He got up, a silly grin on his face, collected some matches from the desk.

'You're not smoking that damn pipe in here,' she said automatically.

'So nothing's going on,' he repeated smugly, and lit his pipe, sucking noisily.

'God, I hate you.'

Woodford shook his head, still grinning. 'Never mind,' he urged, 'just never mind. You said it, my dear, I didn't. I'm not sleeping in the office so everything's fine, isn't it? So I didn't go to Oxford either; I didn't even go to the Ministry; I haven't got a car to bring me home at night.'

She leant forward, her voice suddenly urgent, dangerous. 'What's happening?' she hissed. 'I've got a right to know, haven't I? I'm your wife, aren't I? You tell those little tarts in the office, don't you? Well, tell me!'

'We're putting a man over the border,' Woodford said. It was his moment of victory. 'I'm in charge of the London end. There's a crisis. There could even be a war. It's a damn ticklish thing.' The match had gone out, but he was still swinging it up and

down with long movements of his arm, watching her with triumph in his eyes.

'You bloody liar,' she said. 'Don't give me that.'

Back in Oxford, the pub at the corner was three-quarters empty.
They had the saloon bar to themselves. Leiser sipped a White
Lady while the wireless operator drank best bitter at the De-
partment's expense.

'Just take it gently, that's all you got to do, Fred,' he urged
kindly. 'You came up lovely on the last run through. We'll hear
you, don't worry about that – you're only eighty miles from the
border. It's a piece of cake as long as you remember your procedure. Take it gently on the tuning or we're all done for.'

'I'll remember. Not to worry.'

'Don't get all bothered about the Jerries picking it up; you're
not sending love letters, just a handful of groups. Then a new
call sign and a different frequency. They'll never home in on
that, not for the time you're there.'

'Perhaps they can, these days,' Leiser said. 'Maybe they got
better since the war.'

'There'll be all sorts of other traffic getting in their hair;
shipping, military, air control, Christ knows what. They're not
supermen, Fred; they're like us. A dozy lot. Don't worry.'

'I'm not worried. They didn't get me in the war; not for long.'

'Now listen, Fred, how about this? One more drink and we'll
slip home and just have a nice run through with Mrs Hartbeck.
No lights, mind. In the dark: she's shy, see? Get it a hundred per
cent before we turn in. Then tomorrow we'll take it easy. After
all, it's Sunday tomorrow, isn't it?' he added solicitously.

'I want to sleep. Can't I sleep a little, Jack?'

'Tomorrow, Fred. Then you can have a nice rest.' He nudged
Leiser's elbow. 'You're married now, Fred. Can't always go to
sleep, you know. You've taken the vow, that's what we used to say.'

'All right, forget about it, will you?' Leiser sounded on edge.
'Just leave it alone, see?'

'Sorry, Fred.'

'When do we go to London?'

'Monday, Fred.'

'Will John be there?'

'We meet him at the airport. And the Captain. They wanted us to have a bit more practice . . . on the routine and that.'

Leiser nodded, drumming his second and third fingers lightly on the table as if he were tapping the key.

'Here – why don't you tell us about one of those girls you had on your weekend in London?' Johnson suggested.

Leiser shook his head.

'Come on, then, let's have the other half and you give us a nice game of billiards.'

Leiser smiled shyly, his irritation forgotten. 'I got a lot more money than you, Jack. White Lady's an expensive drink. Not to worry.'

He chalked his cue and put in the sixpence. 'I'll play you double or quits; for last night.'

'Look, Fred,' Johnson pleaded gently. 'Don't always go for the big money, see, trying to put the red into the hundred slot. Just take the twenties and fifties – they mount up, you know. Then you'll be home and dry.'

Leiser was suddenly angry. He put his cue back in the cradle and took down his camel-hair coat from its peg.

'What's the matter, Fred, what the hell's the matter now?'

'For Christ's sake let me loose! Stop behaving like a bloody gaoler. I'm going on a job, like we all did in the war. I'm not sitting in the hanging cell.'

'Don't you be daft,' Johnson said gently, taking his coat and putting it back on the peg. 'Anyway we don't say hanging, we say condemned.'

Carol put the coffee on the desk in front of Leclerc. He looked up brightly and said thank you, tired but well drilled, like a child at the end of a party.

'Adrian Haldane's gone home,' Carol observed. Leclerc went back to the map.

'I looked in his room. He might have said goodnight.'

'He never does,' Leclerc said proudly.

'Is there anything I can do?'

'I never remember how you turn yards into metres.'

'Neither do I.'

'The Circus say this gully is two hundred metres long. That's about two hundred and fifty yards, isn't it?'

'I think so. I'll get the book.'

She went to her room and took a ready-reckoner from the bookcase.

'One metre is thirty-nine point three seven inches,' she read. 'A hundred metres is a hundred and nine yards and thirteen inches.'

Leclerc wrote it down.

'I think we should make a confirmatory telegram to Gorton. Have your coffee first, then come in with your pad.'

'I don't want any coffee.'

'Routine Priority will do, we don't want to haul old Jimmy out of bed.' He ran his small hand briskly over his hair. 'One. Advance party, Haldane, Avery, Johnson and Mayfly arrive BEA flight so and so, such and such a time December nine.' He glanced up. 'Get the details from Administration. Two. All will travel under their own names and proceed by train to Lübeck. For security reasons you will not repeat not meet party at airport but you may discreetly contact Avery by telephone at Lübeck base. We can't put him on to old Adrian,' he observed with a short laugh. 'The two of them don't hit it off at all . . .' He raised his voice: 'Three. Party number two consisting of Director only arriving morning flight December ten. You will meet him at airport for short conference before he proceeds to Lübeck. Four. Your role is discreetly to provide advice and assistance at all stages in order to bring operation Mayfly to successful conclusion.'

She stood up.

'Does John Avery have to go? His poor wife hasn't seen him for weeks.'

'Fortunes of war,' Leclerc replied without looking at her. 'How long does a man take to crawl two hundred and twenty yards?' he muttered. 'Oh, Carol – put another sentence on to that telegram: Five. Good Hunting. Old Jimmy likes a bit of encouragement, stuck out there all on his own.'

He picked a file from the in-tray and looked critically at the cover, aware perhaps of Carol's eyes upon him.

'Ah.' A controlled smile. 'This must be the Hungarian report. Did you ever meet Arthur Fielden in Vienna?'

'No.'

'A nice fellow. Rather your type. One of our best chaps . . . knows his way around. Bruce tells me he's done a very good report on unit changes in Budapest. I must get Adrian to look at it. Such a *lot* going on just now.' He opened the file and began reading.

Control said: 'Did you speak to Hyde?'

'Yes.'

'Well, what did he say? What have they got down there?'

Smiley handed him a whisky and soda. They were sitting in Smiley's house in Bywater Street. Control was in the chair he preferred, nearest the fire.

'He said they'd got first-night nerves.'

'Hyde said that? Hyde used an expression like that? How extraordinary.'

'They've taken over a house in North Oxford. There was just this one agent, a Pole of about forty, and they wanted him documented as a mechanic from Magdeburg, a name like Freiser. They wanted travel papers to Rostock.'

'Who else was there?'

'Haldane and that new man, Avery. The one who came to me about the Finnish courier. And a wireless operator, Jack Johnson. We had him in the war. No one else at all. So much for their big team of agents.'

'What *are* they up to? And whoever gave them all that money just for *training*? We lent them some equipment, didn't we?'

'Yes, a B2.'

'What on earth's that?'

'A wartime set,' Smiley replied with irritation. 'You said it was all they could have. That and the crystals. Why on earth did you bother with the crystals?'

'Just charity. A B2 was it? Oh well,' Control observed with apparent relief. 'They wouldn't get far with *that*, would they?'

'Are you going home tonight?' Smiley asked impatiently.

'I thought you might give me a bed here,' Control suggested. 'Such a *fag* always traipsing home. It's the people . . . They seem to get worse every time.'

Leiser sat at the table, the taste of the White Ladies still in his mouth. He stared at the luminous dial of his watch, the suitcase open in front of him. It was eleven eighteen; the second hand struggled jerkily towards twelve. He began tapping, JAJ, JAJ, – you can remember that, Fred, my name's Jack Johnson, see? – he switched over to receive, and there was Johnson's reply, steady as a rock.

Take your time, Johnson had said, don't rush your fences. We'll be listening all night, there are plenty more schedules. By the beam of a small torch he counted the encoded groups. There were thirty-eight. Putting out the torch he tapped a three and an eight; numerals were easy but long. His mind was very clear. He could hear Jack's gentle repetitions all the time: You're too quick on your shorts, Fred, a dot is one third of a dash, see? That's longer than you think. Don't rush the gaps, Fred; five dots between each word, three dots between each letter. Forearm horizontal, in a straight line with the key lever; elbow just clear of the body. It's like knife-fighting, he thought with a little smile, and began keying. Fingers loose, Fred, relax, wrist clear of the table. He tapped out the first two groups, slurring a little on the gaps, but not as much as he usually did. Now came the third group: put in the safety signal. He tapped an S, cancelled it and tapped the next ten groups, glancing now and then at the dial of his watch. After two and a half minutes he went off the air, groped for the small capsule which contained the crystal, discovered with the tips of his fingers the twin sockets of the housing, inserted it, then stage by stage followed the tuning procedure, moving the dials, flashing his torch on the crescent window to watch the black tongue tremble across it.

He tapped out the second call sign, PRE, PRE, switched quickly to receive and there was Johnson again, QRK4, your signal readable. For the second time he began transmitting, his hand moving slowly but methodically as his eye followed the meaningless letters, until with a nod of satisfaction he heard Johnson's reply: Signal received. QRU: I have nothing for you.

When they had finished Leiser insisted on a short walk. It was bitterly cold. They followed Walton Street as far as the main gates of Worcester, thence by way of Banbury Road once more to the respectable sanctuary of their dark North Oxford house.

16

Take-off

It was the same wind. The wind that had tugged at Taylor's frozen body and drove the rain against the blackened walls of Blackfriars Road, the wind that flailed the grass of Port Meadow now ran headlong against the shutters of the farmhouse.

The farmhouse smelt of cats. There were no carpets. The floors were of stone: nothing would dry them. Johnson lit the tiled oven in the hall as soon as they arrived but the damp still lay on the flagstones, collecting in the dips like a tired army. They never saw a cat all the time they were there, but they smelt them in every room. Johnson left corned beef on the doorstep: it was gone in ten minutes.

It was built on one floor with a high granary roof, of brick, and lay against a small coppice beneath a vast Flemish sky, a long, rectangular building with cattle sheds on the sheltered side. It was two miles north of Lübeck. Leclerc had said they were not to enter the town.

A ladder led to the loft, and there Johnson installed his wireless, stretching the aerial between the beams, thence through a skylight to an elm tree beside the road. He wore plimsolls in the house, brown ones of military issue, and a blazer with a squadron crest. Gorton had had food delivered from the Naafi in Celle. It covered the kitchen floor in old cardboard boxes, with an invoice marked 'Mr Gorton's party'. There were two bottles of gin and three of whisky. They had two bedrooms; Gorton had sent Army beds, two to each room, and reading lights with standard green shades. Haldane was very angry about the beds. 'He must have told every damned department in the area,' he complained. 'Cheap whisky, Naafi food, army beds. I suppose we shall find he requisitioned the house next. God, what a way to mount an operation.'

It was late afternoon when they arrived. Johnson, having put up his set, busied himself in the kitchen. He was a domesticated man; he cooked and washed up without complaint, treading lightly over the flagstones in his neat plimsolls. He assembled a hash of bully beef and egg, and gave them cocoa with a great deal of sugar. They ate in the hall in front of the stove. Johnson did most of the talking; Leiser, very quiet, scarcely touched his food.

'What's the matter, Fred? Not hungry, then?'

'Sorry, Jack.'

'Too many sweets on the plane, that's your trouble.' Johnson winked at Avery. 'I saw you giving that air hostess a look. You shouldn't do it, Fred, you know, you'll break her heart.' He frowned round the table in mock disapproval. 'He really looked her over, you know. A proper tip-to-toe job.'

Avery grinned dutifully. Haldane ignored him.

Leiser was concerned about the moon, so after supper they stood at the back door in a small shivering group, staring at the sky. It was strangely light; the clouds drifted like black smoke, so low that they seemed to mingle with the swaying branches of the coppice and half obscure the grey fields beyond.

'It will be darker at the border, Fred,' said Avery. 'It's higher ground; more hills.'

Haldane said they should have an early night; they drank another whisky and at quarter past ten they went to bed, Johnson and Leiser to one room, Avery and Haldane to the other. No one dictated the arrangement. Each knew, apparently, where he belonged.

It was after midnight when Johnson came into their room. Avery was woken by the squeak of his rubber shoes.

'John, are you awake?'

Haldane sat up.

'It's about Fred. He's sitting alone in the hall. I told him to try and sleep, sir; gave him a couple of tablets, the kind my mother takes; he wouldn't even get into bed at first, now he's gone along to the hall.'

Haldane said, 'Leave him alone. He's all right. None of us can sleep with this damned wind.'

Johnson went back to his room. An hour must have passed; there was still no sound from the hall. Haldane said, 'You'd better go and see what he's up to.'

Avery put on his overcoat and went along the corridor, past tapestries of biblical quotations and an old print of Lübeck harbour. Leiser was sitting on a chair beside the tiled oven.

'Hullo, Fred.'

He looked old and tired.

'It's near here, isn't it, where I cross?'

'About five kilometres. The Director will brief us in the morning. They say it's quite an easy run. He'll give you all your papers and that kind of thing. In the afternoon we'll show you the place. They've done a lot of work on it in London.'

'In London,' Leiser repeated, and suddenly: 'I did a job in Holland in the war. The Dutch were good people. We sent a lot of agents to Holland. Women. They were all picked up. You were too young.'

'I read about it.'

'The Germans caught a radio operator. Our people didn't know. They just went on sending more agents. They said there was nothing else to do.' He was talking faster. 'I was only a kid then; just a quick job they wanted, in and out. They were short of operators. They said it didn't matter me not speaking Dutch, the reception party would meet me at the drop. All I had to do was work the set. There'd be a safe house ready.' He was far away. 'We fly in and nothing moves, not a shot or a searchlight, and I'm jumping. And when I land, there they are: two men and a woman. We say the words and they take me to the road to get the bikes. There's no time to bury the parachute – we aren't bothering by then. We find the house and they give me food. After supper we go upstairs where the set is – no schedules, London listened all the time in those days. They give the message: I'm sending a call sign – "Come in TYR, come in TYR" – then the message in front of me, twenty-one groups, four-letter.'

He stopped.

'Well?'

'They were following the message, you see; they wanted to know where the safety signal came. It was in the ninth letter; a back shift of one. They let me finish the message and then they were on me, one hitting me, men all over the house.'

'But *who*, Fred? Who's *they*?'

'You can't talk about it like that: you never know. It's never that easy.'

'But for God's sake, whose fault was it? Who did it? Fred!'

'Anyone's. You can never tell. You'll learn that.' He seemed to have given up.

'You're alone this time. Nobody has been told. Nobody's expecting you.'

'No. That's right.' His hands were clasped on his lap. He made a hunched figure, small and cold. 'In the war it was easier because, however bad it got, you thought one day we'd win. Even if you were picked up, you thought, "They'll come and get me, they'll drop some men or make a raid." You knew they never would, see, but you could think it. You just wanted to be left alone to think it. But nobody wins this one, do they?'

'It's not the same. But more important.'

'What do you do if I'm caught?'

'We'll get you back. Not to worry, eh, Fred?'

'Yes, but how?'

'We're a big outfit, Fred. A lot goes on you don't know about. Contacts here and there. You can't see the whole picture.'

'Can you?'

'Not all of it, Fred. Only the Director sees it all. Not even the Captain.'

'What's he like, the Director?'

'He's been in it a long time. You'll see him tomorrow. He's a very remarkable man.'

'Does the Captain fancy him?'

'Of course.'

'He never talks about him,' Leiser said.

'None of us talk about him.'

'There was this girl I had. She worked in the bank. I told her I was going away. If anything goes wrong I don't want anything said, see. She's just a kid.'

'What was her name?'

A moment of mistrust. 'Never mind. But if she turns up just keep it all right with her.'

'What do you mean, Fred?'

'Never mind.'

Leiser didn't talk after that. When the morning came Avery returned to his room.

'What's it all about?' Haldane asked.

'He was in some mess in the war, in Holland. He was betrayed.'

'But he's giving us a second chance. How nice. Just what they always said.' And then: 'Leclerc arrives this morning.'

His taxi came at eleven. Leclerc was getting out almost before it had pulled up. He was wearing a duffel coat, heavy brown shoes for rough country and a soft cap. He looked very well.

'Where's Mayfly?'

'With Johnson,' Haldane said.

'Got a bed for me?'

'You can have Mayfly's when he's gone.'

At eleven thirty Leclerc held a briefing; in the afternoon they were to make a tour of the border.

The briefing took place in the hall. Leiser came in last. He stood in the doorway, looking at Leclerc, who smiled at him winningly, as if he liked what he saw. They were about the same height.

Avery said, 'Director, this is Mayfly.'

His eyes still on Leiser, Leclerc replied, 'I think I'm allowed to call him Fred. Hullo.' He advanced and shook him by the hand, both formal, two weather men coming out of a box.

'Hullo,' said Leiser.

'I hope they haven't been working you too hard?'

'I'm all right, sir.'

'We're all very impressed,' Leclerc said. 'You've done a grand job.' He might have been talking to his constituents.

'I haven't started yet.'

'I always feel the training is three-quarters of the battle. Don't you, Adrian?'

'Yes.'

They sat down. Leclerc stood a little away from them. He had hung a map on the wall. By some indefinable means – it may have been his maps, it may have been the precision of his language, or it may have been his strict deportment, which so elusively combined purpose with restraint – Leclerc evoked in that hour that same nostalgic, campaigning atmosphere which had informed the briefing in Blackfriars Road a month before. He had the illusionist's gift, whether he spoke of rockets or wireless transmission, of cover or the point at which the border was to be crossed, of implying great familiarity with his subject.

'Your target is Kalkstadt' – a little grin – 'hitherto famous only for a remarkably fine fourteenth-century church.' They laughed, Leiser too. It was so good, Leclerc knowing about old churches.

He had brought a diagram of the crossing point, done in different inks, with the border drawn in red. It was all very simple. On the western side, he said, there was a low, wooded hill overgrown with gorse and bracken. This ran parallel to the border until the southern end curved eastwards in a narrow arm stopping about two hundred and twenty yards short of the border, directly opposite an observation tower. The tower was set well back from the demarcation line: at its foot ran a fence of barbed wire. It had been observed that this wire was laid out in a single apron and only loosely fixed to its staves. East German guards had been seen to detach it in order to pass through and patrol the undefended strip of territory which lay between the demarcation line and the physical border. That afternoon Leclerc would indicate the precise staves. Mayfly, he said, should not be alarmed at having to pass so close to the tower; experience had shown that the attention of the guards was concentrated on the more distant parts of their area; the night was ideal; a high wind was forecast; there would be no moon. Leclerc had set the crossing time for 0235 hours; the guard changed at midnight, each watch lasted three hours. It was reasonable to suppose that the sentries would not be as alert after two and a half hours on duty as they would be at the start of their watches. The relief guard, which had to approach from a barrack some distance to the north, would not yet be under way.

Much attention had been given, Leclerc continued, to the possibility of mines. They would see from the map – the little forefinger traced the green dotted line from the end of the rise across the border – that there was an old footpath which did indeed follow the very route which Leiser would be taking. The frontier guards had been seen to avoid this path, striking a track of their own some ten yards to the south of it. The assumption was, Leclerc said, that the path was mined, while the area to the side of it had been left clear for the benefit of patrols. Leclerc proposed that Leiser should use the track made by the frontier guards.

Wherever possible over the two hundred-odd yards between the foot of the hill and the tower, Leiser should crawl, keeping his head below the level of the bracken. This eliminated the small danger that he would be sighted from the tower. He would be comforted to hear, Leclerc added with a smile, that there was no record of any patrol operating on the western side of the wire during the hours of darkness. The East German guards seemed to fear that one of their own number might slip away unseen.

Once across the border Leiser should keep clear of any path. The country was rough, partly wooded. The going would be hard but all the safer for that; he was to head south. The reason for this was simple. To the south, the border turned westward for some ten kilometres. Thus Leiser, by moving southwards, would put himself not two but fifteen kilometres from the border, and more quickly escape the zonal patrols which guarded the eastern approaches. Leclerc would advise him thus – he withdrew one hand casually from the pocket of his duffel coat and lit a cigarette, conscious all the time of their eyes upon him – march east for half an hour, then turn due south, making for the Marienhorst lake. At the eastern end of the lake was a disused boathouse. There he could lie up for an hour and give himself some food. By that time Leiser might care for a drink – relieved laughter – and he would find a little brandy in his rucksack.

Leclerc had a habit, when making a joke, of holding himself at attention and lifting his heels from the ground as if to launch his wit upon the higher air.

'I couldn't have something with gin, could I?' Leiser asked. 'White Lady's my drink.'

There was a moment's bewildered silence.

'That wouldn't do at all,' Leclerc said shortly, Leiser's master.

Having rested, he should walk to the village of Marienhorst and look around for transport to Schwerin. From then on, Leclerc added lightly, he was on his own.

'You have all the papers necessary for a journey from Magdeburg to Rostock. When you reach Schwerin, you are on the legitimate route. I don't want to say too much about cover because you have been through that with the Captain. Your name is Fred Hartbeck, you are an unmarried mechanic from Magdeburg with an offer of employment at the State Co-operative ship-building works at Rostock.' He smiled, undeterred. 'I am sure you have all been through every detail of this already. Your love life, your pay, medical history, war service and the rest. There is just one thing that *I* might add about cover. Never *volunteer* information. People don't *expect* you to explain yourself. If you are cornered, play it by ear. Stick as closely to the truth as you can. Cover,' he declared, stating a favourite maxim, 'should never be *fabricated* but only an extension of the truth.' Leiser laughed in a reserved way. It was as if he could have wished Leclerc a taller man.

Johnson brought coffee from the kitchen, and Leclerc said briskly, 'Thank you, Jack,' as if everything were quite as it should be.

Leclerc now addressed himself to the question of Leiser's target; he gave a résumé of the indicators, implying somehow that they only confirmed suspicions which he himself had long harboured. He employed a tone which Avery had not heard in him before. He sought to imply, as much by omission and inference as by direct allusion, that theirs was a Department of enormous skill and knowledge, enjoying in its access to money, its intercourse with other services and in the unchallenged authority of its judgements an unearthly, oracular immunity, so that Leiser might well have wondered why, if all this were so, he need bother to risk his life at all.

'The rockets are in the area now,' Leclerc said. 'The Captain has told you what signs to look for. We want to know what they look like, where they are and above all who mans them.'

'I know.'

'You must try the usual tricks. Pub gossip, tracing an old soldier friend, you know the kind of thing. When you find them, come back.'

Leiser nodded.

'At Kalkstadt there's a workers' hostel.' He unfolded a chart of the town. 'Here. Next to the church. Stay there if you can. You may run into people who have actually been engaged . . .'

'I know,' Leiser repeated. Haldane stirred, glanced at him anxiously.

'You might even hear something of a man who used to be employed at the station, Fritsche. He gave us some interesting details about the rockets, then disappeared. If you get the chance, that is. You could ask at the station, say you're a friend of his . . .'

There was a very slight pause.

'Just disappeared,' Leclerc repeated, for them, not for himself. His mind was elsewhere. Avery watched him anxiously, waiting for him to go on. At last he said, rapidly, 'I have deliberately avoided the question of communication,' indicating by his tone that they were nearly done. 'I imagine you have gone over that enough times already.'

'No worries there,' Johnson said. 'All the schedules are at night. That leaves the frequency range pretty simple. He'll have a clear hand during the day, sir. We've had some very nice dummy runs, haven't we, Fred?'

'Oh yes. Very nice.'

'As regards getting back,' Leclerc said, 'we play the war rules. There are no submarines any more, Fred; not for this kind of thing. When you return, you should report at once to the nearest British Consulate or Embassy, give your proper name and ask to be repatriated. You should represent yourself as a distressed British subject. My instinct would be to advise you to come out the way you went in. If you're in trouble, don't necessarily move west straight away. Lie up for a bit. You're taking plenty of money.'

Avery knew he would never forget that morning, how they had sat at the farmhouse table like sprawling boys at the Nissen-hut desks, their strained faces fixed upon Leclerc as in the stillness of a church he read the liturgy of their devotion, moving his little hand across the map like a priest with the taper. All of them in that room – but Avery perhaps best of all – knew the fatal disproportion between the dream and reality, between motive and action. Avery had talked to Taylor's child, stammered out his half-formed lies to Peersen and the Consul: he had heard that dreadful footfall in the hotel, and returned from a nightmare journey to see his own experiences remade into the images of Leclerc's world. Yet Avery, like Haldane and Leiser, listened to Leclerc with the piety of an agnostic, feeling perhaps that this was how, in some clean and magic place, it really ought to be.

'Excuse me,' said Leiser. He was looking at the plan of Kalk-stadt. He was very much the small man just then. He might have been pointing to a fault in an engine. The station, hostel and church were marked in green; an inset at the bottom left-hand corner depicted the railway warehouses and dumping sheds. At each side, the point of the compass was given adjecti-vally: Western Prospect, Northern Prospect.

'What's a prospect, sir?' Leiser inquired.

'A view, an outlook.'

'What's it for? What's it for on the map, please?'

Leclerc smiled patiently. 'For purposes of orientation, Fred.'

Leiser got up and examined the chart closely. 'And this is the church?'

'That's right, Fred.'

'Why does it face north? Churches go from east to west. You've got the entrance on the eastern side where the altar should be.'

Haldane leant forward, the index finger of his right hand resting on his lip.

'It's only a sketch map,' Leclerc said. Leiser returned to his place and sat to attention, straighter than ever. 'I see. Sorry.'

When the meeting was over Leclerc took Avery on one side. 'Just one point, John, he's not to take a gun. It's quite out of the question. The Minister was adamant. Perhaps you'll mention it to him.'

'No gun?'

'I think we can allow the knife. That could be a general-purpose thing; I mean if anything went wrong we could say it was general purpose.'

After lunch they made a tour of the border – Gorton had pro-vided a car. Leclerc brought with him a handful of notes he had made from the Circus frontier report, and these he kept on his knee, together with a folded map.

The extreme northern part of the frontier which divides the

two halves of Germany is largely a thing of depressing inconse-
quence. Those who look eagerly for dragon's teeth and substantial
fortifications will be disappointed. It crosses land of considerable variety; gullies and small hills overgrown with bracken and
patches of untended forest. Often the Eastern defences are set so
far behind the demarcation line as to be hidden from Western
eyes – only a forward pillbox, crumbling roads, a vacated farmhouse or an occasional observation tower excite the imagination.

By way of emphasis the Western side is adorned with the
grotesque statuary of political impotence: a plywood model of
the Brandenburg Gate, the screws rusting in their sockets, rises
absurdly from an untended field; notice boards, broken by wind
and rain, display fifteen-year-old slogans across an empty valley.
Only at night, when the beam of a searchlight springs from the
darkness and draws its wavering finger across the cold earth,
does the heart chill for the captive crouching like a hare in the
plough, waiting to break cover and run in terror till he fall.

They followed an unmade road along the top of a hill, and
wherever it ran close to the frontier they stopped the car and
got out. Leiser was shrouded in a mackintosh and hat. The day
was very cold. Leclerc wore his duffel coat and carried a shooting stick – Heaven knows where he had found it. The first time
they stopped, and the second, and again at the next, Leclerc said
quietly, 'Not this one.' As they got into the car for the fourth
time he declared, 'The next stop is ours.' It was the kind of brave
joke favoured in battle.

Avery would not have recognised the place from Leclerc's
sketch map. The hill was there, certainly, turning inwards towards the frontier, then descending sharply to the plain below.
But the land beyond it was hilly and partly wooded, its horizon
fringed with trees against which, with the aid of glasses, they
could discern the brown shape of a wooden tower. 'It's the three
staves to the left,' Leclerc said. As they scanned the ground,
Avery could make out here and there the worn mark of the old
path.

'It's mined. The path is mined the whole way. Their territory begins at the foot of the hill.' Leclerc turned to Leiser. 'You start from here.' He pointed with his shooting stick. 'You proceed to the brow of the hill and lie up till take-off time. We'll have you here early so that your eyes grow used to the light. I think we should go now. We mustn't attract attention, you know.'

As they drove back to the farmhouse the rain came bursting against the windscreen, thundering on the roof of the car. Avery, sitting next to Leiser, was sunk in his own thoughts. He realised with what he took to be utter detachment that, whilst his own mission had unfolded as comedy, Leiser was to play the same part as tragedy; that he was witnessing an insane relay race in which each contestant ran faster and longer than the last, arriving nowhere but at his own destruction.

'Incidentally,' he said suddenly, addressing himself to Leiser, 'hadn't you better do something about your hair? I don't imagine they have much in the way of lotions over there. A thing like that could be insecure.'

'He needn't cut it,' Haldane observed. 'The Germans go in for long hair. Just wash it, that's all that's needed. Get the oil out. A nice point, John, I congratulate you.'

17

The rain had stopped. The night came slowly, struggling with the wind. They sat at the table in the farmhouse, waiting; Leiser was in his bedroom. Johnson made tea and attended to his equipment. No one talked. The pretending was over. Not even Leclerc, master of the public-school catchword, bothered any more. He seemed to resent being made to wait, that was all, at the tardy wedding of an unloved friend. They had relapsed into a state of somnolent fear, like men in a submarine, while the lamp over their heads rocked gently. Now and then Johnson would be sent to the door to look for the moon, and each time he announced that there was none.

'The met reports were pretty good,' Leclerc observed, and drifted away to the attic to watch Johnson check his equipment.

Avery, alone with Haldane, said quickly, 'He says the Ministry's ruled against the gun. He's not to take it.'

'And what bloody fool told him to consult the Ministry in the first place?' Haldane demanded, beside himself with anger. Then: 'You'll have to tell him. It depends on you.'

'Tell Leclerc?'

'No, you idiot; Leiser.'

They had some food and afterwards Avery and Haldane took Leiser to his bedroom.

'We must dress you up,' they said.

They made him strip, taking from him piece by piece his warm, expensive clothes: jacket and trousers of matching grey, cream silk shirt, black shoes without toecaps, socks of dark blue nylon. As he loosened the knot of his tartan tie his fingers discovered the gold pin with the horse's head. He unclipped it carefully and held it out to Haldane.

'What about this?'

Haldane had provided envelopes for valuables. Into one of these he slipped the tie-pin, sealed it, wrote on the back, tossed it on the bed.

'You washed your hair?'

'Yes.'

'We had difficulty in obtaining East German soap. I'm afraid you'll have to try and get some when you're over there. I understand it's in short supply.'

'All right.'

He sat on the bed naked except for his watch, crouched forward, his broad arms folded across his hairless thighs, his white skin mottled from the cold. Haldane opened a trunk and extracted a bundle of clothes and half a dozen pairs of shoes.

As Leiser put on each unfamiliar thing, the cheap, baggy trousers of coarse serge, broad at the foot and gathered at the waist, the grey, threadbare jacket with arched pleats, the shoes, brown with a bright unhealthy finish, he seemed to shrink before their eyes, returning to some former estate which they had only guessed at. His brown hair, free from oil, was streaked with grey and fell undisciplined upon his head. He glanced shyly at them, as if he had revealed a secret; a peasant in the company of his masters.

'How do I look?'

'Fine,' Avery said. 'You look marvellous, Fred.'

'What about a tie?'

'A tie would spoil it.'

He tried the shoes one after another, pulling them with difficulty over the coarse woollen socks.

'They're Polish,' Haldane said, giving him a second pair. 'The Poles export them to East Germany. You'd better take these as well – you don't know how much walking you'll have to do.'

Haldane fetched from his own bedroom a heavy cashbox and unlocked it.

First he took a wallet, a shabby brown one with a centre compartment of Cellophane which held Leiser's identity card, fingered and stamped it; it lay open behind its flat frame, so that the photograph of Leiser looked outwards, a little prison picture. Beside it was an authority to travel and a written offer of employment from the State Co-operative for ship-building in Rostock. Haldane emptied one pocket of the wallet and then replaced the contents paper for paper, describing each in turn.

'Food registration card – driving licence ... Party card. How long have you been a Party member?'

'Since 'forty-nine.'

He put in a photograph of a woman and three or four grimy letters, some still in their envelopes.

'Love letters,' he explained shortly.

Next came a Union card and a cutting from a Magdeburg newspaper about production figures at a local engineering works; a photograph of the Brandenburg Gate before the war, a tattered testimonial from a former employer.

'That's the wallet, then,' Haldane said. 'Except for the money. The rest of your equipment is in the rucksack. Provisions and that kind of thing.'

He handed Leiser a bundle of banknotes from the box. Leiser stood in the compliant attitude of a man being searched, his arms raised a little from his sides and his feet slightly apart. He would accept whatever Haldane gave him, put it carefully away, then resume the same position. He signed a receipt for the money. Haldane glanced at the signature and put the paper in a black briefcase which he had put separately on a side table.

Next came the odds and ends which Hartbeck would plausibly have about him: a bunch of keys on a chain – the key to the suitcase was among them – a comb, a khaki handkerchief stained with oil and a couple of ounces of substitute coffee in a twist of newspaper; a screwdriver, a length of fine wire and fragments of metal ends newly turned – the meaningless rubble of a working man's pockets.

'I'm afraid you can't take that watch,' Haldane said.

Leiser unbuckled the gold armband and dropped the watch into Haldane's open palm. They gave him a steel one of Eastern manufacture and set it with great precision by Avery's bedside clock.

Haldane stood back. 'That will do. Now remain there and go through your pockets. Make sure things are where you would naturally keep them. Don't touch anything else in the room, do you understand?'

'I know the form,' said Leiser, glancing at his gold watch on the table. He accepted the knife and hooked the black scabbard into the waistband of his trousers.

'What about my gun?'

Haldane guided the steel clip of the briefcase into its housing and it snapped like the latch of a door.

'You don't take one,' Avery said.

'No gun?'

'It's not on, Fred. They reckon it's too dangerous.'

'Who for?'

'It could lead to a dangerous situation. Politically, I mean. Sending an armed man into East Germany. They're afraid of an incident.'

'Afraid.'

For a long time he stared at Avery, his eyes searching the young, unfurrowed face for something that was not there. He turned to Haldane.

'Is that true?'

Haldane nodded.

Suddenly he thrust out his empty hands in front of him, cupped in a terrible gesture of poverty, the fingers crooked and pressed together as if to catch the last water, his shoulders trembling in the cheap jacket, his face drawn, half in supplication, half in panic.

'The gun, John! You can't send a man without a gun! For mercy's sake, let me have the gun!'

'Sorry, Fred.'

His hands still extended, he swung round to Haldane. 'You don't know what you're doing!'

Leclerc had heard the noise and came to the doorway. Haldane's face was arid as rock; Leiser could have beaten his empty fists upon it for all the charity it held. His voice fell to a whisper. 'What are you doing? God Christ, what are you trying to do?' To both of them he cried in revelation, 'You hate me, don't you! What have I done to you? John, what have I done? We were pals, weren't we?'

Leclerc's voice, when at last he spoke, sounded very pure, as if he were deliberately emphasising the gulf between them.

'What's the trouble?'

'He's worried about the gun,' Haldane explained.

'I'm afraid there's nothing we can do. It's out of our hands. You know how we feel about it, Fred. Surely you know that. It's an order, that's all. Have you forgotten how it used to be?' He added stiffly, a man of duty and decision, 'I can't question my orders: what do you want me to say?'

Leiser shook his head. His hands fell to his sides. The discipline had gone out of his body.

'Never mind.' He was looking at Avery.

'A knife's better in some ways, Fred,' Leclerc added consolingly, 'quieter.'

'Yes.'

Haldane picked up Leiser's spare clothes. 'I must put these into the rucksack,' he said, and with a sideways glance at Avery, walked quickly from the room, taking Leclerc with him. Leiser and Avery looked at one another in silence. Avery was embarrassed to see him so ugly. At last Leiser spoke.

'It was us three. The Captain, you and me. It was all right, then. Don't worry about the others, John. They don't matter.'

'That's right, Fred.'

Leiser smiled. 'It was the best ever, that week, John. It's

funny, isn't it: we spend all our time chasing girls, and it's the men that matter; just the men.'

'You're one of us, Fred. You always were; all the time your card was there, you were one of us. We don't forget.'

'What does it look like?'

'It's two pinned together. One for then, one for now. It's in the index . . . live agents, we call it. Yours is the first name. You're the best man we've got.' He could imagine it now; the index was something they had built together. He could believe in it, like love.

'You said it was alphabetical order,' Leiser said sharply. 'You said it was a special index for the best.'

'Big cases go to the front.'

'And men all over the world?'

'Everywhere.'

Leiser frowned as if it were a private matter, a decision to be privately taken. He stared slowly round the bare room, then at the cuffs on his coarse jacket, then at Avery, interminably at Avery, until, taking him by the wrist, but lightly, more to touch than to lead, he said under his breath, 'Give us something. Give me something to take. From you. Anything.'

Avery felt in his pockets, pulling out a handkerchief, some loose change and a twist of thin cardboard, which he opened. It was the photograph of Taylor's little girl.

'Is that your kid?' Leiser looked over the other's shoulder at the small, bespectacled face; his hand closed on Avery's. 'I'd like that.' Avery nodded. Leiser put it in his wallet, then picked up his watch from the bed. It was gold with a black dial for the phases of the moon. 'You have it,' he said. 'Keep it. I've been trying to remember,' he continued, 'at home. There was this school. A big courtyard like a barracks with nothing but windows and drainpipes. We used to bang a ball round after lunch. Then a gate, and a path to the church, and the river on the other side . . .' He was laying out the town with his hands, placing bricks. 'We went on Sunday, through the side door, the kids last, see?' A smile of success. 'That church was facing north,' he declared, 'not east at all.' Suddenly he asked: 'How long; how long have you been in, John?'

'In the outfit?'

'Yes.'

'Four years.'

'How old were you then?'

'Twenty-eight. It's the youngest they take you.'

'You told me you were thirty-four.'

'They're waiting for us,' Avery said.

In the hall they had the rucksack and the suitcase, green canvas with leather corners. He tried the rucksack on, adjusting the straps until it sat high on his back, like a German school-boy's satchel. He lifted the suitcase and felt the weight of the two things together.

'Not too bad,' he muttered.

'It's the minimum,' Leclerc said. They had begun to whis-per, though no one could hear. One by one they got into the car.

A hurried handshake and he walked away towards the hill. There were no fine words; not even from Leclerc. It was as if they had all taken leave of Leiser long ago. The last they saw of him was the rucksack gently bobbing as he disappeared into the dark-ness. There had always been a rhythm about the way he walked.

18

Leiser lay in the bracken on the spur of the hill, stared at the luminous dial of his watch. Ten minutes to wait. The key chain was swinging from his belt. He put the keys back in his pocket, and as he drew his hand away he felt the links slip between his thumb and finger like the beads of a rosary. For a moment he let them linger there; there was comfort in their touch; they were where his childhood was. St Christopher and all his angels, please preserve us from road accidents.

Ahead of him the ground descended sharply, then evened out. He had seen it; he knew. But now, as he looked down, he could make out nothing in the darkness below him. Suppose it were marshland down there? There had been rain; the water had drained into the valley. He saw himself struggling through mud to his waist, carrying the suitcase above his head, the bullets splashing round him.

He tried to discern the tower on the opposite hill, but if it was there it was lost against the blackness of the trees.

Seven minutes. Don't worry about the noise, they said, the wind will carry it south. They'll hear nothing in a wind like this. Run beside the path, on the south side, that means to the right, keep on the new trail through the bracken, it's narrow but clear. If you meet anyone, use your knife, but for the love of Heaven don't go near the path.

His rucksack was heavy. Too heavy. So was the case. He'd quarrelled about it with Jack. He didn't care for Jack. 'Better be on the safe side, Fred,' Jack had explained. 'These little sets are sensitive as virgins: all right for fifty miles, dead as mutton on sixty. Better to have the margin, Fred, then we know where we are. They're experts, real experts where this one comes from.'

One minute to go. They'd set his watch by Avery's clock.

He was frightened. Suddenly he couldn't keep his mind from it any more. Perhaps he was too old, too tired, perhaps he'd done enough. Perhaps the training had worn him out. He felt his heart pounding in his chest. His body wouldn't stand any more; he hadn't the strength. He lay there, talking to Haldane: Christ, Captain, can't you see I'm past it? The old body's cracking up. That's what he'd tell them; he would stay there when the minute hand came up, he would stay there too heavy to move. 'It's my heart, it's packed in,' he'd tell them. 'I've had a heart attack, skipper, didn't tell you about my dickie heart, did I? It just came over me as I lay here in the bracken.'

He stood up. Let the dog see the rabbit.

Run down the hill, they'd said; in this wind they won't hear a thing; run down the hill, because that's where they may spot you, they'll be looking at that hillside hoping for a silhouette. Run fast through the moving bracken, keep low and you'll be safe. When you reach level ground, lie up and get your breath back, then begin the crawl.

He was running like a madman. He tripped and the rucksack brought him down, he felt his knee against his chin and the pain as he bit his tongue, then he was up again and the suitcase swung him round. He half fell into the path and waited for the flash of a bursting mine. He was running down the slope, the ground gave way beneath his heels, the suitcase rattling like an old car. Why wouldn't they let him take the gun? The pain rose in his chest like fire, spreading under the bone, burning the lungs: he counted each step, he could feel the thump of each footfall and the slowing drag of the case and rucksack. Avery had lied. Lied all the way. Better watch that cough, Captain; better see a doctor, it's like barbed wire in your guts. The ground levelled out; he fell again and lay still, panting like an animal, feeling nothing but fear and the sweat that drenched his woollen shirt.

He pressed his face to the ground. Arching his body, he slid his hand beneath his belly and tightened the belt of his rucksack.

He began crawling up the hill, dragging himself forward with his elbows and his hands, pushing the suitcase in front of him, conscious all the time of the hump on his back rising above the undergrowth. The water was seeping through his clothes; soon it ran freely over his thighs and knees. The stink of leaf mould filled his nostrils; twigs tugged at his hair. It was as if all nature conspired to hold him back. He looked up the slope and caught sight of the observation tower against the line of black trees on the horizon. There was no light on the tower.

He lay still. It was too far: he could never crawl so far. It was quarter to three by his watch. The relief guard would be coming from the north. He unbuckled his rucksack, stood up, holding it under his arm like a child. Taking the suitcase in his other hand he began walking cautiously up the rise, keeping the trodden path to his left, his eyes fixed upon the skeleton outline of the tower. Suddenly it rose before him like the dark bones of a monster.

The wind clattered over the brow of the hill. From directly above him he could hear the slats of old timber banging, and the long creak of a casement. It was not a single apron but double; when he pulled, it came away from the staves. He stepped across, reattached the wire and stared into the forest ahead. He felt even in that moment of unspeakable terror while the sweat blinded him and the throbbing of his temples drowned the rustling of the wind, a full, confiding gratitude towards Avery and Haldane, as if he knew they had deceived him for his own good.

Then he saw the sentry, like the silhouette in the range, not ten yards from him, back turned, standing on the old path, his rifle slung over his shoulder, his bulky body swaying from left to right as he stamped his feet on the sodden ground to keep them from freezing. Leiser could smell tobacco – it was past him in a second – and coffee warm like a blanket. He put down the rucksack and suitcase and moved instinctively towards him; he might have been in the gymnasium at Headington. He felt the haft sharp in his hand, cross-hatched to prevent slip. The sentry was quite a young boy under his greatcoat; Leiser was surprised how young. He killed him hurriedly, one blow, as a fleeing man might shoot into a crowd; shortly; not to destroy but to preserve; impatiently, for he had to get along; indifferently because it was a fixture.

'Can you see anything?' Haldane repeated.

'No.' Avery handed him the glasses. 'He just went into the dark.'

'Can you see a light from the watch-tower? They'd shine a light if they heard him.'

'No, I was looking for Leiser,' Avery answered.

'You should have called him Mayfly,' Leclerc objected from behind. 'Johnson knows his name now.'

'I'll forget it, sir.'

'He's over, anyway,' Leclerc said and walked back to the car. They drove home in silence.

As they entered the house Avery felt a friendly touch upon his shoulder and turned, expecting to see Johnson; instead he found himself looking into the hollow face of Haldane, but so altered, so manifestly at peace, that it seemed to possess the youthful calm of a man who has survived a long illness; the last pain had gone out of him.

'I am not given to eulogies,' Haldane said.

'Do you think he's safely over?'

'You did well.' He was smiling.

'We'd have heard, wouldn't we? Heard the shots or seen the lights?'

'He's out of our care. Well done.' He yawned. 'I propose we go early to bed. There is nothing more for us to do. Until to-morrow night, of course.' At the door he stopped, and without turning his head he remarked, 'You know, it doesn't seem real.

In the war, there was no question. They went or they refused. Why did he go, Avery? Jane Austen said money or love, those were the only two things in the world. Leiser didn't go for money.'

'You said one could never know. You said so the night he telephoned.'

'He told me it was hate. Hatred for the Germans; and I didn't believe him.'

'He went anyway. I thought that was all that mattered to you, you said you didn't trust motive.'

'He wouldn't do it for hatred, we know that. What is he, then? We never knew him, did we? He's near the mark, you know; he's on his deathbed. What does he think of? If he dies now, tonight, what will be in his mind?'

'You shouldn't speak like that.'

'Ah.' At last he turned and looked at Avery and the peace had not left his face. 'When we met him he was a man without love. Do you know what love is? I'll tell you: it is whatever you can still betray. We ourselves live without it in our profession. We don't force people to do things for us. We let them discover love. And, of course, Leiser did, didn't he? He married us for money, so to speak, and left us for love. He took his second vow. I wonder when.'

Avery said quickly, 'What do you mean, for money?'

'I mean whatever we gave to him. Love is what he gave to us. I see you have his watch, incidentally.'

'I'm keeping it for him.'

'Ah. Goodnight. Or good morning, I suppose.' A little laugh. 'How quickly one loses one's sense of time.' Then he commented, as if to himself: 'And the Circus helped us all the way. It's most strange. I wonder why.'

Very carefully Leiser rinsed the knife. The knife was dirty and must be washed. In the boathouse, he ate the food and drank the brandy in the flask. 'After that,' Haldane had said, 'you live off the land; you can't run around with tinned meat and French brandy.' He opened the door and stepped outside to wash his hands and face in the lake.

The water was quite still in the darkness. Its unruffled surface was like a perfect skin shrouded with floating veils of grey mist. He could see the reeds along the bank; the wind, subdued by the approach of dawn, touched them as it moved across the water. Beyond the lake hung the shadow of low hills. He felt rested and at peace. Until the memory of the boy passed over him like a shudder.

He threw the empty meat can and the brandy bottle far out, and as they hit the water a heron rose languidly from the reeds. Stooping, he picked up a stone and sent it skimming across the lake. He heard it bounce three times before it sank. He threw another but he couldn't beat three. Returning to the hut he fetched his rucksack and suitcase. His right arm was aching painfully, it must have been from the weight of the case. From somewhere came the bellow of cattle.

He began walking east, along the track which skirted the lake. He wanted to get as far as he could before morning came.

He must have walked through half a dozen villages. Each was empty of life, quieter than the open road because they gave a moment's shelter from the rising wind. There were no signposts and no new buildings, it suddenly occurred to him. That was where the peace came from, it was the peace of no innovation – it might have been fifty years ago, a hundred. There were no street lights, no gaudy signs on the pubs or shops. It was the darkness of indifference, and it comforted him. He walked into it like a tired man breasting the sea; it cooled and revived him like the wind; until he remembered the boy. He passed a farmhouse. A long drive led to it from the road. He stopped. Half-way up the drive stood a motorbike, an old mackintosh thrown over the saddle. There was no one in sight.

The oven smoked gently.

'When did you say his first schedule was?' Avery asked. He had asked already.

'Johnson said twenty-two twenty. We start scanning an hour before.'

'I thought he was on a fixed frequency,' Leclerc muttered, but without much interest.

'He may start with the wrong crystal. It's the kind of thing that happens under strain. It's safest for base to scan with so many crystals.'

'He must be on the road by now.'

'Where's Haldane?'

'Asleep.'

'How can anyone sleep at a time like this?'

'It'll be daylight soon.'

'Can't you do something about that fire?' Leclerc asked. 'It shouldn't smoke like that, I'm sure.' He shook his head, suddenly, as if shaking off water and said, 'John, there's a most interesting report from Fielden. Troop movements in Budapest. Perhaps when you get back to London . . .' He lost the thread of his sentence and frowned.

'You mentioned it,' Avery said softly.

'Yes, well, you must take a look at it.'

'I'd like to. It sounds very interesting.'

'It does, doesn't it?'

'Very.'

'You know,' he said – he seemed to be reminiscing – 'they *still* won't give that wretched woman her pension.'

He sat very straight on the motorbike, elbows in as if he were at table. It made a terrible noise; it seemed to fill the dawn with sound, echoing across the frosted fields and stirring the roosting poultry. The mackintosh had leather pieces on the shoulders; as he bounced along the unmade road its skirts fluttered behind, rattling against the spokes of the rear wheel. Daylight came.

Soon he would have to eat. He couldn't understand why he was so hungry. Perhaps it was the exercise. Yes, it must be the exercise. He would eat, but not in a town, not yet. Not in a café where strangers came. Not in a café where the boy had been.

He drove on. His hunger taunted him. He could think of nothing else. His hand held down the throttle and drove his ravening body forward. He turned on to a farm track and stopped.

The house was old, falling with neglect; the drive overgrown with grass, pitted with cart tracks. The fences were broken. There was a terraced garden once partly under plough, now left as if it were beyond all use.

A light burnt in the kitchen window. Leiser knocked at the door. His hand was trembling from the motorbike. No one came; he knocked again, and the sound of his knocking frightened him. He thought he saw a face, it might have been the shadow of the boy sinking across the window as he fell, or the reflection of a swaying branch.

He returned quickly to his motorbike, realizing with terror that his hunger was not hunger at all but loneliness. He must lie up somewhere and rest. He thought: I've forgotten how it takes you. He drove on until he came to the wood, where he lay down. His face was hot against the bracken.

It was evening; the fields were still light but the wood in which he lay gave itself swiftly to the darkness, so that in a moment the red pines had turned to columns of black.

He picked the leaves from his jacket and laced up his shoes. They pinched badly at the instep. He never had a chance to wear them in. He caught himself thinking, it's all right for them, and he remembered that nothing ever bridged the gulf between the man who went and the man who stayed behind, between the living and the dying.

He struggled into the harness of his rucksack and once again felt gratefully the hot, raw pain in his shoulders as the straps found the old bruises. Picking up the suitcase he walked across the field to the road where the motorbike was waiting; five kilometres to Langdorn. He guessed it lay beyond the hill: the first of the three towns. Soon he would meet the road block; soon he would have to eat.

He drove slowly, the case across his knees, peering ahead all the time along the wet road, straining his eyes for a line of red lights or a cluster of men and vehicles. He rounded a bend and saw to his left a house with a beer sign propped in the window. He entered the forecourt; the noise of the engine brought an old man to the door. Leiser lifted the bike on to its stand.

'I want a beer,' he said, 'and some sausage. Have you got that here?'

The old man showed him inside, sat him at a table in the front room from which Leiser could see his motorbike parked in the yard. He brought him a bottle of beer, some sliced sausage and a piece of black bread; then stood at the table watching him eat.

'Where are you making for?' His thin face was shaded with beard.

'North.' Leiser knew this game.

'Where are you from?'

'What's the next town?'

'Langdorn.'

'Far?'

'Five kilometres.'

'Somewhere to stay?'

The old man shrugged. It was a gesture not of indifference nor of refusal, but of negation, as if he rejected everything and everything rejected him.

'What's the road like?' Leiser asked.

'It's all right.'

'I heard there was a diversion.'

'No diversion,' the old man said, as if a diversion were hope, or comfort, or companionship; anything that might warm the damp air or lighten the corners of the room.

'You're from the east,' the man declared. 'One hears it in the voice.'

'My parents,' he said. 'Any coffee?'

The old man brought him coffee, very black and sour, tasting of nothing.

'You're from Wilmsdorf,' the old man said. 'You've got a Wilmsdorf registration.'

'Much custom?' Leiser asked, glancing at the door.

The old man shook his head.

'Not a busy road, eh?' Still the old man said nothing. 'I've got a friend near Kalkstadt. Is that far?'

'Not far. Forty kilometres. They killed a boy near Wilmsdorf.'

'He runs a café. On the northern side. The Tom Cat. Know it at all?'

'No.'

Leiser lowered his voice. 'They had trouble there. A fight. Some soldiers from the town. Russians.'

'Go away,' the old man said.

He tried to pay him but he only had a fifty-mark note.

'Go away,' the old man repeated.

Leiser picked up the suitcase and rucksack. 'You old fool,' he said roughly. 'What do you think I am?'

'You are either good or bad, and both are dangerous. Go away.'

There was no road block. Without warning he was in the centre of Langdorn; it was already dark; the only lights in the main street stole from the shuttered windows, barely reaching the wet cobbles. There was no traffic. He was alarmed by the din of his motorbike; it sounded like a trumpet blast across the market square. In the war, Leiser thought, they went to bed early to keep warm; perhaps they still did.

It was time to get rid of the motorbike. He drove through the town, found a disused church and left it by the vestry door. Walking back into the town he made for the railway station. The official wore uniform.

'Kalkstadt. Single.'

The official held out his hand. Leiser took a banknote from his wallet and gave it to him. The official shook it impatiently.

For a moment Leiser's mind went blank while he looked stupidly at the flicking fingers in front of him and the suspicious, angry face behind the grille.

Suddenly the official shouted: 'Identity card!'

Leiser smiled apologetically. 'One forgets,' he said, and opened his wallet to show the card in the Cellophane window.

'Take it out of the wallet,' the official said. Leiser watched him examine it under the light on his desk.

'Travel authority?'

'Yes, of course.' Leiser handed him the paper.

'Why do you want to go to Kalkstadt if you are travelling to Rostock?'

'Our co-operative in Magdeburg sent some machinery by rail to Kalkstadt. Heavy turbines and some tooling equipment. It has to be installed.'

'How did you come this far?'

'I got a lift.'

'The granting of lifts is forbidden.'

'One must do what one can these days.'

'These days?'

The man pressed his face against the glass, looking down at Leiser's hands.

'What's that you're fiddling with down there?' he demanded roughly.

'A chain; a key chain.'

'So the equipment has to be installed. Well? Go on!'

'I can do the job on the way. The people in Kalkstadt have been waiting six weeks already. The consignment was delayed.'

'So?'

'We made inquiries . . . of the railway people.'

'And?'

'They didn't reply.'

'You've got an hour's wait. It leaves at six thirty.' A pause. 'You heard the news? They've killed a boy at Wilmsdorf,' he said. 'Swine.' He handed him his change.

He had nowhere to go; he dared not deposit his luggage.

There was nothing else to do. He walked for half an hour, then returned to the station. The train was late.

'You both deserve great credit,' Leclerc said, nodding gratefully at Haldane and Avery. 'You too, Johnson. From now on there's nothing any of us can do: it's up to Mayfly.' A special smile for Avery: 'How about you, John; you've been keeping very quiet? Do you think you've profited from the experience?' He added with a laugh, appealing to the other two, 'I do hope we shan't have a divorce on our hands; we must get you home to your wife.'

He was sitting at the edge of the table, his small hands folded tidily on his knee. When Avery said nothing he declared brightly, 'I had a ticking-off from Carol, you know, Adrian; breaking up the young home.'

Haldane smiled as if it were an amusing notion. 'I'm sure there's no danger of that,' he said.

'He made a great hit with Smiley, too; we must see they don't poach him away!'

19

When the train reached Kalkstadt, Leiser waited until the other passengers had left the platform. An elderly guard collected the tickets. He looked a kindly man.

'I'm looking for a friend,' Leiser said. 'A man called Fritsche. He used to work here.'

The guard frowned.

'Fritsche?'

'Yes.'

'What was his first name?'

'I don't know.'

'How old, then; how old about?'

He guessed: 'Forty.'

'Fritsche, here, at this station?'

'Yes. He had a small house down by the river; a single man.'

'A whole house? And worked at this station?'

'Yes.'

The guard shook his head. 'Never heard of him.' He peered at Leiser. 'Are you sure?' he said.

'That's what he told me.' Something seemed to come back to him. 'He wrote to me in November ... he complained that Vopos had closed the station.'

'You're mad,' the guard said. 'Goodnight.'

'Goodnight,' Leiser replied; as he walked away he was conscious all the time of the man's gaze upon his back.

There was an inn in the main street called the Old Bell. He waited at the desk in the hall and nobody came. He opened a door and found himself in a big room, dark at the farther end. A girl sat at a table in front of an old gramophone. She was slumped forward, her head buried in her arms, listening to the music. A single light burnt above her. When the record stopped she played it again, moving the arm of the record player without lifting her head.

'I'm looking for a room,' Leiser said. 'I've just arrived from Langdorn.'

There were stuffed birds round the room: herons, pheasants and a kingfisher. 'I'm looking for a room,' he repeated. It was dance music, very old.

'Ask at the desk.'

'There's no one there.'

'They have nothing, anyway. They're not allowed to take you. There's a hostel near the church. You have to stay there.'

'Where's the church?'

With an exaggerated sigh she stopped the record, and Leiser knew she was glad to have someone to talk to.

'It was bombed,' she declared. 'We just talk about it still. There's only the tower left.'

Finally he said, 'Surely they've got a bed here? It's a big place.' He put his rucksack in a corner and sat at the table next to her. He ran a hand through his thick dry hair.

'You look all in,' the girl said.

His blue trousers were still caked with mud from the border. 'I've been on the road all day. Takes a lot out of you.'

She stood up self-consciously and went to the end of the room where a wooden staircase led upwards towards a glimmer of light. She called out but no one came.

'Steinhäger?' she asked him from the dark.

'Yes.'

She returned with a bottle and a glass. She was wearing a mackintosh, an old brown one of military cut with epaulettes and square shoulders.

'Where are you from?' she asked.

'Magdeburg. I'm making north. Got a job in Rostock.' How many more times would he say it? 'This hostel; do I get a room to myself?'

'If you want one.'

The light was so poor that at first he could scarcely make her out. Gradually she came alive. She was about eighteen, and heavily built; quite a pretty face but bad skin. The same age as the boy; older perhaps.

'Who are you?' he asked. She said nothing. 'What do you do?'

She took his glass and drank from it, looking at him precociously over the brim as if she were a great beauty. She put it down slowly, still watching him, touched the side of her hair. She seemed to think her gestures mattered. Leiser began again:

'Been here long?'

'Two years.'

'What do you do?'

'Whatever you want.' Her voice was quite earnest.

'Much going on here?'

'It's dead. Nothing.'

'No boys?'

'Sometimes.'

'Troops?' A pause.

'Now and then. Don't you know it's forbidden to ask that?'

Leiser helped himself to more Steinhäger from the bottle. She took his glass, fumbling with his fingers.

'What's wrong with this town?' he asked. 'I tried to come here six weeks ago. They wouldn't let me in. Kalkstadt, Langdorn, Wolken, all closed, they said. What was going on?'

Her fingertips played over his hand.

'What was up?' he repeated.

'Nothing was closed.'

'Come off it,' Leiser laughed. 'They wouldn't let me near the place, I tell you. Road blocks here and on the Wolken road.' He thought: it's eight twenty; only two hours till the first schedule.

'Nothing was closed.' Suddenly she added, 'So you came from the west: you came by road. They're looking for someone like you.'

He stood up to go. 'I'd better find the hostel.' He put some money on the table. The girl whispered, 'I've got my own room. In a new flat behind the Friedensplatz. A workers' block. They don't mind. I'll do whatever you want.'

Leiser shook his head. He picked up his luggage and went to the door. She was still looking at him and he knew she suspected him.

'Goodbye,' he said.

'I won't say anything. Take me with you.'

'I had a Steinhäger,' Leiser muttered. 'We didn't even talk. You played your record all the time.' They were both frightened.

The girl said, 'Yes. Records all the time.'

'It was never closed, you are sure of that? Langdorn, Wolken, Kalkstadt, six weeks ago?'

'What would anyone close this place for?'

'Not even the station?'

She said quickly, 'I don't know about the station. The area was closed for three days in November. No one knows why. Russian troops stayed, about fifty. They were billeted in the town. Mid November.'

'Fifty? Any equipment?'

'Lorries. There were manoeuvres farther north, that's the rumour. Stay with me tonight. Stay with me! Let me come with you. I'll go anywhere.'

'What colour shoulder-boards?'

'I don't remember.'

'Where did they come from?'

'They were new. Some came from Leningrad, two brothers.'

'Which way did they go?'

'North. Listen, no one will ever know. I don't talk, I'm not the kind. I'll give it to you, anything you want.'

'Towards Rostock?'

'They said they were going to Rostock. They said not to tell. The Party came round all the houses.'

Leiser nodded. He was sweating. 'Goodbye,' he said.

'What about tomorrow, tomorrow night? I'll do whatever you want.'

'Perhaps. Don't tell anyone, do you understand?'

She shook her head. 'I won't tell them,' she said, 'because I don't care. Ask for the Hochhaus behind the Friedensplatz. Apartment nineteen. Come any time. I'll open the door. You give two rings and they know it's for me. You needn't pay. Take care,' she said. 'There are people everywhere. They've killed a boy in Wilmsdorf.'

He walked to the market square, correct again because everything was closing in, looking for the church tower and the hostel. Huddled figures passed him in the darkness; some wore pieces of uniform; forage caps and the long coats they had in the war. Now and then he would glimpse their faces, catching them in the pale glow of a street light and he would seek in their locked, unseeing features the qualities he hated. He would say to himself, 'Hate him – he is old enough,' but it did not stir him. They were nothing. Perhaps in some other town, some other place, he would find them and hate them; but not here. These were old and nothing; poor, like him, and alone. The tower was black and empty. It reminded him suddenly of the turret on the border, and the garage after eleven, of the moment when he killed the sentry: just a kid, like himself in the war; even younger than Avery.

'He should be there by now,' Avery said.

'That's right, John. He should be there, shouldn't he? One hour to go. One more river to cross.' He began singing. No one took him up.

They looked at each other in silence.

'Know the Alias Club at all?' Johnson asked suddenly. 'Off Villiers Street? A lot of the old gang meet up there. You ought to come along one evening, when we get home.'

'Thanks,' Avery replied. 'I'd like to.'

'It gets nice Christmas time,' he said. 'That's when I go. A good crowd. There's even one or two come in uniform.'

'It sounds fine.'

'They have a mixed do at New Year. You could take your wife.'

'Grand.'

Johnson winked. 'Or your fancy-girl.'

'Sarah's the only girl for me,' Avery said.

The telephone was ringing. Leclerc rose to answer it.

20

Homecoming

He put down the rucksack and the suitcase and looked round the walls. There was an electric point beside the window. The door had no lock so he pushed the armchair against it. He took off his shoes and lay on the bed. He thought of the girl's fingers on his hands and the nervous movement of her lips; he remembered her deceitful eyes watching him from the shadows and he wondered how long it would be before she betrayed him.

He remembered Avery: the warmth and English decency of their early companionship; he remembered his young face glistening in the rain, and his shy, dazzled glance as he dried his spectacles, and he thought: he must have said thirty-two all the time. I misheard.

He looked at the ceiling. In an hour he would put up the aerial.

The room was large and bare with a round marble basin in one corner. A single pipe ran from it to the floor and he hoped to God it would do for the earth. He ran some water and to his relief it was cold, because Jack had said a hot pipe was dicey. He drew his knife and carefully scraped the pipe clean on one side. The earth was important; Jack had said so. If you can't do anything else, he'd said, lay your earth wire zig-zag fashion under the carpet, the same length as the aerial. But there was no carpet; the pipe would have to do. No carpet, no curtains.

Opposite him stood a heavy wardrobe with bow doors. The place must once have been the main hotel. There was a smell of

Turkish tobacco and rank, unscented disinfectant. The walls were of grey plaster; the damp had spread over them in dark shadows, arrested here and there by some mysterious inner property of the house which had dried a path across the ceiling. In some places the plaster had crumbled with the damp, leaving a ragged island of white mildew; in others it had contracted and the plasterer had returned to fill the cavities with paste which described white rivers along the corners of the room. Leiser's eye followed them carefully while he listened for the smallest sound outside.

There was a picture on the wall of workers in a field, leading a horse plough. On the horizon was a tractor. He heard Johnson's benign voice running on about the aerial: 'If it's indoors it's a headache, and indoors it'll be. Now listen: zig-zag fashion across the room, quarter the length of your wave and one foot below the ceiling. Space them wide as possible, Fred, and not parallel to metal girders, electric wires and that. And don't double her back on herself, Fred, or you'll muck her up properly, see?' Always the joke, the copulative innuendo to aid the memory of simple men.

Leiser thought: I'll take it to the picture frame, then back and forth to the far corner. I can put a nail into that soft plaster; he looked around for a nail or pin, and noticed a bronze hanger on one of the pelmets. He got up, unscrewed the handle of his razor. The thread began to the right, it was considered an ingenious detail, so that a suspicious man who gave the handle a casual twist to the left would be going against the thread. From the recess he extracted the knot of silk cloth which he smoothed carefully over his knee with his thick fingers. He found a pencil in his pocket and sharpened it, not moving from the edge of his bed because he did not want to disturb the silk cloth. Twice the point broke; the shavings collected on the floor at his feet. He began writing in the notebook, capital letters, like a prisoner writing to his wife, and every time he made a full stop he drew a ring round it the way he was taught long ago.

The message composed, he drew a line after every two letters, and beneath each compartment he entered the numerical
equivalent according to the chart he had memorised: sometimes
he had to resort to a mnemonic rhyme in order to recall the
numbers; sometimes he remembered wrong and had to rub out
and begin again. When he had finished he divided the line of
numbers into groups of four and deducted each in turn from
the groups on the silk cloth; finally he converted the figures
into letters again and wrote out the result, redividing them into
groups of four.

Fear like an old pain had again taken hold of his belly so that
with every imagined sound he looked sharply towards the door,
his hand arrested in the middle of writing. But he heard nothing; just the creaking of an ageing house, like the noise of wind
in the rigging of a ship.

He looked at the finished message, conscious that it was too
long, and that if he were better at that kind of thing, if his mind
were quicker, he could reduce it, but just now he couldn't think
of a way, and he knew, he had been taught, better put in a word
or two too many than make it ambiguous the other end. There
were forty-two groups.

He pushed the table away from the window and lifted the
suitcase; with the key from his chain he unlocked it, praying all
the time that nothing was broken from the journey. He opened
the spares box, discovering with his trembling fingers the silk
bag of crystals bound with green ribbon at the mouth. Loosening the ribbon, he shook the crystals on to the coarse blanket
which covered the bed. Each was labelled in Johnson's handwriting, first the frequency and below it a single figure denoting the
place where it came in the signal plan. He arranged them in line,
pressing them on to the blanket so that they lay flat. The crystals
were the easiest part. He tested the door against the armchair.
The handle slipped in his palm. The chair provided no protection. In the war, he remembered, they had given him steel
wedges. Returning to the suitcase he connected the transmitter

and receiver to the power pack, plugged in the earphones and unscrewed the Morse key from the lid of the spares box. Then he saw it.

Mounted inside the suitcase lid was a piece of adhesive paper with half a dozen groups of letters and beside each its Morse equivalent; they were the international code for standard phrases, the one he could never remember.

When he saw those letters, drawn out in Jack's neat, post-office hand, tears of gratitude started to his eyes. He never told me, he thought, he never told me he'd done it. Jack was all right, after all. Jack, the Captain and young John; what a team to work for, he thought; a man could go through life and never meet a set of blokes like that. He steadied himself, pressing his hands sharply on the table. He was trembling a little, perhaps from the cold; his damp shirt clung to his shoulder-blades; but he was happy. He glanced at the chair in front of the door and thought: when I've got the headphones on I shan't hear them coming, the way the boy didn't hear me because of the wind.

Next he attached aerial and earth to their terminals, led the earth wire to the water pipe and fastened the two strands to the cleaned surface with tabs of adhesive plaster. Standing on the bed, he stretched the aerial across the ceiling in eight lengths, zig-zag as Johnson had instructed, fixing it as best he could to the curtain rail or plaster on either side. This done, he returned to the set and adjusted the waveband switch to the fourth position, because he knew that all the frequencies were in the three-megacycle range. He took from the bed the first crystal in the line, plugged it into the far left-hand corner of the set, and settled down to tune the transmitter, muttering gently as he performed each movement. Adjust crystal selector to 'fundamental all crystals', plug in the coil; anode-tuning and aerial-matching controls to ten.

He hesitated, trying to remember what happened next. A block was forming in his mind. 'PA – don't you know what PA stands for?' He set the meter switch to three to read the Power Amplifier grid current . . . TSR switch to T for tuning. It was coming back to him. Meter switch to six to ascertain total current . . . anode tuning for minimum reading.

Now he turned the TSR switch to S for send, pressed the key briefly, took a reading, manipulated the aerial-matching control so that the meter reading rose slightly; hastily readjusted the anode tuning. He repeated the procedure until to his profound relief he saw the finger dip against the white background of the kidney-shaped dial and knew that the transmitter and aerial were correctly tuned, and that he could talk to John and Jack.

He sat back with a grunt of satisfaction, lit a cigarette, wished it were an English one because if they came in now they wouldn't have to bother about the brand of cigarette he was smoking. He looked at his watch, turning the winder until it was stiff, terrified lest it run down; it was matched with Avery's and in a simple way this gave him comfort. Like divided lovers, they were looking at the same star.

He had killed that boy.

Three minutes to schedule. He unscrewed the Morse key from the spares box because he couldn't manage it properly while it was on that lid. Jack had said it was all right; he said it didn't matter. He had to hold the key base with his left hand so that it didn't slide about, but Jack said every operator had his quirks. He was sure it was smaller than the one they gave him in the war; he was sure of it. Traces of French chalk clung to the lever. He drew in his elbows and straightened his back. The third finger of his right hand crooked over the key. JAJ's my first call sign, he thought, Johnson's my name, they call me Jack, that's easy enough to remember. JA, John Avery; JJ, Jack Johnson. Then he was tapping it out. A dot and three dashes, dot dash, a dot and three dashes, and he kept thinking: it's like the house in Holland, but there's no one with me.

Say it twice, Fred, then get off the air. He switched over to receive, pushed the sheet of paper farther towards the middle of the table and suddenly realised he had nothing to write with when Jack came through.

He stood up and looked around for his notebook and pencil, the sweat breaking out on his back. They were nowhere to be seen. Dropping hastily to his hands and knees he felt in the thick dust under the bed, found the pencil, groped vainly for his notebook. As he was getting up he heard a crackle from the ear-phones. He ran to the table, pressed one phone to his ear, at the same time trying to hold still the sheet of paper so that he could write in a corner of it beside his own message.

'QSA3: hearing you well enough,' that's all they were saying. 'Steady, boy, steady,' he muttered. He settled into the chair, switched to transmit, looked at his own encoded message and tapped out four-two because there were forty-two groups. His hand was coated with dust and sweat, his right arm ached, per-haps from carrying the suitcase. Or struggling with the boy.

You've got all the time in the world, Johnson had said. We'll be listening: you're not passing an exam. He took his handker-chief from his pocket and wiped away the grime from his hands. He was terribly tired; the tiredness was like a physical despair, like the moment of guilt before making love. Groups of four let-ters, Johnson had said, think of four-letter words, eh, Fred. You don't need to do it all at once, Fred, have a little stop in the middle if you like; two and a half minutes on the first frequency, two and a half on the second, that's the way we go; Mrs Hart-beck will wait, I'm sure. With his pencil he drew a heavy line under the ninth letter because that was where the safety device came. That was something he dared think of only in passing.

He put his face in his hands, summoning the last of his con-centration, then reached for the key and began tapping. Keep the hand loose, first and second fingers on top of the key, thumb beneath the edge, no putting the wrist on the table, Fred, breathe regular, Fred, you'll find it helps you to relax.

God, why were his hands so slow? Once he took his fingers from the key and stared impotently at his open palm; once he ran his left hand across his forehead to keep the sweat from his eyes, and he felt the key drifting across the table. His wrist was too stiff: the hand he killed the boy with. All the time he was saying it over to himself – dot, dot, dash, then a K, he always knew that one, a dot between two dashes – his lips were spelling out the letters, but his hand wouldn't follow, it was a kind of stammer that got worse the more he spoke, and always the boy in his mind, only the boy. Perhaps he was quicker than he thought. He lost all notion of time; the sweat was running into his eyes, he couldn't stop it any more. He kept mouthing the dots and dashes, and he knew that Johnson would be angry because he shouldn't be thinking in dots and dashes at all but musically, de-dah, dah, the way the professionals did, but Johnson had not killed the boy. The pounding of his heart outran the weary tapping of the key; his hand seemed to grow heavier and still he went on signalling because it was the only thing left to do, the only thing to hold on to while his body gave way. He was waiting for them now, wishing they'd come – take me, take it all – longing for the footsteps. Give us your hand, John; give us a hand.

When at last he had finished, he went back to the bed. Almost with detachment he caught sight of the line of crystals on the blanket, untouched, still and ready, dressed by the left and numbered; flat on their backs, like dead sentries.

Avery looked at his watch. It was quarter past ten. 'He should come on in five minutes,' he said.

Leclerc announced suddenly: 'That was Gorton on the telephone. He's received a telegram from the Ministry. They have some news for us apparently. They're sending out a courier.'

'What could that be?' Avery asked.

'I expect it's the Hungarian thing. Fielden's report. I may have to go back to London.' A satisfied smile. 'But I think you people can get along without me.'

Johnson was wearing earphones, sitting forward on a high-backed wooden chair carried up from the kitchen. The dark green receiver hummed gently from the mains transformer; the tuning dial, illuminated from within, glowed palely in the half-light of the attic.

Haldane and Avery sat uncomfortably on a bench. Johnson had a pad and pencil in front of him. He lifted the phones above his ears and said to Leclerc who stood beside him, 'I shall take him straight through the routine, sir; I'll do my best to tell you what's going on. I'm recording, too, mind, for safety's sake.'

'I understand.'

They waited in silence. Suddenly – it was their moment of utter magic – Johnson had sat bolt upright, nodded sharply to them, switched on the tape recorder. He smiled, quickly turned to transmission and was tapping. 'Come in, Fred,' he said out loud. 'Hearing you nicely.'

'He's made it!' Leclerc hissed. 'He's on target now!' His eyes were bright with excitement. 'Do you hear that, John? Do you hear?'

'Shall we be quiet?' Haldane suggested.

'Here he comes,' Johnson said. His voice was level, controlled. 'Forty-two groups.'

'Forty-two!' Leclerc repeated.

Johnson's body was motionless, his head inclined a little to one side, his whole concentration given to the earphones, his face impassive in the pale light.

'I'd like silence now, please.'

For perhaps two minutes his careful hand moved briskly across the pad. Now and then he muttered inaudibly, whispered a letter or shook his head, until the message seemed to come more slowly, his pencil pausing while he listened, until it was tracing out each letter singly with agonising care. He glanced at the clock.

'Come on, Fred,' he urged. 'Come on, change over, that's nearly three minutes.' But still the message was coming through, letter by letter, and Johnson's simple face assumed an expression of alarm.

'What's going on?' Leclerc demanded. 'Why hasn't he changed his frequency?'

But Johnson only said, 'Get off the air, for Christ's sake, Fred, get off the air.'

Leclerc touched him impatiently on the arm. Johnson raised one earphone.

'Why's he not changed frequency? Why's he still talking?'

'He must have forgotten! He never forgot on training. I *know* he's slow, but Christ!' He was still writing automatically. 'Five minutes,' he muttered. 'Five bloody minutes. Change the bloody crystal!'

'Can't you tell him?' Leclerc cried.

'Of course I can't. How can I? He can't receive and send at the same time!'

They sat or stood in dreadful fascination. Johnson had turned to them, his voice beseeching. 'I told him; if I told him once I told him a dozen times. It's bloody suicide, what he's doing!' He looked at his watch. 'He's been on damn near six minutes. Bloody, bloody, *bloody* fool.'

'What will they do?' said Haldane.

'If they pick up a signal? Call in another station. Take a fix, then it's simple trigonometry when he's on this long.' He banged his open hands helplessly on the table, indicated the set as if it were an affront. 'A kid could do it. Do it with a pair of compasses. Christ Almighty! Come on, Fred, for Jesus' sake, come on!' He wrote down a handful of letters then threw his pencil aside. 'It's on tape, anyway,' he said.

Leclerc turned to Haldane. 'Surely there's something we can do!'

'Be quiet,' Haldane said.

The message stopped. Johnson tapped an acknowledgement, fast, a stab of hatred. He wound back the tape recorder and began transcribing. Putting the coding sheet in front of him he worked without interruption for perhaps a quarter of an hour, occasionally making simple sums on the rough paper at his elbow. No one spoke. When he had finished he stood up, a half-forgotten gesture of respect. 'Message reads: Area Kalkstadt closed three days mid November when fifty unidentified Soviet troops seen in town. No special equipment. Rumours of Soviet manoeuvres farther north. Troops believed moved to Rostock.

Fritsche not repeat not known Kalkstadt railway station. No road check on Kalkstadt road.' He tossed the paper on to the desk. 'There are fifteen groups after that which I can't unbutton. I think he's muddled his coding.'

The Vopo sergeant in Rostock picked up the telephone; he was an elderly man, greying and thoughtful. He listened for a moment then began dialling on another line. 'It must be a child,' he said, still dialling. 'What frequency did you say?' He put the other telephone to his ear and spoke into it fast, repeating the frequency three times. He walked into the adjoining hut. 'Witmar will be through in a minute,' he said. 'They're taking a fix. Are you still hearing him?' The corporal nodded. The sergeant held a spare headphone to his ear.

'It couldn't be an amateur,' he muttered. 'Breaking the regulations. But what is it? No agent in his right mind would put out a signal like that. What are the neighbouring frequencies? Military or civilian?'

'It's near the military. Very near.'

'That's odd,' the sergeant said. 'That would fit, wouldn't it? That's what they did in the war.'

The corporal was staring at the tapes slowly revolving on their spindles. 'He's still transmitting. Groups of four.'

'Four?' The sergeant was searching in his memory for something that had happened long ago. 'Let me hear again. Listen, listen to the fool! He's as slow as a child.'

The sound struck some chord in his memory – the slurred gaps, the dots so short as to be little more than clicks. He could swear he knew that hand . . . from the war, in Norway . . . but not so slow: nothing had ever been as slow as this. Not Norway . . . France. Perhaps it was only imagination. Yes, it was imagination.

'Or an old man,' the corporal said.

The telephone rang. The sergeant listened for a moment, then ran, ran as fast as he could, through the hut to the officers' mess across the tarmac path.

The Russian captain was drinking beer; his jacket was slung over the back of his chair and he looked very bored.

'You wanted something, Sergeant?' He affected the languid style.

'He's come. The man they told us about. The one who killed the boy.'

The captain put down his beer quickly.

'You heard him?'

'We've taken a fix. With Witmar. Groups of four. A slow hand. Area Kalkstadt. Close to one of our own frequencies. Sommer recorded the transmission.'

'Christ,' he said quietly. The sergeant frowned.

'What's he looking for? Why should they send him here?' the sergeant asked.

The captain was buttoning his jacket. 'Ask them in Leipzig. Perhaps they know that too.'

21

It was very late.

The fire in Control's grate was burning nicely, but he poked at it with effeminate discontent. He hated working at night.

'They want you at the Ministry,' he said irritably. 'Now, of all hours. It really is too bad. Why does everyone get so *agitato* on a Thursday? It will *ruin* the weekend.' He put down the poker and returned to his desk. 'They're in a dreadful state. Some idiot talking about ripples in a pond. It's extraordinary what the night does to people. I do *detest* the telephone.' There were several in front of him.

Smiley offered him a cigarette and he took one without looking at it, as if he could not be held responsible for the actions of his limbs.

'What Ministry?' Smiley asked.

'Leclerc's. Have you *any* idea what's going on?'

Smiley said, 'Yes. Haven't you?'

'Leclerc's so *vulgar*. I admit, I find him vulgar. He thinks we compete. What on earth would I do with his dreadful militia? Scouring Europe for mobile laundries. He thinks I want to gobble him up.'

'Well, don't you? Why *did* we cancel that passport?'

'What a *silly* man. A silly, vulgar man. However did Haldane fall for it?'

'He had a conscience once. He's like all of us. He's learnt to live with it.'

'Oh dear. Is that a dig at me?'

'What does the Ministry want?' Smiley asked sharply.

Control held up some papers, flapping them. 'You've seen these from Berlin?'

'They came in an hour ago. The Americans have taken a fix. Groups of four; a primitive letter code. They say it comes from the Kalkstadt area.'

'Where on *earth's* that?'

'South of Rostock. The message ran six minutes on the same frequency. They said it sounded like an amateur on a first run-through. One of the old wartime sets: they wanted to know if it was ours.'

'And you replied?' Control asked quickly.

'I said no.'

'So I should hope. Good Lord.'

'You don't seem very concerned,' Smiley said.

Control seemed to remember something from long ago. 'I hear Leclerc's in Lübeck. Now *there's* a pretty town. I adore Lübeck. The Ministry wants you immediately. I said you'd go. Some meeting.' He added in apparent earnest, 'You must, George. We've been the most awful fools. It's in every East German newspaper; they're screaming about peace conferences and sabotage.' He prodded at a telephone. 'So is the Ministry. God, how I loathe Civil Servants.'

Smiley watched him with scepticism. 'We could have stopped them,' he said. 'We knew enough.'

'Of course we could,' Control said blandly. 'D'you know why we didn't? Plain, idiot Christian charity. We let them have their war game. You'd better go now. And Smiley . . .'

'Yes?'

'Be gentle.' And in his silly voice: 'I do envy them Lübeck, all the same. There's that restaurant, isn't there; what do they call it? Where Thomas Mann used to eat. So interesting.'

'He never did,' Smiley said. 'The place you're thinking of was bombed.'

Smiley still did not go. 'I wonder,' he said. 'You'll never tell me, will you? I just wonder.' He was not looking at Control.

'My dear George, what *has* come over you?'

'We handed it to them. The passport that was cancelled . . . a courier service they never needed . . . a clapped-out wireless set . . . papers, frontier reports . . . who told Berlin to listen for him? Who told them what frequencies? We even gave Leclerc the crystals, didn't we? Was that just Christian charity too? Plain, idiot Christian charity?'

Control was shocked.

'What *are* you suggesting? How *very* distasteful. Who ever would do a thing like that?'

Smiley was putting on his coat.

'Goodnight, George,' Control said; and fiercely, as if he were tired of sensibility: 'Run along. And preserve the difference between us: your country needs you. It's not *my* fault they've taken so long to die.'

The dawn came and Leiser had not slept. He wanted to wash but dared not go into the corridor. He dared not move. If they were looking for him, he knew he must leave normally, not bolt from the hostel before the morning came. Never run, they used to say: walk like the crowd. He could go at six: that was late enough. He rubbed his chin against the back of his hand: it was sharp and rough, marking the brown skin.

He was hungry and no longer knew what to do, but he would not run.

He half turned on the bed, pulled the knife from inside the waistband of his trousers and held it before his eyes. He was shivering. He could feel across his brow the unnatural heat of incipient fever. He looked at the knife, and remembered the clean, friendly way they had talked: thumb on top, blade parallel to the ground, forearm stiff. 'Go away,' the old man had said. 'You are either good or bad, and both are dangerous.' How should he hold the knife when people spoke to him like that? The way he held it for the boy?

It was six o'clock. He stood up. His legs were heavy and stiff. His shoulders still ached from carrying the rucksack. His clothes, he noticed, smelt of pine and leaf mould. He picked the half-dried mud from his trousers and put on his second pair of shoes.

He went downstairs, looking for someone to pay, the new shoes squeaking on the wooden steps. There was an old woman in a white overall sorting lentils into a bowl, talking to a cat.

'What do I owe?'

'You fill in the form,' she said sourly. 'That's the first thing you owe. You should have done it when you came.'

'I'm sorry.'

She rounded on him, muttering but not daring to raise her voice. 'Don't you know it's forbidden, staying in a town and not reporting your presence to the police?' She looked at his new shoes. 'Or are you so rich that you think you need not trouble?'

'I'm sorry,' Leiser said again. 'Give me the form and I'll sign it now. I'm not rich.'

The woman fell silent, picking studiously among the lentils.

'Where do you come from?' she asked.

'East,' said Leiser. He meant south, from Magdeburg, or west from Wilmsdorf.

'You should have reported last night. It's too late now.'

'What do I pay?'

'You can't,' the woman replied. 'Never mind. You haven't filled in the form. What will you say if they catch you?'

'I'll say I slept with a girl.'

'It's snowing outside,' the woman said. 'Mind your nice shoes.'

Grains of hard snow drifted forlornly in the wind, collecting in the cracks between the black cobbles, lingering on the stucco of the houses. A drab, useless snow, dwindling where it fell.

He crossed the Friedensplatz and saw a new, yellow building, six or seven storeys high, standing on a patch of waste land beside a new estate. There was washing hanging on the balconies, touched with snow. The staircase smelt of food and Russian petrol. The flat was on the third floor. He could hear a child crying and a wireless playing. For a moment he thought he should turn and go away, because he was dangerous for them. He pressed the bell twice, as the girl had told him. She opened the door; she was half asleep. She had put on her mackintosh over the cotton nightdress and she held it at the neck because of the freezing cold. When she saw him she hesitated, not knowing what to do, as if he had brought bad news. He said nothing, just stood there with the suitcase swinging gently at his side. She beckoned with her head; he followed her across the corridor to her room, put the suitcase and rucksack in the corner. There were travel posters on the walls, pictures of desert, palm trees and the moon over a tropical sea. They got into bed and she covered him with her heavy body, trembling a little because she was afraid.

'I want to sleep,' he said. 'Let me sleep first.'

The Russian captain said, 'He stole a motorbike at Wilmsdorf and asked for Fritsche at the station. What will he do now?'

'He'll have another schedule. Tonight,' the sergeant replied. 'If he's got anything to say.'

'At the same time?'

'Of course not. Nor the same frequency. Nor from the same place. He may go to Witmar or Langdorn or Wolken; he may even go to Rostock. Or he may stay in town but go to another house. Or he may not send at all.'

'House? Who would harbour a spy?'

The sergeant shrugged as if to say he might himself. Stung, the captain asked, 'How do you know he's sending from a house? Why not a wood or a field? How can you be so sure?'

'It's a very strong signal. A powerful set. He couldn't get a signal like that from a battery, not a battery you could carry around alone. He's using the mains.'

'Put a cordon round the town,' the captain said. 'Search every house.'

'We want him alive.' The sergeant was looking at his hands. 'You want him alive.'

'Then tell me what we should do?' the captain insisted.

'Make sure he transmits. That's the first thing. And make him stay in town. That is the second.'

'Well?'

'We would have to act quickly,' the sergeant observed.

'Well?'

'Bring some troops into town. Anything you can find. As soon as possible. Armour, infantry, it doesn't matter. Create some movement. Make him pay attention. But be quick!'

'I'll go soon,' Leiser said. 'Don't let me stay. Give me coffee and I'll go.'

'Coffee?'

'I've got money,' Leiser said, as if it were the only thing he had. 'Here.' He climbed out of bed, fetched the wallet from his jacket and drew a hundred-mark note from the wad.

'Keep it.'

She took the wallet and with a little laugh emptied it out on the bed. She had a ponderous, kittenish way which was not quite sane; and the quick instinct of an illiterate. He watched her indifferently, running his fingers along the line of her naked shoulder. She held up a photograph of a woman; a blonde, round head.

'Who is she? What is her name?'

'She doesn't exist,' he said.

She found the letters and read one aloud, laughing at the affectionate passages. 'Who is she?' she kept taunting him. 'Who is she?'

'I tell you, she doesn't exist.'

'Then I can tear them up?' She held a letter before him with both hands, teasing him, waiting for him to protest. Leiser said nothing. She made a little tear, still watching him, then tore it completely, and a second and a third.

She found a picture of a child, a girl in spectacles, eight or nine years old perhaps, and again she asked, 'Who is it? Is it your child? Does *she* exist?'

'Nobody. Nobody's kid. Just a photograph.' She tore that too, scattering the pieces dramatically over the bed, then fell on him, kissing him on the face and neck. 'Who are you? What is your name?'

He wanted to tell her when she pushed him away.

'No!' she cried. 'No!' She lowered her voice. 'I want you with nothing. Alone from it all. You and me alone. We'll make our own names, our own rules. Nobody, no one at all, no father, no mother. We'll print our own newspapers, passes, ration cards; make our own people.' She was whispering, her eyes shining.

'You're a spy,' she said, her lips in his ear. 'A secret agent. You've got a gun.'

'A knife is quieter,' he said. She laughed, on and on, until she noticed the bruises on his shoulders. She touched them curiously, with respect, as a child might touch a dead thing.

She went out carrying a shopping basket, still clutching the mackintosh at her neck. Leiser dressed, shaving in cold water, staring at his lined face in the distorted mirror above the basin. When she returned it was nearly midday and she looked worried.

'The town's full of soldiers. And Army trucks. What do they want here?'

'Perhaps they are looking for someone.'

'They are just sitting about, drinking.'

'What kind of soldiers?'

'I don't know what kind. Russian. How can I tell?'

He went to the door. 'I'll come back in an hour.'

She said, 'You're trying to get away from me.' She held his arm, looking up at him, wanting to make a scene.

'I'll come back. Maybe not till later. Maybe this evening. But if I do . . .'

'Yes?'

'It will be dangerous. I shall have to . . . do something here. Something dangerous.'

She kissed him, a light, silly kiss. 'I like danger,' she said.

'Four hours,' Johnson said. 'If he's still alive.'

'Of course he's alive,' Avery said angrily. 'Why do you talk like that?'

Haldane interrupted. 'Don't be an ass, Avery. It's a technical term. Dead or live agents. It has nothing to do with his physical condition.'

Leclerc was drumming his fingers lightly on the table.

'He'll be all right,' he said. 'Fred's a hard man to kill. He's an old hand.' The daylight had revived him apparently. He glanced at his watch. 'What the devil's happened to that courier, I wonder.'

Leiser blinked at the soldiers like a man emerging from the dark. They filled the cafés, gazed into shop windows, looked at the girls. Trucks were parked in the square, their wheels thick with red mud, a thin surface of snow on their bonnets. He counted them and there were nine. Some had heavy couplings at the rear for pulling trailers; some a line of Cyrillic script on their battered doors, or the imprint of unit insignia and a number. He noted the emblems of the drivers' uniforms, the colour of their shoulder-boards; they came, he realised, from a variety of units.

Walking back to the main street he pushed his way into a café and ordered a drink. Half a dozen soldiers sat disconsolately at a table sharing three bottles of beer. Leiser grinned at them; it was like the encouragement of a tired whore. He lifted his fist in a Soviet salute and they watched him as if he were mad. He left his drink and made his way back to the square; a group of children had gathered round the trucks and the drivers kept telling them to go away.

He made a tour of the town, went into a dozen cafés, but no

one would talk to him because he was a stranger. Everywhere the soldiers sat or stood in groups, aggrieved and bewildered, as if they had been roused to no purpose.

He ate some sausage and drank a Steinhäger, walked to the station to see if anything was going on. The same man was there, watching him, this time without suspicion, from behind his little window; and somehow Leiser knew, though it made no difference, that the man had told the police.

Returning from the station, he passed a cinema. A group of girls had gathered round the photographs and he stood with them pretending to look. Then the noise came, a metallic, irregular drone, filling the street with the piping, rattling of engines, metal and war. He drew back into the cover of the foyer, saw the girls turn and the ticket-seller stand up in her box. An old man crossed himself; he had lost one eye, and wore his hat at an angle. The tanks rolled through the town; they carried troops with rifles. The gun barrels were too long, marked white with snow. He watched them pass, then made his way across the square, quickly.

She smiled as he came in; he was out of breath.

'What are they doing?' she asked. She caught sight of his face. 'You're afraid,' she whispered, but he shook his head. 'You're afraid,' she repeated.

'I killed the boy,' he said.

He went to the basin, examined his face with the great care of a man under sentence. She followed him, clasped him round the chest, pressing herself against his back. He turned and seized her, wild, held her without skill, forced her across the room. She fought him with the rage of a daughter, calling some name, hating someone, cursing him, taking him, the world burning and only they alive; they were weeping, laughing together, falling, clumsy lovers clumsily triumphant, recognising nothing but each himself, each for that moment completing lives half lived, and for that moment the whole damned dark forgotten.

Johnson leant out of the window and gently drew on the aerial to make sure it was still fast, then began looking over his receiver like a racing driver before the start, needlessly touching terminals and adjusting dials. Leclerc watched him admiringly.

'Johnson, that was nobly done last time. Nobly done. We owe you a vote of thanks.' Leclerc's face was shiny, as if he had only recently shaved. He looked oddly fragile in the pale light. 'I propose to hear one more schedule and get back to London.' He laughed. 'We've work to do, you know. This isn't the season for continental holidays.'

Johnson might not have heard. He held up his hand. 'Thirty minutes,' he said. 'I shall be asking you for a little hush soon, gentlemen.' He was like a conjurer at a children's party. 'Fred's a devil for punctuality,' he observed loudly.

Leclerc addressed himself to Avery. 'You're one of those lucky people, John, who have seen action in peacetime.' He seemed anxious to talk.

'Yes. I'm very grateful.'

'You don't have to be. You've done a good job, and we recognise that. There's no question of *gratitude*. You've achieved something very rare in our work; I wonder if you know what it is?'

Avery said he did not.

'You've induced an agent to *like* you. In the ordinary way – Adrian will bear me out – the relationship between an agent and his controllers is clouded with suspicion. He resents them, that's the first thing, for not doing the job themselves. He suspects them of ulterior motives, ineptitude, duplicity. But we're not the Circus, John: that's not the way we do things.'

Avery nodded. 'No, quite.'

'You've done something else, you and Adrian. I would like to feel that if a similar need arose in the future we could use the same technique, the same facilities, the same *expertise* – that means the Avery–Haldane combination. What I'm trying to say is' – Leclerc raised one hand and with his forefinger and thumb lightly touched the bridge of his nose in an unusual gesture of English diffidence – 'the experience you've made is to our mutual advantage. Thank you.'

Haldane moved to the stove and began warming his hands, rubbing them gently as if he were separating wheat.

'That Budapest thing,' Leclerc continued, raising his voice, partly in enthusiasm and partly perhaps to dispel the atmosphere of intimacy which suddenly threatened them, 'it's a complete reorganisation. Nothing less. They're moving their armour to the border, d'you see. The Ministry is talking about forward strategy. They're really most interested.'

Avery said, 'More interested than in the Mayfly area?'

'No, no,' Leclerc protested lightly. 'It's all part of the same complex – they think very big over there, you know – a move here and a move there – it all has to be pieced together.'

'Of course,' Avery said gently. 'We can't see it ourselves, can we? We can't see the whole picture.' He was trying to make it better for Leclerc. 'We haven't the perspective.'

'When we get back to London,' Leclerc proposed, 'you must come and dine with me, John: you and your wife; both come. I've been meaning to suggest it for some time. We'll go to my club. They do a rather good dinner in the Ladies' Room; your wife would enjoy it.'

'You mentioned it. I asked Sarah. We'd love to. My mother-in-law's with us just now. She could baby-sit.'

'How nice. Don't forget.'

'We're looking forward to it.'

'Am I not invited?' Haldane asked coyly.

'Why, of course, Adrian. Then we shall be four. Excellent.' His voice changed. 'Incidentally, the landlords have complained about the house in Oxford. They say we left it in a poor state.'

'Poor state?' Haldane echoed angrily.

'It appears we have been overloading the electrical circuit. Parts of it are quite burnt out. I told Woodford to cope with it.'

'We should have our own place,' said Avery. 'Then we wouldn't have to worry.'

'I agree. I spoke to the Minister about it. A training centre is what we need. He was enthusiastic. He's keen on this kind of thing, now, you know. They have a new phrase for it over there.

They are speaking of ICOs. Immediate Clarification Operations. He suggests we find a place and take it for six months. He
proposes to speak to the Treasury about a lease.'

'That's terrific,' Avery said.

'It could be very useful. We must be sure not to abuse our
trust.'

'Of course.'

There was a draught, followed by the sound of someone cautiously ascending the stairs. A figure appeared in the attic doorway. He wore an expensive overcoat of brown tweed, a little too
long in the sleeve. It was Smiley.

22

Smiley peered round the room, at Johnson, now in earphones, busy with the controls of his set, at Avery staring over Haldane's shoulder at the signal plan, at Leclerc, who stood like a soldier, who alone had noticed him, whose face, though turned to him, was empty and far away.

'What do you want here?' Leclerc said at last. 'What do you want with me?'

'I'm sorry. I was sent.'

'So were we all,' Haldane said, not moving.

A note of warning entered Leclerc's voice. 'This is my operation, Smiley. We've no room for your people here.'

There was nothing in Smiley's face but compassion, nothing in his voice but that dreadful patience with which we speak to the insane.

'It wasn't Control who sent me,' he said. 'It was the Ministry. They asked for me, you see, and Control let me go. The Ministry laid on a plane.'

'Why?' Haldane inquired. He seemed almost amused.

One by one they stirred, waking from a single dream. Johnson laid his earphones carefully on the table.

'Well?' Leclerc asked. 'Why did they send you?'

'They called me round last night.' He managed to indicate that he was as bewildered as they. 'I had to admire the operation, the way you'd conducted it; you and Haldane. All done from nothing. They showed me the files. Scrupulously kept . . .

Library Copy, Operational Copy, sealed minutes: just like in the war. I congratulate you . . . I really do.'

'They showed you the files? *Our* files?' Leclerc repeated. 'That's a breach of security: interconsciousness between Departments. You've committed an offence, Smiley. They must be mad! Adrian, do you hear what Smiley has told me?'

Smiley said, 'Is there a schedule tonight, Johnson?'

'Yes, sir. Twenty-one hundred.'

'I was surprised, Adrian, that you felt the indicators were strong enough for such a *big* operation.'

'Haldane was not responsible,' Leclerc said crisply. 'The decision was a collective one; ourselves on the one side, the Ministry on the other.' His voice changed key. 'When the schedule is finished I shall want to know, Smiley, I have a right to know, how you came to see those files.' It was his committee voice, powerful and fluent; for the first time it had the ring of dignity.

Smiley moved towards the centre of the room. 'Something's happened; something you couldn't know about. Leiser killed a man on the border. Killed him with a knife as he went over, two miles from here, at the crossing point.'

Haldane said, 'That's absurd. It needn't be Leiser. It could have been a refugee coming west. It could have been anyone.'

'They found tracks leading east. Traces of blood in the hut by the lake. It's in all the East German papers. They've been putting it over the wireless since midday yesterday . . .'

Leclerc cried, 'I don't believe it. I don't believe he did it. It's some trick of Control's.'

'No,' Smiley replied gently. 'You've got to believe me. It's true.'

'They killed Taylor,' Leclerc said. 'Have you forgotten that?'

'No, of course not. But we shall never know, shall we? How he died, I mean . . . whether he was murdered . . .' Hurriedly he continued, 'Your Ministry informed the Foreign Office yesterday afternoon. The Germans are bound to catch him, you see; we have to assume that. His transmissions are slow . . . very slow. Every policeman, every soldier is after him. They want him alive. We think they're going to stage a show trial, extract a public confession, display the equipment. It could be very embarrassing. You don't have to be a politician to sympathise with the Minister. So there's the question of what to do.'

Leclerc said, 'Johnson, keep an eye on the clock.' Johnson put his earphones on again, but without conviction.

Smiley appeared to want someone else to speak, but no one did, so he repeated ponderously, 'It's a question of what to do. As I say, we're not politicians, but one can see the dangers. A party of Englishmen in a farmhouse two miles from where the body was found, posing as academics, stores from the Naafi and a house full of radio equipment. You see what I mean? Making your transmissions,' he went on, 'on a single frequency . . . the frequency Leiser receives on . . . There could be a very big scandal indeed. One can imagine even the West Germans getting awfully angry.'

Haldane spoke first again: 'What are you trying to say?'

'There's a military plane waiting at Hamburg. You fly in two hours; all of you. A truck will collect the equipment. You're to leave nothing behind, not even a pin. Those are my instructions.'

Leclerc said, 'What about the target? Have they forgotten why we're here? They're asking a lot, you know, Smiley: a great lot.'

'Yes, the target,' Smiley conceded. 'We'll have a conference in London. Perhaps we could do a joint operation.'

'It's a military target. I shall want my Ministry represented. No monolith; it's a policy decision, you know.'

'Of course. And it'll be your show.'

'I suggest the product go out under our joint title: my Ministry could retain autonomy in the matter of distribution. I imagine that would meet their more obvious objections. How about your people?'

'Yes, I think Control would accept that.'

Leclerc said casually, everyone watching, 'And the schedule? Who takes care of that? We've an agent in the field, you know.' It was only a small point.

'He'll have to manage by himself.'

'The war rules.' Leclerc spoke proudly. 'We play the war rules. He knew that. He was well trained.' He seemed reconciled; the thing was dismissed.

Avery spoke for the first time. 'You can't leave him out there alone.' His voice was flat.

Leclerc intervened: 'You know Avery, my aide?' This time no one came to his rescue. Smiley, ignoring him, observed, 'The man's probably been caught already. It's only a matter of hours.'

'You're leaving him there to die!' Avery was gathering courage.

'We're disowning him. It's never a pretty process. He's as good as caught already, don't you see?'

'You can't do it,' he shouted. 'You can't just leave him there for some squalid diplomatic reason!'

Now Haldane swung round on Avery, furious. 'You of all people should not complain! You wanted a faith, didn't you? You wanted an eleventh Commandment that would match your rare soul!' He indicated Smiley and Leclerc. 'Well, here you have it: here is the law you were looking for. Congratulate yourself; you found it. We sent him because we needed to; we abandon him because we must. That is the discipline you admired.' He turned to Smiley. 'You too: I find you contemptible. You shoot us, then preach to the dying. Go away. We're technicians, not poets. Go away!'

Smiley said, 'Yes. You're a very good technician, Adrian. There's no pain in you any more. You've made technique a way of life . . . like a whore . . . technique replacing love.' He hesitated. 'Little flags . . . the old war piping in the new. There was all that, wasn't there? And then the man . . . he must have been heady wine. Comfort yourself, Adrian, you weren't fit.'

He straightened his back, making a statement. 'A British-naturalised Pole with a criminal record escapes across the border to East Germany. There is no extradition treaty. The Germans will say he is a spy and produce the equipment; we shall say they planted it and point out that it's twenty-five years old. I understand he put out a cover story that he was attending a course in Coventry. That is easily disproved: there is no such course. The conclusion is that he proposed to flee the country; and we shall imply that he owed money. He was keeping some young girl, you know; she worked in a bank. That ties in quite nicely. I mean with the criminal record, since we have to make one up . . .' He nodded to himself. 'As I say, it's not an attractive process. By then we shall all be in London.'

'And he'll be transmitting,' Avery said, 'and no one will listen.'

'To the contrary,' Smiley retorted bitterly. 'They'll be listening.'

Haldane asked: 'Control too, no doubt. Isn't that right?'

'Stop!' Avery shouted suddenly. 'Stop, for God's sake! If anything matters, if anything is real, we've got to hear him now! For the sake of . . .'

'Well?' Haldane inquired with a sneer.

'Love. Yes, love! Not yours, Haldane, mine. Smiley's right! You made me do it for you, made me love him! It wasn't in you any more! I brought him to you, I kept him in your house, made him dance to the music of your bloody war! I piped for him, but there's no breath in me now. He's Peter Pan's last victim, Haldane, the last one, the last love; the last music gone.'

Haldane was looking at Smiley: 'My congratulations to Control,' he said. 'Thank him, will you? Thank him for the help, the *technical* help, Smiley; for the encouragement, thank him for the rope. For the kind words too: for lending you to bring the flowers. So nicely done.'

But Leclerc seemed impressed by the neatness of it.

'Let's not be hard on Smiley, Adrian. He's only doing his job. We must all get back to London. There's the Fielden report . . . I'd like to show you that, Smiley. Troop dispositions in Hungary: something new.'

'And I'd like to see it,' Smiley replied politely.

'He's right, you know, Avery,' Leclerc repeated. His voice was quite eager. 'Be a soldier. Fortunes of war; keep to the rules!

We play the war rules in this game. Smiley, I owe you an apology. And Control too, I fear. I had thought the old rivalry was awake. I'm wrong.' He inclined his head. 'You must dine with me in London. My club is not your mark, I know, but it's quiet there; a good set. Very good. Haldane must come. Adrian, I invite you!'

Avery had buried his face in his hands.

'There's something else I want to discuss with you, Adrian – Smiley, you won't mind this I'm sure, you're practically one of the family – the question of Registry. The system of library files is really out of date. Bruce was on to me about it just before I left. Poor Miss Courtney can hardly keep pace. I fear the answer is more copies . . . top copy to the case officer, carbons for information. There's a new machine on the market, cheap photostats, threepence halfpenny a copy, that seems quite reasonable in these dog days . . . I must speak to the people about it . . . the Ministry . . . they know a good thing when they see one. Perhaps—' he broke off. 'Johnson, I could wish you made less noise, we're still operational, you know.' He spoke like a man intent upon appearances, conscious of tradition.

Johnson had gone to the window. Leaning on the sill he reached outside and with his customary precision began winding in the aerial. He held a spool in his left hand like a bobbin. As he gathered in the wire he gently turned it as an old woman spins her thread. Avery was sobbing like a child. No one heeded him.

23

The green van moved slowly down the road, crossed the Station Square where the empty fountain stood. On its roof the small loop aerial turned this way and that like a hand feeling for the wind. Behind it, well back, were two trucks. The snow was settling at last. They drove on sidelights, twenty yards apart, following each other's tyre marks.

The captain sat in the back of the van with a microphone for speaking to the driver, and beside him the sergeant, lost in private memories. The corporal crouched at his receiver, his hand constantly turning the dial as he watched the line tremble in the small screen.

'The transmission's stopped,' he said suddenly.

'How many groups have you recorded?' the sergeant asked.

'A dozen. The call sign over and over again, then part of a message. I don't think he's getting any reply.'

'Five letters or four?'

'Still four.'

'Did he sign off?'

'No.'

'What frequency was he using?'

'Three six five zero.'

'Keep scanning across it. Two hundred either side.'

'There's nothing there.'

'Keep searching,' he said sharply. 'Right across the band. He's changed the crystal. He'll take a few minutes to tune up.'

The operator began spinning the large dial, slowly, watching the eye of green light in the centre of the set which opened and closed as he crossed one station after another. 'Here he is. Three eight seven zero. Different call sign but the same handwriting. Quicker than yesterday; better.'

The tape recorder wound monotonously at his elbow. 'He's working on alternating crystals,' the sergeant said. 'Like they did in the war. It's the same trick.' He was embarrassed, an elderly man confronted with his past.

The corporal slowly raised his head. 'This is it,' he said. 'Zero. We're right on top of him.'

Quietly the two men dismounted from the van. 'Wait here,' the sergeant told the corporal. 'Keep listening. If the signal breaks, even for a moment, tell the driver to flash the headlights, do you understand?'

'I'll tell him.' The corporal looked frightened.

'If it stops altogether, keep searching and let me know.'

'Pay attention,' the captain warned as he dismounted. The sergeant was waiting impatiently; behind him, a tall building standing on waste land.

In the distance, half hidden in the falling snow, lay row after row of small houses. No sound came.

'What do they call this place?' the captain asked.

'A block of flats; workers' flats. They haven't named it yet.'

'No, beyond.'

'Nothing. Follow me,' the sergeant said.

Pale lights shone in almost every window; six floors. Stone steps, thick with leaves, led to the cellar. The sergeant went first, shining his torch ahead of them on to the shoddy walls. The captain nearly fell. The first room was large and airless, half of brick and half unrendered plaster. At the far end were two steel doors. On the ceiling a single bulb burnt behind a wire cage. The sergeant's torch was still on; he shone it needlessly into the corners.

'What are you looking for?' the captain asked.

The steel doors were locked.

'Find the janitor,' the sergeant ordered. 'Quickly.'

The captain ran up the stairs and returned with an old man, unshaven, gently grumbling; he held a bunch of long keys on a chain. Some were rusty.

'The switches,' said the sergeant. 'For the building. Where are they?'

The old man sorted through the keys. He pushed one into the lock and it would not fit, he tried another and a third.

'Quick, you fool,' the captain shouted.

'Don't fuss him,' said the sergeant.

The door opened. They pushed into the corridor, their torches playing over the whitewash. The janitor was holding up a key, grinning. 'Always the last one,' he said. The sergeant found what he was looking for, hidden on the wall behind the door: a box with a glass front. The captain put his hand to the main lever, had half pulled it when the other struck him roughly away.

'No! Go to the top of the stairs; tell me when the driver flashes his headlights.'

'Who's in charge here?' the captain complained.

'Do as I ask.' He had opened the box and was tugging gently at the first fuse, blinking through his gold-rimmed spectacles; a benign man.

With diligent, surgical fingers the sergeant drew out the fuse, cautiously, as if he were expecting an electric shock, then immediately replaced it, his eyes turning towards the figure at the top of the steps; then a second and still the captain said nothing. Outside the motionless soldiers watched the windows of the block, saw how floor by floor the lights went out, then quickly on again. The sergeant tried another and a fourth and this time he heard an excited cry from above him: 'The head-lights! The headlights have gone out.'

'Quite! Go and ask the driver which floor. But *quietly*.'

'They'll never hear us in this wind,' the captain said irrita-bly, and a moment later: 'The driver says third floor. The third-floor light went out and the transmission stopped at the same time. It's started again now.'

'Put the men round the building,' the sergeant said. 'And pick five men to come with us. He's on the third floor.'

Softly, like animals, the Vopos dismounted from the two trucks, their carbines held loosely in their hands, advancing in a ragged line, ploughing the thin snow, turning it to nothing; some to the foot of the building, some standing off, staring at the windows. A few wore helmets, and their square silhouette was redolent of the war. From here and there came a click as the first bullet was sprung gently into the breech; the sound rose to a faint hail and died away.

Leiser unhooked the aerial and wound it back on the reel, screwed the Morse key into the lid, replaced the earphones in the spares box and folded the silk cloth into the handle of the razor.

'Twenty years,' he protested, holding up the razor, 'and they still haven't found a better place.'

'Why do you do it?'

She was sitting contentedly on the bed in her nightdress, wrapped in the mackintosh as if it gave her company.

'Who do you talk to?' she asked again.

'No one. No one heard.'

'Why do you do it, then?'

He had to say something, so he said, 'For peace.'

He put on his jacket, went to the window and peered outside. Snow lay on the houses. The wind blew angrily across them. He glanced into the courtyard below, where the silhouettes were waiting.

'Whose peace?' she asked.

'The light went out, didn't it, while I was working the set?'

'Did it?'

'A short break, a second or two, like a power cut?'

'Yes.'

'Put it out again now.' He was very still. 'Put the light out.'

'Why?'

'I like to look at the snow.'

She put the light out and he drew the threadbare curtains.

Outside the snow reflected a pale glow into the sky. They were in half-darkness.

'You said we'd love now,' she complained.

'Listen; what's your name?'

He heard the rustle of raincoat.

'What is it?' His voice was rough.

'Anna.'

'Listen, Anna.' He went to the bed. 'I want to marry you,' he said. 'When I met you, in that inn, when I saw you sitting there, listening to the records, I fell in love with you, do you understand? I'm an engineer from Magdeburg, that's what I said. Are you listening?'

He seized her arms and shook her. His voice was urgent.

'Take me away,' she said.

'That's right! I said I'd make love to you, take you away to all the places you dreamt of, do you understand?' He pointed to the posters on the wall. 'To islands, sunny places—'

'Why?' she whispered.

'I brought you back here. You thought it was to make love, but I drew this knife and threatened you. I said if you made a sound, I'd kill you with the knife, like I – I told you I'd killed the boy and I'd kill you.'

'Why?'

'I had to use the wireless. I needed a house, see? Somewhere to work the wireless. I'd nowhere to go. So I picked you up and used you. Listen: if they ask you, that's what you must say.'

She laughed. She was afraid. She lay back uncertainly on her bed, inviting him to take her, as if that were what he wanted.

'If they ask, remember what I said.'

'Make me happy. I love you.'

She put out her arms and pulled his head towards her. Her lips were cold and damp, too thin against her sharp teeth. He drew away but she still held him. He strained his ears for any sound above the wind, but there was none.

'Let's talk a bit,' he said. 'Are you lonely, Anna? Who've you got?'

'What do you mean?'

'Parents, boy friend. Anyone.'

She shook her head in the darkness. 'Just you.'

'Listen; here, let's button your coat up. I like to talk first. I'll tell you about London. You want to hear about London, I'll bet. I went for a walk, once, it was raining and there was this man by the river, drawing on the pavement in the rain. Fancy that! Drawing with chalk in the rain, and the rain just washing it away.'

'Come now. Come.'

'Do you know what he was drawing? Just dogs, cottages and that. And the people, Anna – listen to this! – standing in the rain, watching him.'

'I want you. Hold me. I'm frightened.'

'Listen! D'you know why I went for a walk: they wanted me to make love to a girl. They sent me to London and I went for this walk instead.'

He could make her out as she watched him, judging him according to some instinct he did not understand.

'Are you alone too?'

'Yes.'

'Why did you come?'

'They're crazy people, the English! That old fellow by the river: they think the Thames is the biggest river in the world, you know that? And it's nothing! Just a little brown stream, you could nearly jump across it some places!'

'What's that noise?' she said suddenly. 'I know that noise! It was a gun; the cocking of a gun!'

He held her tightly to stop her trembling.

'It was just a door,' he said, 'the latch of a door. This place is made of paper. How could you hear anything in such a wind?'

There was a footfall in the corridor. She struck at him in terror, the raincoat swinging round her. As they came in he was standing away from her, the knife at her throat, his thumb uppermost, the blade parallel to the ground. His back was very straight and his small face was turned to her, empty, held by some private discipline, a man once more intent upon appearances, conscious of tradition.

The farmhouse lay in darkness, blind and not hearing, motionless against the swaying larches and the running sky.

They had left a shutter open and it banged slowly without rhythm, according to the strength of the storm. Snow gathered like ash and was dispersed. They had gone, leaving nothing behind but tyre tracks in the hardening mud, a twist of wire, and the sleepless tapping of the north wind.

Praise for
THE SPY WHO CAME IN FROM THE COLD

PRAISE FOR JOHN LE CARRÉ

"A brilliant linguistic artist with a keen eye for the exotic and not-so-exotic locale, a crafty moralizer with an occasional bent for sentiment."
—*The Wall Street Journal*

"No other contemporary novelist has more durably enjoyed the twin badges of being both well-read and well-regarded." —Scott Turow

"Le Carré has a great talent for entangling his audience in the sticky tape of complexity, paradox, and irony, and much of the pleasure in his stories is following the same dense, dark path as his characters."
—*Daily News* (New York)

"Any reader who feared that the end of the Cold War would deprive Mr. le Carré of his subject can now feel a measure of relief. If anything, his subject of East-West misunderstanding has grown richer, and he now possesses vast new territories to mine."
—*The New York Times*

"He has reinvented the realistic spy story as the supreme theater of paradox, where heroism breeds vice, and virtue is a quite accidental by-product of impudent crimes."
—*Time*

PENGUIN BOOKS

THE SPY WHO CAME IN FROM THE COLD

JOHN LE CARRÉ was born in 1931. For six decades, he wrote novels that came to define our age. The son of a con man, he spent his childhood between boarding school and the London underworld. At sixteen he found refuge at the university of Bern, then later at Oxford. A spell of teaching at Eton led him to a short career in British Intelligence (MI5&6). He published his debut novel, *Call for the Dead*, in 1961 while still a secret servant. His third novel, *The Spy Who Came in from the Cold*, secured him a worldwide reputation, which was consolidated by the acclaim for his trilogy *Tinker Tailor Soldier Spy*, *The Honourable Schoolboy*, and *Smiley's People*. At the end of the Cold War, le Carré widened his scope to explore an international landscape including the arms trade and the War on Terror. His memoir, *The Pigeon Tunnel*, was published in 2016 and the last George Smiley novel, *A Legacy of Spies*, appeared in 2017. *Silverview* is his twenty-sixth novel. He died on December 12, 2020.

BY JOHN LE CARRÉ

JOHN LE CARRÉ

THE SPY WHO CAME IN FROM THE COLD

PENGUIN BOOKS

PENGUIN BOOKS
An imprint of Penguin Random House LLC
penguinrandomhouse.com

First published in Great Britain by Victor Gollancz Ltd. 1963
First published in the United States of America by Walker Publishing Company, Inc. 1963
Published with a foreword by Joseph Kanon 2005
Published in Penguin Books 2012
This edition with a new introduction published in Penguin Books 2013

ISBN 9780143124757 (paperback)
ISBN 9781101573181 (ebook)
CIP data available

Printed in the United States of America
26th Printing

Designed by Sabrina Bowers

CONTENTS

FIFTY YEARS LATER

I wrote *The Spy Who Came in from the Cold* at the age of thirty under intense, unshared, personal stress and in extreme privacy. As an intelligence officer in the guise of a junior diplomat at the British Embassy in Bonn, I was a secret to my colleagues, and much of the time to myself. I had written a couple of earlier novels, necessarily under a pseudonym, and my employing service had approved them before publication. After lengthy soul-searching, they had also approved *The Spy Who Came in from the Cold*. To this day, I don't know what I would have done if they hadn't.

As it was, they seem to have concluded, rightly if reluctantly, that the book was sheer fiction from start to finish, uninformed by personal experience, and that accordingly it constituted no breach of security. This was not, however, the view taken by the world's press, which with one voice decided that the book was not merely authentic but some kind of revelatory Message from the Other Side, leaving me with nothing to do but sit tight and watch, in a kind of frozen awe, as it climbed the bestseller list and stuck there, while pundit after pundit heralded it as the real thing.

And to my awe, add over time a kind of impotent anger.

Anger, because from the day my novel was published, I realized that now and forever more I was to be branded as the spy turned writer, rather than as a writer who, like scores of his kind, had done a stint in the secret world and written about it.

But journalists of the time weren't having any of that. I was the British spy who had come out of the woodwork and told it how it really was, and anything I said to the contrary only reinforced the myth. And since I was writing for a public hooked on Bond and desperate for the antidote, the myth stuck. Meanwhile, I was receiving the sort of attention writers dream of. My only problem was, I didn't believe my own publicity. I didn't like it even while I was subscribing to it, and there was in the most literal sense nothing I could say to stop the bandwagon, even if I'd wanted to. And I wasn't sure I did.

In the sixties—and right up to the present day—the identity of a member of the British Secret Services was and is, quite rightly, a State secret. To divulge it is a crime. The Services may choose to leak a name when it pleases them. They may showcase an intelligence baron or two to give us a glimpse of their omniscience and—wait for it—openness. But woe betide a leaky former member.

And anyway I had my own inhibitions. I had no quarrel with my former employers; quite the contrary. Presenting myself to the press in New York a few months after the novel had made its mark in the States, I dutifully if nervously mouthed my denials: no, no, I had never been in the spy business; no, it was just a bad dream. Which of course it was.

The paradox was compounded when an American journalist with connections told me out of the corner of his mouth that the reigning chief of my Service had advised a former director of the CIA that I had been his serving officer, and that *he* had told nobody but his very large retinue of best friends, and that anyone in the room who was anyone knew I was lying.

Every interview I have faced in the fifty years since then seems designed to penetrate a truth that isn't there, and perhaps that's one reason why I have become allergic to the process.

The Spy Who Came in from the Cold was the work of a wayward imagination brought to the end of its tether by political disgust and personal confusion. Fifty years on, I don't associate the book with anything that ever happened to me, save for one wordless encounter at London airport when a worn-out middle-aged military kind of man in a stained raincoat slammed a handful of mixed foreign change onto the bar and in a gritty Irish accent ordered himself as much Scotch as it would buy. In that moment, Alec Leamas was born. Or so my memory, not always a reliable informant, tells me.

Today I think of the novel as a not-very-well-disguised internal explosion after which my life would never be the same. It was not the first such explosion, or the last. And yes, yes, by the time I wrote it, I had been caught up in secret work off and on for a decade; a decade the more formative because I had the inherited guilt of being too young to fight in the Second World War and—more important—of being the son of a war profiteer, another secret I felt I had to keep to myself until he died.

But I was never a mastermind, or a mini-mind, and long before I even entered the secret world, I had an instinct toward fiction that made me a dubious fact-gatherer. I was never at personal risk in my secret work; I was frequently bored stiff by it. Had things been otherwise, my employers would not have allowed me to publish my novel, even if later they kicked themselves for doing so. But that was because they decided it was being taken too seriously by too many people, and because any suggestion that the British Secret Service would betray its own was deemed derogatory to its ethical principles, bad for recruitment, and accordingly Bad for Britain, a charge to which there is no effective answer.

The proof that the novel was *not* "authentic"—how many times did I have to repeat this?—had been delivered by the fact that it was published. Indeed, one former head of a department that had employed me has since gone on record to declare that my contribution was negligible, which I can well believe. Another described the novel as "the only bloody double-agent operation that ever worked"—not true, but fun. The trouble is, when professional spies go out of their way to make a definitive statement about one of their own, the public tends to believe the opposite, which puts us all back where we started, myself included.

And if the spies hadn't had me at that age, some equally

luckless institution would have, and after a couple of years I'd have been digging my way out.

And the deep background of the novel? The sights, smells, and voices that, fifteen years after the end of the war, continued to infest every corner of divided Germany? The Berlin in which Leamas had his being was a paradigm of human folly and historical paradox. In the early sixties I had observed it mostly from the confines of the British Embassy in Bonn, and only occasionally in the raw. But I watched the Wall's progress from barbed wire to breeze block; I watched the ramparts of the Cold War going up on the still-warm ashes of the hot one. And I had absolutely no sense of transition from the one war to the other, because in the secret world there barely was one. To the hardliners of East and West the Second World War was a distraction. Now that it was over, they could get on with the real war that had started with the Bolshevik Revolution in 1917 and had been running under different flags and disguises ever since.

No wonder then if Alec Leamas found himself rubbing shoulders with some pretty unsavory colleagues in the ranks of Western intelligence. Former Nazis with attractive qualifications weren't just tolerated by the Allies, they were positively mollycoddled for their anti-Communist credentials. Who was America's first choice to head West Germany's embryonic intelligence service? General Reinhard Gehlen, former chief of Hitler's Foreign Armies East (Russian theater) where he had made himself a corner in the Soviet order of battle. Anticipating Germany's defeat, the general had assembled his files and his people, and at the first opportunity had turned them over to the Americans, who accepted them with open arms. Recruited, Gehlen tactfully dropped the "general" and became *Herr Doktor* instead.

But where to house this precious asset and his crown jewels? The Americans decided to install Gehlen and his people in the cozy Bavarian village of Pullach, eight miles outside Munich and handy for their intelligence headquarters.

And whose handsome country estate, now vacant, did they

select for the *Herr Doktor*? Martin Bormann was Hitler's most trusted confidant and private secretary. When the Führer established himself at his Eagle's Nest just up the road, his buddies scurried to set up house nearby. Gehlen and his people were settled in Martin Bormann's villa, now the subject of a conservation order issued by the Bavarian government. Just a few years ago, in circumstances of extraordinary courtesy, one of the Bundesnachrichtendienst's latter-day luminaries gave me a personal tour. I recommend the 1930s furniture in the conference room and the Jugendstil statues in the gardens at the back. But the main attraction must surely be the great dark staircase winding into the cellars and the fully furnished bunker, just like the Führer's, but smaller.

Was Alec Leamas a regular visitor to Pullach? He had no choice. Few secret operations into East Germany could take place without the connivance of the BND. And did Leamas, on his regular visits, perhaps come across the *Herr Doktor*'s valued chief of counterintelligence, Heinz Felfe, formerly of the SS and Sicherheitsdienst? He must have done. Felfe was a legendary operator. Had he not singlehandedly unmasked a raft of Soviet spies?

Of course he had, and no wonder. When he was finally unmasked himself, he got fourteen years for spying for Moscow, only to be traded for a bunch of hapless West Germans held there.

Did Leamas enjoy access to the ultrasecret "special material" obtained by Operation GOLD, the hugely costly quarter-mile-long Anglo-American audio tunnel that tapped into Russian cables a couple of feet below the surface of a road in the Eastern Sector of Berlin? Before the first spade went into the ground, GOLD had been comprehensively blown by a Soviet agent named George Blake, the heroic ex-prisoner of North Korea and pride of the British Secret Service.

Yet to this day, many of GOLD's architects would have us believe that their operation was not merely an engineering triumph but an intelligence coup as well, on the questionable grounds that, so reluctant were the Russians to blow their agent, they let communications flow as usual.

Dissolve to a couple of years later and Kim Philby, once in line for chief, was also revealed as Moscow's man. No wonder poor Leamas needed that stiff Scotch at London airport. The Service that owned his unflinching allegiance was in a state of corporate rot that would take another generation to heal. Did he know that? I think deep down he did.

And I think I must have known it too, or I wouldn't have written *Tinker, Tailor, Soldier, Spy* a few years down the line.

The novel's merit, then—or its offense, depending where you stood—was not that it was authentic, but that it was credible. The bad dream turned out to be one that a lot of people in the world were sharing, since it asked the same old question that we are asking ourselves fifty years later: how far can we go in the rightful defense of our Western values without abandoning them along the way? My fictional chief of the British Service—I called him Control—had no doubt of the answer:

> *"I mean, you can't be less ruthless than the opposition simply because your government's policy is benevolent, can you now?"*

Today, the same man, with better teeth and hair, and a much smarter suit, can be heard explaining away the catastrophic illegal war in Iraq, or justifying medieval torture techniques as the preferred means of interrogation in the twenty-first century, or defending the inalienable right of closet psychopaths to bear semiautomatic weapons and the use of unmanned drones as a risk-free method of assassinating one's perceived enemies and anybody who has the bad luck to be standing near them. Or, as a loyal servant of his corporation, assuring us that smoking is harmless to the health of the Third World and great banks are there to serve the public.

What have I learned over the last fifty years? Come to think of it, not much. Just that the morals of the secret world are very like our own.

John le Carré

1

Checkpoint

The American handed Leamas another cup of coffee and said, "Why don't you go back and sleep? We can ring you if he shows up."

Leamas said nothing, just stared through the window of the checkpoint, along the empty street.

"You can't wait forever, sir. Maybe he'll come some other time. We can have the polizei contact the Agency: you can be back here in twenty minutes."

"No," said Leamas, "it's nearly dark now."

"But you can't wait forever; he's nine hours over schedule."

"If you want to go, go. You've been very good," Leamas added. "I'll tell Kramer you've been damn' good."

"But how long will you wait?"

"Until he comes." Leamas walked to the observation window and stood between the two motionless policemen. Their binoculars were trained on the Eastern checkpoint.

"He's waiting for the dark," Leamas muttered. "I know he is."

"This morning you said he'd come across with the workmen."

Leamas turned on him.

"Agents aren't aeroplanes. They don't have schedules. He's blown, he's on the run, he's frightened. Mundt's after him, now, at this moment. He's only got one chance. Let him choose his time."

The younger man hesitated, wanting to go and not finding the moment.

A bell rang inside the hut. They waited, suddenly alert. A policeman said in German, "Black Opel Rekord, Federal registration."

"He can't see that far in the dusk, he's guessing," the American whispered and then he added: "How did Mundt know?"

"Shut up," said Leamas from the window. One of the policemen left the hut and walked to the sandbag emplacement two feet short of the white demarcation which lay across the road like the base line of a tennis court. The other waited until his companion was crouched behind the telescope in the emplacement, then put down his binoculars, took his black helmet from the peg by the door, and carefully adjusted it on his head. Somewhere high above the checkpoint the arclights sprang to life, casting theatrical beams on to the road in front of them.

The policeman began his commentary. Leamas knew it by heart.

"Car halts at the first control. Only one occupant, a woman. Escorted to the Vopo hut for document check." They waited in silence.

"What's he saying?" said the American. Leamas didn't reply. Picking up a spare pair of binoculars, he gazed fixedly towards the East German controls.

"Document check completed. Admitted to the second control."

"Mr. Leamas, is this your man?" the American persisted. "I ought to ring the Agency."

"Wait."

"Where's the car now? What's it doing?"

"Currency check, Customs," Leamas snapped.

Leamas watched the car. There were two Vopos at the driver's door, one doing the talking, the other standing off, waiting. A third was sauntering round the car. He stopped at the boot, then walked back to the driver. He wanted the key. He opened the boot, looked inside, closed it, returned the key, and walked thirty yards up the road to where, midway between the two opposing checkpoints, a solitary East German sentry was standing, a squat silhouette in boots and baggy trousers. The two stood together talking, self-conscious in the glare of the arclight.

With a perfunctory gesture they waved the car on. It reached the two sentries in the middle of the road and stopped again. They walked round the car, stood off, and talked again; finally, almost unwillingly, they let it continue across the line to the Western sector.

"It is a man you're waiting for, Mr. Leamas?" asked the American.

"Yes, it's a man."

Pushing up the collar of his jacket, Leamas stepped outside into the icy October wind. He remembered the crowd then. It was something you forgot inside the hut, this group of puzzled faces. The people changed but the expressions were the same. It was like the helpless crowd that gathers round in a traffic accident, no one knowing how it happened, whether you should move the body. Smoke or dust rose through the beam of the arclamps, a constant shifting pall between the margins of light.

Leamas walked over to the car, and said to the woman, "Where is he?"

"They came for him and he ran. He took the bicycle. They can't have known about me."

"Where did he go?"

"We had a room near Brandenburg, over a pub. He kept a few things there, money, papers. I think he'll have gone there. Then he'll come over."

"Tonight?"

"He said he would come tonight. The others have all been caught—Paul, Viereck, Ländser, Salomon. He hasn't got long."

Leamas stared at her for a moment in silence.

"Ländser too?"

"Last night."

A policeman was standing at Leamas' side.

"You'll have to move away from here," he said. "It's forbidden to obstruct the crossing point."

Leamas half turned.

"Go to hell," he snapped. The German stiffened, but the woman said:

"Get in. We'll drive down to the corner."

He got in beside her and they moved slowly down the road to a side turning.

"I didn't know you had a car," he said.

"It's my husband's," she replied indifferently. "Karl never told you I was married, did he?" Leamas was silent. "My husband and I work for an optical firm. They let us over to do business. Karl only told you my maiden name. He didn't want me to be mixed up with . . . you."

Leamas took a key from his pocket.

"You'll want somewhere to stay," he said. His voice sounded flat. "There's an apartment in the Albrecht-Dürer-Strasse, next to the Museum. Number 28A. You'll find everything you want. I'll telephone you when he comes."

"I'll stay here with you."

"I'm not staying here. Go to the flat. I'll ring you. There's no point in waiting here now."

"But he's coming to this crossing point."

Leamas looked at her in surprise.

"He told you that?"

"Yes. He knows one of the Vopos there, the son of his landlord. It may help. That's why he chose this route."

"And he told *you* that?"

"He trusts me. He told me everything."

"Christ."

He gave her the key and went back to the checkpoint hut, out of the cold. The policemen were muttering to each other as he entered; the larger one ostentatiously turned his back.

"I'm sorry," said Leamas. "I'm sorry I bawled you out." He opened a tattered briefcase and rummaged in it until he found what he was looking for: a half bottle of whisky. With a nod the elder man accepted it, half filled each coffee mug and topped them up with black coffee.

"Where's the American gone?" asked Leamas.

"Who?"

"The CIA boy. The one who was with me."

"Bed time," said the elder man and they all laughed.

Leamas put down his mug and said:

"What are your rules for shooting to protect a man coming over? A man on the run."

"We can only give covering fire if the Vopos shoot into our sector."

"That means you can't shoot until a man's over the boundary?"

The older man said, "We can't give covering fire, Mr. . . ."

"Thomas," Leamas replied, "Thomas." They shook hands, the two policemen pronouncing their own names as they did so.

"We can't give covering fire. That's the truth. They tell us there'd be war if we did."

"It's nonsense," said the younger policeman, emboldened by the whisky. "If the allies weren't here the Wall would be gone by now."

"So would Berlin," muttered the elder man.

"I've got a man coming over tonight," said Leamas abruptly.

"Here? At this crossing point?"

"It's worth a lot to get him out. Mundt's men are looking for him."

"There are still places where you can climb," said the younger policeman.

"He's not that kind. He'll bluff his way through; he's got papers, if the papers are still good. He's got a bicycle."

There was only one light in the checkpoint, a reading lamp with a green shade, but the glow of the arclights, like artificial moonlight, filled the cabin. Darkness had fallen, and with it silence. They spoke as if they were afraid of being overheard. Leamas went to the window and waited, in front of him the road and to either side the Wall, a dirty, ugly thing of breeze blocks and strands of barbed wire, lit with cheap yellow light, like the backdrop for a concentration camp. East and west of the Wall lay the unrestored part of Berlin, a half-world of ruin, drawn in two dimensions, crags of war.

That damned woman, thought Leamas, and that fool Karl who'd lied about her. Lied by omission, as they all do, agents the world over. You teach them to cheat, to cover their tracks, and they cheat you as well. He'd only produced her once, after that dinner in the Schürzstrasse last year. Karl had just had his big scoop and Control had wanted to meet him. Control always came in on success. They'd had dinner together—Leamas, Control, and Karl. Karl loved that kind of thing. He turned up looking like a Sunday School boy, scrubbed and shining, doffing his hat and all respectful. Control had shaken his hand for five minutes and said: "I want you to know how pleased we are, Karl, damn' pleased." Leamas had watched and thought, "That'll cost us another couple of hundred a year." When they'd finished dinner Control pumped their hands again, nodded significantly and implying that he had to go off and risk his life somewhere else, got back into his chauffeur-driven car. Then Karl had laughed, and Leamas had laughed with him, and they'd finished the champagne, still laughing about Control. Afterwards they'd gone to the "Alter Fass," Karl had insisted on it, and there Elvira was waiting for them, a forty-year-old blonde, tough as nails.

"This is my best kept secret, Alec," Karl had said, and Leamas was furious. Afterwards they'd had a row.

"How much does she know? Who is she? How did you meet her?" Karl sulked and refused to say. After that things went badly. Leamas tried to alter the routine, change the meeting places and the catch words, but Karl didn't like it. He knew what lay behind it and he didn't like it.

"If you don't trust her it's too late anyway," he'd said, and Leamas took the hint and shut up. But he went carefully after that, told Karl much less, used more of the hocus-pocus of espionage technique. And there she was, out there in her car, knowing everything, the whole network, the safe house, everything; and Leamas swore, not for the first time, never to trust an agent again.

He went to the telephone and dialled the number of his flat. Frau Martha answered.

"We've got guests at the Dürer-Strasse," said Leamas, "a man and a woman."

"Married?" asked Martha.

"Near enough," said Leamas, and she laughed that frightful laugh. As he put down the receiver one of the policemen turned to him.

"Herr Thomas! Quick!" Leamas stepped to the observation window.

"A man, Herr Thomas," the younger policeman whispered, "with a bicycle." Leamas picked up the binoculars.

It was Karl, the figure was unmistakable even at that distance, shrouded in an old Wehrmacht macintosh, pushing his bicycle. He's made it, thought Leamas, he must have made it, he's through the document check, only currency and Customs to go. Leamas watched Karl lean his bicycle against the railing, walk casually to the Customs hut. Don't overdo it, he thought. At last Karl came out, waved cheerfully to the man on the barrier, and the red and white pole swung slowly upwards. He was through, he was coming towards them, he had made it. Only the Vopo in the middle of the road, the line, and safety.

At that moment, Karl seemed to hear some sound, sense danger; he glanced over his shoulder, began to pedal furiously, bending low over the handlebars. There was still the lonely sentry on the bridge, and he had turned and was watching Karl. Then, totally unexpected, the searchlights went on, white and brilliant, catching Karl and holding him in their beam like a rabbit in the headlights of a car. There came the see-saw wail of a siren, the sound of orders wildly shouted. In front of Leamas the two policemen dropped to their knees, peering through the sandbagged slits, deftly flicking the rapid load on their automatic rifles.

The East German sentry fired, quite carefully, away from them, into his own sector. The first shot seemed to thrust Karl forward, the second to pull him back. Somehow he was still moving, still on the bicycle, passing the sentry, and the sentry was still shooting at him. Then he sagged, rolled to the ground, and they heard quite clearly the clatter of the bike as it fell. Leamas hoped to God he was dead.

2

The Circus

He watched the Tempelhof runway sink beneath him. Leamas was not a reflective man and not a particularly philosophical one. He knew he was written off—it was a fact of life which he would henceforth live with, as a man must live with cancer or imprisonment. He knew there was no kind of preparation which could have bridged the gap between then and now. He met failure as one day he would probably meet death, with cynical resentment and the courage of a solitary. He'd lasted longer than most; now he was beaten. It is said a dog lives as long as its teeth; metaphorically, Leamas' teeth had been drawn: and it was Mundt who had drawn them.

Ten years ago he could have taken the other path—there were desk jobs in that anonymous government building in Cambridge Circus which Leamas could have taken and kept till he was God knows how old; but Leamas wasn't made that way. You might as well have asked a jockey to become a totalisator clerk as expect Leamas to abandon operational life for the tendentious theorising and clandestine self-interest of Whitehall. He had stayed on in Berlin, conscious that Personnel had marked his file for review at the end of every year—stubborn,

wilful, contemptuous of instruction, telling himself that something would turn up. Intelligence work has one moral law—it is
justified by results. Even the sophistry of Whitehall paid court
to that law, and Leamas got results. Until Mundt came.

It was odd how soon Leamas had realised that Mundt was
the writing on the wall.

Hans-Dieter Mundt, born forty-two years ago in Leipzig.
Leamas knew his dossier, knew the photograph on the inside of
the cover; the blank, hard face beneath the flaxen hair; knew by
heart the story of Mundt's rise to power as second man in the
Abteilung and effective head of operations. Mundt was hated
even within his own department. Leamas knew that from the evidence of defectors, and from Riemeck, who as a member of the
SED Praesidium sat on security committees with Mundt, and
dreaded him. Rightly as it turned out, for Mundt had killed him.

Until 1959 Mundt had been a minor functionary of the
Abteilung, operating in London under the cover of the East
German Steel Mission. He returned to Germany in a hurry
after murdering two of his own agents to save his skin and was
not heard of for more than a year. Quite suddenly he reappeared at the Abteilung's headquarters in Leipzig as head of
the Ways and Means Department, responsible for allocating
currency, equipment, and personnel for special tasks. At the
end of that year came the big struggle for power within the
Abteilung. The number and influence of Soviet liaison officers
were drastically reduced, several of the old guard were dismissed on ideological grounds and three men emerged: Fiedler
as head of counter intelligence, Jahn took over from Mundt as
head of facilities, and Mundt himself got the plum—deputy
director of operations—at the age of forty-one. Then the new
style began. The first agent Leamas lost was a girl. She was
only a small link in the network; she was used for courier jobs.
They shot her dead in the street as she left a West Berlin cinema. The police never found the murderer and Leamas was at
first inclined to write the incident off as unconnected with her

work. A month later a railway porter in Dresden, a discarded agent from Peter Guillam's network, was found dead and mutilated beside a railway track. Leamas knew it wasn't coincidence any longer. Soon after that two members of another network under Leamas' control were arrested and summarily sentenced to death. So it went on: remorseless and unnerving.

And now they had Karl, and Leamas was leaving Berlin as he had come—without a single agent worth a farthing. Mundt had won.

Leamas was a short man with close, iron-grey hair, and the physique of a swimmer. He was very strong. This strength was discernible in his back and shoulders, in his neck, and in the stubby formation of his hands and fingers.

He had a utilitarian approach to clothes, as he did to most other things, and even the spectacles he occasionally wore had steel rims. Most of his suits were of artificial fibre, none of them had waistcoats. He favoured shirts of the American kind with buttons on the points of the collars, and suede shoes with rubber soles.

He had an attractive face, muscular, and a stubborn line to his thin mouth. His eyes were brown and small; Irish, some said. It was hard to place Leamas. If he were to walk into a London club the porter would certainly not mistake him for a member; in a Berlin night club they usually gave him the best table. He looked like a man who could make trouble, a man who looked after his money, a man who was not quite a gentleman.

The air hostess thought he was interesting. She guessed he was North Country, which he might have been, and rich, which he was not. She put his age at fifty, which was about right. She guessed he was single, which was half true. Somewhere long ago there had been a divorce; somewhere there were children, now in their teens, who received their allowance from a rather odd private bank in the City.

"If you want another whisky," said the air hostess, "you'd better hurry. We shall be at London airport in twenty minutes."

"No more." He didn't look at her; he was looking out of the window at the grey-green fields of Kent.

Fawley met him at the airport and drove him to London.

"Control's pretty cross about Karl," he said, looking sideways at Leamas. Leamas nodded.

"How did it happen?" asked Fawley.

"He was shot. Mundt got him."

"Dead?"

"I should think so, by now. He'd better be. He nearly made it. He should never have hurried, they couldn't have been sure. The Abteilung got to the checkpoint just after he'd been let through. They started the siren and a Vopo shot him twenty yards short of the line. He moved on the ground for a moment, then lay still."

"Poor bastard."

"Precisely," said Leamas.

Fawley didn't like Leamas, and if Leamas knew he didn't care. Fawley was a man who belonged to Clubs and wore representative ties, pontificated on the skills of sportsmen, and assumed a service rank in office correspondence. He thought Leamas suspect, and Leamas thought him a fool.

"What section are you in?" asked Leamas.

"Personnel."

"Like it?"

"Fascinating."

"Where do I go now? On ice?"

"Better let Control tell you, old boy."

"Do you know?"

"Of course."

"Then why the hell don't you tell me?"

"Sorry, old man," Fawley replied, and Leamas suddenly very

nearly lost his temper. Then he reflected that Fawley was probably lying anyway.

"Well, tell me one thing, do you mind? Have I got to look
for a bloody flat in London?"

Fawley scratched at his ear: "I don't think so, old man, no."

"No? Thank God for that."

They parked near Cambridge Circus, at a parking meter,
and went together into the hall.

"You haven't got a pass, have you? You'd better fill in a slip,
old man."

"Since when have we had passes? McCall knows me as well
as his own mother."

"Just a new routine. Circus is growing, you know."

Leamas said nothing, nodded at McCall, and got into the
lift without a pass.

Control shook his hand rather carefully, like a doctor feeling
the bones.

"You must be awfully tired," he said apologetically, "do sit
down." That same dreary voice, the donnish bray.

Leamas sat down in a chair facing an olive green electric
fire with a bowl of water balanced on the top of it.

"Do you find it cold?" Control asked. He was stooping over
the fire rubbing his hands together. He wore a cardigan under
his black jacket, a shabby brown one. Leamas remembered
Control's wife, a stupid little woman called Mandy who seemed
to think her husband was in the Coal Board. He supposed she
had knitted it.

"It's so dry, that's the trouble," Control continued. "Beat
the cold and you patch the atmosphere. Just as dangerous." He
went to the desk and pressed a button. "We'll try and get some
coffee," he said, "Ginnie's on leave, that's the trouble. They've
given me some new girl. It really is too bad."

He was shorter than Leamas remembered him: otherwise,

just the same. The same affected detachment, the same donnish conceits; the same horror of draughts; courteous according to a formula miles removed from Leamas' experience. The same milk-and-water smile, the same elaborate diffidence, the same apologetic adherence to a code of behaviour which he pretended to find ridiculous. The same banality.

He brought a packet of cigarettes from the desk and gave one to Leamas.

"You're going to find these more expensive," he said, and Leamas nodded dutifully. Slipping the cigarettes into his pocket, Control sat down. There was a pause; finally Leamas said:

"Riemeck's dead."

"Yes, indeed," Control declared, as if Leamas had made a good point. "It is very unfortunate. Most . . . I suppose the girl blew him—Elvira?"

"I suppose so." Leamas wasn't going to ask him how he knew about Elvira.

"And Mundt had him shot," Control added.

"Yes."

Control got up and drifted round the room looking for an ashtray. He found one and put it awkwardly on the floor between their two chairs.

"How did you feel? When Riemeck was shot, I mean? You saw it, didn't you?"

Leamas shrugged. "I was bloody annoyed," he said.

Control put his head on one side and half closed his eyes. "Surely you felt more than that? Surely you were upset? That would be more natural."

"I was upset. Who wouldn't be?"

"Did you like Riemeck—as a man?"

"I suppose so," said Leamas helplessly. "There doesn't seem much point in going into it," he added.

"How did you spend the night, what was left of it, after Riemeck had been shot?"

"Look, what is this?" Leamas asked hotly; "what are you getting at?"

"Riemeck was the last," Control reflected, "the last of a series of deaths. If my memory is right it began with the girl, the one they shot in Wedding, outside the cinema. Then there was the Dresden man, and the arrests at Jena. Like the ten little niggers. Now Paul, Vierek, and Ländser—all dead. And finally Riemeck." He smiled deprecatingly; "that is quite a heavy rate of expenditure. I wondered if you'd had enough."

"What do you mean—enough?"

"I wondered whether you were tired. Burnt out." There was a long silence.

"That's up to you," Leamas said at last.

"We have to live without sympathy, don't we? That's impossible of course. We act it to one another, all this hardness; but we aren't like that really, I mean . . . one can't be out in the cold all the time; one has to come in from the cold . . . d'you see what I mean?"

Leamas saw. He saw the long road outside Rotterdam, the long straight road beside the dunes, and the stream of refugees moving along it; saw the little aeroplane miles away, the procession stop and look towards it; and the plane coming in, nearly over the dunes; saw the chaos, the meaningless hell, as the bombs hit the road.

"I can't talk like this, Control," Leamas said at last. "What do you want me to do?"

"I want you to stay out in the cold a little longer." Leamas said nothing, so Control went on: "The ethic of our work, as I understand it, is based on a single assumption. That is, we are never going to be aggressors. Do you think that's fair?"

Leamas nodded. Anything to avoid talking.

"Thus we do disagreeable things, but we are *defensive*. That, I think, is still fair. We do disagreeable things so that ordinary people here and elsewhere can sleep safely in their beds at night. Is that too romantic? Of course, we occasionally do very wicked things"; he grinned like a schoolboy. "And in weighing up the moralities, we rather go in for dishonest comparisons; after all, you can't compare the ideals of one side with the methods of the other, can you, now?"

Leamas was lost. He'd heard the man talked a lot of drivel before getting the knife in, but he'd never heard anything like this before.

"I mean you've got to compare method with method, and ideal with ideal. I would say that since the war, our methods—ours and those of the opposition—have become much the same. I mean you can't be less ruthless than the opposition simply because your government's *policy* is benevolent, can you now?" He laughed quietly to himself: "That would *never* do," he said.

For God's sake, thought Leamas, it's like working for a bloody clergyman. What *is* he up to?

"That is why," Control continued, "I think we ought to try and get rid of Mundt . . . Oh really," he said, turning irritably towards the door, "Where is that damned coffee?"

Control crossed to the door, opened it, and talked to some unseen girl in the outer room. As he returned he said: "I really think we *ought* to get rid of him if we can manage it."

"Why? We've got nothing left in East Germany, nothing at all. You just said so—Riemeck was the last. We've nothing left to protect."

Control sat down and looked at his hands for a while.

"That is not altogether true," he said finally; "but I don't think I need to bore you with the details."

Leamas shrugged.

"Tell me," Control continued, "are you tired of spying? Forgive me if I repeat the question. I mean that is a phenomenon we understand here, you know. Like aircraft designers . . . metal fatigue, I think the term is. Do say if you are."

Leamas remembered the flight home that morning and wondered.

"If you were," Control added, "we would have to find some other way of taking care of Mundt. What I have in mind is a little out of the ordinary."

The girl came in with the coffee. She put the tray on the desk and poured out two cups. Control waited till she had left the room.

"Such a *silly* girl," he said, almost to himself. "It seems extraordinary they can't find good ones anymore. I do wish Ginnie wouldn't go on holiday at times like this." He stirred his coffee disconsolately for a while.

"We really must discredit Mundt," he said. "Tell me, do you drink a lot? Whisky and that kind of thing?"

Leamas had thought he was used to Control.

"I drink a bit. More than most I suppose."

Control nodded understandingly. "What do you know about Mundt?"

"He's a killer. He was here a year or two back with the East German Steel Mission. We had an Adviser here then: Maston."

"Quite so."

"Mundt was running an agent, the wife of an FO man. He killed her."

"He tried to kill George Smiley. And of course he shot the woman's husband. He is a very distasteful man. Ex–Hitler Youth and all that kind of thing. Not at all the intellectual kind of Communist. A practitioner of the cold war."

"Like us," Leamas observed drily. Control didn't smile.

"George Smiley knew the case well. He isn't with us anymore, but I think you ought to ferret him out. He's doing things on seventeenth-century Germany. He lives in Chelsea, just behind Sloane Square. Bywater Street, do you know it?"

"Yes."

"And Guillam was on the case as well. He's in Satellites Four, on the first floor. I'm afraid everything's changed since your day."

"Yes."

"Spend a day or two with them. They know what I have in mind. Then I wondered if you'd care to stay with me for the weekend. My wife," he added hastily, "is looking after her mother, I'm afraid. It will be just you and I."

"Thanks. I'd like to."

"We can talk about things in comfort then. It would be very nice. I think you might make a lot of money out of it. You can have whatever you make."

"Thanks."

"That is, of couse, if you're *sure you want* to . . . no metal fatigue or anything?"

"If it's a question of killing Mundt, I'm game."

"Do you really feel that?" Control enquired politely. And then, having looked at Leamas thoughtfully for a moment he observed: "Yes, I really think you do. But you mustn't feel you *have* to say it. I mean in our world we pass so quickly out of the register of hate or love—like certain sounds a dog can't hear. All that's left in the end is a kind of nausea; you never want to cause suffering again. Forgive me, but isn't that rather what you felt when Karl Riemeck was shot? Not hate for Mundt, nor love for Karl, but a sickening jolt like a blow on a numb body . . . They tell me you walked all night—just walked through the streets of Berlin. Is that right?"

"It's right that I went for a walk."

"All night?"

"Yes."

"What happened to Elvira?"

"God knows . . . I'd like to take a swing at Mundt," he said.

"Good . . . good. Incidentally, if you should meet any old friends in the meantime, I don't think there's any point in discussing this with them. In fact," Control added after a moment, "I should be rather short with them. Let them think we've treated you badly. It's as well to begin as one intends to continue, isn't it?"

3

Decline

It surprised no one very much when they put Leamas on the shelf. In the main, they said, Berlin had been a failure for years, and someone had to take the rap. Besides, he was old for operational work, where your reflexes often had to be as quick as those of a professional tennis player. Leamas had done good work in the war, everyone knew that. In Norway and Holland he had somehow remained demonstrably alive, and at the end of it they gave him a medal and let him go. Later, of course, they got him to come back. It was bad luck about his pension, decidedly bad luck. Accounts Section had let it out, in the person of Elsie. Elsie said in the canteen that poor Alec Leamas would only have £400 a year to live on because of his interrupted service. Elsie felt it was a rule they really ought to change; after all, Mr. Leamas had *done* the service, hadn't he? But there they were with Treasury on their backs, not a bit like the old days, and what could they do? Even in the bad days of Maston they'd managed things better.

Leamas, the new men were told, was the old school; blood, guts and cricket and School Cert. French. In Leamas' case this happened to be unfair, since he was bilingual in German and

English and his Dutch was admirable; he also disliked cricket.
But it was true that he had no degree.

Leamas' contract had a few months to run, and they put
him in Banking to do his time. Banking Section was different
from Accounts; it dealt with overseas payments, financing
agents and operations. Most of the jobs in Banking could have
been done by an office boy were it not for the high degree of
secrecy involved, and thus Banking was one of several Sections
of the Service which were regarded as laying-out places for
officers shortly to be buried.

Leamas went to seed.

The process of going to seed is generally considered to be
a protracted one, but in Leamas this was not the case. In the
full view of his colleagues he was transformed from a man
honourably put aside to a resentful, drunken wreck—and all
within a few months. There is a kind of stupidity among
drunks, particularly when they are sober, a kind of disconnection which the unobservant interpret as vagueness and which
Leamas seemed to acquire with unnatural speed. He developed small dishonesties, borrowed insignificant sums from
secretaries and neglected to return them, arrived late or left
early under some mumbled pretext. At first his colleagues
treated him with indulgence; perhaps his decline scared them
in the same way as we are scared by cripples, beggars, and in-
valids because we fear we could ourselves become them; but in
the end his neglect, his brutal, unreasoning malice isolated
him.

Rather to people's surprise, Leamas didn't seem to mind
being put on the shelf. His will seemed suddenly to have collapsed. The débutante secretaries, reluctant to believe that
Intelligence Services are peopled by ordinary mortals, were
alarmed to notice that Leamas had become definitely seedy.
He took less care of his appearance and less notice of his surroundings, he lunched in the canteen which was normally the
preserve of junior staff, and it was rumoured that he was drink-

ing. He became a solitary, belonging to that tragic class of active men prematurely deprived of activity; swimmers barred from the water or actors banished from the stage.

Some said he had made a mistake in Berlin, and that was why his network had been rolled up; no one quite knew. All agreed that he had been treated with unusual harshness, even by a personnel department not famed for its philanthropy. They would point to him covertly as he went by, as men will point to an athlete of the past, and say: "That's Leamas. He put up a black in Berlin. Pathetic the way he's let himself go."

And then one day he had vanished. He said good-bye to no one, not even, apparently, Control. In itself that was not surprising. The nature of the Service precluded elaborate farewells and the presentation of gold watches, but even by these standards Leamas' departure seemed abrupt. So far as could be judged, his departure occurred before the statutory termination of his contract. Elsie, of Accounts Section, offered one or two crumbs of information: Leamas had drawn the balance of his pay in cash, which, if Elsie knew anything, meant he was having trouble with his bank. His gratuity was to be paid at the turn of the month, she couldn't say how much but it wasn't four figures, poor lamb. His National Insurance card had been sent on. Personnel had an address for him, Elsie added with a sniff, but of course they weren't revealing it, not Personnel.

Then there was the story about the money. It leaked out—no one, as usual, knew where from—that Leamas' sudden departure was connected with irregularities in the accounts of Banking Section. A largish sum was missing (not three figures but four, according to a lady with blue hair who worked in the telephone room) and they'd got it back, nearly all of it, and they'd stuck a lien on his pension. Others said they didn't believe it— if Alec had wanted to rob the till, they said, he'd know better ways of doing it than fiddling with HQ accounts. Not that he wasn't capable of it—he'd just have done it better. But those less impressed by Leamas' criminal potential pointed at his

large consumption of alcohol, at the expense of maintaining a
separate household, at the fatal disparity between pay at home
and allowances abroad and above all at the temptations put in
the way of a man handling large sums of hot money when he
knew that his days in the Service were numbered. All agreed
that if Alec had dipped his hands in the honey pot he was finished for all time—the Resettlement people wouldn't look at
him and Personnel would give him no reference—or one so
icy cold that the most enthusiastic employer would shiver at
the sight of it. Peculation was the one sin Personnel would
never let you forget—and they never forgot it themselves. If it
was true that Alec had robbed the Circus, he would take the
wrath of Personnel with him to the grave—and Personnel
would not so much as pay for the shroud.

For a week or two after his departure, a few people wondered what had become of him. But his former friends had
already learnt to keep clear of him. He had become a resentful
bore, constantly attacking the Service and its administration,
and what he called the "Cavalry boys" who, he said, managed
its affairs as if it were a regimental club. He never missed an
opportunity of railing against the Americans and their intelligence agencies. He seemed to hate them more than the
Abteilung, to which he seldom, if ever, referred. He would hint
that it was they who had compromised his network; this
seemed to be an obsession with him, and it was poor reward
for attempts to console him, it made him bad company, so that
those who had known and even tacitly liked him, wrote him
off. Leamas' departure caused only a ripple on the water; with
other winds and the changing of the seasons it was soon
forgotten.

His flat was small and squalid, done in brown paint with photographs of Clovelly. It looked directly on to the grey backs of
three stone warehouses, the windows of which were drawn, for

aesthetic reasons, in creosote. Above the warehouse there lived an Italian family, quarrelling at night and beating carpets in the morning. Leamas had few possessions with which to brighten his rooms. He bought some shades to cover the light bulbs, and two pairs of sheets to replace the hessian squares provided by the landlord. The rest Leamas tolerated: the flower pattern curtains, not lined or hemmed, the fraying brown carpets, and the clumsy darkwood furniture, like something from a seamen's hostel. From a yellow, crumbling geyser he obtained hot water for a shilling.

He needed a job. He had no money, none at all. So perhaps the stories of embezzlement were true. The offers of resettlement which the Service made had seemed to Leamas lukewarm and peculiarly unsuitable. He tried first to get a job in commerce. A firm of industrial adhesive manufacturers showed interest in his application for the post of assistant manager and personnel officer. Unconcerned by the inadequate reference with which the Service provided him, they demanded no qualifications, and offered him six hundred a year. He stayed for a week, by which time the foul stench of decaying fish oil had permeated his clothes and hair, lingering in his nostrils like the smell of death. No amount of washing would remove it, so that in the end Leamas had his hair cut short to the scalp and threw away two of his best suits. He spent another week trying to sell encyclopaedias to suburban housewives, but he was not a man that housewives liked or understood; they did not want Leamas, let alone his encyclopaedias. Night after night he returned wearily to his flat, his ridiculous sample under his arm. At the end of a week he telephoned the company and told them he had sold nothing. Expressing no surprise, they reminded him of his obligation to return the sample if he discontinued acting on their behalf, and rang off. Leamas stalked out of the telephone booth in a fury, leaving the sample behind him, went to a pub and got very drunk at a cost of twenty-five shillings, which he could not afford. They threw him out for shouting at a woman who tried to pick him up. They told him never to come back, but they'd forgotten all about it a week later. They were beginning to know Leamas there.

They were beginning to know him elsewhere too, the grey, shambling figure from the Mansions. Not a wasted word did he speak, not a friend, neither man, woman, nor beast did he have. They guessed he was in trouble, run away from his wife like as not. He never knew the price of anything, never remembered it when he was told. He patted all his pockets whenever he looked for change, he never remembered to bring a basket, always buying carrier bags. They didn't like him in the Street, but they were almost sorry for him. They thought he was dirty too, the way he didn't shave weekends, and his shirts all grubby.

A Mrs. McCaird from Sudbury Avenue cleaned for him for a week, but having never received a civil word from him withdrew her labour. She was an important source of information in the Street, where tradesmen told one another what they needed to know in case he asked for credit. Mrs. McCaird's advice was against credit. Leamas never had a letter, she said, and they agreed that that was serious. He'd no pictures and only a few books; she thought one of the books was dirty but couldn't be sure because it was in foreign writing. It was her opinion he had a bit to live on, and that that bit was running out. She knew he drew Benefit on Thursdays. Bayswater was warned, and needed no second warning. They heard from Mrs. McCaird that he drank like a fish: this was confirmed by the publican. Publicans and charwomen are not in the way of accommodating their clients with credit; but their information is treasured by those who are.

4

Liz

Finally he took the job in the library. The Labour Exchange had put him on to it each Thursday morning as he drew his unemployment benefit, and he'd always turned it down.

"It's not really your cup of tea," Mr. Pitt said, "but the pay's fair and the work's easy for an educated man."

"What sort of library?" Leamas asked.

"It's the Bayswater Library for Psychic Research. It's an endowment. They've got thousands of volumes, all sorts, and they've been left a whole lot more. They want another helper."

He took his dole and the slip of paper. "They're an odd lot," Mr. Pitt added, "but then you're not a stayer anyway, are you? I think it's time you gave them a try, don't you?"

It was odd about Pitt. Leamas was certain he'd seen him before somewhere. At the Circus, during the war.

The library was like a church hall, and very cold. The black oil stoves at either end made it smell of paraffin. In the middle of the room was a cubicle like a witness-box and inside it sat Miss Crail, the librarian.

It had never occurred to Leamas that he might have to

work for a woman. No one at the Labour Exchange had said anything about that.

"I'm the new help," he said; "my name's Leamas."

Miss Crail looked up sharply from her card index, as if she had heard a rude word. "Help? What do you mean, help?"

"Assistant. From the Labour Exchange. Mr. Pitt." He pushed across the counter a roneoed form with his particulars entered in a sloping hand. She picked it up and studied it.

"You are Mr. Leamas." This was not a question, but the first stage of a laborious fact-finding investigation.

"And you are from the Labour Exchange."

"No. I was sent by the Exchange. They told me you needed an assistant."

"I see." A wooden smile.

At that moment the telephone rang: she lifted the receiver and began arguing with somebody, fiercely. Leamas guessed they argued all the time; there were no preliminaries. Her voice just rose a key and she began arguing about some tickets for a concert. He listened for a minute or two and then drifted towards the bookshelves. He noticed a girl in one of the alcoves standing on a ladder sorting large volumes.

"I'm the new man," he said, "my name's Leamas."

She came down from the ladder and shook his hand a little formally.

"I'm Liz Gold. How d'you do. Have you met Miss Crail?"

"Yes, but she's on the phone at the moment."

"Arguing with her mother I expect. What are you going to do?"

"I don't know. Work."

"We're marking at the moment; Miss Crail's started a new index."

She was a tall girl, ungainly, with a long waist and long legs. She wore flat, ballet-type shoes to reduce her height. Her face, like her body, had large components which seemed to hesitate between plainness and beauty. Leamas guessed she was twenty-two or -three, and Jewish.

"It's just a question of checking that all the books are in the shelves. This is the reference bit, you see. When you've checked you pencil in the new reference and mark it off on the index."

"What happens then?"

"Only Miss Crail's allowed to ink in the reference. It's the rule."

"Whose rule?"

"Miss Crail's. Why don't you start on the archaeology?"

Leamas nodded and together they walked to the next alcove where a shoe-box full of cards lay on the floor.

"Have you done this kind of thing before?" she asked.

"No." He stooped and picked up a handful of cards and shuffled through them. "Mr. Pitt sent me. From the Exchange." He put the cards back.

"Is Miss Crail the only person who can ink the cards, too?" Leamas enquired.

"Yes."

She left him there, and after a moment's hesitation he took out a book and looked at the fly-leaf. It was called *Archaeological Discoveries in Asia Minor*, Volume four. They only seemed to have volume four.

It was one o'clock and Leamas was hungry, so he walked over to where Liz Gold was sorting and said:

"What happens about lunch?"

"Oh, I bring sandwiches." She looked a little embarrassed. "You can have some of mine if that would help. There's no café for miles."

Leamas shook his head.

"I'll go out, thanks. Got some shopping to do." She watched him push his way through the swing doors.

It was half past two when he came back. He smelt of whisky. He had one carrier bag full of vegetables and another containing groceries. He put them down in a corner of the alcove and wearily began again on the archaeology books. He'd been marking for about ten minutes when he became aware that Miss Crail was watching him.

"*Mister* Leamas." He was half-way up the ladder, so he looked down over his shoulder and said:

"Yes?"

"Do you know where these carrier bags come from?"

"They're mine."

"I see. They are yours." Leamas waited. "I regret," she continued at last, "that we do not allow it, bringing shopping into the library."

"Where else can I put it? There's nowhere else I *can* put it."

"Not in the library," she replied. Leamas ignored her, and returned his attention to the archaeology section.

"If you only took the normal lunch break," Miss Crail continued, "you would not have time to go shopping. Neither of *us* does, Miss Gold or myself; *we* do not have time to shop."

"Why don't you take an extra half-hour?" Leamas asked, "you'd have time then. If you're pushed you can work another half-hour in the evening. If you're pressed."

She stayed for some moments, just watching him and obviously thinking of something to say. Finally she announced:

"I shall discuss it with Mr. Ironside," and went away.

At exactly half past five Miss Crail put on her coat and, with a pointed: "Good night, Miss Gold," left. Leamas guessed she had been brooding on the carrier bags all afternoon. He went into the next alcove where Liz Gold was sitting on the bottom rung of her ladder reading what looked like a tract. When she saw Leamas she dropped it guiltily into her handbag and stood up.

"Who's Mr. Ironside?" Leamas asked.

"I don't think he exists," she replied. "He's her big gun

when she's stuck for an answer. I asked her once who he was. She went all shifty and mysterious, and said 'Never mind.' I don't think he exists."

"I'm not sure Miss Crail does," said Leamas and Liz Gold smiled.

At six o'clock she locked up and gave the keys to the curator, a very old man with First War shellshock who, said Liz, sat awake all night in case the Germans made a counterattack. It was bitterly cold outside.

"Got far to go?" asked Leamas.

"Twenty minutes' walk. I always walk it. Have you?"

"Not far," said Leamas. "Good night."

He walked slowly back to the flat. He let himself in and turned the light switch. Nothing happened. He tried the light in the tiny kitchen and finally the electric fire that plugged in by his bed. On the door mat was a letter. He picked it up and took it out into the pale, yellow light of the staircase. It was the electricity company, regretting that the area manager had no alternative but to cut off the electricity until the outstanding account of nine pounds four shillings and eightpence had been settled.

He had become an enemy of Miss Crail, and enemies were what Miss Crail liked. Either she scowled at him or she ignored him, and when he came close, she began to tremble, looking to left and right, either for something with which to defend herself, or perhaps for a line of escape. Occasionally she would take immense umbrage, such as when he hung his macintosh on *her* peg, and she stood in front of it shaking, for fully five minutes, until Liz spotted her and called Leamas. Leamas went over to her and said:

"What's troubling you, Miss Crail?"

"Nothing," she replied in a breathy, clipped way, "nothing at all."

"Something wrong with my coat?"

"Nothing at all."

"Fine," he replied, and went back to his alcove. She quivered all that day, and conducted a telephone call in a stage whisper for half the morning.

"She's telling her mother," said Liz. "She always tells her mother. She tells her about me, too."

Miss Crail developed such an intense hatred for Leamas that she found it impossible to communicate with him. On pay days he would come back from lunch and find an envelope on the third rung of his ladder with his name misspelt on the outside. The first time it happened he took the money over to her with the envelope and said; "It's L-E-A, Miss Crail, and only one S," whereupon she was seized with a veritable palsy, rolling her eyes and fumbling erratically with her pencil until Leamas went away. She conspired into the telephone for hours after that.

About three weeks after Leamas began work at the library Liz asked him to supper. She pretended it was an idea that had come to her quite suddenly, at five o'clock that evening; she seemed to realise that if she were to ask him for tomorrow or the next day he would forget or just not come, so she asked him at five o'clock. Leamas seemed reluctant to accept, but in the end he did.

They walked to her flat through the rain and they might have been anywhere—Berlin, London, any town where paving stones turn to lakes of light in the evening rain, and the traffic shuffles despondently through wet streets.

It was the first of many meals which Leamas had at her flat. He came when she asked him, and she asked him often. He never spoke much. When she discovered he would come, she took to laying the table in the morning before leaving for the library. She even prepared the vegetables beforehand and had the candles on the table, for she loved candlelight. She always knew that there was something deeply wrong with Leamas, and that one day, for some reason she could not understand, he might break and she would never see him again. She tried to tell him she knew; she said to him one evening:

"You must go when you want. I'll never follow you, Alec," and his brown eyes rested on her for a moment: "I'll tell you when," he replied.

Her flat was just a bed-sitting-room and a kitchen. In the sitting-room were two armchairs, a divan bed, and a bookcase full of paper-back books, mainly classics which she had never read.

After supper she would talk to him, and he would lie on the divan, smoking. She never knew how much he heard, she didn't care. She could kneel by the bed holding his hand against her cheek, talking.

Then one evening she said to him:

"Alec, what do you believe in? Don't laugh—tell me." She waited and at last he said:

"I believe an eleven bus will take me to Hammersmith. I don't believe it's driven by Father Christmas."

She seemed to consider this and at last she asked again:

"But what do you believe in?"

Leamas shrugged.

"You must believe in something," she persisted: "something like God—I know you do, Alec; you've got that look sometimes, as if you'd got something special to do, like a priest. Alec, don't smile, it's true."

He shook his head.

"Sorry, Liz, you've got it wrong. I don't like Americans and public schools. I don't like military parades and people who play soldiers." Without smiling he added, "And I don't like conversations about Life."

"But, Alec, you might as well say—"

"I should have added," Leamas interrupted, "that I don't like people who tell me what I ought to think." She knew he was getting angry but she couldn't stop herself anymore.

"That's because you don't *want* to think, you don't dare!

There's some poison in your mind, some hate. You're a fanatic, Alec. I know you are, but I don't know what about. You're a fanatic who doesn't want to convert people, and that's a dangerous thing. You're like a man who's . . . sworn vengeance or something." The brown eyes rested on her. When he spoke she was frightened by the menace in his voice.

"If I were you," he said roughly, "I'd mind my own business."

And then he smiled, a roguish smile. He hadn't smiled like that before and Liz knew he was putting on the charm.

"What does Liz believe in?" he asked, and she replied:

"I can't be had that easy, Alec."

Later that night they talked about it again. Leamas brought it up—he asked her whether she was religious.

"You've got me wrong," she said, "all wrong. I don't believe in God."

"Then what do you believe in?"

"History."

He looked at her in astonishment for a moment, then laughed.

"Oh, Liz . . . oh *no*. You're not a bloody Communist?" She nodded, blushing like a small girl at his laughter, angry and relieved that he didn't care.

She made him stay that night and they became lovers. He left at five in the morning. She couldn't understand it; she was so proud and he seemed ashamed.

He left her flat and turned down the empty street towards the park. It was foggy. Some way down the road—not far, twenty yards, perhaps a bit more—stood the figure of a man in a raincoat, short and rather plump. He was leaning against the railings of the park, silhouetted in the shifting mist. As Leamas approached, the mist seemed to thicken, closing in around the figure at the railings, and when it parted the man was gone.

5

Credit

Then one day about a week later, he didn't come to the library. Miss Crail was delighted; by half-past eleven she had told her mother, and on returning from lunch she stood in front of the archaeology shelves where he had been working since he came. She started with theatrical concentration at the rows of books and Liz knew she was pretending to work out whether Leamas had stolen anything.

Liz entirely ignored her for the rest of the day, failed to reply when she addressed her and worked with assiduous application. When the evening came she walked home and cried herself to sleep.

The next morning she arrived early at the library. She somehow felt that the sooner she got there, the sooner Leamas might come; but as the morning dragged on her hopes faded, and she knew he would never come. She had forgotten to make sandwiches for herself that day so she decided to take a bus to the Bayswater Road and go to the ABC. She felt sick and empty, but not hungry. Should she go and find him? She had promised never to follow him, but he had promised to tell her; should she go and find him?

She hailed a taxi and gave his address.

• • •

She made her way up the dingy staircase and pressed the bell of his door. The bell seemed to be broken; she heard nothing. There were three bottles of milk on the mat and a letter from the electricity company. She hesitated a moment, then banged on the door, and she heard the faint groan of a man. She rushed downstairs to the flat below, hammered and rang at the door. There was no reply so she ran down another flight and found herself in the back room of a grocer's shop. An old woman sat in a corner, rocking back and forth in her chair.

"The top flat," Liz almost shouted, "somebody's very ill. Who's got a key?"

The old woman looked at her for a moment, then called towards the front room, where the shop was.

"Arthur, come in here, Arthur, there's a girl here!"

A man in a brown overall and grey trilby hat looked round the door and said:

"Girl?"

"There's someone seriously ill in the top flat," said Liz, "he can't get to the front door to open it. Have you got a key?"

"No," replied the grocer, "but I've got a hammer," and they hurried up the stairs together, the grocer, still in his trilby, carrying a heavy screwdriver and a hammer. He knocked on the door sharply, and they waited breathless for an answer. There was none.

"I heard a groan before, I promise I did," Liz whispered.

"Will you pay for this door if I bust it?"

"Yes."

The hammer made a terrible noise. With three blows he had wrenched out a piece of the frame and the lock came with it. Liz went in first and the grocer followed. It was bitterly cold in the room and dark, but on the bed in the corner they could make out the figure of a man.

"Oh God," thought Liz, "if he's dead I don't think I can

touch him," but she went to him and he was alive. Drawing the curtains, she knelt beside the bed.

"I'll call you if I need you, thank you," she said without looking back, and the grocer nodded and went downstairs.

"Alec, what is it, what's making you ill? What is it, Alec?"

Leamas moved his head on the pillow. His sunken eyes were closed. The dark beard stood out against the pallor of his face.

"Alec, you must tell me, please, Alec." She was holding one of his hands in hers. The tears were running down her cheeks. Desperately she wondered what to do; then, getting up, she ran to the tiny kitchen and put on a kettle. She wasn't quite clear what she would make, but it comforted her to do something. Leaving the kettle on the gas she picked up her handbag, took Leamas' key from the bedside table and ran downstairs, down the four flights into the street, and crossed the road to Mr. Sleaman, the Chemist. She bought some calves-foot jelly, some essence of beef, and a bottle of aspirin. She got to the door, then went back and bought a packet of rusks. Altogether it cost her sixteen shillings, which left four shillings in her handbag and eleven pounds in her post office book, but she couldn't draw any of that till tomorrow. By the time she returned to his flat the kettle was just boiling.

She made the beef tea like her mother used to, in a glass with a teaspoon in to stop it cracking, and all the time she glanced towards him, as if she were afraid he was dead.

She had to prop him up to make him drink the tea. He only had one pillow and there were no cushions in the room, so taking his overcoat down from the back of the door she made a bundle of it and arranged it behind the pillow. It frightened her to touch him, he was drenched in sweat, so that his short grey hair was damp and slippery. Putting the cup beside the bed she held his head with one hand, and fed him the tea with the other. After he had taken a few spoonfuls, she crushed two aspirin and gave them to him in the spoon. She talked to him as if he were a child, sitting on the edge of the bed looking at him, sometimes letting her fingers run over his head and face, whispering his name over and over again, "Alec, Alec."

Gradually his breathing became more regular, his body more relaxed as he drifted from the taut pain of fever to the calm of sleep; Liz, watching him, sensed that the worst was over. Suddenly she realised it was almost dark.

Then she felt ashamed, because she knew she should have cleaned and tidied. Jumping up, she fetched the carpet sweeper and a duster from the kitchen, and set to work with feverish energy. She found a clean teacloth and spread it neatly on the bedside table and she washed up the odd cups and saucers which lay around the kitchen. When everything was done she looked at her watch and it was half past eight. She put the kettle on and went back to the bed. Leamas was looking at her.

"Alec, don't be cross, please don't," she said. "I'll go. I promise I will, but let me make you a proper meal. You're ill, you can't go on like this, you're . . . oh, Alec," and she broke down and wept, holding both hands over her face, the tears running between her fingers like the tears of a child. He let her cry, watching her with his brown eyes, his hands holding the sheet.

She helped him wash and shave and she found some clean bedclothes. She gave him some calves-foot jelly, and some breast of chicken from the jar she'd bought at Mr. Sleaman's. Sitting on the bed she watched him eat, and she thought she had never been so happy before.

Soon he fell asleep, and she drew the blanket over his shoulders and went to the window. Parting the threadbare curtains, she raised the sash and looked out. Two other windows in the courtyard were lit. In one she could see the flickering blue shadow of a television screen, the figures round it held motionless in its spell; in the other a woman, quite young, was arranging curlers in her hair. Liz wanted to weep at the crabbed delusion of their dreams.

She fell asleep in the armchair and did not wake until it was nearly light, feeling stiff and cold. She went to the bed: Leamas stirred as she looked at him and she touched his lips with the tip of her finger. He did not open his eyes but gently took her arm and drew her down on to the bed and suddenly she wanted him terribly, and nothing mattered, and she kissed him again and again and when she looked at him he seemed to be smiling.

She came every day for six days. He never spoke to her much and once, when she asked him if he loved her, he said he didn't believe in fairy tales. She would lie on the bed, her head against his chest, and sometimes he would put his thick fingers in her hair, holding it quite tight, and Liz laughed and said it hurt. On the Friday evening she found him dressed but not shaved and she wondered why he hadn't shaved. For some imperceptible reason she was alarmed. Little things were missing from the room—his clock and the cheap portable wireless that had been on the table. She wanted to ask and did not dare. She had bought some eggs and ham and she cooked them for their supper while Leamas sat on the bed and smoked one cigarette after another. When it was ready he went to the kitchen and came back with a bottle of red wine.

He hardly spoke at supper, and she watched him, her fear growing until she could bear it no more and she cried out suddenly:

"Alec . . . oh, Alec . . . what is it? Is it good-bye?"

He got up from the table, took her hands, and kissed her in a way he'd never done before and spoke to her softly for a long time, told her things she only dimly understood, only half heard because all the time she knew it was the end and nothing mattered any more.

"Good-bye, Liz," he said. "Good-bye," and then: "Don't follow me. Not again."

Liz nodded and muttered: "Like we said." She was thankful for the biting cold of the street and for the dark which hid her tears.

It was the next morning, the Saturday, that Leamas asked at the grocer's for credit. He did it without much artistry, in a way not calculated to ensure him success. He ordered half a dozen items—they didn't come to more than a pound—and when they had been wrapped and put into the carrier bag he said:

"You'd better send me that account."

The grocer smiled a difficult smile and said:

"I'm afraid I can't do that"; the "Sir" was definitely missing.

"Why the hell not?" asked Leamas, and the queue behind him stirred uneasily.

"Don't know you," replied the grocer.

"Don't be bloody silly," said Leamas, "I've been coming here for four months." The grocer coloured.

"We always ask for a banker's reference before giving credit," he said, and Leamas lost his temper.

"Don't talk bloody cock," he shouted. "Half your customers have never seen the inside of a bank and never bloody well will." This was heresy beyond bearing, since it was true.

"I don't know you," the grocer repeated thickly, "and I don't like you. Now get out of my shop." And he tried to recover the parcel which unfortunately Leamas was already holding. Opinions later differed as to what happened next. Some said the grocer, in trying to recover the bag, pushed Leamas; others say he did not. Whether he did or not, Leamas hit him, most people think twice, without disengaging his right hand, which still held the carrier bag. He seemed to deliver the blow not with the fist but with the side of the left hand, and then, as part of the same phenomenally rapid movement, with the left elbow; and the grocer fell straight over and lay as still as a rock. It was said in court later, and not contested by the defence, that the grocer had two injuries—a fractured cheek bone from the first blow and a dislocated jaw from the second. The coverage in the daily press was adequate, but not over-elaborate.

6

Contact

At night he lay on his bunk listening to the sounds of the prisoners. There was a boy who sobbed and an old lag who sang "On Ilkley Moor bar t' at" beating out the time on his food tin. There was a warder who shouted, "Shut up, George, you miserable sod," after each verse, but no one took any notice. There was an Irishman who sang songs about the IRA, though the others said he was in for rape.

Leamas took as much exercise as he could during the day in the hope that he would sleep at night; but it was no good. At night you knew you were in prison: at night there was nothing, no trick of vision or self-delusion which saved you from the nauseating enclosure of the cell. You could not keep the taste of prison, the smell of prison uniform, the stench of prison sanitation heavily disinfected, the noises of captive men. It was then, at night, that the indignity of captivity became urgently insufferable, it was then that Leamas longed to walk in the friendly sunshine of a London park. It was then that he hated the grotesque steel cage that held him, had to force back the urge to fall upon the bars with his bare fists, to split the skulls of his gaolers and burst into the free, free space of London. Sometimes he thought of Liz. He would direct his mind towards her briefly like the shutter of a camera, recall for a moment the softhard touch of her long body, then put her from his memory. Leamas was not a man accustomed to living on dreams.

He was contemptuous of his cell mates, and they hated him. They hated him because he succeeded in being what each in his heart longed to be: a mystery. He preserved from collectivisation some discernible part of his personality; he could not be drawn at moments of sentiment to talk of his girl, his family or his children. They knew nothing of Leamas; they waited, but he did not come to them. New prisoners are largely of two kinds—there are those who for shame, fear, or shock wait in fascinated horror to be initiated into the lore of prison life, and there are those who trade on their wretched novelty in order to endear themselves to the community. Leamas did neither of these things. He seemed pleased to despise them all, and they hated him because, like the world outside, he did not need them. After about ten days they had had enough. The great had had no homage, the small had had no comfort, so they crowded him in the dinner queue. Crowding is a prison ritual akin to the eighteenth-century practice of jostling. It has the virtue of an apparent accident, in which the prisoner's mess tin is upturned, and its contents spilt on his uniform. Leamas was barged from one side, while from the other an obliging hand descended on his forearm, and the thing was done. Leamas said nothing, looked thoughtfully at the two men on either side of him, and accepted in silence the filthy rebuke of a warder who knew quite well what had happened.

Four days later, while working with a hoe on the prison flower-bed, he seemed to stumble. He was holding the hoe with both hands across his body, the end of the handle protruding about six inches from his right fist. As he strove to recover his balance the prisoner to his right doubled up with a grunt of agony, his arms across his stomach. There was no more crowding after that.

Perhaps the strangest thing of all about prison was the brown paper parcel when he left. In a ridiculous way it reminded him of the marriage service—with this ring I thee wed, with this paper parcel I return thee to society. They handed it to him and made him sign for it, and it contained all he had in the world. There was nothing else. Leamas felt it the most dehumanising moment of the three months, and he determined to throw the parcel away as soon as he got outside.

He seemed a quiet prisoner. There had been no complaints against him. The Governor, who was vaguely interested in his case, secretly put the whole thing down to the Irish blood he swore he could detect in Leamas.

"What are you going to do," he asked, "when you leave here?" Leamas replied, without a ghost of a smile, that he thought he would make a new start, and the Governor said that was an excellent thing to do.

"What about your family?" he asked. "Couldn't you make it up with your wife?"

"I'll try," Leamas had replied indifferently; "but she's remarried."

The probation officer wanted Leamas to become a male nurse at a mental home in Buckinghamshire and Leamas agreed to apply. He even took down the address and noted the train times from Marylebone.

"The rail's electrified as far as Great Missenden, now," the probation officer added, and Leamas said that would be a help. So they gave him the parcel and he left. He took a bus to Marble Arch and walked. He had a bit of money in his pocket and he intended to give himself a decent meal. He thought he would walk through Hyde Park to Piccadilly, then through Green Park and St. James's Park to Parliament Square, then wander down Whitehall to the Strand where he could go to the big café near Charing Cross station and get a reasonable steak for six shillings.

London was beautiful that day. Spring was late and the

parks were filled with crocuses and daffodils. A cool, cleaning wind was blowing from the south; he could have walked all day. But he still had the parcel and he had to get rid of it. The litter baskets were too small; he'd look absurd trying to push his parcel into one of those. He supposed there were one or two things he ought to take out—his wretched pieces of paper—insurance card, driving licence and his E.93 (whatever that was) in a buff OHMS envelope, but suddenly he couldn't be bothered. He sat down on a bench and put the parcel beside him, not too close, and moved a little away from it. After a couple of minutes he walked back towards the footpath, leaving the parcel where it lay. He had just reached the footpath when he heard a shout; he turned, a little sharply perhaps, and saw a man in an army macintosh beckoning to him, holding the brown paper parcel in the other hand.

Leamas had his hands in his pockets and he left them there, and stood, looking back over his shoulder at the man in the macintosh. The man hesitated, evidently expecting Leamas to come to him or give some sign of interest, but Leamas gave none. Instead, he shrugged and continued along the footpath. He heard another shout and ignored it, and he knew the man was coming after him. He heard the footsteps on the gravel, half running, approaching rapidly, and then a voice, a little breathless, a little aggrieved:

"Here, you—I say!" and then he had drawn level, so that Leamas stopped, turned, and looked at him.

"Yes?"

"This is your parcel, isn't it? You left it on the seat. Why didn't you stop when I called you?"

Tall, with rather curly brown hair, orange tie, and pale green shirt; a little bit petulant, a little bit of a pansy, thought Leamas. Could be a schoolmaster, ex–LSE and runs a suburban drama club. Weak-eyed.

"You can put it back," said Leamas. "I don't want it."

The man coloured.

"You can't just leave it there," he said, "it's litter."

"I bloody well can," Leamas replied. "Somebody will find a use for it." He was going to move on, but the stranger was still standing in front of him, holding the parcel in both arms as if it were a baby. "Get out of the light," said Leamas. "Do you mind?"

"Look here," said the stranger, and his voice had risen a key, "I was trying to do you a favour; why do you have to be so damned rude?"

"If you're so anxious to do me a favour," Leamas replied, "why have you been following me for the last half-hour?"

He's pretty good, thought Leamas. He hasn't flinched, but he must be shaken rigid.

"I thought you were somebody I once knew in Berlin, if you must know."

"So you followed me for half an hour?"

Leamas' voice was heavy with sarcasm, his brown eyes never left the other's face.

"Nothing like half an hour. I caught sight of you in Marble Arch and I thought you were Alec Leamas, a man I borrowed some money from. I used to be in the BBC in Berlin and there was this man I borrowed some money from. I've had a conscience about it ever since and that's why I followed you. I wanted to be sure."

Leamas went on looking at him, not speaking, and thought he wasn't all that good but he was good enough. His story was scarcely plausible—that didn't matter. The point was that he'd produced a new one and stuck to it after Leamas had wrecked what promised to be a classic approach.

"I'm Leamas," he said at last, "who the hell are you?"

He said his name was Ashe with an 'E' he added quickly, and Leamas knew he was lying. He pretended not to be quite sure that Leamas really was Leamas, so over lunch they opened the parcel and looked at the National Insurance card like, thought Leamas, a couple of cissies looking at a dirty postcard. Ashe ordered lunch with just a fraction too little regard for expense, and they drank some Frankenwein to remind them of the old days. Leamas began by insisting he couldn't remember Ashe, and Ashe said he was surprised. He said it in the sort of tone that suggested he was hurt. They met at a party, he said, which Derek Williams gave in his flat off the Kudamm (he got that right) and all the press boys had been there; surely Alec remembered that? No, Leamas did not. Well, surely he remembered Derek Williams from the *Observer*, that *nice* man who gave such lovely pizza parties? Leamas had a lousy memory for names, after all they were talking about fifty-four; a lot of water had flowed under the bridge since then . . . Ashe remembered (his christian name was William, by the by, most people called him Bill). Ashe remembered *vividly*. They'd been drinking stingers, brandy and créme de menthe, and were all rather tiddly, and Derek had provided some really gorgeous girls, half the cabaret from the Malkasten, *surely* Alec remembered now? Leamas thought it was probably coming back to him, if Bill would go on a bit.

Bill did go on, *ad lib.* no doubt, but he did it well, playing up the sex side a little, how they'd finished up in a night club with three of these girls; Alec, a chap from the political adviser's office, and Bill, and Bill had been so embarrassed because he hadn't any money on him and Alec had paid, and Bill had wanted to take a girl home and Alec had lent him another tenner . . .

"Christ," said Leamas, "I remember now, of course I do."

"I *knew* you would," said Ashe happily, nodding at Leamas over his glass, "look, do let's have the other half, this is *such* fun."

Ashe was typical of that stratum of mankind which conducts its human relationships according to a principle of challenge and response. Where there was softness, he would advance;

where he found resistance, retreat. Having himself no particular opinions or tastes he relied upon whatever conformed with those of his companion. He was as ready to drink tea at Fortnum's as beer at the Prospect of Whitby; he would listen to military music in St. James's Park or jazz in a Compton Street cellar; his voice would tremble with sympathy when he spoke of Sharpeville, or with indignation at the growth of Britain's coloured population. To Leamas this observably passive role was repellent; it brought out the bully in him, so that he would lead the other gently into a position where he was committed, and then himself withdraw, so that Ashe was constantly scampering back from some cul-de-sac into which Leamas had enticed him. There were moments that afternoon when Leamas was so brazenly perverse that Ashe would have been justified in terminating their conversation—not least since he was paying for it; but he did not. The little sad man with spectacles who sat alone at the neighbouring table, deep in a book on the manufacture of ball bearings, might have deduced, had he been listening, that Leamas was indulging a sadistic nature—or perhaps (if he had been a man of particular subtlety) that Leamas was proving to his own satisfaction that only a man with a strong ulterior motive would put up with that kind of treatment.

It was nearly four o'clock before they ordered the bill and Leamas tried to insist on paying his half. Ashe wouldn't hear of it, paid the bill and took out his cheque book in order to settle his debt to Leamas.

"Twenty of the best," he said, and filled in the date on the cheque form.

Then he looked up at Leamas, all wide-eyed and accommodating.

"I say, a cheque is all right by you, isn't it?"

Colouring a little, Leamas replied:

"I haven't got a bank at the moment—only just back from

abroad, something I've got to fix up. Better give me a cheque and I'll cash it at your bank."

"My dear chap, I wouldn't *dream* of it! You'd have to go to Rotherhithe to cash this one!" Leamas shrugged and Ashe laughed, and they agreed to meet at the same place on the following day, at one o'clock, when Ashe would have the money in cash.

Ashe took a cab at the corner of Compton Street, and Leamas waved at it until it was out of sight. When it was gone, he looked at his watch. It was four o'clock. He guessed he was still being followed, so he walked down to Fleet Street and had a cup of coffee in the Black and White. He looked at bookshops, read the evening papers displayed in the show windows of newspaper offices, and then quite suddenly, as if the thought had occurred to him at the last minute, he jumped on a bus. The bus went to Ludgate Hill, where it was held up in a traffic jam near a tube station; he dismounted and caught a tube. He bought a sixpenny ticket, stood in the end carriage, and alighted at the next station. He caught another train to Euston, trekked back to Charing Cross. It was nine o'clock when he reached the station and it had turned rather cold. There was a van waiting in the forecourt; the driver was fast asleep. Leamas glanced at the number, went over, and called through the window:

"Are you from Clements?" The driver woke up with a start and asked:

"Mr. Thomas?"

"No," replied Leamas. "Thomas couldn't come. I'm Amies from Hounslow."

"Hop in, Mr. Amies," the driver replied, and opened the door. They drove west, towards the King's Road. The driver knew the way.

Control opened the door.

"George Smiley's out," he said. "I've borrowed his house. Come in." Not until Leamas was inside and the front door closed, did Control put on the hall light.

"I was followed till lunch time," Leamas said. They went into the little drawing-room. There were books everywhere. It was a pretty room; tall, with eighteenth-century mouldings, long windows, and a good fireplace.

"They picked me up this morning. A man called Ashe." He lit a cigarette. "A pansy. We're meeting again tomorrow."

Control listened carefully to Leamas' story, stage by stage, from the day he hit Ford, the grocer, to his encounter that morning with Ashe.

"How did you find prison?" Control enquired. He might have been asking whether Leamas had enjoyed his holiday. "I am sorry we couldn't improve conditions for you, provide little extra comforts, but that would never have done."

"Of course not."

"One must be consistent. At every turn one must be consistent. Besides, it would be wrong to break the spell. I understand you were ill. I am sorry. What was the trouble?"

"Just fever."

"How long were you in bed?"

"About ten days."

"How very distressing; and nobody to look after you, of course."

There was a very long silence.

"You know she's in the Party, don't you?" Control asked quietly.

"Yes," Leamas replied. Another silence. "I don't want her brought into this."

"Why should she be?" Control asked sharply and for a moment, just for a moment, Leamas thought he had penetrated the veneer of academic detachment. "Who suggested she should be?"

"No one," Leamas replied, "I'm just making the point. I

know how these things go—all offensive operations. They have by-products, take sudden turns in unexpected directions. You think you've caught one fish and you find you've caught another. I want her kept clear of it."

"Oh, quite, quite."

"Who's that man in the Labour Exchange—Pitt? Wasn't he in the Circus during the war?"

"I know no one of that name. Pitt, did you say?"

"Yes."

"No, not a name to me. In the Labour Exchange?"

"Oh, for God's sake," Leamas muttered audibly.

"I'm sorry," said Control, getting up, "I'm neglecting my duties as deputy host. Would you care for a drink?"

"No. I want to get away tonight, Control. Go down to the country and get some exercise. Is the House open?"

"I've arranged a car," he said. "What time do you see Ashe tomorrow—one o'clock?"

"Yes."

"I'll ring Haldane and tell him you want some squash. You'd better see a doctor, too. About that fever."

"I don't need a doctor."

"Just as you like."

Control gave himself a whisky and began looking idly at the books in Smiley's shelf.

"Why isn't Smiley here?" Leamas asked.

"He doesn't like the operation," Control replied indifferently. "He finds it distasteful. He sees the necessity but he wants no part in it. His fever," Control added with a whimsical smile, "is recurrent."

"He didn't exactly receive me with open arms."

"Quite. He wants no part in it. But he told you about Mundt; gave you the background?"

"Yes."

"Mundt is a very *hard* man," Control reflected. "We should never forget that. And a good intelligence officer."

"Does Smiley know the reason for the operation? The special interest?"

Control nodded and took a sip of whisky.

"And he still doesn't like it?"

"It isn't a question of moralities. He is like the surgeon who has grown tired of blood. He is content that others should operate."

"Tell me," Leamas continued, "how are you so certain this will get us where we want? How do you know the East Germans are on to it—not the Czechs or the Russians?"

"Rest assured," Control said a little pompously, "that that has been taken care of."

As they got to the door, Control put his hand lightly on Leamas' shoulder.

"This is your last job," he said. "Then you can come in from the cold. About that girl—do you want anything done about her, money or anything?"

"When it's over. I'll take care of it myself then."

"Quite. It would be very insecure to do anything now."

"I just want her left alone," Leamas repeated with emphasis. "I just don't want her to be messed about. I don't want her to have a file or anything. I want her forgotten."

He nodded to Control and slipped out into the night air. Into the cold.

7

Kiever

On the following day Leamas arrived twenty minutes late for his lunch with Ashe, and smelt of whisky. Ashe's pleasure on catching sight of Leamas was, however, undiminished. He claimed that he had himself only that moment arrived, he'd been a little late getting to the bank. He handed Leamas an envelope.

"Singles," said Ashe. "I hope that's all right."

"Thanks," Leamas replied, "let's have a drink." He hadn't shaved and his collar was filthy. He called the waiter and ordered drinks, a large whisky for himself and a pink gin for Ashe. When the drinks came Leamas' hand trembled as he poured the soda into the glass, almost slopping it over the side.

They lunched well, with a lot of drink, and Ashe made most of the running. As Leamas had expected he first talked about himself, an old trick but not a bad one.

"To be quite frank, I've got on to rather a good thing recently," said Ashe, "free-lancing English features for the foreign press. After Berlin I made rather a mess of things at first—the Corporation wouldn't renew the contract and I took a job running a dreary toffee-shop weekly about hobbies for the over-sixties. Can you *imagine* anything more frightful? That went under in the first printing strike—I can't tell you how relieved I was. Then I went to live with my mamma in Cheltenham for a time; she runs an antique shop, does very nicely thank you, as a matter of fact. Then I got a letter from an old friend, Sam Kiever his name is actually, who was starting up a new agency for small features on English life specially slanted for foreign papers. You know the sort of thing—six hundred words on Morris dancing. Sam had a new gimmick, though; he sold the stuff already translated and do you know, it makes a hell of a difference. One always imagines anyone can pay a translator to do it themselves, but if you're looking for a half column in-fill for your foreign features you don't *want* to waste time and money on translation. Sam's gambit was to get in touch with the editors direct—he traipsed round Europe like a gypsy, poor thing, but it's paid hands *down*."

Ashe paused, waiting for Leamas to accept the invitation to speak about himself, but Leamas ignored it. He just nodded dully and said: "Bloody good." Ashe had wanted to order wine, but Leamas said he'd stick to whisky and by the time the coffee came he'd had four large ones. He seemed to be in bad shape; he had the drunkard's habit of ducking his mouth towards the rim of his glass just before he drank, as if his hand might fail him and the drink escape.

Ashe fell silent for a moment.

"You don't know Sam, do you?" he asked.

"Sam?"

A note of irritation entered Ashe's voice.

"Sam Kiever, my boss. The chap I was telling you about."

"Was he in Berlin too?"

"No. He knows Germany well, but he's never lived in Berlin. He did a bit of devilling in Bonn, free-lance stuff. You might have met him. He's a dear."

"Don't think so." A pause.

"What do you do these days, old chap?" asked Ashe.

Leamas shrugged.

"I'm on the shelf," he replied, and grinned a little stupidly. "Out of the bag and on the shelf."

"I forget what you were doing in Berlin? Weren't you one of the mysterious cold warriors?" My God, thought Leamas, you're stepping things up a bit.

Leamas hesitated, then coloured and said savagely, "Office boy for the bloody Yanks, like the rest of us."

"You know," said Ashe, as if he had been turning the idea over for some time, "you ought to meet Sam. You'd like him," and then, all of a bother, "I say, Alec—I don't even know where to get hold of you!"

"You can't," Leamas replied listlessly.

"I don't get you, old chap. Where are you staying?"

"Around the place. Roughing it a bit. I haven't got a job. Bastards wouldn't give me a proper pension."

Ashe looked horrified.

"But, Alec, that's awful; why didn't you *tell* me? Look, why not come and stay at my place? It's only tiny but there's room for one more if you don't mind a camp bed. You can't just live in the trees, my dear chap!"

"I'm all right for a bit," Leamas replied, tapping at the pocket which contained the envelope. "I'm going to get a job," he nodded with determination; "get one in a week or so. Then I'll be all right."

"What sort of job?"

"Oh, I don't know. Anything."

"But you can't just throw yourself away, Alec! You speak German like a native, I remember you do. There must be all sorts of things you can do!"

"I've done all sorts of things. Selling encyclopaedias for some bloody American firm, sorting books in a psychic library, punching work tickets in a stinking glue factory. What the hell *can* I do?" He wasn't looking at Ashe but at the table before him, his agitated lips moving quickly. Ashe responded to his animation, leaning forward across the table, speaking with emphasis, almost triumph.

"But Alec, you need *contacts*, don't you see? I know what it's like, I've been on the breadline myself. That's when you need to *know* people. I don't know what you were doing in Berlin, I don't want to know, but it wasn't the sort of job where you could meet people who matter, was it? If I hadn't met Sam at Poznan five years ago I'd *still* be on the breadline. Look, Alec, come and stay with me for a week or so. We'll ask Sam round and perhaps one or two of the old press boys from Berlin if any of them are in town."

"But I can't write," said Leamas. "I couldn't write a bloody thing." Ashe had his hand on Leamas' arm: "Now, don't fuss," he said soothingly; "let's just take things one at a time. Where are your bits and pieces?"

"My what?"

"Your things: clothes, baggage and what not?"

"I haven't got any. I've sold what I had—except the parcel."

"What parcel?"

"The brown paper parcel you picked up in the park. The one I was trying to throw away."

Ashe had a flat in Dolphin Square. It was just what Leamas had expected—small and anonymous with a few hastily assembled curios from Germany: beer mugs, a peasant's pipe, and a few pieces of second-rate Nymphenburg.

"I spend the weekends with my mother in Cheltenham," he said. "I just use this place mid-week. It's pretty handy," he added deprecatingly. They fixed the camp bed up in the tiny drawing-room. It was about four-thirty.

"How long have you been here?" asked Leamas.

"Oh—about a year or more."

"Find it easily?"

"They come and go, you know, these flats. You put your

name down and one day they ring you up and tell you you've made it."

Ashe made tea and they drank it, Leamas sullen, like a man not used to comfort. Even Ashe seemed a little piano. After tea Ashe said: "I'll go out and do a spot of shopping before the shops close, then we'll decide what to do about everything. I might give Sam a tinkle later this evening—I think the sooner you two get together the better. Why don't you get some sleep—you look all in."

Leamas nodded. "It's bloody good of you—" he made an awkward gesture with his hand, "—all this." Ashe gave him a pat on the shoulder, picked up his army macintosh, and left.

As soon as Leamas reckoned Ashe was safely out of the building, he put the front door of the flat carefully on the latch and made his way downstairs to the centre hall where there were two telephone cabins. He dialled a Maida Vale number and asked for Mr. Thomas' secretary. Immediately a girl's voice said, "Mr. Thomas' secretary speaking."

"I'm ringing on behalf of Mr. Sam Kiever," Leamas said, "he has accepted the invitation and hopes to contact Mr. Thomas personally this evening."

"I'll pass that on to Mr. Thomas. Does he know where to get in touch with you?"

"Dolphin Square," Leamas replied, and gave the address. "Good-bye."

After making some enquiries at the reception desk he returned to Ashe's flat, and sat on the camp bed looking at his clasped hands. After a while he lay down. He decided to accept Ashe's advice and get some rest. As he closed his eyes he remembered Liz lying beside him in the flat in Bayswater, and he wondered vaguely what had become of her.

He was woken up by Ashe, accompanied by a small, rather plump man with long, greying hair swept back and a double-breasted suit. He spoke with a slight central European accent; German perhaps, it was hard to tell. He said his name was Kiever—Sam Kiever.

They had a gin and tonic, Ashe doing most of the talking. It was just like old times, he said, in Berlin: the boys together and the night their oyster. Kiever said he didn't want to be too late; he had to work tomorrow. They agreed to eat at a Chinese restaurant that Ashe knew of—it was opposite Limehouse police station and you brought your own wine. Oddly enough Ashe had some Burgundy in the kitchen, and they took that with them in the taxi.

Dinner was very good and they drank both bottles of wine. Kiever opened up a little on the second: he'd just come back from a tour of West Germany and France. France was in a hell of a mess, de Gaulle was on the way out and God alone knew what would happen then. With a hundred thousand demoralised *colons* returning from Algeria he reckoned Fascism was on the cards.

"What about Germany?" asked Alec, prompting him.

"It's just a question of whether the Yanks can hold them." Kiever looked invitingly at Leamas.

"What do you mean?" asked Leamas.

"What I say. Dulles gave them a foreign policy with one hand, Kennedy takes it away with the other. They're getting waspish."

Leamas nodded abruptly and said, "Bloody typical Yank."

"Alec doesn't seem to like our American cousins," said Ashe, stepping in heavily, and Kiever, with complete disinterest, murmured, "Oh, really?" Kiever played it, Leamas reflected, very long. Like someone used to horses, he let you come to him. He conveyed to perfection a man who suspected that he was about to be asked a favour, and was not easily won.

After dinner Ashe said, "I know a place in Wardour Street—you've been there, Sam. They do you all right there. Why don't we summon a barouche and go along?"

"Just a minute," said Leamas, and there was something in his voice which made Ashe look at him quickly; "just tell me something will you? Who's paying for this jolly?"

"I am," said Ashe quickly, "Sam and I."

"Have you discussed it?"

"Well—no."

"Because I haven't got any bloody money; you know that, don't you? None to throw about anyway."

"Of course, Alec. I've looked after you up till now, haven't I?"

"Yes," Leamas replied; "yes, you have."

He seemed to be going to say something else, and then to change his mind. Ashe looked worried, not offended, and Kiever as inscrutable as before.

Leamas refused to speak in the taxi. Ashe attempted some conciliatory remark and he just shrugged irritably. They arrived at Wardour Street and dismounted, neither Leamas nor Kiever making any attempt to pay for the cab. Ashe led them past a shop window full of "girlie" magazines, down a narrow alley, at the far end of which shone a tawdry neon sign: "Pussywillow Club. Members Only." On either side of the door were photographs of girls, and pinned across each was a thin, hand-printed strip of paper which read, "Nature Study. Members only."

Ashe pressed the bell. The door was at once opened by a very large man in a white shirt and black trousers.

"I'm a member," Ashe said. "These two gentlemen are with me."

"See your card?"

Ashe took a buff card from his wallet and handed it over.

"Your guests pay a quid a head temporary membership. Your recommendation, right?" He held out the card and as he did so, Leamas stretched past Ashe and took it. He looked at it for a moment, then handed it back to Ashe.

Taking two pounds from his hip pocket Leamas put them into the waiting hand of the man at the door.

"Two quid," said Leamas, "for the guests," and ignoring the astonished protests of Ashe he guided them through the curtained doorway into the dim hallway of the club. He turned to the doorman.

"Find us a table," said Leamas, "and a bottle of Scotch. And see we're left alone." The doorman hesitated for a moment, decided not to argue, and escorted them downstairs. As they descended they heard the subdued moan of unintelligible music.

They got a table on their own at the back of the room. A two-piece band was playing and girls sat around in twos and threes. Two got up as they came in but the big doorman shook his head.

Ashe glanced at Leamas uneasily while they waited for the whisky. Kiever seemed slightly bored. The waiter brought a bottle and three tumblers and they watched in silence as he poured a little whisky into each glass. Leamas took the bottle from the waiter and added as much again to each. This done, he leant across the table and said to Ashe, "Now perhaps you'll tell me what the bloody hell's going on?"

"What do you mean?" Ashe sounded uncertain. "What *do* you mean, Alec?"

"You followed me from prison the day I was released," he began quietly, "with some bloody silly story of meeting me in Berlin. You gave me money you didn't owe me. You've bought me expensive meals and you're putting me up in your flat."

Ashe coloured and said, "If that's the—"

"Don't interrupt," said Leamas fiercely. "Just damn' well wait till I've finished, do you mind? Your membership card for this place is made out for someone called Murphy. Is that your name?"

"No, it is not."

"I suppose a friend called Murphy lent you his membership card?"

"No he didn't as a matter of fact. If you must know I come

here occasionally to find a girl. I used a phoney name to join the club."

"Then why," Leamas persisted ruthlessly, "is Murphy registered as the tenant of your flat?"

It was Kiever who finally spoke.

"You run along home," he said to Ashe. "I'll look after this."

A girl performed a striptease, a young, drab girl with a dark bruise on her thigh. She had that pitiful, spindly nakedness which is embarrassing because it is not erotic; because it is artless and undesiring. She turned slowly, jerking sporadically with her arms or legs as if she only heard the music in snatches, and all the time she looked at them with the precocious interest of a child in adult company. The tempo of the music increased abruptly, and the girl responded like a dog to the whistle, scampering back and forth. Removing her brassiere on the last note, she held it above her head, displaying her meagre body with its three tawdry patches of tinsel hanging from it like old Christmas decorations.

They watched in silence, Leamas and Kiever.

"I suppose you're going to tell me that we've seen better in Berlin," Leamas suggested at last, and Kiever saw that he was still very angry.

"I expect *you* have," Kiever replied pleasantly. "I have often been to Berlin, but I am afraid I dislike nightclubs."

Leamas said nothing.

"I'm no prude, mind, just rational. If I want a woman I know cheaper ways of finding one; if I want to dance I know better places to do it." Leamas might not have been listening.

"Perhaps you'll tell me why that cissy picked me up," he suggested. Kiever nodded.

"By all means. I told him to."

"Why?"

"I am interested in you. I want to make you a proposition, a journalistic proposition."

There was a pause.

"Journalistic," Leamas repeated, "I see."

"I run an agency, an international feature service. It pays well—very well—for interesting material."

"Who publishes the material?"

"It pays so well, in fact, that a man with your kind of experience of . . . the international scene, a man with your background, you understand, who provided convincing, factual material, could free himself in a comparatively short time from further financial worry."

"Who publishes the material, Kiever?" There was a threatening edge to Leamas' voice, and for a moment, just for a moment, a look of apprehension seemed to pass across Kiever's smooth face.

"International clients. I have a correspondent in Paris who disposes of a good deal of my stuff. Often I don't even know who *does* publish. I confess," he added with a disarming smile, "that I don't awfully care. They pay and they ask for more. They're the kind of people, you see, Leamas, who don't fuss about awkward details; they pay promptly, and they're happy to pay into foreign banks, for instance, where no one bothers about things like tax."

Leamas said nothing. He was holding his glass with both hands, staring into it.

Christ, they're rushing their fences, Leamas thought; it's indecent. He remembered some silly music-hall joke—"This is an offer no respectable girl could accept—and besides, I don't know what it's worth." Tactically, he reflected, they're right to rush it. I'm on my uppers, prison experience still fresh, social resentment strong. I'm an old horse, I don't need breaking in; I don't have to pretend they've offended my honour as an English gentleman. On the other hand they would expect *practical* objections. They would expect him to be afraid; for his Service pursued traitors as the eye of God followed Cain across the desert.

And finally, they would know it was a gamble. They would

know that inconsistency in human decision can make nonsense of the best-planned espionage approach; that cheats, liars, and criminals may resist every blandishment while respectable gentlemen have been moved to appalling treasons by watery cabbage in a Departmental canteen.

"They'd have to pay a hell of a lot," Leamas muttered at last. Kiever gave him some more whisky.

"They are offering a downpayment of fifteen thousand pounds. The money is already lodged at the Banquet Cantonale in Bern. On production of a suitable identification, with which my clients will provide you, you can draw the money. My clients reserve the right to put questions to you over the period of one year on payment of another five thousand pounds. They will assist you with any . . . resettlement problems that may arise."

"How soon do you want an answer?"

"Now. You are not expected to commit all your reminiscences to paper. You will meet my client and he will arrange to have the material . . . ghost written."

"Where am I supposed to meet him?"

"We felt for everybody's sake it would be simplest to meet outside the United Kingdom. My client suggested Holland."

"I haven't got my passport," Leamas said dully.

"I took the liberty of obtaining one for you," Kiever replied suavely; nothing in his voice or his manner indicated that he had done other than negotiate an adequate business arrangement. "We're flying to The Hague tomorrow morning at nine forty-five. Shall we go back to my flat and discuss any other details?"

Kiever paid and they took a taxi to a rather good address not far from St. James's Park.

Kiever's flat was luxurious and expensive, but its contents somehow gave the impression of having been hastily assembled. It is said that there are shops in London which will sell you bound books by the yard, and interior decorators who will harmonise the colour scheme of the walls with that of a painting. Leamas, who was not particularly receptive to such subtleties, found it hard to remember that he was in a private flat and not an hotel. As Kiever showed him to his room (which looked onto a dingy inner courtyard and not onto the street) Leamas asked him:

"How long have you been here?"

"Oh, not long," Kiever replied lightly, "a few months, not more."

"Must cost a packet. Still, I suppose you're worth it."

"Thanks."

There was a bottle of Scotch in his room and a syphon of soda on a silver-plated tray. A curtained doorway at the further end of the room led to a bathroom and lavatory.

"Quite a little love nest. All paid for by the great Worker State?"

"Shut up," said Kiever savagely, and added, "If you want me, there's an internal telephone to my room. I shall be awake."

"I think I can manage my buttons now," Leamas retorted.

"Then good night," said Kiever shortly, and left the room. He's on edge, too, thought Leamas.

Leamas was woken by the telephone at his bedside. It was Kiever.

"It's six o'clock," he said, "breakfast at half past."

"All right," Leamas replied, and rang off. He had a headache.

Kiever must have telephoned for a taxi because at seven o'clock the door bell rang and Kiever asked, "Got everything?"

"I've no luggage," Leamas replied, "except a toothbrush and a razor."

"That is taken care of. Are you ready otherwise?"

Leamas shrugged. "I suppose so. Have you got any cigarettes?"

"No," Kiever replied, "but you can get some on the plane. You'd better look through this," he added, and handed Leamas a British passport. It was made out in his name with his own photograph mounted in it, embossed by the deep press Foreign Office seal running across the corner. It was neither old nor new; it described Leamas as a clerk, and gave his status as single. Holding it in his hand for the first time, Leamas was a little nervous. It was like getting married: whatever happened, things would never be the same again.

"What about money?" Leamas asked.

"You won't need any. It's on the firm."

8

Le Mirage

It was cold that morning; the light mist was damp and grey, pricking the skin. The airport reminded Leamas of the war: machines, half hidden in the fog, waiting patiently for their masters; the resonant voices and their echoes, the sudden shout and the incongruous clip of a girl's heels on a stone floor; the roar of an engine that might have been at your elbow. Everywhere that air of conspiracy which generates among people who have been up since dawn—of superiority almost, derived from the common experience of having seen the night disappear and the morning come. The staff had that look which is informed by the mystery of dawn and animated by the cold, and they treated the passengers and their baggage with the remoteness of men returned from the front: ordinary mortals had nothing for them that morning.

Kiever had provided Leamas with luggage. It was a nice detail: Leamas admired it. Passengers without luggage attracted attention, and it was not part of Kiever's plan to do that. They checked in at the airline desk and followed the signs to passport control. There was a ludicrous moment when they lost the way and Kiever was rude to a porter. Leamas supposed

Kiever was worried about the passport—he needn't be, thought Leamas, there's nothing wrong with it.

The passport officer was a youngish, little man with an Intelligence Corps tie and some mysterious badge in his lapel. He had a ginger moustache, and a North Country accent which was his life's enemy.

"Going to be away for a long time, sir?" he asked Leamas.

"A couple of weeks," Leamas replied.

"You'll want to watch it, sir. Your passport's due for renewal on the 31st."

"I know," said Leamas.

They walked side by side into the passengers' waiting room. On the way Leamas said: "You're a suspicious sod, aren't you, Kiever," and the other laughed quietly.

"Can't have you on the loose, can we! Not part of the contract," he replied.

They still had twenty minutes to wait. They sat down at a table and ordered coffee. "And take these things away," Kiever added to the waiter, indicating the used cups, saucers, and ashtrays on the table. "There's a trolley coming round," the waiter replied.

"Take them," Kiever repeated, angry again. "It's disgusting, leaving dirty crockery there like that."

The waiter just turned and walked away. He didn't go near the service counter and he didn't order their coffee. Kiever was white, ill with anger. "For Christ's sake," Leamas muttered, "let it go. Life's too short."

"Cheeky bastard, that's what he is," said Kiever.

"All right, all right, make a scene; you've chosen a good moment. They'll never forget us here."

The formalities at the airport at The Hague provided no problem. Kiever seemed to have recovered from his anxieties. He became jaunty and talkative as they walked the short distance between the plane and the Customs sheds. The young Dutch officer gave a perfunctory glance at their luggage and passports and announced in awkward throaty English: "I hope you have a pleasant stay in the Netherlands."

"Thanks," said Kiever, almost too gratefully, "thanks very much."

They walked from the Customs shed along the corridor to the reception hall on the other side of the airport buildings. Kiever led the way to the main exit, between the little groups of travellers staring vaguely at kiosk displays of scent, cameras, and fruit. As they pushed their way through the revolving glass door, Leamas looked back. Standing at the newspaper kiosk, deep in a copy of the *Continental Daily Mail*, stood a small, froglike figure in glasses, an earnest, worried little man. He looked like a civil servant. Something like that.

A car was waiting for them in the car park, a Volkswagen with a Dutch registration, driven by a woman who ignored them. She drove slowly, always stopping if the lights were amber, and Leamas guessed she had been briefed to drive that way and that they were being followed by another car. He watched the off-side wing mirror, trying to recognise the car, but without success. Once he saw a black Peugeot with a CD number, but when they turned the corner there was only a furniture van behind them. He knew The Hague quite well from the war, and he tried to work out where they were heading. He guessed they were travelling northwest towards Scheveningen. Soon they had left the suburbs behind them and were approaching a colony of villas bordering the dunes along the sea front.

Here they stopped. The woman got out, leaving them in the car, and rang the front door bell of a small cream-coloured bungalow which stood at the near end of the row. A wrought iron sign hung on the porch with the words "Le Mirage" in pale blue Gothic script. There was a notice in the window, which proclaimed that all the rooms were taken.

The door was opened by a kindly, plump woman who looked past the driver towards the car. Her eyes still on the car, she came down the drive towards them, smiling with pleasure. She reminded Leamas of an old aunt he once had who beat him for wasting string.

"How nice that you have come," she declared; "we are so *pleased* that you have come!" They followed her into the bungalow, Kiever leading the way. The driver got back into the car. Leamas glanced down the road which they had just travelled; three hundred yards away a black car, a Fiat perhaps, or a Peugeot, had parked. A man in a raincoat was getting out.

Once in the hall the woman shook Leamas warmly by the hand. "Welcome, welcome to Le Mirage. Did you have a good journey?"

"Fine," Leamas replied.

"Did you fly or come by sea?"

"We flew," Kiever said; "a very smooth flight." He might have owned the airline.

"I'll make your lunch," she declared; "a special lunch. I'll make you something specially good. What shall I bring you?"

"Oh, for God's sake," said Leamas under his breath, and the door bell rang. The woman went quickly into the kitchen; Kiever opened the front door.

He was wearing a macintosh with leather buttons. He was about Leamas' height, but older. Leamas put him at about fifty-five. His face had a hard, grey hue and sharp furrows; he might have been a soldier. He held out his hand.

"My name is Peters," he said. The fingers were slim and polished.

"Did you have a good journey?"

"Yes," said Kiever quickly, "quite uneventful."

"Mr. Leamas and I have a lot to discuss; I do not think we need to keep you, Sam. You could take the Volkswagen back to town."

Kiever smiled. Leamas saw the relief in his smile.

"Good-bye, Leamas," said Kiever, his voice jocular; "good luck, old man."

Leamas nodded, ignoring Kiever's hand.

"Good-bye," Kiever repeated and let himself quietly out of the front door.

Leamas followed Peters into a back room. Heavy lace curtains hung on the window, ornately fringed and draped. The window sill was covered with potted plants; great cacti, a tobacco plant, and some curious tree with wide, rubbery leaves. The furniture was heavy, pseudo-antique. In the centre of the room was a table with two carved chairs. The table was covered with a rust-coloured counterpane more like a carpet; on it before each chair was a pad of paper and a pencil. On a sideboard there was whisky and soda. Peters went over to it and mixed them both a drink.

"Look," said Leamas suddenly, "from now on I can do without the goodwill; do you follow me? We both know what we're about; both professionals. You've got a paid defector—good luck to you. For Christ's sake don't pretend you've fallen in love with me." He sounded on edge, uncertain of himself.

Peters nodded. "Kiever told me you were a proud man," he observed dispassionately. Then he added without smiling, "After all, why else does a man attack tradesmen?"

Leamas guessed he was Russian, but he wasn't sure. His English was nearly perfect, he had the ease and habits of a man long used to civilised comforts.

They sat at the table.

"Kiever told you what I am going to pay you?" Peters enquired.

"Yes. Fifteen thousand pounds to be drawn on a Bern bank."

"Yes."

"He said you might have follow-up questions during the next year," said Leamas, "you would pay another five thousand if I kept myself available."

Peters nodded.

"I don't accept that condition," Leamas continued. "You know as well as I do it wouldn't work. I want to draw the fifteen thousand and get clear. Your people have a rough way with defected agents; so have mine. I'm not going to sit on my fanny in St. Moritz while you roll up every network I've given you. They're not fools; they'd know who to look for. For all you and I know they're on to us now."

Peters nodded: "You could, of course, come somewhere . . . safer, couldn't you?"

"Behind the Curtain?"

"Yes."

Leamas just shook his head and continued: "I reckon you'll need about three days for a preliminary interrogation. Then you'll want to refer back for a detailed brief."

"Not necessarily," Peters replied.

Leamas looked at him with interest.

"I see," he said, "they've sent the expert. Or isn't Moscow Centre in on this?"

Peters was silent; he was just looking at Leamas, taking him in. At last he picked up the pencil in front of him and said:

"Shall we begin with your war service?"

Leamas shrugged:

"It's up to you."

"That's right. We'll begin with your war service. Just talk."

I enlisted in the Engineers in 1939. I was finishing my training when a notice came round inviting linguists to apply for specialist service abroad. I had Dutch and German and a good deal of French and I was fed up with soldiering, so I applied. I

knew Holland well; my father had a machine tool agency at
Leiden; I'd lived there for nine years. I had the usual interviews and went off to a school near Oxford where they taught
me the usual monkey tricks."

"Who was running that setup?"

"I didn't know till later. Then I met Steed-Asprey, and an
Oxford don called Fielding. They were running it. In forty-one
they dropped me into Holland and I stayed there nearly two
years. We lost agents quicker than we could find them in those
days—it was bloody murder. Holland's a wicked country for
that kind of work—it's got no real rough country, nowhere out
of the way you can keep a headquarters or a radio set. Always
on the move, always running away. It made it a very dirty
game. I got out in forty-three and had a couple of months in
England, then I had a go at Norway—that was a picnic by
comparison. In forty-five they paid me off and I came over
here again, to Holland, to try and catch up on my father's old
business. That was no good, so I joined up with an old friend
who was running a travel agency business in Bristol. That
lasted eighteen months then we were sold up. Then out of the
blue I got a letter from the Department: would I like to go
back? But I'd had enough of all that, I thought, so I said I'd
think about it and rented a cottage on Lundy Island. I stayed
there a year contemplating my stomach, then I got fed up again
so I wrote to them. By late forty-nine I was back on the payroll. Broken service of course—reduction of pension rights
and the usual crabbing. Am I going too fast?"

"Not for the moment," Peters replied, pouring him some
more whisky; "we'll discuss it again of course, with names and
dates."

There was a knock at the door and the woman came in
with lunch, an enormous meal of cold meats and bread and
soup. Peters pushed his notes aside and they ate in silence. The
interrogation had begun.

• • •

Lunch was cleared away. "So you went back to the Circus," said Peters.

"Yes. For a while they gave me a desk job, processing reports, making assessments of military strengths in Iron Curtain countries, tracing units and that kind of thing."

"Which section?"

"Satellites Four. I was there from February fifty to May fifty-one."

"Who were your colleagues."

"Peter Guillam, Brian de Grey, and George Smiley. Smiley left us in early fifty-one and went over to Counter Intelligence. In May fifty-one I was posted to Berlin as DCA—Deputy-Controller of Area. That meant all the operational work."

"Who did you have under you?" Peters was writing swiftly. Leamas guessed he had some homemade shorthand.

"Hackett, Sarrow, and de Jong. De Jong was killed in a traffic accident in fifty-nine. We thought he was murdered but we could never prove it. They all ran networks and I was in charge. Do you want details?" he asked drily.

"Of course, but later. Go on."

"It was late fifty-four when we landed our first big fish in Berlin: Fritz Feger, second man in the DDR Defence Ministry. Up till then it had been heavy going—but in November fifty-four we got on to Fritz. He lasted almost exactly two years, then one day we never heard any more. I hear he died in prison. It was another three years before we found anyone to touch him. Then, in 1959, Karl Riemeck turned up. Karl was on the Praesidium of the East German Communist Party. He was the best agent I ever knew."

"He is now dead," Peters observed.

A look of something like shame passed across Leamas' face.

"I was there when he was shot," he muttered. "He had a

mistress who came over just before he died. He'd told her everything—she knew the whole damned network. No wonder he was blown."

"We'll return to Berlin later. Tell me this. When Karl died you flew back to London. Did you remain in London for the rest of your service?"

"What there was of it, yes."

"What job did you have in London?"

"Banking section; supervision of agents' salaries, overseas payments for clandestine purposes. A child could have managed it. We got our orders and we signed the drafts. Occasionally there was a security headache."

"Did you deal with agents direct?"

"How could we? The Resident in a particular country would make a requisition. Authority would put a hoofmark on it and pass it to us to make the payment. In most cases we had the money transferred to a convenient foreign bank where the Resident could draw it himself and hand it to the agent."

"How were agents described? By cover names?"

"By figures. The Circus calls them combinations. Every network was given a combination; every agent was described by a suffix attached to the combination. Karl's combination was eight A stroke one."

Leamas was sweating. Peters watched him coolly, appraising him like a professional gambler across the table. What was Leamas worth? What would break him, what attract or frighten him? What did he hate, above all, what did he know? Would he keep his best card to the end and sell it dear? Peters didn't think so; Leamas was too much off balance to monkey about. He was a man at odds with himself, a man who knew one life, one confession, and had betrayed them. Peters had seen it before. He had seen it, even in men who had undergone a complete ideological rehearsal, who in the secret hours of the night had found a new creed, and alone, compelled by the internal power of their convictions, had betrayed their calling, their families, their countries. Even they, filled as they were with new zeal and new hope, had had to struggle against the stigma of treachery; even they wrestled with the almost physical anguish of saying that which they had been trained never, never to reveal. Like apostates who feared to burn the Cross, they hesitated between the instinctive and the material; and Peters, caught in the same polarity, must give them comfort and destroy their pride. It was a situation of which they were both aware; thus Leamas had fiercely rejected a human relationship with Peters, for his pride precluded it. Peters knew that for those reasons, Leamas would lie; lie perhaps only by omission, but lie all the same, for pride, from defiance or through the sheer perversity of his profession; and he, Peters, would have to nail the lies. He knew, too, that the very fact that Leamas was a professional could militate against his interests, for Leamas would select where Peters wanted no selection; Leamas would anticipate the type of intelligence which Peters required—and in doing so might pass by some casual scrap which could be of vital interest to the evaluators. To all that, Peters added the capricious vanity of an alcoholic wreck.

"I think," he said, "we will now take your Berlin service in some detail. That would be from May 1951 to March 1961. Have another drink."

Leamas watched him take a cigarette from the box on the table, and light it. He noticed two things: that Peters was left-handed, and that once again he had put the cigarette in his mouth with the maker's name away from him, so that it burnt first. It was a gesture Leamas liked: it indicated that Peters, like himself, had been on the run.

Peters had an odd face, expressionless and grey. The colour must have left it long ago—perhaps in some prison in the early days of the Revolution—and now his features were formed and Peters would look like that till he died. Only the stiff, grey hair might turn to white, but his face would not change. Leamas wondered vaguely what Peters' real name was, whether he was married. There was something very orthodox about him which Leamas liked. It was the orthodoxy of strength, of confidence. If Peters lied there would be a reason. The lie would be a calculated, necessary lie, far removed from the fumbling dishonesty of Ashe.

Ashe, Kiever, Peters; that was a progression in quality, in authority, which to Leamas was axiomatic of the hierarchy of an intelligence network. It was also, he suspected, a progression in ideology. Ashe, the mercenary, Kiever the fellow traveller, and now Peters, for whom the end and the means were identical.

Leamas began to talk about Berlin. Peters seldom interrupted, seldom asked a question or made a comment, but when he did, he displayed a technical curiosity and expertise which entirely accorded with Leamas' own temperament. Leamas even seemed to respond to the dispassionate professionalism of his interrogator—it was something they had in common.

It had taken a long time to build a decent East Zone network from Berlin, Leamas explained. In the earlier days the city had been thronging with second-rate agents: intelligence was discredited and so much a part of the daily life of Berlin that you could recruit a man at a cocktail party, brief him over dinner, and he would be blown by breakfast. For a professional it was a nightmare: dozens of agencies, half of them penetrated by the opposition, thousands of loose ends; too many leads, too few sources, too little space to operate. They had their break with Feger in 1954, true enough. But by '56 when every Service department was screaming for high-grade intelligence, they were becalmed. Feger had spoilt them for second-rate stuff that was only one jump ahead of the news. They needed the real thing—and they had to wait another three years before they got it.

Then one day de Jong went for a picnic in the woods on the edge of East Berlin. He had a British military number plate on his car, which he parked, locked, in an unmade road beside the canal. After the picnic his children ran on ahead, carrying the basket. When they reached the car they stopped, hesitated, dropped the basket and ran back. Somebody had forced the car door—the handle was broken and the door was slightly open. De Jong swore, remembering that he had left his camera in the glove compartment. He went and examined the car. The handle had been forced; de Jong reckoned it had been done with a piece of steel tubing, the kind of thing you can carry in your sleeve. But the camera was still there, so was his coat, so were some parcels, belonging to his wife. On the driving seat was a tobacco tin, and in the tin was a small nickel cartridge. De Jong knew exactly what it contained: it was the film cartridge of a subminiature camera, probably a Minox.

De Jong drove home and developed the film. It contained the minutes of the last meeting of the Praesidium of the East German Communist Party, the SED. By an odd coincidence there was collateral from another source; the photographs were genuine.

Leamas took the case over then. He was badly in need of a success. He'd produced virtually nothing since arriving in Berlin, and he was getting past the usual age limit for full-time operational work. Exactly a week later he took de Jong's car to the same place and went for a walk.

It was a desolate spot that de Jong had chosen for his picnic: a strip of canal with a couple of shell-torn pill-boxes, some parched, sandy fields, and on the Eastern side a sparse pine wood, lying about two hundred yards from the gravel road which bordered the canal. But it had the virtue of solitude—something that was hard to find in Berlin—and surveillance was impossible. Leamas walked in the woods. He made no attempt to watch the car because he did not know from which direction the approach might be made. If he was seen watching the car from the woods, the chances of retaining his informant's confidence were ruined. He need not have worried.

When he returned there was nothing in the car so he drove back to West Berlin, kicking himself for being a damned fool; the Praesidium was not due to meet for another fortnight. Three weeks later he borrowed de Jong's car and took a thousand dollars in twenties in a picnic case. He left the car unlocked for two hours and when he returned there was a tobacco tin in the glove compartment. The picnic case had gone.

The films were packed with first grade documentary stuff. In the next six weeks he did it twice more, and the same thing happened.

Leamas knew he had hit a gold mine. He gave the source the cover name of "Mayfair" and sent a pessimistic letter to London. Leamas knew that if he gave London half an opening they would control the case direct, which he was desperately anxious to avoid. This was probably the only kind of operation which could save him from superannuation and it was just the kind of thing that was big enough for London to want to take over for itself. Even if he kept them at arm's length there was still the danger that the Circus would have theories, make suggestions, urge caution, demand action. They would want him to give only new dollar bills in the hope of tracing them, they would want the film cartridges sent home for examination, they would plan clumsy tailing operations and tell the Departments. Most of all they would want to tell the Departments; and that, said Leamas, would blow the thing sky-high. He worked like a madman for three weeks. He combed the personality files of each member of the Praesidium. He drew up a list of all the clerical staff who might have had access to the minutes. From the distribution list on the pages of the facsimiles he extended the total of possible informants to thirty-one, including clerks and secretarial staff.

Confronted with the almost impossible task of identifying an informant from the incomplete records of thirty-one candidates, Leamas returned to the original material, which, he said, was something he should have done earlier. It puzzled him that in none of the photostat minutes he had so far received were the pages numbered, that none was stamped with a security classification, and that in the second and fourth copy words were crossed out in pencil or crayon. He came finally to an important conclusion: that the photocopies related not to the minutes themselves, but to the *draft* minutes. This placed the source in the Secretariat and the Secretariat was very small. The draft minutes had been well and carefully photographed: that suggested that the photographer had had time and a room to himself.

Leamas returned to the personality index. There was a man called Karl Riemeck in the Secretariat, a former corporal in the Medical Corps, who had served three years as a prisoner of war in England. His sister had been living in Pomerania when the Russians overran it, and he had never heard of her since. He was married and had one daughter named Carla.

Leamas decided to take a chance. He found out from London Riemeck's prisoner of war number, which was 29012, and the date of his release which was November 10th, 1945. He bought an East German children's book of science fiction and wrote in the fly leaf in German in an adolescent hand: "This book belongs to Carla Riemeck, born December 10th, 1945, in Bideford, North Devon. Signed Moonspacewoman 29012," and underneath, he added, "Applicants wishing to make space flights should present themselves for instruction to C. Riemeck in person. An application form is enclosed. Long live the People's Republic of Democratic Space!"

He ruled some lines on a sheet of writing paper, made columns of name, address, and age, and wrote at the bottom of the page:

"Each candidate will be interviewed personally. Write to the usual address stating when and where you wish to be met. Applications will be considered in seven days. C.R."

He put the sheet of paper inside the book. Leamas drove to the usual place, still in de Jong's car, and left the book on the passenger seat with five used one-hundred-dollar bills inside the cover. When Leamas returned the book had gone, and there was a tobacco tin on the seat instead. It contained three rolls of film. Leamas developed them that night: one film contained as usual the minutes of the Praesidium's last meeting; the second showed a draft revision of the East Germans' relationship to COMECON; and the third a breakdown of the East German Intelligence Service, complete with functions of departments and details of personalities.

Peters interrupted: "Just a minute," he said. "Do you mean to say all this intelligence came from Riemeck?"

"Why not? You know how much he saw."

"It's scarcely possible," Peters observed, almost to himself; "he must have had help."

"He did have later on; I'm coming to that."

"I know what you are going to tell me. But did you never have the feeling he got assistance from *above* as well as from the agents he afterwards acquired?"

"No. No, I never did. It never occurred to me."

"Looking back on it now, does it seem likely?"

"Not particularly."

"When you sent all this material back to the Circus, they never suggested that even for a man in Riemeck's position, the intelligence was phenomenally comprehensive."

"No."

"Did they ever ask where Riemeck got his camera from, who instructed him in document photography?"

Leamas hesitated.

"No . . . I'm sure they never asked."

"Remarkable," Peters observed drily. "I'm sorry—do go on. I do not mean to anticipate you."

Exactly a week later, Leamas continued, he drove to the canal and this time he felt nervous. As he turned into the unmade road he saw three bicycles lying in the grass and two hundred yards down the canal, three men fishing. He got out of the car as usual and began walking towards the line of trees on the other side of the field. He had gone about twenty yards when he heard a shout. He looked round and caught sight of one of the men beckoning to him. The other two had turned and were looking at him too. Leamas was wearing an old macintosh; he had his hands in the pockets, and it was too late to take them out. He knew that the men on either side were covering the man in the middle and that if he took his hands out of his pockets they would probably shoot him; they would think he was holding a revolver in his pocket. Leamas stopped ten yards from the centre man.

"You want something?" Leamas asked.

"Are you Leamas?" He was a small, plump man, very steady. He spoke English.

"Yes."

"What is your British national identity number?"

"PRT stroke L 58003 stroke one."

"Where did you spend VJ night?"

"At Leiden in Holland in my father's workshop, with some Dutch friends."

"Let's go for a walk, Mr. Leamas. You won't need your macintosh. Take it off and leave it on the ground where you are standing. My friends will look after it."

Leamas hesitated, shrugged, and took off his macintosh. Then they walked together briskly towards the wood.

"You know as well as I do who he was," said Leamas wearily, "third man in the Ministry of the Interior, Secretary to the SED Praesidium, head of the Co-ordinating Committee for the Protection of the People. I suppose that was how he knew about de Jong and me: he'd seen our counter intelligence files in the Abteilung. He had three strings to his bow: the Praesidium, straightforward internal political and economic reporting, and access to the files of the East German Security Service."

"But only *limited* access. They'd never give an outsider the run of all their files," Peters insisted.

Leamas shrugged.

"They did," he said.

"What did he do with his money?"

"After that afternoon I didn't give him any. The Circus took that over straight away. It was paid into a West German bank. He even gave me back what I'd given him. London banked it for him."

"How much did you tell London?"

"Everything after that. I had to; then the Circus told the Departments. "After that," Leamas added venomously, "it was only a matter of time before it packed up. With the Departments at their backs, London got greedy. They began pressing us for more, wanted to give him more money. Finally we had to suggest to Karl that he recruited other sources and we took them on to form a network. It was bloody stupid, it put a strain on Karl, endangered him, undermined his confidence in us. It was the beginning of the end."

"How much did you get out of him?"

Leamas hesitated.

"How much? Christ, I don't know. It lasted an unnaturally long time. I think he was blown long before he was caught. The standard dropped in the last few months; think they'd begun to suspect him by then and kept him away from the good stuff."

"Altogether, what did he give you?" Peters persisted.

Piece by piece, Leamas recounted the full extent of all Karl Riemeck's work. His memory was, Peters noted approvingly, remarkably precise considering the amount he drank. He could give dates and names, he could remember the reaction from London, the nature of corroboration where it existed. He could remember sums of money demanded and paid, the dates of the conscription of other agents into the network.

"I'm sorry," said Peters at last, "but I do not believe that one man, however well placed, however careful, however industrious, could have acquired such a range of detailed knowledge. For that matter, even if he had he would never have been able to photograph it."

"He *was* able," Leamas persisted, suddenly angry, "he bloody well did and that's all there is to it."

"And the Circus never told you to go into it with him, exactly how and when he saw all this stuff."

"No," snapped Leamas, "Riemeck was touchy about that, and London was content to let it go."

"Well, well," Peters mused.

After a moment Peters said: "You heard about that woman, incidentally?"

"What woman?" Leamas asked sharply.

"Karl Riemeck's mistress, the one who came over to West Berlin the night Riemeck was shot."

"Well?"

"She was found dead a week ago. Murdered. She was shot from a car as she left her flat."

"It used to be my flat," said Leamas mechanically.

"Perhaps," Peters suggested, "she knew more about Riemeck's network than you did."

"What the hell do you mean?" Leamas demanded.

Peters shrugged.

"It's all very strange," he observed. "I wonder who killed her."

When they had exhausted the case of Karl Riemeck, Leamas went on to talk of other less spectacular agents, then of the procedure of his Berlin office, its communications, its staff, its secret ramifications—flats, transport, recording and photographic equipment. They talked long into the night and throughout the next day and when at last Leamas stumbled into bed the following night he knew he had betrayed all that he knew of Allied Intelligence in Berlin, and drunk two bottles of whisky in two days.

One thing puzzled him: Peters' insistence that Karl Riemeck must have had help—must have had a high-level collaborator. Control had asked him the same question—he remembered
now—Control had asked about Riemeck's access. How could
they both be so sure Karl hadn't managed alone? He'd had
helpers, of course; like the guards by the canal the day Leamas
met him. But they were small beer—Karl had told him about
them. But Peters—and Peters, after all, would know precisely
how much Karl had been able to get his hands on—Peters had
refused to believe Karl had managed alone. On this point,
Peters and Control were evidently agreed.

Perhaps it was true. Perhaps there was somebody else. Perhaps this was the Special Interest whom Control was so anxious to protect from Mundt. That would mean that Karl
Riemeck had collaborated with this special interest and provided what both of them had together obtained. Perhaps that
was what Control had spoken to Karl about, alone, that evening in Leamas' flat in Berlin.

Anyway, tomorrow would tell. Tomorrow he would play
his hand.

He wondered who had killed Elvira. And he wondered *why*
they had killed her. Of course—here was a point, here was a
possible explanation—Elvira, knowing the identity of Riemeck's special collaborator, had been murdered *by* that collaborator . . . No, that was too far-fetched. It overlooked the
difficulty of crossing from East to West: Elvira had after all
been murdered in West Berlin.

He wondered why Control had never told him Elvira had
been murdered. So that he would react suitably when Peters
told him? It was useless speculating. Control had his reasons;
they were usually so bloody tortuous it took you a week to
work them out.

As he fell asleep he muttered, "Karl was a damn' fool. That
woman did for him, I'm sure she did." Elvira was dead now,
and serve her right. He remembered Liz.

9

The Second Day

Peters arrived at eight o'clock the next morning, and without ceremony they sat down at the table and began.

"So you came back to London. What did you do there?"

"They put me on the shelf. I knew I was finished when that ass in Personnel met me at the airport. I had to go straight to Control and report about Karl. He was dead—what else was there to say?"

"What did they do with you?"

"They said at first I could hang around in London and wait till I was qualified for a proper pension. They were so bloody decent about it I got angry—I told them that if they were so keen to chuck money at me why didn't they do the obvious thing and count in all my time instead of bleating about broken service. Then they got cross when I told them that. They put me in Banking with a lot of women. I can't remember much about that part—I began hitting the bottle a bit. Had rather a bad patch."

He lit a cigarette. Peters nodded.

"That was why they gave me the push, really. They didn't like me drinking."

"Tell me what you *do* remember about Banking Section," Peters suggested.

"It was a dreary set-up. I never was cut out for desk work, I knew that. That's why I hung on in Berlin. I knew when they recalled me I'd be put on the shelf, but, Christ . . . !"

"What did you do?"

Leamas shrugged.

"Sat on my behind in the same room as a couple of women. Thursby and Larrett. I called them Thursday and Friday." He grinned rather stupidly. Peters looked uncomprehending.

"We just pushed paper. A letter came down from Finance: 'the payment of seven hundred dollars to so and so is authorised with effect from so and so. Kindly get on with it'—that was the gist of it. Thursday and Friday would kick it about a bit, file it, stamp it and I'd sign a cheque or get the bank to make a transfer."

"What bank?"

"Blatt and Rodney, a chichi little bank in the City. There's a sort of theory in the Circus that Etonians are discreet."

"In fact, then, you knew the names of agents all over the world?"

"Not necessarily. That was the cunning thing. I'd sign the cheque, you see, or the order to the bank, but we'd leave a space for the name of the payee. The covering letter or what have you was all signed and then the file would go *back* to Special Despatch."

"Who are they?"

"They're the general holders of agents' particulars. They put in the names and posted the order. Bloody clever, I must say."

Peters looked disappointed.

"You mean you had no way of knowing the names of the payees?"

"Not usually, no."

"But occasionally?"

"We got pretty near the knuckle now and again. All the fiddling about between Banking, Finance, and Special Despatch led to cock-ups, of course. Too elaborate. Then occasionally we came in on special stuff which brightened one's life a bit."

Leamas got up. "I've made a list," he said, "of all the payments I can remember. It's in my room. I'll get it."

He walked out of the room, the rather shuffling walk he had affected since arriving in Holland. When he returned he held in his hand a couple of sheets of lined paper torn from a cheap notebook.

"I wrote these down last night," he said; "I thought it would save time."

Peters took the notes and read them slowly and carefully. He seemed impressed.

"Good," he said, "very good."

"Then I remembered best a thing called Rolling Stone. I got a couple of trips out of it. One to Copenhagen and one to Helsinki. Just dumping money at banks."

"How much?"

"Ten thousand dollars in Copenhagen, forty thousand D-Marks in Helsinki."

Peters put down his pencil.

"Who for?" he asked.

"God knows. We worked Rolling Stone on a system of deposit accounts. The service gave me a phoney British passport; I went to the Royal Scandinavian Bank in Copenhagen and the National Bank of Finland in Helsinki, deposited the money, and drew a pass book on a joint account for me in my alias and for someone else—the agent, I suppose, in his alias. I gave the banks a sample of the co-holder's signature. I'd got that from Head Office. Later the agent was given the pass book and a false passport which he showed at the bank when he drew the money. All I knew was the alias." He heard himself talking and it all sounded so ludicrously improbable.

"Was this procedure common?"

"No. It was a special payment. It had a subscription list."

"What's that?"

"It had a code name known to very few people."

"What was the code name?"

"I told you—Rolling Stone. The operation covered irregular payments of ten thousand dollars in different currencies and in different capitals."

"Always in capital towns?"

"Far as I know. I remember reading in the file that there had been other Rolling Stone payments before I came to the section, but in those cases Banking Section got the local Resident to do it."

"These other payments that took place before you came, where were they made?"

"One in Oslo. I can't remember where the other was."

"Was the alias of the agent always the same?"

"No. That was an added security precaution. I heard later we pinched the whole technique from the Russians. It was the most elaborate payment scheme I'd met. In the same way I used a different alias and of course a different passport for each trip." That would please him; help him to fill in the gaps.

"These faked passports the agent was given so that he could draw the money: did you know anything about them, how they were made out and despatched?"

"No. Oh, except that they had to have visas in them for the country where the money was deposited. And entry stamps."

"*Entry stamps?*"

"Yes. I assumed the passports were never used at the border—only presented at the bank for identification purposes. The agent must have travelled on his own passport, quite legally entered the country where the bank was situated, then used the faked passport at the bank. That was my guess."

"Do you know of a reason why earlier payments were made

by the Residents, and later payments by someone travelling out from London?"

"I know the reason. I asked the women in Banking Section, Thursday and Friday. Control was anxious that—"

"*Control?* Do you mean to say Control himself was running the case?"

"Yes, he was running it. He was afraid the Resident might be recognised at the bank. So he used a postman: me."

"When did you make your journeys?"

"Copenhagen on the fifteenth of June. I flew back the same night. Helsinki at the end of September. I stayed two nights there, flew back around the twenty-eighth. I had a bit of fun in Helsinki." He grinned but Peters took no notice.

"And the other payments—when were they made?"

"I can't remember. Sorry."

"But one was definitely in Oslo?"

"Yes, in Oslo."

"How much time separated the first two payments, the payments made by the Residents?"

"I don't know. Not long, I think. Maybe a month. A bit more perhaps."

"Was it your impression that the agent had been operating for some time before the first payment was made? Did the file show that?"

"No idea. The file simply covered actual payments. First payments early '59. There was no other data on it. That is the principle that operates where you have a limited subscription. Different files handle different bits of a single case. Only some-one with the master file would be able to put it all together."

Peters was writing all the time now. Leamas assumed there was a tape recorder hidden somewhere in the room but the subsequent transcription would take time. What Peters wrote down now would provide the background for this evening's telegram to Moscow, while in the Soviet Embassy in The

Hague the girls would sit up all night telegraphing the verbatim transcript on hourly schedules.

"Tell me," said Peters; "these are large sums of money. The arrangements for paying them were elaborate and very expensive. What did you make of it yourself?"

Leamas shrugged.

"What could I make of it? I thought Control must have a bloody good source, but I never saw the material so I don't know. I didn't like the way it was done—it was too high-powered, too complicated, too clever. Why couldn't they just meet him and give him the money in cash? Did they really let him cross borders on his own passport with a forged one in his pocket? I doubt it," said Leamas. It was time he clouded the issue, let him chase a hare.

"What do you mean?"

"I mean, that for all I know the money was never drawn from the bank. Supposing he was a highly placed agent behind the Curtain—the money would be on deposit for him when he could get at it. That was what I reckoned anyway. I didn't think about it all that much. Why should I? It's part of our work only to know pieces of the whole set-up. You know that. If you're curious, God help you."

"If the money wasn't collected, as you suggest, why all the trouble with passports?"

"When I was in Berlin we made an arrangement for Karl Riemeck in case he ever needed to run and couldn't get hold of us. We kept a bogus West German passport for him at an address in Düsseldorf. He could collect it any time by following a prearranged procedure. It never expired—Special Travel renewed the passport and the visas as they expired. Control might have followed the same technique with this man. I don't know—it's only a guess."

"How do you know for certain that passports were issued?"

"There were minutes on the file between Banking section

and Special Travel. Special Travel is the section which arranges
false identity papers and visas."

"I see." Peters thought for a moment and then he asked:
"What names did you use in Copenhagen and Helsinki?"

"Robert Lang, electrical engineer from Derby. That was in
Copenhagen."

"When exactly were you in Copenhagen?" Peters asked.

"I told you, June the fifteenth. I got there in the morning at
about eleven-thirty."

"Which bank did you use?"

"Oh, for Christ's sake, Peters," said Leamas, suddenly angry,
"the Royal Scandinavian. You've got it written down."

"I just wanted to be sure," the other replied evenly, and
continued writing. "And for Helsinki, what name?"

"Stephen Bennett, marine engineer from Plymouth. I was
there," he added sarcastically, "at the end of September."

"You visited the bank on the day you arrived?"

"Yes. It was the 24th or 25th, I can't be sure, as I told you."

"Did you take the money with you from England?"

"Of course not. We just transferred it to the Resident's
account in each case. The Resident drew it, met me at the airport with the money in a suitcase, and I took it to the bank."

"Who's the Resident in Copenhagen?"

"Peter Jensen, a bookseller in the University bookshop."

"And what were the names which would be used by the
agent?"

"Horst Karlsdorf in Copenhagen. I think that was it, yes it
was, I remember. Karlsdorf. I kept on wanting to say Karlshorst."

"Description?"

"Manager, from Klagenfurt in Austria."

"And the other? The Helsinki name?"

"Fechtmann. Adolf Fechtmann from St. Gallen, Switzerland. He had a title—yes, that's right: Doctor Fechtmann,
archivist."

"I see; both German-speaking?"

"Yes, I noticed that. But it can't be a German."

"Why not?"

"I was head of the Berlin set-up, wasn't I? I'd have been in on it. A high-level agent in East Germany would have to be run from Berlin. I'd have known." Leamas got up, went to the sideboard, and poured himself some whisky. He didn't bother about Peters.

"You said yourself there were special precautions, special procedures in this case. Perhaps they didn't think you needed to know."

"Don't be bloody silly," Leamas rejoined shortly; "of course I'd have known." This was the point he would stick to through thick and thin; it made them feel they knew better, gave credence to the rest of his information. "They will want to deduce *in spite of you*," Control had said. "We must give them the material and remain sceptical to their conclusions. Rely on their intelligence and conceit, on their suspicion of one another— that's what we must do."

Peters nodded as if he were confirming a melancholy truth. "You are a very proud man, Leamas," he observed once more.

Peters left soon after that. He wished Leamas good day and walked down the road along the seafront. It was lunchtime.

10

The Third Day

Peters didn't appear that afternoon, nor the next morning. Leamas stayed in, waiting with growing irritation for some message, but none came. He asked the housekeeper but she just smiled and shrugged her heavy shoulders. At about eleven o'clock the next morning he decided to go out for a walk along the front, bought some cigarettes and stared dully at the sea.

There was a girl standing on the beach throwing bread to the seagulls. Her back was turned to him. The sea wind played with her long black hair and pulled at her coat, making an arc of her body, like a bow strung towards the sea. He knew what it was then that Liz had given him; the thing that he would have to go back and find if ever he got home to England: it was the caring about little things—the faith in ordinary life; the simplicity that made you break up a bit of bread into a paper bag, walk down to the beach, and throw it to the gulls. It was this respect for triviality which he had never been allowed to possess; whether it was bread for the seagulls or love, whatever it was he would go back and find it; he would make Liz find it for him. A week, two weeks perhaps, and he would be home. Control had said he could keep whatever they paid—and that would be enough. With fifteen thousand pounds, a gratuity, and a pension from the Circus, a man—as Control would say—can afford to come in from the cold.

He made a detour and returned to the bungalow at a quarter to twelve. The woman let him in without a word, but when he had gone into the back room he heard her lift the receiver and dial a telephone number. She only spoke for a few seconds. At half past twelve she brought him lunch, and, to his pleasure, some English newspapers, which he read contentedly until three o'clock. Leamas, who normally read nothing, read newspapers slowly and with concentration. He remembered details, like the names and addresses of people who were the subject of small news items. He did it almost unconsciously as a kind of private pelmanism, and it absorbed him entirely.

At three o'clock Peters arrived, and as soon as Leamas saw him he knew that something was up. They did not sit at the table; Peters did not take off his macintosh.

"I've got bad news for you," he said, "they're looking for you in England. I heard this morning. They're watching the ports."

Leamas replied impassively: "On what charge?"

"Nominally for failing to report to a police station within the statutory period after release from prison."

"And in fact?"

"The word is going around that you're wanted for an offence under the Official Secrets Act. Your photograph's in all the London evening papers. The captions are very vague."

Leamas was standing very still.

Control had done it. Control had started the hue and cry. There was no other explanation. If Ashe or Kiever had been pulled in, if they had talked—even then, the responsibility for the hue and cry was still Control's. "A couple of weeks," he'd said; "I expect they'll take you off somewhere for the interrogation—it may even be abroad. A couple of weeks should see you through, though. After that, the thing should run itself. You'll have to lie low over here while the chemistry works itself out; but you won't mind that I'm sure. I've agreed to keep you on operational subsistence until Mundt is eliminated: that seemed the fairest way."

And now this.

This wasn't part of the bargain; this was different. What the hell was he supposed to do? By pulling out now, by refusing to go along with Peters, he was wrecking the operation. It was just possible that Peters was lying, that this was the test—all the more reason that he should agree to go. But if he went, if he agreed to go east, to Poland, Czechoslovakia, or God knows where, there was no good reason why they should ever let him out—there was no good reason (since he was notionally a wanted man in the West) why he should *want* to be let out.

Control had done it—he was sure. The terms had been too generous, he'd known that all along. They didn't throw money about like that for nothing—not unless they thought they might lose you. Money like that was a *douceur* for discomfort and dangers Control would not openly admit to. Money like that was a warning; Leamas had not heeded the warning.

"Now how the devil," he asked quietly, "could they get on to that?" A thought seemed to cross his mind and he said, "Your friend Ashe could have told them, of course, or Kiever ..."

"It's possible," Peters replied. "You know as well as I do that such things are always possible. There is no certainty in our job. The fact is," he added with something like impatience, "that by now every country in Western Europe will be looking for you."

Leamas might not have heard what Peters was saying. "You've got me on the hook now, haven't you, Peters?" he said. "Your people must be laughing themselves sick. Or did they give the tip-off themselves?"

"You overrate your own importance," Peters said sourly.

"Then why do you have me followed, tell me that? I went for a walk this morning. Two little men in brown suits, one twenty yards behind the other, trailed me along the seafront. When I came back the housekeeper rang you up."

"Let us stick to what we know," Peters suggested. "How your own authorities have got on to you does not at the moment acutely concern us. The fact is, they have."

"Have you brought the London evening papers with you?"

"Of course not. They are not available here. We received a telegram from London."

"That's a lie. You know perfectly well your apparatus is only allowed to communicate with Centre."

"In this case a direct link between two outstations was permitted," Peters retorted angrily.

"Well, well," said Leamas with a wry smile, "you must be quite a big wheel. Or"—a thought seemed to strike him—"isn't Centre in on this?"

Peters ignored the question.

"You know the alternative. You let us take care of you, let us arrange your safe passage, or you fend for yourself—with the certainty of eventual capture. You've no false papers, no money, nothing. Your British passport will have expired in ten days."

"There's a third possibility. Give me a Swiss passport and some money and let me run. I can look after myself."

"I am afraid that is not considered desirable."

"You mean you haven't finished the interrogation. Until you have I am not expendable?"

"That is roughly the position."

"When you have completed the interrogation, what will you do with me?"

Peters shrugged. "What do you suggest?"

"A new identity. Scandinavian passport perhaps. Money."

"It's very academic," Peters replied, "but I will suggest it to my superiors. Are you coming with me?" Leamas hesitated then he smiled a little uncertainly and asked:

"If I didn't, what would you do? After all I've quite a story to tell, haven't I?"

"Stories of that kind are hard to substantiate. I shall be gone tonight. Ashe and Kiever . . ." he shrugged, "what do they add up to?"

Leamas went to the window. A storm was gathering over the grey North Sea. He watched the gulls wheeling against the dark clouds. The girl had gone.

"All right," he said at last, "fix it up."

"There's no plane East until tomorrow. There's a flight to Berlin in an hour. We shall take that. It's going to be very close."

Leamas' passive role that evening enabled him once again to admire the unadorned efficiency of Peters' arrangements. The passport had been put together long ago—Centre must have thought of that. It was made out in the name of Alexander Thwaite, travel agent, and filled with visas and frontier stamps—the old, well-fingered passport of the professional traveller. The Dutch frontier guard at the airport just nodded and stamped it for form's sake—Peters was three or four behind him in the queue and took no interest in the formalities.

As they entered the "passengers only" enclosure Leamas caught sight of a bookstall. A selection of international newspapers was on show: *Figaro, Monde, Neue Zürcher Zeitung, Die Welt*, and half a dozen British dailies and weeklies. As he watched, the girl came round to the front of the kiosk and pushed an *Evening Standard* into the rack. Leamas hurried across to the bookstall and took the paper from the rack.

"How much?" he asked. Thrusting his hand into his trouser pocket he suddenly realised that he had no Dutch currency.

"Thirty cents," the girl replied. She was rather pretty; dark and jolly.

"I've only got two English shillings. That's a guilder. Will you take them?"

"Yes, please," she replied, and Leamas gave her the florin. He looked back; Peters was still at the passport desk, his back turned to Leamas. Without hesitation he made straight for the men's lavatory. There he glanced rapidly but thoroughly at each page, then shoved the paper in the litter basket and re-emerged. It was true: there was his photograph with the vague little passage underneath. He wondered if Liz had seen it. He made his way thoughtfully to the passengers' lounge. Ten minutes later they boarded the plane for Hamburg and Berlin. For the first time since it all began, Leamas was frightened.

11

Friends of Alec

The men called on Liz the same evening.

Liz Gold's room was at the northern end of Bayswater. It had two single beds in it, and a gas fire, rather a pretty one in charcoal grey, which made a modern hiss instead of an old fashioned bubble. She used to gaze into it sometimes when Leamas was there, when the gas fire shed the only light in the room. He would lie on the bed, hers, the one furthest from the door, and she would sit beside him and kiss him, or watch the gas fire with her face pressed against his. She was afraid to think of him too much now because then she forgot what he looked like, so she let her mind think of him for brief moments like running her eyes across a faint horizon, and then she would remember some small thing he had said or done, some way he had looked at her, or, more often, ignored her. That was the terrible thing, when her mind dwelled on it: she had nothing to remember him by—no photograph, no souvenir, nothing. Not even a mutual friend—only Miss Crail in the library, whose hatred of him had been vindicated by his spectacular departure. Liz had been round to his room once and seen the landlord. She didn't know why she did it quite, but she plucked up courage and went. The landlord was very kind about Alec; Mr. Leamas had paid his rent like a gentleman, right till the end, then there'd been a week or two owing and a chum of Mr. Leamas had dropped in and paid up handsome, no queries or nothing. He'd always said it of Mr. Leamas, always would, he was a gent. Not public school, mind, nothing arsy-tarsy but a real gent. He liked to scowl a bit occasionally, and of course he drank a drop more than was good for him, though he never acted tight when he came home. But this little bloke who come round, funny little shy chap with specs, *he* said Mr. Leamas had particularly requested, quite particularly, that the rent owing should be settled up. And if that wasn't gentlemanly the landlord was damned if he knew what was. Where he got the money from Heaven knows, but that Mr. Leamas was a deep one and no mistake. He only did to Ford the grocer what a good many had been wanting to do ever since the war. The room? Yes, the room had been taken—a gentleman from Korea, two days after they took Mr. Leamas away.

That was probably why she went on working at the library— because there, at least, he still existed; the ladders, shelves, the books, the card index, were things he had known and touched, and one day he might come back to them. He had said he would never come back, but she didn't believe it. It was like saying you would never get better, to believe a thing like that. Miss Crail thought he would come back: she had discovered she owed him some money—wages underpaid—and it infuriated her that her monster had been so unmonstrous as not to collect it. After Leamas had gone, Liz had never given up asking herself the same question; why had he hit Mr. Ford? She knew he had a terrible temper, but that was different. He had intended to do it right from the start as soon as he had got rid of his fever. Why else had he said good-bye to her the night before? He knew that he would hit Mr. Ford on the following day. She refused to accept the only other possible interpretation: that he had grown tired of her and said good-bye, and the next day, still under the emotional strain of their parting, had lost his temper with Mr. Ford and struck him. She knew, she had always known, that there was something Alec had got to do. He'd even told her that himself. What it was she could only guess.

First, she thought he had a quarrel with Mr. Ford, some deep-rooted hatred going back for years. Something to do with a girl, or Alec's family perhaps. But you only had to look at Mr. Ford and it seemed ridiculous. He was the archetypal *petit-bourgeois*, cautious, complacent, mean. And anyway, if Alec had a vendetta on with Mr. Ford, why did he go for him in the shop on a Saturday, in the middle of the weekend shopping rush, when everyone could see?

They'd talked about it in the meeting of her party branch. George Hanby, the branch treasurer, had actually been passing Ford the grocer's as it happened, he hadn't seen much because of the crowd, but he'd talked to a bloke who'd seen the whole thing. Hanby had been so impressed that he'd rung the *Worker*, and they'd sent a man to the trial—that was why the *Worker* had given it a middle page spread as a matter of fact. It was just a straight case of protest—of sudden social awareness and hatred against the boss class, as the *Worker* said. This bloke that Hanby spoke to (he was just a little ordinary chap with specs, white collar type) said it had been so sudden—spontaneous was what he meant—and it just proved to Hanby once again how incendiary was the fabric of the capitalist system. Liz had kept very quiet while Hanby talked: none of them knew, of course, about her and Leamas. She realised then that she hated George Hanby; he was a pompous, dirty-minded little man, always leering at her and trying to touch her.

Then the men called.

She thought they were a little too smart for policemen: they came in a small black car with an aerial on it. One was short and rather plump. He had glasses and wore odd, expensive clothes; he was a kindly, worried little man and Liz trusted him somehow without knowing why. The other was smoother, but not glossy—rather a boyish figure, although she guessed he wasn't less than forty. They said they came from Special Branch, and they had printed cards with photographs in cellophane cases. The plump one did most of the talking.

"I believe you were friendly with Alec Leamas," he began. She was prepared to be angry, but the plump man was so earnest that it seemed silly.

"Yes," Liz answered. "How did you know?"

"We found out quite by chance the other day. When you go to . . . prison, you have to give next of kin. Leamas said he hadn't any. That was a lie as a matter of fact. They asked him whom they should inform if anything happened to him in prison. He said you."

"I see."

"Does anyone else know you were friendly with him?"

"No."

"Did you go to the trial?"

"No."

"No press men called, creditors, no one at all?"

"No, I've told you. No one else knew. Not even my parents, no one. We worked together in the library, of course—the Psychical Research Laboratory—but only Miss Crail, the librarian, would know that. I don't think it occurred to her that there was anything between us. She's queer," Liz added simply.

The little man peered very seriously at her for a moment, then asked:

"Did it surprise you when Leamas beat up Mr. Ford?"

"Yes, of course."

"Why did you think he did it?"

"I don't know. Because Ford wouldn't give him credit, I suppose. But I think he always meant to." She wondered if she was saying too much, but she longed to talk to somebody about it, she was so alone and there didn't seem any harm.

"But that night, the night before it happened, we talked

together. We had supper, a sort of special one; Alec said we should and I knew that it was our last night. He'd got a bottle of red wine from somewhere; I didn't like it much. Alec drank most of it. And then I asked him, 'Is this good-bye'—whether it was all over."

"What did he say?"

"He said there was a job he'd got to do. I didn't really understand it all, not really."

There was a very long silence and the little man looked more worried than ever. Finally he asked her:

"Do you believe that?"

"I don't know." She was suddenly terrified for Alec, and she didn't know why. The man asked:

"Leamas has got two children by his marriage, did he tell you?" Liz said nothing. "In spite of that he gave your name as next of kin. Why do you think he did that?" The little man seemed embarrassed by his own question. He was looking at his hands, which were pudgy and clasped together on his lap. Liz blushed.

"I was in love with him," she replied.

"Was he in love with you?"

"Perhaps. I don't know."

"Are you still in love with him?"

"Yes."

"Did he ever say he would come back?" asked the younger man.

"No."

"But he did say good-bye to you?" the other asked quickly.

"Did he say good-bye to you?" The little man repeated his question slowly, kindly. "Nothing more can happen to him, I promise you. But we want to help him, and if you have any idea of why he hit Ford, if you have the slightest notion from something he said, perhaps casually, or something he did, then tell us for Alec's sake."

Liz shook her head.

"Please go," she said, "please don't ask any more questions. Please go now."

As he got to the door, the elder man hesitated, then took a card from his wallet and put it on the table, gingerly, as if it might make a noise. Liz thought he was a very shy little man.

"If you ever want any help—if anything happens about Leamas or . . . ring me up," he said. "Do you understand?"

"Who are you?"

"I'm a friend of Alec Leamas." He hesitated. "Another thing," he added, "one last question. Did Alec know you were . . . did Alec know about the Party?"

"Yes," she replied, hopelessly, "I told him."

"Does the Party know about you and Alec?"

"I've told you. No one knew." Then, white-faced, she cried out suddenly, "Where is he; tell me where he is. Why won't you tell me where he is? I can help him, don't you see; I'll look after him . . . even if he's gone mad, I don't care, I swear I don't . . . I wrote to him in prison; I shouldn't have done, I know. I just said he could come back any time. I'd wait for him always . . ." She couldn't speak any more, just sobbed and sobbed, standing there in the middle of the room, her broken face buried in her hands; the little man watching her.

"He's gone abroad," he said gently. "We don't quite know where he is. He isn't mad, but he shouldn't have said all that to you. It was a pity."

The younger man said:

"We'll see you're looked after. For money and that kind of thing."

"Who are you?" Liz asked again.

"Friends of Alec," the young man repeated; "good friends."

She heard them go quietly down the stairs and into the street. From her window she watched them get into the small black car and drive away in the direction of the park.

Then she remembered the card. Going to the table she picked it up and held it to the light. It was expensively done, more than a policeman could afford, she thought. Engraved. No rank in front of the name, no police station or anything. Just the name with "Mister"—and whoever heard of a policeman living in Chelsea?

"Mr. George Smiley. 9 Bywater Street, Chelsea." Then the telephone number underneath.

It was very strange.

12

East

Leamas unfastened his seat belt.

It is said that men condemned to death are subject to sudden moments of elation; as if, like moths in the fire, their destruction were coincidental with attainment. Following directly upon his decision, Leamas was aware of a comparable sensation; relief, short-lived but consoling, sustained him for a time. It was followed by fear and hunger.

He was slowing down. Control was right.

He'd noticed it first during the Riemeck case, early last year. Karl had sent a message: he'd got something special for him and was making one of his rare visits to Western Germany; some legal conference at Karlsruhe. Leamas had managed to get an air passage to Cologne, and picked up a car at the airport. It was still quite early in the morning and he'd hoped to miss most of the autobahn traffic to Karlsruhe but the heavy lorries were already on the move. He drove seventy kilometres in half an hour, weaving between the traffic, taking risks to beat the clock, when a small car, a Fiat probably, nosed its way out into the fast lane forty yards ahead of him. Leamas stamped on the brake, turning his headlights full on and sounding his horn, and by the grace of God he missed it; missed it by a fraction of a second. As he passed the car he saw out of the corner of his eye four children in the back, waving and laughing, and the stupid, frightened face of their father at the wheel. He drove on, cursing, and suddenly it happened; suddenly his hands were shaking feverishly, his face was burning, his heart palpitating wildly. He managed to pull off the road into a lay-by, scrambled out of the car, and stood breathing heavily, staring at the hurtling stream of giant lorries. He had a vision of the little car caught among them, pounded and smashed, until there was nothing left, nothing but the frenetic whine of klaxons and the blue lights flashing; and the bodies of the children, torn, like the murdered refugees on the road across the dunes.

He drove very slowly the rest of the way and missed his meeting with Karl.

He never drove again without some corner of his memory recalling the tousled children waving to him from the back of that car, and their father grasping the wheel like a farmer at the shafts of a hand plough.

Control would call it fever.

He sat dully in his seat over the wing. There was an American woman next to him wearing high-heeled shoes in polythene wrappers. He had a momentary notion of passing her some note for the people in Berlin, but he discarded it at once. She'd think he was making a pass at her, Peters would see it. Besides, what was the point? Control knew what had happened; Control had made it happen. There was nothing to say.

He wondered what would become of him. Control hadn't talked about that—only about the technique:

"Don't give it to them all at once, make them work for it. Confuse them with detail, leave things out, go back on your tracks. Be testy, be cussed, be difficult. Drink like a fish; don't give way on the ideology, they won't trust that. They want to deal with a man they've bought; they want the clash of opposites, Alec, not some half-cock convert. Above all, they want to *deduce*. The ground's prepared; we did it long ago, little things, difficult clues. You're the last stage in the treasure hunt."

He'd had to agree to do it; you can't back out of the big fight when all the preliminary ones have been fought for you.

"One thing I can promise you: it's worth it. It's worth it for our special interest, Alec. Keep alive and we've won a great victory."

He didn't think he could stand torture. He remembered a book by Koestler where the old revolutionary had conditioned himself for torture by holding lighted matches to his fingers. He hadn't read much but he'd read that and he remembered it.

It was nearly dark as they landed at Tempelhof. Leamas watched the lights of Berlin rise to meet them, felt the thud as the plane touched down, saw the Customs and immigration officials move forward out of the half light.

For a moment Leamas was anxious lest some former acquaintance should chance to recognise him at the airport. As they walked side by side, Peters and he, along the interminable corridors, through the cursory Customs and immigration check, and still no familiar face turned to greet him, he realised that his anxiety had in reality been hope; hope that somehow his tacit decision to go on would be revoked by circumstance.

It interested him that Peters no longer bothered to disown him; it was as if Peters regarded West Berlin as safe ground, where vigilance and security could be relaxed; a mere technical staging post to the East.

They were walking through the big reception hall to the main entrance when Peters suddenly seemed to alter his mind, abruptly changed direction and led Leamas to a smaller side entrance which gave on to a car park and taxi rank. There Peters hesitated a second, standing beneath the light over the door, then put his suitcase on the ground beside him, deliberately removed his newspaper from beneath his arm, folded it, pushed it into the left pocket of his raincoat and picked up his suitcase again. Immediately, from the direction of the car park, a pair of headlights sprang to life, were dipped and then extinguished.

"Come on," said Peters and started to walk briskly across the tarmac, Leamas following more slowly. As they reached the first row of cars the rear door of a black Mercedes was opened from the inside, and the courtesy light went on. Peters, ten yards ahead of Leamas, went quickly to the car, spoke softly to the driver, then called to Leamas.

"Here's the car. Be quick."

It was an old Mercedes 180 and he got in without a word. Peters sat beside him in the back. As they pulled out they over-took a small DKW with two men sitting in the front. Twenty yards down the road there was a telephone kiosk. A man was talking into the telephone, and he watched them go by, talking all the time. Leamas looked out of the back window and saw the DKW following them. Quite a reception, he thought.

They drove quite slowly. Leamas sat with his hands on his knees, looking straight in front of him. He didn't want to see Berlin that night. This was his last chance, he knew that. The way he was sitting now he could drive the side of his right hand into Peters' throat, smashing the promontory of the thorax. He could get out and run, weaving to avoid the bullets from the car behind. He would be free—there were people in Berlin who would take care of him—he could get away.

He did nothing.

It was so easy crossing the sector border. Leamas had never expected it to be quite that easy. For about ten minutes they dawdled, and Leamas guessed that they had to cross at a pre-arranged time. As they approached the West German checkpoint, the DKW pulled out and overtook them with the ostentatious roar of a laboured engine, and stopped at the police hut. The Mercedes waited thirty yards behind. Two minutes later the red and white pole lifted to let through the DKW and as it did so both cars drove over together, the Mercedes engine screaming in second gear, the driver pressing himself back against his seat, holding the wheel at arms' length.

As they crossed the fifty yards which separated the two checkpoints, Leamas was dimly aware of the new fortifications on the Eastern side of the wall—dragons' teeth, observation towers, and double aprons of barbed wire. Things had brightened up.

The Mercedes didn't stop at the second checkpoint; the booms were already lifted and they drove straight through, the Vopos just watching them through binoculars. The DKW had disappeared, and when Leamas sighted it ten minutes later it was behind them again. They were driving fast now—Leamas had thought they would stop in East Berlin, change cars perhaps, and congratulate one another on a successful operation, but they drove on eastwards through the city.

"Where are we going?" he asked Peters.

"We are there. The German Democratic Republic. They have arranged accommodation for you."

"I thought we'd be going further east."

"We are. We are spending a day or two here first. We thought the Germans ought to have a talk with you."

"I see."

"After all, most of your work has been on the German side. I sent them details from your statement."

"And they asked to see me?"

"They've never had anything quite like you, nothing quite so . . . near the source. My people agreed that they should have the chance to meet you."

"And from there? Where do we go from Germany?"

"East again."

"Who will I see on the German side?"

"Does it matter?"

"Not particularly. I know most of the Abteilung people by name, that's all. I just wondered."

"Who would you expect to meet?"

"Fiedler," Leamas replied promptly, "deputy head of security. Mundt's man. He does all the big interrogations. He's a bastard."

"Why?"

"A savage little bastard. I've heard about him. He caught an agent of Peter Guillam's and bloody nearly killed him."

"Espionage is not a cricket game," Peters observed sourly and after that they sat in silence. So it is Fiedler, Leamas thought.

Leamas knew Fiedler all right. He knew him from the photographs on the file and the accounts of his former subordinates. A slim, neat man, quite young, smooth-faced. Dark hair, bright brown eyes; intelligent and savage, as Leamas had said. A lithe, quick body containing a patient, retentive mind; a man seemingly without ambition for himself but remorseless in the destruction of others. Fiedler was a rarity in the Abteilung—he took no part in its intrigues, seemed content to live in Mundt's shadow without prospect of promotion. He could not be labelled as a member of this or that clique; even those who had worked close to him in the Abteilung could not say where he stood in its power complex. Fiedler was a solitary; feared, disliked, and mistrusted. Whatever motives he had were concealed beneath a cloak of destructive sarcasm.

"Fiedler is our best bet," Control had explained. They'd been sitting together over dinner—Leamas, Control, and Peter Guillam—in the dreary little seven-dwarfs house in Surrey where Control lived with his beady wife, surrounded by carved Indian tables with brass tops. "Fiedler is the acolyte who one day will stab the high priest in the back. He's the only man who's a match for Mundt"—here Guillam had nodded—"and he hates his guts. Fiedler's a Jew of course, and Mundt is quite the other thing. Not at all a good mixture. It has been our job," he declared, indicating Guillam and himself, "to give Fiedler the weapon with which to destroy Mundt. It will be yours, my dear Leamas, to encourage him to use it. Indirectly, of course, because you'll never meet him. At least I certainly hope you won't."

They'd all laughed then, Guillam too. It had seemed a good joke at the time; good by Control's standards anyway.

It must have been after midnight.

For some time they had been travelling an unmade road, partly through a wood and partly across open country. Now they stopped and a moment later the DKW drew up beside them. As he and Peters got out Leamas noticed that there were now three people in the second car. Two were already getting out. The third was sitting in the back seat looking at some papers by the light from the car roof, a slight figure half in shadow.

They had parked by some disused stables; the building lay thirty yards back. In the headlights of the car Leamas had glimpsed a low farmhouse with walls of timber and white-washed brick. They got out. The moon was up, and shone so brightly that the wooded hills behind were sharply defined against the pale night sky. They walked to the house, Peters and Leamas leading and the two men behind. The other man in the second car had still made no attempt to move; he remained there, reading.

As they reached the door Peters stopped, waiting for the other two to catch them up. One of them carried a bunch of keys in his left hand, and while he fiddled with them the other stood off, his hands in his pockets, covering him.

"They're taking no chances," Leamas observed to Peters, "what do they think I am?"

"They are not paid to think," Peters replied, and turning to one of them he asked in German:

"Is he coming?"

The German shrugged and looked back towards the car.

"He'll come," he said; "he likes to come alone."

They went into the house, the man leading the way. It was got up like a hunting lodge, part old, part new. It was badly lit with pale overhead lights. The place had a neglected, musty air as if it had been opened for the occasion. There were little touches of officialdom here and there—a notice of what to do in case of fire, institutional green paint on the door, and heavy spring-cartridge locks; and in the drawing-room, which was quite comfortably done, dark, heavy furniture, badly scratched, and the inevitable photographs of Soviet leaders. To Leamas these lapses from anonymity signified the involuntary identification of the Abteilung with bureaucracy. That was something he was familiar with in the Circus.

Peters sat down, and Leamas did the same. For ten minutes, perhaps longer, they waited, then Peters spoke to one of the two men standing awkwardly at the other end of the room.

"Go and tell him we're waiting. And find us some food, we're hungry." As the man moved towards the door Peters called, "And whisky—tell them to bring whisky and some glasses." The man gave an uncooperative shrug of his heavy shoulders and went out, leaving the door open behind him.

"Have you been here before?" asked Leamas.

"Yes," Peters replied, "several times."

"What for?"

"This kind of thing. Not the same, but our kind of work."

"With Fiedler?"

"Yes."

"Is he good?"

Peters shrugged. "For a Jew, he's not bad," he replied, and Leamas, hearing a sound from the other end of the room, turned and saw Fiedler standing in the doorway. In one hand he held a bottle of whisky, and in the other, glasses and some mineral water. He couldn't have been more than five foot six. He wore a dark blue single-breasted suit; the jacket was cut too long. He was sleek and slightly animal; his eyes were brown and bright. He was not looking at them but at the guard beside the door.

"Go away," he said. He had a slight Saxonian twang: "Go away and tell the other one to bring us food."

"I've told him," Peters called; "they know already. But they've brought nothing."

"They are great snobs," Fiedler observed drily in English. "They think we should have servants for the food."

Fiedler had spent the war in Canada. Leamas remembered that, now that he detected the accent. His parents had been German Jewish refugees, Marxists, and it was not until 1946 that the family returned home, anxious to take part, whatever the personal cost, in the construction of Stalin's Germany.

"Hello," he added to Leamas, almost by the way, "glad to see you."

"Hello, Fiedler."

"You've reached the end of the road."

"What the hell d'you mean?" asked Leamas quickly.

"I mean that contrary to anything Peters told you, you are not going further east. Sorry." He sounded amused.

Leamas turned to Peters.

"Is this true?" His voice was shaking with rage. "Is it true? Tell me!"

Peters nodded: "Yes. I am the go-between. We had to do it that way. I'm sorry," he added.

"Why?"

"*Force majeure*," Fiedler put in. "Your initial interrogation took place in the West, where only an embassy could provide the kind of link we needed. The German Democratic Republic has no embassies in the West. Not yet. Our liaison section therefore arranged for us to enjoy facilities and communications and immunities which are at present denied to us."

"You bastard," hissed Leamas, "you lousy bastard! You knew I wouldn't trust myself to your rotten Service; that was the reason, wasn't it? That was why you used a Russian."

"We used the Soviet Embassy at The Hague. What else could we do? Up till then it was our operation. That's perfectly reasonable. Neither we nor anyone else could have known that your own people in England would get on to you so quickly."

"No? Not even when you put them on to me yourselves? Isn't that what happened, Fiedler? Well, isn't it?" Always remember to dislike them, Control had said. Then they will treasure what they get out of you.

"That is an absurd suggestion," Fiedler replied shortly. Glancing towards Peters he added something in Russian. Peters nodded and stood up.

"Good-bye," he said to Leamas. "Good luck."

He smiled wearily, nodded to Fiedler, then walked to the door. He put his hand on the door handle, then turned and called to Leamas again:

"Good luck." He seemed to want Leamas to say something, but Leamas might not have heard. He had turned very pale, he held his hands loosely across his body, the thumbs upwards as if he were going to fight. Peters remained standing at the door.

"I should have known," said Leamas, and his voice had the odd, faulty note of a very angry man, "I should have guessed you'd never have the guts to do your own dirty work, Fiedler. It's typical of your rotten little half-country and your squalid little Service that you get big uncle to do your pimping for you. You're not a country at all, you're not a government, you're a fifth-rate dictatorship of political neurotics." Jabbing his finger in Fiedler's direction, he shouted:

"I know you, you sadistic bastard; it's typical of you. You were in Canada in the war, weren't you; a bloody good place to be then, wasn't it? I'll bet you stuck your fat head into Mummy's apron any time an aeroplane flew over. What are you now? A creeping little acolyte to Mundt and twenty-two Russian divisions sitting on your mother's doorstep. Well, I pity you, Fiedler, the day you wake up and find them gone. There'll be a killing then, and not Mummy or big uncle will save you from getting what you deserve."

Fiedler shrugged.

"Regard it as a visit to the dentist, Leamas. The sooner it's all done, the sooner you can go home. Have some food and go to bed."

"You know perfectly well I can't go home," Leamas retorted. "You've seen to that. You blew me sky high in England, you had to, both of you. You knew damn' well I'd never come here unless I had to."

Fiedler looked at his thin, strong fingers.

"This is hardly the time to philosophise," he said, "but you can't really complain, you know. All our work—yours and mine—is rooted in the theory that the whole is more important than the individual. That is why a Communist sees his secret service as the natural extension of his arm, and that is why in your own country intelligence is shrouded in a kind of *pudeur anglaise*. The exploitation of individuals can only be justified by the collective need, can't it? I find it slightly ridiculous that you should be so indignant. We are not here to observe the ethical laws of English country life. After all," he added silkily, "your own behaviour has not, from the purist's point of view, been irreproachable."

Leamas was watching Fiedler with an expression of disgust.

"I know your set-up. You're Mundt's poodle, aren't you? They say you want his job. I suppose you'll get it now. It's time the Mundt dynasty ended; perhaps this is it."

"I don't understand," Fiedler replied.

"I'm your big success, aren't I?" Leamas sneered. Fiedler seemed to reflect for a moment, then he shrugged and said, "The operation was successful. Whether you were worth it is questionable. We shall see. But it was a good operation. It satisfied the only requirement of our profession: it worked."

"I suppose you take the credit?" Leamas persisted, with a glance in the direction of Peters.

"There is no question of credit," Fiedler replied crisply, "none at all." He sat down on the arm of a sofa, looked at Leamas thoughtfully for a moment and then said:

"Nevertheless you are right to be indignant about one thing. Who told your people we had picked you up? We didn't. You may not believe me, but it happens to be true. We didn't tell them. We didn't even want them to know. We had ideas then of getting you to work for us later—ideas which I now realise to be ridiculous. So who told them? You were lost, drifting around, you had no address, no ties, no friends. Then how the devil did they know you'd gone? Someone told them—scarcely Ashe or Kiever, since they are both now under arrest."

"Under arrest?"

"So it appears. Not specifically for their work on your case, but there were other things . . ."

"Well, well."

"It is true, what I said just now. We would have been content with Peters' report from Holland. You could have had your money and gone. But you hadn't told us everything; and I want to know everything. After all, your presence here provides us with problems too, you know."

"Well, you've boobed. I know damn' well—and you're welcome to it."

There was a silence, during which Peters, with an abrupt and by no means friendly nod in Fiedler's direction, quietly let himself out of the room.

Fiedler picked up the bottle of whisky and poured a little into each glass.

"We have no soda, I'm afraid," he said. "Do you like water? I ordered soda, but they brought some wretched lemonade."

"Oh, go to hell," said Leamas. He suddenly felt very tired.

Fiedler shook his head.

"You are a very proud man," he observed, "but never mind. Eat your supper and go to bed."

One of the guards came in with a tray of food—black bread, sausage, and cold green salad.

"It is a little crude," said Fiedler, "but quite satisfying. No potato, I'm afraid. There is a temporary shortage of potato."

They began eating in silence, Fiedler very carefully, like a man who counted his calories.

The guards showed Leamas to his bedroom. They let him carry his own luggage—the same luggage that Kiever had given him before he left England—and he walked between them along the wide central corridor which led through the house from the front door. They came to a large double door, painted dark green, and one of the guards unlocked it; they beckoned to Leamas to go first. He pushed open the door and found himself in a small barrack bedroom with two bunk beds, a chair and a rudimentary desk. It was like something in prison camp. There were pictures of girls on the walls and the windows were shuttered. At the far end of the room was another door. They signalled him forward again. Putting down his baggage he went and opened the door. The second room was identical to the first, but there was one bed and the walls were bare.

"You bring those cases," he said; "I'm tired." He lay on the bed, fully dressed, and within a few minutes he was fast asleep.

A sentry woke him with breakfast: black bread and *ersatz* coffee. He got out of bed and went to the window.

The house stood on a high hill. The ground fell steeply away from beneath his window, the crowns of pine trees visible above the crest. Beyond them, spectacular in their symmetry, unending hills, heavy with trees, stretched into the distance. Here and there a timber gully or fire-break formed a thin brown divide between the pines, seeming like Aaron's rod miraculously to hold apart massive seas of encroaching forest. There was no sign of man; not a house or church, not even the ruin of some previous habitation—only the road, the yellow unmade road, a crayon line across the basin of the valley. There was no sound. It seemed incredible that anything so vast could be so still. The day was cold but clear. It must have rained in the night; the ground was moist, and the whole landscape so sharply defined against the white sky that Leamas could distinguish even single trees on the furthest hills.

He dressed slowly, drinking the sour coffee meanwhile. He had nearly finished dressing and was about to start eating the bread when Fiedler came into the room.

"Good morning," he said cheerfully. "Don't let me keep you from your breakfast." He sat down on the bed. Leamas had to hand it to Fiedler; he had guts. Not that there was anything brave about coming to see him—the sentries, Leamas supposed, were still in the adjoining room. But there was an endurance, a defined purpose in his manner which Leamas could sense and admire.

"You have presented us with an intriguing problem," he observed.

"I've told you all I know."

"Oh no." He smiled. "Oh no, you haven't. You have told us all you are *conscious* of knowing."

"Bloody clever," Leamas muttered, pushing his food aside and lighting a cigarette—his last.

"Let me ask *you* a question," Fiedler suggested with the exaggerated bonhomie of a man proposing a party game. "As an experienced intelligence officer, what would *you* do with the information you have given us?"

"What information?"

"My dear Leamas, you have only given us one piece of intelligence. You have told us about Riemeck: we knew about Riemeck. You have told us about the dispositions of your

Berlin organisation, about its personalities and its agents. That, if I may say so, is old hat. Accurate—yes. Good background, fascinating reading, here and there good collateral, here and there a little fish which we shall take out of the pool. But not—if I may be crude—not fifteen thousand pounds' worth of intelligence. Not," he smiled again, "at current rates."

"Listen," said Leamas, "I didn't propose this deal—you did. You, Kiever, and Peters. I didn't come crawling to your cissy friends, peddling old intelligence. You people made the running, Fiedler; you named the price and took the risk. Apart from that, I haven't had a bloody penny. So don't blame me if the operation's a flop." Make them come to you, Leamas thought.

"It isn't a flop," Fiedler replied, "it isn't finished. It can't be. You haven't told us what you *know*. I said you had given us one piece of intelligence. I'm talking about Rolling Stone. Let me ask you again—what would *you* do if I, if Peters or someone like us, had told *you* a similar story?"

Leamas shrugged:

"I'd feel uneasy," he said; "it's happened before. You get an indication, several perhaps, that there's a spy in some department or at a certain level. So what? You can't arrest the whole government service. You can't lay traps for a whole department. You just sit tight and hope for more. You bear it in mind. In Rolling Stone you can't even tell what country he's working in."

"You are an operator, Leamas," Fiedler observed with a laugh, "not an evaluator. That is clear. Let me ask you some elementary questions."

Leamas said nothing.

"The file—the actual file on operation Rolling Stone. What colour was it?"

"Grey with a red cross on it—that means limited subscription."

"Was anything attached to the outside?"

"Yes, the Caveat. That's the subscription label. With a

legend saying that any unauthorised person not named on this label finding the file in his possession must at once return it unopened to Banking Section."

"Who was on the subscription list?"

"For Rolling Stone?"

"Yes."

"PA to Control, Control, Control's secretary; Banking Section, Miss Bream of Special Registry and Satellites Four. That's all, I think. And Special Despatch, I suppose—I'm not sure about them."

"Satellites Four? What do they do?"

"Iron Curtain countries excluding the Soviet Union and China. The Zone."

"You mean the GDR?"

"I mean the Zone."

"Isn't it unusual for a whole section to be on a subscription list?"

"Yes, it probably is. I wouldn't know—I've never handled limited subscription stuff before. Except in Berlin, of course; it was all different there."

"Who was in Satellites Four at that time?"

"Oh, God. Guillam, Haverlake, de Jong, I think. De Jong was just back from Berlin."

"Were they *all* allowed to see this file?"

"I don't know, Fiedler," Leamas retorted irritably; "and if I were you—"

"Then isn't it odd that a whole section was on the subscription list while all the rest of the subscribers are individuals?"

"I tell you I don't know—how could I know? I was just a clerk in all this."

"Who carried the file from one subscriber to another?"

"Secretaries, I suppose—I can't remember. It's bloody months since—"

"Then why weren't the secretaries on the list? Control's Secretary was." There was a moment's silence.

"No, you're right; I remember now," Leamas said, a note of surprise in his voice; "we passed it by hand."

"Who else in Banking dealt with that file?"

"No one. It was my pigeon when I joined the section. One of the women had done it before, but when I came I took it over and they were taken off the list."

"Then you alone passed the file by hand to the next reader?"

"Yes . . . yes, I suppose I did."

"To whom did you pass it?"

"I . . . I can't remember."

"*Think!*" Fiedler had not raised his voice, but it contained a sudden urgency which took Leamas by surprise.

"To Control's PA, I think, to show what action we had taken or recommended."

"Who brought the file?"

"What do you mean?" Leamas sounded off balance.

"Who brought you the file to read? Somebody on the list must have brought it to you."

Leamas' fingers touched his cheek for a moment in an involuntary nervous gesture.

"Yes, they must. It's difficult, you see, Fiedler; I was putting back a lot of drink in those days." His tone was oddly conciliatory. "You don't realise how hard it is to—"

"I ask you again. Think. Who brought you the file?"

Leamas sat down at the table and shook his head.

"I can't remember. It may come back to me. At the moment I just can't remember, really I can't. It's no good chasing it."

"It can't have been Control's girl, can it? You always handed the file *back* to Control's PA. You said so. So those on the list must all have seen it *before* Control."

"Yes, that's it, I suppose."

"Then there is Special Registry, Miss Bream."

"She was just the woman who ran the strong room for sub-scription list files. That's where the file was kept when it wasn't in action."

"Then," said Fiedler silkily, "it must have been Satellites Four who brought it, mustn't it?"

"Yes, I suppose it must," said Leamas helplessly, as if he were not quite up to Fiedler's brilliance.

"Which floor did Satellites Four work on?"

"The second."

"And Banking?"

"The fourth. Next to Special Registry."

"Do you remember *who* brought it up? Or do you remember, for instance, going downstairs ever to collect the file from them?"

In despair, Leamas shook his head; then suddenly he turned to Fiedler and cried:

"Yes, yes I do! Of course I do! I got it from Peter!" Leamas seemed to have woken up, his face was flushed, excited. "That's it: I once collected the file from Peter in his room. We chatted together about Norway. We'd served there together, you see."

"Peter Guillam?"

"Yes, Peter—I'd forgotten about him. He'd come back from Ankara a few months before. He was on the list! Peter was—of course! That's it. It was Satellite Four and PG in brackets, Peter's initials. Someone else had done it before and Special Registry had glued a bit of white paper over the old name and put Peter's initials."

"What territory did Guillam cover?"

"The Zone. East Germany. Economic stuff; ran a small section, sort of backwater. He was the chap. He brought the file up to me once too, I remember that now. He didn't run agents though: I don't quite know how he came into it—Peter and a couple of others were doing some research job on food shortages. Evaluation really."

"Did you not discuss it with him?"

"No, that's taboo. It isn't done with subscription files. I got a homily from the woman in Special Registry about it—Bream—no discussion, no questions."

"But taking into account the elaborate security precautions surrounding Rolling Stone, it is possible, is it not, that Guillam's so-called research job might have involved the partial running of this agent, Rolling Stone?"

"I've told Peters," Leamas almost shouted, banging his fist on the desk, "it's just bloody silly to imagine that any operation could have been run against East Germany without my knowledge—without the knowledge of the Berlin organisation. I would have known, d'you see? How many times do I have to say that? I would have known!"

"Quite so," said Fiedler softly, "of course you would." He stood up and went to the window.

"You should see it in the Autumn," he said, looking out; "it's magnificent when the beeches are on the turn."

13

Pins or Paper Clips

Fiedler loved to ask questions. Sometimes, because he was a lawyer, he asked them for his own pleasure alone, to demonstrate the discrepancy between evidence and perfective truth. He possessed, however, that persistent inquisitiveness which for journalists and lawyers is an end in itself.

They went for a walk that afternoon, following the gravel road down into the valley, then branching into the forest along a broad, pitted track lined with felled timber. All the time, Fiedler probed, giving nothing. About the building in Cambridge Circus, and the people who worked there. What social class did they come from, what parts of London did they inhabit, did husbands and wives work in the same Department? He asked about the pay, the leave, the morale, the canteen; he asked about their love-life, their gossip, their philosophy. Most of all he asked about their philosophy.

To Leamas that was the most difficult question of all.

"What do you mean, a philosophy?" he replied; "we're not Marxists, we're nothing. Just people."

"Are you Christians, then?"

"Not many, I shouldn't think. I don't know many."

"What makes them do it, then?" Fiedler persisted; "they must have a philosophy."

"Why must they? Perhaps they don't know; don't even care. Not everyone has a philosophy," Leamas answered, a little helplessly.

"Then tell me what is your philosophy?"

"Oh for Christ's sake," Leamas snapped, and they walked on in silence for a while. But Fiedler was not to be put off.

"If they do not know what they want, how can they be so certain they are right?"

"Who the hell said they were?" Leamas replied irritably.

"But what is the justification then? What is it? For us it is easy, as I said to you last night. The Abteilung and organisations like it are the natural extension of the Party's arm. They are in the vanguard of the fight for Peace and Progress. They are to the Party what the Party is to socialism: they *are* the vanguard. Stalin said so"—he smiled drily, "it is not fashionable to quote Stalin—but he said once 'half a million liquidated is a statistic, and one man killed in a traffic accident is a national tragedy.' He was laughing, you see, at the bourgeois sensitivities of the mass. He was a great cynic. But what he meant is still true: a movement which protects itself against counter-revolution can hardly stop at the exploitation—or the elimination, Leamas—of a few individuals. It is all one, we have never pretended to be wholly just in the process of rationalistic society. Some Roman said it, didn't he, in the Christian Bible—it is expedient that one man should die for the benefit of many."

"I expect so," Leamas replied wearily.

"Then what do you think? What is your philosophy?"

"I just think the whole lot of you are bastards," said Leamas savagely.

Fiedler nodded, "That is a viewpoint I understand. It is primitive, negative, and very stupid—but it is a viewpoint, it exists. But what about the rest of the Circus?"

"I don't know. How should I know?"

"Have you never discussed philosophy with them?"

"No. We're not Germans." He hesitated, then added vaguely: "I suppose they don't like Communism."

"And that justifies, for instance, the taking of human life? That justifies the bomb in the crowded restaurant; that justifies your write-off rate of agents—all that?"

Leamas shrugged. "I suppose so."

"You see, for us it does," Fiedler continued, "I myself would have put a bomb in a restaurant if it brought us further along the road. Afterwards I would draw the balance—so many women, so many children; and so far along the road. But Christians—and yours is a Christian society—Christians may not draw the balance."

"Why not? They've got to defend themselves, haven't they?"

"But they believe in the sanctity of human life. They believe every man has a soul which can be saved. They believe in sacrifice."

"I don't know. I don't much care," Leamas added. "Stalin didn't either, did he?"

Fiedler smiled; "I like the English," he said, almost to himself; "my father did too. He was very fond of the English."

"That gives me a nice, warm feeling," Leamas retorted, and relapsed into silence.

They stopped while Fiedler gave Leamas a cigarette and lit it for him.

They were climbing steeply now. Leamas liked the exercise, walking ahead with long strides, his shoulders thrust forward. Fiedler followed, slight and agile, like a terrier behind his master. They must have been walking for an hour, perhaps more, when suddenly the trees broke above them and the sky appeared. They had reached the top of a small hill, and could look down on the solid mass of pine broken only here and there by grey clusters of beech. Across the valley Leamas could glimpse the hunting lodge, perched below the crest of the opposite hill, low and dark against the trees. In the middle of the clearing was a rough bench beside a pile of logs and the damp remnants of a charcoal fire.

"We'll sit down for a moment," said Fiedler, "then we must go back." He paused. "Tell me: this money, these large sums in foreign banks—what did you think they were for?"

"What do you mean? I've told you, they were payments to an agent."

"An agent from behind the Iron Curtain?"

"Yes, I thought so," Leamas replied wearily.

"Why did you think so?"

"First, it was a hell of a lot of money. Then the complications of paying him; the special security. And of course, Control being mixed up in it."

"What did you think the agent did with the money?"

"Look, I've told you—I don't know. I don't even know if he collected it. I didn't know anything—I was just the bloody office boy."

"What did you do with the pass books for the accounts?"

"I handed them in as soon as I got back to London— together with my phoney passport."

"Did the Copenhagen or Helsinki banks ever write to you in London—to your alias, I mean?"

"I don't know. I suppose any letters would have been passed straight to Control anyway."

"The false signatures you used to open the accounts— Control had a sample of them?"

"Yes. I practised them a lot and they had samples."

"More than one?"

"Yes. Whole pages."

"I see. Then letters could have gone to the banks after you had opened the accounts. You need not have known. The signatures could have been forged and the letters sent without your knowledge."

"Yes. That's right. I suppose that's what happened. I signed a lot of blank sheets too. I always assumed someone else took care of the correspondence."

"But you never did actually *know* of such correspondence?"

Leamas shook his head: "You've got it all wrong," he said; "you've got it all out of proportion. There was a lot of paper going around—this was just part of the day's work. It wasn't something I gave much thought to. Why should I? It was hush-hush, but I've been in on things all my life where you only know a little and someone else knows the rest. Besides, paper bores me stiff. I didn't lose any sleep on it. I liked the trips of course—I drew operational subsistence which helped. But I didn't sit at my desk all day, wondering about Rolling Stone. Besides," he added a little shamefacedly, "I was hitting the bottle a bit."

"So you said," Fiedler commented, "and of course, I believe you."

"I don't give a damn whether you believe me or not," Leamas rejoined hotly.

Fiedler smiled.

"I am glad. That is your virtue," he said, "that is your great virtue. It is the virtue of indifference. A little resentment here, a little pride there, but that is nothing: the distortions of a tape recorder. You are objective. It occurred to me," Fiedler continued after a slight pause, "that you could still help us to establish whether any of that money was ever drawn. There is nothing to stop you writing to each bank and asking for a current statement. We could say you were staying in Switzerland; use an accommodation address. Do you see any objection to that?"

"It might work. It depends on whether Control has been corresponding with the bank independently, over my forged signature. It might not fit in."

"I do not see that we have much to lose."

"What have you got to win?"

"If the money has been drawn, which I agree is doubtful,

we shall know where the agent was on a certain day. That seems to be a useful thing to know."

"You're dreaming. You'll never find him, Fiedler, not on that kind of information. Once he's in the West he can go to any Consulate, even in a small town, and get a visa for another country. How are you any the wiser? You don't even know whether the man is East German. What are you after?"

Fiedler did not answer at once. He was gazing distractedly across the valley.

"You said you are accustomed to knowing only a little, and I cannot answer your question without telling you what you should not know." He hesitated. "But Rolling Stone was an operation against us, I can assure you."

"Us?"

"The GDR." He smiled, "the Zone if you prefer. I am not really so sensitive."

He was watching Fiedler now, his brown eyes resting on him reflectively.

"But what about me?" Leamas asked. "Suppose I don't write letters?" His voice was rising. "Isn't it time to talk about me, Fiedler!"

Fiedler nodded.

"Why not?" he replied, agreeably. There was a moment's silence, then Leamas said:

"I've done my bit, Fiedler. You and Peters between you have got all I know. I never agreed to write letters to banks—it could be bloody dangerous, a thing like that. That doesn't worry you, I know. As far as you're concerned I'm expendable."

"Now let me be frank," Fiedler replied. "There are, as you know, two stages in the interrogation of a defector. The first stage in your case is nearly complete: you have told us all we can reasonably record. You have not told us whether your Service favours pins or paper clips because we haven't asked you, and because you did not consider the answer worth volunteering. There is a process on both sides of unconscious selection. Now it is always possible—and this is the worrying thing, Leamas—it is always entirely possible that in a month or two we shall unexpectedly and quite desperately need to know about the pins and paper clips. That is normally accounted for in the second stage—that part of the bargain which you refused to accept in Holland."

"You mean you're going to keep me on ice?"

"The profession of defector," Fiedler observed with a smile, "demands great patience. Very few are suitably qualified."

"How long?" Leamas insisted.

Fiedler was silent.

"Well?"

Fiedler spoke with sudden urgency. "I give you my word that as soon as I possibly can, I will tell you the answer to your question. Look—I could lie to you, couldn't I? I could say one month or less, just to keep you sweet. But I am telling you I don't know because that is the truth. You have given us some indications: until we have run them to earth I cannot listen to talk of letting you go. But afterwards if things are as I think they are, you will need a friend and that friend will be me. I give you my word as a German."

Leamas was so taken aback that for a moment he was silent.

"All right," he said finally, "I'll play, Fiedler, but if you are stringing me along, somehow I'll break your neck."

"That may not be necessary," Fiedler replied evenly.

A man who lives apart, not to others but alone, is exposed to obvious psychological dangers. In itself, the practice of deception is not particularly exacting; it is a matter of experience, of professional expertise, it is a facility most of us can acquire. But while a confidence trickster, a play-actor, or a gambler can return from his performance to the ranks of his admirers, the secret agent enjoys no such relief. For him, deception is first a matter of self-defence. He must protect himself not only from without but from within, and against the most natural of impulses; though he earn a fortune, his role may forbid him the purchase of a razor, though he be erudite, it can befall him to mumble nothing but banalities; though he be an affectionate husband and father, he must under all circumstances withhold himself from those in whom he should naturally confide.

Aware of the overwhelming temptations which assail a man permanently isolated in his deceit, Leamas resorted to the course which armed him best; even when he was alone, he compelled himself to live with the personality he had assumed. It is said that Balzac on his deathbed enquired anxiously after the health and prosperity of characters he had created. Similarly Leamas, without relinquishing the power of invention, identified himself with what he had invented. The qualities he exhibited to Fiedler, the restless uncertainty, the protective arrogance concealing shame, were not approximations but extensions of qualities he actually possessed; hence also the slight dragging of the feet, the aspect of personal neglect, the indifference to food, and an increasing reliance on alcohol and tobacco. When alone, he remained faithful to these habits. He would even exaggerate them a little, mumbling to himself about the iniquities of his Service.

Only very rarely, as now, going to bed that evening, did he allow himself the dangerous luxury of admitting the great lie he lived.

Control had been phenomenally right. Fiedler was walking like a man led in his sleep, into the net which Control had spread for him. It was uncanny to observe the growing identity of interest between Fiedler and Control: it was as if they had agreed on the same plan, and Leamas had been despatched to fulfill it.

Perhaps that was the answer. Perhaps Fiedler was the special interest Control was fighting so desperately to preserve. In matters of that kind he was wholly uninquisitive: he knew that no conceivable good could come of his deductions. Nevertheless, he hoped to God it was true. It was possible, just possible in that case, that he would get home.

14

Letter to a Client

Leamas was still in bed the next morning when Fiedler brought him the letters to sign. One was on the thin, blue writing paper of the Seiler Hotel Alpenblick, Lake Spiez, Switzerland, the other from the Palace Hotel, Gstaad.

Leamas read the first letter:

To the Manager,
The Royal Scandinavian Bank Ltd.,
Copenhagen.

Dear Sir,

I have been travelling for some weeks and have not received any mail from England. Accordingly I have not had your reply to my letter of March 3rd requesting a current statement of the deposit account of which I am a joint signatory with Herr Karlsdorf. To avoid further delay, would you be good enough to forward a duplicate statement to me at the following address, where I shall be staying for two weeks beginning April 21st:

c/o Madame Y. de Sanglot,
13 Avenue des Colombes,
Paris XII,
France.
I apologise for this confusion,

Yours faithfully,
(Robert Lang)

"What's all this about a letter of March 3rd?" he asked. "I didn't write them any letter."

"No, you didn't. As far as we know, no one did. That will worry the bank. If there is any inconsistency between the letter we are sending them now and letters they have had from Control, they will assume the solution is to be found in the *missing* letter of March 3rd. Their reaction will be to send you the statement as you ask, with a covering note regretting that they have not received your letter of the third."

The second letter was the same as the first; only the names were different. The address in Paris was the same. Leamas took a blank piece of paper and his fountain pen and wrote half a dozen times in a fluent hand "Robert Lang"; then signed the first letter. Sloping his pen backwards he practised the second signature until he was satisfied with it, then wrote "Stephen Bennett" under the second letter.

"Admirable," Fiedler observed, "quite admirable."

"What do we do now?"

"They will be posted in Switzerland tomorrow, in Interlaken and Gstaad. Our people in Paris will telegraph the replies to me as soon as they arrive. We shall have the answer in a week."

"And until then?"

"We shall be constantly in one another's company. I know that is distasteful to you, and I apologise. I thought we could go for walks, drive round in the hills a bit, kill time. I want you to relax and talk; talk about London, about Cambridge Circus and working in the Department; tell me the gossip, talk about the pay, the leave, the rooms, the paper, and the people. The pins and the paper clips. I want to know all the little things that don't matter. Incidentally . . ." A change of tone.

"Yes?"

"We have facilities here for people, who . . . for people who are spending some time with us. Facilities for diversion and so on."

"Are you offering me a woman?" he asked.

"Yes."

"No, thank you. Unlike you, I haven't reached the stage where I need a pimp."

Fiedler seemed indifferent to his reply. He went on quickly.

"But you had a woman in England, didn't you—the girl in the library."

Leamas turned on him, his hands open at his sides.

"One thing!" he shouted. "Just that one thing—don't ever mention that again, not as a joke, not as a threat, not even to turn the screws, Fiedler, because it won't work, not ever; I'd dry up, d'you see, you'd never get another bloody word from me as long as I lived. Tell that to them, Fiedler, to Mundt and Stammberger or whichever little alley-cat told you to say it— tell them what I said."

"I'll tell them," Fiedler replied; "I'll tell them. It may be too late."

In the afternoon they went walking again. The sky was dark and heavy, and the air warm.

"I've only been to England once," Fiedler observed casually, "that was on my way to Canada, with my parents before the war. I was a child then of course. We were there for two days."

Leamas nodded.

"I can tell you this now," Fiedler continued. "I nearly went there a few years back. I was going to replace Mundt on the Steel Mission—did you know he was once in London?"

"I knew," Leamas replied cryptically.

"I always wondered what it would have been like, that job."

"Usual game of mixing with the other Bloc Missions I suppose. Certain amount of contact with British business—not much of that." Leamas sounded bored.

"But Mundt got about all right: he found it quite easy."

"So I hear," said Leamas; "he even managed to kill a couple of people."

"So you heard about that too?"

"From Peter Guillam. He was in on it with George Smiley. Mundt bloody nearly killed George as well."

"The Fennan case," Fiedler mused. "It was amazing that Mundt managed to escape at all, wasn't it?"

"I suppose it was."

"You wouldn't think that a man whose photograph and personal particulars were filed at the Foreign Office as a member of a Foreign Mission would have a chance against the whole of British Security."

"From what I hear," Leamas said, "they weren't too keen to catch him anyway."

Fiedler stopped abruptly.

"What did you say?"

"Peter Guillam told me he didn't reckon they wanted to catch Mundt, that's all I said. We had a different set-up then—an Adviser instead of an Operational Control—a man called Maston. Maston had made a bloody awful mess of the Fennan case from the start, that's what Guillam said. Peter reckoned that if they'd caught Mundt it would have made a hell of a stink—they'd have tried him and probably hanged him. The dirt that came out in the process would have finished Maston's career. Peter never knew quite what happened, but he was bloody sure there was no full-scale search for Mundt."

"You are sure of that, you are sure Guillam told you that in as many words? No full-scale search?"

"Of course I am sure."

"Guillam never suggested any other reason why they might have let Mundt go?"

"What do you mean?"

Fiedler shook his head and they walked on along the path.

"The Steel Mission was closed down after the Fennan case," Fiedler observed a moment later, "that's why I didn't go."

"Mundt must have been mad. You may be able to get away with assassination in the Balkans—or here—but not London."

"He did get away with it though, didn't he?" Fiedler put in quickly. "And he did good work."

"Like recruiting Kiever and Ashe? God help him."

"They ran the Fennan woman for long enough."

Leamas shrugged.

"Tell me something else about Karl Riemeck," Fiedler began again. "He met Control once, didn't he?"

"Yes, in Berlin about a year ago, maybe a bit more."

"Where did they meet?"

"We all met together in my flat."

"Why?"

"Control loved to come in on success. We'd got a hell of a lot of good stuff from Karl—I suppose it had gone down well with London. He came out on a short trip to Berlin and asked me to fix up for them to meet."

"Did you mind?"

"Why should I?"

"He was your agent. You might not have liked him to meet other operators."

"Control isn't an operator, he's head of Department. Karl knew that and it tickled his vanity."

"Were you all three together, all the time?"

"Yes. Well, not quite. I left them alone for a quarter of an hour or so—not more. Control wanted that—he wanted a few minutes alone with Karl, God knows why, so I left the flat on some excuse, I forget what. Oh—I know, I pretended we'd run out of Scotch. I actually went and collected a bottle from de Jong in fact."

"Do you know what passed between them while you were out?"

"How could I? I wasn't that interested, anyway."

"Didn't Karl tell you afterwards?"

"I didn't ask him. Karl was a cheeky sod in some ways, always pretending he had something over me. I didn't like the way he sniggered about Control. Mind you, he had every right to snigger—it was a pretty ridiculous performance. We laughed about it together a bit, as a matter of fact. There wouldn't have been any point in pricking Karl's vanity; the whole meeting was supposed to give him a shot in the arm."

"Was Karl depressed then?"

"No, far from it. He was spoilt already. He was paid too much, loved too much, trusted too much. It was partly my fault, partly London's. If we hadn't spoilt him he wouldn't have told that bloody woman of his about his network."

"Elvira?"

"Yes." They walked on in silence for a while, until Fiedler interrupted his own reverie to observe:

"I'm beginning to like you. But there's one thing that puzzles me. It's odd—it didn't worry me before I met you."

"What's that?"

"Why you ever came. Why you defected." Leamas was going to say something when Fiedler laughed. "I'm afraid that wasn't very tactful, was it?" he said.

They spent that week walking in the hills. In the evenings they would return to the lodge, eat a bad meal washed down with a bottle of rank white wine, sit endlessly over their Steinhäger in front of the fire. The fire seemed to be Fiedler's idea—they didn't

have it to begin with, then one day Leamas overheard him telling a guard to bring logs. Leamas didn't mind the evening then;
after the fresh air all day, the fire and the rough spirit, he would
talk unprompted, rambling on about his service. Leamas supposed it was recorded. He didn't care.

As each day passed in this way Leamas was aware of an
increasing tension in his companion. Once they went out in the
DKW—it was late in the evening—and stopped at a call-box.
Fiedler left him in the car with the keys and made a long phone
call. When he came back Leamas said:

"Why didn't you ring from the house?" But Fiedler just
shook his head.

"We must take care," he replied; "you too, you must take
care."

"Why? What's going on?"

"The money you paid into the Copenhagen bank—we
wrote, you remember?"

"Of course I remember."

Fiedler wouldn't say any more, but drove on in silence into
the hills. There they stopped. Beneath them, half screened by
the ghostly patchwork of tall pine trees, lay the meeting point
of two great valleys. The steep wooded hills on either side
gradually yielded their colours to the gathering dusk until
they stood grey and lifeless in the twilight.

"Whatever happens," Fiedler said, "don't worry. It will be
all right, do you understand?" His voice was heavy with emphasis, his slim hand rested on Leamas' arm. "You may have to
look after yourself a little, but it won't last long, do you understand?" he asked again.

"No. And since you won't tell me I shall have to wait and
see. Don't worry too much for my skin, Fiedler." He moved his
arm, but Fiedler's hand still held him. Leamas hated being
touched.

"Do you know Mundt?" asked Fiedler, "do you know about
him?"

"We've talked about Mundt."

"Yes," Fiedler repeated, "we've talked about him. He shoots first and asks questions afterwards. The deterrent principle. It's an odd system in a profession where the questions are always supposed to be more important than the shooting." Leamas knew what Fiedler wanted to tell him. "It's an odd system unless you're frightened of the answers," Fiedler continued under his breath.

Leamas waited. After a moment Fiedler said:

"He's never taken on an interrogation before. He's left it to me before, always. He used to say to me—'You interrogate them, Jens, no one can do it like you. I'll catch them and you make them sing.' He used to say that people who do counter-espionage are like painters—they need a man with a hammer standing behind them to strike when they have finished their work, otherwise they forget what they're trying to achieve. 'I'll be your hammer,' he used to say to me. It was a joke between us, at first, then it began to matter; when he began to kill, kill them before they sang, just as you said: one here, another there, shot or murdered. I asked him, I begged him, 'Why not arrest them? Why not let me have them for a month or two? What good to you are they when they are dead?' He just shook his head at me and said there was a law that thistles must be cut down before they flower. I had the feeling that he'd prepared the answer before I ever asked the question. He's a good operator, very good. He's done wonders with the Abteilung—you know that. He's got theories about it; I've talked to him late at night. Coffee he drinks—nothing else—just coffee all the time. He says Germans are too introspective to make good agents, and it all comes out in counter-intelligence. He says counter-intelligence people are like wolves chewing dry bones—you have to take away the bones and make them find new quarry—I see all that, I know what he means. But he's gone too far. Why did he kill Viereck? Why did he take him away from me? Viereck was fresh quarry, we hadn't even taken the meat from the bone, you see. So why did he take him? Why, Leamas, why?" The hand on Leamas' arm was clasping it tightly; in the total darkness of the car Leamas was aware of the frightening intensity of Fiedler's emotion.

"I've thought about it night and day. Ever since Viereck was shot, I've asked for a reason. At first it seemed fantastic. I told myself I was jealous, that the work was going to my head, that I was seeing treachery behind every tree; we get like that, people in our world. But I couldn't help myself, Leamas, I had to work it out. There'd been other things before. He was afraid—he was afraid that we would catch one who would talk too much!"

"What are you saying? You're out of your mind," said Leamas, and his voice held a trace of fear.

"It all held together, you see. Mundt escaped so easily from England; you told me yourself he did. And what did Guillam say to you? He said they didn't *want* to catch him! Why not? I'll tell you why—he was their man; they turned him, they caught him, don't you see and that was the price of his freedom—that and the money he was paid."

"I tell you you're out of your mind!" Leamas hissed. "He'll kill you if he ever thinks you make up this kind of stuff. It's sugar candy, Fiedler. Shut up and drive us home." At last the hot grip on Leamas' arm relaxed.

"That's where you're wrong. You provided the answer, you yourself, Leamas. That's why we need one another."

"It's not true!" Leamas shouted. "I've told you again and again, they couldn't have done it. The Circus couldn't have run him against the Zone without my knowing! It just wasn't an administrative possibility. You're trying to tell me Control was personally directing the deputy head of the Abteilung without the knowledge of the Berlin station. You're mad, Fiedler, you're just bloody well off your head!" Suddenly he began to laugh quietly. "You may want his job, you poor bastard; that's not unheard of, you know. But this kind of thing went out with bustles." For a moment neither spoke.

"That money," Fiedler said, "in Copenhagen. The bank replied to your letter. The manager is very worried lest there has been a mistake. The money was drawn by your co-signatory exactly one week after you paid it in. The date it was drawn coincides with a two-day visit which Mundt paid to Denmark in February. He went there under an alias to meet an American agent we have who was attending a world scientists' conference." Fiedler hesitated, then added, "I suppose you ought to write to the bank and tell them everything is quite in order?"

15

Come to the Ball

Liz looked at the letter from Party Centre and wondered what it was about. She found it a little puzzling. She had to admit she was pleased, but why hadn't they consulted her first? Had the District Committee put up her name, or was it Centre's own choice? But no one in Centre knew her, so far as she was aware. She'd met odd speakers of course, and at District Congress she'd shaken hands with the Party Organiser. Perhaps that man from Cultural Relations had remembered her—that fair, rather effeminate man who was so ingratiating. Ashe, that was his name. He'd taken a bit of interest in her and she supposed he might have handed her name on, or remembered her when the Scholarship came up. An odd man, he was; took her to the Black and White for coffee after the meeting and asked her about her boyfriends. He hadn't been amorous or anything—she'd thought he was a bit queer to be honest—but he asked her masses of questions about herself. How long had she been in the Party, did she get homesick living away from her parents? Had she lots of boyfriends or was there a special one she carried a torch for? She hadn't cared for him much but his talk had gone down quite well—the worker-state in the

German Democratic Republic, the concept of the worker-poet and all that stuff. He certainly knew all about Eastern Europe, he must have travelled a lot. She'd guessed he was a schoolmaster, he had that rather didactic, fluent way with him. They'd had a collection for the Fighting Fund afterwards, and Ashe had put a pound in; she'd been absolutely amazed. That was it, she was sure now: it was Ashe who'd remembered her. He'd told someone at London District, and District had told Centre or something like that. It still seemed a funny way to go about things, but then the Party always was secretive—it was part of being a revolutionary party, she supposed. It didn't appeal to Liz much, the secrecy, it seemed dishonest. But she supposed it was necessary, and Heaven knows, there were plenty who got a kick out of it.

She read the letter again. It was on Centre's writing paper, with the thick red print at the top, and it began, "Dear Comrade," it sounded so military to Liz, and she hated that; she'd never quite got used to "Comrade."

Dear Comrade,

We have recently had discussions with our Comrades in the Socialist Unity Party of the German Democratic Republic on the possibility of effecting exchanges between party members over here and our comrades in democratic Germany. The idea is to create a basis of exchange at the rank and file level between our two parties. The SUP is aware that the existing discriminatory measures by the British Home Office make it unlikely that their own delegates will be able to come to the United Kingdom in the immediate future, but they feel that an exchange of experiences is all the more important for this reason. They have generously invited us to select five Branch Secretaries with good experience and a good record of stimulating mass action at street level. Each selected comrade will spend three weeks attending

Branch discussions, studying progress in industry and social welfare and seeing at first hand the evidence of fascist provocation by the West. This is a grand opportunity for our comrades to profit from the experience of a young socialist system.

We therefore asked District to put forward the names of young Cadre workers from your areas who might get the biggest advantage from the trip, and your name has been put forward. We want you to go if you possibly can, and carry out the second part of the scheme—which is to establish contact with a Party Branch in the GDR whose members are from similar industrial backgrounds and have the same kind of problems as your own. The Bayswater South Branch has been paired with Neuenhagen, a suburb of Leipzig. Freda Lüman, Secretary of the Neuenhagen branch, is preparing a big welcome. We are sure you are just the Comrade for the job, and that it will be a terrific success. All expenses will be paid by the GDR Cultural Office.

We are sure you realise what a big honour this is, and are confident you will not allow personal considerations to prevent you from accepting. The visits are due to take place at the end of next month, about the 23rd, but the selected Comrades will travel separately as their invitations are not all concurrent. Will you please let us know as soon as possible whether you can accept, and we will let you know further details.

The more she read it, the odder it seemed. Such short notice for a start—how could they know she could get away from the Library? Then to her surprise she recalled that Ashe had asked her what she did for her holidays, whether she had taken her leave this year, and whether she had to give a lot of notice if she wanted to claim free time. Why hadn't they told her who the other nominees were? There was no particular reason why they should, perhaps, but it somehow looked odd

when they didn't. It was such a *long* letter, too. They were so
hard up for secretarial help at Centre they usually kept their
letters short, or asked Comrades to ring up. This was so efficient, so well typed it might not have been done at Centre at
all. But it *was* signed by the Cultural Organiser; it was his signature all right, no doubt of that. She'd seen it at the bottom of
roneoed notices masses of times. And the letter had that awkward, semi-bureaucratic, semi-Messianic style she had grown
accustomed to without ever liking. It was stupid to say she had
a good record of stimulating mass action at street level. She
hadn't. As a matter of fact she hated that side of party work—
the loudspeakers at the factory gates, selling the *Daily Worker*
at the street corner, going from door to door at the local elections. Peace Work she didn't mind so much, it meant something to her, it made sense. You could look at the kids in the
street as you went by, at the mothers pushing their prams and
the old people standing in doorways, and you could say, "I'm
doing it for them." That really *was* fighting for peace.

But she never quite saw the fighting for votes and the fighting for sales in the same way. Perhaps that was because it cut
them down to size, she thought. It was easy when there were a
dozen or so together at a Branch meeting to rebuild the world,
march at the vanguard of socialism, and talk of the inevitability of history. But afterwards she'd go out into the streets with
an armful of *Daily Workers*, often waiting an hour, two hours,
to sell a copy. Sometimes she'd cheat, as the others cheated,
and pay for a dozen herself just to get out of it and go home. At
the next meeting they'd boast about it—forgetting they'd bought
them themselves—"Comrade Gold sold eighteen copies on Saturday night—eighteen!" It would go in the Minutes then, and
the Branch bulletin as well. District would rub their hands, and
perhaps she'd get a mention in that little panel on the front page
about the Fighting Fund. It was such a little world, and she
wished they could be more honest. But she lied to herself about
it all, too. Perhaps they all did. Or perhaps the others understood

more *why* you had to lie so much. It seemed so odd they'd made her Branch Secretary. It was Mulligan who'd proposed it—"Our young, vigorous, *and* attractive comrade—" He'd thought she'd sleep with him if he got her made secretary. The others had voted for her because they liked her, and because she could type. Because she'd do the work and not try and make them go canvassing at weekends. Not too often anyway. They'd voted for her because they wanted a decent little club, nice and revolutionary and no fuss. It was all such a fraud. Alec had seemed to understand that; he just hadn't taken it seriously. "Some people keep canaries, some people join the Party," he'd said once, and it was true. In Bayswater South it was true anyway, and District knew that perfectly well. That's why it was so peculiar that she had been nominated; that was why she was extremely reluctant to believe that District had even had a hand in it. The explanation, she was sure, was Ashe. Perhaps he had a crush on her, perhaps he wasn't queer but just looked it.

Liz made a rather exaggerated shrug, the kind of overstressed gesture people do make when they are excited and alone. It was abroad anyway, it was free and it sounded interesting. She had never been abroad, and she certainly couldn't afford the fare herself. It would be rather fun. She had reservations about Germans, that was true. She knew, she had been told, that West Germany was militarist and revanchist, and that East Germany was democratic and peace-loving. But she doubted whether all the good Germans were on one side and all the bad ones on the other. And it was the bad ones who had killed her father. Perhaps that was why the Party had chosen her—as a generous act of reconciliation. Perhaps that was what Ashe had had in mind when he asked her all those questions. Of course—that was the explanation. She was suddenly filled with a feeling of warmth and gratitude towards the Party. They really were decent people and she was proud and thankful to belong. She went to the desk and opened the drawer where, in an old school satchel, she kept the Branch stationery and the dues stamps. Putting a sheet of paper into her old Underwood typewriter—they'd sent it down from District when they heard she could type: it jumped a bit but otherwise was fine—she typed a neat, grateful letter of acceptance. Centre was such a wonderful thing—stern, benevolent, impersonal, perpetual. They were good, good people. People who fought for peace. As she closed the drawer she caught sight of Smiley's card.

She remembered the little man with the earnest, puckered face, standing at the doorway of her room and saying: "Did the Party know about you and Alec?" How silly she was. Well, this would take her mind off it.

16

Arrest

Fiedler and Leamas drove back the rest of the way in silence. In the dusk the hills were black and cavernous, the pinpoint lights struggling against the gathering darkness like the lights of distant ships at sea.

Fiedler parked the car in a shed at the side of the house and they walked together to the front door. They were about to enter the lodge when they heard a shout from the direction of the trees, followed by someone calling Fiedler's name. They turned, and Leamas distinguished in the twilight twenty yards away three men standing, apparently waiting for Fiedler to come.

"What do you want?" Fiedler called.

"We want to talk to you. We're from Berlin."

Fiedler hesitated. "Where's that damn' guard?" he asked Leamas; "there should be a guard on the front door."

Leamas shrugged.

"Why aren't the lights on in the hall?" he asked again: then, still unconvinced, he began walking slowly towards the men.

Leamas waited a moment, then, hearing nothing, made his

way through the unlit house to the annexe behind it. This was
a shoddy barrack but attached to the back of the building and
hidden from all sides by close plantations of young pine trees.
The hut was divided into three adjoining bedrooms; there was
no corridor. The centre room had been given to Leamas, and
the room nearest to the main building was occupied by two
guards. Leamas never knew who occupied the third. He had
once tried to open the connecting door between it and his own
room, but it was locked. He had only discovered it was a bedroom by peering through a narrow gap in the lace curtains
early one morning as he went for a walk. The two guards, who
followed him everywhere at fifty yards' distance, had not
rounded the corner of the hut, and he looked in at the window.
The room contained a single bed, made, and a small writing-desk
with papers on it. He supposed that someone, with what passes
for German thoroughness, watched him from that bedroom.
But Leamas was too old a dog to allow himself to be bothered
by surveillance. In Berlin it had been a fact of life—if you
couldn't spot it so much the worse: it only meant they were taking greater care, or you were losing your grip. Usually, because
he was good at that kind of thing, because he was observant and
had an accurate memory—because, in short, he was good at his
job—he spotted them anyway. He knew the formations
favoured by a shadowing team, he knew the tricks, the weaknesses, the momentary lapses that could give them away. It
meant nothing to Leamas that he was watched, but as he walked
through the improvised doorway from the lodge to the hut,
and stood in the guards' bedroom, he had the distinct feeling
that something was wrong.

The lights in the annexe were controlled from some central
point. They were put on and off by an unseen hand. In the
mornings he was often woken by the sudden blaze of the single
overhead light in his room. At night he would be hastened to
bed by perfunctory darkness. It was only nine o'clock as he
entered the annexe, and the lights were already out. Usually

they stayed on till eleven, but now they were out and the shutters had been lowered. He had left the connecting door from
the house open, so that the pale twilight from the hallway
reached, but scarcely penetrated, the guards' bedroom, and by
it he could just see the two empty beds. As he stood there peering into the room, surprised to find it empty, the door behind
him closed. Perhaps by itself, but Leamas made no attempt to
open it. It was pitch dark. No sound accompanied the closing
of the door, no click nor footstep. To Leamas, his instinct suddenly alert, it was as if the sound-track had stopped. Then he
smelt the cigar smoke. It must have been hanging in the air but
he had not noticed it till now. Like a blind man, his senses of
touch and smell were sharpened by the darkness.

There were matches in his pocket but he did not use them.
He took one pace sideways, pressed his back against the wall
and remained motionless. To Leamas there could only be one
explanation—they were waiting for him to pass from the
guards' room to his own and therefore he determined to
remain where he was. Then from the direction of the main
building whence he had come he heard clearly the sound of a
footstep. The door which had just closed was tested, the lock
turned and made fast. Still Leamas did not move. Not yet.
There was no pretence: he was a prisoner in the hut. Very
slowly, Leamas now lowered himself into a crouch putting his
hand in the side pocket of his jacket as he did so. He was quite
calm, almost relieved at the prospect of action, but memories
were racing through his mind. "You've nearly always got a
weapon: an ash-tray, a couple of coins, a fountain-pen—anything
that will gouge or cut." It was the favourite dictum of the mild
little Welsh sergeant at that house near Oxford in the war;
"Never use both hands at once, not with a knife, a stick or a
pistol; keep your left arm free, and hold it across the belly. If
you can't find anything to hit with, keep the hands open and
the thumbs stiff." Taking the box of matches in his right hand
he clasped it longways, and deliberately crushed it, so that the

small, jagged edges of boxwood protruded from between his fingers. This done, he edged his way along the wall until he came to a chair which he knew was in the corner of the room. Indifferent now to the noise he made, he shoved the chair into the centre of the floor. Counting his footsteps as he moved back from the chair, he positioned himself in the angle of the two walls. As he did so, he heard the door of his own bedroom flung open. Vainly he tried to discern the figure who must be standing in the doorway, but there was no light from his own room either. The darkness was impenetrable. He dared not move forward to attack, for the chair was now in the middle of the room; it was his tactical advantage, for he knew where it was, and they did not. They must come for him, they must; he could not let them wait until their helper outside had reached the master switch and put on the lights.

"Come on, you windy bastards," he hissed in German; "I'm here, in the corner. Come and get me, can't you?" Not a move, not a sound.

"I'm here, can't you see me? What's the matter then? What's the matter, children, come on, can't you?" And then he heard one stepping forward, and another following; and then the oath of a man as he stumbled on the chair, and that was the sign that Leamas was waiting for. Tossing away the box of matches he slowly, cautiously crept forward, pace by pace, his left arm extended in the attitude of a man warding off twigs in a wood until, quite gently, he had touched an arm and felt the warm prickly cloth of a military uniform. Still with his left hand Leamas deliberately tapped the arm twice—two distinct taps—and heard a frightened voice whisper close to his ear in German:

"Hans, is it you?"

"Shut up, you fool," Leamas whispered in reply, and in that same moment reached out and grasped the man's hair, pulling his head forward and down, then in a terrible cutting blow drove the side of his right hand on to the nape of the neck, pulled him up again by the arm, hit him in the throat with an upward thrust of his open fist, then released him to fall where the force of gravity took him. As the man's body hit the ground, the lights went on.

In the doorway stood a young captain of the People's Police smoking a cigar, and behind him two men. One was in civilian clothes, quite young. He held a pistol in his hand. Leamas thought it was the Czech kind with a loading lever on the spine of the butt. They were all looking at the man on the floor. Somebody unlocked the outer door and Leamas turned to see who it was. As he turned, there was a shout—Leamas thought it was the captain—telling him to stand still. Slowly he turned back and faced the three men.

His hands were still at his side as the blow came. It seemed to crush his skull. As he fell, drifting warmly into unconsciousness, he wondered whether he had been hit with a revolver, the old kind with a swivel on the butt where you fastened the lanyard.

He was woken by the lag singing and the warder yelling at him to shut up. He opened his eyes and like a brilliant light the pain burst upon his brain. He lay quite still, refusing to close them, watching the sharp, coloured fragments racing across his vision. He tried to take stock of himself: his feet were icy cold and he was aware of the sour stench of prison denims. The singing had stopped and suddenly Leamas longed for it to start again, although he knew it never would. He tried to raise his hand and touch the blood that was caked on his cheek, but his hands were behind him, locked together. His feet too must be bound: the blood had left them, that was why they were cold. Painfully he looked about him, trying to lift his head an inch or two from the floor. To his surprise he saw his own knees in front of him. Instinctively he tried to stretch his legs and as he did so his whole body was seized with a pain so sudden and terrible that he screamed out a sobbing agonised cry of self-pity, like the last cry of a man upon the rack. He lay there panting, attempting to master the pain, then through the sheer perversity of his nature, he tried again, quite slowly, to straighten his legs. At once the agony returned, but Leamas had found the cause: his hands and feet were chained together behind his back. As soon as he attempted to stretch his legs the chain tightened, forcing his shoulders down and his damaged head on to the stone floor. They must have beaten him up while he was unconscious, his whole body was stiff and bruised and his groin ached. He wondered if he'd killed the guard. He hoped so.

Above him shone the light, large, clinical, and fierce. No furniture, just whitewashed walls, quite close all round, and the grey steel door, a smart charcoal grey, the colour you see on clever London houses. There was nothing else. Nothing at all. Nothing to think about, just the savage pain.

He must have lain there hours before they came. It grew hot from the light, he was thirsty but he refused to call out. At last the door opened and Mundt stood there. He knew it was Mundt from the eyes. Smiley had told him about them.

17

Mundt

They untied him and let him try to stand. For a moment he almost succeeded, then, as the circulation returned to his hands and feet, and as the joints of his body were released from the contraction to which they had been subject, he fell. They let him lie there, watching him with the detachment of children looking at an insect. One of the guards pushed past Mundt and yelled at Leamas to get up. Leamas crawled to the wall and put the palms of his throbbing hands against the white brick. He was half-way up when the guard kicked him and he fell again. He tried once more and this time the guard let him stand with his back against the wall. He saw the guard move his weight on to his left leg and he knew he would kick him again. With all his remaining strength Leamas thrust himself forward, driving his lowered head into the guard's face. They fell together, Leamas on top. The guard got up and Leamas lay there waiting for the pay-off. But Mundt said something to the guard and Leamas felt himself being picked up by the shoulders and feet and heard the door of his cell close as they carried him down the corridor. He was terribly thirsty.

They took him to a small comfortable room, decently furnished with a desk and armchairs. Swedish blinds half covered the barred windows. Mundt sat at the desk and Leamas in an armchair, his eyes half closed. The guards stood at the door.

"Give me a drink," said Leamas.

"Whisky?"

"Water."

Mundt filled a carafe from a basin in the corner, and put it on the table beside him with a glass.

"Bring him something to eat," he ordered, and one of the guards left the room, returning with a mug of soup and some sliced sausage. He drank and ate, and they watched him in silence.

"Where's Fiedler?" Leamas asked finally.

"Under arrest," Mundt replied curtly.

"What for?"

"Conspiring to sabotage the security of the people."

Leamas nodded slowly. "So you won," he said. "When did you arrest him?"

"Last night."

Leamas waited a moment, trying to focus again on Mundt.

"What about me?" he asked.

"You're a material witness. You will of course stand trial yourself later."

"So I'm part of a put-up job by London to frame Mundt, am I?"

Mundt nodded, lit a cigarette and gave it to one of the sentries to pass to Leamas. "That's right," he said. The sentry came over, and with a gesture of grudging solicitude, put the cigarette between Leamas' lips.

"A pretty elaborate operation," Leamas observed, and added stupidly, "clever chaps these Chinese."

Mundt said nothing. Leamas became used to his silences as the interview progressed. Mundt had rather a pleasant voice, that was something Leamas hadn't expected, but he seldom spoke. It was part of Mundt's extraordinary self-confidence perhaps, that he did not speak unless he specifically wished to, that he was prepared to allow long silences to intervene rather than exchange pointless words. In this he differed from professional interrogators who set store by initiative, by the evocation of atmosphere and the exploitation of that psychological dependency of a prisoner upon his inquisitor. Mundt despised technique: he was a man of fact and action. Leamas preferred that.

Mundt's appearance was fully consistent with his temperament. He looked an athlete. His fair hair was cut short. It lay matt and neat. His young face had a hard, clean line, and a frightening directness; it was barren of humour or fantasy. He looked young but not youthful; older men would take him seriously. He was well built. His clothes fitted him because he was an easy man to fit. Leamas found no difficulty in recalling that Mundt was a killer. There was a coldness about him, a rigorous self-sufficiency which perfectly equipped him for the business of murder. Mundt was a very hard man.

"The other charge on which you will stand trial, if necessary," Mundt added quietly, "is murder."

"So the sentry died, did he?" Leamas replied.

A wave of intense pain passed through his head.

Mundt nodded: "That being so," he said, "your trial for espionage is somewhat academic. I propose that the case against Fiedler should be publicly heard. That is also the wish of the Praesidium."

"And you want my confession?"

"Yes."

"In other words you haven't any proof."

"We shall have proof. We shall have your confession." There was no menace in Mundt's voice. There was no style, no theatrical twist.

"On the other hand, there could be mitigation in your case. You were blackmailed by British Intelligence; they accused you of stealing money and then coerced you into preparing a revanchist trap against myself. The court would have sympathy for such a plea."

Leamas seemed to be taken off his guard.

"How did you know they accused me of stealing money?" But Mundt made no reply.

"Fiedler has been very stupid," Mundt observed. "As soon as I read the report of our friend Peters I knew why you had been sent, and I knew that Fiedler would fall into the trap. Fiedler hates me so much." Mundt nodded, as if to emphasise the truth of his observation. "Your people knew that of course. It was a very clever operation. Who prepared it, tell me. Was it Smiley? Did he do it?" Leamas said nothing.

"I wanted to see Fiedler's report of his own interrogation of you, you see. I told him to send it to me. He procrastinated and I knew I was right. Then yesterday he circulated it among the Praesidium, and did not send me a copy. Someone in London has been very clever."

Leamas said nothing.

"When did you last see Smiley?" Mundt asked casually. Leamas hesitated, uncertain of himself. His head was aching terribly.

"When did you last see him?" Mundt repeated.

"I don't remember," Leamas said at last, "he wasn't really in the outfit any more. He'd drop in from time to time."

"He is a great friend of Peter Guillam, is he not?"

"I think so, yes."

"Guillam, you thought, studied the economic situation in the GDR. Some odd little section in your Service, you weren't quite sure what it did."

"Yes." Sound and sight were becoming confused in the mad throbbing in his brain. His eyes were hot and painful. He felt sick.

"Well, when did you last see Smiley?"

"I don't remember . . . I don't remember."

Mundt shook his head.

"You have a very good memory—for anything that incriminates me. We can all remember when we *last* saw somebody. Did you for instance see him after you returned from Berlin?"

"Yes, I think so. I bumped into him . . . in the Circus once, in London." Leamas had closed his eyes and he was sweating. "I can't go on, Mundt . . . not much longer, Mundt; I'm sick," he said.

"After Ashe had picked you up, after he had walked into the trap that had been set for him, you had lunch together, didn't you?"

"Yes. Lunch together."

"Lunch ended at about four o'clock. Where did you go then?"

"I went down to the City, I think. I don't remember for sure . . . for Christ's sake, Mundt," he said holding his head with his hand, "I can't go on. My bloody head's . . ."

"And after that where did you go? Why did you shake off your followers, why were you so keen to shake them off?"

Leamas said nothing: he was breathing in sharp gasps, his head buried in his hands.

"Answer this one question, then you can go. You shall have a bed. You can sleep if you want. Otherwise you must go back to your cell, do you understand? You will be tied up again and fed on the floor like an animal, do you understand? Tell me where you went."

The wild pulsation of his brain suddenly increased, the room was dancing; he heard voices around him and the sound of footsteps; spectral shapes passed and re-passed, detached from sound and gravity; someone was shouting, but not at him; the door was open, he was sure someone had opened the door. The room was full of people, all shouting now, and then they were going, some of them had gone, he heard them marching away, the stamping of their feet was like the throbbing of his head; the echo died and there was silence. Then like the touch of mercy itself, a cool cloth was laid across his forehead, and kindly hands carried him away.

He woke on a hospital bed, and standing at the foot of it was Fiedler, smoking a cigarette.

18

Fiedler

Leamas took stock. A bed with sheets. A single ward with no bars in the windows, just curtains and frosted glass. Pale green walls, dark green linoleum; and Fiedler watching him, smoking.

A nurse brought him food: an egg, some thin soup and fruit. He felt like death, but he supposed he'd better eat it. So he did and Fiedler watched.

"How do you feel?" he asked.

"Bloody awful," Leamas replied.

"But better?"

"I suppose so." He hesitated, "Those sods beat me up."

"You killed a sentry, you know that?"

"I guessed I had . . . What do they expect if they mount such a damn' stupid operation. Why didn't they pull us both in at once? Why put all the lights out? If anything was over-organised, that was."

"I am afraid that as a nation we tend to over-organise. Abroad that passes for efficiency."

Again there was a pause.

"What happened to you?" Leamas asked.

"Oh, I too was softened for interrogation."

"By Mundt's men?"

"By Mundt's men *and* Mundt. It was a very peculiar sensation!"

"That's one way of putting it."

"No, no; not physically. Physically it was a nightmare, but you see Mundt had a special interest in beating me up. Apart from the confession."

"Because you dreamed up that story about—"

"Because I am a Jew."

"Oh Christ," said Leamas softly.

"That is why I got special treatment. All the time he whispered to me. It was very strange."

"What did he say?"

Fiedler didn't reply. At last he muttered:

"That's all over."

"Why? What's happened?"

"The day we were arrested I had applied to the Praesidium for a civil warrant to arrest Mundt as an enemy of the people."

"But you're mad—I told you, you're raving mad, Fiedler! He'll never—"

"There was other evidence against him apart from yours. Evidence I have been accumulating over the last three years, piece by piece. Yours provided the proof we need; that's all. As soon as that was clear I prepared a report and sent it to every member of the Praesidium except Mundt. They received it on the same day that I made my application for a warrant."

"The day we were pulled in."

"Yes. I knew Mundt would fight. I knew he had friends on the Praesidium, or yes-men at least, people who were sufficiently frightened to go running to him as soon as they got my report. And in the end, I knew he would lose. The Praesidium had the weapon it needed to destroy him; they had the report, and for those few days while you and I were being questioned they read it and re-read it until they knew it was true and each knew the others knew. In the end they acted. Herded together by their common fear, their common weakness, and their common knowledge they turned against him and ordered a Tribunal."

"Tribunal?"

"A secret one, of course. It meets tomorrow. Mundt is under arrest."

"What is this other evidence? The evidence you've collected."

"Wait and see," Fiedler replied with a smile. "Tomorrow you will see."

Fiedler was silent for a time, watching Leamas eat.

"This Tribunal," Leamas asked, "how is it conducted?"

"That is up to the President. It is not a People's Court—it is important to remember that. It is more in the nature of an enquiry—a committee of enquiry, that's it, appointed by the Praesidium to investigate and report upon a certain . . . subject. Its report contains a recommendation. In a case like this the recommendation is tantamount to a verdict, but remains secret, as part of the proceedings of the Praesidium."

"How does it work? Are there counsel and judges?"

"There are three judges," Fiedler said; "and in effect, there are counsel. Tomorrow I myself shall put the case against Mundt. Karden will defend him."

"Who's Karden?"

Fiedler hesitated.

"A very tough man," he said. "Looks like a country doctor, small and benevolent. He was at Buchenwald."

"Why can't Mundt defend himself?"

"It was Mundt's wish. It is said that Karden will call a witness."

Leamas shrugged.

"That's your affair," he said. Again there was silence. At last Fiedler said reflectively:

"I wouldn't have minded—I don't think I would have

minded, not so much anyway—if he had hurt me for myself, for hate or jealousy. Do you understand that? That long, long pain and all the time you say to yourself, 'Either I shall faint or I shall grow to bear the pain, nature will see to that' and the pain just increases like a violinist going up the E string. You think it can't get any higher and it does—the pain's like that, it rises and rises, and all that nature does is bring you on from note to note like a deaf child being taught to hear. And all the time he was whispering Jew . . . Jew. I could understand, I'm sure I could, if he had done it for the idea, for the Party, if you like, or if he had hated *me*. But it wasn't that; he hated—"

"All right," said Leamas shortly, "you should know. He's a bastard."

"Yes," said Fiedler, "he is a bastard." He seemed excited; he wants to boast to somebody, thought Leamas.

"I thought a lot about you," Fiedler added. "I thought about that talk we had—you remember—about the motor."

"What motor?"

Fiedler smiled. "I'm sorry, that is a direct translation. I mean '*Motor*,' the engine, spirit, urge; whatever Christians call it."

"I'm not a Christian."

Fiedler shrugged. "You know what I mean." He smiled again, "the thing that embarrasses you . . . I'll put it another way. Suppose Mundt is right. He asked me to confess, you know; I was to confess that I was in league with British spies who were plotting to murder him. You see the argument—that the whole operation was mounted by British Intelligence in order to entice us—me, if you like—into liquidating the best man in the Abteilung. To turn our own weapon against us."

"He tried that on me," said Leamas indifferently. And he added, "As if I'd cooked up the whole bloody story."

"But what I mean is this: suppose you had done that, suppose it were true—I am taking an example, you understand, a hypothesis, would you kill a man, an innocent man—"

"Mundt's a killer himself."

"Suppose he wasn't. Suppose it were me they wanted to kill: would London do it?"

"It depends . . . it depends on the need . . ."

"Ah," said Fiedler contentedly, "it depends on the need. Like Stalin, in fact. The traffic accident and the statistics. That is a great relief."

"Why?"

"You must get some sleep," said Fiedler. "Order what food you want. They will bring you whatever you want. Tomorrow you can talk." As he reached the door he looked back and said, "We're all the same, you know, that's the joke."

Soon Leamas was asleep, content in the knowledge that Fiedler was his ally and that they would shortly send Mundt to his death. That was something which he had looked forward to for a very long time.

19

Branch Meeting

Liz was happy in Leipzig. Austerity pleased her—it gave her the comfort of sacrifice. The little house she stayed in was dark and meagre, the food was poor and most of it had to go to the children. They talked politics at every meal, she and Frau Ebert, Branch Secretary for the Ward Branch of Leipzig-Hohengrün, a small, grey woman whose husband managed a gravel quarry on the outskirts of the city. It was like living in a religious community, Liz thought; a convent or a kibbutz or something. You felt the world was better for your empty stomach. Liz had some German which she had learnt from her aunt, and she was surprised how quickly she was able to use it. She tried it on the children first and they grinned and helped her. The children treated her oddly to begin with, as if she were a person of great quality or rarity value, and on the third day one of them plucked up courage and asked her if she had brought any chocolate from *"drüben"*—from "over there." She'd never thought of that and she felt ashamed. After that they seemed to forget about her.

In the evenings there was Party Work. They distributed literature, visited Branch members who had defaulted on their dues or lagged behind in their attendance at meetings, called in at District for a discussion on "Problems connected with the centralised distribution of agricultural produce" at which all local Branch Secretaries were present, and attended a meeting of the Workers' Consultative Council of a machine tool factory on the outskirts of the town.

At last, on the fourth day, the Thursday, came their own Branch Meeting. This was to be, for Liz at least, the most exhilarating experience of all; it would be an example of all that her own Branch in Bayswater could one day be. They had chosen a wonderful title for the evening's discussions— "Coexistence after two wars"—and they expected a record attendance. The whole ward had been circularised, they had taken care to see that there was no rival meeting in the neighbourhood that evening; it was not a late shopping day.

Seven people came.

Seven people and Liz and the Branch Secretary and the man from District. Liz put a brave face on it but she was terribly upset. She could scarcely concentrate on the speaker, and when she tried he used long German compounds that she couldn't work out anyway. It was like the meetings in Bayswater, it was like mid-week evensong when she used to go to church— the same dutiful, little group of lost faces, and same fussy self-consciousness, the same feeling of a great idea in the hands of little people. She always felt the same thing—it was awful, really, but she did—she wished no one would turn up, because that was absolute and it suggested persecution, humiliation—it was something you could react to.

But seven people were nothing: they were worse than nothing, because they were evidence of the inertia of the uncapturable mass. They broke your heart.

The room was better than the schoolroom in Bayswater, but even that was no comfort. In Bayswater it had been fun trying to *find* a room. In the early days they had pretended they were something else, not the Party at all. They'd taken back rooms in pubs, a committee room at the Ardena Café, or met secretly in one another's houses. Then Bill Hazel had joined from the Secondary School and they'd used his class-room. Even that was a risk—the headmaster thought Bill ran a drama group, so theoretically at least they might still be chucked out. Somehow that fitted better than this Peace Hall in pre-cast concrete with the cracks in the corners and the pic-ture of Lenin. Why did they have that silly frame thing all round the picture? Bundles of organ pipes sprouting from the corners and the bunting all dusty. It looked like something from a fascist funeral. Sometimes she thought Alec was right—you believed in things because you needed to; what you believed in had no value of its own, no function. What did he say: "A dog scratches where it itches. Different dogs itch in different places." No, it was wrong, Alec was wrong—it was a wicked thing to say. Peace and freedom and equality—they were facts, of course they were. And what about history—all those laws the Party proved. No, Alec was wrong: truth existed outside people, it was demonstrated in history, individuals must bow to it, be crushed by it if necessary. The Party was the vanguard of history, the spearpoint in the fight for Peace . . . she went over the rubric a little uncertainly. She wished more people had come. Seven was so few. They looked so cross; cross and hungry.

The meeting over, Liz waited for Frau Ebert to collect the unsold literature from the heavy table by the door, fill in her attendance book, and put on her coat, for it was cold that eve-ning. The speaker had left—rather rudely, Liz thought—before the general discussion. Frau Ebert was standing at the door with her hand on the light switch when a man appeared out of the darkness, framed in the doorway. Just for a moment Liz thought it was Ashe. He was tall and fair and wore one of those raincoats with leather buttons.

"Comrade Ebert?" he enquired.

"Yes?"

"I am looking for an English Comrade, Gold. She is staying with you?"

"I'm Elizabeth Gold," Liz put in, and the man came into the hall, closing the door behind him, so that the light shone full upon his face.

"I am Holten from District." He showed some paper to Frau Ebert who was still standing at the door, and she nodded and glanced a little anxiously towards Liz.

"I have been asked to give a message to Comrade Gold from the Praesidium," he said. "It concerns an alteration in your programme; an invitation to attend a special meeting."

"Oh," said Liz rather stupidly. It seemed fantastic that the Praesidium should even have heard of her.

"It is a gesture," Holten said. "A gesture of goodwill."

"But I—but Frau Ebert . . ." Liz began helplessly.

"Comrade Ebert, I am sure, will forgive you under the circumstances."

"Of course," said Frau Ebert quickly.

"Where is the meeting to be held?"

"It will necessitate your leaving tonight," Holten replied. "We have a long way to go. Nearly to Görlitz."

"To Görlitz . . . Where's that?"

"East," said Frau Ebert quickly. "On the Polish border."

"We can drive you home now. You can collect your things and we will continue the journey at once."

"Tonight? Now?"

"Yes." Holten didn't seem to consider Liz had much choice.

A large black car was waiting for them. There was a driver in the front and a flagpost on the bonnet. It looked rather a military car.

20

Tribunal

The court was no larger than a schoolroom. At one end, on the mere five or six benches which were provided, sat guards and warders and here and there among them spectators—members of the Praesidium and selected officials. At the other end of the room sat the three members of the Tribunal on tall-backed chairs at an unpolished oak table. Above them, suspended from the ceiling by three loops of wire, was a large red star made of plywood. The walls of the courtroom were white like the walls of Leamas' cell.

On either side, their chairs a little forward of the table, and turned inwards to face one another, sat two men; one was middle-aged, sixty perhaps, in a black suit and a grey tie, the kind of suit they wear in church in German country districts. The other was Fiedler.

Leamas sat at the back, a guard on either side of him. Between the heads of the spectators he could see Mundt, himself surrounded by police, his fair hair cut very short, his broad shoulders covered in the familiar grey of prison uniform. It seemed to Leamas a curious commentary on the mood of the court—or the influence of Fiedler—that he himself should be wearing his own clothes, while Mundt was in prison uniform.

Leamas had not long been in his place when the president of the Tribunal, sitting at the centre of the table, rang the bell. The sound directed his attention towards it, and a shiver passed over him as he realised that the president was a woman. He could scarcely be blamed for not noting it before. She was fiftyish, small-eyed and dark. Her hair was cut short like a man's, and she wore the kind of functional dark tunic favoured by Soviet wives. She looked sharply round the room, nodded to a sentry to close the door, and began at once without ceremony to address the court.

"You all know why we are here. The proceedings are secret, remember that. This is a Tribunal convened expressly by the Praesidium. It is to the Praesidium alone that we are responsible. We shall hear evidence as we think fit." She pointed perfunctorily towards Fiedler. "Comrade Fiedler, you had better begin."

Fiedler stood up. Nodding briefly towards the table he drew from the brief-case beside him a sheaf of papers held together in one corner by a piece of black cord.

He talked quietly and easily, with a diffidence which Leamas had never seen in him before. Leamas considered it a good performance, well adjusted to the role of a man regretfully hanging his superior.

"You should know first, if you do not know already," Fiedler began, "that on the day that the Praesidium received my report on the activities of Comrade Mundt I was arrested, together with the defector Leamas. Both of us were imprisoned and both of us . . . invited, under extreme duress, to confess that this whole terrible charge was a fascist plot against a loyal comrade.

"You can see from the report I have already given you how it was that Leamas came to our notice: we ourselves sought him out, induced him to defect, and finally brought him to

Democratic Germany. Nothing could more clearly demonstrate the impartiality of Leamas than this: that he still refuses, for reasons I will explain, to believe that Mundt was a British agent. It is therefore grotesque to suggest that Leamas is a plant: the initiative was ours, and the fragmentary but vital evidence of Leamas provides only the final proof in a long chain of indications reaching back over the last three years.

"You have before you the written record of this case. I need do no more than interpret for you facts of which you are already aware.

"The charge against Comrade Mundt is that he is the agent of an imperialist power. I could have made other charges—that he passed information to the British Secret Service, that he turned his Department into the unconscious lackey of a bourgeois state, that he deliberately shielded revanchist anti-Party groups and accepted sums of foreign currency in reward. These other charges would derive from the first; that Hans-Dieter Mundt is the agent of an imperialist power. The penalty for this crime is death. There is no crime more serious in our penal code, none which exposes our state to greater danger, nor demands more vigilance of our Party organs." Here he put the papers down.

"Comrade Mundt is forty-two years old. He is deputy head of the Department for the Protection of the People. He is unmarried. He has always been regarded as a man of exceptional capabilities, tireless in serving the Party's interests, ruthless in protecting them.

"Let me tell you some details of his career. He was recruited into the Department at the age of twenty-eight and underwent the customary instruction. Having completed his probationary period he undertook special tasks in Scandinavian countries—notably Norway, Sweden, and Finland—where he succeeded in establishing an intelligence network which carried the battle against fascist agitators into the enemy's camp. He performed this task well, and there is no reason to suppose that at that time he was other than a diligent member of his

Department. But, Comrades, you should not forget this early connection with Scandinavia. The networks established by Comrade Mundt soon after the war provided the excuse, many years later, for him to travel to Finland and Norway, where his commitments became a cover enabling him to draw thousands of dollars from foreign banks in return for his treacherous conduct. Make no mistake: Comrade Mundt has not fallen victim to those who try to disprove the arguments of history. First cowardice, then weakness, then greed were his motives; the acquirement of great wealth his dream. Ironically, it was the elaborate system by which his lust for money was satisfied that brought the forces of justice on his trail."

Fiedler paused, and looked round the room, his eyes suddenly alight with fervour. Leamas watched, fascinated.

"Let that be a lesson," Fiedler shouted, "to those other enemies of the state, whose crime is so foul that they must plot in the secret hours of the night!" A dutiful murmur rose from the tiny group of spectators at the back of the room.

"They will not escape the vigilance of the people whose blood they seek to sell!" Fiedler might have been addressing a large crowd rather than a handful of officials and guards assembled in the tiny, white-walled room.

Leamas realised at that moment that Fiedler was taking no chances: the deportment of the Tribunal, prosecutors, and witnesses must be politically impeccable. Fiedler, knowing no doubt that the danger of a subsequent counter-charge was inherent in such cases, was protecting his own back: the polemic would go down in the record and it would be a brave man who set himself to refute it.

Fiedler now opened the file that lay on the desk before him.

"At the end of 1956 Mundt was posted to London as a member of the East German Steel Mission. He had the additional special task of undertaking counter-subversionary measures against *emigré* groups. In the course of his work he exposed himself to great dangers—of that there is no doubt—and he obtained valuable results."

Leamas' attention was again drawn to the three figures at the centre table. To the President's left a youngish man, dark. His eyes seemed to be half closed. He had lank, unruly hair and the grey, meagre complexion of an ascetic. His hands were slim, restlessly toying with the corner of a bundle of papers which lay before him. Leamas guessed he was Mundt's man; he found it hard to say why. On the other side of the table sat a slightly older man, balding, with an open agreeable face. Leamas thought he looked rather an ass. He guessed that if Mundt's fate hung in the balance the young man would defend him and the woman condemn. He thought the second man would be embarrassed by the difference of opinion and side with the President.

Fiedler was speaking again.

"It was at the end of his service in London that recruitment took place. I have said that he exposed himself to great dangers; in doing so he fell foul of the British secret police, and they issued a warrant for his arrest. Mundt, who had no diplomatic immunity (NATO Britain does not recognise our sovereignty), went into hiding. Ports were watched, his photograph and description were distributed throughout the British Isles. Yet, after two days in hiding, Comrade Mundt took a taxi to London Airport and flew to Berlin. 'Brilliant,' you will say, and so it was. With the whole of Britain's police force alerted, her roads, railways, shipping, and air routes under constant surveillance, Comrade Mundt takes a plane from London Airport. Brilliant indeed. Or perhaps you may feel, Comrades, with the advantage of hindsight, that Mundt's escape from England was a little *too* brilliant, a little *too* easy, that without the connivance of the British authorities it would never have been possible at all!" Another murmur, more spontaneous than the first, rose from the back of the room.

"The truth is this: Mundt *was* taken prisoner by the British; in a short historic interview they offered him the classic alternative. Was it to be years in an imperialist prison, the end of a brilliant career, or was Mundt to make a dramatic return to his home country, against all expectation, and fulfil the promise he had shown? The British, of course, made it a condition of his return that he should provide them with information, and they would pay him large sums of money. With the carrot in front and the stick behind, Mundt was recruited.

"It was now in the British interest to promote Mundt's career. We cannot yet prove that Mundt's success in liquidating minor Western intelligence agents was the work of his imperialist masters betraying their own collaborators—those who were expendable—in order that Mundt's prestige should be enhanced. We cannot prove it, but it is an assumption which the evidence permits.

"Ever since 1960—the year Comrade Mundt became Head of the Counter Espionage section of the Abteilung—indications have reached us from all over the world that there was a highly placed spy in our ranks. You all know Karl Riemeck was a spy; we thought when he was eliminated that the evil had been stamped out. But the rumours persisted.

"In late 1960 a former collaborator of ours approached an Englishman in the Lebanon known to be in contact with their Intelligence Service. He offered him—we found out soon afterwards—a complete breakdown of the two sections of the Abteilung for which he had formerly worked. His offer, after it had been transmitted to London, was rejected. That was a very curious thing. It could only mean that the British already possessed the intelligence they were being offered, *and that it was up to date.*

"From mid-1960 onwards we were losing collaborators abroad at an alarming rate. Often they were arrested within a few weeks of their despatch. Sometimes the enemy attempted to turn our own agents back on us, but not often. It was as if they could scarcely be bothered.

"And then—it was early 1961 if my memory is correct—we

had a stroke of luck. We obtained by means I will not describe, a summary of the information which British Intelligence held about the Abteilung. It was complete, it was accurate, and it was astonishingly up to date. I showed it to Mundt, of course—he was my superior. He told me it came as no surprise to him: he had certain enquiries in hand and I should take no action for fear of prejudicing them. And I confess that at that moment the thought crossed my mind, remote and fantastic as it was, that Mundt himself could have provided the information. There were other indications too . . .

"I need hardly tell you that the last, the very last person to be suspected of espionage is the head of the Counter Espionage section. The notion is so appalling, so melodramatic that few would entertain it, let alone give expression to it! I confess that I myself have been guilty of excessive reluctance in reaching such a seemingly fantastic deduction. That was erroneous.

"But, Comrades, the final evidence has been delivered into our hands. I propose to call that evidence now." He turned, glancing towards the back of the room. "Bring Leamas forward."

The guards on either side of him stood up and Leamas edged his way along the row to the rough gangway which ran, not more than two feet wide, down the middle of the room. A guard indicated to him that he should stand facing the table. Fiedler stood a bare six feet away from him. First the President addressed him.

"Witness, what is your name?" she asked.

"Alec Leamas."

"What is your age?"

"Fifty."

"Are you married?"

"No."

"But you were."

"I'm not married now."

"What is your profession?"

"Assistant librarian."

Fiedler angrily intervened. "You were formerly employed by British Intelligence, were you not?" he snapped.

"That's right. Till a year ago."

"The Tribunal has read the reports of your interrogation," Fiedler continued. "I want you to tell them again about the conversation you had with Peter Guillam some time in May last year."

"You mean when we talked about Mundt?"

"Yes."

"I've told you. It was at the Circus, the office in London, our headquarters in Cambridge Circus. I bumped into Peter in the corridor. I knew he was mixed up with the Fennan case and I asked him what had become of George Smiley. Then we got talking about Dieter Frey, who died, and Mundt, who was mixed up in the thing. Peter said he thought that Maston—Maston was effectively in charge of the case then—had not wanted Mundt to be caught."

"How did you interpret that?" asked Fiedler.

"I knew Maston had made a mess of the Fennan case. I supposed he didn't want any mud raked up by Mundt appearing at the Old Bailey."

"If Mundt had been caught, would he have been legally charged?" the President put in.

"It depends who caught him. If the police got him they'd report it to the Home Office. After that no power on earth could stop him being charged."

"And what if your Service had caught him?" Fiedler enquired.

"Oh, that's a different matter. I suppose they would either have interrogated him and then tried to exchange him for one of our own people in prison over here; or else they'd have given him a ticket."

"What does that mean?"

"Get rid of him."

"Liquidate him?" Fiedler was asking all the questions now, and the members of the Tribunal were writing diligently in the files before them.

"I don't know what they do. I've never been mixed up in that game."

"Might they not have tried to recruit him as their agent?"

"Yes, but they didn't succeed."

"How do you know that?"

"Oh, for God's sake, I've told you over and over again. I'm not a bloody performing seal . . . I was head of the Berlin Command for four years. If Mundt had been one of our people, I would have known. I couldn't help knowing."

"Quite."

Fiedler seemed content with that answer, confident perhaps that the remainder of the Tribunal was not. He now turned his attention to Operation "Rolling Stone"; took Leamas once again through the special security complexities governing the circulation of the file, the letters to the Copenhagen and Helsinki banks and the one reply which Leamas had received. Addressing himself to the Tribunal, Fiedler commented:

"We had no reply from Helsinki. I do not know why. But let me recapitulate for you. Leamas deposited money at Copenhagen on June 15th. Among the papers before you there is the facsimile of a letter from the Royal Scandinavian Bank addressed to Robert Lang. Robert Lang was the name Leamas used to open the Copenhagen deposit account. From that letter (it is the twelfth serial in your files) you will see that the entire sum—ten thousand dollars—was drawn by the co-signatory to the account one week later. I imagine," Fiedler continued, indicating with his head the motionless figure of Mundt in the front row, "that it is not disputed by the Defendant that he was in Copenhagen on June 21st, nominally engaged in secret work on behalf of the Abteilung." He paused and then continued:

"Leamas' visit to Helsinki—the second visit he made to deposit money—took place on about September 24th." Raising his voice he turned and looked directly at Mundt. "On the third of October Comrade Mundt made a clandestine journey to Finland—once more allegedly in the interests of the Abteilung." There was silence. Fiedler turned slowly and addressed himself once more to the Tribunal. In a voice at once subdued and threatening he asked:

"Are you complaining that the evidence is circumstantial? Let me remind you of something more." He turned to Leamas.

"Witness, during your activities in Berlin you became associated with Karl Riemeck, formerly Secretary to the Praesidium of the Socialist Unity Party. What was the nature of that association?"

"He was my agent, until he was shot by Mundt's men."

"Quite so. He was shot by Mundt's men. One of several spies who were summarily liquidated by Comrade Mundt before they could be questioned. But before he was shot by Mundt's men he was an agent of the British Secret Service?"

Leamas nodded.

"Will you describe Riemeck's meeting with the man you call Control."

"Control came over to Berlin from London to see Karl. Karl was one of the most productive agents we had, I think, and Control wanted to meet him."

Fiedler put in: "He was also one of the most trusted?"

"Yes, oh yes. London loved Karl; he could do no wrong. When Control came out I fixed up for Karl to come to my flat and the three of us dined together. I didn't like Karl coming there really, but I couldn't tell Control that. It's hard to explain but they get ideas in London, they're so cut off from it and I was frightened stiff they'd find some excuse for taking over Karl themselves—they're quite capable of it."

"So you arranged for the three of you to meet," Fiedler put in curtly, "what happened?"

"Control asked me beforehand to see that he had a quarter of an hour alone with Karl, so during the evening I pretended

to have run out of Scotch. I left the flat and went over to de
Jong's place. I had a couple of drinks there, borrowed a bottle
and came back."

"How did you find them?"

"What do you mean?"

"Were Control and Riemeck talking still? If so, what were
they talking about?"

"They weren't talking at all when I came back."

"Thank you. You may sit down."

Leamas returned to his seat at the back of the room. Fiedler
turned to the three members of the Tribunal and began:

"I want to talk first about the spy Riemeck, who was shot:
Karl Riemeck. You have before you a list of all the information
which Riemeck passed to Alec Leamas in Berlin, so far as
Leamas can recall it. It is a formidable record of treachery. Let
me summarise it for you. Riemeck gave to his masters a detailed
breakdown of the work and personalities of the whole Abteilung.
He was able, if Leamas is to be believed, to describe the workings of our most secret sessions. As secretary of the Praesidium he gave minutes of its most secret proceedings.

"That was easy for him; he himself compiled the record of
every meeting. But Riemeck's *access* to the secret affairs of the
Abteilung is a different matter. Who at the end of 1959 co-opted
Riemeck onto the Committee for the Protection of the People,
that vital subcommittee of the Praesidium which coordinates
and discusses the affairs of our security organs? Who proposed
that Riemeck should have the privilege of access to the files of
the Abteilung? Who at every stage in Riemeck's career *since*
1959 (the year Mundt returned from England, you remember)
singled him out for posts of exceptional responsibility? I will tell
you," Fiedler proclaimed. "The same man who was uniquely
placed to shield him in his espionage activities: Hans-Dieter
Mundt. Let us recall how Riemeck contacted the Western Intelligence Agencies in Berlin—how he sought out de Jong's car on
a picnic and put the film inside it. Are you not amazed at

Riemeck's foreknowledge? How could he have known where to find that car, and on that very day? Riemeck had no car himself, he could not have followed de Jong from his house in West Berlin. There was only one way he could have known—through the agency of our own Security police, who reported de Jong's presence as a matter of routine as soon as the car passed the Inter Sector checkpoint. That knowledge was available to Mundt, and Mundt made it available to Riemeck. *That* is the case against Hans-Dieter Mundt—I tell you, Riemeck was his creature, the link between Mundt and his imperialist masters!"

Fiedler paused, then added quietly:

"Mundt—Riemeck—Leamas: that was the chain of command, and it is axiomatic of intelligence technique the whole world over that each link of the chain be kept, as far as possible, in ignorance of the others. Thus it is *right* that Leamas should maintain he knows nothing to the detriment of Mundt: that is no more than the proof of good security by his masters in London.

"You have also been told how the whole case known as 'Rolling Stone' was conducted under conditions of special secrecy, how Leamas knew in vague terms of the intelligence section under Peter Guillam which was supposedly concerned with economic conditions in our Republic—a section which surprisingly was on the distribution list of 'Rolling Stone.' Let me remind you that that same Peter Guillam was one of several British security officers who were involved in the investigation of Mundt's activities while he was in England."

The youngish man at the table lifted his pencil, and looking at Fiedler with his hard, cold eyes wide open he asked:

"Then why did Mundt liquidate Riemeck, if Riemeck was his agent?"

"He had no alternative. Riemeck was under suspicion. His mistress had betrayed him by boastful indiscretion. Mundt gave the order that he be shot on sight, got word to Riemeck to run, and the danger of betrayal was eliminated. Later, Mundt assassinated the woman.

"I want to speculate for a moment on Mundt's technique. After his return to Germany in 1959 British Intelligence played a waiting game. Mundt's willingness to cooperate with them had yet to be demonstrated, so they gave him instructions and waited, content to pay their money and hope for the best. At that time Mundt was not a senior functionary of our Service—nor of our Party—but he saw a good deal, and what he saw he began to report. He was, of course, communicating with his masters unaided. We must suppose that he was met in West Berlin, that on his short journeys abroad to Scandinavia and elsewhere he was contacted and interrogated. The British must have been wary to begin with—who would not be?—they weighed what he gave them with painful care against what they already knew, they feared that he would play a double game. But gradually they realised they had hit a gold mine. Mundt took to his treacherous work with the systematic efficiency for which he is renowned. At first—this is my guess, but it is based, Comrades, on long experience of this work and on the evidence of Leamas—for the first few months they did not dare to establish any kind of network which included Mundt. They let him be a lone wolf, they serviced him, paid and instructed him independently of their Berlin organisation. They established in London, under Guillam (for it was he who recruited Mundt in England), a tiny undercover section whose function was not known even within the Service save to a select circle. They paid Mundt by a special system which they called Rolling Stone, and no doubt they treated the information he gave them with prodigious caution. Thus, you see, it is consistent with Leamas' protestations that the existence of Mundt was unknown to him although—as you will see—he not only paid him, but in the end *actually received from Riemeck and passed to London the intelligence which Mundt obtained.*

"Towards the end of 1959 Mundt informed his London masters that he had found within the Praesidium a man who would act as intermediary between them and Mundt. That man was Karl Riemeck.

"How did Mundt find Riemeck? How did he dare to establish Riemeck's willingness to cooperate? You must remember Riemeck's exceptional position: he had access to all the security files, could tap telephones, open letters, employ watchers; he could interrogate anyone with undisputed right, and had before him the most detailed picture of their private life. Above all he could silence suspicion in a moment by turning against the people the very weapon"—Fiedler's voice was trembling with fury—"which was designed for their protection." Returning effortlessly to his former rational style, he continued:

"You can see now what London did. Still keeping Mundt's identity a close secret, they connived at Riemeck's enlistment and enabled indirect contact to be established between Mundt and the Berlin command. That is the significance of Riemeck's contact with de Jong and Leamas. *That* is how you should interpret Leamas' evidence, *that* is how you should measure Mundt's treachery." He turned and, looking Mundt full in the face, he shouted:

"There is your saboteur, terrorist! There is the man who has sold the people's right!

"I have nearly finished. Only one more thing needs to be said. Mundt gained a reputation as a loyal and astute protector of the people, and he silenced for ever those tongues that could betray his secret. Thus he killed in the name of the people to protect his fascist treachery and advanced his own career within our Service. It is not possible to imagine a crime more terrible than this. That is why—in the end—having done what he could to protect Karl Riemeck from the suspicion which was gradually surrounding him he gave the order that Riemeck be shot on sight. That is why he arranged for the assassination of Riemeck's mistress. When you come to give your judgement to the Praesidium, do not shrink from recognising the full bestiality of this man's crime. For Hans-Dieter Mundt, death is a judgement of mercy."

21

The Witness

The President turned to the little man in the black suit sitting directly opposite Fiedler.

"Comrade Karden, you are speaking for Comrade Mundt. Do you wish to examine the witness Leamas?"

"Yes, yes, I should like to in one moment" he replied, getting laboriously to his feet and pulling the end of his gold-rimmed spectacles over his ears. He was a benign figure, a little rustic, and his hair was white.

"The contention of Comrade Mundt," he began—his mild voice was rather pleasantly modulated—"is that Leamas is lying; that Comrade Fiedler either by design or ill chance has been drawn into a plot to disrupt the Abteilung, and thus bring into disrepute the organs for the defence of our socialist state. We do not dispute that Karl Riemeck was a British spy—there is evidence for that. But we dispute that Mundt was in league with him, or accepted money for betraying our Party. We say there is no objective evidence for this charge, that Comrade Fiedler is intoxicated by dreams of power and blinded to rational thought. We maintain that from the moment Leamas returned from Berlin to London he lived a part; that he simulated a swift decline into degeneracy, drunkenness, and debt, that he assaulted a tradesman in full public view and affected anti-American sentiment—all solely in order to attract the attention of the Abteilung. We believe that British Intelligence has deliberately spun around Comrade Mundt a mesh of circumstantial evidence—the payment of money to foreign banks, its withdrawal to coincide with Mundt's presence in this or that country, the casual hearsay evidence from Peter Guillam, the secret meeting between Control and Riemeck at which matters were discussed that Leamas could not hear: these all provided a spurious chain of evidence and Comrade Fiedler, on whose ambitions the British so accurately counted, accepted it; and thus he became party to a monstrous plot to destroy—to murder in fact, for Mundt now stands to lose his life—one of the most vigilant defenders of our Republic.

"Is it not consistent with their record of sabotage, subversion, and human trafficking that the British should devise this desperate plot? What other course lies open to them now that the rampart has been built across Berlin and the flow of Western spies has been checked? We have fallen victim to their plot; at best Comrade Fiedler is guilty of a most serious error; at worst of conniving with imperialist spies to undermine the security of the worker state, and shed innocent blood.

"We also have a witness." He nodded benignly at the court. "Yes. We too have a witness. For do you really suppose that all this time Comrade Mundt has been in ignorance of Fiedler's fevered plotting? Do you really suppose that? For months he has been aware of the sickness in Fiedler's mind. It was Comrade Mundt himself who authorised the approach that was made to Leamas in England: do you think he would have taken such an insane risk if he were himself to be implicated?

"And when the reports of Leamas' first interrogation in The Hague reached the Praesidium, do you suppose Comrade Mundt threw his away unread? And when, after Leamas had arrived in our country and Fiedler embarked on his own interrogation, no further reports were forthcoming, do you suppose Comrade Mundt was then so obtuse that he did not know what Fiedler was hatching? When the first reports came in from Peters in The Hague, Mundt had only to look at the dates of Leamas' visits to Copenhagen and Helsinki to realise that the whole thing was a plant—a plant to discredit Mundt himself. Those dates did indeed coincide with Mundt's visits to Denmark and Finland: they were chosen by London for that very reason. Mundt had known of those 'earlier indications' as well as Fiedler—remember that. Mundt too was looking for a spy within the ranks of the Abteilung . . .

"And so by the time Leamas arrived in Democratic Germany, Mundt was watching with fascination how Leamas nourished Fiedler's suspicions with hints and oblique indications— never overdone, you understand, never emphasised, but dropped here and there with perfidious subtlety. And by then the ground had been prepared . . . the man in the Lebanon, the miraculous scoop to which Fiedler referred, both seeming to confirm the presence of a highly placed spy within the Abteilung . . .

"It was wonderfully well done. It could have turned—it could still turn—the defeat which the British suffered through the loss of Karl Riemeck into a remarkable victory.

"Comrade Mundt took one precaution while the British, with Fiedler's aid, planned his murder.

"He caused scrupulous enquiries to be made in London. He examined every tiny detail of that double life which Leamas led in Bayswater. He was looking, you see, for some human error in a scheme of almost superhuman subtlety. Somewhere, he thought, in Leamas' long sojourn in the wilderness, he would have to break faith with his oath of poverty, drunkenness, degeneracy, above all of solitude. He would need a companion, a mistress perhaps; he would long for the warmth of human contact, long to reveal a part of the other soul within his breast. Comrade Mundt was right you see. Leamas, that skilled, experienced operator, made a mistake so elementary,

so human that . . ." He smiled. "You shall hear the witness, but
not yet. The witness is here; procured by Comrade Mundt. It
was an admirable precaution. Later I shall call—that witness."
He looked a trifle arch, as if to say he must be allowed his little
joke. "Meanwhile I should like, if I may, to put one or two
questions to this reluctant incriminator, Mr. Alec Leamas."

"Tell me," he began, "are you a man of means?"

"Don't be bloody silly," said Leamas shortly; "you know
how I was picked up."

"Yes, indeed," Karden declared, "it was masterly. I may take
it, then, that you have no money at all?"

"You may."

"Have you friends who would lend you money, give it to
you perhaps? Pay your debts?"

"If I had I wouldn't be here now."

"You have none? You cannot imagine that some kindly
benefactor, someone perhaps you have almost forgotten about,
would ever concern himself with putting you on your feet . . .
settling with creditors and that kind of thing?"

"No."

"Thank you. Another question: do you know George
Smiley?"

"Of course I do. He was in the Circus."

"He has now left British Intelligence?"

"He packed it up after the Fennan case."

"Ah—the case in which Mundt was involved. Have you
ever seen him since?"

"Once or twice."

"Have you seen him since you left the Circus?"

Leamas hesitated.

"No," he said.

"He didn't visit you in prison?"

"No. No one did."

"And before you went to prison?"

"No."

"After you left prison—the day of your release in fact—you were picked up, weren't you, by a man called Ashe?"

"Yes."

"You had lunch with him in Soho. After the two of you had parted, where did you go?"

"I don't remember. Probably I went to a pub. No idea."

"Let me help you. You went to Fleet Street eventually and caught a bus. From there you seem to have zigzagged by bus, tube, and private car, rather inexpertly for a man of your experience, to Chelsea. Do you remember that? I can show you the report if you like, I have it here."

"You're probably right. So what?"

"George Smiley lives in Bywater Street, just off the King's Road, that is my point. Your car turned into Bywater Street and our agent reported that you were dropped at number nine. That happens to be Smiley's house."

"That's drivel," Leamas declared. "I should think I went to the Eight Bells; it's a favourite pub of mine."

"By private car?"

"That's nonsense too. I went by taxi, I expect. If I have money I spend it."

"But why all the running about beforehand?"

"That's just cock. They were probably following the wrong man. That would be bloody typical."

"Going back to my original question, you cannot imagine that Smiley would have taken any interest in you after you left the Circus?"

"God, no."

"Nor in your welfare after you went to prison, nor spent money on your dependents, nor wanted to see you after you had met Ashe?"

"No. I haven't the least idea what you're trying to say,

Karden, but the answer's no. If you'd ever met Smiley you wouldn't ask. We're about as different as we could be."

Karden seemed rather pleased with this, smiling and nodding to himself as he adjusted his spectacles and referred elaborately to his file.

"Oh yes," he said, as if he had forgotten something; "when you asked the grocer for credit, how much money had you?"

"Nothing," said Leamas carelessly. "I'd been broke for a week. Longer, I should think."

"What had you lived on?"

"Bits and pieces. I'd been ill; some fever. I'd hardly eaten anything for a week. I suppose that made me nervous too—tipped the scales."

"You were, of course, still owed money at the library, weren't you?"

"How did you know that?" asked Leamas sharply. "Have you been—"

"Why didn't you go and collect it? Then you wouldn't have had to ask for credit, would you, Leamas?"

He shrugged.

"I forget. Probably because the library was closed on Saturday mornings."

"I see. Are you sure it was closed on Saturday mornings?"

"No, it's just a guess."

"Quite. Thank you, that is all I have to ask." Leamas was sitting down as the door opened, and a woman came in. She was large and ugly, wearing a grey overall with chevrons on one sleeve. Behind her stood Liz.

22

The President

She entered the court slowly, looking around her, wide-eyed, like a half-woken child entering a brightly lit room. Leamas had forgotten how young she was. When she saw him sitting between two guards she stopped.

"Alec."

The guard beside her put his hand on her arm and guided her forward to the spot where Leamas had stood. It was very quiet in the courtroom.

"What is your name, child?" the President asked abruptly. Liz's long hands hung at her sides, the fingers straight.

"What is your name?" she repeated, loudly this time.

"Elizabeth Gold."

"You are a member of the British Communist Party?"

"Yes."

"And you have been staying in Leipzig?"

"Yes."

"When did you join the Party?"

"1955. No—fifty-four, I think it was—"

She was interrupted by the sound of movement; the screech

of furniture forced aside, and Leamas' voice, hoarse, high-pitched, ugly, filling the room.

"You bastards! Leave her alone!"

Liz turned in terror and saw him standing, his white face bleeding and his clothes awry, saw a guard hit him with his fist, so that he half fell; then they were both upon him, had lifted him up, thrusting his arms high behind his back. His head fell forward on his chest, then jerked sideways in pain.

"If he moves again, take him out," the President ordered, and she nodded to Leamas in warning, adding: "You can speak again later if you want. Wait." Turning to Liz she said sharply, "Surely you know when you joined the Party?"

Liz said nothing, and after waiting a moment the President shrugged. Then leaning forward and staring at Liz intently she asked:

"Elizabeth, have you ever been told in your Party about the need for secrecy?"

Liz nodded.

"And you have been told never, never to ask questions of another Comrade on the organisation and dispositions of the Party?"

Liz nodded again. "Yes," she said, "of course."

"Today you will be severely tested in that rule. It is better for you, far better, that you should know nothing. Nothing," she added with sudden emphasis. "Let this be enough: we three at this table hold very high rank in the Party. We are acting with the knowledge of our Praesidium, in the interests of Party security. We have to ask you some questions, and your answers are of the greatest importance. By replying truthfully, and bravely, you will help the cause of Socialism."

"But *who*," she whispered, "*who* is on trial? What's Alec done?"

The President looked past her at Mundt and said, "Perhaps no one is on trial. That is the point. Perhaps only the accusers.

It can make no difference *who* is accused," she added, "it is a guarantee of your impartiality that you cannot know."

Silence descended for a moment on the little room; and then, in a voice so quiet that the President instinctively turned her head to catch her words, she asked:

"Is it Alec? Is it Leamas?"

"I tell you," the President insisted, "it is better for you—far better—you should not know. You must tell the truth and go. That is the wisest thing you can do."

Liz must have made some sign or whispered some words the others could not catch, for the President again leant forward and said, with great intensity:

"Listen, child, do you want to go home? Do as I tell you and you shall. But if you ..." She broke off, indicated Karden with her hand and added cryptically, "this Comrade wants to ask you some questions, not many. Then you shall go. Tell the truth."

Karden stood again, and smiled his kindly, churchwarden smile.

"Elizabeth," he enquired, "Alec Leamas was your lover, wasn't he?"

She nodded.

"You met at the library in Bayswater, where you work."

"Yes."

"You had not met him before?"

She shook her head: "We met at the library," she said.

"Have you had many lovers, Elizabeth?"

Whatever she said was lost as Leamas shouted again: "Karden, you swine," but as she heard him she turned and said, quite loud:

"Alec, don't. They'll take you away."

"Yes," observed the President drily; "they will."

"Tell me," Karden resumed smoothly, "was Alec a Communist?"

"No."

"Did he know you were a Communist?"

"Yes. I told him."

"What did he say when you told him then, Elizabeth?"

She didn't know whether to lie, that was the terrible thing. The questions came so quickly she had no chance to think. All the time they were listening, watching, waiting for a word, a gesture, perhaps, that could do terrible harm to Alec. She couldn't lie unless she knew what was at stake; she would fumble on and Alec would die—for there was no doubt in her mind that Leamas was in danger.

"What did he say then?" Karden repeated.

"He laughed. He was above all that kind of thing."

"Do you believe he was above it?"

"Of course."

The young man at the Judges' table spoke for the second time. His eyes were half closed:

"Do you regard that as a valid judgement of a human being? That he is *above* the course of history and the compulsion of dialectic?"

"I don't know. It's what I believed, that's all."

"Never mind," said Karden; "tell me, was he a *happy* person, always laughing and that kind of thing?"

"No. He didn't often laugh."

"But he laughed when you told him you were in the Party. Do you know why?"

"I think he despised the Party."

"Do you think he *hated* it?" Karden asked casually.

"I don't know," Liz replied pathetically.

"Was he a man of strong likes and dislikes?"

"No . . . no; he wasn't."

"But he assaulted a grocer. Now why did he do that?"

Liz suddenly didn't trust Karden any more. She didn't trust the caressing voice and the good-fairy face.

"I don't know."

"But you thought about it?"

"Yes."

"Well, what conclusion did you come to?"

"None," said Liz flatly.

Karden looked at her thoughtfully, a little disappointed perhaps, as if she had forgotten her catechism.

"Did you," he asked—it might have been the most obvious of questions—"did you *know* that Leamas was going to hit the grocer?"

"No," Liz replied, perhaps too quickly, so that in the pause that followed Karden's smile gave way to a look of amused curiosity.

"Until now, until today," he asked finally, "when had you last seen Leamas?"

"I didn't see him again after he went to prison," Liz replied.

"When did you see him last, then?"—the voice was kind but persistent. Liz hated having her back to the court; she wished she could turn and see Leamas, see his face perhaps; read in it some guidance, some sign telling her how to answer. She was becoming frightened for herself; these questions which proceeded from charges and suspicions of which she knew nothing. They must know she wanted to help Alec, that she was afraid, but no one helped her—why would no one help her?

"Elizabeth, when was your last meeting with Leamas until today?" Oh that voice, how she hated it, that silken voice.

"The night before it happened," she replied, "the night before he had the fight with Mr. Ford."

"The fight? It wasn't a fight, Elizabeth. The grocer never hit back, did he—he never had a chance. Very unsporting!" Karden laughed, and it was all the more terrible because no one laughed with him.

"Tell me, where did you meet Leamas that last night?"

"At his flat. He'd been ill, not working. He'd been in bed and I'd been coming in and cooking for him."

"And buying the food? Shopping for him?"

"Yes."

"How kind. It must have cost you a lot of money," Karden observed sympathetically: "could you afford to keep him?"

"I didn't keep him. I got it from Alec. He . . ."

"Oh," said Karden sharply, "so he *did* have some money?"

Oh God, thought Liz, oh God, oh dear God, what have I said?

"Not much," she said quickly, "not much, I know. A pound, two pounds, not more. He didn't have more than that. He couldn't pay his bills—his electric light and his rent—they were all paid afterwards, you see, after he'd gone, by a friend. A friend had to pay, not Alec."

"Of course," said Karden quietly, "a friend paid. Came specially and paid all his bills. Some old friend of Leamas, someone he knew before he came to Bayswater perhaps. Did you ever meet this friend, Elizabeth?"

She shook her head.

"I see. What other bills did this good friend pay, do you know?"

"No . . . no."

"Why do you hesitate?"

"I said I don't know," Liz retorted fiercely.

"But you hesitated," Karden explained, "I wondered if you had second thoughts."

"No."

"Did Leamas ever speak of this friend? A friend with money who knew where Leamas lived?"

"He never mentioned a friend at all. I didn't think he had any friends."

"Ah."

There was a terrible silence in the courtroom, more terrible to Liz because like a blind child among the seeing she was cut off from all those around her, they could measure her answers against some secret standard, and she could not know from the dreadful silence what they had found.

"How much money do you earn, Elizabeth?"

"Six pounds a week."

"Have you any savings?"

"A little. A few pounds."

"How much is the rent of your flat?"

"Fifty shillings a week."

"That's quite a lot, isn't it, Elizabeth? Have you paid your rent recently?"

She shook her head helplessly.

"Why not," Karden continued. "Have you no money?"

In a whisper she replied: "I've got a lease. Someone bought the lease and sent it to me."

"Who?"

"I don't know." Tears were running down her face, "I don't know . . . Please don't ask any more questions. I don't know who it was . . . six weeks ago they sent it, a bank in the City . . . some charity had done it . . . a thousand pounds. I swear I don't know who . . . a gift from a charity they said. You know everything—you tell me who . . ."

Burying her face in her hands she wept, her back still turned to the court, her shoulders moving as the sobs shook her body. No one moved, and at length she lowered her hands but did not look up.

"Why didn't you enquire?" Karden asked simply, "or are you used to receiving anonymous gifts of a thousand pounds?"

She said nothing and Karden continued: "You didn't enquire because you guessed. Isn't that right?"

Raising her hand to her face again, she nodded.

"You guessed it came from Leamas, or from Leamas' friend, didn't you?"

"Yes," she managed to say. "I heard in the street that the grocer had got some money, a lot of money from somewhere after the trial. There was a lot of talk about it, and I knew it must be Alec's friend . . ."

"How very strange," said Karden almost to himself. "How

odd." And then: "Tell me, Elizabeth, did anyone get in touch with you after Leamas went to prison?"

"No," she lied. She knew now, she was sure they wanted to prove something against Alec, something about the money or his friends; something about the grocer.

"Are you sure?" Karden asked, his eyebrows raised above the gold rims of his spectacles.

"Yes."

"But your neighbour, Elizabeth," Karden objected patiently, "says that men called—two men—quite soon after Leamas had been sentenced; or were they just lovers, Elizabeth? Casual lovers, like Leamas, who gave you money?"

"Alec *wasn't* a casual lover," she cried, "how can you . . ."

"But he gave you money. Did the men give you money, too?"

"Oh God," she sobbed, "don't ask . . ."

"Who were they?" She did not reply, then Karden shouted, quite suddenly; it was the first time he had raised his voice.

"*Who?*"

"I don't know. They came in a car. Friends of Alec."

"*More* friends? What did they want?"

"I don't know. They kept asking me what he had told me . . . they told me to get in touch with them if . . ."

"*How? How* get in touch with them?"

At last she replied:

"He lived in Chelsea . . . his name was Smiley . . . George Smiley . . . I was to ring him."

"And did you?"

"No!"

Karden had put down his file. A deathly silence had descended on the court. Pointing towards Leamas Karden said, in a voice more impressive because it was perfectly under control:

"Smiley wanted to know whether Leamas had told her too much. Leamas had done the one thing British Intelligence had never expected him to do: he had taken a girl and wept on her shoulder." Then Karden laughed quietly, as if it were all such a neat joke:

"Just as Karl Riemeck did. He's made the same mistake."

"Did Leamas ever talk about himself?" Karden continued.

"No."

"You know nothing about his past?"

"No. I knew he'd done something in Berlin. Something for the government."

"Then he did talk about his past, didn't he? Did he tell you he had been married?"

There was a long silence. Liz nodded.

"Why didn't you see him after he went to prison? You could have visited him."

"I didn't think he'd want me to."

"I see. Did you write to him?"

"No. Yes, once . . . just to tell him I'd wait. I didn't think he'd mind."

"You didn't think he would want that either?"

"No."

"And when he had served his time in prison, you didn't try and get in touch with him?"

"No."

"Did he have anywhere to go, did he have a job waiting for him—friends who would take him in?"

"I don't know . . . I don't know."

"In fact you were finished with him, were you?" Karden asked with a sneer. "Had you found another lover?"

"No! I waited for him . . . I'll always wait for him." She checked herself. "I wanted him to come back."

"Then why had you not written? Why didn't you try and find out where he was?"

"He didn't want me to, don't you see? He made me promise . . . never to follow him . . . never to . . ."

"*So he expected to go to prison, did he?*" Karden demanded triumphantly.

"No . . . I don't know. How can I tell what I don't know . . ."

"And on that last evening," Karden persisted, his voice harsh and bullying, "on the evening before he hit the grocer, did he make you renew your promise? . . . Well, did he?"

With infinite weariness, she nodded in a pathetic gesture of capitulation. "Yes."

"And you said good-bye?"

"We said good-bye."

"After supper, of course. It was quite late. Or did you spend the night with him?"

"After supper. I went home . . . not straight home . . . I went for a walk first, I don't know where. Just walking."

"What reason did he give for breaking off your relationship?"

"He didn't break it off," she said. "Never. He just said there was something he had to do; someone he had to get even with, whatever it cost, and afterwards, one day perhaps, when it was all over . . . he would . . . come back, if I was still there and . . ."

"And you said," Karden suggested with irony, "that you would always wait for him, no doubt? That you would always love him?"

"Yes," Liz replied simply.

"Did he say he would send you money?"

"He said . . . he said things weren't as bad as they seemed . . . that I would be . . . looked after."

"And that was why you didn't enquire, wasn't it, afterwards, when some charity in the City casually gave you a thousand pounds?"

"Yes! Yes, that's right. Now you know everything—you knew it all already . . . Why did you send for me if you knew?"

Imperturbably Karden waited for her sobbing to stop.

"That," he observed finally to the Tribunal before him, "is the evidence of the defence. I am sorry that a girl whose perception is clouded by sentiment, and whose alertness is blunted by money, should be considered by our British comrades a suitable person for Party office."

Looking first at Leamas and then at Fiedler he added brutally:

"She is a fool. It is fortunate, nevertheless, that Leamas met her. This is not the first time that a revanchist plot has been uncovered through the decadence of its architects."

With a little precise bow towards the Tribunal, Karden sat down.

As he did so, Leamas rose to his feet, and this time the guards left him alone.

London must have gone raving mad. He'd told them—that was the joke—he'd told them to leave her alone. And now it was clear that from the moment, the very moment he left England—before that, even, as soon as he went to prison— some bloody fool had gone round tidying up—paying the bills, settling the grocer, the landlord; above all, Liz. It was insane, fantastic. What were they trying to do—kill Fiedler, kill their agent? Sabotage their own operation? Was it just Smiley—had his wretched little conscience driven him to this? There was only one thing to do—get Liz and Fiedler out of it and carry the can. He was probably written off anyway. If he could save Fiedler's skin—if he could do that—perhaps there was a chance that Liz would get away.

How the hell did they know so much? He was sure, he was absolutely sure, he hadn't been followed to Smiley's house that afternoon. And the money—how did they pick up the story about him stealing money from the Circus? That was designed for internal consumption only . . . then how? For God's sake, how?

Bewildered, angry and bitterly ashamed he walked slowly up the gangway, stiffly, like a man going to the scaffold.

23

Confession

"All right, Karden," his face was white and hard as stone, his head tilted back, a little to one side; in the attitude of a man listening to some distant sound. There was a frightful stillness about him, not of resignation but of self-control, so that his whole body seemed to be in the iron grip of his will.

"All right, Karden, let her go."

Liz was staring at him, her face crumpled and ugly, her dark eyes filled with tears.

"No, Alec . . . no," she said. There was no one else in the room—just Leamas tall and straight like a soldier.

"Don't tell them," she said, her voice rising, "whatever it is, don't tell them just because of me . . . I don't mind anymore, Alec; I promise I don't."

"Shut up, Liz," said Leamas awkwardly. "It's too late now." His eyes turned to the President.

"She knows nothing. Nothing at all. Get her out of here and send her home, I'll tell you the rest."

The President glanced briefly at the men on either side of her. She deliberated, then said:

"She can leave the court; but she cannot go home until the hearing is finished. Then we shall see."

"She knows nothing, I tell you," Leamas shouted. "Karden's right, don't you see? It was an operation, a planned operation. How could she know that! She's just a frustrated little girl from a crackpot library—she's no good to you!"

"She is a witness," replied the President shortly. "Fiedler may want to question her." It wasn't Comrade Fiedler any more.

At the mention of his name, Fiedler seemed to wake from the reverie into which he had sunk, and Liz looked at him consciously for the first time. His deep brown eyes rested on her for a moment, and he smiled very slightly, as if in recognition of her race. He was a small, forlorn figure, oddly relaxed she thought.

"She knows nothing," Fiedler said. "Leamas is right, let her go." His voice was tired.

"You realise what you are saying?" the President asked. "You realise what this means? Have *you* no questions to put to her?"

"She has said what she had to say." Fiedler's hands were folded on his knees and he was studying them as if they interested him more than the proceedings of the court. "It was all most cleverly done." He nodded. "Let her go. She cannot tell us what she does not know." With a certain mock formality he added, "I have no questions for the witness."

A guard unlocked the door and called into the passage outside. In the total silence of the court they heard a woman's answering voice, and her ponderous footsteps slowly approaching. Fiedler abruptly stood up, and taking Liz by the arm, he guided her to the door. As she reached the door she turned and looked back towards Leamas, but he was staring away from her like a man who cannot bear the sight of blood.

"Go back to England," Fiedler said to her. "You go back to England." Suddenly Liz began to sob uncontrollably. The wardress put an arm round her shoulder, more for support than comfort, and led her from the room. The guard closed the door. The sound of her crying faded gradually to nothing.

"There isn't much to say," Leamas began. "Karden's right. It was a put-up job. When we lost Karl Riemeck we lost our only decent agent in the Zone. All the rest had gone already. We couldn't understand it—Mundt seemed to pick them up almost before we'd recruited them. I came back to London and saw Control. Peter Guillam was there and George Smiley. George was in retirement really, doing something clever. Philology or something.

"Anyway, they'd dreamed up this idea. Set a man to trap himself, that's what Control said. Go through the motions and see if they bite. Then we worked it out—backwards so to speak. 'Inductive' Smiley called it. If Mundt *were* our agent how would we have paid him, how would the files look, and so on. Peter remembered that some Arab had tried to sell us a breakdown of the Abteilung a year or two back and we'd sent him packing. Afterwards we found out we'd made a mistake. Peter had the idea of fitting that in—as if we'd turned it down because we already knew. That was clever.

"You can imagine the rest. The pretence of going to pieces; drink, money troubles, the rumours that Leamas had robbed the till. It all hung together. We got Elsie in Accounts to help with the gossip, and one or two others. They did it bloody well," he added with a touch of pride. "Then I chose a morning—a Saturday morning, lots of people about—and broke out. It made the local press—it even made the *Worker* I think—and by that time you people had picked it up. From then on," he added with contempt, "you dug your own graves."

"Your grave," said Mundt quietly. He was looking thoughtfully at Leamas with his pale, pale eyes. "And perhaps Comrade Fiedler's."

"You can hardly blame Fiedler," said Leamas indifferently, "he happened to be the man on the spot; he's not the only man in the Abteilung who'd willingly hang you, Mundt."

"We shall hang you, anyway," said Mundt reassuringly. "You murdered a guard. You tried to murder me."

Leamas smiled drily.

"All cats are alike in the dark, Mundt . . . Smiley always said it could go wrong. He said it might start a reaction we couldn't stop. His nerve's gone—you know that. He's never been the same since the Fennan case—since the Mundt affair in London. They say something happened to him then—that's why he left the Circus. That's what I can't make out, why they paid off the bills, the girl and all that. It must have been Smiley wrecking the operation on purpose, it must have been. He must have had a crisis of conscience, thought it was wrong to kill or something. It was mad after all that preparation, all that work, to mess up an operation that way.

"But Smiley hated you, Mundt. We all did, I think, although we didn't say it. We planned the thing as if it was all a bit of a game . . . it's hard to explain now. We knew we had our backs to the wall: we'd failed against Mundt and now we were going to try and kill him. But it was still a game." Turning to the Tribunal he said: "You're wrong about Fiedler, he's not ours. Why would London take this kind of risk with a man in Fiedler's position? They counted on him, I admit. They knew he hated Mundt—why shouldn't he? Fiedler's a Jew, isn't he? You know, you must know, all of you, what Mundt's reputation is, what he thinks about Jews.

"I'll tell you something, no one else will, so I'll tell you: Mundt had Fiedler beaten up, and all the time, while it was going on, Mundt baited him and jeered at him for being a Jew. You all know what kind of man Mundt is, and you put up with him because he's good at his job. But . . ." he faltered for a second, then continued: "But for God's sake . . . enough people have got mixed up in all this without Fiedler's head going into the basket. Fiedler's all right, I tell you . . . ideologically sound, that's the expression, isn't it?"

He looked at the Tribunal. They watched him impassively, curiously almost, their eyes steady and cold. Fiedler, who had returned to his chair and was listening with rather studied detachment, looked at Leamas blandly for a moment:

"And you messed it all up, Leamas, is that it?" he asked. "An old dog like Leamas, engaged in the crowning operation of his career, falls for a . . . what did you call her? . . . a frustrated little girl in a crackpot library? London must have known; Smiley couldn't have done it alone." Fiedler turned to Mundt: "Here's an odd thing, Mundt; they must have known you'd check up on every part of his story. That was why Leamas lived the life. Yet afterwards they sent money to the grocer, paid up the rent; and they bought the lease for the girl. Of all the extraordinary things for them to do . . . people of their experience . . . to pay a thousand pounds, to a girl—*to a member of the Party*—who was supposed to believe he was broke. Don't tell me Smiley's conscience goes that far. London must have done it. What a risk!"

Leamas shrugged.

"Smiley was right. We couldn't stop the reaction. We never expected you to bring me here—Holland yes—but not here." He fell silent for a moment, then continued. "And I never thought you'd bring the girl. I've been a bloody fool."

"But Mundt hasn't," Fiedler put in quickly. "Mundt knew what to look for—he even knew the girl would provide the proof—very clever of Mundt I must say. He even knew about that lease—amazing really. I mean, how *could* he have found out; she didn't tell anyone. I know that girl; I understand her . . . she wouldn't tell anyone at all." He glanced towards Mundt. "Perhaps Mundt can tell us how he knew?"

Mundt hesitated, a second too long, Leamas thought.

"It was her subscription," he said; "a month ago she increased her Party contribution by ten shillings a month. I heard about it. And so I tried to establish how she could afford it. I succeeded."

"A masterly explanation," Fiedler replied coolly.

There was silence.

"I think," said the President, glancing at her two colleagues, "that the Tribunal is now in a position to make its report to the Praesidium. That is," she added, turning her small, cruel eyes on Fiedler, "unless you have anything more to say."

Fiedler shook his head. Something still seemed to amuse him.

"In that case," the President continued, "my colleagues are agreed that Comrade Fiedler should be relieved of his duties until the disciplinary committee of the Praesidium has considered his position.

"Leamas is already under arrest. I would remind you all that the Tribunal has no executive powers. The people's prosecutor, in collaboration with Comrade Mundt, will no doubt consider what action is to be taken against a British *agent provocateur* and murderer."

She glanced past Leamas at Mundt. But Mundt was looking at Fiedler with the dispassionate regard of a hangman measuring his subject for the rope.

And suddenly, with the terrible clarity of a man too long deceived, Leamas understood the whole ghastly trick.

24

The Commissar

Liz stood at the window, her back to the wardress, and stared blankly into the tiny yard outside. She supposed the prisoners took their exercise there. She was in somebody's office; there was food on the desk beside the telephone but she couldn't touch it. She felt sick and terribly tired; physically tired. Her legs ached, her face felt stiff and raw from weeping. She felt dirty and longed for a bath.

"Why don't you eat?" the woman asked again. "It's all over now." She said this without compassion, as if the girl were a fool not to eat when the food was there.

"I'm not hungry."

The wardress shrugged: "You may have a long journey," she observed, "and not much the other end."

"What do you mean?"

"The workers are starving in England," she declared complacently. "The capitalists let them starve."

Liz thought of saying something but there seemed no point. Besides, she wanted to know; she had to know, and this woman could tell her.

"What is this place?"

"Don't you know?" the wardress laughed. "You should ask them over there," she nodded towards the window. "They can tell you what it is."

"Who are they?"

"Prisoners."

"What kind of prisoners?"

"Enemies of the state," she replied promptly. "Spies, agitators."

"How do you know they are spies?"

"The Party knows. The Party knows more about people than they know themselves. Haven't you been told that?" The wardress looked at her, shook her head and observed, "The English! The rich have eaten your future and your poor have given them the food—that's what's happened to the English."

"Who told you that?"

The woman smiled and said nothing. She seemed pleased with herself.

"And this is a prison for spies?" Liz persisted.

"It is a prison for those who fail to recognise Socialist reality; for those who think they have the right to err; for those who slow down the march. Traitors," she concluded briefly.

"But what have they done?"

"We cannot build Communism without doing away with individualism. You cannot plan a great building if some swine builds his sty on your site."

Liz looked at her in astonishment.

"Who told you all this?"

"I am Commissar here," she said proudly, "I work in the prison."

"You are very clever," Liz observed, approaching her.

"I am a worker," the woman replied acidly. "The concept of brain workers as a higher category must be destroyed. There are no categories, only workers; no antithesis between physical and mental labour. Haven't you read Lenin?"

"Then the people in this prison are intellectuals?"

The woman smiled. "Yes," she said, "they are reactionaries who call themselves progressive: they defend the individual against the state. Do you know what Khrushchev said about the counter-revolution in Hungary?"

Liz shook her head. She must show interest, she must make the woman talk.

"He said it would never have happened if a couple of writers had been shot in time."

"Who will they shoot now?" Liz asked quickly. "After the trial?"

"Leamas," she replied indifferently, "and the Jew, Fiedler." Liz thought for a moment she was going to fall but her hand found the back of a chair and she managed to sit down.

"What has Leamas done?" she whispered. The woman looked at her with her small, cunning eyes. She was very large; her hair was scant, stretched over her head to a bun at the nape of her thick neck. Her face was heavy, her complexion flaccid and watery.

"He killed a guard," she said.

"Why?"

The woman shrugged.

"As for the Jew," she continued, "he made an accusation against a loyal comrade."

"Will they shoot Fiedler for that?" asked Liz incredulously.

"Jews are all the same," the woman commented. "Comrade Mundt knows what to do with Jews. We don't need their kind here. If they join the Party they think it belongs to them. If they stay out, they think it is conspiring against them. It is said that Leamas and Fiedler plotted against Mundt. Are you going to eat that?" she enquired, indicating the food on the desk. Liz shook her head. "Then I must," she declared, with a grotesque attempt at reluctance. "They have given you potato. You must have a lover in the kitchen." The humour of this observation sustained her until she had finished the last of Liz's meal.

Liz went back to the window.

. . .

In the confusion of Liz's mind, in the turmoil of shame and grief and fear there predominated the appalling memory of Leamas, as she had last seen him in the courtroom, sitting stiffly in his chair, his eyes averted from her own. She had failed him and he dared not look at her before he died; would not let her see the contempt, the fear perhaps, that was written on his face.

But how could she have done otherwise? If Leamas had only told her what he had to do—even now it wasn't clear to her—she would have lied and cheated for him, anything, if he had only told her! Surely he understood that; surely he knew her well enough to realise that in the end she would do whatever he said, that she would take on his form and being, his will, life, his image, his pain, if she could; that she prayed for nothing more than the chance to do so? But how could she have known, if she was not told, how to answer those veiled, insidious questions? There seemed no end to the destruction she had caused. She remembered, in the fevered condition of her mind, how, as a child, she had been horrified to learn that with every step she made, thousands of minute creatures were destroyed beneath her foot; and now, whether she had lied or told the truth—or even, she was sure, had kept silent—she had been forced to destroy a human being; perhaps two, for was there not also the Jew, Fiedler, who had been gentle with her, taken her arm and told her to go back to England? They would shoot Fiedler, that's what the woman said. Why did it have to be Fiedler—why not the old man who asked the questions, or the fair one in the front row between the soldiers, the one who smiled all the time; whenever she turned round she had caught sight of his smooth, blond head and his smooth, cruel face smiling as if it were all a great joke. It comforted her that Leamas and Fiedler were on the same side. She turned to the woman again and asked:

"Why are we waiting here?"

The wardress pushed the plate aside and stood up.

"For instructions," she replied. "They are deciding whether you must stay."

"Stay?" repeated Liz blankly.

"It is a question of evidence. Fiedler may be tried, I told you: they suspect conspiracy between Fiedler and Leamas."

"But who against? How could he conspire in England? How did he come here? He's not in the Party."

The woman shook her head.

"It is secret," she replied. "It concerns only the Praesidium. Perhaps the Jew brought him here."

"But *you* know," Liz insisted, a note of blandishment in her voice, "you are Commissar at the prison. Surely they told *you?*"

"Perhaps," the woman replied, complacently. "It is very secret," she repeated.

The telephone rang. The woman lifted the receiver and listened. After a moment she glanced at Liz.

"Yes, Comrade. At once," she said, and put down the receiver.

"You are to stay," she said shortly. "The Praesidium will consider the case of Fiedler. In the meantime you will stay here. That is the wish of Comrade Mundt."

"Who is Mundt?"

The woman looked cunning.

"It is the wish of the Praesidium," she said.

"I don't want to stay," Liz cried. "I want . . ."

"The Party knows more about us than we know ourselves," the woman replied. "You must stay here. It is the Party's wish."

"Who is Mundt?" Liz asked again, but still she did not reply.

Slowly Liz followed her along endless corridors, through grilles manned by sentries, past iron doors from which no sound came, down endless stairs, across whole courtyards far beneath the ground, until she thought she had descended to the bowels of hell itself, and no one would even tell her when Leamas was dead.

She had no idea what time it was when she heard the footsteps in the corridor outside her cell. It could have been five in the evening—it could have been midnight. She had been awake, staring blankly into the pitch darkness, longing for a sound. She had never imagined that silence could be so terrible. Once she had cried out, and there had been no echo, nothing. Just the memory of her own voice. She had visualised the sound breaking against the solid darkness like a fist against a rock. She had moved her hands about her as she sat on the bed, and it seemed to her that the darkness made them heavy, as if she were groping in the water. She knew the cell was small; that it contained the bed on which she sat, a handbasin without taps, and a crude table: she had seen them when she first entered. Then the light had gone out, and she had run wildly to where she knew the bed had stood, and struck it with her shins, and had remained there, shivering with fright. Until she heard the footsteps, and the door of her cell was opened abruptly.

She recognised him at once, although she could only discern his silhouette against the pale blue light in the corridor. The trim, agile figure, the clear line of the cheek and the short fair hair just touched by the light behind him.

"It's Mundt," he said. "Come with me, at once." His voice was contemptuous yet subdued, as if he were not anxious to be overheard.

Liz was suddenly terrified. She remembered the wardress: "Mundt knows what to do with Jews." She stood by the bed, staring at him, not knowing what to do.

"Hurry, you fool." Mundt had stepped forward and seized her wrist. "Hurry." She let herself be drawn into the corridor.

Bewildered, she watched Mundt quietly relock the door of her cell. Roughly he took her arm and forced her quickly along the first corridor, half running, half walking. She could hear the distant whirr of air conditioners; and now and then the sound of other footsteps from passages branching from their own. She noticed that Mundt hesitated, drew back even, when they came upon other corridors, would go ahead and confirm that no one was coming, then signal her forward. He seemed to assume that she would follow, that she knew the reason. It was almost as if he was treating her as an accomplice.

And suddenly he had stopped, was thrusting a key into the keyhole of a dingy metal door. She waited, panic-stricken. He pushed the door savagely outwards and the sweet, cold air of a winter's evening blew against her face. He beckoned to her again, still with the same urgency, and she followed him down two steps on to a gravel path which led through a rough kitchen garden.

They followed the path to an elaborate Gothic gateway which gave on to the road beyond. Parked in the gateway was a car. Standing beside it was Alec Leamas.

"Keep your distance," Mundt warned her as she started to move forward:

"Wait here."

Mundt went forward alone and for what seemed an age she watched the two men standing together, talking quietly between themselves. Her heart was beating madly, her whole body shivering with cold and fear. Finally Mundt returned.

"Come with me," he said, and led her to where Leamas stood. The two men looked at one another for a moment.

"Good-bye," said Mundt indifferently. "You're a fool, Leamas," he added. "She's trash, like Fiedler." And he turned without another word and walked quickly away into the twilight.

She put her hand out and touched him, and he half turned

from her, brushing her hand away as he opened the car door. He nodded to her to get in, but she hesitated.

"Alec," she whispered, "Alec, what are you doing? Why is he letting you go?"

"Shut up!" Leamas hissed. "Don't even think about it, d'you hear? Get in."

"What is it he said about Fiedler? Alec, why is he letting us go?"

"He's letting us go because we've done our job. Get into the car, quick!" Under the compulsion of his extraordinary will she got into the car and closed the door. Leamas got in beside her.

"What bargain have you struck with him?" she persisted, suspicion and fear rising in her voice. "They said you had tried to conspire against him, you and Fiedler. Then why is he letting you go?"

Leamas had started the car and was soon driving fast along the narrow road. On either side, bare fields; in the distance, dark monotonous hills were mingling with the gathering darkness. Leamas looked at his watch.

"We're five hours from Berlin," he said. "We've got to make Köpenick by quarter to one. We should do it easily."

For a time Liz said nothing; she stared through the windscreen down the empty road, confused and lost in a labyrinth of half formed thoughts. A full moon had risen and the frost hovered in long shrouds across the fields. They turned on to an autobahn.

"Was I on your conscience, Alec?" she said at last. "Is that why you made Mundt let me go?"

Leamas said nothing.

"You and Mundt are enemies, aren't you?"

Still he said nothing. He was driving fast now, the needle showed a hundred and twenty kilometres; the autobahn was pitted and bumpy. He had his headlights on full, she noticed, and didn't bother to dip for oncoming traffic on the other lane.

He drove roughly, leaning forward, his elbows almost on the wheel.

"What will happen to Fiedler?" Liz asked suddenly and this time Leamas answered.

"He'll be shot."

"Then why didn't they shoot you?" Liz continued quickly. "You conspired with Fiedler against Mundt, that's what they said. You killed a guard. Why has Mundt let you go?"

"All right!" Leamas shouted suddenly. "I'll tell you. I'll tell you what you were never, never to know, neither you nor I. Listen: Mundt is London's man, their agent; they bought him when he was in England. We are witnessing the lousy end to a filthy, lousy operation to save Mundt's skin. To save him from a clever little Jew in his own department who had begun to suspect the truth. They made us kill him, d'you see, kill the Jew. Now you know, and God help us both."

25

The Wall

"If that is so, Alec," she said at last, "what was my part in all this?" Her voice was quite calm, almost matter-of-fact.

"I can only guess, Liz, from what I know and what Mundt told me before we left. Fiedler suspected Mundt; had suspected him ever since Mundt came back from England; he thought Mundt was playing a double game. He hated him, of course—why shouldn't he—but he was right too: Mundt was London's man. Fiedler was too powerful for Mundt to eliminate alone, so London decided to do it for him. I can see them working it out, they're so damned academic; I can see them sitting round a fire in one of their smart bloody clubs. They knew it was no good just eliminating Fiedler—he might have told friends, published accusations: they had to eliminate *suspicion*. Public rehabilitation, that's what they organised for Mundt."

He swung into the left-hand lane to overtake a lorry and trailer. As he did so the lorry unexpectedly pulled out in front of him, so that he had to brake violently on the pitted road to avoid being forced into the crash-fence on his left.

"They told me to frame Mundt," he said simply; "they said he had to be killed, and I was game. It was going to be my last job. So I went to seed, and punched the grocer . . . you know all that."

"And made love?" she asked quietly. Leamas shook his head. "But this is the point, you see," he continued, "Mundt knew it all; he knew the plan; he had me picked up, he and Fiedler. Then he let Fiedler take over, because he knew in the end Fiedler would hang himself. My job was to let them think what in fact was the truth: that Mundt was a British spy." He hesitated. "Your job was to discredit me. Fiedler was shot and Mundt was saved, mercifully delivered from a fascist plot. It's the old principle of love on the rebound."

"But how could they know about me; how could they know we would come together?" Liz cried. "Heavens above, Alec, can they even tell when people will fall in love?"

"It didn't matter—it didn't depend on that. They chose you because you were young and pretty and in the Party, because they knew you would come to Germany if they rigged an invitation. That man in the Labour Exchange, Pitt, he sent me up there; they knew I'd work at the Library. Pitt was in the Service during the war and they squared him, I suppose. They only had to put you and me in contact, even for a day, it didn't matter; then afterwards they could call on you, send you the money, make it look like an affair even if it wasn't, don't you see? Make it look like an infatuation, perhaps. The only material point was that after bringing us together they should send you money as if it came at my request. As it was, we made it very easy for them . . ."

"Yes, we did." And then she added, "I feel dirty, Alec, as if I'd been put out to stud."

Leamas said nothing.

"Did it ease your Department's conscience at all? Exploiting . . . somebody in the Party, rather than just anybody?" Liz continued.

Leamas said, "Perhaps. They don't really think in those terms. It was an operational convenience."

"I might have stayed in that prison, mightn't I? That's what Mundt wanted, wasn't it? He saw no point in taking the risk—I might have heard too much, guessed too much. After all, Fiedler was innocent, wasn't he? But then he's a Jew," she added excitedly. "So that doesn't matter so much, does it?"

"Oh, for God's sake," Leamas exclaimed.

"It seems odd that Mundt let me go, all the same—even as part of the bargain with you," she mused. "I'm a risk now, aren't I? When we get back to England, I mean: a Party member knowing all this . . . It doesn't seem logical that he should let me go."

"I expect," Leamas replied, "he is going to use our escape to demonstrate to the Praesidium that there are other Fiedlers in his department who must be hunted down."

"And other Jews?"

"It gives him a chance to secure his position," Leamas replied curtly.

"By killing more innocent people? It doesn't seem to worry you much."

"Of course it worries me. It makes me sick with shame and anger and . . . but I've been brought up differently, Liz; I can't see it in black and white. People who play this game take risks. Fiedler lost and Mundt won. London won—that's the point. It was a foul, foul operation. But it's paid off, and that's the only rule." As he spoke his voice rose, until finally he was nearly shouting.

"You're trying to convince yourself," Liz cried. "They've done a wicked thing. How can you kill Fiedler—he was good, Alec; I know he was. And Mundt—"

"What the hell are you complaining about," Leamas demanded roughly. "Your Party's always at war, isn't it? Sacrificing the individual to the mass. That's what it says. Socialist reality: fighting night and day—that relentless battle—that's what they say, isn't it? At least you've survived. I never heard that Communists preached the sanctity of human life—perhaps I've got it wrong," he added sarcastically. "I agree, yes, I agree, you might have been destroyed. That was on the cards. Mundt's a vicious swine; he saw no point in letting you survive. His promise—I suppose he gave a promise to do his best by you— isn't worth a great deal. So you might have died—today, next year, or twenty years on—in a prison in the worker's paradise. And so might I. But I seem to remember the Party is aiming at the destruction of a whole class. Or have I got it wrong?" Extracting a packet of cigarettes from his jacket he handed her two, together with a box of matches. Her fingers trembled as she lit them and passed one back to Leamas.

"You've thought it all out, haven't you?" she asked.

"We happened to fit the mould," Leamas persisted, "and I'm sorry. I'm sorry for the others too—the others who fit the mould. But don't complain about the terms, Liz; they're Party terms. A small price for a big return. One sacrificed for many. It's not pretty, I know, choosing who it'll be—turning the plan into people."

She listened in the darkness, for a moment scarcely conscious of anything except the vanishing road before them, and the numb horror in her mind.

"But they let me love you," she said at last. "And you let me believe in you and love you."

"They used us," Leamas replied pitilessly. "They cheated us both because it was necessary. It was the only way. Fiedler was bloody nearly home already, don't you see? Mundt would have been caught, can't you understand that?"

"How can you turn the world upside down?" Liz shouted suddenly. "Fiedler was kind and decent; he was only doing his job, and now you've killed him. Mundt is a spy and a traitor and you protect him. Mundt is a Nazi, do you know that? He hates Jews . . . what side are you on? How can you . . . ?"

"There's only one law in this game," Leamas retorted. "Mundt is their man; he gives them what they need. That's easy enough to understand, isn't it? Leninism—the expediency of temporary alliances. What do you think spies are: priests, saints, and martyrs? They're a squalid procession of vain fools, traitors too, yes; pansies, sadists, and drunkards, people who play cowboys and Indians to brighten their rotten lives. Do you think they sit like monks in London balancing the rights and wrongs? I'd have killed Mundt if I could, I hate his guts; but not now. It so happens that they need him. They need him so that the great moronic mass that you admire can sleep soundly in their beds at night. They need him for the safety of ordinary, crummy people like you and me."

"But what about Fiedler—don't you feel anything for him?"

"This is a war," Leamas replied. "It's graphic and unpleasant because it's fought on a tiny scale, at close range; fought with a wastage of innocent life sometimes, I admit. But it's nothing, nothing at all besides other wars—the last or the next."

"Oh God," said Liz softly. "You don't understand. You don't want to. You're trying to persuade yourself. It's far more terrible, what they are doing; to find the humanity in people, in me and whoever else they use, to turn it like a weapon in their hands, and use it to hurt and kill . . ."

"Christ Almighty!" Leamas cried. "What else have men done since the world began? I don't believe in anything, don't you see—not even destruction or anarchy. I'm sick, sick of killing but I don't see what else they can do. They don't proselytise; they don't stand in pulpits or on party platforms and tell us to fight for Peace or for God or whatever it is. They're the poor sods who try to keep the preachers from blowing each other sky high."

"You're wrong," Liz declared hopelessly; "they're more wicked than all of us."

"Because I made love to you when you thought I was a tramp?" Leamas asked savagely.

"Because of their contempt," Liz replied; "contempt for what is real and good; contempt for love, contempt for—"

"Yes," Leamas agreed, suddenly weary. "That is the price

they pay; to despise God and Karl Marx in the same sentence.
If that is what you mean."

"It makes you the same," Liz continued; "the same as
Mundt and all the rest . . . I should know, I was the one who
was kicked about, wasn't I? By them, by you because you don't
care. Only Fiedler didn't . . . But the rest of you . . . you all
treated me as if I was . . . nothing . . . just currency to pay
with . . . You're all the same, Alec."

"Oh, Liz," he said desperately, "for God's sake believe me:
I hate it, I hate it all; I'm tired. But it's the world, it's mankind
that's gone mad. We're a tiny price to pay . . . but everywhere's
the same, people cheated and misled, whole lives thrown away,
people shot and in prison, whole groups and classes of men
written off for nothing. And you, your party—God knows it
was built on the bodies of ordinary people. You've never seen
men die as I have, Liz . . ."

As he spoke Liz remembered the drab prison courtyard,
and the wardress saying: "It is a prison for those who slow
down the march . . . for those who think they have the right
to err."

Leamas was suddenly tense, peering forward through the
windscreen. In the headlights of the car Liz discerned a figure
standing in the road. In his hand was a tiny light which he
turned on and off as the car approached. "That's him," Leamas
muttered; switched off the headlights and engine, and coasted
silently forward. As they drew up, Leamas leant back and
opened the rear door.

Liz did not turn round to look at him as he got in. She was
staring stiffly forward, down the street at the falling rain.

"Drive at thirty kilometres," the man said. His voice was taut,
frightened. "I'll tell you the way. When we reach the place you
must get out and run to the wall. The searchlight will be shining at the point where you must climb. Stand in the beam of

the searchlight. When the beam moves away begin to climb.
You will have ninety seconds to get over. You go first," he said
to Leamas; "and the girl follows. There are iron rungs in the
lower part—after that you must pull yourself up as best you
can. You'll have to sit on top and pull the girl up. Do you understand?"

"We understand," said Leamas. "How long have we got?"

"If you drive at thirty kilometres we shall be there in about
nine minutes. The searchlight will be on the wall at five past
one exactly. They can give you ninety seconds. Not more."

"What happens after ninety seconds?" Leamas asked.

"They can only give you ninety seconds," the man repeated;
"otherwise it is too dangerous. Only one detachment has been
briefed. They think you are being infiltrated into West Berlin.
They've been told not to make it too easy. Ninety seconds are
enough."

"I bloody well hope so," said Leamas drily. "What time do
you make it?"

"I checked my watch with the sergeant in charge of the
detachment," the man replied. A light went on and off briefly
in the back of the car. "It is twelve forty-eight. We must leave
at five to one. Seven minutes to wait."

They sat in total silence save for the rain pattering on the
roof. The cobble road reached out straight before them, staged
by dingy street lights every hundred metres. There was no one
about. Above them the sky was lit with the unnatural glow of
arclights. Occasionally the beam of a searchlight flickered
overhead, and disappeared. Far to the left Leamas caught sight
of a fluctuating light just above the sky-line, constantly altering in strength, like the reflection of a fire.

"What's that?" he asked, pointing towards it.

"Information Service," the man replied. "A scaffolding of
lights. It flashes news headlines into East Berlin."

"Of course," Leamas muttered. They were very near the
end of the road.

"There is no turning back," the man continued; "he told you that? There is no second chance."

"I know," Leamas replied.

"If something goes wrong—if you fall or get hurt—don't turn back. They shoot on sight within the area of the wall. You *must* get over."

"We know," Leamas repeated; "he told me."

"From the moment you get out of the car you are in the area."

"We know. Now shut up," Leamas retorted. And then he added: "Are you taking the car back?"

"As soon as you get out of the car I shall drive it away. It is a danger for me, too," the man replied.

"Too bad," said Leamas drily.

Again there was silence; then Leamas asked: "Have you got a gun?"

"Yes," said the man; "but I can't give it to you; he said I shouldn't give it to you . . . that you were sure to ask for it."

Leamas laughed quietly. "He would," he said.

Leamas pulled the starter. With a noise that seemed to fill the street the car moved slowly forward.

They had gone about three hundred yards when the man whispered excitedly, "Go right here, then left." They swung into a narrow side street. There were empty market stalls on either side so that the car barely passed between them.

"Left here, now!"

They turned again, fast, this time between two tall buildings into what looked like a cul-de-sac. There was washing across the street, and Liz wondered whether they would pass under it. As they approached what seemed to be the dead end the man said: "Left again—follow the path." Leamas mounted the curb, crossed the pavement, and they followed a broad footpath bordered by a broken fence to their left, and a tall, windowless building to their right. They heard a shout from somewhere above them, a woman's voice, and Leamas muttered: "Oh, shut up," as he steered clumsily round a right-angle bend in the path and came almost immediately upon a major road.

"Which way?" he demanded.

"Straight across—past the chemist—between the chemist and the post office—there!" The man was leaning so far forward that his face was almost level with theirs. He pointed now, reaching past Leamas, the tips of his fingers pressed against the windscreen.

"Get back," Leamas hissed. "Get your hand away. How the hell can I see if you wave your hand around like that?" Slamming the car into first gear he drove fast across the wide road. Glancing to his left he was astonished to glimpse the plump silhouette of the Brandenburg Gate three hundred yards away, and the sinister grouping of military vehicles at the foot of it.

"Where are we going?" asked Leamas suddenly.

"We're nearly there. Go slowly now . . . left, left, go left!" he cried, and Leamas jerked the wheel in the nick of time; they passed under a narrow archway into a courtyard. Half the windows were missing or boarded up; the empty doorways gaped sightlessly at them. At the other end of the yard was an open gateway. "Through there," came the whispered command, urgent in the darkness; "then hard right. You'll see a street lamp on your right. The one beyond it is broken. When you reach the second lamp switch off the engine and coast until you see a fire hydrant. That's the place."

"Why the hell didn't you drive yourself?"

"He said you should drive; he said it was safer."

They passed through the gate and turned sharply to the right. They were in a narrow street, pitch dark.

"Lights out!"

Leamas switched off the car lights, drove slowly forwards towards the first street lamp. Ahead, they could just see the second. It was unlit. Switching off the engine they coasted silently past it, until twenty yards ahead of them they discerned the dim outline of the fire hydrant. Leamas braked; the car rolled to a standstill.

"Where are we?" Leamas whispered. "We crossed the Lenin-Allee, didn't we?"

"Griefswalder Strasse. Then we turned north. We're north of Bernauerstrasse."

"Pankow?"

"Just about. Look," the man pointed down a side street to the left. At the far end they saw a brief stretch of wall, grey brown in the weary arclight. Along the top ran a triple strand of barbed wire.

"How will the girl get over the wire?"

"It is already cut where you climb. There is a small gap. You have one minute to reach the wall. Good-bye."

They got out of the car, all three of them. Leamas took Liz by the arm, and she started from him as if he had hurt her.

"Good-bye," said the German.

Leamas just whispered: "Don't start the car till we're over."

Liz looked at the German for a moment in the pale light. She had a brief impression of a young, anxious face; the face of a boy trying to be brave.

"Good-bye," said Liz. She disengaged her arm and followed Leamas across the road and into the narrow street that led towards the wall.

As they entered the street they heard the car start up behind them, turn, and move quickly away in the direction they had come.

"Pull up the ladder, you bastard," Leamas muttered, glancing back at the retreating car.

Liz hardly heard him.

26

In from the Cold

They walked quickly, Leamas glancing over his shoulder from time to time to make sure she was following. As he reached the end of the alley, he stopped, drew into the shadow of a doorway and looked at his watch.

"Two minutes," he whispered.

She said nothing. She was staring straight ahead towards the wall, and the black ruins rising behind it.

"Two minutes," Leamas repeated.

Before them was a strip of thirty yards. It followed the wall in both directions. Perhaps seventy yards to their right was a watch tower; the beam of its searchlight played along the strip. The thin rain hung in the air, so that the light from the arclamps was sallow and chalky, screening the world beyond. There was no one to be seen; not a sound. An empty stage.

The watch tower's searchlight began feeling its way along the wall towards them, hesitant; each time it rested they could see the separate bricks and the careless lines of mortar hastily put on. As they watched the beam stopped immediately in front of them. Leamas looked at his watch.

"Ready?" he asked.

She nodded.

Taking her arm he began walking deliberately across the strip. Liz wanted to run, but he held her so tightly that she could not. They were half-way towards the wall now, the brilliant semi-circle of light drawing them forward, the beam directly above them. Leamas was determined to keep Liz very close to him, as if he were afraid that Mundt would not keep his word and somehow snatch her away at the last moment.

They were almost at the wall when the beam darted to the north, leaving them momentarily in total darkness. Still holding Liz's arm, Leamas guided her forward blindly, his left hand reaching ahead of him until suddenly he felt the coarse, sharp contact of the cinder brick. Now he could discern the wall and, looking upwards, the triple-strand of wire and the cruel hooks which held it. Metal wedges, like climbers' pitons, had been driven into the brick. Seizing the highest one, Leamas pulled himself quickly upwards until he had reached the top of the wall. He tugged sharply at the lower strand of wire and it came towards him, already cut.

"Come on," he whispered urgently, "start climbing."

Laying himself flat he reached down, grasped her upstretched hand and began drawing her slowly upwards as her foot found the first metal rung.

Suddenly the whole world seemed to break into flame; from everywhere, from above and beside them, massive lights converged, bursting upon them with savage accuracy.

Leamas was blinded, he turned his head away, wrenching wildly at Liz's arm. Now she was swinging free; he thought she had slipped and he called frantically, still drawing her upwards. He could see nothing—only a mad confusion of colour dancing in his eyes.

Then came the hysterical wail of sirens, orders frantically shouted. Half kneeling astride the wall he grasped both her arms in his, and began dragging her to him inch by inch, himself on the verge of falling.

Then they fired—single rounds, three or four, and he felt her shudder. Her thin arms slipped from his hands. He heard a voice in English from the Western side of the wall:

"Jump, Alec! Jump, man!"

Now everyone was shouting, English, French, and German mixed; he heard Smiley's voice from quite close:

"The girl, where's the girl?"

Shielding his eyes he looked down at the foot of the wall and at last he managed to see her, lying still. For a moment he hesitated, then quite slowly he climbed back down the same rungs, until he was standing beside her. She was dead; her face was turned away, her black hair drawn across her cheek as if to protect her from the rain.

They seemed to hesitate before firing again; someone shouted an order, and still no one fired. Finally they shot him, two or three shots. He stood glaring round him like a blinded bull in the arena. As he fell, Leamas saw a small car smashed between great lorries, and the children waving cheerfully through the window.

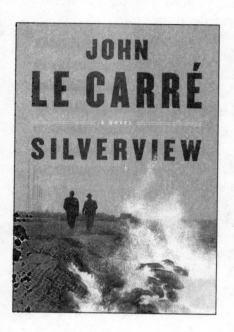

Praise for John le Carré

"There are those writer[s] ... who themselves should be immortal. ... I would suggest immortality for John le Carré, who I believe one of the most intelligent and entertaining writers. ... May he write forever!"
— Alan Cheuse, *Chicago Tribune*

"No other contemporary novelist has more durably enjoyed the twin badges of being both well-read and well-regarded."
— Scott Turow

"A brilliant linguistic artist with a keen eye for the exotic and not-so-exotic locale, a crafty moralizer."
— *The Wall Street Journal*

"Le Carré is simply the world's greatest fictional spymaster."
— *Newsweek*

"Le Carré's work is ... the gold standard of espionage fiction and the author is ... a master of any sort of fiction, no matter the genre."
— *The Seattle Times*

"Le Carré's execution is perfect."
— *The New York Times Book Review*

"Le Carré has a great talent for entangling his audience in the sticky tape of complexity, paradox, and irony, and much of the pleasure in his stories is following the same dense, dark path as his characters."
— *New York Daily News*

"He has reinvented the realistic spy story as the supreme theater of paradox, where heroism breeds vice, and virtue is a quite accidental by-product of impudent crimes."
— *Time*

PENGUIN BOOKS

CALL FOR THE DEAD

JOHN LE CARRÉ was born in 1931. For six decades, he wrote novels that came to define our age. The son of a con man, he spent his childhood between boarding school and the London underworld. At sixteen he found refuge at the university of Bern, then later at Oxford. A spell of teaching at Eton led him to a short career in British Intelligence (MI5&6). He published his debut novel, *Call for the Dead*, in 1961 while still a secret servant. His third novel, *The Spy Who Came in from the Cold*, secured him a worldwide reputation, which was consolidated by the acclaim for his trilogy *Tinker Tailor Soldier Spy*, *The Honourable Schoolboy*, and *Smiley's People*. At the end of the Cold War, le Carré widened his scope to explore an international landscape including the arms trade and the War on Terror. His memoir, *The Pigeon Tunnel*, was published in 2016 and the last George Smiley novel, *A Legacy of Spies*, appeared in 2017. He died on December 12, 2020.

johnlecarre.com
🐦 lecarre_news
f johnlecarreofficial

JOHN LE CARRÉ

CALL FOR THE
DEAD

PENGUIN BOOKS

PENGUIN BOOKS
An imprint of Penguin Random House LLC
penguinrandomhouse.com

First published in Great Britain by Victor Gollancz Ltd 1961
Published in Penguin Books 2012
This edition with a new introduction by the author published in Penguin Books 2021

ISBN 9780143122579 (paperback)
ISBN 9781101603758 (ebook)
CIP data available

Printed in the United States of America
13th Printing

CONTENTS

INTRODUCTION TO THE SIXTIETH ANNIVERSARY EDITION

There are several reasons why I have had so much difficulty re-reading a book of mine that I wrote sixty years ago, none of them to my credit. The first is that my immediate instinct on opening it is to chase around for infelicities: hanging clauses, word repetition, adverbs where a simple verb would have done a better job and—a meaningless aversion—split infinitives.

But then a second reason kicks in. Still in pursuit of my shortcomings, I stumble on passages that are not only free of infelicities but actually, dare I say it, pretty good. Well, I say to myself uneasily, the boy could write a decent paragraph when he put his mind to it. But can he—could he—write like that today? Which in turn brings me to the somber questions of what recognition and money do to a writer, and more particularly what they did to me.

I wrote *Call for the Dead*, my first novel, because I had been boiling to write for twenty years but had never quite had the prompt. I had done book illustrations, I had written bad poetry and one or two stories, and produced a couple of amateur plays, and become a reasonable hand at caricatures. In a bookless household, I had managed to acquire some sort of taste for books, largely because of a master at one of my early schools who read aloud to us beautifully from Conan Doyle and G. K. Chesterton. At sixteen, having fled my English public school,

I took a huge side-step into German language and literature and ended up teaching them at Eton, with the result that English letters always played second fiddle. It took a lurch from Eton into the Intelligence community to get me writing *Call for the Dead*, and the prompt came from John Bingham, novelist, spy, and colleague.

In MI5 the standard of report writing was very high indeed. Registry and senior officers were all pedants and descended on you like eagles if they spotted a sloppy sentence or an unsubstantiated claim: "Too fluffy. Can you actually demonstrate this? If this is hearsay, kindly say so clearly," ran the marginal comments in different handwritings as your report came whistling back to you from the top floor. It was my first experience of having to battle for every sentence I wrote as if it had to stand up in court.

The agent-running section to which I was eventually attached was dominated by two figures, both men: Maxwell Knight, naturalist, broadcaster, and the subject of at least two published biographies, and John Bingham. Knight, allegedly of the far right, though I never heard him on politics, was by the time I knew him tolerated only on account of the agents he had recruited long ago and that were still beholden to him. He was a big, unwashed, silvery boy scout of a man, of great charm and idiosyncratic habits that included bringing ailing small animals such as gerbils into the office in his jacket pocket. Bingham could scarcely have been more different. Everything about Knight suggested that he be enjoyed with caution, but John was approachable, unassuming, quietly spoken, and a kindly shepherd and confessor to his agents, mostly women. He was also a needle-sharp intelligence officer of great experience, as I had good reason to learn when one of my agents was blown and I needed his urgent advice on how to limit the damage. And John of necessity did much of his work in the evenings, when his agents returned home from their high-wire acts needing his consolation and wisdom and a large gin. So by day, when he wasn't writing a report, John was writing a novel. He had written quite a few by then, thrillers, all published by Gollancz and well received. I don't remember that we ever talked about the process of writing. John, once a journalist, didn't see himself as a literary man, just a thorough writer doing a job. The one piece of advice I remember him giving me was to stick a postcard with £100 written on it above my desk and look at it every time I thought of giving up. But far more inspiring than anything he could have said was the simple act of him sitting five yards from me day after day at his desk with his head down and a hangover, writing himself a novel on lined paper. And I suppose, at the most primitive level, I decided that if he could do that, I could.

I lived in Great Missenden in those days and commuted to Marylebone Station, then walked or took the bus to Curzon Street. The train journey was an hour plus, so I wrote in small notebooks supplied, I am ashamed to say, by Her Majesty's Stationery Office. I just wrote. And the first person who came to mind was the man who got me going: John Bingham, one of the meek who do not inherit the earth. But no real character in my experience is drawn directly from life, and for George Smiley I needed a lot of things that John simply hadn't got and didn't wish to have: an obsession with German literature (although he spoke decent German), a miserable private life, a sense of being strapped to the secret treadmill and not knowing how to get off it, and, most importantly, serious moral questions about the work I was doing. John was, to say the least, a nationalist, and doubts of that sort were simply not his thing, particularly when his every evening was spent buoying up women agents who were, in their estimation and his, sacrificing their private lives for England.

So where to turn? Well, my own life had been pretty well supplied with moral doubt, not least by my father, a con man on the run from the law. But I needed more stately concerns for George Smiley, bred in me in part by the unsparing plays of Schiller, Lessing, and Büchner and the anguished cries of seventeenth-century Germany. But Smiley is not at heart an academic. In the beginning was not the word but the deed, Goethe tells us through the agency of his Faust, and Smiley refuses to shirk from action where he believes in the rightness of his cause. And so it seems to me now, with the luxury of hindsight, that for Smiley's conflicted inner life I resorted to my beloved mentor, Dr. Vivian Green, by then Rector of Lincoln College, Oxford: scholar, administrator, closet iconoclast, and Anglican priest whose institutional faith over time gave way to a universal humanism.

I don't know any more whether you will find the seeds of all this theorizing in my first stab at George Smiley, but I do. We have grown up together, changed and matured together, and seen his likeness exquisitely portrayed by two great actors, Alec Guinness and Gary Oldman. But for me he's still the same soul-searching secret sharer that I wrote about in little notebooks on the rattly commuter train from Great Missenden to Marylebone.

John le Carré
2020

CALL FOR THE
DEAD

1

A Brief History of George Smiley

When Lady Ann Sercomb married George Smiley towards the end of the war she described him to her astonished Mayfair friends as breathtakingly ordinary. When she left him two years later in favour of a Cuban motor racing driver, she announced enigmatically that if she hadn't left him then, she never could have done; and Viscount Sawley made a special journey to his club to observe that the cat was out of the bag.

This remark, which enjoyed a brief season as a *mot*, can only be understood by those who knew Smiley. Short, fat, and of a quiet disposition, he appeared to spend a lot of money on really bad clothes, which hung about his squat frame like skin on a shrunken toad. Sawley, in fact, declared at the wedding that "Sercomb was mated to a bullfrog in a sou'wester." And Smiley, unaware of this description, had waddled down the aisle in search of the kiss that would turn him into a Prince.

Was he rich or poor, peasant or priest? Where had she got him from? The incongruity of the match was emphasized by Lady Ann's undoubted beauty, its mystery stimulated by the disproportion between the man and his bride. But gossip must see its characters in black and white, equip them with sins and motives easily conveyed in the shorthand of conversation. And so Smiley, without school, parents, regiment or trade, without wealth or poverty, travelled without labels in the guard's van of the social express, and soon became lost luggage, destined, when the divorce had come and gone, to remain unclaimed on the dusty shelf of yesterday's news.

When Lady Ann followed her star to Cuba, she gave some thought to Smiley. With grudging admiration she admitted to herself that if there were an only man in her life, Smiley would be he. She was gratified in retrospect that she had demonstrated this by holy matrimony.

The effect of Lady Ann's departure upon her former husband did not interest society—which indeed is unconcerned with the aftermath of sensation. Yet it would be interesting to know what Sawley and his flock might have made of Smiley's reaction; of that fleshy, bespectacled face puckered in energetic concentration as he read so deeply among the lesser German poets, the chubby wet hands clenched beneath the tumbling sleeves. But Sawley profited by the occasion with the merest of shrugs by remarking *partir c'est courir un peu*, and he appeared to be unaware that though Lady Ann just ran away, a little of George Smiley had indeed died.

That part of Smiley which survived was as incongruous to his appearance as love, or a taste for unrecognized poets: it was his profession, which was that of intelligence officer. It was a profession he enjoyed, and which mercifully provided him with colleagues equally obscure in character and origin. It also provided him with what he had once loved best in life: academic excursions into the mystery of human behaviour, disciplined by the practical application of his own deductions.

Some time in the twenties when Smiley had emerged from his unimpressive school and lumbered blinking into the murky cloisters of his unimpressive Oxford College, he had dreamed of Fellowships and a life devoted to the literary obscurities of seventeenth-century Germany. But his own tutor, who knew Smiley better, guided him wisely away from the honours that would undoubtedly have been his. On a sweet July morning in 1928, a puzzled and rather pink Smiley had sat before an interviewing board of the Overseas Committee for Academic Research, an organization of which he had unaccountably never heard. Jebedee (his tutor) had been oddly vague about the introduction: "Give these people a try, Smiley, they might have you and they pay badly enough to guarantee you decent company." But Smiley was annoyed and said so. It worried him that Jebedee, usually so precise, was so evasive. In a slight huff he agreed to postpone his reply to All Souls until he had seen Jebedee's "mysterious people."

He wasn't introduced to the Board, but he knew half of its members by sight. There was Fielding, the French medievalist from Cambridge, Sparke from the School of Oriental Languages, and Steed-Asprey, who had been dining at High Table the night Smiley had been Jebedee's guest. He had to admit he was impressed. For Fielding to leave his rooms, let alone Cambridge, was in itself a miracle. Afterwards Smiley always thought of that interview as a fan dance; a calculated progression of disclosures, each revealing different parts of a mysterious entity. Finally Steed-Asprey, who seemed to be Chairman, removed the last veil, and the truth stood before him in all its dazzling nakedness. He was being offered a post in what, for want of a better name, Steed-Asprey blushingly described as the Secret Service.

Smiley had asked for time to think. They gave him a week. No one mentioned pay.

That night he stayed in London at somewhere rather good and took himself to the theatre. He felt strangely light-headed and this worried him. He knew very well that he would accept, that he could have done so at the interview. It was only an instinctive caution, and perhaps a pardonable desire to play the coquette with Fielding, which prevented him from doing so.

Following his affirmation came training: anonymous country houses, anonymous instructors, a good deal of travel and, looming ever larger, the fantastic prospect of working completely alone.

His first operational posting was relatively pleasant: a two-year appointment as *englischer Dozent* at a provincial German university: lectures on Keats and vacations in Bavarian hunting lodges with groups of earnest and solemnly promiscuous German students. Towards the end of each long vacation he brought some of them back to England, having already earmarked the likely ones and conveyed his recommendations by clandestine means to an address in Bonn; during the entire two years he had no idea of whether his recommendations had been accepted or ignored. He had no means of knowing even whether his candidates were approached. Indeed he had no means of knowing whether his messages ever reached their destination; and he had no contact with the Department while in England.

His emotions in performing this work were mixed, and irreconcilable. It intrigued him to evaluate from a detached position what he had learnt to describe as "the agent potential" of a human being; to devise minuscule tests of character and behaviour which could inform him of the qualities of a candidate. This part of him was bloodless and inhuman—Smiley in this role was the international mercenary of his trade, amoral and without motive beyond that of personal gratification.

Conversely it saddened him to witness in himself the gradual death of natural pleasure. Always withdrawn, he now found himself shrinking from the temptations of friendship and human loyalty; he guarded himself warily from spontaneous reaction. By the strength of his intellect, he forced himself to observe humanity with clinical objectivity, and because he was neither immortal nor infallible he hated and feared the falseness of his life.

But Smiley was a sentimental man and the long exile strengthened his deep love of England. He fed hungrily on memories of Oxford; its beauty, its rational ease, and the mature slowness of its judgements. He dreamt of windswept autumn holidays at Hartland Quay, of long trudges over the Cornish cliffs, his face smooth and hot against the sea wind. This was his other secret life, and he grew to hate the bawdy intrusion of the new Germany, the stamping and shouting of uniformed students, the scarred, arrogant faces and their cheapjack answers. He resented, too, the way in which the Faculty had tampered with his subject—*his* beloved German literature. And there had been a night, a terrible night in the winter of 1937, when Smiley had stood at his window and watched a great bonfire in the university court: round it stood hundreds of students, their faces exultant and glistening in the dancing light. And into the pagan fire they threw books in their hundreds. He knew whose books they were: Thomas Mann, Heine, Lessing and a host of others. And Smiley, his damp hand cupped round the end of his cigarette, watching and hating, triumphed that he knew his enemy.

Nineteen thirty-nine saw him in Sweden, the accredited agent of a well-known Swiss small-arms manufacturer, his association with the firm conveniently backdated. Conveniently, too, his appearance had somehow altered, for Smiley had discovered in himself a talent for the part which went beyond the rudimentary change to his hair and the addition of a small moustache. For four years he had played the part, travelling back and forth between Switzerland, Germany, and Sweden. He had never guessed it was possible to be frightened for so long. He developed a nervous irritation in his left eye which remained with him fifteen years later; the strain etched lines on his fleshy cheeks and brow. He learnt what it was never to sleep, never to relax, to feel at any time of day or night the restless beating of his own heart, to know the extremes of solitude and self-pity, the sudden unreasoning desire for a woman, for drink, for exercise, for any drug to take away the tension of his life.

Against this background he conducted his authentic commerce and his work as a spy. With the progress of time the network grew, and other countries repaired their lack of fore-sight and preparation. In 1943 he was recalled. Within six weeks he was yearning to return, but they never let him go.

"You're finished," Steed-Asprey said. "Train new men, take time off. Get married or something. Unwind."

Smiley proposed to Steed-Asprey's secretary, the Lady Ann Sercomb.

The war was over. They paid him off, and he took his beautiful wife to Oxford to devote himself to the obscurities of seventeenth-century Germany. But two years later Lady Ann was in Cuba, and the revelations of a young Russian cypher-clerk in Ottawa had created a new demand for men of Smiley's experience.

The job was new, the threat elusive and at first he enjoyed it. But younger men were coming in, perhaps with fresher minds. Smiley was no material for promotion and it dawned on him gradually that he had entered middle age without ever being young, and that he was—in the nicest possible way—on the shelf.

Things changed. Steed-Asprey was gone; fled from the new world to India, in search of another civilization. Jebedee was dead. He had boarded a train at Lille in 1941 with his radio operator, a young Belgian, and neither had been heard of again. Fielding was wedded to a new thesis on Roland—only Maston remained, Maston the career man, the war-time recruit, the Ministers' Adviser on Intelligence; "the first man," Jebedee had said, "to play power tennis at Wimbledon." The NATO alli-ance, and the desperate measures contemplated by the Ameri-cans, altered the whole nature of Smiley's Service. Gone for ever were the days of Steed-Asprey, when as like as not you took your orders over a glass of port in his rooms at Magdalen; the inspired amateurism of a handful of highly qualified, under-paid men had given way to the efficiency, bureaucracy, and intrigue of a large Government department—effectively at the mercy of Maston, with his expensive clothes and his knight-hood, his distinguished grey hair and silver-coloured ties; Maston, who even remembered his secretary's birthday, whose manners were a by-word among the ladies of the registry; Maston, apologetically extending his empire and regretfully moving to even larger offices; Maston, holding smart house-parties at Henley and feeding on the success of his subordinates.

They had brought him in during the war, the professional civil servant from an orthodox department, a man to handle paper and integrate the brilliance of his staff with the cumbersome machine of bureaucracy. It comforted the Great to deal with a man they knew, a man who could reduce any colour to grey, who knew his masters and could walk among them. And he did it so well. They liked his diffidence when he apologized for the company he kept, his insincerity when he defended the vagaries of his subordinates, his flexibility when formulating new commitments. Nor did he let go the advantages of a cloak and dagger man *malgré lui*, wearing the cloak for his masters and preserving the dagger for his servants. Ostensibly, his position was an odd one. He was not the nominal Head of Service, but the Ministers' Adviser on Intelligence, and Steed-Asprey had described him for all time as the Head Eunuch.

This was a new world for Smiley: the brilliantly lit corridors, the smart young men. He felt pedestrian and old-fashioned, homesick for the dilapidated terrace house in Knightsbridge where it had all begun. His appearance seemed to reflect this discomfort in a kind of physical recession which made him more hunched and frog-like than ever. He blinked more, and acquired the nickname of "Mole." But his débutante secretary adored him, and referred to him invariably as "My darling teddy-bear."

Smiley was now too old to go abroad. Maston had made that clear: "Anyway, my dear fellow, as like as not you're blown after all the ferreting about in the war. Better stick at home, old man, and keep the home fires burning."

Which goes some way to explaining why George Smiley sat in the back of a London taxi at two o'clock on the morning of Wednesday, 4 January, on his way to Cambridge Circus.

2

We Never Closed

He felt safe in the taxi. Safe and warm. The warmth was contraband, smuggled from his bed and hoarded against the wet January night. Safe because unreal: it was his ghost that ranged the London streets and took note of their unhappy pleasure-seekers, scuttling under commissionaires' umbrellas; and of the tarts, gift-wrapped in polythene. It was his ghost, he decided, which had climbed from the well of sleep and stopped the telephone shrieking on the bedside table . . . Oxford Street . . . why was London the only capital in the world that lost its personality at night? Smiley, as he pulled his coat more closely about him, could think of nowhere, from Los Angeles to Berne, which so readily gave up its daily struggle for identity.

The cab turned into Cambridge Circus, and Smiley sat up with a jolt. He remembered why the Duty Officer had rung, and the memory woke him brutally from his dreams. The conversation came back to him word for word—a feat of recollection long ago achieved.

"Duty Officer speaking, Smiley. I have the Adviser on the line . . ."

"Smiley; Maston speaking. You interviewed Samuel Arthur Fennan at the Foreign Office on Monday, am I right?"

"Yes . . . yes I did."

"What was the case?"

"Anonymous letter alleging Party membership at Oxford. Routine interview, authorized by the Director of Security."

(Fennan *can't* have complained, thought Smiley; he knew I'd clear him. There was nothing irregular, nothing.)

"Did you go for him at all? Was it hostile, Smiley, tell me that?"

(Lord, he does sound frightened. Fennan must have put the whole Cabinet on to us.)

"No. It was a particularly friendly interview; we liked one another, I think. As a matter of fact I exceeded my brief in a way."

"How, Smiley, how?"

"Well, I more or less told him not to worry."

"You *what?*"

"I told him not to worry; he was obviously in a bit of a state, and so I told him."

"*What* did you tell him?"

"I said I had no powers and nor had the Service; but I could see no reason why we should bother him further."

"Is that all?"

Smiley paused for a second; he had never known Maston like this, never known him so dependent.

"Yes, that's all. Absolutely all." (He'll never forgive me for this. So much for the studied calm, the cream shirts and silver ties, the smart luncheons with Ministers.)

"He says you cast doubts on his loyalty, that his career in the FO is ruined, that he is the victim of paid informers."

"He said *what?* He must have gone stark mad. He knows he's cleared. What else does he want?"

"Nothing. He's dead. Killed himself at 10:30 this evening. Left a letter to the Foreign Secretary. The police rang one of his secretaries and got permission to open the letter. Then they told us. There's going to be an inquiry. Smiley, you're sure, aren't you?"

"Sure of what?"

". . . never mind. Get round as soon as you can."

It had taken him hours to get a taxi. He rang three cab ranks and got no reply. At last the Sloane Square rank replied, and Smiley waited at his bedroom window wrapped in his overcoat until he saw the cab draw up at the door. It reminded him of the air raids in Germany, this unreal anxiety in the dead of night.

At Cambridge Circus he stopped the cab a hundred yards from the office, partly from habit and partly to clear his head in anticipation of Maston's febrile questioning.

He showed his pass to the constable on duty and made his way slowly to the lift.

The Duty Officer greeted him with relief as he emerged, and they walked together down the bright cream corridor.

"Maston's gone to see Sparrow at Scotland Yard. There's a squabble going on about which police department handles the case. Sparrow says Special Branch, Evelyn says CID and the Surrey police don't know what's hit them. Bad as a will. Come and have coffee in the DO's glory hole. It's out of a bottle but it does."

Smiley was grateful it was Peter Guillam's duty that night. A polished and thoughtful man who had specialized in satellite espionage, the kind of friendly spirit who always has a timetable and a penknife.

"Special Branch rang at 12:05. Fennan's wife went to the theatre and didn't find him till she got back alone at 10:45. She eventually rang the police."

"He lived down in Surrey somewhere."

"Walliston, off the Kingston by-pass. Only just outside the Metropolitan area. When the police arrived they found a letter to the Foreign Secretary on the floor beside the body. The Superintendent rang the Chief Constable, who rang the Duty Officer at the Home Office, who rang the Resident Clerk at the Foreign Office, and eventually they got permission to open the letter. Then the fun started."

"Go on."

"The Director of Personnel at the Foreign Office rang us. He wanted the Adviser's home number. Said this was the last time Security tampered with his staff, that Fennan had been a loyal and talented officer, bla . . . bla . . . bla . . ."

"So he was. So he was."

"Said the whole affair demonstrated conclusively that Security had got out of hand—Gestapo methods which were not even mitigated by a genuine threat . . . bla . . .

"I gave him the Adviser's number and dialled it on the other phone while he went on raving. By a stroke of genius I got the FO off one line and Maston on the other and gave him the news. That was at 12:20. Maston was here by 1:00 in a state of advanced pregnancy—he'll have to report to the Minister tomorrow morning."

They were silent for a moment, while Guillam poured coffee essence into the cups and added boiling water from the electric kettle.

"What was he like?" he asked.

"Who? Fennan? Well, until tonight I could have told you. Now he doesn't make sense. To look at, obviously a Jew. Orthodox family, but dropped all that at Oxford and turned Marxist. Perceptive, cultured . . . a reasonable man. Soft spoken, good listener. Still educated; you know, facts galore. Whoever denounced him was right of course: he *was* in the Party."

"How old?"

"Forty-four. Looks older really." Smiley went on talking as his eyes wandered round the room. ". . . sensitive face—mop of straight dark hair undergraduate fashion, profile of a twenty-year-old, fine dry skin, rather chalky. Very lined too—lines going all ways, cutting the skin into squares. Very thin fingers . . . compact sort of chap; self-contained unit. Takes his pleasures alone. Suffered alone too, I suppose."

They got up as Maston came in.

"Ah, Smiley. Come in." He opened the door and put out his

left arm to guide Smiley through first. Maston's room contained not a single piece of government property. He had once
bought a collection of nineteenth-century watercolours, and
some of these were hanging on the walls. The rest was off the
peg, Smiley decided. Maston was off the peg too, for that matter. His suit was just too light for respectability; the string of
his monocle cut across the invariable cream shirt. He wore a
light grey woollen tie. A German would call him *flott*, thought
Smiley; chic, that's what he is—a barmaid's dream of a real
gentleman.

"I've seen Sparrow. It's a clear case of suicide. The body has
been removed and beyond the usual formalities the Chief
Constable is taking no action. There'll be an inquest within a
day or two. It has been agreed—I can't emphasize this too
strongly, Smiley—that no word of our former interest in Fennan is to be passed to the Press."

"I see." (You're dangerous, Maston. You're weak and frightened. Anyone's neck before yours, I know. You're looking at
me that way—measuring me for the rope.)

"Don't think I'm criticizing, Smiley; after all if the Director of Security authorized the interview you have nothing to
worry about."

"Except Fennan."

"Quite so. Unfortunately the Director of Security omitted
to sign off your minute suggesting an interview. He authorized it verbally, no doubt?"

"Yes. I'm sure he'll confirm that."

Maston looked at Smiley again, sharp, calculating; something was beginning to stick in Smiley's throat. He knew he
was being uncompromising, that Maston wanted him nearer,
wanted him to conspire.

"You know Fennan's office has been in touch with me?"

"Yes."

"There will have to be an inquiry. It may not even be possible to keep the Press out. I shall certainly have to see the

Home Secretary first thing tomorrow." (Frighten me and try again . . . I'm getting on . . . pension to consider . . . unemployable, too . . . but I won't share your lie, Maston.) "I must have all the facts, Smiley. I must do my duty. If there's anything you feel you should tell me about that interview, anything you haven't recorded, perhaps, tell me now and let me be the judge of its significance."

"There's nothing to add, really, to what's already on the file, and what I told you earlier tonight. It might help you to know (the "you" was a trifle strong, perhaps)—it might help you to know that I conducted the interview in an atmosphere of exceptional informality. The allegation against Fennan was pretty thin—university membership in the thirties and vague talk of current sympathy. Half the Cabinet were in the Party in the thirties." Maston frowned. "When I got to his room in the Foreign Office it turned out to be rather public—people trotting in and out the whole time, so I suggested we should go out for a walk in the park."

"Go on."

"Well, we did. It was a sunny, cold day and rather pleasant. We watched the ducks." Maston made a gesture of impatience. "We spent about half an hour in the park—he did all the talking. He was an intelligent man, fluent and interesting. But nervous, too, not unnaturally. These people love talking about themselves, and I think he was pleased to get it off his chest. He told me the whole story—seemed quite happy to mention names—and then we went to an espresso café he knew near Millbank."

"A *what?*"

"An espresso bar. They sell a special kind of coffee for a shilling a cup. We had some."

"I see. It was under these . . . convivial circumstances that you told him the Department would recommend no action."

"Yes. We often do that, but we don't normally record it." Maston nodded. That was the kind of thing he understood, thought Smiley; goodness me, he really is rather contempt-ible. It was exciting to find Maston being as unpleasant as he expected.

"And I may take it therefore that his suicide—and his let-ter, of course—come as a complete surprise to you? You find no explanation?"

"It would be remarkable if I did."

"You have no idea who denounced him?"

"No."

"He was married, you know."

"Yes."

"I wonder . . . it seems conceivable that his wife might be able to fill in some of the gaps. I hesitate to suggest it, but per-haps someone from the Department ought to see her and, so far as good feeling allows, question her on all this."

"Now?" Smiley looked at him, expressionless.

Maston was standing at his big flat desk, toying with the businessman's cutlery—paper knife, cigarette box, lighter—the whole chemistry set of official hospitality. He's showing a full inch of cream cuff, thought Smiley, and admiring his white hands.

Maston looked up, his face composed in an expression of apathy.

"Smiley, I know how you feel, but despite this tragedy you must try to understand the position. The Minister and the Home Secretary will want the fullest possible account of this affair and it is my specific task to provide one. Particularly any information which points to Fennan's state of mind immedi-ately after his interview with . . . with us. Perhaps he spoke to his wife about it. He's not supposed to have done but we must be realistic."

"You want *me* to go down there?"

"Someone must. There's a question of the inquest. The Home Secretary will have to decide about that of course, but at present we just haven't the facts. Time is short and you know the case, you made the background inquiries. There's no time for anyone else to brief himself. If anyone goes it will have to be you, Smiley."

"When do you want me to go?"

"Apparently Mrs. Fennan is a somewhat unusual woman. Foreign. Jewish, too, I gather, suffered badly in the war, which adds to the embarrassment. She is a strong-minded woman and relatively unmoved by her husband's death. Only superficially, no doubt. But sensible and communicative. I gather from Sparrow that she is proving cooperative and would probably see you as soon as you can get there. Surrey police can warn her you're coming and you can see her first thing in the morning. I shall telephone you there later in the day."

Smiley turned to go.

"Oh—and Smiley . . ." He felt Maston's hand on his arm and turned to look at him: Maston wore the smile normally reserved for the older ladies of the Service. "Smiley, you can count on me, you know; you can count on my support."

My God, thought Smiley; you really do work round the clock. A twenty-four-hour cabaret, you are—"We Never Closed." He walked out into the street.

3

Elsa Fennan

Merridale Lane is one of those corners of Surrey where the inhabitants wage a relentless battle against the stigma of suburbia. Trees, fertilized and cajoled into being in every front garden, half obscure the poky "Character dwellings" which crouch behind them. The rusticity of the environment is enhanced by the wooden owls that keep guard over the names of houses, and by crumbling dwarfs indefatigably poised over goldfish ponds. The inhabitants of Merridale Lane do not paint their dwarfs, suspecting this to be a suburban vice, nor, for the same reason, do they varnish the owls; but wait patiently for the years to endow these treasures with an appearance of weathered antiquity, until one day even the beams on the garage may boast of beetle and woodworm.

The lane is not exactly a cul-de-sac although estate agents insist that it is; the further end from the Kingston by-pass dwindles nervously into a gravel path, which in turn degenerates into a sad little mud track across Merries Field—leading to another lane indistinguishable from Merridale. Until about 1920 this path had led to the parish church, but the church now stands on what is virtually a traffic island adjoining the London road, and the path which once led the faithful to worship provides a superfluous link between the inhabitants of Merridale Lane and Cadogan Road. The strip of open land called Merries Field has already achieved an eminence far beyond its own aspirations; it has driven a wedge deep into the District Council, between the developers and the preservers, and so effectively that on one occasion the entire machinery of local government in Walliston was brought to a standstill. A kind of natural compromise has now established itself: Merries Field is neither developed nor preserved by the three steel pylons, placed at regular intervals across it. At the centre is a cannibal hut with a thatched roof called "The War Memorial Shelter," erected in 1951 in grateful memory to the fallen of two wars, as a haven for the weary and old. No one seems to have asked what business the weary and old would have in Merries Field, but the spiders have at least found a haven in the roof, and as a sitting-out place for pylon-builders the hut was unusually comfortable.

Smiley arrived there on foot just after 8:00 that morning, having parked his car at the police station, which was ten minutes' walk away.

It was raining heavily, driving cold rain, so cold it felt hard upon the face.

Surrey police had no further interest in the case, but Sparrow had sent down independently a Special Branch officer to remain at the police station and act if necessary as liaison between Security and the police. There was no doubt about the manner of Fennan's death. He had been shot through the temple at point blank range by a small French pistol manufactured in Lille in 1957. The pistol was found beneath the body. All the circumstances were consistent with suicide.

Number fifteen Merridale Lane was a low, Tudor-style house with the bedrooms built into the gables, and a half-timbered garage. It had an air of neglect, even disuse. It might have been occupied by artists, thought Smiley. Fennan didn't seem to fit here. Fennan was Hampstead and au-pair foreign girls.

He unlatched the gate and walked slowly up the drive to the front door, trying vainly to discern some sign of life through the leaded windows. It was very cold. He rang the bell.

Elsa Fennan opened the door.

"They rang and asked me if I minded. I didn't know what to say. Please come in." A trace of a German accent.

She must have been older than Fennan. A slight, fierce woman with hair cut very short and dyed to the colour of nicotine. Although frail, she conveyed an impression of endurance and courage, and the brown eyes that shone from her crooked little face were of an astonishing intensity. It was a worn face, racked and ravaged long ago, the face of a child grown old on starving and exhaustion, the eternal refugee face, the prison-camp face, thought Smiley.

She was holding out her hand to him—it was scrubbed and pink, bony to touch. He told her his name.

"You're the man who interviewed my husband," she said; "about loyalty." She led him into the low, dark drawing-room. There was no fire. Smiley felt suddenly sick and cheap. Loyalty to whom, to what? She didn't sound resentful. He was an oppressor, but she accepted oppression.

"I liked your husband very much. He would have been cleared."

"Cleared? Cleared of what?"

"There was a prima facie case for investigation—an anonymous letter—I was given the job." He paused and looked at her with real concern. "You have had a terrible loss, Mrs. Fennan . . . you must be exhausted. You can't have slept all night . . ."

She did not respond to his sympathy: "Thank you, but I can scarcely hope to sleep today. Sleep is not a luxury I enjoy." She looked down wryly at her own tiny body; "My body and I must put up with one another twenty hours a day. We have lived longer than most people already.

"As for the terrible loss. Yes, I suppose so. But you know, Mr. Smiley, for so long I owned nothing but a toothbrush, so

I'm not really used to possession, even after eight years of marriage. Besides, I have the experience to suffer with discretion."

She bobbed her head at him, indicating that he might sit,
and with an oddly old-fashioned gesture she swept her skirt
beneath her and sat opposite him. It was very cold in that
room. Smiley wondered whether he ought to speak; he dared
not look at her, but peered vaguely before him, trying desperately in his mind to penetrate the worn, travelled face of Elsa
Fennan. It seemed a long time before she spoke again.

"You said you liked him. You didn't give him that impression, apparently."

"I haven't seen your husband's letter, but I have heard of its
contents." Smiley's earnest, pouchy face was turned towards
her now: "It simply doesn't make sense. I as good as told him
he was . . . that we would recommend that the matter be taken
no further."

She was motionless, waiting to hear. What could he say: "I'm
sorry I killed your husband, Mrs. Fennan, but I was only doing
my duty. (Duty to *whom* for God's sake?) He was in the Communist Party at Oxford twenty-four years ago; his recent promotion
gave him access to highly secret information. Some busybody
wrote us an anonymous letter and we had no option but to follow it up. The investigation induced a state of melancholia in
your husband, and drove him to suicide." He said nothing.

"It was a game," she said suddenly, "a silly balancing trick
of ideas; it had nothing to do with him or any real person.
Why do you bother yourself with us? Go back to Whitehall
and look for more spies on your drawing boards." She paused,
showing no sign of emotion beyond the burning of her dark
eyes. "It's an old illness you suffer from, Mr. Smiley," she continued, taking a cigarette from the box; "and I have seen many
victims of it. The mind becomes separated from the body; it
thinks without reality, rules a paper kingdom and devises
without emotion the ruin of its paper victims. But sometimes

the division between your world and ours is incomplete; the files grow heads and arms and legs, and that's a terrible moment, isn't it? The names have families as well as records, and human motives to explain the sad little dossiers and their make-believe sins. When that happens I am sorry for you." She paused for a moment, then continued:

"It's like the State and the People. The State is a dream too, a symbol of nothing at all, an emptiness, a mind without a body, a game played with clouds in the sky. But States make war, don't they, and imprison people? To dream in doctrines— how tidy! My husband and I have both been tidied now, haven't we?" She was looking at him steadily. Her accent was more noticeable now.

"You call yourself the State, Mr. Smiley; you have no place among real people. You dropped a bomb from the sky: don't come down here and look at the blood, or hear the scream."

She had not raised her voice, she looked above him now, and beyond.

"You seem shocked. I should be weeping, I suppose, but I've no more tears, Mr. Smiley—I'm barren; the children of my grief are dead. Thank you for coming, Mr. Smiley; you can go back, now—there's nothing you can do here."

He sat forward in his chair, his podgy hands nursing one another on his knees. He looked worried and sanctimonious, like a grocer reading the lesson. The skin of his face was white and glistened at the temples and on the upper lip. Only under his eyes was there any colour: mauve half-moons bisected by the heavy frame of his spectacles.

"Look, Mrs. Fennan; that interview was almost a formality. I think your husband enjoyed it, I think it even made him happy to get it over."

"How *can* you say that, how can you, now this . . ."

"But I tell you it's true: why, we didn't even hold the thing in a Government office—when I got there I found Fennan's office was a sort of right of way between two other rooms, so we walked out into the park and finished up at a café—scarcely an inquisition, you see. I even told him not to worry—I told him that. I just don't understand the letter—it doesn't . . ."

"It's not the letter, Mr. Smiley, that I'm thinking of. It's what he said to me."

"How do you mean?"

"He was deeply upset by the interview, he told me so. When he came back on Monday night he was desperate, almost incoherent. He collapsed in a chair and I persuaded him to go to bed. I gave him a sedative which lasted him half the night. He was still talking about it the next morning. It occupied his whole mind until his death."

The telephone was ringing upstairs. Smiley got up.

"Excuse me—that will be my office. Do you mind?"

"It's in the front bedroom, directly above us."

Smiley walked slowly upstairs in a state of complete bewilderment. What on earth should he say to Maston now?

He lifted the receiver, glancing mechanically at the number on the apparatus.

"Walliston 2944."

"Exchange here. Good morning. Your 8:30 call."

"Oh—Oh yes, thank you very much."

He rang off, grateful for the temporary respite. He glanced briefly round the bedroom. It was the Fennans' own bedroom, austere but comfortable. There were two armchairs in front of the gas fire. Smiley remembered now that Elsa Fennan had been bedridden for three years after the war. It was probably a survival from those years that they still sat in the bedroom in the evenings. The alcoves on either side of the fireplace were full of books. In the furthest corner, a typewriter on a desk. There was something intimate and touching about the arrangement, and perhaps for the first time Smiley was filled with an immediate sense of the tragedy of Fennan's death. He returned to the drawing-room.

"It was for you. Your 8:30 call from the exchange."

He was aware of a pause and glanced incuriously towards her. But she had turned away from him and was standing looking out of the window, her slender back very straight and still, her stiff, short hair dark against the morning light.

Suddenly he stared at her. Something had occurred to him which he should have realized upstairs in the bedroom, something so improbable that for a moment his brain was unable to grasp it. Mechanically he went on talking; he must get out of there, get away from the telephone and Maston's hysterical questions, get away from Elsa Fennan and her dark, restless house. Get away and think.

"I have intruded too much already, Mrs. Fennan, and I must now take your advice and return to Whitehall."

Again the cold, frail hand, the mumbled expressions of sympathy. He collected his coat from the hall and stepped out into the early sunlight. The winter sun had just appeared for a moment after the rain, and it repainted in pale, wet colours the trees and houses of Merridale Lane. The sky was still dark grey, and the world beneath it strangely luminous, giving back the sunlight it had stolen from nowhere.

He walked slowly down the gravel path, fearful of being called back.

He returned to the police station, full of disturbing thoughts. To begin with it was not Elsa Fennan who had asked the exchange for an 8:30 call that morning.

4

Coffee at the Fountain

The CID Superintendent at Walliston was a large, genial soul who measured professional competence in years of service and saw no fault in the habit. Sparrow's Inspector Mendel on the other hand was a thin, weasel-faced gentleman who spoke very rapidly out of the corner of his mouth. Smiley secretly likened him to a gamekeeper—a man who knew his territory and disliked intruders.

"I have a message from your Department, sir. You're to ring the Adviser at once." The Superintendent indicated his telephone with an enormous hand and walked out through the open door of his office. Mendel remained. Smiley looked at him owlishly for a moment, guessing his man.

"Shut the door." Mendel moved to the door and pulled it quietly to.

"I want to make an inquiry of the Walliston telephone exchange. Who's the most likely contact?"

"Assistant Supervisor normally. Supervisor's always in the clouds; Assistant Supervisor does the work."

"Someone at 15 Merridale Lane asked to be called by the exchange at 8:30 this morning. I want to know what time the request was made and who by. I want to know whether there's a standing request for a morning call, and if so let's have the details."

"Know the number?"

"Walliston 2944. Subscriber Samuel Fennan, I should think."

Mendel moved to the telephone and dialled 0. While he waited for a reply he said to Smiley: "You don't want anyone to know about this, do you?"

"No one. Not even you. There's probably nothing in it. If we start bleating about murder we'll . . ."

Mendel was through to the exchange, asking for the Assistant Supervisor.

"Walliston CID here, Superintendent's office. We have an inquiry . . . yes, of course . . . ring me back then . . . CID outside line, Walliston 2421."

He replaced the receiver and waited for the exchange to ring him. "Sensible girl," he muttered, without looking at Smiley. The telephone rang and he began speaking at once.

"We're investigating a burglary in Merridale Lane. Number 18. Just possible they used No. 15 as an observation point for a job on the opposite house. Have you got any way of finding out whether calls were originated or received on Walliston 2944 in the last twenty-four hours?"

There was a pause. Mendel put his hand over the mouthpiece and turned to Smiley with a very slight grin. Smiley suddenly liked him a good deal.

"She's asking the girls," said Mendel; "and she'll look at the dockets." He turned back to the telephone and began jotting down figures on the Superintendent's pad. He stiffened abruptly and leaned forward on the desk.

"Oh yes." His voice was casual, in contrast to his attitude; "I wonder when she asked for that?" Another pause . . . "19:55 hours . . . a man, eh? The girl's sure of that, is she? . . . Oh, I see, oh, well, that fixes that. Thanks very much indeed all the same. Well, at least we know where we stand . . . not at all, you've been very helpful . . . just a theory, that's all . . . have to think again, won't we? Well, thanks very much. Very kind, keep it under your hat . . . Cheerio." He rang off, tore the page from the pad, and put it in his pocket.

Smiley spoke quickly: "There's a beastly café down the road. I need some breakfast. Come and have a cup of coffee." The telephone was ringing; Smiley could almost feel Maston on the other end. Mendel looked at him for a moment and seemed to understand. They left it ringing and walked quickly out of the police station towards the High Street.

The Fountain Café (Proprietor Miss Gloria Adam) was all Tudor and horse brasses and local honey at sixpence more than anywhere else. Miss Adam herself dispensed the nastiest coffee south of Manchester and spoke of her customers as "My Friends." Miss Adam did not do business with friends, but simply robbed them, which somehow added to the illusion of genteel amateurism which Miss Adam was so anxious to preserve. Her origin was obscure, but she often spoke of her late father as "The Colonel." It was rumoured among those of Miss Adam's friends who had paid particularly dearly for their friendship that the colonelcy in question had been granted by the Salvation Army.

Mendel and Smiley sat at a corner table near the fire, waiting for their order. Mendel looked at Smiley oddly: "The girl remembers the call clearly; it came right at the end of her shift—7:55 last night. A request for an 8:30 call this morning. It was made by Fennan himself—the girl is positive of that."

"How?"

"Apparently this Fennan had rung the exchange on Christmas Day and the same girl was on duty. Wanted to wish them all a Happy Christmas. She was rather bucked. They had quite a chat. She's sure it was the same voice yesterday, asking for the call. 'Very cultured gentleman,' she said."

"But it doesn't make sense. He wrote a suicide letter at 10:30. What happened between 8:00 and 10:30?"

Mendel picked up a battered old briefcase. It had no lock—more like a music case, thought Smiley. He took from it a plain buff folder and handed it to Smiley. "Facsimile of the letter.

Super said to give you a copy. They're sending the original to the FO and another copy straight to Marlene Dietrich."

"Who the devil's she?"

"Sorry, sir. What we call your Adviser, sir. Pretty general in the Branch, sir. Very sorry, sir."

How beautiful, thought Smiley, how absolutely beautiful. He opened the folder and looked at the facsimile. Mendel went on talking: "First suicide letter I've ever seen that was typed. First one I've seen with the time on it, for that matter. Signature looks OK, though. Checked it at the station against a receipt he once signed for lost property. Right as rain."

The letter was typed, probably a portable. Like the anonymous denunciation; that was a portable too. This one was signed with Fennan's neat, legible signature. Beneath the printed address at the head of the page was typed the date, and beneath that the time: 10:30 P.M.

Dear Sir David,

    After some hesitation I have decided to take my life. I cannot spend my remaining years under a cloud of disloyalty and suspicion. I realize that my career is ruined, that I am the victim of paid informers.

                            Yours sincerely,
                            Samuel Fennan

Smiley read it through several times, his mouth pursed in concentration, his eyebrows raised a little as if in surprise. Mendel was asking him something:

"How d'you get on to it?"

"On to what?"

"This early call business."

"Oh, I took the call. Thought it was for me. It wasn't— it was the exchange with this thing. Even then the penny didn't drop. I assumed it was for her, you see. Went down and told her."

"Down?"

"Yes. They keep the telephone in the bedroom. It's a sort of bed-sitter, really . . . she used to be an invalid, you know, and they've left the room as it was then, I suppose. It's like a study, one end; books, typewriter, desk and so forth."

"Typewriter?"

"Yes. A portable. I imagine he did this letter on it. But you see when I took that call I'd forgotten it couldn't possibly be Mrs. Fennan who'd asked for it."

"Why not?"

"She's an insomniac—she told me. Made a sort of joke of it. I told her to get some rest and she just said: 'My body and I must put up with one another twenty hours a day. We have lived longer than most people already.' There was more of it— something about not enjoying the luxury of sleep. So why should she want a call at 8:30?"

"Why should her husband—why should anyone? It's damn nearly lunch-time. God help the Civil Service."

"Exactly. That puzzles me too. The Foreign Office admittedly starts late—ten o'clock, I think. But even then Fennan would be pushed to dress, shave, breakfast and catch the train on time if he didn't wake till 8:30. Besides, his wife could call him."

"She might have been shooting a line about not sleeping," said Mendel. "Women do, about insomnia and migraine and stuff. Makes people think they're nervous and temperamental. Cock, most of it."

Smiley shook his head: "No, she couldn't have made the call, could she? She wasn't home till 10:45. But even supposing she made a mistake about the time she got back, she couldn't have gone to the telephone without seeing her husband's body first. And you're not going to tell me that her reaction on finding her husband dead was to go upstairs and ask for an early call?"

They drank their coffee in silence for a while.

"Another thing," said Mendel.

"Yes?"

"His wife got back from the theatre at 10:45, right?"

"That's what she says."

"Did she go alone?"

"No idea."

"Bet she didn't. I'll bet she *had* to tell the truth there, and timed the letter to give herself an alibi."

Smiley's mind went back to Elsa Fennan, her anger, her submission. It seemed ridiculous to talk about her in this way. No: not Elsa Fennan. No.

"Where was the body found?" Smiley asked.

"Bottom of the stairs."

"Bottom of the stairs?"

"True. Sprawled across the hall floor. Revolver underneath him."

"And the note. Where was that?"

"Beside him on the floor."

"Anything else?"

"Yes. A mug of cocoa in the drawing-room."

"I see. Fennan decides to commit suicide. He asks the exchange to ring him at 8:30. He makes himself some cocoa and puts it in the drawing-room. He goes upstairs and types his last letter. He comes down again to shoot himself, leaving the cocoa undrunk. It all hangs together nicely."

"Yes, doesn't it. Incidentally, hadn't you better ring your office?"

He looked at Mendel equivocally. "That's the end of a beautiful friendship," he said. As he walked towards the coin box beside a door marked "Private" he heard Mendel saying: "I bet you say that to all the boys." He was actually smiling as he asked for Maston's number.

Maston wanted to see him at once.

He went back to their table. Mendel was stirring another cup of coffee as if it required all his concentration. He was eating a very large bun.

Smiley stood beside him. "I've got to go back to London."

"Well, this will put the cat among the pigeons." The weasel face turned abruptly towards him; "Or will it?" He spoke with the front of his mouth while the back of it continued to deal with the bun.

"If Fennan was murdered, no power on earth can prevent the Press from getting hold of the story," and to himself added: "I don't think Maston would like that. He'd prefer suicide."

"Still, we've got to face that, haven't we?"

Smiley paused, frowning earnestly. Already he could hear Maston deriding his suspicions, laughing them impatiently away. "I don't know," he said, "I really don't know."

Back to London, he thought, back to Maston's Ideal Home, back to the rat-race of blame. And back to the unreality of containing a human tragedy in a three-page report.

It was raining again, a warm incessant rain now, and in the short distance between the Fountain Café and the police station he got very wet. He took off his coat and threw it into the back of the car. It was a relief to be leaving Walliston—even for London. As he turned on to the main road he saw out of the corner of his eye the figure of Mendel stoically trudging along the pavement towards the station, his grey trilby shapeless and blackened by the rain. It hadn't occurred to Smiley that he might want a lift to London, and he felt ungracious. Mendel, untroubled by the niceties of the situation, opened the passenger door and got in.

"Bit of luck," he observed. "Hate trains. Cambridge Circus you going to? You can drop me Westminster way, can't you?"

They set off and Mendel produced a shabby green tobacco tin and rolled himself a cigarette. He directed it towards his mouth, changed his mind and offered it to Smiley, lighting it for him with an extraordinary lighter that threw a two-inch blue flame. "You look worried sick," said Mendel.

"I am."

There was a pause. Mendel said: "It's the devil you don't know that gets you."

They had driven another four or five miles when Smiley drew the car in to the side of the road. He turned to Mendel.

"Would you mind awfully if we drove back to Walliston?"

"Good idea. Go and ask her."

He turned the car and drove slowly back to Walliston, back to Merridale Lane. He left Mendel in the car and walked down the familiar gravel path.

She opened the door and showed him into the drawing-room without a word. She was wearing the same dress, and Smiley wondered how she had passed the time since he had left her that morning.

Had she been walking about the house or sitting motionless in the drawing-room? Or upstairs in the bedroom with the leather chairs? How did she see herself in her new widowhood? Could she take it seriously yet, was she still in that secretly elevated state which immediately follows bereavement? Still looking at herself in mirrors, trying to discern the change, the horror in her own face, and weeping when she could not?

Neither of them sat down—both instinctively avoided a repetition of that morning's meeting.

"There was one thing I felt I must ask you, Mrs. Fennan. I'm very sorry to have to bother you again."

"About the call, I expect; the early morning call from the exchange."

"Yes."

"I thought that might puzzle you. An insomniac asks for an early morning call." She was trying to speak brightly.

"Yes. It did seem odd. Do you often go to the theatre?"

"Yes. Once a fortnight. I'm a member of the Weybridge Repertory Club, you know. I try and go to everything they do. I have a seat reserved for me automatically on the first Tuesday of each run. My husband worked late on Tuesdays. He never came; he'd only go to classical theatre."

"But he liked Brecht, didn't he? He seemed very thrilled with the Berliner Ensemble performances in London."

She looked at him for a moment, and then smiled suddenly— the first time he had seen her do so. It was an enchanting smile; her whole face lit up like a child's.

Smiley had a fleeting vision of Elsa Fennan as a child—a spindly, agile tomboy like George Sand's "Petite Fadette"— half woman, half glib, lying girl. He saw her as a wheedling *Backfisch*, fighting like a cat for herself alone, and he saw her too, starved and shrunken in prison camp, ruthless in her fight for self-preservation. It was pathetic to witness in that smile the light of her early innocence, and a steeled weapon in her fight for survival.

"I'm afraid the explanation of that call is very silly," she said. "I suffer from a terrible memory—really awful. Go shopping and forget what I've come to buy, make an appointment on the telephone and forget it the moment I replace the receiver. I ask people to stay the week-end and we are out when they arrive. Occasionally, when there is something I simply have to remember, I ring the exchange and ask for a call a few minutes before the appointed time. It's like a knot in one's handkerchief, but a knot can't ring a bell at you, can it?"

Smiley peered at her. His throat felt rather dry, and he had to swallow before he spoke.

"And what was the call for this time, Mrs. Fennan?"

Again the enchanting smile: "There you are. I completely forget."

5

Maston and Candlelight

As he drove slowly back towards London Smiley ceased to be conscious of Mendel's presence.

There had been a time when the mere business of driving a car was a relief to him; when he had found in the unreality of a long, solitary journey a palliative to his troubled brain, when the fatigue of several hours' driving had allowed him to forget more sombre cares.

It was one of the subtler landmarks of middle age, perhaps, that he could no longer thus subdue his mind. It needed sterner measures now: he even tried on occasion to plan in his head a walk through a European city—to record the shops and buildings he would pass, for instance, in Berne on a walk from the Münster to the university. But despite such energetic mental exercise, the ghosts of time present would intrude and drive his dreams away. It was Ann who had robbed him of his peace, Ann who had once made the present so important and taught him the habit of reality, and when she went there was nothing.

He could not believe that Elsa Fennan had killed her husband. Her instinct was to defend, to hoard the treasures of her life, to build about herself the symbols of normal existence. There was no aggression in her, no will but the will to preserve.

But who could tell? What did Hesse write? "Strange to wander in the mist, each is alone. No tree knows his neighbour. Each is alone." We know nothing of one another, nothing, Smiley mused. However closely we live together, at whatever time of day or night we sound the deepest thoughts in one another, we know nothing. How am I judging Elsa Fennan? I think I understand her suffering and her frightened lies, but what do I know of her? Nothing.

Mendel was pointing at a sign-post.

". . . That's where I live. Mitcham. Not a bad spot really. Got sick of bachelor quarters. Bought a decent little semi-detached down here. For my retirement."

"Retirement? That's a long way off."

"Yes. Three days. That's why I got this job. Nothing to it; no complications. Give it to old Mendel; he'll muck it up."

"Well, well. I expect we shall both be out of a job by Monday."

He drove Mendel to Scotland Yard and went on to Cambridge Circus.

He realized as he walked into the building that everyone knew. It was the way they looked; some shade of difference in their glance, their attitude. He made straight for Maston's room. Maston's secretary was at her desk and she looked up quickly as he entered.

"Adviser in?"

"Yes. He's expecting you. He's alone. I should knock and go in." But Maston had opened the door and was already calling him. He was wearing a black coat and pinstripe trousers. Here goes the cabaret, thought Smiley.

"I've been trying to get in touch with you. Did you not receive my message?" said Maston.

"I did, but I couldn't possibly have spoken to you."

"I don't quite follow?"

"Well, I don't believe Fennan committed suicide—I think he was murdered. I couldn't say that on the telephone."

Maston took off his spectacles and looked at Smiley in blank astonishment.

"Murdered? Why?"

"Well, Fennan wrote his letter at 10:30 last night, if we are to accept the time on his letter as correct."

"Well?"

"Well, at 7:55 he rang up the exchange and asked to be called at 8:30 the next morning."

"How on earth do you know that?"

"I was there this morning when the exchange rang. I took the call thinking it might be from the Department."

"How can you possibly say that it was Fennan who ordered the call?"

"I had inquiries made. The girl at the exchange knew Fennan's voice well; she was sure it was he, and that he rang at 7:55 last night."

"Fennan and the girl knew each other, did they?"

"Good heavens no. They just exchanged pleasantries occasionally."

"And how do you conclude from this that he was murdered?"

"Well I asked his wife about this call . . ."

"And?"

"She lied. Said she ordered it herself. She claimed to be frightfully absent-minded—she gets the exchange to ring her occasionally, like tying a knot in a handkerchief, when she has an important appointment. And another thing—just before shooting himself he made some cocoa. He never drank it."

Maston listened in silence. At last he smiled and got up.

"We seem to be at cross-purposes," he said. "I send you down to discover why Fennan shot himself. You come back and say he didn't. We're not policemen, Smiley."

"No. I sometimes wonder what we are."

"Did you hear of anything that affects our position here—anything that explains his action at all? Anything to substantiate the suicide letter?"

Smiley hesitated before replying. He had seen it coming.

"Yes. I understood from Mrs. Fennan that her husband was

very upset after the interview." He might as well hear the whole story. "It obsessed him, he couldn't sleep after it. She had to give him a sedative. Her account of Fennan's reaction to my interview entirely substantiates the letter." He was silent for a minute, blinking rather stupidly before him. "What I am trying to say is that I don't believe her. I don't believe Fennan wrote that letter, or that he had any intention of dying." He turned to Maston. "We simply cannot dismiss the inconsistencies. Another thing," he plunged on, "I haven't had an expert comparison made but there's a similarity between the anonymous letter and Fennan's suicide note. The type looks identical. It's ridiculous, I know, but there it is. We must bring the police in—give them the facts."

"Facts?" said Maston. "What facts? Suppose she did lie—she's an odd woman by all accounts, foreign, Jewish. Heaven knows the tributaries of her mind. I'm told she suffered in the war, persecuted and so forth. She may see in you the oppressor, the inquisitor. She spots you're on to something, panics and tells you the first lie that comes into her head. Does that make her a murderess?"

"Then why did Fennan make the call? Why make himself a nightcap?"

"Who can tell?" Maston's voice was richer now, more persuasive. "If you or I, Smiley, were ever driven to that dreadful point where we were determined to destroy ourselves, who can tell what our last thoughts on earth would be? And what of Fennan? He sees his career in ruins, his life has no meaning. Is it not conceivable that he should wish, in a moment of weakness or irresolution, to hear another human voice, feel again the warmth of human contact before he dies? Fanciful, sentimental, perhaps; but not improbable in a man so overwrought, so obsessed that he takes his own life."

Smiley had to give him credit—it was a good performance and he was no match for Maston when it came to this. Abruptly he felt inside himself the rising panic of frustration beyond endurance. With panic came an uncontrollable fury with this posturing sycophant, this obscene cissy with his greying hair and his reasonable smile. Panic and fury welled up in a sudden tide, flooding his breast, suffusing his whole body. His face felt hot and red, his spectacles blurred, and tears sprang to his eyes, adding to his humiliation.

Maston went on, mercifully unaware: "You cannot expect me to suggest to the Home Secretary on this evidence that the police have reached a false conclusion; you know how tenuous our police liaison is. On the one hand we have your suspicions: that in short Fennan's behavior last night was not consistent with the intent to die. His wife has apparently lied to you. Against that we have the opinion of trained detectives, who found nothing disturbing in the circumstances of death, and we have Mrs. Fennan's statement that her husband was upset by his interview. I'm sorry, Smiley, but there it is."

There was complete silence. Smiley was slowly recovering himself, and the process left him dull and inarticulate. He peered myopically before him, his pouchy, lined face still pink, his mouth slack and stupid. Maston was waiting for him to speak, but he was tired and suddenly utterly disinterested. Without a glance at Maston he got up and walked out.

He reached his own room and sat down at the desk. Mechanically he looked through his work. His in-tray contained little— some office circulars and a personal letter addressed to G. Smiley Esq., Ministry of Defence. The handwriting was unfamiliar; he opened the envelope and read the letter.

Dear Smiley,

It is essential that I should lunch with you tomorrow at the Compleat Angler at Marlow. Please do your best to meet me there at one o'clock. There is something I have to tell you.

Yours,
Samuel Fennan

The letter was handwritten and dated the previous day, Tuesday, 3 January. It had been postmarked in Whitehall at 6:00 P.M.

He looked at it stodgily for several minutes, holding it stiffly before him and inclining his head to the left. Then he put the letter down, opened a drawer of the desk and took out a single clean sheet of paper. He wrote a brief letter of resignation to Maston, and attached Fennan's invitation with a pin. He pressed the bell for a secretary, left the letter in his out-tray and made for the lift. As usual it was stuck in the basement with the registry's tea trolley, and after a short wait he began walking downstairs. Halfway down he remembered that he had left his mackintosh and a few bits and pieces in his room. Never mind, he thought, they'll send them on.

He sat in his car in the car park, staring through the drenched windscreen.

He didn't care, he just damn well didn't care. He was surprised certainly. Surprised that he had so nearly lost control. Interviews had played a great part in Smiley's life, and he had long ago come to consider himself proof against them all: disciplinary, scholastic, medical, and religious. His secretive nature detested the purpose of all interviews, their oppressive intimacy, their inescapable reality. He remembered one deliriously happy dinner with Ann at Quaglino's when he had described to her the Chameleon-Armadillo system for beating the interviewer.

They had dined by candlelight; white skin and pearls— they were drinking brandy—Ann's eyes wide and moist, only for him; Smiley playing the lover and doing it wonderfully well; Ann loving him and thrilled by their harmony.

". . . and so I learned first to be a chameleon."

"You mean you sat there burping, you rude toad?"

"No, it's a matter of colour. Chameleons change colour."

"Of course they change colour. They sit on green leaves and go green. Did you go green, toad?"

His fingers ran lightly over the tips of hers. "Listen, minx, while I explain the Smiley Chameleon-Armadillo technique for the impertinent interviewer." Her face was very close to his and she adored him with her eyes.

"The technique is based on the theory that the interviewer, loving no one as well as himself, will be attracted by his own image. You therefore assume the exact social, temperamental, political and intellectual colour of your inquisitor."

"Pompous toad. But intelligent lover."

"Silence. Sometimes this method founders against the idiocy or ill-disposition of the inquisitor. If so, become an armadillo."

"And wear linear belts, toad?"

"No, place him in a position so incongruous that you are superior to him. I was prepared for confirmation by a retired bishop. I was his whole flock, and received on one half holiday sufficient guidance for a diocese. But by contemplating the bishop's face, and imagining that under my gaze it became covered in thick fur, I maintained the ascendancy. From then on the skill grew. I could turn him into an ape, get him stuck in sash windows, send him naked to Masonic banquets, condemn him, like the serpent, to go about on his belly . . ."

"*Wicked* lover-toad."

And so it had been. But in his recent interviews with Maston the power of detachment had left him; he was getting too involved. When Maston made the first moves, Smiley had been too tired and disgusted to compete. He supposed Elsa Fennan had killed her husband, that she had some good reason and it just did not bother him any more. The problem no longer existed; suspicion, experience, perception, common sense—for Maston these were not the organs of fact. Paper was fact, Ministers were fact, Home Secretaries were hard fact. The Department did not concern itself with the vague impressions of a single officer when they conflicted with policy.

Smiley was tired, deeply, heavily tired. He drove slowly

homewards. Dinner out tonight. Something rather special. It was only lunch-time now—he would spend the afternoon pursuing Olearius across the Russian continent on his Hansa voyage. Then dinner at Quaglino's, and a solitary toast to the successful murderer, to Elsa perhaps, in gratitude for ending the career of George Smiley with the life of Sam Fennan.

He remembered to collect his laundry in Sloane Street, and finally turned into Bywater Street, finding a parking space about three houses down from his own. He got out carrying the brown paper parcel of laundry, locked the car laboriously, and walked all round it from habit, testing the handles. A thin rain was still falling. It annoyed him that someone had parked outside his house again. Thank goodness Mrs. Chapel had closed his bedroom window, otherwise the rain would have . . .

He was suddenly alert. Something had moved in the drawing-room. A light, a shadow, a human form; something, he was certain. Was it sight or instinct? Was it the latent skill of his own tradecraft which informed him? Some fine sense or nerve, some remote faculty of perception warned him now and he heeded the warning.

Without a moment's thought he dropped his keys back into his overcoat pocket, walked up the steps to his own front door and rang the bell.

It echoed shrilly through the house. There was a moment's silence, then came to Smiley's ears the distinct sound of footsteps approaching the door, firm and confident. A scratch of the chain, a click of the Ingersoll latch and the door was opened, swiftly, cleanly.

Smiley had never seen him before. Tall, fair, handsome, thirty-five odd. A light grey suit, white shirt and silver tie— *habillé en diplomate*. German or Swede. His left hand remained nonchalantly in his jacket pocket.

Smiley peered at him apologetically:

"Good afternoon. Is Mr. Smiley in, please?"

The door was opened to its fullest extent. A tiny pause.

"Yes. Won't you come in?"

For a fraction of a second he hesitated. "No thanks. Would you please give him this?" He handed him the parcel of laundry, walked down the steps again, to his car. He knew he was still being watched. He started the car, turned and drove into Sloane Square without a glance in the direction of his house. He found a parking space in Sloane Street, pulled in and rapidly wrote in his diary seven sets of numbers. They belonged to the seven cars parked along Bywater Street.

What should he do? Stop a policeman? Whoever he was, he was probably gone by now. Besides there were other considerations. He locked the car again and crossed the road to a telephone kiosk. He rang Scotland Yard, got through to Special Branch and asked for Inspector Mendel. But it appeared that the Inspector, having reported back to the Superintendent, had discreetly anticipated the pleasures of retirement and left for Mitcham. Smiley got his address after a good deal of prevarication, and set off once more in his car, covering three sides of a square and emerging at Albert Bridge. He had a sandwich and a large whisky at a new pub overlooking the river, and a quarter of an hour later was crossing the bridge on the way to Mitcham, the rain still beating down on his inconspicuous little car. He was worried, very worried indeed.

6

Tea and Sympathy

It was still raining as he arrived. Mendel was in his garden wearing the most extraordinary hat Smiley had ever seen. It had begun life as an Anzac hat but its enormous brim hung low all the way round, so that he resembled nothing so much as a very tall mushroom. He was brooding over a tree stump, a wicked looking pick-axe poised obediently in his sinewy right hand.

He looked at Smiley sharply for a moment, then a grin slowly crossed his thin face as he extended his hand.

"Trouble," said Mendel.

"Trouble."

Smiley followed him up the path and into the house. Suburban and comfortable.

"There's no fire in the living-room—only just got back. How about a cup of tea in the kitchen?"

They went into the kitchen. Smiley was amused to notice the extreme tidiness, the almost feminine neatness of everything about him. Only the police calendar on the wall spoilt the illusion. While Mendel put a kettle on and busied himself with cups and saucers, Smiley related dispassionately what had happened in Bywater Street. When he had finished Mendel looked at him for a long time in silence.

"But why did he ask you in?"

Smiley blinked and coloured a little. "That's what I

wondered. It put me off my balance for a moment. It was lucky I had the parcel."

He took a drink of tea. "Though I don't believe he was taken in by the parcel. He may have been, but I doubt it. I doubt it very much."

"Not taken in?"

"Well, I wouldn't have been. Little man in a Ford delivering parcels of linen. Who could I have been? Besides, I asked for Smiley and then didn't want to see him—he must have thought that was pretty queer."

"But what was he after? What would he have done with you? Who did he think you were?"

"That's just the point, that's just it, you see. I think it was me he was waiting for, but of course he didn't expect me to ring the bell. I put him off balance. I think he wanted to kill me. That's why he asked me in: he recognized me but only just, probably from a photograph."

Mendel looked at him in silence for a while.

"Christ," he said.

"Suppose I'm right," Smiley continued, "all the way. Suppose Fennan *was* murdered last night and I *did* nearly follow him this morning. Well, unlike your trade, mine doesn't normally run to a murder a day."

"Meaning what?"

"I don't know. I just don't know. Perhaps before we go much further you'd check on these cars for me. They were parked in Bywater Street this morning."

"Why not do it yourself?"

Smiley looked at him, puzzled, for a second. Then it dawned on him that he hadn't mentioned his resignation.

"Sorry. I didn't tell you, did I? I resigned this morning. Just managed to get it in before I was sacked. So I'm free as air. And about as employable."

Mendel took the list of numbers from him and went into the hall to telephone. He returned a couple of minutes later.

"They'll ring back in an hour," he said. "Come on. I'll show you round the estate. Know anything about bees, do you?"

"Well, a very little, yes. I got bitten with the natural history bug at Oxford." He was going to tell Mendel how he had wrestled with Goethe's metamorphoses of plants and animals in the hope of discovering, like Faust, "what sustains the world at its inmost point." He wanted to explain why it was impossible to understand nineteenth-century Europe without a working knowledge of the naturalistic sciences, he felt earnest and full of important thoughts, and knew secretly that this was because his brain was wrestling with the day's events, that he was in a state of nervous excitement. The palms of his hands were moist.

Mendel led him out of the back door: three neat beehives stood against the low brick wall which ran along the end of the garden. Mendel spoke as they stood in the fine rain.

"Always wanted to keep them, see what it's all about. Been reading it all up—frightens me stiff, I can tell you. Odd little beggars." He nodded a couple of times in support of this statement, and Smiley looked at him again with interest. His face was thin but muscular, its expression entirely uncommunicative; his iron grey hair was cut very short and spiky. He seemed quite indifferent to the weather, and the weather to him. Smiley knew exactly the life that lay behind Mendel, had seen in policemen all over the world the same leathern skin, the same reserves of patience, bitterness, and anger. He could guess the long, fruitless hours of surveillance in every kind of weather, waiting for someone who might never come . . . or come and go too quickly. And he knew how much Mendel and the rest of them were at the mercy of personalities—capricious and bullying, nervous and changeful, occasionally wise and sympathetic. He knew how intelligent men could be broken by the stupidity of their superiors, how weeks of patient work night and day could be cast aside by such a man.

Mendel led him up the precarious path laid with broken

stone to the beehives and, still oblivious of the rain, began taking one to pieces, demonstrating and explaining. He spoke in jerks, with quite long pauses between phrases, indicating precisely and slowly with his slim fingers.

At last they went indoors again, and Mendel showed him the two downstairs rooms. The drawing-room was all flowers: flowered curtains and carpet, flowered covers on the furniture. In a small cabinet in one corner were some Toby jugs and a pair of very handsome pistols beside a cup for target shooting.

Smiley followed him upstairs. There was a smell of paraffin from the stove on the landing, and a surly bubbling from the cistern in the lavatory.

Mendel showed him his own bedroom.

"Bridal chamber. Bought the bed at a sale for a quid. Box spring mattress. Amazing what you can pick up. Carpets are ex–Queen Elizabeth. They change them every year. Bought them at a store in Watford."

Smiley stood in the doorway, somehow rather embarrassed. Mendel turned back and passed him to open the other bedroom door.

"And that's your room. If you want it." He turned to Smiley. "I wouldn't stay at your place tonight if I were you. You never know, do you? Besides, you'll sleep better here. Air's better."

Smiley began to protest.

"Up to you. You do what you like." Mendel grew surly and embarrassed. "Don't understand your job, to be honest, any more than you know police work. You do what you like. From what I've seen of you, you can look after yourself."

They went downstairs again. Mendel had lit the gas fire in the drawing-room.

"Well, at least you must let me give you dinner tonight," said Smiley.

The telephone rang in the hall. It was Mendel's secretary about the car numbers.

Mendel came back. He handed Smiley a list of seven names and addresses. Four of the seven could be discounted; the registered addresses were in Bywater Street. Three remained: a hired car from the firm of Adam Scarr and Sons of Battersea; a trade van belonging to the Severn Tile Company, Eastbourne; and the third was listed specially as the property of the Panamanian Ambassador.

"I've got a man on the Panamanian job now. There'll be no difficulty there—they've only got three cars on the Embassy strength."

"Battersea's not far," Mendel continued. "We could pop over there together. In your car."

"By all means, by all means," Smiley said quickly, "and we can go in to Kensington for dinner. I'll book a table at the Entrechat."

It was 4:00. They sat for a while talking in a rather desultory way about bees and house-keeping. Mendel quite at ease and Smiley still bothered and awkward, trying to find a way of talking, trying not to be clever. He could guess what Ann would have said about Mendel. She would have loved him, made a person of him, had a special voice and face for imitating him, would have made a story of him until he fitted into their lives and wasn't a mystery any more: "Darling, who'd have thought he could be so *cosy!* The last man I'd ever thought would tell me where to buy cheap fish. And what a darling little house—*no bother*—he must know Toby jugs are hell and he just doesn't care. I think he's a pet. Toad, do ask him to dinner. You must. Not to giggle at but to *like*." He wouldn't have asked him, of course, but Ann would be content—she'd found a way to like him. And having done so, forgotten him.

That was what Smiley wanted, really—a way to like Mendel. He was not as quick as Ann at finding one. But Ann was Ann—she practically murdered an Etonian nephew once for drinking claret with fish, but if Mendel had lit a pipe over her *crêpe Suzette*, she probably would not have noticed.

Mendel made more tea and they drank it. At about 5:15 they set off for Battersea in Smiley's car. On the way Mendel bought an evening paper. He read it with difficulty, catching the light from the street lamps. After a few minutes he spoke with sudden venom:

"Krauts. *Bloody* Krauts. God, I hate them!"

"Krauts?"

"Krauts. Huns. Jerries. Bloody Germans. Wouldn't give you sixpence for the lot of them. Carnivorous ruddy sheep. Kicking Jews about again. Us all over. Knock 'em down, set 'em up. Forgive and forget. *Why* bloody well forget, I'd like to know? Why forget theft, murder, and rape just because millions committed it? Christ, one poor little sod of a bank clerk pinches ten bob and the whole of the Metropolitan's on to him. But Krupp and all that mob—oh no. Christ, if I was a Jew in Germany I'd . . ."

Smiley was suddenly wide awake: "What would you do? What would you do, Mendel?"

"Oh, I suppose I'd sit down under it. It's statistics now, politics. It isn't sense to give them H-bombs so it's politics. And there's the Yanks—millions of ruddy Jews in America. What do they do? Damn all: give the Krauts more bombs. All chums together—blow each other up."

Mendel was trembling with rage, and Smiley was silent for a while, thinking of Elsa Fennan.

"What's the answer?" he asked, just for something to say.

"Christ knows," said Mendel savagely.

They turned into Battersea Bridge Road and drew up beside a constable standing on the pavement. Mendel showed his police card.

"Scarr's garage? Well it isn't hardly a garage, sir, just a yard. Scrap metal he handles mostly, and secondhand cars. If they won't do for one they'll do for the other, that's what Adam says. You want to go down Prince of Wales Drive till you come to the hospital. It's tucked in there between a couple of pre-fabs. Bomb site it is really. Old Adam straightened it out with some cinders and no one's ever moved him."

"You seem to know a lot about him," said Mendel.

"I should do, I've run him in a few times. There's not much in the book that Adam hasn't been up to. He's one of our hardy perennials, Scarr is."

"Well, well. Anything on him at present?"

"Couldn't say, sir. But you can have him any time for illegal betting. And Adam's practically under the Act already."

They drove towards Battersea Hospital. The park on their right looked black and hostile behind the street lamps.

"What's under the Act?" asked Smiley.

"Oh, he's only joking. It means your record's so long you're eligible for Preventive Detention—years of it. He sounds like my type," Mendel continued. "Leave him to me."

They found the yard as the constable had described, between two dilapidated pre-fabs in an uncertain row of hutments erected on the bomb site. Rubble, clinker, and refuse lay everywhere. Bits of asbestos, timber, and old iron, presumably acquired by Mr. Scarr for resale or adaptation, were piled in a corner, dimly lit by the pale glow which came from the farther pre-fab. The two men looked round them in silence for a moment. Then Mendel shrugged, put two fingers in his mouth and whistled shrilly.

"Scarr!" he called. Silence. The outside light on the far pre-fab went on, and three or four pre-war cars in various stages of dilapidation became dimly discernible.

The door opened slowly and a girl of about twelve stood on the threshold.

"Your dad in, dear?" asked Mendel.

"Nope. Gone to the Prod, I 'spect."

"Righto, dear. Thanks."

They walked back to the road.

"What on earth's the Prod, or daren't I ask?" said Smiley.

"Prodigal's Calf. Pub round the corner. We can walk it—only a hundred yards. Leave the car here."

It was only just after opening time. The public bar was empty, and as they waited for the landlord to appear the door swung open and a very fat man in a black suit came in. He walked straight to the bar and hammered on it with a half-crown.

"Wilf," he shouted. "Take your finger out, you got customers, you lucky boy." He turned to Smiley; "Good evening, friend."

From the rear of the pub a voice replied: "Tell 'em to leave their money on the counter and come back later."

The fat man looked at Mendel and Smiley blankly for a moment, then suddenly let out a peal of laughter: "Not them, Wilf—they're busies!" The joke appealed to him so much that he was finally compelled to sit on the bench that ran along the side of the room, with his hands on his knees, his huge shoulders heaving with laughter, the tears running down his cheeks. Occasionally he said "Oh dear, oh dear," as he caught his breath before another outburst.

Smiley looked at him with interest. He wore a very dirty stiff white collar with rounded edges, a flowered red tie carefully pinned outside the black waistcoat, army boots and a shiny black suit, very threadbare and without a vestige of a crease in the trousers. His shirt cuffs were black with sweat, grime, and motor oil and held in place by paper-clips twisted into a knot.

The landlord appeared and took their orders. The stranger bought a large whisky and ginger wine and took it at once to the saloon bar, where there was a coal fire. The landlord watched with disapproval.

"That's him all over, mean sod. Won't pay saloon prices, but likes the fire."

"Who is he?" asked Mendel.

"Him? Scarr, his name is. Adam Scarr. Christ knows why Adam. See him in the Garden of Eden: bloody grotesque, that's what it is. They say round here that if Eve gave him an apple he'd eat the ruddy core." The landlord sucked his teeth and shook his head. Then he shouted to Scarr. "Still, you're good for business, aren't you, Adam? They come bloody miles to see you, don't they? Teenage monster from outer space, that's what you are. Come and see. Adam Scarr: one look and you'll sign the pledge."

More hilarious laughter. Mendel leant over to Smiley. "You go and wait in the car—you're better out of this. Got a fiver?"

Smiley gave him five pounds from his wallet, nodded his agreement and walked out. He could imagine nothing more frightful than dealing with Scarr.

"You Scarr?" said Mendel.

"Friend, you are correct."

"TRX 0891. That your car?"

Mr. Scarr frowned at his whisky and ginger. The question seemed to sadden him.

"Well?" said Mendel.

"She was, squire, she was."

"What the hell do you mean?"

Scarr raised his right hand a few inches then let it gently fall. "Dark waters, squire, murky waters."

"Listen, I've got bigger fish to fry than ever you dreamed of. I'm not made of glass, see? I couldn't care bloody less about your racket. Where's that car?"

Scarr appeared to consider this speech on its merits. "I see the light, friend. You wish for information."

"Of course I bloody well do."

"These are hard times, squire. The cost of living, dear boy, is a rising star. Information is an item, a saleable item, is it not?"

"You tell me who hired that car and you won't starve."

"I don't starve now, friend. I want to eat better."

"A fiver."

Scarr finished his drink and replaced his glass noisily on the table. Mendel got up and bought him another.

"It was pinched," said Scarr. "I had it a few years for self-drive, see. For the deepo."

"The *what?*"

"The deepo—the deposit. Bloke wants a car for a day. You take twenty quid deposit in notes, right? When he comes back he owes you forty bob, see? You give him a cheque for thirty-eight quid, show it on your books as a loss and the job's worth a tenner. Got it?"

Mendel nodded.

"Well, three weeks ago a bloke come in. Tall Scotsman. Well-to-do, he was. Carried a stick. He paid the deepo, took the car, and I never see him nor the car again. Robbery."

"Why not report it to the police?"

Scarr paused and drank from his glass. He looked at Mendel sadly.

"Many factors would argue against, squire."

"Meaning you'd pinched it yourself?"

Scarr looked shocked. "I have since heard distressing rumours about the party from which I obtained the vehicle. I will say no more," he added piously.

"When you rented him the car he filled in forms, didn't he? Insurance, receipt, and so on? Where are they?"

"False, all false. He gave me an address in Ealing. I went there and it didn't exist. I have no doubt the name was also fictitious."

Mendel screwed the money into a roll in his pocket, and handed it across the table to Scarr. Scarr unfolded it and, quite unselfconscious, counted it in full view of anyone who cared to look.

"I know where to find you," said Mendel; "and I know a few things about you. If that's a load of cock you've sold me I'll break your bloody neck."

*   *   *

It was raining again and Smiley wished he had brought a hat. He crossed the road, entered the side street which accommodated Mr. Scarr's establishment and walked towards the car. There was no one in the street, and it was oddly quiet. Two hundred yards down the road Battersea General Hospital, small and neat, shed multiple beams of light from its uncurtained windows. The pavement was very wet and the echo of his own footsteps was crisp and startling.

He drew level with the first of the two pre-fabs which bordered Scarr's yard. A car was parked in the yard with its sidelights on. Curious, Smiley turned off the street and walked towards it. It was an old MG saloon, green probably, or that brown they went in for before the war. The numberplate was barely lit, and caked in mud. He stopped to read it, tracing the letters with his forefinger: TRX 0891. Of course—that was one of the numbers he had written down this morning.

He heard a footstep behind him and stood up, half turning. He had begun to raise his arm as the blow fell.

It was a terrible blow—it seemed to split his skull in two. As he fell he could feel the warm blood running freely over his left ear. Not again, oh Christ, not again, thought Smiley. But he hardly felt the rest—just a vision of his own body, far away, being slowly broken like rock; cracked and split into fragments, then nothing. Nothing but the warmth of his own blood as it ran over his face into the cinders, and far away the beating of the stonebreakers. But not here. Far away.

7

Mr. Scarr's Story

Mendel looked at him and wondered whether he was dead. He emptied the pockets of his own overcoat and laid it gently over Smiley's shoulders, then he ran, ran like a madman towards the hospital, crashed through the swing-doors of the out-patients' department into the bright, twenty-four-hour interior of the hospital. A young coloured doctor was on duty. Mendel showed him his card, shouted something to him, took him by the arm, tried to lead him down the road. The doctor smiled patiently, shook his head and telephoned for an ambulance.

Mendel ran back down the road and waited. A few minutes later the ambulance arrived and skilful men gathered Smiley up and took him away.

"Bury him," thought Mendel; "I'll make the bastard pay."

He stood there for a moment, staring down at the wet patch of mud and cinders where Smiley had fallen; the red glow of the car's rear lights showed him nothing. The ground had been hopelessly churned by the feet of the ambulance men and a few inhabitants from the pre-fabs who had come and gone like shadowy vultures. Trouble was about. They didn't like trouble.

"Bastard," Mendel hissed, and walked slowly back towards the pub.

The saloon bar was filling up. Scarr was ordering another drink. Mendel took him by the arm. Scarr turned and said:

"Hello, friend, back again. Have a little of what killed Auntie."

"Shut up," said Mendel; "I want another word with you. Come outside."

Mr. Scarr shook his head and sucked his teeth sympathetically.

"Can't be done, friend, can't be done. Company." He indicated with his head an eighteen-year-old blonde with off-white lipstick and an improbable bosom, who sat quite motionless at a corner table. Her painted eyes had a permanently startled look.

"Listen," whispered Mendel; "in just two seconds I'll tear your bloody ears off, you lying sod."

Scarr consigned his drinks to the care of the landlord and made a slow, dignified exit. He didn't look at the girl.

Mendel led him across the street towards the pre-fabs. The sidelights of Smiley's car shone towards them eighty yards down the road.

They turned into the yard. The MG was still there. Mendel had Scarr firmly by the arm, ready if necessary to force the forearm back and upwards, breaking or dislocating the shoulder joint.

"Well, well," cried Scarr with apparent delight. "She's returned to the bosom of her ancestors."

"Stolen, was it?" said Mendel. "Stolen by a tall Scotsman with a walking stick and an address in Ealing. Decent of him to bring it back, wasn't it? Friendly gesture, after all this time. You've mistaken your bloody market, Scarr." Mendel was shaking with anger. "And why are the sidelights on? Open the door."

Scarr turned to Mendel in the dark, his free hand slapping his pockets in search of keys. He extracted a bunch of three or four, felt through them and finally unlocked the car door.

Mendel got in, found the passenger light in the roof and switched it on. He began methodically to search the inside of the car. Scarr stood outside and waited.

He searched quickly but thoroughly. Glove tray, seats, floor, rear window-ledge: nothing. He slipped his hand inside the map pocket on the passenger door, and drew out a map and an envelope. The envelope was long and flat, grey-blue in colour with a linen finish. Continental, thought Mendel. There was no writing on it. He tore it open. There were ten used five-pound notes inside and a piece of plain postcard. Mendel held it to the light and read the message printed on it with a ball-point pen:

FINISHED NOW. SELL IT.

There was no signature.

He got out of the car, and seized Scarr by the elbows. Scarr stepped back quickly. "What's your problem, friend?" he asked.

Mendel spoke softly. "It's not my problem, Scarr, it's yours. The biggest bloody problem you ever had. Conspiracy to murder, attempted murder, offences under the Official Secrets Act. And you can add to that contravention of the Road Traffic Act, conspiracy to defraud the Inland Revenue, and about fifteen other charges that will occur to me while you nurse your problem on a cell bed."

"Just a minute, copper, let's not go over the moon. What's the story? Who the hell's talking about murder?"

"Listen, Scarr, you're a little man, come in on the fringe of the big spenders, aren't you? Well now you're the big spender. I reckon it'll cost you fifteen years."

"Look, shut up, will you."

"No I won't, little man. You're caught between two big ones, see, and you're the mug. And what will I do? I'll bloody well laugh myself sick while you rot in the Scrubs and contemplate your fat belly. See that hospital, do you? There's a bloke dying there, murdered by your tall Scotsman. They found him half an hour ago bleeding like a pig in your yard. There's another one dead in Surrey, and for all I know there's one in every bloody home county. So it's your problem, you poor sod, not mine. Another thing—you're the only one who knows who he is, aren't you? He might want to tidy that up a bit, mightn't he?"

Scarr walked slowly round to the other side of the car.

Mendel sat in the driving seat and unlocked the passenger door from the inside. Scarr sat himself beside him. They didn't put the light on.

"I'm in a nice way of business round here," said Scarr quietly, "and the pickings is small but regular. Or was till this bloke come along."

"What bloke?"

"Bit by bit, copper, don't rush me. That was four years ago. I didn't believe in Father Christmas till I met him. Dutch, he said he was, in the diamond business. I'm not pretending I thought he was straight, see, because you're not barmy and nor am I. I never asked what he done and he never told me, but I guessed it was smuggling. Money to burn he had, came off him like leaves in autumn. 'Scarr,' he said; 'you're a man of business. I don't like publicity, never did, and I hears we're birds of a feather. I want a car. Not to keep, but to borrow.' He didn't put it quite like that because of the lingo, but that's the sense of it. 'What's your proposition?' I says. 'Let's have a proposition.'

"'Well,' he says; 'I'm shy. I want a car that no one can ever get on to, supposing I had an accident. Buy a car for me, Scarr, a nice old car with something under the bonnet. Buy it in your own name,' he says, 'and keep it wrapped up for me. There's five hundred quid for a start, and twenty quid a month for garaging. And there's a bonus, Scarr, for every day I take it out. But I'm shy, see, and you don't know me. That's what the money's for,' he says. 'It's for not knowing me.'

"I'll never forget that day. Raining cats and dogs it was, and me bent over an old taxi I'd got off a bloke in Wandsworth. I owed a bookie forty quid, and the coppers were sensitive about a car I'd bought on the never never and flogged in Clapham."

Mr. Scarr drew breath, and let it out again with an air of comic resignation.

"And there he was, standing over me like my own conscience, showering old singles on me like used tote tickets."

"What did he look like?" asked Mendel.

"Quite young he was. Tall, fair chap. But cool—cool as charity. I never saw him after that day. He sent me letters posted in London and typed on plain paper. Just 'Be ready Monday night,' 'Be ready Thursday night,' and so on. We had it all arranged. I left the car out in the yard, full of petrol and teed up. He never said when he'd be back. Just ran it in about closing time or later, leaving the lights on and the doors locked. He'd put a couple of quid in the map pocket for each day he'd been away.'

"What happened if anything went wrong, if you got pinched for something else?"

"We had a telephone number. He told me to ring and ask for a name."

"What name?"

"He told me to choose one. I chose Blondie. He didn't think that was very funny but we stuck to it. Primrose 0098."

"Did you ever use it?"

"Yes, a couple of years ago I took a bint to Margate for ten days. I thought I'd better let him know. A girl answered the phone—Dutch too, by the sound of her. She said Blondie was in Holland, and she'd take a message. But after that I didn't bother."

"Why not?"

"I began to notice, see. He came regular once a fortnight, the first and third Tuesdays except January and February. This was the first January he come. He brought the car back

Thursday usually. Odd him coming back tonight. But this is the end of him, isn't it?" Scarr held in his enormous hand the piece of postcard he had taken from Mendel.

"Did he miss at all? Away long periods?"

"Winters he kept away more. January he never come, nor February. Like I said."

Mendel still had the £50 in his hand. He tossed them into Scarr's lap.

"Don't think you're lucky. I wouldn't be in your shoes for ten times that lot. I'll be back."

Mr. Scarr seemed worried.

"I wouldn't have peached," he said; "but I don't want to be mixed up in nothing, see. Not if the old country's going to suffer, eh, squire?"

"Oh, shut up," said Mendel. He was tired. He took the postcard back, got out of the car and walked away towards the hospital.

There was no news at the hospital. Smiley was still unconscious. The CID had been informed. Mendel would do better to leave his name and address and go home. The hospital would telephone as soon as they had any news. After a good deal of argument Mendel obtained from the sister the key to Smiley's car.

Mitcham, he decided, was a lousy place to live.

8

Reflections in a Hospital Ward

He hated the bed as a drowning man hates the sea. He hated the sheets that imprisoned him so that he could move neither hand nor foot.

And he hated the room because it frightened him. There was a trolley by the door with instruments on it, scissors, bandages, and bottles, strange objects that carried the terror of the unknown, swathed in white linen for the last Communion. There were jugs, tall ones half covered with napkins, standing like white eagles waiting to tear at his entrails, little glass ones with rubber tubing coiled inside them like snakes. He hated everything, and he was afraid. He was hot and the sweat ran off him, he was cold and the sweat held him, trickling over his ribs like cold blood. Night and day alternated without recognition from Smiley. He fought a relentless battle against sleep, for when he closed his eyes they seemed to turn inwards on the chaos of his brain; and when sometimes by sheer weight his eyelids drew themselves together he would summon all his strength to tear them apart and stare again at the pale light wavering somewhere above him.

Then came a blessed day when someone must have drawn the blinds and let in the grey winter light. He heard the sound of traffic outside and knew at last that he would live.

So the problem of dying once more became an academic one—a debt he would postpone until he was rich and could pay in his own way. It was a luxurious feeling, almost of purity. His mind was wonderfully lucid, ranging like Prometheus over his whole world; where had he heard that: "the mind becomes separated from the body, rules a paper kingdom . . ."? He was bored by the light above him, and wished there was more to look at. He was bored by the grapes, the smell of honeycomb and flowers, the chocolates. He wanted books, and literary journals; how could he keep up with his reading if they gave him no books? There was so little research done on his period as it was, so little creative criticism on the seventeenth century.

It was three weeks before Mendel was allowed to see him. He walked in holding a new hat and carrying a book about bees. He put his hat on the end of the bed and the book on the bedside table. He was grinning.

"I bought you a book," he said; "about bees. They're clever little beggars. Might interest you."

He sat on the edge of the bed. "I got a new hat. Daft really. Celebrate my retirement."

"Oh yes, I forgot. You're on the shelf too." They both laughed, and were silent again.

Smiley blinked. "I'm afraid you're not very distinct at the moment. I'm not allowed to wear my old glasses. They're getting me some new ones." He paused. "You don't know who did this to me, do you?"

"May do. Depends. Got a lead, I think. I don't know enough, that's the trouble. About your job, I mean. Does the East German Steel Mission mean anything to you?"

"Yes, I think so. It came here four years ago to try and get a foot in the Board of Trade."

Mendel gave an account of his transactions with Mr. Scarr. ". . . Said he was Dutch. The only way Scarr had of getting in touch with him was by ringing a Primrose telephone number. I checked the subscriber. Listed as the East German Steel Mission, in Belsize Park. I sent a bloke to sniff round. They've cleared out. Nothing there at all, no furniture, nothing. Just the telephone, and that's been ripped out of its socket."

"When did they go?"

"The third of January. Same day as Fennan was murdered." He looked at Smiley quizzically. Smiley thought for a minute and said:

"Get hold of Peter Guillam at the Ministry of Defence and bring him here tomorrow. By the scruff of the neck."

Mendel picked up his hat and walked to the door.

"Good-bye," said Smiley; "thank you for the book."

"See you tomorrow," said Mendel, and left.

Smiley lay back in bed. His head was aching. Damn, he thought, I never thanked him for the honey. It had come from Fortnums, too.

Why the early morning call? That was what puzzled him more than anything. It was silly, really, Smiley supposed, but of all the unaccountables in the case, that worried him most.

Elsa Fennan's explanation had been so stupid, so noticeably unlikely. Ann, yes; she would make the exchange stand on its head if she'd felt like it, but not Elsa Fennan. There was nothing in that alert, intelligent little face, nothing in her total independence to support the ludicrous claim to absent-mindedness. She could have said the exchange had made a mistake, had called the wrong day, anything. Fennan, yes; he had been absent-minded. It was one of the odd inconsistencies about Fennan's character which had emerged in the inquiries before the interview. A voracious reader of Westerns and a passionate chess player, a musician and a spare-time philosopher, a deep thinking man—but absent-minded. There had been a frightful row once about him taking some secret papers out of the Foreign Office, and it turned out that he had put them in his despatch case with his *Times* and the evening paper before going home to Walliston.

Had Elsa Fennan, in her panic, taken upon herself the mantle of her husband? Or the *motive* of her husband? Had Fennan asked for the call to remind *him* of something, and had Elsa borrowed the motive? Then what did Fennan need to be reminded of—and what did his wife so strenuously wish to conceal?

Samuel Fennan. The new world and the old met in him. The eternal Jew, cultured, cosmopolitan, self-determinate, industrious and perceptive: to Smiley, immensely attractive. The child of his century; persecuted, like Elsa, and driven from his adopted Germany to university in England. By the sheer weight of his ability he had pushed aside disadvantage and prejudice, finally to enter the Foreign Office. It had been a remarkable achievement, owed to nothing but his own brilliance. And if he was a little conceited, a little disinclined to bide the decision of minds more pedestrian than his own, who could blame him? There had been some embarrassment when Fennan pronounced himself in favour of a divided Germany, but it had all blown over, he had been transferred to an Asian desk, and the affair was forgotten. For the rest, he had been generous to a fault, and popular both in Whitehall and in Surrey, where he devoted several hours each week-end to charity work. His great love was skiing. Every year he took all his leave at once and spent six weeks in Switzerland or Austria. He had visited Germany only once, Smiley remembered—with his wife about four years ago.

It had been natural enough that Fennan should join the Left at Oxford. It was the great honeymoon period of university Communism, and its causes, heaven knows, lay close enough to his heart. The rise of Fascism in Germany and Italy, the Japanese invasion of Manchuria, the Franco rebellion in Spain, the slump in America, and above all the wave of anti-Semitism that was sweeping across Europe: it was inevitable that Fennan should seek an outlet for his anger and revulsion. Besides, the Party was respectable then; the failure of the Labour Party and the Coalition Government had convinced many intellectuals that the Communists alone could provide an effective alternative to Capitalism and Fascism. There was the excitement, an air of conspiracy and comradeship which must have appealed to the flamboyance in Fennan's character and given him comfort in his loneliness. There was talk of going to Spain; some *had* gone, like Cornford from Cambridge, never to return.

Smiley could imagine Fennan in those days—volatile and earnest, no doubt bringing to his companions the experience of real suffering, a veteran among cadets. His parents had died—his father had been a banker with the foresight to keep a small account in Switzerland. There had not been much, but enough to see him through Oxford, and protect him from the cold wind of poverty.

Smiley remembered so well that interview with Fennan; one among many, yet different. Different because of the language. Fennan was so articulate, so quick, so sure. "Their greatest day," he had said, "was when the miners came. They came from the Rhondda, you know, and to the comrades it seemed the spirit of Freedom had come down with them from the hills. It was a hunger march. It never seemed to occur to the Group that the marchers might actually *be* hungry, but it occurred to me. We hired a truck and the girls made stew— tons of it. We got the meat cheap from a sympathetic butcher in the market. We drove the truck out to meet them. They ate the stew and marched on. They didn't like us really, you know, didn't trust us." He laughed. "They were so small—that's what I remember best—small and dark like elves. We hoped they'd sing and they did. But not for us—for themselves. That was the first time I had met Welshmen.

"It made me understand my own race better, I think—I'm a Jew, you know."

Smiley had nodded.

"They didn't know what to do when the Welshmen had gone. What do you do when a dream has come true? They realized then why the Party didn't much care about intellectuals. I think they felt cheap, mostly, and ashamed. Ashamed of their beds and their rooms, their full bellies and their clever essays. Ashamed of their talents and their humour. They were always saying how Keir Hardie taught himself shorthand with a piece of chalk on the coal face, you know. They were ashamed of having pencils and paper. But it's no good just throwing them away, is it? That's what I learnt in the end. That's why I left the Party, I suppose."

Smiley wanted to ask him how Fennan himself had felt, but Fennan was talking again. He had shared nothing with them, he had come to realize that. They were not men, but children, who dreamed of freedom-fires, gipsy music, and one world tomorrow, who rode on white horses across the Bay of Biscay or with a child's pleasure bought beer for starving elves from Wales; children who had no power to resist the Eastern sun, and obediently turned their tousled heads towards it. They loved each other and believed they loved mankind, they fought each other and believed they fought the world.

Soon he found them comic and touching. To him, they might as well have knitted socks for soldiers. The disproportion between the dream and reality drove him to a close examination of both; he put all his energy into philosophical and historical reading, and found, to his surprise, comfort and peace in the intellectual purity of Marxism. He feasted on its intellectual ruthlessness, was thrilled by its fearlessness, its academic reversal of traditional values. In the end it was this and not the Party that gave him strength in his solitude, a philosophy which exacted total sacrifice to an unassailable formula, which humiliated and inspired him; and when he finally found success, prosperity, and integration, he turned his back sadly upon it as a treasure he had outgrown and must leave at Oxford with the days of his youth.

This was how Fennan had described it and Smiley had understood. It was scarcely the story of anger and resentment that Smiley had come to expect in such interviews, but (perhaps because of that) it seemed more real. There was another thing about that interview: Smiley's conviction that Fennan had left something important unsaid.

Was there any *factual* connection between the incident in Bywater Street and Fennan's death? Smiley reproached himself for being carried away. Seen in perspective, there was nothing but the sequence of events to suggest that Fennan and Smiley were part of a single problem.

The sequence of events, that is, and the weight of Smiley's intuition, experience or what you will—the extra sense that had told him to ring the bell and not use his key, the sense that did not, however, warn him that a murderer stood in the night with a piece of lead piping.

The interview had been informal, that was true. The walk in the park reminded him more of Oxford than of Whitehall. The walk in the park, the café in Millbank—yes, there had been a procedural difference too, but what did it amount to? An official of the Foreign Office walking in the park, talking earnestly with an anonymous little man . . . Unless the little man was *not* anonymous!

Smiley took a paper-back book and began to write in pencil on the fly-leaf:

"Let us assume what is by no means proven: that the murder of Fennan and the attempted murder of Smiley are related. What circumstances connected Smiley with Fennan *before* Fennan's death?

1. Before the interview on Monday, 2 January, I had never met Fennan. I read his file at the Department and I had certain preliminary inquiries made.

2. On 2 January I went alone to the Foreign Office by taxi. The FO arranged the interview, but did not, repeat not, know in advance who would conduct it. Fennan therefore had no prior knowledge of my identity, nor had anyone else outside the Department.

3. The interview fell into two parts; the first at the FO, when people wandered through the room and took no notice of us at all, the second outside when anyone could have seen us.

What followed? Nothing, unless . . .

Yes, that was the only possible conclusion: unless whoever saw them together recognized not only Fennan but Smiley as well, and was violently opposed to their association.

Why? In what way was Smiley dangerous? His eyes suddenly opened very wide. Of course—in one way, in one way only—*as a security officer.*

He put down his pencil.

And so whoever killed Sam Fennan was anxious that he should not talk to a security officer. Someone in the Foreign Office, perhaps. But essentially someone who knew Smiley too. Someone Fennan had known at Oxford, known as a communist, someone who feared exposure, who thought that Fennan would talk, had talked already, perhaps? And if he had talked already, then of course Smiley would have to be killed—killed quickly before he could put in his report.

That would explain the murder of Fennan and the assault on Smiley. It made some sense, but not much. He had built a card-house as high as it would go, and he still had cards in his hand. What about Elsa, her lies, her complicity, her fear? What about the car and the 8:30 call? What about the anonymous letter? If the murderer was frightened of contact between

Smiley and Fennan, he would scarcely call attention to Fennan by denouncing him. Who then? Who?

He lay back and closed his eyes. His head was throbbing again. Perhaps Peter Guillam could help. He was the only hope. His head was going round. It hurt terribly.

9

Tidying Up

Mendel showed Peter Guillam into the ward, grinning hugely.

"Got him," he said.

The conversation was awkward; strained for Guillam at least, by the recollection of Smiley's abrupt resignation and the incongruity of meeting in a hospital ward. Smiley was wearing a blue bedjacket, his hair was spiky and untidy above the bandages and he still had the trace of a heavy bruise on his left temple.

After a particularly awkward pause, Smiley said: "Look, Peter, Mendel's told you what happened to me. You're the expert—what do we know about the East German Steel Mission?"

"Pure as the driven snow, dear boy, except for their sudden departure. Only about three men and a dog in the thing. They hung out in Hampstead somewhere. No one quite knew why they were here when they first came but they've done quite a decent job in the last four years."

"What are their terms of reference?"

"God knows. I think they thought when they arrived that they were going to persuade the Board of Trade to break the European steel rings, but they got the cold shoulder. Then they went in for consular stuff with the accent on machine tools and finished products, exchange of industrial and technical information and so on. Nothing to do with what they came for but rather more acceptable, I gather."

"Who were they?"

"Oh—couple of technicians—Professor Doktor someone and Doktor someone else—couple of girls and a general dogsbody."

"Who was the dogsbody?"

"Don't know. Some young diplomat to iron out the wrinkles. We have them recorded at the Department. I can send you details, I suppose."

"If you don't mind."

"No, of course not."

There was another awkward pause. Smiley said: "Photographs would be a help, Peter. Could you manage that?"

"Yes, yes, of course." Guillam looked away from Smiley in some embarrassment. "We don't know much about the East Germans, really, you know. We get odd bits here and there, but on the whole they're something of a mystery. If they operate at all they don't do it under Trade or Diplomatic cover—that's why, if you're right about this chap, it's so odd him coming from the Steel Mission."

"Oh," said Smiley flatly.

"How do they operate?" asked Mendel.

"It's hard to generalize from the very few isolated cases we do know of. My impression is that they run their agents direct from Germany with no contact between controller and agent in the operational zone."

"But that must limit them terribly," cried Smiley. "You may have to wait months before your agent can travel to a meeting place outside his own country. He may not have the necessary cover to make the journey at all."

"Well, obviously it does limit him, but their targets seem to be so insignificant. They prefer to run foreign nationals—Swedes, expatriate Poles and what not, on short-term missions, where the limitations of their technique don't matter. In exceptional cases where they have an agent resident in the target country, they work on a courier system, which corresponds to the Soviet pattern."

Smiley was listening now.

"As a matter of fact," Guillam went on, "the Americans intercepted a courier quite recently, which is where we learnt the little we do know about GDR technique."

"Such as what?"

"Oh well, never waiting at a rendezvous, never meeting at the stated time but twenty minutes before; recognition signals—all the usual conjuring tricks that give a gloss to low-grade information. They muck about with names, too. A courier may have to contact three or four agents—a controller may run as many as fifteen. They never invent cover names for themselves."

"What do you mean? Surely they must."

"They get the agent to do it for them. The agent chooses a name, any name he likes, and the controller adopts it. A gimmick really—" He stopped, looking at Mendel in surprise.

Mendel had leapt to his feet.

Guillam sat back in his chair and wondered if he were allowed to smoke. He decided reluctantly that he wasn't. He could have done with a cigarette.

"Well?" said Smiley. Mendel had described to Guillam his interview with Mr. Scarr.

"It fits," said Guillam. "Obviously it fits with what we know. But then we don't know all that much. If Blondie was a courier, it is exceptional—in my experience at least—that he should use a trade delegation as a staging post."

"You said the Mission had been here four years," said Mendel. "Blondie first came to Scarr four years ago."

No one spoke for a moment. Then Smiley said earnestly:

"Peter, it is possible, isn't it? I mean they might under certain operational conditions need to have a station over here as well as couriers."

"Well, of course, if they were on to something really big they might."

"Meaning if they had a highly placed resident agent in play?"

"Yes, roughly."

"And assuming they had such an agent, a Maclean or Fuchs, it is conceivable that they would establish a station here under trade cover with no operational function except to hold the agent's hand?"

"Yes, it's conceivable. But it's a tall order, George. What you're suggesting is that the agent is run from abroad, serviced by courier and the courier is serviced by the Mission, which is also the agent's personal guardian angel. He'd have to be some agent."

"I'm not suggesting quite that—but near enough. And I accept that the system demands a high-grade agent. Don't forget we only have Blondie's word for it that he came from abroad."

Mendel chipped in: "This agent—would he be in touch with the Mission direct?"

"Good lord, no." said Guillam. "He'd probably have an emergency procedure for getting in touch with them—a telephone code or something of the sort."

"How does that work?" asked Mendel.

"Varies. Might be on the wrong number system. You dial the number from a call box and ask to speak to George Brown. You're told George Brown doesn't live there so you apologize and ring off. The time and the rendezvous are prearranged— the emergency signal is contained in the name you ask for. Someone will be there."

"What else would the Mission do?" asked Smiley.

"Hard to say. Pay him probably. Arrange a collecting place

for reports. The controller would make all those arrangements for the agent, of course, and tell him his part of it by courier. They work on the Soviet principle a good deal, as I told you—even the smallest details are arranged by control. The people in the field are allowed very little independence."

There was another silence. Smiley looked at Guillam and then at Mendel, then blinked and said:

"Blondie didn't come to Scarr in January and February, did he?"

"No," said Mendel; "this was the first year."

"Fennan always went skiing in January and February. This was the first time in four years he'd missed."

"I wonder," said Smiley, "whether I ought to go and see Maston again."

Guillam stretched luxuriously and smiled: "You can always try. He'll be thrilled to hear you've been brained. I've a sneaking feeling he'll think Battersea's on the coast, but not to worry. Tell him you were attacked while wandering about in someone's private yard—he'll understand. Tell him about your assailant, too, George. You've never seen him, mind, and you don't know his name, but he's a courier of the East German Intelligence Service. Maston will back you up; he always does. Specially when he's got to report to the Minister."

Smiley looked at Guillam and said nothing.

"After your bang on the head, too," Guillam added; "he'll understand."

"But, Peter—"

"I know, George, I know."

"Well, let me tell you another thing. Blondie collected his car on the first Tuesday of each month."

"So?"

"Those were the nights Elsa Fennan went to the Weybridge Rep. Fennan worked late on Tuesdays, she said."

Guillam got up. "Let me dig about, George. Cheerio,

Mendel, I'll probably give you a ring tonight. I don't see what we can do now, anyway, but it would be nice to know, wouldn't it?" He reached the door. "Incidentally, where are Fennan's possessions—wallet, diary, and so forth? Stuff they found on the body?"

"Probably still at the Station," said Mendel; "until after the inquest."

Guillam stood looking at Smiley for a moment, wondering what to say.

"Anything you want, George?"

"No thanks—oh, there is one thing."

"Yes?"

"Could you get the CID off my back? They've visited me three times now and of course they've got nowhere locally. Could you make this an Intelligence matter for the time being? Be mysterious and soothing?"

"Yes, I should think so."

"I know it's difficult, Peter, because I'm not—"

"Oh, another thing just to cheer you up. I had that comparison made between Fennan's suicide note and the anonymous letter. They were done by different people on the same machine. Different pressures and spacing but identical typeface. So long, old dear. Tuck into the grapes."

Guillam closed the door behind him. They heard his footsteps echoing crisply down the bare corridor.

Mendel rolled himself a cigarette.

"Lord," said Smiley; "does nothing frighten you? Haven't you seen the Sister here?"

Mendel grinned and shook his head.

"You can only die once," he said, putting the cigarette between his thin lips. Smiley watched him light it. He produced his lighter, took the hood off it and rotated the wheel with his stained thumb, swiftly cupping both hands around it and nursing the flame towards the cigarette. There might have been a hurricane blowing.

"Well, you're the crime expert," said Smiley. "How are we doing?"

"Messy," said Mendel. "Untidy."

"Why?"

"Loose ends everywhere. No police work. Nothing checked. Like algebra."

"What's algebra got to do with it?"

"You've got to prove what *can* be proved, first. Find the constants. Did she really go to the theatre? Was she alone? Did the neighbours hear her come back? If so, what time? Was Fennan really late Tuesdays? Did his Missus go to the theatre regularly *every* fortnight like she said?"

"And the 8:30 call. Can you tidy that for me?"

"You've got that call on the brain, haven't you?"

"Yes. Of all the loose ends, that's the loosest. I brood over it, you know, and there just isn't any sense in it. I've been through his train timetable. He was a punctual man—often got to the FO before anyone else, unlocked his own cupboard. He would have caught the 8:54, the 9:08, or at worst the 9:14. The 8:54 got him in at 9:38—he liked to be at his office by a quarter to ten. He couldn't possibly want to be woken at 8:30."

"Perhaps he just liked bells," said Mendel, getting up.

"And the letters," Smiley continued. "Different typists but the same machine. Discounting the murderer two people had access to that machine: Fennan and his wife. If we accept that Fennan typed the suicide note—and he certainly signed it— we must accept that it was Elsa who typed the denunciation. Why did she do that?"

Smiley was tired out, relieved that Mendel was going.

"Off to tidy up. Find the constants."

"You'll need money," said Smiley, and offered him some from the wallet beside his bed. Mendel took it without ceremony, and left.

Smiley lay back. His head was throbbing madly, burning hot. He thought of calling the nurse and cowardice prevented him. Gradually the throbbing eased. He heard from outside the ringing of an ambulance bell as it turned off Prince of Wales Drive into the hospital yard. "Perhaps he just liked bells," he muttered, and fell asleep.

He was woken by the sound of argument in the corridor—he heard the Sister's voice raised in protest; he heard footsteps and Mendel's voice, urgent in contradiction. The door opened suddenly and someone put the light on. He blinked and sat up, glancing at his watch. It was a quarter to six. Mendel was talking to him, almost shouting. What was he trying to say? Something about Battersea Bridge . . . the river police . . . missing since yesterday . . . He was wide awake. Adam Scarr was dead.

10

The Virgin's Story

Mendel drove very well, with a kind of schoolma'amish ped-
antry that Smiley would have found comic. The Weybridge road was packed with traffic as usual. Mendel hated
motorists. Give a man a car of his own and he leaves humility
and common sense behind him in the garage. He didn't care
who it was—he'd seen bishops in purple doing seventy in a
built-up area, frightening pedestrians out of their wits. He
liked Smiley's car. He liked the fussy way it had been maintained, the sensible extras, wing mirrors and reversing light. It
was a decent little car.

He liked people who looked after things, who finished
what they began. He liked thoroughness and precision. No
skimping. Like this murderer. What had Scarr said? "Young,
mind, but cool. Cool as charity." He knew that look, and
Scarr had known it too . . . the look of complete negation
that reposes in the eyes of a young killer. Not the look of a
wild beast, not the grinning savagery of a maniac, but the
look born of supreme efficiency, tried and proven. It was a
stage beyond the experience of war. The witnessing of death in
war brings a sophistication of its own; but beyond that, far
beyond, is the conviction of supremacy in the heart of the professional killer. Yes, Mendel had seen it before: the one that
stood apart from the gang, pale eyed, expressionless, the one

the girls went after, spoke of without smiling. Yes, he was a cool one all right.

Scarr's death had frightened Mendel. He made Smiley promise not to go back to Bywater Street when he was released from the hospital. With any luck they'd think he was dead, anyway. Scarr's death proved one thing, of course: the murderer was still in England, still anxious to tidy up. "When I get up," Smiley had said last night, "we must get him out of his hole again. Put out bits of cheese." Mendel knew who the cheese would be: Smiley. Of course if they were right about the motive there would be other cheese too: Fennan's wife. In fact, Mendel thought grimly, it doesn't say much for her that she hasn't been murdered. He felt ashamed of himself and turned his mind to other things. Such as Smiley again.

Odd little beggar, Smiley was. Reminded Mendel of a fat boy he'd played football with at school. Couldn't run, couldn't kick, blind as a bat but played like hell, never satisfied till he'd got himself torn to bits. Used to box, too. Came in wide open swinging his arms about: got himself half killed before the referee stopped it. Clever bloke, too.

Mendel stopped at a roadside café for a cup of tea and a bun, then drove into Weybridge. The Repertory Theatre was in a one-way street leading off the High Street where parking was impossible. Finally he left the car at the railway station and walked back into the town.

The front doors of the theatre were locked. Mendel walked round to the side of the building under a brick archway. A green door was propped open. It had push bars on the inside and the words "stage door" scribbled in chalk. There was no bell; a faint smell of coffee issued from the dark green corridor within. Mendel stepped through the doorway and walked down the corridor, at the end of which he found a stone staircase with a metal handrail leading upwards to another green door. The smell of coffee was stronger, and he heard the sound of voices.

"Oh rot, darling, frankly. If the culture vultures of blissful

Surrey want Barrie three months running let them have it, say I. It's either Barrie or *A Cuckoo in the Nest* for the third year running and for me Barrie gets it by a short head"—this from a middle-aged female voice.

A querulous male replied: "Well, Ludo can always do Peter Pan, can't you, Ludo?"

"Bitchie, bitchie," said a third voice, also male, and Mendel opened the door.

He was standing in the wings of the stage. On his left was a piece of thick hardboard with about a dozen switches mounted on a wooden panel. An absurd rococo chair in gilt and embroidery stood beneath it for the prompter and factotum.

In the middle of the stage two men and a woman sat on barrels smoking and drinking coffee. The décor represented the deck of a ship. A mast with rigging and rope ladders occupied the centre of the stage, and a large cardboard cannon pointed disconsolately towards a backcloth of sea and sky.

The conversation stopped abruptly as Mendel appeared on the stage. Someone murmured: "My dear, the ghost at the feast," and they all looked at him and giggled.

The woman spoke first: "Are you looking for someone, dear?"

"Sorry to butt in. Wanted to talk about becoming a subscriber to the theatre. Join the club."

"Why yes, of course. How nice," she said, getting up and walking over to him. "How *very* nice." She took his left hand in both of her own and squeezed it, stepping back at the same time and extending her arms to their full length. It was her chatelaine gesture—Lady Macbeth receives Duncan. She put her head on one side and smiled girlishly, retained his hand and led him across the stage to the opposite wing. A door led into a tiny office littered with old programmes and posters, greasepaint, false hair and tawdry pieces of nautical costume.

"Have you seen our panto this year? *Treasure Island.* Such a *gratifying* success. And so much more *social content*, don't you think, than those vulgar nursery tales?"

Mendel said: "Yes, wasn't it," without the least idea of what she was talking about, when his eye caught a pile of bills rather neatly assembled and held together by a bulldog clip. The top one was made out to Mrs. Ludo Oriel and was four months overdue.

She was looking at him shrewdly through her glasses. She was small and dark, with lines on her neck and a great deal of make-up. The lines under her eyes had been levelled off with greasepaint but the effect had not lasted. She was wearing slacks and a chunky pullover liberally splashed with distemper. She smoked incessantly. Her mouth was very long, and she held her cigarette in the middle of it in a direct line beneath her nose, her lips formed an exaggerated convex curve, distorting the lower half of her face and giving her an ill-tempered and impatient look. Mendel thought she would probably be difficult and clever. It was a relief to think she couldn't pay her bills.

"You *do* want to join the club, don't you?"

"No."

She suddenly flew into a rage: "If you're another bloody tradesman you can get out. I've said I'll pay and I will, just don't pester me. If you let people think I'm finished I *will* be and you'll be the losers, not me."

"I'm not a creditor, Mrs. Oriel. I've come to offer you money."

She was waiting.

"I'm a divorce agent. Rich client. Like to ask you a few questions. We're prepared to pay for your time."

"Christ," she said with relief. "Why didn't you say so in the first place?" They both laughed. Mendel put five pounds on top of the bills, counting them down.

"Now," said Mendel; "how do you keep your club subscription list? What are the benefits of joining?"

"Well, we have watery coffee on stage every morning at

eleven sharp. Members of the club can mix with the cast during the break between rehearsals from 11:00 to 11:45. They pay for whatever they have, of course, but entry is strictly limited to club members."

"Quite."

"That's probably the part that interests you. We seem to get nothing but pansies and nymphos in the morning."

"It may be. What else goes on?"

"We put on a different show each fortnight. Members can reserve seats for a particular day of each run—the second Wednesday of each run, and so on. We always begin a run on the first and third Mondays of the month. The show begins at 7:30 and we hold the club reservations until 7:20. The girl at the box office has the seating plan and strikes off each seat as it's sold. Club reservations are marked in red and aren't sold off till last."

"I see. So if one of your members doesn't take his usual seat, it will be marked off on the seating plan."

"Only if it's sold."

"Of course."

"We're not often full after the first week. We're trying to do a show a week, you see, but it's not easy to get the—er—facilities. There isn't the support for two-week runs really."

"No, no, quite. Do you keep old seating plans?"

"Sometimes, for the accounts."

"How about Tuesday the third of January?"

She opened a cupboard and took out a sheaf of printed seating plans. "This is the second fortnight of our pantomime, of course. Tradition."

"Quite," said Mendel.

"Now who is it you're so interested in?" asked Mrs. Oriel, picking up a ledger from the desk.

"Small blonde party, aged about forty-two or three. Name of Fennan, Elsa Fennan."

Mrs. Oriel opened her ledger. Mendel quite shamelessly

looked over her shoulder. The names of club members were entered neatly in the left-hand column. A red tick on the extreme left of the page indicated that the member had paid his subscription. On the right-hand side of the page were notes of standing reservations made for the year. There were about eighty members.

"Name doesn't ring a bell. Where does she sit?"

"No idea."

"Oh yes, here we are. Merridale Lane, Walliston. Merridale!—I *ask* you. Let's look. A rear stall at the end of a row. Very odd choice, don't you think? Seat number R2. But God knows whether she took it on the third of January. I shouldn't think we've got the plan any more, though I've never thrown anything away in my life. Things just evaporate, don't they?" She looked at him out of the corner of her eye, wondering whether she'd earned her five pounds. "Tell you what, we'll ask the Virgin." She got up and walked to the door; "Fennan . . . Fennan . . ." she said. "Half a sec, that does ring a bell. I wonder why. Well I'm damned—of course—the music case." She opened the door. "Where's the Virgin?" she said, talking to someone on the stage.

"God knows."

"Helpful pig," said Mrs. Oriel, and closed the door again. She turned to Mendel: "The Virgin's our white hope. English rose, local solicitor's stage-struck daughter, all lisle stockings and get-me-if-you-can. We loathe her. She gets a part occasionally because her father pays tuition fees. She does seating in the evenings sometimes when there's a rush—she and Mrs. Torr, the cleaner, who does cloaks. When things are quiet, Mrs. Torr does the whole thing and the Virgin mopes about in the wings hoping the female lead will drop dead." She paused. "I'm damned sure I remember 'Fennan.' Damn sure I do. I wonder where that cow *is*." She disappeared for a couple of minutes and returned with a tall and rather pretty girl with fuzzy blonde hair and pink cheeks—good at tennis and swimming.

"This is Elizabeth Pidgeon. She may be able to help. Darling, we want to find out a Mrs. Fennan, a club member. Didn't you tell me something about her?"

"Oh *yes*, Ludo." She must have thought she sounded sweet. She smiled vapidly at Mendel, put her head on one side and twined her fingers together. Mendel jerked his head towards her.

"Do you know her?" asked Mrs. Oriel.

"Oh *yes*, Ludo. She's madly musical; at least I think she must be because she always brings her music. She's madly thin and odd. She's foreign, isn't she, Ludo?"

"Why odd?" asked Mendel.

"Oh, well, last time she came she got in a frightful pet about the seat next to her. It was a club reservation you see and simply hours after twenty past. We'd just started the panto season and there were millions of people wanting seats so I let it go. She kept on saying she was sure the person would come because he always did."

"Did he?" asked Mendel.

"No. I let the seat go. She must have been in an awful pet because she left after the second act, and forgot to collect her music case."

"This person she was sure would turn up," said Mendel, "is he friendly with Mrs. Fennan?"

Ludo Oriel gave Mendel a suggestive wink.

"Well, gosh, I should think *so*, he's her husband, isn't he?"

Mendel looked at her for a minute and then smiled: "Couldn't we find a chair for Elizabeth?" he said.

"Gosh, thanks," said the Virgin, and sat on the edge of an old gilt chair like the prompter's chair in the wings. She put her red, fat hands on her knees and leaned forward, smiling all the time, thrilled to be the centre of so much interest. Mrs. Oriel looked at her venomously.

"What makes you think he was her husband, Elizabeth?" There was an edge to his voice which had not been there before.

"Well, I know they arrive separately, but I thought that as

they had seats apart from the rest of the club reservations, they must be husband and wife. And of course he always brings a music case too."

"I see. What else can you remember about that evening, Elizabeth?"

"Oh, well, lots really because you see I felt awful about her leaving in such a pet and then later that night she rang up. Mrs. Fennan did, I mean. She said her name and said she'd left early and forgotten her music case. She'd lost the ticket for it, too, and was in a frightful state. It sounded as if she was crying. I heard someone's voice in the background, and then she said someone would drop in and get it if that would be all right without the ticket. I said of course, and half an hour later the man came. He's rather super. Tall and fair."

"I see," said Mendel; "thank you very much, Elizabeth, you've been very helpful."

"Gosh, that's OK." She got up.

"Incidentally," said Mendel. "This man who collected her music case—he wasn't by any chance the same man who sits beside her in the theatre, was he?"

"Rather. Gosh, sorry, I should have said that."

"Did you talk to him?"

"Well, just to say here you are, sort of thing."

"What kind of voice had he?"

"Oh, foreign, like Mrs. Fennan's—she *is* foreign, isn't she? That's what I put it down to—all her fuss and state—foreign temperament."

She smiled at Mendel, waited a moment, then walked out like Alice.

"Cow," said Mrs. Oriel, looking at the closed door. Her eyes turned to Mendel. "Well, I hope you've got your five quids' worth."

"I think so," said Mendel.

11

The Unrespectable Club

Mendel found Smiley sitting in an armchair fully dressed. Peter Guillam was stretched luxuriously on the bed, a pale green folder held casually in his hand. Outside, the sky was black and menacing.

"Enter the third murderer," said Guillam as Mendel walked in. Mendel sat down at the end of the bed and nodded happily to Smiley, who looked pale and depressed.

"Congratulations. Nice to see you on your feet."

"Thank you. I'm afraid if you did see me on my feet you wouldn't congratulate me. I feel as weak as a kitten."

"When are they letting you go?"

"I don't know when they expect me to go—"

"Haven't you asked?"

"No."

"Well, you'd better. I've got news for you. I don't know what it means but it means something."

"Well, well," said Guillam; "everyone's got news for everyone else. Isn't that exciting. George has been looking at my family snaps"—he raised the green folder a fraction of an inch—"and recognizes all his old chums."

Mendel felt baffled and rather left out of things. Smiley intervened: "I'll tell you all about it over dinner tomorrow evening. I'm getting out of here in the morning, whatever they say. I think we've found the murderer and a lot more besides.

Now let's have your news." There was no triumph in his eyes.
Only anxiety.

Membership of the club to which Smiley belonged is not
quoted among the respectable acquisitions of those who adorn
the pages of *Who's Who*. It was formed by a young renegade of
the Junior Carlton named Steed-Asprey, who had been warned
off by the Secretary for blaspheming within the hearing of a
South African bishop. He persuaded his former Oxford landlady to leave her quiet house in Hollywell and take over two
rooms and a cellar in Manchester Square which a monied relative put at his disposal. It had once had forty members who
each paid fifty guineas a year. There were thirty-one left.
There were no women and no rules, no secretary and no bishops. You could take sandwiches and buy a bottle of beer, you
could take sandwiches and buy nothing at all. As long as you
were reasonably sober and minded your own business, no one
gave twopence what you wore, did, or said, or whom you
brought with you. Mrs. Sturgeon no longer devilled at the bar,
or brought you your chop in front of the fire in the cellar, but
presided in genial comfort over the ministrations of two
retired sergeants from a small border regiment.

Naturally enough, most of the members were approximate
contemporaries of Smiley at Oxford. It had always been agreed
that the club was to serve one generation only, that it would
grow old and die with its members. The war had taken its toll
of Jebedee and others, but no one had ever suggested they
should elect new members. Besides, the premises were now
their own, Mrs. Sturgeon's future had been taken care of, and
the club was solvent.

It was a Saturday evening and only half a dozen people
were there. Smiley had ordered their meal, and a table was set
for them in the cellar, where a bright coal fire burned in a brick
hearth. They were alone, there was sirloin and claret; outside
the rain fell continuously. For all three of them the world

seemed an untroubled and decent place that night, despite the strange business that brought them together.

"To make sense of what I have to tell you," began Smiley at last, addressing himself principally to Mendel, "I shall have to talk at length about myself. I'm an intelligence officer by trade as you know—I've been in the Service since the Flood, long before we were mixed up in power politics with Whitehall. In those days we were understaffed and underpaid. After the usual training and probation in South America and Central Europe, I took a job lecturing at a German university, talent spotting for young Germans with an agent potential." He paused, smiled at Mendel and said: "Forgive the jargon." Mendel nodded solemnly and Smiley went on. He knew he was being pompous, and didn't know how to prevent himself.

"It was shortly before the last war, a terrible time in Germany then, intolerance run mad. I would have been a lunatic to approach anyone myself. My only chance was to be as nondescript as I could, politically and socially colourless, and to put forward candidates for recruitment by someone else. I tried to bring some back to England for short periods on students' tours. I made a point of having no contact at all with the Department when I came over because we hadn't any idea in those days of the efficiency of German Counter Intelligence. I never knew who was approached, and of course it was much better that way. In case I was blown, I mean.

"My story really begins in 1938. I was alone in my rooms one summer evening. It had been a beautiful day, warm and peaceful. Fascism might never have been heard of. I was working in my shirt sleeves at a desk by my window, not working very hard because it was such a wonderful evening."

He paused, embarrassed for some reason, and fussed a little with the port. Two pink spots appeared high on his cheeks. He felt slightly drunk though he had very little wine.

"To resume," he said, and felt an ass. "I'm sorry, I feel a little inarticulate . . . Anyway, as I sat there, there was a knock on the door and a young student came in. He was nineteen, in fact, but he looked younger. His name was Dieter Frey. He was a pupil of mine, an intelligent boy and remarkable to look at." Smiley paused again, staring before him. Perhaps it was his illness, his weakness, which brought the memory so vividly before him.

"Dieter was a very handsome boy, with a high forehead and a lot of unruly black hair. The lower part of his body was deformed, I think by infantile paralysis. He carried a stick and leaned heavily upon it when he walked. Naturally he cut a rather romantic figure at a small university; they thought him Byronic and so on. In fact I could never find him romantic myself. The Germans have a passion for discovering young genius, you know, from Herder to Stefan George—somebody lionized them practically from the cradle. But you couldn't lionize Dieter. There was a fierce independence, a ruthlessness about him which scared off the most determined patron. This defensiveness in Dieter derived not only from his deformity, but his race, which was Jewish. How on earth he kept his place at university I could never understand. It was possible that they didn't know he was a Jew—his beauty might have been southern, I suppose, Italian, but I don't really see how. To me he was obviously Jewish.

"Dieter was a socialist. He made no secret of his views even in those days. I once considered him for recruitment, but it seemed futile to take on anyone who was so obviously earmarked for concentration camp. Besides he was too volatile, too swift to react, too brightly painted, too vain. He led all the societies at the university—debating, political, poetry and so on. In all the athletic guilds he held honorary positions. He had the nerve not to drink in a university where you proved your manhood by being drunk most of your first year.

"That was Dieter, then: a tall, handsome, commanding cripple, the idol of his generation; a Jew. And that was the man who came to see me that hot summer evening.

"I sat him down and offered him a drink, which he refused. I made some coffee, I think, on a gas ring. We spoke in a desultory way about my last lecture on Keats. I had complained about the application of German critical methods to English poetry, and this had led to some discussion—as usual—on the Nazi interpretation of 'decadence' in art. Dieter dragged it all up again and became more and more outspoken in his condemnation of modern Germany and finally of Nazism itself. Naturally, I was guarded—I think I was less of a fool in those days than I am now. In the end he asked me point blank what I thought of the Nazis. I replied rather pointedly that I was disinclined to criticize my hosts, and that anyway I didn't think politics were much fun. I shall never forget his reply. He was furious, struggled to his feet and shouted at me: *'Von Freude ist nicht die Rede!'*—'We're not talking about fun!'" Smiley broke off and looked across the table to Guillam: "I'm sorry, Peter, I'm being rather long-winded."

"Nonsense, old dear. You tell the story in your own way." Mendel grunted his approval; he was sitting rather stiffly with both hands on the table before him. There was no light in the room now except the bright glow of the fire, which threw tall shadows on the roughcast wall behind them. The port decanter was three parts empty; Smiley gave himself a little and passed it on.

"He raved at me. He simply did not understand how I could apply an independent standard of criticism to art and remain so insensitive to politics, how I could bleat about artistic freedom when a third of Europe was in chains. Did it mean nothing to me that contemporary civilization was being bled to death? What was so sacred about the eighteenth century that I could throw the twentieth away? He had come to me because he enjoyed my seminars and thought me an enlightened man, but he now realized that I was worse than all of them.

"I let him go. What else could I do? On paper he was suspect anyway—a rebellious Jew with a university place still mysteriously free. But I watched him. The term was nearly over and the long vacation soon to begin. In the closing debate of the term three days later he was dreadfully outspoken. He really frightened people, you know, and they grew silent and apprehensive. The end of the term came and Dieter departed without a word of farewell to me. I never expected to see him again.

"It was about six months before I did. I had been visiting friends near Dresden, Dieter's home town, and I arrived half an hour early at the station. Rather than hang around on the platform I decided to go for a stroll. A couple of hundred metres from the station was a tall, rather grim seventeenth-century house. There was a small courtyard in front of it with tall iron railings and a wrought-iron gate. It had apparently been converted into a temporary prison: a group of shaven prisoners, men and women, were being exercised in the yard, walking round the perimeter. Two guards stood in the centre with tommy guns. As I watched I caught sight of a familiar fig-ure, taller than the rest, limping, struggling to keep up with them. It was Dieter. They had taken his stick away.

"When I thought about it afterwards, of course, I realized that the Gestapo would scarcely arrest the most popular mem-ber of the university while he was still up. I forgot about my train, went back into the town and looked for his parents in the telephone book. I knew his father had been a doctor so it wasn't difficult. I went to the address and only his mother was there. The father had died already in a concentration camp. She wasn't inclined to talk about Dieter, but it appeared that he had not gone to a Jewish prison but to a general one, and ostensibly for 'a period of correction' only. She expected him back in about three months. I left him a message to say I still had some books of his and would be pleased to return them if he would call on me.

"I'm afraid the events of 1939 must have got the better of me, because I don't believe I gave Dieter another thought that year. Soon after I returned from Dresden my Department ordered me back to England. I packed and left within forty-eight hours, to find London in a turmoil. I was given a new assignment which required intensive preparation, briefing, and training. I was to go back to Europe at once and activate almost untried agents in Germany who had been recruited against such an emergency. I began to memorize the dozen odd names and addresses. You can imagine my reaction when I discovered Dieter Frey among them.

"When I read his file I found he had more or less recruited himself by bursting in on the consulate in Dresden and demanding to know why no one lifted a finger to stop the persecution of the Jews." Smiley paused and laughed to himself; "Dieter was a great one for getting people to do things." He glanced quickly at Mendel and Guillam. Both had their eyes fixed on him.

"I suppose my first reaction was pique. The boy had been right under my nose and I hadn't considered him suitable—what was some ass in Dresden up to? And then I was alarmed to have this firebrand on my hands, whose impulsive temperament could cost me and others our lives. Despite the slight changes in my appearance and the new cover under which I was operating, I should obviously have to declare myself to Dieter as plain George Smiley from the university, so he could blow me sky high. It seemed a most unfortunate beginning, and I was half resolved to set up my network without Dieter. In the event I was wrong. He was a magnificent agent.

"He didn't curb his flamboyance, but used it skilfully as a kind of double bluff. His deformity kept him out of the Services and he found himself a clerical job on the railways. In no time he worked his way to a position of real responsibility and the quantity of information he obtained was fantastic. Details of troop and ammunition transports, their destination and date of transit. Later he reported on the effectiveness of our bombing, pinpointed key targets. He was a brilliant organizer

and I think that was what saved him. He did a wonderful job
on the railways, made himself indispensable, worked all hours
of the night and day; became almost inviolate. They even gave
him a civilian decoration for exceptional merit and I suppose
the Gestapo conveniently lost his file.

"Dieter had a theory that was pure Faust. Thought alone
was valueless. You must act for thought to become effective.
He used to say that the greatest mistake man ever made was to
distinguish between the mind and the body: an order does not
exist if it is not obeyed. He used to quote Kleist a great deal: 'If
all eyes were made of green glass, and if all that seems white
was really green, who would be the wiser?' Something like
that.

"As I say, Dieter was a magnificent agent. He even went so
far as to arrange for certain freights to be transported on good
flying nights for the convenience of our bombers. He had
tricks all his own—a natural genius for the nuts and bolts of
espionage. It seemed absurd to suppose it could last, but the
effect of our bombing was often so widespread that it would
have been childish to attribute it to one person's betrayal—let
alone a man so notoriously outspoken as Dieter.

"Where he was concerned my job was easy. Dieter put in a
lot of travelling as it was—he had a special pass to get him
around. Communication was child's play by comparison with
some agents. Occasionally we would actually meet and talk in
a café, or he would pick me up in a Ministry car and drive me
sixty or seventy miles along a main road, as if he were giving
me a lift. But more often we would take a journey in the
same train and swap briefcases in the corridor or go to the theatre with parcels and exchange cloakroom tickets. He seldom
gave me actual reports but just carbon copies of transit orders.
He got his secretary to do a lot—he made her keep a special
float which he 'destroyed' every three months by emptying it
into his briefcase in the lunch hour.

"Well, in 1943 I was recalled. My trade cover was rather thin by then I think, and I was getting a bit shopsoiled." He stopped and took a cigarette from Guillam's case.

"But don't let's get Dieter out of perspective," he said. "He was my best agent, but he wasn't my only one. I had a lot of headaches of my own—running him was a picnic by comparison with some. When the war was over I tried to find out from my successor what had become of Dieter and the rest of them. Some were resettled in Australia and Canada, some just drifted away to what was left of their home towns. Dieter hesitated, I gather. The Russians were in Dresden, of course, and he may have had doubts. In the end he went—he had to really, because of his mother. He hated the Americans, anyway. And of course he was a socialist.

"I heard later that he had made his career there. The administrative experience he had picked up during the war got him some Government job in the new republic. I suppose that his reputation as a rebel and the suffering of his family cleared the way for him. He must have done pretty well for himself."

"Why?" asked Mendel.

"He was over here until a month ago running the Steel Mission."

"That's not all," said Guillam quickly. "In case you think your cup is full, Mendel, I spared you another visit to Weybridge this morning and called on Elizabeth Pidgeon. It was George's idea." He turned to Smiley: "She's a sort of Moby Dick, isn't she—big white man-eating whale."

"Well?" said Mendel.

"I showed her a picture of that young diplomat by the name of Mundt they kept in tow there to pick up the bits. Elizabeth recognized him at once as the nice man who collected Elsa Fennan's music case. Isn't that jolly?"

"But—"

"I know what you're going to ask, you clever youth. You

want to know whether George recognized him too. Well,
George did. It's the same nasty fellow who tried to lure him
into his house in Bywater Street. Doesn't he get around?"

Mendel drove to Mitcham. Smiley was dead tired. It was
raining again and cold. Smiley hugged his greatcoat round
him and, despite his tiredness, watched with quiet pleasure the
busy London night go by. He had always loved travelling. Even
now, if he had the choice, he would cross France by train rather
than fly. He could still respond to the magic noises of a night
journey across Europe, the oddly cacophonous chimes and the
French voices suddenly waking him from English dreams.
Ann had loved it too and they had twice travelled overland to
share the dubious joys of that uncomfortable journey.

When they got back Smiley went straight to bed while
Mendel made some tea. They drank it in Smiley's bedroom.

"What do we do now?" asked Mendel.

"I thought I might go to Walliston tomorrow."

"You ought to spend the day in bed. What do you want to
do there?"

"See Elsa Fennan."

"You're not safe on your own. You'd better let me come. I'll
sit in the car while you do the talking. She's a Yid, isn't she?"

Smiley nodded.

"My dad was Yid. He never made such a bloody fuss
about it."

12

Dream for Sale

She opened the door and stood looking at him for a moment in silence.

"You could have let me know you were coming," she said.

"I thought it safer not to."

She was silent again. Finally she said: "I don't know what you mean." It seemed to cost her a good deal.

"May I come in?" said Smiley. "We haven't much time."

She looked old and tired, less resilient perhaps. She led him into the drawing-room and with something like resignation indicated a chair.

Smiley offered her a cigarette and took one himself. She was standing by the window. As he looked at her, watched her quick breathing, her feverish eyes, he realized that she had almost lost the power of self-defence.

When he spoke, his voice was gentle, concessive. To Elsa Fennan it must have seemed like a voice she had longed for, irresistible, offering all strength, comfort, compassion and safety. She gradually moved away from the window and her right hand, which had been pressed against the sill, trailed wistfully along it, then fell to her side in a gesture of submission. She sat opposite him, her eyes upon him in complete dependence, like the eyes of a lover.

"You must have been terribly lonely," he said. "No one can stand it for ever. It takes courage, too, and it's hard to be brave alone. They never understand that, do they? They never know what it costs—the sordid tricks of lying and deceiving, the isolation from ordinary people. They think you can run on their kind of fuel—the flag waving and the music. But you need a different kind of fuel, don't you, when you're alone? You've got to hate, and it needs strength to hate all the time. And what you must love is so remote, so vague when you're not part of it." He paused. Soon, he thought, soon you'll break. He prayed desperately that she would accept him, accept his comfort. He looked at her. Soon she would break.

"I said we hadn't much time. Do you know what I mean?"

She had folded her hands on her lap and was looking down at them. He saw the dark roots of her yellow hair and wondered why on earth she dyed it. She showed no sign of having heard his question.

"When I left you that morning a month ago I drove to my home in London. A man tried to kill me. That night he nearly succeeded—he hit me on the head three or four times. I've just come out of the hospital. As it happens I was lucky. Then there was the garage man he hired the car from. The river police recovered his body from the Thames not long ago. There were no signs of violence—he was just full of whisky. They can't understand it—he hadn't been near the river for years. But then we're dealing with a competent man, aren't we? A trained killer. It seems he's trying to remove anyone who can connect him with Samuel Fennan. Or his wife, of course. Then there's that young blonde girl at the Repertory Theatre . . ."

"What are you saying?" she whispered. "What are you trying to tell me?"

Smiley suddenly wanted to hurt her, to break the last of her will, to remove her utterly as an enemy. For so long she had haunted him as he had lain helpless, had been a mystery and a power.

"What games did you think you were playing, you two? Do

you think you can flirt with power like theirs, give a little and not give all? Do you think that *you* can stop the dance—control the strength you give them? What dreams did you cherish, Mrs. Fennan, that had so little of the world in them?"

She buried her face in her hands and he watched the tears run between her fingers. Her body shook with great sobs and her words came slowly, wrung from her.

"No, no dreams. I had no dream but him. He had one dream, yes . . . one great dream." She went on crying, helpless, and Smiley, half in triumph, half in shame, waited for her to speak again. Suddenly she raised her head and looked at him, the tears still running down her cheeks. "Look at me," she said. "What dream did they leave me? I dreamed of long golden hair and they shaved my head, I dreamed of a beautiful body and they broke it with hunger. I have seen what human beings are, how could I believe in a formula for human beings? I said to him, oh I said to him a thousand times, 'only make no laws, no fine theories, no judgements, and the people may love, but give them one theory, let them invent one slogan, and the game begins again.' I told him that. We talked whole nights away. But no, that little boy must have his dream, and if a new world was to be built, Samuel Fennan must build it. I said to him, 'Listen,' I said. 'They have given you all you have, a home, money, and trust. Why do you do it to them?' And he said to me: 'I do it *for* them. I am the surgeon and one day they will understand.' He was a child, Mr. Smiley, they led him like a child."

He dared not speak, dared put nothing to the test.

"Five years ago he met that Dieter. In a ski hut near Garmisch. Freitag told us later that Dieter had planned it that way—Dieter couldn't ski anyway because of his legs. Nothing seemed real then; Freitag wasn't a real name. Fennan christened him Freitag like Man Friday in *Robinson Crusoe*. Dieter found that so funny and afterwards we never talked of Dieter but always of Mr. Robinson and Freitag." She broke off now and looked at him with a very faint smile: "I'm sorry," she said; "I'm not very coherent."

"I understand," said Smiley.

"That girl—what did you say about that girl?"

"She's alive. Don't worry. Go on."

"Fennan liked you, you know. Freitag tried to kill you . . . why?"

"Because I came back, I suppose, and asked you about the 8:30 call. You told Freitag that, didn't you?"

"Oh God," she said, her fingers at her mouth.

"You rang him up, didn't you? As soon as I'd gone?"

"Yes, yes. I was frightened. I wanted to warn him to go, him and Dieter, to go away and never come back, because I knew you'd find out. If not today then one day, but I knew you'd find out in the end. Why would they never leave me alone? They were frightened of me because they knew I had no dreams, that I only wanted Samuel, wanted him safe to love and care for. They relied on that."

Smiley felt his head throbbing erratically. "So you rang him straight away," he said. "You tried the Primrose number first and couldn't get through."

"Yes," she said vaguely. "Yes, that's right. But they're both Primrose numbers."

"So you rang the *other* number, the alternative . . ."

She drifted back to the window, suddenly exhausted and limp; she seemed happier now—the storm had left her reflective and, in a way, content.

"Yes. Freitag was a great one for alternative plans."

"What was the other number?" Smiley insisted. He watched her anxiously as she stared out of the window into the dark garden.

"Why do you want to know?"

He came and stood beside her at the window, watching her profile. His voice was suddenly harsh and energetic.

"I said the girl was all right. You and I are alive, too. But don't think that's going to last."

She turned to him with fear in her eyes, looked at him for a moment, then nodded. Smiley took her by the arm and guided her to a chair. He ought to make her a hot drink or something. She sat down quite mechanically, almost with the detachment of incipient madness.

"The other number was 9747."

"Any address—did you have an address?"

"No, no address. Only the telephone. Tricks on the telephone. No address," she repeated, with unnatural emphasis, so that Smiley looked at her and wondered. A thought suddenly struck him—a memory of Dieter's skill in communication.

"Freitag didn't meet you the night Fennan died, did he? He didn't come to the theatre?"

"No."

"That was the first time he had missed, wasn't it? You panicked and left early."

"No . . . yes, yes, I panicked."

"No you didn't! You left early because you had to, it was the arrangement. *Why* did you leave early? Why?"

Her hands hid her face.

"Are you still mad?" Smiley shouted. "Do you still think you can control what you have made? Freitag will kill you, kill the girl, kill, kill, kill. Who are you trying to protect, a girl or a murderer?"

She wept and said nothing. Smiley crouched beside her, still shouting.

"I'll tell you why you left early, shall I? I'll tell you what I think. It was to catch the last post that night from Weybridge. He hadn't come, you hadn't exchanged cloakroom tickets, had you, so you obeyed the instructions, you posted your ticket to him and you *have* got an address, not written down but remembered, remembered for ever: 'If there is a crisis, if I do not come, this is the address': is that what he said? An address never to be used or spoken of, an address forgotten and remembered for ever? Is that right? Tell me!"

She stood up, her head turned away, went to the desk and found a piece of paper and a pencil. The tears still ran freely over her face. With agonizing slowness she wrote the address, her hand faltering and almost stopping between the words.

He took the paper from her, folded it carefully across the middle and put it in his wallet.

Now he would make her some tea.

She looked like a child rescued from the sea. She sat on the edge of the sofa holding the cup tightly in her frail hands, nursing it against her body. Her thin shoulders were hunched forward, her feet and ankles pressed tightly together. Smiley, looking at her, felt he had broken something he should never have touched because it was so fragile. He felt an obscene, coarse bully, his offerings of tea a futile recompense for his clumsiness.

He could think of nothing to say. After a while, she said: "He liked you, you know. He really liked you . . . he said you were a clever little man. It was quite a surprise when Samuel called anyone clever." She shook her head slowly. Perhaps it was the reaction that made her smile: "He used to say there were two forces in the world, the positive and the negative. 'What shall I do then?' he would ask me. 'Let them ruin their harvest because they give me bread? Creation, progress, power, the whole future of mankind waits at their door: shall I not let them in?' And I said to him: 'But Samuel, maybe the people are happy without these things?' But you know he didn't think of people like that.

"But I couldn't stop him. You know the strangest thing about Fennan? For all that thinking and talking, he had made up his mind long ago what he would do. All the rest was poetry. He wasn't coordinated, that's what I used to tell him . . ."

". . . and yet you helped him," said Smiley.

"Yes, I helped him. He wanted help so I gave it him. He was my life."

"I see."

"That was a mistake. He was a little boy, you know. He forgot things just like a child. And so vain. He had made up his mind to do it and he did it so badly. He didn't think of it as you do, or I do. He simply didn't think of it like that. It was his work and that was all.

"It began so simply. He brought home a draft telegram one night and showed it to me. He said: 'I think Dieter ought to see that'—that was all. I couldn't believe it to begin with—that he was a spy, I mean. Because he was, wasn't he? And gradually, I realized. They began to ask for special things. The music case I got back from Freitag began to contain orders, and sometimes money. I said to him: 'Look at what they are sending you—do you want this?' We didn't know what to do with the money. In the end we gave it away mostly, I don't know why. Dieter was very angry that winter, when I told him."

"What winter was that?" asked Smiley.

"The second winter with Dieter—1956 in Mürren. We met him first in January 1955. That was when it began. And shall I tell you something? Hungary made no difference to Samuel, not a tiny bit of difference. Dieter was frightened about him then, I know, because Freitag told me. When Fennan gave me the things to take to Weybridge that November I nearly went mad. I shouted at him: 'Can't you see it's the same? The same guns, the same children dying in the streets? Only the dream has changed, the blood is the same colour. Is that what you want?' I asked him: 'Would you do this for Germans, too? It's me who lies in the gutter, will you let them do it to *me?*' But he just said: 'No, Elsa, this is different.' And I went on taking the music case. Do you understand?"

"I don't know. I just don't know. I think perhaps I do."

"He was all I had. He was my life. I protected myself,

I suppose. And gradually I became a part of it, and then it was too late to stop . . . And then you know," she said, in a whisper; "there were times when I was glad, times when the world seemed to applaud what Samuel was doing. It was not a pretty sight for us, the new Germany. Old names had come back, names that had frightened us as children. The dreadful, plump pride returned, you could see it even in the photographs in the papers, they marched with the old rhythm. Fennan felt that too, but then thank God he hadn't seen what I saw.

"We were in a camp outside Dresden, where we used to live. My father was paralysed. He missed tobacco more than anything and I used to roll cigarettes from any rubbish I could find in the camp—just to pretend with. One day a guard saw him smoking and began laughing. Some others came and they laughed too. My father was holding the cigarette in his paralysed hand and it was burning his fingers. He didn't know, you see.

"Yes, when they gave guns to the Germans again, gave them money and uniforms, then sometimes—just for a little while—I was pleased with what Samuel had done. We are Jews, you know, and so . . ."

"Yes, I know, I understand," said Smiley. "I saw it too, a little of it."

"Dieter said you had."

"Dieter said that?"

"Yes. To Freitag. He told Freitag you were a very clever man. You once deceived Dieter before the war, and it was only long afterwards that he found out, that's what Freitag said. He said you were the best he'd ever met."

"When did Freitag tell you that?"

She looked at him for a long time. He had never seen in any face such hopeless misery. He remembered how she had said to him before: "The children of my grief are dead." He understood that now, and heard it in her voice when at last she spoke:

"Why, isn't it obvious? The night he murdered Samuel.

"That's the great joke, Mr. Smiley. At the very moment when Samuel could have done so much for them—not just a piece here and a piece there, but all the time—so many music cases—at that moment their own fear destroyed them, turned them into animals and made them kill what they had made.

"Samuel always said: 'They will win because they *know* and the others will perish because they do not: men who work for a dream will work for ever'—that's what he said. But I knew their dream, I knew it would destroy us. What has not destroyed? Even the dream of Christ."

"It was Dieter then, who saw me in the park with Fennan?"

"Yes."

"And thought—"

'Yes. Thought that Samuel had betrayed him. Told Freitag to kill Samuel."

"And the anonymous letter?"

"I don't know. I don't know who wrote it. Someone who knew Samuel, I suppose, someone from the office who watched him and knew. Or from Oxford, from the Party. I don't know. Samuel didn't know either."

"But the suicide letter—"

She looked at him, and her face crumpled. She was almost weeping again. She bowed her head:

"I wrote it. Freitag brought the paper, and I wrote it. The signature was already there. Samuel's signature."

Smiley went over to her, sat beside her on the sofa and took her hand. She turned on him in a fury and began screaming at him:

"Take your hands off me! Do you think I'm yours because I don't belong to them? Go away! Go away and kill Freitag and Dieter, keep the game alive, Mr. Smiley. But don't think I'm on *your* side, d'you hear? Because I'm the wandering Jewess, the no-man's land, the battlefield for your toy soldiers. You can kick me and trample on me, see, but never, never touch me, never tell me you're sorry, d'you hear? Now get out! Go away and kill."

She sat there, shivering as if from cold. As he reached the door he looked back. There were no tears in her eyes.

Mendel was waiting for him in the car.

13

The Inefficiency of Samuel Fennan

They arrived at Mitcham at lunch-time. Peter Guillam was waiting for them in his car.

"Well, children; what's the news?"

Smiley handed him the piece of paper from his wallet. "There was an emergency number, too—Primrose 9747. You'd better check it but I'm not hopeful of that either."

Peter disappeared into the hall and began telephoning. Mendel busied himself in the kitchen and returned ten minutes later with beer, bread, and cheese on a tray. Guillam came back and sat down without saying anything. He looked worried. "Well," he said at last, "what did she say, George?"

Mendel cleared away as Smiley finished the account of his interview that morning.

"I see," said Guillam. "How very worrying. Well, that's it, George, I shall have to put this on paper today, and I'll have to go to Maston at once. Catching dead spies is a poor game really—and causes a lot of unhappiness."

"What access did he have at the FO?" asked Smiley.

"Recently a lot. That's why they felt he should be interviewed, as you know."

"What kind of stuff, mainly?"

"I don't know yet. He was on an Asian desk until a few months ago but his new job was different."

"American, I seem to remember," said Smiley. "Peter?"

"Yes."

"Peter, have you thought at all *why* they wanted to kill Fennan so much. I mean, supposing he *had* betrayed them, as they thought, why kill him? They had nothing to gain."

"No; no, I suppose they hadn't. That does need some explaining, come to think of it . . . or does it? Suppose Fuchs or Maclean had betrayed them, I wonder what would have happened. Suppose they had reason to fear a chain reaction—not just here but in America—all over the world? Wouldn't they kill him to prevent that? There's so much we shall just never know."

"Like the 8:30 call?" said Smiley.

"Cheerio. Hang on here till I ring you, will you? Maston's bound to want to see you. They'll be running down the corridors when I tell them the glad news. I shall have to wear the special grin I reserve for bearing really disastrous tidings."

Mendel saw him out and then returned to the drawing-room. "Best thing you can do is put your feet up," he said. "You look a ruddy mess, you do."

"Either Mundt's here or he's not," thought Smiley as he lay on the bed in his waistcoat, his hands linked under his head. "If he's not, we're finished. It will be for Maston to decide what to do with Elsa Fennan, and my guess is he'll do nothing.

"If Mundt *is* here, it's for one of three reasons: A, because Dieter told him to stay and watch the dust settle; B, because he's in bad odour and afraid to go back; C, because he has unfinished business.

"A is improbable because it's not like Dieter to take needless risks. Anyway, it's a woolly idea.

"B is unlikely because, while Mundt may be afraid of Dieter he must also, presumably, be frightened of a murder charge here. His wisest plan would be to go to another country.

"C is more likely. If I was in Dieter's shoes I'd be worried

sick about Elsa Fennan. The Pidgeon girl is immaterial—
without Elsa to fill in the gaps she presents no serious danger.
She was not a conspirator and there is no reason why she should
particularly remember Elsa's friend at the theatre. No, Elsa
constitutes the real danger."

There was, of course, a final possibility, which Smiley was
quite unable to judge: the possibility that Dieter had other
agents to control here through Mundt. On the whole he was
inclined to discount this, but the thought had no doubt crossed
Peter's mind.

No . . . it still didn't make sense—it wasn't tidy. He decided
to begin again.

What do we know? He sat up to look for pencil and paper and
at once his head began throbbing. Obstinately he got off the
bed and took a pencil from the inside pocket of his jacket.
There was a writing pad in his suitcase. He returned to the
bed, shaped the pillows to his satisfaction, took four aspirin
from the bottle on the table and propped himself against the
pillows, his short legs stretched before him. He began writing.
First he wrote the heading in a neat, scholarly hand, and underlined it.

<u>What do we know?</u>

Then he began, stage by stage, to recount as dispassionately as
possible the sequence of events hitherto:

"On Monday, 2 January, Dieter Frey saw me in the park
talking to his agent and concluded . . ." Yes, what *did* Dieter
conclude? That Fennan had confessed, was going to confess?
That Fennan was *my* agent? ". . . and concluded that Fennan
was dangerous, for reasons still unknown. The following evening, the first Tuesday in the month, Elsa Fennan took her
husband's reports in a music case to the Weybridge Repertory
Theatre, in the agreed way, and left the case in the cloakroom

in exchange for a ticket. Mundt was to bring his own music case and do the same thing. Elsa and Mundt would then exchange tickets during the performance. Mundt did not appear. Accordingly she followed the emergency procedure and posted the ticket to a prearranged address, having left the theatre early to catch the last post from Weybridge. She then drove home to be met by Mundt, who had, by then, murdered Fennan, probably on Dieter's orders. He had shot him at point blank range as soon as he met him in the hall. Knowing Dieter, I suspect that he had long ago taken the precaution of keeping in London a few sheets of blank writing paper signed with samples, forged or authentic, of Sam Fennan's signature, in case it was ever necessary to compromise or blackmail him. Assuming this to be so, Mundt brought a sheet with him in order to type the suicide letter over the signature on Fennan's own typewriter. In the ghastly scene which must have followed Elsa's arrival, Mundt realized that Dieter had wrongly interpreted Fennan's encounter with Smiley, but relied on Elsa to preserve her dead husband's reputation—not to mention her own complicity. Mundt was therefore reasonably safe. Mundt made Elsa type the letter, perhaps because he did not trust his English. (Note: But who the devil typed the *first* letter, the denunciation?)

"Mundt then, presumably, demanded the music case he had failed to collect, and Elsa told him that she had obeyed standing instructions and posted the cloakroom ticket to the Hampstead address, leaving the music case at the theatre. Mundt reacted significantly: he forced her to telephone the theatre and to arrange for him to collect the case that night on his way back to London. Therefore either the address to which the ticket was posted was no longer valid, or Mundt intended at that stage to return home early the next morning without having time to collect the ticket and the case.

"Smiley visits Walliston early on the morning of Wednesday, 4 January, and during the *first* interview takes an 8:30 call from the exchange which (beyond reasonable doubt) Fennan requested at 7:55 the previous evening. WHY?

"Later that morning S. returns to Elsa Fennan to ask about the 8:30 call—which she knew (on her own admission) would 'worry me' (no doubt Mundt's flattering description of my powers had had its effect). Having told S. a futile story about her bad memory she panics and rings Mundt.

"Mundt, presumably equipped with a photograph or a description from Dieter, decides to liquidate S. (on Dieter's authority?) and later that day nearly succeeds. (Note: Mundt did not return the car to Scarr's garage till the night of the 4th. This does not necessarily prove that Mundt had no plans for flying earlier in the day. If he had originally meant to fly in the morning he might well have left the car at Scarr's earlier and gone to the airport by bus.)

"It does seem pretty likely that Mundt changed his plans after Elsa's telephone call. It is not clear that he changed them *because* of her call." Would Mundt really be panicked by Elsa? Panicked into staying, panicked into murdering Adam Scarr, he wondered.

The telephone was ringing in the hall . . .

"George, it's Peter. No joy with the address or the telephone number. Dead end."

"What do you mean?"

"The telephone number and the address both led to the same place—furnished apartment in Highgate village."

"Well?"

"Rented by a pilot in Lufteuropa. He paid his two months' rent on the fifth of January and hasn't come back since."

"Damn."

"The landlady remembers Mundt quite well. The pilot's friend. A nice polite gentleman he was, for a German, very open-handed. He used to sleep on the sofa quite often."

"Oh God."

"I went through the room with a toothcomb. There was a desk in the corner. All the drawers were empty except one, which contained a cloakroom ticket. I wonder where that came from . . . Well, if you want a laugh, come round to the Circus. The whole of Olympus is seething with activity. Oh, incidentally—"

"Yes?"

"I dug around at Dieter's flat. Another lemon. He left on the fourth of January. Didn't tell the milkman."

"What about his mail?"

"He never received any, apart from bills. I also had a look at Comrade Mundt's little nest: couple of rooms over the Steel Mission. The furniture went out with the rest of the stuff. Sorry."

"I see."

"I'll tell you an odd thing though, George. You remember I thought I might get on to Fennan's personal possessions—wallet, notebook, and so on? From the police."

"Yes."

"Well, I did. His diary's got Dieter's full name entered in the address section with the Mission telephone number against it. Bloody cheek."

"It's more than that. It's lunacy. Good Lord."

"Then for the fourth of January the entry is 'Smiley C.A. Ring 8:30.' That was corroborated by an entry for the third which ran 'request call for Wed. morning.' There's your mysterious call."

"Still unexplained." A pause.

"George, I sent Felix Taverner round to the FO to do some ferreting. It's worse than we feared in one way, but better in another."

"Why?"

"Well, Taverner got his hands on the registry schedules for the last two years. He was able to work out what files have been marked to Fennan's section. Where a file was particularly requested by that section they still have a requisition form."

"I'm listening."

"Felix found that three or four files were usually marked in to Fennan on a Friday afternoon and marked out again on Monday morning; the inference is that he took the stuff home at week-ends."

"Oh my Lord!"

"But the odd thing is, George, that during the last six months, since his posting in fact, he tended to take home *unclassified* stuff which wouldn't have been of interest to anyone."

"But it was during the last months that he began dealing mainly with secret files," said Smiley. "He could take home anything he wanted."

"I know, but he didn't. In fact you'd almost say it was deliberate. He took home very low-grade stuff barely related to his daily work. His colleagues can't understand it now they think about it—he even took back some files handling subjects outside the scope of his section."

"And unclassified."

"Yes—of no conceivable intelligence value."

"How about earlier, before he came into his new job? What kind of stuff went home then?"

"Much more what you'd expect—files he'd used during the day, policy and so on."

"Secret?"

"Some were, some weren't. As they came."

"But nothing unexpected—no particularly delicate stuff that didn't concern him?"

"No. Nothing. He had opportunity galore quite frankly and didn't use it. Windy, I suppose."

"So he ought to be if he puts his controller's name in his diary."

"And make what you like of this: he'd arranged at the FO to

take a day off on the fourth—the day after he died. Rather an event apparently—he was a glutton for work, they say."

"What's Maston doing about all this?" asked Smiley, after a pause.

"Going through the files at the moment and rushing in to see me with bloody fool questions every two minutes. I think he gets lonely in there with hard facts."

"Oh, he'll beat them down, Peter, don't worry."

"He's already saying that the whole case against Fennan rests on the evidence of a neurotic woman."

"Thanks for ringing, Peter."

"Be seeing you, dear boy. Keep your head down."

Smiley replaced the receiver and wondered where Mendel was. There was an evening paper on the hall table, and he glanced vaguely at the headline "Lynching: World Jewry Protests" and beneath it the account of the lynching of a Jewish shopkeeper in Düsseldorf. He opened the drawing-room door—Mendel was not there. Then he caught sight of him through the window wearing his gardening hat, hacking savagely with a pick-axe at a tree stump in the front garden. Smiley watched him for a moment, then went upstairs again to rest. As he reached the top of the stairs the telephone began ringing again.

"George—sorry to bother you again. It's about Mundt."

"Yes?"

"Flew to Berlin last night by BEA. Travelled under another name but was easily identified by the air hostess. That seems to be that. Hard luck, chum."

Smiley pressed down the cradle with his hand for a moment, then dialled Walliston 2944. He heard the number ringing the other end. Suddenly the dialling tone stopped and instead he heard Elsa Fennan's voice:

"Hullo . . . Hullo . . . *Hullo?*"

Slowly he replaced the receiver. She was alive.

Why on earth *now?* Why should Mundt go home *now,* five

weeks after murdering Fennan, three weeks after murdering
Scarr; why had he eliminated the lesser danger—Scarr—and
left Elsa Fennan unharmed, neurotic and embittered, liable at
any moment to throw aside her own safety and tell the whole
story? What effect might that terrible night not have had upon
her? How could Dieter trust a woman now so lightly bound to
him? Her husband's good name could no longer be presented;
might she not, in God knows what mood of vengeance or
repentance, blurt out the whole truth? Obviously, a little time
must elapse between the murder of Fennan and the murder of
his wife, but what event, what information, what danger, had
decided Mundt to return last night? A ruthless and elaborate
plan to preserve the secrecy of Fennan's treason had now
apparently been thrown aside unfinished. What had happened
yesterday that Mundt could know of? Or was the timing of his
departure a coincidence? Smiley refused to believe it was. If
Mundt had remained in England after the two murders and
the assault on Smiley, he had done so unwillingly, waiting
upon some opportunity or event that would release him. He
would not stay a moment longer than he need. Yet what had he
done since Scarr's death? Hidden in some lonely room, locked
away from light and news. Then why did he now fly home so
suddenly?

And Fennan—what spy was this who selected innocuous
information for his masters when he had such gems at his fingertips? A change of heart, perhaps? A weakening of purpose?
Then why did he not tell his wife, for whom his crime was a
constant nightmare, who would have rejoiced at his conversion? It seemed now that Fennan had never shown any preference for secret papers—he had simply taken home whatever
files currently might occupy him. But certainly a weakening of
purpose would explain the strange summons to Marlow and
Dieter's conviction that Fennan was betraying him. And who
wrote the anonymous letter?

Nothing made sense, nothing. Fennan himself—brilliant,

fluent, and attractive—had deceived so naturally, so expertly. Smiley had really liked him. Why then had this practised deceiver made the incredible blunder of putting Dieter's name in his diary—and shown so little judgement or interest in the selection of intelligence?

Smiley went upstairs to pack the few possessions which Mendel had collected for him from Bywater Street. It was all over.

14

The Dresden Group

He stood on the doorstep and put down his suitcase, fumbling for his latchkey. As he opened the door he recalled how Mundt had stood there looking at him, those very pale blue eyes calculating and steady. It was odd to think of Mundt as Dieter's pupil. Mundt had proceeded with the inflexibility of a trained mercenary—efficient, purposeful, narrow. There had been nothing original in his technique: in everything he had been a shadow of his master. It was as if Dieter's brilliant and imaginative tricks had been compressed into a manual which Mundt had learnt by heart, adding only the salt of his own brutality.

Smiley had deliberately left no forwarding address and a heap of mail lay on the door mat. He picked it up, put it on the hall table and began opening doors and peering about him, a puzzled, lost expression on his face. The house was strange to him, cold and musty. As he moved slowly from one room to another he began for the first time to realize how empty his life had become.

He looked for matches to light the gas fire, but there were none. He sat in an armchair in the living-room and his eyes wandered over the bookshelves and the odds and ends he had collected on his travels. When Ann had left him he had begun by rigorously excluding all trace of her. He had even got rid of her books. But gradually he had allowed the few remaining symbols that linked his life with hers to reassert themselves: wedding presents from close friends which had meant too much to be given away. There was a Watteau sketch from Peter Guillam, a Dresden group from Steed-Asprey.

He got up from his chair and went over to the corner cupboard where the group stood. He loved to admire the beauty of those figures, the tiny rococo courtesan in shepherd's costume, her hands outstretched to one adoring lover, her little face bestowing glances on another. He felt inadequate before that fragile perfection, as he had felt before Ann when he first began the conquest which had amazed society. Somehow those little figures comforted him: it was as useless to expect fidelity of Ann as of this tiny shepherdess in her glass case. Steed-Asprey had bought the group in Dresden before the war, it had been the prize of his collection and he had given it to them. Perhaps he had guessed that one day Smiley might have need of the simple philosophy it propounded.

Dresden: of all German cities, Smiley's favourite. He had loved its architecture, its odd jumble of medieval and classical buildings, sometimes reminiscent of Oxford, its cupolas, towers, and spires, its copper-green roofs shimmering under a hot sun. Its name meant "town of the forest-dwellers" and it was there that Wenceslas of Bohemia had favoured the minstrel poets with gifts and privilege. Smiley remembered the last time he had been there, visiting a university acquaintance, a Professor of Philology he had met in England. It was on that visit that he had caught sight of Dieter Frey, struggling round the prison courtyard. He could see him still, tall and angry, monstrously altered by his shaven head, somehow too big for that little prison. Dresden, he remembered, had been Elsa's birthplace. He remembered glancing through her personal particulars at the ministry: Elsa *neé* Freimann, born 1917 in Dresden, Germany, of German parents; educated Dresden: imprisoned 1938–45. He tried to place her against the background of her home, the patrician Jewish family living out its life amid insult and persecution. "I dreamed of long golden hair and they shaved my head." He realized with sickening accuracy why she dyed her hair. She might have been like this shepherdess, round-bosomed and pretty. But the body had been broken with hunger so that it was frail and ugly, like the carcass of a tiny bird.

He could picture her on the terrible night when she found her husband's murderer standing by his body; hear her breath-less, sobbing explanation of why Fennan had been in the park with Smiley; and Mundt unmoved, explaining and reasoning, compelling her finally to conspire once more against her will in this most dreadful and needless of crimes, dragging her to the telephone and forcing her to ring the theatre, leaving her finally tortured and exhausted to cope with the enquiries that were bound to follow, even to type that futile suicide letter over Fennan's signature. It was inhuman beyond belief and, he added to himself, for Mundt a fantastic risk.

She had, of course, proved herself a reliable enough accom-plice in the past, cool-headed and, ironically, more skilful than Fennan in the techniques of espionage. And, heaven knows, for a woman who had been through such a night as that, her performance at their first meeting had been a marvel.

As he stood gazing at the little shepherdess, poised eter-nally between her two admirers, he realized dispassionately that there was another quite different solution to the case of Samuel Fennan, a solution which matched every detail of cir-cumstance, reconciled the nagging inconsistencies apparent in Fennan's character. The realization began as an academic exer-cise without reference to personalities; Smiley manoeuvred the characters like pieces in a puzzle, twisting them this way and that to fit the complex framework of established facts and then, in a moment, the pattern had suddenly re-formed with such assurance that it was a game no more.

His heart beat faster, as with growing astonishment Smiley retold to himself the whole story, reconstructed scenes and incidents in the light of his discovery. Now he knew why

Mundt had left England that day, why Fennan chose so little that was of value to Dieter, had asked for the 8:30 call, and why his wife had escaped the systematic savagery of Mundt. Now at last he knew who had written the anonymous letter. He saw how he had been the fool of his own sentiment, had played false with the power of his mind.

He went to the telephone and dialled Mendel's number. As soon as he had finished speaking to him he rang Peter Guillam. Then he put on his hat and coat and walked round the corner to Sloane Square. At a small newsagent's beside Peter Jones he bought a picture postcard of Westminster Abbey. He made his way to the underground station and travelled north to Highgate, where he got out. At the main post office he bought a stamp and addressed the postcard in stiff, continental capitals to Elsa Fennan. In the panel for correspondence he wrote in spiky longhand: "Wish you were here." He posted the card and noted the time, after which he returned to Sloane Square. There was nothing more he could do.

He slept soundly that night, rose early the following morning, a Saturday, and walked round the corner to buy croissants and coffee beans. He made a lot of coffee and sat in the kitchen reading *The Times* and eating his breakfast. He felt curiously calm and when the telephone rang at last he folded his paper carefully together before going upstairs to answer it.

"George, it's Peter"—the voice was urgent, almost triumphant: "George, she's bitten, I swear she has!"

"What happened?"

"The post arrived at exactly 8:35. By 9:30 she was walking briskly down the drive, booted and spurred. She made straight for the railway station and caught the 9:52 to Victoria. I put Mendel on the train and hared up by car, but I was too late to meet the train this end."

"How will you make contact with Mendel again?"

"I gave him the number of the Grosvenor Hotel and I'm

there now. He's going to ring me as soon as he gets a chance and I'll join him wherever he is."

"Peter, you're taking this gently, aren't you?"

"Gentle as the wind, dear boy. I think she's losing her head. Moving like a greyhound."

Smiley rang off. He picked up his *Times* and began studying the theatre column. He must be right . . . he must be.

After that the morning passed with agonizing slowness. Sometimes he would stand at the window, his hands in his pockets, watching leggy Kensington girls going shopping with beautiful young men in pale blue pullovers, or the car-cleaning brigade toiling happily in front of their houses, then drifting away to talk motoring shop and finally setting off purposefully down the road for the first pint of the week-end.

At last, after what seemed an interminable delay, the front door bell rang and Mendel and Guillam came in, grinning cheerfully, ravenously hungry.

"Hook, line, and sinker," said Guillam. "But let Mendel tell you—he did most of the dirty work. I just got in for the kill."

Mendel recounted his story precisely and accurately, looking at the ground a few feet in front of him, his thin head slightly on one side.

"She caught the 9:52 to Victoria. I kept well clear of her on the train and picked her up as she went through the barrier. Then she took a taxi to Hammersmith."

"A taxi?" Smiley interjected. "She must be out of her mind."

"She's rattled. She walks fast for a woman anyway, mind, but she damn nearly ran going down the platform. Got out at the Broadway and walked to the Sheridan Theatre. Tried the doors to the box office but they were locked. She hesitated a moment then turned back and went to a café a hundred yards down the road. Ordered coffee and paid for it at once. About forty minutes later she went back to the Sheridan. The box office was open and I ducked in behind her and joined the queue. She bought two rear stalls for next Thursday, Row T, 27 and 28. When she got outside the theatre she put one ticket in an envelope and sealed it up. Then she posted it. I couldn't see the address but there was a sixpenny stamp on the envelope."

Smiley sat very still. "I wonder," he said; "I wonder if he'll come."

"I caught up with Mendel at the Sheridan," said Guillam. "He saw her into the café and then rang me. After that he went in after her."

"Felt like a coffee myself," Mendel went on. "Mr. Guillam joined me. I left him there when I joined the ticket queue, and he drifted out of the café a bit later. It was a decent job and no worries. She's rattled, I'm sure. But not suspicious."

"What did she do after that?" asked Smiley.

"Went straight back to Victoria. We left her to it."

They were silent for a moment, then Mendel said:

"What do we do now?"

Smiley blinked and gazed earnestly into Mendel's grey face. "Book tickets for Thursday's performance at the Sheridan."

They were gone and he was alone again. He still had not begun to cope with the quantity of mail which had accumulated in his absence. Circulars, catalogues from Blackwells, bills and the usual collection of soap vouchers, frozen pea coupons, football pool forms and a few private letters still lay unopened on the hall table. He took them into the drawing-room, settled in an armchair and began opening the personal letters first. There was one from Maston, and he read it with something approaching embarrassment.

My dear George,

I was so sorry to hear from Guillam about your accident, and I do hope that by now you have made a full recovery.

You may recall that in the heat of the moment you wrote me a letter of resignation before your misfortune, and I just wanted to let you know that I am not, of course, taking this seriously. Sometimes when events crowd in upon us our sense of perspective suffers. But old campaigners like ourselves, George, are not so easily put off the scent. I look forward to seeing you with us again as soon as you are strong enough, and in the meantime we continue to regard you as an old and loyal member of the staff.

Smiley put this on one side and turned to the next letter. Just for a moment he did not recognize the handwriting; just for a moment he looked bleakly at the Swiss stamp and the expensive hotel writing paper. Suddenly he felt slightly sick, his vision blurred and there was scarcely strength enough in his fingers to tear open the envelope. What did she want? If money, she could have all he possessed. The money was his own, to spend as he wished; if it gave him pleasure to squander it on Ann, he would do so. There was nothing else he had to give her—she had taken it long ago. Taken his courage, his love, his compassion, carried them jauntily away in her little jewel case to fondle occasionally on odd afternoons when the time hung heavy in the Cuban sun, to dangle them perhaps before the eyes of her newest lover, to compare them even with similar trinkets which others before or since had brought her.

Darling George,

    I want to make you an offer which no gentleman could accept. I want to come back to you.

    I'm staying at the Baur-au-Lac at Zurich till the end of the month. Let me know.

                                         Ann

Smiley picked up the envelope and looked at the back of it: "Madame Juan Alvida." No, no gentleman could accept that offer. No dream could survive the daylight of Ann's departure with her saccharine Latin and his orange-peel grin. Smiley had once seen a news film of Alvida winning some race in Monte Carlo. The most repellent thing about him, he remembered, had been the hair on his arms. With his goggles and the motor oil and that ludicrous laurel-wreath he had looked exactly like an anthropoid ape fallen from a tree. He was wearing a white tennis shirt with short sleeves, which had somehow remained spotlessly clean throughout the race, setting off those black monkey arms with repulsive clarity.

That was Ann: Let me know. Redeem your life, see whether it can be lived again and let me know. I have wearied my lover, my lover has wearied me, let me shatter your world again: my own bores me. I want to come back to you . . . I want, I want . . .

Smiley got up, the letter still in his hand, and stood again before the porcelain group. He remained there several minutes, gazing at the little shepherdess. She was so beautiful.

15

The Last Act

The Sheridan's three-act production of *Edward II* was playing to a full house. Guillam and Mendel sat in adjacent seats at the extreme end of the circle, which formed a wide U facing the stage. The left-hand end of the circle afforded a view of the rear stalls, which were otherwise concealed. An empty seat separated Guillam from a party of young students buzzing with anticipation.

They looked down thoughtfully on a restless sea of bobbing heads and fluttering programmes, stirring in sudden waves as later arrivals took their places. The scene reminded Guillam of an Oriental dance, where the tiny gestures of hand and foot animate a motionless body. Occasionally he would glance towards the rear stalls, but there was still no sign of Elsa Fennan or her guest.

Just as the recorded overture was ending he looked again briefly towards the two empty stalls in the back row and his heart gave a sudden leap as he saw the slight figure of Elsa Fennan sitting straight and motionless, staring fixedly down the auditorium like a child learning deportment. The seat on her right, nearest the gangway, was still empty.

Outside in the street taxis were drawing up hastily at the theatre entrance and an agreeable selection of the established and the disestablished hurriedly over-tipped their cabmen and spent five minutes looking for their tickets. Smiley's taxi took him past the theatre and deposited him at the Clarendon Hotel, where he went straight downstairs to the dining-room and bar.

"I'm expecting a call any moment," he said. "My name's Savage. You'll let me know, won't you?"

The barman turned to the telephone behind him and spoke to the receptionist.

"And a small whisky and soda, please; will you have one yourself?"

"Thank you sir, I never touch it."

The curtain rose on a dimly lit stage and Guillam, peering towards the back of the auditorium, tried at first without success to penetrate the sudden darkness. Gradually his eyes accustomed themselves to the faint glow cast by the emergency lamps, until he could just discern Elsa in the half light; and still the empty seat beside her.

Only a low partition separated the rear stalls from the gangway which ran along the back of the auditorium, and behind it were several doors leading to the foyer, bar, and cloakrooms. For a brief moment one of these opened and an oblique shaft of light was cast as if by design upon Elsa Fennan, illuminating with a thin line one side of her face, making its hollows black by contrast. She inclined her head slightly, as if listening to something behind her, half rose in her seat, then sat down again, deceived, and resumed her former attitude.

Guillam felt Mendel's hand on his arm, turned, and saw his lean face thrust forward, looking past him. Following Mendel's gaze, he peered down into the well of the theatre, where a tall figure was slowly making his way towards the back of the stalls; he was an impressive sight, erect and handsome, a lock of black hair tumbling over his brow. It was he whom Mendel watched with such fascination, this elegant giant limping up the gangway. There was something different about him, something arresting and disturbing. Through his glasses Guillam watched his slow and deliberate progress, admired the grace and measure of his uneven walk. He was a man apart, a man you remember, a man who strikes a chord deep in your experience, a man with the gift of universal familiarity: to Guillam he was a living component of all our romantic dreams, he stood at the mast with Conrad, sought the lost Greece with Byron, and with Goethe visited the shades of classical and medieval hells.

As he walked, thrusting his good leg forward, there was a defiance, a command, that could not go unheeded. Guillam noticed how heads turned in the audience, and eyes followed him obediently.

Pushing past Mendel, Guillam stepped quickly through the emergency exit into the corridor behind. He followed the corridor down some steps and arrived at last at the foyer. The box office had closed down, but the girl was still poring hopelessly over a page of laboriously compiled figures, covered with alterations and erasures.

"Excuse me," said Guillam; "but I must use your telephone—it's urgent, do you mind?"

"Ssh!" She waved her pencil at him impatiently, without looking up. Her hair was mousy, her oily skin glistened from the fatigue of late nights and a diet of chipped potatoes. Guillam waited a moment, wondering how long it would be before she found a solution to that tangle of spidery numerals which would match the pile of notes and silver in the open cash box beside her.

"Listen," he urged; "I'm a police officer—there's a couple of heroes upstairs who are after you cash. Now will you let me use that telephone?"

"Oh Lord," she said in a tired voice, and looked at him for the first time. She wore glasses and was very plain. She was neither alarmed nor impressed. "I wish they'd perishing well take the money. It sends me up the wall." Pushing her accounts to one side she opened a door beside the little kiosk and Guillam squeezed in.

"Hardly decent, is it?" the girl said with a grin. Her voice was nearly cultured—probably a London undergraduate earning pin-money, thought Guillam. He rang the Clarendon and asked for Mr. Savage. Almost immediately he heard Smiley's voice.

"He's here," said Guillam, "been here all the time. Must have bought an extra ticket; he was sitting in the front stalls. Mendel suddenly spotted him limping up the aisle."

"Limping?"

"Yes, it's not Mundt. It's the other one, Dieter."

Smiley did not reply and after a moment Guillam said: "George—are you there?"

"We've had it, I'm afraid, Peter. We've got nothing against Frey. Call the men off, they won't find Mundt tonight. Is the first act over yet?"

"Must be just coming up for the interval."

"I'll be round in twenty minutes. Hang on to Elsa like grim death—if they leave and separate, Mendel's to stick to Dieter. You stay in the foyer for the last act in case they leave early."

Guillam replaced the receiver and turned to the girl. "Thanks," he said, and put four pennies on her desk. She hastily gathered them together and pressed them firmly into his hand.

"For God's sake," she said, "don't add to my troubles."

He went outside into the street and spoke to a plain clothes man loitering on the pavement. Then he hurried back and rejoined Mendel as the curtain fell on the first act.

Elsa and Dieter were sitting side by side. They were talking happily together, Dieter laughing, Elsa animated and articulate like a puppet brought to life by her master. Mendel watched them in fascination. She laughed at something Dieter said, leant forward and put her hand on his arm. He saw her thin fingers against his dinner jacket, saw Dieter incline his head and whisper something to her, so that she laughed again. As Mendel watched, the theatre lights dimmed and the noise of conversation subsided as the audience quickly prepared for the second act.

Smiley left the Clarendon and walked slowly along the pavement towards the theatre. Thinking about it now, he realized that it was logical enough that Dieter should come, that it would have been madness to send Mundt. He wondered how long it could be before Elsa and Dieter discovered that it was not Dieter who had summoned her, not Dieter who had sent the postcard by a trusted courier. That, he reflected, should be an interesting moment. All he prayed for now was the opportunity of one more interview with Elsa Fennan.

A few minutes later he slipped quietly into the empty seat beside Guillam. It was a long time since he had seen Dieter.

He had not changed. He was the same improbable romantic with the magic of a charlatan; the same unforgettable figure which had struggled over the ruins of Germany, implacable of purpose, satanic in fulfilment, dark and swift like the Gods of the North. Smiley had lied to them that night in his club; Dieter *was* out of proportion, his cunning, his conceit, his strength and his dream—all were larger than life, undiminished by the moderating influence of experience. He was a man who thought and acted in absolute terms, without patience or compromise.

Memories returned to Smiley that night as he sat in the dark theatre and watched Dieter across a mass of motionless faces, memories of dangers shared, of mutual trust when each had held in his hand the life of the other . . . Just for a second Smiley wondered whether Dieter had seen him, had the feeling that Dieter's eyes were upon him, watching him in the dim half light.

Smiley got up as the second half drew to a close; as the curtain fell he made quickly for the side exit and waited discreetly in the corridor until the bell rang for the last act. Mendel joined him shortly before the end of the interval, and Guillam slipped past them to take up his post in the foyer.

"There's trouble," Mendel said. "They're arguing. She looks frightened. She keeps on saying something and he just shakes his head. She's panicking, I think, and Dieter looks worried. He's started looking round the theatre as if he was trapped, getting the measure of the place, making plans. He glanced up to where you'd been sitting."

"He won't let her leave alone," said Smiley. "He'll wait and get out with the crowd. They won't leave before the end. He probably reckons he's surrounded: he'll bargain on flustering us by parting from her suddenly in the middle of a crowd—just losing her."

"What's our game? Why can't we go down there and get them?"

"We just wait; I don't know what for. We've no proof. No proof of murder and none of espionage until Maston decides to do something. But remember this: Dieter doesn't know that. If Elsa's jumpy and Dieter's worried, they'll do *something*—that's certain. So long as *they* think the game is up, we've a chance. Let them bolt, panic, anything. So long as they do something . . ."

It was dark in the theatre again, but out of the corner of his eye Smiley saw Dieter leaning over Elsa whispering to her. His left hand held her arm, his whole attitude was one of urgent persuasion and reassurance.

The play dragged on, the shouts of soldiers and the screams of the demented king filled the theatre, until the dreadful climax of his foul death, when an audible sigh rose from the stalls beneath them. Dieter had his arm round Elsa's shoulders now, he had gathered the folds of her thin wrap about her neck and protected her as if she were a sleeping child. They remained like this until the final curtain. Neither applauded, Dieter looked about for Elsa's handbag, said something reassuring to her and put it on her lap. She nodded very slightly. A warning roll of the drums brought the audience to its feet for the national anthem—Smiley rose instinctively and noticed to his surprise that Mendel had vanished. Dieter slowly stood up and as he did so Smiley realized that something had happened. Elsa was still sitting and though Dieter gently prevailed on her to rise, she made no answering sign. There was something oddly dislocated in the way she sat, in the way her head lolled forward on her shoulders . . .

The last line of the anthem was beginning as Smiley rushed to the door, ran down the corridor, down the stone stairs to the foyer. He was just too late—he was met by the first crowd of anxious theatre-goers hastening towards the street in search of taxis. He looked wildly among the crowd for Dieter and knew it was hopeless—that Dieter had done what he himself would have done, had chosen one of the dozen emergency exits which led to the street and safety. He pushed his bulky frame gradually through the middle of the crowd towards the entrance to the stalls. As he twisted this way and that, forcing himself between oncoming bodies, he caught sight of Guillam at the edge of the stream searching hopelessly for Dieter and Elsa. He shouted to him, and Guillam turned quickly.

Struggling on, Smiley at last found himself against the low partition and he could see Elsa Fennan sitting motionless as all around her men stood up and women felt for their coats and handbags. Then he heard the scream. It was sudden, short and utterly expressive of horror and disgust. A girl was standing in the gangway looking at Elsa. She was young and very pretty, the fingers of her right hand were raised to her mouth, her face was deathly white. Her father, a tall cadaverous man, stood behind her. He grasped her shoulders quickly and drew her back as he caught sight of the dreadful thing before him.

Elsa's wrap had slipped from her shoulders and her head was lolling on to her chest.

Smiley had been right. "Let them bolt, panic, anything . . . so long as they do *something* . . ." And this was what they had done: this broken, wretched body was witness to their panic.

"You'd better get the police, Peter. I'm going home. Keep me out of it, if you can. You know where to find me." He nodded, as if to himself; "I'm going home."

It was foggy, and a fine rain was falling as Mendel quickly darted across the Fulham Palace Road in pursuit of Dieter. The headlights of cars came suddenly out of the wet mist twenty yards from him; the noise of traffic was high-pitched and nervous as it groped its uncertain way.

He had no choice but to keep close on Dieter's heels, never more than a dozen paces behind him. The pubs and cinemas had closed but the coffee bars and dance halls still attracted noisy groups crowding the pavements. As Dieter limped ahead of him Mendel staged his progression by the street lamps, watching his silhouette suddenly clarify each time it entered the next cone of light.

Dieter was walking swiftly despite his limp. As his stride lengthened his limp became more pronounced, so that he seemed to swing his left leg forward by a sudden effort of his broad shoulders.

There was a curious expression on Mendel's face, not of hatred or iron purpose but of frank distaste. To Mendel, the frills of Dieter's profession meant nothing. He saw in his quarry only the squalor of a criminal, the cowardice of a man who paid others to do his killing. When Dieter had gently disengaged himself from the audience and moved towards the side exit, Mendel saw what he had been waiting for: the stealthy act of a common criminal. It was something he expected and understood. To Mendel there was only one criminal class, from pickpocket and sneak-thief to the big operator tampering with company law; they were outside the law and it was his distasteful but necessary vocation to remove them to safe keeping. This one happened to be German.

The fog grew thick and yellow. Neither of them wore a coat. Mendel wondered what Mrs. Fennan would do now. Guillam would take care of her. She hadn't even looked at Dieter when he slinked off. She was an odd one that, all skin and bones and good works by the look of her. Lived on dry toast and Bovril.

Dieter turned abruptly down a side street to the right then another to the left. They had been walking for nearly an hour and he showed no sign of slowing down. The street seemed empty: certainly Mendel could hear no other footsteps but their own, crisp and short, the echo corrupted by the fog. They were in a narrow street of Victorian houses with hastily contrived Regency-style façades, heavy porches and sash windows. Mendel guessed they were somewhere near Fulham Broadway, perhaps beyond it, nearer the King's Road. Still Dieter's pace did not flag, still the crooked shadow thrust forward into the fog, confident of its path, urgent in its purpose.

As they approached a main road Mendel heard again the plaintive whine of traffic, brought almost to a standstill by the fog. Then from somewhere above them a yellow street light shed a pale glow, its outline clearly drawn like the aura of a winter sun. Dieter hesitated a moment on the kerb, then, chancing the ghostly traffic that nosed its way past them from nowhere, he crossed the road and plunged at once into one of the innumerable side streets that led, Mendel was certain, towards the river.

Mendel's clothes were soaking wet, and the thin rain ran over his face. They must be near the river now; he thought he could detect the smell of tar and coke, feel the insidious cold of the black water. Just for a moment he thought Dieter had vanished. He moved forward quickly, nearly tripped on a kerb, went forward again and saw the railings of the embankment in front of him. Steps led upwards to an iron gate in the railings and this was slightly open. He stood at the gate and peered beyond, down into the water. There was a stout wooden gangway and Mendel heard the uneven echo as Dieter, hidden by the fog, followed his strange course to the water's edge. Mendel waited, then, wary and silent, he made his way down the gangway. It was a permanent affair with heavy pine handrails on either side. Mendel reckoned it had been there some time. The low end of the gangway was joined to a long raft made of duckboard and oil-drums. Three dilapidated houseboats loomed in the fog, rocking gently on their moorings.

Noiselessly Mendel crept on to the raft, examining each of the houseboats in turn. Two were close together, connected by a plank. The third was moored some fifteen feet away, and a light was burning in her forward cabin. Mendel returned to the embankment, closing the iron gate carefully behind him.

He walked slowly down the road, still uncertain of his bearings. After about five minutes the pavement took him suddenly to the right and the ground rose gradually. He guessed he was on a bridge. He lit his cigarette lighter, and its long flame cast a glow over the stone wall on his right. He moved the lighter back and forth, and finally came upon a wet and dirty metal plate bearing the words "Battersea Bridge." He made his way back to the iron gate and stood for a moment, orientating himself in the light of his knowledge.

Somewhere above him and to his right the four massive chimneys of Fulham Power Station stood hidden in the fog. To his left was Cheyne Walk with its row of smart little boats reaching to Battersea Bridge. The place where he now stood marked the dividing line between the smart and the squalid, where Cheyne Walk meets Lots Road, one of the ugliest streets in London. The southern side of this road consists of vast warehouses, wharves, and mills, and the northern side presents an unbroken line of dingy houses typical of the side streets of Fulham.

It was in the shadow of the four chimneys, perhaps sixty feet from the Cheyne Walk mooring, that Dieter Frey had found a sanctuary. Yes, Mendel knew the spot well. It was only a couple of hundred yards up river from where the earthly remains of Mr. Adam Scarr had been recovered from the unyielding arms of the Thames.

16

Echoes in the Fog

It was long after midnight when Smiley's telephone rang. He got up from the armchair in front of the gas fire and plodded upstairs to his bedroom, his right hand gripping the banisters tightly as he went. It was Peter, no doubt, or the police, and he would have to make a statement. Or even the Press. The murder had taken place just in time to catch today's papers and mercifully too late for last night's news broadcast. What would this be? "Maniac killer in theatre?" "Death-lock murder— woman named?" He hated the Press as he hated advertising and television, he hated mass-media, the relentless persuasion of the twentieth century. Everything he admired or loved had been the product of intense individualism. That was why he hated Dieter now, hated what he stood for more strongly than ever before: it was the fabulous impertinence of renouncing the individual in favour of the mass. When had mass philosophies ever brought benefit or wisdom? Dieter cared nothing for human life: dreamed only of armies of faceless men bound by their lowest common denominators; he wanted to shape the world as if it were a tree, cutting off what did not fit the regular image; for this he fashioned blank, soulless automatons like Mundt. Mundt was faceless like Dieter's army, a trained killer born of the finest killer breed.

He picked up the telephone and gave his number. It was Mendel.

"Where are you?"

"Near Chelsea Embankment. Pub called the Balloon, in Lots Road. Landlord's a chum of mine. I knocked him up . . . Listen, Elsa's boy friend is lying up in a houseboat by Chelsea flour mill. Bloody miracle in the fog, he is. Must have found his way by Braille."

"*Who?*"

"Her boy friend, her escort at the theatre. Wake up, Mr. Smiley; what's eating you?"

"You followed Dieter?"

"Of course I did. That was what you told Mr. Guillam, wasn't it? He was to stick to the woman and me the man . . . How did Mr. Guillam get on, by the way? Where did Elsa get to?"

"She didn't get anywhere. She was dead when Dieter left. Mendel, are you there? Look, for God's sake, how do I find you? Where is this place, will the police know it?"

"They'll know. Tell them he's in a converted landing craft called *Sunset Haven*. She's lying against the eastern side of Sennen Wharf, between the flour mills and Fulham Power Station. They'll know . . . but the fog's thick, mind, very thick."

"Where can I meet you?"

"Cut straight down to the river. I'll meet you where Battersea Bridge joins the north bank."

"I'll come at once, as soon as I've rung Guillam."

He had a gun somewhere, and for a moment he thought of looking for it. Then, somehow, it seemed pointless. Besides, he reflected grimly, there'd be the most frightful row if he used it. He rang Guillam at his flat and gave him Mendel's message: "And Peter, they must cover all ports and airfields; order a special watch on river traffic and seabound craft. They'll know the form."

He put on an old mackintosh and a pair of thick leather gloves and slipped quickly out into the fog.

Mendel was waiting for him by the bridge. They nodded to

one another and Mendel led him quickly along the embankment, keeping close to the river wall to avoid the trees that grew along the road. Suddenly Mendel stopped, seizing Smiley by the arm in warning. They stood motionless, listening. Then Smiley heard it too, the hollow ring of footsteps on a wooden floor, irregular like the footsteps of a limping man. They heard the creak of an iron gate, the clang as it was closed, then the footsteps again, firm now upon the pavement, growing louder, coming towards them. Neither moved. Louder, nearer, then they faltered, stopped. Smiley held his breath, trying desperately at the same time to see an extra yard into the fog, to glimpse at the waiting figure he knew was there.

Then suddenly he came, rushing like a massive wild beast, bursting through them, knocking them apart like children and running on, lost again, the uneven echo fading in the distance. They turned and chased after him, Mendel in front and Smiley following as best he could, the image vivid in his mind of Dieter, gun in hand, bursting on them out of the night fog. Ahead, the shadow of Mendel turned abruptly to the right, and Smiley followed blindly. Then suddenly the rhythm had changed to the scuffle of fighting. Smiley ran forward, heard the unmistakable sound of a heavy weapon striking a human skull, and then he was upon them: saw Mendel on the ground, and Dieter stooping over him, raising his arm to hit him again with the heavy butt of an automatic pistol.

Smiley was out of breath. His chest was burning from the bitter, rank fog, his mouth hot and dry, filled with a taste like blood. Somehow he summoned breath, and he shouted desperately:

"Dieter!"

Frey looked at him, nodded and said:

"*Servus*, George," and hit Mendel a hard, brutal blow with the pistol. He got up slowly, holding the pistol downwards and using both hands to cock it.

Smiley ran at him blindly, forgetting what little skill he had ever possessed, swinging with his short arms, striking with his open hands. His head was against Dieter's chest and he pushed forward, punching Dieter's back and sides. He was mad and, discovering in himself the energy of madness, pressed Dieter back still further towards the railing of the bridge while Dieter, off balance and hindered by his weak leg, gave way. Smiley knew Dieter was hitting him, but the decisive blow never came. He was shouting at Dieter; "Swine, swine!" and as Dieter receded still further Smiley found his arms free and once more struck at his face with clumsy, childish blows. Dieter was leaning back and Smiley saw the clean curve of his throat and chin, as with all his strength he thrust his open hand upwards. His fingers closed over Dieter's jaw and mouth and he pushed further and further. Dieter's hands were at Smiley's throat, then suddenly they were clutching at his collar to save himself as he sank slowly backwards. Smiley beat frantically at his arms, and then he was held no more and Dieter was falling, falling into the swirling fog beneath the bridge, and there was silence. No shout, no splash. He was gone; offered like a human sacrifice to the London fog and the foul black river lying beneath it.

Smiley leant over the bridge, his head throbbing wildly, blood pouring from his nose, the fingers of his right hand feeling broken and useless. His gloves were gone. He looked down into the fog and could see nothing.

"Dieter!" he cried in anguish. "Dieter!"

He shouted again, but his voice choked and tears sprang to his eyes. "Oh dear God what have I done, Oh Christ, Dieter, why didn't you stop me, why didn't you hit me with the gun, why didn't you shoot?" He pressed his clenched hands to his face, tasting the salt blood in the palms mixed with the salt of his tears. He leant against the parapet and cried like a child. Somewhere beneath him a cripple dragged himself through the filthy water, lost and exhausted, yielding at last to the stenching blackness till it held him and drew him down.

* * *

He woke to find Peter Guillam sitting on the end of his bed pouring out tea.

"Ah, George. Welcome home. It's two in the afternoon."

"And this morning—?"

"This morning, dear boy, you were carolling on Battersea Bridge with Comrade Mendel."

"How is he ... Mendel, I mean?"

"Suitably ashamed of himself. Recovering fast."

"And Dieter—?"

"Dead."

Guillam handed him a cup of tea and some ratafia biscuits from Fortnum's.

"How long have you been here, Peter?"

"Well, we came here in a series of tactical bounds, as it were. The first was to Chelsea Hospital where they licked your wounds and gave you a fairly substantial tranquillizer. Then we came back here and I put you to bed. That was disgusting. Then I did a spot of telephoning and, so to speak, went round with a pointed stick tidying up the mess. I looked in on you now and again. Cupid and Psyche. You were either snoring like a saddleback or reciting Webster."

"God."

"*Duchess of Malfi*, I think it was. 'I bade thee, when I was distracted of my wits, go kill my dearest friend, and thou hast done it!' Dreadful nonsense, George, I'm afraid."

"How did the police find us—Mendel and me?"

"George, you may not know it but you were bellowing pejoratives at Dieter as if—"

"Yes, of course. You heard."

"We heard."

"What about Maston? What does Maston say about all this?"

"I think he wants to see you. I have a message from him asking you to drop in as soon as you feel well enough. I don't know what he thinks about it. Nothing at all, I should imagine."

"What do you mean?"

Guillam poured out more tea.

"Use your loaf, George. All three principals in this little fairy tale have now been eaten by bears. No secret information has been compromised for the last six months. Do you really think Maston wants to dwell on the details? Do you really think he is bursting to tell the Foreign Office the good tidings—and admit that we only catch spies when we trip over their dead bodies?"

The front-door bell rang and Guillam went downstairs to answer it. In some alarm Smiley heard him admit the visitor to the hall, then the subdued sound of voices, footsteps coming up the stairs. There was a knock on the door and Maston came in. He was carrying an absurdly large bunch of flowers and looked as though he had just been to a garden party. Smiley remembered it was Friday: no doubt he was going to Henley this week-end. He was grinning. He must have been grinning all the way up the stairs.

"Well, George, in the wars again!"

"Yes, I'm afraid so. Another accident."

He sat on the edge of the bed, leaning across it, one arm supporting him the other side of Smiley's legs.

There was a pause and then he said:

"You got my note, George?"

"Yes."

Another pause.

"There has been talk of a new section in the Department, George. We (your Department, that is) feel we should devote more energy to technique research, with particular application to satellite espionage. That is also the Home Office view, I'm pleased to say. Guillam has agreed to advise on terms of reference. I wondered if you'd take it on for us. Running it. I mean, with the necessary promotion of course and the option of extending your service after the statutory retirement age. Our personnel people are right behind me on this."

"Thank you . . . perhaps I could think about it, may I?"

"Of course . . . of course," Maston looked slightly put out.

"When will you let me know? It may be necessary to take on some new men and the question of space arises . . . Have the week-end to think about it, will you, and let me know on Monday. The Secretary was quite willing for you to—"

"Yes, I'll let you know. It's very good of you."

"Not at all. Besides I am only the Adviser, you know, George. This is really an internal decision. I'm just the bringer of good news, George; my usual function of errand boy."

Maston looked at Smiley hard for a moment, hesitated and then said: "I've put the Ministers in the picture . . . as far as is necessary. We discussed what action should be taken. The Home Secretary was also present."

"When was this?"

"This morning. Some very grave issues were raised. We considered a protest to the East Germans and an extradition order for this man Mundt."

"But we don't recognize East Germany."

"Precisely. That was the difficulty. It is however possible to lodge a protest with an intermediary."

"Such as Russia?"

"Such as Russia. In the event, however, certain factors militated against this. It was felt that publicity, whatever form it took, would ultimately rebound against the nation's interests. There is already considerable popular hostility in this country to the rearmament of Western Germany. It was felt that any evidence of German intrigue in Britain—whether inspired by the Russians or not—might encourage this hostility. There is, you see, no positive evidence that Frey was operating for the Russians. It might well be represented to the public that he was operating on his own account or on behalf of a united Germany."

"I see."

"So far very few people indeed are aware of the facts at all.

That is most fortunate. On behalf of the police the Home Secretary has tentatively agreed that they will do their part in playing the affair down as far as possible . . . Now this man Mendel, what's he like? Is he trustworthy?"

Smiley hated Maston for that.

"Yes," he said.

Maston got up. "Good," he said, "good. Well, I must get along. Anything you want at all, anything I can do?"

"No, thank you. Guillam is looking after me admirably."

Maston reached the door. "Well good luck, George. Take the job if you can." He said this quickly in a subdued voice with a pretty, sidelong smile as if it meant rather a lot to him.

"Thank you for the flowers," said Smiley.

Dieter was dead, and he had killed him. The broken fingers of his right hand, the stiffness of his body and the sickening headache, the nausea of guilt, all testified to this. And Dieter had let him do it, had not fired the gun, had remembered their friendship when Smiley had not. They had fought in a cloud, in the rising stream of the river, in a clearing in a timeless forest: they had met, two friends rejoined, and fought like beasts. Dieter had remembered and Smiley had not. They had come from different hemispheres of the night, from different worlds of thought and conduct. Dieter, mercurial, absolute, had fought to build a civilization. Smiley, rationalistic, protective, had fought to prevent him. "Oh God," said Smiley aloud, "who was then the gentleman . . . ?"

Laboriously he got out of bed and began to dress. He felt better standing up.

17

Dear Adviser

Dear Adviser,

I am at last able to reply to Personnel's offer of a higher appointment in the Department. I am sorry that I have taken so long to do this, but as you know, I have not been well recently, and have also had to contend with a number of personal problems outside the scope of the Department.

As I am not entirely free of my indisposition, I feel it would be unwise for me to accept their offer. Kindly convey this decision to Personnel.

I am sure you will understand.

Yours,
George Smiley

Dear Peter,

I enclose a note on the Fennan Case. This is the only copy. Please pass it to Maston when you have read it. I thought it would be valuable to record the events—even if they did not take place.

Ever,
George

The Fennan Case

On Monday, 2 January, I interviewed Samuel Arthur Fennan, a senior member of the Foreign Office, in order to clarify certain allegations made against him in an anonymous letter. The interview was arranged in accordance with the customary procedure, that is to say with the consent of the FO. We knew of nothing adverse to Fennan beyond communist sympathy while at Oxford in the thirties, to which little significance was attached. The interview was therefore in a sense a strictly routine affair.

Fennan's room at the Foreign Office was found to be unsuitable and we agreed to continue our discussion in St. James's Park, availing ourselves of the good weather.

It has subsequently transpired that we were recognized and observed in this by an agent of the East German Intelligence Service, who had cooperated with me during the war. It is not certain whether he had placed Fennan under some kind of surveillance, or whether his presence in the park was coincidental.

On the night of 3 January it was reported by Surrey police that Fennan had committed suicide. A typewritten suicide note signed by Fennan claimed that he had been victimized by the security authorities.

The following facts, however, emerged during investigation, and suggested foul play:

1. At 7:55 P.M. on the night of his death Fennan had asked the Walliston exchange to call him at 8:30 the following morning.
2. Fennan had made himself a cup of cocoa shortly before his death, and had not drunk it.
3. He had supposedly shot himself in the hall, at the bottom the stairs. The note was beside the body.
4. It seemed inconsistent that he should type his last letter, as he seldom used a typewriter, and even more remarkable

that he should come downstairs to the hall to shoot himself.

5. On the day of his death he posted a letter inviting me in urgent terms to lunch with him at Marlow the following day.

6. Later it also transpired that Fennan had requested a day's leave for Wednesday, 4 January. He did not apparently mention this to his wife.

7. It was also noted that the suicide letter had been typed on Fennan's own machine—and that it contained certain peculiarities in the typescript similar to those in the anonymous letter. The laboratory report concluded, however, that the two letters had not been typed by the same hand, though originating from the same machine.

Mrs. Fennan, who had been to the theatre on the night her husband died, was invited to explain the 8:30 call from the exchange and falsely claimed to have requested it herself. The exchange was positive that this was not the case. Mrs. Fennan claimed that her husband had been nervous and depressed since his security interview, which corroborated the evidence of his final letter.

On the afternoon of 4 January, having left Mrs. Fennan earlier in the day, I returned to my house in Kensington. Briefly observing somebody at the window, I rang the front-door bell. A man opened the door who has since been identified as a member of the East German Intelligence Service. He invited me into the house but I declined his offer and returned to my car, noting at the same time the numbers of cars parked nearby.

That evening I visited a small garage in Battersea to inquire into the origin of one of these cars which was registered in the name of the proprietor of the garage. I was attacked by an unknown assailant and beaten senseless. Three weeks later the proprietor himself, Adam Scarr, was found dead in the Thames near Battersea Bridge. He had been drunk at the time of drowning. There were no signs of violence and he was known as a heavy drinker.

It is relevant that Scarr had for the last four years provided an anonymous foreigner with the use of a car, and had received generous rewards for doing so. Their arrangements were designed to conceal the identity of the borrower even from Scarr himself, who only knew his client by the nickname "Blondie" and could only reach him through a telephone number. The telephone number is of importance—it was that of the East German Steel Mission.

Meanwhile, Mrs. Fennan's alibi for the evening of the murder had been investigated and significant information came to light:

1. Mrs. Fennan attended the Weybridge Repertory Theatre twice a month, on the first and third Tuesdays. (N.B. Adam Scarr's client had collected his car on the first and third Tuesdays of each month.)
2. She always brought a music case and left it in the cloakroom.
3. When visiting the theatre she was always joined by a man whose description corresponded with that of my assailant and Scarr's client. It was even mistakenly assumed by a member of the theatre staff that this man was Mrs. Fennan's husband. He too brought a music case and left it in the cloakroom.
4. On the evening of the murder Mrs. Fennan had left the theatre early after her friend had failed to arrive and had forgotten to reclaim her music case. Late that night she telephoned the theatre to ask if the case could be called for at once. She had lost her cloakroom ticket. The case was collected—by Mrs. Fennan's usual friend.

At this point the stranger was identified as an employee of the East German Steel Mission named Mundt. The principal of the Mission was Herr Dieter Frey, a war-time collaborator of our Service, with extensive operational experience. After the war he had entered Government service in the Soviet zone of Germany. I should mention that Frey had operated with me during the war in enemy territory and had shown himself to be a brilliant and resourceful agent.

I now decided to conduct a third interview with Mrs. Fennan. She broke down and confessed to having acted as an intelligence courier for her husband, who had been recruited by Frey on a skiing holiday five years ago. She herself had cooperated unwillingly, partly in loyalty to her husband and partly to protect him from his own carelessness in performing his espionage role. Frey had seen Fennan talking to me in the park. Assuming I was still operationally employed, he had concluded that Fennan was either under suspicion or a double agent. He instructed Mundt to liquidate Fennan, and his wife had been compelled into silence by her own complicity. She had even typed the text of the suicide letter on Fennan's typewriter over a specimen of her husband's signature.

The means whereby she passed to Mundt the intelligence procured by her husband is relevant. She placed notes and copied documents in a music case, which she took to the theatre. Mundt brought a similar case containing money and instructions and, like Mrs. Fennan, left it in the cloakroom. They had only to exchange cloakroom tickets. When Mundt failed to appear at the theatre on the night in question, Mrs. Fennan obeyed standing instructions and posted the ticket to an address in Highgate. She left the theatre in order to catch the last post from Weybridge. When later that night Mundt demanded the music case she told him what she had done. Mundt insisted on collecting the case that night, for he did not wish to make another journey to Weybridge.

When I interviewed Mrs. Fennan the following morning, one of my questions (about the 8:30 call) alarmed her so much that she telephoned Mundt. This accounts for the assault upon me later that day.

Mrs. Fennan provided me with the address and telephone number she used when contacting Mundt—whom she knew by the cover name of Freitag. Both led to the apartment of a "Lufteuropa" pilot who often entertained Mundt and provided accommodation for him when he required it. The pilot (presumably a courier of the East German Intelligence Service) has not returned to this country since 5 January.

This, then, was the sum of Mrs. Fennan's revelations, and in a sense they led nowhere. The spy was dead, his murderers had vanished. It only remained to assess the extent of the damage. An official approach was now made to the Foreign Office and Mr. Felix Taverner was instructed to calculate from Foreign Office schedules what information had been compromised. This involved listing all files to which Fennan had had access since his recruitment by Frey. Remarkably, this revealed no systematic acquisition of secret files. Fennan had drawn no secret files except those which directly concerned him in his duties. During the last six months, when his access to sensitive papers was substantially increased, he had actually taken home *no* files of secret classification. The files he took home over this period were of universally low grade, and some treated subjects actually outside the scope of his section. This was not consistent with Fennan's role as a spy. It was, however, possible that he had lost heart for his work, and that his luncheon invitation to me was a first step to confession. With this in mind he might also have written the anonymous letter which could have been designed to put him in touch with the Department.

Two further facts should be mentioned at this point. Under an assumed name and with a fake passport, Mundt left the country by air on the day after Mrs. Fennan made her confession. He evaded the notice of the airport authorities, but was retrospectively identified by the air hostess. Secondly, Fennan's diary contained the full name and official telephone number of Dieter Frey—a flagrant breach of the most elementary rule of espionage.

It was hard to understand why Mundt had waited three weeks in England after murdering Scarr, and even harder to reconcile Fennan's activities as described by his wife with the obviously unplanned and unproductive selection of files. Re-examination of the facts led repeatedly to this conclusion: the only evidence that Fennan was a spy came from his wife. If the facts were as she described them, why had she been allowed to survive the determination of Mundt and Frey to eliminate those in possession of dangerous knowledge?

On the other hand, might she not herself be the spy?

This would explain the date of Mundt's departure: he left as soon as he had been reassured by Mrs. Fennan that I had accepted her ingenious confession. It would explain the entry in Fennan's diary: Frey was a chance skiing acquaintance and an occasional visitor to Walliston. It would make sense of Fennan's choice of files—if Fennan deliberately chose unclassified papers at a time when his work was mainly secret there could be only one explanation: he had come to suspect his wife. Hence the invitation to Marlow, following naturally upon our encounter the previous day. Fennan had decided to tell me of his apprehensions and had taken a day's leave to do so—a fact of which his wife was not apparently aware. This would also explain why Fennan denounced himself in an anonymous letter: he wished to put himself in touch with us *as a preliminary to denouncing his wife.*

Continuing the supposition it was remarkable that in matters of tradecraft Mrs. Fennan alone was efficient and conscientious. The technique used by herself and Mundt recalled that of Frey during the war. The secondary arrangement to post the cloakroom ticket if no meeting took place was typical of his scrupulous planning. Mrs. Fennan, it seemed, had acted with a precision scarcely compatible with her claim to be an unwilling party to her husband's treachery.

While logically Mrs. Fennan now came under suspicion as a spy, there was no reason to believe that her account of what happened on the night of Fennan's murder was necessarily untrue. Had she known of Mundt's intention to murder her husband she would not have taken the music case to the theatre, and would not have posted the cloakroom ticket.

There seemed no way of proving the case against her unless it was possible to reactivate the relationship between Mrs. Fennan and her controller. During the war Frey had devised an ingenious code for emergency communication by the use of snapshots and picture postcards. The actual subject of the photograph contained the message. A religious subject such as a painting of a Madonna or a church conveyed a request for an early meeting. The recipient would send in reply an entirely unrelated letter, making sure to date it. A meeting would take place at a prearranged time and place exactly five days after the date on the letter.

It was just possible that Frey, whose tradecraft had evidently altered so little since the war, might have clung to this system—which, after all, would only seldom be needed. Relying on this I therefore posted to Elsa Fennan a picture postcard depicting a church. The card was posted from Highgate. I hoped somewhat forlornly that she would assume it had come to her through the agency of Frey. She reacted at once by sending to an unknown address abroad a ticket for a London theatre performance five days ahead. Mrs. Fennan's communication reached Frey, who accepted it as an *urgent summons*. Knowing that Mundt had been compromised by Mrs. Fennan's "confession" he decided to come himself.

They therefore met at the Sheridan Theatre, Hammersmith, on Tuesday, 15 February.

At first each assumed that the other had initiated the meeting, but when Frey realized they had been brought together by a deception he took drastic action. It may be that he suspected Mrs. Fennan of luring him into a trap, that he realized he was under surveillance. We shall never know. In any event, he murdered her. His method of doing this is best described in the coroner's report at the inquest: "a single degree of pressure had been applied on the larynx, in particular to the horns of the thyroid cartilage, causing almost immediate death. It would appear that Mrs. Fennan's assailant was no layman in these matters."

Frey was pursued to a houseboat moored near Cheyne Walk, and while violently resisting arrest he fell into the river, from which his body has now been recovered.

18

Between Two Worlds

Smiley's unrespectable club was usually empty on Sundays, but Mrs. Sturgeon left the door unlocked in case any of her gentlemen chose to call in. She adopted the same stern, possessive attitude towards her gentlemen as she had done in her landlady days at Oxford, when she had commanded from her fortunate boarders more respect than the entire assembly of dons and proctors. She forgave everything, but somehow managed to suggest on each occasion that her forgiveness was unique, and would never, never happen again. She had once made Steed-Asprey put ten shillings in the poor box for bringing seven guests without warning, and afterwards provided the dinner of a lifetime.

They sat at the same table as before. Mendel looked a shade sallower, a shade older. He scarcely spoke during the meal, handling his knife and fork with the same careful precision which he applied to any task. Guillam supplied most of the conversation, for Smiley, too, was less talkative than usual. They were at ease in their companionship and no one felt unduly the need to speak.

"Why did she do it?" Mendel asked suddenly.

Smiley shook his head slowly: "I think I know, but we can only guess. I think she dreamed of a world without conflict, ordered and preserved by the new doctrine. I once angered her, you see, and she shouted at me: 'I'm the wandering

Jewess,' she said; 'the no-man's land, the battlefield for your toy soldiers.' As she saw the new Germany rebuilt in the image of the old, saw the plump pride return, as she put it, I think it was just too much for her; I think she looked at the futility of her suffering and the prosperity of her persecutors and rebelled. Five years ago, she told me, they met Dieter on a skiing holiday in Germany. By that time the reestablishment of Germany as a prominent western power was well under way."

"Was she a communist?"

"I don't think she liked labels. I think she wanted to help build one society which could live without conflict. Peace is a dirty word now, isn't it? I think she wanted peace."

"And Dieter?" asked Guillam.

"God knows what Dieter wanted. Honour, I think, and a socialist world." Smiley shrugged. "They dreamed of peace and freedom. Now they're murderers and spies."

"Christ Almighty," said Mendel.

Smiley was silent again, looking into his glass. At last he said: "I can't expect you to understand. You only saw the end of Dieter. I saw the beginning. He went the full circle. I don't think he ever got over being a traitor in the war. He had to put it right. He was one of those world-builders who seem to do nothing but destroy: that's all."

Guillam gracefully intervened: "What about the 8:30 call?"

"I think it's pretty obvious. Fennan wanted to see me at Marlow and he'd taken a day's leave. He can't have told Elsa he was having a day off or she'd have tried to explain it away to me. He staged a phone call to give himself an excuse for going to Marlow. That's my guess, anyway."

The fire crackled in the wide hearth.

He caught the midnight plane to Zurich. It was a beautiful night, and through the small window beside him he watched the grey wing, motionless against the starlit sky, a glimpse of eternity between two worlds. The vision soothed him, calmed his fears and his doubts, made him fatalistic towards the inscrutable purpose of the universe. It all seemed to matter so little—the pathetic quest for love, or the return to solitude.

Soon the lights of the French coast came in sight. As he watched, he began to sense vicariously the static life beneath him; the rank smell of Gauloises Bleues, garlic and good food, the raised voices in the bistro. Maston was a million miles off, locked away with his arid paper and his shiny politicians.

Smiley presented an odd figure to his fellow passengers—a little fat man, rather gloomy, suddenly smiling, ordering a drink. The young, fair-haired man beside him examined him closely out of the corner of his eye. He knew the type well—the tired executive out for a bit of fun. He found it rather disgusting.

Praise for John le Carré

"There are those writer[s] . . . who themselves should be immortal. . . . I would suggest immortality for John le Carré, who I believe one of the most intelligent and entertaining writers. . . . May he write forever!"
—Alan Cheuse, *Chicago Tribune*

"No other contemporary novelist has more durably enjoyed the twin badges of being both well-read and well-regarded."
—Scott Turow

"A brilliant linguistic artist with a keen eye for the exotic and not-so-exotic locale, a crafty moralizer."
—*The Wall Street Journal*

"Le Carré is simply the world's greatest fictional spymaster."
—*Newsweek*

"Le Carré's work is . . . the gold standard of espionage fiction and the author is . . . a master of any sort of fiction, no matter the genre."
—*The Seattle Times*

"Le Carré's execution is perfect."
—*The New York Times Book Review*

"Le Carré has a great talent for entangling his audience in the sticky tape of complexity, paradox, and irony, and much of the pleasure in his stories is following the same dense, dark path as his characters."
—*New York Daily News*

"He has reinvented the realistic spy story as the supreme theater of paradox, where heroism breeds vice, and virtue is a quite accidental by-product of impudent crimes."
—*Time*

PENGUIN BOOKS

A MURDER OF QUALITY

JOHN LE CARRÉ was born in 1931. For six decades, he wrote novels that came to define our age. The son of a con man, he spent his childhood between boarding school and the London underworld. At sixteen he found refuge at the university of Bern, then later at Oxford. A spell of teaching at Eton led him to a short career in British Intelligence (MI5&6). He published his debut novel, *Call for the Dead*, in 1961 while still a secret servant. His third novel, *The Spy Who Came in from the Cold*, secured him a worldwide reputation, which was consolidated by the acclaim for his trilogy *Tinker Tailor Soldier Spy*, *The Honourable Schoolboy*, and *Smiley's People*. At the end of the Cold War, le Carré widened his scope to explore an international landscape including the arms trade and the War on Terror. His memoir, *The Pigeon Tunnel*, was published in 2016 and the last George Smiley novel, *A Legacy of Spies*, appeared in 2017. He died on December 12, 2020.

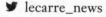

johnlecarre.com
🐦 lecarre_news
f johnlecarreofficial

JOHN LE CARRÉ

A MURDER OF QUALITY

PENGUIN BOOKS

PENGUIN BOOKS
Published by the Penguin Group
Penguin Group (USA) Inc., 375 Hudson Street, New York, New York 10014, U.S.A.
Penguin Group (Canada), 90 Eglinton Avenue East, Suite 700,
Toronto, Ontario, Canada M4P 2Y3 (a division of Pearson Penguin Canada Inc.)
Penguin Books Ltd, 80 Strand, London WC2R 0RL, England
Penguin Ireland, 25 St Stephen's Green, Dublin 2, Ireland (a division of Penguin Books Ltd)
Penguin Group (Australia), 250 Camberwell Road, Camberwell, Victoria 3124, Australia
(a division of Pearson Australia Group Pty Ltd)
Penguin Books India Pvt Ltd, 11 Community Centre,
Panchsheel Park, New Delhi – 110 017, India
Penguin Group (NZ), 67 Apollo Drive, Rosedale, Auckland 0632,
New Zealand (a division of Pearson New Zealand Ltd)
Penguin Books (South Africa) (Pty) Ltd, 24 Sturdee Avenue,
Rosebank, Johannesburg 2196, South Africa

Penguin Books Ltd, Registered Offices:
80 Strand, London WC2R 0RL, England

First published in Great Britain by Victor Gollancz Ltd 1962
First published in the United States of America by Walker and Company 1963
Published in Penguin Books 2012

10th Printing

PUBLISHER'S NOTE
This is a work of fiction. Names, characters, places, and incidents either are the product of the author's imagination or are used fictitiously, and any resemblance to actual persons, living or dead, businesses, companies, events, or locales is entirely coincidental.

LIBRARY OF CONGRESS CATALOGING-IN-PUBLICATION DATA
Le Carré, John, 1931–
A murder of quality / John Le Carré.
p. cm.
ISBN 978-0-14-312258-6
1. Smiley, George (Fictitious character)—Fiction. 2. Boarding schools—Fiction.
3. Murder—Investigation—Fiction. 4. Dorset (England)—Fiction. I. Title.
PR6062.E33M8 2012
823'.914—dc23 2012019593

Printed in the United States of America

To Ann

FOREWORD

There are probably a dozen great schools of whom it will be confidently asserted that Carne is their deliberate image. But he who looks among their common rooms for the D'Arcys, Fieldings, and Hechts will search in vain.

JOHN LE CARRÉ

CONTENTS

INTRODUCTION

JOHN LE CARRÉ
December 1989

The origins of most of my books are by now a mystery to me, even if they were not at the time, but *A Murder of Quality* is clearly set in my memory. It was my second book and I wrote it in the flush of the modest success enjoyed by my first, *Call for the Dead*. I began it in 1961 when I arrived in Bonn ahead of my family to take up a junior post at the British Embassy, and by the time it appeared I had *The Spy Who Came in from the Cold* in my sights.

I still had a notion in those days of writing a thriller a year and adding a much-needed few hundred pounds to my Foreign Service salary. Or so I told myself, even if my ambitions were secretly larger. I wrote *A Murder of Quality* first in the gloomy *pension* in Bad Godesberg where junior British diplomats were stabled while they awaited accommodation, then in the tiny house in the Gringstrasse where we lived with our two children and our au pair. In consequence, I wrote the book lying down, on beds, in notebooks, in the few snatched hours that were left to me by family and diplomatic life.

My sources were extremely present to me, as they will be to the reader. I hated English boarding schools. I found them monstrous and still do, probably because I began my boarding school career at the age of five, at a place called St. Martin's, Northwood, and did not end it till I was sixteen, when I flatly refused to return to Westcott House, Sherborne, on the solid grounds that I would take no more of such institutions.

Yet as life would have it, eight years later I was banged up once again, this time at Eton as a junior Modern Languages master.

Eton was not Sherborne at all. Sherborne in my day had been rustic, colonialist, chauvinist, militarist, religious, patriotic and repressive. Boys beat other boys, housemasters beat boys, and even the headmaster turned his hand to beating boys when the crime was held to be sufficiently heinous or school discipline was thought to be slipping. I don't know whether masters beat masters but, in any case, I loathed them, and I loathed their grotesque allegiances most of all. To this day, I can find no forgiveness for their terrible abuse of the charges entrusted to them.

Only adults had nervous breakdowns in those days, so the methods of survival for boys who refused to join the system were animal cunning, "internal immigration" as the Germans call it, or simply getting the hell out. I practised the first two, then opted for the third and took myself to Switzerland.

But Eton was an English social class of its own. A graduate of Eton is an Etonian first and a citizen second. He enjoys, during his schooling, more personal access to the staff than in any other school I am aware of, and an extremely high standard of teaching. Certainly the system had its barbarisms, but it awarded more privacy, more sovereignty to its pupils, more self-esteem—some would say arrogance—than I had imagined possible. As a young schoolmaster, I had the sensation of embarking on a second, vicarious education of my own, reacting sometimes against it, sometimes for it, but never calmly, never with any sense of integration or acceptance. Probably, since I had not yet begun to write, I had not realised quite how much of an outsider I was anyway, constantly repelled by the institutions that drew me.

So the components are there for you to dissect as you will:

an outrage at my Sherborne schooling, a fascination with the mores of the Etonian class, an attraction to it all, a revulsion from it, a bestiary of frightening adults drawn from the timid chambers of my institutional and largely parentless childhood; and a spiritual brutality towards young minds that in this far-from-perfect story takes the form of bloody violence.

As to poor Stella Rode and her non-conformism, they came from even further back, from the days when my brother and I spent our Sundays in the chapels and tabernacles of coastal Dorset, listening to the counsel of a far humbler God than He who guided the untroubled conscience of the British ruling classes.

Rereading the book now, I find a flawed thriller redeemed by ferocious and quite funny social comment. Most of all I recognise the dankness of those old stone walls that formed the limits of my childhood and left me for the rest of my life with an urge to fight off whatever threatened to enclose me.

A MURDER OF
QUALITY

1

Black Candles

The greatness of Carne School has been ascribed by common consent to Edward VI, whose educational zeal is ascribed by history to the Duke of Somerset. But Carne prefers the respectability of the monarch to the questionable politics of his adviser, drawing strength from the conviction that Great Schools, like Tudor Kings, were ordained in Heaven.

And indeed its greatness is little short of miraculous. Founded by obscure monks, endowed by a sickly boy king, and dragged from oblivion by a Victorian bully, Carne had straightened its collar, scrubbed its rustic hands and face and presented itself shining to the courts of the twentieth century. And in the twinkling of an eye, the Dorset bumpkin was London's darling: Dick Whittington had arrived. Carne had parchments in Latin, seals in wax, and Lammas Land behind the Abbey. Carne had property, cloisters and woodworm, a whipping block and a line in the Doomsday Book—then what more did it need to instruct the sons of the rich?

And they came; each Half they came (for terms are not elegant things), so that throughout a whole afternoon the trains would unload sad groups of black-coated boys on to the station platform. They came in great cars that shone with mournful purity. They came to bury poor King Edward, trundling handcarts over the cobbled streets or carrying tuck boxes like little coffins. Some wore gowns, and when they walked they looked like crows, or black angels come for the burying. Some followed singly like undertakers' mutes, and you could hear the clip of their boots as they went. They were always in mourning at Carne; the small boys because they must stay and the big boys because they must leave, the masters because respectability was underpaid; and now, as the Lent Half (as the Easter term was called) drew to its end, the cloud of gloom was as firmly settled as ever over the grey towers of Carne.

Gloom and the cold. The cold was crisp and sharp as flint. It cut the faces of the boys as they moved slowly from the deserted playing fields after the school match. It pierced their black top-coats and turned their stiff, pointed collars into icy rings round their necks. Frozen, they plodded from the field to the long walled road which led to the main tuck shop and the town, the line gradually dwindling into groups, and the groups into pairs. Two boys who looked even colder than the rest crossed the road and made their way along a narrow path which led towards a distant but less populated tuck shop.

"I think I shall die if ever I have to watch one of those beastly rugger games again. The noise is fantastic," said one. He was tall with fair hair, and his name was Caley.

"People only shout because the dons are watching from the pavilion," the other rejoined; "that's why each house has to stand together. So that the house dons can swank about how loud their houses shout."

"What about Rode?" asked Caley. "Why does he stand with us and make us shout, then? He's not a house don, just a bloody usher."

"He's sucking up to house dons all the time. You can see him in the quad between lessons buzzing round the big men. All the junior masters do." Caley's companion was a cynical red-haired boy called Perkins, Captain of Fielding's house.

"I've been to tea with Rode," said Caley.

"Rode's hell. He wears brown boots. What was tea like?"

"Bleak. Funny how tea gives them away. Mrs. Rode's quite decent, though—homely in a plebby sort of way: doyleys and china birds. Food's good: Women's Institute, but good."

"Rode's doing Corps next Half. That'll put the lid on it. He's so *keen*, bouncing about all the time. You can tell he's not a gentleman. You know where he went to school?"

"No."

"Branxome Grammar. Fielding told my Mama, when she came over from Singapore last Half."

"God. Where's Branxome?"

"On the coast. Near Bournemouth. I haven't been to tea with anyone except Fielding." Perkins added after a slight pause, "You get roast chestnuts and crumpets. You're never allowed to thank him, you know. He says emotionalism is only for the lower classes. That's typical of Fielding. He's not like a don at all. I think boys bore him. The whole house goes to tea with him once a Half, he has us in turn, four at a time, and that's about the only time he talks to most men."

They walked on in silence for a while until Perkins said:

"Fielding's giving another dinner party tonight."

"He's pushing the boat out these days," Caley replied, with disapproval. "Suppose the food in your house is worse than ever?"

"It's his last Half before he retires. He's entertaining every don and all the wives separately by the end of the Half. Black candles every evening. For mourning. Hells extravagant."

"Yes. I suppose it's a sort of gesture."

"My Pater says he's a queer."

They crossed the road and disappeared into the tuck shop, where they continued to discuss the weighty affairs of Mr. Terence Fielding, until Perkins drew their meeting reluctantly to a close. Being a poor hand at science, he was unfortunately obliged to take extra tuition in the subject.

The dinner party to which Perkins had alluded that afternoon was now drawing to a close. Mr. Terence Fielding, senior housemaster of Carne, gave himself some more port and pushed the decanter wearily to his left. It was his port, the best he had. There was enough of the best to last the Half—and after that, be damned. He felt a little tired after watching the match, and a little drunk, and a little bored with Shane Hecht and her husband. Shane was so hideous. Massive and enveloping, like a faded Valkyrie. All that black hair. He should have asked someone else. The Snows for instance, but he was too clever. Or Felix D'Arcy, but D'Arcy interrupted. Ah well, a little later he would annoy Charles Hecht, and Hecht would get in a pet and leave early.

Hecht was fidgeting, wanting to light his pipe, but Fielding damn well wouldn't have it. Hecht could have a cigar if he wanted to smoke. But his pipe could stay in his dinner-jacket pocket, where it belonged, or didn't belong, and his athletic profile could remain unadorned.

"Cigar, Hecht?"

"No thanks, Fielding. I say, do you mind if I . . ."

"I can recommend the cigars. Young Havelake sent them from Havana. His father's ambassador there, you know."

"Yes, dear," said Shane tolerantly; "Vivian Havelake was in Charles's troop when Charles was commandant of the Cadets."

"Good boy, Havelake," Hecht observed, and pressed his lips together to show he was a strict judge.

"It's amusing how things have changed." Shane Hecht said this rapidly with a rather wooden smile, as if it weren't really amusing. "Such a grey world we live in, now.

"I remember before the war when Charles inspected the Corps on a white horse. We don't do that kind of thing now, do we? I've got nothing against Mr. Iredale as commandant, nothing at all. What *was* his regiment, Terence, do you know? I'm sure he does it very nicely, whatever they do now in the Corps—he gets on so well with the boys, doesn't he? His wife's such a nice person . . . I wonder why they can never keep their servants. I hear Mr. Rode will be helping out with the Corps next Half."

"Poor little Rode," said Fielding slowly; "running about like a puppy, trying to earn his biscuits. He tries so hard; have you seen him cheering at school matches? He'd never seen a game of rugger before he came here, you know. They don't play rugger at grammar schools—it's all soccer. Do you remember when he first came, Charles? It was fascinating. He lay very low at first, drinking us in: the games, the vocabulary, the manners. Then, one day it was as if he had been given the power of speech, and he spoke in our language. It was amazing, like plastic surgery. It was Felix D'Arcy's work of course—I've never seen anything quite like it before."

"Dear Mrs. Rode," said Shane Hecht in that voice of abstract vagueness which she reserved for her most venomous pronouncements: "So sweet . . . and such simple taste, don't you think? I mean, whoever would have dreamed of putting those china ducks on the wall? Big ones at the front and little ones at the back. Charming, don't you think? Like one of those teashops. I wonder where she bought them. I must ask her. I'm told her father lives near Bournemouth. It must be so lonely for him, don't you think? Such a vulgar place; no one to talk to."

Fielding sat back and surveyed his own table. The silver was good. The best in Carne, he had heard it said, and he was inclined to agree. This Half he had nothing but black candles. It was the sort of thing people remembered when you'd gone: "Dear old Terence—marvellous host. He dined every member of the staff during his last Half, you know, wives too. Black candles, rather touching. It broke his heart giving up his house." But he must annoy Charles Hecht. Shane would like that. Shane would egg him on because she hated Charles, because within her great ugly body she was as cunning as a snake.

Fielding looked at Hecht and then at Hecht's wife, and she

smiled back at him, the slow rotten smile of a whore. For a moment Fielding thought of Hecht pasturing in that thick body: it was a scene redolent of Lautrec . . . yes, that was it! Charles pompous and top-hatted, seated stiffly upon the plush coverlet; she massive, pendulous and bored. The image pleased him: so perverse to consign that fool Hecht from the Spartan cleanliness of Carne to the brothels of nineteenth-century Paris . . .

Fielding began talking, pontificating rather, with an air of friendly objectivity which he knew Hecht would resent.

"When I look back on my thirty years at Carne, I realise I have achieved rather less than a road sweeper." They were watching him now—"I used to regard a road sweeper as a person inferior to myself. Now, I rather doubt it. Something is dirty, he makes it clean, and the state of the world is advanced. But I—what have *I* done? Entrenched a ruling class which is distinguished by neither talent, culture, nor wit; kept alive for one more generation the distinctions of a dead age."

Charles Hecht, who had never perfected the art of not listening to Fielding, grew red and fussed at the other end of the table.

"Don't we teach them, Fielding? What about our successes, our scholarships?"

"I have never taught a boy in my life, Charles. Usually the boy wasn't clever enough; occasionally, I wasn't. In most boys, you see, perception dies with puberty. In a few it persists, though where we find it we take good care at Carne to kill it. If it survives our efforts the boy wins a scholarship . . . Bear with me, Shane; it's my last Half."

"Last Half or not, you're talking through your hat, Fielding," said Hecht, angrily.

"That is traditional at Carne. These successes, as you call them, are the failures, the rare boys who have not learned the lessons of Carne. They have ignored the cult of mediocrity. We can do nothing for them. But for the rest, for the puzzled little clerics and the blind little soldiers, for them the truth of Carne is written on the wall, and they hate us."

Hecht laughed rather heavily.

"Why do so many come back, then, if they hate us so much? Why do they remember us and come and see us?"

"Because we, dear Charles, are the writing on the wall! The one lesson of Carne they never forget. They come back to read *us*, don't you see? It was from us they learnt the secret of life: that we grow old without growing wise. They realised that nothing happened when we grew up: no blinding light on the road to Damascus, no sudden feeling of maturity." Fielding put his head back and gazed at the clumsy Victorian moulding on the ceiling, and the halo of dirt round the light rose.

"We just got a little older. We made the same jokes, thought the same thoughts, wanted the same things. Year in, year out, Hecht, we were the same people, not wiser, not better; we haven't had an original thought between us for the last fifty years of our lives. They saw what a trick it all was, Carne and us: our academic dress, our schoolroom jokes, our wise little offerings of guidance. And that's why they come back year after year of their puzzled, barren lives to gaze fascinated at you and me, Hecht, like children at a grave, searching for the secret of life and death. Oh, yes, they have learned *that* from us."

Hecht looked at Fielding in silence for a moment.

"Decanter, Hecht?" said Fielding, in a slightly conciliatory way, but Hecht's eyes were still upon him.

"If that's a joke . . ." he began, and his wife observed with satisfaction that he was very angry indeed.

"I wish I knew, Charles," Fielding replied with apparent earnestness. "I really wish I knew. I used to think it was clever to confuse comedy with tragedy. Now I wish I could distinguish them." He rather liked that.

They had coffee in the drawing-room, where Fielding resorted to gossip, but Hecht was not to be drawn. Fielding rather wished he had let him light his pipe. Then he recalled his vision of the Hechts in Paris, and it restored him. He had been rather good this evening. There were moments when he convinced himself.

While Shane fetched her coat, the two men stood together in the hall, but neither spoke. Shane returned, an ermine stole, yellow with age, draped over her great white shoulders. She inclined her head to the right, smiled and held out her hand to Fielding, the fingers down.

"Terence, darling," she said, as Fielding kissed her fat knuckles; "so kind. And in your last Half. You must dine with us before you go. So sad. So few of us left." She smiled again, half closing her eyes to indicate emotional disturbance, then followed her husband into the street. It was still bitterly cold and snow was in the air.

Fielding closed and carefully bolted the door behind them—perhaps a fraction earlier than courtesy required—and returned to the dining-room. Hecht's port glass was still about half full. Fielding picked it up and carefully poured the contents back into the decanter. He hoped Hecht wasn't too upset; he hated people to dislike him. He snuffed the black candles and damped their wicks between his forefinger and thumb. Switching on the light, he took from the sideboard a sixpenny notebook, and opened it. It contained his list of dining guests for the remainder of the Half. With his fountain pen he placed a neat tick against the name Hecht. They were done. On Wednesday he would have the Rodes. The husband was quite good value, but she, of course, was hell . . . It was not always the way with married couples. The wives as a rule were so much more sympathetic.

He opened the sideboard and took from it a bottle of brandy and a tumbler. Holding them both in the same hand, he shuffled wearily back to the drawing-room, resting his other hand on the wall as he went. God! He felt old, suddenly; that thin line of pain across the chest, that heaviness in the legs and feet. Such an effort being with people—on stage all the time. He hated to be alone, but people bored him. Being alone was like being tired, but unable to sleep. Some German poet had said that; he'd quoted it once, "You may sleep but I must dance." Something like that.

"That's how I am," thought Fielding. "That's how Carne is, too; an old satyr dancing to the music." The music grew faster and their bodies older, but they must dance on—there were young men waiting in the wings. It had been funny once dancing the old dances in a new world. He poured himself some more brandy. He'd be pleased to leave in a way, even though he'd have to go on teaching somewhere else.

But it had its beauty, Carne . . . The Abbey Close in spring . . . the flamingo figures of boys waiting for the ritual of worship . . . the ebb and flow of children, like the seasons of the year, and the old men dying among them. He wished he could paint; he would paint the pageant of Carne in the fallow browns of autumn . . . What a shame, thought Fielding, that a mind so perceptive of beauty had no talent for creation.

He looked at his watch. Quarter to twelve. Nearly time to go out . . . to dance, and not to sleep.

2

The Thursday Feeling

It was Thursday evening and the *Christian Voice* had just been put to bed. This was scarcely a historic event in Fleet Street. The pimply boy from Dispatch who took away the ragged pile of page-proofs showed no more ceremony than was strictly demanded by the eventual prospect of his Christmas bonus. And even in this respect he had learned that the secular journals of Unipress were more provident of material charity than the *Christian Voice*; charity being in strict relationship to circulation.

Miss Brimley, the journal's editor, adjusted the air cushion beneath her and lit a cigarette. Her secretary and sub-editor—the appointment carried both responsibilities—yawned, dropped the aspirin bottle into her handbag, combed out her ginger hair and bade Miss Brimley good night, leaving behind her as usual the smell of strongly scented powder and an empty paper-tissue box. Miss Brimley listened contentedly to the clipping echo of her footsteps as it faded down the corridor. It pleased her to be alone at last, tasting the anticlimax. She never failed to wonder at herself, how every Thursday morning brought the same slight uneasiness as she entered the vast Unipress building and stood a little absurdly on one escalator after the other, like a drab parcel on a luxury liner. Heaven knows, she had run the *Voice* for fourteen years, and there were those who said its layout was the best thing Unipress did. Yet the Thursday feeling never left her, the wakeful anxiety that one day, perhaps today, they wouldn't be ready when the dispatch boy came. She often wondered what would happen then. She had heard of failures elsewhere in that vast combine, of features disapproved and staff rebuked. It was a mystery to her why they kept the *Voice* at all, with its expensive room on the seventh floor and a circulation which, if Miss Brimley knew anything, hardly paid for the paper-clips.

The *Voice* had been founded at the turn of the century by old Lord Landsbury, together with a Nonconformist daily newspaper and the *Temperance Gazette*. But the *Gazette* and the daily were long since dead, and Landsbury's son had woken one morning not long ago to find his whole business and every man and woman of it, every stick of furniture, ink, paper-clips, and galley-pins, bought by the hidden gold of Unipress.

That was three years ago and every day she had waited for her dismissal. But it never came; no directive, no question, no word. And so, being a sensible woman, she continued exactly as before and ceased to wonder.

And she was glad. It was easy to sneer at the *Voice*. Every week it offered humbly and without fanfares evidence of the Lord's intervention in the world's affairs, retold in simple and somewhat unscientific terms the early history of the Jews, and provided over a fictitious signature motherly advice to whomever should write and ask for it. The *Voice* scarcely concerned itself with the fifty-odd millions of the population who had never heard of it. It was a family affair, and rather than abuse those who were not members, it did its best for those who were. For them it was kind, optimistic, and informative. If a million children were dying of the plague in India, you may be sure that the weekly editorial described the miraculous escape from fire of a Methodist family in Kent. The *Voice* did not advise you how to disguise the encroaching wrinkles round your eyes, or control your spreading figure; did not dismay you, if you were old, by its own eternal youth. It was itself middle-aged and middle class, counselled caution to girls and charity to all.

Nonconformity is the most conservative of habits and families which took the *Voice* in 1903 continued to take it in 1960.

Miss Brimley was not quite the image of her journal. The fortunes of war and the caprice of Intelligence work had thrown her into partnership with the younger Lord Landsbury, and for the six years of war they had worked together efficiently and inconspicuously in an unnamed building in Knightsbridge. The fortunes of peace rendered both unemployed, but Landsbury had the good sense, as well as the generosity, to offer Miss Brimley a job. The *Voice* had ceased publication during the war, and no one seemed anxious to renew it. At first Miss Brimley had felt a little ashamed at reviving and editing a journal which in no way expressed her own vague deism, but quite soon, as the touching letters came in and the circulation recovered, she developed an affection for her job—and for her readers—which outweighed her earlier misgivings. The *Voice* was her life and its readers her preoccupation. She struggled to answer their odd, troubled questions, sought advice of others where she could not provide it herself, and, in time, under a handful of pseudonyms, became, if not their philosopher, their guide, friend, and universal aunt.

Miss Brimley put out her cigarette, absently tidied the pins, paper-clips, scissors, and paste into the top right-hand drawer of her desk, and gathered together the afternoon mail from her in-tray which, because it was Thursday, she had left untouched. There were several letters addressed to Barbara Fellowship, under which name the *Voice* had, since its foundation, answered both privately and through its published columns the many problems of its correspondents. They could wait until tomorrow. She rather enjoyed the "problem post," but Friday morning was when she read it. She opened the little filing cabinet at her elbow and dropped the letters into a box file at the front of the compartment. As she did so, one of them fell on its back and she noticed with surprise that the sealed flap was embossed with an elegant blue dolphin. She picked the envelope out of the cabinet and looked at it curiously, turning it over several times. It was of pale grey paper, very faintly lined. Expensive— perhaps hand-made. Beneath the dolphin was a tiny scroll on which she could just discern the legend, *Regem defendere diem videre*. The postmark was Carne, Dorset. That must be the school crest. But why was Carne familiar to her? Miss Brimley was proud of her memory, which was excellent, and she was vexed when it failed her. As a last resort she opened the enve- lope with her faded ivory paper knife and read the letter.

> Dear Miss Fellowship,
>
> I don't know if you are a real person but it doesn't matter, because you always give such good, kind answers. It was me who wrote last June about the pastry mix. I am not mad and I know my husband is trying to kill me. Could I please come and see you as soon as it's convenient? I'm sure you'll believe me, and understand that I am normal. Could it be *as soon as possible* please, I am so afraid of the long nights. I don't know who else to turn to. I could try Mr. Cardew at the Tabernacle but he wouldn't believe me and Dad's too sensible. I might as well be dead. There's something not quite right about him. At night sometimes when he thinks I'm asleep he just lies watching the darkness. I know it's wrong to think such wicked things and have fear in our hearts, but I can't help it.
>
> I hope you don't get many letters like this.
>
> Yours faithfully,
> Stella Rode (Mrs.)
> *née* Glaston

She sat quite still at her desk for a moment, looking at the address in handsome blue engraving at the top of the page: "North Fields, Carne School, Dorset." In that moment of shock and astonishment one phrase forced itself upon her mind. "The value of intelligence depends on its breeding." That was

John Landsbury's favourite dictum. Until you know the pedigree of the information you cannot evaluate a report. Yes, that was what he used to say: "We are not democratic. We close the door on intelligence without parentage." And she used to reply: "Yes, John, but even the best families had to begin somewhere."

But Stella Rode *had* parentage. It all came back to her now. She was the Glaston girl. The girl whose marriage was reported in the editorial, the girl who won the summer competition; Samuel Glaston's daughter from Branxome. She had a card in Miss Brimley's index.

Abruptly she stood up, the letter still in her hand, and walked to the uncurtained window. Just in front of her was a contemporary window-box of woven white metal. It was odd, she reflected, how she could never get anything to grow in that window-box. She looked down into the street, a slight, sensible figure leaning forward a little and framed by the incandescent fog outside; fog made yellow from the stolen light of London's streets. She could just distinguish the street lamps far below, pale and sullen. She suddenly felt the need for fresh air, and on an impulse quite alien to her usual calm, she opened the window wide. The quick cold and the angry surge of noise burst in on her, and the insidious fog followed. The sound of traffic was constant, so that for a moment she thought it was the turning of some great machine. Then above its steady growl she heard the newsboys. Their cries were like the cries of gulls against a gathering storm. She could see them now, sentinels among the hastening shadows.

It might be true. That had always been the difficulty. Right through the war it was the same restless search. It might be true. It was no use relating reports to probability when there was no quantum of knowledge from which to start. She remembered the first intelligence from France on flying bombs, wild talk of concrete runways in the depths of a forest. You had to resist the dramatic, you had to hold out against it. Yet it might be true. Tomorrow, the day after, those newsboys down there might be shouting it, and Stella Rode *née* Glaston might be dead. And if that was so, if there was the remotest chance that this man was plotting to kill this woman, then she, Ailsa Brimley, must do what she could to prevent it. Besides, Stella Glaston had a claim on her assistance if anyone did: both her father and her grandfather had taken the *Voice*, and when Stella married five years ago Miss Brimley had put a couple of lines about it in the editorial. The Glastons sent her a Christmas card every year. They were one of the original families to subscribe . . .

It was cold at the window, but she remained there, still fascinated by the half hidden shadows joining and parting beneath her, and the useless street lights burning painfully among them. She began to imagine him as one of those shadows, pressing and jostling, his murderer's eyes turned to sockets of dark. And suddenly she was frightened and needed help.

But not the police, not yet. If Stella Rode had wanted that she would have gone herself. Why hadn't she? For love? For fear of looking a fool? Because instinct was not evidence? They wanted fact. But the fact of murder was death. Must they wait for that?

Who would help? She thought at once of Landsbury, but he was farming in Rhodesia. Who else had been with them in the war? Fielding and Jebedee were dead, Steed-Asprey vanished. Smiley—where was he? George Smiley, the cleverest and perhaps the oddest of them all. Of course, Miss Brimley remembered now. He made that improbable marriage and went back to research at Oxford. But he hadn't stayed there . . . The marriage had broken up . . . What *had* he done after that?

She returned to her desk and picked up the S-Z directory. Ten minutes later she was sitting in a taxi, heading for Sloane Square. In her neatly gloved hand she held a cardboard folder containing Stella Rode's card from the index and the correspondence which had passed between them at the time of the summer competition. She was nearly at Piccadilly when she remembered she'd left the office window open. It didn't seem to matter much.

"With other people it's Persian cats or golf. With me it's the *Voice* and my readers. I'm a ridiculous spinster, I know, but there it is. I won't go to the police until I've tried *something*, George."

"And you thought you'd try me?"

"Yes."

She was sitting in the study of George Smiley's house in Bywater Street; the only light came from the complicated lamp on his desk, a black spider of a thing shining brightly on to the manuscript notes which covered the desk.

"So you've left the Service?" she said.

"Yes, yes, I have." He nodded his round head vigorously, as if reassuring himself that a distasteful experience was really over, and mixed Miss Brimley a whisky and soda. "I had another spell there after . . . Oxford. It's all very different in peacetime, you know," he continued.

Miss Brimley nodded.

"I can imagine it. More time to be bitchy." Smiley said nothing, just lit a cigarette and sat down opposite her.

"And the people have changed. Fielding, Steed, Jebedee. All gone." She said this in a matter-of-fact way as she took from her large sensible handbag Stella Rode's letter. "This is the letter, George."

When he had read it, he held it briefly towards the lamp, his round face caught by the light in a moment of almost comic earnestness. Watching him, Miss Brimley wondered what impression he made on those who did not know him well. She used to think of him as the most forgettable man she had ever met; short and plump, with heavy spectacles and thinning hair, he was at first sight the very prototype of an unsuccessful middle-aged bachelor in a sedentary occupation. His natural diffidence in most practical matters was reflected in his clothes, which were costly and unsuitable, for he was clay in the hands of his tailor, who robbed him.

He had put down the letter on the small marquetry table beside him, and was looking at her owlishly.

"This other letter she sent you, Brim. Where is it?"

She handed him the folder. He opened it and after a moment read aloud Rode's other letter:

Dear Miss Fellowship,

I would like to submit the following suggestion for your "Kitchen Hints" competition.

Make your basic batch of cake mixture once a month. Cream equal quantities of fat and sugar and add one egg for every six ounces of the mixture. For puddings and cakes, add flour to the required quantity of basic mixture.

This will keep well for a month.

I enclose stamped addressed envelope.

Yours sincerely,
Stella Rode (*née* Glaston)

PS—Incidentally, you can prevent wire wool from rusting by keeping it in a jar of soapy water. Are we allowed two suggestions? If so, please can this be my second?

"She won the competition," Miss Brimley observed, "but that's not the point. This is what I want to tell you, George. She's a Glaston, and the Glastons have been reading the *Voice* since it started. Stella's grandfather was old Rufus Glaston, a Lancashire pottery king; he and John Landsbury's father built chapels and tabernacles in practically every village in the Midlands. When Rufus died the *Voice* put out a memorial edition and old Landsbury himself wrote the obituary. Samuel Glaston took on his father's business, but had to move south because of his health. He ended up near Bournemouth, a widower with one daughter, Stella. She's the last of all that family. The whole lot are as down to earth as you could wish, Stella included, I should think. I don't think any of them is likely to be suffering from delusions of persecution."

Smiley was looking at her in astonishment.

"My dear Brim, I can't possibly take that in. How on earth do you know all this?"

Miss Brimley smiled apologetically.

"The Glastons are easy—they're almost part of the magazine. They send us Christmas cards, and boxes of chocolates on the anniversary of our foundation. We've got about five hundred families who form what I call our Establishment. They were in on the *Voice* from the start and they've kept up ever since. They write to us, George; if they're worried they write and say so; if they're getting married, moving house, retiring from work, if they're ill, depressed, or angry, they write. Not often, Heaven knows; but enough."

"How do you remember it all?"

"I don't. I keep a card index. I always write back you see . . . only . . ."

"Yes?"

Miss Brimley looked at him earnestly.

"This is the first time anyone has written because she's frightened."

"What do you want me to do?"

"I've only had one bright idea so far. I seem to remember Adrian Fielding had a brother who taught at Carne . . ."

"He's a housemaster there, if he hasn't retired."

"No, he retires this Half—it was in *The Times* some weeks ago, in that little bit on the Court page where Carne always announces itself. It said: 'Carne School reassembles today for the Lent Half. Mr. T. R. Fielding will retire at the end of the Half, having completed his statutory fifteen years as a housemaster.'"

Smiley laughed.

"Really, Brim, your memory is absurd!"

"It was the mention of Fielding . . . Anyway, I thought you could ring him up. You must know him."

"Yes, yes. I know him. At least, I met him once at Magdalen High Table. But—" Smiley coloured a little.

"But what, George?"

"Well, he's not quite the man his brother was, you know."

"How could he be?" Miss Brimley rejoined a little sharply. "But he can tell you something about Stella Rode. And her husband."

"I don't think I could do that on the telephone. I think I'd rather go and see him. But what's to stop you ringing up Stella Rode?"

"Well, I can't tonight, can I? Her husband will be in. I thought I'd put a letter in the post to her tonight telling her she can come to see me any time. But," she continued, making a slight, impatient movement with her foot, "I want to do something *now*, George."

Smiley nodded and went to the telephone. He rang directory inquiries and asked for Terence Fielding's number. After a long delay he was told to ring Carne School central exchange, who would connect him with whomever he required. Miss Brimley, watching him, wished she knew a little more about George Smiley, how much of that diffidence was assumed, how vulnerable he was.

"The best," Adrian had said. "The strongest and the best."

But so many men learnt strength during the war, learnt terrible things, and put aside their knowledge with a shudder when it ended.

The number was ringing now. She heard the dialling tone and for a moment was filled with apprehension. For the first time she was afraid of making a fool of herself, afraid of becoming involved in unlikely explanations with angular, suspicious people.

"Mr. Terence Fielding, please . . ." A pause.

"Fielding, good evening. My name is George Smiley; I

knew your brother well in the war. We have in fact met . . . Yes, yes, quite right—Magdalen, was it not, the summer before last? Look, I wonder if I might come and see you on a personal matter . . . it's a little difficult to discuss on the telephone. A friend of mine has received a rather disturbing letter from the wife of a Carne master . . . Well, I—Rode, Stella Rode; her husband . . ."

He suddenly stiffened, and Miss Brimley, her eyes fixed upon him, saw with alarm how his chubby face broke into an expression of pain and disgust. She no longer heard what he was saying. She could only watch the dreadful transformation of his face, the whitening knuckles of his hand clutching the receiver. He was looking at her now, saying something . . . it was too late. Stella Rode was dead. She had been murdered late on Wednesday night. They'd actually been dining with Fielding the night it happened.

3

The Night of the Murder

The seven-five from Waterloo to Yeovil is not a popular train, though it provides an excellent breakfast. Smiley had no difficulty in finding a first-class compartment to himself. It was a bitterly cold day, dark and the sky heavy with snow. He sat huddled in a voluminous travelling coat of Continental origin, holding in his gloved hands a bundle of the day's papers. Because he was a precise man and did not care to be hurried, he had arrived thirty minutes before the train was due to depart. Still tired after the stresses of the previous night, when he had sat up talking with Ailsa Brimley until Heaven knew what hour, he was disinclined to read. Looking out of the window on to an almost empty station, he caught sight, to his great surprise, of Miss Brimley making her way along the platform, peering in at the windows, a carrier bag in her hand. He lowered the window and called to her.

"My dear Brim, what are you doing here at this dreadful hour? You should be in bed."

She sat down opposite him and began unpacking her bag and handing him its contents: thermos, sandwiches, and chocolate.

"I didn't know whether there was a breakfast car," she explained; "and besides, I wanted to come and see you off. You're such a dear, George, and I wish I could come with you, but

Unipress would go mad if I did. The only time they notice you is when you're not there."

"Haven't you seen the papers?" he asked.

"Just briefly, on the way here. They seem to think it wasn't him, but some madman . . ."

"I know, Brim. That's what Fielding said, wasn't it?" There was a moment's awkward silence.

"George, am I being an awful ass, letting you go off like this? I was sure last night, but now I wonder . . ."

"After you left I rang Ben Sparrow of Special Branch. You remember him, don't you? He was with us in the war. I told him the whole story."

"George! At three in the morning?"

"Yes. He's ringing the Divisional Superintendent at Carne. He'll tell him about the letter, and that I'm coming down. Ben had an idea that a man named Rigby would be handling the case. Rigby and Ben were at police college together." He looked at her kindly for a moment. "Besides, I'm a man of leisure, Brim. I shall enjoy the change."

"Bless you, George," said Miss Brimley, woman enough to believe him. She got up to go, and Smiley said to her:

"Brim, if you should need any more help or anything, and can't get hold of me, there's a man called Mendel who lives in Mitcham, a retired police inspector. He's in the book. If you get hold of him and mention me, he'll do what he can for you. I've booked a room at the Sawley Arms."

Alone again, Smiley surveyed uneasily the assortment of food and drink which Miss Brimley had provided. He had promised himself the luxury of breakfast in the restaurant car. He would keep the sandwiches and coffee for later, that would be the best thing; for lunch, perhaps. And he would breakfast properly.

In the restaurant car Smiley read first the less sensational reports on the death of Stella Rode. It appeared that on Wednesday evening Mr. and Mrs. Rode had been guests at dinner of

Mr. Terence Fielding, the senior housemaster at Carne and brother of the late Adrian Fielding, the celebrated French scholar who had vanished during the war while specially employed by the War Office. They had left Mr. Fielding's house together at about ten to eleven and walked the half mile from the centre of Carne to their house, which stood alone at the edge of the famous Carne playing fields. As they reached their house Mr. Rode remembered that he had left at Mr. Fielding's house some examination papers which urgently required correction that night. (At this point Smiley remembered that he had failed to pack his dinner jacket, and that Fielding would almost certainly ask him to dine.) Rode determined to walk back to Fielding's house and collect the papers, therefore, starting back at about five past eleven. It appears that Mrs. Rode made herself a cup of tea and sat down in the drawing-room to await his return.

Adjoining the back of the house is a conservatory, the inner door of which leads to the drawing-room. It was there that Rode eventually found his wife when he returned. There were signs of a struggle, and certain inexpensive articles of jewellery were missing from the body. The confusion in the conservatory was terrible. Fortunately there had been a fresh fall of snow on Wednesday afternoon, and detectives from Dorchester were examining the footprints and other traces early on Thursday morning. Mr. Rode had been treated for shock at Dorchester Central Hospital. The police wished to interview a woman from the adjacent village of Pylle who was locally known as "Mad Janie" on account of her eccentric and solitary habits. Mrs. Rode, who was well known in Carne for her energetic work on behalf of the International Refugee Year, had apparently shown a charitable interest in her welfare, and she had vanished without trace since the night of the murder. The police were currently of the opinion that the murderer had caught sight of Mrs. Rode through the drawing-room window (she had not drawn the curtains) and that Mrs. Rode had admitted the murderer at the front door in the belief that it was her husband returning from Mr. Fielding's house. The Home Office pathologist had been asked to conduct a post-mortem examination.

The other reports were not so restrained: "Murder most foul has desecrated the hallowed playing fields of Carne" one article began, and another, "Science teacher discovers murdered wife in blood-spattered conservatory." A third screamed, "Mad woman sought in Carne murder." With an expression of distaste, Smiley screwed up all the newspapers except the *Guardian* and *The Times* and tossed them on to the luggage rack.

He changed at Yeovil for a local line to Sturminster, Okeford and Carne. It was something after eleven o'clock when he finally arrived at Carne station.

He telephoned the hotel from the station and sent his luggage ahead by taxi. The Sawley Arms was only full at Commemoration and on St. Andrew's Day. Most of the year it was empty; sitting like a prim Victorian lady, its slate roof in the mauve of half-mourning, on ill-tended lawns midway between the station and Carne Abbey.

Snow still lay on the ground, but the day was fine and dry, and Smiley decided to walk into the town and arrange to meet the police officer conducting the investigation of the murder. He left the station, with its foretaste of Victorian austerity, and walked along the avenue of bare trees which led towards the great Abbey tower, flat and black against the colourless winter sky. He crossed the Abbey Close, a serene and beautiful square of medieval houses, the roofs snow-covered, the white lawns shaded with pin strokes of grass. As he passed the west door of the Abbey, the soft snow creaking where he trod, the clock high above him struck the half-hour, and two knights on horseback rode out from their little castle over the door, and slowly raised their lances to each other in salute. Then, as if it were all part of the same clockwork mechanism, other doors all round the Close opened too, releasing swarms of black-coated boys who stampeded across the snow towards the Abbey. One boy passed so close that his gown brushed against Smiley's sleeve. Smiley called to him as he ran past:

"What's going on?"

"Sext," shouted the boy in reply, and was gone.

He passed the main entrance to the school and came at once upon the municipal part of the town, a lugubrious nineteenth-century fairyland in local stone, stitched together by a complexity of Gothic chimneys and crenel windows. Here was the town hall, and beside it, with the flag of St. George floating at its masthead, the Carne Constabulary Headquarters, built ninety years ago to withstand the onslaughts of archery and battering rams.

He gave his name to the Duty Sergeant, and asked to see the officer investigating the death of Mrs. Rode. The Sergeant, an elderly, inscrutable man, addressed himself to the telephone with a certain formality, as if he were about to perform a difficult conjuring trick. To Smiley's surprise, he was told that Inspector Rigby would be pleased to see him at once, and a police cadet was summoned to show him the way. He was led at a spanking pace up the wide staircase in the centre of the hall, and in a matter of moments found himself before the Inspector.

He was a very short man, and very broad. He could have been a Celt from the tin-mines of Cornwall or the collieries of Wales. His dark grey hair was cut very close; it came to a point in the centre of his brow like a devil's cap. His hands were large and powerful, he had the trunk and stance of a wrestler, but he spoke slowly, with a Dorset burr to his soft voice. Smiley quickly noticed that he had one quality rare among small men: the quality of openness. Though his eyes were dark and bright and the movements of his body swift, he imparted a feeling of honesty and straight dealing.

"Ben Sparrow rang me this morning, sir. I'm very pleased you've come. I believe you've got a letter for me."

Rigby looked at Smiley thoughtfully over his desk, and decided that he liked what he saw. He had got around in the war and had heard a little, just a very little, of the work of George

Smiley's Service. If Ben said Smiley was all right, that was good enough for him—or almost. But Ben had said more than that.

"Looks like a frog, dresses like a bookie, and has a brain I'd give my eyes for. Had a very nasty war. Very nasty indeed."

Well, he looked like a frog, right enough. Short and stubby, round spectacles with thick lenses that made his eyes big. And his clothes *were* odd. Expensive, mind, you could see that. But his jacket seemed to drape where there wasn't any room for drape. What did surprise Rigby was his shyness. Rigby had expected someone a little brash, a little too smooth for Carne, whereas Smiley had an earnest formality of manner which appealed to Rigby's conservative taste.

Smiley took the letter from his wallet and put it on the desk, while Rigby extracted an old pair of gold-rimmed spectacles from a battered metal case and adjusted the ends carefully over his ears.

"I don't know if Ben explained," said Smiley, "but this letter was sent to the correspondence section of a small Nonconformist journal to which Mrs. Rode subscribed."

"And Miss Fellowship is the lady who brought you the letter?"

"No; her name is Brimley. She is the editor of the magazine. Fellowship is just a pen-name for the correspondence column."

The brown eyes rested on him for a moment.

"When did she receive this letter?"

"Yesterday, the seventeenth. Thursday's the day they go to press, their busy day. The afternoon mail doesn't get opened till the evening, usually. This was opened about six o'clock, I suppose."

"And she brought it straight to you?"

"Yes."

"Why?"

"She worked for me during the war, in my department. She was reluctant to go straight to the police—I was the only person she could think of who wasn't a policeman," he added stupidly. "Who could help, I mean."

"May I ask what you yourself, sir, do for a living?"

"Nothing much. A little private research on seventeenth-century Germany." It seemed a very silly answer.

Rigby didn't seem bothered.

"What's this earlier letter she talks about?"

Smiley offered him the second envelope, and again the big, square hand received it.

"It appears she won this competition," Smiley explained. "That was her winning entry. I gather she comes from a family which has subscribed to the magazine since its foundation. That's why Miss Brimley was less inclined to regard the letter as nonsense. Not that it follows."

"Not that what follows?"

"I meant that the fact that her family had subscribed to a journal for fifty years does not logically affect the possibility that she was unbalanced."

Rigby nodded, as if he saw the point, but Smiley had an uncomfortable feeling that he did not.

"Ah," said Rigby, with a slow smile. "Women, eh?"

Smiley, completely bewildered, gave a little laugh. Rigby was looking at him thoughtfully.

"Know any of the staff, do you, sir?"

"Only Mr. Terence Fielding. We met at an Oxford dinner some time ago. I thought I'd call round and see him. I knew his brother pretty well."

Rigby appeared to stiffen slightly at the mention of Fielding, but he said nothing, and Smiley went on:

"It was Fielding I rang when Miss Brimley brought me the letter. He told me the news. That was last night."

"I see."

They looked at one another again in silence. Smiley discomfited and slightly comic, Rigby appraising him, wondering how much to say.

"How long are you staying?" he said at last.

"I don't know," Smiley replied. "Miss Brimley wanted to come herself, but she has her paper to run. She attached great importance, you see, to doing all she could for Mrs. Rode, even though she was dead. Because she was a subscriber, I mean. I promised to see that the letter arrived quickly in the right hands. I don't imagine there's much else I can do. I shall probably stay on for a day or two just to have a word with Fielding . . . go to the funeral, I suppose. I've booked in at the Sawley Arms."

"Fine hotel, that."

Rigby put his spectacles carefully back into their case and dropped the case into a drawer.

"Funny place, Carne. There's a big gap between the Town and Gown, as we say; neither side knows nor likes the other. It's fear that does it, fear and ignorance. It makes it hard in a case like this. Oh, I can call on Mr. Fielding and Mr. D'Arcy and they say, 'Good day, Sergeant,' and give me a cup of tea in the kitchen, but I can't get among them. They've got their own community, see, and no one outside it can get in. No gossip in the pubs, no contacts, nothing . . . just cups of tea and bits of seed cake, and being called Sergeant." Rigby laughed suddenly, and Smiley laughed with him in relief. "There's a lot I'd like to ask them, a lot of things; who liked the Rodes and who didn't, whether Mr. Rode's a good teacher and whether his wife fitted in with the others. I've got all the facts I want, but I've got no clothes to hang on them." He looked at Smiley expectantly. There was a very long silence.

"If you want me to help, I'd be delighted," said Smiley at last. "But give me the facts first."

"Stella Rode was murdered between about ten past eleven and quarter to twelve on the night of Wednesday the sixteenth. She must have been struck fifteen to twenty times with a cosh or bit of piping or something. It was a terrible murder . . . terrible. There are marks all over her body. At a guess I would say she came from the drawing-room to the front door to answer the bell or something, when she opened the door she was struck down and dragged to the conservatory. The conservatory door was unlocked, see?"

"I see . . . It's odd that he should have known that, isn't it?"

"The murderer may have been hiding there already: we can't tell from the prints just there. He was wearing boots—Wellington boots, size 10 ½. We would guess from the spacing of the footprints in the garden that he was about six foot tall. When he had got her to the conservatory he must have hit her again and again—mainly on the head. There's a lot of what we call travelled blood in the conservatory, that's to say, blood spurted from an open artery. There's no sign of that anywhere else."

"And no sign of it on her husband?"

"I'll come to that later, but the short answer is, no." He paused a moment and continued:

"Now, I said there were footprints, and so there were. The murderer came through the back garden. Where he came from and went to, Heaven alone knows. You see, there are no tracks leading away—not Wellingtons. None at all. Of course, it's possible the outgoing tracks followed the path to the front gate and got lost in all the to-ing and fro-ing later that night. But I don't think we'd have lost them even then." He glanced at Smiley, then went on:

"He left one thing behind him in the conservatory—an old cloth belt, navy blue, from a cheap overcoat by the look of it. We're working on that now."

"Was she . . . robbed or anything?"

"No sign of interference. She was wearing a string of green beads round her neck, and they've gone, and it looks as though he tried to get the rings off her finger, but they were too tight." He paused.

"I need hardly tell you that we've had reports from every corner of the country about tall men in blue overcoats and gumboots. But none of them had wings as far as I know. Or seven-league boots for jumping from the conservatory to the road."

They paused, while a police cadet brought in tea on a tray. He put it on the desk, looked at Smiley out of the corner of his eye and decided to let the Inspector pour out. He guided the teapot round so that the handle was towards Rigby and withdrew. Smiley was amused by the immaculate condition of the tray cloth, by the matching china and tea-strainer, laid before them by the enormous hands of the cadet. Rigby poured out the tea and they drank for a moment in silence. There was, Smiley reflected, something devastatingly competent about Rigby. The very ordinariness of the man and his room identified him with the society he protected. The nondescript furniture, the wooden filing cupboards, the bare walls, the archaic telephone with its separate earpiece, the brown frieze round the wall and the brown paint on the door, the glistening linoleum and the faint smell of carbolic, the burbling gas-fire, and the calendar from the Prudential—these were the evidence of rectitude and moderation; their austerity gave comfort and reassurance. Rigby continued:

"Rode went back to Fielding's house for the examination papers. Fielding confirms that, of course. He arrived at Fielding's house at about 11:35, near as Fielding can say. He hardly spent any time there at all—just collected his papers at the door—they were in a small writing-case he uses for carrying exercise books. He doesn't remember whether he saw anyone on the road. He thinks a bicycle overtook him, but he can't be sure. If we take Rode's word for it, he walked straight home. When he got there he rang the bell. He was wearing a dinner-jacket and so he hadn't got his key with him. His wife was expecting him to ring the bell, you see. That's the devil of it. It was a moonlit night, mind, and snow on the ground, so you could see a mighty long way. He called her, but she didn't answer. Then he saw footprints going round to the side of the house. Not just footprints, but blood marks and the snow all churned up where the body had been dragged to the conservatory. But he didn't know it was blood in the moonlight, it just showed up dark, and Rode said afterwards he thought it was the dirty water from the gutters running over on to the path.

"He followed the prints round until he came to the conservatory. It was darker in there and he fumbled for the light switch, but it didn't work."

"Did he light a match?"

"No, he didn't have any. He's a non-smoker. His wife didn't approve of smoking. He moved forward from the door. The conservatory walls are mainly glass except for the bottom three feet, but the roof is tiled. The moon was high that night, and not much light got in at all, except through the partition window between the drawing-room and the conservatory—but she'd only had the little table light on in the drawing-room. So he groped his way forward, talking all the time, calling Stella, his wife. As he went, he tripped over something and nearly fell. He knelt down and felt with his hands, up and down her body. He realised that his hands were covered in blood. He doesn't remember much after that, but there's a senior master living a hundred yards up the road—Mr. D'Arcy his name is, lives with his sister, and he heard him screaming on the road. D'Arcy went out to him. Rode had blood all over his hands and face and seemed to be out of his mind. D'Arcy rang the police and I got there at about one o'clock that morning. I've seen some nasty things in my time, but this is the worst. Blood everywhere. Whoever killed her must have been covered in it. There's an outside tap against the conservatory wall. The tap had been turned on, probably by the murderer to rinse his hands. The boffins have found traces of blood in the snow underneath it. The tap was lagged recently by Rode I gather . . ."

"And fingerprints?" Smiley asked. "What about them?"

"Mr. Rode's were everywhere. On the floor, the walls and windows, on the body itself. But there were other prints; smudges of blood, little more, made with a gloved hand probably."

"And they were the murderer's?"

"They had been made *before* Rode made his. In some cases Rode's prints were partly superimposed on the glove prints."

Smiley was silent for a moment.

"These examination papers he went back for. Were they as important as all that?"

"Yes. I gather they were. Up to a point anyway. The marks had to be handed in to Mr. D'Arcy by midday on Friday."

"But why did he take them to Fielding's in the first place?"

"He didn't. He'd been invigilating exams all afternoon and the papers were handed in to him at six o'clock. He put them in his little case and had them taken to Fielding's by a boy—head boy in Mr. Fielding's house, name of Perkins. Rode was on Chapel duty last week, so he didn't have time to return home before dinner."

"Where did he change then?"

"In the Tutors' Robing Room, next to the Common Room. There are facilities there, mainly for games tutors who live some distance from Carne."

"The boy who brought this case to Fielding's house—who was he?"

"I can't tell you much more than I've said. His name is Perkins; he's head of Mr. Fielding's house. Fielding has spoken to him and confirmed Rode's statement . . . House tutors are very possessive about their boys, you know . . . don't like them to be spoken to by rough policemen." Rigby seemed to be slightly upset.

"I see," Smiley said at last, helplessly, and then: "But how do you explain the letter?"

"It isn't only the letter we've got to explain."

Smiley looked at him sharply.

"What do you mean?"

"I mean," said Rigby slowly, "that Mrs. Rode did several pretty queer things in the last few weeks."

4

Town and Gown

"Mrs. Rode was Chapel, of course," Rigby continued, "and we've quite a community in Carne. Truth to tell," he added with a slow smile, "my wife belongs to it.

"A couple of weeks ago our Minister called round to see me. It was in the evening, about half past six, I suppose. I was just thinking of going home, see. He walked in here and sat himself down where you're sitting now. He's a big fellow, the Minister, a fine man; comes from up North, where Mrs. Rode came from. Cardew, his name is."

"The Mr. Cardew in the letter?"

"That's him. He knew all about Mrs. Rode's family before the Rodes ever came here. Glaston's quite a name up North, and Mr. Cardew was very pleased when he heard that Stella Rode was Mr. Glaston's daughter; very pleased indeed. Mrs. Rode came to the Tabernacle regular as clockwork, you can imagine, and they like to see that round here. My wife was pleased as Punch, I can tell you. It was the first time, I suppose, that anyone from the School had done that. Most of the Chapel people here are tradespeople—what we call the locals." Rigby smiled again. "It isn't often that Town and Gown come together, so to speak. Not here."

"How about her husband? Was he Chapel too?"

"Well, he had been, so she told Mr. Cardew. Mr. Rode was born and bred in Branxome, and all his family were Chapel people. That's how Mr. and Mrs. Rode first met, I gather—at Branxome Tabernacle. Ever been there, have you? A fine church, Branxome, right up on the hill there, overlooking the sea."

Smiley shook his head and Rigby's wide brown eyes rested on him thoughtfully for a moment.

"You should," he said, "you should go and see that. It seems," he continued, "that Mr. Rode turned Church of England when he came to Carne. Even tried to persuade his wife to do the same. They're very strong at the School. I heard that from my wife, as a matter of fact. I never let her gossip as a rule, being a policeman's wife and that, but Mr. Cardew told her that himself."

"I see," said Smiley.

"Well now, Cardew came and saw me. He was all worried and bothered with himself. He didn't know what he should make of it, but he wanted to talk to me as a friend and not as a policeman." Rigby looked sour, "When people say that to me, I always know that they want to talk to me as a policeman. Then he told me his story. Mrs. Rode had called to see him that afternoon. He'd been out visiting a farmer's wife over in Okeford and didn't come home until half past five or thereabouts, so Mrs. Cardew had had to talk to her and hold the fort until the Minister came home. Mrs. Rode was white as a sheet, sitting very still by the fire. As soon as the Minister arrived, Mrs. Cardew left them alone and Stella Rode started talking about her husband."

He paused. "She said Mr. Rode was going to kill her. In the long nights. She seemed to have a kind of fixation about being murdered in the long nights. Cardew didn't take it too seriously at first, but thinking about it afterwards, he decided to let me know."

Smiley looked at him sharply.

"He couldn't make out what she meant. He thought she was out of her mind. He's a down-to-earth man, see, although he's a Minister. I think he was probably a bit too firm with her.

He asked her what put this dreadful thought into her head, and she began to weep. Not hysterical, apparently, but just crying quietly to herself. He tried to calm her down, promised to help her any way he could, and asked her again what had given her this idea. She just shook her head, then got up, walked over to the door, still shaking her head in despair. She turned to him, and he thought she was going to say something, but she didn't. She just left."

"How very curious," said Smiley, "that she lied about that in her letter. She went out of her way to say she *hadn't* told Cardew."

Rigby shrugged his great shoulders.

"If you'll pardon me," he said, "I'm in a darned awkward position. The Chief Constable would sooner cut his throat than call in Scotland Yard. He wants an arrest and he wants one quick. We've got enough clues to cover a Christmas tree; footprints, time of the murder, indication of murderer's cloth- ing, and even the weapon itself."

Smiley looked at him in surprise.

"You've *found* the weapon, then?"

Rigby hesitated. "Yes, we've found it. There's hardly a soul knows this, sir, and I'll trouble you to remember that. We found it the morning after the murder, four miles north of Carne on the Okeford road, tossed into a ditch. Eighteen inches of what they call coaxial cable. Know what that is, do you? It comes in all sizes, but this piece is about two inches in diameter. It has a copper rod running down the middle and plastic insulation between the rod and the outer cover. There was blood on it: Stella Rode's blood group, and hairs from her head, stuck to the blood. We're keeping that very dark indeed. By the Grace of God, it was found by one of our own men. It pinpoints the line of the murderer's departure."

"There's no doubt, I suppose, that it *is* the weapon?" Smiley asked lamely.

"We found particles of copper in the wounds on the body."

"It's odd, isn't it," Smiley suggested reflectively, "that the murderer should have carried the weapon so far before getting rid of it? Specially if he was walking. You'd think he'd want to get rid of it as soon as he could."

"It is odd. Very odd. The Okeford road runs beside the canal for half of those four miles; he could have pitched the cable into the canal anywhere along there. We'd never have been the wiser."

"Was the cable old?"

"Not particularly. Just standard type. It could have come from almost anywhere." Rigby hesitated a minute, then burst out:

"Look, sir, this is what I am trying to say. The circumstances of this case demand a certain type of investigation: wide-scale search, detailed laboratory work, mass inquiry. That's what the Chief wants, and he's right. We've no case against the husband at all, and to be frank he's precious little use to us. He seems a bit lost, a bit vague, contradicting himself on little things that don't matter, like the date of his marriage or the name of his doctor. It's shock, of course, I've seen it before. I know all about your letter, sir, and it's damned odd, but if you can tell me how he could have produced Wellington boots out of a hat and got rid of them afterwards, battered his wife to death without leaving more than a few smudges of blood on himself, and got the weapon four miles from the scene of the crime, all within ten minutes of being at Fielding's house, I'll be grateful to you. We're looking for a stranger, six foot tall, wearing newish Dunlop Wellington boots size 10 ½, leather gloves and an old blue overcoat stained with blood. A man who travels on foot, who was in the area of North Fields between 11:10 and 11:45 on the night of the murder, who left in the direction of Okeford, taking with him one and a half feet of coaxial cable, a string of green beads and an imitation diamond clip, valued at twenty-three and six. We're looking for a maniac, a man who kills for pleasure or the price of a meal." Rigby paused, smiled wistfully and added, "Who can fly fifty feet through the air? But with information like this how else should we spend our time? What else can we look for? I can't put men on to chasing shadows when there's work like that to be done."

"I understand that."

"But I'm an old policeman, Mr. Smiley, and I like to know what I'm about. I don't like looking for people I can't believe in, and I don't like being cut off from witnesses. I like to meet people and talk to them, nose about here and there, get to know the country. But I can't do that, not at the school. Do you follow me? So we've got to rely on laboratories, tracker dogs, and nation-wide searches, but somehow in my bones I don't think it's altogether one of those cases."

"I read in the paper about a woman, a Mad Janie . . ."

"I'm coming to that. Mrs. Rode was a kindly woman, easy to talk to. I always found her so, anyway. Some of the women at Chapel took against her, but you know what women are. It seems she got friendly with this Janie creature. Janie came begging, selling herbs and charms at the back door; you know the kind of thing. She's queer, talks to birds and all that. She lives in a disused Norman chapel over Pylle. Stella Rode used to give her food and clothes—the poor soul was often as not half-starved. Now Janie's disappeared. She was seen early Wednesday night on the lane towards North Fields and hasn't been seen since. That don't mean a thing. These people come and go in their own way. They'll be all over the neighbourhood for years, then one day they're gone like snow in the fire. They've died in a ditch, maybe, or they've took ill and crept away like a cat. Janie's not the only queer one round here. There's a lot of excitement because we found a spare set of footprints running along the fringe of trees at the far end of the garden. They were a woman's prints by the look of them, and at one point they come quite close to the conservatory. Could be a gypsy or a beggar woman. Could be anything, but I expect it's

Janie right enough. I hope to Heaven it was, sir; we could do with an eyewitness, even a mad one."

Smiley stood up. As they shook hands, Rigby said, "Good-bye, sir. Ring me any time, any time at all." He scribbled a telephone number on the pad in front of him, tore off the sheet and gave it to Smiley. "That's my home number." He showed Smiley to the door, seemed to hesitate, then he said, "You're not a Carnian yourself by any chance, are you, sir?"

"Good heavens, no."

Again Rigby hesitated. "Our Chief's a Carnian. Ex-Indian Army. Brigadier Havelock. This is his last year. He's very interested in this case. Doesn't like me messing around the school. Won't have it."

"I see."

"He wants an arrest quickly."

"And outside Carne, I suppose?"

"Good-bye, Mr. Smiley. Don't forget to ring me. Oh, another thing I should have mentioned. That bit of cable . . ."

"Yes?"

"Mr. Rode used a length of the same stuff in a demonstration lecture on elementary electronics. Mislaid it about three weeks ago."

Smiley walked slowly back to his hotel.

My dear Brim,

As soon as I arrived I handed your letter over to the CID man in charge of the case—it was Rigby, as Ben had supposed: he looks like a mixture of Humpty-Dumpty and a Cornish elf—very short and broad—and I don't think he's anyone's fool.

To begin at the middle—our letter didn't have quite the effect we expected; Stella Rode evidently told Cardew, the local Baptist Minister, two weeks ago, that her husband was trying to kill her in the long nights, whatever they are. As for the circumstances of the murder—the account in the *Guardian* is substantially correct.

In fact, the more Rigby told me, the less likely it became that she was killed by her husband. Almost everything pointed away from him. Quite apart from motive, there is the location of the weapon, the footprints in the snow (which indicate a tall man in Wellingtons), the presence of unidentified glove-prints in the conservatory. Add to that the strongest argument of all: whoever killed her must have been covered in blood—the conservatory was a dreadful sight, Rigby tells me. Of course, there *was* blood on Rode when he was picked up by his colleague in the lane, but only smears which could have resulted from stumbling over the body in the dark. Incidentally, the footprints only go into the garden and not out.

As things stand at the moment, there is, as Rigby points out, only one interpretation—the murderer was a stranger, a tramp, a madman perhaps, who killed her for pleasure or for her jewellery (which was worthless) and made off along the Okeford road, throwing the weapon into a ditch. (But why carry it four miles—and why not throw it into the canal the other side of the ditch? The Okeford road crosses Okemoor, which is all cross-dyked to prevent flooding.) If this interpretation is correct, then I suppose we attribute Stella's letter and her interview with Cardew to a persecuted mind, or the premonition of death, depending on whether we're superstitious. If that is so, it is the most monstrous coincidence I have ever heard of. Which brings me to my final point.

I rather gathered from what Rigby *didn't* say that his Chief Constable was treading on his tail, urging him to scour the country for tramps in bloodstained blue overcoats (you remember the belt). Rigby, of course, has no alternative but to follow the signs and do as his Chief expects—but he is clearly uneasy about something—either something he hasn't

told me, or something he just feels in his bones. I think he
was sincere when he asked me to tell him anything I found
out about the *School* end—the Rodes themselves, the way they
fitted in, and so on. Carne's monastery walls are still pretty
high, he feels . . .

So I'll just sniff around a bit, I think, and see what goes
on. I rang Fielding when I got back from the police station
and he's asked me to supper tonight. I'll write again as soon
as I have anything to tell you.

George.

Having carefully sealed the envelope, pressing down the corners with his thumbs, Smiley locked his door and made his
way down the wide marble staircase, treading carefully on the
meagre coconut matting that ran down the centre. There was
a red wooden letter box in the hall for the use of residents, but
Smiley, being a cautious man, avoided it. He walked to the
pillar box at the corner of the road, posted his letter and wondered what to do about lunch. There were, of course, the sandwiches and coffee provided by Miss Brimley. Reluctantly he
returned to the hotel. It was full of journalists, and Smiley
hated journalists. It was also cold, and he hated the cold. And
there was something very familiar about sandwiches in a hotel
bedroom.

5

Cat and Dog

It was just after seven o'clock that evening when George Smiley climbed the steps which led up to the front door of Mr. Terence Fielding's house. He rang, and was admitted to the hall by a little plump woman in her middle fifties. To his right a log fire burned warmly on a pile of wood ash and above him he was vaguely aware of a minstrel gallery and a mahogany staircase, which rose in a spiral to the top of the house. Most of the light seemed to come from the fire, and Smiley could see that the walls around him were hung with a great number of paintings of various styles and periods, and the chimney-piece was laden with all manner of *objets d'art*. With an involuntary shudder, he noticed that neither the fire nor the pictures quite succeeded in banishing the faint smell of school—of polish bought wholesale, of cocoa and community cooking. Corridors led from the hall, and Smiley observed that the lower part of each wall was painted a dark brown or green according to the inflexible rule of school decorators. From one of these corridors the enormous figure of Mr. Terence Fielding emerged.

He advanced on Smiley, massive and genial, with his splendid mane of grey hair falling anyhow across his forehead, and his gown billowing behind him.

"Smiley? Ah! You've met True, have you—Miss Truebody, my housekeeper? Marvellous this snow, isn't it? Pure Bruegel! Seen the boys skating by the Eyot? Marvellous sight! Black suits, coloured scarves, pale sun; all there, isn't it, all there! Bruegel to the life. Marvellous!" He took Smiley's coat and flung it on to a decrepit deal chair with a rush seat which stood in the corner of the hall.

"You like that chair—you recognise it?"

"I don't think I do," Smiley replied in some confusion.

"Ah, you should, you know, you should! Had it made in Provence before the war. Little carpenter I knew. Place it now? Facsimile of Van Gogh's yellow chair; some people recognise it." He led the way down a corridor and into a large comfortable study adorned with Dutch tiles, small pieces of Renaissance sculpture, mysterious bronzes, china dogs and unglazed vases; and Fielding himself towering magnificent among them.

As senior housemaster of Carne, Fielding wore, in place of the customary academic dress, a wonderful confection of heavy black skirts and legal bib, like a monk in evening dress. All this imparted a suggestion of clerical austerity in noted contrast to the studied flamboyance of his personality. Evidently conscious of this, he sought to punctuate the solemnity of his uniform and give to it a little of his own temperament, by adorning it with flowers carefully chosen from his garden. He had scandalised the tailors of Carne, whose frosted windows carried the insignia of royal households, by having buttonholes let into his gown. These he would fill according to his mood with anything from hibernia to bluebells. This evening he wore a rose, and from its freshness Smiley deduced that he had this minute put it into place, having ordered it specially.

"Sherry wine or Madeira?"

"Thank you; a glass of sherry."

"Tart's drink, Madeira," Fielding called, as he poured from a decanter, "but boys like it. Perhaps that's why. They're frightful flirts." He handed Smiley a glass and added, with a dramatic modification of his voice:

"We're all rather subdued at the moment by this dreadful

business. We've never had anything quite like it, you know. Have you seen the evening papers?"

"No, I'm afraid I haven't. But the Sawley Arms is packed with journalists of course."

"They've really gone to town. They've got the Army out in Hampshire, playing about with mine-detectors. God knows what they expect to find."

"How have the boys taken it?"

"They adore it! My own house has been particularly fortunate, of course, because the Rodes were dining here that night. Some oaf from the police even wanted to question one of my boys."

"Indeed," said Smiley innocently. "What on earth about?"

"Oh, God knows," Fielding replied abruptly, and then, changing the subject, he asked, "You knew my brother well, didn't you? He talked about you, you know."

"Yes, I knew Adrian very well. We were close friends."

"In the war, too?"

"Yes."

"Were you in his crowd, then?"

"What crowd?"

"Steed-Asprey, Jebedee. All those people."

"Yes."

"I never really heard how he died. Did you?"

"No."

"We didn't see much of one another in later years, Adrian and I. Being a fraud, I can't afford to be seen beside the genuine article," Fielding declared, with something of his earlier panache. Smiley was spared the embarrassment of a reply by a quiet knock at the door, and a tall red-haired boy came timidly into the room.

"I've called the Adsum, sir, if you're ready, sir."

"Damn," said Fielding, emptying his glass. "Prayers." He turned to Smiley.

"Meet Perkins, my head prefect. Musical genius, but a problem in the schoolroom. That right, Tim? Stay here or come as you like. It only lasts ten minutes."

"Rather less tonight, sir," said Perkins. "It's the Nunc Dimittis."

"Thank God for small mercies," Fielding declared, tugging briefly at his bib, as he led Smiley at a spanking pace out into the corridor and across the hall, with Perkins stalking along behind them. Fielding was speaking all the time without bothering to turn his head:

"I'm glad you've chosen this evening to come. I never entertain on Fridays as a rule because everyone else does, though none of us quite knows what to do about entertaining at the moment. Felix D'Arcy will be coming tonight, but that's hardly entertaining. D'Arcy's a professional. Incidentally, we normally dress in the evening, but it doesn't matter."

Smiley's heart sank. They turned a corner and entered another corridor.

"We have prayers at all hours here. The Master's revived the seven Day Hours for the Offices: Prime, Terce, Sext and so on. A surfeit during the Half, abstinence during the holidays, that's the system, like games. Useful in the house for roll-calls, too." He led the way down yet another corridor, flung open a double door at the end of it and marched straight into the dining-room, his gown filling gracefully behind him. The boys were waiting for him.

"More sherry? What did you think of prayers? They sing quite nicely, don't they? One or two good tenors. We tried some plainsong last Half; quite good, really quite good. D'Arcy will be here soon. He's a frightful toad. Looks like a Sickert model fifty years after—all trousers and collar. However, you're lucky his sister isn't accompanying him. She's worse!"

"What's his subject?" They were back in Fielding's study.

"Subject! I'm afraid we don't have subjects here. None of us has read a word on any subject since we left university." He lowered his voice and added darkly, "That's if we *went* to university. D'Arcy teaches French. D'Arcy is Senior Tutor by election, bachelor by profession, sublimated pansy by inclination . . ." he was standing quite still now, his head thrown back and his right hand stretched out towards Smiley, ". . . and his subject is other people's shortcomings. He is principally, however, self-appointed major-domo of Carne protocol. If you wear a gown on a bicycle, reply incorrectly to an invitation, make a fault in the *placement* of your dinner guests or speak of a colleague as 'Mister,' D'Arcy will find you out and admonish you."

"What are the duties of Senior Tutor, then?" Smiley asked, just for something to say.

"He's the referee between the classics and the scientists; arranges the timetable and vets the exam results. But principally, poor man, he must reconcile the Arts with the Sciences." He shook his head sagely. "And it takes a better man than D'Arcy to do that. Not, mind you," he added wearily, "that it makes the least difference who wins the extra hour on Friday evenings. Who cares? Not the boys, poor dears, that's certain."

Fielding talked on, at random and always in superlatives, sometimes groping in the air with his hand as if to catch the more elusive metaphors; now of his colleagues with caustic derision, now of boys with compassion if not with understanding; now of the Arts with fervour—and the studied bewilderment of a lonely disciple.

"Carne isn't a school. It's a sanatorium for intellectual lepers. The symptoms began when we came down from university; a gradual putrefaction of our intellectual extremities. From day to day our minds die, our spirits atrophy and rot. We watch the process in one another, hoping to forget it in ourselves." He paused, and looked reflectively at his hands.

"In me the process is complete. You see before you a dead soul, and Carne is the body I live in." Much pleased by this confession, Fielding held out his great arms so that the sleeves of his gown resembled the wings of a giant bat; "the Vampire of Carne," he declared, bowing deeply. *"Alcoholique et poète!"* A bellow of laughter followed this display.

Smiley was fascinated by Fielding, by his size, his voice, the wanton inconstancy of his temperament, by his whole big-screen style; he found himself attracted and repelled by this succession of contradictory poses; he wondered whether he was supposed to take part in the performance, but Fielding seemed so dazzled by the footlights that he was indifferent to the audience behind them. The more Smiley watched, the more elusive seemed the character he was trying to comprehend: changeful but sterile, daring but fugitive; colourful, unbounded, ingenuous, yet deceitful and perverse. Smiley began to wish he could acquire the material facts of Fielding—his means, his ambitions and disappointments.

His reverie was interrupted by Miss Truebody. Felix D'Arcy had arrived.

No candles, and a cold supper admirably done by Miss Truebody. Not claret, but hock, passed round like port. And at last, at long last, Fielding mentioned Stella Rode.

They had been talking rather dutifully of the Arts and the Sciences. This would have been dull (for it was uninformed) had not D'Arcy constantly been goaded by Fielding, who seemed anxious to exhibit D'Arcy in his worst light. D'Arcy's judgements of people and problems were largely coloured by what he considered "seemly" (a favourite word) and by an effeminate malice towards his colleagues. After a while Fielding asked who was replacing Rode during his absence, to which D'Arcy said, "No one," and added unctuously:

"It was a terrible shock to the community, this affair."

"Nonsense," Fielding retorted. "Boys love disaster. The

further we are from death the more attractive it seems. They find the whole affair most exhilarating."

"The publicity has been most unseemly," said D'Arcy, "most. I think that has been prominent in the minds of many of us in the Common Room." He turned to Smiley:

"The press, you know, is a constant worry here. In the past it could never have happened. Formerly our great families and institutions were not subjected to this intrusion. No, indeed not. But today all that is changed. Many of us are compelled to subscribe to the cheaper newspapers for this very reason. One Sunday newspaper mentioned no fewer than four of Hecht's old boys in one edition. All of them in an unseemly context, I may say. And of course such papers never fail to mention that the boy is a Carnian. You know, I suppose, that we have the young Prince here. (I myself have the honour to supervise his French studies.) The young Sawley is also at Carne. The activity of the press during his parents' divorce suit was deplorable. Quite deplorable. The Master wrote to the Press Council, you know. I drafted the letter myself. But on this tragic occasion they have excelled themselves. We even had the press at Compline last night, you know, waiting for the Special Prayer. They occupied the whole of the two rear pews on the west side. Hecht was doing Chapel Duty and tried to have them removed." He paused, raised his eyebrows in gentle reproach and smiled. "He had no business to, of course, but that never stopped the good Hecht." He turned to Smiley, "One of our *athletic* brethren," he explained.

"Stella was too common for you, Felix, wasn't she?"

"Not at all," said D'Arcy quickly. "I would not have you say that of me, Terence. I am by no means discriminatory in the matter of class; merely of manners. I grant you, in that particular field, I found her wanting."

"In many ways she was just what we needed," Fielding continued, addressing Smiley and ignoring D'Arcy. "She was everything we're forced to ignore—she was red-brick, council

estates, new towns, the very antithesis of Carne!" He turned
suddenly to D'Arcy and said, "But to you, Felix, she was just
bad form."

"Not at all; merely unsuitable."

Fielding turned to Smiley in despair.

"Look," he said. "We talk academic here, you know, wear
academic dress and hold high table dinners in the Common
Room; we have long graces in Latin that none of us can translate. We go to the Abbey and the wives sit in the hencoop in
their awful hats. But it's a charade. It means nothing."

D'Arcy smiled wanly.

"I cannot believe, my dear Terence, that anyone who keeps
such an excellent table as yourself can have so low an opinion
of the refinements of social conduct." He looked to Smiley for
support and Smiley dutifully echoed the compliment. "Besides,
we know Terence of old at Carne. I am afraid we are accustomed to his roar."

"I know why you disliked that woman, Felix. She was honest, and Carne has no defence against that kind of honesty."

D'Arcy suddenly became very angry indeed.

"Terence, I will not have you say this. I simply will not have
it. I feel I have a certain duty at Carne, as indeed we all have,
to restore and maintain those standards of behaviour which
suffered so sadly in the war. I am sensible that this determination has made me on more than one occasion unpopular. But
such comment or advice as I offer is never—I beg you to notice
this—is *never* directed against personalities, only against
behaviour, against unseemly lapses in conduct. I will acknowledge that more than once I was compelled to address Rode on
the subject of his wife's conduct. That is a matter quite divorced
from personalities, Terence. I will not have it said that I disliked Mrs. Rode. Such a suggestion would be disagreeable at
all times, but under the present tragic circumstances it is
deplorable. Mrs. Rode's own . . . background and education
did not naturally prepare her for our ways; that is quite a

different matter. It does, however, illustrate the point that I wish to emphasise, Terence: it was a question of enlightenment, not of criticism. Do I make myself clear?"

"Abundantly," Fielding answered dryly.

"Did the other wives like her?" Smiley ventured.

"Not entirely," D'Arcy replied crisply.

"The wives! My God!" Fielding groaned, putting his hand to his brow. There was a pause.

"Her clothes, I believe, were a source of distress to some of them. She also frequented the public laundry. This, too, would not make a favourable impression. I should add that she did not attend our church . . ."

"Did she have any close friends among the wives?" Smiley persisted.

"I believe young Mrs. Snow took to her."

"And you say she was dining here the night she was murdered?"

"Yes," said Fielding quietly, "Wednesday. And it was Felix and his sister who took in poor Rode afterwards . . ." He glanced at D'Arcy.

"Yes, indeed," said D'Arcy abruptly. His eyes were on Fielding, and it seemed to Smiley that something had passed between them. "We shall never forget, never . . . Terence, if I may talk shop for just one moment, Perkins's construe is abysmal; I declare I have never seen work like it. Is he unwell? His mother is a most cultured woman, a cousin of the Samfords, I am told."

Smiley looked at him and wondered. His dinner-jacket was faded, green with age. Smiley could almost hear him saying it had belonged to his grandfather. The skin of his face was so unlined that he somehow suggested fatness without being fat. His voice was pitched on one insinuating note, and he smiled all the time, whether he was speaking or not. The smile never left his smooth face, it was worked into the malleable fabric of his flesh, stretching his lips across his perfect teeth and opening the corners of his red mouth, so that it seemed to be held in place by the invisible fingers of his dentist. Yet D'Arcy's face was far from unexpressive; every mark showed. The smallest movement of his mouth or nose, the quickest glance or frown, were there to read and interpret. And he wanted to change the subject. Not away from Stella Rode (for he returned to discussing her himself a moment later), but away from the particular evening on which she died, away from the precise narration of events. And what was more, there was not a doubt in Smiley's mind that Fielding had seen it too, that in that look which passed between them was a pact of fear, a warning perhaps, so that from that moment Fielding's manner changed, he grew sullen and preoccupied, in a way that puzzled Smiley long afterwards.

D'Arcy turned to Smiley and addressed him with cloying intimacy.

"*Do* forgive my deplorable descent into Carne gossip. You find us a little cut off, here, do you not? We are often held to be cut off, I know. Carne is a 'Snob School,' that is the cry. You may read it every day in the gutter press. And yet, despite the claims of the *avant-garde*," he said, glancing slyly at Fielding, "I may say that *no one* could be less of a snob than Felix D'Arcy." Smiley noticed his hair. It was very fine and ginger, growing from the top and leaving his pink neck bare.

"Take poor Rode, for instance. I certainly don't hold Rode's background against him in any way, poor fellow. The grammar schools do a splendid job, I am sure. Besides, he settled down here very well. I told the Master so. I said to him that Rode had settled down well; he does Chapel duty quite admirably—that was the very point I made. I hope I have played my part, what is more, in helping him to fit in. With careful instruction, such people can, as I said to the Master, learn our customs and even our manners; and the Master agreed."

Smiley's glass was empty and D'Arcy, without consulting

Fielding, filled it for him from the decanter. His hands were polished and hairless, like the hands of a girl.

"But," he continued, "I must be honest. Mrs. Rode did not adapt herself so willingly to our ways." Still smiling, he sipped delicately from his glass. He wants to put the record straight, thought Smiley.

"She would never really have fitted in at Carne; that is my opinion—though I am sure I never voiced it while she was alive. Her background was against her. The fault was not hers—it was her background which, as I say, was unfortunate. Indeed, if we may speak frankly and in confidence, I have reason to believe it was her past that brought about her death."

"Why do you say that?" asked Smiley quickly, and D'Arcy replied with a glance at Fielding, "It appears she was expecting to be attacked."

"My sister is devoted to dogs," D'Arcy continued. "You may know that already perhaps. King Charles spaniels are her *forte*. She took a first at the North Dorset last year and was commended at Cruft's shortly afterwards for her 'Queen of Carne.' She sells to America, you know. I dare say there are few people in the country with Dorothy's knowledge of the breed. The Master's wife found occasion to say the very same thing a week ago. Well, the Rodes were our neighbours, as you know, and Dorothy is not a person to neglect her neighbourly duties. Where duty is concerned, you will not find her discriminatory, I assure you. The Rodes also had a dog, a large mongrel, quite an intelligent animal, which they brought with them. (I have little idea where they came from, but that is another matter.) They appeared quite devoted to the dog, and I have no doubt they were. Rode took it with him to watch the football until I had occasion to advise him against it. The practice was giving rise to unseemly humour among the boys. I have found the same thing myself when exercising Dorothy's spaniels.

"I shall come to the point presently. Dorothy uses a vet called Harriman, a superior type of person who lives over toward Sturminster. A fortnight ago she sent for him. 'Queen of Carne' was coughing badly and Dorothy asked Harriman to come over. A bitch of her quality is not to be taken lightly, I assure you."

Fielding groaned, and D'Arcy continued, oblivious:

"I happened to be at home, and Harriman stayed for a cup of coffee. He is, as I say, a superior type of person. Harriman made some reference to the Rodes' dog and then the truth came out; Mrs. Rode had had the dog destroyed the previous day. She said it had bitten the postman. Some long and confused story; the Post Office would sue, the police had been round, and I don't know what else. And, anyway, she said, the dog couldn't really protect, it could only warn. She had said so to Harriman, 'It wouldn't do any good.'"

"Wasn't she upset about losing the dog?" asked Smiley.

"Oh, indeed, yes. Harriman said she was in tears when she arrived. Mrs. Harriman had to give her a cup of tea. They suggested she should give the dog another chance, put it in kennels for a while, but she was adamant, quite adamant. Harriman was most perplexed. So was his wife. When they discussed it afterwards they agreed that Mrs. Rode's behaviour had not been quite normal. Not normal at all, in fact. Another curious fact was the condition of the dog: it had been maltreated, seriously so. Its back was marked as if from beatings."

"Did Harriman follow up this remark she made? About not doing any good? What did Harriman make of it?" Smiley was watching D'Arcy intently.

"She repeated it to Mrs. Harriman, but she wouldn't explain it. However, I think the explanation is obvious enough."

"Oh?" said Fielding.

D'Arcy put his head on one side and plucked coyly at the lobe of his ear.

"We all have a little of the detective in us," he said.

"Dorothy and I talked it over after the—death. We decided that Stella Rode had formed some unsavoury association before coming to Carne, which had recently been revived . . . possibly against her will. Some violent ruffian—an old admirer— who would resent the improvement in her station."

"How badly was the postman bitten by the dog?" Smiley asked.

D'Arcy turned to him again.

"That is the extraordinary thing. That is the very crux of the story, my dear fellow: the postman hadn't been bitten at all. Dorothy inquired. Her whole story was an absolute string of lies from beginning to end."

They rose from the table and made their way to Fielding's study, where Miss Truebody had put the coffee. The conversation continued to wander back and forth over Wednesday's tragedy. D'Arcy was obsessed with the indelicacy of it all—the persistence of journalists, the insensitivity of the police, the uncertainty of Mrs. Rode's origin, the misfortune of her husband. Fielding was still oddly silent, sunk in his own thoughts, from which he occasionally emerged to glance at D'Arcy with a look of hostility. At exactly a quarter to eleven D'Arcy pronounced himself tired, and the three of them went into the great hall, where Miss Truebody produced a coat for Smiley and a coat and muffler and cap for D'Arcy. Fielding accepted D'Arcy's thanks with a sullen nod. He turned to Smiley:

"That business you rang me about. What was it exactly?"

"Oh—a letter from Mrs. Rode just before she was murdered," said Smiley vaguely, "the police are handling it now, but they do not regard it as . . . significant. Not significant at all. She seems to have had a sort of"—he gave an embarrassed grin—"persecution complex. Is that the expression? However, we might discuss it some time. You must dine with me at the Sawley before I go back. Do you come to London at all? We might meet in London perhaps, at the end of the Half."

D'Arcy was standing in the doorway, looking at the new fall of snow which lay white and perfect on the pavement before him.

"Ah," he said, with a little knowing laugh, "the long nights, eh, Terence, the long nights."

6

Holly for the Devil

"What are the long nights?" Smiley asked, as he and D'Arcy walked briskly away from Fielding's house through the new snow towards the Abbey Close.

"We have a proverb that it always snows at Carne in the long nights. That is the traditional term here for the nights of Lent," D'Arcy replied. "Before the Reformation the monks of the Abbey kept a vigil during Lent between the Offices of Compline and Lauds. You may know that already perhaps. As there is no longer a religious order attached to the Abbey, the custom has fallen into disuse. We continue to observe it, however, by the saying of Compline during Lent. Compline was the last of the Canonical Day Hours and was said before retiring for the night. The Master, who has a great respect for traditions of this kind, has reintroduced the old words for our devotions. Prime was the dawn Office, as you are no doubt aware. Terce was at the third hour of daylight—that is to say at 9:00 A.M. Thus we no longer refer to Morning Prayer, but to Terce. I find it delightful. Similarly, during Advent and Lent we say Sext at midday in the Abbey."

"Are all these services compulsory?"

"Of course. Otherwise it would be necessary to make arrangements for those boys who did not attend. That is not desirable. Besides, you forget that Carne is a religious foundation."

It was a beautiful night. As they crossed the Close, Smiley looked up at the tower. It seemed smaller and more peaceful in the moonlight. The whiteness of the new snow lit the very sky itself; the whole Abbey was so sharply visible against it that even the mutilated images of saints were clear in every sad detail of their defacement, wretched figures, their purpose lost, with no eyes to see the changing world.

They reached the cross-roads to the south of the Abbey.

"The parting of the ways, I fear," said D'Arcy, extending his hand.

"It's a beautiful night," Smiley replied quickly, "let me come with you as far as your house."

"Gladly," said D'Arcy dryly.

They turned down North Fields Lane. A high stone wall ran along one side; and on the other the great expanse of playing fields, twenty or more rugby pitches, bordered the road for over half a mile. They walked this distance in silence, until D'Arcy stopped and pointed with his stick past Smiley towards a small house on the edge of the playing fields.

"That's North Fields, the Rodes' house. It used to belong to the head groundsman, but the school added a wing a few years ago, and now it's a staff house. My own house is rather larger, and lies farther up the road. Happily, I am fond of walking."

"Was it along here that you found Stanley Rode that night?"

There was a pause, then D'Arcy said: "It was nearer to my house, about a quarter of a mile farther on. He was in a terrible condition, poor fellow, terrible. I am myself unable to bear the sight of blood. If I had known how he would look when I brought him into the house, I do not think I could have done it. Mercifully, my sister Dorothy is a most competent woman."

They walked on in silence, until Smiley said: "From what you were saying at dinner, the Rodes were a very ill-assorted couple."

"Precisely. If her death had happened any other way, I

would describe it as providential: a blessed release for Rode. She was a thoroughly mischievous woman, Smiley, who made it her business to hold her husband up to ridicule. I believe it was intentional. Others do not. I do, and I have my reasons. She took pleasure in deriding her husband."

"And Carne too, no doubt."

"Just so. This is a critical moment in Carne's development. Many public schools have conceded to the vulgar clamour for change—change at any price. Carne, I am pleased to say, has not joined these Gadarene swine. That makes it more important than ever that we protect ourselves from within as well as from without." He spoke with surprising vehemence.

"But was she really such a problem? Surely her husband could have spoken to her?"

"I never encouraged him to do so, I assure you. It is not my practice to interfere between man and wife."

They reached D'Arcy's house. A high laurel hedge entirely concealed the house from the road, except for two multiple chimney-stacks which were visible over the top of it, confirming Smiley's impression that the house was large and Victorian.

"I am not ashamed of the Victorian taste," said D'Arcy as he slowly opened the gate; "but then, I am afraid we are not close to the modern idiom at Carne. This house used to be the rectory for North Fields Church, but the church is now served by a priest-in-charge from the Abbey. The vicarage is still within the school's gift, and I was fortunate enough to receive it. Good night. You must come for sherry before you go. Do you stay long?"

"I doubt it," Smiley replied, "but I am sure you have enough worries at the moment."

"What do you mean?" D'Arcy said sharply.

"The press, the police and all the attendant fuss."

"Ah yes, just so. Quite so. Nevertheless, our community life must continue. We always have a small party in the middle of the Half, and I feel it is particularly important that we should do so on this occasion. I will send a note to the Sawley tomorrow. My sister would be charmed. Good night." He clanged the gate to, and the sound was greeted by the frantic barking of dogs from somewhere behind the house. A window opened and a harsh female voice called:

"Is that you, Felix?"

"Yes, Dorothy."

"Why do you have to make such a bloody noise? You've woken those dogs again." The window closed with a significant thud, and D'Arcy, without so much as a glance in Smiley's direction, disappeared quickly into the shadow of the house.

Smiley set off along the road again, back towards the town. After walking for about ten minutes he stopped and looked again towards the Rodes' house a hundred yards across the playing fields. It lay in the shadow of a small coppice of fir trees, dark and secret against the white fields. A narrow lane led towards the house; there was a brick pillar-box on one corner and a small oak sign-post, quite new, pointed along the lane, which must, he decided, lead to the village of Pylle. The legend upon the sign was obscured by a film of snow, and Smiley brushed it away with his hand, so that he could read the words "North Fields," done in a contrived suburban Gothic script which must have caused D'Arcy considerable discomfort. The snow in the lane was untrodden; obviously more had fallen recently. There could not be much traffic between Pylle and Carne. Glancing quickly up and down the main road he began making his way along the lane. The hedge rose high on either side, and soon Smiley could see nothing but the pale sky above him, and the straggling willow wands reaching towards it. Once he thought he heard the sound of a footstep, close behind him, but when he stopped he heard nothing but the furtive rustle of the laden hedges. He grew more conscious of the cold:

it seemed to hang in the still damp of the sunken road, to clutch
and hold him like the chill air of an empty house. Soon the
hedge on his left gave way to a sparse line of trees, which Smiley judged to belong to the coppice he had seen from the road.
The snow beneath the trees was patchy, and the bare ground
looked suddenly ugly and torn. The lane took him in a gradual
curve to the left and, quite suddenly the house stood before
him, gaunt and craggy in the moonlight. The walls were brick
and flint, half obscured by the mass of ivy which grew in profusion across them, tumbling over the porch in a tangled
mane.

He glanced towards the garden. The coppice which bordered
the lane encroached almost as far as the corner of the house,
and extended to the far end of the lawn, screening the house from
the playing fields. The murderer had reached the house by a
path which led across the lawn and through the trees to the
lane at the farthest end of the garden. Looking carefully at
the snow on the lawn, he was able to discern the course of the
path. The white glazed door to the left of the house must lead
to the conservatory . . . And suddenly he knew he was afraid—
afraid of the house, afraid of the sprawling dark garden. The
knowledge came to him like an awareness of pain. The ivy
walls seemed to reach forward and hold him, like an old woman
cosseting an unwilling child. The house was large, yet dingy,
holding to itself unearthly shapes, black and oily in the sudden
contrasts of moonlight. Fascinated despite his fear, he moved
towards it. The shadows broke and reformed, darting swiftly
and becoming still, hiding in the abundant ivy, or merging
with the black windows.

He observed in alarm the first involuntary movement of
panic. He was afraid, then suddenly the senses joined in one
concerted cry of terror, where sight and sound and touch could
no longer be distinguished in the frenzy of his brain. He
turned round and ran back to the gate. As he did so, he looked
over his shoulder towards the house.

A woman was standing in the path, looking at him, and behind her the conservatory door swung slowly on its hinges.

For a second she stood quite still, then turned and ran back towards the conservatory. Forgetting his fear, Smiley followed. As he reached the corner of the house he saw to his astonishment that she was standing at the door, rocking it gently back and forth in a thoughtful, leisurely way, like a child. She had her back to Smiley, until suddenly she turned to him and spoke, with a soft Dorset drawl, and the childish lilt of a simpleton:

"I thought you was the Devil, Mister, but you'm got no wings."

Smiley hesitated. If he moved forward, she might take fright again and run. He looked at her across the snow, trying to make her out. She seemed to be wearing a bonnet or shawl over her head, and a dark cape over her shoulders. In her hand she held a sprig of leaves, and these she gently waved back and forth as she spoke to him.

"But you'm carn't do nothin', Mister, 'cos I got the holly fer to hold yer. So you do bide there, Mister, for little Jane can hold yer." She shook the leaves vehemently towards him and began laughing softly. She still had one hand upon the door, and as she spoke her head lolled to one side.

"You bide away from little Jane, Mister, however pretty she'm do be."

"Yes, Jane," said Smiley softly, "you're a very pretty girl, I can see that; and that's a pretty cape you're wearing, Jane."

Evidently pleased with this, she clutched the lapels of her cape and turned slowly round, in a child's parody of a fine lady.

As she turned, Smiley saw the two empty sleeves of an overcoat swinging at her sides.

"There's some do laugh at Janie," she said, a note of petulance in her voice, "but there's not many seen the Devil fly,

Mister. But Janie seed 'im, Janie seed 'im. Silver wings like fishes 'e done 'ad, Janie saw."

"Where did you find that coat, Janie?"

She put her hands together and shook her head slowly from side to side.

"He'm a bad one. Ooh, he'm a bad one, Mister," and she laughed softly. "I seed 'im flying, riding on the wind," she laughed again, "and the moon be'ind 'im, lightin' up the way! They'm close as sisters, moon and Devil."

On an impulse Smiley seized a handful of ivy from the side of the house and held it out to her, moving slowly forward as he did so.

"Do you like flowers, Janie? Here are flowers for Janie; pretty flowers for pretty Janie." He had nearly reached her when with remarkable speed she ran across the lawn, disappeared into the trees and ran off down the lane. Smiley let her go. He was drenched in sweat.

As soon as he reached the hotel he telephoned Detective Inspector Rigby.

7

King Arthur's Church

The coffee lounge of the Sawley Arms resembles nothing so much as the Tropical Plants Pavilion at Kew Gardens. Built in an age when cactus was the most fashionable of plants and bamboo its indispensable companion, the lounge was conceived as the architectural image of a jungle clearing. Steel pillars, fashioned in segments like the trunk of a palm tree, supported a high glass roof whose regal dome replaced the African sky. Enormous urns of bronze or green-glazed earthenware contained all that was elegant and prolific in the cactus world, and between them very old residents could relax on sofas of spindly bamboo, sipping warm coffee and re-living the discomforts of safari.

Smiley's efforts to obtain a bottle of whisky and a syphon of soda at half past eleven at night were not immediately rewarded. It seemed that, like carrion from the carcass, the journalists had gone. The only sign of life in the hotel was the night porter, who treated his request with remote disapproval and advised him to go to bed. Smiley, by no means naturally persistent, discovered a half-crown in his overcoat pocket and thrust it a little irritably into the old man's hand. The result, though not magical, was effective, and by the time Rigby had made his way to the hotel, Smiley was seated in front of a bright gas fire in the coffee lounge with glasses and a whisky bottle before him.

Smiley retold his experiences of the evening with careful accuracy.

"It was the coat that caught my eye. It was a heavy overcoat like a man's," he concluded. "I remembered the blue belt and . . ." He left the sentence unfinished. Rigby nodded, got up and walked briskly across the lounge and through the swing doors to the porter's desk. Ten minutes later, he returned.

"I think we'd better go and pull her in," he said simply. "I've sent for a car."

"We?" asked Smiley.

"Yes, if you wouldn't mind. What's the matter? Are you frightened?"

"Yes," he replied. "Yes, I am."

The village of Pylle lies to the south of North Fields, upon a high spur which rises steeply from the flat, damp pastures of the Carne valley. It consists of a handful of stone cottages and a small inn where you may drink beer in the landlord's parlour. Seen from Carne playing fields, the village could easily be mistaken for an outcrop of rock upon a tor, for the hill on which it stands appears conical from the northern side. Local historians claim that Pylle is the oldest settlement in Dorset, that its name is Anglo-Saxon for harbour, and that it served the Romans as a port when all the low-lands around were covered by the sea. They will tell you, too, that King Arthur rested there after seven months at sea, and paid homage to Saint Andrew, the patron saint of sailors, on the site of Pylle Church, where he burned a candle for each month he had spent afloat; and that in the church, built to commemorate his visit and standing to this day lonely and untended on the hillside, there is a bronze coin as witness to his visit—the very one King Arthur gave to the verger before he set sail again for the Isle of Avalon.

Inspector William Rigby, himself a keen local historian, gave Smiley a somewhat terse précis of Pylle's legendary past as he drove cautiously along the snow-covered lanes.

"These small, out-of-the-way villages are pretty strange places," he concluded. "Often only three or four families, all so inbred you can no more sort them out than a barnful of cats. That's where your village idiots come from. They call it the Devil's Mark; I call it incest. They hate to have them in the village, you know—they'll drive them away at any price, like trying to wash away their shame, if you follow me."

"I follow you."

"This Jane's the religious sort. There's one or two of them turn that way. The villagers at Pylle are all Chapel now, see, so there's been no use for King Arthur's Church since Wesley. It's empty, falling to bits. There's few from the valley go up to see it, for its history, like, but no one cares for it, or didn't not till Janie moved in."

"Moved in?"

"Yes. She's taken to cleaning the church out night and day, bringing in wild flowers and such. That's why they say she's a witch."

They passed Rode's house in silence and after turning a sharp bend began climbing the long steep hill that led to Pylle village. The snow in the lane was untouched and apart from occasional skidding they progressed without difficulty. The lower slopes of the hill were wooded, and the lane dark, until suddenly they emerged to find themselves on a smooth plateau, where a savage wind blew the fine snow like smoke across the fields, whipping it against the car. The snow had risen in drifts to one side of the lane, and the going became increasingly difficult.

Finally Rigby stopped the car and said:

"We'll walk from here, sir, if you don't mind."

"How far is it?"

"Short and sour, I'd say. That's the village straight ahead."

Through the windscreen, Smiley could discern behind the drifting veils of blown snow two low buildings about a quarter of a mile away. As he looked, a tall, muffled figure advanced towards them along the lane.

"That's Ted Mundy," said Rigby with satisfaction, "I told him to be here. He's the sergeant from Okeford." He leaned out of the car window and called merrily:

"Hullo, Ted there, you old buzzard, how be?" Rigby opened the back door of the car and the sergeant climbed in. Smiley and Mundy were briefly introduced.

"There's a light in the church," said Mundy, "but I don't know whether Janie's there. I can't ask no one in the village, see, or I'd have the whole lot round me. They thought she'd gone for good."

"Does she sleep there then, Ted? She got a bed there or something?" Rigby asked, and Smiley noticed with pleasure that his Dorset accent was more pronounced when he spoke to Mundy.

"So they say, Bill. I couldn't find no bed when I looked in there Saturday. But I tell you an odd thing, Bill. It seems Mrs. Rode used to come up here sometimes, to the chapel, to see Janie."

"I heard about that," said Rigby shortly. "Now which way's the church, Ted?"

"Over the hill," said Mundy. "Outside the village, in a paddock." He turned to Smiley. "That's quite common round here, sir, as I expect you know." Mundy spoke very slowly, choosing his words. "You see, when they had the plague they left their dead in the villages and moved away; not far though, on account of their land and the church. Terrible it was, terrible." Somehow Mundy managed to imply that the Black Death was a fairly recent disaster in those parts, if not actually within living memory.

They got out of the car, forcing the doors against the strong wind, and made their way towards the village, Mundy leading and Smiley in third place. The driven snow, fine and hard, stung their faces. It was an unearthly walk, high on that white hill on such a night. The curve of the bleak hill's crest and the moaning of the wind, the snow cloud which sped across the moon, the dismal, unlit cottages so cautiously passed, belonged to another corner of the world.

Mundy led them sharply to the left, and Smiley guessed that by avoiding the centre of the village he hoped to escape the notice of its inhabitants. After about twenty minutes' walking, often through deep snow, they found themselves following a low hedge between two fields. In the furthest corner of the right-hand field they saw a pale light glimmering across the snow, so pale that at first Smiley had to look away from it, then run his eyes back along the line of that distant hedge to make sure he was not deceived. Rigby stopped, beckoning to the others.

"I'll take over now," he said. He turned to Smiley. "I'd be obliged, sir, if you'd stand off a little. If there's any trouble we don't want you mixed up in it, do we?"

"Of course."

"Ted Mundy, you come up by me."

They followed the hedge until they came to a stile. Through the gap in the hedge they saw the church clearly now, a low building more like a tithe barn than a church. At one end a pale glow, like the uncertain light of a candle, shone dimly through the leaded windows.

"She's there," said Mundy, under his breath, as he and Rigby moved forward, Smiley following some distance behind.

They were crossing the field now, Rigby leading, and the church drawing ever closer. New sounds disturbed the moaning of the storm: the parched creak of a door, the mutter of a crumbling roof, the incessant sigh of wind upon a dying house. The two men in front of Smiley had stopped, almost in the shadow of the church wall, and were whispering together. Then Mundy walked quietly away, disappearing round the corner of the church. Rigby waited a moment, then approached the narrow entrance in the rear wall, and pushed the door.

It opened slowly, creaking painfully on its hinges. Then he disappeared into the church. Smiley was waiting outside when suddenly above all the sounds of night he heard a scream, so taut and shrill and clear that it seemed to have no source, but to ride everywhere upon the wind, to mount the ravaged sky on wings; and Smiley had a vision of Mad Janie as he had seen her earlier that night, and he heard again in her demented cry the dreadful note of madness. For a moment he waited. The echo died. Then slowly, terrified, he walked through the snow to the open doorway.

Two candles and an oil lamp on the bare altar shed a dim light over the tiny chapel. In front of the altar, on the sanctuary step, sat Jane, looking vaguely towards them. Her vacuous face was daubed with stains of green and blue, her filthy clothes were threaded with sprigs of evergreen and all about her on the floor were the bodies of small animals and birds.

The pews were similarly decorated with dead creatures of all kinds; and on the altar, broken twigs and little heaps of holly leaves. Between the candles stood a crudely-fashioned cross. Stepping forward past Rigby, Smiley walked quickly down the aisle, past the lolling figure of Jane, until he stood before the altar. For a moment he hesitated, then turned and called softly to Rigby.

On the cross, draped over its three ends like a crude diadem, was a string of green beads.

8

Flowers for Stella

He woke with the echo of her scream in his ears. He had meant to sleep late, but his watch said half past seven. He put on his bedside lamp, for it was still half-dark, and peered owlishly round the room. There were his trousers, flung over the chair, the legs still sodden from the snow. There were his shoes; he'd have to buy another pair. And there beside him were the notes he had made early that morning before going to sleep, transcriptions from memory of some of Mad Jane's monologue on the journey back to Carne, a journey he would never forget. Mundy had sat with her in the back. She spoke to herself as a child does, asking questions and then in the patient tones of an adult for whom the reply is self-evident, providing the answer.

One obsession seemed to fill her mind: she had seen the devil. She had seen him flying on the wind, his silver wings stretched out behind him. Sometimes the recollection amused her, sometimes inflated her with a sense of her own importance or beauty, and sometimes it terrified her, so that she moaned and wept and begged him to go away. Then Mundy would speak kindly to her, and try to calm her. Smiley wondered whether policemen grew accustomed to the squalor of such things, to clothes that were no more than stinking rags wound round wretched limbs, to puling imbeciles who clutched and screamed and wept. She must have been living on the run for nights on end, finding her food in the fields and dustbins since the night of the murder . . . What had she done that night? What had she seen? Had she killed Stella Rode? Had she seen the murderer, and fancied *him* to be the devil flying on the wind? Why should she think that? If Janie did not kill Stella Rode, what had she seen that so frightened her that for three long winter nights she prowled in terror like an animal in the forest? Had the devil within taken hold of Janie and given power to her arm as she struck down Stella? Was that the devil who rode upon the wind?

But the beads and the coat and the footprints which were not hers—what of them? He lay there thinking, and achieving nothing. At last it was time to get up: it was the morning of the funeral.

As he was getting out of bed the telephone rang. It was Rigby. His voice sounded strained and urgent. "I want to see you," he said. "Can you call round?"

"Before or after the funeral?"

"Before, if possible. What about now?"

"I'll be there in ten minutes."

Rigby looked, for the first time since Smiley had met him, tired and worried.

"It's Mad Janie," he said. "The Chief thinks we should charge her."

"What for?"

"Murder," Rigby replied crisply, pushing a thin file across the table. "The old fool's made a statement . . . a sort of confession."

They sat in silence while Smiley read the extraordinary statement. It was signed with Mad Janie's mark—J.L.—drawn in a childish hand in letters an inch high. The constable who had taken it down had begun by trying to condense and simplify her account, but by the end of the first page he had obviously despaired. At last Smiley came to the description of the murder:

"So I tells my darling, I tells her: 'You are a naughty creature to go with the devil,' but her did not hearken, see, and I took angry with her, but she paid no call. I can't abide them as go with devils in the night, and I told her. She ought to have had holly, mister, there's the truth. I told her, mister, but she never would hearken, and that's all Janie's saying, but she drove the devil off, Janie did, and there's one will thank me, that's my darling and I took her jewels for the saints I did, to pretty out the church, and a coat for to keep me warm."

Rigby watched him as he slowly replaced the statement on the desk.

"Well, what do you think of it?"

Smiley hesitated. "It's pretty good nonsense as it stands," he replied at last.

"Of course it is," said Rigby, with something like contempt. "She saw something, Lord knows what, when she was out on the prowl; stealing, I shouldn't wonder. She may have robbed the body, or else she picked up the beads where the murderer dropped them. We've traced the coat. Belonged to a Mr. Jardine, a baker in Carne East. Mrs. Jardine gave it to Stella Rode last Wednesday morning for the refugees. Janie must have pinched it from the conservatory. That's what she meant by 'a coat for to keep me warm.' But she no more killed Stella Rode than you or I did. What about the footprints, the glove-marks in the conservatory? Besides, she's not strong enough, Janie isn't, to heave that poor woman forty feet through the snow. This is a man's work, as anyone can see."

"Then what exactly . . . ?"

"We've called off the search, and I'm to prepare a case against one Jane Lyn of the village of Pylle for the wilful murder of Stella Rode. I wanted to tell you myself before you read it all over the papers. So that you'd know how it was."

"Thanks."

"In the meantime, if there's any help I can give you, we're still willing." He hesitated, seemed about to say something, then to change his mind.

As he made his way down the wide staircase Smiley felt useless and very angry, which was scarcely the right frame of mind in which to attend a funeral.

It was an admirably conducted affair. Neither the flowers nor the congregation exceeded what was fitting to the occasion. She was not buried at the Abbey, out of deference perhaps to her simplicity of taste, but in the parish churchyard not far from North Fields. The Master was detained that day, as he was on most days, and had sent instead his wife, a small, very vague woman who had spent a long time in India. D'Arcy was much in evidence, fluttering here and there before the ceremony like an anxious beadle; and Mr. Cardew had come to guide poor Stella through the unfamiliarities of High Anglican procedure. The Hechts were there, Charles all in black, scrubbed and shining, and Shane in dramatic weeds, and a hat with a very broad brim.

Smiley, who, like the others, had arrived early in anticipation of the unwholesome public interest which the ceremony might arouse, found himself a seat near the entrance of the church. He watched each new arrival with interest, waiting for his first sight of Stanley Rode.

Several tradesmen arrived, pressed into bulging serge and black ties, and formed a small group south of the aisle, away from the staff and their wives. Soon they were joined by other members of the town community, women who had known Mrs. Rode at the Tabernacle; and then by Rigby, who looked straight at Smiley and gave no sign. Then on the stroke of three a tall old man walked slowly through the doorway, looking straight before him, neither knowing nor seeing anyone. Beside him was Stanley Rode.

It was a face which at first sight meant nothing to Smiley, seeming to have neither the imprint of temperament nor the components of character; it was a shallow, ordinary face, inclining to plumpness, and lacking quality. It matched his short, ordinary body and his black, ordinary hair; it was suitably compressed into an expression of sorrow. As Smiley watched him turn into the centre aisle and take his place among the principal mourners, it occurred to him that Rode's very walk and bearing successfully conveyed something entirely alien to Carne. If it is vulgar to wear a pen in the breast pocket of your jacket, to favour Fair Isle pullovers and brown ties, to bob a little and turn your feet out as you walk, then Rode beyond a shadow of doubt was vulgar, for though he did not now commit these sins, his manner implied them all.

They followed the coffin into the churchyard and gathered round the open grave. D'Arcy and Fielding were standing together, seemingly intent upon the service. The tall, elderly figure who had entered the churchyard with Rode was now visibly moved, and Smiley guessed that he was Stella's father, Samuel Glaston. As the service ended, the old man walked quickly away from the crowd, nodding briefly to Rode, and disappeared into the church. He seemed to struggle as he went, like a man walking against a strong wind.

The little group moved slowly away from the graveside, until only Rode remained, an oddly stiff figure, taut and constrained, his eyes wide but somehow sightless, his mouth set in a strict, pedagogic line. Then, as Smiley watched, Rode seemed to wake from a dream; his body suddenly relaxed and he too walked slowly but quite confidently away from the grave towards the small group which by now had reassembled at the churchyard gate. As he did so, Fielding, at the edge of the group, caught sight of him approaching and, to Smiley's astonishment, walked deliberately and quite quickly away with an expression of strong distaste. It was not the calculated act of a man wishing to insult another, for it attracted the notice neither of Rode nor of anyone else standing by. Terence Fielding, for once, appeared to be in the grip of a genuine emotion, and indifferent to the impression he created.

* * *

Reluctantly Smiley approached the group. Rode was rather to one side, the D'Arcys were there, and three or four members of the staff. No one was talking much.

"Mr. Rode?" he inquired.

"That's right, yes." He spoke slowly, a trace of an accent carefully avoided.

"I'm representing Miss Brimley of the *Christian Voice*."

"Oh, yes."

"She was most anxious that the journal should be represented. I thought you would like to know that."

"I saw your wreath; very kind, I am sure."

"Your wife was one of our most loyal supporters," Smiley continued. "We regarded her almost as one of the family."

"Yes, she was very keen on the *Voice*." Smiley wondered whether Rode was always as impassive as this, or whether bereavement had made him listless.

"When did you come?" Rode asked suddenly.

"Yesterday."

"Making a week-end of it, eh?"

Smiley was so astonished that for a moment he could think of nothing to say. Rode was still looking at him, waiting for an answer.

"I have one or two friends here . . . Mr. Fielding . . ."

"Oh, Terence." Smiley was convinced that Rode was not on Christian-name terms with Fielding.

"I would like, if I may," Smiley ventured, "to write a small obituary for Miss Brimley. Would you have any objection?"

"Stella would have liked that."

"If you are not too upset, perhaps I could call round tomorrow for one or two details?"

"Certainly."

"Eleven o'clock?"

"It will be a pleasure," Rode replied, almost pertly, and they walked together to the churchyard gate.

9

The Mourners

It was a cheap trick to play on a man who had suddenly lost his wife. Smiley knew that. As he gently unlatched the gate and entered the drive, where two nights ago he had conducted his strange conversation with Jane Lyn, he acknowledged that in calling on Rode under any pretext at such a time he was committing a thoroughly unprincipled act. It was a peculiarity of Smiley's character that throughout the whole of his clandestine work he had never managed to reconcile the means to the end. A stringent critic of his own motives, he had discovered after long observation that he tended to be less a creature of intellect than his tastes and habits might suggest; once in the war he had been described by his superiors as possessing the cunning of Satan and the conscience of a virgin, which seemed to him not wholly unjust.

He pressed the bell and waited.

Stanley Rode opened the door. He was very neatly dressed, very scrubbed.

"Oh hullo," he said, as if they were old friends. "I say, you haven't got a car, have you?"

"I'm afraid I left it in London."

"Never mind." Rode sounded disappointed. "Thought we might have gone out for a drive, had a chat as we went. I get a bit fed-up, kicking around here on my own. Miss D'Arcy asked me to stay over at their place. Very good people they are, very good indeed; but somehow I didn't wish it, not yet."

"I understand."

"Do you?" They were in the hall now, Smiley was getting out of his overcoat, Rode waiting to receive it. "I don't think many do—the loneliness I mean. Do you know what they've done, the Master and Mr. D'Arcy? They meant it well, I know. They've farmed out all my correcting—my exam correcting, you understand. What am I supposed to do here, all on my own? I've no teaching, nothing; they've all taken a hand. You'd think they wanted to get rid of me."

Smiley nodded vaguely. They moved towards the drawing-room, Rode leading the way.

"I know they did it for the best, as I said. But after all, I've got to spend the time somehow. Simon Snow got some of my division to correct. Have you met him by any chance? Sixty-one per cent he gave one boy—sixty-one. The boy's an absolute fool; I told Fielding at the beginning of the Half that he wouldn't possibly get his remove. Perkins his name is, a nice enough boy; head of Fielding's house. He'd have been lucky to get thirty per cent . . . sixty-one, Snow gave him. I haven't seen the papers yet, of course, but it's impossible, quite impossible."

They sat down.

"Not that I don't want the boy to get on. He's a nice enough boy, nothing special, but well-mannered. Mrs. Rode and I meant to have him here to tea this Half. We would have done, in fact, if it hadn't been for . . ." There was a moment's silence. Smiley was going to speak when Rode stood up and said:

"I've a kettle on the stove, Mr. . . ."

"Smiley."

"I've a kettle on the stove, Mr. Smiley. May I make you a cup of coffee?" That little stiff voice with the corners carefully defined, like a hired morning suit, thought Smiley.

Rode returned a few minutes later with a tray and measured their coffee in precise quantities, according to their taste.

Smiley found himself continually irritated by Rode's social assumptions, and his constant struggle to conceal his origin. You could tell at the time, from every word and gesture, what he was; from the angle of his elbow as he drank his coffee, from the swift, expert pluck at the knee of his trouser leg as he sat down.

"I wonder," Smiley began, "whether perhaps I might now . . ."

"Go ahead, Mr. Smiley."

"We are, of course, largely interested in Mrs. Rode's association with . . . our Church."

"Quite."

"You were married at Branxome, I believe."

"Branxome Hill Tabernacle; fine church." D'Arcy wouldn't have liked the way he said that; cocksure lad on a motor-bike. Pencils in the outside pocket.

"When was that?"

"September, fifty-one."

"Did Mrs. Rode engage in charitable work in Branxome? I know she was very active here."

"No, not at Branxome, but a lot here. She had to look after her father at Branxome, you see. It was refugee relief she was keen on here. That didn't get going much until late 1956—the Hungarians began it, and then this last year . . ."

Smiley peered thoughtfully at Rode from behind his spectacles, forgot himself, blinked, and looked away.

"Did she take a large part in the social activities of Carne? Does the staff have its own Women's Institute and so on?" he asked innocently.

"She did a bit, yes. But, being Chapel, she kept mainly with the Chapel people from the town . . . you should ask Mr. Cardew about that; he's the Minister."

"But may I say, Mr. Rode, that she took an active part in school affairs as well?"

Rode hesitated.

"Yes, of course," he said.

"Thank you."

There was a moment's silence, then Smiley continued: "Our readers will, of course, remember Mrs. Rode as the winner of our Kitchen Hints competition. Was she a good cook, Mr. Rode?"

"Very good, for plain things, not fancy."

"Is there any little fact that you would specially like us to include, anything she herself would like to be remembered by?"

Rode looked at him with expressionless eyes. Then he shrugged.

"No, not really. I can't think of anything. Oh, you could say her father was a magistrate up North. She was proud of that."

Smiley finished his coffee and stood up.

"You've been very patient with me, Mr. Rode. We're most grateful, I assure you. I'll take care to send you an advance copy of our notice . . ."

"Thanks. I did it for her, you see. She liked the *Voice*; always did. Grew up with it."

They shook hands.

"By the way, do you know where I can find old Mr. Glaston? Is he staying in Carne or has he returned to Branxome?"

"He was up here yesterday. He's going back to Branxome this afternoon. The police wanted to see him before he left."

"I see."

"He's staying at the Sawley."

"Thank you. I might try and see him before I go."

"When do you leave, then?"

"Quite soon, I expect. Good-bye, then, Mr. Rode. Incidentally—" Smiley began.

"Yes?"

"If ever you're in London and at a loose end, if ever you want a chat . . . and a cup of tea, we're always pleased to see you at the *Voice*, you know. Always."

"Thanks. Thanks very much, Mr.—"

"Smiley."

"Thanks, that's very decent. No one's said that to me for a long time. I'll take you up on that one day. Very good of you."

"Good-bye." Again they shook hands; Rode's was dry and cool. Smooth.

He returned to the Sawley Arms, sat himself at a desk in the empty residents' lounge and wrote a note to Mr. Glaston:

Dear Mr. Glaston,

I am here on behalf of Miss Brimley of the *Christian Voice*. I have some letters from Stella which I think you would like to see. Forgive me for bothering you at this sad moment: I understand you are leaving Carne this afternoon and wondered if I might see you before you left.

He carefully sealed the envelope and took it to the reception desk. There was no one there, so he rang the bell and waited. At last a porter came, an old turnkey with a grey, bristly face, and after examining the envelope critically for a long time, he agreed, against an excessive fee, to convey it to Mr. Glaston's room. Smiley stayed at the desk, waiting for his answer.

Smiley himself was one of those solitaries who seem to have come into the world fully educated at the age of eighteen. Obscurity was his nature, as well as his profession. The byways of espionage are not populated by the brash and colourful adventurers of fiction. A man who, like Smiley, has lived and worked for years among his country's enemies learns only one prayer: that he may never, never be noticed. Assimilation is his highest aim, he learns to love the crowds who pass him in the street without a glance; he clings to them for his anonymity and his safety. His fear makes him servile—he could embrace the shoppers who jostle him in their impatience, and force him from the pavement. He could adore the officials, the police, the bus conductors, for the terse indifference of their attitudes.

But this fear, this servility, this dependence, had developed in Smiley a perception for the colour of human beings: a swift, feminine sensitivity to their characters and motives. He knew mankind as a huntsman knows his cover, as a fox the wood. For a spy must hunt while he is hunted, and the crowd is his estate. He could collect their gestures and their words, record the interplay of glance and movement, as a huntsman can record the twisted bracken and the broken twig, or as a fox detects the signs of danger.

Thus, while he waited patiently for Glaston's reply and recalled the crowded events of the last forty-eight hours, he was able to order and assess them with detachment. What was the cause of D'Arcy's attitude to Fielding, as if they were unwilling partners to a shabby secret? Staring across the neglected hotel gardens towards Carne Abbey, he was able to glimpse behind the lead roof of the Abbey the familiar battlements of the school: keeping the new world out and the old world secure. In his mind's eye he saw the Great Court now, as the boys came out of Chapel: the black-coated groups in the leisured attitudes of eighteenth-century England. And he remembered the other school beside the police station: Carne High School; a little tawdry place like a porter's lodge in an empty graveyard, as detached from the tones of Carne as its brick and flint from the saffron battlements of School Hall.

Yes, he reflected, Stanley Rode had made a long, long journey from the grammar school at Branxome. And if he killed his wife, then the motive, Smiley was sure, and even the means, were to be found in that hard road to Carne.

"It was kind of you to come," said Glaston; "kind of Miss Brimley to send you. They're good people at the *Voice*; always were." He said this as if "good" were an absolute quality with which he was familiar.

"You'd better read the letters, Mr. Glaston. The second one will shock you, I'm afraid, but I'm sure you'll agree that it would be wrong of me not to show it to you." They were sitting in the lounge, the mammoth plants like sentinels beside them.

He handed Glaston the two letters, and the old man took them firmly and read them. He held them a good way from him to read, thrusting his strong head back, his eyes half closed, the crisp line of his mouth turned down at the corners. At last he said:

"You were with Miss Brimley in the war, were you?"

"I worked with John Landsbury, yes."

"I see. That's why she came to you?"

"Yes."

"Are you Chapel?"

"No."

He was silent for a while, his hands folded on his lap, the letters before him on the table.

"Stanley was Chapel when they married. Then he went over. Did you know that?"

"Yes."

"Where I come from in the North, we don't do that. Chapel was something we'd stood up for and won. Almost like the Vote."

"I know."

His back was as straight as a soldier's. He looked stern rather than sad. Quite suddenly, his eyes turned towards Smiley, and he looked at him long and carefully.

"Are you a schoolmaster?" he asked, and it occurred to Smiley that in his day Samuel Glaston had been a very shrewd man of business.

"No . . . I'm more or less retired."

"Married?"

"I was."

Again the old man fell silent, and Smiley wished he had left him alone.

"She was a great one for chatter," he said at last.

Smiley said nothing.

"Have you told the police?"

"Yes, but they knew already. That is, they knew that Stella thought her husband was going to murder her. She'd tried to tell Mr. Cardew . . ."

"The Minister?"

"Yes. He thought she was overwrought and . . . deluded."

"Do you think she wasn't?"

"I don't know. I just don't know. But from what I have heard of your daughter I don't believe she was unbalanced. *Something* roused her suspicions, something frightened her very much. I don't believe we can just disregard that. I don't believe it was a coincidence that she was frightened before she died. And therefore I don't believe that the beggar-woman murdered her."

Samuel Glaston nodded slowly. It seemed to Smiley that the old man was trying to show interest, partly to be polite, and partly because if he did not it would be a confession that he had lost interest in life itself.

Then, after a long silence, he carefully folded up the letters and gave them back. Smiley waited for him to speak, but he said nothing.

After a few moments Smiley got up and walked quietly from the room.

10

Little Women

Shane Hecht smiled, and drank some more sherry. "You must be dreadfully important," she said to Smiley, "for D'Arcy to serve decent sherry. What are you, *Almanach de Gotha?*"

"I'm afraid not. D'Arcy and I were both dining at Terence Fielding's on Friday night and D'Arcy asked me for sherry."

"Terence is *wicked*, isn't he? Charles loathes him. I'm afraid they see Sparta in *quite* different ways . . . Poor Terence. It's his last Half, you know."

"I know."

"So sweet of you to come to the funeral yesterday. I hate funerals, don't you? Black is so insanitary. I always remember King George V's funeral. Lord Sawley was at Court in those days, and gave Charles two tickets. So kind. I always think it's *spoilt* us for ordinary funerals in a way. Although I'm never quite *sure* about funerals, are you? I have a suspicion that they are largely a lower-class recreation; cherry brandy and seed cake in the parlour. I think the tendency of people like ourselves is for a *quiet* funeral these days; no flowers, just a short obituary and a memorial service later." Her small eyes were bright with pleasure. She finished her sherry and held out her empty glass to Smiley.

"Would you mind, dear? I hate sherry, but Felix is so mean." Smiley filled her glass from the decanter on the table.

"Dreadful about the murder, wasn't it? That beggar-woman

must be mad. Stella Rode was such a nice person, I always thought . . . and so *unusual*. She did such clever things with the same dress . . . But she had such curious friends. All for Hans the woodcutter and Pedro the fisherman, if you know what I mean."

"Was she popular at Carne?"

Shane Hecht laughed gently: "No one is popular at Carne . . . but she wasn't easy to like . . . She would wear black crêpe on Sundays . . . Forgive me, but do the lower classes always do that? The townspeople liked her, I believe. They adore anyone who betrays Carne. But then she was a Christian Scientist or something."

"Baptist, I understand," said Smiley unthinkingly.

She looked at him for a moment with unfeigned curiosity. "How sweet," she murmured. "Tell me, what *are* you?"

Smiley made some facetious reply about being unemployed, and realised that it was only by a hair's-breadth that he had avoided explaining himself to Shane Hecht like a small boy. Her very ugliness, her size and voice, coupled with the sophisticated malice of her conversation, gave her the dangerous quality of command. Smiley was tempted to compare her with Fielding, but for Fielding other people scarcely existed. For Shane Hecht they did exist: they were there to be found wanting in the minute tests of social behaviour, to be ridiculed, cut off and destroyed.

"I read in the paper that her father was quite well off. From the North. Second generation. Remarkable really how *unspoilt* she was . . . so natural . . . You wouldn't think she *needed* to go to the launderette or to make friends with beggars . . . Though, of course, the Midlands are different, aren't they? Only about three good families between Ipswich and Newcastle. Where did you say you came from, dear?"

"London."

"How nice. I went to tea with Stella once. Milk in first and Indian. So different," and she looked at Smiley suddenly and said, "I'll tell you something. She almost aroused an admiration in me, I found her so insufferable. She was one of those tiresome little snobs who think that only the humble are virtuous." Then she smiled and added, "I even agreed with Charles about Stella Rode, and that's saying something. If you're a student of mankind, do go and have a look at him, the contrast is riveting." But at that moment they were joined by D'Arcy's sister, a bony, virile woman with untidy grey hair and an arrogant, hunting mouth.

"Dorothy darling," Shane murmured; "such a lovely party. So *kind*. And so *exciting* to meet somebody from London, don't you think? We were talking about poor Mrs. Rode's funeral."

"Stella Rode may have been damn' bad form, Shane, but she did a lot for my refugees."

"Refugees?" asked Smiley innocently.

"Hungarians. Collecting for them. Clothes, furniture, money. One of the few wives who *did* anything." She looked sharply at Shane Hecht, who was smiling benignly past her towards her husband: "Busy little creature, she was; didn't mind rolling her sleeves up, going from door to door. Got her little women on to it too at the Baptist chapel and brought in a mass of stuff. You've got to hand it to them, you know. They've got *spirit*. Felix, more sherry!"

There were about twenty in the two rooms, but Smiley, who had arrived a little late, found himself attached to a group of about eight who stood nearest the door: D'Arcy and his sister; Charles and Shane Hecht; a young mathematician called Snow and his wife; a curate from the Abbey and Smiley himself, bewildered and mole-like behind his spectacles. Smiley looked quickly round the room, but could see no sign of Fielding.

". . . Yes," Dorothy D'Arcy continued, "she was a good little worker, very . . . right to the end. I went over there on Friday with that parson man from the tin tabernacle—Cardew—to see if there was any refugee stuff to tidy up. There wasn't a thing out of place—every bit of clothing she had was all packed up and addressed; we just had to send it off. She was a damn' good little worker, I will say. Did a splendid job at the bazaar, you know."

"Yes, darling," said Shane Hecht sweetly. "I remember it well. It was the day I presented her to Lady Sawley. She wore such a *nice* little hat—the one she wore on Sundays, you know. And *so* respectful. She called her 'my lady.'" She turned to Smiley and breathed: "Rather feudal, don't you think, dear? I always like that: so few of us left."

The mathematician and his wife were talking to Charles Hecht in a corner and a few minutes later Smiley managed to extricate himself from the group and join them.

Ann Snow was a pretty girl with a rather square face and a turned-up nose. Her husband was tall and thin, with an agreeable stoop. He held his sherry glass between straight, slender fingers as if it were a chemical retort and when he spoke he seemed to address the sherry rather than his listener; Smiley remembered them from the funeral. Hecht was looking pink and rather cross, sucking at his pipe. They talked in a desultory way, their conversation dwarfed by the exchanges of the adjoining group. Hecht eventually drifted away from them, still frowning and withdrawn, and stood ostentatiously alone near the door.

"Poor Stella," said Ann Snow after a moment's silence. "Sorry," she added. "I can't get her out of my mind yet. It seems mad, just mad. I mean why should she *do* it, that Janie woman?"

"Did you like Stella?" Smiley asked.

"Of course we did. She was sweet. We've been here four Halves now, but she was the only person here who's ever been *kind* to us." Her husband said nothing, just nodded at his sherry. "Simon wasn't a boy at Carne, you see—most of the staff were—so we didn't know anyone and no one was really interested. They all pretended to be terribly pleased with us, of course, but it was Stella who really . . ."

Dorothy D'Arcy was descending on them. "Mrs. Snow," she said crisply, "I've been meaning to talk to you. I want you to take over Stella Rode's job on the refugees." She cast an appraising look in Simon's direction: "The Master's very keen on refugees."

"Oh, my goodness!" Ann Snow replied, aghast. "I couldn't possibly, Miss D'Arcy, I . . ."

"Couldn't? Why couldn't you? You helped Mrs. Rode with her stall at the bazaar, didn't you?"

"So that's where she got her clothes from," breathed Shane Hecht behind them. Ann was fumbling on:

"But . . . well I haven't quite got Stella's nerve, if you understand what I mean; and besides, she was a Baptist: all the locals helped her and gave her things, and they all liked her. With me it would be different."

"Lot of damn' nonsense," declared Miss D'Arcy, who spoke to all her juniors as if they were grooms or erring children; and Shane Hecht beside her said: "Baptists are the people who don't like private pews, aren't they? I do so agree—one feels that if one's paid one simply has to go."

The curate, who had been talking cricket in a corner, was startled into mild protest: "Oh, come, Mrs. Hecht, the private pew had many advantages . . ." and embarked on a diffuse apologia for ancient custom, to which Shane listened with every sign of the most assiduous interest. When at last he finished she said: "Thank you, William dear, so sweet," turned her back on him and added to Smiley in a stage whisper: "William Trumper—one of Charles's old pupils—such a triumph when he passed his Certificate."

Smiley, anxious to dissociate himself from Shane Hecht's vengeance on the curate, turned to Ann Snow, but she was still at the mercy of Miss D'Arcy's charitable intentions, and Shane was still talking to him:

"The only Smiley I ever heard of married Lady Ann Sercomb at the end of the war. She left him soon afterwards, of

course. A very curious match. I understand he was quite unsuitable. She was Lord Sawley's cousin, you know. The Saw-
leys have been connected with Carne for four hundred years.
The present heir is a pupil of Charles; we often dine at the
Castle. I never did hear what became of Ann Sercomb . . . she
went to Africa, you know . . . or was it India? No, it was America. So tragic. One doesn't talk about it at the Castle." For a
moment the noise in the room stopped. For a moment, no
more, he could discern nothing but the steady gaze of Shane
Hecht upon him, and knew she was waiting for an answer. And
then she released him as if to say: "I could crush you, you see.
But I won't, I'll let you live," and she turned and walked away.

He contrived to take his leave at the same time as Ann and
Simon Snow. They had an old car and insisted on running
Smiley back to his hotel. On the way there, he said:
    "If you have nothing better to do, I would be happy to give
you both dinner at my hotel. I imagine the food is dreadful."
    The Snows protested and accepted, and a quarter of an
hour later they were all three seated in a corner of the enormous dining-room of the Sawley Arms, to the great despondency of three waiters and a dozen generations of Lord Sawley's
forebears, puffy men in crumbling pigment.
    "We really got to know her our second Half," Ann Snow
ran on. "Stella didn't do much mixing with the other wives—
she'd learnt her lesson by then. She didn't go to coffee parties
and things, so it was really luck that we did meet. When we
first came there wasn't a staff house available for us: we had to
spend the first Half in a hotel. We moved in to a little house
in Bread Street at the end of our second Half. Moving was
chaos—Simon was examining for the scholarships and we
were terribly broke, so we had to do everything we possibly
could for ourselves. It was a wet Thursday morning when we
moved. The rain was simply teeming down; but none of our
good pieces would get in through the front door, and in the

end Mulligan's just dumped me on the doorstep and let me sort it out." She laughed, and Smiley thought what an agreeable child she was. "They were absolutely foul. They would have just driven off, I think, but they wanted a cheque as soon as they'd done the delivery, and the bill was pounds more than the estimate. I hadn't got the cheque-book, of course. Simon had gone off with it. Mulligan's even threatened to take all the stuff away again. It was monstrous. I think I was nearly in tears." She nearly is now, thought Smiley. "Then out of the blue Stella turned up. I can't think how she even knew we were moving—I'm sure no one else did. She'd brought an overall and an old pair of shoes and she'd come to help. When she saw what was going on she didn't bother with the men at all, just went to a phone and rang Mr. Mulligan himself. I don't know what she said to him, but she made the foreman talk to him afterwards and there was no more trouble after that. She was terribly happy—happy to *help*. She was that sort of person. They took the door right out and managed to get everything in. She was marvellous at helping without managing. The rest of the wives," she added bitterly, "are awfully good at managing, but don't help at all."

Smiley nodded, and discreetly filled their glasses.

"Simon's leaving," Ann said, suddenly confidential. "He's got a grant and we're going back to Oxford. He's going to do a DPhil and get a university job."

They drank to his success, and the conversation turned to other things until Smiley asked: "What's Rode himself like to work with?"

"He's a good schoolmaster," said Simon, slowly, "but tiring as a colleague."

"Oh, he was *quite* different from Stella," said Ann; "terribly Carne-minded. D'Arcy adopted him and he got the bug. Simon says all the grammar school people go that way—it's the fury of the convert. It's sickening. He even changed his religion when he got to Carne. Stella didn't, though; she wouldn't dream of it."

"The Established Church has much to offer Carne," Simon observed, and Smiley enjoyed the dry precision of his delivery.

"Stella can't exactly have hit it off with Shane Hecht," Smiley probed gently.

"Of *course* she didn't!" Ann declared angrily. "Shane was horrid to her, always sneering at her because she was honest and simple about the things she liked. Shane hated Stella—I think it was because Stella didn't *want* to be a lady of quality. She was quite happy to be herself. That's what really worried Shane. Shane likes people to compete so that she can make fools of them."

"So does Carne," said Simon, quietly.

"She was awfully good at helping out with the refugees. That was how she got into real trouble." Ann Snow's slim hands gently rocked her brandy glass.

"Trouble?"

"Just before she died. Hasn't anyone told you? About her frightful row with D'Arcy's sister?"

"No."

"Of course, they wouldn't have done. Stella never gossiped."

"Let me tell you," said Simon. "It's a good story. When the Refugee Year business started, Dorothy D'Arcy was fired with charitable enthusiasm. So was the Master. Dorothy's enthusiasms always seem to correspond with his. She started collecting clothes and money and packing them off to London. All very laudable, but there was a perfectly good town appeal going, launched by the Mayor. That wasn't good enough for Dorothy, though: the school must have its own appeal; you can't mix your charity. I think Felix was largely behind it. Anyway, after the thing had been going for a few months the refugee centre in London apparently wrote to Dorothy and asked whether anyone would be prepared to accommodate a refugee couple. Instead of publicising the letter, Dorothy wrote straight back and said she would put them up herself. So far so good. The couple turned up, Dorothy and Felix pointed a proud finger at them and the local press wrote it all up as an example of British humanity.

"About six weeks later, one afternoon, these two turned up on Stella's doorstep. The Rodes and the D'Arcys are neighbours, you see, and anyway Stella had tried to take an interest in Dorothy's refugees. The woman was in floods of tears and the husband was shouting blue murder, but that didn't worry Stella. She had them straight into the drawing-room and gave them a cup of tea. Finally, they managed to explain in basic English that they had run away from the D'Arcys because of the treatment they received. The girl was expected to work from morning till night in the kitchen, and the husband was acting as unpaid kennel-boy for those beastly spaniels that Dorothy breeds. The ones without noses."

"King Charles," Ann prompted.

"It was about as awful as it could be. The girl was pregnant and he was a fully qualified engineer, so neither of them were exactly suited to domestic service. They told Stella that Dorothy was away till the evening—she'd gone to a dog show. Stella advised them to stay with her for the time being, and that evening she went round and told Dorothy what had happened. She had quite a nerve, you see. Although it wasn't nerve really. She just did the simple thing. Dorothy was furious, and demanded that Stella should return 'her refugees' immediately. Stella replied that she was sure that they wouldn't come, and went home. When Stella got home she rang up the refugee people in London and asked their advice. They sent a woman down to see Dorothy and the couple, and the result was that they returned to London the following day . . . You can imagine what Shane Hecht would have made of that story."

"Didn't she ever find out?"

"Stella never told anyone except us, and we didn't pass it on. Dorothy just let it be known that the refugees had gone to some job in London, and that was that."

"How long ago did this happen?"

"They left exactly three weeks ago," said Ann to her husband. "Stella told me about it when she came to supper the night you were in Oxford for your interview. That was three weeks ago tonight." She turned to Smiley:

"Poor Simon's been having an awful time. Felix D'Arcy unloaded all Rode's exam correcting on to him. It's bad enough doing one person's correction—two is frantic."

"Yes," replied Simon reflectively. "It's been a bad week. And rather humiliating in a way. Several of the boys who were up to me for science last Half are now in Rode's forms. I'd regarded one or two of them as practically unteachable, but Rode seems to have brought them on marvellously. I corrected one boy's paper—Perkins—sixty-one per cent for elementary science. Last Half he got fifteen per cent in a much easier paper. He only got his remove because Fielding raised hell. He was in Fielding's house."

"Oh I know—a red-haired boy, a prefect."

"Good Lord," cried Simon. "Don't say you know him?"

"Oh, Fielding introduced us," said Smiley vaguely. "Incidentally—no one else ever mentioned that incident to you about Miss D'Arcy's refugees, did they? Confirmed it, as it were?"

Ann Snow looked at him oddly. "No. Stella told us about it, but of course Dorothy D'Arcy never referred to it at all. She must have *hated* Stella, though."

He saw them to their car, and waited despite their protests while Simon cranked it. At last they drove off, the car bellowing down the silent street. Smiley stood for a moment on the pavement, an odd, lonely figure peering down the empty road.

11

A Coat to Keep Her Warm

A dog that had not bitten the postman; a devil that rode upon the wind; a woman who knew that she would die; a little, worried man in an overcoat standing in the snow outside his hotel, and the laborious chime of the Abbey clock telling him to go to bed.

Smiley hesitated, then with a shrug crossed the road to the hotel entrance, mounted the step and entered the cheap, yellow light of the residents' hall. He walked slowly up the stairs.

He detested the Sawley Arms. That muted light in the hall was typical: inefficient, antiquated and smug. Like the waiters in the dining-room and the lowered voices in the residents' lounge, like his own hateful bedroom with its blue and gilt urns, and the framed tapestry of a Buckinghamshire garden.

His room was bitterly cold; the maid must have opened the window. He put a shilling in the meter and lit the gas. The fire bubbled grumpily and went out. Muttering, Smiley looked around for some paper to write on, and discovered some, much to his surprise, in the drawer of the writing desk. He changed into his pyjamas and dressing-gown and crawled miserably into bed. After sitting there uncomfortably for some minutes he got up, fetched his overcoat and spread it over the eiderdown. A coat for to keep her warm . . .

How did her statement read? "There's one will thank me, that's my darling and I took her jewels for the saints I did, and a coat for to keep me warm . . ." The coat had been given to Stella last Wednesday for the refugees. It seemed reasonable to assume from the way the statement read that Janie had taken the coat from the outhouse at the same time as she took the beads from Stella's body. But Dorothy D'Arcy had been round there on Friday morning—of course she had, with Mr. Cardew—she was talking about it at her party that very evening: "There wasn't a thing out of place—every bit of clothing she had was all packed up and addressed—a damn' good little worker, I will say . . ." Then why hadn't Stella packed the overcoat? If she packed everything else, why not the overcoat too?

Or had Janie stolen the coat earlier in the day, before Stella made her parcel? If that was so, it went some way to weakening the case against her. But it was not so. It was not so because it was utterly improbable that Janie should steal a coat in the afternoon and return to the house the same evening.

"Start at the beginning," Smiley muttered, a little sententiously, to the crested paper on his lap. "Janie stole the coat at the same time as she stole the beads—that is, after Stella was dead. Therefore either the coat was not packed with the other clothes, or . . ."

Or what? *Or somebody else, somebody who was not Stella Rode, packed up the clothes after Stella had died and before Dorothy D'Arcy and Mr. Cardew went round to North Fields on Friday morning. And why the devil,* thought Smiley, *should anyone do that?*

It had been one of Smiley's cardinal principles in research, whether among the incunabula of an obscure poet or the laboriously gathered fragments of intelligence, not to proceed beyond the evidence. A fact, once logically arrived at, should not be extended beyond its natural significance. Accordingly he did not speculate with the remarkable discovery he had made, but turned his mind to the most obscure problem of all: motive for murder.

He began writing:

"Dorothy D'Arcy—resentment after refugee fiasco. As a motive for murder—definitely thin." Yet why did she seem to go out of her way to sing Stella's praises?

"Felix D'Arcy—resented Stella Rode for not observing Carne's standards. As a motive for murder—ludicrous.

"Shane Hecht—hatred.

"Terence Fielding—in a sane world, no conceivable motive."

Yet was it a sane world? Year in year out they must share the same life, say the same things to the same people, sing the same hymns. They had no money, no hope. The world changed, fashion changed; the women saw it second-hand in the glossy papers, took in their dresses and pinned up their hair, and hated their husbands a little more. Shane Hecht—did she kill Stella Rode? Did she conceal in the sterile omniscience of her huge body not only hatred and jealousy, but the courage to kill? Was she frightened for her stupid husband, frightened of Rode's promotion, of his cleverness? Was she really so angry when Stella refused to take part in the rat race of gentility?

Rigby was right—it was impossible to know. You had to be ill, you had to be sick to understand, you had to be there in the sanatorium, not for weeks, but for years, had to be one in the line of white beds, to know the smell of their food and the greed in their eyes. You had to hear it and see it, to be part of it, to know their rules and recognise their transgressions. This world was compressed into a mould of anomalous conventions: blind, pharisaical but real.

Yet some things were written plain enough: the curious bond which tied Felix D'Arcy and Terence Fielding despite their mutual dislike; D'Arcy's reluctance to discuss the night of the murder; Fielding's evident preference for Stella Rode rather than her husband; Shane Hecht's contempt for everyone.

He could not get Shane out of his mind. If Carne were a rational place, and somebody had to die, then Shane Hecht should clearly be the one. She was a depository of other people's secrets, she had an infallible sense of weakness. Had she not found even Smiley out? She had taunted him with his wretched marriage, she had played with him for her own pleasure. Yes, she was an admirable candidate for murder.

But why on earth should Stella die? Why and how? Who tied up the parcel after her death? And why?

He tried to sleep, but could not. Finally, as the Abbey clock chimed three, he put the light on again and sat up. The room was much warmer and at first Smiley wondered if someone had switched on the central heating in the middle of the night, after it had been off all day. Then he became aware of the sound of rain outside; he went to the window and parted the curtains. A steady rain was falling; by tomorrow the snow would be washed away. Two policemen walked slowly down the road; he could hear the squelch of their boots as they trod in the melting snow. Their wet capes glistened in the arc of the street lamp.

And suddenly he seemed to hear Rigby's voice: "Blood everywhere. Whoever killed her must have been covered in it." And then Mad Janie calling to him across the moonlit snow: "Janie seed 'im . . . silver wings like fishes . . . flying on the wind . . . there's not many seen the Devil fly . . ." Of course: the parcel! He remained a long time at the window, watching the rain. Finally, content at last, he climbed back into bed and fell asleep.

He tried to telephone Miss Brimley throughout the morning. Each time she was out and he left no message. Eventually, at about midday, he spoke to her:

"George, I'm terribly sorry—some missionary is in London—I had to go for an interview and I've got a Baptist Conference this afternoon. They've both got to be in this week. Will first thing tomorrow do?"

"Yes," said Smiley. "I'm sure it will." There was no particular hurry. There were one or two ends he wanted to tie up that afternoon, anyway.

12

Uncomfortable Words

He enjoyed the bus. The conductor was a very surly man with a great deal to say about the bus company, and why it lost money. Gently encouraged by Smiley, he expanded wonderfully so that by the time they arrived at Sturminster he had transformed the Directors of the Dorset and General Traction Company into a herd of Gadarene swine charging into the abyss of voluntary bankruptcy. The conductor directed Smiley to the Sturminster kennels, and when he alighted in the tiny village, he set out confidently towards a group of cottages which stood about a quarter of a mile beyond the church, on the Okeford road.

He had a nasty feeling he wasn't going to like Mr. Harriman. The very fact that D'Arcy had described him as a superior type of person inclined Smiley against him. Smiley was not opposed to social distinctions but he liked to make his own.

A notice stood at the gate: *"Sturminster Kennels, proprietor, C. J. Reid-Harriman, Veterinary Surgeon. Breeder of Alsatian and Labrador Dogs. Boarding."*

A narrow path led to what seemed to be a backyard. There was washing everywhere, shirts, underclothes, and sheets, most of it khaki. There was a rich smell of dog. There was a rusted hand-pump with a dozen or so dog leads draped over it, and there was a small girl. She watched him sadly as he picked his way through the thick mud towards the door. He pulled on the bell-rope and waited. He tried again, and the child said:

"It doesn't work. It's bust. It's been bust for years."

"Is anyone at home?" Smiley asked.

"I'll see," she replied coolly, and after another long look at him she walked round the side of the house and disappeared from view. Then Smiley heard from inside the house the sound of someone approaching, and a moment later the door opened.

"Good day to you." He had sandy hair and a moustache. He wore a khaki shirt and a khaki tie of a lighter shade; old Service dress trousers and a tweed jacket with leather buttons.

"Mr. Harriman?"

"Major," he replied lightly. "Not that it matters, old boy. What can we do for you?"

"I'm thinking of buying an Alsatian," Smiley replied, "as a guard dog."

"Surely. Come in, won't you. Lady wife's out. Ignore the child: she's from next door. Just hangs around; likes the dogs." He followed Harriman into the living-room and they sat down. There was no fire.

"Where are you from?" Harriman asked.

"I'm staying at Carne at the moment; my father lives over at Dorchester. He's getting on and he's nervous, and he wants me to find him a good dog. There's a gardener to look after it in the daytime, feed it and exercise it and so on. The gardener doesn't live in at night, of course, and it's at night that the old man gets so worried. I've been meaning to get him a dog for some time—this recent business at Carne rather brought it home to me." Harriman ignored the hint.

"Gardener good chap?"

"Yes, very."

"You don't want anything brilliant," said Harriman. "You want a good, steady type. I'd take a bitch if I were you." His hands were dark brown, his wrists too. His handkerchief was tucked into his cuff. Smiley noticed that his wrist-watch faced inwards, conforming with the obscure rites of the military *demi-monde* from which he seemed to come.

"What will it do, a dog like that? Will it attack, or what?"

"Depends how she's trained, old boy; depends how she's trained. She'll warn, though; that's the main thing. Frighten the fellers away. Shove a notice up, 'Fierce Dog,' let her sniff at the tradesmen a bit and the word will get around. You won't get a burglar within a mile of the place."

They walked out into the garden again, and Harriman led the way to an enclosure with half a dozen Alsatian puppies yapping furiously at them through the wire.

"They're good little beasts, all of them," he shouted. "Game as hell." He unlocked the door and finally emerged with a plump bitch puppy chewing fiercely at his jacket.

"This little lady might do you," he said. "We can't show her—she's too dark."

Smiley pretended to hesitate, allowed Harriman to persuade him and finally agreed. They went back into the house.

"I'd like to pay a deposit," said Smiley, "and collect her in about ten days. Would that be all right?" He gave Harriman a cheque for five pounds and again they sat down, Harriman foraging in his desk for inoculation certificates and pedigrees. Then Smiley said:

"It's a pity Mrs. Rode didn't have a dog, isn't it? I mean, it might have saved her life."

"Oh, she *had* a dog, but she had it put down just before she was killed," said Harriman. "Damned odd story between ourselves. She was devoted to the beast. Odd little mongrel, bit of everything, but she loved it. Brought it here one day with some tale about it biting the postman, got me to put it down—said it was dangerous. It wasn't anything of the sort. Some friends of mine in Carne made inquiries. No complaints anywhere. Postman liked the brute. Damned silly sort of lie to tell in a small community. Bound to be found out."

"Why on earth did she tell it then?"

Harriman made a gesture which particularly irritated Smiley. He ran his forefinger down the length of his nose, then flicked either side of his absurd moustache very quickly. There was something shamefaced about the whole movement, as if he were assuming the ways of senior officers, and fearful of rebuke.

"She was trouble," he said crisply. "I can spot 'em. I've had a few in the regiment, wives who are trouble. Little simpering types. Butter-wouldn't-melt, holier-than-thou. Arrange the flowers in the church and all that—pious as you please. I'd say she was the hysterical kind, self-dramatising, weeping all over the house for days on end. Anything for a bit of drama."

"Was she popular?" Smiley offered him a cigarette.

"Shouldn't think so. Thanks. She wore black on Sundays, I gather. Typical. We used to call them 'crows' out East, the ones who wore black—Sunday virgins. They were OD mostly—other denominations. Not C of E—some were Romans, mind . . . I hope I'm not . . ."

"Not at all."

"You never know, do you? Can't stand 'em myself; no prejudice, but I don't like Romans—that's what my old father used to say."

"Did you know her husband?"

"Not so well, poor devil, not so well."

Harriman, Smiley reflected, seemed to have a great deal more sympathy for the living than the dead. Perhaps soldiers were like that. He wouldn't know.

"He's terribly cut up, I hear. Dreadful shock—fortunes of war, eh?" he added and Smiley nodded. "He's the other type. Humble origin, good officer qualities, credit to the mess. Those are the ones that cut up most, the ones women get at."

They walked along the path to the gate. Smiley said goodbye, and promised to return in a week or so to collect the puppy. As he walked away Harriman called to him:

"Oh—incidentally . . ."

Smiley stopped and turned round.

"I'll pay that cheque in, shall I, and credit you with the amount?"

"Of course," said Smiley. "That will do very well," and he made his way to the bus stop pondering on the strange byways of the military mind.

The same bus took him back to Carne, the same conductor railed against his employers, the same driver drove the entire distance in second gear. He got out at the station and made his way to the red-brick Tabernacle. Gently opening the Gothic door, made of thickly-varnished ochre pine, he stepped inside. An elderly woman in an apron was polishing the heavy brass chandelier which hung over the centre aisle. He waited a moment, then tiptoed up to her and asked for the Minister. She pointed towards the vestry door. Obeying her mimed directions, he crossed to it, knocked and waited. A tall man in a clerical collar opened the door.

"I'm from the *Christian Voice*," said Smiley quietly. "Can I have a word with you?"

Mr. Cardew led him through the side entrance and into a small vegetable garden, carefully tilled, with bright yellow paths running between the empty beds. The sun shone through the crisp air. It was a cold, beautiful day. They crossed the garden and entered a paddock. The ground was hard despite last night's rain, and the grass short. They strolled side by side, talking as they went.

"This is Lammas Land, belonging to the School. We hold our fêtes here in the summer. It's very practical."

Cardew seemed a little out of character. Smiley, who had a rather childish distrust of clergymen, had expected a Wesleyan hammer, a wordy, forbidding man with a taste for imagery.

"Miss Brimley, our editor, sent me," Smiley began. "Mrs. Rode subscribed to our journal; her family has taken it since it began. She was almost a part of the family. We wanted to write an obituary about her work for the Church."

"I see."

"I managed to have a word with her husband; we wanted to be sure to strike the right note."

"What did he say?"

"He said I should speak to you about her work—her refugee work particularly."

They walked on in silence for a while, then Cardew said, "She came from up North, near Derby. Her father used to be a man of substance in the North—though money never altered him."

"I know."

"I've known the family for years, off and on. I saw her old father before the funeral."

"What may I say about her work for the Church, her influence on the Chapel community here? May I say she was universally loved?"

"I'm afraid," said Cardew, after a slight pause, "that I don't hold much with that kind of writing, Mr. Smiley. People are never universally loved, even when they're dead." His North Country accent was strong.

"Then what may I say?" Smiley persisted.

"I don't know," Cardew replied evenly. "And when I don't know, I usually keep quiet. But since you're good enough to ask me, I've never met an angel, and Stella Rode was no exception."

"But was she not a leading figure in refugee work?"

"Yes. Yes, she was."

"And did she not encourage others to make similar efforts?"

"Of course. She was a good worker."

They walked on together in silence. The path across the field led downwards, then turned and followed a stream which was almost hidden by the tangled gorse and hawthorn on either side. Beyond the stream was a row of stark elm trees, and behind them the familiar outline of Carne.

"Is that all you wanted to ask me?" said Cardew suddenly.

"No," replied Smiley. "Our editor was very worried by a

letter she received from Mrs. Rode just before her death. It was a kind of . . . accusation. We put the matter before the police. Miss Brimley reproaches herself in some way for not having been able to help her. It's illogical, perhaps, but there it is. I would like to be able to assure her that there was no connexion between Stella Rode's death and this letter. That is another reason for my visit . . ."

"Whom did the letter accuse?"

"Her husband."

"I should tell your Miss Brimley," said Cardew slowly, and with some emphasis, "that she has nothing whatever for which to reproach herself."

13

The Journey Home

It was Monday evening. At about the time that Smiley returned to his hotel after his interview with Mr. Cardew, Tim Perkins, the Head of Fielding's house, was taking his leave of Mrs. Harlowe, who taught him the 'cello. She was a kindly woman, if neurotic, and it distressed her to see him so worried. He was quite the best pupil that Carne had sent her, and she liked him.

"You played foully today, Tim," she said as she wished him good-bye at the door, "quite foully. You needn't tell me—you've only got one more Half and you still haven't got three passes in A Level and you've got to get your remove, and you're in a fizz. We won't practise next Monday if you don't want—just come and have buns and we'll play some records."

"Yes, Mrs. Harlowe." He strapped his music-case on to the carrier of his bicycle.

"Lights working, Tim?"

"Yes, Mrs. Harlowe."

"Well, don't try and beat the record tonight, Tim. You've plenty of time till Boys' Tea. Remember the lane's still quite slippery from the snow."

Perkins said nothing. He pushed the bicycle on to the gravel path and started towards the gate.

"Haven't you forgotten something, Tim?"

"Sorry, Mrs. Harlowe."

He turned back and shook hands with her in the doorway. She always insisted on that.

"Look, Tim, what *is* the matter? Have you done something silly? You can tell me, can't you? I'm not Staff, you know."

Perkins hesitated, then said:

"It's just exams, Mrs. Harlowe."

"Are your parents all right? No trouble at home?"

"No, Mrs. Harlowe; they're fine." Again he hesitated, then: "Good night, Mrs. Harlowe."

"Good night."

She watched him close the gate behind him and cycle off down the narrow lane. He would be in Carne in a quarter of an hour; it was downhill practically all the way.

Usually he loved the ride home. It was the best moment of the week. But tonight he hardly noticed it. He rode fast, as he always did; the hedge raced against the dark sky and the rabbits scuttled from the beam of his lamp, but tonight he hardly noticed them.

He would have to tell somebody. He should have told Mrs. Harlowe; he wished he had. She'd know what to do. Mr. Snow would have been all right, but he wasn't up to him for science any longer, he was up to Rode. That was half the trouble. That and Fielding.

He could tell True—yes, that's who he'd tell, he'd tell True. He'd go to Miss Truebody tonight after evening surgery and he'd tell her the truth. His father would never get over it, of course, because it meant failure and perhaps disgrace. It meant not getting to Sandhurst at the end of next Half, it meant more money they couldn't afford . . .

He was coming to the steepest part of the hill. The hedge stopped on one side and instead there was a marvellous view of Sawley Castle against the night sky, like a backcloth for *Macbeth*. He loved acting—he wished the Master let them act at Carne.

He leant forward over the handlebars and allowed himself to gather speed to go through the shallow ford at the bottom of the hill. The cold air bit into his face, and for a moment he almost forgot . . . Suddenly he braked; felt the bike skid wildly beneath him.

Something was wrong; there was a light ahead, a flashing light, and a familiar voice calling to him urgently across the darkness.

14

The Quality of Mercy

T he Public Schools Committee for Refugee Relief (Patroness: Sarah, Countess of Sawley) has an office in Belgrave Square. It is not at all clear whether this luxurious situation is designed to entice the wealthy or encourage the dispossessed—or, as some irreverent voices in Society whispered, to provide the Countess of Sawley with an inexpensive *pied-à-terre* in the West End of London. The business of assisting refugees has been suitably relegated to the south of the river, to one of those untended squares in Kennington which are part of London's architectural schizophrenia. York Gardens, as the square is called, will one day be discovered by the world, and its charm lost, but go there now, and you may see real children playing hopscotch in the road, and their mothers, shod in bedroom slippers, abusing them from doorways.

Miss Brimley, dispatched on her way by Smiley's telephone call the previous morning, had the rare gift of speaking to children as if they were human beings, and thus discovered without difficulty the dilapidated, unnamed house which served the Committee as a collecting centre. With the assistance of seven small boys, she pulled on the bell and waited patiently. At last she heard the clatter of feet descending an uncarpeted staircase, and the door was opened by a very beautiful girl. They looked at one another with approval for a moment.

"I'm sorry to be a nuisance," Miss Brimley began, "but a friend of mine in the country has asked me to make some inquiries about a parcel of clothes that was sent up a day or two ago. She's made rather a stupid mistake."

"Oh, goodness, how awful," said the girl pleasantly. "Would you like to come in? Everything's frightfully chaotic, I'm afraid, and there's nothing to sit on, but we can give you powdered coffee in a mug."

Miss Brimley followed her in, closing the door firmly on the seven children, who were edging gently forward in her wake. She was in the hall, and everywhere she looked there were parcels of every kind, some wrapped in jute with smart labels, some in brown paper, torn and clumsy, some in crates and laundry baskets, old suitcases and even an antiquated cabin trunk with a faded yellow label on it which read: "Not wanted on voyage."

The girl led the way upstairs to what was evidently the office, a large room containing a deal table littered with correspondence, and a kitchen chair. An oil stove sputtered in one corner, and an electric kettle was steaming in a melancholy way beside it. "I'm sorry," said the girl as they entered the room, "but there just isn't anywhere to talk downstairs. I mean, one can't talk on one leg like the Incas. Or isn't it Incas? Perhaps it's Afghans. However did you find us?"

"I went to your West End office first," Miss Brimley replied, "and they told me I should come and see you. I think they were rather cross. After that I relied on children. They always know the way. You are Miss Dawney, aren't you?"

"Lord, no. I'm the sort of daily help. Jill Dawney's gone to see the Customs people at Rotherhithe—she'll be back at tea time if you want to see her."

"Gracious, my dear, I'm sure I shan't keep you two minutes. A friend of mine who lives in Carne—("Goodness! How grand," said the girl) she's a sort of cousin really, but it's simpler to call her a friend, isn't it?—gave an old grey dress to the refugee people last Thursday and now she's convinced she left her brooch pinned to the bodice. I'm sure she hasn't done anything of the sort, mind you—she's a scatter-brain creature—but she rang me yesterday morning in a dreadful state and made me promise to come round at once and ask. I couldn't come yesterday, unfortunately—tied to my little paper from dawn till dusk. But I gather you're a bit behind, so it won't be too late?"

"Gosh, no! We're miles behind. That's all the stuff downstairs, waiting to be unpacked and sorted. It comes from the voluntary reps at each school—sometimes boys and sometimes Staff—and they put all the clothes together and send them up in big parcels, either by train or ordinary mail, usually by train. We sort them here before sending abroad."

"That's what I gathered from Jane. As soon as she realised she'd made this mistake she got hold of the woman doing the collecting and sending, but of course it was too late. The parcel had gone."

"How frantic . . . Do you know when the parcel was sent off?"

"Yes. On Friday morning."

"From Carne? Train or post?"

Miss Brimley had been dreading this question, but she made a guess:

"Post, I believe."

Darting past Miss Brimley, the girl foraged among the pile of papers on her desk and finally produced a stiff-backed exercise book with a label on it marked "Ledger." Opening it at random, she whisked quickly back and forth through the pages, licking the tip of one finger now and then in a harassed sort of way.

"Wouldn't have arrived till yesterday at the earliest," she said. "We certainly won't have opened it yet. Honestly, I don't know how we shall *ever* cope, and with Easter coming up we shall just get worse and worse. On top of that, half our stuff is rotting in the Customs sheds—hullo, here we are!" She pushed the ledger over to Miss Brimley, her slim finger pointing to a pencilled entry in the central column: "Carne, parcel post, 27 lb."

"I wonder," said Miss Brimley, "whether you would mind awfully if we had a quick look inside?"

They went downstairs to the hall.

"It's not quite as hideous as it looks," the girl called over her shoulder. "All the Monday lot will be nearest the door."

"How do you know where they come from if you can't read the postmark?" asked Miss Brimley as the girl began to forage among the parcels.

"We issue volunteer reps with our printed labels. The labels have an originator's number on. In other cases we just ask them to write the name of the school in capitals on the outside. You see, we simply can't allow covering letters; it would be *too* desperate. When we get a parcel all we have to do is send off a printed card acknowledging with thanks receipt of a parcel of such and such a date weighing so and so much. People who aren't reps won't send parcels to this address, you see—they'll send to the advertised address in Belgrave Square."

"Does the system work?"

"No," replied the girl, "it doesn't. The reps either forget to use our labels or they run out and can't be bothered to tell us. Ten days later they ring up in a rage because they haven't had an acknowledgement. Reps change, too, without letting us know, and the packing and labelling instructions don't get passed on. Sometimes the boys will suddenly decide to do it themselves, and no one tells them the way to go about it. Lady Sarah gets as mad as a snake if parcels turn up at Head Office— they all have to be carted over here for repacking and inventories."

"I see." Miss Brimley watched anxiously as the girl foraged among the parcels, still talking.

"Did you say your friend actually *taught* at Carne? She must be terribly grand. I wonder what the Prince is like: he looks rather soft in his photographs. My cousin went to Carne—he's an utter wet. Do you know what he told me? During Ascot week they all . . . Hello! Here we are!" The girl stood up, a large square parcel in her arms, and carried it to a table which stood in the shadow of the staircase. Miss Brimley, standing beside her as she began carefully to untie the stout twine, looked curiously at the printed label. In its top left-hand corner was stamped the symbol which the Committee had evidently allocated to Carne: C4. After the four the letter B had been written in with ballpoint pen.

"What does the B mean?" asked Miss Brimley.

"Oh, that's a local arrangement at Carne. Miss D'Arcy's the rep there, but they've done so well recently that she coopted a friend to help with dispatch. When we acknowledge we always mention whether it was A or B. B must be terribly keen, whoever she is."

Miss Brimley forbore from inquiring what proportion of the parcels from Carne had originated from Miss D'Arcy, and what proportion from her anonymous assistant.

The girl removed the string and turned the parcel upside down in order to liberate the overlap of wrapping paper. As she did so Miss Brimley caught sight of a faint brown smudge, no more, about the size of a shilling, near the join. It was consistent with her essential rationalism that she should search for any explanation other than that which so loudly presented itself. The girl continued the work of unwrapping, saying suddenly: "I say, Carne was where they had that dreadful murder, wasn't it—that master's wife who got killed by the gipsy? It really *is* awful, isn't it, how much of that kind of thing goes on? Hm! Thought as much," she remarked, suddenly interrupting herself. She had removed the outer paper, and was about to unwrap the bundle inside when her attention was evidently arrested by the appearance of the inner parcel.

"What?" Miss Brimley said quickly.

The girl laughed. "Oh, only the packing," she said. "The C4Bs are usually so neat—quite the best we get. This is quite different. Not the same person at all. Must be a stand-in. I thought so from the outside."

"How can you be so sure?"

"Oh, it's like handwriting. We can tell." She laughed again, and without more ado removed the last wrapping. "Grey dress, you said, didn't you? Let's see." With both hands she began picking clothes from the top of the pile and laying them to either side. She was nearly half-way through when she exclaimed, "Well, *honestly!* They must be having a brain-storm," and drew from the bundle of partworn clothes a transparent plastic mack-intosh, a very old pair of leather gloves, and a pair of rubber overshoes.

Miss Brimley was holding the edge of the table very tightly. The palms of her hands were throbbing.

"Here's a cape. Damp, too," the girl added in disgust, and tossed the offending articles on to the floor beside the table. Miss Brimley could only think of Smiley's letter: "Whoever killed her must have been covered in blood." Yes, and who-ever killed her wore a plastic cape and a hood, rubber overshoes and those old leather gloves with the terra-cotta stains. Who-ever killed Stella Rode had not chanced upon her in the night, but had plotted long ahead, had waited. "Yes," thought Miss Brimley, "had waited for the long nights."

The girl was talking to her again: "I'm afraid it really isn't here."

"No, my dear," Miss Brimley replied, "I see that. Thank you. You've been very sweet." Her voice faltered for a moment, then she managed to say: "I think, my dear, you should leave the parcel exactly as it is now, the wrapping and everything in it. Something very dreadful has happened, and the police will want to . . . know about it and see the parcel . . . You must trust me, my dear—things aren't quite what they seem . . ." And somehow she escaped to the comforting freedom of York Gardens and the large-eyed wonder of its waiting children.

She went to a telephone box. She got through to the Sawley Arms and asked a very bored receptionist for Mr. Smiley. Total silence descended on the line until the Trunks operator asked her to put in another three and sixpence. Miss Brimley replied sharply that all she had so far had for her money was a three-minute vacuum; this was followed by the unmistakable sound of the operator sucking her teeth, and then, quite suddenly, by George Smiley's voice:

"George, it's Brim. A plastic mackintosh, a cape, rubber overshoes, and some leather gloves that look as though they're stained with blood. Smudges on some of the wrapping paper too by the look of it."

A pause.

"Handwriting on the outside of the parcel?"

"None. The Charity organisers issue printed labels."

"Where is the stuff now? Have you got it?"

"No. I've told the girl to leave everything exactly as it is. It'll be all right for an hour or two . . . George, are you there?"

"Yes."

"Who did it? Was it the husband?"

"I don't know. I just don't know."

"Do you want me to do anything—about the clothes, I mean? Phone Sparrow or anything?"

"No. I'll see Rigby at once. Good-bye, Brim. Thanks for ringing."

She put back the receiver. He sounded strange, she thought. He seemed to lose touch sometimes. As if he'd switched off.

She walked north-west towards the Embankment. It was long after ten o'clock—the first time she'd been late for Heaven knows how long. She had better take a taxi. Being a frugal woman, however, she took a bus.

Ailsa Brimley did not believe in emergencies, for she enjoyed a discipline of mind uncommon in men and even rarer in women. The greater the emergency, the greater her calm. John Landsbury had remarked upon it: "You have sales resistance to the dramatic, Brim; the rare gift of contempt for what is urgent. I know of a dozen people who would pay you five thousand a year for telling them every day that what is important is seldom urgent. Urgent equals ephemeral, and ephemeral equals unimportant."

She got out of the bus, carefully putting the ticket in the rubbish compartment. As she stood in the warm sunlight of the street she caught sight of the hoardings advertising the first edition of the evening papers. If it hadn't been for the sun, she might never have looked; but the sun dazzled her and made her glance downwards. And so she did see; she read it in the plump black of the wet newsprint, in the prepacked hysteria of Fleet Street: "All-night search for missing Carne boy."

15

The Road to Fielding

Smiley put down the receiver and walked quickly past the reception desk towards the front door. He must see Rigby at once. Just as he was leaving the hotel he heard his name called. Turning, he saw his old enemy, the night porter, braving the light of day, beckoning to him like Charon with his grey hand.

"They've been on to you from the police station," he observed with undisguised pleasure. "Mr. Rigby wants you, the Inspector. You're to go there at once. At once, see?"

"I'm on my way there now," Smiley replied irritably, and as he pushed his way through the swing doors he heard the old man repeat; "At once, mind; they're waiting for you."

Making his way through the Carne streets, he reflected for the hundredth time on the obscurity of motive in human action: there is no true thing on earth. There is no constant, no dependable point, not even in the purest logic or the most obscure mysticism; least of all in the motives of men when they are moved to act violently.

Had the murderer, now so near discovery, found contentment in the meticulous administration of his plans? For now it was clear beyond a doubt; this was a murder devised to the last detail, even to the weapon inexplicably far from the place of its use; a murder with clues cast to mislead, a murder planned to look unplanned, a murder for a string of beads. Now the mystery of the footprints was solved: having put the overshoes into the parcel, the murderer had walked down the path to the gate, and his own prints had been obscured by the subsequent traffic of feet.

Rigby looked tired.

"You've heard the news, sir, I suppose?"

"What news?"

"About the boy, the boy in Fielding's house, missing all night?"

"No." Smiley felt suddenly sick. "No, I've heard nothing."

"Good Lord, I thought you knew! Half past eight last night Fielding rang us here. Perkins, his head boy, hadn't come back from a music lesson with Mrs. Harlowe, who lives over to Longemede. We put out an alert and started looking for him. They sent a patrol car along the road he should have come back on—he was cycling, you see. The first time they didn't see anything, but on the way back the driver stopped the car at the bottom of Longemede Hill, just where the water-splash is. It occurred to him the lad might have taken a long run at the water-splash from the top of the hill, and come to grief in the dip. They found him half in the ditch, his bike beside him. Dead."

"Oh, my dear God."

"We didn't let on to the press at first. The boy's parents are in Singapore. The father's an Army officer. Fielding sent them a telegram. We've got on to the War Office, too."

They were silent for a moment, then Smiley asked, "How did it happen?"

"We've closed the road and we've been trying to reconstruct the accident. I've got a detective over there now, just having a look. Trouble is, we couldn't do much till the morning. Besides, the men trampled everywhere; you can't blame them. It looks as though he must have fallen near the bottom of the hill and hit his head on a stone: his right temple."

"How did Fielding take it?"

"He was very shaken. Very shaken indeed. I wouldn't have believed it, to be quite honest. He just seemed to . . . give up. There was a lot that had to be done—telegraph the parents, get in touch with the boy's uncle at Windsor, and so on. But he just left all that to Miss Truebody, his housekeeper. If it hadn't been for her, I don't know how he'd have managed. I was with him for about half an hour, then he just broke down, completely, and asked to be left alone."

"How do you mean, broke down?" Smiley asked quickly.

"He cried. Wept like a child," said Rigby evenly. "I'd never have thought it."

Smiley offered Rigby a cigarette and took one himself.

"I suppose," he ventured, "it was an accident?"

"I suppose so," Rigby replied woodenly.

"Perhaps," said Smiley, "before we go any farther, I'd better give you my news. I was on my way to see you when you rang. I've just heard from Miss Brimley." And in his precise, rather formal way he related all that Ailsa Brimley had told him, and how he had become curious about the contents of the parcel.

Smiley waited while Rigby telephoned to London. Almost mechanically, Rigby described what he wanted done: the parcel and its contents were to be collected and arrangements made to subject them immediately to forensic examination; the surfaces should be tested for fingerprints. He would be coming up to London himself with some samples of a boy's handwriting and an examination paper; he would want the opinion of a handwriting expert. No, he would be coming by train on the 4:25 from Carne, arriving at Waterloo at 8:05. Could a car be sent to the station to collect him? There was silence, then Rigby said testily, "All right, I'll take a ruddy taxi," and rang off rather abruptly. He looked at Smiley angrily for a moment, then grinned, plucked at his ear and said:

"Sorry, sir; getting a bit edgy." He indicated the far wall

with his head and added, "Fighting on too many fronts, I suppose. I shall have to tell the Chief about that parcel, but he's out shooting at the moment—only pigeon, with a couple of friends, he won't be long—but I haven't mentioned your presence here in Carne, as a matter of fact, and if you don't mind I'll . . ."

"Of course," Smiley cut in quickly. "It's much simpler if you keep me out of it."

"I shall tell him it was just a routine inquiry. We shall have to mention Miss Brimley later . . . but there's no point in making things worse, is there?"

"No."

"I shall have to let Janie go, I suppose . . . She was right, wasn't she? Silver wings in the moonlight."

"I wouldn't—no, I wouldn't let her go, Rigby," said Smiley with unaccustomed vehemence. "Keep her with you as long as you can possibly manage. No more accidents, for heaven's sake. We've had enough."

"Then you don't believe Perkins's death was an accident?"

"Good Lord, no," cried Smiley suddenly, "and nor do you, do you?"

"I've put a detective on to it," Rigby replied coolly. "I can't take the case myself. I shall be needed on the Rode murder. The Chief will have to call the Yard in now; there'll be hell to pay, I can tell you. He thought it was all over bar the shouting."

"And in the meantime?"

"In the meantime, sir, I'm going to do my damnedest to find out who killed Stella Rode."

"If," said Smiley slowly, "if you find fingerprints on that mackintosh, which I doubt, will you have anything . . . local . . . to compare them with?"

"We've got Rode's, of course, and Janie's."

"But not Fielding's?"

Rigby hesitated.

"As a matter of fact, we have," he said at last. "From long ago. But nothing to do with this kind of thing."

"It was during the war," said Smiley. "His brother told me. Up in the North. It was hushed up, wasn't it?"

Rigby nodded. "So far as I heard, only the D'Arcys knew; and the Master, of course. It happened in the holidays—some Air Force boy. The Chief was very helpful . . ."

Smiley shook hands with Rigby and made his way down the familiar pine staircase. He noticed again the vaguely institutional smell of floor polish and carbolic soap, like the smell at Fielding's house.

He walked slowly back towards the Sawley Arms. At the point where he should have turned left to his hotel, however, he hesitated, then seemed to change his mind. Slowly, almost reluctantly, he crossed the road to the Abbey Close, and walked along the southern edge towards Fielding's house. He looked worried, almost frightened.

16

A Taste for Music

Miss Truebody opened the door. The rims of her eyes were pink, as though she had been weeping.

"I wonder if I might see Mr. Fielding? To say good-bye."

She hesitated: "Mr. Fielding's very upset. I doubt whether he'll want to see anyone." He followed her into the hall and watched her go to the study door. She knocked, inclined her head, then gently turned the handle and let herself in. It was a long time before she returned. "He'll be out shortly," she said, without looking at him. "Will you take off your coat?" She waited while he struggled out of his overcoat, then took it from him and hung it beside the Van Gogh chair. They stood together in silence, both looking towards the study door.

Then, quite suddenly, Fielding was standing in the half-open doorway, unshaven and in his shirt-sleeves. "For Christ's sake," he said thickly. "What do you want?"

"I just wanted to say good-bye, Fielding, and to offer you my condolences."

Fielding looked at him hard for a moment; he was leaning heavily against the doorway. "Well, good-bye. Thank you for calling." He waved one hand vaguely in the air. "You needn't have bothered really, need you?" he added rudely. "You could have sent me a card, couldn't you?"

"I could have done, yes; it just seemed so very tragic, when he was so near success."

"What do you mean? What the devil do you mean?"

"I mean in his work . . . the improvement. Simon Snow was telling me all about it. Amazing really, the way Rode brought him on."

A long silence, then Fielding spoke: "Good-bye, Smiley. Thanks for coming." He was turning back into the study as Smiley called:

"Not at all . . . not at all. I suppose poor Rode must have been bucked with those exam results, too. I mean it was more or less a matter of life and death for Perkins, passing that exam, wasn't it? He wouldn't have got his remove next Half if he'd failed in science. They might have superannuated him, I suppose, even though he was head of the house; then he couldn't have sat for the Army. Poor Perkins, he had a lot to thank Rode for, didn't he? And you, too, Fielding, I'm sure. You must have helped him wonderfully . . . both of you did, you and Rode; Rode and Fielding. His parents ought to know that. They're rather hard up, I gather; the father's in the Army, isn't he, in Singapore? It must have been a great effort keeping the boy at Carne. It will comfort them to know how much was done for him, won't it, Fielding?"

Smiley was very pale. "You've heard the latest, I suppose," he continued. "About that wretched gipsy woman who killed Stella Rode? They've decided she's fit to plead. I suppose they'll hang her. That'll be the third death, won't it? You know, I'll tell you an odd thing—just between ourselves, Fielding. I don't believe she did it. Do you? I don't believe she did it at all."

He was not looking at Fielding. He had clasped his little hands tightly behind his back, and he stood with his shoulders bowed and his head inclined to one side, as though listening for an answer.

Fielding seemed to feel Smiley's words like a physical pain. Slowly he shook his head:

"No," he said; "no. Carne killed them; it was Carne. It could only happen here. It's the game we play: the exclusion game. Divide and rule!" He looked Smiley full in the face, and shouted: "Now for God's sake go! You've got what you want, haven't you? You can pin me on your little board, can't you?" And then, to Smiley's distress, he began sobbing in great uncontrollable gulps, holding his hand across his brow. He appeared suddenly grotesque, stemming the childish tears with his chalky hand, his cumbersome feet turned inwards. Gently, Smiley coaxed him back into the study, gently sat him before the dead fire. Then he began talking to him softly and with compassion.

"If what I think is true, there isn't much time," he began. "I want you to tell me about Tim Perkins—about the exam."

Fielding, his face buried in his hands, nodded.

"He would have failed, wouldn't he? He would have failed and not got his remove; he'd have had to leave." Fielding was silent. "After the exam that day, Rode gave him the writing-case to bring here, the case that contained the papers; Rode was doing chapel duty that week and wouldn't be going home before dinner, but he wanted to correct the papers that night, after his dinner with you."

Fielding took his hands from his face and leant back in his chair, his great head tilted back, his eyes closed. Smiley continued:

"Perkins came home, and that evening he brought the case to you, as Rode told him to, for safe keeping. Perkins, after all, was head of your house, a responsible boy . . . He gave you the case and you asked him how he'd done in the exam."

"He wept," said Fielding suddenly. "He wept as only a child can."

"And after breaking down he told you he had cheated? That he had looked up the answers and copied them on to his paper. Is that right? And after the murder of Stella Rode he remembered what else he had seen in the suitcase?"

Fielding was standing up. "No! Don't you see? Tim wouldn't

have cheated to save his life! That's the whole point, the whole bloody irony of it," he shouted. "He never cheated at all. *I* cheated for him."

"But you couldn't! You couldn't copy his handwriting!"

"He wrote with a ball-pen. It was only formulae and diagrams. When he'd gone, and left me alone with the case, I looked at his paper. It was hopeless—he'd only done two out of seven questions. So I cheated for him. I just cribbed them from the science book, and wrote them with blue ballpoint, the kind we all use. Abbots' sell them. I copied his hand as best I could. It only needed about three lines of figures. The rest was diagrams."

"Then it was you who opened the case? You who saw . . ."

"Yes. It was me, I tell you, not Tim! He couldn't cheat to save his life! But Tim paid for it, don't you see? When the marks were published. Tim must have known something was wrong with them. After all, he'd only attempted two questions out of seven and yet he'd got sixty-one per cent. But he knew *nothing* else, *nothing!*"

For a long time neither spoke. Fielding was standing over Smiley, exultant with the relief of sharing his secret, and Smiley was looking vaguely past him, his face drawn in deep concentration.

"And of course," he said finally, "when Stella was murdered, you knew who had done it."

"Yes," replied Fielding. "I knew that Rode had killed her."

Fielding poured himself a brandy and gave one to Smiley. He seemed to have recovered his self-control. He sat down and looked at Smiley thoughtfully for a time.

"I've got no money," he said at last. "None. Nobody knows that except the Master. Oh, they know I'm more or less broke, but they don't know *how* broke. Long ago I made an ass of myself. I got into trouble. It was in the war, when staff was impossible. I had a boys' house and was practically running the school—D'Arcy and I. We were running it together, and the Master running us. Then I made an ass of myself. It was during the holidays. I was up North at the time, giving a course of talks at an RAF educational place. And I stepped out of line. Badly. They pulled me in. And along came D'Arcy wearing his country overcoat and bringing the Master's terms: Come back to Carne, my dear fellow, and we'll say no more about it; go on running your house, my dear fellow, and giving of your wisdom. There's been no publicity. We know it will never happen again, my dear fellow, and we're dreadfully hard up for staff. Come back as a temporary. So I did, and I've been one ever since, going cap in hand to darling D'Arcy every December asking for my contract to be renewed. And, of course—no pension. I shall have to teach at a crammer's. There's a place in Somerset where they'll take me. I'm seeing their Headmaster in London on Thursday. It's a sort of breaker's yard for old dons. The Master had to know, because he gave me a reference."

"That was why you couldn't tell anyone? Because of Perkins?"

"In a way, yes. I mean they'd want to know all sorts of things. I did it for Tim, you see. The Governors wouldn't have liked that much . . . inordinate affection . . . It looks bad, doesn't it? But it wasn't that kind of affection, Smiley, not any more. You never heard him play the 'cello. He wasn't marvellous, but just sometimes he would play so beautifully, with a kind of studious simplicity, that was indescribably good. He was an awkward boy, and when he played well it was such a surprise. You should have heard him play."

"You didn't want to drag him into it. If you told the police what you had seen it would ruin Tim too?"

Fielding nodded. "In the whole of Carne, he was the one thing I loved."

"Loved?" asked Smiley.

"For God's sake," said Fielding in an exhausted voice, "why not?"

* * *

"His parents wanted him to go to Sandhurst; I didn't, I'm afraid. I thought that if I could keep him here another Half or two I might be able to get him a music scholarship. That's why I made him Head of House: I wanted his parents to keep him on because he was doing so well." Fielding paused. "He was a rotten Head of House," he added.

"And what exactly was in the writing-case," Smiley asked, "when you opened it that evening to look at Tim's exam paper?"

"A sheet of transparent plastic . . . it may have been one of those pack-away cape things—an old pair of gloves, and a pair of home-made galoshes."

"Home-made?"

"Yes. Hacked from a pair of Wellington boots, I should think."

"That's all?"

"No. There was a length of heavy cable, I presumed for demonstrating something in his science lessons. It seemed natural enough in winter to carry waterproofs about. Then, after the murder, I realised how he had done it."

"Did you know," Smiley asked him, "*why* he had done it?"

Fielding seemed to hesitate: "Rode's a guinea-pig," he began, "the first man we've had from a grammar school. Most of us are old Carnians ourselves, in fact. Focused when we start. Rode wasn't, and Carne thrilled him. The very name Carne means quality, and Rode loved quality. His wife wasn't like that. She had her standards and they were different, but just as good. I used to watch Rode in the Abbey sometimes on Sunday mornings. Tutors sit at the end of pews, right by the aisle, you know. I used to watch his face as the choir processed past him in white and scarlet, and the Master in his doctor's robes and the Governors and Guardians behind him. Rode was drunk—drunk with the pride of Carne. We're heady wine for the grammar school men, you know. It must have hurt him terribly that Stella wouldn't share any of that. You could see it did. The night they came to dinner with me, the night she died, they argued. I never told anyone, but they did. The Master had preached a sermon at Compline that evening: 'Hold fast to that which is good.' Rode talked about it at dinner; he couldn't take much drink, you know, he wasn't used to it. He was full of this sermon and of the eloquence of the Master. She never came to the Abbey—she went to that drab tabernacle by the station. He went on and on about the beauty of the Abbey service, the dignity, the reverence. She kept quiet till he'd finished, then laughed, and said: 'Poor old Stan. You'll always be Stan to me.' I've never seen anyone so angry as he was then. He went quite pale."

Fielding swept his white hair from his eyes and went on, with something like the old panache: "I've watched her, too, at meals. Not just here, but at dinner parties elsewhere, when we've both been invited. I've watched her do the simplest things—like eating an apple. She'd peel it in one piece, round and round till the whole peel fell off. Then she'd cut the apple and dice the quarters, getting it all ready before she ate it. She might have been a miner's wife preparing it for her husband. She must have *seen* how people do things here, but it never occurred to her that she ought to copy them. I admire that. So do you, I expect. But Carne doesn't—and Rode didn't; above all, Rode didn't. He'd watch her, and I think he grew to hate her for not conforming. He came to see her as the bar to his success, the one factor which would deprive him of a great career. Once he'd reached that conclusion, what could he do? He couldn't divorce her—that would do him more harm than remaining married to her. Rode knew what Carne would think of divorce; we're a Church foundation, remember. So he killed her. He plotted a squalid murder, and with his little scientist's mind he gave them all the clues they wanted. Fabricated clues. Clues that would point to a murderer who didn't exist. But something went wrong; Tim Perkins got sixty-one per cent. He'd got an impossible mark—he must have cheated. He'd had the opportunity—he'd had the papers in the case. Rode put his little mind to it and decided what had happened: Tim had opened the case and he'd seen the cape and the boots and the gloves. And the cable. So Rode killed him too."

With surprising energy, Fielding got up and gave himself more brandy. His face was flushed, almost exultant.

Smiley stood up. "When did you say you'll be coming to London? Thursday, wasn't it?"

"Yes. I had arranged to lunch with my crammer man at one of those dreadful clubs in Pall Mall. I always go into the wrong one, don't you? But I'm afraid there's not much point in my seeing him now, is there, if all this is going to come out? Not even a crammer's will take me then."

Smiley hesitated.

"Come and dine with me that evening. Spend the night if you want. I'll ask one or two other people. We'll have a party. You'll feel better by then. We can talk a bit. I might be able to help you . . . for Adrian's sake."

"Thank you. I should like to. Interview apart, I've got some odds and ends to clear up in London, anyway."

"Good. Quarter to eight. Bywater Street, Chelsea, number 9A." Fielding wrote it down in his diary. His hand was quite steady.

"Black tie?" asked Fielding, his pen poised, and some imp made Smiley reply:

"I usually do, but it doesn't matter." There was a moment's silence.

"I suppose," Fielding began tentatively, "that all this *will* come out in the trial, about Tim and me? I'll be ruined if it does, you know, ruined."

"I don't see how they can prevent it."

"I feel much better now, anyway," said Fielding, "much."

With a cursory good-bye, Smiley left him alone. He walked quickly back to the police station, reasonably confident that Terence Fielding was the most accomplished liar he had met for a long time.

17

Rabbit Run

He knocked on Rigby's door and walked straight in.

"I'm awfully afraid you'll have to arrest Stanley Rode," he began, and recounted his interview with Fielding.

"I shall have to tell the Chief," said Rigby doubtfully. "Would you like to repeat all that in front of him? If we're going to pull in a Carne master, I think the Chief had better know first. He's just come back. Hang on a minute." He picked up the telephone on his desk and asked for the Chief Constable. A few minutes later they were walking in silence down a carpeted corridor. On either wall hung photographs of rugby and cricket teams, some yellow and faded from the Indian sun, others done in a sepia tint much favoured by Carne photographers in the early part of the century. At intervals along the corridor stood empty buckets of brilliant red, with FIRE printed carefully in white on the outside. At the far end of the corridor was a dark oak door. Rigby knocked and waited. There was silence. He knocked again and was answered with a cry of "Come!"

Two very large spaniels watched them come in. Behind the spaniels, at an enormous desk, Brigadier Havelock, O.B.E., Chief Constable of Carne, sat like a water rat on a raft.

The few strands of white hair which ran laterally across his otherwise bald head were painstakingly adjusted to cover the maximum area. This gave him an oddly wet look, as if he had just emerged from the river. His moustache, which lavishly compensated for the scarcity of other hair, was yellow and appeared quite solid. He was a very small man, and he wore a brown suit and a stiff white collar with rounded corners.

"Sir," Rigby began, "may I introduce Mr. Smiley from London?"

He came out from behind his desk as if he were giving himself up, unconvinced but resigned. Then he pushed out a little, knobbly hand and said, "From London, eh? How d'you do, sir," all at once, as if he'd learnt it by heart.

"Mr. Smiley's here on a private visit, sir," Rigby continued. "He is an acquaintance of Mr. Fielding."

"Quite a card, Fielding, quite a card," the Chief Constable snapped.

"Yes, indeed, sir," said Rigby, and went on:

"Mr. Smiley called on Mr. Fielding just now, sir, to take his leave before returning to London." Havelock shot a beady glance at Smiley, as if wondering whether he were fit to make the journey.

"Mr. Fielding made a kind of statement, which he substantiated with new evidence of his own. About the murder, sir."

"Well, Rigby?" he said challengingly. Smiley intervened:

"He said that the husband had done it; Stanley Rode. Fielding said that when his head boy brought him Rode's writing-case containing the examination papers . . ."

"What examination papers?"

"Rode was invigilating that afternoon, you remember. He was also doing chapel duty before going on to dinner at Fielding's house. As an expediency, he gave the papers to Perkins to take . . ."

"The boy who had the accident?" Havelock asked.

"Yes."

"You know a lot about it," said Havelock darkly.

"Fielding said that when Perkins brought him the case, Fielding opened it. He wanted to see how Perkins had done in the science paper. It was vital to the boy's future that he should get his remove," Smiley went on.

"Oh, work's the only thing now," said Havelock bitterly. "Wasn't the way when I was a boy here, I assure you."

"When Fielding opened the case, the papers were inside. So was a plastic cape, an old pair of leather gloves, and a pair of rubber overshoes, cut from Wellingtons."

A pause.

"Good God! Good God! Hear that, Rigby? That's what they found in the parcel in London. Good God!"

"Finally, there was a length of cable, heavy cable, in the case as well. It was this writing-case that Rode went back for, you remember, on the night of the murder," Smiley concluded. It was like feeding a child—you couldn't overload the spoon.

There was a very long silence indeed. Then Rigby, who seemed to know his man, said:

"Motive was self-advancement in the profession, sir. Mrs. Rode showed no desire to improve her station, dressed in a slovenly manner and took no part in the religious life of the school."

"Just a minute," said Havelock. "Rode planned the murder from the start, correct?"

"Yes, sir."

"He wanted to make it look like robbery with violence."

"Yes, sir."

"Having collected the writing-case, he walked back to North Fields. Then what does he do?"

"He puts on the plastic cape and hood, overshoes and gloves. He arms himself with the weapon, sir. He lets himself in by the garden gate, crosses the back garden, goes to the front door and rings the bell, sir. His wife come to the door. He knocks her down, drags her to the conservatory and murders her. He rinses the clothes under the tap and puts them in the parcel. Having sealed the parcel, he walks down the drive this time to the front gate, following the path, sir, knowing that his own footprints will soon be obscured by other people's. Having got to the road, where the snow was hard and showed no prints, he turned round and reentered the house, playing the part of the distressed husband, taking care, when he discovers the body, sir, to put his own fingerprints over the glove-marks. There was one article that was too dangerous to send, sir. The weapon."

"All right, Rigby. Pull him in. Mr. Borrow will give you a warrant if you want one; otherwise I'll ring Lord Sawley."

"Yes, sir. And I'll send Sergeant Low to take a full statement from Mr. Fielding, sir?"

"Why the devil didn't he speak up earlier, Rigby?"

"Have to ask him that, sir," said Rigby woodenly, and left the room.

"You a Carnian?" Havelock asked, pushing a silver cigarette-box across the desk.

"No. No, I'm afraid not," Smiley replied.

"How d'you know Fielding?"

"We met at Oxford after the war."

"Queer card, Fielding, very queer. Say your name was Smiley?"

"Yes."

"There was a fellow called Smiley married Ann Sercomb, Lord Sawley's cousin. Damned pretty girl, Ann was, and went and married this fellow. Some funny little beggar in the Civil Service with an OBE and a gold watch. Sawley was damned annoyed." Smiley said nothing. "Sawley's got a son at Carne. Know that?"

"I read it in the press, I think."

"Tell me—this fellow Rode. He's a grammer school chap, isn't he?"

"I believe so, yes."

"Damned odd business. Experiments never pay, do they? You can't experiment with tradition."

"No. No, indeed."

"That's the trouble today. Like Africa. Nobody seems to understand you can't build society overnight. It takes centuries to make a gentleman." Havelock frowned to himself and fiddled with the paper-knife on his desk.

"Wonder how he got his cable into that ditch, the thing he killed her with. He wasn't out of our sight for forty-eight hours after the murder."

"That," said Smiley, "is what puzzles me. So does Jane Lyn."

"What d'you mean?"

"I don't believe Rode would have had the nerve to walk back to the house after killing his wife knowing that Jane Lyn had seen him do it. Assuming, of course, that he *did* know, which seems likely. It's too cool . . . too cool altogether."

"Odd, damned odd," muttered Havelock. He looked at his watch, pushing his left elbow outwards to do so, in a swift equestrian movement which Smiley found comic, and a little sad. The minutes ticked by. Smiley wondered if he should leave, but he had a vague feeling that Havelock wanted his company.

"There'll be a hell of a fuss," said Havelock. "It isn't every day you arrest a Carne tutor for murder." He put down the paper-knife sharply on the desk.

"These bloody journalists ought to be horsewhipped!" he declared. "Look at the stuff they print about the Royal Family. Wicked, wicked!" He got up, crossed the room and sat himself in a leather armchair by the fire. One of the spaniels went and sat at his feet.

"What made him do it, I wonder. What the devil made him do it? His own wife, I mean; a fellow like that." Havelock said this simply, appealing for enlightenment.

"I don't believe," said Smiley slowly, "that we can ever entirely know what makes anyone do anything."

"My God, you're dead right . . . What do you do for a living, Smiley?"

"After the war I was at Oxford for a bit. Teaching and research. I'm in London now."

"One of those clever coves, eh?"

Smiley wondered when Rigby would return.

"Know anything about this fellow's family? Has he got people, or anything?"

"I think they're both dead," Smiley answered, and the telephone on Havelock's desk rang sharply. It was Rigby. Stanley Rode had disappeared.

18

After the Ball

He caught the 1:30 train to London. He just made it after an argument at his hotel about the bill. He left a note for Rigby giving his address and telephone number in London and asking him to telephone that night when the laboratory tests were completed. There was nothing else for him to do in Carne.

As the train pulled slowly out of Carne and one by one the familiar landmarks disappeared into the cold February mist, George Smiley was filled with a feeling of relief. He hadn't wanted to come, he knew that. He'd been afraid of the place where his wife had spent her childhood, afraid to see the fields where she had lived. But he had found nothing, not the faintest memory, neither in the lifeless outlines of Sawley Castle, nor in the surrounding countryside, to remind him of her. Only the gossip remained, as it would while the Hechts and the Havelocks survived to parade their acquaintance with the first family in Carne.

He took a taxi to Chelsea, carried his suitcase upstairs and unpacked with the care of a man accustomed to living alone. He thought of having a bath, but decided to ring Ailsa Brimley first. The telephone was by his bed. He sat on the edge of the bed and dialled the number. A tinny model-voice sang: "Unipress, good afternoon," and he asked for Miss Brimley. There was a long silence, then, "Ah'm afraid Miss Brimley is in conference. Can someone else answer your query?"

Query, thought Smiley. Good God! Why on earth query—why not question or inquiry?

"No," he replied. "Just tell her Mr. Smiley rang." He put back the receiver and went into the bathroom and turned on the hot tap. He was fiddling with his cuff-links when the telephone rang. It was Ailsa Brimley:

"George? I think you'd better come round at once. We've got a visitor. Mr. Rode from Carne. He wants to talk to us." Pulling on his jacket, he ran out into the street and hailed a taxi.

19

Disposal of a Legend

The descending escalator was packed with the staff of Unipress, homebound and heavy-eyed. To them, the sight of a fat, middle-aged gentleman bounding up the adjoining staircase provided unexpected entertainment, so that Smiley was hastened on his way by the jeers of office-boys and the laughter of typists. On the first floor he paused to study an enormous board carrying the titles of a quarter of the national dailies. Finally, under the heading of "Technical and Miscellaneous," he spotted the *Christian Voice*, Room 619. The lift seemed to go up very slowly. Formless music issued from behind its plush, while a boy in a monkey jacket flicked his hips on the heavier beats. The golden doors parted with a sigh, the boy said "Six," and Smiley stepped quickly into the corridor. A moment or two later he was knocking on the door of Room 619. It was opened by Ailsa Brimley.

"George, how nice," she said brightly. "Mr. Rode will be dreadfully pleased to see you." And without any further introduction she led him into her office. In an armchair near the window sat Stanley Rode, tutor of Carne, in a neat black overcoat. As Smiley entered he stood up and held out his hand. "Good of you to come, sir," he said woodenly. "Very." The same flat manner, the same cautious voice.

"How can I help you?" asked Smiley.

They all sat down. Smiley offered Miss Brimley a cigarette and lit it for her.

"It's about this article you're writing about Stella," he began. "I feel awful about it really, because you've been so good to her, and her memory, if you see what I mean. I know you wish well, but I don't want you to write it."

Smiley said nothing, and Ailsa was wise enough to keep quiet. From now on it was Smiley's interview. The silence didn't worry him, but it seemed to worry Rode.

"It wouldn't be right; it wouldn't do at all. Mr. Glaston agreed; I spoke to him yesterday before he left and he agreed. I just couldn't let you write that stuff."

"Why not?"

"Too many people know, you see. Poor Mr. Cardew, I asked him. He knows a lot; and a lot about Stella, so I asked him. He understands why I gave up Chapel too; I couldn't bear to see her going there every Sunday and going down on her knees." He shook his head. "It was all wrong. It just made a fool of your faith."

"What did Mr. Cardew say?"

"He said we should not be the judges. We should let God judge. But I said to him it wouldn't be right, those people knowing her and knowing what she'd done, and then reading all that stuff in the *Voice*. They'd think it was crazy. He didn't seem to see that, he just said to leave it to God. But I can't, Mr. Smiley."

Again no one spoke for a time. Rode sat quite still, save for a very slight rocking movement of his head. Then he began to talk again:

"I didn't believe old Mr. Glaston at first. He said she was bad, but I didn't believe it. They lived up on the hill then, Gorse Hill, only a step from the Tabernacle; Stella and her father. They never seemed to keep servants for long, so she did most of the work. I used to call in Sunday mornings sometimes after church. Stella looked after her father, cooked for him and everything, and I always wondered how I'd ever have the nerve to ask Mr. Glaston for her. The Glastons were big people in Branxome. I was teaching at grammar school in those days. They let me teach part-time while I read for my degree, and I made up my mind that if I passed the exam I'd ask her to marry me.

"The Sunday after the results came out I went round to the house after morning service. Mr. Glaston opened the door himself. He took me straight into the study. You could see half the potteries in Poole from the window, and the sea beyond. He sat me down and he said: 'I know what you're here for, Stanley. You want to marry Stella. But you don't know her,' he said, 'you don't know her.' 'I've been visiting two years, Mr. Glaston,' I said, 'and I think I know my mind.' Then he started talking about her. I never thought to hear a human being talk like that of his own child. He said she was bad—bad in her heart. That she was full of malice. That was why no servants would stay at the Hill. He told me how she'd lead people on, all kind and warm, till they'd told her everything, then she'd hurt them, saying wicked, wicked things, half true, half lies. He told me a lot more besides, and I didn't believe it, not a word. I think I lost my head; I called him a jealous old man who didn't want to lose his housekeeper, a lying, jealous old man who wanted his child to wait on him till he died. I said it was him who was bad, not Stella, and I shouted at him liar. He didn't seem to hear, just shook his head, and I ran out into the hall and called Stella. She'd been in the kitchen, I think, and she came to me and put her arms round me and kissed me.

"We were married a month later, and the old man gave her away. He shook my hand at the wedding and called me a fine man, and I thought what an old hypocrite he was. He gave us money—to me, not her—two thousand pounds. I thought perhaps he was trying to make up for the dreadful things he'd said, and later I wrote to him and said I forgave him. He never answered and I didn't see him often after that.

"For a year or more we were happy enough at Branxome.

She was just what I thought she'd be, neat and simple. She liked to go for walks and kiss at the stiles; she liked to be a bit grand sometimes, going to the Dolphin for dinner all dressed up. It meant a lot to me then, I don't mind admitting, going to the right places with Mr. Glaston's daughter. He was Rotary and on the Council and quite a figure in Branxome. She used to tease me about it—in front of other people too, which got me a bit. I remember one time we went to the Dolphin, one of the waiters there was a bloke called Johnnie Raglan. We'd been to school together. Johnnie was a bit of a tear-about and hadn't done anything much since he'd left school except run after girls and get into trouble. Stella knew him, I don't know how, and she waved to him as soon as we'd sat down. Johnnie came over and Stella made him bring another chair and sit with us. The Manager looked daggers, but he didn't dare to do anything because she was Samuel Glaston's daughter. Johnnie stayed there all the meal and Stella talked to him about school and what I was like. Johnnie was pleased as punch and got cheeky, saying I'd been a swat and a good boy and all the rest, and how Johnnie had knocked me about—lies most of it, and she egged him on. I went for her afterwards and said I didn't pay good money at the Dolphin to hear Johnnie Raglan tell a lot of tall stories, and she turned on me fast like a cat. It was her money, she said, and Johnnie was as good as me any day. Then she was sorry and kissed me and I pretended to forgive her."

Sweat was forming on his face; he was talking fast, the words tripping over each other. It was like a man recalling a nightmare, as if the memory were still there, the fear only half gone. He paused and looked sharply at Smiley as if expecting him to speak, but Smiley seemed to be looking past him, his face impassive, its soft contours grown hard.

"Then we went to Carne. I'd just started reading *The Times* and I saw the advert. They wanted a science tutor and I applied. Mr. D'Arcy interviewed me and I got the job. It wasn't till we got to Carne that I knew that what her father had said was true. She hadn't been very keen on Chapel before, but as soon as she got here she went in for it in a big way. She knew it would look wrong, that it would hurt me. Branxome's a fine big church, you see; there was nothing funny about going to Branxome Tabernacle. But at Carne it was different; Carne Tabernacle's a little out-of-the-way place with a tin roof. She wanted to be different, to spite the school and me, by playing the humble one. I wouldn't have minded if she'd been sincere, but she wasn't, Mr. Cardew knew that. He got to know Stella, Mr. Cardew did. I think her father told him; anyway, Mr. Cardew was up North before, and he knew the family well. For all I know he wrote to Mr. Glaston, or went and saw him or something.

"She began there well enough. The townspeople were all pleased enough to see her—a wife from the School coming to the Tabernacle, that had never happened before. Then she took to running the appeal for the refugees—to collecting clothes and all that. Miss D'Arcy was running it for the school, Mr. D'Arcy's sister, and Stella wanted to beat her at her own game—to get more from the Chapel people than Miss D'Arcy got from the School. But I knew what she was doing, and so did Mr. Cardew, and so did the townspeople in the end. She listened. Every drop of gossip and dirt, she hoarded it away. She'd come home of an evening sometimes—Wednesdays and Fridays she did her Chapel work—and she'd throw off her coat and laugh till I thought she'd gone mad.

"'I've got them! I've got them all,' she'd say, 'I know all their little secrets and I've got them in the hollow of my hand, Stan.' That's what she'd say. And those that realised grew to be frightened of her. They all gossiped, Heaven knows, but not to profit from it, not like Stella. Stella was cunning; anything decent, anything good, she'd drag it down and spoil it. There were a dozen she'd got the measure of. There was Mulligan the furniture man; he's got a daughter with a kid near Leamington. Somehow she found out the girl wasn't married—they'd sent her to an aunt to have her baby and begin again up there.

She rang up Mulligan once, something to do with a bill for moving Simon Snow's furniture, and she said 'Greetings from Leamington Spa, Mr. Mulligan. We need a little cooperation.' She told me that—she came home laughing her head off and told me. But they got her in the end, didn't they? They got their own back!"

Smiley nodded slowly, his eyes now turned fully upon Rode.

"Yes," he said at last, "they got their own back!"

"They thought Mad Janie did it, but I didn't. Janie'd as soon have killed her own sister as Stella. They were as close as moon and stars, that's what Stella said. They'd talk together for hours in the evenings when I was out late on Societies or Extra Tuition. Stella cooked food for her, gave her clothes and money. It gave her a feeling of power to help a creature like Janie, and have her fawning round. Not because she was kind, but because she was cruel.

"She'd brought a little dog with her from Branxome, a mongrel. One day a few months ago I came home and found it lying in the garage whimpering, terrified. It was limping and had blood on its back. She'd beaten it. She must have gone mad. I knew she'd beaten it before, but never like that; never. Then something happened—I shouted at her and she laughed and then I hit her. Not hard, but hard enough. In the face. I gave her twenty-four hours to have the dog destroyed or I'd tell the police. She screamed at me—it was her dog and she'd damn' well do what she liked with it—but next day she put on her little black hat and took the dog to the vet. I suppose she told him some tale. She could spin a good tale about anything, Stella could. She kind of stepped into a part and played it right through. Like the tale she told the Hungarians. Miss D'Arcy had some refugees to stay from London once and Stella told them such a tale they ran away and had to be taken back to London. Miss D'Arcy paid for their fares and everything, even had the welfare officer down to see them and try and put things right. I don't think Miss D'Arcy ever knew who'd got at them, but I did—Stella told me. She laughed, always that same laugh: 'There's your fine lady, Stan. Look at her charity now.'

"After the dog, she took to pretending I was violent, cringing away whenever I came near, holding her arm up as though I was going to hit her again. She even made out I was plotting to murder her: she went and told Mr. Cardew I was. She didn't believe it herself; she'd laugh about it sometimes. She said to me: 'It's no good killing me now, Stan; they'll all know who's done it.' But other times she'd whine and stroke me, begging me not to kill her. 'You'll kill me in the long nights!' She'd scream it out—it was the words that got her, the long nights, she liked the sound of them the way an actor does, and she'd build a whole story round them. 'Oh, Stan,' she'd say, 'keep me safe in the long nights.' You know how it is when you never meant to do anything anyway, and someone goes on begging you not to do it? You think you might do it after all, you begin to consider the possibility."

Miss Brimley drew in her breath rather quickly. Smiley stood up and walked over to Rode.

"Why don't we go back to my house for some food?" he said. "We can talk this over quietly. Among friends."

They took a taxi to Bywater Street. Rode sat beside Ailsa Brimley, more relaxed now, and Smiley, opposite him on a drop-seat, watched him and wondered. And it occurred to him that the most important thing about Rode was that he had no friends. Smiley was reminded of Büchner's fairy tale of the child left alone in an empty world who, finding no one to talk to, went to the moon because it smiled at him, but the moon was made of rotten wood. And when the sun and moon and stars had all turned to nothing, he tried to go back to the earth, but it had gone.

Perhaps because Smiley was tired, or perhaps because he was getting a little old, he felt a movement of sudden compassion towards Rode, such as children feel for the poor and parents for their children. Rode had tried so hard—he had used Carne's language, bought the right clothes, and thought as best he could the right thoughts, yet remained hopelessly apart, hopelessly alone.

He lit the gas-fire in the drawing-room while Ailsa Brimley went to the delicatessen in the King's Road for soup and eggs. He poured out whisky and soda and gave one to Rode, who drank it in short sips, without speaking.

"I had to tell somebody," he said at last. "I thought you'd be a good person. I didn't want you to print that article, though. Too many knew, you see."

"How many really knew?"

"Only those she'd gone for, I think. I suppose about a dozen townspeople. And Mr. Cardew, of course. She was terribly cunning, you see. She didn't often pass on gossip. She knew to a hair how far she could go. Those who knew were the ones she'd got on the hook. Oh, and D'Arcy, Felix D'Arcy, he knew. She had something special there, something she never told me about. There were nights when she'd put on her shawl and slip out, all excited as if she was going to a party. Quite late sometimes, eleven or twelve. I'd never ask her where she was going because it only bucked her, but sometimes she'd nod at me all cunning and say, 'You don't know, Stan, but D'Arcy does. D'Arcy knows and he can't tell,' and then she'd laugh again and try and look mysterious, and off she'd go."

Smiley was silent for a long time, watching Rode and thinking. Then he asked suddenly: "What was Stella's blood group, do you know?"

"Mine's B. I know that. I was a donor at Branxome. Hers was different."

"How do you know that?"

"She had a test before we were married. She used to suffer from anaemia. I remember hers being different, that's all. Probably A. I can't remember for sure. Why?"

"Where were you registered as a donor?"

"North Poole Transfusion Centre."

"Will they know you there still? Are you still recorded there?"

"I suppose so."

The front door bell rang. It was Ailsa Brimley, back from her shopping.

Ailsa installed herself in the kitchen, while Rode and Smiley sat in the warm comfort of the drawing-room.

"Tell me something else," said Smiley, "about the night of the murder. Why did you leave the writing-case behind? Was it absent-mindedness?"

"No, not really. I was on Chapel duty that night, so Stella and I arrived separately at Fielding's house. She got there before I did and I think Fielding gave the case to her—right at the start of the evening so that it wouldn't get forgotten. He said something about it later that evening. She'd put the case beside her coat in the hall. It was only a little thing about eighteen inches by twelve. I could have sworn she was carrying it as we stood in the hall saying good-bye, but I must have been mistaken. It wasn't till we got to the house that she asked me what I'd done with it."

"*She* asked *you* what you'd done with it?"

"Yes. Then she threw a temper and said I expected her to remember everything. I didn't particularly want to go back, I could have rung Fielding and arranged to collect it first thing next morning, but Stella wouldn't hear of it. She made me go. I didn't like to tell the police all this stuff about us quarrelling, it didn't seem right."

Smiley nodded. "When you got back to Fielding's you rang the bell?"

"Yes. There's the front door, then a glass door inside, a sort of french window to keep out draughts. The front door was still open, and the light was on in the hall. I rang the bell and collected the case from Fielding."

*   *   *

They had finished supper when the telephone rang.

"Rigby here, Mr. Smiley. I've got the laboratory results. They're rather puzzling."

"The exam paper first: it doesn't tally?"

"No, it doesn't. The boffins here say all the figures and writing were done with the same ballpoint pen. They can't be sure about the diagrams but they say the legend on all the diagrams corresponds to the rest of the script on the sheet."

"All done by the boy after all in fact?"

"Yes. I brought up some other samples of his hand-writing for comparison. They match the exam paper right the way through. Fielding couldn't have tinkered with it."

"Good. And the clothing? Nothing there either?"

"Traces of blood, that's all. No prints on the plastic."

"What was her blood group, by the way?"

"Group A."

Smiley sat down on the edge of the bed. Pressing the receiver to his ear, he began talking quietly. Ten minutes later he was walking slowly downstairs. He had come to the end of the chase, and was already sickened by the kill.

It was nearly an hour before Rigby arrived.

20

The Dross of the River

Albert Bridge was as preposterous as ever; bony steel, rising to Wagnerian pinnacles, against the patient London sky; the Thames crawling beneath it with resignation, edging its filth into the wharves of Battersea, then sliding towards the mist down river.

The mist was thick. Smiley watched the driftwood, as it touched it, turning first to white dust, then seeming to lift, dissolve and vanish.

This was how it would end, on a foul morning like this when they dragged the murderer whimpering from his cell and put the hempen rope round his neck. Would Smiley have the courage to recall this two months from now, as the dawn broke outside his window and the clock rang out the time? When they broke a man's neck on the scaffold and put him away like the dross of the river?

He made his way along Beaumont Street towards the King's Road. The milkman chugged past him in his electric van. He would breakfast out this morning, then take a cab to Curzon Street and order the wine for dinner. He would choose something good. Fielding would like that.

Fielding closed his eyes and drank, his left hand held lightly across his chest.

"Divine," he said, "divine!" And Ailsa Brimley, opposite him, smiled gently.

"How are you going to spend your retirement, Mr. Fielding?" she asked. "Drinking Frankenwein?"

His glass still held before his lips, he looked into the candles. The silver was good, better than his own. He wondered why they were only dining three. "In peace," he replied at last. "I have recently made a discovery."

"What's that?"

"That I have been playing to an empty house. But now I'm comforted to think that no one remembers how I forgot my words or missed an entry. So many of us wait patiently for our audience to die. At Carne no one will remember for more than a Half or two what a mess I've made of life. I was too vain to realise that until recently." He put the glass down in front of him and smiled suddenly at Ailsa Brimley. "That is the peace I mean. Not to exist in anyone's mind, but my own; to be a secular monk, safe and forgotten."

Smiley gave him more wine: "Miss Brimley knew your brother Adrian well in the war. We were all in the same department," he said. "She was Adrian's secretary for a while. Weren't you, Brim?"

"It's depressing how the bad live on," Fielding declared. "Rather embarrassing. For the bad, I mean." He gave a little gastronomic sigh. "The moment of truth in a good meal! *Übergangsperiode* between *entremets* and dessert," and they all laughed, and then were silent. Smiley put down his glass, and said:

"The story you told me on Thursday, when I came and saw you . . ."

"Well?" Fielding was irritated.

"About cheating for Tim Perkins . . . how you took the paper from the case and altered it . . ."

"Yes?"

"It isn't true." He might have been talking about the

weather. "They've examined it and it isn't true. The writing was all one person's . . . the boy's. If anyone cheated, it must have been the boy."

There was a long silence. Fielding shrugged.

"My dear fellow, you can't expect me to believe that. These people are practically moronic."

"Of course, it doesn't necessarily signify anything. I mean you could be protecting the boy, couldn't you? By lying for him, for his honour so to speak. Is that the explanation?"

"I've told you the truth," he replied shortly. "Make what you want of it."

"I mean, I can see a situation where there might have been collusion, where you were moved by the boy's distress when he brought you the papers; and on the spur of the moment you opened the case and took out his paper and told him what to write."

"Look here," said Fielding hotly, "why don't you keep off this? What's it got to do with you?" And Smiley replied with sudden fervour:

"I'm trying to help, Fielding. I beg you to believe me, I'm trying to help. For Adrian's sake. I don't want there to be . . . more trouble than there need, more pain. I want to get it straight before Rigby comes. They've dropped the charge against Janie. You know that, don't you? They seem to think it's Rode, but they haven't pulled him in. They could have done, but they haven't. They just took more statements from him. So you see, it matters terribly about the writing-case. Everything hangs by whether you really saw inside it; and whether Perkins did. Don't you see that? If it was Perkins who cheated after all, if it was only the boy who opened the case and not you, then they'll want to know the answer to a very important question: *they'll want to know how you knew what was inside it.*"

"What are you trying to say?"

"They're not really moronic, you know. Let's start from the other end for a moment. Suppose it was you who killed

Stella Rode, suppose you had a reason, a terribly good reason, and they knew what that reason might be; suppose you went ahead of Rode after giving him the case that night—by bicycle, for instance, like Janie said, riding on the wind. If that were really so, none of those things you saw would have been in the case at all. You could have made it up. And when later the exam results came out and you realised that Perkins had cheated, then you guessed he had seen inside the case, had seen that it contained nothing, *nothing but exam papers*. I mean that would explain why you had to kill the boy." He stopped and glanced towards Fielding. "And in a way," he added almost reluctantly, "it makes better sense, doesn't it?"

"And what, may I ask, was the reason you speak of?"

"Perhaps she blackmailed you. She certainly knew about your conviction in the war from when she was up North. Her father was a magistrate, wasn't he? I understand they've looked up the files. The police, I mean. It was her father who heard the case. She knew you're broke and need another job and she kept you on a hook. It seems D'Arcy knew too. She told him. She'd nothing to lose; he was in on the story from the start, he'd never allow the papers to get hold of it; she knew that, she knew her man. Did *you* tell D'Arcy as well, Fielding? I think you may have done. When she came to you and told you she knew, jeered and laughed at you, you went to D'Arcy and told him. You asked him what to do. And he said—what would he say?—perhaps he said find out what she wants. But she wanted nothing; not money at least, but something more pleasing, more gratifying to her twisted little mind: she wanted to command and own you. She loved to conspire, she summoned you to meetings at absurd times and places; in woods, in disused churches, and above all at night. And she wanted nothing from you but your will, she made you listen to her boasts and her mad intrigues, made you fawn and cringe, then let you run away till the next time." He looked up again. "They might think along those lines, you see. That's why we need to know who saw inside the case. And who cheated in the exam." They were both looking at him, Ailsa in horror, Fielding motionless, impassive.

"If they think that," asked Fielding at last, "how do they suppose I knew Rode would come back for the case that night?"

"Oh, they knew she was expecting you to meet her that night, after the dinner at your house." Smiley threw this off as if it were a tedious detail, "It was part of the game she liked to play."

"How do they know that?"

"From what Rode says," Smiley continued, "Stella was carrying the case in the hall, actually had it in her hand. When they arrived at North Fields she was without it; she flew into a rage and accused him of forgetting it. She made him go back for it. You see the inference?"

"Oh, clearly," said Fielding, and Smiley heard Ailsa Brimley whisper his name in horror.

"In other words, when Stella devised this trick to gratify her twisted will, you saw it as an opportunity to kill her, putting the blame on a non-existent tramp, or, failing that, on Rode, as a second line of defence. Let us suppose you had been meaning to kill her. You had meant, I expect, to ride out there one night when Rode was teaching late. You had your boots and your cape, even the cable stolen from Rode's room, and you meant to lay a false trail. But what a golden opportunity when Perkins turned up with the hand-case! Stella wanted her meeting—the forgotten hand-case was agreed upon as the means of achieving it. That, I fear, is the way their minds may work. And you see, they *know* it wasn't Rode."

"How do they know? How *can* they know? He's got no alibi." Smiley didn't seem to hear. He was looking towards the window, and the heavy velvet curtains stirring uneasily.

"What's that? What are you looking at?" Fielding asked with sudden urgency, but Smiley did not answer.

"You know, Fielding," he said at last, "we just don't know

what people are like, we can never tell; there isn't any truth about human beings, no formula that meets each one of us. And there are some of us—aren't there?—who are nothing, who are so labile that we astound ourselves; we're the chameleons. I read a story once about a poet who bathed himself in cold fountains so that he could recognise his own existence in the contrast. He had to reassure himself, you see, like a child being hateful to its parents. You might say he had to make the sun shine on him so that he could see his shadow and feel alive."

Fielding made an impatient movement with his hand. "How do you know it wasn't Rode?"

"The people who are like that—there really are some, Fielding—do you know their secret? They can't feel anything inside them, no pleasure or pain, no love or hate; they're ashamed and frightened that they can't feel. And their shame, this shame, Fielding, drives them to extravagance and colour; they must make themselves feel that cold water, and without that they're nothing. The world sees them as showmen, fantasists, liars, as sensualists perhaps, not for what they are: the living dead."

"How do you know? How do you know it wasn't Rode?" Fielding cried with anger in his voice, and Smiley replied: "I'll tell you."

"If Rode murdered his wife, he had planned to do so long ago. The plastic cape, the boots, the weapon, the intricate timing, the use of Perkins to carry the case to your house—these are evidence of long premeditation. Of course one could ask: if that's so, why did he bother with Perkins at all—why didn't he keep the case with him all the time? But never mind. Let's see how he does it. He walks home with his wife after dinner, having deliberately forgotten the writing-case. Having left Stella at home, he returns to your house to collect it. It was a risky business, incidentally, leaving that case behind. Quite apart from the fact that one would expect him to have locked it, his wife might have noticed he hadn't got it as they left—or you might have noticed, or Miss Truebody—but luckily no one did. He collects the case, hurries back, kills her, fabricating the clues which mislead the police. He thrusts the cape, boots and gloves into the refugees' parcel, ties it up and prepares to make good his escape. He is alarmed by Mad Janie, perhaps, but reaches the lane and re-enters the house as Stanley Rode. Five minutes later he is with the D'Arcys. From then on for the next forty-eight hours he is under constant supervision. Perhaps you didn't know this, Fielding, but the police found the murder weapon four miles down the road in a ditch. They found it within ten hours of the murder being discovered, long before Rode had a chance to throw it there.

"This is the point, though, Fielding. This is what they can't get over. I suppose it would be possible to make a phoney murder weapon. Rode could have taken hairs from Stella's comb, stuck them with human blood to a length of coaxial cable and planted the thing in a ditch *before* he committed the murder. But the only blood he could use was his own—which belongs to a different blood group. The blood on the weapon they found belonged to Stella's blood group. He didn't do it. There's a rather more concrete piece of evidence, to do with the parcel. Rigby had a word with Miss Truebody yesterday. It seems she telephoned Stella Rode on the morning of the day she was murdered. Telephoned at your request, Fielding, to say a boy would be bringing some old clothes up to North Fields on Thursday morning—would she be sure to keep the parcel open till then? . . . What did Stella threaten to do, Fielding? Write an anonymous letter to your next school?"

Then Smiley put his hand on Fielding's arm and said: "Go now, in God's name go now. There's very little time, for Adrian's sake go now," and Ailsa Brimley whispered something he could not hear.

Fielding seemed not to hear. His great head was thrown back, his eyes half closed, his wine glass still held between his thick fingers.

And the front-door bell rang out, like the scream of a woman in an empty house.

Smiley never knew what made the noise, whether it was Fielding's hands on the table as he stood up, or his chair, falling backwards. Perhaps it was not a noise at all, but simply the shock of violent movement when it was least expected; the sight of Fielding, who a moment before had sat lethargic in his chair, springing forward across the room. Then Rigby was holding him, had taken Fielding's right arm and done something to it so that Fielding cried out in pain and fear, swinging round to face them under the compulsion of Rigby's grip. Then Rigby was saying the words, and Fielding's terrified gaze fell upon Smiley.

"Stop him, stop him, Smiley, for God's sake! They'll hang me." And he shouted the last two words again and again: "Hang me, hang me," until the detectives came in from the street and shoved him without ceremony into a waiting car.

Smiley watched the car go. It didn't hurry, just picked its way down the wet street and disappeared. He remained there long after it had gone, looking towards the end of the road, so that passers-by stared oddly at him, or tried to follow his gaze. But there was nothing to see. Only the half-lit street, and the shadows moving along it.